Tom Clancy

THREE COMPLETE NOVELS

Also by Tom Clancy

THE HUNT FOR RED OCTOBER

RED STORM RISING

THE CARDINAL OF THE KREMLIN

WITHOUT REMORSE

Nonfiction

SUBMARINE:
A Guided Tour Inside a Nuclear Warship

Tom Clancy

THREE COMPLETE NOVELS

Patriot Games

Clear and Present Danger

The Sum of All Fears

G. P. PUTNAM'S SONS
New York

G. P. Putnam's Sons
Publishers Since 1838
200 Madison Avenue
New York, NY 10016

Library of Congress Cataloging-in-Publication Data

Clancy, Tom, date
[Patriot games]
Three complete novels / Tom Clancy.
p. cm.
Contents: Patriot games—Clear and present danger—The sum of all fears.
ISBN 0-399-13935-4
1. Ryan, Jack (Fictitious character)—Fiction. 2. Spy stories,
American. I. Clancy, Tom, date. Clear and present danger.
1994. II. Title.
PS3553.L245A6 1994 93-31270 CIP
813'.54—dc20

Printed in the United States of America
3 4 5 6 7 8 9 10

Contents

Tom Clancy

THREE COMPLETE NOVELS

Patriot Games

For Wanda

1. A Sunny Day in Londontown

Ryan was nearly killed twice in half an hour. He left the taxi a few blocks short of his destination. It was a fine, clear day, the sun already low in the blue sky. Ryan had been sitting for hours in a series of straight-back wooden chairs, and he wanted to walk a bit to work the kinks out. Traffic was relatively light on the streets and sidewalks. That surprised him, but he looked forward to the evening rush hour. Clearly these streets had not been laid out with automobiles in mind, and he was sure that the afternoon chaos would be something to behold. Jack's first impression of London was that it would be a fine town to walk in, and he moved at his usual brisk pace, unchanged since his stint in the Marine Corps, marking time unconsciously by tapping the edge of his clipboard against his leg.

Just short of the corner the traffic disappeared, and he moved to cross the street early. He automatically looked left, right, then left again as he had since childhood, and stepped off the curb—

And was nearly crushed by a two-story red bus that screeched past him with a bare two feet to spare.

"Excuse me, sir." Ryan turned to see a police officer—they call them constables over here, he reminded himself—in uniform complete to the Mack Sennett hat. "Please do be careful and cross at the corners. You might also mind the painted signs on the pavement to look right or left. We try not to lose too many tourists to the traffic."

"How do you know I'm a tourist?" He would now, from Ryan's accent.

The cop smiled patiently. "Because you looked the wrong way, sir, and you dress like an American. Please be careful, sir. Good day." The bobby moved off with a friendly nod, leaving Ryan to wonder what there was about his brand-new three-piece suit that marked him as an American.

Chastened, he walked to the corner. Painted lettering on the blacktop warned him to LOOK RIGHT, along with an arrow for the dyslexic. He waited for the light to change, and was careful to stay within the painted lines. Jack remembered that he'd have to pay close attention to the traffic, especially when he rented the car Friday. England was one of the last places in the world where the people drove on the wrong side of the road. He was sure it would take some getting used to.

But they did everything else well enough, he thought comfortably, already drawing universal observations one day into his first trip to Britain. Ryan was a practiced observer, and one can draw many conclusions from a few glances. He was walking in a business and professional district. The other people on the sidewalk were better dressed than their American counterparts would be—aside from the punkers with their spiked orange and purple hair, he thought. The architecture here was a hodgepodge ranging from Octavian Augustus to Mies van der Rohe, but most of the buildings had an old, comfortable look that in Washington or Baltimore would long since have been replaced with an unbroken row of new and soulless glass boxes.

Both aspects of the town dovetailed nicely with the good manners he'd encountered so far. It was a working vacation for Ryan, but first impressions told him that it would be a very pleasant one nonetheless.

There were a few jarring notes. Many people seemed to be carrying umbrellas. Ryan had been careful to check the day's weather forecast before setting out on his research trip. A fair day had been accurately predicted—in fact it had been called a hot day, though temperatures were only in the upper sixties. A warm day for this time of year, to be sure, but "hot"? Jack wondered if they called it Indian summer here. Probably not. Why the umbrellas, though? Didn't people trust the local weather service? Was *that* how the cop knew I was an American?

Another thing he ought to have anticipated was the plethora of Rolls-Royces on the streets. He hadn't seen more than a handful in his entire life, and while the streets were not exactly crowded with them, there were quite a few. He himself usually drove around in a five-year-old VW Rabbit. Ryan stopped at a newsstand to purchase a copy of *The Economist,* and had to fumble with the change from his cab fare for several seconds in order to pay the patient dealer, who doubtless also had him pegged for a Yank. He paged through the magazine instead of watching where he was going as he went down the street, and presently found himself halfway down the wrong block. Ryan stopped dead and thought back to the city map he'd inspected before leaving the hotel. One thing Jack could not do was remember street names, but he had a photographic memory for maps. He walked to the end of the block, turned left, proceeded two blocks, then right, and sure enough there was St. James's Park. Ryan checked his watch; he was fifteen minutes early. It was downhill past the monument to a Duke of York, and he crossed the street near a longish classical building of white marble.

Yet another pleasant thing about London was the profusion of green spaces. The park looked big enough, and he could see that the grass was tended with care. The whole autumn must have been unseasonably warm. The trees still bore plenty of leaves. Not many people around, though. Well, he shrugged, it's Wednesday. Middle of the week, the kids were all in school, and it was a normal business day. So much the better, he thought. He'd deliberately come over after the tourist season. Ryan did not like crowds. The Marine Corps had taught him that, too.

"*Daddee!*" Ryan's head snapped around to see his little daughter running toward him from behind a tree, heedless as usual of her safety. Sally arrived with her customary thump against her tall father. Also as usual, Cathy Ryan trailed behind, never quite able to keep up with their little white tornado. Jack's wife did look like a tourist. Her Canon 35mm camera was draped over one shoulder, along with the camera case that doubled as an oversized purse when they were on vacation.

"How'd it go, Jack?"

Ryan kissed his wife. Maybe the Brits don't do that in public either, he thought. "Great, babe. They treated me like I owned the place. Got all my notes tucked away." He tapped his clipboard. "Didn't you get anything?" Cathy laughed.

"The shops here deliver." She smiled in a way that told him she'd parted with a fairish bit of the money they had allocated for shopping. "And we got something really nice for Sally."

"Oh?" Jack bent over to look his daughter in the eye. "And what might that be?"

"It's a surprise, Daddy." The little girl twisted and giggled like a true four-year-old. She pointed to the park. "Daddy, they got a lake with swans and peccalins!"

"Pelicans," Jack corrected.

"Big white ones!" Sally loved peccalins.

"Uh-huh," Ryan observed. He looked up to his wife. "Get any good pictures?"

Cathy patted her camera. "Oh, sure. London is already Canonized—or would you prefer that we spent the whole day shopping?" Photography was Cathy Ryan's only hobby, and she was good at it.

"Ha!" Ryan looked down the street. The pavement here was reddish, not black, and the road was lined with what looked like beech trees. The Mall, wasn't it? He couldn't remember, and would not ask his wife, who'd been to London many times. The Palace was larger than he'd expected, but it seemed a dour building, three hundred yards away, hidden behind a marble monument of some sort. Traffic was a little thicker here, but moved briskly. "What do we do for dinner?"

"Catch a cab back to the hotel?" She looked at her watch. "Or we can walk."

"They're supposed to have a good dining room. Still early, though. These civilized places make you wait until eight or nine." He saw another Rolls go by in the direction of the Palace. He was looking forward to dinner, though not really to having Sally there. Four-year-olds and four-star restaurants didn't go well together. Brakes squealed off to his left. He wondered if the hotel had a baby-sitting—

BOOM!

Ryan jumped at the sound of an explosion not thirty yards away. *Grenade,* something in his mind reported. He sensed the whispering sound of fragments in the air and a moment later heard the chatter of automatic weapons fire. He spun around to see the Rolls turned crooked in the street. The front end seemed lower than it should be, and its path was blocked by a black sedan. There was a man standing at its right front fender, firing an AK-47 rifle into the front end, and another man was racing around to the car's left rear.

"Get down!" Ryan grabbed his daughter's shoulder and forced her to the ground behind a tree, yanking his wife roughly down beside her. A dozen cars were stopped raggedly behind the Rolls, none closer than fifty feet, and these shielded his family from the line of fire. Traffic on the far side was blocked by the sedan. The man with the Kalashnikov was spraying the Rolls for all he was worth.

"Sonuvabitch!" Ryan kept his head up, scarcely able to believe what he saw. "It's the goddamned IRA—they're killing somebody right—" Ryan moved slightly to his left. His peripheral vision took in the faces of people up and down the street, turning and staring, in each face the black circle of a shock-opened mouth. *This is really happening!* he thought, *right in front of me, just like that, just like some Chicago gangster movie. Two bastards are committing murder. Right here. Right now. Just like* that. "Son of a *bitch*!"

Ryan moved farther left, screened by a stopped car. Covered by its front fender, he could see one man standing at the left rear of the Rolls, just standing there, his pistol hand extended as though expecting someone to bolt from the passenger door. The bulk of the Rolls screened Ryan from the AK gunner, who was crouched down to control his weapon. The near gunman had his back to Ryan. He was no more than fifty feet away. He didn't move, concentrating on the passenger door. His back was still turned. Ryan would never remember making any conscious decision.

He moved quickly around the stopped car, head down, keeping low and accelerating rapidly, his eyes locked on his target—the small of the man's back—just as he'd been taught in high school football. It took only a few seconds to cover the distance, with Ryan's mind reaching out, willing the man to stay dumb just a moment longer. At five feet Ryan lowered his shoulder and drove off both legs. His coach would have been proud.

The blind-side tackle caught the gunman perfectly. His back bent like a bow and Ryan heard bones snap as his victim pitched forward and down. A satisfying *klonk* told him that the man's head had bounced off the bumper on the way to the pavement. Ryan got up instantly—winded but full of adrenaline—and crouched beside the body. The man's pistol had dropped from his hand and lay beside the body. Ryan grabbed it. It was an automatic of some sort he had never handled. It looked like a 9mm Makarov or some other East Bloc military issue. The hammer was back and the safety off. He fitted the gun carefully in his right hand—his left hand didn't seem to be working right, but Ryan ignored that. He looked down at the man he'd just tackled and shot him once in the hip. Then he brought the gun up to eye level and moved to the right rear corner of the Rolls. He crouched lower still and peeked around the edge of the bodywork.

The other gunman's AK was lying on the street and he was firing into the car with his own pistol, something else in his other hand. Ryan took a deep breath and stepped from behind the Rolls, leveling his automatic at the man's chest. The other gunman turned his head first, then swiveled off-balance to bring his own gun around. Both men fired at the same instant. Ryan felt a fiery thump in his left shoulder and saw his own round take the man in the chest. The 9mm slug knocked the man backward as though from a hard punch. Ryan brought his own pistol down from recoil and squeezed off another round. The second bullet caught the man under the chin and exploded out the back of his head in a wet, pink cloud. Like a puppet with severed strings, the gunman fell to the pavement without a twitch. Ryan kept his pistol centered on the man's chest until he saw what had happened to his head.

"Oh, God!" The surge of adrenaline left him as quickly as it had come. Time slowed back down to normal, and Ryan found himself suddenly dizzy and breathless. His mouth was open and gasping for air. Whatever force had been holding his body erect seemed to disappear, leaving his frame weak, on the verge of collapse. The black sedan backed up a few yards and accelerated past him, racing down the street, then turning left up a side street. Ryan didn't think to take the number. He was stunned by the flashing sequence of events with which his mind had still not caught up.

The one he'd shot twice was clearly dead, his eyes open and surprised at fate, a foot-wide pool of blood spreading back from his head. Ryan was chilled to see a grenade in his gloved left hand. He bent down to ensure that the cotter pin was still in place on the wooden stick handle, and it was a slow, painful process to straighten up. Next he looked to the Rolls.

The first grenade had torn the front end to shreds. The front wheels were askew, and the tires flat on the blacktop. The driver was dead. Another body was slumped over in the front seat. The thick windshield had been blasted to fragments. The driver's face was—gone, a red spongy mass. There was a red smear on the glass partition separating the driver's seat from the passenger compartment. Jack moved around the car and looked in the back. He saw a man lying prone on the floor, and under him the corner of a woman's dress. He tapped the pistol butt against the glass. The man stirred for a moment, then froze. At least he was alive.

Ryan looked at his pistol. It was empty, the slide locked back on a dry clip. His breath was coming in shudders now. His legs were wobbling under him and his hands were beginning to shake convulsively, which gave his wounded shoulder brief, sharp waves of intense pain. He looked around and saw something to make him forget that—

A soldier was running toward him, with a police officer a few yards behind. One of the Palace guards, Jack thought. The man had lost his bearskin shako but still had an automatic rifle with a half-foot of steel bayonet perched on the muzzle. Ryan quickly wondered if the rifle might be loaded and decided it might be expensive to find out. This was a guardsman, he told himself, a professional soldier from a crack regiment who'd had to prove he had real balls before they sent him to the finishing school that made windup toys for tourists to gawk at. Maybe as good as a Sea Marine. *How did you get here so fast?*

Slowly and carefully, Ryan held the pistol out at arm's length. He thumbed the clip-release button, and the magazine clattered down to the street. Next he twisted the gun so that the soldier could see it was empty. Then he set it down on the pavement and stepped away from it. He tried to raise his hands, but the left one wouldn't move. The guardsman all the time ran smart, head up, eyes tracing left and right but never leaving Ryan entirely. He stopped ten feet away with his rifle at low-guard, its bayonet pointed right at Jack's throat, just like it said in the manual. His chest was heaving, but the soldier's face was a blank mask. The policeman hadn't caught up, his face bloody as he shouted into a small radio.

"At ease, Trooper," Ryan said as firmly as he could. It was not impressive. "We got two bad guys down. I'm one of the good guys."

The guardsman's face didn't change a whit. The boy was a pro, all right. Ryan could hear his thinking—how easy to stick the bayonet right out his target's back. Jack was in no shape to avoid that first thrust.

"DaddeeDaddeeDaddee!" Ryan turned his head and saw his little girl racing past the stalled cars toward him. The four-year-old stopped a few feet away from him, her eyes wide with horror. She ran forward to wrap both arms around her father's leg and screamed up at the guardsman: *"Don't you hurt my daddy!"*

The soldier looked from father to daughter in amazement as Cathy approached more carefully, hands in the open.

"Soldier," she announced in her voice of professional command, "I'm a doctor, and I'm going to treat that wound. So you can put that gun down, right now!"

The police constable grabbed the guardsman's shoulder and said something Jack couldn't make out. The rifle's angle changed fractionally as the soldier relaxed ever so slightly. Ryan saw more cops running to the scene, and a white car with its siren screaming. The situation, whatever it was, was coming under control.

"You lunatic." Cathy surveyed the wound dispassionately. There was a dark stain on the shoulder of Ryan's new suit jacket that turned the gray wool to purple-crimson. His whole body was shaking now. He could barely stand and the weight of Sally hanging on his leg was forcing him to weave. Cathy grabbed his right arm and eased him down to the pavement, sitting him back against the side of the car. She moved his coat away from the wound and probed gently at his shoulder. It didn't feel gentle at all. She reached around to his back pocket for a handkerchief and pressed it against the center of the wound.

"That doesn't feel right," she remarked to no one.

"Daddy, you're all bloody!" Sally stood an arm's length away, her hands fluttering like the wings of a baby bird. Jack wanted to reach out to her, to tell her everything was all right, but the three feet of distance might as well have been a thousand miles—and his shoulder was telling him that things were definitely not all right.

There were now about ten police officers around the car, many of them panting for breath. Three had handguns out, and were scanning the gathering crowd. Two more red-coated soldiers appeared from the west. A police sergeant approached. Before he could say anything Cathy looked up to bark an order.

"Call an ambulance *right now*!"

"On the way, mum," the Sergeant replied with surprising good manners. "Why don't you let us look after that?"

"I'm a doctor," she answered curtly. "You have a knife?"

The Sergeant turned to remove the bayonet from the first guardsman's rifle and stooped down to assist. Cathy held the coat and vest clear for him to cut away, then both cut the shirt free from his shoulder. She tossed the handkerchief clear. It was already blood-sodden. Jack started to protest.

"Shut up, Jack." She looked over to the Sergeant and jerked her chin toward Sally. "Get her away from here."

The Sergeant gestured for a guardsman to come over. The Private scooped Sally up in his arms. He took her a few feet away, cradling her gently to his chest. Jack saw his little girl crying pitifully, but somehow it all seemed to be very far away. He felt his skin go cold and moist—shock?

"Damn," Cathy said gruffly. The Sergeant handed her a thick bandage. She pressed it against the wound and it immediately went red as she tried to tie it in place. Ryan groaned. It felt as though someone had taken an ax to his shoulder.

"Jack, what the hell were you trying to do?" she demanded through clenched teeth as she fumbled with the cloth ties.

Ryan snarled back, the sudden anger helping to block out the pain. "I didn't try—I fucking did it!" The effort required to say that took half his strength away with it.

"Uh-huh," Cathy grunted. "Well, you're bleeding like a pig, Jack."

More men ran in from the other direction. It seemed that a hundred sirens were converging on the scene with men—some in uniform, some not—leaping out to join the party. A uniformed policeman with more ornate shoulder boards began to shout orders at the others. The scene was impressive. A separate, detached part of Ryan's brain catalogued it. There he was, sitting against the Rolls, his shirt soaked red as though blood had been poured from a pitcher. Cathy, her hands covered with her husband's blood, was still trying to arrange the bandage correctly. His daughter was gasping out tears in the arms of a burly young soldier who seemed to be singing to her in a language that Jack couldn't make out. Sally's eyes were locked on him, full of desperate anguish. The detached part of his mind found all this very amusing until another wave of pain yanked him back to reality.

The policeman who'd evidently taken charge came up to them after first checking the perimeter. "Sergeant, move him aside."

Cathy looked up and snapped angrily: "Open the other side, dammit, I got a bleeder here!"

"The other door's jammed, ma'am. Let me help." Ryan heard a different kind of siren as they bent down. The three of them moved him aside a foot or so, and the senior officer made to open the car door. They hadn't moved him far enough. When the door swung open, its edge caught Ryan's shoulder. The last thing he heard before passing out was his own scream of pain.

Ryan's eyes focused slowly, his consciousness a hazy, variable thing that reported items out of place and out of time. For a moment he was inside a vehicle of some sort. The lateral movements of its passage rippled agony through his chest, and there was an awful atonal sound in the distance, though not all that far away. He thought he saw two faces he vaguely recognized. Cathy was there, too, wasn't she—no, there were some people in green. Everything was soft and vague except the burning pain in his shoulder and chest, but when he blinked his eyes all were gone. He was someplace else again.

The ceiling was white and nearly featureless at first. Ryan knew somehow that he was under the influence of drugs. He recognized the feelings, but could not remember why. It required several minutes of lazy concentration for him to determine that the ceiling was made of white acoustical tiles on a white metal framework. Some of the tiles were waterstained and served to give him a reference. Others were translucent plastic for the soft fluorescent lighting. There was something tied under his nose, and after a moment he began to feel a cool gas tracing into his nostrils—oxygen? His other senses began to report in one at a time. Expanding radially down from his head, they began to explore his body and reported reluctantly to his brain. Some unseen things were taped to his chest. He could feel them pulling at the hairs that Cathy liked to play with when she was drunk. His left shoulder felt . . . didn't really feel at all. His whole body was far too heavy to move even an inch.

A hospital, he decided after several minutes. *Why am I in a hospital . . . ?* It took an indeterminate period of concentration for Jack to remember why he was here. When it came to him, it was just as well that he could contemplate the taking of a human life from within the protective fog of drugs.

I was shot, too, wasn't I? Ryan turned his head slowly to the right. A bottle of IV fluids was hanging on a metal stand next to the bed, its rubber hose trailing down under the sheet where his arm was tied down. He tried to feel the prick of the catheter that had to be inside the right elbow, but couldn't. His mouth was cottony dry. *Well, I wasn't shot on the right side . . .* Next he tried to turn his head to the left. Something soft but very firm prevented it. Ryan wasn't able to care very much about it. Even his curiosity for his condition was a tenuous thing. For some reason his surroundings seemed much more interesting than his own body. Looking directly up, he saw a TV-like instrument, along with some other electronic stuff, none of which he could make out at the acute angle. *EKG readout? Something like that,* he decided. It all figured. He was in a surgical recovery room, wired up like an astronaut while the staff decided if he'd live or not. The drugs helped him to consider the question with marvelous objectivity.

"Ah, we're awake." A voice other than the distant, muffled tone of the PA system. Ryan dropped his chin to see a nurse of about fifty. She had a Bette Davis face crinkled by years of frowns. He tried to speak to her, but his mouth seemed glued shut. What came out was a cross between a rasp and a croak. The nurse disappeared while he tried to decide what exactly the sound was.

A man appeared a minute or so later. He was also in his fifties, tall and spare, dressed in surgical greens. There was a stethoscope hanging from his neck, and he seemed to be carrying something that Ryan couldn't quite see. He seemed rather tired, but wore a satisfied smile.

"So," he said, "we're awake. How are we feeling?" Ryan managed a full-fledged croak this time. The doctor—?—gestured to the nurse. She came forward to give Ryan a sip of water through a glass straw.

"Thanks." He sloshed the water around his mouth. It was not enough to swallow. His mouth tissues seemed to absorb it all at once. "Where am I?"

"You are in the surgical recovery unit of St. Thomas's Hospital. You are recovering from surgery on your upper left arm and shoulder. I am your surgeon. My team and I have been working on you for, oh, about six hours now, and it would appear that you will probably live,'' he added judiciously. He seemed to regard Ryan as a successful piece of work.

Rather slowly and sluggishly Ryan thought to himself that the English sense of humor, admirable as it might otherwise be, was a little too dry for this sort of situation. He was composing a reply when Cathy came into view. The Bette Davis nurse moved to head her off.

''I'm sorry, Mrs. Ryan, but only medical person—''

''I'm a doctor.'' She held up her plastic ID card. The man took it.

''Wilmer Eye Institute, Johns Hopkins Hospital.'' The surgeon extended his hand and gave Cathy a friendly, colleague-to-colleague smile. ''How do you do, Doctor? My name is Charles Scott.''

''That's right,'' Ryan confirmed groggily. ''She's the surgeon doctor. I'm the historian doctor.'' No one seemed to notice.

''Sir Charles Scott? Professor Scott?''

''The same.'' A benign smile. *Everyone likes to be recognized,* Ryan thought as he watched from his back.

''One of my instructors knows you—Professor Knowles.''

''Ah, and how is Dennis?''

''Fine, Doctor. He's associate professor of orthopedics now.'' Cathy shifted gears smoothly, back to medical professional. ''Do you have the X-rays?''

''Here.'' Scott held up a manila envelope and extracted a large film. He held it up in front of a lighting panel. ''We took this prior to going in.''

''Damn.'' Cathy's nose wrinkled. She put on the half-glasses she used for close work, the ones Jack hated. He watched her head move slowly from side to side. ''I didn't know it was *that* bad.''

Professor Scott nodded. ''Indeed. We reckon the collarbone was broken before he was shot, then the bullet came crashing through here—just missed the brachial plexus, so we expect no serious nerve damage—and did all this damage.'' He traced a pencil across the film. Ryan couldn't see any of it from the bed. ''Then it did this to the top of the humerus before stopping here, just inside the skin. Bloody powerful thing, the nine millimeter. As you can see, the damage was quite extensive. We had a jolly time finding all these fragments and jigsawing them back into proper place, but—we were able to accomplish this.'' Scott held a second film up next to the first. Cathy was quiet for several seconds, her head swiveling back and forth.

''That is nice work, Doctor!''

Sir Charles' smile broadened a notch. ''From a Johns Hopkins surgeon, yes, I think I'll accept that. Both these pins are permanent, this screw also, I'm afraid, but the rest should heal rather nicely. As you can see, all the large fragments are back where they belong, and we have every reason to expect a full recovery.''

''How much impairment?'' A detached question. Cathy could be maddeningly unemotional about her work.

''We're not sure yet,'' Scott said slowly. ''Probably a little, but it should not be overly severe. We can't guarantee a complete restoration of function—the damage was far too extensive for that.''

''You mind telling me something?'' Ryan tried to sound angry, but it hadn't come out right.

''What I mean, Mr. Ryan, is that you'll probably have some permanent loss of use of your arm—precisely how much we cannot determine as yet—and from now on you'll have a permanent barometer. Henceforth, whenever the weather is about to change for the worse, you'll know it before anyone else.''

''How long in this cast?'' Cathy wanted to know.

''At least a month.'' The surgeon seemed apologetic. ''It is awkward, I know, but the shoulder must be totally immobilized for at least that long. After that we'll have to reevaluate the injury and we can probably revert to a normal cast for another . . . oh, another month or so, I expect. I presume he heals well, no allergies. Looks to be in good health, decent physical shape.''

''Jack's in good physical shape, except for a few loose marbles in his head,'' Cathy nodded, an edge on her weary voice. ''He jogs. No allergies except ragweed, and he heals rapidly.''

''Yeah,'' Ryan confirmed. ''Her teethmarks go away in under a week, usually.'' He thought this uproariously funny, but no one laughed.

''Good,'' Sir Charles said. ''So, Doctor, you can see that your husband is in good hands. I will leave the two of you together for five minutes. After that, I wish that he should get some rest, and you look as though you could use some also.'' The surgeon moved off with Bette Davis in his wake.

Cathy moved closer to him, changing yet again from cool professional to concerned wife. Ryan told himself for perhaps the millionth time how lucky he was to have this girl. Caroline Ryan had a small, round face, short butter-blond hair, and the world's prettiest blue eyes. Behind those eyes was a person with intelligence at least the equal of his own, someone he loved as much as a man could. He would never understand how he'd won her. Ryan was painfully aware that on his best day his own undistinguished features, a heavy beard and a lantern jaw, made him look like a dark-haired Dudley Do-Right of the Mounties. She played pussycat to his crow. Jack tried to reach out for her hand, but was foiled by straps. Cathy took his.

''Love ya, babe,'' he said softly.

''Oh, Jack.'' Cathy tried to hug him. She was foiled by the cast that he couldn't even see. ''Jack, why the hell did you do that?''

He had already decided how to answer that. ''It's over and I'm still alive, okay? How's Sally?''

''I think she's finally asleep. She's downstairs with a policeman.'' Cathy did look tired. ''How do you think she is, Jack? Dear God, she saw you killed almost. You scared us both to death.'' Her china-blue eyes were rimmed in red, and her hair looked terrible, Jack saw. Well, she never was able to do much of anything with her hair. The surgical caps always ruined it.

''Yeah, I know. Anyway, it doesn't look like I'll be doing much more of that for a while,'' he grunted. ''Matter of fact, it doesn't look like I'll be doing much of anything for a while.'' That drew a smile. It was good to see her smile.

''Fine. You're supposed to conserve your energy. Maybe this'll teach you a lesson—and don't tell me about all those strange hotel beds going to waste.'' She squeezed his hand. Her smile turned impish. ''We'll probably work something out in a few weeks. How do I look?''

''Like hell.'' Jack laughed quietly. ''I take it the doc was a somebody?''

He saw his wife relax a little. ''You might say that. Sir Charles Scott is one of the best orthopods in the world. He trained Professor Knowles—he did a super job on you. You're lucky to have an arm at all, you know—my God!''

''Easy, babe. I'm going to live, remember?''

''I know, I know.''

''It's going to hurt, isn't it?''

Another smile. "Just a bit. Well. I've got to put Sally down. I'll be back tomorrow." She bent down to kiss him. Skin full of drugs, oxygen tube, dry mouth, and all, it felt good. *God,* he thought, *God, how I love this girl.* Cathy squeezed his hand one more time and left.

The Bette Davis nurse came back. It was not a satisfactory trade.

"I'm 'Doctor' Ryan, too, you know," Jack said warily.

"Very good, Doctor. It is time for you to get some rest. I'll be here to look after you all night. Now sleep, Doctor Ryan."

On this happy note Jack closed his eyes. Tomorrow would be a real bitch, he was sure. It would keep.

2. Cops and Royals

Ryan awoke at 6:35 A.M. He knew that because it was announced by a radio disc-jockey whose voice faded to an American Country & Western song of the type which Ryan avoided at home by listening to all-news radio stations. The singer was admonishing mothers not to allow their sons to become cowboys, and Ryan's first muddled thought of the day was, *Surely they don't have that problem over here . . . do they?* His mind drifted along on this tangent for half a minute, wondering if the Brits had C&W bars with sawdust on the floors, mechanical bull rides, and office workers who strutted around with pointy-toed boots and five-pound belt buckles. . . . *Why not?* he concluded. *Yesterday I saw something right out of a Dodge City movie.*

Jack would have been just as happy to slide back into sleep. He tried closing his eyes and willing his body to relax, but it was no use. The flight from Dulles had left early in the morning, barely three hours after he'd awakened. He hadn't slept on the plane—it was something he simply could not do—but flying always exhausted him, and he'd gone to bed soon after arriving at the hotel. Then how long had he been unconscious in the hospital? Too long, he realized. Ryan was all slept out. He would have to begin facing the day.

Someone off to his right was playing a radio just loudly enough to hear. Ryan turned his head and was able to see his shoulder—

Shoulder, he thought, *that's why I'm here. But* where's *here?* It was a different room. The ceiling was smooth plaster, recently painted. It was dark, the only illumination coming from a light on the table next to the bed, perhaps enough to read by. There seemed to be a painting on the wall—at least a rectangle darker than the wall, which wasn't white. Ryan took this in, consciously delaying his examination of his left arm until no excuses remained. He turned his head slowly to the left. He saw his arm first of all. It was sticking up at an angle, wrapped in a plaster and fiberglass cast that went all the way to his hand. His fingers stuck out like an afterthought, about the same shade of gray as the plaster-gauze wrappings. There was a metal ring at the back of the wrist, and in the ring was a hook whose chain led to a metal frame that arced over the bed like a crane.

First things first. Ryan tried to wiggle his fingers. It took several seconds before they acknowledged their subservience to his central nervous system. Ryan let out a long breath and closed his eyes to thank God for that. About where his elbow was, a metal rod angled downward to join the rest of the cast, which, he finally appreciated, began at his neck and went diagonally to his waist. It left his arm sticking out entirely on its own and made Ryan look like half a bridge. The cast was not tight on his chest, but touched almost everywhere, and already he had itches where he couldn't scratch. The surgeon had said something about immobilizing the shoulder, and, Ryan thought glumly, he hadn't been kidding. His shoulder ached in a distant sort of way with the promise of more to come. His mouth tasted like a urinal, and the rest of his body was stiff and sore. He turned his head the other way.

"Somebody over there?" he asked softly.

"Oh, hello." A face appeared at the edge of the bed. Younger than Ryan, mid-twenties or so, and lean. He was dressed casually, his tie loose in his collar, and the edge of a shoulder holster showed under his jacket. "How are you feeling, sir?"

Ryan attempted a smile, wondering how successful it was. "About how I look, probably. Where am I, who are you—first, is there a glass of water in this place?"

The policeman poured ice water from a plastic jug into a plastic cup. Ryan reached out with his right hand before he noticed that it wasn't tied down as it had been the last time he awoke. He could now feel the place where the IV catheter had been. Jack greedily sucked the water from the straw. It was only water, but no beer ever tasted better after a day's yardwork. "Thanks, pal."

"My name is Anthony Wilson. I'm supposed to look after you. You are in the VIP suite of St. Thomas's Hospital. Do you remember why you're here, sir?"

"Yeah, I think so," Ryan nodded. "Can you unhook me from this thing? I have to go." The other reminder of the IV.

"I'll ring the sister—here." Wilson squeezed the button that was pinned to the edge of Ryan's pillow.

Less than fifteen seconds later a nurse came through the door and flipped on the overhead lights. The blaze of light dazzled Jack for a moment before he saw it was a different nurse. Not Bette Davis, this one was young and pretty, with the eager, protective look common to nurses. Ryan had seen it before, and hated it.

"Ah, we're awake," she observed brightly. "How are we feeling?"

"Great," Ryan grumped. "Can you unhook me? I have to go to the john."

"We're not supposed to move just yet, Doctor Ryan. Let me fetch you something." She disappeared out the door before he could object. Wilson watched her leave with an appraising look. Cops and nurses, Ryan thought. His dad had married a nurse; he'd met her after bringing a gunshot victim into the emergency room.

The nurse—her name tag said KITTIWAKE—returned in under a minute bearing a stainless steel urinal as though it were a priceless gift, which under the circumstances, it was, Ryan admitted to himself. She lifted the covers on the bed and suddenly Jack realized that his hospital gown was not really on, but just tied loosely around his neck—worse, the nurse was about to make the necessary adjustments for him to use the urinal. Ryan's right hand shot downward under the covers to take it away from her. He thanked God for the second time this morning that he was able, barely, to reach down far enough.

"Could you, uh, excuse me for a minute?" Ryan willed the girl out of the room, and she went, smiling her disappointment. He waited for the door to close completely before continuing. In deference to Wilson he stifled his sigh of relief. Kittiwake was back through the door after counting to sixty.

"Thank you." Ryan handed her the receptacle and she disappeared out the door.

It had barely swung shut when she was back again. This time she stuck a thermometer in his mouth and grabbed his wrist to take his pulse. The thermometer was one of the new electronic sort, and both tasks were completed in fifteen seconds. Ryan asked for the score, but got a smile instead of an answer. The smile remained fixed as she made the entries on his chart. When this task was fulfilled, she made a minor adjustment in the covers, beaming at Ryan. *Little Miss Efficiency,* Ryan told himself. *This girl is going to be a real pain in the ass.*

"Is there anything I might get you, Doctor Ryan?" she asked. Her brown eyes belied the wheat-colored hair. She was cute. She had that dewy look. Ryan was unable to remain angry with pretty women, and hated them for it. Especially young nurses with that dewy look.

"Coffee?" he asked hopefully.

"Breakfast is not for another hour. Can I fetch you a cup of tea?"

"Fine." It wasn't, but it would get rid of her for a little while. Nurse Kittiwake breezed out the door with her ingenuous smile.

"Hospitals!" Ryan snarled when she was gone.

"Oh, I don't know," Wilson observed, the image of Nurse Kittiwake fresh in his mind.

"You ain't the one getting your diapers changed." Ryan grunted and leaned back into the pillow. It was useless to fight it, he knew. He smiled in spite of himself. *Useless to fight it.* He'd been through this twice before, both times with young, pretty nurses. Being grumpy only made them all the more eager to be overpoweringly nice—they had time on their side, time and patience enough to wear anyone down. He sighed out his surrender. It wasn't worth the waste of energy. "So, you're a cop, right? Special Branch?"

"No, sir. I'm with C-13, Anti-Terrorist Branch."

"Can you fill me in on what happened yesterday? I kinda missed a few things."

"How much do you remember, Doctor?" Wilson slid his chair closer. Ryan noted that he remained halfway facing the door, and kept his right hand free.

"I saw—well, I *heard* an explosion, a hand grenade, I think—and when I turned I saw two guys shooting the hell out of a Rolls-Royce. IRA, I guess. I took two of them out, and another one got away in a car. The cavalry arrived, and I passed out and woke up here."

"Not IRA. ULA—Ulster Liberation Army, a Maoist offshoot of the Provos. Nasty buggers. The one you killed was John Michael McCrory, a very bad boy from Londonderry—one of the chaps who escaped from the Maze last July. This is the first time he's surfaced since. And the last"—Wilson smiled coldly—"we haven't identified the other chap yet. That is, not as of when I came on duty three hours ago."

"ULA?" Ryan shrugged. He remembered hearing the name, though he couldn't talk about that. "The guy I—killed. He had an AK, but when I came around the car he was using a pistol. How come?"

"The fool jammed it. He had two full magazines taped end to end, like you see all the time in the movies, but like they trained us specifically *not* to do in the paras. We reckon he bashed it, probably when he came out of the car. The second magazine was bent at the top end—wouldn't feed the rounds properly, you see. Damn good luck for you. You *knew* you were going after a chap with a Kalashnikov?" Wilson examined Ryan's face closely.

Jack nodded. "Doesn't sound real smart, does it?"

"You bloody fool." Wilson said this just as Kittiwake came through the door with a tea tray. The nurse flashed the cop an emphatically disapproving look as she set the tray on the bedstand and wheeled it over. Kittiwake arranged things just so, and poured Ryan a cup with delicacy. Wilson had to do his own.

"So who was in the car, anyway?" Ryan asked. He noted strong reactions.

"You didn't know?" Kittiwake was dumbfounded.

"There wasn't much time to find out." Ryan dropped two packets of brown sugar into his cup. His stirring stopped abruptly when Wilson answered his question.

"The Prince and Princess of Wales. And their new baby."

Ryan's head snapped around. "What?"

"You really didn't know?" the nurse asked.

"You're serious," Ryan said quietly. *They wouldn't kid about this, would they?*

"Too bloody right, I'm serious," Wilson went on, his voice very even. Only his choice of words betrayed how deeply the affair disturbed him. "Except for you, they would all three be quite dead, and that makes you a bloody hero, Doctor Ryan." Wilson sipped his tea neatly and fished out a cigarette.

Ryan set his cup down. "You mean you let them drive around here without a police or secret service—whatever you call it—without an escort?"

"Supposedly it was an unscheduled trip. Security arrangements for the Royals are not my department in any case. I would speculate, however, that those whose department it is will be rethinking a few things," Wilson commented.

"They weren't hurt?"

"No, but their driver was killed. So was their security escort from DPG—Diplomatic Protection Group—Charlie Winston. I knew Charlie. He had a wife, you know, and four children, all grown."

Ryan observed that the Rolls should have had bulletproof glass.

Wilson grunted. "It *did* have bulletproof glass. Actually plastic, a complex polycarbonate material. Unfortunately, no one seems to have read what it said on the box. The guarantee is only for a year. Turns out that sunlight breaks the material down somehow or other. The windshield was no more use than ordinary safety glass. Our friend McCrory put thirty rounds into it, and it quite simply shattered, killing the driver first. The interior partition, thank God, had not been exposed to sunlight, and remained intact. The last thing Charlie did was push the button to put it up. That probably saved them, too—didn't do Charlie much good, though. He had enough time to draw his automatic, but we don't think he was able to get a shot off."

Ryan thought back. There had been blood in the back of the Rolls—not just blood. The driver's head had been blown apart, and his brains had scattered into the passenger compartment. Jack winced thinking about it. The escort had probably leaned over to push the button before defending himself. . . . *Well,* Jack thought, *that's what they pay them for. What a hell of a way to earn a living.*

"It was fortunate that you intervened when you did. They both had hand grenades, you know."

"Yeah, I saw one." Ryan sipped away the last of his tea. "What the hell was I thinking about?" *You weren't thinking at all, Jack.* That'*s what you were thinking about.*

Kittiwake saw Ryan go pale. "You feel quite all right?" she asked.

"I guess." Ryan grunted in wonderment. "Dumb as I was, I must feel pretty good—I ought to be dead."

"Well, that most emphatically will not happen here." She patted his hand. "Please ring me if you need anything." Another beaming smile and she left.

Ryan was still shaking his head. ''The other one got away?''

Wilson nodded. ''We found the car near a tube station a few blocks away. It was stolen, of course. No real problem for him to get clean away. Disappear into the underground. Go to Heathrow, perhaps, and catch a plane to the continent—Brussels, say—then a plane to Ulster or the Republic, and a car the rest of the way home. That's one route; there are others, and it's impossible to cover them all. He was drinking beer last night, watching the news coverage on television in his favorite pub, most likely. Did you get a look at him?''

''No, just a shape. I didn't even think to get the tag number—dumb. Right after that the redcoat came running up to me.'' Ryan winced again. ''Christ, I thought he'd put that pigsticker right through me. For a second there I could see it all—I do something right, then get wasted by a good guy.''

Wilson laughed. ''You don't know how lucky you were. The current guard force is from the Welsh Guards.''

''So?''

''His Royal Highness's own regiment, as it were. He's their colonel-in-chief. There you were with a pistol—how would you expect him to react?'' Wilson stubbed out his cigarette. ''Another piece of good luck, your wife and daughter came running up to you, and the soldier decides to wait a bit, just long enough for things to sort themselves out. Then our chap catches up with him and tells him to stand easy. And a hundred more of my chaps come swooping in.

''I hope you can appreciate this, Doctor. Here we were with three men dead, two others wounded, a Prince and Princess looking as though they'd been shot—your wife examined them on the scene, by the way, and pronounced them fit just before the ambulance arrived—a baby, a hundred witnesses each with his own version of what had just taken place. A bloody Yank—an Irish-American to boot!—whose wife claims he's the chap in the white hat.'' Wilson laughed again. ''Total chaos!

''First order of business, of course, was to get the Royals to safety. The police and guardsmen handled that, probably praying by this time that someone would make trouble. They're still in an evil mood, they tell me, angrier even than from the bandstand bombing incident. Not hard to understand. Anyway, your wife flatly refused to leave your side until you were under doctor's care here. Quite a forceful woman, they tell me.''

''Cathy's a surgeon,'' Ryan explained. ''When she plays doc, she's used to having her own way. Surgeons are like that.''

''After she was quite satisfied we drove her down to the Yard. Meanwhile we had a merry time identifying you. They called your Legal Attaché at the American Embassy and he ran a check through your FBI, plus a backup check through the Marine Corps.'' Ryan stole a cigarette from Wilson's pack. The policeman lit it with a butane lighter. Jack gagged on the smoke, but he needed it. Cathy would give him hell for it, he knew, but one thing at a time. ''Mind you, we never really thought you were one of them. Have to be a maniac to bring the wife and child along on this sort of job. But one must be careful.''

Ryan nodded agreement, briefly dizzy from the smoke. *How'd they know to check through the Corps . . . oh, my Marine Corps Association card. . . .*

''In any event we have things pretty well sorted out. Your government are sending us everything we need—probably here by now, actually.'' Wilson checked his watch.

''My family's all right?''

Wilson smiled in rather an odd way. "They are being very well looked after, Doctor Ryan. You have my word on that."

"The name's Jack."

"Fine. I'm known to my friends as Tony." They finally got around to shaking hands. "And as I said, you're a bloody hero. Care to see what the press have to say?" He handed Ryan a *Daily Mirror* and a *Times*.

"Dear God!"

The tabloid *Mirror*'s front page was almost entirely a color photograph of himself, sitting unconscious against the Rolls. His chest was a scarlet mass.

ATTEMPT ON HRH—MARINE TO THE RESCUE

> A bold attempt to assassinate Their Royal Highnesses the Prince and Princess of Wales within sight of Buckingham Palace was thwarted today by the courage of an American tourist.
>
> John Patrick Ryan, an historian and formerly a lieutenant in the United States Marines, dashed barehanded into a pitched battle on The Mall as over a hundred Londoners watched in shocked disbelief. Ryan, 31, of Annapolis, Maryland, successfully disabled one gunman and, taking his weapon, shot another dead. Ryan himself was seriously wounded in the exchange. He was taken by ambulance to St. Thomas's Hospital, where emergency surgery was successfully performed by Sir Charles Scott.
>
> A third terrorist is reported to have escaped the scene, by running east on The Mall, then turning north on Marlborough Road.
>
> Senior police officials were unanimous in their opinion that, but for Ryan's courageous intervention, Their Highnesses would certainly have been slain.

Ryan turned the page to see another color photograph of himself in happier circumstances. It was his graduation photo from Quantico, and he had to smile at himself, resplendent, then, in blue high-necked blouse, two shiny gold bars, and the Mamaluke sword. It was one of the few decent photographs ever taken of him.

"Where did they get this?"

"Oh, your Marine chaps were most helpful. In fact, one of your Marine ships—helicopter carrier, or something like that—is at Portsmouth right now. I understand that your former colleagues are getting all the free beer they can swill."

Ryan laughed at that. Next he picked up the *Times,* whose headline was marginally less lurid.

> The Prince and Princess of Wales escaped certain death this afternoon. Three, possibly four terrorists armed with hand grenades and Kalashnikov assault rifles lay in wait for their Rolls-Royce; only to have their carefully-laid plans foiled by the bold intervention of J. P. Ryan, formerly a second lieutenant in the United States Marine Corps, and now an historian. . . .

Ryan flipped to the editorial page. The lead item, signed by the publisher, screamed for vengeance while praising Ryan, America, and the United States Marine Corps, and thanked Divine Providence with a flourish worthy of a Papal Encyclical.

"Reading about yourself?" Ryan looked up. Sir Charles Scott was standing at the foot of his bed with an aluminum chart.

"First time I ever made the papers." Ryan set them down.

"You've earned it, and it would seem that the sleep did you some good. How do you feel?"

"Not bad, considering. How am I?" Ryan asked.

"Pulse and temperature normal—almost normal. Your color isn't bad at all. With luck we might even avoid a postoperative infection, though I should not wish to give odds on that," the doctor said. "How badly does it hurt?"

"It's there, but I can live with it," Ryan answered cautiously.

"It is only two hours since your last medication. I trust you are not one of those thickheaded fools who do not want pain medications?"

"Yes, I am," Ryan said. He went on slowly. "Doctor, I've been through this twice before. The first time, they gave me too much of the stuff, and coming off was—I'd just as soon not go through that again, if you know what I mean."

Ryan's career in the Marine Corps had ended after a mere three months with a helicopter crash on the shores of Crete during a NATO exercise. The resulting back injury had sent Ryan to Bethesda Naval Medical Center, outside Washington, where the doctors had been a little too generous with their pain medications, and Ryan had taken two weeks to get over them. It was not an experience he wanted to repeat.

Sir Charles nodded thoughtfully. "I think so. Well, it's your arm." The nurse came back in as he made some notations on the chart. "Rotate the bed a bit."

Ryan hadn't noticed that the rack from which his arm hung was actually circular. As the head of the bed came up, his arm dropped to a more comfortable angle. The doctor looked over his glasses at Ryan's fingers.

"Would you wiggle them, please?" Ryan did so. "Good, that's very good. I didn't think there'd be any nerve damage. Doctor Ryan, I am going to prescribe something mild, just enough to keep the edge off it. I will require that you take the medications which I prescribe." Scott's head came around to face Ryan directly. "I've never yet got a patient addicted to narcotics, and I do not propose to start with you. Don't be pigheaded: pain, discomfort will retard your recovery—unless, that is, you *want* to remain in hospital for several months?"

"Message received, Sir Charles."

"Right." The surgeon smiled. "If you should feel the need for something stronger, I shall be here all day. Just ring nurse Miss Kittiwake here." The girl beamed in anticipation.

"How about something to eat?"

"You think you can keep something down?"

If not, Kittiwake will probably love to help me throw up. "Doc, in the last thirty-six hours I've had a continental breakfast and a light lunch."

"Very well. We'll try some soft foods." He made another notation on the chart and flashed a look to Kittiwake: *Keep an eye on him.* She nodded.

"Your charming wife told me that you are quite obstinate. We'll see about that. Still and all you are doing rather nicely. You can thank your physical condition for that—and my outstanding surgical skill, of course." Scott chuckled to himself. "After breakfast an orderly will help you freshen up for your more, ah, official visitors. Oh, don't expect to see your family soon. They were quite exhausted last night. I gave your wife something to help her sleep; I hope she took it. Your darling little daughter was all done in." Scott gave Ryan a serious look. "I was not misleading you earlier. Discomfort *will* slow your recovery. Do what I tell you and we'll have you out of that bed in a week, and discharged in two—perhaps. But you must do exactly as I say."

"Understood, sir. And thanks. Cathy said you did a good job on the arm."

Scott tried to shrug it off. The smile showed only a little. "One must take proper care of one's guests. I'll be back late this afternoon to see how you are progressing." He left, mumbling instructions to the nurse.

The police arrived in force at 8:30. By this time Ryan had been able to eat his hospital breakfast and wash up. Breakfast had been a huge disappointment, with Wilson collapsing in laughter at Ryan's comment on its appearance—but Kittiwake had been so downcast from this that Ryan had felt constrained to eat all of it, even the stewed prunes that he'd loathed since childhood. Only after finishing had he realized that her demeanor had probably been a sham, a device to get him to eat all the slop. *Nurses,* he reminded himself, *are tricky.* At eight the orderly had arrived to help him clean up. Ryan shaved himself, with the orderly holding the mirror and clucking every time he nicked himself. Four nicks—Ryan customarily used an electric shaver, and hadn't faced a bare blade in years. By 8:30 Ryan felt and looked human again. Kittiwake had brought in a second cup of coffee. It wasn't very good, but it was still coffee.

There were three police officers, very senior ones, Ryan thought, from the way Wilson snapped to his feet and scurried about to arrange chairs for them before excusing himself out the door.

James Owens appeared to be the most senior, and inquired as to Ryan's condition—politely enough that he probably meant it. He reminded Ryan of his own father, a craggy, heavyset man, and, judging from his large, gnarled hands, one who had earned his way to commander's rank after more than a few years of walking the streets and enforcing the law the hard way.

Chief Superintendent William Taylor was about forty, younger than his Anti-Terrorist Branch colleague, and neater. Both senior detectives were well dressed, and both had the red-rimmed eyes that came from an uninterrupted night's work.

David Ashley was the youngest and best-dressed of the three. About Ryan's size and weight, perhaps five years older. He described himself as a representative of the Home Office, and he looked a great deal smoother than either of the others.

"You're quite certain you're up to this?" Taylor asked.

Ryan shrugged. "No sense waiting."

Owens took a cassette tape recorder from his portfolio and set it on the bedstand. He plugged in two microphones, one facing Ryan, the other toward the officers. He punched the record button and announced the date, time, and place.

"Doctor Ryan," Owens asked formally, "do you know that this interview is being recorded?"

"Yes, sir."

"And do you have any objection to this?"

"No, sir. May I ask a question?"

"Certainly," Owens answered.

"Am I being charged with anything? If so, I would like to contact my embassy and have an attor—" Ryan was more than a little uneasy to be the focus of so much high-level police attention, but was cut off by the chuckles of Mr. Ashley. He noted that the other police officers deferred to him for the answer.

"Doctor Ryan, you may just have things the wrong way 'round. For the record, sir, we have no intention whatever of charging you with anything. Were we to do so, I dare say we'd be looking for new employment by day's end."

Ryan nodded, not showing his relief. He'd not yet been sure of this, sure only that the law doesn't have to make sense. Owens began reading his questions from a yellow pad.

"Can you give us your name and address, please?"

"John Patrick Ryan. Our mailing address is Annapolis, Maryland. Our home is at Peregrine Cliff, about ten miles south of Annapolis on the Chesapeake Bay."

"And your occupation?" Owens checked off something on his pad.

"I guess you could say I have a couple of jobs. I'm an instructor in history at the U.S. Naval Academy in Annapolis. I lecture occasionally at the Naval War College in Newport, and from time to time I do a little consulting work on the side."

"That's all?" Ashley inquired with a friendly smile—or was it friendly? Ryan asked himself. Jack wondered just how much they'd managed to find out about him in the past—what? fifteen hours or so—and exactly what Ashley was hinting at. *You're no cop,* Ryan thought. *What exactly are you?* Regardless, he had to stick to his cover story, that he was a part-time consultant to the Mitre Corporation.

"And the purpose of your visit to this country?" Owens went on.

"Combination vacation and research trip. I'm gathering data for a new book, and Cathy needed some time off. Sally is still a preschooler, so we decided to head over now and miss the tourist season." Ryan took a cigarette from the pack Wilson had left behind. Ashley lit it from a gold lighter. "In my coat—wherever that is—you'll find letters of introduction to your Admiralty and the Royal Naval College at Dartmouth."

"We have the letters," Owens replied. "Quite illegible, I'm afraid, and I fear your suit is a total loss also. What the blood did not ruin, your wife and our sergeant finished off with a knife. So when did you arrive in Britain?"

"It's still Thursday, right? Well, we got in Tuesday night from Dulles International outside Washington. Arrived about seven-thirty, got to the hotel about nine-thirty or so, had a snack sent up, and went right to sleep. Flying always messes me up—jet lag, whatever. I conked right out." That was not exactly true, but Ryan didn't think they needed to know *everything*.

Owens nodded. They had already learned why Ryan hated flying. "And yesterday?"

"I woke up about seven, I guess, had breakfast and a paper sent up, then just kinda lazed around until about eight-thirty. I arranged to meet Cathy and Sally in the park around four, then caught a cab to the Admiralty building—close, as it turned out, I could have walked it. As I said, I had a letter of introduction to see Admiral Sir Alexander Woodson, the man in charge of your naval archives—he's retired, actually. He took me down to a musty sub-sub-basement. He had the stuff I wanted all ready for me.

"I came over to look at some signal digests. Admiralty signals between London and Admiral Sir James Somerville. He was commander of your Indian Ocean fleet in the early months of 1942, and that's one of the things I'm writing about. So I spend the next three hours reading over faded carbon copies of naval dispatches and taking notes."

"On this?" Ashley held up Ryan's clipboard. Jack snatched it from his hands.

"Thank God!" Ryan exclaimed. "I was sure it got lost." He opened it and set it up on the bedstand, then typed in some instructions. "Ha! It still works!"

"What exactly is that thing?" Ashley wanted to know. All three got out of their chairs to look at it.

"This is my baby." Ryan grinned. On opening the clipboard he revealed a typewriter-style keyboard and a yellow Liquid Crystal Diode display. Outwardly it looked like an expensive clipboard, about an inch thick and bound in leather. ''It's a Cambridge Datamaster Model-C Field Computer. A friend of mine makes them. It has an MC-68000 microprocessor, and two megabytes of bubble memory.''

''Care to translate that?'' Taylor asked.

''Sorry. It's a portable computer. The microprocessor is what does the actual work. Two megabytes means that the memory stores up to two million characters—enough for a whole book—and since it uses bubble memory, you don't lose the information when you switch it off. A guy I went to school with set up a company to make these little darlings. He hit on me for some start-up capital. I use an Apple at home, this one's just for carrying around.''

''We knew it was some sort of computer, but our chaps couldn't make it work,'' Ashley said.

''Security device. The first time you use it, you input your user's code and activate the lockout. Afterward, unless you type in the code, it doesn't work—period.''

''Indeed?'' Ashley observed. ''How foolproof?''

''You'd have to ask Fred. Maybe you could read the data right off the bubble chips. I don't know how computers work. I just use 'em,'' Ryan explained. ''Anyway, here are my notes.''

''Getting back to your activities of yesterday,'' Owens said, giving Ashley a cool look. ''We now have you to noon.''

''Okay. I broke for lunch. A guy on the ground floor directed me to a—a pub, I guess, two blocks away. I don't remember the name of the place. I had a sandwich and a beer while I played with this thing. That took about half an hour. I spent another hour at the Admiralty building before I checked out. Left about quarter of two, I suppose. I thanked Admiral Woodson—very good man. I caught a cab to—don't remember the address, it was on one of my letters. North of—Regent's Park, I think. Admiral Sir Roger DeVere. He served under Somerville. He wasn't there. His housekeeper said he got called out of town suddenly due to a death in the family. So I left a message that I'd been there and flagged another cab back downtown. I decided to get out a few blocks early and walk the rest of the way.''

''Why?'' Taylor asked.

''Mainly I was stiff from all the sitting—in the Admiralty building, the flight, the cab. I needed a stretch. I usually jog every day, and I get restless when I miss it.''

''Where did you get out?'' Owens asked.

''I don't know the name of the street. If you show me a map I can probably point it out.'' Owens nodded for him to go on. ''Anyway, I nearly got run over by a double-decker bus, and one of your uniformed cops told me not to jaywalk—'' Owens looked surprised at that and scribbled some notes. Perhaps they hadn't learned of that encounter. ''I picked up a magazine at a street stand and met Cathy about, oh, three-forty or so. They were early, too.''

''And how had she spent her day?'' Ashley inquired. Ryan was certain that they had this information already.

''Shopping, mainly. Cathy's been over here a few times, and likes to shop in London. She was last here about three years ago for a surgical convention, but I couldn't make the trip.''

''Left you with the little one?'' Ashley smiled thinly again. Ryan sensed that Owens was annoyed with him.

"Grandparents. That was before her mom died. I was doing comps for my doctorate at Georgetown, couldn't get out of it. As it was I got my degree in two and a half years, and I sweated blood that last year between the university and seminars at the Center for Strategic and International Studies. This was supposed to be a vacation." Ryan grimaced. "The first real vacation since our honeymoon."

"What were you doing when the attack took place?" Owens got things back on track. All three inquisitors seemed to lean forward in their seats.

"Looking the wrong way. We were talking about what we'd do for dinner when the grenade went off."

"You knew it was a grenade?" Taylor asked.

Ryan nodded. "Yeah. They make a distinctive sound. I hate the damned things, but that's one of the little toys the Marines trained me to use at Quantico. Same thing with the machine-gunner. At Quantico we were exposed to East Bloc weapons. I've handled the AK-47. The sound it makes is different from our stuff, and that's a useful thing to know in combat. How come they didn't both have AKs?"

"As near as we can determine," Owens said, "the man you wounded disabled the car with a rifle-launched antitank grenade. Forensic evidence points to this. His rifle, therefore, was probably one of the new AK-74s, the small-caliber one, fitted to launch grenades. Evidently he didn't have time to remove the grenade-launcher assembly and decided to press on with his pistol. He had a stick grenade also, you know." Jack didn't know about the rifle grenade, but the type of hand grenade he'd seen suddenly leaped out of his memory.

"The antitank kind?" Ryan asked.

"You know about that, do you?" Ashley responded.

"I used to be a Marine, remember? Called the RKG-something, isn't it? Supposed to be able to punch a hole in a light armored vehicle or rip up a truck pretty good." *Where the hell did they get those little rascals—and why didn't they use them . . . ? You're missing something, Jack.*

"Then what?" Owens asked.

"First thing, I got my wife and kid down on the deck. The traffic stopped pretty quick. I kept my head up to see what was happening."

"Why?" Taylor inquired.

"I don't know," Ryan said slowly. "Training, maybe. I wanted to see what the hell was going on—call it stupid curiosity. I saw the one guy hosing down the Rolls and the other one hustling around the back, like he was trying to bag anyone who tried to jump out of the car. I saw that if I moved to my left I could get closer. I was screened by the stopped cars. All of a sudden I was within fifty feet or so. The AK gunner was screened behind the Rolls, and the pistolero had his back to me. I saw that I had a chance, and I guess I took it."

"Why?" It was Owens this time, very quiet.

"Good question. I don't know, I really don't." Ryan was silent for half a minute. "It made me mad. Everyone I've met over here so far has been pretty nice, and all of a sudden I see these two cocksuckers committing murder right the hell in front of me."

"Did you guess who they were?" Taylor asked.

"Doesn't take much imagination, does it? That pissed me off, too. I guess that's it—anger. Maybe that's what motivates people in combat," Ryan mused. "I'll have to think about that. Anyway, like I said, I saw the chance and I took it.

"It was easy—I was very lucky." Owens' eyebrows went up at that understatement. "The guy with the pistol was dumb. He should have checked his back.

Instead he just kept looking at his kill zone—*very* dumb. You always 'check-six.' I blindsided him.'' Ryan grinned. ''My coach would have been proud—I really stuck him good. But I guess I ought to have had my pads on, 'cause the doc says I broke something up here when I hit him. He went down pretty hard. I got his gun and shot him—you want to know why I did that, right?''

''Yes,'' Owens replied.

''I didn't want him to get up.''

''He was unconscious—he didn't wake up for two hours, and had a nasty concussion when he did.''

If I'd known he had that grenade, I wouldn't have shot him in the ass! ''How was I supposed to know that?'' Ryan asked reasonably. ''I was about to go up against somebody with a light machine gun, and I didn't need a bad guy behind me. So I neutralized him. I could have put one through the back of his head—at Quantico when they say 'neutralize,' they mean *kill.* My dad was the cop. Most of what I know about police procedures comes from watching TV, and I *know* most of that's wrong. All I knew was that I couldn't afford to have him come at me from behind. I can't say I'm especially proud of it, but at the time it seemed like a good idea.

''I moved around the right-rear corner of the car and looked around. I saw the guy was using a pistol. Your man Wilson explained that to me—that was lucky, too. I wasn't real crazy about taking an AK on with a dinky little handgun. He saw me come around. We both fired about the same time—I just shot straighter, I guess.''

Ryan stopped. He hadn't meant it to sound like that. *Is that how it was? If* you *don't know, who does?* Ryan had learned that in a crisis, time compresses and dilates—seemingly at the same time. *It also fools your memory, doesn't it? What else could I have done?* He shook his head.

''I don't know,'' he said again. ''Maybe I should have tried something else. Maybe I should have said, 'Drop it!' or 'Freeze!' like they do on TV—but there just wasn't time. Everything was *right now*—him or me—do you know what I mean? You don't . . . you don't reason all this out when you only have half a second of decision time. I guess you go on training and instinct. The only training I've had was in the Green Machine, the Corps. They don't teach you to arrest people—Christ's sake, I didn't *want* to kill anybody, I just didn't have a hell of a choice in the matter.'' Ryan paused for a moment.

''Why didn't he—quit, run away, something! He saw I had him. He must have known I had him cold.'' Ryan slumped back into the pillow. Having to articulate what had happened brought it back all too vividly. *A man is dead because of you, Jack. All the way dead. He had his instincts, too, didn't he? But yours worked better—so why doesn't that make you feel good?*

''Doctor Ryan,'' Owens said calmly, ''we three have personally interviewed six people, all of whom had a clear view of the incident. From what they have told us, you have related the circumstances to us with remarkable clarity. Given the facts of the matter, I—we—do not see that you had any choice at all. It is as certain as such things can possibly be that you did precisely the right thing. And your second shot did not matter, if that is troubling you. Your first went straight through his heart.''

Jack nodded. ''Yeah, I could see that. The second shot was completely automatic, like my hand did it without being told. The gun came back down and zap! No thought at all . . . funny how your brain works. It's like one part does the doing and another part does the watching and advising. The 'watching' part saw the first round go right through his ten-ring, but the 'doing' part kept going till he went down. I might have tried to squeeze off another round for all I know, but the gun was empty.''

"The Marines taught you to shoot very well indeed,'' Taylor observed.

Ryan shook his head. "Dad taught me when I was a kid. The Corps doesn't make a big deal about pistols anymore—they're just for show. If the bad guys get that close, it's time to leave. I carried a rifle. Anyway, the guy was only fifteen feet away.'' Owens made some more notes.

"The car took off a few seconds later. I didn't get much of a look at the driver. It could have been a man or a woman. He or she was white, that's all I can say. The car went whippin' up the street and turned, last I saw of it.''

"It was one of our London taxis—did you notice that?'' Taylor asked.

Ryan blinked. "Oh, you're right. I didn't really think about that—that's dumb! Hell, you have a million of the damned things around. No wonder they used one of those.''

"Eight thousand six hundred seventy-nine, to be exact,'' Owens said. "Five thousand nine hundred nineteen of which are painted black.''

A light went off in Ryan's head. "Tell me, was this an assassination attempt or were they trying to kidnap them?''

"We're not sure about that. You might be interested to know that Sinn Fein, the political wing of the PIRA, released a statement completely disowning the incident.''

"You believe that?'' Ryan asked. With pain medications still coursing through his system, he didn't quite notice how skillfully Taylor had parried his question.

"Yes, we are leaning in that direction. Even the Provos aren't this crazy, you know. Something like this has far too high a political price. They learned that much from killing Lord Mountbatten—wasn't even the PIRA who did that, but the INLA, the Irish National Liberation Army. Regardless, it cost them a lot of money from their American sympathizers,'' Taylor said.

"I see from the papers that your fellow citizens—''

"Subjects,'' Ashley corrected.

"Whatever, your people are pretty worked up about this.''

"Indeed they are, Doctor Ryan. It is rather remarkable how terrorists can always seem to find a way to shock us, no matter what horrors have gone before,'' Owens noted. His voice was wholly professional, but Ryan sensed that the chief of Anti-Terrorist Branch was willing to rip the head right off the surviving terrorist with his bare hands. They looked strong enough to do just that. "So what happened next?''

"I made sure the guy I shot—the second one—was dead. Then I checked the car. The driver—well, you know about that, and the security officer. One of your people, Mr. Owens?''

"Charlie was a friend of mine. He's been with the Royal Family's security detail for three years now. . . .'' Owens spoke almost as though the man were still alive, and Ryan wondered if they had ever worked together. Police make especially close friendships, he knew.

"Well, you guys know the rest. I hope somebody gives that redcoat a pat on the head. Thank God he took the time to think it all out—at least long enough for your guy to show up and calm him down. Would have been embarrassing for everybody if he'd stuck that bayonet out my back.''

Owens grunted agreement. "Indeed it would."

"Was that rifle loaded?" Ryan asked.

"If it was," Ashley replied, "why didn't he shoot?"

"A crowded street isn't the best place to use a high-powered rifle, even if you're sure of your target," Ryan answered. "It was loaded, wasn't it?"

"We cannot discuss security matters," Owens said.

I knew *it was loaded,* Ryan told himself. "Where the hell did he come from, anyway? The Palace is a good ways off."

"Clarence House—the white building adjoining St. James's Palace. The terrorists picked a bad time—or perhaps a bad place—for their attack. There is a guard post at the southwest corner of the building. The guard changes every two hours. When the attack took place, the change was just under way. That meant that four soldiers were there at the time, not just one. The police on duty at the Palace heard the explosion and automatic fire. The Sergeant in charge ran to the gate to see what was going on and yelled for a guardsman to follow."

"He's the one who sounded the alarm, right? That's how the rest of them arrived so fast?"

"Charlie Winston," Owens said. "The Rolls has an electronic attack alarm—you don't need to tell anyone that. That alerted headquarters. Sergeant Price acted entirely on his own initiative. Unfortunately for him, the guardsman was a hurdler—the lad runs track and field—and vaulted the barriers there. Price tried to do it also, but he fell down and broke his nose. He had a devil of a time catching up, plus sending out his own alarm on his portable radio."

"Well, I'm glad he caught up when he did. That trooper scared the hell out of me. I hope your Sergeant gets a pat on the head, too."

"The Queen's Police Medal for starters, and the thanks of Her Majesty," Ashley said. "One thing that has confused us, Doctor Ryan. You left the military with a physical disability, yet you evidenced none of this yesterday."

"You know that after I left the Corps, I went into the brokerage business. I made something of a name for myself, and Cathy's father came down to talk to me. That's when I met Cathy. I passed on the invitation to move to New York, but Cathy and I hit it right off. One thing led to another, and pretty soon we were engaged. I wore a back brace then, because every so often my back would go bad on me. Well, it happened again right after we got engaged, and Cathy took me into Johns Hopkins to have one of her teachers check me out. One was Stanley Rabinowisz, professor of neurosurgery there. He ran me through three days of tests and said he could fix me good as new.

"It turned out that the docs at Bethesda had goofed my myelogram. No reflection on them, they were sharp young docs, but Stan's about the best there is. Good as his word, too. He opened me up that Friday, and two months later I *was* almost as good as new," Ryan said. "Anyway, that's the story of Ryan's back. I just happened to fall in love with a pretty girl who was studying to be a surgeon."

"Your wife is certainly a most versatile and competent woman," Owens agreed.

"And you found her pushy," Ryan observed.

"No, Doctor Ryan. People under stress are never at their best. Your wife also examined Their Royal Highnesses on the scene, and that was most useful to us. She refused to leave your side until you were under competent medical care; one can hardly fault her for that. She did find our identification procedures a touch longwinded, I think, and she was quite naturally anxious about you. We might have moved things along more quickly—"

"No need to apologize, sir. My dad was a cop. I know the score. I understand you had trouble identifying us."

"Just over three hours—a timing problem, you see. We had your passport out of your coat, and your driving license, which, we were glad to see, had your photograph. Our initial request to your Legal Attaché was just before five, and that made it noon in America. Lunchtime, you see. He called the FBI's Baltimore field office, who in turn called their Annapolis office. The identification business is fairly straightforward—first they had to find some chaps at your Naval Academy who knew who you were, when you came over, and so forth. Next they found the travel agent who booked your flight and hotel. Another agent went to your motor vehicle registration agency. Many of these people were off eating lunch, and we reckon that cost us roughly an hour. Simultaneously he—the Attaché—sent a query to your Marine Corps. Within three hours we had a fairly complete history on you—including fingerprints. We had your fingerprints from your travel documents and the hotel registration, and they matched your military records, of course."

"Three hours, eh?" *Dinnertime here, and lunchtime at home, and they did it all in three hours. Damn.*

"While all that was going on we had to interview your wife several times to make sure that she related everything she saw—"

"And she gave it to you exactly the same way every time, right?" Ryan asked.

"Correct," Owens said. He smiled. "That is quite remarkable, you know."

Ryan grinned. "Not for Cathy. Some things, medicine especially, she's a real machine. I'm surprised she didn't hand you a roll of film."

"She said that herself," Owens replied. "The photographs in the paper are from a Japanese tourist—that's a cliché, isn't it?—half a block away with a telephoto lens. You might be interested to know that your Marine Corps thinks rather highly of you, by the way." Owens consulted his notes. "Tied for first in your class at Quantico, and your fitness reports were excellent."

"So, you're satisfied I'm a good guy?"

"We were convinced of that from the first moment," Taylor said. "One must be thorough in major felony cases, however, and this one obviously had more than its share of complications."

"There's one thing that bothers me," Jack said. There was more than one, but his brain was working too slowly to classify them all.

"What's that?" Owens asked.

"What the hell were they—the Royals, you call them?—doing out on the street with only one guard—wait a minute." Ryan's head cocked to one side. He went on, speaking rather slowly as his mind struggled to arrange his thoughts. "That ambush was planned—this wasn't any accidental encounter. But the bad guys caught 'em on the fly. . . . They had to hit a particular car in a particular place. Somebody timed this one out. There were some more people involved in this, weren't there?" Ryan heard a lot of silence for a moment. It was all the answer he needed. "Somebody with a radio . . . those characters had to know that they were coming, the route they'd take, and exactly when they got into the kill zone. Even then it wouldn't be all that easy, 'cause you have to worry about traffic. . . ."

"Just an historian, Doctor Ryan?" Ashley asked.

"They teach you how to do ambushes in the Marines. If you want to ambush a specific target . . . first, you have to have intelligence information; second, you choose your ground; third, you put your own security guys out to tell you when the target is coming—that's just the bare-bones requirements. Why here—why St.

James's Park, The Mall?'' *The terrorist is a political creature. The target and the place are chosen for political effect,* Ryan told himself. ''You didn't answer my question before: was this an assassination or an attempted kidnapping?''

''We are not entirely sure,'' Owens answered.

Ryan looked over his guests. He'd just touched an open nerve. *They disabled the car with an antitank rifle-grenade, and both of them had the hand-thrown kind, too. If they just wanted to kill . . . the grenades would defeat any armor on the car, why use guns at all? No, if this was a straight assassination attempt, they would not have taken so long, would they? You just fibbed to me, Mr. Owens. This was definitely a kidnap attempt and you know it.*

''Why just the one security officer in the car, then? You have to protect your people better than that.'' *What was it Tony said? An unscheduled trip? The first requirement for a successful ambush is good* intelligence. . . . *You can't pursue this, idiot!* The Commander solved the problem for Jack.

''Well, I believe we covered everything rather nicely. We'll probably be back tomorrow,'' Owens said.

''How are the terrorists—the one I wounded, I mean.''

''He has not been terribly cooperative. Won't speak to us at all, not even to tell us his name—old story dealing with this lot. We've only identified him a few hours ago. No previous criminal record at all—his name appeared as a possible player in two minor cases, but nothing more than that. He is recovering quite nicely, and in three weeks or so,'' Taylor said coldly, ''he will be taken before the Queen's Bench, tried before a jury of twelve good men and true, convicted, and sentenced to spend the remainder of his natural life at a secure prison.''

''Only three weeks?'' Ryan asked.

''The case is clear-cut,'' Owens said. ''We have three photographs from our Japanese friend that show this lad holding his gun behind the car, and nine good eyewitnesses. There will be no mucking about with this lad.''

''And I'll be there to see it,'' Ryan observed.

''Of course. You will be our most important witness, Doctor. A formality, but a necessary one. And no claim of lunacy like the chap who tried to kill your President. This boy is a university graduate, with honors, and he comes from a good family.''

Ryan shook his head. ''Ain't that a hell of a thing? But most of the really bad ones are, aren't they?''

''You know about terrorists?'' Ashley asked.

''Just things I've read,'' Ryan answered quickly. *That was a mistake, Jack. Cover it.* ''Officer Wilson said the ULA were Maoists.''

''Correct,'' Taylor said.

''That really is crazy. Hell, even the Chinese aren't Maoists anymore, at least the last time I checked they weren't. Oh—what about my family?''

Ashley laughed. ''About time you asked, Doctor. We couldn't very well leave them at the hotel, could we? It was arranged for them to be put up at a highly secure location.''

''You need not be concerned,'' Owens agreed. ''They are quite safe. My word on it.''

''Where, exactly?'' Ryan wanted to know.

''A security matter, I'm afraid,'' Ashley said. The three inquisitors shared an amused look. Owens checked his watch and shot a look to the others.

''Well,'' Owens said. He switched off the tape recorder. ''We do not wish to trouble you further the day after surgery. We will probably be back to check a few additional details. For the moment, sir, you have the thanks of all of us at the Yard for doing our job for us.''

''How long will I have Mr. Wilson here?''

''Indefinitely. The ULA are likely to be somewhat annoyed with you,'' Owens said. ''And it would be most embarrassing for us if they were to make an attempt on your life and find you unprotected. We do not regard this as likely, mind, but one must be careful.''

''I can live with that,'' Ryan agreed. *I make a hell of a target here, don't I? A third-grader could kill me with a Popsicle stick.*

''The press want to see you,'' Taylor said.

''I'm thrilled.'' *Just what I need,* Ryan thought. ''Could you hold them off a bit?''

''Simple enough,'' Owens agreed. ''Your medical condition does not permit it at the moment. But you should get used to the idea. You are now something of a public figure.''

''Like hell!'' Ryan snorted. ''I like being obscure.'' *Then you should have stayed behind the tree, dumbass! Just what have you got yourself into?*

''You can't refuse to see them indefinitely, you know,'' Taylor said gently.

Jack let out a long breath. ''You're correct, of course. But not today. Tomorrow is soon enough.'' *Let the hubbub die down some first,* Ryan thought stupidly.

''One cannot always stay in the shadows, Doctor Ryan,'' Ashley said, standing. The others took their cue from him.

The cops and Ashley—Ryan now had him pegged as some kind of spook, intelligence or counterintelligence—took their leave. Wilson came back in, with Kittiwake trailing behind.

''Did they tire you out?'' the nurse asked.

''I think I'll live,'' Ryan allowed. Kittiwake thrust a thermometer in his mouth to make sure.

Forty minutes after the police had left, Ryan was typing happily away on his computer-toy, reviewing notes and drafting some fresh copy. Cathy Ryan's most frequent (and legitimate) complaint about her husband was that while he was reading—or worse, writing—the world could end around him without his taking notice. This was not entirely true. Jack did notice Wilson jumping to attention out the corner of his eye, but he did not look up until he had finished the paragraph. When he did, he saw that his new visitors were Her Majesty, the Queen of the United Kingdom of Great Britain and Northern Ireland, and her husband, the Duke of Edinburgh. His first coherent thought was a mental curse that no one had warned him. His second, that he must look very funny with his mouth hanging open.

''Good morning, Doctor Ryan,'' the Queen said agreeably. ''How are you feeling?''

''Uh, quite well, thank you, uh, Your Majesty. Won't you, uh, please sit down?'' Ryan tried to sit more erect in his bed, but was halted by a flash of pain from his shoulder. It helped to center his thoughts and reminded him that his medication was nearly due.

''We have no wish to impose,'' she said. Ryan sensed that she didn't wish to leave right away, either. He took a second to frame his response.

''Your Majesty, a visit from a head of state hardly qualifies as an imposition. I would be most grateful for your company.'' Wilson hustled to get two chairs and excused himself out the door as they sat.

The Queen was dressed in a peach-colored suit whose elegant simplicity must have made a noteworthy dent even in her clothing budget. The Duke was in a dark blue suit which finally made Ryan understand why his wife wanted him to buy some clothes over here.

''Doctor Ryan,'' she said formally, ''on our behalf, and that of our people, we wish to express to you our most profound gratitude for your action of yesterday. We are very much in your debt.''

Ryan nodded soberly. He wondered just how awful he looked. ''For my own part, ma'am, I am glad that I was able to be of service—but the truth of the matter is that I didn't really do all that much. Anyone could have done the same thing. I just happened to be the closest.''

''The police say otherwise,'' the Duke observed. ''And after viewing the scene myself, I am inclined to agree with them. I'm afraid you're a hero whether you like it or not.'' Jack remembered that this man had once been a professional naval officer—probably a good one. He had the look.

''Why did you do it, Doctor Ryan?'' the Queen asked. She examined his face closely.

Jack made a quick guess. ''Excuse me, ma'am, but are you asking why I took the chance, or why an Irish-American would take the chance?'' Jack was still ordering his own thoughts, examining his own memories. *Why* did *you do it? Will you ever know?* He saw that he'd guessed right and went on quickly.

''Your Majesty, I cannot speak to your Irish problem. I'm an American citizen, and my country has enough problems of its own without having to delve into someone else's. Where I come from we—that is, Irish-Americans—have made out pretty well. We're in all the professions, business, and politics, but your prototypical Irish-American is still a basic police officer or firefighter. The cavalry that won the West was a third Irish, and there are still plenty of us in uniform—especially the Marine Corps, as a matter of fact. Half of the local FBI office lived in my old neighborhood. They had names like Tully, Sullivan, O'Connor, and Murphy. My dad was a police officer for half his life, and the priests and nuns who educated me were mostly Irish, probably.

''Do you see what I mean, Your Majesty? In America we are the forces of order, the glue that holds society together—so what happens?

''Today, the most famous Irishmen in the world are the maniacs who leave bombs in parked cars, or assassins who kill people to make some sort of political point. I don't like that, and I know my dad wouldn't like it. He spent his whole working life taking animals like that off the street and putting them in cages where they belong. We've worked pretty hard to get where we are—too hard to be happy about being thought of as the relatives of terrorists.'' Jack smiled. ''I guess I understand how Italians feel about the Mafia. Anyway, I can't say that all this stuff paraded through my head yesterday, but I did kind of figure what was going on. I couldn't just sit there like a dummy and let murder be committed before my eyes and not do *something*. So I saw my chance and I took it.''

The Queen nodded thoughtfully. She regarded Ryan with a warm, friendly smile for a few moments and turned to look at her husband. The two communicated without words. They'd been married long enough for that, Ryan thought. When she turned back, he could see that a decision had been reached.

"So, then. How shall we reward you?"

"Reward, ma'am?" Ryan shook his head. "Thank you very much, but it's not necessary. I'm glad I was able to help. That's enough."

"No, Doctor Ryan, it is not enough. One of the nicer things about being Queen is that one is permitted to recognize meritorious conduct, then to reward it properly. The Crown cannot appear to be ungrateful." Her eyes sparkled with some private joke. Ryan found himself captivated by the woman's humanity. He'd read that some people found her to be less than intelligent. He already knew they were far off the mark. There was an active brain behind those eyes, and an active wit as well. "Accordingly, it has been decided that you shall be invested as a Knight Commander of the Victorian Order."

"What—er, I beg your pardon, ma'am?" Ryan blinked a few times as his brain tried to catch up with his ears.

"The Victorian Order is a recent development intended to reward those persons who have rendered personal service to the Crown. Certainly you qualify. This is the first case in many years that an heir to the throne has been saved from almost certain death. As an historian yourself, you might be interested to learn that our own scholars are in disagreement as to when was our most recent precedent—in any event, you will henceforth be known as Sir John Ryan."

Again Jack thought that he must look rather funny with his mouth open.

"Your Majesty, American law—"

"We know," she interrupted smoothly. "The Prime Minister will be discussing this with your President later today. We believe that in view of the special nature of this case, and in the interest of Anglo-American relations, the matter will be settled amicably."

"There is ample precedent for this," the Duke went on. "After the Second World War a number of American officers were accorded similar recognition. Your Fleet Admiral Nimitz, for example, became a Knight Commander of the Bath, along with Generals Eisenhower, Bradley, Patton, and a number of others.

"For the purposes of American law, it will probably be considered honorary—but for our purposes it will be quite real."

"Well." Ryan fumbled for something to say. "Your Majesty, insofar as this does not conflict with the laws of my country, I will be deeply honored to accept." The Queen beamed.

"That's settled, then. Now, how are you feeling—really feeling?"

"I've felt worse, ma'am. I have no complaints—I just wish I'd moved a little faster."

The Duke smiled. "Being wounded makes you appear that much more heroic—nothing like a little drama."

Especially if it's someone else's shoulder, my Lord Duke, Ryan thought. A small bell went off in his head. "Excuse me, this knighthood, does it mean that my wife will be called—"

"Lady Ryan? Of course." The Queen flashed her Christmas-tree smile again.

Jack grinned broadly. "You know, when I left Merrill Lynch, Cathy's father was madder than—he was very angry with me, said I'd never amount to anything writing history books. Maybe this will change his mind." He was sure that Cathy would not mind the title—*Lady Ryan*. No, she wouldn't mind that one little bit.

"Not so bad a thing after all?"

"No, sir, and please forgive me if I gave that impression. I'm afraid you caught me a little off balance.'' Ryan shook his head. *This whole damned affair has me a lot off balance.* ''Might I ask a question, sir?''

''Certainly.''

''The police wouldn't tell me where they're keeping my family.'' This drew a hearty laugh. The Queen answered.

''It is the opinion of the police that there might exist the possibility of a reprisal against you or your family. Therefore it was decided that they should be moved to a more secure location. Under the circumstances, we decided that they might most easily be moved to the Palace—it was the least thing we could do. When we left, your wife and daughter were fast asleep, and we left strict instructions that they should not be disturbed.''

''The Palace?''

''We have ample room for guests, I assure you,'' the Queen replied.

''Oh, Lord!'' Ryan muttered.

''You have an objection?'' the Duke asked.

''My little girl, she—''

''Olivia?'' the Queen said, rather surprised. ''She's a lovely child. When we saw her last night she was sleeping like an angel.''

''Sally''—Olivia had been a peace offering to Cathy's family that hadn't worked; it was the name of her grandmother—''is a little angel, asleep, but when she wakes up she's more like a little tornado, and she's very good at breaking things. Especially valuable things.''

''What a dreadful thing to say!'' Her Majesty feigned shock. ''That lovely little girl. The police told us that she broke hearts throughout Scotland Yard last evening. I fear you exaggerate, Sir John.''

''Yes, ma'am.'' There was no arguing with a queen.

3. Flowers and Families

Wilson had been mistaken in his assessment. The escape had taken longer than anyone at the Yard had thought. Six hundred miles away, a Sabena flight was landing outside of Cork. The passenger in seat 23-D of the Boeing 737 was entirely unremarkable; his sandy hair was cut medium-close, and he was dressed like a middle-level executive in a neat but rumpled suit that gave the entirely accurate impression of a man who'd spent a long day on the job and gotten too little sleep before catching a flight home. An experienced traveler to be sure, with one carry-on flight bag. If asked, he could have given a convincing discourse on the wholesale fish business in the accent of Southwestern Ireland. He could change accents as easily as most men changed shirts; a useful skill, since TV news crews had made the patois of his native Belfast recognizable the world over. He read the *London Times* on the flight, and the topic of discussion in his seat row, as with the rest of the aircraft, was the story which covered the front page.

''A terrible thing, it is,'' he'd agreed with the man in 23-E, a Belgian dealer in machine tools who could not have known how an event might be terrible in more than one way.

All the months of planning, the painstakingly gathered intelligence, the rehearsals carried out right under the Brit noses, the three escape routes, the radiomen—all for nothing because of this bloody meddler. He examined the photo on the front page.

Who are you, Yank? he wondered. *John Patrick Ryan. Historian—a bloody academic! Ex-Marine—trust a damned bootneck to stick his nose where it doesn't belong!* John Patrick Ryan. *You're a bloody Catholic, aren't you? Well, Johnny nearly put paid on your account. . . . Too bad about Johnny. Good man Johnny was, dependable, loved his guns, and true to the Cause.*

The plane finally came to a stop at the jetway. Forward, the stewardess opened the door, and the passengers rose to get their bags from the overhead stowage. He got his, and joined the slow movement forward. He tried to be philosophical about it. In his years as a "player," he'd seen operations go awry for the most ridiculous of reasons. But this op was so important. So *much* planning. He shook his head as he tucked the paper under his arm. *We'll just have to try again, that's all. We can afford to be patient.* One failure, he told himself, didn't matter in the great scheme of things. The other side had been lucky this time. *We only have to be lucky once.* The men in the H-blocks weren't going anywhere.

What about Sean? A mistake to have taken him along. He'd helped plan the operation from the beginning. Sean knows a great deal about the Organization. He set that worry aside as he stepped off the aircraft. *Sean would never talk. Not Sean, not with his girl in her grave these past five years, from a para's stray bullet.*

He wasn't met, of course. The other men who had been part of the operation were already back, their equipment left behind in rubbish bins, wiped clean of fingerprints. Only he had the risk of exposure, but he was sure that this Ryan fellow hadn't got a good look at his face. He thought back again to be sure. No. The look of surprise on his face, the look of pain he'd seen there. The American couldn't have gotten much of a look—if he had, an identikit composite picture would be in the press already, complete with the moppy wig and fake glasses.

He walked out of the terminal building to the parking lot, his travel bag slung over his shoulder, searching in his pocket for the keys that had set off the airport metal detector in Brussels—what a laugh that was! He smiled for the first time in nearly a day. It was a clear, sunny day, another glorious Irish fall it was. He drove his year-old BMW—a man with a business cover had to have a full disguise, after all—down the road to the safehouse. He was already planning two more operations. Both would require a lot of time, but time was the one thing he had in unlimited quantity.

It was easy enough to tell when it was time for another pain medication. Ryan was unconsciously flexing his left hand at the far end of the cast. It didn't reduce the pain, but did seem to move it about somewhat as the muscles and tendons changed place slightly. It bothered his concentration however much he tried to shut it out. Jack remembered all the TV shows in which the detective or otherwise employed hero took a round in the shoulder but recovered fully in time for the last commercial. The human shoulder—his, at any rate—was a solid collection of bones that bullets—*one* bullet—all too easily broke. As the time for another medication approached it seemed that he could feel every jagged edge of every broken bone grating against its neighbor as he breathed, and even the gentle tapping of his right-hand fingers on the keyboard seemed to ripple across his body to the focus of his pain until he had to stop and watch the wall clock—for the first time he wanted Kittiwake to appear with his next installment of chemical bliss.

Until he remembered his fear. The pain of his back injury had made his first week at Bethesda a living hell. He knew that his present injury paled by comparison, but the body does not remember pain, and the shoulder was *here and now*. He forced himself to remember that pain medications had made his back problem almost tolerable . . . except that the doctors had gotten just a little too generous with his dosages. More than the pain, Ryan dreaded withdrawal from morphine sulphate. That had lasted a week, the wanting that seemed to draw his entire body into some vast empty place, someplace where his innermost self found itself entirely alone and *needing*. . . . Ryan shook his head. The pain rippled through his left arm and shoulder and he forced himself to welcome it. *I'm not going to go through that again. Never again.*

The door opened. It wasn't Kittiwake—the med was still fourteen minutes away. Ryan had noticed a uniform outside the door when it had opened before. Now he was sure. A thirtyish uniformed officer came in with a floral arrangement and he was followed by another who was similarly loaded. A scarlet and gold ribbon decorated the first, a gift from the Marine Corps, followed by another from the American Embassy.

"Quite a few more, sir," one uniformed officer said.

"The room isn't all that big. Can you give me the cards and spread these around some? I'm sure there's people around who'd like them." *And who wants to live in a jungle?* Within ten minutes Ryan had a pile of cards, notes, and telegrams. He found that reading the words of others was better than reading his own when it came to blocking out the ache of his damaged shoulder.

Kittiwake arrived. She gave the flowers only a fleeting glance before administering Ryan's medication, and hustled out with scarcely a word. Ryan learned why five minutes later.

His next visitor was the Prince of Wales. Wilson snapped to his feet again, and Jack wondered if the kid's knees were tiring of this. The med was already working. His shoulder was drifting farther away, but along with this came a slight feeling of light-headedness as from a couple of stiff drinks. Maybe that was part of the reason for what happened next.

"Howdy." Jack smiled. "How are you feeling, sir?"

"Quite well, thank you." The answering smile contained no enthusiasm. The Prince looked very tired, his thin face stretched an extra inch or so, with a lingering sadness around the eyes. His shoulders drooped within the conservative gray suit.

"Why don't you sit down, sir?" Ryan invited. "You look as though you had a tougher night than I did."

"Yes, thank you, Doctor Ryan." He made another attempt to smile. It failed. "And how are you feeling?"

"Reasonably well, Your Highness. And how is your wife—excuse me, how is the Princess doing?"

The Prince's words did not come easily, and he had trouble looking up to Ryan from his chair. "We both regret that she could not come with me. She's still somewhat disturbed—in shock, I believe. She had a very . . . bad experience."

Brains splattered over her face. I suppose you might call that a bad experience. "I saw. I understand that neither of you was physically injured, thank God. I presume your child also?"

"Yes, all thanks to you, Doctor."

Jack tried another one-armed shrug. The gesture didn't hurt so much this time. "Glad to help, sir—I just wish I hadn't got myself shot in the process." His attempt at levity died on his lips. He'd said the wrong thing in the wrong way. The Prince looked at Jack very curiously for a moment, but then his eyes went flat again.

"We would all have been killed except for you, you know—and on behalf of my family and myself—well, thank you. It's not enough just to say that—" His Highness went on, then halted again and struggled to find a few more words. "But it's the best I can manage. I wasn't able to manage very much yesterday, come to that," he concluded, staring quietly at the foot of the bed.

Aha! Ryan thought. The Prince stood and turned to leave. *What do I do now?*

"Sir, why don't you sit down and let's talk this one over for a minute, okay?"

His Highness turned back. For a moment he looked as though he would say something, but the drawn face changed again and turned away.

"Your Highness, I really think . . ." No effect. *I can't let him go out of here like this. Well, if* good *manners won't work*—Jack's voice became sharp.

"Hold it!" The Prince turned with a look of great surprise. *"Sit down, goddammit!"* Ryan pointed to the chair. *At least I have his attention now. I wonder if they can take a knighthood back. . . .*

By this time the Prince flushed a bit. The color gave his face life that it had lacked. He wavered for a moment, then sat with reluctance and resignation.

"Now," Ryan said heatedly, "I think I know what's eating at you, sir. You feel bad because you didn't do a John Wayne number yesterday and handle those gunmen all by yourself, right?" The Prince didn't nod or make any other voluntary response, but a hurt expression around his eyes answered the question just as surely.

"Aw, crap!" Ryan snorted. In the corner, Tony Wilson went pale as a ghost. Ryan didn't blame him.

"You oughta have better sense . . . sir," Ryan added hastily. "You've been through the service schools, right? You've qualified as a pilot, parachuted out of airplanes, and even had command of your own ship?" He got a nod. Time to step it up. "Then you've got no excuse, you damned well ought to have better sense than to think like that! You're not really that dumb, are you?"

"What exactly do you mean?" *A trace of anger,* Ryan thought. *Good.*

"Use your head. You've been trained to think this sort of thing out, haven't you? Let's critique the exercise. Examine what the tactical situation was yesterday. You were trapped in a stopped car with two or three bad guys outside holding automatic weapons. The car is armor-plated, but you're stuck. What can you do? The way I see it, you had three choices:

"One. You can just freeze, just sit there and wet your pants. Hell, that's what most normal people would do, caught by surprise like that. That's probably the normal reaction. But you didn't do that.

"Two. You can try to get out of the car and *do something,* right?"

"Yes, I should have."

"Wrong!" Ryan shook his head emphatically. "Sorry, sir, but that's not a real good idea. The guy I tackled was waiting for you to do just that. That guy could have put a nine-millimeter slug in your head before you had both feet on the pavement. You look like you're in pretty good shape. You probably move pretty good—but ain't nobody yet been able to outrun a bullet, sir! That choice might have gotten you killed, and the rest of your family along with you.

"Three. Your last choice, you tough it out and pray the cavalry gets there in time. You know you're close to home. You know there's cops and troops around. So you know that time is on your side if you can survive for a couple of minutes. In the meantime you try to protect your family as best you can. You get them down on the floor of the car and get overtop of them so the only way the terrorists can get them is to go through you first. And *that,* my friend, is what you did.'' Ryan paused for a moment to let him absorb this.

''You did *exactly* the right thing, dammit!'' Ryan leaned forward until his shoulder pulled him back with a gasp. It wasn't all that much of a pain medication. ''Jesus, this hurts. Look, sir, you were stuck out in the open—with a lousy set of alternatives. But you used your head and took the best one you had. From where I sit, you could not have done any better than you did. So there is nothing, repeat *nothing,* for you to feel bad about. And if you don't believe me, ask Wilson. He's a cop.'' The Prince turned his head.

The Anti-Terrorist Branch officer cleared his throat. ''Excuse me, Your Royal Highness, but Doctor Ryan is quite correct. We were discussing this, this problem yesterday, and we reached precisely the same conclusion.''

Ryan looked over to the cop. ''How long did you fellows kick the idea around, Tony?''

''Perhaps ten minutes,'' Wilson answered.

''That's six *hundred* seconds, Your Highness. But you had to think and act in—what? Five? Maybe three? Not much time to make a life-and-death decision, is it? Mister, I'd say you did damned well. All that training you've picked up along the line worked. And if you were evaluating someone else's performance instead of your own, you'd say the same thing, just like Tony and his friends did.''

''But the press—''

''Oh, screw the press!'' Ryan snapped back, wondering if he'd gone too far. ''What do reporters know about anything? They don't *do* anything, for crying out loud, they just report what other people do. You can fly an airplane, you've jumped out of them—flying scares the hell out of me; I don't even want to think about jumping out of one—and commanded a ship. Plus you ride horses and keep trying to break your neck—and now, finally, you're a father, you got a kid of your own now, right? Isn't that enough to prove to the world that you've got balls? You're not some dumb kid, sir. You're a trained pro. Start acting like one.''

Jack could see his mind going over what he'd just been told. His Highness was sitting a little straighter now. The smile that began to form was an austere one, but at least it had some conviction behind it.

''I am not accustomed to being addressed so forcefully.''

''So cut my head off.'' Ryan grinned. ''You looked like you needed a little straightening out—but I had to get your attention first, didn't I? I'm not going to apologize, sir. Instead, why don't you look in that mirror over there. I bet the guy you see now looks better than the one who shaved this morning.''

''You really believe what you said?''

''Of course. All you have to do is look at the situation from the outside, sir. The problem you had yesterday was tougher than any exercise I had to face at Quantico, but you gutted it out. Listen, I'll tell you a story.

''My first day at Quantico, first day of the officer's course. They line us up, and we meet our Drill Instructor, Gunnery Sergeant Willie King—humongous black guy, we called him Son of Kong. Anyway, he looks us up and down and says, 'Girls, I got some good news, and I got some bad news. The good news is, if you prove that you're good enough to get through this here course, you ain't got nothin' left to prove as long as you live.' And he waits for a couple of seconds. 'The bad news is, you gotta prove it to *me*!' ''

''You were top in your class,'' the Prince said. He'd been briefed, too.

''I was third in that one. I tied for first in the Basic Officer's Course later on. Yeah, I did okay. That course was a gold-plated sonuvabitch. The only easy thing was sleeping—by the time your day was finished, falling asleep was easy enough. But, you know, Son of Kong was almost right.

''If you make it through Quantico, you know you've done something. After that there *was* only one more thing left for me to prove, and the Corps didn't have anything to do with that.'' Ryan paused for a moment. ''Her name is Sally. Anyway, you and your family are alive, sir. Okay, I helped—but so did you. And if any reporter-expert says different, you still have the Tower of London, right? I remember that stuff in the press about your wife last year. Damn, if anybody'd talked that way about Cathy I'd have changed his voice for him.''

''Changed his voice?'' His Highness asked.

''The *hard* way!'' Ryan laughed. ''I guess that's a problem with being important—you can't shoot back. Too bad. People in that business could use some manners, and people in your business are entitled to some privacy, just like the rest of us.''

''And what of your manners, Sir John?'' A real smile now.

''*Mea maxima culpa,* my Lord Prince, you got me there.''

''Still, we might not be here except for you.''

''I couldn't just sit there and watch some people get murdered. If situations had been reversed, I'll bet you'd have done the same thing I did.''

''You really think so?'' His Highness was surprised.

''Sir, are you kidding? Anybody dumb enough to jump out of an airplane is dumb enough to try anything.''

The Prince stood and walked over to the mirror on the wall. Clearly he liked what he saw there. ''Well,'' he murmured to the mirror. He turned back to voice his last self-doubt.

''And if you had been in my place?''

''I'd probably just've wet my pants,'' Ryan replied. ''But you have an advantage over me, sir. You've thought about this problem for a few years, right? Hell, you practically grew up with it, and you've been through basic training—Royal Marines, too, maybe?''

''Yes, I have.''

Ryan nodded. ''Okay, so you had your options figured out beforehand, didn't you? They caught you by surprise, sure, but the training shows. You did all right. Honest. Sit back down, and maybe Tony can pour us some coffee.''

Wilson did so, though he was clearly uneasy to be close to the heir. The Prince of Wales sipped at his cup while Ryan lit up one of Wilson's cigarettes. His Highness looked on disapprovingly.

''That's not good for you, you know,'' he pointed out.

Ryan just laughed. ''Your Highness, since I arrived in this country, I nearly got run over by one of those two-story buses, I almost got my head blown off by a damned Maoist, then I nearly get myself shish-kabobed by one of your redcoats.'' Ryan waved the cigarette in the air. ''This is the *safest* damned thing I've done since I got here! What a vacation this's turned out to be.''

''You do have a point,'' the Prince admitted. ''And quite a sense of humor, Doctor Ryan.''

''I guess the Valium—or whatever they're giving me—helps. And the name's Jack.'' He held out his hand. The Prince took it.

''I was able to meet your wife and daughter yesterday—you were unconscious at the time. I gather that your wife is an excellent physician. Your little daughter is quite wonderful.''

''Thanks. How do you like being a daddy?''

''The first time you hold your newborn child . . .''

''Yeah,'' Jack said. ''Sir, that's what it's all about.'' He stopped talking abruptly.

Bingo, Ryan thought. *A four-month-old baby. If they kidnap the Prince and Princess, well, no government can cave in to terrorism. The politicians and police* have to *have a contingency plan already set up for this, don't they? They'd take this town apart one brick at a time, but they wouldn't—couldn't—negotiate anything, and that was just too bad for the grown-ups, but a little baby* . . . damn, *there's a bargaining chip! What kind of people would—*

''Bastards,'' Ryan whispered to himself. Wilson blanched, but the Prince suspected what Jack was thinking about.

''Excuse me?''

''They weren't trying to kill you. Hell, I bet you weren't even the real objective. . . .'' Ryan nodded slowly. He searched his mind for the data he'd seen on the ULA. There hadn't been much—it hadn't been his area of focus in any case—a few tidbits of shadowy intelligence reports, mixed with a lot of pure conjecture. ''They didn't want to kill you at all, I bet. And when you covered the wife and kid, you burned their plan . . . maybe, or maybe you just—yeah, maybe you just threw them a curve, and that blew their timing a little bit.''

''What do you mean?'' the Prince asked.

''Goddamned medications slow your brain down,'' Ryan said mainly to himself. ''Have the police told you what the terrorists were up to?''

His Highness sat upright in the chair. ''I can't—''

''You don't have to,'' Ryan cut him off. ''Did they tell you that what you did definitely—*definitely*—saved all of you?''

''No, but—''

''Tony?''

''They told me you were a very clever chap, Jack,'' Wilson said. ''I'm afraid I can't comment further. Your Royal Highness, Doctor Ryan may be correct in his assessment.''

''What assessment?'' The Prince was puzzled.

Ryan explained. It only took a few minutes.

''How did you arrive at this conclusion, Jack?''

Ryan's mind was still churning through the hypothesis. ''Sir, I'm an historian. My business is figuring things out. Before that I was a stockbroker—doing essentially the same thing. It's not all that hard when you think about it. You look for apparent inconsistencies and then you try to figure out why they're not really inconsistent.'' He concluded, ''It's all speculation on my part, but I'm willing to bet that Tony's colleagues are pursuing it.'' Wilson didn't say anything. He cleared his throat—which was answer enough.

The Prince looked deep into his coffee cup. His face was that of a man who had recovered from fear and shame. Now he contemplated cold anger at what might have been.

''Well, they've had their chance, haven't they?''

''Yes, sir. I imagine if they ever try again, it'll be a lot harder. Right, Tony?''

"I seriously doubt that they will ever try again," Wilson replied. "We should develop some rather good intelligence from this incident. The ULA have stepped over an invisible line. Politically, success might have enhanced their position, but they didn't succeed, did they? This will harm them, harm their 'popular' support. Some people who know them will now consider talking—not to us, you understand, but some of what they say will get to us in due course. They were outcasts before, they will be outcasts even more now."

Will they learn from this? Ryan wondered. *If so, what will they have learned? There's a question.* Jack knew that it had only two possible answers, and that those answers were diametrically opposed. He made a mental note. He'd follow up on this when he got home. It wasn't a merely academic exercise now. He had a bullet hole in his shoulder to prove that.

The Prince rose to his feet. "You must excuse me, Jack. I'm afraid I have rather a full day ahead."

"Going back out, eh?"

"If I hide, they've won. I understand that fact better now than when I came in here. And I have something else to thank you for."

"You would have figured it out sooner or later. Better it should be sooner, don't you think?"

"We must see more of each other."

"I'd like that, sir. Afraid I'm stuck here for a while, though."

"We are traveling out of the country soon—the day after tomorrow. It's a state visit to New Zealand and the Solomon Islands. You may be gone before we get back."

"Is your wife up to it, Your Highness?"

"I think so. A change of scenery, the doctor said, is just the ticket. She had a very bad experience yesterday, but"—he smiled—"I think it was harder on me than on her."

I'll buy that, Ryan thought. *She's young, she'll bounce back, and at least she has something good to remember. Putting your body between your family and the bullets ought to firm up any relationship.* "Hey, she sure as hell knows you love her, sir."

"I do, you know," the Prince said seriously.

"It's the customary reason to get married, sir," Jack replied, "even for us common folk."

"You're a most irreverent chap, Jack."

"Sorry about that." Ryan grinned. So did the Prince.

"No, you're not." His Highness extended his hand. "Thank you, Sir John, for many things."

Ryan watched him leave with a brisk step and a straight back.

"Tony, you know the difference between him and me? I can say that I used to be a Marine, and that's enough. But that poor guy's got to prove it every damned day, to everybody he meets. I guess that's what you have to do when you're in the public eye all the time." Jack shook his head. "There's no way in hell they could pay me enough to take his job."

"He's born to it," Wilson said.

Ryan thought about that. "That's one difference between your country and mine. You think people are born to something. We know that they have to grow into it. It's not the same thing, Tony."

"Well, you're part of it now, Jack."

* * *

''I think I should go.'' David Ashley looked at the telex in his hand. The disturbing thing was that he'd been requested by name. The PIRA knew who he was, and they knew that he was the Security Service executive on the case. *How the hell did they know* that*!*

''I agree,'' James Owens said. ''If they're this anxious to talk with us, they might be anxious enough to tell us something useful. Of course, there is an element of risk. You could take someone with you.''

Ashley thought about that one. There was always the chance that he'd be kidnapped, but . . . The strange thing about the PIRA was that they did have a code of conduct. Within their own definitions, they were honorable. They assassinated their targets without remorse, but they wouldn't deal in drugs. Their bombs would kill children, but they'd never kidnapped one. Ashley shook his head.

''No, people from the Service have met with them before and there's never been a problem. I'll go alone.'' He turned for the door.

''Daddy!'' Sally ran into the room and stopped cold at the side of the bed as she tried to figure a way to climb high enough to kiss her father. She grabbed the side rails and set one foot on the bedframe as if it were the monkey bars at her nursery school and sprang upward. Her diminutive frame bent over the edge of the mattress as she scrambled for a new foothold, and Ryan pulled her up.

''Hi, Daddy.'' Sally kissed him on the cheek.

''And how are you today?''

''Fine. What's that, Daddy?'' She pointed.

''It's called a cast,'' Cathy Ryan answered. ''I thought you had to go to the bathroom.''

''Okay.'' Sally jumped back off the bed.

''I think it's in there,'' Jack said. ''But I'm not sure.''

''I thought so,'' Cathy said after surveying Jack's attachment to the bed. ''Okay, come on, Sally.''

A man had entered behind his family, Ryan saw. Late twenties, very athletic, and nicely dressed, of course. He was also rather good-looking, Jack reflected.

''Good afternoon, Doctor Ryan,'' he said. ''I'm William Greville.''

Jack made a guess. ''What regiment?''

''Twenty-second, sir.''

''Special Air Service?'' Greville nodded, a proud but restrained smile on his lips.

''When you care enough to send the very best,'' Jack muttered. ''Just you?''

''And a driver, Sergeant Michaelson, a policeman from the Diplomatic Protection Group.''

''Why you and not another cop?''

''I understand your wife wishes to see a bit of the countryside. My father is something of an authority on various castles, and Her Majesty thought that your wife might wish to have an, ah, escort familiar with the sights. Father has dragged me through nearly every old house in England, you see.''

''Escort'' is the right word, Ryan thought, remembering what the ''Special Air Service'' really was. The only association they had with airplanes was jumping out of them—or blowing them up.

Greville went on. ''I am also directed by my colonel to extend an invitation to our regimental mess.''

Ryan gestured at his suspended arm. "Thanks, but that might have to wait a while."

"We understand. No matter, sir. Whenever you have the chance, we'll be delighted to have you in for dinner. We wanted to extend the invitation before the bootnecks, you see." Greville grinned. "What you did was more our sort of op, after all. Well, I had to extend the invitation. You want to see your family, not me."

"Take good care of them . . . Lieutenant?"

"Captain," Greville corrected. "We will do that, sir." Ryan watched the young officer leave as Cathy and Sally emerged from the bathroom.

"What do you think of him?" Cathy asked.

"His daddy's a count, Daddy!" Sally announced. "He's nice."

"What?"

"His father's Viscount-something-or-other," his wife explained as she walked over. "You look a lot better."

"So do you, babe." Jack craned his neck up to meet his wife's kiss.

"Jack, you've been smoking." Even before they'd gotten married, Cathy had bullied him into stopping.

Her damned sense of smell, Jack thought. "Be nice, I've had a hard day."

"Wimp!" she observed disgustedly.

Ryan looked up at the ceiling. *To the whole world I'm a hero, but I smoke a couple of cigarettes and to Cathy that makes me a wimp.* He concluded that the world was not exactly overrun with justice.

"Gimme a break, babe."

"Where'd you get them?"

"I have a cop baby-sitting me in here—he had to go someplace a few minutes ago."

Cathy looked around for the offending cigarette pack so that she could squash it. Jack had it stashed under his pillow. Cathy Ryan sat down. Sally climbed into her lap.

"How do you feel?"

"I know it's there, but I can live with it. How'd you make out last night?"

"You know where we are now, right?"

"I heard."

"It's like being Cinderella." Caroline Muller Ryan, MD, grinned.

John Patrick Ryan, PhD, wiggled the fingers of his left hand. "I guess I'm the one who turned into the pumpkin. I guess you're going to make the trips we planned. Good."

"Sure you don't mind?"

"Half the reason for the vacation was to get you away from hospitals, Cathy, remember? No sense taking all the film home unused, is it?"

"It'd be a lot more fun with you."

Jack nodded. He'd looked forward to seeing the castles on the list, too. Like many Americans, Ryan could not have abided the English class system, but that didn't stop him from being fascinated with its trappings. *Or something like that,* he thought. His knighthood, he knew, might change that perspective if he allowed himself to dwell on it.

"Look on the bright side, babe. You've got a guide who can tell you everything you ever wanted to know about Lord Jones's castle on the coast of whatever. You'll have plenty of time for it, too."

"Yeah," she said, "the police said we'd be staying over a while longer than we planned. I'll have to talk to Professor Lewindowski about that." She shrugged. "They'll understand."

"How do you like the new place? Better than the hotel?"

"You're going to have to see—no, you'll have to *experience* it." She laughed. "I think hospitality is the national sport over here. They must teach it in the schools, and have quarterly exams. And guess who we're having dinner with tonight?"

"I don't have to guess."

"Jack, they're so *nice*."

"I noticed. Looks like you're really getting the VIP treatment."

"What's the Special Air Service—he's some kind of pilot?"

"Something like that," Jack said diffidently. Cathy might feel uncomfortable sitting next to a man who had to be carrying a gun. And was trained to use it with as little compunction as a wolf might use his teeth. "You're not asking how I feel."

"I got hold of your chart on the way in," Cathy explained.

"And?"

"You're doing okay, Jack. I see you can move your fingers. I was worried about that."

"How come?"

"The brachial plexus—it's a nerve junction inside your shoulder. The bullet missed it by about an inch and a half. That's why you can move your fingers. The way you were bleeding, I thought the brachial artery was cut, and that runs right next to the nerves. It would have put your arm out of business for good. But"—she smiled—"you lucked out. Just broken bones. They hurt but they heal."

Doctors are so wonderfully objective, Ryan told himself, even the ones you marry. *Next thing, she'll say the pain is good for me.*

"Nice thing about pain," Cathy went on. "It tells you the nerves are working."

Jack closed his eyes and shook his head. He opened them when he felt Cathy take his hand.

"Jack, I'm so proud of you."

"Nice to be married to a hero?"

"You've always been a hero to me."

"Really?" She'd never said *that* before. What was heroic about being an historian? Cathy didn't know the other stuff he did, but that wasn't especially heroic either.

"Ever since you told Daddy to—well, you know. Besides, I love you, remember?"

"I seem to recall a reminder of that the other day."

Cathy made a face. "Better get your mind off that for a while."

"I know." Ryan made a face of his own. "The patient must conserve his energy—or something. What ever happened to that theory about how a happy attitude speeds recovery?"

"That's what I get for letting you read my journals. Patience, Jack."

Nurse Kittiwake came in, saw the family, and made a quick exit.

"I'll try to be patient," Jack said, and looked longingly at the closing door.

"You turkey," Cathy observed. "I know you better than that."

She did, Jack knew. He couldn't even make that threat work. *Oh, well—that's what you get for loving your wife.*

Cathy stroked his face. "What did you shave with this morning, a rusty nail?"

"Yeah—I need my razor. Maybe my notes, too?"

"I'll bring them over or have somebody do it." She looked up when Wilson came back in.

"Tony, this is Cathy, my wife, and Sally, my daughter. Cathy, this is Tony Wilson. He's the cop who's baby-sitting me."

"Didn't I see you last night?" Cathy never forgot a face—so far as Jack could tell, she never forgot much of anything.

"Possibly, but we didn't speak—rather a busy time for all of us. You are well, Lady Ryan?"

"Excuse me?" Cathy asked. "Lady Ryan?"

"They didn't tell you?" Jack chuckled.

"Tell me what?"

Jack explained. "How do you like being married to a knight?"

"Does that mean you have to have a horse, Daddy?" Sally asked hopefully. "Can I ride it?"

"Is it legal, Jack?"

"They told me that the Prime Minister and the President would discuss it today."

"My God," Lady Ryan said quietly. After a moment, she started smiling.

"Stick with me, kid." Jack laughed.

"What about the horse, Daddy!" Sally insisted.

"I don't know yet. We'll see." He yawned. The only practical use Ryan acknowledged for horses was running at tracks—or maybe tax shelters. *Well, I already have a sword,* he told himself.

"I think Daddy needs a nap," Cathy observed. "And I have to buy something for dinner tonight."

"Oh, God!" Ryan groaned. "A whole new wardrobe."

Cathy grinned. "Whose fault is that, Sir John?"

They met at Flanagan's Steakhouse on O'Connell Street in Dublin. It was a well-regarded establishment whose tourist trade occasionally suffered from being too close to a McDonald's. Ashley was nursing a whiskey when the second man joined him. A third and fourth took a booth across the room and watched. Ashley had come alone. This wasn't the first such meeting, and Dublin was recognized—most of the time—as neutral ground. The two men on the other side of the room were to keep a watch for members of the Garda, the Republic's police force.

"Welcome to Dublin, Mr. Ashley," said the representative of the Provisional Wing of the Irish Republican Army.

"Thank you, Mr. Murphy," the counterintelligence officer answered. "The photograph we have in the file doesn't do you justice."

"Young and foolish, I was. And very vain. I didn't shave very much then," Murphy explained. He picked up the menu that had been waiting for him. "The beef here is excellent, and the vegetables are always fresh. This place is full of bloody tourists in the summer—those who don't want French fries—driving prices up as they always do. Thank God they're all back home in America now, leaving so much money behind in this poor country."

"What information do you have for us?"

"Information?"

"You asked for the meeting, Mr. Murphy," Ashley pointed out.

"The purpose of the meeting is to assure you that we had no part in that bloody fiasco yesterday."

"I could have read that in the papers—I did, in fact."

"It was felt that a more personal communiqué was in order, Mr. Ashley."

"Why should we believe you?" Ashley asked, sipping at his whiskey. Both men kept their voices low and level, though neither man had the slightest doubt as to what they thought of each other.

"Because we are not as crazy as that," Murphy replied. The waiter came, and both men ordered. Ashley chose the wine, a promising Bordeaux. The meal was on his expense account. He was only forty minutes off the flight from London's Gatwick airport. The request for a meeting had been made before dawn in a telephone call to the British Ambassador in Dublin.

"Is that a fact?" Ashley said after the waiter left, staring into the cold blue eyes across the table.

"The Royal Family are strictly off limits. As marvelous a political target as they all are"—Murphy smiled—"we've known for some time that an attack on them would be counterproductive."

"Really?" Ashley pronounced the word as only an Englishman can do it. Murphy flushed angrily at this most elegant of insults.

"Mr. Ashley, we are enemies. I would as soon kill you as have dinner with you. But even enemies can negotiate, can't they, now?"

"Go on."

"We had no part of it. You have my word."

"Your word as a Marxist-Leninist?" Ashley inquired with a smile.

"You are very good at provoking people, Mr. Ashley." Murphy ventured his own smile. "But not today. I am here on a mission of peace and understanding."

Ashley nearly laughed out loud, but caught himself and grinned into his drink.

"Mr. Murphy, I would not shed a single tear if our lads were to catch up with you, but you are a worthy adversary, I'll say that. And a charming bastard."

Ah, the English sense of fair play, Murphy reflected. *That's why we'll win eventually, Mr. Ashley.*

No, you won't. Ashley had seen that look before.

"How can I make you believe me?" Murphy asked reasonably.

"Names and addresses," Ashley answered quietly.

"No. We cannot do that and you know it."

"If you wish to establish some sort of quid pro quo, that's how you must go about it."

Murphy sighed. "Surely you know how we are organized. Do you think we can punch up a bloody computer command and print out our roster? We're not even sure ourselves who they are. Some men, they just drop out. Many come south and simply vanish, more afraid of us than of you, they are—and with reason," Murphy added. "The one you have alive, Sean Miller—we've never even heard the name."

"And Kevin O'Donnell?"

"Yes, he's probably the leader. He dropped off the earth four years ago, as you well know, after—ah, you know the story as well as I."

Kevin Joseph O'Donnell, Ashley reminded himself. *Thirty-four now. Six feet, one hundred sixty pounds, unmarried—this data was old and therefore suspect. The all-time Provo champion at "own-goals." Kevin had been the most ruthless chief of security the Provos had ever had, thrown out after it had been proven that he'd used his power as counterintelligence boss to purge the Organization of political elements he disapproved of. What was the figure—ten, fifteen solid members that he'd had killed or maimed before the Brigade Commander'd found him out? The amazing thing,* Ashley thought, *was that he'd escaped alive at all.* But Murphy was wrong on one thing, Ashley didn't know what had finally tipped the Brigade that O'Donnell was outlaw.

"I fail to see why you feel the urge to protect him and his group." He knew the reason, but why not prod the man when he had the chance?

"And if we turn 'grass,' what becomes of the Organization?" Murphy asked.

"Not my problem, Mr. Murphy, but I do see your point. Still and all, if you want us to believe you—"

"Mr. Ashley, you demonstrate the basis of the entire problem we have, don't you? Had your country ever dealt with Ireland in mutual good faith, surely we would not be here now, would we?"

The intelligence officer reflected on that. It took no more than a couple of seconds, so many times had he examined the historical basis of the Troubles. Some deliberate policy acts, mixed with historical accidents—who could have known that the onset of the crisis that erupted into World War I would prevent a solution to the issue of "Home [or "Rome"] Rule," that the Conservative Party of the time would use this issue as a hammer that would eventually crush the Liberal Party—and who was there to blame now? They were all dead and forgotten, except by hard-core academics who knew that their studies mattered for nothing. It was far too late for that. *Is there a way out of this bloody quagmire?* he wondered. Ashley shook his head. That was not his brief. That was something for politicians. The same sort, he reminded himself, who'd built the Troubles, one small brick at a time.

"I'll tell you this much, Mr. Ashley—" The waiter showed up with dinner. It was amazing how quick the service was here. The waiter uncorked the wine with a flourish, allowing Ashley to smell the cork and sample a splash in his glass. The Englishman was surprised at the quality of the restaurant's cellar.

"This much you will tell me . . ." Ashley said after the waiter left.

"They get very good information. So good, you would not believe it. And their information comes from your side of the Irish Sea, Mr. Ashley. We don't know who, and we don't know how. The lad who found out died, four years ago, you see." Murphy sampled the broccoli. "There, I told you the vegetables were fresh."

"Four years?"

Murphy looked up. "You don't know the story, then? That is a surprise, Mr. Ashley. Yes. His name was Mickey Baird. He worked closely with Kevin. He's the lad who—well, you can guess. He was talking with me over a jar in Derry and said that Kevin had a bloody good new intelligence source. Next day he was dead. The day after, Kevin managed to escape us by an hour. We haven't seen him since. If we find Kevin again, Mr. Ashley, we'll do your work for you, and leave the body for your SAS assassins to collect. Would that be fair enough, now? We cannot exactly tout to the enemy, but he's on our list, too, and if you manage to find the lad, and you don't wish to bring him in yourselves, we'll handle the job for you—assuming, of course, that you don't interfere with the lads who do the work. Can we agree on that?"

"I'll pass that along," Ashley said. "If I could approve it myself, I would. Mr. Murphy, I think we can believe you on this."

"Thank you, Mr. Ashley. That wasn't so painful, was it?" Dinner was excellent.

4. Players

Ryan tried to blink away the blue dots that swirled around his eyes as the television crews set up their own lights. Why the newspaper photographers couldn't wait for the powerful TV lights, he didn't know, and didn't bother asking. Everyone was kind enough to ask how he felt—but nothing short of respiratory arrest would have gotten them out of the room.

It could have been worse, of course. Dr. Scott had told the newspeople rather forcefully that his patient needed rest to recover speedily, and Nurse Kittiwake was there to glower at the intruders. So press access to Ryan was being limited to no more than the number of people who would fit into his room. This included the TV crew. It was the best sort of bargain Jack could get. The cameramen and sound technicians took up space that would otherwise be occupied by more inquisitorial reporters.

The morning papers—Ryan had been through the *Times* and the *Daily Telegraph*—had carried reports that Ryan was a former (or current) employee of the Central Intelligence Agency, something that was technically not true, and that Jack had not expected to become public in any case. He found himself remembering what the people at Langley said about leaks, and how pleased they'd been with his offhand invention of the Canary Trap. *A pity they couldn't use it in my case,* Ryan told himself wryly. *I really need this complication to my life, don't I? For crying out loud, I turned their offer* down. *Sort of.*

"All ready here," the lighting technician said. A moment later he proved this was true by turning on the three klieg lights that brought tears to Jack's squinted eyes.

"They are awfully bright, aren't they?" a reporter sympathized, while the still photographers continued to snap-and-whir away with their strobe-equipped Nikons.

"You might say that," Jack replied. A two-headed mike was clipped to his robe.

"Say something, will you?" the sound man asked.

"And how are you enjoying your first trip to London, Doctor Ryan?"

"Well, I better not hear any complaints about how American tourists are staying away due to panic over the terrorism problem!" Ryan grinned. *You jerk.*

"Indeed," the reporter laughed. "Okay?"

The cameraman and sound man pronounced themselves ready.

Ryan sipped at his tea and made certain that the ashtray was out of sight. One print journalist shared a joke with a colleague. A TV correspondent from NBC was there, along with the London correspondent of the *Washington Post,* but all the others were British. Everything would be pooled with the rest of the media, it had been agreed. There just wasn't room here for a proper press conference. The camera started rolling tape.

They ran through the usual questions. The camera turned to linger on his arm, hanging from its overhead rack. They'd run that shot with the voice-over of Jack's story on when he was shot, he was sure. Nothing like a little drama, as he'd already been told. He wiggled his fingers for the camera.

"Doctor Ryan, there are reports in the American and British press that you are an employee of the Central Intelligence Agency."

"I read that this morning. It was as much a surprise to me as it was to anyone else." Ryan smiled. "Somebody made a mistake. I'm not good-looking enough to be a spy."

"So you deny that report?" asked the *Daily Mirror*.

"Correct. It's just not true. I teach history at the Naval Academy, in Annapolis. That ought to be easy enough to check out. I just gave an exam last week. You can ask my students." Jack waved his left hand at the camera again.

"The report comes from some highly placed sources," observed the *Post*.

"If you read a little history, you'll see that highly placed folks have been known to make mistakes. I think that's what happened here. I teach. I write books. I lecture—okay, I did give a lecture at CIA once, but that was just a repeat of one I delivered at the Naval War College and one other symposium. It wasn't even classified. Maybe that's where the report comes from. Like I said, check it out. My office is in Leahy Hall, at the Naval Academy. I think somebody just goofed." *Somebody goofed, all right.* "I can get you guys a copy of the lecture. It's no big deal."

"How do you like being a public figure, now?" one of the Brit TV people asked.

Thanks for changing the subject. "I think I can live without it. I'm not a movie star, either—again, not good-looking enough."

"You're far too modest, Doctor Ryan," a female reporter observed.

"Please be careful how you say that. My wife will probably see this." There was general laughter. "I suppose I'm good-looking enough for her. That's enough. With all due respect, ladies and gentlemen, I'll be perfectly glad to descend back into obscurity."

"Do you think that likely?"

"That depends on how lucky I am, ma'am. And on whether you folks will let me."

"What do you think we should do with the terrorist, Sean Miller?" the *Times* asked.

"That's for a judge and jury to decide. You don't need me for that."

"Do you think we should have capital punishment?"

"We have it where I live. For your country, that is a question for your elected representatives. We both live in democracies, don't we? The people you elect are supposed to do what the voters ask them to do." *Not that it always works that way, but that's the theory. . . .*

"So you support the idea?" the *Times* persisted.

"In appropriate cases, subject to strict judicial review, yes. Now you're going to ask me about this case, right? It's a moot point. Anyway, I'm no expert on criminal justice. My dad was a cop but I'm just a historian."

"And what of your perspective, as an Irish-American, on the Troubles?" the *Telegraph* wanted to know.

"We have enough problems of our own in America without having to borrow yours."

"So you say we should solve it, then?"

"What do you think? Isn't that what problems are for?"

"Surely you have a suggestion. Most Americans do."

"I think I teach history. I'll let other people make it. It's like being a reporter." Ryan smiled. "I get to criticize people long after they make their decisions. That doesn't mean I know what to do today."

"But you knew what to do on Tuesday," the *Times* pointed out. Ryan shrugged.

"Yeah, I guess I did," Ryan said on the television screen.

"You clever bastard," Kevin Joseph O'Donnell muttered into a glass of dark Guinness beer. His base of operations was much farther from the border than any might have suspected. Ireland is a small country, and distances are but relative things—particularly to those with all the resources they need. His former colleagues in the PIRA had extensive safehouses along the border, convenient to a quick trip across from either direction. Not for O'Donnell. There were numerous practical reasons. The Brits had their informers and intelligence people there, always creeping about—and the SAS raiders, who were not averse to a quick snatch—or a quiet kill—of persons who had made the mistake of becoming too well known. The border could be a convenience to either side. A more serious threat was the PIRA itself, which also watched the border closely. His face, altered as it was with some minor surgery and a change in hair color, might still be recognizable to a former colleague. But not here. And the border wasn't all that far a drive in a country barely three hundred miles long.

He turned away from the Sony television and gazed out the leaded-glass windows to the darkness of the sea. He saw the running lights of a car ferry inbound from Le Havre. The view was always a fine one. Even in the limited visibility of an ocean storm, one could savor the fundamental force of nature as the gray waves battered the rocky cliff. Now, the clear, cold air gave him a view to the star-defined horizon, and he spied another merchant ship heading eastward for an unknown port. It pleased O'Donnell that this stately house on the headlands had once belonged to a British lord. It pleased him more that he'd been able to purchase it through a dummy corporation; that there were few questions when cash and a reputable solicitor were involved. So vulnerable this society—all societies were when you had the proper resources . . . and a competent tailor. So shallow they were. So lacking in political awareness. *One must know who one's enemies are,* O'Donnell told himself at least ten times every day. Not a liberal "democratic" society, though. Enemies were people to be dealt with, compromised with, to be civilized, brought into the fold, co-opted.

Fools, self-destructive, ignorant fools who earned their own destruction.

Someday they would all disappear, just as one of those ships slid beneath the horizon. History was a science, an inevitable process. O'Donnell was sure of that.

He turned again to stare into the fire burning under the wide, stone mantel. There had once been stag heads hanging over it, perhaps the lord's favorite fowling piece—from Purdey's, to be sure. And a painting or two. Of horses, O'Donnell was sure—they had to be paintings of horses. The country gentleman who had built this house, he mused, would have been someone who'd been given everything he had. No ideology would have intruded in his empty, useless head. He would have sat in a chair very like this one and sipped his malt whiskey and stared into the fire—his favorite dog at this feet—while he chatted about the day's hunting with a neighbor and planned the hunting for the morrow. *Will it be birds again, or fox, Bertie? Haven't had a good fox hunt in weeks, time we did it again, don't you think?* Or something like that, he was sure. O'Donnell wondered if there was a seasonal aspect to it, or had the lord just done whatever suited his mood. The current owner of the country house never hunted animals. What was the point of killing something that could not harm you or your cause, something that had no ideology? Besides, that was something the Brits did, something the local gentry still did. He didn't hunt the local Irish gentry, they weren't worth his contempt, much less his action. At least, not yet. *You don't hate trees,* he told himself. *You ignore the things until you have to cut them down.* He turned back to the television.

That Ryan fellow was still there, he saw, talking amiably with the press idiots. Bloody hero. *Why did you stick your nose in where it doesn't belong?* Reflex, sounds like, O'Donnell judged. *Bloody meddling fool. Don't even know what's going on, do you? None of you do.*

Americans. The Provo fools still like to talk it up with your kind, telling their lies and pretending that they represent Ireland. What do you Yanks know about anything? *Oh, but we can't afford to offend the Americans,* the Provos still said. Bloody Americans, with all their money and all their arrogance, all their ideas on right and wrong, their childish vision of Irish destiny. Like children dressed up for First Communion. So pure. So naive. So useless with their trickle of money—for all that the Brits complained about NORAID, O'Donnell knew that the PIRA had not netted a million dollars from America in the past three years. All the Americans knew of Ireland came from a few movies, some half-remembered songs for St. Paddy's Day, and the occasional bottle of whiskey. What did they know of life in Ulster, of the imperialist oppression, the way all Ireland was still enslaved to the decaying British Empire, which was, in turn, enslaved to the American one? What did they know about anything? *But we can't offend the Americans.* The leader of the ULA finished off his beer and set it on the end table.

The Cause didn't require much, not really. A clear ideological objective. A few good men. Friends, the right friends, with access to the right resources. That was all. Why clutter things up with bloody Americans? And a public political wing—Sinn Fein electing people to Parliament, what rubbish! They were waiting, *hoping* to be co-opted by the Brit imperialists. Valuable political targets declared off-limits. And people wondered why the Provos were getting nowhere. Their ideology was bankrupt, and there were too many people in the Brigade. When the Brits caught some, a few were bound to turn tout and inform on their comrades. The kind of commitment needed for this sort of job demanded an elite few. O'Donnell had that, all right. *And you need to have the right plan,* he told himself with a wispy smile. O'Donnell had his plan. This Ryan fellow hadn't changed that, he reminded himself.

"Bastard's bloody pleased with himself, isn't he?"

O'Donnell turned to see a fresh bottle of Guinness offered. He took it and refilled his glass. "Sean should have watched his back. Then this bloody hero would be a corpse." *And the mission would have been successful. Damn!*

"We can still do something about that, sir."

O'Donnell shook his head. "We do not waste our energy on the insignificant. The Provos have been doing that for ten years and look where it has gotten them."

"What if he is CIA? What if we've been infiltrated and he was there—"

"Don't be a bloody fool," O'Donnell snapped. "If they'd been tipped, every peeler in London would have been there in plain clothes waiting for us." *And I would have known beforehand,* he didn't say. Only one other member of the Organization knew of his source, and he was in London. "It was luck, good for them, bad for us. Just luck. We were lucky in your case, weren't we, Michael?" Like any Irishman he still believed in luck. Ideology would never change that.

The younger man thought of his eighteen months in the H-Blocks at Long Kesh prison, and was silent. O'Donnell shrugged at the television as the news program changed to another story. Luck. That was all. Some monied Yank with too long a nose who'd gotten very lucky. Any random event, like a punctured tire, a defective radio battery, or a sudden rainstorm, could have made the operation fail, too. And his advantage over the other side was that they had to be lucky all the time. O'Donnell only had to be lucky once. He considered what he had just seen on the television and decided that Ryan wasn't worth the effort.

Mustn't offend the Americans, he thought to himself again, this time with surprise. *Why? Aren't they the enemy, too? Patrick, me boy, now you're thinking like those idiots in the PIRA. Patience is the most important quality in the true revolutionary. One must wait for the proper moment—and then strike decisively.*

He waited for his next intelligence report.

The rare book shop was in the Burlington Arcade, a century-old promenade of shops off the most fashionable part of Piccadilly. It was sandwiched between one of London's custom tailors—this one catered mainly to the tourists who used the arcade to shelter from the elements—and a jeweler. It had the sort of smell that draws bibliophiles as surely as the scent of nectar draws a bee, the musty, dusty odor of dried-out paper and leather binding. The shop's owner-operator was contrastingly young, dressed in a suit whose shoulders were sprinkled with dust. He started every day by running a feather duster over the shelves, and the books were ever exuding new quantities of it. He had grown to like it. The store had an ambience that he dearly loved. The store did a small but lucrative volume of business, depending less on tourists than on a discreet number of regular customers from the upper reaches of London society. The owner, a Mr. Dennis Cooley, traveled a great deal, often flying out on short notice to participate in an auction of some deceased gentleman's library, leaving the shop to the custody of a young lady who would have been quite pretty if she'd worked at it a little harder. Beatrix was off today.

Mr. Cooley had an ancient teak desk in keeping with the rest of the shop's motif, and even a cushionless swivel chair to prove to the customers that nothing in the shop was modern. Even the bookkeeping was done by hand. No electronic calculators here. A battered ledger book dating back to the 1930s listed thousands of sales, and the shop's book catalog was made of simple filing cards in small wooden boxes, one set listing books by title, and another by author. All writing was done with a gold-nibbed fountain pen. A no-smoking sign was the only modern touch. The smell of tobacco might have ruined the shop's unique aroma. The store's stationery bore the "by appointment to" crests of four Royal Family members. The arcade was but a ten-minute uphill walk from Buckingham Palace. The glass door had a hundred-year-old silver bell hanging on the top of the frame. It rang.

"Good morning, Mr. Cooley."

"And to you, sir," Dennis answered one of his regulars as he stood. He had an accent so neutral that his customers had him pegged as a native of three different regions. "I have the first-edition Defoe. The one you called about earlier this week. Just came in yesterday."

"Is this the one from that collection in Cork you spoke about?"

"No, sir. I believe it's originally from the estate of Sir John Claggett, near Swaffham Prior. I found it at Hawstead's in Cambridge."

"A first edition?"

"Most certainly, sir." The book dealer did not react noticeably. The code phrase was both constant and changing. Cooley made frequent trips to Ireland, both north and south, to purchase books from the estates of deceased collectors or from dealers in the country. When the customer mentioned any county in the Irish Republic, he indicated the destination for his information. When he questioned the edition of the book, he also indicated its importance. Cooley pulled the book off the shelf and set it on his desk. The customer opened it with care, running his finger down the title page.

"In an age of paperbacks and half-bound books. . . ."

"Indeed." Cooley nodded. Both men's love for the art of bookbinding was genuine. Any good cover becomes more real than its builders expect. "The leather is in remarkable shape." His visitor grunted agreement.

"I must have it. How much?"

The dealer didn't answer. Instead Cooley removed the card from the box and handed it to his customer. He gave the card only a cursory look.

"Done." The customer sat down in the store's only other chair and opened his briefcase. "I have another job for you. This is an early copy of *The Vicar of Wakefield*. I found it last month at a little shop in Cornwall." He handed the book over. Cooley needed only a single look at its condition.

"Scandalous."

"Can your chap restore it?"

"I don't know. . . ." The leather was cracked, some of the pages had been dog-eared, and the binding was frayed almost to nonexistence.

"I'm afraid the attic in which they found it had a leaky roof," the customer said casually.

"Oh?" *Is the information* that *important?* Cooley looked up. "A tragic waste."

"How else can you explain it?" The man shrugged.

"I'll see what I can do. He's not a miracle worker, you know." *Is it that important?*

"I understand. Still, the best you can arrange." *Yes, it's that important.*

"Of course, sir." Cooley opened his desk drawer and withdrew the cashbox.

This customer always paid cash. Of course. He removed the wallet from his suitcoat and counted out the fifty-pound notes. Cooley checked the amount, then placed the book in a stout cardboard box, which he tied with string. No plastic bags for this shop. Seller and buyer shook hands. The transfer was complete. The customer walked south toward Piccadilly, then turned right, heading west toward Green Park and downhill to the Palace.

Cooley took the envelope that had been hidden in the book and tucked it away in a drawer. He finished making his ledger entry, then called his travel agent to book a flight to Cork, where he would meet a fellow dealer in rare books and have lunch at the Old Bridge restaurant before catching a flight home. Beatrix would have to manage the shop tomorrow. It did not occur to him to open the envelope. That was not his job. The less he knew, the less was vulnerable if he were caught. Cooley had been trained by professionals, and the first rule pounded into his head had been *need-to-know*. He ran the intelligence operation, and he needed to know how to do that. He didn't always need to know what specific information he gathered.

"Hello, Doctor Ryan." It was an American voice, with a South Bay Boston accent that Jack remembered from his college days. It sounded good. The man was in his forties, a wiry, athletic frame, with thinning black hair. He had a flower box tucked under his arm. Whoever he was, the cop outside had opened the door for him.

"Howdy. Who might you be?"

"Dan Murray. I'm the Legal Attaché at the embassy. FBI," he explained. "Sorry I couldn't get down sooner, but things have been a little busy." Murray showed his ID to the cop sitting in with Ryan—Tony Wilson was off duty. The cop excused himself. Murray took his seat.

"Lookin' good, ace."

"You could have left the flowers at the main desk." Ryan gestured around the room. Despite all his efforts to spread the flowers about, he could barely see the walls for all the roses.

"Yeah, I figured that. How's the grub?"

"Hospital food is hospital food."

"Figured that, too." Murray removed the red ribbon and opened the box. "How does a Whopper and fries grab you? You have a choice of vanilla or chocolate shakes."

Jack laughed—and grabbed.

"I've been over here three years," Murray said. "Every so often I have to hit the fast-food joints to remind myself where I come from. You can get tired of lamb. The local beer's pretty good, though. I'd have brought a few of those but—well, you know."

"You just made a friend for life, Mr. Murray, even without the beer."

"Dan."

"Jack." Ryan was tempted to wolf down the burger for fear of having a nurse come through the door and throw an immediate institutional fit. *No,* he decided, *I'll enjoy this one*. He selected the vanilla shake. "The local guys say you broke records identifying me."

"No big deal." Murray poked a straw into the chocolate one. "By the way, I bring you greetings from the Ambassador—he wanted to come over, but they have a big-time party for later tonight. And my friends down the hall send their regards, too."

"Who down the hall?"

"The people you have never worked for." The FBI agent raised his eyebrows.

"Oh." Jack swallowed a few fries. "Who the hell broke that story?"

"Washington. Some reporter was having lunch with somebody's aide—doesn't really matter whose, does it? They all talk too much. Evidently he remembered your name in the back of the final report and couldn't keep his trap shut. Apologies from Langley, they told me to tell you. I saw the TV stuff. You dodged that pretty good."

"I told the truth—barely. All my checks came through Mitre Corporation. Some sort of bookkeeping thing, and Mitre had the consulting contract."

"I understand all your time was at Langley, though."

"Yeah, a little cubbyhole on the third floor with a desk, a computer terminal, and a scratchpad. Ever been there?"

Murray smiled. "Once or twice. I'm in the terrorism business, too. The Bureau has a much nicer decorator. Helps to have a PR department, don't you know?" Murray affected a caricatured London accent. "I saw a copy of the report. Nice work. How much of it did you do?"

"Most. It wasn't all that hard. I just came up with a new angle to look at it from."

"It's been passed along to the Brits—I mean, it came over here two months ago for the Secret Intelligence Service. I understand they liked it."

"So their cops know."

"I'm not sure—well, you can probably assume they do now. Owens is cleared all the way on this stuff."

"And so's Ashley."

"He's a little on the snotty side, but he's damned smart. He's 'Five.' "

"What?" Ryan didn't know that one.

"He's in MI-5, the Security Service. We just call it Five. Has a nice insider feel that way." Murray chuckled.

"I figured him for something like that. The other two started as street cops. It shows."

"It struck a few people as slightly curious—the guy who wrote *Agents and Agencies* gets stuck in the middle of a terrorist op. That's why Ashley showed up." Murray shook his head. "You wouldn't believe all the coincidences you run into in my business. Like you and me."

"I know you come from New England—oh, don't tell me. Boston College?"

"Hey, I always wanted to be an FBI agent. It was either BC or Holy Cross, right?" Murray grinned. That in-house FBI joke went back two generations, and was not without a few grains of truth. Ryan leaned back and sucked the shake up the straw. It tasted wonderful.

"How much do we know about these ULA guys?" Jack asked. "I never saw very much at Langley."

"Not a hell of a lot. The boss-man's a chap named Kevin O'Donnell. He used to be in the PIRA. He started throwing rocks in the streets and supposedly worked his way up to head counterintelligence man. The Provos are pretty good at that. Have to be. The Brits are always working to infiltrate the Organization. The word is that he got a little carried away cleansing the ranks, and barely managed to skip out before they gave him Excedrin Headache number three-five-seven. Just plain disappeared and hasn't been spotted since. A few sketchy reports, like maybe he spent some time in Libya, like maybe he's back in Ulster with a new face, like maybe he has a lot of money—want to guess where from?—to throw around. All we know for sure is that he's one malignant son of a bitch.

"His organization?" Murray set the milkshake down. "It's gotta be small, probably less than thirty. We think he had part of the breakout from Long Kesh last summer. Eleven hard-core Provos got out. The RUC bagged one of 'em two days later and he said that six of the eleven went south, probably to Kevin's outfit. He was a little pissed by that. They were supposed to come back to the PIRA fold, but somebody convinced them to try something different. Some very bad boys—they had a total of fifteen murders among them. The one you killed is the only one to show up since."

"Are they that good?" Ryan asked.

"Hey, the PIRA are the best terrorists in the world, unless you count those bastards in Lebanon, and those are mostly family groups. Hell of a way to describe them, isn't it? But they are the best. Well organized, well trained, and they *believe,* if you know what I mean. They really care about what they're doing. The level of commitment these characters have to the Cause is something you have to see to believe."

"You've been in on it?"

"Some. I've been able to sit in on interrogations—the other side of the two-way mirror, I mean. One of these guys wouldn't talk—wouldn't even give 'em his name!—for a week. Just sat there like a sphinx. Hey, I've chased after bank robbers, kidnappers, mob guys, spies, you name it. These fellows are real pros—and that's the PIRA, maybe five hundred real members, not even as big as a New York Mafia family, and the RUC—that's the Royal Ulster Constabulary, the local cops—is lucky to convict a handful in a year. They have a law of *omertà* up there that would impress the old-time Sicilians. But at least the cops have a handle on who the bastards are. The ULA—we got a couple of names, a few pictures, and that's it. It's almost like the Islamic Jihad bums. You only know them from what they do.''

''What do they do?'' Ryan asked.

''They seem to specialize in high-risk, high-profile operations. It took over a year to confirm that they exist at all; we thought they were a special-action group of the PIRA. They're an anomaly within the terrorist community. They don't make press releases, they don't take public credit for what they do. They go for the big-time stuff and they cover their tracks like you wouldn't believe. It takes resources to do that. Somebody is bankrolling them in a pretty big way. They've been identified for nine jobs we're sure of, maybe two others. They've only had three operations go bad—quite a track record. They missed killing a judge in Londonderry because the RPG round was a dud—it still took his bodyguard out. They tried to hit a police barracks last February. Somebody saw them setting up and phoned in—but the bastards must have been monitoring the police radio. They skipped before the cavalry arrived. The cops found an eighty-two-millimeter mortar and a box of rounds—high-explosive and white phosphorus, to be exact. And you got in the way of the last one.

''These suckers are getting pretty bold,'' Murray said. ''On the other hand, we got one now.''

''We?'' Ryan said curiously. ''It's not our fight.''

''We're talking terrorists, Jack. Everybody wants them. We swap information back and forth with the Yard every day. Anyway, the guy they have in the can right now, they'll keep talking at him. They have a hook on this one. The ULA is an outcast outfit. He is going to be a pariah and he knows it. His colleagues from PIRA and INLA won't circle wagons around him. He'll go to a maximum-security prison, probably to one on the Isle of Wight, populated with some real bad boys. Not all of them are political types, and the ordinary robbers and murderers will probably—well, it's funny how patriotic these guys are. Spies, for example, have about as much fun in the joint as child molesters. This guy went after the Royal Family, the one thing over here that everybody loves. We're talking some serious hard time with this kid. You think the guards are going to bust their ass looking out for his well-being? He's going to learn a whole new sport. It's called *survival*. After he has a taste of it, people will talk to him. Sooner or later that kid's going to have to decide just how committed he is. He just might break down a little. Some have. That's what we play for, anyway. The bad guys have the initiative, we have organization and procedures. If they make a mistake, give us an opportunity, we can act on it.''

Ryan nodded. ''Yeah, it's all intelligence.''

''That's right. Without the right information we're crippled. All we can do is plod along and hope for a break. But give us one solid fact and we'll bring the whole friggin' world down on 'em. It's like taking down a brick wall. The hard part's getting that first brick loose.''

''And where do they get their information?''

"They told me you tumbled to that," Murray observed with a smile.

"I don't think it was a chance encounter. Somebody had to tip them. They hit a moving target making an unscheduled trip."

"How the hell did you know that?" the agent demanded.

"Doesn't matter, does it? People talk. Who knew that they were coming in?"

"That is being looked at. The interesting thing is what they were coming in for. Of course, that could just be a coincidence. The Prince gets briefed on political and national security stuff, same as the Queen does. Something happened with the Irish situation, negotiations between London and Dublin. He was coming in for the briefing. All I can tell you."

"Hey, if you checked me out, you know how I'm cleared," Ryan sniffed.

Murray grinned. "Nice try, ace. If you weren't cleared TS, I wouldn't have told you this much. We're not privy to it yet anyway. Like I said, it might just have been a coincidence, but you guessed right on the important part. It was an unscheduled trip and somebody got the word out for the ambush. Only way it could have happened. You will consider that classified information, Doctor Ryan. It doesn't go past that door." Murray was affable. He was also very serious about his job.

Jack nodded agreement. "No problem. It was a kidnap, too, wasn't it?"

The FBI agent grimaced and shook his head. "I've handled about a half-dozen kidnappings and closed every case with a conviction. We only lost one hostage—they killed that kid the first day. Those two were executed. I watched," Murray said coldly. "Kidnapping is a high-risk crime all the way down the line. They have to be at a specific place to get their money—that's usually what gets 'em caught. We can track people like you wouldn't believe, then bring in the cavalry hard and fast. In this case . . . we're talking some impressive bargaining chips, and there would not be a money transfer—the public release of some 'political' prisoners is the obvious objective. The evidence does lean that way, except that these characters have never done one of those. It makes the escape procedures a lot more complex, but these ULA characters have always had their escape routes well planned beforehand. I'd say you're probably right, but it's not as clear-cut as you think. Owens and Taylor aren't completely sure, and our friend isn't talking. Big surprise."

"They've never made a public announcement, you said? Was this supposed to be their break into the big time? Their first public announcement, they might as well do it with something spectacular," Ryan said thoughtfully.

"That's a fair guess." Murray nodded. "It certainly would have put them on the map. Like I said, our intel on these chaps is damned thin; almost all of it's secondhand stuff that comes through the PIRA—which is why we thought they were actually part of it. We haven't exactly figured what they're up to. Every one of their operations has—how do I say this? There seems to be a pattern there, but nobody's ever figured it out. It's almost as though the political fallout isn't aimed at us at all, but that doesn't make any sense—not that it *has* to make sense," the agent grunted. "It's not easy trying to psychoanalyze the terrorist mind."

"Any chance they'll come after me, or—"

Murray shook his head. "Unlikely, and the security's pretty tight. You know who they have taking your wife and kid around?"

"SAS—I asked."

"That youngster's on their Olympic pistol team, and I hear that he has some field experience that never made the papers. The DPG escort is also one of the varsity, and they'll have a chase car everywhere they go. The security on you is pretty impressive, too. You have some big-league interest in your safety. You can relax. And after you get home it's all behind you. None of these groups has *ever* operated in the U.S. We're too important to them. NORAID means more to them psychologically than financially. When they fly to Boston, it's like crawling back into the womb, all the beers people buy for them, it tells them that they're the good guys. No, if they started raising hell out our side of the pond—I don't think they could take being persona non grata in Boston. It's the only real weak point the PIRA and the rest have, and unfortunately it's not one that we can exploit all that well. We've pretty much cut down on the weapons pipeline, but, hell, they get most of their stuff from the other side now. Or they make their own. Like explosives. All you need is a bag of ammonia-based fertilizer and you can make a respectable bomb. You can't arrest a farmer for carrying fertilizer in his truck, can you? It's not as sexy as some good plastique, but it's a hell of a lot easier to get. For guns and heavier stuff—anybody can get AK-47s and RPGs, they're all over the place. No, they depend on us for moral support, and there's quite a few people who'll give it, even in Congress. Remember the fight over the extradition treaty? It's amazing. These bastards kill people.

"Both sides." Murray paused for a moment. "The Protestant crazies are just as bad. The Provisionals waste a prod. Then the Ulster Volunteer Force sends a car through a Catholic neighborhood and pops the first convenient target. A lot of the killing is purely random now. Maybe a third of the kills are people who were walking down the wrong street. The process feeds on itself, and there's not much of a middle ground left anymore. Except the cops—I know, the RUC used to be the bad guys, too, but they've just about ended that crap. The Law has got to be the Law for everyone—but that's too easy to forget sometimes, like in Mississippi back in the sixties, and that's essentially what happened in Northern Ireland. Sir Jack Hermon is trying to turn the RUC into a professional police force. There are plenty of people left over from the bad old days, but the troops are coming around. They must be. The cops are taking casualties from both sides, the last one was killed by prods. They firebombed his house." Murray shook his head. "It's amazing. I was just over there two weeks ago. Their morale's great, especially with the new kids. I don't know how they do it—well, I do know. They have their mission, too. The cops and the courts have to reestablish justice, and the people have to see that they're doing it. They're the only hope that place has, them and a few of the church leaders. Maybe common sense'll break out someday, but don't hold your breath. It's going to take a long time. Thank God for Tom Jefferson and Jim Madison, bub. Sometimes I wonder how close we came to that sectarian stuff. It's like a Mafia war that everybody can play in."

"Well, Judge?" Admiral James Greer hit the off switch on the remote control as the Cable News Network switched topics. The Director of Central Intelligence tapped his cigar on the cut-glass ashtray.

"We know he's smart, James, and it looks like he knows how to handle himself with reporters, but he's impetuous," Judge Arthur Moore said.

"Come on, Arthur. He's young. I want somebody in here with some fresh ideas. You going to tell me now that you didn't like his report? First time at bat, and he turns out something that good!"

Judge Moore smiled behind his cigar. It was drizzling outside the seventh-floor window of the office of the Deputy Director, Intelligence, of the Central Intelligence

Agency. The rolling hills of the Potomac Valley prevented his seeing the river, but he could spy the hills a mile or so away on the far side. It was a far prettier view than that of the parking lots.

"Background check?"

"We haven't done a deep one yet, but I'll bet you a bottle of your favorite bourbon that he comes up clean."

"No bet, James!" Moore had already seen Jack's service record from the Marine Corps. Besides, he hadn't come to the Agency. They had gone to him and he'd turned them down on the first offer. "You think he can handle it, eh?"

"You really ought to meet the kid, Judge. I had him figured out the first ten minutes he was in here last July."

"You arranged the leak?"

"Me? Leak?" Admiral Greer chuckled. "Nice to know how he can handle himself, though, isn't it? Didn't even blink when he fielded the question. The boy takes his clearance seriously, and"—Greer held up the telex from London—"he's asking good questions. Emil says his man Murray was fairly impressed, too. It's just a damned shame to waste him teaching history."

"Even at your alma mater?"

Greer smiled. "Yes, that does hurt a little. I want him, Arthur. I want to teach him, I want to groom him. He's our kind of people."

"But he doesn't seem to think so."

"He will." Greer was quietly positive.

"Okay, James. How do you want to approach him?"

"No hurry. I want a very thorough background check done first—and who knows? Maybe he'll come to us."

"No chance," Judge Moore scoffed.

"He'll come to us requesting information on this ULA bunch," Greer said.

The Judge thought about that one. One thing about James Greer, Moore knew, was his ability to see into things and people as though they were made of crystal. "That makes sense."

"You bet it does. It'll be a while—the Attaché says he has to stay over for the trial and all—but he'll be in this office two weeks after he gets back, asking for a chance to research this ULA outfit. If he does, I'll pop the offer—if you agree, Arthur. I also want to talk to Emil Jacobs at FBI and compare files on these ULA characters."

"Okay."

They turned to other matters.

5. Perqs and Plots

The day Ryan was released from the hospital was the happiest in his life, at least since Sally had been born at Johns Hopkins, four years before. It was after six in the evening when he finally finished dressing himself—the cast made that a very tricky exercise—and plopped down in the wheelchair. Jack had groused about that, but it was evidently a rule as inviolable in British hospitals as in American ones: patients are not allowed to walk out—somebody might think they were cured. A uniformed policeman pushed him out of the room into the hall. Ryan didn't look back.

Virtually the whole floor staff was lined up in the hall, along with a number of the patients Ryan had met the past week and a half as he'd relearned how to walk up and down the drab corridors—with a ten-degree list from the heavy cast. Jack flushed red at the applause, the more so when people reached out to shake his hand. *I'm not an Apollo astronaut,* he thought. *The Brits are supposed to be more dignified than this.*

Nurse Kittiwake gave a little speech about what a model patient he was. *What a pleasure and an honor . . .* Ryan blushed again when she finished, and gave him some flowers, to take to his lovely wife, she said. Then she kissed him, on behalf of everyone else. Jack kissed back. It was the least he could do, he told himself, and she really was a pretty girl. Kittiwake hugged him, cast and all, and tears started running out of her eyes. Tony Wilson was at her side and gave Jack a surreptitious wink. That was no surprise. Jack shook hands with another ten or so people before the cop got him into the elevator.

"Next time you guys find me wounded in the street," Ryan said, "let me die there."

The policeman laughed. "Bloody ungrateful fellow you are."

"True."

The elevator opened at the lobby and he was grateful to see that it had been cleared except for the Duke of Edinburgh and a gaggle of security people.

"Good evening, My Lord." Ryan tried to stand, but was waved back down.

"Hello, Jack! How are you feeling?" They shook hands, and for a moment he was afraid that the Duke himself would wheel him out the door. That would have been intolerable, but the police officer resumed his pushing as the Duke walked alongside. Jack pointed forward.

"Sir, I will improve at least fifty percent when we make it through that door."

"Hungry?"

"After hospital food? I just might eat one of your polo horses."

The Duke grinned. "We'll try to do a little better than that."

Jack noticed seven security people in the lobby. Outside was a Rolls-Royce . . . and at least four other cars, along with a number of people who did not look like ordinary passersby. It was too dark to see anyone prowling the roofs, but they'd be there, too. *Well,* Ryan thought, *they've learned their lessons on security. Still a damned shame, though, and it means the terrorists have won a victory. If they make society change, even a little, they've won something. Bastards.* The cop brought him right to the Rolls.

"Can I get up now?" The cast was so heavy that it ruined his balance. Ryan stood a little too fast and nearly smashed into the car, but caught himself with an angry shake of the head before anyone had to grab for him. He stood still for a moment, his left arm sticking out like the big claw on a fiddler crab, and tried to figure how to get into the car. It turned out that the best way was to stick the cast in first, then rotate clockwise as he followed it. The Duke had to enter from the other side, and it turned out to be rather a snug fit. Ryan had never been in a Rolls before, and found that it wasn't all that spacious.

"Comfortable?"

"Well—I'll have to be careful not to punch a window out with this damned thing." Ryan leaned back and shook his head with an eyes-closed smile.

"You really are glad to be out of hospital."

"My Lord, on that you can wager one of your castles. This makes three times I've been in the body and fender shop, and that's enough." The Duke motioned for the driver to pull out. The convoy moved slowly into the street, two lead cars and two chase cars surrounding the Rolls-Royce. "Sir, may I ask what's happening this evening?"

"Very little, really. A small party in your honor, with just a few close friends."

Jack wondered what "a few close friends" meant. Twenty? Fifty? A hundred? He was going to dinner at . . . *Scotty, beam me up!* "Sir, you know that you've really been too kind to us."

"Bloody rubbish. Aside from the debt we owe you—not exactly what one would call a small debt, Jack. Aside from that, it's been entirely worthwhile to meet some new people. I even finished your book Sunday night. I thought it was excellent; you must send me a copy of your next one. And the Queen and your wife have got on marvelously. You are a very lucky chap to have a wife like that—and that little imp of a daughter. She's a gem, Jack, a thoroughly wonderful little girl."

Ryan nodded. He often wondered what he had done to be so lucky. "Cathy says that she's seen about every castle in the realm, and thanks a lot for the people you put with her. It made me feel much better about having them run all over the place."

The Duke waved his hand dismissively. It wasn't worth talking about. "How did the research go on your new book?"

"Quite well, sir." The one favorable result of his being in the hospital was that he'd had the time to sift through all of it in detail. His computer had two hundred new pages of notes stored in its bubble chips, and Ryan had a new perspective on judging the actions of others. "I guess I've learned one thing from my little escapade. Sitting in front of a keyboard isn't quite the same as looking into the front end of a gun. Decisions are a little different from that perspective." Ryan's tone made a further statement.

The Duke clapped him on the knee. "I shouldn't think that anyone will fault yours."

"Maybe. The thing is, my decision was made on pure instinct. If I'd known what I was doing—what if I had done the *wrong* thing on instinct?" He looked out the window. "Here I am, supposed to be an expert on naval history, with special emphasis on how decisions are made under stress, and I'm still not satisfied with my own. Damn." Jack concluded quietly: "Sir, you don't forget killing somebody. You just don't."

"You oughtn't to dwell on it, Jack."

"Yes, sir." Ryan turned back from the window. The Duke was looking at him much the same way his father had, years before. "A conscience is the price of morality, and morality is the price of civilization. Dad used to say that many criminals don't have a conscience, not much in the way of feelings at all. I guess that's what makes us different from them."

"Exactly. Your introspection is a fundamentally healthy thing, but you should not overdo it. Put it behind you, Jack. It was my impression of Americans that you prefer to look to the future rather than the past. If you cannot do that professionally, at least try to do it personally."

"Understood, sir. Thank you." *Now if I could just make the dreams stop.* Nearly every night Jack relived the shoot-out on The Mall. Almost three weeks now. Something else they didn't tell you about on TV. The human mind has a way of punishing itself for killing a fellow man. It remembers and relives the incident again and again. Ryan hoped it would stop someday.

The car turned left onto Westminster Bridge. Jack hadn't known exactly where the hospital was, just that it was close to a railway station and close enough to Westminster to hear Big Ben toll the hours. He looked up at the gothic stonework. "You know, besides the research I wanted to do, I actually wanted to see part of your country, sir. Not much time left for that."

"Jack, do you really think that we will let you return to America without experiencing British hospitality?" The Duke was greatly amused. "We are quite proud of our hospitals, of course, but tourists don't come here to see those. Some small arrangements have been made."

"Oh."

Ryan had to think a moment to figure where they were, but the maps he'd studied before coming over came back to him. It was called Birdcage Walk—he was only three hundred yards from where he'd been shot . . . there was the lake that Sally liked. He could see Buckingham Palace past the head of the security officer in the left front seat. Knowing that he was going there was one thing, but now the building loomed in front of him and the emotional impact started to take hold.

They entered the Palace grounds at the northeast gate. Jack hadn't seen the Palace before except from a distance. The perimeter security didn't seem all that impressive, but the Palace's hollow-square design hid nearly everything from outside view. There could easily be a company of armed troops inside—and who could tell? More likely civilian police, Ryan knew, backed up by a lot of electronic hardware. But there would be some surprises hidden away, too. After the scares in the past, and this latest incident, he imagined that this place was as secure as the White House—or even better, given greater space in and around the buildings.

It was too dark to make out many details, but the Rolls pulled through an archway into the building's courtyard, then under a canopy, where a sentry snapped to present-arms in the crisp three-count movement the Brits used. As the car stopped, a footman in livery pulled the door open.

Getting out was the reverse of getting in. Ryan turned counterclockwise, stepped out backwards, and pulled his arm out behind. The footman grabbed his arm to help. Jack didn't want the help, but this wasn't a good time to object.

"You'll need a little practice on that," the Duke observed.

"I think you're right, sir." Jack followed him to the door, where another servant did his duty.

"Tell me, Jack—the first time we visited you, you seemed far more intimidated by the presence of the Queen than of me. Why is that?"

"Well, sir, you used to be a naval officer, right?"

"Of course." The Duke turned and looked rather curious.

Ryan grinned. "Sir, I work at Annapolis. The Academy crawls with naval officers, and remember I used to be a Marine. If I let myself get intimidated by every swabbie who crossed my path, the Corps would come and take my sword back."

"You cheeky bugger!" They both had a laugh.

Ryan had expected to be impressed by the Palace. Even so, it was all he could manage to keep from being overwhelmed. Half the world had once been run from this house, and in addition to what the Royal Family had acquired over the centuries had come gifts from all over the world. Everywhere he looked the wide corridors were decorated with too many masterpieces of painting and sculpture to count. The walls were mainly covered with ivory-colored silk brocaded with gold thread. The carpets, of course, were imperial scarlet over marble or parquet hardwood. The money manager that Jack had once been tried to calculate the value of it all. He overloaded after about ten seconds. The paintings alone were so valuable that any attempt to sell them off would distort the world market in fine art. The gilt frames alone. . . . Ryan shook his head, wishing he had the time to examine every painting. *You could live here five years and not have time to appreciate it all.* He almost fell behind, but managed to control his gawking and kept pace with the older man. Ryan's discomfiture was growing. To the Duke this was home—perhaps one so large as to be something of a nuisance, but nonetheless home, routine. The Rubens masterpieces on the wall were part of the scenery, as familiar to him as the photographs of wife and kids on any man's office desk. To Ryan the impact of where he was, an impact made all the more crushing by the trappings of wealth and power, made him want to shrink away to nothingness. It was one thing to take his chance on the street—the Marines, after all, had prepared and trained him for that—but . . . *this.*

Get off it, Jack, he told himself. *They're a royal family, but they're not* your *royal family.* This didn't work. They were *a* royal family. That was enough to lacerate most of his ego.

"Here we are," the Duke said after turning right through an open door. "This is the Music Room."

It was about the size of the living/dining room in Ryan's house, the only thing he had seen thus far that could be so compared with any part of his $300,000 home on Peregrine Cliff. The ceiling was higher here, domed with gold-leaf trim. There were about thirty people, Ryan judged, and the moment they entered all conversation stopped. Everyone turned to stare at Ryan—Jack was sure they'd seen the Duke before—and his grotesque cast. He had a terrible urge to slink away. He needed a drink.

"If you'll excuse me for a moment, Jack, I must be off. Back in a few minutes."

Thanks a lot, Ryan thought as he nodded politely. *Now what do I do?*

"Good evening, Sir John," said a man in the uniform of a vice admiral of the Royal Navy. Ryan tried not to let his relief show. Of course, he'd been handed off to another custodian. He realized belatedly that lots of people came here for the first time. Some would need a little support while they got used to the idea of being in a palace, and there would be a procedure to take care of them. Jack took a closer look at the man's face as they shook hands. There was something familiar about it. "I'm Basil Charleston."

Aha! "Good evening, sir." His first week at Langley he'd seen the man, and his CIA escort had casually noted that this was "B.C." or just "C," the chief of the British Secret Intelligence Service, once known as MI-6. *What are you doing here?*

"You *must* be thirsty." Another man arrived with a glass of champagne. "Hello. I'm Bill Holmes."

"You gentlemen work together?" Ryan sipped at the bubbling wine.

"Judge Moore told me you were a clever chap," Charleston observed.

"Excuse me? Judge who?"

"Nicely done, Doctor Ryan," Holmes smiled as he finished off his glass. "I understand that you used to play football—the American kind, that is. You were on the junior varsity team, weren't you?"

"Varsity and junior varsity, but only in high school. I wasn't big enough for college ball," Ryan said, trying to mask his uneasiness. "Junior Varsity" was the project name under which he'd been called in to consult with CIA.

"And you wouldn't happen to know anything about the chap who wrote *Agents and Agencies*?" Charleston smiled. Jack went rigid.

"Admiral, I cannot talk about that without—"

"Copy number sixteen is sitting on my desk. The good judge told me to tell you that you were free to talk about the 'smoking word-processor.' "

Ryan let out a breath. The phrase must have come originally from James Greer. When Jack had made the Canary Trap proposal to the Deputy Director, Intelligence, Admiral James Greer had made a joke about it, using those words. Ryan was free to talk. Probably. His CIA security briefing had not exactly covered this situation.

"Excuse me, sir. Nobody ever told me that I was free to talk about that."

Charleston went from jovial to serious for a moment. "Don't apologize, lad. One is supposed to take matters of classification seriously. That paper you wrote was an excellent bit of detective work. One of our problems, as someone doubtless told you, is that we take in so much information now that the real problem is making sense of it all. Not easy to wade through all the muck and find the gleaming nugget. For the first time in the business, your report was first-rate. What I didn't know about was this thing the Judge called the Canary Trap. He said you could explain it better than he." Charleston waved for another glass. A footman, or some sort of servant, came over with a tray. "You know who I am, of course."

"Yes, Admiral. I saw you last July at the Agency. You were getting out of the executive elevator on the seventh floor when I was coming out of the DDI's office, and somebody told me who you were."

"Good. Now you know that all of this remains in the family. What the devil is this Canary Trap?"

"Well, you know about all the problems CIA has with leaks. When I was finishing off the first draft of the report, I came up with an idea to make each one unique."

"They've been doing that for years," Holmes noted. "All one must do is misplace a comma here and there. Easiest thing in the world. If the newspeople are foolish enough to print a photograph of the document, we can identify the leak."

"Yes, sir, and the reporters who publish the leaks know that, too. They've learned not to show photographs of the documents they get from their sources, haven't they?" Ryan answered. "What I came up with was a new twist on that. *Agents and Agencies* has four sections. Each section has a summary paragraph. Each of those is written in a fairly dramatic fashion."

"Yes, I noticed that," Charleston said. "Didn't read like a CIA document at all. More like one of ours. We use people to write our reports, you see, not computers. Do go on."

"Each summary paragraph has six different versions, and the mixture of those paragraphs is unique to each numbered copy of the paper. There are over a thousand possible permutations, but only ninety-six numbered copies of the actual document. The reason the summary paragraphs are so—well, lurid, I guess—is to entice a reporter to quote them verbatim in the public media. If he quotes something from two or three of those paragraphs, we know which copy he saw and, therefore, who leaked it. They've got an even more refined version of the trap working now. You can do it by computer. You use a thesaurus program to shuffle through synonyms, and you can make every copy of the document totally unique."

"Did they tell you if it worked?" Holmes asked.

"No, sir. I had nothing to do with the security side of the Agency." *And thank God for that.*

"Oh, it worked." Sir Basil paused for a moment. "That idea is bloody simple—and bloody brilliant! Then there was the substantive aspect of the paper. Did they tell you that your report agreed in nearly every detail with an investigation we ran last year?"

"No, sir, they didn't. So far as I know, all the documents I worked with came from our own people."

"Then you came up with it entirely on your own? Marvelous."

"Did I goof up on anything?" Ryan asked the Admiral.

"You should have paid a bit more attention to that South African chap. That is more our patch, of course, and perhaps you didn't have enough information to fiddle with. We're giving him a very close look at the moment."

Ryan finished off his glass and thought about that. There had been a good deal of information on Mr. Martens . . . *What did I miss?* He couldn't ask that, not now. Bad form. But he could ask—

"Aren't the South African people—"

"I'm afraid the cooperation they give us isn't quite as good now as it once was, and Erik Martens is quite a valuable chap for them. One can hardly blame them, you know. He does have a way of procuring what their military need, and that rather limits the pressure his government are willing to put on him," Holmes pointed out. "There is also the Israeli connection to be considered. They occasionally stray from the path, but we—SIS and CIA—have too many common interests to rock the boat severely." Ryan nodded. The Israeli defense establishment had orders to generate as much income as possible, and this occasionally ran contrary to the wishes of Israel's allies. *I remember Martens' connections, but I must have missed something important . . . what?*

"Please don't take this as criticism," Charleston said. "For a first attempt your report was excellent. The CIA must have you back. It's one of the few Agency reports that didn't threaten to put me to sleep. If nothing else, perhaps you might teach their analysts how to write. Surely they asked if you wanted to stay on?"

"They asked, sir. I didn't think it was a very good idea for me."

"Think again," Sir Basil suggested gently. "This Junior Varsity idea was a good one, like the Team-B program back in the seventies. We do it also—get some outside academics into the shop—to take a new look at all the data that cascades in the front door. Judge Moore, your new DCI, is a genuine breath of fresh air. Splendid chap. Knows the trade quite well, but he's been away from it long enough to have some new ideas. You are one of them, Doctor Ryan. You belong in the business, lad."

"I'm not so sure about that, sir. My degree's history and—"

"So is mine," Bill Holmes said. "One's degree doesn't matter. In the intelligence trade we look for the right sort of mind. You appear to have it. Ah, well, *we* can't recruit you, can we? I would be rather disappointed if Arthur and James don't try again. Do think about it."

I have, Ryan didn't say. He nodded thoughtfully, mulling over his own thoughts. *But I* like *teaching history.*

"The hero of the hour!" Another man joined the group.

"Good evening, Geoffrey," Charleston said. "Doctor Ryan, this is Geoffrey Watkins of the Foreign Office."

"Like David Ashley of the 'Home Office'?" Ryan shook the man's hand.

"Actually I spend much of my time right here," Watkins said.

"Geoff's the liaison officer between the Foreign Office and the Royal Family. He handles briefings, dabbles in protocol, and generally makes a nuisance of himself," Holmes explained with a smile. "How long now, Geoff?"

Watkins frowned as he thought that over. "Just over four years, I think. Seems like only last week. Nothing like the glamour one might expect. Mainly I carry the dispatch box and try to hide in corners." Ryan smiled. He could identify with that.

"Nonsense," Charleston objected. "One of the best minds in the Office, else they wouldn't have kept you here."

Watkins made an embarrassed gesture. "It does keep me rather busy."

"It must," Holmes observed. "I haven't seen you at the tennis club in months."

"Doctor Ryan, the Palace staff have asked me to express their appreciation for what you have done." He droned on for a few more seconds. Watkins was an inch under Ryan's height and pushing forty. His neatly trimmed black hair was going gray at the sides, and his skin was pale in the way of people who rarely saw the sun. He looked like a diplomat. His smile was so perfect that he must have practiced it in front of a mirror. It was the sort of smile that could have meant anything. Or more likely, nothing. There was interest behind those blue eyes, though. As had happened many times in the past few weeks, this man was trying to decide what Dr. John Patrick Ryan was made of. The subject of the investigation was getting very tired of this, but there wasn't much Jack could do about it.

"Geoff is something of an expert on the Northern Ireland situation," Holmes said.

"No one's an 'expert,' " Watkins said with a shake of his head. "I was there at the beginning, back in 1969. I was in uniform then, a subaltern with—well, that hardly matters now, does it? How do you think we should handle the problem, Doctor Ryan?"

"People have been asking me that question for three weeks, Mr. Watkins. How the hell should I know?"

"Still looking for ideas, Geoff?" Holmes asked.

"The right idea is out there somewhere," Watkins said, keeping his eyes on Ryan.

"I don't have it," Jack said. "And even if someone did, how would you know? I teach history, remember, I don't make it."

"Just a history teacher, and these two chaps descend on you?"

"We wanted to see if he really works for CIA, as the papers say," Charleston responded.

Jack took the signal from that. Watkins wasn't cleared for everything, and was not to know about his past association with the Agency—not that he couldn't draw his own conclusions, Ryan reminded himself. Regardless, rules were rules. *That's why I turned Greer's offer down,* Jack remembered. *All those idiot rules. You can't talk to anybody about this or that, not even to your wife. Security. Security. Security . . . Crap! Sure,* some *things have to stay secret, but if nobody gets to see them, how is anyone supposed to make use of them—and what good is a secret you can't use?*

"You know, it'll be nice to get back to Annapolis. At least the mids believe I'm a teacher!"

"Quite," Watkins noted. *And the head of SIS is asking you for an opinion on Trafalgar. What exactly are you, Ryan?* After leaving military service in 1972 and joining the Foreign Office, Watkins had often played the foreign service officer's embassy game: *Who's the spook?* He was getting mixed signals from Ryan, and this made the game all the more interesting. Watkins loved games. All sorts.

"How do you keep yourself busy now, Geoff?" Holmes asked.

"You mean, aside from the twelve-hour days? I do manage to read the occasional book. I just started going through *Moll Flanders* again."

"Really?" Holmes asked. "I just started *Robinson Crusoe* a few days ago. One sure way of getting one's mind off the world is to return to the classics."

"Do you read the classics, Doctor Ryan?" Watkins asked.

"Used to. Jesuit education, remember? They don't let you avoid the old stuff." *Is* Moll Flanders *a classic*? Jack wondered. *It's not in Latin or Greek, and it's not Shakespeare. . . .*

" 'Old stuff.' What a terrible attitude!" Watkins laughed.

"Did you ever try to read Virgil in the original?" Ryan asked.

"Arma virumque cano, trojae qui primus ab oris . . . ?"

"Geoff and I attended Winchester together," Holmes explained. *"Contiquere omnes, intenteque ora tenebant. . . ."* Both public school graduates had a good chuckle.

"Hey, I got good marks in Latin, I just don't remember any of it," Ryan said defensively.

"Another colonial philistine," Watkins observed.

Ryan decided that he didn't like Mr. Watkins. The foreign-service officer was deliberately hitting him to get reactions, and Ryan had long since tired of this game. Ryan was happy with what he was, and didn't need a bunch of amateur pshrinks, as he called them, to define his personality for him.

"Sorry. Where I live we have slightly different priorities."

"Of course," Watkins replied. The smile hadn't changed a whit. This surprised Jack, though he wasn't sure why.

"You live not far from the Naval Academy, don't you? Wasn't there some sort of incident there recently?" Sir Basil asked. "I read about it in some report somewhere. I never did get straight on the details."

"It wasn't really terrorism—just your basic crime. A couple of midshipmen saw what looked like a drug deal being made in Annapolis, and called the police. The people who got arrested were members of a local motorcycle gang. A week later, some of the gang members decided to take the mids out. They got past the Jimmy Legs—the civilian security guards—about three in the morning and sneaked into Bancroft Hall. They must have assumed that it was just another college dorm—not hardly. The kids standing midwatch spotted them, got the alarm out, and then everything came apart. The intruders got themselves lost—Bancroft has a couple of miles of corridors—and cornered. It's a federal case since it happened on government property, and the FBI takes a very dim view of people who try to tamper with witnesses. They'll be gone for a while. The good news is that the Marine guard force at the Academy has been beefed up, and it's a lot easier to get in and out now."

"Easier?" Watkins asked. "But—"

Jack smiled. "With Marines on the perimeter, they leave a lot more gates open—a Marine guard beats a locked gate any day."

"Indeed. I—" Something caught Charleston's eye. Ryan was facing the wrong way to see what it was, but the reactions were plain enough. Charleston and Holmes began to disengage, with Watkins making his way off first. Jack turned in time to see the Queen appear at the door, coming past a servant.

The Duke was at her side, with Cathy trailing a diplomatically defined distance behind and to the side. The Queen came first to him.

"You are looking much better."

Jack tried to bow—he thought he was supposed to—without endangering the Queen's life with his cast. The main trick was standing still, he'd learned. The weight of the thing tended to induce a progressive lean to the left. Moving around helped him stay upright.

"Thank you, Your Majesty. I feel much better. Good evening, sir."

One thing about shaking hands with the Duke, you knew there was a man at the other end. "Hello again, Jack. Do try to be at ease. This is completely informal. No receiving line, no protocol. Relax."

"Well, the champagne helps."

"Excellent," the Queen observed. "I think we'll let you and Caroline get reacquainted for the moment." She and the Duke moved off.

"Easy on the booze, Jack." Cathy positively glowed in a white cocktail dress so lovely that Ryan forgot to wonder what it had cost. Her hair was nicely arranged and she had makeup on, two things that her profession regularly denied her. Most of all, she was Cathy Ryan. He gave his wife a quick kiss, audience and all.

"All these people—"

"Screw 'em," Jack said quietly. "How's my favorite girl?"

Her eyes sparkled with the news, but her voice was deadpan-professional: "Pregnant."

"You sure—*when*?"

"I'm sure, darling, because, A, I'm a doctor, and B, I'm two weeks late. As to when, Jack, remember when we got here, as soon as we put Sally down to bed. . . . It's those strange hotel beds, Jack." She took his hand. "They do it every time."

There wasn't anything for Jack to say. He wrapped his good arm around her shoulders and squeezed as discreetly as his emotions would allow. If she was two weeks late—well, he knew Cathy to be as regular as her Swiss watch. *I'm going to be a daddy—again!*

"We'll try for a boy this time," she said.

"You know that's not important, babe."

"I see you've told him." The Queen returned as quietly as a cat. The Duke, Jack saw, was talking to Admiral Charleston. About what? he wondered. "Congratulations, Sir John."

"Thank you, Your Majesty, and thank you for a lot of things. We'll never be able to repay you for all your kindness."

The Christmas-tree smile again. "It is we who are repaying you. From what Caroline tells me, you will now have at least one positive reminder of your visit to our country."

"Indeed, ma'am, but more than one." Jack was learning how the game was played.

"Caroline, is he always so gallant?"

"As a matter of fact, ma'am, no. We must have caught him at a weak moment," Cathy said. "Or maybe being over here is a civilizing influence."

"That is good to know, after all the horrid things he said about your little Olivia. Do you know that she refused to go to bed without kissing me goodnight? Such a lovely, charming little angel. And *he* called her a menace!"

Jack sighed. It wasn't hard for him to get the picture. After three weeks in this environment, Sally was probably doing the cutest curtsies in the history of Western

Civilization. By this time the Palace staff was probably fighting for the right to look after her. Sally was a true daddy's girl. The ability to manipulate the people around her came easily. She'd practiced on her father for years.

"Perhaps I exaggerated, ma'am."

"Libelously." The Queen's eyes flared with amusement. "She has not broken a single thing. Not one. And I'll have you know that she's turning into the best equestrienne we have seen in years."

"Excuse me?"

"Riding lessons," Cathy explained.

"You mean on a horse?"

"What else would she ride?" the Queen asked.

"Sally, on a horse?" Ryan looked at his wife. He didn't like that idea very much.

"And doing splendidly." The Queen sprang to Cathy's defense. "It's quite safe, Sir John. Riding is a fine skill for a child to learn. It teaches discipline, coordination, and responsibility."

Not to mention a fabulous way to break her pretty little neck, Ryan thought. Again he remembered that one does not argue with a queen, especially under her own roof.

"You could even try to ride yourself," the Queen said. "Your wife rides."

"We have enough land now, Jack," Cathy said. "You'd love it."

"I'd fall off," Ryan said bleakly.

"Then you climb back on again until you get it right," said a woman with over fifty years of riding behind her.

It's the same with a bike, except you don't fall as far off a bike, and Sally's too little *for a bike,* Ryan told himself. He got nervous watching Sally move her Hotwheels trike around the driveway. *For God's sake, she's so little the horse wouldn't even know if she was there or not.* Cathy read his mind.

"Children do have to grow up. You can't protect her from everything," his wife pointed out.

"Yes, dear, I know." *The hell I can't. That's my job.*

A few minutes later everyone headed out the room for dinner. Ryan found himself in the Blue Drawing Room, a breathtaking pillared hall, and then passed through mirrored double doors into the State Dining Room.

The contrast was incredible. From a room of muted blue they entered one ablaze with scarlet, fabric-covered walls. Overhead the vaulted ceiling was ivory and gold, and over the snow-white fireplace was a massive portrait—of whom? Ryan wondered. It had to be a king, of course, probably 18th or 19th century, judging by his white . . . pantyhose, or whatever they'd called them then, complete with garter. Over the door they'd entered was the royal cipher of Queen Victoria, VR, and he wondered how much history had passed through—or been made right in this single room.

"You will sit at my right hand, Jack," the Queen said.

Ryan took a quick look at the table. It was wide enough that he didn't have to worry about clobbering Her Majesty with his left arm. That wouldn't do.

The worst thing about the dinner was that Ryan would be forever unable to remember—and too proud to ask Cathy—what it was. Eating one-handed was something he'd had a lot of practice at, but never had he had such an audience, and Ryan was sure that everyone was watching him. After all, he was a Yank and would have been something of a curiosity even without his arm. He constantly reminded himself to be careful, to go easy on the wine, to watch his language. He shot the occasional glance at Cathy, sitting at the other end of the table next to the Duke and clearly enjoying herself. It made her husband slightly angry that she was more at ease than he was. *If there was ever a pig in the manger,* Ryan thought while chewing on something he immediately forgot, *it's me*. He wondered if he would be here now, had he been a rookie cop or a private in the Royal Marines who just happened to be at the right place. Probably not, he thought. *And why is that?* Ryan didn't know. He did know that something about the institution of nobility went against his American outlook. At the same time, being knighted—even honorarily—was something he liked. It was a contradiction that troubled him in a way he didn't understand. All this attention was too seductive, he told himself. *It'll be good to get away from it. Or will it?* He sipped at a glass of wine. *I know I don't belong here, but do I* want *to belong here? There's a good question*. The wine didn't give him an answer. He'd have to find it somewhere else.

He looked down the table to his wife, who did seem to fit in very nicely. She'd been raised in a similar atmosphere, a monied family, a big house in Westchester County, lots of parties where people told one another how important they all were. It was a life he'd rejected, and that she had walked away from. They were both happy with what they had, each with a career, but did her ease with this mean that she missed . . . Ryan frowned.

"Feeling all right, Jack?" the Queen asked.

"Yes, ma'am, please excuse me. I'm afraid it will take me a while to adjust to all of this."

"Jack," she said quietly, "the reason everyone likes you—and we all do, you know—is because of who and what you are. Try to keep that in mind."

It struck Ryan that this was probably the kindest thing he'd ever been told. Perhaps nobility was supposed to be a state of mind rather than an institution. His father-in-law could learn from that, Ryan thought. His father-in-law could learn from a lot of things.

Three hours later Jack followed his wife into their room. There was a sitting room off to the right. In front of him the bed had already been turned down. He pulled the tie loose from his collar and undid the button, then let out a long, audible breath.

"You weren't kidding about turning into pumpkins."

"I know," his wife said.

Only a single dim light was lit, and his wife switched it off. The only illumination in the room was from distant streetlights that filtered through the heavy curtains. Her white dress stood out in the darkness, but her face showed only the curve of her lips and the sparkle of her eyes as she turned away from the light. Her husband's mind filled in the remaining details. Jack wrapped his good arm around his wife and cursed the monstrosity of plaster that encased his left side as he pulled her in close. She rested her head on his healthy shoulder, and his cheek came down to the softness of her fine blond hair. Neither said anything for a minute or two. It was enough to be alone, together in the quiet darkness.

"Love ya, babe."

"How are you feeling, Jack?" The question was more than a simple inquiry.

"Not bad. Pretty well rested. The shoulder doesn't hurt very much anymore. Aspirin takes care of the aches." This was an exaggeration, but Jack was used to the discomfort.

"Oh, I see how they did it." Cathy was exploring the left side of his jacket. The tailors had put snap closures on the underside so that it would not so much conceal the cast as make it look dressed. His wife removed the snaps quickly and pulled the coat off. The shirt went next.

"I am able to do this myself, you know."

"Shut up, Jack. I don't want to have to wait all night for you to undress." He next heard the sound of a long zipper.

"Can I help?"

There was laughter in the darkness. "I might want to wear this dress again. And be careful where you put that arm."

"I haven't crunched anyone yet."

"Good. Let's try to keep a perfect record." A whisper of silk. She took his hand. "Let's get you sitting down."

After he sat on the edge of the bed, the rest came easy. Cathy sat beside him. He felt her, cool and smooth at his side, a hint of perfume in the air. He reached around her shoulder, down to the soft skin of her abdomen.

It's happening right now, growing away while we sit here. "You're going to have my baby," Jack said softly. *There really is a God, and there really are miracles.*

Her hand came across his face. "That's right. I can't have anything to drink after tonight—but I wanted to enjoy tonight."

"You know, I really do love you."

"I know," she said. "Lie back."

6. Trials and Troubles

Preliminary testimony lasted for about two hours while Ryan sat on a marble bench outside Old Bailey's number two courtroom. He tried to work on his computer, but he couldn't seem to keep his mind on it, and found himself staring around the hundred-sixty-year-old building.

Security was incredibly tight. Outside, numerous uniformed police constables stood about in plain sight, small zippered pistol cases dangling from their hands. Others, uniformed and not, stood on the buildings across Newgate Street like falcons on the watch for rabbits. Except rabbits don't carry machine guns and RPG-7 bazookas, Ryan thought. Every person who entered the building was subjected to a metal detector sensitive enough to *ping* on the foil inside a cigarette pack, and nearly everyone was given a pat-down search. This included Ryan, who was surprised enough at the intimacy of the search to tell the officer that he went a bit far for a first date. The grand hall was closed off to anyone not connected with the case, and less prominent trials had been switched among the building's nineteen courtrooms to accommodate *Crown v Miller*.

Ryan had never been in a courthouse before. He was amused by the fact that he'd never even had a speeding ticket, his life had been so dull until now. The marble floor—nearly everything in sight was marble—gave the hall the aspect of a cathedral, and the walls were decorated with aphorisms such as Cicero's THE WELFARE OF THE PEOPLE IS THE HIGHEST LAW, a phrase he found curiously—or at least potentially—expedient in what was certainly designed as a temple to the idea of law. He wondered if the members of the ULA felt the same way, and justified their activities in accordance with their view of the welfare of the people. *Who doesn't?* Jack asked himself. *What tyrant ever failed to justify his crimes?* Around him were a half-dozen other witnesses. Jack didn't talk with them. His instructions were quite specific: even the appearance of conversation might give cause to the defense attorneys to speculate that witnesses had coached one another. The prosecution team had bent every effort to make their case a textbook example of correct legal procedure.

The case was being handled on a contradictory basis. The ambush had taken place barely four weeks ago, and the trial was already under way—an unusually speedy process even by British standards. Security was airtight. Admittance to the public gallery (visitors entered from another part of the building) was being strictly controlled. But at the same time, the trial was being handled strictly as a criminal matter. The name ''Ulster Liberation Army'' had not been mentioned. The prosecutor had not once used the word terrorist. The police ignored—publicly—the political aspects of the case. Two men were dead, and this was a trial for first-degree murder—period. Even the press was playing along, on the theory that there was no more contemptuous way to treat the defendant than to call him a simple criminal, and not sanctify him as a creature of politics. Jack wondered about additional political or intelligence-related motives in this treatment, but no one was talking along those lines, and the defense attorney certainly couldn't defend his client better by calling him a member of a terrorist group. In the media, and in the courtroom, this was a case of murder.

The truth was different, of course, and everyone knew it. But Ryan knew enough about the law to remember that lawyers rarely concern themselves with truth. The rules were far more important. There would therefore be no official speculation on the goal of the criminals, and no involvement of the Royal Family, aside from depositions that they could not identify the living conspirator and hence had no worthwhile evidence to offer.

It didn't matter. From the press coverage of the evidence it seemed clear enough that the trial was as airtight as was possible without a videotape of the entire event. Similarly, Cathy was not to testify. In addition to forensic experts who had testified the day before, the Crown had eight eyewitnesses. Ryan was number two. The trial was expected to last a maximum of four days. As Owens had told him in the hospital, there would be no mucking about with this lad.

''Doctor Ryan? Would you please follow me, sir?'' The VIP treatment continued here also. A bailiff in short sleeves and tie came over and led him into the courtroom through a side door. A police officer took his computer after opening the door. ''Showtime,'' Ryan whispered to himself.

Old Bailey #2 was an extravagance of 19th-century woodworking. The large room was paneled with so much solid oak that the construction of a similar room in America would draw a protest from the Sierra Club for all the trees it required. The actual floorspace was surprisingly small, scarcely as much as the dining room in his house, a similarity made all the more striking by a table set in the center. The judge's bench was a wooden fortress adjacent to the witness box. The Honorable Mr. Justice Wheeler sat in one of the five high-backed chairs behind it. He was resplendent in a scarlet robe and sash, and a horsehair wig, called a ''peruke,'' Ryan had been told, that fell to his narrow shoulders and clearly looked like something from another age. The jury box was to Ryan's left. Eight women and four men sat in two even rows, each face full of anticipation. Above them was the public gallery, perched like a choir loft and angled so that Ryan could barely see the people there. The barristers were to Ryan's right, across the small floorspace, wearing black robes, 18th-century cravats, and their own, smaller wigs. The net effect of all this was a vaguely religious atmosphere that made Ryan slightly uneasy as he was sworn in.

William Richards, QC, the prosecutor, was a man of Ryan's age, similar in height and build. He began with the usual questions: your name, place of residence, profession, when did you arrive, for what purpose? Richards predictably had a flair for the dramatic, and by the time the questions carried them to the shooting, Ryan could sense the excitement and anticipation of the audience without even looking at their faces.

"Doctor Ryan, could you describe in your own words what happened next?"

Jack did exactly this for ten minutes, without interruption, all the while half-facing the jury. He tried to avoid looking into their faces. It seemed an odd place to get stage fright, but this was precisely what Ryan felt. He focused his eyes on the oak panels just over their heads as he ran through the events. It was almost like living it again, and Ryan could feel his heart beating faster as he concluded.

"And, Doctor Ryan, can you identify for us the man whom you first attacked?" Richards finally asked.

"Yes, sir." Ryan pointed. "The defendant, right there, sir."

It was Ryan's first really good look at him. His name was Sean Miller—not a particularly Irish name to Ryan's way of thinking. He was twenty-six, short, slender, dressed neatly in a suit and tie. He was smiling up at someone in the visitors' gallery, a family member perhaps, when Ryan pointed. Then his gaze shifted, and Ryan examined the man for the first time. What sort of person, Jack had wondered for weeks, could plan and execute such a crime? What was missing in him, or what terrible thing lived in him that most civilized people had the good fortune to lack? The thin, acne-scarred face was entirely normal. Miller could have been an executive trainee at Merrill Lynch or any other business concern. Jack's father had spent his life dealing with criminals, but their existence was a puzzlement to Ryan. *Why are you different? What makes you what you are?* Ryan wanted to ask, knowing that even if there were an answer the question would remain. Then he looked at Miller's eyes. He looked for . . . something, a spark of life, humanity—something that would say that this was indeed another human being. It could only have been two seconds, but for Ryan the moment seemed to linger into minutes as he looked into those pale gray eyes and saw . . .

Nothing. Nothing at all. And Jack began to understand a little.

"The record will show," the Lord Justice intoned to the court reporter, "that the witness identified the defendant, Sean Miller."

"Thank you, My Lord," Richards concluded.

Ryan took the opportunity to blow his nose. He'd acquired a head cold over the preceding weekend.

"Are you quite comfortable, Doctor Ryan?" the judge inquired. Jack realized that he'd been leaning on the wooden rail.

"Excuse me, your hon—My Lord. This cast is a little tiring." Every time Sally came past her father, she had taken to singing, "I'm a little teapot . . ."

"Bailiff, a stool for the witness," the judge ordered.

The defense team was seated adjacent to the prosecution, perhaps fifteen feet farther away in the same row of seats, green leather cushions on the oak benches.

In a moment the bailiff arrived with a simple wooden stool, and Ryan settled down on it. What he really needed was a hook for his left arm, but he was gradually becoming used to the weight. It was the constant itching that drove him crazy, though there was nothing anybody could do about that.

The defense attorney—barrister—rose with elegant deliberation. His name was Charles Atkinson, more commonly known as Red Charlie, a lawyer with a penchant for radical causes and radical crimes. He was supposed to be an embarrassment to the Labour Party, which he had served until recently in Parliament. Red Charlie was about thirty pounds overweight, his wig askew atop a florid, strangely thin face for the ample frame. Defending terrorists must have paid well enough, Ryan thought. *There's a question Owens must be looking into,* Ryan told himself. *Where is your money coming from, Mr. Atkinson?*

"May it please Your Lordship," he said formally to the bench. He walked slowly towards Ryan, a sheaf of notes in his hand.

"Doctor Ryan—or should I say Sir John?"

Jack waved his hand. "Whatever is convenient to you, sir," he answered indifferently. They had warned him about Atkinson. *A very clever bastard,* they'd said. Ryan had known quite a few clever bastards in the brokerage business.

"You were, I believe, a *left*enant in the United States Marine Corps?"

"Yes, sir, that is correct."

Atkinson looked down at his notes, then over at the jury. "Bloodthirsty mob, the U.S. Marines," he muttered.

"Excuse me, sir? Bloodthirsty?" Ryan asked. "No, sir. Most of the Marines I know are beer drinkers."

Atkinson spun back at Ryan as a ripple of laughter came down from the gallery. He gave Jack a thin, dangerous smile. They'd warned Jack most of all to beware his word games and tactical skill in the courtroom. *To hell with it,* Ryan told himself. He smiled back at the barrister. *Go for it, asshole. . . .*

"Forgive me, Sir John. A figure of speech. I meant to say that the U.S. Marines have a reputation for aggressiveness. Surely this is true?"

"Marines are light infantry troops who specialize in amphibious assault. We were pretty well trained, but when you get down to it we weren't all that different from any other kind of soldier. It's just a matter of specialization in a particularly tough field," Ryan answered, hoping to throw him a little off balance. Marines were supposed to be arrogant, but that was mostly movie stuff. If you're really good, they'd taught him at Quantico, you don't have to be arrogant. Just letting people know you're a Marine was usually enough.

"Assault troops?"

"Yes, sir. That's basically correct."

"So, you commanded assault troops, then?"

"Yes, sir."

"Try not to be too modest, Sir John. What sort of man is selected to lead such troops. Aggressive? Decisive? Bold? Certainly he would have more of these qualities than the average foot soldier?"

"As a matter of fact, sir, in my edition of *The Marine Officer's Guide,* the foremost of the qualities that the Corps looks for in an officer is *integrity.*" Ryan smiled again. Atkinson hadn't done his homework on that score. "I commanded a platoon, sure, but as my captain explained to me when I came aboard, my principal job was to carry out the orders he gave me, and to lean on my gunny—my platoon sergeant—for his practical experience. The job I was in was supposed to be as much a learning experience as a command slot. I mean, in business it's called an entry-level position. You don't start shaking the world your first day on the job in any business.''

Atkinson frowned a bit. This was not going as he'd expected.

''Ah, then, Sir John, a *lef*tenant of American Marines is really a leader of Boy Scouts. Surely you don't mean that?'' he asked, a sarcastic edge on his voice.

''No, sir. Excuse me, I did not mean to give that impression, but we're not a bunch of hyperaggressive barbarians either. My job was to carry out orders, to be as aggressive as the situation called for, and to exercise some amount of judgment, like any officer. But I was only there three months, and I was still learning how to be an officer when I was injured. Marines follow orders. Officers give orders, of course, but a second lieutenant is the lowest form of officer. You take more than you give. I guess you've never been in the service,'' Ryan tagged on the barb at the end.

''So, what sort of training *did* they give you?'' Atkinson demanded, either angry or feigning it.

Richards looked up to Ryan, a warning broadcast from his eyes. He'd emphasized several times that Jack shouldn't cross swords with Red Charlie.

''Really, basic leadership skills. They taught us how to lead men in the field,'' Ryan replied. ''How to react to a given tactical situation. How to employ the platoon's weapons, and to a lesser extent, the weapons in a rifle company. How to call in outside support from artillery and air assets—''

''To react?''

''Yes, sir, that is part of it.'' Ryan kept his answers as long as he thought he could get away with, careful to keep his voice even, friendly, and informative. ''I've never been in anything like a combat situation—unless you count this thing we're talking about, of course—but our instructors were very clear about telling us that you don't have time to think very much when bullets are flying. You have to know what to do, and you have to do it fast—or you get your own people killed.''

''Excellent, Sir John. You were trained to react quickly and decisively to tactical stimuli, correct?''

''Yes, sir.'' Ryan thought he saw the ambush coming.

''So, in the unfortunate incident before this court, when the initial explosion took place, you have testified that you were looking in the wrong direction?''

''I was looking away from the explosion, yes, sir.''

''How soon afterwards did you turn to see what was happening?''

''Well, sir, as I said earlier, the first thing I did was to get my wife and daughter down under cover. Then I looked up. How long did that take?'' Ryan cocked his head. ''At least one second, sir, maybe as many as three. Sorry, but as I said earlier, it's hard to recall that sort of thing—you don't have a stopwatch on yourself, I mean.''

''So, when you *finally* did look up, you had not seen what had immediately transpired?''

''Correct, sir.'' *Okay, Charlie, ask the next question.*

''You did not, therefore, see my client fire his pistol, nor throw a hand grenade?''

Cute, Ryan thought, surprised that he'd try this ploy. *Well, he has to try something, doesn't he?* ''No, sir. When I first saw him, he was running around the corner of the car, from the direction of the other man, the one who was killed—the one with the rifle. A moment later he was at the right-rear corner of the Rolls, facing away from me, with the pistol in his right hand, pointed forward and down, as if—''

"Assumption on your part," Atkinson interrupted. "As if what? It could have been any one of several things. But what things? How could you tell what he was doing there? You did not see him get out of the car, which later drove off. For all you know he might have been another pedestrian racing to the rescue, just as you did, mightn't he?"

Jack was supposed to be surprised by this.

"Assumption, sir? No, I'd call it a judgment. For him to have been racing to the rescue as you suggest, he would have had to come from across the street. I doubt that anyone could have reacted anywhere near fast enough to do that at all, not to mention the fact that there was a guy there with a machine gun to make you think twice about it. Also, the direction I saw him running from was directly away from the guy with the AK-47. If he was running to the rescue, why away from him? If he had a gun, why not shoot him? At the time I never considered this possibility, and it seems pretty unlikely now, sir."

"Again, a *conclusion,* Sir John," Atkinson said as though to a backward child.

"Sir, you asked me a question, and I tried to answer it, with the reasons to back up my answer."

"And you expect us to believe that all this flashed through your mind in a brief span of seconds?" Atkinson turned back to the jury.

"Yes, sir, it did," Ryan said with conviction. "That's all I can say—it did."

"I don't suppose you've been told that my client has never been arrested, or accused of any crime?"

"I guess that makes him a first offender."

"It's for the jury to decide that," the lawyer snapped back. "You did not see him fire a single shot, did you?"

"No, sir, but his automatic had an eight-shot clip, and there were only three rounds in it. When I fired my third shot, it was empty."

"So what? For all you know someone else could have fired that gun. You did not see him fire, did you?"

"No, sir."

"So it might have been dropped by someone in the car. My client might have picked it up and, I repeat, been doing the same thing you were doing—this could all be true, but you have no way of knowing this, do you?"

"I cannot testify about things I didn't see, sir. However, I *did* see the street, the traffic, and the other pedestrians. If your client did what you say, where did he come from?"

"Precisely—you don't know, do you?" Atkinson said sharply.

"When I saw your client, sir, he was coming from the direction of the stopped car." Jack gestured to the model on the evidence table. "For him to have come off the sidewalk, then gotten the gun, and then appeared where I saw him—there's just no way unless he's an Olympic-class sprinter."

"Well, we'll never know, will we—you fixed that. You reacted precipitously, didn't you? You reacted as you were trained to by the U.S. Marines, never stopping to assess the situation. You raced into the fray quite recklessly, attacked my client and knocked him unconscious, then tried to kill him."

"No, sir, I did not try to kill your client. I've already—"

"Then why did you shoot an unconscious, helpless man?"

"My Lord," prosecutor Richards said, standing up, "we have already asked that question."

"The witness may answer on further reflection," Justice Wheeler intoned. No one would say that this trial was unfair.

"Sir, I did not know he was unconscious, and I didn't know how long it would be before he got up. So, I shot to disable him. I just didn't want him to get back up for a while."

"I'm sure that's what they said at My Lai."

"That wasn't the Marines, Mr. Atkinson," Ryan shot back.

The lawyer smiled up at Jack. "I suppose your chaps were better trained at keeping quiet. Indeed, perhaps you yourself have been trained in such things. . . ."

"No, sir, I have not." *He's making you angry, Jack.* He took his handkerchief out and blew his nose again. The two deep breaths helped. "Excuse me, I'm afraid the local weather has given me a bit of a head cold. What you just said—if the Marines trained people in that sort of stuff, the newspapers would have plastered it on their front pages years ago. No, moral issues aside for the moment, the Corps has a much better sense of public relations than that, Mr. Atkinson."

"In*deed.*" The barrister shrugged. "And what about the Central Intelligence Agency?"

"Excuse me?"

"What of the press reports that you've worked for the CIA?"

"Sir, the only times I've been paid by the U.S. government," Jack said, choosing his words very carefully, "the money came from the Navy Department, first as a Marine, then later—now, that is, as an instructor at the United States Naval Academy. I have never been employed by any other government agency, period."

"So you are not an agent of the CIA? I remind you that you are under oath."

"No, sir. I am not now, and I never have been any kind of agent—unless you count being a stockbroker. I don't work for the CIA."

"And these news reports?"

"I'm afraid that you'll have to ask the reporters. I don't know where that stuff comes from. I teach history. My office is in Leahy Hall on the Naval Academy grounds. That's kind of a long way from Langley."

"Langley? You know where CIA is, then?"

"Yes, sir. It's on record that I have delivered a lecture there. It was the same lecture I delivered the month before at the Naval War College at Newport, Rhode Island. My paper dealt with the nature of tactical decision-making. I have never worked for the Central Intelligence Agency, but I did, once, give a lecture there. Maybe that's where all these reports started."

"I think you're lying, Sir John," Atkinson observed.

Not quite, Charlie. "I can't help what you think, sir. I can only answer your questions truthfully."

"And you never wrote an official report for the government entitled *Agents and Agencies*?"

Ryan did not allow himself to react. *Where did you get that bit of data, Charlie?* He answered the question with great care.

"Sir, last year—that is, last summer, at the end of the last school year—I was asked to be a contract consultant to a private company that does government work. The company is the Mitre Corporation, and I was hired on a temporary basis as part of one of their consulting contracts with the U.S. government. The work involved was classified, but it obviously had nothing at all to do with this case."

"Obviously? Why don't you let the jury decide that?"

"Mr. Atkinson," Justice Wheeler said tiredly, "are you suggesting that this work in which the witness was involved has a direct connection with the case before the court?"

"I think we might wish to establish that, My Lord. It is my belief that the witness is misleading the court."

"Very well." The judge turned. "Doctor Ryan, did this work in which you were engaged have anything whatever to do with a case of murder in the city of London, or with any of the persons involved in this case?"

"No, sir."

"You are quite certain?"

"Yes, sir."

"Are you now or have you ever been an employee of any intelligence or security agency of the American government?"

"Except for the Marine Corps, no, sir."

"I remind you of your oath to tell the truth—the whole, complete truth. Have you misled the court in any way, Doctor Ryan?"

"No, sir, absolutely not."

"Thank you, Doctor Ryan. I believe that question is now settled." Mr. Justice Wheeler turned back to his right. "Next question, Mr. Atkinson."

The barrister had to be angry at that, Ryan thought, but he didn't let it show. He wondered if someone had briefed the judge.

"You say that you shot my client *merely* in the hope that he would not get up?"

Richards stood. "My Lord, the witness has already—"

"If His Lordship will permit me to ask the next question, the issue will be more clear," Atkinson interrupted smoothly.

"Proceed."

"Doctor Ryan, you said that you shot my client in the hope that he would not get up. Do the U.S. Marine Corps teach one to shoot to disable, or to kill?"

"To kill, sir."

"And you are telling us, therefore, that you went against your training?"

"Yes, sir. It is pretty clear that I was not on a battlefield. I was on a city street. It never occurred to me to kill your client." *I wish it* had, *then I probably wouldn't be here,* Ryan thought, wondering if he really meant it.

"So you reacted in accordance with your training when you leaped into the fray on The Mall, but then you *disregarded* your training a moment later? Do you think it reasonable that all of us here will believe *that*?"

Atkinson had finally succeeded in confusing Ryan. Jack had not the slightest idea where this was leading.

"I haven't thought of it that way, sir, but, yes, you are correct," Jack admitted. "That is pretty much what happened."

"And next you crept to the corner of the automobile, saw the second person whom you had seen earlier, and instead of trying to disable him, you shot him dead without warning. In this case, it is clear that you reverted again to your Marine training, and shot to kill. Don't you find this inconsistent?"

Jack shook his head. "Not at all, sir. In each case I used the force necessary to—well, the force I had to use, as I saw things."

"I think you are wrong, Sir John. I think that you reacted like a hotheaded officer of the United States Marines throughout. You raced into a situation of which you had no clear understanding, attacked an innocent man, and tried then to kill him while he lay helpless and unconscious on the street. Next you coldly gunned down someone else without the first thought of trying to disarm him. You did not know then, and you do not know now what was really happening, do you?''

''No, sir, I do not believe that was the case at all. What was I supposed to have done with the second man?''

Atkinson saw an opening and used it. ''You just told the court that you only wished to disable my client—when in fact you tried to kill him. How do you expect us to believe that when your next action had not the first thing to do with such a *peaceful* solution?''

''Sir, when I saw McCrory, the second gunman, for the first time, he had an AK-47 assault rifle in his hands. Going up against a light machine gun with a pistol—''

''But by this time you saw that he didn't have the Kalashnikov, didn't you?''

''Yes, sir, that's true. If he'd still had it—I don't know, maybe I wouldn't have stepped around the car, maybe I would have shot from cover, from behind the car, that is.''

''Ah, I see!'' Atkinson exclaimed. ''Instead, here was your chance to confront and kill the man in true cowboy fashion.'' His hands went up in the air. ''Dodge City on The Mall!''

''I wish you'd tell me what you think I should have done,'' Jack said with some exasperation.

''For someone able to shoot straight through the heart on his first shot, why not shoot the gun from his hand, Sir John?''

''Oh, I see.'' Atkinson had just made a mistake. Ryan shook his head and smiled. ''I wish you'd make up your mind.''

''What?'' The barrister was caught by surprise.

''Mr. Atkinson, a minute ago you said that I tried to kill your client. I was at arm's-length range, but I *didn't* kill him. So I'm a pretty lousy shot. But you expect me to be able to hit a man in the hand at fifteen or twenty feet. It doesn't work that way, sir. I'm either a good shot or a bad shot, sir, but not both. Besides, that's just TV stuff, shooting a gun out of somebody's hand. On TV the good guy can do that, but TV isn't real. With a pistol, you aim for the center of your target. That's what I did. I stepped out from behind the car to get a clear shot, and I aimed. If McCrory had not turned his gun towards me—I can't say for sure, but probably I would not have shot. But he did turn and fire, as you can see from my shoulder—and I did return fire. It is true that I might have done things differently. Unfortunately I did not. I had—I didn't have much time to take action. I did the best I could. I'm sorry the man was killed, but that was his choice, too. He saw I had the drop on him, but he turned and fired—and he fired first, sir.''

''But you never said a word, did you?''

''No, I don't think I did,'' Jack admitted.

''Don't you wish you'd done things differently?''

''Mr. Atkinson, if it makes you feel any better, I have gone over that again and again for the past four weeks. If I'd had more time to think, perhaps I would have done something different. But I'll never know, because I didn't have more time.'' Jack paused. ''I suppose the best thing for all concerned would be if all this had never happened. But I didn't make it happen, sir. He did.'' Jack allowed himself to look at Miller again.

Miller was sitting in a straight-back wooden chair, his arms crossed in front of him, and head cocked slightly to the left. A smile started to take shape at one corner of his mouth. It didn't go very far, and wasn't supposed to. It was a smile for Ryan alone . . . or maybe not me alone, Jack realized. Sean Miller's gray eyes didn't blink—he must have practiced that—as they bored in on him from thirty feet away. Ryan returned the stare, careful to keep his face without expression, and while the court reporter finished up his transcription of Jack's testimony, and the visitors in the overhead gallery shared whispered observations, Ryan and Miller were all alone, testing each other's wills. *What's behind those eyes?* Jack wondered again. No weakling, to be sure. This was a game—Miller's game that he'd practiced before, Ryan thought with certainty. There was strength in there, like something one might encounter in a predatory animal. But there was nothing to mute the strength. There was none of the softness of morality or conscience, only strength and will. With four police constables around him, Sean Miller was as surely restrained as a wolf in a cage, and he looked at Ryan as a wolf might from behind the bars, without recognition of his humanity. He was a predator, looking at a . . . thing—and wondering how he might reach it. The suit and the tie were camouflage, as had been his earlier smile at his friends in the gallery. He wasn't thinking about them now. He wasn't thinking about what the court would decide. He wasn't thinking about prison, Jack knew. He was thinking only about something named Ryan, something he could see just out of his reach. In the witness box, Jack's right hand flexed in his lap as though to grasp the pistol which lay in sight on the evidence table a few feet away.

This wasn't an animal in a cage, after all. Miller had intelligence and education. He could think and plan, as a human could, but he would not be restrained by any human impulses when he decided to move. Jack's academic investigation of terrorists for the CIA had dealt with them as abstractions, robots that moved about and did things, and had to be neutralized one way or another. He'd never expected to meet one. More important, Jack had never expected to have one look at him in this way. Didn't he know that Jack was just doing his civic duty?

You could care less about that. I'm something that got in your way. I hurt you, killed your friend, and defeated your mission. You want to get even, don't you? A wounded animal will always seek out its tormentor, Jack told himself. *And this wounded animal has a brain. This one has a memory.* Out of sight to anyone else, he wiped a sweaty hand on his pants. *This one is* thinking.

Ryan was frightened in a way that he'd never known before. It lasted several seconds before he reminded himself that Miller *was* surrounded by four cops, that the jury would find him guilty, that he would be sentenced to prison for the remainder of his natural life, and that prison life would change the person or thing that lived behind those pale gray eyes.

And I used to be a Marine, Jack told himself. *I'm not afraid of you. I can handle you, punk. I took you out once, didn't I?* He smiled back at Sean Miller, just a slight curve at the corner of his own mouth. *Not a wolf—a weasel. Nasty, but not that much to worry about,* he told himself. Jack turned away as though from an exhibit in the zoo. He wondered if Miller had seen through his quiet bravado.

"No further questions," Atkinson said.

"The witness may step down," Mr. Justice Wheeler said.

Jack stood up from the stool and turned to find the way out. As he did so, his eyes swept across Miller one last time, long enough to see that the look and the smile hadn't changed.

Jack walked back out to the grand hall as another witness passed in the other direction. He found Dan Murray waiting for him.

"Not bad," the FBI agent observed, "but you want to be careful locking horns with a lawyer. He almost tripped you up."

"You think it'll matter?"

Murray shook his head. "Nah. The trial's a formality, the case is airtight."

"What'll he get?"

"Life. Normally over here 'life' doesn't mean any more than it does stateside—six or eight years. For this kid, 'life' means *life*. Oh, there you are, Jimmy."

Commander Owens came down the corridor and joined them. "How did our lad perform?"

"Not an Oscar winner, but the jury liked him," Murray said.

"How can you tell that?"

"That's right, you've never been through this, have you? They sat perfectly still, hardly even breathed while you were telling your story. They believed everything you said, especially the part about how you've thought and worried about it. You come across as an honest guy."

"I am," Ryan said. "So?"

"Not everybody is," Owens pointed out. "And juries are actually quite good at noticing it. That is, some of the time."

Murray nodded. "We both have some good—well, not so good—stories about what a jury can do, but when you get down to it, the system works pretty well. Commander Owens, why don't we buy this gentleman a beer?"

"A fine idea, Agent Murray." Owens took Ryan's arm and led him to the staircase.

"That kid's a scary little bastard, isn't he?" Ryan said. He wanted a professional opinion.

"You noticed, eh?" Murray observed. "Welcome to the wonderful world of the international terrorist. Yeah, he's a tough little son of a bitch, all right. Most of 'em are, at first."

"A year from now he'll have been changed a bit. He's a hard one, mind, but the hard ones are often rather brittle," Owens said. "They sometimes crack. Time is very much on our side, Jack. And even if he doesn't, that's one less to worry about."

"A very confident witness," the TV news commentator said. "Doctor Ryan fended off a determined attack by the defense counsel, Charles Atkinson, and identified defendant Sean Miller quite positively in the second day of The Mall Murder trial in Old Bailey Number Two." The picture showed Ryan walking down the hill from the courthouse with two men in attendance. The American was gesturing about something, then laughed as he passed the TV news camera.

"Our old friend Owens. Who's the other one?" O'Donnell asked.

"Daniel E. Murray, FBI representative at Grosvenor Square," replied his intelligence officer.

"Oh. Never saw his face. So that's what he looks like. Going out for a jar, I'll wager. The hero and his coat-holders. Pity we couldn't have had a man with an RPG right there. . . ." They'd scouted James Owens once, trying to figure a way to assassinate him, but the man always had a chase car and never used the same route twice. His house was always watched. They could have killed him, but the getaway would have been too risky, and O'Donnell was not given to sending his men on suicide missions. "Ryan goes home either tomorrow or next day."

"Oh?" The intelligence officer hadn't learned that. *Where does Kevin get all his special information . . . ?*

"Too bad, isn't it? Wouldn't it be grand to send him home in a coffin, Michael?"

"I thought you said he was not a worthwhile target," Mike McKenney said.

"Ah, but he's a proud one, isn't he? Crosses swords with our friend Charlie and prances out of the Bailey for a pint of beer. Bloody American, so sure of everything." *Wouldn't it be nice to . . .* Kevin O'Donnell shook his head. "We have other things to plan. Sir John can wait, and so can we."

"I practically had to hold a gun on somebody to get to do this," Murray said over his shoulder. The FBI agent was driving his personal car, with a Diplomatic Protection Group escort on the left front seat, and a chase car of C-13 detectives trying to keep up.

Keep your eyes on the damned road, Ryan wished as hard as he could. His exposure to London traffic to this point had been minimal, and only now did he appreciate that the city's speed limit was considered a matter of contempt by the drivers. Being on the wrong side of the road didn't help either.

"Tom Hughes—he's the Chief Warder—told me what he had planned, and I figured you might want an escort who talks right."

And drives right, Ryan thought as they passed a truck—lorry—on the wrong side. *Or was it the right side? How do you tell?* He could tell that they'd missed the truck's taillights by about eighteen inches. English roads were not impressive for their width.

"Damned shame you didn't get to see very much."

"Well, Cathy did, and I caught a lot of TV."

"What did you watch?"

Jack laughed. "I caught a lot of the replays of the cricket championships."

"Did you ever figure out the rules?" Murray asked, turning his head again.

"It has rules?" Ryan asked incredulously. "Why spoil it with rules?"

"They say it does, but damn if I ever figured them out. But we're getting even now."

"How's that?"

"Football is becoming pretty popular over here. Our kind, I mean. I gave Jimmy Owens a big runaround last year on the difference between offside and illegal procedure."

"You mean encroachment and false start, don't you?" the DPG man inquired.

"See? They're catching on."

"You mean I could have gotten football on TV, and nobody told me!"

"Too bad, Jack," Cathy observed.

"Well, here we are." Murray stood on the brakes as he turned downhill toward the river. Jack noticed that he seemed to be heading the wrong way down a one-way street, but at least he was going more slowly now. Finally the car stopped. It was dark. The sunset came early this time of year.

"Here's your surprise." Murray jumped out and got the door, allowing Ryan to repeat his imitation of a fiddler crab exiting from a car. "Hi, there, Tom!"

Two men approached, both in Tudor uniforms of blue and red. The one in the lead, a man in his late fifties, came directly to Ryan.

"Sir John, Lady Ryan, welcome to Her Majesty's Tower of London. I am Thomas Hughes, this is Joseph Evans. I see that Dan managed to get you here on time." Everyone shook hands.

"Yeah, we didn't even have to break mach-1. May I ask what the surprise is?"

"But then it wouldn't be a surprise," Hughes pointed out. "I had hoped to conduct you around the grounds myself, but there's something I must attend to. Joe will see to your needs, and I will rejoin you shortly.'' The Chief Warder walked off with Dan Murray in his wake.

''Have you been to the Tower before?'' Evans asked. Jack shook his head.

''I have, when I was nine,'' Cathy said. ''I don't remember very much.''

Evans motioned for them to come along with him. ''Well, we'll try to implant the knowledge more permanently this time.''

''You guys are all soldiers, right?''

''Actually, Sir John, we are all ex–sergeant majors—well, two of us were warrant officers. I was sergeant major in 1 Para when I retired. I had to wait four years to get accepted here. There is quite a bit of interest in this job, as you might imagine. The competition is very keen.''

''So, you were what we call a command sergeant-major, sir?''

''Yes, I think that's right.''

Ryan gave a quick look to the decorations on Evans' coat—it looked more like a dress, but he had no plans to say that. Those ribbons didn't mean that Evans had come out of the dentist's office with no cavities. It didn't take much imagination to figure what sort of men got appointed to this job. Evans didn't walk; he marched with the sort of pride that took thirty years of soldiering to acquire.

''Is your arm troubling you, sir?''

''My name's Jack, and my arm's okay.''

''I had a cast just like that one back in sixty-eight, I think it was. Training accident,'' Evans said with a rueful shake of his head. ''Landed on a stone fence. Hurt like the very devil for weeks.''

''But you kept jumping.'' *And did your push-ups one-handed, didn't you?*

''Of course.'' Evans stopped. ''Right, now this imposing edifice is the Middle Tower. There used to be an outer structure right there where the souvenir shop is. They called it the Lion Tower, because that's where the royal menagerie was kept until 1834.''

The speech was delivered as perfectly as Evans had done, several times per day, for the past four years. *My first castle,* Jack thought, looking at the stone walls.

''Was the moat for-real?''

''Oh, yes, and a very unpleasant one at that. The problem, you see, was that it was designed so that the river would wash in and out every day, thereby keeping it fresh and clean. Unfortunately the engineer didn't do his sums quite right, and once the water came in, it stayed in. Even worse, everything that got thrown away by the people living here was naturally enough thrown into the moat—and stayed there, and rotted. I suppose it served a tactical purpose, though. The smell of the moat alone must have been sufficient to keep all but the most adventurous chaps away. It was finally drained in 1843, and now it serves a really useful purpose—the children can play football there. On the far side are swings and jungle gyms. Do you have children?''

''One and a ninth,'' Cathy answered.

''Really?'' Evans smiled in the darkness. ''Bloody marvelous! I suppose that's one Yank who will be forever—at least a little—British! Moira and I have two, both of them born overseas. Now this is the Byward Tower.''

''These things all had drawbridges, right?'' Jack asked.

''Yes, the Lion and Middle towers were essentially islands with twenty or so feet of smelly water around them. You'll also notice that the path into the grounds has a right-angle turn. The purpose of that, of course, was to make life difficult for the chaps with the battering ram."

Jack looked at the width of the moat and the height of the walls as they passed into the Tower grounds proper. "So nobody ever took this place?"

Evans shook his head. "There has never been a serious attempt, and I wouldn't much fancy trying today."

"Yeah," Ryan agreed. "You sweat having somebody come in and bomb the place?"

"That's happened, I am sorry to say, in the White Tower, over ten years ago—terrorists. Security is somewhat tighter now," Evans said.

In addition to the Yeoman Warders there were uniformed guards like those Ryan had encountered on The Mall, wearing the same red tunics and bearskin hats, and carrying the same kind of modern rifle. It was rather an odd contrast to Evans' period uniform, but no one seemed to notice.

"You know, of course, that this facility served many purposes over the years. It was the royal prison, and as late as World War Two, Rudolf Hess was kept here. Now, do you know who was the first Queen of England to be executed here?"

"Anne Boleyn," Cathy answered.

"Very good. They teach our history in America?" Evans asked.

"*Masterpiece Theatre,*" Cathy explained. "I saw the TV show."

"Well, then you know that all the private executions were carried out with an ax—except hers. King Henry had a special executioner imported from France; he used a sword instead of an ax."

"He didn't want it to hurt?" Cathy asked with a twisted smile. "Nice of him."

"Yes, he was a considerate chap, wasn't he? And this is Traitor's Gate. You might be interested to know that it was originally called the Water Gate."

Ryan laughed. "Lucky for you guys too, eh?"

"Indeed. Prisoners were taken through this gate by boat to Westminster for trial."

"Then back here for their haircuts?"

"Only the really important ones. Those executions—they were private instead of public—were done on the Tower Green. The public executions were carried out elsewhere." Evans led them through the gate in the Bloody Tower, after explaining its history. Ryan wondered if anyone had ever put all this place's history into one book, and if so, how many volumes it required.

The Tower Green was far too pleasant to be the site of executions. Even the signs to keep people off the grass said *Please*. Two sides were lined with Tudor-style (of course) houses, but the northern edge was the site where the scaffolding was erected for the high-society executions. Evans went through the procedure, which included having the executionee pay the headsman—in advance—in the hope that he'd do a proper job.

"The last woman to be executed here," Evans went on, "was Jane, Viscountess Rochford, 13 February, 1542."

"What did she do?" Cathy asked.

"What she didn't do, actually. She neglected to tell King Henry the Eighth that his fifth wife, Catherine Howard, was, uh, amorously engaged with someone other than her husband," Evans said delicately.

"That was a real historic moment," Jack chuckled. "That's the last time a woman was ever executed for keeping her mouth *shut*."

Cathy smiled at her husband. "Jack, how about I break your other arm?"

"And what would Sally say?"

"She'd understand," his wife assured him.

"Sergeant major, isn't it amazing how women stick together?"

"I did not survive thirty-one years as a professional soldier by being so foolish as to get involved in domestic disputes," Evans said sensibly.

I lose, Ryan told himself. The remainder of the tour lasted about twenty minutes. The Yeoman led them downhill past the White Tower, then left toward an area roped off from the public. A moment later Ryan and his wife found themselves in another of the reasons that men applied for the job.

The Yeoman Warders had their own little pub hidden away in the 14th-century stonework. Plaques from every regiment in the British Army—and probably gifts from many others—lined the walls. Evans handed them off to yet another man. Dan Murray reappeared, a glass in his hand.

"Jack, Cathy, this is Bob Hallston."

"You must be thirsty," the man said.

"You could talk me into a beer," Jack admitted. "Cathy?"

"Something soft."

"You're sure?" Hallston asked.

"I'm not a temperance worker, I just don't drink when I'm pregnant," Cathy explained.

"Congratulations!" Hallston took two steps to the bar and returned with a glass of lager for Jack, and what looked like ginger ale for his wife. "To your health, and your baby's."

Cathy beamed. There was something about pregnant women, Jack thought. His wife wasn't just pretty anymore. She glowed. He wondered if it was only for him.

"I understand you're a doctor?"

"I'm an ophthalmic surgeon."

"And you teach history, sir?"

"That's right. I take it you work here, too."

"Correct. There are thirty-nine of us. We are the ceremonial guardians of the Sovereign. We have invited you here to thank you for doing our job, and to join us in a small ceremony that we do every night."

"Since 1240," Murray said.

"The year 1240?" Cathy asked.

"Yeah, it's not something they cooked up for the tourists. This is the real thing," Murray said. "Right, Bob?"

"Quite real. When we lock up for the night, this museum collection becomes the safest place in England."

"I'll buy that," Jack tossed off half his beer. "And if they get past those kids out there, the bad guys have you fellows to worry about."

"Yes." Hallston smiled. "One or two of us might remember our basic skills. I was in the original SAS, playing hare and hounds with Rommel in the Western Desert. Dreadful place, the desert. Left me with a permanent thirst."

They never lose it, Ryan thought. They never lose the look, not the real professionals. They get older, add a few pounds, mellow out a little, but beneath all that you can still see the discipline and the essential toughness that makes them different. And the pride, the understated confidence that comes from having done it all, and not having to talk about it very much, except among themselves. It never goes away.

"Do you have any Marines in here?"

"Two," Hallston said. "We try to keep them from holding hands."

"Right! Be nice, I used to be a Marine."

"No one's perfect," Hallston sympathized.

"So, what's this Key Ceremony?"

"Well, back in the year 1240, the chap whose job it was to lock up for the night was set upon by some ruffians. Thereafter, he refused to do his duty without a military escort. Every night since, without interruption, the Chief Warder locks the three principal gates, then places the keys in the Queen's House on the Tower Green. There's a small ceremony that goes along with this. We thought that you and your wife might like to see it." Hallston sipped his beer. "You were in court today, I understand. How did it go?"

"I'm glad it's behind me. Dan says I did all right." Ryan shrugged. "When Mr. Evans showed us the block topside—I wonder if it still works," Ryan said thoughtfully, remembering the look on that young face. *Is Miller sitting in his cell right now, thinking about me?* Ryan drank the last of his beer. *I'll bet he is.*

"Excuse me?"

"That Miller kid. It's a shame you can't take him up there for a short haircut."

Hallston smiled coldly. "I doubt anyone here would disagree with you. We might even find a volunteer to swing the ax."

"You'd have to hold a lottery, Bob." Murray handed Ryan another glass. "You still worrying about him, Jack?"

"I've never seen anybody like that before."

"He's in jail, Jack," Cathy pointed out.

"Yeah, I know." *So why are you still thinking about him?* Jack asked himself. *The hell with it. The hell with him.* "This is great beer, Sar-major."

"That's the real reason they apply for the job," Murray chuckled.

"One of the reasons." Hallston finished his glass. "Almost time."

Jack finished off his second glass with a gulp. Evans reappeared, now wearing street clothes, and led them back out to the chilled night air. It was a clear night, with a three-quarters moon casting muted shadows on the stone battlements. A handful of electric lights added a few isolated splashes of light. Jack was surprised how peaceful it was for being in the center of a city, like his own home over the Chesapeake. Without thinking, he took his wife's hand as Evans led them west toward the Bloody Tower. A small crowd was already there, standing by Traitor's Gate, and a Warder was giving them instructions to be as quiet as possible, and not, of course, to take any photographs. A sentry was posted there, plus four other men under arms, their breath illuminated by the blue-white floodlights. It was the only sign of life. Otherwise they might have been made of stone.

"Right about now," Murray whispered.

Jack heard a door close somewhere ahead. It was too dark to see very much, and the few lights that were turned on only served to impair his night vision. He heard the sound of jingling keys first of all, like small bells rattling to the measured tread of a walking man. Next he saw a point of light. It grew into a square lantern with a candle inside, carried by Tom Hughes, the Chief Warder. The sound of his footsteps was as regular as a metronome as he approached, his back ramrod-straight from a lifetime of practice. A moment later the four soldiers formed up on him, the warder between them, and they marched off, back into the tunnel-like darkness to the fading music of the rattling keys and cleated shoes clicking on the pavement, leaving the sentry at the Bloody Tower.

Jack didn't hear the gates close, but a few minutes later the sound of the keys returned, and he glimpsed the returning guards in the irregular splashes of light. For some reason the scene was overpoweringly romantic. Ryan reached around his wife's waist and pulled her close. She looked up.

Love you, he said with his lips as the keys approached again. Her eyes answered.

To their right, the sentry snapped to on-guard: "Halt! Who goes there?" His words reverberated down the corridor of ancient stone.

The advancing men stopped at once, and Tom Hughes answered the challenge: "The keys!"

"Whose keys?" the sentry demanded.

"Queen Anne's keys!"

"Pass, Queen Anne's keys!" The sentry brought his rifle to present-arms.

The sentries, with Hughes in their midst, resumed their march and turned left, up the slope to the Tower Green. Ryan and his wife followed close behind. At the steps that capped the upward slope waited a squad of riflemen. Hughes and his escort stopped. The squad on the steps came to present-arms, and the Chief Warder removed his uniform bonnet.

"God preserve Queen Anne!"

"Amen!" the guard force replied.

Behind them, a bugler stood. He blew Last Post, the British version of Taps. The notes echoed against the stones in a way that denoted the end of day, and when necessary, the end of life. Like the circular waves that follow a stone's fall into the water, the last mournful note lingered until it faded to nothingness in the still air. Ryan bent down to kiss his wife. It was a magical moment that they would not soon forget.

The Chief Warder proceeded up the steps to secure the keys for the night, and the crowd withdrew.

"Every night since 1240, eh?" Jack asked.

"The ceremony was interrupted during the Blitz. A German bomb fell into the Tower grounds while things were under way. The warder was bowled over by the blast, and the candle in his lantern was extinguished. He had to relight it before he could continue," Evans said. That the man had been wounded was irrelevant. Some things are more important than that. "Shall we return to the pub?"

"We don't have anything like this at home," Cathy said quietly.

"Well, America isn't old enough, is she?"

"It would be nice if we had something like this, maybe at Bunker Hill or Fort McHenry," Jack said quietly.

Murray nodded agreement. "Something to remind us why we're here."

"Tradition is important," Evans said. "For a soldier, tradition is often the reason one carries on when there are so many reasons not to. It's more than just yourself, more than just your mates—but it's not just something for soldiers, is it? It is true—or should be true—of any professional community."

"It is," Cathy said. "Any good medical school beats that into your head. Hopkins sure did."

"So does the Corps," Jack agreed. "But we don't express it as well as you just did."

"We've had more practice." Evans opened the door to the pub. "And better beer to aid in our contemplation."

"Now, if you guys could only learn how to fix beef properly. . . ." Jack said to Evans.

"That's telling 'em, ace," the FBI agent chuckled.

"Another beer for a brother Marine." A glass was handed to Ryan by another of the warders. "Surely you've had enough of this para prima donna by now."

"Bert's one of the Marines I told you about," Evans explained.

"I never say bad things about somebody who buys the drinks," Ryan told Bert.

"That is an awfully sensible attitude. Are you sure you were only a lieutenant?"

"Only for three months." Jack explained about the helicopter crash.

"That *was* bad luck. Bloody training accidents," Evans said. "More dangerous than combat."

"So you guys work as tour guides here?"

"That's part of it," the other warder said. "It's a good way to keep one's hand in, and also to educate the odd lieutenant. Just last week I spoke to one of the Welsh Guards chaps—he was having trouble getting things right, and I gave him a suggestion."

"The one thing you really miss," Evans agreed. "Teaching those young officers to be proper soldiers. Who says the best diplomats work at Whitehall?"

"I never got the feeling that I was completely useless as a second lieutenant," Jack observed with a smile.

"All depends on one's point of view," the other yeoman said. "Still and all, you might have worked out all right, judging by what you did on The Mall."

"I don't know, Bert. A lieutenant with a hero complex is not the sort of chap you want to be around. They keep doing the damnedest things. But I suppose the ones who survive, and learn, do work out as you say. Tell me, Lieutenant Ryan, what have you learned?"

"Not to get shot. The next time I'll just shoot from cover."

"Excellent." Bob Hallston rejoined them. "And don't leave one alive behind you," he added. The SAS wasn't noted for leaving people alive by accident.

Cathy didn't like this sort of talk. "Gentlemen, you can't just kill people like that."

"The Lieutenant took rather a large chance, ma'am, not the sort of chance that one will walk away from very often. If there is ever a next time—and there won't be, of course. But if there is, you can act like a policeman or a soldier, but not both. You're very lucky to be alive, young man. You have that arm to remind you just how lucky you are. It is good to be brave, Lieutenant. It is better to be smart, and much less painful for those around you," Evans said. He looked down at his beer. "Dear God, how *many* times have I said that!"

"How many times have we all said it?" Bert said quietly. "And the pity is, so many of them didn't listen. Enough of that. This lovely lady doesn't want to hear the ramblings of tired old men. Bob tells me that you are expecting another child. In two months, I shall be a grandfather for the first time."

"Yes, he can hardly wait to show us the pictures." Evans laughed. "A boy or a girl this time?"

"Just so all the pieces are attached, and they all work." There was general agreement on the point. Ryan finished off his third beer of the evening. It was pretty strong stuff, and he was getting a buzz from it. "Gentlemen, if any of you come to America, and happen to visit the Washington area, I trust you will let us know."

"And the next time you are in London, the bar is open," Tom Hughes said. The Chief Warder was back in civilian clothes, but carrying his uniform bonnet, a hat whose design went back three or four centuries. "And perhaps you'll find room in your home for this. Sir John, with the thanks of us all."

"I'll take good care of this." Ryan took the hat, but couldn't bring himself to put it on. He hadn't earned that right.

"Now, I regret to say that if you don't leave now, you'll be stuck here all night. At midnight all the doors are shut, and that is that."

Jack and Cathy shook hands all around, then followed Hughes and Murray out the door.

The walk between the inner and outer walls was still quiet, the air still cold, and Jack found himself wondering if ghosts walked the Tower Grounds at night. It was almost—

"What's that?" He pointed to the outer wall. A spectral shape *was* walking up there.

"A sentry," Hughes said. "After the Ceremony of the Keys, the guards don their pattern-disruptive clothing." They passed the sentry at the Bloody Tower, now dressed in camouflage fatigues, with web gear and ammo pouches.

"Those rifles are loaded now, aren't they?" Jack asked.

"Not very much use otherwise, are they? This is a very safe place," Hughes replied.

Nice to know that some places are, Ryan thought. *Now why did I think that?*

7. Speedbird Home

The Speedway Lounge at Heathrow Airport's Terminal 4 was relaxing enough, or would have been had Jack not been nervous about flying. Beyond the floor-to-ceiling windows he could see the Concorde he'd be taking home in a few minutes. The designers had given their creation the aspect of a living creature, like some huge, merciless bird of prey, a thing of fearful beauty. It sat there at the end of the jetway atop its unusually high landing gear, staring at Ryan impassively over its daggerlike nose.

"I wish the Bureau would let me commute back and forth on that baby," Murray observed.

"It's pretty!" Sally Ryan agreed.

It's just another goddamned airplane, Jack told himself. *You can't see what holds it up.* Jack didn't remember whether it was Bernoulli's Principle or the Venturi Effect, but he knew that it was something *inferred,* not actually seen, that enabled aircraft to fly. He remembered that something had interrupted the Principle or Effect over Crete and nearly killed him, and that nineteen months later that same something had reached up and killed his parents five thousand feet short of the runway at Chicago's O'Hare International Airport. Intellectually he knew that his Marine helicopter had died of a mechanical failure, and that commercial airliners were simpler and easier to maintain than CH-46s. He also knew that bad weather had been the main contributing factor in his parents' case—and the weather here was clear—but to Ryan there was something outrageous about flying, something unnatural.

Fine, Jack. Why not go back to living in caves and hunting bear with a pointed stick? What's natural about teaching history, or watching TV, or driving a car? Idiot.

But I hate to fly, Ryan reminded himself.

"There has never been an accident in the Concorde," Murray pointed out. "And Jimmy Owens's troops gave the bird a complete checkout." The possibility of a bomb on that pretty white bird was a real one. The explosives experts from C-13 had spent over an hour that morning making sure that nobody had done that, and now police dressed as British Airways ground crewmen stood around the airliner. Jack wasn't worried about a bomb. Dogs could find bombs.

"I know," Jack replied with a wan smile. "Just a basic lack of guts on my part."

"It's only lack of guts if you don't go, ace," Murray pointed out. He was surprised that Ryan was so nervous, though he concealed it well, the FBI agent thought. Murray enjoyed flying. An Air Force recruiter had almost convinced him to become a pilot, back in his college days.

No, it's lack of brains if I do, Jack told himself. *You really are a wimp,* another part of his brain informed him. *Some Marine you turned out to be!*

"When do we blast off, Daddy?" Sally asked.

"One o'clock," Cathy told her daughter. "Don't bother Daddy."

Blast off, Jack thought with a smile. *Dammit, there is* nothing *to be afraid of and you know it!* Ryan shook his head and sipped at his drink from the complimentary bar. He counted four security people in the lounge, all trying to look inconspicuous. Owens was taking no chances on Ryan's last day in England. The rest was up to British Airways. He wasn't even being billed for the extra cost. Ryan wondered if that was good luck or bad.

A disembodied female voice announced the flight. Jack finished off the drink and rose to his feet.

"Thanks for everything, Dan."

"Can we go now, Daddy?" Sally asked brightly. Cathy took her daughter's hand.

"Wait a minute!" Murray stooped down to Sally. "Don't I get a hug and a kiss?"

"Okay." Sally obliged with enthusiasm. "G'bye, Mr. M'ray."

"Take good care of our hero," the FBI man told Cathy.

"He'll be all right," she assured him.

"Enjoy the football, ace!" Murray nearly crushed Jack's hand. "That's the one thing I really miss."

"I can send you tapes."

"It's not the same. Back to teaching history, eh?"

"That's what I do," Ryan said.

"We'll see," Murray observed cryptically. "How the hell do you walk with that thing on?"

"Badly," Ryan chuckled. "I think the doc installed some lead weights, or maybe he left some tools in there by mistake. Well, here we are." They reached the entrance to the jetway.

"Break a leg." Murray smiled and moved off.

"Welcome aboard, Sir John," a flight attendant said. "We have you in 1-D. Have you flown Concorde before?"

"No." It was all Jack could muster. Ahead of him, Cathy turned and grinned. The tunnel-like jetway looked like the entrance to the grave.

"Well, you are in for the thrill of your life!" the stewardess assured him.

Thanks a lot! Ryan nearly choked at the outrage, and remembered that he couldn't strangle her with one hand. Then he laughed. There wasn't anything else to do.

He had to duck to avoid crunching his head at the door. It was tiny inside; the cabin was only eight or nine feet across. He looked forward quickly and saw the flight crew in impossibly tight quarters—getting into the pilot's left seat must have been like putting on a boot, it seemed so cramped. Another attendant was hanging up coats. He had to wait until she saw him, and walked sideways, his plaster-encased arm leading the way into the passenger cabin.

"Right here," his personal guide said.

Jack got into the right-side window seat in the front row. Cathy and Sally were already in their seats on the other side. Jack's cast stuck well over seat 1-C. No one could have sat there. It was just as well that British Airways wasn't charging the difference between this and their L-1011 tickets; there would have been an extra seat charge. He immediately tried to snap on his seat belt and found that it wasn't easy with only one hand. The stewardess was ready for this, and handled it for him.

"You are quite comfortable?"

"Yes," Jack lied. *I am quite terrified.*

"Excellent. Here is your Concorde information kit." She pointed toward a gray vinyl folder. "Would you like a magazine?"

"No, thank you, I have a book in my pocket."

"Fine. I'll be back after we take off, but if you need anything, please ring."

Jack pulled the seat belt tighter as he looked forward and left at the airplane's door. It was still open. He could still escape. But he knew he wouldn't do that. He leaned back. The seat was gray, too, a little on the narrow side but comfortable. His placement in the front row gave him all the legroom he needed. The airplane's inside wall—or whatever they called it—was off-white, and he had a window to look out of. Not a very large one, about the size of two paperback books, but better than no window at all. He looked around. The flight was about three-quarters full. These were seasoned travelers, and wealthy ones. Business types mostly, Jack figured, many were reading their copies of the *Financial Times*. And none of them were afraid of flying. You could tell from their impassive faces. It never occurred to Jack that his face was set exactly the same.

"Ladies and gentlemen, this is Captain Nigel Higgins welcoming you aboard British Airways Flight 189, Concorde Service to Washington, D.C., and Miami, Florida. We'll begin taxiing in approximately five minutes. Weather at our first stop, Washington's Dulles International Airport, is excellent, clear, with a temperature of fifty-six degrees. We will be in the air a total of three hours and twenty-five minutes. Please observe that the no-smoking sign is lighted, and we ask that while you are seated you keep your seat belts fastened. Thank you," the clipped voice concluded.

The door had been closed during the speech, Ryan noted sourly. A clever distraction, as their only escape route was eliminated. He leaned back and closed his eyes, resigning himself to fate. One nice thing about being up front was that no one could see him except Cathy—Sally had the window seat—and his wife understood, or at least pretended to. Soon the cabin crew was demonstrating how to put on and inflate life jackets stowed under the seats. Jack watched without interest. Concorde's perfect safety record meant that no one had the first idea on how to ditch one safely, and his position near the nose, so far from the delta-shaped wing, ensured that if they hit the water he'd be in the part of the fuselage that broke off and sank like a cement block. Not that this would matter. The impact itself would surely be fatal.

Asshole, if this bird was dangerous, they would have lost one by now.

The whine of the jet turbines came next, triggering the acid glands in Jack's stomach. He closed his eyes again. *You can't run away.* He commanded himself to control his breathing and relax. That was strangely easy. Jack had never been a white-knuckled flier. He was more likely to be limp.

Some unseen tractor-cart started pushing the aircraft backward. Ryan looked out of the window and watched the scenery move slowly forward. Heathrow was quite a complex. Aircraft from a dozen airlines were visible, mainly sitting at the terminal buildings like ships at a dock. *Wish we could take a ship home,* he thought, forgetting that he'd been one seasick Marine on *Guam,* years ago. The Concorde stopped for a few seconds, then began moving under its own power. Ryan didn't know why the landing gear was so high, but this factor imparted an odd sort of movement as they taxied. The captain came on the intercom again and said something about taking off on afterburners, but Ryan didn't catch it, instead watching a Pan Am 747 lift off. The Concorde was certainly prettier, Ryan thought. It reminded him of the models of fighter planes he'd assembled as a kid. *We're going first class.*

The plane made a sweeping turn at the end of the runway and stopped, bobbing a little on the nose gear. *Here we go.*

"Departure positions," the intercom announced. Somewhere aft the cabin crew strapped into their jump seats. In 1-D, Jack fitted himself into his seat much like a man awaiting electrocution. His eyes were open now, watching out the window.

The engine sounds increased markedly, and Speedbird started to roll. A few seconds later the engine noise appeared to pick up even more, and Ryan was pressed back into the fabric and vinyl chair. *Damn,* he told himself. The acceleration was impressive, about double anything he'd experienced before. He had no way of measuring it, but an invisible hand was pressing him backward while another pushed at his cast and tried to turn him sideways. The stew had been right. It was a thrill. The grass was racing by his window, then the nose came up sharply. A final bump announced that the main gear was off the ground. Jack listened for its retraction into the airframe, but the sheer power of the takeoff blocked it out. Already they were at least a thousand feet off the ground and rocketing upward at what seemed an impossible angle. He looked over to his wife. Wow, Cathy mouthed at him. Sally had her nose against the plastic inside window.

The angle of climb eased off slightly. Already the cabin attendants were at work, with a drink cart. Jack got himself a glass of champagne. He wasn't in a celebrating mood, but bubbly wines always affected him fast. Once Cathy had offered to prescribe some Valium for his flying jitters. Ryan had an ingrained reluctance to take drugs. But booze was different, he told himself. He looked out the window. They were still going up. The ride was fairly smooth, no bumps worse than going over the tar strip on a concrete highway.

Jack felt every one, mindful of the fact that he was several thousand feet over—he checked—still the ground.

He fished the paperback out of his pocket and started reading. This was his one sure escape from flying. Jack slouched to his right, his head firmly wedged into the place where the seat and white plastic wall met. He was able to rest his left arm on the aisle seat, and that took the weight off the place on his waist where the cast dug in hard. His right elbow was planted on the armrest, and Ryan made himself a rigid part of the airframe as he concentrated on his book. He'd selected well for the flight, one of Alistair Horne's books on the Franco-German conflicts. He soon found another reason to hate his cast. It was difficult to read and turn pages one-handed. He had to set the book down first to do it.

A brief surge of power announced that first one, then the other pair of afterburners had been activated on the Concorde's Olympus engines. He felt the new acceleration, and the aircraft began to climb again as she passed through mach-1, and the airliner gave meaning to her call sign prefix: "Speedbird." Jack looked out the window—they were over water now. He checked his watch: less than three hours to touchdown at Dulles. *You can put up with anything for three hours, can't you?*

Like you have a choice. A light caught his eye. *How did I miss that before?* On the bulkhead a few feet from his head was a digital speed readout. It now read 1024, the last number changing upward rapidly.

Damn! I'm going a thousand miles per hour. What would Robby say about this? I wonder how Robby's doing. . . . He found himself mesmerized by the number. Soon it was over 1300. The rate of change dropped off nearly to zero, and the display stopped at 1351. *One thousand three hundred fifty-one miles per hour.* He did the computation in his head: nearly two thousand feet per second, almost as fast as a bullet, about twenty miles per minute. *Damn.* He looked out the window again. *But why is it still noisy? If we're going supersonic, how come the sound isn't all behind us? I'll ask Robby. He'll know.*

The puffy, white, fair-weather clouds were miles below and sliding by at a perceptible rate nevertheless. The sun glinted off the waves, and they stood out like shiny blue furrows. One of the things that annoyed Jack about himself was the dichotomy between his terror of flying and his fascination with what the world looked like from up here. He pulled himself back to the book and read of a period when a steam locomotive was the leading edge of human technology, traveling at a thirtieth of what he was doing now. *This may be terrifying, but at least it gets you from place to place.*

Dinner arrived a few minutes later. Ryan found that the champagne had given him an appetite. Jack was rarely hungry on an airplane, but much to his surprise he was now. The menu carried on the annoying, and baffling, English habit of advertising their food in French, as if language had any effect on taste. Jack soon found that the taste needed no amplification. Salmon gave way to a surprisingly good steak—something the Brits have trouble with—a decent salad, strawberries and cream for dessert, and a small plate of cheese. A good port replaced the champagne, and Ryan found that forty minutes had slipped by. Less than two hours to home.

"Ladies and gentlemen, this is the captain speaking. We are now cruising at fifty-three thousand feet, with a ground speed of thirteen hundred fifty-five miles per hour. As we burn off fuel, the aircraft will float up to a peak altitude of roughly fifty-nine thousand feet. The outside air temperature is sixty degrees below zero Celsius, and the aircraft skin temperature is about one hundred degrees Celsius, this caused by friction as we pass through the air. One side effect of this is that the aircraft expands, becoming roughly eleven inches longer in midflight—"

Metal fatigue! Ryan thought bleakly. *Did you* have *to tell me that?* He touched the window. It felt warm, and he realized that one could boil water on the outside aluminum skin. He wondered what effect that had on the airframe. *Back to the 19th century,* he commanded himself again. Across the aisle his daughter was asleep, and Cathy was immersed in a magazine.

The next time Jack checked his watch there was less than an hour to go. The captain said something about Halifax, Nova Scotia, to his right. Jack looked but saw only a vague dark line on the northern horizon. *North America—we're getting there.* That was good news. As always, his tension and the airliner seat conspired to make his back stiff, and the cast didn't help at all. He felt a need to stand up and walk a few steps, but that was something he tried not to do on airplanes. The steward refilled his port glass, and Jack noticed that the angle of the sun through the window had not changed since London. They were staying even, the aircraft keeping up with the earth's rotation as it sped west. They would arrive at Dulles at about noon, the pilot informed them. Jack looked at his watch again: forty minutes. He stretched his legs and went back to the book.

The next disturbance was when the cabin crew handed out customs and immigration forms. As he tucked his book away, Jack watched his wife go to work listing all the clothes she'd bought. Sally was still asleep, curled up with an almost angelic peace on her face. They made landfall a minute later somewhere over the coast of New Jersey, heading west into Pennsylvania before turning south again. The aircraft was lower now. He'd missed the transonic deceleration, but the cumulus clouds were much closer than they'd been over the ocean. *Okay, Captain Higgins, let's get this bird back on the ground in one solid piece*. He found a silver luggage tag that he was evidently supposed to keep. In fact, he decided to keep the whole package, complete with a certificate that identified him as a Concorde passenger—*or veteran,* he thought wryly. *I survived the British Airways Concorde.*

Dumbass, if you'd flown the 747 back home, you'd still be over the ocean.

They were low enough to see roads now. The majority of aircraft accidents came at landing, but Ryan didn't see it that way. They were nearly home. His fear was nearly at an end. That was good news as he looked out the window at the Potomac. Finally the Concorde took a large nose-high angle again, coming in awfully fast, Jack thought, as she dropped gently toward the ground. A second later he saw the airport perimeter fence. The heavy bumps on the airliner's main gear followed at once. They were down. They were safe. Anything that happened now was a vehicle accident, not an aircraft one, he told himself. Ryan felt safe in cars, mainly because he was in control. He remembered that Cathy would have to drive today, however.

The seat belt sign came off a moment after the aircraft stopped, and the forward door was opened. Home. Ryan stood and stretched. It was good to be stationary. Cathy had their daughter in her lap, running a brush through her hair as Sally rubbed the sleep from her eyes.

"Okay, Jack?"

"Are we home *already*?" Sally asked.

Her father assured her that they were. He walked forward. The stewardess who'd led him aboard asked if he'd enjoyed the ride, and Jack replied, truthfully, that he had. *Now that it's over*. He found a seat in the mobile lounge, and his family joined him.

"Next time we go across, that's how we do it," Ryan announced quietly.

"Why? Did you like it?" Cathy was surprised.

"You better believe I like it. You only have to be up there half as long." Jack laughed, mainly at himself. As with every flight he took, being back on the ground alive carried its own thrill. He had survived what was patently an unnatural act, and the exhilaration of being alive, and home, gave him a quiet glow of his own. The stride of passengers off an airplane is always jauntier than the stride on. The lounge pulled away. The Concorde looked very pretty indeed as they drew away from it and turned toward the terminal.

"How much money did you spend on clothes?" Jack asked as the lounge stopped at the arrival gate. His wife just handed him the form. "That much?"

"Well, why not?" Cathy grinned. "I can pay for it out of *my* money, can't I?"

"Sure, babe."

"And that's three suits for you, too, Jack," his wife informed him.

"What? How did you—"

"When the tailor set you up for the tux, I had him do three suits. Your arms are the same length, Jack. They'll fit, as soon as we get that damned cast off you, that is."

Another nice thing about the Concorde: the airliner carried so few people, compared to a wide-body, that getting the luggage back was a snap. Cathy got a wheeled cart—which Sally insisted on pushing—while Jack retrieved their bags. The last obstacle was customs, where they paid over three hundred dollars' worth of penance for Cathy's purchases. Less than thirty minutes after leaving the aircraft, Jack proceeded to his left out the door, helping Sally with the luggage cart.

"Jack!" It was a big man, taller than Jack's six-one, and broader across the shoulders. He walked badly due to a prosthetic leg that extended above where he had once had a left knee, a gift from a drunken driver. His artificial left foot was a squared-off aluminum band instead of something that looked human. Oliver Wendell Tyler found it easier to walk on. But his hand was completely normal, if rather large. He grabbed Ryan's and squeezed. "Welcome home, buddy!"

"How's it goin', Skip?" Jack disengaged his hand from the grip of a former offensive tackle and mentally counted his fingers. Skip Tyler was a close friend who never fully appreciated his strength.

"Good. Hi, Cathy." His wife got a kiss. "And how's Sally?"

"Fine." She held up her arms, and got herself picked up as desired. Only briefly, though; Sally wriggled free to get back to the luggage cart.

"What are you doing here?" Jack asked. *Oh, Cathy must have called. . . .*

"Don't worry about the car," Dr. Tyler said. "Jean and I retrieved it for you, and dropped it off home. We decided we'd pick you up in ours—more room. She's getting it now."

"Taking a day off, eh?"

"Something like that. Hell, Jack, Billings has been covering your classes for a couple of weeks. Why can't I take an afternoon off?" A skycap approached them, but Tyler waved him off.

"How's Jean?" Cathy asked.

"Six more weeks."

"It'll be a little longer for us," Cathy announced.

"Really?" Tyler's face lit up. "Outstanding!"

It was cool, with a bright autumn sun, as they left the terminal. Jean Tyler was already pulling up with the Tyler family's full-size Chevy wagon. Dark-haired, tall, and willowy, Jean was pregnant with their third and fourth children. The sonogram had confirmed the twins right before the Ryans had left for England. Her otherwise slender frame would have seemed grotesque with the bulge of the babies except for the glow on her face. Cathy went right to her as she got out of the car and said something. Jack knew what it was immediately—their wives immediately hugged: Me, too. Skip wrenched the tailgate open and tossed the luggage inside like so many sheets of paper.

"I gotta admire your timing, Jack. You made it back almost in time for Christmas break," Skip observed as everyone got in the car.

"I didn't exactly plan it that way," Jack objected.

"How's the shoulder?"

"Better'n it was, guy."

"I believe it," Tyler laughed as he pulled away from the terminal. "I was surprised they got you on the Concorde. How'd you like it?"

"It's over a lot faster."

"Yeah, that's what they say."

"How are things going at school?"

"Ah, nothing ever changes. You heard about The Game?" Tyler's head came around.

"No, as a matter of fact." *How did I ever forget about that?*

"Absolutely great. Five points down with three minutes left, we recover a fumble on our twelve. Thompson finally gets it untracked and starts hitting sideline patterns—boom, boom, boom, eight–ten yards a pop. Then he pulls a draw play that gets us to the thirty. Army changes its defense, right? So we go to a spread. I'm up in the press box, and I see their strong-side safety is favoring the outside—figures we gotta stop the clock—and we call a post for the tight end. Like a charm! Thompson couldn't have *handed* him the ball any better! Twenty-one to nineteen. What a way to end the season."

Tyler was an Annapolis graduate who'd made second-string All-American at offensive tackle before entering the submarine service. Three years before, when he'd been on the threshold of his own command a drunk driver had left him without half his leg. Amazingly, Skip hadn't looked back. After taking his doctorate in engineering from MIT, he'd joined the faculty at Annapolis, where he was also able to scout and do a little coaching in the football program. Jack wondered how much happier Jean was now. A lovely girl who had once worked as a legal secretary, she must have resented Skip's enforced absences on submarine duty. Now she had him home—surely he wasn't straying far; it seemed that Jean was always pregnant—and they were rarely separated. Even when they walked in the shopping malls, Skip and Jean held hands. If anyone found it humorous, he kept his peace about it.

"What are you doing about a Christmas tree, Jack?"

"I haven't thought about it," Ryan admitted.

"I found a place where we can cut 'em fresh. I'm going over tomorrow. Wanna come?"

"Sure. We have some shopping to do, too," he added quietly.

"Boy, you've really been out of it. Cathy called last week. Jean and I finished up the, uh, the important part. Didn't she tell you?"

"No." Ryan turned to see his wife smile at him. *Gotcha!* "Thanks, Skip."

"Ah." Tyler waved his hand as they pulled onto the D.C. beltway. "We're going up to Jean's family's place—last chance for her to travel before the twins arrive. And Professor Billings says you have a little work waiting for you."

A little, Ryan thought. *More like two months' worth.*

"When are you going to be able to start back to work?"

"It'll have to wait until he gets the cast off," Cathy answered for Jack. "I'll be taking Jack to Baltimore tomorrow to see about that. We'll get Professor Hawley to check him out."

"No sense hurrying with that kind of injury," Skip acknowledged. He had ample personal experience with that sort of thing. "Robby says hi. He couldn't make it. He's down at Pax River today on a flight simulator, learning to be an airedale again. Rob and Sissy are doing fine, they were just over the house night before last. You picked a good weather day, too. Rained most of last week."

Home, Jack told himself as he listened. Back to the mundane, day-to-day crap that grates on you so much—until somebody takes it away from you. It was so nice to be back to a situation where rain was a major annoyance, and one's day was marked by waking up, working, eating, and going back to bed. Catching things on television, and football games. The comics in the daily paper. Helping his wife with the wash. Curling up with a book and a glass of wine after Sally was put to bed. Jack promised himself that he'd never find this a dull existence again. He'd just spent over a month on the fast track, and was grateful that he'd left it three thousand miles behind him.

"Good evening, Mr. Cooley." Kevin O'Donnell looked up from his menu.

"Hello, Mr. Jameson. How nice to see you," the book dealer replied with well-acted surprise.

"Won't you join me?"

"Why, yes. Thank you."

"What brings you into town?"

"Business. I'm staying overnight with friends at Cobh." This was true; it also told O'Donnell—known locally as Michael Jameson—that he had the latest message with him.

"Care to look at the menu?" O'Donnell handed it over. Cooley inspected it briefly, closed it, and handed it back. No one could have seen the transfer. "Jameson" let the small envelope inside the folder drop to his lap. The conversation which ensued over the next hour drifted through various pleasantries. There were four Gardai in the next booth, and in any case Mr. Cooley did not concern himself with operational matters. His job was that of contact agent and cutout. A weak man, O'Donnell thought, though he'd never told this to anyone. Cooley didn't have the right qualities for real operations; he was better suited to the role of intelligence. Not that he'd ever asked, and surely the smaller man had passed through training well enough. His ideology was sound, but O'Donnell had always sensed within him a weakness of character that accompanied his cleverness. No matter. Cooley was a man with no record in any police station. He'd never even thrown a rock, much less a cocktail, at a Saracen. He'd preferred to watch and let his hate fester without an emotional release. Quiet, bookish, and unobtrusive, Dennis was perfect for his job. If Cooley was unable to shed blood, O'Donnell knew, he was also unlikely to shed tears. *You bland little fellow, you can organize a superb intelligence-gathering operation, and so long as you don't have to do any of the wet-work yourself, you can—you have helped cause the death of . . . ten or twelve, wasn't it?* Did the man have any emotions at all? Probably not, the leader judged. Perfect. He had his own little Himmler, O'Donnell told himself—or maybe Dzerzhinsky would be a more apt role model. Yes, "Iron Feliks" Dzerzhinsky: that malignant, effective little man. It was only the round, puffy face that reminded him of the Nazi Himmler—and a man couldn't choose his looks, could he? Cooley had a future in the Organization. When the time came, they'd need a real Dzerzhinsky.

They finished their talking over after-dinner coffee. Cooley picked up the check. He insisted: business was excellent. O'Donnell pocketed the envelope and left the restaurant. He resisted the urge to read the report. Kevin was a man to whom patience came hard, and as a consequence he forced himself to it. Impatience had ruined more operations than the British Army ever had, he knew. Another lesson from his early days with the Provos. He drove his BMW through the old streets at the legal limit, leaving the town behind as he entered the narrow country roads to his home on the headlands. He did not take a direct route, and kept an eye on his mirror. O'Donnell knew that his security was excellent. He also knew that continued vigilance was the reason it remained so. His expensive car was registered to his corporation's head office in Dundalk. It was a real business, with nine blue-water trawlers that dragged purse-seine nets through the cold northern waters that surrounded the British Isles. The business had an excellent general manager, a man who had never been involved in the Troubles and whose skills allowed O'Donnell to live the life of a country gentleman far to the south. The tradition of absentee ownership was an old one in Ireland—like O'Donnell's home, a legacy from the English.

It took just under an hour to reach the private driveway marked by a pair of stone pillars, and another five minutes to reach the house over the sea. Like any common man, O'Donnell parked his car in the open; the carriage house that was attached to the manor had been converted to offices by a local contractor. He went at once to his study. McKenney was waiting for him there, reading a recent edition of Yeats' poetry. Another bookish lad, though he did not share Cooley's aversion to the sight of blood. His quiet, disciplined demeanor concealed an explosive capacity for action. A man very like O'Donnell himself, Michael was. Like the O'Donnell of ten or twelve years before, his youth needed tempering; hence his assignment as chief of intelligence so that he could learn the value of deliberation, of gathering all the information he could get before he committed himself to action. The Provos never really did that. They used tactical intelligence, but not the strategic kind—a fine explanation, O'Donnell thought, for the mindlessness of their overall strategy. Another of the reasons he had left the Provisionals—but he would return to the fold. Or more properly, the fold would return to him. Then he would have his army. Kevin already had his plan, though not even his closest associates knew it—at least not all of it.

O'Donnell sat in the leather chair behind the desk and took the envelope from his coat pocket. McKenney discreetly went to the corner bar and got his superior a glass of whiskey. With ice, a taste Kevin had acquired in hotter climes several years before. He set the glass on the desk, and O'Donnell took it, sipping off a tiny bit without a word.

There were six pages to the document, and O'Donnell read through the single-spaced pages as slowly and deliberately as McKenney had just been doing with the words of Yeats. The younger man marveled at the man's patience. For all his reputation as a fighter capable of ruthless action, the chief of the ULA often seemed a creature made of stone, the way he would assemble and process data. Like a computer, but a malignant one. He took fully twenty minutes to go through the six pages.

"Well, our friend Ryan is back in America, where he belongs. Flew the Concorde home, and his wife arranged for a friend to meet them at the airport. Next Monday I expect he'll be back teaching those fine young men and women at their Naval Academy." O'Donnell smiled at the humor of his words. "His Highness and his lovely bride will be back home two days late. It seems that their aircraft developed electrical problems, and a new instrument had to be flown in all the way from England—or so the public story will go. In reality, it would seem that they like New Zealand so much that they wanted some additional time to enjoy their privacy. Security on their arrival will be impressive.

"In fact, looking this over, it would seem that their security for the next few months at least will be impenetrable."

McKenney snorted. "No security's impenetrable. We've proven that ourselves."

"Michael, we do not wish to kill them. Any fool can do that," he said patiently. "Our objective demands that we take them alive."

"But—"

Would they never learn? "No buts, Michael. If I wanted to kill them, they would already be dead, and this Ryan bastard along with them. It is easy to kill, but that will not achieve what we wish."

"Yes, sir." McKenney nodded his submission. "And Sean?"

"They will be processing him in Brixton Prison for another two weeks or so—our friends in C-13 don't want him far from their reach for the moment."

"Does that mean that Sean—"

"Most unlikely," O'Donnell cut him off. "Still and all, I think the Organization is stronger with him than without him, don't you?"

"But how will we know?"

"There is a great deal of high-level interest in our comrade," O'Donnell half-explained.

McKenney nodded thoughtfully. He concealed his annoyance that the Commander would not share his intelligence source with his own intelligence chief. McKenney knew how valuable the information was, but where it came from was the deepest of all the ULA's secrets. The younger man shrugged it off. He had his own information sources, and his skill at using their information was growing on a daily basis. Having always to wait so long to act on it chafed on him, but he admitted to himself—grudgingly at first, but with increasing conviction—that full preparation had allowed several tricky operations to go perfectly. Another operation that had not gone so well had landed him in the H-Blocks of Long Kesh prison. The lesson he'd learned from this miscued op was that the revolution needed more competent hands. He'd come to hate the PIRA leadership's ineffectiveness even more than he did the British Army. The revolutionary often had more to fear from friends than enemies.

"Anything new with our colleagues?" O'Donnell asked.

"Yes, as a matter of fact," McKenney answered brightly. *Our colleagues* were the Provisional Wing of the Irish Republican Army. "One of the cells of the Belfast Brigade is going to go after a pub, day after tomorrow. Some UVF chaps have been using it of late—not very smart of them, is it?"

"I think we can let that one pass," O'Donnell judged. It would be a bomb, of course, and it would kill a number of people, some of whom might be members of the Ulster Volunteer Force, whom he regarded as the reactionary forces of the ruling bourgeoisie—no more than thugs, since they lacked any ideology at all. So much the better that some UVF would be killed, but really any prod would suffice, since then other UVF gunmen would slink into a Catholic neighborhood and kill one or two people on the street. And the detectives of the RUC's Criminal Investigation Division would investigate, as always, and no one would admit to having seen much of anything, as usual, and the Catholic neighborhoods would retain their state of revolutionary instability. Hate was such a useful asset. Even more than fear, hate was what sustained the Cause. "Anything else?"

"The bombmaker, Dwyer, has dropped out of sight again," McKenney went on.

"The last time that happened . . . yes, England, wasn't it? Another campaign?"

"Our man doesn't know. He's working on it, but I have told him to be careful."

"Very good." O'Donnell would think about this one. Dwyer was one of the best PIRA bombers, a genius with delayed fuses, someone Scotland Yard's C-13 branch wanted as badly as they wanted anyone. Dwyer's capture would be a serious blow to the PIRA leadership. . . . "We want our chap to be very careful indeed, but it would be useful to know where Dwyer is."

McKenney got the message loud and clear. It was too bad about Dwyer, but that colleague had picked the wrong side. "And the Belfast brigadier?"

"No." The chief shook his head.

"But he'll slip away again. We needed a month to—"

"No, Michael. Timing—remember the importance of timing. The operation is an integrated whole, not a mere collection of events." The commander of the PIRA's Belfast Brigade—*Brigade, less than two hundred men,* O'Donnell thought wryly—was the most wanted man in Ulster. Wanted by more than one side, though for the moment the Commander perforce had to let the Brits have him. *Too bad. I will dearly love to make you pay personally for casting me out, Johnny Doyle, for putting a price on* my *head. But on this I, too, must be patient. After all, I want more than your head.* "You might also keep in mind that our chaps have their own skins to protect. The reason timing is so important is that what we have planned can only work once. That is why we must be patient. We must wait for exactly the right moment."

What right moment? *What plan?* McKenney wanted to know. Only weeks before, O'Donnell had announced that "the moment" was at hand, only to call things off with a last-second telephone call from London. Sean Miller knew, as did one or two others, but McKenney didn't even know who those privileged fellows were. If there was anything the Commander believed in, it was security. The intelligence officer acknowledged its importance, but his youth chafed at the frustration of knowing the importance of what was happening without knowing *what it was.*

"Difficult, isn't it, Mike?"

"Yes, sir, it is," McKenney admitted with a smile.

"Just keep in mind where impatience has gotten us," the leader said.

8. Information

"I guess that about covers it, Jimmy. Thanks from the Bureau for tracking that guy down."

"I really don't think he's the sort of tourist we need, Dan," Owens replied. A Floridian who'd embezzled three million dollars from an Orlando bank had made the mistake of stopping off in Britain on his way to another European country, one with slightly different banking laws. "I think the next time we'll let him do some shopping on Bond Street before we arrest him, though. You can call that a fee—a fee for apprehending him."

"Ha!" The FBI representative closed the last folder. It was six o'clock local time. Dan Murray leaned back in his chair. Behind him, the brick Georgian buildings across the street paled in the dusk. Men were discreetly patrolling the roofs there, as with all the buildings on Grosvenor Square. The American Embassy was not so much heavily guarded as minorly fortified, so many terrorist threat warnings had come and gone over the past six years. Uniformed police officers stood in front of the building, where North Audley Street was closed off to traffic. The sidewalk was decorated with concrete "flowerpots" that a tank could surmount only with difficulty, and the rest of the building had a sloped concrete glacis to fend off car bombs. Inside, behind bullet-resistant glass, a Marine corporal stood guard beside a wall safe containing a .357 Magnum Smith & Wesson revolver. *A hell of a thing,* Murray thought. *A hell of a thing. The wonderful world of the international terrorist.* Murray hated working in a building that seemed part of the Maginot Line, hated wondering if there might be some Iranian, or Palestinian, or Libyan, or whatever madman of a terrorist, with an RPG-7 rocket launcher in a building across the street from his office. It wasn't fear for his life. Murray had put his life at risk more than once. He hated the injustice, the insult to his profession, that there were people who would kill their fellow men as a part of some form of political expression. *But they're not madmen at all, are they? The behavioral specialists say that they're not. They're romantics—believers, people willing to commit themselves to an ideal, and to commit any crime to further it.* Romantics*!*

"Jimmy, remember the good old days when we hunted bank bandits who were just in the business for a fast buck?"

"I've never done any of those. I was mainly concerned with ordinary thievery until they sent me to handling murders. But terrorism does make one nostalgic for the day of the common thug. I can even remember when *they* were fairly civilized." Owens refilled his glass with port. A growing problem for the Metropolitan Police was that the criminal use of firearms was no longer so rare as it had once been, this new tool made more popular by the evening news reports on terrorism within the U.K. And while the streets and parks of London were far safer than their American counterparts, they were not as safe as they'd only recently been. The times were changing in London, too, and Owens didn't like it at all.

The phone rang. Murray's secretary had just left for the night, and the agent lifted it.

"Murray. Hi, Bob. Yeah, he's right here. Bob Highland for you, Jimmy." He handed the phone over.

"Commander Owens here." The officer sipped at his port, then set the glass down abruptly and waved for a pen and pad. "Where exactly? And you've already—good, excellent. I'm coming straightaway."

"What gives?" Murray asked quickly.

"We've just had a tip on a certain Dwyer. Bomb factory in a flat on Tooley Street."

"Isn't that right across the river from the Tower?"

"Too bloody right. I'm off." Owens rose and grabbed for his coat.

"You mind if I tag along?"

"Dan, you must remember—"

"To keep out of the way." Murray was already on his feet. One hand unconsciously checked his left hip, where his service revolver would be, had the agent not been in a foreign country. Owens had never carried a gun. Murray wondered how you could be a cop and not be armed with something. Together they left Murray's office and trotted up the corridor, turning left for the elevators. Two minutes later they were in the Embassy's basement parking garage. The two officers from Owens' chase car were already in their vehicle, and the Commander's driver followed them out.

Owens was on the radio the instant the car hit the street, with Murray in the back seat.

"You have people rolling?" Murray asked.

"Yes. Bob will have a team there in a few minutes. Dwyer, by God! The description fits perfectly." As much as he tried to hide it, Owens was as excited as a kid on Christmas morning.

"Who tipped you?"

"Anonymous. A male voice, claimed to have seen wiring, and something that was wrapped up in small blocks, when he looked in the window."

"I love it! Peeping Tom cues the cops—probably afraid his wife'll find out what he's been up to. Well, you take what you get." Murray grinned. He'd had cases break on slimmer stuff than this.

The evening traffic was curb-to-curb, and the police siren could not change that. It took fully twenty frustrating minutes to travel the five miles to Tooley Street, with Owens listening to the radio, his fist beating softly on the front door's armrest while his men arrived at the suspect house. Finally the car darted across the Tower Bridge and turned right. The driver parked it on the sidewalk alongside two other police cars.

It was a three-story building of drab, dirty brick, in a working class neighborhood. Next door was a small pub with its daily menu scrawled on a blackboard. Several patrons were standing at the door, pints in their fists as they watched the police, and more stood across the street. Owens ran to the door. A plainclothes detective was waiting for him.

"All secure, sir. We have the suspect in custody. Top floor, in the rear."

The Commander trotted up the stairs with Murray on his heels. Another detective met him on the top-floor landing. Owens proceeded the last thirty feet with a cruel, satisfied smile on his face.

"It's all over, sir," Highland said. "Here's the suspect."

Maureen Dwyer was stark naked, spread-eagled on the floor. Around her was a puddle of water, and a trail of wet footprints coming from the adjacent bathroom.

"She was taking a bath," Highland explained. "And she'd left her pistol on the kitchen table. No trouble at all."

"Do you have a female detective on the way?"

"Yes, sir. I'm surprised she's not here already."

"Traffic is bloody awful," Owens noted.

"Any evidence of a companion?"

"No, sir. None at all," Highland answered. "Only this."

The bottom drawer of the only bureau in the shabby apartment was lying on the floor. It contained several blocks of what looked like plastic explosive, some blasting caps, and what were probably electronic timers. Already a detective was doing a written inventory while another was busily photographing the entire room with a Nikon camera and strobe. A third was breaking open an evidence kit. Everything in the room would be tagged, dropped in a clear plastic bag, and stored for use in yet another terrorist trial in the Old Bailey. There were smiles of satisfaction everywhere—except for Maureen Dwyer's face, which was pressed to the floor. Two detectives stood over the girl, their service revolvers holstered as they watched the naked, wet figure without a trace of sympathy.

Murray stood in the doorway to keep out of everyone's way while his eyes took in the way Owens' detectives handled the scene. There wasn't much to criticize. The suspect was neutralized, the area secured, and now evidence was being collected; everything was going by the book. He noted that the suspect was kept stationary. A woman officer would perform a cavity search to ensure that she wasn't "holding" something that might be dangerous. This was a little hard on Miss Dwyer's modesty, but Murray didn't think a judge would object. Maureen Dwyer was a known bomber, with at least three years' work behind her. Nine months before, she'd been seen leaving the site of a nasty one in Belfast that minutes later had killed four people and maimed another three. No, there wouldn't be all that much sympathy for Miss Dwyer. After another several minutes, a detective took the sheet off the bed and draped it over her, covering her from her knees to her shoulders. Through it all, the suspect didn't move. She was breathing rapidly, but made no sound.

"This is interesting," one man said. He pulled a suitcase from under the bed. After checking it for booby traps, he opened it and extracted a theatrical makeup case complete with four wigs.

"Goodness, I could use one of those myself." The female detective squeezed past Murray and approached Owens. "I came as fast as I could, Commander."

"Carry on." Owens smiled. He was too happy to let something this minor annoy him.

"Spread 'em, dearie. You know the drill." The detective put on a rubber glove for her search. Murray didn't watch. This was one thing he'd always been squeamish about. A few seconds later, the glove came off with a snapping sound. A detective handed Dwyer some clothes to put on. Murray watched the suspect dress herself as unselfconsciously as if she'd been alone—no, he thought, alone she'd show more emotion. As soon as her clothes were on, a police officer snapped steel handcuffs on her wrists. The same man informed Dwyer of her rights, not very differently from the way American cops did it. She did not acknowledge the words. Maureen Dwyer looked about at the police, no expression at all on her face, not even anger, and was taken out without having said a single word.

That's a cold piece of work, Murray told himself. Even with her hair wet, with no makeup, she was pretty enough, he thought. Nice complexion. It wouldn't hurt her to knock off eight or ten pounds, but in nice clothes that wouldn't matter very much. *You could pass her on the street, or sit next to her in a bar and offer to buy her a drink, and you'd never suspect that she was carrying two pounds of high explosives in her purse. Thank God we don't have anything like that at home. . . .* He wondered how well the Bureau would do against such a threat. Even with all their resources, the scientific and forensic experts who back up the special agents in the field, this was no easy crime to deal with. For any police force, the name of the game was wait for the bad guys to make a mistake. You had to play for the breaks, just like a football team waited for a turnover. The problem was, the crooks kept getting better, kept learning from their mistakes. It was like any sort of competition. Both sides became increasingly sophisticated. But the criminals always had the initiative. The cops were always playing catchup ball.

"Well, Dan, any critique? Do we measure up to FBI standards?" Owens inquired with the slightest amount of smugness.

"Don't give me that crap, Jimmy!" Murray grinned. Things were settled down now. The detectives were fully engaged in cataloging the physical evidence in the confidence that they already had a solid criminal case. "I'd say you have this one pretty cold. You know how lucky you are not to have our illegal-search-and-seizure rules?" *Not to mention some of our judges.*

"Finished," the photographer said.

"Excellent," replied Sergeant Bob Highland, who was running the crime scene.

"How'd you get here so fast, Bob?" Murray wanted to know. "You take the tube, or what?"

"Why didn't I think of that?" Highland laughed. "Perhaps we caught the traffic right. We were here within eleven minutes. You weren't that far behind us. We booted the door and had Dwyer in custody in under five seconds. Isn't it amazing how easy it can be—if you have the bloody information you need!"

"Can I come in now?"

"Certainly." Owens waved him into the apartment.

Murray went right to the bureau drawer with the explosives. The FBI man was an expert on explosive devices. He and Owens crouched over the collection.

"Looks like Czech," Murray muttered.

"It is," another detective said. "From Skoda works, you can tell from the wrapping. These are American, though. California Pyronetics, model thirty-one electronic detonator." He tossed one—in a plastic bag—to Murray.

"Damn! They're turning up all over the place—a shipment of these little babies got hijacked a year and a half ago. They were heading for an oil field in Venezuela, and got taken outside Caracas," Murray explained. He gave the small black device a closer look. "The oil field guys love 'em. Safe, reliable, and damned near foolproof. This is as good as the stuff the Army uses. State of the art."

"Where else have they turned up?" Owens asked.

"We're sure about three or four. The problem is, they're so small that it's not always possible to identify what's left. A bank in Puerto Rico, a police station in Peru—those were political. The other one—maybe two—were drug related. Until now they've all been on the other side of the Atlantic. As far as I know, this is the first time they've showed up here. These detonators have lot numbers. You'll want to check them against the stolen shipment. I can get a telex off tonight, have you an answer inside an hour."

"Thank you, Dan."

Murray counted five one-kilo blocks of explosive. The Czech plastique had a good reputation for quality. It was as potent as the stuff Du Pont made for American military use. One block, properly placed, could take a building down. With the Pyronetics timers, Miss Dwyer could have placed five separate bombs, set them for delayed detonation—as much as a month—and been a thousand miles away when they went off.

"You saved some lives tonight, gentlemen. Good one." Murray looked up. The apartment had a single window facing to the rear. The window had a pull-down blind that was all the way down, and some cheap, dirty curtains. Murray wondered what this flat cost to rent. Not much, he was sure. The heat was turned way up, and the room was getting stuffy. "Anybody mind if I let some air in here?"

"Excellent idea, Dan," Owens answered.

"Let me do it, sir." A detective with gloves on put up the blind and then the window. Everything in the room would be dusted for fingerprints also, but opening the window wouldn't harm anything. A breeze cooled things off in an instant.

"That's better." The FBI representative took a deep breath, scarcely noticing the smell of diesel exhaust from the London cabs. . . .

Something was wrong.

It hit Murray as a surprise. Something *was* wrong. *What?* He looked out the window. To the left was a—probably a warehouse, a blank four-story wall. Past it on the right, he could see the outline of the Tower of London, standing over the River Thames. That was all. He turned his head to see Owens, also staring out the window. The Commander of C-13 turned his head and looked at Murray, a question on his face also.

"Yes," Owens said.

"What was it that guy on the phone said?" Murray muttered.

Owens' head bobbed. "Exactly. Sergeant Highland?"

"Yes, Commander?"

"The voice on the phone. What exactly did it say, and what exactly did it sound like?" Owens kept looking out the window.

"The voice had . . . a Midlands accent, I should think. A man's voice. He said that he was looking in the window, and saw explosives and some wires. We have it all on tape, of course."

Murray reached through the open window and ran a finger along the outside surface of the glass. It came back dirty. "It sure wasn't a window-washer who called in." He leaned out the window. There was no fire escape.

"Someone atop the warehouse, perhaps—no," Owens said at once. "The angle isn't right, unless she had the material spread out on the floor. That is rather odd."

"Break-in? Maybe someone got in here, saw the stuff, and decided to call in like a good citizen?" Murray asked. "That doesn't sound very likely."

Owens shrugged. "No telling, is there? A boyfriend she dumped—I think for the moment we can be content with counting our blessings, Dan. There are five bombs that will never hurt anyone. Let's get out of everyone's way and send that telex off to Washington. Sergeant Highland, gentlemen, this was well done! Congratulations to you all for some splendid police work. Carry on."

Owens and Murray left the building quietly. Outside they found a small crowd being restrained by about ten uniformed constables. A TV news crew was on the scene with its bright lights. These were enough to keep them from seeing across the street. This block had three small pubs. In the doorway of one stood a soft-looking man with a pint of bitter in his hand. He showed no emotion, not even curiosity, as he looked across the street. His memory recorded the faces he saw. His name was Dennis Cooley.

Murray and Owens drove to New Scotland Yard headquarters, where the FBI agent made his telex to Washington. They didn't discuss the one anomaly that the case had unexpectedly developed, and Murray left Owens to his work. C-13 had broken yet another bomb case—and done so in the best way, without a single casualty. It meant that Owens and his people would have a sleepless night of paperwork, and preparing reports for the Home Office bureaucracy, and press releases for Fleet Street, but that was something they would gladly accept.

Ryan's first day back at work was easier than he had expected. His prolonged absence had forced the History Department to reassign his classes, and in any case it was almost time for Christmas break, and nearly all of the mids were looking forward to being home for the holidays. Class routine was slightly relaxed, and even the plebes enjoyed a respite from the upperclassmen's harassment in the wake of the win over Army. For Ryan, the result was a fairish collection of letters and documents piled on his In tray, and a quiet day with which to deal with them. He'd arrived in his office at 7:30; by quarter to five he'd dealt with most of his paperwork, and Ryan felt that he'd delivered an honest day's work. He was finishing a series of test questions for the semester's final exam when he smelled cheap cigar smoke and heard a familiar voice.

"Did you enjoy your vacation, boy?" Lieutenant Commander Robert Jefferson Jackson was leaning against the door frame.

"It had a few interesting moments, Robby. The sun over—or under—the yardarm yet?"

"Damn straight!" Jackson set his white cap on top of Ryan's filing cabinet and collapsed unceremoniously into the leather chair opposite his friend's desk.

Ryan closed the file folder on his draft exam and shoved it into a desk drawer. One of the personal touches in his office was a small refrigerator. He opened it and took out a two-liter bottle of 7-Up, along with an empty bottle of Canada Dry ginger ale, then removed a bottle of Irish whiskey from his desk. Robby got two cups from the table by the door and handed them to Jack. Ryan mixed two drinks to the approximate color of ginger ale. It was against Academy policy to have liquor in one's office—a stance Ryan found curious, given the naval orientation of the institution—but drinking "ginger ale" was a winked-upon subterfuge. Besides, everyone recognized that the Officer and Faculty Club was only a minute's walk away. Jack handed one drink over and replaced everything but the empty ginger ale bottle.

"Welcome home, pal!" Robby held his drink up.

"Nice to be back." The two men clicked their cups together.

"Glad you made it, Jack. You kind of worried us. How's the arm?" Jackson gestured with his cup.

"Better than it was. You oughta see the cast I started out with. They took it off at Hopkins last Friday. I learned one thing today, though, driving a stick shift through Annapolis with one arm is a bitch."

"I'll bet," Robby chuckled. "Damn if you ain't crazy, boy."

Ryan nodded agreement. He'd met Jackson the previous March at a faculty tea. Robby wore the gold wings of a naval aviator. He'd been assigned to the nearby Patuxent River Naval Air Test Center, Maryland, as an instructor in the test pilot school until a faulty relay had unexpectedly blasted him clear of the Buckeye jet trainer he'd been flying one fine, clear morning. Unprepared for the event, he'd broken his leg badly. The injury had been serious enough to take him off flight status for six months, and the Navy had assigned him to temporary duty as an instructor in Annapolis, where he was currently in the engineering department. It was an assignment which Jackson regarded as one step above pulling oars in a galley.

Jackson was shorter than Ryan, and much darker. He was the fourth son of a Baptist preacher in southern Alabama. When they'd first met, the officer was still in a cast, and Jackson had asked Ryan if he might want to try his hand at kendo. It was something that Ryan had never tried, the Japanese fencing sport in which bamboo staves are used in place of samurai swords. Ryan had used pugil sticks in the Marines and figured it wouldn't be too different. He'd accepted the invitation, thinking that his longer reach would be a decisive advantage, particularly on top of Jackson's reduced mobility. It hadn't occurred to him that Jackson would first have asked a brother officer for a kendo match. In fact, Ryan later learned, he had. He'd also learned by then that Robby had the blinding quickness and killer instinct of a rattlesnake. By the time the bruises had faded, they were fast friends.

For his part, Ryan had introduced the pilot to the smoky flavor of good Irish whiskey, and they'd evolved the tradition of an afternoon drink or two in the privacy of Jack's office.

"Any news on campus?" Ryan asked.

"Still teachin' the boys and girls," Jackson said comfortably.

"And you've started to like it?"

"Not exactly. The leg's finally back in battery, though. I've been spending my weekends down at Pax River to prove I still know how to fly. You know, you made one hell of a flap hereabouts."

"When I was shot?"

"Yeah, I was in with the Superintendent when the call came in. The 'soop' put it on speaker, and we got this FBI-guy askin' if we got a nut-case teacher in London playing cops and robbers. I said, sure, I know the jerk, but they wanted somebody in the History Department to back me up—mainly they wanted the name of your travel agent, I suppose. Anyway, everybody was out to lunch, and I had to track Professor Billings down in the O-Club, and the superintendent did some runnin' around, too. You almost ruined the boss's last golf day with the Governor."

"Damned near ruined my day, too."

"Was it like they said in the papers?"

"Probably. The Brit papers got it pretty straight."

Jackson nodded as he tapped the cigar on Ryan's ashtray. "You're lucky you didn't come home parcel post, boy," he said.

"Don't you start, Robby. One more guy tells me I'm a hero, and I'll flatten him—"

"Hero? Hell, no! If all you honkies were that dumb, my ancestors would have imported yours." The pilot shook his head emphatically. "Didn't anybody ever tell you, that hand-to-hand stuff is *dangerous*?"

"If you'd been there, I bet you'd have done the same—"

"No chance! God Almighty, is there anything dumber than a Marine? This hand-to-hand stuff, Jeez, you get blood on your clothes, mess up the shine on your shoes. No way, boy! When I do my killin', it'll be with cannon shells and missiles—you know, the civilized way." Jackson grinned. "The safe way."

"Not like flying an airplane that decides to blast you loose without warning you first," Ryan scoffed.

"I dinged my leg some, sure, but when I got my Tomcat strapped to my back, I'm hummin' along at six hundred-plus knots. Anybody who wants to put a bullet in me, fella, he can do it, but he's gonna have to work at it."

Ryan shook his head. He was hearing a safety lecture from someone who just happened to be in the most dangerous business there was—a carrier aviator *and* a test pilot.

"How's Cathy and Sally?" Robby asked, more seriously. "We meant to come over Sunday, but we had to drive up to Philadelphia on short notice."

"It was kinda tough on them, but they came through all right."

"You got a family to worry about, Jack," Jackson pointed out. "Leave that rescue stuff to the professionals." The funny thing about Robby, Jack knew, was his caution. For all the down-home bantering about his life as a fighter pilot, Jackson never took a risk he didn't have to. He'd known pilots who had. Many were dead. There was not a single man wearing those gold wings who had not lost a friend, and Jack wondered how deeply that had affected Jackson over the years. Of one thing he was sure, though Robby was in a dangerous business, like all successful gamblers he thought things over before he moved his chips. Wherever his body went, his mind had already gone.

"It's all over, Rob. It's all behind me, and there won't be a next time."

"We'll put a big roger on that. Who else am I gonna drink with? So how'd you like it over there?"

"I didn't see very much, but Cathy had a great time, all things considered. I think she saw every castle in the country—plus the new friends we made."

"That must have been right interesting," Robby chuckled. The flyer stubbed out his cigar. They were cheap, crooked, evil-smelling little things, and Jack figured that Jackson puffed on them only as part of the Image of the Fighter Pilot. "Not hard to understand why they took a liking to you."

"They took a liking to Sally, too. They got her started riding horses," Jack added sourly.

"Oh, yeah? So what are they like?"

"You'd like 'em," Ryan assured him.

Jackson smiled. "Yeah, I imagine I would. The Prince used to drive Phantoms, so he must be a right guy, and his dad's supposed to know his way around a cockpit, too. I hear you took the Concorde back. How'd you like it?"

"I meant to ask you about that. How come it was so noisy? I mean, if you're doing mach-2-plus, why isn't all the noise behind you?"

Jackson shook his head sadly. "What's the airplane made out of?"

"Aluminum, I suppose."

"You suppose the speed of sound is faster in metal than it is in air, maybe?" Jackson asked.

"Oh. The sound travels through the body of the airplane."

"Sure, engine noise, noise from the fuel pumps, various other things."

"Okay." Ryan filed that away.

"You didn't like it, did you?" Robby was amused at his friend's attitude toward flying.

"Why does everybody pick on me for that?" Ryan asked the ceiling.

"Because it's so funny, Jack. You're the last person in the world who's afraid to fly."

"Hey, Rob, I do it, okay? I get aboard, and strap in, and do it."

"I know. I'm sorry." Jackson eased off. "It's just that it's so easy to needle you on this—I mean, what are friends for? You done good, Jack. We're proud of you. But for Christ's sake, be careful, okay? This hero shit gets people killed."

"I hear you."

"Is it true about Cathy?" Robby asked.

"Yep. The doc confirmed it the same day they took the cast off."

"Way to go, pop! I'd say that calls for another—a light one." Robby held his cup out, and Jack poured. "Looks like the bottle's about had it, too."

"It's my turn to buy the next one, isn't it?"

"It's been so long, I don't remember," Robby admitted. "But I'll take your word for it."

"So they have you back in airplanes?"

"Next Monday they'll let me back in a Tomcat," Jackson replied. "And come summer, it's back to the work they pay me for."

"You got orders?"

"Yeah, you're looking at the prospective XO of VF-41." Robby held his cup up in the air.

The executive officer of Fighter Squadron 41, Ryan translated. "That's all right, Rob!"

"Yeah, it's not bad, considering I've been a black shoe for the past seven months."

"Right out on carriers?"

"No, we'll be on the beach for a while, down at Oceana, Virginia. The squadron's deployed now on *Nimitz*. When the boat comes back for refit, the fighters stay on the beach for refresher training. Then we'll probably redeploy on *Kennedy*. They're reshuffling the squadron assignments. Jack, it'll be good to strap that fighter back on! I've been here too long."

"We're gonna miss you and Sissy."

"Hey, we don't leave till summer—they're making me finish out the school year—and Virginia Beach isn't all that far away. Come on down and visit, for crying out loud. You don't have to fly, Jack. You can drive," Jackson pointed out.

"Well, you'll probably be around for the new kid."

"Good." Jackson finished off his drink.

"Are you and Sissy going anywhere for Christmas?"

"Not that I know of. I can't, really; most of the holidays I'm gonna be flying down at Pax."

"Okay, come on over to our place for dinner—three-ish."

"Cathy's family isn't—"

"No," Ryan said as he tucked everything back where it belonged. Robby shook his head.

"Some folks just don't catch on," the pilot observed.

"Well, you know how it is. I don't worship at the temple of the Almighty Dollar anymore."

"But you managed to do a job on the collection basket."

Jack grinned. "Yeah, you might say that."

"That reminds me. There's a little outfit outside Boston that's gonna hit it big."

"Oh?" Jack's ears perked up.

"It's called Holoware, Ltd., I think. They came up with new software for the computers on fighter planes—really good stuff, cuts a third off the processing time, generates intercept solutions like magic. It's set up on the simulator down at Pax, and the Navy's going to buy it real soon."

"Who knows?"

Jackson laughed as he got his things. "The company doesn't know yet. Captain Stevens down at Pax just got the word from the guys out at Topgun. Bill May out there—I used to fly with Bill—ran the stuff for the first time a month ago, and he liked it so much that he almost got the Pentagon boys to cut through all the bullshit and just buy the stuff. It got hung up, but DCNO-Air is on it now, and they say Admiral Rendall is really hot for it. Thirty more days, and that little company is going to get a Christmas present. A little late," Robby said, "but it'll fill one big stocking. Just for the hell of it, I checked the paper this morning, and sure enough, they're listed on the American Exchange. You might want to check it out."

"What about you?"

The pilot shook his head. "I don't play the market, but you still fool around there, right?"

"A little. Is this classified or anything?" Jack asked.

"Not that I know of. The classified part is how the software is written, and they got a real good classification system on that—nobody understands it. Maybe Skip Tyler could figure it out, but I never will. You have to be a nuc to think in ones and zeros. Pilots don't think digital. We're analog." Jackson chuckled. "Gotta run. Sissy's got a recital tonight."

" 'Night, Rob."

"Low and slow, Jack." Robby closed the door behind him. Jack leaned back in his chair for a moment. He smiled to himself, then rose and packed some papers into his briefcase.

"Yeah," he said to himself. "Just to show him that I still know how."

Ryan got his coat on and left the building, walking downhill past the Preble Memorial. His car was parked on Decatur Road. Jack drove a five-year-old VW Rabbit. It was a very practical car for the narrow streets of Annapolis, and he refused to have a Porsche like his wife used for commuting back and forth to Baltimore. It was dumb, he'd told Cathy about a thousand times, for two people to have three cars. A Rabbit for him, a 911 for her, and a station wagon for the family. Dumb. Cathy's suggestion that he should sell the Rabbit and drive the wagon was, of course, unacceptable. The little gas engine fired up at once. It sounded too noisy. He'd have to check the muffler. Jack pulled out, turning right, as always, onto Maryland Avenue through Gate Three in the grimly undecorous perimeter wall that surrounded the Academy. A Marine guard saluted him on the way out. Ryan was surprised by that—they'd never done it before.

Driving wasn't easy. When he shifted, Ryan twisted his left hand inside the sling to grab the wheel while his right hand worked the gearshift. The rush-hour traffic didn't help. Several thousand state workers were disgorging themselves from various government buildings, and the crowded streets gave Ryan plenty of opportunity to stop and restart from first gear. His Rabbit had five, plus reverse, and by the time he got to the Central Avenue light he was asking himself why he hadn't gotten the Rabbit with an automatic. Fuel efficiency was the answer—*is this worth an extra two miles per gallon*? Ryan laughed at himself as he headed east toward the Chesapeake Bay, then right onto Falcon's Nest Road.

There was rarely any traffic back here. Falcon's Nest Road came to a dead end not too far down from Ryan's place, and on the other side of the road were several farms, also dormant at the beginning of winter. The stubby remains of cornstalks lay in rows on the brown, hard fields. He turned left into his driveway. Ryan had thirty acres on Peregrine Cliff. His nearest neighbor, an engineer named Art Palmer, was half a mile away through heavily wooded slopes and across a murky stream. The cliffs on the western shore of the Chesapeake Bay were nearly fifty feet high where Jack lived—those farther south got a little higher, but not much—and made of crumbly sandstone. They were a paleontologist's delight. Every so often a team from a local college or museum would scour at the base and find fossilized shark teeth that had once belonged to a creature as large as a midget submarine, along with the bones of even more unlikely creatures that had lived here a hundred million years earlier.

The bad news was that the cliffs were prone to erosion. His house was built a hundred feet back from the edge, and his daughter was under strict orders—twice enforced with a spanking—not to go anywhere near the edge. In an attempt to protect the cliff face, the state environmental-protection people had persuaded Ryan and his neighbors to plant kudzu, a prolific weed from the American South. The weed had thoroughly stabilized the cliff face, but it was now attacking the trees near the cliff, and Jack periodically had to go after them with a weed-eater to save the trees from being smothered. But that wasn't a problem this time of year.

Ryan's lot was half open and half wooded. The part near the road had once been farmed, though not easily, as the ground was not flat enough to drive a tractor across it safely. As he approached his house, the trees began, some gnarled old oaks, and other deciduous trees whose leaves were gone now, leaving skeletal branches to reach out into the thin, cold air. As he approached the carport, he saw that Cathy was already home, her Porsche and the family wagon parked in the carport. He had to leave his Rabbit in the open.

"Daddy!" Sally yanked open the door and ran out without her jacket to meet her father.

"It's too cold out here," Jack told his daughter.

"No, isn't," Sally replied. She grabbed his briefcase and carried it with two hands, puffing as she climbed up the three steps into the house.

Ryan got out of his coat and hung it in the entry closet. As with everything else, it was hard to do with one hand. He was cheating a little now. As with steering the car, he was starting to use his left hand, careful to avoid putting any strain on his shoulder. The pain was completely gone now, but Ryan was sure that he could bring it back quickly enough if he did something dumb. Besides which, Cathy would yell at him. He found his wife in the kitchen. She was looking at the pantry and frowning.

"Hi, honey."

"Hi, Jack. You're late."

"So are you." Ryan kissed his wife. Cathy smelled his breath. Her nose crinkled. "How's Robby?"

"Fine—and I just had two very light ones."

"Uh-huh." She turned back to the pantry. "What do you want for dinner?"

"Surprise me," Jack suggested.

"You're a big help! I ought to let you fix it."

"It's not my turn, remember?"

"I knew I should have stopped at the Giant," Cathy groused.

"How was work?"

"Only one procedure. I assisted Bernie on a cornea transplant, then I had to take the residents around for rounds. Dull day. Tomorrow'll be better. Bernie says hi, by the way. How does franks and beans grab you?"

Jack laughed. Ever since they came back, their diet had consisted mainly of basic American staples, and it was a little late for something fancy.

"Okay. I'm going to change and punch up something on the computer for a few minutes."

"Careful with the arm, Jack."

Five times a day she warns me. Jack sighed. *Never marry a doctor*. The Ryan home was a deckhouse design. The living/dining room had a cathedral ceiling that peaked sixteen feet over the carpeted floor with an enormous wood beam. A wall of triple-paned windows faced the bay, with a large deck beyond the sliding glass doors. Opposite the glass was a massive brick fireplace that reached through the roof. The master bedroom was half a level above the living room, with a window that enabled one to look down into it. Ryan trotted up the steps. The house design accommodated large closets. Ryan selected casual clothes, and went through the annoying ritual of changing himself one-handed. He was still experimenting, trying to find an efficient way to do it.

Finished, he went back down, and curved around the stairs to the next level down, his library. It was a large one. Jack read a lot, and also purchased books he didn't have time to read, banking against the time when he would. He had a large desk up against the windows on the bay side of the house. Here was his personal computer, an Apple, and all of its peripheral equipment. Ryan flipped it on and started typing in instructions. Next he put his modem on line and placed a call into

CompuServe. The time of day guaranteed easy access, and he selected MicroQuote II from the entry menu.

A moment later he was looking at Holoware, Ltd.'s stock performance over the past three years. The stock was agreeably unimpressive, fluctuating from two dollars to as much as six, but that was two years back—it was a company which had once held great promise, but somewhere along the way investors had lost confidence. Jack made a note, then exited the program and got into another, Disclosure II, to look at the company's SEC filings and last annual report. *Okay,* Ryan told himself. The company was making money, but not very much. One problem with hi-tech issues was that so many investors wanted big returns very quickly, or they'd move on to something else, forgetting that things didn't necessarily happen that way. This company had found a small though somewhat precarious niche, and was ready to try something bold. Ryan made a mental estimate of what the Navy contract would be worth and compared it with the company's total revenues. . . .

"Okay!" he told himself before exiting the system completely and shutting his computer down. Next he called his broker. Ryan worked through a discount brokerage firm that had people on duty around the clock. Jack always dealt with the same man.

"Hi, Mort, it's Jack. How's the family?"

"Hello again, Doctor Ryan. Everything's fine with us. What can we do for you tonight?"

"An outfit called Holoware, one of the hi-tech bunch on Highway 128 outside Boston. It's on the AMEX."

"Okay." Ryan heard tapping on a keyboard. Everyone used computers. "Here it is. Going at four and seven-eighths, not a very active issue . . . until lately. There has been some modest activity over the past month."

"What kind?" Ryan asked. This was another sign to look for.

"Oh, I see. The company is buying itself back a little. No big deal, but they're buying their own stock out."

Bingo! Ryan smiled to himself. *Thank you, Robby. You gave me a tip on a real live one.* Jack asked himself if this constituted trading on inside information. His initial tip might be called that, but his decision to buy was based on confirmation made legally, on the basis of his experience as a stock trader. *Okay, it's legal.* He could do whatever he wanted.

"How much do you think you can get for me?"

"It's not a very impressive stock."

"How often am I wrong, Mort?"

"How much do you want?"

"At least twenty-K, and if there's more, I want all of it you can find." There was no way he'd get hold of more than fifty thousand shares, but Ryan made a snap decision to grab all he could. If he lost, it was only money, and it had been over a year since he'd last had a hunch like this one. If they got the Navy contract, that stock would increase in value tenfold. The company must have had a tip, too. Buying back their own stock on the slim resources they had would, if Ryan was guessing right, dramatically increase the firm's capital, enabling a rapid expansion of operations. Holoware was betting on the future, and betting big.

There was five seconds of silence on the phone.

"What do you know, Jack?" the broker asked finally.

"I'm playing a hunch."

"Okay . . . twenty-K plus . . . I'll call you at ten tomorrow. You think I should . . . ?"

"It's a toss of the dice, but I think it's a good toss."

"Thanks. Anything else?"

"No. I have to go eat dinner. Good night, Mort."

"See ya." Both men hung up. At the far end of the phone, the broker decided that he'd go in for a thousand shares, too. Ryan was occasionally wrong, but when he was right, he tended to be very right.

"Christmas Day," O'Donnell said quietly. "Perfect."

"Is that the day they're moving Sean?" McKenney asked.

"He leaves London by van at four in the morning. That's bloody good news. I was afraid they'd use a helicopter. No word on the route they'll use. . . ." He read on. "But they're going to take him across on the Lymington ferry at eight-thirty Christmas morning. Excellent timing, when you think about it. Too early for heavy traffic. Everyone'll be opening his presents and getting dressed for church. The van might even have the ferry to itself—who'd expect a prisoner transfer on Christmas Day?"

"So, we are going to break Sean out, then?"

"Michael, our men do us little good when they're inside, don't they? You and I are flying over tomorrow morning. I think we'll drive down to Lymington and look at the ferry."

9. A Day for Celebration

"God, it'll be nice to have two arms again," Ryan observed.

"Two more weeks, maybe three," Cathy reminded him. "And keep your hand still inside the damned sling!"

"Yes, dear."

It was about two in the morning, and things were going badly—and well. Part of the Ryan family tradition—a tradition barely three years old, but a tradition nevertheless—was that after Sally was in bed and asleep, her parents would creep down to the basement storage area—a room with a padlocked door—and bring the toys upstairs for assembly. The previous two years, this ceremony had been accompanied by a couple of bottles of champagne. Assembling toys was a wholly different sort of exercise when the assemblers were half blasted. It was their method of relaxing into the Christmas spirit.

So far things had gone well. Jack had taken his daughter to the seven o'clock children's mass at St. Mary's, and gotten her to bed a little after nine. His daughter had slid her head around the fireplace wall only twice before a loud command from her father had banished her to her bedroom for good, her arm clasping an overly talkative AG Bear to her chest. By midnight it was decided that she was asleep enough for her parents to make a little noise. This had begun the toy trek, as Cathy called it. Both parents removed their shoes to minimize noise on the hardwood steps and went downstairs. Of course, Jack forgot the key to the padlock, and had to climb back upstairs to the master bedroom to search for it. Five minutes later the door was opened and the two of them made four trips each, setting up a lavish pile of multicolored boxes near the tree, next to Jack's tool kit.

"You know what the two most obscene words in the English language are, Cathy?" Ryan asked nearly two hours later.

" 'Assembly required,' " his wife answered with a giggle. "Honey, last year I said that."

"A small Phillips." Jack held his hand out. Cathy smacked the screwdriver into his hand like a surgical instrument. Both of them were sitting on the rug, fifteen feet from the eight-foot tree. Around them was a crescent of toys, some in boxes, some already assembled by the now-exasperated father of a little girl.

"You ought to let me do that."

"This is man's work," her husband said. He sat the screwdriver down and sipped at a glass of champagne.

"You chauvinist pig! If I let you do this by yourself, you wouldn't be finished by Easter."

She was right, Jack told himself. Doing it half-drunk wasn't all that hard. Doing it one-handed was hard but not insurmountable. Doing it one-handed *and* half-drunk was . . . The damned screws didn't want to stay in the plastic, and the instructions for putting a V-8 engine together had to be easier than this!

"Why is it that a doll needs a house?" Jack asked plaintively. "I mean, the friggin' doll's already *in* a house, isn't she?"

"It must be hard, being a chauvinist pig. You dodos just don't understand anything," Cathy noted sympathetically. "I guess men never get over baseball bats—all those simple, one-piece toys."

Jack's head turned slowly. "Well, the least you could do is have another glass of wine."

"One's the weekly limit, Jack. I did have a big glass," she reminded him.

"And made me drink the rest."

"You bought the bottle, Jack." She picked it up. "Big one, too."

Ryan turned back to the Barbie Doll house. He thought he remembered when the Barbie Doll had been invented, a simple, rather curvy doll, but still just a damned doll, something that girls played with. It hadn't occurred to him then that he might someday have a little girl of his own. *The things we do for our kids,* he told himself. Then he laughed quietly at himself. *Of course we do, and we enjoy it. Tomorrow this will be a funny memory, like the Christmas morning last year when I nearly put this very screwdriver through the palm of my hand.* If he didn't enlist his wife's assistance, Ryan told himself, Santa would be planning next year's flight before he finished. Jack took a deep breath and swallowed his pride.

"Help."

Cathy checked her watch. "That took about forty minutes longer than I expected."

"I must be slowing down."

"Poor baby, having to drink all that champagne all by himself." She kissed him on the forehead. "Screwdriver."

He handed it to her. Cathy took a quick look at the plans. "No wonder, you dummy. You're using a short screw when you're supposed to use a long one."

"I keep forgetting that I'm married to a high-priced mechanic."

"That's real Christmas spirit, Jack." She grinned as she turned the screw into place.

"A very pretty, smart, and extremely lovable high-priced mechanic." He ran a finger down the back of her neck.

"That's a *little* better."

"Who's better with tools than I am, one-handed."

Her head turned to reveal the sort of smile a wife saves only for the husband she loves. "Give me another screw, Jack, and I'll forgive you."

"Don't you think you should finish the doll house first?"

"Screw, dammit!" He handed her one. "You have a one-track gutter, but I forgive you anyway."

"Thanks. If it didn't work, though, I had something else planned."

"Oh, did Santa come for me, too?"

"I'm not sure. I'll check in a few minutes."

"You didn't do bad, considering," his wife said, finishing off the orange plastic roof. "That's it, isn't it?"

"Last one," Jack confirmed. "Thanks for the assist, babe."

"Did I ever tell you what—no, I didn't. It was one of the ladies-in-waiting. I never did find out what they were waiting for. Anyway, this one countess . . . she was right out of *Gone With the Wind,*" Cathy said with a chuckle. It was his wife's favorite epithet for useless women. "She asked me if I did needlepoint."

Not the sort of thing you ask my wife. Jack grinned at the windows. "And you said . . ."

"Only on eyeballs." A sweet, nasty smile.

"Oooh. I hope that wasn't over lunch."

"Jack! You know me better than that. She was nice enough, and she played a pretty good piano."

"Good as yours?"

"No." His wife smiled at him. Jack reached out to squeeze the tip of her nose.

"Caroline Ryan, MD, liberated woman, instructor in ophthalmic surgery, world-famous player of classical piano, wife and mother, takes no crap off anybody."

"Except her husband."

"When's the last time I ever won an exchange with you?" Jack asked.

"Jack, we're not in competition. We're in love." She leaned toward him.

"I won't argue with you on that," he said quietly before kissing his wife's offered lips. "How many people do you suppose are still in love after all the time we've been married?"

"Just the lucky ones, you old fart. 'All the time we've been married'!"

Jack kissed her again and rose. He walked carefully around the sea of toys toward the tree and returned with a small box wrapped in green Christmas paper. He sat down beside his wife, his shoulder against hers as he dropped the box in her lap.

"Merry Christmas, Cathy."

She opened the box as greedily as a child, but neatly, using her nails to slit the paper. She found a white cardboard box, and inside it, a felt-covered one. This she opened slowly.

It was a necklace of fine gold, more than a quarter-inch wide, designed to fit closely around the neck. You could tell the price by the workmanship and the weight. Cathy Ryan took a deep breath. Her husband held his. Figuring out women's fashions was not his strongest point. He'd gotten advice from Sissy Jackson, and a very patient clerk at the jewelry store. *Do you like it?*

"I better not swim with this on."

"But you won't have to take it off when you scrub," Jack said. "Here." He took it from the box and put it around her neck. He managed to clasp it one-handed on the first try.

"You practiced." One hand traced over the necklace while her eyes looked deeply into his. "You practiced, just so you could put it on me yourself, didn't you?"

"For a week at the office." Jack nodded. "Wrapping it was a bitch, too."

"It's wonderful. Oh, Jack!" Both her arms darted around his neck, and he kissed the base of hers.

"Thanks, babe. Thanks for being my wife. Thanks for having my kids. Thanks for letting me love you."

Cathy blinked away a tear or two. They gave her blue eyes a gleam that made him happier than any man on earth. *Let me count the ways . . .*

"Just something I saw," he explained casually, lying. It was something he'd seen after looking for nine hours, through seven stores in three shopping malls. "And it just said to me, 'I was made for her.' "

"Jack, I didn't get you anything like—"

"Shut up. Every morning I wake up, and I see you next to me, I get the best present there is."

"You are a sentimental jerk right out of some book—but I don't mind."

"You do like it?" he asked carefully.

"You dummy—I love it!" They kissed again. Jack had lost his parents years before. His sister lived in Seattle, and most of the rest of his relations were in Chicago. Everything he loved was in this house: a wife, a child—and a third of another. He'd made his wife smile on Christmas, and now this year went into the ledger book as a success.

About the time Ryan started assembling the doll house, four identical blue vans left the Brixton Prison at five-minute intervals. For each, the first thirty minutes involved driving through the side streets of suburban London. In each, a pair of police officers sat looking out the small windows in the rear doors, watching to see if there might be a car trailing the truck on its random path through the city.

They'd picked a good day for it. It was a fairly typical morning for the English winter. The vans drove through patches of fog and cold rain. There was a moderate storm blowing in from the Channel, and best of all, it was dark. The island's northern latitude guaranteed that the sun would not be up for some hours yet, and the dark blue vans were invisible in the early morning.

Security was so strict that Sergeant Bob Highland of C-13 didn't even know that he was in the third van to leave the jail. He did know that he was sitting only a few feet from Sean Miller, and that their destination was the small port of Lymington. They had a choice of three ports to take them to the Isle of Wight, and three different modes of transport: ordinary ferry, hovercraft, and hydrofoil. They might also have chosen a Royal Navy helicopter out of Gosport, but Highland needed only a quick look at the starless sky to rule that one out. *Not a good idea,* he thought to himself. Besides, security is airtight. Not more than thirty people knew that Miller was being moved this morning. Miller himself hadn't known until three hours before, and he still didn't know what prison he was heading to. He'd only learn when he got to the island.

Embarrassments to the British prison system had accumulated over the years. The old, forbidding structures that inhabited such desolate places as Dartmoor in Cornwall had turned out to be amazingly easy to escape from, and as a result two new maximum-security facilities, Albany and Parkhurst, had been built on the Isle of Wight. There were many advantages to this. An island by definition was easier to secure, and this one had only four regular entry points. More importantly, this island was a clannish place even by English standards, and any stranger on the loose would at least be noticed, and might even be commented upon. The new prisons were somewhat more comfortable than those constructed in the previous century. It was an accident, but one to which Highland did not object. Along with the better living conditions for the prisoners came facilities designed to make escape very difficult—nothing made them impossible, but these new prisons had television cameras to cover every inch of wall, electronic alarms in the most unlikely of places, and guards armed with automatic weapons.

Highland stretched and yawned. With luck he'd get home by early afternoon and still salvage something of Christmas Day with his family.

"I don't see anything at all to concern us," the other constable said, his nose against the small glass rectangle in the door. "Only a handful of vehicles on the street, and none are following us."

"I shouldn't complain," Highland observed. He turned around to look at Miller.

The prisoner sat all the way forward on the left-hand bench. His hands were manacled, a chain running from the cuffs to a similar pair on his ankles. With luck and a little assistance, a man so restrained might be able to keep pace with a crawling infant, but he'd have little chance of outracing a two-year-old. Miller just sat there, his head back against the wall of the van, his eyes closed as the vehicle bounced and jolted over the road. He looked to be asleep, but Highland knew better. Miller had withdrawn into himself again, lost in some kind of contemplation.

What are you thinking about, Mr. Miller? the policeman wanted to ask. It wasn't that he'd failed to ask questions. Almost every day since the incident on The Mall, Highland and several other detectives had sat across a rugged wood table from this young man and tried to start some kind of conversation. He was a strong one, Highland admitted to himself. He had spoken but one unnecessary word, and that only nine days before. A jailer with more indignation than professionalism had used the excuse of a plumbing problem in Miller's cell to move him temporarily to another. In the other were two ODCs, as they were called: Ordinary Decent Criminals, as opposed to the political kind that C-13 dealt with. One was awaiting sentencing for a series of vicious street robberies, the other for the gun-murder of a shop owner in Kensington. Both knew who Miller was, and hated him enough to look at the small young man as a way to atone for the crimes which they little regretted in any case. When Highland had shown up for yet another fruitless interrogation session, he'd found Miller facedown on the floor of the cell, his pants gone, and the robber sodomizing him so brutally that the policeman had actually felt sympathy for the terrorist.

The Ordinary Decent Criminals had withdrawn at Highland's command, and when the cell door was opened, Highland had himself picked Miller up and helped him to the dispensary. And there Miller had actually spoken to him as though to another human being. A single word from the puffy, split lips: "Thanks."

Cop rescues terrorist, Highland thought to himself, *some headline that would be*. The jailer had pleaded innocence, of course. There *was* a problem with the plumbing in Miller's cell—somehow the work order had got mislaid, you see—and the jailer had been called to quell a disturbance elsewhere. Hadn't heard a sound from that end of the cell block. Not a sound. Miller's face had been beaten to a bloody pulp, and certainly he'd have no toilet problems for a few more days. His sympathy for Miller had been short-lived. Highland was still angry with the jailer. It was his professionalism that was offended. What the jailer had done was, quite simply, wrong, and potentially the first step on a path that could lead back to the rack and hot pincers. The law was not so much designed to protect society from the criminals, but more profoundly to protect society from itself. This was a truth that not even all policemen understood fully, but it was the single lesson that Highland had learned from five years in the Anti-Terrorist Branch. It was a hard lesson to believe when you'd seen the work of the terrorists.

Miller's face still bore some of the marks, but he was a young man and he was healing quickly. Only for a brief few minutes had he been a victim, a human victim. Now he was an animal again. Highland was hard-pressed to think of him as a fellow man—but that was what his professionalism was for. *Even for the likes of you*. The policeman looked back out the rear window.

It was a boring drive, as it had to be with no radio, no conversation, only vigilance for something that almost certainly wasn't out there. Highland wished that he'd put coffee in his thermos instead of tea. They watched the truck pass out of Woking, then Aldershot and Farnham. They were in the estate country of Southern England now. All around them were stately homes belonging to the horse crowd, and the less stately homes of those whom they employed. It was a pity it was dark, Highland thought, this could be a very pleasant drive. As it was, the fog hung in the numerous valleys, and rain pelted the flat metal top of the van, and the van's driver had to be especially careful as he negotiated the narrow, twisting roads that characterize the English countryside. The only good news was the near-total absence of traffic. Here and there Highland saw a solitary light over some distant door, but there was little more than that.

An hour later, the van used the M-27 motorway to bypass Southampton, then turned south on a secondary—"Class A"—road for Lymington. Every few miles they passed through a small village. There were the beginnings of life here and there. A few bakeries had cars parked outside while their owners got fresh, hot bread for the day's dinner. Early church services were under way already, but the real traveling wouldn't start until the sun was up, and that was still over two hours off. The weather was worsening. They were only a few miles from the coast now, and the wind was gusting at thirty miles per hour. It blew away the fog, but also drove sheets of cold rain and rocked the van on its wheels.

"Miserable bloody day to take a boat ride," the other cop in the back commented.

"Only supposed to be thirty minutes," Highland said, his own stomach already queasy at the thought. Born in a nation of seamen, Bob Highland detested traveling on the water.

"On a day like this? An hour, more like." The man started humming "A Life on the Rolling Wave" while Highland started regretting the large breakfast he'd fixed before leaving home.

Nothing for it, he told himself. *After we deliver young Mr. Miller, it's home for Christmas and two days off. I've bloody earned it*. Thirty minutes later they arrived in Lymington.

Highland had been there once before, but he remembered more than he could see. The wind off the water was now a good forty miles per hour, a full gale out of the southwest. He remembered from the map that most of the boat ride to the Isle of Wight was in sheltered waters—a relative term, but something to depend on nonetheless. The ferry *Cenlac* waited at the dock for them. Only half an hour before, the boat's captain had been told that a special passenger was en route. That explained the four armed officers who stood or sat in various places around the ferry. A low-profile operation, to be sure, and it didn't interfere with the ferry's other passengers, many of them carrying bundles whose identity didn't need to be guessed at.

The Lymington to Yarmouth ferry cast off her lines at 8:30 exactly. Highland and the other officer remained in the van while the driver and another armed constable who'd ridden in front stood outside. *Another hour,* he told himself, *then a few more minutes to deliver Miller to the prison, and then a leisurely drive back to London. I might even stretch out and get a few winks.* Christmas Dinner was scheduled for four in the afternoon—his contemplation of that event stopped abruptly.

The *Cenlac* entered the Solent, the channel between the English mainland and the Isle of Wight. If these waters were sheltered, Highland didn't want to think what the open ocean was like. The *Cenlac* wasn't all that large, and the ferry lacked the weatherly lines of a blue-water craft. The channel gale was broad on her starboard beam, as were the seas, and the boat was already taking fifteen-degree rolls.

"Bloody hell," the Sergeant observed to himself. He looked at Miller. The terrorist's demeanor hadn't changed a whit. He sat there like a statue, head still against the van's wall, eyes still closed, hands in his lap. Highland decided to try the same thing. There was nothing to be gained by staring out the back window. There wasn't any traffic to worry about now. He sat back and propped his feet on the left-side bench. Somewhere he'd once read that closing one's eyes was an effective defense against motion sickness. He had nothing to fear from Miller. Highland was not carrying a gun, of course, and the keys to the prisoner's manacles were in the driver's pocket. So he did close his eyes, and let his inner ear come to terms with the rolling motion of the ferry without the confusion that would come from staring at the unmoving interior of the truck. It helped a little. His stomach soon started to inform him of its dissatisfaction with the current scheme of things, but it didn't get too bad. Highland hoped that the rougher seas farther out wouldn't change this. They wouldn't.

The sound of automatic weapons fire jerked his head up a moment later. The screams came next, from women and children, followed by the rough shouts of men. Somewhere an automobile horn started blaring and didn't stop. More guns started. Highland recognized the short bark of some detective's service automatic—answered at once by the staccato of a submachine gun. It couldn't have lasted more than a minute. The *Cenlac*'s own horn started blowing short, loud notes, then stopped after a few seconds while the auto's horn kept going. The screams diminished. No longer shrill cries of alarm, they were now the deeper cries of comprehended terror. A few more bursts of machine-gun fire crashed out, then stopped. Highland feared the silence more than the noise. He looked out the window and saw nothing but a car and the dark sea beyond. There would be more, and he knew what it would be. Uselessly his hand went inside his jacket for the pistol that wasn't there.

How did they know—how did the bastards know we'd be here!

Now came more shouts, the sound of orders that would not be disobeyed by anyone who wanted to live through this Christmas Day. Highland's hands balled into fists. He turned to look again at Miller. The terrorist was staring at him now. The Sergeant would have preferred a cruel smile to the empty expression he saw on that young, pitiless face.

The metal door shook to the impact of an open hand.

"Open the bloody door or we'll blow it off!"

"What do we do?" the other cop asked.

"We open the door."

"But—"

"But *what*? Wait for them to hold a gun at some baby's head? They've won." Highland twisted the handles. Both doors were yanked open.

There were three men there, ski masks pulled down over their faces. They held automatic weapons.

"Let's see your guns," the tall one said. Highland noted the Irish accent, not that he was very surprised by it.

"We are both unarmed," the Sergeant answered. He held both hands up.

"Out. One at a time, and flat on the deck." The voice didn't bother to make any threats.

Highland stepped out of the truck and got to his knees, then was kicked down on his face. He felt the other cop come down beside him.

"Hello, Sean," another voice said. "You didn't think we'd forget you, did you now?"

Still Miller didn't say anything, Highland thought in wonderment. He listened to the flat jingle of his chains as he hobbled out of the van. He saw the shoes of a man step to the doors, probably to help him down.

The driver must be dead, Highland thought. The gunmen had his keys. He heard the manacles come off, then a pair of hands lifted Miller to his feet. Miller was rubbing his wrists, finally showing a little emotion. He smiled at the deck before looking up at the Sergeant.

There wasn't much point in looking at the terrorist. Around them he saw at least three men dead. One of the black-clad gunmen pulled a shattered head off a car's wheel, and the horn finally stopped. Twenty feet away a man was grasping at a bloody stomach and moaning, a woman—probably his wife—trying to minister to him. Others lay about on the deck in small knots, each watched by an armed terrorist as their hands sweated on the backs of their necks. There was no unnecessary noise from the gunmen, Highland noted. They were trained men. All the noise came from the civilians. Children were crying, and their parents were faring better than the childless adults. Parents had to be brave to protect their kids, while the single had only their own lives to fear for. Several of these were whimpering.

"You are Robert Highland," the tall one said quietly. "Sergeant Highland of the famous C-13?"

"That's right," the policeman answered. He knew that he was going to die. It seemed a terrible thing to die on Christmas Day. But if he was going to die, there was nothing left to lose. He wouldn't plead, he wouldn't beg. "And who might you be?"

"Sean's friends, of course. Did you really think that we'd abandon him to your kind?" The voice sounded educated despite the simple diction. "Do you have anything to say?"

Highland wanted to say something, but he knew that nothing would really matter. He wouldn't even entertain them with a curse—and it came to him that he understood

Miller a little better now. The realization shocked him out of his fear. Now he knew why Miller hadn't spoken. *What damned fool things go through your head at a time like this,* he thought. It was almost funny, but more than that it was disgusting.

"Get on with it and be on your way."

He could only see the tall one's eyes, and was robbed of the satisfaction he might have had from seeing the man's reactions. Highland became angry at that. Now that death was certain, he found himself enraged by the irrelevant. The tall one took an automatic pistol from his belt and handed it to Miller.

"This one's yours, Sean."

Sean took the gun in his left hand and looked one last time at Highland.

I might as well be a rabbit for all that little fucker cares.

"I should have left you in that cell," Highland said, his own voice now devoid of emotion.

Miller considered that for a moment, waiting for a fitting reply to spring from his brain as he held the gun at his hip. A quote from Josef Stalin came to mind. He raised his gun. "Gratitude, Mr. Highland . . . is a disease of dogs." He fired two rounds from a distance of fifteen feet.

"Come on," O'Donnell said from behind his mask. Another black-clad man appeared on the vehicle deck. He trotted to the leader.

"Both engines are disabled."

O'Donnell checked his watch. Things had gone almost perfectly. A good plan, it was—except for the bloody weather. Visibility was under a mile, and—

"There it is, coming up aft," one man called.

"Patience, lads."

"Just who the hell are you?" the cop at their feet asked.

O'Donnell fired a short burst for an answer, correcting this oversight. Another chorus of screams erupted, then trailed quickly away into the shriek of the winds. The leader took a whistle from inside his sweater and blew it. The assault group formed up on the leader. There were seven of them, plus Sean. Their training showed, O'Donnell noted with satisfaction. Every man of them stood facing outward around him, gun at the ready in case one of these terrified civilians might be so foolish as to try something. The ferry's captain stood on the ladder sixty feet away, clearly worrying about his next hazard, handling his craft in a storm without engine power. O'Donnell had considered killing all aboard and sinking the boat, but rejected the idea as counterproductive. Better to leave survivors behind to tell the tale, otherwise the Brits might not know of his victory.

"Ready!" the man at the stern announced.

One by one the gunmen moved aft. There was an eight-foot sea rolling, and it would get worse farther out beyond the shelter of Sconce Point. It was a hazard that O'Donnell could accept more readily than the *Cenlac*'s captain.

"Go!" he ordered.

The first of his men jumped into the ten-meter Zodiac. The man at the controls of the small boat took alee from the ferry and used the power of his twin outboards to hold her in close. The men had all practiced that in three-foot seas, and despite the more violent waves, things went easily. As each man jumped aboard, he rolled to starboard to clear a path for the next. It took just over a minute. O'Donnell and Miller went last, and as they hit the rubber deck, the boat moved alee, and the throttles cracked open to full power. The Zodiac raced up the side of the ferry, out of her wind shadow, and then southwest toward the English Channel. O'Donnell looked back at the ferry. There were perhaps six people watching them pull away. He waved to them.

"Welcome back to us, Sean," he shouted to his comrade.

"I didn't tell them a bloody thing," Miller replied.

"I know that." O'Donnell handed the younger man a flask of whiskey. Miller lifted it and swallowed two ounces. He'd forgotten how good it could taste, and the cold sheets of rain made it all the better.

The Zodiac skimmed over the wavetops, almost like a hovercraft, driven by a pair of hundred-horsepower engines. The helmsman stood at his post 'midships, his knees bent to absorb the mild buffeting as he piloted the craft through the wind and rain toward the rendezvous. O'Donnell's fleet of trawlers gave him a wide choice of seamen, and this wasn't the first time he'd used them in an operation. One of the gunmen crawled around to pass out life jackets. In the most unlikely event that someone saw them, they would look like a team from the Royal Marines' Special Boat Service, running an exercise on Christmas morning. O'Donnell's operations always covered the angles, were always planned down to the last detail. Miller was the only man he'd ever had captured; and now his perfect record was reestablished. The gunmen were securing their weapons in plastic bags to minimize corrosion damage. A few were talking to each other, but it was impossible to hear them over the howl of wind and outboard motors.

Miller had hit the boat pretty hard. He was rubbing his backside.

"Bloody faggots!" he snarled. It was good to be able to talk again.

"What's that?" O'Donnell asked over the noise. Miller explained for a minute. He was sure it had all been Highland's idea, something to soften him up, make him grateful to the cop. That was why both his shots had gone into Highland's guts. There was no sense in letting him die fast. But Miller didn't tell his boss that. That sort of thing was not professional. Kevin might not approve.

"Where's that Ryan bastard?" Sean asked.

"Home in America." O'Donnell checked his watch and subtracted six hours. "Fast asleep in his bed, I wager."

"He set us back a year, Kevin," Miller pointed out. "A whole bloody year!"

"I thought you'd say that. Later, Sean."

The younger man nodded and took another swig of whiskey. "Where are we going?"

"Someplace warmer than this!"

The *Cenlac* drifted before the wind. As soon as the last terrorist had left, the captain had sent his crew below to check for bombs. They'd found none, but the Captain knew that could just mean they were hidden, and a ship was the perfect place to hide anything. His engineer and another sailor were trying to repair one of his diesels while his three deckhands rigged a sea anchor that now streamed over the stern to steady the ferry on the rolling seas. The wind drove the boat closer to land. That did give them more moderate seas, but to touch the coast in this weather was death for all aboard. He thought he might launch one of his lifeboats, but even that entailed dangers that he prayed he might yet avoid.

He stood alone in the pilothouse and looked at his radios—smashed. With them he could call for help, a tug, a merchantman, anything that could put a line on his bow and pull him to safe harbor. But all three of his radio transmitters were wrecked beyond repair by a whole clip of machine gun bullets.

Why did the bastards leave us alive? he asked himself in quiet, helpless rage. His engineer appeared at the door.

"Can't fix it. We just don't have the tools we need. The bastards knew exactly what to break."

"They knew exactly what to do, all right," the Captain agreed.

"We're late for Yarmouth. Perhaps—"

"They'll write it off to the weather. We'll be on the rocks before they get their thumbs out." The Captain turned and opened a drawer. He withdrew a flare pistol and a plastic box of star shells. "Two-minute intervals. I'm going to see to the passengers. If nothing happens in . . . forty minutes, we launch the boats."

"But we'll kill the wounded getting them in—"

"We'll lose bloody everyone if we don't!" The Captain went below.

One of the passengers was a veterinarian, it turned out. Five people were wounded, and the doctor was trying to treat them, assisted by a member of the crew. It was wet and noisy on the vehicle deck. The ferry was rolling twenty degrees, and a window had been smashed by the seas. One of his deck crew was struggling to put canvas over the hole. The Captain saw that he would probably succeed, then went to the wounded.

"How are they?"

The veterinarian looked up, the anguish plain on his face. One of his patients was going to die, and the other four . . .

"We may have to move them to the lifeboats soon."

"It'll kill them. I—"

"Radio," one of them said through his teeth.

"Lie still," the doctor said.

"Radio," he persisted. The man's hands were clasping bandages to his abdomen, and it was all he could do not to scream out his agony.

"The bastards wrecked them," the Captain said. "I'm sorry—we don't have one."

"The truck—a radio in the fucking truck!"

"What?"

"Police," Highland gasped. "Police van—prisoner transport . . . *radio*. . . ."

"Holy Jesus!" He looked at the van—the radio might not work from inside the ferry. The Captain ran back to the pilothouse and gave an order to his engineer.

It was an easy enough task. The engineer used his tools to remove the VHF radio from the truck. He was able to hook it up to one of the ferry's antennas, and the Captain was using it within five minutes.

"Who is this?" the police dispatcher asked.

"This is the *Cenlac,* you bloody fool. Our marine radios are out. We are disabled and adrift, three miles south of Lisle Court, and we need assistance at once!"

"Oh. Very well. Stand by." The desk sergeant in Lymington was no stranger to the sea. He lifted his telephone and ran his finger down a list of emergency numbers till he found the right one. Two minutes later he was back to the ferry.

"We have a tugboat heading towards you right now. Please confirm your position three miles south of Lisle Court."

"That is correct, but we are drifting northeast. Our radar is still operating. We can guide the tug in. For Christ's good sake, tell him to hurry. We have wounded aboard."

The Sergeant bolted upright in his chair. "Say again—repeat your last."

The Captain explained in as few words as possible now that help was en route to his ship. Ashore, the Sergeant called his superior, then the local superintendent. Another call went to London. Fifteen minutes later, a Royal Navy flight crew was warming up a Sea King rescue helicopter at Gosport. They flew first to the naval hospital at Portsmouth to pick up a doctor and a medical orderly, then reversed course into the teeth of the gale. It took twenty dreadful minutes to find her, the pilot fighting his aircraft through the buffeting winds while the copilot used the look-down radar to pick the ferry's profile out from the sea return on the scope. That was the easy part.

He had to give his aircraft more than forty knots of forward speed just to hold her steady over the boat—and the wind never stayed the same for more than a few seconds, veering a few degrees in direction, changing ten knots in speed as he struggled with the controls to maintain something like a hover over her. Aft, the crew chief wrapped the rescue sling around the doctor first, holding him at the open door. Over the intercom, the pilot told the chief to lower away. At least they had a fairly large target. Two crewmen waited on the top deck of the ferry to receive the doctor. They'd never done it before, but the helicopter crew had, dropping him rapidly to ten feet over the rocking deck, then more easily the last few feet. One crewman tackled the doctor and detached the collar. The medical orderly came next, cursing fate and nature all the way down. He too arrived safely, and the helicopter shot upward to get away from the dangerous surface.

''Surgeon Lieutenant Dilk, Doctor.''

''Welcome. I'm afraid my practice is usually limited to horses and dogs,'' the vet replied at once. ''One sucking chest, the other three are belly wounds. One died—I did my best, but—'' there wasn't much else to say. ''Fucking murderers!''

The sound of a diesel horn announced the arrival of the tugboat. Lieutenant Dilk didn't bother looking while the Captain and crew caught the messenger line and hauled in a towing wire. Together, the doctors administered morphine and worked to stabilize the wounded.

The helicopter was already gone southwest, a grimmer purpose to their second mission for the day. Another helicopter, this one with armed Marines aboard, was lifting off from Gosport while the first searched the surface with radar and eyes for a black ten-meter zodiac-type rubber boat. Orders had come from the Home Office with record speed, and for once they were orders that men in uniform were trained and equipped to handle: *Locate and destroy.*

''The radar's hopeless,'' the copilot reported over the intercom.

The pilot nodded agreement. On a calm day they'd have a good chance to pick the rubber boat out, but the return from the confused seas and the flying spray made radar detection impossible.

''They can't have gone too far, and visibility isn't all that bad from up here. We'll do a quartering search and eyeball the bastards.''

''Where do we start?''

''Off the Needles, then inward to Christchurch Bay, then we'll work west if we have to. We'll catch the bastards before they make landfall and have the bootnecks meet them on the beach. You heard the orders.''

''Indeed.'' The copilot activated his tactical navigation display to set up the search pattern. Ninety minutes later it was plain that they'd searched in the wrong place. Surprised—baffled—the helicopters returned to Gosport empty-handed. The pilot went into the ready shack and found two very senior police officers.

''Well?''

''We searched from the Needles to Poole Bay—we didn't miss a thing.'' The pilot traced his flight path on the chart. ''That type of boat can make perhaps twenty knots in these sea conditions—at most, and then only with an expert crew. We should not have missed them.'' The pilot sipped at a mug of tea. He stared at the chart and shook his head in disbelief. ''No *way* we could have missed them! Not with two machines up.''

''What if they went seaward, what if they went south?''

''But where? Even if they carried enough fuel to cross the Channel, which I doubt, only a madman would try it. There will be twenty-foot seas out there, and the gale is still freshening. Suicide,'' the pilot concluded.

''Well, we know that they're not madmen, they're too damned smart for that. No way they could have gotten past you, made landfall before you caught up with them?''

''Not a chance. None.'' The flyer was emphatic.

''Then where the hell are they?''

''I'm sorry, sir, but I haven't a clue. Perhaps they sank.''

''Do you believe that?'' the cop demanded.

''No, sir.''

Commander James Owens turned away. He looked out the windows. The pilot was right; the storm was worsening. The phone rang.

''For you, sir.'' A petty officer held it up.

''Owens. Yes?'' His face changed from sadness to rage and back. ''Thank you. Please keep us posted. That was the hospital. Another of the wounded died. Sergeant Highland's in surgery now. One of the bullets hit his spine. That's a total of nine dead, I believe. Gentlemen, is there anything you can suggest to us? I'd be quite willing to hire a gypsy fortune teller at the moment.''

''Perhaps they made south from the Needles, then curved east and made landfall on the Isle of Wight.''

Owens shook his head. ''We have people there. Nothing.''

''Then they might have rendezvoused with a ship. There is the usual amount of traffic in the Channel.''

''Any way to check that?''

The pilot shook his head. ''No. There's a ship-traffic-control radar at Dover Strait, but not here. We can't board every ship, can we?''

''Very well. Gentlemen, thank you for your efforts, particularly getting your surgeon out as quickly as you did. I was told that this action saved several lives.'' Commander Owens walked out of the building. Those left behind marveled at his self-control. Outside, the senior detective looked up into the leaden sky and swore a mental curse at fortune, but he was too consumed by anger to show what he felt. Owens was a man accustomed to concealing what he thought and felt. Emotions, he often lectured his men, had no place in police work. Of course that was false, and like many cops Owens only succeeded in turning his rage inward. That accounted for the packet of antacid pills always in his coat pocket, and the quiet spells at home that his wife had learned to live with. He reached in his shirt pocket for a cigarette that wasn't there, then snorted to himself—*how did you ever break that habit, Jimmy*? He stood alone in the parking lot for a moment, as though the cold rain would dampen his anger. But it only gave him a chill, and he couldn't afford that. He'd have to answer for this, answer to the Commissioner of the Metropolitan Police, answer to the Home Office. Someone—*not me, thank God*—would also have to answer to the Crown.

That thought hammered home. He had failed *them*. He'd failed them twice. He had failed to detect and prevent the original attack on The Mall, and only the incredible luck of that Yank's intervention had saved the day. Then, when everything had subsequently gone right, this failure. Nothing like this had ever happened before. Owens was responsible. It had all happened on his watch. He had personally set up the transport scheme. The method was of his choosing. He had established the security procedures. Picked the day. Picked the routes. Picked the men, all dead now, except for Bob Highland.

How did they know? Owens demanded of himself. *They knew when, they knew where. How did they know? Well,* he told himself, *that's one place to start looking.* The number of people who had this information was known to Owens. Somehow it had been leaked. He remembered the report Ashley had brought back from Dublin. "So good, you would not believe it," that PIRA bastard had said of O'Donnell's intelligence source. Murphy was wrong, the detective thought. Everyone will believe it now.

"Back to London," he told the driver.

"Great day, Jack," Robby observed on the couch.

"Not bad at all," Ryan agreed. *Of course the house looks like a Toys 'Я Us that got nuked. . . .*

In front of them, Sally was playing with her new toys. She particularly liked the doll house, Jack was gratified to see. His daughter was winding down, having gotten her parents up at seven that morning. Jack and Cathy were winding down also after only five hours of sleep. That was a little tough on a pregnant wife, Jack had thought an hour earlier, and he and Robby had cleared away the dishes, now being processed by the dishwasher in the kitchen. Now their wives were on the other couch talking while the menfolk sipped at some brandy.

"Not flying tomorrow?"

Jackson shook his head. "The bird went tits-up, take another day or so to fix. Besides, what's Christmas without a good brandy? I'll be back in the simulator tomorrow, and regs don't prevent me from drinking before I do that. I don't strap in until three tomorrow, I ought to be fairly sober by then." Robby'd had one glass of wine with dinner, and had limited himself to only one Hennessy.

"God, I need a stretch." Jack stood up and beckoned his friend to the stairs.

"How late were you up last night, sport?"

"I think we hit the sack a little after two."

Robby checked to see that Sally was out of earshot. "Being Santa is a bitch, isn't it? If you can put all those toys together, maybe I ought to turn you loose on my broke airplane."

"Wait till I have both arms back." Jack pulled his arm out of the sling and moved it around as they went down to the library level.

"What's Cathy say about that?"

"What docs always say—hell, if you get well too soon, they lose money!" He moved his wrist around. "This thing knots up like you wouldn't believe."

"How's it feel?"

"Pretty good. I think I might get full use back. At least I haven't had it quit on me yet." Jack checked his watch. "Want to catch the news?"

"Sure."

Ryan flipped on the small TV on his deck. Cable had finally made it down his road, and he was already hooked on CNN. It was so nice to get the national and world news whenever you wanted. Jack dropped into his swivel chair while Robby selected another in the corner. It was a few minutes short of the hourly headlines. Jack left the sound down.

"How's the book coming?"

"Getting there. I have all the information in line, finally. Four more chapters to write, and two I have to change around some, and it's done."

"What did you change?"

"Turned out that I got bum data. You were right about that deck-spotting problem on the Japanese carriers."

"I didn't think that sounded right," Robby replied. "They were pretty good, but they weren't that good—I mean, we took 'em at Midway, didn't we?"

"What about today?"

"The Russians? Hey, Jack, anybody wants to fool with me and my Tomcat better have his will fixed up. They don't pay me to lose, son." Jackson grinned like a sleepy lion.

"Nice to see such confidence."

"There's better pilots than me," Robby admitted. "Three, as a matter of fact. Ask me again in a year, when I'm back in the groove."

"Oh, yeah!" Jack laughed. The laugh died when he saw the picture on the TV screen. "That's him—I wonder why—" He turned the sound up.

". . . killed, including five police officers. An intensive land, sea, and air search is under way for the terrorists who snatched their convicted comrade while en route to a British prison on the Isle of Wight. Sean Miller was convicted only three weeks ago in the daring attack on the Prince and Princess of Wales within sight of Buckingham Palace. Two police officers and one of the terrorists were killed before the attack was broken up by American tourist Jack Ryan of Annapolis, Maryland."

The picture changed to show the weather on the Channel and a Royal Navy helicopter, evidently searching for something. It changed again to a file tape of Miller being taken out of the Old Bailey. Just before he was put in the police van, Miller turned to face the camera, and now weeks later his eyes stared again into those of John Patrick Ryan.

"Oh, my God . . ." Jack muttered.

10. Plans and Threats

"You shouldn't blame yourself, Jimmy," Murray said. "And Bob's going to make it. That's something."

"Certainly," Owens replied sardonically. "There's even a fifty-percent chance that he'll learn to walk again. What of the others, Dan? Five good men gone, and four civilians along with them."

"And maybe the terrorists, too," Murray pointed out.

"You don't believe that any more than I do!"

It had come as a piece of blind luck. A Royal Navy mine-hunter ship conducting an ongoing sonar survey of the English Channel had found a new object on the bottom and immediately sent a camera sled down to classify it. The videotape showed the remains of a ten-meter zodiac-type inflatable boat, with two hundred-horse outboard motors. It had clearly sunk as the result of an explosion near the gas tanks, but there was no evidence of the men who'd been aboard, or their weapons. The vessel's skipper had immediately grasped the importance of the discovery and informed his superiors. A salvage crew was preparing now to go out and raise the wreck.

"It's a possibility. One of them might have screwed up, the boat blew, the bad guys get dumped in the drink . . ."

"And the bodies?"

"Fish food." Murray smirked. "Makes a nice image, doesn't it?"

"You are so fond of punting, Dan. Just what percentage of your salary would you wager on that hypothesis?" Owens wasn't in the mood for humor. Murray could see that the head of C-13 still looked on this as a very personal defeat.

"Not very much," the FBI representative conceded. "So you think a ship picked them up."

"It's the only thing that makes the least bit of sense. Nine merchant vessels were close enough to have been involved. We have the list."

So did Murray. It had already been forwarded to Washington, where the FBI and CIA would both work on it. "But why not recover the boat, too?"

"Obvious, isn't it? What if one of our helicopters saw them doing it? Or it might have been too difficult for the weather conditions. Or they might just not have wished to trouble themselves. They do have ample financial resources, don't they?"

"When will the Navy raise the wreck?"

"If the weather holds, day after tomorrow," Owens said. That was the one thing to be happy about. Then they'd have physical evidence. Everything made in the world carried trademarks and serial numbers. Somewhere there would be records of sale. That was how many successful investigations had started—a single sales slip in a single shop had often led to the conviction of the most dangerous criminals. From the videotape, the outboards on the boat looked like American Mercury motors. The Bureau had already been alerted to run that lead down as soon as the engine numbers were in. Murray had already learned that Mercury motors were a favorite all over the world. It would make matters harder, but it was still something; and something was always better than nothing. The resources of the Metropolitan Police and the Bureau were designed for precisely such a task.

"Any breaks on the leak?" Murray asked. This touched the rawest nerve of all.

"He'd better pray we don't find him," Owens said quietly. There was as yet no danger that this would happen. There had been a total of thirty-one people who'd known the time and route for the prisoner transfer, and five of them were dead—even the driver of the van hadn't known beforehand. That left twenty-six, ranging from a few members of C-13, two more high officials in the Metropolitan Police, ten in the Home Office, a few more in MI-5, the Security Service, and various others. Every one of them had a top-drawer security clearance. *Not that a clearance matters a damn,* Owens told himself again. *By definition a leak had to come from some bastard with a top-drawer clearance.*

But this was different. This was treason—it was *worse* than treason—a concept that Owens hadn't even thought possible until the last week. Whoever had leaked this had also to have been involved in the attack on the Royal Family. To betray national security secrets to a foreign power was sufficiently heinous to make the Commander think in unprofessional terms. But deliberately to endanger the Royal Family itself was so incomprehensible a crime that Owens had scarcely been able to believe it possible. This wasn't someone of dubious mental state. This was a person with intelligence and considerable skill at dissimulation, someone who had betrayed a trust both personal and national. There had been a time in his country when such people died by torture. It was not a fact that Owens was proud of, but now he understood why it had happened, how easily one might countenance such punishment. The Royal Family served so many functions for the United Kingdom, was so greatly loved by the people. And someone, probably someone very close to them, was quite willing to betray them to a small band of terrorists. Owens wanted that person. Wanted to see him dead, wanted to watch him die. There could be no other punishment for this kind of crime.

His professionalism returned after the few seconds of grim revelry. *We won't find the bastard by wishing him dead. Finding him means police work—careful, painstaking, thorough investigation.* Owens knew how to do that. Neither he nor the elite team of men on the investigation would rest until they succeeded. But none of them doubted that they would ultimately succeed.

"That's two breaks you have, Jimmy," Murray said after reading his friend's mind. It wasn't hard to do. Both men had handled hard cases, and police differ little over the world.

"Indeed," Owens said, almost smiling. "They ought not to have tipped their hand. They should have bent every effort to protect their source. We can compare the lists of who knew that His Highness was coming in that afternoon, and who knew that young Mr. Miller was going to Lymington."

"And the telephone operators who put the calls through," Murray reminded him. "And the secretaries and co-workers who might have overheard, and the girlfriends, or boyfriends, who might have heard during some horizontal conversation."

"Thank you ever so much for that, Dan. One needs encouragement at a time like this." The Englishman walked over to Murray's cabinet and found a bottle of whiskey—a Christmas present, still unopened on New Year's Eve.

"You're right that they should have protected their intel source. I know you'll get him, Jimmy. I will put some money down on that."

Owens poured the drinks. It was gratifying to see that the American had finally learned to drink his whiskey decently. In the past year Owens had broken Murray of the need to put ice in everything. It was shameful to contaminate single-malt Scotch whiskey. He frowned at another recurring thought. "What does that tell us about Sean Miller?"

Murray stretched his arms out. "More important than you thought, maybe? Maybe they were afraid you'd break information out of him. Maybe they just wanted to keep their perfect record. Maybe something else?"

Owens nodded. In addition to the close working relationship Scotland Yard had with the FBI, Owens valued the opinions of his colleague. Though both were experienced cops, Murray could always be trusted to have a slightly different slant on things. Two years before Owens had been surprised to learn how valuable this might be. Though he never had thought about it, Murray had used his colleague's brain the same way on several occasions.

"So what might that make Miller?" Owens wondered aloud.

"Who can say? Chief of operations?" Murray waved his glass.

"Awfully young for that."

"Jimmy, the guy who dropped the atomic bomb on Hiroshima was a full colonel in the Air Force, and twenty-nine years old. Hell, how old is this O'Donnell character?"

"That's what Bob Highland thinks." Owens stared into his glass for a moment, frowning again.

"Bob's a smart kid, too. God, I hope you can put him back on the street."

"If not, we can still use him in the office," Commander Owens said positively. "He does have a fine brain for the business of investigations—too good to be lost now. Well, I must be off. New Year's Eve, Dan. What do we drink to?"

"That's obvious. A successful investigation. You're going to get that source, Jimmy, and he's going to give you the information you need." Murray held his glass up. "To a closed case."

"Yes." Both men emptied their glasses.

"Jimmy, do yourself a favor and give it a night off. Clear the old head out and start fresh in the morning."

Owens smiled. "I'll try." He picked up his overcoat and walked toward the door. "One last thing. It hit me on the drive over. These chaps, the ULA, have broken all the rules, haven't they?"

"That's true enough," Murray replied as he locked up his files.

"There's only one rule they haven't broken."

Murray turned. "Oh? What's that?"

"They've never done anything in America."

"None of them do that." Murray dismissed the idea.

"None have had much of a reason before."

"So?"

"Dan, the ULA might have a reason now—and they've never been reticent about breaking the rules. It's just a feeling, no more than that." Owens shrugged. "Well. Good night, and a happy New Year to you, Special Agent Murray."

They shook hands ceremonially. "And to you, Commander Owens. Give my love to Emily."

Dan saw him to the door, locked it, and returned to his office to make sure all his secure files were locked up properly. It was pitch dark outside at—he checked his watch—quarter to six.

"Jimmy, why did you say that?" Murray asked the darkness. He sat back down in his swivel chair.

No Irish terrorist group had ever operated in the United States. Sure, they raised money there, in the Irish neighborhoods and saloons of Boston and New York, made the odd speech about their vision for the future of a free, united Ireland—never bothering to say that as committed Marxist-Leninists, their vision of Ireland was of another Cuba. They had always been shrewd enough to know that Irish-Americans might not feel comfortable with that little detail. And there was the gun-running. That was largely something in the past. The PIRA and INLA currently got most of their weapons on the open world market. There were also reports that some of their people had gotten training in Soviet military camps—you couldn't tell a man's nationality from a satellite photograph, nor could you recognize a specific face. These reports had never been confirmed sufficiently to be released to the press. The same was true of the camps in Libya, and Syria, and Lebanon. Some people, fair-skinned people, were being trained there—but who? The intelligence got a little confused on this point. It was different with the European terrorists. The Arabs who got caught often sang like canaries, but the captured members of the PIRA and INLA, and the Red Army Faction, and *Action-Directe* of France, and all the other shadowy groups gave up their information far more grudgingly. A cultural thing, or maybe they could simply be more certain that their captors would not—could not—use interrogation measures still common in the Middle East. They'd all been raised under democratic rules, and knew precisely the weaknesses of the societies they sought to topple. Murray thought of them as strengths, but recognized the inconveniences that they imposed on law-enforcement professionals. . . .

The bottom line was still that PIRA and INLA had never committed a violent crime in America. Never. Not once.

But Jimmy's right. The ULA has never hesitated to break a rule. The Royal Family was off-limits to everyone else, but not the ULA. The PIRA and INLA never hesitated to advertise its operations—every terrorist group advertises its operations. But not the ULA. He shook his head. There wasn't any evidence to suggest that they'd break this rule. It was simply the one thing that they hadn't done . . . yet. Not the sort of thing to start an investigation with.

"But what are they up to?" he said aloud. Nobody knew that. Even their name was an anomaly. Why did they call themselves the *Ulster* Liberation Army? The nationalist movement always focused on its Irishness, it was an Irish nationalist movement, but the ULA's very name was a regional expression. "Ulster" was invariably the prefix of the reactionary *Protestant* groups. Terrorists didn't have to make all that much sense in what they did, but they did have to make *some* sense. Everything about the ULA was an anomaly. They did the things no one else would do, called themselves something no one else would.

They did the things no one else would. That's what was chewing on Jimmy, Murray knew. Why did they operate that way? There had to be a reason. For all the madness of their actions, terrorists were rational by their own standards. However twisted their reasoning appeared to an outsider, it did have its own internal logic. The PIRA and INLA had such logic. They had even announced their rationales, and their actions could be seen to fit with what they said: To make Northern Ireland ungovernable. If they succeeded, the British would finally have enough of it and leave. Their objective, therefore, was to sustain a low-level conflict indefinitely and wait for the other side to walk away. It did make conceptual sense.

But the ULA has never said what it's up to. Why not? Why should their objective be a secret? Hell, why should the existence of a terrorist group be a secret—if they're running operations, how *can it be a secret; then why have they never even announced their existence, except within the PIRA/INLA community itself? This can't be completely unreasoned action,* he reminded himself. *They can't be acting completely without reason and still be as effective as they've been.*

"Damn!" The answer was there. Murray could feel it floating at the edge of his consciousness, but his mind couldn't quite reach that far. The agent left his office. Two Marines were already patrolling the corridors, checking that the doors were locked. Dan waved to them on the way to the elevator, his mind still trying to assemble the pieces into a unified picture. He wished that Owens hadn't left so soon. He wanted to talk this one over with Jimmy. Maybe the two of them could make sense of it all. No, he told himself, not "maybe." They'd find it. It was there, waiting to be found.

I bet Miller knew, Murray thought.

"What a dreadful place," Sean Miller said. The sunset was magnificent, almost like one at sea. The sky was clear of the usual urban pollution, and the distant dunes gave a crisp, if crenelated, line for the sun to slide behind. The odd thing was the temperature range, of course. The noon temperature had reached ninety-two—and the locals thought of this as a cool day!—but now as the sun sank, a cool wind came up, and soon the temperature would drop to freezing. The sand couldn't hold the heat, and with the clear, dry air, it would just radiate away, back to the stars.

Miller was tired. It had been that sort of day: refresher training. He hadn't touched a weapon in nearly two months. His reactions were off, his marksmanship abysmal, his physical condition little better. He'd actually gained a few pounds on prison food, something that had come as quite a surprise. In a week he'd have that run off. The desert was good for that. Like most men born in the higher latitudes, Miller had trouble tolerating this sort of climate. His physical activity made him thirsty, but he found it difficult to eat when it was so hot. So he drank water and allowed his body to turn in on itself. He'd lose the weight and harden his body more quickly here than anywhere else. But that didn't make him like the place.

Four more of their men were here also, but the remainder of the rescue force had immediately flown home via Rome and Brussels, putting a new string of entry stamps on their "travel" passports.

"It's not Ireland," O'Donnell agreed. His nose crinkled at the smell of dust, and his own sweat. Not like home. No smell of the mist over the peat, or coke fires on the hearths, or the alcoholic ambience of the local pub.

That was an annoying development: no liquor. The locals had got another attack of Allah and decided that even the fellow members of the international revolutionary community could not break God's law. *What a bloody nuisance.*

It wasn't much of a camp. Six buildings, one of them a garage. An unused helicopter pad, a road half-covered with sand from the last storm. One deep well for water. A firing range. Nothing else. In the past as many as fifty people had cycled through here at a time. Not now. This was the ULA's own camp, well separated from camps used by other groups. Every one of them had learned the importance of security. On a blackboard in hut #1 was a schedule provided by other fair-skinned friends that gave the pass-over times for American reconnaissance satellites; everyone knew when to be out of sight, and the camp's vehicles were under cover.

Two headlights appeared on the horizon, heading south toward the camp. O'Donnell noted their appearance, but said nothing about it. The horizon was far away. He put his arms into the sleeves of his jacket to ward off the gathering chill as he watched the lights slide left and right, their conical beams tracing over the dunes. The driver was taking his time, Kevin saw. The lights weren't bouncing about. The climate made it hard for a man to push himself hard. Things would get done tomorrow, God willing. *Insh'Allah,* a Latin colleague had once told him, meant the same thing as mañana—but without the urgency.

The vehicle was a Toyota Land Cruiser, the four-wheel-drive that had replaced the Land-Rover in most places. The driver took it right into the garage before getting out. O'Donnell checked his watch. The next satellite pass was in thirty minutes. Close enough. He rose and walked into hut #3. Miller followed, waving to the man who'd just come into the camp. A uniformed soldier from the camp's permanent force closed the garage door, and otherwise ignored them.

"Glad to see you got out, Sean," the visitor said. He carried a small satchel.

"Thank you, Shamus."

O'Donnell held open the door. He was not one to stand on ceremony.

"Thank you, Kevin."

"You're just in time for dinner," the chief of the ULA said.

"Well, one can't always be lucky," Shamus Padraig Connolly said. He looked around the inside of the hut. "No wogs about?"

"Not in here," O'Donnell assured him.

"Good." Connolly opened his satchel and brought out two bottles. "I thought you might like a drop of the pure."

"How did you get it past the bastards?" Miller asked.

"I heard about the new rule. I told them I was bringing in a gun, of course." Everyone laughed as Miller fetched three glasses and ice. You always used ice in this place.

"When are you supposed to arrive at the camp?" O'Donnell referred to the one forty miles away used by the PIRA.

"I'm having some car trouble, and staying the night with our uniformed friends. The bad news is that they've confiscated my whiskey."

"Bloody heathens!" Miller laughed. The three men toasted one another.

"How was it inside, Sean?" Connolly asked. The first round of drinks was already gone.

"Could have been worse. A week before Kevin came for me, I had a bad time with some thugs—the peelers put them up to it, of course, and they had a merry time. Bloody faggots. Aside from that, ah, it is so entertaining to sit there and watch them talk and talk and talk like a bunch of old women."

"You didn't think that Sean would talk, did you?" O'Donnell asked reprovingly. The smile covered his feelings—of course they had all worried about that; they had worried most of all what might happen when the PIRA and INLA lads in Parkhurst Prison got hold of him.

"Good lad!" Connolly refilled the glasses.

"So, what's the news from Belfast?" the chief asked.

"Johnny Doyle is not very pleased with having lost Maureen. The men are becoming restless—not much, mind, but there is talk. Your op in London, Sean, in case you've not been told, had glasses filled and raised throughout the Six Counties." That most citizens in Northern Ireland, Protestant and Catholic, had been disgusted by the operation mattered not to Connolly. His small community of revolutionaries was the entire world.

"One does not get drunk for a failure," Miller observed sourly. *That bastard Ryan!*

"But it was a splendid attempt. It is clear enough that you were unlucky, no more than that, and we are all slaves to fortune."

O'Donnell frowned. His guest was too poetic for Kevin's way of thinking, despite the fact, as Connolly was fond of pointing out, that Mao himself had written poetry.

"Will they try to spring Maureen?"

Connolly laughed at that one. "After what you did with Sean here? Not bloody likely. How ever did you pull that off, Kevin?"

"There are ways." O'Donnell let it go at that. His intelligence source was under strict orders not to do a thing for two months. Dennis's bookstore was closed so far as he was concerned. The decision to use him to get information for the rescue operation hadn't come easy. That was the problem with good intelligence, his teachers had hammered into his head years before. The really valuable stuff was always a risk to the source itself. It was a paradox. The most useful material was often too dangerous to use, but at the same time intelligence information that could not be used had no value at all.

"Well, you've gotten everyone's attention. The reason I'm here is to brief our lads on your operation."

"Really!" Kevin laughed. "And what does Mr. Doyle think of us?"

The visitor crooked a comically accusing finger. "You are a counterrevolutionary influence whose objective is to wreck the movement. The op on The Mall has had serious repercussions on the other side of the Atlantic. We'll—excuse me, *they'll* be sending some of their chaps to Boston in another month or so to set things right, to tell the Yanks that they had nothing to do with it," Connolly said.

"Money—we don't need their bloody money!" Miller objected. "And they can put their 'moral support' up—"

"Mustn't offend the Americans," Connolly pointed out.

O'Donnell raised his glass for a toast: "The devil with the bloody Americans."

As he drank off the last of his second whiskey, Miller's eyes snapped open sharply enough to make a *click*.

"Kevin, we won't be doing much in the U.K. for a while. . . ."

"Nor in the Six Counties," O'Donnell said thoughtfully. "This is a time to lie low, I think. We'll concentrate on our training for the moment and await our next opportunity."

"Shamus, how effective might Doyle's men be in Boston?"

Connolly shrugged his shoulders. "Get enough liquor into them and they'll believe anything they're told, and toss their dollars into the hat as always."

Miller smiled for a moment. He refilled his own glass this time as the other two talked on. His own mind began assembling a plan.

Murray had had a number of assignments in the Bureau over his many years of service, ranging from junior agent involved in chasing down bank robbers to instructor in investigation procedures at the FBI Academy at Quantico, Virginia. One thing he'd always told the youngsters in the classroom was the importance of intuition. Law enforcement was still as much art as science. The Bureau had immense scientific resources to process evidence, had written procedures for everything, but when you got down to it, there was never a substitute for the mind of an experienced agent. It was mostly experience, Murray knew, the way you fitted evidence together, the way you got a feel for the mind of your target and tried to predict his next move. But more than experience, there was intuition. The two qualities worked together until you couldn't separate them in your own mind.

That's the hard part, Murray told himself on the drive home from the embassy. *Because intuition can run a little wild if there's not enough evidence to hold on to.*

"You will learn to trust your instincts," Murray told the traffic, quoting from his memorized class notes. "Instinct is never a substitute for evidence and procedure, but it can be a very useful tool in adapting one to another—oh, Dan, you would have made a hell of a Jesuit." He chuckled to himself, oblivious of the stare he was getting from the car on his right.

If it's so damned funny, why does it bother you?

Murray's instinct was ringing a quiet but persistent bell. Why had Jimmy said that? Obviously it was bothering him, too—but what the hell was it?

The problem was, it wasn't just one thing. He saw that now. It was several things, and they were interrelated like some kind of three-dimensional crossword puzzle. He didn't know the number of blanks, and he didn't have any of the clues to the words, but he did know roughly the way they fitted together. That was something. Given time, it might even be enough, but—

"Damn!" His hands gripped tight on the steering wheel as good humor again gave way to renewed frustration. He could talk it over with Owens tomorrow or the next day, but the bell told him that it was more urgent than that.

Why is it so damned urgent? There is no *evidence of anything to get excited about.*

Murray reminded himself that the first case that he'd broken more or less on his own, ten months after hitting the street as a special agent, had begun with a feeling like this one. In retrospect the evidence had seemed obvious enough once he'd put the right twist on it, but that twist hadn't occurred to anyone else. And with Murray himself it had begun as nothing more than the same sort of intellectual headache he was suffering through in his car. Now he was really mad at himself.

Fact: The ULA broke all the rules. Fact: No Irish terrorist organization had ever run an operation in the U.S. There were no more Facts. If they ran an op in America . . . well, they were undoubtedly mad at Ryan, but they hadn't made a move against him over here, and that would have been a hell of a lot easier than staging one in the U.S. What if Miller really was their chief of operations—no, Murray told himself, terrorists don't usually take things personally. It's unprofessional, and the bastards *are* professional. They'd have to have a better reason than that.

Just because you don't know what the reason is doesn't mean they don't have one, Danny. Murray found himself wondering if his intuition hadn't transformed itself into paranoia with increasing age. *What if there's more than one reason to do it?*

"There's a thought," he said to himself. One could be an excuse for the other—but what's the *it* that they want to do? *Motive,* all the police procedure manuals said, was the main thing to look for. Murray didn't have a clue on their motive. "I could go crazy doing this."

Murray turned left off Kensington Road, into the upscale neighborhood of flats where he had his official residence. Parking was the usual problem. Even when he'd been assigned to the counterespionage section of the New York City Field Office, parking hadn't been this bad. He found a space perhaps two feet longer than his car and spent nearly five minutes fitting the vehicle into it.

Murray hung his coat on the peg beside the door and walked right into the living room. His wife found him dialing the phone, a ferocious scowl on his face. She wondered what was wrong.

It took a few seconds for the overseas call to go into the proper office.

"Bill, this is Dan Murray . . . we're fine," his wife heard him say. "I want you to do something. You know that guy Jack Ryan? Yeah, that's the one. Tell him—hell, how do I say this? Tell him that maybe he should watch his back. . . . I know that, Bill. . . . I can't say, something's bothering me, and I can't—something like that, yeah. . . . I know they've never done it before, Bill, but it's still bothering me. . . . No, nothing specific that I can point to, but Jimmy Owens brought it up, and now he's got me worrying about it. Oh, you got the report already? Good, then you know what I mean."

Murray leaned back and stared at the ceiling for a moment. "Call it feeling, or instinct—call it anything you want, it's bothering me. I want somebody to act on it. . . . Good man. How's the family? Oh, yeah? Great! Well, I guess it'll be a happy New Year for you. Okay. Take care. 'Bye." He set the phone down. "Well, that feels a little better," he said quietly to himself.

"The party starts at nine," his wife said. She was used to his bringing work home. He was used to having her remind him of his social obligations.

"I guess I better get dressed, then." Murray rose and kissed his wife. He did feel better now. He'd done *something*—probably no more than having people in the Bureau wonder what was happening to him over here, but he could live with that. "Bill's oldest is engaged. He's going to marry her off to a young agent in the D.C. Field Office."

"Anyone we know?"

"New kid."

"We have to leave soon."

"Okay, okay." He walked to the master bedroom and started to change for the big embassy party.

11. Warnings

"As you see, ladies and gentlemen, the decision Nelson made in this case had the long-term effect of finally putting an end to the stultifying influence of the Royal Navy's formal tactics." Ryan closed his note folder. "There is nothing like a decisive victory to teach people a lesson. Questions?"

It was Jack's first day back at teaching class. The room had forty students, all third classmen (that title included the six female mids in the class), or sophomores in civilian terms, taking Ryan's introductory course in naval history. There were no questions. He was surprised. Jack knew he was a pretty good teacher, but not that good. After a moment, one of the students stood up. It was George Winton, a football player from Pittsburgh.

"Doctor Ryan," he said stiffly, "I've been asked to make a presentation on behalf of the class."

"Uh-oh." Jack took half a step backward and scanned the body of students theatrically for the advancing threat.

Mid/3 Winton walked forward and produced a small box from behind his back. There was a typed sheet on the top. The young man stood at attention.

"Attention to orders: For service above and beyond the duty of a tourist—even a brainless Marine—the class awards Doctor John Ryan the Order of the Purple Target, in the hope that he will duck the next time, lest he become a part of history rather than a teacher of it."

Winton opened the box and produced a purple ribbon three inches across on which was inscribed in gold: SHOOT ME. Below it was a brass bull's-eye of equal size. The mid pinned it to Ryan's shoulder so that the target portion almost covered where he'd been shot. The class stood and applauded as Ryan shook hands with the class spokesman.

Jack fingered the "decoration" and looked up at his class. "Did my wife put you up to this?" They started converging on him.

"Way to go, Doc!" said an aspiring submarine driver.

"Semper fi!" echoed a would-be Marine.

Ryan held up his hands. He was still getting used to the idea of having his left arm back. The shoulder ached now that he was really using it, but the surgeon at Hopkins had told him that the stiffness would gradually fade away, and the net impairment to his left shoulder would be less than five percent.

"Thank you, people, but you still have to take the exam next week!"

There was general laughter as the kids filed out of the room to their next class. This was Ryan's last for the day. He gathered up his books and notes and trailed out of the room for the walk uphill to his office in Leahy Hall.

There was snow on the ground this frigid January day. Jack had to watch for patches of ice on the brick sidewalk. Around him the campus of the Naval Academy was a beautiful place. The immense quadrangle bordered by the chapel to the south, Bancroft Hall to the east, and classroom buildings on the other sides, was a glistening white blanket with pathways shoveled from one place to another. The kids—Ryan thought of them as kids—marched about as they always did, a little too earnest and serious for Jack's liking. They saved their smiles for places where no outsiders might notice. Each of them had his (or her) shoes spit-shined, and they moved about with straight backs, books tucked under the left arm so as not to interfere with saluting. There was a lot of that here. At the top of the hill, at Gate #3, a Marine lance corporal stood with the "Jimmy Legs" civilian guard. A normal day at the office, Jack told himself. It was a good place to work. The mids were easily the equal of the students of any school in the country, always ready with questions, and, once you earned their trust, capable of some astonishing horseplay. This was something a visitor to the Academy might never suspect, so serious was the kids' public demeanor.

Jack got into the steam-heated warmth of Leahy Hall and bounded up the steps to his office, laughing to himself at the absurd award that dangled from his shoulder. He found Robby sitting opposite his desk.

"What in the hell is that?" the pilot inquired. Jack explained as he set his books down. Robby started laughing.

"It's nice to see the kids can unwind a little, even in exam season. So what's new with you?" Jack asked his friend.

"Well, I'm a Tomcat driver again," Robby announced. "Four hours over the weekend. Oh, man! Jack, I'm telling you, I had that baby talking to me. Took her offshore, had her up to mach one-point-four, did a midair refueling, then I came back for some simulated carrier landings, and—it was good, Jack," the pilot concluded. "Two more months and I'll be back where I belong."

"That long, Rob?"

"Flying this bird is not supposed to be easy or they wouldn't need people of my caliber to do it," Jackson explained seriously.

"It must be hard to be so humble."

Before Robby could respond, there came a knock on the opened door and a man stuck his head in. "Doctor Ryan?"

"That's right. Join us."

"I'm Bill Shaw, FBI." The visitor came all the way in and held up his ID card. About Robby's height, he was a slender man in his mid-forties with eyes so deep set that they almost gave him the look of a raccoon, the kind of eyes that got that way from sixteen-hour days. A sharp dresser, he looked like a very serious man. "Dan Murray asked me to come over to see you."

Ryan rose to take his hand. "This is Lieutenant Commander Jackson."

"Howdy." Robby shook his hand, too.

"I hope I'm not interrupting anything."

"Not at all—we're both finished teaching for the day. Grab a chair. What can I do for you?"

Shaw looked at Jackson but didn't say anything.

"Well, if you guys have to talk, I can mosey on over to the O-Club—"

"Relax, Rob. Mr. Shaw, you're among friends. Can I offer you anything?"

"No, thank you." The FBI agent pulled the straight-back chair from next to the door. "I work in the counterterrorism unit at FBI headquarters. Dan asked me to—well, you know that the ULA rescued their man Miller from police custody."

Now Ryan was completely serious. "Yeah—I caught that on TV. Any idea where they took him to?"

Shaw shook his head. "They just disappeared."

"Quite an operation," Robby noted. "They escaped to seaward, right? Some ship pick them up maybe?" This drew a sharp look. "You notice my uniform, Mr. Shaw? I earn my living out there on the water."

"We're not sure, but that is a possibility."

"Whose ships were out there?" Jackson persisted. This wasn't a law-enforcement problem to Robby. It was a naval matter.

"That's being looked at."

Jackson and Ryan traded a look. Robby fished out one of his cigars and lit it.

"I got a call last week from Dan. He's a little—I wish to emphasize this, only a little—concerned that the ULA might . . . well, they don't have much of a reason to like you, Doctor Ryan."

"Dan said that none of these groups has ever operated over here," Ryan said cautiously.

"That's entirely correct." Shaw nodded. "It's never happened. I imagine Dan explained why this is true. The Provisional IRA continues to get money from over here, I am sorry to say, not much, but some. They still get some weapons. There is even reason to believe that they have some surface-to-air missiles—"

"What the hell!" Jackson's head snapped around.

"There have been several thefts of Redeye missiles—the man-portable one the Army's phasing out now. They were stolen from a couple of National Guard armories. This isn't new. The RUC has captured M-60 machine guns that got over to Ulster the same way. These weapons were either stolen or bought from some supply sergeants who forgot who they were working for. We've convicted several of them in the past year, and the Army's setting up a new system to keep track of things. Only one missile has turned up. They—the PIRA—tried to shoot down a British Army helicopter a few months back. It never made the papers over here, mainly because they missed, and the Brits were able to hush it up.

"Anyway," Shaw went on, "if they were to conduct actual terrorist operations over here, the money and the weapons would probably dry up quite a bit. The PIRA knows that, and it stands to reason that the ULA does, too."

"Okay," Jack said. "They've never operated over here. But Murray asked you to come here and warn me. How come?"

"There isn't any reason. If this had come from anyone except Dan, I wouldn't even be here, but Dan's a very experienced agent, and he's a little bit concerned that maybe you should be made aware of his—it's not even enough to be a suspicion, Doctor Ryan. Call it insurance, like checking the tires on your car before a long drive."

"Then what the hell are you telling me?" Ryan said testily.

"The ULA has dropped out of sight—that's not saying much, of course. I guess it's the way they dropped out of sight. They pulled a pretty bold operation, and"—he snapped his fingers—"disappeared back under their rock."

"Intel," Jack muttered.

"What's that?" Shaw asked.

"It happened again. The thing in London that I got in the way of, it resulted from very good intelligence information. This did, too, didn't it? They were moving Miller secretly, but the bad guys penetrated Brit security, didn't they?"

"I honestly don't know the specifics, but I'd say you probably had that one figured out pretty well," Shaw conceded.

Jack picked up a pencil in his left hand and started twirling it. "Do we know anything about what we're up against here?"

"They're professionals. That's bad news for the Brits and the RUC, of course, but it's good news for you."

"How's that?" Robby asked.

"Their disagreement with Doctor Ryan here is more or less a 'personal' matter. To take action against him would be unprofessional."

"In other words," the pilot said, "when you tell Jack that there's nothing for him to really worry about, you're betting on the 'professional' conduct of terrorists."

"That's one way to put it, Commander. Another way is to say that we have long experience dealing with this type of person."

"Uh-huh." Robby stabbed out his cigar. "In mathematics that's called inductive reasoning. It's a conclusion inferred, rather than deduced from specific evidence. In engineering we call it a WAG."

"Wag?" Shaw shook his head.

"A Wild-Ass Guess." Jackson turned to stare into the FBI man's eyes. "Like most operational intelligence reports—you can't tell the good ones from the bad ones until it's too damned late. Excuse me, Mr. Shaw, I'm afraid that we operators aren't always impressed with the stuff we get from the intelligence community."

"I knew it was a mistake to come here," Shaw observed. "Look, Dan told me over the phone that he doesn't have a single piece of evidence to suggest that there is any chance something unusual will happen. I've spent the last couple of days going over what we have on this outfit, and there just isn't any real evidence. He's responding to instinct. When you're a cop, you learn to do that."

Robby nodded at that one. Pilots trust their instinct, too. Now, his were telling him something.

"So," Jack leaned back. "What should I do?"

"The best defense against terrorists—what the security schools teach business executives, for example—is to avoid patterns. Take a slightly different route to work every day. Alter your time of departure somewhat. When you drive in, keep an eye on the mirror. If you see the same vehicle three or more days in a row, take the tag number and call me. I'll be glad to have it run through the computer—no big deal. It's probably nothing to be worried about, just be a little bit more alert. With luck, in a few days or weeks we'll be able to call you and tell you to forget the whole thing. What I am almost certainly doing is alarming you unnecessarily, but you know the rule about how it's better to be safe than sorry, right?"

"And if you get any information the other way?" Jack asked.

"I'll be on the phone to you five minutes later. The Bureau doesn't like the idea of having terrorists operate here. We work damned hard to keep it from happening, and we've been very effective so far."

"How much of that is luck?" Robby asked.

"Not as much as you think," Shaw replied. "Well, Doctor Ryan, I'm really sorry to have worried you about what is probably nothing at all. Here's my card. If there is anything we can do for you, don't hesitate to call me."

"Thank you, Mr. Shaw." Jack took the card and watched the man leave. He was silent for a few seconds. Then he flipped open his phone list and dialed 011-44-1-499-9000. It took a few seconds for the overseas call to get through.

"American Embassy," the switchboard operator answered after the first ring.

"Legal Attaché, please."

"Thank you. Wait, please." Jack waited. The operator was back in fifteen seconds. "No answer. Mr. Murray has gone home for the day—no, excuse me, he's out of town for the remainder of the week. Can I take a message?"

Jack frowned for a moment. "No, thank you. I'll call back next week."

Robby watched his friend hang up. Jack drummed his fingers on the phone and again remembered what Sean Miller's face had looked like. *He's three thousand miles away, Jack,* Ryan told himself. "Maybe," he breathed aloud.

"Huh?"

"I never told you about the one I . . . captured, I guess."

"The one they sprung? The one we saw on TV?"

"Rob, you ever seen—how do I say it? You ever see somebody that you're just automatically afraid of?"

"I think I know what you mean," Robby said to avoid the question. Jackson didn't know how to answer that. As a pilot, he'd known fear often enough, but always there was training and experience to deal with it. There was no *man* in the world he'd ever been afraid of.

"At the trial, I looked at him, and I just knew that—"

"He's a terrorist, and he kills people. That would bother me, too." Jackson stood up and looked out the window. "Jesus, and they call 'em professionals! *I'm* a professional. I have a code of conduct, I train, I practice, I adhere to standards and rules."

"They're real good at what they do," Jack said quietly. "That's what makes them dangerous. And this ULA outfit is unpredictable. That's what Dan Murray told me." Jackson turned away from the window.

"Let's go see somebody."

"Who?"

"Just come along, boy." Jackson's voice had the ring of command when he wanted it to. He set his white officer's cap on his head just so.

They took the stairs down and walked east, past the chapel and Bancroft Hall's massive, prisonlike bulk. Ryan liked the Academy campus except for that. He supposed it was necessary for all the mids to experience the corporate identity of military life, but Jack would not have cared to live that way as a college student. The odd mid snapped a salute at Robby, who returned each with panache as he proceeded in total silence with Jack trying to keep up. Ryan could almost hear the thoughts whirring through the aviator's head. It took five minutes to reach the new LeJeune Annex across from the Halsey field house.

The large glass and marble edifice contrasted with Bancroft's stolid gray stone. The United States Naval Academy was a government complex, and hence exempt from the normal standards of architectural good taste. They entered the ground floor past a gaggle of midshipmen in jogging suits, and Robby led him down a staircase into the basement. Jack had never been here before. They ended up in a dimly lit corridor whose block walls led to a dead end. Ryan imagined he heard the crack of small-bore pistol fire, and it was confirmed when Jackson opened a heavy steel door to the Academy's new pistol range. They saw a lone figure standing in the center lane, a .22 automatic steady in his extended right hand.

Sergeant Major Noah Breckenridge was the image of the Marine noncommissioned officer. Six-three, the only fat on his two-hundred-pound frame was in the hot dogs he'd had for lunch in the adjacent Dalgren Hall. He was wearing a short-sleeved khaki shirt. Ryan had seen but never met him, though Breckenridge's reputation was well known. In twenty-eight years as a Marine, he had been everywhere a Marine can go, done everything a Marine can do. His "salad bar" of decorations covered five even rows, topmost among them the Navy Cross, which he'd won while a sniper in Vietnam, part of 1st Force Recon. Beneath the ribbons were his marksmanship medals—"shooting iron"—the least of which was a "Master" rating. Breckenridge was known for his weapons proficiency. Every year he went to the national championships at Camp Perry, Ohio, and in two of the past five years he had won the President's Cup for his mastery of the .45 Colt automatic. His shoes were so shiny that one could determine only with difficulty that the underlying leather was actually black. His brass shone like stainless steel, and his hair was cut so close that if any gray were in there, the casual observer could never have seen it. He had begun his career as an ordinary rifleman, been an Embassy Marine and a Sea Marine. He had taught marksmanship at the sniper school, been a drill instructor at Parris Island and an officer instructor at Quantico.

When the Marine detail at the Academy had been augmented, Breckenridge had been the divisional Sergeant Major at Camp LeJeune, and it was said that when he left Annapolis, he would complete his thirty-year tour of duty as Sergeant Major of the Corps, with an office adjoining that of the Commandant. His presence at Annapolis was no accident. As he walked about the campus, Breckenridge was himself an eloquent and unspoken challenge to whichever midshipman might still be undecided on his career goals: *Don't even think about being a Marine officer unless you are fit to command a man like this.* It was the sort of challenge that few mids could walk away from. The Marine force that backed up the civilian guards was technically under the command of a captain. In fact, as was so often the case with the Corps, the Captain had the good sense to let Breckenridge run things. The traditions of the Corps were not passed on by officers, but rather by the professional NCOs who were the conservators of it all.

As Ryan and Jackson watched, the Sergeant Major took a fresh pistol from a cardboard box and slipped a clip into it. He fired two rounds, then checked his target through a spotting scope. Frowning, he pulled a tiny screwdriver from his shirt pocket and made an adjustment to the sights. Two more rounds, check, another adjustment. Two more shots. The pistol was now perfectly sighted, and went back into the manufacturer's box.

"How's it going, Gunny?" Robby asked.

"Good afternoon, Commander," Breckenridge said agreeably. His southern Mississippi accent spilled across the naked concrete floor. "And how are you today, sir?"

"No complaints. I got somebody I want you to meet. This here's Jack Ryan."

They shook hands. Unlike Skip Tyler, Breckenridge was a man who understood and disciplined his strength.

"Howdy. You're the guy was in the papers." Breckenridge examined Ryan like a fresh boot.

"That's right."

"Pleased to meet you, sir. I know the guy who ran you through Quantico."

Ryan laughed. "And how is Son of Kong?"

"Willie's retired now. He runs a sporting goods store down in Roanoke. He remembers you. Says you were pretty sharp for a college boy, and I imagine you remember mosta what he taught you.'' Breckenridge gazed down at Jack with a look of benign satisfaction, as though Ryan's action in London was renewed proof that everything the Marine Corps said and did, everything to which he had dedicated his life, really meant something. He would not have believed otherwise in any case, but incidents like this further enhanced his belief in the image of the Corps. ''If the papers got things straight, you did right well, Lieutenant.''

''Not all that well, Sergeant Major—''

''Gunny,'' Breckenridge corrected. ''Everybody calls me Gunny.''

''After it was all over,'' Ryan went on, ''I shook like a baby's rattle.''

Breckenridge was amused by this. ''Hell, sir, we all do that. What counts is gettin' the job done. What comes after don't matter a damn. So, what can I do for you gentlemen? You want a few rounds of small-bore practice?''

Jackson explained what the FBI agent had said. The Sergeant Major's face darkened, the jaw set. After a moment he shook his head.

''You're sweatin' this, eh? Can't say that I blame you, Lieutenant. 'Terrorists!' '' he snorted. ''A 'terrorist' is a punk with a machine gun. That's all, just a well-armed punk. It doesn't take much to shoot somebody in the back or hose down an airport waiting room. So. Lieutenant, you'll be thinkin' about carrying some protection, right? And maybe something at home.''

''I don't know . . . but I guess you're the man to see.'' Ryan hadn't thought about it yet, but it was clear that Robby had.

''How'd you do at Quantico?''

''I qualified with the .45 automatic and the M-16. Nothing spectacular, but I qualified.''

''Do you do any shootin' now, sir?'' Breckenridge asked with a frown. Just qualifying wasn't a very hopeful sign to a serious marksman.

''I usually get my quota of ducks and geese. I missed out this season, though,'' Jack admitted.

''Uplands game?''

''I had two good afternoons after dove in September. I'm a pretty fair wing-shot, Gunny. I use a Remington 1100 automatic, 12-gauge.''

Breckenridge nodded. ''Good for a start. That's your at-home gun. Nothing beats a shotgun at close range—short of a flamethrower, that is.'' The Sergeant Major smiled. ''You have a deer/slug barrel? No? Well, you're gonna get one of those. It's twenty inches or so, with a cylinder bore and rifle-type sights. You pull the magazine plug, and you got five-round capacity. Now most people'll tell you to use double-ought buck, but I like number four better. More pellets, and you're not giving any range away. You can still hit out to eighty, ninety yards, and that's all you'll ever need. The important thing is, anything you hit with buckshot's goin' down—period.'' He paused. ''As a matter of fact, I might be able to get you some flechette rounds.''

''What's that?'' Ryan asked.

''It's an experimental thing they foolin' with down at Quantico for military police use, and maybe at the embassies. Instead of lead pellets, you shoot sixty or so darts, about three-caliber diameter, like little arrows. You gotta see what those little buggers do to believe it. Nasty. So that'll take care of home. Now, you gonna want to carry a handgun with you?''

Ryan thought about that. It would mean getting a permit. He thought he could apply to the state police for one . . . or maybe to a certain federal agency. Already his mind was mulling over *that* question.

"Maybe," he said finally.

"Okay. Let's do a little experiment." Breckenridge walked into his office. He returned a minute later with a cardboard box.

"Lieutenant, this here's a High-Standard target pistol, a .22 built on a .45 frame." The Sergeant Major handed it over. Ryan took it, ejected the magazine, and pulled the slide back to make sure the pistol was unloaded. Breckenridge watched and nodded approvingly. Jack had been taught range safety by his father twenty years before. After that he fitted the weapon in his hand, then sighted down the range to get used to the feel. Every gun is a little different. This was a target pistol, with nice balance and pretty good sights.

"Feels okay," Ryan said. "Little lighter than a Colt, though."

"This'll make it heavier." Breckenridge handed over a loaded clip. "That's five rounds. Insert the clip in the weapon, but do not chamber a round until I tell you, sir." The Sergeant Major was accustomed to giving orders to officers, and knew how to do so politely. "Step to lane four. Relax. It's a nice day in the park, okay?"

"Yeah. That's how this whole mess started," Ryan observed wryly.

The Gunny walked over to the switch panel and extinguished most of the lights in the room.

"Okay, Lieutenant, let's keep the weapon pointed downrange and at the floor, if you please, sir. Chamber your first round, and relax."

Jack pulled the slide back with his left hand, then let it snap forward. He didn't turn around. He told himself to relax and play the game. He heard a cigarette lighter snap shut. Maybe Robby was lighting up one of his cigars.

"I saw a picture of your little girl in the papers, Lieutenant. She's a pretty little thing."

"Thank you, Gunny. I've seen one of yours on campus, too. Cute, but not very little. I heard she's engaged to a mid."

"Yes, sir. That's my little baby," Breckenridge said, like a father rather than a Marine. "The last of my three. She'll be married—"

Ryan nearly jumped out of his skin as a string of firecrackers began exploding at his feet. He started to turn when Breckenridge screamed at him:

"There, there, there's your target!"

A light snapped on to illuminate a silhouette target fifty feet away. One small part of Ryan's mind knew this was a test—but most of him didn't care. The .22 came up and seemed to aim itself at the paper target. He loosed all five rounds in under three seconds. The noise was still echoing when his trembling hands set the automatic down on the table.

"Jesus Christ, Sar-major!" Ryan nearly screamed.

The rest of the lights came back on. The room stank of gunpowder, and paper fragments from the firecrackers littered the floor. Robby, Jack saw, was standing safely at the entrance to the Gunny's office, while Breckenridge was right behind him, ready to grab Ryan's gun hand if he did anything foolish.

"One of the other things I do is moonlight as an instructor for the Annapolis City Police. You know, it's a real pain in the ass trying to figure a way to simulate the stress of combat conditions. This here's what I came up with. Okay, let's get a look at the target." Breckenridge punched a button, and a hidden electric motor turned the pulley for lane four.

"Damn!" Ryan growled, looking at the target.

"Not so bad," Breckenridge judged. "We got four rounds on the paper. Two snowbirds. Two in the black, both in the chest. Your target is on the ground, Lieutenant, and he's hurt pretty bad.''

''Two rounds out of five—must be the last two. I settled down on them and took some more time.''

''I noticed that.'' Breckenridge nodded. ''Your first round was high and to the left, missed the card. Your next two came in here and here. The last two were on the money fairly well. That's not too bad, Lieutenant.''

''I did a hell of a lot better in London.'' Ryan was not convinced. The two holes outside the black target silhouette mocked at him, and one round hadn't even found the target at all. . . .

''In London, if the TV got it right, you had a second or two to figure out what you were gonna do,'' the Gunny said.

''That's pretty much the way it was,'' Ryan admitted.

''You see, Lieutenant, that's the real important part. That one or two seconds makes all the difference, because you have a little time to think things over. The reason so many cops get killed is because they don't have that little bit of time to think it out—but the crooks have done that already. That one second lets you figure what's happening, select your target, and decide what you're gonna do about it. Now, what I just made you do was go through all three steps, all at once. Your first round went wild. The second and third were better, and your last two were good enough to put the target on the ground. That's not bad, son. That's about as well as a trained cop does—but you gotta do better than that.''

''What do you mean?''

''A cop's job is to keep the peace. Your job is just staying alive, and that's a little easier. That's the good news. The bad news is, those bad guys ain't gonna give you two seconds to think unless you make them, or you're real lucky.'' Breckenridge waved for the men to follow him into his office. The Sergeant Major plopped down in his cheap swivel chair. Like Jackson, he was a cigar smoker. He lit up something better than what Robby smoked, but it still stank up the room.

''Two things you gotta do. One, I want to see you here every day for a box of .22; that's every day for a month, Lieutenant. You have to learn to shoot better. Shootin' is just like golf. You want to be good at it, you gotta do it every day. You have to work at it, and you need somebody to teach you right.'' The Gunny smiled. ''That's no problem; I'll teach you right. The second thing, you have to buy time for yourself if the bad guys come lookin' for you.''

''The FBI told him to drive like the embassy guys do,'' Jackson offered.

''Yeah, that's good for starters. Same as in Nam—you don't settle into patterns. What if they try to hit you at home?''

''Pretty isolated, Gunny,'' Robby said.

''You got an alarm?'' Breckenridge asked Ryan.

''No, but I can fix that pretty easy,'' Ryan said.

''It's a good idea. I don't know the layout of your place, but if you can buy yourself a few seconds, and you got that shotgun, Lieutenant, you can make 'em wish they never came calling—at least you can hold them off till the police come. Like I said, the name of the game's just staying alive. Now, what about your family?''

''My wife's a doc, and she's pregnant. My little girl—well, you saw her on TV, I guess.''

''Does your wife know how to shoot?''

"I don't think she's ever touched a gun in her life."

"I teach a class in firearms safety for women—part of the work I do with the local police."

Ryan wondered how Cathy would react to all this. He put that one off. "What sort of handgun you think I oughta get?"

"If you come by tomorrow, I'll try you out on a couple of 'em. Mainly you want something you're comfortable with. Don't go out and get a .44 Magnum, okay? I like automatics, myself. The springs eat up a lot of the recoil, so they're easier to get comfortable with. You want to buy something that's fun to shoot, not something that beats up on your hand and wrist. Me, I like the .45 Colt, but I been shooting that little baby for twenty-some years." Breckenridge grabbed Ryan's right hand and flexed it around roughly. "I think I'll start you off on a 9-millimeter Browning. Your hand looks big enough to hold it right—the Browning's got a thirteen-shot clip, you need a fair-sized hand to control it proper. Got a nice safety, too. If you have a kid in the house, Lieutenant, you'd better think about safety, okay?"

"No problem," Ryan said. "I can keep it where she can't reach it—we got a big closet, and I can keep them there, seven feet off the floor. Can I practice with a big-bore handgun in here?"

The Sergeant Major laughed. "That backstop we got used to be the armor plate on a heavy cruiser. Mainly we use .22's in here, but my guards practice with .45's all the time. Sounds to me like you know shotgunnin' pretty good. Once you have that skill with pistol too, you'll be able to do it with any gun you pick up. Trust me, sir, this is what I do for a living."

"When do you want me here?"

"Say about four, every afternoon?"

Ryan nodded. "Okay."

"About your wife—look, just bring her over some Saturday maybe. I'll sit her down and talk to her about guns. Lots of women, they're just afraid of the noise—and there's all that crap on TV. If nothing else, we'll get her used to shotgunning. You say she's a doc, so she's gotta be pretty smart. Hell, maybe she'll like it. You'd be surprised how many of the gals I teach really get into it."

Ryan shook his head. Cathy had never once touched his shotgun, and whenever he cleaned it, kept Sally out of the room. Jack hadn't thought much about it, and hadn't minded having Sally out of the way. Little kids and firearms were not a happy mixture. At home he usually had the Remington disassembled and the ammunition locked away in the basement. How would Cathy react to having a loaded gun in the house?

What if you start carrying a gun around? How will she react to that? What if the bad guys are interested in going after them, too . . . ?

"I know what you're thinkin', Lieutenant," Breckenridge said. "Hey, the Commander said the FBI didn't think any of this crap was gonna happen, right?"

"Yeah."

"So what you're doin' is buyin' insurance, okay?"

"He said that, too," Ryan replied.

"Look—we get intel reports here, sir. Yeah, that's right. Ever since those bike bums broke in, we get stuff from the cops and the FBI, and from some other places—even the Coast Guard. Some of their guys come here for firearms training, 'cause of the drug stuff they got 'em doing now. I'll keep an ear out, too," Breckenridge assured him.

Information—it's all a battle for information. You have to know what's happening if you're going to do anything about it. Jack turned back to look at Jackson while he made a decision that he'd been trying to avoid ever since he got back from England. He still had the number in his office.

"And if they tell you those bike bums are coming back?" Ryan asked with a smile.

"They'll wish they didn't," the Sergeant Major said seriously. "This is a U.S. Navy reservation, guarded by the United States Marine Corps."

And that's the name of that tune, Ryan thought. "Well, thanks, Gunny. I'll get out of your way."

Breckenridge saw them to the door. "Sixteen hundred tomorrow, Lieutenant. How about you, Commander Jackson?"

"I'll stick to missiles and cannons, Gunny. Safer that way. G'night."

"Good night, sir."

Robby walked Jack back to his office. They had to pass on the daily drinks. Jackson had to do some shopping on the way home. After his friend left, Jack stared at his telephone for several minutes. Somehow he'd managed to avoid doing this for several weeks despite his wish to track down information on the ULA. But it wasn't just curiosity anymore. Ryan flipped open his telephone book and turned to the "G" page. He was able to call the D.C. area direct, though his finger hesitated before it jabbed down on each button.

"This is Mrs. Cummings," a voice answered after the first ring. Jack took a deep breath.

"Hello, Nancy, this is Doctor Ryan. Is the boss in?"

"Let me check. Can you hold for a second?"

"Yes."

They didn't have one of the new musical hold buttons there, Ryan noted. There was just the muted chirp of electronic noise for him to listen to. *Am I doing the right thing?* he wondered. He admitted to himself that he didn't know.

"Jack?" a familiar voice said.

"Hello, Admiral."

"How's the family?"

"Fine, thank you, sir."

"They came through all the excitement all right?"

"Yes, sir."

"And I understand that your wife's expecting another baby. Congratulations."

And how did you know that, Admiral? Ryan did not ask. He didn't have to. The DDI was supposed to know everything, and there were at least a million ways he might have found out.

"Thank you, sir."

"So, what can I do for you?"

"Admiral, I . . ." Jack hesitated. "I want to look into this ULA bunch."

"Yeah, I thought you might. I have here on my desk a report from the FBI's terrorism unit about them, and we've been coordinating lately with the SIS. I'd like to see you back here, Jack. Maybe even on a more permanent basis. Have you thought our offer over any more since we last spoke?" Greer inquired innocently.

"Yes, sir, I have, but . . . well, I am committed to the end of the school year." Jack temporized. He didn't want to have to face that particular question. If forced, he'd just say no, and that would kill his chance to get into Langley.

"I understand. Take your time. When do you want to come over?"

Why are you making it so easy? "Could I come over tomorrow morning? My first class isn't until two in the afternoon."

"No problem. Be at the main gate at eight in the morning. They'll be waiting for you. See ya."

"Goodbye, sir." Jack hung up.

Well, that was easy. Too easy, Jack thought. *What's he up to?* Ryan dismissed the thought. He wanted to look at what CIA had. They might have stuff the FBI didn't; at the least he'd get a look at more data than he had now, and Jack wanted to do that.

Nevertheless the drive home was a troubled one. Jack watched his rearview mirror after remembering that he'd left the Academy the same way he always did. The hell of it was, he *did* see familiar cars. That was a problem with making your commute about the same time every day. There were at least twenty cars that he had learned to recognize. There was someone's secretary driving her Camaro Z-28. She had to be a secretary. She was dressed too well to be anything else. Then there was the young lawyer in his BMW—the car made him a lawyer, Ryan thought, wondering how he had ever assigned tags to his fellow commuters. *What if a new one shows up?* he wondered. *Will you be able to tell which one is a terrorist?* Fat chance, he knew. Miller, for all the danger that lay on his face, would look ordinary enough with a jacket and tie, just another state employee fighting his way up Route 2 into Annapolis. . . .

"Paranoid, all this is paranoid," Ryan murmured to himself. Pretty soon he'd check the rear seat in his car before he got in, to see if someone might be lurking back there like on TV, with a pistol or garrote! He wondered if the whole thing might be a stupid, paranoid waste of time. What if Dan Murray just had a bug up his ass or was simply being cautious? The Bureau probably taught its men to be cautious on these things, he was sure. Do I scare Cathy over this? What if that's all there is to it?

What if it's not?

That's why I'm going to go to Langley tomorrow, Ryan answered himself.

They sent Sally to bed at 8:30, dressed in her bunny-rabbit sleeper, the flannel pajamas with feet that keep kids warm through the night. She was getting a little old for that, Jack thought, but his wife insisted on them, since their daughter had a habit of kicking the blankets on the floor in the middle of the night.

"How was work today?" his wife asked.

"The mids gave me a medal," he said, and explained on for a few minutes. Finally he pulled the Order of the Purple Target out of his briefcase. Cathy found it amusing. The smiling stopped when he related the visit from Mr. Shaw of the FBI. Jack ran through the information, careful to include everything the agent had said.

"So, he doesn't really think it'll be a problem?" she asked hopefully.

"We can't ignore it."

Cathy turned away for a moment. She didn't know what to make of this new information. *Of course,* her husband thought. *Neither do I.*

"So what are you going to do?" she asked finally.

"For one thing I'm going to call an alarm company and have the house wired. Next, I've already put my shotgun back together, and it's loaded—"

"No, Jack, not in this house, not with Sally around," Cathy said at once.

"It's on the top shelf in my closet. It's loaded, but it doesn't have a round chambered. She can't possibly get to it, not even with a stool to stand on. It stays loaded, Cathy. I'm also going to start practicing some with it, and maybe get a pistol, too. And"—he hesitated—"I want you to start shooting, too."

"No! I'm a doctor, Jack. I don't use guns."

"They don't bite," Jack said patiently. "I just want you to meet a guy I know who teaches women to shoot. Just meet the guy."

"No." Cathy was adamant. Jack took a deep breath. It would take an hour to persuade her, that was the usual time required for her common sense to overcome her prejudices. The problem was, he didn't want to spend an hour on the subject right now.

"So you're going to call the alarm company tomorrow morning?" she asked.

"I have to go somewhere."

"Where? You don't have any classes until after lunch."

Ryan took a deep breath. "I'm going over to Langley."

"What's at Langley?"

"The CIA," Jack answered simply.

"What?"

"Remember last summer? I got that consulting money from Mitre Corporation?"

"Yeah."

"All the work was at CIA headquarters."

"But—you said over in England that you never—"

"That's where the checks came from. That's who I was working for. But CIA was where I was working *at.*"

"You lied?" Cathy was astounded. "You lied in a courtroom?"

"No. I said that I was never employed by CIA, and I wasn't."

"But you never told me."

"You didn't need to know," Jack replied. *I knew this wasn't a good idea. . . .*

"I'm your wife, dammit! What were you doing there?"

"I was part of a team of academics. Every few years they bring in outsiders to look at some of their data, just as sort of a check on the regular people who work there. I'm not a spy or anything. I did all the work sitting at a little desk in a little room on the third floor. I wrote a report, and that was that." There was no sense in explaining the rest to her.

"What was the report about?"

"I can't say."

"Jack!" She was really mad now.

"Look, babe, I signed an agreement that I would never discuss the work with anybody who wasn't cleared—I gave my word, Cathy." That calmed her down a bit. She knew that her husband was a real stickler for keeping his word. It was actually one of the things she loved about him. It annoyed her that he used this as a defense, but she knew that it was a wall she couldn't breach. She tried another tack.

"So why are you going back?"

"I want to see some information they have. You ought to be able to figure out what that information is."

"About these ULA people, then."

"Well, let's just say that I'm not worried about the Chinese right now."

"You really are worried about them, aren't you?" She was starting to worry, finally.

"Yeah, I guess I am."

"But why? You said the FBI said they weren't—"

"I don't know—hell, yes, I *do* know. It's that Miller bastard, the one at the trial. He wants to kill me." Ryan looked down at the floor. It was the first time he'd said it aloud.

"How do you know that?"

"Because I saw his face, Cathy. I saw it, and I'm scared—not just for me."

"But Sally and I—"

"Do you really think he cares about that?" Ryan snapped angrily. "These bastards kill people they don't even know. They almost do it for fun. They want to change the world into something they like, and they don't give a damn who's in the way. *They just don't care.*"

"So why go to the CIA? Can they protect you—us—I mean. . . ."

"I want a better feel for what these guys are all about."

"But the FBI knows that, don't they?"

"I want to see the information for myself. I did pretty good when I worked there," Jack explained. "They even asked me to, well, to take a permanent position there. I turned them down."

"You never told me any of this," Cathy grumped.

"You know now." Jack went on for a few minutes, explaining what Shaw had told him. Cathy would have to be careful driving to and from work. She finally started smiling again. She drove a six-cylinder bomb of a Porsche 911. Why she never got a speeding ticket was always a source of wonderment to her husband. Probably her looks didn't hurt, and maybe she flashed her Hopkins ID card, with a story that she was heading to emergency surgery. However she did it, she was in a car with a top speed of over a hundred twenty miles per hour and the maneuverability of a jackrabbit. She'd been driving Porsches since her sixteenth birthday, and Jack admitted to himself that she knew how to make the little green sports car streak down a country road—enough to make him hold on pretty tight. This, Ryan told himself, was probably a better defense than carrying a gun.

"So, you think you can remember to do that?"

"Do I really have to?"

"I'm sorry I got us into this. I never—I never knew that anything like this would happen. Maybe I just should have stayed put."

Cathy ran her hand across his neck. "You can't change it now. Maybe they're wrong. Like you said, probably they're just acting paranoid."

"Yeah."

12. Homecoming

Ryan left home well before seven. First he drove to U.S. Route 50 and headed west toward D.C. The road was crowded, as usual, with the early morning commuters heading to the federal agencies that had transformed the District of Columbia from a picturesque plot of real estate into a pseudo-city of transients. He got off onto I-

495, the beltway that surrounds the town, heading north through even thicker traffic whose more congested spots were reported on by a radio station's helicopter. It was nice to know why the traffic was moving at fifteen miles per hour on a road designed for seventy.

He wondered if Cathy was doing what she was supposed to do. The problem was that there weren't that many roads for her to use to get to Baltimore. The nursery school that Sally attended was on Ritchie Highway, and that precluded use of the only direct alternate route. On the other hand, Ritchie Highway was always a crowded and fast-moving road, and intercepting her wouldn't be easy there. In Baltimore itself, she had a wide choice of routes into Hopkins, and she promised to switch them around. Ryan looked out at the traffic in front of him and swore a silent curse. Despite what he'd told Cathy, he didn't worry overly much about his family. He was the one who'd gotten in the way of the terrorists, and if their motivation was really personal, then he was the only target. Maybe. Finally he crossed the Potomac River and got on the George Washington Parkway. Fifteen minutes later he took the CIA exit.

He stopped his Rabbit at the guard post. A uniformed security officer came out and asked his name, though he'd already checked Ryan's license plate against a computer-generated list on his clipboard. Ryan handed his driver's license to the guard, who scrupulously checked the photograph against Jack's face before giving him a pass.

"Sir, the visitors' parking lot is to the left, then the second right—"

"Thanks, I've been here before."

"Very well, sir." The guard waved him on.

The trees were bare. CIA headquarters was built behind the first rank of hills overlooking the Potomac Valley, in what had once been a lush forest. Most of the trees remained, to keep people from seeing the building. Jack took the first left and drove uphill on a curving road. The visitor parking lot was also attended by a guard—this one was a woman—who waved him to an open slot and made another check of Ryan before directing him toward the canopied main entrance. To his right was "the Bubble," an igloo-shaped theater that was connected to the building by a tunnel. He'd once delivered a talk there, a paper on naval strategy. Before him, the CIA building was a seven-story structure of white stone, or maybe prestressed concrete. He'd never checked that closely. As soon as he got inside, the ambience of spook-central hit him like a club. He saw eight security officers, all in civilian clothes now, their jackets unbuttoned to suggest the presence of sidearms. What they really carried was radios, but Jack was sure that men with guns were only a few feet away. The walls had cameras that fed into some central monitoring room—Ryan didn't know where that was; in fact, the only parts of the building he actually knew were the path to his erstwhile cubbyhole of an office, from there to the men's room, and the route to the cafeteria. He'd been to the top floor several times, but each time he'd been escorted since his security pass didn't clear him for that level.

"Doctor Ryan." A man approached. He looked vaguely familiar, but Jack couldn't put a name on the face. "I'm Marty Cantor—I work upstairs."

The name came back as they shook hands. Cantor was Admiral Greer's executive assistant, a preppy type from Yale. He gave Jack a security pass.

"I don't have to go through the visitor room?" Jack waved to his left.

"All taken care of. You can follow me."

Cantor led him to the first security checkpoint. He took the pass from the chain around his neck and slid it into a slot. A small gate with orange and yellow stripes, like those used for parking garages, snapped up, then down again as Ryan stuck his card in the slot. A computer in a basement room checked the electronic code on the pass and decided that it could safely admit Ryan to the building. The gate went back up. Already Jack was uncomfortable here. *Just like before,* he thought, *like being in a prison—no, security in a prison is nothing compared to this.* There was something about this place that made Jack instantly paranoid.

Jack slung the pass around his neck. He gave it a quick look. It had a color photograph, taken the previous year, and a number, but no name. None of the CIA passes had names on them. Cantor led off at a brisk walk to the right, then left toward the elevators. Ryan noticed the kiosk where you could buy a Coke and a Snickers bar. It was staffed by blind workers, yet another of the oddly sinister things about the CIA. Blind people were less likely to be security risks, he supposed, though he wondered how they drove in to work every day. The building was surprisingly shabby, the floor tile never quite shiny, the walls a drab shade of yellow-beige; even the murals were second-rate. It surprised a lot of people that the Agency spent little on the outward trappings of importance. The previous summer Jack had learned that the people here took a perverse pride in the place's seediness.

Everywhere people walked about with anonymous haste. They walked so fast in the building that most corners had hubcap-shaped mirrors to warn you of possible collision with a fellow spook . . . or to alert you that someone might be lurking and listening around the corner.

Why did you come here?

Jack shook the thought off as he entered the elevator. Cantor pushed the button for the seventh floor. The door opened a minute later to expose yet another drab corridor. Ryan vaguely remembered the way now. Cantor turned left, then right, as Ryan watched people walking about with a speed that would impress a recruiter for the Olympic Team's heel-and-toe crew. He had to smile at it until he realized that none of them were smiling. A serious place, the Central Intelligence Agency.

The executive row of CIA had its own private corridor—this one had a rug—that paralleled the main one and led to offices facing the east. As always, there were people just standing about and watching. They inspected Ryan and his pass, but showed no reaction, which was good enough news for Jack. Cantor took his charge to the proper door and opened it.

Admiral James Greer was in civilian clothes, as usual, leaning back in a high-backed swivel chair, reading an inevitable folder and sipping at inevitable coffee. Ryan had never seen him otherwise. He was in his middle sixties, a tall, patrician-looking man whose voice could be as courtly or harsh as he wished. His accent was that of Maine, and for all his sophistication, Ryan knew him to be a farmer's son who'd earned his way into the Naval Academy, then spent forty years in uniform, first as a submarine officer, then as a full-time intelligence specialist. Greer was one of the brightest people Ryan had ever met. And one of the trickiest. Jack was convinced that this gray-haired old gentleman could read minds. Surely that was part of the job description for the Deputy Director, Intelligence, of the Central Intelligence Agency. All the data gathered by spies and satellites, and God only knew what else, came across his desk. If Greer didn't know it, it wasn't worth knowing. He looked up after a moment.

"Hello, Doctor Ryan." The Admiral rose and came over. "I see you're right on time."

"Yes, sir. I remembered what a pain the commute was last summer." Without being asked, Marty Cantor got everyone coffee as they sat on chairs around a low table. One nice thing about Greer was that he always had good coffee, Jack remembered.

"How's the arm, son?" the Admiral asked.

"Almost normal, sir. I can tell you when it's going to rain, though. They say that may go away eventually, but it's like arthritis."

"And how's your family?"

The man doesn't miss a trick, Jack thought. But Jack had one of his own. "A little tense at the moment, sir. I broke the news to Cathy last night. She's not real happy about it, but then neither am I." *Let's get down to business, Admiral.*

"So what exactly can we do for you?" Greer's demeanor changed from pleasant old gentleman to professional intelligence officer.

"Sir, I know this is asking a lot, but I'd like to see what the Agency has on these ULA characters."

"Not a hell of a lot." Cantor snorted. "These boys cover their tracks like real pros. They're being bankrolled in a pretty big way—that's inferred, of course, but it has to be true."

"Where does your data come from?"

Cantor looked over to Greer and got a nod. "Doctor, before we go any further, we have to talk about classification."

Resignedly: "Yeah. What do I have to sign?"

"We'll take care of that before you leave. We'll show you just about everything we've got. What you have to know now is that this stuff is classified SI-codeword."

"Well, that's no surprise." Ryan sighed. Special-Intelligence-Codeword was a level of classification higher than top secret. People had to be individually cleared for the data, which was identified by a special codeword. Even the codeword itself was secret. Ryan had only twice before seen data of this sensitivity. *But now they're going to lay it all out in front of me,* he thought as he looked at Cantor. *Greer must really want me back to open a door like this.* "So, like I said, where does it come from?"

"Some from the Brits—actually from the PIRA via the Brits. Some new stuff from the Italians—"

"Italians?" Ryan was surprised for a moment, then realized what the implications of that were. "Oh. Okay, yeah, they have a lot of people down in sand-dune country, don't they?"

"One of them ID'd your friend Sean Miller last week. He was getting off a certain ship that was, miraculously enough, in the English Channel on Christmas Day," Greer said.

"But we don't know where he is?"

"He and an unknown number of associates headed south." Cantor smiled. "Of course the whole country is south of the Med, so that's not much of a help."

"The FBI has everything we have, and so do the Brits," Greer said. "It's not much to go on, but we do have a team sifting through it."

"Thanks for letting me take a look, Admiral."

"We're not doing this out of charity, Doctor Ryan," the Admiral pointed out. "I'm hoping that you might find something useful. And this thing has a price for you, too. If you want in, you will be an Agency employee by the end of the day. We can even arrange for you to have a federal pistol permit."

"How did you know—"

"It's my job to know, sonny." The old man grinned at him. Ryan didn't think this situation was the least bit funny, but he granted the Admiral his points.

"When can I start?"

"How does your schedule look?"

"I can work on that," Jack said cautiously. "I can be here Tuesday morning, and maybe work one full day per week, plus two half-days. In the mornings. Most of my classes are in the afternoon. Semester break is coming up, and then I can give you a full week."

"Very well. You can work out the details with Marty. Go take care of the paperwork. Nice to see you again, Jack."

Jack shook his hand once more. "Thank you, sir."

Greer watched the door close before he went back to the desk. He waited a few seconds for Ryan and Cantor to clear the corridor, then walked out to the corner office that belonged to the Director of Central Intelligence.

"Well?" Judge Arthur Moore asked.

"We got him," Greer reported.

"How's the clearance procedure going?"

"Clean. He was a little too sharp doing his stock deals a few years back, but, hell, he was supposed to be sharp."

"Nothing illegal?" Judge Moore asked. The Agency didn't need someone who might be investigated by the SEC. Greer shook his head.

"Nah, just very smart."

"Fine. But he doesn't see anything but this terrorist stuff until the clearance procedures are complete."

"Okay, Arthur!"

"And I don't have Deputy Directors to do our recruiting," the DCI pointed out.

"You're taking this awfully hard. Does a bottle of bourbon put that much of a dent in your bank account?"

The Judge laughed. The day after Miller had been sprung from British custody, Greer had made the gentlemanly wager. Moore didn't like losing at anything—he'd been a trial lawyer before becoming a jurist—but it was nice to know that his DDI had a head for prognostication.

"I'm having Cantor get him a gun permit, too," Greer added.

"You sure that's a good idea?"

"I think so."

"So it's decided, then?" Miller asked quietly.

O'Donnell looked over at the younger man, knowing why the plan had been formulated. It was a good plan, he admitted to himself, an effective plan. It had elements of brilliance in its daring. But Sean had allowed personal feelings to influence his judgment. That wasn't so good.

He turned toward the window. The French countryside was dark, thirty thousand feet below the airliner. All those peaceful people, sleeping in their homes, safe and secure. They were on a red-eye flight, and the plane was nearly empty. The stewardess dozed a few rows aft, and there was no one about to hear what they were saying. The whine of the jet engines would keep any electronic listening device from working, and they'd been very careful to cover their tracks. First the flight to Bucharest, then to Prague, then to Paris, and now the flight home to Ireland, with only French entry stamps on their passports. O'Donnell was a careful man, to the point of carrying notes on his fictitious business meetings in France. They'd get through customs easily enough, O'Donnell was sure. It was late, and the clerks at passport control were scheduled to go home right after this flight arrived.

Sean had a completely new passport, with the proper stamps, of course. His eyes were now brown, courtesy of some contact lenses, his hair changed in color and style, a neatly trimmed beard changing the shape of his face. Sean hated the beard for its itching. O'Donnell smiled at the darkness. Well, he'd have to get used to that.

Sean didn't say anything else. He sat back and pretended to read through the magazine he'd found in the seat pocket. The pretended patience was gratifying to his chief. The young man had gone through his refresher training (O'Donnell thought in military terms for this sort of thing) with a passion, trimming off the excess weight, reacquainting himself with his weapons, conferring with the intelligence officers from other fair-skinned nations, and living through their critique of the failed operation in London. These "friends" had not acknowledged the luck factor, and pointed out that another car of men had been needed to ensure success. Through all of it, Sean had kept his peace and listened politely. And now he waited patiently for the decision on his proposed operation. Perhaps the young man had learned something in that English jail.

"Yes."

Ryan signed the form, acknowledging receipt of the cartful of information. He was back in the same cubbyhole office he'd had the previous summer, a windowless, closet-sized room on the third floor of CIA's main building. His desk was about the smallest size made—in federal prison workshops—for office use, and the swivel chair was a cheap one. CIA chic.

The messenger stacked the documents on the corner of Ryan's desk and wheeled the cart back out of the room. Jack went to work. He took the top off a Styrofoam cup of coffee bought at the kiosk around the corner, dumped in the whole container of creamer and two envelopes of sugar, and stirred it with a pencil as he often did. It was a habit his wife loathed.

The pile was about nine inches high. The files were in oversized envelopes, each of which had an alpha-numeric code stamped on in block figures. The file folders he removed from the top envelope were trimmed with red tape so as to look important—the visual cues were designed to be noticed, to stand out visually. Such files had to be locked up in secure cabinets every night, never left on a desk where someone might take an unauthorized look at them. The papers inside each were held in place with Acco fasteners, and all had numbers. The cover of the first file had its codeword neatly typed on a paper label: FIDELITY. Ryan knew that the code names were assigned at random by a computer, and he wondered how many such files and names there were, if the dictionary of the English language that resided in the computer's memory had been seriously depleted by the elimination of words for the thousands of secret files that sat in cabinets throughout the building. He hesitated for a moment before opening it, as though doing so would irrevocably commit him to employment at CIA; as though the first step on that path had not already been taken. . . .

Enough of that, he told himself, and opened the file. It was the first official CIA report on the ULA, barely a year old.

"Ulster Liberation Army," the title of the report read. "Genesis of an Anomaly."

"Anomaly." That was the word Murray had used, Ryan remembered. The first paragraph of the report stated with disarming honesty that the information contained in the following thirty single-spaced pages was more speculation than fact, based principally on data gotten from convicted PIRA members—specifically on denials they'd made. *That wasn't* our *operation,* some of them had said after being caught for another. Ryan frowned. Not exactly the most reliable of evidence. The two men who'd done the report, however, had done a superb job of cross-referencing. The most unlikely story, heard from four separate sources, changed to something else. It was particularly true since the PIRA was, technically speaking, a professional outfit. Jack knew from his own research the previous year that the Provisional Wing of the Irish Republican Army was superbly organized, along the classic cellular lines. It was just like any intelligence agency. With the exception of a handful of top people, the specifics of any particular operation were compartmentalized: known only to those who really needed to know. ''Need-to-know'' was the catch phrase in any intelligence agency.

Therefore, if the details of an operation are *widely known,* the report argued, *it can only be because it was not a PIRA op. Otherwise they would not have known or talked about the details, even among themselves.* This was twisted logic, Jack thought, but fairly convincing nonetheless. The theory held insofar as the PIRA's main rival, the less well organized Irish National Liberation Army, the gang that had killed Lord Louis Mountbatten, had often had its operations identified in the same way. The rivalry between PIRA and INLA had turned vicious often enough, though the latter, with its lack of internal unity and generally amateurish organization, was not nearly as effective.

It was barely a year since the ULA had emerged from the shadows to take some kind of shape. For the first year they'd operated, it was thought by the British that they were a PIRA Special Action Group, a Provo hit squad, a theory broken when a captured PIRA member had indignantly denied complicity in what had turned out to be a ULA assassination. The authors of the report then examined suspected ULA operations, pointing to operational patterns. These, Ryan saw, were quite real. For one thing, they involved more people, on average, than PIRA ops.

That's interesting. . . . Ryan walked out of the room, heading down the corridor to the kiosk, where he bought a pack of cigarettes. In under a minute he was back to his office, fumbling with the cipher lock on the door.

More people per operation. Ryan lit one of the low-tar smokes. That was a violation of ordinary security procedures. The more people involved in an operation, the greater the risk of its being blown. What did this mean? Ryan examined three separate operations, looking for his own patterns.

It was clear after ten minutes of examination. The ULA was more of a military organization than PIRA. Instead of the small, independent groups typical of urban terrorists, the ULA organized itself more on classic military lines. The PIRA often depended on a single ''cowboy'' assassin, less often on the special action groups. There were many cases Ryan knew of, where the one ''designated hitter''—a term popular in CIA the previous year—had his own special gun, and lay in wait like a deer hunter, often for days, to kill a specific target. But the ULA was different. For one thing they didn't generally go for individual targets. They relied, it seemed, on a reconnaissance team and an assault team that worked in close cooperation—the operative word here was ''seemed,'' Ryan read, since this, again, was something inferred from scanty evidence. When they did something, they usually got away cleanly. Planning and resources.

Classic military lines. That implied a great deal of confidence by the ULA in its people—and in its security. Jack started making notes. The actual facts in the report were thin—he counted six—but the analysis was interesting. The ULA showed a very high degree of professionalism in its planning and execution of operations, more so than the PIRA, which was itself proficient enough. Instead of a small number of really sharp operatives, it appeared that weapons expertise was uniform throughout the small organization. The uniformity of expertise was interesting.

Military training? Ryan wrote down. *How good? Where done? What source?* He looked at the next report. It was dated some months after "Genesis" and showed a greater degree of institutional interest. CIA had begun to take a closer look at the ULA, starting seven months previously. *Right after I left here,* Jack noted. *Coincidence.*

This one concentrated on Kevin O'Donnell, the suspected leader of the ULA. The first thing Ryan saw was a photograph taken from a British intelligence-gathering team. The man was fairly tall, but otherwise ordinary. The photo was dated years before, and the next thing Jack read was that the man had reportedly had plastic surgery to change his face. Jack studied the photo anyway. He'd been at a funeral for a PIRA member killed by the Ulster Defense Regiment. The face was solemn enough, with a hardness around the eyes. He wondered how much he could draw from a single photo of a man at a funeral for a comrade, and set the picture aside to read the biography of the man.

A working-class background. His father had been a truck driver. His mother had died when he was nine. Catholic schools, of course. A copy of his college transcript showed him to be bright enough. O'Donnell had graduated from university with honors, and his degree was in political science. He'd taken every course on Marxism that the institution had offered, and been involved on the fringes of civil-rights groups in the late sixties and early seventies. This had earned him attention from the RUC and British intelligence agencies. Then, after graduating, he'd dropped out of sight for a year, reappearing in 1972 after the Bloody Sunday fiasco when British Army paratroopers had gotten out of control and fired into a crowd of demonstrators, killing fourteen people, none of whom had been proven to have a gun.

"There's a coincidence," Ryan whispered to himself. The paratroopers still claimed that they'd been fired upon from someone in the crowd and merely returned fire to defend themselves. An official government report done by the British backed this up—of course, what else could they say? Ryan shrugged. It might even have been true. The biggest mistake the English had ever made was to send troops into Northern Ireland. What they'd needed was good cops to reestablish law and order, not an army of occupation. But with the RUC out of control then, and supplemented by the B-Special thugs, there hadn't been a real alternative. So soldiers had been sent in, to a situation for which they were unsuited by training . . . and vulnerable to provocation.

Ryan's antennae twitched at that.

Political-science major, heavy course-load in Marxism. O'Donnell had dropped out of sight, then reappeared about a year later immediately after the Bloody Sunday disaster, and soon thereafter was identified by an informer as the PIRA's chief of internal security. He didn't get that job on the basis of college classwork. He'd had to work to earn that. Terrorism, like any other profession, has its apprenticeship. Somehow this Kevin Joseph O'Donnell had earned his spurs. *How did you do that? Were you one of the guys who stage-managed the provocations? If so, where did you learn how, and does that missing year have anything to do with it? Were you trained in urban insurgency tactics . . . in the Crimea maybe . . . ?*

Too much of a coincidence, Jack told himself. The idea of Soviet training for the hard-core members of the PIRA and INLA had been bandied about so much that it had lost credibility. Besides, it didn't have to be something that dramatic. They might just have figured out the proper tactics for themselves, or read them in books. There were plenty of books on the subject of how to be an urban guerrilla. Jack had read several of them.

He flipped forward in time to O'Donnell's second disappearance. Here the information from British sources was fairly complete for once. O'Donnell had been remarkably effective as chief of internal security. Nearly half the people he'd killed really had been informers of one sort or another, not a bad percentage in this sort of business. He found a couple of new pages at the end of the report, and read the information that David Ashley had gathered a few months before in Dublin. . . . *He got a little carried away.* . . . O'Donnell had used his position to eliminate Provos whose politics didn't quite agree with his. It had been discovered, and he'd vanished for a second time. Again the data was speculative, but it tracked with what Murray had told him in London. O'Donnell *had* gone somewhere.

Surely he'd convinced someone to provide his nascent organization with financing, training, and support. *His nascent organization,* Ryan thought. *Where had it come from?* There was a lapse of two years before O'Donnell's disappearance from Ulster and the first positively identified operation of the ULA. Two complete years. The Brit intel data suggested plastic surgery. Where? Who paid for it? *He didn't do that in some jerkwater third-world country,* Ryan told himself. He wondered if Cathy could ask her colleagues at Hopkins about the availability of good face-cutters. *Two years to change his face, get financial backing, recruit his troops, establish a base of operations, and begin to make his impact. . . . Not bad,* Ryan thought with grudging admiration. All that in two years.

Another year before the name of the outfit surfaces. . . .

Ryan turned when he heard someone working the lock on his office door. It was Marty Cantor.

"I thought you stopped smoking." He pointed at the cigarette.

Ryan crushed it out. "So does my wife. Have you seen all this stuff?"

"Yeah." Cantor nodded. "The boss had me run through it over the weekend. What do you think?"

"I think this O'Donnell character is one formidable son of a bitch. He's got his outfit organized and trained like a real army. It's small enough that he knows every one of them. His ideological background tells me he's a careful recruiter. He has an unusually high degree of trust in his troops. He's a political animal, but he knows how to think and plan like a soldier. Who trained him?"

"Nobody knows," Cantor replied. "I think you can overestimate that factor, though."

"I know that," Ryan agreed. "What I'm looking for is . . . flavor, I guess. I'm trying to get a feel for how he thinks. It would also be nice to know who's bankrolling him." Ryan paused, and something else leaped into his mind. "What are the chances that he has people inside the PIRA?"

"What do you mean?"

"He runs for his life when he finds out that the PIRA leadership is out for his ass. Two years later, he's back in business with his own organization. Where did the troops come from?"

"Some pals from inside the PIRA, obviously," Cantor said.

"Sure." Jack nodded. "People he knew to be reliable. But we also know that he's a counterintelligence type, right?"

"What do you mean?" Cantor hadn't been down this road yet.

"Who's the main threat to O'Donnell?"

"Everybody wants him—"

"Who wants to kill him?" Jack refocused the question. "The Brits don't have capital punishment—but the PIRA does."

"So?"

"So if you were O'Donnell, and you recruited people from inside the PIRA, and you knew that the PIRA was interested in having your head on a wall plaque, you think you'd leave people inside to cue you in?"

"Makes sense," Cantor said thoughtfully.

"Next, who is the ULA's political target?"

"We don't know that."

"Don't give me that crap, Marty!" Ryan snapped. "Most of the information in these documents comes from inside the Provos, doesn't it? How the hell do these people know what the ULA is up to? How does the data get to them?"

"You're pushing, Jack," Cantor warned. "I've seen the data, too. It's mainly negative. The Provos who had the information sweated out of them mainly said that certain operations weren't theirs. The conclusion that ULA did 'em is inferential—circumstantial. I don't think that this stuff is as clear as you do."

"No, the two guys who did this report make a good case for putting the ULA fingerprint on these ops. What the ULA has is its own *style,* Marty! We can identify that, can't we?"

"You've constructed a circular argument," Cantor pointed out. "O'Donnell comes from the Provos, therefore he must have recruited from there, therefore he must have people in there, et cetera. Your basic arguments are logical, but try to remember that they're based on a very shaky foundation. What if the ULA really is a special-action group of the Provisionals? Isn't it in their interest to have something like that?" Cantor was a splendid devil's advocate, one of the reasons he was Greer's executive assistant.

"Okay, there is some truth to that," Ryan admitted. "Still, everything I say makes sense, assuming that the ULA is real."

"Granted that it's logical. But not proven."

"So it's the first logical thing we have for these characters. What else does that tell us?"

Cantor grinned. "Let me know when you figure it out."

"Can I talk to anybody about this?"

"Like who—I just want to ask before I say no."

"The Legal Attaché in London—Dan Murray," Ryan said. "He's supposed to be cleared all the way on this material, isn't he?"

"Yeah, he is, and he works with our people, too. Okay, you can talk with him. That keeps it in the family."

"Thanks."

Five minutes later Cantor was sitting across from Admiral Greer's desk.

"He really knows how to ask the right questions."

"So what did he tumble to?" the Admiral asked.

"The same questions that Emil Jacobs and his team have been asking: What's O'Donnell up to? Does he have the PIRA infiltrated? If so, why?"

"And Jack says . . . ?"

"Same as Jacobs and the FBI evaluation: O'Donnell is a counterintelligence type by training. The Provos want his hide on the barn door, and the best way to keep his hide where it belongs is to have people inside to warn him if they get too close."

The Admiral nodded agreement, then looked away for a moment. That was only part of an answer, his instincts told him. There had to be more. "Anything else?"

"The training stuff. He hasn't sifted through all the data yet. I think we should give him some time. But you were right, sir. He's pretty sharp."

Murray lifted his phone and pushed the right button without paying much attention. "Yeah?"

"Dan? This is Jack Ryan," the voice on the phone said.

"How's it going, teacher?"

"Not bad. Something I want to talk over with you."

"Shoot."

"I think the ULA has the PIRA infiltrated."

"What?" Murray snapped upright in his chair. "Hey, ace, I can't—" He looked at the telephone. The line he was talking on was— "What the hell are you doing on a secure line?"

"Let's say that I'm back in government service," Ryan replied coyly.

"Nobody told me."

"So what do you think?"

"I think it's a possibility. Jimmy came up with the idea about three months back. The Bureau agrees that it makes sense. There is no objective evidence to support the theory, but everybody thinks it's a logical—I mean, it would be a smart thing for our friend Kevin to do, if he can. Remember that the PIRA has very good internal security, Jack."

"You told me that most of what we know about the ULA comes from PIRA sources. How do they get the info?" Ryan asked rapidly.

"What? You lost me."

"How does the PIRA find out what the ULA is doing?"

"Oh, okay. That we don't know." It was something that bothered Murray, and James Owens, but cops deal all the time with anonymous information sources.

"Why would they be doing that?"

"Telling the Provos what they're up to? We have no idea. If you have a suggestion, I'm open to it."

"How about recruiting new members for his team?" Ryan asked.

"Why don't you think that one over for a few seconds," Murray replied immediately. Ryan had just rediscovered the flat earth theory.

There was a moment of silence. "Oh—then he'd risk being infiltrated by the Provisionals."

"Very good, ace. If O'Donnell's got them infiltrated as a security measure to protect himself, why invite members of the group that wants his ass into his own fold? If you want to kill yourself, there're simpler ways, Jack." Murray had to laugh. He could hear Ryan deflate over the phone.

"Okay, I guess I had that coming. Thanks."

"Sorry to rain on your parade, but we buried that idea a couple of months ago."

"But he must have recruited his people from the Provisionals to begin with," Ryan objected belatedly. He cursed himself for being so slow, but remembered that Murray had been an expert on this subject for years.

"Yeah, I'll buy that, but he kept the numbers very low," Murray said. "The bigger the organization gets, the greater the risk that the Provos will infiltrate—and destroy—him. Hey, they really want his ass on a platter, Jack.'' Murray stopped short of revealing the deal David Ashley had cut with the PIRA. CIA didn't know about that yet.

''How's the family?'' he asked, changing the subject.

''Fine.''

''Bill Shaw says he talked to you last week. . . .'' Murray said.

''Yeah. That's why I'm here now. You've got me looking over my shoulder, Dan. Anything else that you've cued in on?''

It was Murray's turn to deflate. ''The more I think about it, the more it looks like I got worried over nothing. No evidence at all, Jack. It was just instinct, you know, like from an old woman. Sorry. I think I just overreacted to something Jimmy said. Hope I didn't worry you too much.''

''Don't sweat it,'' Jack replied. ''Well, I have to clear out of here. See ya.''

''Yeah. 'Bye, Jack.'' Murray replaced the phone in the holder and went back to his paperwork.

Ryan did much the same. He had to leave by noon in order to make his first class of the day. The messenger came back with his cart and took the files away, along with Jack's notes, which, of course, were also classified. He left the building a few minutes later, his mind still sifting through the data he'd read.

What Jack didn't know was that in the new annex to the CIA headquarters building was the headquarters of the National Reconnaissance Office. This was a joint CIA–Air Force agency that managed the data from satellites and, to a lesser degree, high-altitude reconnaissance aircraft.

The new generation of satellites used television-type scanning cameras instead of photographic film. One consequence of this was that they could be used almost continuously instead of husbanding their film for coverage of the Soviet Union and its satellites. This allowed the NRO to assemble a much better data base on world trends and events, and had generated scores of new projects for hundreds of new analysts—explaining the newly built annex behind the original CIA building.

One junior analyst's brief was coverage on camps suspected to be used for the training of terrorists. The project had not yet shown enough results to be treated more importantly, though the data and photographs were passed on to the Task Force on Combating Terrorism. TFCT used the satellite photos, as was the norm in government circles. The staffers *ooh*ed and *ahh*ed over the clarity of the shots, were briefed on the new charge-coupled devices that enabled the cameras to get high-resolution pictures despite atmospheric disturbances, noted that, despite all the hoopla, you really couldn't read the numbers on a license plate—and promptly forgot about them as anything more than pictures of camps where terrorists might be training. Photoreconnaissance interpretation had always been a narrow field for experts only. The analysis work was simply too technical.

And as was so often the case, here was the rub. The junior analyst was better described as a technician. He collected and collated data, but didn't really analyze it. That was someone else's job, for when the project was finished. In this particular case the data being processed noted infrared energy. The camps he examined on a daily basis—there were over two hundred—were mainly in deserts. That was remarkably good luck. While everyone knew that deserts suffer from blistering daylight heat, it was less appreciated that they can get quite cold at night—falling below freezing in many cases. So the technician was trying to determine the occupancy of the camps from the number of buildings that were heated during the cool nights. These showed up quite well on the infrared: bright blobs of white on a cold, black background.

A computer stored the digital signals from the satellite. The technician called up the camps by code number, noted the number of heated buildings in each, and transferred the data to a second data file. Camp 11-5-18, located at 28° 32′ 47″ North Latitude, 19° 07′ 52″ East Longitude, had six buildings, one of which was a garage. This one had at least two vehicles in it; though the building was unheated, the thermal signatures of two internal-combustion engines radiated clearly through the corrugated steel roofs. Of the other five buildings, only one had its heater on, the technician noted. The previous week—he checked—three had been warm. The warm one now, the data sheet said, was occupied by a small guard and maintenance group, thought to be five men. It evidently had its own kitchen, since one part of the building was always a little warmer than the rest. Another building was a full-sized dining hall. That and the dormitories were now empty. The technician made the appropriate notations, and the computer assigned them to a simple line graph that peaked when occupancy was high and fell when it was low. The technician didn't have the time to check the patterns on the graph, but he assumed, wrongly, that someone else did.

"You remember, Lieutenant," Breckenridge said. "Deep breath, let it half out, and squeeze gently."

The 9mm Browning automatic had excellent sights. Ryan centered them on the circular target and did what the Gunny said. He did it right. The flash and sound of the shot came almost as a surprise to him. The automatic ejected the spent round and was ready to fire again as Jack brought the pistol down from recoil. He repeated the procedure four more times. The pistol locked open on the empty clip and Ryan set it down. Next he took off the muff-type ear protectors. His ears were sweaty.

"Two nines, three tens, two of them in the X-ring." Breckenridge stood away from the spotting scope. "Not as good as the last time."

"My arm's tired," Ryan explained. The pistol weighed almost forty ounces. It didn't seem like much weight until you had to hold it stone-steady at arm's length for an hour.

"You can get some wrist weights—you know, like joggers use. It'll build up your forearm and wrist muscles." Breckenridge slipped five rounds into the clip of Ryan's pistol and stepped to the line to aim at a fresh target.

The Sergeant Major fired all five in under three seconds. Ryan looked in the spotting scope. There were five holes within the target's X-ring, clustered like the petals on a flower.

"Damn, I forgot how much fun a nice Browning could be." He ejected the clip and reloaded. "The sights are right on, too."

"I noticed," Jack replied lamely.

"Don't feel too bad, Lieutenant," Breckenridge said. "I've been doin' this since you were in diapers." Five more rounds and the center was effectively removed from the target, fifty feet away.

"Why are we doing round targets anyway?" Jack asked.

"I want you to get used to the idea of placing your shots exactly where you want them to go," the Gunny explained. "We'll sweat the fancy stuff later. For now we'll work on basic skills. You look a little looser today, Lieutenant."

"Yeah, well, I talked to the FBI guy who originated the warning. Now he says he might have overreacted—maybe I did, too."

Breckenridge shrugged. "You never been in combat, Lieutenant. I have. One thing you learn: the first twitch you have is usually right. Keep that in mind."

Jack nodded, not believing it. He'd accomplished much today. His look at the ULA data told him a lot about the organization, but there was not the first inkling that they had ever operated at all in America. The Provisional IRA had plenty of American connections, but no one believed that the ULA did. Even if they planned to do something here, Ryan judged, they'd need the connections. It was possible that O'Donnell might call on some of his previous PIRA friends, but that seemed most unlikely. He was a dangerous man, but only on his own turf. And America wasn't his turf. That's what the data said. Jack knew that this was too broad a conclusion to base on one day's work, of course. He'd keep looking—it seemed that his investigation would last two or three weeks, the way he was going. If nothing else, he wanted to look into the relationship between O'Donnell and the Provos. He did have a feeling that something odd was going on, just as Murray evidently did, and he wanted to examine the data fully, in the hope of coming up with a plausible theory. He owed CIA something for its courtesy.

The storm was magnificent. Miller and O'Donnell stood by the leaded-glass windows and watched as the Atlantic gale beat the sea to foaming waves that slammed against the base of the cliff on which the house stood. The crash of the breaking waves provided the bass notes, while the wind howled and whistled through the trees and raindrops beat their tattoo against the house itself.

"Not a day to be sailing, Sean," O'Donnell said as he sipped at a whiskey.

"When do our colleagues go to America?"

"Three weeks. Not much time. Do you still want to do it?" The chief of the ULA thought the timing marginal for what Sean planned.

"This is not an opportunity to be missed, Kevin," Miller answered evenly.

"Do you have another motive?" O'Donnell asked. Better to get it in the open, he decided.

"Consider the ramifications. The Provisionals go over to proclaim their innocence and—"

"Yes, I know. It is a fine opportunity. Very well. When do you want to leave?"

"Wednesday morning. We must move quickly. Even with our contacts, it won't be easy."

13. Visitors

The two men hunched over the blow-up of the map, flanked by several eight-by-ten photographs.

"This is going to be the hard one," Alex said. "This one I can't help you with."

"What's the problem?" Sean could see it, but by asking the question he could also gauge the skill of his new associate. He'd never worked with a black before, and though he'd met Alex and members of his group the year before, both were unknown quantities, at least in an operational sense.

"He always comes out by Gate Three, here. This street, as you see, is a dead end. He has to go straight west or turn north coming out. He has done both. This street here is wide enough to do the job from a car, but this one—too narrow, and it leads the wrong way. That means the only sure spot is right here, at the corner. Traffic lights here and here." Alex pointed. "Both these streets are narrow and always have cars parked on both sides. This building is apartments. These are houses—expensive ones. There isn't much pedestrian traffic here, oddly enough. One man can probably get by. Two or more, uh-uh." He shook his head. "And it's a white area. A black man would be conspicuous. Your guy has to wing this one alone, pal, and he's gotta be on foot. Probably inside this door is the best place, but he'll have to be on his toes or the target will get away."

"How does he get out?" Sean asked.

"I can park a car around this corner, or this one. Timing for that is not a concern. We can wait all day for the right slot. We have a choice of escape routes. That's no problem either. At rush hour the streets are crowded. That actually works for us. The cops will have trouble responding, and we can use a car that looks ordinary, like a state-owned one. They can't stop all of them. Getaway is easy. The problem is your man. He has to be right here."

"Why not catch him in his car at a different place?"

Alex shook his head. "Too hard. The roads are too crowded to be sure, and it'd be too easy to lose him. You've seen the traffic, Sean, and he never goes exactly the same way twice. If you want my opinion, you should split the operation, do it one part at a time."

"No." Miller was adamant. "We'll do it the way I want."

"Okay, man, but I'm telling you, this man is exposed."

Miller thought that one over for a moment. Finally he smiled. "I have just the right man for it.

"The other part?"

Alex switched maps. "Easy. The target can take any route at all, but they all come to this place here at exactly four forty-five. We've checked six days in the past two weeks, never been off by more than five minutes. We'll do the job right along here, close to the bridge. Anybody could handle this one. We can even rehearse it for you."

"When?"

"This afternoon good enough?" Alex smiled.

"Indeed. Escape route?"

"We'll show you. We might as well make it a real rehearsal."

"Excellent." Miller was well pleased. Getting here had been complicated enough. Not difficult, just complicated, involving six separate flights. It hadn't been without humor, though. Sean Miller was traveling on a British passport at the moment, and the immigration clerk at Miami had taken his Belfast accent for Scottish. It hadn't occurred to him that to an American ear there isn't much difference between a brogue and a burr. *If that's the skill level in American law-enforcement officials,* Miller told himself, *this op should go easily enough.*

They'd do the run-through today. If it looked good he'd summon the team, and they'd go in . . . four days, he judged. The weapons were already in place.

* * *

"Conclusions?" Cantor asked.

Ryan picked up a sixty-page sheaf of paper. "Here's my analysis, for what it's worth—not much," Jack admitted. "I didn't turn up anything new. The reports you already have are pretty good, given the lack of real evidence to go on. The ULA is a really kinky bunch. On one hand their operations don't seem to have a real purpose that we can discern—but this kind of skill. . . . They're too professional to be operating without an objective, dammit!"

"True enough," Cantor said. They were in his office, across the hall from the DDI's. Admiral Greer was out of town. "You come up with anything at all?"

"I've mapped their operations geographically and against time. No pattern there that I can see. The only visible pattern is in the type of operation, and the execution, but that doesn't mean anything. They like high-profile targets, but—hell, what terrorist doesn't? That's the whole point of being a terrorist, going after the really big game, right? They mostly use East Bloc weapons, but most of the groups do. We infer that they're well financed. That's logical, given the nature of their activity, but again there isn't any substantive evidence to confirm it.

"O'Donnell has a real talent for dropping out of sight, both personally and professionally. There are three whole years we can't account for, one before he turned up around the time of Bloody Sunday and two years after the Provos tried to punch his ticket. They're both complete blanks. I talked to my wife about the plastic surgery angle—"

"What?" Cantor didn't react favorably to that.

"She doesn't know why I wanted the information. Give me a break, Marty. I'm married to a surgeon, remember? One of her classmates is a reconstructive surgeon, and I had Cathy ask her where you can get a new face. Not many places that can really do it—I was surprised. I have a list of where they are in here. Two are behind the Curtain. It turns out that some of the real pioneering work was done in Moscow before World War Two. Hopkins people have been to the institute—it's named for the guy, but I can't recall the name—and they found a few odd things about the place."

"Like what?" Cantor asked.

"Like two floors that you can't get onto. Annette DiSalvi—Cathy's classmate—was there two years ago. The top two floors of the place can be reached only by special elevators, and the stairways have barred gates. Odd sort of thing for a hospital. I thought that was a funny bit of information. Maybe it'll be useful to somebody else."

Cantor nodded. He knew something about this particular clinic, but the closed floors were something new. It was amazing, he thought, how new bits of data could turn up so innocently. He also wondered why a surgical team from Johns Hopkins had been allowed into the place. He made a mental note to check that out.

"Cathy says this 'getting a new face' thing isn't what it's cracked up to be. Most of the work is designed to correct damage from trauma—car accidents and things like that. The job isn't so much to change as to repair. There is a lot of cosmetic work—I mean aside from nose jobs and face-lifts—but that you can accomplish almost as well with a new hair style and a beard. They can change chins and cheekbones pretty well, but if the work is too extensive it leaves scars. This place in Moscow is good, Annette says, almost as good as Hopkins or even UCLA. A lot of the best reconstructive surgeons are in California," Jack explained. "Anyway, we're not talking a face-lift or a nose job here. Extensive facial surgery involves multiple procedures and takes several months. If O'Donnell was gone for two years, a lot of the time was spent in the body shop."

"Oh." Cantor got the point. "He really is a fast worker, then?"

Jack grinned. "That's what I was really after. He was out of sight for two years. At least six months of that time must have been spent in some hospital or other. So in the other eighteen months, he recruited his people, set up a base of operations, started collecting operational intelligence, and ran his first op."

"Not bad," Cantor said thoughtfully.

"Yeah. So he had to have recruited people from in the Provos. They must have brought some stuff with them, too. I'll bet that his initial operations were things the PIRA had already looked at and set aside for one reason or another. That's why the Brits thought they were actually part of the PIRA to begin with, Marty."

"You said you didn't find anything important," Cantor said. "This sounds like pretty sharp analysis to me."

"Maybe. All I did was reorder stuff you already had. Nothing new is in here, and I still haven't answered my own question. I don't have much of an idea what they're really up to." Ryan's hand flipped through the pages of manuscript. His voice showed his frustration. Jack was not accustomed to failure. "We still don't know where these bastards are coming from. They're up to something, but damned if I know what it is."

"American connections?"

"None—none at all that we know of. That makes me feel a lot better. There's no hint of a contact with American organizations, and lots of reasons for them not to have any. O'Donnell is too slick to play with his old PIRA contacts."

"But his recruiting—" Cantor objected. Jack cut him off.

"Over here, I mean. As chief of internal security, he could know who was who in Belfast and Londonderry. But the American connections to the Provisionals all run through Sinn Fein, the Provos' political wing. He'd have to be crazy to trust them. Remember, he did his best to restructure the political leanings in the outfit and failed."

"Okay. I see what you mean. Possible connections with other groups?"

Ryan shook his head. "No evidence. I wouldn't bet against contact with some of the European groups, maybe some of the Islamic ones even, but not over here. O'Donnell's a smart cookie. To come over here means too many complications—hey, they don't like me, I can dig that. The good news is that the FBI's right. We're dealing with professionals. I am not a politically significant target. Coming after me has no political value, and these are political animals," Jack observed confidently. "Thank God."

"Did you know that the PIRA—well, Sinn Fein—has a delegation coming over day after tomorrow?"

"What for?"

"The thing in London hurt them in Boston and New York. They've denied involvement about a hundred times, and they have a bunch coming over for a couple of weeks to tell the local Irish communities in person."

"Aw, crap!" Ryan snarled. "Why not keep the bastards out of the friggin' country?"

"Not that easy. The people coming over aren't on the Watch List. They've been here before. They're clean, technically. We live in a free democracy, Jack. Remember what Oliver Wendell Holmes said: the Constitution was written for people of fundamentally differing views—or something like that. The short name is Freedom of Speech.''

Ryan had to smile. The outside view of the Central Intelligence Agency people was often one of bumbling fascists, threats to American freedom, corrupt but incompetent schemers, a cross between the Mafia and the Marx brothers. In fact, Ryan had found them to be politically moderate—more so than he was. If the truth ever got out, of course, the press would think it was a sinister ruse. Even he found it very odd.

''I hope somebody will keep an eye on them,'' Jack observed.

''The FBI will have people in every bar, swilling their John Jameson and singing 'The Men Behind the Wire.' And keeping an eye on everything. The Bureau's pretty good at that. They've just about ended the gun-running. The word's gotten out on that—must be a half-dozen people who got sent up the river for sending guns and explosives over.''

''Fine. So now the bad guys use Kalashnikovs, or Armalites made in Singapore.''

''That,'' Cantor said, ''is not our responsibility.''

''Well, this here's all that I was able to come up with, Marty. Unless there's other data around, that's all I can give you.'' Jack tossed the report in Cantor's lap.

''I'll read this over and get back to you. Back to teaching history?''

''Yep.'' Ryan stood and got his coat from the back of the chair. He paused. ''What if something about these guys turns up in a different place?''

''This is the only compartment you can see, Jack—''

''I know that. What I'm asking is, the way this place is set up, how do you connect things from different compartments?''

''That's why we have supervisory oversight teams, and computers,'' Cantor answered. *Not that the system always works. . . .*

''If anything new turns up—''

''It's flagged,'' Cantor said. ''Both here and at the FBI. If we get any sort of twitch on these fellows, you'll be warned the day we get it.''

''Fair enough.'' Ryan made sure his pass was hanging in plain view before going out into the corridor. ''Thanks—and please thank the Admiral for me. You guys didn't have to do this. I wouldn't feel this good if somebody else had told me what I saw for myself. I owe you.''

''You'll be hearing from us,'' Cantor promised him.

Ryan nodded and went out the door. He'd be hearing from them, all right. They'd make the offer again, and he'd turn it down again—with the greatest reluctance, of course. He'd gone out of his way to be humble and polite with Cantor. In truth, he thought his sixty-page report did a pretty good job of organizing what data they did have on the ULA. That squared matters. He didn't really think he owed anybody.

Caroline Muller Ryan, MD, FACS, lived a very controlled and structured life. She liked it that way. In surgery she always worked with the same team of doctors, nurses, and technicians. They knew how she liked to work, how she liked her instruments arranged. Most surgeons had their peculiarities, and the ophthalmic specialists were unusually fastidious. Her team tolerated it because she was one of the best technical surgeons of her age group and also one of the easiest to like. She rarely had problems with her temper, and got along well with her nurses—something that female doctors often had trouble with. Her current problem was her pregnancy, which forced her to limit her exposure to certain operating-room chemicals. Her swelling abdomen was beginning to alter her stance at the table—actually eye surgeons usually sit, but the principle was the same. Cathy Ryan had to reach a little farther now, and joked about it constantly.

These traits carried over to her personal life also. She drove her Porsche with mechanistic precision, always shifting the gears at exactly the right RPM setting, taking corners on a line as regular as a Formula One driver's. Doing things the same way every time wasn't a rut for Cathy Ryan; it was perfection. She played the piano that way also. Sissy Jackson, who played and taught professionally, had once remarked that her playing was too perfect, lacking in soul. Cathy took that as a compliment. Surgeons don't autograph their work; they do it the right way, every time.

Which was why she was annoyed with life at the moment. It was a minor annoyance having to take a slightly different route to work every day—in fact it was something of a challenge, since she gave herself the goal of not allowing it to affect her schedule. Driving to and from work never took more than fifty-seven minutes, nor less than forty-nine (unless she came in on a weekend, when different traffic rules applied). She always picked up Sally at exactly quarter to five. Taking new routes, mainly inside Baltimore, threatened to change this segment of her life, but there weren't many driving problems that a Porsche 911 couldn't solve.

Her route this day was down state Route 3, then across a secondary road. That brought her out onto Ritchie Highway, six miles above the Giant Steps Nursery School. She caught the light just right and took the turn in second gear, working quickly up to third, then fourth. The feline growl of the six-cylinder engine reached through the sound insulation as a gentle purr. Cathy Ryan loved her Porsche. She'd never driven anything else until after she was married—a station wagon was useful for shopping and family drives, unfortunately—and wondered what she'd do when her second child arrived. That, she sighed, would be a problem. It depended on where the sitter was, she decided. Or maybe she could finally convince Jack to get a nanny. Her husband was a little too working-class in that respect. He'd resisted the idea of hiring a part-time maid to help with the housework—that was all the more crazy since Cathy knew her husband tended to be something of a slob, slow to hang up his clothing. Getting the maid had changed that a little. Now, nights before the maid was due in, Jack scurried around picking things up so that she wouldn't think the Ryans were a family of slovens. Jack could be so funny. *Yes,* she thought, *we'll get a nanny. After all, Jack's a knight now.* Cathy smiled at the traffic. Pushing him in the right direction wouldn't be all that hard. Jack was very easy to manipulate. She changed lanes and darted past a dump truck in third gear. The Porsche made it so easy to accelerate around things.

She turned right into the Giant Steps parking lot two minutes later. The sports car bumped over the uneven driveway and she brought it to a stop in the usual spot. Cathy locked the car on getting out, of course. Her Porsche was six years old, but meticulously maintained. It had been her present to herself on getting through her intern year at Hopkins. There wasn't a single scratch on the British Racing Green finish, and only a Hopkins parking sticker marred the gleaming chrome bumper.

"Mommy!" Sally met her at the door.

Cathy bent to pick her up. It was getting harder to bend over, and harder still to stand up with Sally around her neck. She hoped that their daughter would not feel threatened by the arrival of the baby. Some kids were, she knew, but she had already explained to the little girl what was going on, and Sally seemed to like the idea of a new brother or sister.

"So what did my big girl do today?" Dr. Ryan asked. Sally liked being called a Big Girl, and this was Cathy's subterfuge for ensuring that sibling rivalry would be minimized by the arrival of a ''little'' boy or girl.

Sally wriggled free to drop back to the floor, and held up a finger painting done on what looked like wide-carriage computer paper. It was a credible abstract work of purple and orange. Together, mother and daughter went to the back and got her coat and lunch box. Cathy made sure that Sally's coat was zipped and the hood up—it was only a few degrees above freezing outside, and they didn't want Sally to get another cold. It took a total of five minutes from the time Cathy stopped the car until she was back out the door, walking toward it again.

She didn't really notice the routineness of her daily schedule. Cathy unlocked the door, got Sally into her seat, and made sure the seat belt was fastened snugly before closing and locking the door and going around to the left side of the car.

She looked up briefly. Across Ritchie Highway was a small shopping center, a 7-Eleven Store, a cleaners, a video store, and a hardware dealer. There was a blue van parked at the 7-Eleven again. She'd noticed it twice the previous week. Cathy shrugged it off. 7-Eleven was a convenience store, and lots of people made it a regular stop on the way home.

''Hello, Lady Ryan,'' Miller said inside the van. The two windows in the rear doors—they reminded Miller of the police transport van; he smiled to himself at that—were made of coated glass so that an outsider couldn't see in. Alex was in the store getting a six-pack of Cokes, as he'd done on a fairly regular basis the previous two weeks.

Miller checked his watch: She'd arrived at 4:46 and was leaving at 4:52. Next to him, a man with a camera was shooting away. Miller raised binoculars. The green Porsche would be easy to spot, plus it had a customized license plate, CR-SRGN. Alex had explained how license plates in Maryland could be bought to individual specifications, and Sean wondered who'd be using that code next year. Surely there was another surgeon with the initials CR.

Alex got back in and started the engine. The van left the parking lot just as the target's Porsche did. Alex did his own driving. He went north on Ritchie Highway, hung a quick U-turn, and raced south to keep the Porsche in sight. Miller joined him in the right-side seat.

''She takes this road south to Route 50, across the Severn River bridge, then gets off 50 onto Route 2. We want to hit her before she does that. We'll proceed, take the same exit, and switch cars where I showed you. Too bad,'' Alex said. ''I was beginning to like this here van.''

''You can buy another with what we're paying you.''

A grin split the black face. ''Yeah, I 'spect so. Have a better interior on the next one, too.'' He turned right, taking the exit onto Route 50. It was a divided, multilane highway. Traffic was moderate to heavy. Alex explained that this was normal.

''No problem getting the job done,'' he assured Miller.

''Excellent,'' Miller agreed. ''Good work, Alex.'' *Even if you do have a big mouth.*

Cathy always drove more sedately with Sally aboard. The little girl craned her neck to see over the dashboard, her left hand fiddling with the seat belt buckle as it usually did. Her mother was relaxing now. It generally took her about this length of time to settle down from a hard day—there were few easy ones—at the Wilmer Eye Institute. It wasn't stress so much. She'd had two procedures today and would have two more the next day. She loved her work. There were a lot of people now who could see only because of her professional skill, and the satisfaction of that was not something easily communicated, even to Jack. The price of it was that her days were rarely easy ones. The minute precision demanded by ophthalmic surgery denied her coffee—she couldn't risk the slight tremor in her hands that might come from caffeine—and imposed a degree of concentration on her that few professions demanded. There were more difficult medical skills, but not many. This was the main reason she drove her 911. It was as though in pushing through the air, or taking a tight corner at twenty-five in second gear, the car drained the excess energy from the driver and spread it into the environment. She almost always got home in a good mood. Tonight would be better still since it was Jack's turn to fix dinner. If the car had been built with a brain, it would have noticed the reduced pressure on accelerator and brakes as they took the Route 2 exit. It was being pampered now, like a faithful horse that had jumped all the fences properly.

"Okay?" Alex asked, keeping west on Route 50 toward Washington.

The other man in the back handed Miller the clipboard with the new time notation. There was a total of seven entries, all but the last complete with photographs. Sean looked at the numbers. The target was on a beautifully regular schedule.

"Fine," he said after a moment.

"I can't give you a precise spot for the hit—traffic can make things go a little funny. I'd say we should try on the east side of the bridge."

"Agreed."

Cathy Ryan walked into her house fifteen minutes later. She unzipped Sally's coat and watched her little—"big"—girl struggle out of the sleeves, a skill she was just beginning to acquire. Cathy took it and hung it up before getting out of her coat. Mother and daughter then proceeded to the kitchen, where they heard the unmistakable noise of a husband trying to fix dinner and a television tuned to the *MacNeil-Lehrer Report*.

"Daddy, look what I did!" Sally said first.

"Oh, great!" Jack took the picture and examined it with great care. "I think we'll hang this one up." All of them got hung up. The art gallery in question was the front of the family refrigerator. A magnetized holder gave the finger painting a semipermanent place over the ice and cold-water dispenser. Sally never noticed that there was a new hanging spot every day. Nor did she know that every such painting was saved, tucked away in a box in the foyer closet.

"Hi, babe." Jack kissed his wife next. "How were things today?"

"Two cornea replacements. Bernie assisted on the second one—it was a bear. Tomorrow, I'm scheduled for a vitrectomy. Bernie says hi, by the way."

"How's his kid?" Jack asked.

"Just an appendectomy, she'll be climbing the monkey bars next week," Cathy replied, surveying the kitchen. She often wondered if having Jack fix dinner was worth the wreckage he made of her room. It appeared that he was fixing pot roast, but she wasn't sure. It wasn't that Jack was a bad cook—with some things he was pretty good—he was just so damned sloppy about it. Never kept his utensils neat. Cathy always had her knives, forks, and everything else arranged like a surgical instrument tray. Jack would just set them anywhere and spent half of his time looking for where they were.

Sally left the room and found a TV that didn't have a news show on.

"Good news," Jack said.

"Oh?"

"I finished up at CIA today."

"So what are you smiling about?"

"There just isn't anything I see to make me suspect that we have anything to worry about." Jack explained for several minutes, keeping within the bounds of classification—mostly. "They've never operated over here. They don't have any contacts over here that we know of. The real thing is that we're not good targets for them."

"Why?"

"We're not political. The people they go after are soldiers, police, judges, mayors, stuff like that—"

"Not to mention the odd prince," Cathy observed.

"Yeah, well, we're not one of those either, are we?"

"So what are you telling me?"

"They're a scary bunch. That Miller kid—well, we've talked about that. I'll feel a little better when they have him back in the can. But these guys are pros. They're not going to mount an op three thousand miles from home for revenge."

Cathy took his hand. "You're sure?"

"Sure as I can be. The intelligence biz isn't like mathematics, but you get a feel for the other guy, the way his head works. A terrorist kills to make a political point. We ain't political fodder."

Cathy gave her husband a gentle smile. "So I can relax now?"

"I think so. Still, keep an eye on the mirror."

"And you're not going to carry that gun anymore," she said hopefully.

"Babe, I like shooting. I forgot what fun a pistol can be. I'm going to keep shooting at the Academy, but, no, I won't be wearing it anymore."

"And the shotgun?"

"It hasn't hurt anybody."

"I don't *like* it, Jack. At least unload it, okay?" She walked off to the bedroom to change.

"Okay." It wasn't that important. He'd keep the box of shells right next to the gun, on the top shelf of the closet. Sally couldn't reach it. Even Cathy had to stretch. It would be safe there. Jack reconsidered all his actions over the past three and a half weeks and decided that they had been worthwhile, really. The alarm system on the house wasn't such a bad idea, and he liked his new 9mm Browning. He was getting pretty good scores. If he kept at it for a year, maybe he could give Breckenridge a run for his money.

He checked the oven. Another ten minutes. Next he turned up the TV. The current segment on the *MacNeil-Lehrer News Hour* was—*I'll be damned.*

"Joining us from our affiliate WGBH in Boston is Padraig—did I pronounce that right?—O'Neil, a spokesman for Sinn Fein and an elected member of the British Parliament. Mr. O'Neil, why are you visiting America at this time?"

"I and many of my colleagues have visited America many times, to inform the American people of the oppression inflicted upon the Irish people by the British government, the systematic denial of economic opportunity and basic civil rights, the total abrogation of the judicial process, and the continuing brutality of the British army of occupation against the people of Ireland," O'Neil said in a smooth and reasonable voice. He had done all this before.

"Mr. O'Neil," said someone from the British Embassy in Washington, "is the political front-man for the Provisional Wing of the so-called Irish Republican Army. This is a terrorist organization that is illegal both in Northern Ireland and in the Irish Republic. His mission in the United States is, as always, to raise money so that his organization can buy arms and explosives. This source of income for the IRA was damaged by the cowardly attack against the Royal Family in London last year, and his reason for being here is to persuade Irish-Americans that the IRA had no part in that.''

"Mr. O'Neil,'' MacNeil said, "how do you respond to that?''

The Irishman smiled at the camera as benignly as Bob Keeshan's Captain Kangaroo. "Mr. Bennett, as usual, skirts over the legitimate political issues here. Are Northern Ireland's Catholics denied economic and political opportunity—yes, they are. Have the legal processes in Northern Ireland been subverted for political reasons by the British government—yes, they have. Are we any closer to a political settlement of this dispute that goes back, in its modern phase, to 1969—no, I regret to say we are not. If I am a terrorist, why have I been allowed into your country? I am, in fact, a member of the British Parliament, elected by the people of my parliamentary district.''

"But you don't take your seat in Parliament,'' MacNeil objected.

"And join the government that is killing my constituents?''

"Jesus,'' Ryan said, "what a mess.'' He turned the TV off.

"Such a reasonable man,'' Miller said. Alex's house was outside the D.C. beltway. "Tell your friends how reasonable you are, Paddy. And when you get to the pubs tonight, be sure to tell your friends that you have never hurt anyone who was not a genuine oppressor of the Irish people.'' Sean watched the whole segment, then placed an overseas call to a pay phone outside a Dublin pub.

The next morning—only five hours later in Ireland—four men boarded a plane for Paris. Neatly dressed, they looked like young executives traveling with their soft luggage to business appointments overseas. At Charles de Gaulle International Airport they made connections to a flight to Caracas. From there they flew Eastern Air Lines to Atlanta, and another Eastern flight to National Airport, just down the Potomac from the memorial to Thomas Jefferson. The four were jet-lagged out and sick of airliner seats when they arrived. They took an airport limousine to a local hotel to sleep off their travel shock. The young businessmen checked out the next morning and were met by a car.

14. Second Chances

There ought to be a law against Mondays, Ryan thought. He stared at what had to be the worst way to start any day: a broken shoelace that dangled from his left fist. Where were the spares? he asked himself. He couldn't ask Cathy; she and Sally had left the house ten minutes before on the way to Giant Steps and Hopkins. Damn. He started rummaging through his dresser drawers. Nothing. The kitchen. He walked downstairs and across the house to the kitchen drawer that held everything that wasn't someplace else. Hidden beneath the notepads and magnets and scissors he found a spare pair—no, one white lace for a sneaker. He was getting warmer. Several minutes of digging later, he found something close enough. He took one and left the other. After all, shoelaces broke one at a time.

Next Jack had to select a tie for the day. That was never easy, though at least he didn't have his wife around to tell him he'd picked the wrong one. He was wearing a gray suit, and picked a dark blue tie with red stripes. Ryan was still wearing white, button-down shirts made mostly of cotton. Old habits die hard. The suit jacket slid on neatly. It was one of the suits Cathy had bought in England. It was painful to admit that her taste in clothing was far better than his. That London tailor wasn't too bad, either. He smiled at himself in the mirror—*you handsome devil!*—before heading downstairs. His briefcase was waiting on the foyer table, full of the draft quizzes he'd be giving today. Ryan took his overcoat from the closet, checked to see his keys were in the right pocket, got the briefcase, and went out the door.

"Oops!" He unlocked the door and set the burglar alarm before going back outside.

Sergeant Major Breckenridge walked down the double line of Marines, and his long-practiced eyes didn't miss a thing. One private had lint on his blue, high-necked blouse. Another's shoes needed a little more work, and two needed haircuts; you could barely see their scalps under the quarter-inch hair. All in all, there wasn't much to be displeased with. Every one would have passed a normal inspection, but this wasn't a normal post, and normal rules didn't apply. Breckenridge was not a screamer. He'd gotten past that. His remonstrations were more fatherly now. They carried the force of a command from God nevertheless. He finished the inspection and dismissed the guard detail. Several marched off to their gate posts. Others rode in pickups to the more remote posts to relieve the current watch standers at eight o'clock exactly. Each Marine wore his dress blues and a white pistol belt. Their pistols were kept at the posts. They were unloaded, in keeping with the peaceful nature of their duty, but full clips of .45 ACP cartridges were always nearby, in keeping with the nature of the Marines.

Did I really look forward to this? It took all of Ryan's energy just to think that question of himself. But he didn't have any further excuses. In London his injuries had prevented him from doing it. The same had been true of the first few weeks at home. Then he'd spent the early mornings traveling to CIA. That had been his last excuse. None were left.

Rickover Hall, he told himself. *I'll stop when I get to Rickover Hall.* He had to stop soon. Breathing the cold air off the river was like inhaling knives. His nose and mouth were like sandpaper and his heart threatened to burst from his chest. Jack hadn't jogged in months, and he was paying the price for his sloth.

Rickover Hall seemed a thousand miles away, though he knew it was only a few hundred more yards. As recently as the previous October, he'd been able to make three circuits of the grounds and come away with nothing more than a good sweat. Now he was only at the halfway mark of his first lap, and death seemed amazingly attractive. His legs were already rubbery with fatigue. His stride was off; Ryan was weaving slightly, a sure sign of a runner who was beyond his limit.

Another hundred yards. About fifteen seconds more, he told himself. All the time he'd spent on his back, all the time sitting down, all the cigarettes he'd sneaked at CIA were punishing him now. The runs he'd had to do at Quantico had been nothing like this. *You were a lot younger then,* Ryan's mind pointed out gleefully.

He turned his head left and saw that he was lined up on the building's east wall. Ryan leaned back and slowed to a walk, hands supported on his hips as his chest heaved to catch up on the oxygen it needed.

"You okay, Doc?" A mid stopped—his legs still pumping in double-time—to look Jack over. Ryan tried to hate him for his youth and energy, but couldn't summon enough energy.

"Yeah, just out of training," Jack gasped out over three breaths.

"You gotta work back into it slowly, sir," the twenty-year-old pointed out, and sped off, leaving his history teacher scornfully in his dust. Jack started laughing at himself, but it gave him a coughing fit. The next one to pass him was a girl. Her grin really made things worse.

Don't sit down. Whatever you do, don't sit down.

He turned and moved away from the seawall. Just walking on his wobbly legs was an effort. He took the towel from around his neck to wipe the sweat from his face before he got too much of a chill. Jack held the towel taut between his hands and stretched his arms high. He'd caught his breath by now. A renewed supply of oxygen returned to his limbs, and most of the pain left. The rubberiness would go next, he knew. In another ten minutes he'd feel pretty good. Tomorrow he'd make it a little farther—to the Nimitz Library, he promised himself. By May he wouldn't have the mids—at least not the girls—racing past him. Well, not all of the girls, anyway. He was spotting a minimum of ten years to the midshipmen, something that would only get worse. Jack had already passed thirty. Next stop: forty.

Cathy Ryan was in her greens, scrubbing at the special basin outside the surgical suite. The elastic waistband of the pants was high, above the curve of her abdomen, and that made the pants overly short, like the clamdiggers that had been fashionable in her teenage years. A green cap was over her hair, and she wondered yet again why she bothered to brush it out every morning. By the time the procedure was finished, her hair would look like the snaky locks of the Medusa.

"Game time," she said quietly to herself. She hit the door-opening switch with her elbow, keeping her hands high, just like it was done in the movies. Bernice, the circulating nurse, had her gloves ready, and Cathy reached her hands into the rubber until the tops of the gloves came far up on her forearms. Because of this, she was rarely able to wear her engagement ring, though her simple wedding band posed no problem. "Thanks."

"How's the baby?" Bernice asked. She had three of her own.

"At the moment he's learning to jog." Cathy smiled behind her mask. "Or maybe he's lifting weights."

"Nice necklace."

"Christmas present from Jack."

Dr. Terri Mitchell, the anesthesiologist, hooked the patient up to her various monitors and went to work as the surgeons looked on. Cathy gave the instruments a quick look, knowing that Lisa-Marie always got things right. She was one of the best scrub nurses in the hospital and was picky on the doctors she'd work with.

"All ready, Doctor?" Cathy asked the resident. "Okay, people, let's see if we can save this lady's eyesight." She looked at the clock. "Starting at eight forty-one."

* * *

Miller assembled the submachine gun slowly. He had plenty of time. The weapon had been carefully cleaned and oiled after being test fired the night before at a quarry twenty miles north of Washington. This one would be his personal weapon. Already he liked it. The balance was perfect, the folding stock, when extended, had a good, solid feel to it. The sights were easy to use, and the gun was fairly steady on full-automatic fire. All in all, a nice combination of traits for such a small, deadly weapon. He palmed back the bolt and squeezed the trigger to get a better feel for where it broke. He figured it at about twelve pounds—perfect, not too light and not too heavy. Miller left the bolt closed on an empty chamber and loaded the magazine of thirty 9mm rounds. Then he folded the stock and tried the hanging hook inside his topcoat. A standard modification to the Uzi, it allowed a person to carry it concealed. That probably wouldn't be necessary, but Miller was a man who planned for all the contingencies. He'd learned that lesson the hard way.

"Ned?"

"Yes, Sean?" Eamon Clark, known as Ned, hadn't stopped going over the maps and photographs of his place since arriving in America. One of the most experienced assassins in Ireland, he was one of the men the ULA had broken from Long Kesh Prison the previous year. A handsome young man, Clark had spent the previous day touring the Naval Academy grounds, carrying his own camera as he'd photographed the statue of Tecumseh . . . and carefully examined Gate Three. Ryan would drive straight uphill, giving him roughly fifteen seconds to get ready. It would demand vigilance, but Ned had the necessary patience. Besides, they knew the target's schedule. His last class ended at three that afternoon and he hit the gate at a predictable time. Alex was even now parking the getaway car on King George Street. Clark had misgivings, but kept them to himself. Sean Miller had masterminded the prison break that had made him a free man. This was his first real operation with the ULA. Clark decided that he owed them loyalty. Besides, his look at the Academy's security had not impressed him. Ned Clark knew that he was not the brightest man in the room, but they needed a man able to work on his own, and he did know how to do that. He'd proven this seven times.

Outside the house were three cars, the van and two station wagons. The van would be used for the second part of the operation, while the station wagons would take everyone to the airport when the operation was finished.

Miller sat down in an overstuffed chair and ran over the entire operation in his mind. As always, he closed his eyes and visualized every event, then he inserted variables. What if the traffic were unusually heavy or unusually light? What if . . .

One of Alex's men came through the front door. He tossed Miller a Polaroid.

"Right on time?" Sean Miller asked.

"You got it, man."

The photograph showed Cathy Ryan leading her daughter by the hand into—what was the name of the place? Oh, yes, Giant Steps. Miller smiled at that. Today would be a giant step indeed. Miller leaned back again, eyes closed, to make sure.

"But there wasn't a threat," a mid objected.

"That's correct. Which is to say we know that *now*. But how did it look to Spruance? He knew what the Japanese fleet had in surface ships. What if they *had* come east, what if the recall order had never been issued?" Jack pointed to the diagram he'd drawn on the blackboard. "There would have been contact at about oh-three-hundred hours. Who do you think would have won that one, mister?"

"But he blew his chance for a good air strike the next day," the midshipman persisted.

"With what? Let's look at the losses in the air groups. With all the torpedo craft lost, just what losses do you think he could have inflicted?" Jack asked.

"But—"

"You remember the Kenny Rogers song: You have to know when to walk away, and know when to run. Buck fever is a bad thing in a hunter. In an admiral commanding a fleet it can be disastrous. Spruance looked at his information, looked at his capabilities, and decided to call it a day. A secondary consideration was—what?"

"To cover Midway?" another mid asked.

"Right. What if they had carried on with the invasion? That was gamed out at Newport once and the invasion was successful. Please note that this is a manifestation of logic overpowering reality, but it was a possibility that Spruance could not afford to dismiss. His primary mission was to inflict damage on a superior Japanese fleet. His secondary mission was to prevent the occupation of Midway. The balance he struck here is a masterpiece of operational expertise. . . ." Ryan paused for a moment. What was it that he'd just said? *Logic overcoming reality*. Hadn't he just come to the logical conclusion that the ULA wouldn't—no, no, a different situation entirely. He shook off the thought and kept going on the lessons from the Battle of Midway. He had the class going now, and ideas were crackling across the room like lightning.

"Perfect," Cathy said as she pulled her mask down around her neck. She stood up from the stool and stretched her arms over her head. "Nice one, folks."

The patient was wheeled out to the recovery room while Lisa-Marie made a final check of her instruments. Cathy Ryan pulled off her mask and rubbed her nose. Then her hands went down to her belly. The little guy really was kicking up a storm.

"Football player?" Bernice asked.

"Feels like a whole backfield. Sally wasn't this active. I think this one's a boy," Cathy judged, knowing that there was no such correlation. It was good enough that the baby was very active. That was always a positive sign. She smiled, mostly to herself, at the miracle and the magic of motherhood. Right there inside her was a brand-new human being waiting to be born, and by the feel of it, rather impatient. "Well. I have a family to talk to."

She walked out of the operating room, not bothering to change out of her greens. It always looked more dramatic to keep them on. The waiting room was a mere fifty feet away. The Jeffers family—the father and one of their daughters—was waiting on the inevitable couch, staring at the inevitable magazines but not reading them. The moment she came through the swinging door, both leaped to their feet. She gave them her best smile, always the quickest way to convey the message.

"Okay?" the husband asked, his anxiety a physical thing.

"Everything went perfectly," Cathy said. "No problems at all. She'll be fine."

"When will she be able—"

"A week. We have to be patient on this. You'll be able to see her in about an hour and a half. Now, why don't you get yourselves something to eat. There's no sense having a healthy patient if the family is worn out, I—"

"Doctor Ryan," the public address speaker said. "Doctor Caroline Ryan."

"Wait a minute." Cathy walked to the nurses' station and lifted the phone. "This is Doctor Ryan."

"Cathy, this is Gene in the ER. I've got a major eye trauma. Ten-year-old black male, he took his bike through a store window," the voice said urgently. "His left eye is badly lacerated."

"Send him up to six." Cathy hung up and went back to the Jeffers family. "I have to run, there's an emergency case coming up. Your wife will be fine. I'll be seeing you tomorrow." Cathy walked as quickly as she could to the OR.

"Heads up, we have an emergency coming in from ER. Major eye trauma to a ten-year-old." Lisa-Marie was already moving. Cathy walked to the wall phone and punched the number for surgeons' lounge. "This is Ryan in Wilmer six. Where's Bernie?"

"I'll get him." A moment later: "Doctor Katz."

"Bernie, I have a major eye trauma coming into six. Gene Wood in ER says it's a baddie."

"On the way." Cathy Ryan turned.

"Terri?"

"All ready," the anesthesiologist assured her.

"Give me another two minutes," Lisa-Marie said.

Cathy went into the scrub room to rewash her hands. Bernie Katz arrived before she started. He was a thoroughly disreputable-looking man, only an inch taller than Cathy Ryan, with longish hair and a Bismarck mustache. He was also one of the best surgeons at Hopkins.

"You'd better lead on this one," she said. "I haven't done a major trauma in quite a while."

"No problem. How's the baby coming?"

"Great." A new sound arrived, the high-pitched shrieks of a child in agony. The doctors moved into the OR. They watched dispassionately as two orderlies were strapping the child down. *Why weren't you in school?* Cathy asked him silently. The left side of the boy's face was a mess. The reconstructive teams would have to work on that later. Eyes came first. The child had already tried to be brave, but the pain was too great for that. Terri did the first medication, with both orderlies holding the child's arm in place. Cathy and Bernie hovered over the kid's face a moment later.

"Bad," Dr. Katz observed. He looked to the circulating nurse. "I have a procedure scheduled for one o'clock. Have to bump it. This one's going to take some time."

"All ready on this side," the scrub nurse said.

"Two more minutes," the anesthesiologist advised. You had to be careful medicating kids.

"Gloves," Cathy said. Bernie came over with them a moment later. "What happened?"

"He was riding his bike down the sidewalk on Monument Street," the orderly said. "He hit something and went through an appliance-store window."

"Why wasn't he in school?" she asked, looking back at the kid's left eye. She saw hours of work and an uncertain outcome.

"President's Day, Doc," the orderly replied.

"Oh. That's right." She looked at Bernie Katz. His grimace was visible around the mask.

"I don't know, Cathy." He was examining the eye through the magnifying-glass headset. "Must have been a cheap window—lots of slivers. I count five penetrations. Jeez, look at how that one's extended into the cornea. Let's go."

The Chevy pulled into one of Hopkins' high-rise parking garages. From the top level the driver had a perfect view of the door leading from the hospital to the doctors' parking area. The garage was guarded, of course, but there was plenty of traffic in and out, and it was not unusual for someone to wait in a car while another visited a family member inside. He settled back and lit a cigarette, listening to music on the car radio.

Ryan put roast beef on his hard roll and selected iced tea. The Officer and Faculty Club had an unusual arrangement for charging: he set his tray on a scale and the cashier billed him by weight. Jack paid up his two dollars and ten cents. The price for lunch was hardly exorbitant, but it did seem an odd way to set the price. He joined Robby Jackson in a corner booth.

"Mondays!" he observed to his friend.

"Are you kidding? I can relax today. I was up flying Saturday and Sunday."

"I thought you liked that."

"I do," Robby assured him. "But both days I got off before seven. I actually got to sleep until six this morning. I needed the extra two hours. How's the family?"

"Fine. Cathy had a big procedure today—had to be up there early. The one bad thing about being married to a surgeon, they always start early. Sometimes it's a little hard on Sally."

"Yeah, early to bed, early to rise—might as well be dead," Robby agreed. "How's the baby coming?"

"Super." Jack smiled. "He's an active little bugger. I never figured how women can take that—having the kid kick, turn and like that, I mean."

"Mind if I join you?" Skip Tyler slipped into the booth.

"How are the twins?" Jack asked at once.

The reply was a low moan, and a look at the circles under Tyler's eyes provided the answer. "The trick is getting both of them asleep. You just get one quieted down, then the other one goes off like a damned fire alarm. I don't know how Jean does it. Of course"—Tyler grinned—"she can walk the floor with them. When I do it it's step-*thump,* step-*thump.*"

All three men laughed. Skip Tyler had never been the least sensitive about losing his leg.

"How's Jean holding up?" Robby asked.

"No problem—she sleeps when they do and I get to do all the housework."

"Serves you right, turkey," Jack observed. "Why don't you give it a rest?"

"Can I help it if I'm hot-blooded?" Skip demanded.

"No, but your timing sucks," Robby replied.

"My timing," Tyler said with raised eyebrows, "is perfect."

"I guess that's one way to look at it," Jack agreed.

"I heard you were out jogging this morning." Tyler changed subjects.

"So did I." Robby laughed.

"I'm still alive, guys."

"One of my mids said tomorrow they're going to follow you around with an ambulance just in case.'' Skip chuckled. ''I suppose it's nice for you to remember that most of the kids know CPR.''

''Why are Mondays always like this?'' Jack asked.

Alex and Sean Miller made a final run along Route 50. They were careful to keep just under the speed limit. The State Police radar cars were out in force today for some reason or other. Alex assured his colleague that this would end around 4:30. Rush hour had too many cars on the road for efficient law enforcement. Two other men were in the back of the van, each with his weapon.

''Right about here, I think,'' Miller said.

''Yeah, it's the best place,'' Alex agreed.

''Escape route.'' Sean clicked on a stopwatch.

''Okay.'' Alex changed lanes and kept heading west. ''Remember, it's gonna be slower tonight.''

Miller nodded, getting the usual pre-op butterflies in his stomach. He ran through his plan, thinking over each contingency as he sat in the right-front seat of the van, watching the way traffic piled up at certain exits off the highway. The road was far better than the roads he was accustomed to in Ireland, but people drove on the wrong side here, he thought, though with pretty good traffic manners compared to Europe. Especially France and Italy . . . he shook off the thought and concentrated on the situation at hand.

Once the attack was completed, they would reach the getaway vehicles in under ten minutes. The way it was timed, Ned Clark would be waiting for them. Miller completed his mental run-through, satisfied that his plan, though a hasty one, was effective.

''You're early,'' Breckenridge said.

''Yeah, well, I have a couple of mids coming in this afternoon to go over their term papers. Any problem?'' Jack took the Browning from his briefcase.

The Sergeant Major grabbed a box of 9mm rounds. ''Nope. Mondays are supposed to be screwed up.''

Ryan walked to lane three and pulled the gun from the holster. First he ejected the empty clip and pulled the slide back. Next he checked the barrel for obstructions. He knew the weapon was fine mechanically, of course, but Breckenridge had range-safety rules that were inviolable. Even the Superintendent of the Academy had to follow them.

''Okay, Gunny.''

''I think today we'll try rapid fire.'' The Sergeant Major clipped the appropriate target on the rack, and the motorized pulley took it fifty feet downrange. Ryan loaded five rounds into the clip.

''Get your ears on, Lieutenant.'' Breckenridge tossed the muff-type protectors. Ryan put them on. He slid the clip into the pistol and thumbed down the slide release. The weapon was now ''in battery,'' ready to fire. Ryan pointed it downrange and waited. A moment later the light over the target snapped on. Jack brought the gun up and set the black circle right on the top of his front sight blade before he squeezed. Rapid-fire rules gave him one second per shot. This was more time than it sounded like. He got the first round off a little late, but most people did. The gun ejected the spent case and Ryan pulled it down for the next shot, concentrating on the target and his sights. By the time he counted to five, the gun was locked open. Jack pulled off the ear protectors.

"You're getting there, Lieutenant," Breckenridge said at the spotting scope. "All in the black: a nine, four tens, one of 'em in the X-ring. Again."

Ryan reloaded with a smile. He'd allowed himself to forget how much fun a pistol could be. This was a pure physical skill, a man's skill that carried the same sort of satisfaction as a just-right golf shot. He had to control a machine that delivered a .357-inch bullet to a precise destination. Doing this required coordination of eye and hand. It wasn't quite the same as using a shotgun or a rifle. Pistol was much harder than either of those, and hitting the target carried a subintellectual pleasure that was not easily described to someone who hadn't done it. His next five rounds were all tens. He tried the two-hand Weaver stance, and placed four out of five in the X-ring, a circle half the diameter of the ten-ring, used for tie-breaking in competition shoots.

"Not bad for a civilian," Breckenridge said. "Coffee?"

"Thanks, Gunny." Ryan took the cup.

"I want you to concentrate a little more on your second round. You keep letting that one go off to the right some. You're rushing it a little." The difference, Ryan knew, was barely two inches at fifty feet. Breckenridge was a stone perfectionist. It struck him that the Sergeant Major and Cathy had very similar personalities: either you were doing it exactly right or you were doing it completely wrong. "Doc, it's a shame you got hurt. You would have made a good officer, with the right sergeant to bring you along—they all need that of course."

"You know something, Gunny? I met a couple of guys in London that you'd just love." Jack slipped the magazine back into his automatic.

"Ryan is rather a clever lad, isn't he?" Owens handed the document back to Murray.

"Nothing really new in here," Dan admitted, "but at least it's well organized. Here's the other thing you wanted."

"Oh, our friends in Boston. How is Paddy O'Neil doing?" Owens was more than just annoyed at this. Padraig O'Neil was an insult to the British parliamentary system, an elected mouthpiece for the Provisional IRA. In ten years of trying, however, neither Owens' Anti-Terrorist Branch nor the Royal Ulster Constabulary had ever linked him to an illegal act.

"Drinking a lot of beer, talking to a lot of folks, and raising a little money, just like always." Murray sipped at his port. "We have agents following him around. He knows they're there, of course. If he spits on the sidewalk, we'll put him on the next bird home. He knows that, too. He hasn't broken a single law. Even his driver—the guy's a teetotaler. I hate to say it, Jimmy, but the bum's clean, and he's making points."

"Oh, yes, he's a charming one, Paddy is." Owens flipped a page and looked up. "Let me see that thing your Ryan fellow did again."

"The guys at Five glommed your copy. I expect they'll give it to you tomorrow."

Owens grunted as he flipped to the summary at the back of the document. "Here it is. . . . Good God above!"

"What?" Murray snapped forward in his chair.

"The link, the bloody link. It's right here!"

"What are you talking about, Jimmy? I've read the thing twice myself."

" 'The fact that ULA personnel seem to have been drawn almost entirely from "extreme" elements within the PIRA itself,' " he read aloud, " 'must have a significance beyond that established by existing evidence. It seems likely that since the ULA membership has been so recruited, some ULA "defectors-in-place" remain within the PIRA, serving as information sources to their actual parent organization. It follows that such information may be of an operational nature in addition to its obvious counterintelligence value.' *Operational,*" Owens said quietly. "We've always assumed that O'Donnell was simply trying to protect himself . . . but he could be playing another game entirely."

"I still haven't caught up with you, Jimmy." Murray set his glass down and frowned for a moment. "Oh. Maureen Dwyer. You never did figure out that tip, did you?"

Owens was thinking about another case, but Murray's remark exploded like a flashbulb in front of his eyes. The detective just stared at his American colleague for a moment while his brain raced down a host of ideas.

"But why?" Murray asked. "What do they gain?"

"They can do great embarrassment to the leadership, inhibit operations."

"But what material good does that do for the ULA? O'Donnell's too professional to screw his old friends just for the hell of it. The INLA might, but they're just a bunch of damned-fool cowboys. The ULA is too sophisticated for that sort of crap."

"Yes. We've just surmounted one wall to find another before us. Still, that's one more wall behind us. It gives us something to question young Miss Dwyer about, doesn't it?"

"Well, it's an idea to run down. The ULA has the PIRA penetrated, and sometimes they feed information to you to make the Provos look bad." Murray shook his head. *Did I just say that one terrorist outfit was trying to make another one look bad?* "Do you have enough evidence to back that idea up?"

"I can name you three cases in the last year where anonymous tips gave us Provos who were at the top of our list. In none of the three did we ever learn who the source was."

"But if the Provos suspect it—oh, scratch that idea. They want O'Donnell anyway, and that's straight revenge for all the people he did away with within the organization. Okay, embarrassing the PIRA leadership may be an objective in itself—*if* O'Donnell was trying to recruit some new members. But you've already discarded that idea."

Owens swore under his breath. Criminal investigation, he often said, was like doing a jigsaw puzzle when you didn't have all the pieces and never really knew their shapes. But telling that to his subordinates wasn't the same thing as experiencing it himself. If only they hadn't lost Sean Miller. Maybe they might have gotten something from him by now. His instinct told him that one small, crucial fact would make a complete picture of all the rubbish he was sorting through. Without that fact, his reason told Owens, everything he thought he knew was nothing more than speculation. But one thought kept repeating itself in his mind:

"Dan, if you wanted to embarrass the Provisionals' leadership politically, how and where would you do it?"

"Hello, this is Doctor Ryan."

"This is Bernice Wilson at Johns Hopkins. Your wife asked me to tell you that she's in an emergency procedure and she'll be about a half hour late tonight."

"Okay, thank you." Jack replaced the phone. *Mondays,* he told himself. He went back to discussing the term paper projects with his two mids. His desk clock said four in the afternoon. Well, there was no hurry, was there?

* * *

The watch changed at Gate Three. The civilian guard was named Bob Riggs. He was a retired Navy chief master at arms, past fifty, with a beer belly that made it hard for him to see his shoes. The cold affected him badly, and he spent as much time as possible in the guardhouse. He didn't see a man in his late twenties approach the opposite corner and disappear into a doorway. Neither did Sergeant Tom Cummings of the Marine guard force, who was checking some paperwork just after relieving the previous watch-stander. The Academy was good duty for the young Marine NCO. There were a score of good saloons within easy walking distance, and plenty of unattached womenfolk to be sampled, but the duty at Annapolis was pretty boring when you got down to it, and Cummings was young enough to crave some action. It had been a typical Monday. The previous guard had issued three parking citations. He was already yawning.

Fifty feet away, an elderly lady approached the entrance to the apartment building. She was surprised to see a handsome young man there and dropped her shopping bag while fumbling for her key.

"Can I help you with that, now?" he asked politely. His accent made him sound different, but rather kind, the lady thought. He held the bag while she unlocked the door.

"I'm afraid I'm a little early—waiting to meet my young lady, you see," he explained with a charming smile. "I'm sorry if I startled you, ma'am—just trying to keep out of this bitter wind."

"Would you like to wait inside the door?" she offered.

"That's very kind indeed, ma'am, but no. I might miss her and it's a bit of a surprise, you see. Good day to you." His hand relaxed around the knife in his coat pocket.

Sergeant Cummings finished going over the papers and walked outside. He noticed the man in the doorway for the first time. Looked like he was waiting for someone, the Sergeant judged, and trying to keep out of the cold north wind. That seemed sensible enough. The Sergeant checked his watch. Four-fifteen.

"I think that does it," Bernie Katz said.

"We did it," Cathy Ryan agreed. There were smiles all around the OR. It had taken over five hours, but the youngster's eye was back together. He might need another operation, and certainly he'd wear glasses for the rest of his life, but that was better than having only one eye.

"For somebody who hasn't done one of these in four months, not bad, Cath. This kid will have both his eyes. You want to tell the family? I have to go to the john."

The boy's mother was waiting exactly where the Jeffers family had been, the same look of anxiety on her face. Beside her was someone with a camera.

"We saved the eye," Cathy said at once. After she sat down beside the woman, the photographer—he said he was from the *Baltimore Sun*—fired away with his Nikon for several minutes. The surgeon explained the procedure to the mother for several minutes, trying to calm her down. It wasn't easy, but Cathy'd had lots of practice.

Finally someone from Social Services arrived, and Cathy was able to head for the locker room. She pulled off her greens, tossing them in the hamper. Bernie Katz was sitting on the bench, rubbing his neck.

"I could use some of that myself," Cathy observed. She stood there in her Gucci underwear and stretched. Katz turned to admire the view.

"Getting pretty big, Cath. How's the back?"

"Stiff. Just like it was with Sally. Avert your gaze, Doctor, you're a married man."

"Can I help it if pregnant women look sexy?"

"I'm glad I look it, 'cause I sure as hell don't feel like it at the moment." She dropped to the bench in front of her locker. "I didn't think we could do that one, Bernie."

"We were lucky," Katz admitted. "Fortunately the dear Lord looks after fools, drunks, and little children. Some of the time, anyway."

Cathy pulled open the locker. In the mirror she had inside, she saw that her hair did indeed look like the Medusa's. She made a face at herself. "I need another vacation."

"But you just had one," Katz observed.

"Right," Dr. Ryan snorted. She slid her legs into her pants and reached for her blouse.

"And when that fetus decides to become a baby, you'll have another."

The jacket came next. "Bernie, if you were in OB, your patients would kill you for that sort of crap."

"What a loss to medicine that would be," Katz thought aloud.

Cathy laughed. "Nice job, Bern. Kiss Annie for me."

"Sure, and you take it a little easy, eh, or I'll tell Madge North to come after you."

"I see her Friday, Bernie. She says I'm doing fine." Cathy breezed out the door. She waved to her nurses, complimenting them yet again for a superb job in the OR. The elevator was next. Already she had her car keys in her hand.

The green Porsche was waiting for her. Cathy unlocked the door and tossed her bag in the back before settling in the driver's seat. The six-cylinder engine started in an instant. The tachymeter needle swung upward to the idle setting. She let the engine warm up for a minute while she buckled her seat belt and slipped off the parking brake. The throaty rumble of the engine echoed down the concrete walls of the parking garage. When the temperature needle started to move, she shifted into reverse. A moment later she dropped the gear lever into first and moved toward Broadway. She checked the clock on the dashboard and winced—worse, she had to make a stop at the store on the way home. Well, she did have her 911 to play catch-up with.

"The target is moving," a voice said into a radio three levels up. The message was relayed by telephone to Alex's safehouse, then by radio again.

"About bloody time," Miller growled a few minutes later. "Why the hell is she late?" The last hour had been infuriating for him. First thirty minutes of waiting for her to be on time, then another thirty minutes while she wasn't. He told himself to relax. She had to be at the day-care center to pick up the kid.

"She's a doc. It happens, man," Alex said. "Let's roll."

The pickup car led off first, followed by the van. The Ford would be at the 7-Eleven across from Giant Steps in exactly thirty minutes.

"He must be waiting for somebody pretty," Riggs said when he got back into the guard shack.

''Still there?'' Cummings was surprised. Three weeks before, Breckenridge had briefed the guard force about the possible threat to Dr. Ryan. Cummings knew that the history teacher always went out this gate—he was late today, though. The Sergeant could see that the light in his office was still on. Though the duty here was dull, Cummings was serious about it. Three months in Beirut had taught him everything he would ever need to know about that. He walked outside and took a place on the other side of the road.

Cummings watched the cars leaving. Mostly they were driven by civilians, but those driven by naval officers got a regulation Marine salute. The wind only got colder. He wore a sweater under his blouse. This kept his torso warm, but the white kid gloves that went with the dress-blue uniform were the next thing to useless. He made a great show of clapping his hands together as he turned around periodically. He never stared at the apartment building, never acted as though he knew anybody were there. It was getting dark now, and it wasn't all that easy to see him anyway. But somebody was there.

''That was fast,'' the man in the pickup car said. He checked his watch. She'd just knocked five minutes off her fastest time. *Damn,* he thought, *must be nice to have one of those little Porsches.* He checked the tag: CR-SRGN. Yep, that was the one. He grabbed the radio.

''Hi, Mom, I'm home,'' he said.

''It's about time,'' a male voice answered. The van was half a mile away, sitting on Joyce Lane, west of Ritchie Highway.

He saw the lady come out of the day-care center less than two minutes later. She was in a hurry.

''Rolling.''

''Okay,'' came the answer.

''Come on, Sally, we're late. Buckle up.'' Cathy Ryan hated to be late. She restarted the engine. She hadn't been this late in over a month, but she could still make it home before Jack if she hustled.

The rush hour was under way in earnest, but the Porsche was small, fast, and agile. In a minute from sitting in the parking lot she was doing sixty-five, weaving through traffic like a race driver at Daytona.

For all their preparation, Alex almost missed her. An eighteen-wheeler was laboring up the hill in the right lane when the distinctive shape of the Porsche appeared next to it. Alex floored the van and darted out onto the road, causing the semi to jam his brakes and horn at the same time. Alex didn't look back. Miller got out of the right-front seat and went back to the window on the sliding door.

''Whooee, this lady's in a hurry tonight!''

''Can you catch her?'' Miller asked.

Alex just smiled. ''Watch.''

''Damn, look at that Porsche!'' Trooper First Class Sam Waverly was driving J-30, a State Police car coming off an afternoon of pursuit-radar work on U.S. Route 50. He and Larry Fontana of J-19 were heading back to the Annapolis police barracks off Rowe Boulevard after a long day's work when they saw the green sports car take the entrance ramp off Ritchie Highway. Both troopers were driving about sixty-five miles per hour, a privilege that accrued only to police officers.

Their cars were unmarked. This made them and their radar guns impossible to spot until it was too late. They usually worked in pairs, and took turns, with one working his radar gun and the other a quarter mile down the road to wave the speeders over for their tickets.

''Another one!'' Fontana said over the radio. A van swerved into the highway's left lane, forcing somebody in a Pontiac to jam on his brakes. ''Let's get 'em.'' They were both young officers and while, contrary to legend, the State Police didn't assign ticket quotas to its officers, everyone knew that one sure way to promotion was to write a lot of them. It also made the roads safer, and that was their mission as state troopers. Neither officer really enjoyed giving out traffic citations, but they enjoyed responding to major accidents far less.

''Okay, I got the Porsche.''

''You get all the fun,'' Fontana noted. He'd gotten a quick look at the driver.

It was a lot harder than one might imagine. First they had to clock the speeding vehicles to establish how far over the limit they were going—the greater the speed, the greater the fine, of course—then they had to close and switch on their lights to pull them over. Both subject vehicles were two hundred yards ahead of the police cruisers now.

Cathy checked her clock again. She'd managed to cut nearly ten minutes off her trip time. Next she checked her rearview mirror for a police car. She didn't want to get a ticket. There was nothing that looked like a cop car, only ordinary cars and trucks. She had to slow as the traffic became congested approaching the Severn River bridge. She debated getting over into the left lane, but decided against it. Sometimes it was hard to get back into the right lane in time to take the Route 2 exit. Beside her, Sally was craning her neck to see over the dash, as usual, and playing with the seat-belt buckle. Cathy didn't say anything this time, but concentrated on the traffic as she eased off the pedal.

Miller slipped the door latch and moved the door an inch backward. Another man took hold of the door as he knelt and thumbed the safety forward on his weapon.

He couldn't get her for speeding now, Trooper Waverly noted sourly. She'd slowed before he could establish her speed. He was a hundred yards back. Fontana could, however, ticket the van for improper lane-changing, and one out of two wasn't bad. Waverly checked his mirror. J-19 was catching up, about to pull even with his J-30. There was something odd about the blue van, he saw . . . like the side door wasn't quite right.

''Now!'' Alex called.

Cathy Ryan noted that a van was pulling up on her left side. She took a casual look in time to see the van's door slide back. There was a man kneeling, holding something. There came a chilling moment of realization. She stomped her foot on the brake a fraction of a second before she saw the white flash.

''What!'' Waverly saw a foot-long tongue of flame spit out from the side of the van. The windshield of the Porsche went cloudy and the car swerved sideways, straightened out, then slammed into the bridge's concrete work at over fifty miles per hour. Instantly cars in both lanes slammed on their brakes. The van kept going.

''Larry, shots fired—shots fired from the van. The Porsche was hit!'' Waverly flipped on his lights and stood on his brakes. The police car skidded right and nearly slid sideways into the wrecked Porsche. "Get the van, get the van!"

"I'm on him," Fontana replied. He suddenly realized that the gout of flame he'd seen could only mean some kind of machine gun. "Holy shit," he said to himself.

Waverly returned his attention to the Porsche. Steam poured from the rear engine compartment. "J-30, Annapolis, officer reports shots fired—looked like automatic weapons fire—and a PI accident westbound Route 50 on Severn River bridge. Appears to be serious PI. J-19 in pursuit of vehicle 2. Stand by."

"Standing by," the dispatcher acknowledged. *What the hell . . .*

Waverly grabbed his fire extinguisher and ran the fifteen feet to the wreck. Glass and metal were scattered as far as he could see. The engine, thank God, wasn't on fire. He checked the passenger compartment next.

"Oh, Jesus!" He ran back to his car. "J-30, Annapolis. Call fireboard, officer requests helicopter response. Serious PI, two victims, a white female adult and a white female child, repeat we have a serious PI accident westbound Route 50 east side of Severn River bridge. Officer requests helicopter response."

"J-19, Annapolis," Fontana called in next. "I am in pursuit of a dark van, with handicap tag number Henry Six-Seven-Seven-Two. I am westbound on Route 50 just west of the Severn River bridge. Shots fired from this vehicle. Officer requests assistance," he said coolly. He decided against turning his lights on for the moment. *Holy shit . . .*

"You get her?" Alex called back.

Miller was breathing heavily. He wasn't sure—he wasn't sure about his shots. The Porsche had slowed suddenly just as he squeezed the trigger, but he saw the car hit the bridge and spring up into the air like a toy. No way they could walk away from that sort of accident, he was sure of that.

"Yes."

"Okay, let's boogie." Alex didn't let his emotions interfere with his work. This job meant weapons and money for his movement. It was too bad about the woman and the kid, but it wasn't his fault that they made the wrong kind of enemies.

The Annapolis dispatcher was already on his UHF radio to the State Police helicopter. Trooper-1, a Bell JetRanger-II, was just lifting off from a refueling stop at Baltimore-Washington International Airport.

"Roger that," the helicopter pilot replied, turning south and twisting the throttle control to full power. The paramedic in the left seat leaned forward to change the transponder "squawk" setting from 1200 to 5101. This would inform air traffic controllers that the helicopter was on an emergency medevac mission.

"Trooper-1, J-30, we are en route to your position, ETA four minutes."

Waverly didn't acknowledge. He and two civilians were prying the driver's side window off the car with a tire iron. The driver and passenger were both unconscious, and there was blood all over the interior of the car. She was probably pretty, Waverly thought, looking at the driver, but her head was covered with glistening blood. The child lay like a broken doll, half on the seat, half on the floor. His stomach was a tight cold ball just below his pounding heart. *Another dead kid,* he thought. *Please, God, not another one.*

"Trooper-2, Annapolis," came the next call to the dispatcher.

"Annapolis, Trooper-2, where are you?"

"We are over Mayo Beach, northbound. I copied your medevac call. I have the Governor and Attorney General aboard. Can we help, over."

The dispatcher made a quick decision. Trooper-1 would be at the accident scene in three more minutes. J-19 needed backup in a hurry. This was real luck. Already he had six state vehicles converging on the area, plus three more from the Anne Arundel County Police station at Edgewater. "Trooper-2, contact J-19."

"Trooper-2, J-19, please advise your location," the radio squawked in Fontana's car.

"Westbound Route 50, just passing Rowe Boulevard. I am in pursuit of a dark van with a handicap tag. J-30 and I observed automatic weapons fire from this vehicle, repeat automatic weapons fire. I need some help, people."

It was easy to spot. The Sergeant flying Trooper-2 saw the other helicopter circling over the accident to the east, and Route 50 was nearly bare of cars from west of the accident to Rowe Boulevard. The police car and the van were on the back edge of the moving traffic.

"What gives?" the Governor asked from the back. The paramedic in the left-front seat filled them in as the pilot continued his visual search for . . . there! *Okay, sucker . . .*

"J-19, this is Trooper-2, I got you and the subject car visual." The pilot dropped altitude to five hundred feet. "Trooper-2, Annapolis, I got 'em. Black, or maybe blue van westbound on 50, with an unmarked car in pursuit."

Alex was wondering who the car was. It was unmarked, but a cheap-body car, with dull, monocolor paintwork. *Uh-oh.*

"That's a cop behind us!" he shouted. One of Miller's men looked out the window. Unmarked cars were nothing new where they came from.

"Get rid of him!" Alex snarled.

Fontana held at fifty yards from the van. This was far enough, he thought, to keep himself out of danger. The trooper was listening to continuous chatter on his radio as additional cars announced that they were inbound on the call. The distraction of the radio made him a second late on seeing the van's door fly open. Fontana blanched and hit the brakes.

Miller handled this one too. The moment the door was open, he leveled his machine gun and loosed ten rounds at the police car. He saw it dip when the driver tried to panic-stop, swerve sideways in the road, and flip over. He was too excited even to smile, though inwardly he was awash with glee. The door came back shut as Alex changed lanes.

Fontana felt the bullet hit his chest before he realized that the car's windshield was shattering around him. His right arm jerked down, turning the car too rapidly to the right. The locked-up rear wheels gave the car a broadside skid, a tire blew out, and the car flipped over. Fontana watched in fascination the world rotate around him as the car's top crumpled. Like most policemen he never bothered with his seat belt, and he fell on his neck. The collapsing car top broke it. It didn't matter. A car that had been following his crashed into the police cruiser, finishing the work begun by Miller's submachine gun.

* * *

''Shit!'' the pilot of Trooper-2 cursed. ''Trooper-2, Annapolis, J-19 is wrecked with serious PI on 50 west of the Route 2 exit. Where the hell are the other cars!''

''Trooper-2, advise condition of J-19.''

''He's dead, man—I'm on that fucking van! Where's the goddamned backup!''

''Trooper-2, be advised we have eleven cars converging. We have a roadblock setting up now on 50 at South Haven Road. There are three cars westbound on 50 about half a mile back of you and two more eastbound approaching the exit to General's Highway.''

''Roger that, I am on the van,'' the pilot responded.

''Come on, Alex!'' Miller shouted.

''Almost there, man,'' the black man said, changing to the right lane exit. About a mile ahead he saw the blue and red flashing lights of two police cars coming east toward him, but there was no eastbound exit here. *Tough luck, pigs.* He didn't feel very happy about doing the Porsche, but a dead cop was always something to feel good about. ''Here we go!''

''Annapolis, Trooper-2,'' the pilot called, ''the subject van is turning north off of Route 50.'' It took a moment to register. ''Oh, no!'' He gave a quick order. The eastbound police cars slowed, then darted across the grass median strip into the westbound lanes. These were clear, blocked by a second major accident, but the median was uneven. One car bogged down in the grass and mud while the other bounded up onto the pavement and ran the wrong way on the highway toward the exit.

Alex hit the traffic light exactly right, crossing West Street and heading north. His peripheral vision caught a county police car stuck in the rush-hour traffic on West Street two hundred yards to his right, despite his lights and siren. *Too late, pig.* He proceeded two hundred yards and turned left.

The Sergeant flying Trooper-2 started cursing, oblivious to the Governor and Attorney General in the back. As he watched, the van pulled into the hundred-acre parking lot that surrounded Annapolis Mall. The vehicle proceeded toward the inner ring of parking spaces as three cars turned off West Street in pursuit.

''Son of a *bitch*!'' He pushed down on his collective control and dove at the parking lot.

Alex pulled into a handicap parking slot and stopped the van. His passengers were ready, and opened the doors as soon as the vehicle stopped. They walked slowly and normally to the entrance to the mall. The driver looked up in surprise when he heard the whine and flutter of the helicopter. It hovered at about a hundred feet. Alex made sure his hat was in place and waved as he went through the door.

The helicopter pilot looked at the paramedic in the left seat, whose hand was clenched in rage at his shoulder-holstered .357 revolver while the pilot needed both of his on the controls.

''They're gone,'' the paramedic said quietly over the intercom.

''What do you mean they're gone!'' the Attorney General demanded.

Below them, a county and a State Police car screeched to a halt outside the entrance. But inside those doors were about three thousand shoppers, and the police didn't know what the suspects looked like. The officers stood there, guns drawn, not knowing what to do next.

Alex and his men were inside a public rest room. Two members of Alex's organization were waiting there with shopping bags. Each man from the van got a new coat. They broke up into pairs and walked out into the shopping concourse, heading for an exit at the west end of the mall. They took their time. There was no reason to hurry.

"He waved at us," the Governor said. "Do something!"

"What?" the pilot asked. "What do you want us to do? Who do we stop? They're gone, they might as well be in California now."

The Governor was slow to catch on, though faster than the Attorney General, who was still blubbering. What had begun as a routine political meeting in Salisbury, on Maryland's eastern shore, had turned into an exciting pursuit, but one with a most unsatisfactory ending. He'd watched one of his state troopers killed right before his eyes, and neither he nor his people could do a single thing about it. The Governor swore, finally. The voters would have been shocked at his language.

Trooper-1 was sitting on the Severn River bridge, its rotor turning rapidly to stay above the concrete barriers. The paramedic, Trooper Waverly, and a motorist who turned out to be a volunteer fireman, were loading the two accident victims into Stokes litters for transport on the helicopter. The other motorist who had assisted was standing alone by the police car, over a puddle of his own vomit. A fire engine was pulling up to the scene, and two more state troopers were preparing to get traffic moving, once the helicopter took off. The highway was already backed up at least four miles. As they prepared to start directing traffic, they heard on their radios what had happened to J-19 and its driver. The police officers exchanged looks, but no words. They would come later.

As first officer on the scene, Waverly took the driver's purse and started looking for identification. He had lots of forms to fill out, and people to notify. Inside the purse, he saw, was some kind of finger painting. He looked up as the little girl's litter was loaded into the top rack of the helicopter's passenger bay. The paramedic went in behind it, and less than thirty seconds later, Waverly's face stung with the impact of gravel, thrown up by the helicopter's rotor. He watched it lift into the air, and whispered a prayer for the little girl who'd done a painting of something that looked like a blue cow. *Back to work,* he told himself. The purse had a red address book. He checked the driver's license to get a name, then looked in the book under the same letter. Someone with the first name of Jack, but no last name written in, had a number designated "work." It was probably her husband's. Somebody had to call him.

"Baltimore Approach, this is Trooper-1 on a medevac inbound to Baltimore."

"Trooper-1, roger, you are cleared for direct approach, come left to course three-four-seven and maintain current altitude," the air controller at Baltimore-Washington International responded. The 5101 squawk number was clear on his scope, and medical emergencies had unconditional priority.

"Hopkins Emergency, this is Trooper-1, inbound with a white female child accident victim."

"Trooper-1, Hopkins. Divert to University. We're full up here."
"Roger. University, Trooper-1, do you copy, over."
"Trooper-1, this is University, we copy, and we're ready for you."
"Roger, ETA five minutes. Out."

"Gunny, this is Cummings at Gate Three," the Sergeant called on the telephone.

"What is it, Sergeant?" Breckenridge asked.

"There's this guy, he's been standing on the corner across the street for about forty-five minutes. It just feels funny, you know? He's off the grounds, but it doesn't feel right."

"Call the cops?" the Sergeant Major asked.

"What for?" Cummings asked reasonably. "He ain't even spit far as I can tell."

"Okay, I'll walk on up." Breckenridge stood. He was bored anyway. The Sergeant Major donned his cap and walked out of the building, heading north across the campus. It took five minutes, during which he saluted six officers and greeted a larger number of mids. He didn't like the cold. It had never been like this during his childhood on a Mississippi dirt farm. But spring was coming. He was careful not to look too obviously out of the gate as he crossed the street.

He found Cummings in the guardhouse, standing inside the door. A good young sergeant, Cummings was. He had the new look of the Corps. Breckenridge was built along the classic John Wayne lines, with broad shoulders and imposing bulk. Cummings was a black kid, a runner who had the frame of a Frank Shorter. The boy could run all day, something that the Gunny had never been able to do. But more than all of that, Cummings was a lifer. He understood what the Marine Corps was all about. Breckenridge had taken the young man under his wing, imparting a few important lessons along the way. The Sergeant Major knew that he would soon be part of the Corps' past. Cummings was its future, and he told himself that the future looked pretty good.

"Hey, Gunny," the Sergeant greeted him.

"The guy in the doorway?"

"He's been there since a little after four. He don't live here." Cummings paused for a moment. He was, after all, only a "buck" sergeant with no rockers under his stripes, talking to a man whom generals addressed with respect. "It just feels funny."

"Well, let's give him a few minutes," Breckenridge thought aloud.

"God, I hate grading quizzes."

"So go easy on the boys and girls," Robby chuckled.

"Like you do?" Ryan asked.

"I teach a difficult, technical subject. I have to give quizzes."

"Engineers! Shame you can't read and write as well as you multiply."

"You must have taken a tough-pill this afternoon, Jack."

"Yeah, well—" The phone rang. Jack picked it up. "Doctor Ryan. Yes—who?" His face changed, his voice became guarded.

"Yes, that's right." Robby saw his friend go stiff in the chair. "Are you sure? Where are they now? Okay—ah, okay, thank you . . . I, uh, thank you." Jack stared at the phone for a second or two before hanging it up.

"What's the matter, Jack?" Robby asked.

It took him a moment to answer. "That was the police. There's been an accident."

''Where are they?'' Robby said immediately.

''They flew them—they flew them to Baltimore.'' Jack stood shakily. ''I have to get there.'' He looked down at his friend. ''God, Robby . . .''

Jackson was on his feet in an instant. ''Come on, I'll take you up there.''

''No, I'll—''

''Stuff it, Jack. I'm driving.'' Robby got his coat and tossed Jack's over the desk. ''Move it, boy!''

''They took them by helicopter . . .''

''Where? Where to, Jack?''

''University,'' he said.

''Get it together, Jack.'' Robby grabbed his arm. ''Settle down some.'' The flyer led his friend down the stairs and out of the building. His red Corvette was parked a hundred yards away.

''Still there,'' the civilian guard reported when he came back in.

''Okay,'' Breckenridge said, standing. He looked at the pistol holster hanging in the corner, but decided against that. ''This is what we're going to do.''

Ned Clark hadn't liked the mission from the first moment. Sean was too eager on this one. But he hadn't said so. Sean had masterminded the prison break that had made him a free man. If nothing else, Ned Clark was loyal to the Cause. He was exposed here and didn't like that either. His briefing had told him that the guards at the Academy gate were lax, and he could see that they were unarmed. They had no authority at all off the grounds of the school.

But it was taking too long. His target was thirty minutes late. He didn't smoke, didn't do anything to make himself conspicuous, and he knew that he'd be hard to spot. The doorway of the tired old apartment building had no light—one of Alex's people had taken care of that with a pellet gun the previous night.

Ought to call this one off, Clark told himself. But he didn't want to do that. He didn't want to fail Sean. He saw a pair of men leave the Academy. Bootnecks, bloody Marines in their Sunday clothes. They looked so pretty without their guns, so vulnerable.

''So the Captain, he says,'' the big one was saying loudly, ''get that goddamned gook off my chopper!'' And the other one started laughing.

''I love it!''

''How about a couple of beers?'' the big one said next. They crossed the street, heading his way.

''Okay by me, Gunny. You buyin'?''

''My turn, isn't it? I have to get some money first.'' The big one reached in his pocket for some keys and turned toward Clark. ''Excuse me, sir, can I help you?'' His hand came out of his pocket without any keys.

Clark reacted quickly, but not quickly enough. The right hand inside his overcoat started moving up, but Breckenridge's own right grabbed it like a vise.

''I asked if I could help you, sir,'' the Sergeant Major said pleasantly. ''What do you have in that hand?'' Clark tried to move, but the big man pushed him against the brick wall.

''Careful, Tom,'' Breckenridge warned.

Cummings' hand searched downward and found the metallic shape of a pistol. ''Gun,'' he said sharply.

"It better not go off," the Gunny announced, his left arm across Clark's throat. "Let the man have it, sonny, real careful, like."

Clark was amazed at his stupidity, letting them get so close to him. His head tried to turn to look up the street, but the man waiting for him in the car was around the corner. Before he could think of anything to do, the black man had disarmed him and was searching his pockets. Cummings removed the knife next.

"Talk to me," Breckenridge said. Clark didn't say anything, and the forearm slid roughly across his throat. "*Please* talk to me, *sir*."

"Get your bloody hands off of me! Who do you think you are?"

"Where you from, boy?" Breckenridge didn't need an answer to that one. The Sergeant wrenched Clark's arm out of the pocket and twisted it behind his back. "Okay, sonny, we're going to walk through that gate over yonder, and you're gonna sit down and be a good boy while we call the police. If you make any trouble, I'm going to tear this arm off and shove it right up your ass. Let's go, boy."

The driver who'd been waiting for Clark was standing at the far corner. He took one look at what had happened and walked to his car. Two minutes later he was blocks away.

Cummings handcuffed the man to a chair while Breckenridge established that he carried no identification—aside from an automatic pistol, which was ID enough. First he called his captain, then the Annapolis City police. It started there, but, though the Gunny didn't know, it wouldn't stop there.

15. Shock and Trauma

If Jack had ever doubted that Robby Jackson really was a fighter pilot, this would have cured him. Jackson's personal toy was a two-year-old Chevrolet Corvette, painted candy-apple red, and he drove it with a sense of personal invincibility. The flyer raced out the Academy's west gate, turned left, and found his way to Rowe Boulevard. The traffic problems on Route 50 west were immediately apparent, and he changed lanes to head east. In a minute he was streaking across the Severn River bridge. Jack was too engrossed in his thoughts to see much of anything, but Robby saw what looked like the remains of a Porsche on the other side of the roadway. Jackson's blood went cold as he turned away. He cast the thoughts aside and concentrated on his driving, pushing the Corvette past eighty. There were too many cops on the other side of the road for him to worry about a ticket. He took the Ritchie Highway exit a minute later and curved around north toward Baltimore. Rush-hour traffic was heavy, though most of it was heading in the other direction. This gave him gaps to exploit, and the pilot used every one. He worked up and down through the gears, rarely touching the brakes.

To his right, Jack simply stared straight ahead, not seeing much of anything. He managed to wince when Robby paused behind two tractor-trailers running side by side—then shot up right between them with scant inches of clearance on either side. The outraged screams of the two diesel horns faded irrelevantly behind the racing 'Vette, and Jack returned to the emptiness of his thoughts.

* * *

Breckenridge allowed his captain, Mike Peters, to handle the situation. He was a pretty good officer, the Sergeant Major thought, who had the common sense to let his NCOs run things. He'd managed to get to the guard shack about two minutes ahead of the Annapolis City police, long enough for Breckenridge and Cummings to fill him in.

"So what gives, gentlemen?" the responding officer asked. Captain Peters nodded for Breckenridge to speak.

"Sir, Sergeant Cummings here observed this individual to be standing over at the corner across the street. He did not look like a local resident, so we kept an eye on him. Finally Cummings and I walked over and asked if we might be of assistance to him. He tried to pull this on us"—the Gunny lifted the pistol carefully, so as not to disturb the fingerprints—"and he had this knife in his pocket. Carrying a concealed weapon is a violation of local law, so Cummings and I made a citizen's arrest and called you. This character does not have any identification on him, and he declined to speak with us."

"What kind of gun is that?" the cop asked.

"It's an FN nine-millimeter," Breckenridge answered. "It's the same as the Browning Hi-Power, but a different trademark, with a thirteen-round magazine. The weapon was loaded, with a live round in the chamber. The hammer was down. The knife is a cheap piece of shit. Punk knife."

The cop had to smile. He knew Breckenridge from the department firearms training unit.

"Can I have your name, please," the cop said to Eamon Clark. The "suspect" just stared at him. "Sir, you have a number of constitutional rights which I am about to read to you, but the law does not allow you to withhold your identity. You have to tell me your name."

The cop stared at Clark for another minute. At last he shrugged and pulled a card from his clipboard. "Sir, you have the right to remain silent. . . ." He read the litany off the card. "Do you understand these rights?"

Still Clark didn't say anything. The police officer was getting irritated. He looked at the other three men in the room. "Gentlemen, will you testify that I read this individual his rights?"

"Yes, sir, we certainly will," Captain Peters said.

"If I may make a suggestion, officer," Breckenridge said. "You might want to check this boy out with the FBI."

"How come?"

"He talks funny," the Sergeant Major explained. "He don't come from here."

"Great—two crazy ones in one day."

"What do ya mean?" Breckenridge asked.

"Little while ago a car got machine-gunned on 50, sounds like some kind of drug hit. A trooper got killed by the same bunch a few minutes later. The bad guys got away." The cop leaned down to look Clark in the face. "You better start talkin', sir. The cops in this town are in a mean mood tonight. What I'm tellin' you, man, is that we don't want to put up with some unnecessary shit. You understand me?"

Clark didn't understand. In Ireland carrying a concealed weapon was a serious crime. In America it was rather less so since so many citizens owned guns. Had he said he was waiting for someone and carried a gun because he was afraid of street criminals, he might have gotten out on the street before identification procedures were complete. Instead, his intransigence was only making the policeman angry and ensuring that the identification procedures would be carried out in full before he was arraigned.

Captain Peters and Sergeant Major Breckenridge exchanged a meaningful look.

"Officer," the Captain said, "I would most strongly recommend that you check this character's ID with the FBI. We've, uh, we had a sort of an informal warning about terrorist activity a few weeks back. This is still your jurisdiction since he was arrested in the city, but . . ."

"I hear you, Cap'n," the cop said. He thought for a few seconds and concluded that there was something more here than met the eye. "If you gentlemen will come to the station with me, we'll find out who Mr. Doe here really is."

Ryan charged through the entrance of the Shock-Trauma Center and identified himself to the reception desk, whose occupant directed him to a waiting room where, she said firmly, he would be notified as soon as there was anything to report. The sudden change from action to inaction disoriented Jack enormously. He stood at the entrance to the waiting room for some minutes, his mind a total blank as it struggled with the situation. By the time Robby arrived from parking his car, he found his friend sitting on the cracked vinyl of an old sofa, mindlessly reading through a brochure whose stiff paper had become as soft as chamois from the numberless hands of parents, wives, husbands, and friends of the patients who had passed through this building.

The brochure explained in bureaucratic prose how the Maryland Institute for Emergency Medical Services was the first and best organization of its kind, devoted exclusively to the most sophisticated emergency care for trauma victims. Ryan knew all this. Johns Hopkins managed the more recent pediatric unit and provided many of the staff surgeons for eye injuries. Cathy had spent some time doing that during her residency, an intense two months that she'd been happy to leave behind. Jack wondered if she were now being treated by a former colleague. *Would he recognize her? Would it matter?*

The Shock-Trauma Center—so known to everyone but the billing department—had begun as the dream of a brilliant, aggressive, and supremely arrogant heart surgeon who had bludgeoned his way through a labyrinth of bureaucratic empires to build this 21st-century emergency room.

It had blossomed into a dazzling, legendary success. Shock-Trauma was the leading edge of emergency medical technology. It had already pioneered many techniques for critical care, and in doing so had overthrown many historical precepts of conventional medicine—which had not endeared its founder to his medical brethren. That would have been true in any field, and Shock-Trauma's founder had not helped the process with his brutally outspoken opinions. His greatest—but unacknowledged—crime, of course, was being right in nearly all details. And while this prophet was without honor in the mainstream of his profession, its younger members were easier to convert. Shock-Trauma attracted the best young surgical talent in the world, and only the finest of them were chosen.

But will they be good enough? Ryan asked himself.

He lost all track of time, waiting, afraid to look at his watch, afraid to speculate on the significance of time's flight. Alone, completely alone in his circumscribed world, he reflected that God had given him a wife he loved and a child he treasured more than his own life; that his first duty as husband and father was to protect them from an often hostile world; that he had failed; that, because of this, their lives were now in strangers' hands. All his knowledge, all his skills were useless now. It was worse than impotence, and some evil agency in his mind kept repeating over and over the thoughts that made him cringe as he retreated further and further into catatonic numbness. For hours he stared at the floor, then the wall, unable even to pray as his mind sought the solace of emptiness.

Jackson sat beside his friend, silent, in his own private world. A naval aviator, he had seen close friends vanish from a trivial mistake or a mechanical glitch—or seemingly nothing at all. He'd felt death's cold hand brush his own shoulder less than a year before. But this wasn't a danger to a mature man who had freely chosen a dangerous profession. This was a young wife and an innocent child whose lives were at risk. He couldn't joke about how ''old Dutch'' would luck this one out. He knew nothing at all he could say, no encouragement he could offer other than just sitting there, and though he gave no sign of it, Robby was sure that Jack knew his friend was close at hand.

After two hours Jackson quietly left the waiting room to call his wife and check discreetly at the desk. The receptionist fumbled for the names, then identified them as: a Female, Blond, Age Thirty or so, Head; and a Female, Blond, Age Four or so, Flailed Chest. The pilot was tempted to throttle the receptionist for her coldness, but his discipline was sufficient to allow him to turn away without a word. Jackson rejoined Ryan a moment later, and together they stared at the wall through the passage of time. It started to rain outside, a cold rain that perfectly matched what they both felt.

Special Agent Shaw was walking through the door of his Chevy Chase home when the phone rang. His teen-age daughter answered it and just held it out to him. This sort of thing was not the least unusual.

''Shaw here.''

''Mr. Shaw, this is Nick Capitano from the Annapolis office. The city police here have in custody a man with a pistol, a knife, but no ID. He refuses to talk at all, but earlier he did speak to a couple of Marines, and he had an accent.''

''That's nice, he has an accent. What kind?'' Shaw asked testily.

''Maybe Irish,'' Capitano replied. ''He was apprehended just outside Gate Three of the U.S. Naval Academy. There's a Marine here who says that some teacher named Ryan works there, and he got some sort of warning from the Anti-Terrorism Office.''

What the hell. ''Have you ID'd the suspect yet?''

''No, sir. The local police just fingerprinted him, and they faxed a copy of the prints and photo to the Bureau. The suspect refuses to say anything. He just isn't talking at all, sir.''

''Okay,'' Shaw thought for a moment. *So much for dinner.* ''I'll be back in my office in thirty minutes. Have them send a copy of the mug shot and the prints there. You stay put, and have somebody find Doctor Ryan and stay with him.''

''Right.''

Shaw hung up and dialed his office at the Bureau. ''Dave, Bill. Call London, and tell Dan Murray I want him in his office in half an hour. We may have something happening over here.''

''Bye, Daddy,'' his daughter said. Shaw hadn't even had time to take off his coat.

He was at his desk twenty-seven minutes later. First he called Nick Capitano in Annapolis.

''Anything new?''

"No, sir. The security detail at Annapolis can't find this Ryan guy. His car is parked on the Academy grounds, and they've got people looking for him. I've asked the Anne Arundel County Police to send a car to his home in case he got a ride—car broke down, or something like that. Things are a little wild here at the moment. Something crazy happened about the same time this John Doe gunman got picked up. A car got hosed down with a machine gun just outside the city."

"What the hell was that?"

"The State Police are handling it. We haven't been called in," Capitano explained.

"Get a man over there!" Shaw said at once. A secretary came into the office and handed him a folder. Inside was a facsimile copy of the suspect's mug shot. It showed full face and profile.

"Hold it!" He caught the secretary before the door was closed. "I want this faxed to London right now."

"Yes, sir."

Shaw next dialed the tie line to the embassy in London.

"I just got to sleep," the voice answered after the first ring.

"Hi, Dan. I just missed dinner. It's a tough world. I have a photo being faxed to you now." Shaw filled Murray in on what had happened.

"Oh, my God." Murray gulped down some coffee. "Where's Ryan?"

"We don't know. Probably just wandering around somewhere. His car's still parked in Annapolis—at the Academy, I mean. The security guys are looking for him. He's gotta be all right, Dan. If I read this right, the suspect in Annapolis was probably waiting for him."

The photograph of Eamon Clark was already in the embassy. The Bureau's communications unit worked on the same satellite net used by the intelligence services. The embassy communications officers were actually employees of the National Security Agency, which never slept. The facsimile had arrived with a FLASH-priority header, and a messenger ran it up to the Legal Attaché's office. But the door was locked. Murray had to set the phone down to open it.

"I'm back," Murray said. He opened the folder. The photo had suffered somewhat from twice being broken into electronic bits and broadcast, but for all of that it was recognizable. "This one's familiar. I can't put a name on him, but he's a bad guy."

"How fast can you ID him?"

"I can call Jimmy Owens real quick. You in your office?"

"Yeah," Shaw answered.

"I'll be back." Murray changed buttons on his phones. He didn't have Owens' home number memorized and had to look it up.

"Yes?"

"Hi, Jimmy, it's Dan." Murray's voice was actually chipper now. *Have I got something for you.*

Owens didn't know that yet. "Do you know what time it is?"

"Our guys have somebody in custody that you may be interested in."

"Who?" Owens asked.

"I got a picture but no name. He was arrested in Annapolis, outside the Naval Academy—"

"Ryan?"

"Maybe." Murray was worried about that.

"Meet me at the Yard," Owens said.

"On the way." Murray headed downstairs for his car.

It was easier for Owens. His house was always watched by a pair of armed detectives in a police car. All he had to do was step outside and wave, and the Land-Rover came to his door. He beat Murray by five minutes. By the time the FBI agent arrived, Owens had already consumed a cup of tea. He poured two more.

"This guy look familiar?" The FBI agent tossed the photo over. Owens' eyes went wide.

"Ned Clark," he breathed. "In America, you say?"

"I thought he looked familiar. He got picked up in Annapolis."

"This is one of the lads who broke out of Long Kesh, a very bad boy with several murders to his name. Thank you, Mr. Murray."

"Thank the Marines." Murray grabbed a cup of tea. He really needed the caffeine. "Can I make a call?" Within a minute he was back to FBI headquarters. The desk phone was on speaker so that Owens could listen in.

"Bill, the suspect is one Ned Clark, a convicted murderer who escaped from prison last year. He used to be a big-time assassin with the Provos."

"I got some bad news, Dan," Shaw replied. "It appears that there was an attack on this Ryan fellow's family. The State Police are investigating what looks like a machine-gun attack on a car belonging to Doctor Caroline Ryan, MD. The suspects were in a van and made a clean escape after killing a state trooper."

"Where is Jack Ryan?" Murray asked.

"We don't know yet. He was seen leaving the Naval Academy grounds in the car of a friend. The troopers are looking for the car now."

"What about his family?" It was Owens this time.

"They were flown to the Shock-Trauma Center in Baltimore. The local police have been notified to keep an eye on the place, but it's usually guarded anyway. As soon as we find Ryan we'll put some people with him. Okay, on this Clark kid, I'll have him in federal custody by tomorrow morning. I expect that Mr. Owens wants him back?"

"Yes." Owens leaned back in his chair. He had his own call to make now. As often happened in police work, there was bad news to accompany the good.

"Mr. Ryan?" It was a doctor. Probably a doctor. He wore a pink paper gown and strange-looking pink booties over what were probably sneakers. The gown was bloodstained. He couldn't be much over thirty, Ryan judged. The face was tired and dark. DR. BARRY SHAPIRO, the name tag announced, DEPUTY TRAUMA-SURGEON-IN-CHIEF. Ryan tried to stand but found that his legs would not work. The doctor waved for him to remain seated. He came over slowly and fell into the chair next to the sofa.

What news do you bring me? Ryan thought. His mind both screamed for information and dreaded learning what had happened to his family.

"I'm Barry Shapiro. I've been working on your daughter." He spoke quickly, with a curious accent that Ryan noted but discarded as irrelevant. "Okay, your wife is fine. She had a broken and lacerated upper left arm and a nasty cut on her head. When the helicopter paramedic saw the head wound—heads bleed a lot—he brought her here as a precaution. We ran a complete head protocol on her, and she's fine. A mild concussion, but nothing to worry about. She'll be fine."

"She's pregnant. Do—"

"We noticed." Shapiro smiled. "No problem with that. The pregnancy has not been compromised in any way."

"She's a surgeon. Will there be any permanent damage?"

"Oh? I didn't know that. We don't bother very much with patient identification," Shapiro explained. "No, there should be no problem. The damage to her arm is extensive but routine. It should heal completely."

Ryan nodded, afraid to ask the next question. The doctor paused before going on. *Does the bad news come next. . . .*

"Your daughter is a very sick little girl."

Jack nearly choked with his next breath. The iron fist that had clutched his stomach relaxed a millimeter. *At least she's alive. Sally's alive!*

"Apparently she wasn't wearing her seat belt. When the car hit she was thrown forward, very hard." Jack nodded. Sally liked to play with her seat belt buckle—*we thought it was cute,* Ryan reminded himself bitterly. "Okay, tib and fib are broken in both legs, along with the left femur. All of the left-side ribs are broken, and six on the right side—a classic flailed chest. She can't breathe for herself, but she's on respirator; that is under control. She arrived with extensive internal injuries and hemorrhaging, severe damage to the liver and spleen, and the large bowel. Her heart stopped right after she got here, probably—almost certainly—from loss of blood volume. We got it restarted at once and immediately started replacing the blood loss." Shapiro went on quickly. "That problem is also behind us.

"Doctor Kinter and I have been working on her for the best part of five hours. We had to remove the spleen—that's okay, you can live without a spleen." Shapiro didn't say that the spleen was an important part of the body's defense against infections. "The liver had a moderately extensive stellate fracture and damage to the main artery that feeds blood into the organ. We had to remove about a quarter of the liver—again no problem with that—and I *think* we fixed the arterial damage, and I *think* the repair will hold. The liver is important. It has a great deal to do with blood formation and the body's biochemical balance. You can't live without it. If liver function is maintained . . . she'll probably make it. The damage to the bowel was easy to repair. We removed about thirty centimeters. The legs are immobilized. We'll repair them later. The ribs—well, that's painful but not life-threatening. And the skull is relatively minor. I guess her chest took the main impact. She has a concussion, but there's no sign of intercranial bleeding." Shapiro rubbed his hands over his heavily-bearded face.

"The whole thing revolves around her liver function. If the liver continues to work, she will probably recover fully. We're keeping a very close watch on her blood chemistry, and we'll know something in, oh, maybe eight or nine hours."

"Not till then?" Ryan's face twisted into an agonized mass. The fist tightened its grip yet again. *She still might die . . . ?*

"Mr. Ryan," Shapiro said slowly, "I know what you are going through. If it hadn't been for the helicopter bringing your little girl in, well, right now I'd be telling you that she had died. Another five minutes getting here—maybe not that long—and she would not have made it this far. That's how close it was. But she *is* alive now, and I promise you that we're doing our very best to keep her that way. And our best is the best there is. My team of doctors and nurses is the best of its kind in the world—period. Nobody comes close. If there's a way, we'll find it." *And if there's not,* he didn't say, *we won't.*

"Can I see them?"

"No." Shapiro shook his head. "Right now both of them are in the CCRU—the Critical Care Recovery Unit. We keep that as clean as an OR. The smallest infection can be lethal for a trauma patient. I'm sorry, but it would be too dangerous to them. My people are watching them constantly. A nurse—an experienced trauma nurse—is with each of them every second, with a team of doctors and nurses thirty feet away."

"Okay." He almost gasped the word. Ryan leaned his head back against the wall and closed his eyes. *Eight more hours? But you have no choice. You have to wait. You have to do what they say.* "Okay."

Shapiro left and Jackson followed after him, catching him by the elevator.

"Doc, can't Jack see his little girl? She—"

"Not a chance." Shapiro half fell against the wall and let out a long breath. "Look, right now the little girl—what's her name anyway?"

"Sally."

"Okay, right now she's in a bed, stark naked, with IV tubes running into both arms and one leg. Her head's partially shaved. She's wired up to a half-dozen monitors, and we have an Engstrom respirator breathing for her. Her legs are wrapped—all you can see of her is one big bruise from her hips to the top of her head." Shapiro looked down at the pilot. He was too tired to show any emotion. "Look, she might die. I don't think so, but there's no way we can be sure. With liver injuries, you can't tell until the blood-chemistry readings come in, you just can't. If she does die, would you want your friend to see her like that? Would you want him to remember her like that, for the rest of his life?"

"I guess not," Jackson said quietly, surprised at how much he wanted this little girl to live. His wife could not have children, and somehow Sally had become like their own. "What are her chances?"

"I'm not a bookie, I don't quote odds. Numbers don't mean a thing in a case like this. Sorry, but either she makes it or she doesn't. Look, that wasn't a song and dance I gave—Jack, you said? She could not be in a better place." Shapiro's eyes focused on Jackson's chest. He jabbed a finger at the wings of gold. "You a pilot?"

"Yeah. Fighters."

"Phantoms?"

"No, the F-14. Tomcat."

"I fly." Shapiro smiled. "I used to be a flight surgeon in the Air Force. Last year I got a sailplane. Nice and peaceful up there. When I can get away from this madhouse, I go up every time I can. No phones. No hassles. Just me and the clouds." The doctor was not talking to Jackson so much as himself. Robby set his hand on the surgeon's arm.

"Doc, tell you what—you save that little girl, and I'll get you a checkride in any bird you want. Ever been up in a T-38?"

"What's that?" Shapiro was too tired to remember that he'd seen them before.

"A spiffy little supersonic trainer. Two seats, dual controls, and she handles like a wet dream. I can disguise you as one of ours and get you up, no sweat. Ever been past mach-1?"

"No. Can you do some aerobatics?" Shapiro smiled like a tired little boy.

"Sure, Doc." Jackson grinned, knowing that he could do maneuvers to make a quail lose its lunch.

"I'll take you up on that. We work the same way with every patient, but I'll take you up on that anyway. Keep an eye on your friend. He looks a little rocky. That's normal. This sort of thing can be harder on the family than it is on the victims. If he doesn't come around some, tell the receptionist. We have a staff psychiatrist who specializes in working with—the *other* victims, he calls 'em." Yet another new idea at Shock-Trauma was a specialist in helping people cope with the injuries to family and friends.

"Cathy's arm. She's an eye surgeon, lots of fine work, you know? You sure there's no problem with that?"

Shapiro shook his head. "No big deal. It was a clean break to the humerus. Must have been a jacketed slug. The bullet went in clean, went out clean. Pretty lucky, really."

Robby's hand clamped shut on the doctor's arm as the elevator arrived. *"Bullet?"*

"Didn't I say that? God, I must be tireder than I thought. Yeah, it was a gunshot wound, but very clean. Hell, I wish they were all that clean. A nine-millimeter, maybe a thirty-eight, 'bout that size. I have to get back to work." The doctor went into the elevator.

"Shit," Jackson said to the wall. He turned when he heard a man with an English accent—two of them, it turned out—whom the receptionist directed to the waiting room. Robby followed them in.

The taller one approached Ryan and said, "Sir John?"

Ryan looked up. *Sir John?* Robby thought. The Brit drew himself to attention and went on briskly.

"My name is Geoffrey Bennett. I am Chargé d'Affaires at the British Embassy." He produced an envelope from his pocket and handed it to Ryan. "I am directed by Her Majesty to deliver this personally into your hand and to await your reply."

Jack blinked his eyes a few times, then tore open the envelope and extracted a yellow message form. The cable was brief, kind, and to the point. *What time is it over there?* Ryan wondered. *Two in the morning? Three? Something like that.* That meant that she'd been awakened with the news, probably, and cared enough to send a personal message. And was waiting for a reply.

How about that.

Ryan closed his eyes and told himself that it was time to return to the world of the living. Too drained for the tears he needed to shed, he swallowed a few times and rubbed his hands across his face before standing.

"Please tell Her Majesty that I am most grateful for her concern. My wife is expected to recover fully, but my daughter is in critical condition and we will have no definitive word on her for another eight or nine hours. Please tell Her Majesty that . . . that I am deeply touched by her concern, and that all of us value her friendship very highly indeed."

"Thank you, Sir John." Bennett made some notes. "I will cable your reply immediately. If you have no objection, I will leave a member of the embassy staff here with you." Jack nodded, puzzled, as Bennett made his exit.

Robby took all this in with a raised eyebrow and a dozen unasked questions. *Who was this guy?* He introduced himself as Edward Wayson, and took a seat in the corner facing the doorway. He looked over at Jackson. Their eyes met briefly and each man evaluated the other. Wayson had cool, detached eyes, and a wispy smile at the corners of his mouth. Robby gave him a closer look. There was a slight bulge under his left arm. Wayson affected to read a paperback novel, which he held in his left hand, but his eyes kept flickering to the door every few seconds, and his right hand stayed free in his lap. He caught Jackson's glance and nodded. So, Robby concluded, a spook, or at least a security officer. *So that's what this is all about.* The realization came as a blast of cold air. The pilot's hands flexed as he considered the type of person who would deliberately attempt to murder a woman and her child.

Five minutes later three State Police officers made their belated arrival. They talked to Ryan for ten minutes. Jackson watched with interest and saw his friend's face go pale with anger as he stammered answers to numerous questions. Wayson didn't look but heard it all.

"You were right, Jimmy," Murray said. He was standing at the window, watching the early morning traffic negotiate the corner of Broadway and Victoria.

"Paddy O'Neil in Boston likes to say what wonderful chaps Sinn Fein are," Owens said speculatively. "And our friend O' Donnell decides to embarrass them. We could not have known, Dan. A possibility of a suspicion is not evidence and you know it. There was no basis in fact for giving them a more serious warning than what you did. And you *did* warn them, Dan."

"She's a pretty little girl. Gave me a hug and a kiss before they flew home." Murray looked at his watch again and subtracted five hours. "Jimmy, there are times . . . Fifteen years ago we arrested this—this person who went after kids, little boys. I interrogated him. Sang like a canary, he couldn't be happier with himself. He copped to six cases, gave me all the details with a big shit-eatin' grin. It was right after the Supreme Court struck down all the death-penalty laws, so he knew that he'd live to a ripe old age. Do you know how close I came to—" He stopped for a moment before going on. "Sometimes we're too damned civilized."

"The alternative, Dan, is to become like them."

"I know that's true, Jimmy, but I just don't like it right now."

When Barry Shapiro next checked his watch it was five in the morning. *No wonder I feel so tired,* he thought. *Twenty hours on duty. I'm too old for this.* He was senior staff. He was supposed to know better.

The first sign was staying on duty too long, taking on too much personal responsibility, taking too keen an interest in patients who in the final analysis were nothing more or less than bruised and broken pieces of meat. Some of them died. No matter how great his skill, how refined his technique, how determined the efforts of his team, some would always die. And when you got this tired, you couldn't sleep. Their injuries—and worse, their faces—were too fresh in your memory, too haunting to go away. Doctors need sleep more than most men. Persistent loss of sleep was the last and most dangerous warning. That was when you had to leave—or risk a breakdown, as had happened all too often to the Shock-Trauma staffers.

It was their grimmest institutional joke: how their patients arrived with broken bodies and mostly went home whole—but the staff doctors and nurses who came in with the greatest energy and highest personal ideals would so often leave broken in spirit. It was the ultimate irony of his profession that success would engender the expectation of still greater success; that failure in this most demanding of medical disciplines could leave almost as much damage on the practitioner as the patient. Shapiro was cynic enough to see the humor of it.

The surgeon reread the print-out that the blood-analyzer unit had spat out a minute before, and handed it back to the nurse-practitioner. She attached it to the child's chart, then sat back down, stroking her dirty hair outside the oxygen mask.

"Her father is downstairs. Get relief here and go down and tell him. I'm going upstairs for a smoke." Shapiro left the CCRU and got his overcoat, fishing in his pockets for his cigarettes.

He wandered down the hall to the fire stairs, then climbed slowly up the six flights to the roof. *God,* he thought. *Dear God, I'm tired.* The roof was flat, covered with tar and gravel, spotted here and there with the UHF antennas for the center's SYSCOM communications net, and a few air-conditioning condensers. Shapiro lit a cigarette in the lee of the stairway tower, cursing himself for his inability to break the noxious habit. He rationalized that, unlike most of his colleagues, he never saw the degenerative effects of smoking. Most of his patients were too young for chronic diseases. Their injuries resulted from the miracles of a technical society: automobiles, motorcycles, firearms, and industrial machinery.

Shapiro walked to the edge of the roof, rested his foot on the parapet as though on a bar rail, and blew smoke into the early-morning air. It wafted away to appear and disappear as a gentle morning breeze carried it past the rooftop lights. The doctor stretched his tired arms and neck. The night's rain had washed the sky clean of its normal pollution, and he could see stars overhead in the pre-dawn darkness.

Shapiro's curious accent resulted from his background. His early childhood had been spent in the Williamsburg section of New York, the son of a rabbi who had taken his family to South Carolina. Barry had had good private schooling there, but emerged from it with a mixture of Southern drawl and New York quip. It was further damaged by a prairie twang acquired during his medical training at Baylor University in Texas. His father was a distinguished man of letters in his own right, a frequent lecturer at the University of South Carolina at Columbia. An expert in 19th-century American literature, Rabbi Shapiro's specialty was the work of Edgar Allan Poe. Barry Shapiro loathed Poe. A scribbler of death and perversity, the surgeon called him whenever the subject came up, and he'd been surprised to learn that Poe had died in Baltimore long before, after falling asleep, drunk, in a gutter; and that Poe's home was only a few blocks from the University Hospital complex, a demi-shrine for the local literati.

It seemed to the surgeon that everything about Poe was dark and twisted, always expecting the inevitability of death—violent, untimely death, Shapiro's own very personal enemy. He had come to think of Poe as the embodiment of that enemy, sometimes beaten, sometimes not. It was not something he talked about to the staff psychiatrist, who also kept a close eye on the hospital staff—but now, alone, he looked north to the Poe house.

"You son of a bitch," he whispered. To himself. To Poe. To no one. "*You son of a bitch!* Not this time—you don't get this one! This one goes home." He flicked the cigarette away and watched the point of orange light fall all the way to the shining, empty street. He turned back to the stairs. It was time to get some sleep.

16. Objectives and Patriots

Like most professional officers, Lieutenant Commander Robby Jackson had little use for the press. The irony of it was that Jack had tried many times to tell him that his outlook was wrong, that the press was as important to the preservation of American democracy as the Navy was. Now, as he watched, reporters were hounding his friend with questions that alternated between totally inane and intrusively personal. Why did everyone need to know how Jack felt about his daughter's condition? What would *any* normal person feel about having his child hovering near death—did they need such feelings explained? How was Jack supposed to know who'd done the shooting—if the police didn't know, how could he?

"And what's *your* name?" one finally asked Robby. He gave the woman his name and rank, but not his serial number.

"What are you doing here?" she persisted.

"We're friends. I drove him up here." *You dumbass.*

"And what do you think of all this?"

"What do you think I think? If that was your friend's little girl up there, what the hell would you think?" the pilot snapped back at her.

"Do you know who did it?"

"I fly airplanes for a living, I'm not a cop. Ask them."

"They're not talking."

Robby smiled thinly. "Well, score one for the good guys. Lady, why don't you leave that man alone? If you were going through what he is, do you think you would want a half-dozen strangers asking you these kind of questions? That's a human being over there, y'know? And he's my friend and I don't like what you people are doing to him."

"Look, Commander, we know that his wife and daughter were attacked by terrorists—"

"Says who?" Jackson demanded.

"Who else would it be? Do you think we're stupid?" Robby didn't answer that. "This is news—it's the first attack by a foreign terrorist group on American soil, if we're reading this right. That is important. The people have a right to know what happened and why," the reporter said reasonably.

She's right, Robby admitted reluctantly to himself. He didn't like it, but she was right. *Damn.*

"Would it make you feel any better to know that I do have a kid about that age? Mine's a boy," she said. The reporter actually seemed sympathetic.

Jackson searched for something to dislike about her. "Answer me this: if you have a chance to interview the people who did this, would you do it?"

"That's my job. We need to know where they're coming from."

"Where they're comin' from, lady, is they kill people for the fun of it. It's all part of their game." Robby remembered intelligence reports he'd seen while in the Eastern Med. "Back a couple of years ago—you never heard this from me, okay?"

"Off the record," she said solemnly.

"I was on a carrier off Beirut, okay? We had intelligence reports—and pictures—of people from Europe who flew in to do some killing. They were mainly kids, musta been from good families—I mean, from the way they dressed. No shit, this is for-real, I saw the friggin' pictures. They joined up with some of the crazies, got guns, and just started blasting away, at random, for the pure hell of it. They shot from those high-rise hotels and office buildings into the streets. With a rifle you can hit from a thousand yards away. Something moves—boom, they blast it with automatic weapons fire. Then they got to go home. They were killing people, for fun! Maybe some of them grew up to be real terrorists, I don't know. It was pretty sickening stuff, not the sort of thing you forget. That's the kind of people we're talking about here, okay?

"I don't give a good goddamn about their point of view, lady! When I was a little kid in Alabama, we had problems with people like that, those assholes in the Klan. I don't give a damn about their point of view, either. The only good thing about the Klan was they were idiots. The terrorists we got running around now are a lot more efficient. Maybe that makes them more legitimate in your eyes, but not mine."

"That thing in Beirut never made the papers," the reporter said.

"I know for a fact that one reporter saw it. Maybe he figured that nobody would believe it. I don't know that I would have without the photos. But I saw 'em. You got my word on that, lady."

"What kind of pictures?"

"That I can't say—but they were good enough to see their shiny young faces." The photos had been made by U.S. and Israeli reconnaissance aircraft.

"So what do you do about it?"

"If you could arrange to have all these bastards in one place, I think we and the Marines could figure something out," Robby replied, voicing a wish common to professional soldiers throughout the world. "We might even invite you newsies to the wake. Who the hell is that?" Two new people came into the room.

Jack was too tired to be fully coherent. The news that Sally was out of immediate danger had been like a giant weight leaving his shoulders, and he was waiting for the chance to see his wife, who would soon be moved to a regular hospital floor. A few feet away, Wayson, the British security officer, watched with unconcealed contempt, refusing even to give his name to the reporters who asked. The State Police officers were unable to keep the press away, though hospital personnel flatly refused to let the TV equipment in the front door, and were able to make that stick. The question that kept repeating was, Who did it? Jack said he didn't know, though he thought he did. It was probably the people he'd decided not to worry about.

It could have been worse, he told himself. At least it was now probable that Sally would be alive at the end of the week. His daughter was not dead because of his misjudgment. That was some consolation.

"Mr. Ryan?" one of the new visitors asked.

"Yeah?" Jack was too exhausted to look up. He was awake only because of adrenaline now. His nerves were too ragged to allow him sleep, much as he needed it.

"I'm Special Agent Ed Donoho, Boston Field Office of the FBI. I have somebody who wants to say something to you."

Nobody ever said that Paddy O'Neil was stupid, Donoho thought. As soon as the report had made the Eleven O'Clock News, the man from Sinn Fein had asked his

FBI "escort" if he might fly down to Baltimore. Donoho was in no position to deny him the right, and had been co-opted into bringing the man himself on the first available plane into BWI.

"Mr. Ryan," O'Neil said with a voice that dripped sympathy, "I understand that the condition of your child has been upgraded. I hope that my prayers had something to do with it, and . . ."

It took Ryan over ten seconds to recognize the face that he'd seen a few days before on TV. His mouth slowly dropped open as his eyes widened. For some reason he didn't hear what the man was saying. The words came through his ears, but, as though they were in some unknown tongue, his brain did not assemble them into speech. All he saw was the man's throat, five feet away. *Just about five feet,* was what his brain told him.

"Uh-oh," Robby said on the other side of the room. He stood as his friend went beet-red. Two seconds later, Ryan's face was as pale as the collar on his white cotton shirt. Jack's feet shifted, sliding straight beneath his body as he leaned forward on the couch.

Robby pushed past the FBI agent as Ryan launched himself from the couch, hands stretching out for O'Neil's neck. Jackson's shoulder caught his friend's chest, and the pilot wrapped Jack up in a bear hug, trying to push him backward as three photographers recorded the scene. Jack didn't make a sound, but Robby knew exactly what he wanted to do. Jackson had leverage going for him, and pushed Ryan back, hurling him onto the couch. He turned quickly.

"Get that asshole outa here before *I* kill him!" Jackson was four inches shorter than the Irishman, but his rage was scarcely less than Ryan's. "Get that terrorist bastard out of here!"

"Officer!" Special Agent Donoho pointed to a state trooper, who grabbed O'Neil and dragged him from the room in an instant. For some reason the reporters followed as O'Neil loudly protested his innocence.

"Are you out of your fucking mind!" Jackson snarled at the FBI agent.

"Cool down, Commander. I'm on your side, okay? Cool it down some."

Jackson sat down beside Ryan, who was breathing like a horse at the end of a race while he stared at the floor. Donoho sat down on the other side.

"Mr. Ryan, I couldn't keep him from coming down. I'm sorry, but we can't do that. He wanted to tell you—shit, all the way down on the plane, he told me that his outfit had nothing to do with this; that it would be a disaster for them. He wanted to extend his sympathy, I guess." The agent hated himself for saying that, even though it was true enough. He hated himself even more because he'd almost started to like Paddy O'Neil over the past week. The front man for Sinn Fein was a person of considerable charm, a man with a gift for presenting his point of view in a reasonable way. Ed Donoho asked himself why he'd been assigned to this job. *Why couldn't they have picked an Italian?* He knew the answer to that, of course, but just because there was a reason didn't mean that he had to like it. "I'll make sure he doesn't bother you anymore."

"You do that," Robby said.

Donoho went back into the hall, and unsurprisingly found O'Neil giving his spiel to the reporters. *Mr. Ryan is distraught,* he was saying, *as any family man would be in similar circumstances.* His first exposure to the man the previous week had given him a feeling of distaste. Then he'd started to admire his skill and charm. Now Donoho's reaction to the man's words was one of loathing. An idea blinked on in his head. He wondered if the Bureau would approve and decided it was worth the risk. First the agent grabbed a state trooper by the arm and made sure that the man wouldn't get close to Ryan again. Next he got hold of a photographer and talked to him briefly. Together they found a doctor.

"No, absolutely not," the surgeon replied to the initial request.

"Hey, Doc," the photojournalist said. "My wife's pregnant with our first. If it'll help this guy, I'm for it. This one doesn't make the papers. You got my word, Doc."

"I think it'll help," the FBI agent said. "I really do."

Ten minutes later Donoho and the photographer stripped off their scrub clothing. The FBI agent took the film cassette and tucked it in his pocket. Before he took O'Neil back to the airport, he made a call to headquarters in Washington, and two agents drove out to Ryan's home on Peregrine Cliff. They didn't have any problem with the alarm system.

Jack had been awake for more than twenty-four hours now. If he'd been able to think about it, he would have marveled at the fact that he was awake and functional, though the latter observation would have been a matter of dispute to anyone who saw him walking. He was alone now. Robby was off attending to something that he couldn't remember.

He would have been alone in any case. Twenty minutes earlier, Cathy had been moved into the main University Hospital complex, and Jack had to go see her. He walked like a man facing execution down a drab corridor of glazed institutional brick. He turned a corner and saw what room it had to be. A pair of state troopers was standing there. They watched him approach, and Jack watched their eyes for a sign that they knew all of this was his fault, that his wife and daughter had nearly died because he'd decided that there was nothing to worry about. Not once in his life had Jack experienced failure, and its bitter taste made him think that the whole world would hold him in the same contempt he felt for himself.

You're so fucking smart.

It seemed to his senses that he did not so much approach the door—it approached him, looming ever larger in his sight. Behind the door was the woman he loved. The woman who had nearly died because of his confidence in himself. What would she say to him? Did he dare to find out? Jack stood at the door for a moment. The troopers tried not to stare at him. Perhaps they felt sympathy, Jack thought, knowing that he didn't deserve it. The doorknob was cold, accusing metal in his hand as he entered the room.

Cathy was lying in her single-bed room. Her arm was in a cast. An enormous purple bruise covered the right side of her face and there was a bandage over half her forehead. Her eyes were open but almost lifeless, staring at a television that wasn't on. Jack moved toward her as though asleep. A nurse had set a chair alongside the bed. He sat in it, and took his wife's hand while he tried to think of something he could say to the wife he had failed. Her face turned toward his. Her eyes were blackened and full of tears.

"I'm sorry, Jack," she whispered.

"What?"

"I knew she was fooling with the seat belt, but I didn't do anything because I was in a hurry—and then that truck came, and I didn't have time to—if I had made sure she was strapped in, Sally would be fine . . . but I was in a hurry," she finished, and looked away. "Jack, I'm so sorry."

My God, she thinks it's her *fault . . . what do I say now?*

"She's going to be okay, babe," Ryan managed to say, stunned at what he'd just heard. He held Cathy's hand to his face and kissed it. "And so are you. That's the only thing that matters now."

"But—" She stared at the far wall.

"No 'buts.' "

Her face turned back. Cathy tried to smile but tears were rolling from her eyes. "I talked to Doctor Ellingstone at Hopkins—he came over and saw Sally. He says—he says she'll be okay. He says that Shapiro saved her life."

"I know."

"I haven't even seen her—I remember seeing the bridge and then I woke up two hours ago, and—*oh, Jack*!" Her hand closed on his like a claw. He leaned forward to kiss her, but before their lips touched, both started weeping.

"It's okay, Cathy," Jack said, and he started to believe that it really was, or at least that it would be so again. His world had not ended, not quite.

But someone else's will, Ryan told himself. The thought was a quiet, distant one, voiced in a part of his mind that was already looking at the future while the present occupied his sight. Seeing his wife weeping tears caused by someone else started a cold rage in him which only that someone's death could ever warm.

The time for grief was already ending, carried away by his own tears. Though it had not yet happened, Ryan's intellect was already beginning to think of the time when his emotions would be at rest—most of them. One would remain. He would control it, but it would also control him. He would not feel like a whole man again until he was purged of it.

One can only weep for so long; it is as though each tear carries a finite amount of emotion away with it. Cathy stopped first. She used her hand to wipe her husband's face. She managed a real smile now. Jack hadn't shaved. It was like rubbing sandpaper.

"What time is it?"

"Ten-thirty." Jack didn't have to check his watch.

"You need sleep, Jack," she said. "You have to stay healthy, too."

"Yeah." Jack rubbed his eyes.

"Hi, Cathy," Robby said as he came through the door. "I've come to take him away from you."

"Good."

"We're checked into the Holiday Inn over on Lombard Street."

"We? Robby, you don't—"

"Stuff it, Jack," Robby said. "How are you, Cathy?"

"I have a headache you wouldn't believe."

"Good to see you smile," Robby said softly. "Sissy'll be up after lunch. Is there anything she can get for you?"

"Not right now. Thanks, Rob."

"Hang in there, Doc." Robby took Jack's arm and hauled him to his feet. "I'll have him back to you later today."

Twenty minutes later Robby led Jack into their motel room. He pulled a pill container from his pocket. "The doc said you should take one of these."

"I don't take pills."

"You're taking one of these, sport. It's a nice yellow one. That's not a request, Jack, it's an order. You need sleep. Here." Robby tossed them over and stared until Jack swallowed one. Ryan was asleep in ten minutes. Jackson made certain that the door was secured before settling down on the other bed. The pilot dreamed of seeing the people who had done all this. They were in an airplane. Four times he fired a missile into their bird and watched their bodies spill out of the hole it made so that he could blast them with his cannon before they fell into the sea.

The Patriots Club was a bar across the street from Broadway Station in one of South Boston's Irish enclaves. Its name harkened not back to the revolutionaries of the 1770s, but rather to the owner's image of himself. John Donoho had served in the First Marine Division on the bitter retreat from the Chosin Reservoir. Wounded twice, he'd never left his squad on the long, cold march to the port of Hungnam. He still walked with a slight limp from the four toes that frostbite had taken from his right foot. He was prouder of this than of his several decorations, framed under a Marine Corps standard behind the bar. Anyone who entered the bar in a Marine uniform always got his first drink free, along with a story or two about the Old Corps, which Corporal John Donoho, USMC (ret.), had served at the ripe age of eighteen.

He was also a professional Irishman. Every year he took an Aer Lingus flight from Boston's Logan International Airport to the old sod, to brush up on his roots and his accent, and sample the better varieties of whiskey that somehow were never exported to America in quantity. Donoho also tried to keep current on the happenings in the North, "the Six Counties," as he called them, to maintain his spiritual connection with the rebels who labored courageously to free their people from the British yoke. Many a dollar had been raised in his bar, to aid those in the North, many a glass raised to their health and to the Cause.

"Hello, Johnny!" Paddy O'Neil called from the door.

"And good evening to you, Paddy!" Donoho was already drawing a beer when he saw his nephew follow O'Neil through the door. Eddie was his dead brother's only son, a good boy, educated at Notre Dame, where he'd played second string on the football team before joining up with the FBI. It wasn't quite as good as being a Marine, but Uncle John knew that it paid a lot better. He'd heard that Eddie was following O'Neil around, but was vaguely sad to see that it was true. Perhaps it was to protect Paddy from a Brit assassin, the owner rationalized.

John and Paddy had a beer together before the latter joined a small group waiting for him in the back room. His nephew stayed alone at the end of the bar, where he drank a cup of coffee and kept an eye on things. After ten minutes O'Neil went back to give his talk. Donoho went to say hello to his nephew.

"Hi, Uncle John," Eddie greeted him.

"Have you set the date yet, now?" John asked, affecting an Irish accent, as he usually did when O'Neil was around.

"Maybe next September," the younger man allowed.

"And what would your father say, you living with the girl for almost a year? And the good fathers at Notre Dame?"

"Probably the same thing they'd say to you for raising money for terrorists," the young agent replied. Eddie was sick and tired of being told how to live his life.

"I don't want to hear any of that in my place." He'd heard that line before, too.

"That's what O'Neil does, Uncle John."

"They're freedom fighters. I know they bend some of our laws from time to time, but the English laws they break are no concern of mine—or yours," John Donoho said firmly.

"You watch TV?" The agent didn't need an answer to that. A wide-screen TV in the opposite corner was used for baseball and football games. The bar's name had also made it an occasional watering hole for the New England Patriots football players. Uncle John's interest in TV was limited to the Patriots, Red Sox, Celtics, and Bruins. His interest in politics was virtually nil. He voted for Teddy Kennedy every six years and considered himself a staunch proponent of national defense. "I want to show you a couple of pictures."

He set the first one on the bar. "This is a little girl named Sally Ryan. She lives in Annapolis."

His uncle picked it up and smiled. "I remember when my Kathleen looked like that."

"Her father is a teacher at the Naval Academy, used to be a Marine lieutenant. He went to Boston College. His father was a cop."

"Sounds like a good Irishman. Friend of yours?"

"Not exactly," Eddie said. "Paddy and I met him earlier today. This is what his daughter looked like then." The second photo was laid on the bar.

"Jesus, Mary, and Joseph." It wasn't easy to discern that there was a child under all the medical equipment. Her feet stuck out from heavy wrappings. An inch-wide plastic pipe was in her mouth, and what parts of her body were visible formed a horribly discolored mass that the photographer had recorded with remarkable skill.

"She's the lucky one, Uncle John. The girl's mother was there, too." Two more photos went onto the bar.

"What happened, car accident—what are you showing me?" John Donoho asked. He really didn't know what this was all about.

"She's a surgeon—she's pregnant, too, the pictures don't show that. Her car was machine-gunned yesterday, right outside of Annapolis, Maryland. They killed a State Police officer a few minutes later." Another picture went down.

"What? Who did it?" the older man asked.

"Here's the father, Jack Ryan." It was the same picture that the London papers had used, Jack's graduation shot from Quantico. Eddie knew that his uncle always looked at Marine dress blues with pride.

"I've seen him before somewhere . . ."

"Yeah. He stopped a terrorist attack over in London a few months back. It looks like he offended the terrorists enough that they came after him and his family. The Bureau is working on that."

"Who did it?"

The last photo went down on the bar. It showed Ryan's hands less than a foot from Paddy O'Neil, and a black man holding him back.

"Who's the jig?" John asked. His nephew almost lost his temper.

"Goddammit, Uncle John! That *man* is a Navy fighter pilot."

"Oh." John was briefly embarrassed. He had little use for blacks, though one who wore a Marine uniform into his bar got his first drink free, too. It was different with the ones in uniform, he told himself. Anyone who served the flag as he had done was okay in his book, John Donoho always said. *Some of my best friends in the Corps. . . .* He remembered how Navy strike aircraft had supported his outfit all the way back to the sea, holding the Chinese back with rockets and napalm. Well, maybe this one was different, too. He stared at the rest of the picture for a few seconds. "So, you say Paddy had something to do with this?"

"I've been telling you for years who the bastard fronts for. If you don't believe me, maybe you want to ask Mr. Ryan here. It's bad enough that O'Neil spits on our whole country every time he comes over here. His friends damned near killed this whole family yesterday. We got one of 'em. Two Marine guards at the Naval

Academy grabbed him, waiting to shoot Ryan. His name's Eamon Clark, and we know that he used to work for the Provisional Wing of the IRA—we *know* it, Uncle John, he's a convicted murderer. They caught him with a loaded pistol in his pocket. You still think they're good guys? Dammit, they're going after Americans now! If you don't believe me, believe this!'' Eddie Donoho rearranged the photos on the wooden surface. ''This little girl, and her mother, and a kid not even born yet almost died yesterday. This state trooper did. He left a wife and a kid behind. That friend of yours in the back room raises the money to buy the guns, he's connected with the people who did this.''

''But why?''

''Like I said, this girl's dad got in the way of a murder over in London. I guess the people he stopped wanted to get even with him—not just him, though, they went for his whole family,'' the agent explained slowly.

''The little girl didn't—''

''Goddammit,'' Eddie swore again. ''That's why they're called terrorists!'' It was getting through. He could see that he was finally getting the message across.

''You're sure that Paddy is part of this?'' his uncle asked.

''He's never lifted a gun that we know of. He's their mouthpiece, he comes over here and raises money so that they can do things like this at home. Oh, he never gets his hands bloody. He's too smart for that. But this is what the money goes for. We are absolutely sure of that. And now they're playing their games over here.'' Agent Donoho knew that the money-raising was secondary to the psychological reasons for coming over, but now wasn't the time to clutter the issue with details. He watched his uncle stare at the photos of the little girl. His face showed the confusion that always accompanies a completely new thought.

''You're sure? Really sure?''

''Uncle John, we have over thirty agents on the case now, plus the local police. You bet we're sure. We'll get 'em, too. The Director's put the word out on this case. We want 'em. Whatever it takes, we'll get these bastards,'' Edward Michael Donoho, Jr., said with cold determination.

John Donoho looked at his nephew, and for the first time he saw a man. Eddie's FBI post was a source of family pride, but John finally knew why this was so. He wasn't a kid anymore. He was a man with a job about which he was deadly serious. More than the photographs, it was this that decided things. John had to believe what he'd been told.

The owner of the Patriots Club stood up straight and walked down the bar to the folding gate. He lifted it and made for the back room, with his nephew trailing behind.

''But our boys are fighting back,'' O'Neil was telling the fifteen men in the room. ''Every day they fight back to—joining us, Johnny?''

''Out,'' Donoho said quietly.

''What—I don't understand, John,'' O'Neil said, genuinely puzzled.

''You must think I'm pretty stupid. I guess maybe I was. Leave.'' The voice was more forceful now, and the feigned accent was gone. ''Get out of my club and don't ever come back.''

''But, Johnny—what are you talking about?''

Donoho grabbed the man by his collar and lifted him off his chair. O'Neil's voice continued to protest as he was propelled all the way out the front door. Eddie Donoho waved to his uncle as he followed his charge out onto the street.

''What was that all about?'' one of the men from the back room asked. Another of them, a reporter for the *Boston Globe,* started making notes as the bar owner stumbled through what he had finally learned.

To this point no police agency had implicated any terrorist group by name, and in fact neither had Special Agent Donoho done so. His instructions from Washington on that score had been carefully given and carefully followed. But in the translation through Uncle John and a reporter, the facts got slightly garbled—as surprised no one—and within hours the story was on the AP wire that the attack on Jack Ryan and his family had been made by the Provisional Wing of the Irish Republican Army.

Sean Miller's mission in America had been fully accomplished by an agency of the United States government.

Miller and his party were already back home. As many people in this line of work had done before, Sean reflected on the value of rapid international air travel. In this case it had been off to Mexico from Washington's Dulles International, from there to the Netherlands Antilles, to Schiphol International Airport on a KLM flight, and then to Ireland. All one needed were correct travel documents and a little money. The travel documents in question were already destroyed, and the money untraceable cash. He sat across from Kevin O'Donnell's desk, drinking water to compensate for the dehydration normal to flying.

''What about Eamon?'' One rule of ULA operations was that no overseas telephone calls ever came to his house.

''Alex's man says he was picked up.'' Miller shrugged. ''It was a risk I felt worth taking. I selected Ned for it because he knows very little about us.'' He knew that O'Donnell had to agree with that. Clark was one of the new men brought into the Organization, and more of an accident than a recruit. He'd come south because one of his friends from the H-blocks had come. O'Donnell had thought him of possible use, since they had no experienced work-alone assassins. But Clark was stupid. His motivations came from emotion rather than ideology. He was, in fact, a typical PIRA thug, little different from those in the UVF for that matter, useful in the same sense that a trained dog was useful, Kevin told himself. He knew but a few names and faces within the Organization. Most damning of all, he had failed. Clark's one redeeming characteristic was his doglike loyalty. He hadn't broken in Long Kesh prison and he probably wouldn't break now. He lacked the imagination.

''Very well,'' Kevin O'Donnell said after a moment's reflection. Clark would be remembered as a martyr, gaining greater respect in failure than he had managed to earn in success. ''The rest?''

''Perfect. I saw the wife and child die, and Alex's people got us away cleanly.'' Miller smiled and poured some whiskey to follow his liter of ice water.

''They're not dead, Sean,'' O'Donnell said.

''What?'' Miller had been on an airplane less than three hours after the shooting, and hadn't seen or heard a snippet of news since. He listened to his boss's explanation in incredulous silence.

''But it doesn't matter,'' O'Donnell concluded. He explained that, too. The AP story that had originated in the *Boston Globe* had been picked up by the *Irish Times* of Dublin. ''It was a good plan after all, Sean. Despite everything that went wrong, the mission is accomplished.''

Sean didn't allow himself to react. Two operations in a row had gone wrong for him. Before the fiasco in London, he'd never failed at all. He'd written that off to random chance, pure luck, nothing more. He didn't even think of that in this case.

Two in a row, that wasn't luck. He knew that Kevin would not tolerate a third failure. The young operations officer took a deep breath and told himself to be objective. He'd allowed himself to think of Ryan as a personal target, not a political one. That had been his first mistake. Though Kevin hadn't said it, losing Ned had been a serious mistake. Miller reviewed his plan, rethinking every aspect of the operation. Just going after the wife and child would have been simple thuggery, and he'd never approved of that; it was not professional. Just going after Ryan himself, however, would not have carried the same political impact, which was the whole point of the operation. The rest of the family was—had been necessary. So his objectives had been sound enough, but . . .

"I should have taken more time on this one," he said finally. "I tried to be too dramatic. Perhaps we should have waited."

"Yes," his boss agreed, pleased that Sean saw his errors.

"Any help we can give you," Owens said, "is yours. You know that, Dan."

"Yeah, well, this has attracted some high-level interest." Murray held a cable from Director Emil Jacobs himself. "Well, it was only a matter of time. It had to happen sooner or later." *And if we don't bag these sons of bitches,* he thought, *it'll happen again. The ULA just proved that terrorists could operate in the U.S.* The emotional shock of the event had come as a surprise to Murray. As a professional in the field, he knew that it was mere luck that it hadn't happened already. The inept domestic terrorist groups had set off some bombs and murdered a few people, but the Bureau had experienced considerable success running them to ground. None of them had ever gotten much in the way of foreign support. But that had changed, too. The helicopter pilot had identified one of the escaping terrorists as black, and there weren't many of them in Ireland.

It was a new ball game, and for all his experience in the FBI, Murray was worried about how well the Bureau would be able to handle it. Director Jacobs was right on one thing: this was a top-priority mission. Bill Shaw would run the case personally, and Murray knew him to be one of the best intellects in the business. The thirty agents initially assigned to the case would treble in the next few days, then treble again. The only way to keep this from happening again was to demonstrate that America was too dangerous a place for terrorists. In his heart, Murray knew that this was impossible. No place was too dangerous, certainly no democracy.

But the Bureau did have formidable resources, and it wouldn't be the only agency involved.

17. Recriminations and Decisions

Ryan awoke to find Robby waving a cup of coffee under his nose. Jack had managed to sleep without dreams this time, and the oblivion of undisturbed slumber had worked wonders on him.

"Sissy was over the hospital earlier. She says Cathy looks all right, considering. It's all set up so you can get in to see Sally. She'll be asleep, but you can see her."

"Where is she?"

"Sissy? She's out runnin' some errands."

"I need a shave."

"Me, too. She's getting what we need. First I'm gonna get some food in ya'," Robby said.

"I owe you, man," Jack said as he stood.

"Give it a rest, Jack. That's what the Lord put us here for, like my pappy says. Now, eat!" Robby commanded.

Jack realized that he'd not eaten anything for a long time, and once his stomach reminded itself of this, it cried out for nourishment. Within five minutes he'd disposed of two eggs, bacon, hash-browns, four slices of toast, and two cups of coffee.

"Shame they don't have grits here," Robby observed. A knock came to the door. The pilot answered it. Sissy breezed in with a shopping bag in one hand and Jack's briefcase in the other.

"You better freshen up, Jack," she said. "Cathy looks better than you do."

"Nothing unusual about that," Jack replied—cheerfully, he realized with surprise. Sissy had baited him into it.

"Robby?"

"Yeah?"

"What the hell are grits?"

"You don't want to know," Cecilia Jackson answered.

"I'll take your word for it." Jack walked into the bathroom and started the shower. By the time he got out, Robby had shaved, leaving the razor and cream on the sink. Jack scraped his beard away and patched the bloody spots with toilet paper. A new toothbrush was sitting there too, and Ryan emerged from the room looking and feeling like a human being.

"Thanks, guys," he said.

"I'll take you home tonight," Robby said. "I have to teach class tomorrow. You don't. I fixed it with the department."

"Okay."

Sissy left for home. Jack and Robby walked over to the hospital. Visiting hours were under way and they were able to walk right up to Cathy's room.

"Well, if it isn't our hero!" Joe Muller was Cathy's father. He was a short, swarthy man—Cathy's hair and complexion came from her mother, now dead. A senior VP with Merrill Lynch, he was a product of the Ivy League, and had started in the brokerage business much as Ryan had, though his brief stint in the military had been two years of drafted service in the Army that he'd long since put behind him. He'd once had big plans for Jack and had never forgiven him for leaving the business. Muller was a passionate man who was also well aware of his importance in the financial community. He and Jack hadn't exchanged a civil word in over three years. It didn't look to Jack as though that was going to change.

"Daddy," Cathy said, "we don't need that."

"Hi, Joe." Ryan held out his hand. It hung there for five seconds, all by itself. Robby excused himself out the door, and Jack went to kiss his wife. "Lookin' better, babe."

"What do you have to say for yourself?" Muller demanded.

"The guy who wanted to kill me was arrested yesterday. The FBI has him,"

Jack said carefully. He amazed himself by saying it so calmly. Somehow it seemed a trivial matter compared with his wife and daughter.

"This is all your fault, you know." Muller had been rehearsing this for hours.

"I know," Jack conceded the point. He wondered how much more he could back up.

"Daddy—" Cathy started to say.

"You keep out of this," Muller said to his daughter, a little too sharply for Jack.

"You can say anything you want to me, but don't snap at her," he warned.

"Oh, you want to protect her, eh? So where the hell were you yesterday!"

"I was in my office, just like you were."

"You had to stick your nose in where it didn't belong, didn't you? You had to play hero—and you damned near got your family killed," Muller went on through his lines.

"Look, Mr. Muller." Jack had told himself all these things before. He could accept the punishment from himself. But not from his father-in-law. "Unless you know of a company on the exchange that makes a time machine, we can't very well change that, can we? All we can do now is help the authorities find the people who did this."

"Why didn't you think about all this before, dammit!"

"Daddy, that's enough!" Cathy rejoined the conversation.

"Shut up—this is between us!"

"If you yell at her again, mister, you'll regret it." Jack needed a release. He hadn't protected his family the previous day, but he could now.

"Calm down, Jack." His wife didn't know that she was making things worse, but Jack took the cue after a moment. Muller didn't.

"You're a real big guy now, aren't you?"

Keep going, Joe, and you might find out. Jack looked over to his wife and took a deep breath. "Look, if you came down here to yell at me, that's fine, we can do that by ourselves, okay?—but that's your daughter over there, and maybe she needs you, too." He turned to Cathy. "I'll be outside if you need me."

Ryan left the room. There were still two very serious state troopers at the door, and another at the nurses' station down the hall. Jack reminded himself that a trooper had been killed, and that Cathy was the only thing they had that was close to being a witness. She was safe, finally. Robby waved to his friend from down the hall.

"Settle down, boy," the pilot suggested.

"He has a real talent for pissing me off," Jack said after another deep breath.

"I know he's an asshole, but he almost lost his kid. Try to remember that. Taking it out on him doesn't help things."

"It might," Jack said with a smile, thinking about it. "What are you, a philosopher?"

"I'm a PK, Jack. Preacher's Kid. You can't imagine the stuff I used to hear from the parlor when people came over to talk with the old man. He isn't so much mad at you as scared by what almost happened," Robby said.

"So am I, pal." Ryan looked down the hall.

"But you've had more time to deal with it."

"Yeah." Jack was quiet for a moment. "I still don't like the son of a bitch."

"He gave you Cathy, man. That's something."

"Are you sure you're in the right line of work? How come you're not a chaplain?"

"I am the voice of reason in a chaotic world. You don't accomplish as much when you're pissed off. That's why we train people to be professionals. If you want to get the job done, emotions don't help. You've already gotten even with the man, right?''

''Yeah. If he'd had his way, I'd be living up in Westchester County, taking the train in every day, and—crap!'' Jack shook his head. ''He still makes me mad.''

Muller came out of the room just then. He looked around for a moment, spotted Jack, and walked down. ''Stay close,'' Ryan told his friend.

''You almost killed my little girl.'' Joe's mood hadn't improved.

Jack didn't reply. He'd told himself that about a hundred times, and was just starting to consider the possibility that he was a victim, too.

''You ain't thinking right, Mr. Muller,'' Robby said.

''Who the hell are you!''

''A friend,'' Robby replied. He and Joe were about the same height, but the pilot was twenty years younger. The look he gave the broker communicated this rather clearly. The voice of reason didn't like being yelled at. Joe Muller had a talent for irritating people. On Wall Street he could get away with it, and he assumed that meant that he could do it anywhere he liked. He was a man who had not learned the limitations of his power.

''We can't change what has happened,'' Jack offered. ''We can work to see that it doesn't happen again.''

''If you'd done what I wanted, this never would have happened!''

''If I'd done what *you* wanted, I'd be working with you every day, moving money from Column A to Column B and pretending it was important, like all the other Wall Street wimps—and hating it, and turning into another miserable bastard in the financial world. I proved that I could do that as well as you, but I made my pile, and so now I do something I like. At least we're trying to make the world a better place instead of trying to take it over with leveraged buyouts. It's not my fault that you don't understand that. Cathy and I are doing what we like to do.''

''Something you *like,*'' Muller snapped, rejecting the concept that making money wasn't something to be enjoyed in and of itself. ''Make the world a better place, eh?''

''Yeah, because I'm going to help catch the bastards who did this.''

''And how is a punk history teacher going to do that!''

Ryan gave his father-in-law his best smile. ''That's something I can't tell you, Joe.''

The stockbroker swore and stalked away. *So much for reconciliation,* Jack told himself. He wished it had gone otherwise. His estrangement with Joe Muller was occasionally hard on Cathy.

''Back to the Agency, Jack?'' Robby asked.

''Yeah.''

Ryan spent twenty minutes with his wife, long enough to learn what she'd told the police and to make sure that she really was feeling better. She was dozing off when he left. Next he went across the street to the Shock-Trauma Center.

Getting into scrubs reminded him of the only other time he'd done so, the night Sally was born. A nurse took him into the Critical Care Recovery Unit, and he saw his little girl for the first time in thirty-six hours, a day and a half that had stretched into an eternity. It was a thoroughly ghastly experience. Had he not been told positively that her survival chances were good, he might have broken down on the spot. The bruised little shape was unconscious from the combination of drugs and injuries. He watched and listened as the respirator breathed for her. She was being fed from bottles and tubes that ran into her veins. A doctor explained that her condition looked far worse than it was. Sally's liver was functioning well, under the circumstances. In two or three more days the broken legs would be set.

"Is she going to be crippled?" Jack asked quietly.

"No, there isn't any reason to worry about that. Kids' bones—what we say is, if the broken pieces are in the same room, they'll heal. It looks far worse than it is. The trick with cases like this is getting them through the first hour—in her case, the first twelve or so. Once we get kids through the initial crisis, once we get the system working again, they heal fast. You'll have her home in a month. In two months, she'll be running around like it never happened. As crazy as that sounds, it's true. Nothing heals like a kid. She's a very sick little girl right now, but she's going to get well. Hey, I was here when she arrived."

"What's your name?"

"Rich Kinter. Barry Shapiro and I did most of the surgery. It was close—God, it was so close! But we won. Okay? We won. You will be taking her home."

"Thanks—that doesn't cover it, Doc." Jack stumbled over a few more words, not knowing what to say to the people who had saved his daughter's life.

Kinter shook his head. "Bring her back sometime and we're even. We have a party for ex-patients every few months. Mr. Ryan, there is nothing you can do that comes close to what we all feel when we see our little patients come back—walk back. That's why we're here, man, to make sure they come back for cake and juice. Just let us bounce her on our knees after she's better."

"Deal." Ryan wondered how many people were alive because of the people in this room. He was certain that this surgeon could be a rich man in private practice. Jack understood him, understood why he was here, and knew that his father-in-law wouldn't. He sat for a few minutes at Sally's side, listening to the machine breathe for her through the plastic tube. The nurse-practitioner overseeing the case smiled at him around her mask. He kissed Sally's bruised forehead before leaving. Jack felt better now, better about almost everything. But one item remained. The people who had done this to his little girl.

"It had wheelchair tags," the clerk in the 7-Eleven was saying, "but the dude who drove it didn't look crippled or anything."

"You remember what he looked like?" Special Agent Nick Capitano and a major from the Maryland State Police were interviewing the witness.

"Yeah, he was 'bout as black as me. Tall dude. He wore sunglasses, the mirror kind. Had a beard, too. There was always at least one other dude in the truck, but I never got a look at him—black man, that's all I can say."

"What did he wear?"

"Jeans and a brown leather jacket, I think. You know, like a construction worker."

"Shoes or boots?" the Major asked.

"Never did see that," the clerk said after a moment.

"How about jewelry, T-shirt with a pattern, anything special or different about him?"

"No, nothin' I remember."

"What did he do here?"

"He always bought a six-pack of Coke Classic. Once or twice he got some Twinkies, but he always got hisself the Cokes."

"What did he sound like? Anything special?"

The clerk shook her head. "Nah, just a dude, y'know?"

"Do you think you could recognize him again?" Capitano asked.

"Maybe—we get a lot of folks through here, lotta regulars, lotta strangers, y'know?"

"Would you mind looking through some pictures?" the agent went on.

"Gotta clear it with the boss. I mean, I need the job, but you say this chump tried to kill a little girl—yeah, sure, I'll help ya."

"We'll clear it with the boss," the Major assured her. "You won't lose pay over it."

"Gloves," she said, looking up. "Forgot to say that. He wore work gloves. Leather ones, I think." *Gloves,* both men wrote in their notebooks.

"Thank you, ma'am. We'll call you tonight. A car will pick you up tomorrow morning so you can look at some pictures for us," the FBI agent said.

"Pick me up?" The clerk was surprised.

"You bet." Manpower was not a factor on this case. The agent who picked her up would pick her brain again on the drive into D.C. The two investigators left. The Major drove his unmarked State Police car.

Capitano checked his notes. This wasn't bad for a first interview. He, the Major, and fifteen others had spent the day interviewing people in stores and shops up and down five miles of Ritchie Highway. Four people thought they remembered the van, but this was the first person who had seen one of its occupants closely enough for a description. It wasn't much, but it was a start. They already had the shooter ID'd. Cathy Ryan had recognized Sean Miller's face—thought she did, the agent corrected himself. If it had been Miller, he had a beard now, on the brown side of black and neatly trimmed. An artist would try to re-create that.

Twenty more agents and detectives had spent their day at the three local airports, showing photos to every ticket agent and gate clerk. They'd come up blank, but they hadn't had a description of Miller then. Tomorrow they would try again. A computer check was being made of international flights that connected to flights to Ireland, and domestic flights that connected to international ones. Capitano was happy that he didn't have to run all of those down. It would take weeks, and the chance of getting an ID from an airport worker diminished measurably every hour.

The van had been identified for more than a day, off the FBI's computer. It had been stolen a month before in New York City, repainted—professionally, by the look of it—and given new tags. Several sets of them, since the handicap tags found on it yesterday had been stolen less than two days before from a nursing home's van in Hagerstown, Maryland, a hundred miles away. Everything about the crime said it was a professional job from start to finish. Switching cars at the shopping center had been a brilliant finale to a perfectly planned and executed operation. Capitano and the Major were able to restrain their admiration, but they had to make an objective assessment of the people they were after. These weren't common thugs. They were professionals in every perverted sense of the word.

"You suppose they got the van themselves?" Capitano asked the Major.

The State Police investigator grunted. "There's some outfit in Pennsylvania that steals them from all over the Northeast, paints them, reworks the interior, and sells 'em. You guys are looking for them, remember?"

"I've heard a few things about the investigation, but that's not my territory. It's being looked at. Personally, I think they did it themselves. Why risk a connection with somebody else?"

"Yeah," the Major agreed reluctantly. The van had already been checked out by state and federal forensic experts. Not a single fingerprint had been found. The vehicle had been thoroughly cleaned, down to the knobs on the window handles. The technicians found nothing that could lead them to the criminals. Now the dirt and fabric fibers vacuumed from the van's carpet were being analyzed in Washington, but this was the sort of clue that worked reliably only on TV. If the people had been smart enough to clean out the van, they were almost certainly smart enough to burn the clothing they'd worn. Everything was being checked out anyway, because even the smartest people did make mistakes.

"You heard anything on the ballistics yet?" the Major asked, turning the car onto Rowe Boulevard.

"Oughta be waiting for us." They'd found almost twenty nine-millimeter cartridge cases to go along with the two usable bullets recovered from the Porsche, and the one that had gone through Trooper Fontana's chest and lodged in the back seat of his wrecked car. These had gone directly to the FBI laboratory in Washington for analysis. The evidence would tell them that the weapon was a submachine gun, which they already knew, but might give them a type, which they didn't yet know. The cartridge cases were Belgian-made, from the Fabrique Nationale at Liège. They might be able to identify the lot number, but FN made so many millions of such rounds per year, which were shipped and reshipped all over the world, that the lead was a slim one. Very often such shipments simply disappeared, mainly from sloppy—or creative—bookkeeping.

"How many black groups are known to have contact with these ULA characters?"

"None," Capitano replied. "That's something we are going to have to establish."

"Great."

Ryan arrived home to find an unmarked car and a liveried State Police cruiser in his driveway. Jack's own FBI interview wasn't a long one. It hadn't taken long to confirm the fact that he quite simply knew nothing about the attempt on his family or himself.

"Any idea where they are?" he asked finally.

"We're checking airports," the agent answered. "If these guys are as smart as they look, they're long gone."

"They're smart, all right," Ryan noted sourly. "What about the one you caught?"

"He's doing one hell of a good imitation of a clam. He has a lawyer now, of course, and the lawyer is telling him to keep his mouth shut. You can depend on lawyers for that."

"Where'd the lawyer come from?"

"Public defender's office. It's a rule, remember. You hold a suspect for any length of time, he has to have a lawyer. I don't think it matters. He probably isn't talking to the lawyer either. We have him on a state weapons violation and federal immigration laws. He goes back to the U.K. as soon as the paperwork gets done. Maybe two weeks or so, depending on if the attorney contests things." The agent closed his notebook. "You never know, maybe he'll start talking, but don't count on it. The word we get from the Brits is that he's not real bright anyway. He's the Irish version of a street hood, very good with weapons but a little slow upstairs."

"So if he's dumb, how come—"

"How come he's good at what he does? How smart do you have to be to kill somebody? Clark's a sociopathic personality. He has very little in the way of feelings. Some people are like that. They don't relate to the people around them as being real people. They see them as objects, and since they're only objects, whatever happens to them is not important. Once I met a hit man who killed four people—just the ones we know about—and didn't bat an eye, far as I could tell; but he cried like a baby when we told him his cat died. People like that don't even understand why they get sent to prison; they really don't understand,'' he concluded. ''Those are the scary ones.''

''No,'' Ryan said. ''The scary ones are the ones with brains, the ones who believe in it.''

''I haven't met one of those yet,'' he admitted.

''I have.'' Jack walked him to the door and watched him pull away. The house was an empty, quiet place without Sally running around, without the TV on, without Cathy talking about her friends at Hopkins. For several minutes Jack wandered around aimlessly, as though expecting to find someone. He didn't want to sit down, because that would somehow be an admission that he was all alone. He walked into the kitchen and started to fix a drink, but before he was finished, he dumped it all down the sink. He didn't want to get drunk. It was better to keep his mind unimpaired. Finally he lifted the phone and dialed.

''Yes,'' a voice answered.

''Admiral, Jack Ryan.''

''I understand that your girl's going to be all right,'' James Greer said. ''I'm glad to hear that, son.''

''Thank you, sir. Is the Agency involved in this?''

''This is an unsecure line, Jack,'' the Admiral replied.

''I want in,'' Ryan said.

''Be here tomorrow morning.''

Ryan hung up and went looking for his briefcase. He opened it and took out the Browning automatic pistol. After setting it on the kitchen table, he got out his shotgun and cleaning kit. He spent the next hour cleaning and oiling first the pistol, then the shotgun. When he was satisfied, he loaded both.

He left for Langley at five the next morning. Ryan had managed to get four more hours of sleep before rising and going through the usual morning ritual of coffee and breakfast. His early departure allowed him to miss the worst of the traffic, though the George Washington Parkway was never really free of the government workers heading to and from the agencies that were always more or less awake. After getting into the CIA building, he reflected that he had never called here and found Admiral Greer absent. *Well,* he told himself, *that's one thing in this world that I can depend on.* A security officer escorted him to the seventh floor.

''Good morning, sir,'' Jack said on entering the room.

''You look better than I expected,'' the DDI observed.

''It's an illusion mostly, but I can't solve my problem by hiding in a corner, can I? Can we talk about what's going on?''

''Your Irish friends have gotten a lot of attention. The President himself wants action on this. We've never had international terrorists play games in our country—at least, not things that ever made the press,'' Greer said cryptically. ''It is now a high-priority case. It's getting a lot of resources.''

''I want to be one of them,'' Ryan said simply.

''If you think that you can be part of an operation—''

"I know better than that, Admiral."

Greer smiled at the younger man. "That's good to see, son. I thought you were smart. So what do you want to do for us?"

"We both know that the bad guys are part of the network. The data you let me look at was pretty limited. Obviously you're going to be trying to collate data on all the groups, searching for leads on the ULA. Maybe I can help."

"What about your teaching?"

"I can be here when I'm not teaching. There isn't much to hold me at home at the moment, sir."

"It isn't good practice to use people who are personally involved in the investigation," Greer pointed out.

"This isn't the FBI, sir. I'm not going out into the field. You just told me that. I know you want me back here on a permanent basis, Admiral. If you really want me, let me start off doing something that's important to both of us." Jack paused, searching for another point. "If I'm good enough, let's find out now."

"Some people aren't going to like it."

"There's things happening to me that I don't like very much, sir, and I have to live with it. If I can't fight back somehow, I might as well stay at home. You're the only chance I have to do something to protect my family, sir."

Greer turned to refill his coffee cup from the drip machine behind his desk. He'd liked Jack almost from the first moment he'd met him. This was a young man accustomed to having his way, though he was not arrogant about it. That was a point in his favor: Ryan knew what he wanted, but wasn't overly pushy. He wasn't a person driven by ambition, another point in his favor. Finally, he had a lot of raw talent to be shaped and trained and directed. Greer was always looking for talent. The Admiral turned back.

"Okay, you're on the team. Marty's coordinating the information. You'll work directly with him. I hope you don't talk in your sleep, son, because you're going to see stuff that you're not even allowed to dream about."

"Sir, there's only one thing that I'm going to dream about."

It had been a very busy month for Dennis Cooley. The death of an earl in East Anglia had forced his heirs to sell off a massive collection of books to pay the death duties, and Cooley had used up nearly all of his available capital to secure no less than twenty-one items for his shop. But it was worth it: among them was a rare first-folio of Marlowe's plays. Better still, the dead earl had been assiduous in protecting his treasures. The books had been deep-frozen several times to kill off the insects that desecrated these priceless relics of the past. The Marlowe was in remarkably good shape, despite the waterstained cover that had put off a number of less perceptive buyers. Cooley was stooped over his desk, reading the first act of *The Jew of Malta,* when the bell rang.

"Is that the one I heard about?" his visitor asked at once.

"Indeed." Cooley smiled to cover his surprise. He hadn't seen this particular visitor for some time, and was somewhat disturbed that he'd come back so soon. "Printed in 1633, forty years after Marlowe's death. Some parts of the text are suspect, of course, but this is one of the few surviving copies of the first printed edition."

"It's quite authentic?"

"Of course," Cooley replied, slightly put off at the question. "In addition to my own humble expertise, it has authentication papers from Sir Edmund Grey of the British Museum.''

''One cannot argue with that,'' the customer agreed.

''I'm afraid I have not yet decided upon a price for it.'' *Why are you here?*

''Price is not an object. I understand that you may wish to enjoy it for yourself, but I must have it.'' This told Cooley why he was here. He leaned to look over Cooley's shoulder at the book. ''Magnificent,'' he said, placing a small envelope in the book dealer's pocket.

''Perhaps we can work something out,'' Cooley allowed. ''In a few weeks, perhaps.'' He looked out the window. A man was window-shopping at the jewelry store on the opposite side of the arcade. After a moment he straightened up and walked away.

''Sooner than that, please,'' the man insisted.

Cooley sighed. ''Come see me next week and we may be able to discuss it. I do have other customers, you know.''

''But none more important, I hope.''

Cooley blinked twice. ''Very well.''

Geoffrey Watkins continued to browse the store for another few minutes. He selected a Keats that had also come from the dead earl's estate and paid six hundred pounds for it before leaving. On leaving the arcade he failed to notice a young lady at the newsstand outside and could not have known that another was waiting at the arcade's other end. The one who followed him was dressed in a manner guaranteed to garner attention, including orange hair that would have fluoresced if the sun had been out. She followed him west for two blocks and kept going in that direction when he crossed the street. Another police officer was on the walk down Green Park.

That night the daily surveillance reports came to Scotland Yard where, as always, they were put on computer. The operation being run was a joint venture between the Metropolitan Police and the Security Service, once known as MI-5. Unlike the American FBI, the people at ''Five'' did not have the authority to arrest suspects, and had to work through the police to bring a case to a conclusion. The marriage was not entirely a happy one. It meant that James Owens had to work closely with David Ashley. Owens entirely concurred with his FBI colleague's assessment of the younger man: ''a snotty bastard.''

''Patterns, patterns, patterns,'' Ashley said, sipping his tea while he looked at the print-out. They had identified a total of thirty-nine people who knew, or might have known, information common to the ambush on The Mall and Miller's transport to the Isle of Wight. One of them had leaked the information. Every one of them was being watched. Thus far they had discovered a closet homosexual, two men and one woman who were having affairs not of state, and a man who got considerable enjoyment watching pornographic movies in the Soho theaters. Financial records gotten from Inland Revenue showed nothing particularly interesting, nor did living habits. There was the usual spread of hobbies, taste in theatrical plays, and television shows. Several of the people had wide collections of friends. A few had none at all. The investigators were grateful for these sad, lonely people—many of the other people's friends had to be checked out, too, and this took time and manpower. Owens viewed the entire operation as something necessary but rather distasteful. It was the police equivalent of peering through windows. The tapes of telephone conversations—especially those between lovers—made him squirm on occasion. Owens was a man who appreciated the individual's need for privacy. No one's life could survive this sort of scrutiny. He told himself that one person's life wouldn't, and that was the point of the exercise.

"I see Mr. Watkins visited a rare book shop this afternoon," Owens noted, reading over his own print-out.

"Yes. He collects them. So do I," Ashley said. "I've been in that shop once or twice myself. There was an estate sale recently. Perhaps Cooley bought a few things that Geoffrey wants for himself." The security officer made a mental note to look at the shop for himself. "He was in there for ten minutes, spoke with Dennis—"

"You know him?" Owens looked up.

"One of the best men in the trade," Ashley said. He smiled at his own choice of words: *the Trade*. "I bought a Brontë there for my wife, Christmas two years ago, I think. He's a fat little poof, but he's quite knowledgeable. So Geoffrey spoke with him for about ten minutes, made a purchase, and left. I wonder what he bought." Ashley rubbed his eyes. He'd been on a strict regimen of fourteen-hour days for longer than he cared to remember.

"The first new person Watkins has seen in several weeks," Owens noted. He thought about it for a moment. There were better leads than this to follow up on, and his manpower was limited.

"So can we deal on this immigration question?" the public defender asked.

"Not a chance," Bill Shaw said from the other side of the table. *You think we're going to give him political asylum?*

"You're not offering us a thing," the lawyer observed. "I bet I can beat the weapons charge, and there's no way you can make the conspiracy stick."

"That's fine, counselor. If it will make you any happier we'll cut him loose and give him a plane ticket, and even an escort, home."

"To a maximum-security prison." The public defender closed his file folder on the case of Eamon Clark. "You're not giving me anything to deal with."

"If he cops to the gun charge and conspiracy, and if he helps us, he gets to spend a few years in a much nicer prison. But if you think we're going to let a convicted murderer just walk, mister, you are kidding yourself. What do you think you have to deal with?"

"You might be surprised," the attorney said cryptically.

"Oh, yeah? I'm willing to bet that he hasn't said anything to you either," the agent challenged the young attorney, and watched closely for his reaction. Bill Shaw, too, had passed the bar exam, though he devoted his legal expertise to the safety of society rather than the freedom of criminals.

"Conversations between attorney and client are privileged." The lawyer had been practicing for exactly two and a half years. His understanding of his job was limited largely to keeping the police away from his charges. At first he'd been gratified that Clark hadn't said much of anything to the police and FBI, but he was surprised that Clark wouldn't even talk to him. After all, maybe he could cut a deal, despite what this FBI fellow said. But he had nothing to deal with, as Shaw had just told him. He waited a few moments for a reaction from the agent and got nothing but a blank stare. The public defender admitted defeat to himself. Well, there hadn't been much of a chance on this.

"That's what I thought." Shaw stood. "Tell your client that unless he opens up by the day after tomorrow, he's flying home to finish out a life sentence. Make sure you tell him that. If he wants to talk after he gets back, we'll send people to him. They say the beer's pretty good over there, and I wouldn't mind flying over myself to find out.'' The only thing the Bureau could use over Clark was fear. The mission he'd been part of had hurt the Provos, and young, dumb Ned might not like the reception he got. He'd be safer in a U.S. penitentiary than he would be in a British one, but Shaw doubted that he understood this, or that he'd crack in any case. Maybe after he got back, something might be arranged.

The case was not going well; not that he'd expected otherwise. This sort of thing either cracked open immediately, or took months—or years. The people they were after were too clever to have left an immediate opening to be exploited. What remained to him and his men was the day-by-day grind. But that was the textbook definition of investigative police work. Shaw knew this well enough: he had written one of the standard texts.

18. Lights

Ashley entered the bookshop at four in the afternoon. A true bibliophile, he paused on opening the door to appreciate the aroma.

''Is Mr. Cooley in today?'' he asked the clerk.

''No, sir,'' Beatrix replied. ''He's abroad on business. May I help you?''

''Yes. I understand that you've made some new acquisitions.''

''Ah, yes. Have you heard about the Marlowe first folio?'' Beatrix looked remarkably like a mouse. Her hair was exactly the proper drab shade of brown and ill-kept. Her face was puffy, whether from too much food or too much drink, Ashley couldn't say. Her eyes were hidden behind thick glasses. She dressed in a way that fitted the store exactly—everything she had on was old and out of date. Ashley remembered buying his wife the Brontë here, and wondered if those two sad, lonely sisters had looked like this girl. It was too bad, really. With a little effort she might actually have been attractive.

''A Marlowe?'' the man from ''Five'' asked. ''First folio, you said?''

''Yes, sir, from the collection of the late Earl of Crundale. As you know, Marlowe's plays were not actually printed until forty years after his death.'' She went on, displaying something that her appearance didn't begin to hint at. Ashley listened with respect. The mouse knew her business as well as an Oxford don.

''How do you find such things?'' Ashley asked when she'd finished her discourse.

She smiled. ''Mr. Dennis can smell them. He is always traveling, working with other dealers and lawyers and such. He's in Ireland today, for example. It's amazing how many books he manages to obtain over there. Those horrid people have the most marvelous collections.'' Beatrix did not approve of the Irish.

''Indeed,'' David Ashley noted. He didn't react to this bit of news at all. At least not physically, but a switch in the back of his head flipped on. ''Well, that is one of the contributions our friends across the water have made. A few rather good writers, and whiskey.''

''And bombers,'' Beatrix noted. ''I shouldn't want to travel there so much myself.''

''Oh, I take my holiday there quite often. The fishing is marvelous.''

''That's what Lord Louis Mountbatten thought,'' the clerk observed.

''How often does Dennis go over?''

''At least once a month.''

''Well, on this Marlowe you have—may I see it?'' Ashley asked with an enthusiasm that was only partially feigned.

''By all means.'' The girl took the volume from a shelf and opened it with great care. ''As you see, though the cover is in poor condition, the pages are in a remarkable state of preservation.''

Ashley hovered over the book, his eyes running down the opened page. ''Indeed they are. How much for this one?''

''Mr. Dennis hasn't set a price yet. I believe another customer is already very interested in it, however.''

''Do you know who that is?''

''No, sir, I do not, and I would not be able to reveal his name in any case. We respect our customers' confidentiality,'' Beatrix said primly.

''Quite so. That is entirely proper,'' Ashley agreed. ''So when will Mr. Cooley be back? I want to talk to him about this myself.''

''He'll be back tomorrow afternoon.''

''Will you be here also?'' Ashley asked with a charming smile.

''No, I'll be at my other job.''

''Too bad. Well, thank you very much for showing me this.'' Ashley made for the door.

''My pleasure, sir.''

The security officer walked out of the arcade and turned right. He waited for the afternoon traffic to clear before crossing the street. He decided to walk back to Scotland Yard instead of taking a cab, and went downhill along St. James's Street, turning left to go around the Palace to the east, then down Marlborough Road to The Mall.

It happened right there, he thought. *The getaway car turned here to make its escape. The ambush was a mere hundred yards west of where I'm standing now.* He stood and looked for a few seconds, remembering.

The personality of a security officer is much the same all over the world. They do not believe in coincidences, though they do believe in accidents. They lack any semblance of a sense of humor where their work is concerned. This comes from the knowledge that only the most trusted of people have the ability to be traitors; before betraying their countries, they must first betray the people who trust them. Beneath all his charm, Ashley was a man who hated traitors beyond all things, who suspected everyone and trusted no one.

Ten minutes later Ashley got past the security checkpoint at Scotland Yard and took the elevator to James Owens' office.

''That Cooley chap,'' he said.

''Cooley?'' Owens was puzzled for a moment. ''Oh, the book dealer Watkins visited yesterday. Is that where you were?''

''A fine little shop. Its owner is in Ireland today,'' Ashley said deadpan.

Commander Owens nodded thoughtfully at that. What had been unimportant changed with a word. Ashley outlined what he had learned over several minutes. It wasn't even a real lead yet, but it was something to be looked at. Neither man said anything about how significant it might be—there had been many such things to run down, all of which to date had ended at blank walls. Many of the walls had also been checked out in every possible detail. The investigation wasn't at a standstill. People were still out on the street, accumulating information—none of which was the least useful to the case. This was something new to be looked at, nothing more than that; but for the moment that was enough.

It was eleven in the morning at Langley. Ryan was not admitted to the meetings between CIA and FBI people coordinating information on the case. Marty Cantor had explained to him that the FBI might be uneasy to have him there. Jack didn't mind. He'd get the information summaries after lunch, and that was enough for the moment. Cantor would come away both with the information FBI had developed, plus the thoughts and ideas of the chief investigators. Ryan didn't want that. He preferred to look at the raw data. His unprejudiced outsider's perspective had worked before and it might work again, he thought—hoped.

The wonderful world of the international terrorist, Murray had said to him outside the Old Bailey. It wasn't very wonderful, Jack thought, but it was a fairly complete world, including all of what the Greeks and Romans thought the civilized world was. He was going over satellite reconnaissance data at the moment. The bound report he was looking at contained no less than sixteen maps. In addition to the cities and roads shown on them were little red triangles designating suspected terrorist training camps in four countries. These were being photographed on almost a daily basis by the photoreconnaissance satellites (Jack was not allowed to know their number) orbiting the globe. He concentrated on the ones in Libya. They did have that report from an Italian agent that Sean Miller had been seen leaving a freighter in Bengazi harbor. The freighter had been of Cypriot registry, owned by a network of corporations sufficiently complex that it didn't really matter, since the ship was under charter to yet another such network. An American destroyer had photographed the ship in what certainly seemed a chance encounter in the Straits of Sicily. The ship was old but surprisingly well maintained, with modern radar and radio gear. She was regularly employed on runs from Eastern European ports to Libya and Syria, and was known to carry arms and military equipment from the East Bloc to client states on the Mediterranean. This data had already been set aside for further use.

Ryan found that the CIA and National Reconnaissance Office were looking at a number of camps in the North African desert. A simple graph accompanied the dated photos of each, and Ryan was looking for a camp whose apparent activity had changed the day that Miller's ship had docked at Bengazi. He was disappointed to find that four had done so. One was known to be used by the Provisional Wing of the IRA—this datum had come from the interrogation of a convicted bomber. The other three were unknowns. The people there—aside from the maintenance staff provided by the Libyan armed forces—could be identified from the photos as Europeans from their fair skin, but that was all. Jack was disappointed to see that you couldn't recognize a face from these shots, just color of skin, and if the sun was right, color of hair. You could also determine the make of a car or truck, but not its identifying tag numbers. Strangely, the clarity of the photos was better at night. The cooler night air was less roiled and did not interfere with imaging as much as in the shimmering heat of the day.

The pictures in the heavy binder that occupied his attention were of camps 11-5-04, 11-5-18, and 11-5-20. Jack didn't know how the number designators had been arrived at and didn't really care. The camps were all pretty much the same; only the spacing of the huts distinguished one from another.

Jack spent the best part of an hour looking over the photos, and concluded that this miracle of modern technology told him all sorts of technical things, none of which were pertinent to his purpose. Whoever ran those camps knew enough to keep people out of sight when a reconsat was overhead—except for one which was not known to have photographic capability. Even then, the number of people visible was almost never the same, and the actual occupancy of the camps was therefore a matter for uncertain estimation. It was singularly frustrating.

Ryan leaned back and lit another low-tar cigarette bought from the kiosk on the next floor down. It went well with the coffee that was serving to keep him awake. He was up against another blank wall. It made him think of the computer games he occasionally played at home when he was tired of writing—Zork and Ultima. The business of intelligence analysis was so often like those computer ''head games.'' You had to figure things out, but you never quite knew what it was that you were figuring out. The patterns you had to deduce could be very different from anything one normally dealt with, and the difference could be significant or mere happenstance.

Two of the suspected ULA camps were within forty miles of the known IRA outpost. *Less than an hour's drive,* Jack thought. *If they only knew.* He would have settled for having the Provos clean out the ULA, as they evidently wanted to do. There were indications that the Brits were thinking along similar lines. Jack wondered what Mr. Owens thought of that one and concluded that he probably didn't know. It was a surprising thought that he now had information that some experienced players did not. He went back to the pictures.

One, taken a week after Miller had been seen in Bengazi, showed a car—it looked like a Toyota Land Cruiser—about a mile from 11-5-18, heading away. Ryan wondered where it was going. He wrote down the date and time on the bottom of the photo and checked the cross-reference table in the front. Ten minutes later he found the same car, the next day, at Camp 11-5-09, a PIRA camp forty miles from 11-5-18.

Jack told himself not to get overly excited: 11-5-18 could belong to the Red Army Faction of West Germany, Italy's resurgent Red Brigade, or any number of other organizations with which the PIRA cross-pollinated. He still made some notes. It was a ''datum,'' a bit of information that was worth checking out.

Next he checked the occupancy graph for the camp. This showed the number of camp buildings occupied at night, and went back for over two years. He compared it with a list of known ULA operations, and discovered . . . nothing, at first. The instances where the number of occupied buildings blipped up did not correlate with the organization's known activities . . . but there was some sort of pattern, he saw.

What kind of pattern? Jack asked himself. Every three months or so the occupancy went up by one. Regardless of the number of the people at the camp, the number of huts being used went up by one, for a period of three days. Ryan swore when he saw that the pattern didn't quite hold. Twice in two years the number didn't change. *And what does* that *mean?*

''You are in a maze of twisty passages, all alike,'' Jack murmured to himself. It was a line from one of his computer games. Pattern-recognition was not one of his strong points. Jack left the room to get a can of Coke, but more to clear his head. He was back in five minutes.

He pulled the occupancy graphs from the three ''unknown'' camps to compare the respective levels of activity. What he really needed to do was to make Xerox copies of the graphs, but CIA had strict rules on the use of copying machines. Doing it would take time that he didn't want to lose at the moment. The other two camps showed no recognizable pattern at all, while Camp -18 did seem to lean in that direction. He spent an hour doing this. By the end of it he had all three graphs memorized. He had to get away from it. Ryan tucked the graphs back where they belonged and returned to examining the photographs themselves.

Camp 11-5-20, he saw, showed a girl in one photo. At least there was someone there wearing a two-piece bathing suit. Jack stared at the image for a few seconds, then turned away in disgust. He was playing voyeur, trying to discern the figure of someone who was probably a terrorist. There were no such attractions at camps -04 and -18, and he wondered at the significance of this until he remembered that only one satellite was giving daylight photos with people in them. Ryan made a note to himself to check at the Academy's library for a book on orbital mechanics. He decided that he needed to know how often a single satellite passed over a given spot in a day.

''You're not getting anywhere,'' he told himself aloud.

''Neither is anybody else,'' Marty Cantor said. Ryan spun around.

''How did you get in here?'' Jack demanded.

''I'll say one thing for you, Jack, when you concentrate you really concentrate. I've been standing here for five minutes.'' Cantor grinned. ''I like your intensity, but if you want an opinion, you're pushing a little hard, fella.''

''I'll survive.''

''You say so,'' Cantor said dubiously. ''How do you like our photo album?''

''The people who do this full-time must go nuts.''

''Some do,'' Cantor agreed.

''I might have something worth checking out,'' Jack said, explaining his suspicions on Camp -18.

''Not bad. By the way, number -20 may be *Action-Directe,* the French group that's picked up lately. DGSE—the French foreign intelligence service—thinks they have a line on it.''

''Oh. That may explain one of the photos.'' Ryan flipped to the proper page.

''Thank God Ivan doesn't know what that bird does,'' Cantor nodded. ''Hmm. We may be able to ID from this.''

''How?'' Jack asked. ''You can't make out her face.''

''You can tell her hair length, roughly. You can also tell the size of her tits.'' Cantor grinned ear to ear.

''What?''

''The guys in photointerpretation are—well, they're very technical. For cleavage to show up in these photos, a girl has to have C-cup breasts—at least that's what they told me once. I'm not kidding, Jack. Somebody actually worked the math out, because you can identify people from a combination of factors like hair color, length, and bust size. *Action-Directe* has lots of female operatives. Our French colleagues might find this interesting.'' *If they're willing to deal,* he didn't say.

''What about -18?''

''I don't know. We've never really tried to identify that one. The thing about the car may count against it, though.''

''Remember that our ULA friends have the Provos infiltrated,'' Jack said.

''You're still on that, eh? Okay, it's something to be considered,'' Cantor conceded. ''What about this pattern thing you talked about?''

"I haven't got anything to point to yet," Jack admitted.

"Let's see the graph."

Jack unfolded it from the back of the binder. "Every three months, mostly, the occupancy rate picks up."

Cantor frowned at the graph for a moment. Then he flipped through the photographs. On only one of the dates did they have a daylight photo that showed anything. Each of the camps had what looked like a shooting range. In the photo Cantor selected, there were three men standing near it.

"You might have something, Jack."

"What?" Ryan had looked at the photo and made nothing of it.

"What's the distinguishing feature of the ULA?"

"Their professionalism," Ryan answered.

"Your last paper on them said they were more militarily organized than some of the others, remember? Every one of them, as far as we can tell, is skilled with weapons."

"So?"

"Think!" Cantor snapped. Ryan gave him a blank look. "Periodic weapons-refresher training, maybe?"

"Oh. I hadn't thought of that. How come nobody ever—"

"Do you know how many satellite photos come through here? I can't say exactly, but you may safely assume that it's a fairly large number, thousands per month. Figure it takes a minimum of five minutes to examine each one. Mostly we're interested in the Russians—missile silos, factories, troop movements, tank parks, you name it. That's where most of the analytical talent goes, and they can't keep up with what comes in. The guys we have on this stuff here are technicians, not analysts." Cantor paused. "Camp -18 looks interesting enough that we might try to figure a way to check it out, see who really lives there. Not bad."

"He's violated security," Kevin O'Donnell said by way of greeting. He was quiet enough that no one in the noisy pub would have heard him.

"Perhaps this is worth it," Cooley replied. "Instructions?"

"When are you going back?"

"Tomorrow morning, the early flight."

O'Donnell nodded, finishing off his drink. He left the pub and walked directly to his car. Twenty minutes later he was home. Ten minutes after that, his operations and intelligence chiefs were in his study.

"Sean, how did you like working with Alex's organization?"

"They're like us, small but professional. Alex is a very thorough technician, but an arrogant one. He hasn't had a great deal of formal training. He's clever, very clever. And he's hungry, as they say over there. He wants to make his mark."

"Well, he may just have his chance next summer." O'Donnell paused, holding up the letter Cooley had delivered. "It would seem that His Royal Highness will be visiting America next summer. The Treasure Houses exhibit was such a success that they are going to stage another one. Nearly ninety percent of the works of Leonardo Da Vinci belong to the Royal Family, and they'll be sending them over to raise money for some favored charities. The show opens in Washington on August the first, and the Prince of Wales will be going over to start things off. This will not be announced until July, but here is his itinerary, including the proposed security arrangements. It is as yet undecided whether or not his lovely bride will accompany His Highness, but we will proceed on the assumption that she will."

''The child?'' Miller asked.

''I rather suspect not, but we will allow for that possibility also.'' He handed the letter to Michael McKenney. The intelligence officer for the ULA skimmed over the data.

''The security at the official functions will be airtight. The Americans have had a number of incidents, and they've learned from each of them,'' McKenney said. Like all intelligence officers, he saw his potential opponents as overwhelmingly powerful. ''But if they go forward with this one . . .''

''Yes,'' O'Donnell said. ''I want you two to work together on this. We have plenty of time and we'll use all of it.'' He took the letter back and reread it before giving it to Miller. After they left, he wrote his instructions for their agent in London.

At the airport the next morning Cooley saw his contact and walked into the coffee shop. He was early for his flight, seasoned traveler that he was, and had a cup while he waited for it to be announced. Finished, he walked outside. His contact was just walking in. The two men brushed by each other, and the message was passed, just as was taught in every spy school in the world.

''He does travel about a good deal,'' Ashley observed. It had taken Owens' detectives less than an hour to find Cooley's travel agent and to get a record of his trips for the past three years. Another pair was assembling a biographical file on the man. It was strictly routine work. Owens and his men knew better than to get excited about a new lead. Enthusiasm all too easily got in the way of objectivity. His car—parked at Gatwick Airport—had considerable mileage on the clock for its age, and that was explained by his motoring about buying books. This was the extent of the data assembled in eighteen hours. They would patiently wait for more.

''How often does he travel to Ireland?''

''Quite frequently, but he does business in English-language books, and we are the only two countries in Europe that speak English, aren't we?'' Ashley, too, was able to control himself.

''America?'' Owens asked.

''Once a year, looks like. I rather suspect it's to an annual trade show. I can check that myself.''

''They speak English, too.''

Ashley grinned. ''Shakespeare didn't live or print books there. There aren't many examples of American publishing old enough to excite a person like Cooley. What he might do is buy up books of ours that have found their way across the water, but more likely he's looking for buyers. No, Ireland fits beautifully with his cover—excuse me, if it is that. My own dealer, Samuel Pickett and Sons, travel there often also . . . but not as much, I should think,'' he added.

''Perhaps his biography will tell us something,'' Owens noted.

''One can hope.'' Ashley was looking for a light at the end of this tunnel, but saw only more tunnel.

''It's okay, Jack,'' Cathy said.

He nodded. Ryan knew that his wife was right. The nurse-practitioner had positively beamed at the news she gave them on their arrival. Sally was bouncing back like any healthy child should. The healing process had already begun.

Yet there was a difference between the knowledge of the mind and the knowledge of the heart. Sally had been awake this time. She was unable to speak, of course, with the respirator hose in her mouth, but the murmurs that tried to come out could only have meant: *It hurts*. The injuries inflicted on the body of his child did not appear any less horrific, despite his knowledge that they would heal. If anything they seemed worse now that she was occasionally conscious. The pain would eventually go away—but his little girl was in pain now. Cathy might be able to tell herself that only the living could feel pain, that it was a positive sign for all the discomfort it gave. Jack could not. They stayed until she dozed off again. He took his wife outside.

"How are you?" he asked her.

"Better. You can take me home tomorrow night."

Jack shook his head. He hadn't thought about that. Stupid, Ryan told himself. Somehow he'd assumed that Cathy would stay here, close to Sally.

"The house is pretty empty without you, babe," he said after a moment.

"It'll be empty without her," his wife answered, and the tears started again. She buried her face in her husband's shoulder. "She's so little . . ."

"Yeah." Jack thought of Sally's face, the two little blue eyes surrounded by a sea of bruises, the hurt there, the pain there. "She's going to get better, honey, and I don't want to hear any more of that 'it's my fault' crap."

"But it is!"

"No, it isn't. Do you know how lucky I am to have you both alive? I saw the FBI's data today. If you hadn't stomped on the brakes when you did, you'd both be dead." The supposition was that this had thrown off Miller's aim by a few inches. At least two rounds had missed Cathy's head by a whisker, the forensic experts said. Jack could close his eyes and recite that information word for word. "You saved her life and yours by being smart."

It took Cathy a moment to react. "How did you find that out?"

"CIA. They're cooperating with the police. I asked to be part of the team and they let me join up."

"But—"

"A lot of people are working on this, babe. I'm one of them," Jack said quietly. "The only thing that matters now is finding them."

"Do you think . . ."

"Yeah, I do." *Sooner or later.*

Bill Shaw had no such hopes at the moment. The best potential lead they had was the identity of the black man who'd driven the van. This was being kept out of the media. As far as the TV and newspapers were concerned, all the suspects were white. The FBI hadn't so much lied to the press as allowed them to draw a false conclusion from the partial data that had been released—as happened frequently enough. It might keep the suspect from being spooked. The only person who'd seen him at close range was the 7-Eleven clerk. She had spent several hours going over pictures of blacks thought to be members of revolutionary groups and come up with three possibles. Two of these were in prison, one for bank robbery, the other for interstate transport of explosives. The third had dropped out of sight seven years before. He was only a picture to the Bureau. The name they had for him was known to be an alias, and there were no fingerprints. He'd cut himself loose from his former associates—a smart move, since most of them had been arrested and convicted for various criminal acts—and simply disappeared. The best bet, Shaw told himself, was that he was now part of society, living a normal life somewhere with his past activities no more than a memory.

The agent looked over the file once again. "Constantine Duppens," his alias had been. Well-spoken on the few occasions when he'd spoken at all, the informant had said of him. Educated, probably. Attached to the group the Bureau had been watching, but never really part of it, the file went on. He'd never participated in a single illegal act, and had drifted away when the leaders of the little band had started talking about supporting themselves with bank robberies and drug trafficking. Maybe a dilettante, Shaw thought, a student with a radical streak who'd gotten a look at one of the groups and recognized them for what they were—what Shaw thought they were: ineffective dolts, street hoods with a smattering of Marxist garbage or pseudo-Hitlerism.

A few fringe groups occasionally managed to set off a bomb somewhere, but these cases were so rare, so minor, that the American people scarcely knew that they'd happened at all. When a group robbed a bank or armored car to support itself, the public remembered that one need not be politically motivated to rob a bank; greed was enough. From a high of fifty-one terrorist incidents in 1982, the number had been slashed to seven in 1985. The Bureau had managed to run down many of these amateurish groups, preventing more than twenty incidents the previous year, with good intelligence followed by quick action. Fundamentally, the small cells of crazies had been done in by their own amateurism.

America didn't have any ideologically motivated terrorist groups, at least not in the European sense. There were the Armenian groups whose main objective was murdering Turkish diplomats, and the white-supremacist people in the Northwest, but in both cases the only ideology was hatred—of Turks, blacks, Jews, or whatever. These were vicious but not really dangerous to society, since they lacked a shared vision of their political objective. To be really effective, the members of such a group had to believe in something more than the negativity of hate. The most dangerous terrorists were the idealists, of course, but America was a hard place to see the benefits of Marxism or Nazism. When even welfare families had color televisions, how much attraction could there be to collectivism? When the country lacked a system of class distinctions, what group could one hate with conviction? And so most of the small groups found that they were guerrilla fish swimming not in a sea of peasants, but rather a sea of apathy. Not a single group had been able to overcome that fact before being penetrated and destroyed by the Bureau—then to learn that their destruction was granted but a few column inches on page eleven, their defiant manifesto not printed at all. They were judged by faceless editors not to be newsworthy. In so many ways this was the perfect conclusion to a terrorist trial.

In that sense the FBI was a victim of its own success. So well had the job been done that the possibility of terrorist activity in America was not a matter of general public concern. Even the Ryan Case, as it was now being called, was regarded as nothing more than a nasty crime, not a harbinger of something new in America. To Shaw it was both. As a matter of institutional policy, the FBI regarded terrorism as a crime without any sort of political dimension that might lend a perverted respectability to the perpetrators. The importance of this distinction was not merely semantic. Since by their nature, terrorists struck at the foundations of civilized society, to grant them the thinnest shred of respectability was the equivalent of a suicide note for the targeted society. The Bureau recognized, however, that these were not mere criminals chasing after money. Their objective was far more dangerous than that. For this reason, crimes that otherwise would have been in the domain of local police departments were immediately taken under charge by the federal government.

Shaw returned to the photo of "Constantine Duppens" one more time. It was expecting too much for a convenience-store clerk to remember one face from the hundred she saw every day, or at least to remember it well enough to pick out a photo that might be years old. She'd certainly tried to help, and had agreed to tell no one of what she'd done. They had a description of the suspect's clothing—almost certainly burned—and the van, which they had. It was being dismantled piece by piece not far from Shaw's office. The forensic experts had identified the type of gun used. For the moment, that was all they had. All Inspector Bill Shaw could do was wait for his agents in the field to come up with something new. A paid informant might overhear something, or a new witness might turn up, or maybe the forensics team would discover something unexpected in the van. Shaw told himself to be patient. Despite twenty-two years in the FBI, patience was something he still had to force on himself.

"Aw, I was starting to like the beard," a co-worker said.

"Damned thing itched too much." Alexander Constantine Dobbens was back at his job. "I was spending half my time just scratching my face."

"Yeah, same thing when I was on subs," his roommate agreed. "Different when you're young."

"Speak for yourself, grandpop!" Dobbens laughed. "You old married turkey. Just because you're chained doesn't mean I have to be."

"You oughta settle down, Alex."

"The world is full of interesting things to do, and I haven't done them all yet." *Not hardly*. He was a field engineer for Baltimore Gas and Electric Company and usually worked nights. The job forced him to spend much of his time on the road, checking equipment and supervising line crews. Alex was a popular fellow who didn't mind getting his hands dirty, who actually enjoyed the physical work that many engineers were too proud to do. A man of the people, he called himself. His pro-union stance was a source of irritation to management, but he was a good engineer, and being black didn't hurt either. A man who was a good engineer, popular with his people, *and* black was fireproof. He'd done a good deal of minority recruiting, moreover, having brought a dozen good workers into the company. A few of them had shaky backgrounds, but Alex had brought them around.

It was often quiet working nights, and as was usually the case, Alex got the first edition of the *Baltimore Sun*. The case was already off the front page, now back in the local news section. The FBI and State Police, he read, were continuing to investigate the case. He was still amazed that the woman and kid had survived—testimony, his training told him, to the efficacy of seat belts, not to mention the work of the Porsche engineers. *Well,* he decided, *that's okay*. Killing a little kid and a pregnant woman wasn't exactly something to brag about. They had wasted the state trooper, and that was enough for him. Losing that Clark boy to the cops continued to rankle Dobbens, though. *I told the dumb fuck that the man was too exposed there, but no, he wanted to waste the whole family at once*. Alex knew why that was so, but saw it as a case of zeal overcoming realism. *Damned political-science majors, they think you can make something happen if you wish hard enough*. Engineers knew different.

Dobbens took comfort from the fact that all the known suspects were white.

Waving to the helicopter had been his mistake. Bravado had no place in revolutionary activity. It was his own lesson to be learned, but this one hadn't hurt anyone. The gloves and hat had denied the pigs a description. The really funny thing was that despite all the screwups, the operation had been a success. That IRA punk, O-something, had been booted out of Boston with his honky tail between his legs. At least the operation had been politically sound. And that, he told himself, was the real measure of success.

From his point of view, success meant earning his spurs. He and his people had provided expert assistance to an established revolutionary group. He could now look to his African friends for funding. They really weren't African to his way of thinking, but they liked to call themselves that. There were ways to hurt America, to get attention in a way that no revolutionary group ever had. What, for example, if he could turn out the lights in fifteen states at once? Alex Dobbens knew how. The revolutionary had to know a way of hitting people where they lived, and what better way, he thought, than to make unreliable something that they took for granted? If he could demonstrate that the corrupt government could not even keep their lights on reliably, what doubts might he put in people's heads next? America was a society of things, he thought. What if those things stopped working? What then would people think? He didn't know the answer to that, but he knew that something would change, and change was what he was after.

19. Tests and Passing Grades

"He is an odd duck," Owens observed. The dossier was the result of three weeks of work. It could have gone faster, of course, but when you don't want the news of an inquiry to reach its subject, you had to be more circumspect.

Dennis Cooley was a Belfast native, born to a middle-class Catholic family, although neither of his deceased parents had been churchgoers, something decidedly odd in a region where religion defines both life and death. Dennis had attended church—a necessity for one who'd been educated at the parish school—until university, then stopped at once and never gone back. No criminal record at all. None. Not even a place in a suspected associates file. As a university student he'd hung around the fringes of a few activist groups, but never joined, evidently preferring his studies in literature. He'd graduated with the highest honors. A few courses in Marxism, a few more in economics, always with a teacher whose leanings were decidedly left of center, Owens saw. The police commander snorted to himself. There were enough of those at the London School of Economics, weren't there?

For two years all they had were tax records. He'd worked in his father's bookshop, and so far as the police were concerned, simply did not exist. That was a problem with police work—you noticed only the criminals. A few very discreet inquiries made in Belfast hadn't turned up anything. All sorts of people had visited the shop, even soldiers of the British Army, who'd arrived there about the time Cooley had graduated university. The shop's window had been smashed once or twice by marauding bands of Protestants—the reason the Army had been called in in the first place—but nothing more serious than that. Young Dennis hadn't frequented the local pubs enough that anyone had noticed, hadn't belonged to any church organization, nor any political club, nor any sports association. "He was always reading something," someone had told one of the detectives. *There's a bloody revelation,* Owens told himself. *A bookshop owner who reads . . .*

Then his parents had died in an auto accident.

Owens was struck by the fact that they'd died in a completely ordinary way. A lorry's brakes had failed and smashed into their Mini one Saturday afternoon. It was hard to remember that some people in Ulster actually died "normally," and were just as dead as those blown up or shot by the terrorists who prowled the night. Dennis Cooley had taken the insurance settlement and continued to operate the store as before after the quiet, ill-attended funeral ceremony at the local church. Some years later he'd sold out and moved to London, first setting up a shop in Knightsbridge and soon thereafter taking over a shop in the arcade where he continued to do business.

Tax records showed that he made a comfortable living. A check of his flat showed that he lived within his means. He was well-regarded by his fellow dealers. His one employee, Beatrix, evidently liked working with him part-time. Cooley had no friends, still didn't frequent local pubs—rarely drank at all, it seemed—lived alone, had no known sexual preferences, and traveled a good deal on business.

"He's a bloody cipher, a zero," Owens said.

"Yes," Ashley replied. "At least it explains where Geoff met him—he was a lieutenant with one of the first regiments to go over, and probably wandered into the shop once or twice. You know what a talker Geoff Watkins is. They probably started talking books—can't have been much else. I doubt that Cooley has any interest beyond that."

"Yes, I believe he's what the Yanks call a nerd. Or at least it's an image he's cultivating. What about his parents?"

Ashley smiled. "They are remembered as the local Communists. Nothing serious, but decidedly bolshie until the Hungarian uprising of 1956. That seems to have disenchanted them. They remained outspokenly left-wing, but their political activities effectively ended then. Actually they're remembered as rather pleasant people, but a little odd. Evidently they encouraged the local children to read—made good business sense, if nothing else. Paid their bills on time. Other than that, nothing."

"This girl Beatrix?"

"Somehow she got an education from our state schools. Didn't attend university, but self-taught in literature and the history of publishing. Lives with her elderly father—he's a retired RAF sergeant. She has no social life. She probably spends her evenings watching the telly and sipping Dubonnet. She rather intensely dislikes the Irish, but doesn't mind working with 'Mr. Dennis' because he's an expert in his field. Nothing there at all."

"So, we have a dealer in rare books with a Marxist family, but no known ties with any terrorist group," Owens summarized. "He was in university about the same time as our friend O'Donnell, wasn't he?"

"Yes, but nobody remembers if they ever met. In fact, they lived only a few streets apart, but again no one remembers if Kevin ever frequented the bookshop." Ashley shrugged. "That goes back before O'Donnell attracted any serious attention, remember. If there were a lead of some sort then, it was never documented. They shared this economics instructor. That might have been a useful lead, but the chap died two years ago—natural causes. Their fellow students have scattered to the four winds, and we've yet to find one who knew both of them.''

Owens walked to the corner of his office to pour a cup of tea. *A chap with a Marxist background who attended the same school at the same time as O'Donnell.* Despite the total lack of a connection with a terrorist group, it was enough to follow up. If they could find something to suggest that Cooley and O'Donnell knew each other, then Cooley was the likely bridge between Watkins and the ULA. That did not mean there was any evidence to suggest the link was real, but in several months they had discovered nothing else even close.

''Very well, David, what do you propose to do?''

''We'll plant microphones in his shop and his home, and tap all of his telephone calls, of course. When he travels, he'll have a companion.''

Owens nodded approval. That was more than he could do legally, but the Security Service didn't operate under the same rules as did the Metropolitan Police. ''How about watching his shop?''

''Not easy, when you remember where it is. Still, we might try to get one of our people hired in one of the neighboring shops.''

''The one opposite his is a jewelry establishment, isn't it?''

''Nicholas Reemer and Sons,'' Ashley nodded. ''Owner and two employees.''

Owens thought about that. ''I could find an experienced burglary detective, someone knowledgeable in the field. . . .''

''Morning, Jack,'' Cantor said.

''Hi, Marty.''

Ryan had given up on the satellite photographs weeks before. Now he was trying to find patterns within the terrorist network. Which group had connections with which other? Where did their arms come from? Where did they train? Who helped with the training? Who provided the money? Travel documents? What countries did they use for safe transits?

The problem with these questions was not a lack of information, but a glut of it. Literally thousands of CIA field officers and their agents, plus those of every other Western intelligence service, were scouring the world for such information. Many of the agents—foreign nationals recruited and paid by the Agency—would make reports on the most trivial encounter in the hope of delivering The One Piece of Information that would crack open Abu Nidal, or Islamic Jihad, or one of the other high-profile groups, for a substantial reward. The result was thousands of communiqués, most of them full of worthless garbage that was indistinguishable from the one or two nuggets of real information. Jack had not realized the magnitude of the problem. The people working on this were all talented, but they were being overwhelmed by a sea of raw intelligence data that had to be graded, collated, and cross-referenced before proper analysis could begin. The difficulty of finding any single organization was inversely proportional to its size, and some of these groups were composed of a mere handful of people—in extreme cases composed of family members only.

''Marty,'' Jack said, looking away from the papers on his desk, ''this is the closest thing to impossible I've ever seen.''

''Maybe, but I've come to deliver a well-done,'' Cantor replied.

''What?''

"Remember that satellite photo of the girl in the bikini? The French think they've ID'd her: Françoise Theroux. Long, dark hair, a striking figure, and she was thought to be out of the country when the photo was made. That confirms that the camp belongs to *Action-Directe*."

"So who's the girl?"

"An assassin," Marty replied. He handed Jack a photograph taken at closer range. "And a good one. Three suspected kills, two politicians and an industrialist, all with a pistol at close range. Imagine how it's done: you're a middle-aged man walking down the street; you see a pretty girl; she smiles at you, maybe asks for directions or something; you stop, and the next thing you know, there's a pistol in her hand. Goodbye, Charlie."

Jack looked at the photograph. She didn't look dangerous—she looked like every man's fantasy. "Like we used to say in college, not the sort of girl you'd kick out of bed. Jesus, what sort of world do we live in, Marty?"

"You know that better than I do. Anyway, we've been asked to keep an eye on the camp. If we spot her there again, the French want us to real-time the photo to them."

"They're going to go in after her?"

"They didn't say, but you might recall that the French have troops in Chad, maybe four hundred miles away. Airborne units, with helicopters."

Jack handed the picture back. "What a waste."

"Sure is." Cantor pocketed the photo and the issue. "How's it going with your data?"

"So far I have a whole lot of nothing. The people who do this full-time . . ."

"Yeah, for a while there they were working around the clock. We had to make them stop, they were burning out. Computerizing it was a little helpful. Once we had the head of one group turn up at six airports in one day, and we knew the data was for crap, but every so often we get a live one. We missed that guy by a half hour outside Beirut last March. Thirty goddamned minutes," Cantor said. "You get used to it."

Thirty minutes, Jack thought. *If I'd left my office thirty minutes earlier, I'd be dead. How am I supposed to get used to that?*

"What would you have done to him?"

"We wouldn't have read him his constitutional rights," Cantor replied. "So, any connections that you've been able to find?"

Ryan shook his head. "This ULA outfit is so goddamned small. I have sixteen suspected contacts between the IRA and other groups. Some of them could be our boys, but how can you tell? The reports don't have pictures, the written descriptions could be anybody. Even when we have a reported IRA contact with a bunch they're not supposed be talking to—one that might actually be the ULA—then, A, our underlying information could easily be wrong, and B, it could be the first time they talked with the IRA! Marty, how in the hell is somebody supposed to make any sense out of this garbage?"

"Well, the next time you hear somebody ask what the CIA is doing about terrorism—you won't be able to tell him." Cantor actually smiled at that. "These people we're looking for aren't dumb. They know what'll happen if they get caught. Even if we don't do it ourselves—which we might not want to do—we can always tip the Israelis. Terrorists are tough, nasty bastards, but they can't stand up to real troops and they know it.

"That's the frustrating part. My brother-in-law's an Army major, part of the

Delta Force down at Fort Bragg. I've seen them operate. They could take out this camp you looked at in under two minutes, kill everybody there, and be gone before the echo fades. They're deadly and efficient, but without the right information, they don't know *where* to be deadly and efficient *at*. Same with police work. Do you think the Mafia could survive if the cops knew exactly where and when they did their thing? How many bank robberies would be successful if the SWAT team was waiting inside the doors? But you gotta know where the crooks are. It's all about intelligence, and intelligence comes down to a bunch of faceless bureaucrats sifting through all this crap. The people who gather the intel give it to us, and we process it and give it to the operations teams. The battle is fought here, too, Jack. Right here in this building, by a bunch of GS-9s and -10s who go home to their families every night.''

But the battle is being lost, Jack told himself. *It sure as hell isn't being won.*

''How's the FBI doing?'' he asked.

''Nothing new. The black guy—well, he might as well not exist so far as anyone can tell. They have a crummy picture that's several years old, an alias with no real name or prints to check, and about ten lines of description that mainly says he's smart enough to keep his mouth shut. The Bureau's checking through people who used to be in the radical groups—funny how they have mostly settled down—without any success so far.''

''How about the bunch who flew over there two years back?'' Not so long ago members of several radical American groups had flown to Libya to meet with ''progressive elements'' of the third-world community. The echoes of that event still reverberated through the antiterrorism community.

''You've noticed that we don't have any pictures from Bengazi, right? Our agent got picked up—one of those horrible accidents. It cost us the photos and it cost him his neck. Fortunately they never found out he was working for us. We know some of the names of the people who were there, but not all.''

''Passport records?''

Cantor leaned against the doorframe. ''Let's say Mr. X flew to Europe, an American on vacation—we're talking tens of thousands of people per month. He makes contact with someone on the other side, and they get him the rest of the way without going through the usual immigration-control procedures. It's easy—hell, the Agency does it all the time. If we had a name we could see if he was out of the country at the right time. That would be a start—but we don't have a name to check.''

''We don't have anything!'' Ryan snapped.

''Sure we do. We have all that''—he waved at the documents on Ryan's desk—''and lots more where that came from. Somewhere in there is the answer.''

''You really believe that?''

''Every time we crack one of these things, we find that all the information was under our nose for months. The oversight committees in Congress always hammer us on that. Sitting in that pile right now, Jack, is a crucial lead. That's almost a statistical certainty. But you probably have two or three hundred such reports sitting there, and only one matters.''

''I didn't expect miracles, but I did expect to make some progress,'' Jack said quietly, the magnitude of the problem finally sinking in.

''You did. You saw something that no one else did. You may have found Françoise Theroux. And now if a French agent sees something that might be useful to us, maybe they'll pass it along. You didn't know this, but the intel business is like the old barter economy. We give them, and then they give us, or we'll never give to them again. If this pans out, they'll owe us big-time. They really want that gal. She popped a close friend of their President, and he took it personally.

"Anyway, you get a well-done from the Admiral and the DGSE. The boss says you should take it a little easier, by the way."

"I'll take it easy when I find the bastards," Ryan replied.

"Sometimes you have to back off. You look like hell. You're tired. Fatigue makes for errors. We don't like errors. No more late hours, Jack, that comes from Greer, too. You're out of here by six." Cantor left, denying Jack a chance to object.

Ryan turned back toward his desk, but stared at the wall for several minutes. Cantor was right. He was working so late that half the time he couldn't drive up to Baltimore to see how his daughter was doing. Jack rationalized that his wife was with her every day, frequently spending the night at Hopkins to be close to their daughter. *Cathy has her job and I have mine.*

So, he told the wall, *at least I managed to get something right.* He remembered that it had been an accident, that Marty had made the real connection; but it was also true that he'd done what an analyst was supposed to do, find something odd and bring it to someone's attention. He could feel good about that. He'd found a terrorist maybe, but certainly not the right one.

It's a start. His conscience wondered what the French would do if they found that pretty girl, and how he'd feel about it if he found out. It would be better, he decided, if terrorists were ugly, but pretty or not, their victims were just as dead. He promised himself that he wouldn't go out of his way to find out if anyone got her. Jack went back into the pile, looking for that one piece of hard information. The people he was looking for were somewhere in the pile. He had to find them.

"Hello, Alex," Miller said as he entered the car.

"How was the trip?" He still had his beard, Dobbens saw. Well, nobody had gotten much of a look at him. This time he'd flown to Mexico, driven across the border, then taken a domestic flight into D.C., where Alex had met him.

"Your border security over here's a bloody joke."

"Would it make you happy if they changed it?" Alex inquired. "Let's talk business." The abruptness of his tone surprised Miller.

Aren't you a proud one, with one whole operation under your belt, Miller thought. "We have another job for you."

"You haven't paid me for the last one yet, boy."

Miller handed over a passbook. "Numbered account, Bahamian bank. I believe you'll find the amount correct."

Alex pocketed the book. "That's more like it. Okay, we have another job. I hope you don't expect to go with it as fast as before."

"We have several months to plan it," Miller replied.

"I'm listening." Alex sat through ten minutes of information.

"Are you out of your fucking mind?" Dobbens asked when he was finished.

"How hard would it be to gather the information we need?"

"That's not the problem, Sean. The problem is getting your people in and out. No way I could handle that."

"That is my concern."

"Bullshit! If my people are involved, it's my concern, too. If that Clark turkey broke to the cops, it would have burned a safehouse—and me!"

"But he didn't break, did he? That's why we chose him."

"Look, what you do with your people, I don't give a rat's ass. What happens to my people, I do. That last little game we played for you was bush league, Sean."

Miller figured out what "bush league" meant from context. "The operation was politically sound, and you know it. Perhaps you've forgotten that the objective is always political. Politically, the operation was a complete success."

"I don't need you to tell me that!" Alex snapped back in his best intimidating tone. Miller was a proud little twerp, but Alex figured he could pinch his head off with one good squeeze. "You lost a troop because you were playing this personal, not professional—and I know what you're thinking. It was our first big play, right? Well, son, I think we proved that we got our shit together, didn't we? And I warned you up front that your man was too exposed. If you'd listened to me, you wouldn't have a man on the inside. I know your background is pretty impressive, but this is my turf, and I know it."

Miller knew that he had to accept that. He kept his face impassive. "Alex, if we were in any way displeased, we would not have come back to you. Yes, you do have your shit together," *you bloody nigger,* he didn't say. "Now, can you get us the information we need?"

"Sure, for the right price. You want us in the op?"

"We don't know yet," Miller replied honestly. *Of course the only issue here is money. Bloody Americans.*

"If you want us in, I'm part of the planning. Number one, I want to know how you get in and out. I might have to go with you. If you shitcan my advice this time, I walk and I take my people with me."

"It's a little early to be certain, but what we hope to arrange is really quite simple. . . ."

"You think you can set that up?" For the first time since he'd arrived, Sean had Alex nodding approval. "Slick. I'll give you that. It's slick. Now let's talk price."

Sean wrote a figure on a piece of paper and handed it to Alex. "Fair enough?" People interested in money were easy to impress.

"I sure would like an account at *your* bank, brother."

"If this operation comes off, you will."

"You mean that?"

Miller nodded emphatically. "Direct access. Training facilities, help with travel documents, the lot. Your skill in helping us last time attracted attention. Our friends like the idea of an active revolutionary cell in America." *If they really want to do business with you, it's their problem.* "Now, how quickly can you get the information?"

"End of the week good enough?"

"Can you do it that fast without attracting attention?"

"Let me worry about that," Alex replied with a smile.

"Anything new on your end?" Owens asked.

"Not much," Murray admitted. "We have plenty of forensic evidence, but only one witness who got a clear look at one face, and she can't give us a real ID."

"The local help?"

"That's who we almost ID'd. Nothing yet. Maybe they've learned from the ULA. No manifesto, no announcement claiming credit for the job. The people we have inside some other radical groups—that is, those that still exist—have drawn a big blank. We're still working on it, and we have a lot of money out on the street, but so far we haven't got anything to show for it." Murray paused. "That'll change.

Bill Shaw is a genius, one of the real brains we have in the Bureau. They switched him over from counterintelligence to terrorism a few years back, and he's done really impressive work. What's new on your end?''

''I can't go into specifics yet,'' Owens said. ''But we might have a small break. We're trying to decide now if it's real or not. That's the good news. The bad is that His Royal Highness is traveling to America this coming summer. A number of people were informed of his itinerary, including six on our list of possible suspects.''

''How the hell did you let that happen, Jimmy?''

''No one asked me, Dan,'' Owens replied sourly. ''In several cases, if the people hadn't been informed it would have told them that something odd was happening—you can't simply stop trusting people, can you? For the rest, it was just another balls-up. Some secretary put out the plans on the normal list without consulting the security officers.'' This wasn't a new story for either man. There was always someone who didn't get the word.

''Super. So call it off. Let him get the flu or something when the time comes,'' Murray suggested.

''His Highness won't do that. He's become quite adamant on the subject. He won't allow a terrorist threat to affect his life in any way.''

Murray grunted. ''You gotta admire the kid's guts, but—''

''Quite so,'' Owens agreed. He didn't really care for having his next king referred to as ''the kid,'' but he'd long since gotten used to the American way of expressing things. ''It doesn't make our job any easier.''

''How firm are the travel plans?'' Murray asked, getting back to business.

''Several items on the itinerary are tentative, of course, but most are set in stone. Our security people will be meeting with yours in Washington. They're flying over next week.''

''Well, you know that you'll get all the cooperation you want, Secret Service, the Bureau, local police, everything. We'll take good care of him for you,'' Murray assured him. ''He and his wife are pretty popular back home. Will they be taking the baby with them?''

''No. We were able to prevail on him about that.''

''Okay. I'll call Washington tomorrow and get things rolling. What's happening with our friend Ned Clark?''

''Nothing as yet. His colleagues are evidently giving him rather a bad time, but he's too bloody stupid to break.''

Murray nodded. He knew the type.

Well, they wanted me to take off early, Ryan thought. He decided to accept an invitation to a lecture at Georgetown University. Unfortunately, it was something of a disappointment. Professor David Hunter was Columbia's *enfant terrible,* America's ranking authority on political affairs in Eastern Europe. His book of the previous year, *Revolution Postponed,* had been a penetrating study of the political and economic problems of the Soviet's unsteady empire, and Ryan, like others, had been eager to hear his new information on the subject. The speech had turned out to be little more than a rehash of the book, with the rather startling suggestion at the end that the NATO countries should be more aggressive in trying to separate the Soviet Union from her captives. Ryan considered that to be lunacy, even if it did guarantee lively discussions at the reception.

At the end of the talk, Ryan moved quickly to the reception. He'd skipped dinner to make it here on time. There was a wide table of hors d'oeuvres, and Jack filled his plate as patiently as he could before drifting off to a sedate corner by the elevators. He let others form knots of conversation around Professor Hunter. On the whole, it was nice to be back at Georgetown, if only for a few hours. The "Galleria" in the Intercultural Center was quite a contrast to the CIA institutional drab. The four-story atrium of the language building was lined with the glass windows of offices, and a pair of potted trees reached toward the glass roof. The plaza outside was paved with bricks, and known to the students as Red Square. To the west was the old quadrangle, and the cemetery where rested the priests who had taught here for nearly two hundred years. It was a thoroughly civilized setting, except for the discordant shriek of jets coming out of National Airport, a few miles downriver. Someone jostled Ryan just as he was finishing his snacks.

"Excuse me, Doctor." Ryan turned to see a man shorter than himself. He had a florid complexion and was dressed in a cheap-looking suit. His blue eyes seemed to sparkle with amusement. His voice had a pronounced accent. "Did you enjoy the lecture?"

"It was interesting," Ryan said diffidently.

"So. I see that capitalists can lie as well as we poor socialists." The man had a jolly, overpowering laugh, but Jack decided that his eyes were sparkling with something other than amusement. They were measuring eyes, playing yet another variation of the game he'd been part of in England. Already Ryan disliked him.

"Have we met?"

"Sergey Platonov." They shook hands after Ryan set his plate on a table. "I am Third Secretary of the Soviet Embassy. Perhaps my photograph at Langley does not do me justice."

A Russian—Ryan tried not to look too surprised—*who knows I've been working at CIA*. Third Secretary could easily mean that he was KGB, perhaps a diplomatic intelligence specialist, or maybe a member of the CPSU's Foreign Department—as though it made a difference. A "legal" intelligence officer with a diplomatic cover. *What do I do now?* For one thing, he knew that he'd have to write up a contact report for CIA tomorrow, explaining how they'd met and what they'd talked about, perhaps an hour's work. It took an effort to remain polite.

"You must have the wrong guy, Mr. Platonov. I'm a history teacher. I work at the Naval Academy in Annapolis. I was invited to this because I got my degree here."

"No, no." The Russian shook his head. "I recognize you from the photograph on your book jacket. You see, I purchased ten copies of it last summer."

"Indeed." Jack was surprised again and unable to conceal it. "My publisher and I thank you, sir."

"Our Naval Attaché was much taken by it, Doctor Ryan. He felt that it should be brought to the attention of the Frunze Academy, and, I think, the Grechko Naval Academy in Leningrad." Platonov applied his considerable charm. Ryan knew it for what it was, but . . . "To be honest, I merely skimmed the book myself. It seemed quite well organized, and the Attaché said that your analysis of the way decisions are made in the heat of battle was highly accurate."

"Well." Jack tried not to be overly flattered, but it was hard. Frunze was *the* Soviet staff academy, the finishing school for young field-grade officers who were tagged for stardom. The Grechko Academy was only slightly less prestigious.

"Sergey Nikolay'ch," boomed a familiar voice, "it is not *kulturny* to prey upon the vanity of helpless young authors.'' Father Timothy Riley joined them. A short, plump Jesuit priest, Riley had headed the history department at Georgetown while Ryan had gotten his doctorate. He was a brilliant intellect with a series of books to his credit, including two penetrating works on the history of Marxism—neither of which, Ryan was certain, had found their way into the library at Frunze. ''How's the family, Jack?''

''Cathy's back to work, Father. They moved Sally over to Hopkins. With luck we'll have her home early next week.''

''She will recover fully, your little daughter?'' Platonov asked. ''I read about the attack on your family in the newspaper.''

''We think so. Except for losing her spleen, there seems to be no permanent damage. The docs say she's recovering nicely, and with her at Hopkins, Cathy's able to see her every day,'' Ryan said more positively than he felt. Sally was a different child. Her legs weren't fully healed yet, but worst of all, his bouncing little girl was a sad thing now. She'd learned a lesson that Ryan had hoped to hold off for at least ten more years—that the world is a dangerous place even when you have a mother and a father to take care of you. A hard lesson for a child, it was harder still for a parent. *But she's alive,* Jack told himself, unaware of the expression on his face. *With time and love, you can recover from anything, except death.* The doctors and nurses at Hopkins were taking care of her like one of their own. That was a tangible advantage of having a doctor in the family.

''A terrible thing.'' Platonov shook his head in what seemed to be genuine disgust. ''A terrible thing to attack innocent people for no reason.''

''Indeed, Sergey,'' Riley said in the astringent voice that Ryan had known so well. When he wanted, ''Father Tim'' had a tongue that could saw through wood. ''I seem to recall that V. I. Lenin said the purpose of terrorism is to terrorize, and that sympathy in a revolutionary is as reprehensible as cowardice on the field of battle.''

''Those were hard times, good Father,'' Platonov said smoothly. ''My country has no business with those IRA madmen. They are not revolutionaries, however much they pretend to be. They have no revolutionary ethic. It is madness, what they do. The working classes should be allies, contesting together against the common enemy that exploits them both, instead of killing one another. Both sides of the conflict are victimized by bosses who play them off against each other, but instead of recognizing this they kill one another like mad dogs, and with as little point. They are bandits, not revolutionaries,'' he concluded with a distinction lost on the other two.

''Maybe so, but if I ever get my hands on them, I'll give them a lesson in revolutionary justice.'' It was good to let his hatred out in the open for once.

''You have no sympathy for them, either of you?'' Platonov baited them. ''After all, you are both related to the victims of British imperialism. Did not both your families flee to America to escape it?''

Ryan was caught very short by that remark. It seemed an incredible thing to say until he saw that the Russian was watching for his reaction.

''Or perhaps the direct victim of Soviet imperialism,'' Jack responded with his own look. ''Those two guys in London had Kalashnikov rifles. So did the ones who attacked my wife,'' he lied. ''You don't buy one of those at the local hardware store. Whether you choose to admit it or not, most of the terrorists over there profess to be Marxists. That makes them your allies, not mine, and it makes it appear more than a coincidence that they use Soviet arms.''

''Do you know how many countries manufacture weapons of Soviet design? It is sadly inevitable that some will fall into the wrong hands.''

''In any case, my sympathy for their aim is, shall we say, limited by their choice of technique. You can't build a civilized country on a foundation of murder,'' Ryan concluded. ''Much as some people have tried.''

''It would be well if the world worked in more peaceful ways.'' Platonov ignored the implicit comment on the Soviet Union. ''But it is an historical fact that nations are born in blood, even yours. As countries grow, they mature beyond such conduct. It is not easy, but I think we can all see the value of peaceful coexistence. For myself, Doctor Ryan, I can sympathize with your feelings. I have two fine sons. We once had a daughter also, Nadia. She died long ago, at age seven, from leukemia. I know it is a hard thing to see your child in pain, but you are more fortunate than I. Your daughter will live.'' He allowed his voice to soften. ''We disagree on many things, but no man can fail to love his children.

''So.'' Platonov changed gears smoothly. ''What did you really think of Professor Hunter's little speech? Should America seek to foment counterrevolution in the socialist states of Europe?''

''Why don't you ask the State Department? That's not my part of the world, remember? I teach naval history. But if you want a personal opinion, I don't see how we can encourage people to rebel if we have no prospect of helping them directly when your country reacts.''

''Ah, good. You understand that we must act to protect our fraternal socialist brothers from aggression.''

The man was good, Ryan saw, but he'd had a lot of practice at this. ''I wouldn't call the encouragement of people to seek their own freedom a form of aggression, Mr. Platonov. I was a stockbroker before I got my history degree, and that doesn't make me much of a candidate for sympathizing with your political outlook. What I am saying is that your country used military force to crush democratic feelings in Czechoslovakia and Hungary. To encourage people toward their own suicide is both immoral and counterproductive.''

''Ah, but what does your government think?'' the Russian asked with another jolly laugh.

''I'm a historian, not a soothsayer. In this town they all work for the *Post*. Ask them.''

''In any case,'' the Russian went on, ''our Naval Attaché is most interested to meet you and discuss your book. We are having a reception at the embassy on the twelfth of next month. The good Father is coming, he can watch over your soul. Might you and your wife attend?''

''For the next few weeks I plan to be at home with my family. My girl needs me there for a while.''

The diplomat was not to be put off. ''Yes, I can understand that. Some other time, perhaps?''

''Sure, give me a call sometime this summer.'' *Are you kidding?*

''Excellent. Now if you will excuse me, I wish to speak to Professor Hunter.'' The diplomat shook hands again and walked off to the knot of historians who were hanging on Hunter's every word.

Ryan turned to Father Riley, who'd watched the exchange in silence while sipping at his champagne.

''Interesting guy, Sergey,'' Riley said. ''He loves to hit people for reactions.

I wonder if he really believes in his system or if he's just playing the game for points . . . ?''

Ryan had a more immediate question. ''Father, what in the hell was that all about?''

Riley chuckled. ''You're being checked out, Jack.''

''Why?''

''You don't need me to answer that. You're working at CIA. If I guess right, Admiral Greer wants you on his personal staff. Marty Cantor is taking a job at the University of Texas next year, and you're one of the candidates for his job. I don't know if Sergey's aware of that, but you probably looked like the best target of opportunity in the room, and he wanted to get a feel for you. Happens all the time.''

''Cantor's job? But—nobody told me that!''

''The world's full of surprises. They probably haven't finished the full background check on you yet, and they won't pop the offer until they do. I presume the information you're looking at is still pretty limited?''

''I can't discuss that, Father.''

The priest smiled. ''Thought so. The work you've done over there has impressed the right people. If I have things right, they're going to bring you along like a good welterweight prospect.'' Riley got another glass of champagne. ''If I know James Greer, he'll just sort of ease you into it. What did it, you see, was that Canary Trap thing. It really impressed some folks.''

''How do you know all this?'' Ryan asked, shocked at what he'd just heard.

''Jack, how do you think you got over there in the first place? Who do you think got you that Center for Strategic and International Studies fellowship? The people there liked your work, too. Between what I said and what they said, Marty thought you were worth a look last summer, and you worked out better than anyone expected. There are some people around town who respect my opinion.''

''Oh.'' Ryan had to smile. He'd allowed himself to forget the first thing about the Society of Jesus: they know everyone, from whom they can learn nearly everything. The President of the university belonged to both the Cosmos and University clubs, with which came access to the most important ears and mouths in Washington. That's how it would start. Occasionally a man would need advice on something, and being unable to consult the people he worked with, he might try to discuss it with a clergyman. No one was better qualified for this than a Jesuit, meticulously educated, well versed in the ways of the world, but not spoiled by it—most of the time. Like any clergyman, each was a good listener. So effective was the Society at gathering information that the State Department's code-breakers had once been tasked to break the Jesuits' own cipher systems; the assignment had started a small revolt in the ''Black Chamber'' . . . until they'd realized what sort of information was finding its way to them.

When Saint Ignatius Loyola had founded the order, the ex-soldier set it on a path to do only two things: to send out missionaries and to build schools. Both had been done extraordinarily well. The influence passed on by the schooling would never be lost on the men who'd graduated. It wasn't Machiavellian, not really. The colleges and universities plied its students with philosophy and ethics and theology—all required courses—to mute their baser tendencies and sharpen their wits. For centuries the Jesuits had built ''men for others,'' and wielded a kind of invisible temporal power, mainly for the good. Father Riley's intellectual credentials were widely known, and his opinions would be sought, just as from any distinguished academic, added to which was his moral authority as a graduate theologian.

"We're good security risks, Jack," Riley said benignly. "Can you imagine one of us being a Communist agent? So, are you interested in the job?"

"I don't know." Ryan looked at his reflection in a window. "It would mean more time away from the family. We're expecting another one this summer, you know."

"Congratulations, that's good news. I know you're a family man, Jack. The job would mean some sacrifices, but you're a good man for it."

"Think so?" *I haven't exactly set the world on fire yet.*

"I'd rather see people like you over there than some others I know. Jack, you're plenty smart enough. You know how to make decisions, but more importantly, you're a pretty good fellow. I know you're ambitious, but you've got ethics, values. I'm one of those people who thinks that still matters for something in the world, regardless of how nasty things get."

"They get pretty nasty, Father," Ryan said after a moment.

"How close are you to finding them?"

"Not very close at—" Jack stopped himself too late. "You did that one pretty well."

"I didn't mean it that way," Father Tim said very sincerely. "It would be a better world if they were off the street. There must be something wrong with the way they think. It's hard to understand how anyone could deliberately hurt a child."

"Father, you really don't have to understand them. You just have to know where to find them."

"That's work for the police, and the courts, and a jury. That's why we have laws, Jack," Riley said gently.

Ryan turned to the window again. He examined his own image and wondered what it was that he saw. "Father, you're a good man, but you've never had kids of your own. I can forgive somebody who comes after me, maybe, but not anyone who tries to hurt my little girl. If I find him—hell, I won't. But I sure would like to," Jack told the image of himself. *Yes,* it agreed.

"It's not a good thing, hate. It might do things to you that you'll regret, things that can change you from the person you are."

Ryan turned back, thinking about the person he'd just looked at. "Maybe it already has."

20. Data

It was a singularly boring tape. Owens was used to reading police reports, transcripts of interrogations, and, worst of all, intelligence documents, but the tape was even more boring than that. The microphone which the Security Service had hidden in Cooley's shop was sound-activated and sensitive enough to pick up any noise. The fact that Cooley hummed a lot made Owens regret this feature. The detective whose job it was to listen to the unedited tape had included several minutes of the awful, atonal noise to let his commander know what he had to suffer through. The bell finally rang.

Owens heard the clatter, made metallic by the recording system, of the door opening and closing, then the sound of Cooley's swivel chair scraping across the floor. It must have had a bad wheel, Owens noted.

"Good morning, sir!" It was Cooley's voice.

"And to you," said the second. "Well, have you finished the Marlowe?"

"Yes, I have."

"So what's the price?"

Cooley didn't say it aloud, but Ashley had told Owens that the shop owner never spoke a price. He handed it to his customers on a file card. That, Owens thought, was one way to keep from haggling.

"That is quite steep, you know," Watkins' voice observed.

"I could get more, but you are one of our better clients," Cooley replied.

The sigh was audible on the tape. "Very well, it is worth it."

The transaction was made at once. They could hear the rasping sound of new banknotes being counted.

"I may soon have something new from a collection in Kerry," Cooley said next.

"Oh?" There was interest in the reply.

"Yes, a signed first edition of *Great Expectations*. I saw it on my last trip over. Might you be interested in that?"

"Signed, eh?"

"Yes, sir, 'Boz' himself. I realize that the Victorian period is rather more recent than most of your acquisitions, but the author's signature . . ."

"Indeed. I would like to see it, of course."

"That can be arranged."

"At this point," Owens told Ashley, "Watkins leaned over, and our man in the jewelry shop lost sight of him."

"So he could have passed a message."

"Possibly." Owens switched off the tape machine. The rest of the conversation had no significance.

"The last time he was in Ireland, Cooley didn't go to County Kerry. He was in Cork the whole time. He visited three dealers in rare books, spent the night in a hotel, and had a few pints at a local pub," Ashley reported.

"A pub?"

"Yes, he drinks in Ireland, but not in London."

"Did he meet anyone there?"

"Impossible to tell. Our man wasn't close enough. His orders were to be discreet, and he did well not to be spotted." Ashley was quiet for a moment as he tried to pin down something on the tape. "It sounded to me as though he paid cash for the book."

"He did, and it is out of pattern. Like most of us he uses checks and credit cards for the majority of his transactions, but not for this. His bank records show no checks to this shop, though he does occasionally make large cash withdrawals. They may or may not match with his purchases there."

"How very odd," Ashley thought aloud. "Everyone—well, someone must know that he goes there."

"Checks have dates on them," Owens suggested.

"Perhaps." Ashley wasn't convinced, but he'd done enough investigations of this kind to know that you never got all the answers. Some details were always left hanging. "I took another look at Geoff's service record last night. Do you know that when he was in Ireland, he had four men killed in his platoon?"

"What? That makes him a fine candidate for our investigation!" Owens didn't think this was good news.

"That's what I thought," Ashley agreed. "I had one of our chaps in Germany—his former regiment's assigned to the BAOR at the moment—interview one of Watkins's mates. Had a platoon in the same company, the chap's a half-colonel now. He said that Geoff took it quite hard, that he was quite vociferous on the point that they were in the wrong place, doing the wrong thing, and losing people in the process. Rather puts a different spin on things, doesn't it?"

"Another lieutenant with the solution to the problem." Owens snorted.

"Yes—we leave and let the bloody Irish sort things out. That's not exactly a rare sentiment in the Army, you know."

It wasn't exactly a rare sentiment throughout England, Commander Owens knew. "Even so, it's not much of a basis for motive, is it?"

"Better than nothing at all."

The cop grunted agreement. "What else did the Colonel tell your chap?"

"Obviously Geoff had a rather busy tour of duty in the Belfast area. He and his men saw a lot. They were there when the Army was welcomed in by the Catholics, and they were there when the situation reversed. It was a bad time for everyone," Ashley added unnecessarily.

"It's still not very much. We have a former subaltern, now in the striped-pants brigade, who didn't like being in Northern Ireland; he happens to buy rare books from a chap who grew up there and now runs a completely legitimate business in central London. You know what any solicitor would say: pure coincidence. We don't have one single thing that can remotely be called evidence. The background of each man is pure enough to qualify him for sainthood."

"These are the people we've been looking for," Ashley insisted.

"I know that." Owens almost surprised himself when he said it for the first time. His professionalism told him that this was a mistake, but his instincts told him otherwise. It wasn't a new feeling for the Commander of C-13, but one that always made him uneasy. If his instincts were wrong, he was looking in the wrong place, at the wrong people. But his instincts were almost never wrong. "You know the rules of the game, and by those rules, I don't even have enough to go to the Commissioner. He'd boot me out of the office, and be right to do so. We have nothing but unsupported suspicions." The two men stared at each other for several seconds.

"I never wanted to be a policeman." Ashley smiled and shook his head.

"I didn't get my wish, either. I wanted to be an engine driver when I was six, but my father said there were enough railway people in the family. So I became a copper." Both men laughed. There wasn't anything else to do.

"I'll increase the surveillance on Cooley's trips abroad. I don't think there's much more to be done on your side," Ashley said finally.

"We have to wait for them to make a mistake. Sooner or later they all do, you know."

"But soon enough?" That was the question.

"Here we are," Alex said.

"How did you get these?" Miller asked in amazement.

"Routine, man. Power companies shoot aerial photographs of their territory all the time. They help us plan the surveys we have to do. And here"—he reached into his briefcase—"is a topographic map. There's your target, boy." Alex handed him a magnifying glass borrowed from his company. It was a color shot, taken on a bright sunny day. You could tell the makes of the cars. It must have been done the previous summer—the grass had just been cut. . . .

"How tall is the cliff?"

"Enough that you don't want to fall off it. Tricky, too. I forget what it's made of, sandstone or something crumbly, but you want to be careful with it. See that fence here? The man knows to keep away from the edge. We have the same problem at our reactor plant at Calvert Cliff. It's the same geological structure, and a lot of work went into giving the plant a solid foundation."

"Only one road in," Miller noted.

"Dead end, too. That *is* a problem. We have these gullies here and here. Notice that the power line comes in cross-country, from this road over here. It looks like there was an old farm road that connected with this one, but they let it go to seed. That's going to be helpful."

"How? No one can use it."

"I'll tell you later. Friday, you and me are going fishing."

"What?" Miller looked up in surprise.

"You want to eyeball the cliff, right? Besides, the blues are running. I love bluefish."

Breckenridge had silhouette targets up, finally. Jack's trips to the range were less frequent now, mainly in the mornings before class. If nothing else, the incident outside the gate had told the Marine and civilian guards that their jobs were valuable. Two Marines and one of the civilians were also firing their service pieces. They didn't just shoot to qualify now. They were all shooting for scores. Jack hit the button to reel his target in. His rounds were all clustered in the center of the target.

"Pretty good, Doc." The Sergeant Major was standing behind him. "If you want, we can run a competition string. I figure you'll qualify for a medal now."

Ryan shook his head. He still had to shower after his morning jog. "I'm not doing this for score, Gunny."

"When does the little girl come home?"

"Next Wednesday, I hope."

"That's good, sir. Who's going to look after her?"

"Cathy's taking a few weeks off."

"My wife asked if y'all might need any help," Breckenridge said.

Jack turned in surprise. "Sissy—Commander Jackson's wife—will be over most of the time. Please thank your wife for us, Gunny, that's damned nice of her."

"No big deal. Any luck finding the bastards?" Ryan's day-hops to CIA were not much of a secret.

"Not yet."

"Good morning, Alex," the field superintendent said. "You're staying in a little late. What can I do for you?" Bert Griffin was always in early, but he rarely saw Dobbens before he went home at seven every morning.

"I've been looking over the specifications on that new Westinghouse transformer."

"Getting dull working nights?" Griffin asked with a smile. This was a fairly easy time of year for the utility company. In the summer, with all the air conditioners up and running, things would be different, of course. Spring was the time of year for new ideas.

"I think we're ready to give it a try."

"Have they ironed the bugs out?"

"Pretty much, enough for a field test, I think."

"Okay." Griffin sat back in his chair. "Tell me about it."

"Mainly, sir, I'm worried about the old ones. The problem's only going to get worse as we start retiring the old units. We had that chemical spill last month—"

"Oh, yeah." Griffin rolled his eyes. Most of the units in use contained PBBs, polybrominated biphenyls, as a cooling element within the power transformer. These were dangerous to the linemen, who were supposed to wear protective clothing when working on them, but, despite company rules, often didn't bother. PBBs were a serious health hazard to the men. Even worse, the company had to dispose of the toxic liquid periodically. It was expensive and ran the risk of spills, the paperwork for which was rapidly becoming as time-consuming as that associated with the company's nuclear reactor plant. Westinghouse was experimenting with a transformer that used a completely inert chemical in place of the PBBs. Though expensive, it held great promise for long-term economies—and would help get the environmentalists off their backs, which was even more attractive than the monetary savings. "Alex, if you can get those babies up and working, I will personally get you a new company car!"

"Well, I want to try one out. Westinghouse will lend us one for free."

"This is really starting to sound good," Griffin noted. "But have they really ironed the bugs out yet?"

"They say so, except for some occasional voltage fluctuations. They're not sure what causes that, and they want to do some field tests."

"How bad are the fluctuations?"

"Marginal." Alex pulled out a pad and read off the numbers. "It seems to be an environmental problem. Looks like it only happens when the ambient air temperature changes rapidly. If that's the real cause, it shouldn't be too hard to beat."

Griffin considered that for a few seconds. "Okay, where do you want to set it up?"

"I have a spot picked out down in Anne Arundel County, south of Annapolis."

"That's a long ways away. Why there?"

"It's a dead-end line. If the transformer goes bad, it won't hurt many houses. The other thing is, one of my crews is only twenty miles away, and I've been training them on the new unit. We'll set up the test instrumentation, and I can have them check it every day for the first few months. If it works out, we can make our purchase order in the fall and start setting them up next spring."

"Okay. Where exactly is this?"

Dobbens unfolded his map on Griffin's table. "Right here."

"Expensive neighborhood," the field superintendent said dubiously.

"Aw, come on, boss!" Alex snorted. "How would it look in the papers if we did all our experiments on poor folk? Besides"—he smiled—"all those environmental freaks are rich, aren't they?"

Dobbens had chosen his remark with care. One of Griffin's personal hobbyhorses was the "Park Avenue Environmentalist." The field superintendent owned a small farm, and didn't like having some condo-owning dilettante tell him about nature.

"Okay, you can run with it. How soon can you set it up?"

"Westinghouse can have the unit to us the end of next week. I can have it up and running three days after that. I want my crew to check the lines—in fact, I'll be going down myself to set it up if you don't mind."

Griffin nodded approval. "You're my kind of engineer, son. Most of the schoolboys we get now are afraid to get their hands dirty. You'll keep me posted?"

"Yes, sir."

"Keep up the good work, Alex. I've been telling management about you."

"I appreciate that, Mr. Griffin."

Dobbens left the building and drove home in his two-year-old company Plymouth. Most of the rush-hour traffic was heading in while he headed out. He was home in under an hour. Sean Miller was just waking up, drinking tea and watching television. Alex wondered how anyone could start the day with tea. He made some instant coffee for himself.

"Well?" Miller asked.

"No problem." Alex smiled, then stopped. It occurred to him that he'd miss his job. After all the talk in college about bringing Power to the People, he'd realized with surprise after starting with BG&E that a utility company engineer did exactly that. In a funny sort of way, he was now serving the ordinary people, though not in a manner that carried much significance. Dobbens decided that it was good training for his future ambitions. He'd remember that even those who served humbly still served. An important lesson for the future. "Come on, we'll talk about it in the boat."

Wednesday was a special day. Jack was away from both his jobs, carrying the bear while Cathy wheeled their daughter out. The bear was a gift from the midshipmen of his history classes, an enormous monster that weighed sixty pounds and was nearly five feet tall, topped off with a Smokey Bear hat—actually that of a Marine drill instructor courtesy of Breckenridge and the guard detail. A police officer opened the door for the procession. It was a windy March day, but the family wagon was parked just outside. Jack scooped up his daughter in both arms while Cathy thanked the nurses. He made sure she was in her safety seat and buckled the belt himself. The bear had to go in the back.

"Ready to go home, Sally?"

"Yes." Her voice was listless. The nurses reported that she still cried out in her sleep. Her legs were fully healed, finally. She could walk again, badly and awkwardly, but she could walk. Except for the loss of her spleen, she was whole again. Her hair was trimmed short to compensate for what had been shaved, but that would grow out soon enough. Even the scars, the surgeons said, would fade, and the pediatricians assured him that in a few months the nightmares would end. Jack turned to run his hand along the little face, and got a smile for his efforts. It wasn't the smile he was accustomed to getting. Behind his own smile, Ryan's mind boiled with rage yet again, but he told himself that this wasn't the time. Sally needed a father now, not an avenger.

"We have a surprise waiting for you," he said.

"What?" Sally asked.

"If I told you, it wouldn't be a surprise," her father pointed out.

"Daddy!" For a moment his little girl was back.

"Wait and see."

"What's that?" Cathy asked on getting in the car.

"The surprise."

"What surprise?"

"See," Jack told his daughter. "Mommy doesn't know either."

"Jack, what's going on?"

"Doctor Schenk and I had a little talk last week," was all Ryan would say. He released the parking brake and headed off onto Broadway.

"I want my bear," Sally said.

"He's too big to sit there, honey," Cathy responded.

"But you can wear his Smokey hat. He said it was okay." Jack handed it back. The wide-brimmed campaign hat dropped over her head.

"Did you thank the people for the bear?" Cathy asked.

"You bet." Ryan smiled for a moment. "Nobody flunks this term. But don't tell anybody that." Jack had a reputation as a tough marker. That might not survive this semester. *Principles be damned,* he told himself. The mids in his classes had sent Sally a steady stream of flowers, toys, puzzles, and cards that had entertained his little girl, then circulated around the pediatric floor and brightened the days of fifty more sick kids. Smokey Bear was the crowning achievement. The nurses had told Cathy that it had made a difference. The monster toy had often sat at the top of Sally's bed, with the little girl clinging to it. It would be a tough act to follow, but Jack had that one figured out. Skip Tyler was making the final arrangements now.

Jack took his time, driving as though he were carrying a cargo of cracked eggs. His recent habits at CIA made him yearn for a cigarette, but he knew that he'd have to stop that now, with Cathy home all the time. He was careful to avoid the route Cathy had taken the day that— His hands tightened on the wheel as they had for weeks now. He knew he had to stop thinking about it so much. It had become an obsession, and that wasn't going to help anything.

The scenery had changed since the . . . accident. What had been bare trees now had the green edges of buds and leaves with the beginning of spring. Horses and cows were out on the farms. Some calves and colts were visible, and Sally's nose pressed against the car window as she looked at them. As it did every year, life was renewing itself, Ryan told himself. His family was whole again, and he'd keep it that way. The last turn onto Falcon's Nest Road finally came. Jack noted that the utility trucks were still around, and he wondered briefly what they had been up to as he turned left into his driveway.

"Skip's here?" Cathy asked.

"Looks like it," Jack replied with a suppressed grin.

"They're home," Alex said.

"Yeah," Louis noted. Both men were perched at the top of the utility pole, ostensibly stringing new power lines to accommodate the experimental transformer. "You know, the day after the job," the lineman said, "there was a picture of the lady in the papers. Some kid went through a window and got his face all cut up. It was a little brother, Alex. The lady saved his eyes, man."

"I remember, Louis." Alex raised his camera and snapped off a string of shots.

"An' I don't like fucking with kids, man," Louis said. "A cop's a different thing," he added defensively. He didn't have to say that so was the kid's father. That was business. Like Alex, he had a few remaining scruples, and hurting children was not something he could do without some internal turmoil.

"Maybe we were all lucky." Alex knew objectively that this was a stupid way for a revolutionary to think. Sentimentality had no place in his mission; it got in the way of what he had to do, prolonging the task and causing more deaths in the process. He also knew that the taboos against injuring children were part of the genetic programming of any human being. Mankind had progressed in its knowledge since Marx and Lenin. So whenever possible he'd avoid injuring kids. He rationalized that this would enhance his sympathy in the community he was seeking to liberate.

"Yeah."

"So what have you seen?"

"They got a maid—black o'course. Fine-lookin' woman, drives a Chevy. There's somebody else in there now. He's a white dude, big guy, an' he walks funny."

"Right." Alex made note of the former and dismissed the latter. The man was probably a family friend.

"The cops—state cops—are back here every two hours minimum. One of them asked me what we were doing yesterday afternoon. They're keeping an eye on this place. There's an extra phone line into the house—gotta be for an alarm company. So they got a house alarm and the cops are always close."

"Okay. Keep your eyes open but don't be too obvious."

"You got it."

"Home," Ryan breathed. He stopped the car and got out, walking around to Sally's door. He saw that the little girl wasn't playing with the seat-belt buckle. He took care of it himself, then lifted his daughter out of the car. She wrapped her arms around his neck, and for a moment life was perfect again. He carried Sally to the front door, both arms clasping her to his chest.

"Welcome back." Skip had the door open already.

"Where's my surprise?" Sally demanded.

"Surprise?" Tyler was taken aback. "I don't know about any surprise."

"Daddy!" Her father got an accusing look.

"Come on in," Tyler said.

Mrs. Hackett was there, too. She'd gotten lunch ready for everyone. A single mother of two sons, she worked hard to support them. Ryan set his girl down, and she walked to the kitchen. Skip Tyler and her father watched her stiff legs negotiate the distance.

"God, it's amazing how kids heal," Tyler observed.

"What?" Jack was surprised.

"I broke a leg playing ball once—damned if I bounced back that fast. Come on," Tyler beckoned Jack out the door. First he checked out the stuffed animal in the car. "I heard it was some kind of bear. That one must have played in Chicago!"

Then they went into the trees north of Ryan's house. Here they found the surprise, tied to a tree. Jack loosed the chain and picked him up.

"Thanks for bringing him over."

"Hey, no big deal. It's good to see her home, pal."

The two men walked back into the house. Jack peeked around the corner and saw that Sally was already demolishing a peanut-butter sandwich.

"Sally . . ." he said. His wife was already looking at him with an open mouth. His daughter's head came around just as Jack set the puppy on the floor.

It was a black Labrador, just old enough to be separated from his mother. The puppy needed a single look to know to whom he belonged. He scampered across the floor, mostly sideways, with his tail gyrating wildly. Sally was on the floor, and grabbed him. A moment later, the dog was cleaning her face.

"She's too little for a puppy," Cathy said.

"Okay, you can take him back this afternoon," Jack replied quietly. The remark got him an angry look. His daughter squealed when the dog started chewing on the heel of one shoe. "She's not big enough for a pony yet, but I think this is just the right thing."

"You train it!"

"That'll be easy. He comes from good stock. Champion Chesapeake's Victor Hugo Black for a father, would you believe? The Lab's got a soft mouth, and they like kids," Jack went on. "I've already scheduled him for classes."

"Classes in what?" Cathy was really befuddled now.

"The breed is called the Labrador *Retriever,*" Jack noted.

"How big does it get?"

"Oh, maybe seventy pounds."

"That's bigger than she is!"

"Yeah, they love to swim, too. He can look after her in the pool."

"We don't have a pool."

"They start in three weeks." Jack smiled again. "Doctor Schenk also said that swimming is good therapy for this kind of injury."

"You've been busy," his wife observed. She was smiling now.

"I was going to get a Newfoundland, but they're just too big—one-fifty." Jack didn't say that his first wish had been to get a dog big and tough enough to tear the head off anyone who came close to his daughter, but that his common sense had prevented it.

"Well, there's your first job," Cathy pointed. Jack got a paper towel to clean up the puddle on the tile. Before he could do it, his daughter nearly strangled him with a ferocious hug. It was all he could do to control himself, but he had to. Sally would not have understood why her daddy was crying. The world was back in its proper shape. *Now if we can just keep it that way.*

"I'll have the pictures tomorrow. I wanted to get them done before the trees fill in. When they do, you won't be able to see the house from the road very well." Alex summarized the results of his reconnaissance.

"What about the alarm?"

Alex read off the data from his notes.

"How the bloody hell did you get that?"

Dobbens chuckled as he popped open the beer. "It's easy. If you want the data for any kind of burglar alarm, you call the company that did it and say you work for an insurance company. You give them a policy number—you make that up, of course—and they give you all the information you want. Ryan has a perimeter system, and a backup intruder system 'with keys,' which means that the alarm company has keys to the house. Somewhere on the property they have infrared beams. Probably on the driveway in the trees. This guy isn't dumb, Sean."

"It doesn't matter."

"Okay, I'm just telling you. One more thing."

"Yes?"

"The kid doesn't get hurt this time, not the wife either if we can help it."

"That is not part of the plan," Miller assured him. *You bloody wimp.* Sean had learned a new word in America. *What sort of revolutionary do you think you are?* he didn't say.

"That's from my people," Alex continued, telling only part of the truth. "You gotta understand, Sean, child abuse looks bad over here. It's not the kind of image we want to have, you dig?"

"And you want to come out with us?"

Dobbens nodded. "It might be necessary."

"I think we can avoid that. It just means eliminating all the people who see your faces."

You're a cold little cocksucker, Dobbens thought, though his words made perfect sense. Dead men told no tales.

"Very well. All we have to do now is find a way to make the security people relax a bit," the Irishman said. "I'd prefer to avoid brute force."

"I've been thinking about that." Alex took a moment before going on. "How do armies succeed?"

"What do you mean?" Miller asked.

"I mean, the great plans, the ones that really work. They all work because you show the other guy something he expects to see, right? You make him go for the fake, but it's gotta be a really good fake. We have to make them look for the wrong thing in the wrong place, and they have to put the word out."

"And how do we do that?" After two minutes: "Ah."

Alex retired to his bedroom a few minutes later, leaving Miller in front of the television to go over his material. On the whole, it had been a very useful trip. The plan was already beginning to take shape. It would require a lot of people, but that came as no surprise.

Curiously, his respect for Alex was now diminished. The man was competent, certainly, even brilliant in his plan for a diversion—but that absurd sentimentality! It was not that Miller reveled in the idea of hurting children, but if that was what the revolution took, then it was a necessary price to pay. Besides, it got people's attention. It told them that he and his organization were serious. Until Alex got over that, he'd never be successful. But that wasn't Miller's problem. Part One of the operation was now outlined in his mind. Part Two was already drawn up, already had been aborted once. *But not this time,* Miller promised himself.

By noon the following day, Alex had handed him the photos and driven him to an outlying station of the D.C. Metro. Miller took the subway train to National Airport to catch the first of four flights that would take him home.

Jack walked into Sally's bedroom just before eleven. The dog—his daughter had named him Ernie—was an invisible shape in the corner. This was one of the smartest things he had ever done. Sally was too much in love with Ernie to dwell on her injuries, and she chased after him as fast as her weakened legs would allow. That was enough to make her father overlook the chewed shoes and occasional mistakes with which the dog was littering the house. In a few weeks she'd be back to normal. Jack adjusted the covers slightly before leaving. Cathy was already in bed when he got there.

"Is she okay?"

"Sleeping like an angel," Jack replied as he slid in beside her.

"And Ernie?"

"He's in there somewhere. I could hear his tail hitting the wall." He wrapped his arms around her. It was hard getting close to her now. He ran one hand down to her abdomen, feeling the shape of his unborn child. "How's the next one?"

"Quiet, finally. God, he's an active one. Don't wake him up."

It struck Jack as an absurd idea that babies were awake before they were born, but you couldn't argue with a doctor. "He?"

"That's what Madge says."

"What's she say about you?" He felt her ribs next. They were too prominent. His wife had always been slender, but this was too much.

"I'm gaining the weight back," Cathy answered. "You don't have to worry. Everything's fine."

"Good." He kissed her.

"Is that all I get?" he heard from the darkness.

"You think you can handle more?"

"Jack, I don't have to go to work tomorrow," she pointed out.

"But some of us do," he protested, but soon found that his heart wasn't in it.

21. Plans

"He is thorough," O'Donnell observed. Miller had returned with the aerial photographs that Dobbens had copied, topographic maps, and photos of Ryan's home from the land and water sides. Added to these were typed notes of the observations made by his people and other data thought to be of interest.

"Unfortunately he allows his personal feelings to interfere with his activities," Miller observed coolly.

"And you don't, Sean?" O'Donnell chided gently.

"It won't happen again," his operations officer promised.

"That's good. The important thing about mistakes is that we learn from them. So let's go over your proposed operation."

Sean took out two other maps and spent twenty minutes running through his ideas. He concluded with Dobbens' suggestion for a diversion.

"I like it." He turned to his intelligence chief. "Michael?"

"The opposition will be formidable, of course, but the plan allows for that. The only thing that worries me is that it will take nearly all of our people to do it."

"Nothing else looks feasible," Miller replied. "It's not so much a question of getting close enough, but of leaving the area after the mission is accomplished. Timing is crucial—"

"And when timing is crucial, simplicity is a must." O'Donnell nodded. "Is there anything else that the opposition might try?"

"I think not," McKenney said. "This is the worst-case expectation."

"Helicopters," Miller said. "They nearly did for us the last time. No real problem if we're prepared for it, but we must be prepared."

"Very well," O'Donnell said. "And the second part of the operation?"

"Obviously we need to know where all the targets will be," McKenney said. "When do you want me to activate our people?" On orders, the intelligence chief's penetration agents had been quiescent for some weeks.

"Not just yet," the Commander replied thoughtfully. "Again a question of timing. Sean?"

"I think we should wait until the mission is fully accomplished before moving."

"Yes, it proved to be a good idea the last time," the Commander agreed. "How many people are needed for your operation?"

"No less than fifteen. I think we can depend on Alex for three trained men, himself included. More than that—no, we should limit his participation as much as possible."

"Agreed," McKenney said.

"And training?" O'Donnell asked.

"The most we've ever done."

"To start when?"

"A month beforehand," Miller answered. "Any more time would be a waste of resources. For the moment I have quite a lot of work to do."

"So here are the plans," Murray said. "You can either let them stay at your embassy or we'll put them in Blair House, right across the street from the President."

"With all due respect to your Secret Service chaps—" The head of the Diplomatic Protection Group didn't have to go on. Their safety was his responsibility and he wouldn't trust it to foreigners any more than he had to.

"Yeah, I understand. They'll get a full security detail from the Secret Service plus a couple of FBI liaison people and the usual assistance from the local police. Finally we'll have two HRT groups on alert the whole time they're over, one in D.C., and a backup team at Quantico."

"How many people know?" Ashley asked.

"The Secret Service and Bureau people are already fully briefed. When your advance men go over, they ought to have most of the events scouted for you already. The local cops will not be notified until they have to know."

"You said most of the locations have been scouted, but not all?" Owens asked.

"Do you want us to check out the unannounced points this early, too?"

"No." The man from DPG shook his head. "It's bad enough that the public functions have to be exposed this early. It's still not official that they're going, you know. The element of surprise is our best defense."

Owens looked at his colleague, but didn't react. The head of the DPG was on his suspects list, and his orders were not to allow anyone to know the details of his investigation. Owens thought him to be in the clear, but his detectives had discovered a few irregularities in the man's personal life that had somehow gotten past all the previous security screenings. Until it was certain that he was not a possible blackmail risk, he would not be allowed to know that some possible suspects had already seen the itinerary. The Commander of C-13 gave Murray an ironic look.

"I think you're overdoing this, gentlemen, but that's your business," the FBI man said as he stood. "Your people are flying over tomorrow?"

"That's right."

"Okay, Chuck Avery of the Secret Service will meet your people at Dulles. Tell them not to be bashful about asking for things. You will have our total cooperation." He watched them leave. Five minutes later Owens was back.

"What gives, Jimmy?" Murray wasn't surprised.

"What further progress have you made on the chaps who attacked Ryan?"

"Not a thing for the past two weeks," Murray admitted. "You?"

"We have a possible link—let me be precise, we suspect that there might be a possible link."

The FBI man grinned. "Yeah, I know what that's like. Who is it?"

"Geoffrey Watkins." That got a reaction.

"The foreign-service guy? Damn! Anybody else on the list that I know?"

''The chap you were just talking to. Ashley's people discovered that he's not entirely faithful to his wife.''

''Boys or girls?'' Murray took a cue from the way Owens had said that. ''You mean that he doesn't know, Jimmy?''

''He doesn't know that the itinerary has been leaked, possibly to the wrong people. Watkins is among them, but so is our DPG friend.''

''Oh, that's real good! The plans may be leaked, and you can't tell the head of the security detail because he may be the one—''

''It's most unlikely, but we must allow for the possibility.''

''Call the trip off, Jimmy. If you have to break his leg, call it the hell off.''

''We can't. He won't. I spoke with His Highness day before yesterday and told him the problem. He refuses to allow his life to be managed that way.''

''Why are you telling me this?'' Murray rolled his eyes.

''I must tell someone, Dan. If I can't tell my chaps, then . . .'' Owens waved his hands.

''You want us to call the trip off for you, is that it?'' Murray demanded. He knew that Owens couldn't answer that one. ''Let's spell this one out nice and clear. You want our people to be alert to the chance that an attack is a serious possibility, and that one of the good guys might be a bad guy.''

''Correct.''

''This isn't going to make our folks real happy.''

''I'm not terribly keen on it myself, Dan,'' Owens replied.

''Well, it gives Bill Shaw something else to think about.'' Another thought struck him. ''Jimmy, that's one expensive piece of live bait you have dangling on the hook.''

''He knows that. It's our job to keep the sharks away, isn't it?''

Murray shook his head. The ideal solution would be to find a way to cancel the trip, thereby handing the problem back to Owens and Ashley. That meant involving the State Department. The boys at Foggy Bottom would spike that idea, Murray knew. You couldn't un-invite a future chief of state because the FBI and Secret Service didn't think they could guarantee his safety—the reputation of American law-enforcement would be laid open to ridicule, they'd say, knowing that his protection wasn't the responsibility of the people at State.

''What do you have on Watkins?'' he asked after a moment. Owens outlined his ''evidence.''

''That's all?''

''We're still digging, but so far there is nothing more substantive. It could all be coincidence, of course . . .''

''No, it sounds to me like you're right.'' Murray didn't believe in coincidences either. ''But there's nothing that I could take to a grand jury at home. Have you thought about flushing the game?''

''You mean running through a change in the schedule? Yes, we have. But then what? We could do that, see if Watkins goes to the shop, and arrest both men there—if we can confirm that what is happening is what we think it to be. Unfortunately, that means throwing away the only link we've ever had with the ULA, Dan. At the moment, we're watching Cooley as closely as we dare. He is still traveling. If we can find out whom he is contacting, then perhaps we can wrap up the entire operation. What you suggest is an option, but not the best one. We do have time, you know. We have several months before we need to do something so drastic as that.''

Murray nodded, not so much in agreement as in understanding. The possibility of finding and destroying O'Donnell's bunch had to be tantalizing to Scotland Yard. Bagging Cooley now would quash that. It wasn't something that they'd simply toss off. He knew that the Bureau would think much the same way.

"Jack, I want you to come along with me," Marty Cantor said. "No questions."

"What?" Ryan asked, and got an accusing look. "All right, all right." He took the files he was working on and locked them in his file cabinet, then grabbed his jacket. Cantor led him around the corner to the elevator. After arriving on the first floor, he walked rapidly west into the annex behind the headquarters building. Once in the new structure, they passed through five security checkpoints. This was an all-time record for Ryan, and he wondered if Cantor had had to reprogram the pass-control computer to get him into this building. After ten minutes he was on the fourth floor in a room identified only by its number.

"Jack, this is Jean-Claude. He's one of our French colleagues."

Ryan shook hands with a man twenty years older than himself, whose face was the embodiment of civilized irony. "What gives, Marty?"

"Professor Ryan," Jean-Claude said. "I am informed that you are the man we must thank."

"What for—" Ryan stopped. *Uh-oh.* The Frenchman led him to a TV monitor.

"Jack, you never saw this," Cantor said as a picture formed on the screen. It had to be satellite photography. Ryan knew it at once from the viewing angle, which changed very slowly.

"When?" he asked.

"Last night, our time, about three A.M. local."

"Correct." Jean-Claude nodded, his eyes locked on the screen.

It was Camp -20, Ryan thought. The one that belonged to *Action-Directe*. The spacing of the huts was familiar. The infrared picture showed that three of the huts had their heaters on. The brightness of the heat signals told him that ground temperature must have been about freezing. South of the camp, behind a dune, two vehicles were parked. Jack couldn't tell if they were jeeps or small trucks. On closer inspection, faint figures were moving on the cold background: men. From the way they moved: soldiers. He counted eight of them split into two equal groups. Near one of the huts was a brighter light. There appeared to be a man standing there. *Three in the morning, when one's body functions are at the lowest ebb.* One of the camp guards was smoking on duty, doubtless trying to stay awake. That was a mistake, Ryan knew. The flare of the match would have destroyed his night vision. *Oh, well. . . .*

"Now," Jean-Claude said.

There was a brief flash from one of the eight intruders; it was strange to see but not hear it. Ryan couldn't tell if the guard moved as a result, but his cigarette did, flying perhaps two yards, after which both images remained stationary. *That's a kill,* he told himself. *Dear God, what am I watching?* The eight pale shapes closed on the camp. First they entered the guard hut—it was always the same one. A moment later they were back outside. Next, they redeployed into the two groups of four, each group heading toward one of the "lighted" huts.

"Who are the troops?" Jack asked.

"Paras," Jean-Claude answered simply.

Some of the men reappeared thirty seconds later. After another minute, the rest emerged—more than had gone in, Ryan saw. Two seemed to be carrying something.

Then something else entered the picture. It was a bright glow that washed out other parts of the picture, but the new addition was a helicopter, its engines blazing in the infrared picture. The picture quality deteriorated and the camera zoomed back. Two more helicopters were in the area. One landed near the vehicles, and the jeeps were driven into it. After that helicopter lifted off, the other skimmed the ground, following the vehicle tracks for several miles and erasing them with its downdraft. By the time the satellite lost visual lock with the scene, everyone was gone. The entire exercise had taken less than ten minutes.

"Quick and clean," Marty breathed.

"You got her?" Jack had to ask.

"Yes," Jean-Claude replied. "And five others, four of them alive. We removed all of them, and the camp guards who, I regret to say, did not survive the evening." The Frenchman's regrets were tossed in for good manners only. His face showed what he really felt.

"Any of your people hurt?" Cantor asked.

An amused shake of his head: "No. They were all asleep, you see. One slept with a pistol next to his cot, and made the mistake of reaching for it."

"You pulled everybody out, even the camp guards?"

"Of course. All are now in Chad. The living are being questioned."

"How did you arrange the satellite coverage?" Jack asked.

This answer came with a Gallic shrug. "A fortunate coincidence."

Right, Jack thought. *Some coincidence. I just watched the instant-replay of the death of three or four people. Terrorists,* he corrected himself. *Except for the camp guards, who only helped terrorists. The timing could not have been an accident. The French wanted us to know that they were in counterterrorist operations for-real.*

"Why am I here?"

"But you made this possible," Jean-Claude said. "It is my pleasure to give you the thanks of my country."

"What's going to happen to the people you captured?" Jack wanted to know.

"Do you know how many people they have assassinated? For those crimes they will answer. Justice, that will happen to them."

"You wanted to see a success, Jack," Cantor said. "You just did."

Ryan thought that one over. Removing the bodies of the camp guards told him how the operation would end. No one was supposed to know what had happened. Sure, some bullet holes were left behind, and a couple of bloodstains, but no bodies. The raiders had quite literally covered their tracks. The whole operation was "deniable." There was nothing left behind that would point to the French. In that sense it had been a perfect covert operation. And if that much effort had gone into making it so, then there was little reason to suspect that the *Action-Directe* people would ever face a jury. *You wouldn't go to that much trouble and then go through the publicity of a trial,* Ryan told himself. *Goodbye, Françoise Theroux. . . .*

I condemned these people to death, he realized finally. Just the one of them was enough to trouble his conscience. He remembered the police-style photograph he'd seen of her face and the fuzzy satellite image of a girl in a bikini.

"She's murdered at least three people," Cantor said, reading Jack's face.

"Professor Ryan, she has no heart, that one. No feelings. You must not be misled by her face," Jean-Claude advised. "They cannot all look like Hitler."

But that was only part of it, Ryan knew. Her looks merely brought into focus that hers was a human life whose term was now unnaturally limited. *As she has limited those of others,* Jack told himself. He admitted to himself that he would have no qualms at all if her name had been Sean Miller.

"Forgive me," he said. "It must be my romantic nature."

"But of course," the Frenchman said generously. "It is something to be regretted, but those people made their choice, Professor, not you. You have helped to avenge the lives of many innocent people, and you have saved those of people you will never know. There will be a formal note of thanks—a secret one, of course—for your assistance."

"Glad to help, Colonel," Cantor said. Hands were shaken all around, and Marty led Jack back to the headquarters building.

"I don't know that I want to see anything like that again," Ryan said in the corridor. "I mean, I don't want to know their faces. I mean—hell, I don't know what I mean. Maybe—it's just . . . different when you're detached from it, you know? It was too much like watching a ball game on TV, but it wasn't a ball game. Who was that guy, anyway?"

"Jean-Claude's the head of the DGSE's Washington Station, and he was the liaison man. We got the first new picture of her a day and a half ago. They had the operation all ready to roll, and he got things going inside of six hours. Impressive performance."

"I imagine they wanted us to be impressed. They're not bringing 'em in, are they?"

"No. I seriously doubt those people are going back to France to stand trial. Remember the problem they had the last time they tried a public trial of *Action-Directe* members? The jurors started getting midnight phone calls, and the case got blown away. Maybe they don't want to put up with the hassle again." Cantor frowned. "Well, it's not our call to make. Their system isn't the same as ours. All we did was forward information to an ally."

"An American court could call that accessory to murder."

"Possibly," Cantor admitted. "Personally, I prefer what Jean-Claude called it."

"Then why are you leaving in August?" Ryan asked.

Cantor delivered his answer without facing him. "Maybe you'll find out someday, Jack."

Back alone in his office, Ryan couldn't get his mind off what he'd seen. Five thousand miles away, agents of the DGSE's "action" directorate were now questioning that girl. If this had been a movie, their techniques would be brutal. What they used in real life, Ryan didn't want to know. He told himself that the members of *Action-Directe* had brought it on themselves. First, they had made a conscious choice to be what they were. Second, in subverting the French legal system the previous year, they'd given their enemies an excuse to bypass whatever constitutional guarantees . . . but was that truly an excuse?

"What would Dad think?" he murmured to himself. Then the next question hit him. Ryan lifted his phone and punched in the right number.

"Cantor."

"Why, Marty?"

"Why what, Jack?"

"Why did you let me see that?"

"Jean-Claude wanted to meet you, and he also wanted you to see what your data accomplished."

"That's bull, Marty! You let me into a real-time satellite display—okay, taped, but essentially the same thing. There can't be many people cleared for that. I don't need-to-know how good the real-time capability is. You could have told him I wasn't cleared for it and that would have been that."

"Okay, you've had some time to think it over. Tell me what you think."

"I don't like it."

"Why?" Cantor asked.

"It broke the law."

"Not ours. Like I told you twenty minutes ago, all we did was provide intelligence information to a friendly foreign nation."

"But they used it to kill people."

"What do you think intel is *for,* Jack? What should they have done? No, answer this first: what if they were foreign nationals who had murdered French nationals in—in Liechtenstein, say, and then boogied back to their base?"

"That's not the same thing. That's more . . . more like an act of war—like doing the guards at the camp. The people they *were* after were their own citizens who committed crimes in their own country, and—and are subject to French law."

"And what if it had been a different camp? What if those paratroopers had done a job for us, or the Brits, and taken out your ULA friends?"

"That's different!" Ryan snapped back. *But why?* he asked himself a moment later. "It's personal. You can't expect me to feel the same way about that."

"Can't I?" Cantor hung up the phone.

Ryan stared at the telephone receiver for several seconds before replacing it in the cradle. What was Marty trying to tell him? Jack reviewed the events in his own mind, trying to come to a conclusion that made sense.

Did any of it make sense? Did it make sense for political dissidents to express themselves with bombs and machine guns? Did it make sense for small nations to use terrorism as a short-of-war weapon to change the policies of larger ones? Ryan grunted. That depended on which side of the issue you were on—or at least there were people who thought that way. Was this something completely new?

It was, and it wasn't. State-sponsored terrorism, in the form of the Barbary pirates, had been America's first test as a nation. The enemy objective then had been simple greed. The Barbary states demanded tribute before they would give right of passage to American-flag trading ships, but it had finally been decided that enough was enough. Preble took the infant U.S. Navy to the Mediterranean Sea to put an end to it—no, to put an end to America's victimization by it, Jack corrected himself.

God, it was even the same place, Ryan thought. "To the shores of Tripoli," the Marine Hymn said, where First Lieutenant Presley O'Bannon, USMC, had attacked the fort at Derna. Jack wondered if the place still existed. Certainly the problem did.

The violence hadn't changed. What had changed were the rules under which the large nations acted, and the objectives of their enemies. Two hundred years earlier, when a small nation offended a larger one, ships and troops would settle matters. No longer was this simple wog-bashing, though. The smaller countries now had arsenals of modern weapons that could make such punitive expeditions too expensive for societies that had learned to husband the lives of their young men. A regiment of troops could no longer settle matters, and moving a whole army was no longer such a simple thing. Knowing this, the small country could inflict wounds itself, or even more safely, sponsor others to do so—"deniably"—in order to move its larger opponent in the desired direction. There wasn't even much of a hurry. Such low-level conflict could last years, so small were the expenditures of resources and so different the perceived value of the human lives taken and lost.

What was new, then, was not the violence, but the safety of the nation that either performed or sponsored it. Until that changed, the killing would never stop.

So, on the international level, terrorism was a form of war that didn't even have to interrupt normal diplomatic relations. America itself had embassies in some of the nations, even today. Nearer to home, however, it was being treated as a crime. He'd faced Miller in the Old Bailey, Ryan remembered, not a military court-martial. *They can even use that against us.* It was a surprising realization. *They can fight their kind of war, but we can't recognize it as such without giving up something our society needs. If we treat terrorists as politically motivated activists, we give them an honor they don't deserve. If we treat them as soldiers, and kill them as such, we both give them legitimacy and violate our own laws.* By a small stretch of the imagination, organized crime could be thought of as a form of terrorism, Ryan knew. The terrorists' only weakness was their negativity. They were a political movement with nothing to offer other than their conviction that their parent society was unjust. So long as the people in that society felt otherwise, it was the terrorists who were alienated from it, not the population as a whole. The democratic processes that benefited the terrorists were also their worst political enemy. Their prime objective, then, had to be the elimination of the democratic process, converting justice to injustice in order to arouse members of the society to sympathy with the terrorists.

The pure elegance of the concept was stunning. Terrorists could fight a war and be protected by the democratic processes of their enemy. If those processes were obviated, the terrorists would win additional political support, but so long as those processes were not obviated, it was extremely difficult for them to lose. They could hold a society hostage against itself and its most important precepts, daring it to change. They could move around at will, taking advantage of the freedom that defined a democratic state, and get all the support they needed from a nation-state with which their parent society was unwilling or unable to deal effectively.

The only solution was international cooperation. The terrorists had to be cut off from support. Left to their own resources, terrorists would become little more than an organized-crime network. . . . But the democracies found it easier to deal with their domestic problems singly than to band together and strike a decisive blow at those who fomented them, despite all the rhetoric to the contrary. Had that just changed? The CIA had given data on terrorists to someone else, and action had been taken as a result. What he had seen earlier, therefore, was a step in the right direction, even if it wasn't necessarily the right kind of step. Ryan told himself that he'd just witnessed one of the world's many imperfections, but at least one aimed in the proper direction. That it had disturbed him was a consequence of his civilization. That he was now rationalizing it was a result of . . . what?

Cantor walked into Admiral Greer's office.

"Well?" the DDI asked.

"We'll give him a high B, maybe an A-minus. It depends on what he learns from it."

"Conscience attack?" the DDI asked.

"Yeah."

"It's about time he found out what the game's really like. Everybody has to learn that. He'll stay," Greer said.

"Probably."

The pickup truck tried to pull into the driveway that passed under the Hoover building, but a guard waved him off. The driver hesitated, partly in frustration, partly in rage while he tried to figure something else out. The heavy traffic didn't help. Finally he started circling the block until he was able to find a way into a public parking garage. The attendant held up his nose at the plebeian vehicle—he was more accustomed to Buicks and Cadillacs—and burned rubber on the way up the ramp to show his feelings. The driver and his son didn't care. They walked downhill and across the street, going by foot on the path denied their truck. Finally they got to the door and walked in.

The agent who had desk duty noted the entrance of two people somewhat disreputably dressed, the elder of whom had something wrapped in his leather jacket and tucked under his arm. This got the agent's immediate and full attention. He waved the visitors over with his left hand. His right was somewhere else.

"Can I help you, sir?"

"Hi," the man said. "I got something for you." The man raised the jacket and pulled out a submachine gun. He quickly learned that this wasn't the way to get on the FBI's good side.

The desk agent snatched the weapon and yanked it off the desk, standing and reaching for his service revolver. The panic button under the desk was already pushed, and two more agents in the room converged on the scene. The man behind the desk immediately saw that the gun's bolt was closed—the gun was safe, and there wasn't a magazine in the pistol grip.

"I found it!" the kid announced proudly.

"What?" one of the arriving agents said.

"And I figured I'd bring it here," the lad's father said.

"What the hell?" the desk agent observed.

"Let's see it." A supervisory agent arrived next. He came from a surveillance room whose TV cameras monitored the entrance. The man behind the desk rechecked to make sure the weapon was safe, then handed it across.

It was an Uzi, the 9mm Israeli submachine gun used all over the world because of its quality, balance, and accuracy. The cheap-looking (the Uzi is anything but cheap, though it does look that way) metal stampings were covered with red-brown rust, and water dripped from the receiver. The agent pulled open the bolt and stared down the barrel. The gun had been fired and not cleaned since. It was impossible to tell how long ago that had been, but there weren't all that many FBI cases pending in which a weapon of this type had been used.

"Where did you find this, sir?"

"In a quarry, about thirty miles from here," the man said.

"*I* found it!" the kid pointed out.

"That's right, he found it," his father conceded. "I figured this was the place to bring it."

"You thought right, sir. Will both of you come with me, please?"

The agent on the desk gave both of them "visitor" passes. He and the other two agents on entrance-guard duty went back to work, wondering what the hell that had been all about.

On the building's top floor, those few people in the corridor were surprised to see a man walking around with a machine gun, but it would not have been in keeping with Bureau chic to pay too much attention—the man with the gun did have an FBI pass, and he was carrying it properly. When he walked into an office, however, it did get a reaction from the first secretary he saw.

"Is Bill in?" the agent asked.

"Yes, I'll—" Her eyes didn't leave the gun.

The man waved her off, motioned for the visitors to follow him, and walked toward Shaw's office. The door was open. Shaw was talking with one of his people. Special Agent Richard Alden went straight to Shaw's desk and set the gun on the blotter.

"Christ, Richie!" Shaw looked up at the agent, then back down at the gun. "What's this?"

"Bill, these two folks just walked in the door downstairs and gave it to us. I thought it might be interesting."

Shaw looked at the two people with visitor passes and invited them to sit on the couch against the wall. He called for two more agents to join them, plus someone from the ballistics laboratory. While things were being organized, his secretary got a cup of coffee for the father and a Dr Pepper for the son.

"Could I have your names, please?"

"I'm Robert Newton and this here's my son Leon." He gave his address and phone number without being asked.

"And where did you find the gun?" Shaw asked while his subordinates were taking notes.

"It's called Jones Quarry. I can show you on a map."

"What were you doing there?"

"I was fishing. I found it," Leon reminded them.

"I was getting in some firewood," his father said.

"This time of year?"

"Beats doing it during the summer, when it's hot, man," Mr. Newton pointed out reasonably. "Also lets the wood season some. I'm a construction worker. I walk iron, and it's a little slow right now, so I went out for some wood. The boy's off from school today, so I brought him along. While I cut the wood, Leon likes to fish. There's some big ones in the quarry," he added with a wink.

"Oh, okay." Shaw grinned. "Leon, you ever catch one?"

"No, but I got close last time," the youngster responded.

"Then what?"

Mr. Newton nodded for his son.

"My hook got caught on sumthin' heavy, you know, an' I pulled and pulled and pulled. It come loose, and I tried real hard, but I couldn't reel it up. So I called my daddy."

"I reeled it in," Mr. Newton explained. "When I saw it was a gun, I almost crapped my drawers. The hook was snagged on the trigger guard. What kinda gun is that, anyway?"

"Uzi. It's made in Israel, mostly," the ballistics expert said, looking up from the weapon. "It's been in the water at least a month."

Shaw and another agent shared a look at that bit of news.

"I'm afraid I handled it a lot," Newton said. "Hope I didn't mess up any fingerprints."

''Not after being in the water, Mr. Newton,'' Shaw replied. ''And you brought it right here?''

''Yeah, we only got it, oh''—he checked his watch—''an hour and a half ago. Aside from handling it, we didn't do anything. It didn't have no magazine in it.''

''You know guns?'' the ballistics man asked.

''I spent a year in Nam. I was a grunt with the 173rd Airborne. I know M-16s pretty good.'' Newton smiled. ''And I used to do a little hunting, mostly birds and rabbits.''

''Tell us about the quarry,'' Shaw said.

''It's off the main road, back maybe three-quarters of a mile, I guess. Lots of trees back there. That's where I get my firewood. I don't really know who owns it. Lots of cars go back there. You know, it's a parking spot for kids on Saturday nights, that sorta place.''

''Have you ever heard shooting there?''

''No, except during hunting season. There's squirrels in there, lotsa squirrels. So what's with the gun? Does it mean anything to ya?''

''It might. It's the kind of gun used in the murder of a police officer, and—''

''Oh, yeah! That lady and her kid over Annapolis, right?'' He paused for a moment. ''Damn.''

Shaw looked at the boy. He was about nine, the agent thought, and the kid had smart eyes, scanning the items Shaw had on his walls, the memorabilia from his many cases and posts. ''Mr. Newton, you have done us a very big favor.''

''Oh, yeah?'' Leon responded. ''What you gonna do with the gun?''

The ballistics expert answered. ''First we'll clean it and make sure it's safe. Then we'll fire it.'' He looked at Shaw. ''You can forget any other forensic stuff. The water in the quarry must be chemically active. This corrosion is pretty fierce.'' He looked at Leon. ''If you catch any fish there, son, you be sure you don't eat them unless your dad says it's all right.''

''Okay,'' the boy assured him.

''Fibers,'' Shaw said.

''Yeah, maybe that. Don't worry. If they're there, we'll find 'em. What about the barrel?''

''Maybe,'' the man replied. ''By the way, this gun comes from Singapore. That makes it fairly new. The Israelis just licensed them to make the piece eighteen months ago. It's the same outfit that makes the M-16 under license from Colt's.'' He read off the number. It would be telexed to the FBI's Legal Attaché in Singapore in a matter of minutes. ''I want to get to work on this right now.''

''Can I watch?'' Leon asked. ''I'll keep out of the way.''

''Tell you what,'' Shaw said. ''I want to talk to your dad a little longer. How about I have one of our agents take you through our museum. You can see how we caught all the old-time bad guys. If you wait outside, somebody will come and take you around.''

''Okay!''

''We can't talk about this, right?'' Mr. Newton asked after his son had left.

''That's correct, sir.'' Shaw paused. ''That's important for two reasons. First, we don't want the perpetrators to know that we've had a break in the case—and this could be a major break, Mr. Newton; you've done something very important. The other reason is to protect you and your family. The people involved in this are very dangerous. Put it this way: you know that they tried to kill a pregnant woman and a four-year-old girl.''

That got the man's attention. Robert Newton, who had five children, three of them girls, didn't like hearing that.

''Now, have you ever seen people around the quarry?'' Shaw asked.

''What do you mean?''

''Anybody.''

''There's maybe two or three other folks who cut wood back there. I know the names—I mean their first names, y'know? And like I said, kids like to go parking back there.'' He laughed. ''Once I had to help one out. I mean, the road's not all that great, and this one kid was stuck in the mud, and . . .'' Newton's voice trailed off. His face changed. ''Once, it was a Tuesday . . . I couldn't work that day 'cause the crane was broke, and I didn't much feel like sitting around the house, y'know? So I went out to chop some wood. There was this van coming outa the road. He was having real trouble in the mud. I had to wait like ten minutes 'cause he blocked the whole road, slippin' and slidin', like.''

''What kind of van?''

''Dark, mostly. The kind with the sliding door—musta been customized some, it had that dark stuff on the windows, y'know?''

Bingo! Shaw told himself. ''Did you see the driver or anybody inside?''

Newton thought for a moment. ''Yeah . . . it was a black dude. He was—yeah, I remember, he was yellin', like. I guess he was pissed at getting stuck like that. I mean, I couldn't hear him, but you could tell he was yelling, y'know? He had a beard, and a leather jacket like the one I wear to work.''

''Anything else about the van?''

''I think it made noise, like it had a big V-8. Yeah, it must have been a custom van to have that.''

Shaw looked at his men, too excited to smile as they scribbled their notes.

''The papers said all the crooks were white,'' Newton said.

''The papers don't always get things right,'' Shaw noted.

''You mean the bastard who killed that cop was black?'' Newton didn't like that. So was he. ''And he tried to do that family, too. . . . Shit!''

''Mr. Newton, that is secret. Do you understand me? You can't tell anybody about that, not even your son—was he there then?''

''Nah, he was in school.''

''Okay, you can't tell anyone. That is to protect you and your family. We're talking about some very dangerous people here.''

''Okay, man.'' Newton looked at the table for a moment. ''You mean we got people running around with machine guns, killing people—here? Not in Lebanon and like that, but here?''

''That's about the size of it.''

''Hey, man, I didn't spend a year in the Nam so we could have that shit where I live.''

Several floors downstairs, two weapons experts had already detail-stripped the Uzi. A small vacuum cleaner was applied to every part in the hope there might be cloth fibers that matched those taken from the van. A final careful look was taken at the parts. The damage from water immersion had done no good to the stampings, made mostly of mild steel. The stronger, corrosion-resistant ballistic steel of the barrel and bolt were in somewhat better shape. The lab chief reassembled the gun himself, just to show his technicians that he still knew how. He took his time, oiling the pieces with care, finally working the action to make sure it functioned properly.

"Okay," he said to himself. He left the weapon on the table, its bolt closed on an empty chamber. Next he pulled an Uzi magazine from a cabinet and loaded twenty 9-millimeter rounds. This he stuck in his pocket.

It always struck visitors as somewhat incongruous. The technicians usually wore white laboratory coats, like doctors, when they fired the guns. The man donned his ear protectors, stuck the muzzle into the slot, and fired a single round to make certain that the gun really worked. It did. Then he held the trigger down, emptying the magazine in a brief span of seconds. He pulled out the magazine, checked that the weapon was safe, and handed it to his assistant.

"I'm going to wash my hands. Let's get those bullets checked out." The chief ballistics technician was a fastidious person.

By the time he was finished drying his hands, he had a collection of twenty spent bullets. The metal jacket on each showed the characteristic marks made by the rifling of the machine gun's barrel. The marks were roughly the same on each bullet, but slightly different, since the gun barrel expanded when it got hot.

He took a small box from the evidence case. This bullet had gone completely through the body of a police officer, he remembered. It seemed such a puny thing to have taken a life, he thought, not even an ounce of lead and steel, hardly deformed at all from its deadly passage. It was hard not to dwell on such thoughts. He placed it on one side of the comparison microscope and took another from the set he'd just fired. Then he removed his glasses and bent down to the eyepieces. The bullets were . . . close. They'd definitely been fired by the same kind of gun. . . . He switched samples. Closer. The third bullet was closer still. He carefully rotated the sample, comparing it with the round that was kept in the evidence case, and it . . .

"We got a match." He backed away from the 'scope and another technician bent down to check.

"Yeah, that's a match. One hundred percent," the man agreed. The boss ordered his men to check other rounds and walked to the phone.

"Shaw."

"It's the same gun. One-hundred-percent sure. I have a match on the round that killed the trooper. They're checking the ones from the Porsche now."

"Good work, Paul!"

"You bet. I'll be back to you in a little while."

Shaw replaced the phone and looked at his people. "Gentlemen, we just had a break in the Ryan case."

22. Procedures

Robert Newton took the agents to the quarry that night. By dawn the next day a full team of forensic experts was sifting through every speck of dirt at the site. A pair of divers went into the murky water, and ten agents were posted in the woods to watch for company. Another team located and interviewed Newton's fellow woodcutters. More spoke with the residents of the farms near the road leading back into the woods. Dirt samples were taken to be matched with those vacuumed from the van. The tracks were photographed for later analysis.

The ballistics people had already made further tests on the Uzi. The ejected cartridge cases were compared with those recovered from the van and the crime scene, and showed perfect matches in extractor marks and firing-pin penetrations. The match of the gun with the crime and the van was now better than one hundred percent. The serial number had been confirmed with the factory in Singapore, and records were being checked to determine where the gun had been shipped. The name of every arms dealer in the world was in the Bureau's computer.

The whole purpose of the FBI's institutional expertise was to take a single piece of information and develop it into a complete criminal case. What it could not entirely prevent was having someone see them. Alex Dobbens drove past the quarry road on his way to work every day. He saw a pair of vehicles pulling out onto the highway from the dirt and gravel path. Though both the car and van from the FBI laboratory were unmarked, they had federal license plates, and that was all he needed to see.

Dobbens was not an excitable man. His professional training permitted him to look at the world as a collection of small, discrete problems, each of which had a solution; and if you solved enough of the small ones, then the large ones would similarly be solved, one at a time. He was also a meticulous person. Everything he did was part of a larger plan, both part of, and isolated from, the next planned step. It was not something that his people had easily come to understand, but it was hard to argue with success, and everything Dobbens did was successful. This had earned him respect and obedience from people who had once been too passionate for what Alex deemed their mission in life.

It was unusual, Dobbens thought, for two cars at once to come out of that road. It was out of the ordinary realm of probability that both should have government license plates. Therefore he had to assume that somehow the feds had learned that he'd used the quarry for weapons training. How had it been blown? he wondered. A hunter, perhaps, one of the rustics who went in there after squirrels and birds? Or one of the people who chopped wood, maybe? Or some kid from a nearby farm? How big a problem was this?

He'd taken his people to shoot there only four times, the most recent being when the Irish had come over. *Hmm, what does that tell me?* he asked the road in front of his car. *That was weeks ago*. Each time, they'd done all the shooting during rush hour, mostly in the morning. Even this far from D.C., there were a lot of cars and trucks on the road in the morning and late afternoon, enough to add quite a bit of noise to the environment. It was therefore unlikely that anyone had heard them. *Okay*.

Every time they had shot there, Alex had been assiduous about picking up the brass, and he was certain that they'd left nothing behind, not even a cigarette butt, to prove that they'd been there. They could not avoid leaving tire marks, but one of the reasons he'd picked the place was that kids went back there to park on weekends—there were plenty of tire marks.

They had dumped the gun there, he remembered, but who could have discovered that? The water in the quarry was over eighty feet deep—he'd checked—and looked about as uninviting as a rice paddy, murky from dirt that washed in, and whatever kind of scum it was that formed on the surface. Not a place to go swimming. They had dumped only the gun that had been fired, but as unlikely as it seemed, he had to assume they'd found it. How that had happened didn't matter for the moment. *Well, we have to dispose of the others too, now,* Alex told himself. *You can always get new guns.*

What is the most the cops can learn? he asked himself. He was well versed on police procedures. It seemed only reasonable that he should know his enemy, and Alex owned a number of texts on investigative techniques, the books used to train cops in their various academies, like Snyder's *Homicide Investigation* and the *Law Enforcement Bible.* He and his people studied them as carefully as the would-be cops with their shiny young faces. . . .

There could be no fingerprints on the gun. After being in water, the skin oil that makes the marks would long since have been gone. Alex had handled and cleaned it, but he didn't need to worry about that.

The van was gone. It had been stolen to begin with, then customized by one of Alex's own people, and had used four different sets of tags. The tags were long gone, underneath a telephone/power pole in Anne Arundel County. If something had resulted from that, he'd have known it long before now, Alex thought. The van itself had been fully sanitized, everything had been wiped clean, the dirt from the quarry road . . . that was something to think about, but the van still led to a dead end. They'd left nothing in it to connect it with his group.

Had any of his people talked, perhaps a man with an aching conscience because of the kid who'd almost died? Again, had that happened, he would have awakened this afternoon to see a badge and gun in front of his face. So that was out. Probably. He'd talk to his people about that, remind them that they could never talk with anyone about what they did.

Might his face have been seen? Alex chided himself again for having waved at the helicopter. But he'd been wearing a hat, sunglasses, and a beard, all of which were now gone, along with the jacket, jeans, and boots that he'd worn. He still had the work gloves, but they were so common an item that you could buy them in any hardware store. *So dump 'em and buy another pair, asshole!* he said to himself. *Make sure they're the same color, and keep the sales receipt.*

His mind ran through the data again. He might even be overreacting, he thought. The feds could be investigating some totally unrelated thing, but it was stupid to take any unnecessary risks. Everything that they'd used at the quarry would be disposed of. He'd make a complete list of possible connections and eliminate every one of them. They'd never go back there again. Cops had their rules and procedures, and he'd unhesitatingly copied the principle to deny its advantage to his opponents. He had established the rules for himself after seeing what catastrophes resulted from having none. The radical groups he'd hovered around in his college days had died because of their arrogance and stupidity, their underestimation of the skill of their enemies. Fundamentally, they'd died because they were unworthy of success. *Victory comes only to those prepared to make it, and* take *it,* Alex thought. He was even able to keep from congratulating himself on spotting the feds. It was simple prudence, not genius. His route had been chosen with an eye to taking note of such things. He already had another promising site for weapons training.

"Erik Martens," Ryan breathed. "We meet again."

All of the FBI's data had been forwarded to the Central Intelligence Agency's working group within hours of its receipt. The Uzi that had been recovered—Ryan marveled at how that had happened!—had, he saw, been fabricated in Singapore, at a plant that also made a version of the M-16 rifle that he'd carried in the Corps, and a number of other military arms, both East and West, for sale to third-world countries . . . and other interested parties. From his work the previous summer, Ryan knew that there were quite a few such factories, and quite a few governments whose only measure for the legitimacy of an arms purchaser was his credit rating. Even those who paid lip-service to such niceties as "end-user certificates" often turned a blind eye to the reputation of a dealer who never quite proved to be on the wrong side of the shadowy line that was supposed to distinguish the honest from the others. Since it was the dealer's government that generally made this determination, yet another variable was added to an already inexact equation.

Such was the case with Mr. Martens. A very competent man in his business, a man with remarkable connections, Martens had once worked with the CIA-backed UNITA rebels in Angola until a more regular pipeline had been established. His principal asset, however, was his ability to obtain items for the South African government. His last major coup had been obtaining the manufacturing tools and dies for the Milan antitank missile, a weapon that could not be legally shipped to the Afrikaner government due to the Western embargo. After three months' creative effort on his part, the government's own armaments factories would be making it themselves. His fee for that had doubtless been noteworthy, Ryan knew, though the CIA had been unable to ascertain just how noteworthy. The man owned his own business jet, a Grumman G-3 with intercontinental range. To make sure that he could fly it anywhere he wished, Martens had obtained weapons for a number of black African nations, and even missiles for Argentina. He could go to any corner of the world and find a government that was in his debt. The man would have been a sensation on Wall Street or any other marketplace, Ryan smiled to himself. He could deal with anyone, could market weapons the way that people in Chicago traded wheat futures.

The Uzis from Singapore had come to him. Everyone loved the Uzi. Even the Czechs had tried to copy it, but without great commercial success. The Israelis sold them by the thousands to military and security forces, always—most of the time—following the rules that the United States insisted upon. Quite a few had found their way to South Africa, Ryan read, until the embargo had made it rather more difficult. *Is that the reason they finally let someone make the gun under license?* Jack wondered. *Let someone else broaden the market for you, and just keep the profits. . . .*

The shipment had been five thousand units . . . about two million dollars, wholesale. Not very much, really, enough to equip a city police force or a regiment of paratroopers, depending on the receiving government's orientation. Large enough to show a profit for Mr. Martens, small enough not to attract a great deal of attention. One truckload, Ryan wondered, maybe two? The pallets of boxes would be tucked into a corner of his warehouse, technically supervised by his government, but more likely in fact to be Martens' private domain. . . .

That's what Sir Basil Charleston told me at the dinner, Ryan reminded himself. *You didn't pay enough attention to that South African chap. . . .* So the Brits think he deals to terrorists . . . directly? No, his government wouldn't tolerate that. *Probably wouldn't,* Ryan corrected himself. The guns might find their way to the African National Congress, which might not be very good news for the government they were pledged to destroy. So now Ryan had to find an intermediary. It took thirty minutes to get that file, involving a call to Marty Cantor.

The file was a disaster. Martens had eight known and fifteen suspected intermediary agents . . . one or two in every country he sold to—of course! Ryan punched Cantor's number again.

"I take it we've never talked to Martens?" Ryan asked.

"Not for a few years. He ran some guns into Angola for us, but we didn't like the way he handled things."

"How so?"

"The man's something of a crook," Cantor replied. "That's not terribly unusual in the arms business, but we try to avoid the type. We set up our own pipeline after the Congress took away the restriction on those operations."

"I got twenty-three names here," Ryan said.

"Yeah, I'm familiar with the file. We thought he was passing arms to an Iranian-sponsored group last November, but it turned out he wasn't. It took us a couple of months to clear him. It would have been a whole lot easier if we'd been able to talk to him."

"What about the Brits?" Jack asked.

"Stone wall," Marty said. "Every time they try to talk with him, some big ol' Afrikaner soldier says no. You can't blame them, really, if the West treats them like pariahs, they're sure as hell going to act like pariahs. The other thing to remember is, pariahs stick together."

"So we don't know what we need to know about this guy and we're not going to find out."

"I didn't say that exactly."

"Then we're sending people in to check a few things out?" Ryan asked hopefully.

"I didn't say that either."

"Dammit, Marty!"

"Jack, you are not cleared to know anything about field operations. In case you haven't noticed, not one of the files you've seen tells you how the information gets in here."

Ryan had noticed that. Informants weren't named, meeting places weren't specified, and the methods used to pass the information were nowhere to be found. "Okay, may I safely assume that we will, by some unknown means, get more data on this gentleman?"

"You may safely assume that the possibility is being considered."

"He may be the best lead we have," Jack pointed out.

"I know."

"This can be pretty frustrating stuff, Marty," Ryan said, getting that off his chest.

"Tell me about it," Cantor chuckled. "Wait till you get involved with something really important—sorry, but you know what I mean. Like what the Politburo people really think about something, or how powerful and accurate their missiles are, or whether they have somebody planted in this building."

"One problem at a time."

"Yeah, that must be nice, sport, just to have one problem at a time."

"When can I expect something on Martens?" Ryan asked.

"You'll know when it comes in," Cantor promised. " 'Bye."

"Great." Jack spent the rest of the day and part of another looking through the list of people Martens had dealt with. It was a relief to have to go back to teaching class the next two days, but he did find one possible connection. The Mercury motors found on the Zodiac used by the ULA had probably—the bookkeeping had broken down in Europe—gone through a Maltese dealer with whom Martens had done a little business.

The good news of the spring was that Ernie was a quick study. The dog got the hang of relieving himself outside within the first two weeks, which relieved Jack of a message from his daughter, "Daaaaddy, there's a little proooblem . . ." invariably followed by a question from his wife: "Having fun, Jack?" In fact, even his wife admitted that the dog was working out nicely. Ernie could only be separated from their daughter with a hard tug on his leash. He now slept in her bed, except when he patrolled the house every few hours. It was somewhat unnerving at first to see the dog—rather, to see a black mass darker than the night a few inches from one's face—when Ernie seemed to be reporting that everything was clear before he headed back to Sally's room for two more hours of protective slumber. He was still a puppy, with impossibly long legs and massive webbed feet, and he still liked to chew things. When that had included the leg of one of Sally's Barbie dolls, it resulted in a furious scolding from his owner that ended when he started licking Sally's face by way of contrition.

Sally was finally back to normal. As the doctors had promised her parents, her legs were fully healed, and she was running around now as she had before. This day would mark her return to Giant Steps. Her way of knocking glasses off tables as she ran past them was the announcement that things were right again, and her parents were too pleased by this to bring themselves to scold the girl for her unladylike behavior. For her part, Sally endured an abnormally large number of spontaneous hugs which she didn't really understand. She'd been sick and she was now better. She'd never really known that an attack had happened, Jack was slow to realize. The handful of times she referred to it, it had always been "the time the car broke." She still had to see the doctors every few weeks for tests. She both hated and dreaded these, but children adapt to a changing reality far more readily than their parents.

One of these changes was her mother. The baby was really growing now. Cathy's petite frame seemed poorly suited to such abuse. After every morning shower, she looked at herself, naked, in a full-length mirror that hung on the back of the closet door and came away with an expression that was both proud and mournful as her hands traced over the daily alterations.

"It's going to get worse," her husband told her as he emerged from the shower next.

"Thanks, Jack, I really need to hear that."

"Can you see your feet?" he asked with a grin.

"No, but I can feel them." They were swelling, too, along with her ankles.

"You look great to me, babe." Jack stood behind her, reaching his arms around to hold her bulging abdomen. He rested his cheek on the top of her head. "Love ya."

"That's easy for you to say!" She was still looking in the mirror. Jack saw her face in the glass, a tiny smile on her lips. An invitation? He moved his hands upward to find out. "Ouch! I'm sore."

"Sorry." He softened his grip to provide nothing more than support. "Hmph. Has something changed here?"

"It took you this long to notice?" The smile broadened a tad. "It's a shame that I have to go through this for that to happen."

"Have you ever heard me complain? Everything about you has always been A-plus. I guess pregnancy drops you to a B-minus. But only in one subject," he added.

"You've been teaching too long, Professor." Her teeth were showing now. Cathy leaned back, rubbing her skin against her husband's hairy chest. For some reason she loved to do that.

"You're beautiful," he said. "You glow."

"Well, I have to glow my way to work." Jack didn't move his hands. "I have to get dressed, Jack."

" 'How do I love thee, let me count the ways . . .' " he murmured into her damp hair. "One . . . two . . . three . . ."

"Not *now,* you lecher!"

"Why?" His hands moved very gently.

"Because I have to operate in three hours, and you have to go to spook city." She didn't move, though. There weren't all that many moments that they could be alone.

"I'm not going there today. I got stuck with a seminar at the Academy. I'm afraid the department is a little miffed with me." He kept looking in the mirror. Her eyes were closed now. *Screw the department* . . . "God, I love you!"

"Tonight, Jack."

"Promise?"

"You've sold me on the idea, okay? Now I—" She reached up to grab his hands, pulled them downward, and pressed them against the taut skin of her belly.

He—the baby was definitely a he, insofar as that was what they called him—was wide awake, rolling and kicking, pushing at the dark envelope that defined his world.

"Wow," his father observed. Cathy's hands were over his, moving them about every few seconds to follow the movements of the baby. "What does that feel like?"

Her head leaned back a fraction. "It feels good—except when I'm trying to sleep or when he kicks my bladder during a procedure."

"Was Sally this—this strong?"

"I don't think so." She didn't say that it wasn't the sort of thing you remember in terms of strength. It was just the singular feeling that your baby is alive and healthy, something that no man would ever understand. Not even Jack. Cathy Ryan was a proud woman. She knew that she was one of the best eye surgeons around. She knew that she was attractive, and worked hard to keep herself that way; even now, misshapen by her pregnancy, she knew that she was carrying it well. She could tell that from her husband's biological reaction, in the small of her back. But more than that, she knew that she was a woman, doing something that Jack could neither duplicate nor fully comprehend. *Well,* she told herself, *Jack does things I don't much understand either*. "I have to get dressed."

"Okay." Jack kissed the base of her neck. He took his time. It would have to last until this evening. "I'm up to eleven," he said as he stepped back.

She turned. "Eleven what?"

"Counting the ways," Jack laughed.

"You turkey!" She swung her bra at him. "*Only* eleven?"

"It's early. My brain isn't fully functional yet."

"I can tell it doesn't have enough of a blood supply." The funny thing, she thought, was that Jack didn't think he was very good-looking. She liked the strong jaw, except when he forgot to shave it, and his kind, loving eyes. She looked at the scars on his shoulder, and remembered her horror as she'd watched her husband run into harm's way, then her pride in him for what he had accomplished. Cathy knew that Sally had almost died as a direct result, but there was no way Jack could have foreseen it. It was her fault, too, she knew, and Cathy promised herself that Sally would never play with her seat belt again. Each of them had paid a price for the turns their lives had taken. Sally was almost fully recovered from hers, as was she. Cathy knew it wasn't true of her husband, who'd been awake through it all while she slept.

When that *happened, at least I had the blessing of unconsciousness. Jack had to live through it. He's still paying that price for it,* she thought. *Working two jobs now, his face always locked into a frown of concentration, worrying over something he can't talk about.* She didn't know exactly what he was doing, but she was certain that it was not yet done.

The medical profession had unexpectedly given her a belief in fate. Some people simply had their time. If it was not yet that time, chance or a good surgeon would save the life in question, but if the time had come, all the skilled people in the world could not change it. Caroline Ryan, MD, knew that this was a strange way for a physician to think, and she balanced the belief with the professional certainty that she was the instrument which would thwart the force that ruled the world—but she had also chosen a field in which life-and-death was rarely the issue. Only she knew that. A close friend had gone into pediatric oncology, the treatment of children stricken with cancer. It was a field that cried out for the best people in medicine, and she'd been tempted, but she knew that the effect on her humanity would be intolerable. How could she carry a child within her while she watched other children die? How could she create life while she was unable to prevent its loss? Her belief in fate could never have made that leap of imagination, and the fear of what it might have done to her psyche had turned her to a field that was demanding in a different way. It was one thing to put your life on the line—quite another to wager your soul.

Jack, she knew, had the courage to face up to that. This, too, had its price. The anguish she occasionally saw in him could only be that kind of question. She was sure that his unspoken work at CIA was aimed at finding and killing the people who had attacked her. She felt it necessary, and she would shed no tears for those who had nearly killed her little girl, but it was a task which, as a physician, she could not herself contemplate. Clearly it wasn't easy for her man. Something had just happened a few days ago. He was struggling with whatever it was, unable to discuss it with anyone while he tried to retain the rest of his world in an undamaged state, trying to love his family while he labored . . . to bring others to their death? It could not have come easily to him. Her husband was a genuinely good man, in so many ways the ideal man—*at least for me,* she thought. He'd fallen in love with her at their first meeting, and she could recount every step of their courtship. She remembered his clumsy—in retrospect, hilarious—proposal of marriage, the terror in his eyes as she'd hesitated over the answer, as though he felt himself unworthy of her, the idiot. Most of all, she remembered the look on his face when Sally had been born. The man who had turned his back on the dog-eat-dog world of investments—the world that since the death of her mother had made her father into a driven, unhappy man—who had returned to teaching eager young minds, was now trapped in something he didn't like. But she knew that he was doing his best, and she knew just how good his best was. She'd just experienced that. Cathy wished that she could share it, as he occasionally had to share with her the depression following a failed procedure. As much as she had needed him a few painful weeks past, now he needed her. She couldn't do that—or could she?

"What's been bothering you? Can I help?"

"I can't really talk about it," Jack said as he knotted his tie. "It was the right thing, but not something you can feel very good about."

"The people who—"

"No, not them. If it was them . . ." He turned to face his wife. "If it was them, I'd be all smiles. There's been a break. The FBI—I shouldn't be telling you this, and it doesn't go any farther than this room—they found the gun. That might be important, but we don't know for sure yet. The other thing—well, I can't talk about that at all. Sorry. I wish I could."

"You haven't done anything wrong?" His face changed at that question.

"No. I've thought that one over the past few days. Remember the time you had to take that lady's eye out? It was necessary, but you still felt pretty bad about it. Same thing." He looked in the mirror. *Sort of the same thing.*

"Jack, I love you and I believe in you. I know that you'll do the right thing."

"I'm glad, babe, because sometimes I'm not so sure." He held out his arms and she came to him. At some French military base in Chad, another young woman was experiencing something other than a loving embrace, Ryan thought. *Whose fault is that? One thing for sure, she isn't the same as my wife. She's not like this girl of mine.*

He felt her against himself, felt the baby move again, and finally he was sure. As his wife had to be protected, so did all the other wives, and all the children, and all the living people who were judged as mere abstractions by the ones who trained in those camps. Because they weren't abstractions, they were real. It was the terrorists who had cast themselves out of the civilized community and had to be hunted down one way or another. *If we can do it by civilized rules, well and good—but if not, then we have to do the best we can, and rely on our consciences to keep us from going over the edge.* He thought that he could trust his conscience. He was holding it in his arms. Jack kissed his wife gently on the cheek.

"Thanks. That's twelve."

The seminar led to the final two weeks of classes which led in turn to final exams and Commissioning Week: yet another class of midshipmen graduated to join the fleet, and the Corps. The plebes were plebes no longer, and were finally able to smile in public once or twice per day. The campus became quiet, or nearly so, as the underclassmen went home for brief vacations before taking cruises with the fleet, and preparing for Plebe Summer, the rough initiation for a new class of mids. Ryan was incongruously trapped in his real job for a week, finishing up a mountain of paperwork. Neither the Academy's history department nor the CIA was very happy with him now. His attempt to serve two masters had not been a total success. Both jobs, he realized, had suffered somewhat, and he knew that he'd have to choose between them. It was a decision that he consciously tried to avoid while the proof of its necessity piled up around him.

"Hey, Jack!" Robby came in wearing his undress whites.

"Grab a seat, Commander. How's the flying business?"

"No complaints. The kid is back in the saddle," Jackson said, sitting down. "You should have been up in the Tomcat with me last week. Oh, man, I'm finally back in the groove. I was hassling with a guy in an A-4 playing aggressor, and I ruined his day. It was so fine.'' He grinned like a lion surveying a herd of crippled antelope. ''I'm ready!''

''When do you leave?''

''I report for duty 5 August. I guess I'll be heading out of here on the first.''

''Not before we have you and Sissy over for dinner.'' Jack checked his calendar. ''The thirtieth is a Friday. Seven o'clock. Okay?''

''Aye aye, sir.''

''What's Sissy going to do down there?''

''Well, they have a little symphony in Norfolk. She's going to be their number-two piano soloist, plus doing her teachin' on the side.''

''You know they have the in-vitro center down there. Maybe you guys can have a kid after all.''

''Yeah, Cathy told her about that. We're thinking about it, but—well, Sissy's had a lot of disappointments, you know?''

''You want Cathy to talk to her about it some more?''

Robby thought about that. ''Yeah, she knows how. How's she making out with this one?''

''She's bitching about her figure a lot,'' Jack chuckled. ''Why is it that they never understand how pretty they look pregnant?''

''Yeah.'' Robby grinned his agreement, wondering if Sissy would ever look the same way to him. Jack felt guilty for touching a sensitive topic, and changed the subject.

''By the way, what's with all the boats? I saw a bunch of yardbirds parked on the waterfront this morning.''

''That's 'moored,' you dumb jarhead,'' Robby corrected his friend. ''They're replacing the pilings over at the naval station across the river. It's supposed to take two months. Something went wrong with the old ones—the preservative didn't work or some such bullcrap. Your basic government-contractor screwup. No big deal. The job's supposed to be finished in time for the next school year—not that I care one way or another, of course. By that time, boy, I'll be spending my mornings at twenty-five thousand feet, back where I belong. What are you going to be doing?''

''What do you mean?''

''Well, you're either gonna be here or at Langley, right?''

Ryan looked out the window. ''Damned if I know. Rob, we got a baby on the way and a bunch of other things to think about.''

''You haven't found 'em yet?''

Jack shook his head. ''We thought we had a break, but it didn't work out. These guys are pros, Robby.''

Jackson reacted with surprising passion. ''Bull-shit, man! Professionals don't hurt kids. Hey, they want to take a shot at a soldier or a cop, okay, I can understand that—it ain't right, but I can understand it, okay?—soldiers and cops have guns to shoot back with, and they got training. So it's an even match, surprise on one side and procedure on the other, and that makes it a fair game. Going after noncombatants, they're just fucking street hoods, Jack. Maybe they're clever, but they sure as hell ain't professionals! Professionals got balls. Professionals put it on the line for-real.''

Jack shook his head. Robby was wrong, but he knew of no way to persuade his friend otherwise. His code was that of the warrior, who had to live by civilized rules. Rule Number One was: You don't deliberately harm the helpless. It was bad enough when that happened by accident. To do so on purpose was cowardly, beneath contempt; those who did so merited only death. They were beyond the pale.

"They're playing a goddamned game, Jack," the pilot went on. "There's even a song about it. I heard it at Riordan's on St. Patrick's Day. 'I've learned all my heroes and wanted the same/To try out my hand at the patriot game.' Something like that." Jackson shook his head in disgust. "War isn't a game, it's a profession. They play their little *games,* and call themselves patriots, and go out and kill little kids. Bastards. Jack, out in the fleet, when I'm driving my Tomcat, we play *our* games with the Russians. Nobody gets killed, because both sides are professionals. I don't much like the Russians, but the boys that fly the Bears know their stuff. We know our stuff, and both sides respect the other. There's rules, and both sides play by 'em. That's the way it's supposed to be."

"The world isn't that simple, Robby," Jack said quietly.

"Well, it damned well ought to be!" Jack was surprised at how worked up his friend was about this. "You tell those guys at CIA: find 'em for us, then get somebody to give the order, and I'll escort the strike in."

"The last two times we did that we lost people," Ryan pointed out.

"We take our chances. That's what they pay us for, Jack."

"Yeah, but before you toss the dice again, we want you over for dinner."

Jackson grinned sheepishly. "I won't bring my soap box with me, I promise. Dressy?"

"Robby, am I ever dressy?"

"I told 'em it wasn't dressy," Jack said afterward.

"Good," his wife agreed.

"I thought you'd say that." He looked up at his wife, her skin illuminated by moonlight. "You really are pretty."

"You keep saying that—"

"Don't move. Just stay where you are." He ran his hand across her flanks.

"Why?"

"You said this is the last time for a while. I don't want it to be over yet."

"The next time you can be on top," she promised.

"It'll be worth waiting for, but you won't be as beautiful as you are now."

"I don't feel beautiful at the moment."

"Cathy, you are talking to an expert," her husband pronounced. "I am the one person in this house who can give out a dispassionate appraisal of the pulchritude of any female human being, living or dead, and *I* say that you are beautiful. End of discussion."

Cathy Ryan took her own appraisal. Her belly was disfigured by gross-looking stretch marks, her breasts were bloated and sore, her feet and ankles swollen, and her legs were knotting up from her current position. "Jack, you are a dope."

"She never listens," he told the ceiling.

"It's just pheromones," she explained. "Pregnant women smell different and it must tickle your fancy somehow or other."

"Then how come you're beautiful when my nose is stuffy? Answer me that!"

She reached down to twist her fingers in the hair on his chest. Jack started squirming. It tickled. "Love is blind."

"When I kiss you, my eyes are always open."

"I didn't know that!"

"I know," Jack laughed quietly. "Your eyes are always closed. Maybe your love is blind, but mine isn't." He ran his fingertips over her abdomen. It was still slick from the baby oil she used to moisturize her skin. Jack found this a little kinky. His fingertips traced circles on the taut, smooth surface.

"You're a throwback. You're something out of a thirties movie." She started squirming now. "Stop that."

"Errol Flynn never did this in the movies," Jack noted, without stopping that.

"They had censors then."

"Spoilsports. Some people are just no fun." His hands expanded their horizons. The next target was the base of her neck. It was a long reach, but worth the effort. She was shivering now. "Now, I, on the other hand . . ."

"Mmmmm."

"I thought so."

"Uh-oh. He's awake again."

Jack felt him almost as soon as his wife. He—she, it—was rotating. Jack wondered how a baby could do that, without anything to latch on to, but the evidence was clear, his hands felt a lump shift position. The lump was his child's head, or the opposite end. Moving. Alive. Waiting to be born. He looked up to see his wife, smiling down at him and knowing what he felt.

"You're beautiful, and I love you very much. Whether you like it or not." He was surprised to find that there were tears in his eyes. He was even more surprised by what happened next.

"Love you, too, Jack—again?"

"Maybe that wasn't the last time for a while after all. . . ."

23. Movement

"We got these last night." Priorities had changed somewhat at CIA. Ryan could tell. The man going over the photos with him was going gray, wore rimless glasses and a bow tie. Garters on his sleeves would not have seemed out of place. Marty stood in the corner and kept his mouth shut. "We figure it's one of these three camps, right?"

"Yeah, the others are identified." Ryan nodded. This drew a snort.

"You say so, son."

"Okay, these two are active, this one as of last week, and this one two days ago."

"What about -20, the *Action-Directe* camp?" Cantor asked.

"Shut down ever since the Frenchies went in. I saw the tape of that." The man smiled in admiration. "Anyway, here."

It was one of the rare daylight photographs, even in color. The firing range adjacent to the camp had six men standing in line. The angle prevented them from seeing if the men held guns or not.

"Weapons training?" Ryan asked cautiously.

"Either that or they're taking a leak by the numbers." This was humor.

"Wait a minute, you said these came in last night."

"Look at the sun angle," the man said derisively.

"Oh. Early morning."

"Around midnight our time. Very good," the man observed. *Amateurs,* he thought. *Everybody thinks he can read a recon photo!* "You can't see any guns, but see these little points of light here? That might be sunlight reflecting off ejected cartridge brass. Okay, we have six people here. Probably Northern Europeans because they're so pale—see this one here with the sunburn, his arm looks a little pink? All appear to be male, from the short hair and style of dress. Okay, now the question is, who the hell are they?"

"They're not *Action-Directe,*" Marty said.

"How do you know that?" Ryan asked.

"The ones who got picked up are no longer with us. They were given trials by military tribunal and executed two weeks ago."

"Jesus!" Ryan turned away. "I didn't want to know that, Marty."

"Those who asked had clergy in attendance. I thought that was decent of our colleagues." He paused for a moment, then went on: "It turns out that French law allows for that sort of trial under very special circumstances. So despite what we both thought all the time, it was all done by the book. Feel better?"

"Some," Ryan admitted on reflection. It might not have made a great deal of difference to the terrorists, but at least the formality of law had been observed, and that was one of the things "civilization" meant.

"Good. A couple sang like canaries beforehand, too. DGSE was able to bag two more members outside of Paris—this hasn't made the papers yet—plus a barnful of guns and explosives. They may not be out of business, but they've been hurt."

"All right," the man in the bow tie acknowledged. "And this is the guy who tumbled to it?"

"All because he likes to see tits from three hundred miles away," Cantor replied.

"How come nobody else saw that first?" Ryan would have preferred that someone else had done all this.

"Because there aren't enough people in my section. I just got authority to hire ten new ones. I've already got them picked out. They're people who're leaving the Air Force. Pros."

"Okay, what about the other camp?"

"Here." A new photo came into view. "Pretty much the same thing. We have two people visible—"

"One's a girl," Ryan said at once.

"One appears to have shoulder-length hair," the photo expert agreed. He went on: "That doesn't necessarily mean it's a girl." Jack thought about that, looking at the figure's stance and posture.

"If we assume it's a girl, what does that tell us?" he asked Marty.

"You tell me."

"We have no indication that the ULA has female members, but we know that the PIRA does. This is the camp—remember that jeep that was driving from one to the other and was later seen parked at this camp?" Ryan paused before going on. *Oh, what the hell . . .* He grabbed the photo of the six people on the gun range. "This is the one."

"And what the hell are you basing that on?" the photo-intel man asked.

"Call it a strong hunch," Ryan replied.

"That's fine. The next time I go to the track I'll bring you along to pick my horses for me. Listen, the thing about these photos is, what you see is all you got.

If you read too much into these photos, you end up making mistakes. Big ones. What you have here is six people lined up, *probably* firing guns. That's all.''

''Anything else?'' Cantor asked.

''We'll have a night pass at about 2200 local time—this afternoon our time. I'll have the shots to you right after they come in.''

''Very good. Thanks,'' Cantor said. The man left the room to go back to his beloved photo equipment.

''I believe you call that sort of person an empiricist,'' Ryan observed after a moment.

Cantor chuckled. ''Something like that. He's been in the business since we had U-2s flying over Russia. He's a real expert. The important thing about that is, he doesn't say he's sure about something until he's *really* sure. What he said's true, you can easily read too much into these things.''

''Fine, but you agree with me.''

''Yeah.'' Cantor sat on the desk next to Ryan and examined the photo through a magnifying glass.

The six men lined up on the firing line were not totally clear. The hot air rising off the desert even in early morning was disturbed enough to ruin the clarity of the image. It was like looking through the shimmering mirage on a flat highway. The satellite camera had a very high ''shutter'' speed—actually the photoreceptors were totally electronic—that canceled most of the distortion, but all they really had was a poorly focused, high-angle image that showed man-shapes. You could tell what they were wearing—tan short-sleeved shirts and long pants—and the color of their hair with total certainty. A glimmer off one man's wrist seemed to indicate a watch or bracelet. The face of one man was darker than it should have been—his uncovered forearm was quite pale—and that probably indicated a short beard. . . . *Miller has a beard now,* Ryan reminded himself.

''Damn, if this was only a little better . . .''

''Yeah,'' Marty agreed. ''But what you see here is the result of thirty years of work and God only knows how much money. In cold climates it comes out a little better, but you can't ever recognize a face.''

''This is it, Marty. This is the one. We have to have something that confirms that, or at least confirms something.''

'' 'Fraid not. Our French colleagues asked the people they captured. The answer they got was that the camps are totally isolated from one another. When the groups meet, it's almost always on neutral ground. They didn't even know for sure that there was a camp here.''

''*That* tells us something!''

''The thing about the car? It could have been somebody from the Army, you know. The guy who oversees the guards, maybe. It didn't have to be one of the players who drove from this one to the Provisionals' camp. In fact, there is ample reason to believe that it wasn't. Compartmentalization is a logical security measure. It makes sense for the camps to be isolated from one another. These people know about the importance of security, and even if they didn't before, the French op was a gilt-edge reminder.''

Ryan hadn't thought about that. The raid on the *Action-Directe* camp had to have an effect on the others, didn't it?

''You mean we shot ourselves in the foot?''

''No, we sent a message that was worth sending. So far as we can determine, nobody knows what actually happened there. We have reason to believe that the suspicion on the ground is that a rival outfit settled a score—not all of these groups like each other. So, if nothing else, we've fostered some suspicions among the groups themselves, and vis-à-vis their hosts. That sort of thing could break some information loose for us, but it'll take time to find out.''

''Anyway, now that we know that this camp is likely to be the one we want, what are we going to do about it?''

''We're working on that. I can't say any more.''

''Okay.'' Ryan gestured to his desk. ''You want some coffee, Marty?''

Cantor's face took on a curious expression. ''No, I'm off coffee for a while.''

What Cantor didn't say was that a major operation had been laid on. It was fairly typical in that very few of the participants actually knew what was going on. A Navy carrier battle group centered on USS *Saratoga* was due to sail west out of the Mediterranean Sea, and would pass north of the Gulf of Sidra in several days. As was routine, the formation was being trailed by a Soviet AGI—a fishing trawler that gathers electronic intelligence instead of mackerel—which would give information to the Libyans. When the carrier was directly north of Tripoli, in the middle of the night, a French-controlled agent would interrupt electrical power to some radar installations soon after the carrier started conducting nighttime flight operations. This was expected to get some people excited, although the carrier group Commander had no idea that he was doing anything other than routine flight ops. It was hoped that the same team of French commandos that had raided Camp -20 would also be able to slip into Camp -18. Marty couldn't tell Ryan any of this, but it was a measure of how well *Action-Directe* had been damaged that the French were willing to give the Americans such cooperation. While it hadn't exactly been the first example of international cooperation, it was one of three such operations that had actually been successful. The CIA had helped to avenge the murder of a friend of the French President. Whatever the differences between the two countries, debts of honor were still paid in full. It appealed to Cantor's sense of propriety, but was something known to only twenty people within the Agency. The op was scheduled to run in four days. A senior case officer from the Operations Directorate was even now working with the French paratroopers who, he reported, were eager to demonstrate their prowess yet again. With luck, the terrorist group that had had the temerity to commit murder within the United States and the United Kingdom would be hurt by the troops of yet another nation. If successful, the precedent would signal a new and valuable development in the struggle against terrorism.

Dennis Cooley was working on his ledger book. It was early. The shop wasn't open for business yet, and this was the time of day for him to set his accounts straight. It wasn't very hard. His shop didn't have all that many transactions. He hummed away to himself, not knowing what annoyance this habit caused for the man listening to the microphone planted behind one of his bookshelves. Abruptly his humming stopped and his head came up. What was wrong . . . ?

The little man nearly leaped from his chair when he smelled the acrid smoke. He scanned the room for several seconds before looking up. The smoke was coming from the ceiling light fixture. He darted to the wall switch and slapped his hand on it. A blue flash erupted from the wall, giving him a powerful electric shock that numbed his arm to the elbow. He stared at his arm in surprise, flexing his fingers and looking at the smoke that seemed to be trailing off. He didn't wait to see it stop. Cooley had a fire extinguisher in the back room. He got it and came back, pulled the safety pin, and aimed the device at the switch. No smoke there anymore.

Next he stood on his chair to get close to the ceiling fixture, but already the smoke was nearly gone. The smell remained. Cooley stood on the chair for over a minute, his knees shaking as the chair moved slightly under him, holding the extinguisher and trying to decide what to do. Call the fire brigade? But there wasn't any fire—was there? All his valuable books. . . . He'd been trained in many things, but fighting fires was not one of them. He was breathing heavily now, nearly panicked until he finally decided that there wasn't anything to be panicked about. He turned to see three people staring at him through the glass with curious expressions.

He lowered the extinguisher with a shamefaced grin and gestured comically to the spectators. The light was off. The switch was off. The fire, if it had been a fire, was gone. He'd call the building's electrician. Cooley opened the door to explain what was wrong to his fellow shop owners. One remarked that the wiring in the arcade was horribly out of date. It was something Cooley hadn't ever thought about. Electricity was electricity. You flipped the switch and the light went on, and that was that. It annoyed him that something so reliable, wasn't. A minute later he called the building manager, who promised that an electrician would be there in half an hour.

The man arrived forty minutes later, apologizing for being held up in traffic. He stood for a moment, admiring the bookshelves.

"Smells like a wire burned out," he judged next. "You're lucky, sir. That frequently causes a fire."

"How difficult will it be to fix?"

"I expect that I'll have to replace the wiring. Ought to have been done years ago. This old place—well, the electric service is older than I am, and that's too old by half." He smiled.

Cooley showed him to the fuse box in the back room, and the man went to work. Dennis was unwilling to use his table lamp, and sat in the semidarkness while the tradesman went to work.

The electrician flipped off the outside master switch and examined the fuse box. It still had the original inspection tag, and when he rubbed off the dust, he read off the date: 1919. The man shook his head in amazement. Almost seventy bloody years! He had to remove some items to get at the wall, and was surprised to see that there was some recent plasterwork. It was as good a place to start as any. He didn't want to damage the wall any more than he had to. With hammer and chisel he broke into the new plaster, and there was the wire. . . .

But it wasn't the right one, he thought. It had plastic insulation, not the gutta-percha used in his grandfather's time. It wasn't in quite the right place, either. Strange, he thought. He pulled on the wire. It came out easily.

"Mr. Cooley, sir?" he called. The shop owner appeared a moment later. "Do you know what this is?"

"Bloody hell!" the detective said in the room upstairs. "Bloody fucking hell!" He turned to his companion, a look of utter shock on his face. "Call Commander Owens!"

"I've never seen anything like this." He cut off the end and handed it over. The electrician did not understand why Cooley was so pale.

Neither had Cooley, but he knew what it was. The end of the wire showed nothing, just a place where the polyvinyl insulation stopped, without the copper core that one expects to see in electrical circuitry. Hidden in the end was a highly sensitive microphone. The shop owner composed himself after a moment, though his voice was somewhat raspy.

"I have no idea. Carry on."

"Yes, sir." The electrician resumed his search for the power line.

Cooley had already lifted his telephone and dialed a number.

"Hello?"

"Beatrix?"

"Good morning, Mr. Dennis. How are you today?"

"Can you come into the shop this morning? I have a small emergency."

"Certainly." She lived only a block from the Holloway Road tube station. The Piccadilly Line ran almost directly to the shop. "I can be there in fifteen minutes."

"Thank you, Beatrix. You're a love," he added before he hung up. By this time Cooley's mind was racing at mach-1. There was nothing in the shop or his home that could incriminate him. He lifted the phone again and hesitated. His instructions under these circumstances were to call a number he had memorized—but if there were a microphone in his office, his phone . . . and his home phone . . . Cooley was sweating now despite the cool temperature. He commanded himself to relax. He'd never said anything compromising on either phone—had he? For all his expertise and discipline, Cooley had never faced danger, and he was beginning to panic. It took all of his concentration to focus on his operational procedures, the things he had learned and practiced for years. Cooley told himself that he had never deviated from them. Not once. He was sure of that. By the time he stopped shaking, the bell rang.

It was Beatrix, he saw. Cooley grabbed his coat.

"Will you be back later?"

"I'm not sure. I'll call you." He went right out the door, leaving his clerk with a very curious look.

It had taken ten minutes to locate James Owens, who was in his car south of London. The Commander gave immediate orders to shadow Cooley and to arrest him if it appeared that he was attempting to leave the country. Two men were already watching the man's car and were ready to trail him. Two more were sent to the arcade, but the detectives arrived just as he walked out, and were on the wrong side of the street. One hopped out of the car and followed, expecting him to turn onto Berkeley Street toward his travel agent. Instead, Cooley ducked into the tube station. The detective was caught off guard and raced down the entrance on his side of the street. The crowd of morning commuters made spotting his short target virtually impossible. In under a minute, the officer was sure that his quarry had caught a train that he had been unable to get close to. Cooley had escaped.

The detective ran back to the street and put out a radio call to alert the police at Heathrow airport, where this underground line ended—Cooley always flew, unless he drove his own car—and to get cars to all the underground stations on the Piccadilly Line. There simply wasn't enough time.

Cooley got off at the next station, as his training had taught him, and took a cab to Waterloo Station. There he made a telephone call.

"Five-five-two-nine," the voice answered.

"Oh, excuse me, I was trying to get six-six-three-zero. Sorry." There followed two seconds of hesitation on the other side of the connection.

"Oh . . . That's quite all right," the voice assured him in a tone that was anything but all right.

Cooley replaced the phone and walked to a train. It was everything he could do not to look over his shoulder.

"This is Geoffrey Watkins," he said as he lifted the phone.

"Oh, I beg your pardon," the voice said. "I was trying to get Mr. Titus. Is this six-two-nine-one?" *All contacts are broken until further notice,* the number told him. *Not known if you are in danger. Will advise if possible.*

"No, this is six-two-one-nine," he answered. *Understood.* Watkins hung the phone up and looked out his window. His stomach felt as though a ball of refrigerated lead had materialized there. He swallowed twice, then reached for his tea. For the rest of the morning, it was hard to concentrate on the Foreign Office white paper he was reading. He needed two stiff drinks with lunch to settle himself down.

By noon, Cooley was in Dover, aboard a cross-channel ferry. He was fully alert now, and sat in a corner seat on the upper deck, looking over the newspaper in his hands to see if anyone was watching him. He'd almost boarded the hovercraft to Calais, but decided against it at the last moment. He had enough cash for the Dover-Dunkerque ferry, but not the more expensive hovercraft, and he didn't want to leave a paper trail behind. It was only two and a quarter hours in any case. Once in France, he could catch a train to Paris, then start flying. He started to feel secure for the first time in hours, but was able to suppress it easily enough. Cooley had never known this sort of fear before, and it left a considerable aftertaste. The quiet hatred that had festered for years now ate at him like an acid. They had made him run. *They* had spied on *him!* Because of all his training, all the precautions that he'd followed assiduously, and all the professional skill that he'd employed, Cooley had never seriously considered the possibility that he would be turned. He had thought himself too skillful for that. That he was wrong enraged him, and for the first time in his life, he wanted to lash out himself. He'd lost his bookshop and with it all the books he loved, and this, too, had been taken from him by the bloody Brits! He folded the paper neatly and set it down in his lap while the ferry pulled into the English Channel, placid with the summer sun overhead. His bland face stared out at the water with a gaze as calm as a man in contemplation of his garden while he fantasized images of blood and death.

Owens was as furious as anyone had ever seen him. The surveillance of Cooley had been so easy, so routine—but that was no excuse, he told his men. That harmless-looking little poof, as Ashley had called him, had slipped away from his shadowers as adroitly as someone trained at Moscow Center itself. There were men at every international airport in Britain clutching pictures of Cooley, and if he used his credit card to purchase any kind of ticket, the computers would notify Scotland Yard at once, but Owens had a sickening feeling that the man was already out of the country. The Commander of C-13 dismissed his people.

Ashley was in the room, too, and his people had been caught equally off guard. He and Owens shared a look of anger mixed with despair.

A detective had left the tape of a phone call to Geoffrey Watkins made less than an hour after Cooley disappeared. Ashley played it. It lasted all of twenty seconds. And it wasn't Cooley's voice. If it had been, they would have arrested Watkins then and there. For all their effort, they still did not have a single usable piece of evidence on Geoffrey Watkins.

"There is a Mr. Titus in the building. The voice even gave the correct number. By all rights it could have been a simple wrong number."

"But it wasn't, of course."

"That is how it's done, you know. You have pre-set messages that are constructed to sound entirely harmless. Whoever trained these chaps knew what they were about. What about the shop?"

"The girl Beatrix knows absolutely nothing. We have people searching the shop at this moment, but so far they've found nothing but old bloody books. Same story at his flat." Owens stood and spoke in a voice full of perverse wonder. "An electrician. . . . Months of work, gone because he yanks the wrong wire."

"He'll turn up. He could not have had a great deal of cash. He must use his credit card."

"He's out of the country already. Don't say he isn't. If he's clever enough for what we know he's done—"

"Yes." Ashley nodded reluctant agreement. "One doesn't always win, James."

"It is so nice to hear that!" Owens snapped out his reply. "These bastards have outguessed us every step of the way. The Commissioner is going to ask me how it is that we couldn't get our thumbs out in time, and there is no answer to that question."

"So what's the next step, then?"

"At least we know what he looks like. We . . . we share what we know with the Americans, all of it. I have a meeting scheduled with Murray this evening. He's hinted that they have something operating that he's not able to talk about, doubtless some sort of CIA op."

"Agreed. Is it here or there?"

"There." Owens paused. "I am getting sick of this place."

"Commander, you should measure your successes against your failures," Ashley said. "You're the best man we've had in this office in some years."

Owens only grunted at that remark. He knew it was true. Under his leadership, C-13 had scored major coups against the Provisionals. But in this job, as in so many others, the question one's superiors always asked was, *What have you accomplished today?* Yesterday was ancient history.

"Watkins' suspected contact has flown," he announced three hours later.

"What happened?" Murray closed his eyes halfway through the explanation and shook his head sadly. "We had the same sort of thing happen to us," he said after Owens finished. "A renegade CIA officer. We were watching his place, and let things settle into a comfortable routine, and then—zip! He snookered the surveillance team. He turned up in Moscow a week later. It happens, Jimmy."

"Not to me," Owens almost snarled. "Not until now, that is."

"What's he look like?" Owens handed a collection of photographs across the desk. Murray flipped through them. "Mousy little bastard, isn't he? Almost bald." The FBI man considered this for a moment, then lifted his phone and punched in four numbers. "Fred? Dan. You want to come down to my office for a minute?"

The man arrived a minute later. Murray didn't identify him as a member of the CIA and Owens didn't ask. He didn't have to. He'd given over two copies of each photo.

Fred—one of the men from "down the hall"—took his photos and looked at them. "Who's he supposed to be?"

Owens explained briefly, ending, "He's probably out of the country by now."

"Well, if he turns up in any of our nets, we'll let you know," Fred promised, and left.

"Do you know what they're up to?" Owens asked Murray.

"No. I know something is happening. The Bureau and the Agency have a joint task force set up, but it's compartmented, and I don't need to know all of it yet."

"Did your chaps have a part in the raid on *Action-Directe*?"

"I don't know what you're talking about," Murray said piously. *How the hell did you hear about that, Jimmy?*

"I thought as much," Owens replied. *Bloody security!* "Dan, we are concerned here with the personal safety of—"

Murray held his hands up like a man at bay. "I know, I know. And you're right, too. We ought to cut your people in on this. I'll call the Director myself."

The phone rang. It was for Owens.

"Yes?" The Commander of C-13 listened for a minute before hanging up. "Thank you." A sigh. "Dan, he's definitely on the continent. He used a credit card to purchase a railway ticket. Dunkerque to Paris, three hours ago."

"Have the French pick him up?"

"Too late. The train arrived twenty minutes ago. He's completely gone now. Besides, we have nothing to arrest him for, do we?"

"And Watkins has been warned off."

"Unless that was a genuinely wrong number, which I rather doubt, but try to prove *that* in a court of law!"

"Yeah." Judges didn't understand any instinct but their own.

"And don't tell me that you can't win them all! That's what they pay me to do." Owens looked down at the rug, then back up. "Please excuse me for that."

"Aah!" Murray waved it off. "You've had bad days before. So have I. It's part of the business we're in. What we both need at a time like this is a beer. Come on downstairs, and I'll treat you to a burger."

"When will you call your Director?"

"It's lunchtime over there. He always has a meeting going over lunch. We'll let it wait a few hours."

Ryan had lunch with Cantor that day in the CIA cafeteria. It could have been the eating place in any other government building. The food was just as unexciting. Ryan decided to try the lasagna, but Marty stuck with fruit salad and cake. It seemed an odd diet until Jack watched him take a tablet before eating. He washed it down with milk.

"Ulcers, Marty?"

"What makes you say that?"

"I'm married to a doc, remember? You just took a Tagamet. That's for ulcers."

"This place gets to you after a while," Cantor explained. "My stomach started acting up last year and didn't get any better. Everyone in my family comes down with it sooner or later. Bad genes, I guess. The medication helps some, but the doctor says that I need a less stressful environment." A snort.

"You do work long hours," Ryan observed.

"Anyway, my wife got offered a teaching position at the University of Texas—she's a mathematician. And to sweeten the deal they offered me a place in the Political Science Department. The pay's better than it is here, too. I've been here twelve years," he said quietly. "Long time."

"So what do you feel bad about? Teaching's great. I love it, and you'll be good at it. You'll even have a good football team to watch."

"Yeah, well, she's already down there, and I leave in a few weeks. I'm going to miss this place."

"You'll get over it. Imagine being able to walk into a building without getting permission from a computer. Hey, I walked away from my first job."

"But this one's important." Cantor drank his milk and looked across the table. "What are you going to do?"

"Ask me after the baby is born." Ryan didn't want to dwell on this question.

"The Agency needs people like you, Jack. You've got a feel for things. You don't think and act like a bureaucrat. You say what you think. Not everyone in this building does that, and that's why the Admiral likes you."

"Hell, I haven't talked to him since—"

"He knows what you're doing." Cantor smiled.

"Oh." Ryan understood. "So that's it."

"That's right. The old man really wants you, Jack. You still don't know how important that photo you tripped over was, do you?"

"All I did was show it to you, Marty," Ryan protested. "You're the one who really made the connection."

"You did exactly the right thing, exactly what an analyst is supposed to do. There was more brains in that than you know. You have a gift for this sort of work. If you can't see it, I can." Cantor examined the lasagna and winced. How could anybody eat that greasy poison? "Two years from now you'll be ready for my job."

"One bridge at a time, Marty." They let it go at that.

An hour later Ryan was back in his office. Cantor came in.

"Another pep talk?" Jack smiled. *Full-court press time . . .*

"We have a picture of a suspected ULA member and it's only a week old. We got it in from London a couple of hours ago."

"Dennis Cooley." Ryan examined it and laughed. "He looks like a real wimp. What's the story?"

Cantor explained. "Bad luck for the Brits, but maybe good luck for us. Look at the picture again and tell me something important."

"You mean . . . he's lost most of his hair. Oh! We can ID the guy if he turns up at one of the camps. None of the other people are bald."

"You got it. And the boss just cleared you for something. There's an op laid on for Camp -18."

"What kind?"

"The kind you watched before. Is that still bothering you?"

"No, not really." *What bothers me is that it* doesn't *bother me,* Ryan thought. *Maybe it should. . . .* "Not with these guys, I don't. When?"

"I can't tell you, but soon."

"So why did you let me know—nice one, Marty. Not very subtle, though. Does the Admiral want me to stay that bad?"

"Draw your own conclusions."

An hour after that the photo expert was back. Another satellite had passed over the camp at 2208 local time. The infrared image showed eight people standing at line on the firing range. Bright tongues of flame marked two of the shapes. They were firing their weapons at night, and there were now at least eight of them there.

* * *

"What happened?" O'Donnell asked. He'd met Cooley at the airport. A cutout had gotten word out that Cooley was on the run, but the reason for it had had to wait until now.

"There was a bug in my shop."

"You're sure?" O'Donnell asked.

Cooley handed it over. The wire had been in his pocket for thirty hours. O'Donnell pulled the Toyota Land Cruiser over to examine it.

"Marconi make these for intelligence use. Quite sensitive. How long might it have been there?"

Cooley could not remember having anyone go into his back room unsupervised. "I've no idea."

O'Donnell put the vehicle back into gear, heading out into the desert. He pondered the question for over a mile. Something had gone wrong, but what . . . ?

"Did you ever think you were being followed?"

"Never."

"How closely did you check, Dennis?" Cooley hesitated, and O'Donnell took this for an answer. "Dennis, did you ever break tradecraft—*ever?*"

"No, Kevin, of course not. It isn't possible that—for God's sake, Kevin, it's been weeks since I've been in contact with Watkins."

"Since your last trip to Cork." O'Donnell squinted in the bright sun.

"Yes, that's right. You had a security man watching me then—was there anyone following me?"

"If there were, he must have been a damnably clever one, and he could not have been too close. . . ." The other possibility that O'Donnell was considering, of course, was that Cooley had turned traitor. *But if he'd done that, he wouldn't have come here, would he?* the chief of the ULA thought. *He knows me, knows where I live, knows McKenney, knows Sean Miller, knows about the fishing fleet at Dundalk.* O'Donnell realized that Cooley knew quite a lot. No, if he'd gone tout, he wouldn't be here. Cooley was sweating despite the air conditioning in the car. Dennis didn't have the belly to risk his life that way. He could see that.

"So, Dennis, what are we to do with you?"

Cooley's heart was momentarily irregular, but he spoke with determination. "I want to be part of the next op."

"Excuse me?" O'Donnell's head came around in surprise.

"The fucking Brits—Kevin, they came after *me!*"

"That is something of an occupational hazard, you know."

"I'm quite serious," Cooley insisted.

It wouldn't hurt to have another man. . . . "Are you in shape for it?"

"I will be."

The chief made his decision. "Then you can start this afternoon."

"What is it, then?"

O'Donnell explained.

"It would seem that your hunch was correct, Doctor Ryan," the man with the rimless glasses said the next afternoon. "Maybe I will take you to the track."

He was standing outside one of the huts, a dumpy little man with a head that shone from the sunlight reflecting off his sweaty, hairless dome. Camp -18 was the one.

''Excellent,'' Cantor observed. ''Our English friends have really scored on this one. Thanks,'' he said to the photo expert.

''When's the op?'' Ryan asked after he left.

''Early morning, day after tomorrow. Our time . . . eight in the evening, I think.''

''Can I watch in real time?''

''Maybe.''

''This is a secret that's hard to keep,'' he said.

''Most of the good ones are,'' Cantor agreed. ''But—''

''Yeah, I know.'' Jack put his coat on and locked up his files. ''Tell the Admiral that I owe him one.''

Driving home, Ryan thought about what might be happening. He realized that his anticipation was not very different from . . . Christmas? No, that was not the right way to think about this. He wondered how his father had felt right before a big arrest after a lengthy investigation. It was something he'd never asked. He did the next best thing. He forgot about it, as he was supposed to do with everything that he saw at Langley.

There was a strange car parked in front of the house when he got there, just beyond the nearly completed swimming pool. On inspection he saw that it had diplomatic tags. He went inside to find three men talking to his wife. He recognized one but couldn't put a name on him.

''Hello, Doctor Ryan, I'm Geoffrey Bennett from the British Embassy. We met before at—''

''Yeah, I remember now. What can we do for you?''

''Their Royal Highnesses will be visiting the States in a few weeks. I understand that you offered an invitation when you met, and they wish to see if it remains open.''

''Are you kidding?''

''They're not kidding, Jack, and I already said yes,'' his wife informed him. Even Ernie was wagging his tail in anticipation.

''Of course. Please tell them that we'd be honored to have them down. Will they be staying the night?''

''Probably not. It was hoped that they could come in the evening.''

''For dinner? Fine. What day?''

''Friday, 30th July.''

''Done.''

''Excellent. I hope you won't mind if our security people—plus your Secret Service chaps—conduct a security sweep in the coming week.''

''Do I have to be home for that?''

''I can do it, Jack. I'm off work now, remember?''

''Oh, of course,'' Bennett said. ''When is the baby due?''

''First week of August—that might be a problem for this,'' Cathy realized belatedly.

''If something unexpected happens, you may be sure that Their Highnesses will understand. One more thing. This is a private matter, not one of the public events for the trip. We must ask that you keep this entirely confidential.''

''Sure, I understand,'' Ryan said.

''If they're going to be here for dinner, is there anything we shouldn't serve?'' Cathy asked.

"What do you mean?" Bennett responded.

"Well, some people are allergic to fish, for example."

"Oh, I see. No, I know of nothing along those lines."

"Okay, the basic Ryan dinner," Jack said. "I—uh-oh."

"What's the matter?" Bennett asked.

"We're having company that night."

"Oh," Cathy nodded. "Robby and Sissy."

"Can't you cancel?"

"It's a going-away party. Robby—he's a Navy fighter pilot, we both teach at the Academy—is transferring back to the fleet. Would they mind?"

"Doctor Ryan, His Highness—"

"His Highness is a good guy. So's Robby. He was there that night we met. I can't cancel him out, Mr. Bennett. He's a friend. The good news is, His Highness will like him. He used to fly fighter planes, too, right?"

"Well, yes, but—"

"Do you remember the night we met? Without Robby I might not have gotten through it. Look, this guy's a lieutenant commander in the United States Navy who happens to fly a forty-million-dollar fighter airplane. He probably is not a security risk. His wife plays one hell of a piano." Ryan saw that he hadn't quite gotten through yet. "Mr. Bennett, check Rob out through your attaché and ask His Highness if it's all right."

"And if he objects?"

"He won't. I've met him. Maybe he's a better guy than you give him credit for," Jack observed. *He won't object, you dummy. It's the security pukes who'll throw a fit.*

"Well." That remark took him somewhat aback. "I cannot fault your sense of loyalty, Doctor. I will pass this through His Highness's office. But I must insist that you do not tell Commander Jackson anything."

"You have my word." Jack nearly laughed. He couldn't wait to see the look on Robby's face. This would finally even the score for that kendo match.

"Contraction peaks," Jack said that night. They were practicing the breathing exercises in preparation for the delivery. His wife started panting. Jack knew that this was a serious business. It merely looked ridiculous. He checked the numbers on his digital watch. "Contraction ends. Deep, cleansing breath. I figure steaks on the grill, baked potatoes, and fresh corn on the cob, with a nice salad."

"It's too plain," Cathy protested.

"Everywhere they go over here, people will be hitting them with that fancy French crap. Somebody ought to give them a decent American meal. You know I do a mean steak on the grill, and your spinach salad is famous from here to across the road."

"Okay." Cathy started laughing. It was becoming uncomfortable for her to do so. "If I stand over a stove for more than a few minutes, I get nauseous anyway."

"It must be tough, being pregnant."

"You should try it," she suggested.

Her husband went on: "It's the *only* hard thing women have to do, of course."

"What!" Cathy's eyes nearly popped out.

"Look at history. Who has to go out and kill the buffalo? The man. Who has to carry the buffalo back? The man. Who has to drive off the bear? The man. We do all the hard stuff. I still have to take out the garbage every night! Do I ever complain about that?'' He had her laughing again. He'd read her mood right. She didn't want sympathy. She was too proud of herself for that.

''I'd hit you on the head, but there's no sense in breaking a perfectly good club over something worthless.''

''Besides, I was there the last time, and it didn't look all that hard.''

''If I could move, Jack, I'd kill you for that one!''

He moved from opposite his wife to beside her. ''Nah, I don't think so. I want you to form a picture in your mind.''

''Of what?''

''Of the look on Robby's face when he gets here for dinner. I'm going to jiggle the time a little.''

''I'll bet you that Sissy handles it better than he does.''

''How much?''

''Twenty.''

''Deal.'' He looked at his watch. ''Contraction begins. Deep breath.'' A minute later, Jack was amazed to see that he was breathing the same way as his wife. That got them both laughing.

24. Connections Missed and Made

There were no new pictures of Camp -18 the day of the raid. A sandstorm had swept over the area at the time of the satellite pass, and the cameras couldn't penetrate it, but a geosynchronous weather satellite showed that the storm had left the site. Ryan was cued after lunch that day that the raid was on, and spent his afternoon in fidgety anticipation. Careful analysis of the existing photos showed that between twelve and eighteen people were at the camp, over and above the guard force. If the higher number were correct, and the official estimate of the ULA's size was also accurate, that represented more than half of its membership. Ryan worried a little about that. If the French were sending in only eight paratroopers . . . but then he remembered his own experiences in the Marine Corps. They'd be hitting the objective at three in the morning. Surprise would be going for them. The assault team would have its weapons loaded and locked—and aimed at people who were asleep. The element of surprise, in the hands of elite commandos, was the military equivalent of a Kansas tornado. Nothing could stand up to it.

They're in their choppers now, Ryan thought. He remembered his own experience in the fragile, ungainly aircraft. *There you are, all your equipment packed up, clean utilities, your weapons ready, and despite it all you're as vulnerable as a baby in the womb.* He wondered what sort of men they were, and realized that they wouldn't be too very different from the Marines he'd served with: all would be volunteers, doubly so since you also had to volunteer for parachute training. They'd opted a third time to be part of the antiterror teams. It would be partly for the extra pay they got and partly for the pride that always came with membership in a small, very special force—like the Marine Corps' Force Recon—but mostly they'd be there because they knew that this was a mission worth doing. To a man, professional soldiers despised terrorists, and each would dream about getting them in an even-up-battle—the idea of the Field of Honor had never died for the real professionals. It was the place where the ultimate decision was made on the basis of courage and skill, on the basis of manhood itself, and it was this concept that marked the professional soldier as a romantic, a person who truly believed in the rules.

They'd be nervous in their helicopter. Some would fidget and be ashamed of it. Others would make a great show of sharpening their knives. Some would joke quietly. Their officers and sergeants would sit quietly, setting an example and going over the plans. All would look about the helicopter and silently hate being trapped within it. For a moment Jack was there with them.

"Good luck, guys," he whispered to the wall. "*Bonne chance.*"

The hours crept by. It seemed to Ryan that the numbers on his digital watch were reluctant to change at all, and it was impossible for him to concentrate on his work. He was going over the photos of the camp again, counting the man-figures, examining the ground to predict for himself how the final approach would be made. He wondered if their orders were to take the terrorists alive. He couldn't decide on that question. From a legal perspective, he didn't think it really mattered. If terrorism were the modern manifestation of piracy—the analogy seemed apt enough—then the ULA was fair game for any nation's armed forces. On the other hand, taken alive, they could be put on trial and displayed. The psychological impact on other such groups might be real. If it didn't put the fear of God in them, it would at least get their attention. It would frighten them to know that they were not safe even in their most remote, most secure sanctuary. Some members might drift away, and maybe one or two of them would talk. It didn't take much intelligence information to hammer them. Ryan had seen that clearly enough. You needed to know where they were, that was all. With that knowledge you could bring all the forces of a modern nation to bear, and for all their arrogance and brutality, they couldn't hope to stand up to that.

Marty came into the office. "Ready to go over?"

"Hell, yes!"

"Did you have dinner?"

"No. Maybe later."

"Yeah." Together they walked to the annex. The corridors were nearly empty now. For the most part, CIA worked like any other place. At five the majority of the workers departed for home and dinner and evening television.

"Okay, Jack, this is real-time. Remember that you can't discuss any aspect of this." Cantor looked rather tired, Jack thought.

"Marty, if this op is successful, I will tell my wife that the ULA is out of business. She has a right to know that much."

"I can understand that. Just so she doesn't know how it happens."

"She wouldn't even be interested," Jack assured him as they entered the room with the TV monitor. Jean-Claude was there again.

"Good evening, Mr. Cantor, Professor Ryan," the DGSE officer greeted them both.

"How's the op going?"

''They are under radio silence,'' the Colonel replied.

''What I don't understand is how they can do it the same way twice,'' Ryan went on.

''There is a risk. A little disinformation has been used,'' Jean-Claude said cryptically. ''In addition, your carrier now has their full attention.''

''*Saratoga* has an alpha-strike up,'' Marty explained. ''Two fighter squadrons and three attack ones, plus jamming and radar coverage. They're patrolling that 'Line of Death' right now. According to our electronics listening people, the Libyans are going slightly ape. Oh, well.''

''The satellite comes over the horizon in twenty-four minutes,'' the senior technician reported. ''Local weather looks good. We ought to get some clear shots.''

Ryan wished he had a cigarette. They made the waiting easier, but every time Cathy smelled them on his breath, there was hell to pay. At this point the raiding force would be crawling across the last thousand yards. Ryan had done the drill himself. They'd come away with bloody hands and knees, sand rubbed into the wounds. It was an incredibly tiring thing to do, made more difficult still by the presence of armed soldiers at the objective. You had to time your moves for when they were looking the other way, and you had to be quiet. They'd be carrying the bare minimum of gear, their personal weapons, maybe some grenades, a few radios, slinking across the ground the way a tiger did, watching and listening.

Everyone was staring at the blank TV monitor now, each of them bewitched by his imagination's picture of what was happening.

''Okay,'' the technician said, ''cameras coming on line, attitude and tracking controls in automatic, programming telemetry received. Target acquisition in ninety seconds.''

The TV picture lit up. It showed a test pattern. Ryan hadn't seen one of those in years.

''Getting a signal.''

Then the picture appeared. Disappointingly, it was in infrared again. Somehow Ryan had expected otherwise. The low angle showed very little of the camp. They could discern no movement at all. The technician frowned and increased the viewing field. Nothing more, not even the helicopters.

The viewing angle changed slowly, and it was hard to believe that the reconnaissance satellite was racing along at over eighteen thousand miles per hour. Finally they could see all of the huts. Ryan blinked. Only one was lit up on the infrared picture. *Uh-oh.* Only one hut—the guards' one—had had its heater on. What did that mean? *They're gone—nobody's home . . . and the assault force isn't there either.*

Ryan said what the others didn't want to say: ''Something's gone wrong.''

''When can they tell us what happened?'' Cantor asked.

''They cannot break silence for several hours.''

Two more hours followed. They were spent in Marty's office. Food was sent up. Jean-Claude didn't say anything, but he was clearly disappointed by it. Cantor didn't touch his at all. The phone rang. The Frenchman took the call, and spoke in his native tongue. The conversation lasted four or five minutes. Jean-Claude hung up and turned.

''The assault force came upon a regular army unit a hundred kilometers from the camp, apparently a mechanized unit on an exercise. This was not expected. Coming in low, they encountered them quite suddenly. It opened fire on the helicopters. Surprise was lost, and they had to turn back.'' Jean-Claude didn't have to explain that, at best, operations like this were successful barely more than half the time.

"I was afraid of that." Jack stared at the floor. He didn't need to have anyone tell him that the mission could not be repeated. They had run a serious risk, trying a covert mission the same way twice. There would be no third attempt. "Are your people safe?"

"Yes, one helicopter was damaged, but managed to return to base. No casualties."

"Please thank your people for trying, Colonel." Cantor excused himself and walked to his private bathroom. Once in there, he threw up. His ulcers were bleeding again. Marty tried to stand, but found himself faint. He fell against the door with a hard rap on the head.

Jack heard the noise and went to see what it was. It was hard to open the door, but he finally saw Marty lying there. Ryan's first instinct was to tell Jean-Claude to call for a doctor, but Jack himself didn't know how to do that here. He helped Marty to his feet and led him back into his office, setting him in a chair.

"What's the matter?"

"He just tossed up blood—how do you call . . ." Ryan said the hell with it and dialed Admiral Greer's line.

"Marty's collapsed—we need a doctor here."

"I'll take care of it. Be there in two minutes," the Admiral answered.

Jack went into the bathroom and got a glass of water and some toilet paper. He used this to wipe Cantor's mouth, then held up the glass. "Wash your mouth out."

"I'm okay," the man protested.

"Bullshit," Ryan replied. "You jerk. You've been working too damned late, trying to finish up all your stuff before you leave, right?"

"Got—got to."

"What you got to do, Marty, is get the hell out of here before it eats you up."

Cantor gagged again.

You weren't kidding, Marty, Jack thought. *The war is being fought here, too, and you're one of the casualties. You wanted that mission to score as much as I did.*

"What the hell!" Greer entered the room. He even looked a little disheveled.

"His ulcers let go," Jack explained. "He's been puking blood."

"Aw, Jesus, Marty!" the Admiral said.

Ryan hadn't known that there was a medical dispensary at Langley. Someone identifying himself as a paramedic arrived next. He examined Cantor quickly, then he and a security guard loaded the man on a wheelchair. They took him out, and the three men left behind stared at each other.

"How hard is it to die from ulcers?" Ryan asked his wife just before midnight.

"How old is he?" she asked. Jack told her. Cathy thought about it for a moment. "It can happen, but it's fairly rare. Somebody at work?"

"My supervisor at Langley. He's been on Tagamet, but he vomited blood tonight."

"Maybe he tried going without it. That's one of the problems. You give people medications, and as soon as they start feeling better, they stop taking the meds. Even smart people," Cathy noted. "Is it *that* stressful over there?"

"I guess it was for him."

"Super." It was the kind of remark that should have been followed by a rollover, but Cathy hadn't been able to do that for some time. "He'll probably be all right. You really have to work at it to be in serious trouble from ulcers nowadays. Are you sure you want to work there?"

"No. They want me, but I won't decide until you lose a little weight."

"You'd better not be that far away when I go into labor."

"I'll be there when you need me."

"Almost got 'em," Murray reported.

"The same mob who raided *Action-Directe,* eh? Yes, I've heard that was a nicely run mission. What happened?" Owens asked.

"The assault group was spotted seventy miles out and had to turn back. On reexamination of the photos, it may be that our friends were already gone anyway."

"Marvelous. I see our luck is holding. Where did they go, you reckon?"

Murray grunted. "I've got to make the same assumption you have, Jimmy."

"Quite." He looked out the window. The sun would be rising soon. "Well, we've cleared the DPG man and told him the story."

"How'd he take it?"

"He immediately offered his resignation, but the Commissioner and I prevailed upon him to withdraw it. We all have our little foibles," Owens said generously. "He's a very good chap at what he does. You'll be pleased to learn that his reaction was precisely the same as yours. He said we should arrange for His Highness to fall off one of his polo ponies and break his leg. Please don't quote either of us on that!"

"It's a hell of a lot easier to protect cowards, isn't it? It's the brave ones who complicate our lives. You know something? He's going to be a good king for you someday. If he lives long enough," Murray added. It was impossible not to like the kid, he thought. And his wife was dynamite. "Well, if it makes you feel any better, the security on 'em in the States will be *tight.* Just like what we give the President. Even some of the same people are involved."

That's supposed to make me feel happy? Owens asked himself silently, remembering how close several American Presidents had come to death at the hands of madmen, not to mention John F. Kennedy. It could be, of course, that the ULA was back wherever it lived, but all his instincts told him otherwise. Murray was a close friend, and he also knew and respected the Secret Service agents who'd formed the security detail. But the security of Their Highnesses was properly the responsibility of the Yard, and he didn't like the fact that it was now largely in others' hands. Owens had been professionally offended the last time the American President had been in the U.K., when the Secret Service had made a big show of shoving the locals as far aside as they dared. Now he understood them a little better.

"How much is the rent?" Dobbens asked.

"Four-fifty a month," the agent answered. "That's furnished."

"Uh-huh." The furnishings weren't exactly impressive, Alex saw. They didn't have to be.

"When can my cousin move in?"

"It's not for you?"

"No, it's my cousin. He's in the same business I am," Alex explained. "He's new to the area. I'll be responsible for the rent, of course. A three-month deposit, you said?"

"Okay." The agent had specified two months' rent up-front.

"Cash all right?" Dobbens asked.

"Sure. Let's go back to the office and get the paperwork done."

"I'm running a little late, I'm afraid. Don't you have the contract with you?"

The agent nodded. "Yeah, I can do it right here." He walked out to his car and came back with a clipboard and a boilerplate rental contract. He didn't know that he was condemning himself to death, that no one else from his office had seen this man's face.

"My mail goes to a box—I get it on the way into work." That took care of the address.

"What sort of work, did you say?"

"I work at the Applied Physics Laboratory, electrical engineer. I'm afraid I can't be more specific than that. We do a lot of government work, you understand." Alex felt vaguely sorry for the man. He was pleasant enough, and hadn't given him a runaround like many real estate people did. It was too bad. *That's life.*

"You always deal in cash?"

"That's one way to make sure you can afford it," Alex chuckled.

"Could you sign here, please?"

"Sure thing." Alex did so with his own pen, left-handed as he'd practiced. "And that's thirteen-fifty." He counted off the bills.

"That was easy," the agent said as he handed over the keys and a receipt.

"It sure was. Thank you, sir." Alex shook his hand. "He'll probably be moving in next week, certainly by the week after that."

The two men walked out to their cars. Alex wrote down the agent's tag number: he drove his own car, not one belonging to the brokerage. Alex noted his description anyway, just to be sure that his people didn't kill the wrong man. He was glad he hadn't drawn a woman agent. Alex knew that he'd have to overcome that prejudice sooner or later, but for the moment it was an issue he was just as happy to avoid. He followed the agent for a few blocks, then turned off and doubled back to the house.

It wasn't exactly perfect, but close enough. Three small bedrooms. The eat-in kitchen was all right, though, as was the living room. Most important, it had a garage, and sat on nearly an acre of ground. The lot was bordered by hedges, and sat in a semirural working-class neighborhood where the houses were separated by about fifty feet. It would do just fine as a safehouse.

Finished, he drove to Washington National Airport, where he caught a flight to Miami. There was a three-hour layover until he took another airplane to Mexico City. Miller was waiting for him in the proper hotel.

"Hello, Sean."

"Hello, Alex. Drink?"

"What do you have?"

"Well, I brought a bottle of decent whiskey, or you can have some of the local stuff. The beer isn't bad, but I personally stop short of drinking something with a worm in the bottle."

Alex selected a beer. He didn't bother with a glass.

"So?"

Dobbens drained the beer in one long pull. It was good to be able to relax—really relax. Play-acting all the time at home could be a strain. "I got the safehouse all set up. Did that this morning. It'll do fine for what we want. What about your people?"

"They're on the way. They'll arrive as planned."

Alex nodded approval as he got a second beer. "Okay, let's see how the operation's going to run."

"In a very real sense, Alex, you inspired this." Miller opened his briefcase and extracted the maps and charts. They went on the coffee table. Alex didn't smile. Miller was trying to stroke him, and Dobbens didn't like being stroked. He listened for twenty minutes.

"Not bad, that's pretty fair, but you're going to have to change a few things."

"What?" Miller asked. He was already angered by Dobbens' tone.

"Look, man, there's going to be at least fifteen security guys right here." Alex tapped the map. "And you're going to have to do them right quick, y'know? We're not talking street cops here. These guys are trained and well-armed. They're not exactly dumb, either. If you want this to work, man, you have to land the first punch harder. Your timing is off some, too. No, we have to tighten this up some, Sean."

"But they'll be in the wrong place!" Miller objected as dispassionately as he could manage.

"And you want them to be running around loose? No way, boy! You'd better think about taking them out in the first ten seconds. Hey, think of them as soldiers. This ain't no snatch-and-run job. We're talking combat here."

"But if the security is going to be as tight as you say—"

"I can handle that, man. Don't you pay attention to what I'm doing? I can put your shooters in exactly the right spot at exactly the right time."

"And how the hell will you do that!" Miller was unable to calm himself anymore. There was just something about Alex that set him off.

"It's easy, man." Dobbens smiled. He enjoyed showing this hotshot how things were done. "All you gotta do . . ."

"And you really think you can get past them just like that!" Miller snapped after he finished.

"Easy. I can write my own work orders, remember?"

Miller struggled with himself again, and this time he won. He told himself to view Alex's idea dispassionately. He hated admitting to himself that the plan made sense. This amateur black was telling him how to run an op, and the fact that he was right just made it worse.

"Hey, man, it's not just better, it's easier to do." Alex backed off somewhat. Even arrogant whities needed their pride. This boy was used to having his own way. He was smart enough, Dobbens admitted to himself, but too inflexible. Once he got himself set on an idea, he didn't want to change a thing. He never would have made a good engineer, Alex knew. "Remember the last op we ran for you? Trust me, man. I was right then, wasn't I?"

For all his technical expertise, Alex did not have tremendous skills for handling people. This last remark almost set Miller off again, but the Irishman took a deep breath as he continued to stare at the map. *Now I know why the Yanks love their niggers so much.*

"Let me think about it."

"Sure. Tell you what. I'm going to get some sleep. You can pray over the map all you want."

"Who else besides the security and the targets?"

Alex stretched. "Maybe they're going to cater it. Hell—I don't know. I imagine they'll have their maid. I mean, you don't have that kind of company without one servant, right? She doesn't get hurt either, man. She's a sister, handsome woman. And remember what I said about the lady and the kid. If it's necessary, I can live with it, but if you pop 'em for fun, Sean, you'll answer to me. Let's try to keep this one professional. You have three legitimate political targets. That's enough. The rest are bargaining chips, we can use 'em to show good will. That might not be important to you, boy, but it's fucking well important to me. You dig?''

''Very well, Alex.'' Sean decided then and there that Alex would not see the end of this operation. It shouldn't be too hard to arrange. With his absurd sentimentality, he was unfit to be a revolutionary. *You'll die a brave death. At least we can make a martyr of you.*

Two hours later Miller admitted to himself that this was unfortunate. The man did have a flair for operations.

The security people were late enough that Ryan pulled into the driveway right behind them. There were three of them, led by Chuck Avery of the Secret Service.

''Sorry, we got held up,'' Avery said as he shook hands. ''This is Bert Longley and Mike Keaton, two of our British colleagues.''

''Hello, Mr. Longley,'' Cathy called from the door.

His eyes went wide as he saw her condition. ''My goodness, perhaps we should bring a physician in with us! I'd no idea you were so far along.''

''Well, this one will be part English.'' Jack explained. ''Come on in.''

''Mr. Longley arranged our escort when you were in the hospital,'' Cathy told her husband. ''Nice to see you again.''

''How are you feeling?'' Longley asked.

''A little tired, but okay,'' Cathy allowed.

''Have you cleared the problem about Robby?'' Jack asked.

''Yes, we have. Please excuse Mr. Bennett. I'm afraid he took his instructions a bit too literally. We have no problems with a naval officer. In fact, His Highness is looking forward to meeting him. So, may we look around?''

''If it's all right with you, I want to see that cliff of yours,'' Avery said.

''Follow me, gentlemen.'' Jack led the three through the sliding-glass doors onto the deck that faced Chesapeake Bay.

''Magnificent!'' Longley observed.

''The only thing we did wrong is that the living and dining room aren't separated, but that's how the design was drawn, and we couldn't figure a graceful way to change it. But all those windows do give us a nice view, don't they?''

''Indeed, also one that gives our chaps good visibility,'' Keaton observed, surveying the area.

Not to mention decent fields of fire, Ryan thought.

''How many people will you be bringing?'' Jack asked.

''I'm afraid that's not something we can discuss,'' Longley replied.

''More than twenty?'' Jack persisted. ''I plan to have coffee and sandwiches for your troops. Don't worry, I haven't even told Robby.''

''Enough for twenty will be more than ample,'' Avery said after a moment. ''Just coffee will be fine.'' They'd be drinking a lot of coffee, the Secret Service man thought.

''Okay, let's see the cliff.'' Jack went down the steps from the deck to the grass. ''You want to be very careful here, gentlemen.''

''How unstable is it?'' Avery asked.

"Sally has been past where the fence is twice. Both times she got smacked for it. The problem's erosion. The cliff's made out of something real soft—sandstone, I think. I've been trying to stabilize it. The state conservation people talked me into planting this damned kudzu, and—stop right there!"

Keaton had stepped over the low fence.

"Two years ago I watched a twenty-square-foot piece drop off. That's why I planted these vines. You don't think somebody's going to climb that, do you?"

"It's one possibility," Longley answered.

"You'd think different if you looked at it from a boat. The cliff won't take the weight. A squirrel can make it up, but that's all."

"How high is it?" Avery asked.

"Forty-three feet over there, almost fifty here. The kudzu vines just make it worse. The damned stuff's nearly impossible to kill, but if you try grabbing on to it, you're in for a big surprise. Like I said, if you want to check it, do it from a boat," Ryan said.

"We'll do that," Avery replied.

"Coming in, that driveway must be three hundred yards," Keaton said.

"Just over four hundred, counting the curves. It cost an arm and a leg to pave it."

"What about the swimming pool people?" It was Longley this time.

"The pool's supposed to be finished next Wednesday."

Avery and Keaton walked around the north side of the house. There were trees twenty yards from there, and a swarm of brambles that went on forever. Ryan had planted a long row of shrubs to mark the border. Sally didn't go in there either.

"This looks pretty secure," Avery said. "There's two hundred yards of open space between the road and the trees, then more open ground between the pool and the house."

"Right." Ryan chuckled. "You can set up your heavy machine guns in the treeline and put the mortars over by the pool."

"Doctor Ryan, we are quite serious about this," Longley pointed out.

"I'm sure. But it's an unannounced trip, right? They can't—" Jack stopped short. He didn't like the look on their faces.

Avery said, "We always assume that the other side knows what we're up to."

"Oh." *Is that all of it, or is there more?* He knew it wouldn't do any good to ask. "Well, speaking as a has-been Marine, I wouldn't want to hit this place cold. I know a little about how you guys are trained. I wouldn't want to mess with you."

"We try," Avery assured him, still looking around. The way the driveway came through the trees, he could use his communications van to block vehicles out entirely. He reminded himself that there would be ten people from his agency, six Brits, a liaison guy from the Bureau, and probably two or three State Police for traffic control on the road. Each of his men would have both a service revolver and a submachine gun. They practiced at least once a week.

Avery still was not happy, not with the possibility of an armed terrorist group running around loose. But all the airports were being watched, all the local police forces alerted. There was only one road in here. The surrounding terrain would be difficult even for a platoon of soldiers to penetrate without making all kinds of noise, and as nasty as terrorists were, they'd never fought a set-piece battle. This wasn't London, and the potential targets weren't driving blithely about with a single armed guard.

"Thank you, Doctor Ryan. We will check the cliff out from the water side. If you see a Coast Guard cutter, that'll be us."

"You know how to get to the station at Thomas Point? You take Forest Drive east to Arundel-on-the-Bay and hang a right. You can't miss it."

"Thanks, we'll do that."

The real estate agent came out of the office just before ten. It was his turn to shut down. In his briefcase was an envelope for the bank's night depository and some contracts he'd go over the next morning before going in to work. He set the case on the seat beside him and started the car. Two headlights pulled right in behind him.

"Can I talk to you?" a voice called in the darkness. The agent turned to see a shape coming toward him.

"I'm afraid we're closed. The office opens at—" He saw that he was looking at a gun.

"I want your money, man. Just be cool, and everything'll be okay," the gunman said. There was no sense terrifying the man. He might do something crazy, and he might get lucky.

"But I don't have any—"

"The briefcase and the wallet. Slow and easy and you'll be home in half an hour."

The man got his wallet first. It took three attempts to loosen the button on his hip pocket, and his hands were quivering as he handed it over. The briefcase came next.

"It's just checks—no cash."

"That's what they all say. Lie down on the seat and count to one hundred. Don't stick your head up till you finish, and everything'll be just fine. Out loud, so's I can hear you." *Let's see, the heart's right about there. . . .* He reached his gun hand inside the open window. The man got to seven. When it went off, the sound of the silenced automatic was further muffled by being inside the car. The body jerked a few times, but not enough to require a second round. The gunman opened the door and wound up the window, then killed the engine and the lights before going back to his car. He pulled back onto the road and drove at the legal limit. Ten minutes later the empty briefcase and wallet were tossed into a shopping center dumpster. He got back onto the highway and drove in the opposite direction. It was dangerous to hold on to the gun, but that had to be disposed of more carefully. The gunman drove the car back to where it belonged—the family that owned it was on vacation—and walked two blocks to get his own. *Alex was right,* as always, the gunman thought. *If you plan everything, think it all out, and most important, don't leave any evidence behind, you can kill all the people you want. Oh,* he remembered, *one more thing: you don't talk about it.*

"Hi, Ernie," Jack said quietly. The dog showed up as a dark spot on the light-colored carpet in the living room. It was four in the morning. Ernie had heard a noise and come out of Sally's room to see what it was. One thing about dogs, they never slept the way people did. Ernie looked at him for several minutes, his tail gyrating back and forth until he got a scratch between his ears, then he moved off, back to Sally's room. It was amazing, Jack thought. The dog had entirely supplanted AG Bear. He found it hard to believe that anything could do that.

They're coming back, aren't they? he asked the night. Jack rose off the leather couch and walked to the windows. It was a clear night. Out on the Chesapeake Bay, he could see the running lights of ships plying their way to or from the Port of Baltimore, and the more ornate displays of tug-barge combinations that plodded along more slowly.

He didn't know how he could have been so slow on the uptake. Perhaps because the activity at Camp -18 almost tracked with the pattern that he'd tried repeatedly to discern. It was about the right time for them to show up for refresher training. But it was equally likely that they were planning something big. *Like maybe right here. . . .*

"Jesus. You were too close to the problem, Jack," he whispered. It was public knowledge—had been for a couple of weeks—that they were coming over, and the ULA had already demonstrated its ability to operate in America, he remembered. *And we're bringing known targets into our home! Real smart, Jack.* In retrospect it was amazing enough. They'd accepted the backward invitation without the first thought . . . and even when the security people had been here the previous day, he'd made jokes. *You asshole!*

He thought over the security provisions, taking himself back again to his time in the Corps. As an abstract battle problem, his house was a tough objective. You couldn't do anything from the east—the cliff was a more dangerous obstacle than a minefield. North and south, the woods were so thick and tangled that even the most skilled commando types would be hard-pressed to come through without making a horrendous racket—and they sure as hell couldn't practice that kind of skill in a barren, treeless desert! So they had to come from the west. *How many people did Avery say—well, he didn't say, but I got the impression of about twenty.* Twenty security people, armed and trained. He remembered the days from the Basic Officer's Course at Quantico, and the nights. Twenty-two years old, invincible and immortal, drinking beer at local bars. There'd been one night at a place called the Command Post, the one with a picture of Patton on the wall, when he'd started talking to a couple of instructors from the FBI Academy, just south of the Marine base. They were every bit as proud as his brother Marines. *They never bothered to say "we are the best." They simply assumed that everyone knew it. Just like us.* The next day he'd accepted the invitation to shoot on their range and settle a gentlemanly wager. It had cost him ten dollars to learn that one of them was the chief firearms instructor. *God, I wonder if Breckenridge could beat him!* The Secret Service wouldn't be very different, given their mission. *Would* you *want to tangle with them? Hell, no!*

If I assume that the ULA is as smart as it seems to be . . . and it is an unannounced trip, a private sort of thing. . . . They won't know to come here, and even if they did, if they're too smart to take this one on . . . it should be safe, shouldn't it?

But that was a word whose meaning was forever changed. Safe. It was something no longer real.

Jack walked around the fireplace into the house's bedroom wing. Sally was sleeping, with Ernie curled up on the foot of the bed. His head came up when Jack entered the room, as if to say, "Yes?"

His little girl was lying there, at peace, dreaming a child's dreams while her father contemplated the nightmare that still hovered over his family, the one he'd allowed himself to forget for a few hours. He straightened the covers and patted the dog on the head before leaving the room.

Jack wondered how public figures did it. They lived with the nightmare all the time. He remembered congratulating the Prince for not letting such a threat dominate his life: *Well done, old boy, that'll show them! Be a fearless target!* It was a very different thing when you were yourself the target, Ryan admitted to the night, when your family was the target. You put on the brave face, and followed your instructions, and wondered if every car on the street could hold a man with a machine gun who was bent on making *your* death into a very special political statement. You could keep your mind off it during the day when you had work to do, but at night, when the mind wanders and dreams begin . . .

The dualism was incredible. You couldn't dwell on it, but neither could you allow yourself to forget it. You couldn't let your life be dominated by fear, but you couldn't ever lapse into a feeling of security. A sense of fatalism would have helped, but Ryan was a man who had always deemed himself the master of his fate. He would not admit that anything else could be true. He wanted to lash out, if not at *them,* then at destiny, but both were as far beyond his reach as the ships whose lights passed miles from his windows. The safety of his family had almost been assured—

We came so close! he cried silently to the night.

They'd almost done it. They'd almost won that one battle, and they had helped others win another. He *could* fight back, and he knew that he could do it best by working at that desk in Langley, by joining the team full-time. He would not be the master of his fate, but at least he could play a part. He had played a part. It had been important enough—if only an accident—to Françoise Theroux, that pretty, malignant thing now dead. And so the decision was made. The people with guns would play their part, and the man behind the desk would play his. Jack would miss the Academy, miss the eager young kids, but that was the price he'd have to pay for getting back into the game. Jack got a drink of water before going back to bed.

Plebe Summer started on schedule. Jack watched with impassive sympathy as the recently graduated high school seniors were introduced to the rigors of military life. The process was consciously aimed at weeding out the weak as early as possible, and so it was largely in the hands of upperclassmen who had only recently been through the same thing. The new youngsters were at the debatable mercy of the older ones, running around with their closely cropped hair to the double-time cadence of students only two years their senior.

"Morning, Jack!" Robby came over to watch with him from the parking lot.

"You know, Rob, Boston College was never like this."

"If you think this is a Plebe Summer," Jackson snorted, "you should have seen what it was like when I was here!"

"I bet they've been saying that for a hundred years," Jack suggested.

"Probably so." The white-clad plebes passed like a herd of buffalo, all gasping for air on the hot, humid morning. "We kept better formations, though."

"The first day?"

"The first few days were a blur," Jackson admitted.

"Packing up?"

Jackson nodded. "Most of the gear's already in boxes. I have to get my relief settled in."

"Me, too."

"You're leaving?" Robby was surprised.

"I told Admiral Greer that I wanted in."

"Admiral—oh, the guy at CIA. You're going to do it, eh? How did the department take it?"

"I think you can say that they managed to restrain their tears. The boss isn't real happy about all the time I missed this year. So it looks like we're both having a going-away dinner.''

''Jeez, it's this Friday, isn't it?''

''Yeah. Can you show up about eight-fifteen?''

''You got it. You said not dressy, right?''

''That's right.'' Jack smiled. *Gotcha.*

The RAF VC-10 aircraft touched down at Andrews Air Force Base at eight in the evening and taxied to the same terminal used by Air Force One. The reporters noted that security was very tight, with what looked to be a full company of Air Police in view, plus the plainclothes Secret Service agents. They told themselves that security at this particular part of the base was always strict. The plane came to a halt at exactly the right place, and the stairs were rolled to the forward door, which opened after a moment.

At the foot of the stairs waited the Ambassador and officials from the State Department. Inside the aircraft, security men made a final check out the windows. Finally His Highness appeared in the doorway, joined by his young wife, waving to the distant spectators, and descending the stairs gingerly despite legs that were stiff from the flight. At the bottom a number of military officers from two nations saluted, and the State Department protocol officer curtsied. This would earn her a reprimand from the *Washington Post*'s arbiter of manners in the morning edition. The six-year-old granddaughter of the base commander presented Her Highness with a dozen yellow roses. Strobes flashed, and both royal personages smiled dutifully at the cameras while they took the time to say something pleasant to everyone in the receiving line. The Prince shared a joke with a naval officer who had once commanded him, and the Princess said something about the oppressive, muggy weather that had persisted into the evening. The Ambassador's wife pointed out that the climate here was such that Washington D.C. had once been considered a hazardous-duty station. The malarial mosquitoes were long gone, but the climate hadn't changed very much. Fortunately, everyone had air conditioning. Reporters noted the color, style, and cut of the Princess's outfit, especially her ''daring'' new hat. She stood with the poise of a professional model while her husband looked as casual as a Texas cowboy, as incongruous as that might have seemed, one hand in his pocket and a relaxed grin on his face. The Americans who'd never met the couple before found him wonderfully easygoing, and of course every man there had long since fallen in love with the Princess, along with most of the Western world.

The security people saw none of this. They all had their backs to the scene, their eyes scanning the crowd, their faces stamped into the same serious expression while each with various degrees of emphasis thought: *Please, God, not while I'm on duty.* Every one had a radio earpiece constantly providing information that their brains monitored while their eyes were otherwise occupied.

Finally they moved to the embassy's Rolls-Royce, and the motorcade formed up. Andrews had a number of gates, and the one they took had been decided upon only an hour before. The route into town was its own traffic jam of marked and unmarked cars. Two additional Rolls-Royce automobiles, of exactly the same model and color, were dispersed through the procession, each with a lead- and chase-car, and a helicopter was overhead. If anyone had taken the time to count the firearms present, the total would have been nearly a hundred. The arrival had been timed to allow swift passage through Washington, and twenty-five minutes later the motorcade got to the British Embassy. A few minutes after that, Their Highnesses were safely in the building, and for the moment the responsibility of someone else. Most of the local security people dispersed, heading back to their homes or stations, but ten men and women stayed around the building, most invisibly hidden in cars and vans, while a few extra uniformed police walked the perimeter.

"America," O'Donnell said. "The land of opportunity." The television news coverage came on at eleven, and had tape of the arrival.

"What do you suppose they're doing now?" Miller asked.

"Working on their jet lag, I imagine," his chief observed. "Getting a good night's sleep. So, all ready here?"

"Yes, the safehouse is all prepared for tomorrow. Alex and his people are ready, and I've gone over the changes in the plan."

"They're from Alex, too?"

"Yes, and if I hear one more bit of advice from that arrogant bastard—"

"He is one of our revolutionary brethren," O'Donnell noted with a smile. "But I know what you mean."

"Where's Mike?"

"Belfast. He'll run Phase Two."

"The timing is all set?"

"Yes. Both brigade commanders, and the whole Army Council. We should be able to get them all. . . ." O'Donnell finally revealed his plan in toto. McKenney's penetration agents either worked closely with all of the senior PIRA people or knew those who did. On command from O'Donnell, they would assassinate them all, completely removing the Provisionals' military leadership. There would be no one left to run the Organization . . . except one man whose masterstroke mission would catapult him back to respectability with rank-and-file Provos. With his hostages, he'd get the release of all the men "behind the wire" even if it meant mailing the Prince of Wales to Buckingham Palace one cubic centimeter at a time. O'Donnell was certain of this. For all the brave, pious talk in Whitehall, it was centuries since an English king had faced death, and the idea of martyrdom sat better with revolutionaries than with those in power. Public pressure would see to that. They would *have* to negotiate to save the life of the heir to the throne. The scope of this operation would enliven the Movement, and Kevin Joseph O'Donnell would lead a revolution reborn in boldness and blood. . . .

"Changing of the guard, Jack?" Marty observed. He, too, had packed up his things. A security officer would check the box before he left.

"How are you feeling?"

"Better, but you can get tired of watching daytime TV."

"Taking all your pills?" Ryan asked.

"I'll never forget again, Mom," was the answer.

"I see there's nothing new on our friends."

"Yeah. They dropped back into that black hole they live in. The FBI is worried that they're over here, of course, but there hasn't even been a hint of it. Of course, whenever anybody's felt secure dealing with these bastards, they've gotten bit on the ass. Still, about the only outfit that isn't on alert is the Delta Force. All kinds of assets are standing by. If they're over here and they show anybody a whisker, the whole world is going to come crashing in on them. 'Call in the whole world.'

We used to say that in Vietnam.'' Cantor grunted. ''I'll be in Monday and Tuesday. You don't have to say goodbye yet. Have a good weekend.''

''You too.'' Ryan walked out, with a new security pass hanging around his neck and his jacket draped over his shoulder. It was hot outside, and his Rabbit didn't have air conditioning. The drive home along Route 50 was complicated by all the people heading to Ocean City for the weekend, anything to get away from the heat that had covered the area like an evil spell for two weeks. They were in for a surprise, Jack thought. A cold front was supposed to come through.

''Howard County Police,'' the Desk Sergeant said. ''Can I help you?''

''This is 911, right?'' It was a male voice.

''Yes, sir. What seems to be the problem?''

''Hey, uh, my wife said I shouldn't get involved, you know, but—''

''Can you give me your name and phone number, please?''

''No way—look, this house, uh, down the street. There's people there with guns, you know? Machine guns.''

''Say that again.'' The Sergeant's eyes narrowed.

''Machine guns—no shit, I saw an M-60 machine gun, like in the Army—y'know, thirty caliber, feeds off a belt, heavy bitch to pack along, a real friggin' machine gun. I saw some other stuff, too.''

''Where?''

The voice became rapid. ''Eleven-sixteen Green Cottage Lane. There's maybe—I mean I saw four of 'em, one black and three white. They were unloading the guns from a van. It was three in the morning. I had to get up an' take a leak, and I looked out the bathroom window, y'know? The garage door was open, and the light was on, and when they passed the gun across, it was in the light, like, and I could tell it was a sixty. Hey, I used to carry one in the Army, y'know? Anyway, that's it, man, you wanna do something about it, that's your lookout.'' The line clicked off. The Sergeant called his captain at once.

''What is it?'' The Sergeant handed over his notes. ''Machine gun? M-60?''

''He said it was—he said it was a thirty-caliber that feeds off a belt. That's the M-60. That alert we got from the FBI, Captain . . .''

''Yeah.'' The Station Commander had visions of promotion dangling before his eyes—but also visions of his men in a pitched battle where the perpetrators had better weapons. ''Get a car out there. Tell them to keep out of sight and take no action. I'm going to request a SWAT callup and get hold of the feds.''

Less than a minute later a police car was heading to the area. The responding officer was a six-year veteran of the county police who very much wanted to be a seven-year veteran. It took him almost ten minutes to reach the scene. He parked his car a block away, behind a large shrub, and was able to watch the house without exposing himself as a police officer. The shotgun that usually hung under the dashboard was in his sweating hands now, with a double-ought buck round chambered. Another car was four minutes behind his, and two more officers joined him. Then the whole world really did seem to arrive. First a patrol sergeant, then a lieutenant, then two captains, and finally, two agents from the FBI's Baltimore office. The officer who had first responded was now one of the Indians in a tribe top-heavy with chiefs.

The FBI Special Agent in Charge for the Baltimore office set up a radio link with the Washington headquarters, but left the operation in the hands of the local police.

The county police had its own SWAT team, like most local forces did, and they quickly went to work. The first order of business was to evacuate the people from the area's homes. To everyone's relief, they were able to do that from the rear in every case. The people removed from their homes were immediately interviewed. Yes, they had seen people in that house. Yes, they were mostly white, but there had been at least one black person. No, they hadn't seen any guns—in fact, they hardly saw the people at all. One lady thought they had a van, but if so, it was usually kept in the garage. The interviews went on while the SWAT team moved in. The neighborhood houses were all of the same style and design, and the men made a quick check through one to establish its layout. Another set up a scope-sighted rifle in the house directly across the street and used his sight to examine the target home's windows.

The SWAT team might have waited, but the longer they did that, the greater was the risk of alerting their quarry. They moved in slowly and carefully, skillfully using cover and concealment until they were within fifty feet of the target house. Anxious, sharp eyes scanned the windows for movement and saw none. *Could they all be asleep?* The team leader went in first, sprinting across the yard and stopping under a window. He held up a stick-on microphone and attached it to the corner of the window, listening to an earpiece for a sign of occupancy. The second-in-command watched the man's head cock almost comically to one side, then he spoke into a radio that all his team members could hear: "The TV's on. No conversation, I—something else, can't make it out." He motioned for his team to approach, one at a time, while he crouched under the window, gun at the ready. Three minutes later the team was ready.

"Team leader," the radio crackled. "This is Lieutenant Haber. We have a young man here who says a van went tearing out of that house about quarter to five—that's about the time the police radio call went out."

The team leader waved acknowledgment and treated the message as something that mattered not a bit. The team executed a forced entry maneuver. Two simultaneous shotgun blasts blew the hinges off the windowless side door and it hadn't even hit the floor before the team leader was through the opening, training his gun around the kitchen. Nothing. They proceeded through the house in movements that looked like a kind of evil ballet. The entire exercise was over in a minute. The radio message went out: "The building is secure."

The team leader emerged on the front porch, his shotgun pointed at the floor, and pulled off his black mask before he waved the others in. His hands moved back and forth across his chest in the universal wave-off signal. The Lieutenant and the senior FBI agent ran across the street as he wiped the sweat away from his eyes.

"Well?"

"You're gonna love it," the team leader said. "Come on."

The living room had a small-screen color TV on, sitting on a table. The floor was covered with wrappers from McDonald's, and the kitchen sink held what looked like fifty neatly stacked paper cups. The master bedroom—it was a few square feet larger than the other two—was the armory. Sure enough, there was an American M-60 machine gun, with two 250-round ammo boxes, along with a dozen AK-47 assault rifles, three of them stripped down for cleaning, and a bolt-action rifle with a telescopic sight. On the oaken dresser, however, was a scanner radio. Its indicator lights skipped on and off. One of them was on the frequency of the Howard County Police. Unlike the FBI, the local police did not use secure—that is, scrambled—

radio circuits. The FBI agent walked out to his vehicle and got Bill Shaw on the radio.

"So they monitored the police call and split," Shaw said after a couple of minutes.

"Looks like it. The locals have a description of the van out. At least they bugged out so fast that they had to leave a bunch of weapons behind. Maybe they're spooked. Anything new coming in at your end?"

"Negative." Shaw was in the FBI's emergency command center, Room 5005 of the J. Edgar Hoover Building. He knew of the French attempt to hit their training camp. *Twice now they've escaped by sheer luck.* "Okay, I'll get talking to the State Police forces. The forensic people are on the way. Stay put and coordinate with the locals."

"Right. Out."

The security people were already setting up. Discreetly, he saw, their cars were by the pool, which had been filled up only a couple of days before, and there was a van which evidently contained special communications gear. Jack counted eight people in the open, two of them with Uzis. Avery was waiting for him when he pulled into the carport.

"Good news for a change—well, good and bad."

"How so?" Ryan asked.

"Somebody phoned the cops and said he saw some people with guns. They rolled on it real quick. The suspects split—they were monitoring the police radio—but we captured a bunch of guns. Looks like our friends had a safehouse set up. Unfortunately for them it didn't quite work out. We may have 'em on the run. We know what kind of car they're using, and the local cops have this area completely sealed off, and we're sweeping the whole state. The Governor has even authorized the use of helicopters from the National Guard to help with the search."

"Where were they?"

"Howard County, a little community south of Columbia. We missed them by a whole five minutes, but we have them moving and out in the open. Just a matter of time."

"I hope the cops are careful," Ryan said.

"Yes, sir."

"Any problems here?"

"No, everything's going just fine. Your guests should be here about quarter to eight. What's for dinner?" Avery asked.

"Well, I picked up some fresh white corn on the way home—you passed the place coming in. Steaks on the grill, baked potatoes, and Cathy's spinach salad. We'll give 'em some good, basic American food." Jack opened the hatch on the Rabbit and pulled out a bag of freshly picked corn.

Avery grinned. "You're making me hungry."

"I got a caterer coming in at six-thirty. Cold cuts and rolls. I'm not going to let you guys work all that time without food, okay?" Ryan insisted. "You can't stay alert if you're hungry."

"We'll see. Thanks."

"My dad was a cop."

"By the way, I tried the lights around the pool, but they don't work."

"I know, the electricity's been acting up the last couple of days. The power company says they have a new transformer up, and it needs work—something like that.'' Ryan shrugged. ''Evidently it damaged the breaker on the pool line, but so far nothing's gone bad in the house. You weren't planning to go swimming, were you?''

''No. We wanted to use one of the plugs here, but it's out too.''

''Sorry. Well, I have some stuff to do.''

Avery watched him leave, and went over his own deployment plans one last time. A pair of State Police cars would be a few hundred yards down the road to stop and check anyone coming back here. The bulk of his men would be covering the road. Two would watch each side of the clearing—the woods looked too inhospitable to penetrate, but they'd watch them anyway. This was called Team One. The second team would consist of six men. There would be three people in the house. Three more, one of them a communicator in the radio van, in the trees by the pool.

The speed trap was well known to the locals. Every weekend a car or two was set up on this stretch of Interstate 70. There had even been something about it in the local paper. But people from out of state didn't read that, of course. The trooper had his car just behind a small crest, which allowed cars heading up to Pennsylvania to fly by, right past his radar gun before they knew it. The pickings were so good that he never bothered chasing after anyone who did under sixty-five, and at least twice a night he nailed people for doing over eighty.

Be on the lookout for a black van, make and year unknown, the all-points call had said a few minutes before. The trooper estimated that there were at least five thousand such vans in the state of Maryland, and they'd all be on the road on a Friday night. Somebody else would have to worry about that. *Approach with extreme caution.*

His patrol car rocked like a boat crossing a wake as a vehicle zoomed past. The radar gun readout said 83. Business. The trooper dropped his car into gear and started moving after it before he saw that it was a black van. *Approach with extreme caution. . . . They didn't give a tag number. . . .*

''Hagerstown, this is Eleven. I am following a van, black in color, that I clocked at eighty-three. I am westbound on I-70, about three miles east of exit thirty-five.''

''Eleven, get the tag number but do not—repeat *do not*—attempt to apprehend. Get the number, back off, and stay in visual contact. We'll get some backup for you.''

''Roger. Moving in now.'' *Damn.*

He floored his accelerator and watched his speedometer go to ninety. The van had slowed a little, it seemed. He was now two hundred yards back. His eyes squinted. He could see the plate but not the number. He closed the distance more slowly now. At fifty yards he could make out the plate—it was a handicap one. The trooper lifted his radio microphone to call in the tag numbers when the rear doors flew open.

It all hit him in a moment: *This was how Larry Fontana got it!* He slammed on his brakes and tried to turn the wheel, but the microphone cable got caught on his arm. The police officer cringed and slid down behind the dashboard as the car slowed, and then he saw the flash, a sun-white tongue of flame that reached directly at him. As soon as he understood what that was, he heard the impacting rounds. One of his tires blew, and his radiator exploded, sending a shower of steam and water into the air. More rounds walked up the hood into the right side of the car, and the trooper dived under the steering wheel while the car bounced up and down on the flattened tire. Then the noise stopped. The State Police officer stuck his head up and saw the van was a hundred yards away, accelerating up the hill. He tried to make a call on the radio, but it didn't work. He discovered soon after that two bullets had blasted through the car's battery, now leaking acid on the pavement. He stood there for several minutes, wondering why he was alive, before another police car arrived.

The trooper was shaking badly enough that he had to hold the microphone in both hands. "Hagerstown, the bastard machine-gunned my car! It's a Ford van, looks like an eighty-four, handicap tag Nancy two-two-nine-one, last seen westbound on I-70 east of exit thirty-fi-five."

"Were you hit?"

"Negative, but the car's b-beat to shit. They used a goddamned machine gun on me!"

That really got things rolling. The FBI was again notified, and every available State Police helicopter converged on the Hagerstown area. For the first time, the choppers held men with automatic weapons. In Annapolis, the Governor wondered if he should use National Guard units. An infantry company was put on alert—it was already engaged in its weekend drill—but for the moment, he limited the Guard's active involvement to helicopter support of the State Police. The hunt was on in the central Maryland hill country. Warnings went out over commercial radio and TV stations for people to be on the alert. The President was spending the weekend in the country, and that was another major complication. Marines at nearby Camp David and a few other highly secret defense installations tucked away in the rolling hills hung up their usual dress blues and pistol belts. They substituted M-16 rifles and camouflage greens.

25. Rendezvous

They arrived exactly on time. A pair of State Police cars remained on the road, and three more loaded with security people accompanied the Rolls up the driveway to the Ryan house. The chauffeur, one of the security force, pulled right to the front and jumped out to open the passenger door. His Highness came out first, and helped his wife. The security people were already swarming all over the place. The leader of the British contingent conferred with Avery, and the detail dispersed to their predetermined stations. As Jack came down the steps to greet his guests, he had the feeling that his home had been subjected to an armed invasion.

"Welcome to Peregrine Cliff."

"Hello, Jack!" The Prince took his hand. "You're looking splendid."

"You, too, sir." He turned to the Princess, whom he'd never actually met. "Your Highness, this is a great pleasure."

"And for us, Doctor Ryan."

He led them into the house. "How's your trip been so far?"

"Awfully hot," the Prince answered. "Is it always like this in the summer?"

"We've had two pretty bad weeks," Jack answered. The temperature had hit ninety-five a few hours earlier. "They say that's going to change by tomorrow. It isn't supposed to go much past eighty for the next few days.'' This did not get an enthusiastic response.

Cathy was waiting inside with Sally. The weather was especially hard on her, this close to delivery. She shook hands, but Sally remembered how to curtsy from England, and performed a beautiful one, accompanied by a giggle.

''Are you quite all right?'' Her Highness asked Cathy.

''Fine, except for the heat. Thank God for air conditioning!''

''Can we show you around?'' Jack led the party into the living/dining room.

''The view is marvelous,'' the Prince observed.

''Okay, the first thing is, nobody wears a coat in my house,'' Ryan pronounced. ''I think you call this 'Planter's Rig' over in England.''

''Excellent idea,'' said the Prince. Jack took his jacket and hung it in the foyer closet next to his old Marine parka, then got rid of his own. By this time Cathy had everyone seated. Sally perched next to her mother, her feet high off the floor as she tried to keep her dress down on her knees. Cathy found it almost impossible to sit comfortably.

''How much longer?'' the Princess asked.

''Eight days—of course with number two, that means any time.''

''I shall find that out myself in seven more months.''

''Really? Congratulations!'' Both women beamed.

''Way to go, sir,'' Ryan observed.

''Thank you, Jack. How have you been?''

''I suppose you know the work I'm doing?''

''Yes, I heard last night from one of our security people. I've been told that you located and identified a terrorist camp that has since been . . . neutralized,'' the Prince said quietly.

Ryan nodded discreetly. ''I'm afraid that I'm not able to discuss that.''

''Understood. And how has your little girl done after . . .''

''Sally?'' Jack turned. ''How's my little girl?''

''I'm a *big* girl!'' she replied forcefully.

''What do you think?''

''I think you've been damned lucky.''

''I'd settle for a little bit more. I presume you've heard?''

''Yes.'' He paused. ''I hope your chaps are careful.''

Jack voiced agreement, then rose as he heard a car pull up. He opened the door to see Robby and Sissy Jackson getting out of the pilot's Corvette. The Secret Service's communications van moved to block the driveway behind them. Robby stormed up the steps.

''What gives? Who's here, the President?''

Cathy must have warned them, Jack saw. Sissy was dressed in a simple but very nice blue dress, and Robby had a tie on. Too bad.

''Come on in and join the party,'' Jack said with a nasty grin.

Robby looked at the two men by the pool, their jackets unbuttoned, and gave Jack a puzzled look, but followed. As they came around the brick fireplace, the pilot's eyes went wide.

''Commander Jackson, I presume.'' His Highness rose.

''Jack,'' Robby whispered. ''I'm going to kill you!'' Louder: ''How do you do, sir. This is my wife, Cecilia.'' As usually happened, the people immediately split into male and female groups.

''I understand you're a naval aviator.''

"Yes, sir. I'm going back to a fleet squadron now. I fly the F-14." Robby struggled to keep his voice under control. He was successful, mostly.

"Yes, the Tomcat. I've flown the Phantom. Have you?"

"I have a hundred twenty hours in them, sir. My squadron transitioned into fourteens a few months after I joined up. I was just getting the Phantom figured out when they took 'em away. I—uh—sir, aren't you a naval officer also?"

"Yes, Commander, I have the rank of captain," His Highness answered.

"Thank you. Now I know what to call you, Captain," Robby said with visible relief. "That's okay, isn't it?"

"Of course. You know, it does get rather tiresome when people act so awkwardly around one. This friend of yours here actually read me off some months ago."

Robby smiled finally. "You know Marines, sir. Long on mouth and short on brains."

Jack realized that it was going to be that kind of night. "Can I get anyone something to drink?"

"I gotta fly tomorrow, Jack," Robby answered. He checked his watch. "I'm under the twelve-hour rule."

"You really take that so seriously?" the Prince asked.

"You bet you do, Captain, when the bird costs thirty or forty mil. If you break one, booze better not be the reason. I've been through that once."

"Oh? What happened?"

"An engine blew when I put her in burner. I tried to get back but I lost hydraulic pressure five miles from the boat and had to punch out. That's twice I've ejected, and that's by-God enough."

"Oh?" This question got Robby started on how his test-pilot days at Pax River had ended. *There I was at ten thousand . . .* Jack went into the kitchen to get everyone some iced tea. He found two security types, an American and a Brit.

"Everything okay?" Ryan asked.

"Yeah. It looks like our friends got spotted near Hagerstown. They blasted a State Police car and split. The trooper's okay, they missed this one. Anyway, they were last seen heading west." The Secret Service agent seemed very pleased by that. Jack looked outside to see another one standing on the outside deck.

"You sure it's them?"

"It was a van, and it had handicap tags. They usually fall into patterns," the agent explained. "Sooner or later it catches up with them. The area's been sealed off. We'll get 'em."

"Good." Jack lifted a tray of glasses.

By the time he got back, Robby was discussing some aspect of flying with the Prince. He could tell since it involved elaborate hand movements.

"So if you fire the Phoenix inside that radius, he just can't evade it. The missile can pull more gees than any pilot can," Jackson concluded.

"Ah, yes, the same thing with the Sparrow, isn't it?"

"Right, Cap'n, but the radius is smaller." Robby's eyes really lit up. "Have you ever been up in a Tomcat?"

"No, I wish I could."

"For crying out loud, that's no big deal. Hell, we take *civilians* up all the time—I mean it has to be cleared and all that, but we've even had Hollywood actors up. Getting you a hop ought to be a snap. I mean, it's not like you're a security risk, is it?" Robby laughed and grabbed a glass of tea. "Thanks, Jack. Captain, if you've got the time, I've got the bird."

"I'd love to be there. We do have a little free time. . . ."

"Then let's do it," Jackson said.

"I see you two are getting along."

"Indeed," the Prince replied. "I've wanted to meet an F-14 pilot for years. Now, you say that telescopic camera arrangement is really effective?"

"Yes, sir! It's not that big a deal. It's a ten-power lens on a dinky little TV camera. You can identify your target fifty miles out, and it's Phoenix time. If you play it right, you can splash the guy before he knows you're in the same county, and that's the idea, isn't it?"

"So you try to avoid the dogfight?"

"ACM, you mean—air-combat maneuvering, Jack," Robby explained to the ignorant bystander. "That'll change when we get the new engines, Cap'n, but, yeah, the farther away you can take him, the better, right? Sometimes you have to get wrapped up in the fur-ball, but if you do that you're giving away your biggest advantage. Our mission is to engage the other guy as far from the boat as we can. That's why we call it the Outer Air Battle."

"It would have been rather useful at the Falklands," His Highness observed.

"That's right. If you engage the enemy over your own decks, he's already won the biggest part of the battle. We want to start scoring three hundred miles out, and hammer their butts all the way in. If your Navy'd had a full-size carrier, that useless little war never would have happened. Excuse me, sir. That wasn't your fault."

"Can I show you around the house?" Jack asked. It always seemed to happen. You worked to have one of your guests meet another, and all of a sudden you were cut out of the conversation.

"How old is it, Jack?"

"We moved in a few months before Sally was born."

"The woodwork is marvelous. Is that the library down there?"

"Yes, sir." The way the house was laid out, you could look down from the living room into the library. The master bedroom was perched over it. There had been a rectangular hole in the wall, which allowed someone in there to see into the living room, but Ryan had placed a print over it. The picture was mounted on a rail and could be slid aside, Jackson noticed. The purpose of that was clear enough. Jack led them to his library next. Everyone liked that the only window was over his desk and looked out over the bay.

"No servants, Jack?"

"No, sir. Cathy's talking about getting a nanny, but she hasn't sold me on that idea yet. Is everyone ready for dinner?"

The response was enthusiastic. The potatoes were already in the oven, and Cathy was ready to start the corn. Jack took the steaks from the refrigerator and led the menfolk outside.

"You'll like this, Cap'n. Jack does a mean steak."

"The secret's in the charcoal," Ryan explained. He had six gorgeous-looking sirloins, and a hamburger for Sally. "It helps to have good meat, too."

"I know it's too late to ask, Jack, but where do you get those?"

"One of my old stock clients has a restaurant-supply business. These are Kansas City strips." Jack transferred them to the grill with a long-handled fork. A gratifying sizzle rose to their ears. He brushed some sauce on the meat.

"The view is spectacular," His Highness observed.

"It's nice to be able to watch the boats go by," Jack agreed. "Looks a little thin now, though."

"They must be listening to the radio," Robby observed. "There's a severe thunderstorm warning on for tonight."

"I didn't hear that."

"It's the leading edge of that cold front. They develop pretty fast over Pittsburgh. I'm going up tomorrow, like I said, and I called Pax Weather right before we left. They told me that the storms look pretty ferocious on radar. Heavy rain and gusts. Supposed to hit around ten or so."

"Do you get many of those here?" His Highness asked.

"Sure do, Captain. We don't get tornadoes like in the Midwest, but the thunder-boomers we get here'll curl your hair. I was bringing a bird back from Memphis last—no, two years ago, and it was like being on a pogo stick. You just don't have control of the airplane. Those suckers can be scary. Down at Pax, they're taking all the birds they can inside the hangars, and they'll be tying the rest down tight."

"It'll be worth it to cool things off," Jack said as he turned the steaks.

"Roger that. It's just your basic thunderstorm, Captain. We get the big ones three or four times a year. It'll knock down some trees, but as long as you're not in the air or out in a small boat, it's no big deal. Down in Alabama with this kind of storm coming across, we'd be sweating tornadoes. Now that's scary!"

"You've seen one?"

"More 'n one, Cap'n. You get those mostly in the spring down home. When I was ten or so, I watched one come across the road, pick up a house like it was part of a Christmas garden, and drop it a quarter mile away. They're weird, though. It didn't even take the weathervane off my pappy's church. They're like that. It's something to see, all right—but you want to do it from a safe distance."

"Turbulence is the main flying hazard, then?"

"Right. But the other thing is water. I know of cases where jets have ingested enough water through the intakes to snuff the engines right out." Robby snapped his fingers. "All of a sudden you're riding in a glider. Definitely not fun. So you keep away from them when you can."

"And when you can't?"

"Once, Cap'n, I had to land on a carrier in one—at night. That's about as close as I've come to wetting my pants since I was two." He even threw in a shudder.

"Your Highness, I have to thank you for getting all of this out of Robby. I've known him for over a year and he's never admitted to being mildly nervous up there." Jack grinned.

"I didn't want to spoil the image," Jackson explained. "You have to put a gun to Jack's head to get him aboard a plane, and I didn't want to scare him any more than he already is." *Zing!* And Robby took the point.

It helped that the deck was now in the shade, and there was a slight northerly breeze. Jack manipulated the steaks over the coals. There were a few boats out on the bay, but most of them seemed to be heading back to harbor. Jack nearly jumped out of his skin when a jet fighter screamed past the cliff. He turned in time to see the white-painted aircraft heading south.

"Robby, what the hell is that all about? They've been doing that for two weeks."

Jackson watched the plane's double tail vanish in the haze. "They're testing a new piece of gear on the F-18. What's the big deal?"

"The noise!" Ryan flipped the steaks over.

Robby laughed. "Aw, Jack, that's not noise. That's the sound of freedom."

"Not bad, Commander," His Highness judged.

"Well, how about the sound of dinner?" Ryan asked.

Robby grabbed the platter, and Jack piled the meat on it. The salads were already on the table. Cathy made a superb spinach salad, with homemade dressing. Jack noted that Sissy was bringing the corn and potatoes out, wearing an apron to protect her dress. He distributed the steaks and put Sally's hamburger on a roll. Next he got their daughter in a booster seat. The one awkward thing was that nobody was drinking. He'd gotten four bottles of a choice California red to go with the steaks, but it seemed that everyone was in a teetotaling mood.

"Jack, the electricity is acting up again," his wife reported. "For a while there I didn't think we'd get the corn finished."

The Secret Service agent stood in the middle of the road, forcing the van to stop.

"Yes, sir?" the driver said.

"What are you doing here?" The agent's coat was unbuttoned. No gun was visible, but the driver knew it was there somewhere. He counted six more men within ten yards of the van and another four readily visible.

"Hey, I just told the cop." The man gestured backward. The two State Police cars were only two hundred yards away.

"Could you tell me, please?"

"There's a problem with the transformer at the end of the road. I mean, you can see this is a BG and E truck, right?"

"Could you wait here, please?"

"Okay with me, man." The driver exchanged a look with the man in the right-front seat. The agent returned with another. This one held a radio.

"What seems to be the problem?"

The driver sighed. "Third time. There's a problem with the electrical transformer at the end of the road. Have the people here been complaining about the electricity?"

"Yeah," the second man, Avery, said. "I noticed, too. What gives?"

The man in the right seat answered. "I'm Alex Dobbens, field engineer. We have a new, experimental transformer on this line. There's a test monitor on the box, and it's been sending out some weird signals, like the box is going to fail. We're here to check it out."

"Could we see some ID, please?"

"Sure." Alex got out of the truck and walked around. He handed over his BG&E identification card. "What the hell's going on here?"

"Can't say." Avery examined the pass and handed it back. "You have a work order?"

Dobbens gave the man his clipboard. "Hey, if you want to check it out, you can call that number up top. That's the field-operations office at company headquarters in Baltimore. Ask for Mr. Griffin."

Avery talked into his radio, ordering his men to do just that. "Do you mind if we look at the truck?"

"Be my guest," Dobbens replied. He led the two agents around. He noted also that four men were keeping a very close eye on things, and that they were widely separated, with their hands free. Others were scattered across the yard. He yanked open the sliding door and waved the two agents inside.

The agents saw a mass of tools and cables and test equipment. Avery let his subordinate do the searching. "Do you have to go back there now?"

"The transformer might go out, man. I could let it, but the folks in the neighborhood might be upset if the lights went off. People are like that, you know? Do you mind if I ask who you are?"

"Secret Service." Avery held up his ID. Dobbens was taken aback.

"Jeez! You mean the President's back there?"

"I can't say," Avery replied. "What's the problem with the transformer—you said it was new?"

"Yeah, it's an experimental model. It uses an inert cooling agent instead of PBBs, and it has a built-in surge-suppressor. That's probably the problem. It looks like the unit's temperature-sensitive for some reason. We've adjusted it several times, but we can't seem to get it dialed in right. I've been on the project for a couple of months. Usually I let my people do it, but this time the boss wanted me to eyeball it myself." He shrugged. "It's my project."

The other agent came out of the van and shook his head. Avery nodded. Next the chief agent called the radio van, whose occupants had called Baltimore Gas & Electric and confirmed what Alex had told them.

"You want to send a guy to watch us?" Dobbens asked.

"No, that's okay. How long will it take?" Avery asked.

"Your guess is as good as mine, sir. It's probably something simple, but we haven't figured it out yet. The simple ones are the ones that kill you."

"There's a storm coming in. I wouldn't want to be up on a pole in one of those," the agent observed.

"Yeah, well, while we're sitting here, we're not getting much work done. Everything okay with you guys?"

"Yeah, go ahead."

"You really can't tell me who's in the neighborhood?"

Avery smiled. "Sorry."

"Well, I didn't vote for him anyway." Dobbens laughed.

"Hold it!" the second agent called.

"What's the matter?"

"That left-front tire." The man pointed.

"Goddammit, Louis!" Dobbens growled at the driver. The steel belt was showing on part of the tire.

"Hey, boss, it's not my fault. They were supposed to change it this morning. I wrote it up Wednesday," the driver protested. "I got the order slip right here."

"All right, just take it easy." Dobbens looked over to the agent. "Thanks, man."

"Can't you change it?"

"We don't have a jack. Somebody lifted it. That's a problem with company trucks. Something is always missing. It'll be all right. Well, we got a transformer to fix. See ya." Alex reboarded the truck and waved as the vehicle pulled off.

"Good one, Louis."

The driver smiled. "Yeah, I thought the tire was a nice touch. I counted fourteen."

"Right. Three in the trees. Figure four more in the house. They're not our problem." He paused, looking at the clouds that were building on the horizon. "I hope Ed and Willy made out all right."

"They did. All they had to do was hose down one pigmobile and switch cars. The pigs here were more relaxed than I expected," Louis observed.

"Why not? They think we're someplace else." Alex opened a toolbox and removed his transceiver. The agent had seen it and not questioned it. He couldn't tell that the frequency range had been altered. There were no guns in the van, of course, but radios were far deadlier. He radioed what he'd learned and got an acknowledgment. Then he smiled. The agents hadn't even asked about the two extension ladders on the roof. He checked his watch. Rendezvous was scheduled in ninety minutes. . . .

''The problem is, there really isn't a civilized way to eat corn on the cob,'' Cathy said. ''Not to mention buttering it.''

''It was excellent, though,'' the Prince noted. ''From a local farm, Jack?''

''Picked 'em off the stalk this afternoon,'' Ryan confirmed. ''That's the best way to get it.''

Sally'd become a slow eater of late. She was still laboring at her food, but nobody seemed anxious to leave the table.

''Jack, Cathy, that was a wonderful dinner,'' His Highness pronounced.

His wife agreed. ''And no after-dinner speechmaking!''

''I guess all that formal stuff gets to be tiresome,'' Robby noted, trying to ask a question that he couldn't voice: *What's it like to be a prince?*

''It wouldn't be so bad if the speeches could be original, but I've been listening to the same one for years!'' he said wryly. ''Excuse me. I mustn't say such things, even around friends.''

''It's not all that different at a History Department meeting,'' Jack said.

At Quantico, Virginia, the phone rang. The FBI's Hostage Rescue Team had its own private building, located at the end of the long line of firing ranges that served the Bureau's training center. An engineless DC-4 sat behind it, and was used to practice assault techniques on hijacked aircraft. Down the hill was the ''Hostage House'' and other facilities used every day for the team members to hone their skills. Special Agent Gus Werner picked up the phone.

''Hi, Gus,'' Bill Shaw said.

''Have they found 'em yet?'' Werner asked. He was thirty-five, a short, wiry man with red hair and a brushy mustache that never would have been allowed under Hoover's directorship.

''No, but I want you to assemble an advance team and fly them up. If something breaks, we may have to move fast.''

''Fair enough. Where are we going, exactly?''

''Hagerstown, the State Police barracks. S-A-C Baltimore will be waiting for you.''

''Okay, I'll take six men. We can probably get moving in thirty or forty minutes, as soon as the chopper gets here. Buzz me if anything happens.''

''Will do. See ya.'' Shaw hung up.

Werner switched buttons on the phone and alerted the helicopter crew. Next he walked across the building to the classroom on the far side. The five men of his ready-response group were lounging about, mostly reading. They'd been on alert status for several days. This had increased their training routines somewhat, but it was mainly to defend against boredom that came from waiting for something that probably wouldn't happen. Nighttimes were devoted to reading and television. The Red Sox were playing the Yankees on TV. These were not Brooks Brothers FBI agents. The men were in baggy jumpsuits lavishly equipped with pockets. In addition to being experienced field agents, nearly all were veterans of combat or peacetime military service, and each man was a match-quality marksman who fired several boxes of ammunition per week.

''Okay, listen up,'' Werner said. ''They want an advance team in Hagerstown. The chopper'll be here in half an hour.''

"There's a severe thunderstorm warning," one objected lightly.

"So take your airsick pills," Werner advised.

"They find 'em yet?" another asked.

"No, but people are getting a little nervous."

"Right." The questioner was a long-rifleman. His custom-made sniper rifle was already packed in a foam-lined case. The team's gear was in a dozen duffle bags. The men buttoned their shirts. Some headed off to the bathroom for a preflight pitstop. None were especially excited. Their job involved far more waiting than doing. The Hostage Rescue Team had been in existence for years, but it had yet to rescue a single hostage. Instead its members were mainly used as a special SWAT team, and they had earned a reputation as awesome as it was little known, except within the law-enforcement community.

"Wow," Robby said. "Here it comes. This one's going to be a beauty." In the space of ten minutes, the wind had changed from gentle breezes to gusts that made the high-ceilinged house resonate.

"It was a dark and stormy night," Jack chuckled. He went into the kitchen. Three agents were making sandwiches to take out to the men by the road. "I hope you guys have raincoats."

"We're used to it," one assured him.

"At least it will be a warm rain," his British colleague thought. "Thank you very much for the food and coffee." The first rumble of distant thunder rolled through the house.

"Don't stand under any trees," Jack suggested. "Lightning can ruin your whole day." He returned to the dining room. Conversation was still being made around the table. Robby was back to discussing flying. The current war-story was about catapults.

"You never get used to the thrill," he was saying. "In a couple of seconds you go from a standstill to a hundred fifty knots."

"And if something goes wrong?" the Princess asked.

"You go swimming," Robby answered.

"Mr. Avery," the hand-held radio squawked.

"Yeah," he answered.

"Washington's on the line."

"Okay, I'll be there in a minute." Avery walked down the driveway toward the communications van. Longley, the leader of the British contingent, tagged along. Both had left their raincoats there anyway, and they'd need them in a few minutes. They could see lightning flashes a few miles away, and the jagged strokes of light were approaching fast.

"So much for the weather," Longley said.

"I was hoping it would miss us." The wind lashed at them again, blowing dust from the plowed field on the other side of Falcon's Nest Road. They passed the two men carrying a covered plate of sandwiches. A black puppy trotted along behind in the hope that they'd drop one.

"This Ryan fellow's a decent chap, isn't he?"

"He's got a real nice kid. You can tell a lot about a man from his kids," Avery thought aloud. They got to the van just as the first sprinkles started. The Secret Service agent got on the radiophone.

"Avery here."

"Chuck, this is Bill Shaw at the Bureau. I just got a call from our forensics people at that house in Howard County."

"Okay."

At the other end of the connection, Shaw was looking at a map and frowning. "They can't find any prints, Chuck. They have guns, they have ammo, some of the guns were being cleaned, but no prints. Not even on the hamburger wrappers. Something feels bad."

"What about the car that got shot up in western Maryland?"

"Nothing, not a damned thing. Like the bad guys jumped in a hole and pulled it in behind them."

That was all Shaw had to say. Chuck Avery had been a Secret Service agent all of his adult life, and was normally on the Presidential detail. He thought exclusively in terms of threats. This was an inevitable consequence of his job. He guarded people whom other people wanted to kill. It had given him a limited and somewhat paranoid outlook on life. Avery's mind reviewed his threat briefing. *The enemy here is extremely clever. . . .*

"Thanks for the tip, Bill. We'll keep our eyes open." Avery got into his coat and picked up his radio. "Team One, this is Avery. Heads up. Assemble at the entrance. We have a possible new threat." *The full explanation will have to wait.*

"What's the matter?" Longley asked.

"There's no real evidence at the house, the lab people haven't found any prints."

"They couldn't have had time to wipe everything before they left." Longley didn't need much of a hint either. "It might all have been planned to—"

"Exactly. Let's get out and talk to the troops. First thing, I'm going to get the perimeter spread out some. Then I'll call for more police backup." The rain was pelting the van now. "I guess we're all going to get wet."

"I want two more people at the house," Longley said.

"Agreed, but let's brief the people first." He slid the door open and both men went back up the driveway.

The agents on perimeter duty came together where the driveway met the road. They were alert, but it was hard to see with the wind-driven rain in their faces and the stinging dust blowing from the field on the other side of the road. Several were trying to finish sandwiches. One agent did a head count and came up one short. He sent a fellow agent to fetch the man whose radio was evidently out. Ernie tagged along with him; this agent had given him half a sandwich.

"You want to retire to the living room?" Cathy waved at the seats a few feet away. "I'd like to clear these dishes away."

"I'll do it, Cath," Sissy Jackson said. "You go sit down." She went into the kitchen and got the apron. Ryan knew for certain that Cathy had warned the Jacksons—Sissy at least, since she was wearing what on further inspection seemed an expensive dress. Everyone stood, and Robby walked off to the bathroom for a head call.

"Here we go," Alex said. He was at the wheel now. "All ready?"

"Go!" O'Donnell said. Like Alex, he wanted to be out in front with his troops. "Thank God for the weather!"

"Right," Alex agreed. He flipped the van's headlights to high-beam. He saw two groups of agents, standing a few yards apart.

* * *

The security force saw the approaching lights, and, being trained men, they kept a close eye on it despite knowing who it was and what it had been doing. Thirty yards from them there was a flash and a bang. Some men reached instinctively for their guns, then stopped when they saw that the vehicle's left-front tire had blown and was fluttering on the road as the driver struggled to get the truck back under control. It stopped right in front of the driveway. No one had commented on the ladders before. No one noticed their absence now. The driver got out and looked at the wheel.

"Aw, shit!"

Two hundred yards away, Avery saw the truck sitting on the road, and his instincts set off an alarm. He started running.

The van's door slid back, revealing four men with automatic weapons.

The agents a few feet away reacted in a moment, but too late. Barely had the door moved when the first weapon fired. A cylindrical silencer hung on the muzzle, which muffled the noise, but not the tongue of white flame that hovered in the darkness, and five men were down in the first second. The other gunmen had already joined in, and the first group of agents was wiped out without having fired a single return shot. The terrorists leaped out of the side and back doors of the van and engaged the second group. One Secret Service agent got his Uzi up and fired a short burst that killed the first man out of the back of the van, but the man behind him killed the agent with his weapon. Two more of the guards were now dead, and the other four of the group dropped to the ground and tried to return fire.

"What the hell is that?" Ryan said. The sound was hard to distinguish through the noise of the rain and the recurring thunder. Heads throughout the room turned. There was a British security officer in the kitchen and two Secret Service agents on the deck outside the room. Their heads had already turned, and one man was reaching for his radio.

Avery's service revolver was out. As team leader he didn't bother carrying anything but his Smith & Wesson .357 Magnum. His other hand was in any case busy with his radio.

"Call Washington, we are under attack! We need backup right the hell now! Unknown gunmen on the west perimeter. Officers down, officers need help!"

Alex reached back into the truck and pulled out an RPG-7 rocket launcher. He could just make out the two State Police cars two hundred yards down the road. He couldn't see the cops, but they had to be there. He elevated the weapon to the proper mark on the steel sight and squeezed the trigger, adding yet another thundering noise to the flashing sky. The round fell a few feet short of the target, but its explosion lanced hot fragments through one gas tank. It exploded, bathing both cars in burning fuel.

"Hot damn!"

Behind him, the gunmen had spread out and flanked the Secret Service officers. Only one was still shooting back. Two more of the ULA shooters were down, Alex saw, but the rest closed in on the agent from behind and finished him with a barrage of fire.

"Oh, God!" Avery saw it, too. He and Longley looked at each other and each knew what the other thought. *They won't get them, not while I'm alive.*

"Shaw." The radio-telephone circuit crackled with static.

"We are under attack. We have officers down," the wall speaker said. "Unknown number of—it sounds like a fucking war out there! We need help and we need it now."

"Okay, stand by, we're working on it." Shaw gave quick orders and phone lines started lighting up. The first calls to go out went to the nearest state and county police stations. Next, the Hostage Rescue Team group on alert in Washington was ordered out. Their Chevy Suburban was sitting in the garage. He checked the wall clock and called Quantico on the direct line.

"The chopper's just landing now," Gus Werner answered.

"Do you know where the Ryan house is?" Shaw asked.

"Yeah, it's on the map. That's where our visitors are now, right?"

"It's under attack. How fast can you get there?"

"What's the situation?" Werner watched his men out the window, loading their gear into the helicopter.

"Unknown—we just rolled the team from here, but you may be the first ones in. The communications guy just called in, says they're under attack, officers down."

"If there's any additional information, get it to us. We'll be up in two minutes." Werner ran outside to his men. He had to shout at them to be heard under the turning rotor, then ran back to the building, where the watch officers were ordered to summon the rest of the team to the HRT headquarters. By the time he got back in the chopper, his men had their weapons out of their duffles. Then the helicopter lifted off into the approaching storm.

Ryan noted the flurry of activity outside as the British officer from the kitchen ran outside and conferred briefly with the Secret Service agents. He was just coming back inside when a series of lightning flashes illuminated the deck. One of the agents turned and brought his gun out—then fell backward. The glass behind him shattered. The other two men both dived for the deck. One rose up to fire and fell beside his comrade. The last came inside and shouted for everyone to lie flat. Jack had barely enough time to be horrified when another window shattered and the last security man was down. Four armed figures appeared where the broken glass was. They were all dressed in black, except for the mud on their boots and chests. One pulled off his mask. It was Sean Miller.

Avery and Longley were alone, lying in the middle of the yard. The Brit watched as a number of armed men checked the bodies of the fallen agents. Then they formed into two groups and started moving toward the house.

"We're too bloody exposed here," Longley said. "If we're to do any good at all, we must be back in the trees."

"You go first." Avery held his revolver in both hands and sighted on a black-clad figure visible only when the lightning flashed. They were still over a hundred yards away, very long range for a handgun. The next flash gave him a target, and Avery fired, missing and drawing a storm of fire at himself. Those rounds missed, too, but the sound of thuds in the wet ground was far too close. The fire shifted. Perhaps they saw Longley running back to the trees. Avery fired another carefully aimed shot and saw a man go down with a leg wound. The return fire was more accurate this time. The Secret Service agent emptied his gun. He thought he might have hit another of them when everything stopped.

Longley made it to the trees and looked back. Avery's prone figure didn't move despite the gunmen fifty yards away. The British security officer shouted a curse and gathered the remaining people. The FBI liaison agent had only his revolver, the three British officers had automatic pistols, and the one Secret Service agent had an Uzi with two spare magazines. Even if there weren't people to protect, there wasn't anyplace to run.

"So we meet again," Miller said. He held an Uzi submachine gun and bent down to pick up another from one of the fallen guards. Five more men came in behind him. They spread out in a semicircle to cover Ryan and his guests. "Get up! Hands where we can see them."

Jack stood, with the Prince next to him. Cathy came up next, holding Sally in her arms, and finally Her Highness. Three men spun around when the kitchen door swung open. It was Sissy Jackson, trying to hold some plates while a gunman held on to her arm. Two plates fell to the floor and broke when he jerked her arm up.

They have a maid, Miller remembered, seeing the dark dress and the apron. *Black, handsome woman.* He was smiling now. The disgrace of his failed missions was far behind him. He had all his targets before him, and in his hands was the instrument to eliminate them.

"You get over here with the rest," he ordered.

"What the hell—"

"Move, nigger!" Another of the gunmen, the shortest of the bunch, roughly propelled her toward the others. Jack's eyes fixed on him for a moment—where had he seen that face before. . . .

"You trash!" Sissy's eyes flared in outrage at that, her fear momentarily forgotten as she wheeled to snap back at the man.

"You should be more careful who you work for," Miller said. He gestured with his weapon. "Move."

"What are you going to do?" Ryan asked.

"Why spoil the surprise?"

Forty feet away, Robby was in the worst part of the house to hear anything. He'd been washing his hands, ignoring the thunder when the gunfire had erupted at the home's deck. Jackson slipped out of the bathroom and peered down the corridor to the living room, but saw nothing. What he heard was enough. He turned and went upstairs to the master bedroom. His first instinct was to call the police on the telephone, but the line was dead. His mind searched for something else to do. This wasn't like flying a fighter plane.

Jack has guns . . . but where the hell does he keep them . . . ? It was dark in the bedroom and he didn't dare to flip on a light.

Outside, the line of gunmen advanced toward the woods. Longley deployed his men to meet them. His military service was too far in the past, and his work as a security officer hadn't prepared him for this sort of thing, but he did his best. They had good cover in the trees, some of which were thick enough to stop a bullet. He ordered his only automatic weapon to the left.

* * *

''FBI, this is Patuxent River Approach. Squawk four-zero-one-niner, over.''

Aboard the helicopter, the pilot turned the transponder wheels until the proper code number came up. Next he read off the map coordinates of his destination. He knew what it looked like from aerial photographs, but they'd been taken in daylight. Things could look very different at night, and there was also the problem of controlling the aircraft. He was flying with a forty-knot crosswind, and weather conditions deteriorated with every mile. In the back the HRT members were trying to get into their night-camouflage clothing.

''Four-zero-one-niner, come left to heading zero-two-four. Maintain current altitude. Warning, it looks like a pretty strong thunder cell is approaching your target,'' the controller said. ''Recommend you do not exceed one thousand feet. I'll try to steer you around the worst of it.''

''Roger.'' The pilot grimaced. It was plain that the weather ahead was even worse than he'd feared. He lowered his seat as far as it would go, pulled his belts tighter, and turned on his storm lights. The only other thing he could do was sweat, and that came automatically. ''You guys in back, strap down tight!''

O'Donnell called for his men to stop. The treeline was a hundred yards ahead, and he knew that it held guns. One group moved left, the other right. They'd attack by echelons, with each group alternately advancing and providing fire support for the other. All his men wore black and carried submachine guns, except for one man who trailed a few yards behind the rest. He found himself wishing that they'd brought heavier weapons. There was still much to do, including removing the bodies of his fallen men. One was dead and two more wounded. But first—he lifted his radio to order one of his squads in.

On O'Donnell's right, the single remaining Secret Service agent tucked his left side against an oak tree and shouldered his Uzi. For him and his comrades in the trees, there was no retreat. The black metal sights were hard to use in the dark, and his targets were nearly invisible. Lightning again played a part, strobe-lighting the lawn for an instant that showed the green grass and black-clad men. He selected a target and fired a short burst, but missed. Both groups of attackers returned fire, and the agent cringed as he heard a dozen rounds hit the tree. The whole countryside seemed alive with the flashes of gunfire. The Secret Service agent came around again and fired. The group that had been approaching him directly was running to his left into the brambles. He was going to be flanked—but then they reappeared, firing their weapons into the bushes, and there were flashes firing *out*. Everyone was surprised by that, and suddenly no one had control of the situation.

O'Donnell had planned to advance his teams on either side of the clearing, but unexpectedly there was fire coming from the woodline to the south, and one of his squads was exposed and flanked from two directions. He evaluated the new tactical situation in an instant and started giving orders.

Ryan watched in mute rage. The gunmen knew exactly what they were doing, and that reduced his number of options to exactly zero. There were six guns on him and his guests, and not a chance that he could do anything about it. To his right, Cathy held on to their daughter, and even Sally kept quiet. Neither Miller nor his men made any unnecessary sound.

''Sean, this is Kevin,'' Miller's radio crackled with static. ''We have opposition in the treeline. Do you have them?''

"Yes, Kevin, the situation is under control."

"I need help out here."

"We're coming." Miller pocketed his radio. He pointed to his comrades. "You three, get them ready. If they resist, kill them all. You two come with me." He led them out the broken glass doors and disappeared.

"Come on." The remaining three gunmen had their masks off now. Two were tall, about Ryan's height, one with blond hair, the other black. The other was short and going bald—*I know you, but from where?* He was the most frightening. His face was twisted with emotions that Jack didn't want to guess at. Blondie threw him a bundle of rope. An instant later it was plain that it was a collection of smaller pieces already cut and meant to tie them up.

Robby, where the hell are you? Jack looked over to Sissy, who was thinking the same thing. She nodded imperceptibly, and there was still hope in her eyes. The short one noticed.

"Don't worry," Shorty said. "You'll get paid." He set his weapon on the dinner table and moved forward while Blondie and Blackie backed off to cover them all. Dennis Cooley took the rope to the Prince first, yanking his hands down behind his back.

There! Robby looked up. Jack had set his shotgun on the top shelf of the walk-in closet, along with a box of shells. He had to reach to get them, and when he did so, a holstered pistol dropped to the floor. Jackson winced at the sound it made, but grabbed it from the holster and tucked it into his belt. Next he checked the shotgun, pulling back the bolt—there was a round in the chamber and the gun was on safe. *Okay.* He filled his pockets with additional rounds and went back into the bedroom.

Now what? This wasn't like flying his F-14, with radar to track targets a hundred miles away and a wingman to keep the bandits off his tail.

The picture . . . You had to kneel on the bed to see out of it—*Why the hell did Jack arrange his furniture like this!* the pilot raged. He set the shotgun down and used both hands to slide the picture aside. He moved it only a few inches, barely enough to see out. *How many . . . one, two . . . three. Are there any others . . . ? What if I leave one alive . . . ?*

As he watched, Jack was being tied up. The Prince—*the Captain,* Robby thought—already was tied, and was sitting with his back to the pilot. The short one finished Jack next and pushed him back onto the couch. Jackson next watched the man put hands on his wife.

"What are you going to do with us?" Sissy asked.

"Shut up, nigger!" Shorty replied.

Even Robby knew that this was a trivial thing to get angry about; the problem at hand was far worse than some white asshole's racist remark, but his blood turned to fire as he watched the woman he loved being handled by that . . . *little white shit!*

Use your head, boy, something in the back of his brain said. *Take your time. You have to get it right on the first try. Cool down.*

Longley was beginning to hope. There were friendlies in the trees to his left. Perhaps they'd come from the house, he thought. At least one of them had an automatic weapon, and he counted three of the terrorists dead, or at least not moving on the grass. He had fired five rounds and missed with every one—the range was just too great for a pistol in the dark—but they'd stopped the terrorists cold. And help was coming. It had to be. The radio van was empty, but the FBI agent to his right had been there. All they had to do was wait, hold on for a few more minutes. . . .

"I got flashes on the ground ahead," the pilot said. "I—"

Lightning revealed the house for a brief moment in time. They couldn't see people on the ground, but that was the right house, and there were flashes that had to be gunfire, half a mile off as the helicopter buffeted through the wind and rain. It was about all the pilot could see. His instrument lights were turned up full-white, and the lightning had decorated his vision with a stunning collection of blue and green spots.

"Jesus," Gus Werner said over the intercom. "What are we getting into?"

"In Vietnam," the pilot replied coolly, "we called it a hot LZ." *And I was scared then, too.*

"Get Washington." The copilot switched frequencies on the radio and waved to the agent in the back while both men orbited the helicopter. "This is Werner."

"Gus, this is Bill Shaw. Where are you?"

"We have the house in sight, and there's a goddamned battle going on down there. Do you have contact with our people?"

"Negative, they're off the air. The D.C. team is still thirty minutes away. The state and county people are close but not there yet. The storm's knocking trees down all over the place and traffic is tied up something fierce. You're the man on the scene, Gus, you'll have to call it."

The mission of the Hostage Rescue Team was to take charge of an existing situation, stabilize it, and rescue the hostages—peacefully if possible, by force if not. They were not assault troops; they were special agents of the FBI. But there were brother agents down there.

"We're going in now. Tell the police that federal officers are on the scene. We'll try to keep you informed."

"Right. Be careful, Gus."

"Take us in," Werner told the pilot.

"Okay. I'll skirt the house first, then come around in and land you to windward. I can't put you close to the house. The wind's too bad, I might lose it down there."

"Go." Werner turned. Somehow his men had all their gear on. Each carried an automatic pistol. Four had MP-5 machine guns, as did he. The long-rifleman and his spotter would be the first men out the door. "We're going in." One of the men gave a thumbs-up that looked a lot jauntier than anyone felt.

The helicopter lurched toward the ground when a sudden downdraft hammered at it. The pilot wrenched upward on his collective and bottomed the aircraft out a scant hundred feet from the trees. The house was only a few hundred yards away now. They skimmed over the southern edge of the clearing, allowing everyone a close look at the situation.

"Hey, the spot between the house and the cliff might be big enough after all," the pilot said. He increased power as the chopper swept to windward.

"Helicopter!" someone screamed to O'Donnell's right. The chief looked up, and there it was, a spectral shape and a fluttering sound. That was a hazard he'd prepared for.

Back near the road, one of his men pulled the cover off a Redeye missile launcher purchased along with the rest of their weapons.

"I have to use landing lights—my night vision is wasted," the pilot said over the intercom. He turned the aircraft half a mile west of the Ryan house. He planned to head straight past the house; then he'd drop and turn into the wind and slide up behind what he hoped was a wind shadow in its lee. *God,* he thought, *this* is *like Vietnam.* From the pattern of the flashes on the ground, it seemed that the house was in friendly hands. The pilot reached down and flipped on his landing lights. It was a risk, but one he had to accept.

Thank God I can see again, he told himself. The ground was visible through a shimmering curtain of rain. He realized that the storm was still worsening. He had to approach from windward. Flying into the rain would reduce his visibility to a few feet. At least this way he could see a couple of hundred or so—*what the hell!*

He saw a man standing all alone in the center of the field, aiming something. The pilot pushed down on the collective just as a streak of red light rocketed toward the helicopter, his eyes locked on what could only be a surface-to-air missile. The two seconds it took seemed to stretch into an hour as the missile passed through his rotor blades and disappeared overhead—he immediately pulled back on the control, but there was no time to recover from his evasion maneuver. The helicopter slammed into the middle of a plowed field, four hundred yards from the Ryan house. It wouldn't move again until a truck came to collect the wreckage.

Miraculously, only two men were hurt. Werner was one of them. It felt as though he'd been shot in the back. The rifleman pulled the door open and ran out with his spotter behind. The others went next, one of them helping Werner while another hobbled on a sprained ankle.

The Princess was next. She was taller than Cooley, and managed a look that contained more than mere contempt. The little man spun her around roughly to tie her hands.

"We have big plans for you," he promised when he finished.

"You little scum, I bet you don't even know how," Sissy said. It earned her a vicious slap. Robby watched, waiting for the blond-haired one to get in the clear. Finally he did, moving back toward the others. . . .

26. The Sound of Freedom

Pellets fired from a shotgun disperse radially at a rate of one inch per yard of linear travel. A lightning flash blazed through the windows, and Ryan cringed on hearing the thunder immediately after—then realized it had followed too quickly to be thunder. The shot pattern had missed his head by three feet, and before he understood what had passed by him, Blondie's head snapped back, exploding into a cloud of red as his body fell backward to crash against a table leg. Blackie was looking out the window in the corner and turned to see his comrade go down without knowing how or why. His eyes searched frantically for a second, then a red circle the size of a 45-rpm record appeared in his chest and he was flung against the wall. Shorty was tying up Cathy's hands and concentrating a little too much. He hadn't recognized the first shot for what it was. He did with the second—too late.

The Prince sprang at him, knocking him down with a lowered shoulder before himself falling on the floor. Jack leaped over the coffee table and kicked wildly at Shorty's head. He connected, but lost his balance doing so and fell backward. Shorty was stunned for a moment, then shook it off and moved toward the dinner table, where his gun was. Ryan lurched to his feet too, and threw himself on the terrorist's legs. The Prince was back up now. Shorty threw a wild punch at him and tried to kick Ryan off his legs—then stopped when the warm muzzle of a shotgun pressed against his nose.

"You hold it right there, sucker, or I'll blow your head off."

Cathy already had the ropes shucked off her hands, and untied Jack first. He went over to Blondie. The body was still twitching. Blood was still pumping from the surreal nightmare that had been a human face thirty seconds before. Jack took the Uzi from his hands, and a spare magazine. The Prince did the same with Blackie, whose body was quite still.

"Robby," Jack said as he examined the safety-selector switch on the gun. "Let's get the hell away from here."

"Second the motion, Jack, but where to?" Jackson pushed Shorty's head against the floor. The terrorist's eyes crossed almost comically on the business end of the Remington shotgun. "I expect he might know something useful. How'd you plan to get away, boy?"

"No." It was all Cooley could muster at the moment. He realized that he was, after all, the wrong man for this kind of job.

"That the way it is?" Jackson asked, his voice a low, angry rasp. "You listen to me, boy. That lady over there, the one you called *niggah*—that's my wife, boy, that's my lady. I saw you hit her. So, I already got one good reason to kill you, y'dig?" Robby smiled wickedly, and let the shotgun trace a line down to Shorty's crotch. "But I ain't gonna kill ya. I'll do somethin' lots worse—

"I'll make a girl outa you, punk." Robby pushed the muzzle against the man's zipper. "Think fast, boy."

Jack listened to his friend in amazement. Robby never talked like this. But it was convincing. Jack believed that he'd do it.

So did Cooley: "Boats . . . boats at the base of the cliff."

"That's not even clever. Say goodbye to 'em, boy." The angle of the shotgun changed fractionally.

"*Boats! Two boats at the base of the cliff.* There are two ladders—"

"How many watching them?" Jack demanded.

"One, that's all."

Robby looked up. "Jack?"

"People, I suggest we go steal some boats. That firefight outside is getting closer." Jack ran to his closet and got coats for everyone. For Robby he picked up his old Marine field jacket that Cathy hated so much. "Put this on, that white shirt is too damned visible."

"Here." Robby handed over Jack's automatic. "I got a box of rounds for the shotgun." He started transferring them from his pants to the jacket pockets and then hefted the last Uzi over his shoulder. ''We're leaving friendlies behind, Jack,'' he added quietly.

Ryan didn't like it either. ''I know, but if they get him, they win—and this ain't no place for women and kids, man.''

''Okay, you're the Marine.'' Robby nodded. That was that.

''Let's get outa here. I have the point. I'm going to take a quick look-see. Rob, you take Shorty for now. Prince, you take the women.'' Jack reached down and grabbed Dennis Cooley by the throat. ''You screw up, you're dead. No fartin' around with him, Robby, just waste him.''

''That's a rog.'' Jackson backed away from the terrorist. ''Up slow, punk.''

Jack led them through the shattered doors. The two dead agents lay crumpled on the wood deck, and he hated himself for not doing something about it, but Ryan was proceeding on some sort of automatic control that the Marine Corps had programmed into him ten years before. It was a combat situation, and all the lectures and field exercises were flooding back into his consciousness. In a moment he was drenched by the falling sheets of rain. He trotted down the stairs and looked around the house.

Longley and his men were too busy dealing with the threat to their front to notice what was approaching from behind. The British security officer fired four rounds at an advancing black figure and had the satisfaction of seeing him react from at least one hit when a hammering impact hurled him against a tree. He rebounded off the rough bark and half turned to see yet another black-clad shape holding a gun ten feet away. The gun flashed again. Within seconds the woodline was quiet.

''Dear God,'' the rifleman muttered. Running in a crouch, he passed the bodies of five agents, but there wasn't time for that. He and his spotter went down next to a bush. The rifleman activated his night scope and tracked on the woodline a few hundred yards ahead. The green picture he got on the imaging tube showed men dressed in dark clothes heading into the woodline.

''I count eleven,'' the spotter said.

''Yeah,'' the rifleman agreed. His bolt-action sniper rifle was loaded with .308 caliber match rounds. He could hit a moving three-inch target the first time, every time, at over two hundred yards, but his mission for the moment was reconnaissance, to gather information and forward it to the team leader. Before the team could act, they had to know what the hell was going on, and all they had now was chaos.

''Werner, this is Paulson. I count what looks like eleven bad guys moving into the trees between us and the house. They appear to be armed with light automatic weapons.'' He pivoted the rifle around. ''Looks like six of them down in the yard. Lots of good guys down—Jesus, I hope there's ambulances on the way.''

''Do you see any friendlies around?''

''Negative. Recommend that you move in from the other side. Can you give me a backup here?''

''Sending one now. When he gets there, move in carefully. Take your time, Paulson.''

''Right.''

To the south, Werner and two other men advanced along the treeline. Their night-camouflage clothing was a hatchwork of light green, designed by computer, and even in the lightning they were nearly invisible.

* * *

Something had just happened. Jack saw a sudden flurry of fire, then nothing. Despite what he'd told Robby, he didn't like running away from the scene. But what else could he do? There was an unknown number of terrorists out there. He had only three armed men to protect three women and a child, with their backs to a cliff. Ryan swore and returned to the others.

"Okay, Shorty, show me the way down," Ryan said, pressing the muzzle of his Uzi against the man's chest.

"Right there." The man pointed, and Ryan swore again.

In all the time they'd lived here, Jack's only concern with the cliff was to keep away from it, lest it crumble under him or his daughter. The view from his house was magnificent enough, but the cliff's height meant that from the house there was an unseen dead zone a thousand yards wide which the terrorists had used to approach. And they'd used ladders to climb up—*of course, that's what ladders are for!* Their placements were marked the way it said in every field manual in the world, with wooden stakes wrapped with white gauze bandaging, to be seen easily in the dark.

"Okay, people," Ryan began, looking around. "Shorty and I go first. Your Highness, you come next with the women. Robby, stay ten yards back and cover the rear."

"I am adept with light weapons," the Prince said.

Jack shook his head emphatically. "No, if they get you, they win. If something goes wrong, I'm depending on you to take care of my wife and kid, sir. If something happens, go south. About half a mile down you'll find a gully. Take that inland and don't stop till you find a hard-surface road. It's real thick cover, you should be okay. Robby, if anything gets close, blast it."

"But what if—"

"But, hell! Anything that moves is the enemy." Jack looked around one last time. *Give me five trained men, maybe Breckenridge and four others, and I could set up one pisser of an ambush . . . and if pigs had wings . . .* "Okay, Shorty, you go down first. If you fuck us up, the first thing happens, I'll cut you in half. Do you believe me?"

"Yes."

"Then move."

Cooley moved to the ladder and proceeded down backward, with Ryan several feet above him. The aluminum rungs were slippery with the rain, but at least the wind was blocked by the body of the cliff. The extension ladder—*how the hell did they get that here?*—wobbled under him. Ryan tried to keep an eye on Shorty and slipped once halfway down. Above him, the second group was beginning its descent. The Princess had taken charge of Sally, and was coming down with Ryan's daughter between her body and the ladder to keep her from falling. He could hear his little girl whimpering anyway. Jack had to ignore it. There wasn't room in his consciousness for anger or pity now. He had to do this one right the first time. There would be no second. A flash of lightning revealed the two boats a hundred yards to the north. Ryan couldn't tell if anyone was there or not. Finally they reached the bottom. Cooley moved a few feet to the north and Ryan jumped down the next few feet, gun at the ready.

"Let's just stay put for a minute."

The Prince arrived next, then the women. Finally Robby started down, his Marine parka making him invisible against the black sky. He came down quickly, also jumping the last five feet.

"They got to the house just as I started down. Maybe this'll slow them some." He held the white-wrapped stakes. It might make the ladders harder to find.

"Good one, Rob." Jack turned. The boats were out there, invisible again in the rain and shadows. Shorty had said that only one man was guarding them. *What if he's lying?* Ryan asked himself. *Is this guy willing to die for his cause? Will he sacrifice himself to shout a warning and get us killed? Does it make a difference—do we have a choice? No!*

"Move out, Shorty." Ryan gestured with his gun. "Just remember who dies first."

It was high tide, and the water came to within a few feet of the base of the cliff. The sand was wet and hard under his feet as Ryan stayed three feet behind the terrorist. *How far were they—a hundred yards? How* far *can one hundred yards be?* Ryan asked himself. He was discovering that now. The people behind him kept close to the kudzu-covered cliff. That made them extremely hard to see, though if there was someone in the boat, he'd know that people were coming toward him.

Krak!

Everyone's heart stopped for a moment. A lightning stroke had shattered a tree on the cliff's edge not two hundred yards behind them. For a brief instant he saw the boats again—and there was a man in each.

"Just one, eh?" Jack muttered. Shorty hesitated, then proceeded, hands at his side. With the return of darkness, he again lost sight of the boats, and Jack reasoned that everyone's night vision was equally ruined by the lightning. His mind returned to the image he'd just seen. The man in the near boat was standing at the near side, amidships, and appeared to be holding a weapon—one that needed two hands. Ryan was enraged that Shorty had lied to him. It seemed absurd as he watched the emotion flare and fade in his consciousness.

"What's the password?"

"There isn't one," Dennis Cooley replied, his voice unsteady as he contemplated the situation from rather a different perspective. He was between the loaded guns of two sides, each of which was likely to shoot. Cooley's mind was racing, too, looking for something he could do to turn the tables.

Was he telling the truth now? Ryan wondered, but there wasn't time to puzzle that one out. "Keep moving."

The boat reappeared now. At first it was just something different from the darkness and the beach. In five more yards it was a shape. The rain was pouring down hard enough to distort everything he saw, but there was a white, almost rectangular shape ahead. Ryan guessed the range at fifty yards. He prayed for the lightning to hold off now. If they were lighted, the men in the boats might be able to recognize a face, and if they saw that Shorty was in front . . .

How do I do this . . . ?

You can be a policeman or a soldier, but not both. Joe Evans' words at the Tower came back, and told him what he had to do.

Forty yards to go. There were rocks on the beach, too, and Jack had to be careful not to trip over one. He reached forward with his left hand and unscrewed the bulky silencer. He stuck it in his belt. He didn't like what it did to the gun's balance.

Thirty yards. He searched for and found the stock release switch on the Uzi. Jack extended the stock, planting the metal buttplate in his armpit and snugging the weapon in tight. *Just a few more seconds . . .*

Twenty-five yards. He could see the boat clearly now, twenty feet or so, with a blunt bow, and another just like it perhaps twenty yards beyond. There was definitely a man in the near boat, standing amidships on its port side, looking straight at the people approaching him. Jack's right thumb pushed the Uzi's selector switch all the way forward, to full automatic fire, and he tightened his fist on the pistol grip. He hadn't fired an Uzi since a brief familiarization at Quantico. It was small but nicely balanced. The black metal sights were nearly useless in the dark, though, and what he had to do . . .

Twenty yards. *The first burst has to be right on, Jack, right the hell on . . .*

Ryan took half a step to his right and dropped to one knee. He brought the weapon up, placing the front sight low and left of his target before he held the trigger down for a four-round burst. The gun jerked up and to the right as the bullets left, tracing a diagonal line across the target's outline. The man dropped instantly from sight, and Ryan was again dazzled, this time by his own muzzle flashes. Shorty had dived to the ground at the sound.

"Come on!" Ryan yanked Cooley up and threw him forward, but Jack stumbled in the sand and recovered to see that the terrorist was indeed running for the boat—*where there was a gun to turn against them all!* He was yelling something Ryan couldn't understand.

Jack had nearly caught up when Shorty got there first—

And died. The man in the other boat fired a long, wild burst in their direction just as Cooley was leaping aboard. Ryan saw his head snap over and Shorty fell into the boat like a sack of groceries. Jack knelt at the gunnel and fired his own burst, and the other man went down. Hit or not, Ryan couldn't tell. It was just like the exercises at Quantico, he told himself, total chaos, and the side that makes the fewest mistakes wins.

"Get aboard!" He stayed up, holding his gun on the other boat. He didn't turn his head, but felt the others board. Lightning flashed, and Ryan saw the man he'd shot, three red spots on his chest, his eyes and mouth agape in surprise. Shorty was beside him, the side of his head horribly opened. Between the two it seemed a gallon of blood had been poured onto the fiberglass deck. Robby finally arrived and jumped aboard. A head appeared in the other boat, and Ryan fired again, then clambered aboard.

"Robby, get us the hell outa here!" Jack moved on hands and knees to the other side, making sure that everyone's head was down.

Jackson moved into the driver's seat and searched for the ignition. It was set up just like a car, and the keys were in. He turned them, and the engine coughed to life as yet another burst of fire came from the other boat. Ryan heard the sound of bullets hitting the fiberglass. Robby cringed but didn't move as his hand found the shift lever. Jack brought the gun up and fired again.

"Men on the cliff!" the Prince shouted.

O'Donnell gathered his men quickly and gave out new orders. All the security men were dead, he was sure, but that helicopter had probably landed to the west. He didn't think the missile had hit, though it was impossible to be sure.

"Thanks for the help, Sean, they were better than I expected. You have them in the house?"

"I left Dennis and two others. I think we should leave."

"You got that right!" Alex said. He pointed west. "I think we have some more company."

"Very well. Sean, you collect them and bring them to the cliff."

Miller got his two men and ran back to the house. Alex and his man tagged along.

The front door was open, and all five raced inside, turned around the fireplace, and stopped cold.

Paulson, his spotter, and another agent were running too. He led them along the woodline to where the driveway turned, and dropped again, setting his rifle up on the bipod. There were sirens in the distance now, and he wondered what had taken so goddamned long as he tracked his night-sight in a search for targets. He caught a glimpse of men running around the northern side of the house.

"Something feels wrong about this," the sniper said.

"Yeah," his spotter agreed. "They sure as hell didn't plan to leave by the road—but what else is there?"

"Somebody better find out," Paulson thought aloud, and got on his radio.

Werner struggled forward on the south side of the yard, trying his best to ignore his throbbing back as he led his group forward. The radio squawked again, and he ordered his other team to advance with extreme caution.

"Well, where are they, man?" Alex asked.

Miller looked around in stunned amazement. Two of his men were dead on the floor, their guns were gone—and so were . . .

"Where the hell are they!" Alex repeated.

"Search the house!" Miller screamed. He and Alex stayed in the room. The black man looked at him with an unforgiving stare.

"Did I go through all this to watch you fuck up again?"

The three men returned a few seconds later and reported the house empty. Miller had already determined that his men's guns were gone. Something had gone wrong. He took his people outside.

Paulson had a new spot and finally could see his targets again. He counted twelve, then more joined from the house. They seemed to be confused as he watched the images on his night-sight gesture at one another. Some men were talking while others just milled around waiting for orders. Several appeared to be hurt, but he couldn't tell for sure.

"They're gone." Alex said it before Miller had a chance.

O'Donnell couldn't believe it. Sean explained in a rapid, halting voice while Dobbens looked on.

"Your boy fucked up," Dobbens said.

It was just too much. Miller slipped his own Uzi behind his back and retrieved the one he'd taken from the Secret Service agent. He brought it up in one smooth motion and fired into Alex's chest from a distance of three feet. Louis looked at his fallen boss for a second, then tried to bring his pistol up, but Miller cut him down, too.

"What the hell!" the spotter said.

Paulson flipped the rifle's safety off and centered his sight on the man who had just fired, killing two men—but whom had he killed? He could shoot only to save the lives of friendlies, and the dead men had almost certainly been bad guys. There weren't any hostages to be saved, as far as he could tell. *Where the hell are they?* One of the men near the cliff's edge appeared to shout something, and the others ran to join him. The marksman had his choice of targets, but without positive identification, he couldn't dare to fire a shot.

"Come on, baby," Jackson said to the engine. The motor was still cold and ran unevenly as he shifted to reverse. The boat moved slowly backward, away from the beach. Ryan had his Uzi trained on the other boat. The man there appeared again, and Ryan fired three rounds before the gun stopped. He cursed and switched magazines before firing a number of short bursts again to keep his head down.

"Men on the cliff," the Prince repeated. He'd taken the shotgun and had it aimed, but didn't fire. He didn't know who it was up there, and the range was too great in any case. Then flashes appeared. Whoever it was, they were firing at the boat. Ryan turned when he heard bullets hitting the water, and two thudded into the boat itself. Sissy Jackson screamed and grabbed at herself, while the Prince fired three rounds back.

Robby had the boat thirty yards from the beach now, and savagely brought the wheel around as he shifted the selector back into drive. When he rammed the throttle forward, the engine coughed again for one long, terrible moment, but then it caught and the boat surged forward.

"*All right!*" the aviator hooted. "Jack—where to? How about Annapolis?"

"Do it!" Ryan agreed. He looked aft. There were men coming down the ladder. Some were still shooting at them but missing wildly. Next he saw that Sissy was holding her foot.

"Cathy, see if you can find a first-aid kit," His Highness said. He'd already inspected the wound, but was now in the stern, facing aft with the shotgun at the ready. Jack saw a white plastic box under the driver's seat and slid it toward his wife.

"Rob, Sissy took a round in the foot," Jack said.

"I'm okay, Rob," his wife said at once. She didn't sound okay.

"How is it, Sis?" Cathy asked, moving to take a look.

"It hurts, but it's no big deal," she said through her teeth, trying to smile.

"You sure you're okay, honey?" Robby asked.

"Just *go,* Robby!" she gasped. Jack moved aft and looked. The bullet had gone straight through the top of her foot, and her light-colored shoe was bathed in dark blood. He looked around to see if anyone else was hurt, but aside from the mere terror that each felt, everyone else seemed all right.

"Commander, do you want me to take the wheel for you?" the Prince asked.

"Okay, Cap'n, come on forward." Robby slid away from the controls as His Highness joined him. "Your course is zero-three-six magnetic. Watch it, it's going to get rough when we're out of the cliff's lee, and there's lots of merchant traffic out there." They could already see four feet of chop building a hundred yards ahead, driven by the gusting winds.

"Right. How do I know when we've arrived at Annapolis?" The Prince settled behind the wheel and started checking out the controls.

"When you see the lights on the Bay Bridges, call me. I know the harbor, I'll take her in."

The Prince nodded agreement. He throttled back to half power as they entered the heavy chop, and kept moving his eyes from the compass to the water. Jackson moved to check his wife.

Sissy waved him away. "You worry about *them!*"

In another moment they were roller-coastering over four- and five-foot waves.

The boat was a nineteen-foot cathedral-hull lake boat of a type favored by local fishermen for her good calm-seas speed and shallow draft. Her blunt nose didn't handle the chop very well. They were taking water over the bow, but the forward snap-on cover was in place, and the windshield deflected most of the water over the side. That water which did get into the back emptied down a self-bailing hole next to the engine box. Ryan had never been in a boat like this, but knew what it was. Its hundred-fifty-horse engine drove an inboard-outdrive transmission whose movable propeller eliminated the need for a rudder. The bottom and sides of the boat were filled with foam for positive flotation. You could fill it with water and it wouldn't sink—but more to the point, the fiberglass and the foam would probably stop the bullets from a submachine gun. Jack checked his fellow passengers again. His wife was ministering to Sissy. The Princess held his daughter. Except for himself, Robby, and the Prince at the wheel, everyone's head was down. He started to relax slightly. They were away, and their fate was back in their own hands. Jack promised himself that this would never change again.

"They're coming after us," Robby said as he fed two rounds into the bottom of the shotgun. " 'Bout three hundred yards back. I saw them in the lightning, but they'll lose us in this rain if we're lucky."

"What would you call the visibility?"

"Except for the lightning"—Robby shrugged—"maybe a hot hundred yards, tops. We're not leaving a wake for them to follow, and they don't know where we're going." He paused. "God, I wish we had a radio! We could get the Coast Guard in on this, or maybe somebody else, and set up a nice little trap for them."

Jack sat all the way down, facing aft on the opposite side of the engine box from his friend. He saw that his daughter was asleep in the arms of the Princess. *It must be nice to be a kid,* he reflected.

"Count your blessings, Commander."

"Bet your ass, boy! I guess I picked a good time to take a leak."

Ryan grunted agreement. "I didn't know you could handle a shotgun."

"Back when I was a kid, the Klan had this little hobby. They'd get boozed up every Tuesday night and burn down a nigger church—just to keep us in line, y'know? Well, one night, the sheetheads decided to burn my pappy's church. We got word—a liquor-store owner called; not all rednecks are assholes. Anyway, Pappy and me were waiting for them. Didn't kill any, but we must have scared them as white as their sheets. I blew the radiator right out of one car." Robby chuckled at the memory. "They never did come back for it. The cops didn't arrest anybody, but that's the last time anybody tried to burn a church in our town, so I guess they learned their lesson." He paused again. When he went on, his voice was more sober. "That's the first time I ever killed a man, Jack. Funny, it doesn't feel like anything, not anything at all."

"It will tomorrow."

Robby looked over at his friend. "Yeah."

Ryan looked aft, his hands tight on the Uzi. There was nothing to be seen. The sky and water merged into an amorphous gray mass, and the wind-driven rain stung at his face. The boat surged up and down on the breaking swells, and for a moment Jack wondered why he wasn't seasick. Lightning flashed again, and still he saw nothing, as though they were under a gray dome on a sparkling, uneven floor.

They were gone. After the sniper team reported that all the terrorists had disappeared over the cliff, Werner's men searched the house and found nothing but dead men. The second HRT group was now on the scene, plus over twenty police, and another crowd of firemen and paramedics. Three of the Secret Service agents were still alive, plus a terrorist who'd been left behind. All were being transported to hospitals. That made for seventeen security people dead, and a total of four terrorists, two of them apparently killed by their own side.

"They all crowded into the boat and took off that way," Paulson said. "I could have taken a few out, but there just wasn't any way to figure who was who." He'd done the right thing. The sniper knew it, and so did Werner. You don't shoot without knowing what your target is.

"So now what the hell do we do?" This question came from a captain of the State Police. It was a rhetorical question insofar as there was no immediate answer.

"Do you suppose the good guys got away?" Paulson asked. "I didn't see anything that looked like a friendly, and the way the bad guys were acting . . . something went wrong," he said. "Something went wrong for everybody."

Something went wrong, all right, Werner thought. *A goddamned battle was fought here. Twenty-some people dead and nobody in sight.*

"Let's assume that the friendlies escaped somehow—no, let's just assume that the bad guys got away in a boat. Okay. Where would they go?" Werner asked.

"Do you know how many boatyards there are around here?" the State Police Captain asked. "Jesus, how many houses with private slips? Hundreds—we can't check them all out!"

"Well, we have to do something!" Werner snapped back, his anger amplified by his sprained back. A black dog came up to them. He looked as confused as everyone else.

"I think they lost us."

"Could be," Jackson replied. The last lightning flash had revealed nothing. "The bay's right big, and visibility isn't worth a damn—but the way the rain's blowing, they can see better than we can. Twenty yards, maybe, just enough to matter."

"How about we go farther east?" Jack asked.

"Into the main ship channel? It's a Friday night. There'll be a bunch of ships coming out of Baltimore, knocking down ten-twelve knots, and as blind as we are." Robby shook his head. "Uh-uh, we didn't make it this far to get run down by some Greek rustbucket. This is hairy enough."

"Lights ahead," the Prince reported.

"We're home, Jack!" Robby went forward. The lights of the twin Chesapeake Bay Bridges winked at them unmistakably in the distance. Jackson took the wheel, and the Prince took up his spot in the stern. All were long since soaked through by the rain, and they shivered in the wind. Jackson brought the boat around to the west. The wind was on the bow now, coming straight down the Severn River valley, as it usually did here. The waves moderated somewhat as he steered past the Annapolis town harbor. The rain was still falling in sheets, and Robby navigated the boat mostly by memory.

The lights along the Naval Academy's Sims Drive were a muted, linear glow through the rain and Robby steered for them, barely missing a large can buoy as he fought the boat through the wind. In another minute they could see the line of gray YPs—Yard Patrol boats—still moored to the concrete seawall while their customary slips were being renovated across the river. Robby stood to see better, and brought the boat in between a pair of the wood-hulled training craft. He actually wanted to enter the Academy yacht basin, but it was too full at the moment. Finally he nosed the boat to the seawall, holding her to the concrete with engine power.

"Y'all stop that!" A Marine came into view. His white cap had a plastic cover over it, and he wore a raincoat. "Y'all can't tie up here."

"This is Lieutenant Commander Jackson, son," Robby replied. "I work here. Stand by. Jack, you get the bowline."

Ryan ducked under the windshield and unsnapped the bow cover. A white nylon line was neatly coiled in the right place, and Ryan stood as Robby used engine power to bring the boat's port side fully against the seawall. Jack jumped up and tied the line off. The Prince did the same at the stern. Robby killed the engine and went up to face the Marine.

"You recognize me, son?"

The Marine saluted. "Beg pardon, Commander, but—" He flashed his light into the boat. "Holy Christ!"

About the only good thing that could be said about the boat was that the rain had washed most of the blood down the self-bailing hole. The Marine's mouth dropped open as he saw two bodies, three women, one of them apparently shot, and a sleeping child. Next he saw a machine gun draped around Ryan's neck. A dull, wet evening of walking guard came to a screeching end.

"You got a radio, Marine?" Robby asked. He held it up and Jackson snatched it away. It was a small Motorola CC unit like those used by police. "Guardroom, this is Commander Jackson."

"Commander? This is Sergeant Major Breckenridge. I didn't know you had the duty tonight, sir. What can I do for you?"

Jackson took a long breath. "I'm glad it's you, Gunny. Listen up: Alert the command duty officer. Next, I want some armed Marines on the seawall west of the yacht basin *immediately!* We got big trouble here, Gunny, so let's shag it!"

"Aye aye, sir!" The radio squawked. Orders had been given. Questions could wait.

"What's your name, son?" Robby asked the Marine next.

"Lance Corporal Green, sir!"

"Okay, Green, help me get the womenfolk out of the boat." Robby reached out his hand. "Let's go, ladies."

Green leaped down and helped Sissy out first, then Cathy, then the Princess, who was still holding Sally. Robby got them all behind the wood hull of one of the YPs.

"What about them, sir?" Green gestured at the bodies.

"They'll keep. Get back up here, Corporal!"

Green gave the bodies a last look. "Reckon so," he muttered. He already had his raincoat open and the flap loose on his holster.

"What's going on here?" a woman's voice asked. "Oh, it's you, Commander."

"What are you doing here, Chief?" Robby asked her.

"I have the duty section out keeping an eye on the boats, sir. The wind could beat 'em to splinters on this seawall if we don't—" Chief Bosun's Mate Mary Znamirowski looked at everyone on the dock. "Sir, what the hell . . ."

"Chief, I suggest you get your people together and put them under cover. No time for explanations."

A pickup truck came next. It halted in the parking lot just behind them. The driver jumped out and sprinted toward them with three others trailing behind. It was Breckenridge. The Sergeant Major gave the women a quick look, then turned to Jackson and asked the night's favorite question—

"What the hell is going on, sir?"

Robby gestured to the boat. Breckenridge gave it a quick look that lingered into four or five seconds. "Christ!"

"We were at Jack's place for dinner," Robby explained. "And some folks crashed the party. They were after him—" Jackson gestured to the Prince of Wales, who turned and smiled. Breckenridge's eyes went wide in recognition. His mouth flapped open for a moment, but he recovered and did what Marines always do when they don't know what else—he saluted, just as prescribed in the *Guide Book.* Robby went on: "They killed a bunch of security troops. We got lucky. They planned to escape by boat. We stole one and came here, but there's another boat out there, full of the bastards. They might have followed us."

"Armed with what?" the Sergeant Major asked.

"Like this, Gunny." Ryan held up his Uzi.

The Sergeant Major nodded and reached into his coat. His hand came out with a radio. "Guardroom, this is Breckenridge. We have a Class-One Alert: Wake up all the people. Call Captain Peters. I want a squad of riflemen on the seawall in five minutes. Move out!"

"Roger," the radio answered. "Class-One Alert."

"Let's get the women the hell outa here," Ryan urged.

"Not yet, sir," Breckenridge replied. He looked around, his professional eye making a quick evaluation. "I want some more security here first. Your friends might have landed upriver and be coming overland—that's how I'd do it. In ten minutes I'll have a platoon of riflemen sweepin' the grounds, maybe a full squad here in five. If my people ain't too drunked out," he concluded quietly, reminding Ryan that it was indeed a Friday night—Saturday morning—and Annapolis had many bars. "Cummings and Foster, look after the ladies. Mendoza, get on one of these boats and keep a lookout. Y'all heard the man, so stay awake!"

Breckenridge walked up and down the seawall for a minute, checking fields of view and fields of fire. The .45 Colt automatic looked small in his hands. They could see in his face that he didn't like the situation, and wouldn't until he had more people here and the civilians tucked safely away. Next he checked the women out.

"You ladies all right—oh, sorry, Mrs. Jackson. We'll get you to the sick bay real quick, ma'am."

"Any way to turn the lights off?" Ryan asked.

"Not that I know of—I don't like being under 'em either. Settle down, Lieutenant, we got all this open ground behind us, so nobody's going to sneak up this way. Soon as I get things organized, we'll get the ladies off to the dispensary and put a guard on 'em. You ain't as safe as I'd like, but we're gettin' there. How did you get away?"

"Like Robby said, we got lucky. He did two of them with the shotgun. I got one in the boat. The other one got popped by his own man." Ryan shivered, this time not from wind or rain. "It was kinda hairy there for a while."

"I believe it. These guys any good?"

"The terrorists? You tell me. They had surprise going for them before, and that counts for a lot."

"We'll see about that." Breckenridge nodded.

"There's a boat out there!" It was Mendoza, up on one of the YPs.

"Okay, boys," the Sergeant Major breathed, holding his .45 up alongside his head. "Just wait another couple of minutes, till we get some real weapons here."

"They're coming in slow," the Marine called.

Breckenridge's first look was to make sure the women were safely behind cover. Then he ordered everyone to spread out and pick an open spot between the moored boats. "And for Christ's sake keep your damned heads down!"

Ryan picked a spot for himself. The others did the same, at intervals of from ten to over a hundred feet apart. He felt the reinforced-concrete seawall with his hand. He was sure it would stop a bullet. The four sailors from the YP duty section stayed with the women, with a Marine on either side. Breckenridge was the only one moving, crouching behind the seawall, following the white shape of the moving boat. He got to Ryan.

"There, about eighty yards out, going left to right. They're trying to figure things out, too. *Just give me a couple more minutes, people,*" he whispered.

"Yeah." Ryan thumbed off the safety, one eye above the lip of the concrete. It was just a white outline, but he could hear the muted sputter of the engine. The boat turned in toward where Robby had tied up the one they'd stolen. It was their first real mistake, Jack thought.

"Great." The Sergeant Major leveled his automatic, shielded by the stern of a boat. "Okay, gentlemen. Come on if you're coming. . . ."

Another pickup truck approached on Sims Drive. It came up without lights and stopped right by the women. Eight men jumped off the back. Two Marines ran along the seawall, and were illuminated by a light between two of the moored YPs. Out on the water, the small boat lit up with muzzle flashes, and both Marines went down. Bullets started hitting the moored boats around them. Breckenridge turned and yelled.

"Fire!" The area exploded with noise. Ryan spotted on the flashes and depressed his trigger with care. The submachine gun fired four rounds before locking open on an empty magazine. He cursed and stared stupidly at the weapon before he realized that he had a loaded pistol in his belt. He got the Browning up and fired a single shot before he realized that the target wasn't there anymore. The noise from the boat's motor increased dramatically.

"Cease fire! Cease fire! They're buggin' out," Breckenridge called. "Anybody hit?"

"Over here!" someone called to the right, where the women were.

Ryan followed the Sergeant Major over. Two Marines were down, one with a flesh wound in the arm, but the other had taken a round right through the hip and was screaming like a banshee. Cathy was already looking at him.

"Mendoza, what's happening?" Breckenridge called.

"They're heading out—wait—yeah, they're moving east!"

"Move your hands, soldier," Cathy was saying. The Private First-Class had taken a painful hit just below the belt on his left side. "Okay, okay, you're going to be all right. It hurts, but we can fix it." Breckenridge reached down to take the man's rifle. He tossed it to Sergeant Cummings.

"Who's in command here?" demanded Captain Mike Peters.

"I guess I am," Robby said.

"Christ, Robby, what's going on?"

"What the hell does it look like!"

Another truck arrived, carrying another six Marines. They took one collective look at the wounded men and yanked at the charging handles on their rifles.

"Goddammit, Robby—sir!" Captain Peters yelled.

"Terrorists. They tried to get us at Jack's place. They were trying to get—well, look!"

"Good evening, Captain," the Prince said after checking his wife. "Did we get any? I didn't have a clear shot." His voice showed real disappointment at that.

"I don't know, sir," Breckenridge answered. "I saw some rounds go short, and pistol stuff won't penetrate a boat like that." Another series of lightning flashes illuminated the area.

"I see 'em, they're going out to the bay!" Mendoza called.

"Damn!" Breckenridge growled. "You four, get the ladies over to the dispensary." He bent down to help the Princess to her feet as Robby lifted his wife. "You want to give the little girl to the Private, ma'am? They're going to take you to the hospital and get you all dried off."

Ryan saw that his wife was still trying to help one of the wounded Marines, then looked at the patrol boat in front of him. "Robby?"

"Yeah, Jack?"

"Does this boat have radar?"

Chief Znamirowski answered. "They all do, sir."

A Marine lowered the tailgate on the one pickup and helped Jackson load his wife aboard. "What are you thinking, Jack?"

"How fast are they?"

"About thirteen—I don't think they're fast enough."

Chief Bosun's Mate Znamirowski looked over the seawall at the boat Robby had steered in. "In the seas we got now, you bet I can catch one of those little things! But I need someone to work the radar. I don't have an operator in my section right now."

"I can do that," the Prince offered. He was tired of being a target, and no one would keep him out of this. "It would be a pleasure in fact."

"Robby, you're senior here," Jack said.

"Is it legal?" Captain Peters asked, fingering his automatic.

"Look," Ryan said quickly, "we just had an armed attack by *foreign* nationals on a U.S. government reservation—that's an act of war and posse comitatus doesn't apply." *At least I don't think it does,* he thought. "Can you think of a good reason not to go after them?"

He couldn't. "Chief Z, you have a boat ready?" Jackson asked.

"Hell, yes, we can take the seventy-six boat."

"Crank her up! Captain Peters, we need some Marines."

"Sar-Major Breckenridge, secure the area, and bring along ten men."

The Sergeant Major had left the officers to their arguments while getting the civilians loaded onto the truck. He grabbed Cummings.

"Sergeant, take charge of the civilians, get 'em to sick bay, and put a guard on 'em. Beef up the guard force, but your primary mission is to take care of these people here. Their safety is your responsibility—and you ain't relieved till *I* relieve you! Got it?"

"Aye, Gunny."

Ryan helped his wife to the truck. "We're going after them."

"I know. Be careful, Jack. Please."

"I will, but we're going to get 'em this time, babe." He kissed his wife. There was a funny sort of look on her face, something more than concern. "Are you okay?"

"I'll be fine. You worry about you. Be careful!"

"Sure, babe. I'll be back." *But* they *won't!* Jack turned away to jump aboard the boat. He went inside the deckhouse and found the ladder to the bridge.

"I am Chief Znamirowski, and I have the conn," she announced. Mary Znamirowski didn't look like a chief bosun's mate, but the young seaman—was seawoman the proper term for her? Jack wondered—on the wheel jumped as though she were. "Starboard back two thirds, port back one third, left full rudder."

"Stern line is in," a seaman—this one was a man—reported.

"Very well," she acknowledged, and continued her terse commands to get the YP away from the dock. Within seconds they were clear of the seawall and the other boats.

"Right full rudder, all ahead full! Come to new course one-three-five." She turned. "How's the radar look?"

The Prince was looking over the controls on the unfamiliar set. He found the clutter-suppression switch and bent down to the viewing hood. "Ah! Target bearing one-one-eight, range thirteen hundred, target course northeasterly, speed . . . about eight knots."

"That's about right, it can get choppy by the point," Chief Z thought. "What's our mission, Commander?"

"Can we stay with them?"

"They shot up *my* boats! I'll ram the turkeys if you want, sir," the chief replied. "I can give you thirteen knots as long as you want. I doubt they can do more than ten in the seas we got."

"Okay. I want us to follow as close as we can without being spotted."

The chief opened one of the pilothouse doors and looked at the water. "We'll close to three hundred. Anything else?"

"Go ahead and close up. For the rest of it, I am open to ideas," Robby replied.

"How about we see where they're going?" Jack suggested. "Then we can call in the cavalry."

"That makes sense. If they try to run for shore . . . Christ, I'm a fighter pilot, not a cop." Robby lifted the radio microphone. The set showed the boat's call sign: NAEF. "Naval Station Annapolis, this is November Alfa Echo Foxtrot. Do you read, over." He had to repeat the call twice more before getting an acknowledgment.

"Annapolis, give me a phone patch to the Superintendent."

"He just called us, sir. Stand by." A few clicks followed, plus the usual static.

"This is Admiral Reynolds, who is this?"

"Lieutenant Commander Jackson, sir, aboard the seventy-six boat. We are one mile southeast of the Academy in pursuit of the boat that just shot up our waterfront."

"Is that what happened? All right, who do you have aboard?"

"Chief Znamirowski and the duty boat section, Captain Peters and some Marines, Doctor Ryan, and, uh, Captain Wales, sir, of the Royal Navy," Robby answered.

"Is *that* where he is? I have the FBI on the other phone—Christ, Robby! Okay, the civilians are under guard at the hospital, and the FBI and police are on the way here. Repeat your situation and then state your intentions."

"Sir, we are tracking the boat that attacked the dock. Our intentions are to close and track by radar to determine its destination, then call in the proper law-enforcement agencies, sir." Robby smiled into the mike at his choice of words. "My next call is to Coast Guard Baltimore, sir. Looks like they're heading in that direction at the moment."

"Roger that. Very well, you may continue the mission, but the safety of your guests is your responsibility. Do not, repeat do not take any unnecessary chances. Acknowledge."

''Yes, sir, we will not take any unnecessary chances.''

''Use your head, Commander, and report as necessary. Out.''

''Now there's a vote of confidence,'' Jackson thought aloud. ''Carry on.''

''Left fifteen degrees rudder,'' Chief Z ordered, rounding Greenbury Point. ''Come to new course zero-two-zero.''

''Target bearing zero-one-four, range fourteen hundred, speed still eight knots,'' His Highness told the quartermaster on the chart table. ''They took a shorter route around this point.''

''No problem,'' the chief noted, looking at the radar plot. ''We have deep water all the way up from here.''

''Chief Z, do we have any coffee aboard?''

''I got a pot in the galley, sir, but I don't have anybody to work it.''

''I'll take care of that,'' Jack said. He went below, then to starboard and below again. The galley was a small one, but the coffee machine was predictably of the proper size. Ryan got it started and went back topside. Breckenridge was passing out life jackets to everyone aboard, which seemed a sensible enough precaution. The Marines were deployed on the bridgewalk outside the pilothouse.

''Coffee in ten minutes,'' he announced.

''Say again, Coast Guard,'' Robby said into the microphone.

''Navy Echo Foxtrot, this is Coast Guard Baltimore, do you read, over.''

''That's better.''

''Can you tell us what's going on?''

''We are tracking a small boat, about a twenty-footer—with ten or more armed terrorists aboard.'' He gave position, course, and speed. ''Acknowledge that.''

''Roger, you say a boat full of bad guys and machine guns. Is this for real? Over.''

''That's affirmative, son. Now let's cut the crap and get down to it.''

The response was slightly miffed. ''Roger that, we have a forty-one boat about to leave the dock and a thirty-two-footer'll be about ten minutes behind it. These are small harbor-patrol boats. They are not equipped to fight a surface gun action, mister.''

''We have ten Marines aboard,'' Jackson replied. ''Do you request assistance?''

''Hell, yes—that's affirmative, Echo Foxtrot. I have the police and the FBI on the phone, and they are heading to this area.''

''Okay, have your forty-one boat call us when they clear the dock. Let's have your boat track from in front and we'll track from behind. If we can figure where the target is heading, I want you to call in the cops.''

''We can do that easy enough. Let me get some things rolling here, Navy. Stand by.''

''A ship,'' the Prince said.

''It's gotta be,'' Ryan agreed. ''The same way they did it when they rescued that Miller bastard. . . . Robby, can you get the Coast Guard to give us a list of the ships in the harbor?''

Werner and both Hostage Rescue groups were already moving. He wondered what had gone wrong—and right—tonight, but that would be determined later. For the moment he had agents and police heading toward the Naval Academy to protect the people he was supposed to have rescued, and his men were split between an FBI Chevy Suburban and two State Police cars, all heading north on Ritchie Highway toward Baltimore. If only they could use helicopters, he thought, but the weather was too bad, and everyone had had enough of that for one night. They were back to being a SWAT team, a purpose for which they were well suited. Despite everything that had gone wrong tonight, they now had a large group of terrorists flushed and in the open. . . .

"Here's the list of the ships in port," the Coast Guard Lieutenant said over the radio. "We had a lot of them leave Friday night, so the list isn't too long. I'll start off at the Dundalk Marine Terminal. *Nissan Courier,* Japanese registry, she's a car carrier out of Yokohama delivering a bunch of cars and trucks. *Wilhelm Schörner,* West German registry, a container boat out of Bremen with general cargo. *Costanza,* Cypriot registry, out of Valetta, Malta—"

"Bingo!" Ryan said.

"—scheduled to sail in about five hours, looks like. *George McReady,* American, arrived with a cargo of lumber from Portland, Oregon. That's the last one there."

"Tell me about the *Costanza,*" Robby said, looking at Jack.

"She arrived in ballast and loaded up a cargo mainly of farm equipment and some other stuff. Sails before dawn, supposed to be headed back for Valetta."

"That's probably our boy," Jack said quietly.

"Stand by, Coast Guard." Robby turned away from the radio. "How do you know, Jack?"

"I don't *know,* but it's a solid guess. When these bastards pulled that rescue on Christmas Day, they were probably picked up in the Channel by a Cypriot-registered ship. We think their weapons get to them through a Maltese dealer who works with a South African, and a lot of terrorists move back and forth through Malta—the local government's tight with a certain country due south of there. The Maltese don't get their own hands dirty, but they're real good at looking the other way if the money's right." Robby nodded and keyed his mike.

"Coast Guard, have you gotten things straightened out with the local cops?"

"That's a rog, Navy."

"Tell them that we believe the target's objective is the *Costanza.*"

"Roger that. We'll have our thirty-two boat stake her out and call in the cops."

"Don't let them see you, Coast Guard!"

"Understood, Navy. We can handle that part easy enough. Stand by. . . . Navy, be advised that our forty-one boat reports radar contact with you and the target, rounding Bodkin Point. Is this correct? Over."

"Yes!" called the Quartermaster at the chart table. He was making a precise record of the course tracks from the radar plot.

"That's affirm, Coast Guard. Tell your boat to take station five hundred yards forward of the target. Acknowledge."

"Roger, five-zero-zero yards. Okay, let's see if we can get the cops moving. Stand by."

"We got 'em," Ryan thought aloud.

"Uh, Lieutenant, keep your hands still, sir." It was Breckenridge. He reached into Ryan's belt and extracted the Browning automatic. Jack was surprised to see that he'd stuck it in there with the hammer back and safety off. Breckenridge lowered the hammer and put the pistol back where it was. "Let's try to think 'safe,' sir, okay? Otherwise you might lose something important."

Ryan nodded rather sheepishly. "Thanks, Gunny."

"Somebody has to protect the lieutenants." Breckenridge turned. "Okay, Marines—let's stay awake out there!"

"You got a man on the Prince?" Jack asked.

"Even before the Admiral said so." The Sergeant Major gestured to where a corporal was standing, rifle in hand, three feet from His Highness, with orders to stay between him and the gunfire.

Five minutes later a trio of State Police cars drove without lights to Berth Six of the Dundalk Marine Terminal. The cars were parked under one of the gantry cranes used for transferring cargo containers, and five officers walked quietly to the ship's accommodation ladder. A crewman stationed there stopped them—or tried to. A language barrier prevented proper communications. He found himself accompanying the troopers, with his hands cuffed behind his back. The senior police officer bounded up three more ladders and arrived at the bridge.

"What is this!"

"And who might you be?" the cop inquired from behind a shotgun.

"I am the master of this ship!" Captain Nikolai Frenza proclaimed.

"Well, Captain, I am Sergeant William Powers of the Maryland State Police, and I have some questions for you."

"You have no authority on my ship!" Frenza answered. His accent was a mixture of Greek and some other tongue. "I will talk to the Coast Guard and no one else."

"I want to make this real clear." Powers walked the fifteen feet to the Captain, his hands tight around the Ithaca 12-gauge shotgun. "That shore you're tied to is the State of Maryland, and this shotgun says I got all the authority I need. Now we have information that a boatload of terrorists is coming here, and the word is they've killed a bunch of people, including three state troopers." He planted the muzzle against Frenza's chest. "Captain, if they do come here, or if you fuck with me any more tonight, *you are in a whole shitpot full of trouble—do you understand me!*"

The man wilted before his eyes, Powers saw. *So the information is correct. Good.*

"You would be well advised to cooperate, 'cause pretty soon we're going to have more cops here 'n you ever saw. You just might need some friends, mister. If you have something to tell me, I want to hear it right now."

Frenza hesitated, his eyes shifting toward the bow and back. He was in deep trouble, more than his advance payment would ever cover. "There are four of them aboard. They are forward, starboard side, near the bow. We didn't know—"

"Shut up." Powers nodded to a corporal, who got on his portable radio. "What about your crew?"

"The crew is below, preparing to take the ship to sea."

"Sarge, the Coast Guard says they're three miles off and heading in."

"All right." Powers pulled a set of handcuffs from his belt. He and his men took the four men standing bridge watch and secured them to the ship's wheel and two other fittings. "Captain, if you or your people make any noise at all, I'll come back here and splatter you all over this ship. I am not kidding."

Powers took his men down to the main deck and forward on the port side. The *Costanza*'s superstructure was all aft. Forward of it, the deck was a mass of cargo containers, each the size of a truck-trailer, piled three- and four-high. Between each pile was an artificial alleyway, perhaps three feet wide, which allowed them to approach the bow unobserved. The Sergeant had no SWAT experience, but all of his men had shotguns and he did know something of infantry tactics.

It was like walking alongside a building, except that the street was made of rusty steel. The rain had abated, finally, but it still made noise, clattering on the metal container boxes. They passed the last of these to find that the ship's forward hold was open and a crane was hanging over the starboard side. Powers peeked around the corner and saw two men standing at the far side of the deck. They appeared to be looking southeast, toward the entrance to the harbor. There was no easy way to approach. He and his men crouched and went straight toward them. They'd gotten halfway when one turned.

"Who are you?"

"State Police!" Powers noted the accent and brought his gun up, but he tripped on a deck fitting and his first shot went into the air. The man on the starboard side came up with a pistol and fired, also missing, then ducked behind the container. The fourth state trooper went forward around the deck hatch and fired at the container edge, covering his comrades. Powers heard a flurry of conversation and the sound of running feet. He took a deep breath and ran to the starboard side.

No one was in sight. The men who'd run aft were nowhere to be seen. There was an accommodation ladder leading from an opening in the rail down to the water, and nothing else but a radio that someone had dropped.

"Oh, shit." The tactical situation was lousy. He had armed criminals close by but out of sight and a boatload of others on the way. He sent one of his men to the port side to watch that line of approach, and another to train his shotgun down the starboard side. Then he got on the radio and learned that plenty more help was on the way. Powers decided to sit tight and take his chances. He'd known Larry Fontana, helped carry his coffin out of the church, and he was damned if he'd pass up the chance to get the people who'd killed him.

A State Police car had taken the lead. The FBI was now on the Francis Scott Key Bridge, crossing over Baltimore Harbor. The next trick was to get from the expressway to the marine terminal. A trooper said he knew a shortcut, and he led the procession of three cars. A twenty-foot boat was going under the bridge at that very moment.

"Target coming right, appears to be heading towards a ship tied to the quay, bearing three-five-two," His Highness reported.

"That's it," Ryan said. "We got 'em."

"Chief, let's close up some," Jackson ordered.

"They might spot us, sir—the rain's slacking off. If they're heading to the north, I can close up on their port side. They're heading for that ship—you want us to hit them right when they get there?" Chief Znamirowski asked.

"That's right."

"Okay. I'll get somebody on the searchlight. Captain Peters, you'll want to get your Marines on the starboard side. Looks like surface action starboard," Chief Z noted. Navy regulations prohibited her from serving on a combatant ship, but she'd beaten the game after all!

"Right." Peters gave the order and Breckenridge got the Marines in place. Ryan left the pilothouse and went to the main deck aft. He had already come to his decision. Sean Miller was out there.

"I hear a boat," one of the troopers said quietly.

"Yeah." Powers fed a round into his shotgun. He looked aft. There were people there with guns. He heard footsteps behind him—more police!

"Who's in charge here?" a corporal asked.

"I am," Powers replied. "You stay here. You two, move aft. If you see a head come out from behind a container, blow it the hell off."

"I see it!" So did Powers. A white fiberglass boat appeared a hundred yards off, coming slowly up to the ship's ladder.

"Jesus." It seemed full of people, and every one, he'd been told, had an automatic weapon. Unconsciously he felt the steel plating on the ship's side. He wondered if it would stop a bullet. Most troopers now wore protective body armor, but Powers didn't. The Sergeant flipped off the safety on his shotgun. It was just about time.

The boat approached like a car edging into a parking space. The helmsman nosed the boat to the bottom of the accommodation ladder and someone in the bow tied it off. Two men got out onto the small lower platform. They helped someone off the boat, then started to carry him up the metal staircase. Powers let them get halfway.

"*Freeze!* State Police!" He and two others pointed shotguns straight down at the boat. "Move and you're dead," he added, and was sorry for it. It sounded too much like TV.

He saw heads turn upward, a few mouths open in surprise. A few hands moved, too, but before anything that looked like a weapon moved in his direction, a two-foot searchlight blazed down on the boat from seaward.

Powers was thankful for the light. He saw their heads snap around, then up at him. He could see their expressions now. They were trapped and knew it.

"Hi, there." A voice came across the water. It was a woman's voice on a loudspeaker. "If anybody moves, I have ten Marines to blow you to hell-and-gone. Make my day," the voice concluded. Sergeant Powers winced at that.

Then another light came on. "This is the U.S. Coast Guard. You are all under arrest."

"Like hell!" Powers screamed. "I got 'em!" It took another minute to establish what was going on to everyone's satisfaction. The big, gray Navy patrol boat came right alongside the smaller boat, and Powers was relieved to see ten rifles pointed at his prisoners.

"Okay, let's put all the guns down, people, and come up one at a time." His head jerked around as a single pistol shot rang out, followed by a pair of shotgun blasts. The Sergeant winced, but ignored it as best he could and kept his gun zeroed on the boat.

"I seen one!" a trooper said. "About a hundred feet back of us!"

"Cover it," Powers ordered. "Okay, you people get the hell up here and flat down on the deck."

The first two arrived, carrying a third man who was wounded in the chest. Powers got them stretched out, facedown on the deck, forwards of the front rank of containers. The rest came up singly. By the time the last was up, he'd counted twelve, several more of them hurt. They'd left behind a bunch of guns and what looked like a body.

"Hey, Marines, we could use a hand here!"

It was all the encouragement he needed. Ryan was standing on the YP's afterdeck, and jumped down. He slipped and fell on the deck. Breckenridge arrived immediately behind him and looked at the body the terrorists had left behind. A half-inch hole had been drilled in the man's forehead.

"I thought I got off one good round. Lead on, Lieutenant." He gestured at the ladder. Ryan charged up the steps, pistol in hand. Behind him, Captain Peters was screaming something at him, but Jack simply didn't care.

"Careful, we have bad guys down that way in the container stacks," Powers warned.

Jack went around the front rank of metal boxes and saw the men facedown on the deck, hands behind their necks, with a pair of troopers standing over them. In a moment there were six Marines there, too.

Captain Peters came up and went to the police Sergeant, who seemed to be in command.

"We have at least two more, maybe four, hiding in the container rows," Powers said.

"Want some help flushing them out?"

"Yeah, let's go do it." Powers grinned in the darkness. He assembled all of his men, leaving Breckenridge and three Marines to guard the men on the deck. Ryan stayed there, too. He waited for the others to move aft.

Then he started looking at faces.

Miller was looking, too, still hoping to find a way out. He turned his head to the left and saw Ryan staring at him from twenty feet away. They recognized each other in an instant, and Miller saw something, a look that he had always reserved for his own use.

I am Death, Ryan's face told him.

I have come for you.

It seemed to Ryan that his body was made of ice. His fingers flexed once around the butt of his pistol as he walked slowly to port, his eyes locked on Miller's face. He still looked like an animal to Jack, but he was no longer a predator on the loose. Jack reached him and kicked Miller's leg. He gestured with the pistol for him to stand, but didn't say a word.

You don't talk to snakes. You kill snakes.

"Lieutenant . . ." Breckenridge was a little slow to catch on.

Jack pushed Miller back against the metal wall of a container, his forearm across the man's neck. He savored the feel of the man's throat on his wrist.

This is the little bastard who nearly killed my family. Though he didn't know it, his face showed no emotion at all.

Miller looked into his eyes and saw . . . nothing. For the first time in his life, Sean Miller knew fear. He saw his own death, and remembered the long-past lessons in Catholic school, remembered what the sisters had taught him, and his fear was that they might have been right. His face broke out in a sweat and his hands trembled as, despite all his contempt for religion, he feared the eternity in hell that surely awaited him.

Ryan saw the look in Miller's eyes, and knew it for what it was. *Goodbye, Sean. I hope you like it there. . . .*

"Lieutenant!"

Jack knew that he had little time. He brought up the pistol and forced it into Miller's mouth as his eyes bored in on Sean's. He tightened his finger on the trigger just as he'd been taught. A gentle squeeze, so you never know when the trigger will break. . . .

But nothing happened, and a massive hand came down on the gun.

"He ain't worth it, Lieutenant, he just ain't worth it." Breckenridge withdrew his hand, and Ryan saw that the gun's hammer was down. He'd have to cock it before the weapon could fire. "Think, son."

The spell was broken. Jack swallowed twice and took a breath. What he saw now was something less monstrous than before. Fear had given Miller the humanity that he'd lacked before. He was no longer an animal, after all. He was a human being, an evil example of what could happen when a man lost something that all men needed. Miller's breath was coming in gasps as Ryan pulled the gun out of his mouth. He gagged, but couldn't bend over with Jack's arm across his throat. Ryan backed away and the man fell to the deck. The Sergeant Major put his hand on Ryan's right arm, forcing the gun downward.

"I know what you're thinking, what he did to your little girl, but it isn't worth what you'd have to go through. I could tell the cops you shot him when he tried to run. My boys would back me up. You'd never go to trial, but it ain't worth what it would do to you, son. You're not cut out to be a murderer," Breckenridge said gently. "Besides, look what you did to him. I don't know what that is down there, but it's not a man, not anymore."

Jack nodded, as yet unable to speak. Miller was still on all fours, looking down at the deck, unable to meet Ryan's eyes. Jack could feel his body again; the blood coursing through his veins told him that he was alive and whole. *I've won,* he thought, as his mind regained control of his emotions. *I've won. I've defeated him and I haven't destroyed myself doing it.* His hands relaxed around the pistol grip.

"Thanks, Gunny. If you hadn't—"

"If you'd really wanted to kill him, you would have remembered to cock it. Lieutenant, I had you figured out a long time ago." Breckenridge nodded to reinforce his words. "Back on the deck, you," he told Miller, who slowly complied.

"Before any of you people think you're lucky, I got a hot flash for you," the Sergeant Major said next. "You have committed murder in a place that has a gas chamber. You can die by the numbers over here, people. Think about it."

The Hostage Rescue Team arrived next. They found the Marines and state troopers on the deck, working their way aft. It took a few minutes to determine that no one was in the container stacks. The remaining four ULA members had used an alleyway to head aft, and were probably in the superstructure. Werner took over. He had a solid perimeter. Nobody was going anywhere. Another group of FBI agents went forward to collect the terrorists.

Three TV news trucks arrived on the scene, adding their lights to the ones turning night into day on the dock. The police were keeping them back, but already live news broadcasts were being sent worldwide. A colonel of the State Police was giving out a press release at the moment. The situation, he told the cameras, was under control, thanks to a little luck and a lot of good police work.

By this time all the terrorists forward were handcuffed and had been searched. The agents read off their constitutional rights while three of their number went into the boat to collect their weapons and other evidence. The Prince finally came up the ladder, with a heavy guard. He came to where the terrorists were sitting, now. He looked at them for a minute or so but didn't say a word. He didn't have to.

"Okay, we have things contained aft. There seems to be four of them. That's what the crew says," one of the HRT people said. "They're below somewhere, and we'll have to talk them out. It shouldn't be too hard, and we have all the time in the world."

"How do we get these characters off?" Sergeant Powers asked.

"We haven't worked that out yet, but let's get the civilians off. We'd prefer you did it from here. It might be a little dangerous to use the aft ladder. That means the Marines, too. Thanks for the assist, Captain."

"I hope we didn't screw anything up, joining in, I mean."

The agent shook his head. "You didn't break any laws that I know of. We got all the evidence we need, too."

"Okay, then we head back to Annapolis."

"Fine. There'll be a team of agents waiting to interview you there. Please thank the boat crew for us."

"Sar-Major, let's get the people moving."

"Okay, Marines, saddle up," Breckenridge called. Two minutes later everyone was aboard the patrol boat, heading out of the harbor. The rain had finally ended and the sky was clearing, the cooler Canadian air finally breaking the heat wave that had punished the area. The Marines took the opportunity to climb into the boat's bunks. Chief Znamirowski and her crew handled the driving. Ryan and the rest congregated in the galley and started drinking the coffee that no one had touched to this point.

"Long day," Jackson said. He checked his watch. "I'm supposed to fly in a few hours. Well, I was, anyway."

"Looks like we finally won a round," Captain Peters observed.

"It wasn't cheap." Ryan stared into his cup.

"It's never cheap, sir," Breckenridge said after a few seconds.

The boat rumbled with increased engine power. Jackson lifted a phone and asked why they were speeding up. He smiled at the answer, but said nothing.

Ryan shook his head to clear it and went topside. Along the way he found a crewman's pack of cigarettes on a table and stole one. He proceeded out onto the fantail. Baltimore Harbor was already low on the horizon, and the boat was turning south toward Annapolis, chugging along at thirteen knots—about fifteen miles per hour, but on a boat it seemed fast enough. The smoke he blew out made its own trail as he stared aft. *Was Breckenridge right?* he asked the sky. The answer came in a moment. *He got one part right. I'm not cut out to be a murderer. Maybe he was right on the other part, too. I sure hope so. . . .*

"Tired, Jack?" the Prince asked, standing beside him.

"I ought to be, but I guess I'm still too pumped up."

"Indeed," His Highness observed quietly. "I wanted to ask them why. When I went up to look at them, I wanted—"

"Yeah." Ryan took a last drag and flipped the butt over the side. "You could ask, but I doubt the answer would mean much of anything."

"Then how are we supposed to solve the problem?"

We did solve my *problem,* Jack thought. *They won't be coming after my family anymore. But that's not the answer you want, is it?* "I guess maybe it comes down to justice. If people believe in their society, they don't break its rules. The trick's making them believe. Hell, we can't always accomplish that." Jack turned. "But you try your best, and you don't quit. Every problem has a solution if you work at it long enough. You have a pretty good system over there. You just have to make it work for everybody, and do it well enough that they believe. It's not easy, but I think you can do it. Sooner or later, civilization always wins over barbarism." *I just proved that, I think.* I hope.

The Prince of Wales looked aft for a moment. "Jack, you're a good man."

"So are you, pal. That's why we'll win."

It was a grisly scene, but not one to arouse pity in any of the men who surveyed it. Geoffrey Watkins' body was quite warm, and his blood was still dripping from the ceiling. After the photographer finished up, a detective took the gun from his hands. The television remained on, and "Good Morning, Britain" continued to run its live report from America. All the terrorists were now in custody. *That's what must have done it,* Murray thought.

"Bloody fool," Owens said. "We didn't have a scrap of usable evidence."

"We do now." A detective held three sheets of paper in his hand. "This is quite a letter, Commander." He slid the sheets into a plastic envelope.

Sergeant Bob Highland was there, too. He was still learning to walk again, with a leg brace and a cane, and looked down at the body of the man whose information had almost made orphans of his children. Highland didn't say a word.

"Jimmy, you've closed the case," Murray observed.

"Not the way I would have liked," Owens replied. "But now I suppose Mr. Watkins is answering to a higher authority."

The boat arrived in Annapolis forty minutes later. Ryan was surprised when Chief Znamirowski passed the line of moored boats and proceeded straight to Hospital Point. She conned the boat expertly alongside the seawall, where a couple of Marines were waiting. Ryan and everyone but the boat's crew jumped off.

"All secure," Sergeant Cummings reported to Breckenridge. "We got a million cops and feds here, Gunny. Everybody's just fine."

"Very well, you're relieved."

"Doctor Ryan, will you come along with me? You want to hustle, sir," the young Sergeant said. He led off at a slow trot.

It was well that the pace was an easy one. Ryan's legs were rubbery with fatigue as the Sergeant led him up the hill and into the old Academy hospital.

"Hold it!" A federal agent took the pistol from Ryan's belt. "I'll keep this for you, if that's okay."

"Sorry," Jack said with embarrassment.

"It's all right. You can go in." There was no one in sight. Sergeant Cummings motioned for him to follow.

"Where is everybody?"

"Sir, your wife's in the delivery room at the moment." Cummings turned to grin at him.

"Nobody told me!" Ryan said in alarm.

"She said not to worry you, sir." They reached the proper floor. Cummings pointed. "Down there. Don't toss your cookies, Doc."

Jack ran down the corridor. A corpsman stopped him and waved Ryan into a dressing room, where Ryan tore off his clothes and got into surgical greens. It took a few minutes. Ryan was clumsy from fatigue. He walked to the waiting room and saw that all his friends were there. Then the corpsman walked him into the delivery room.

"I haven't done this in a long time," the doctor was saying.

"It's been a few years for me, too," Cathy reproached him. "You're supposed to inspire confidence in your patient." Then she started blowing again, fighting off the impulse to push. Jack grabbed her hand.

"Hi, babe."

"Your timing is pretty good," the doctor observed.

"Five minutes earlier would have been better. Are you all right?" she asked. As it had been the last time, her face was bathed in sweat, and very tired. And she looked beautiful.

"It's all over. *All* over," he repeated. "I'm fine, how about you?"

"Her water broke two hours ago, and she'd be in a hurry if we weren't all waiting for you to get back from your boat ride. Otherwise everything looks good," the doctor answered. He seemed far more nervous than the mother. "Are you ready to push?"

"Yes!"

Cathy squeezed his hand. Her eyes closed and she summoned her strength for the effort. Her breath came out slowly.

"There's the head. Everything's fine. One more push and we're home," the doctor said. His gloved hands were poised to make the catch.

Jack turned as the rest of the newborn appeared. His position allowed him to tell even before the doctor did. The infant had already started screaming, as a healthy baby should. *And that, too,* Jack thought, *is the sound of freedom.*

"Boy," John Patrick Ryan Sr. told his wife just before he kissed her, "I love you."

The nearest corpsman assisted the doctor as he clamped off the cord and swaddled the infant in a white blanket to take him away a few feet. The placenta came next with an easy push.

"A little tearing," the doctor reported. He reached for a painkiller before he started the stitching.

"I can tell," Cathy replied with a slight grimace. "Is he okay?"

"Looks okay to me," the corpsman said. "Eight pounds even, and all the pieces are in the right places. Airway's fine, and the kid's got a great little heart."

Jack picked up his son, a small, noisy package of red flesh with an absurd little button of a nose.

"Welcome to the world. I'm your father," he said quietly. *And your father isn't a murderer. That might not sound like much, but it's a lot more than most people think.* He cradled the newborn to his chest for a moment and reminded himself that there really was a God. After a moment he looked down at his wife. "Do you want to see your son?"

"I'm afraid he doesn't have much of a mother left."

"She looks pretty good to me." Jack placed his son in Cathy's arms. "Are you all right?"

"Except for Sally, I think I have everything here that I need, Jack."

"Finished," the doctor said. "I may not be much of an OB, but I do one hell of a good stitch." He looked up to see the usual aftermath of a birth, and he wondered why he'd decided against obstetrics. It had to be the happiest discipline of them all. But the hours were lousy, he reminded himself.

The corpsman reclaimed the infant, and took John Patrick Ryan Jr. to the nursery, where he'd be the only baby for a while. It would give the pediatric people something to do.

Jack watched his wife drift off to sleep after—he checked his watch—a twenty-three-hour day. She needed it. So did he, but not quite yet. He kissed his wife one more time before another corpsman wheeled her away to the recovery room. There was one thing left for him to do.

Ryan walked out to the waiting room to announce the birth of his son, a handsome young man who would have two complete, but very different, sets of godparents.

Clear and Present Danger

ACKNOWLEDGMENTS

As always, there are many people to thank. To "The Great Geraldo" for his friendship; to Russ for his second installment of wise counsel and amazing breadth of knowledge; to Carl and Colin, who never knew what they were starting, but then, neither did I; to Bill for his wisdom; to Rich for his contemplation of what matters; to Tim, Ninja-Six, for more than a few tips on fieldcraft; to Ed, commander of warriors, and Patricia, who named the Cabbage Patch Hat, for their gracious hospitality; to Pete, former headmaster of the world's most exciting school (the passing grade is life); to Pat, who teaches the same course at yet another school; to Harry, mentee, for his most serious irreverence; to W.H., who does his best in a hopeless, thankless job; and of course to a dozen or so warrant officers who could teach astronauts a thing or two; and so many others—would that America served you as faithfully as you serve her.

To the memory of John Ball,
Friend and teacher,
The professional who took the last plane out

Law, without force, is impotent.

—PASCAL

It is the function of police to exercise force, or to threaten it, in execution of the state's purpose, internally and under normal conditions. It is the function of armed forces to exercise force, or the threat of it, externally in normal times and internally only in times that are abnormal. . . .

[T]he degree of force which the state is prepared to apply in the execution of its purpose . . . is as much as the government of the day considers it necessary or expedient to use to avoid a breakdown in its function and a surrender of its responsibilities.

—GENERAL SIR JOHN HACKETT

Prologue: Situation

The room was still empty. The Oval Office is in the southeast corner of the White House West Wing. Three doors lead into it, one from the office of the President's personal secretary, another from a small kitchen which leads in turn to the President's study, and a third into a corridor, directly opposite the entrance to the Roosevelt Room. The room itself is of only medium size for a senior executive, and visitors always remark afterward that it seemed smaller than they expected. The President's desk, set just in front of thick windows of bullet-resistant polycarbonate that distort the view of the White House lawn, is made from the wood of HMS *Resolute*, a British ship that sank in American waters during the 1850s. Americans salvaged and returned it to the United Kingdom, and a grateful Queen Victoria ordered a desk made from its oaken timbers by way of official thanks. Made in an age when men were shorter than today, the desk was increased somewhat in height during the Reagan presidency. The President's desk was laden with folders and position papers capped with a printout of his appointment schedule, plus an intercom box, a conventional push-button multiline telephone, and another ordinary-looking but highly sophisticated secure instrument for sensitive conversations.

The President's chair was custom-made to fit its user, and its high back included sheets of DuPont Kevlar—lighter and tougher than steel—as additional protection against bullets that some madman might fire through the heavy windows. There were, of course, about a dozen Secret Service agents on duty in this part of the Presidential Mansion during business hours. To get here most people had to pass through a metal detector—in fact all did, since the obvious ones were a little *too* obvious—and everyone had to pass the quite serious scrutiny of the Secret Service detail, whose identity was plain from the flesh-toned earpieces that coiled out from under their suit jackets, and whose politeness was secondary to their real mission of keeping the President alive. Beneath the jacket of each was a powerful handgun, and each of these agents was trained to view everyone and everything as a potential threat to WRANGLER, which was the President's current code-name. It had no meaning beyond being easy to say and easily recognizable on a radio circuit.

Vice Admiral James Cutter, USN, was in an office on the opposite, northwest corner of the West Wing and had been since 6:15 that morning. The job of Special Assistant to the President for National Security Affairs requires a man to be an early riser. At a quarter to eight he finished off his second cup of morning coffee—it was good here—and tucked his briefing papers into a leather folder. He walked through the empty office of his vacationing deputy, turned right down the corridor past the similarly vacant office of the Vice President, who was in Seoul at the moment, and turned left past the office of the President's Chief of Staff. Cutter was one of the handful of real Washington insiders—the Vice President was not among them—who didn't need the permission of the Chief of Staff to walk into the Oval Office whenever he felt the need, though he'd generally call ahead first to give the secretaries a heads-up. The Chief of Staff didn't like anyone to have that privilege, but that made his unlimited access all the more pleasant for Cutter to exercise. Along the way four security personnel nodded good morning to the Admiral, who returned the gestures as he would greet any skilled menial. Cutter's official code-name was LUMBERJACK, and though he knew that the Secret Service agents called him something else among themselves, Cutter was past caring what little people thought of him. The secretaries' anteroom was already up and running, with three secretaries and a Secret Service agent sitting in their appointed places.

"Chief on time?" he asked.

"WRANGLER is on the way down, sir," Special Agent Connor said. He was forty, a section chief of the Presidential Detail, didn't give a goddamn who Cutter was, and could care less what Cutter thought of him. Presidents and aides came and went, some liked, some loathed, but the professionals of the Secret Service served and protected them all. His trained eyes swept over the leather folder and Cutter's suit. No guns there today. He was not being paranoid. A king of Saudi Arabia had been killed by a family member, and a former prime minister of Italy had been betrayed by a daughter to the terrorist kidnappers who'd ultimately murdered him. It wasn't just kooks he had to worry about. Anyone could be a threat to the President. Connor was fortunate, of course, that he only had to worry about physical security. There were other sorts; those were the concerns of others less professional than he.

Everyone stood when the President arrived, of course, followed by his personal bodyguard, a lithe, thirtyish woman whose dark tresses neatly concealed the fact that she was one of the best pistol shots in government service. "Daga"—her Service nickname—smiled good morning at Pete. It would be an easy day. The President wasn't going anywhere. His appointment list had been thoroughly checked—the Social Security numbers of all nonregulars are run through the FBI's crime computers—and the visitors themselves would, of course, be subjected to the most thorough searches that can be made without an actual pat-down. The President waved for Admiral Cutter to follow him in. The two agents went over the appointment list again. It was routine, and the senior agent didn't mind that a man's job had been taken by a woman. Daga had earned her job on the street. If she were a man, everyone agreed, she'd have two big brass ones, and if any would-be assassin mistook her for a secretarial type, that was his bad luck. Every few minutes, until Cutter left, one or the other of the agents would peer through the spy-hole in the white-painted door to make sure that nothing untoward was happening. The President had held office for over three years, and was used to the constant observation. It hardly occurred to the agents that a normal man might find it oppressive. It was their job to know everything there was to know about the President, from how often he visited the bathroom to those with whom he slept. They didn't call the agency the Secret Service for nothing. Their antecedents had concealed all manner of peccadillos. The President's wife was not entitled to know what he did every hour of the day—at least, some presidents had so decided—but his security detail was.

Behind the closed door, the President took his seat. From the side door a Filipino mess steward carried in a tray with coffee and croissants and came to attention before leaving. With this the morning's preliminary routine was complete, and Cutter began his morning intelligence briefing. This had been delivered from CIA to his Fort Myer, Virginia, home before dawn, which allowed the Admiral to paraphrase it. The brief didn't take long. It was late spring, and the world was a relatively quiet place. Those wars underway in Africa and elsewhere were not of great import to American interests, and the Middle East was as tranquil as it ever seemed to be. That left time for other issues.

"What about SHOWBOAT?" the President asked while buttering his croissant.

"It's underway, sir. Ritter's people are already at work," Cutter replied.

"I'm still worried about security on the operation."

"Mr. President, it's as tight as one could reasonably expect. There are risks—you can't avoid them all—but we're keeping the number of people involved to an absolute minimum, and those people have been carefully selected and recruited."

That earned the National Security Adviser a grunt. The President was trapped—and as with nearly every president, it had come about from his own words. Presidential promises and statements . . . the people had this annoying way of remembering them. And even if they didn't there were journalists and political rivals who never passed on a chance to make the necessary reminders. So many things had gone right in this presidency. But so many of those were secret—and, annoyingly to Cutter, those secrets had somehow been kept. Well, they had to be, of course. Except that in the political arena no secret was truly sacred, most especially in an election year. Cutter wasn't supposed to be concerned with that. He was a professional naval officer, and therefore supposed to be apolitical in his outlook on the ins and outs of national security, but whoever had formulated that particular guideline must have been a monk. Members of the senior executive service did not take vows of poverty and chastity, however—and obedience was also a sometime thing.

"I promised the American people that we'd do something about this problem," the President observed crossly. "And we haven't accomplished shit."

"Sir, you cannot deal with threats to national security through police agencies. Either our national security is threatened or it is not." Cutter had been hammering that point for years. Now, finally, he had a receptive audience.

Another grunt: "Yeah, well, I said that, too, didn't I?"

"Yes, Mr. President. It's time they learned a lesson about how the big boys play." That had been Cutter's position from the beginning, when he'd been Jeff Pelt's deputy, and with Pelt now gone it was his view that had finally prevailed.

"Okay, James. It's your ball. Run with it. Just remember that we need results."

"You'll get 'em, sir. Depend on that."

"It's time those bastards were taught a lesson," the President thought aloud. He was certain that the lessons would be hard ones. On that he was correct. Both men sat in a room in which was focused and from which emanated the ultimate power of the most powerful nation in the history of civilization. The people who selected the man who occupied that room did so above all for their protection. Protection against the vagaries of foreign powers and domestic bullies, against all manner of enemies. Those enemies came in many forms, some of which the founding fathers had not quite anticipated. But one sort that had been anticipated existed in this very room . . . though it was not the one the President had in mind.

The sun rose an hour later on the Caribbean coast, and unlike the climate-controlled comfort of the White House, here the air was thick and heavy with humidity on what promised to be yet another sultry day under a lingering high-pressure system. The forested hills to the west reduced the local winds to a bare whisper, and the owner of *Empire Builder* was past being ready to go to sea, where the air was cooler and the breezes unrestricted.

His crewmen arrived late. He didn't like their looks, but he didn't have to. Just so long as they behaved themselves. After all, his family was aboard.

"Good morning, sir. I am Ramón. This is Jesús," the taller one said. What troubled the owner was that they were so obviously tidied-up versions of . . . of what? Or had they merely wanted to look presentable?

"You think you can handle this?" the owner asked.

"*Sí*. We have experience with large motor craft." The man smiled. His teeth were even and brushed. This was a man who took care with his appearance at all times, the owner thought. He was probably being overly cautious. "And Jesús, you will see, is a fine cook."

Charming little bastard. "Okay, crew quarters are forward. She's tanked up, and the engines are already warm. Let's get out where it's cool."

"Muy bien, Capitán." Ramón and Jesús unloaded their gear from the jeep. It took several trips to get it all stowed, but by nine in the morning, MY *Empire Builder* slipped her mooring lines and stood out to sea, passing a handful of party boats heading out with *yanqui* tourists and their fishing rods. Once in open waters, the yacht turned north. It would take three days.

Ramón already had the wheel. That meant he sat in a wide, elevated chair while the autopilot—"George"—handled the steering. It was an easy ride. The Rhodes had fin stabilizers. About the only disappointment was in the crew accommodations, which the owner had neglected. So typical, Ramón thought. A multimillion-dollar yacht with radar and every possible amenity, but the crew who operated it didn't have so much as a television set and VCR to amuse themselves when off duty. . . .

He moved forward on the seat, craning his neck to look on the fo'c'sle. The owner was there, asleep and snoring, as though the work of taking the yacht out to sea had exhausted him. Or perhaps his wife had tired him out? She was beside her husband, lying facedown on her towel. The string for her bikini top was untied so as to give her back an even tan. Ramón smiled. There were many ways for a man to amuse himself. But better to wait. Anticipation made it all the better. He heard the sound of a taped movie in the main salon, aft of the bridge, where their children were watching some movie or other. It never occurred to him to feel pity for any of the four. But he was not completely heartless. Jesús was a good cook. They both approved of giving the condemned a hearty meal.

It was just light enough to see without the night-vision goggles, the dawn twilight that the helicopter pilots hated because the eye had to adapt itself to a lightening sky and ground that was still in shadows. Sergeant Chavez's squad was seated and strapped in with four-point safety belts, and between the knees of each was a weapon. The UH-60A Blackhawk helicopter swooped high over one of the hills and then dropped hard when past the crest.

"Thirty seconds," the pilot informed Chavez over the intercom.

It was supposed to be a covert insertion, which meant that the helicopters were racing up and down the valleys, careful that their operational pattern should confuse any possible observer. The Blackhawk dove for the ground and pulled up short as the pilot eased back on the cyclic control stick, which gave the aircraft a nose-up attitude, signaling the crew chief to slide the right-side door open and the soldiers to twist the release dials on their safety-belt buckles. The Blackhawk could touch down only for a moment.

"Go!"

Chavez went out first, moving perhaps ten feet from the door before he fell flat to the ground. The squad did the same, allowing the Blackhawk to lift off immediately, and rewarding each of its former passengers with a faceful of flying grit as it clawed its way back into the sky. It would reappear around the southern end of a hill as though it had never stopped. Behind it, the squad assembled and moved out into the treeline. Its work had just begun. The sergeant gave his commands with hand motions and led them off at a dead run. It would be his last mission, then he could relax.

At the Navy's weapons testing and development facility, China Lake, California, a team of civilian technicians and some Navy ordnance experts hovered over a new bomb. Built with roughly the same dimensions as the old two-thousand-pounder, it weighed nearly seven hundred pounds less. This resulted from its construction. Instead of a steel skin, the bombcase was made of Kevlar-reinforced cellulose—an idea borrowed from the French, who made shell casings from the naturally produced fibers—with only enough metal fittings to allow attachment of fins, or the more extensive hardware that would convert it into an "LGB," able to track in on a specific point target. It was little known that a smart-bomb is generally a mere iron bomb with the guidance equipment bolted on.

"You're not going to get fragments worth a damn," a civilian objected.

"What's the point of having a Stealth bomber," another technician asked, "if the bad guys get a radar return off the ordnance load?"

"Hmph," observed the first. "What's the point of a bomb that just pisses the other guy off?"

"Put it through his front door and he won't live long enough to get pissed, will he?"

"Hmph." But at least he knew what the bomb was actually for. It would one day hang on the ATA, the Advanced Tactical Aircraft, a carrier-based attack bomber with stealth technology built in. Finally, he thought, the Navy's getting on board that program. About time. For the moment, however, the job at hand was to see if this new bomb with a different weight and a different center of gravity would track in on a target with a standard LGB guidance pack. The bomb hoist came over and lifted the streamlined shape off its pallet. Next the operator maneuvered it under the center-line hard-point of an A-6E Intruder attack bomber.

The technicians and officers walked over to the helicopter that would take them to the bombing range. There was no rush. An hour later, safely housed in a bunker that was clearly marked, one of the civilians trained an odd-looking device at a target four miles away. The target was an old five-ton truck that the Marines had given up on, and which would now, if everything went according to plan, die a violent and spectacular death.

"Aircraft is inbound over the range. Start the music."

"Roger," the civilian replied, squeezing the trigger on the GLD. "On target."

"Aircraft reports acquisition—stand by . . ." the communicator said.

At the other end of the bunker, an officer was watching a television camera locked onto the inbound Intruder. "Breakaway. We have a nice, clean release off the ejector rack." He'd check that view later with one off an A-4 Skyhawk fighter-bomber that was flying chase on the A-6. Few people realized that the mere act of dropping a bomb off an airplane was a complex and potentially dangerous exercise. A third camera followed the bomb down.

"Fins are moving just fine. Here we go . . ."

The camera on the truck was a high-speed one. It had to be. The bomb was falling too fast for anyone to catch it on the first run-through, but by the time the crushing bass note of the detonation reached the bunker, the operator had already started rewinding the tape. The replay was done one frame at a time.

"Okay, there's the bomb." Its nose appeared forty feet over the truck. "How was it fused?"

"VT," one of the officers answered. VT stood for variable time. The bomb had a miniradar transceiver in its nose, and was programmed to explode within a fixed distance of the ground; in this case, five feet, or almost the instant it hit the truck. "Angle looks just fine."

"I thought it would work," an engineer observed quietly. He'd suggested that since the bomb was essentially a thousand pounder, the guidance equipment could be programmed for the lighter weight. Though it was slightly heavier than that, the reduced density of the cellulose bombcase made for a similar ballistic performance. "Detonation."

As with any high-speed photos of such an event, the screen flashed white, then yellow, then red, then black, as the expanding gasses from the high-explosive filler cooled in the air. Just in front of the gas was the blast wave: air compressed to a point at which it was denser than steel, moving faster than any bullet. No machine press could duplicate the effect.

"We just killed another truck." It was a wholly unnecessary observation. Roughly a quarter of the truck's mass was pounded straight down into a shallow crater, perhaps a yard deep and twenty across. The remainder was hurled laterally as shrapnel. The gross effect was not terribly different, in fact, from a large car bomb of the sort delivered by terrorists, but a hell of a lot safer for the deliverymen, one of the civilians thought.

"Damn—I didn't think it'd be that easy. You were right, Ernie, we don't even have to reprogram the seeker," a Navy commander observed. They'd just saved the Navy over a million dollars, he thought. He was wrong.

And so began something that had not quite begun and would not soon end, with many people in many places moving off in directions and on missions which they all mistakenly thought they understood. That was just as well. The future was too fearful for contemplation, and beyond the expected, illusory finish lines were things fated by the decisions made this morning—and, once decided, best unseen.

1. The King of SAR

You couldn't look at her and not be proud, Red Wegener told himself. The Coast Guard cutter *Panache* was one of a kind, a design mistake of sorts, but she was his. Her hull was painted the same gleaming white found on an iceberg—except for the orange stripe on the bow that designated the ship as part of the United States Coast Guard. Two hundred eighty feet in length, *Panache* was not a large ship, but she was his ship, the largest he'd ever commanded, and certainly the last he would ever have. Wegener was the oldest lieutenant-commander in the Coast Guard, but Wegener was The Man, the King of Search-and-Rescue missions.

His career had begun the same way many Coast Guard careers had. A young man from a Kansas wheat farm who'd never seen the sea, he'd walked into a Coast Guard recruiting station the day after graduating from high school. He hadn't wanted to face a life driving tractors and combines, and he'd sought out something as different from Kansas as he could find. The Coast Guard petty officer hadn't made much of a sales pitch, and a week later he'd begun his career with a bus ride that ended at Cape May, New Jersey. He could still remember the chief petty officer that first morning who'd told them of the Coast Guard creed. "You have to go out. You don't have to come back."

What Wegener found at Cape May was the last and best true school of seamanship in the Western world. He learned how to handle lines and tie sailor knots, how to extinguish fires, how to go into the water after a disabled or panicked boater, how to do it right the first time, every time—or risk not coming back. On graduation he was assigned to the Pacific Coast. Within a year he had his rate, Boatswain's Mate Third Class.

Very early on it was recognized that Wegener had that rarest of natural gifts, the seaman's eye. A catch-all term, it meant that his hands, eyes, and brain could act in unison to make his boat perform. Guided along by a tough old chief quartermaster, he soon had "command" of his "own" thirty-foot harbor patrol boat. For the really tricky jobs, the chief would come along to keep a close eye on the nineteen-year-old petty officer. From the first Wegener had shown the promise of someone who only needed to be shown things once. His first five years in uniform now seemed to have passed in the briefest instant as he learned his craft. Nothing really dramatic, just a succession of jobs that he'd done as the book prescribed, quickly and smoothly. By the time he'd considered and opted for re-enlistment, it was evident that when a tough job had to be done, his name was the one that came up first. Before the end of his second hitch, officers routinely asked his opinion of things. By this time he was thirty, one of the youngest chief bosun's mates in the service, and he was able to pull a few strings, one of which ended with command of *Invincible*, a forty-eight-footer which had already garnered a reputation for toughness and dependability. The stormy California coast was her home, and it was here that Wegener's name first became known outside of his service. If a fisherman or a yachtsman got into trouble,

Invincible always seemed to be there, often roller-coastering across thirty-foot seas with her crewmen held in place with ropes and safety belts—but there and ready to do the job with a red-haired chief at the wheel, an unlit briar pipe in his teeth. In that first year he saved the lives of at least fifteen people.

The number grew to fifty before he'd ended his tour of duty at the lonely station. After a couple of years, he was in command of his own station, and the holder of a title craved by all seamen—Captain—though his rate was that of Senior Chief. Located on the banks of a small stream that fed into the world's largest ocean, he ran his station as tautly as any ship, and inspecting officers had come there not so much to see how Wegener ran things as to see how things should be run.

For good or ill, Wegener's career plan had changed with one epic winter storm on the Oregon Coast. Commanding a larger rescue station now near the mouth of the Columbia River and its infamous bar, he'd received a frantic radio call from a deep-sea fisherman named *Mary-Kat:* engines and rudder disabled, being driven toward a lee shore that devoured ships. His personal flagship, the eighty-two-foot *Point Gabriel* was away from the dock in ninety seconds, her mixed crew of veterans and apprentices hooking their safety belts into place while Wegener coordinated the rescue efforts on his own radio channels.

It had been an epic battle. After a six-hour ordeal, Wegener had rescued the *Mary-Kat*'s six fishermen, but just barely, his ship assaulted by wind and furious seas. Just as the last man had been brought in, the *Mary-Kat* had grounded on a submerged rock and snapped in half.

As luck would have it, Wegener had had a reporter on board that day, a young feature writer for the *Portland Oregonian* and an experienced yachtsman, who thought he knew what there was to know about the sea. As the cutter had tunneled through the towering breakers at the Columbia bar, the reporter had vomited on his notebook, then wiped it on his Mustang suit and kept writing. The series of articles that had followed was entitled "The Angel of the Bar," and won the journalist a Pulitzer Prize for feature writing.

The following month, in Washington, the senior United States Senator from the State of Oregon, whose nephew had been a crewman on the *Mary-Kat,* wondered aloud why someone as good as Red Wegener was not an officer, and since the commandant of the Coast Guard was in that room to discuss the service's budget, it was an observation to which a four-star admiral had decided to pay heed. By the end of the week Red Wegener was commissioned as lieutenant—the senator had also observed that he was a little too old to be an ensign. Three years later he was recommended for the next available command.

There was only one problem with that, the commandant considered. He did have an available command—*Panache*—but it might seem a mixed blessing. The cutter was nearly completed. She was to have been the lead ship for a new class, but funding had been cut, the yard had gone bankrupt, and the commissioning skipper had been relieved for bungling his job. That left the Coast Guard with an unfinished ship whose engines didn't work, in an out-of-business shipyard. But Wegener was supposed to be a miracle worker, the commandant decided at his desk. To make it a fair chance, he made sure that Wegener got some good chiefs to back up the inexperienced wardroom.

His arrival at the shipyard gate had been delayed by the picket line of disgruntled workers, and by the time he'd gotten through that, he was sure things couldn't get worse. Then he'd seen what was supposed to have been a ship. It was a steel artifact, pointed at one end and blunt at the other, half painted, draped with cables, piled with crates, and generally looking like a surgical patient who'd died on the table and been left there to rot. If that hadn't been bad enough, *Panache* couldn't even be towed from her berth—the last thing a worker had done was to burn out the motor on a crane, which blocked the way.

The previous captain had already left in disgrace. The commissioning crew, assembled on the helicopter deck to receive him, looked like children forced to attend the funeral of a disliked uncle, and when Wegener tried to address them, the microphone didn't work. Somehow that broke the evil spell. He waved them toward himself with a smile and a chuckle.

"People," he'd said, "I'm Red Wegener. In six months this will be the best ship in the United States Coast Guard. In six months you will be the best crew in the United States Coast Guard. I'm not the one who's going to make that happen. You will—and I'll help a little. For right now, I'm cutting everybody as much liberty as we can stand while I get a handle on what we have to do. Have yourselves a great time. When you get back, we all go to work. Dismissed."

There was a collective "oh" from the assembled multitude, which had expected shouts and screams. The newly arrived chiefs regarded one another with raised eyebrows, and the young officers who'd been contemplating the abortion of their service careers retired to the wardroom in a state of bemused shock. Before meeting with them, Wegener took his three leading chiefs aside.

"Engines first," Wegener said.

"I can give you fifty-percent power all day long, but when you try to use the turbochargers, everything goes to hell in fifteen minutes," Chief Owens announced. "An' I don't know why." Mark Owens had been working with marine diesels for sixteen years.

"Can you get us to Curtis Bay?"

"As long as you don't mind taking an extra day, Cap'n."

Wegener dropped the first bomb. "Good—'cause we're leaving in two weeks, and we'll finish the fitting-out up there."

"It'll be a month till the new motor's ready for that crane, sir," Chief Boatswain's Mate Bob Riley observed.

"Can the crane turn?"

"Motor's burned out, Cap'n."

"When the time comes, we'll snake a line from the bow to the back end of the crane. We have seventy-five feet of water in front of us. We set the clutch on the crane and pull forward real gentle-like, and turn the crane ourselves, then back out," the captain announced. Eyes narrowed.

"Might break it," Riley observed after a moment.

"That's not my crane, but, by God, this is my ship."

Riley let out a laugh. "Goddamn, it's good to see you again, Red—excuse me, Captain Wegener!"

"Mission Number One is to get her to Baltimore for fitting-out. Let's figure out what we have to do, and take it one job at a time. I'll see you oh-seven-hundred tomorrow. Still make your own coffee, Portagee?"

"Bet your ass, sir," Chief Quartermaster Oreza replied. "I'll bring a pot."

And Wegener had been right. Twelve days later, *Panache* had indeed been ready for sea, though not much else, with crates and fittings lashed down all over the ship. Moving the crane out of the way was accomplished before dawn, lest anyone

Somebody said something. Wilcox's head turned quickly one way, then back the other. Obrecki stepped to the side and brought the shotgun down. Both men went down on their faces, dropping from view.

"Looks like a bust, sir," Ensign O'Neil noted. Wegener took one step into the wheelhouse.

"Radio!" A crewman tossed him a Motorola portable. Wegener listened but didn't make a call. Whatever his people had just found, he didn't want to distract them. Obrecki stayed with the two men while Wilcox went inside the yacht. Riley had sure as hell found something. The shotgun was definitely aimed at them, and the tension in the boy's arms radiated across the water to the cutter. The captain turned to the machine-gunner, whose weapon was still aimed at the yacht.

"Safe that gun!"

"Aye!" the sailor answered at once, and dropped his hands to point it at the sky. The officer next to him winced with embarrassment. Another lesson learned. A few words would accompany it in an hour or two. This had been a mistake with a gun.

Wilcox reappeared a moment later, with Chief Riley behind him. The bosun handed over two pairs of handcuffs to the officer, who bent down to work them. They had to be the only two aboard; Riley holstered his pistol a moment later, and Obrecki's shotgun went up to the sky again. Wegener thought he saw the youngster reset the safety. The farm boy knew his guns, all right, had learned to shoot the same way his skipper had. Why had he taken the safety off . . . ? The radio crackled just as Wegener's mind asked the question.

"Captain, this is Wilcox." The lieutenant stood to speak, and both men faced each other, a hundred yards apart.

"I'm here."

"It's a bad one, sir . . . sir, there's blood all over the place. One of 'em was scrubbing the salon down, but—it's a real mess here, sir."

"Just the two of them?"

"Affirmative. Only two people aboard. We've cuffed 'em both."

"Check again," Wegener ordered. Wilcox read the captain's mind: he stayed with the prisoners and let Chief Riley do the search. The bosun appeared three minutes later, shaking his head. His face looked pale through the binoculars, Wegener saw. What would make Bob Riley go pale?

"Just these two, sir. No ID on them. I don't think we want to do much of a search, I think—"

"Correct. I'll send you another man and leave you Obrecki. Can you get the yacht to port?"

"Sure, Captain. We got plenty of fuel."

"There's going to be a little blow tonight," Wegener warned.

"I checked the weather this morning. No sweat, sir."

"Okay, let me call this one in and get things organized. Stand by."

"Roger that. Sir, I recommend that you send the TV camera across for a permanent record to back up the stills."

"Okay, it'll be over in a few minutes."

It took half an hour for the Coast Guard base to get the FBI and DEA agreed on things. While they waited for word, the Zodiac took another crewman over with a portable TV camera and tape recorder. One of the boarding party shot off sixty frames with a Polaroid camera, while the TV recorded everything on half-inch tape. The Coast Guardsmen restarted *Empire Builder*'s engines and headed northwest for Mobile, with the cutter holding station on her portside. It was finally decided that

Wilcox and Obrecki could take the yacht back to Mobile, and that a helicopter would pick up the two ''yachtsmen'' that afternoon—weather permitting. It was a long way to the helicopter base. *Panache* was supposed to have her own helicopter, but the Coast Guard didn't have the funding to buy enough. A third seaman was landed on the yacht, and it was time to bring the prisoners back to *Panache*.

Chief Riley took the prisoners aft. Wegener watched the bosun fairly throw them into the Zodiac. Five minutes later it was hoisted aboard. The yacht headed northwest, and the cutter turned away to continue her patrol. The first man from the boarding party to reach the bridge was the seaman who'd worked the Polaroid. He handed over half a dozen of the color frames.

''The chief collected some stuff for you to look at, Cap'n. It's worse'n it looks here. Wait till you see the TV tape. It's already set up for copying.''

Wegener handed the photos back. ''Okay—it all goes into the evidence locker. You join up with the others. Have Myers set up a new tape in the VCR, and I want you all to tell the camera what you saw. You know how it goes. Let's make sure we get it all right.''

''Yes, sir!''

Riley appeared a minute later. Robert Timothy Riley was a man in the traditional pattern of the chief boatswain's mate. Six-two and over two hundred pounds, he had the hairy arms of a gorilla, the gut of a man who knew his way around a beer can, and the rumbling voice to outscream a winter gale. His oversized right hand grasped a couple of plastic food bags. His face showed that anger was now replacing the shock.

''It's a fuckin' slaughterhouse, sir. Like somebody exploded a couple cans of brown paint—'cept it ain't paint. Jesus.'' One bag came up. ''The little one was cleaning up when we pulled 'em over. There's a trash can in the saloon with maybe a half dozen cartridge cases. I pulled these two off the rug—just like they taught us, Cap'n. Picked 'em up with my ball-point and shuffled 'em into the baggie. Two guns I left aboard. I bagged them, too. That ain't the worst of it.''

The next baggie contained a small, framed photograph. It had to be the yacht's owner and his family. The baggie after that contained a . . .

''Found it under a table. Rape, too. She must've been havin' her period, but they didn't let that stop 'em. Maybe just the wife. Maybe the little girl, too. In the galley there's some butcher knives, all bloodied up. I figure they carved the bodies up and tossed 'em over the side. These four people are shark-shit now.''

''Drugs?''

''Twenty or so keys of white powder stowed in the crew's quarters. Some marijuana, too, but that just looks like a personal stash.'' Riley shrugged. ''I didn't even bother using the test kit, sir. Don't matter. This is straight piracy-and-murder. I saw one bullet hole in the deck, a through-and-through. Red, I ain't seen nothing like this in my whole life. Like something in a movie, but worse.'' He let out a long breath. ''You have to have been there, sir.''

''What do we know about the prisoners?''

''Nothing. They ain't done nothing more'n grunt, leastways not when I was around. No ID on them, and I didn't want to go messing around things looking for passports an' stuff. Figured I'd leave that for the real cops. The wheelhouse is clean. So's one of the heads. Mr. Wilcox won't have much trouble taking her back, and I heard him tell Obrecki and Brown not to touch anything. Plenty of fuel aboard, he can run her at full speed. He'll have her in Mobile 'fore midnight if the weather holds off. Nice boat.'' Another shrug.

"Bring 'em up here," Wegener said after a moment.

"Aye aye." Riley went aft.

Wegener filled his pipe, then had to remember where he'd left his matches. The world had changed while he'd been off doing other things, and Wegener didn't like it. It was dangerous enough out here. Wind and wave were as deadly an enemy as man needed. The sea was always waiting for her chance. It didn't matter how good you thought you were; you only had to forget once, just once, that you could never trust her. Wegener was a man who never forgot, and devoted his life to protecting those who had. Remembering that one hazard, and protecting those who forgot, had given him a full and satisfying life. He liked being the guardian angel in the snow-white boat. You were never lost if Red Wegener was around. You always had a chance, a good chance, that he could reach into the wet, stormy grave and pull you out with his bare hands . . . but sharks were feasting on four people now. Wegener loved the sea for all her moods, but sharks were something to loathe, and the thought that they were now eating people that he might have saved . . . four people who'd forgotten that not all sharks live in the sea, Wegener told himself. That's what had changed. Piracy. He shook his head. That's what you called it on the water. Piracy. Something that Errol Flynn had made movies about in Wegener's boyhood. Something that had ended two centuries earlier. Piracy and murder, the part that the movies had usually left out. Piracy and murder and rape, each of them a capital offense in the old days. . . .

"Stand up straight!" Riley snarled. He had both by the arm. Both were still cuffed, and Riley's hands kept them from straying. Chief Oreza had come along to keep an eye on things.

Both were in their mid-twenties, both were thin. One was tall, about six feet, and arrogant, which struck the captain as odd. He had to know the trouble he was in, didn't he? His dark eyes burned at Wegener, who regarded the younger man dispassionately from behind his pipe. There was something odd about his eyes, but Wegener didn't know what it was.

"What's your name?" the captain asked. There was no reply. "You have to tell me your name," Wegener pointed out quietly.

Then something very unusual happened. The tall one spat on Wegener's shirt. There was a strangely long fragment of time in which the captain refused to believe what had happened, his face not even showing surprise. Riley was the first to react to the blasphemy.

"You son of a bitch!" The bosun lifted the prisoner up like a rag doll, spinning him in the air and smashing him down on the bridge rail. The young man landed on his belt, and for a second it seemed that he'd break in half. The air whooshed out of his mouth, and his legs kicked, trying to find the deck before he dropped into the water.

"Christ, Bob!" Wegener managed to say as Riley picked him back up. The bosun spun him around, his left hand clamped on the man's throat as he lifted him clear of the deck with one arm. "Put him down, Riley!"

If nothing else, Riley had broken through the arrogance. For a moment there was genuine fear in those eyes as the prisoner fought for breath. Oreza had the other one on the deck already. Riley dropped his man beside him. The pirate—Wegener was already thinking of him in those terms—pitched forward until his forehead touched the deck. He gagged and struggled for breath while Chief Riley, just as pale, rediscovered his self-control.

"Sorry, Captain. Guess I just lost it for a second." The bosun made it clear that he was apologizing only for embarrassing his commanding officer.

"Brig," Wegener said. Riley led both aft.

"Damn." Oreza observed quietly. The quartermaster fished out his handkerchief and wiped his captain's shirt. "Jesus, Red, what's the world comin' to?"

"I don't know, Portagee. I think we're both too old to answer that one." Wegener finally found his matches and managed to light his pipe. He stared out at the sea for several seconds before finding the right words. "When I joined up I got broke in by an old chief who told stories about Prohibition. Nothing nasty like this—he made it all sound like a great big game."

"Maybe people were more civilized back then," Oreza thought.

"More likely you couldn't carry a million bucks' worth of booze on a motorboat. Didn't you ever watch The Untouchables'? The gang wars they had back then were as nasty as the ones we read about now. Maybe worse. Hell, I don't know. I didn't join up to be a cop, Chief."

"Me neither, Cap'n." Oreza grunted. "We went an' got old, and the world went an' changed on us. One thing I wish didn't change, though."

"What's that, Portagee?"

The master chief quartermaster turned to look at his commanding officer. "Something I picked up at New London a few years back. I used to sit in on some classes when I had nothing better to do. In the old days when they caught a couple of pirates, they had the option of doing a court-martial on the spot and settlin' things right then an' there—and you know something? It worked." Oreza grunted again. "I s'pose that's why they stopped doin' it that way."

"Give 'em a fair trial—then hang 'em?"

"Hell, why not, sir?"

"That's not the way we do things anymore. We're civilized now."

"Yeah, civilized." Oreza opened the door to the wheelhouse. "I can tell. I seen the pictures."

Wegener smiled, then wondered why. His pipe had gone out. He wondered why he didn't just quit entirely as he fished for his matches again, but the pipe was part of the image. The old man of the sea. He'd gotten old, all right, Wegener thought. A puff of wind caught the match as he tried to toss it, dropping it on the deck. How did you ever forget to check the wind? he asked himself as he bent down to retrieve it.

There was a pack of cigarettes there, halfway out the scupper. Wegener was a fanatic on ship-cleanliness and was ready to snarl at whoever had tossed the empty pack when he realized that it hadn't come from one of his crewmen. The name on the pack was "Calvert," and that, he remembered vaguely, was a Latin American brand-name from a U.S. tobacco company. It was a hard pack, with a flip-top, and out of simple curiosity he opened it.

They weren't cigarettes. At least, they weren't tobacco cigarettes. Wegener fished one out. They weren't hand-rolled, but neither were they as neatly manufactured as something from a real American cancer factory. The captain smiled in spite of himself. Some clever entrepreneur had come up with a cute way of disguising—joints, wasn't it?—as real cigarettes. Or maybe it was just more convenient to carry them this way. It must have pitched out of his shirt when Riley flipped him around, Wegener realized belatedly. He closed the pack and pocketed it. He'd turn it over to the evidence locker when he got a chance. Oreza returned.

"Weather update. That squall line'll be here no later'n twenty-one hundred. The squalls are upgraded some. We can expect gusts up to forty knots. Gonna be a fair blow, sir."

"Any problem for Wilcox and the yacht?" There was still time to recall him.

"Shouldn't be, sir. It turned south. A high-pressure system is heading down from Tennessee. Mr. Wilcox oughta have it pretty smooth all the way in, Cap'n, but it might be a little dicey for the helicopter. They didn't plan to get it to us until eighteen hundred, and that's cutting it a little close. They'll be bucking the front edge of the line on the way back."

"What about tomorrow?"

"Supposed to clear off about dawn, then the high-pressure system takes over. We're in for some rollin' tonight, but then we got four days of good weather." Oreza didn't actually voice his recommendation. He didn't have to. The two old pros communicated with glances.

Wegener nodded agreement. "Advise Mobile to put the pickup off until noon tomorrow."

"Aye aye, Cap'n. No sense risking a helicopter to haul garbage."

"Right on that, Portagee. Make sure Wilcox gets the word on the weather in case that system changes course." Wegener checked his watch. "Time for me to get my paperwork done."

"Pretty full day already, Red."

"True enough."

Wegener's stateroom was the largest aboard, of course, and the only private accommodation aboard, since privacy and loneliness were the traditional luxuries accorded a skipper. But *Panache* wasn't a cruiser, and Wegener's room was barely over a hundred square feet, albeit with a private head, which on any ship was something worth fighting for. Throughout his Coast Guard career, paperwork was something Wegener had avoided whenever possible. He had an executive officer, a bright young lieutenant whom the captain stuck with as much of it as his conscience could justify. That left him with two or three hours' worth per day. The captain attacked it with the enthusiasm of a man on his way to a hanging. Half an hour later he realized that it seemed harder than usual. The murders were pulling at his consciousness. Murder at sea, he thought, as he looked at the porthole on the starboard bulkhead. It wasn't unknown, of course. He'd heard of a few during his thirty years, though he'd never been directly involved. There had been a case off the Oregon coast when a crewman had gone berserk and nearly killed a mate—turned out that the poor guy had developed a brain tumor and he'd later died from it, Red remembered. *Point Gabriel* had gone out and collected the man, already hog-tied and sedated. That was the extent of Wegener's experience with violence at sea. At least the man-made kind. The sea was dangerous enough without the need for that sort of thing. The thought came back to him like the recurring theme of a song. He tried to get back to his work, but failed.

Wegener frowned at his own indecision. Whether he liked paperwork or not, it was part of the job. He relit the pipe in the hope that it would aid his concentration. That didn't work either. The captain muttered a curse at himself, partly in amusement, partly in annoyance, as he walked into his head for a drink of water. The paperwork still beckoned. He looked at himself in the mirror and realized that he needed a shave. And the paperwork wasn't getting done.

"You're getting old, Red," he told the face in the mirror. "Old and senile."

He decided that he had to shave. He did it in the old-fashioned way, with a shaving cup and brush, the disposable razor his only concession to modernity. He had his face lathered and halfway shaved when someone knocked at the door.

"Come!" It opened to reveal Chief Riley.

"Sorry, Cap'n, didn't know you were—"

"No problem, Bob, what's up?"

"Sir, I got the first-draft of the boarding report. Figured you'd want to go over it. We got everyone's statement on tape, audio, and TV. Myers made a copy of the tape from the boarding. The original's in with the evidence, in a lockbox inside the classified-materials safe, as per orders. I got the copy if you wanna see it."

"Okay, just leave it. Anything from our guests?"

"No, sir. Turned into a pretty day outside."

"And me stuck with all this damned paper."

"A chief may work from sun to sun, but the skipper's work is never done," Riley observed.

"You're not supposed to pick on your commanding officer, Master Chief." Wegener managed to stop himself from laughing only because he still had the razor to his throat.

"I humbly beg the captain's pardon. And, by your leave, sir, I also have work to do."

"The kid we had on the fifty-cal this morning was part of the deck division. He needs a talk about safety. He was slow taking his gun off the yacht this morning. Don't tear his head all the way off," Wegener said as he finished shaving. "I'll talk to Mr. Peterson myself."

"We sure don't need people fucking around with those things. I'll talk with the lad, sir, right after I do my walk-around."

"I'm going to do one after lunch—we have some weather coming in tonight."

"Portagee told me. We'll have everything lashed down tight."

"See you later, Bob."

"Aye." Riley withdrew.

Wegener stowed his shaving gear and went back to his desk. The preliminary draft of the boarding and arrest report was on the top of his pile. The full version was being typed now, but he always liked to see the first version. It was generally the most accurate. Wegener scanned it as he sipped at some cold coffee. The Polaroid shots were tucked into pockets on a plastic page. They hadn't gotten any better. Neither had the paperwork. He decided to slip the videotape into his personal VCR and view it before lunch.

The quality of the tape was several steps down from anything that could be called professional. Holding the camera still on a rolling yacht was nearly impossible, and there hadn't been enough light for decent picture quality. For all that, it was disturbing. The sound caught snippets of conversations, and the screen occasionally flared when the Polaroid's flash went off.

It was plain that four people had died aboard *Empire Builder,* and all they had left behind were bloodstains. It didn't seem very much of a legacy, but imagination supplied the rest. The bunk in what had probably been the son's cabin was sodden with blood—a lot of it—at the top end of the bed. Head shot. Three other sets of bloodstains decorated the main salon. It was the part of the yacht with the most space, the place where the entertainment had gone on. *Entertainment,* Wegener thought. Three sets of bloodstains. Two close together, one distant. The man had an attractive wife, and a daughter of thirteen . . . they'd made him watch, hadn't they?

"Jesus," Wegener breathed. That had to be it, didn't it? *They made him watch, and then they killed them all . . . carved up the bodies and tossed them over the side.*

"Bastards."

2. Creatures of the Night

The name on this passport said J. T. Williams, but he had quite a few passports. His current cover was as a representative for an American pharmaceuticals firm, and he could give a lengthy discourse on various synthetic antibiotics. He could similarly discuss the ins and outs of the heavy-equipment business as a special field representative for Caterpillar Tractor, and had two other "legends" that he could switch in and out of as easily as he changed his clothes. His name was not Williams. He was known in CIA's Operations Directorate as Clark, but his name wasn't Clark either, even though that was the name under which he lived and raised his family. Mainly he was an instructor at CIA's school for field officers, known as "The Farm," but he was an instructor because he was pretty good at what he did, and for the same reason he often returned to the field.

Clark was a solidly built man, over six feet tall, with a full head of black hair and a lantern jaw that hinted at his ancestry, along with the blue eyes that twinkled when he wanted them to, and burned when he did not. Though well over forty, Clark did not have the usual waistline flab that went along with a desk job, and his shoulders spoke volumes about his exercise program. For all that, in an age of attention to physical fitness he was unremarkable enough, save for one distinguishing mark. On his forearm was the tattoo of a grinning red seal. He ought to have had it removed, but sentiment did not allow it. The seal was part of the heritage he'd once chosen for himself. When asked about it during a flight, he'd reply, honestly, that he'd once been in the Navy, then go on to lie about how the Navy had financed his college education in pharmaceuticals, mechanical engineering, or some other field. Clark actually had no college or graduate degree, though he'd accumulated enough special knowledge along the way to qualify for a half dozen of them. The lack of a degree would have—should have—disqualified him for the position which he held in the Agency, but Clark had a skill that is curiously rare in most of the Western intelligence agencies. The need for it was also rare, but the need *was* occasionally real, and a senior CIA official had once recognized that someone like Clark was useful to have on the payroll. That he'd blossomed into a very effective field officer—mainly for special, short, dangerous jobs—was all the better for the Agency. Clark was something of a legend, though only a handful of people at Langley knew why. There was only one Mr. Clark.

"What brings you to our country, Señor Williams?" the immigration official asked.

"Business. And I'm hoping to do a little fishing before I go home," Clark replied in Spanish. He was fluent in six languages, and could pass for a native with three of them.

"Your Spanish is excellent."

"Thank you. I grew up in Costa Rica," Clark lied. He was particularly good at that, too. "My father worked there for years."

"Yes, I can tell. Welcome to Colombia."

Clark went off to collect his bags. The air was thin here, he noted. His daily jogging helped him with that, but he reminded himself to wait a few days before he tried anything really strenuous. It was his first time in this country, but something told him that it wouldn't be the last. All the big ones started with reconnaissance. That was his current mission. Exactly what he was supposed to recon told him what the real mission would probably be. He'd done such things before, Clark told himself. In fact, one such mission was the reason that CIA had picked him up, changed his name, and given him the life that he'd led for nearly twenty years.

One of the singular things about Colombia was that the country actually allowed people to bring firearms in with very little in the way of hassle. Clark had not bothered this time. He wondered if the next time might be a little different. He knew that he couldn't work through the chief of station for that. After all, the chief of station didn't even know that he was here. Clark wondered why, but shrugged it off. That didn't concern him. The mission did.

The United States Army had reinstituted the idea of the Infantry Division (Light) only a few years before. The units had not been all that hard to make. It was simply a matter of selecting an Infantry Division (Mechanized) and removing all of its (Mechanized) equipment. What then remained behind was an organization of roughly 10,500 people whose TOE (Table of Organization and Equipment) was even lighter than that of an airborne division, traditionally the lightest of them all, and therefore able to be air-transported by a *mere* five hundred flights of the Air Force's Military Airlift Command. But the light infantry divisions, or "LIDs" as they came to be known, were not as useless as the casual observer might imagine, however. Far from it.

In creating the "light-fighters," the Army had decided to return to the timeless basics of history. Any thinking warrior will testify that there are two kinds of fighters: the infantry, and those who in one way or another support the infantry. More than anything else, the LIDs were postgraduate institutions for advanced infantry skills. Here was where the Army grew its sergeants the old-fashioned way. In recognizing this, the Army had carefully assigned some of its best officers to command them. The colonels commanding the brigades, and the generals commanding the divisions, were veterans of Vietnam whose memories of that bitter conflict included admiration for their enemies—most especially the way in which the Viet Cong and NVA had converted their lack of equipment and firepower into an asset. There was no reason, the Army's thinkers decided, that American soldiers should not have the same degree of skill in fieldcraft that Vo Nguyen Giap's soldiers had developed; better still that those skills should be mated to America's traditional fascination with equipment and firepower. What had resulted were four elite divisions, the 7th in the green hills of Fort Ord, California, the 10th Mountain at Fort Drum, New York, the 25th at Schofield Barracks, Hawaii, and the 6th at Fort Wainwright, Alaska. Perversely, each had problems holding on to its sergeants and company-grade officers, but that was part of the overall plan. Light-fighters live a strenuous life, and on reaching thirty even the best of them would think longingly of being able to ride to battle in a helicopter or an armored personnel carrier, and maybe being able to spend a reasonable amount of time with their young wives and children instead of climbing hills. Thus the best of them, the ones that stayed and completed the difficult NCO schools that each division ran, having learned that sergeants must occasionally act without their lieutenants' direction, then joined the heavy formations that comprised the rest of the Army, bringing with them skills that they'd never quite forget. The LIDs were, in short, factory institutions, where the Army built sergeants with exceptional leadership ability and mastery of the unchanging truths of warfare—it always came down to a few people with muddy boots and smelly uniforms who could use the land and the night as allies to visit death on their fellowmen.

Staff Sergeant Domingo Chavez was one of these. Known as "Ding" by his squad, he was twenty-six. Already a nine-year veteran, he'd begun as a gang kid in Los Angeles whose basic common sense had overcome his ineffectual education—he'd decided that there was no future in the *Bandidos* when a close friend had died in a drive-by shooting whose purpose he'd never quite figured out. The following Monday morning he'd taken the bus to the nearest Army Recruiting Office after the Marines had turned him down. Despite his near illiteracy, the recruiting sergeant had signed him up in a moment—his quota had been short, and the kid had expressed a willingness to go infantry, thus fulfilling two blank spots on the sergeant's monthly reporting sheet. Most of all, the youngster wanted to go right in. It could not have been better for the recruiter.

Chavez hadn't had many ideas what military service would be like, and most of those had turned out to be wrong. After losing his hair and a rat-faced beard, he'd learned that toughness is worthless without discipline, and that the Army doesn't tolerate insolence. That lesson had come behind a white-painted barracks at the hands of a drill sergeant whose face was as black as a jungle night. But Chavez's life had never known an easy lesson; as a result he hadn't learned to resent the hard ones. Having discovered that the Army was also a hierarchy with strict hierarchical rules, he stayed within them and gradually turned into an above-average recruit. Former gang kid that he was, he'd already known about camaraderie and teamwork, and redirecting these traits into positive directions had come easily enough. By the time basic training had ended, his small frame was as lean and taut as a steel cable, his physical appearance was something in which he took inordinate pride, and he was already well on his way to mastering every weapon that an infantryman can carry. Where else, he asked himself once a day, do they give you a machine gun and pay you to shoot it?

But soldiers are grown, not born. Chavez's first posting was to Korea, where he learned about hills, and just how deadly enemy gangs could be, since duty on the DMZ has never been anything that one might call safe. Discipline, he learned there once and for all, had a real purpose. It kept you alive. A small team of North Korean infiltrators had picked a rainy night to go through his unit's piece of the line for purposes known only to their commanders. On the way they'd stumbled on an unmarked listening post whose two American occupants had decided to sleep through the night, and never awoke. ROK units had later intercepted and killed the invaders, but Chavez was the one who'd discovered the men from his own platoon, throats cut in the same way he'd seen in his own neighborhood. Soldiering, he'd decided then and there, was a serious business, and one which he wanted to master. The platoon sergeant noticed first, then the lieutenant. Chavez paid attention to lectures, even trying to take notes. On realizing his inability to read and write beyond things he'd carefully memorized in advance, the platoon leader had gotten the young PFC help. Working hard on his own time, before the end of the year Chavez had passed a high-school equivalency test—on his first try! he told everyone who would listen that night—and made Specialist Fourth Class, which earned him an extra $58.50 per month. His lieutenant didn't fully understand, though the platoon sergeant did, that Domingo Chavez had been forever changed by that combination of events. Though he'd always had the Latino's deep pride, part of the eighteen-year-old soldier now understood that he had truly done something to be proud about. For this he deemed himself to be in the Army's debt, and with the deep sense of personal honor which was also part of his cultural heritage, it was a debt that he would forever after work to repay.

Some things never left. He cultivated physical toughness. Part of that came from his small size—just five-eight—but he also came to understand that the real world was not a football field: the tough ones who made the long haul were most often the compact, lean fighters. Chavez came to love running, and enjoyed a good sweat. Because of this, assignment to the 7th Infantry Division (Light) was almost inevitable. Though based at Fort Ord, near Monterey on the California coast, the 7th trains farther down the coast at Hunter-Liggett Military Reservation, once the sprawling rancho of the Hearst family. A place of magnificent green hills in the moist winters, Hunter-Liggett becomes a blistering moonscape in the California summer, a place of steep, topless hills, gnarled, shapeless trees, and grass that crumbles to dust under one's boots. For Chavez it was home. He arrived as a brand-new buck sergeant E-5, and was immediately sent to the division's two-week Combat Leaders Course, a prep school for squad sergeants that also paved the way for his entry into Ranger School at Fort Benning, Georgia. On his return from that most rigorous of Army training courses, Chavez was leaner and more confident than ever. His return to Fort Ord coincided with the arrival of a new "cohort" of recruits for his battalion. Ding Chavez was assigned to command a squad of slick-sleeved privates fresh from Advanced Infantry Training. It was the first payback time for the young sergeant. The Army had invested considerable time and training in him, and now it was time for him to pass it along to nine raw recruits—and also time for the Army to see if Chavez had the stuff that leaders are made of. He took command of his squad as a stepfather of a large and unruly family faces his newly acquired children. He wanted them to turn out properly because they were his, and because they were his, he was damned sure going to see that they did.

At Fort Ord, he'd also learned the real art of soldiering, for infantry tactics are precisely that for the light-fighters—an art form. Assigned to Bravo Company, 3rd Battalion of the 17th Infantry Regiment, whose somewhat ambitious motto was "Ninja! We Own the Night!" Chavez went into the field with his face coated in camouflage paint—in the 7th LID even the helicopter pilots wear camouflage paint—and learned his profession in full even while he taught his men. Most of all, he came to love the night. Chavez learned to move himself and his squad through cover as quietly as a whispering breeze. The objective of such missions was generally the same. Unable to match a heavy formation force-on-force, Chavez trained to do the close, nasty work that has always characterized light infantrymen: raids and ambushes, infiltration and intelligence gathering. Stealth was their means, and surprise was their tool, to appear where least expected, to strike with close-quarter ferocity, then to escape into the darkness before the other side could react. Such things had been tried on Americans once, and it was only fair that Americans should learn to return the favor. All in all, SSG Domingo Chavez was a man whom the Apaches or the Viet Cong would have recognized as one of their own—or one of their most dangerous enemies.

"Hey, Ding!" the platoon sergeant called. "The ell-tee wants you."

It had been a long one at Hunter-Liggett, ending at the dawn now two hours old. The exercise had lasted nearly nine days, and even Chavez was feeling it. He wasn't seventeen anymore, his legs were telling him with some amusement. At least it was his last such job with the Ninjas. He was rotating out, and his next assignment was to be a drill sergeant with the Army's basic-training school at Fort Benning, Georgia. Chavez was immensely proud of that. The Army thought enough of him that he would now be an example to young recruits. The sergeant got to his feet, but before walking over to where the lieutenant was, he reached into his pocket and took out a throwing star. Ever since the colonel had taken to calling his men Ninjas, the nasty little steel projectiles had become *de rigueur* to the men—somewhat to the concern of the powers-that-were. But there was always a little slack cut for the good ones, and Chavez was one of these. He flipped the star with a deceptively powerful flick of the wrist and buried it an inch deep in a tree fifteen feet away. He collected it on the way to see the boss.

"Yes, sir!" Chavez said, standing at attention.

"At ease, Sergeant," Lieutenant Jackson said. He was sitting against a tree to take the strain off his blistered feet. A West Point graduate and only twenty-three, he was learning how hard it could be to keep up with the soldiers he was supposed to lead. "Got a call. They need you back at headquarters. Something to do with the paperwork on your transfer. You can go in on a resupply flight out of battalion trains. The chopper'll be down there in an hour. Nice work last night, by the way. I'm going to be sorry to lose you, Ding."

"Thank you, sir." Jackson wasn't bad for a young officer, Chavez thought. Green, of course, but he tried pretty hard and learned fast. He saluted the younger man snappily.

"You take care of yourself, Sergeant." Jackson rose to return it properly.

"We own the night, sir!" Chavez replied in the manner of the Ninjas, 3rd Battalion, 17th Infantry. Twenty-five minutes later he climbed aboard a Sikorsky UH-60A Blackhawk helicopter for the fifty-minute ride back to Ord. The battalion sergeant-major handed him a message as he got aboard. Chavez had an hour to get cleaned up before appearing at the divisional G-1 or personnel office. It took a long shower to erase the salt and "war paint," but he managed to arrive early in his best set of BDU camouflage fatigues.

"Hey, Ding," said another staff sergeant, who was working in G-1 while his broken leg healed. "The man's waiting for you in the conference room, end of the hall on the second floor."

"What's it all about, Charlie?"

"Damned if I know. Some colonel asked to see you is all."

"Damn—I need a haircut, too," Chavez muttered as he trotted up the wooden stairs. His boots could have used a little more work also. Hell of a way to appear before some friggin' colonel, but then Chavez was entitled to a little more warning than he'd been given. That was one of the nice things about the Army, the sergeant thought. The rules applied to everyone. He knocked on the proper door, too tired to be worried. He wouldn't be around much longer, after all. His orders for Fort Benning were already cut, and he was wondering what the loose womenfolk in

Georgia were like. He'd just broken up with a steady girlfriend. Maybe the more stable life-style that went with a drill sergeant would allow him to—

"Come!" a voice boomed in reply to his knock.

The colonel was sitting behind a cheap wooden desk. He was dressed in a black sweater over a lime-green shirt, and had a name tag that said SMITH. Ding came to attention.

"Staff Sergeant Domingo Chavez reporting as ordered, sir."

"Okay, relax and sit down, Sergeant. I know you've been on the go for a while. There's coffee in the corner if you want."

"No, thank you, sir." Chavez sat down and almost relaxed a bit until he saw his personnel jacket lying on the desk. Colonel Smith picked it up and flipped it open. Having someone rip through your personnel file was usually worrisome, but the colonel looked up with a relaxed smile. Chavez noticed that Colonel Smith had no unit crest above his name tag, not even the hourglass-bayonet symbol of the 7th LID. Where did he come from? Who was this guy?

"This looks pretty damned good, Sergeant. I'd say you're a good bet for E-7 in two or three years. You've been down south, too, I see. Three times, is it?"

"Yes, sir. We been to Honduras twice and Panama once."

"Did well all three times. It says here your Spanish is excellent."

"It's what I was raised with, sir." As his accent told everyone he met. He wanted to know what this was all about, but staff sergeants do not ask such questions of bird-colonels. He got his wish in any case.

"Sergeant, we're putting a special group together, and we want you to be part of it."

"Sir, I got new orders, and—"

"I know that. We're looking for people with a combination of good language skills and—hell, we're looking for the best light-fighters we can find. Everything I see about you says you're one of the best in the division." There were other criteria that "Colonel Smith" did not go into. Chavez was unmarried. His parents were both dead. He had no close family members, or at least was not known to write or call anyone with great frequency. He didn't fit the profile perfectly—there were some other things that they wished he had—but everything they saw looked good. "It's a special job. It might be a little dangerous, but probably not. We're not sure yet. It'll last a couple of months, six at the most. At the end, you make E-7 and have your choice of assignments."

"What's this special job all about, sir?" Chavez asked brightly. The chance of making E-7 a year or two early got his full and immediate attention.

"That I can't say, Sergeant. I don't like recruiting people blind," "Colonel Smith" lied, "but I have my orders, too. I can say that you'll be sent somewhere east of here for intensive training. Maybe it'll stop there, maybe not. If it does stop there, the deal holds on the promotion and the assignment. If it goes farther, you will probably be sent somewhere to exercise your special kind of skills. Okay, I *can* say that we're talking some covert intelligence-gathering. We're not sending you to Nicaragua or anything like that. You're not being sent off to fight a secret war." That statement was technically not a lie. "Smith" didn't know exactly what the job was all about, and he wasn't being encouraged to speculate. He'd been given the mission requirements, and his nearly completed job was to find people who could do it—whatever the hell it was.

"Anyway, that's all I can say. What we have discussed to this point does not leave the room—meaning that you do not discuss it with anybody without my authorization, understood?'' the man said forcefully.

''Understood, sir!''

''Sergeant, we've invested a lot of time and money in you. It's payback time. The country needs you. We need what you know. We need what you know how to do.''

Put that way, Chavez knew he had little choice. ''Smith'' knew that, too. The young man waited about five seconds before answering, which was less than expected.

''When do I leave, sir?''

Smith was all business now. He pulled a large manila envelope from the desk's center drawer. CHAVEZ was scrawled on it in Magic Marker. ''Sergeant, I've taken the liberty of doing a few things for you. In here are your medical and finance records. I've already arranged to clear you through most of the post agencies. I've also scratched in a limited power of attorney form so that you can have somebody ship your personal effects—where 'to' shows on the form.''

Chavez nodded, though his head swam slightly. Whoever this Colonel Smith was, he had some serious horsepower to run paperwork through the Army's legendary bureaucracy so quickly. Clearing post ordinarily took five days of sitting and waiting. He took the envelope from the colonel's hand.

''Pack your gear and be back here at eighteen hundred. Don't bother getting a haircut or anything. You're going to let it grow for a while. I'll handle things with the people downstairs. And remember: you do not discuss this with anybody. If someone asks, you got orders to report to Fort Benning a little early. That's your story, and I expect you to stick to it.'' ''Colonel Smith'' stood and extended his hand while he told another lie, mixed with some truth. ''You did the right thing. I knew we could count on you, Chavez.''

''We own the night, sir!''

''Dismissed.''

''Colonel Smith'' replaced the personnel folder in his briefcase. That was that. Most of the men were already on their way to Colorado. Chavez was one of the last. ''Smith'' wondered how things would work out. His real name was Edgar Jeffries, and he had once been an Army officer, long since seconded to, then hired by, the Central Intelligence Agency. He found himself hoping that things would go as planned, but he'd been with the Agency too long to place much store in that train of thought. This wasn't his first recruiting job. Not all of them had gone well, and fewer still had gone as planned. On the other hand, Chavez and all the rest had volunteered to join the country's military service, had voluntarily re-enlisted, and had voluntarily decided to accept his invitation to do something new and different. The world was a dangerous place, and these forty men had made an informed decision to join one of its more dangerous professions. It was some consolation to him, and because Edgar Jeffries still had a conscience, he needed the consolation.

''Good luck, Sarge,'' he said quietly to himself.

Chavez had a busy day. First changing into civilian clothes, he washed his field uniform and gear, then assembled all of the equipment which he'd be leaving behind. He had to clean the equipment also, because you were supposed to give it back better than you got it, as Sergeant First Class Mitchell expected. By the time the rest of the platoon arrived from Hunter-Liggett at 1300, his tasks were well underway. The activity was noted by the returning NCOs, and soon the platoon sergeant appeared.

"Why you packed up, Ding?" Mitchell asked.

"They need me at Benning early—that's, uh, that's why they flew me back this morning."

"The lieutenant know?"

"They musta told him—well, they musta told the company clerk, right?" Chavez was a little embarrassed. Lying to his platoon sergeant bothered him. Bob Mitchell had been a friend and a teacher for his nearly four years at Fort Ord. But his orders came from a colonel.

"Ding, one thing you still have to learn about is paperwork. Come on, son. The ell-tee's in his office."

Lieutenant Timothy Washington Jackson, Infantry, hadn't cleaned up yet, but was almost ready to leave for his place in the bachelor officers' quarters, called the BOQ, or merely The Q. He looked up to see two of his senior NCOs.

"Lieutenant, Chavez here's got orders to skip off to Fort Benning PDQ. They're picking him up this evening."

"So I hear. I just got a call from the battalion sergeant major. What the hell gives? We don't do things this way," Jackson growled. "How long?"

"Eighteen hundred, sir."

"Super. I gotta go and get cleaned up before I see the S-3. Sergeant Mitchell, can you handle the equipment records?"

"Yes, sir."

"Okay, I'll be back at seventeen hundred to finish things up. Chavez, don't leave before I get back."

The rest of the afternoon passed quickly. Mitchell was willing to handle shipping—there wasn't that much to ship—and squared the younger man away, with a few lessons tossed in on the better ways to expedite paperwork. Lieutenant Jackson was back on time, and brought both men into his office. It was quiet. Most of the platoon was already gone for a well-deserved night on the town.

"Ding, I ain't ready to lose you yet. We haven't decided who takes the squad over. You were talking about Ozkanian, Sergeant Mitchell?"

"That's right, sir. What d'you think, Chavez?"

"He's about ready," Ding judged.

"Okay, we'll give Corporal Ozkanian a shot at it. You're lucky, Chavez," Lieutenant Jackson said next. "I got caught up on all my paperwork right before we went into the field. You want me to go over your evaluation with you?"

"Just the high spots'll be fine, sir." Chavez grinned. The lieutenant liked him, and Chavez knew it.

"Okay, I say you're damned good, which you are. Sorry to lose you this quick. You going to need a lift?" Jackson asked.

"No problem, sir. I was planning to walk over."

"Crap. We all did enough walking last night. Load your stuff into my car." The lieutenant tossed him the keys. "Anything else, Sergeant Mitchell?"

"Nothin' that can't wait until Monday, sir. I figure we earned ourselves a nice restful weekend."

"As always, your judgment is impeccable. My brother's in town, and I'm gone till 0600 Monday morning."

"Roger that. Have a good one, sir."

Chavez didn't have much in the way of personal gear, and, unusually, didn't even have a car. In fact he was saving his money to buy a Chevy Corvette, the car that had fascinated him since boyhood, and was within five thousand dollars of being able to pay cash for one. His baggage was already loaded into the back of Jackson's Honda CVCC when the lieutenant emerged from the barracks. Chavez tossed him the keys back.

"Where they picking you up?"

"Division G-1 is what the man said, sir."

"Why there? Why not Martinez Hall?" Jackson asked as he started up. Martinez was the customary processing facility.

"Lieutenant, I just go where they tell me."

Jackson laughed at that. "Don't we all?"

It only took a couple of minutes. Jackson dropped Chavez off with a handshake. There were five other soldiers there, the lieutenant noted briefly. All sergeants, which was something of a surprise. All looked hispanic, too. He knew two of them. León was in Ben Tucker's platoon, 4th of the 17th, and Muñoz was with divisional recon. Those were two good ones, too. Lieutenant Jackson shrugged it off as he drove away.

3. The *Panache* Procedure

Wegener's inspection came before lunch instead of after. There wasn't much to complain about. Chief Riley had been there first. Except for some paint cans and brushes that were actually in use—painting a ship is something that never begins or ends; it just is—there was no loose gear in view. The ship's gun was properly trained in and secured, as were the anchor chains. Lifelines were taut, and hatches dogged down tight in anticipation of the evening storm. A few off-duty sailors lounged here and there, reading or sunning themselves. These leapt to their feet at Riley's rumbling "Attention on deck!" One third-class was reading a *Playboy*. Wegener informed him good-naturedly that he'd have to watch out for that on the next cruise, as three female crewmen were scheduled to join the ship in less than two weeks' time, and it wouldn't do to offend their sensibilities. That *Panache* had none aboard at the moment was a statistical anomaly, and the change didn't trouble the captain greatly, though his senior chiefs were skeptical to say the least. There was also the problem of who got to use the plumbing when, since female crewmen had not been anticipated by the cutter's designers. It was the first time today that Red Wegener had had something to smile about. The problems of taking women to sea . . . and the smile died again as the images from the videotape came back to him. Those two women—no, a woman and a little girl—had gone to sea, too, hadn't they . . . ?

It just wouldn't go away.

Wegener looked around and saw the questions forming on the faces of the men around him. The skipper was pissed about something. They didn't know what it was, but knew that you don't want to be around the captain when he was mad about something. Then they saw his face change. The captain had just asked himself a question, they thought.

"Looks all right to me, people. Let's make sure we keep it that way." He nodded and walked forward to his stateroom. Once there he summoned Chief Oreza.

The quartermaster arrived within a minute. *Panache* wasn't big enough to allow a longer walk than that. "You called, Captain?"

"Close the door, Portagee, and grab a seat."

The master chief quartermaster was of Portuguese extraction, but his accent was New England. Like Bob Riley he was a consummate seaman, and like his captain he was also a gifted instructor. A whole generation of Coast Guard officers had learned the use of the sextant from this swarthy, overweight professional. It was men like Manuel Oreza who really ran the Coast Guard, and Wegener occasionally regretted leaving their ranks for officer status. But he hadn't left them entirely, and in private Wegener and Oreza still communicated on a first-name basis.

"I saw the tape of the boarding, Red," Oreza said, reading his captain's mind. "You shoulda let Riley snap the little fucker in half."

"That's not the way we're supposed to do things," Wegener said somewhat lamely.

"Piracy, murder, and rape—toss in the drugs for fun." The quartermaster shrugged his shoulders. "I know what we oughta do with people like that. Problem is, nobody ever does."

Wegener knew what he meant. Although there was a new federal death-penalty law to deal with drug-related murders, it had only rarely been invoked. The problem was simply that every drug dealer arrested knew someone bigger who was even more desirable a target—the really big ones never placed themselves in a position where the supposed long arm of the law could reach. Federal law-enforcement agencies might have been omnipotent within U.S. borders, and the Coast Guard might have plenipotentiary powers at sea—even to the point where they were allowed to board and search numerous foreign-flag ships at will—but there were always limits. There had to be. The enemy knew what those limits were, and it was really a simple thing to adapt to them. This was a game whose fixed rules applied only to one side; the other was free to redefine its own rules at will. It was simple for the big boys in the drug trade to keep clear, and there were always plenty of smaller fry to take their chances on the dangerous parts—especially since their pay exceeded that of any army in history. These foot soldiers were dangerous and clever enough to make the contest difficult—but even when you caught them, they were always able to trade their knowledge for partial immunity.

The result was that nobody ever seemed to pay in full. Except the victims, of course. Wegener's train of thought was interrupted by something even worse.

"You know, Red, these two might get off entirely."

"Hold it, Portagee, I can't—"

"My oldest girl is in law school, skipper. You want to know the really bad news?" the chief asked darkly.

"Go on."

"We get these characters to port—well, the helo brings them in tomorrow—and they ask for a lawyer, right? Anybody who watches American TV knows that much. Let's say that they keep their mouths shut till then. Then their lawyer says that his clients saw a drifting yacht yesterday morning and boarded it. The boat they were on headed back to wherever it came from, and they decide to take it to port to claim the salvage rights. They didn't use the radio because they didn't know how to work it—you see that on the tape? It was one of those gollywog computer-driven scanners with the hundred-page manual—and our friends don't reada da Eenglish so good.

Somebody on the fishing boat will corroborate part of the story. It's all a horrible misunderstanding, see? So the U.S. Attorney in Mobile decides that he might not have a good-enough case, and our friends cop to a lesser charge. That's how it works.'' He paused.

''That's hard to believe.''

''We got no bodies. We got no witnesses. We have weapons aboard, but who can say who fired them? It's all circumstantial evidence.'' Oreza smiled for a grim moment. ''My daughter gave me a good brief last month on how all this stuff works. They whistle up someone to back up their version of how they got aboard—somebody clean, no criminal record—and all of a sudden the only real witnesses are on the other side, and we got shit, Red. They cop to some little piddly-ass charge, and that's it.''

''But if they're innocent, why don't they—''

''Talk very much? Oh, hell, that's the easy part. A foreign-flag warship pulls up alongside and puts an armed boarding party aboard. The boarding party points a bunch of guns at them, roughs them up a bit, and they're so scared that they didn't say anything—that's what the lawyer'll say. Bet on it. Oh, they prob'ly won't walk, but the prosecutor will be so afraid of losing the case that he'll look for an easy way out. Our friends will get a year or two in the can, then they get a free plane ticket home.''

''But they're murderers.''

''Sure as hell,'' Portagee agreed. ''To get off, all they have to be is smart murderers. And there might even be some other things they can say. What my girl taught me, Red, is that it's never as simple as it looks. Like I said, you shoulda let Bob handle it. The kids would have backed you up, Captain. You oughta hear what they're saying about this thing.''

Captain Wegener was quiet for a moment. That made sense, didn't it? Sailors didn't change much over the years, did they? On the beach they'd work mightily to get into every pair of female pants in sight, but on the question of murder and rape, the ''kids'' felt the same way the old-timers did. Times hadn't changed all that much after all. Men were still men. They knew what justice was, courts and lawyers to the contrary.

Red thought about that for a few seconds. Then he rose and walked to his bookshelf. Next to his current copy of the *Uniform Code of Military Justice* and *The Manual of Courts Martial* was a much older book better known by its informal title, ''Rocks and Shoals.'' It was the old reference book of regulations whose ancestry went back to the 18th century, and which had been replaced by the UCMJ soon after World War II. Wegener's copy was an antique. He'd found it gathering dust in a cardboard box fifteen years before at an old boat station on the California coast. This one had been published in 1879, when the rules had been very different. It had been a safer world then, the captain told himself. It wasn't hard to understand why. All you had to do was read what the rules had once been. . . .

''Thanks, Portagee. I've got a little work to do. I want you and Riley here at fifteen hundred.''

Oreza stood. ''Aye aye, sir.'' The quartermaster wondered for a moment what the captain had thanked him for. He was skilled at reading the skipper's mind, but it didn't work this time. He knew that something was going on in there. He just didn't know what it was. He also knew that he'd find out at fifteen hundred. He could wait.

Wegener had lunch with his officers a few minutes later. He sat quietly at the end of the table reading over some message traffic. His wardroom was young and informal. Table talk was as lively as usual. The talk today was on the obvious subject, and Wegener allowed it to go on as he flipped through the yellow sheets generated by the ship's printer. The thought that had come to him in his stateroom was taking shape. He weighed the pluses and minuses in silence. What could they really do to him? Not much, he judged. Would his people go along with him?

"I heard Oreza say that in the old days, they knew what to do about bastards like this," a lieutenant (j.g.) observed at the far end of the table. There were affirmative grunts all around the table.

"Ain't 'progress' a bitch?" another noted. The twenty-four-year-old officer didn't know that he had just made a decision for his commanding officer.

It would work, Wegener decided. He glanced up from his messages to look at the faces of his officers. He'd trained them well, the captain thought. He'd had them for ten months now, and their performance was as nearly perfect as any commander could ask. They'd been a sorry, dejected lot when he'd arrived at the shipyard, but now they sparkled with enthusiasm. Two had grown mustaches, the better to look like the seamen they'd become. All of them lounged in their hard-backed chairs, radiating competence. They were proud of their ship and proud of their captain. They'd back him up. Red joined the conversation, just to make sure, just to test the waters, just to decide who would play a part and who would not.

He finished his lunch and returned to his cabin. The paperwork was still there, and he raced through it as quickly as he could, then opened his "Rocks and Shoals." At fifteen hundred Oreza and Riley arrived, and he outlined his plan. The two master chiefs were surprised at first, but fell into line quickly.

"Riley, I want you to take this down to our guests. One of 'em dropped it on the bridge." Wegener fished the cigarette pack out of his pocket. "There's a vent in the brig, isn't there?"

"Sure is, skipper," the bosun answered in some surprise. He didn't know about the "Calverts."

"We start at twenty-one hundred," the captain said.

"About the time the weather gets here," Oreza observed. "Fair enough, Red. You know you wanna be real careful how you—"

"I know, Portagee. What's life without a few risks?" he asked with a smile.

Riley left first. He walked forward to a ladder, then down two levels and aft until he got to the brig. The two were there, inside the ten-foot-square cage. Each lay on a bunk. They might have been speaking before, but stopped when the door to the compartment opened. It seemed to the bosun that someone might have included a microphone in the brig, but the district legal officer had once explained that such an installation would be a violation of constitutional rights, or a violation of search-and-seizure, or some such legalistic bullshit, the chief thought.

"Hey, Gomer," he said. The one on the lower bunk—the one he'd cracked across the bridge rail—looked around to see who it was. He was rewarded with widening eyes. "You guys get lunch?" the bosun asked.

"Yes." There was an accent there, but a funny one, the master chief thought.

"You dropped your smokes on the bridge awhile back." Riley tossed the pack through the bars. They landed on the deck, and Pablo—the chief thought he looked like a Pablo—snatched them up with a surprised look on his face.

"Thank you," the man said.

"Uh-huh. Don't you boys go anywhere without letting me know, hear?" Riley chuckled and walked away. It was a real brig. The designers had gotten that part right, the master chief thought. Even had its own head. That offended Riley. A prison cell on a Coast Guard cutter. Hmph. But at least that meant you didn't have to detail a couple of men to guard the gomers. At least not yet, Riley smiled to himself. *Are you boys in for a surprise.*

Weather at sea is always impressive. Perhaps it looks that way sweeping across a uniform surface, or maybe the human mind simply knows that weather has a power at sea that it lacks on land. There was a three-quarter moon tonight, allowing Wegener to watch the line squalls approach at over twenty knots. There were sustained twenty-five-knot winds in there, and gusts almost double that. Experience told him that the gentle four-foot swells that *Panache* rode through would soon be whipped to a maniacal series of breaking waves and flying spray. Not all that much, really, but enough to give his cutter an active ride. Some of his younger crewmen would presently regret dinner. Well, that was something you had to learn about the sea. She didn't like people to overeat.

Wegener welcomed the storm. In addition to giving him the atmosphere he wanted, it also gave him an excuse to fiddle with his watch bill. Ensign O'Neil had not yet conned the ship through heavy weather and tonight would be his chance.

"Any problems, Mister?" the skipper asked the junior officer.

"No, sir."

"Okay, just remember that if anything comes up, I'll be in the wardroom." One of Wegener's standing orders read: *No watch officer will ever be reprimanded for calling the captain to the bridge. Even if you only want to check the correct time: CALL ME!* It was a common hyperbole. You had to say such things, lest your junior officers be so afraid to bother the skipper that they rammed a tanker by way of protecting his sleep—and ending his career. The mark of a good officer, Wegener repeatedly told his youngsters, was willingness to admit he had something yet to learn.

O'Neil nodded. Both men knew that there was nothing to worry about. It was just that the kid had never learned first-hand that a ship handles a little differently with sea and wind on the beam. Besides, Chief Owens was standing by. Wegener walked aft, and the boatswain's mate of the watch announced, "Captain off the bridge."

In the crew's mess the enlisted men were settling down to watch a movie. It was a new tape, with a "Hard R" notation on the plastic box. Riley had seen to that. Lots of T&A to keep their attention. The same movie was available to the wardroom TV; young officers had the same hormonal drives, but they wouldn't be exercised tonight.

The onrushing storm would serve to keep people off the weather decks, and the noise wouldn't hurt either. Wegener smiled to himself as he pulled open the door to the wardroom. He couldn't have planned it any better.

"Are we ready?" the captain asked.

The initial enthusiasm for the plan was gone. The reality of things had sunk in a little. That was to be expected, Wegener thought. The youngsters were sober, but they weren't backing away either. They needed someone to say something, and they got it.

"Ready here, sir," Oreza said from his seat at the far end of the table. The officers all nodded agreement. Red walked to his seat in the center of the mess table. He looked at Riley.

"Bring 'em up here."

"Aye aye, sir."

The bosun left the room and proceeded down to the brig. On opening the door again, he caught the acrid stink that made him think at first that there was a fire in the rope locker—but an instant later the truth sprang on him.

"Shit," he growled disgustedly. *On my ship!* "Stand up, Gomer!" his voice boomed, adding, "Both of ya'!"

The one on the lower bunk flipped his butt into the toilet and stood slowly, an arrogant smile on his face. Riley answered it, and produced a key. That changed Pablo's smile, but didn't erase it.

"We're taking a little walk, children." The bosun also produced a pair of handcuffs. He figured that he could handle both of them easily enough, especially stoned, but the skipper had been clear on his instructions. Riley reached through the bars to yank one toward him. On a rough order to turn around, the man complied, and allowed himself to be cuffed. So did the other. The lack of resistance surprised the master chief. Next Riley unlocked the brig door and waved them out. As "Pablo" passed, Riley removed the pack from his pocket and for want of something better, tossed it back on the lower bunk.

"Come on." Riley grabbed each by the arm and led them forward. They walked unevenly—the increased rolling of the ship didn't help, but there was more to it than that. It took three or four minutes to reach the wardroom.

"The prisoners will be seated," Wegener announced when they arrived. "The court is called to order."

Both of them stopped cold on hearing that, which told everybody something. Riley steered them to their seats at the defense table after a moment. It is hard for a person to endure the stares of his fellowman in silence, particularly when one knows that something is going on, but not quite what it is. The big one broke the silence after a minute or so.

"What's happening?"

"Sir," Wegener replied evenly, "we are holding a summary court-martial." That only earned him a curious look, and he went on, "The trial judge advocate will read the charges."

"Mr. President, the defendants are charged under the Eleventh Article of War with piracy, rape, and murder. Each of these is a capital offense. Specifications: that on or about the fourteenth of this month, the defendants did board the motor yacht *Empire Builder;* that while aboard they did murder the four people aboard the vessel, that is, the owner and master, his wife, and their two minor children; further, that in the course of these events the defendants did rape the wife and daughter of the owner and master; further that the defendants did dismember and dispose of the bodies of the victims prior to our boarding the vessel on the morning of the fifteenth. The prosecution will show that these actions took place in the course of drug-running operations. Murder in the course of drug-related activities is a capital offense under United States Code, Annotated. Further, murder in the course of piracy, and rape in the course of piracy, are capital crimes under the Articles of War. As the court is aware, piracy is a crime under the doctrine of *jus gentium,* and falls under the jurisdiction of any interested warship. Further, murder attending piracy is, as I have stated, a capital crime. Although as a ship of the United States Coast Guard we have *de jure* rights to board and seize any American-flag vessel, that authority is not strictly necessary in a case of this kind. Therefore, this court has full jurisdiction to try and, if necessary, execute the prisoners. The prosecution announces herewith its intention to request the death penalty in this case."

"Thank you," Wegener said, turning to the defense table. "Do you understand the charges?"

"Huh?"

"What the trial judge advocate just said was that you are being tried for piracy, rape, and murder. If you are found guilty, the court will then decide whether or not to execute you. You have the right to legal counsel. Lieutenant Alison, sitting there at the table with you, is your defending officer. Do you understand?" It took a few more seconds for things to sink in, but he understood all right. "Does the defense waive full reading of charges and specifications?"

"Yes, Mr. President. Sir, the defense moves that the cases be tried individually, and begs the indulgence of the court to confer with his clients."

"Sir, the prosecution objects to splitting the cases."

"Argument?" the captain asked. "Defense first."

"Sir, since, as the trial judge advocate has told us, this is to be a capital case, I beg the court's indulgence to allow me to defend my clients as best I can under the circumstances, and—"

Wegener stopped him with a wave of the hand. "The defense correctly points out that, since this is a capital case, it is customary to grant the utmost leeway to the defense. The court finds this a persuasive argument and grants the motion. The court also grants the defense five minutes to confer with his clients. The court suggests that the defense might instruct his clients to identify themselves properly to the court."

The lieutenant took them to a corner of the room, still in handcuffs, and started talking to them quietly.

"Look, I'm Lieutenant Alison, and I'm stuck with the job of keeping you two characters alive. For starters, you'd better damned sight tell me who the hell you are!"

"What is this bullshit?" the tall one asked.

"This bullshit is a court-martial. You're at sea, mister, and in case nobody ever told you, the captain of an American warship can do any goddamned thing he wants. You shouldn't have pissed him off."

"So?"

"So, this is a *trial,* you asshole! You know, a judge, a jury. They can sentence you to death and they can do it right here aboard the ship."

"Bullshit!"

"What's your name, for God's sake?"

"Yo' mama," the tall one said contemptuously. The other one looked somewhat less sure of himself. The lieutenant scratched the top of his head. Eighteen feet away, Captain Wegener took note of it.

"What the hell did you do aboard that yacht?"

"Get me a real lawyer!"

"Mister, I'm all the lawyer you're gonna get," the lieutenant said. "Haven't you figured that out yet?"

The man didn't believe him, which was precisely what everyone had expected. The defending officer led his clients back to their table.

"The court is back in session," Wegener announced. "Do we have a statement for the defense?"

"May it please the court, neither defendant chooses to identify himself."

"That does not please the court, but we must take that fact at face value. For the purposes of the trial, we will identify your clients as John Doe and James Doe."

Wegener pointed to designate which was which. "The court chooses to try John Doe first. Is there any objection? Very well, the trial judge advocate will begin presenting his case."

Which he did over the next twenty minutes, calling only one witness, Master Chief Riley, who recounted the boarding and gave a color commentary to the videotape record of the boarding.

"Did the defendant say anything?"

"No, sir."

"Could you describe the contents of this evidence bag?" the prosecutor asked next.

"Sir, I think that's called a tampon. It appears to be used, sir," Riley said with some embarrassment. "I found that under the coffee table in the yacht's main salon, close to a bloodstain—actually these two on the photograph, sir. I don't use the things myself, you understand, sir, but in my experience women don't leave them around on the floor. On the other hand, if someone was about to rape a lady, this thing would be in the way, sort of, and he might just remove it and toss it out of the way so's he could get on with it, like. If you see where I picked it up, and where the bloodstains are, well, it's pretty obvious what happened there, sir."

"No further questions. The prosecution rests."

"Very well. Before the defense begins its case, the court wishes to ask if the defense intends to call any witnesses other than the defendant."

"No, Mr. President."

"Very well. At this point the court will speak directly to the defendant." Wegener shifted his gaze and leaned forward slightly in his chair. "In your own defense, sir, you have the right to do one of three things. First, you can choose not to make any statement at all, in which case the court will draw no inferences from your action. Second, you are allowed to make a statement not under oath and not subject to cross-examination. Third, you may make a statement under oath and subject to cross-examination by the trial judge advocate. Do you understand these rights, sir?"

"John Doe," who had watched the preceding hour or so in amused silence, came awkwardly to his feet. With his hands cuffed behind his back, he leaned slightly forward, and since the cutter was now rolling like a log in a flume, he had quite a bit of trouble keeping his feet.

"What is all this shit?" he demanded, again making people wonder about his accent. "I want to go back to my room and be left alone till I can get my own fucking lawyer."

"Mr. Doe," Wegener replied, "in case you haven't figured it out yet, you are on trial for piracy, rape, and murder. This book"—the captain lifted his "Rocks and Shoals"—"says I can try you here and now, and this book says that if we find you guilty, we can decide to hang you from the yardarm. Now, the Coast Guard hasn't done this in over fifty years, but you better believe that I can damned well do it if I want to! They haven't bothered changing the law. So now things are different from what you expected, aren't they? You want a lawyer—you have Mr. Alison right there. You want to defend yourself? Here's your chance. But, Mr. Doe, there is no appeal from this court, and you'd better think about that real hard and real fast."

"I think this is all bullshit. Go fuck yourself!"

"The court will disregard the defendant's statement," Wegener said, struggling to keep his face straight and sober, as befitting the presiding officer in a capital case.

Counsel for the defense spoke for fifteen minutes, making a valiant but futile attempt to counter the weight of evidence already presented by the trial judge advocate. Case summaries took five minutes each. Then it was time for Captain Wegener to speak again.

''Having heard the evidence, the members of the court will now vote on the verdict. This will be by secret written ballot. The trial judge advocate will pass out the voting papers, and collect them.''

This took less than one minute. The prosecutor handed each of the five members a slip of note paper. The members of the court all looked at the defendant before and after marking their votes. The prosecutor then collected the ballots, and after shuffling them in his hand about as adroitly as a five-year-old with his Old Maid cards, handed them to the captain. Wegener unfolded the ballots and set them on the table in front of him. He made a note in his yellow pad before speaking.

''Defendant will stand and face the court. Mr. Doe, do you have anything to say before sentence is passed?''

He didn't, an amused, disbelieving smirk on his face.

''Very well. The court having voted, two-thirds of the members concurring, finds the defendant guilty, and sentences him to death by hanging. Sentence to be carried out within the hour. May God have mercy on your soul. Court is adjourned.''

''Sorry, sir,'' the defense counsel said to his client. ''You didn't give me much to work with.''

''Now get me a lawyer!'' Mr. Doe snarled.

''Sir, you don't need a lawyer just now. You need a priest.'' As if to emphasize that fact, Chief Riley took him by the arm.

''Come on, sweetheart. You got a date with a rope.'' The master chief led him out of the room.

The other prisoner, known as James Doe, had watched the entire proceeding in fascinated disbelief. The disbelief was still there, everyone saw, but it was more the sort of disbelief that you'd expect to see on the face of a man stuck in front of an onrushing train.

''Do *you* understand what's going on here?'' the lieutenant asked.

''This ain't real, man,'' the prisoner said, his voice lacking much of the conviction it might have held an hour or so earlier.

''Hey, man, aren't you paying attention? Didn't they tell you guys that some of your kind just sort of disappear out here? We've been doing this for almost six months. The prisons are all full up, and the judges just don't want to be bothered. If we bag somebody and we have the evidence we need, they let us handle things at sea. Didn't anybody tell you that the rules have changed some?''

''You can't do this!'' he almost screamed in reply.

''Think so? Tell you what. In about ten minutes I'll take you topside, and you can watch. I'm telling you, if you don't cooperate, we are not going to fuck around with you, pal. We're tired of that. Why don't you just sit quiet and think it over, and when the time comes, I'll let you see how serious we are.'' The lieutenant helped himself to a cup of coffee to pass the time, not speaking at all to his client. About the time he finished, the door opened again.

''Hands topside to witness punishment,'' Chief Oreza announced.

''Come on, Mr. Doe. You'd better see this.'' The lieutenant took him by the arm and led him forward. Just outside the wardroom door was a ladder that led upward. At the top of it was a narrow passageway, and both men headed aft toward the cutter's vacant helicopter deck.

The lieutenant's name was Rick Alison. A black kid from Albany, New York, and the ship's navigator, Alison thanked God every night for serving under Red Wegener, who was far and away the best commander he'd ever met. He'd thought about leaving the service more than once, but now planned on staying in as long as he could. He led Mr. Doe aft, about thirty feet from the festivities.

The seas were really rough now, Alison noted. He gauged the wind at over thirty knots, and the seas at twelve or fourteen feet. *Panache* was taking twenty-five-degree rolls left and right of the vertical, snapping back and forth like a kids' seesaw. Alison remembered that O'Neil had the conn, and hoped that Chief Owens was keeping an eye on the boy. The new ensign was a good enough kid, but he still had a lot to learn about ship handling, thought the navigator, who was a bare six years older himself. Lightning flashed occasionally to starboard, flash-lighting the sea. Rain was falling in solid sheets, the drops flying across the deck at a sharp angle and driven hard enough by the wind to sting the cheeks. All in all it was the sort of night to make Edgar Allan Poe salivate at its possibilities. There were no lights visible, though the cutter's white paint gave them a sort of ghostly outline as a visual reference. Alison wondered if Wegener had decided to do this because of the weather, or was it just a fortunate coincidence?

Captain, you've pulled some crazy shit since you came aboard, but this one really takes it.

There was the rope. Someone had snaked it over the end of the cutter's radio/radar mast. That must have been fun, Alison thought. Had to have been Chief Riley. Who else would be crazy enough to try?

Then the prisoner appeared. His hands were still behind his back. The captain and XO were there, too. Wegener was saying something official, but they couldn't hear it. The wind whistled across the deck, and through the mast structure with its many signal halyards—oh, that's what Riley did, Alison realized. He'd used a halyard as a messenger line to run the one-inch hemp through the block. Even Riley wasn't crazy enough to crawl the mast top in this weather.

Then some lights came on. They were the deck floods, used to help guide a helo in. They had the main effect of illuminating the rain, but did give a slightly clearer picture of what was happening. Wegener said one more thing to the prisoner, whose face was still set in an arrogant cast. He still didn't believe it, Alison thought, wondering if that would change. The captain shook his head and stepped back. Riley then placed the noose around his neck.

John Doe's expression changed at that. He still didn't believe it, but all of a sudden things were slightly more serious. Five people assembled on the running end of the line. Alison almost laughed. He'd known that was how it was done, but hadn't quite expected the skipper to go that far. . . .

The final touch was the black hood. Riley turned the prisoner to face aft toward Alison and his friend—there was another reason, as well—before surprising him with it. And finally it got through to Mr. Doe.

"*Noooooo!*" The scream was perfect, a ghostly sort of cry that matched the weather and the wind better than anyone might have hoped. His knees buckled as expected, and the men on the running end of the line took the strain and ran aft. The prisoner's feet rose clear of the black no-skid deck as the body jerked skyward. The legs kicked a few times, then were still before the line was tied off on a stanchion.

"Well, that's that," Alison said. He took the other Mr. Doe by the arm and led him forward. "Now it's your turn, sport."

Lightning flashed close aboard just as they reached the door leading back into the superstructure. The prisoner stopped cold, looking up one last time. There was his companion, body limp, swinging like a pendulum below the yard, hanging there dead in the rain.

"You believe me now?" the navigator asked as he pulled him inside. Mr. Doe's trousers were already soaked from the falling rain, but they were wet for another reason as well.

The first order of business was to get dried off. When the court reconvened, everyone had changed to fresh clothing. James Doe was now in a set of blue Coast Guard coveralls. His handcuffs had been taken off and left off, and he found a hot cup of coffee waiting for him on the defense table. He failed to note that Chief Oreza was no longer at the head table, nor was Chief Riley in the wardroom at the moment. The entire atmosphere was more relaxed than it had been, but the prisoner scarcely noticed that. James Doe was anything but calm.

"Mr. Alison," the captain intoned, "I would suggest that you confer with your client."

"This one's real simple, sport," Alison said. "You can talk or you can swing. The skipper doesn't give a shit one way or the other. For starters, what's your name?"

Jesús started talking. One of the officers of the court picked up a portable TV camera—the same one used in the boarding, in fact—and they asked him to start again.

"Okay—do you understand that you are not required to say anything?" someone asked. The prisoner scarcely noticed, and the question was repeated.

"Yeah, right, I understand, okay?" he responded without turning his head. "Look, what do you want to know?"

The questions were already written down, of course. Alison, who was also the cutter's legal officer, ran down the list as slowly as he could, in front of the video camera. His main problem was in slowing the answers down enough to be intelligible. The questioning lasted forty minutes. The prisoner spoke rapidly, but matter-of-factly, and didn't notice the looks he was getting from the members of the court.

"Thank you for your cooperation," Wegener said when things were concluded. "We'll try to see that things go a little easier for you because of your cooperation. We won't be able to do much for your colleague, of course. You do understand that, don't you?"

"Too bad for him, I guess," the man answered, and everyone in the room breathed a little easier.

"We'll talk to the U.S. Attorney," the captain promised. "Lieutenant, you can return the prisoner to the brig."

"Aye aye, sir." Alison took the prisoner out of the room as the camera followed. On reaching the ladder to go below, however, the prisoner tripped. He didn't see the hand that caused it, and didn't have time to look, as another unseen hand crashed down on the back of his neck. Next Chief Riley broke the unconscious man's forearm, while Chief Oreza clamped a patch of ether-soaked gauze over his mouth. The two chiefs carried him to sick bay, where the cutter's medical corpsman splinted the arm. It was a simple green-stick fracture and required no special assistance. His undamaged arm was secured to the bunk in sick bay, and he was allowed to sleep there.

The prisoner slept late. Breakfast was brought in to him from the wardroom, and he was allowed to clean himself up before the helicopter arrived. Oreza came to collect him, leading him topside again, and aft to the helo deck, where he found Chief Riley, who was delivering the other prisoner to the helicopter. What James Doe—his real name had turned out to be Jesús Castillo—found remarkable was the fact that John Doe—Ramón José Capati—was alive. A pair of DEA agents seated them as far apart as possible, and had instructions to keep the prisoners separate. One had confessed, the captain explained, and the other might not be overly pleased with that. Castillo couldn't take his eyes off Capati, and the amazement in his eyes looked enough like fear that the agents—who liked the idea of a confession in a capital case—resolved to keep the prisoners as far apart as circumstances allowed. Along with them went all the physical evidence and several videotape cassettes. Wegener watched the Coast Guard Dolphin helo power up, wondering how the people on the beach would react. The sober pause that always follows a slightly mad act had set in, but Wegener had anticipated that also. In fact, he figured that he'd anticipated everything. Only eight members of the crew knew what had taken place, and they knew what they were supposed to say. The executive officer appeared at Wegener's side.

"Nothing's ever quite what it seems, is it?"

"I suppose not, but three innocent people died. Instead of four." *Sure as hell the owner wasn't any angel,* the captain reflected. *But did they have to kill his wife and kids, too?* Wegener stared out at the changeless sea, unaware of what he had started or how many people would die because of it.

4. Preliminaries

Chavez's first indication of how unusual this job really was came at San José airport. Driven there in an unmarked rental van, they ended up in the general-aviation part of the facility and found a private jet waiting for them. Now, that was really something. "Colonel Smith" didn't board. He shook every man's hand, told them that they'd be met, and got back into the van. The sergeants all boarded the aircraft which, they saw, was less an executive jet than a mini-airliner. It even had a stewardess who served drinks. Each man stowed his gear and availed himself of a drink except Chavez, who was too tired even to look at the young lady. He barely noted the plane's takeoff, and was asleep before the climb-out was finished. Something told him that he ought to sleep while he had the time. It was a common instinct for soldiers, and usually a correct one.

Lieutenant Jackson had never been at the Monterey facility, but his older brother had given him the necessary instructions, and he found the O-Club without difficulty. He felt suddenly lonely. As he locked his Honda he realized that his was the only Army uniform in view. At least it wasn't hard to figure out whom to salute. As a second lieutenant, he had to salute damned near everybody.

"Yo, Timmy!" his brother called, just inside the door.

"Hiya, Rob." The two men embraced. Theirs was a close family, but Timmy hadn't seen his big brother, Commander Robert Jefferson Jackson, USN, in almost a year. Robby's mother had died years before. Only thirty-nine, she'd complained of a headache, decided to lie down for a few minutes, and never stirred again, the victim of a massive stroke. It had later been determined that she was an undiagnosed hypertensive, one of many American blacks cursed by the symptomless malady. Her husband, the Reverend Hosiah Jackson, mourned her loss along with the community in which both had raised their family. But pious man that Reverend Jackson was, he was also a father whose children needed a mother. Four years later he'd remarried, to a twenty-three-year-old parishioner, and started afresh. Timothy was the first child of his second union. His fourth son had followed a path similar to the first's. An Annapolis graduate, Robby Jackson flew fighter aircraft for the Navy. Timmy had won an appointment at West Point, and looked forward to a career in the infantry. Another brother was a physician, and the fourth was a lawyer with political ambitions. Times had changed in Mississippi.

It would have been hard for an observer to determine which brother was prouder of the other. Robby, with three gold stripes on his shoulder boards, bore on his breast pocket the gold star that denoted a former command at sea—in his case, VF-41, a squadron of F-14 Tomcat fighters. Now working in the Pentagon, Robby was on his way to command of a Carrier Air Wing, and after that perhaps his own carrier. Timothy, on the other hand, had been the family runt for quite a few years, but West Point had changed that with a vengeance. He had two solid inches on his older brother, and at least fifteen more pounds of muscle. There was a Ranger flash on his shoulder above the hourglass insignia of his division. Another boy had been turned into a man, the old-fashioned way.

"Lookin' good, boy," Robby observed. "How 'bout a drink?"

"Not too many, I've been up for a while."

"Long day?"

"Long week, as a matter of fact," Tim replied, "but I did get a nap yesterday."

"Nice of 'em," the elder Jackson observed with some fraternal concern.

"Hey, if I wanted an easy life, I woulda joined the Navy." The brothers had a good laugh on the way to the bar. Robby ordered John Jameson, a taste introduced to him by a friend. Tim settled for a beer. Conversation over dinner, of course, began with catching up on family matters, then turned to shop talk.

"Not real different from what you do," Timmy explained. "You try to get in close and smoke a guy with a missile before he knows you're there. We try to get in close and shoot him in the head before he knows where we are. You know about that, don't you, big brother?" Timmy asked with a smile that was touched with envy. Robby had been there once.

"Once was enough," Robby answered soberly. "I leave that close-quarter crap to idiots like you."

"Yeah, well, last night we were the forward element for the battalion. My lead squad went in beautiful. The OPFOR—excuse me, Opposing Force—was a bunch from the California Guard, mainly tanks. They got careless about how they set up, and Sergeant Chavez was inside the laager before they knew about it. You oughta see this guy operate. I swear, Rob, he's nearly invisible when he wants to be. It's going to be a bitch to replace him."

"Huh?"

"Just transferred out this afternoon. I was going to lose him in a couple weeks anyway, but they lifted him early to go to Fort Benning. Whole bunch of good sergeants moved out today." Tim paused for a moment. "All Spanish ones. Coincidence.'' Another pause. ''That's funny, wasn't León supposed to go to Fort Benning, too?''

''Who's León?''

''Sergeant E-6. He was in Ben Tucker's platoon—Ben and I played ball together at the Point. Yeah, he was supposed to be going to Ranger School as an instructor in a couple of weeks. I wonder why him and Chavez left together? Ah, well, that's the Army for you. So how do you like the Pentagon?''

''Could be worse,'' Robby allowed. ''Twenty-five more months, and thank God Almighty, I'll be free at last. I'm in the running for a CAG slot,'' the elder brother explained. He was at the career stage where things got really sticky. There were more good men than jobs to be filled. As with combat operations, one of the determining factors now was pure luck. Timmy, he saw, didn't know about that yet.

The jet landed after a flight of just under three hours. Once on the ground it taxied to the cargo terminal at the small airport. Chavez didn't know which one. He awoke still short of the sleep he needed when the plane's door was wrenched open. His first impression was that there wasn't much air here. It seemed an odd observation to make, and he wrote it off to the usual confusion following a nap.

''Where the hell are we?'' another sergeant asked.

''They'll tell you outside,'' the attendant replied. ''Y'all have a nice time here.'' The smile that accompanied the answer was too charming to merit a further challenge.

The sergeants collected their bags and shuffled out of the aircraft, finding yet another van waiting for them. Chavez got his question answered before he boarded it. The air was very thin here, all right, and in the west he saw why. The last glow of sunset illuminated the jagged outline of mountains to the west. Easterly course, three hours' flight time, and mountains: he knew at once they were somewhere in the Rockies, even though he'd never really been there. His last view of the aircraft as the van rolled off showed a fueling truck moving toward it. Chavez didn't quite put it together. The aircraft would be leaving in less than thirty minutes. Few people would have noticed that it had even been there, much less trouble themselves to wonder why.

Clark's hotel room was a nice one, befitting his cover. There was an ache at the back of his head to remind him that he was still not fully adjusted to the altitude, but a couple of Tylenol caplets went to work on that, and he knew that his job didn't involve much in the way of physical activity. He ordered breakfast sent up and went through some setting-up exercises to work the kinks out of his muscles. The morning jog was definitely out, however. Finished, he showered and shaved. Service was good here. Just as he got his clothes on, breakfast arrived, and by nine o'clock he was ready for work. Clark took the elevator down to the lobby, then went outside. The car was waiting. He got in the front.

''*Buenos días,*'' the driver said. ''There may be rain this afternoon.''

''If so, I have my coat.''

''A cold rain, perhaps.''

''The coat has a liner,'' Clark said, finishing the code sequence.

''Whoever thought that one up was bright enough,'' the man said. ''There is rain in the forecast. The name's Larson.''

''Clark.'' They didn't shake hands. It just wasn't done. Larson, which probably wasn't his real name either, Clark thought, was about thirty, with dark hair that belied his vaguely Nordic surname. Locally, Carlos Larson was thought to be the son of a Danish father and a Venezuelan mother, and he ran a flying school, a service much in demand. He was a skilled pilot who taught what he knew and didn't ask many questions, which appealed to his clientele. He didn't really need to ask questions—pilots, especially student pilots, talk a good deal—and he had a good memory for every sort of detail, plus the sort of professional expertise that invited lots of requests for advice. It was also widely believed that he'd financed his business by making a few highly illegal flights, then semiretired to a life of luxury. This legend created bona fides for the people in whom he had interest, but did so without making him any sort of adversary. He was a man who'd done what was needed to get what he wanted, and now lived the sort of life that he'd wanted to live. That explained the car, which was the most powerful BMW made, and the expensive apartment, and the mistress, a stewardess for Avianca whose real job was as a courier for CIA. Larson thought it all a dream assignment, the more so because the stewardess really was his lover, a fringe benefit that might not have amused the Agency's personnel directorate. The only thing that bothered him was that his placement in Colombia was also unknown to the station chief. A relatively inexperienced agent, Larson—Clark would have been surprised to learn that that was his real name—knew enough about how the Agency worked to realize that separate command loops generally denoted some sort of special operation. His cover had been established over a period of eighteen months, during which he'd been required to do not very much in return. Clark's arrival was probably the signal that all of that was about to change. Time to earn his pay.

"What's the plan of the day?" Clark asked.

"Do a little flying. We'll be down before the weather goes bad," Larson added.

"I know you have an instrument rating."

"I will take that as a vote of confidence," the pilot said with a smile as he drove toward the airport. "You've been over the photos, of course."

"Yeah, about three days' worth. I'm just old-fashioned enough that I like to eyeball things myself. Maps and photos don't tell you everything."

"They told me the mission profile is just to fly around straight and level, no buzzing or circling to get people mad." The nice thing about having a flying school was that its aircraft were expected to be all over the place, but if one showed specific interest in specific people, they might take note of your registration number, and they might come down to the airport to ask why. The people who lived in Medellín were not known to ask such questions politely. Larson was not afraid of them. So long as he maintained his cover, he knew that he had little to worry about. At the same time, he was a pro, and pros are careful, especially if they want to last.

"Sounds okay to me." Clark knew the same things. He'd gotten old in a dangerous business by taking only the necessary risks. Those were bad enough. It wasn't very different from playing the lottery. Even though the odds were against one's hitting the number, if you played the game long enough, the right—or wrong—number would appear, no matter how careful you were. Except in this lottery the prize wasn't money. It was an unmarked, shallow grave, and you got that only if the opposition remembered something about religion.

He couldn't decide if he liked the mission or not. On the one hand, the objective was worthy enough. On the other . . . But Clark wasn't paid to make that sort of evaluation. He was paid to do, not to think very much about it. That was the main problem with covert operations. You had to risk your life on the judgment of others. It was nice to know why, but the decision-makers said knowing why often had the effect of making the job all the more dangerous. The field operators didn't always believe that. Clark had that problem right now.

The Twin-Beech was parked in the general-aviation section of El Dorado International Airport. It didn't require too much in the way of intelligence to make an accurate assessment of what the aircraft were used for. There were too many expensive cars, and far too many expensive aircraft to be explained by the Colombian gentry. These were toys for the newly rich. Clark's eyes swept over them, his face showing neutral interest.

"Wages of sin ain't bad, are they?" Larson chuckled.

"What about the poor bastards who're paying the wages?"

"I know about that, too. I'm just saying that they're nice airplanes. Those Gulfstreams—I'm checked out on 'em—that's one sweethandlin' bird."

"What do they cost?" Clark asked.

"A wise man once said, if you have to ask the price, you can't afford it."

"Yeah." Clark's mouth twisted into a smile. *But some things carry a price that's not measured in dollars.* He was already getting into the proper frame of mind for the mission.

Larson preflighted the Beech in about fifteen minutes. He'd just flown in ninety minutes earlier, and few private pilots would have bothered to run through the whole checklist, but Larson was a good pilot, which meant he was before all things a careful one. Clark took the right-side cockpit seat, strapping in as though he were a student pilot on his first hop. Commercial traffic was light at this hour, and it was easy to taxi into the takeoff pattern. About the only surprise was the long takeoff roll.

"It's the altitude," Larson explained over the intercom headset as he rotated off the runway. "It makes the controls a little mushy at low speed, too. No problem. Like driving in the snow—you just have to pay attention." He moved the lever to bring the gear up, leaving the aircraft at full power to claw up to altitude as quickly as possible. Clark scanned the instruments and saw nothing obviously awry, though it did seem odd to show nine thousand feet of altitude when you could still pick out individual people on the ground.

The aircraft banked to the left, taking a northwesterly heading. Larson backed off on the throttles, commenting that you also had to pay close attention to engine temperatures here, though the cooling systems on the twin Continental engines were beefed up to allow for it. They were heading toward the country's mountainous spine. The sky was clear and the sun was bright.

"Beautiful, isn't it?"

"It is that," Clark agreed. The mountains were covered with emerald-green trees whose leaves shimmered with moisture from the night's rain. But Clark's trained eyes saw something else. Walking these hills would be a cast-iron bitch. About the only good thing to be said was that there was good cover under which people could conceal themselves. The combination of steep hills and thin air would make this place an arduous one. He hadn't been briefed on what exactly was going to happen, but he knew enough to be glad that the hard part of the job would not be his.

The mountain ranges in Colombia run on a southwest-to-northeast vector. Larson picked a convenient pass to fly over, but the winds off the nearby Pacific Ocean made the crossing bumpy.

"Get used to it. Winds are picking up today because of the weather front that's moving in. They really boil around these hills. You ought to see what real bad weather is like."

"Thanks, but no thanks! Not much in the way of places to land in case things—"

"Go bad?" Larson asked. "That's why I pay attention to the checklist. Besides, there are more little strips down there than you might imagine. Of course, you don't always get a welcome when you decide to use one. Don't sweat it. I just put new engines on this bird a month ago. Sold the old ones to one of my students for his old King Air. It belongs to the Bureau of Customs now," Larson explained.

"Did you have any part in that?"

"Negative! Look, they expect me to know why all these kids are taking lessons. I'm not supposed to be dumb, right? So I also teach them standard evasion tactics. You can read them in any decent book, and they expect me to be able to do that. Pablo wasn't real big on reading. Hell of a natural pilot, though. Too bad, really, he was a nice enough kid. They bagged him with fifty keys. I understand he didn't talk much. No surprise there. Gutsy little bastard."

"How well motivated are these folks?" Clark had seen lots of combat once, and he knew that the measure of an enemy is not to be found by counting his weapons.

Larson frowned at the sky. "Depends on what you mean. If you change the word from 'motivated' to 'macho,' that about covers it. You know, the cult of manliness, that sort of thing. Part of it's kinda admirable. These people have a funny sense of honor. For example, the ones I know socially treat me just fine. Their hospitality is impressive, especially if you show a little deference, which everyone does. Besides, I'm not a business rival. What I mean is, I know these people. I've taught a bunch of them to fly. If I had a money problem, I could probably go to them for help and get it. I'm talking like half a million in cash on a handshake—and I'd walk out of the hacienda with the cash in a briefcase. I'd have to make some courier flights to square things, of course. And I'd never have to pay the money back. On the other hand, if I screwed them, well, they'd make damned sure that I paid for that, too. They have rules. If you live by them, you're fairly safe. If not, you'd better have your bags packed."

"I know about the ruthlessness. What about the brains?"

"They're as smart as they have to be. What smarts they don't have, they buy. They can buy anything, anybody. Don't underestimate them. Their security systems are state-of-the-art, like what we put on ICBM silos—shit, maybe better than that. They're protected as tightly as we protect the President, except their shooters are less restrained by rules of engagement. I suppose the best indicator on how smart they are is the fact that they've banded together to form the cartel. They're smart enough to know that gang wars cost everybody, so they formed a loose alliance. It ain't perfect, but it works. People who try to break into the business mostly end up dead. Medellín is an easy town to die in."

"Cops? Courts?"

"The locals have tried. Lots of dead cops, lots of dead judges to prove it," Larson said with a shake of the head. "Takes a lot for people to keep plugging away when they can't see any results. Then toss in the money angle. How often can a man walk away from a suitcase full of tax-free hundred-dollar bills? Especially when the alternative is certain death for himself and his family. The cartel is smart, my friend, and it's patient, and it has all the resources it needs, and it's ruthless enough to scare a veteran Nazi. All in all, that's some enemy." Larson pointed to a gray smudge in the distance. "There's Medellín. Drugs 'R Us, all in that one little city in the valley. One nuke could settle things, say about two megatons, airburst four thousand feet AGL. I wonder if the rest of the country would really mind . . . ?"

That earned Larson a glance from his passenger. Larson lived here, knew a lot of these people, and even liked some, as he'd just said. But his hatred for them occasionally peeked through his professional detachment. The best sort of duplicity. This kid had a real future in the Agency, Clark decided. Brains and passion both. If he knew how to maintain a proper balance of the two, he could go places. Clark reached into his bag for a camera and a pair of binoculars. His interest wasn't in the city itself.

"Nice places, aren't they?"

The drug chieftains were growing increasingly security-conscious. The hilltops around the city were all being cleared of trees. Clark counted over a dozen new homes already. Homes, he thought with a snort. Castles was more like it. Walled fortresses. Enormous dwelling structures surrounded by low walls, surrounded in turn by hundreds of yards of clear, steep slopes. What people found picturesque about Italian villages and Bavarian castles was always the elegant setting. Always on the top of a hill or mountain. You could easily imagine the work that went into such a beautiful place—clearing the trees, hauling the stone blocks up the slopes, and ending up with a commanding view of the countryside that extended for miles. But the castles and villages hadn't been built in such places for fun, and neither had these houses. The heights meant that no one could approach them unobserved. The cleared ground around those houses was known in terse military nomenclature as a killing zone, a clear field of fire for automatic weapons. Each house had a single road up to a single gate. Each house had a helipad for a fast evacuation. The wall around each was made of stone that would stop any bullet up to fifty caliber. His binoculars showed that immediately inside each wall was a gravel or concrete path for guards to walk. A company of trained infantrymen would have no easy time assaulting one of these haciendas. *Maybe a helicopter assault, supported by mortars and gunships . . . Christ,* Clark thought to himself, *what am I thinking about?*

"What about house plans?"

"No problem. Three architectural firms have designed these places. Security isn't all that good there. Besides, I've been in that one for a party—just two weeks ago, as a matter of fact. I guess that's one area they're not too smart in. They like to show their places off. I can get you floor plans. The satellite overheads will show guard strength, vehicle garaging, all that sort of thing."

"They do." Clark smiled.

"Can you tell me exactly what you're here for?"

"Well, they want an evaluation of the physical characteristics of the terrain."

"I can see that. Hell, I could do that easy enough from memory." Larson's question was not so much curiosity as his slight offense at not being asked to do this job himself.

"You know how it is at Langley," was the statement Clark used to dismiss the observation.

You're a pilot, Clark didn't say. *You've never humped a field pack in the boonies. I have.* If Larson had known his background, he could have made an intelligent guess, but what Clark did for the Agency, and what he'd done before joining, were not widely known. In fact, they were hardly known at all.

"Need-to-know, Mr. Larson," Clark said after another moment.

"Roger that," the pilot agreed over the intercom.

"Let's do a photo pass."

"I'll do a touch-and-go at the airport first. We want to make it look good."

"Fair enough," Clark agreed.

"What about the refining sites?" Clark asked after they headed back to El Dorado.

"Mainly southwest of here," Larson answered, turning the Beech away from the valley. "I've never seen one myself—I'm not in that part of the business, and they know it. If you want to scout them out, you go around at night with imaging IR equipment, but they're hard to track in on. Hell, they're portable, easy to set up, and easy to move. You can load the whole assembly on a medium truck and set it up ten miles away the next day."

"Not that many roads. . . ."

"What you gonna do, search every truck that comes along?" Larson asked. "Besides, you can man-pack it if you want. Labor's cheap down here. The opposition is smart, and adaptable."

"How much does the local army get involved?" Clark had been fully briefed, of course, but he also knew that a local perspective might not agree with Washington's—and might be correct.

"They've tried. Biggest problem they have is sustaining their forces—their helicopters don't spend twenty percent of their time in the air. That means they don't do many ops. It means that if anyone gets hit he might not get medical attention very fast—and that hurts performance when they do run ops. Even then—you can guess what the government pays a captain, say. Now imagine that somebody meets that captain at a local bar, buys him a drink, and talks to him. He tells the captain that he might want to be in the southwestern corner of his sector tomorrow night—well, *anywhere but* the northeastern sector, okay? If he decides to patrol one part of his area, but not another, he gets a hundred thousand dollars. Okay, the other side has enough money that they can pay him up front just to see if he'll cooperate. Seed money, kind of. Once he shows he can be bought, they settle down to a smaller but regular payment. Also, the other side has enough product that they can let him do some real seizures once in a while, once they know he's theirs, to make him look good. Someday that captain grows up and becomes a colonel who controls a lot more territory. . . . It's not because they're bad people, it's just that things are so fucking hopeless. Legal institutions are fragile down here and—hell, look at the way things are at home, for Christ's sake. I—"

"I'm not criticizing anybody, Larson," Clark said. "Not everybody can take on a hopeless mission and keep at it." He turned to look out the side window and smiled to himself. "You have to be a little crazy to do that."

5. Beginnings

Chavez awoke with the headache that accompanies initial exposure to a thin atmosphere, the sort that begins just behind the eyes and radiates around the circumference of one's head. For all that, he was grateful. Throughout his career in the Army, he'd never failed to awaken a few minutes before reveille. It allowed him an orderly transition from sleep to wakefulness and made the waking-up process easier to tolerate. He turned his head left and right, inspecting his environment in the orange twilight that came through the uncurtained windows.

The building would be called a barracks by anyone who did not regularly live in one. To Chavez it seemed more of a hunting camp, a guess that was wholly accurate. Perhaps two thousand square feet in the bunk room, he judged, and he counted a total of forty single metal-frame bunks, each with a thin GI mattress and brown GI blanket. The sheets, however, were fitted, with elastic at the corners; so he decided that there wouldn't be any of the bouncing-quarter bullshit, which was fine with him. The floor was bare, waxed pine, and the vaulted ceiling was supported by smoothed-down pine trunks in lieu of finished beams. It struck the sergeant that in hunting season people—rich people—actually paid to live like this: proof positive that money didn't automatically confer brains on anyone. Chavez didn't like barracks life all that much, and the only reason he'd not opted for a private apartment in or near Fort Ord was his desire to save up for that Corvette. To complete the illusion, at the foot of each bed was a genuine Army-surplus footlocker.

He thought about getting up on his elbows to look out the windows, but knew that the time for that would come soon enough. It had been a two-hour drive from the airport, and on arrival each man had been assigned a bunk in the building. The rest of the bunks had already been filled with sleeping, snoring men. Soldiers, of course. Only soldiers snored like that. It had struck him at the time as ominous. The only reason why young men would be asleep and snoring just after ten at night was fatigue. This was no vacation spot. Well, that was no surprise either.

Reveille came in the form of an electric buzzer, the kind associated with a cheap alarm clock. That was good news. No bugle—he hated bugles in the morning. Like most professional soldiers, Chavez knew the value of sleep, and waking up was not a cause for celebration. Bodies stirred around him at once, to the accompaniment of the usual wake-up grumbles and profanity. He tossed off the blanket and was surprised to learn how cold the floor was.

"Who're you?" the man in the next bunk said while staring at the floor.

"Chavez, Staff Sergeant. Bravo, 3rd of the 17th."

"Vega. Me, too. Headquarters Company, 1st/22nd. Get in last night?"

"Yep. What gives here?"

"Well, I don't really know, but they sure did run us ragged yesterday," Staff Sergeant Vega said. He stuck his hand out. "Julio."

"Domingo. Call me Ding."

"Where you from?"

"L.A."

"Chicago. Come on." Vega rose. "One good thing about this place, you got all the hot water you want, and no Mickey Mouse on the housekeeping. Now, if they could just turn the fucking heat on at night—"

"Where the hell are we?"

"Colorado. I know that much. Not much else, though." The two sergeants joined a loose trail of men heading for the showers.

Chavez looked around. Nobody was wearing glasses. Everybody looked pretty fit, even accounting for the fact that they were soldiers. A few were obvious iron-pumpers, but most, like Chavez, had the lean, wiry look of distance runners. One other thing that was so obvious it took him half a minute to notice it. They were all Latinos.

The shower helped. There was a nice, tall pile of new towels, and enough sinks that everyone had room to shave. And the toilet stalls even had doors. Except for the thin air, Chavez decided, this place had real possibilities. Whoever ran the place gave them twenty-five minutes to get it together. It was almost civilized.

Civilization ended promptly at 0630. The men got into their uniforms, which included stout boots, and moved outside. Here Chavez saw four men standing in a line. They had to be officers. You could tell from the posture and the expressions. Behind the four was another, older man, who also looked and acted like an officer, but . . . not quite, Chavez told himself.

"Where do I go?" Ding asked Vega.

"You're supposed to stick with me. Third squad, Captain Ramirez. Tough mother, but a good guy. Hope you like to run, *'mano.*"

"I'll try not to crap out on ya'," Chavez replied.

Vega turned with a grin. "That's what I said."

"Good morning, people!" boomed the voice of the older one. "For those of you who don't know me, I am Colonel Brown. You newcomers, welcome to our little mountain hideaway. You've already gotten to your proper squads, and for everyone's information, our TO and E is now complete. This is the whole team."

It didn't surprise Chavez that Brown was the only obvious non-Latino to be seen. But he didn't know why he wasn't surprised. Four others were walking toward the assembly. They were PT instructors. You can always tell from the clean, white T-shirts and the confidence that they could work anyone into the ground.

"I hope everyone got a good night's sleep," Brown went on. "We will start our day with a little exercise—"

"Sure," Vega muttered, "might as well die before breakfast."

"How long you been here?" Ding asked quietly.

"Second day. Jesus, I hope it gets easier. The officers musta been here a week at least—they don't barf after the run."

"—and a nice little three-mile jog through the hills," Brown ended.

"That's no big deal," Chavez observed.

"That's what I said yesterday," Vega replied. "Thank God I quit smokin'."

Ding didn't know how to react to that. Vega was another light infantryman from the 10th Mountain, and like himself was supposed to be able to move around all day with fifty pounds of gear on his back. But the air was pretty thin, thin enough that Chavez wondered just how high they were.

They started off with the usual daily dozen, and the number of repeats wasn't all that bad, though Chavez found himself breaking a slight sweat. It was the run that told him how tough things would get. As the sun rose above the mountains, he got a feel for what sort of country it was. The camp was nestled in the bottom of a valley, and comprised perhaps fifty acres of almost flat ground. Everything else looked vertical, but on inspection proved to be slopes of less than forty-five degrees, dotted with scruffy-looking little pine trees that would never outgrow the height for Christmas decorations. The four squads, each led by an instructor and a captain, moved in different directions, up horse trails worn into the mountainside. In the first mile, Chavez reckoned, they had climbed over five hundred feet, snaking their way along numerous switchbacks toward a rocky knoll. The instructor didn't bother with the usual singing that accompanied formation running. There wasn't much of a formation anyway, just a single-file of men struggling to keep pace with a faceless robot whose white shirt beckoned them on toward destruction. Chavez, who hadn't run a distance less than three miles, every day for the last two years of his life, was gasping for breath after the first. He wanted to say something, like, "There isn't any fuckin' air!" But he didn't want to waste the oxygen. He needed every little molecule for his bloodstream. The instructor stopped at the knoll to make sure everyone was there, and Chavez, jogging doggedly in place, had the chance to see a vista worthy of an Ansel Adams photograph—all the better in the full light of a morning sun. But his only thought on being able to see over forty miles was terror that he'd have to run it all.

God, I thought I was in shape!

Hell, I am *in shape!*

The next mile traced a ridgeline to the east, and the sun punished eyes that had to stay alert. This was a narrow trail, and going off it could involve a painful fall. The instructor gradually picked up the pace, or so it seemed, until he stopped again at another knoll.

"Keep those legs pumpin'!" he snarled at those who'd kept up. There were two stragglers, both new men, Chavez thought, and they were only twenty yards back. You could see the shame on their faces, and the determination to catch up. "Okay, people, it's downhill from here."

And it was, mostly, but that only made it more dangerous. Legs rubbery from the fatigue that comes from oxygen deprivation had to negotiate a downward slope that alternated from gradual to perilously steep, with plenty of loose rocks for the unwary. Here the instructor eased off on the pace, for safety as everyone guessed. The captain let his men pass, and took up the rear to keep an eye on things. They could see the camp now. Five buildings. Smoke rose from a chimney to promise breakfast. Chavez saw a helipad, half a dozen vehicles—all four-wheel-drives—and what could only be a rifle range. There was no other sign of human habitation in sight, and the sergeant realized that even the wide view he'd had earlier hadn't shown any buildings closer than five or six miles. It wasn't hard to figure out why the area was sparsely settled. But he didn't have time or energy for deep thoughts at the moment. His eyes locked on the trail, Ding Chavez concentrated on his footing and the pace. He took up a position alongside one of the erstwhile stragglers and kept an eye on him. Already Chavez was thinking of this as his squad, and soldiers are supposed to look out for one another. But the man had firmed up. His head was high now, his hands balled into tight, determined fists, and his powerfully exhaled breaths had purpose in them as the trail finally flattened out and they approached the camp. Another group was coming in from the far side.

"Form up, people!" Captain Ramirez called out for the first time. He passed his men and took the place of the instructor, who peeled off to let them by. Chavez noted that the bastard wasn't even sweating. Third Squad formed into a double line behind their officer.

"Squad! Quick-time, march!" Everyone slowed to a regular marching pace. This took the strain off lungs and legs, told them that they were now the custody of their captain, and reminded them that they were still part of the Army. Ramirez delivered them in front of their barracks. The captain didn't order anyone to sing a cadence, though. That made him smart, Chavez thought, smart enough to know that nobody had enough breath to do so. Julio was right, probably. Ramirez might be a good boss.

"Squad, halt!" Ramirez turned. "At ease, people. Now, that wasn't so bad, was it?"

"Madre de Dios!" a voice noted quietly. From the back rank, a man tried to vomit but couldn't find anything to bring up.

"Okay." Ramirez grinned at his men. "The altitude is a real bitch. But I've been here two weeks. You get used to it right quick. Two weeks from now, we'll be running five miles a day with packs, and you'll feel just fine."

Bullshit. Chavez shared the thought with Julio Vega, knowing that the captain was right, of course. The first day at boot camp had been harder than this . . . hadn't it?

"We're taking it easy on you. You have an hour to unwind and get some breakfast. Go easy on the chow: we'll have another little run this afternoon. At 0800 we assemble here for training. Dismissed."

"Well?" Ritter asked.

They sat on the shaded veranda of an old planter's house on the island of St. Kitts. Clark wondered what they'd planted here once. Probably sugarcane, though there was nothing now. What had once been a plantation manor was obviously supposed to look like the island retreat of a top-drawer capitalist and his collection of mistresses. In fact it belonged to CIA, which used it as an informal conference center, a particularly nice safe house for the debriefing of VIP defectors, and other, more mundane uses—like a vacation spot for senior executives.

"The background info was fairly accurate, but it underestimated the physical difficulties. I'm not criticizing the people who put the package together. You just have to see it to believe it. It's very tough country." Clark stretched in the wicker chair and reached for his drink. His personal seniority at the Agency was many levels below Ritter's, but Clark was one of a handful of CIA employees whose position was unique. That, plus the fact that he often worked personally for the Deputy Director (Operations), gave him the right to relax in the DDO's presence. Ritter's attitude toward the younger man was not one of deference, but he did show Clark considerable respect. "How's Admiral Greer doing?" Clark asked. It was James Greer who'd actually recruited him, many years before.

"Doesn't look very good. Couple of months at most," Ritter replied.

"Damn." Clark stared into his drink, then looked up. "I owe that man a lot. Like my whole life. They can't do anything?"

"No, it's spread too much for that. They can keep him comfortable, that's about all. Sorry. He's my friend, too."

"Yes, sir, I know." Clark finished off his drink and went back to work. "I still don't know exactly what you have in mind, but you can forget about going after them in their houses."

"That tough?"

Clark nodded. "That tough. It's a job for real infantry with real support, and even then you're going to take real casualties. From what Larson tells me, the security troops these characters have are pretty good. I suppose you might try to buy a few off, but they're probably well paid already, so that might just backfire." The field officer didn't ask what the real mission was, but he assumed it was to snatch some warm bodies and whisk them off stateside, where they'd arrive gift-wrapped in front of some FBI office, or maybe a U.S. courthouse. Like everyone else, he was making an incorrect guess. "Same thing with bagging one on the move. They take the usual precautions—irregular schedules, irregular routes, and they have armed escorts everywhere they go. So bagging one on the fly means having good intel, which means having somebody on the inside. Larson is as close to being inside as anybody we've ever run, and he's not close enough. Trying to get him in closer will get him killed. He's gotten us some good data—Larson's a pretty good kid—and the risks of trying that are just too great. I presume the local people have tried to—''

''They have. Six of them ended up dead or missing. Same thing with informers. They disappear a lot. The locals are thoroughly penetrated. They can't run any sort of op for long without risking their own. You do that long enough and people stop volunteering.''

Clark shrugged and looked out to seaward. There was a white-hulled cruise ship inbound on the horizon. ''I suppose I shouldn't have been surprised at how tough these bastards are. Larson was right, what brains they don't already have they can buy. Where do they hire their consultants?''

''Open market, mainly Europe, and—''

''I mean the intel pros. They must have some real spooks.''

''Well, there's Félix Cortez. That's only a rumor, but the name's come up half a dozen times in the past few months.''

''The DGI colonel who disappeared,'' Clark observed. The DGI was Cuba's intelligence service, modeled on the Soviet KGB. Cortez had been reported working with the Macheteros, a Puerto Rican terrorist group that the FBI had largely run to ground in the past few years. Another DGI colonel named Filiberto Ojeda had been arrested by the Bureau, after which Cortez had disappeared. So he'd decided to remain outside his country's borders. Next question: had Cortez decided to opt for this most vigorous branch of the free-enterprise system or was he still working under Cuban control? Either way, DGI was Russian-trained. Its senior people were graduates of the KGB's own academy. They were, therefore, opponents worthy of respect. Certainly Cortez was. His file at the Agency spoke of a genius for compromising people to get information.

''Larson know about this?''

''Yeah. He caught the name at a party. Of course, it would help if we knew what the hell Cortez looks like, but all we have is a description that fits half the people south of the Rio Grande. Don't worry. Larson knows how to be careful, and if anything goes wrong, he's got his own airplane to get out of Dodge with. His orders are fairly specific on that score. I don't want to lose a trained field officer doing police work.'' Ritter added, ''I sent you down for a fresh appraisal. You know what the overall objective is. Tell me what you think is possible.''

''Okay. You're probably right to go after the airfields and to keep it an intelligence-gathering operation. Given the necessary surveillance assets, we *could* finger processing sites fairly easily, but there's a lot of them and their mobility demands a rapid reaction time to get there. I figure that'll work maybe a half-dozen times, max, before the other side wises up. Then we'll take casualties, and if the bad guys get lucky, we might lose a whole assault force—if you've got people thinking in those terms. Tracking the finished product from the processing sites is probably impossible without a whole lot of people on the ground—too many to keep it a covert op for very long—and it wouldn't buy us very much anyway. There are a lot of little airfields on the northern part of the country to keep an eye on, but Larson thinks that they may be victims of their own success. They've been so successful buying off the military and police in that district that they might be falling into a regular pattern of airfield use. If the insertion teams keep a low profile, they could conceivably operate for two months—that may be a little generous—before we have to yank them out. I need to see the teams, see how good they are.''

''I can arrange that,'' Ritter said. He'd already decided to send Clark to Colorado. Clark was the best man to evaluate their capabilities. ''Go on.''

''What we're setting up will go all right for a month or two. We can watch their aircraft lift off and call it ahead to whoever else is wrapped up in this.'' This was the only part of the op that Clark knew about. ''We can inconvenience them for that long, but I wouldn't hope for much more.''

''You're painting a fairly bleak picture, Clark.''

Clark leaned forward. ''Sir, if you want to run a covert operation to gather usable tactical intelligence against an adversary who's this decentralized in his own operations—yes, it's possible, but only for a limited period of time and only for a limited return. If you increase the assets to try and make it more effective, you're going to get blown sure as hell. You can run an operation like that, but it can't be for long. I don't know why we're even bothering.'' That wasn't quite true. Clark figured, correctly, that the reason was that it was an election year, but that wasn't the sort of observation a field officer was allowed to make—especially when it was a correct one.

''Why we're bothering isn't strictly your concern,'' Ritter pointed out. He didn't raise his voice. He didn't have to, and Clark was not a man to be intimidated.

''Fine, but this is not a serious undertaking. It's an old story, sir. Give us a mission we can do, not one we can't. Are we serious about this or aren't we?''

''What do you have in mind?'' Ritter asked.

Clark told him. Ritter's face showed little in the way of emotion at the answer to his question. One of the nice things about Clark, Ritter thought to himself, was that he was the only man in the Agency who could discuss these topics calmly and dispassionately—and really mean it. There were quite a few for whom such talk was an interesting intellectual exercise, unprofessional speculation, really, gotten consciously or subconsciously from reading spy fiction. *Gee, wouldn't it be nice if we could* . . . It was widely believed in the general public that the Central Intelligence Agency employed a goodly number of expert professionals in this particular field. It didn't. Even the KGB had gotten away from such things, farming this kind of work out to the Bulgarians—regarded by their own associates as uncouth barbarians—or genuine third-parties like terrorist groups in Europe and the Middle East. The political cost of such operations was too high, and despite the mania for secrecy cultivated by every intelligence service in the world, such things always got out eventually. The world had gotten far more civilized since Ritter had graduated from The Farm on the York River, and while he thought that a genuinely good thing, there were times when a return to the good old days beckoned with solutions to problems that hadn't quite gone away.

''How hard would it be?'' Ritter asked, interested.

''With the proper backup and some additional assets—it's a snap.'' Clark explained what special assets were needed. ''Everything they've done plays into our hands. That's the one mistake they've made. They're conventional in their defensive outlook. Same old thing, really. It's a matter of who determines the rules of the game. As things now stand, we both play by the same rules, and those rules, as applied here, give the advantage to the opposition. We never seem to learn that. We always let the other side set the rules. We can annoy them, inconvenience them, take away some of their profit margin, but, hell, given what they already make, it's a minor business loss. I only see one thing changing that.''

''Which is?''

''How'd you like to live in a house like that one?'' Clark asked, handing over one of his photographs.

''Frank Lloyd Wright meets Ludwig the Mad,'' Ritter observed with a chuckle.

Unions—neutralized with hired thugs. Governments—bribed and subverted. The press—allowed to bray on . . . until too many people listened. He'd learned from that example. The local press was no longer terribly outspoken, not after learning that its members were mortal. The railroad barons had built themselves palatial homes—winter ones in New York, and summer "cottages" at Newport. Of course, he had problems that they'd not faced, but any historical model broke down if you took it too far. He also chose to ignore the fact that the Goulds and the Harrimans had built something that was useful, not destructive, to their societies. One other lesson he had learned from the previous century was that cutthroat competition was wasteful. He had persuaded his father to seek out his competitors. Even then his powers of persuasion had been impressive. Cleverly, it had been done at a time when danger from outside forces made cooperation attractive. Better to cooperate, the argument had gone, than to waste time, money, energy, and blood—and increase their own personal vulnerabilities. And it had worked.

His name was Ernesto Escobedo. He was one of many within the Cartel, but most of his peers would acknowledge that his was a voice to which all listened. They might not all agree, not all bend to his will, but his ideas were always given the attention they deserved because they had proven to be effective ones. The Cartel had no head as such, since the Cartel was not a single enterprise, but rather a collection of leaders who operated in close confederation—almost a committee, but not quite; almost friends, but not that either. The comparison to the American Mafia suggested itself, but the Cartel was both more civilized and more savage than that. Escobedo would have chosen to say that the Cartel was more effectively organized, and more vigorous, both attributes of a young and vital organization, as opposed to one that was older and feudal.

He knew that the sons of the robber barons had used the wealth accumulated by their antecedents to form a power elite, coming to rule their nation with their "service." He was unwilling to leave such a legacy to his sons, however. Besides, he himself was technically one of the second generation. Things moved more quickly now. The accumulation of great wealth no longer demanded a lifetime, and, therefore, Ernesto told himself, he didn't have to leave that to his sons. He could have it all. The first step in accomplishing any goal was deciding that it was possible. He had long since come to that decision.

It was his goal to see it done. Escobedo was forty, a man of uncommon vigor and confidence. He had never used the product which he provided for others, instead altering his consciousness with wine—and that rarely, now. A glass or two with dinner; perhaps some hard liquor at business meetings with his peers, but more often Perrier. This trait earned him more respect among his associates. Escobedo was a sober, serious man, they all knew. He exercised regularly, and paid attention to his appearance. A smoker in his youth, he'd broken the habit young. He watched his diet. His mother was still alive and vigorous at seventy-three; her mother was the same at ninety-one. His father would have been seventy-five last week, he knew, except for . . . but the people who'd ended his father's life had paid a savage price for their crime, along with all of their families, mostly at Escobedo's own hand. It was something he remembered with filial pride, taking the last one's wife while her dying husband watched, killing her and the two little ones before his eyes closed for the last time. He took no pleasure in killing women and children, of course, but such things were necessary. He'd shown that one who was the better man, and as word of the feat spread, it had become unlikely that his family would ever be troubled again. He took no pleasure from it, but history taught that harsh lessons

"The man who commissioned that house is growing quite an ego, sir. They hav manipulated whole governments. Everyone says that they *are* a government for al practical purposes. They said the same thing in Chicago during Prohibition, tha Capone really ran the town—just one city, right? Well, these people are on thei way to running their own *country,* and renting out others. So let's say that they do have the *de facto* power of a government. Factor ego into that. Sooner or later they're going to start acting like one. I know we won't break the rules. But it wouldn't surprise me if they stepped outside them once or twice, just to see what they might get away with. You see what I mean? They keep expanding their own limits, and they haven't found the brick wall yet, the one that tells them where to stop."

"John, you're turning into a psychologist," Ritter noted with a thin smile.

"Maybe so. These guys peddle addictive drugs, right? Mostly they do not use the stuff themselves, but I think they're getting themselves hooked on the most powerful narcotic there is."

"Power."

Clark nodded. "Sooner or later, they're going to OD. At that point, sir, somebody's going to think seriously about what I just proposed. When you get into the majors, the rules change some. That's a political decision, of course."

He was master of all he surveyed. At least that was the phrase that came to mind, and with all such aphorisms it could be both true and false at the same time. The valley into which he looked did not all belong to him; the parcel of land on which he stood was less than a thousand hectares, and his vista included a million. But not one person who lived within his view could continue to live were he to decide otherwise. That was the only sort of power that mattered, and it was a form of power that he had exercised on occasions too numerous to count. A flick of the wrist, a casual remark to an associate, and it was done. It wasn't that he had ever been casual about it—death was a serious business—but he knew that he could be. It was the sort of power that might make a man mad, he knew. He'd seen it happen among his own business associates, to their sorrow on several occasions. But he was a student of the world, and a student of history. Unusually, for someone in his chosen trade, he was the beneficiary of a good education, something forced on him by his late father, one of the pioneers. One of the greatest regrets of his life was that he'd never expressed his gratitude for it. Because of it he understood economics as well as any university professor. He understood market forces and trends. And he understood the historical forces that brought them about. He was a student o Marxism; though he rejected the Marxist outlook for a multiplicity of reasons, h knew that it contained more than one grain of truth intermixed with all the politica gibberish. The rest of his professional education had been what Americans calle "on-the-job training." While his father had helped invent a whole new way c doing business, he had watched and advised, and taken action. He'd explored ne markets, under his father's direction, and formed the reputation of a careful, tho ough planner, often sought after but never apprehended. He'd been arrested on once, but after two of the witnesses had died, the others had grown forgetful, endi his direct experience with police and courts.

He deemed himself a carry-over from another age—a classic robber-baron capit ist. A hundred years before, they'd driven railroads across the United States— was a genuine expert on that country—and crushed anything in their path. Ind tribes—treated like a two-legged version of the plains buffalo and swatted asi made for long memories. It also taught that those who failed to teach such lessons would not be respected. Escobedo demanded respect above all things. His personal involvement in settling that particular account, instead of leaving it to hirelings, had earned him considerable prestige within the organization. Ernesto was a thinker, his associates said, but he knew how to get things done.

His wealth was so great that counting it had no point. He had the godlike power of life and death. He had a beautiful wife and three fine sons. When the marriage bed palled, he had a choice of mistresses. Every luxury that money could purchase, he had. He had homes in the city below him, this hilltop fortress, and ranches near the sea—both seas, in fact, since Colombia borders on two great oceans. At the ranches were stables full of Arabian horses. Some of his associates had private bull rings, but that sport had never interested him. A crack shot, he had hunted everything that his country offered—including men, of course. He told himself that he ought to be satisfied. But he was not.

The American robber barons had traveled the world, had been invited to the courts of Europe, had married off their progeny to that of noble houses—a cynical exercise, he knew, but somehow a worthy one that he fully understood. The freedoms were denied him, and though the reason for it was plain enough, he was nevertheless offended that a man of his power and wealth could be denied anything. Despite everything that he had accomplished, there were still limits on his life—worse still, the limits were placed there by others of lesser power. Twenty years earlier he had chosen his path to greatness, and despite his obvious success, the fact that he'd chosen that particular path denied him the fruits that he wanted, because lesser men did not approve of it.

It had not always been so. "Law?" one of the great railroad men had said once. "What do I care about law?" And he had gotten away with it, had traveled about at will, had been recognized as a great man.

So why not me? Escobedo asked himself. Part of him knew the answer, but a more powerful part rejected it. He was not a stupid man, far less a foolish one, but he had not come so far to have others set rules upon his life. Ernesto had, in fact, violated every rule he wished, and prospered from it. He had gotten here by making his own rules, the businessman decided. He would have to learn to make some new ones. They would learn to deal with him, on terms of his own choosing. He was tired of having to accommodate the terms of others. Having made the decision, he began to explore methods.

What had worked for others?

The most obvious answer was—success. That which one could not defeat, one had to acknowledge. International politics had as few rules as any other major enterprise, except for the only one that mattered—success. There was not a country in the world that failed to make deals with murderers, after all; it was just that the murderers in question had to be effective ones. Kill a few million people and one was a statesman. Did not every nation in the world kowtow to the Chinese—and had they not killed millions of their own? Didn't America seek to accommodate the Russians—and had they not killed millions of their own? Under Carter, the Americans had supported the regime of Pol Pot, which had killed millions of its own. Under Reagan, America had sought to reach a *modus vivendi* with the same Iranians who had killed so many of their own, including most of those who thought of America as a friend—and been abandoned. America befriended dictators with bloody hands—some on the right and some on the left—in the name of *realpolitik,* while refusing to support moderates—left or right—because they might not be quite moderate enough. Any country so lacking in principle could come to recognize him and his associates, couldn't it? That was the central truth about America in Ernesto's view. While he had principles from which he would not deviate, America did not.

The corruption of America was manifest to Ernesto. He, after all, fed it. For years now, forces in his largest and most important market had lobbied to legalize his business there. Fortunately they had all failed. That would have been disaster for the Cartel, and was yet another example of how a government lacked the wit to act in its own self-interest. The American government could have made billions from the business—as he and his associates did—but lacked the vision and the good sense to do so. And they called themselves a great power. For all their supposed strength, the *yanquis* had no will, no manhood. He could regulate the goings-on where he lived, but they could not. They could range over oceans, fill the air with warplanes—but use them to protect their own interests? He shook his head with amusement.

No, the Americans were not to be respected.

6. Deterrence

Felix Cortez traveled with a Costa Rican passport. If someone noted his Cuban accent, he'd explain that his family had left that country when he was a boy, but by carefully selecting his port of entry, he avoided that notice. Besides, he was working on the accent. Cortez was fluent in three languages—English and Russian in addition to his native Spanish. A raffishly handsome man, his tropical complexion was barely different from a vacationer's tan. The neat mustache and custom-tailored suit proclaimed him a successful businessman, and the gleaming white teeth made him a pleasant one at that. He waited in the immigration line at Dulles International Airport, chatting with the lady behind him until he got to the INS inspector, as resignedly unhurried as any frequent traveler.

"Good afternoon, sir," the inspector said, barely looking up from the passport. "What brings you to America?"

"Business," Cortez replied.

"Uh-huh," the inspector grunted. He flipped through the passport and saw numerous entry stamps. The man traveled a lot, and about half his trips in the previous . . . four years were to the States. The stamps were evenly split between Miami, Washington, and Los Angeles. "How long will you be staying?"

"Five days."

"Anything to declare?"

"Just my clothes, and my business notes." Cortez held up his briefcase.

"Welcome to America, Mr. Díaz." The inspector stamped the passport and handed it back.

"Thank you." He moved off to collect his bag, a large and well-used two-suiter. He tried to come through American airports at slack hours. This was less for convenience than because it was unusual for someone who had something to hide. At slack times the inspectors had all the time they needed to annoy people, and the sniffer dogs weren't rushed along the rows of luggage. It was also easier to spot surveillance when the airport concourses were uncrowded, of course, and Cortez/Díaz was an expert at countersurveillance.

His next stop was the Hertz counter, where he rented a full-size Chevy. Cortez had no love for Americans, but he did like their big cars. The routine was down pat. He used a Visa card. The young lady at the counter asked the usual question about joining the Hertz Number One Club, and he took the proffered brochure with feigned interest. The only reason he used a rental car company more than once was that there weren't enough to avoid repetition. Similarly, he never used the same passport twice, nor the same credit cards. At a place near his home he had an ample supply of both. He had come to Washington to see one of the people who made that possible.

His legs were still stiff as he walked out to get his car—he could have taken the courtesy van, but he'd been sitting for too long. The damp heat of a late spring day reminded him of home. Not that he remembered Cuba all that fondly, but his former government had, after all, given him the training that he needed for his current job. All the school classes on Marxism-Leninism, telling people who scarcely had food to eat that they lived in paradise. In Cortez's case, they'd had the effect of telling him what he wanted out of life. His training in the DGI had given him the first taste of privilege, and the unending political instruction had only made his government look all the more grotesque in its claims and its goals. But he'd played the game, and learned what he'd needed to learn, exchanging his time for training and field work, learning how capitalist societies work, learning how to penetrate and subvert them, learning their strong points and weak ones. The contrast between the two was entertaining to the former colonel. The relative poverty in Puerto Rico had looked like paradise to him, even while working along with fellow Colonel Ojeda and the Machetero savages to overthrow it—and replace it with Cuba's version of socialist realism. Cortez shook his head in amusement as he walked toward the parking lot.

Twenty feet over the Cuban's head, Liz Murray dropped her husband off behind a vanload of travelers. There was barely time for a kiss. She had errands to run, and they'd call Dan's flight in another ten minutes.

"I ought to be back tomorrow afternoon," he said as he got out.

"Good," Liz replied. "Remember the movers."

"I won't." Dan closed the door and took three steps. "I mean, I won't forget, honey . . ." He turned in time to see his wife laughing as she drove off; she'd done it to him again. "It's not fair," he grumbled to himself. "Bring you back from London, big promotion, and second day on the job they drop you in the soup." He walked through the self-opening doors into the terminal and found a TV monitor with his flight information. He had only one bag, and that was small enough to carry on. He'd already reviewed the paperwork—it had all been faxed to Washington by the Mobile Field Office and was the subject of considerable talk in the Hoover Building.

The next step was getting through the metal detector. Actually he bypassed it. The attendant gave out the usual, "Excuse me, sir," and Murray held up his ID folder, identifying himself as Daniel E. Murray, Deputy Assistant Director of the Federal Bureau of Investigation. There was no way he could have passed through the magnetometer, not with the Smith & Wesson automatic clipped to his belt, and people in airports tended to get nervous if he showed what he was carrying. Not that he shot that well with it. He hadn't even requalified yet. That was scheduled for the next week. They weren't so strict about that with top-level FBI management—his main workplace hazard now came from staple pullers—but though Murray was a man with few vanities, shooting skill was one of them. For no particular reason, Murray was worried about that. After four years in London as the legal attaché, he knew that he needed some serious practice before he would shoot "expert" with either hand again, especially with a new gun. His beloved stainless-steel Colt Python .357 was in retirement. The Bureau was switching over to automatics, and on his arrival in his new office he'd found the engraved S&W gift-wrapped on his desk, a present arranged by his friend Bill Shaw, the newly appointed executive assistant director (Investigations). Bill always had been a class act. Murray switched the bag to his left hand and surreptitiously checked to see that the gun was in place, much as an ordinary citizen might check for his wallet. The only bad thing about his London duty was being unarmed. Like any American cop, Murray felt slightly naked without a gun, even though he'd never had cause to use one in anger. If nothing else, he could make sure that this flight didn't go to Cuba. He wouldn't have much chance to do hands-on law enforcement anymore, of course. Now he was part of management, another way of saying that he was too old to be useful, Murray told himself as he selected a seat close to the departure gate. The problem at hand was about as close as he was going to get to handling a real case, and it was happening only because the Director had got hold of the file and called in Bill Shaw who, in turn, had decided that he wanted someone he knew to take a look at it. It promised to be ticklish. They were really starting him off with a cute one.

The flight took just over two hours of routine boredom and a dry meal. Murray was met at the gate by Supervisory Special Agent Mark Bright, assistant special-agent-in-charge of the Mobile Field Office.

"Any other bags, Mr. Murray?"

"Just this one—and the name's Dan," Murray replied. "Has anybody talked to them yet?"

"Not in yet—that is, I don't think so." Bright checked his watch. "They were due in about ten, but they got called in on a rescue last night. Some fishing boat blew up and the cutter had to get the crew off. It made the morning TV news. Nice job, evidently."

"Super," Murray observed. "We're going in to grill a friggin' hero, and he's gone and done it again."

"You know this guy's background?" Bright asked. "I haven't had much chance to—"

"I've been briefed. Hero's the right word. This Wegener's a legend. Red Wegener's called the King of SAR—that means search-and-rescue. Half the people who've ever been to sea, he's saved at one time or another. At least that's the word on the guy. He's got some big-time friends on The Hill, too."

"Like?"

"Senator Billings of Oregon." Murray explained why briefly.

"Chairman of Judiciary. Why couldn't he just have stayed with Transportation?" Bright asked the ceiling. The Senate Judiciary Committee had oversight duties for the FBI.

"How new are you on this case?"

"I'm here because DEA liaison is my job. I didn't see the file until just before lunch. Been out of the office for a couple of days," Bright said as he walked through the door. "We just had a baby."

''Oh,'' Murray noted. You couldn't blame a man for that. ''Congratulations. Everyone all right?''

''Brought Marianne home this morning, and Sandra is the cutest thing I ever saw. Noisy, though.''

Murray laughed. It had been quite a while since he'd had to handle an infant. Bright's car turned out to be a Ford whose engine purred like a well-fed tiger. Some paperwork on Captain Wegener lay on the front seat. Murray leafed through it while Bright picked his way out of the airport parking lot. It fleshed out what he'd heard in Washington.

''This is some story.''

''How 'bout that.'' Bright nodded. ''You don't suppose this is all true, do you?''

''I've heard some crazy ones before, but this one would be the all-time champ.'' Murray paused. ''The funny thing is—''

''Yeah,'' the younger agent agreed. ''Me, too. Our DEA colleagues believe it, but what broke loose out of this—I mean, even if the evidence is all tossed, what we got out of this is so—''

''Right.'' Which was the other reason Murray was involved in the case. ''How important was the victim?''

''Big-time political connections, directorships of banks, the University of Alabama, the usual collection of civic groups—you name it. This guy wasn't just a solid member of the community, he was goddamned Stone Mountain.'' Both men knew that was in Georgia, but the point was made. ''Old family, back to a Civil War general. His grandfather was a governor.''

''Money?''

Bright grunted. ''More than I'd ever need. Big place north of town, still a working farm—plantation, I guess you'd call it, but that's not where it comes from. He put all the family money into real-estate development. Very successfully as far as we can tell. The development stuff is a maze of small corporations—the usual stuff. We've got a team working, but it'll take awhile to sort through it. Some of the corporate veils are overseas, though, and we may never get it all. You know how that goes. We've barely begun to check things out.''

'' 'Prominent local businessman tied to drug kingpins.' Christ, he hid things real well. Never had a sniff?''

''Nary a one,'' Bright admitted. ''Not us, not DEA, not the local cops. Nothing at all.''

Murray closed the file and nodded at the traffic. This was only the opening crack in a case that could develop into man-years of investigative work. *Hell, we don't even know exactly what we're looking for yet,* the deputy assistant director told himself. *All we do know is that there was a cold million dollars in used twenties and fifties aboard the good ship* Empire Builder. So much cash could only mean one thing—but that wasn't true. It could mean lots of things, Murray thought.

''Here we are.''

Getting onto the base was easy enough, and Bright knew the way to the pier. *Panache* looked pretty big from the car, a towering white cliff with a bright-orange stripe and some dark smudgemarks near midships. Murray knew that she was a small ship, but one needed a big ocean to tell. By the time he and Bright got out of the car, someone got on the phone at the head of the gangway, and another man appeared there within seconds. Murray recognized him from the file. It was Wegener.

The man had the muddy remains of what had once been red hair, but was now sprinkled with enough gray to defy an accurate description. He looked fit enough, the FBI agent thought as he came up the aluminum brow, a slight roll at the waist, but little else. A tattoo on his forearm marked him for a sailorman, and the impassive eyes marked the face of a man unaccustomed to questioning of any kind.

"Welcome aboard. I'm Red Wegener," the man said with enough of a smile to be polite.

"Thank you, Captain. I'm Dan Murray and this is Mark Bright."

"They told me you were FBI," the captain observed.

"I'm a deputy assistant director, down from Washington. Mark's the assistant special-agent-in-charge of the Mobile Office." Wegener's face changed a bit, Murray saw.

"Well, I know why you're here. Let's go to my cabin to discuss things."

"What's with all the scorching?" Dan asked as the captain led off. There was something about the way he'd said that. Something . . . odd.

"Shrimp boat had an engine fire. Happened five miles away from us last night while we were on the way in. The fuel tanks blew just as we came alongside. Got lucky. Nobody killed, but the mate was burned some."

"How about the boat?" Bright asked.

"Couldn't save her. Getting the crew off was pretty tricky." Wegener held open the door for his visitors. "Sometimes that's the best you can do. You gentlemen want any coffee?"

Murray declined. His eyes really bored in on the captain now. More than anything else, Dan thought, he looked embarrassed. Wrong emotion. Wegener got his guests seated, then took his chair behind the desk.

"I know why you're here," Red announced. "It's all my fault."

"Uh, Captain, before you go any farther—" Bright tried to say.

"I've pulled some dumb ones in my time, but this time I really fucked up," Wegener went on as he lit his pipe. "You don't mind if I smoke, do you?"

"No, not at all," Murray lied. He didn't know what was coming, but he knew that it wasn't what Bright thought. He knew several other things that Bright didn't know, also. "Why don't you tell us about it?"

Wegener reached into his desk drawer and pulled something out. He tossed it to Murray. It was a pack of cigarettes.

"One of our friends dropped this on the deck and I had one of my people give this back to them. I figured—well, look at it. I mean, it looks like a pack of cigarettes, right? And when we have people in custody, we're supposed to treat 'em decent, right? So, I let 'em have their smokes. They're joints, of course. So, when we questioned them—especially the one who talked—well, he was high as a kite. That screws it all up, doesn't it?"

"That's not all, Captain, is it?" Murray asked innocently.

"Chief Riley roughed one of 'em up. My responsibility. I talked to the chief about it. The, uh, I forget his name—the obnoxious one—well, he spit on me, and Riley was there, and Riley got a little pissed and roughed him up some. He should not have done it, but this is a military organization, and when you spit on the boss, well, the troops might not like it. So Riley got a little out of hand—but it happened on my ship and it's my responsibility."

Murray and Bright exchanged a look. The suspects hadn't talked about that at all.

"Captain, that's not why we're here exactly," Murray said after a moment.

"Oh?" Wegener said. "Then why?"

"They say that you executed one of them," Bright replied. The stateroom was quiet for a moment. Murray could hear someone hammering on something, but the loudest noise came from the air-conditioning vent.

"They're both alive, aren't they? There were only two of them, and they're both alive. I sent that tape on the helicopter when we searched the yacht. I mean, if they're both alive, which one did we shoot?"

"Hanged," Murray said. "They say you hanged one."

"Wait a minute." He lifted the phone and punched a button. "Bridge, captain speaking. Send the XO to my stateroom. Thank you." The phone went back into place, and Wegener looked up. "If it's all right with you, I want my executive officer to hear this also."

Murray managed to keep his face impassive. *You should have known, Danny,* he told himself. *They've had plenty of time to work out the little details, and Mr. Wegener is nobody's fool. He's got a U.S. senator to hide behind, and he handed us two cold-blooded killers. Even without the confession, there's enough evidence for a capital murder case, and if you trash Wegener, you run the risk of losing that. The prominence of the victim—well, the U.S. Attorney won't go for it. No chance.* . . . There wasn't a United States Attorney in all of America who lacked political ambition, and putting these two in the electric chair was worth half a million votes. Murray couldn't run the risk of screwing this case up. FBI Director Jacobs had been a federal prosecutor, and he'd understand. Murray decided that it might make things a lot easier.

The XO appeared a moment later, and after introductions were exchanged, Bright went on with his version of what the subjects had told the local FBI office. It took about five minutes during which Wegener puffed on his pipe and let his eyes go slightly wide.

"Sir," the XO told Bright when he was finished. "I've heard a couple of good sea stories, but that one's the all-time champ."

"It's my fault," Wegener grumbled with a shake of the head. "Lettin' 'em have their pot back."

"How come nobody noticed what they were smoking?" Murray asked, less with curiosity for the answer than for the skill with which it was delivered. He was surprised when the XO replied.

"There's an A/C return right outside the brig. We don't keep a constant watch on prisoners—these were our first, by the way—because that's supposed to be unduly intimidating or something. Anyway, it's in our procedure book that we don't. Besides, we don't have all that many people aboard that we can spare 'em. What with the smoke getting sucked out, nobody noticed the smell until that night. Then it was too late. When we brought them into the wardroom for questioning—one at a time; that's in the book, too—they were both kinda glassy-eyed. The first one didn't talk. The second one did. You have the tape, don't you?"

"Yes, I've seen it," Bright answered.

"Then you saw that we read them their rights, right off the card we carry, just like it says. But—hung 'em? Damn. That's crazy. I mean, that's really crazy. We don't—I mean, we can't. I don't even know when it was legal to do it."

"The last time I know about was 1843," the captain said. "The reason there's a Naval Academy at Annapolis is because some people got strung up on USS *Somers*. One of them was the son of the Secretary of War. Supposedly it was an attempted mutiny, but there was quite a stink about it. We don't hang people anymore,'' Wegener concluded wryly. ''I've been in the service a long time, but I don't go that far back.''

''We can't even have a general court-martial,'' the XO added. ''Not by ourselves, I mean. The manual for that weighs about ten pounds. Gawd, you need a judge, and real lawyers, all that stuff. I've been in the service for almost nine years, and I've never even seen a real one—just the practice things in law classes at the Academy. All we ever do aboard is Captain's Mast, and not much of that.''

''Not a bad idea, though. I wouldn't have minded hanging those sons of bitches,'' Wegener observed. It struck Murray as a very strange, and very clever, thing to say. He felt a little sorry for Bright, who'd probably never had a case go this way. In that sense Murray was grateful for his time as legal attaché in London. He understood politics better than most agents.

''Oh?''

''When I was a little kid, they used to hang murderers. I grew up in Kansas. And you know, there weren't many murders back then. Course, we're too civilized to do that now, and so we got murders every damned day. Civilized,'' Wegener snorted. ''XO, did they ever hang pirates like this?''

''I don't think so. Blackbeard's crew was tried at Williamsburg—ever been there?—the old courthouse in the tourist part of the place. I remember hearing that they were actually hung where one of the Holiday Inns is. And Captain Kidd was taken home to England for hanging, wasn't he? Yeah, they had a place called Execution Dock or something like that. So—no, I don't think they really did it aboard ship, even in the old days. Damn sure we didn't do it. Christ, what a story.''

''So it never happened,'' Murray said, not in the form of a question.

''No, sir, it did not,'' Wegener replied. The XO nodded to support his captain.

''And you're willing to say that under oath.''

''Sure. Why not?''

''If it's all right with you, I also need to speak to one of your chiefs. It's the one who 'assaulted' the—''

''Is Riley aboard?'' Wegener asked the XO.

''Yeah. Him and Portagee were working on something or other down in the goat locker.''

''Okay, let's go see 'em.'' Wegener rose and waved for his visitors to follow.

''You need me, sir? I have some work to do.''

''Sure thing, XO. Thanks.''

''Aye aye. See you gentlemen later,'' the lieutenant said, and disappeared around a corner.

The walk took longer than Murray expected. They had to detour around two work parties who were repainting bulkheads. The chiefs' quarters—called the goat locker for reasons ancient and obscure—was located aft. Riley and Oreza, the two most senior chiefs aboard, shared the cabin nearest the small compartment where they and their peers ate in relative privacy. Wegener got to the open door and found a cloud of smoke. The bosun had a cigar clamped in his teeth while his oversized hands were trying to manipulate a ridiculously small screwdriver. Both men came to their feet when the captain appeared.

''Relax. What the hell you got there?''

''Portagee found it.'' Riley handed it over. ''It's a real old one and we've been trying to fix it.''

''How does 1778 grab you, sir?'' Oreza asked. ''A sextant made by Henry

Edgworth. Found it in an old junk shop. It might be worth a few bucks if we can get it cleaned up.''

Wegener gave it a close look. ''1778, you said?''

''Yes, sir. That makes it one of the oldest-model sextants. The glass is all broke, but that's easy to fix. I know a museum that pays top dollar for these—but then I might just keep it myself, of course.''

''We got some company,'' Wegener said, getting back to business. ''They want to talk about the two people we picked up.''

Murray and Bright held up their ID cards. Dan noticed a phone in the compartment. The XO, he realized, might have called to warn them what was coming. Riley's cigar hadn't dropped an ash yet.

''No problem,'' Oreza said. ''What are you guys going to do with the bastards?''

''That's up to the U.S. Attorney,'' Bright said. ''We're supposed to help put the case together, and that means we have to establish what you people did when you apprehended them.''

''Well, you want to talk to Mr. Wilcox, sir. He was in command of the boarding party,'' Riley said. ''We just did what he told us.''

''Lieutenant Wilcox is on leave,'' the captain pointed out.

''What about after you brought them aboard?'' Bright asked.

''Oh, that,'' Riley admitted. ''Okay, I was wrong, but that little cocksucker—I mean, he spit on the captain, sir, and you just don't do that kinda shit, y'know? So I roughed him up some. Maybe I shouldn't have done it, but maybe that little prick oughta have manners, too.''

''That's not what we're here about,'' Murray said after a moment. ''He says you hanged him.''

''Hung him? What from?'' Oreza asked.

''I think you call it the yardarm.''

''You mean—hang, like in, well, *hang?* Around the neck, I mean?'' Riley asked.

''That's right.''

The bosun's laugh rumbled like an earthquake. ''Sir, if I ever hung somebody, he wouldn't go around bitchin' about it the next day.''

Murray repeated the story as he'd heard it, almost word for word. Riley shook his head.

''That's not the way it's done, sir.''

''What do you mean?''

''You say that the little one said that the last thing he saw was his friend swinging back and forth, right? That ain't the way it's done.''

''I still don't understand.''

''When you hang somebody aboard ship, you tie his feet together and run a downhaul line—you tie that off to the rail or a stanchion so he don't swing around. You gotta do that, sir. You have something that weight—well, over a hundred pounds—swinging around like that, it'll break things. So what you do is, you two-block him—that means you run him right up to the block—that's the pulley, okay?—and you got the downhaul to keep him in place real snug like. Otherwise it just ain't shipshape. Hell, everybody knows that.''

''How do *you* know that?'' Bright asked, trying to hide his exasperation.

''Sir, you lower boats into the water, or you rig stuff on this ship, and that's my job. We call it seamanship. I mean, say you had some piece of gear that weighs as much as a man, okay? You want it swinging around loose like a friggin' chandelier on a long chain? Christ, it'd eventually hit the radar, tear it right off the mast. We had a storm that night, too. Nah, the way they did it in the old days was just like a signal hoist—line on top of the hoist and a line on the bottom, tie it off nice and tight so it don't go noplace. Hey, somebody in the deck division leaves stuff flapping around like that, I tear him a new asshole. Gear is expensive. We don't go around breaking it for kicks, sir. What do you think, Portagee?''

''He's right. That was a pretty good blow we had that night—didn't the captain tell you?—the only reason we still had the punks aboard was that we waved off the helo pickup 'cause of the weather. We didn't have any work parties out on deck that night, did we?''

''No chance,'' Riley said. ''We buttoned up tight that night. What I mean, sir, is we can go out and work even in a damned hurricane if we have to, but unless you gotta, you don't go screwin' around on the weather decks during a gale. It's dangerous. You lose people that way.''

''How bad was it that night?'' Murray asked.

''Some of the new kids spent the night with their heads in the thunderjugs. The cook decided to serve chops that night, too.'' Oreza laughed. ''That's how we learned, ain't it, Bob?''

''Only way,'' Riley agreed.

''So there wasn't a court-martial that night either?''

''Huh?'' Riley appeared genuinely puzzled for a moment, then his face brightened. ''Oh, you mean we gave 'em a fair trial, then hung 'em, like in the old beer commercial?''

''Just one of them,'' Murray said helpfully.

''Why not both? They're both fuckin' murderers, ain't they? Hey, sir, I was aboard that yacht, all right? I seen what they did—have you? It's a real mess. You see something like that all the time, maybe. I never have, and—well, I don't mind tellin' you, sir, it shook me up some. You want 'em hung, yeah, I'll do it and they won't bitch about it the next day, either. Okay, maybe I shouldn't 'a snapped the one over the rail—lost my cool, and I shouldn't have—okay, I'm sorry about that. But those two little fucks took out a whole family, probably did some rapin', too. I got a family, too, y'know? I got daughters. So does Portagee. You want us to shed tears over those two fuckers, you come to the wrong place, sir. You sit 'em in the electric chair and I'll throw the switch for you.''

''So you didn't hang him?'' Murray asked.

''Sir, I wish I'd'a thought of it,'' Riley announced. It was, after all, Oreza who'd thought of it.

Murray looked at Bright, whose face was slightly pink by this time. It had gone even more smoothly than he'd expected. Well, he'd been told that the captain was a clever sort. You didn't give command of a ship to a jerk—at least you weren't supposed to.

''Okay, gentlemen, I guess that answers all the questions we have for the moment. Thank you for your cooperation.'' A moment later, Wegener was leading them away.

The three men stopped at the gangway for a moment. Murray motioned for Bright to head for the car, then turned to the captain.

''You actually operate helicopters off that deck up there?''

''All the time. I just wish we had one of our own.''

''Could I see it before I leave? I've never been aboard a cutter before.''

''Follow me.'' In less than a minute, Murray was standing in the center of the deck, directly on the crossed yellow lines painted on the black no-skid deck coating. Wegener was explaining how the lights at the control station worked, but Murray was looking at the mast, drawing an imaginary line from the yardarm to the deck. *Yeah,* he decided, *you could do it easy enough.*

"Captain, for your sake I hope you never do anything this crazy again."

Wegener turned in surprise. "What do you mean?"

"We both know what I mean."

"You believe what those two—"

"Yes, I do. A jury wouldn't—at least I don't think one would, though you can never really tell what a jury will believe. But you did it. I know—you can't say anything. . . ."

"What makes you think—"

"Captain, I've been in the Bureau for twenty-six years. I've heard lots of crazy stories, some real, some made up. You gradually get a feel for what's real and what isn't. The way it looks to me, you could run a piece of rope from that pulley up there, down to here pretty easy, and if you're taking the seas right, having a man swing wouldn't matter much. It sure wouldn't hurt the radar antenna that Riley was so worried about. Like I said, don't do it again. This one's a freebie because we can prosecute the case without the evidence you got for us. Don't push it. Well, I'm sure you won't. You found out that there was more to this one than you thought, didn't you?"

"I was surprised that the victim was—"

"Right. You opened a great big can of worms without getting your hands too dirty. You were lucky. Don't push it," Murray said again.

"Thank you, sir."

One minute after that, Murray was back in the car. Agent Bright was still unhappy.

"Once upon a time, when I was a brand-new agent fresh out of the Academy, I was assigned to Mississippi," Murray said. "Three civil-rights workers disappeared, and I was a very junior member of the team that cleared the case. I didn't do much of anything other than hold Inspector Fitzgerald's coat. Ever hear about Big Joe?"

"My dad worked with him," Bright answered.

"Then you know that Joe was a character, a real old-time cop. Anyway, the word got to us that the local Klukkers were mouthing off about how they were gonna kill a few agents—you know the stories, how they were harassing some families and stuff like that. Joe got a little pissed. Anyway, I drove him out to see—forget the mutt's name, but he was the Grand Kleagle of the local Klavern and he was the one with the biggest mouth. He was sitting under a shady tree in his front lawn when we pulled up. He had a shotgun next to the chair, and he was half in the bag from booze already. Joe walks up to him. The mutt starts to pick up the shotgun, but Joe just stared him down. Fitzgerald could do that; he put three guys in the ground and you could see in his face that he'd done it. I got a little worried, had my hand on my revolver, but Joe just stared him down and told him if there was any more talk about offing an agent, or any more shitty phone calls to wives and kids, Big Joe was going to come back and kill him, right there in his front yard. Didn't shout or anything, just said it like he was ordering breakfast. The Kleagle believed him. So did I. Anyway, all that loose talk ended.

"What Joe did was illegal as hell," Murray went on. "Sometimes the rules get bent. I've done it. So have you."

"I've never—"

"Don't get your tits in a flutter, Mark. I said 'bent,' not broken. The rules do not anticipate all situations. That's why we expect agents to exercise judgment. That's how society works. In this case, those Coasties broke loose some valuable information, and the only way we can use it is if we ignore how they got it. No real harm was done, because the subjects will be handled as murderers, and all the evidence we need is physical. Either they fry or they cop to the murders and cooperate by again giving us all the information that the good Captain Wegener scared out of 'em. Anyway, that's what they decided in D.C. It's too embarrassing to everyone to make an issue of what we discussed aboard the cutter. Do you really think a local jury would—"

"No," Bright admitted at once. "It wouldn't take much of a lawyer to blow it apart, and even if he didn't—"

"Exactly. We'd just be spinning our wheels. We live in an imperfect world, but I don't think that Wegener will ever make that mistake again."

"Okay." Bright didn't like it, but that was beside the point.

"So what we do now is figure out exactly why this poor bastard and his family got themselves murdered by a *sicario* and his spear-carrier. You know, when I was chasing wise guys up in New York, nobody messed with families. You didn't even kill a guy in front of his family except to make a special kind of point."

"Not much in the way of rules for the druggies," Bright pointed out.

"Yeah—and I used to think terrorists were bad."

It was so much easier than his work with the Macheteros, Cortez thought. Here he was, sitting in the corner booth of a fine, expensive restaurant with a ten-page wine list in his hands—Cortez thought himself an authority on wines—instead of a rat-infested barrio shack eating beans and mouthing revolutionary slogans with people whose idea of Marxism was robbing banks and making heroic taped pronouncements that the local radio stations played between the rock songs and commercials. America had to be the only place in the world, he thought, where poor people drove their own cars to demonstrations and the longest lines they stood in were at the supermarket check-out.

He selected an obscure estate label from the Loire Valley for dinner. The wine steward clicked his ballpoint in approval as he retrieved the list.

Cortez had grown up in a place where the poor people—which category included nearly everyone—scrounged for shoes and bread. In America, the poor areas were the ones where people indulged drug habits that required hundreds of cash dollars per week. It was more than bizarre to the former colonel. In America drugs spread from the slums to the suburbs, bringing prosperity to those who had what others wanted.

Which was essentially what happened on the international scale also, of course. The *yanquis,* ever niggardly in their official aid to their less prosperous neighbors, now flooded them with money, but on what the Americans liked to call a people-to-people basis. That was good for a laugh. He didn't know or care how much the *yanqui* government gave to its friends, but he was sure that ordinary citizens—so bored with their comfortable lives that they needed chemical stimulation—gave far more, and did so without strings on "human rights." He'd spent so many years as a professional intelligence officer, trying to find a way to demean America, to damage its stature, lessen its influence. But he'd gone about it in the wrong way, Félix had come to realize. He'd tried to use Marxism to fight capitalism despite all the evidence that showed what worked and what did not. He could, however, use capitalism against itself, and fulfill his original mission while enjoying all the benefits of the very system that he was hurting. And the oddest part of all: his former employers thought him a traitor because he had found a way that worked. . . .

The man opposite him was a fairly typical American, Cortez thought. Overweight from too much good food, careless about cleaning his expensive clothing. Probably didn't polish his shoes either. Cortez remembered going barefoot for much of his youth, and thinking himself fortunate to have three shirts to call his own. This man drove an expensive car, lived in a comfortable flat, had a job that paid enough for ten DGI colonels—and it wasn't enough. That was America right there—whatever one had, it was never enough.

"So what do you have for me?"

"Four possible prospects. All the information is in my briefcase."

"How good are they?" Cortez asked.

"They all meet your guidelines," the man answered. "Haven't I always—"

"Yes, you are most reliable. That is why we pay you so much."

"Nice to be appreciated, Sam," the man said with a trace of smugness.

Félix—Sam to his dinner partner—had always appreciated the people with whom he worked. He appreciated what they could do. He appreciated the information they provided. But he despised them for the weaklings they were. Still, an intelligence officer—and that remained the way he thought of himself—couldn't be too picky. America abounded with people like this one. Cortez did not reflect on the fact that he, too, had been bought. He deemed himself a skilled professional, perhaps something of a mercenary, but that was in keeping with an honored tradition, wasn't it? Besides, he was doing what his former masters had always wanted him to do, more effectively than had ever been possible with the DGI, and someone else was doing the paying. In fact, ultimately the Americans themselves paid his salary.

Dinner passed without incident. The wine was every bit as excellent as he'd expected, but the meat was overdone and the vegetables disappointing. Washington, he thought, was overrated as a city of restaurants. On his way out he simply picked up his companion's briefcase and walked to his car. The drive back to his hotel took twenty leisurely minutes. After that, he spent several hours going over the documents. The man was reliable, Cortez reflected, and earned his appreciation. Each of the four was a solid prospect.

His recruiting effort would begin tomorrow.

7. Knowns and Unknowns

It had taken a week to get accustomed to the altitude, as Julio had promised. Chavez eased out of the suspenders pack. It wasn't a fully loaded one yet, only twenty-five pounds, but they were taking their time, almost easing people into the conditioning program instead of using a more violent approach. That suited the sergeant, still breathing a little hard after the eight-mile run. His shoulders hurt some, and his legs ached in the usual way, but around him there was no sound of retching, and there hadn't been any dropouts this time around. Just the usual grumbles and curses.

"That wasn't so bad," Julio said without gasping. "But I still say that getting laid is the best workout there is."

"You got that one right," Chavez agreed with a laugh. "All those unused muscle groups, as the free-weight guys say."

The best thing about the training camp was the food. For lunch in the field they had to eat MRE packs—"Meal Ready to Eat," which was three lies for the price of one—but breakfast and supper selections were always well prepared in the camp's oversized kitchen. Chavez invariably selected as large a bowl of fresh fruits as he could get away with, heavily laced with white sugar for energy, along with the usual Army coffee whose caffeine content always seemed augmented to give you that extra wake-up punch. He laid into his bowl of diced grapefruit, oranges, and damned near everything else with gusto while his tablemates attacked their greasy eggs and bacon. Chavez went back to the line for some hash-browns. He'd heard that carbohydrates were also good for energy, and now that he was almost accustomed to the altitude, the thought of grease for breakfast didn't bother him that much.

Things were going well. Work here was hard, but there was nothing in the way of Mickey Mouse bullshit. Everyone here was an experienced pro, and they were being treated as such. No energy was being wasted on bed-making; the sergeants all knew how, and if a blanket corner wasn't quite tucked in, peer pressure set things right without the need for shouting from a superior officer. They were all young men, as serious about their work as they knew how to be, but there was a spirit of fun and adventure. They still didn't know exactly what they were training for. There was the inevitable speculation, whispering between bunks that gradually transformed to a symphony of snoring at night after agreement on some wildly speculative idea.

Though an uneducated man, Chavez was not a stupid one. Somehow he knew that all of the theories were wrong. Afghanistan was all over; they couldn't be going there. Besides, everyone here spoke fluent Spanish. He mulled over it again while chewing a mouthful of kiwi fruit—a treat he hadn't known to exist a week before. High altitude—they weren't training them here for the fun of it. That eliminated Cuba and Panama. Nicaragua, perhaps. How high were the mountains there? Mexico and the other Central American nations had mountains, too. Everyone here was a sergeant. Everyone here had led a squad, and had done training at one level or other. Everyone here was a light infantryman. Probably they'd be dispatched on some special training mission, therefore, training other light-fighters. That made it counterinsurgency. Of course, every country south of the Rio Grande had one sort of guerrilla problem or other. They resulted from the inequities of the individual governments and economies, but to Chavez the explanation was simpler and to the point—those countries were all fucked up. He'd seen enough of that in his trips with his battalion to Honduras and Panama. The local towns were dirty—they'd made his home barrio seem paradise on earth. The police—well, he'd never thought that he would come to admire the LAPD. But it was the local armies that had earned his *especial* contempt. Bunch of lazy, incompetent bullies. Not much different from street gangs, as a matter of fact, except that they all carried the same sort of guns (the L.A. gangs tended toward individualism). Weapons skills were about the same. It didn't require very much for a soldier to buttstroke some poor bastard with his rifle. The officers—well, he hadn't seen anyone to compare with Lieutenant Jackson, who loved to run with his men and didn't mind getting all dirty and smelly like a real soldier. But inevitably it was the sergeants down there who earned his fullest contempt. It had been that paddy Sergeant McDevitt in Korea who'd shown Ding Chavez the light—skill and professionalism equaled pride. And, when you got down to it, pride truly earned was all there was to a man. Pride was what kept you going, what kept you from caving in on those goddamned mountainside runs. You couldn't let down your friends. You couldn't let your friends see you for something less than you wanted to be. That was the short version of everything he had learned in the Army, and he knew that the same could be said of all the men in this room. What they were preparing for, therefore, was to train others to do the same. So their mission was a fairly conventional Army mission. For some reason or other—probably political, but Chavez didn't worry about political stuff; never made much sense anyway—it was a secret mission. He was smart enough to know that this kind of hush-hush preparation meant CIA. He was correct on that judgment. It was the mission he was wrong on.

Breakfast ended at the normal time. The men rose from their tables, taking their trays and dishes to the stacking table before proceeding outside. Most made pit stops and many, including Chavez, changed into clean, dry T-shirts. The sergeant wasn't overly fastidious, but he did prefer the crisp, clean smell of a newly washed shirt. There was an honest-to-God laundry service here. Chavez decided that he'd miss the camp, altitude and all. The air, if thin, was clean and dry. Each day they'd hear the lonely wail of diesel horns from the trains that entered the Moffat Tunnel, whose entrance they'd see on their twice-daily runs. Often in the evening they'd catch the distant sight of the double-deck cars of an Amtrak train heading east to Denver. He wondered what hunting was like here. What did they hunt? Deer, maybe? They'd seen a bunch of them, big mule deer, but also the curious white shapes of mountain goats racing up sheer rock walls as the soldiers approached. Now, *those* fuckers were really in shape, Julio had noted the previous day. But Chavez dismissed the thought after a moment. The animals he hunted had only two legs. And shot back if you weren't careful.

The four squads formed up on time. Captain Ramirez called them to attention and marched them off to their separate area, about half a mile east of the main camp at the far end of the flat bottom of the high valley. Waiting for them was a black man dressed in T-shirt and dark shorts, both of which struggled to contain bulging muscles.

"Good morning, people," the man said. "I am Mr. Johnson. Today we will begin some real mission-oriented training. All of you have had training in hand-to-hand combat. My job is to see how good you are, and to teach you some new tricks that your earlier training may have left out. Killing somebody silently isn't all that hard. The tricky part is getting close enough to do it. We all know that." Johnson's hands slipped behind his back as he talked on for a moment. "This is another way to kill silently."

His hands came into view holding a pistol with a large, canlike device affixed to the front. Before Chavez had told himself that it was a silencer, Johnson brought it around in both hands and fired it three times. It was a very good silencer, Ding noted immediately. You could barely hear the metallic clack of the automatic's slide—quieter, in fact, than the tinkle of glass from the three bottles that disintegrated twenty feet away—and you couldn't hear the sound of the shot at all. Impressive.

Johnson gave them all a mischievous grin. "You don't get your hands all bruised, either. Like I said, you all know hand-to-hand, and we're going to work on that. But I've been around the block a few times, just like you people, and let's not dick around the issue. Armed combat beats unarmed any day of the week. So today we're going to learn a whole new kind of fighting: silent *armed* combat.'' He bent down and flipped the blanket off a submachine gun. It, too, appeared to have a silencer on the muzzle. Chavez reproached himself for his earlier speculation. Whatever the mission was, it wasn't about training.

Vice Admiral James Cutter, USN, was a patrician. At least he looked like one, Ryan thought—tall and spare, his hair going a regal silver, and a confident smile forever fixed on his pink-scrubbed face. Certainly he acted like one—or thought he did, Jack corrected himself. It was Ryan's view that truly important people didn't go out of their way to act like it. It wasn't as though being the President's Special Assistant for National Security Affairs was the same as a peerage. Ryan knew a few people who actually had them. Cutter came from one of those old swamp-Yankee families which had grown rocks on their New England farmsteads for generations, then turned to the mercantile trade, and, in Cutter's case, sent its surplus sons to sea. But Cutter was the sort of sailor for whom the sea was a means to an end. More than half of his career had been spent in the Pentagon, and that, Ryan thought, was no place for a proper sailor. He'd had all the necessary commands, Jack knew. First a destroyer, then a cruiser. Each time he'd done his job well—well enough to be noticed, which must have been the important part. Plenty of outstanding officers' careers stopped cold at captain's rank because they'd failed to be noticed by a high-enough patron. What had Cutter done to make him stick out from the crowd . . . ?

Polished up the knocker faithfully, perhaps? Jack wondered as he finished his briefing.

Not that it mattered now. The President had noticed him on Jeff Pelt's staff, and on Pelt's return to academia—the International Relations chair at the University of Virginia—Cutter had slipped into the job as neatly as a destroyer coming alongside the pier. He sat behind his desk in a neatly tailored suit, sipping his coffee from a mug with USS BELKNAP engraved on it, the better to remind people that he'd commanded that cruiser once. In case the casual visitor missed that one—there were few casual visitors to the National Security Adviser's office—the wall on the left was liberally covered with plaques of the ships he'd served on, and enough signed photographs for a Hollywood agent's office. Naval officers call this phenomenon the I LOVE ME! wall, and while most of them have one, they usually keep it at home.

Ryan didn't like Cutter very much. He hadn't liked Pelt either, but the difference was that Pelt was almost as smart as he thought he was. Cutter was not even close. The three-star Admiral was in over his head, but had not the sense to know it. The bad news was that while Ryan was also a Special Assistant To, it was not To the President. That meant he had to report to Cutter whether he liked it or not. With his boss in the hospital, that task would be a frequent occurrence.

''How's Greer?'' the man asked. He spoke with a nasal New England accent that ought to have died a natural death long before, though it was one thing that Ryan didn't mind. It reminded him of his undergraduate days at Boston College.

''They're not through with the tests yet.'' Ryan's voice betrayed his worries. It looked like pancreatic cancer, the survival rate for which was just about zero. He'd checked with Cathy about that, and had tried to get his boss to Johns Hopkins, but

Greer was Navy, which meant going to Bethesda. Though Bethesda Naval Medical Center was the Navy's number-one hospital, it wasn't Johns Hopkins.

"And you're going to take over for him?" Cutter asked.

"That is in rather poor taste, Admiral," Bob Ritter answered for his companion. "In Admiral Greer's absence, Dr. Ryan will represent him from time to time."

"If you handle that as well as you've handled this briefing, we ought to get along just fine. Shame about Greer. Hope things work out." There was about as much emotion in his voice as one needed to ask directions.

You're a warm person, aren't you? Ryan thought to himself as he closed his briefcase. *I bet the crew of the* Belknap *just loved you.* But Cutter wasn't paid to be warm. He was paid to advise the President. And Ryan was paid to brief him, not to love him.

Cutter wasn't a fool. Ryan had to admit that also. He was not an expert in the area of Ryan's own expertise, nor did he have Pelt's cardsharp's instinct for political wheeling and dealing behind the scene—and, unlike Pelt, Cutter liked to operate without consulting the State Department. He sure as hell didn't understand how the Soviet Union worked. The reason he was sitting in that high-back chair, behind that dark-oak desk, was that he was a reputed expert in other areas, and evidently those were the areas in which the President had most of his current interest. Here Ryan's intellect failed him. He came back to his brief on what KGB was up to in Central Europe instead of following that idea to its logical conclusion. Jack's other mistake was more basic. Cutter knew that he wasn't the man Jeff Pelt had been, and Cutter wanted to change all that.

"Nice to see you again, Dr. Ryan. Good brief. I'll bring that matter to the President's attention. Now if you'll excuse us, the DDO and I have something to discuss."

"See you back at Langley, Jack," Ritter said. Ryan nodded and left. The other two waited for the door to close behind him. Then the DDO presented his own brief on Operation SHOWBOAT. It lasted twenty minutes.

"So how do we coordinate this?" the Admiral asked Ritter.

"The usual. About the only good thing that came out of the Desert One fiasco was that it proved how secure satellite communications were. Ever see the portable kind?" the DDO asked. "It's standard equipment for the light forces."

"No, just the ones aboard ship. They're not real portable."

"Well, it has a couple of pieces, an X-shaped antenna and a little wire stand that looks like it's made out of a couple of used coat hangers. There's a new backpack only weighs fifteen pounds, including the handset, and it even has a Morse key in case the sender doesn't want to talk too loud. Single sideband, super-encrypted UHF. That's as secure as communications get."

"But what about keeping them covert?" Cutter was worried about that.

"If the region was heavily populated," Ritter explained tiredly, "the opposition wouldn't be using it. Moreover, they operate mainly at night for the obvious reason. So our people will belly-up during the day and only move around at night. They are trained and equipped for that. Look, we've been thinking about this for some time. These people are very well trained already, and we're—"

"Resupply?"

"Helicopter," Ritter said. "Special-ops people down in Florida."

"I still think we should use Marines."

"The Marines have a different mission. We've been over this, Admiral. These kids are better trained, they're better equipped, most of them have been into areas like this one, and it's a hell of a lot easier to get them into the program without anybody noticing,'' Ritter explained for what must have been the twentieth time. Cutter wasn't one to listen to the words of others. His own opinions were evidently too loud. The DDO wondered how the President fared, but that question needed no answer. A presidential whisper carried more weight than a scream from anyone else. The problem was, the President so often depended on idiots to make his wishes a reality. Ritter would not have been surprised to learn that his opinion of the National Security Adviser matched that of Jack Ryan; it was just that Ryan could not know why.

''Well, it's your operation,'' Cutter said after a moment. ''When does it start?''

''Three weeks. Just had a report last night. Things are going along just fine. They already had all the basic skills we needed. It's only a matter of honing a few special ones and adding a few refinements. We've been lucky so far. Haven't even had anybody hurt up there.''

''How long have you had that place, anyway?''

''Thirty years. It was supposed to have been an air-defense radar installation, but the funding got cut off for some reason or other. The Air Force turned it over to us, and we've been using it to train agents ever since. It doesn't show up on any of the OMB site lists. It belongs to an offshore corporation that we use for various things. During the fall we occasionally lease it out as a hunting camp, would you believe? It even shows a profit for us, which is another reason why it doesn't show on the OMB list. Is that covert enough? Came in real useful during Afghanistan, though, doing the same thing we're doing now, and nobody ever found out about it. . . .''

''Three weeks.''

Ritter nodded. ''Maybe a touch longer. We're still working on coordinating the satellite intelligence, and our assets on the ground.''

''Will it all work?'' Cutter asked rhetorically.

''Look, Admiral, I've told you about that. If you want some magical solution to give to the President, we don't have it. What we can do is sting them some. The results will look good in the papers, and, hell, maybe we'll end up saving a life or two. Personally, I think it's worth doing even if we don't get much of a return.''

The nice thing about Ritter, Cutter thought, was that he didn't state the obvious. There would be a return. Everyone knew what that was all about. The mission was not an exercise in cynicism, though some might see it as such.

''What about the radar coverage?''

''There are only two aircraft coming on line. They're testing a new system called LPI—Low Probability of Intercept—radar. I don't know all the details, but because of a combination of frequency agility, reduced side-lobes, and relatively low power output, it's damned hard to detect the emissions from the set. That will invalidate the ESM equipment that the opposition has started using. So we can use our assets on the ground to stake out between four and six of the covert airfields, and let us know when a shipment is en route. The modified E-2s will establish contact with them south of Cuba and pace them all the way in till they're intercepted by the F-15 driver I told you about. He's a black kid—hell of a fighter jock, they say. Comes from New York. His mother got mugged by a druggie up there. It was a bad one. She got all torn up, and eventually died. She was one of those ghetto success stories that you never hear about. Three kids, all of them turned out pretty well. The fighter pilot is a very angry kid at the moment. He'll work for us, and he won't talk.''

"Right," Cutter said skeptically. "What about if he develops a conscience later on and—"

"The boy told me that he'd shoot all the bastards down if we wanted him to. A druggie killed his *mother*. He wants to get even, and he sees this as a good way. There are a lot of sensitive projects underway at Eglin. His fighter is cut loose from the rest as part of the LPI Radar project. It's two Navy airplanes carrying the radar, and we've picked the flight crews—pretty much the same story on them. And remember—after we have lock-on from the F-15, the radar aircraft shuts down and leaves. So if Bronco—that's the kid's name—does have to splash the inbound druggie, nobody'll know about it. Once we get them on the ground, the flight crews will have the living shit scared out of them. I worked out the details on that part myself. If some people have to disappear—I don't expect it—that can be arranged, too. The Marines there are all special-ops types. One of my people will pretend he's a fed, and the judge we take them to is the one the President—"

"I know that part." It was odd, Cutter thought, how ideas grow. First the President had made an intemperate remark after learning that the cousin of a close friend had died of a drug overdose. He'd talked about it with Ritter, gotten an idea, and mentioned it to the President. A month after that, a plan had started to grow. Two months more and it was finalized. A secret Presidential Finding was written and in the files—there were only four copies of it, each of which was locked up tight. Now things were starting to move. It was past the time for second thoughts, Cutter told himself weakly. He'd been involved in all the planning discussions, and still the operation had somehow leaped unexpectedly to full flower. . . .

"What can go wrong?" he asked Ritter.

"Look, in field operations anything can go wrong. Just a few months ago a crash operation went bad because of an illegal turn—"

"That was KGB," Cutter said. "Jeff Pelt told me about that one."

"We are not immune. Shit happens, as they say. What we can do, we've done. Every aspect of the operation is compartmentalized. On the air part, for example, the fighter pilot doesn't know the radar aircraft or its people—for both sides it's just call signs and voices. The people on the ground don't know what aircraft are involved. The people we're putting in-country will get instructions from satellite radios—they won't even know where from. The people who insert them won't know why they're going or where the orders come from. Only a handful of people will know everything. The total number of people who know anything at all is less than a hundred, and only ten know the whole story. I can't make it any tighter than that. Now, either it's a Go-Mission or it's not. That's your call, Admiral Cutter. I presume," Ritter added for effect, "that you've fully briefed the President."

Cutter had to smile. It was not often, even in Washington, that a man could speak the truth and lie at the same time: "Of course, Mr. Ritter."

"In writing," Ritter said next.

"No."

"Then I call the operation off," the DDO said quietly. "I won't be left hanging on this one."

"But I will?" Cutter observed. He didn't allow anger to creep into his voice, but his face conveyed the message clearly enough. Ritter made the obvious maneuver.

"Judge Moore requires it. Would you prefer that he ask the President himself?"

Cutter was caught short. His job, after all, was to insulate the President. He'd tried to pass that onus to Ritter and/or Judge Moore, but found himself outmaneuvered in his own office. Someone had to be responsible for everything; bureaucracy or not, it always came down to one person. It was rather like a game of musical chairs. Someone was always left standing. That person was called the loser. For all his skills, Vice Admiral Cutter had found himself without a seat on that last chair. His naval training, of course, had taught him to take responsibilities, but though Cutter called himself a naval officer, and thought of himself as one—without wearing the uniform, of course—responsibility was something he'd managed to avoid for years. Pentagon duty was good for that, and White House duty was better still. Now responsibility was his again. He hadn't been this vulnerable since his cruiser had nearly rammed a tanker during replenishment operations—his executive officer had saved him with a timely command to the helmsman, Cutter remembered. A pity that his career had ended at captain's rank, but Ed just hadn't had the right stuff to make Flag. . . .

Cutter opened a drawer to his desk and pulled out a sheet of paper whose letterhead proclaimed "The White House." He took a gold Cross pen from his pocket and wrote a clear authorization for Ritter in his best Palmer Method penmanship. *You are authorized by the President . . .* The Admiral folded the sheet, tucked it into an envelope, and handed it across.

"Thank you, Admiral." Ritter tucked the envelope into his coat pocket. "I'll keep you posted."

"You be careful who sees that," Cutter said coldly.

"I do know how to keep secrets, sir. It's my job, remember?" Ritter rose and left the room, finally with a warm feeling around his backside. His ass was covered. It was a feeling craved by many people in Washington. It was one he didn't share with the President's National Security Adviser, but Ritter figured it wasn't his fault that Cutter hadn't thought this one through.

Five miles away, the DDI's office seemed a cold and lonely place to Ryan. There was the credenza and the coffee machine where James Greer made his Navy brew, there the high-backed judge's chair in which the old man leaned back before making his professorial statements of fact and theory, and his jokes, Jack remembered. His boss had one hell of a sense of humor. What a fine teacher he might have made—but then he really was a teacher to Jack. What was it? Only six years since he'd started with the Agency. He'd known Greer for less than seven, and the Admiral had in large part become the father he'd lost in that airplane crash at Chicago. It was here he had come for advice, for guidance. How many times?

The trees outside the seventh-floor windows were green with the leaves of summer, blocking the view of the Potomac Valley. The really crazy things had all happened when there were no leaves, Ryan thought. He remembered pacing around on the lush carpet, looking down at the piles of snow left by the plows while trying to find answers to hard questions, sometimes succeeding, sometimes not.

Vice Admiral James Greer would not live to see another winter. He'd seen his last snow, his last Christmas. Ryan's boss lay in a VIP suite at Bethesda Naval Medical Center, still alert, still thinking, still telling jokes. But his weight was down by fifteen pounds in the last three weeks, and the chemotherapy denied him any sort of food other than what came through tubes stuck in his arms. And the pain. There was nothing worse, Ryan knew, than to watch the pain of others. He'd seen his wife and daughter in pain, and it had been far worse than his own hospital stays. It was hard to go and see the Admiral, to see the tightness around the face, the occasional stiffening of limbs as the spasms came and went, some from the cancer, some from the medications. But Greer was as much a part of his family as—God, Ryan thought, I am thinking of him like my father. And so he would, until the end.

"Shit," Jack said quietly, without knowing it.

"I know what you mean, Dr. Ryan."

"Hmph?" Jack turned. The Admiral's driver (and security guard) stood quietly by the door while Jack retrieved some documents. Even though Ryan was the DDI's special assistant and *de facto* deputy, he had to be watched when going over documents cleared DDI-eyes-only. CIA's security rules were tough, logical, and inviolable.

"I know what you mean, sir. I've been with him eleven years. He's as much a friend as a boss. Every Christmas he has something for the kids. Never forgets a birthday, either. You think there's any hope at all?"

"Cathy had one of her friends come down. Professor Goldman. Russ is as good as they come, professor of oncology at Hopkins, consultant to NIH, and a bunch of other things. He says one chance in thirty. It's spread too far, too fast, Mickey. Two months, tops. Anything else would be a miracle." Ryan almost smiled. "I got a priest working on that."

Murdock nodded. "I know he's tight with Father Tim over at Georgetown. He was just at the hospital for some chess last night. The Admiral took him in forty-eight moves. You ever play chess with him?"

"I'm not in his class. Probably never will be."

"Yes, sir, you are," Murdock said after a moment or two. "Leastways, that's what he says."

"He would." Ryan shook his head. Damn it, Greer wouldn't want either of them to talk like this. There was work to be done. Jack took the key and unlocked the file drawer in the desk. He set the key chain on the desk blotter for Mickey to retrieve and reached down to pull the drawer, but goofed. Instead he pulled out the sliding board you could use as a writing surface, though this one was marked with brown rings from the DDI's coffee mug. Near the inside end of it, Ryan saw, was a file card, taped in place. Written on the card, in Greer's distinctive hand, were two safe combinations. Greer had a special office safe and so did Bob Ritter. Jack remembered that his boss had always been clumsy with combination locks, and he probably needed the combination written down so he wouldn't forget it. He found it odd that the Admiral should have combinations for both his and Ritter's, but decided after a moment that it made sense. If somebody had to get into the DDO's safe in a hurry—for example, if Ritter were kidnapped, and someone had to see what really classified material was in the current file—it had to be someone very senior, like the DDI. Probably Ritter had the combination to the DDI's personal safe, as well. Jack wondered who else did. Shrugging off the thought, he slid the board back into place and opened the drawer. There were six files there. All related to long-term intelligence evaluations that the Admiral wanted to see. None were especially critical. In fact, they weren't all that sensitive, but it would give the Admiral something to occupy his mind. A rotating team of CIA security personnel guarded his room, with two on duty at all times, and he could still do work in the time he had left.

Damn! Jack snarled at himself. *Get your mind off of it. Hell, he does have a chance. Some chance is better than none at all.*

Chavez had never handled a submachine gun. His personal weapon had always been the M-16 rifle, often with an M-203 grenade launcher slung under the barrel.

He also knew how to use the SAW—the Belgian-made squad automatic weapon that had recently been added to the Army's inventory—and had shot expert with pistol once. But submachine guns had long since gone out of favor in the Army. They just weren't serious weapons of the sort a soldier would need.

Which was not to say that he didn't like it. It was a German gun, the MP-5 SD2 made by Heckler & Koch. It was decidedly unattractive. The matte-black finish was slightly rough to the touch, and it lacked the sexy compactness of the Israeli Uzi. On the other hand, it wasn't made to look good, he thought, it was made to shoot good. It was made to be reliable. It was made to be accurate. Whoever had designed this baby, Chavez decided as he brought it up for the first time, knew what shooting was all about. Unusually for a German-made weapon, it didn't have a huge number of small parts. It broke down easily and quickly for cleaning, and reassembly took less than a minute. The weapon nestled snugly against his shoulder, and his head dropped automatically into the right place to peer through the ring-aperture sight.

"Commence firing," Mr. Johnson commanded.

Chavez had the weapon on single-shot. He squeezed off the first round, just to get a feel for the trigger. It broke cleanly at about eleven pounds, the recoil was straight back and gentle, and the gun didn't jump off the target the way some weapons did. The shot, of course, went straight through the center of the target's silhouetted head. He squeezed off another, and the same thing happened, then five in rapid fire. The repeated shots rocked him back an inch or two, but the recoil spring ate up most of the kick. He looked up to see seven holes in a nice, tight group, like the nose carved into a jack-o'-lantern. Okay. Next he flipped the selector switch to the burst position—it was time for a little rock and roll. He put three rounds at the target's chest. This group was larger, but any of the three would have been fatal. After another one Chavez decided that he could hold a three-round burst dead on target. He didn't need full-automatic fire. Anything more than three rounds just wasted ammunition. His attitude might have seemed strange for a soldier, but as a light infantryman he understood that ammunition was something that had to be carried. To finish off his thirty-round magazine he aimed bursts at unmarked portions of the target card, and was rewarded with hits exactly where he'd wanted them.

"Baby, where have you been all my life?" Best of all, it wasn't much noisier than the rustle of dry leaves. It wasn't that it had a silencer; the barrel *was* a silencer. You heard the muted clack of the action, and the swish of the bullet. They were using a subsonic round, the instructor told them. Chavez picked one out of the box. The bullet was a hollow-point design; it looked like you could mix a drink in it, and on striking a man it probably spread out to the diameter of a dime. Instant death from a head shot, nearly as quick in the chest—but if they were training him to use a silencer, he'd be expected to go for the head. He figured that he could take head shots reliably from fifty or sixty feet—maybe farther under ideal circumstances, but soldiers don't expect ideal circumstances. On the face of it, he'd be expected to creep within fifteen or twenty yards of his target and drop him without a sound.

Whatever they were preparing for, he thought again, it sure as hell wasn't a training mission.

"Nice groups, Chavez," the instructor observed. Only three other men were on the firing line. There would be two submachine gunners per squad. Two SAWs—Julio had one of those—and the rest had M-16s, two of them with grenade launchers attached. Everyone had pistols, too. That seemed strange, but despite the weight Chavez didn't mind.

''This baby really shoots, sir.''

''It's yours. How good are you with a pistol?''

''Just fair. I don't usually—''

''Yeah, I know. Well, you'll all get practice. Pistol ain't really good for much, but there's times when it comes in right handy.'' Johnson turned to address the whole squad. ''All right, you four come on up. We want everyone to know how all these here weapons work. Everybody's gotta be an expert.''

Chavez relinquished his weapon to another squad member and walked back from the firing line. He was still trying to figure things out. Infantry combat is the business of death, at the personal level, where you could usually see what you were doing and to whom you were doing it. The fact that Chavez had not actually done it yet was irrelevant; it was still his business, and the organization of his unit told him what form the mission would take. Special ops. It had to be special ops. He knew a guy who'd been in the Delta Force at Bragg. Special operations were merely a refinement of straight infantry stuff. You had to get in real close, usually you had to chop down the sentries, and then you hit hard and fast, like a bolt of lightning. If it wasn't over in ten seconds or less—well, then things got a little too exciting. The funny part to Chavez was the similarity with street-gang tactics. There was no fair play in soldiering. You sneaked in and did people in the back without warning. You didn't give them a chance to protect themselves—none at all. But what was called cowardly in a gang kid was simply good tactics to a soldier. Chavez smiled to himself. It hardly seemed fair, when you looked at it like that. The Army was just better organized than a gang. And, of course, its targets were selected by others. The whole point to an Army, probably, was that what it did made sense to someone. That was true of gangs, too, but Army activity was supposed to make sense to someone important, someone who knew what he was really doing. Even if what he was doing didn't make much sense to him—a frequent occurrence for soldiers—it did make sense to somebody.

Chavez wasn't old enough to remember Vietnam.

Seduction was the saddest part of the job.

With this, as with all parts of his profession, Cortez had been trained to be coldly objective and businesslike. but there wasn't a way to be coldly intimate—at least not if you wanted to accomplish anything. Even the KGB Academy had recognized that. There had been hours of lectures on the pitfalls, he remembered with an ironic smile—Russians trying to tell a Latin about romantic entanglements. Probably the climate worked against them. You adapted your approach to the individual peculiarities of your target subject, in this case a widow who at forty-six retained surprising good looks, who had enough remaining of her youth to need companionship after the children retired for the evening or went out on their own dates, whose bed was a lonely place of memories grown cold. It wasn't his first such subject, and there was always something brave about them, as well as something pathetic. He was supposed to think—as his training had taught him—that their problems were their business and his opportunity. But how does a man become intimate with such a woman without feeling her pain? The KGB instructors hadn't had an answer to that one, though they did give him the proper technique. He, too, had to have suffered a recent loss.

His ''wife'' had also died of cancer, he'd told her. He'd married late in life, the story went, after getting the family business back on track—all that time working, flying around to secure the business his father had spent his life founding—and then married his María only three years before. She'd become pregnant, but when she'd visited the doctor to confirm the joyous news, the routine tests . . . only six months. The baby hadn't had a chance, and Cortez had nothing left of María. Perhaps, he'd told his wineglass, it was God's punishment on him for marrying so young a girl, or for his many dalliances as a footloose playboy.

At that point Moira's hand had come across the table to touch his. Of course it wasn't his fault, the woman told him. And he looked up to see the sympathy in the eyes of someone who'd asked herself questions not so different from those he'd just ostensibly addressed to himself. People were so predictable. All you had to do was press the right buttons—and have the proper feelings. When her hand had come to his, the seduction was accomplished. There had been a flush of warmth from the touch, the feeling of simple humanity. But if he thought of her as a simple target, how could he return the emotions—and how could he accomplish the mission? He felt her pain, her loneliness. He would be good to her.

And so he was, now two days later. It would have been comical except for how touching it was, how she'd prepared herself like a teenage girl on a date—something she hadn't done for over twenty years; certainly her children had found it entertaining, but there had been enough time since the death of their father that they didn't resent their mother's needs and had smiled bemused encouragement at her as she walked out to her car. A quick, nervous dinner, then the short ride to his hotel. Some more wine to get over the nerves that were real for both of them, if more so for her. But it had certainly been worth the wait. She was out of practice, but her responses were far more genuine than those he got from his usual bedmates. Cortez was very good at sex. He was proud of his abilities and gave her an above-average performance: an hour's work, building her up slowly, then letting her back down as gently as he knew how.

Now they lay side by side, her head on his shoulder, tears dripping slowly from her eyes in the silence. A fine woman, this one. Even dying young, her husband had been a lucky man to have a woman who knew that silence could be the greatest passion of all. He watched the clock on the end table. Ten minutes of silence before he spoke.

"Thank you, Moira . . . I didn't know . . . it's been." He cleared his throat. "This is the first time since . . . since . . ." Actually it had been a week since the last one, which had cost him thirty thousand pesos. A young one, a skilled one. But—

The woman's strength surprised him. He was barely able to take his next breath, so powerful was her embrace. Part of what had once been his conscience told him that he ought to be ashamed, but the greater part reported that he'd given more than he'd taken. This was better than purchased sex. There were feelings, after all, that money couldn't buy; it was a thought both reassuring and annoying to Cortez, and one which amplified his sense of shame. Again he rationalized that there would be no shame without her powerful embrace, and the embrace would not have come unless he had pleased her greatly.

He reached behind himself to the other end table and got his cigarettes.

"You shouldn't smoke," Moira Wolfe told him.

He smiled. "I know. I must quit. But after what you have done to me," he said with a twinkle in his eye, "I must gather myself." Silence.

"*Madre de Dios,*" he said after another minute.

"What's the matter?"

Another mischievous smile. "Here I have given myself to you, and I hardly know who you are!"

"What do you want to know?"

A chuckle. A shrug. "Nothing important—I mean, what could be more important than what you have already done?" A kiss. A caress. More silence. He stubbed out the cigarette at the halfway point to show that her opinion was important to him. "I am not good at this."

"Really?" It was her turn to chuckle, his turn to blush.

"It is different, Moira. I—when I was a young man, it was understood that when—it was understood that there was no importance, but . . . now I am grown, and I cannot be so . . ." Embarrassment. "If you permit it, I wish to know about you, Moira. I come to Washington frequently, and I wish . . . I am tired of the loneliness. I am tired of . . . I wish to know you," he said with conviction. Then, tentatively, haltingly, hopeful but afraid, "If you permit it."

She kissed his cheek gently. "I permit it."

Instead of his own powerful hug, Cortez let his body go slack with relief not wholly feigned. More silence before he spoke again.

"You should know about me. I am wealthy. My business is machine tools and auto parts. I have two factories, one in Costa Rica, the other in Venezuela. The business is complicated and—not dangerous, but . . . it is complicated dealing with the big assemblers. I have two younger brothers also in the business. So . . . what work do you do?"

"Well, I'm an executive secretary. I've been doing that kind of work for twenty years."

"Oh? I have one myself."

"And you must chase her around the office . . ."

"Consuela is old enough to be my mother. She worked for my father. Is that how it is in America? Does your boss chase you?" A hint of jealous outrage.

Another chuckle. "Not exactly. I work for Emil Jacobs. He's the Director of the FBI."

"I do not know the name." A lie. "The FBI, that is your *federales,* this I know. And you are the chief secretary for them all, then?"

"Not exactly. Mainly my job is to keep Mr. Jacobs organized. You wouldn't believe his schedule—all the meetings and conferences to keep straight. It's like being a juggler."

"Yes, it is that way with Consuela. Without her to watch over me . . ." Cortez laughed. "If I had to choose between her and one of my brothers, I would choose her. I can always hire a factory manager. What sort of man is this—Jacobs, you say? You know, when I was a boy, I wanted to be a policeman, to carry the gun and drive the car. To be the chief police officer, that must be a grand thing."

"Mainly his job is shuffling papers—I get to do a lot of the filing, and dictation. When you are the head, your job is mainly doing budgets and meetings."

"But surely he gets to know the—the good things, yes? The best part of being a policeman—it must be the best thing, to know the things that other people do not. To know who are the criminals, and to hunt them."

"And other things. It isn't just police work. They also do counterespionage. Chasing spies," she added.

"That is CIA, no?"

"No. I can't talk about it, of course, but, no, that is a Bureau function. It's all the same, really, and it's not like television at all. Mainly it's boring. I read the reports all the time.''

''Amazing,'' Cortez observed comfortably. ''All the talents of a woman, and also she educates me.'' He smiled encouragement so that she would elaborate. That idiot who'd put him onto her, he remembered, suggested that he'd have to use money. Cortez thought that his KGB training officers would have been proud of his technique. The KGB was ever parsimonious with funds.

''Does he make you work so hard?'' Cortez asked a minute later.

''Some of the days can go long, but really he's pretty good about that.''

''If he makes you work too hard, we will speak, Mr. Jacobs and I. What if I come to Washington and I cannot see you because you are working?''

''You really want . . . ?''

''Moira.'' His voice changed its timbre. Cortez knew that he'd pressed too hard for a first time. It had gone too easily, and he'd asked too many questions. After all, lonely widow or not, this was a woman of substance and responsibility—therefore a woman of intellect. But she was also a woman of feelings, and of passion. He moved his hands and his head. He saw the question on her face: Again? He smiled his message: Again.

This time he was less patient, no longer a man exploring the unknown. There was familiarity now. Having established what she liked, his ministrations had direction. Within ten minutes she'd forgotten all of his questions. She would remember the smell and the feel of him. She would bask in the return of youth. She would ask herself where things might lead, but not how they had started.

Assignations are conspiratorial by their nature. Just after midnight he returned her to where her car was parked. Yet again she amazed him with her silence. She held his hand like a schoolgirl, yet her touch was in no way so simple. One last kiss before she left the car—she wouldn't let him get out.

''Thank you, Juan,'' she said quietly.

Cortez spoke from the heart. ''Moira, because of you I am again a man. You have done more for me. When next I come to Washington, we must—''

''We will.''

He followed her most of the way home, to let her know that he wished to protect her, breaking off before getting so close to her home that her children—surely they were waiting up—would notice. Cortez drove back to the apartment with a smile on his face, only partly because of his mission.

Her co-workers knew at once. With little more than six hours' sleep, Moira bounced into the office wearing a suit she hadn't touched in a year. There was a sparkle in her eye that could not be hidden. Even Director Jacobs noticed, but no one said anything. Jacobs understood. He'd buried his wife only a few months after Moira's loss, and learned that such voids in one's life could never quite be filled with work. *Good for her,* he thought. She still had children at home. He'd have to go easier on her schedule. She deserved another chance at a real life.

8. Deployment

The amazing thing was how smoothly things had gone, Chavez thought. After all, they were all sergeants, but whoever had set this thing up had been a clever man because there had been no groping around for which man got which function. There was an operations sergeant in his squad to assist Captain Ramirez with planning. There was a medical corpsman, a good one from the Special Forces who already had his weapons training. Julio Vega and Juan Piscador had once been machine-gunners, and they got the SAWs. The same story applied to their radioman. Each member of the team fit neatly into a preselected slot, all were sufficiently trained that they respected the expertise of one another, and further cross-training enhanced that respect even more. The rugged regime of exercises had extended the pride with which each had arrived, and within two weeks the team had meshed together like a finely made machine. Chavez, a Ranger School graduate, was point man and scout. His job was to probe ahead, to move silently from one place of concealment to another, to watch and listen, then report his observations to Captain Ramirez.

"Okay, where are they?" the captain asked.

"Two hundred meters, just around that corner," Chavez whispered in reply. "Five of them. Three asleep, two awake. One's sitting by the fire. The other one's got an SMG, walking around some."

It was cool in the mountains at night, even in summer. A distant coyote howled at the moon. There was the occasional whisper from a deer moving through the trees, and the only sound associated with man was the distant noise of jets. The clear night made for surprisingly good visibility, even without the low-light goggles with which they were normally equipped. In the thin mountain air, the stars overhead didn't sparkle, but shone as constant, discrete points of light. Ordinarily Chavez would have noticed the beauty, but this was a work night.

Ramirez and the rest of the squad were wearing four-color camouflage fatigues of Belgian manufacture. Their faces were painted with matching tones from sticks of makeup (understandably the Army didn't call it that) so that they blended into the shadows as perfectly as Wells' invisible man. Most importantly, they were totally at home in the darkness. Night was their best and most powerful friend. Man was a day-hunter. All of his senses, all of his instincts, and all of his inventions worked best in the light. Primordial rhythms made him less efficient at night—unless he worked very hard to overcome them, as these soldiers had. Even American Indian tribes living in close partnership with nature had feared the night, had almost never fought at night, had not even guarded their encampments at night—thus giving the U.S. Army its first useful doctrine for operations in darkness. At night man built fires as much for vision as for warmth, but in doing so reduced that vision to mere feet, whereas the human eye, properly conditioned, can see quite well in the darkness.

"Only five?"

"That's all I counted, sir."

Ramirez nodded and gestured for two more men to come forward. A few quiet orders were given. He went with the other two, moving to the right to get above the encampment. Chavez went back forward. His job was to take the sentry down, along with the one dozing at the fire. Moving quietly in the dark is harder than seeing. The human eye is better at spotting movement in the dark than in identifying stationary objects. He put each foot down carefully, feeling for something that might slide or break, thus making noise—the human ear is much underestimated. In daylight his method of moving would have appeared comical, but stealth has its price. Worst of all, he moved slowly, and Ding was no more patient than any man still in his twenties. It was a weakness against which he'd trained himself. He walked in a tight crouch. His weapon was up and ready to guard against surprise, and as the moment approached, his senses were fully alerted, as though an electric current ran across his skin. His head swiveled slowly left and right, his eyes never quite locking on anything, because when one stares at an object in the darkness, it tends to disappear after a few seconds.

Something bothered Chavez, but he didn't know what it was. He stopped for a moment, looking around, searching with all his senses over to his left for about thirty seconds. Nothing. For the first time tonight he found himself wishing for his night goggles. Ding shook it off. Maybe a squirrel or some other night forager. Not a man, certainly. No one could move in the dark as well as a Ninja, he smiled to himself, and got back to the business at hand. He reached his position several minutes later, just behind a scrawny pine tree, and eased down to a kneeling position. Chavez slid the cover off the green face of his digital watch, watching the numbers march slowly toward the appointed moment. There was the sentry, moving in a circle around the fire, never more than thirty feet from it, trying to keep his eyes turned away from it to protect his night vision. But the light reflected off the rocks and the pines would damage his perceptions badly enough—he looked straight at Chavez twice, but saw nothing.

Time.

Chavez brought up his MP-5 and loosed a single round into the target's chest. The man flinched with the impact, grasped the spot where he'd been hit, and dropped to the ground with a surprised gasp. The MP-5 made only a slight metallic clack, like a small stone rolling against another, but in the still mountain night, it was something out of the ordinary. The drowsy one by the fire turned around, but only made it halfway when he too was struck. Chavez figured himself to be on a roll and was taking aim on one of the sleeping men when the distinctive ripping sound of Julio's squad automatic weapon jolted them from their slumber. All three leapt to their feet, and were dead before they got there.

"Where the hell did you come from?" the dead sentry demanded. The place on his chest where the wax bullet had struck was very sore, all the more so from surprise. By the time he was standing again, Ramirez and the others were in the camp.

"Kid, you are very good," a voice said behind Chavez, and a hand thumped down on his shoulder. The sergeant nearly jumped out of his skin as the man walked past him into the encampment. "Come on."

A rattled Chavez followed the man to the fire. He cleared his weapon on the way—the wax bullets could do real harm to a man's face.

"We'll score that one a success," the man said. "Five kills, no reaction from the bad guys. Captain, your machine-gunner got a little carried away. I'd go easier on the rock and roll; the sound of an automatic weapon carries an awful long way.

I'd also try to move in a little closer, but—I guess that rock there was about the best you could do. Okay, forget that one. My mistake. We can't always pick the terrain. I liked your discipline on the approach march, and your movement into the objective was excellent. This point man you have is terrific. He almost picked me up.'' The last struck Chavez as faint praise indeed.

''Who the fuck are you!'' Ding asked quietly.

''Kid, I was doing this sort of thing for-real when you were playing with guns made by Mattel. Besides, I cheated.'' Clark held up his night goggles. ''I picked my route carefully, and I froze every time you turned your head. What you heard was my breathing. You almost had me. I thought I blew the exercise. Sorry. My name's Clark, by the way.'' A hand appeared.

''Chavez.'' The sergeant took it.

''You're pretty good, Chavez. Best I've seen in a while. I especially like the footwork. Not many have the patience you do. We could have used you in the 3rd SOG.'' It was Clark's highest praise, and rarely given.

''What's that?''

A grunt and a chuckle. ''Something that never existed—don't worry about it.''

Clark walked over to examine the two men Chavez had shot. Both were rubbing identical places on their flak jackets, right over their hearts.

''You know how to shoot, too.''

''Anybody can hit with this.''

Clark turned to look at the young man. ''Remember, when it's for-real, it's not quite the same.''

Chavez recognized genuine meaning in that statement. ''What should I do different, sir?''

''That's the hard part,'' Clark admitted as the rest of the squad approached the fire. He spoke as a teacher to a gifted pupil. ''Part of you has to pretend it's the same as training. Another part has to remember that you don't get many mistakes anymore. You have to know which part to listen to, 'cause it changes from one minute to the next. You got good instincts, kid. Trust 'em. They'll keep you alive. If things don't feel right, they probably aren't. Don't confuse that with fear.''

''Huh?''

''You're going to be afraid out there, Chavez. I always was. Get used to the idea, and it can work for you 'stead of against you. For Christ's sake, don't be ashamed of it. Half the problem out in Indian Country is people afraid of being afraid.''

''Sir, what the hell are we training for?''

''I don't know yet. Not my department.'' Clark managed to conceal his feelings on that score. The training wasn't exactly in accord with what he thought the mission was supposed to be. Ritter might be having another case of the clevers. There was nothing more worrisome to Clark than a clever superior.

''You're going to be working with us, though.''

It was an exceedingly shrewd observation, Clark thought. He'd asked to come out here, of course, but realized that Ritter had maneuvered him into asking. Clark was the best man the Agency had for this sort of thing. There weren't many men with similar experience anywhere in government service, and most of those, like Clark, were getting a little old for the real thing. Was that all? Clark didn't know. He knew that Ritter liked to keep things under his hat, especially when he thought he was being clever. Clever men outsmart themselves, Clark thought, and Ritter wasn't immune from that.

"Maybe," he admitted reluctantly. It wasn't that he minded associating with these men, but Clark worried about the circumstances that might make it necessary, later on. *Can* you *still cut it, Johnny boy?*

"So?" Director Jacobs asked. Bill Shaw was there, too.

"So he did it, sure as hell," Murray replied as he reached for his coffee. "But taking it to trial would be nasty. He's a clever guy, and his crew backed him up. If you read up on his file, you'll see why. He's some officer. The day I went down, he rescued the crew of a burning fishing boat—talk about perfect timing. There were scorch marks on the hull, he went in so close. Oh, sure, we could get them all apart and interview them, but just figuring out who was involved would be tricky. I hate to say this, but it probably isn't worth the hassle, especially with the senator looking over our shoulder, and the local U.S. Attorney probably won't spring for it either. Bright wasn't all that crazy about it, but I calmed him down. He's a good kid, by the way."

"What about the defense for the two subjects?" Jacobs asked.

"Slim. On the face of it the case against them is pretty damned solid. Ballistics has matched the bullet Mobile pulled out of the deck to the gun recovered on the boat, with both men's fingerprints on it—that was a real stroke of luck. The blood type around where the bullet was found was AB-positive, which matches the wife. A carpet stain three feet away from that confirms that she was having her period, which along with a couple of semen stains suggests rape rather strongly. Right now they're doing the DNA match downstairs on semen samples recovered from the rug—anybody here want to bet against a positive match? We have a half-dozen bloody fingerprints that match the subjects ten points' worth or more. There's a lot of good physical evidence. It's more than enough to convict already," Murray said confidently, "and the lab boys haven't got halfway through their material yet. The U.S. Attorney is going to press for capital punishment. I'll think he'll get it. The only question is whether or not we allow them to trade information for a lighter sentence. But it's not exactly my case." That earned Murray a smile from the Director.

"Pretend it is," Jacobs ordered.

"We'll know in a week or so if we need anything they can tell us. My instincts say no. We ought to be able to figure out who the victim was working for, and that'll be the one who ordered the hit—we just don't know why yet. But it's unlikely that the subjects know why either. I think we have a couple of *sicarios* who hoped to parlay their hit into an entrée to the marketing side of the business. I think they're throwaways. If that's correct, they don't know anything that we can't figure out for ourselves. I suppose we have to give them a chance, but I would recommend against mitigation of sentence. Four murders—bad ones at that. We have a death-penalty statute, and to this brick-agent, I think the chair would fit them just fine."

"Getting nasty in your old age?" Shaw asked. It was another inside joke. Bill Shaw was one of the Bureau's leading intellectuals. He had won his spurs cracking down on domestic terrorist groups, and had accomplished that mission by carefully rebuilding the FBI's intelligence-gathering and analysis procedures. A quintessential chess player with a quiet, organized demeanor, this tall, spare man was also a former field agent who advocated capital punishment in a quiet, organized, and well-reasoned way. It was a point on which police opinion was almost universal. All you had to do to understand capital punishment was to see a crime scene in all its vile spectacle.

"The U.S. Attorney agrees, Dan," Director Jacobs said. "These two druggies are out of the business for keeps."

As if it matters, Murray thought to himself. What mattered to him was that two murderers would pay the price. Because a sufficiently large stash of drugs had been found aboard the yacht, the government could invoke the statute that allowed the death penalty in drug-related murders. The relationship was probably a loose one in this case, but that didn't matter to the three men in the room. The fact of murder—brutal and premeditated—was enough. But to say, as both they and the United States Attorney for the Southern District of Alabama would tell the TV cameras, that this was a fight against the drug trade, was a cynical lie.

Murray's education had been a classical one at Boston College, thirty years before. He could still recite passages in Latin from Virgil's *Aeneid,* or Cicero's opening salvo against Catiline. His study of Greek had been only in translation—foreign languages were one thing to Murray; different alphabets were something else—but he remembered the legend of the Hydra, the mythical beast that had seven or more heads. Each time you cut one off, two would grow to take its place. So it was with the drug trade. There was just too much money involved. Money beyond the horizon of greed. Money to purchase anything a simple man—most of them were—could desire. A single deal could make a man wealthy for life, and there were many who would willingly and consciously risk their lives for that one deal. Having decided to wager their lives on a toss of the dice—what value might they attach to the lives of others? The answer was the obvious one. And so they killed as casually and as brutally as a child might stamp down his foot on an anthill. They killed their competitors because they didn't wish to have competition. They killed their competitors' families whole because they didn't want a wrathful son to appear five, ten, twenty years later with vendetta on his mind; and also because, like nation-states armed with nuclear weapons, the principle of deterrence came into play. Even a man willing to wager his own life might quail before the prospect of wagering those of his children.

So in this case they'd cut off two heads from the Hydra. In three months or so the government would present its case in Federal District Court. The trial would probably last a week. The defense would do its best, but as long as the feds were careful with their evidence, they'd win. The defense would try to discredit the Coast Guard, but it wasn't hard to see what the prosecutor had already decided: the jury would look at Captain Wegener and see a hero, then look at the defendants and see scum. The only likely tactic of the defense would almost certainly be counterproductive. Next, the judge had to make the proper rulings, but this was the South, where even federal judges were expected to have simple, clear ideas about justice. Once the defendants had been found guilty, the penalty phase of the trial would proceed, and again, this was the South, where people read their Bibles. The jury would listen to the aggravating circumstances: mass murder of a family, probability of rape, murder of children, and drugs. But there was a million dollars aboard, the defense would counter. The principal victim was involved in the drug trade. What proof of that is there? the prosecutor would inquire piously—and what of the wife and children? The jury would listen quietly, soberly, almost reverently, would get their instructions from the same judge who had told them how to find the defendants guilty in the first place. They'd deliberate a reasonable period of time, going through the motions of thorough consideration for a decision made days earlier, and report back: death. The criminals, no longer defendants, would be remanded to federal custody. The case would automatically be appealed, but a reversal was unlikely so long as the judge hadn't made any serious procedural errors, which the physical evidence made unlikely. It would take years of appeals. People would object to the sentence on philosophical grounds—Murray disagreed but respected them for their views. The Supreme Court would have to rule sooner or later, but the Supremes, as the police called them, knew that, despite earlier rulings to the contrary, the Constitution clearly contemplated capital punishment, and the will of the People, expressed through Congress, had directly mandated death in certain drug-related cases, as the majority opinion would make clear in its precise, dry use of the language. So, in about five years, after all the appeals had been heard and rejected, both men would be strapped into a wooden chair and a switch would be thrown.

That would be enough for Murray. For all his experience and sophistication, he was before all things a cop. He was an adulthood beyond his graduation from the FBI Academy, when he'd thought that he and his classmates—mostly retired now—would really change the world. The statistics said that they had in many ways, but statistics were too dry, too remote, too inhuman. To Murray the war on crime was an endless series of small battles. Victims were robbed alone, kidnapped alone, or killed alone, and were individuals to be saved or avenged by the warrior-priests of the FBI. Here, too, his outlook was shaped by the values of his Catholic education, and the Bureau remained a bastion of Irish-Catholic America. Perhaps he hadn't changed the world, but he had saved lives, and he had avenged deaths. New criminals would arise as they always did, but his battles had all ended in victories, and ultimately, he had to believe, there would be a net difference for his society, and the difference would be a positive one. He believed as truly as he believed in God that every felon caught was probably a life saved, somewhere down the line.

In this case he had helped to do so again.

But it wouldn't matter a damn to the drug business. His new post forced him to assume a longer view that ordinary agents contemplated only over drinks after their offices closed. With these two out of circulation, the Hydra had already grown two new heads, Murray knew, perhaps more. His mistake was in not pursuing the myth to its conclusion, something others were already doing. Heracles had slain the Hydra by changing tactics. One of the people who had remembered that fact was in this room. What Murray had not yet learned was that at the policy-making level, one's perspective gradually changed one's views.

Cortez liked the view also, despite the somewhat thinner air of this eyrie. His newly acquired boss knew the superficial ways to communicate his power. His desk faced away from the wide window, making it hard for those opposite the massive desk to read the expression on his face. He spoke with the calm, quiet voice of great power. His gestures were economical, his words generally mild. In fact he was a brutal man, Cortez knew, and despite his education a less sophisticated man than he deemed himself to be, but that, Félix knew, was why he'd been hired. So the former colonel trained in Moscow Center adjusted the focus of his eyes to examine the green vista of the valley. He allowed Escobedo to play his eye-power games. He'd played them with far more dangerous men than this one.

"So?"

"I have recruited two people," Cortez replied. "One will feed us information for monetary considerations. The other will do so for other reasons. I also examined two other potential prospects, but discarded them as unsuitable."

"Who are they—who are the ones you will use?"

"No." Cortez shook his head. "I have told you that the identity of my agents must remain secret. This is a principle of intelligence operations. You have informers within your organization, and loose talk would compromise our ability to gather the information which you require. *Jefe,*" he said fawningly. This one needed that sort of thing. "*Jefe,* you have hired me for my expertise and experience. You must allow me to do my work properly. You will know the quality of my sources from the information which I give you. I understand how you feel. It is normal. Castro himself has asked me that question, and I gave him the same answer. It must be so."

That earned Cortez a grunt. Escobedo liked to be compared with a chief of state, better still one who had defied the *yanquis* so successfully for a generation. There would be a satisfied smile now on the handsome face, Félix knew without bothering to check for it. His answer was a lie for two reasons: Castro had never asked the question, and neither Félix nor anyone else on that island would ever have dared to deny him the information.

"So what have you learned?"

"Something is afoot," he said in a matter-of-fact voice that was almost taunting. After all, he had to justify his salary. "The American government is putting together a new program designed to enhance their interdiction efforts. My sources have no specifics as yet, though what they have heard has come from multiple sources and is probably true. My other source will be able to confirm what information I receive from the first." The lesson was lost on Escobedo, Félix knew. Recruiting two complementary sources on a single mission would have earned him a flowery commendation letter from any real intelligence service.

"What will the information cost us?"

Money. It is always money with him, Cortez told himself with a stifled sigh. No wonder he needed a professional with his security operations. Only a fool thinks that he can buy everything. On the other hand, there were times when money was helpful, and though he didn't know it, Escobedo paid more money to his American hirelings and traitors than the entire Communist intelligence network.

"It is better to spend a great deal of money on one person at a high level than to squander it on a large number of minor functionaries. A quarter of a million dollars will do nicely to get the information which we require." Cortez would be keeping most of that, of course. He had expenses of his own.

"That is all?" Escobedo asked incredulously. "I pay more than that to—"

"Because your people have never used the proper approach, *jefe*. Because you pay people on the basis of where they are, not what they know. You have never adopted a systematic approach to dealing with your enemies. With the proper information, you can utilize your funds much more efficiently. You can act strategically instead of tactically," Cortez concluded by pushing the proper button.

"Yes! They must learn that we are a force to be reckoned with!"

Not for the first time, Félix thought that his main objective was to take the money and run . . . perhaps a house in Spain . . . or, perhaps, to supplant this egomaniacal buffoon. That was a thought. . . . But not for now. Escobedo was an egomaniac, but he was also a shrewd one, capable of rapid action. One difference between this man and those who ran his former agency was that Escobedo wasn't afraid to make a decision, and do it quickly. No bureaucracy here, no multiplicity of desks for messages to pass. For that he respected *El Jefe*. At least he knew how to make a decision. KGB had probably been that way once, maybe even the American intelligence organs. But no longer.

* * *

"One more week," Ritter told the National Security Adviser.

"Nice to hear that things are moving," the Admiral observed. "Then what?"

"Why don't you tell me? Just to keep things clear," the DDO suggested. He followed it with a reminder. "After all, the operation was your idea in the first place."

"Well, I sold Director Jacobs on the idea," Cutter replied with a smile at his own cleverness. "When we're ready to proceed—and I mean ready to push the button—Jacobs will fly down there to meet with their Attorney General. The ambassador says that the Colombians will go along with almost anything. They're even more desperate than we are and—"

"You didn't—"

"No, Bob, the ambassador doesn't know. Okay?" *I'm not the idiot you take me for,* his eyes told the CIA executive. "If Jacobs can sell the idea to them, we insert the teams ASAP. One change I want to make."

"What's that?"

"The air side of it. Your report says that practice tracking missions are already turning up targets."

"Some," Ritter admitted. "Two or three per week."

"The wherewithal to handle them is already in place. Why not activate that part of the operation? I mean, it might actually help to identify the areas we want to send the insertion teams to, develop operational intelligence, that sort of thing."

"I'd prefer to wait," Ritter said cautiously.

"Why? If we can identify the most frequently used areas, it cuts down on the amount of moving around they'll have to do. That's your greatest operational risk, isn't it? This is a way to develop information that enhances the entire operational concept."

The problem with Cutter, Ritter told himself, was that the bastard knew just enough about operations to be dangerous. Worse, he had the power to enforce his will—and a memory of the Operations Directorate's recent history. What was it he'd said a few months back? *Your best operations in the last couple of years actually came out of Greer's department. . . .* By which he meant Jack Ryan, James's bright rising star—possibly the new DDI the way things looked. That was too bad. Ritter was genuinely fond of his counterpart at the head of the Intelligence Directorate, but less so of Greer's ingratiating protégé. But it was nevertheless true that the Agency's two best coups in recent years had begun in the "wrong" department, and it was time for Operations to reassert its primacy. Ritter wondered if Cutter was consciously using that as a prod to move him to action. Probably not, he decided. Cutter didn't know enough about infighting yet. Not that he wouldn't learn, of course.

"Going too early is a classic error in field operations," the DDO offered lamely.

"But we're not. Essentially we have two separate operations, don't we?" Cutter asked. "The air part can operate independently of the in-country part. I admit it'll be less effective, but it can still operate. Doesn't this give us a chance to check out the less tricky side of the plan before we commit to the dangerous part? Doesn't it give us something to take to the Colombians to show that we're really serious?"

Too soon, the voice in Ritter's head said urgently, but his face showed indecision.

"Look, do you want me to take it to the President?" Cutter asked.

"Where is he today—California?"

"Political trip. I would prefer not to bother him with this sort of thing, but—"

It was a curious situation, the DDO thought. He had underestimated Cutter, while the National Security Adviser seemed quite able to overestimate himself. "Okay, you win. EAGLE EYE starts day after tomorrow. It'll take that long to get everyone up and running."

"And SHOWBOAT?"

"One more week to prep the teams. Four days to get them to Panama and meet up with the air assets, check communications systems and all that."

Cutter grinned as he reached for his coffee. It was time to smooth some ruffled feathers, he thought. "God, it's nice to work with a real pro. Look on the bright side, Bob. We'll have two full weeks to interrogate whatever turns up in the air net, and the insertion teams will have a much better idea of where they're needed."

You've already won, you son of a bitch. Do you have to rub it in? Ritter wanted to ask. He wondered what would have happened if he'd called Cutter's cards. What would the President have said? Ritter's position was a vulnerable one. He'd grumbled long and loud within the intelligence community that CIA hadn't run a serious field operation in . . . fifteen years? It depended on what you meant by "serious," didn't it? Now he was being given the chance, and what had been a nice line to be spoken at the coffee sessions during high-level government conferences was now a gray chicken come home to roost. Field operations like this were dangerous. Dangerous to the participants. Dangerous to those who gave the orders. Dangerous to the governments that sponsored them. He'd told Cutter that often enough, but like many, the National Security Adviser was mesmerized by the glamour of field ops. It was known in the trade as the *Mission: Impossible* Syndrome. Even professionals could confuse a TV drama with reality, and, throughout government, people tended to hear only that which they wished to hear, and to ignore the unpleasant parts. But it was somewhat late for Ritter to give out his warnings. After all, he'd complained for years that such a mission was possible, and occasionally a desirable adjunct to international policy. And he'd said often enough that his directorate still knew how to do it. The fact that he'd had to recruit field operatives from the Army and Air Force had escaped notice. Time had been when the Agency had been able to use its own private air force and its own private army . . . and if this worked out, perhaps those times would come again. It was a capability the Agency and the country needed, Ritter thought. Here, perhaps, was his chance to make it all happen. If putting up with amateur power-vendors like Cutter was the price of getting it, then that was the price he'd have to pay.

"Okay, I'll get things moving."

"I'll tell the boss. How soon do you expect we'll have results . . . ?"

"Impossible to say."

"But before November," Cutter suggested lightly.

"Yeah, probably by then." Politics, too, of course. Well, that was what kept traffic circling around the beltway.

The 1st Special Operations Wing was based at Hurlburt Field, at the west end of the Eglin Air Force Base complex in Florida. It was a unique unit, but any military unit with "Special" in its name was unique by its very nature. The adjective was used for any number of meanings. "Special weapons" most often meant nuclear weapons, and here the word was used to avoid offending the sensibilities of those for whom "nuclear" connoted mushroom clouds and megadeaths; it was as though a change of wording could effect a change of substance, yet another characteristic of governments all over the world. "Special Operations," on the other hand, meant something else. Generally it denoted covert business, getting people into places where they ought not to be, supporting them while they were there, and getting them out after concluding business that they ought not to have done in the first place. That, among other things, was the business of the 1st.

Colonel Paul Johns—"PJ"—didn't know everything the wing did. The 1st was rather an odd grouping where authority didn't always coincide with rank, where the troops provided support for the aircraft and crews without always knowing why they did so, where aircraft came and went on irregular schedules, and where people weren't encouraged to speculate or ask questions. The wing was divided into individual fiefdoms that interacted with others on an *ad hoc* basis. PJ's fiefdom included half a dozen MH-53J "Pave Low III" helicopters. Johns had been around for quite a while, and somehow had managed to spend nearly all of his Air Force career in the air. It was a career path that guaranteed him both a fulfilling, exciting career, and precisely zero chance at ever wearing general's stars. But on that score he didn't give much of a damn. He'd joined the Air Force to fly; something generals don't get to do very much. He'd kept his part of the bargain, and the service had kept its, which wasn't quite as common an arrangement as some would imagine. Johns had early on eschewed fixed-wing aircraft, the fast-movers that dropped bombs or shot down other aircraft. A people-person all of his life, Johns had started off in the Jolly Green Giants, the HH-3 rescue helicopters of Vietnam fame, then graduated to the Super Jolly HH-53, part of the Air Rescue Service. As a brash young captain he'd flown in the Song Tay Raid, copilot of the aircraft that had deliberately crashed into the prison camp twenty miles west of Hanoi as part of the effort to rescue people who, it turned out, had been moved just a short time before. That had been one of the few failures in his life. Colonel Johns was not a man accustomed to such things. If you went down, PJ would come get you. He was the third-ranking all-time rescue specialist in the Air Force. The current Chief of Staff and two other general officers had been excused a stay in the Hanoi Hilton because of him and his crews. PJ was a man who only rarely had to buy himself a drink. He was also a man whom general officers saluted first. It was a tradition that went along with the Medal of Honor.

Like most heroes, he was grossly ordinary. Only five-six and a hundred thirty pounds, he looked like any other middle-aged man picking up a loaf of bread in the base exchange. The reading glasses he now had to wear made him look rather like a friendly suburban banker, and he did not often raise his voice. He cut his own grass when he had the time, and his wife did it when he didn't. His car was a fuel-efficient Plymouth Horizon. His son was studying engineering at Georgia Tech, and his daughter had won a scholarship to Princeton, leaving him and his wife an overly quiet house on post in which to contemplate the retirement that lay a few years in the future.

But not now. He sat in the left seat of the Pave Low helicopter checking out a bright young captain who, everyone thought, was ready to be a command pilot himself. The multimillion-dollar helicopter was skimming treetops at a hair under two hundred knots. It was a dark, cloudy night over the Florida panhandle, and this part of the Eglin complex wasn't brightly lit, but that didn't matter. Both he and the captain wore special helmets with built-in low-light goggles, not terribly unlike what Darth Vader wore in *Star Wars*. But these worked, converting the vague darkness ahead into a green and gray display. PJ kept his head moving around, and made sure that the captain did the same. One danger with the night-vision gear was that your depth perception—a matter of life and death to a low-level flyer—was degraded by the artificial picture generated by the masks. Perhaps a third of the squadron's operational losses, Johns thought, could be traced to that particular hazard, and the technical wizards hadn't come up with a decent fix yet. One problem with the Pave Lows was that operational and training losses were relatively high. It was a price of the mission for which they trained, and there was no answer to that but more training.

The six-bladed rotor spun overhead, driven by the two turboshaft engines. Pave Low was about as big as helicopters got, with a full combat crew of six and room for over forty combat-equipped passengers. The nose bulged at various places with radar, infrared, and other instruments—the general effect was of an insect from another planet. At doors on each side of the airframe were mounts for rotary miniguns, plus another at the tail cargo door, because their primary mission, covert insertion and support of special-operations forces, was a dangerous business—as was the secondary role they practiced tonight, combat search-and-rescue. During his time in Southeast Asia, PJ had worked with A-1 Skyraider attack bombers, the Air Force's last piston-engine attack aircraft, called SPADs or Sandys. Exactly who would support them today was still something of an open question. To protect herself, in addition to the guns the aircraft carried flare and chaff pods, IR jamming and suppression gear . . . and her crew of madmen.

Johns smiled within his helmet. This was real flying, and there wasn't much of that left. They had the option of flying with the aid of an autopilot-radar-computer system that hedgehopped automatically, but tonight they were simulating a system failure. Autopilot or not, the pilot was responsible for flying the airplane, and Willis was doing his best to keep the helicopter down on the treetops. Every so often Johns would have to stop himself from flinching as an errant tree branch seemed certain to slap against the chopper's underside, but Captain Willis was a competent young man, keeping the aircraft low, but not too low. Besides, as PJ knew from long experience, the top branches on trees were thin, fragile things that did nothing more than mar the paint. More than once he'd brought home a helicopter whose underside bore green stains like those on a child's jeans.

"Distance?" Willis asked.

Colonel Johns checked the navigation display. He had a choice of Doppler, satellite, or inertial, plus the old-fashioned plotting board that he still used, and still insisted that all his people learn.

"Two miles, zero-four-eight."

"Roger." Willis eased off on the throttle.

For this training mission, an honest-to-God fighter pilot had "volunteered" to be trucked out to the boonies, where another helicopter had draped a parachute over a tree to simulate a genuinely shot-down airman, who had in turn activated a genuine rescue-beacon radio. One of the new tricks was that the chute was coated with a chemical that fluoresced on ultraviolet light. Johns did the copilot's job of activating a low-power UV laser that scanned ahead, looking for the return signal. Whoever had come up with this idea deserved a medal, PJ thought. The worst, scariest, and always seemingly the longest part of any rescue mission was actually getting eyeballs on the victim. That was when the gomers on the ground, who were also out hunting, would hear the sound of the rotor and decide that they might as well bag two aircraft on the same day. . . . His Medal of Honor had come on such a mission over eastern Laos, when the crew of an F-105 Wild Weasel had attracted a platoon of NVA. Despite aggressive support from the Sandy team, the downed airmen hadn't dared to reveal their position. But Johns had coldly decided not to go home empty, and his Jolly had absorbed two hundred rounds in a furious gunfight before getting both men out. Johns often wondered if he'd ever have the courage—lunacy—to try that again.

"I got a chute at two o'clock."

"X-Ray Two-Six, this is Papa Lima; we have your chute. Can you mark your position?"

"Affirmative, tossing smoke, tossing green smoke."

The rescuee was following proper procedure in telling the chopper crew what sort of smoke grenade he was using, but you couldn't tell in the dark. On the other hand, the heat of the pyrotechnic device blazed like a beacon on the infrared display, and they could see their man.

"Got him?"

"Yep," Willis answered, and spoke next to the crew chief. "Get ready, we have our victim."

"Standing by, sir." In the back the flight engineer, Senior Master Sergeant Buck Zimmer—he and the colonel went way back together—activated his winch controls. At the end of the steel cable was a heavy steel device called a penetrator. Heavy enough to fall through the foliage of any forest, its bottom unfolded like the petals of a flower, providing a seat for the victim, who would then be pulled back up through the branches, an experience which remarkably enough had never quite killed anyone. In the event that the victim was injured, it was the job of Sergeant Zimmer or a rescue paramedic to ride it down, attach the victim to the penetrator, and take the elevator ride himself. That job sometimes entailed physically searching for the victim, often under fire. It was for this reason that the people who flew the rescue choppers treated their crewmen with considerable respect. Nothing so horrifies a pilot as the idea of being on the ground, with people shooting at you.

But not this time. Since it was peacetime and safety rules applied, training or not, the pickup was being made from a small clearing. Zimmer worked the winch controls. The victim unfolded the seat-petals and hooked himself securely aboard, knowing what was to follow. The flight engineer started hoisting the cable, made sure that the victim was firmly attached, and so notified the flight crew.

On the flight deck, forward, Captain Willis immediately twisted the throttle control to full power and moved upward. Within fifteen seconds, the "rescued" fighter pilot was three hundred feet over the ground, hanging by a quarter-inch steel cable and wondering why in the hell he'd been so fucking idiotic to volunteer for this. Five seconds later, the burly arm of Sergeant Zimmer yanked him into the aircraft.

"Recovery complete," Zimmer reported.

Captain Willis pushed his cyclic control forward, diving the helicopter at the ground. He'd climbed too much on the extraction, he knew, and tried to compensate by showing Colonel Johns that he could get back down to the safety of the treetops very quickly. He accomplished this, but he could feel the eyes of his commander on the side of his head. He'd made a mistake. Johns did not tolerate mistakes. People died of mistakes, the colonel told them every goddamned day, and he was tired of having people die.

"Can you take it for a minute?" Willis asked.

"Copilot's airplane," Johns acknowledged, taking the stick and easing the Sikorsky down another foot or so. "You don't want to climb so much winching the guy in, not with possible SAMs out there."

"At night you'd expect more guns than SAMs." Willis was right, sort of. It was a hard call. And he knew the answer that would come.

"We're protected against small-caliber guns. The big ones are as dangerous as SAMs. You keep it closer to the ground next time, Captain."

"Yes, sir."

"Other than that, not bad. Arm a little stiff?"

"Yes, sir."

"It might be the gloves. Unless your fingers fit in just right, you end up gripping too hard, and that translates back into the wrist and upper arm after a while. You end up with a stiff arm, stiff movements on the stick, and sloppy handling. Get yourself a good set of gloves. My wife makes mine for me special. You might not always have a copilot to take the airplane, and this sort of thing is tough enough that you don't want any more distractions than you gotta have."

"Yes, sir."

"By the way, you passed."

It wouldn't do to thank the colonel, Captain Willis knew. He did the next best thing after flexing his hand for a minute.

"I got the airplane."

PJ took his hand off the stick. "Pilot's airplane," he acknowledged. "By the way . . ."

"Yes, sir?"

"I've got a special job coming up in a week or so. Interested?"

"Doing what?"

"You're not supposed to ask that," the colonel told him. "A little TDY. Not too far away. We'll be flying this bird down. Call it Spec-Ops."

"Okay," Willis said. "Count me in. Who's cleared to—"

"In simple terms, nobody is. We're taking Zimmer, Childs, and Bean, and a support team. Far as everybody knows, we're TDY for some practice missions out on the California coast. That's all you need to know for now."

Inside his helmet, Willis's eyebrow went up. Zimmer had worked with PJ all the way back to Thailand and the Jolly Green days, one of the few enlisted men left with real combat experience. Sergeant Bean was the squadron's best gunner. Childs was right behind him. Whatever this TDY—temporary detached duty—assignment was, it was for-real. It also meant that Willis would remain a copilot for a little while longer, but he didn't mind. It was always a treat flying with the champion of Combat Search and Rescue. That was where the colonel got his call sign. C-SAR, in PJ's lexicon, it came out "Caesar."

Chavez traded a look with Julio Vega: *Jesucristo!*

"Any questions?" the briefer asked.

"Yes, sir," a radio operator said. "What happens after we call it in?"

"The aircraft will be intercepted."

"For-real, sir?"

"That's up to the flight crew. If they don't do what they're told, they're going swimming. That's all I can say. Gentlemen, everything you've heard is Top Secret. Nobody—I mean *nobody!*—ever hears what I just said. If the wrong folks ever learn about this, people will get hurt. The objective of this mission is to put a crimp in the way people move drugs into the United States. It may get a little rough."

"About fucking time," a quiet voice observed.

"Okay, now you know. I repeat, gentlemen, this mission is going to be dangerous. We are going to give each of you some time to think about it. If you want out, we'll understand. We're dealing with some pretty bad folks. Of course"—the man smiled and went on after a moment—"we got some pretty bad people here, too."

"Fuckin' A!" another voice said.

"Anyway, you have the rest of the night to think this one over. We move out at eighteen-hundred hours tomorrow. There is no turning back at that point. Everybody understand? Good. That is all for now."

"Ten-Hut!" Captain Ramirez snapped. Everyone in the room jumped to attention as the briefer left. Then it was the captain's turn: "Okay, you heard the man. Give this one a real good think, people. I want you to come along on this one—hell, I need every one of you—but if you're not comfortable with the idea, I don't want you. You got any questions for me?" There weren't. "Okay. Some of you know people who got fucked up because of drugs. Maybe friends, maybe family, I don't know. What we have here is a chance to get even. Those bastards are fucking up our country, and it's time we taught 'em a little lesson. Think it over. If anyone has any problems, let me know right away. If anybody wants out, that's okay." His face and tone said something else entirely. Anyone who opted out would be seen by his officer as something less than a man, and that would be doubly painful since Ramirez had led his men, shared every hardship, and sweated with them through every step of training. He turned and left.

"Damn," Chavez observed finally. "I figured this was going to be a strange one, but . . . damn."

"I had a friend died of an OD," Vega said. "He was just playing around, y'know, not a regular user like, but I guess it was bad stuff. Scared the shit outa me. I never touched it again. I was pissed when that happened. Tomás was a friend, '*mano*. The fucker sold him the shit, man, I wouldn't mind introducin' him to my SAW."

Chavez nodded as thoughtfully as his age and education allowed. He remembered the gangs who had been vicious enough in his early childhood, but that activity seemed almost playful in retrospect. Now the turf fights were not the mere symbolism over who dwelt on what block. Now it was over marketing position. There was serious money involved, more than enough to kill for. That was what had transformed his old neighborhood from a zone of poverty to an area of open combat. Some people he knew were afraid to walk their own streets because of other people with drugs and guns. Wild rounds came through windows and killed people in front of televisions, and the cops were often afraid to visit the projects unless they came with the numbers and weapons of an invading army . . . all because of drugs. And the people who caused it all were living high and safe, fifteen hundred miles away. . . .

Chavez didn't begin to grasp how skillfully he and his fellows—even Captain Ramirez—had been manipulated. They were all soldiers who trained constantly to protect their country against its enemies, products of a system that took their youth and enthusiasm and gave it direction; that rewarded hard work with achievement and pride; that most of all gave their boundless energy purpose; that asked only for allegiance in return. Since enlisted soldiers most often come from the poorer strata of society, they all had learned that minority status did not matter—the Army rewarded performance without consideration to one's color or accent. All of these men were intimately aware of the social problems caused by drugs, and were part of a subculture in which drugs were not tolerated—the military's effort to expunge its ranks of drug users had been painful, but it had succeeded. Those who stayed in were people for whom the use of drugs was beyond the pale. They were the achievers from their neighborhoods. They were the success stories. They were the adventurous, the brave, the disciplined graduates of the mean streets for whom obstacles were things to be overcome, and for whom every instinct was to help others to do the same.

And that was the mission they all contemplated. Here was a chance to protect not only their country, but also the barrios from which they had all escaped. Already marked as achievers within the ranks of the Army's most demanding units, then given training to make them prouder still, they could no more decline participation in this mission than they could deny their manhood. There was not a man here who had not once in his life contemplated taking down a drug dealer. But the Army was letting them do something even better. Of course they'd do it.

"Blow the fuckers right out of the sky!" the squad's radio operator said. "Put a Sidewinder missile right up his ass! You got the right to remain *dead,* sucker!"

"Yeah," Vega agreed. "I wouldn't mind seeing that. Hell, I wouldn't mind it if we got to go after the big shots where they fucking live! Think we could get them, Ding?"

Chavez grinned. "You shittin' me, Julio? Who you suppose they got working for them, soldiers? Shit. Punks with machine guns, probably don't even keep 'em clean. Against us? Shit. Maybe against what they got down there, maybe, but against us? No chance, man. I'm talking dead meat. I just get in close, pop the sentries nice an' quiet with my H and K, an' let you turkeys do the easy stuff."

"More Ninja shit," a rifleman said lightly.

Ding pulled one of his throwing stars from his shirt pocket and flicked it into the doorframe fifteen feet away.

"Smile when you say that, boy." Chavez laughed.

"Hey, Ding, could you teach me to do that?" the rifleman asked. There was no further discussion of the mission's dangers, only of its opportunities.

They called him Bronco. His real name was Jeff Winters, and he was a newly promoted captain in the United States Air Force, but because his job was flying fighter aircraft he had to have a special name, known as a call sign. His resulted from a nearly forgotten party in Colorado—he'd graduated from the United States Air Force Academy—at which he'd fallen from a horse so gentle that the animal had nearly died of fright. The six-pack of Coors had contributed to the fall, along with the laughter that followed from his amused classmates, and one of them—the asshole was flying trash-haulers now, Winters told himself with a tight smile—assigned him the name on the spot. The classmate knew how to ride horses, Bronco told the night, but he hadn't made the grade to fly F-15-Charlies. The world wasn't exactly overrun with justice, but there was some to be found.

Which was the whole purpose of his special mission.

Winters was a small man, and a young one. Twenty-seven, to be exact, he already had seven hundred hours in the McDonnell-Douglas fighter. As some men were born to play baseball, or to act, or to drive race cars, Bronco Winters had entered the world for the single purpose of flying fighter planes. He had the sort of eyesight to make an ophthalmologist despair, coordination that combined the best of a concert pianist and the man on the flying trapeze, and a much rarer quality known in his tight community as SA—situational awareness. Winters always knew what was happening around him. His airplane was as natural a part of the young man as the muscles in his arm. He transmitted his wishes to the airplane and the F-15C complied at once, precisely mimicking the mental image in the pilot's mind. Where his mind went, the airplane followed.

At the moment he was orbiting two hundred miles off the Florida Gulf Coast. He'd taken off from Eglin Air Force Base forty minutes earlier, topped off his fuel from a KC-135 tanker, and now he had enough JP-5 aboard to fly for five hours if he took things easy, as he had every intention of doing. FAST-pack conformal fuel cells were attached along the sides of his aircraft. Ordinarily they were hung with missiles as well—the F-15 can carry as many as eight—but for this evening's mission the only ordnance aboard were the rounds for his 20mm rotary cannon, and these were always kept aboard the aircraft because their weight was a convenience in maintaining the Eagle's flying trim.

He flew in a racetrack pattern, his engines throttled down to loitering speed. Bronco's dark, sharp eyes swept continuously left and right, searching for the running lights of other aircraft but finding none among the stars. He wasn't the least bit bored. He was, rather, a man quietly delighted that the taxpayers of his country were actually foolish enough to give him over $30,000 per year to do something for which he would have been grateful to pay. Well, he told himself, I guess that's what I'm doing tonight.

"Two-Six Alpha, this is Eight-Three Quebec, do you read, over?" his radio crackled. Bronco squeezed the trigger on his stick.

"Eight-Three Quebec, this is Two-Six Alpha. I read you five by five, over." The radio channel was encrypted. Only the two aircraft were using the unique encoding algorithm for this evening; all that anyone trying to listen in would hear would be the warbling rasp of static.

"We have a target on profile, bearing one-nine-six, range two-one-zero your position. Angels two. Course zero-one-eight. Speed two-six-five. Over." There was no command to accompany this information. Despite the secure radios, chatter was kept to a minimum.

"Roger, copy. Out."

Captain Winters moved his stick left. The proper course and speed for his intercept sprang into his mind unbidden. The Eagle changed over to a southerly heading. Winters dropped the nose a touch as he brought the fighter to a course of one hundred eighty degrees and increased power a fraction to bring his speed up. It actually seemed that he was abusing the airplane to fly her this slow, but that was not actually the case.

It was a twin-engined Beech, Captain Winters saw, the most common aircraft used by the druggies. That meant cocaine rather than the bulkier marijuana, and that suited him, since it was probably a cokehead who'd mugged his mom. He pulled his F-15 level behind it, about half a mile back.

This was the eighth time he'd intercepted a drug runner, but it was the first time he'd be allowed to do something about it. On the previous occasions he'd not even been allowed to call the information in to the Customs boys. Bronco verified the course of the target—for fighter pilots anything other than a friendly was a target—and checked his systems. The directional radio transmitter hanging in the streamlined container under the fighter's centerline slaved itself to the radar tracking Beech. He made his first radio call, and flipped on his landing lights, transfixing the small executive aircraft in the night. Immediately the Beech dived for the wave tops, and the Eagle followed it down. He called again, giving his order and getting no response. He moved the button on the top of his stick to the "guns" position. The next call was accompanied by a burst from his cannon. This started the Beech in a series of radical evasive turns. Winters decided that the target was not going to do what it was told.

Okay.

An ordinary pilot might have been startled by the lights and turned to evade a collision, but an ordinary pilot would not do what the druggies did. The Beech dived for the wave tops, reduced power, and popped his flaps, slowing the aircraft down to approach speed, which was far slower than the F-15 could do without stalling out. This maneuver often forced the DEA and Coast Guard planes to break contact. But Bronco's job wasn't to follow the guy in. As the Beech turned west to run for the Mexican coast, Captain Winters killed his lights, added power, and zoomed up to five thousand feet. There he executed a smart hammerhead turn and took a nose-down attitude, the Eagle's radar sweeping the surface of the sea. There: heading due west, speed 85 knots, only a few feet over the water. A gutsy pilot, Bronco thought, holding that close to a stall and that low. Not that it mattered.

Winters extended his own speed brakes and flaps, taking the fighter down. He felt to make sure that the selector button was still in the "guns" position and watched the Head-Up Display, bringing the pipper right on the target and holding it there. It might have been harder if the Beech had kept speed up and tried to maneuver, but it wouldn't really have mattered. Bronco was just too good, and in his Eagle, he was nearly invincible. When he got within four hundred yards, his finger depressed the button for a fraction of a second.

A line of green tracers lanced through the sky.

Several rounds appeared to miss the Beech ahead, but the rest hit right in the cockpit area. He heard no sound from the kill. There was only a brief flash of light, followed by a phosphorescent splash of white foam when the aircraft hit.

Winters reflected briefly that he had just killed one man, maybe two. That was all right. They wouldn't be missed.

9. Meeting Engagement

"So?" Escobedo eyed Larson as coldly as a biology professor might look at a caged white rat. He had no special reason to suspect Larson of anything, but he was angry, and Larson was the nearest target for that anger.

But Larson was used to that. "So I don't know, *jefe*. Ernesto was a good pilot, a good student. So was the other one, Cruz. The engines in the aircraft were practically new—two hundred hours on each. The airframe was six years old, but that's nothing unusual; the aircraft was well maintained. Weather was okay all the way north, some scattered high clouds over the Yucatan Channel, nothing worse than that." The pilot shrugged. "Aircraft disappear, *jefe*. One cannot always know why."

"He is my cousin! What do I tell his mother?"

"Have you checked with any airfields in Mexico?"

"Yes! And Cuba, and Honduras, and Nicaragua!"

"No distress calls? No reports from ships or aircraft in the vicinity?"

"No, nothing." Escobedo moderated somewhat as Larson went through the possibilities, professional as ever.

"If it was some sort of electrical failure, he might be down somewhere, but . . . I would not be hopeful, *jefe*. If they had landed safely, they would have let us know by now. I am sorry, *jefe*. He is probably lost. It has happened before. It will happen again."

One other possibility was that Ernesto and Cruz had made their own arrangements, had landed somewhere other than their intended destination, had sold their cargo of forty kilograms, and had decided to disappear, but that was not seriously considered. The question of drugs had not even been mentioned, because Larson was not really part of the operation, merely a technical consultant who had asked to be cut out of that aspect of the business. Escobedo trusted Larson to be honest and objective because he had always been so in the past, taking his money and doing his job well, and also because Larson was no fool—he knew the consequences of lying and double-dealing.

They were in Escobedo's expensive condominium in Medellín. It occupied the entire top floor of the building. The floor immediately under this was occupied by Escobedo's vassals and retainers. The elevator was controlled by people who knew who could pass and who could not. The street outside the building was watched. Larson reflected that at least he didn't have to worry about somebody stealing the hubcaps off his car. He also wondered what the hell had happened to Ernesto. Was it simply an accident of some sort? Such things had happened often enough. One reason for his position as flying instructor was that past smuggling operations had lost quite a few airplanes, often through the most prosaic of causes. But Larson was not a fool. He was thinking about recent visitors and recent orders from Langley; training at The Farm didn't encourage people to believe in coincidences. Some sort of op was about to run. Might this have been the opening move?

Larson didn't think so. CIA was years past that sort of thing, which was too bad, he thought, but a fact nonetheless.

"He was a good pilot?" Escobedo asked again.

"I taught him myself, *jefe*. He had four hundred hours, good mechanical skills, and he was as good on instruments as a young pilot can be. The only thing that worried me about him was that he liked flying low."

"Yes?"

"Flying low over water is dangerous, especially at night. It is too easy to become disoriented. You forget where the horizon is, and if you keep looking out of the windows instead of checking your instruments . . . Experienced pilots have driven their airplanes right into the water that way. Unfortunately, flying very low is fun and many pilots, especially the young ones, think that it is also a test of manhood. That is foolish, as pilots learn with time."

" 'A good pilot is a cautious pilot'?" Escobedo asked.

"That is what I tell every student," Larson replied seriously. "Not all of them believe me. It is true everywhere. You can ask instructors in any air force in the world. Young pilots make foolish mistakes because they are young and inexperienced. Judgment comes with experience—most often through a frightening experience. Those who survive learn, but some do not survive."

Escobedo considered that for a few seconds.

"He was a proud one, Ernesto." To Larson it sounded like an epitaph.

"I will recheck the maintenance log of the aircraft," the pilot offered. "And I will also review the weather data."

"Thank you for coming in so quickly, Señor Larson."

"I am at your service, *jefe*. If I learn anything, I will let you know."

Escobedo saw him to the door, then returned to his desk. Cortez entered the room from a side door.

"Well?"

"I like Larson," Cortez said. "He speaks the truth. He has pride, but not too much."

Escobedo nodded agreement. "A hireling, but a good one."

. . . *like you*. Cortez didn't react to the implied message. "How many flights have been lost over the years?"

"We didn't even kept records until eighteen months ago. Since then, nine. That's one reason we took Larson on. I felt that the crashes were due to pilot error and poor maintenance. Carlos has proven to be a good instructor."

"But never wished to become involved himself?"

"No. A simple man. He has a comfortable life doing what he enjoys. There is much to be said for that," Escobedo observed lightly. "You have been over his background?"

"*Sí*. Everything checks out, but . . ."

"But?"

"But if he were something other than what he appears to be, things would also check out." This was the point at which an ordinary man would say something like, *But you can't suspect everyone*. Escobedo did not, and that was a measure of his sophistication, Cortez noted. His employer had ample experience with conspiracy and knew that you had to suspect everyone. He wasn't exactly a professional, but he wasn't exactly a fool either.

"Do you think—"

"No. He was nowhere near the place the flight left from, had no way of knowing that it was happening that night. I checked: he was in Bogotá with his lady friend. They had dinner alone and retired early. Perhaps it was a flying accident, but coming so soon after we learn that the *norteamericanos* are planning something, I do not think we should call it such a thing. I think I should return to Washington."

"What will you find out?"

"I will attempt to discover something of what they are doing."

"Attempt?"

"Señor, gathering sensitive intelligence information is an art—"

"You can buy anything you need!"

"There you are incorrect," Cortez said with a level stare. "The best sources of information are never motivated by money. It is dangerous—foolish—to assume that allegiance can be purchased."

"And what of you?"

"That is a question you must consider, but I am sure you already have." The best way to earn trust with this man was always to say that trust did not exist. Escobedo thought that whatever allegiance money could not buy could be maintained with fear instead. In that sense, his employer was foolish. He assumed that his reputation for violence could cow anyone, and rarely considered that there were those who could give him lessons in applied violence. There was much to admire about this man, but so much also to merit disdain. Fundamentally he was an amateur—though a gifted one—who learned from his mistakes readily enough, but lacked the formal training that might have enabled him to learn from the mistakes of others—and what was intelligence training but the institutional memory of lessons from the mistakes of others? He didn't so much need an intelligence and security adviser as one in covert operations per se, but that was an area in which none of these men would solicit or accept advice. They came from generations of smugglers, and their expertise in corrupting and bribing was real enough. It was just that they'd never learned how to play the game against a truly organized and formidable adversary—the Colombians didn't count. That the *yanquis* had not yet discovered within themselves the courage to act in accordance with their power was nothing more than good fortune. If there was one thing the KGB had drilled into Cortez, it was that good fortune did not exist.

Captain Winters viewed his gunsight videotape with the men from Washington. They were in a corner office of one of the Special Ops buildings—Eglin had quite a few—and the other two wore Air Force uniforms, both bearing the rank of lieutenant colonel, a convenient middle grade of officer, many of whom came and went in total anonymity.

"Nice shooting, son," one observed.

"He could have made it harder," Bronco replied without much in the way of emotion. "But he didn't."

"How about traffic on the surface?"

"Nothing within thirty miles."

"Put up the Hawkeye tape," the senior man ordered. They were using three-quarter-inch tape, which was preferred by the military for its higher data capacity. The tape was already cued. It showed the inbound Beechcraft, marked as XX1 on the alphanumeric display, one of many contacts, most of which were clearly marked as airliners, and had been high over the shoot-down. There were also numerous surface contacts, but all of them were a good distance away from the area of the attack, and this tape ended prior to the shoot-down. The Hawkeye crew, as planned, had no direct knowledge of what had transpired after handing over the contact to the fighter. The guidelines for the mission were clear, and the intercept area was calculated to avoid frequently used shipping channels. The low-altitude path taken by the drug smugglers helped, of course, insofar as it limited the distance at which someone might see a flash or an explosion, neither of which had happened here.

"Okay," said the senior one. "That was well within mission parameters." They switched tapes again.

"How many rounds expended?" the junior one asked Winters.

"A hundred 'n eight," the captain replied. "With a Vulcan it's kinda hard to keep it down, y'know? The critter shoots right quick."

"It did that plane like a chainsaw."

"That's the idea, sir. I could have been a little faster on the trigger, but you want me to try 'n avoid the fuel tanks, right?"

"That's correct." The cover story, in case anyone saw a flash, was that there was a Shoot-Ex out of Eglin—exercises killing target drones are not uncommon there—but so much the better if no one noticed at all.

Bronco didn't like the secrecy stuff. As far as he was concerned, shooting the bastards down made perfectly good sense. The point of the mission, they'd told him during the recruiting phase, was that drug trafficking was a threat to U.S. national security. That phrasing made everything legitimate. As an air-defense fighter pilot, he was trained to deal with threats to national security in this specific way—to shoot them out of the sky with as much emotion as a skeet-shooter dispatched clay birds thrown out from the traps. Besides, Bronco thought, if it's a real threat to national security, why shouldn't the people know about it? But that wasn't his department. He was only a captain, and captains are operators, not thinkers. Somebody up the line had decided that this was okay, and that was all he needed to know. Dispatching this Twin-Beech had been the next thing to murder, but that was as accurate a description of combat operations as any other. After all, giving people a fair chance was what happened at the Olympics, not where your life was on the line. If somebody was dumb enough to let his ass get killed, that wasn't Bronco's lookout, especially if he happened to be committing an act of war against Bronco's country. And *that* was what "threat to national security" meant, wasn't it?

Besides, he *had* given Juan—or whatever the bastard's name had been—a fair warning, hadn't he? If the asshole'd thought he could outfly the best fucking fighter plane in the whole world, well, he'd learned different. Tough.

"You got any problems to this point, Captain?" the senior one asked.

"Problems with what, sir?" *What a dumbass question!*

The airstrip at which they had arrived wasn't big enough for a proper military transport. The forty-four men of Operation SHOWBOAT traveled by bus to Peterson Air Force Base, a few miles east of the Air Force Academy at Colorado Springs. It was dark, of course. The bus was driven by one of the "camp counselors," as the men had taken to calling them, and the ride was a quiet one, with many of the soldiers asleep after their last day's PT. The rest were alone with their own thoughts. Chavez watched the mountains slide by as the bus twisted its way down the last range. The men were ready.

"Pretty mountains, man," Julio Vega observed sleepily.

"Especially in a bus heading downhill."

"Fuckin' A!" Vega chuckled. "You know, someday I'm gonna come back here and do some skiing." The machine-gunner adjusted himself in the seat and faded out.

They were roused thirty-five minutes later after passing through the gate at Peterson. The bus pulled right up to the aft ramp of an Air Force C-141 Starlifter transport. The soldiers rose and assembled their gear in an orderly fashion, with each squad captain checking to make sure that everyone had everything he'd been issued as they filed off. A few looked around on the way to the aircraft. There was nothing unusual about the departure, no special security guards, merely the ground crew fueling and preflighting the aircraft for an immediate departure. In the distance a KC-135 aerial tanker was lifting off, and though no one thought much about it, they'd be meeting that bird in a little while. The Air Force sergeant who was loadmaster for this particular aircraft took them aboard and seated them as comfortably as the spartan appointments allowed—this mainly involved giving everyone ear protectors.

The flight crew went through the usual startup procedures, and presently the Starlifter began moving. The noise was grating despite the earmuffs, but the aircraft had an Air Force Reserve crew, all airline personnel, who gave them a decent ride. Except for the midair refueling, that is. As soon as the C-141 had climbed to altitude, it rendezvoused with the KC-135 to replace the fuel burned off during the climb-out. For the passengers this involved the usual roller-coaster buffet which, amplified by the near total absence of windows, made a few stomachs decidedly queasy, though all looked quietly inured to it. Half an hour after lifting off, the C-141 settled down on a southerly course, and from a mixture of fatigue and sheer boredom, the soldiers drifted off to sleep for the remainder of the ride.

The MH-53J left Eglin Air Force Base at about the same time, all of its fuel tanks topped off after engine warm-up. Colonel Johns took it to one thousand feet and a course of two-one-five for the Yucatan Channel. Three hours out, an MC-130E Combat Talon tanker/support aircraft caught up with the Pave Low, and Johns decided to let the captain handle the midair refueling. They'd have to tank thrice more, and the tanker would accompany them all the way down, bringing a maintenance and support crew and spare parts.

"Ready to plug," PJ told the tanker commander.

"Roger," answered Captain Montaigne in the MC-130E, holding the aircraft straight and level.

Johns watched Willis ease the nose probe into the drogue. "Okay, we got plug."

In the cockpit of the -130E, Captain Montaigne took note of the indicator light and keyed the microphone. *"Ohhh!"* she said in her huskiest voice. "*Nobody* does it like you, Colonel!"

Johns laughed out loud and keyed his switch twice, generating a *click-click* signal, which meant Affirmative. He switched to intercom. "Why spoil it for her?" he asked Willis, who was regrettably straitlaced. The fuel transfer took six minutes.

"How long do you think we'll be down there?" Captain Willis wondered after it was done.

"They didn't tell me that, but if it goes too long, they say we'll get relief."

"That's nice," the captain observed. His eyes shifted back and forth from his flight instruments to the world outside the armored cockpit. The aircraft had more than its full load of combat gear aboard—Johns was a firm believer in firepower—and the electronic countermeasures racks were gone. Whatever they'd be doing, they wouldn't have to worry about unfriendly radar coverage, and that meant that the job, whatever it was, didn't involve Nicaragua or Cuba. It also made for more passenger room in the aircraft and deleted the second flight engineer from the crew. "You were right about the gloves. My wife made up a set and it does make a difference."

"Some guys just fly without 'em, but I don't like to have sweaty hands on the stick."

"Is it going to be that warm?"

"There's warm, and there's warm," Johns pointed out. "You don't get sweaty hands just from the outside temperature."

"Oh. Yes, sir." *Gee, he gets scared, too—just like the rest of us?*

"Like I keep telling people, the more thinking you do before things get exciting, the less exciting things will be. And they get plenty exciting enough."

Another voice came onto the intercom circuit: "You keep talking like that, sir, and *we* might get a little scared."

"Sergeant Zimmer, how are things in the back?" Johns asked. Zimmer's regular spot was just aft of the two pilots, hovering over an impressive array of instruments.

"Coffee, tea, or milk, sir? The meals for this flight are Chicken Kiev with rice, Roast Beef au Jus with baked potato, and for the weight-watchers among us, Orange Ruffy and stir-fried veggies—and if you believe that, sir, you've been staring at the instrument panel too long. Why the hell don't we have a stewardess along with us?''

" 'Cause you and I are both too old for that shit, Zimmer!'' PJ laughed.

"It ain't bad in a chopper, sir. What with all the vibration and all . . .''

"I've been trying to reform him since Korat,'' Johns explained to Captain Willis. "How old are the kids now, Buck?''

"Seventeen, fifteen, twelve, nine, six, five, and three, sir.''

"Christ,'' Willis noted. "Your wife must be some gal, Sarge.''

"She's afraid I'll run around, so she robs me of my energy,'' Zimmer explained. "I fly to get away from her. It's the only thing that keeps me alive.''

"Her cooking must be all right, judging by your uniform.''

"Is the colonel picking on his sergeant again?'' Zimmer asked.

"Not exactly. I just want you to look as good as Carol does.''

"No chance, sir.''

"Roger that. Some coffee would be nice.''

"On the way, Colonel, sir.'' Zimmer was on the flight deck in less than a minute. The instrument console for the Pave Low helicopter was large and complex, but Zimmer had long since installed gimbaled cup holders suitable for the spillproof cups that Colonel Johns liked. PJ took a quick sip.

"She makes good coffee, too, Buck.''

"Funny how things work out, isn't it?'' Carol Zimmer knew that her husband would share it with his colonel. Carol wasn't her original given name. Born in Laos thirty-six years earlier, she was the daughter of a Hmong warlord who'd fought long and hard for a country that was no longer his. She was the only survivor of a family of ten. PJ and Buck had lifted her and a handful of others off a hilltop at the final stages of a North Vietnamese assault in 1972. America had failed that man's family, but at least it hadn't failed his daughter. Zimmer had fallen in love with her from the first moment, and it was generally agreed that they had the seven cutest kids in Florida.

"Yep.''

It was late in Mobile, somewhere between the two southbound aircraft, and jails—especially Southern jails—are places where the rules are strictly applied. For lawyers, however, the rules are often rather lenient, and paradoxically they were very lenient indeed in the case of these two. These two had an as-yet-undetermined date with "Old Sparky,'' the electric chair at Admore Prison. The jailors at Mobile therefore didn't want to do anything to interfere with the prisoners' constitutional rights, access to counsel, or general comfort. The attorney, whose name was Edward Stuart, had been fully briefed going in, and was fully fluent in Spanish.

"How did they do it?''

"I don't know.''

"You screamed and kicked, Ramón,'' Jesús said.

"I know. And you sang like a canary.''

"It doesn't matter,'' the attorney told them. "They're not charging you with anything but drug-related murder and piracy. The information Jesús gave them is not being used at all in this case.''

"So do your lawyer shit and get us off!''

The look on Stuart's face was all the response either man needed.

"You tell our friends that if we don't get off on this one, we start talking.''

The jail guards had already told both men in loving detail what fate had in store for them. One had even shown Ramón a poster of the chair itself with the caption REGULAR OR EXTRA CRISPY. Though a hard man and a brutal one, the idea of being strapped into a hard-backed wooden chair, then having a copper band affixed to his left leg, and a small metal cap set on a bald spot that the prison barber would shave on his head the day before, and the small sponge soaked in a saline solution to facilitate electrical conductivity, the leather mask to keep his eyes from flying out of his head . . . Ramón was a brave man when he had the upper hand, and that hand held a gun or a knife directed at an unarmed or bound person. Then he was quite brave. It had never occurred to him that one day he might be the helpless one. Ramón had lost five pounds in the preceding week. His appetite was virtually nil and he took an inordinate interest in light bulbs and wall sockets. He was afraid, but more than that he was angry, at himself for his fear, at the guards and police for giving him that fear, and at his former associates for not getting him free of this mess.

"I know many things, many useful things."

"It does not matter. I have spoken with the *federales,* and they do not care what you know. The U.S. Attorney claims to have no interest in what you might tell him."

"That is ridiculous. They always trade for information, they always—"

"Not here. The rules have changed."

"What do you tell us?"

"I will do my best for you." *I'm supposed to tell you to die like men,* Stuart could not say. "There are many things that can happen in the next few weeks."

The attorney was rewarded with skeptical expressions not entirely devoid of hope. He himself had no hope at all. The U. S. Attorney was going to handle this one himself, the better to get his face on the 5:30 and 11:00 Eyewitness News broadcasts. This would be a very speedy trial, and a U.S. Senate seat would be available in just over two years. So much the better that the prosecutor could point to his law-and-order record. Frying some druggie-pirate-rapist-murderers would surely appeal to the citizens of the sovereign state of Alabama, Stuart knew. The defense attorney objected to capital punishment on principle, and had spent much of his time and money working against it. He'd successfully taken one case to the Supreme Court and on a five-to-four decision managed to get his client a new trial, where the death sentence had been bargained down to life plus ninety-nine years. Stuart regarded that as a victory even though his client had survived precisely four months in the prison's general population until someone who disliked child-murderers had put a shank into his lumbar spine. He didn't have to like his clients—and most often he didn't. He was occasionally afraid of them, especially the drug runners. They quite simply expected that in return for however much cash—it was generally cash—they paid for his services they would get their freedom in return. They did not understand that in law there are no guarantees, especially for the guilty. And these two were guilty as hell. But they did not deserve death. Stuart was convinced that society could not afford to debase itself to the level of . . . his clients. It was not a popular opinion in the South, but Stuart had no ambition to run for public office.

In any case, he was their lawyer, and his job was to provide them with the best possible defense. He'd already explored the chances of a plea-bargain; life imprisonment in exchange for information. He'd already examined the government's case. It was all circumstantial—there were no witnesses except his own clients, of course—but the physical evidence was formidable, and that Coast Guard crew had scrupulously left the crime scene intact except for removing some evidence, all of which had been carefully locked up for a proper chain-of-evidence. Whoever had briefed and trained those people had done it right. Not much hope there. His only real hope, therefore, was to impeach their credibility. It was a slim hope, but it was the best he had.

Supervisory Special Agent Mark Bright was also working late. The crew had been busy. For starters there had been an office and a home to search, a lengthy procedure that was just the opening move in a process to last months, probably, since all the documents found, all the phone numbers scribbled in any of eleven places, all the photographs on desks and walls, and everything else found would have to be investigated. Every business acquaintance of the deceased would be interviewed, along with neighbors, people whose offices adjoined his, members of his country club, and even parishioners at his church. For all that, the major break in the case had come in the second hour of the fourth home search, fully a month after the case had begun. Something had told them all that there *had to be* something else. In his den, the deceased had a floor safe—with no record of its purchase or installation—neatly hidden by an untacked segment of the wall-to-wall carpeting. Discovering it had required thirty-two days. Tickling it open took nearly ninety minutes, but an experienced agent had done it by first experimenting with the birthdays of the deceased's whole family, then playing variations on the theme. It turned out that the three-element combination came from taking the month of the man's birth and adding one, taking the day of his birth and adding two, then taking the year of his birth and adding three. The door of the expensive Mosler came open with a whisper as it rubbed against the rug flap.

No money, no jewels, no letter to his attorney. Inside the safe had been five computer disks of a type compatible with the businessman's IBM personal computer. That told the agents all they wanted. Bright had at once taken the disks and the deceased's computer to his office, which was also equipped with IBM-compatible machines. Mark Bright was a good investigator, which meant that he was a patient one. His first move had been to call a local computer expert who assisted the FBI from time to time. A free-lance software consultant, he'd first protested that he was busy, but he'd only needed to hear that there was a major criminal investigation underway to settle that. Like many such people who informally assist the FBI, he found police work most exciting, though not quite exciting enough to take a full-time job for the FBI Laboratory. Government service didn't come close to paying what he earned on the outside. Bright had anticipated his first instruction: bring in the man's own computer and hard-disk.

After first making exact copies of the five disks using a program called CHASTITY BELT, he had Bright store the originals while he went to work on the copies. The disks were encrypted, of course. There were many ways of accomplishing that, and the consultant knew them all. As he and Bright had anticipated, the encrypting algorithm was permanently stored on the deceased's hard disk. From that point it was merely a question of what option and what personal encrypting key had been used to secure the data on the disks. That took nine nonstop hours, with Bright feeding coffee and sandwiches to his friend and wondering why he did it all for free.

"Gotcha!" A scruffy hand punched the PRINT command, and the office laser printer started humming and disgorging papers. All five disks were packed with data, totaling over seven hundred single-spaced pages of text. By the time the third one was printed, the consultant had left. Bright read it all, over a period of three days. Then he made six Xerox copies for the other senior agents in the case. They were now flipping through the pages around the conference table.

"Christ, Mark, this stuff is fantastic!"

"That's what I said."

"Three hundred million dollars!" another exclaimed. "Christ, I shop there myself . . ."

"What's the total involved?" a third asked more soberly.

"I just skimmed through this stuff," Bright answered, "but I got close to seven hundred million. Eight shopping malls spread from Fort Worth to Atlanta. The investments go through eleven different corporations, twenty-three banks, and—"

"My life insurance is with this company! They do my IRA, and—"

"The way he set it up, he was the only one who knew. Talk about an artist, this guy was like Leonardo. . . ."

"Sucker got greedy, though. If I read this right, he skimmed off about thirty million . . . God almighty . . ."

The plan, as with all great plans, was an elegantly simple one. There were eight real-estate-development projects. In each case the deceased had set up himself as the general partner representing foreign money—invariably described as Persian Gulf oil money or Japanese industrial money, with the funds laundered through an incredible maze of non-American banks. The general partner had used the "Oil Money"—the term was almost generic in the venture capital field—to purchase land and set the project in motion, then solicited further development funds from limited partners who had no say in the executive management of the individual projects, but whose profits were almost guaranteed by the syndicate's previous performance. Even the one in Fort Worth had made money, despite the recent slowdown in the local oil industry. By the time ground was broken on every project, actual ownership was further disguised by majority investment from banks, insurance companies, and wealthy private investors, with much of the original overseas investment fully recovered and gone back to the Bank of Dubai and numerous others—but with a controlling interest remaining in the project itself. In this way, the overseas investors speedily recouped their initial investment with a tidy profit, and continued to get much of the profits from the project's actual operations, further looking forward to the eventual sale of the project to local interests for more profit still. For each hundred million dollars invested, Bright estimated, one hundred fifty million fully laundered dollars were extracted. And that was the important part. The hundred million put in, and the fifty million profit taken out were as clean as the marble on the Washington Monument.

Except for these computer disks.

"Every one of these projects, and every dime of investment and profits, went through IRS, SEC, and enough lawyers to fill the Pentagon, and *nobody* ever caught a sniff. He kept these records in case somebody ever burned him—but he must have expected to trade this information for a crack at the Witness Protection Program—"

"And he'd be the richest guy in Cody, Wyoming," Mike Schratz observed. "But the wrong people got a sniff. I wonder what tipped them off? What did our friends say?"

"They don't know. Just that they pulled the job of killing them all off and making it look like a disappearance. The bosses clearly anticipated losing them and compartmentalized the information. How hard is it to get one of these mutts to take a contract? It's like filling out a girl's dance card at the cotillion."

"Roger that. Headquarters know about this yet?"

"No, Mike, I wanted you guys to see it first," Bright said. "Opinions, gentlemen?"

"If we move fast . . . we could seize a whole shitload of money . . . unless they've moved the money on us," Schratz thought aloud. "I wonder if they have? As clever as this stuff is . . . I got a buck says they haven't. Takers?"

"Not from me," another agent announced. This one was a CPA and a lawyer. "Why should they bother? This is the closest thing I've ever seen to—hell, it *is* a perfect plan. I suppose we ought to show some appreciation, what with all the help they're giving our balance-of-payments problem. In any case, folks, this money is exposed. We can bag it all."

"There's the Bureau's budget for the next two years—"

"And a squadron of fighters for the Air Force. This is big enough to sting them pretty good. Mark, I think you ought to call the Director," Schratz concluded. There was general agreement. "Where's Pete today?" Pete Mariano was the special-agent-in-charge of the Mobile Field Office.

"Probably Venice," an agent said. "He's going to be pissed he was away for this one."

Bright closed the ring binder. He was already booked on an early-morning flight to Dulles International Airport.

The C-141 landed ten minutes early at Howard Field. After the clean, dry air of the Colorado Rockies, and the cleaner, thinner, and drier air of the flight, the damp oven of the Isthmus of Panama was like walking into a door. The soldiers assembled their gear and allowed themselves to be herded off by the loadmaster. They were quiet and serious. The change in climate was a physical sign that playtime was over. The mission had begun. They immediately boarded yet another green bus which took them to some dilapidated barracks on the grounds of Fort Kobbe.

The MH-53J helicopter landed several hours later at the same field, and was rolled unceremoniously into a hangar, which was surrounded with armed guards. Colonel Johns and the flight crew were taken to nearby quarters and told to stay put.

Another helicopter, this one a Marine CH-53E Super Stallion, lifted off the deck of USS *Guadalcanal* just before dawn. It flew west over the Bay of Panama to Corezal, a small military site near the Gaillard Cut, the most difficult segment of the original Panama Canal construction project. The helicopter-carrier's flight-deck crew attached a bulky item to a sling dangling from the helicopter's underside, and the CH-53E headed awkwardly toward shore. After a twenty-minute flight, the helicopter hovered over its predetermined destination. The pilot killed his forward speed and gently eased toward the ground, coached by instructions from the crew chief, until the communications van touched down on a concrete pad. The sling was detached and the helicopter flew off at once to make room for a second aircraft, a smaller CH-46 troop carrier which deposited four men before returning to its ship. The men went immediately to work setting up the van.

The van was quite ordinary, looking most of all like a cargo container with wheels, though it was painted in the mottled green camouflage scheme of most military vehicles. That changed rapidly as the communications technicians began erecting various radio antennas, including one four-foot satellite dish. Power cables were run in from a generator vehicle already in place, and the van's air-conditioning systems were turned on to protect the communications gear, rather than the technicians. They wore military-style dress, though none of them were soldiers. All the pieces were now in place.

Or almost all. At Cape Canaveral, a Titan-IIID rocket began its final countdown. Three senior Air Force officers and half a dozen civilians watched the hundred or so technicians go through the procedure. They were unhappy. Their cargo had been bumped at the last minute for this less important one (they thought). The explanation for the change was not to their collective satisfaction, and there weren't enough launch rockets to play this sort of game. But nobody had bothered telling them what the game actually was.

"Tallyho, tallyho. I have eyeballs on target," Bronco reported. The Eagle bottomed out half a mile astern and slightly below the target. It seemed to be a four-engined Douglas. A DC-4, -6, or -7, a big one—the biggest he'd yet intercepted. Four piston engines and a single rudder made it a Douglas product, certainly older than the man who was now chasing it. Winters saw the blue flames from the exhaust ports on the big radial engines, along with the moonlight shimmering from the propellers. The rest was mainly guesswork.

The flying became harder now. He was closing on the target and had to slough off his airspeed lest he overtake it. Bronco throttled his Pratt & Whitney engines back and put on some flaps to increase both lift and drag as he watched his airspeed drop to a scant two-hundred forty knots.

He matched speed when he was a hundred yards aft of the target. The heavy fighter rocked slightly—only the pilot would have noticed—from the larger plane's wake turbulence. Time. He took a deep breath and flexed his fingers once around the stick. Captain Winters switched on his powerful landing lights. They were alert, he saw. The wingtips rocked a second after his lights transfixed the former airliner in the sky.

"Aircraft in view, please identify, over," he called over the guard frequency.

It started turning—it was a DC-7B, he thought now, the last of the great piston-engine liners, so quickly brushed aside by the advent of the jetliners in the late fifties. The exhaust flames grew brighter as the pilot added power.

"Aircraft in view, you are in restricted airspace. Identify immediately, over," Bronco called next. *Immediately* is a word that carries a special meaning for flyers.

The DC-7B was diving now, heading for the wave tops. The Eagle followed almost of its own accord.

"Aircraft in view, I repeat—you are in restricted airspace. Identify *at once!*"

Turning away now, heading east for the Florida peninsula. Captain Winters eased back on the stick and armed his gun system. He checked the surface of the ocean to make sure that there were no ships or boats about.

"Aircraft in view, if you do not identify I will open fire, over." No reaction.

The hard part now was that the Eagle's gun system, once armed, did everything possible to facilitate the pilot's task of hitting the target. But they wanted him to bring one in alive, and Bronco had to concentrate to make sure he'd miss, then squeezed the trigger for a fraction of a second.

Half the rounds in the magazine were tracers, and the six-barrel cannon spat them out at a rate of almost a hundred per second. What resulted was a streak of green-yellow light that looked like one of the laser beams in a science-fiction movie, and hung for a sizable portion of infinity a bare ten yards from the DC-7B's cockpit window.

"Aircraft in view: level out and identify or you'll eat the next burst. Over."

"Who is this? What the hell are you doing?" The DC-7B leveled out.

"Identify!" Winters commanded tersely.

"Carib Cargo—we're a special flight, inbound from Honduras."

"You are in restricted airspace. Come left to new course three-four-seven."

"Look, we didn't know about the restriction. Tell us where to go and we're out of here, okay? Over."

"Come left to three-four-seven. I will be following you in. You got some big-league explaining to do, Carib. You picked a bad place to be flying without lights. I hope you got a good story, 'cause the colonel is not pleased with you. Bring that fat-assed bird left—now!"

Nothing happened for a moment. Bronco was a little bit peeved that they were not taking him seriously enough. He eased his fighter over to the right and triggered off another burst to encourage the target.

And it came left to a heading of three-four-seven. And the anticollision lights came on.

"Okay, Carib, maintain course and altitude. Stay off your radio. I repeat, maintain radio silence until instructed otherwise. Don't make it any worse than it already is. I'll be back here to keep an eye on you. Out."

It took nearly an hour—each second like driving a Ferrari in Manhattan rush-hour traffic. Clouds were rolling in from the north, he saw as they approached the coast, and there was lightning in them. They'd land first, Winters thought. On cue, a set of runway lights came on.

"Carib, I want you to land on that strip right in front of you. You do exactly what they tell you. Out." Bronco checked his fuel state. Enough for several more hours. He indulged himself by throttling up and rocketing to twenty thousand as he watched the DC-7's strobe lights enter the blue rectangle of the old airstrip.

"Okay, he's ours," the radio told the fighter pilot.

Bronco did not acknowledge. He brought the Eagle around for Eglin AFB, and figured that he'd beat the weather in. Another night's work.

The DC-7B rolled to a stop at the end of the runway. As it halted, a number of lights came on. A jeep rolled to within fifty yards of the aircraft's nose. On the back of the jeep was an M-2 .50-caliber machine gun, on the left side of which hung a large box of ammunition. The gun was pointed right at the cockpit.

"Out of the fuckin' airplane, *amigo!*" an angry voice commanded over some loudspeakers.

The forward door opened on the left side of the aircraft. The man who looked down was white and in his forties. Blinded by the lights that were aimed at his face, he was still disoriented. Which was part of the plan, of course.

"Down on the pavement, *amigo,*" a voice said from behind a light.

"What gives? I—"

"Down on the fuckin' pavement—right the fuck now!"

There were no stairs. The pilot was joined by another man, and one at a time they sat down on the doorsill, and stretched down to hang from their hands, then dropped the four feet or so to the cracked concrete. They were met by strong arms in rolled-up camouflage fatigues.

"Face on the cement, you fuckin' commie spy!" a young voice screamed at them.

"Hot diggity damn, we finally bagged one!" another voice called. "We got us a fuckin' Cuban spy plane!"

"What the hell—" one of the men on the cement started to say. He stopped talking when the three-pronged flash suppressor on an M-16 rifle came to rest on the back of his neck. Then he felt a hot breath on the side of his face.

"I want any shit out of you, *amigo,* I'll fuckin' blow it outa ya'!" said the other voice. It sounded older than the first one. "Anybody else on the airplane, *amigo?*"

"No. Look, we're—"

"Check it out! And watch your ass!" the gunnery sergeant added.

"Aye aye, Gunny," answered the Marine corporal. "Give me some cover on the door."

"You got a name?" the gunnery sergeant asked. He punctuated the question by pressing his muzzle into the pilot's neck.

"Bert Russo. I'm—"

"You picked a bad time to spy on the exercise, Ro*bert*o. We was ready for y'all this time, boy! I wonder if Fidel'll want your ass back . . . ?"

"He don't look Cuban to me, Gunny," a young voice observed. "You s'pose he's a Russian?"

"Hey, I don't know what you're talking about," Russo objected.

"Sure, Ro*bert*o. I—over here, Cap'n!" Footsteps approached. And a new voice started talking.

"Sorry I'm late, Gunny Black."

"We got it under control, sir. Putting people into the plane now. Finally bagged that Cuban snooper, we did. This here's Ro*bert*o. Ain't talked to the other one yet."

"Roll him over."

A rough hand flipped the pilot faceup like a rag doll, and he saw what the hot breath came from. The biggest German Shepherd dog he'd ever seen in his life was staring at him from a distance of three inches. When he looked at it, it started growling.

"Don't you go scarin' my dog, Roberto," Gunnery Sergeant Black warned him unnecessarily.

"You have a name?"

Bert Russo couldn't see any faces. Everyone was backlit by the perimeter lights. He could see the guns, and the dogs, one of which stood next to his copilot. When he started to speak, the dog over his face moved, and that froze the breath in his throat.

"You Cubans ought to know better. We warned you not to come snooping into our exercise last time, but you had to come bother us again, didn't you?" the captain observed.

"I'm not a Cuban—I'm an American. And I don't know what you're talking about," the pilot finally managed to say.

"You got some ID?" the captain asked.

Bert Russo started moving his hand toward his wallet, but then the dog really let loose a snarl.

"Don't scare the dog," the captain warned. "They're a little high-strung, y'know?"

"Fuckin' Cuban spies," Gunny Black observed. "We could just waste them, sir. I mean, who really gives a damn?"

"Hey, Gunny!" a voice called from the airplane. "This ain't no spy-bird. It's full of drugs! We got us a drug runner!"

"Son of a bitch!" The gunny sounded disappointed for a moment. "Fuckin' druggie is all? Shit!"

The captain just laughed. "Mister, you really picked the wrong place to drive that airplane tonight. How much, Corp?"

"A whole goddamned pisspot full, sir. Grass and coke both. Plane's like full of it, sir."

"Fuckin' druggie," the gunny observed. He was quiet for a moment. "Cap'n?"

"Yeah?"

"Sir, all the time, sir, these planes land, and the crew just bugs the hell out, and nobody ever finds 'em, sir."

As though on cue, they all heard a guttural sound from the swamp that surrounded the old airstrip. Albert Russo came from Florida and knew what the sound was.

"I mean, sir, who'd ever know the difference? Plane landed, and the crew ran off 'fore we could catch up, and they got into the swamp over yonder, and like we heard some screams, y'know . . . ?" A pause. "I mean, they're just druggies. Who's really gonna care, sir? Make the world a better place, y'know? Hell, it even feeds them 'gators. They sound right hungry to me, sir."

"No evidence . . ." the captain mused.

"Ain't nobody gonna give a good goddamn, sir," the sergeant persisted. "Just us be out here, sir."

"No!" the copilot screamed, speaking for the first time and startling the dog at the back of his neck.

"Y'all be quiet now, we be talking business here," the gunny observed.

"Gentlemen, I find that the sergeant makes a pretty good case," the captain said after a moment's contemplation. "And the 'gators do sound hungry. Kill 'em first, Sergeant. No sense being cruel about it, and the 'gators don't care one way or the other. Be sure you take all their IDs, though."

"Aye aye, skipper," the gunnery sergeant replied. He and the remainder of the duty section—there were only eight of them—came from the Special Operations Center at MacDill. They were Recon Marines, for whom unusual activities were the rule rather than the exception. Their helicopter was half a mile away.

"Okay, sport," Black said as he bent down. He hoisted Russo to his feet with one brutal jerk. "You sure did pick the wrong time to run drugs, boy."

"Wait a minute!" the other one screamed. "We didn't—I mean, we can tell you—"

"You talk all you want, boy. I *got* my orders. Come on, now. Y'all want to pray or something, now be the time."

"We came in from Colombia—"

"That's a real surprise, ain't it?" Black observed as he frog-marched the man toward the trees. "You best be doing your talking to the Lord, boy. He might listen. Then again, He might not. . . ."

"I can tell you everything," Russo said.

"I ain't *int'rested!"*

"But you can't—"

"Sure I can. What do you think I do for a livin', boy?" Black said with amusement. "Don't worry. It'll be quick and clean. I don't make people suffer like your kind does with drugs. I just do it."

"I have a family . . ." Russo was whimpering now.

"Most people do," Black agreed. "They'll get along. You got insurance, I 'spect. Lookie there!"

Another Marine pointed his flashlight into the bushes. It was as large an alligator as Russo had ever seen, over twelve feet long. The large eyes blazed yellow in the darkness, while the rest of the reptile's body looked like a green log. With a mouth.

"This is far enough," Black judged. "Keep them dogs back, goddammit!"

The alligator—they called him Nicodemus—opened his mouth and hissed. It was a thoroughly evil sound.

"Please . . ." Russo said.

"I can tell you everything!" the copilot offered again.

"Like *what?*" the captain asked disgustedly. *Why can't you just die like a man?* he seemed to ask instead.

"Where we came from. Who gave us the load. Where we're going. Radio codes. Who's supposed to meet us. Everything!"

"Sure," the captain noted. "Get their IDs. Pocket change, car keys, everything. As a matter of fact, just strip 'em naked before you shoot 'em. Let's try to be neat."

"I know everything!" Russo screamed.

"He knows everything," Gunny Black said. "Isn't that nice? Take off your clothes, boy."

"Hold it a minute, Gunny." The captain came forward and shined his light right in Russo's face.

"What do you know that would interest us?" It was a voice they hadn't heard before. Though dressed in fatigues, he was not a Marine.

Ten minutes later it was all on tape. They already knew most of the names, of course. The location of the airstrip was new information, however, as were the radio codes.

"Do you waive the right to counsel?" the civilian asked.

"Yes!"

"You willing to cooperate?"

"Yes!"

"Good." Russo and the copilot, whose name was Bennett, were blindfolded and led to a helicopter. By noon the next day they'd be taken before a U.S. Magistrate, then a judge of the Federal District Court; by sundown to a remote part of Eglin Air Force Base, a newly built structure with a high fence. It was guarded by serious-looking men in uniform.

They didn't know that they were the lucky ones. Five downed planes qualified a pilot as an ace. Bronco was well on his way there.

10. Dry Feet

Mark Bright checked in with Deputy Assistant Director Murray, just as a matter of courtesy, before going in to see the Director.

"You must have caught the first bird out. How's the case coming?"

"The Pirates Case—that's how the papers are treating it—is just fine. I'm up here because of what spun off of it. The victim was dirtier than we thought." Bright explained on for several minutes, pulling one of the ring binders from his briefcase.

''How much?''

''We're not sure. This one's going to take some careful analysis by people with expertise in the world of high finance, but . . . well, probably on the order of seven hundred million dollars.''

Murray managed to set down his coffee without spilling any. ''Say that again?''

''You heard right. I didn't know that until day before yesterday, and I didn't finish reading this until about twenty-four hours ago. Christ, Dan, I just skimmed it. If I'm wrong, I'm off on the low side. Anyway, I figured the Director needed to see this PDQ.''

''Not to mention the AG and the President. What time you going in to see Emil?''

''Half an hour. Want to tag along? You know this international shuffle better than I do.''

The Bureau had a lot of deputy assistant directors, and Murray's post had a vague definition that he jokingly called ''utility outfielder.'' The Bureau's leading authority on terrorism, Murray was also the agency's in-house expert on how various international groups moved people, arms, and money from point to point. That, added to his wide experience as a street agent, gave him the brief of overseeing certain important cases for the Director or for Bill Shaw, the executive assistant director (Investigations). Bright hadn't walked into this office entirely by accident.

''How solid is your information?''

''Like I said, it's not all collated yet, but I got a bunch of account numbers, transaction dates, amounts, and a solid trail all the way back to the point of origin.''

''And all of this because that Coast Guard—''

''No, sir.'' Bright hesitated. ''Well, maybe. Knowing the victim was dirty made us search his background a little more thoroughly. We probably would have gotten this stuff eventually anyway. As it was, I kept going back to the house. You know how it is.''

''Yeah.'' Murray nodded. One mark of a good agent was tenacity. Another was instinct. Bright had returned to the home of the victims for as long as his mind kept telling him that something else had to be there. ''How'd you find the safe?''

''The guy had one of those Rubbermaid sheets for his swivel chair to ride on. You know how they tend to drift away when you move your chair back and forth? I must have sat at that desk for an hour, all told, and I noticed that it had moved. I rolled the chair away, so I could slide the mat back, and then it hit me—what a perfect hiding place. I was right.'' Bright grinned. He had every right to do so.

''You should write that one up for *The Investigator*''—that was the Justice Department's in-house newsletter—''so everybody'll know to look for it.''

''We have a good safe-man in the office. After that, it was just a matter of cracking the code on the disks. We have a guy in Mobile who helps us out on that—and, no, he doesn't know what's on the disks. He knows not to pay close attention, and he's not all that interested anyway. I figure we'll want to keep this one pretty tight until we move to seize the funds.''

''You know, I don't think we've ever owned a shopping mall. I remember when we seized that topless bar, though.'' Murray laughed as he lifted his phone and tapped in the number for the Director's office. ''Morning, Moira, this is Dan Murray. Tell the boss that we have something really hot for him. Bill Shaw will want to come in for this, too. Be there in two minutes.'' Murray hung up. ''Come on, Agent Bright. It's not often that you hit a grand slam on your first major-league at-bat. You ever meet the Director?''

"Just to say hi to him twice at receptions."

"He's good people," Murray assured him on the way out the door. It was a short walk down the carpeted corridor. Bill Shaw met them on the way.

"Hi, Mark. How's your dad?"

"Catching a lot of fish."

"Living down in the Keys now, isn't he?"

"Yes, sir."

"You're going to love this one, Bill," Murray observed as he opened the door. He led them in and stopped cold when he saw the Director's secretary. "My God, Moira, you're beautiful!"

"You watch that, Mr. Murray, or I'll tell your wife!" But there was no denying it. Her suit was lovely, her makeup was perfect, and her face positively glowed with what could only be new love.

"I most humbly beg your pardon, ma'am," Murray said gallantly. "This handsome young man is Mark Bright."

"You're five minutes early, Agent Bright," Mrs. Wolfe noted without checking the appointment calendar. "Coffee?"

"No, thank you, ma'am."

"Very well." She checked to see that the Director wasn't on the phone. "You can go right in."

The Director's office was large enough for conferences. Emil Jacobs had come to the Bureau after a distinguished career as a United States Attorney in Chicago, and to take this job he'd declined a seat on the U.S. Circuit Court of Appeals there. It went without saying that he could have held a partner's chair in any criminal-law firm in America, but from the day he'd passed the bar exam, Emil Jacobs had dedicated his life to putting criminals in jail. Part of that resulted from the fact that his father had suffered during the beer wars of Prohibition. Jacobs never forgot the scars his father bore for once having talked back to a South Side Gang enforcer. A small man, like his father, Emil Jacobs viewed his mission in life as protecting the weak from the evil. He pursued that mission with a religious fervor that hid behind a brilliant analytical mind. A rare Jew in a largely Irish-Catholic agency, he'd been made an honorary member of seventeen Hibernian lodges. While J. Edgar Hoover had been known in the field as "Director Hoover," to the current crop of agents, Director Jacobs was "Emil."

"Your dad worked for me once," Jacobs said as he extended his hand to Agent Bright. "He's down on Marathon Key, isn't he? Still fishing for tarpon?"

"Yes, sir. How'd you know?"

"Every year he sends me a Chanukah card." Jacobs laughed. "It's a long story. I'm surprised he hasn't told you that one. So what's the story?"

Bright sat down and opened his briefcase, handing out the bound copies of his documents. He started talking, awkwardly at first, but in ten minutes he was fully warmed to the subject. Jacobs was flipping rapidly through the binder, but didn't miss a spoken word.

"We're talking over half a billion dollars," Bright concluded.

"More than that from what I see here, son."

"I haven't had time to give it a detailed analysis, sir. I figured you'd want to see this right quick."

"You figured right," Jacobs replied without looking up. "Bill, who's the best guy at Justice to get in on this?"

"Remember the guy who headed the savings-and-loan thing? He's a whiz for following money from place to place. Marty something,'' Shaw said. ''Young guy. He has a real nose for it. I think Dan ought to be involved also.''

Jacobs looked up. ''Well?''

''Fine with me. Shame we can't get a commission on what we seize. We're going to want to move fast on this. The first inkling they have . . . ''

''That might not matter,'' Jacobs mused. ''But there's no reason to drag our feet. This sort of loss will sting them pretty good. And with the other things we're . . . excuse me. Right, Dan, let's set this up to move fast. Any complications on the piracy case?''

''No, sir. The physical evidence is enough for a conviction. The U.S. Attorney tossed the confession entirely when the defense lawyer started grumbling about how it had been obtained. Says he smiled when he did it. Told the other guy no deals of any kind, that he had enough evidence to fry them, which is exactly what he plans to do. He's pressing for an early trial date, going to try the case himself. The whole thing.''

''Sounds like we have a budding political career on our hands,'' Jacobs observed. ''How much show and how much substance?''

''He's been pretty good to us down in Mobile, sir,'' Bright said.

''You can never have too many friends on The Hill,'' Jacobs agreed. ''You're fully satisfied with the case?''

''Yes, sir. It's solid. What's spun off of it can stand pretty much on its own.''

''Why was there so much money on the boat if they just planned to kill him?'' Murray asked.

''Bait,'' Agent Bright answered. ''According to the confession that we trashed, they were actually supposed to deliver it to a contact in the Bahamas. As you can see from this document, the victim occasionally handled large cash transactions himself. That's probably the reason he bought the yacht in the first place.''

Jacobs nodded. ''Fair enough. Dan, you did tell that captain—''

''Yes, sir. He learned his lesson.''

''Fine. Back to the money. Dan, you coordinate with Justice and keep me informed through Bill. I want a target date to start the seizures—give you three days for that. Agent Bright and the Mobile Field Office are to get full credit for turning this one—*but,* this one is code-word until we're ready to move.'' Code-word meant that the case would be classified right up with CIA operations. It wasn't all that unusual for the Bureau, which ran most of America's counterintelligence operations. ''Mark, pick a code-word.''

''*Tarpon*. Dad always has been crazy about chasing after them, and they're good fighters.''

''I'm going to have to go down there and see. I've never caught anything bigger than a pike.'' Jacobs was quiet for a moment. He was thinking about something, Murray thought, wondering what it was. Whatever it was, it gave Emil a very crafty look. ''The timing couldn't be better. Shame I can't tell you why. Mark, say hi to your dad for me.'' The Director stood, ending the meeting.

Mrs. Wolfe noted that everyone was smiling when they came out of the room. Shaw even gave her a wink. Ten minutes later she'd opened a new file in the secure cabinet, an empty folder with the name TARPON typed on the paper label. It went in the drug section, and Jacobs told her that further documentation would follow in a few days.

Murray and Shaw walked Agent Bright down to his car and saw him off.

''What's with Moira?'' Dan asked as the car pulled out.

"They think she's got a boyfriend."

"About time."

At 4:45, Moira Wolfe placed the plastic cover over her computer keyboard and another over her typewriter. Before leaving the office, she checked her makeup one last time and then walked out with a spring in her step. The oddest thing was that she didn't realize that everyone else in the office was rooting for her. The other secretaries and executive assistants, even the Director's security detail, had avoided comment for fear of making her self-conscious. But tonight had to be a date. The signs were clear, even though Moira thought that she was concealing it all.

As a senior executive secretary, Mrs. Wolfe rated a reserved parking space, one of many things that made her life easier. She drove out a few minutes later onto 10th Street, Northwest, then turned right onto Constitution Avenue. Instead of her normal southward course toward Alexandria and home, she headed west across the Theodore Roosevelt Bridge into Arlington. It seemed as though the rush-hour traffic was parting before her, and twenty-five minutes later she pulled up to a small Italian restaurant in Seven Corners. Before going in she checked her makeup again in the rearview mirror. Her children would be getting dinner from McDonald's tonight, but they understood. She told them that she'd be working very late, and she was sure that they believed her, though she ought to have known that they saw through her lies as easily as she had once seen through theirs.

"Excuse me," she said to the hostess upon entering.

"You must be Mrs. Wolfe," the young lady replied at once. "Please come with me. Mr. Díaz is waiting for you."

Félix Cortez—Juan Díaz—was sitting in a corner booth at the rear of the restaurant. Moira was sure that he'd picked the dark place for privacy, and that he had his back to the wall so that he could see her coming. She was partially correct on both counts. Cortez was wary of being in this area. CIA headquarters was less than five miles away, thousands of FBI personnel lived in this area, and who could say whether a senior counterintelligence officer might also like this restaurant? He didn't think that anyone there knew what he looked like, but intelligence officers do not live to collect their pensions by assuming anything. His nervousness was not entirely feigned. On the other hand, he was unarmed. Cortez was in a business where firearms caused far more problems than they solved, public perceptions to the contrary.

Félix rose as she approached. The hostess departed as soon as she realized the nature of this "business dinner," leaving the two lovers—she thought it was kind of cute—to grab each other's hands and exchange kisses that were oddly passionate despite their being restrained for so public a place. Cortez seated his lady, pouring her a glass of white wine before resuming his place opposite her. His first words were delivered with sheepish embarrassment.

"I was afraid you wouldn't come."

"How long have you been waiting?" Moira asked. There were a half-dozen stubbed-out cigarettes in the ashtray.

"Almost an hour," he answered with a funny look. Clearly he was amused at himself, she thought.

"But I'm early."

"I know." This time he laughed. "You make me a fool, Moira. I do not act in such a way at home."

She misread what he was trying to say. "I'm sorry, Juan, I didn't mean—"

A perfect response, Cortez's mind reported. *Exactly right.* He took her hand across the table and his eyes sparkled. "Do not trouble yourself. Sometimes it is good for a man to be a fool. Forgive me for calling you so abruptly. A small business problem. I had to fly to Detroit on short notice, and since I was in the neighborhood, as you say, I wanted to see you before I went home."

"Problem . . . ?"

"A change in the design for a carburetor. Something to do with fuel economy, and I must change some tools in my factories." He waved his hand. "The problem is solved. These things are not uncommon—and, it gave me an excuse to make an extra trip here. Perhaps I should thank your EPA, or whatever government office complains about air pollution."

"I will write the letter myself, if you wish."

His voice changed. "It is *so* good to see you again, Moira."

"I was afraid that—"

The emotion on his face was manifest. "No, Moira, it was I who was afraid. I am a foreigner. I come here so seldom, and surely there must be many men who—"

"Juan, where are you staying?" Mrs. Wolfe asked.

"At the Sheraton."

"Do they have room service?"

"Yes, but why—"

"I won't be hungry for about two hours," she told him, and finished off her wine. "Can we leave now?"

Félix dropped a pair of twenties on the table and led her out. The hostess was reminded of a song from *The King and I.* They were in the lobby of the Sheraton in less than six minutes. Both walked quickly to the elevators, and both looked warily about, both hoping that they wouldn't be spotted, but for different reasons. His tenth-floor room was actually an expensive suite. Moira scarcely noticed on entering, and for the next hour knew of nothing but a man whose name she mistakenly thought was Juan Díaz.

"So wonderful a thing," he said at last.

"What's that?"

"So wonderful a thing that there was a problem with the new carburetor."

"Juan!"

"I must now create quality-control problems so that they call me every week to Detroit," he suggested lightly, stroking her arm as he did so.

"Why not build a factory here?"

"The labor costs are too high," he said seriously. "Of course, drugs would be less of a problem."

"There, too?"

"Yes. They call it *basuco,* filthy stuff, not good enough for export, and too many of my workers indulge." He stopped talking for a moment. "Moira, I try to make a joke, and you force me to speak of business. Have you lost interest in me?"

"What do you think?"

"I think I need to return to Venezuela while I can still walk."

Her fingers did some exploring. "I think you will recover soon."

"That is good to know." He turned his head to kiss her, and let his eyes linger, examining her body in the rays of the setting sun that spilled through the windows. She noticed his stares and reached for the sheet. He stopped her.

"I am no longer young," she said.

''Every child in all the world looks upon his mother and sees the most beautiful woman in the world, even though many mothers are not beautiful. Do you know why this is so? The child looks with love, and sees love returned. Love is what makes beauty, Moira. And, truly, you are beautiful to me.''

And there it was. The word was finally out in the open. He watched her eyes go somewhat wider, her mouth move, and her breaths deepen for a moment. For the second time, Cortez felt shame. He shrugged it off. Or tried to. He'd done this sort of thing before, of course. But always with young women, young, single ones with an eye for adventure and a taste for excitement. This one was different in so many ways. Different or not, he reminded himself, there was work to be done.

''Forgive me. Do I embarrass you?''

''No,'' she answered softly. ''Not now.''

He smiled down at her. ''And now, are you ready for dinner?''

''Yes.''

''That is good.''

Cortez rose and got the bathrobes from the back of the bathroom door. Service was good. Half an hour later, Moira stayed in the bedroom while the dinner cart was rolled into the sitting room. He opened the connecting door as soon as the waiter left.

''You make of me a dishonest man. The look he gave me!''

She laughed. ''Do you know how long it's been since I had to hide in the other room?''

''And you didn't order enough. How can you live on this tiny salad?''

''If I grow fat, you will not come back to me.''

''Where I come from, we do not count a woman's ribs,'' Cortez said. ''When I see someone who grows too thin, I think it is the *basuco* again. Where I live, they are the ones who forget even to eat.''

''Is it that bad?''

''Do you know what *basuco* is?''

''Cocaine, according to the reports I see.''

''Poor quality, not good enough for the criminals to send to the *norteamericanos,* and mixed with chemicals that poison the brain. It is becoming the curse of my homeland.''

''It's pretty bad here,'' Moira said. She could see that it was something that really worried her lover. Just like it was with the Director, she thought.

''I have spoken to the police at home. How can my workers do their jobs if their minds are poisoned by this thing? And what do the police do? They shrug and mumble excuses—and people die. They die from the *basuco*. They die from the guns of the dealers. And no one does anything to stop it.'' Cortez made a frustrated gesture. ''You know, Moira, I am not merely a capitalist. My factories, they give jobs, they bring money into my country, money for the people to build houses and educate their children. I am rich, yes, but I help to build my country—with these hands, I do it. My workers, they come to me and tell me that their children—ah! I can do nothing. Someday, the dealers, they will come to me and try to take my factory,'' he went on. ''I will go to the police, and the police will do nothing. I will go to the army, and the army will do nothing. You work for your *federales,* yes? Is there nothing anyone can do?'' Cortez nearly held his breath, wondering what the answer would be.

''You should see the reports I have to type for the Director.''

''Reports,'' he snorted. ''Anyone can write reports. At home, the police write many reports, and the judges do their investigations—and nothing happens. If I ran my factory in this way, soon I would be living in a hillside shack and begging for money in the street! Do your *federales* do anything?''

''More than you might think. There are things going on right now that I cannot speak about. What they're saying around the office is that the rules are changing. But I don't know what that means. The Director is flying down to Colombia soon to meet with the Attorney General, and—oh! I'm not supposed to tell anybody that. It's supposed to be a secret.''

''I will tell no one,'' Cortez assured her.

''I really don't know that much anyway,'' she went on carefully. ''Something new is about to start. I don't know what. The Director doesn't like it very much, whatever it is.''

''If it hurts the criminals, why should he not like it?'' Cortez asked in a puzzled voice. ''You could shoot them all dead in the street, and I would buy your *federales* dinner afterwards!''

Moira just smiled. ''I'll pass that along. That's what all the letters say—we get letters from all sorts of people.''

''Your director should listen to them.''

''So does the President.''

''Perhaps he will listen,'' Cortez suggested. *This is an election year . . .*

''Maybe he already is. Whatever just changed, it started there.''

''But your director doesn't like it?'' He shook his head. ''I do not understand the government in my country. I should not try to understand yours.''

''It *is* funny, though. This is the first time that I don't know—well, I couldn't tell you anyway.'' Moira finished her salad. She looked at her empty wineglass. Félix/Juan filled it for her.

''Can you tell me one thing?''

''What?''

''Call me when your director leaves for Colombia,'' he said.

''Why?'' She was too taken aback to say no.

''For state visits one spends several days, no?''

''Yes, I suppose. I don't really know.''

''And if your director is away, and you are his secretary, you will have little work to do, no?''

''No, not much.''

''Then I will fly to Washington, of course.'' Cortez rose from his chair and took three steps around the table. Moira's bathrobe hung loosely around her. He took advantage of that. ''I must fly home early tomorrow morning. One day with you is no longer enough, my love. Hmm, you are ready, I think.''

''Are you?''

''We will see. There is one thing I will never understand,'' he said as he helped her from the chair.

''What is that?''

''Why would any fool use powder for pleasure when he can have a woman?'' It was, in fact, something that Cortez never would understand. But it wasn't his job to understand it.

''Any woman?'' she said, heading for the door.

Cortez pulled the robe from her. ''No, not any woman.''

''My God,'' Moira said, half an hour later. Her chest glistened with perspiration, hers and his.

"I was mistaken," he gasped facedown at her side.

"What?"

"When your director of *federales* flies to Colombia, do not call me!" He laughed to show that he was kidding. "Moira, I do not know that I can do this for more than one day a month."

A giggle. "Perhaps you should not work so hard, Juan."

"How can I not?" He turned to look at her. "I have not felt like this since I was a boy. But I am no longer a boy. How can women stay young when men cannot?" She smiled with amusement at the obvious lie. He had pleased her greatly.

"I cannot call you."

"What?"

"I do not have your number." She laughed. Cortez leaped from the bed and pulled the wallet from his coat pocket, then muttered something that sounded profane.

"I have no cards—ah!" He took the pad from the night table and wrote the number. "This is for my office. Usually I am not there—I spend my days on the shop floor." A grunt. "I spend my nights in the factory. I spend weekends in the factory. Sometimes I sleep in the factory. But Consuela will reach me, wherever I might be."

"And I must leave," Moira said.

"Tell your director that he must make it a weekend trip. We will spend two days in the country. I know of a small, quiet place in the mountains, just a few hours from here."

"Do you think you can survive it?" she asked with a hug.

"I will eat sensibly and exercise," he promised her. A final kiss, and she left.

Cortez closed the door and walked into the bathroom. He hadn't learned all that much, but what he had found out might be crucial. "The rules are changing." Whatever they were changing to, Director Jacobs didn't like it, but was evidently going along. He was going to Colombia to discuss it with the Attorney General. Jacobs, he remembered, knew the Attorney General quite well. They had been classmates together in college, over thirty years before. The Attorney General had flown to America for the funeral of Mrs. Jacobs. Something with a presidential seal on it, also. Well. Two of Cortez's associates were in New Orleans to meet with the attorney for the two fools who'd botched the killing on the yacht. The FBI had certainly played a part in that, and whatever had happened there would give him a clue.

Cortez looked up from washing his hands to see the man who had obtained those intelligence tidbits and decided that he didn't like the man who had done it. He shrugged off the feeling. It wasn't the first time. Certainly it wouldn't be the last.

The shot went off at 23:41 hours. The Titan-IIID's two massive solid-rocket boosters ignited at the appointed time, over a million pounds of thrust was generated, and the entire assembly leapt off the pad amid a glow that would be seen from Savannah to Miami. The solid boosters burned for 120 seconds before being discarded. At this point the liquid-fuel engines on the booster's center section ignited, hurling the remaining package higher, faster, and farther downrange. All the while onboard instruments relayed data from the booster to ground station at the Cape. In fact, they were also radioing their data to a Soviet listening post located on the northern tip of Cuba, and to a "fishing trawler" which kept station off Cape Canaveral, and also flew a red flag. The Titan-IIID was a bird used exclusively for

and listening as much as looking. Chavez waited, switching off the scope and removing it from his head. Then he removed his fighting knife from its sheath. Closer, only about fifty yards now, and the sergeant coiled up, drawing his legs under his chest. At thirty feet, he stopped breathing. If he could have willed his heart to stop, he'd have done that to reduce the noise. This was for fun. If this had been for-real, a 9mm bullet would now reside in the man's head.

The sentry walked right past Ding's position, looking but not seeing the form under the bush. He made it another step before he heard a swishing sound, but then it was too late. By that time, he was facedown on the gravel, and he felt the hilt of a knife at the back of his neck.

"Ninja owns the night, boy! You're history."

"You got me, sure as hell," the man whispered in reply.

Chavez rolled him over. It was a major, and his headgear was a beret. Maybe the OPFOR wasn't MPs after all.

"Who are you?" the victim asked.

"Staff Sergeant Domingo Chavez, sir."

"Well, you just killed a jungle-warfare instructor, Chavez. Good job. Mind if I get a drink? It's been a long night." Chavez allowed the man to roll into the bushes, where he, too, took a pull off his canteen. "What outfit you from—wait a minute, 3rd of the 17th, right?"

"We own the night, sir," Chavez agreed. "You been there?"

"Going there, for a battalion staff job." The major wiped some blood from his face. He'd hit the road a little hard.

"Sorry about that, sir."

"My fault, Sergeant, not yours. We have twenty guys out there. I never thought you'd make it this far without being spotted."

The sound of a vehicle came down the road. A minute later the wide-set lights of a Hummer—the new and larger incarnation of the venerable jeep—appeared, announcing that the exercise was over. The "dead" major marched off to collect his men, while Captain Ramirez did the same.

"That was the final exam, people," he told the squad. "Get a good day's sleep. We go in tonight."

"I don't believe it," Cortez said. He'd hopped the first flight from Dulles to Atlanta. There he met an associate in a rented car, and now they discussed their information in the total anonymity of an automobile driving at the posted limit on the Atlanta beltway.

"Call it psychological warfare," the man answered. "No plea-bargain, no nothing. It's being handled as a straight murder trial. Ramón and Jesús will not get any consideration."

Cortez looked at the passing traffic. He didn't give a damn about the two *sicarios,* who were as expendable as any other terrorists and who didn't know the reason for the killings. What he was considering now was a series of seemingly disjointed and unconnected bits of information on American interdiction operations. An unusual number of courier aircraft were disappearing. The Americans were treating this legal case in an unusual way. The Director of the FBI was doing something that he didn't like, and that his personal secretary didn't know about yet. "The rules are changing." That could mean anything at all.

Something fundamental. It had to be. But what?

There were a number of well-paid and highly reliable informants throughout the

American government, in Customs, DEA, the Coast Guard, none of whom had reported a single thing. The law-enforcement community was in the dark—except for the FBI Director, who didn't like it, but would soon go to Colombia. . . .

Some sort of intelligence operation was—no. Active Measures? The phrase came from KGB, and could mean any of several things, from feeding disinformation to reporters to "wet" work. Would the Americans do anything like that? They never had. He glowered at the passing scenery. He was an experienced intelligence officer, and his profession was to determine what people were doing from bits and pieces of random data. That he was working for someone he detested was beside the point. This was a matter of pride and besides, he detested the Americans even more.

What were they doing now?

Cortez had to admit to himself that he didn't know, but in one hour he'd board a plane, and in six hours he'd have to tell his employer that he didn't know. That did not appeal to him.

Something fundamental. The rules are changing. The FBI Director didn't like it. His secretary didn't know. The trip to Colombia was clandestine.

Cortez relaxed. Whatever it was, it was not an immediate threat. The Cartel was too secure. There would be time to analyze and respond. There were many people in the smuggling chain who could be sacrificed, who would fight for the chance, in fact. And after a time, the Cartel would adapt its operations to the changing conditions as it always had. All he had to do was convince his employer of that simple fact. What did *el jefe* really care about Ramón and Jesús or any of the underlings who ran the drugs and did the killings that became necessary? It was continuing the supply of drugs to the consumers that mattered.

His mind came back to the vanishing airplanes. Historically, the Americans had managed to intercept one or two per month, that small a number despite all their radars and aircraft. But recently—four in the last two weeks, wasn't it?—had disappeared. What did that mean? Unknown to the Americans, there had always been "operational" losses, a military term that meant nothing more mysterious than flying accidents. One of the reasons that his boss had taken Carlos Larson on was to mitigate that wastage of resources, and it had, initially, shown promise—until very recently. Why the sudden jump in losses? If the Americans had somehow intercepted them, the air crews would have shown up in courtrooms and jails, wouldn't they? Cortez had to dismiss that thought.

Sabotage, perhaps? What if someone were placing explosives in the aircraft, like the Arab terrorists did . . . ? Unlikely . . . or was it? Did anyone check for that? It wouldn't take much. Even minor damage to a low-flying aircraft could face the pilot with a problem whose solution required more time than he had in altitude. Even a single blasting cap could do it, not even a cubic centimeter . . . he'd have to check that out. But, then, who would be doing it? The Americans? But what if it became known that the Americans were placing bombs on aircraft? Would they take that political risk? Probably not. Who else, then? The Colombians might. Some senior Colombian military officer, operating entirely on his own . . . or in the pay of the *yanquis?* That was possible. It couldn't be a government operation, Cortez was sure. There were too many informants there, too.

Would it have to be a bomb? Why not contaminated gasoline? Why not minor tampering with an engine, a frayed control cable . . . or a flight instrument. What was it that Larson had said about having to watch instruments at low level? What if some mechanic had altered the setting on the artificial horizon . . . ? Or merely arranged for it to stop working . . . something in the electrical system, perhaps? How hard was it to make a small airplane stop flying? Whom to ask? Larson?

Cortez grumbled to himself. This was undirected speculation, decidedly unprofessional. There were countless possibilities. He knew that *something* was probably happening, but not what it was. And only probably, he admitted to himself. The unusually large number of missing aircraft could merely be a statistical anomaly—he didn't believe that, but forced himself to consider the possibility. A series of coincidences—there was not an intelligence academy in the world that encouraged its students to believe in coincidences, and yet how many strange coincidences had he encountered in his professional career?

"The rules are changing," he muttered to himself.

"What?" the driver asked.

"Back to the airport. My Caracas flight leaves in less than an hour."

"Sí, jefe."

Cortez lifted off on time. He had to travel to Venezuela first for the obvious reasons. Moira might get curious, might want to see his ticket, might ask his flight number, and besides, American agents would be less interested in people who flew there than those who flew directly to Bogotá. Four hours later he made his Avianca connection to El Dorado International Airport, where he met a private plane for the last hop over the mountains.

Equipment was issued as always, with a single exception. Chavez noted that nobody was signing for anything. That was a real break from routine. The Army always had people sign for their gear. If you broke it or lost it, well, though they might not make you pay for it, you had to account for it in one way or another.

But not now.

The load-outs differed slightly from one man to the next. Chavez, the squad scout, got the lightest load, while Julio Vega, one of the machine-gunners, got the heaviest. Ding got eleven magazines for his MP-5 submachine gun, a total of 330 rounds. The M-203 grenade launchers that two squad members had attached to their rifles were the only heavy firepower they'd be carrying in.

His uniform was not the usual stripe-and-splotch Army fatigue pattern, but rather rip-stop khaki because they weren't supposed to look like Americans to the casual observer, if any. Khaki clothing was not the least unusual in Colombia. Jungle fatigues were. A floppy green hat instead of a helmet, and a scarf to tie over his hair. A small can of green spray paint and two sticks of facial camouflage "makeup." A waterproof map case with several maps; Captain Ramirez got one also. Twelve feet of rope and a snaplink, issued to everyone. A short-range FM radio of an expensive commercial type that was nonetheless better and cheaper than the one the Army used. Seven-power compact binoculars, Japanese. American-style web gear of the type used by every Army in the world, actually made in Spain. Two one-quart canteens to hang on the web belt, and a third two-quart water bottle for his rucksack, American, commercial. A large supply of water-purification tablets—they'd resupply their own water, which wasn't a surprise.

Ding got a strobe light with an infrared cover lens because one of his jobs would be to select and mark helicopter landing zones, plus a VS-17 panel for the same purpose. A signaling mirror for times when a radio might not be appropriate (steel mirrors, moreover, do not break). A small flashlight; and a butane cigarette lighter, which was far better than carrying matches. A large bottle of extra-strength Tylenol, also known as "light-fighter candy." A bottle of prescription cough medicine, heavily laced with codeine. A small bottle of Vaseline petroleum jelly. A small squeeze bottle of concentrated CS tear gas. A weapons-cleaning kit, which included a toothbrush. Spare batteries for everything. A gas mask.

Chavez would travel light with but four hand grenades—Dutch NR-20 C1 type—and two smokes, also of Dutch manufacture. The rest of the squad got the Dutch frags, and some CS tear-gas grenades, also Dutch. In fact, all of the weapons carried by the squad and all of their ammunition had been purchased at Colón, Panama, in what was fast becoming the hemisphere's most convenient arms market. For anyone with cash there were weapons to be had.

Rations were the normal MREs. Water was the main hygienic concern, but they'd already been fully briefed about using their water-purification tablets. Whoever forgot had a supply of antidiarrhea pills that would follow a serious chewing from Captain Ramirez. Every man had gotten a new series of booster shots while still in Colorado against the spectrum of tropical diseases endemic to the area, and all carried an odorless insect repellent made for the military by the same company that produced the commercial product called "Off." The squad medic carried a full medical kit, and each rifleman had his own morphine Syrette and a plastic bottle of IV fluids for use as a blood-expander.

Chavez had a razor-sharp machete, a four-inch folding knife, and, of course, his three nonregulation throwing stars that Captain Ramirez didn't know about. With other sundry items, Chavez would be carrying a load of exactly fifty-eight pounds. That made his load the lightest in the squad. Vega and the other SAW gunner had the heaviest, with seventy-one pounds. Ding jostled the load around on his shoulders to get a feel for it, then adjusted the straps on his ruck to make it as comfortable as possible. It was a futile exercise. He was packing a third of his body weight, which is about as much as a man can carry for any length of time without risking a physical breakdown. His boots were well broken-in, and he had extra pairs of dry socks.

"Ding, could you give me a hand with this?" Vega asked.

"Sure, Julio." Chavez took some slack in on one of the machine gunner's shoulder straps. "How's that?"

"Just right, '*mano*. Jeez, carrying the biggest gun do have a price."

"Roger that, *Oso*." Julio, who'd demonstrated the ability to pack more than anyone in the squad, had a new nickname, *Oso:* Bear.

Captain Ramirez came down the line, walking around each man to check the loads. He adjusted a few straps, bounced a few rucks, and generally made sure that every man was properly loaded, and that all weapons were clean. When he was finished, Ding checked the captain's load, and Ramirez took his place in front of the squad.

"Okay—anybody got aches, pains, or blisters?"

"No, sir!" the squad replied.

"We ready to go do it?" Ramirez asked with a wide grin that belied the fact that he was as nervous as everyone else in the squad bay.

"Yes, sir!"

One more thing left to do. Ramirez walked down the line and collected dog tags from each man. Each set went into a clear plastic bag along with wallets and all other forms of identification. Finished, he removed his own, counted the bags a last time, and left them on the table in the squad bay. Outside, each squad boarded a separate five-ton truck. Few waves were exchanged. Though friendships had sprouted up in training, they were mainly limited within the structure of the squads.

Each eleven-man unit was a self-contained community. Every member knew every other, knew all there was to know, from stories of sexual performance to marksmanship skills. Some solid friendships had blossomed, and some even more valuable rivalries. They were, in fact, already closer than friends could ever be. Each man knew that his life would depend on the skill of his fellows, and none of them wished to appear weak before his comrades. Argue as they might among themselves, they were now a team; though they might trade barbed comments, over the past weeks they had been forged into a single complex organism with Ramirez as their brain, Chavez as their eyes, Julio Vega and the other machine-gunner as their fists, and all the others as equally vital components. They were as ready for their mission as any soldiers had ever been.

The trucks arrived together behind the helicopter and the troops boarded by squads. The first thing Chavez noticed was the 7.62mm minigun on the right side of the aircraft. There was an Air Force sergeant standing next to it, his green coveralls topped by a camouflage-painted flight helmet, and a massive feed line of shells leading to an even larger hopper. Ding had no particular love for the Air Force—a bunch of pansy truck drivers, he'd thought until now—but the man on that gun looked serious and competent as hell. Another such gun was unmanned on the opposite side of the aircraft, and there was a spot for another at the rear. The flight engineer—his name tag said ZIMMER—moved them all into their places and made sure that each soldier was properly strapped down to his particular piece of floor. Chavez didn't trade words with him, but sensed that this man had been around the block a few times. It was, he belatedly realized, the biggest goddamned helicopter he'd ever seen.

The flight engineer made one final check before going forward and plugging his helmet into the intercom system. A moment later came the whine from the helicopter's twin turbine engines.

"Looking good," PJ observed over the headset. The engines had been prewarmed and the fuel tanks topped off. Zimmer had repaired a minor hydraulic problem, and the Pave Low III was as ready as his skilled men could make it. Colonel Johns keyed his radio.

"Tower, this is Night Hawk Two-Five requesting permission to taxi. Over."

"Two-Five, tower, permission granted. Winds are one-zero-niner at six knots."

"Roger. Two-Five is rolling. Out."

Johns twisted the throttle grip on his collective control and eased the cyclic stick forward. Due to the size and engine power of the big Sikorsky, it was customary to taxi the aircraft toward the runway apron before actually lifting off. Captain Willis swiveled his neck around, checking for other ground traffic, but there was none this late at night. One ground crewman walked backward in front of them as a further safety measure, waving for them to follow with lighted wands. Five minutes later they were at the apron. The wands came together and pointed to the right. Johns gave the man a last look, returning the ceremonial salute.

"Okay, let's get this show on the road." PJ brought the throttle to full power, making a last check of his engine instruments as he did so. Everything looked fine. The helicopter lifted at the nose a few feet, then dipped forward as it began to move forward. Next it started to climb, leaving behind a small tornado of dust, visible only in the blue runway perimeter lights.

Captain Willis put the navigations systems on line, adjusting the electronic terrain display. There was a moving map display not unlike that used by James Bond in *Goldfinger*. Pave Low could navigate from a Doppler-radar system that interrogated the ground, from an inertial system using laser-gyroscopes, or from navigational satellites. The helicopter initially flew straight down the Canal's length, simulating the regular security patrol. They unknowingly flew within a mile of the SHOWBOAT's communications nexus at Corezal.

"Lot of pick-and-shovel work down there," Willis observed.

"Ever been here before?"

"No, sir, first time. Quite a job for eighty-ninety years ago," he said as they flew over a large container ship. They caught a little buffet from the hot stack-gas of the ship. PJ came to the right to get out of it. It would be a two-hour flight, and there was no sense in jostling the passengers any more than necessary. In an hour their MC-130E tanker would lift off to refuel them for the return leg.

"Lot of dirt to move," Colonel Johns agreed after a moment. He moved a little in his seat. Twenty minutes later they went "feet wet," passing over the Caribbean Sea for the longest portion of the flight on a course of zero-nine-zero, due east.

"Look at that," Willis said half an hour later. On their night-vision sets, they spotted a twin-engine aircraft on a northerly heading, perhaps six miles away. They spotted it from the infrared glow of the two piston engines.

"No lights," PJ agreed.

"I wonder what he's carrying?"

"Sure as hell isn't Federal Express." *More to the point, he can't see us unless he's wearing the same goggles we got.*

"We could pull up alongside and take the miniguns—"

"Not tonight." *Too bad. I wouldn't especially mind. . . .*

"What do you suppose our passengers—"

"If we were supposed to know, Captain, they would have told us," Johns replied. He was wondering, too, of course. *Christ, but they're loaded for bear,* the colonel thought. Not wearing standard-issue uniforms . . . obviously a covert insertion—*hell, I've known that part of the mission for weeks*—but they were clearly planning to stay awhile. Johns hadn't heard that the government had ever done that. He wondered if the Colombians were playing ball . . . *probably not. And we're staying down here for at least a month, so they're planning for us to support them, maybe extract them if things get a little hot . . . Christ, it's Laos all over again,* he concluded. *Good thing I brought Buck along. We're the only real vets left.* Colonel Johns shook his head. Where had his youth gone?

You spent it with a helicopter strapped to your back, doing all sorts of screwy things.

"I got a ship target on the horizon at about eleven o'clock," the captain said, and altered course a few degrees to the right. The mission brief had been clear on that. Nobody was supposed to see or hear them. That meant avoiding ships, fishing boats, and inquisitive dolphins, staying well off the coast, no more than a thousand feet up, and keeping their anticollision lights off. The mission profile was precisely what they'd fly in wartime, with some flight-safety rules set aside. Even in the special-operations business, that last fact was somewhat out of the ordinary, Johns reminded himself. Hot guns and all.

They made the Colombian coast without further incident. As soon as it was in view, Johns alerted his crew. Sergeants Zimmer and Bean powered up their electrically driven miniguns and slid open the doors next to them.

"Well, we just invaded a friendly foreign country," Willis noted as they went "feet dry" north of Tolú. They used their low-light instruments to search for vehicular traffic, which they were also supposed to avoid. Their course track was plotted to avoid areas of habitation. The six-bladed rotor didn't make the fluttering *whops* associated with smaller helicopters. Its sound, at a distance, wasn't terribly different from turbopowered aircraft; it was also directionally deceptive—even if you heard the noise, it was hard to figure where it came from. Once past the Pan American Highway, they curved north, passing east of Plato.

"Zimmer, LZ One in five minutes."

"Right, PJ," the flight engineer replied. It had been decided to leave Bean and Childs on the guns, while Zimmer handled the dropoff.

It must be a combat mission. Johns smiled to himself. *Buck only calls me that when he expects to get shot at.*

Aft, Sergeant Zimmer walked down the center of the aircraft, telling the first two squads to unbuckle their safety belts and holding up his hand to show how many more minutes there were. Both captains nodded.

"LZ One in sight," Willis said soon thereafter.

"I'll take her."

"Pilot's airplane."

Colonel Johns orbited the area, spiraling into the clearing selected from satellite photos. Willis scanned the ground for the least sign of life, but there was none.

"Looks clear to me, Colonel."

"Going in now," Johns said into the intercom.

"Get ready!" Zimmer shouted as the helicopter's nose came up.

Chavez stood up with the rest of his squad, facing aft to the opening cargo door. His knees buckled slightly as the Sikorsky touched down.

"*Go!*" Zimmer waved them out, patting each man on the shoulder to keep a proper count.

Chavez went out behind his captain, turning left to avoid the tail rotor as soon as his feet were on the dirt. He went ten steps and dropped to his face. Above his head, the rotor was still turning at full power, holding the lethal blades a safe fifteen feet off the ground.

"Clear, clear, clear!" Zimmer said when he'd seen them all off.

"Roger," Johns replied, twisting the throttle again to lift off.

Chavez turned his head as the whine of the engines increased. The blacked-out helicopter was barely visible, but he saw the spectral outline lift off and felt the dirt stinging his face as the hundred-knot downwash from the rotor subsided, and stopped. It was gone.

He ought to have expected it, but the feeling came to Chavez as a surprise. He was in enemy territory. It was real, not an exercise. The only way he had out—had just flown away, already invisible. Despite the fact that there were ten men around him, he was momentarily awash in a sense of loneliness. But he was a trained man, a professional soldier. Chavez grasped his loaded weapon and took strength from it. He wasn't quite alone.

"Move out," Captain Ramirez told him quietly.

Chavez moved toward the treeline in the knowledge that behind him the squad would follow.

11. In-Country

Three hundred miles away from SSG Ding Chavez, Colonel Félix Cortez, formerly of the Cuban DGI, sat dozing in *el jefe*'s office. *El jefe,* he'd been told on his arrival several hours before, was occupied at present—probably entertaining a mistress. *Maybe even his wife,* Cortez thought; unlikely but possible. He'd drunk two cups of the fine local coffee—previously Colombia's most valuable export crop—but it hadn't helped. He was tired from the previous night's exertions, from the travel, and now from readjusting yet again to the high altitude of the region. Cortez was ready for sleep, but had to stay awake to debrief his boss. Inconsiderate bastard. At least in the DGI he could have submitted a hastily written report and taken a few hours to freshen up before normal office hours began. But the DGI was composed of professionals, and he'd chosen to work for an amateur.

Just after 1:30 in the morning he heard feet coming down the corridor. Cortez stood and shook off the sleep. The door opened, and there was *el jefe,* his visage placid and happy. One of his mistresses.

"What have you learned?" Escobedo asked without preamble.

"Nothing specific as of yet," Cortez replied with a yawn. He proceeded to speak for about five minutes, going over what things he had discovered.

"I pay you for results, Colonel," Escobedo pointed out.

"That is true, but at high levels such results require time. Under the methods for gathering information which you had in place before I arrived, you would still know nothing other than the fact that some aircraft are missing, and that two of your couriers have been apprehended by the *yanquis.*"

"Their story about the interrogation aboard the ship?"

"Most unusual, perhaps all a fabrication on their part." Cortez settled into his chair, wishing for another cup of coffee. "Or perhaps true, though I doubt it. I do not know either man and cannot evaluate the reliability of their claims."

"Two men from Medellín. Ramón's older brother served me well. He was killed in the battles with M-19. He died bravely. Ramón has also served me. I had to give him a chance," Escobedo said. "It was a matter of honor. He is not very intelligent, but he is faithful."

"And his death is not overly troublesome?"

Escobedo shook his head without a moment's pause. "No. He knew what the chances were. He did not know why it was necessary to kill the American. He can tell them nothing about that. As for the American—he was a thief, and a foolish thief. He thought that we would not discover his thievery. He was mistaken. So we eliminated him."

And his family, Cortez noted. Killing people was one thing. Raping children . . . that was something else. But such things were not his concern.

"You are sure that they cannot tell the Americans—"

"They were told to get aboard the yacht, using the money as their bona fides and concealing their cache of drugs. Once the killings were accomplished, they were instructed to go to the Bahamas, turn the money over to one of my bankers, destroy the yacht discreetly, and then smuggle the drugs in normally, into Philadelphia. They knew that the American had displeased me, but not how he had done so."

"They must know that he was laundering money, and they must have told the Americans this," Cortez pointed out patiently.

"*Sí*. Fortunately, however, the American was very clever in how he did this. We were careful, Colonel. Beforehand we made sure that no one could learn exactly what the thief had done." Escobedo smiled, still in the afterglow of Pinta's services. "He was so very clever, that American."

"What if he left behind a record?"

"He did not. A police officer in that city searched his office and home for us—so carefully that the American *federales* never noticed that he had been there—*before* I authorized the killings."

Cortez took a deep breath before speaking. "*Jefe,* do you not understand that you *must tell me about such things as this beforehand!* Why do you employ me if you have no wish to make use of my knowledge?"

"We have been doing things such as this for years. We can manage our affairs without—"

"The Russians would send you to Siberia for such idiocy!"

"You forget your place, Señor Cortez!" Escobedo snarled back.

Félix bit off his own reply and managed to speak reasonably. "You think the *norteamericanos* are fools because they are unable to stop your smuggling. Their weakness is a political failing, not one of professional expertise. You do not understand that, and so I will explain it to you. Their borders are easy to violate because the Americans have a tradition of open borders. You confuse that with inefficiency. It is not. They have highly efficient police with the best scientific methods in the world—do you know that the Russian KGB reads American police textbooks? And copies their techniques? The American police are hamstrung because their political leadership does not allow them to act as they wish to act—and as they could act, in a moment, if those restrictions were ever eased. The American FBI—the *federales*—have resources beyond your comprehension. I know—they hunted me in Puerto Rico and came within a hair of capturing me along with Ojeda—and I am a trained intelligence officer."

"Yes, yes," Escobedo said patiently. "So what are you telling me?"

"Exactly what did this dead American do for you?"

"He laundered vast sums of money for us, and it continues to generate clean income for us. He set up a laundering scheme that we continue to use and—"

"Get your money out at once. If this *yanqui* was as efficient as you say, it is very likely that he left evidence behind. If he did so, then it is likely that those records were found."

"If so, then why have the *federales* not acted? They've had over a month now." Escobedo turned around to grab a bottle of brandy. He rarely indulged, but this was a time for it. Pinta had been especially fine tonight, and he enjoyed telling Cortez that his expertise, while useful, was not entirely crucial.

"*Jefe,* perhaps it will not happen this time, but someday you will learn that chances such as you took in this case are foolish."

Escobedo waved the snifter under his nose. "As you say, Colonel. Now, what about these new rules you speak of?"

* * *

Chavez was already fully briefed, of course. They'd had a "walk-through/talk-through" on a sand table as part of their mission brief, and every man in the unit had the terrain and their way through it committed to memory. The objective was an airfield designated RENO. He'd seen satellite and low-oblique photos of the site. He didn't know that it had been fingered by someone named Bert Russo, confirming an earlier intelligence report. It was a gravel strip about five thousand feet long, easy enough for a twin-engine aircraft, and marginally safe for a larger one, if it were lightly loaded—with grass, for instance, which was bulky but not especially heavy. The sergeant navigated by the compass strapped to his wrist. Every fifty yards he'd check the compass, sight on a tree or other object on the proper line of bearing, and head for it, at which time the procedure would begin again. He moved slowly and quietly, listening for any vaguely human noise and looking around with the night-vision scope that he wore on his head. His weapon was loaded and locked, but the selector switch was on "safe." Vega, the second or "slack" man in the line, was the buffer between Chavez's point position and the main body of the unit, fifty meters behind Vega. His machine gun made for a formidable buffer. If contact were made, their first thought would be evasion, but if evasion proved impossible, then they were to eliminate whatever stood in their path as quickly and violently as possible.

After two hours and two kilometers, Ding picked a spot to rest, a preselected rally point. He raised his hand and twirled it around in a lasso-motion to communicate what he was doing. They could have pushed a little harder, but the flight, as all lengthy helicopter flights, had been tiring, and the captain hadn't wanted to press too hard. They were not in fact expected to reach the objective until the following night. Every other word in the mission brief had been "Caution!" He remembered smirking every time he'd heard that. Now the amusement had left him. That guy Clark had been right. It was different in Indian Country. The price of failure here would not be the embarrassment of having your "MILES" beeper go off.

Chavez shook his head to clear away the thought. He had a job. It was a job for which he was fully trained and equipped, and it was a job which he wanted to do.

His rest spot was a small, dry knoll, which he scanned for snakes before sitting down. He made one last scan of the area before switching off his goggles to save battery time, and pulled out his canteen for a drink. It was hot, but not terribly so. High eighties, he thought, and the humidity was well up there also. If it was this hot at night, he didn't want to think about the daytime heat. At least they'd be bellied up during daylight. And Chavez was accustomed to heat. At Hunter-Liggett he'd marched over hills through temperatures over a hundred-ten degrees. He didn't much like it, but he could do it easily enough.

"How we doin', Chavez?"

"*Muy bien, Capitán,*" Chavez replied. "I figure we've made two miles, maybe two and a half—three klicks. That's Checkpoint WRENCH right over there, sir."

"Seen anything?"

"Negative. Just birds and bugs. Not even a wild pig or anything . . . you suppose people hunt here?"

"Good bet," Ramirez said after a moment's thought. "That's something we'll want to keep in mind, Ding."

Chavez looked around. He could see one man, but the rest blended in with the ground. He'd worried about the khaki clothing—not as effective camouflage as what he was accustomed to—but in the field it seemed to disappear just fine. Ding took another drink, then shook his canteen to see how noisy it was. That was a nice thing about the plastic canteens. Water sloshing around wasn't as noisy as with the old aluminum ones. It was still something to worry about. Any kind of noise was, in the bush. He popped a cough drop to keep his mouth moist and made ready to head out.

"Next stop, Checkpoint CHAINSAW. Captain, who thinks those dumbass names up?"

Ramirez chuckled quietly. "Why, I do, Sergeant. Don't feel bad. My ex didn't much like my taste either, so she went and married a real-estate hustler."

"Ain't broads a bitch?"

"Mine sure was."

Even the captain, Chavez thought. *Christ, nobody has a girl or a family behind. . . .* The thought was distantly troubling, but the issue at hand was getting past WRENCH to CHAINSAW in less than two hours.

The next hop involved crossing a road—what they called a road. It was a straight dirt-gravel track that stretched off to infinity in both directions. Chavez took his time approaching and crossing it. The rest of the squad halted fifty meters from the roadway, allowing the point man to move left and right of the crossing point to make sure it was secure. That done, he made a brief radio transmission to Captain Ramirez, in Spanish:

"The crossing is clear." His answer was a double click of static as the captain keyed the transmit key on his radio, but without saying anything. Chavez answered in kind and waited for the squad to cross.

The terrain here was agreeably flat, enough so that he was wondering why their training had been in towering, airless mountains. Probably because it was well hidden, he decided. The forest, or jungle, was thick, but not quite as bad as it had been in Panama. There was ample evidence that people occasionally farmed here, probably slash-and-burn operations, judging from the numerous small clearings. He'd seen half a dozen crumbling shacks where some poor bastard had tried to raise a family, or farm for beans, or something that hadn't worked out. The poverty that such evidence spoke of was depressing to Chavez. The people who lived in this region had names not unlike his, spoke a language differing only in accent from that spoken in his childhood home. Had his great-grandfather not decided to come to California and pick lettuce, might he have grown up in such a place? If so, how might he have turned out? Might Ding Chavez have ended up running drugs or being a shooter for the Cartel bigshots? That was a truly disturbing thought. His personal pride was too great to consider the possibility seriously, but its basic truth hovered at the edges of his conscious thoughts. There was poverty here, and poor people seized at whatever opportunity presented itself. How could you face your children and say that you could not feed them without doing something illegal? You could not, of course. What would a child understand other than an empty belly? Poor people had poor options. Chavez had found the Army almost by accident, and had found in it a true home of security and opportunity and fellowship and respect. But down here . . . ?

Poor bastards. But what about the people from his own barrio? Their lives poisoned, their neighborhoods corrupted. Who was to blame for it all?

Less thinkin' and more workin', 'mano, he told himself. Chavez switched on his night scope for the next part of the trek.

He moved standing straight up, not crouched as one would expect. His feet caressed the ground carefully, making sure that there wasn't a twig to snap, and he avoided bushes that might have leaves or thorns to grasp at his clothing and make their own rustling noise. Wherever possible he cut across clearings, skirting the treelines to keep from being silhouetted against the cloudy sky. But the main enemy at night was noise, not sight. It was amazing how acute your hearing got in the bush. He thought he could hear every bug, every birdcall, each puff of breeze in the leaves far over his head. But there were no human sounds. No coughs or mutters, none of the distinctive metallic noises that only men make. While he didn't exactly relax, he moved with confidence, just like on field-training exercises, he realized. Every fifty meters he'd stop and listen for those behind him. Not a whisper, not even *Oso* with his machine gun and heavy load. In their quiet was safety.

How good was the opposition? he wondered. Well equipped, probably. With the sort of money they had, you could buy any sort of weapons—in America or anyplace else. But trained soldiers? No way.

So how good are they? Ding asked himself. Like the members of his old gang, perhaps. They'd cultivate physical toughness, but not in a structured way. They'd be bullies, tough when they had the edge in weapons or numbers. Because of that they wouldn't be skilled in weapons use or fieldcraft; they'd rely on intimidation, and they'd be surprised when people failed to be intimidated. Some might be good hunters, but they wouldn't know how to move as a team. They wouldn't know about overwatch, mutual support, and grazing fire. They might know ambushes, but the finer points of reconnaissance would be lost on them. They would not have proper discipline. Chavez was sure that when they got to their objective, he'd find men smoking on guard. The arts of soldiering took time to acquire—time and discipline and desire. No, he was up against bullies. And bullies were cowards. These were mercenaries who acted for money. Chavez, on the other hand, took great pride that he performed his *duties* for love of country and, though he didn't quite think of it in those terms, for love of his fellow soldiers. His earlier uneasiness at the departure of the helicopter faded away. Though his mission was reconnaissance—intelligence-gathering—he found himself hoping that he'd have his chance to use the MP-5 SD2.

He reached CHAINSAW right on schedule. There the squad rested again, and Chavez led off to the final objective for the night's march, Checkpoint RASP. It was a small wooded knoll, five kilometers from their objective. Ding took his time checking RASP out. He looked especially for evidence of animals that might be hunted, and the tracks of men who might be doing the hunting. He found nothing. The squad arrived twenty minutes after he called them in by radio, having "hooked" and reversed their path to make sure that there were no trailers. Captain Ramirez examined the site as carefully as Chavez had done and came to the same positive conclusion. The squad members paired off to find places to eat and sleep. Ding teamed with Sergeant Vega, taking a security position along the most likely threat axis—northeast—to site one of the squad's two SAW machine guns. The squad medic—Sergeant Olivero—took a man to a nearby stream to replenish canteens, taking special care that everyone used his water-purification tablets. A latrine site was agreed upon, and men used that as well to dump the trash left over from their daily rations. But cleaning weapons came first, even though they hadn't been used. Each pair of soldiers cleaned their weapons one at a time, then worried about food.

"That wasn't so bad," Vega said as the sun climbed over the trees.

"Nice and flat," Chavez agreed with a yawn. "Gonna be a hot fucker down here, though."

"Have one o' these, *'mano*." Vega passed over an envelope of Gatorade concentrate.

"All right!" Chavez loved the stuff. He tore open the envelope and dumped the contents into his canteen, swishing it around to get the powder mixed in properly. "Captain know about this?"

"Nah—why worry him?"

"Right." Chavez pocketed the empty envelope. "Shame they don't make instant beer, isn't it?" They traded a chuckle. Neither man would do something so foolish, but both agreed that a cold beer wasn't all that bad an idea in the abstract.

"Flip you for first sleep," Vega said next. It turned out that he had a single U.S. quarter for the task. They'd each been issued five hundred dollars' equivalent in local currency, but all in paper, since coins make noise. It came up heads. Chavez got to stand watch on the gun while Vega curled up for sleep.

Ding settled down in the position. Julio had selected a good one. It was behind a spreading bush of one kind or another, with a shallow berm of dirt in front of him that could stop bullets but didn't obstruct his view, and the SAW had a good field of fire out to nearly three hundred meters. Ding checked that the weapon had a round chambered, but that the selector switch was also on "safe." He took out his binoculars to survey the area.

"How do things look, Sergeant?" Captain Ramirez asked quietly.

"Nothing moving at all, sir. Why don't you catch some Zs? We'll keep watch for ya'." Officers, Ding knew, have to be looked after. And if sergeants didn't do it, who would?

Ramirez surveyed the position. It had been well selected. Both men had eaten and refreshed themselves as good soldiers do, and would be well rested by sundown—over ten hours away. The captain patted Chavez on the shoulder before returning to his own position.

"All ready, sir," the communications sergeant—Ingeles—reported. The satellite-radio antenna was set up. It was only two bits of steel, about the size and shape of grade-school rulers, linked together in a cross, with a bit of wire for a stand. Ramirez checked his watch. It was time to transmit.

"VARIABLE, this is KNIFE, over." The signal went twenty-two thousand miles to a geosynchronous communications satellite, which relayed it back down toward Panama. It took about one-third of a second, and two more seconds passed before the reply came down. The circuit was agreeably free of static.

"KNIFE, this is VARIABLE. Your signal is five by five. Over."

"We are in position, Checkpoint RASP. All is quiet, nothing to report, over."

"Roger, copy. Out."

In the hilltop communications van, Mr. Clark occupied a seat in the corner by the door. He wasn't running the operation—far from it—but Ritter wanted his tactical expertise available in case it was needed. On the wall opposite the racks of communications gear was a large tactical map which showed the squads and their various checkpoints. All had made them on schedule. At least whoever had set this operation up had known—or listened to people who did—what men in the bush could and could not do. The expectations for time and distance were reasonable.

That's nice for a change, Clark thought. He looked around the van. Aside from the two communicators, there were two senior people from the Directorate of Operations, neither of whom had what Clark would call expertise in this particular sort of operation—though they were close to Ritter and dependable. *Well,* he admitted, *people with my sort of experience are mostly retired now.*

Clark's heart was out there in the field. He'd never operated in the Americas, at least not in the jungles of the Americas, but for all that he'd "been there"—out in the boonies, alone as a man could be, your only lifeline back to friendly forces a helicopter that might or might not show, tethered by an invisible thread of radio energy. The radios were far more reliable now; that was one positive change. For what it was worth. If something went wrong, these radios would not, however, bring in a flight of "fast-movers" whose afterburning engines rattled the sky and whose bombloads shook the ground fifteen minutes after you called for help. No, not this time.

Christ, do they know that? Do they really know what that fact means?

No, they don't. They can't. They're all too young. Kids. They're all little kids. That they were older, bigger, and tougher than his own children was for the moment beside the point. Clark was a man who'd operated in Cambodia and Vietnam—North and South. Always with small teams of men with guns and radios, almost always trying to stay hidden, looking for information and trying to get the hell away without being noticed. Mostly succeeding, but some of them had been very, very close.

"So far, so good," the senior Operations guy observed as he reached for a coffee mug. His companion nodded agreement.

Clark merely raised an eyebrow. *And what the hell do you two know about this?*

The Director, Moira saw, was excited about TARPON. As well he might be, she thought as she made her notes. It would take about a week, but already the seizure notices were being scratched in. Four Justice Department specialists had spent more than a day going through the report Mark Bright had delivered. Electronic banking, she realized, had made the job much easier. Somewhere in the Department of Justice there was someone who could access the computerized records of every bank in the world. Or maybe not in Justice. Maybe one of the intelligence agencies, or maybe a private contractor, because the legality of the matter was slightly vague. In any case, comparing records of the Securities and Exchange Commission with the numerous bank transactions, they had already identified the drug money used to finance the projects in which the "victim"—at least his family had been real victims, Moira told herself—had sought to launder it. She'd never known the wheels of justice to turn so quickly.

What arrogant people they must be, thinking they can invest and launder their dirty money right here! Juan was right about them and their arrogance, Moira thought. Well, this would wipe the smiles off their faces. There was at least six hundred million dollars of equity that the government could seize, and that didn't count the profits that they expected to make when the properties were rolled over. Six hundred million dollars! The amount was astounding. Sure, she'd heard about how "billions" in drug money poured out of the country, but the actual estimates were about as reliable as weather reports. It was plain, the Director said in dictation, that the Cartel was unhappy with its previous laundering arrangements and/or found that bringing the cash directly back to their own country created as many problems as it solved. Therefore, it appeared that after laundering the primary funds—plus making a significant profit on their money—they were setting up their accounts in such a way as to establish an enormous investment trust fund which could legitimately begin to take over all commercial businesses in their home country or any other country in which they wished to establish a political or economic position. What made this interesting, Emil went on, was that it might presage an attempt to launder themselves—the old American criminal phraseology: "to go legit"—to a degree that would be fully acceptable in the local, Latin American political context.

"How soon do you need this, sir?" Mrs. Wolfe asked.

"I'm seeing the President tomorrow morning."

"Copies?"

"Five, all numbered. Moira, this is code-word material," he reminded her.

"Soon as I finish, I'll eat the computer disk," she promised. "You have Assistant Director Grady coming in for lunch, and the AG canceled on dinner tomorrow night. He has to go out to San Francisco."

"What does the Attorney General want in San Francisco?"

"His son decided to get married on short notice."

"That's short, all right," Jacobs agreed. "How far away are you from that?"

"Not very. Your trip to Colombia—do you know when yet, so I can rework your appointments?"

"Sorry, still don't know. It shouldn't hurt the schedule too much, though. It'll be a weekend trip. I'll get out early Friday, and I ought to be back by lunch on the following Monday. So it shouldn't hurt anything important."

"Oh, okay." Moira left the room with a smile.

"Good morning." The United States Attorney was a thirty-seven-year-old man named Edwin Davidoff. He planned to be the first Jewish United States senator from Alabama in living memory. A tall, fit, two hundred pounds of former varsity wrestler, he'd parlayed a Presidential appointment into a reputation as a tough, effective, and scrupulously honest champion of the people. When handling civil-rights cases, his public statement always referred to the Law Of The Land, and all the things that America Stands For. When handling a major criminal case, he talked about Law And Order, and the Protection That The People Expect. He spoke a lot, as a matter of fact. There was scarcely a Rotary or Optimists group in Alabama to which he had not spoken in the past three years, and he hadn't missed any police departments at all. His post as the chief government lawyer for this part of Alabama was mainly administrative, but he did take the odd case, which always seemed to be a high-profile one. He'd been especially keen on political corruption, as three state legislators had discovered to their sorrow. They were now raking the sand traps at the Officers' Club Golf Course at Eglin Air Force Base.

Edward Stuart took his seat opposite the desk. Davidoff was a polite man, standing when Stuart arrived. Polite prosecutors worried Stuart.

"We finally got confirmation on your clients' identity," Davidoff said in a voice that might have feigned surprise, but instead was fully businesslike. "It turns out that they're both Colombian citizens with nearly a dozen arrests between them. I thought you said that they came from Costa Rica."

Stuart temporized: "Why did identification take so long?"

"I don't know. That factor doesn't really matter anyway. I've asked for an early trial date."

"What about the consideration the Coast Guard offered my client?"

"That statement was made after his confession—and in any case, we are not using the confession because we don't need it."

"Because it was obtained through flagrantly—"

"That's crap and you know it. Regardless, it will not play in this case. Far as

I'm concerned, the confession does not exist, okay? Ed, your clients committed mass murder and they're going to pay for that. They're going to pay in full."

Stuart leaned forward. "I can give you information—"

"I don't care what information they have," Davidoff said. "This is a murder case."

"This isn't the way things are done," Stuart objected.

"Maybe that's part of the problem. We're sending a message with this case."

"You're going to try to execute my clients just to send a message." It was not a question.

"I know we disagree on the deterrent value of capital punishment."

"I'm willing to trade a confession to murder and all their information for life."

"No deal."

"Are you really that sure you'll win the case?"

"You know what our evidence is," Davidoff replied. Disclosure laws required the prosecution to allow the defense team to examine everything they had. The same rule was not applied in reverse. It was a structural means of ensuring a fair trial to the defendants, though it was not universally approved of by police and prosecutors. It was, however, a rule, and Davidoff always played by the rules. That, Stuart knew, was one of the things that made him so dangerous. He had never once lost a case or an appeal on procedural grounds. Davidoff was a brilliant legal technician.

"If we kill these two people, we've sunk to the same level that we say they live at."

"Ed, we live in a democracy. The people ultimately decide what the laws should be, and the people approve of capital punishment."

"I will do everything I can to prevent that."

"I would be disappointed in you if you didn't."

Christ, but you'll be a great senator. So evenhanded, so tolerant of those who disagree with you on principle. No wonder the papers love you.

•

"So that's the story on Eastern Europe for this week," Judge Moore observed. "Sounds to me like things are quieting down."

"Yes, sir," Ryan replied. "It does look that way for the present."

The Director of Central Intelligence nodded and changed subjects. "You were in to see James last night?"

"Yes, sir. His spirits are still pretty good, but he knows." Ryan hated giving these progress reports. It wasn't as though he were a physician.

"I'm going over tonight," Ritter said. "Anything he needs, anything I can take over?"

"Just work. He still wants to work."

"Anything he wants, he gets," Moore said. Ritter stirred slightly at that, Ryan saw. "Dr. Ryan, you are doing quite well. If I were to suggest to the President that you might be ready to become the next DDI—look, I know how you feel about James; remember that I've worked with him longer than you have, all right?—and—"

"Sir, Admiral Greer isn't dead," Jack objected. He'd almost said *yet,* and cursed himself for even having thought that word.

"He's not going to make it, Jack," Moore said gently. "I'm sorry about that. He's my friend, too. But our business here is to serve our country. That is more important than personalities, even James. What's more, James is a pro, and he would be disappointed in your attitude.''

Ryan managed not to flinch at the rebuke. But it wounded him, all the more so because the Judge was correct. Jack took a deep breath and nodded agreement.

''James told me last week that he wants you to succeed him. I think you might be ready. What do you think?''

''Judge, I think I am fitted technically, but I lack the political sophistication needed for the office.''

''There's only one way to learn that part of the job—and, hell, politics aren't supposed to have much place in the Intelligence Directorate.'' Moore smiled to punctuate the irony of that statement. ''The President likes you, and The Hill likes you. As of now you're acting Deputy Director (Intelligence). The slot won't be officially filled until after the election, but as of now the job is yours on a provisional basis. If James recovers, well and good. The additional seasoning you get from working under him won't hurt. But even if he recovers, it will soon be time for him to leave. We are all replaceable, and James thinks you're ready. So do I.''

Ryan didn't know what to say. Still short of forty, he now had one of the premier intelligence posts in the world. As a practical matter, he'd had it for several months—even for several years, some might say—but now it was official, and somehow that made it different. People would now come to him for opinions and judgments. That had been going on for a long time, but he'd always had someone to fall back on. Now he would not. He'd present his information to Judge Moore and await final judgment, but from this moment the responsibility for being right was his. Before, he'd presented opinions and options to his superiors. Beginning now, he'd present policy decisions directly to the ultimate decision-makers. The increase in responsibility, though subtle, was vast.

''Need-to-know still applies,'' Ritter pointed out.

''Of course,'' Ryan said.

''I'll tell Nancy and your department heads,'' Moore said. ''James ginned up a letter I'll read. Here's your copy.''

Ryan stood to take it.

''I believe you have work to do, Dr. Ryan,'' Moore said.

''Yes, sir.'' Jack turned and left the room. He knew that he should have felt elated, but instead felt trapped. He thought he knew why.

''Too soon, Arthur,'' Ritter said after Jack had left.

''I know what you're saying, Bob, but we can't have Intelligence go adrift just because you don't want him in on SHOWBOAT. We'll keep him out of that, at least isolated from what Operations is doing. He'll have to get in on the information that we're developing. For Christ's sake, his knowledge of finance will be useful to us. He just doesn't have to know how the information gets to us. Besides, if the President says 'go' on this, and he gets approval from The Hill, we're home free.''

''So when do you go to The Hill?''

''I have four of them coming here tomorrow afternoon. We're invoking the special- and hazardous-operations rule.''

SAHO was an informal codicil of the oversight rules. While Congress had the right under law to oversee all intelligence operations, in a case two years earlier, a leak from one of the select committees had caused the death of a CIA station chief and a high-ranking defector. Instead of going public, Judge Moore had approached the members of both committees and gotten written agreement that in special cases the chairman and co-chairman of each committee would alone be given access to the necessary information. It was then their responsibility to decide if it should be shared with the committees as a whole. Since members of both political parties were present, it had been hoped that political posturing could be avoided. In fact, Judge Moore had created a subtle trap for all of them. Whoever tried to decide that information had to be disseminated ran the risk of being labeled as having a political agenda. Moreover, the higher selectivity of the four SAHO-cleared members had already created an atmosphere of privilege that militated directly against spreading the information out. So long as the operation was not politically sensitive, it was a virtual guarantee that Congress would not interfere. The remarkable thing was that Moore had managed to get the committees to agree to this. But bringing the widow and children of the dead station chief to the executive hearings hadn't hurt one bit. It was one thing to carp abstractly about the majesty of law, quite another to have to face the results of a mistake—the more so if one of them was a ten-year-old girl without a father. Political theater was not solely the domain of elected officials.

"And the Presidential Finding?" Ritter asked.

"Already done. 'It is determined that drug-smuggling operations are a clear and present danger to U.S. national security. The President authorizes the judicious use of military force in accord with established operational guidelines to protect our citizens,' *et cetera.*"

"The political angle is the one I don't like."

Moore chuckled. "Neither will the people from The Hill. So we have to keep it all secret, don't we? If the President goes public to show that he's 'really doing something,' the opposition will scream that he's playing politics. If the opposition burns the operation, then the President can do the same thing. So both sides have a political interest in keeping this one under wraps. The election-year politics work in our favor. Clever fellow, that Admiral Cutter."

"Not as clever as he thinks," Ritter snorted. "But who is?"

"Yeah. Who is? You know, it's a shame that James never got in on this."

"Gonna miss him," Ritter agreed. "God, I wish there was something I could take him, something to make it a little easier."

"I know what you mean," Judge Moore agreed. "Sooner or later, Ryan has to get in on this."

"I don't like it."

"What you don't like, Bob, is the fact that Ryan's been involved in two highly successful field operations in addition to all the work he's done at his desk. Maybe he did poach on your territory, but in both cases he had your support when he did so. Would you like him better if he'd failed? Robert, I don't have Directorate chiefs so that they can get into pissing contests like Cutter and those folks on The Hill."

Ritter blinked at the rebuke. "I've been saying for a long time that we brought him along too fast—which we have. I'll grant you that he's been very effective. But it's also true that he doesn't have the necessary political savvy for this sort of thing. He's yet to establish the capacity needed for executive oversight. He has to fly over to Europe to represent us at the NATO intel conference. No sense dropping SHOWBOAT on him before he leaves, is there?"

Moore almost replied that Admiral Greer was out of the loop because of his physical condition, which was mainly, but only partly, true. The presidential directive mandated an extremely tight group of people who really knew what the counter-drug operations were all about. It was an old story in the intelligence game: sometimes security was so tight that people who might have had something important to offer were left out of the picture. It was not unknown, in fact, for those left out to have had knowledge crucial to the operation's successful conclusion. But it was equally true that history was replete with examples of the disasters that resulted from making an operation so broadly based as to paralyze the decision-making process and compromise its secrecy. Drawing the line between operational security and operational efficiency was historically the most difficult task of an intelligence executive. There were no rules, Judge Moore knew, merely the requirement that such operations must succeed. One of the most persistent elements of spy fiction was the supposition that intelligence chiefs had an uncanny, infallible sixth sense of how to run their ops. But if the world's finest surgeons could make mistakes, if the world's best test pilots most often died in crashes—for that matter, if a pro-bowl quarterback could throw interceptions—why should a spymaster be any different? The only real difference between a wise man and a fool, Moore knew, was that the wise man tended to make more serious mistakes—and only because no one trusted a fool with really crucial decisions; only the wise had the opportunity to lose battles, or nations.

"You're right about the NATO conference. You win, Bob. For now." Judge Moore frowned at his desk. "How are things going?"

"All four teams are within a few hours' march of their surveillance points. If everything goes according to plan, they'll be in position by dawn tomorrow, and the following day they'll begin feeding us information. The flight crew we bagged the other day coughed up all the preliminary information we need. At least two of the airfields we staked out are 'hot.' Probably at least one of the others is also."

"The President wants me over tomorrow. It seems that the Bureau has tumbled to something important. Emil's really hot about it. Seems that they've identified a major money-laundering operation."

"Something we can exploit?"

"It would seem so. Emil's treating it as code-word material."

"Sauce for the goose," Ritter observed with a smile. "Maybe we can put a real crimp in their operations."

Chavez awoke from his second sleep period an hour before sundown. Sleep had come hard. Daytime temperatures were well over a hundred, and the high humidity made the jungle seem an oven despite being in shade. His first considered act was to drink over a pint of water—Gatorade—from his canteen to replace what he'd sweated off while asleep. Next came a couple of Tylenol. Light-fighters lived off the things to moderate the aches and pains that came with their normal physical regimen of exertion. In this case, it was a heat-induced headache that felt like a low-grade hangover.

"Why don't we let 'em keep this fucking place?" he muttered to Julio.

"Roger that, *'mano.*" Vega chuckled in return.

Sergeant Chavez wrenched himself to a sitting position, shaking off the cobwebs as he did so. He rubbed a hand over his face. The heavy beard he'd had since puberty was growing with its accustomed rapidity, but he wouldn't shave today. That merited a grunt. Normal Army routine was heavy on personal hygiene, and light infantrymen, as elite soldiers, were supposed to be "pretty" troops. Already he stank like a basketball team after double overtime, but he wouldn't wash, either. Nor would he don a clean uniform. But he would, of course, clean his weapon again. After making sure that Julio had already serviced his SAW, Chavez stripped his MP-5 down to six pieces and inspected them all visually. The matte-black finish resisted rust quite well. Regardless, he wiped everything down with oil, ran a toothbrush along all operation parts, checked to see that all springs were taut and magazines were not fouled with dirt or grit. Satisfied, he reassembled the weapon and worked the action quietly to make certain that it functioned smoothly. Finally, he inserted the magazine, chambered a round, and set the safety. Next he checked that his knives were clean and sharp. This included his throwing stars, of course.

"The captain's gonna be pissed if he sees them," Vega observed quietly.

"They're good luck," Chavez replied as he put them back in his pocket. " 'Sides, you never know. . . ." He checked the rest of his gear. Everything was as it should be. He was ready for the day's work. Next the maps came out.

"That where we're goin'?"

"RENO." Chavez pointed to the spot on the tactical map. "Just under five klicks." He examined the map carefully, making several mental notes and again committing the details to memory. The map had no marks on it, of course. If lost or captured, such marks would tell the wrong people things that they ought not to know.

"Here." Captain Ramirez joined the two, handing over a satellite photograph.

"These maps must be new, sir."

"They are. DMA"—he referred to the Defense Mapping Agency—"didn't have good maps of this area until recently. They were drawn up from the satellite photos. See any problems?"

"No, sir." Chavez looked up with a smile. "Nice and flat, lots of thinned-out trees—looks easier than last night, Cap'n."

"When we get in close, I want you to approach from this angle here into the objective rally point." Ramirez traced his hand across the photo. "I'll make the final approach with you for the leader's recon.' "

"You the boss, sir," Ding agreed.

"Plan the first break point right here, Checkpoint SPIKE."

"Right."

Ramirez stuck his head up, surveying the area. "Remember the briefing. These guys may have very good security, and be especially careful for booby traps. You see something, let me know immediately—as long as it's safe to do so. When in doubt, remember the mission is covert."

"I'll get us there, sir."

"Sorry, Ding," Ramirez apologized. "I must sound like a nervous woman."

"You ain't got the legs for it, sir," Chavez pointed out with a grin.

"You up to carrying that SAW another night, *Oso?*" Ramirez asked Vega.

"I carried heavier toothpicks, *jefe*."

Ramirez laughed and made off to check the next pair.

"I've known worse captains than that one," Vega observed when he was gone.

"Hard worker," Chavez allowed. Sergeant Olivero appeared next.

"How's your water?" the medic asked.

"Both a quart low," Vega replied.

"Both of you, drink a quart down right now."

"Come on, doc," Chavez protested.

"No dickin' around, people. Somebody gets heatstroke and it's my ass. If you ain't gotta piss, you ain't been drinking enough. Pretend it's a Corona," he suggested as both men took out their canteens. "Remember that: if you don't have to piss, you need a drink. Damn it, Ding, you oughta know that, you spent time at

Hunter-Liggett. This fucking climate'll dry your ass out in a heartbeat, and I ain't carrying your ass, dried-out or not.''

Olivero was right, of course. Chavez emptied a canteen in three long pulls. Vega followed the medic off to the nearby stream to replenish the empty containers. He reappeared several minutes later. *Oso* surprised his friend with a couple more envelopes of Gatorade concentrate. The medic, he explained, had his own supply. About the only bad news was that the water-purification pills did not mix well with the Gatorade, but that was for electrolytes, not taste.

Ramirez assembled his men just at sundown, repeating the night's brief already delivered to the individual guard posts. Repetition was the foundation of clarity—some manual said that, Chavez knew. The squad members were all dirty. The generally heavy beards and scraggly hair would enhance their camouflage, almost obviating the need for paint. There were a few aches and pains, mainly from the rough sleeping conditions, but everyone was fit and rested. And eager. Garbage was assembled and buried. Olivero sprinkled CS tear-gas powder before the dirt was smoothed over the hole. That would keep animals from scratching it up for a few weeks. Captain Ramirez made a final check of the area while there was still light. By the time Chavez moved out at point, there was no evidence that they'd ever been here.

Ding crossed the clearing as quickly as safety allowed, scanning ahead with his low-light goggles. Again using compass and landmarks, he was able to travel rapidly, now that he had a feel for the country. As before, there was no sound other than what nature provided, and better still, the forest wasn't quite as dense. He made better than a kilometer per hour. Best of all, he had yet to spot a snake.

He made Checkpoint SPIKE in under two hours, feeling relaxed and confident. The walk through the jungle had merely served to loosen up his muscles. He stopped twice along the way for water breaks, more often to listen, and still heard nothing unexpected. Every thirty minutes he checked in by radio with Captain Ramirez.

After Chavez picked a place to belly-up, it took ten minutes for the rest of the squad to catch up. Ten more minutes and he was off again for the final checkpoint, MALLET. Chavez found himself hoping that they'd run out of tool names.

He was more careful now. He had the map committed to memory, and the closer he got to the objective, the more likely that he'd encounter somebody. He slowed down almost without thinking about it. Half a klick out of SPIKE he heard something moving off to his right. Something quiet, but a land creature. He waved the squad to halt while he checked it out—Vega did the same, aiming his SAW in that direction—but whatever it was, it moved off heading southwest. Some animal or other, he was sure, though Ding waited another few minutes before he felt totally safe moving off. He checked the wind, which was blowing from his left rear, and wondered if his pungent odor was detectable to men—probably not, he decided. The rank smells of the jungle were pretty overpowering. On the other hand, maybe washing once in a while was worth the effort. . . .

He arrived at MALLET without further incident. He was now one kilometer off the objective. Again the squad assembled. There was a creek less than fifty meters from the checkpoint, and water was again replenished. The next stop was the objective rally point, picked for its easy identifiability. Ding got them there in just under an hour. The squad formed yet another defensive perimeter while the point man and commander got together.

Ramirez took out his map again. Chavez and his captain turned on the infrared lights that were part of the goggle-sets and traced ideas on the map and the accompanying photos. Also present was the operations sergeant, appropriately named Guerra. The road to the airfield came in from the opposite direction, looping around a stream that the squad had followed into the rally point. The only building visible on the photo was also on the far side of the objective.

"I like this way in, sir," Chavez observed.

"I think you're right," Ramirez replied. "Sergeant Guerra?"

"Looks pretty good to me, sir."

"Okay, people, if there's going to be contact, it'll be in this here neighborhood. It is now post time. Chavez, I'm going in with you. Guerra, you bring the rest of the squad in behind us if there's any trouble."

"Yes, sir," both sergeants replied.

Out of habit, Ding pulled out his camouflage stick and applied some green and black to his face. Next he put on his gloves. Though sweaty hands were a nuisance, the dark leather shells would darken his hands. He moved out, with Captain Ramirez close behind. Both men had their goggles on, and both moved very slowly now.

The stream they'd followed in for the last half a klick made for good drainage in the area, and that made for dry, solid footing—the same reason that someone had decided to bulldoze a landing strip here, of course. Chavez was especially wary for booby traps. With every step he checked the ground for wires, then up at waist and eye level. He also checked for any disturbance of ground. Again he wondered about game in the area. If there were some, it, too, would set off the booby traps, wouldn't it? So how would the bad guys react if one got set off? Probably they'd send somebody out to look . . . that would be bad news regardless of what he expected to find, wouldn't it?

Let's be cool, 'mano, Chavez told himself.

Finally: noise. It carried against the breeze. The low, far-off murmuring of talking men. Though too sporadic and confused even to guess the language, it was human speech.

Contact.

Chavez turned to look at his captain, pointing to the direction from which it seemed to come and tapping his ear with a finger. Ramirez nodded and motioned for the sergeant to press on.

Not real smart, people, Chavez thought at his quarry. *Not real smart talking so's a guy can hear you a couple hundred meters away. You are making my job easier.* Not that the sergeant minded. Just being here was hard enough.

Next, a trail.

Chavez knelt down and looked for human footprints. They were here, all right, coming out and going back. He took a very long step to pass over the narrow dirt path, and stopped. Ramirez and Chavez were now a tight two-man formation, far enough apart that the same burst wouldn't get both, close enough that they could provide mutual support. Captain Ramirez was an experienced officer, just off his eighteen-month tour in command of a light-infantry company, but even he was in awe of Chavez's woodcraft skills. It was now post time, as he'd told them a few minutes earlier, and his were the greatest worries of the unit. He was in command. That meant that the mission's success was his sole responsibility. He was similarly responsible for the lives of his men. He'd brought ten men in-country, and he was supposed to bring all ten men out. As the single officer, moreover, he was supposed to be at least as good as any of his men—preferably better—in every specialty. Even though that was not realistic, it was expected by everyone. Including Captain

Ramirez, who was old enough to know better. But watching Chavez, ten meters ahead, in the gray-green image of his night goggles, moving like a ghost, as quietly as a puff of breeze, Ramirez had to shake off a feeling of inadequacy. It was replaced a moment later with one of elation. This was better than command of a company. Ten elite specialists, each one of them among the best the Army had, and they were his to command. . . . Ramirez distantly realized that he was experiencing the emotional roller-coaster common to combat operations. A bright young man, he was now learning another lesson that history talked about but never quite conveyed: it was one thing to talk and think and read about this sort of thing, but there would never be a substitute for doing it. Training could attenuate the stress of combat operations, but never remove it. It amazed the young captain that everything seemed so clear to him. His senses were as fully alert as they had ever been, and his mind was working with speed and clarity. He recognized the stress and danger, but he was ready for it. In that recognition came elation as the roller coaster rolled on. A far-off part of his intellect watched and evaluated his performance, noting that as in a contact sport, every member of the squad needed the shock of real contact before settling down fully to work. The problem was simply that they were supposed to avoid that contact.

Chavez's hand went up, Ramirez saw, and then the scout crouched down behind a tree. The captain passed around a thicket of bushes and saw why the sergeant had stopped.

There was the airfield.

Better yet, there was an aircraft, several hundred yards away, its engines off but glowing on the infrared image generated by the goggles.

"Looks like we be in business, Cap'n," Ding noted in a whisper.

Ramirez and Chavez moved left and right, well inside the treeline, to search for security forces. But there were none. The objective, RENO, was agreeably identical to what they'd been told to expect. They took their time making sure, of course, then Ramirez went back to the rally point, leaving Chavez to keep an eye on things. Twenty minutes later the squad was in place on a small hill just northwest of the airfield, covering a front of two hundred yards. This had probably once been some peasant's farm, with the burned-off fields merely extended into the strip. They all had a clear view of the airstrip. Chavez was on the extreme right with Vega, Guerra on the far left with the other SAW gunner, and Ramirez stayed in the center, with his radio operator, Sergeant Ingeles.

12. The Curtain on SHOWBOAT

"VARIABLE, this is KNIFE. Stand by to copy, over."

The signal off the satellite channel was as clear as a commercial FM station. The communications technician stubbed out his cigarette and keyed his headset.

"KNIFE, this is VARIABLE, your signal is five by five. We are ready to copy, over." Behind him, Clark turned in his swivel chair to look at the map.

"We are at Objective RENO, and guess what—there's a twin-engine aircraft in view with some people loading cardboard boxes into it. Over."

Clark turned to look in surprise at the radio rack. Was their operational intel *that good?*

"Can you read the tail number, over."

"Negative, the angle's wrong. But he's going to take off right past us. We are right in the planned position. No security assets are evident at this time."

"Damn," observed one of the Operations people. He lifted a handset. "This is VARIABLE. RENO reports bird in the nest, time zero-three-one-six Zulu . . . Roger. Will advise. Out." He turned to his companion. "The stateside assets are at plus-one hour."

"That'll do just fine," the other man thought.

As Ramirez and Chavez watched through their binoculars, two men finished loading their boxes into the aircraft. It was a Piper Cheyenne, both men determined, a midsize corporate aircraft with reasonably long range, depending on load weights and flight profile. Local shops could fit it with ferry tanks, extending the range designed into the aircraft. The cargo flown into America by drug smugglers had little to do with weight or—except in the case of marijuana—bulk. The limiting factor was money. A single aircraft could carry enough refined cocaine, even at wholesale value, to wipe out the cash holdings of most federal reserve banks.

The pilots boarded the aircraft after shaking hands with the ground crews—that part seemed to their covert observers just as routine as any aircraft departure. The engines began turning, and their roar swept across the open land toward the light-fighters.

"Jesus," Sergeant Vega noted with bemusement. "I could smoke the bird right here and now. Damn." His gun was on "safe," of course.

"Might make our life a little too exciting," Chavez noted. "Yeah, that makes sense, *Oso*. The security guys were all around the airplane. They're spreading out now." He grabbed his radio. "Captain—"

"I see it. Heads up in case we have to move out."

The Piper taxied to the end of the runway, moving like a crippled bird, bouncing and bobbing on the landing-gear shocks. The airstrip was illuminated by a mere handful of small flares, far fewer lights than were normally used to outline a real runway. It struck all who looked as dangerous, and suddenly Chavez realized that if the aircraft crashed on takeoff, some squad members would end up eating the thing. . . .

The aircraft's nose dropped as the pilot pushed the engines to full throttle preparatory to takeoff, then reduced power to make sure the motors wouldn't quit when he did so. Satisfied, they ran up again, and the aircraft slipped its brakes and started moving. Chavez set his binoculars down to watch. Heavily loaded with fuel, it cleared the trees to his right by a mere twenty yards. Whoever the pilot was, he was a daredevil. The term that sprang into the sergeant's mind seemed appropriate enough.

"Just took off now. It's a Piper Cheyenne," Ramirez's voice read off the tail number. It had American registration. "Course about three-three-zero." Which headed for the Yucatan Channel, between Cuba and Mexico. The communicator took the proper notes. "What can you tell me about RENO?"

* * *

"I count six people. Four carry rifles, can't tell about the rest. One pickup truck and a shack, like on the satellite overheads. Truck's moving now, and I think—yeah, they're putting out the runway lights. They're using flares, just putting dirt over on top of them. Stand by, we have a truck heading this way."

Off to Ramirez's left, Vega had his machine gun up on its bipod, the sight tracking the pickup as it moved down the east side of the runway. Every few hundred meters, it stopped, and the passenger jumped out and shoveled dirt on one of the sputtering flares.

"Reach out, reach out and touch someone . . . " Julio murmured.

"Be cool, *Oso,*" Ding cautioned.

"No problem." Vega's thumb was on the selector switch—still set on "safe"—and his finger was on the trigger guard, not the trigger itself.

The flares went out one by one. The truck was briefly within one hundred fifty meters of the two soldiers, but never approached them directly. They merely happened to be in a place the truck had to pass by. Vega's gun stayed on the truck until well after it turned away. As he set the buttstock back down on the dirt, he turned to his comrade.

"Aw, shit!" he whispered in feigned disappointment.

Chavez had to stifle a giggle. Wasn't this odd, he thought. Here they were in enemy territory, loaded for fucking bear, and they were playing a game no different from what children did on Christmas Eve, peeking around corners. The game was serious as hell, they all knew, but the form it took was almost laughable. They also knew that could change in an instant. There wasn't anything funny about training a machine gun on two men in a truck. Was there?

Chavez reactivated his night goggles. At the far end of the runway, people were lighting cigarettes. The faint images on his display flared white with the heat energy. That would kill their night vision, Ding knew. He could tell from the way they moved that they were just bullshitting around now. Their day's—night's—work was complete. The truck drove off, leaving two men behind. These, it would seem, were the security troops for this airstrip. Only two, and they smoked at night. Armed or not—they seemed to be carrying AK-47s or a close copy thereof—they were not serious opposition.

"What do you suppose they're smoking?" Vega asked.

"I didn't think about that," Chavez admitted with a grunt. "You don't suppose they're that dumb, do you?"

"We ain't dealing with soldiers, man. We coulda moved in and snuffed those fuckers no sweat. Maybe ten seconds' worth of firefight."

"Still gotta be careful," Chavez whispered in reply.

"Roge-o," Vega agreed. "That's where you get the edge."

"KNIFE, this is Six," Ramirez called on the radio net. "Fall back to the rally point."

"Move, I'll cover," Chavez told Vega.

Julio stood and shouldered his weapon. There was a slight but annoying tinkle from the metal parts as he did so—the ammo belt, Ding thought. *Have to keep that in mind.* He waited in place for several minutes before moving out.

The rally point was a particularly tall tree close to the stream. Again, people replenished their canteens at Olivero's persistent urging. It turned out that one man had had his face slashed by a low branch, requiring attention from the medic, but otherwise the squad was fully intact. They'd camp five hundred meters from the airfield, leaving two men at an observation point—the one Chavez had staked out for himself—around the clock. Ding took the first watch, again with Vega, and would be relieved at dawn by Guerra and another man armed with a silenced MP-5. Either a SAW or a soldier armed with a grenade launcher would always be at the OP in case the opposition got rambunctious. If there was to be a firefight, the idea was to end it as quickly as possible. Light-fighters weren't especially big on tanks and heavy guns, but American soldiers think in terms of firepower, which, after all, had been largely an American invention in the first place.

It amazed Chavez how easily one could slip into a routine. An hour before dawn, he and Vega surveyed the landing strip from their little knoll. Of the two men in the permanent security team, only one was moving around. The other was sitting with his back against the shack, still smoking something or other. The one up and moving didn't stray far.

"What's happening, Ding?" the captain asked.

"I heard you coming, sir," Chavez said.

"I tripped. Sorry."

Chavez ran down the situation briefly. Ramirez put his binoculars on the enemy to check things for himself.

"Supposedly they aren't being bothered by the local police and army," the captain observed.

"Bought off?" Vega asked.

"No, just they got discouraged, mainly. So the druggies have settled down to a half-dozen or so regular airfields. Like this one. We're gonna be here awhile." A pause. "Anything happens—"

"We'll call you right off, sir," Vega promised.

"See any snakes?" Ramirez asked.

"No, thank God." The captain's teeth flared in the darkness. He clapped Chavez on the shoulder and disappeared back into the bushes.

"What's wrong with snakes?" Vega asked.

Captain Winters felt the pangs of disappointment as he watched the Piper touch down. It was two in a row now. The big one from the other night was gone already. Exactly where they flew them off to, he didn't know. Maybe the big boneyard in the desert. One more old piston bird would hardly be noticed. On the other hand, you could sell one of these Pipers easily enough.

The .50-caliber machine gun looked even more impressive at eye level, though with dawn coming up, the spotlights were less overpowering. They didn't use the spy-plane ploy this time. The Marines treated the smugglers just as roughly as before, however, and their actions again had the desired effect. The CIA officer running the operation had formerly been with DEA, and he enjoyed the difference in interrogation methods. Both pilots were Colombians, the aircraft's registration to the contrary. Despite their machismo, it took only one look at Nicodemus. To be brave in the face of a bullet, or even an attack dog, was one thing. To be brave before a living carnosaur was something else entirely. It took less than an hour for them to be processed, then taken off to the tame federal district judge.

"How many planes don't make it here?" Gunnery Sergeant Black asked as they were driven away.

"What d'you mean, Gunny?"

"I seen the fighter, sir. It figures that he told the dude, 'Fly this way or else!'

An' we been called here more times 'n airplanes have showed up, right? What I'm saying, sir, is it stands to reason, like, that some folks didn't take the hint, and the boy driving the fighter showed them the 'or else.' "

"You don't need to know that, Gunny Black," the CIA officer pointed out.

"Fair enough. Either way, it's cool with me, sir. My first tour in 'Nam, I seen a squad get wiped because some of 'em were doped up. I caught a punk selling drugs in my squad, back in '74–75, and I damned near beat the little fuck to death. Almost got in trouble over it, too."

The CIA officer nodded as though that statement surprised him. It didn't.

" 'Need-to-know,' Gunny," he repeated.

"Aye aye, sir." Gunnery Sergeant Black assembled his men and walked off toward the waiting helicopter.

That was the problem with "black" operations, the CIA officer thought as he watched the Marines leave. You want good people, reliable people, smart people, to be part of the op. But the good, reliable, and smart people all had brains and imagination. And it really wasn't all that hard for them to figure things out. After enough of that happened, "black" operations tended to become gray ones. Like the dawn that had just risen. Except that light wasn't always a good thing, was it?

Admiral Cutter met Directors Moore and Jacobs in the lobby of the office wing, and took them straight to the Oval Office. Agents Connor and D'Agostino were on duty in the secretarial office and gave all three the usual once-over out of habit. Unusually, for the White House, they walked straight in to see WRANGLER.

"Good afternoon, Mr. President," all three said in turn.

The President rose from his desk and took his place in an antique chair by the fireplace. This was where he usually sat for "intimate" conversations. The President regretted this. The chair he sat in was nowhere near as comfortable as the custom-designed one behind his desk, and his back was acting up, but even presidents have to play by the rules of others' expectations.

"I take it that this is to be a progress report. You want to start off, Judge?"

"SHOWBOAT is fully underway. We've had a major stroke of luck, in fact. Just as we got a surveillance team in place, they spotted an aircraft taking off." Moore favored everyone with a smile. "Everything worked exactly as planned. The two smugglers are in federal custody. That was luck, pure and simple, of course. We can't expect that to happen too often, but we intercepted ninety kilos of cocaine, and that's a fair night's work. All four covert teams are on the ground and in place. None have been spotted."

"How's the satellite working out?"

"Still getting parts of it calibrated. That's mainly a computer problem, of course. The thing we're planning to use the Rhyolite for will take another week or so. As you know, that element of the plan was set up rather late, and we're playing it by ear at the moment. The problem, if I can call it that, is setting up the computer software, and they need another couple of days."

"What about The Hill?"

"This afternoon," Judge Moore answered. "I don't expect that to be a problem."

"You've said that before," Cutter pointed out.

Moore turned and examined him with a tired eye. "We've laid quite a bit of groundwork. I don't invoke SAHO very often, and I've never had any problems from them when I did."

"I don't expect any active opposition there, Jim," the President agreed. "I've laid some groundwork, too. Emil, you're quiet this morning."

"We've been over that aspect of the operation, Mr. President. I have no special legal qualms, because there really is no law on this issue. The Constitution grants you plenipotentiary powers to use military force to protect our national security once it is determined—by you, of course—that our security is, in fact, threatened. The legal precedents go all the way back to the Jefferson presidency. The political issues are something else, but that's not really my department. In any case, the Bureau has broken what appears to be a major money-laundering operation, and we're just about ready to move on it."

"How major?" Admiral Cutter asked, annoying the President, who wanted to ask the same question.

"We can identify a total of five hundred eighty-eight million dollars of drug money, spread through twenty-two different banks all the way from Liechtenstein to California, invested in a number of real-estate ventures, all of which are here in the United States. We've had a team working 'round the clock all week on this."

"How much?" the President asked, getting in first this time. He wasn't the only person in the room who wanted that number repeated.

"Almost six hundred million," the FBI Director repeated. "It was just over that figure two days ago, but a sizable block of funds was transferred on Wednesday—it looks like it was a routine transfer, but we are keeping an eye on the accounts in question."

"And what will you be doing?"

"By this evening we'll have complete documentation on all the accounts. Starting tomorrow, the legal attachés in all our embassies overseas, and the field divisions covering the domestic banks, will move to freeze the accounts and—"

"Will the Swiss and the Europeans cooperate?" Cutter interrupted.

"Yes, they will. The mystique about numbered accounts is overrated, as President Marcos found out a few years ago. If we can prove that the deposits result from criminal operations, the governments in question will freeze the funds. In Switzerland, for example, the money goes to the state—'canton'—government for domestic applications. Aside from the moral issue, it's simple self-interest, and we have treaties to cover this. It hardly hurts the Swiss economy, for example, to keep that money in Switzerland, does it? If we're successful, as I have every right to expect, the total net loss to the Cartel will be on the order of one billion dollars. That figure is just an estimate on our part which includes loss of equity in the investments and the expected profits from rollover. The five eighty-eight, on the other hand, is a hard number. We're calling this Operation TARPON. Domestically, the law is entirely on our side, and on close inspection, it's going to be very hard for anyone to liberate the funds, ever. Overseas the legal issues are more muddied, but I think we can expect fairly good cooperation. The European governments are starting to notice drug problems of their own, and they have a way of handling the legal issues more . . . oh, I guess the word is pragmatically," Jacobs concluded with a smile. "I presume you'll want the Attorney General to make the announcement."

You could see the sparkle in the President's eyes. The press release would be made in the White House Press Room. He'd let the Justice Department handle it, of course, but it would be done in the White House so that journalists could get the right spin. *Good morning, ladies and gentlemen. I have just informed the President that we have made a major break in the continuing war against . . .*

"How badly will this hurt them?" the President asked.

"Sir, exactly how much money they have has always been a matter of speculation on our part. What's really interesting about this whole scheme is that the laundering operation may actually be designed to legitimize the money once it gets into Colombia. That's hard to read, but it would seem that the Cartel is trying to find a less overtly criminal way in which to infiltrate their own national economy. Since that is not strictly necessary in economic terms, the presumptive goal of the operation would seem to be political. To answer your question, the monetary loss will sting them rather badly, but will not cripple them in any way. The political ramifications, however, may be an extra bonus whose scope we cannot as yet evaluate."

"A billion dollars. . . ." the President said. "That really gives you something to tell the Colombians about, doesn't it?"

"I do not think they'll be displeased. The political rumblings they've been getting from the Cartel are very troubling to them."

"Not troubling enough to take action," Cutter observed.

Jacobs didn't like that at all. "Admiral, their Attorney General is a friend of mine. He travels with a security detail that's double the size of the President's, and he has to deal with a security threat that'd make most people duck for cover every time a car backfired. Colombia is trying damned hard to run a real democracy in a region where democracies are pretty rare—which historically happens to be our fault, in case you've forgotten—and you expect them to do—what? Trash what institutions they do have, do what Argentina did? For Christ's sake, the Bureau and DEA combined don't have the manpower to go after the drug rings that we already know about, and we have a thousand times their resources. So what the hell do you expect, that they'll go fascist again to hunt down the druggies just because it suits us? We *did* expect that and we *got* that, for over a hundred years, and look where it's gotten *us!" This clown is supposed to be an expert on Latin America,* Jacobs didn't say out loud. *Says who? I bet you couldn't even drive boats worth a damn!*

The bottom line, Judge Moore noted, *is that Emil doesn't like this whole operation, does he?* On the other hand, it did rock Cutter back in his chair. A small man, Jacobs had dignity and moral authority measured in megaton quantities.

"You're trying to tell us something, Emil," the President said lightly. "Spit it out."

"Terminate this whole operation," the FBI Director said. "Stop it before it goes too far. Give me the manpower I need, and I can accomplish more right here at home, entirely within the law, than we'll ever accomplish with all this covert-operations nonsense. TARPON is the proof of that. Straight police work, and it's the biggest success we've ever had."

"Which happened only because some Coast Guard skipper got a little off the reservation," Judge Moore noted. "If that Coastie hadn't broken the rules himself, your case would have looked like simple piracy and murder. You left that part out, Emil."

"Not the first time something like that has happened, and the difference, Arthur, is that that wasn't planned by anyone in Washington."

"That captain isn't going to be hurt, is he?" the President asked.

"No, sir. That's already been taken care of," Jacobs assured him.

"Good. Keep it that way. Emil, I respect your point of view," the President said, "but we have to try something different. I can't sell Congress on the funding to double the size of the FBI, or DEA. You know that."

You haven't tried, Jacobs wanted to say. Instead he nodded submission.

"And I thought we had your agreement on this operation."

"You do, Mr. President." *How did I ever rope myself into this?* Jacobs asked himself. This road, like so many others, was paved with good intentions. What they were doing wasn't quite illegal; in the same sense that skydiving wasn't quite dangerous—so long as everything went according to plan.

"And when are you heading down to Bogotá?"

"Next week, sir. I've messengered a letter to the legal attaché, and he'll deliver it by hand to the AG. We'll have good security for the meeting."

"Good. I want you to be careful, Emil. I need you. I especially need your advice," the President said kindly. "Even if I don't always take it."

The President has to be the world's champ at setting people down easy, Moore told himself. But part of that was Emil Jacobs. He'd been a team player since he joined the U.S. Attorney's office in Chicago, lo, those thirty years ago.

"Anything else?"

"I've made Jack Ryan the acting DDI," Moore said. "James recommended him, and I think he's ready."

"Will he be cleared for SHOWBOAT?" Cutter asked immediately.

"He's not that ready, is he, Arthur?" the President opined.

"No, sir, your orders were to keep this one tight."

"Any change with Greer?"

"It does not look good, Mr. President," Moore replied.

"Damned shame. I have to go into Bethesda to have my blood pressure looked at next week. I'll stop in to see him."

"That would be very kind of you, sir."

Everyone was supportive as hell, Ryan noted. He felt like a trespasser in this office, but Nancy Cummings—secretary to the DDI from long before the time Greer arrived here—did not treat him as an interloper, and the security detail that he now rated called him "sir" even though two of them were older than Jack was. The really good news, he didn't realize until someone told him, was that he now rated a driver also. The purpose of this was simply that the driver was a security officer with a Beretta Model 92-F automatic pistol under his left armpit (there was something even more impressive under the dash), but for Ryan it meant that he'd no longer have to make the fifty-eight-minute drive himself. From now on he'd be one of those Important People who sat in the back of the speeding car talking on a secure mobile phone, or reading over Important Documents, or, more likely, reading the paper on the way into work. The official car would be parked in CIA's underground garage, in a reserved space near the executive elevator, which would whisk him directly to the seventh floor without having to pass through the customary security-gate routine, which was such a damned nuisance. He'd eat in the executive dining room with its mahogany furniture and discreetly elegant silverware.

The increase in salary was also impressive, or would have been if it had matched what his wife, Cathy, was making from the surgical practice that supplemented her associate professorship at Johns Hopkins. But there was not a single government salary—not even the President's—that matched what a good surgeon made. Ryan also had the equivalent rank of a three-star general or admiral, even though his capacity in the job was merely "acting."

His first task of the day, after closing the office door, had been to open the DDI safe. There was nothing in it. Ryan memorized the combination, again noting that the DDO's combination was scribbled on the same sheet of paper. His office had that most precious of government perks: a private bathroom; a high-definition TV monitor on which he could watch satellite imagery come in without going to the viewing room in the building's new north wing; a secure computer terminal over which he could communicate to other offices if he so wished—there was dust on the keys; Greer had almost never used it. Most of all, there was *room*. He could get up and pace if he wanted. His job gave him unlimited access to the Director. When the Director was away—and even if he were not—Ryan could call the White House for an immediate meeting with the President. He'd have to go through the Chief of Staff—bypassing Cutter, if he felt the need—but if Ryan now said, "I have to see the President, right now!" he'd get in, right now. Of course he'd have to have a very good reason for doing so.

Jack sat in the high-backed chair, facing away from the plate-glass windows, and realized that he had gotten there. This was as far as he had ever expected to rise in the Agency. Not even forty yet. He'd made his money in the brokerage business—and the money was still growing; he needed his CIA salary about as much as he needed a third shoe—gotten his doctor's degree, written his books, taught some history, made himself a new and interesting career, and worked his way to the top. Not even forty yet. He would have awarded himself a gentle, satisfied smile except for the fatherly gentleman who was now at Bethesda Naval Medical Center, dying the lingering and painful death that had put him in this chair, in this office, in this position.

It's not worth it. It sure as hell isn't worth that, Jack told himself. He'd lost his parents to an airliner crash at Chicago, and remembered the sudden, wrenching loss, the impact that had come like a thrown punch. For all that, it had come with merciful speed. He hadn't realized it at the time, but he did now. Ryan made a point of seeing Admiral Greer three times a week, watching his body shrink, draw in on itself like a drying plant, watching the pain lines deepen in his dignified face as the man fought valiantly in a battle he knew to be hopeless. He'd been spared the ordeal of watching his parents fade away, but Greer had become a new father to him, and Ryan was now observing his filial duty for his surrogate parent. Now he understood why his wife had chosen eye surgery. It was tough, technically demanding work in which a slip could cause blindness, but Cathy didn't have to watch people die. What could be harder than this—but Ryan knew that answer. He'd seen his daughter hover near death, saved by chance and some especially fine surgeons.

Where do they get the courage? Jack wondered. It was one thing to fight against people. Ryan had done that. But to fight against Death itself, knowing that they must ultimately lose, but still fighting. Such was the nature of the medical profession.

Jesus, you're a morbid son of a bitch this morning.

What would the Admiral say?

He'd say to get on with the goddamned job.

The point of life was to press on, to do the best you can, to make the world a better place. Of course, Jack admitted, CIA might seem to some a most peculiar place in which to do that, but not to Ryan, who had done some very odd but also very useful things here.

A smell got his attention. He turned to see that the coffee machine on the credenza was turned on. Nancy must have done it, he realized. But Admiral Greer's mugs were gone, and some "generic" CIA-logoed cups sat on the silver tray. Just then came a knock on the door. Nancy's head appeared.

"Your department-head meeting starts in two minutes, Dr. Ryan."

"Thanks, Mrs. Cummings. Who did the coffee?" Jack asked.

''The Admiral called in this morning. He said you would need some on your first day.''

''Oh. I'll thank him when I go over tonight.''

''He sounded a little better this morning,'' Nancy said hopefully.

''Hope you're right.''

The department heads appeared right on schedule. He poured himself a cup of coffee, offering the same to his visitors, and in a minute was down to work. The first morning report, as always, concerned the Soviet Union, followed by the others as CIA's interests rotated around the globe. Jack had attended these meetings as a matter of routine for years, but now he was the man behind the desk. He knew how the meetings were supposed to be run, and he didn't break the pattern. Business was still business. The Admiral wouldn't have had it any other way.

With presidential approval, things moved along smartly. Overseas communications were handled, as always, by the National Security Agency, and only the time zones made things inconvenient. An earlier heads-up signal had been dispatched to the legal attachés in several European embassies, and at the appointed time, first in Bern, teletype machines operating off encrypted satellite channels began punching out paper. In the communications rooms in all the embassies, the commo-techs took note of the fact that the systems being used were the most secure lines available. The first, or register, sheet prepped the technicians for the proper one-time-pad sequence, which had to be retrieved from the safes which held the cipher keys.

For especially sensitive communications—the sort that might accompany notice that war was about to start, for example—conventional cipher machines simply were not secure enough. The Walker-Whitworth spy ring had seen to that. Those revelations had forced a rapid and radical change in American code policy. Each embassy had a special safe—actually a safe within yet another, larger safe—which contained a number of quite ordinary-looking tape cassettes. Each was encased in a transparent but color-coded plastic shrink-wrap. Each bore two numbers. One number—in this case 342—was the master registration number for the cassette. The other—in the Bern embassy; it was 68—designated the individual cassette within the 342 series. In the event that the plastic wrap on any of the cassettes, anywhere in the world, was determined to be split, scratched, or even distorted, all cassettes on that number series were immediately burned on the assumption that the cassette might have been compromised.

In this case, the communications technician removed the cassette from its storage case, examined its number, and had his watch supervisor verify that it had the proper number: ''I read the number as three-four-two.''

''Concur,'' the watch supervisor confirmed. ''Three-four-two.''

''I am opening the cassette,'' the technician said, shaking his head at the absurd solemnity of the event.

The shrink-wrap was discarded in the low-tech rectangular plastic waste can next to his desk, and the technician inserted the cassette in an ordinary-looking but expensive player that was linked electronically to another teletype machine ten feet away.

The technician set the original printout on the clipboard over his own machine and started typing.

The message, already encrypted on the master 342 cassette at NSA headquarters, Fort Meade, Maryland, had been further encrypted for satellite transmission on the current maximum-security State Department cipher, called STRIPE, but even if someone had the proper keys to read STRIPE, all he would have gotten was a message that read DEERAMO WERAC KEWJRT, and so on, due to the super-encipherment imposed by the cassette system. That would at the least annoy anyone who thought that he'd broken the American communications systems. It certainly annoyed the communications technician, who had to concentrate as hard as he knew on how to type things like DEERAMO WERAC KEWJRT instead of real words that made some sort of sense.

Each letter passed through the cassette player, which took note of the incoming letter and treated it as a number from 1 (A) to 26 (Z), and then added the number on the tape cassette. Thus, if 1 (A) on the original text corresponded to another 1 (A) on the cassette, 1 was added to 1, making 2 (B) on the clear-text message. The transpositions on the cassette were completely random, having been generated from atmospheric radio noise by a computer at Fort Meade. It was a completely unbreakable code system, technically known as a One-Time Pad. There was, by definition, no way to order or predict random behavior. So long as the tape cassettes were uncompromised, no one could break this cipher system. The only reason that this system, called TAPDANCE, was not used for all communications was the inconvenience of making, shipping, securing, and keeping track of the thousands of cassettes that would be required, but that would soon be made easier when a laser-disc format replaced the tape cassettes. The code-breaking profession had been around since Elizabethan times, and this technical development threatened to render it as obsolete as the slide rule.

The technician pounded away on the keyboard, trying to concentrate as he grumbled to himself about the late hours. He ought to have been off work at six, and was looking forward to dinner in a nice little place a couple of blocks from the embassy. He could not, of course, see the clear-text message coming up ten feet away, but the truth was that he didn't give a good goddamn. He'd been doing this sort of thing for nine years, and the only reason he stuck with it was the travel opportunity. Bern was his third posting overseas. It wasn't as much fun as Bangkok had been, but it was far more interesting than his childhood home in Ithaca, New York.

The message had seventeen thousand characters, which probably corresponded to about twenty-five hundred words, the technician thought. He blazed through the message as quickly as he could.

"Okay?" he asked when he was finished. The last "word" had been ERYTPESM.

"Yep," the legal attaché replied.

"Great." The technician took the telex printout he'd just typed from and fed it into the code room's own shredder. It came out as flat pasta. Next he removed the tape cassette from the player and, getting a nod from the watch supervisor, walked to the corner of the room. Here, tied to a cable fixed to the wall—actually it was just a spiraled telephone cord—was a large horseshoe magnet. He moved this back and forth over the cassette to destroy the magnetic information encoded on the tape inside. Then the cassette went into the burn-bag. At midnight, one of the Marine guards, supervised by someone else, would carry the bag to the embassy's incinerator, where both would watch a day's worth of paper and other important garbage burned to ashes by a natural-gas flame. Mr. Bernardi finished scanning the message and looked up.

"I wish my secretary could type that fast, Charlie. I count two—only two!—mistakes. Sorry we kept you late." The legal attaché handed over a ten-franc note. "Have a couple of beers on me."

"Thank you, Mr. Bernardi."

Chuck Bernardi was a senior FBI agent, whose civil-service rank was equivalent to that of brigadier general in the United States Army, in which he had served as an infantry officer, long ago and far away. He had two more months to serve here, after which he'd rotate home to FBI Headquarters and maybe a job as special-agent-in-charge of a medium-sized field division. His specialty was in the Bureau's OC—Organized Crime—Directorate, which explained his posting to Switzerland. Chuck Bernardi was an expert on tracking mob money, and a lot of it worked its way through the Swiss banking system. His job, half police officer and half diplomat, put him in touch with all of the top Swiss police officials, with whom he had developed a close and friendly working relationship. The local cops were smart, professional, and damned effective, he thought. A little old lady could walk the streets of Bern with a shopping bag full of banknotes and feel perfectly secure. And some of them, he chuckled to himself on the walk to his office, probably did.

Once in his office, Bernardi flipped on his reading light and reached for a cigar. He hadn't shaken off the first ash when he leaned back in his chair to stare at the ceiling.

"Son of a *bitch!*" He reached for his telephone and called the most senior cop he knew.

"This is Chuck Bernardi. Could I speak to Dr. Lang, please? Thank you. . . . Hi, Karl, Chuck here. I need to see you . . . right away if possible . . . it's pretty important, Karl, honest. . . . In your office would be better. . . . Not over the phone, Karl, if you don't mind. . . . Okay, thanks, pal. It's worth it, believe me. I'll be there in fifteen minutes."

He hung up the phone. Next he walked out to the office Xerox machine and made a copy of the document, signing off that it was he who had used the machine and how many copies had been run off. Before leaving, he put the original in his personal safe and tucked the copy in his coat pocket. Karl might be pissed about missing dinner, he thought, but it wasn't every day that somebody enriched your national economy to the tune of two hundred million dollars. The Swiss would freeze the accounts. That meant that six of their banks would, by law, keep all the accrued interest—and maybe the principal also, as the identity of the government which was entitled to get the funds might never be clear, "forcing" the Swiss to keep the funds, which would ultimately be turned over to the canton governments. And people wondered why Switzerland was such a wealthy, peaceful, charming little country. It wasn't just the skiing and the chocolate.

Within an hour, six embassies had the word, and as the sun marched across the earth, special agents of the FBI also visited the executive suites of several American commercial—"full-service"—banks. They handed over the identifying numbers or names of several accounts, all of whose considerable funds would be immediately frozen by the simple expedient of putting a computer lock on them. In all cases, it was done quietly. No one had to know, and the importance of secrecy was conveyed in very positive terms—in America and elsewhere—by serious, senior government employees, to bank presidents who were fully cooperative in every instance. (After all, it wasn't *their* money, was it?) In nearly all cases, the police officials learned, the accounts were not terribly active, averaging two or three transactions per month; always large ones, of course. Deposits would still be accepted, and it was suggested by a Belgian official that if the FBI had the account information for other such accounts, transfers from one monitored account to another would be allowed—only within the same country, of course, the Belgian pointed out—to prevent tipping off the depositors. After all, he said, drugs were the common enemy of all civilized men, and most certainly of all police officers. That suggestion was immediately ratified by Director Jacobs, with the concurrence of the AG. Even the Dutch went along, despite the fact that the Netherlands government itself sold drugs in approved stores to its more jaded younger citizens. It was, all in all, a clear case of capitalism in action. There was dirty money around, money that had not been rightly earned, and governments did not approve of such money. Which was why they seized it for their own approved ends. In the case of the banks, the secrecy to which they were sworn was every bit as sacred as that by which they guarded the identity of their depositors.

By the close of business hours on Friday, all had been accomplished. The banks' computer systems stayed up and running. The law-enforcement people now had two full additional days to give the money trails further examination. If they found any more money related to the accounts already seized, those funds would also be frozen, and, in the case of the European banks, confiscated. The first hit here was in Luxembourg. Though Swiss banks are those known internationally for their confidentiality laws, the only real difference in security between their operation and those of banks in most other European countries was the fact that Belgium, for example, wasn't surrounded by the Alps, and that Switzerland hadn't been overrun by foreign armies quite as recently as her European neighbors. Otherwise, the integrity of the banks was identical, and accordingly the non-Swiss bankers actually resented the Alps for giving their Swiss brethren such an additional and accidental business advantage. But in this case, international cooperation was the rule. By Sunday evening, six new "dirty" accounts had been identified, and one hundred thirty-five million additional dollars were put under computer lock.

Back in Washington, Director Jacobs, Deputy Assistant Director Murray, the specialists from the organized-crime office, and the Justice Department left their offices for a well-deserved dinner at the Jockey Club Restaurant. While the Director's security detail watched, the ten men proceeded to have themselves a superb meal at government expense. Perhaps a passing reporter or Common Cause staffer might have objected, but this one had been well and truly earned. Operation TARPON was the greatest single success in the War on Drugs. It would go public, they agreed, by the end of the week.

"Gentlemen," Dan Murray said, rising with his—he didn't remember how many glasses of Chablis had accompanied this fish—of course—dinner. "I give you the United States Coast Guard!"

They all rose with a chorus of laughter that annoyed the other customers in the restaurant. "The United States Coast Guard!" It was a pity, one of the Justice Department attorneys noted, that they didn't know the words to "Semper Paratus."

The party broke up about ten o'clock. The Director's security men shared looks. Emil didn't hold his liquor all that well, and he'd be a gruff, hungover little bear tomorrow morning—though he'd apologize to them all before lunch.

"We'll be flying down to Bogotá Friday afternoon," he told them in the sanctity of his official car, an Oldsmobile. "Make your plans but don't tell the Air Force until Wednesday. I don't want any leaks on this."

"Yes, sir," the chief of the detail answered. He wasn't looking forward to this one either. Especially now. The druggies were going to be pissed. But this visit would catch them unawares. The news stories would say that Jacobs was remaining in D.C. to work on the case, and they wouldn't expect him to show up in Colombia.

Even so, the security for this one would be tight. He and his fellow agents would be spending some extra time in the Hoover Building's own weapons range, honing their skills with their automatic pistols and submachine guns. They couldn't let anything happen to Emil.

Moira found out Tuesday morning. By this time she, too, knew all about TARPON, of course. She knew that the trip was supposed to be secret, and she had no doubt that it would also be dangerous. She wouldn't tell Juan until Thursday night. After all, she had to be careful. She spent the rest of the week wondering what special place he had in the Blue Ridge Mountains.

It no longer mattered that the uniform clothing was khaki instead of woodland pattern Battle Dress Uniform. Between the sweat stains and the dirt, the squad members were now exactly the same color as the ground on which they hid. They had all washed once in the stream from which they took their water, but no one had used soap for fear that suds or smell or something might alert someone downstream. Under the circumstances, washing without soap wasn't even as good as kissing your sister. It had cooled them off, however, and that for Chavez was a most pleasant memory. For—what was it?—ten glorious minutes he'd been comfortable. Ten minutes after which, he'd sweated again. The climate was beastly, with temperatures reaching to one hundred twenty degrees on one cloudless afternoon. If this was a goddamned jungle, Chavez asked himself, why the hell doesn't it rain? The good news was that they didn't have to move around a great deal. The two jerks who guarded this airstrip spent most of their time sleeping, smoking—probably grass, Chavez thought—and generally jerking off. They had, once, startled him by firing their weapons at tin cans that they'd set up on the runway. That might have been dangerous, but the direction of fire hadn't been toward the observation post, and Chavez had used the opportunity to evaluate the weapons skills of the opposition. Shitty, he'd told Vega at once. Now they were up to it again. They set up three bean cans—big ones—perhaps a hundred meters from the shack, and just blazed away, shooting from the hip like movie actors.

"Christ, what fuck-ups," he observed, watching through his binoculars.

"Lemme see." Vega got to watch just as one of them knocked a can down on his third try. "Hell, I could hit the damned things from here. . . ."

"Point, this is Six, what the fuck is going on!" the radio squawked a moment later. Vega answered the call.

"Six, this is Point. Our friends are doing some plinkin' again. Their axis of fire is away from us, sir. They're punchin' holes in some tin cans. They can't shoot for shit, Cap'n."

"I'm coming over."

"Roger." Ding set down the radio. "The Cap'n's coming. I think the noise made him nervous."

"He sure does worry a lot," Vega noted.

"That's what they pay officers for, ain't it?"

Ramirez appeared three minutes later. Chavez made to hand over his binoculars, but the captain had brought his own pair this time. He fell to a prone position and got his glasses up just in time to watch another can go down.

"Oh."

"Two cans, two full magazines," Chavez explained. "They like to go rock-and-roll. I guess ammo's cheap down here."

Both of the guards were still smoking. The captain and the sergeant watched them laugh and joke as they shot. Probably, Ramirez thought, they're as bored as we are. After the first aircraft, there had been no activity at all here at RENO, and soldiers like boredom even less than ordinary citizens. One of them—it was hard to tell them apart since they were roughly the same size and wore the same sort of clothing—inserted another magazine into his AK-47 and blazed off a ten-round burst. The little fountains of dirt walked up to the remaining can, but didn't quite hit it.

"I didn't know it would be this easy, sir," Vega observed from behind the sights of his machine gun. "What a bunch of fuck-ups!"

"You think that way, *Oso,* you turn into one yourself," Ramirez said seriously.

"Roger that, Cap'n, but I can't help seein' what I'm seein'."

Ramirez softened his rebuke with a smile. "I suppose you're right."

The third can finally went down. They were averaging thirty rounds per target. Next the guards used their weapons to push the cans around the runway.

"You know," Vega said after a moment, "I ain't seen 'em clean their weapons yet." For the squad members, cleaning their weapons was as regular a routine as morning and evening prayers were for clergymen.

"The AK'll take a lot of abuse. It's good for that," Ramirez pointed out.

"Yes, sir."

Finally the guards, too, grew bored. One of them retrieved the cans. As he was doing so, a truck appeared. With little in the way of warning, Chavez was surprised to note. The wind was wrong, but even so it hadn't occurred to him that he wouldn't have at least a minute or two worth of warning. Something to remember. There were three people in the truck, one of whom was riding in the back. The driver dismounted and walked out to the two guards. In a moment he was pointing at the ground and yelling—they could hear it from five hundred yards away even though they hadn't heard the truck, which really seemed strange.

"What's that all about?" Vega asked.

Captain Ramirez laughed quietly. "FOD. He's pissed off at the FOD."

"Huh?" Vega asked.

"Foreign Object Damage. You suck one of those cartridge cases into an aircraft engine, like a turbine engine, and it'll beat the hell out of it. Yeah—look, they're picking up their brass."

Chavez turned his binoculars back to the truck. "I see some boxes there, sir. Maybe we got a pickup tonight. How come no fuel cans—yeah! Captain, last time we were here, they didn't fuel the airplane, did they?"

"The flight originates from a regular airstrip twenty miles off," Ramirez explained. "Maybe they don't have to top off . . . Does seem odd, though."

"Maybe they got fuel drums in the shack . . . ?" Vega wondered.

Captain Ramirez grunted. He wanted to send a couple of men in close to check the area out, but his orders didn't permit that. Their only patrolling was to check the airfield perimeter for additional security troops. They never got closer than four hundred meters to the cleared area, and it was always done with an eye on the two guards. His operational orders were not to take the slightest risk of making contact with the opposition. So they weren't supposed to patrol the area even though it would have told them more about the opposition than they knew—would tell them things that they might need to know. That was just good basic soldiering, he thought, and the order not to do it was a dumb order, since it ran as many—or more—risks than it was supposed to avoid. But orders were still orders. Whoever had generated them didn't know much about soldiering. It was Ramirez's first experience with that phenomenon, since he, too, was not old enough to remember Vietnam.

"They're gonna be out there all day," Chavez said. It appeared that the truck driver was making them count their brass, and you never could find all of the damned things. Vega checked his watch.

"Sundown in two hours. Anybody wanna bet we'll have business tonight? I got a hundred pesos says we get a plane before twenty-two hundred."

"No bet," Ramirez said. "The tall one by the truck just opened a box of flares." The captain left. He had a radio call to make.

It had been a quiet couple of days at Corezal. Clark had just returned from a late lunch at the Fort Amador Officers' Club—curiously, the head of the Panamanian Army had an office in the same building; most curious, since he was not overly popular with the U.S. military at the moment—followed by a brief siesta. Local customs, he decided, made sense. Especially sleeping through the hottest part of the day. The cold air of the van—the air conditioning was to protect the electronics gear, mainly from the oppressive humidity here—gave him the wakeup shock he needed.

Team KNIFE had scored on their first night with a single aircraft. Two of the other squads had also had hits, but one of the aircraft had made it all the way to its destination when the F-15 had lost its radar ten minutes after takeoff, much to everyone's chagrin. But that was the sort of problem you had to expect with an operation this short of assets. Two for three wasn't bad at all, especially when you considered what the odds had been like a bare month before, when the Customs people were lucky to bag a single aircraft in a month. One of the squads, moreover, had drawn a complete blank. Their airfield seemed totally inactive, contradicting intelligence data that had looked very promising only a week before. That also was a hazard of real-world operations.

"VARIABLE, this is KNIFE, over," the speaker said without preamble.

"KNIFE, this is VARIABLE. We read you loud and clear. We are ready to copy, over."

"We have activity at RENO. Possible pickup this evening. We will keep you advised. Over."

"Roger, copy. We'll be here. Out."

One of the Operations people lifted the handset to another radio channel.

"EAGLE'S NEST, this is VARIABLE . . . Stand to . . . Roger. We'll keep you posted. Out." He set the instrument down and turned. "They'll get everyone up. The fighter is back on line. Seems the radar was overdue for some part replacement or other. It's up and running, and the Air Force offers its apology."

"Damned well ought to," the other Operations man grumbled.

"You guys ever think that maybe an operation can go too right?" Clark asked from his seat in the corner.

The senior one wanted to say something snotty, Clark saw, but knew better.

"They must know that something odd is happening. You don't want to make it too obvious," Clark explained for the other one. Then he leaned back and closed his eyes. Might as well get another piece of that siesta, he told himself. It might be a long night.

Chavez got his wish just after sundown. It started to rain lightly, and clouds moving in from the west promised an even heavier downpour. The airfield crew set out their flares—quite a few more than the last time, he saw—and the aircraft arrived soon after that.

Rain made visibility difficult. It seemed to Chavez that someone ran a fuel hose out from the shack. Maybe there were some fuel drums in there, and maybe a hand-crank pump, but his ability to see the five or six hundred yards came and went with the rain. Something else happened. The truck drove down the center of the strip, and the driver tossed out at least ten additional flares to mark the centerline. The aircraft took off twenty minutes after it arrived, and Ramirez was already on his satellite radio.

"Did you get the tail number?" VARIABLE asked.

"Negative," the captain replied. "It's raining pretty heavy now. Visibility is dogshit. But he got off at twenty-fifty-one Lima, heading north-northwest."

"Roger, copy. Out."

Ramirez didn't like the effect that the reduced visibility might have on his unit. He took another pair of soldiers forward to the OP, but he just as well might not have bothered. The guards didn't bother extinguishing the flares this time, letting the rain wet things down. The truck left soon after the aircraft took off, and the two chastised runway guards retired to the shack to keep dry. All in all, he thought, it couldn't be much easier.

Bronco was bored, too. It wasn't that he minded what he was doing, but there really wasn't much challenge in it. And besides, he was stuck at four kills, and needed only one more to be an ace. The fighter pilot was sure that the mission was better accomplished with live prisoners—but, damn it, killing the sons of bitches was . . . satisfying, even though there wasn't much challenge to it. He was flying an aircraft designed to mix it up with the best fighters the Russians could make. Taking out a Twin-Beech was about as difficult as driving to the O-Club for a couple of brews. Maybe tonight he'd do something different . . . but what?

That gave him something to think about as he orbited north of the Yucatan Channel, just behind the E-2C, and of course out of normal airliner tracks. The contact call came in at about the right time. He turned south to get on the target, which took just over ten minutes.

"Tallyho," he told the Hawkeye. "I have eyeballs on target."

Another two-engine, therefore another coke smuggler. Captain Winters was still angry about the other night. Someone had forgotten to check the maintenance schedule on his Eagle, and sure enough, that damned widget had failed right when the contractor said it would, at five hundred three hours. Amazing that they could figure it that close. Amazing that an umpty-million-dollar fighter plane went tits-up because of a five-dollar widget, or diode, or chip, or whatever the hell it was. It cost five bucks. He knew that because the sergeant had told him.

Well, there he was. Twin engines, looked like a Beech King Air. No lights, cruising a lot lower than his most efficient cruise altitude.

Okay, Bronco thought, slowing his fighter down, then lighting him up and making the first radio call.

It was a druggie, all right. He did the same dumbass thing they all did, reducing power, lowering flaps, and diving for the deck. Winters had never gotten past the fourth level of Donkey Kong, but popping a real airplane under these circumstances was a hell of a lot easier than that, and you didn't even have to put in a quarter . . . but he was bored.

Okay, let's try something different.

He let the aircraft go down, maintaining his own altitude and power setting to pass well ahead of it. He checked to make sure that all of his flying lights were off, then threw the Eagle into a tight left-hand turn. This brought his fire-control radar in on the target, and that allowed him to spot the King Air on his infrared scanner, which was wired in to a videotape recorder the same way his gun systems were.

You think you've lost me, don't you. . . .

Now for the fun part. It was a really dark one tonight. No stars, no moon, solid overcast at ten or twelve thousand feet. The Eagle was painted in a blue-gray motif that was supposed to blend in with the sky anyway, and at night it was even better than flat-matte black. He was invisible. The crew in the Beech must be looking all over creation for him, he knew. Looking everywhere but directly forward.

They were flying at fifty feet, and on his screen Captain Winters saw that their propwash was throwing up spray from the waves—five- or six-footers, he thought—just over a mile away. He came straight in at one hundred feet and five hundred knots. Exactly a mile from the target, he put on his lights again.

It was so predictable. The Beech pilot saw the incoming, sun-bright lights, seemingly dead-on, and instinctively did what any pilot would do. He banked hard right and dove—*exactly fifty feet*—cartwheeling spectacularly into the sea. Probably didn't even have time to realize what he'd done wrong, Bronco thought, then he laughed out loud as he yanked back on the stick and rolled to give it a last look. *Now that was a class kill,* Captain Winters told himself as he turned for home. The Agency people would really love that one. And best of all, he was now an ace. You didn't have to shoot them down for it to count. You just had to get the kill.

13. The Bloody Weekend

It really wasn't fair to make him wait, was it? Moira thought on her drive home Wednesday afternoon. What if he couldn't come? What if he needed notice in advance? What if he had something important scheduled in for the weekend? What if he couldn't make it?

She had to call him.

Mrs. Wolfe reached into the purse at her side and felt for the scrap of hotel stationery—it was still there in the zipper pocket—and the numbers written on it seemed to burn into her skin. She had to call him.

Traffic was confused today. Somebody had blown a tire on the 14th Street Bridge, and her hands sweated on the plastic steering wheel. What if he couldn't make it?

What about the kids? They were old enough to look after themselves, that was the easy part—but how to explain to them that their mother was going off for a weekend to—what was the phrase they used? To "get laid." *Their mother*. How would they react? It hadn't occurred to her that her horrible secret was nothing of the kind, not to her children, not to her co-workers, not to her boss, and she would have been dumbfounded to know that all of them were rooting for her . . . *to get laid*. Moira Wolfe had missed the sexual revolution by only a year or two. She'd taken her fearful-hopeful-passionate-frightened virginity to the marriage bed, and always thought that her husband had done the same. He must have, she'd told herself then and later, because they'd both botched things so badly the first time. But within three days they'd had the basics figured out—youthful vigor and love could handle almost anything—and over the next twenty-two years the two newlyweds had truly become one.

The void left in her life by the loss of her husband was like an open sore that would not heal. His picture was at her bedside, taken only a year before his death, working on his sailboat. No longer a young man when it had been taken, love handles at his waist, much of his hair gone, but the smile. What was it Juan said? You look with love, and see love returned. *Such a fine way of putting it,* Moira thought.

My God, What would Rich think? She'd asked herself that question more than once. Every time she looked at the photograph before sleep. Every time she looked at her children on the way in or out of the house, hoping that they didn't suspect, knowing in a way conscious thought did not touch that they must know. But what choice did she have? Was she supposed to wear widow's weeds—that was a custom best left in the distant past. She'd mourned for the appropriate time, hadn't she? She'd wept alone in her bed when a phrase crossed her mind, on the anniversaries of all the special dates that acquire meaning in the twenty-two years that two lives merge into one, and, often enough, just from looking at that picture of Rich on the boat that they'd saved years for. . . .

What do people expect of me? she asked herself in sudden anguish. *I still have a life. I still have needs.*

What would Rich say?

He hadn't had time to say anything at all. He'd died on his way to work, two months after a routine physical that had told him that he should lose a few pounds, that his blood pressure was a touch high, but nothing to worry about really, that his cholesterol was pretty good for somebody in his forties, and that he should come back for the same thing next year. Then, at 7:39 in the morning, his car had just run off the road into a guardrail and stopped. A policeman only a block away had come and been puzzled to see the driver still in the car, and wondered whether or not someone might be driving drunk this early in the morning, then realized that there was no pulse. An ambulance had been summoned, its crew finding the officer pounding on Rich's chest, making the assumption of a heart attack that they'd made themselves, doing everything they'd been trained to do. But there had never been a chance. Aneurysm in the brain. A weakening in the wall of a blood vessel, the doctor had explained after the postmortem. Nothing that could have been done. Why did it happen . . . ? Maybe hereditary, probably not. No, blood pressure had nothing to do with it. Almost impossible to diagnose under the best of circumstances. Did he complain of headaches? Not even that much warning? The doctor had walked away quietly, wishing he could have said more, not so much angry as saddened by the fact that medicine didn't have all the answers, and that there never was much you could say. (*Just one of those things,* was what doctors said among themselves, but you couldn't say that to the family, could you?) There hadn't been much pain, the doctor had said—not knowing if it were a lie or not—but that hardly mattered now, so he'd said confidently that, no, she could take comfort in the fact that there would not have been much pain. Then the funeral. Emil Jacobs there, already anticipating the death of his wife; she'd come from the hospital herself to attend the event with the husband she'd soon leave. All the tears that were shed. . . .

It wasn't fair. Not fair that he'd been forced to leave without saying goodbye. A kiss that tasted of coffee on the way to the door, something about stopping at the Safeway on the way home, and she'd turned away, hadn't even seen him enter the car that last time. She'd punished herself for months merely because of that.

What would Rich say?

But Rich was dead, and two years was long enough.

The kids already had dinner going when she got home. Moira walked upstairs to change her clothes, and found herself looking at the phone that sat on the night table. Right next to the picture of Rich. She sat down on the bed, looking at it, trying to face it. It took a minute or so. Moira took the paper from her purse, and with a deep breath began punching the number into the phone. There were the normal chirps associated with an international call.

"Díaz y Díaz," a voice answered.

"Could I speak to Juan Díaz, please?" Moira asked the female voice.

"Who is calling, please?" the voice asked, switching over to English.

"This is Moira Wolfe."

"Ah, Señora Wolfe! I am Consuela. Please hold for a *momento*." There followed a minute of static on the line. "Señora Wolfe, he is somewhere in the factory. I cannot locate him. Can I tell him to call you?"

"Yes. I'm at home."

"*Sí,* I will tell him—Señora?"

"Yes?"

"Please excuse me, but there is something I must say. Since the death of his María—Señor Juan, he is like my son. Since he has met you, Señora, he is happy again. I was afraid he would never—please, you must not say I tell you this, but, thank you for what you have done. It is a good thing you have done for Señor Juan. We in the office pray for both of you, that you will find happiness."

It was exactly what she needed to hear. "Consuela, Juan has said so many wonderful things about you. Please call me Moira."

"I have already said too much. I will find Señor Juan, wherever he is."

"Thank you, Consuela. Goodbye."

Consuela, whose real name was María—from which Félix (Juan) had gotten the name for his dead wife—was twenty-five and a graduate of a local secretarial school who wanted to make better money than that, and who, as a consequence, had smuggled drugs into America, through Miami and Atlanta, on half a dozen occasions before a close call had decided her on a career change. Now she handled odd jobs for her former employers while she operated her own small business outside Caracas. For this task, merely waiting for the phone to ring, she was being paid five thousand dollars per week. Of course, that was only one half of the job. She proceeded to perform the other half, dialing another number. There was an unusual series of chirps as, she suspected, the call was skipped over from the number she'd dialed to another she didn't know about.

"Yes?"

"Señor Díaz? This is Consuela."

"Yes?"

"Moira called a moment ago. She wishes for you to call her at home."

"Thank you." And the connection broke.

Cortez looked at his desk clock. He'd let her wait . . . twenty-three minutes. His place was yet another luxury condominium in Medellín, two buildings down from that of his boss. Was this the call? he wondered. He remembered when patience had come hard to him, but it was a long time since he'd been a fledgling intelligence officer, and he went back to his papers.

Twenty minutes later he checked the time again and lit a cigarette, watching the hands move around the dial. He smiled, wondering what it was like for her to have to wait, two thousand miles away. What was she thinking? Halfway through the cigarette, it was time to find out. He lifted the phone and dialed in the number.

Dave got to the phone first. "Hello?" He frowned. "We have a bad connection. Could you repeat that? Oh, okay, hold on." Dave looked over to see his mother's eyes on him. "For you, Mom."

"I'll take it upstairs," she said at once, and moved toward the stairs as slowly as she could manage.

Dave put his hand over the receiver. "Guess who?" There were knowing looks around the dining room.

"Yes," Dave heard her say on the other phone. He discreetly hung up. *Good luck, Mom.*

"Moira, this is Juan."

"Are you free this weekend?" she asked.

"This weekend? Are you sure?"

"I'm free from lunch Friday to Monday morning."

"So . . . let me think . . . " Two thousand miles away, Cortez stared out the window at the building across the street. *Might it be a trap? Might the FBI Intelligence Division . . . might the whole thing be a . . . ?* Of course not. "Moira, I must talk to someone here. Please hold for another minute. Can you?"

"Yes!"

The enthusiasm in her voice was unmistakable as he punched the hold button. He let her wait two minutes by his clock before going back on the line.

"I will be in Washington Friday afternoon."

"You'll be getting in about the time—about the right time."

"Where can we meet? At the airport. Can you meet me at the airport?"

"Yes."

"I don't know what flight I'll be on. I'll meet you at . . . at the Hertz counter at three o'clock. You will be there, yes?"

"I will be there."

"As will I, Moira. Goodbye, my love."

Moira Wolfe looked again at the photograph. The smile was still there, but she decided it was not an accusing smile.

Cortez got up from his desk and walked out of the room. The guard in the hall stood when he came out of the door.

"I am going to see *el jefe,*" he said simply. The guard lifted his cellular phone to make the call.

The technical problems were very difficult. The most basic one was power. While the base stations cranked out about five hundred watts, the mobile stations were allowed less than seven, and the battery-powered hand-held sets that everyone likes to use were three hundred milliwatts, and even with a huge parabolic dish receiving antenna, the signals gathered were like whispers. But the Rhyolite-J was a highly sophisticated instrument, the result of uncounted billions of research-and-development dollars. Supercooled electronics solved part of the problem. Various computers worked on the rest. The incoming signals were broken down into digital code—ones and zeroes—by a relatively simple computer and downlinked to Fort Huachuca, where another computer of vastly greater power examined the bits of raw information and tried to make sense of them. Random static was eliminated by a mathematically simple but still massively repetitive procedure—an algorithm—that compared neighboring bits to one another and through a process of averaging numerical values filtered out over 90 percent of the noise. That enabled the computer to spit out a recognizable conversation from what it had downloaded from the satellite. But that was only the beginning.

The reason the Cartel used cellular phones for its day-to-day communications was security. There were roughly six hundred separate frequencies, all in the UHF band from 825 to 845 and 870 to 890 megahertz. A small computer at the base station would complete a call by selecting an available frequency at random, and in the case of a call from a mobile phone, changing that frequency to a better one when performance wavered. Finally, the same frequency could be used simultaneously for different calls on neighboring "cells" (hence the name of the system) of the same overall network. Because of this operating feature, there was not a police force in the world that could monitor phone calls made on cellular-phone equipment. Even without scrambling, the calls could be made in the clear, without even the need for code.

Or that's what everyone thought.

The United States government had been in the business of intercepting foreign radio communications since the days of Yardley's famous Black Chamber. Technically known as comint or sigint—for communications or signals intelligence—there was no better form of information possible than your enemy's own words to his own people. It was a field in which America had excelled for generations. Whole constellations of satellites were deployed to eavesdrop on foreign nations, catching snippets of radio calls, side-lobe signals from microwave relay towers. Often encoded in one way or another, the signals were most often processed at the headquarters of the National Security Agency, on the grounds of Fort Meade, Maryland, between Washington and Baltimore, whose acres of basement held most of the supercomputers in the world.

The task here was to keep constant track of the six hundred frequencies used by the cellular phone net in Medellín. What was impossible for any police agency in the world was less than a light workout for NSA, which monitored literally tens of thousands of radio and other electronic channels on a continuous basis. The National Security Agency was far larger than CIA, far more secretive, and much better funded. One of its stations was on the grounds of Fort Huachuca, Arizona. It even had its own supercomputer, a brand-new Cray connected by fiberoptic cable to one of many communications vans, each of which performed functions that those in the loop knew not to ask about.

The next problem was making the computer work. The names and identities of many Cartel figures were fully known to the U.S. government, of course. Their voices had been recorded, and the programmers had started there. Using voiceprints of the known voices, they established an algorithm to recognize those voices, whichever cellular frequency they used. Next, those who called *them* had their voices electronically identified. Soon the computer was automatically keying and recording over thirty known voices, and the number of known voice-targets was expanding on a daily basis. Source-power considerations made voice identification difficult on occasion, and some calls were inevitably missed, but the chief technician estimated that they were catching over 60 percent, and that as their identification data-base grew larger, that their performance would grow to 85 percent.

Those voices that did not have names attached were assigned numbers. Voice 23 had just called Voice 17. Twenty-three was a security guard. He had been identified because he had called 17, who was also known to be a security guard for Subject ECHO, as Escobedo was known to the comint team. "He's coming over to see him," was all the recorded signal told them. Exactly who "he" was they didn't know. It was a voice they had either not yet heard or, more likely, not yet identified. The intelligence specialists were patient. This case had gone a lot quicker than normal. For all their sophistication, the targets never dreamed that someone could tap in on them in this way and as a consequence had taken no precautions against it. Within a month the comint team would have enough experience with the targets to develop all sorts of usable tactical intelligence. It was just a matter of time. The technicians wondered when actual operations would begin. After all, setting up the sigint side was always the precursor to putting assets in the field.

"What is it?" Escobedo asked as Cortez entered the room.

"The American FBI Director will be flying to Bogotá tomorrow. He leaves Washington sometime after noon. It is to be a covert visit. I would expect him to be using an official aircraft. The Americans have a squadron of such aircraft at Andrews Air Force Base. There will be a flight plan filed, probably covered as something else. Anything from four tomorrow afternoon to eight in the evening could be the flight. I expect it to be a twin-engine executive jet, the G-Three, although another type is possible. He will be meeting with the Attorney General, undoubtedly to discuss something of great importance. I will fly to Washington immediately to find out what I can. There is a flight to Mexico City in three hours. I'll be on it."

"Your source is a good one," Escobedo observed, impressed for once.

Cortez smiled. "*Sí, jefe*. Even if you are unable to determine what is being discussed here, I hope to find out over the weekend. I make no promises, but I will do my best."

"A woman," Escobedo observed. "Young and beautiful, I am sure."

"As you say. I must be off."

"Enjoy your weekend, Colonel. I will enjoy mine."

Cortez had been gone only an hour when a telex came in, informing him that last night's courier flight had failed to arrive at its destination in southwestern Georgia. The amusement that invariably accompanies receipt of top-secret information changed at once to anger. *El jefe* thought to call Cortez on his mobile phone, but remembered that his hireling refused to discuss substantive matters over what he called a "nonsecure" line. Escobedo shook his head. This *colonel* of the DGI—he was an old woman! *El jefe*'s phone twittered its own signal.

"Bingo," a man said in a van, two thousand miles away.

VOX IDENT, his computer screen announced: SUBJECT BRAVO INIT CALL TO SUBJECT ECHO FRQ 848.970MHZ CALL INIT 2349Z INTERCEPT IDENT 345.

"We may have our first big one here, Tony."

The senior technician, who'd been christened Antonio forty-seven years earlier, put on his headphones. The conversation was being taken down on high-speed tape—it was actually a three-quarter-inch videotape because of the nature of the system used to intercept the signal. Four separate machines recorded the signal.

They were Sony commercial recorders, only slightly modified by the NSA technical staff.

"Ha! Señor Bravo is pissed!" Tony observed as he caught part of the conversation. "Tell Meade that we finally caught a frozen rope down the left-field line." A "frozen rope" was the current NSA nickname for a very important signal intercept. It was baseball season, and the Baltimore Orioles were coming back.

"How's the signal?"

"Clear as a church bell. Christ, why don't I ever buy TRW stock?" Antonio paused, struggling not to laugh. "God, is he pissed!"

The call ended a minute later. Tony switched his headphone input to one of the tape machines and crab-walked his swivel chair to a teleprinter, where he started typing.

FLASH
TOP SECRET ***** CAPER
2358Z
SIGINT REPORT
INTERCEPT 345 INIT 2349Z FRQ 836.970 MHZ
INIT: SUBJECT BRAVO
RECIP: SUBJECT ECHO
B: WE'VE LOST ANOTHER DELIVERY. [AGITATION]
E: WHAT HAPPENED?
B: THE CURSED THING DIDN'T APPEAR. WHAT DO YOU THINK? [AGITATION].
E: THEY'RE DOING SOMETHING DIFFERENT. I TOLD YOU THAT. WE'RE TRYING TO FIND OUT WHAT IT IS.
B: SO WHEN ARE YOU GOING TO KNOW?
E: WE'RE WORKING ON THAT. OUR MAN IS TRAVELING TO WASHINGTON TO FIND OUT. THERE ARE SOME OTHER THINGS HAPPENING ALSO.
B: WHAT? [AGITATION]
E: I PROPOSE WE MEET TOMORROW TO DISCUSS IT.
B: THE REGULAR MEETING IS TUESDAY.
E: THIS IS IMPORTANT, EVERYONE MUST HEAR IT, PABLO.
B: CAN'T YOU TELL ME ANYTHING?
E: THEY ARE CHANGING THE RULES, THE NORTH AMERICANS. EXACTLY HOW THEY ARE CHANGING THEM WE DO NOT YET KNOW.
B: WELL, WHAT ARE WE PAYING THAT CUBAN RENEGADE FOR? [AGITATION]
E: HE IS DOING VERY WELL. PERHAPS HE WILL LEARN MORE ON HIS TRIP TO WASHINGTON. BUT WHAT WE HAVE LEARNED TO THIS POINT WILL BE THE SUBJECT OF OUR MEETING.
B: VERY WELL. I WILL SET UP THE MEETING.
E: THANK YOU, PABLO.
END CALL. DISCONNECT SIGNAL. END INTERCEPT.

"What's this 'agitation' business?"

"I can't put 'pissed' in an official TWX," Antonio pointed out. "This one's hot. We have some operational intel here." He pressed the transmit key on his terminal. The signal was addressed to a code-word destination—CAPER—which was all anyone who worked in the van knew.

* * *

Bob Ritter had just left for home, and was only a mile up on the George Washington Parkway when his secure carphone made its distinctive and, to him, irritating noise.

"Yeah?"

"CAPER traffic," the voice said.

"Right," the Deputy Director (Operations) said with a suppressed sigh. To his driver: "Take me back."

"Yes, sir."

Getting back, even for a top CIA executive, meant finding a place to reverse course, and then fight the late D.C. rush-hour traffic which, in its majesty, allows rich, poor, and important to crawl at an equal twenty miles per hour. The gate guard waved the car through, and he was in his seventh-floor office five minutes after that. Judge Moore was already gone. There were only four watch officers cleared for this operation. That was the minimum number required merely to wait for and evaluate signal traffic on the operation. The current watch officer had just come on duty. He handed over the signal.

"We have something hot," the officer said.

"You're not kidding. It's Cortez," Ritter observed after scanning the message form.

"Good bet, sir."

"Coming here . . . but we don't know what he looks like. If only the Bureau had gotten a picture of the bastard when he was in Puerto Rico. You know the description we have of him." Ritter looked up.

"Black and brown. Medium height, medium build, sometimes wears a mustache. No distinguishing marks or characteristics," the officer recited from memory. It wasn't hard to memorize nothing, and nothing was exactly what they had on Félix Cortez.

"Who's your contact at the Bureau?"

"Tom Burke, middle-level guy in the Intelligence Division. Pretty good man. He handled part of the Henderson case."

"Okay, get this to him. Maybe the Bureau can figure a way to bag the bastard. Anything else?"

"No, sir."

Ritter nodded and resumed his trip home. The watch officer returned to his own office on the fifth floor and made his call. He was in luck this night; Burke was still at his office. They couldn't discuss the matter over the phone, of course. The CIA watch officer, Paul Hooker, drove over to the FBI Building at 10th and Pennsylvania.

Though CIA and FBI are sometimes rivals in the intelligence business, and always rivals for federal budget funds, at the operational level their employees get along well enough; the barbs they trade are good-natured ones.

"There's a new tourist coming into D.C. in the next few days," Hooker announced once the door was closed.

"Like who?" Burke inquired, gesturing to his coffee machine.

Hooker declined. "Félix Cortez." The CIA officer handed over a Xerox of the telex. Portions of it had been blacked out, of course. Burke didn't take offense at this. As a member of the Intelligence Division, charged with catching spies, he was accustomed to "need-to-know."

"You're assuming that it's Cortez," the FBI agent pointed out. Then he smiled. "But I wouldn't bet against you. If we had a picture of this clown, we'd stand a fair chance of bagging him. As it is . . ." A sigh. "I'll put people at Dulles, National, and BWI. We'll try, but you can guess what the odds are." *If the Agency had gotten a photo of this mutt while he was in the field—or while he was at the KGB Academy—it would make our job a hell of a lot easier. . . .* "I'll assume that he's coming in over the next four days. We'll check all flights directly in from down there, and all connecting flights."

The problem was more one of mathematics than anything. The number of direct flights from Colombia, Venezuela, Panama, and other nearby countries directly into the D.C. area was quite modest and easy to cover. But if the subject made a connecting flight through Puerto Rico, the Bahamas, Mexico, or any number of other cities, including American ones, the number of possible connections increased by a factor of ten. If he made one more intermediary stop in the United States, the number of possible flights for the FBI to monitor took a sudden jump into the hundreds. Cortez was a KGB-trained pro, and he knew that fact as well as these two men did. The task wasn't a hopeless one. Police play for breaks all the time, because even the most skilled adversaries get careless or unlucky. But that was the game here. Their only real hope was a lucky break.

Which they would not get. Cortez caught an Avianca flight to Mexico City, then an American Airlines flight to Dallas–Fort Worth, where he cleared customs and made yet another American connection to New York City. He checked into the St. Moritz Hotel on Central Park South. By this time it was three in the morning, and he needed some rest. He left a wakeup call for ten and asked the concierge to have him a first-class ticket for the eleven o'clock Metroliner into Union Station, Washington, D.C. The Metroliners, he knew, had their own phones. He'd be able to call ahead if something went wrong. Or maybe . . . no, he decided, he didn't want to call her at work; surely the FBI tapped its own phones. The last thing Cortez did before collapsing onto the bed was to shred his plane-ticket receipts and the baggage tags on his luggage.

The phone awoke him at 9:56. *Almost seven hours' sleep,* he thought. It seemed like only a few seconds, but there was no time to dawdle. Half an hour later he appeared at the desk, tossed in his express check-out form, and collected his train ticket. The usual Manhattan midtown traffic nearly caused him to miss the train, but he made it, taking a seat in the last row of the three-across club-car smoking section. A smiling, red-vested attendant started him off with decaffeinated coffee and a copy of *USA Today,* followed by a breakfast that was no different—though a little warmer—from what he'd have gotten on an airliner. By the time the train stopped in Philadelphia, he was back asleep. Cortez figured that he'd need his rest. The attendant noted the smile on his sleeping face as he collected the breakfast tray and wondered what dreams passed through the passenger's head.

At one o'clock, while Metroliner 111 approached Baltimore, the TV lights were switched on in the White House Press Room. The reporters had already been prepped with a "deep background, not for attribution" briefing that there would be a major announcement from the Attorney General, and that it would have something to do with drugs. The major networks did not interrupt their afternoon soap operas—it was no small thing to cut away from "The Young and the Restless"—but CNN, as usual, put up their "Special Report" graphic. This was noticed at once by the intelligence watch officers in the Pentagon's National Military Command Center, each of whom had a TV on his desk tuned in to CNN. That was perhaps the most eloquent comment possible on the ability of America's intelligence agencies to keep its government informed, but one on which the major networks, for obvious reasons, had never commented.

The Attorney General strode haltingly toward the lectern. For all his experience as a lawyer, he was not an effective public speaker. You didn't need to be if your practice was corporate law and political campaigning. He was, however, photogenic and a sharp dresser, and always good for a leak on a slow news day, which explained his popularity with the media.

"Ladies and gentlemen," he began, fumbling with his notes. "You will soon be getting handouts concerning Operation TARPON. This represents the most effective operation to date against the international drug cartel." He looked up, trying to see the reporters' faces past the glare of the lights.

"Investigation by the Department of Justice, led by the FBI, has identified a number of bank accounts both in the United States and elsewhere which were being used for money-laundering on an unprecedented scale. These accounts range over twenty-nine banks from Liechtenstein to California, and their deposits exceed, at our current estimates, over six hundred fifty million dollars." He looked up again as he heard a *Goddamn!* from the assembled multitude. That elicited a smile. It was never easy to impress the White House press corps. The autowind cameras were really churning away now.

"In cooperation with six foreign governments, we have initiated the necessary steps to seize all of those funds, and also to seize eight real-estate joint-venture investments here in the United States which were the primary agency in the actual laundering operation. This is being done under the RICO—the Racketeer-Influenced and Corrupt Organization—statute. I should emphasize on that point that the real-estate ventures involve the holdings of many innocent investors; their holdings will not—I repeat *not*—be affected in any way by the government's action. They were used as dupes by the Cartel, and they will not be harmed by these seizures."

"Excuse me," Associated Press interrupted. "You did say six hundred fifty *million* dollars?"

"That is correct, more than half a *billion* dollars." The AG described generally how the information had been found, but not the way in which the first lead had been obtained, nor the precise mechanisms used to track the money. "As you know, we have treaties with several foreign governments to cover cases such as this. Those funds identified as drug-related and deposited in foreign banks will be confiscated by the governments in question. In Swiss accounts, for example, are approximately . . ." He checked his notes again. "It looks like two hundred thirty-seven million dollars, all of which now belongs to the Swiss government."

"What's our take?" *The Washington Post* asked.

"We don't know yet. It's difficult to describe the complexity of this operation—just the accounting is going to keep us busy for weeks."

"What about cooperation from the foreign governments?" another reporter wanted to know.

You gotta be kidding, the journalist next to him thought.

"The cooperation we've received on this case is simply outstanding." The Attorney General beamed. "Our friends overseas have moved with dispatch and professionalism."

Not every day you can steal this much money and call it something for the Public Good, the quiet journalist told herself.

CNN is a worldwide service. The broadcast was monitored in Colombia by two men whose job it was to keep track of the American news media. They were journalists themselves, in fact, who worked for the Colombian TV network, Inravision. One of them excused himself from the control room and made a telephone call before returning.

Tony and his partner had just come back on duty in the van, and there was a telex clipped to the wall, telling them to expect some activity on the cellular-phone circuits at about 1800 Zulu time. They weren't disappointed.

"Can we talk to Director Jacobs about this?" a reporter asked.

"Director Jacobs is taking a personal interest in the case, but is not available for comment," the AG answered. "You'll be able to talk to him next week, but at the moment he and his team are all pretty busy." That didn't break any rules. It gave the impression that Emil was in town, and the reporters, recognizing exactly what the Attorney General had said and how he had said it, collectively decided to let it slide. It fact, Emil had taken off from Andrews Air Force Base twenty-five minutes earlier.

"*Madre de Dios!*" Escobedo observed. The meeting had barely gotten past the usual social pleasantries so necessary for a conference of cutthroats. All the members of the Cartel were in the same room, which happened rarely enough. Even though the building was surrounded with a literal wall of security people, they were nervous about their safety. The building had a satellite dish on the roof, and this was immediately tuned into CNN. What was supposed to have been a discussion of unexpected happenings in their smuggling operations was suddenly sidetracked onto something far more troubling. It was especially troubling for Escobedo, moreover, since he'd been one of the three Cartel members who had urged this money-laundering scheme on his colleagues. Though all had complimented him on the efficiency of the arrangement over the last two years, the looks he was getting now were somewhat less supportive.

"There is nothing we can do?" one asked.

"It is too early to tell," replied the Cartel's equivalent of a chief financial officer. "I remind you that the money we have already taken completely through the arrangements nearly equals what our normal returns would be. So you can say that we have lost very little other than the gain we expected to reap from our investments." That sounded lame even to him.

"I think we have tolerated enough interference," Escobedo said forcefully. "The Director of the American *federales* will be here in Bogotá later today."

"Oh? And how did you discover this?"

"Cortez. I told you that hiring him would be to our benefit. I called this meeting to give you the information that he has gotten for us."

"This is too much to accept," another member agreed. "We should take action. It must be forceful."

There was general agreement. The Cartel had not yet learned that important decisions ought never to be taken in anger, but there was no one to counsel moderation. These men were not known for that quality in any case.

* * *

Train 111, Metroliner Service from New York, arrived a minute early at 1:48 P.M. Cortez walked off, carrying his two bags, and walked at once to the taxi stand at the front of the station. The cabdriver was delighted to have a fare to Dulles. The trip took just over thirty minutes, earning the cabbie what for Cortez was a decent tip: $2.00. He entered the upper level, walked to his left, took the escalator down, where he found the Hertz counter. Here he rented another large Chevy and took the spare time to load his bags. By the time he returned inside, it was nearly three. Moira was right on time. They hugged. She wasn't one to kiss in so public a place.

"Where did you park?"

"In the long-term lot. I left my bags in the car."

"Then we will go and get them."

"Where are we going?"

"There is a place on Skyline Drive where General Motors occasionally holds important conferences. There are no phones in the rooms, no televisions, no newspapers."

"I know it! How did you ever get a reservation at this late notice?"

"I've been reserving a suite for every weekend since we were last together," Cortez explained truthfully. He stopped dead in his tracks. "That sounds . . . that sounds improper?" He had the halting embarrassment down pat by this time.

Moira grabbed his arm. "Not to me."

"I can tell that this will be a long weekend." Within minutes they were on Interstate 66, heading west toward the Blue Ridge Mountains.

Four embassy security officers dressed in airline coveralls gave the area a final look, then one of them pulled out a sophisticated satellite-radio phone and gave the final clearance.

The VC-20A, the military version of the G-III executive jet, flew in with a commercial setting on its radar transponder, landing at 5:39 in the afternoon at El Dorado International Airport, about eight miles outside of Bogotá. Unlike most of the VC-20As belonging to the 89th Military Airlift Wing at Andrews Air Force Base, Maryland, this one was specially modified to fly into high-threat areas and carried jamming gear originally invented by the Israelis to counter surface-to-air missiles in the hands of terrorists . . . or businessmen. The aircraft flared out and made a perfect landing into gentle westerly winds, then taxied to a distant corner of the cargo terminal, the one the cars and jeeps were heading for. The aircraft's identity was no longer a secret to anyone who'd bothered to look, of course. It had barely stopped when the first jeeps formed up on its left side. Armed soldiers dismounted and spread out, their automatic weapons pointed at threats that might have been imaginary, or might not. The aircraft's door dropped down. There were stairs built into it, but the first man off the plane didn't bother with them. He jumped, with one hand hidden in the right side of a topcoat. He was soon joined by another security guard. Each man was a special agent of the FBI, and the job of each was the physical safety of their boss, Director Emil Jacobs. They stood within the ring of Colombian soldiers, each of whom was a member of an elite counterinsurgency unit. Every man there was nervous. There was nothing routine about security in this country. Too many had died proving otherwise.

Jacobs came out next, accompanied by his own special assistant, and Harry Jefferson, Administrator of the Drug Enforcement Administration. The last of the three stepped down just as the ambassador's limousine pulled up. It didn't stop for long. The ambassador did step out to greet his guests, but all of them were inside the car a minute later. Then the soldiers remounted their jeeps, which moved off to escort the ambassador. The aircraft's crew chief closed the Gulfstream's door, and the VC-20A, whose engines had never stopped turning, immediately taxied to take off again. Its destination was the airfield at Grenada, thoughtfully built for the Americans by the Cubans only a few years before. It would be easier to guard it there.

"How was the flight, Emil?" the ambassador asked.

"Just over five hours. Not bad," the Director allowed. He leaned back on the velvet seat of the stretch limo, which was filled to capacity. In front were the ambassador's driver and bodyguard. That made a total of four machine guns in the car, and he was sure Harry Jefferson carried his service automatic. Jacobs had never carried a gun in his life, didn't wish to bother with the things. And besides, if his two bodyguards and his assistant—another crack shot—didn't suffice to protect him, what would? It wasn't that Jacobs was an especially courageous man, just that after nearly forty years of dealing with criminals of all sorts—the Chicago mob had once threatened him quite seriously—he was tired of it all. He'd grown as comfortable as any man can be with such a thing: it was part of the scenery now, and like a pattern in the wallpaper or the color of a room's paint, he no longer noticed it.

He did notice the altitude. The city of Bogotá sits at an elevation of nearly 8,700 feet, on a plain among towering mountains. There was no air to breathe here and he wondered how the ambassador tolerated it. Jacobs was more comfortable with the biting winter winds off Lake Michigan. Even the humid pall that visited Washington every summer was better than this, he thought.

"Tomorrow at nine, right?" Jacobs asked.

"Yep." The ambassador nodded. "I think they'll go along with nearly anything we want." The ambassador, of course, didn't know what the meeting was about, which did not please him. He'd worked as chargé d'affaires at Moscow, and the security *there* wasn't as tight as it was here.

"That's not the problem," Jefferson observed. "I know they mean well—they've lost enough cops and judges proving that. Question is, will they play ball?"

"Would we, under similar circumstances?" Jacobs mused, then steered the conversation in a safer direction. "You know, we've never been especially good neighbors, have we?"

"How do you mean?" the ambassador asked.

"I mean, when it suited us to have these countries run by thugs, we let it happen. When democracy finally started to take root, we often as not stood at the sidelines and bitched if their ideas didn't agree fully with ours. And now that the druggies threaten their governments because of what our own citizens want to buy—we blame them."

"Democracy comes hard down here," the ambassador pointed out. "The Spanish weren't real big on—"

"If we'd done our job a hundred years ago—or even fifty years ago—we wouldn't have half the problems we have now. Well, we didn't do it then. We sure as hell have to do it now."

"If you have any suggestions, Emil—"

Jacobs laughed. "Hell, Andy, I'm a cop—well, a lawyer—not a diplomat. That's your problem. How's Kay?"

"Just fine." Ambassador Andy Westerfield didn't have to ask about Mrs. Jacobs. He knew Emil had buried his wife nine months earlier after a courageous fight with cancer. He'd taken it hard, of course, but there were so many good things to remember about Ruth. And he had a job to keep him busy. Everyone needed that, and Jacobs more than most.

In the terminal, a man with a 35mm Nikon and a long lens had been snapping pictures for the past two hours. When the limousine and its escorts started moving off the airport grounds, he removed the lens from the body, set both in his camera case, and walked off to a bank of telephones.

The limousine moved quickly, with one jeep in front and another behind. Expensive cars with armed escorts were not terribly unusual in Colombia, and they moved out from the airport at a brisk clip. You had to spot the license plate to know that the car was American. The four men in each jeep had not known of their escort job until five minutes before they left, and the route, though predictable, wasn't a long one. There shouldn't have been time for anyone to set up an ambush—assuming that anyone would be crazy enough to consider such a thing.

After all, killing an American ambassador was crazy; it had only happened recently in the Sudan, Afghanistan, Pakistan. . . . And no one had ever made a serious attempt on an FBI Director.

The car they drove in was a Cadillac Fleetwood chassis. Its special equipment included thick Lexan windows that could stop a machine-gun bullet, and Kevlar armor all around the passenger compartment. The tires were foam-filled against flattening, and the gas tank of a design similar to that used on military aircraft as protection against explosion. Not surprisingly, the car was known in the embassy motor pool as the Tank.

The driver knew how to handle it as skillfully as a NASCAR professional. He had engine power to race at over a hundred miles per hour; he could throw the three-ton vehicle into a bootlegger turn and reverse directions like a movie stunt driver. His eyes flickered between the road ahead and the rearview mirror. There had been one car following them, for two or three miles, but it turned off. Probably nothing, he judged. Somebody else coming home from the airport. . . . The car also had sophisticated radio gear to call for help. They were heading to the embassy. Though the ambassador had a separate residence, a pretty two-story house set on six sculpted acres of garden and woodland, it wasn't secure enough for his visitors. Like most contemporary American embassies, this one looked to be a cross between a low-rise office block and part of the Siegfried Line.

VOX IDENT, his computer screen read, two thousand miles away: VOICE 34 INIT CALL TO UNKNOWN RECIP FRQ 889.980MHZ CALL INIT 2258Z INTERCEPT IDENT 381.

Tony donned the headphones and listened in on the tape-delay system.

"Nothing," he said a moment later. "Somebody's taking a drive."

At the embassy, the legal attaché paced nervously in the lobby. Special Agent Pete Morales of the FBI should have been at the airport. It was *his* director coming in, but the security pukes said only one car because it was a surprise visit—and surprise, everyone knew, was better than a massive show of force. The everybodies who knew did not include Morales, who believed in showing force. It was bad enough having to live down here. Morales was from California; though his surname was Hispanic, his family had been in the San Francisco area when Major Frémont had arrived, and he'd had to brush up on his somewhat removed mother tongue to take his current job, which job also meant leaving his wife and kids behind in the

States. As his most recent report had told headquarters, it was dangerous down here. Dangerous for the local citizens, dangerous for Americans, and very dangerous indeed for American cops.

Morales checked his watch. About two more minutes. He started moving to the door.

"Right on time," a man noted three blocks from the embassy. He spoke into a hand-held radio.

Until recently, the RPG-7D had been the standard-issue Soviet light antitank weapon. It traces its ancestry to the German Panzerfaust, and was only recently replaced by the RPG-18, a close copy of the American M-72 LAW rocket. The adoption of the new weapon allowed millions of the old ones to be disposed of, adding to the already abundant supply in arms bazaars all over the world. Designed to punch holes in battle tanks, it is not an especially easy weapon to use. Which was why there were four of them aimed at the ambassador's limousine.

The car proceeded south, down Carrera 13 in the district known as Palermo, slowing now because of the traffic. Had the Director's bodyguards known the name of the district and designation of the street, they might have objected merely on grounds of superstition. The slow speed of the traffic here in the city itself made everyone nervous, especially the soldiers in the escort jeeps who craned their necks looking up into the windows of various buildings. It is a fact so obvious as to be misunderstood that one cannot ordinarily look into a window from outside. Even an open window is merely a rectangle darker than the exterior wall, and the eye adjusts to ambient light, not to light in a specific place. There was no warning.

What made the deaths of the Americans inevitable was something as prosaic as a traffic light. A technician was working on a balky signal—people had been complaining about it for a week—and while checking the timing mechanism, he flipped it to red. Everyone stopped on the street, almost within sight of the embassy. From third-floor windows on both sides of the street, four separate RPG-7D projectiles streaked straight down. Three hit the car, two of them on the roof.

The flash was enough. Morales was moving even before the noise reached the embassy gates, and he ran with full knowledge of the futility of the gesture. His right hand wrenched his Smith & Wesson automatic from the waist holster, and he carried it as training prescribed, pointed straight up. It took just over two minutes.

The driver was still alive, thrown from the car and bleeding to death from holes that no doctor could ever patch in time. The soldiers in the lead jeep were nowhere to be seen, though there was blood on a rear seat. The trail jeep's driver was still at the wheel, his hands clutching at a face shredded with broken glass, and the man next to him was dead, but again the other two were gone—

Then Morales knew why. Automatic weapons fire erupted in a building to his left. It started, stopped, then began again. A scream came from a window, and that also stopped. Morales wanted to race into the building, but he had no jurisdiction, and was too much a professional to risk his life so foolishly. He moved up to the smashed limousine. He knew that this, too, was futile.

They'd all died instantly, or as quickly as any man might die. The Director's two bodyguards had worn Kevlar armor. That would stop bullets, but not fragments from a high-explosive warhead, and had proven no more effective than the armor in the Tank. Morales knew what had hit the car—weapons designed to destroy tanks. Real ones. For those inside, the only remarkable thing was that you could tell that they had once been human. There was nothing anyone could do, except a priest . . . or rabbi. Morales turned away after a few seconds.

He stood alone in the street, still operating on his professional training, not letting his humanity affect his judgment. The one living soldier in view was too injured to move—probably had no idea where he was or what had happened to him. None of the people on the sidewalk had come to help . . . but some of them, he saw, were hurt, too, and their injuries occupied the attention of the others. Morales realized that the damage to the car told everyone else in view where they might best spend their efforts. The agent turned to scan up and down the street. He didn't see the technician at the light-control box. The man was already gone.

Two soldiers came out of a building, one carrying what looked like an RPG-7 launcher unit. Morales recognized one of them, Captain Edmundo Garza. There was blood on his khaki shirt and pants, and in his eyes the wild look that Morales hadn't seen since his time in the Marine Corps. Behind him, two more men dragged yet another who'd been shot in the arms and the groin. Morales holstered his automatic before going over, slowly, his hands visible until he was sure he'd been recognized.

''*Capitán* . . .'' Morales said.

''One more dead upstairs, and one of mine. Four teams. Getaway cars in the alleys.'' Garza looked at the blood on his upper arm with annoyance that was rapidly changing to appreciation of his wounds. But there was something more than shock to postpone the pain. The captain looked at the car for the first time in several minutes, hoping that his immediate impression might have been wrong and knowing that it could not be. His handsome, bloody face looked at the American and received a shake by way of reply. Garza was a proud man, a professional soldier dedicated to his country as thoroughly as any man could be, and he'd been chosen for this assignment for his combination of skill and integrity. A man who did not fear death, he had just suffered the thing all soldiers fear more. He had failed in his mission. Not knowing why only made it worse.

Garza continued to ignore his wounds, turning to their one prisoner. ''We will talk,'' the captain promised him just before he collapsed into Morales' arms.

''Hi, Jack!'' Dan and Liz Murray had just arrived at the Ryan house. Dan had to remove his automatic and holster, which he set on the shelf in the closet with something of a sheepish look.

''I figured you for a revolver,'' Jack said with a grin. It was the first time that they'd had the Murrays over.

''I miss my Python, but the Bureau's switching over to automatics. Besides, I don't chase bad guys anymore. I chase memos, and position papers, and budget estimates.'' A rueful shake of the head. ''What fun.''

''I know the feeling,'' Ryan agreed, leading Murray to the kitchen. ''Beer?''

''Sounds good to me.''

They'd first met in London, at St. Thomas's Hospital to be precise, some years earlier when Murray had been legal attaché to the American Embassy, and Ryan had been a shooting victim. Still tall and spare, his hair a little thinner but not yet gray, Murray was an affable, free-spirited man whom one would never pick for a cop, much less one of the best around. A gifted investigator, he'd hunted down every sort of criminal there was, and though he now chafed at his absence from hands-on police work, he was handling his administrative job as skillfully as all his others.

"What's this sting I heard about?" Jack asked.

"TARPON? The Cartel murdered a guy who was laundering money for them on a very big scale—and doing some major-league skimming, too. He left records behind. We found them. It's been a busy couple of weeks running all the leads down."

"I heard six-hundred-plus-million bucks."

"It'll go higher. The Swiss cracked open a new account this afternoon."

"Ouch." Ryan popped open a couple of beers. "That's a real sting, isn't it?"

"I think they'll notice this one," Murray agreed. "What's this I hear about your new job?"

"You probably heard right. It's just that you don't want to get a promotion this way."

"Yeah. I've never met Admiral Greer, but the Director thinks a lot of him."

"Two of a kind. Old-fashioned honorable gentlemen," Jack observed. "Endangered species."

"Hello, Mr. Murray," Sally Ryan said from the door.

"Mister Murray?"

"Uncle Dan!" Sally raced up and delivered a ferocious hug. "Aunt Liz says that you and Daddy better get out there," she said with a giggle.

"Why do we let them push us warriors around, Jack?"

" 'Cause they're tougher than we are?" Ryan wondered.

Dan laughed. "Yeah, that explains it. I—" Then his beeper went off. Murray pulled the small plastic box from his belt. In a moment the LCD panel showed the number he was supposed to call. "You know, I'd like to waste the bastard who invented these things."

"He's already dead," Jack replied deadpan. "He came into a hospital emergency room with chest pains, and after the doc figured out who he was, they were a little slow getting around to treating him. The doc explained later that he had had an important phone call come in, and . . . oh, well. . . ." Ryan's demeanor changed. "You need a secure line? I have one in the library."

"Color me important," Murray observed. "No. Can I use this one?"

"Sure, the bottom button's a D.C. line."

Murray punched in the number without referring to his beeper. It was Shaw's office. "Murray here. You rang, Alice? Okay . . . Hi, Bill, what gives?"

It was as though the room took a sudden chill. Ryan felt it before he understood the change in Murray's face.

"No chance that—oh, yeah, I know Pete." Murray checked his watch. "Be there in forty minutes." He hung up.

"What happened?"

"Somebody killed the Director," Dan answered simply.

"What—where?"

"Bogotá. He was down for a quiet meeting, along with the head of DEA. Flew down this afternoon. They kept it real quiet."

"No chance that—"

Murray shook his head. "The attaché down there's Pete Morales. Good agent, I worked OC with him once. He said they were all killed instantly. Emil, Harry

Jefferson, the ambassador, all the security guys.'' He stopped and read the look on Jack's face. ''Yeah, somebody had some pretty good intel on this.''

Ryan nodded. ''This is where I came in. . . .''

''I don't think there's a street agent in the Bureau who doesn't love that man.'' Murray set his beer down on the counter.

''Sorry, pal.''

''What was it you said? Endangered species?'' Murray shook his head and went to collect his wife. Ryan hadn't even closed the door behind them when his secure phone started ringing.

The Hideaway, located only a few miles from the Luray Caverns, was a modern building despite its deliberate lack of some modern amenities. While there was no in-room cable television, no pay-for-view satellite service, no complimentary paper outside the door every morning, there was air conditioning, running water, and the room-service menu was six pages long, supplemented by ten full pages of wine listings. The hotel catered to newlyweds who needed few distractions and to others trying to save their marriages from distractions. Service was on the European model. The guest wasn't expected to do anything but eat, drink, and rumple the linen, though there were saddle horses, tennis courts, and a swimming pool for those few whose suite didn't include a bathtub large enough for the purpose. Moira watched her lover tip the bellman ten dollars—far more than he ever tipped anyone—before she thought to ask the most obvious question.

''How did you register?''

''Mr. and Mrs. Juan Díaz.'' Another embarrassed look. ''Forgive me, but I didn't know what else to say. I didn't think''—he lied haltingly. ''And I didn't want—what could I say without embarrassing myself?'' he finally asked with a frustrated gesture.

''Well, I need a shower. Since we are husband and wife, you may join me. It looks big enough for two.'' She walked from the room, dropping her silk blouse on the bed as she went.

Five minutes later, Cortez decided that the shower was easily big enough for four. But as things turned out, that was just as well.

The President had flown to Camp David for the weekend, and had barely showered himself when his junior military aide—a Marine lieutenant had the duty—brought him the cordless phone.

''Yes—what is it?''

The lieutenant's first reaction on seeing the President's expression was to wonder where his pistol was.

''I want the Attorney General, Admiral Cutter, Judge Moore, and Bob Ritter flown here immediately. Tell the press secretary to call me in fifteen minutes to work on the statement. I'll be staying here for the time being. What about bringing them back home? Okay—we have a couple of hours to think about that. For now, the usual protocol. That's right. No, nothing from State. I'll handle it from here, then the secretary can have his say. Thank you.'' The President pushed the kill button on the phone and handed it back to the Marine.

''Sir, is there anything that the guard detail needs—''

''No.'' The President explained briefly what had happened. ''Carry on, Lieutenant.''

"Aye aye, sir." The Marine left.

The President put on his bathrobe and walked over to the mirror to comb his hair. He had to use the terrycloth of his sleeve to wipe the condensation off the glass. Had he noticed, he would have wondered why the look in his eyes didn't shatter it.

"Okay," the President of the United States told the mirror. "So you bastards want to play. . . ."

The flight from Andrews to Camp David was made in one of the new VH-60 Blackhawk helicopters that the 89th Military Airlift Wing had just acquired. Plushly appointed to carry VIPs from place to place, it was still too noisy for anything approximating a normal conversation. Each of the four passengers stared out the windows on the sliding doors, watching the western Maryland hills slide beneath the aircraft, each alone with his grief and his anger. The trip took twenty minutes. The pilot had been told to hurry.

On touching down, the four men were loaded into a car for the short drive to the President's cabin on the grounds. They found him hanging up the phone. It had taken half an hour to locate his press secretary, further exacerbating the President's already stormy mood.

Admiral Cutter started to say something about how sorry everyone was, but the President's expression cut him short.

The President sat down on a couch opposite the fireplace. In front of him was what most people ordinarily took to be a coffee table, but now, with the top removed, it was a set of computer screens and quiet thermal printers that tapped into the major news wire services and other government information channels. Four television sets were in the next room, tuned in to CNN and the major networks. The four visitors stared down at him, watching the anger come off the President like steam from a boiling pot.

"We will not let this one slip past with us standing by and deploring the event," the President said quietly as he looked up. "They killed my friend. They killed my ambassador. They have directly challenged the sovereign power of the United States of America. They want to play with the big boys," the President went on in a voice that was grotesquely calm. "Well, they're going to have to play by the big boys' rules. Peter," he said to the AG, "there is now an informal Presidential Finding that the drug Cartel has initiated an undeclared war against the government of the United States. They have chosen to act like a hostile nation-state. We will treat them as we would treat a hostile nation-state. As President, I am resolved to carry the fight to the enemy as we would carry it to any other originator of state-sponsored terrorism."

The AG didn't like that, but nodded agreement anyway. The President turned to Moore and Ritter.

"The gloves come off. I just made the usual wimpy-ass statement for my press secretary to deliver, but the fucking gloves come off. Come up with a plan. I want these bastards hurt. No more of this 'sending a message' crap. I want them to get the message whether the phone rings or not. Mr. Ritter, you have your hunting license, and there's no bag limit. Is that sufficiently clear?"

"Yes, sir," the DDO answered. Actually, it wasn't. The President hadn't said "kill" once, as the tape recorders that were surely somewhere in this room would show. But there were some things that you didn't do, and one of them was that you did not force the President to speak clearly when clarity was something he wished to avoid.

"Find yourselves a cabin and come up with a plan. Peter, I want you to stay here with me for a while." The next message: the Attorney General, once having acceded to the President's desire to Do Something, didn't need to know exactly what was going to be done. Admiral Cutter, who was more familiar with Camp David than the other two, led the way to one of the guest cabins. Since he was in front, Moore and Ritter could not see the smile on his face.

Ryan was just getting to his office, having driven himself in, a habit which he had just unlearned. The senior intelligence watch officer was waiting for him in the corridor as Jack got off the elevator. The briefing took a whole four minutes, after which Ryan found himself sitting in the office with nothing at all to do. It was strange. He was now privy to everything the U.S. government knew about the assassination of its people—not much more than what he'd heard on the car radio coming in, actually, though he now had names to put on the "unnamed sources." Sometimes that was important, but not this time. The DCI and DDO, he learned at once, were up at Camp David with the President.

Why not me? Jack asked himself in surprise.

It should have occurred to him immediately, of course, but he was not yet used to being a senior executive. With nothing to do, his mind went along that tangent for several minutes. The conclusion was an obvious one. He didn't need to know what was being talked about—but that had to mean that something was *already* happening, didn't it . . .? If so, what? And for how long?

By noon the next day, an Air Force C-141B Starlifter transport had landed at El Dorado International. Security was like nothing anyone had seen since the funeral of Anwar Sadat. Armed helicopters circled overhead. Armored vehicles sat with their gun tubes trained outward. A full battalion of paratroops ringed the airport, which was shut down for three hours. That didn't count the honor guard, of course, all of whom felt as though they had no honor at all, that it had been stripped away from their army and their nation by . . . *them*.

Esteban Cardinal Valdéz prayed over the coffins, accompanied by the chief rabbi of Bogotá's small Jewish community. The Vice President attended on behalf of the American government, and one by one the Colombian Army handed the caskets over to enlisted pallbearers from all of the American uniformed services. The usual, predictable speeches were made, the most eloquent being a brief address by Colombia's Attorney General, who shed unashamed tears for his friend and college classmate. The Vice President boarded his aircraft and left, followed by the big Lockheed transport.

The President's statement, already delivered, spoke of reaffirming the rule of law to which Emil Jacobs had dedicated his life. But that statement seemed as thin as the air at El Dorado International even to those who didn't know better.

In the town of Eight Mile, Alabama, a suburb of Mobile, a police sergeant named Ernie Braden was cutting his front lawn with a riding mower. A burglary investigator, he knew all the tricks of the people whose crimes he handled, including how to bypass complex alarm systems, even the sophisticated models used by wealthy investment bankers. That skill, plus the information he picked up from office chatter—the narcs' bullpen was right next to the burglary section—enabled him to offer his services to people who had money with which to pay for the orthodonture and education of his children. It wasn't so much that Braden was a corrupt cop as that he'd simply been on the job for over twenty years and no longer gave much of a damn. If people wanted to use drugs, then the hell with them. If druggies wanted to kill one another off, then so much the better for the rest of society. And if some arrogant prick of a banker turned out to be a crook among crooks, then that also was too bad; all Braden had been asked to do was shake the man's house to make sure that he'd left no records behind. It was a shame about the man's wife and kids, of course, but that was called playing with fire.

Braden rationalized the damage done to society simply by continuing to investigate his burglaries, and even catching a real hood from time to time, though that was rare enough. Burglary was a pretty safe crime to commit. It never got the attention it deserved. Neither did the people whose job it was to track them down—probably the most unrewarded segment of the law-enforcement profession. He'd been taking the lieutenant's exam for nine years, and never quite made it. Braden needed or at least wanted the money that the promotion would bring, only to see the promotions go to the hotshots in Narcotics and Homicide while he slaved away . . . and why not take the goddamned money? More than anything else, Ernie Braden was tired of it all. Tired of the long hours. Tired of the crime victims who took their frustration out on him when he was just trying to do his job. Tired of being unappreciated within his own community of police officers. Tired of being sent out to local schools for the *pro forma* anticrime lectures that nobody ever listened to. He was even tired of coaching little-league baseball, though that had once been the single joy of his life. Tired of just about everything. But he couldn't afford to retire, either. Not yet, anyway.

The noise from the Sears riding mower crackled through the hot, humid air of the quiet street on which he and his family lived. He wiped a handkerchief across his sweaty brow and contemplated the cold beer he'd have as soon as he was finished. It could have been worse. Until three years ago he'd pushed a goddamned Lawn-Boy across the grass. At least now he could sit down as he did his weekly chore, cutting the goddamned grass. His wife had a real thing about the lawn and garden. As if it mattered, Braden grumbled.

He concentrated on the job at hand, making sure that the spinning blades had at least two sweeps over every square inch of the green crap that, this early in the season, grew almost as fast as you cut it. He didn't notice the Plymouth minivan coming down the street. Nor did he know that the people who paid him his supplementary income were most unhappy with a recent clandestine effort he'd made on their behalf.

Braden had several eccentricities, as do many men and most police officers. In his case, he never went anywhere unarmed. Not even to cut the grass. Under the back of his greasy shirt was a Smith & Wesson Chief's Special, a five-shot stainless steel revolver that was as close as he'd ever get to something with "chief" written on it. When he finally noticed the minivan pull up behind his Chevy Citation, he took little note of it, except that there were two men in it, and they seemed to be looking at him.

His cop's instinct didn't entirely fail him, however. They were looking real hard at him. That made him look back, mainly in curiosity. Who'd be interested in him on a Saturday afternoon? When the passenger-side door opened and he saw the gun, that question faded away.

When Braden rolled off the mower, his foot came off the brake pedal, which had the opposite effect as in a car. The mower stopped in two feet, its blades still churning away on the bluegrass-and-fescue mix of the policeman's front yard.

Braden came off just at the ejection port of the mower assembly, and felt tiny bits of grit and sand peppering his knees, but that, too, was not a matter of importance at the moment. His revolver was already out when the man from the van fired his first round.

He was using an Ingram Mac-10, probably a 9-millimeter, and the man didn't know how to use it well. His first round was roughly on target, but the next eight merely decorated the sky as the notoriously unstable weapon jerked out of control, not even hitting the mower. Sergeant Braden fired two rounds back, but the range was over ten yards, and the Chief's Special had only a two-inch barrel, which gave it an effective combat range measured in feet, not yards. With the instant and unexpected stress added to his poorly selected weapon, he managed to hit the van behind his target with only one round.

But machine-gun fire is a highly distinctive sound—not the least mistakable for firecrackers or any other normal noise—and the neighborhood immediately realized that something very unusual was happening. At a house across the street a fifteen-year-old boy was cleaning his rifle. It was an old Marlin .22 lever-action that had once belonged to his grandfather, and its proud owner had learned to play third base from Sergeant Braden, whom he thought to be a really neat guy. The young man in question, Erik Sanderson, set down his cleaning gear and walked to the window just in time to see his former coach shooting from behind his mower at somebody. In the clarity that comes in such moments, Erik Sanderson realized that people were trying to kill his coach, a police officer, that he had a rifle and cartridges ten feet away, and that it Would Be All Right for him to use the rifle to come to the aid of the policeman. The fact that he'd spent the morning plinking away at tin cans merely meant that he was ready. Erik Sanderson's main ambition in life was to become a U.S. Marine, and he seized the chance to get an early feel for what it was all about.

While the sound of gunfire continued to crackle around the wooded street, he grabbed the rifle and a handful of the small copper-colored rimfire cartridges and ran out to the front porch. First he twisted the spring-loaded rod that pushed rounds down the magazine tube which hung under the barrel. He pulled it out too far, dropping it, but the young man had the good sense to ignore that for the moment. He fed the .22 rounds into the loading slot one at a time, surprised that his hands were already sweaty. When he had fourteen rounds in, he bent down to get the rod, and two rounds fell out the front of the tube. He took the time to reload them, reinserted the rod, twisting it shut, then slammed his hand down and up on the lever, loading the gun and cocking the exposed hammer.

He was surprised to see that he didn't have a shot, and ran down the sidewalk to the street, taking a position across the hood of his father's pickup truck. From this point he could see two men, each firing a submachine gun from the hip. He looked just in time to see Sergeant Braden fire off his last round, which missed as badly as the first four had. The police officer turned to run for the safety of his house, but tripped over his own feet and had trouble getting up. Both gunmen advanced on Braden, loading new magazines into their weapons. Erik Sanderson's hands were trembling as he shouldered his rifle. It had old-fashioned iron sights, and he had to stop and remind himself how to line them up as he'd been taught in Boy Scouts, with the front-sight post centered in the notch of the rear-sight leaf, the top of the post even with the top of the leaf as he maneuvered it on a target.

He was horrified to be too late. Both men blew his little-league coach to shreds with extended bursts at point-blank range. Something snapped inside Erik's head at that moment. He sighted on the head of the nearer gunman and jerked off his round.

Like most young and inexperienced shooters, he immediately looked up to see what had happened. Nothing. He'd missed—with a rifle at a range of only thirty yards, he'd missed. Amazed, he sighted again and squeezed the trigger, but nothing happened. The hammer was down. He'd forgotten to cock the rifle. Swearing something his mother would have slapped him to hear, he reloaded the Marlin .22 and took exquisitely careful aim, squeezing off his next shot.

The murderers hadn't heard his first shot, and with their ears still ringing from their own shots, they didn't hear the second, but one man's head jerked to the side with the wasp's-sting impact of the round. The man knew what had happened, turned to his left, and fired off a long burst despite the crushing pain that seized his head in an instant. The other one saw Erik and fired as well.

But the young man was now jacking rounds into the breech of his rifle as fast as he could fire them. He watched in rage as he kept missing, unconsciously flinching as bullets came his way, trying to kill both men before they could get back into their car. He had the satisfaction of seeing them duck behind cover, and wasted his last three rounds trying to shoot through the car body to get them. But a .22 can't accomplish that, and the minivan pulled away.

Erik watched it pull away, wishing he'd loaded more rounds into his rifle, wishing that he could try a shot through the back window before the car turned right and disappeared.

The young man didn't have the courage to go over and see what had happened to Sergeant Braden. He just stayed there, leaning across the truck, cursing himself for letting them get away. He didn't know, and would never believe, that he had, in fact, done better than many trained police officers could have done.

In the minivan, one of the gunmen took more note of the bullet in his chest than the one in his head. But it was the head shot that would kill him. As the man bent down, a lacerated artery let go completely and showered the inside of the car with blood, much to the surprise of the dying man, who had but a few seconds to realize what had happ—

Another Air Force flight, as luck had it, also a C-141B, took Mr. Clark out of Panama, heading for Andrews, where rapid preparations were being made for the arrival ceremony. Before the funeral flight arrived, Clark was in Langley talking to his boss, Bob Ritter. For the first time in a generation, the Operations Directorate had been granted a presidential hunting license. John Clark, carried on the personnel rolls as a case-officer instructor, was the CIA chief hunter. He hadn't been asked to exercise that particular talent in a very long time, but he still knew how.

Ritter and Clark didn't watch the TV coverage of the arrival. All that was part of history now, and while both men had an interest in history, it was mainly in the sort that is never written down.

"We're going to take another look at the idea you handed me at St. Kitts," the Deputy Director (Operations) said.

"What's the objective?" Clark asked carefully. It wasn't hard to guess why this was happening, or the originator of the directive. That was the reason for his caution.

"The short version is revenge," Ritter answered.

"Retribution is a more acceptable word," Clark pointed out. Lacking in formal education though he was, he did read a good deal.

"The targets represent a clear and present danger to the security of the United States."

"The President said that?"

''His words,'' Ritter affirmed.

''Fine. That makes it all legal. Not any less dangerous, but legal.''

''Can you do it?''

Clark smiled in a distant, smoky way. ''I run my side of the op my way. Otherwise, forget it. I don't want to die from oversight. No interference from this end. You give me the target list and the assets I need. I do the rest, my way, my schedule.''

''Agreed,'' Ritter nodded.

Clark was more than surprised by that. ''Then I can do it. What about the kids we have running around in the jungle?''

''We're pulling them out tonight.''

''To be reinserted where?'' Clark asked.

Ritter told him.

''That's really dangerous,'' the case officer observed, though he was not surprised by the answer. It had probably been planned all along. But, if it had . . .

''We know that.''

''I don't like it,'' Clark said after a moment's thought. ''It complicates things.''

''We don't pay you to like it.''

Clark had to agree to that. He was honest enough with himself, though, to admit that part of it he did like. A job such as this, after all, had gotten him into the protective embrace of the Central Intelligence Agency in the first place, so many years before. But that job had been on a free-agent basis. This one was legal, but arguably. Once that would not have mattered to Mr. Clark, but with a wife and kids, it did now.

''Do I get to see the family for a couple of days?''

''Sure. It'll take a while to get things in place. I'll have all the information you need messengered down to The Farm.''

''What do we call this one?''

''RECIPROCITY.''

''I guess that about covers it.'' Clark's face broke into a grin. He walked out of the room toward the elevator. The new DDI was there, Dr. Ryan, heading to Judge Moore's office. They'd never quite met, Clark and Ryan, and this wasn't the time, though their lives had already touched on two occasions.

14. Snatch and Grab

''I must thank your Director Jacobs,'' Juan said. ''Perhaps we will meet someday.'' He'd taken his time with this one. Soon, he judged, he'd be able to extract any information he wanted from her with the same intimate confidence that might be expected of husband and wife—after all, true love did not allow for secrets, did it?

''Perhaps,'' Moira replied after a moment. Already part of her was thinking that the Director would come to her wedding. It wasn't too much to hope for, was it?

''What did he travel to Colombia for, anyway?'' he asked while his fingertips did some more exploring over what was now very familiar ground.

"Well, it's public information now. They called it Operation TARPON." Moira explained on for several minutes during which Juan's caresses didn't miss a beat.

Which was only due to his experience as an intelligence officer. He actually found himself smiling lazily at the ceiling. *The fool. I warned him. I warned him more than once in his own office, but no—he was too smart, too confident in his own cleverness to take my advice. Well, maybe the stupid bastard will heed my advice now. . . .* It took another few moments before he found himself asking how his employer would react. That was when the smiling and the caresses stopped.

"Something wrong, Juan?"

"Your director picked a dangerous time to visit Bogotá. They will be very angry. If they discover that he is there—"

"The trip is a secret. Their attorney general is an old friend—I think they went to school together, and they've known each other for forty years."

The trip was a secret. Cortez told himself that they couldn't be so foolish as to—but they could. He was amazed that Moira didn't feel the chill that swept over his body. But what could he do?

As was true of the families of military people and sales executives, Clark's family was accustomed to having him away at short notice and for irregular intervals. They were also used to having him reappear without much in the way of warning. It was almost a game, and one, strangely enough, to which his wife didn't object. In this case he took a car from the CIA pool and made the two-and-a-half-hour drive to Yorktown, Virginia, by himself to think over the operation he was about to undertake. By the time he turned off Interstate 64, he'd answered most of the procedural questions, though the exact details would wait until he'd had a chance to go over the intelligence package that Ritter had promised to send down.

Clark's house was that of a middle-level executive, a four-bedroom split-foyer brick dwelling set in an acre of the long-needled pines common to the American South. It was a ten-minute drive from The Farm, the CIA's training establishment whose post-office address is Williamsburg, Virginia, but which is actually closer to Yorktown, adjacent to an installation in which the Navy keeps both submarine-launched ballistic missiles and their nuclear warheads. The development in which he lived was mainly occupied by other CIA instructors, obviating the need for elaborate stories for the neighbors' benefit. His family, of course, had a pretty good idea what he did for a living. His two daughters, Maggie, seventeen, and Patricia, fourteen, occasionally called him "Secret Agent Man," which they'd picked up from the revival of the Patrick McGoohan TV series on one of the cable channels, but they knew not to discuss it with their schoolmates—though they would occasionally warn their boyfriends to behave as responsibly as possible around their father. It was an unnecessary warning. On instinct, most men watched their behavior around Mr. Clark. John Clark did not have horns and hooves, but it seldom took more than a single glance to know that he was not to be trifled with, either. His wife, Sandy, knew even more, including what he had done before joining the Agency. Sandy was a registered nurse who taught student nurses in the operating rooms of the local teaching hospital. As such she was accustomed to dealing with issues of life and death, and she took comfort from the fact that her husband was one of the few "laymen" who understood what that was all about, albeit from a reversed perspective. To his wife and children, John Terence Clark was a devoted husband and father, if somewhat overly protective at times. Maggie had once complained that he'd scared off one prospective "steady" with nothing more than a look. That the boy in question had later been arrested for drunken driving had only proved her father correct, rather to her chagrin. He was also a far easier touch than their mother on issues like privileges and had a ready shoulder to cry on, when he was home. At home, his counsel was invariably quiet and reasoned, his language mild, and his demeanor relaxed, but his family knew that away from home he was something else entirely. They didn't care about that.

He pulled into the driveway just before dinnertime, taking his soft two-suiter in through the kitchen to find the smells of a decent dinner. Sandy had been surprised too many times to overreact on the matter of how much food she'd prepared.

"Where have you been?" Sandy asked rhetorically, then went into her usual guessing game. "Not much work done on the tan. Someplace cold or cloudy?"

"Spent most of my time indoors," Clark replied honestly. *Stuck with a couple of clowns in a damned commo van on a hilltop surrounded by jungle. Just like the bad old days. Almost.* For all her intelligence, she almost never guessed where he'd been. But then, she wasn't supposed to.

"How long . . . ?"

"Only a couple of days, then I have to go out again. It's important."

"Anything to do with—" Her head jerked toward the kitchen TV.

Clark just smiled and shook his head.

"What do you think happened?"

"From what I see, the druggies got real lucky," he said lightly.

Sandy knew what her husband thought of druggies, and why. Everyone had a pet hate. That was his—and hers; she'd been a nurse too long, had too often seen the results of substance abuse, to think otherwise. It was the one thing he'd lectured the girls on, and though they were as rebellious as any pair of healthy adolescents, it was one line they didn't approach, much less cross.

"The President sounds angry."

"How would you feel? The FBI Director was his friend—as far as a politician has friends." Clark felt the need to qualify the statement. He was wary of political figures, even the ones he'd voted for.

"What is he going to do about it?"

"I don't know, Sandy." *I haven't quite figured it out yet.* "Where are the kids?"

"They went to Busch Gardens with their friends. There's a new coaster, and they're probably screaming their brains out."

"Do I have time to shower? I've been traveling all day."

"Dinner in thirty minutes."

"Fine." He kissed her again and headed for the bedroom with his bag. Before entering the bathroom, he emptied his dirty laundry into the hamper. Clark would give himself one restful day with the family before starting on his mission planning. There wasn't that much of a hurry. For missions of this sort, haste made death. He hoped the politicians would understand that.

Of course, they wouldn't, he told himself on the way to the shower. They never did.

"Don't feel bad," Moira told him. "You're tired. I'm sorry I've worn you out." She cradled his face to her chest. A man was not a machine, after all, and five times in just over one day's time . . . what could she fairly expect of her lover? He had to sleep, had to rest. As did she, Moira realized, drifting off herself.

Within minutes, Cortez gently disengaged himself, watching her slow, steady breathing, a dreamy smile on her placid face while he wondered what the hell he could do. If anything. Place a phone call—risk everything for a brief conversation on a nonsecure line? The Colombian police or the Americans, or *somebody* had to have taps on all those phones. No, that was more dangerous than doing nothing at all.

His professionalism told him that the safest course of action was to do nothing. Cortez looked down at himself. Nothing was precisely what he had just accomplished. It was the first time that had happened in a very long time.

Team KNIFE, of course, was completely—if not blissfully—unaware of what had transpired the previous day. The jungle had no news service, and their radio was for official use only. That made the new message all the more surprising. Chavez and Vega were again on duty at the observation post, enduring the muggy heat that followed a violent thunderstorm. There had been two inches of rain in the previous hour, and their observation point was now a shallow puddle, and there would be more rain in the afternoon before things cleared off.

Captain Ramirez appeared, without much in the way of warning this time, even to Chavez, whose woodcraft skills were a matter of considerable pride. He rationalized to himself that the captain had learned from watching him.

''Hey, Cap'n,'' Vega greeted their officer.

''Anything going on?'' Ramirez asked.

Chavez answered from behind his binoculars. ''Well, our two friends are enjoying their morning siesta.'' There would be another in the afternoon, of course. He was pulled away from the lenses by the captain's next statement.

''I hope they like it. It's their last one.''

''Say again, Cap'n?'' Vega asked.

''The chopper's coming in to pick us up tonight. That's the LZ right there, troops.'' Ramirez pointed to the airstrip. ''We waste this place before we leave.''

Chavez evaluated that statement briefly. He'd never liked druggies. Having to sit here and watch the lazy bastards go about their business as matter-of-factly as a man on a golf course hadn't mitigated his feelings a dot.

Ding nodded. ''Okay, Cap'n. How we gonna do it, sir?''

''Soon as it's dark, you and me circle around the north side. Rest of the squad forms up in two fire teams to provide fire support in case we need it. Vega, you and your SAW stay here. The other one goes down about four hundred meters. After we do the two guards, we booby-trap the fuel drums in the shack, just as a farewell present. The chopper'll pick us up at the far end at twenty-three hundred. We bring the bodies out with us, probably dump 'em at sea.''

Well, how about that, Chavez thought. ''We'll need like thirty-forty minutes to get around to them, just to play it safe and all, but the way those two fuckers been actin', no sweat, sir.'' The sergeant knew that the killing would be his job. He had the silenced weapon.

''You're supposed to ask me if this is for-real,'' Captain Ramirez pointed out. He had done just that over the satellite radio.

''Sir, you say do it, I figure it's for-real. It don't bother me none,'' Staff Sergeant Domingo Chavez assured his commander.

''Okay—we'll move out as soon as it's dark.''

''Yes, sir.''

The captain patted both men on the shoulder and withdrew to the rally point. Chavez watched him leave, then pulled out his canteen. He unscrewed the plastic top and took a long pull before looking over at Vega.

"*Fuck!*" the machine-gunner observed quietly.

"Whoever's runnin' this party musta grown a pair o' balls," Ding agreed.

"Be nice to get back to a place with showers and air conditioning," Vega said next. That two people would have to die to make that possible was, once it was decided, a matter of small consequence. It bemused both men somewhat that after years of uniformed service they were finally being told to do the very thing for which they'd trained endlessly. The moral issue never occurred to them. They were soldiers of their country. Their country had decided that those two dozing men a few hundred meters away were enemies worthy of death. That was that, though both men wondered what it would actually be like to do it.

"Let's plan this one out," Chavez said, getting back to his binoculars. "I want you to be careful with that SAW, *Oso*."

Vega considered the situation. "I won't fire to the left of the shack unless you call in."

"Yeah, okay. I'll come in from the direction of that big-ass tree. Shouldn't be no big deal," he thought aloud.

"Nah, shouldn't be."

Except that this time it was all real. Chavez stayed on the glasses, examining the men whom he would kill in a few hours.

Colonel Johns got his stand-to order at roughly the same time as all of the field teams, along with a whole new set of tactical maps that were for further study. He and Captain Willis went over the plan for this night in the privacy of their room. There was a snatch-and-grab tonight. The troops they'd inserted were coming back out far earlier than scheduled. PJ suspected that he knew why. Part of it, anyway.

"Right on the airfields?" the captain wondered.

"Yeah, well, either all four were dry holes, or our friends are going to have to secure them before we land for the snatch-and-grab."

"Oh." Captain Willis understood after a moment's thought.

"Get ahold of Buck and have him check the miniguns out again. He'll get the message from that. I want to take a look at the weather for tonight."

"Pickup order reverse from the drop-off?"

"Yeah—we'll tank fifty miles off the beach and then again after we make the pickup."

"Right." Willis walked out to find Sergeant Zimmer. PJ went in the opposite direction, heading for the base meteorological office. The weather for tonight was disappointing: light winds, clear skies, and a crescent moon. Perfect flying weather for everyone else, it was not what special-ops people hoped for. Well, there wasn't much you could do about that.

They checked out of The Hideaway at noon. Cortez thanked whatever fortune smiled down on him that it had been her idea to cut the weekend short, claiming that she had to get back to her children, though he suspected that she had made a conscious decision to go easy on her weary lover. No woman had ever felt the need to take pity on him before, and the insult of it was balanced against his need to find out what the hell was going on.

They drove up Interstate 81, in silence as usual. He'd rented a car with an ordinary bench seat, and she sat in the center, leaning against him with his right arm wrapped warmly around her shoulder. Like teenagers, almost, except for the silence, and again he found himself appreciating her for it. But it wasn't for the quiet passion now. His mind was racing far faster than the car, which he kept exactly at the posted limit. He could have turned on the car radio, but that would have been out of character. He couldn't risk that, could he? If his employer had only exercised intelligence—and he had plenty of that, Cortez compelled himself to admit—then he still had his arm draped over a supremely valuable source of strategic intelligence. Escobedo took an appropriately long view of his business operations. He understood—but Cortez remembered the man's arrogance, too. How easily he took offense—it wasn't enough for him to win, Escobedo also felt the need to humiliate, crush, utterly destroy those who offended him in the slightest way. He had power, and the sort of money normally associated only with governments, but he lacked perspective. For all his intelligence, he was a man ruled by childish emotions, and that thought merely grew in Cortez's mind as he turned onto I-66, heading east now, for Washington. It was so strange, he mused with a thin, bitter smile, that in a world replete with information, he was forced to speculate like a child when he could have all he needed merely from the twist of a radio knob, but he commanded himself to do without.

They reached the airport parking lot right on time. He pulled up to Moira's car and got out to unload her bags.

"Juan . . ."

"Yes?"

"Don't feel badly about last night. It was my fault," she said quietly.

He managed a grin. "I already told you that I am no longer a young man. I have proved it true. I will rest for the next time so that I will do better."

"When—"

"I don't know. I will call you." He kissed her gently. She drove off a minute later, and he stood there in the parking lot watching her leave, as she would have expected. Then he got into his car. It was nearly four o'clock, and he flipped on the radio to get the hourly news broadcast. Two minutes after that he'd driven the car to the return lot, taken out his bags, and walked into the terminal, looking for the first plane anywhere. A United flight to Atlanta was the next available, and he knew that he could make the necessary connections at that busy terminal. He barely squeezed aboard at the last call.

Moira Wolfe drove home with a smile tinged with guilt. What had happened to Juan the previous night was one of the most humiliating things a man could experience, and it was all her fault. She'd demanded too much of him and he was, as he'd said himself, no longer young. She'd let her enthusiasm take charge of her own judgment, and hurt a man whom she—loved. She was certain now. Moira had thought she'd never know the emotion again, but there it was, with all the carefree splendor of her youth, and if Juan lacked the vigor of those years, he more than compensated with his patience and fantastic skill. She reached down and turned on her radio to an oldies FM channel, and for the remainder of her drive basked in the glow of the most pleasant of emotions, her memories of youthful happiness brought further to the fore by the sounds of the teenage ballads to which she'd danced thirty years before.

She was surprised to see what looked like a Bureau car parked across the street from her house, but it might just as easily have been a cheap rental or something else—except for the radio antenna, she realized. It was a Bureau car. That was odd, she thought. She parked against the curb and got out her bags, walking up the sidewalk, but when the door was opened, she saw Frank Weber, one of the Director's security detail.

"Hi, Frank." Special Agent Weber helped her with the bags, but his expression was serious. "Something wrong?"

There wasn't any easy way of telling her, though Weber felt guilty for spoiling what must have been a very special weekend for her.

"Emil was killed Friday evening. We've been trying to reach you since then."

"What?"

"They got him on the way to the embassy. The whole detail—everybody. Emil's funeral's tomorrow. The rest of 'em are Tuesday."

"Oh, my God." Moira sat on the nearest chair. "Eddie—Leo?" She thought of the young agents on Emil's protection detail as her own kids.

"All of them," Weber repeated.

"I didn't know," she said. "I haven't seen a paper or turned on a TV in—since Friday night. Where—?"

"Your kids went out to the movies. We need you to come down to help us out with a few things. We'll have somebody here to look after them for you."

It was several minutes before she was able to go anywhere. The tears started as soon as the reality of Weber's words got past her newly made storehouse of other feelings.

Captain Ramirez didn't like the idea of accompanying Chavez. It wasn't cowardice, of course, but a question of what his part of the job actually was. His command responsibilities were muddled in some ways. As a captain who had recently commanded a company, he had learned that "commanding" isn't quite the same thing as "leading." A company commander is supposed to stay a short distance back from the front line and manage—the Army doesn't like that word—the combat action, maneuvering his units and keeping an overview of the battle underway so that he could control matters while his platoon leaders handled the actual fighting. Having learned to "lead from the front" as a lieutenant, he was supposed to apply his lessons at the next higher level, though there would be times when the captain was expected to take the lead. In this case he was commanding only a squad, and though the mission demanded circumspection and command judgment, the size of his unit demanded personal leadership. Besides, he could not very well send two men out on their first killing mission without being there himself, even though Chavez had far superior movement skills than Captain Ramirez ever expected to attain. The contradiction between his command and leadership responsibilities troubled the young officer, but he came down, as he had to, on the side of leading. He could not exercise command, after all, if his men didn't have confidence in his ability to lead. Somehow he knew that if this one went right, he'd never have the same problem again. Maybe that's how it always worked, he told himself.

After setting up his two fire teams, he and Chavez moved out, heading around the northern side of the airstrip with the sergeant in the lead. It went smoothly. The two targets were still lolling around, smoking their joints—or whatever they were—and talking loudly enough to be heard through a hundred meters of trees. Chavez had planned their approach carefully, drawing on previous nights' perimeter patrolling which Captain Ramirez had ordered. There were no surprises, and after twenty minutes they curved back in and again saw where the airstrip was. Now they moved more slowly.

Chavez kept the lead. The narrow trail that the trucks followed to get in here was a convenient guide. They stayed on the north side of it, which would keep them out of the fire lanes established for the squad's machine guns. Right on time, they sighted the shack. As planned, Chavez waited for his officer to close up from his approach interval of ten meters. They communicated with hand signals. Chavez would move straight in with the captain to his right front. The sergeant would do the shooting, but if anything went wrong, Ramirez would be in position to support him at once. The captain tapped out four dashes on the transmit key of his radio and got two signals back. The squad was in place on the far side of the strip, aware of what was about to happen and ready to play its part in the action if needed.

Ramirez waved Ding forward.

Chavez took a deep breath, surprised at how rapidly his heart was beating. After all, he'd done this a hundred times before. He jerked his arms around just to get loose, then adjusted the fit of his weapon's sling. His thumb went down on the selector switch, putting the MP-5 on the three-round-burst setting. The sights were painted with small amounts of tritium, and glowed just enough to be visible in the near-total darkness of the equatorial forest. His night-vision goggles were stowed in a pocket. They'd just get in the way if he tried to use them.

He moved very slowly now, moving around trees and bushes, finding firm, uncluttered places for his feet or pushing the leaves out of his way with his toe before setting his boot down for the next step. It was all business. The obvious tension in his body disappeared, though there was something like a buzz in his ear that told him that this was not an exercise.

There.

They were standing in the open, perhaps two meters apart, twenty meters from the tree against which Chavez leaned. They were still talking, and though he could understand their words easily enough, for some reason it was as foreign to him as the barking of dogs. Ding could have gotten closer, but didn't want to take the chance, and twenty meters was close enough—sixty-six feet. It was a clear shot past another tree to both of them.

Okay.

He brought the gun up slowly, centering the ringed forward sight in the aperture rear sight, making sure that he could see the white circle all around, and putting the center post right on the black, circular mass that represented the back of a human head that was no longer part of a human being—it was just a target, just a thing. His finger squeezed gently on the trigger.

The weapon jerked slightly in his grip, but the double-looped sling kept it firmly in place. The target dropped. He moved the gun right even as it fell. The next target was spinning around in surprise, giving him a dull white circle of reflected moonlight to aim at. Another burst. There had hardly been any noise at all. Chavez waited, moving his weapon back and forth across the two bodies, but there was no movement.

Chavez darted out of the trees. One of the bodies clutched an AK-47. He kicked it loose and pulled a penlight from his breast pocket, shining it on the targets. One had taken all three rounds in the back of the head. The other had only caught two, but both through the forehead. The second one's face showed surprise. The first one no longer had a face. The sergeant knelt by the bodies and looked around for further movement and activity. Chavez's only immediate emotion was one of elation. Everything he'd learned and practiced—it all worked! Not exactly easy, but it wasn't a big deal, really.

Ninja really does *own the night.*

Ramirez came over a moment later. There was only one thing he could say.

"Nice work, Sergeant. Check out the shack." He activated his radio. "This is Six. Targets down, move in."

The squad was over to the shack in a couple of minutes. As was the usual practice with armies, they clustered around the bodies of the dead guards, getting their first sample of what war was really all about. The intelligence specialist went through their pockets while the captain got the squad spread out in a defensive perimeter.

"Nothing much here," the intel sergeant told his boss.

"Let's go see the shack." Chavez had made sure that there was no additional guard whom they might have overlooked. Ramirez found four gasoline drums and a hand-crank pump. A carton of cigarettes was sitting on one of the gasoline drums, evoking a withering comment from the captain. There was some canned food on a few rough-cut shelves, and a two-roll pack of toilet paper. No books, documents, or maps. A well-thumbed deck of cards was the only other thing found.

"How you wanna booby-trap it?" the intelligence sergeant asked. He was also a former Green Beret, and an expert on setting booby traps.

"Three-way."

" 'Kay." It was easily done. He dug a small depression in the dirt floor with his hands, taking some wood scraps to firm up the sides. A one-pound block of C-4 plastic explosive—the whole world used it—went snugly into the hole. He inserted two electrical detonators and a pressure switch like the one used for a land mine. The control wires were run along the dirt floor to switches at the door and window, and were set as to be invisible to outside inspection. The sergeant buried the wires under an inch of dirt. Satisfied, he rocked the drum around, bringing it down gently on the pressure switch. If someone opened the door or the window, the C-4 would go off directly underneath a fifty-five-gallon drum of aviation gasoline, with predictable results. Better still, if someone were very clever indeed and defeated the electrical detonators on the door and window, he would then follow the wires to the oil drums in order to recover the explosives for his own later use . . . and that very clever person would be removed from the other team. Anyone could kill a dumb enemy. Killing the smart ones required artistry.

"All set up, sir. Let's make sure nobody goes near the shack from now on, sir," the intelligence sergeant told his captain.

"Roger that." The word went out at once. Two men dragged the bodies into the center of the field, and after that, they all settled down to wait for the helicopter. Ramirez redeployed his men to keep the area secured, but the main object of concern now was to have every man inventory his gear to make sure that nothing was left behind.

PJ handled the refueling. The good visibility helped, but would also help if there were anyone on the surface looking for them. The drogue played out from the wing tank of the MC-130E Combat Talon on the end of a reinforced rubber hose, and the Pave Low's refueling probe extended telescopically, stabbing into the center of it. Though it was often observed that having a helicopter refuel in this way seemed a madly unnatural act—the probe and drogue met twelve feet under the edge of the rotor arc, and contact between blade tips and hose meant certain death for the helicopter crew—the Pave Low crews always responded that it was a very natural act indeed, and one in which, of course, they had ample practice. That didn't alter the fact that Colonel Johns and Captain Willis concentrated to a remarkable degree for the whole procedure, and didn't utter a single unnecessary syllable until it was over:

"Breakaway, breakaway," PJ said as he backed off the drogue and withdrew his probe. He pulled up on the collective and eased back on the stick to pull his rotors up and away from the hose. On command, the MC-130E climbed to a comfortable cruising altitude, where it would circle until the helicopter returned for another fill-up. The Pave Low III turned for the beach, heading down to cross at an unpopulated point.

"Uh-oh," Chavez whispered to himself when he heard the noise. It was the laboring sound of a V-8 engine that needed service, and a new muffler. It was getting louder by the second.

"Six, this is Point, over," he called urgently.

"Six here. Go," Captain Ramirez replied.

"We got company coming in. Sounds like a truck, sir."

"KNIFE, this is Six," Ramirez reacted immediately. "Pull back to the west side. Take your covering positions. Point, fall back now!"

"On the way." Chavez left his listening post on the dirt road and raced back past the shack—he gave it a wide berth—and across the landing strip. There he found Ramirez and Guerra pulling the dead guards toward the far treeline. He helped the captain carry his burden into cover, then came back to assist the operations sergeant. They made the shelter of the trees with twenty seconds to spare.

The pickup traveled with lights ablaze. The glow snaked left and right along the trail, glowing through the underbrush before coming out just next to the shack. The truck stopped, and you could almost see the puzzlement even before the engine was switched off and the men dismounted. As soon as the lights were off, Chavez activated his night goggles. As before, there were four, two from the cab and two from the back. The driver was evidently the boss. He looked around in obvious anger. A moment later he shouted something, then pointed to one of the people who'd jumped out of the back of the truck. One of them walked straight to the shack—

—"Oh, shit!" Ramirez keyed his radio switch. "Everybody get down!" he ordered unnecessarily—

—and wrenched open the door.

A gasoline drum rocketed upward like a space launch, leaving a cone of white flame behind as it blasted through the top of the shack. Flames from the other drums spread laterally. The one who'd opened the door was a silhouette of black, as though he'd just opened the front door of hell, but only for an instant before he vanished in the spreading flames. Two of his companions vanished into the same white-yellow mass. The third was on the edge of the initial blast, and started running away, directly toward the soldiers, before the falling gasoline from the flying drum splashed on him and he became a stick figure made of fire who lasted only ten steps. The circle of flames was forty yards wide, its center composed of four men whose high-pitched screams were distinct above the low-frequency roar of the blaze. Next the truck's fuel tank added its own punctuation to the explosion. There were perhaps two hundred gallons of gasoline afire, sending up a mushroom cloud illuminated by the flames below. In less than a minute the ammunition in various firearms cooked off, sounding like firecrackers within the roaring flames. Only the afternoon's heavy rain prevented the fire from spreading rapidly into the forest.

Chavez realized that he was lying next to the intelligence specialist.

"Nice work on the booby trap."

"Wish the fuckers coulda waited." The screaming was over by now.

"Yeah."

"Everybody check in," Ramirez ordered over the radio. They all did. Nobody was hurt.

The fire died down quickly. The aviation gasoline had been spread thinly over a wide area, and burned rapidly. Within three minutes all that was left was a wide scorched area defined by a perimeter of burning grass and bushes. The truck was a blackened skeleton, its loadbed still alight from the box of flares. They'd continue to burn for quite a while.

"What the hell was that?" Captain Willis wondered in the left seat of the helicopter. They'd just made their first pickup, and on climbing back to cruising altitude, the glow on the horizon looked like a sunrise on their infrared vision systems.

"Plane crash, maybe—that's right on the bearing to the last pickup," Colonel Johns realized belatedly.

"Super."

"Buck, be advised we have possible hostile activity at Pickup Four."

"Right, Colonel," Sergeant Zimmer replied curtly.

With that observation, Colonel Johns continued the mission. He'd find out what he needed to know soon enough. One thing at a time.

Thirty minutes after the explosion, the fire was down enough that the intelligence sergeant donned his gloves and moved in to try to recover his triggering devices. He found part of one, but the idea, though good, was hopeless. The bodies were left in place, and no attempt was made to search them. Though IDs might have been recovered—leather wallets resist fire reasonably well—their absence would have been noticed. Again the airfield guards were dragged to the center of the northern part of the runway, which was to have been the pickup point anyway. Ramirez redeployed his men to guard against the possibility that someone might have noticed the fire and reported it to someone else. The next concern was the courier flight that was probably heading in tonight. Their experience told them that it was still over two hours away—but they'd seen only one full cycle, and that was a thin basis for making any sort of prediction.

What if the airplane comes in? Ramirez asked himself. He'd already considered the possibility, but now it was an immediate threat.

The crew of that aircraft could not be allowed to report to anyone that they'd seen a large helicopter. On the other hand, leaving bullet holes in the airplane would be almost as clear a message of what had happened.

For that matter, Ramirez asked himself, *why the hell were we ordered to kill those two poor bastards and leave from here instead of the preplanned exfiltration point?*

So, what if an airplane comes in?

He didn't have an answer. Without the flares to mark the strip it wouldn't land. Moreover, one of the new arrivals had brought a small VHF radio. The druggies were smart enough that they'd have radio codes to assure the flight crew that the airfield was safe. So, what if the aircraft just orbited? Which it probably would do. Might the helicopter shoot it down? What if it tried and missed? What if? What if?

Before insertion, Ramirez had thought that the mission had been exquisitely planned, with every contingency thought out—as it had, but halfway through their planned stay they were being yanked out, and the plan had been trashed. What dickhead had decided to do that?

What the hell is going on? he demanded of himself. His men looked to him for information and knowledge and leadership and assurance. He had to pretend that everything was all right, that he was in control. It was all a lie, of course. His greater overall knowledge of the operation only increased his ignorance of the real situation. He was used to being moved around like a chess piece. That was the job of a junior officer—but this was *real*. There were six dead men to prove it.

"KNIFE, this is NIGHT HAWK, over," his high-frequency radio crackled.

"HAWK, this is KNIFE. LZ is the northern edge of RENO. Standing by for extraction, over."

"Bravo X-Ray, over."

Colonel Johns was interrogating for possible trouble. Juliet Zulu was the coded response indicating that they were in enemy hands and that a pickup was impossible. Charlie Foxtrot meant that there was active contact, but that they could still be gotten out. Lima Whiskey was the all-clear signal.

"Lima Whiskey, over."

"Say again, KNIFE, over."

"Lima Whiskey, over."

"Roger, copy. We are three minutes out."

"Hot guns," PJ ordered his flight crew. Sergeant Zimmer left his instruments to take the right-side gun position. He activated the power to his six-barreled minigun. The newest version of the Gatling gun of yore began spinning, ready to draw shells from the hopper to Zimmer's left.

"Ready right," he reported over the intercom.

"Ready left," Bean said on the other side.

Both men scanned the trees with their night-vision goggles, looking for anything that might be hostile.

"I got a strobe light at ten o'clock," Willis told PJ.

"I see it. Christ—what happened here?"

As the Sikorsky slowed, the four bodies were clearly visible around what had once been a simple wooden shack . . . and there was a truck, too. Team KNIFE was right where it was supposed to be, however. And they had two bodies as well.

"Looks clear, Buck."

"Roger, PJ." Zimmer left his gun on and headed aft. Sergeant Bean could jump to the opposite gun station if he had to, but it was Zimmer's job to get a count on the last pickup. He did his best to avoid stepping on people as he moved, but the soldiers understood when his feet landed on several of them. Soldiers are typically quite forgiving toward those who lift them out of hostile territory.

Chavez kept his strobe on until the helicopter touched down, then ran to join his squad. He found Captain Ramirez standing by the ramp, counting them off as they raced aboard. Ding waited his turn, then the captain's hand thumped down on his shoulder.

"Ten!" he heard as he leaped over several bodies on the ramp. He heard the number again from the big Air Force sergeant, then: "Eleven! Go-go-go!" as the captain came aboard.

The helicopter lifted off immediately. Chavez fell hard onto the steel deck, where

Vega grabbed him. Ramirez came down next to him, then rose and followed Zimmer forward.

"What happened here?" PJ asked Ramirez a minute later. The infantry officer filled him in quickly. Colonel Johns increased power somewhat and kept low, which he would have done anyway. He ordered Zimmer to stay at the ramp for two minutes, watching for a possible aircraft, but it never appeared. Buck came forward, killed power to his gun, and resumed his vigil with the flight instruments. Within ten minutes they were "feet-wet," over the water, looking for their tanker to top off for the flight back to Panama. In the back, the infantrymen buckled into place and promptly began dropping off to sleep.

But not Chavez and Vega, who found themselves sitting next to six bodies, lying together on the ramp. Even for professional soldiers—one of whom had done some of the killing—it was a grisly sight. But not as bad as the explosions. Neither had ever seen pictures of people burning to death, and even for druggies, they agreed, it was a bad way out.

The helicopter ride became rough as the Pave Low entered the propwash from the tanker, but it was soon over. A few minutes after that, Sergeant Bean—the little one, as Chavez thought of him—came aft, walking carefully over the soldiers. He clipped his safety belt to a fitting on the deck, then spoke into his helmet microphone. Nodding, he went aft to the ramp. Bean motioned to Chavez for a hand. Ding grabbed the man's belt at the waist and watched him kick the bodies off the edge of the ramp. It seemed kind of cold, but then, the scout reflected, it no longer mattered to the druggies. He didn't look aft to see them hit the water, but instead settled back down for a nap.

A hundred miles behind them, a twin-engined private plane circled over where the landing strip—known to the flight crew simply as Number Six—was still marked by a vaguely circular array of flames. They could see where the clearing was, but the airstrip itself wasn't marked with flares, and without that visual reference a landing attempt would have been madness. Frustrated, yet also relieved because they knew what had happened to a number of flights over the previous two weeks, they turned back for their regular airfield. On landing they made a telephone call.

Cortez had risked a direct flight from Panama to Medellín, though he did place the charge on an as-yet unused credit card so that the name couldn't be tracked. He drove his personal car to his home and immediately tried to contact Escobedo, only to discover that he was at his hilltop hacienda. Félix didn't have the energy to drive that far this late on a long day, nor would he entrust a substantive conversation to a cellular phone, despite all the assurances about how safe those channels were. Tired, angry, and frustrated for a dozen reasons, he poured himself a stiff drink and went off to bed. All that effort wasted, he swore at the darkness. He'd never be able to use Moira again. Would never call her, never talk to her, never see her. And the fact that his last "performance" with her had ended in failure, caused by his fears at what he'd thought—correctly!—his boss had done, merely put more genuine emotion into his profanities.

Before dawn a half-dozen trucks visited a half-dozen different airfields. Two groups of men died fiery deaths. A third entered the airfield shack and found exactly what they'd expected to find: nothing. The other three found their airstrips entirely normal, the guards in place, content and bored with the monotony of their duties.

When two of the trucks failed to return, others were sent out after them, and the necessary information quickly found its way to Medellín. Cortez was awakened by the phone and given new travel orders.

In Panama, all of the infantrymen were still asleep. They'd be allowed to stand down for a full day, and sleep in air-conditioned comfort—under heavy blankets—after hot showers and meals which, if not especially tasty, were at least different from the MREs they'd had for the preceding week. The four officers, however, were awakened early and taken elsewhere for a new briefing. Operation SHOWBOAT, they learned, had taken a very serious turn. They also learned why, and the source of their new orders was as exhilarating as it was troubling.

The new S-3, operations officer, for the 3rd Battalion of the 17th Infantry, which formed part of the First Brigade, 7th Infantry Division (Light), checked out his office while his wife struggled with the movers. Already sitting on his desk was a Mark-2 Kevlar helmet, called a Fritz for its resemblance to the headgear of the old German Wehrmacht. For the 7th LID, the camouflage cloth cover was further decorated with knotted shreds of the same material used for their battle-dress uniform fatigues. Most of the wives referred to it as the Cabbage Patch Hat, and like a cabbage, it broke up the regular outline of the helmet, making it harder to spot. The battalion commander was off at a briefing, along with the XO, and the new S-3 decided to meet with the S-1, or personnel officer. It turned out that they'd served together in Germany five years before, and they caught up on personal histories over coffee.

"So how was Panama?"

"Hot, miserable, and I don't need to fill you in on the political side. Funny thing—just before I left I ran into one of your Ninjas."

"Oh, yeah? Which one?"

"Chavez. Staff sergeant, I think. Bastard wasted me on an exercise."

"I remember him. He was a good one with, uh . . . Sergeant Bascomb?"

"Yes, Major?" A head appeared at the office door.

"Staff Sergeant Chavez—who was he with?"

"Bravo Company, sir. Lieutenant Jackson's platoon . . . second squad, I think. Yeah, Corporal Ozkanian took it over. Chavez transferred out to Fort Benning, he's a basic-training instructor now," Sergeant Bascomb remembered.

"You sure about that?" the new S-3 asked.

"Yes, sir. The paperwork got a little ruffled. He's one of the guys who had to check out in a hurry. Remember, Major?"

"Oh, yeah. That was a cluster-fuck, wasn't it?"

"Roge-o, Major," the NCO agreed.

"What the hell was he doing running an FTX in the Canal Zone?" the operations officer wondered.

"Lieutenant Jackson might know, sir," Bascomb offered.

"You'll meet him tomorrow," the S-1 told the new S-3.

"Any good?"

"For a new kid fresh from the Hudson, yeah, he's doing just fine. Good family. Preacher's kid, got a brother flies fighter planes for the Navy—squadron commander, I think. Bumped into him at Monterey a while back. Anyway, Tim's got a good platoon sergeant to teach him the ropes."

"Well, that was one pretty good sergeant, that Chavez kid. I'm not used to having people sneak up on me!'' The S-3 fingered the scab on his face. ''Damn if he didn't, though.''

''We got a bunch of good ones, Ed. You're gonna like it here. How 'bout lunch?''

''Sounds good to me. When do we start PT in the morning?''

''Zero-six-fifteen. The boss likes to run.''

The new S-3 grunted on his way out the door. Welcome back to the real Army.

''Looks like our friends down there are a little pissed,'' Admiral Cutter observed. He held a telex form that had emanated from the CAPER side of the overall operation. ''Who was it came up with the idea of tapping into their communications?''

''Mr. Clark,'' the DDO replied.

''The same one who—''

''The same.''

''What can you tell me about him?''

''Ex–Navy SEAL, served nineteen months in Southeast Asia in one of those special operations groups that never officially existed. Got shot up a few times,'' Ritter explained. ''Left the service as a chief bosun's mate, age twenty-eight. He was one of the best they ever had. He's the guy who went in and saved Dutch Maxwell's boy.''

Cutter's eyes went active at that. ''I knew Dutch Maxwell, spent some time on his staff when I was a j.g. So, he's the guy who saved Sonny's ass? I never did hear the whole story on that.''

''Admiral Maxwell made him a chief on the spot. That's when he was COMAIRPAC. Anyway, he left the service and got married, went into the commercial diving business—the demolitions side; he's an expert with explosives, too. But his wife got killed in a car accident down in Mississippi. That's when things started going bad for him. Met a new girl, but she was kidnapped and murdered by a local drug ring—seems she was a mule for them before they met. Our former SEAL decided to go big-game hunting on his own hook. Did pretty well, but the police got a line on him. Anyway, Admiral Maxwell was OP-03 by then. He caught a rumble, too. He knew James Greer from the old days, and one thing led to another. We decided that Mr. Clark had some talents we needed. So the Agency helped stage his 'death' in a boating accident. We changed his name—new identity, the whole thing, and now he works for us.''

''How—''

''It's not hard. His service records are just gone. Same thing we did with the SHOWBOAT people. His fingerprints in the FBI file were changed—that was back when Hoover still ran things and, well, there were ways. He died and got himself reborn as John Clark.''

''What's he done since?'' Cutter asked, enjoying the conspiratorial aspects of this.

''Mainly he's an instructor down at The Farm. Every so often we have a special job that requires his special talents,'' Ritter explained. ''He's the guy who went on the beach to get Gerasimov's wife and daughter, for example.''

''Oh. And this all started because of a drug thing?''

''That's right. He has a special, dark place in his heart for druggies. Hates the bastards. It's about the only thing he's not professional about.''

''Not pro—''

''I don't mean it that way. He'll enjoy doing this job. It won't affect how he does it, but he will enjoy it. I don't want you to misunderstand me. Clark is a very capable field officer. He's got great instincts, and he's got brains. He knows how to plan it, and he knows how to run it."

"So what's his plan?"

"You'll love it." Ritter opened his portfolio and started taking papers out. Most of them, Cutter saw, were "overhead imagery"—satellite photographs.

"Lieutenant Jackson?"

"Good morning, sir," Tim said to the new battalion operations officer after cracking off a book-perfect salute. The S-3 was walking the battalion area, getting himself introduced.

"I've heard some pretty good things about you." That was always something that a new second lieutenant wanted to hear. "And I met one of your squad leaders."

"Which one, sir?"

"Chavez, I think."

"Oh, you just in from Fort Benning, Major?"

"No, I was an instructor at the Jungle Warfare School, down in Panama."

"What was Chavez doing down there?" Lieutenant Jackson wondered.

"Killing me," the major replied with a grin. "All your people that good?"

"He was my best squad leader. That's funny, they were supposed to send him off to be a drill sergeant."

"That's the Army for you. I'm going out with Bravo Company tomorrow night for the exercise down at Hunter-Liggett. Just thought I'd let you know."

"Glad to have you along, sir," Tim Jackson told the Major. It wasn't strictly true, of course. He was still learning how to be a leader of men, and oversight made him uncomfortable, though he knew that it was something he'd have to learn to live with. He was also puzzled by the news on Chavez, and made a mental note to have Sergeant Mitchell check that out. After all, Ding was still one of "his" men.

"Clark." That was how he answered the phone. And this one came in on his "business" line.

"It's a Go. Be here at ten tomorrow morning."

"Right." Clark replaced the phone.

"When?" Sandy asked.

"Tomorrow."

"How long?"

"A couple of weeks. Not as long as a month." *Probably,* he didn't add.

"Is it—"

"Dangerous?" John Clark smiled at his wife. "Honey, if I do my job right, no, it's not dangerous."

"Why is it," Sandra Burns Clark wondered, "that I'm the one with gray hair?"

"That's because I can't go into the hair parlor and have it fixed. You can."

"It's about the drug people, isn't it?"

"You know I can't talk about that. It would just get you worried anyway, and there's no real reason to worry," he lied to his wife. Clark did a lot of that. She knew it, of course, and for the most part she wanted to be lied to. But not this time.

Clark returned his attention to the television. Inwardly he smiled. He hadn't gone after druggies for a long, long time, and he'd never tried to go this far up the ladder—back then he hadn't known how, hadn't had the right information. Now he had everything he needed for the job. Including presidential authorization. There were advantages to working for the Agency.

Cortez surveyed the airfield—what was left of it—with a mixture of satisfaction and anger. Neither the police nor the army had come to visit yet, though eventually they would. Whoever had been here, he saw, had done a thorough, professional job.

So what am I supposed to think? he asked himself. Did the Americans send some of their Green Berets in? This was the last of five airstrips that he'd examined today, moved about by a helicopter. Though not a forensic detective by training, he had been thoroughly schooled in booby traps and knew exactly what to look for. Exactly what he would have done.

The two guards who'd been here, as at the other sites, were simply gone. That surely meant that they were dead, of course, but the only real knowledge he had was that they were gone. Perhaps he was supposed to think that they had set the explosives, but they were simple peasants in the pay of the Cartel, untrained ruffians who probably hadn't even patrolled around the area to make certain that . . .

"Follow me." He left the helicopter with one of his assistants in trail. This one was a former police officer who did have some rudimentary intelligence; at least he knew how to follow simple orders.

If I wanted to keep watch of a place like this . . . I'd think about cover, and I'd think about the wind, and I'd think about a quick escape. . . .

One thing about military people was that they were predictable.

They'd want a place from which they could watch the length of the airstrip, and also keep an eye on the refueling shack. That meant one of two corners, Cortez judged, and he walked off toward the northwest one. He spent a half hour prowling the bushes in silence with a confused man behind him.

"Here is where they were," Félix said to himself. The dirt just behind the mound of dirt was smoothed down. Men had lain there. There was also the imprint from the bipod of a machine gun.

He couldn't tell how long they'd watched the strip, but he suspected that here was the explanation for the disappearing aircraft. Americans? If so, what agency did they work for? CIA? DEA? Some special-operations group from the military, perhaps?

And why were they pulled out?

And why had they made their departure so obvious?

What if the guards were not dead? What if the Americans had bought them off?

Cortez stood and brushed the mud off his trousers. They were sending a message. Of course. After the murder of their FBI Director—he hadn't had time to talk to *el jefe* about that act of lunacy yet—they wanted to send a message so that such things were not to be repeated.

That the Americans had done anything at all was unusual, of course. After all, kidnapping and/or killing American citizens was about the safest thing any international terrorist could do. The CIA had allowed one of their station chiefs to be tortured to death in Lebanon—and done nothing. All those Marines blown up—and the Americans had done nothing. Except for the occasional attempt at sending a message. The Americans were fools. They'd tried to send messages to the North Vietnamese for nearly ten years, and failed, and *still* they hadn't learned better. So this time, instead of doing nothing at all, they'd done something that was less useful than nothing. To have so much power and have so little appreciation of it, Cortez thought. Not like the Russians. When some of their people had been kidnapped in Lebanon, the KGB's First Directorate men had snatched their own hostages off the street and returned them—one version said headless, another with more intimate parts removed—immediately after which the missing Russians had been returned with something akin to an apology. For all their crudeness, the Russians understood how the game was played. They were predictable, and played by all the classic rules of clandestine behavior so that their enemies knew what would not be tolerated. They were serious. And they were taken seriously.

Unlike the Americans. As much as he warned his employer to be wary of them, Cortez was sure that they wouldn't answer even something as outrageous as the murder of senior officials of their government.

That was too bad, Cortez told himself. He could have made it work for him.

"Good evening, boss," Ryan said as he took his seat.

"Hi, Jack." Admiral Greer smiled as much as he could. "How do you like the new job?"

"Well, I'm keeping your chair warm."

"It's your chair now, son," the DDI pointed out. "Even if I do get out of here, I think it's time to retire."

Jack didn't like the way he pronounced the word *if*.

"I don't think I'm ready yet, sir."

"Nobody's ever ready. Hell, when I was still a naval officer, about the time I actually learned how to do the job, it was time to leave. That's the way life is, Jack."

Ryan thought that one over as he surveyed the room. Admiral Greer was getting his nourishment through clear plastic tubes. A blue-green gadget that looked like a splint kept the needles in his arm, but he could see where previous IV lines had "infiltrated" and left ugly bruises. That was always a bad sign. Next to the IV bottle was a smaller one, piggybacked with the D5W. That was the medication he was being given, the chemotherapy. It was a fancy name for poison, and poison was exactly what it was, a biocide that was supposed to kill the cancer a little faster than it killed the patient. He didn't know what this one was, some acronym or other that designated a compound developed at the National Institutes of Health instead of the Army's Chemical Warfare Center. Or maybe, Jack thought, they cooperated on such concoctions. Certainly Greer looked as though he were the victim of some dreadful, vicious experiment.

But that wasn't true. The best people in the field were doing everything they knew to keep him alive. And failing. Ryan had never seen his boss so thin. It seemed that every time he came—never less than three times per week—he'd lost additional weight. His eyes burned with defiant energy, but the light at the end of this painful tunnel was not recovery. He knew it. So did Jack. There was only one thing he could do to ease the pain. And this he did. Jack opened his briefcase and took out some documents.

"You want to look these over." Ryan handed them over.

They nearly tangled on the IV lines, and Greer grumbled his annoyance at the plastic spaghetti.

"You're leaving for Belgium tomorrow night, right?"

"Yes, sir."

"Give my regards to Rudi and Franz from the BND. And watch the local beer, son."

Ryan laughed. "Yes, sir."

Admiral Greer scanned through the first folder. "The Hungarians are still at it, I see."

"They got the word to cool it down, and they have, but the underlying problem isn't going to go away. I think it's in the interests of everyone concerned that they should cool it. Our friend Gerasimov has given us some tips on how to get word to a few people ourselves."

Greer nearly laughed at that. "It figures. How is the former KGB Director adapting to life in America?"

"Not as well as his daughter is. Turns out that she always wanted a nose job. Well, she got her wish." Jack grinned. "Last time I saw her she was working on a tan. She restarts college next fall. The wife is still a little antsy, and Gerasimov is still cooperating. We haven't figured out what to do with him when we're finished, though."

"Tell Arthur to show him my old place up in Maine. He'll like the climate, and it ought to be easy to guard."

"I'll pass that along."

"How do you like being let in on all the Operations stuff?" James Greer asked.

"Well, what I've seen is interesting enough, but there's still 'need-to-know' to worry about."

"Says who?" the DDI asked in surprise.

"Says the Judge," Jack replied. "They have a couple of things poppin' that they don't want me in on."

"Oh, really?" Greer was quiet for a moment. "Jack, in case nobody ever told you, the Director, the Deputy Director—they still haven't refilled that slot, have they?—and the directorate chiefs are cleared for everything. You are now a chief of directorate. There isn't anything you aren't supposed to know. You *have* to know. You brief Congress."

Ryan waved it off. It wasn't important, really. "Well, maybe the Judge doesn't see things that way and—"

The DDI tried to sit up in bed. "Listen up, son. What you just said is bullshit! You *have* to know, and you tell Arthur I said so. That 'need-to-know' crap stops at the door to my office."

"Yes, sir. I'll take care of that." Ryan didn't want his boss to get upset. He was only an acting chief of directorate, after all, and he was accustomed to being cut out of operational matters which, for the past six years, he'd been quite content to leave to others. Jack wasn't ready to challenge the DCI on something like this. His responsibility for the Intelligence Directorate's output to Congress, of course, was something he would make noise over.

"I'm not kidding, Jack."

"Yes, sir." Ryan pointed to another folder. He'd fight that battle after he got back from Europe. "Now, this development in South Africa is especially interesting and I want your opinion. . . ."

15. Deliverymen

Clark walked off the United flight in San Diego and rented a car for the drive to the nearby naval base. It didn't take very long. He felt the usual pang of nostalgia when he saw the towering gray-blue hulls. He'd once been a part of this team, and though he'd been young and foolish then, he remembered it fondly as a time in which things were simpler.

USS *Ranger* was a busy place. Clark parked his car at the far end of the area used by the enlisted crewmen and walked toward the quay, dodging around the trucks, cranes, and other items of mobile hardware that cycled in and out from their numerous tasks. The carrier was preparing to sail in another eight hours, and her thousands of sailors were on-loading all manner of supplies. Her flight deck was empty save for a single old F-4 Phantom fighter which no longer had any engines and was used for training new members of the flight-deck crew. The carrier's air wing was scattered among three different naval air stations and would fly out after the carrier sailed. That fact spared the pilots of the wing from the tumult normal to a carrier's departure. Except for one.

Clark walked up to the officer's brow, guarded by a Marine corporal who had his name written down on his clipboard list of official visitors. The Marine checked off the line on his list and lifted the dock phone to make the call that was mandated by his instructions. Clark just kept going up the steps, entering the carrier at the hangar-deck level, then looking around for a way topside. Finding one's way around a carrier is not easy for the uninitiated, but if you kept going up you generally found the flight deck soon enough. This he did, heading for the forward starboard-side elevator. Standing there was an officer whose khaki collar bore the silver leaf of a Commander, USN. There was also a gold star over one shirt pocket that denoted command at sea. Clark was looking for the CO of a squadron of Grumman A-6E Intruder medium attack bombers.

"Your name Jensen?" he asked. He'd flown down early to make this appointment.

"That's right, sir. Roy Jensen. And you are Mr. Carlson?"

Clark smiled. "Something like that." He motioned to the officer to follow him forward. The flight deck here was idle. Most of the loading activity was aft. They walked toward the bow across the black no-skid decking material, little different from the blacktop on any country road. Both men had to talk loudly to be heard. There was plenty of noise from the dock, plus a fifteen-knot onshore wind. Several people could see the two men talking, but with all the activity on the carrier's flight deck, there was little likelihood that anyone would notice. And you couldn't bug a flight deck. Clark handed over an envelope and let Jensen read its contents before taking it back. By this time they were nearly at the bow, standing between the two catapult tracks.

"This for-real?"

"That's right. Can you handle it?"

Jensen thought for a moment, staring off into the naval base.

"Sure. Who's going to be on the ground?"

"Not supposed to tell you—but it's going to be me."

"The battle group's not supposed to be going down there, you know—"

"That's already been changed."

"What about the weapons?"

"They're being loaded aboard *Shasta* tomorrow. They'll be painted blue, and they're light for—"

"I know. I did one of the drops a few weeks ago over at China Lake."

"Your CAG will get the orders three days from now. But he won't know what's happening. Neither will anybody else. We'll have a 'tech-rep' flown aboard with the weapons. He'll baby-sit the mission from this side. Your BDA cassettes go to him. Nobody else sees them. He's bringing his own set, and they're color-coded with orange-and-purple tape so they don't get mixed up with anything else. You got a B/N you can trust to keep his mouth shut?"

"With these orders?" Commander Jensen asked. "No sweat."

"Fair enough. The 'tech-rep' will have the details when he gets aboard. He reports to the CAG first, but he'll ask to see you. From there on it's eyes-only. The CAG'll know that it's a quiet project. If he asks about it, just tell him it's a Drop-Ex to evaluate a new weapon." Clark raised an eyebrow. "It really is a Drop-Ex, isn't it?"

"The people we're—"

"What people? You do not need to know. You do not want to know," Clark said. "If you have a problem with that, I want you to tell me right now."

"Hey, I told you we could do it. I was just curious."

"You're old enough to know better." Clark delivered the line gently. He didn't want to insult the man, though he did have to get the message across.

"Okay."

USS *Ranger* was about to deploy for an extended battle-group exercise whose objective was work-ups: battle practice to prepare the group for a deployment to the Indian Ocean. They were scheduled for three weeks of intensive operations that involved everything from carrier landing practice to underway-replenishment drills, with a mock attack from another carrier battle group returning from WestPac. The operations would be carried out, Commander Jensen had just learned, about three hundred miles from Panama instead of farther west. The squadron commander wondered who had the juice to reroute a total of thirty-one ships, some of them outrageous fuelhogs. That confirmed the source of the orders he'd just been given. Jensen was a careful man; though he'd gotten a very official telephone call, and the orders hand-delivered by Mr. Carlson said everything they needed to say, it was nice to have outside confirmation.

"That's it. You'll get notice when you need it. Figure eight hours or so of warning time. That enough?"

"No sweat. I'll make sure the ordies put the weapons in a convenient place. You be careful on the ground, Mr. Carlson."

"I'll try." Clark shook hands with the pilot and walked aft to find his way off the ship. He'd be catching another plane in two hours.

The Mobile cops were in a particularly foul mood. Bad enough that one of their own had been murdered in such an obvious, brutal way, Mrs. Braden had made the mistake of coming to the door to see what was wrong and caught two rounds herself.

The surgeons had almost saved her, but after thirty-six hours that too was over, and all the police had to show for it was a kid not yet old enough to drive who claimed to have hit one of the killers with his granddad's Marlin '39, and some bloodstains that might or might not have supported the story. The police preferred to believe that Braden had scored for the points, of course, but the experienced homicide investigators knew that a two-inch belly gun was the next thing to useless unless the shoot-out were held inside a crowded elevator. Every cop in Mississippi, Alabama, Florida, and Louisiana was looking for a blue Plymouth Voyager minivan with two male Caucs, black hair, medium, medium, armed and dangerous, suspected cop-killers.

The van was found Monday afternoon by a concerned citizen—there really were some in Alabama—who called the local county sheriff's office, who in turned called the Mobile force.

"The kid was right," the lieutenant in charge of the case observed. The body on the back of the van was about as distasteful to behold as any cadaver would be after two days locked inside a car, in Alabama, in June, but for all that the hole near the base of the skull, just at the hairline, was definitely a .22. It was also clear that the killer had died in the right-front seat, hemorrhaging explosively from the head wound. There was one more thing.

"I've seen this guy. He's a druggie," another detective observed.

"So what was Ernie wrapped up with?"

"Christ knows. What about his kids?" the detective asked. "They lose their mom and dad—we gonna tell the whole fucking world that their dad was a dirty cop? Do that to a couple of orphaned kids?"

It merely required a single look for both men to agree that, no, you couldn't do something like that. They'd find a way to make Ernie a hero, and damned sure somebody'd give the Sanderson kid a pat on the head.

"Do you realize what you have done?" Cortez asked. He'd steeled himself going in to restrain his temper. In an organization of Latins, his would be—had to be—the only voice of reason. They would respect that in the same sense that the Romans valued chastity: a rare and admirable commodity best found in others.

"I have taught the *norteamericanos* a lesson," Escobedo replied with arrogant patience that nearly defeated Félix's self-discipline.

"And what did they do in reply?"

Escobedo made a grand gesture with his hand, a gesture of power and satisfaction. "The sting of an insect."

"You also know, of course, that after all the effort I made to establish a valuable information source, you have pissed it away like—"

"What source?"

"The secretary of the FBI Director," Cortez answered with his own self-satisfied smile.

"And you cannot use her again?" Escobedo was puzzled.

Fool! "Not unless you wish me to be arrested, *jefe*. Were that to happen, my services would cease to be useful to you. We could have used information from this woman, carefully, over years. We could have identified attempts to infiltrate the organization. We could have discovered what new ideas the *norteamericanos* have, and countered them, again carefully and thoughtfully, protecting our operations while allowing them enough successes to think that they were accomplishing something.'' Cortez almost said that he'd just figured out why all those aircraft had disappeared, but didn't. His anger wasn't under that much control. Félix was just beginning to realize that he really could supplant the man who sat behind the desk. But first he would have to demonstrate his value to the organization and gradually prove to all of the criminals that he was more useful than this buffoon. Better to let them stew in their own juice for a while, the better to appreciate the difference between a trained intelligence professional and a pack of self-taught and over-rich smugglers.

Ryan gazed down at the ocean, forty-two thousand feet below him. The VIP treatment wasn't hard to get used to. As a directorate chief he also rated a special flight from Andrews direct to a military airfield outside of the NATO headquarters at Mons, Belgium. He was representing the Agency at a semiannual conference with his intelligence counterparts from the European Alliance. It would be a major performance. He had a speech to give, and favorable impressions to make. Though he knew many of the people who'd be there, he'd always been an upscale gofer for James Greer. Now he had to prove himself. But he'd succeed. Ryan was sure of that. He had three of his own department heads along, and a comfortable seat on a VC-20A to remind him how important he was. He didn't know that it was the same bird that had taken Emil Jacobs to Colombia. That was just as well. For all his education, Ryan remained superstitious.

As Executive Assistant Director (Investigations), Bill Shaw was the Bureau's senior official, and until a new Director was appointed by the President and confirmed by the Senate, he'd be acting Director. That might last for a while. It was a presidential election year, and with the coming of summer, people were thinking about conventions, not appointments. Perversely, Shaw didn't mind a bit. That meant that he'd be running things, and for a case of this magnitude, the Bureau needed an experienced cop at the helm. ''Political realities'' were not terribly important to William Shaw. Crime cases were something that agents solved, and to him the case was everything. His first act on learning of the death of Director Jacobs had been to recall his friend, Dan Murray. It would be Dan's job to oversee the case from his deputy assistant director's office, since there were at least two elements to it: the investigation in Colombia and the one in Washington. Murray's experience as legal attaché in London gave him the necessary political sensitivity to understand that the overseas aspect of the case might not be handled to the Bureau's satisfaction. Murray entered Shaw's office at seven that morning. Neither had gotten much sleep in the previous two days, but they'd sleep on the plane. Director Jacobs would be buried in Chicago today, and they'd be flying out on the plane with the body to attend the funeral.

''Well?''

Dan flipped open his folder. ''I just talked to Morales in Bogotá. The shooter they bagged is a stringer for M-19, and he doesn't know shit. Name is Héctor Buente, age twenty, college dropout from the University of the Andes—bad marks. Evidently the locals leaned on him a little bit—Morales says they're pretty torqued about this—but the kid doesn't know much. The shooters got a heads-up for an important job several days ago, but they didn't know what or where until four hours before it actually took place. They didn't know who was in the car aside from the ambassador. There was another team of shooters, by the way, staked out on a different route. They have some names, and the local cops're taking the town apart looking for them. I think that's a dead end. It was a contract job, and the people who know anything are long gone.''

''What about places they fired from?''

''Broke in both apartments. They undoubtedly had the places surveyed beforehand. When the time came, they got in, tied up—actually cuffed—the owners, and sat it out. A real professional job from beginning to end,'' Murray said.

''Four hours' warning?''

''Correct.''

''That makes it after the time the plane lifted off Andrews,'' Shaw observed.

Murray nodded. ''That makes it clear that the leak was on our side. The airplane's flight plan was filed for Grenada—where the bird actually ended up. That was changed two hours out from the destination. The Colombian Attorney General was the only guy who knew that Emil was going down, and he didn't spread the word until *three* hours before the landing. Other senior government members knew that something was up, and that could explain the alert order to our M-19 friends, but the timing just isn't right. The leak was here unless their AG himself blew the cover off. Morales says that's very unlikely. The man is supposed to be the local Oliver Cromwell, honest as God and the balls of a lion. No mistress to blab to or anything like that. The leak was on our end, Bill.''

Shaw rubbed his eyes and thought about some more coffee, but he had enough caffeine in his system already to hyperactivate a statue. ''Go on.''

''We've interviewed everyone who knew about the trip. Needless to say, nobody claims to have talked. I've ordered a subpoena to check phone records, but I don't expect anything there.''

''What about—''

''The guys at Andrews?'' Dan smiled. ''They're on the list. Maybe forty people, tops, who could have known that the Director was taking a flight. That includes people who found out up to an hour *after* the bird lifted off.''

''Physical evidence?''

''Well, we have one of the RPG launchers and assorted other weapons. The Colombian Army troops reacted damned well—Christ, running into a building where you *know* there's heavy weapons, that's real balls. The M-19ers were carrying Soviet-bloc light weapons also, probably from Cuba, but that's incidental. I'd like to ask the Sovs to help us identify the RPG lot and shipment.''

''You think we'll get any cooperation?''

''The worst thing they can say is no, Bill. We'll see if this *glasnost* crap is for-real or not.''

''Okay, ask.''

''The rest of the physical side is pretty straightforward. It'll confirm what we already know, but that's about it. Maybe the Colombians will be able to work their way back through M-19, but I doubt it. They've been working on that group for quite a while, and it's a tough nut.''

''Okay.''

''You look a little punked out, Bill,'' Murray observed. ''We got young agents to burn both ends of the candle. Us old farts are supposed to know about pacing ourselves.''

''Yeah, well, I have all this other stuff to get current with.'' Shaw waved at his desk.

''When's the plane leave?''

"Ten-thirty."

"Well, I'm going to go back to my office and grab a piece of the couch. I suggest you do the same."

Shaw realized that it wasn't such a bad idea. Ten minutes later, he'd done the same, asleep despite all the coffee he'd drunk. An hour after that, Moira Wolfe came to his door minutes ahead of the time his own executive secretary showed up. She knocked but got no answer. She didn't want to open the door, didn't want to disturb Mr. Shaw, even though there was something important that she wanted to tell him. It could wait until they were all on the airplane.

"Hi, Moira," Shaw's secretary said, catching her on the way out. "Anything wrong?"

"I wanted to see Mr. Shaw, but I think he's asleep. He's been working straight through since—"

"I know. You look like you could use some rest, too."

"Tonight, maybe."

"Want me to tell him—"

"No, I'll see him on the airplane."

There was a mix-up on the subpoena. The agent who'd made the arrangements had gotten the name of the wrong judge from the U.S. Attorney, and found himself sitting in the anteroom until 9:30 because the judge was also late coming in this Monday morning. Ten minutes after that, he had everything he needed. The good news was that it was but a short drive to the phone company, and that the local Bell office could access all the billing records it needed. The total list was nearly a hundred names, with over two hundred phone numbers and sixty-one credit cards, some of which were not AT&T. It took an hour to get a hard copy of all the records, and the agent rechecked the numbers he had written down to make sure that there hadn't been any garbles or overlooks. He was a new agent, only a few months out of the Academy, on his first assignment to the Washington Field Division, essentially running an important errand for his supervisor as he learned the ropes, and he hadn't paid all that much attention to the data he'd just received. He didn't know, for example, that a 58 prefix on a certain telephone number denoted an overseas call to Venezuela. But he was young, and he'd know that before lunch.

The aircraft was a VC-135, the military version of the old 707. It was windowless, which the passengers always enjoyed, but had a large cargo door that was necessary for loading Director Jacobs aboard for his last trip to Chicago. The President was in another aircraft, scheduled to arrive at O'Hare International a few minutes ahead of this one. He would speak both at the temple and the graveside.

Shaw, Murray, and several other senior FBI officials rode in the second aircraft, which was often used for similar missions, and had the appropriate hardware to keep the casket in place in the forward section of the cabin. It gave them a chance to stare at the polished oak box for the entire flight, without even a small window to distract them. Somehow that brought it home more than anything else might have done. It was a very quiet flight, only the whine of the turbofan engines to keep the living and the dead company.

But the aircraft was part of the President's own fleet, and had all of the communications gear needed for that duty. An Air Force lieutenant came aft, asking for Murray, then led him forward to the communications console.

Mrs. Wolfe was in an aisle seat thirty feet aft of the senior executives. There were tears streaming down her face, and while she remembered that there was something she ought to tell Mr. Shaw, this wasn't the time or place, was it? It didn't really matter anyway—just that she'd made a mistake when the agent had interviewed her the previous afternoon. It was the shock of the event, really. It was so—hard. Her life had known too many losses in the past few years, and the mental whiplash of the weekend had . . . what? Confused her? She didn't know. But this wasn't the right time. Today was a time to remember the best boss she'd ever had, a man who was every bit as thoughtful to her as he'd ever been to the agents who lionized him. She saw Mr. Murray walk forward for something or other, past the coffin that her hand had brushed on the way in, her last goodbye to the Director.

The call didn't take more than a minute. Murray emerged from the small radio compartment, his face as much under control as it ever was. He didn't look again at the casket, just looked aft, Moira saw, straight down the aisle before he took his place next to his wife.

"Oh, shit!" Dan muttered to himself after he was seated. His wife's head snapped around. It wasn't the sort of thing you say at a funeral. She touched his arm, but Murray shook his head. When he looked at his wife, the expression she saw was sadness, but not grief.

The flight lasted just over an hour. The honor guard came up from the rear of the aircraft to take charge of the Director, all polished and scrubbed in their dress uniforms. After they were out, the passengers exited to find the rest of the assembly waiting for them on the tarmac, watched by distant TV news cameras. The honor guard marched their burden behind two flags, that of their nation and the banner of the FBI, emblazoned with the "Fidelity—Bravery—Integrity" motto of the Bureau. Murray watched as the wind played with the flag, watched the words curl and flap in the breeze, and realized just how intangible such words really were. But he couldn't tell Bill just yet. It would be noticed.

"Well, now we know why we wasted the airfield." Chavez watched the ceremony in the squad bay of the barracks. It was all very clear to him now.

"But why'd they yank us out?" Vega asked.

"We're going back, *Oso*. An' the air's gonna be thin where we're goin' back to."

Larson didn't need to watch the TV coverage. He hovered over a map, plotting known and suspected processing sites southwest of Medellín. He knew the areas—who didn't?—but isolating individual locations . . . that was harder, but, again, it was a technological question. The United States had invented modern reconnaissance technology and spent almost thirty years perfecting it. He was in Florida, having flown to the States ostensibly to take delivery of a new aircraft, which had unaccountably developed engine problems.

"How long have we been doing this?"

"Only a couple of months," Ritter answered.

Even with so thin a data base, it wasn't all that hard. All of the towns and villages in the area were plotted, of course, even individual houses. Since nearly all had electricity, they were easy to spot, and once identified, the computer simply erased them electronically. That left energy sources that were not towns, villages, and individual farmsteads. Of these, some were regular or fairly so. It had been arbitrarily decided that anything that appeared more than twice in a week was too obvious to be of real interest, and these, too, were erased. That left sixty or so locations that appeared and disappeared in accordance with a chart next to the map and photographs. Each was a possible site where raw coca leaves began the refining process. They were not encampments for the Colombian Boy Scouts.

"You can't track in on them chemically," Ritter said. "I checked. The ether and acetone concentrations released into the air aren't much more than you'd expect from the spillage of nail-polish remover, not to mention the usual biochemical processes in this sort of environment. It's a jungle, right? Lots of stuff rots on the ground, and they give off all sorts of chemicals when they do. So all we have off the satellite is the usual infrared. They still do all their processing at night? I wonder why?"

Larson grunted agreement. "It's a carry-over from when the Army was actively hunting them. They still do it mainly from habit, I suppose."

"Well, it gives us something, doesn't it?"

"What are we going to do with it?"

Murray had never been to a Jewish funeral. It wasn't very different from a Catholic one. The prayers were in a language he couldn't understand, but the message wasn't very different. *Lord, we're sending a good man back to You. Thanks for letting us have him for a while.* The President's eulogy was particularly impressive, having been drafted by the best White House speechwriter, quoting from the Torah, the Talmud, and the New Testament. Then he started talking about Justice, the secular god that Emil had served for all of his adult life. When, toward the end, he talked about how men should turn their hearts away from vengeance, however, Murray thought that . . . it wasn't the words. The speech was as poetically written as any he'd ever heard. It was just that the President started sounding like a politician at that point, Dan thought. *Is that my own cynicism talking?* the agent thought. He was a cop, and justice to him meant that the bastards who committed crimes had to pay. Evidently the President thought the same way, despite the statesmanlike stuff he was saying. That was fine with Murray.

The soldiers watched the TV coverage in relative silence. A few men worked knives across sharpening stones, but mainly they just sat there, listening to their President speak, knowing who had killed the man whose name few had heard until after he was dead. Chavez had been the first to make the correct observation, but it hadn't been all that great a leap of imagination, had it? They accepted the as-yet-unspoken news phlegmatically. Here was merely additional proof that their enemy had struck out directly against one of the most important symbols of their nation. There was their country's flag, draped across the coffin. There was the banner of the man's own agency, but this wasn't a job for cops, was it? So the soldiers traded looks in silence while their Commander-in-Chief had his say. When it was all over, the door to the squad bay opened, and there was their commander.

"We're going back in tonight. The good news is, it's going to be cooler where we're going," Captain Ramirez told his men. Chavez cocked an eyebrow at Vega.

USS *Ranger* sailed on the tide, assisted away from the dock by a flotilla of tugs while her escorts formed up, already out of the harbor and taking rolls from the broad Pacific swells. Within an hour she was clear of the harbor, doing twenty knots. Another hour, and it was time to begin flight operations. First to arrive were the helicopters, one of which refueled and took off again to take plane-guard station off the carrier's starboard quarter. The first fixed-wing aircraft aboard were the

Intruder attack bombers, led, of course, by the skipper, Commander Jensen. On the way out he'd seen the ammunition ship, USS *Shasta,* just beginning to get up steam. She'd join the underway-replenishment group that was to sail two hours behind the battle group. *Shasta* had the weapons that he'd be dropping. He already knew the sort of targets. Not the exact places yet, but he had the rough idea, and that, he realized as he climbed down from his aircraft, was all the idea he wanted to have. Worrying about "Collateral Damage" wasn't strictly his concern, as somebody had told him earlier in the day. *What an odd term,* he thought. *Collateral Damage.* What an offhand way of condemning people whom fate had already selected to be in the wrong place. He felt sorry for them, but not all that sorry.

Clark arrived in Bogotá late that afternoon. No one met him, and he rented a car as he usually did. One hour out of the airport he stopped to park on a secondary road. He waited several annoying minutes for another car to pull up alongside. The driver, a CIA officer assigned to the local station, handed him a package and drove off without a word. Not a large package, it weighed about twenty pounds, half of which was a stout tripod. Clark set it gently on the floor of the passenger compartment and drove off. He'd been asked to "deliver" quite a few messages in his time, but never quite so emphatically as this. It was all his idea. Well, he thought, mostly his idea. That made it somewhat more palatable.

The VC-135 lifted off two hours after the funeral. It was too bad they didn't have a wake in Chicago. That was an Irish custom, not one for the children of Eastern European Jews, but Emil would have approved, Dan Murray was sure. He would have understood that many a beer or whiskey would be lifted to his memory tonight, and somewhere, in his quiet way he'd laugh in the knowledge of it. But not now. Dan had gotten his wife to maneuver Mrs. Shaw onto the other side of the airplane so that he could sit next to Bill. Shaw noticed that immediately, of course, but waited until the aircraft leveled off to make the obvious question.

"What is it?"

Murray handed over the sheet he pulled off the aircraft's facsimile printer a few hours earlier.

"Oh, shit!" Shaw swore quietly. "Not Moira. Not her."

16. Target List

"I'm open to suggestions," Murray said. He regretted his tone at once.

"Christ's sake, Dan!" Shaw's face had gone gray for a moment, and his expression was now angry.

"Sorry, but—damn it, Bill, do we handle it straight or do we candy-ass our way around the issue?"

"Straight."

"One of the kids from WFO asked her the usual battery of questions, and she said that she didn't tell anybody . . . well, maybe so, but who the hell did she call in Venezuela? They rechecked going back a year, no such calls ever before. The boy I left behind to run things did some further checking—the number she called is an apartment, and the phone there rang someplace in Colombia within a few minutes of Moira's call.''

''Oh, God.'' Shaw shook his head. From anyone else he would merely have felt anger, but Moira had worked with the Director since before he'd returned to D.C., from his command of the New York Field Division.

''Maybe it's an innocent thing. Maybe even a coincidence,'' Murray allowed, but that didn't improve Bill's demeanor very much.

''Care to do a probability assessment of that statement, Danny?''

''No.''

''Well, we're all going back to the office after we land. I'll have her into my place an hour after we get back. You be there, too.''

''Right.'' It was time for Murray to shake his head. She'd shed as many tears at the graveside as anyone else. He'd seen a lifetime's worth of duplicity in his law-enforcement career, but to think that of Moira was more than he could stomach. *It has to be a coincidence. Maybe one of her kids has a pen pal down there. Or something like that,* Dan told himself.

The detectives searching Sergeant Braden's home found what they were looking for. It wasn't much, just a camera case. But the case had a Nikon F-3 body and enough lenses that the entire package had to be worth eight or nine thousand dollars. More than a Mobile detective sergeant could afford. While the rest of the officers continued the search, the senior detective called Nikon's home office and checked the number on the camera to see if the owner had registered it for warranty purposes. He had. And with the name that was read off to him, the officer knew that he had to call the FBI office as well. It was part of a federal case, and he hoped that somehow they could protect the name of a man who had certainly been a dirty cop. Dirty or not, he did leave kids behind. Perhaps the FBI would understand that.

He was committing a federal crime to do this, but the attorney considered that he had a higher duty to his clients. It was one of those gray areas which decorate not so much legal textbooks, but rather the volumes of written court decisions. He was sure a crime had been committed, was sure that nothing was being done to investigate it, and was sure that its disclosure was important to the defense of his clients on a case of capital murder. He didn't expect to be caught, but if he were, he'd have something to take to the professional ethics panel of the state bar association. Edward Stuart's professional duty to his clients, added to his personal distaste for capital punishment, made the decision an inevitable one.

They didn't call it Happy Hour at the base NCO club anymore, but nothing had really changed. Stuart had served his time in the U.S. Navy as a legal officer aboard an aircraft carrier—even in the Navy, a mobile city of six thousand people needed a lawyer or two—and knew about sailors and suds. So he'd visited a uniform store and gotten the proper outfit of a Coast Guard chief yeoman complete with the appropriate ribbons and just walked onto the base, heading for the NCO club where, as long as he paid for his drinks in cash, nobody would take great note of his presence. He'd been a yeoman himself while aboard USS *Eisenhower,* and knew the lingo well enough to pass any casual test of authenticity. The next trick, of course, was finding a crewman from the cutter *Panache*.

The cutter was finishing up the maintenance period that always followed a deployment, preparatory to yet another cruise, and her crewmen would be hitting the club after working hours to enjoy their afternoon beers while they could. It was just a matter of finding the right ones. He knew the names, and had checked tape archives at the local TV stations to get a look at the faces. It was nothing more than good luck that the one he found was Bob Riley. He knew more about that man's career than the other chiefs.

The master chief boatswain's mate strolled in at 4:30 after ten hot hours supervising work on various topside gear. He'd had a light lunch and sweated off all of that and more, and now figured that a few mugs of beer would replace all the fluids and electrolytes that he'd lost under the hot Alabama sun. The barmaid saw him coming and had a tall one of Samuel Adams all ready by the time he selected a stool. Edward Stuart got there a minute and half a mug later.

"Ain't you Bob Riley?"

"That's right," the bosun said before turning. "Who're you?"

"Didn't think you'd remember me. Matt Stevens. You near tore my head off on the *Mellon* awhile back—said I'd never get my shit together."

"Looks like I was wrong," Riley noted, searching his memory for the face.

"No, you were right. I was a real punk back then, but you—well, I owe you one, Master Chief. I did get my shit together. Mainly 'causa what you said." Stuart stuck out his hand. "I figure I owe you a beer at least."

It wasn't all that unusual a thing for Riley to hear. "Hell, we all need straightenin' out. I got bounced off a coupla bulkheads when I was a kid, too, y'know?"

"Done a little of it myself." Stuart grinned. "You make chief an' you gotta be respectable and responsible, right? Otherwise who keeps the officers straightened out?"

Riley grunted agreement. "Who you workin' for?"

"Admiral Hally. He's at Buzzard's Point. Had to fly down with him to meet with the base commander. I think he's off playing golf right now. Never did get the hang of that game. You're on *Panache,* right?"

"You bet."

"Captain Wegener?"

"Yep." Riley finished off his beer and Stuart waved to the barmaid for refills.

"Is he as good as they say?"

"Red's a better seaman 'n I am," Riley replied honestly.

"Nobody's that good, Master Chief. Hey, I was there when you took the boat across—what was the name of that container boat that snapped in half . . . ?"

"*Arctic Star.*" Riley smiled, remembering. "Jesus, if we didn't earn our pay that afternoon."

"I remember watching. Thought you were crazy. Well, shit. All I do now is drive a word processor for the Admiral, but I did a little stuff in a forty-one boat before I made chief, working outa Norfolk. Nothing like *Arctic Star,* of course."

"Don't knock it, Matt. One of those jobs's enough for a couple years of sea stories. I'll take an easy one any day. I'm gettin' a little old for that dramatic stuff."

"How's the food here?"

"Fair."

"Buy you dinner?"

"Matt, I don't even remember what I said to you."

"I remember," Stuart assured him. "God knows how I woulda turned out if you hadn't turned me around. No shit, man. I owe you one. Come on." He waved Riley over to a booth against the wall. They were quickly going through their third beer when Chief Quartermaster Oreza arrived.

"Hey, Portagee," Riley called to his fellow master chief.

"I see the beer's cold, Bob."

Riley waved to his companion. "This here's Matt Stevens. We were on the *Mellon* together. Did I ever tell you about the *Arctic Star* job?"

"Only about thirty times," Oreza noted.

"You wanna tell the story, Matt?" Riley asked.

"Hey, I didn't even see it all, you know—"

"Yeah, half the crew was puking their guts out. I'm talking a real gale blowing. No way the helo could take off, and this container boat—the after half of her, that is; the fo'ard part was already gone—look like she was gonna roll right there an' then . . ."

Within an hour, two more rounds had been consumed, and the three men were chomping their way through a disk of knockwurst and sauerkraut, which went well with beer. Stuart stuck with stories about his new Admiral, the Chief Counsel of the Coast Guard, in which legal officers are also line officers, expected to know how to drive ships and command men.

"Hey, what's with these stories I been hearing about you an' those two drug pukes?" the attorney finally asked.

"What d'ya mean?" Oreza asked. Portagee still had some remaining shreds of sobriety.

"Hey, the FBI guys went in to see Hally, right? I had to type up his reports on my Zenith, y'know?"

"What did them FBI guys say?"

"I'm not supposed—oh, fuck it! Look, you're all in the clear. The Bureau isn't doing a fuckin' thing. They told your skipper 'go forth and sin no more,' okay? The shit you got outa those pukes—didn't you hear? Operation TARPON. That whole sting operation came from you guys. Didn't you know that?"

"What?" Riley hadn't seen a paper or turned on a TV in days. Though he did know about the death of the FBI Director, he had no idea of the connection with his Hang-Ex, as he had taken to calling it in the goat locker.

Stuart explained what he knew, which was quite a lot.

"Half a billion dollars?" Oreza observed quietly. "That oughta build us a few new hulls."

"Christ knows we need 'em," Stuart agreed.

"You guys didn't really—I mean, you didn't really . . . hang one of the fuckers, did you?" Stuart extracted a Radio Shack mini–tape recorder from his pocket and thumbed the volume switch to the top.

"Actually it was Portagee's idea," Riley said.

"Couldn't have done it without you, Bob," Oreza said generously.

"Yeah, well, the trick was how to do the hangin'," Riley explained. "You see, we had to make it look real if we was gonna scare the piss outa the little one. Wasn't really all that hard once I thought it over. After we got him alone, the pharmacist mate gave him a shot of ether to knock him out for a few minutes, and I rigged a rope harness on his back. When we took him topside, the noose had a hook on the back, so when I looped the noose around his neck, all I hadda do was attach the hook to an eye I put on the harness, so we was hoistin' him by the harness, not the neck. We didn't really wanna kill the fucker—well, I did," Riley said. "But Red didn't think it was a real good idea." The bosun grinned at the quartermaster.

"The other trick was baggin' him," Oreza said. "We put a black hood over his head. Well, there was a gauze pad inside soaked in ether. The bastard screamed bloody murder when he smelled it, but it had him knocked out as soon as we ran his ass up to the yardarm.''

''The little one believed the whole thing. Fucker wet his pants, it was beautiful! Sang like a canary when they got him back to the wardroom. Soon as he was outa sight, of course, we lowered the other one and got him woke back up. They were both half in the bag from smokin' grass all day. I don't think they ever figured out what we did to them.''

No, they didn't. ''Grass?''

''That was Red's idea. They had their own pot stash—looked like real cigarettes. We just gave 'em back to 'em, and they got themselves looped. Throw in the ether and everything, and I bet they never figured out what really happened.''

Almost right, Stuart thought, hoping that his tape recorder was getting this.

''I wish we really could have hung 'em,'' Riley said after a few seconds. ''Matt, you ain't never seen anything like what that yacht looked like. Four people, man—butchered 'em like cattle. Ever smell blood? I didn't know you could. You can,'' the bosun assured him. ''They raped the wife and the little girl, then cut 'em up like they was—God! You know, I been having nightmares from that? Nightmares—me! Jesus, that's one sea story I wish I could forget. I got a little girl that age. Those fuckers raped her an' killed her, and cut her up an' fed her to the fuckin' sharks. Just a little girl, not even big enough to drive a car or go out on a date.

''We're supposed to be professional cops, right? We're supposed to be cool about it, don't get personally involved. All that shit?'' Riley asked.

''That's what the book says,'' Stuart agreed.

''The book wasn't written for stuff like this,'' Portagee said. ''People who do this sort of thing—they ain't really people. I don't know what the hell they are, but people they ain't. You can't do that kinda shit and be people, Matt.''

''Hey, what d'you want me to say?'' Stuart asked, suddenly defensive, and not acting a part this time. ''We got laws to deal with people like that.''

''Laws ain't doin' much good, are they?'' Riley asked.

The difference between the people he was obliged to defend and the people he had to impeach, Stuart told himself through the fog of alcohol, was that the bad ones were his clients and the good ones were not. And now, by impersonating a Coast Guard chief, he too had broken a law, just as these men had done, and like them, he was doing it for some greater good, some higher moral cause. So he asked himself who was right. Not that it mattered, of course. Whatever was ''right'' was lost somewhere, not to be found in lawbooks or canons of ethics. Yet if you couldn't find it there, then where the hell was it? But Stuart was a lawyer, and his business was law, not right. Right was the province of judges and juries. Or something like that. Stuart told himself that he shouldn't drink so much. Drink made confused things clear, and the clear things confused.

The ride in was far rougher this time. Westerly winds off the Pacific Ocean hit the slopes of the Andes and boiled upward, looking for passes to go through. The resulting turbulence could be felt at thirty thousand feet, and here, only three hundred feet AGL—above ground level—the ride was a hard one, all the more so with the helicopter on its terrain-following autopilot. Johns and Willis were strapped in tight to reduce the effects of the rough ride, and both knew that the people in back were having a bad time indeed as the big Sikorsky jolted up and down in twenty-foot bounds at least ten times per minute. PJ's hand was on the stick, following the motions of the autopilot but ready to take instant command if the system showed the first sign of failure. This was real flying, as he liked to say. That generally meant the dangerous kind.

Skimming through this pass—it was more of a saddle, really—didn't make it any easier. A ninety-six-hundred-foot peak was to the south, and one of seventy-eight hundred feet to the north, and a lot of Pacific air was being funneled through as the Pave Low roared at two hundred knots. They were heavy, having tanked only a few minutes earlier just off Colombia's Pacific Coast.

"There's Mistrato," Colonel Johns said. The computer navigation system had already veered them north to pass well clear of the town and any roads. The two pilots were also alert for anything on the ground that hinted at a man or a car or a house. The route had been selected off satellite photographs, of course, both daylight and nighttime infrared shots, but there was always the chance of a surprise.

"Buck, LZ One in four minutes," PJ called over the intercom.

"Roger."

They were flying over Risaralda Province, part of the great valley that lay between two enormous ridgelines of mountains flung into the sky by a subductal fault in the earth's crust. PJ's hobby was geology. He knew how much effort it took to bring his aircraft to this altitude, and he boggled at the forces that could push mountains to the same height.

"LZ One in sight," Captain Willis said.

"Got it." Colonel Johns took the stick. He keyed his microphone. "One minute. Hot guns."

"Right." Sergeant Zimmer left his position to head aft. Sergeant Bean activated his minigun in case there was trouble. Zimmer slipped and nearly fell on a pool of vomit. That wasn't unusual. The ride smoothed out now that they were in the lee of the mountains, but there were some very sick kids in back who would be glad to get on firm, unmoving ground. Zimmer had trouble understanding that. It was dangerous on the ground.

The first squad was up as the helicopter flared to make its first landing, and as before, the moment it touched down, they ran out the back. Zimmer made his count, watched to be certain that everyone got off safely, and notified the pilot to lift off as soon as they were clear.

Next time, Chavez told himself, *next time I fucking walk in and out!* He had had some rough chopper rides in his time, but nothing like that one. He led off to the treeline and waited for the remainder of the squad to catch up.

"Glad to be on the ground?" Vega asked as soon as he got there.

"I didn't know I ate that much," Ding groaned. Everything he'd eaten in the last few hours was still aboard the helicopter. He opened a canteen and drank a pint of water just to wash away the vile taste.

"I usta love roller coasters," *Oso* said. "No more, *'mano!*"

"Fuckin' A!" Chavez remembered standing in line for the big ones at Knott's Berry Farm and other California theme parks. Never again!

"You okay, Ding?" Captain Ramirez asked.

"Sorry, sir. That never happened to me—ever! I'll be okay in a minute," he promised his commander.

"Take your time. We picked a nice, quiet spot to land." *I hope.*

Chavez shook his head to clear it. He didn't know that motion sickness started in the inner ear, had never known what motion sickness was until half an hour earlier. But he did the right thing, taking deep breaths and shaking his head to get his equilibrium back. The ground wasn't moving, he told himself, but part of his brain wasn't sure.

"Where to, Cap'n?"

"You're already heading in the right direction." Ramirez clapped him on the shoulder. "Move out."

Chavez put on his low-light goggles and started moving off through the forest. God, but that was embarrassing. He'd never do anything that dumb again, the sergeant promised himself. With his head still telling him that he was probably moving in a way that his legs couldn't possibly cause, he concentrated on his footing and the terrain, rapidly moving two hundred meters ahead of the main body of the squad. The first mission into the swampy lowlands had just been practice, hadn't really been serious, he thought now. But this was the real thing. With that thought foremost in his mind, he batted away the last remnants of his nausea and got down to work.

Everyone worked late that night. There was the investigation to run, and routine office business had to be kept current as well. By the time Moira came into Mr. Shaw's office, she'd managed to organize everything he'd need to know, and it was also time to tell him what she'd forgotten. She wasn't surprised to see Mr. Murray there, too. She was surprised when he spoke first.

"Moira, were you interviewed about Emil's trip?" Dan asked.

She nodded. "Yes. I forgot something. I wanted to tell you this morning, Mr. Shaw, but when I came in early you were asleep. Connie saw me," she assured him.

"Go on," Bill said, wondering if he should feel a little better about that or not.

Mrs. Wolfe sat down, then turned to look at the open door. Murray walked over to close it. On the way back he placed his hand on her shoulder.

"It's okay, Moira."

"I have a friend. He lives in Venezuela. We met . . . well, we met a month and a half ago, and we—this is hard to explain." She hesitated, staring at the rug for a moment before looking up. "We fell in love. He comes up to the States on business every few weeks, and with the Director away, we wanted to spend a weekend—at The Hideaway, in the mountains near Luray Caverns?"

"I know it," Shaw said. "Nice place to get away from it all."

"Well, when I knew that Mr. Jacobs was going to be away and we had a chance for a long weekend, I called him. He has a factory. He makes auto parts—two factories, actually, one in Venezuela and one in Costa Rica. Carburetors and things like that."

"Did you call him at his home?" Murray asked.

"No. He works such long hours that I called him at his factory. I have the number here." She handed over the scrap of Sheraton note paper that he'd written it down on. "Anyway, I got his secretary—her name's Consuela—because he was out on the shop floor, and he called me back, and I told him that we could get together, so he came up—we met at the airport Friday afternoon. I left early after Mr. Jacobs did."

"Which airport?"

"Dulles."

"What's his name?" Shaw asked.

"Díaz. Juan Díaz. You can call him there at the factory and—"

"That phone number goes to an apartment, not a factory, Moira," Murray said. And it was that clear, that fast.

"But—but he—" She stopped. "No. No. He isn't—"

''Moira, we need a complete physical description.''

''Oh, no.'' Her mouth fell open and wouldn't close. She looked from Shaw to Murray and back again as the horror of it all closed in on her. She was dressed in black, of course, probably the same outfit she'd worn to bury her own husband. For a few weeks she'd been a bright, beautiful, happy woman again. No more. Both FBI executives felt her pain, hating themselves for having brought it to her. She was a victim, too. But she was also a lead, and they needed a lead.

Moira Wolfe summoned what little dignity she had left and gave them as complete a description as they had ever had of any man in a voice as brittle as crystal before she lost control entirely. Shaw had his personal assistant drive her home.

''Cortez,'' Murray said as soon as the door closed behind her.

''That's a pretty solid bet,'' the Executive Assistant Director (Investigations) agreed. ''The book on him says that he's a real ace at compromising people. Jesus, did he ever prove that right.'' Shaw's head went from side to side as he reached for some coffee. ''But he couldn't have known what they were doing, could he?''

''Doesn't make much sense to have come here if he did,'' Murray said. ''But since when are criminals logical? Well, we start checking immigration control points, hotels, airlines. See if we can track this cocksucker. I'll get on it. What are we going to do about Moira?''

''She didn't break any laws, did she?'' That was the really odd part. ''Find a place where she doesn't have to see classified material, maybe in another agency. Dan, we can't destroy her, too.''

''No.''

Moira Wolfe got home just before eleven. Her kids were all still up waiting for her. They assumed that her tears were a delayed reaction from the funeral. They'd all met Emil Jacobs, too, and mourned his passing as much as anyone else who worked for the Bureau. She didn't say very much, heading upstairs for bed while they continued to sit before the television. Alone in the bathroom she stared in the mirror at the woman who'd allowed herself to be seduced and *used* like . . . like a fool, something worse than a fool, a stupid, vain, lonely old woman looking for her youth. So desperate to be loved again that . . . That she had condemned—how many? Seven people? She couldn't remember, staring at her empty face in the glass. The young agents on Emil's security detail had families. She'd knitted a sweater for Leo's firstborn son. He was still too young—he'd never remember what a nice, handsome young man his father had been.

It's all my fault.

I helped kill them.

She opened the mirrored door to the medicine cabinet. Like most people, the Wolfes never threw out old medicine, and there it was, a plastic container of Placidyls. There were still—she counted six of them. Surely that would be enough.

''What brings you out this time?'' Timmy Jackson asked his big brother.

''I gotta go out on *Ranger* to observe a Fleet-Ex. We're trying out some new intercept tactics I helped work up. And a friend of mine just got command of *Enterprise,* so I came out a day early to watch the ceremony. I go down to D'ego tomorrow and catch the COD out to *Ranger.*''

''COD?''

''The carrier's delivery truck,'' Robby explained. ''Twin-engine prop bird. So how's life in the light infantry?''

"We're still humpin' hills. Got our clock cleaned on the last exercise. My new squad leader really fucked up. It isn't fair," Tim observed.

"What do you mean?"

Lieutenant Jackson tossed off the last of his drink. " 'A green lieutenant and a green squad leader is too much burden for any platoon to bear'—that's what the new S-3 said. He was out with us. Of course, the captain didn't exactly see it that way. Lost a little weight yesterday—he chewed off a piece of my ass for me. God, I wish I had Chavez back."

"Huh?"

"Squad leader I lost. He—that's the odd part. He was supposed to go to a basic-training center as an instructor, but seems he got lost. The S-3 says he was in Panama a few weeks ago. Had my platoon sergeant try to track him down, see what the hell was going on—he's still my man, you know?" Robby nodded. He understood. "Anyway, his paperwork is missing, and the clerks are runnin' in circles trying to find it. Fort Benning called to ask where the hell he was, 'cause they were still waiting for him. Nobody knows where the hell Ding got to. That sort of thing happen in the Navy?"

"When a guy goes missing, it generally means that he wants to be missing."

Tim shook his head. "Nah, not Ding. He's a lifer, I don't even think he'll stop at twenty. He'll retire as a command sergeant major. No, he's no bugout."

"Then maybe somebody dropped his file in the wrong drawer," Robby suggested.

"I suppose. I'm still new at this," Tim reminded himself. "Still, it is kind of funny, turning up down there in the jungle. Enough of that. How's Sis?"

About the only good thing to say was that it wasn't hot. In fact, it was pretty cool. Maybe there wasn't enough air to be hot, Ding told himself. The altitude was marginally less than they'd trained at in Colorado, but that was weeks behind them, and it would be a few days before the soldiers were reacclimated. That would slow them down some, but on the whole Chavez thought that heat was more debilitating than thin air, and harder to get used to.

The mountains—nobody called these mothers hills—were about as rugged as anything he'd ever seen, and though they were well forested, he was paying particularly close attention to his footing. The thick trees made for limited visibility, which was good news. His night scope, hanging on his head like a poorly designed cap, allowed him to see no more than a hundred meters, and usually less than that, but he could see something, while the overhead cover eliminated the light needed for the unaided eye to see. It was scary, and it was lonely, but it was home for Sergeant Chavez.

He did not move in a straight line to the night's objective, following instead the Army's approved procedure of constantly veering left and right of the direction in which he was actually traveling. Every half hour he'd stop, double back, and wait until the rest of the squad was in view. Then it was their turn to rest for a few minutes, checking their own back for people who might take an interest in the new visitors to the jungle highlands.

The sling on his MP-5 was double-looped so that he could carry it slung over his head, always in firing position. There was electrician's tape over the muzzle to keep it from being clogged, and more tape was wrapped around the sling swivels to minimize noise. Noise was their enemy. Chavez concentrated on that, and seeing, and a dozen other things. This one was for-real. The mission brief had told them all about that. Their job wasn't reconnaissance anymore.

After six hours, the RON—remain overnight—site was in view. Chavez radioed back—five taps on the transmit key answered by three—for the squad to remain in place while he checked it out. They'd picked a real eyrie—he knew the word for an eagle's nest—from which, in daylight, they could look down on miles of the main road that snaked its way from Manizales to Medellín, and off of which the refining sites were located. Six of them, supposedly, were within a night's march of the RON site. Chavez circled it carefully, looking for footprints, trash, anything that hinted at human activity. It was too good a site for someone not to have used it for something or other, he thought. Maybe a photographer for *National Geographic* who wanted to take shots of the valley. On the other hand, getting here was a real bitch. They were a good three thousand feet above the road, and this wasn't the sort of country that you could drive a tank across, much less a car. He spiraled in, and still found nothing. Maybe it was too far out of the way. After half an hour he keyed his radio again. The rest of the squad had had ample time to check its rear, and if anyone had been following them, there would have been contact by now. The sun outlined the eastern wall of the valley in red by the time Captain Ramirez appeared. It was just as well that the covert insertion had shortened the night. With only half a night's march behind them they were tired, but not too tired, and would have a day to get used to the altitude all over again. They'd come five linear miles from the LZ—more like seven miles actually walked, and two thousand feet up.

As before, Ramirez spread his men out in pairs. There was a nearby stream, but nobody was dehydrated this time. Chavez and Vega took position over one of the two most likely avenues of approach to their perch, a fairly gentle slope with not too many trees and a good field of fire. Ding hadn't come in this way, of course.

''How you feelin', *Oso?''*

''Why can't we ever go to a place with plenty of air and it's cool and flat?'' Sergeant Vega slipped out of his web gear, setting it in a place where it would make a comfortable pillow. Chavez did the same.

''People don't fight wars there, man. That's where they build golf courses.''

''Fuckin' A!'' Vega set up his Squad Automatic Weapon next to a rocky outcropping. A camouflage cloth was set across the muzzle. He could have torn up a shrub to hide the gun behind, but they didn't want to disturb anything they didn't have to. Ding won the toss this time, and fell off to sleep without a word.

''Mom?'' It was after seven o'clock, and she was always up by now, fixing breakfast for her family of early risers. Dave knocked at the door, but heard nothing. That was when he started being afraid. He'd already lost a father, and knew that even parents were not the immortal, unchanging beings that all children need at the center of their growing universe. It was the constant nightmare that each of Moira's children had but never spoke about, even among themselves, lest their talk somehow make it more likely to happen. *What if something happens to Mom?* Even before his hand felt for the doorknob, Dave's eyes filled with tears at the anticipation of what he might find.

''Mom?'' His voice quavered now, and he was ashamed of it, fearful also that his siblings would hear. He turned the knob and opened the door slowly.

The shades were open, flooding the room with morning light. And there she was, lying on the bed, still wearing her black mourning dress. Not moving.

Dave just stood there, the tears streaming down his cheeks as the reality of his personal nightmare struck him with physical force.

". . . Mom?"

Dave Wolfe was as courageous as any teenager, and he needed all of it this morning. He summoned what strength he had and walked to the bedside, taking his mother's hand. It was still warm. Next he felt for a pulse. It was there, weak and slow, but there. That galvanized him into action. He lifted the bedside phone and punched 911.

"Police emergency," a voice answered immediately.

"I need an ambulance. My mom won't wake up."

"What is your address?" the voice asked. Dave gave it. "Okay, now describe your mother's condition."

"She's asleep, and she won't wake up, and—"

"Is your mother a heavy drinker?"

"No!" he replied in outrage. "She works for the FBI. She went right to bed last night, right after she got home from work. She—" And there it was, right on the night table. "Oh, God. There's a pill bottle here . . ."

"Read the label to me!" the voice said.

"P-l-a-c-i-d-y-l. It's my dad's, and he—" That was all the operator needed to hear.

"Okay—we'll have an ambulance there in five minutes."

Actually, it was there in just over four minutes. The Wolfe house was only three blocks from a firehouse. The paramedics were in the living room before the rest of the family knew anything was wrong. They ran upstairs to find Dave still holding his mother's hand and shaking like a twig in a heavy wind. The leading fireman pushed him aside, checked the airway first, then her eyes, then the pulse.

"Forty and thready. Respiration is . . . eight and shallow. It's Placidyl," he reported.

"Not that shit!" The second one turned to Dave. "How many were in there?"

"I don't know. It was my dad's, and—"

"Let's go, Charlie." The first paramedic lifted her by the arms. "Move it, kid, we gotta roll." There wasn't time to fool around with the Stokes litter. He was a big, burly man and carried Moira Wolfe out of the room like a baby. "You can follow us to the hospital."

"How—"

"She's still breathin', kid. That's the best thing I can tell you right now," the second one said on the way out the door.

What the hell is going on? Murray wondered. He'd come by to pick Moira up—her car was still in the FBI garage—and maybe help ease the guilt she clearly felt. She'd violated security rules, she'd done something very foolish, but she was also a victim of a man who'd searched and selected her for her vulnerabilities, then exploited them as professionally as anyone could have done. Everybody had vulnerabilities. That was another lesson he'd picked up over his years in the Bureau.

He'd never met Moira's kids, though he did know about them, and it wasn't all that hard to figure out who would be there, following the paramedic out of the house. Murray double-parked his Bureau car and hopped out.

"What gives?" he asked the second paramedic. Murray held up his ID so that he'd get an answer.

"Suicide attempt. Pills. Anything else you need?" the paramedic asked on his way to the driver's seat.

"Get moving." Murray turned to make sure he wasn't in the ambulance's way.

When he turned back to look at the kids, it was plain that "suicide" hadn't yet been spoken aloud, and the ugliness of that word made them wilt before his eyes.

That fucker Cortez! You'd better hope that I never get my hands on you!

"Kids, I'm Dan Murray. I work with your mom. You want me to take you to the hospital?" The case could wait. The dead were dead, and they could afford to be patient. Emil would understand.

He let them off in front of the emergency entrance and went off to find a parking place and use his car phone. "Get me Shaw," he told the watch officer. It didn't take long.

"Dan, this is Bill. What gives?"

"Moira tried to kill herself last night. Pills."

"What are you going to do?"

"Somebody has to sit with the kids. Does she have any friends we can bring out?"

"I'll check."

"Until then I'm going to hang around, Bill. I mean—"

"I understand. Okay. Let me know what's happening."

"Right." Murray replaced the phone and walked over to the hospital. The kids were sitting together in the waiting room. Dan knew about emergency-room waiting. He also knew that the gold badge of an FBI agent could open nearly any door. It did this time, too.

"You just brought a woman in," he told the nearest doctor. "Moira Wolfe."

"Oh, she's the OD."

She's a person, *not a goddamned OD!* Murray didn't say. Instead he nodded. "Where?"

"You can't—"

Murray cut him off cold. "She's part of a major case. I want to see what's happening."

The doctor led him to a treatment cubicle. It wasn't pretty. Already there was a respirator tube down her throat, and IV lines in each arm—on second inspection, one of the tubes seemed to be taking her blood out and running it through something before returning it to the same arm. Her clothing was off, and EKG sensors were taped to her chest. Murray hated himself for looking at her. Hospitals robbed everyone of dignity, but life was more important than dignity, wasn't it?

Why didn't Moira know that?

Why didn't you catch the signal, Dan? Murray demanded of himself. *You should have thought to have somebody keep an eye on her. Hell, if you'd put her in custody, she couldn't have done this!*

Maybe we should have yelled at her instead of going so easy. Maybe she took it the wrong way. Maybe. Maybe. Maybe.

Cortez, you are fucking dead. I just haven't figured out when yet.

"Is she going to make it?" Murray asked.

"Who the hell are you?" a doctor asked without turning.

"FBI, and I need to know."

The doctor still didn't look around. "So do I, sport. She took Placidyl. That's a pretty potent sleeping pill, not too many docs prescribe it anymore, 'cause it's too easy to OD on. LD-50 is anywhere from five to ten caps. LD-50 means the dose that'll kill half the people that take it. I don't know how much she took. At least she isn't completely gone, but her vitals are too goddamned low for comfort. We're dialyzing her blood to keep any more from getting into her, hope it's not a waste of time. We've put her on hundred-percent oxygen, then we'll zap her full of IV fluids and wait it out. She'll be out for at least another day. Maybe two, maybe three. Can't tell yet. I can't tell you what the odds are either. Now you know as much as I do. Get out of here, I got work to do."

"There are three kids in the waiting room, Doctor."

That turned his head around for about two seconds. "Tell 'em we got a pretty good chance, but it's going to be tough for a while. Hey, I'm sorry, but I just don't know. The good news is, if she comes back, she'll come all the way back. This stuff doesn't usually do permanent damage. Unless it kills you," the doctor added.

"Thanks."

Murray left to tell the kids what he could. Within an hour, some neighbors showed up to take their place with the Wolfe children. Dan left quietly after an agent arrived to keep his own vigil in the waiting room. Moira was probably their only link with Cortez, and that meant that her life was potentially in danger from hands other than her own. Murray got to the office just after nine, his mood still quiet and angry when he arrived. There were three agents waiting for him, and he waved them to follow.

"Okay, what have you found out?"

" 'Mr. Díaz' used an American Express card at The Hideaway. We've identified the number at two airline ticket counters—thank God for those credit-checking computers. Right after he dropped Mrs. Wolfe off, he caught a flight out of Dulles to Atlanta, and from there to Panama. That's where he disappeared. He must have paid cash for the next ticket, 'cause there's no record of a Juan Díaz on any flight that evening. The counter clerk at Dulles remembers him—he was in a hurry to catch the Atlanta flight. The description matches the one we already have. However he got into the country last week, it wasn't Dulles. We're running computer records now, ought to have an answer later this morning—call it an even-money chance to figure his route in. I'm betting on one of the big hubs, Dallas–Fort Worth, Kansas City, Chicago, one of them. But that's not the interesting thing we've discovered.

"American Express just discovered that it has a bunch of cards for Juan Díaz. Several have been generated recently, and they don't know how."

"Oh?" Murray poured some coffee. "How come they weren't noticed?"

"For one thing, the statements are paid on time and in full, so that dog didn't bark. The addresses are all slightly different, and the name itself isn't terribly unusual, so a casual look at the records won't tip anyone off. What it looks like is that somebody has a way to tap into their computer system—all the way into the executive programming, and that might be another lead for us to run down. He's probably been staying with the name in case Moira gets a look at the card. But what it has told us is that he's made five trips to the D.C. area in the past four months. Somebody is playing with the AmEx computer system, somebody good. Somebody," the agent went on, "good enough to tap into a lot of computers. This guy can generate complete credit lines for Cortez or anyone else. There ought to be a way to check that out, but I wouldn't be real hopeful about running him down fast."

There was a knock at the door, and another young agent came in. "Dallas–Fort Worth," he said, handing over a fax sheet. "The signatures match. He came in there and took a late flight to New York–La Guardia, got in after midnight local time on Friday. Probably caught the Shuttle down to D.C. to meet Moira. They're still checking."

"Beautiful," Murray said. "He's got all the moves. Where'd he come in from?"

"Still checking, sir. He got the New York ticket at the counter. We're talking with Immigration to see when he passed through customs control."

"Okay, next?"

"We have prints on him now. We have what looks like a left forefinger on the note paper he left Mrs. Wolfe, and we've matched that with the credit receipt from the airline counter at Dulles. It was tough, but the lab guys used their lasers to bring 'em out. We sent a team to The Hideaway, but nothing yet. The cleanup crew there is pretty good—too damned good for our purposes, but our guys are still working on it."

"Everything but a picture on the bastard. Everything but a picture," Murray repeated. "What about after Atlanta?"

"Oh, thought I said that. He caught a flight to Panama after a short layover."

"Where's the AmEx card addressed to?"

"It's in Caracas, probably just a letterdrop. They all are."

"How come Immigration doesn't—oh." Murray grimaced. "Of course his passport is under a different name or he has a collection of them to go with his cards."

"We're dealing with a real pro. We're lucky to have gotten this much so fast."

"What's new in Colombia?" he asked the next agent.

"Not much. The lab work is going nicely, but we're not developing anything we didn't already know. The Colombians now have names on about half of the subjects—the prisoner says he didn't know all of them, and that's probably the truth. They've launched a major operation to try an' find 'em, but Morales isn't real hopeful. They're all names of people the Colombian government's been after for quite a while. All M-19 types. It was a contract job, just as we thought."

Murray checked his watch. Today was the funeral for the two agents on Emil's protection detail. It would be held at the National Cathedral, and the President would be speaking there, too. His phone rang.

"Murray."

"This is Mark Bright down at Mobile. We have some additional developments."

"Okay."

"A cop got himself blown away Saturday. It was a contract job, Ingrams at close range, but a local kid popped a subject with his trusty .22, right in the back of the head. Killed him; they found the body and the vehicle yesterday. The shooter was positively ID'd as a druggie. The local cops searched the victim's—Detective Sergeant Braden—house and found a camera that belonged to the victim in the Pirates Case. The new victim is a burglary sergeant. I am speculating that he was working for the druggies and probably checked out the victim's place prior to the killings, looking for the records that we ultimately found."

Murray nodded thoughtfully. That added something to their knowledge. So they'd wanted to make sure that the victim hadn't left any records behind before they'd taken him and his family out, but their guy wasn't good enough, and they killed him for it. It was also part of the murder of Director Jacobs, additional fallout from Operation TARPON. *Those bastards are really flexing their muscles, aren't they?* "Anything else?"

"The local cops are in a pretty nasty mood about this. First time somebody's put a hit on a cop that way. It was a 'public' hit, and his wife got taken out by a stray round. Local cops are pretty pissed. A drug dealer got taken all the way out last night. It'll come out as a righteous shoot, but I don't think it was a coincidence. That's it for now."

"Thanks, Mark." Murray hung up. "The bastards have declared war on us, all right," he murmured.

"What's that, sir?"

"Nothing. Have you back-checked on the earlier trips Cortez made—hotels, car rentals?"

"We have twenty people out there on it. Ought to have some preliminary information in two hours."

"Keep me posted."

Stuart was the first morning appointment for the U.S. Attorney, and he looked unusually chipper this morning, the secretary thought. She couldn't see the hangover.

"Morning, Ed," Davidoff said without rising. His desk was a mass of papers. "What can I do for you?"

"No death penalty," Stuart said as he sat down. "I'll trade a guilty plea for twenty years, and that's the best deal you're going to get."

"See ya' in court, Ed," Davidoff replied, looking back down at his papers.

"You want to know what I've got?"

"If it's good, I'm sure you'll let me know at the proper time."

"May be enough to get my people off completely. You want 'em to walk on this?"

"Believe that when I see it," Davidoff said, but he was looking up now. Stuart was an overly zealous defense lawyer, the United States Attorney thought, but an honest one. He didn't lie, at least not in chambers.

Stuart habitually carried an old-fashioned briefcase, the wedge-shaped kind made of semistiff leather instead of the newer and trimmer attaché case that most lawyers toted now. From it he extracted a tape recorder. Davidoff watched in silence. Both men were trial lawyers and both were experts at concealing their feelings, able to say what they had to say, regardless of what they felt. But since both had this ability, like professional poker players they knew the more subtle signs that others couldn't spot. Stuart knew that he had his adversary worried when he punched the play button. The tape lasted several minutes. The sound quality was miserable, but it was audible, and with a little cleaning up in a sound laboratory—the defendants could afford it—it would be as clear as it needed to be.

Davidoff's ploy was the obvious one: "That has no relevance to the case we're trying. All of the information in the confession is excluded from the proceedings. We agreed on that."

Stuart eased his tone now that he had the upper hand. It was time for magnanimity. "You agreed. I didn't say anything. The government committed a gross violation of my clients' constitutional rights. A simulated execution constitutes mental torture at the very least. It's sure as hell illegal. You have to put these two guys on the stand to make your case, and I'll crucify those Coast Guard sailors when you do. It might be enough to impeach everything they say. You never know what a jury's going to think, do you?"

"They might just stand up and cheer, too," Davidoff answered warily.

"That's the chance, isn't it? One way to find out. We try the case." Stuart replaced the player in his briefcase. "Still want an early trial date? With this as background information I can attack your chain of evidence—after all, if they were crazy enough to pull this number, what if my clients claim that they were forced to masturbate to give you the semen samples that you told the papers about, or were forced to hold the murder weapons to make prints—I haven't yet discussed any of those details with them, by the way—and I link all that in with what I know about the victim? I think I have a fighting chance to send them home alive and free." Stuart leaned forward, resting his arms on Davidoff's desk. "On the other hand, as you say, it's hard to predict how a jury'll react. So what I'm offering you is, they plead guilty to twenty years' worth of whatever charge you want, with no unseemly recommendation from the judge about how they have to serve all twenty—so they're out in, say, eight years. You tell the press that there's problems with the evidence, and you're pretty mad about that, but there's nothing you can do. My clients are out of circulation for a fairly long time. You get your conviction but nobody else dies. Anyway, that's my deal. I'll give you a couple of days to think it over." Stuart rose to his feet, picked up his briefcase, and left without another word. Once outside, he looked for the men's room. He felt an urgent need to wash his hands, but he wasn't sure why. He was certain that he'd done the right thing. The criminals—they really were criminals—would be found guilty, but they wouldn't die in the electric chair—and who knows, he thought, maybe they'll straighten out. That was the sort of lie that lawyers tell themselves. He wouldn't have to destroy the careers of some Coast Guard types who had probably stepped over the line only once and would never do so again. That was something he was prepared to do, but didn't relish. This way, he thought, everybody won something, and for a lawyer that was as successful an exercise as you generally got. But he still felt a need to wash his hands.

For Edwin Davidoff, it was harder. It wasn't just a criminal case, was it? The same electric chair that would deliver those two pirates to hell would deliver him to a suite in the Dirksen Senate Office Building. Since he had read *Advise and Consent* as a freshman in high school, Davidoff had lusted for a place in the United States Senate. And he'd worked very hard to earn it: top of his class at Duke Law School, long hours for which he was grossly underpaid by the Department of Justice, speaking engagements all over the state that had nearly wrecked his family life. He had sacrificed his own life on the altar of justice . . . and ambition, he admitted to himself. And now when it was all within his grasp, when he could rightfully take the lives of two criminals who had forfeited their rights to them . . . this could blow it all, couldn't it? If he wimped out on the prosecution, plea-bargaining down to a trifling twenty years, all his work, all his speeches about Justice would be forgotten. Just like that.

On the other hand, what if he disregarded what Stuart had just told him and took the case to trial—and risked being remembered as the man who lost the case entirely. He might blame the Coast Guardsmen for what they had done—but then he would be sacrificing their careers and possibly their freedom on what altar? Justice? Ambition? How about revenge? he asked himself. Whether he won or lost the Pirates Case, those men would suffer even though what they had done had also given the government its strongest blow yet against the Cartel.

Drugs. It all came down to that. Their capacity to corrupt was like nothing he'd ever known. Drugs corrupted people, clouded their thoughts at the individual level, and ultimately ended their lives. Drugs generated the kinds of money to corrupt those who didn't partake. Drugs corrupted institutions at every level and in every way imaginable. Drugs corrupted whole governments. So what was the answer? Davidoff didn't have that answer, though he knew that if he ever ran for that Senate seat he'd prance about in front of the TV cameras and announce that he did—

or at least part of it, if only the people of Alabama would trust him to represent them. . . .

Christ, he thought. *So now what do I do?*

Those two pirates deserve *to die for what they have done. What about my duty to the victims?* It wasn't all a lie—in fact none of it was. Davidoff did believe in Justice, did believe that law was what men had built to protect themselves from the predators, did believe that his mission in life was to be an instrument of that justice. Why else had he worked so hard for so little? *It wasn't entirely ambition, after all, was it?*

No.

One of the victims had been dirty, but what of the other three? What did the military call that? "Collateral damage." That was the term when an act against an individual target incidentally destroyed the other things that happened to be close by. Collateral damage. It was one thing when the State did it in time of war. In this case it was simply murder.

No, it wasn't simple murder, was it? Those bastards took their time. They enjoyed *themselves. Is eight years of time enough to pay for them?*

But what if you lose the case entirely? Even if you win, can you sacrifice those Coasties to get justice? Is that "collateral damage," too?

There had to be a way out. There usually was, anyway, and he had a couple of days to figure that one out.

They'd slept well, and the thin mountain air didn't affect them as badly as they'd expected. By sundown the squad was up and eager. Chavez drank his instant coffee as he went over the map, wondering which of the marked targets they'd stake out tonight. Throughout the day, squad members had kept a close eye on the road below, knowing more or less what they were looking for. A truck with containers of acid. Some cheap local labor would off-load the jars and head into the hills, followed by people with backpacks of coca leaves and some other light equipment. Around sundown a truck stopped. Light failed before they could see all of what happened, and their low-light goggles had no telescopic features, but the truck moved off rather soon, and it was within three kilometers of HOTEL, one of the locations on the target list, four miles away.

Show time. Each man sprayed a goodly bit of insect repellent onto his hands, then rubbed it on face, neck, and ears. In addition to keeping the bugs off, it also softened the camouflage paint that went on next like some ghastly form of lipstick. The members of each pair assisted one another in putting it on. The darker shades went on forehead, nose, and cheekbones, while the lighter ones went to the normal shadow areas under the eyes and in the hollow of cheeks. It wasn't war paint, as one might think from watching movie representations of soldiers. The purpose was invisibility, not intimidation. With the naturally bright spots dulled, and the normally dark ones brightened, their faces no longer looked like faces at all.

It was time to earn their pay for real. Approach routes and rally points were preselected and made known to every member of the squad. Questions were asked and answered, contingencies examined, alternate plans made, and Ramirez had them up and moving while there was still light on the eastern wall of the valley, heading downhill toward their objective.

17. Execution

The standard Army field order for a combat mission follows an acronym known as SMESSCS: Situation; Mission; Execution; Service and Support; Command and Signal.

Situation is the background information for the mission, what is going on that the soldiers need to know about.

Mission is a one-sentence description of the task at hand.

Execution is the methodology for *how* the mission is to be accomplished.

Service and Support covers the support functions that might aid the men in the performance of their job.

Command defines who gives the orders through every step of the chain, theoretically all the way back up to the Pentagon, and all the way down to the most junior member of the unit who in the final exigency would be commanding himself alone.

Signal is the general term for communications procedures to be followed.

The soldiers had already been briefed on the overall situation, which had hardly been necessary. Both that and their current mission had changed somewhat, but they already knew that, too. Captain Ramirez had briefed them on the execution of their current mission, also giving his men the other information they needed for this evening. There was no outside support; they were on their own. Ramirez was in tactical command, with subordinate leaders identified in case of his disablement, and he'd already issued radio codes. His last act before leading his men down from their perch was to radio his intentions to VARIABLE, whose location he didn't know, but whose approval he receipted.

As always Staff Sergeant Domingo Chavez had the point, now one hundred meters ahead of Julio Vega, again ''walking slack'' fifty meters ahead of the main body, whose men were spread out at ten-meter intervals for the approach. Going downhill made it tougher on the legs, but the men hardly noticed. They were too pumped up. Every few hundred meters Chavez angled for a clear spot from which they could look down at the objective—the place they were going to hit—and through his binoculars he could see the vague glow of gasoline lanterns. With the sun behind him he didn't have to worry about a reflection off the glasses. The spot was right where the map said it was—he wondered how that information had been developed—and they were following exactly the procedure that he'd been briefed about. Somebody, he thought, had really done his homework on this job. They expected ten to fifteen people at HOTEL. He hoped they had that right, too.

The going wasn't so bad. The cover was not as dense as it had been in the lowlands, and there were fewer bugs. Maybe, he thought, the air was too thin for them, too. There were birds calling to one another, the usual forest chatter to mask the sounds of his unit's approach—but there was damned little of that. Chavez had heard one guy slip and fall a hundred meters back, but only a Ninja would have noticed. He was able to cover half the distance in under an hour, stopping at a preplanned rally point for the rest of the squad to catch up.

"So far, so good, *jefe,*" he told Ramirez. "I ain't seen nothing, not even a llama," he added to show that he was at ease. "Little over three thousand more meters to go."

"Okay. Stop at the next checkpoint. Remember there might be folks out taking a stroll."

"Roger that, Cap'n." Chavez took off at once. The rest started moving two minutes later.

Ding moved more slowly now. The probability of contact increased with every step he took toward HOTEL. The druggies couldn't be all that dumb, he warned himself. They had to have a little brains, and the people they used would be locals, people who'd grown up in this valley and knew its ways. And lots of them would have weapons. He was surprised how different it felt from the last time, but then he'd watched and evaluated his targets over a period of days. He didn't even have a proper count on them, didn't know how they were armed, didn't know how good they were.

Christ, this is real combat. We don't know shit.

But that's what Ninja are for! he told himself, taking small comfort in his bravado.

Time started doing strange things. Each single step seemed to take forever, but when he got to the final rally point, it hadn't been all that long at all, had it? He could see the glow of the objective now, a vague green semicircle on the goggle display, but still there was no movement to be seen or heard on the woods. When he got to the last checkpoint, Chavez picked a tree and stood beside it, keeping his head up, swiveling left and right to gather as much information as possible. He thought he could hear things now. It came and went, but occasionally there was an odd, not-natural sound from the direction of the objective. It worried him that he didn't really see anything as yet. Just that glow, but nothing else.

"Anything?" Captain Ramirez asked in a whisper.

"Listen."

"Yeah," the captain said after a moment.

The squad members dropped off their rucksacks and divided according to plan. Chavez, Vega, and Ingeles would advance directly toward HOTEL while the rest circled around to the left. Ingeles, the communications sergeant, had an M-203 grenade launcher slung under his rifle, Vega had the machine gun, and Chavez still had his silenced MP-5. Their job was overwatch. They would get in as close as possible to provide fire support for the actual assault. If anyone was in the way, it was Chavez's job to drop him quietly. Ding led his group off first, while Captain Ramirez moved off a minute later. In the case of both groups, the interval between the men was tightened up to five meters. Another real danger now was confusion. If any of the soldiers lost contact with his comrades, or if an enemy sentry somehow got mixed up with their group, the results could be lethal to the mission and the men.

The last five hundred meters took over half an hour. Ding's overwatch position was clear on the map, but not so clear in the woods at night. Things always looked different at night, and even with the low-light goggles, things were just . . . different. In a distant sort of way, Chavez knew that he was having an attack of the jitters. It wasn't so much that he was afraid, just that he felt much less certain now. He told himself every two or three minutes that he knew exactly what he was doing, and each time it worked—but only for a few minutes before the uncertainty hit him again. Logic told him that he was having what the manuals called a normal anxiety reaction. Chavez didn't like it, but found that he could live with it. Just like the manuals said.

He saw movement and froze. His left hand swung around his back, palm perpendicular to warn the two behind him to stop also. Again he kept his head up, trusting to his training. The human eye sees only movement at night, the manuals and his experience told him. Unless the opposition had goggles. . . .

And this one didn't. The man-shape was almost a hundred meters away, moving slowly and casually through the trees between Chavez and the place where Chavez wanted to be. So simple a thing as that gave the man an early death sentence. Ding waved for Ingeles and Vega to stay put while he moved right, opposite his target's current path to get behind him. Perversely, he moved quickly now. He had to be in place in another fifteen minutes. Using his goggles to select clear places, he set his feet as lightly as he could, moving almost at a normal walking speed. Pride surged past the anxiety now that he could see what he had to do. He made no sound at all, moving alone, crouched down, swiveling his head from his path to his target and back again. Within a minute he was in a good place. There was a worn path there. This was a path for the guard. The idiot stuck to a path, Chavez recognized. You didn't do things like that and expect to live.

He was coming back now, moving with slow, almost childish steps, his legs snapping out from the knees—but he moved quietly enough by walking on the worn path, Ding noticed belatedly. Maybe he wasn't a total fool. His head was looking uphill. But his rifle was slung over his shoulder. Chavez let him approach, taking off his goggles when the man was looking away. The sudden loss of the display made him lose his target for a few seconds, and the edges of panic appeared in his consciousness, but Ding commanded them to be still. The man would reappear presently as he walked back to the south.

He did, first as a spectral outline, then as a black mass walking down the worn corridor in the jungle. Ding crouched at the base of a tree, his weapon aimed at the man's head, and let him come closer. Better to wait and get a sure kill. His selector switch was on the single-shot position. The man was ten meters away. Chavez wasn't even breathing now. He aimed for the center of the man's head and squeezed off a single round.

The metallic sound of the H&K's action cycling back and forth seemed incredibly loud, but the target dropped at once, just a muted clack from his own rifle as it hit the ground alongside the body. Chavez leaped forward, his submachine gun fixed on the target, but the man—it had been a man, after all—didn't move. With his goggles back on, he could see the single hole right in the center of the nose, and the bullet had angled upward, ripping through the bottom of the brain for an instant, noiseless kill.

Ninja! his mind exulted.

He stood beside the body and looked uphill, holding his weapon high. *All clear.* A moment later the shapes of Vega and Ingeles appeared on the green image display, heading downhill. He turned, found a spot from which to observe the objective, and waited for them.

There it was, seventy meters away. The glow from the gasoline lanterns blazed on his goggles, and he realized that he could take them off once and for all. There were more voices now. He could even catch the odd word. It was the bored, day-to-day talk of people doing a job. There was a splashing sound, almost like . . . what? Ding didn't know, and it didn't matter for the present. Their fire-support position was in view. There was just one little problem.

It was oriented the wrong way. The trees that should have provided cover to their right flank instead prevented them from covering the objective. They'd planned the overwatch position in the wrong place, he decided. Chavez grimaced and made other plans, knowing that the captain would do the same. They found a spot almost as good fifteen meters away and oriented in the proper direction. He checked his watch. Nearly time. It was time to make his final, vital inspection of the objective.

He counted twelve men. The center of the site was . . . what looked like a portable bathtub. Two men were walking in it, crushing or stirring up or doing something to the curious-looking soup of coca leaves and . . . *what was it they told us?* he asked himself. *Water and sulfuric acid?* Something like that. *Christ,* he thought. *Walking in fucking acid!* The men doing that distasteful task took turns. He watched one change, and those who got out poured fresh water over their feet and calves. It must have hurt or burned or something, Ding realized. But their banter was good-natured enough, thirty meters away. One was talking about his girlfriend in rather crude terms, boasting of what she did for him and what he did to her.

There were six men with rifles, all AKs. *Christ, the whole world carries those goddamned things.* They stood at the perimeter of the site, watching inward, however, rather than outward. One was smoking. There was a backpack by the lantern. One of the walkers said something to one of the gunmen and pulled a beer bottle out of it for himself, and another for the one who'd given him permission.

Idiots! Ding told himself. The radio earpiece made three rasping dashes of static. Ramirez was in place and asking if Ding was ready. He keyed his radio two times in reply, then looked left and right. Vega had his SAW up on the bipod, and the canvas ammo pouch unzipped. Two hundred rounds were all ready, and a second pouch lay next to the first.

Chavez again nestled himself as close to a thick tree as he could and selected the farthest target. He figured the range to him at about eighty meters, a touch long for his weapon, too long for a head shot, he decided. He thumbed the selector to the burst setting, tucked the weapon in tight, and took careful aim through the diopter sight.

Three rounds were ejected from the side of his weapon. The man's face was surprised when two of them struck his chest. His breath came out in a rasping scream that caused heads to turn in his direction. Chavez shifted aim to another rifleman, whose gun was already coming off his shoulder. This one also took two or three hits, but that didn't stop him from trying to get his weapon around.

As soon as it appeared that fire might be returned, Vega opened up, transfixing that man with tracers from his machine gun, then shifting fire to two more armed men. One of them got a couple of rounds off, but they went high. The other, unarmed men reacted more slowly than the guards. Two started to run but were cut down by Vega's stream of fire. The others fell to the ground and crawled. Two more armed men appeared—or their weapons did. The flaming signatures of automatic weapons appeared in the trees on the far side of the site, aimed up at the fire-support team. Exactly as planned.

The assault element, led by Captain Ramirez, opened up from their right flank. The distinctive chatter of M-16 fire tore through the trees as Chavez, Vega, and Ingeles continued to pour fire into the objective and away from the incoming assault element. One of the people firing from the trees must have been hit. The muzzle flash from his weapon changed direction, blazing straight up. But two others turned and fired into the assault element before they went down. The soldiers were shooting at anything that moved now. One of the men who'd been walking in the tub tried to pick up a discarded rifle and didn't make it. One stood and might have been trying to surrender, but his hands never got high enough before the squad's other SAW lanced a line of tracers through his chest.

Chavez and his team ceased fire to allow the assault element to enter the objective safely. Two of them finished off people who were still moving despite their wounds. Then everything stopped for a moment. The lantern still hissed and illuminated the area, but there was no other sound but the echoes of the shooting and the calls of outraged birds.

Four soldiers checked out the dead. The rest of the assault element would now have formed a perimeter around the objective. Chavez, Vega, and Ingeles safed their weapons, collected their things, and moved in.

What Chavez saw was thoroughly horrible. Two of the enemy were still alive, but wouldn't be for long. One had fallen victim to Vega's machine gun, and his abdomen was torn open. Both of the other's legs had been nearly shot off and were bleeding rapidly onto the beaten dirt. The squad medic looked on without pity. Both died within a minute. The squad's orders were a little vague on the issue of prisoners. No one could lawfully order American soldiers not to take prisoners, and the circumlocutions had been a problem for Captain Ramirez, but the message had gotten through. It was too fucking bad. But these people were involved in killing American kids with drugs, and that wasn't exactly under the Rules of Land Warfare either, was it? It was too fucking bad. Besides, there were other things to worry about.

Chavez had barely gotten into the site when he heard something. Everyone did. Someone was running away, straight downhill. Ramirez pointed to Ding, who immediately ran after him.

He reached for his goggles and tried to hold them in his hand as he ran, then realized that running was probably a stupid thing to do. He stopped, held the goggles to his eyes, and spotted both a path and the running man. There were times for caution, and times for boldness. Instinct told him that this was one of the latter. Chavez raced down the path, trusting to his skills to keep his footing and rapidly catching up with the sound that was trying to get away. Inside three minutes he could hear the man's thrashing and falling through the cover. Ding stopped and used his goggles again. Only a hundred meters ahead. He started running again, the blood hot in his veins. Fifty meters now. The man fell again. Ding slowed his approach. More attention to noise now, he told himself. This guy wasn't going to get away. He left the path, moving at a tangent to his left, his movements looking like an elaborate dance step as he picked his way as quickly as he could. Every fifty yards he stopped and used his night scope. Whoever the man was, he'd tired and was moving more slowly. Chavez got ahead of him, curving back to his right and waiting on the path.

Ding had nearly miscalculated. He'd just gotten his weapon up when the shape appeared, and the sergeant fired on instinct from a range of ten feet into his chest. The man fell against Chavez with a despairing groan. Ding threw the body off and fired another burst into his chest. There was no other sound.

"Jesus," the sergeant said. He knelt to catch his breath. Whom had he killed? He put the scope back on his head and looked down.

The man was barefoot. He wore the simple cotton shirt and pants of . . . Chavez had just killed a peasant, one of those poor dumb bastards who danced in the coca soup. Wasn't that something to be proud of?

The exhilaration that often follows a successful combat operation left him like the air released from a toy balloon. Some poor bastard—didn't even have shoes on.

The druggies hired 'em to hump their shit up the hills, paid 'em half of nothing to do the dirty, nasty work of pre-refining the leaves.

His belt was unbuckled. He'd been off in the bushes taking a dump when the shooting started, and only wanted to get away, but his half-mast pants had made it a futile effort. He was about Ding's age, smaller and more lightly built, but puffy around the face from the starchy diet of the local peasant farmers. An ordinary face, it still bore the signs of the fear and panic and pain with which his death had come. He hadn't been armed. He'd been part of the casual labor. He'd died because he'd been in the wrong place, at the wrong time.

It was not something for Chavez to be proud of. He keyed his radio.

"Six, this is Point. I got him. Just one."

"Need help?"

"Negative. I can handle it." Chavez hoisted the body on his shoulder for the climb back to the objective. It took ten exhausting minutes, but that was part of the job. Ding felt the man's blood oozing from the six holes in his chest, staining the back of his khaki shirt. Maybe staining more than that.

By the time he got back, the bodies had all been laid side by side and searched. There were many sacks of coca leaves, several additional jars of acid, and a total of fourteen dead men when Chavez dumped his at the end of the line.

"You look a little punked out," Vega observed.

"Ain't as big as you, *Oso,*" Ding gasped out in reply.

There were two small radios, and various other personal things to catalog, but nothing of real military value. A few men cast eyes on the pack full of beers, but no one made the expected "Miller Time!" joke. If there had been radio codes, they were in the head of whoever had been the boss here. There was no way of telling who he might have been; in death all men look alike. The bodies were all dressed more or less the same, except for the webbed pistol belts of the armed men. All in all, it was rather a sad thing to see. Some people who had been alive half an hour earlier were no longer so. Beyond that, there wasn't much to be said about the mission.

Most importantly, there were no casualties to the squad, though Sergeant Guerra had gotten a scare from a close burst. Ramirez completed his inspection of the site, then got his men ready to leave. Chavez again took the lead.

It was a tough uphill climb, and it gave Captain Ramirez time to think. It was, he realized, something that he ought to have thought about a hell of a lot sooner:

What is this mission all about? To Ramirez, *Mission* now meant the purpose for their being here in the Colombian highlands, not just the job of taking this place out.

He understood that watching the airfields had the direct effect of stopping flights of drugs into the United States. They'd performed covert reconnaissance, and people were making tactical use of the intelligence information which they'd developed. Not only was it simple—but it also made sense. But what the hell were they doing now? His squad had just executed a picture-perfect small-unit raid. The men could not have done better—aided by the inept performance of the enemy, of course.

That was going to change. The enemy was going to learn damned fast from this. Their security would be better. They would learn that much even before they figured out what was going on. A blown-away processing site was all the information they needed to learn that they had to improve their physical security arrangements.

What had the attack actually accomplished? A few hundred pounds of coca leaves would not be processed tonight. He didn't have instructions to cart the leaves away, and even if he had, there was no ready means of destroying them except by fire, and he wasn't stupid enough to light a fire on a mountainside at night, orders or not. What they had accomplished tonight was . . . nothing. Nothing at all, really. There were tons of coca leaves, and scores—perhaps hundreds—of refining sites. They hadn't made a dent in the trade tonight, not even a dimple.

So what the hell are we risking our lives for? he asked himself. He ought to have asked that question in Panama, but like his three fellow officers, he'd been caught up in the institutional rage accompanying the assassination of the FBI Director and the others. Besides, he was only a captain, and he was more an order-follower than an order-giver. As a professional officer, he was used to being given orders from battalion or brigade commanders, forty-or-so-year-old professional soldiers who knew what the hell they were doing, most of the time. But his orders now were coming from someplace else—where? Now he wasn't so sure—and he'd allowed himself to be lulled in the complacency that assumed whoever generated the orders knew what the hell *he* was doing.

Why didn't you ask more questions!

Ramirez had seen success in his mission tonight. Prior to it his thought had been directed toward a fixed goal. But he'd achieved that goal, and seen nothing beyond it. He ought to have realized that earlier. Ramirez knew that now. But it was too late now.

The other part of the trap was even more troubling. He had to tell his men that everything was all right. They'd done as well as any commander could have asked. But—

What the hell are we doing here? He didn't know, because no one had ever told him, that he was not the first young captain to ask that question all too late, that it was almost a tradition of American arms for bright young officers to wonder why the hell they were sent out to do things. But almost always they asked the question too late.

He had no choice, of course. He had to assume, as his training and experience told him to assume, that the mission really did make sense. Even though his reason—Ramirez was far from being a stupid man—told him otherwise, he commanded himself to have faith in his command leadership. His men had faith in him. He had to have the same faith in those above himself. An army could work no other way.

Two hundred meters ahead, Chavez felt the stickiness on the back of his shirt and asked himself other questions. It had never occurred to him that he'd have to carry the dead, bleeding body of an enemy halfway up a mountain. He'd not anticipated how this physical reminder of what he had done would wear on his conscience. He'd killed a peasant. Not an armed man, not a real enemy, but some poor bastard who had just taken a job with the wrong side, probably just to feed his family, if he had one. But what else could Chavez have done? Let him get away?

It was simpler for the sergeant. He had an officer who told him what to do. Captain Ramirez knew what he was doing. He was an officer, and that was his job: to know what was going on and give the orders. That made it a little easier as he climbed back up the mountain to the RON site, but his bloodied shirt continued to cling to his back like the questions of a nagging conscience.

Tim Jackson arrived back at his office at 2230 hours after a short squad-training exercise right on the grounds of Fort Ord. He'd just sat down in his cheap swivel chair when the phone rang. The exercise hadn't gone well. Ozkanian was a little slow catching on in his leadership of second squad. This was the second time in a row that he'd screwed up and made his lieutenant look bad. That offended Sergeant Mitchell, who had hopes for the young officer. Both knew that you didn't make a good squad sergeant in less than four years, and only then if you had a man as sharp as Chavez had been. But it was Ozkanian's job to lead the squad, and Mitchell was now explaining a few things to him. He was doing so in the way of platoon sergeants, with vigor, enthusiasm, and a few speculative observations about Ozkanian's ancestry. If any.

"Lieutenant Jackson," Tim answered after the second ring.

"Lieutenant, this is Colonel O'Mara at Special Ops Command."

"Yes, sir!"

"I hear you've been making some noise about a staff sergeant named Chavez. Is that correct?" Jackson looked up to see Mitchell walk in, his cabbage-patch helmet tucked under his sweaty arm and a whimsical smile on his lips. Ozkanian had gotten the message this time.

"Yes, sir. He didn't show up where he's supposed to be. He's one of mine, and—"

"Wrong, Lieutenant! He's one of mine now. He's doing something that you do not need to know about, and you will not, repeat *not* burn up any more phone lines *fucking around into something that does not concern you. IS THAT CLEAR, LIEUTENANT?"*

"But, sir, excuse me, but I—"

"You got bad ears or something, son?" The voice was quieter now, and that was really frightening to a lieutenant who'd already had a bad day.

"No, sir. It's just that I got a call from—"

"I know about that. I took care of that. Sergeant Chavez is doing something that you do not need to know about. Period. End. Is that clear?"

"Yes, sir."

The line clicked off.

"Shit," Lieutenant Jackson observed.

Sergeant Mitchell hadn't caught any words from the conversation, but the buzz from the phone line had made it to the doorway he was standing in.

"Chavez?"

"Yeah. Some colonel at Special Ops—Fort MacDill, I guess—says that they have him and he's off doing something. And I don't need to know about that. Says he took care of Fort Benning for us."

"Oh, horseshit," Mitchell observed, taking his place in the seat opposite the lieutenant's desk, after which he asked: "Mind if I sit down, sir?"

"What do you suppose is going on?"

"Beats the hell outa me, sir. But I know a guy at MacDill. Think I'll make a phone call tomorrow. I don't like one of my guys getting lost like that. It's not supposed to work like that. He didn't have no place chewing your ass either, sir. You're just doin' your job, looking after your people that way, and you don't come down on people for doing their job. In case nobody ever told you, sir," Mitchell explained, "you don't chew some poor lieutenant's ass over something like this. You make a quiet call to the battalion commander, or maybe the S-1, and have him settle things nice 'n quiet. Lieutenants get picked on enough by their own colonels without needin' to get chewed on by strange ones. That's why things go through channels, so you know who's chewing' ya'."

"Thank you, Sergeant," Jackson said with a smile. "I needed that."

"I told Ozkanian that he ought to concentrate a little more on leadin' his squad instead of trying to be Sergeant Rock. I think this time he'll listen. He's a pretty good kid, really. Just needs a little seasoning." Mitchell stood. "See you at PT tomorrow, sir. Good night."

"Right. 'Night, Sergeant." Tim Jackson decided that sleep made more sense than paperwork and headed off to his car. On the drive to the BOQ, he was still pondering the call he'd gotten from Colonel O'Mara, whoever the hell he was. Lieutenants didn't interact with bird-colonels very much—he'd made his (required) New Year's Day appearance at the brigade commander's home, but that was it. New lieutenants were supposed to maintain a low profile. On the other hand, one of the many lessons remembered from West Point was that he was responsible for his men. The fact that Chavez hadn't arrived at Fort Benning, that his departure from Ord had been so . . . irregular, and that his natural and responsible inquiry into his man's situation had earned him nothing more than a chewing only made the young officer all the more curious. He'd let Mitchell make his calls, but he'd stay out of it for the moment, not wanting to draw additional attention to himself until he knew what the hell he was doing. In this Tim Jackson was fortunate. He had a big brother on Pentagon duty who knew how things were supposed to work and was pushing hard for O-6—captain's or colonel's—rank, even if he was a squid. Robby could give him some good advice, and advice was what he needed.

It was a nice, smooth flight in the COD. Even so, Robby Jackson didn't like it much. He didn't like sitting in an aft-facing seat, but mainly he didn't like being in an airplane unless he had the stick. A fighter pilot, test pilot, and most recently commander of one of the Navy's elite Tomcat squadrons, he knew that he was about the best flyer in the world, and didn't like trusting his life to the lesser skills of another aviator. Besides, on Navy aircraft the stewardesses weren't worth a damn. In this case it was a pimply-faced kid from New York, judging by his accent, who'd managed to spill coffee on the guy next to him.

"I hate these things," the man said.

"Yeah, well, it ain't Delta, is it?" Jackson noted as he tucked the folder back in his bag. He had the new tactical scheme committed to memory. As well he might. It was mainly his idea.

The man wore khaki uniform clothing, with a "U.S." insignia on his collar. That made him a tech-rep, a civilian who was doing something or other for the Navy. There were always some aboard a carrier—electronics specialists or various sorts of engineers who either provided special service to a new piece of gear or helped train the Navy personnel who did. They were given the simulated rank of warrant officer, but treated more or less as commissioned officers, eating in the officers' mess and quartered in relative luxury—a very relative term on a U.S. Navy ship unless you were a captain or an admiral, and tech-reps did not rate that sort of treatment.

"What are you going out for?" Robby asked.

"Checking out performance on a new piece of ordnance. I'm afraid I can't say any more than that."

"One of them, eh?"

" 'Fraid so," the man said, examining the coffee stain on his knee.

"Do this a lot?"

"First time," the man said. "You?"

"I fly off boats for a living, but I'm serving time in the Pentagon now. OP-05's office, fighter-tactics desk."

"Never made a carrier landing," the man added nervously.

"Not so bad," Robby assured him. "Except at night."

"Oh?" The man wasn't too scared to know that it was dark outside.

"Yeah, well, carrier landings aren't all that bad in daylight. Flying into a regular airfield, you look ahead and pick the spot you're gonna touch on. Same thing on a carrier, just the runway's smaller. But at night you can't really see where you're gonna touch. So that makes it a little twitchy. Don't sweat it. The gal we got driving—"

"A girl?"

"Yeah, a lot of the COD drivers are girls. The one up front is pretty good, instructor pilot, they tell me." It always made people safer to think that the pilot was an instructor, except: "She's breaking in a new ensign tonight," Jackson added maliciously. He loved to needle people who didn't like flying. It was always something he bothered his friend Jack Ryan about.

"New ensign?"

"You know, a kid out of P-cola. Guess he wasn't good enough for fighters or attack bombers, so he flies the delivery truck. They gotta learn, right? Everybody makes a first night carrier landing. I did. No big deal," Jackson said comfortably. Then he checked to make sure his safety belts were nice and tight. Over the years he'd found that one sure way of alleviating fear was to hand it over to someone else.

"Thanks."

"You part of the Shoot-Ex?"

"Huh?"

"The exercise we're running. We get to shoot some real missiles at target drones. 'Shoot-Ex.' Missile-Firing Exercise."

"I don't think so."

"Oh, I was hoping you were a guy from Hughes. We want to see if the fix on the Phoenix guidance package really works or not."

"Oh, sorry—no. I work with something else."

"Okay." Robby pulled a paperback from his pocket and started reading. Now that he was sure there was somebody on the COD more uncomfortable than he was, he could concentrate on the book. He wasn't really frightened, of course. He just hoped that the new nugget sitting in the copilot's right seat wouldn't splatter the COD and its passengers all over the ramp. But there wasn't much that he could do about that.

The squad was tired when they got back to the RON site. They took their positions while the captain made his radio call. One of each pair immediately stripped his weapon down for cleaning, even those few who hadn't gotten a shot off.

"Well, *Oso* and his SAW got on the scoreboard tonight," Vega observed as he pulled a patch through the twenty-one-inch barrel. "Nice work, Ding," he added.

"They weren't very good."

"Hey, *'mano,* we do our thing right, they don't have the chance to be very good."

"It's been awful easy so far, man. Might change."

Vega looked up for a moment. "Yeah. That's right."

* * *

At geosynchronous height over Brazil, a weather satellite of the National Oceanic and Atmospheric Administration had its low-resolution camera pointed forever downward at the planet it had left eleven months before and to which it would never return. It seemed to hover almost in a fixed position, twenty-two thousand six hundred miles over the emerald-green jungles of the Amazon valley, but in fact it was moving at a speed of about seven thousand miles per hour, its easterly orbital path exactly matching the rotation speed of the earth below. The satellite had other instruments, of course, but this particular color-TV camera had the simplest of jobs. It watched clouds that floated in the air like distant balls of cotton. That so prosaic a function could be important was so obvious as to be hard to recognize. This satellite and its antecedents had saved thousands of lives and were arguably the most useful and efficient segment of America's space program. The lives saved were those of sailors for the most part, sailors whose ships might otherwise stray into the path of an undetected storm. From its perch, the satellite could see from the great Southern Ocean girdling Antarctica to beyond the North Cape of Norway, and no storm escaped its notice.

Almost directly below the satellite, conditions still not fully understood gave birth to cyclonic storms in the broad, warm Atlantic waters off the West Coast of Africa, from which they were carried westward toward the New World, where they were known by the West Indian name, hurricane. Data from the satellite was downlinked to NOAA's National Hurricane Center at Coral Gables, Florida, where meteorologists and computer scientists were working as part of a multiyear project to determine how the storms began and why they moved as they did. The busy season for these scientists was just beginning. Fully a hundred people, some with their doctor's degrees years behind them, others summer interns from a score of universities, examined the photographs for the first storm of the season. Some hoped for many, that they might study and learn from them. The more experienced scientists knew that feeling, but also knew that those massive oceanic storms were the most destructive and deadly force of nature, and regularly killed thousands who lived too close to the sea. They also knew that the storms would come in their own good time, for no one had a provable model for explaining exactly why they formed. All man could do was see them, track them, measure their intensity, and warn those in their path. The scientists also named them. The names were chosen years in advance, always starting at the top of the alphabet and proceeding downward. The first name on the list for the current year was *Adele*.

As the camera watched, clouds grew skyward five hundred miles from the Cape Verde islands, cradle of hurricanes. Whether it would become an organized tropical cyclone or simply be just another large rainstorm, no one could say. It was still early in the season. But it had all the makings of a big season. The West African desert was unusually hot for the spring, and heat there had a demonstrable connection with birth of hurricanes.

The truck driver appeared at the proper time to collect the men and the paste processed from the coca leaves, but they weren't there as expected. He waited an hour, and still they weren't there. There were two men with him, of course, and these he sent up to the processing site. The driver was the "senior" man of the group and didn't want to be bothered climbing those cursed mountains anymore. So while he smoked his cigarettes, they climbed. He waited another hour. There was quite a bit of traffic on the highway, especially big diesel trucks whose mufflers and pollution controls were less well attended to than was the case in other, more prosperous regions—besides, their removal made for improved fuel economy in addition to the greater noise and smoke. Many of the big tractor-trailer combinations roared past, vibrating the roadbed and rocking his own truck in the rush of air. That was why he missed the sound. After waiting a total of ninety minutes, it was clear that he'd have to go up himself. He locked the truck, lit yet another cigarette, and began his way up the path.

The driver found it hard going. Though he'd grown up in these hills, and could remember a boyhood in which a thousand-foot climb was just another footrace with his playmates, he'd been driving the truck for some time, and his leg muscles were more accustomed to pushing down pedals than this sort of thing. What would once have taken forty minutes now took over an hour, and with the place almost in sight he was venomously angry, too angry and too tired to pay attention to things that ought to have been obvious by now. He could still hear the traffic sounds on the road below, could hear the birds twittering in the trees around him, but nothing else when he should have been hearing something. He paused, bending over to catch his breath when he got his first warning. It was a dark spot on the trail. Something had turned the brown earth to black, but that could have been anything, and he was in a hurry to see what the problem was up the hill and didn't ponder it. After all, there hadn't been any problem lately with the army or the police, and he wondered why the refining work was done so far up the mountainside in any case. It was no longer necessary.

Five minutes more and he could see the little clearing, and only now he noticed that there were no sounds coming from it, though there was an odd, acrid smell. Doubtless the acid used in the prerefining process, he was sure. Then he made the last turn and saw.

The truck driver was not a man unaccustomed to violence. He'd been involved in the pre-Cartel fighting and had also killed a few M-19 sympathizers in the wars because of which the Cartel had actually been formed. He'd seen blood, therefore, and had spilled some himself.

But not like this. All fourteen of the men he'd driven in the previous night were lined up shoulder to shoulder in a neat little row on the ground. The bodies were already bloated, and animals had been picking at several of the open wounds. The two men he'd dispatched up the mountainside were more freshly dead. Though the driver didn't fathom it, they'd been killed by a claymore mine triggered when they'd examined the bodies, and their bodies were newly shredded, with major sections missing where the ball-bearing-sized fragments had struck, and with the blood still trickling out. One's face showed the surprise and shock. The other man was face-down, with a section about the size of a shoe box messily removed from his back.

The driver stood still for a minute or so, afraid to move in any direction, his quivering hands reaching for another cigarette, then dropping two which he was too terrified to reach for. Before he could get a third, he turned and moved carefully down the path. A hundred meters after that, he was running for his life as every bird call and every breeze through the trees sounded to him like an approaching soldier. They had to be soldiers. He was sure of that. Only soldiers killed with that sort of precision.

"That was a splendid paper you delivered this afternoon. We hadn't considered the Soviet 'nationalities' question as thoroughly as you have. Your analytical skills are as sharp as ever.'' Sir Basil Charleston raised his glass in salute. ''Your promotion was well earned. Congratulations, Sir John.''

''Thanks, Bas'. I just wish it could have happened another way,'' Ryan said.

''That bad?''

Jack nodded. ''I'm afraid so.''

''And Emil Jacobs, too. Bloody bad time for your chaps.''

Ryan smiled rather grimly. ''You might say that.''

''So, what are you going to do about it?''

''I'm afraid there's not much I can say about that,'' Jack replied carefully. *I don't know, but I can't exactly say* that, *can I?*

''Quite so.'' The head of Her Majesty's Secret Intelligence Service nodded sagely. ''Whatever your response is, I'm sure it will be appropriate.''

At that moment he knew that Greer had been right. He had to know such things or risk being taken for a fool by his counterparts here and everywhere else in the world. He'd get home in a few more days and talk things over with Judge Moore. Ryan was supposed to have some bureaucratic muscle now. Might as well flex it a little to see if it worked.

Commander Jackson woke after six hours' sleep. He, too, enjoyed that greatest of luxuries aboard a warship, privacy. His rank and former station as a squadron commander put him high on the list of VIPs, and there happened to be a spare one-man stateroom in this floating city. His was just under the flight deck foreward. Close to the bow catapults by the sound of things, which explained why one of *Ranger*'s own squadron commanders didn't want it. On arrival, he'd made the necessary courtesy calls, and he didn't have any official duties to attend to for another . . . three hours. After washing and shaving and morning coffee, he decided to do a few things on his own. Robby headed below for the carrier's magazine.

This was a large compartment with a relatively low ceiling where the bombs and missiles were kept. Several rooms, really, with nearby shops so that the ''smart'' weapons could be tested and repaired by ordnance technicians. Jackson's personal concern was with the AIM-54C Phoenix air-to-air missiles. There had been problems with the guidance systems, and one purpose of the battle-group exercise was to see if the contractor's fix really worked or not.

Entry into the space was restricted, for obvious reasons. Robby identified himself to a senior chief petty officer, and it turned out that they'd both served on the *Kennedy* a few years before. Together they entered a work space where some ''ordies'' were playing with the missiles, with an odd-looking box hanging on the pointed nose of one.

''What d'ya think?'' one asked.

''Reads out okay to me, Duke,'' the one on the oscilloscope replied. ''Let me try some simulated jamming.''

''That's the bunch we're prepping for the Shoot-Ex, sir,'' the senior chief explained. ''So far they seem to be working all right, but . . .''

''But wasn't it you who found the problem in the first place?'' Robby asked.

''Me and my old boss, Lieutenant Frederickson.'' The chief nodded. The discovery had resulted in several million dollars in penalties to the contractor. And all the AIM-54C missiles in the fleet had been decertified for several months, taking away what should have been the most capable air-to-air missile in the Navy. He led Jackson to the rack of test equipment. ''How many we supposed to shoot?''

"Enough to tell whether the fix works or not," Robby replied. The chief grunted. "That could be quite a Shoot-Ex, sir."

"Drones are cheap!" Robby pointed out in a most outrageous lie. But the chief knew what he meant. It was cheaper than going to the Indian Ocean and maybe having a shoot-out with *Iranian* F-14A Tomcats (they had them, too) and then finding out that the goddamned missiles didn't work properly. That was a most efficient way of killing off pilots whose training went for a million dollars a pop. The good news was that the fix was working, at least as far as the test equipment could tell. To make sure, Robby told the chief, between ten and twenty of the Phoenix-Cs would be shot off, plus a larger number of Sparrows and Sidewinders. Jackson started to leave. He'd seen what he needed to see, and the ordies all had work to do.

"Looks like we're really going to be emptying this here locker out, sir. You know about the new bombs we're checking out?"

"No. I met with a tech-rep on the COD flight in. He didn't talk a hell of a lot. So what the hell is new? Just a bomb, right?"

The senior chief laughed. "Come on, I'll show you the Hush-A-Bomb."

"What?"

"Didn't you ever watch Rocky and Bullwinkle, sir?"

"Chief, you have really lost me."

"Well, when I was a kid I used to watch Rocky the Flying Squirrel and Bullwinkle the Moose, and one of the stories was about how Boris and Natasha—they were the bad guys, Commander—were trying to steal something called Hush-A-Boom. That was an explosive that blew stuff up without making any noise. Looks like the guys at China Lake came up with the next-best thing!"

The chief opened a door to the bomb-storage area. The streamlined shapes—they didn't have any fins or fuses attached until they were taken topside—sat on storage pallets securely chained down to the steel deck. On a pallet close to the rectangular elevator that delivered them topside was a group of blue-painted bombs. The blue color made them exercise units, but from the tag on the pallet it was clear that they were also loaded with the customary explosive filler. Robby Jackson was a fighter pilot, and hadn't dropped very many bombs, but that was just another side of his profession. The weapons he looked at appeared to be standard two-thousand-pound low-drag cases, which translated to nine hundred eighty-five pounds of high explosives, and just over a thousand pounds of steel bombcase. The only difference between a "dumb" or "iron" bomb and a guided "smart" bomb was the attachment of a couple of hardware items: a seeker head on the nose, and movable fins on the tail. Both units attached to the normal fusing points, and in fact the fuses were part of the guidance-package attachments. For obvious reasons these were kept in a different compartment. On the whole, however, the blue bombcases appeared grossly ordinary.

"So?" he asked.

The chief tapped the nearest bombcase with his knuckle. There was an odd sound. Odd enough that Robby did the same.

"That's not steel."

"Cellulose, sir. They made the friggin' things outa paper! How you like that?"

"Oh." Robby understood. "Stealth."

"These babies gotta be guided, though. They ain't gonna make fragments worth a damn." The purpose of the steel bombcase, of course, is to transform itself into thousands of high-speed razors, ripping into whatever lay within their ballistic range after detonation. It wasn't the explosion that killed people—which was, after all, the reason to build bombs—but rather the fragments they generated. "That's why we call it the Hush-A-Bomb. Fucker's gonna be right loud, sir, but after the smoke clears you're gonna wonder what the hell it was."

"New wonders from China Lake," Robby observed. What the hell good was a bomb that—but then, it was probably something for the new Stealth tactical bomber. He didn't know all that much about Stealth yet. It wasn't part of his brief in the Pentagon. Fighter tactics were, and Robby went off to go over his notes with the air-group commander. The first part of the battle-group exercise would begin in just over twenty-four hours.

The word got to Medellín fairly quickly, of course. By noon it was known that two refining operations had been eliminated and a total of thirty-one people killed. The loss of manpower was incidental. In each case more than half had been local peasants who did the coolie work, and the rest had been scarcely more important permanent employees whose guns kept the curious away, generally by example rather than persuasion. What was troubling was the fact that if word of these events got out, there might be some difficulties in recruiting new people to do the refining.

But most troubling of all was the simple fact that nobody knew what was going on. Was the Colombian Army going back into the hills? Was it M-19, breaking its word, or FARC, doing the same thing? Or something else? No one knew. That was most annoying, since they paid a good deal of money to get information. But the Cartel was a group of people, and action was taken only after consensus was reached. It was agreed that there must be a meeting. But then people began to worry if that might be dangerous. After all, clearly there were armed people about, people with little regard for human life, and that was also troubling for the senior Cartel officials. Most of all, these people had heavy weapons and the skill to use them. It was decided, therefore, that the meeting should be held at the most secure location possible.

FLASH
TOP SECRET ***** CAPER
1914Z
SIGINT REPORT
INTERCEPT 1993 INIT 1904Z FRQ 887.020MHZ
INIT: SUBJECT FOXTROT
RECIP: SUBJECT UNIFORM

F IT IS AGREED. WE'LL MEET AT YOUR HOUSE TOMORROW NIGHT AT [2000L].

U: WHO WILL COME?

F: [SUBJECT ECHO] CANNOT ATTEND, BUT PRODUCTION IS NOT HIS CONCERN ANYWAY. [SUBJECT ALPHA], [SUBJECT GOLF], AND [SUBJECT WHISKEY] WILL COME WITH ME. HOW IS YOUR SECURITY?

U: AT MY [EMPHASIS] CASTLE? [LAUGHTER.] FRIEND WE COULD HOLD OFF A REGIMENT THERE, AND MY HELICOPTER IS ALWAYS READY. HOW ARE YOU COMING?

F: HAVE YOU SEEN MY NEW TRUCK?

U: OUR GREAT FEET [MEANING UNKNOWN]? NO I HAVE NOT SEEN YOUR MARVELOUS NEW TOY.

F: I GOT IT BECAUSE OF YOU, PABLO. WHY DON'T YOU EVER REPAIR THE ROAD TO YOUR CASTLE?

U: THE RAIN KEEPS DESTROYING IT. YES, I SHOULD PAVE IT, BUT I USE A HELICOPTER TO GET HERE.

F: AND YOU COMPLAIN ABOUT MY TOYS! [LAUGHTER.] SEE YOU TOMORROW NIGHT, FRIEND.

U: GOODBYE.

END CALL. DISCONNECT SIGNAL. END INTERCEPT.

The intercept was delivered to Bob Ritter's office within minutes of its receipt. So here was the chance, the whole purpose of the exercise. He got his own signals out at once, without checking with Cutter or the President. After all, he was the one with the hunting license.

Aboard *Ranger,* the "tech-rep" got the encrypted message less than an hour later. He immediately placed a telephone call to the Office of Commander Jensen, then headed off to see him personally. It wasn't all that hard. He was an experienced field officer and particularly good with maps. That was very useful on a carrier where even experienced sailors got lost in the gray-painted maze all the time. Commander Jensen was surprised he got there so quickly, but already had his personal bombardier-navigator in his office for the mission briefing.

Clark got his signal about the same time. He linked up with Larson and immediately arranged a flight down the valley south of Medellín to make a final reconnaissance of the objective.

Whatever problems his conscience gave Ding Chavez washed out when he did his shirt. There was a nice little creek a hundred meters from their patrol base, and one by one the squad members washed their things out and cleaned themselves up as best they could without soap. After all, he reasoned, poor, dumb peasant or not, he was doing something that he shouldn't have been doing. To Chavez the main concern was that he'd used up a magazine and a half of ammo, and the squad was short one claymore mine which, they'd heard a few hours earlier, went off exactly as planned. Their intel specialist was a real whiz with booby traps. Finished with his abbreviated personal hygiene routine, Ding returned to the unit perimeter. They'd lay up tonight, putting a listening post out a few hundred meters and running a routine patrol to make sure that there was nobody hunting them, but this would be a night of rest. Captain Ramirez had explained that they didn't want to be too active in this area. It might spook the game sooner than they wanted.

18. Force Majeure

The easiest thing for Sergeant Mitchell to do was to call his friend at Fort MacDill. He'd served with Ernie Davis in the 101st Air Assault Division, lived right next to him in a duplex, and crumpled many an empty beer can after charcoaled franks and burgers in the backyard. They were both E-7s, well schooled in the ways of the

Army, which was really run by the sergeants, after all. The officers got more money and all of the worries while the long-service NCOs kept things on an even keel. He had an Army-wide phone directory at his desk and called the proper AUTOVON number.

"Ernie? Mitch."

"Yo, how's life out in wine country?"

"Humpin' the hills, boy. How's the family?"

"Doing fine, Mitch. And yours?"

"Annie's turning into quite a little lady. Hey, the reason I called, I wanted to check up to make sure one of our people got out to you. Staff Sergeant named Domingo Chavez. You'd like him, Ernie, he's a real good kid. Anyway, the paperwork got fucked up on this end, and I just wanted to make sure that he showed up in the right place."

"No problem," Ernie said. "Chavez, you said?"

"Right." Mitchell spelled it.

"Don't ring a bell. Wait a minute. I gotta switch phones." A moment later Ernie's voice came back, accompanied by the clicking sound that denoted a computer keyboard. What was the world coming to? Mitchell wondered. Even infantry sergeants had to know how to use the goddamned things. "Run that name past me again?"

"Chavez, first name Domingo, E-6." Mitchell read off his service number, which was the same as his Social Security number.

"He ain't here, Mitch."

"Huh? We got a call from this Colonel O'Mara of yours—"

"Who?"

"Some bird named O'Mara. My ell-tee took the call and got a little flustered. New kid, still got a lot to learn," Mitchell explained.

"I never heard of no Colonel O'Mara. I think maybe you got the wrong post, Mitch."

"No shit?" Mitchell was genuinely puzzled. "My ell-tee must have really booted this one. Okay, Ernie, I'll take it from here. You give my love to Hazel now."

"Roge-o, Mitch. You have a good one, son. 'Bye."

"Hmph." Mitchell stared at the phone for a moment. What the hell was going on? Ding wasn't at Benning, and wasn't at MacDill. So where the fuck was he? The platoon sergeant flipped to the number for the Military Personnel Center, located in Alexandria, Virginia. The sergeants' club is a tight one, and the community of E-7s was especially so. His next call was to Sergeant First Class Peter Stankowski. It took two tries to get him.

"Hey, Stan! Mitch here."

"You looking for a new job?" Stankowski was a detailer. His job was to assign his fellow sergeants to new jobs. As such, he was a man with considerable power.

"Nah, I just love being a light-fighter. What's this I hear about you turning track-toad on us?" Stankowski's next job, Mitchell had recently learned, was in the 1st Cavalry Division at Fort Hood, where he'd lead his squad from inside an M-2 Bradley Fighting Vehicle.

"Hey, Mitch, my knees are goin'. Ever think it might be nice to fight sittin' down once in a while? Besides, that twenty-five-millimeter chain gun makes for a nice equalizer. What can I do for you?"

"Trying to track somebody down. One of my E-6s checked out a couple of weeks back, and we have to ship some shit to him, and he ain't where we thought he was."

"Oooo-kay. Wait while I punch up my magic machine and we'll find the lad for you. What's his name?" Stankowski asked. Mitchell gave him the information.

"Eleven-Bravo, right?" 11-B was Chavez's Military Occupation Specialty, or MOS. That designated Chavez as a light infantryman. Mechanized infantry was Eleven-Mike.

"Yep." Mitchell heard some more tapping.

"C-h-a-v-e-z, you said?"

"Right."

"Okay, he was supposed to go to Benning and wear the Smokey Bear hat—"

"That's the guy!" Mitchell said, somewhat relieved.

"—but they changed his orders an' sent him down to MacDill."

But he ain't at *MacDill!* Mitchell managed not to say.

"That's a spooky bunch down there. You know Ernie Davis, don't you? He's there. Why don't you give him a call?"

"Okay," Mitchell said, really surprised by that one. *I just did!* "When you going to Hood?"

"September."

"Okay, I'll, uh, call Ernie. You take it easy, Stan."

"Stay in touch, Mitch. Say hi to the family. 'Bye."

"Shit," Mitchell observed after he hung up. He'd just proved that Chavez didn't exist anymore. That was decidedly strange. The Army wasn't supposed to lose people, at least not like this. The sergeant didn't know what to do next, except maybe talk to his lieutenant about it.

"We had another hit last night," Ritter told Admiral Cutter. "Our luck's holding. One of our people got scratched, but nothing serious, and that's three sites taken out, forty-four enemy KIAs—"

"And?"

"And tonight, four senior Cartel members are going to have a sit-down, right here." Ritter handed over a satellite photograph, along with the text of the intercept. "All people on the production end: Fernández, d'Alejandro, Wagner, and Untiveros. Their ass is ours."

"Fine. Do it," Cutter said.

Clark was examining the same photo at that moment, along with a few obliques that he'd shot himself and a set of blueprints for the house.

"You figure this room, right here?"

"I've never been in this one, but that sure looks like a conference room to me," Larson said. "How close you have to be?"

"I'd prefer under four thousand meters, but the GLD is good to six."

"How about this hilltop right here? We've got a clear line of sight into the compound."

"How long to get there?"

"Three hours. Two to drive, one to walk. You know, you could almost do this from an airplane. . . ."

"Yours?" Clark asked with a sly grin.

"Not on a bet!" They'd use a four-wheel-drive Subaru for the drive. Larson had several different sets of plates, and the car didn't belong to him anyway. "I got the phone number and I got a cellular phone."

Clark nodded. He was really looking forward to this. He'd done jobs against people like this before, but never with official sanction, and never this high up the line. "Okay, I gotta get final approval. Pick me up at three."

Murray hustled over from his office as soon as he got the news. Hospitals never made people look glamorous, but Moira appeared to have aged ten years in the past sixty hours. Hospitals weren't especially big on dignity, either. Her hands were in restraints. She was on suicide watch. Murray knew that it was necessary—could scarcely be more so—but her personality had taken enough battering already, and this didn't make things any better.

The room was already bedecked with flowers. Only a handful of FBI agents knew what had transpired, and the natural assumption at the office was that she'd taken Emil's death too hard. Which wasn't far off, after all.

"You gave us quite a scare, kiddo," he observed.

"It's all my fault." She couldn't bring her eyes to look at him for more than a few seconds at a time.

"You're a victim, Moira. You got taken in by one of the best in the business. It happens, even to the smarties. Trust me, I know."

"I let him *use* me. I acted like a whore—"

"I don't want to hear that. You made a mistake. That happens. You didn't mean to hurt anybody, and you didn't break any laws. It's not worth dying for. It's damned sure not worth dying over when you got kids to worry about."

"What'll they think? What'll they think when they find out. . . ."

"You've already given them all the scare they need. They love you, Moira. Can anything erase that?" Murray shook his head. "I don't think so."

"They're ashamed of me."

"They're scared. They're ashamed of themselves. They think it's partly their fault." That struck a nerve.

"But it's not! It's all my fault—"

"I just told you it isn't. Moira, you got in the way of a truck named Félix Cortez."

"Is that his real name?"

"He used to be a colonel in the DGI. Trained at the KGB Academy, and he's very, very good at what he does. He picked you because you're a widow, a young, pretty one. He scouted you, figured out that you're lonely, like most widows, and he turned on the charm. He probably has a lot of inborn talent, and he was educated by experts. You never had a chance. You got hit by a truck you never saw coming. We're going to have a shrink come down, Dr. Lodge from Temple University. And he's going to tell you the same thing I am, but he's going to charge a lot more. Don't worry, though. It comes under Workers Comp."

"I can't stay with the Bureau."

"That's true. You're going to have to give up your security clearance," Dan told her. "That's no great loss, is it? You're going to get a job at the Department of Agriculture, right down the street, same pay grade and everything," Murray said gently. "Bill set it all up for you."

"Mr. Shaw? But—why?"

" 'Cause you're a good guy, Moira, not a bad guy. Okay?"

"So what exactly are we going to do?" Larson asked.

"Wait and see," Clark replied, looking at the road map. There was a place called Don Diego not too far from where they were going. He wondered if somebody named Zorro lived there. "What's your cover story in case somebody sees us together?"

"You're a geologist, and I've been flying you around looking for new gold deposits."

"Fine." It was one of the stock cover-stories Clark used. Geology was one of his hobbies, and he could discuss the subject well enough to fool a professor in the subject. In fact, that's exactly what he'd done a few times. That cover would also explain some of the gear in the back of the four-wheel-drive station wagon, at least to the casual or unschooled observer. The GLD, they'd explain, was a surveying instrument, which was pretty close.

The drive was not terribly unusual. The local roads lacked the quality of paving common in America, and there weren't all that many guard rails, but the main hazard was the way the locals drove, which was a little on the passionate side, Clark thought. He liked it. He liked South America. For all the social problems, the people down here had a zest for life and an openness that he found refreshing. Perhaps the United States had been this way a century before. The old West probably had. There was much to admire. It was a pity that the economy hadn't developed along proper lines, but Clark wasn't a social theorist. He, too, was a child of his country's working class, and in the important things working people are the same everywhere. Certainly the ordinary folk down here had no more love for the druggies than he did. Nobody likes criminals, especially the sort that flaunt their power, and they were probably angry that their police and army couldn't do anything about it. Angry and helpless. The only "popular" group that had tried to deal with them was M-19, a Marxist guerrilla group—actually more an elitist collection of city-bred and university-educated intellectuals. After kidnapping the sister of a major cocaine trafficker, the others in the business had banded together to get her back, killing over two hundred M-19 members and actually forming the Medellín Cartel in the process. That allowed Clark to admire the Cartel. Bad guys or not, they had made a Marxist revolutionary group back off by playing the urban guerrilla game by M-19's own rules. Their mistake—aside from being in a business which Clark abhorred—had been in assuming that they had the ability to play against another, larger enemy by the same set of rules, and that their new enemy wouldn't respond in kind. Turnabout was fair play, Clark thought. He settled back in his seat to catch a nap. Surely they'd understand.

Three hundred miles off the Colombian coast, USS *Ranger* turned into the wind to commence flight operations. The battle group was composed of the carrier, the Aegis-class cruiser *Thomas S. Gates,* another missile cruiser, four missile-armed destroyers and frigates, and two dedicated antisubmarine destroyers. The underway replenishment group, with a fleet oiler, the ammunition ship *Shasta,* and three escorts, was fifty miles closer to the South American coast. Five hundred miles to seaward was another similar group returning from a lengthy deployment at "Camel Station" in the Indian Ocean. The returning fleet simulated an oncoming enemy formation—pretending to be Russians, though nobody said that anymore in the age of *glasnost*.

The first aircraft off, as Robby Jackson watched from Pri-Fly, the control position high up on the carrier's island structure, were F-14 Tomcat interceptors, loaded out to maximum takeoff weight, squatting at the catapults with cones of fire trailing from each engine. As always, it was exciting to watch. Like a ballet of tanks, the massive, heavily loaded aircraft were choreographed about the four acres of flight deck by teenaged kids in filthy, color-coded shirts who gave instructions in pantomime while keeping out of the way of the jet intakes and exhausts. It was for them a game more dangerous than racing across city streets at rush hour, and more stimulating. Crewmen in purple shirts fueled the aircraft, and were called "grapes." Other kids, red-shirted ordnancemen called "ordies," were loading blue-painted exercise weapons aboard aircraft. The actually shooting part of the Shoot-Ex didn't start for another day. Tonight they'd practice interception tactics against fellow Navy aviators. Tomorrow night, Air Force C-130s would lift out of Panama to rendezvous with the returning battle group and launch a series of target drones which, everyone hoped, the Tomcats would blast from the sky with their newly repaired AIM-54C Phoenix missiles. It was not to be a contractor's test. The drones would be under the control of Air Force NCOs whose job it was to evade fire as though their lives depended on it, for whom every successful evasion involved a stiff penalty to be paid in beer or some other medium of exchange by the flight crew who missed.

Robby watched twelve aircraft launch before heading down to the flight deck. Already dressed in his olive-green flight suit, he carried his personal flight helmet. He'd ride tonight in one of the E-2C Hawkeye airborne-early-warning aircraft, the Navy's own diminutive version of the larger E-3A AWACS, from which he'd see if his new tactical arrangement worked any better than current fleet procedures. It had in all the computer simulations, but computers weren't reality, a fact often lost upon people who worked in the Pentagon.

The E-2C crew met him at the door to the flight deck. A moment later the Hawkeye's plane captain, a First-Class Petty Officer who wore a brown shirt, arrived to take them to the aircraft. The flight deck was too dangerous a place for pilots to walk unattended, hence the twenty-five-year-old guide who knew these parts. On the way aft Robby noticed an A-6E Intruder being loaded with a single blue bombcase to which guidance equipment had been attached, converting it into a GBU-15 laser-guided weapon. It was, he saw, the squadron-skipper's personal bird. That, he thought, must be part of the system-validation test, called a Drop-Ex. It wasn't that often you got to drop a real bomb, and squadron commanders like to have their fair share of fun. Robby wondered for a moment what the target was—probably a raft, he decided—but he had other things to worry about. The plane captain had them at their aircraft a minute later. He said a few things to the pilot, then saluted him smartly and moved off to perform his next set of duties. Robby strapped into the jump seat in the radar compartment, again disliking the fact that he was in an airplane as a passenger rather than a driver.

After the normal preflight ritual, Commander Jackson felt vibration as the turboprop engines fired up. Then the Hawkeye started moving slowly and jerkily toward one of the waist catapults. The engines were run up to full power after the nosewheel attachment was fixed to the catapult shuttle and the pilot spoke over the intercom to warn his crew that it was time. In three stunning seconds, the Grumman-built aircraft went from a standing start to one hundred forty knots. The tail sank as it left the ship, then the aircraft leveled out and tipped up again for its climb to twenty thousand feet. Almost immediately, the radar controllers in back started their systems checks, and in twenty minutes the E-2C was on station, eighty miles from the carrier, its rotodome turning, sending radar beams through the sky to start the exercise. Jackson was seated so as to observe the entire "battle" on the radar screens, his helmet plugged into the command circuit so that he could see how well the *Ranger*'s air wing executed his plan, while the Hawkeye flew a racetrack pattern in the sky.

From their position they could also see the battle group, of course. Half an hour after taking off, Robby noted a double launch from the carrier. The radar-computer system tracked both new contacts as a matter of course. They climbed to thirty thousand feet and rendezvoused. A tanker exercise, he realized at once. One of the aircraft immediately returned to the carrier, while the other flew east-southeast. The intercept exercise began in earnest right about then, but every few seconds Robby noted the course of the new contact, until it disappeared off the screen, still heading toward the South American mainland.

''Yes, yes, I will go,'' Cortez said. ''I am not ready yet, but I will go.'' He hung up his phone with a curse and reached for his car keys. Félix hadn't even had the chance to visit one of the smashed refining sites yet and they wanted him to address the—''The Production Committee,'' *el jefe* called it. That was amusing. The fools were so bent on taking over the national government that they were starting to use quasi-official terminology. He swore again on the way out the door. Drive all the way down to that fat, pompous lunatic's castle on the hill. He checked his watch. It would take two hours. And he would get there late. And he would not be able to tell them anything because he hadn't had time to learn anything. And they would be angry. And he would have to be humble again. Cortez was getting tired of abasing himself to these people. The money they paid him was incredible, but no amount of money was worth his self-respect. That was something he should have thought about before he signed up, Cortez reminded himself as he started his car. Then he swore again.

The newest CAPER intercept was number 2091 and was an intercept from a mobile phone to the home of Subject ECHO. The text came up on Ritter's personal computer printer. Then came 2092, not thirty seconds later. He handed both to his special assistant.

''Cortez . . . going right there? Christmas in June.''

''How do we get the word to Clark?'' Ritter wondered.

The man thought for a moment. ''We can't.''

''Why not?''

''We don't have a secure voice channel we can use. Unless—we can get a secure VOX circuit to the carrier, and from there to the A-6, and from the A-6 to Clark.''

It was Ritter's turn to swear. No, they couldn't do that. The weak link was the carrier. The case officer they had aboard to oversee that end of the mission would have to approach the carrier's commanding officer—it might not start there, but it would sure as hell end there—and ask for a cleared radio compartment to handle the messages by himself on an ears-only basis. That would risk too much, even assuming that the CO went along. Too many questions would be asked, too many new people in the information loop. He swore again, then recovered his senses. Maybe Cortez would get there in time. Lord, wouldn't it be nice to tell the Bureau that they'd nailed the bastard! Or, more properly, that someone had, plausibly deniably. Or maybe not. He didn't know Bill Shaw very well, and didn't know how he might react.

* * *

Larson had parked the Subaru a hundred yards off the main road in a preselected spot that made detection unlikely. The climb to their perch was not a difficult one, and they arrived well before sundown. The photos had identified a perfect place, right on the crest of a ridge, with a direct line of sight toward a house that took their breath away. Twenty thousand square feet it was—a hundred-foot square, two stories, no basement—set within a fenced six-acre perimeter four kilometers away, perhaps three hundred feet lower than their position. Clark had a pair of seven-power binoculars and took note of the guard force while light permitted. He counted twenty men, all armed with automatic weapons. Two crew-served heavy machine guns were sited in built-for-the-purpose strongpoints on the wall. Bob Ritter had called it right on St. Kitts, he thought: *Frank Lloyd Wright meets Ludwig the Mad.* It was a beautiful house, if you went for the neoclassical-Spanish-modern style, fortified in hi-tech fashion to keep the unruly peasants away. There was also the *de rigueur* helicopter pad with a new Sikorsky S-76 sitting on it.

"Anything else I need to know about the house?" Clark asked.

"Pretty massive construction, as you can see. I'd worry about that. This is earthquake country, you know. Personally, I'd prefer something lighter, wood-post and beam, but they like concrete construction—to stop bullets and mortar rounds, I suppose."

"Better and better," Clark observed. He reached into his backpack. First he removed the heavy tripod, setting it up quickly and expertly on solid ground. Then came the GLD, which he attached and sighted in. Finally, he removed a Varo Noctron-V night-sighting device. The GLD had the same capability, of course, but once it was set up he didn't want to fool with it. The Noctron had only five-power magnification—Clark preferred the binocular lens arrangement—but was small, light, and handy. It also amplified ambient light about fifty thousand times. This technology had come a long way since his time in Southeast Asia, but it still struck him as a black art. He remembered being out in the boonies with nothing better than a Mark-1 eyeball. Larson would handle the radio traffic, and had his unit all set up. Then there was nothing left to do but wait. Larson produced some junk food and both men settled down.

"Well, now you know what 'Great Feet' means," Clark chuckled an hour later. The cryppies should have known. He handed the Noctron over.

"Gawd! Only difference between a man and a boy . . ."

It was a Ford three-quarter-ton pickup with optional four-wheel drive. Or at least that was how it had left the factory. Since then it had visited a custom-car shop where four-foot-diameter tires had been attached. It wasn't quite grotesque enough to be called "Big Foot," after the monster trucks so popular at auto shows, but it had the same effect. It was also quite practical, and that was the really strange part. The road up to the *casa* did need some serious help, but this truck didn't notice—though the chieftain's security pukes did, struggling to keep up with their boss's new and wonderful toy.

"I bet the mileage sucks," Larson observed as it came through the gate. He handed the night-sight back.

"He can afford it." Clark watched it maneuver around the house. It was too much to hope for, but it happened. The dickhead parked the truck right next to the house, right next to the windows to the conference room. Perhaps he didn't want to take his eyes off his new toy.

Two men alighted from the vehicle. They were greeted at the veranda—Clark couldn't remember the Spanish name for that—by their host with handshakes and hugs while armed men stood about as nervously as the President's Secret Service detail. He could see them relax when their charges went inside, spreading out, mixing with their counterparts—after all, the Cartel was one big, happy family, wasn't it?

For now, anyway, Clark told himself. He shook his head in amazement at the placement of the truck.

"Here comes the last one." Larson pointed to headlights struggling up the gravel road.

This car was a Mercedes, a stretch job, doubtless armored like a tank—*Just like the ambassador's car,* Clark thought. How poetic. This VIP was also met with pomp and circumstance. There were now at least fifty guards visible. The wall perimeter was fully manned, with other teams constantly patrolling the grounds. The odd thing, he thought, was that there were no guards outside the wall. There had to be a few, but he couldn't spot them. It didn't matter. Lights went on in the room behind the truck. That did matter.

"Looks like you guessed right, boy."

"That's what they pay me for," Larson pointed out. "How close do you think that truck—"

Clark had already checked, keying the laser in on both the house and the truck. "Three meters from the wall. Close enough."

Commander Jensen finished tanking his aircraft, disconnecting from the KA-6 as soon as his fuel gauges pegged. He recovered the refueling probe and maneuvered downward to allow the tanker to clear the area. The mission profile could hardly have been easier. He eased the stick to the right, taking a heading of one-one-five and leveling off at thirty thousand feet. His IFF transponder was switched off at the moment, and he was able to relax and enjoy the ride, something he almost always did. The pilot's seat in the Intruder is set rather high for good visibility during a bomb run—it did make you feel a little exposed when you were being shot at, he remembered. Jensen had done a few missions before the end of the Vietnam War, and he could vividly recall the 100-mm flak over Haiphong, like black cotton balls with evil red hearts. But not tonight. The seat placement now was like a throne in the sky. The stars were bright. The waning moon would soon rise. And all was right with the world. Added to that was his mission. It didn't get any better than this.

With only starlight to see by they could pick out the coast from over two hundred miles away. The Intruder was cruising along at just under five hundred knots. Jensen brought the stick to the right as soon as he was beyond the radar coverage from the E-2C, taking a more southerly heading toward Ecuador. On crossing the coast he turned left to trace along the spine of the Andes. At this point he flipped on his IFF transponder. Neither Ecuador nor Colombia had an air-defense radar network. It was an extravagance that neither country needed. As a result, the only radars that were now showing up on the Intruder's ESM monitors were the usual air-traffic-control type. They were quite modern. A little-known paradox of radar technology was that these new, modern radars didn't really detect aircraft at all. Instead they detected radar transponders. Every commercial aircraft in the world carried a small "black box"—as aircraft electronic equipment is invariably known—that noted receipt of a radar signal and replied with its own signal, giving aircraft identification and other relevant information which was then "painted" on the control scopes at the radar station—most often an airport down here—for the controllers to use. It was cheaper and more reliable than the older radars that did "skin-paints," detecting the aircraft merely as nameless blips whose identity, course, and speed then had to be established by the chronically overworked people on the ground. It was an odd footnote in the history of technology that the new scheme was a step both forward and backward.

The Intruder soon entered the air-control zone belonging to El Dorado International Airport outside Bogotá. A radar controller there called the Intruder as soon as its alphanumeric code appeared on his scope.

"Roger, El Dorado," Commander Jensen replied at once. "This is Four-Three Kilo. We are Inter-America Cargo Flight Six out of Quito, bound for LAX. Altitude three-zero-zero, course three-five-zero, speed four-nine-five. Over."

The controller verified the track with his radar data and replied in English, which is the language of international air travel. "Four-Three Kilo, roger, copy. Be advised no traffic in your area. Weather CAVU. Maintain course and altitude. Over."

"Roger, thank you, and good night, sir." Jensen killed the radio and spoke over his intercom to his bombardier-navigator. "That was easy enough, wasn't it? Let's get to work."

In the right seat, set slightly below and behind the pilot's, the naval flight officer got on his own radio after he activated the TRAM pod that hung on the Intruder's center-line hardpoint.

At T minus fifteen minutes, Larson lifted his cellular phone and dialed the proper number. *"Señor Wagner, por favor."*

"Momento," the voice replied. Larson wondered who it was.

"Wagner," another voice replied a moment later. "Who is this?"

Larson took the cellophane from off a pack of cigarettes and crumpled it over the receiver while he spoke garbled fragments of words, then finally: "I can't hear you, Carlos. I will call back in a few minutes." Larson pressed the kill button on the phone. This location was at the far edge of the cellular system anyway.

"Nice touch," Clark said approvingly. "Wagner?"

"His dad was a sergeant in the *Allgemeine-SS*—worked at Sobibor—came over in forty-six, married a local girl and went into the smuggling business, died before anyone caught up with him. Breeding tells," Larson said. "Carlos is a real prick, likes his women with bruises on them. His colleagues aren't all that wild about him, but he's good at what he does."

"Christmas," Mr. Clark observed. The radio made the next sound, five minutes later.

"Bravo Whiskey, this is Zulu X-Ray, over."

"Zulu X-Ray, this is Bravo Whiskey. I read you five-by-five. Over," Larson answered at once. His radio was the sort used by forward air controllers, encrypted UHF.

"Status report, over."

"We are in place. Mission is go. Say again, mission is go."

"Roger, copy, we are go-mission. We are ten minutes out. Start the music."

Larson turned to Clark. "Light her up."

The GLD was already powered up. Mr. Clark flipped the switch from standby to active. The GLD was more fully known as the Ground Laser Designator. Designed for use by soldiers on the battlefield, it projected a focused infrared (hence invisible) laser beam through a complex but rugged series of lenses. Bore-sighted with the laser system was a separate infrared sensor that told the operator where he was aiming—essentially a telescopic sight. "Great Feet" had a fiberglass cargo box over its load area, and Clark trained the crosshairs on one of its small windows, using the fine-adjustment knobs on the tripod with some delicacy. The laser spot appeared as desired, but then he rethought his aiming point and took advantage of the fact that they were slightly higher than their target, respotting his aim on the center of the vehicle's roof. Finally he turned on the videotape recorder that took its feed from the GLD. The big boys in D.C. wanted to count coup on this one.

"Okay," he said quietly. "The target is lit."

"The music is playing, and it sounds just fine," Larson said over the radio.

Cortez was driving up the hill, having already passed a security checkpoint manned by two people drinking beer, he noted disgustedly. The road was about on a par with what he'd grown up with in Cuba, and the going was slow. They'd still blame him for being late, of course.

It was too easy, Jensen thought as he heard the reply. Tooling along at thirty thousand feet, clear night, no flak or missiles to evade. Even a contractor's validation test wasn't this easy.

"I got it," the B/N noted, staring down at his own scope. You can see a very, very long way at thirty thousand feet on a clear night, especially with a multimillion-dollar system doing the looking. Underneath the Intruder, the Target Recognition and Attack Multisensor pod noted the laser dot that was still sixty miles away. It was a modulated beam, of course, and its carrier signal was known to the TRAM. They now had positive identification of the target.

"Zulu X-Ray confirms music sounds just fine," Jensen said over the radio. Over intercom: "Next step."

On the port inboard weapon station, the bomb's seeker head was powered up. It immediately noted the laser dot as well. Inside the aircraft, a computer was keeping track of the aircraft's position, altitude, course, and speed, and the bombardier-navigator programmed in the position of the target to an accuracy of two hundred meters. He could have dialed it in even closer, of course, but didn't need to. The bomb release would be completely automatic, and at this altitude the laser "basket" into which the bomb had to be dropped was miles wide. The computer took note of all these facts and decided to make an optimum drop, right in the most favorable portion of the basket.

Clark's eyes were now fixed to the GLD. He was perched on his elbows, and no part of his body was touching the instrument except for his eyebrow on the rubber cup that protected the eyepiece.

"Any second now," the B/N said.

Jensen kept the Intruder straight and level, heading straight down the electronic path defined by various computer systems aboard. The entire exercise was now out of human hands. On the ejector rack, a signal was received from the computer. Several shotgun shells—that's precisely what was used—fired, driving down the "ejector feet" onto small steel plates on the upper side of the bombcase. The bomb separated cleanly from the aircraft.

The aircraft jerked upward a bit at the loss of just over eleven hundred pounds of weight.

"Breakaway, breakaway," Jensen reported.

There, finally. Cortez saw the wall. His car—he'd have to buy a jeep if he were going to come here very often—was still losing its grip on the gravel, but he'd be through the gate in a moment, and if he remembered right, the road inside the perimeter was paved decently—probably leftover materials from the helipad, he thought.

"On the way," Larson told Clark.

The bomb was still traveling at five hundred knots. Once clear of the aircraft, gravity took over, arcing it down toward the ground. It actually accelerated somewhat in the rarefied air as the seeker head moved fractionally to correct for wind drift. The seeker head was made of fiberglass and looked like a round-nose bullet with some small fins attached. When the laser dot on which it tracked moved out of the center of its field of view, the entire seeker body moved itself and the plastic tail fins in the appropriate direction to bring the dot back where it belonged. It had to fall exactly twenty-two thousand feet, and the microchip brain in the guidance package was trying to hit the target exactly. It had plenty of time to correct for mistakes.

Clark didn't know what to expect, exactly. It had been too long a time since he'd called air strikes in, and he'd forgotten some of the details—when you had to call in air support, you generally didn't have time to notice the small stuff. He found himself wondering if there'd be the whistle—something he never remembered from his war service. He kept his eye on the target, still careful not to touch the GLD lest he screw things up. There were several men standing close to the truck. One lit a cigarette, and it appeared that several were talking about something or other. On the whole, it seemed like this was taking an awfully long time. When it happened, there was not the least warning. Not a whistle, not anything at all.

Cortez felt his front wheels bump upward as they got on solid pavement.

The GBU-15 laser-guided bomb had a "guaranteed" accuracy of under three meters, but that was under combat conditions, and this was a far easier test of the system. It landed within inches of its target point, striking the top of the truck. Unlike the first test shot, this bomb was impact-fused. Two detonators, one in the nose and one in the tail, were triggered by a computer chip within a microsecond of the instant when the seeker head struck the fiberglass top of the truck. There were mechanical backups to the electronic triggers. Neither proved necessary, but even explosives take time, and the bomb fell an additional thirty inches while the detonation process got underway. The bombcase had barely penetrated the cargo cover when the bomb filler was ignited by both detonators. Things happened more quickly now. The explosive filler was Octol, a very expensive chemical explosive also used to trigger nuclear weapons, with a detonation rate of over eight thousand meters per second. The combustible bombcase vaporized in a few microseconds. Then expanding gas from the explosion hurled fragments of the truck body in all directions—except up—immediately behind which was the rock-hard shock wave.

Both the fragments and the shock wave struck the concrete-block walls of the house in well under a thousandth of a second. The effects were predictable. The wall disintegrated, transformed into millions of tiny fragments traveling at bullet speed, with the remainder of the shock wave still behind to attack other parts of the house. The human nervous system simply doesn't work quickly enough for such events, and the people in the conference room never had the first hint that their deaths were underway.

The low-light sensor on the GLD went white (with a touch of green). Clark cringed on instinct and looked away from the eyepiece to see an even whiter flash in the target area. They were too far away to hear the noise at once. It wasn't often that you could *see* sound, but large bombs make that possible. The compressed air of the shock wave was a ghostly white wall that expanded radially from where the truck had been, at a speed of over a thousand feet per second. It took about twelve seconds for the noise to reach Clark and Larson. Everyone who had been in the conference room was dead by that time, of course, and the *crump* of the pressure wave sounded like the outraged cry of lost souls.

"Christ," Larson said, awed by the event.

"Think you used enough dynamite there, Butch?" Clark asked. It was all he could do not to laugh. That was a first. He'd killed his share of enemies, and never taken joy from it. But the nature of the target combined with the method of the attack made the whole thing seem like a glorious prank. *Son of a BITCH!* The sober pause followed a moment later. His "prank" had just ended the lives of over twenty people, only four of whom were listed targets, and that was no joke. The urge to laugh died. He was a professional, not a psychopath.

Cortez had been less than two hundred meters from the explosion, but being downhill from it saved his life since most of the fragments sailed well over his head. The blast wave was bad enough, hurling his windshield backward into his face, where it fractured but didn't shatter, held together by the polymer filler of the safety-glass sandwich. His car was flipped on its back, but he managed to crawl free even before his mind had decided what his eyes had just witnessed. It was fully six seconds before the word "explosion" occurred to him. At that his reactions were far more rapid than that of the security guards, half of whom were dead or dying in any case. His first considered action was to draw his pistol and advance toward the house.

Except that there wasn't a house there anymore. He was too deafened to hear the screams of the injured. Several guards wandered aimlessly about with their guns held ready—for what, they didn't know. The ones from the far corner of the perimeter wall were the least affected. The body of the house had absorbed most of the blast, protecting them from everything but the projectiles, which had been quite lethal enough.

"Bravo Whiskey, this is Zulu X-Ray requesting BDA, over." BDA was bomb-damage assessment. Larson keyed his microphone one last time.

"I evaluate CEP as zero, I repeat, zero, with high-order detonation. Score this one-four-point-oh. Over."

"Roger that. Out." Jensen switched his radio off again. "You know," he said over the intercom, "I can remember back when I was a lieutenant I made a Med cruise on *Kennedy* and us officers were afraid to go into some spaces because the troops were fuckin' around with drugs.''

''Yeah,'' the bombardier/navigator answered. ''Fuckin' drugs. Don't worry, skipper. I ain't likely to have a conscience attack. Hey, the White House says it's okay, that means that it's really okay.''

''Yep.'' Jensen lapsed back into silence. He'd proceed on his current heading until he was out of El Dorado's radar coverage, then turn southwest for the *Ranger*. It really was a pretty night. He wondered how the air-defense exercise was going. . . .

Cortez had little experience with explosions, and the vagaries of such events were new to him. For example, the fountain in front of the house was still running. The electrical power cables to the *casa* were buried and unharmed, and the breaker box inside hadn't been totally destroyed. He lowered his face into the water to clear it. When he came back up, he felt almost normal except for the ache in his head.

There had been a dozen or so vehicles inside the wall when the explosion happened. About half of them were shredded, and their gas tanks had ruptured, illuminating the area with isolated fires. Untiveros' new helicopter was a smashed wreck against the fractured wall. There were other people rushing about. Cortez stood still and started thinking.

He remembered seeing a truck, one with huge wheels, parked right next to . . . He walked over that way. Though the entire three-hectare area around the house was littered with rubble, here it was clear, he saw as he approached. Then he saw the crater, fully two meters deep and six meters wide.

Car bomb.

A big one. Perhaps a thousand kilos, he thought, looking away from the hole while his brain went to work.

''I think that's all we really need to see,'' Clark observed. He made a last look through the eyepiece of the GLD and switched it off. Repacking took less than three minutes.

''Who do you suppose that is?'' Larson asked while he put his backpack on. He handed the Noctron over to Clark.

''Must be the guy who showed up late in the BMW. Suppose he's important or something?''

''Don't know. Maybe next time.''

''Right.'' Clark led the way down the hill.

It was the Americans, of course. CIA, without doubt. They'd made some financial arrangements and somehow managed to place a ton of explosives in the back of that monstrous truck. Cortez admired the touch. It was Fernández's truck—he'd heard about it but never seen it. *Now I never will,* he thought. Fernández had loved his new truck and had kept it parked right in front of . . . That had to be it. The Americans had gotten lucky. Okay, he thought, how did they do it? They wouldn't have gotten their own hands involved, of course. So they must have arranged for someone else . . . who? Somebody—no, more than one, at least four or five from M-19 or FARC . . . ? Again, that made sense. Might it have been indirect? Have the Cubans or KGB arrange it. With all the changes between East and West, might CIA have managed to get such cooperation? Unlikely, Félix thought, but possible.

A direct attack on high government officials such as the Cartel had executed was the sort of thing to generate the most unlikely of bedfellows.

Was the bomb placement here an accident? Might the Americans have learned of the meeting?

There were voices from inside the rubble pile that had once been a castle. Security people were nosing around, and Cortez joined them. Untiveros' family had been here. His wife and two children, and a staff of eight or more people. Probably treated them like serfs, Cortez thought. The Cartel chieftains all did. Perhaps he'd offended one greatly—gone after a daughter, maybe. They all did that. *Droit du seigneur*. A French term, but one which the chieftains understood. The fools, Cortez told himself. Was there no perversion beneath them?

Security guards were already scrambling through the rubble. It was amazing that anyone could be alive in there. His hearing was coming back now. He caught the shrill screams of some poor bastard. He wondered what the body count would be. Perhaps. Yes. He turned and walked back to his overturned BMW. It was leaking gasoline out the filler cap, but Cortez reached in and got his cellular phone. He walked twenty meters from the car before switching it on.

"*Jefe,* this is Cortez. There has been an explosion here."

It was ironic, Ritter thought, that his first notification of the mission's success should come from another CAPER intercept. The really good news, the NSA guys reported, was that they now had a voiceprint on Cortez. That greatly improved their chances of locating him. It was better than nothing, the DDO thought as his visitor arrived for the second time today.

"We missed Cortez," he told Admiral Cutter. "But we got d'Alejandro, Fernández, Wagner, and Untiveros, plus the usual collateral damage."

"What do you mean?"

Ritter looked again at the satellite photo of the house. He'd have to get a new one to quantify the damage. "I mean there were a bunch of security guards around, and we probably got a bunch of them. Unfortunately there was also Untiveros' family—wife, a couple of kids, and various domestic servants."

Cutter snapped erect in his chair. "You didn't tell me anything about that! This was supposed to be a surgical strike."

Ritter looked up in considerable annoyance. *"Well, for Christ's sake, Jimmy!* What the hell do you expect? You are still a naval officer, aren't you? Didn't anybody ever tell you that there are *always* extraneous people standing around? We used a *bomb,* remember? You don't do surgery with bombs, despite what all the 'experts' say. Grow up!" Ritter himself took no pleasure from the extraneous deaths, but it was a cost of doing business—as the Cartel's own members well understood.

"But I told the President—"

"The President told *me* that I had a hunting license, and no bag limit. This is my op to run, remember?"

"It wasn't supposed to be this way! What if the papers get hold of it? This is cold-blooded murder!"

"As opposed to taking out the druggies and their shooters? That's murder, too, isn't it? Or it would be, if the President hadn't said that the gloves were off. You said it's a war. The President told us to treat it as a war. Okay, we are. I'm sorry there were extraneous people around, but, damn it, there always are. If there were a way to bag these jokers without hurting innocent people, we'd use it—but there isn't.'' To say that Ritter was amazed didn't begin to explain matters. This guy was supposed to be a professional military officer. The taking of human life was part of his job description. Of course, Ritter told himself, Cutter'd spent most of his career driving a desk in the Pentagon—he probably hadn't seen much blood since he learned how to shave. A pussycat hiding in tiger's stripes. No, Ritter corrected himself. Just a pussy. Thirty years in uniform and he'd allowed himself to forget that real weapons killed people somewhat less precisely than in the movies. Some professional officer. And he was advising the President on issues of national security. Great.

''Tell you what, Admiral. If you don't tell the newsies, neither will I. Here's the intercept. Cortez says it was a car bomb. Clark must have rigged it just the way we hoped.''

''But what if the local police do an investigation?''

''First of all, we don't know if the local cops will even be allowed there. Second, what makes you think they have the resources to figure it out? I worked pretty hard setting this up to look like a car-bombing, and it looks like Cortez got faked out. Third, what makes you think that the local cops'll give a flying fuck one way or another?''

''But the media!''

''You've got media on the brain. You're the one who's been arguing for turning us loose on these characters. So now you're changing your mind? It's a little late for that,'' Ritter said disgustedly. This was the best op his Directorate had run in years, and the guy whose idea it had been was now wetting his pants.

Admiral Cutter wasn't paying enough attention to Ritter's invective to be angry. He'd promised the President a surgical removal of the people who had killed Jacobs and the rest. He hadn't bargained for the deaths of ''innocent'' people. More importantly, neither had WRANGLER.

Chavez was too far south to have heard the explosion. The squad was staked out on another processing site. Evidently the sites were set up in relays. As he watched, two men were erecting the portable bathtub under the supervision of several armed men, and he could hear the grunts and gripes of others who were climbing up the mountainside. Four peasants appeared, their backpacks containing jars of acid. They were accompanied by two more riflemen.

Probably the word hadn't gotten out yet, Ding thought. He'd been certain that what the squad had done the other night would discourage people from supplementing their income this way. The sergeant didn't consider the possibility that they had to run such risks to feed their families.

Ten minutes later the third relay of six brought the coca leaves, and five more armed men. The laborers all had collapsible canvas buckets. They went off to a nearby stream for water. The boss guard ordered two of his people to walk into the woods to stand sentry, and that's where things went wrong. One of them walked straight toward the assault element, fifty meters away.

''Uh-oh,'' Vega observed quietly.

Chavez tapped four dashes on his radio button, the danger signal.

I see it, the captain replied with two dashes. Then three dashes. *Get ready.*

Oso got his machine gun up and flipped off the safety.

Maybe they'll drop him quietly, Chavez hoped.

The guys with the buckets were just coming back when Chavez heard a scream over to his left. The riflemen below him reacted at once. Vega started firing then.

The sudden shooting from another direction confused the guards, but they reacted as people with automatic weapons invariably reacted to surprise—they started shooting in all directions.

"Shit!" Ingeles snarled, and fired his grenade into the objective. It landed among the jars and exploded, showering everyone in the area with sulfuric acid. Tracers flew everywhere, and people dropped, but it was too confused, too unplanned for the soldiers to keep track of what was happening. The shooting stopped in a few seconds. Everyone in view was down. The assault group appeared soon thereafter, and Chavez ran down to join them. He counted bodies and came up three short.

"Guerra, Chavez, find 'em!" Captain Ramirez ordered. He didn't have to say *Kill 'em!*

But they didn't. Guerra stumbled across one and killed him on the spot. Chavez came up dry, neither seeing nor hearing anything. He found the stream and one bucket, three hundred meters from the objective. If they'd been right there when the shooting started, that meant they had four or five minutes head start in the country they'd grown up in. Both soldiers spent half an hour rushing and stopping, looking and listening, but two men were away clean.

When they got back to the objective they learned that this was the good news. One of their men was dead. Rocha, one of their riflemen, had taken a burst full in the chest from one of the guards and died instantly. The squad was very quiet.

Jackson was also in an angry mood. The aggressor force had beaten him. *Ranger*'s fighters hadn't gotten it right. His tactical scheme had come apart when one of the squadrons turned the wrong way, and what should have been a masterful trap had turned into a clear avenue for the "Russians" to blaze in and get close enough to the carrier to launch missiles. That was embarrassing, if not completely unexpected. New ideas took time to work out, and maybe he had to rethink some of his arrangements. Just because it had all worked on the computer simulation didn't mean that the plan was perfect, Jackson reminded himself. He continued to stare at the radar screen, trying to remember the patterns and how they had moved. While he watched, a single blip reappeared on the screen, heading southwest toward the carrier. He wondered who that was as the Hawkeye prepared for landing.

The E-2C made a perfect trap, catching the number-three wire and rolling forward to clear the deck for the next aircraft. Robby dismounted in time to see the next one land. It was an Intruder, the same one he'd noticed before boarding the Hawkeye a few hours earlier. The squadron commander's personal bird, he noticed. The one that had flown toward the beach. But that wasn't important. Commander Jackson immediately headed for the CAG's office to start the debrief.

Commander Jensen also taxied clear of the landing area. The Intruder's wings folded up to minimize its deck space as it took its parking place forward. By the time he and his B/N dismounted, his plane captain was there waiting for them. He'd already pulled the videotape from its compartment in the nose instrument bay. This he handed to the skipper—squadron commanders are given that title—before leading them into the island and safety. The "tech-rep" was there to meet them, and Jensen handed the tape over to him.

"Four-oh, the man said," the pilot reported. Jensen just kept walking.

The "tech-rep" carried the tape cassette to his cabin, where he put it in a metal container with a lock. He sealed it further with multicolored tape and affixed a Top Secret label to both sides. It was then placed in yet another shipping box, which the man carried to a compartment on the O-3 level. There was a COD flight scheduled out in thirty minutes. The box would go on it in a courier's pocket and get flown to Panama, where an Agency field officer would take custody of it and fly to Andrews Air Force Base for final delivery to Langley.

19. Fallout

Intelligence services pride themselves on getting information from Point A to Points B, C, D, and so forth with great speed. In the case of highly sensitive information, or data that can be gathered only by covert means, they are highly effective. But for data that is open for all the world to see, they generally fall well short of the commercial news media, hence the fascination of the American intelligence community—and probably many others—with Ted Turner's Cable News Network.

As a result, Ryan was not overly surprised to see that his first notice of the explosion south of Medellín was captioned as having been copied from CNN and other news services. It was breakfast time in Mons. His quarters were in the American VIP section of the NATO complex and had access to CNN's satellite service. He switched the set on halfway through his first cup of coffee to see a TV shot obviously taken from a helicopter with a low-light rig. The caption underneath said, MEDELLÍN, COLOMBIA.

''Lord,'' Jack breathed, setting his cup down. The chopper didn't get very close, probably worried about being shot at by the people milling about on the ground, but it didn't need to be all that clear. What had been a massive house was now a disordered array of rubble set next to a hole in the ground. The ground signature was unmistakable. Ryan had said *car bomb* to himself even before the voice-over of the reporter gave the same evaluation. That meant the Agency wasn't involved, Jack was sure. Car bombs were not the American way. Americans believed in single aimed bullets. Precision firepower was an American invention.

His feelings changed on reflection, however. First, the Agency had to have the Cartel leadership under some sort of surveillance by now, and surveillance was something that CIA was exceedingly good at. Second, if a surveillance operation was underway, he ought to have heard of the explosion through Agency channels, not as a copy of a news report. Something did not compute.

What was it Sir Basil had said? Our response would surely be appropriate. And what does that mean? The intelligence game had become rather civilized over the past decade. In the 1950s, toppling governments had been a standard exercise in the furtherance of national policy. Assassinations had been a rare but real alternative to more complex exercises of diplomatic muscle. In the case of CIA, the Bay of Pigs fiasco and bad press over some operations in Vietnam—which had been a war after all, and wars were violent enterprises at best—had largely terminated such things for everyone. It was odd but true. Even the KGB rarely involved itself in ''wet work'' any longer—a Russian phrase from the thirties, denoting the fact that blood made one's hands wet—instead leaving it to surrogates like the Bulgarians, or more commonly to terrorist groups who performed such irregular services as a *quid pro quo* for arms and training assistance. And remarkably enough, that, too, was dying out. The funny part was that Ryan believed such vigorous action was occasionally necessary—and likely to become all the more so now that the world was turning away from open warfare and drifting to a twilight contest of state-sponsored terrorism and low-intensity conflict. ''Special-operations'' forces offered a real and semicivilized alternative to the more organized and destructive forms of violence associated with conventional armed forces. *If war is nothing more or less than sanctioned murder on an industrial scale, then was it not more humane to apply violence in a much more focused and discrete way?*

That was an ethical question that didn't need contemplation over breakfast.

But what *was* right and what was wrong at this level? Ryan asked himself. It was accepted in law, ethics, and religion that a soldier who killed in war was not a criminal. That only begged the question: What is war? A generation earlier that question had been an easy one. Nation-states would assemble their armies and navies and send them off to do battle over some damned-fool issue or other—afterward it would usually appear that there had been a peaceful alternative—and that was morally acceptable. But war itself was changing, wasn't it? And who decided what war was? Nation-states. So, could a nation-state determine what its vital interests were and act accordingly? How did terrorism enter into the equation? Years earlier, when he'd been a target himself, Ryan had determined that terrorism could be seen as the modern manifestation of piracy, whose practitioners had always been seen as the common enemies of mankind. So, historically, there was a not-quite-war situation in which military forces could be used directly.

And where did that put international drug traffickers? Was it a civil crime, to be dealt with as such? What if the traffickers could subvert a nation to their own commercial will? Did that nation then become mankind's common enemy, like the Barbary Pirates of old?

''Damn,'' Ryan observed. He didn't know what the law said. An historian by training, his degrees didn't help. The only previous experience with such trafficking had been at the hands of a powerful nation-state, fighting a ''real'' war to enforce its ''right'' to sell opium to people whose government objected—but who had lost the war and with it the right to protect its own citizens against illegal drug use.

That was a troubling precedent, wasn't it?

Jack's education compelled him to look for justification. He was a man who believed that Right and Wrong really existed as discrete and identifiable values, but since law books didn't always have the answers, he sometimes had to find his answers elsewhere. As a parent, he regarded drug dealers with loathing. Who could guarantee that his own children might not someday be tempted to use the goddamned stuff? Did he not have a duty to protect his own children? As a representative of his country's intelligence community, what about extending that protective duty to all his nation's children? And what if the enemy started challenging his country directly? Did that change the rules? In the case of terrorism, he had already reached that answer: Challenge a nation-state in that way, and you run a major risk. Nation-states, like the United States, had capabilities that are almost impossible to comprehend. They had people in uniform who did nothing but practice the fine art of visiting death on their fellowman. They had the ability to deliver fearsome tools of that art. Everything from drilling a bullet into one particular man's chest from a thousand yards away to putting a two-thousand-pound smart-bomb right through somebody's bedroom window. . . .

''Christ.''

There was a knock at his door. Ryan found one of Sir Basil's aides standing there. He handed over an envelope and left.

When you get home, do tell Bob that the job was nicely done. Bas.

Jack folded the note back into the envelope and slid it into his coat pocket. He was correct, of course. Ryan was sure of it. Now he had to decide if it was *right* or not. He soon learned that it was much easier to second-guess such decisions when they were made by others.

They had to move, of course. Ramirez had them all doing something. The more work to be done, the fewer things had to be thought about. They had to erase any trace of their presence. They had to bury Rocha. When the time came, if it did, his family, if any, would get a sealed metal casket with one hundred fifty pounds of ballast inside to simulate the body that wasn't there. Chavez and Vega got the job of digging the grave. They went down the customary six feet, not liking the fact that they were going to leave one of their own behind like this. There was the hope that someone might come back to recover their comrade, but somehow neither expected that the effort would ever be made. Even coming from a peacetime army, neither was a stranger to death. Chavez remembered the two kids in Korea, and others killed in training accidents, helicopter crashes and the like. The life of the soldier is dangerous, even when there are no wars to fight. So they tried to rationalize it along the lines of an accidental death. But Rocha had not died by accident. He'd lost his life doing his job, soldiering at the behest of the country which he had volunteered to serve, whose uniform he'd worn with pride. He'd known what the hazards were, taken his chances like a man, and now he was being planted in the ground of a foreign land.

Chavez knew that he'd been irrational to assume that something like this would never happen. The surprise came from the fact that Rocha, like the rest of the squad members, had been a real pro, smart, tough, good with his weapons, quiet in the bush, an intense and very serious soldier who really liked the idea of going after druggies—for reasons he'd never explained to anyone. Oddly, that helped. Rocha had died doing his job. Ding figured that was a good enough epitaph for anyone. When the hole was finished, they lowered the body as gently as they could. Captain Ramirez said a few words, and the hole was filled in partway. As always, Olivero sprinkled his CS tear-gas powder to keep animals from digging it up, and the sod was replaced to erase any trace of what had been done. Ramirez made a point of recording the position, however, in case anyone ever did come back for his man. Then it was time to move.

They kept moving past dawn, heading for an alternate patrol base five miles from the one that Rocha now guarded alone. Ramirez planned to rest his men, then lead them on another mission as soon as possible. Better to have them working than thinking too much. That's what the manuals said.

An aircraft carrier is as much a community as a warship, home for over six thousand men, with its own hospital and shopping center, church and synagogue, police force and videoclub, even its own newspaper and TV network. The men work long hours, and the services they enjoyed while off duty were nothing more than they deserved—and more to the point, the Navy had found that the sailors worked far better when they received them.

Robby Jackson rose and showered as he always did, then found his way to the wardroom for coffee. He'd be having breakfast with the captain today, but wanted to be fully awake before he did so. There was a television set mounted on brackets in the corner, and the officers watched it just as they did at home, and for the same reason. Most Americans start off the day with TV news. In this case the announcer wasn't paid half a million dollars per year, and didn't have to wear makeup. He did have to write his own copy, however.

"At about nine o'clock last night—twenty-one hundred hours to us on the *Ranger*—an explosion ripped through the home of one Esteban Untiveros. *Señor* Untiveros was a major figure in the Medellín Cartel. Looks like one of his friends wasn't quite as friendly as he thought. News reports indicate that a car bomb totally destroyed his expensive hilltop residence, along with everyone in it.

"At home, the first of the summer's political conventions kicks off in Chicago next week. Governor J. Robert Fowler, the leading candidate for his party's nomination, is still a hundred votes short of a majority and is meeting today with representatives from . . ."

Jackson turned to look around. Commander Jensen was thirty feet away, motioning to the TV and chuckling with one of his people, who grinned into his cup and said nothing.

Something in Robby's mind simply went *click*.

A Drop-Ex.

A tech-rep who didn't want to talk very much.

An A-6E that headed to the beach on a heading of one-one-five toward Ecuador and returned to *Ranger* on a heading of two-zero-five. The other side of that triangle must—might—have taken the bird over . . . Colombia.

A report of a car bomb.

A bomb with a combustible case. A *smart*-bomb with a combustible case, Commander Jackson corrected himself.

Well, son of a bitch. . . .

It was amusing in more than one way. Taking out a drug dealer didn't trouble his conscience very much. Hell, he wondered why they didn't just shoot those drug-courier flights down. All that loose politician talk about threats to national security and people conducting chemical warfare against the United States—well, shit, he thought, why not have a for-real Shoot-Ex? You wouldn't even have to spend money for target drones. There was not a man in the service who wouldn't mind taking a few druggies out. Enemies are where you find them—where National Command Authority said they were, that is—and dealing with his country's enemies was what Commander Robert Jefferson Jackson, USN, did for a living. Doing them with a smart-bomb, and making it look like something else, well, that was just sheer artistry.

More amusing was the fact that Robby thought he knew what had happened. That was the trouble with secrets. They were impossible to keep. One way or another, they always got out. He wouldn't tell anyone, of course. And that really was too bad, wasn't it?

But why bother keeping it a secret? Robby wondered. The way the druggies killed the FBI Director—that was a declaration of war. Why not just go public and say, *We're coming for you!* In a political year, too. When had the American people *ever* failed to support their President when he declared the necessity to go after people?

But Jackson's job was not political. It was time to see the skipper. Two minutes later he arrived at the CO's stateroom. The Marine standing guard opened the door for him, and Robby found the captain reading dispatches.

"You're out of uniform!" the man said sternly.

"What—excuse me, Cap'n?" Robby stopped cold, looking to see that his fly was zipped.

"Here." *Ranger*'s CO rose and handed over the message flimsy. "You just got frocked, Robby—excuse *me,* Captain Jackson. Congratulations, Rob. Sure beats coffee for startin' off the day, doesn't it?"

"Thank you, sir."

"Now if we can just get those charlie-fox fighter tactics of yours to work. . . ."

"Yes, sir."

"Ritchie."

"Okay, Ritchie."

"You can still call me 'sir' on the bridge and in public, though," the captain pointed out. Newly promoted officers always got razzed. They also had to pay for the "wetting down" parties.

The TV news crews arrived in the early morning. They, too, had difficulty with the road up to the Untiveros house. The police were already there, and it didn't occur to any of the crews to wonder if these police officers might be of the "tame" variety. They wore uniforms and pistol belts and seemed to be acting like real cops. Under Cortez's supervision, the real search for survivors had been completed already, and the two people found taken off, along with most of the surviving security guards and almost all of the firearms. Security guards per se were not terribly unusual in Colombia, though fully automatic weapons and crew-served machine guns were. Of course, Cortez was also gone before the news crews arrived, and by the time they started taping, the police search was fully underway. Several of the crews had direct satellite feeds, though one of the heavy ground-station trucks had failed to make the hill.

The easiest part of the search, lovingly recorded for posterity by the portacams, began in what had been the conference room, now a three-foot pile of gravel. The largest piece of a Production Committee member found (that title was also not revealed to the newsies) was a surprisingly intact lower leg, from just below the knee to a shoe still laced on the right foot. It would later be established that this "remain" belonged to Carlos Wagner. Untiveros's wife and two young children had been in the opposite side of the house on the second floor, watching a taped movie. The VCR, still plugged in and on play, was found right before the bodies. Yet another TV camera followed the man—a security guard temporarily without his AK-47—who carried the limp, bloody body of a dead child to an ambulance.

"Oh, my God," the President said, watching one of the several televisions in the Oval Office. "If anybody figures this out . . ."

"Mr. President, we've dealt with this sort of thing before," Cutter pointed out. "The Libyan bombing under Reagan, the air strikes into Lebanon and—"

"And we caught hell for it every time! Nobody cares why we did it, all they care about is that we killed the wrong people. Christ, Jim, that was a kid! What are we going to say? 'Oh, that's too bad, but he was in the wrong place'?"

"It is alleged," the TV reporter was saying, "that the owner of this house was a member of the Medellín Cartel, but local police sources tell us that he was never officially charged with any crime, and, well . . ." The reporter paused in front of the camera. "You saw what this car bomb did to his wife and children."

"Great," the President growled. He lifted the controller and punched off the TV set. "Those bastards can do whatever the hell they want to our kids, but if we go after them on their turf, all of a sudden *they're* the goddamned victims! Has Moore told Congress about this yet?"

"No, Mr. President. CIA doesn't have to tell them until forty-eight hours after such an operation begins, and, for administrative purposes, the operation didn't actually begin until yesterday afternoon."

"They don't find out," the President said. "If we tell 'em, then it'll leak sure as hell. You tell Moore and Ritter that."

"Mr. President, I can't—"

"The hell you can't! I just gave you an order, mister." The President walked to the windows. "It wasn't supposed to be this way," he muttered.

Cutter knew what the real issue was, of course. The opposition's political convention would begin shortly. Their candidate, Governor Bob Fowler of Ohio, was leading the President in the polls. That was normal, of course. The incumbent had run through the primaries without serious opposition, resulting in a dull, predetermined result, while Fowler had fought a tooth-and-nail campaign for his party's nomination and was still an eyelash short of certain nomination. Voters always responded to the lively candidates, and while Fowler was personally about as lively as a dishrag, his contest had been the interesting one. And like every candidate since Nixon and the first war on drugs, he was saying that the President hadn't made good on his promise to restrict drug traffic. That sounded familiar to the current occupant of the Oval Office. He'd said the same thing four years earlier, and ridden that issue, and others, into the house on Pennsylvania Avenue. So now he'd actually tried something radical. And this had happened. The government of the United States had just used its most sophisticated military weapons to murder a couple of kids and their mother. That's what Fowler would say. After all, it was an election year.

"Mr. President, it would be unsound to terminate the operations we have running at this point. If you are serious about avenging the deaths of Director Jacobs and the rest, and serious about putting a dent in drug trafficking, you cannot stop things now. We're just about to show results. Drug flights into the country are down twenty percent," Cutter pointed out. "Add that to the money-laundering bust and we can say that we've achieved a real victory."

"How do we explain the bombing?"

"I've been thinking about that, sir. What if we say that we don't know, but it could be one of two things. First, it might be an attack by M-19. That group's political rhetoric lately has been critical of the drug lords. Second, we could say that it results from an internecine dispute within the Cartel itself."

"How so?" he asked without turning around. It was a bad sign when WRANGLER didn't look you in the eye, Cutter knew. He was really worried about this. Politics were such a pain in the ass, the Admiral thought, but they were also the most interesting game in town.

"Killing Jacobs and the rest was an irresponsible action on their part. Everyone knows that. We can leak the argument that some parts of the Cartel are punishing their own peers for doing something so radical as to endanger their whole operation." Cutter was rather proud of that argument. It had come from Ritter, but the President didn't know that. "We know that the druggies aren't all that reticent about killing off family members—it's practically their trademark. This way we can explain what 'they' are doing. We can have our cake and eat it, too," he concluded, smiling at the President's back.

The President turned away from the windows. His mien was skeptical, but . . . "You really think you can bring that off?"

"Yes, sir, I do. It also allows us at least one more RECIPROCITY attack."

"I have to show that we're doing *something,*" the President said quietly. "What about those soldiers we have running around in the jungle?"

"They have eliminated a total of five processing sites. We've lost two people killed, and have two more wounded, but not seriously. That's a cost of doing business, sir. These people are professional soldiers. They knew what the risks were going in. They are proud of what they are doing. You won't have any problems on that score, sir. Pretty soon the word's going to get out that the local peasants ought not to work for the druggies. That will put a serious dent in the processing operations. It'll be temporary—only a few months, but it'll be real. It'll be something you can point to. The street price of cocaine is going to go up soon. You can point to that, too. That's how we gauge success or failure in our interdiction operations. The papers will run that bit of news before we have to announce it."

"So much the better," the President observed with his first smile of the day. "Okay—let's just be more careful."

"Of course, Mr. President."

Morning PT for the 7th Division commenced at 0615 hours. It was one explanation for the puritanical virtue of the unit. Though soldiers, especially young soldiers, like to drink as much as any other segment of American society, doing physical training exercises with a hangover is one step down from lingering death. It was already warm at Fort Ord, and by seven o'clock, at the finish of the daily three-mile run, every member of the platoon had worked up a good sweat. Then it was time for breakfast.

The officers ate together this morning and table talk was on the same subject being contemplated all over the country.

"About fucking time," one captain noted.

"They said it was a car bomb," another pointed out.

"I'm sure the Agency knows how to arrange it. All the experience from Lebanon an' all," a company XO offered.

"Not as easy as you think," the battalion S-2, intelligence officer, observed. A former company commander in the Rangers, he knew a thing or two about bombs and booby traps. "But whoever did it, it was a pretty slick job."

"Shame we can't go down there," a lieutenant said. The junior officers grunted agreement. The senior ones were quiet. Plans for that contingency had been the subject of division and corps staff discussion for some years. Deploying units for war—and that's exactly what it was—was not to be discussed lightly, though the general consensus was that it could be done . . . if the local governments approved. Which they would not, of course. That, the officers thought, was understandable but most unfortunate. It was difficult to overstate the level of loathing in the Army for drugs. The senior battalion officers, major and above, could remember the drug problems of the seventies, when the Army had been every bit as hollow as critics had said it was, and it hadn't been unknown for officers to travel in certain places only with armed guards. Conquering that particular enemy had required years of effort. Even today every member of the American military was liable to random drug testing. For senior NCOs and all officers, there was no forgiveness. One positive test and you were gone. For E-5s and below, there was more leeway: one positive test resulted in an Article 15 and a very stern talking to; a second positive, and out they went. The official slogan was a simple one: NOT IN MY ARMY! Then there was the other dimension. Most of the men around this table were married, with children whom some drug dealer might approach sooner or later as a potential client. The general agreement was that if anyone sold drugs to the child of a professional soldier, that dealer's life was in mortal danger. Such events rarely took place because soldiers are above all disciplined people, but the desire was there. As was the ability.

And the odd dealer had disappeared from time to time, his death invariably ascribed to turf wars. Many of those murders went forever unsolved.

And that's where Chavez is, Tim Jackson realized. There were just too many coincidences. He and Muñoz and León. All Spanish-speakers. All checked out the same day. So they were doing a covert operation, probably at CIA bequest. It was dangerous work in all likelihood, but they were soldiers and that was their business. Lieutenant Jackson breathed easier now that he "knew" what he didn't need to know. Whatever Chavez was doing, it was okay. He wouldn't have to follow that up anymore. Tim Jackson hoped that he'd be all right. Chavez was damned good, he remembered. If anyone could do it, he could.

The TV crews soon got bored, leaving to write their copy and do their voice-overs. Cortez returned as soon as the last of their vehicles went up the road toward Medellín. This time he drove a jeep up the hill. He was tired and irritable, but more than that he was curious. Something very odd had happened and he wasn't sure what it was. He wouldn't be satisfied until he did. The two survivors from the house had been taken to Medellín, where they would be treated privately by a trusted physician. Cortez would be talking to them, but there was one more thing he had to do here. The police contingent at the house was commanded by a captain who had long since come to terms with the Cartel. Félix was certain that he'd shed no tears over the deaths of Untiveros and the rest, but that was beside the point, wasn't it? The Cuban parked his jeep and walked over to where the police commander was talking with two of his men.

"Good morning, *Capitán*. Have you determined what sort of bomb it was?"

"Definitely a car bomb," the man replied seriously.

"Yes, I suspected that myself," Cortez said patiently. "The explosive agent?"

The man shrugged. "I have no idea."

"Perhaps you might find out," Félix suggested. "As a routine part of your investigation."

"Fine. I can do that."

"Thank you." He walked back to his jeep for the ride north. A locally fabricated bomb might use dynamite—there was plenty of that available from local mining operations—or a commercial plastic explosive, or even something made from nitrated fertilizer. If made by M-19, however, Cortez would expect Semtex, a Czech-made variant of RDX currently favored by Marxist terrorists all over the world for its power and ready, cheap supply. Determining what had actually been used would tell him something, and it amused Cortez to have the police run that information down. It was one thing to smile about as he drove down the mountainside.

And there were others. The elimination of four senior Cartel chieftains did not sadden him any more than it had the policeman. After all, they were just businessmen, not a class of individual for which Cortez had great regard. He took their money, that was all. Whoever had done the bombing had done a marvelous, professional job. That started him thinking that it could not have been CIA. They didn't know very much about killing people. Cortez was less offended than one might imagine that he'd come so close to being killed. Covert operations were his business, after all, and he understood the risks. Besides, if he had been the primary target of so elegant a plan, clearly he'd not be trying to analyze it now. In any case, the removal of Untiveros, Fernández, Wagner, and d'Alejandro meant that there were four openings at the top of the Cartel, four fewer people with the power and prestige to stand in his way if . . . If, he told himself. Well, why not? A seat at the table, certainly. Perhaps more than that. But there was work to do, and a "crime" to solve.

By the time he reached Medellín, the two survivors from Untiveros' hilltop house had been treated and were ready for questioning, along with a half-dozen servants from the dead lord's Medellín condominium. They were in a top-floor room of a sturdy, fire-resistive high-rise building, which was also quite soundproof. Cortez walked into the room to find the eight trusted servants all sitting, handcuffed to straight-back chairs.

"Which of you knew about the meeting last night?" he asked pleasantly.

There were nods. They all did, of course. Untiveros was a talker, and servants were invariably listeners.

"Very well. Which of you told, and whom did you tell?" he asked in a formal, literate way. "No one will leave this room until I know the answer to that," he promised them.

The immediate response was a confused flood of denials. He'd expected that. Most of them were true. Cortez was sure of that, too.

It was too bad.

Félix looked to the head guard and pointed to the one in the left-most chair.

"We'll start with her."

Governor Fowler emerged from the hotel suite in the knowledge that the goal to which he had dedicated the last three years of his life was now in his grasp. *Almost,* he told himself, remembering that in politics there are no certainties. But a congressman from Kentucky who'd run a surprisingly strong campaign had just traded his pledged delegates for a cabinet post, and that put Fowler over the top, with a safety margin of several hundred votes. He couldn't say that, of course. He had to let the man from Kentucky make his own announcement, scheduled for the second day of the convention to give him one last day in the sun—or more properly the klieg lights. It would be leaked by people in both camps, but the congressman would smile in his aw-shucks way and tell people to speculate all they wanted—but that he was the only one who knew. Politics, Fowler thought, could be so goddamned phony. This was especially odd since above all things Fowler was a very sincere man, which did not, however, allow him to violate the rules of the game.

And he played by those rules now, standing before the bright TV lights and saying nothing at all for about six minutes of continuous talking. There had been "interesting discussions" of "the great issues facing our country." The Governor and the congressman were "united in their desire to see new leadership" for a country which, both were sure, though they couldn't say it, would prosper whichever man won in November, because petty political differences of presidents and parties generally got lost in the noise of the Capitol Building, and because American parties were so disorganized that every presidential campaign was increasingly a beauty contest. Perhaps that was just as well, Fowler thought, though it was frustrating to see that the power for which he lusted might really be an illusion, after all. Then it was time for questions.

He was surprised by the first one. Fowler didn't see who asked it. He was dazzled by the lights and the flashing strobes—after so many months of it, he wondered if his vision would ever recover—but it was a male voice who asked, from one of the big papers, he thought.

"Governor, there is a report from Colombia that a car bomb destroyed the home of a major figure in the Medellín Cartel, along with his family. Coming so soon after the assassination of the FBI Director and our ambassador to Colombia, would you care to comment?"

"I'm afraid I didn't get a chance to catch the news this morning because of my breakfast with the congressman. What are you suggesting?" Fowler asked. His demeanor had changed from optimistic candidate to careful politician who hoped to become a statesman—whatever the hell that was, he thought. It had seemed so clear once, too.

"There is speculation, sir, that America might have been involved," the reporter amplified.

"Oh? You know the President and I have many differences, and some of them are very serious differences, but I can't remember when we've had a President who was willing to commit cold-blooded murder, and I certainly will not accuse our President of that," Fowler said in his best statesman's voice. He'd meant to say nothing at all—that's what statesmen's voices are for, after all, either nothing or the obvious. He'd kept a fairly high road for most of his presidential campaign. Even Fowler's bitterest enemies—he had several in his own party, not to mention the opposition's—said that he was an honorable, thoughtful man who concentrated on issues and not invective. His statement reflected that. He hadn't meant to change United States government policy, hadn't meant to trap his prospective opponent. But he had, without knowing it, done both.

The President had scheduled the trip well in advance. It was a customary courtesy for the chief executive to maintain a low profile during the opposition's convention. It was just as easy to work at Camp David—easier in fact since it was far easier to shoo reporters away. But you had to run the gauntlet to get there. With the Marine VH-3 helicopter sitting and waiting on the White House lawn, the President emerged from the ground-level door with the First Lady and two other functionaries in tow, and there they were again, a solid phalanx of reporters and cameras. He wondered if the Russians with their *glasnost* knew what they were in for.

"Mister President!" called a senior TV reporter. *"Governor Fowler says that he hopes we weren't involved in the bombing in COLOMBIA! Do you have any comment?"*

Even as he walked over to the roped enclosure of journalists, the President knew that it was a mistake, but he was drawn to them and the question as a lemming is drawn to the sea. He couldn't *not* do it. The way the question was shouted, everyone would know that he'd heard it, and no answer would itself be seen as an answer of sorts. *The President ducked the question of* . . . And he couldn't leave Washington for a week of low-profile existence, leaving the limelight to the other side—not with that question lying unanswered behind him on the White House lawn, could he?

"The United States," the President said, "does not kill innocent women and children. The United States fights *against* people who do that. We do not sink down to their bestial level. Is that a clear enough answer?'' It was delivered in a quiet, reasoned voice, but the look the President gave the reporter made that experienced journalist wilt before his eyes. It was good, the President thought, to see that his power occasionally reached the bastards.

It was the second major political lie of the day—a slow news day to be sure. Governor Fowler well remembered that John and Robert Kennedy had plotted the deaths of Castro and others with a kind of elitist glee born of Ian Fleming's novels, only to learn the hard way that assassination was a messy business. Very messy indeed, for there were usually people about whom you didn't especially want to kill. The current President knew all about ''collateral damage,'' a term which he found distasteful but indicative of something both necessary and impossible to explain to people who didn't understand how the world really worked: terrorists, criminals, and all manner of cowards—brutal people are most often cowards, after all—regularly hid behind or among the innocent, daring the mighty to act, using the altruism of their enemies as a weapon against those enemies. *You cannot touch me. We are the ''evil'' ones. You are the ''good'' ones. You cannot attack us without casting away your self-image.* It was the most hateful attribute of those most hateful of people, and sometimes—rarely, but sometimes—they had to be shown that it didn't work. And that was messy, wasn't it? Like some sort of international auto accident.

But how the hell do I explain that to the American people? In an election year? *Vote to re-elect the President who just killed a wife, two kids, and various domestic servants to protect your children from drugs . . . ?* The President wondered if Governor Fowler understood just how illusory presidential power was—and about the awful noise generated when one principle crashed hard up against another. That was even worse than the noise of the reporters, the President thought. It was something to shake his head about as he walked to his helicopter. The Marine sergeant saluted at the steps. The President returned it—a tradition despite the fact that no sitting President had ever worn a uniform. He strapped in and looked back at the assembled mob. The cameras were still on him, taping the takeoff. The networks wouldn't run that particular shot, but just in case the chopper blew up or crashed, they wanted the cameras rolling.

The word got to the Mobile police a little late. The clerk of the court handled the paperwork, and when information leaks from a courthouse, that is usually the hole. In this case the clerk was outraged. He saw the cases come and go. A man in his middle fifties, he'd gotten his children educated and through college, managing to avoid the drug epidemic. But that had not been true of every child in the clerk's neighborhood. Right next door to his house, the family's youngest had bought a ''rock'' of crack cocaine and promptly driven his car into a bridge abutment at over a hundred miles per hour. The clerk had watched the child grow up, had driven him to school once or twice, and paid the child to mow his lawn. The coffin had been sealed for the funeral at Cypress Hill Baptist Church, and he'd heard that the mother was still on medications after having had to identify what was left of the body. The minister talked about the scourge of drugs like the scourging of Christ's own passion. He was a fine minister, a gifted orator in the Southern Baptist tradition, and while he led them in prayer for the dead boy's soul his personal and wholly genuine fury over the drug problem merely amplified the outrage already felt by his congregation. . . .

The clerk couldn't understand it. Davidoff was a superb prosecuting attorney.

Jew or not, this man was one of God's elect, a true hero in a profession of charlatans. How could this be? *Those two* scum *were going to get off!* the clerk thought. It was *wrong!*

The clerk was unaccustomed to bars. A Baptist serious about his religious beliefs, he had never tasted spiritous liquors, had tried beer only once as a boy on a dare, and was forever guilt-ridden for that. That was one of only two narrow aspects to this otherwise decent and honorable citizen. The other was justice. He believed in justice as he believed in God, a faith that had somehow survived his thirty years of clerking in the federal courts. Justice, he thought, came from God, not from man. Laws came from God, not from man. Were not all Western laws based on Holy Scripture in one way or another? He revered his country's Constitution as a divinely inspired document, for freedom was surely the way in which God intended man to live, that man could learn to know and serve his God not as a slave, but as a positive choice for Right. That was the way things were supposed to be. The problem was that the Right did not always prevail. Over the years he'd gotten used to that idea. Frustrating though it was, he also knew that the Lord was the ultimate Judge, and His Justice would always prevail. But there were times when the Lord's Justice needed help, and it was well known that God chose His Instruments though Faith. And so it was this hot, sultry Alabama afternoon. The clerk had his Faith, and God had His Instrument.

The clerk was in a cop bar, half a block from police headquarters, drinking club soda so that he could fit in. The police knew who he was, of course. He appeared at all the cop funerals. He headed a civic committee that looked after the families of cops and firemen who died in the line of duty. Never asked for anything in return, either. Never even asked to fix a ticket—he'd never gotten one in his life, but no one had ever thought to check.

"Hi, Bill," he said to a homicide cop.

"How's life with the feds?" the detective lieutenant asked. He thought the clerk slightly peculiar, but far less so than most. All he really needed to know was that the clerk of the court took care of cops. That was enough.

"I heard something that you ought to know about."

"Oh?" The lieutenant looked up from his beer. He, too, was a Baptist, but wasn't *that* Baptist. Few cops were, even in Alabama, and like most he felt guilty about it.

"The 'pirates' are getting a plea-bargain," the clerk told him.

"What?" It wasn't his case, but it was a symbol of all that was going wrong. And the pirates were in the same jail in which his prisoners were guests.

The clerk explained what he knew, which wasn't much. Something was wrong with the case. Some technicality or other. The judge hadn't explained it very well. Davidoff was enraged by it all, but there was nothing he could do. That was too bad, they both agreed. Davidoff was one of the Good Guys. That's when the clerk told his lie. He didn't like to tell lies, but sometimes Justice required it. He'd learned that much in the federal court system. It was just a practical application of what his minister said: "God moves in mysterious ways, His wonders to perform."

The funny part was that it wasn't entirely a lie: "The guys who killed Sergeant Braden were connected with the pirates. The feds think that the pirates may have ordered his murder—and his wife's."

"How sure are you of that?" the detective asked.

"Sure as I can be." The clerk emptied his glass and set it down.

"Okay," the cop said. "Thanks. We never heard it from you. Thanks for what you guys did for the Braden kids, too."

The clerk was embarrassed by that. What he did for the families of cops and firemen wasn't done for thanks. It was Duty, pure and simple. His Reward would come from Him who assigned that Duty.

The clerk left, and the lieutenant walked to a corner booth to join a few of his colleagues. It was soon agreed that the pirates would not—could not—be allowed to cop a plea on this one. Federal case or not, they were guilty of multiple rape and murder—and, it would seem, guilty of another double murder in which the Mobile police had direct interest. The word was already on the street: the lives of druggies were at risk. It was another case of sending a message. The advantage that police officers had over more senior government officials was that they spoke in a language that criminals fully understood.

But who, another detective asked, would deliver the message?

"How about the Patterson boys?" the lieutenant answered.

"Ahh," the captain said. He considered the question for a moment, then: "Okay." It was, on the whole, a decision far more easily arrived at than the great and weighty decisions reached by governments. And far more easily implemented.

The two peasants arrived in Medellín around sundown. Cortez was thoroughly frustrated by this time. Eight bodies to be disposed of—not all that difficult a thing to do in Medellín—for no good reason. He was sure of that now. As sure as he'd been of the opposite thing six hours earlier. So where was the information leak? Three women and five men had just died proving that they weren't it. The last two had just been shot in the head, uselessly catatonic after watching the first six die under less merciful circumstances. The room was a mess, and Cortez felt soiled by it. All that effort wasted. Killing people for no good reason. He was too angry to be ashamed.

He met with the peasants in another room on another floor after washing his hands and changing his clothes. They were frightened, but not of Cortez, which surprised Félix greatly. It took several minutes to understand why. They told their stories in an overly rapid and disjointed manner, which he allowed, memorizing the details—some of them conflicting, but that was not unexpected since there were two of them—before he began asking his own, directed questions.

"The rifles were not AK-47s," one said positively. "I know the sound. It was not that one." The other shrugged. He didn't know one weapon from another.

"Did you see anyone?"

"No, señor. We heard the noise and the shouting, and we ran."

Very sensible of you, Cortez noted. "Shouting, you say? In what language?"

"Why, in our language. We heard them chasing after us, but we ran. They didn't catch us. We know the mountains," the weapons expert explained.

"You saw and heard nothing else?"

"The shooting, the explosions, lights—flashes from the guns, that is all."

"The place where it happened—how many times had you been there?"

"Many times, señor, it is where we make the paste."

"Many times," the other confirmed. "For over a year we have gone there."

"You will tell no one that you came here. You will tell no one anything that you know," Félix told them.

"But the families of—"

"You will tell no one," Cortez repeated in a quiet, serious voice. Both men knew danger when they saw it. "You will be well rewarded for what you have done, and the families of the others will be compensated."

Cortez deemed himself a fair man. These two mountain folk had served his purposes well, and they would be properly rewarded. He still didn't know where the leak was, but if he could get ahold of one of those—what? M-19 bands? Somehow he didn't think so.

Then who?

Americans?

If anything, the death of Rocha had only increased their resolve, Chavez knew. Captain Ramirez had taken it pretty hard, but that was to be expected from a good officer. Their new patrol base was only two miles from one of the many coffee plantations in the area, and two miles in a different direction from yet another processing site. The men were in their normal daytime routine. Half asleep, half standing guard.

Ramirez sat alone. Chavez was correct. He had taken it hard. In an intellectual sense, the captain knew that he should accept the death of one of his men as a simple cost of doing business. But emotions are not the same as intellect. It was also true, though Ramirez didn't think along these precise lines, that historically there is no way to predict which officers are suited for combat operations and which are not. Ramirez had committed a typical mistake for combat leaders. He had grown too close to his men. He was unable to think of them as expendable assets. His failure had nothing to do with courage. The captain had enough of that; risking his own life was a part of the job he readily accepted. Where he failed was in understanding that risking the lives of his men—which he also knew to be part of the job—inevitably meant that some would die. Somehow he'd forgotten that. As a company commander he'd led his men on countless field exercises, training them, showing them how to do their jobs, chiding them when their laser-sensing Miles gear went off to denote a simulated casualty. But Rocha hadn't been a simulation, had he? And it wasn't as though Rocha had been a slick-sleeved new kid. He'd been a skilled pro. That meant that he'd somehow failed his men, Ramirez told himself, knowing that it was wrong even as he thought it. If he'd deployed better, if he'd paid more attention, if, if, if. The young captain tried to shake it off but couldn't. But he couldn't quit either. So he'd be more careful next time.

The tape cassettes arrived together just after lunch. The COD flight from *Ranger*, unbeknownst to anyone involved, had been coordinated with a courier flight from Bogotá. Larson had handled part of it, flying the tape from the GLD to El Dorado where he handed it off to another CIA officer. Both cassettes were tucked in the satchel of an Agency courier who rode in the front cabin of the Air Force C-5A transport, catching a few hours' sleep in one of the cramped bunks on the right side of the aircraft, a few feet behind the flight deck. The flight came directly into Andrews, and, after its landing, the forty-foot ladder was let down into the cavernous cargo area and the courier walked out the opened cargo door to a waiting Agency car which sped directly to Langley.

Ritter had a pair of television sets in his office, each with its own VCR. He watched them alone, cueing the tapes until they were roughly synchronized. The one from the aircraft didn't show very much. You could see the laser dot and the rough outline of the house, but little else until the flash of the detonation. Clark's tape was far better. There was the house, its lighted windows flaring in the light-amplified picture, and the guards wandering about—those with cigarettes looked like lightning bugs; each time they took a drag their faces were lit brightly by the glow. Then the bomb. It was very much like watching a Hitchcock movie, Ritter thought. He knew what was happening, but those on the screen did not. They wandered around aimlessly, unaware of the part they played in a drama written in the office of the Deputy Director (Operations) of the Central Intelligence Agency. But—

"That's funny . . ." Ritter said to himself. He used his remote control to back up the tape. Seconds before the bomb went off, a new car appeared at the gate. "Who might you be?" he asked the screen. Then he fast-forwarded the tape past the explosion. The car he'd been driving—a BMW—had been flipped over by the shock wave, but seconds later the driver got out and pulled a pistol.

"Cortez . . ." He froze the frame. The picture didn't tell him much. It was a man of medium dimensions. While everyone else around the wrecked house raced about without much in the way of purpose, this man just stood there for a little while, then revived himself at the fountain—wasn't it odd that it still worked! Ritter thought—and next went to where the bomb had gone off. He couldn't have been a retainer of one of the Cartel members. They were all plowing through the rubble by this time. No, this one was already trying to figure out what had happened. It was right before the tape changed over to blank noise that he got the best picture. That had to be Félix Cortez. Looking around, already thinking, already trying to figure things out. That was a real pro.

"Damn, that was close," Ritter breathed. "One more minute and you would have parked your car over with the others. One more damned minute!" Ritter pulled both tapes and tucked them in his office safe along with all of the EAGLE EYE, SHOWBOAT, and RECIPROCITY material. *Next time,* he promised the tape cassette. Then he started thinking. Was Cortez really involved in the assassination?

"Gawd," Ritter said aloud in his office. He'd assumed that, but . . . Would he have set up the crime and then come to America . . . ? Why do such a thing? According to the statement that secretary had made, he'd not even pumped her very hard for information. Instead it had been a basic get-away-with-your-lover weekend. The technique was a classic one. First, seduce the target. Second, determine if you can get information from her (usually *him* the way Western intelligence services handled sexual recruitments, but the other way around for the Eastern bloc). Third, firm up the relationship—and then use it. If Ritter understood the evidence properly, Cortez hadn't yet gotten to the point . . .

It wasn't Cortez at all, was it? He'd probably forwarded what information he had as a matter of course, not knowing about the FBI operation against the Cartel's money operations. He hadn't been there when the decision to whack the Director had been made. And he would have recommended against it. Why lash out when you have just developed a good intel source? No, that wasn't professional at all.

So, Félix, how do you feel about all this? Ritter would have traded much for the ability to ask that question, though the answer was plain enough. Intelligence officers were regularly betrayed by their political superiors. It wouldn't be the first time for him, but he'd be angry just the same. Just as angry as Ritter was with Admiral Cutter.

For the first time, Ritter found himself wondering what Cortez was really doing. Probably he had simply defected away from Cuba and made a mercenary of himself. The Cartel had hired him on for his training and experience, thinking that they were buying just another mercenary—a very good one to be sure, but a mercenary nonetheless. Just like they bought local cops—hell, American cops—and politicians. But a police officer wasn't the same thing as a professional spook educated at Moscow Center. He was giving them his advice, and he'd think they had betrayed him—well, acted very stupidly, because killing Emil Jacobs had been an act of emotion, not of reason.

Why didn't I see that before! Ritter growled at himself. The answer: because not seeing had given him an excuse to do something he'd always wanted to do. He hadn't thought because somehow he'd known that thinking would have prevented him from taking action.

Cortez wasn't a terrorist, was he? He was an intelligence officer. He'd worked with the Macheteros because he'd been assigned to the job. Before that his experience had been straight espionage, and merely because he'd worked with that loony Puerto Rican group, they'd just assumed . . . That was probably one reason why he'd defected.

It was clearer now. The Cartel had hired Cortez for his expertise and experience. But in doing so they had adopted a pet wolf. And wolves made for dangerous pets, didn't they?

For the moment there was one thing he could do. Ritter summoned an aide and instructed him to take the best frame they had of Cortez, run it through the photo-enhancing computer, and forward it to the FBI. That was something worth doing, so long as they isolated the figure from the background, but that was just another task for the imaging computer.

Admiral Cutter remained at his White House office while the President was away in the western Maryland hills. He'd fly up every day for his usual morning briefing—delivered at a somewhat later hour while the President was on his "vacation" regime—but for the most part he'd stay here. He had his own duties, one of which was being "a senior administration official." ASAO, as he thought of the title, was his name when he gave off-the-record press briefings. Such information was a vital part of presidential policymaking, all part of an elaborate game played by the government and the press: Official Leaking. Cutter would send up "trial balloons," what people in the consumer-products business called test-marketing. When the President had a new idea that he was not too sure about, Cutter—or the appropriate cabinet secretary, each of whom was also an ASAO—would speak on background, and a story would be written in the major papers, allowing Congress and others to react to the idea before it was given an official presidential *imprimatur*. It was a way for elected officials and other players in the Washington scene to dance and posture without the need for anyone to lose face—an Oriental concept that translated well inside the confines of the Capital Beltway.

Bob Holtzman, the senior White House correspondent for one of the Washington papers, settled into his chair opposite Cutter for the deep-background revelations. The rules were fully understood by both sides. Cutter could say anything he wished without fear that his name, title, or the location of his office would be used. Holtzman would feel free to write the story any way he wished, within reason, so long as he did not compromise his source to anyone except his editor. Neither man especially liked the other. Cutter's distaste for journalists was about the only thing he still had in common with his fellow military officers, though he was certain that he concealed it. He thought them all, especially the one before him now, to be lazy, stupid people who couldn't write and didn't think. Holtzman felt that Cutter was the wrong man in the wrong place—the reporter didn't like the idea of having a military officer giving such intimate advice to the President; more importantly, he thought Cutter was a shallow, self-serving apple-polisher with delusions of grandeur, not to mention an arrogant son of a bitch who looked upon reporters as a semiuseful form of domesticated vulture. As a result of such thoughts, they got along rather well.

"You going to be watching the convention next week?" Holtzman asked.

"I try not to concern myself with politics," Cutter replied. "Coffee?"

Right! the reporter told himself. "No, thanks. What the hell's going on down in coca land?"

"Your guess is as good as—well, that's not true. We've had the bastards under surveillance for some time. My guess is that Emil was killed by one faction of the Cartel—no surprise—but without their having made a really official decision. The bombing last night might be indicative of a faction fight inside the organization."

"Well, somebody's pretty pissed," Holtzman observed, scribbling notes on his pad under his personal heading for Cutter. "A Senior Administration Official" was transcribed as *ASO'l.* "The word is that the Cartel contracted M-19 to do the assassination, and that the Colombians really worked over the one they caught."

"Maybe they did."

"How'd they know that Director Jacobs was going down?"

"I don't know," Cutter replied.

"Really? You know that his secretary tried to commit suicide. The Bureau isn't talking at all, but I find that a remarkable coincidence."

"Who's running the case over there? Believe it or not, I don't know."

"Dan Murray, a deputy assistant director. He's not actually doing the field work, but he's the guy reporting to Shaw."

"Well, that's not my turf. I'm looking at the overseas aspects of the case, but the domestic stuff is in another office," Cutter pointed out, erecting a stone wall that Holtzman couldn't breach.

"So the Cartel was pretty worked up about Operation TARPON, and some senior people acted without the approval of the whole outfit to take Jacobs out. Other members, you say, think that their action was precipitous and decided to eliminate those who put out the contract?"

"That's the way it looks now. You have to understand, our intel on this is pretty thin."

"Our intel is always pretty thin," Holtzman pointed out.

"You can talk to Bob Ritter about that." Cutter set his coffee mug down.

"Right." Holtzman smiled. If there were two people in Washington whom you could trust never to leak anything, it was Bob Ritter and Arthur Moore. "What about Jack Ryan?"

"He's just settling in. He's been in Belgium all week anyway, at the NATO intel conference."

"There are rumbles on The Hill that somebody ought to do something about the Cartel, that the attack on Jacobs was a direct attack on—"

"I watch C-SPAN, too, Bob. Talk is cheap."

"And what Governor Fowler said this morning . . . ?"

"I'll leave politics to the politicians."

"You know that the price of coke is up on the street?"

"Oh? I'm not in that market. Is it?" Cutter hadn't heard that yet. *Already . . .*

"Not much, but some. There's word on the street that incoming shipments are off a little."

"Glad to hear it."

"But no comment?" Holtzman asked. "You're the one who's been saying that this is a for-real war and we ought to treat it as such."

Cutter's smile froze on his face for a moment. "The President decides about things like war."

"What about Congress?"

"Well, that, too, but since I've been in government service there hasn't been a congressional declaration along those lines."

"How would you feel personally if we were involved in that bombing?"

"I don't know. We weren't involved." The interview wasn't going as planned. What did Holtzman know?

"That was a hypothetical," the reporter pointed out.

"Okay. We go off the record—completely—at this point. Hypothetically, we could kill all the bastards and I wouldn't shed many tears. How about you?"

Holtzman snorted. "Off the record, I agree with you. I grew up here. I can remember when it was safe to walk the streets. Now I look at the body count every morning and wonder if I'm in D.C. or Beirut. So it wasn't us, then?"

"Nope. Looks more like the Cartel is shaking itself out. That's speculation, but it's the best we have at the moment."

"Fair enough. I suppose I can make a story out of that."

20. Discoveries

It was amazing. But it was also true. Cortez had been there for over an hour. There were six armed men with him, and a dog that sniffed around for signs of the people who had assaulted this processing site. The empty cartridge cases were mostly of the 5.56mm round now used by most of the NATO countries and their surrogates all over the world, but which had begun as the .223 Remington sporting cartridge. In America. There were also a number of 9mm cases, and a single empty hull from a 40mm grenade launcher. One of the attackers had been wounded, perhaps severely. The method of the attack was classic, a fire unit uphill and an assault group on the same level, to the north. They'd left hastily, not booby-trapping the bodies as had happened in two other cases. Probably because of the injured man, Cortez judged. Also because they knew—suspected? No, they probably knew—that two men had gotten away to summon help.

Definitely more than one team was roaming the mountains. Maybe three or four, judging by the number and location of sites that had so far been attacked. That eliminated M-19. There weren't enough trained men in that organization to do something like this—not without his hearing of it, he corrected himself. The Cartel had done more than suborn the local guerrilla factions. It also had paid informants in each unit, something the Colombian government had signally failed to do.

So, he told himself, *now you have probable American covert-action teams working in the hills. Who and what are they? Probably soldiers, or very high-quality mercenaries. More likely the former.* The international mercenary community wasn't what it had once been—and truthfully had never been especially effective. Cortez had been to Angola and seen what African troops were like. Mercenaries hadn't had to be all that effective to defeat them, though that was now changing along with everything else in the world.

Whoever they were, they'd be far away—far enough that he didn't feel uncomfortable at the moment, though he'd leave the hunting to others. Cortez was an intelligence officer, and had no illusions about being a soldier. For now, he gathered his evidence almost like a policeman. The rifle and machine-gun cartridges, he saw, came from a single manufacturer. He didn't have such information committed to memory, but he noted that the 9mm cases had the same lot codes—stamped on the case heads—as those he'd gotten from one of the airfields on Colombia's northern coast. The odds against that being a coincidence were pretty high, he thought. So whoever had been watching the airfields had moved here . . . ? How would that have been done? The simple way would be by truck or bus, but that was a little too simple; that's how M-19 would have done it. Too great a risk for Americans, however. The *yanquis* would use helicopters. Staging from where? A ship, perhaps, or more likely one of their bases in Panama. He knew of no American naval exercises within helicopter range of the coast. Therefore a large aircraft capable of midair refueling. Only the Americans did that. And it would have to be based in Panama. And he had assets in Panama. Cortez pocketed the cartridges and started walking down the hill. Now he had a starting place, and that was all someone with his training needed.

Ryan's VC-20A—thinking of it as his airplane still required a stretch of the imagination—lifted off from the airfield outside Mons in the early afternoon. His first official foray into the big leagues of the international intelligence business had gone well. His paper on the Soviets and their activities in Eastern Europe had met with general approval and agreement, and he'd been gratified to learn that the analysis chiefs of all the NATO intelligence agencies held exactly the same opinion of the changes in their enemy's policies as he did: nobody knew what the hell was going on. There were theories ranging all the way from the peace-is-breaking-out-and-now-what-do-we-do? view to the equally unlikely it's-all-a-trick opinion, but when it came down to doing a formal intelligence estimate, people who'd been in the business since before Jack was born just shook their heads and muttered into their beer—exactly what Ryan did some of the time. The really good news for the year, of course, was the signal success that the counterintelligence groups had had turning KGB operations throughout Europe, and while CIA had not told anyone (except Sir Basil, who'd been there when the plan had been hatched) exactly how that had come about, the Agency enjoyed considerable prestige for its work in that area. The bottom line that Jack had often cited in the investment business was fairly clear: militarily NATO was in its best-ever condition, its security services were riding higher than anyone thought possible—it was just that the alliance's overall mission was now in doubt politically. To Ryan that looked like success, so long as politicians didn't let things go to their heads, which was enough of a caveat for anyone.

So there was a lot to smile about as the Belgian countryside fell farther and farther below him until it looked like a particularly attractive quilt from Pennsylvania Dutch country. At least on the actual NATO side.

Possibly the truest testimony to NATO's present happy condition, however, was that talk around the banquet tables and over coffee in the break periods between the plenary sessions was not on "business" as most of the conference attendees normally viewed it. Intelligence analysts from Germany and Italy, Britain and Norway, Denmark and Portugal, all of them expressed their concern at the growing problems of drugs in their countries. The Cartel's activities were expanding eastward, no longer content with marketing their wares to America alone. The intelligence professionals had noted the assassination of Emil Jacobs and the rest and wondered aloud if international narcoterrorism had taken a wholly new and dangerous turn—and what had to be done about it. The French, with their history of vigorous action to protect their land, were especially approving of the bomb blast outside Medellín, and nonplussed by Ryan's puzzled and somewhat exasperating response: *No comment. I don't know anything*. Their reaction to that was predictable, of course. Had an equivalent French official been so publicly murdered, DGSE would have mounted an immediate operation. It was something the French were especially good at. It was something that the French media and, more to the point, the French people understood and approved. And so the DGSE representatives had expected Ryan to respond with a knowing smile to accompany his lack of comment, not blank embarrassment. That wasn't part of the game as it was played in Europe, and just another odd thing about the Americans for their Old World allies to ponder. *Must they be* so *unpredictable?* they would ask themselves. Being that way to the Russians had strategic value, but not to one's allies.

And not to its own government officials, Ryan thought. *What the hell is going on?*

Being three thousand miles from home had given Jack a properly detached perspective to the affair. In the absence of a viable legal mechanism to deal with such crimes, maybe direct action was the right thing to do. Challenge directly the power of a nation-state and you risked a direct response from that nation-state. If we could bomb a foreign country for sponsoring action against American soldiers in a Berlin disco, then why not—

—kill people on the territory of a fellow American democracy?

What about that *political dimension?*

That was the rub, wasn't it? Colombia had its own laws. It wasn't Libya, ruled by a comic-opera figure of dubious stability. It wasn't Iran, a vicious theocracy ruled by a bitter testimonial to the skill of gerontologists. Colombia was a country with real democratic traditions, one that had put its own institutions at risk, fighting to protect the citizens of another land from—themselves.

What the hell are we doing?

Right and wrong assumed different values at this level of statecraft, didn't they? Or did they? What were the rules? What was the law? Were there any of either? Before he could answer those questions, Ryan knew that he'd have to learn the facts. That would be hard enough. Jack settled back into his comfortable seat and looked down at the English Channel, widening out like a funnel as the aircraft headed west toward Land's End. Beyond that lonely point of ship-killing rocks lay the North Atlantic, and beyond that lay home. He had seven hours to decide what he should do once he got there. *Seven whole hours,* Jack thought, wondering how many times he could ask himself the same questions, and how many times he'd only come up with new questions instead of answers.

Law was a trap, Murray told himself. It was a goddess to worship, a lovely bronze lady who held up her lantern in the darkness to show one the way. But what if the way led nowhere? They now had a dead-bang case against the one "suspect" in the assassination of the Director. The Colombians had gotten the confession and its thirty single-spaced pages of text were lying on his desk. There was ample physical evidence, which had been duly processed through the Bureau's legendary forensic laboratories. There was just one little problem. The extradition treaty the United States had with Colombia was not operative at the moment. Colombia's Supreme Court—more precisely, those justices who remained alive after twelve of their colleagues had been murdered by M-19 raiders not so long ago; all of whom, coincidentally, had been supporters of the extradition treaty before their violent deaths—had decided that the treaty was somehow in opposition to their country's constitution. No treaty. No extradition. The assassin would be tried locally and doubtless sent away for a lengthy prison term, but at the very least Murray and the Bureau wanted him caged in Marion, Illinois—the maximum-security federal prison for really troublesome offenders; Alcatraz without the ambience—and the Justice Department thought it could make a case for invoking the death statute that related to drug-related murders. But—the confession the Colombians had gotten hadn't exactly followed with American rules of evidence, and, the lawyers admitted, might be thrown out by an American judge; which would eliminate the death penalty. And the guy who took out the Director of the FBI might actually become something of a celebrity at Marion, Illinois, most of whose prisoners did not regard the FBI with the same degree of affection accorded by most U.S. citizens. The same thing, he'd learned the day before, was true of the Pirates Case. Some tricky bastard of a defense lawyer had uncovered what the Coast Guard had pulled, blowing that death case away also. And the only good news around was that Murray was sure his government had struck back in a way that was highly satisfying, but fell under the general legal category of cold-blooded murder.

It worried Dan Murray that he did view that development as good news. It wasn't the sort of thing that they'd lectured him—and he had later lectured others—about during his stint as a student and later an instructor at the FBI Academy, was it? What happened when governments broke the law? The textbook answer was anarchy—at least that's what happened when it became known that the government was breaking its own laws. But that was the really operative definition of a criminal, wasn't it—one who got caught breaking the law.

"No," Murray told himself quietly. He'd spent his life following that light because on dark nights that one beacon of sanity was all society had. His mission and the Bureau's was to enforce the laws of his country faithfully and honestly. There was leeway—there had to be, because the written words couldn't anticipate everything—but when the letter of the law was insufficient one was guided by the principle upon which the law was based. Maybe the situation wasn't always a satisfying one, but it beat the alternative, didn't it? But what did you do when the law didn't work? Was that just part of the game, too? Was it, after all was said and done, just a game?

Clark held a somewhat different view. Law had never been his concern—at least not his immediate concern. To him "legal" meant that something was "okay," not that some legislators had drafted a set of rules, and that some President or other had signed it. To him it meant that the sitting President had decided that the continued existence of someone or something was contrary to the best interests of his country. His government service had begun in the United States Navy as part of the SEALs, the Navy's elite, secretive commandos. In that tight, quiet community he'd made himself a name that was still spoken with respect: *Snake,* they'd called him, because you couldn't hear his footsteps. To the best of his knowledge, no enemy had ever seen him and lived to tell the tale. His name had been different then, of course, but only because after leaving the Navy he'd made the mistake—he truly thought of it as a mistake, but only in the technical sense—of applying his skills on a free-agent basis. And done quite well, of course, until the police had discovered his identity. The lesson from that adventure was that while people didn't really investigate happenings on the battlefield, they did elsewhere, requiring far greater circumspection on his part. A foolish error in retrospect, one result of his almost-discovery by a local police force was that he'd come to the attention of CIA, which occasionally needed people with his unique skills. It was even something of a joke: "When there's killing to be done, get someone who kills for a living." At least it had been funny back then, almost twenty years earlier.

Others decided who needed to die. Those others were the properly selected representatives of the American people, whom he'd served in one way or another for most of his adult life. The law, as he'd once bothered to find out, was that there was no law. If the President said "kill," then Clark was merely the instrument of properly defined government policy, all the more so now, since selected members of Congress had to agree with the executive branch. The rules which from time to time prohibited such acts were Executive Orders from the President's office, which orders the President could freely violate—or more precisely, redefine to suit the situation. Of course, Clark did very little of that. Mainly his jobs for the Agency involved his other skills—getting in and out of places without being detected, for example, at which he was the best guy around. But killing was the reason he'd been hired in the first place, and for Clark, who'd been baptized John Terrence Kelly at St. Ignatius Parish in Indianapolis, Indiana, it was simply an act of war sanctioned both by his country and also by his religion, about which he was moderately serious. Vietnam had never been granted the legal sanction of a declared war, after all, and if killing his country's enemies back then had been all right, why not now? Murder to the renamed John T. Clark was killing people without just cause. Law he left to lawyers, in the knowledge that his definition of just cause was far more practical, and far more effective.

His immediate concern was his next target. He had two more days of availability on the carrier battle group, and he wanted to stage another stealth-bombing if he could.

Clark was domiciled in a frame house in the outskirts of Bogotá, a safe house the CIA had set up a decade earlier, officially owned by a corporate front and generally rented out commercially to visiting American businessmen. It had no obvious special features. The telephone was ordinary until he attached a portable encrypting device—a simple one that wouldn't have passed muster in Eastern Europe, but sufficient for the relatively low-intercept threat down here—and he also had a satellite dish that operated just fine through a not very obvious hole in the roof and also ran through an encrypting system that looked much the same as a portable cassette player.

So what to do next? he asked himself. The Untiveros bombing had been carefully executed to look like a car bomb. Why not another, a real one? The trick was setting it up to scare hell out of the intended targets, flushing them into a better target area. To accomplish that it had to appear an earnest attempt, but at the same time it couldn't be earnest enough to injure innocent people. That was the problem with car bombs.

Low-order detonation? he thought. That was an idea. Make the bomb look like an earnest attempt that fizzled. *Too hard to do,* he decided.

Best of all would be a simple assassination with a rifle, but that was too hard to set up. Just getting a perch overlooking the proper place would be difficult and dangerous. The Cartel overlords kept tabs on every window with a line of sight to their own domiciles. If an American rented one, and soon thereafter a shot was fired from it—well, that wouldn't exactly be covert, would it? The whole point was for them not to know exactly what was happening.

Clark's operational concept was an elegantly simple one. So elegant and so simple that it hadn't occurred to the supposed experts in "black" operations at Langley. What Clark wanted to do, simply, was to kill enough of the people on his list to increase the paranoia within his targeted community. Killing them all, desirable though it might be, was a practical impossibility. What he wanted to do was merely to kill enough of them, and to do so in such a way as to spark another reaction entirely.

The Cartel was composed of a number of very ruthless people whose intelligence was manifested in the sort of cunning most often associated with a skilled enemy on the battlefield. Like good soldiers they were always alert to danger, but unlike soldiers they looked for danger from within in addition to from without. Despite the success of their collaborative enterprise, these men were rivals. Flushed with money and power, they didn't and would never have enough. There was never enough of either for men like this, but power most of all. It seemed to Clark and others that their ultimate goal was to assume political control of their country, but countries are not run by committees, at least not by large ones. All Clark needed to accomplish was to make the Cartel chieftains think that there was a power grab underway within their own hierarchy, at which point they would merrily start killing one another off in a new version of the Mafia wars of the 1930s.

Maybe, he admitted to himself. He gave the plan about a 30 percent chance of total success. But even if it failed, some major players would be removed from the field, and that, too, counted as a tactical success if not a strategic one. Weakening the Cartel might increase Colombia's chances of dealing with it, which was another possible strategic outcome, but not the only one. There was also the chance that the war he was hoping to start could have the same result as the final act of the Castellammare Wars, remembered as the Night of the Italian Vespers, in which scores of mafiosi had been killed by their own colleagues. What had grown out of that bloody night was a stronger, better-organized, and more dangerous organized-crime network under the far more sophisticated leadership of Carlo Luchiano and Vito Genovese. That was a real danger, Clark thought. But things couldn't get much worse than they already were. Or so Washington had decided. It was a gamble worth the taking.

Larson arrived at the house. He'd come here only once before, and while it was in keeping with Clark's cover as a visiting prospector of sorts—there were several boxes of rocks lying around the house—it was one aspect of the mission that bothered him.

"Catch the news?"

"Everyone says car bomb," Larson replied with a sly smile. "We won't be that lucky next time."

"Probably not. The next one has to be really spectacular."

"Don't look at me! You don't expect that *I'm* going to find out when the next meet is, do you?"

It would be nice, Clark told himself, but he didn't expect it, and would have disapproved any order requiring it. "No, we have to pray for another intercept. They have to meet. They have to get together and discuss what's happened."

"Agreed. But it might not be up in the mountains."

"Oh?"

"They all have places in the lowlands, too."

Clark had forgotten about that. It would make targeting very difficult. "Can we spot in the laser from an aircraft?"

"I don't see why not. But then I land, refuel, and fly the hell out of this country forever."

Henry and Harvey Patterson were twin brothers, twenty-seven years of age, and were proof of whatever social theory a criminologist might hold. Their father had been a professional, if not especially proficient, criminal for all of his abbreviated life—which had ended at age thirty-two when a liquor-store owner had shot him with a 12-gauge double at the range of eleven feet. That was important to adherents of the behavioral school, generally populated by political conservatives. They were also products of a one-parent household, poor schooling, adverse peer-group pressure, and an economically depressed neighborhood. Those factors were important to the environmental school of behavior, whose adherents are generally political liberals.

Whatever the reason for their behavior, they were career criminals who enjoyed their life-style and didn't give much of a damn whether their brains were preprogrammed into it or they had actually learned it in childhood. They were not stupid. Had intelligence tests not been biased toward the literate, their IQs would have tested slightly above average. They had animal cunning sufficient to make their apprehension by police a demanding enterprise, and a street-smart knowledge of law that had allowed them to manipulate the legal system with remarkable success. They also had principles. The Patterson brothers were drinkers—each was already a borderline alcoholic—but not drug users. This marked them as a little odd, but since neither brother cared a great deal for law, the discontinuity with normal criminal profiles didn't trouble them either.

Together, they had robbed, burglarized, and assaulted their way across southern Alabama since their mid-teens. They were treated by their peers with considerable respect. Several people had crossed one or both—since they were identical twins, crossing one inevitably meant crossing both—and turned up dead. Dead by blunt trauma (a club), or dead by penetrating trauma (knife or gun). The police suspected them of five murders. The problem was, which one of them? The fact that they were identical twins was a technical complication to every case which their lawyer—a good one they had identified quite early in their careers—had used to great effect. Whenever the victim of a Patterson was killed, the police could bet their salaries on the fact that one of the brothers—generally the one who had the motive to kill the victim—would be ostentatiously present somewhere miles away. In addition, their victims were never honest citizens, but members of their own criminal community, which fact invariably cooled the ardor of the police.

But not this time.

It had taken fourteen years since their first officially recorded brush with the law, but Henry and Harvey had finally fucked up big-time, cops all over the state learned from their watch commanders: the police had finally gotten them on a major felony rap and, they noted with no small degree of pleasure, it was because of another pair of identical twins. Two whores, lovely ones of eighteen years, had smitten the hearts of the Patterson brothers. For the past five weeks Henry and Harvey had not been able to get enough of Noreen and Doreen Grayson, and as the patrol officers in the neighborhood had watched the romance blossom, the general speculation in the station was how the hell they kept one another straight—the behavioralist cops pronounced that it wouldn't actually matter, which observation was dismissed by the environmentalist cops as pseudoscientific bullshit, not to mention sexually perverse, but both sides of the argument found it roundly entertaining speculation. In either case, true love had been the downfall of the Patterson brothers.

Henry and Harvey had decided to liberate the Grayson sisters from their drug-dealing pimp, a very disreputable but even more formidable man with a long history of violence, and a suspect in the disappearance of several of his girls. What had brought it to a head was a savage beating to the sisters for not turning over some presents—jewelry—given them by the Pattersons as one-month anniversary presents. Noreen's jaw had been broken, and Doreen had lost six teeth, plus other indignities that had enraged the Pattersons and put both girls in the University of South Alabama Medical Center. The twin brothers were not people to bear offense lightly, and one week later, from the unlit shadows of an alley, the two of them had used identical Smith & Wesson revolvers to end the life of Elrod McIlvane. It was their misfortune that a police radio car had been half a block away at the time. Even the cops thought that, in this case, the Pattersons had rendered a public service to the city of Mobile.

The police lieutenant had both of them in an interrogation room. Their customary defiance was a wilted flower. The guns had been recovered less than fifty yards from the crime scene. Though there had been no usable fingerprints on either—firearms do not always lend themselves to this purpose—the four rounds recovered from McIlvane's body did match up with both; the Pattersons had been apprehended four blocks away; their hands bore powder signatures from having fired guns of some sort; and their motive for eliminating the pimp was well known. Criminal cases didn't get much better than that. The only thing the police didn't have was a confession. The twins' luck had finally run out. Even their lawyer had told them that. There was no hope of a plea-bargain—the local prosecutor hated them even more than the police did—and while they stood to do hard time for murder, the good news was that they probably wouldn't get the chair, since the jurors probably would not want to execute people for killing a drug-dealing pimp who'd put two of his whores in the hospital and probably killed a few more. This was arguably a crime of passion, and under American law such motives are generally seen as mitigating circumstances.

In identical prison garb, the Pattersons sat across the table from the senior police officer. The lieutenant couldn't even tell them apart, and didn't bother asking which was which, because they would probably have lied about it out of pure spite.

"Where's our lawyer?" Henry or Harvey asked.

"Yeah," Harvey or Henry emphasized.

"We don't really need him here for this. How'd you boys like to do a little favor for us?" the lieutenant asked. "You do us a little favor and maybe we can do you a little favor." That settled the problem of legal counsel.

"Bullshit!" one of the twins observed, just as a bargaining position, of course. They were at the straw-grasping stage. Prison beckoned, and while neither had ever served a serious stretch, they'd done enough county time to know that it wouldn't be fun.

"How do you like the idea of life imprisonment?" the lieutenant asked, unmoved by the show of strength. "You know how it works, seven or eight years before you're rehabilitated and they let you out. If you're lucky, that is. Awful long time, eight years. Like that idea, boys?"

"We're not fools. Watchu here for?" the other Patterson asked, indicating that he was ready to discuss terms.

"You do a job for us, and, well, something nice might happen."

"What job's that?" Already both brothers were amenable to the arrangement.

"You seen Ramón and Jesús?"

"The pirates?" one asked. "Shit." In the criminal community as with any other, there is a hierarchy of status. The abusers of women and children are at the bottom. The Pattersons were violent criminals, but had never abused women. They only assaulted men—men much smaller than themselves for the most part, but men nonetheless. That was important to their collective self-image.

"Yeah, we seen the fucks," the other said to emphasize his brother's more succinct observation. "Actin' like king shit last cupla days. Fuckin' spics. Hey, man, we bad dudes, but we ain't never raped no little girl, ain't never killed no little girl neither—and they be gettin' off, they say? Shit! We waste a fuckin' pimp likes to beat on his ladies, and we lookin' at life. What kinda justice you call that, mister po-liceman? Shit!"

"If something were to happen to Ramón and Jesús, something really serious," the lieutenant said quietly, "maybe something else might happen. Something beneficial to you boys."

"Like what?"

"Like you get to see Noreen and Doreen on a very regular basis. Maybe even settle down."

"Shit!" Henry or Harvey said.

"That's the best deal in town, boys," the lieutenant told them.

"You want us to kill the motherfuckers?" It was Harvey who asked this question, disappointing his brother, who thought of himself as the smart one.

The lieutenant just stared at them.

"We hear you," Henry said. "How we know you keep your word?"

"What word is that?" The lieutenant paused. "Ramón and Jesús killed a family of four, raped the wife and the little girl first, of course, and they probably had a hand in the murder of a Mobile police officer and his wife. But something went wrong with the case against them, and the most they'll get is twenty years, walk in seven or eight, max. For killing six people. Hardly seems fair, does it?"

By this time both twins had gotten the message. The lieutenant could see the recognition, an identical expression in both pairs of eyes. Then came the decision. The two pairs of eyes were guarded for a moment as they considered how to do it. Then they became serene. Both Pattersons nodded, and that was that.

"You boys be careful now. Jail can be a very dangerous place." The lieutenant rose to summon the jailer. If asked, he'd say that—after getting their permission to talk to them without a lawyer present, of course—he'd wanted to ask them about a robbery in which the Pattersons had not been involved, but about which they might have some knowledge, and that he had offered them some help with the DA in return for their assistance. Alas, they'd professed no knowledge of the robbery in question, and after less than five minutes of conversation, he'd sent them back to their cell. Should they ever refer to the actual content of the conversation, it would be the word of two career criminals with an open-and-shut murder charge hanging over their heads against the word of a police lieutenant. At most that would result in a page-five story in the *Mobile Register,* which took rather a stern line on violent crime. And they could scarcely confess to a double murder whether done at police behest or not, could they?

The lieutenant was an honorable man, and immediately went to work to hold up his end of the bargain in anticipation of the fact that the Pattersons would do the same. Of the four bullets removed from the body of Elrod McIlvane, one was unusable for ballistic-matching purposes due to its distortion—unjacketed lead bullets are very easily damaged—and the others, though good enough for the criminal case, were borderline. The lieutenant ordered the bullets removed from evidence storage for re-examination, along with the examiner's notes and the photographs. He had to sign for them, of course, to maintain "chain of evidence." This legal requirement was written to ensure that evidence used in a trial, once taken from the crime scene or elsewhere and identified as significant, was always in a known location and under proper custody. It was a safeguard against the illicit manufacture of incriminating evidence. When a piece of evidence got lost, even if it were later recovered, it could never be used in a criminal case, since it was then tainted. He walked down to the laboratory area, but found the technicians leaving to go home. He asked the ballistics expert if he could recheck the Patterson Case bullets first thing Monday morning, and the man replied, sure, one of the matches was a little shaky, but, he thought, close enough for trial purposes. He didn't mind doing a recheck, though.

The policeman walked back to his office with the bullets. The manila envelope which held them was labeled with the case number, and since it was still in proper custody, duly signed for by the lieutenant, chain of evidence had not yet been violated. He made a note on his desk blotter that he didn't want to leave them in his desk over the weekend, and would take them home, keeping the whole package locked in his combination-locked briefcase. The lieutenant was fifty-three years old, and within four months of retirement with full benefits. Thirty years of service was enough, he thought, looking forward to getting full use from his fishing boat. He could scarcely retire in good conscience leaving two cop-killers with eight years of soft time.

The influx of drug money to Colombia has produced all manner of side effects and one of them, in a stunningly ironic twist, is that the Colombian police had obtained a new and very sophisticated crime lab. Residue from the Untiveros house was run through the usual series of chemical tests, and within a few hours it had been determined that the explosive agent had been a mixture of cyclotetramethylenetetranitramine and trinitrotoluene. Known more colloquially as HMX and TNT, when combined in a 70-30 mixture, the chemist wrote, they formed an explosive compound called Octol, which, he wrote on, was a rather expensive, very stable, and extremely violent high explosive made principally in the United States, but available commercially from American, European, and one Asian chemical company. And that ended his work for the day. He handed over his report to his secretary, who faxed it to Medellín, where another secretary made a Xerox copy, which found its way twenty minutes later to Félix Cortez.

The report was yet another piece in the puzzle for the former intelligence officer. No local mining operation used Octol. It was too expensive, and simple nitrate-based explosive gels were all that commercial applications required. If you needed a larger explosive punch to loosen rocks, you simply drilled a wider hole and crammed in more explosives. The same option did not exist, however, for military forces. The size of an artillery shell was limited by the diameter of the gun barrel, and the size of a bomb was limited by the aerodynamic drag it imposed on the aircraft that carried it. Therefore, military organizations were always looking for more powerful explosives to get better performance from their size-limited weapons. Cortez lifted a reference book from his library shelf and confirmed the fact that Octol was almost exclusively a military explosive . . . and was used as a triggering agent for nuclear devices. That evoked a short bark of a laugh.

It also explained a few things. His initial reaction to the explosion was that a ton of dynamite had been used. The same result could be explained by less than five hundred kilos of this Octol. He pulled out another reference book and learned that the actual explosive weight in a two-thousand-pound bomb was under one thousand pounds.

But why were there no fragments? More than half the weight of a bomb was in the steel case. Cortez set that aside for the moment.

An aircraft bomb explained much. He remembered his training in Cuba, when North Vietnamese officers had briefed his class on ''smart-bombs'' that had been the bane of their country's bridges and electrical generating plants during the brief but violent Linebacker-II bombing campaign in 1972. After years of costly failures, the American fighter-bombers had destroyed scores of heavily defended targets in a matter of days, using their new precision-guided munitions.

If targeted on a truck, such a bomb would give every appearance of a car bomb, wouldn't it?

But why were there no fragments? He reread the lab report. There had also been cellulose residue which the lab tech explained away as the cardboard containers in which the explosives had been packed.

Cellulose? That meant paper or wood fibers, didn't it? Make a bomb out of paper? Cortez lifted one of his reference books—*Jane's Weapons Systems*. It was a heavy book with a hard, stiff cover . . . cardboard, covered with cloth. It really was that simple, wasn't it? If you could make paper that strong for so prosaic a purpose as a book binding . . .

Cortez leaned back in his chair and lit a cigarette to congratulate himself—and the *norteamericanos*. It was brilliant. They'd sent a bomber armed with a special smart-bomb, targeted it on that absurd truck, and left nothing behind that could remotely be called evidence. He wondered who had come up with this plan, amazed that the Americans had done something so intelligent. The KGB would have assembled a company of *Spetznaz* commandos and fought a conventional infantry battle, leaving all manner of evidence behind and ''delivering the message'' in a typically Russian way, which was effective but lacking in subtlety. The Americans for once had managed the sort of subtlety worthy of a Spaniard—of a Cortez, Félix chuckled. That was remarkable.

Now he had the ''How.'' Next he had to figure out the ''What For.'' But of course! There had been that American newspaper story about a possible gang war. There had been fourteen senior Cartel lords. Now there were ten. The Americans would try to reduce that number further by . . . what? Might they assume that the single bombing incident would ignite a savage war of infighting? No, Cortez decided. One such incident wasn't enough. Two might be, but not one.

So the Americans had commando teams prowling the mountains south of Medellín, had dropped one bomb, and were doing something else to curtail the drug flights. That became clear as well. They were shooting the airplanes down, of course. They had people watching airfields and forwarding their intelligence information elsewhere for action. It was a fully integrated operation. The most incredible thing of all was that it was actually working. The Americans had decided to do something that worked. Now, *that* was miraculous. For all the time he had been an intelligence officer, CIA had been reasonably effective at gathering information, but not for actually doing something.

Félix rose from his desk and walked over to his office bar. This called for serious contemplation, and that meant a good brandy. He poured a triple portion into a balloon glass, swirling it around, letting his hand warm the liquid so that the aromatic vapors would caress his senses even before he took the first sip.

The Chinese language was ideographic—Cortez had met his share of Chinese intelligence types as well—and its symbol for ''crisis'' was a combination of the symbols denoting ''danger'' and ''opportunity.'' The dualism had struck him the first time he'd heard it, and he'd never forgotten it. Opportunities like this one were exceedingly rare, and equally dangerous. The principal danger, he knew, was the simple fact that he didn't know how the Americans were developing their intelligence information. Everything he knew pointed to a penetration agent within the organization. Someone high up, but not as high as he wished to be. The Americans had compromised someone just as he had so often done. Standard intelligence procedure, and that was something CIA excelled at. Someone. Who? Someone who had been deeply offended, and wanted to get even while at the same time acquiring a seat around the table of chieftains. Quite a few people fell into that category. Including Félix Cortez. And instead of having to initiate his own operation to achieve that goal, he could now depend on the Americans to do it for him. It struck him as very odd indeed that he was trusting the Americans to do his work, but it was also hugely amusing. It was, in fact, almost the definition of the perfect covert operation. All he had to do was let the Americans carry out their own plan, and stand by the sidelines to watch it work. It would require patience and confidence in his enemy—not to mention the degree of danger involved—but Cortez felt that it was worth the effort.

In the absence of knowing how to get the information to the Americans, he decided, he'd just have to trust to luck. No, not luck. They seemed to be getting the word somehow, and they'd probably get it this time, too. He lifted his phone and made a call, something very uncharacteristic for him. Then, on reflection, he made one other arrangement. After all, he couldn't expect that the Americans would do exactly what he wanted exactly when he wanted. Some things he had to do for himself.

Ryan's plane landed at Andrews just after seven in the evening. One of his assistants—it was so nice having assistants—took custody of the classified documents and drove them back to Langley while Jack tossed his bags in the back of his XJS and drove home. He'd get a decent night's sleep to slough off the effects of jet lag, and tomorrow he'd be back at his desk. First order of business, he told himself as he took the car onto Route 50, was to find out what the Agency was up to in South America.

Ritter shook his head in wonder and thanksgiving. CAPER had come through for them again. Cortez himself this time, too. They just hadn't twigged to the fact that their communications were vulnerable. It wasn't a new phenomenon, of course. The same thing had happened to the Germans and Japanese in World War II, and had been repeated time and again. It was just something that Americans were good at. And the timing could hardly have been better. The carrier was available for only thirty more hours, barely time enough to get the message to their man on *Ranger*. Ritter typed up the orders and mission requirements on his personal computer. They were printed, sealed in an envelope, and handed to one of his senior subordinates, who caught an Air Force supply flight to Panama.

Captain Robby Jackson was feeling a little better. If nothing else, he thought he could just barely feel the added weight of the fourth stripe on the shoulders of his undress-white shirt, and the silver eagle that had replaced the oak leaf on the collar of his khakis was so much nicer a symbol for a pilot, wasn't it? The below-the-zone promotion meant that he was seriously in the running for CAG, command of his own carrier air wing—that would be his last real flying job, Jackson knew, but it was the grandest of all. He'd have to check out in several different types of aircraft, and would be responsible for over eighty birds, their flight crews, and the maintenance personnel, without which the aircraft were merely attractive ornaments for a carrier's flight deck.

The bad news was that his tactical ideas hadn't worked out as well as planned, but he consoled himself with the knowledge that all new ideas take time. He'd seen that a few of his original ideas were flawed, and the fixes suggested by one of *Ranger*'s squadron commanders had almost worked—had actually improved the idea markedly. And that, too, was normal. The same could also be said of the Phoenix missiles, whose guidance-package fixes had performed fairly well; not quite as well as the contractor had promised, but that wasn't unusual either, was it?

Robby was in the carrier's Combat Information Center. No flight operations were underway at the moment. The battle group was in some heavy weather that would clear in a few hours, and while the maintenance people were tinkering with their airplanes, Robby and the senior air-defense people were reviewing tapes of the fighter engagements for the sixth time. The "enemy" force had performed remarkably well, diagnosing *Ranger*'s defense plans and reacting to them quickly and effectively to get its missile-shooters within range. That *Ranger*'s fighters had clobbered them on the way out was irrelevant. The whole point of the Outer Air Battle was to clobber the Backfires on the way in.

The tape recording had been made from the radar coverage of the E-2C Hawkeye which Robby had ridden for the first engagement, but six times really were enough. He'd learned all he could learn, and his mind was wandering now. There was the Intruder again, mating up with the tanker, then heading off toward Ecuador and disappearing off the screen just before it made the coast. Captain Jackson settled back in his chair while the discussion went on around him. They fast-forwarded the tape for the approach phase, spent over an hour replaying the actual battle—what there had been of it, Jackson noted with a frown—then fast-forwarded it again. *Ranger*'s CAG was particularly annoyed with the lackadaisical manner in which his squadrons had re-formed for the return to the carrier. The poor organization of the fighters elicited some scathing comments from the captain who had the title that Robby now looked forward to. Listening to his remarks was a good education, though it was a touch profane. The ensuing discussion kept the tape running until—there, again, the A-6 reappeared, heading into the carrier after having done whatever the hell it had done. Robby knew that he was making an assumption, and for professional officers assumptions were dangerous things. But there it was.

"Cap'n Jackson, sir?"

Robby turned to see a yeoman with a clipboard. It was an action message for which he had to sign, which he did before accepting the form and reading it.

"What gives, Rob?" the carrier's operations officer asked.

"Admiral Painter is flying out to the PG School. He wants me to meet him there instead of flying back to D.C. I s'pose he wants an early reading on how my wonderful new tactics worked out," Jackson replied.

"Don't sweat it. They ain't going to take the shoulder boards back."

"I didn't think this all the way through," Robby replied, gesturing at the screen.

"Nobody ever does."

Ranger cleared the bad weather an hour later. The first plane off was the COD, which headed off to Panama to drop off mail and pick up various things. It returned in four hours. The "tech-rep" was waiting for it, already prepped by an innocuous signal over a clear channel. When he'd finished reading the message, he called Commander Jensen's stateroom.

Copies of the photo were being taken to The Hideaway, but the closest witness was in Alexandria, and he took it there himself.

Murray knew better than to ask where the photo had come from. That is, he knew that it came from CIA, and that it was some sort of surveillance photo, but the circumstances that surrounded it were things he didn't need to know—or so he would have been told had he asked, which he hadn't. It was just as well, since he might not have accepted the "need-to-know" explanation in this case.

Moira was improving. The restraints were off, but she was still being treated for some side effects of the sleeping pills she'd taken. Something to do with her liver function, he'd heard, but she was responding well to treatment. He found her sitting up, the motorized bed elevated at the command of a button. Visiting hours were over—her kids had been in tonight, and that, Murray figured, was the best treatment she could possibly get. The official story was an accidental OD. The hospital knew different, and that had leaked, but the Bureau took the public position that it had been an accident since she hadn't quite taken a lethal dose of the drug. The Bureau's own psychiatrist saw her twice a day, and his report was optimistic. The suicide attempt, while real, had been based on impulse, not prolonged contemplation. With care and counseling, she'd come around and would probably fully recover. The psychiatrist also thought that what Murray was about to do would help.

"You look a hell of a lot better," he told her. "How are the kids?"

"I'll never do this to them again," Moira Wolfe replied. "What a stupid, selfish thing to do."

"I keep telling you, you got hit by the truck." Murray took the chair by her bedside and opened the manila envelope he'd carried in. "Is this the truck?"

She took the photo from his hand and stared at it for a moment. It wasn't a very good photograph. Taken at a distance of over two miles, even with the high-power lens and computer enhancement of the image, it didn't show anything approaching the detail of an amateur photographer's action shot of his child. But there is more to a picture than the expression on a person's face. The shape of the head, the style of the hair, the posture, the way he held his hands, the tilt of the head. . . .

"It's him," she said. "That's Juan Díaz. Where did you get it?"

"It came from another government agency," Murray replied, his choice of words telling her nothing—the exact nothing that meant CIA. "They had a discreet surveillance of some place or other—I don't know where—and got this. They thought it might be our boy. For your information, this is the first confirmed shot we have of Colonel Félix Cortez, late of the DGI. At least now we know what the bastard looks like."

"Get him," Moira said.

"Oh, we'll get him," Murray promised her.

"I know what I'll have to do—testify and all that. I know what the lawyers will do to me. I can handle it. I can, Mr. Murray."

She isn't kidding, Dan realized. It wasn't the first time that revenge had been part of saving a life, and Murray was glad to see it. It was one more purpose, one more thing Moira had to live for. His job was to see that she and the Bureau got their revenge. The approved term at the FBI was retribution, but the hundreds of agents on the case weren't using that word now.

Jack arrived at his office early the next morning to find the expected pile of work, on top of which was a note from Judge Moore.

"The convention closes tonight," it read. "You're booked on the last flight to Chicago. Tomorrow morning you will brief Gov. Fowler. This is a normal procedure for presidential candidates. Guidelines for your briefing are attached, along with a copy of the national-security brief done in the 1984 presidential campaign. 'Restricted' and 'Confidential' information may be discussed, but nothing 'Secret' or higher. I need to see your written presentation before five."

And that completely blew the day away. Ryan called home to let his family know that he'd be gone yet another night. Then he got to work. Now he wouldn't be able to quiz Ritter and Moore until the following Monday. And Ritter, he learned, would be spending most of the day over at the White House anyway. Jack's next call was to Bethesda, to check in with Admiral Greer and get some guidance. He was surprised to learn that Greer had done the last such briefing personally. He wasn't surprised that the old man's voice was measurably weaker than the last time they'd talked. The good cheer was still there, but, welcome sound that it was, the image in Jack's mind was of an Olympic skater giving a medal-winning performance on thin, brittle ice.

21. Explanations

He'd never thought of the COD as the busiest aircraft in the carrier's air wing. It was, of course, and he'd always known it, but the machinations of the ugly, slow, prop-driven aircraft had hardly been a matter of interest to a pilot who'd been "born" in an F-4N Phantom-II and soon thereafter moved up in class to the F-14A Tomcat. He hadn't flown a fighter in weeks, and as he walked out toward the COD—officially the C-2A Greyhound, which was almost appropriate since it did indeed fly like a dog—he resolved that he'd sneak down to Pax River for a few hours of turnin' and burnin' in a proper airplane just as soon as he could. "I feel the need," he whispered to himself with a smile. "The need for speed." The COD was spotted for a shot off the starboard bow catapult, and as Robby headed toward it he again saw an A-6E Intruder, again the squadron commander's personal aircraft, parked next to the island. Outboard from the structure was a narrow area called the Bomb Farm, used for ordnance storage and preparation. It was a convenient spot, too small an area for airplanes to be parked and agreeably close to the edge of the deck so that bombs could easily be jettisoned over the side if the need arose. The bombs were moved about on small, low-slung carts, and just as he boarded the COD, he saw one, carrying a blue "practice" bomb toward the Intruder. On the bomb were the odd attachments for laser guidance.

So, another Drop-Ex tonight, eh? It was something else to smile about. *You put that one right down the pickle barrel, too, Jensen,* Robby thought. Ten minutes later he was off, heading for Panama, where he'd hop a ride with the Air Force for California.

Ryan was over West Virginia on a commercial flight, sitting in coach on an American Airlines DC-9. It was quite a comedown from the Air Force VIP group, but there hadn't been sufficient cause for that sort of treatment this time. He was accompanied by a security guard, which Jack was gradually getting used to. This one was a case officer who'd been injured on duty—he'd fallen off something and badly injured his hip. After recovering, he'd probably rotate back to Operations. His name was Roger Harris. He was thirty or so and, Jack thought, pretty smart.

"What did you do before you joined up?" he asked Harris.

"Well, sir, I—"

"Name's Jack. They don't issue a halo along with the job title."

"Would you believe? A street cop in Newark. I decided that I wanted to try something safer, so I came here. And then look what happened," he chuckled.

The flight was only half booked. Ryan looked around and saw that no one was close, and listening devices invariably had trouble with the whine of the engines.

"Where'd it happen?"

"Poland. A meet went down bad—I mean, something just felt bad and I blew it off. My guy got away clean and I boogied the other way. Two blocks from the embassy I hopped over a wall. Tried to. There was a cat, just a plain old alley cat. I stepped on it, and it screeched, and I tripped and broke my fucking hip like some little old lady falling in the bathtub." A rueful smile. "This spy stuff ain't like the movies, is it?"

Jack nodded. "Sometime I'll tell you about a time when the same sort of thing happened to me."

"In the field?" Harris asked. He knew that Jack was Intelligence, not Operations.

"Hell of a good story. Shame I can't tell it to anyone."

"So what are you gonna tell J. Robert Fowler?"

"That's the funny part. It's all stuff he can get in the papers, but it isn't official unless it comes from one of us."

The stewardess came by. It was too short a flight for a meal, but Ryan ordered a couple of beers.

"Sir, I'm not supposed to drink on duty."

"You just got a dispensation," Ryan told him. "I don't like drinking alone, and I always drink when I fly."

"They told me you don't like it up here," Harris observed.

"I got over that," Jack replied, almost truthfully.

* * *

"So what is going on?" Escobedo asked.

"Several things," Cortez answered slowly, carefully, speculatively, to show *el jefe* that he was still somewhat in the dark, but working hard to use his impressive analytical talents to find the correct answer. "I believe the Americans have two or perhaps three teams of mercenaries in the mountains. They are, as you know, attacking some of the processing sites. The objective here would appear to be psychological. Already the local peasants have shown reluctance to assist us. It is not hard to frighten such people. Do it enough and we have problems producing our product."

"Mercenaries?"

"A technical term, *jefe*. A mercenary, as you know, is anyone who performs services for money, but the term most often denotes paramilitary services. Exactly who are they? We know that they speak Spanish. They could be Colombian citizens, disaffected Argentines—you know that the *norteamericanos* used people from the Argentine Army to train the *contras,* correct? Dangerous ones from the time of the Junta. Perhaps with all the turmoil in their home country, they have decided to enter American employ on a semipermanent basis. That is only one of many possibilities. You must understand, *jefe,* that operations such as this must be plausibly deniable. Wherever they come from, they may not even know that they are working for the Americans."

"Whoever they may be, what do you propose to do about them?"

"We will hunt them down and kill them, of course," Cortez said matter-of-factly. "We need about two hundred armed men, but certainly we can assemble such a force. I have people scouting the area already. I need your permission to gather the necessary forces together to sweep the hills properly."

"You'll get it. And what of the Untiveros bombing?"

"Someone loaded four hundred kilos of a very high-grade explosive into the back of his truck. Very cleverly done, *jefe*. In any other vehicle it would have been impossible, but that truck . . ."

"*Sí*. The tires each weighed more than that. Who did it?"

"Not the Americans, nor any of their hirelings," Cortez replied positively.

"But—"

"*Jefe,* think for a moment," Félix suggested. "Who could possibly have had access to the truck?"

Escobedo chewed on that one for a while. They were in the back of his stretch Mercedes. It was an old 600, lovingly maintained and in new-car condition. Mercedes-Benz is the type of car favored by people who need to worry about violent enemies. Already heavy, and with a powerful engine, it easily carried over a thousand pounds of Kevlar armor embedded in vital areas, and thick polycarbonate windows that would stop a .30-caliber machine-gun round. Its tires were filled with foam, not air, so that a puncture wouldn't flatten them—at least not very quickly. The fuel tank was filled with a honeycombed metal lattice that could not prevent a fire, but would prevent a more dangerous explosion. Fifty meters ahead and behind were BMW M3s, fast, powerful cars filled with armed men, much in the way that chiefs of state had lead- and chase-cars for security purposes.

"One of us, you think?" Escobedo asked after a minute's contemplation.

"It is possible, *jefe*." Cortez's tone of voice said that it was more than merely possible. He was pacing his disclosures carefully, keeping an eye on the roadside signs.

"But who?"

"That is a question for you to answer, is it not? I am an intelligence officer, not a detective." That Cortez got away with his outrageous lie was testimony to Escobedo's paranoia.

"And the missing aircraft?"

"Also unknown," Cortez reported. "Someone was watching the airfields, perhaps American paramilitary teams, but more likely the same mercenaries who are now in the mountains. They probably sabotaged aircraft somehow, possibly with the connivance of the airport guards. I speculate that when they left, they killed off the guards so that no one could prove what they had been doing, then booby-trapped the fuel dumps to make it appear to be something else entirely. A very clever operation, but one to which we could have adapted except for the assassinations in Bogotá." Cortez took a deep breath before going on.

"The attack on the Americans in Bogotá was a mistake, *jefe*. It forced the Americans to change what had been a nuisance operation to one which threatens our activities directly. They have suborned someone in the organization, executing their own wish for revenge through the ambition or anger of one of your own senior colleagues." Cortez spoke throughout in the same quiet, reasoned voice that he'd used to brief his seniors in Havana, like a tutor to an especially bright student. His method of delivery reminded people of a doctor, and was an exceedingly effective way of persuading people, particularly Latins, who are given to polemics but conversely respect those who control their passions. By reproaching Escobedo for the death of the Americans—Escobedo did not like to be reproached; Cortez knew it; Escobedo knew that Cortez knew it—Félix merely added to his own credibility. "The Americans have foolishly said so themselves, perhaps in a clumsy attempt to mislead us, speaking of a 'gang war' within the organization. That is a trick the Americans invented, by the way, to use the truth to deny the truth. It is clever, but they have used it too often. Perhaps they feel that the organization is not aware of this trick, but anyone in the intelligence community knows of it." Cortez was winging it, and had just made that up—but, he thought, it certainly sounded good. And it had the proper effect. Escobedo was looking out through the thick windows of the car, his mind churning over the new thought.

"Who, I wonder . . ."

"That is something I cannot answer. Perhaps you and Señor Fuentes can make some progress on that tonight." The hardest part for Cortez was to keep a straight face. For all his cleverness, for all his ruthlessness, *el jefe* was a child to be manipulated once you knew the right buttons to push.

The road traced down the floor of a valley. There was also a rail line, and both followed a path carved into the rock by a mountain-fed river. From a strictly tactical point of view, it was not something to be comfortable with, Cortez knew. Though he had never been a soldier—aside from the usual paramilitary classes in the Cuban school system—he recognized the disadvantage of low ground. You could be seen a long way off from people on the heights. The highway signs assumed a new and ominous significance now. Félix knew everything he needed to know about the car. It had been modified by the world's leading provider of armored transport, and was regularly checked by technicians from that firm. The windows were replaced twice annually, because sunlight altered the crystalline structure of the polycarbonate—all the faster near the equator and at high altitude. The windows *would* stop a 7.62 NATO machine-gun bullet, and the Kevlar sheets in the doors and around the engines could, under favorable circumstances, stop larger rounds than that. He was still nervous, but through force of will did not allow himself to react visibly to the danger.

"Who might it be . . . ?" Escobedo asked as the car came around a sweeping turn.

There were five teams of two men each, gunners and loaders. They were armed with West German MG3 squad machine guns, which the Colombian Army had just adopted because it used the same 7.62mm round as their standard infantry weapon, the G3, also of German manufacture. These five had recently been "stolen"—actually purchased from a greedy supply sergeant—out of an army depot. Based on the earlier German MG-42 of World War II fame, the MG3 retained the older weapon's 1,200-round-per-minute cyclic rate of fire—twenty rounds per second. The gun positions were spaced thirty meters apart, with two guns tasked to engage the chase car, two on the lead car, but only one on the Mercedes. Cortez didn't trust the car's armor quite that much. He looked at the digital clock. They were exactly on time. Escobedo had a fine set of drivers. But then, Untiveros had had a fine set of servants, too.

On the muzzle of each gun was a cone-shaped extension called a flash-hider. Often misunderstood by the layman, its purpose was to shield the flash from the gunner—to prevent him from being blinded by his own shots. Hiding the flash from anyone else is a physical impossibility.

The gunners began firing at the same instant, and five separate yard-long cylinders of pure white flame appeared on the right side of the road. From each muzzle flash sprang a line of tracers, allowing the gunners to walk their fire right into their targets without the need to use the metal sights on their weapons.

None of the occupants of the cars heard the sound of the guns, but all did hear the sound of the impacts—at least those who lived long enough.

Escobedo's body went as rigid as a bar of steel when he saw the yellow line of tracers attach itself to the leading M-3. That car was not as heavily armored as his. The taillights wavered left, then right, and then the car left the road at an angle, rolling over like one of his son's toys. Before that had happened, both he and Cortez felt the impacts of twenty rounds on their own car. It sounded like hail on a tin roof. But it was 150-grain bullets, not hail, impacting steel and Kevlar, not tin. His driver, well trained and always nervously alert, fishtailed the long Mercedes for a moment to avoid the BMW ahead, at the same time flooring the accelerator. The six-liter Mercedes engine responded at once—it, too, was protected by armor—doubling both horsepower and torque in a second and hurling all of the passengers back in their seats. By this time Escobedo's head had turned to see the threat, and it seemed that the tracers were aimed straight at his face, stopped by some apparent miracle by the thick windows—which, he saw, were breaking under the impact.

Cortez hurled his own body against Escobedo's, knocking him down to the floor. Neither man had time to speak a word. The car had been doing seventy miles per hour when the first round was fired. It was already approaching ninety, escaping from the kill zone more rapidly than the gunners could adjust fire as the car body absorbed a total of over forty hits. In two minutes, Cortez looked up.

He was surprised to see that two rounds had hit the left-side windows from the inside. The gunners had been a little too good; had managed to drive repeated rounds through the armored windows. There was no sign of either the lead- or the chase-car. Félix took a very deep breath. He had just won the most daring gamble of his life.

"Take the next turn anywhere!" he shouted at the driver.

"No!" Escobedo said an instant later. "Straight to—"

"Fool!" Cortez turned *el jefe* over. "Do you wish to find another ambush ahead of us! How do you suppose they knew to kill us! *Take the next turn!*" he shouted at the driver again.

The driver, who had a good appreciation of ambush tactics, stood on the brakes and took the next turn. It was a right, leading to a small network of side roads serving local coffee farms.

"Find a quiet place to stop," Cortez ordered next.

"But—"

"They will expect us to run, not to think. They will expect us to do what all the antiterrorist manuals say to do. Only a fool is predictable," Cortez said as he brushed polycarbonate fragments from his hair. His pistol was out now, and he ostentatiously replaced it in his shoulder holster. "José, your driving was magnificent!"

"Both cars are gone," the driver reported.

"I'm not surprised," Cortez replied. Quite honestly. "*Jesús María*—that was close."

Whatever Escobedo might have been, coward was not among them. He too saw the damage to the window that had been inches from his head. Two bullets had come through the car—they were half-buried in the glass. *El jefe* pried one loose and rattled it around in his hand. It was still warm.

"We must speak to the people who make the windows," Escobedo observed coolly. Cortez had saved his life, he realized.

The odd part was that he was right. But Cortez was more impressed with the fact that his reflexes—even forewarned, he had reacted with commendable speed—had saved his own life. It had been a long time since he'd had to pass the physical fitness test required by the DGI. It was moments like this that can make the most circumspect of men feel invincible.

"Who knew that we were going to see Fuentes?" he asked.

"I must—" Escobedo lifted the phone receiver and started to punch in a number. Cortez gently took it away from him and replaced it in the holder.

"Perhaps that would be a serious mistake, *jefe*," he said quietly. "With all respect, señor, please let me handle this. This is a professional matter."

Escobedo had never been so impressed with Cortez than at that moment.

"You will be rewarded," he told his faithful vassal. Escobedo reproached himself for having occasionally mistreated him, and worse, for having occasionally disregarded Cortez's wise counsel. "What should we do?"

"José," Cortez told the driver, "find a high spot from which we can see the Fuentes house."

Within a minute, the driver found a switchback overlooking the valley. He pulled the car off the road and all three got out. José inspected the damage to the car. Fortunately neither the tires nor the engine had been damaged. Though the car's body would have to be totally reworked, its ability to move and maneuver was unimpaired. José truly loved this car, and though he mourned for its defacement, he nearly burst with pride that it and his own skill had saved all their lives.

In the trunk were several rifles—German G3s like those the Army carried, but legally purchased—and a pair of binoculars. Cortez let the others have the rifles. He took the field glasses and trained them in on the well-lit home of Luis Fuentes, about six miles away.

"What are you looking for?" Escobedo asked.

"*Jefe,* if he had part in the ambush, he will know by now that it might have failed, and there will be activity. If he had no such knowledge, we will see no activity at all."

"What of those who fired on us?"

"You think they know that we escaped?" Cortez shook his head. "No, they will not be sure, and first they will try to prove that they succeeded, that our car struggled on for a short while—so they will first of all try to find us. José, how many turns did you take to get us here?"

"Six, señor, and there are many roads," the driver answered. He looked quite formidable with his rifle.

"Do you see the problem, *jefe?* Unless they have a great number of men, there are too many roads to check. We are not dealing with a police or military force. If we were, we'd still be moving. Ambushes like this one—no, *jefe,* once they fail, they fail completely. Here." He handed the glasses over. It was time for a little machismo. He opened the car door and pulled out a few bottles of Perrier—Escobedo liked the stuff. He opened them by inserting the bottlecaps into bullet holes in the trunk lid and snapping down. Even José grunted with amusement at that, and Escobedo was one who admired such panache.

"Danger makes me thirsty," Cortez explained, passing the other bottles around.

"It has been an exciting night," Escobedo agreed, taking a long pull on his bottle.

But not for Commander Jensen and his bombardier/navigator. The first one, as with the first time for anything, had been a special occasion, but already it was routine. The problem was simply that things were too damned easy. Jensen had faced surface-to-air missiles and radar-directed flak in his early twenties, testing his courage and skill against that of North Vietnamese gunners with their own experience and cunning. This mission was about as exciting as a trip to the mailbox, but, he reminded himself, important things often go through the mail. The mission went exactly according to plan. The computer ejected the bomb right on schedule, and the B/N tracked his TRAM sight around to keep an eye on the target. This time Jensen let his right eye wander down to the TV screen.

"I wonder what held Escobedo up?" Larson asked.

"Maybe he got here early?" Clark thought aloud, his eye on the GLD.

"Maybe," the other field officer allowed. "Notice how no cars are parked near the house this time?"

"Yeah, well, this one is fused for one-hundredth-of-a-second delay," Clark told him. "Should go off just about the time it gets to the conference table."

It was even more impressive from this distance, Cortez thought. He didn't see the bomb fall, didn't hear the aircraft that had dropped it—which, he told himself, was rather strange—and he saw the flash long before the sound reached him. *The Americans and their toys,* he thought. *They can be dangerous.* Most dangerous of all, whatever their intelligence source, it was a very, very good one, and Félix didn't have a clue what it might be. That was a continuing source of concern.

"It would seem that Fuentes was not involved," Cortez noted even before the sound reached them.

"That could have been us in there!"

"Yes, but it was not. I think we should leave, *jefe.*"

"What's that?" Larson asked. Two automobile headlights appeared on a hillside three miles away. Neither man had noticed the Mercedes pull into the overlook. They'd been concentrating on the target then, but Clark reproached himself for not remembering to check around further. That sort of mistake was often fatal, and he'd allowed himself to forget just how serious it was.

Clark put his Noctron on it as soon as the lights had turned away. It was a big—

"What kind of car does Escobedo have?"

"Take your pick," Larson replied. "It's like the horse collection at Churchill Downs. Porsches, Rolls, Benzes . . ."

"Well, that looked like a stretch limo, maybe a big Mercedes. Kinda odd place for one, too. Let's get the hell out of here. I think two trips to this particular well is enough. We're out of the bomb business."

Eighty minutes later their Subaru had to slow down. A collection of ambulances and police cars was parked on the shoulder while uniformed men appeared and disappeared in the pinkish light from hazard flares. A pair of black BMWs were lying on their sides just off the road. Whoever owned them, somebody didn't like them, Clark saw. There wasn't much traffic, but here as with every other place in the world where people drove cars, the drivers slowed down to give it all a look.

"Somebody blew the shit out of them," Larson noted. Clark's evaluation was more professional.

"Thirty-cal fire. Heavy machine guns at close range. Pretty slick ambush. Those are M3 BMWs."

"The big, fast one? Somebody with big-time money, then. You don't suppose . . . ?"

"You don't 'suppose' very often in this business. How fast can you get a line on what happened here?"

"Two hours after we get back."

"Okay." The police were looking at the passing cars, but not searching them. One shined his flashlight into the back of the Subaru. There were some curious things there, but not the right size and shape to be machine guns. He waved them on. Clark took that in and did some supposing. Had the gang war he'd hoped to start already begun?

Robby Jackson had a two-hour layover before boarding the Air Force C-141B, which with its refueling housing looked rather like a green, swept-wing snake. Also aboard were sixty or so soldiers with full gear. The fighter pilot looked at them with some amusement. This was what his little brother did for a living. A major sat down next to him after asking permission—Robby was two grades higher.

"What outfit?"

"Seventh Light." The major leaned back, trying to get as much comfort as he could. His helmet rested on his lap. Robby lifted it. Shaped much like the German helmet of World War II, it was made of Kevlar, with a cloth camouflage cover around it, and around that, held in place by a green elasticized cloth band, was a medusa-like collection of knotted cloth strips.

"You know, my brother wears one of these things. Heavy enough. What the hell good is it?"

"The Cabbage Patch Hat?" The major smiled, his eyes closed. "Well, the Kevlar's supposed to stop stuff from tearing your skull apart, and the mop we wrap around it breaks up your outline—makes you harder to see in the bush, sir. Your brother's with us, you said?"

"He's a new nugget—second lieutenant I guess you call him—in the, uh, they call it Ninja-something . . ."

"Three-Seventeen. First Brigade. I'm brigade intel, Second Brigade. What do you do?"

"Serving two-to-three in the Pentagon at the moment. I fly fighter planes when I'm not driving a desk."

"Must be nice to do all your work sitting down," the major observed.

"No." Robby chuckled. "The best part is I can get the hell outa Dodge right quick if I got to."

"Roger that, Captain. What brings you to Panama?"

"We got a carrier group operating offshore. I was down to watch. You?"

"Regular training rotation for one of our battalions. Jungle and tight country is where we work. We hide a lot," the major explained.

"Guerrilla stuff?"

"Roughly similar tactics. This was mainly a reconnaissance exercise, trying to get inside to gather information, conduct a few raids, that sort of thing."

"How'd it go?"

The major grunted. "Not as well as we hoped. We lost some good people out of some important slots—same with you, right? People rotate in, rotate out, and it takes a while to get the new ones up to speed. Anyway, the reconnaissance units in particular lost some good ones, and it cost us some. That's why we train," the major concluded. "Never stops."

"It's different with us. We deploy as a unit and usually don't lose anybody that way until we come back home."

"Always figured the Navy was smart, sir."

"Is it that bad? My brother told me he lost a really good—squad leader? Anyway, is it that big a deal?"

"Can be. I had a guy named Muñoz, really good man for going in the bushes and finding stuff out. Just disappeared one day, off doing some special-ops shit, they told me. The guy who's in his slot now just isn't that good. It happens. You live with it."

Jackson remembered the name Muñoz, but couldn't remember where from. "How do I arrange transport down to Monterey?"

"Hell, it's right next door. You want to catch a ride with us, Captain? We don't have all the amenities of the Navy, of course."

"We do occasionally rough it, Major. Hell, once I didn't even get my bedsheets changed for three whole days. Same week, they made us eat hot dogs for dinner—never forget that cruise. Real bitch that one was. I presume your jeeps have air conditioning?" The two men looked at each other and laughed.

Ryan was given a suite of rooms one floor up from the Governor's entourage, actually paid for by the campaign, which was quite a surprise. That made security easier. Fowler now had a full Secret Service detail, and would keep it until November, and if he were successful, for four years after that. It was a very nice, modern hotel with thick concrete floors, but the sound of the parties down below made its way through.

There came a knock on Jack's door just as he got out of the shower. The hotel had a monogrammed robe hanging there. Ryan put it on to answer the door. It was a fortyish woman dressed to kill—in red, again the current "power" color. No expert on women's fashions, he wondered how the color of one's clothing imparted anything other than visibility.

"Are you Dr. Ryan?" she asked. It was the way she asked that Jack immediately disliked, rather as though he were a disease carrier.

"Yes. Who might you be?"

"I'm Elizabeth Elliot," she replied.

"Ms. Elliot," Jack said. She looked like a *Mizz*. "You have me at a disadvantage. I don't know who you are."

"I'm the assistant adviser for foreign policy."

"Oh. Okay. Come on in, then." Ryan pulled the door all the way open and waved her in. He should have remembered. This was "E.E.," professor of political science at Bennington, whose geopolitical views, Ryan thought, made Lenin look like Theodore Roosevelt. He'd walked several feet before he realized that she hadn't followed. "You coming in or aren't you?"

"Like *this?*" She just stood there for another ten seconds before speaking again. Jack continued to towel off his hair without saying anything, more curious than anything else.

"I know who you are," she said defiantly. What the hell she was defying, Jack didn't know. In any case, Ryan had had a long day and was still suffering jetlag from his European trip, added to which was one more hour of Central Time Zone. That partly explained his reply.

"Look, doc, you're the one who caught me coming out of the shower. I have two children, and a wife, who also graduated Bennington, by the way. I'm not James Bond and I don't fool around. If you want to say something to me, just be nice enough to say it. I've been on the go for the past week, and I'm tired, and I need my sleep."

"Are you always this impolite?"

Jesus! "Dr. Elliot, if you want to play with the big kids in D.C., Lesson Number One is, Business is Business. You want to tell me something, tell. You want to ask me something, ask."

"What the hell are you doing in Colombia?" she snapped at him.

"What are you talking about?" Jack asked in a more moderate tone.

"You know what I'm talking about. I know that you know."

"In that case would you please refresh my memory?"

"Another drug lord just got blown up," she said, casting a nervous glance up and down the corridor as though a passerby might wonder if she was negotiating price with someone. There is a lot of that at political conventions, and E.E. was not physically unattractive.

"I have no knowledge of any such operation being conducted by the American government or any other. That is to say, I have zero information on the subject of your inquiry. I am not omniscient. Believe it or not, even when you are sanctified by employment in the Central Intelligence Agency, you do not automatically know everything that happens on every rock, puddle, and hilltop in the world. What does the news say?"

"But you're supposed to know," Elizabeth Elliot protested. Now she was puzzled.

"Dr. Elliot, two years ago you wrote a book about how pervasive we are. It reminded me of an old Jewish story. Some old guy on the *shtetl* in Czarist Russia who owned two chickens and a broken-down horse was reading the hate rag of the antisemites—you know, the Jews are doing *this,* the Jews are doing *that.* So a neighbor asked him why he got it, and the old guy answered that it was nice to see how powerful he was. That's what your book was, if you'll pardon me: about one percent fact and ninety-nine percent invective. If you really want to know what we can and cannot do, I can tell you a few things, within the limits of classification. I promise that you'll be as disappointed as I regularly am. I wish we were half as powerful as you think."

"But you've *killed* people."

"You mean me personally?"

"Yes!"

Maybe that explained her attitude, Jack thought. "Yes, I have killed people. Someday I'll tell you about the nightmares, too." Ryan paused. "Am I proud of it? No. Am I glad that I did it? Yes, I am. Why? you ask. My life, the lives of my wife and daughter, or the lives of other innocent people were at risk at the times in question, and I did what I had to do to protect my life and those other lives. You do remember the circumstances, don't you?"

Elliot wasn't interested in those. "The Governor wants to see you at eight-fifteen."

Six hours' sleep was what that meant to Ryan. "I'll be there."

"He is going to ask you about Colombia."

"Then you can make points with your boss by giving him the answer early: I do not know."

"If he wins, Dr. Ryan, you're—"

"Out?" Jack smiled benignly at her. "You know, this is like something from a bad movie, Dr. Elliot. If your man wins, maybe you will have the power to fire me. Let me explain to you what that means to me.

"You will then have the power to deny me a total of two and a half hours in a car every working day; the power to fire me from a difficult, stressful job that keeps me away from my family much more than I would like; and the power to compel me to live a life commensurate with the money that I earned ten or so years ago; the power to force me to go back to writing my history books, or maybe to teach again, which is why I got my doctorate in the first place. Dr. Elliot, I've seen loaded machine guns pointed at my wife and daughter, and I managed to deal with *that* threat. If you want to threaten me in a serious way, you'll need something better than taking my job away. I'll see you in the morning, I suppose, but you should know that my briefing is only for Governor Fowler. My orders are that no one else can be in the room." Jack closed, bolted, and chained the door. He'd had too many beers on the airplane, and knew it, but nobody had ever pushed Ryan's buttons that hard before.

Dr. Elliot took the stairs down instead of the elevator. Unlike most of the people in the entourage, Governor Fowler's chief aide was cold sober—he rarely drank in any case—and already at work planning a campaign that would start in a week instead of the customary wait until Labor Day. "Well?" he asked E.E.

"He says he doesn't know. I think he's lying."

"What else?" Arnold van Damm asked.

"He's arrogant, offensive, and insulting."

"So are you, Beth." They both laughed. They didn't really like each other, but political campaigns make for the strangest of bedfellows. The campaign manager was reading over a briefing paper about Ryan from Congressman Alan Trent, new chairman of the House Select Committee for Intelligence Oversight. E.E. hadn't seen it. She had told him, though he already knew (though neither of them knew what it had really all been about), that Ryan had confronted Trent in a Washington social gathering and called him a queer in public. Trent had never forgiven or forgotten an insult in his life. Nor was he one to give gratuitous praise. But Trent's report on Ryan used words like *bright, courageous,* and *honest.* Now what the hell, van Damm wondered, did *that* mean?

It was going to be their third no-hit night, Chavez was sure. They'd been out since sundown and had just passed through the second suspected processing site—the signs had been there. The discoloration of the soil from acid spills, the beaten earth, discarded trash, everything to show that men had been there and probably went there regularly—but not tonight, and not for the two preceding nights. Ding knew that he ought to have expected it. All the manuals, all the lectures of his career, had emphasized the fact that combat operations were some crazy mixture of boredom and terror, boredom because for the most part nothing happened, terror because "it" could happen at any second. Now he understood how men got sloppy out in the field. On exercises you always knew what—well, you knew that something would happen. The Army rarely wasted time on no-contact exercises. Training time cost too much. And so he was faced with the irksome fact that real combat operations were less *exciting* than training, but infinitely more dangerous. The dualism was enough to give the young man a headache.

Aches were something he already had enough of. He was now gobbling a couple of his Tylenol caplets every four hours because of muscle aches and low-order sprains—and simple tension and stress. A young man, he was learning that the combination of strenuous exercise and real mental stress made you old in a hurry. In fact he was no more tired than an office worker after a slightly long day at his desk, but the mission and the environment combined to amplify everything he felt. Joy or sadness, elation or depression, fear or invincibility were all much greater down here. In a word, combat operations were not fun. But then, why did he—not like it, not that, really, but . . . what? Chavez shook the thought away. It was affecting his concentration.

And though he didn't know it, that was the answer. Ding Chavez was a born combat soldier. Just as a trauma surgeon took no pleasure from seeing the broken bodies of accident victims, Chavez would easily have preferred sitting on a barstool next to a pretty girl or watching a football game with his friends. But the surgeon knew that his skills at the table were crucial to the lives of his patients, and Chavez knew that his skills on point were crucial to the mission. This was his place. On the mission, everything was so wonderfully clear—except when he was confused, and even *that* was clear in a different, very strange way. His senses searched out through the trees like radar, filtering out the twitters of birds and the rustle of animals—except when there was a special message in that sort of noise. His mind was a perfect balance of paranoia and confidence. He was a weapon of his country. That much he understood, and fearful though he was, fighting off boredom, struggling to keep alert, concerned for his comrades, Chavez was now a breathing, thinking machine whose single purpose was the destruction of his nation's enemies. The job was hard, but he was the man for it.

But there was still nothing out here to be found this night. The trails were cold. The processing sites unoccupied. Chavez stopped at a preplanned rally point and waited for the rest of the squad to catch up. He switched off his night goggles—you only used them about a third of the time in any case—and had himself a drink of water. At least the water was good here, coming off clear mountain streams.

"Whole lot of nothin', Captain," he told Ramirez when the officer arrived at his side. "Ain't seen nothing, ain't heard nothing."

"Tracks, trails?"

"Nothing less'n two, maybe three days old."

Ramirez knew how to determine the age of a trail, but couldn't do it as well as Sergeant Chavez. He breathed in a way that almost seemed relieved.

"Okay, we start heading back. Take a couple more minutes to relax, then lead off."

"Right. Sir?"

"Yeah, Ding?"

"This area's dryin' up on us."

"You may be right, but we'll wait a few more days to be sure," Ramirez said. Part of him was glad that there had been no contact since the death of Rocha, and that part was blanking out warning signals that he ought to have been getting. Emotion was telling him that something was good, while intelligence and analysis should have told him that something was bad.

Chavez didn't quite catch that one either. There was a distant rumble at the edge of his consciousness, like the strangely noticeable quiet that precedes an earthquake, or the first hint of clouds on a clear horizon. Ding was too young and inexperienced to notice. He had the talents. He was the right man in the right place, but he hadn't been there long enough. He didn't know that, either.

But there was work to do. He led off five minutes later, climbing back up the mountainside, avoiding all trails, taking a path different from any path they had taken to this point, alert to any present danger but oblivious to a danger that was distant but just as clear.

The C-141B touched down hard, Robby thought, though the soldiers didn't seem to notice. In fact, most of them were asleep and had to be roused. Jackson rarely slept on airplanes. It was, he thought, a bad habit for a pilot to acquire. The transport slowed and taxied around every bit as awkwardly as a fighter on the tight confines of a carrier's deck until finally the clamshell cargo doors opened at the tail.

"You come along with me, Captain," the major said. He stood and hefted his rucksack. It looked heavy. "I had the wife bring my personal car here."

"How'd she get home?"

"Car pool," the major explained. "This way the battalion commander and I can discuss the exercise some more on the way down to Ord. We'll drop you off at Monterey."

"Can you take me right into the Fort? I'll kick my little brother's door down."

"Might be out in the field."

"Friday night? I'll take the chance." Robby's real reason was that his conversation with the major had been his first talk with an Army officer in years. Now that he was a captain, the next step was making flag. If he wanted to make that—Robby was as confident as any other fighter pilot, but the step from captain to rear admiral (lower half) is the most treacherous in the Navy—having a somewhat broader field of knowledge wouldn't hurt. It would make him a better staff officer, and after his CAG job, if he got it, he'd go back to being a staff puke again.

"Okay."

The two-hour drive down from Travis Air Force Base to Fort Ord—Ord has only a small airfield, not large enough for transports—was an interesting one, and Robby was in luck. After two hours of swapping sea stories for war stories and learning things that he'd never known about, he found that Tim was just arriving home from a long night on the town. The elder brother found that the couch was all he needed. It wasn't what he was used to, of course, but he figured he could rough it.

Jack and his bodyguard arrived at the Governor's suite right on time. He didn't know any of the Secret Service detail, but they'd been told to expect him, and he still had his CIA security pass. A laminated plastic ID about the size of a playing card with a picture and a number, but no name, it ordinarily hung around his neck on a chain like some sort of religious talisman. This time he showed it to the agents and tucked it back into his coat pocket.

The briefing was set up as that most cherished of political institutions, the working breakfast. Not as socially important as a lunch, much less a dinner, breakfasts were for some reason or other perceived to be matters of great import. Breakfasts were serious.

The Honorable J. (for Jonathan, which he didn't like) Robert (call me Bob) Fowler, Governor of Ohio, was a man in his middle fifties. Like the current President, Fowler was a former state's attorney with an impressive record of law enforcement behind him. He'd ridden the reputation of the man who'd cleaned up Cleveland into six terms in the U.S. House of Representatives, but you didn't go from that House to the White House, and the Senate seats in his state were too secure. So he'd become Governor six years before, and by all reports an effective one. His ultimate political goal had been formed over twenty years before, and now he'd made it to the finals.

He was a trim five-eleven, with brown eyes and hair showing the first signs of gray over the ears. And he was weary. America demands much of her presidential candidates. Marine Corps boot camp was a tryst by comparison. Ryan looked at a man almost twenty years his senior who for the past six months had lived on too much coffee and bad political-dinner food, yet somehow managed to smile at all the bad jokes told by people he didn't like and, most remarkably of all, to make a speech given no less than four times per day sound new and fresh and exciting to everyone who heard it. He also had about as much appreciation of foreign policy, Ryan thought, as Jack did of Einstein's General Theory of Relativity, which wasn't a hell of a lot.

"You're Dr. John Ryan, I take it." Fowler looked up from his morning paper.

"Yes, sir."

"Excuse me for not getting up. I sprained my ankle last week, and it hurts like a son of a bitch." Fowler waved to the cane beside him. Jack hadn't seen that on the morning news broadcasts. He'd given his acceptance speech, danced around the stage . . . on a bum ankle. The man had sand. Jack walked over to shake hands with him.

"They tell me that you are the acting Deputy Director of Intelligence."

"Excuse me, Governor, but the title is Deputy Director (Intelligence). That means I currently head one of the Agency's principal directorates. The others are Operations, Science and Technology, and Administration. Admin is what it sounds like. The Ops guys gather data the old-fashioned way; they're the real field spooks.

The S and T guys run the satellite programs and other scientific stuff. The Intel guys try to figure out what Ops and S and T deliver to us. That's what I try to do. The real DDI is Admiral James Greer, and he's—''

"I've heard. Too bad. I hear he is a fine man. Even his enemies say he's honest. That's probably the best compliment any man can have. How about some breakfast?'' Fowler fulfilled the first requirement of political life. He was pleasant. He was charming.

"Sounds okay to me, sir. Can I give you a hand?''

"No, I can manage.'' Fowler used the cane to rise. "You are an ex-Marine, ex-broker, ex-history teacher. I know about the business with the terrorists a few years back. My people—my informants, I should say,'' he added with a grin as he sat back down, "tell me that you've moved up the ladder at CIA very quickly, but they will not tell me why. It's not in the press either. I find that puzzling.''

"We do keep some secrets, sir. I am not at liberty to discuss all the things you might like to know, and in any case you'd have to depend on others to tell you about me. I'm not objective.''

The Governor nodded pleasantly. "You and Al Trent had one pisser of a fight a while back, but he says things about you that ought to make you blush. How come?''

"You'll have to ask Mr. Trent that, sir.''

"I did. He won't say. He doesn't actually like you very much, either.''

"I am not at liberty to discuss that at all. Sorry, sir. If you win in November, you can find that out.'' How to explain that Al Trent had helped CIA arrange the defection of the head of KGB—to get even with the people who had put a very close Russian friend of his in a labor camp. Even if he could tell the story, who would ever believe it?

"And you really pissed Beth Elliot off last night.''

"Sir, do you want me to talk like a politician, which I am not, or like what I am?''

"Tell it straight, son. That's one of the rarest pleasures a man in my position has.'' Ryan missed that signal entirely.

"I found Dr. Elliot arrogant and abusive. I'm not used to being jacked around. I may owe her an apology, but maybe she owes me one, too.''

"She wants your ass, and the campaign hasn't even started yet.'' This observation was delivered with a laugh.

"It belongs to someone else, Governor. Maybe she can kick it, but she can't *have* it.''

"Don't ever run for public office, Dr. Ryan.''

"Don't get me wrong, sir, but there is no way in hell that I would ever subject myself to what people like you have to put up with.''

"How do you like being a government employee? That's a question, not a threat,'' Fowler explained.

"Sir, I do what I do because I think it's important, and because I think I'm good at it.''

"The country needs you?'' the presidential candidate asked lightly. That one rocked the acting DDI back in his chair. "That's a tough answer to have to make, isn't it? If you say no, then you ought not to have the job because somebody can do it better. If you say yes, then you're an arrogant son of a bitch who thinks he's better than everybody else. Learn something from that, Dr. Ryan. That's my lesson for the day. Now let me hear yours. Tell me about the world—your version of it, that is.''

Jack took out his notes and talked for just under an hour and just over two cups of coffee. Fowler was a good listener. The questions he asked were pointed ones.

"If I read you right, you say you do not know what the Soviets are up to. You've met the General Secretary, haven't you?"

"Well—" Ryan stopped cold. "Sir, I cannot—that is, I shook hands with him twice at diplomatic receptions."

"You've met him for more than a handshake, but you can't talk about it? That is most interesting. You're no politician, Dr. Ryan. You tell the truth before you think to lie. It would appear that you think the world is in pretty good shape at the moment."

"I can remember when it was in far worse shape, Governor," Jack said, grateful for having been let off the hook.

"So why not ease back, cut arms, like I propose?"

"I think it's too soon for that."

"I don't."

"Then we disagree, Governor."

"What is going on in South America?"

"I don't know."

"Does that mean that you do not know what we are doing, or that you do not know if we are doing anything, or that you do know and have been ordered not to discuss it?"

He sure talks like a lawyer. "As I told Ms. Elliot last night, I have no knowledge on that subject. That is the truth. I have already indicated areas in which I do have knowledge which I am not allowed to discuss."

"I find that very strange, given your position."

"I was in Europe for a NATO intelligence meeting when all this started, and I'm a European and Soviet specialist."

"What do you think we ought to do about the killing of Director Jacobs?"

"In the abstract, we should react forcefully to the murder of any of our citizens, even more so in a case like this. But I'm Intelligence, not Operations."

"Including cold-blooded murder?" Fowler pressed.

"If the government decides that killing people is the correct course of action in the pursuit of our national interests, then such killing falls outside the legal definition of murder, doesn't it?"

"That's an interesting position. Go on."

"Because of the way our government works, such decisions have to be made . . . have to reflect the way the American people want things to be, or would want them to be, if they had the knowledge available to the people who make the decisions. That's why we have congressional oversight of covert operations, both to ensure that the operations are appropriate, and to depoliticize them."

"So you're saying that that sort of decision depends upon reasonable men making a reasoned decision—to commit murder."

"That's overly simplified, but, yes."

"I disagree. The American people support capital punishment; that's wrong, too. We demean ourselves and we betray the ideals of our country when we do things like that. What do you think of that?"

"I think you are wrong, Governor, but I don't make government policy. I provide information to those who do."

Bob Fowler's voice changed to something Jack had not yet heard this morning. "Just so we know where we stand. You've lived up to your billing, Dr. Ryan. You are indeed honest, but despite your youth I think that your views reflect times past. People like you *do* make government policy, by casting your analysis in directions of your own choosing—hold it!'' Fowler held up his hand. ''I'm not questioning your integrity. I do not doubt that you do the best job you can, but to tell me that people like you do not make government policy is arrant nonsense.''

Ryan flushed red at that, feeling it, trying to control it, but failing miserably. Fowler wasn't questioning Jack's integrity, just the second-brightest star in his personal constellation, his intelligence. He wanted to snarl back what he thought, but couldn't.

''Now you're going to tell me that if I knew what you knew, I'd think differently, right?'' Fowler asked.

''No, sir. I don't use that argument. It sounds and smells like bullshit. Either you believe me or you do not. All I can do is persuade, not convince. Maybe I am wrong sometimes,'' Jack allowed as he cooled off. ''All I can do is give you the best I have. May I pass along a lesson, too, sir?''

''Go on.''

''The world is not always what we wish it to be, but wishes don't change it.''

Fowler was amused. ''So I should listen to you even when you're wrong? What if I know you're wrong?''

A marvelous philosophical discussion might have followed, but Ryan knew when he was beaten. He'd just wasted ninety minutes. Perhaps one final try.

''Governor, there are tigers in the world. Once I saw my daughter lying near death in a hospital because somebody who hated me tried to kill her. I didn't like it, and I tried to wish it away, but it didn't work. Maybe I just learned a harder lesson. I hope you never have to.''

''Thank you. Good morning, Dr. Ryan.''

Ryan collected his papers and left. It was like something dimly remembered from the Bible. He'd been measured and found wanting by the man who might be his country's next President. He was even more disturbed by his reaction to it: *Fuck him.* He'd fulfilled Fowler's own observation. It was a very dumb thing to think.

''Kick it loose, big brother!'' Tim Jackson said. Robby cracked open one eye to see Timmy clad in his multicolored uniform and boots. ''It's time for our morning run.''

''I remember changing your diapers.''

''You gotta catch me first. Come on, you got five minutes to get ready.''

Captain Jackson grinned up at his little brother. He was in pretty good shape, and a kendo master. ''I'm gonna run your ass right into the ground.''

Pride goeth before the fall, Captain Jackson told himself fifteen minutes later. He would have settled for a fall. If he fell down, he might rest for a few seconds. When he started staggering, Tim backed the pace off.

''You win,'' Robby gasped. ''I ain't gonna change your diapers again.''

''Hey, we've barely done two miles.''

''A carrier's only a thousand feet long!''

''Yeah, and I bet the steel deck's bad on the knees, too. Go on, head back and get breakfast ready, sir. I got two more miles to do.''

''Aye aye, sir.'' *Where are my kendo sticks?* Robby thought, *I can still whip his ass at that!*

It took Robby five minutes to find his way back to the right BOQ building. He passed a number of officers heading to or from their runs, and for the first time in his life, Robby Jackson felt old. It was hardly fair. He was one of the youngest captains in the Navy, and still one hell of a fighter pilot. He also knew how to fix breakfast. It was all on the table when Timmy got back.

"Don't feel too bad, Rob. This is what I do for a living. I can't fly airplanes."

"Shut up and drink your juice."

"Where the hell did you say you were?"

"Aboard *Ranger*—that's a carrier, boy. Observing ops off Panama. My boss gets into Monterey this afternoon and I'm s'posed to meet him there."

"Down where the bombs are going off," Tim observed as he buttered his toast.

"Another one last night?" Robby asked. Well, that made sense, didn't it?

"Looks like we bagged us another druggie. Nice to see the CIA, or somebody, grew hisself a pair of balls for a change. Love to know how the guys are getting the bombs in."

"What do you mean?" Robby asked. Something wasn't right.

"Rob, I *know* what's going down. It's some of our people down there doin' it."

"Tim, you've lost me."

Second Lieutenant Timothy Jackson, Infantry, leaned across the breakfast table in the conspiratorial way of junior officers. "Look, I know it's a secret and all, but, hell, how smart do you have to be? One of my people is down there right now. Figure it out, man. One of my best people disappears, don't show up where he's supposed to be—where the Army thinks he is, for Christ's sake. He's a Spanish speaker. So are some others who checked out funny, Muñoz out of recon, León, two others I heard about. All Spanish speakers, okay? Then all of a sudden there's some serious ass-kickin' going on down in banana land. Hey, how smart you gotta be?"

"Have you told anyone about this?"

"Why tell anybody? I'm a little worried about Chavez—he's one of my people, and I worry a little about him, but he's one good fucking soldier. Far as I'm concerned, he can kill all the druggies he wants. I just want to know how they did the bombs. That might come in handy someday. I'm thinking about going special-ops."

The Navy did the bombs, Timmy, Robby thought very loudly indeed.

"How much talk is there about this?"

"About the first bombing, everybody thought that was pretty good, but talk about our people bein' involved? Uh-uh. Maybe some folks're thinking the same way I am, but you don't talk about shit like that. Security, right?"

"That's right, Tim."

"You know a senior Agency guy, right?"

"Sort of. Godfather for Jack Junior."

"Tell him for us, kill all you want."

"I'll do that," Robby said quietly. It had to be an Agency operation. A very "black" Agency operation, but it wasn't nearly as black as they wanted it to be. If some nugget a year out of the academy could figure it out. . . . The ordies on *Ranger,* personnel officers and NCOs all over the Army—lots of people must have put it together by now. Not all of those who heard the talk would be on the good side.

"Let me give you a tip. You hear talk about this, you tell people to clam up. You get talk started about an operation like this, people start disappearing."

"Hey, Rob, anybody wants to mess with Chavez and Muñoz and—"

"Listen to me, boy! I've *been* there. I've been shot at by machine guns, and my

Tomcat ate a missile once, damned near killed the best RIO I ever had. It's dangerous out there, and talk gets people dead. You remember that. This isn't college anymore, Tim."

Tim considered that for a moment. His brother was right. His brother was also wondering what, if anything, he should do about it. Rob considered just sitting on it, but he was a Tomcat driver, a man of action, not the sort to do nothing at all. If nothing else, he decided, he'd have to warn Jack that the security on the operation wasn't as secure as it ought to be.

22. Disclosures

Unlike Air Force and Army generals, most Navy admirals do not have personal aircraft to chauffeur them around, and for the most part they fly commercial. A coterie of aides and drivers waiting at the gates helps ease the pain, of course, and Robby Jackson was not above making points with his boss by appearing at San José Airport just as the 727 pulled up to the jetway that evening. He had to wait for the first-class passengers to deplane, of course, since even flag officers fly coach.

Vice Admiral Joshua Painter was the current Assistant Chief of Naval Operations for Air Warfare, known to insiders by his "designator," OP-05, or just "oh-five." His three-star rank was a miracle. Painter was first of all an honest man; second, an outspoken one; third, someone who thought the real Navy was at sea, not alongside the Potomac River; finally and most damagingly, he was that rarest of naval officers, the author of a book. The Navy does not encourage its officers to commit their thoughts to paper, except for the odd piece on thermodynamics or the behavior of neutrons within a reactor vessel. An intellectual, a maverick, and a warrior in a service that was increasingly anti-intellectual, conformist, and bureaucratized, he thought of himself as the token exception in what was turning into The Corporate Navy. Painter was a crusty, acerbic Vermont native, short and slight of build, with pale, almost colorless blue eyes and a tongue sharp enough to chip stone. He was also the living god of the aviation community. He'd flown more than four hundred missions over North Vietnam in several different models of the F-4 Phantom, and had two MiGs to his credit—the side panel from his jet, with two red stars painted on it, hung in his Pentagon office, along with the caption, SIDEWINDER MEANS NOT HAVING TO SAY YOU'RE SORRY. Though a perfectionist and a very demanding boss, he deemed nothing too good for his pilots or his enlisted crews, especially the latter.

"I see you got the message," Josh Painter observed, reaching a finger out to tap Robby's bright new shoulder boards.

"Yes, sir."

"I also hear your new tactics were a disaster."

"They could have worked out a little better," Captain Jackson admitted.

"Yeah, it does help if the carrier survives. Maybe a CAG slot will reinforce that in your mind. I just approved you for one," OP-05 announced. "You get Wing Six. It chops to *Abe Lincoln* when *Indy* goes in for overhaul. Congratulations,

Robby. Try not to screw up too badly in the next eighteen months. Now, what went wrong with the Fleet-Ex?" he asked as they walked off toward the waiting car.

"The 'Russians' cheated," Robby answered. "They were smart." That earned him a laugh from his boss. Though crusty, Painter did have a lively sense of humor. The discussion took care of the drive to flag quarters at the Naval Post-Graduate School on the California coast at Monterey.

"Any more on the news about those drug bastards?" Painter asked while his aide carried his bags in.

"We're sure giving them a hard time, aren't we?" Jackson observed.

The Admiral stopped dead in his tracks. "What the hell do you mean?"

"I know that I'm not supposed to know, sir, but I mean, I was there, and I did see what was going on."

Painter waved Jackson inside. "Check the fridge. See if you can put a martini together while I pump bilges. Fix whatever you want for yourself."

Robby made the proper arrangements. Whoever set up flag quarters for them knew what Painter liked to drink. Jackson opened a Miller Lite for himself.

Painter reappeared without his uniform shirt and took a sip from his glass. Then he dismissed his aide and gave Jackson a very close look.

"I want you to repeat what you said on the way in, Captain."

"Admiral, I know I'm not cleared for this, but I'm not blind. I watched the A-6 head for the beach on radar, and I don't figure it was a coincidence. Whoever set up security on the op could have done a better job, sir."

"Jackson, you're going to have to forgive me, but I just spent five and a half hours sitting too close to the engines on a beat-up old 727. You're telling me that those two bombs that took druggies out fell off one of *my* A-6s?"

"Yes, sir. You didn't know?"

"No, Robby, I didn't." Painter knocked off the rest of his drink and set the glass down. "Jesus Christ. What lunatic set up this abortion?"

"But that new bomb, it had to—I mean, the orders and everything—shit, for this sort of thing, the orders have to chop through -05."

"*What* new bomb?" Painter nearly shouted that out, but managed to control himself.

"Some kind of plastic, fiberglass, whatever, some kind of new bombcase. It looks like a stock, low-drag two-thousand-pounder with the usual attachment points for the smart-bomb gear, but it's not made out of steel or any other kind of metal, and it's painted blue like an exercise bomb."

"Oh, okay. There has been a little work on a low-observable bomb for the ATA"—Painter referred to the new Stealth attack plane the Navy was working on—"but, hell, we've just done a little preliminary testing, maybe a dozen drops. Whole program's experimental. They don't even use the regular bomb filler, and I'm probably going to shit-can the program, 'cause I don't think it's worth the money. They haven't even taken those things off China Lake yet."

"Sir, there were several in *Ranger*'s bomb locker. I saw 'em, Admiral, I touched 'em. I saw one attached to an A-6. I watched that A-6 on radar while I was up in the E-2 for the Fleet-Ex. It flew off to the beach and came back from a different direction. The timing might be a coincidence, but I'd be careful putting money down on that. The night I flew back, I saw another one attached to the same aircraft. Next day I hear that another druggie got his house knocked flat. It stands to reason that half a ton of HE'll do just fine for that, and a combustible bombcase won't leave shit behind for evidence."

"Nine hundred eighty-five pounds of Octol—that's what they use in those things." Painter snorted. "It'll do a house, all right. You know who flew the mission?"

"Roy Jensen, he's skipper of—"

"I know him. We were shipmates on—Robby, what the hell is going on here? I want you to start over from the beginning and tell me everything you saw."

Captain Jackson did just that. It took ten uninterrupted minutes.

"Who was the 'tech-rep' from?" Painter asked.

"I didn't ask, sir."

"How much you want to bet he isn't even aboard anymore? Son, we've been had. *I've* been had. Goddammit! Those orders should have come through my office. Somebody's been using my fucking airplanes and not telling me."

It wasn't about the bombings, Robby understood, it was about propriety. And it was about security. Had the Navy planned the job, it would have been done better. Painter and his senior A-6 expert would have set it up so that there would have been no awkward evidence for other people—like Robby in the E-2C—to notice. What Painter feared was the simple fact that now his people could be left holding the bag for an operation imposed from above, bypassing the regular chain of command.

"Get Jensen up here?" Robby wondered.

"I thought of that. Too obvious. Might get Jensen in too much trouble. But I've got to find out where the hell his orders came from. *Ranger*'s out for another ten days or so, right?"

"I believe so, sir."

"Has to be an Agency job," Josh Painter observed quietly. "Authorized higher up than that, but it has to be Agency."

"For what it's worth, sir, I got a good friend who's pretty senior there. I'm godfather for one of his kids."

"Who's that?"

"Jack Ryan."

"Oh, yeah, I've met him. He was with me on *Kennedy* for a day or two back when—you're sure to remember that cruise, Rob." Painter smiled. "Right before you took that missile hit. By that time he was off on HMS *Invincible*."

"*What?* Jack was aboard then? But—why the hell didn't he come down to see me?"

"You never did find out what that op was all about, did you?" Painter shook his head, thinking of the *Red October* affair. "Maybe he can tell you about it. I can't."

Robby accepted it without questioning and turned back to the matter at hand. "There's a land side to this operation, too, Admiral," he said, and explained on for another couple of minutes.

"Charlie-Fox," Painter said when he was done. That was the Navy's shorthand and sanitized version of an expression that had begun in the Marine Corps to denote a confused and self-destructive military operation: Cluster-Fuck. "Robert, you get your ass on the first plane back to D.C. and tell your friend that his operation is going to hell in a basket. Jesus, don't those Agency clowns ever learn? If this gets out, and from what you're telling me, it's sure as hell going to, it's going to hurt us. It's going to hurt the whole country. We don't need this kind of shit, not in an election year with that asshole Fowler running. Also tell him that the next time the Agency decides to play soldier, it *might help* if they asked somebody who knows something about it ahead of time."

* * *

The Cartel had an ample supply of people who were accustomed to carrying guns, and assembling them took only a few hours. Cortez was detailed to run the operation. He'd coordinate it from the village of Anserma, which was in the center of the area in which the "mercenary" teams seemed to be operating. He hadn't told his boss everything he knew, of course, nor did he reveal his full objective. The Cartel was a cooperative enterprise. Nearly three hundred men had been brought in by cars, trucks, and buses, personal retainers from all of the Cartel chieftains, all of them reasonably fit and accustomed to violence. Their presence here reduced the security details of the remaining drug lords. That would allow Escobedo a sizable advantage as he tried to discover which of his colleagues was making the "power play," while Cortez dealt with the "mercenaries." He had every intention of running the American soldiers to ground and killing them all, of course, but there was no special hurry in that. Félix had every reason to suspect that he was up against elite troops, perhaps even American Green Berets, formidable opponents for whom he had due respect. Casualties among his force, therefore, were to be expected. Félix wondered how many he'd have to kill off in order to alter the overall balance of power within the Cartel to his personal advantage.

There was no point in telling the assembled multitude, of course. These harsh, brutal men were used to brandishing their weapons like the Japanese samurai warriors of all those bad movies that they liked to watch, and like those actors playing at killers, these men were accustomed to having people cower before them, the omnipotent, invincible warriors of the Cartel, armed with their AK-47s, swaggering down village streets. *Comical scum,* Cortez thought.

It was all rather comical, really. Cortez would not mind a bit. It was to be a diverting and entertaining exercise, something from half a millennium before, when brutal men would tether a bear in a pit and let dogs at it. Eventually the bear died, and though it was frequently rather hard on the dogs, you could always get new ones. Those new dogs would be trained differently, to be loyal to a new master. . . . It was marvelous, Cortez realized after a moment. He'd be playing a game, with men instead of bears and dogs, a game that hadn't been played since the time of the Caesars. He understood now why some of the drug lords had gotten the way they were. This sort of Godlike power was destructive to one's soul. He'd have to remember that. But first there was work to do.

The chain of command was established. There were five groups of fifty or so men. They were assigned operating areas. Communications would be by radio, coordinated through Cortez, in the safety of a house outside the village. About the only complication was the possible interference of the Colombian Army. Escobedo was taking care of that. M-19 and FARC would start making trouble elsewhere. That would keep the Army occupied.

The "soldiers," as they immediately took to calling themselves, moved off into the hills in trucks. *Buena suerte,* Cortez told their leaders: Good luck. Of course, he wished them nothing of the kind. Luck was no longer a factor in the operation, which suited the former colonel of the DGI. In a properly planned operation, it never was.

It was a quiet day in the mountains. Chavez heard the pealing of church bells echoing up and down the valley, calling the faithful to Sunday liturgy. Was it Sunday? Chavez wondered. He'd lost track. Whichever day it was, traffic sounds were less than normal. Except for the loss of Rocha, things were in rather good shape. They hadn't even expended much of their ammunition, though in another few days they were due for a resupply drop from the helicopter supporting the operation. You could never have too much ammunition. That was one truth Chavez had learned. Happiness is a full bandolier. And a full canteen. And hot food.

The topography of the valley allowed them to hear things especially well. Sound carried up the slopes with a minimum of attenuation, and the air, though thin, seemed to give every noise a special bell-like clarity. Chavez heard the trucks well off, and put his binoculars on a bend in the road, several miles away, to see what it was. He wasn't the least concerned. Trucks were targets, not things to worry about. He adjusted the focus on the binoculars to get the sharpest possible image, and the sergeant had a good pair of eyes. After a minute or so he spotted three of them, flatbed trucks like farmers used, with removable wooden sides. But they were filled with men, and the men appeared to be carrying rifles. The trucks stopped, and the men jumped out. Chavez punched his sleeping companion.

"*Oso,* get the captain here right now!"

Ramirez was there in less than a minute, with his own pair of binoculars.

"You're standing up, sir!" Chavez growled. "Get the fuck down!"

"Sorry, Ding."

"You see 'em?"

"Yeah."

They were just milling around, but it was impossible to miss their rifles, slung over their shoulders. As both men watched, they divided into four groups and started moving off the road. A moment later, they were lost in the trees.

"It'll take 'em about three hours to get here, Cap'n," Ding estimated.

"By that time we'll be six miles north. Get ready to move."

Ramirez set up his satellite radio.

"VARIABLE, this is KNIFE, over." He got a reply on the first call.

"KNIFE, this is VARIABLE. We read you loud and clear. Over."

"KNIFE reports armed men entering the woods five miles east-southeast our position. Estimate reinforced platoon in strength, and heading our way."

"Are they soldiers, over."

"Negative—say again, negative. Weapons in evidence, but no uniforms. I repeat, they do not appear to be wearing uniforms. We are getting ready to move."

"Roger that, KNIFE. Move immediately, check in when you can. We'll try to find out what's going on."

"Roger. KNIFE out."

"What's that all about?" one of the case officers asked.

"I don't know. I wish Clark was here," the other said. "Let's check in with Langley."

Jackson managed to catch a United red-eye flight out of San Francisco direct to Dulles International Airport. Admiral Painter had called ahead, and a Navy sedan took him to Washington National, where his Corvette had been parked, and remarkably enough, not stolen. Robby had played it all back and forth in his mind during the entire flight. In the abstract, CIA operations were fun things to think about: spies skulking about and doing whatever the hell it was that they did. He didn't especially mind what this one was doing, but, damn it, the Navy was being used, and you didn't do that without letting people know. His first stop was at his home to change clothes. Then he made a phone call.

Ryan was home, and enjoying it. He'd managed to get home Friday evening a few minutes ahead of his wife's return from Hopkins and slept in late Saturday to shake off the lingering effects of travel shock. The remainder of the day had been devoted to playing with his kids and taking them to Saturday-night mass so that he could get another long night's sleep, plus reacquainting himself with his wife. Now he was sitting on his John Deere lawn tractor. He might be one of the top people in CIA, but he still cut his own grass. Others seeded and fertilized, but for Jack the pastoral act of cutting was therapy. It was a three-hour ritual done every two weeks—somewhat more often in the spring, but by now the growth rate was down to a reasonable level. He enjoyed the smell of the cut grass. For that matter, he enjoyed the greasy smell of the tractor and the vibration of the motor. He couldn't entirely escape reality, of course. Clipped to his belt was a portable telephone whose electronic chiming was noticeable over the rumble of the tractor. Jack switched off as he hit the activation button on the phone.

"Hello."

"Jack? Rob."

"How you doing, Robby?"

"Just got myself frocked."

"Congratulations, *Captain* Jackson! Aren't you a little young for that?"

"Call it affirmative action, lettin' the aviators catch up with the bubbleheads. Hey, Sissy and I are heading over to Annapolis. Any problem we stop by on the way?"

"Hell, no. How about lunch?"

"Sure it's no trouble?" Jackson asked.

"Robby, give me a break," Ryan replied. "Since when did you get humble on me?"

"Ever since you got important and all."

Ryan violated an FCC rule with his retort.

"Little over an hour okay?"

"Yeah, I'll be finished with the grass by then. See ya', bud." Ryan terminated the call and placed one to his house, which had three lines. It was, perversely, a long-distance call. He needed a D.C. line for his work. Cathy needed a Baltimore connection for hers, plus a local line for other matters.

"Hello?" Cathy answered.

"Rob and Sis are coming over for lunch," Jack told his wife. "How about hot dogs on the grill?"

"My hair's a mess!" Caroline Ryan announced.

"Okay, I'll grill that, too. Can you set up the charcoal for me? I ought to be finished out here in twenty minutes or so."

In fact, it took just over thirty. Ryan parked the mower in the garage next to his Jaguar and went into the house to wash up. He had to shave, too, which he barely finished doing when Robby pulled into the driveway.

"How the hell did you make it this fast?" Jack demanded. He was still wearing his dingy cut-offs.

"You prefer I should be late, Dr. Ryan?" Robby asked as he and his wife got out of the car. Cathy appeared at the door. Handshakes and kisses were exchanged as everyone caught up on what they'd been doing since the last time they'd gotten together. Cathy and Sissy went into the living room while Jack and Robby got the hot dogs and walked out to the deck. The charcoal wasn't quite ready yet.

"So how do you like being a captain?"

"Be even better when they pay me what I am most clearly worth." Being frocked meant that Robby could wear the four stripes of a captain, but still drew the pay of a mere commander. "I'm getting a CAG slot, too. Admiral Painter told me last night."

"Shit hot!" Jack clapped Robby on the shoulder. "That's the next big step, isn't it?"

"So long as I don't step on my weenie. The Navy giveth, and the Navy taketh away. I don't get it for a year and a half, which means giving up part of my delightful tour in the Pentagon, sob." Robby stopped for a moment and got serious. "That's not why I came."

"Oh?"

"Jack, what the hell have you guys got going in Colombia?"

"Rob, I don't know."

"Look, Jack, this is cool, okay? I fucking know! Your security on the op sucks. Hey, I know you got need-to-know rules, but my admiral is kinda pissed that you're using his assets without telling him about it."

"Who's that?"

"Josh Painter," Jackson answered. "You met him on *Kennedy,* remember?"

"Who told you that!"

"A reliable source. I've been thinking about it. The story back then was that Ivan lost a sub and we were out to help 'em find it, but things got a little rough for a while, explaining why my RIO had to have brain surgery and my Tomcat needed three weeks before it could fly again. I guess there was more to that than met the eye, and it never made the papers. Shame I can't hear the story. Anyway, we'll set that one aside for a while. This is why I'm here:

"Those two druggie houses that got blown up—the bombs came off of an A-6E Intruder medium attack bomber belonging to the United States Navy. I'm not the only one who knows. Whoever set up this operation, well, the security's for shit, Jack. You also got a bunch of light-infantry soldiers running around. Doing what, I don't know, but people also know that they're down there. Maybe you can't tell me what's happening. Okay, it's compartmented and all that, and you can't tell me anything, but I'm telling *you,* Jack, the word's leaking out, and some folks in the Pentagon are going to be big-league angry when this sucker hits the networks. Whatever dickhead set this thing up is in way the hell over his head, and the word from on high is that us guys in blue and green suits will not repeat *not* get left holding the bag this time."

"Cool off, Rob." Ryan popped open a can of beer for Robby and one for himself.

"Jack, we're friends, and ain't nothing gonna change that. I know you'd never do anything this dumb, but—"

"I don't know what you're talking about. I don't fucking know, okay? I was in Belgium last week and I told them I didn't know. I was in Chicago Friday morning with that Fowler guy, and I told him and his aide that I don't know. And I'm telling *you* that I don't know."

Jackson was quiet for a moment. "You know, anybody else, I'd call him a liar. I know what your new job is, Jack. You're telling me that you're serious? Honest to God, Jack, this here is important."

"Word of honor, Captain, I don't know dick."

Robby drained his beer and crushed the can flat. "Ain't that the way it always is?" he said. "We got people out there killing, maybe getting hurt, too, and nobody knows anything. God, I love being a fucking pawn. You know, I don't mind taking my chances, but it's nice to know why."

"I'll do my best to find out."

"Good idea. They really haven't told you what's happening, eh?"

"They haven't told me shit, but I'm going to damned well find out. You might want to drop a hint on your boss," Jack added.

"What's that?"

"Tell him to keep a low profile until I get back to you."

Whatever doubt the Patterson brothers had about what they should do ended that Sunday afternoon. The Grayson sisters came for visitors' day, sitting across from their men—neither pair had trouble distinguishing who was who—and proclaiming their undying love for the men who'd liberated them from their pimp. It was no longer just a question of getting out of jail. The final decision was made on the way back to their cell.

Henry and Harvey were in the same cell, mainly for security reasons. Had they been separated, then by the simple expedient of changing shirts, they could have swapped cells and somehow—the jailers knew that the Pattersons were clever bastards—done something to screw things up for everybody. The additional advantage was that the brothers didn't fight each other, as was hardly uncommon with the rest of the jail population, and the fact that they were quiet and untroublesome allowed them to work in undisturbed peace.

Jails are necessarily buildings designed to take abuse. The floors are of bare reinforced concrete, since carpets or tile would just be ripped up to start a fire or some other mischief. The resulting hard, smooth concrete floor made a good grinding surface. Each brother had a simple length of heavy metal wire taken from the bedstead. No one has yet designed a prison bed that doesn't require metal, and metal makes good weapons. In prison such weapons are called shanks, an ugly word completely suitable to their ugly purpose. Law requires that jails and prisons cannot be mere cages for housing prisoners like animals in a zoo, and this jail, like others, had a crafts shop. An idle mind, judges have ruled for decades, is the devil's workshop. The fact that the devil is already a resident in the criminal mind simply means that the craft shops provide tools and material for making shanks more effective. In this case, each brother had a small, grooved piece of wood doweling and some electrician's tape. Henry and Harvey took turns, one rubbing his shank on the concrete to get a needlelike point while the other stood guard for an approaching uniform. It was high-quality wire, and the sharpening process took some hours, but people in jail have lots of idle time. Finished, each wire was inserted in the groove in the dowel—miraculously enough, the groove, cut by a craft-shop router, was exactly the right size and length. The electrician's tape secured the wire in place, and now each brother had a six-inch shank, capable of inflicting a deep, penetrating trauma upon a human body.

They hid their weapons—prison inmates are very effective at it—and discussed tactics. Any graduate of a guerrilla or terrorist school would have been impressed. Though the language was coarse and the discussion lacking in the technical jargon preferred by trained professionals in the field of urban warfare, the Patterson brothers had a clear understand of the idea of *Mission*. They understood covert approach, the importance of maneuver and diversion, and they knew about clearing the area after the mission was successfully executed. In this they expected the tacit assistance of their cellmates, but jails and prisons, though violent and evil places, remain communities of men, and the pirates were decidedly unpopular, whereas the Pattersons were fairly high in the hierarchical chain as tough, ''honest'' hoods. Besides, everyone knew that they were not people to cross, which encouraged cooperation and discouraged informants.

Jails are also places with hygienic rules. Since criminals are frequently the type to defer bathing, and brushing and flossing their teeth, and since such behavior lends itself to epidemic, showers are part of an unbending routine. The Patterson brothers were counting on it.

''What do you mean?'' the man with a Spanish accent asked Mr. Stuart.

''I mean they'll be out in eight years. Considering they murdered a family of four and got caught red-handed with a large supply of cocaine, it's one hell of a good deal,'' the attorney replied. He didn't like doing business on Sunday, and especially didn't like doing business with this man in the den of his home with his family in the backyard, but he had chosen to do business with drug types. He told himself at least ten times with every single case that he'd been a fool to have taken the first one—and gotten him off, of course, because the DEA agents had screwed up their warrant, tainting all the evidence and tossing the case on a classic ''legal technicality.'' That success, which had earned him fifty thousand dollars for four days' work, had given him a ''name'' within the drug community, which had money to burn—or to hire good criminal lawyers. You couldn't easily say no to such people. They were genuinely frightening. They had *killed* lawyers who displeased them. And they paid so well, well enough that he could take time to apply his considerable talents to indigent clients who couldn't pay. At least that was one of the arguments he used on sleepless nights to justify dealing with the animals. ''Look, these guys were looking at a seat in the electric chair—life at minimum—and I knocked that down to twenty years and out in eight. For Christ's sake, that's a goddamned good deal.''

''I think you could do better,'' the man replied with a blank look and in a voice so devoid of emotion as to be mechanistic. And decidedly frightening to a lawyer who had never owned or shot a gun.

That was the other side of the equation. They didn't merely hire him. Somewhere else was another lawyer, one who gave advice without getting directly involved. It was a simple security provision. It also made perfect professional sense, of course, to get a second opinion of anything. It also meant that in special cases the drug community could make sure that its own attorney wasn't making some sort of arrangement with the state, as was not entirely unknown in the countries from which they came. And as was the case here, some might say. Stuart could have played his information from the Coasties for all it was worth, gambling to have the whole case thrown out. He estimated a fifty-fifty chance of that. Stuart was good, even brilliant in a courtroom, but so was Davidoff, and there is not a trial lawyer in the world who would have predicted the reaction of a jury—a south Alabama, law-and-order jury—to a case like this one. Whoever was in the shadows giving advice to the man in his den, he was not as good as Stuart in a courtroom. Probably an academic, the trial lawyer thought, maybe a professor supplementing his teaching income with some informal consulting. Whoever he—she?—was, Stuart hated him on instinct.

"If I do what you want me to do, we run the risk of blowing the whole case. They really could end up in the chair." It also would mean wrecking the careers of Coast Guard sailors who had done wrong, but not nearly so wrong as Stuart's clients had most certainly done. His ethical duty as a lawyer was to give his clients the best possible defense within the law, within the Standards of Professional Conduct, but most of all, within the scope of his knowledge and experience—instinct, which was as real and important as it was impossible to quantify. Exactly how a lawyer balanced his duty on that three-cornered scale was the subject of endless class hours in law school, but the answers arrived at in the theaterlike lecture halls were always clearer than in the real legal world found beyond the green campus lawns.

"They could also go free."

The man's thinking reversal on appeal, Stuart realized. It *was* an academic lawyer giving advice.

"My professional advice to my clients is to accept the deal that I have negotiated."

"Your clients will decline that advice. Your clients will tell you tomorrow morning to—what is the phrase? Go for broke?" The man smiled like a dangerous machine. "Those are your instructions. Good day, Mr. Stuart. I can find the door." The machine left.

Stuart stared at his bookcases for a few minutes before making his telephone call. He might as well do it now. No sense making Davidoff wait. No public announcement had yet been made, though the rumors were out on the street. He wondered how the U.S. Attorney would take it. It was easier to predict what he'd say. The outraged *I thought we had a deal!* would be followed by a resolute *Okay, we'll see what the jury says!* Davidoff would muster his considerable talents, and the battle in Federal District Court would be an epic duel. But that was what courts were all about, wasn't it? It would be a fascinating and exciting technical exercise in the theory of the law, but like most such exercises, it would have little to do with right and wrong, less to do with what had actually happened aboard the good ship *Empire Builder,* and nothing at all to do with justice.

Murray was in his office. Moving into their townhouse had been a formality. He slept there—most of the time—but he saw far less of it than he'd seen of his official apartment in the Kensington section of London while legal attaché to the embassy on Grosvenor Square. It was hardly fair. For what it had cost him to move back to the D.C. area—the city that provided a home for the United States government denied decent housing to those on government salaries—one would have thought that he'd have gotten some real use from it.

His secretary was not in on Sunday, of course, and that meant Murray had to answer his own phone. This one came in on his direct, private line.

"Yeah, Murray here."

"Mark Bright. There's been a development on the Pirates Case that you need to know about. The lawyer for the subjects just called the U.S. Attorney. He's tossing the deal they made. He's going to fight it out; he's going to put those Coasties on the stand and try to blow away the whole case on the basis of that stunt they pulled. Davidoff's worried."

"What do you think?" Murray asked.

"Well, he'll reinstate the whole case: drug-related capital murder. If it means clobbering the Coast Guard, well, that's the price of justice. His words, not mine," Bright pointed out. Like many FBI agents, the agent was also a member of the bar.

"Going on my experience, not his, I'd say it's real gray, Dan. Davidoff's good—I mean, he's really good in front of a jury—but so's the defense guy, Stuart. The local DEA hates his guts, but he's an effective son of a bitch. The law is pretty muddled. What'll the judge say? Depends on the judge. What'll the jury say—depends on what the judge says and does. It's like putting a bet down on the next Super Bowl right now, before the season starts, and that doesn't even take into account what'll happen in the U.S. Court of Appeals after the trial's over in District Court. Whatever happens, the Coasties are going to get raped. Too bad. No matter what, Davidoff is going to tear each of 'em a new asshole for getting him into this mess."

"Warn 'em," Murray said. He told himself that it was an impulsive statement, but it wasn't. Murray believed in law, but he believed in justice more.

"You want to repeat that, sir?"

"They gave us TARPON."

"Mr. Murray"—he wasn't "Dan" now—"I might have to arrest them. Davidoff just might set up a grand jury on this and—"

"Warn them. That is an order, Mr. Bright. I presume the local cops have a good attorney who represents them. Recommend that attorney to Captain Wegener and his men."

Bright hesitated before replying. "Sir, what you just told me to do might be seen as—"

"Mark, I've been in the Bureau a long time. Maybe too damned long," Murray's fatigue—and some other things—said. "But I won't stand by and watch these men get ambushed for doing something that helped us. They'll have to take their chances with the law—but by God, they'll have the same advantages that those fucking pirates have! We owe them that much. Log that one in as my order and carry it out."

"Yes, sir." Murray could hear Bright thinking the rest of the answer: *Damn!*

"On the case, anything else you need from our end that you need help with?"

"No, sir. The forensics are all in. From that side the case is tight as hell. DNA matches on both semen samples to the subjects, DNA blood matches to two of the victims. The wife was a blood donor, and we found a quart of her stuff in a Red Cross freezer; the other one's to the daughter. Davidoff might just bring this one off on that basis alone." The new DNA-match technology was rapidly becoming one of the Bureau's deadliest forensic weapons. Two California men who'd thought themselves to have committed the perfect rape-murder were now contemplating the gas chamber due to the work of two Bureau biochemists and a relatively inexpensive laboratory test.

"Anything else you need, you call me direct. This one is directly tied in with Emil's murder, and I've got all the horsepower I need."

"Yes, sir. Sorry to bother you on a Sunday."

"Right." It was one small thing to chuckle about as he hung up. Murray turned in his swivel chair to stare out the windows onto Pennsylvania Avenue. A pleasant Sunday afternoon, and people were walking up the street of presidents like pilgrims, stopping along the way to purchase ice-creams and T-shirts from vendors. Farther down the street, beyond the Capitol, in the areas that tourists were careful to avoid, there were other places that people entered, also like pilgrims, also stopping to buy things.

"Fucking drugs," he observed quietly. Just how much more damage would they do?

* * *

The Deputy Director (Operations) was also in his office. Three signals from VARIABLE had come in within the space of two hours. Well, it was not entirely unexpected that the opposition would react. They were acting more rapidly and in a more organized way—it appeared—than he had expected, but it wasn't something that he'd neglected to consider beforehand. The whole point of using the troops he was using, after all, was for their field skills . . . and their anonymity. Had he selected Green Berets from the John F. Kennedy Special Warfare Center at Fort Bragg, North Carolina, or Rangers from Fort Stewart, Georgia, or people from the new Special Operations Command at MacDill—it would have been too many people from too small a community. That would have been noticed. But light-fighters had four nearly complete and widely separated divisions, over forty thousand men spread from New York to Hawaii, with the same field skills as soldiers in higher-profile units; and taking forty people out of forty thousand was a far more concealable exercise. Some would be lost. He'd known that going in and so, he was sure, did the soldiers themselves. They were assets, and assets sometimes get expended. That was harsh, but it was reality. If the infantrymen had wanted a safe life, they would not have chosen to be infantrymen, to have re-enlisted at least once each, and to volunteer for a job that was advertised as being potentially dangerous. These weren't government clerks tossed into the jungle and told to fend for themselves. They were professional soldiers who knew what the score was.

At least, that's what Ritter told himself. *But,* his mind asked him, *if you don't know what the score is, how can they?*

The craziest part of all was that the operation was working out exactly as planned—in the field. Clark's brilliant idea, using a few disconnected violent acts to instigate a gang war within the Cartel, appeared to be happening. How else to explain the attempted ambush of Escobedo? He found himself glad that Cortez and his boss had escaped. Now there would be revenge and confusion and turmoil from which the Agency could step back and cover its tracks.

Who, us? the Agency would ask by way of answer to reporters' questions, which would start the following day, Ritter was certain. He was, in fact, surprised that they hadn't started already. But the pieces of the puzzle were coming apart now instead of together. The *Ranger* battle group would sail back north, continuing its Fleet-Ex during the slow trip back to San Diego. The CIA representative was already off the ship and on his way home with the second and final tape cassette. The rest of the "exercise" bombs would be dropped at sea, targeted on discarded life-rafts as normal Drop-Ex's. The fact that they'd never been officially released from the Navy weapons-testing base in California would never be noticed. If it were? Some paperwork screwup—they happened all the time. No, the only tricky part was with those troops in the field. He could have made immediate arrangements to lift them out. Better to leave them there for a few more days. There might be more work for them to do, and as long as they were careful, they'd be all right. The opposition would not be all that good.

"So?" Colonel Johns asked Zimmer.

"Gotta change engines. This one's shot. The burner cans are all right, but the compressor failed big-time. Maybe the boys back home can rebuild it. No way we can fix it with what we've got here, sir."

"How long?"

"Six hours, if we start now, Colonel."

"Okay, Buck."

They'd brought two spare engines, of course. The hangar that held the Pave Low III helicopter wasn't big enough for both it and the MC-130 which provided aerial tanking and spare parts, however, and Zimmer waved to another NCO to punch the button to open the door. They needed a special cart and hoist to handle the T-64 turboshaft engines in any case.

The hangar doors rolled on their metal tracks just as a roach wagon drove onto the flight line. Immediately men descended on the truck. It was a hot day at the Canal Zone—a place where snow is something one sees on television—and it was time for cold drinks. Everyone knew the truck driver, a Panamanian who'd been doing this since God knew when and made a pretty good living at it.

He was also a serious airplane buff. From his own years of observations, plus casual conversations with the enlisted men who serviced them, he'd acquired a familiarity with everything in the inventory of the United States Air Force, and would have been a useful intelligence asset had anyone bothered trying to recruit him. He would never have done anything to hurt them in any case. Though often overbearing, more than once he'd had trouble with his truck and had it fixed on the spot for free by a green-clad mechanic, and around Christmas—everyone knew he had children—there would be presents for him and his sons. He'd even managed a few helicopter rides for them, showing them what the family house outside the base looked like. It was not every father who could do that for his children! The *norteamericanos* were not perfect, he knew, but they were fair and they were generous if you dealt with them honestly, since honesty wasn't something they expected from "natives." That was all the more true now that they were having trouble with the pineapple-faced buffoon who was running his country's government.

As he passed out his Cokes and munchies, he noticed that there was a Pave Low III in the hangar across the way, a large, formidable and in its peculiar way, a very beautiful helicopter. Well, that explained the Combat Talon transport/tanker, and the armed guards who kept him from taking his normal route. He knew much about both aircraft, and while he would never reveal what he knew of their capabilities, telling someone the simple fact that they were here, that was no crime, was it?

But next time, after the money was passed, he'd be asked to take note of the times they came and went.

They'd moved very rapidly for the first hour, then slowed to their normal slow, careful, and very alert pace. Even so, moving in daylight wasn't something they preferred to do. While the Ninja might well own the night, day was something for all, a far easier time to teach people to hunt than in the dark. While the soldiers still had practical advantages over anyone who might come hunting them—even other soldiers—those advantages were minimized by daytime operations. Like gamblers, the light-fighters preferred to use every card in the deck. Doing so, they consciously avoided what some sportsman might call a "fair" fight, but combat had stopped being a sport when a gladiator named Spartacus decided to kill on a free-agent basis, though it had taken the Romans a few more generations to catch on.

Everyone had his war paint on. They wore gloves despite the fact that it was warm. They knew that the nearest other SHOWBOAT team was fifteen klicks to the south, and anyone they saw was either an innocent or a hostile, not a friendly, and to soldiers trying to stay covert, "innocent" was rather a thin concept. They were to avoid contact with anything and anyone, and if contact were made, it would be an on-the-spot call.

The other rules were also different now. They didn't move in single file. Too many people following a single path made for tracks. Though Chavez was at point, with *Oso* twenty meters behind, the rest of the squad was advancing in line abreast, with frequent changes of direction, shifting almost like a football backfield, but over a much larger area. Soon they'd start looping their path, waiting to see if someone might be following. If so, that someone was in for a surprise. For the moment, the mission was to move to a preselected location and evaluate the opposition. And wait for orders.

The police lieutenant didn't often go to evening services at Grace Baptist Church, but he did this time. He was late, but the lieutenant had a reputation for being late, even though he customarily drove his unmarked radio car wherever he went. He parked on the periphery of the well-filled parking lot, walked in, and sat in the back, where he made sure his miserable singing would be noticed.

Fifteen minutes later, another plain-looking car stopped right next to his. A man got out with a tire iron, smashed the window on the right-side front door, and proceeded to remove the police radio, the shotgun clipped under the dash—and the locked, evidence-filled attaché case on the floor. In less than a minute he was back in his car and gone. The case would be found again only if the Patterson brothers didn't keep their word. Cops are honest folk.

23. The Games Begin

The morning routine was exactly the same despite the fact that Ryan had been away from it for a week. His driver awoke early and drove his own car to Langley, where he switched over to the official Buick and also picked up some papers for his passenger. These were in a metal case with a cipher lock and a self-destruct device. No one had ever tried to interfere with the car or its occupants, but that wasn't to say that it would never happen. The driver, one of the official CIA security detail, carried his own 9mm Beretta 92-F pistol, and there was an Uzi submachine gun under the dash. He had trained with the Secret Service and was an expert on protecting his "principal," as he thought of the acting DDI. He also wished that the guy lived closer to D.C., or that he was entitled to mileage pay for all the driving he did. He drove around the inner loop of the Capital Beltway, then took the cloverleaf east on Maryland Route 50.

Jack Ryan rose at 6:15, an hour that seemed increasingly early as he marched toward forty, and followed the same kind of morning routine as most other working people, though his being married to a physician guaranteed that his breakfast was composed of healthy foods, as opposed to those he liked. What was wrong with grease, sugar, and preservatives, anyway?

By 6:55 he was finished with breakfast, dressed, and about halfway through his paper. It was Cathy's job to get the children off to school. Jack kissed his daughter on his way to the door, but Jack Jr. thought himself too old for that baby stuff. The Agency Buick was just arriving, as regular and reliable as airlines and railroads tried to be.

"Good morning, Dr. Ryan."

"Good morning, Phil." Jack preferred to open his own doors, and slid into the right-rear seat. First he would finish his *Washington Post,* ending, as always, with the comics, and saving Gary Larson for last. If there was anything an Agency person needed it was his daily dose of *The Far Side,* far and away the most popular cartoon at Langley. It wasn't hard to understand why. By that time the car was back on Route 50, in the heavy Washington-bound traffic. Ryan worked the lock on the letter case. After opening it he used his Agency ID card to disarm the destruct device. The papers within were important, but anyone who attacked the car now would be more interested in him than in any written material, and no one at the Agency had illusions about Ryan's—or any other person's—ability to resist attempts to extract information. He now had forty minutes to catch up on developments that had taken place overnight—in this case over the weekend—so that he'd be able to ask intelligent questions of the section chiefs and night watch officers who'd brief him when he got in.

Reading the newspaper first always put a decent spin on the official CIA reports. Ryan had his doubts about journalists—their analysis was often faulty—but the fact of the matter was that they were in the same basic job as the Agency: information-gathering and -dissemination, and except for some very technical fields—which were, however, vitally important in matters like arms control—their performance was often as good as and sometimes better than the trained government employees who reported to Langley. Of course, a good foreign correspondent was generally paid better than a GS-12-equivalent case officer, and talent often went where the money was. Besides, reporters were allowed to write books, too, and that's where you could make real money, as many Moscow correspondents had done over the years. All a security clearance really meant, Ryan had learned over the years, was sources. Even at his level in the Agency, he often had access to information little different in substance than any competent newspaper reported. The difference was that Jack knew the sources for that information, which was important in gauging its reliability. It was a subtle but often crucial difference.

The briefing folders began with the Soviet Union. All sorts of interesting things were happening there, but still no one knew what it meant or where it was leading. Fine. Ryan and CIA had been reporting that analysis for longer than he cared to remember. People expected better. Like that Elliot woman, Jack thought, who hated the Agency for what it did—actually, for things it never did anymore—but conversely expected it to know everything. When would they wake up and realize that predicting the future was no easier for intelligence analysts than for a good sportswriter to determine who'd be playing in the Series? Even after the All-Star break, the American League East had three teams within a few percentage points of the lead. That was a question for bookmakers. It was a pity, Ryan grunted to himself, that Vegas didn't set up a betting line on the Soviet Politburo membership, or *glasnost,* or how the "nationalities question" was going to turn out. It would have given him some guidance. By the time they got to the beltway, he was reading through reports from Latin and South America. Sure enough, some drug lord named Fuentes had gotten himself blown up by a bomb.

Well, isn't that too bad? was Jack's initial observation. He was thinking abstractly, but came down to earth. No, it wasn't all that bad that he was dead. It was very worrisome that he'd been killed by an American aircraft bomb. That was the sort of thing that Beth Elliot hated CIA for, Jack reminded himself. All that judge-jury-and-executioner stuff. It had nothing to do with right or wrong. The question, to her, was political expediency and maybe aesthetics. Politicians are more concerned with "issues" than "principles," but talked as though the two nouns had the same meaning.

Jesus, you're really into Monday-morning cynicism, aren't you?

How the hell did Robby Jackson tumble to this? Who set up the operation? What will happen if the word really does get out?

Better yet: *Am I supposed to care about that? If yes, why? If not,* why *not?*

It's political, Jack. How do politics enter into your job? Are politics even supposed to enter into your job?

As with many things, this would have been a superb topic for a philosophical discussion, something for which Ryan's Jesuit education had both prepared him and given him a taste. But the case at hand wasn't an abstract examination of principles and hypotheticals. He was supposed to have answers. What if a member of the Select Committee asked him a question that he *had* to answer? That could happen at any time. He could defer such a question only for as long as it took to drive from Langley to The Hill.

And if Ryan lied, he'd go to jail. That was the downside of his promotion.

For that matter, if he honestly said that he didn't know, he might not be believed, probably not by the committee members, maybe not by a jury. Even honesty might not be real protection. Wasn't that a fun thought?

Jack looked out the window as they passed the Mormon temple, just outside the beltway near Connecticut Avenue. A decidedly odd-looking building, it had grandeur with its marble columns and gilt spires. The beliefs represented by that impressive structure seemed curious to Ryan, a lifelong Catholic, but the people who held them were honest and hardworking, and fiercely loyal to their country, because they believed in what America stood for. And that was what it all came down to, wasn't it? Either you stand *for* something, or you don't, Ryan told himself. Any jackass could be against things, like a petulant child claiming to hate an untasted vegetable. You could tell what these people stood for. The Mormons tithed their income, which allowed their church to construct this monument to faith, just as medieval peasants had taken from their need to build the cathedrals of their age, for precisely the same purpose. The peasants were forgotten by all but the God in Whom they believed. The cathedrals—testimony to those beliefs—remained in their glory, still used for their intended purpose. Who remembered the political issues of that age? The nobles and their castles had crumbled away, the royal bloodlines had mostly ended, and all that age had left behind were memorials to faith, belief in something more important than man's corporeal existence, expressed in stonework crafted by the hands of men. What better proof could there be of what really mattered? Jack knew he wasn't the first to wonder at the fact, not by a very long shot indeed, but it wasn't often that anyone perceived Truth so clearly as Ryan did on this Monday morning. It made expediency seem a shallow, ephemeral, and ultimately useless commodity. He still had to figure out what he would do, and knew that his action would possibly be decided by others, but he knew what sort of guide, what sort of measure he would use to determine his action. That was enough for now, he told himself.

The car pulled through the gate fifteen minutes later, then around the front of the building and into the garage. Ryan tucked all of his material back into the case and took the elevator to the seventh floor. Nancy already had his coffee machine perking as he walked in. His people would arrive in five minutes to complete his morning brief. Ryan had a few more moments for thought.

What had been enough on the beltway faded in the confines of his office. Now he had to *do* something, and while his guide would be principle, his actions would be tactically drawn. And Jack didn't have a clue.

His department chiefs arrived on schedule and began their briefings. They found the acting DDI curiously withdrawn and quiet this morning. Normally he asked questions and had a humorous remark or two. This time he nodded and grunted, hardly saying anything. Maybe he'd had a tough weekend.

For others, Monday morning meant going to court, seeing lawyers, and facing juries. Since the defendant in a criminal trial had the right to put his best face before a jury, it was shower time for the residents of the Mobile jail.

As with all aspects of prison life, security was the foremost consideration. The cell doors were opened, and the prisoners, wearing towels and sandals, trooped toward the end of the corridor under the watchful eyes of three experienced guards. The morning banter among the prisoners was normal: grumbling, jokes, and the odd curse. On their own or during their exercise or eating periods, the prisoners tended to form racially polarized groups, but jail policy forbade such segregation in the blocks—the guards knew it merely guaranteed violence, but the judges who'd made the rules were guided by principle, not reality. Besides, if somebody got killed, it was the guards' fault, wasn't it? The guards were the most cynical of all law-enforcement people, shunned by street cops as mere custodians, hated by the inmates, and not terribly well regarded by the community. It was hard for them to care greatly about their jobs, and their foremost concern was personal survival. The danger involved in working here was very real. The death of an inmate was no small matter to be sure—a serious criminal investigation was conducted both by the guards and the police, or in some cases, federal officers—but the life of a criminal was a smaller concern than the life of a guard—to the guards themselves.

For all that, they did their best. They were mostly experienced men and they knew what to look for. The same was true of the inmates, of course, and what went on here was no different in principle from what happened on a battlefield or in the shadow wars between intelligence agencies. Tactics evolved as measures and countermeasures changed over time. Some prisoners were craftier than others. Some were goddamned geniuses. Others, especially the young, were frightened, meek people whose only objective was exactly the same as the guards': personal survival in a dangerous environment. Each class of prisoner required a slightly different form of scrutiny, and the demands on the guards were severe. It was inevitable that some mistakes would be made.

Towels were hung on numbered hooks. Each prisoner had his own personal bar of soap, and a guard watched them parade naked into the shower enclosure, which had twenty shower heads. He made sure that no weapons were visible. But he was a young guard, and he'd not yet learned that a really determined man always has one place in which he can hide something.

Henry and Harvey Patterson picked neighboring shower heads directly across from the pirates, who had foolishly selected places that could not be seen from the guard's position at the door. The brothers traded a happy look. The bastards might be king shit, but they weren't real swift in the head. Neither brother was particularly comfortable at the moment. The electrician's tape on the three-quarter-inch wood dowels was smooth, but had edges, and walking to the shower in a normal manner had required all their determination. It hurt. The hot water started all at once, and the enclosure started filling up with steam. The Patterson brothers applied their soap bars in the obvious place to facilitate getting their shanks, part of which were visible to a careful onlooker in any case, but they knew that the guard was new. Harvey nodded to a couple of people at the end of the enclosure. The act began with rather an uninspired bit of extemporaneous dialogue.

"Give me my fuckin' soap back, motherfucker!"

"Yo' *momma,*" the other replied casually. He'd thought about his line.

A blow was delivered, and returned.

"Knock it the fuck off—get the fuck out here!" the guard shouted. That's when two more people entered the fray, one knowing why, the other a young first-timer who only knew that he was scared and fighting back to protect himself. The chain reaction expanded almost at once to include the entire shower area. Outside, the guard backed off, calling for help.

Henry and Harvey turned, their shanks concealed in their hands. Ramón and Jesús were watching the fighting, looking the wrong way, fairly certain that they'd stay out of it; not knowing that it had been staged.

Harvey took Jesús, and Henry took Ramón.

Jesús never saw it coming, just a brown shape approaching him like a shadow and a punch in the chest, followed by another. He looked down to see blood spouting from a hole that went all the way into his heart—with each beat the holes tore further open—then a brown hand struck again, and a third red arc of blood joined the first two. He panicked, trying to hold his hand over the wounds to stop the bleeding, not knowing that most of the blood went into the pericardial sac, where it was already causing his death by congestive heart failure. He fell back against the wall and slid to the floor. Jesús died without knowing why.

Henry, who knew that he was the smart one, went for a faster kill. Ramón only made it easier, seeing the danger coming and turning away. Henry drove him against the tiled wall and smashed his shank into the side of the man's head, at the temple, where he knew the bone was eggshell-thin. Once in, he wiggled it left-right, up-down twice. Ramón wriggled like a caught fish for a few seconds, then went limp as a rag doll.

Each Patterson put his weapon in the hand of his brother's victim—they didn't have to worry about fingerprints in the shower—pushed the two bodies together, and stepped back to their own shower streams, where both washed down vigorously and cooperatively to remove any blood that might have splattered on them. By this time things had quieted down. The two men who'd disagreed over ownership of a bar of Dial had shaken hands, apologized to the guard, and were completing their morning ablutions. The steam continued to cloud the enclosure, and the Pattersons continued their thorough washdown. Cleanliness was especially next to godliness where evidence was concerned. After five minutes the water stopped and the men trooped out.

The guard did his count—if there is anything a jail guard knows how to do, it is count—and came up two short while the other eighteen started drying off and playing grab-ass in the way of prisoners in an all-male environment. He stuck his head into the shower, ready to shout something in high-school Spanish, but saw at the bottom of the steam cloud what looked like a body.

"Oh, fuck!" He turned and screamed for the other guards to return. "Nobody fucking move!" he screamed at the prisoners.

"What's the problem?" an anonymous voice asked.

"Hey, man, I gotta be in court in an hour," another pointed out.

The Patterson brothers dried themselves off, put their sandals back on, and stood quietly. Other conspirators might have exchanged a satisfied look—they had just committed a perfect double murder with a cop standing fifteen feet away—but the twins didn't need to. Each knew exactly what the other was thinking: Freedom. They'd just dodged one murder by doing two more. They knew that the cops would play ball. That lieutenant was a righteous cop, and righteous cops kept their word.

Word of the pirates' deaths spread with speed that would have done any news organization proud. The lieutenant was sitting at his desk filling out an incident report when it reached him. He nodded at the news and went back to the embarrassing task of explaining how his personal police radio car had been violated, and an expensive radio, his briefcase, and, worst of all, a shotgun removed. That last item required all kinds of paperwork.

"Maybe that's God's way of telling you to stay home and watch TV," another lieutenant observed.

"You agnostic bastard, you know I finally decided to—oh, shit!"

"Problem?"

"The Patterson Case. I had all the bullets in my briefcase, forgot to take them out. They're gone. Duane, the bullets are gone! The examiner's notes, the photos, everything!"

"The DA's gonna love you, boy. You just put the Patterson boys back on the street."

It was worth it, the police lieutenant didn't say.

At his office four blocks away, Stuart took the call and breathed a sigh of relief. He ought to have been ashamed, of course, and knew it, but this time he just couldn't bring himself to mourn for his clients. For the system that had failed them, yes, but not for their lives, which had manifestly benefited no one. Besides, he'd gotten his fee paid up-front, as any smart attorney did with druggies.

Fifteen minutes later, the U.S. Attorney had a statement out saying that he was outraged that federal prisoners had died in such a way, and that their deaths would be investigated by the appropriate federal authorities. He added that he'd hoped to arrange their deaths within the law, but death under law was a far different thing from death at the unknown hand of a murderer. All in all, it was an excellent statement which would make the noon and evening news broadcasts, which delighted Edward Davidoff even more than the deaths. Losing that case might have ended his chance for a Senate seat. Now people would say that justice had in fact been done, and they'd associate his statement and his face with it. It was almost as good as a conviction.

The Pattersons' lawyer was in the room, of course. They never spoke to a police officer without their attorney present—or so he thought, anyway.

"Hey," Harvey said. "Nobody fuck with me, I don't fuck with nobody. I heard a scuffle, like. That was it, man. You hear something like that in a place like this, smart move is you don't even look, y'know? You be better off not knowin'."

"It would appear that my clients have nothing to contribute to your investigation," the lawyer told the detectives. "Is it possible that the two men killed each other?"

"We don't know. We are just interviewing those who were present when it happened."

"I understand, then, that you do not contemplate charging my clients with anything having to do with this regrettable incident?"

"Not at this time, counselor," the senior detective said.

"Very well, I want that on the record. Also, for the record, my clients have no knowledge that is pertinent to your investigation. Finally, and this, too, is for the record, you will not question my clients except in my presence."

"Yes, sir."

"Thank you. Now, if you will excuse me, I would like to confer with my clients in private."

That conference lasted for about fifteen minutes, after which the attorney knew what had taken place. Which is to say that he didn't "know" in the metaphysical or legal sense, or in any way that had anything to do with legal ethics—but he knew. Under the Canons of Ethics, of course, he could not act on his speculation without betraying his oath as an officer of the court. And so he did what he could do. He filed a new discovery motion on his clients' murder case. By the end of the day he would have added proof of what he did not know.

"Good morning, Judge," Ryan said.

" 'Morning, Jack. This'll have to be fast. I'm going out of town in a few minutes."

"Sir, if somebody asks me what the hell's going on in Colombia, what do I tell 'em?"

"We have kept you out of this one, haven't we?" Moore said.

"Yes, sir, you have."

"I have orders to do that. You can guess where the orders come from. What I can tell you is, the Agency hasn't blown anybody up, okay? We do have an op running down there, but we haven't planted any car bombs."

"That's good to know, Judge. I really didn't think that we were in the car-bomb business," Ryan said as casually as he could. *Oh, shit! The Judge, too?* "So, if I get a call from The Hill, I tell them that, right?"

Moore smiled as he rose. "You're going to have to get used to dealing with them, Jack. It's not easy, and it's often not fun, but I think you'll find that they do business—better than Fowler and his people do, from what I heard this morning."

"It could have gone better, sir," Ryan admitted. "I understand the Admiral handled the last one. I suppose I ought to have spoken more with him before I flew out."

"We don't expect you to be perfect, Jack."

"Thank you, sir."

"And I have to catch a flight out to California."

"Safe trip, Judge," Ryan said as he walked out of the room. Jack entered his office and closed the door before he let his face slip out of neutral.

"Oh, my God," he breathed to himself. If it had been a simple, straight lie from Judge Moore, it would have been easier to take. But it hadn't been. The lie had been carefully crafted, and must have been planned, must have been rehearsed. *We haven't planted any car bombs.*

they were the nearest thing to invisible, well concealed in ground cover and sapling trees. Each man had his war paint on, and even from fifty feet away they would look like part of the environment. They had to keep still, since the human eye is very effective at detecting movement, but as long as they did, they were invisible. This was a very practical demonstration of why the Army trained people to be disciplined. Both sergeants wished they had their camouflage fatigues, but it was a little late to worry about that, and the khaki cloth was brown with rain and mud anyway. By unspoken agreement, each man watched a discrete sector so that they wouldn't have to turn their heads very much. They knew that they could speak if they did so in whispers, but they would do so only for really important information.

"I hear something behind us," Chavez said ten minutes later.

"Better look," Guerra answered.

Ding had to take his time, over thirty seconds to rotate his body and head.

"Uh-oh." There were several men putting bedrolls down on the ground. "Stayin' for the night."

It was clear what had happened. The people they'd been watching had continued their patrol routine and ended up straddling the observation post with their night camp. They could now see or hear over twenty men.

"This is gonna be a fun night," Guerra whispered.

"Yeah, and I gotta take a leak, too." It was a feeble attempt at a joke. Ding looked up at the sky. The rainfall was down to sprinkles now, but the clouds were just as thick. It would be dark a little early, maybe in two hours.

The enemy was spread out in three groups, which wasn't entirely stupid, but each group built fires for cooking, which was. They were also noisy, talking as though they were sitting down for a meal in some village *cantina*. That was good news for Chavez and Guerra. It allowed them to use their radio again.

"Six, this is Point, over."

"Six here."

"Six, uh . . ." Chavez hesitated. "The bad guys have set up their camp all around us. They don't know we're here."

"Tell me what you want to do."

"Nothin' right now. I think maybe we can walk on out when it gets dark. We'll let you know when."

"Roger. Out."

"Walk on out?" Guerra whispered.

"No sense gettin' him all worried, Paco."

"Hey, *'mano,* I'm fucking worried."

"Bein' worried don't help."

There were still no answers. Ryan left his office after what appeared to have been a normal day's work of catching up on correspondence and reports. Not much work had actually been accomplished, however. There were too many distractions that simply hadn't gone away.

He told his driver to head for Bethesda. He hadn't called ahead, but going there would not seem to be too much out of the ordinary. The security watch on the VIP suite was as strong as ever, but they all knew Ryan. The one by the door gave him a sorrowful shake of the head as he reached for the door. Ryan caught that signal clearly enough. He stopped and composed himself before going in. Greer didn't need to see shock on the faces of his visitors. But shock was what Jack felt.

He was barely a hundred pounds now, a scarecrow that had once been a man, a professional naval officer who'd commanded ships and led men in the service of their country. Fifty years of government service lay wasting away on the hospital bed. It was more than the death of a man. It was the death of an age, of a standard of behavior. Fifty years of experience and wisdom and judgment were slipping away. Jack took his seat next to the bed and waved the security officer out of the room.

"Hey, boss."

His eyes opened.

Now what do I say? How are you feeling? There's something to say to a dying man!

"How was the trip, Jack?" the voice was weak.

"Belgium was okay. Everybody sends regards. Friday I got to brief Fowler, like you did the last time."

"What do you think of him?"

"I think he needs some help on foreign policy."

A smile: "So do I. Gives a nice speech, though."

"I didn't exactly hit it off with one of his aides, Elliot, the gal from Bennington. Obnoxious as hell. If her man wins, she says, I retire." That was really the wrong thing to say. Greer tried to move but couldn't.

"Then you find her, and kiss and make up. If you have to kiss her ass at noon on the Bennington quad, you do that. When are you going to learn to bend that stiff Irish neck of yours? Ask Basil sometime how much he likes the people he has to work for. Your duty is to serve the *country,* Jack, not just the people you happen to like." A blow from a professional boxer could not have stung worse.

"Yes, sir. You're right. I still have a lot to learn."

"Learn fast, boy. I haven't got many lessons left."

"Don't say that, Admiral." The line was delivered like the plea of a child.

"It's my time, Jack. Some men I served with died off Savo Island fifty years ago, or at Leyte, or lots of other parts of ocean. I've been a lot luckier than they were, but it's my time. And it's your turn to take over for me. I want you to take my place, Jack."

"I do need some advice, Admiral."

"Colombia?"

"I could ask how you know, but I won't."

"When a man like Arthur Moore won't look you in the eye, you know that something is wrong. He was in here Saturday and he wouldn't look me in the eye."

"He lied to me today." Ryan explained on for five minutes, outlining what he knew, what he suspected, and what he feared.

"And you want to know what to do?" Greer asked.

"I could sure use a little guidance, Admiral."

"You don't need guidance, Jack. You're smart enough. You have all the contacts you need. And you know what's right."

"But what about—"

"Politics? All that shit?" Greer almost laughed. "Jack, you know, when you lay here like this, you know what you think about? You think about all the things you'd like another chance at, all the mistakes, all the people you might have treated better, and you thank God that it wasn't worse. Jack, you will never regret honesty, even if it hurts people. When they made you a Marine lieutenant you swore an oath before God. I understand why we do that now. It's a help, not a threat. It's something to remind you how important words are. Ideas are important. Principles are important. Words are important. Your word is the most important of all. Your word is who you are. That's the last lesson, Jack. You have to carry on from here.'' He paused, and Jack could see the pain coming through the heavy medications. ''You have a family, Jack. Go home to them. Give 'em my love and tell them that I think their daddy is a pretty good guy, and they ought to be proud of him. Good night, Jack.'' Greer drifted off to sleep.

Jack didn't get up for several minutes. It took that long for him to regain control of himself. He dried his eyes and walked out of the room. The doctor was on his way in. Jack stopped him and identified himself.

''Not much longer. Less than a week. I'm sorry, but there never was much hope.''

''Keep him comfortable,'' Ryan said quietly. Another plea.

''We are,'' the oncologist replied. ''That's why he's out most of the time. He's still quite lucid when he's awake. I've had some nice talks with him. I like him, too.'' The doctor was used to losing patients, but had never grown to enjoy it. ''In a few years, we might have saved him. Progress isn't fast enough.''

''Never is. Thanks for trying, doc. Thanks for caring.'' Ryan took the elevator back down to ground level and told the driver to take him home. On the way they passed the Mormon temple again, the marble lit with floodlights. Jack still didn't know exactly what he'd do, but now he was certain of what he had to accomplish. He'd made his silent promise to a dying man, and no promise could be more important than that.

The clouds were breaking up and there would be moonlight soon. It was time. The enemy had sentries out. They paced around the same as the ones who'd guarded the processing sites. The fires were still burning, but conversation had died off as weary men fell asleep.

''Just walk out together,'' Chavez said. ''They see us creep or crawl, they know we're bad guys. They see us walkin', we're some of them.''

''Makes sense,'' Guerra agreed.

Both men slung their weapons across their chests. The profile of each would be distinctively wrong to the enemy, but close up against their bodies the outlines would be obscured and the weapons could still be ready for immediate use. Ding could depend on his MP5 SD2 to kill quietly if the necessity arose. Guerra took out his machete. The metal blade was black-anodized, of course, and the only shiny part was the razor-sharp edge itself. Guerra was especially good with edged weapons, and was ever sharpening his steel. He was also ambidextrous, and held it loosely in his left hand while his right was on the pistol grip of his M-16.

The squad had already moved to a line roughly a hundred meters from the camp past which they'd be walking, ready to provide support if it were needed. It would be a tricky exercise at best, and everyone hoped that it wouldn't be necessary.

'' 'Kay, Ding, you lead off.'' Guerra actually ranked Chavez, but this was a situation where expertise counted for more than seniority.

Chavez headed down the hill, keeping to cover as long as he could, then angling left and north toward safety. His low-light goggles were in his rucksack, back at the squad's hideout because he was supposed to have been relieved before nightfall. Ding missed the night scope. A lot.

The two men moved as quietly as they could, and the soaked ground helped, but the cover got very thick along the path they took. It was only three or four hundred meters to safety, but this time it was too far.

They didn't use paths, of course, but they couldn't entirely avoid them, and one of the paths twisted around. Just as Chavez and Guerra crossed it, two men appeared a mere ten feet away.

"What are you doing out?" one asked. Chavez just waved in a friendly sort of way, hoping that the gesture would stop him, but he approached, trying to see who it was, his companion at his side. About the time he noticed that Ding was carrying the wrong sort of weapon it was too late for everyone.

Chavez had both hands back on his submachine gun, and swiveled it around on the double-looped sling, delivering a single round under the man's chin that exploded out the top of his head. Guerra turned and brought his machete around, and just like in the movies, the whole head came off. Both he and Chavez leaped to catch both victims before they made too much noise.

Shit! Ding thought. Now they'd know that somebody was here. There wasn't time to remove the bodies to a hiding place—they might bump into someone else. If that was true, he reasoned, better to get full value from the kills. He found the loose head and set it on the chest of Guerra's victim, held in both lifeless hands. The message was a clear one: *Don't fuck with us!*

Guerra nodded approval and Ding led off again. It took ten more minutes before they heard a spitting sound just to the right.

"I been watchin' ya' half of forever," *Oso* said.

"You okay?" Ramirez whispered.

"Met two guys. They're dead," Guerra said.

"Let's get moving before they find 'em."

That was not to be. A moment later they heard the thud of a falling body, followed by a shout, followed by a scream, followed by a wild burst of AK-47 fire. It went in the wrong direction, but it sufficed to awaken any sleeping soul within a couple of klicks. The squad members activated their low-light gear, the better to pick their way through the cover as quickly as possible while the camp behind them exploded with noise and shouts and curses aimed in all directions. They didn't stop for two hours. It was as official as orders off their satellite net: they were now the hunted.

It had happened with unaccustomed rapidity, one hundred miles from the Cape Verde Islands. The satellite cameras had been watching for some days now, scanning the storm on several different light frequencies. The photos were downlinked to anyone with the right equipment, and already ships were altering course to get clear of it. Very hot, dry air had spilled off the West African desert in what was already a near-record summer and, driven by the easterly trade winds, combined with moist ocean air to form towering thunderheads, hundreds of them that had begun to merge. The clouds reached down into the warm surface water, drawing additional heat upward into the air to add that energy to what the clouds already contained. When some critical mass of heat and rain and cloud was reached, the storm began to organize itself. The people at the National Hurricane Center still didn't understand why it happened—or why, given the circumstances, it happened so seldom—but it was happening now. The chief scientist manipulated his computer controls to fast-forward the satellite photos, rewind, and fast-forward again. He could see it clearly. The clouds had begun their counterclockwise orbit around a single point in space. It was becoming an organized storm, using its circular motion to increase its own coherence and power as though it knew that such activity would give it life. It wasn't the earliest that such a storm had begun, but conditions were unusually "good" this year for their formation. How lovely they appeared on the satellite photographs, like some kind of modern art, feathery pinwheels of gossamer cloud. *Or,* the chief scientist thought, *that's how they would look if they didn't kill so many people.* When you got down to it, the reason they gave the storms names was that it was unseemly for hundreds or thousands of human lives to be ended by a number. This one would be such a storm, the meteorologist thought. For the moment they'd call it a tropical depression, but if it kept growing in size and power, it would change to a tropical storm. At that point they'd start calling it *Adele.*

About the only thing that the movies got right, Clark thought, was that they often had spies meeting in bars. Bars were useful things in civilized countries. They were places for men to go and have a few, and meet other men, and strike up casual conversations in dimly lit, anonymous rooms, usually with the din of bad music to mute out their words beyond a certain, small radius. Larson arrived a minute late, sliding up to Clark's spot. This *cantina* didn't have stools, just a real brass bar on which to rest one's foot. Larson ordered a beer, a local one, which was something the Colombians were good at. They were good at a lot of things, Clark thought. Except for the drug problem this country could really be going places. This country was suffering—as much as? No, more than his own. Colombia's government was having to face the fact that it had fought a war against the druggies and was losing . . . unlike America? the CIA officer wondered. Unlike America, the Colombian government was threatened? Yeah, sure, he told himself, we're *so* much better off than this place.

"Well?" he asked when the owner moved to the other end of the bar.

Larson spoke quietly, in Spanish. "It's definite. The number of troops the big shots have out on the street has dropped way the hell off."

"Gone where?"

"A guy told me southwest. They were talking about a hunting expedition in the hills."

"Oh, Christ," Clark muttered in English.

"What gives?"

"Well, there's about forty light-infantry soldiers . . ." He explained on for several minutes.

"We've *invaded?"* Larson looked down at the bar. "Jesus Christ, what lunatic came up with that idea?"

"We both work for him—for them, I suppose."

"Goddammit, there is one thing we cannot do to these people, and that's *fucking* it!"

"Fine. You fly back to D.C. and tell the DDO. If Ritter still has a brain, he'll pull them out quick, before anybody really gets hurt." Clark turned. He was thinking very hard at the moment, and didn't like some of the ideas he was getting. He remembered a mission in "Eye" Corps, when . . . "How about you and me take a look down that way tomorrow?"

"You really want me to blow my cover, don't you?" Larson observed.

"You got a bolt-hole?" Clark meant what every field officer sets up when he goes covert, a safe place to run to and hide in if it becomes necessary.

Larson snorted. "Is the Pope Polish?"

"What about your lady friend?"

"We don't take care of her, too, and I'm history with this outfit." The Agency encouraged loyalty to one's agents, even when one didn't sleep with them, and Larson was a man with the normal affection for his year-long lovers.

"We'll try to cover it like a prospecting trip, but after this one, on my authorization, your cover is officially blown, and you will return to D.C. for reassignment. Her, too. That's an official order."

"I didn't know you had—"

Clark smiled. "Officially I don't, but you'll soon discover that Mr. Ritter and I have an understanding. I do the field work and he doesn't second-guess me."

"Nobody has that much juice." All Larson got for a reply was a raised eyebrow and a look into eyes that appeared far more dangerous than he had ever appreciated.

Cortez sat in the one decent room in the house. It was the kitchen, a large one by local standards, and he had a table on which to set his radios and his maps, and a ledger sheet on which he kept a running tally. So far he had lost eleven men in short, violent, and for the most part noiseless encounters—and gotten nothing in return. The "soldiers" he had in the field were still too angry to be afraid, but that wholly suited his purpose. There was a clear acetate cover on the main tactical map, and he used a red grease pencil to mark areas of activity. He had made contact with two—maybe three—of the American teams. He determined contact, of course, by the fact that he had lost eleven men. He chose to believe that he'd lost eleven stupid ones. That was a relative measure, of course, since luck was always a factor on the battlefield, but by and large history taught that the dumb ones die off first, that there was a Darwinian selection process on the field of combat. He planned to lose another fifty or so men before doing anything different. At that point he'd call for reinforcements, further stripping the lords of their retainers. Then he would call his boss and say that he'd identified two or three fellow lords whose men were behaving rather oddly in the field—he already knew whom he would accuse, of course—and the next day he would warn one of those—also preselected—that his own boss was behaving rather oddly, and that his—Cortez's—loyalty was to the organization as a whole which paid him, not to single personalities. His plan was for Escobedo to be killed off. It was necessary, and not especially regrettable. The Americans had already killed off two of the really smart members, and he would help to eliminate the remaining two intellects. The surviving lords would need Cortez, and would know that they needed him. His position as chief of security and intelligence would be upgraded to a seat around the table while the rest of the Cartel was restructured in accordance with his ideas for a streamlined and more secure organization. Within a year he'd be first among equals; another year and he'd merely be first. He wouldn't even have to kill the rest off. Escobedo was one of the smart ones, and he'd proven so easy to manipulate. The rest would be as children, more interested in their money and their expensive toys than with what the organization could really accomplish. His ideas in that area were vague. Cortez was not one to think ten steps ahead. Four or five were enough.

He reexamined the maps. Soon the Americans would become alert to the danger of his operation and would react. He opened his briefcase and compared aerial photographs with the maps. He now knew that the Americans had been brought in and were supported probably by a single helicopter. That was so daring as to be foolish. Hadn't the Americans learned about helicopters on the plains of Iran? He had to identify likely landing zones . . . or did he?

Cortez closed his eyes and commanded himself to return to first principles. That was the real danger in operations like this. One got so caught up in what was going on that one lost sight of the overall situation. Perhaps there was another way. The Americans had already helped him. Perhaps they might help him again. How might he bring that about? What could he do to and for them? What might they do for him? It gave him something to ponder for the rest of the sleepless night.

Bad weather had prevented them from testing out the new engine the previous night, and for the same reason they had to wait until 0300 local time to try this night. The Pave Low was not allowed to show itself by day under any circumstances, without a direct order from on high.

A cart pulled the chopper out of the hangar, and the rotor was unfolded and locked into place before the engines were started. PJ and Captain Willis applied power, with Sergeant Zimmer at his engineer's console. They taxied normally to the runway and started their takeoff in the way of helicopters, with an uneven lurch as the reluctant tons of metal and fuel climbed into the air like a child on his first ladder.

It was hard to say what happened first. A terrible screech reached the pilot's ears, coming through the protective foam of his Darth Vader helmet. At the same time, perhaps a millisecond earlier, Zimmer shouted a warning too loudly over the intercom circuit. Whatever happened first, Colonel Johns' eyes flicked down to his instrument panel and saw that his Number One engine dials were all wrong. Willis and Zimmer both killed the engine while PJ slewed the chopper around, thankful that he was only fifty feet off the pavement. In less than three seconds, he was back on the ground, powering his single working engine down to idle.

''Well?''

''The new engine, sir. It just came apart on us—looks like a total compressor failure. Sounds worse. I'm going to have to give it a look to see if it damaged anything else,'' Zimmer reported.

''Did you have any problem putting it in?''

''Negative. It went just like the book says, sir. That's the second time with this lot of engines, sir. The contractor's fucking up somewhere with those new composite turbine blades. That's going to down-check the whole engine run until we identify the problem, ground every bird that's using them, us, the Navy, Army, everybody.'' The new engine design used turbine-compressor blades made from ceramic instead of steel. It was lighter—you could carry a little more gas—and cheaper—you could buy a few more engines—than the old way, and contractor tests had shown the new version to be just as reliable—until they had reached line service, that is. The first failure had been blamed on an ingested bird, but two Navy choppers using this engine had gone down at sea without a trace. Zimmer was right. Every aircraft with this engine installed would be grounded until the problem was understood and fixed.

''Oh, that's just great, Buck,'' Johns said. ''The other spare we brought down?''

''Take a guess, sir,'' Zimmer suggested. ''I can have 'em send us an old rebuilt one down.''

''Tell me what you think.''

''I think we go for a rebuilt, or maybe yank one from another bird back at Hurlburt.''

''Get on the horn as soon as I cool her down,'' the colonel ordered. ''I want *two* good engines down here ASAP.''

''Yes, sir.'' The crewmen shared looks on the other issue. What about the people they were supposed to support?

His name was Esteves, and he, too, was a staff sergeant, Eleven-Bravo, U.S. Army. Before all this had started, he'd also been part of the recon unit of the 5th

Battalion, 14th Infantry Regiment, First Brigade of the 25th "Tropical Lightning" Infantry Division (Light), based at Schofield Barracks, Hawaii. Young, tough, and proud like every other SHOWBOAT soldier, he was also tired and frustrated. And at the moment, sick. Something he'd eaten, or maybe drunk. When the time came, he'd check in with the squad medic and get some pills to handle it, but right now his bowels rumbled and his arms felt weaker than he would have liked. They'd been in the field exactly twenty-seven minutes less than Team KNIFE, but they hadn't made any contact at all since trashing that little airfield. They'd found six processing sites, four of them very recently used, but all of them devoid of people. Esteves wanted to get on the scoreboard, as he was sure the other squads were doing. Like Chavez he'd grown up in a gang area, and unlike him had been deeply involved with one until fate had shaken him loose long enough to join the Army. Also unlike Chavez, he'd once used drugs, until his sister had OD'd on a needle of overrich heroin. He'd been there, seen her life just stop as though someone had pulled the plug from a wall socket. He'd found that dealer the next night, and joined the Army to escape the murder rap, not ever thinking that he'd become a professional soldier, never dreaming that there were opportunities in life beyond car washes and family-assistance checks. He'd leapt at this chance to get even with the scum who had killed his sister and enslaved his people. But he hadn't yet killed one, hadn't yet gotten on the scoreboard. Fatigue and frustration were a deadly combination in the face of the enemy.

Finally, he thought. He saw the glow of the fire from half a klick away. He did what he was supposed to do, calling his sighting in to his captain, waiting for the squad to form up in two teams, then moving in to take out the ten or so men who were doing their idiot dance in acid. Tired and eager though he was, discipline was still the central fact of his life. He led his section of two other men to a good fire-support position while the captain took charge of the assault element. The very moment he was certain that tonight would be different, it became so.

There was no bathtub, no backpacks full of leaves, but there were fifteen men with weapons. He tapped the danger signal on his radio but got no reply. Though he didn't know it, a branch had broken the antenna off his radio ten minutes earlier. He stood, trying to decide what to do, looking around for some sign, some clue, while the two soldiers at his side wondered what the hell was the matter. Then his stomach cramped up on him again. Esteves doubled over, tripped on a root, and dropped his weapon. It didn't go off, but the buttstock hit the ground hard enough that the bolt jerked back and forth one time with a metallic *clack.* That was when he discovered that twenty feet away was another man whose presence he hadn't yet detected.

This man was awake, massaging his aching calves so that he could get some sleep. He was startled by the noise. A man who liked to hunt, his first reaction was disbelief. How could anyone be out there? He'd made sure that none of his fellows had gone beyond his lookout position, but that sound was man-made and could have come only from a weapon of some sort. His team had already been warned of some brushes with—whoever the hell they were, they had killed the people who were supposed to kill them, which surprised and worried this one. The sudden noise had startled him at first, but that emotion was immediately followed by fright. He moved his rifle to his left and fired off a whole magazine. Four rounds hit Esteves, who died slowly enough to scream a curse at destiny. His two teammates hosed down the area from which the fire had come, killing the man loudly and messily, but by that time the others around the fire were up and running, and the assault element wasn't yet in place. The captain's reaction to the noise was the logical one. His support team had been ambushed, and he had to get in to the objective to take the heat off of them. The fire-support element shifted fire to the encampment, and soon learned that there were other men about. Most of them ran away from the fire and blundered into the assault element, which was racing in the opposite direction.

Had there been a proper after-action report, the first comment would have been that control was lost on both sides. The captain leading the squad had reacted precipitously, and, leading from the front instead of laying back to think about it, he was one of the first men killed. The rest of the squad was now leaderless but didn't know it. The prowess of the individual soldiers was undiminished, of course, but soldiers are first, last, always, members of teams, each a living, thinking organism whose total strength is far greater than the sum of its parts. Without leadership to direct them, they fell back on training, but that was confused by the sound and the dark. Both groups of men were now intermixed, and the Colombians' lack of training and leadership was less important now as the battle was fought by individuals on one side, and by mutually supporting pairs on the other. It lasted under five confused and bloody minutes. The pairs "won." They killed with abandon and efficiency, then crawled away, eventually rising to race to their rally point while those enemies left alive continued to shoot, mostly at each other. Only five made it to the rally point, three from the assault element and Esteves' two from the support element. Half of the squad was dead, including the captain, the medic, and the radioman. The soldiers still didn't know what they'd run into—through a communications foul-up they hadn't been warned of the Cartel's operations against them. What they did know was bad enough. They headed back to their base camp, collected their packs, and moved out.

The Colombians knew less and more. They knew that they had killed five Americans—they hadn't found Esteves yet—and that they had lost twenty-six, some of them probably to their own fire. They didn't know if any had gotten away, didn't know the strength of the unit that had attacked them, didn't even know that they had in fact been attacked by Americans at all—the weapons they recovered were mainly American, but the M-16 was popular throughout South America. They, like the men they'd chased away, knew that something terrible had happened. Mainly they grouped together and sat down and threw up and experienced postcombat shock, having learned for the first time that the mere possession of an automatic weapon didn't make one into a god. Shock was gradually replaced by rage as they collected their dead.

Team BANNER—what was left of it—didn't have that luxury. They didn't have time to think about who had won and who had lost. Each of them had learned a shocking lesson about combat. Someone with a better education might have pointed out that the world was not deterministic, but each of the five men from BANNER consoled himself with the bleakest of soldierly observations: Shit happens.

24. Ground Rules

Clark and Larson started off well before dawn, heading south again in their borrowed Subaru four-wheel-drive wagon. In the front was a briefcase. In the back were a few boxes of rocks, under which were two Beretta automatics whose muzzles were threaded for silencers. It was a pity to abuse the guns by placing all those rocks in the same box, but neither man figured to take the weapons home after the job was completed, and both fervently hoped that they wouldn't be needed in any way.

"What exactly are we looking for?" Larson asked after an hour or so of silence.

"I was kind of hoping that you'd know. Something unusual."

"Seeing people walk around with guns down here isn't terribly unusual, in case you haven't noticed."

"Organized activity?"

"That, too, but it does give us something to think about. We won't be seeing much military activity," Larson said.

"Why?"

"Guerrillas raided a small army post again last night—heard it on the radio this morning. Either M-19 or FARC is getting frisky."

"Cortez," Clark said at once.

"Yeah, that makes sense. Pull all the official heat in a different direction."

"I'm going to have to meet that boy," Mr. Clark told the passing scenery.

"And?" Larson asked.

"And what do you think? The bastard was part of a plot to kill one of our ambassadors, the Director of the FBI, and the Administrator of DEA, plus a driver and assorted bodyguards. He's a terrorist."

"Take him back?"

"Do I look like a cop?" Clark responded.

"Look, man, we don't—"

"I do. By the way, have you forgotten those two bombs? I believe you were there."

"That was—"

"Different?" Clark chuckled. "That's what they always say, 'But that's different.' Larson, I didn't go to Dartmouth like you did, and maybe the difference is lost on me."

"This isn't the fucking movies!" Larson said angrily.

"Carlos, if this was the movies, you'd be a blond with big tits and a loose blouse. You know, I've been in this business since you were driving cars made by Matchbox, and I've never got laid on the job. Never. Not once. Hardly seems fair." He might have added that he was married and took it seriously, but why confuse the lad? He had accomplished what he'd intended. Larson smiled. The tension was broken.

"I guess maybe I got you there, Mr. Clark."

"Where is she?"

"Gone till the end of the week—European run. I left a message in three places—

I mean, *the* message for her to bug out. Soon as she gets back, she hops the next bird for Miami.''

''Good. This one is complicated enough. When it's all over, marry the girl, settle down, raise a family.''

''I've thought about that. What about—I mean, is it fair to—''

''The job you're in is less dangerous statistically than running a liquor store in a big city. They all raise families. What holds you together on a big job in a faraway place is the knowledge that there is somebody to come back to. You can trust me on that one, son.''

''But for the moment we're in the area you want to look at. Now what do we do?''

''Start prowling the side roads. Don't go too fast.'' Clark cranked down his window and started smelling the air. Next he opened his briefcase and pulled out a topographical map. He grew quiet for several minutes, getting his brain in synch with the situation. There were soldiers up there, trained men in Indian country, being hunted and trying to evade contact. He had to get himself in the proper frame of mind, alternately looking at the terrain and the map. ''God, I'd kill for the right kind of radio right now.'' *Your fault, Johnny,* Clark told himself. *You should have demanded it. You should have told Ritter that there had to be someone on the ground to liaise with the soldiers instead of trying to run it through a satellite link like it was a goddamned staff study.*

''Just to talk to them?''

''Look, kid, how much security you seen so far?''

''Why, none.''

''Right. With a radio I could call them down out of the hills and we could pick them up, clean them up, and drive 'em to the fucking airport for the flight home,'' Clark said, the frustration manifest in his voice.

''That's craz—Jesus, you're right. This situation really is crazy.'' The realization dawned on Larson, and he was amazed that he'd misinterpreted the situation so completely.

''Make a note—this is what happens when you run an op out of D.C. instead of running it from the field. Remember that. You might be a supervisor someday. Ritter thinks like a spymaster instead of a line-animal like me, and he's been out of the field too long. That's the biggest problem at Langley: the guys who run the show have forgotten what it's like out here, and the rules have changed a lot since they serviced all their dead-drops in Budapest. Moreover, this is a very different situation from what they think it is. This isn't intelligence-gathering. It's low-intensity warfare. You gotta know when not to be covert, too. This sort of thing is a whole new ball game.''

''They didn't cover this sort of thing at The Farm.''

''That's no surprise. Most of the instructors there are a bunch of old—'' Clark stopped. ''Slow down some.''

''What is it?''

''Stop the car.''

Larson did as he was told, pulling off the gravel surface. Clark jumped out with his briefcase, which seemed very strange indeed, and took the ignition keys as he did so. His next move was open the back, then to toss the keys back to Larson. Clark dug into one of the boxes, past the samples of gold-bearing rock, and came out with his Beretta and silencer. He was wearing a bush jacket, and the gun disappeared nicely in the small of his back, silencer and all. Then he waved to

Larson to stay put and follow him slowly in the car. Clark started walking with his map and a photograph in his hands. There was a bend in the road; just around it was a truck. Near the truck were some armed men. He was looking at his map when they shouted, and his head came up in obvious surprise. A man jerked his AK in a way that required no words: *Come here at once or be shot.*

Larson was overcome with the urge to wet his pants, but Clark waved for him to follow and walked confidently to the truck. Its loadbed was covered with a tarp, but Clark already knew what was under it. He'd smelled it. That was why he'd stopped around the bend.

"Good day," he said to the nearest one with a rifle.

"You have picked a bad day to be on the road, my friend."

"He told me you would be out here. I have permission," Clark replied.

"What? Permission? Whose permission?"

"Señor Escobedo, of course," Larson heard him say.

Jesus, this isn't happening, please tell me this isn't happening!

"Who are you?" the man said with a mixture of anger and wariness.

"I am a prospector. I am looking for gold. Here," Clark said, turning his photo around. "This area I have marked, I think there is gold here. Of course I would not come here without permission of Señor Escobedo, and he told me to tell those I met that I am here under his protection."

"Gold—you look for gold?" another man said as he came up. The first one deferred to him, and Clark figured he was talking to the boss now.

"*Sí*. Come, I will show you." Clark led them to the back of the Subaru and pulled two rocks from the cardboard box. "My driver there is Señor Larson. He introduced me to Señor Escobedo. If you know Señor Escobedo—you must know him, no?"

The man clearly didn't know what to do or think. Clark was speaking in good Spanish, with a trace of accent, and talking as normally as though he were asking directions from a policeman.

"Here, you see this?" Clark said, pointing to the rock. "That is gold. This may be the biggest find since Pizarro. I think Señor Escobedo and his friends will buy all of this land."

"They did not tell me of this," the man temporized.

"Of course. It is a secret. And I must warn you, señor, not to speak of it to anyone or you will surely speak to Señor Escobedo!"

Bladder control was a major problem for Larson now.

"When are we leaving?" someone called from the truck.

Clark looked around while the two gunmen tried to decide what to do. A driver and perhaps one other in the truck. He didn't hear or see anyone else. He started walking toward it. Two more steps and he saw what he'd needed and feared to see. Sticking out from under the edge of the tarp was the front sight assembly of an M-16A2 rifle. What he had to do was decided in less than a second. Even to Clark it was amazing how the old habits kept coming back.

"Stop!" the leader said.

"Can I load my samples on your truck?" Clark asked without turning. "To take to Señor Escobedo? He will be very pleased to see what I have found, I promise you," Clark added.

The two men ran to catch up with him, their rifles dangling from their hands as they did so. They'd gotten within ten feet when he turned. As he did so, his right hand remained fixed in space, and took the Beretta from his waistband while his left hand fluttered the map and photo. Neither one saw it coming, Larson realized. He was so smooth. . . .

"Not this truck, señor, I—"

It was just one more thing to surprise him, but it would be the last. Clark's hand came up and fired into the man's forehead at a range of five feet. Before the leader had even started to fall, the second was also dead from the same cause. Without pause he moved around the right side of the truck. He hopped up on the running board and saw that there was just a driver. He, too, took a silenced round in the head. By this time Larson was out of the car. Approaching Clark from the rear, he came close to getting a round for his trouble.

"Don't do that!" Clark said as he safed his pistol.

"Christ, I just—"

"You announce your presence in a situation like this. You almost died 'cause you didn't. Remember that. Come on." Clark hopped onto the back of the truck and pulled back the tarp.

Most of the dead were locals, judging by their clothes, but there were two faces that Clark vaguely recognized. It took a moment for him to remember. . . .

"Captain Rojas. Sorry, kid," he said quietly to the body.

"Who?"

"He had command of Team BANNER. One of ours. These fuckers killed some of our people." His voice seemed quite tired.

"Looks like our guys did all right, too—"

"Let me explain something to you about combat, kid. There are two kinds of people in the field: your people and other people. The second category can include noncombatants, and you try to avoid hurting them if you have the time, but the only ones who really matter are your own people. You got a handkerchief?"

"Two."

"Give 'em to me, then load those two in the truck."

Clark pulled the cap of the gas tank that hung under the cab. He tied the handkerchiefs together and fed them in. The tank was full and the cloth was immediately saturated with gasoline.

"Come on, back to the car." Clark disassembled his pistol and put it back in the rock box, then closed the back hatch and got back into the front seat. He punched the cigarette lighter. "Pull up close."

Larson did so, getting there about the time the lighter popped out. Clark took it out and touched it to the soaked handkerchiefs. They ignited at once. Larson didn't have to be told to take off. They were around the next bend before the fire started in earnest.

"Back to the city, fast as you can," Clark ordered next. "What's the fastest way to get to Panama?"

"I can have you there in a couple of hours, but it means—"

"Do you have the radio codes to get onto an Air Force base?"

"Yes, but—"

"You are now out of country. Your cover is completely blown," Mr. Clark said. "Get a message to your girl before she gets back. Have her desert, or jump ship, or whatever you call it with an airline so that she doesn't have to come back here. She's blown, too. Both your lives are in danger—no-shit danger. There might have been somebody watching us. Somebody might have noticed that you drove me down here. Somebody might have noticed that you borrowed this car twice. Probably not, but you don't get old in this business by taking unnecessary chances. You have nothing more to contribute to this operation, so get your asses clear."

"Yes, sir." They reached the highway before Larson spoke again. "What you did . . ."

"What about it?"

"You were right. We can't let people do that and—"

"You're wrong. You don't know why I did that, do you?" Clark asked. He spoke like a man teaching a class, but gave only one of the reasons. "You're thinking like a spy, and this is no longer an intelligence operation. We have people, soldiers, running and hiding up in those hills. What I did was to create a *diversion*. If they think our guys came down to avenge their dead, it may pull some of the bad guys down off the mountain, get them to look in the wrong place, take some of the heat off our guys. Not much, but it's the best I could do." He paused for a moment. "I won't say it didn't feel good. I don't like seeing our people killed, and I fucking well don't like not being allowed to do anything about it. That's been happening for too many years—Middle East, everywhere—we lose people and don't do a goddamned thing about it. This time I just had an excuse. It's been a long time. And you know something—it *did* feel good," Clark admitted coldly. "Now shut up and drive. I have some thinking to do."

Ryan was in his office, still quiet, still thinking. Judge Moore was finding all sorts of excuses to be away. Ritter was spending a lot of time out of the office. Jack couldn't ask questions and demand answers if they weren't here. That also made Ryan the senior executive present, and gave him all sorts of extraneous paper to shuffle and telephone calls to return. Maybe he could make that work for him. Of one thing he was certain. He had to find out what the hell was happening. It was also plain that Moore and Ritter had made two mistakes of their own. First, they thought that Ryan didn't know anything. They ought to have known better. He'd only gotten this far in the Agency because he was good at figuring things out. Their second mistake was in their likely assumption that his inexperience would prevent him from pressing too hard even if he did start figuring things out. Fundamentally they were both thinking like bureaucrats. People who spent their lives in bureaucracies were typically afraid of breaking rules. That was a sure way to get fired, and it cowed people to think of tossing their careers away. But that was an issue Jack had decided on long before. He didn't know what his profession was. He'd been a Marine, a stockbroker, an assistant professor of history, and then joined CIA. He could always go back to teaching. The University of Virginia had already talked to Cathy about becoming a full professor at their medical school, and even Jeff Pelt wanted Ryan to come and liven up the history department as a visiting lecturer. It would be nice to teach again, Jack thought. It would certainly be easier than what he was doing here. Whatever he saw in his future, he didn't feel trapped by his job. And James Greer had given him all the guidance he needed: *Do what you think is right*.

"Nancy." Jack keyed his intercom. "When is Mr. Ritter going to be back?"

"Tomorrow morning. He had to meet with somebody down at The Farm."

"Okay, thanks. Could you call my wife and leave a message that I'm going to be pretty late tonight?"

"Surely, Doctor."

"Thanks. I need the file on INF verification, the OSWR preliminary report."

"Dr. Molina is out at Sunnyvale with the Judge," Nancy said. Tom Molina was the head of the Office of Strategic Weapons Research, which was back-checking two other departments on the Intermediate Nuclear Forces Treaty verification procedures.

"I know. I just want to look the report over so I can discuss it with him when he gets back."

"Take about fifteen minutes to get it."

"No rush," Jack replied and killed the intercom. That document could tie up King Solomon himself for three days, and it gave him a wholly plausible excuse for staying late. Congress had gotten antsy about some technical issues as both sides worked to destroy the last of their launchers. Ryan and Molina would have to testify there in the next week. Jack pulled the writing panel out from the side of his desk, knowing what he'd do after Nancy and the other clerical people left.

Cortez was a very sophisticated political observer. That was one reason he'd made colonel so young in an organization as bureaucratized as the DGI. Based on the Soviet KGB model, it had already grown a collection of clerks and inspectors and security officers to make the American CIA look like a mom-and-pop operation—which made the relative efficiencies of the agencies all the more surprising. For all their advantages, the Americans lacked political will, always fighting over issues that ought to have been quite clear. At the KGB Academy, one instructor had compared them to the Polish parliament of old, a collection of over five hundred barons, *all* of whom had had to agree before anything happened—and because of which nothing ever happened, allowing Poland to be raped by anyone with the ability to make a simple decision.

The Americans had acted in this case, however, acted decisively and well. What had changed?

What had changed—what had to have changed in this case—was that the Americans were breaking their own laws. They had responded emotionally . . . no, that wasn't fair, Félix told himself. They had responded forcefully to a direct and arrogant challenge, just as the Soviets would have reacted, though with minor tactical differences. The emotional aspect to the reaction was that they had done the proper thing only by violating their incredible intelligence-oversight laws. And it was an election year in America. . . .

"Ah," Cortez said aloud. It really was that simple, wasn't it? The Americans, who had already helped him, would do so again. He just had to identify the proper target. That took only ten minutes more. So fitting, he thought, that his military rank had been that of colonel. For a century of Latin American history, it was always the colonels who did this sort of thing.

What would Fidel say? Cortez nearly laughed out loud at the thought. For as long as that bearded ideologue had breathed, he'd hated the *norteamericanos* as an evangelist hated sin, enjoyed every small sting he'd been able to inflict on them, dumped his criminals and lunatics on the unsuspecting Carter—*Anyone could have taken advantage of that fool,* Cortez thought with amusement—played every possible gambit of guerrilla diplomacy against them. He really would have enjoyed this one. Now Félix just had to figure a way to pass the message along. It was a high-risk play on his part, but he'd won every toss to this point, and the dice were hot in his hand.

Perhaps it had been a mistake, Chavez reflected. Perhaps leaving the head on the man's chest had merely enraged them. Whatever the cause, the Colombians were prowling the woods with gusto now. They hadn't caught Team KNIFE's trail, and the soldiers were working very hard not to leave one, but one thing was clear to him: there would be a knock-down, drag-out firefight, and it wouldn't be long in coming.

But that wasn't clear to Captain Ramirez. His orders were still to evade and avoid, and he was following them. Most of the men didn't question that, but Chavez did—or more precisely, wanted to. But sergeants don't question captains, at least not very often, and then only if you were a first sergeant and had the opportunity to take the man aside. If there was going to be a fight, and it sure as hell looked that way, why not set it up on favorable terms? Ten good men, armed with automatic weapons and grenades, plus two SAWs, made for one hell of an ambush. Give them a trail to follow, lead them right into the killzone. They were still carrying a couple of claymores. With luck, they'd drop ten or fifteen men in the first three seconds. Then the other side—those few who ran away fast enough—wouldn't be pissed. They'd be pissing in their pants. Nobody would be crazy about hot pursuit then. Why didn't Ramirez see that? Instead he was keeping everyone on the move, wearing them out, not looking for a good place to rest up, prepare a major ambush, duke it out, and *then* take off again. There was a time for caution. There was a time to fight. What that most favored word in any military lexicon, "initiative," meant was who did the deciding on which time was which. Chavez knew it on instinct. Ramirez, he suspected, was thinking too much. About what, Chavez didn't know, but the captain's thinking was starting to worry the sergeant.

Larson returned the car and drove Clark to the airport in his own BMW. He'd miss the car, he realized, as they walked to his aircraft. Clark was carrying all of his classified or sensitive equipment out with him, and nothing else. He hadn't stopped to pack, not even his razor, though his Beretta 92-F, with silencer, was again tucked into the small of his back. He walked coolly and normally, but Larson now knew what tension looked like in Mr. Clark. He appeared even more relaxed than usual, even more offhand, even more absentminded, all the more to appear harmless to the people around him. This, Larson told himself, was one very dangerous cat. The pilot played back the shooting at the truck, the way he'd put the two gunmen at ease, confused them, asked for their help. He'd never known that the Agency had people like this, not after the Church Committee hearings.

Clark climbed up into the aircraft, tossing his gear in the back, and managed to look a little impatient as Larson ran through his preflight procedures. He didn't return to normal until the wheels were retracted.

"How long to Panama?"

"Two hours."

"Take us out over the water as soon as you can."

"You're nervous?"

"Now—only about your flying," Clark said over his headset. He looked over and smiled. "What I'm worried about is thirty or so kids who may just be hung out to dry."

Forty minutes later they left Colombian airspace. Once over the Bay of Panama, Clark reached back for his gear, then forced open the door and dumped it into the sea.

"You mind if I ask . . .?"

"Let's assume for the moment that this whole operation is coming apart. Just how much evidence do you want to be carrying into the Senate hearing room?'' Clark paused. ''Not much danger of that, of course, but what if people see us carrying stuff and wonder what it is and why we're carrying it?''

''Oh. Okay.''

''Keep thinking, Larson. Henry Kissinger said it: Even paranoids have enemies. If they're willing to hang those soldiers out, what about us?''

''But . . . Mr. Ritter—''

''I've known Bob Ritter for quite a while. I have a few questions for him. I want to see if he has good enough answers. It's for goddamned sure he didn't keep us informed of things we needed to know. Maybe that's just another example of D.C. perspective. Then again, maybe it's not.''

''You don't really think—''

''I don't know what to think. Call in,'' Clark ordered. There was no sense getting Larson thinking about it. He hadn't been in the Agency long enough to understand the issues.

The pilot nodded and did what he was told. He switched his radio over to a seldom-used frequency and began transmitting. ''Howard Approach, this is special flight X-Ray Golf Whiskey Delta, requesting permission to land, over.''

''Whiskey Delta, this is Howard Approach, stand by,'' replied some faceless tower controller, who then checked his radio codes. He didn't know who XGWD was, but those letters were on his ''hot'' list. CIA, he thought, or some other agency that put people where they didn't belong, which was all he needed to know. ''Whiskey Delta, squawk one-three-one-seven. You are cleared for a direct visual approach. Winds are one-nine-five at ten knots.''

''Roger, thank you. Out.'' At least one thing had gone well today, Larson thought. Ten minutes later he put the Beech on the ground and followed a jeep to a parking place on the ramp. Air Force Security Police were waiting for them there, and whisked both officers over to Base Operations. The base was on security-alert drill; everyone was wearing green and most had sidearms. This included the operations staff, most of whom were in flight suits to look militant.

''Next flight stateside?'' Clark asked a young female captain. Her uniform ''poopy suit'' bore the silver wings of a pilot, and Clark wondered what she flew.

''We have a -141 inbound to Charleston,'' she replied. ''But if you want to get on it—''

''Young lady, check your ops orders for this.'' Clark handed over his ''J. T. Williams'' passport. ''In the SI section,'' he added helpfully.

The captain rose from her seat and pulled open the top drawer of her classified file cabinet, the one with the double combination lock. She extracted a red-bordered ring binder and flipped to the last divider. This was the ''Special Intelligence'' section, which identified certain things and people that were more closely guarded than mere ''top'' secrets. It took only a couple of seconds before she returned.

''Thank you, Colonel Williams. The flight leaves in twenty minutes. Is there anything that you and your aide require, sir?''

''Have Charleston arrange to have a puddle-jumper standing by to take us to D.C., if you would, please, Captain. Sorry to have to drop in on you so unexpectedly. Thank you for your assistance.''

''Any time, sir,'' she replied, smiling at this polite colonel.

''Colonel?'' Larson asked on the way out the door.

''Special Ops, no less. Pretty good for a beat-up old chief bosun's mate, isn't it?'' A jeep had them to the Lockheed Starlifter in five minutes. The tunnel-like cargo compartment was empty. This was an Air Force Reserve flight, the loadmaster explained. They dropped some cargo off but were deadheading back home. That was fine with Clark, who stretched out as soon as the bird lifted off. It was amazing, he thought as he dozed off, all the things his countrymen did well. You could transition from being in mortal danger to being totally safe in a matter of hours. The same country that put people into the field and failed to support them properly treated them like VIPs—so long as they had the right ID notification in the right book, as though that could make it all better. It was crazy, the things we could do, and the things we couldn't. A moment later he was snoring next to an amazed Carlos Larson. He didn't wake until just before the landing, five hours later.

As with any other government agency, CIA had regular business hours. By 3:30, those who came in early on "flex-time" were already filing out to beat the traffic, and by 5:30 even the seventh floor was quiet. Outside Jack's office, Nancy Cummings put the cover over her IBM typewriter—she used a word processor, too, but Nancy still liked typewriters—and hit a button on her intercom.

"Anything else you need me for, Dr. Ryan?"

"No, thank you. See you in the morning."

"Okay. Good night, Dr. Ryan."

Jack turned in his chair, back to staring out at the trees that walled the complex off from outside view. He was trying to think, but his mind was a blank void. He didn't know what he'd find. Part of him hoped that he'd find nothing. He knew that what he would do was going to cost him his career at the Agency, but he didn't really give much of a damn anymore. If this was what his job required, then the job wasn't really worth having, was it?

But what would the Admiral say about that?

Jack didn't have that answer. He pulled a paperback out of his desk drawer and started reading. A few hundred pages later it was seven o'clock.

Time. Ryan lifted his phone and called the floor security desk. When the secretaries were gone home, it was the security guys who ran errands.

"This is Dr. Ryan. I need some documents from central files." He read off three numbers. "They're big ones," he warned the desk man. "Better take somebody else to help."

"Yes, sir. We'll head down in a minute."

"Not that much of a hurry," Ryan said as he hung up. He already had a reputation as an easygoing boss. As soon as the phone was back in its cradle, he jumped to his feet and switched on his personal Xerox machine. Then he walked out his door to Nancy's outer office space, listening for the diminishing sound of the two security officers walking out to the main corridor.

They didn't lock office doors up here. There was no point. You had to pass through about ten security zones to get here, each guarded by armed officers, each supervised by a separate central security office on the first floor. There were also roving patrols. Security at CIA was tighter than at a federal prison, and about as oppressive. But it didn't really apply to the senior executives, and all Jack had to do was walk across the corridor and open the door to Bob Ritter's office.

The DDO's office safe—vault was a better term—was set up the same way as Ryan's, behind a false panel in the wall. It was less for secrecy—any competent burglar would find it in under a minute—than for aesthetics. Jack opened the panel and dialed the combination for the safe. He wondered if Ritter knew that Greer had the combination. Perhaps he did, but certainly he didn't know that the Admiral had written it down. It was so odd a thing for the Agency, so odd that no one had ever considered the possibility. The smartest people in the world still had blind spots.

The safe doors were all alarmed, of course. The alarm systems were foolproof, and worked the same way as the safety locks on nuclear weapons—and they were the best kind available, weren't they? You dialed in the right combination or the alarm went off. If you goofed doing it the first time, a light would go on above the dial, indicating that you had ten seconds to get it right or another light would go on at two separate security desks. A second goof would set off more alarms. A third would put the safe in lock-down for two hours. Several CIA executives had learned to curse the system and become the subject of jokes in the security department. But not Ryan, who was not intimidated by combination locks. The computer that kept track of such things decided that, well, it must be Mr. Ritter, and that was that.

Jack's heart beat faster now. There were over twenty files in here, and his time was measured in minutes. But again Agency procedures came to his rescue. Inside the front cover of each file was a summary sheet telling what "Operation WHAT-EVER" was all about. He didn't really pay attention to what they said, but used the summary sheets only to identify items of interest. In less than two minutes, Jack had files labeled EAGLE EYE, SHOWBOAT-I and SHOWBOAT-II, CAPER, and RECIPROCITY. The total stack was nearly eighteen inches high. Jack made careful note of where the folders went, then closed the safe door without locking it. Next he returned to his office, setting the papers on the floor behind his desk. He started reading EAGLE EYE first of all.

"Holy Christ!" "Detection and interdiction of incoming drug flight," he saw, meant . . . shooting them down. Someone knocked on his door.

"Come on in." It was the security guys with the files he'd requested. Ryan had them set the files on a chair and dismissed them.

Jack figured he had an hour, two at most, to do what he had to do. That meant he had time to scan, not to read. Each operation had a more detailed summary of objectives and methods plus an event log and daily progress report. Jack's personal Xerox machine was a big, sophisticated one that organized and collated sheets, and most importantly, zipped them through very rapidly. He started feeding sheets into the hopper. The automatic feed allowed him to read and copy at the same time. Ninety minutes later he had copied over six hundred sheets, maybe a quarter of what he'd taken. It wasn't enough, but it would have to do. He summoned the security guards to return the files they'd brought up—he took the time to ruffle them up first. As soon as they were gone, he assembled the files he'd . . .

. . . stolen? Jack asked himself. It suddenly dawned on him that he'd just violated the law,. He hadn't thought of that. He really hadn't. As he loaded the files back in the safe, Ryan told himself that really he hadn't violated anything. As a senior executive, he was entitled to know these things, and the rules didn't *really* apply to him . . . but that, he remembered, was a dangerous way to think. He was serving a higher cause. He was doing What Was Right. He was—

"Shit!" Ryan said aloud when he closed the safe door. "You don't know what the hell you're doing." He was back in his office a minute later.

It was time to leave. First he made a notation on the Xerox count sheet. You didn't make Xerox copies anywhere in this building without signing off for them, but he'd thought ahead on that. Roughly the right number of sheets were assembled in a pile and placed in his safe, ostensibly a copy of the OSWR report that Nancy had retrieved. Making such copies was something that directorate chiefs were allowed to do fairly freely. Inside his safe, he found, was the manual for its operation. The copies he'd made went into his briefcase. The last thing Ryan did before leaving was to change his combination to something nobody would ever guess. He nodded to the security officer at the desk next to the elevator on his way out. The Agency Buick was waiting when he got to the basement garage.

"Sorry to make you stay in so late, Fred," Jack said as he got in. Fred was his evening driver.

"No problem, sir. Home?"

"Right." It required all of his discipline not to start reading on the way. Instead he leaned back and commanded himself to take a nap. It would be the only sleep he would get tonight, he was sure.

Clark got into Andrews just after eight. His first call was to Ritter's office, but it was shortstopped elsewhere and he learned that the DDO was unavailable until morning. With nothing better to do, Clark and Larson checked into a motel near the Pentagon. After picking up shaving gear and a toothbrush from the Marriott's gift shop, Clark again went to sleep, again surprising the younger officer, who was far too keyed up to do so.

"How bad is it?" the President asked.

"We've lost nine people," Cutter replied. "It was inevitable, sir. We knew going in that this was a dangerous operation. So did they. What we can do—"

"What we can do is shut this operation down, and do it at once. And keep a nice tight lid on it forever. This one never happened. I didn't bargain for any of this, not for the civilian casualties, and sure as hell not for losing nine of our own people. Damn it, Admiral, you told me that these kids were so good—"

"Mr. President, I never—"

"The hell you didn't!" the President said loudly enough to startle the Secret Service agent outside his upstairs office. "How the hell did you get me into this mess?"

Cutter's patrician face went pale as a corpse. Everything he'd worked for, the action he'd been proposing for three years. . . . Ritter was proclaiming success. That was the maddest part of all.

"Sir, our objective was to hurt the Cartel. We have accomplished that. The CIA officer who's running RECIPROCITY, in Colombia, right now, said that he could start a gang war within the Cartel—and we have done just that! They just tried to assassinate one of their own people—Escobedo. Drug shipments coming in are down. We haven't announced it yet, but the papers are already talking about how prices are going up on the street. We're winning."

"Fine. You tell Fowler that!" The President slammed a file folder down on his desk. His own private polls showed Fowler ahead by fourteen points.

"Sir, after the convention, the opposition candidate always—"

"Now you're giving me political advice? Mister, you haven't shown me a hell of a lot of competence in your supposed area of expertise."

"Mr. President, I—"

"I want this whole thing shut down. I want it kept quiet. I want you to do it, and I want you to do it fast. This is your mess and you will clean it up."

Cutter hesitated. "Sir, how do you want me to go about it?"

"I don't want to know. I just want to know when it's done."

"Sir, that may mean that I'll have to disappear for a while."

"Then *disappear!*"

''People might notice.''

''Then you are on a special, classified mission for the President. Admiral, I want this thing closed out. I don't care what you have to do. Just do it!''

Cutter came to attention. He still remembered how to do that. ''Yes, Mr. President.''

''Reverse your rudder,'' Wegener said. USCGC *Panache* pivoted with the change of rudder and engine settings, pointing herself down the channel.

''Midships.''

''Rudder amidships, aye. Sir, my rudder is amidships,'' the young helmsman announced under the watchful eye of Master Chief Quartermaster Oreza.

''Very well. All ahead one-third, steady up on course one-nine-five.'' Wegener looked at the junior officer of the deck. ''You have the conn. Take her out.''

''Aye aye, sir, I have the conn,'' the ensign acknowledged in some surprise. ''Take her out'' generally means that you start from the dock, but the skipper was unusually cautious today. The kid on the wheel could handle it from here. Wegener lit his pipe and headed out for the bridge wing. Portagee followed him there.

''That's about as happy as I've ever been to head out to sea,'' Wegener said.

''I know what you mean, Cap'n.''

It had been one scary day. Only one, but that had been enough. The FBI agent's warning had come as quite a shock. Wegener had grilled his people one by one—something that he'd found as distasteful as it had been unfruitful—to find out who had spilled the beans. Oreza thought he knew but wasn't sure. He was thankful that he'd never have to be. That danger had died with the pirates in Mobile jail. But both men had learned their lesson. From now on they'd abide by the rules.

''Skipper, why d'ya suppose that FBI guy warned us?''

''That's a good question, Portagee. It figures that what we choked out of the bastards turned that money seizure they pulled off. I guess they figured they owed us some. Besides, the local guy says that it was his boss in Washington who ordered him to warn us.''

''I think we owe him one,'' Oreza said.

''I think you're right.'' Both men stayed out to savor yet another sunset at sea, and *Panache* took a heading of one-eight-one, heading for her patrol station in the Yucatan Channel.

Chavez was down to his last set of batteries. The situation, if anything, had gotten worse. There was a group somewhere behind them, necessitating a rear guard. It was something that he, on point, couldn't concern himself about, but it was there, a nagging concern as real as the sore muscles that had him popping Tylenol every few hours. Maybe they were being followed. Maybe it was just accidental—or maybe Ramirez had gotten predictable in his evasion tactics. Chavez didn't think so, but he was becoming too tired to think coherently, and knew it. Maybe the captain had the same problem, he realized. That was especially worrisome. Sergeants were paid to fight. Captains were paid to think. But if Ramirez was too tired to do that, then they might as well not have him.

Noise. A whisper from a branch swishing through the air. But there was no wind blowing at the moment. Maybe an animal. Maybe not.

Chavez stopped. He held his hand straight up. Vega, walking slack fifty meters back, relayed the signal. Ding moved alongside a tree and stayed standing for the best possible visibility. He started to lean against it and found himself drifting. The sergeant shook his head to clear it. Fatigue was really getting to him now.

There. Movement. It was a man. Just a spectral green shape, barely more than a stick figure on the goggle display, nearly two hundred meters to Ding's right front. He was moving uphill and—another one, about twenty meters behind. They were moving like . . . soldiers, with the elaborate footwork that looked so damned crazy when somebody else was doing it. . . .

There was one way to check. On the bottom side of his PVS-7 goggles was a small infrared light for use in reading maps. Invisible to the human eye, it would show up like a beacon to anyone wearing another PVS-7. He didn't even have to make a noise. They'd be looking around constantly.

It was still a risk, of course.

Chavez stepped away from the tree. It was too far to see if they were wearing their headsets, if they were. . . .

Yes. The lead figure was turning his head left and right. It stopped dead on where Chavez was standing. Ding tipped his goggles up to expose the IR light and blinked it three times. He dropped his night scope back into place just in time to see the other one do the same.

"I think they're our guys," Chavez whispered into his radio mike.

"Then they're pretty lost," Ramirez replied through his earpiece. "Be careful, Sergeant."

Click-Click. Okay.

Chavez waited for *Oso* to set his SAW up in a convenient place, then walked toward the other man, careful to keep where Vega could cover him. It seemed an awfully long way to walk, farther still without being able to put his weapon on the target, but he couldn't exactly do that, could he? He spotted one more, and there would be others out there also, watching him over the sights of their weapons. If that wasn't a friendly, his chances of seeing the sunrise were somewhere between zero and not much.

"Ding, is that you?" a whisper called the remaining ten meters. "It's León."

Chavez nodded. Both men took very deep breaths as they walked together and hugged. Somehow a handshake just wasn't enough under the circumstances.

"You're lost, 'Berto."

"No shit, man. I know where the fuck we are, but we're fucking lost all right."

"Where's Cap'n Rojas?"

"Dead. Esteves, Delgado, half the team."

"Okay. Hold it." Ding punched his radio button. "Six, this is Point. We just made contact with BANNER. They've had a little trouble, sir. You better get up here."

Click-click.

León waved for his men to come in. Chavez didn't even think to count. It was enough to see that half weren't there. Both men sat on a fallen tree.

"What happened?"

"We walked right into it, man. Thought it was a processing site. It wasn't. Musta been thirty-forty guys there. I think Esteves fucked up and it all came apart. Like a bar fight with guns, man. Then Captain Rojas went down, and—it was pretty bad, *'mano*. Been on the run ever since."

"We got people chasing us, too."

"What's the good news?" León asked.

"I ain't heard any lately, 'Berto," Ding said. "I think it's time for us to get our asses outa this place."

"Roge-o," Sergeant León said just as Ramirez appeared. He made his report to the captain.

"Cap'n," Chavez said when he was finished, "we're all pretty beat. We need a place to belly up."

"The man's right," Guerra agreed.

"What about behind us?"

"They ain't heard nothin' in two hours, sir," Guerra reminded him. "That knoll over there looks like a good spot to me." That was about as hard as he could press his officer, but finally it was enough.

"Take the men up. Set up the perimeter and two outposts. We'll try to rest up till sundown, and maybe I can call in and get us some help."

"Sounds good to me, Cap'n." Guerra took off to get things organized. Chavez left at once to sweep the area while the rest of the squad moved to its new RON site—except, Chavez thought, this was an ROD—remain-over-day—site. It was a bleak attempt at humor, but it was all he could manage under the circumstances.

"My God," Ryan breathed. It was four in the morning, and he was awake only because of coffee and apprehension. Ryan had uncovered his share of things with the Agency. But never anything like this. The first thing he had to do was . . . what?

Get some sleep, even a few hours, he told himself. Jack lifted the phone and called the office. There was always a watch officer on duty.

"This is Dr. Ryan. I'm going to be late. Something I ate. I've been throwing up all night . . . no, I think it's over now, but I need a few hours of sleep. I'll drive myself in tomorr—today," he corrected himself. "Yeah, that's right. Thanks. 'Bye."

He left a note on the refrigerator door for his wife and crawled into a spare bed to avoid disturbing her.

Passing the message was the easiest part for Cortez. It would have been hard for anyone else, but one of the first things he'd done after joining the Cartel was to get a list of certain telephone numbers in the Washington, D.C., area. It hadn't been hard. As with any task, it was just a matter of finding someone who knew what you needed to know. That was something Cortez excelled at. Once he had the list of numbers—it had cost him $10,000, the best sort of money well spent, that is to say, someone's else's well-spent money—it was merely a matter of knowing schedules. That was tricky, of course. The person might not be there, which risked disclosure, but the right sort of eyes-only prefix would probably serve to warn off the casual viewer. The secretaries of such people typically were disciplined people who risked their jobs when they showed too much curiosity.

But what really made it easy was a new bit of technology, the facsimile printer. It was a brand-new status symbol. Everyone had to have one, just as everyone, especially the important, had to have a direct private telephone line that bypassed his secretary. That and the fax went together. Cortez had driven to Medellín to his private office and typed the message himself. He knew what official U.S. government messages looked like, of course, and did his best to reproduce it here. EYES-ONLY NIMBUS was the header, and the name in the FROM slot was bogus, but that in the To place was quite genuine, which ought to have been sufficient to get the attention of the addressee. The body of the message was brief and to the point, and indicated a coded reply-address. How would the addressee react? Well, there was no telling, was there? But this, too, Cortez felt was a good gamble. He inserted the single sheet in his fax, dialed the proper number, and waited. The machine did the rest. As soon as it heard the warbling electronic love-call of another fax machine, it transmitted the message form. Cortez removed the original and folded it away into his wallet.

The addressee turned in surprise when he heard the whir of his fax printing out a message. It had to be official, because only half a dozen people knew that private line. (It never occurred to him that the telephone company's computer knew about it, too.) He finished what he was doing before reaching over for the message.

What the hell is NIMBUS? he wondered. Whatever it was, it was eyes-only to him, and therefore he started to read the message. He was sipping his third cup of morning coffee while he did so, and was fortunate that his cough deposited some of it onto his desk and not his trousers.

Cathy Ryan was nothing if not punctual. The phone in the guest room rang at precisely 8:30. Jack's head jerked off the pillow as though from an electric shock, and his hand reached out to grab the offensive instrument.

"Hello?"

"Good morning, Jack," his wife said brightly. "What's the problem with you?"

"I had to stay up late with some work. Did you take the other thing with you?"

"Yes, what's the—"

Jack cut her off. "I know what it says, babe. Could you just make the call? It's important." Dr. Caroline Ryan was also bright enough to catch the meaning of what he said.

"Okay, Jack. How do you feel?"

"Awful. But I have work to do."

"So do I, honey. 'Bye."

"Yeah." Jack hung up and commanded himself to get out of the bed. First a shower, he told himself.

Cathy was on her way to Surgery, and had to hurry. She lifted her office phone and called the proper number on the hospital's D.C. line. It rang only once.

"Dan Murray."

"Dan, this is Cathy Ryan."

"Morning! What can I do for you this fine day, Doctor?"

"Jack said to tell you that he'd be in to see you just after ten. He wants you to let him park in the drive-through, and he said to tell you that the folks down the hall aren't supposed to know. I don't know what that means, but that's what he told me to say." Cathy didn't know whether to be amused or not. Jack did like to play funny little games—she thought they were pretty dumb little games—with people who shared his clearances, and wondered if this was some sort of joke or not. Jack especially liked to play games with his FBI friend.

"Okay, Cath', I'll take care of that."

"I have to run off to fix somebody's eyeball. Say hi to Liz for me."

"Will do. Have a good one."

* * *

Murray hung up with a puzzled look on his face. *Folks down the hall aren't supposed to know.* "The folks down the hall" was a phrase Murray had used the first time they'd met, in St. Thomas's Hospital in London when Dan had been the legal attaché at the U.S. Embassy on Grosvenor Square. The folks down the hall were CIA.

But Ryan was one of the top six people at Langley, arguably one of the top three. What the hell did that mean?

"Hmph." He called his secretary and had her notify the security guards to allow Ryan into the driveway that passed under the main entrance to the Hoover Building. Whatever it meant, he could wait.

Clark arrived at Langley at nine that morning. He didn't have a security pass—not the sort of thing you carry into the field—and had to use a code-word to get through the main gate, which seemed very conspiratorial indeed. He parked in the visitors' lot—CIA has one of those—and walked in the main entrance, heading immediately to the left where he quickly got what looked like a visitor's badge which, however, worked just fine in the electronically controlled gates. Now he angled off to the right, past the wall murals that looked as though some enormous child had daubed mud all over the place. The decorator for this place, Clark was sure, had to have been a KGB plant. Or maybe they'd just picked the lowest bidder. An elevator took him to the seventh floor, and he walked around the corridor to the executive offices that have their own separate corridor on the face of the building. He ended up in front of the DDO's secretary.

"Mr. Clark to see Mr. Ritter," he said.

"Do you have an appointment?" the secretary asked.

"No, I don't, but I think he wants to see me," Clark said politely. There was no sense in abusing her. Besides, Clark had been raised to show deference to women. She lifted her phone and passed the message. "You can go right in, Mr. Clark."

"Thank you." He closed the door behind him. The door, of course, was heavy and soundproof. That was just as well.

"What the hell are you doing here?" the DDO demanded.

"You're going to have to shut SHOWBOAT down," Clark said without preamble. "It's coming apart. The bad guys are hunting those kids down and—"

"I know. I heard late last night. Look, I never figured this would be a no-loss operation. One of the teams got clobbered pretty good thirty-six hours ago, but based on intercepts, looks like they gave better than they took, and then they got even with some others who—"

"That was me," Clark said.

"What?" Ritter asked in surprise.

"Larson and I took a little drive about this time yesterday, and I found three of those—whatevers. They were just finished loading up the bodies into the back of a truck. I didn't see any point in letting them live," Mr. Clark said in a normal tone of voice. It had been a very long time since anyone at CIA had said something like that.

"Christ, John!" Ritter was even too surprised to blast Clark for violating his own security by stepping into a separate operation.

"I recognized one of the bodies," Clark went on. "Captain Emilio Rojas, United States Army. He was a hell of a nice kid, by the way."

"I'm sorry about that. Nobody ever said this was safe."

"I'm sure his family, if any, will appreciate that. This operation is blown. It's time to cut our losses. What are we doing to get them out?" Clark asked.

"I'm looking at that. I have to coordinate with somebody. I'm not sure that he'll agree."

"In that case, sir," Clark told his boss, "I suggest that you make your case rather forcefully."

"Are you threatening me?" Ritter asked quietly.

"No, sir, I would prefer not to have you read me that way. I am telling you, on the basis of my experience, that this operation must be terminated ASAP. It is your job to make that necessity plain to the people who authorized the operation. Failing to get such permission, I would advise you to terminate the operation anyway."

"I could lose my job for that," the DDO pointed out.

"After I identified the body of Captain Rojas, I set fire to the truck. Couple reasons. I wanted to divert the enemy somewhat, and, of course, I also wanted to render the bodies unrecognizable. I've never burned the body of a friendly before. I did not like doing that. Larson still doesn't know why I did it. He's too young to understand. You're not, sir. You sent those people into the field and you are responsible for them. If you are telling me that your job is more important than that, I am here to tell you that you are wrong, sir." Clark hadn't yet raised his voice above the level of a reasonable man discussing ordinary business, but for the first time in a very long time, Bob Ritter feared for his personal safety.

"Your diversion attempt was successful, by the way. The opposition has forty people looking in the wrong place now."

"Good. That will make the extraction effort all the easier to accomplish."

"John, you can't give me orders like this."

"Sir, I am not giving you orders. I am telling you what has to be done. You told me that the operation was mine to run."

"That was RECIPROCITY, not SHOWBOAT."

"This is not a time for semantics, sir. If you do not pull those people out, more—possibly all of them—will be killed. That, sir, is your responsibility. You can't put people in the field and not support them. You know that."

"You're right, of course," Ritter said after a moment. "I can't do it on my own. I have to inform—well, you know. I'll take care of that. We'll pull them out as quickly as we can."

"Good." Clark relaxed. Ritter was a sharp operator, often too sharp in his dealings with subordinates, but he was a man of his word. Besides, the DDO was too smart to cross him on a matter like this. Clark was sure of that. He had made his own position pretty damned clear, and Ritter had caught the signal five-by-five.

"What about Larson and his courier?"

"I've pulled them both out. His plane's at Panama, and he's at the Marriott down the road. He's pretty good, by the way, but he's probably blown as far as Colombia is concerned. I'd say they could both use a few weeks off."

"Fair enough. What about you?"

"I can head back tomorrow if you want. You might want me to help with the extraction."

"We may have a line on Cortez."

"Really?"

"And you're the guy who got the first picture of him."

"Oh. Where—the guy at the Untiveros house, the guy we just barely missed?"

"The same. Positive ID from the lady he seduced. He's running the people they have in the field from a little house near Anserma."

"I'd have to take Larson back for that."

"Think it's worth the risk?"

"Getting Cortez?" Clark thought for a moment. "Depends. It's worth a look. What do we know about his security?"

"Nothing," Ritter admitted, "just a rough idea where the house is. We got that from an intercept. Be nice to get him alive. He knows a lot of things we want to find out. We bring him back here and we can hang a murder rap over his head. Death-penalty kind."

Clark nodded thoughtfully. Another element of spy fiction was the canard about how people in the intelligence business were willing to take their cyanide capsules or face a firing squad with a song in their hearts. The facts were to the contrary. Men faced certain death courageously only when there was no attractive alternative. The trick was to give them such an alternative, which didn't require the mind of a rocket scientist, as the current aphorism went. If they got Cortez, the normal form would be take him all the way through a trial, sentence him to death—just a matter of picking the right judge, and in national-security matters, there was always lots of leeway—and take it from there. Cortez would crack in due course, probably even before the trial started. Cortez was no fool, after all, and would know when and how to strike a bargain. He'd already sold out on his own country. Selling out on the Cartel was trivial beside that.

Clark nodded. "Give me a few hours to think about it."

Ryan turned left off 10th Street, Northwest, into the drive-through. There were uniformed and plainclothes guards, one of whom held a clipboard. He approached the car.

"Jack Ryan to see Dan Murray."

"Could I see some ID, please?"

Jack pulled out his CIA pass. The guard recognized it for what it was and waved to another guard. This one punched the button to lower the steel barrier that was supposed to prevent people with car bombs from driving under the headquarters of the FBI. He pulled over it and found a place to park the car. A young FBI agent met him in the lobby and handed him a pass that would work the Bureau's electronic gate. If someone invented the right sort of computer virus, Jack thought, half of the government would be prevented from going to work. And maybe the country would be safe until the problem was fixed.

The Hoover Building has a decidedly unusual layout, a maze of diagonal corridors intersecting with squared-off corridors. It is even worse than the Pentagon for the uninitiated to find their way about. In this case, Ryan was well and truly disoriented by the time they found the right office. Dan was waiting for him and led him into his private office. Jack closed the door behind him.

"What gives?" Murray asked.

Ryan set his briefcase on Murray's desk and opened it.

"I need some guidance."

"About what?"

"About what is probably an illegal operation—several of them, as a matter of fact."

"How illegal?"

"Murder," Jack said as undramatically as he could manage.

"The car bombs in Colombia?" Murray asked from his swivel chair.

"Not bad, Dan. Except they weren't car bombs."

Oh? Dan sat down and thought for a few seconds before speaking. He remembered that whatever was being done was retribution for the murder of Emil and the rest. "Whatever they were, the law on this is fairly muddled, you know. The prohibition against killing people in intelligence operations is an Executive Order, promulgated by the President. If he writes *except in this case* on the bottom of the order, then it's legal—sort of. The law on this issue is really strange. More than anything else, it's a constitutional matter, and the Constitution is nice and vague where it has to be."

"Yeah, I know about that. What makes it illegal is that I've been told to give incorrect information to Congress. If the oversight people were in on it, it wouldn't be murder. It would be properly formulated government policy. In fact, as I understand the law, it would not be murder even if we did it first and then told Congress, because we have a lead time to start a covert op if the oversight folks are out of town. But if the DCI tells me to give false information to Congress, then we're committing murder, because we're not following the law. That's the good news, Dan."

"Go on."

"The bad news is that too many people know what's going on, and if the story gets out, some people we have out in the field are in a world of hurt. I'll set the political dimension aside for the moment except to say that there's more than one. Dan, I don't know what the hell I'm supposed to do." Ryan's analysis, as usual, was very accurate. He'd made only a single mistake. He didn't know what the real bad news was.

Murray smiled, not because he wanted to, but because his friend needed it. "What makes you think I do?"

Ryan's tension eased a bit. "Well, I could go to a priest for guidance, but they ain't cleared SI. You are, and the FBI's the next best thing to the priesthood, isn't it?" It was an inside joke between the two. Both were Boston College graduates.

"Where's the operation being run out of?"

"Guess. It isn't Langley, not really. It's being run out of a place exactly six blocks up the street."

"That means I can't even go to the AG."

"Yeah, he just might tell his boss, mightn't he?"

"So I get in trouble with my bureaucracy," Murray observed lightly.

"Is government service really worth the hassle?" Jack asked bleakly, his depression returning. "Hell, maybe we can retire together. Who can you trust?"

That answer came easily. "Bill Shaw." Murray rose. "Let's go see him."

"Loop" is one of those computer words that has gained currency in society. It identifies things that happen and the people who make them happen, an action- or decision-cycle that exists independently of the things around it. Any government has a virtually infinite collection of such loops, each defined by its own special set of ground rules, understood by the players. Within the next few hours a new loop had been established. It included selected members of the FBI, but not the U.S. Attorney General, who had authority over the Bureau. It would also include members of the Secret Service, but not their boss, the Secretary of the Treasury. Investigations of this sort were mainly exercises in paper-chasing and analysis, and Murray—who was also tasked to head this one up—was surprised to see that one of his ''subjects'' was soon on the move. It didn't help him at all to learn that he was driving to Andrews Air Force Base.

By that time, Ryan was back at his desk, looking slightly wan, everyone thought, but everyone had heard that he'd been sick the night before. Something he ate. He now knew what to do: nothing. Ritter was gone, and the Judge still wasn't back. It wasn't easy to do nothing. It was harder still to do things that didn't matter a damn right now. He did feel better, however. Now the problem wasn't his alone. He didn't know that this was nothing to feel better about.

25. The ODYSSEY File

Murray had a senior agent drive to Andrews immediately, of course, and he got there just in time to watch the small jet taxi off to the end of runway One-Left. The agent used his ID to get himself into the office of the colonel who commanded the 89th Military Airlift Wing. That got the agent the flight plan for the aircraft that had just taken off. He used the colonel's phone to call Murray, then admonished the colonel that he, the agent, had never been there, had never made an official inquiry; that this was part of a major criminal investigation and was code-word material. The code-word for the case was ODYSSEY.

Murray and Shaw were together within a minute of taking the call. Shaw had found that he could handle the duties of acting Director. He was sure that it was not a permanent job, and after the proper political figurehead was found, he'd revert to Executive Assistant Director (Investigations). Part of him thought that too bad. What was wrong with having a career cop running the Bureau? Of course, that was politics, not police work, and in over thirty years of police work he'd discovered that politics was not his cup of tea.

''We gotta get somebody there,'' Shaw observed. ''But *how,* for God's sake?''

''Why not the Panama legal attaché?'' Murray asked. ''I know him. Solid guy.''

''He's out doing something with DEA. Won't be back in the office for a couple of days. His number-two's not up to it. Too inexperienced to run this himself.''

''Morales is available in Bogotá—but somebody'd notice. . . . We're playing catch-up again, Bill, and that guy is flying down there at five hundred miles per hour. . . . How about Mark Bright? Maybe he can steal a jet from the Air Guard.''

''Do it!''

''Special Agent Bright,'' he said as he picked up the phone.

''Mark, this is Dan Murray. I need you to do something. Start taking notes, Mark.'' Murray kept talking. Two minutes later Bright muttered a mild obscenity and pulled out his phone book. The first call went to Eglin Air Force Base, the second to the local Coast Guard, and the third to his home. He sure as hell wouldn't be home for dinner. Bright grabbed a few items on his way out the door and had another agent drive him to the Coast Guard yard, where a helicopter was already waiting. It took off a minute after he got aboard and headed east to Eglin Air Force Base.

The Air Force had only three F-15E Strike-Eagles, all prototypes for a ground-attack version of the big, twin-engined fighter, and two of those were at Eglin for technical tests while Congress decided if the service would actually put the aircraft into serial production. Aside from some training birds located elsewhere, this was the only two-seat version of the Air Force's prime air-superiority fighter. The major who'd be flying him was standing at the side of the aircraft when Bright stepped out of the helicopter. A couple of NCOs assisted the agent into his flight suit, parachute harness, and life vest. The helmet was sitting on the top of the rear ejection seat. In ten minutes the aircraft was ready to roll.

''What gives?'' the pilot asked.

''I need to be at Panama, just as fast as you can arrange it.''

''Gee, you mean you're going to make me fly fast?'' the major responded, then laughed. ''Then there's no rush.''

''Say again?''

''The tanker took off three minutes ago. We'll let him get up to thirty thousand before we lift off. He'll top us off up there, and we go balls to the wall. Another tanker is taking off from Panama to meet us—so we'll have enough fuel to land, sir. That way we can go supersonic most of the flight. You did say you were in a hurry?''

''Uh-huh.'' Bright was struggling to adjust his helmet. It didn't fit very well. It was also quite warm in the cockpit, and the air-conditioning system hadn't taken hold yet. ''What if the other tanker doesn't show up?''

''The Eagle is a very good glider,'' the major assured him. ''We won't have to swim *too* far.''

A radio message crackled in Bright's ears. The major answered it, then spoke to his passenger. ''Grab your balls, sir. It is now post time.'' The Eagle taxied to the end of the runway, where it sat still for a moment while the pilot brought the engines to full, screaming, vibrating power, and then slipped his brakes. Ten seconds later Bright wondered if a catapult shot off a carrier could be more exciting than this. The F-15E held a forty-degree angle of climb and just kept accelerating, leaving Florida's gulf coast far behind. They tanked a hundred miles offshore—Bright was too fascinated to be frightened, though the buffet was noticeable—and after separating, the Eagle climbed to forty thousand feet and the pilot punched burners. The aft cockpit was mainly concerned with delivering bombs and missiles on target, but did have a few instruments. One of them told the agent that they had just topped a thousand miles per hour.

''What's the hurry?'' the pilot asked.

''I want to get to Panama ahead of somebody.''

''Can you give me some details? Might help, you know.''

''One of those business jets—G-Three, I think. Left Andrews eighty-five minutes ago.''

The pilot laughed. ''Is that all? Hell, you can check into a hotel 'fore he gets down. We're already ahead of him. We're wasting fuel going this fast.''

''So waste it,'' Bright said.

''Fine with me, sir. Mach-2 or sittin' still, they pay me the same. Okay, figure we'll get in ninety minutes ahead of your guy. How do you like the ride?''

''Where's the drink cart?''

"Should be a bottle down by your right knee. A nice domestic vintage, good nose, but not the least pretentious."

Bright got it and had a drink out of sheer curiosity.

"Salt and electrolytes, to keep you alert," the pilot explained a few seconds later. "You're FBI, right?"

"Correct."

"What gives?"

"Can't say. What's that?" He heard a beeping sound in his headphones.

"SAM radar," the major said.

"What?"

"That's Cuba over there. There's a SAM battery on that point that doesn't like American military aircraft. I can't imagine why. We're out of range anyway. Don't sweat it. It's normal. We use them to calibrate our systems, too. Part of the game."

Murray and Shaw were reading over the material Jack had dropped off. Their immediate problems were, first, to determine what was supposed to be going on; next, to determine what was actually going on; next, to determine if it was legal or not; next, if not, then to take appropriate action, once they could figure what appropriate action was. This wasn't a mere can of worms. It was a can of poisonous snakes that Ryan had spilled over Murray's desk.

"You know how this might end up?"

Shaw turned away from the desk. "The country doesn't need another one." *Not by my hands,* he didn't say.

"We got one whether we need it or not," Murray said. "I admit, part of me says, 'Right on!' about why they're doing it, but from what Jack tells me, we have at the very least a technical violation of the oversight laws, and definitely a violation of the Executive Order."

"Unless there's a classified codicil that we don't know about. What if the AG knows?"

"What if he's part of it? The day Emil got hit, the AG flew to Camp David along with the rest of 'em, remember?"

"What I want to know is, what the hell our friend is going to Panama for?"

"Maybe we'll find out. He's going down alone. No security troops, everybody sworn to secrecy. Who'd you send over to Andrews to choke it out of 'em?"

"Pat O'Day," Murray answered. That explained matters. "I want him to handle the liaison with the Secret Service guys, too. He's done a lot of work with them. When the time comes, that is. We're a mile away from being ready for that."

"Agreed. We have eighteen people working ODYSSEY. That's not enough."

"We have to keep it tight for the moment, Bill. I think the next step is getting somebody over from Justice to cover our asses for us. Who?"

"Christ, I don't know," Shaw replied in exasperation. "It's one thing to run an investigation that the AG knows about but is kept out of, but I can't remember ever running one completely unknown to him."

"Let's take our time, then. The main thing right now is to figure out what the plan was, then branch out from there." It was a logical observation from Murray. It was also wrong. It was to be a day of errors.

The F-15E touched down at Howard Field right on time, eighty minutes before the scheduled arrival of the flight from Andrews. Bright thanked the pilot, who refueled and took off at once for a more leisurely return to Eglin. The base intelligence officer met Bright, along with the most senior agent from the legal attaché's office in Panama City, who was young, sharp, but too new in his post for a case of this sensitivity. The arriving agent briefed his two colleagues on what little he knew and swore both to secrecy. It was enough to get things going. His first stop was the post exchange, where he got some nondescript clothing. The intelligence officer supplied a very plain automobile with local tags that they left outside the gate. On base they'd use an anonymous blue Air Force sedan. The Plymouth sat near the flight line when the VC-20A landed. Bright pulled his Nikon out of the bag and attached a 1000mm telephoto lens. The aircraft taxied to a stop at one of the hangars, and the stairs folded down with the hatch. Bright snugged his camera in and started shooting close-ups from several hundred yards away as the single passenger stepped out of the plane and into a waiting car.

"Jesus, it's really him." Bright rewound and removed the film cassette. He handed it to the other FBI agent and reloaded another thirty-six-frame spool.

The car they followed was a twin to their Air Force sedan. It drove straight off post. Bright and the rest barely had time to switch cars, but the Air Force colonel driving had ambitions to race the NASCAR circuit and took up a surveillance position a hundred yards behind it.

"Why no security?" he asked.

"He generally doesn't bother, they told me," Bright told him. "Sounds odd, doesn't it?"

"Hell, yes, given who he is, what he knows, and where the hell he happens to be at the moment."

The trip into town was unremarkable. The Air Force sedan dropped Cutter off at a luxury hotel on the outskirts of Panama City. Bright hopped out and watched him check in, just like a man on a business trip. The other agent came in a few minutes later while the colonel stayed with the car.

"Now what?"

"Anybody you can trust on the local PD?" Bright asked.

"Nope. I know a few, some of them pretty good guys. But trust? Not down here, man."

"Well, there's always the old-fashioned way," Bright observed.

" 'Kay." The assistant legal attaché reached for his wallet and walked to the registration desk. He came back two minutes later. "The Bureau owes me twenty bucks. He's registered as Robert Fisher. Here's the American Express number." He handed over a crumpled carbon sheet that also had the scrawled signature.

"Call the office and run it. We need to keep an eye on his room. We need—Christ, how many assets do we have?" Bright waved him outside.

"Not enough for this."

Bright's face twisted into an ugly shape for a moment. This was no easy call to make. ODYSSEY was a code-word case, and one thing that Murray had impressed on him was the need for security, but—there was always a "but," wasn't there?—this was something that needed doing. So he was the senior man on the scene and he had to make the call. Of such things, he knew, careers were made and broken. It was murderously hot and humid, but that wasn't the only reason Mark Bright was sweating.

"Okay, tell him we need a half-dozen good people to help us with the surveillance."

"You sure—"

"I'm not sure of anything right now! The man we're supposed to be shadowing—if we suspect him—Christ Almighty, *if* we suspect him—" Bright stopped talking. There wasn't much else to say, was there?

"Yeah."

"I'll hang out here. Tell the colonel to get things organized."

It turned out that they needn't have hurried. The subject—that's what he was now, Bright told himself—appeared in the lobby three hours later, looking fresh and scrubbed in his tropical-weight suit. Four cars waited outside for him, but Cutter only knew about the small, white Mercedes into which he climbed and which drove off to the north. The other three kept it in visual contact.

It was getting dark. Bright had shot only three frames on his second roll of film. He ejected that one and replaced it with some super-high-speed black and white film. He shot a few pictures of the car just to make sure that he got the license number. The driver at this point wasn't the colonel, but a sergeant from the criminal-investigation detachment who knew the area and was impressed as hell to be working a code-word case with the Bureau. He identified the house the Mercedes pulled into. They ought to have guessed it.

The sergeant knew a place that overlooked the house, not a thousand yards away, but they were too late getting there and the car couldn't stay on the highway. Bright and the local FBI representative jumped out and found a wet, smelly place to lie down and wait. The sergeant left them a radio with which to summon him and wished them luck.

The owner of the house was away attending to matters of state, of course, but he had been kind enough to give them free use of it. That included a small but discreet staff which served light snacks and drinks, then withdrew, leaving the tape recorders, both men were sure, to record events. Well, that didn't matter, did it?

The hell it doesn't! Both men realized the sensitivity of the conversation that was about to take place, and it was Cortez who surprised his guest by graciously suggesting that they speak outside, despite the weather. Both men dropped off their suitcoats and went through the French doors to the garden. About the only good news was the impressive collection of blue bug-lights which crackled and sparkled as they attracted and electrocuted thousands of insects. The noise would make hash out of most recording attempts, and who would have expected either of them to eschew the house's air conditioning?

"Thank you for responding to my message," Cortez said pleasantly. It was not a time for bluster or posturing. It was time for business, and he'd have to appear appropriately humble before this man. It didn't bother him. Dealing with people of his rank required it, and it was something he'd have to get used to, Félix expected. They needed deference. It made surrendering all the easier.

"What do you want to talk about?" Admiral Cutter asked.

"Your operations against the Cartel, of course." Cortez waved toward a cane chair. He disappeared for a moment, then returned with the tray of drinks and glasses. For tonight, Perrier was the drink of choice. Both men left the alcohol untouched. For Félix, that was the first good sign.

"What operations are you talking about?"

"You should know that I had nothing personally to do with the death of Mr. Jacobs. It was an act of madness."

"Why should I believe that?"

"I was in America at the time. Didn't they tell you?" Cortez filled in some details. ''An information source like Mrs. Wolfe,'' he concluded, ''is worth far more than stupid, emotional revenge. It is more foolish still to challenge a powerful nation in so obvious a way. Your response was quite well done. In fact, the operations you are running are most impressive. I didn't even suspect your airport-surveillance operations until after they were terminated, and the way you simulated the car bomb—a work of *art,* if I may say so. Can you tell me what the strategic objective of your operation is?''

''Come now, Colonel.''

''Admiral, I have the power to expose the totality of your activities to the press,'' Félix said almost sadly. ''Either you tell me or you tell the members of your own Congress. You will find me far more accommodating. We are, after all, men of the same profession.''

Cutter thought for a moment, and told him. He was greatly irritated to see his interlocutor start laughing.

''Brilliant!'' Cortez said when he was able to. ''One day I would wish to meet this man, the one who proposed this idea. Truly he is a professional!''

Cutter nodded as though accepting the compliment. For a moment Félix wondered if that might be true . . . it was easy enough to find out.

''You must forgive me, Admiral Cutter. You think I am making light of your operation. I say to you honestly that I am not. You have, in fact, accomplished your goal.''

''We know. We know that somebody tried to kill you and Escobedo.''

''Yes,'' Félix replied. ''Of course. I would also like to know how you are developing such fine intelligence on us, but I know that you will not tell me.''

Cutter played the card for all he thought it was worth. ''We have more assets than you think, Colonel.'' It wasn't worth that much.

''I am sure,'' Cortez allowed. ''I think we have an area of agreement.''

''What might that be?''

''You wish to initiate a war within the Cartel. So do I.''

Cutter betrayed himself by the way he stopped breathing. ''Oh? How so?''

Already Cortez knew that he had won. And this fool was advising the American President?

''Why, I will become a *de facto* part of your operation and restructure the Cartel. That means eliminating some of the more offensive members, of course.''

Cutter wasn't a total fool, but made the further mistake of stating the obvious as a question: ''With yourself as the new head?''

''Do you know what sort of people these 'drug lords' are? Vicious peasants. Barbarians without education, drunk with power, yet they complain like spoiled children that they are not *respected.*'' Cortez smiled up at the stars. ''They are not people to be taken seriously by men such as ourselves. Can we agree that the world will be better when they have left it?''

''The same thought has occurred to me, as you have already pointed out.''

''Then we are in agreement.''

''Agreement on what?''

''Your 'car bombs' have already eliminated five of the chieftains. I will further reduce the number. Those eliminated will include all who approved the murder of your ambassador and the others, of course. Such actions cannot go unpunished or the world is plunged into chaos. Also, to show good faith, I will unilaterally reduce cocaine shipments to your country by half. The drug trade is disordered and overly violent,'' the former DGI colonel said judiciously. ''It needs restructuring.''

"We want it stopped!" Even as he said it, Cutter knew that it was a foolish thing to say.

Cortez sipped at his Perrier and continued to speak reasonably. "It will never be stopped. So long as your citizens wish to destroy their brains, someone will make this possible. The question, then, is how do we make the process more orderly? Your education efforts will eventually reduce the demand for drugs to tolerable levels. Until then, I can regularize the trade to minimize the dislocation of your society. I will reduce exports. I can even give you some major arrests so that your police can take credit for the reductions. This is an election year, is it not?"

Cutter's breathing took another hiatus. They were playing high-stakes poker, and Cortez had just announced that the deck was marked.

"Go on," was all he managed to say.

"Was this not the objective of your operations in Colombia? To sting the Cartel and reduce drug trafficking? I offer you success, the sort of success to which your President can point. Reduction in exports, some dramatic seizures and arrests, an intramural war within the Cartel for which you will not be blamed, yet for which you will also take credit. I give you victory," Cortez said.

"In return for . . . ?"

"I, too, must have a small victory to establish my position with the chieftains, yes? You will withdraw support for the Green Berets you have climbing those horrible mountains. You know—the men you are supporting with that large black helicopter in Hangar Three at Howard Air Force Base. You see, those chieftains whom I wish to displace have large groups of retainers, and the best way for me to reduce their numbers is to have your men kill them for me. At the same time, unfortunately, in order to gain standing with my *superiors*"—this word was delivered with Richter-scale irony—"my bloody and costly operation must ultimately be successful. It is a regrettable necessity, but from your point of view it also eliminates a potential security problem, does it not?"

My God. Cutter looked away from Cortez, out past the bug lights into the jungle.

"What do you suppose they're talking about?"

"Beats the hell out of me," Bright replied. He was on his last roll of film. Even with the high-speed setting, to get a good shot he had to bring the shutter speed way down, and that meant holding the camera as still as a hunting rifle on a distant pronghorn.

What was it the President said? Close the operation out, and I don't care how. . . .

But I can't do that.

"Sorry," Cutter said. "Impossible."

Cortez made a helpless, shrugging gesture with both hands. "In that case we will inform the world that your government has invaded Colombia and has committed murder on a particularly epic scale. You are aware, of course, of what will probably happen to you, your President, and many senior members of your government. It took so long for you to get over all those other scandals. It must be very troubling to serve a government that has so many problems with its own laws and then uses them against its own servants."

"You can't blackmail the United States government."

"Why not, Admiral? Our mutual profession carries risks, does it not? You nearly killed me with your first 'car bomb,' and yet I have taken no personal offense. Your risk is exposure. Untiveros's family was there, you know, his wife and two little ones, eleven domestic servants, I believe. All dead from your bomb. I will not count those who were carrying guns, of course. A soldier must take a soldier's chance. As did I. As must you, Admiral, except that yours is not a soldier's chance. Your chance will be before your courts and television reporters, and congressional committees." *What was the old soldier's code?* Cortez asked himself. *Death before dishonor*. He knew that his guest had no stomach for either.

"I need time to—"

"Think? Excuse me, Admiral, but I must be back in four hours, which means I must leave here in fifteen minutes. My superiors do not know that I am gone. I have no time. Neither do you. I offer you the victory for which you and your President hoped. I require something in return. If we cannot agree, then the consequences will be unpleasant for both of us. It is that simple. Yes or no, Admiral?"

"What do you suppose they just shook hands about?"

"Cutter doesn't look real happy about it. Call the car! Looks like they're buggin' out."

"Who the hell was he meeting with, anyway? I don't recognize him. If he's a player, he's not a local one."

"I don't know." The car was late getting back, but the backup followed Cutter right back to his hotel. By the time Bright got back to the airfield, he learned that the subject was planning a good night's sleep for himself. The VC-20A was scheduled for a noon departure right back to Andrews. Bright planned to beat it there by taking an early commercial flight to Miami and connecting into Washington National. He'd arrive half dead from fatigue, but he'd get there.

Ryan took the call for the Director—Judge Moore was finally on his way back, but was still three hours out of Dulles. Jack's driver was ready as the executive elevator opened onto the garage, and they immediately left for Bethesda. They got there too late. Jack opened the door to see the bed covered with a sheet. The doctors had already left.

"I was there at the end. He went out easy," one of the CIA people told him. Jack didn't recognize him, though he gave the impression that he'd been waiting for Jack to appear. "You're Dr. Ryan, right?"

"Yes," Jack said quietly.

"About an hour before he faded out, he said something about—to remember what you two talked about. I don't know what he meant, sir."

"I don't know you."

"John Clark." The man came over to shake Ryan's hand. "I'm Operations, but Admiral Greer recruited me, too, long time ago." Clark let out a breath. "Like losing a father. Twice."

"Yeah," Ryan said huskily. He was too tired, too wrung out to hide his emotions.

"Come on, I'll buy you a cup of coffee and tell you a few stories about the old guy." Clark was sad, but he was a man accustomed to death. Clearly Ryan was not, which was his good luck.

The cafeteria was closed, and they got coffee from a waiting-room pot. It was reheated and full of acid, but Ryan didn't want to go home just yet, and was late remembering that he'd driven his own car in. He'd have to drive himself home tonight. He was too tired for that. He decided to call home and tell Cathy that he'd be staying over in town. CIA had an arrangement with one of the local Marriotts.

Clark offered to drive him down, and Jack dismissed his driver. By this time both men decided that a drink wasn't a bad idea.

Larson was gone from the room. He'd left a note saying that Maria would be coming in later that night, and he was going to pick her up. Clark had a small bottle of bourbon, and this Marriott had real glasses. He mixed two and handed one over to Jack Ryan.

"James Greer, the last of the good guys," Clark said as he raised his glass.

Jack took a sip. Clark had mixed it a little strong, and he nearly coughed.

"If he recruited you, how come—"

"Operations?" Clark smiled. "Well, sir, I never went to college, but Greer spotted me through some of his Navy contacts. It's a long story, and parts of it I'm not supposed to tell, but our paths have crossed three times."

"Oh?"

"When the French went in to bag those *Action Directe* folks you found on the satellite photos, I was the liaison officer in Chad. The second time they went in, after the ULA people who took that dislike to you, I was on the chopper. And I'm the fool who went on the beach to bring Mrs. Gerasimov and her daughter out. And that, sir, was all your fault. I do the crazy stuff," Clark explained. "All the field work that the espionage boys wet their pants over. Of course, maybe they're just smarter than I am."

"I didn't know."

"You weren't supposed to know. Sorry we missed on bagging those ULA pukes. I've always wanted to apologize to you for that. The French were really good about it. They were so happy with us for fingering *Action Directe* that they wanted to give us the ULA heads on plaques. But there was this damned Libyan unit out on maneuvers, and the chopper just stumbled on them—that's a problem when you go zooming in low—and it turned out that the camp was probably empty anyway. Everybody was real sorry it didn't work out as planned. Might have saved you a little grief. We tried, Dr. Ryan. We surely tried."

"Jack." Ryan held out his glass for a refill.

"Fine. Call me John." Clark topped both drinks off. "The Admiral said I could tell you all that. He also said that you tumbled to what was happening down south. I was down there," Clark said. "What do you want to know?"

"You sure you can tell me that?"

"The Admiral said so. He's—excuse me, he *was* a deputy director, and I figure that means I can do what he told me to do. This bureaucratic stuff is a little confusing to a humble line-animal, but I figure you can never go far wrong by telling the truth. Besides, Ritter told me that everything we did was legal, that he had all the permission he needed for this hunting expedition. That permission had to come from one place. Somebody decided that this drug stuff was a 'clear and present danger'—that's a quote—to the security of the United States. Only one man has the power to say that for-real, and if he does, he has the authority to do something about it. Maybe I never went to college, but I do read a lot. Where do you want me to start?"

"At the beginning," Jack replied. He listened for over an hour.

"You're going back?" Ryan asked when he was finished.

"I think a chance at bagging Cortez is worth it, and I might be able to help with the extraction of those kids up in the mountains. I don't really like the idea, but it is what I do for a living. I don't suppose your wife likes all the things she has to do as a doc."

"One thing I gotta ask. How did you feel about guiding those bombs in?"

"How did you feel about shooting people, back when you did it?"

Jack nodded. "Sorry—I had that coming."

"I joined up as a Navy SEAL. Lot of time in Southeast Asia. I got orders to go and kill people, and I went and killed 'em. That wasn't a declared war either, was it? You don't go around braggin' about it, but it's the job. Since I joined the Agency I haven't done very much of that—there have been times when I wished I could have done more of it, 'cause it might have saved a few lives in the long run. I had the head of Abu Nidal in my gunsights, but I never got permission to take the fucker out. Same story with two other people just as bad. It would have been deniable, clean, everything you want, but the lace-panty section at Langley couldn't make up their minds. They told me to see if it was possible, and it's just as dangerous to do that as it is to pull the trigger, but I never got the green light to complete the mission. From where I sit, it's a good mission. Those bastards are the enemies of our country, they kill our citizens—taken out a couple Agency people, too, and not real pretty how they did it—but we don't do anything about it. Tell me that makes sense. But I follow orders like I'm supposed to. Never violated one since I joined up."

"How do you feel about talking to the FBI?"

"You gotta be kidding. Even if I felt like it, which I don't, my main concern is those kids up in the hills. You hold me up on that, Jack, and some of them might get killed. Ritter called me earlier this evening and asked if I was willing to go back. I leave eight-forty tomorrow morning for Panama, and I stage from there back into Colombia."

"You know how to get in touch with me?"

"That might be a good idea," Clark agreed.

The rest had done everyone good. Aches had eased, and all hoped that the remaining stiffness would be worked out by the first few hours of movement. Captain Ramirez assembled his men and explained the new situation to them. He'd called in via his satellite link and requested extraction. The announcement was met with general approval. Unfortunately, he went on, the request had to be booted upstairs—with a favorable endorsement, VARIABLE had told him—and in any case the helicopter was down for an engine change. They'd be in-country at least one more night, possibly two. Until then, their mission was to evade contact and head for a suitable extraction point. These were already identified, and Ramirez had indicated the one he was heading for. It was fifteen kilometers away to the south. So the job for tonight was to skirt past the group that had been hunting for them. That would be tricky, but once past them it should be clear sailing through an area already swept. They'd try to cover eight or nine klicks tonight and the rest the following night. In any case the mission was over and they were pulling out. The recent arrivals from Team BANNER would form a third fire-team, augmenting KNIFE's already formidable firepower. Everyone still had at least two-thirds of his original ammo load-out. Food was running short, but they had enough for two days if nobody minded a few stomach rumbles. Ramirez ended his briefing on a confident note. It hadn't been cheap, and it hadn't been easy, but they had accomplished their mission and put a real hurtin' on the druggies. Now everybody had to keep it together for the trip out. The squad members exchanged nods and prepared to leave.

Chavez led off twenty minutes later. The idea was to keep as high on the mountain as they could. The opposition had shown a tendency to camp out lower down, and this way they stood the best chance of keeping clear. As always he was to avoid anything that looked like habitation. That meant giving a wide berth to the coffee plantations and associated villages, but that was what they had been doing anyway. They also had to move as fast as caution allowed, which meant that caution was downgraded. It was something often done in exercises, always with confidence. Ding's confidence in that sort of thing had also been downgraded by his experience in the field. The good news, as far as he was concerned, was that Ramirez was acting like an officer again. Probably he'd just been tired, too.

One nice thing about being close to the coffee plantations was that the cover wasn't so thick. People went into the woods to get fuel for their fires, and that thinned things out quite a bit. What effects it had on erosion wasn't Chavez's concern. That helped him to go faster, and he was covering nearly two kilometers per hour, which was far faster than he'd expected. By midnight his legs were telling him about every meter. Fatigue, he was learning again, was a cumulative factor. It took more than one day's rest to slough off all of its effects, no matter what sort of shape you were in. He wondered if the altitude wasn't also to blame. In any case he was still fighting to keep up the pace, to keep alert, to remember the path he was supposed to follow. Infantry operations are far more demanding intellectually than most people realize, and intellect is ever the first victim of fatigue.

He remembered a small village on the map, about half a klick from where he was at the moment, downhill. He'd taken the right turn at a landmark a klick back—he'd rechecked it at the rally point where they'd rested forty minutes earlier. He could hear noise from that direction. It seemed odd. The local peasants worked hard on the coffee plantations, he'd been told. They should have been asleep by now. Ding missed the obvious signal. He didn't miss the scream—more of a pant, really, the sort of sound made when—

He switched on his night scope and saw a figure running toward him. He couldn't tell—then he could. It was a girl, moving with considerable skill through the cover. Behind her was the noise of someone running after her with less skill. Chavez tapped the danger signal on his radio. Behind him everyone stopped and waited for his all-clear.

There wouldn't be one. The girl tripped and changed directions. A few seconds later she tripped again and landed right at Chavez's feet.

The sergeant clamped his left hand across her mouth. His other hand put a finger to his lips in the universal sign to be quiet. Her eyes went wide and white as she saw him—or more properly, didn't see him, just a mélange of camouflage paint that looked like something from a horror movie.

"Señorita, you have nothing to fear from me. I am a soldier. I do not molest women. Who is chasing you?" He removed his hand and hoped that she wouldn't scream.

But she couldn't even if she had wanted to, instead gasping out her reply. She'd run too far too fast. "One of their 'soldiers,' the men with guns. I—"

His hand went back on her mouth as the crashing sound came closer.

"Where are you?" the voice crooned.

Shit!

"Run that way," Chavez told her, pointing. "Do not stop and do not look back. Go!"

The girl took off and the man made for the noise. He ran right past Ding Chavez and precisely one foot farther. The sergeant clasped his hand across the man's face and took him down, pulling the head back as he did so. Just as both men hit the ground, Ding's combat knife made a single lateral cut. He was surprised by the noise. Escaping air from the windpipe combined with the spurting blood to make a gurgling sound that made him cringe. The man struggled for a few futile seconds, then went limp. The victim had a knife of his own, and Chavez set it in the wound. He hoped the girl wouldn't be blamed for it, but he'd done all that he could as far as she was concerned. Captain Ramirez showed up a minute later and was not very pleased.

"Didn't have much choice, sir," Chavez said in his own defense. Actually he felt rather proud of himself. After all, protecting the weak was the job of the soldier, wasn't it?

"Move your ass outa here!"

The squad moved especially fast to clear the area, but if anyone came looking for the amorous sleepwalker, no one heard anything to suggest it. It was the last incident of the night. They arrived at the preplanned stopover point just before dawn. Ramirez set up his radio and called in.

"Roger, KNIFE, we copy your position and your objective. We do not as yet have confirmation for the extraction. Please call back around eighteen hundred Lima. We ought to have things set up by then. Over."

"Roger, will call back at eighteen hundred. KNIFE out."

"Shame about BANNER," one communicator said to the other.

"These things do happen."

"Your name Johns?"

"That's right," the colonel said without turning at once. He'd just come back from a test flight. The new—actually rebuilt five-year-old—engine worked just fine. The Pave Low III was back in business. Colonel Johns turned to see to whom he was talking.

"Do you recognize me?" Admiral Cutter asked curtly. He was wearing his full uniform for a change. He hadn't done that in months, but the three stars on each braided shoulder board gleamed in the morning sun, along with his ribbons and surface-warfare officer's badge. In fact, the general effect of the undress-white uniform was quite overpowering, right down to the white buck shoes. Just as he had planned.

"Yes, sir, I do. Please excuse me, sir."

"Your orders have been changed, Colonel. You are to return to your stateside base as soon as possible. That means today," Cutter emphasized.

"But what about—"

"That will be taken care of through other means. Do I have to tell you whose authority I speak with?"

"No, sir, you do not."

"You will not discuss this matter with anyone. That means nobody, anywhere, ever. Do you require any further instructions, Colonel?"

"No, sir, your orders are quite clear."

"Very well." Cutter turned and walked back to the staff car, which drove off at once. His next stop was a hilltop near the Gaillard Cut. There was a communications van there. Cutter walked right past the armed guard—he wore a Marine uniform but was a civilian—and into the van, where he made a similar speech. Cutter was surprised to learn that moving the van would be difficult and would require a helicopter, since the van was too large to be pulled down the little service road. He was, however, able to order them to shut down, and he'd see about getting a helicopter to lift the van out. Until then they would stay put and not do anything. Their security was blown, he explained, and further transmissions would only further endanger the people with whom they communicated. He got agreement on that, too, and left. He boarded his aircraft at eleven in the morning. He'd be home in Washington for supper.

Mark Bright was there just after lunch. He handed his film cassettes over to a lab expert and proceeded to Dan Murray's busy office, where he reported what he had seen.

"I don't know who he met with, but maybe you'll recognize the face. How about the Amex number?"

"It's a CIA account that he's had access to for the past two years. This is the first time he's used it, though. The local guy faxed us a copy so we could run the signature. Forensics has already given us a handwriting match," Murray said. "You look a little tuckered."

"I don't know why—hell, I must have slept three hours in the past day and a half. I've done my D.C. time. Mobile was supposed to be a nice vacation."

Murray grinned. "Welcome back to the unreal world of Washington."

"I had to get some help to pull this off," Bright said next.

"Like what?" Murray wasn't smiling anymore.

"Air Force personnel, intel and CID types. I told 'em this was code-word material, and, hell, even if I had told them everything I know, which I didn't, I don't know what the story is myself. I take responsibility, of course, but if I hadn't done it, I probably wouldn't have gotten the shots."

"Sounds to me like you did the right thing," Murray said. "I don't suppose you had much choice in the matter. It happens like that sometimes."

Bright acknowledged the official forgiveness. "Thanks."

They had to wait five more minutes for the photographs. Decks had been cleared for this case, but even priority cases took time, much to the annoyance of everyone. The technician—actually a section chief—arrived with the moist prints.

"I figured you'd want these babies in a hurry."

"You figured right, Marv—Holy Christ!" Murray exclaimed. "Marv, this is code-word."

"You already told me, Dan. Lips are zipped. We can enhance them some, but that'll take another hour. Want me to get that started?"

"Fast as you can." Murray nodded, and the technician left. "Christ," Murray said again when he reexamined the photos. "Mark, you take a mean picture."

"So who the hell is it?"

"Félix Cortez."

"Who's that?"

"Used to be a DGI colonel. We missed him by a whisker when we bagged Filiberto Ojeda."

"The Macheteros case?" That didn't make any sense.

"No, not exactly." Murray shook his head. He spoke almost reverently, thought for a minute, and called for Bill Shaw to come down. The acting Director was there within a minute. Agent Bright was still in the dark when Murray pointed his boss to the photographs. "Bill, you ain't going to believe this one."

"So who the hell is Félix Cortez?" Bright asked.

Shaw answered the question. "After he skipped out of Puerto Rico, he went to work for the Cartel. He had a piece of Emil's murder, how much we don't know, but he sure as hell was involved. And here he is, sitting with the President's National Security Adviser. Now what do you suppose they had to talk about?''

''It's not with this batch, but I got a picture of them shaking hands,'' the junior agent announced.

Shaw and Murray just stared at him when he said that. Then at each other. *The President's head national-security guy shook hands with somebody who works for the drug Cartel . . . ?*

''Dan,'' Shaw said, ''what the hell is going on? Has the whole world just gone crazy?''

''Sure looks that way, doesn't it?''

''Put a call in to your friend Ryan. Tell him . . . Tell his secretary that there's a terrorism thing—no, we can't risk that. Pick him up on the way home?''

''He's got a driver.''

''That's a big help.''

''I got it.'' Murray lifted his phone and dialed a Baltimore number. ''Cathy? Dan Murray. Yeah, we're fine, thanks. What time does Jack's driver usually get him home? Oh, he didn't? Okay, I need you to do something, and it's important, Cathy. Tell Jack to stop off at Danny's on the way home to, uh, to pick the books up. Just like that, Cathy. This isn't a joke. Can you do that? Thanks, doc.'' He replaced the phone. ''Isn't that conspiratorial?''

''Who's Ryan—isn't he CIA?''

''That's right,'' Shaw answered. ''He's also the guy who dumped this case in our laps. Unfortunately, Mark, you are not cleared for it.''

''I understand, sir.''

''Why don't you see how quick you can fly home and find out how much that new baby's grown. Damned nice work you did here. I won't forget,'' the acting Director promised him.

Pat O'Day, a newly promoted inspector working out of FBI Headquarters, watched from the parking lot as a subordinate stood on the flight line in the soiled uniform of an Air Force technical sergeant. It was a clear, hot day at Andrews Air Force Base, and a D.C. Air National Guard F-4C landed right ahead of the VC-20A. The converted executive jet taxied to the 89th's terminal on the west side of the complex. The stairs dropped and Cutter walked out wearing civilian clothes. By this time—through Air Force intelligence personnel—the Bureau knew that he'd visited a helicopter crew and a communications van in the morning. So far no one had approached either of them to find out why, because headquarters was still trying to figure things out, and, O'Day thought, failing miserably—but that was headquarters for you. He wanted to go back out to the field where the real cops were, though this case did have its special charm. Cutter walked across to where his personal car was parked, tossed his bag in the back seat, and drove off, with O'Day and his driver in visual pursuit. The National Security Adviser got onto Suitland Parkway heading toward D.C., then, after entering the city, onto I-395. They expected him to get off at the Maine Avenue exit, possibly heading toward the White House, but instead the man just kept going to his official residence at Fort Myer, Virginia. A discreet surveillance didn't get more routine than that.

''Cortez? I know that name. Cutter met with a former DGI guy?'' Ryan asked.

''Here's the photo.'' Murray handed it over. The lab troops had run it through their computerized enhancement process. One of the blackest of the Bureau's many forensic arts, it had converted a grainy photographic frame to glossy perfection. Moira Wolfe had again verified Cortez's identity, just to make everyone sure. "Here's another." The second one showed them shaking hands.

"This'll look good in court," Ryan observed as he handed the frames back.

"It's not evidence," Murray replied.

"Huh?"

Shaw explained. "High government officials meet with . . . with strange people all the time. Remember the time when Kissinger made the secret flight to China?"

"But that was—" Ryan stopped when he realized how dumb his objection sounded. He remembered a clandestine meeting with the Soviet Party chairman that he couldn't tell the FBI about. How would *that* look to some people?

"It isn't evidence of a crime, or even a conspiracy, unless we know that what they talked about was illegal," Murray told Jack. "His lawyer will argue, probably successfully, that his meeting with Cortez, while appearing to be irregular, was aimed at the execution of sensitive but proper government policy."

"Bullshit," Jack observed.

"The attorney would object to your choice of words, and the judge would have it stricken from the record, instruct the jury to disregard it, and admonish you about your language in court, Dr. Ryan," Shaw pointed out. "What we have here is a piece of interesting information, but it is not evidence of a crime until we know that a crime is being committed. Of course, it is bullshit."

"Well, I met with the guy who guided the 'car bombs' into the targets."

"Where is he?" Murray asked at once.

"Probably back in Colombia by now." Ryan explained on for a few minutes.

"Christ, who is this guy?" Murray asked.

"Let's leave his name out of it for a while, okay?"

"I really think we should talk to him," Shaw said.

"He's not interested in talking to you. He doesn't want to go to jail."

"He won't." Shaw rose and paced around the room. "In case I never told you, I'm a lawyer, too. In fact, I have a J.D. If we were to attempt to try him, his lawyer would throw Martinez-Barker at us. You know what that is? A little-known result of the Watergate case. Martinez and Barker were Watergate conspirators, right? Their defense, probably an honest one, was that they thought the burglary was sanctioned by properly constituted authority as part of a national-security investigation. In a rather wordy majority opinion, the appeals court ruled that there had been no criminal intent, the defendants had acted in good faith throughout, and therefore no actual crime had been committed. Your friend will say on the stand that once he'd heard the 'clear and present danger' pronouncement from his superiors, and been told that authorization came from way up the chain of command, he was merely following orders given by people who had sufficient constitutional authority to do so. I suppose Dan already told you, there really isn't any law in a case like this. Hell, the majority of my agents would probably like to buy your guy a beer for avenging Emil's death."

"What I can tell you about this guy is that he's a serious combat vet, and as far as I could tell, he's a very straight guy."

"I don't doubt it. As far as the killing is concerned—we've had lawyers say that the actions of police snipers come awfully close to cold-blooded murder. Drawing a distinction between police work and combat action isn't always as easy as we would like. In this case, how do you draw the line between murder and a legitimate counterterrorist operation? What it'll come down to—hell, it will mainly reflect the political beliefs of the judges who try the case, and the appeal, and every other part of the proceeding. Politics. You know,'' Shaw said, ''it was a hell of a lot easier chasing bank robbers. At least then you knew what the score was.''

''There's the key to it right there,'' Ryan said. ''How much you want to bet that this whole thing started because it was an election year?''

Murray's phone rang. ''Yeah? Okay, thanks.'' He hung up. ''Cutter just got in his car. He's heading up the G.W. Parkway. Anybody want to guess where he's going?''

26. Instruments of State

Inspector O'Day thanked his lucky stars—he was an Irishman and believed in such things—that Cutter was such an idiot. Like previous National Security Advisers he'd opted against having a Secret Service detail, and the man clearly didn't know the first thing about countersurveillance techniques. The subject drove right onto the George Washington Parkway and headed north in the firm belief that nobody would notice. No doubling back, no diversion into a one-way street, nothing that one could learn from watching a TV cop show or better yet, reading a Philip Marlowe mystery, which was how Patrick O'Day amused himself. Even on surveillances, he'd play Chandler tapes. He had more problems figuring those cases out than the real ones, but that was merely proof that Marlowe would have made one hell of a G-Man. This sort of case didn't require that much talent. Cutter might have been a Navy three-star, but he was a babe in the woods as far as conspiracy went. His personal car didn't even change lanes, and took the exit for CIA unless, O'Day thought, he had an unusual interest in the Federal Highway Administration's Fairbanks Highway Research Station, which was probably closed in any case. About the only bad news was that picking Cutter up when he left would be tough to do. There wasn't a good place to hide a car here—CIA security was pretty good. O'Day dropped his companion off to keep watch in the woods by the side of the road and whistled up another car to assist. He fully expected that Cutter would reappear shortly and drive right home.

The National Security Adviser never noticed the tail and parked in a VIP slot. As usual, someone held open the door and escorted him to Ritter's office on the seventh floor. The Admiral took his seat without a friendly word.

''Your operation is really coming apart,'' he told the DDO harshly.

''What do you mean?''

''I mean I met with Félix Cortez last night. He knows about the troops. He knows about the recon on the airfields. He knows about the bombs, and he knows about the helicopter we've been using to support SHOWBOAT. I'm shutting everything down. I've already had the helicopter fly back to Eglin, and I ordered the communications people at VARIABLE to terminate operations.''

''The hell you have!'' Ritter shouted.

''The hell I haven't. You're taking your orders from me, Ritter. Is that clear?''

"What about our people?" the DDO demanded.

"I've taken care of that. You don't need to know how. It's all going to quiet down," Cutter said. "You got your wish. There is a gang war underway. Drug exports are going to be cut by half. We can let the press report that the drug war is being won."

"And Cortez takes over, right? Has it occurred to you that as soon as he's settled in, things change back?"

"Has it occurred to you that he can blow the operation wide open? What do you suppose will happen to you and the Judge if he does that?"

"The same thing that'll happen to you," Ritter snarled back.

"Not to me. I was there, so was the Attorney General. The President never authorized you to kill anybody. He never said anything about invading a foreign country."

"This whole operation was your idea, Cutter."

"Says who? Do you have my signature on a single memo?" the Admiral asked. "If this gets blown, the *best* thing you can hope for is that we'll be on the same cellblock. If that Fowler guy wins, we're both fucked. That means we can't let it get blown, can we?"

"I do have your name on a memo."

"That operation is already terminated, and there's no evidence left behind, either. So what can you do to expose me without exposing yourself and the Agency to far worse accusations?" Cutter was rather proud of himself. On the flight back from Panama he'd figured the whole thing out. "In any case, I'm the guy giving the orders. The CIA's involvement in this thing is over. You're the only guy with records. I suggest that you do away with them. All the traffic from SHOWBOAT, VARIABLE, RECIPROCITY, and EAGLE EYE gets destroyed. We can hold on to CAPER. That's one part of the op that the other side hasn't cottoned to. Convert that into a straight covert operation and we can still use it. You have your orders. Carry them out."

"There will be loose ends."

"Where? You think people are going to volunteer for a stretch in federal prison? Will your Mr. Clark announce the fact that he killed over thirty people? Will that Navy flight crew write a book about dropping two smart-bombs on private homes in a friendly country? Your radio people at VARIABLE never actually saw anything. The fighter pilot splashed some airplanes, but who's he going to tell? The radar plane that guided him in never saw him do it, because they always switched off first. The special-ops people who handled the land side of the operation at Pensacola won't talk. And there are only a few people from the flight crews we captured. I'm sure we can work something out with them."

"You forgot the kids we have in the mountains," Ritter said quietly. He knew that part of the story already.

"I need information on where they are so that I can arrange for a pickup. I'm going to handle that through my own channels, if you don't mind. Give me the information."

"No."

"That wasn't a request. You know, I just could be the guy who exposes you. Then your attempts to tie me in with all this would merely look like a feeble effort at exculpating yourself."

"It would still wreck the election."

"And guarantee your imprisonment. Hell, Fowler doesn't even believe in putting serial killers in the chair. How do you think he'll react to dropping bombs on people who haven't even been indicted—and what about that 'collateral damage' you were so cavalier about? This is the only way, Ritter."

"Clark is back in Colombia. I'm sending him after Cortez. That would also tie things up." It was Ritter's last play, and it wasn't good enough.

Cutter jerked in his chair. "And what if he blows it? It is not worth the risk. Call off your dog. That, too, is an order. Now give me that information—and shred your files."

Ritter didn't want to. But he didn't see an alternative. The DDO walked to his wall safe—the panel was open at the moment—and pulled out the files. In SHOWBOAT-II was a tactical map showing the programmed exfiltration sites. He gave it to Cutter.

"I want it all done tonight."

Ritter let out a breath. "It will be."

"Fine." Cutter folded the map into his coat pocket. He left the office without another word.

It all came down to this, Ritter told himself. Thirty years of government service, running agents all over the world, doing things that his country needed to have done, and now he had to follow an outrageous order or face Congress, and courts, and prison. And the best alternative would be to take others there with him. It wasn't worth it. Bob Ritter worried about those kids in the mountains, but Cutter said that he'd take care of it. The Deputy Director (Operations) of the Central Intelligence Agency told himself that he could trust the man to keep his word, knowing that he wouldn't, knowing that it was cowardice to pretend that he would.

He lifted the files off the steel shelves himself, taking them to his desk. Against the wall was a paper shredder, one of the more important instruments of contemporary government. These were the only copies of the documents in question. The communications people on that hilltop in Panama shredded everything as soon as they uplinked copies to Ritter's office. CAPER went through NSA, but there was no operational traffic there, and those files would be lost in the mass of data in the basement of the Fort Meade complex.

The machine was a big one, with a self-feeding hopper. It was entirely normal for senior government officials to destroy records. Extra copies of sensitive files were liabilities, not assets. No notice would be taken of the fact that the clear plastic bag that had been empty was now filled with paper pasta that had once been important intelligence documents. CIA burned tons of the stuff every day, and used some of the heat that was generated to make hot water for the washrooms. Ritter set the papers in the hopper in half-inch lots, watching the entire history of his field operations turn to rubbish.

"There he is," the junior agent said into his portable radio. "Southbound."

O'Day picked the man up three minutes later. The backup car was already on Cutter, and by the time O'Day had caught up, it was clear that he was merely returning to Fort Myer, the VIP section off Sherman Road, east of the officers' club. Cutter lived in a red brick house with a screen porch overlooking Arlington National Cemetery, the garden of heroes. To Inspector O'Day, who'd served in Vietnam, what little he knew of the man and the case made it seem blasphemous that he should live here. The FBI agent told himself that he might be jumping to an inaccurate conclusion, but his instincts told him otherwise as he watched the man lock his car and walk into the house.

* * *

One benefit of being part of the President's staff was that he had excellent personal security when he wanted it, and the best technical security services as a matter of course. The Secret Service and other government agencies worked very hard and very regularly to make sure that his phone lines were secure. The FBI would have to clear any tap with them, and would also have to get a court order first, neither of which had been done. Cutter called a WATS line number—with a toll-free 800 prefix—and spoke a few words. Had anyone recorded the conversation he would have had a problem explaining it, but then so would the listener. Each word he spoke was the first word on a dictionary page, and the number of each page had three digits. The old paperback dictionary had been given him before he left the house in Panama, and he would soon discard it. The code was as simple and easy to use as it was effective, and the few words he spoke indicated pages whose numbers combined to indicate map coordinates for a few locations in Colombia. The man on the other end of the line repeated them back and hung up. The WATS-line call would not show up on Cutter's phone bill as a long-distance call. The WATS account would be terminated the next day. His final move was to take the small computer disk from his pocket. Like many people he had magnets holding messages to his refrigerator door. Now he waved one of them over the disk a few times to destroy the data on it. The disk itself was the last existing record of the soldiers of Operation SHOWBOAT. It was also the last means of reopening the satellite radio link to them. It went into the trash. SHOWBOAT had never happened.

Or that's what Vice Admiral James A. Cutter, USN, told himself. He mixed himself a drink and walked out onto his porch, looking down across the green carpet to the countless headstones. Many times he'd walked over to the Tomb of the Unknown Soldier, watching the soldiers of the President's Guard go through their mechanistic routine before the resting places of men who had served their country to the utmost. It occurred to him now that there would be more unknown soldiers, fallen on some nameless field. The original unknown soldier had died in France in World War I, and had known what he fought for—or thought he did, Cutter corrected himself. Most often they never really understood what it was all about. What they were told wasn't always the truth, but their country called, and off they went to do their duty. But you really needed a perspective to understand what it was all about, how the game was played. And that didn't always—ever?—jibe with what the soldiers were told. He remembered his own service off the coast of Vietnam, a junior officer on a destroyer, watching five-inch-gun rounds pound the beach, and wondering what it was like to be a soldier, living in the mud. But still they went to serve their country, not knowing that the country herself didn't know what service she needed or wanted. An army was composed of young kids who did their job without understanding, serving with their lives, and in this case, with their deaths.

''Poor bastards,'' he whispered to himself. It really was too bad, wasn't it? But it couldn't be helped.

It surprised everyone that they couldn't get the radio link working. The communications sergeant said that his transmitter was working just fine, but there was no answer from VARIABLE at six o'clock local time. Captain Ramirez didn't like it, but decided to press on to the extraction point. There had been no fallout from Chavez's little adventure with the would-be rapist, and the young sergeant led off for what he expected would be the last time. The enemy forces had swept this area, stupidly and oafishly, and wouldn't be back soon. The night went easily. They moved south in one-hour segments, stopping off at rally points, looping their path of advance to check for trailers, and detecting none. By four the following morning, they were at the extraction site. It was a clearing just downhill from a peak of eight thousand feet, lower than the really big crests, and conducive to a covert approach. The chopper could have picked them up nearly anywhere, of course, but their main consideration was still stealth. They'd be picked up, and no one would ever be the wiser. It was a shame about the men they'd lost, but no one would ever really know what they'd been here for, and the mission, though a costly one, had been a success. Captain Ramirez had said so.

He set his men in a wide perimeter to cover all approaches, with fallback defensive positions in case something untoward and unexpected happened. When that task was completed, he again set up his satellite radio and started transmitting. But again, there was no reply from VARIABLE. He didn't know what the problem was, but to this point there had been no hint of trouble, and communications foul-ups were hardly unknown to any infantry officer. He wasn't very worried about this one. Not yet, anyway.

Clark was caught rather short by the message. He and Larson were just planning their flight back to Colombia when it arrived. Just a message form with a few code-words, it was enough to ignite Clark's temper, so vile a thing that he labored hard to control it in the knowledge that it was his most dangerous enemy. He wanted to call Langley, but decided against it, fearing that the order might be restated in a way difficult to ignore. As he cooled off, his brain started working again. That was the danger of his temper, Clark reminded himself, it stopped him from thinking. He sure as hell needed to think now. In a minute he decided that it was time for a little initiative.

"Come on, Larson, we're going to take a little ride." That was easily accomplished. He was still "Colonel Williams" to the Air Force, and got himself a car. Next came a map, and Clark picked his brain to remember the path to that hilltop. . . . It took an hour, and the last few hundred yards were a potholed nightmare of a twisted, half-paved road. The van was still there, as was the single armed guard, who came forward to give them a less than eager greeting.

"Stand down, mister, I was here before."

"Oh, it's you—but, sir, I'm under orders to—"

Clark cut him off. "Don't argue with me. I know about your orders. Why the hell do you think I'm here? Now be a good boy and safe that weapon before you hurt yourself." Clark walked right past him, again amazing Larson, who was far more impressed with loaded and pointed guns.

"What gives?" Clark asked as soon as he was inside. He looked around. All the gear was turned off. The only noise was from the air-conditioning units.

"They shut us down," the senior communicator answered.

"Who shut you down?"

"Look, I can't say, all right, I got orders that we're shut down. That's it. You want answers, go see Mr. Ritter."

Clark walked right up to the man. "He's too far away."

"I got my orders."

"What orders?"

"To shut down, damn it! We haven't transmitted or received anything since lunchtime yesterday," the man said.

"Who gave you the orders?"

"I can't say!"

"Who's looking after the field teams?"

"I don't know. Somebody else. He said our security was blown and it was being handed over to somebody else."

"Who—you can tell me this time," Clark said in an eerily calm voice.

"No, I can't."

"Can you call up the field teams?"

"No."

"Why not?"

"Their satellite radios are encoded. The algorithm is on computer disk. We downloaded all three copies of the encryption keys and erased two of 'em. He watched us do it and took the third disk himself."

"How do you reestablish the link?"

"You can't. It's a unique algorithm that's based on the time transmissions from NAVSTAR satellites. Secure as hell, and just about impossible to duplicate."

"In other words those kids are completely cut off?"

"Well, no, he took the third disk, and there's somebody else who's—"

"Do you really believe that?" Clark asked. The man's hesitation answered the question. When the field officer spoke again, it was in a voice that didn't brook resistance. "You just told me that the commo link was unbreakable, but you accepted a statement from somebody you never saw before that it had been compromised. We got thirty kids down there, and it sounds like they've been abandoned. Now, who gave the orders to do it?"

"Cutter."

"He was *here?*"

"Yesterday."

"Jesus." Clark looked around. The other officer couldn't bring himself to look up. Both men had speculated over what was really happening, and had come to the same conclusion that he had. "Who set up the commo plan for this mission?"

"I did."

"What about their tactical radios?"

"Basically they're commercial sets, a little customized. They have a choice of ten SSB frequencies."

"You have the freqs?"

"Well, yeah, but—"

"Give them to me right now."

The man thought to say that he couldn't do that, but decided against it. He'd just say that Clark threatened him, and it didn't seem like the right time to start a little war in the van. That was accurate enough. He was very much afraid of Mr. Clark at this moment. He pulled the sheet of frequencies from a drawer. It hadn't occurred to Cutter to destroy that, too, but he had the radio channels memorized anyway.

"If anybody asks . . ."

"You were never here, sir."

"Very good." Clark walked out into the darkness. "Back to the air base," Clark told Larson. "We're looking for a helicopter."

Cortez had made it back to Anserma without note having been taken of his seven-hour absence, and had left behind a communications link that knew how to find him, and now, rested and bathed, he waited for the phone to ring. He congratulated himself, first, on having set up a communications net in America as soon as he'd taken the job with the Cartel; next on his performance with Cutter, though not as much for this. He could scarcely have lost, though the American had made it easier through his own stupidity, not unlike Carter and the *marielitos,* though at least the former President had been motivated by humanitarian aims, not political advantage. Now it was just a matter of waiting. The amusing part was the book code that he was using. It was backwards from the usual thing. Normally a book code was transmitted in numbers to identify words, but this time words indicated numbers. Cortez already had the American tactical maps—anyone could buy American military maps from their Defense Mapping Agency, and he'd been using them himself to run his operation against the Green Berets. The book-code system was always a secure method of passing information; now it was even more so.

Waiting was no easier for Cortez than for anyone else, but he amused himself with further planning. He knew what his next two moves were, but what about after that? For one thing, Cortez thought, the Cartel had neglected the European and Japanese markets. Both regions were flush with hard currency, and while Japan might be hard to crack—it was hard to import things legally into that market—Europe would soon get much easier. With the EEC beginning its integration of the continent into a single political entity, trade barriers would soon start to come down. That meant opportunity for Cortez. It was just a matter of finding ports of entry where security was either lax or negotiable, and then setting up a distribution network. Reducing exports to America could not be allowed to interfere with Cartel income, after all. Europe was a market barely tapped, and there he would begin to expand the Cartel horizons with his surplus product. In America, reduced demand would merely increase price. In fact, he expected that his promise to Cutter—a temporary one to be sure—would have a small but positive effect on Cartel income. At the same time, the disorderly American distribution networks would sort themselves out rapidly after the supply was reduced. The strong and efficient would survive, and once firmly established, would conduct business in a more orderly way. Violent crime was more troublesome to the *yanquis* than the actual drug addiction that caused it. Once the violence abated, drug addiction itself would lose some of the priority in the pantheon of American social problems. The Cartel wouldn't suffer. It would grow in riches and power so long as people desired its product.

While that was happening, Colombia itself would be further subverted, but more subtly. That was one more area in which Cortez had been given professional training. The current lords used a brute-force approach, offering money while at the same time threatening death. No, that would also have to stop. The lust in the developed countries for cocaine was a temporary thing, was it not? Sooner or later it would become unfashionable, and demand would gradually diminish. That was one thing that the lords didn't see. When it began to happen, the Cartel had to have a solid political base and a diversified economic foundation if it wished to survive the diminution of its power. That demanded a more accommodating stance with its parent country. Cortez was prepared to establish that, too. Eliminating some of the more obnoxious lords would be a major first step toward that goal. History taught that you could reach a *modus vivendi* with almost anybody. And Cortez had just proven it to be true.

The phone rang. He answered it. He wrote down the words given him and after hanging up, picked up the dictionary. Within a minute he was making marks on his tactical map. The American Green Berets were not fools, he saw. Their encampments were all set on places difficult to approach. Attacking and destroying them would be very costly. Too bad, but all things had their price. He summoned his staff and started getting radio messages out. Within an hour, the hunter groups were coming down off the mountains to redeploy. He'd hit them one at a time, he decided. That would guarantee sufficient strength to overwhelm each detachment, and also guarantee sufficient losses that he'd have to draw further on the retainers of the lords. He would not accompany the teams up the mountains, of course, but that was also too bad. It might have been amusing to watch.

Ryan hadn't slept at all well. A conspiracy was one thing when aimed at an external enemy. His career at CIA had been nothing more than that, an effort to bring advantage to his own country, often by inflicting disadvantage, or harm, upon another. That was his job as a servant of his country's government. But now he was in a conspiracy that was arguably against the government itself. The fact denied him sleep.

Jack was sitting in his library, a single reading lamp illuminating his desk. Next to him were two phones, one secure, one not. It was the latter which rang.

"Hello?"

"This is John," the voice said.

"What's the problem?"

"Somebody cut off support for the field teams."

"But why?"

"Maybe somebody wants them to disappear."

Ryan felt a chill at the back of his neck. "Where are you?"

"Panama. Communications have been shut down and the helicopter is gone. We have thirty kids on hilltops waiting for help that ain't gonna come."

"How can I reach you?" Clark gave him a number. "Okay, I'll be back to you in a few hours."

"Let's not screw around." The line clicked off.

"Jesus." Jack looked into the shadows of his library. He called his office to say that he'd drive himself into work. Then he called Dan Murray.

Ryan was back in the FBI building underpass sixty minutes later. Murray was waiting for him and took him back upstairs. Shaw was there, too, and much-needed coffee was passed out.

"Our field guy called me at home. VARIABLE has been shut down, and the helicopter crew that was supposed to bring them out has been pulled. He thinks they're going to be—hell, he thinks—"

"Yeah," Shaw observed. "If so, we now have a probable violation of the law. Conspiracy to commit murder. Proving it might be a little tough, though."

"Stuff your law—what about those soldiers?"

"How do we get them out?" Murray asked. "Get help from—no, we can't get the Colombians involved, can we?"

"How do you think they'd react to an invasion from a foreign army?" Shaw noted. "About the same way we would."

"What about confronting Cutter?" Jack asked. Shaw answered.

"Confront him with what? What do we have? Zip. Oh, sure, we can get those communications guys and the helicopter crews and talk to them, but they'll stonewall for a while, and then what? By the time we have a case, those soldiers are dead."

"And if we can bring them out, then what case do we have?" Murray asked. "Everybody runs for cover, papers get shredded. . . ."

"If I may make a suggestion, gentlemen, why don't we forget about courtrooms for the moment and try to concentrate on getting those grunts the hell out of Indian country?"

"Getting them out is fine, but—"

"You think your case will get better with thirty or forty new victims?" Ryan snapped. "What is the objective here?"

"That was a cheap shot, Jack," Murray said.

"Where's your case? What if the President authorized the operation, with Cutter as his go-between, and there's no written orders? CIA acted in accordance with verbal orders, and the orders are arguably legal, except that I got told to mislead Congress if they ask, *which they haven't done yet!* There's also that little kink in the law that says we can start a covert operation without telling them, no matter what it is—the limits on our covert ops come from a White House Executive Order, remember—as long as we do get around to telling them. Therefore a killing authorized by the guy who puts out the Executive Order can only become a murder *retroactively* if something extraneous to the murder itself does *not* happen! What bonehead ever set these statutes up? Have they ever really been tested in court?"

"You left something out," Murray observed.

"Yeah, the most obvious reply from Cutter is that this isn't a covert operation at all, but a paramilitary counterterrorist op. That evades the whole issue of intelligence-oversight. Now we come under the War Powers Resolution, which has another lead-time factor. Have any of these laws ever been tested in court?"

"Not really," Shaw answered. "There's been a lot of dancing around, but nothing actually on point. War-Powers especially is a constitutional question that both sides are afraid to put in front of a judge. Where are you coming from, Ryan?"

"I got an agency to protect, don't I? If this adventure goes public, the CIA reverts back to what it was in the seventies. For example, what happens to your counterterrorist programs if the info we feed you dries up?" That one scored points, Jack saw. CIA was the silent partner in the war on terrorism, feeding most of its data to the Bureau, as Shaw had every reason to know. "On the other hand, from what we've talked about the last couple of days, what real case do you have?"

"If by withdrawing support for SHOWBOAT, Cutter made it easier for Cortez to kill them, we have a violation of the District of Columbia law against conspiracy to commit murder. In the absence of a federal law, a crime committed on federal property can be handled by the municipal law that applies to the violation. Some part of what he did was accomplished here or on other federal property, and that's where the jurisdiction comes from. That's how we investigated the cases back in the seventies."

"What cases were they?" Jack asked Shaw.

"It spun out of the Church Committee hearings. We investigated assassination plots by CIA against Castro and some others—they never came to trial. The law we would have used was the conspiracy statute, but the constitutional issues were so murky that the investigation died a natural death, much to everyone's relief."

"Same thing here, isn't it? Except while we fiddle . . ."

"You've made your point," the acting Director said. "Number one priority is getting them out, any way we can. Is there a way to do it covertly?"

"I don't know yet."

"Look, for starters let's get in touch with your field officer," Murray suggested.

"He doesn't—"

"He gets immunity, anything he wants," Shaw said at once. "My word on it. Hell, far as I can tell he hasn't really broken any laws anyway—because of Martinez-Barker—but you have my word, Ryan, no harm comes to him."

"Okay." Jack pulled the slip of paper from his shirt pocket. The number Clark had given him wasn't a real number, of course, but by adding and subtracting to the digits in a prearranged way, the call went through.

"This is Ryan. I'm calling from FBI Headquarters. Hold on and listen." Jack handed the phone over.

"This is Bill Shaw. I'm acting Director. Number one, I just told Ryan that you are in the clear. My word: no action goes against you. Will you trust me on that? Good." Shaw smiled in no small surprise. "Okay, this is a secure line, and I presume that your end is the same way. I need to know what you think is going on, and what you think we can do about it. We know about the kids, and we're looking for a way to get them out. From what Jack tells us, you might have some ideas. Let's hear them." Shaw punched the speaker button on his phone, and everyone started taking notes.

"How fast do you think we can have the radios set up?" Ryan wondered when Clark had finished.

"The technicians start getting in around seven-thirty, figure by lunch. What about transport?"

"I think I can handle that," Jack said. "If you want covert, I can arrange covert. It means letting somebody else in, but it's somebody we can trust."

"No way we can talk to them?" Shaw asked Clark, whose name he didn't yet know.

"Negative," the speaker said. "You sure you can pull it off on your end?"

"No, but we can give it a pretty good try," Shaw replied.

"See you tonight, then." The line clicked off.

"Now all we have to do is steal some airplanes," Murray thought aloud. "Maybe a ship, too? So much the better if we bring it off covertly, right?"

"Huh?" That one threw Ryan. Murray explained.

Admiral Cutter emerged from his house at 6:15 for his daily jog. He headed downhill toward the river and chugged along the path paralleling the George Washington Parkway. Inspector O'Day followed. A reformed smoker, the inspector had no problems keeping up, and watched for anything unusual, but nothing appeared. No messages passed, no dead-drops laid, just a middle-aged man trying to keep fit. Another agent picked him up as Cutter turned for home. O'Day would change and be ready to follow Cutter into work, wondering if he'd spot some unusual behavior there.

Jack showed up for work at the usual hour, looking as tired as he felt. The morning conference in Judge Moore's office began at 8:30, and for once there was a full crew, though there might as well not have been. The DCI and DDO, he saw, were quiet, nodding but not taking very many notes.

These were—well, not friends, Ryan thought. Admiral Greer had been a friend and mentor. But Judge Moore had been a good boss, and though he and Ritter had never really gotten along, the DDO had never treated him unfairly. He had to give them one more chance, Jack told himself impulsively. When the conference ended, he was slow picking up his things while the others left. Moore caught the cue, as did Ritter.

"Jack, you want to say something?"

"I'm not sure I'm right for DDI," Ryan opened.

"Why do you say that?" Judge Moore asked.

"Something's happening that you aren't telling me about. If you don't trust me, I shouldn't have the job."

"Orders," Ritter said. He was unable to hide his discomfort.

"Then you look me straight in the eye and tell me it's all legitimate. I'm supposed to know. I have a right to know." Ritter looked to Judge Moore.

"I wish we were able to let you in on this, Dr. Ryan," the DCI said. He tried to bring his eyes up to meet Jack's, but they wavered and fixed on a spot of wall. "But I have to follow orders, too."

"Okay. I've got some leave coming. I want to think a few things over. My work is all caught up. I'm out of here for a few days, starting in an hour."

"The funeral's tomorrow, Jack."

"I know. I'll be there, Judge," Ryan lied. Then he left the room.

"He knows," Moore said after the door closed.

"No way."

"He knows and he wants to be out of the office."

"So what do we do about it if you're right?"

The Director of Central Intelligence looked up this time. "Nothing. That's the best thing we can do right now."

That was clear. Cutter had done better than he knew. In destroying the radio encryption codes needed to communicate with the four teams, KNIFE, BANNER, FEATURE, and OMEN, he'd eliminated the Agency's ability to affect the turn of events. Neither Ritter nor Moore really expected the National Security Adviser to get the men out, but they had no alternative that would not damage themselves, the Agency, and their President—and, incidentally, their country. If Ryan wanted out of the way if things came apart—well, Moore thought, maybe he had sensed something. The DCI didn't blame him for wanting to stay clear.

There were still things he had to tie up, of course. Ryan left the building just after eleven that morning. He had a car phone in his Jaguar and placed a call to a Pentagon number. "Captain Jackson, please," he said when it was picked up. "Jack Ryan calling." Robby picked up a few seconds later.

"Hey, Jack!"

"How's lunch grab you?"

"Fine with me. My place or yours, boy?"

"You know Artie's Deli?"

"K Street at the river. Yeah."

"Be there in half an hour."

"Right."

Robby spotted his friend at a corner table and came right over. There was already a place set for him, and another man was at the table.

"I hope you like corned beef," Jack said. He waved to the other man. "This is Dan Murray."

"The Bureau guy?" Robby asked as they shook hands.

"Correct, Captain. I'm a deputy assistant director."

"Doing what?"

"Well, I'm supposed to be in the Criminal Division, but ever since I got back I've been stuck supervising two major cases. You ought to be able to guess which ones they are."

"Oh." Robby started working on his sandwich.

"We need some help, Rob," Jack said.

"Like what?"

"Like we need you to get us somewhere quietly."

"Where?"

"Hurlburt Field. That's part of—"

"Eglin, I know. Hurlburt's where the Special Operations Wing works out of; it's right next to P-cola. Whole lot of people been borrowing Navy airplanes lately. The boss doesn't like it."

"You can tell him about this," Murray said. "Just so it doesn't leave his office. We're trying to clean something up."

"What?"

"I can't say, Rob," Jack replied. "But part of it is what you brought to me. It's a worse mess than you think. We have to move real fast, and nobody can know about it. We just need a discreet taxi service for the moment."

"I can do that, but I want to clear it with Admiral Painter."

"Then what?"

"Meet me at Pax River at two o'clock, down the hill at Strike. Hell, I've wanted to do a little proficiency flying anyway."

"Might as well finish your lunch."

Jackson left them five minutes later. Ryan and Murray did the same, driving to the latter's house. Here Jack made a phone call to his wife, telling her that he had to be out of town for a few days and not to worry. They drove away in Ryan's car.

Patuxent River Naval Air Test Center is located about an hour's drive from Washington, on the western shore of the Chesapeake Bay. Formerly one of the nicer plantations of antebellum Maryland, it was now the Navy's primary flight-test and evaluation center, fulfilling most of the functions of the better-known Edwards Air Force Base in California. It is the home of the Navy's Test Pilot School, where Robby had been an instructor, and houses various test directorates, one of which, located a mile or two downhill from the main flight line, is called Strike. The Strike Directorate is concerned with fighter and attack planes, the sexy fast-movers. Murray's FBI identification was sufficient to get them on base, and after checking in with the Strike security shack, they found a place to wait, listening to the bellow of afterburning jet engines. Robby's Corvette arrived twenty minutes later. The new captain led them into the hangar.

"You're in luck," he told them. "We're taking a couple of Tomcats down to Pensacola. The Admiral called ahead, and they're preflighting the birds already. I, uh—"

Another officer came into the room. "Cap'n Jackson? I'm Joe Bramer," the lieutenant said. "I hear we're heading down south, sir."

"Correct, Mr. Bramer. These gents are going with us. Jack Murphy and Dan Tomlinson. They're government employees who need some familiarization with Navy flight procedures. Think you can rustle up some poopy suits and hard hats?"

"No problem, sir. Be back in a minute."

"You wanted covert. You got covert." Jackson chuckled. He pulled his flight suit and helmet from a bag. "What gear you guys bringing along?"

"Shaving kits," Murray replied. "And one bag."

"We can handle that."

Fifteen minutes later, everyone climbed up ladders to board the aircraft. Jack got to fly with his friend. Five minutes after that, the Tomcats were taxiing to the end of the runway.

"Go easy, Rob," Ryan said as they awaited clearance for takeoff.

"Like an airliner," Jackson promised. It wasn't quite that way. The fighters leapt off the ground and streaked to cruising altitude about twice as fast as a 727, but Jackson kept the ride smooth and level once he got there.

"What gives, Jack?" he asked over the intercom.

"Robby, I can't—"

"Did I ever tell you all the things I can make this baby do for me? Jack, my boy, I can make this baby sing. I can turn inside a virgin quail."

"Robby, what we're trying to do is rescue some people who may be cut off. And if you tell that to anyone, even your Admiral, you might just screw things up for us. You ought to be able to figure it out from there."

"Okay. What about your car?"

"Just leave it there."

"I'll get somebody to put the right sticker on it."

"Good idea."

"You're getting better about flying, Jack. You haven't whimpered once."

"Yeah, well, I got one more flight today, and that one's in a fucking helicopter. I haven't ridden one of those since the day my back got broken on Crete." It felt good to tell him that. The real question, of course, was whether or not they'd get the chopper. But that was Murray's job. Jack turned his head to look around and was stunned to see the other Tomcat only a few feet off their right wingtip. Murray waved at him. "Christ, Robby!"

"Huh?"

"The other plane!"

"Hell, I told him to ease it off some, must be twenty feet away. We always fly in formation."

"Congratulations, you just got your whimper."

The flight lasted just over an hour. The Gulf of Mexico appeared first as a blue ribbon on the horizon, then grew into an oceanic mass of water as the two fighters headed down to land. Pensacola's strips were visible to the east, then got lost in the haze. It struck Ryan as odd that he feared flying less when he rode in a military aircraft. You could see better, and somehow that made a difference. But the fighters even landed in formation, which seemed madly dangerous, though nothing happened. The wingman touched first, and then Robby's a second or two later. Both Tomcats rolled out and turned at the end of the runway, stopping near a pair of automobiles. Some groundcrew men had ladders.

"Good luck, Jack," Robby said as the canopy came up.

"Thanks for the ride, man." Jack managed to detach himself from the airplane without help and climbed down. Murray was beside him a minute later. Both entered the waiting cars, and behind them the Tomcats taxied away to complete their flight to nearby Pensacola Naval Air Station.

Murray had called ahead. The officer who met them was the intelligence chief for the 1st Special Operations Wing.

"We need to see Colonel Johns," Murray said after identifying himself. That was the only conversation needed for the moment. The car took them past the biggest helicopters Ryan had ever seen, then to a low block building with cheap windows. The wing intelligence officer took them in. He handled the introduction of the visitors, thinking erroneously that Ryan was also FBI, then left the three alone in the room.

''What can I do for you?'' PJ asked warily.

''We want to talk about trips you made to Panama and Colombia,'' Murray replied.

''Sorry, we don't discuss what we do here very freely. That's what special ops are all about.''

''A couple of days ago you were given some orders by Vice Admiral Cutter. You were in Panama then,'' Murray said. ''Before that you had flown armed troops into Colombia. First you took them into the coastal lowlands, then you pulled them out and reinserted them into the hill country, correct?''

''Sir, I cannot comment on that, and whatever inference you draw is yours, not mine.''

''I'm a cop, not a reporter. You've been given illegal orders. If you carry them out, you may be an accessory to a major felony charge.'' Best to get things immediately on the table, Murray thought. It had the desired effect. Hearing from a senior FBI official that his orders might be illegal forced Johns to respond, though only a little bit.

''Sir, you're asking me something I don't know how to respond to.''

Murray reached into his bag and pulled out a manila envelope. He removed a photograph and handed it to Colonel Johns. ''The man who gave you those orders, of course, was the President's National Security Adviser. Before he met with you, he met with this guy. That is Colonel Félix Cortez. He used to be with the DGI, but now he's working for the Drug Cartel as chief of security. He was instrumental in the Bogotá murders. Exactly what they agreed on we do not know, but I can tell you what we do know. There is a communications van over the Gaillard Cut that had been the radio link with the four teams on the ground. Cutter visited it and shut it down. Then he came to see you and ordered you to fly home and never talk about the mission. Now, you put all three of those things together and tell me if what you do come up with sounds like something you want to be part of.''

''I don't know, sir.'' Johns' response was automatic, but his face had gone pink.

''Colonel, those teams have already taken casualties. It appears likely that the orders you were given might have been aimed at getting them all killed. People are out hunting them right now,'' Ryan said. ''We need your help to go get them out.''

''Who exactly are you, anyway?''

''CIA.''

''But it's your goddamned operation!''

''No, it isn't, but I won't bore you with the details,'' Jack said. ''We need your help. Without it, those soldiers aren't going to make it home. It's that simple.''

''So you're sending us back to clean up your mess. That's the way it always is with you people, you send us out—''

''Actually,'' Murray said, ''we were planning to go with you. Part of the way anyway. How soon can you be in the air?''

''Tell me exactly what you want.'' Murray did just that. Colonel Johns nodded and checked his watch.

''Ninety minutes.''

* * *

The MH-53J was far larger than the CH-46 that had nearly ended Ryan's life at twenty-three, but no less frightening to him. He looked at the single rotor and remembered that they were making a long, over-water flight. The flight crew was businesslike and professional, hooking both civilians up to the intercom and telling them where to sit and what to do. Ryan was especially attentive to the ditching instructions. Murray kept looking at the miniguns, the impressive six-barrel gatlings set next to enormous hoppers of live shells. There were three for this flight. The helicopter lifted off just after four and headed southwest. As soon as they were airborne, Murray had a crewman attach him to the floor with a twenty-foot safety line so that he could walk around. The hatch at the rear of the aircraft was half open, and he walked back to watch the ocean pass beneath them. Ryan stayed put. The ride was better than the Marine Corps helicopters he remembered, but it still felt like sitting on a chandelier during an earthquake as the aircraft vibrated and oscillated beneath its enormous six-bladed rotor. He could look forward and see one of the pilots, just sitting there as comfortably as though at the wheel of a car. But, Ryan told himself, it wasn't a car.

What he hadn't anticipated was the midair refueling. He felt the aircraft increase power and take a slightly nose-up attitude. Then through the front window he saw the wing of another aircraft. Murray hastened forward to watch, standing behind the crew chief, Sergeant Zimmer. He and Ryan were both hooked into the intercom.

"What happens if you tangle with the hose?" Murray asked as they neared the drogue.

"I don't know," Colonel Johns answered coolly. "It's never happened to me yet. You want to keep it quiet now, sir?"

Ryan looked around for "facilities." He saw what looked like a camper's john, but getting to it meant taking his seat belt off. Jack decided against it. The refueling ended without incident, entirely due, Jack was sure, to his prayers.

Panache was cruising on her station in the Yucatan Channel, between Cuba and the Mexican Coast, following a racetrack pattern. There hadn't been much in the way of activity since the cutter had gotten here, but the crew took comfort from the fact that they were back at sea. The great adventure at the moment was observing the new female crewmen. They had a new female ensign fresh from the Coast Guard Academy in Connecticut, and a half dozen others, mainly unrated seamen, but two petty officers, both electronics types, who, their peers grudgingly admitted, knew their jobs. Captain Wegener was watching the new ensign stand watch as junior officer of the deck. Like all new ensigns she was nervous and eager and a little scared, especially with the skipper on the bridge. She was also cute as a button, and that was something Wegener had never thought of an ensign before.

"Commanding officer, commanding officer," the bulkhead speaker called. Wegener picked up the phone next to his bridge chair.

"Captain here. What is it?"

"Need you in the radio room, sir."

"On the way." Red Wegener rose from his chair. "Carry on," he said on his way aft.

"Sir," the petty officer told him in the radio shack, "we just got a transmission from an Air Force helo, says he's got a person he has to drop off here. Says it's secret, sir. I don't have anything on my board about it, and . . . well, sir, I didn't know what to do, sir. So I called you."

"Oh?" The woman handed him the microphone. Wegener depressed the transmit button. "This is *Panache*. Commanding officer speaking. Who am I talking to?"

"*Panache,* this is CAESAR. Helicopter inbound your position on a Sierra-Oscar. I have a drop-off for you, over."

Sierra-Oscar meant some sort of special operation. Wegener thought for a moment, then decided that there wasn't all that much to think about.

"Roger, CAESAR, say your ETA."

"ETA one-zero minutes."

"Roger, one-zero minutes. We'll be waiting. Out." Wegener handed the microphone back and returned to the bridge.

"Flight quarters," he told the OOD. "Miss Walters, bring us to Hotel Corpin."

"Aye aye, sir."

Things started happening quickly and smoothly. The bosun's mate of the watch keyed the 1-MC: "Flight quarters, flight quarters, all hands man your flight-quarter stations. Smoking lamp is out topside." Cigarettes sailed into the water and hands removed their caps, lest they be sucked into somebody's engines. Ensign Walters looked to see where the wind was, and altered course accordingly, also increasing the cutter's speed to fifteen knots, thus bringing the ship to Hotel Corpin, the proper course for flight operations. And all, she told herself proudly, without having to be told. Wegener turned away and grinned. It was one of many first steps in the career of a new officer. She'd actually known what to do and done it without help. For the captain it was like watching his child take a first step. Eager and smart.

"Christ, it's a big one," Riley said on the bridge wing. Wegener went out to watch.

The helicopter, he saw, was an Air Force -53, far larger than anything the Coast Guard had. The pilot brought it in from aft, then pivoted to fly sideways. Someone was attached to the rescue cable and lowered down to the waiting arms of four deck crewmen. The instant he was detached from the harness, the helicopter lowered its nose and moved off to the south. Quick and smooth, Red noted.

"Didn't know we were getting company, sir," Riley observed as he pulled out a cigar.

"We're still at flight quarters, Chief!" Ensign Walters snapped from the wheelhouse.

"Yes, ma'am, beg pardon, I forgot," the bosun responded with a crafty look at Wegener. Another test passed. She wasn't afraid to yell at the master chief, even if he was older than her father.

"You can secure from flight quarters," the CO told her. "I didn't know either," Wegener told Riley. "I'm going aft to see who it is." He heard Ensign Walters give her orders, under the supervision of a lieutenant and a couple of chiefs.

The visitor, he saw as he approached the helo deck door, was stripping off a green flight suit, but didn't appear to be carrying anything, which seemed odd. Then the man turned around, and it just got stranger.

"Howdy, Captain," Murray said.

"What gives?"

"You got a nice quiet place to talk?"

"Come along." They were in Wegener's cabin shortly thereafter.

"I figure I owe you for a couple of favors," he said. "You could have given me a bad time over that dumb stunt we pulled. Thanks for the tip on the lawyer, too.

What he told me was pretty scary—but it turns out that I didn't talk to him until after the two bastards were killed. Last time I ever do something that dumb," Wegener promised. "You're here to collect, right?"

"Good guess."

"So what's going on? You don't just borrow one of those special-ops helos for a personal favor."

"I need you to be someplace tomorrow night."

"Where?"

Murray pulled an envelope from his pocket. "These coordinates. I have the radio plan, too." Murray gave him a few more details.

"You did this yourself, didn't you?" the captain said.

"Yeah, why?"

"Because you ought to have checked the weather."

27. The Battle of Ninja Hill

Armies have habits. These often appear strange or even downright crazy to outsiders, but for all of them there is an underlying purpose, learned over the four millennia in which men have fought one another in an organized fashion. Mainly the lessons learned are negative ones. Whenever men are killed for no good purpose, it is the business of armies to learn from the mistake and ensure that it will never happen again. Of course, such mistakes are repeated as often in the profession of arms as in any other, but also as in all professions, the really good practitioners are those who never forget fundamentals. Captain Ramirez was one of these. Though the captain had learned that he had too much sentiment, that the loss of life which was part and parcel of his chosen way of life was too difficult a burden to bear, he still remembered the other lessons, one of which was reinforced by the most recent and unpleasant discovery. He still expected to be picked up tonight by the Air Force helicopter, and felt reasonably sure that he had evaded the teams set out to hunt Team KNIFE, but he remembered all the lessons of the past when soldiers died because the unexpected happened, because they took things for granted, because they forgot the fundamentals.

The fundamental rule here was that a unit in a fixed location was always vulnerable, and to reduce that vulnerability, the intelligent commander prepared a defense plan. Ramirez remembered that, and hadn't lost a keen eye for terrain. He didn't think that anyone would come to trouble his men that night, but he had already prepared for that eventuality.

His deployments reflected the threat, which he evaluated as a very large but relatively untrained force, and his two special advantages: first, that all of his men had radios, and second, that there were three silenced weapons at his disposal. Ramirez hoped that they wouldn't come calling, but if they did, he planned to give them a whole series of nasty surprises.

Each of his men was part of a two-man team for mutual support—there is nothing so fearful as to be alone in a combat action, and the effectiveness of any soldier is multiplied many times over merely by having a single comrade at his side. Each pair had dug three holes—called Primary, Alternate, and Supplementary—as part of three separate defensive networks, all of them camouflaged and carefully sited to be mutually supporting. Where possible, fire lanes were cleared, but always on oblique lines so that the fire would take the attacker from the side, not the front, and part of the plan was to force the attacker to move in a direction anticipated by the Team. Finally, if everything broke down, there were three preplanned escape routes and corresponding rally points. His men kept busy all day, digging their holes, preparing their positions, siting their remaining claymore mines, until their rest periods were occupied only with sleep and not conversation. But he couldn't keep himself quite that busy, and couldn't keep himself from thinking.

Through the day things kept getting worse. The radio link was never reestablished, and every time Ramirez came up at a scheduled time and heard nothing, the thinner became his explanations for it. He could no longer wave it off as an equipment or power failure at the downlink. Throughout the afternoon he told himself that it was impossible they were cut off, and he never even considered the possibility that they had *been* cut off, but the nagging thought grew louder in the back of his mind that he and his men were alone, far from home, facing a potential threat with only what they had carried in on their own backs.

The helicopter landed back at the same facility it had only left two days before, taxiing into the hangar whose door was immediately closed. The MC-130 that had accompanied them down was similarly hidden. Ryan was exhausted by the flight and walked off with wobbly legs to find Clark waiting. The one really good piece of news was that Cutter had neglected to take the simple expedient of meeting with the base commander, never thinking that his orders would be disregarded. As a result, the reappearance of the special-operations aircraft was just another odd occurrence, and one green helicopter—in shadows they looked black—was pretty much the same as another.

Jack returned to the aircraft after making a trip to the rest room and drinking about a quart of water from the cooler. Introductions had already been explained, and he saw that Colonel Johns had hit it off with Mr. Clark.

"Third SOG, eh?"

"That's right, Colonel," Clark said. "I never made it into Laos myself, but you guys saved a few of our asses. I've been with the Agency ever since—well, almost," Clark corrected himself.

"I don't even know where to go. That Navy prick had us destroy all our maps. Zimmer remembers some of the radio freqs, but—"

"I got the freqs," Clark said.

"Fine, but we still have to find 'em. Even with tanker support, I don't have the legs to do a real search. There's a lot of country down there, and the altitude murders our fuel consumption. What's the opposition like?"

"Lots of people with AKs. Oughta sound familiar."

PJ grimaced. "It does. I got three minis. Without any air support . . ."

"You guessed right: you are the air support. I'd hold on to the miniguns. Okay, the exfiltration sites were agreed upon beforehand?" Clark asked.

"Yeah—a primary and two backups for each team, total of twelve."

"We have to assume that they are known to the enemy. The job for tonight is finding 'em and getting them somewhere else that we know about and they don't. Then tomorrow night you can fly in for the pickup."

"And from there out. . . . The FBI guy wants us to land on that little boat. I'm worried about *Adele*. The last weather report I saw at noon had it heading north towards Cuba. I want to update that."

"I just did," Larson said as he rejoined the group. "*Adele* is heading west again, and she made hurricane an hour ago. Core winds are now seventy-five."

"Oh, shit," Colonel Johns observed. "How fast is she moving?"

"It's going to be close for tomorrow night, but no problem for our flight this evening."

"What flight is that, now?"

"Larson and I are going to hop down to locate the teams." Clark pulled a radio out of what had been Murray's bag. "We fly up and down the valley, talking on these. With luck we'll get contact."

"You must really believe in luck, son," Johns said.

O'Day reflected that the life of an FBI agent wasn't always as glamorous as people thought. There was also the little problem that with less than twenty agents on the case he couldn't assign this distasteful task to a junior agent. But the case had enough of those problems. They hadn't even considered getting a search warrant yet, and sneaking into Cutter's quarters without legal authorization—something that the Bureau seldom did anymore—was impossible. Cutter's wife had just gotten back and was bossing her staff of stewards around like a woman to the manor born. On the other hand, the Supreme Court had ruled a few years before that trash-searching didn't require the sanction of a court. That fact enabled Pat O'Day to get the best upper-body workout he'd had in years. Now he could barely raise his arms after having loaded a few tons of malodorous garbage bags into the back of a white-painted trash truck. It might have been one of several cans. The VIP section of Fort Myer was still a military post; even the trash cans had to be set up just so, and in this case, two homes shared each stopping place for the equally well organized trash contractor. O'Day had marked the bags before loading them into the back of the truck, and as a result, fifteen garbage bags were now sitting in one of the Bureau's many laboratories, though not one that was part of the tourist route, since the FBI shows only its best face to those who tour the Hoover Building, the nice, clean, antiseptic labs. The only good news was that the ventilation system was good, and there were several cans of air freshener around to disguise the smells that got past the technicians' surgical masks. O'Day himself felt as though a squadron of bluebottle flies would follow him for the rest of his life. The search took an hour as the garbage was processed across a white tabletop of imitation marble, about four days' worth of coffee grinds and half-eaten croissants, decomposing merengue, and several diapers—those were from the wrong house: the officer next door to the Cutters had his new granddaughter visiting.

"Bingo," a technician said. His gloved hand held up a computer disk. Even with the gloves, he held it on opposite corners and dropped it into an extended plastic baggie. O'Day took the bag and walked upstairs to latent prints.

Two senior technicians were working overtime tonight. They'd cheated somewhat, of course. They already had a copy of Admiral Cutter's fingerprints from the central print index—all military personnel are printed as a matter of course upon their enlistment—along with their entire bag of tricks, which included a laser.

"What was it in?" one of them asked.

"On top of some newspapers," O'Day replied.

"Aha! No extraneous grease, and good insulation against the heat. There may be a chance.'' The technician removed the disk from the clear bag and went to work. It took ten minutes, while O'Day paced the room.

''I got a thumbprint with eight points on the front side, and what is probably a smudged ring finger on the back side with one good point and one very marginal one. There is one completely different set, but it's too smudged to identify. It's a different pattern, though, has to be a different person.''

O'Day figured that that was more than he'd had the right to expect under the circumstances. A fingerprint identification ordinarily required ten individual points—the irregularities that constituted the art of fingerprint identification—but that number had always been arbitrary. The inspector was certain that Cutter had handled this computer disk, even if a jury might not be completely sure, if that time ever came. Now it was time to see what was on it, and for that he headed to a different lab.

Since personal computers had entered the marketplace, it was only a matter of time until they were used in criminal enterprises. To investigate such use, the Bureau had its own department, but the most useful people of all were private consultants whose real business was ''hacking,'' and for whom computers were marvelous toys and their use the most entertaining of games. To have an important government agency pay them for playing the game was their equivalent of a pro-football career. The one O'Day found waiting for him was one of the champs. He was twenty-five, and still a student at a local community college despite over two hundred hours of credits, the lowest grade for which had been a B+. He had longish red hair and a beard, both of which needed washing. O'Day handed it over.

''This is a code-word case,'' he said.

''That's nice,'' the consultant said. ''This is a Sony MFD-2DD microfloppy, double-sided, double-density, 135TPI, probably formatted for 800K. What's supposed to be on it?''

''We're not sure, but probably an encipherment algorithm.''

''Ah! Russian communications systems? The Sovs getting sophisticated on us?''

''You don't need to know that,'' O'Day pointed out.

''You guys are no fun at all,'' the man said as he slid the disk into the drive. The computer to which it was attached was a new Apple Macintosh IIx, each of whose expander slots was occupied by a special circuit board, two of which the technician had personally designed. O'Day had heard that he'd work on an IBM only if someone put a gun to his head.

The programs he used for this task had been designed by other hackers to recover data from damaged disks. The first one was called Rescuedata. The operation was a delicate one. First the read heads mapped each magnetic zone on the disk, copying the data over to the eight-megabyte memory of the IIx and making a permanent copy on the hard drive, plus a floppy-disk copy. That allowed him to eject the original, which O'Day immediately reinserted in the baggie.

''It's been wiped,'' the man said next.

''What?''

''It's been wiped, not erased or initialized, but wiped. Probably with a little toy magnet.''

''Shit,'' O'Day observed. He knew enough about computers to realize that the magnetically stored data was destroyed by magnetic interference.

''Don't get excited.''

''Huh?''

''If this guy had initialized the disk, we'd be screwed, but he just swiped a magnet around. Some of the data is gone, but some probably isn't. Give me a couple of hours and maybe I can get some of this data back for you—there's a smidge right there. It's in machine language, but I don't recognize the format . . . looks like a transposition algorithm. I don't know any of that cryppie stuff, sir. Looks fairly complex.'' He looked around. ''This is going to take some time.''

''How long?''

''How long to paint the Mona Lisa? How long to build a cathedral. How long . . .'' O'Day was out of the room before he heard the third one. He dropped the disk off in the secure file in his office, then headed for the gym for a shower and a half hour in the Jacuzzi. The shower removed the stink, and while the whirlpool went to work on the aches, O'Day reflected that the case against the son of a bitch was shaping up rather nicely.

''Sir, they just ain't there.''

Ramirez handed the headset back and nodded. There was no denying it now. He looked over to Guerra, his operations sergeant.

''I think somebody forgot about us.''

''Well, that's good news, Cap'n. What are we gonna do about it?''

''Our next check-in time is zero-one-hundred. We give 'em one more chance. If nothing by then, I guess we move out.''

''Where to, sir?''

''Head down off the mountain, see if we can borrow some transport and—Christ, I don't know. We probably have enough cash we can use to fly out of here—''

''No passports, no ID.''

''Yeah. Make it to the Embassy in Bogotá?''

''That violates about a dozen different orders, sir,'' Guerra pointed out.

''First time for everything,'' Captain Ramirez observed. ''Have everybody eat their last rations, rest up as best they can. We stand-to in two hours, and stay alert all night. I want Chavez and León to patrol down the hill, say two klicks' worth.'' Ramirez didn't have to say what he was worried about. As unlikely as intellect told them it had to be, he and Guerra were on the same wavelength.

''It's cool, Cap'n,'' the sergeant assured him. ''We're going to be all right, just as soon as those REMFs get their shit together.''

The mission briefing took fifteen minutes. The men were angry and restive at the losses they had taken, not fully appreciative of the danger that lay ahead, only of their rage at what had already happened to their numbers. Such bravado, Cortez thought, such machismo. *The fools.*

The first target was only thirty kilometers away—for the obvious reasons he wanted to deal with the nearest one first—and twenty-two of them could be covered by truck. They had to wait for darkness, of course, but sixteen trucks rolled out, each with fifteen or so men aboard. Cortez watched them depart, muttering to one another as they pulled out of sight. His own people stayed behind, of course. He had so far recruited ten men, and their loyalty was to him alone. He'd recruited well, of course. No nonsense about who their parents were or how faithfully they had killed. He'd selected them for their skills. Most were dropouts from M-19 and FARC, men for whom five years of playing at guerrilla warfare had been enough. Some had received training in Cuba or Nicaragua and had basic soldier skills—actually terrorist skills, but that put them ahead of the ''soldiers'' of the Cartel, most of whom had never received formal training at all. They were mercenaries.

Their only interest in Cortez was in the money he'd paid them, but he'd also promised them more. More to the point, there was nowhere else for them to go. The Colombian government had no use for them. The Cartel would not have trusted them. And they had forsworn their loyalty to the two Marxist groups which were so politically bankrupt that they allowed themselves to be hired out by the Cartel. That left Cortez. He was the man they would kill for. He hadn't confided in them, since he didn't yet trust them to do any more than that, but all great movements began with small groups of people whose methods were as murky as their objectives, who knew only loyalty to a single man. At least that's what Cortez had been taught. He didn't fully believe that himself, but it was enough for the moment. He had no illusions about leading a revolution. He was merely executing—what was it called? A hostile takeover. Yes, that was right. Cortez chuckled to himself as he walked back inside and started looking at his maps.

"Good thing neither one of us is a smoker," Larson said as the wheels came up. In the cabin behind them was an auxiliary fuel tank. They had a two-hour flight down to their patrol area, and two hours back, with three hours of loiter time on station. "You suppose this is going to work?"

"If it doesn't, somebody's going to pay," Clark replied. "What about the weather?"

"We'll sneak back in ahead of it. Don't make any bets on tomorrow, though."

Chavez and León were two kilometers away from the team's farthest listening post. Both carried silenced weapons. León hadn't been the point scout for BANNER, but had woodcraft skills that Chavez liked. The best news of all was that they found nothing. Captain Ramirez had briefed them on what he was worried about. So far they hadn't detected it, which was fine with the two sergeants. They'd gone down to the north initially, then gradually come south while covering an arc of several kilometers, looking for signs, listening for noise. They were just turning for the climb back to the LZ when Chavez stopped and turned.

It was a metallic sound. He waved for León to freeze and pivoted his head around, hoping—what? he asked himself. Hoping that he'd really heard something? Hoping that he'd imagined it? He switched his goggles and scanned downhill. There was a road down there somewhere. If somebody came calling, it would be from that direction.

It was hard to tell at first. There was thick overhead cover here, and the relative absence of light forced him to turn the brightness control to the maximum. That made the picture fuzzy, like a pre-cable TV signal from a distant city, and what he was looking for was far off—at least five hundred meters, which was as far as he could see down a thinned-out area of the forest. The tension only made him more alert, but that made his imagination work all the harder, and he had to guard against seeing things that weren't there.

But something was there. He could feel it even before the noise returned. There were no more metallic sounds, but there was . . . there was the over-loud whisper of leaves, and then it was a calm night again in the lee of the mountain. Chavez looked over to León, who also had his goggles on, was also looking that way, a green image on the tube. The goggled face turned toward Chavez and nodded. There was no emotion in the gesture, just the professional communication of an unpleasant thought. Chavez knelt to activate his radio.

"Six, this is Point," Ding called.

"Six here."

"We're at the turn-back point. We got movement down here, about half a klick below us. We're gonna wait to see what it is."

"Roger. Be careful, Sergeant," Ramirez said.

"Will do. Out." León came over to join him.

"How d'you want to play this?" 'Berto asked.

"Let's stay close, try not to move too much till we see what they're up to."

"You got it. Better cover about fifty meters uphill."

"Go ahead, I'll be right behind you." Chavez took one more look downhill before following his comrade up to a stand of thick trees. Still nothing he could really identify on the speckled screen. Two minutes later he was at the new perch.

'Berto saw it first and pointed down a trail. The moving specks were larger than the noise generated by the viewing system. Heads. Four or five hundred meters off. Coming straight up the hill.

Okay, Chavez said to himself. *Let's get a count.* He felt himself relaxing. This was business. He'd done it all before. The great unknown was now behind him. There would be a fight. He knew how to do that.

"Six, this is Point, estimate company strength, heading right up to you."

"Anything else?"

"They're moving kinda slow. Careful, like."

"How long can you stay there?"

"Maybe a couple minutes."

"Stay as long as it's safe, then move. Try to pace them for another klick or so. We want to get as many as possible into the sack."

"Roger."

"These numbers suck, man," León whispered.

"We sure as hell want to whittle 'em down some 'fore we run, don't we?" Chavez returned his eyes to the advancing enemy. He saw no obvious organization. They were taking their time, moving slowly up the hill, though he could easily hear them now. They moved in little bands of three or four, probably groups of friends, he thought, like street gangs did. You wanted a friend at your back.

Street gang, he thought. They didn't bother with colors down here like in his barrio, just those damned AK-47s. No real plan, no fire and maneuver teams. He wondered if they had radios to coordinate with. Probably not. He realized, a little late, that they did know where they were going. He didn't understand how they knew, but it only meant that they were heading into one hell of an ambush. But there were still a lot of 'em. An awful lot.

"Time to move," Ding told 'Berto.

They raced uphill, or went as fast as their training allowed, choosing one good observation point after another and keeping their commander posted on their position and the enemy's. Ahead of them, up the hill, the squad had nearly two hours to reorient itself and prepare its ambush. Chavez and León copied his radio message on their own sets. The squad was moving forward to meet the attackers well in front of the primary defensive line. It was set between two particularly steep sections, anchored at those points with the SAWs, covering an approach route less than three hundred meters wide. If the enemy was dumb enough to come through there, well, that was their problem, wasn't it? So far they had taken a direct route to the LZ. Maybe they'd been told that KNIFE probably was there, not certainly, Chavez thought, as he and León picked their spot, just below one of the SAWs.

"Six, this is Point, we are in position. Enemy is three hundred meters below us."

Click-click.

"I see 'em," another voice called over the radio net. "Grenade One sees 'em."

"Medic has 'em."

"SAW One has 'em."

"Grenade Two. We got 'em."

"KNIFE, this is Six. Let's everybody be cool," Ramirez said calmly. "Looks like they're coming right in the front door. Remember the signal, people. . . ."

It took another ten minutes. Chavez switched off his scope both to save batteries and to get his eyes back to normal. His mind played and replayed the squad fire-plan. He and León had specific areas of responsibility. Each soldier was supposed to limit his fire to an individual arc. All the arcs interlocked and overlapped somewhat, but they were supposed to hunt in their own little patch and not hose down the entire area. Even the two SAWs on line were so limited. The third was well behind the firing line with the small reserve force, ready to support the squad as it pulled back or to react to something unexpected.

They were within a hundred meters of the line now. The front rank of the advancing enemy was perhaps eighteen or twenty men, with others struggling behind to keep up. They moved slowly, careful of their footing, weapons held at port across their chests. Chavez counted three in his area of responsibility. León kept watch downhill as he brought his weapon up.

In the old days it was done with volley fire. Napoleonic infantry formed up shoulder-to-shoulder in ranks of two or four, leveling their muskets on command and firing on one another in one dreadful blast of power and ball. The purpose was shock. The purpose still is. Shock to unsettle those enemies fortunate enough to escape instant death, shock to tell them that this was not a place they wanted to be, shock to interfere with their performance, to stop them, to confuse them. It is no longer done with massed columns of muskets. Today it is done by letting them get very, very close, but the impact remains as much psychological as physical.

Click-click-click. Get ready, Ramirez ordered. Across the line, the riflemen snugged their weapons into their shoulders. The machine guns came up on their bipods. Safeties went off. In the center of the line, the captain wrapped his hand around a length of communications wire. It was fifty yards long, and attached to its other end was a tin can containing a few pebbles. Slowly, carefully, he pulled the wire taut. Then he yanked it hard.

The sudden sound froze the moment in time. It was as if everything stopped for an instant that seemed to last for hours. The men in front of the light-fighters turned instinctively toward the sound in their midst, away from the unknown threat that lay to their front and their flanks, away from the fingers that had just begun to press down.

The moment ended with the white muzzle flashes of the squad. The leading fifteen attackers dropped in an instant. Behind them five more died or were wounded before fire was returned. Then the firing from above stopped. The attackers responded late. Many of them emptied whole magazines in the general direction of uphill, but the soldiers were down in their holes, denying the attackers targets.

"Who fired? Who fired? What is going on here?" It was the voice of Sergeant Olivero, whose accent was perfect.

Confusion is the ally of the prepared. More men rushed forward into the killing zone to see what was happening, wondering who had shot at whom. Chavez and all the others counted to ten before coming back up. Ding had two men within thirty meters of his position. On "Ten!" he dropped one with a three-round burst and wounded the other. Maybe a dozen more enemies were down now.

Click-click-click-click-click. "Everybody move out," Ramirez called over the radios.

The drill was the same across the line. One man from each pair took off at once, racing fifty meters uphill before stopping at a preselected spot. The SAWs, which had thus far fired only short bursts as though they were mere rifles, now fired long ones to cover the disengagement. Within a minute, KNIFE had moved away from the area now being beaten with late and inaccurate fire. One man was grazed by a stray round, but ignored it. As usual, Chavez was the last to leave and the slowest to move, picking his way from one thick tree to another as the returning fire became heavier. He reactivated his goggles to get a view of things. Perhaps thirty men were down in the kill zone, only half of them moving. Too late, the enemy was looping around the south side, trying to envelop a position already deserted. He watched them come into the position he and León had occupied only minutes before, and they just stood there in confusion, still wondering what had happened. There were screams from the wounded now, and then the curses started, obscene, powerful curses of enraged men who were accustomed to inflicting death, not receiving it. New voices became clear over the din of sporadic rifle fire and curses and screams. Those would be the leaders, giving orders loudly and in a language all of the soldiers understood. Chavez had just started believing that this battle would be easily won when he took his final look.

"Oh, shit." He keyed his radio. "Six, this is Point. This is greater than company strength, sir. Say again, more than company strength. I estimate three-zero enemy casualties at this time. They just started moving up again. I got thirty or so moving south. Somebody's telling 'em to try 'n surround us."

"Roger, Ding. Get moving uphill."

"On the way." Chavez ran hard, leapfrogging past León's position.

"Mr. Clark, you've got me believing in miracles," Larson said at the wheel of his Beechcraft. They'd made contact with Team OMEN on the third try, and ordered them to move five klicks to a clearing barely large enough for the Pave Low. The next attempt took longer, nearly forty minutes. Now they were looking for BANNER. What was left of it, Clark reminded himself. He didn't know that its survivors had linked up with KNIFE, which was the last team on his list.

The second defense position was of necessity more dispersed than the first, and Ramirez was starting to worry. His men had handled the first ambush so perfectly that someone at the Infantry School might one day write a paper about it, but one immutable law of military operations was that successful tricks can rarely be repeated. There was nothing like death to teach someone a lesson. The enemy would maneuver now, would spread out, trying to coordinate or at least to make better use of his larger numbers. And the enemy was doing something smart. He was moving faster. Now that they knew that they had a real enemy with real teeth, they knew on instinct that the best thing to do was to push, to take the initiative and force the pace of the combat action. That was the one thing that Ramirez could not really prevent. But he, too, had cards to play.

His flank scouts kept him posted on enemy movements. There were now three groups of about forty men each. Ramirez couldn't deal with all three, but he could hurt them one at a time. He also had three fire teams of five men each. One—the remains of BANNER—he left in the center, with a scout on the left to keep track of the third enemy group while he slid the bulk of his force south and deployed on an oblique uphill-downhill line, almost an L-shaped ambush line anchored at the uphill side with both SAWs.

They didn't have to wait very long. The enemy was moving faster than Ramirez hoped, and there was barely time for his men to select good firing positions, but the attackers were still moving predictably over the terrain, which was again to be their misfortune. Chavez was at the bottom end and gave warning as they approached. Again, they allowed the enemy to close to fifty meters' distance. Chavez and León were several meters apart, looking for leaders. Their job was to fire first, silently, to remove anyone who might try to coordinate and lead the attackers. There was one, Ding thought, someone gesturing to others. He leveled his MP-5 and squeezed off a burst which missed. Despite the silenced weapon, its cycling made enough noise to draw a shot, and the whole squad opened up. Five more attackers fell. The rest returned fire accurately this time and formed up to assault the defenders' position, but when their muzzle flashes revealed their position, both SAW machine guns raked up and down their line.

The theater of combat was horrible and fascinating to watch. As soon as people started firing, night vision fell away. Chavez tried to protect his by keeping one eye shut as he'd been drilled, but found that it didn't work. The forest was alive with bright cylindrical tongues of flame, some of which became small globes of light that illuminated the moving men like a series of strobe lights. Tracers from the machine guns walked fire into living men. Tracers from the riflemen meant something else. The last three rounds in every magazine were lit to tell them that it was time to load new magazines. The noise was unlike anything Chavez had ever heard, the chatter of the M-16s, and the lower, slower rattle of the AK-47s. The shouted orders, the screams of rage and pain and despairing death.

"Run!" It was Captain Ramirez's voice, shouting in Spanish. Again they disengaged by pairs. Or tried to. Two squad members had been hit in this exchange. Chavez tripped on one, who was trying to crawl away. He lifted the man on his shoulders and ran up the hill while he tried to ignore the pain in his legs. The man—it was Ingeles—died at the rally point. There was no time for grief; his unused magazines were passed out among the other riflemen. While Captain Ramirez tried to get things organized again, all of them heard the mixed notes of gunfire down the hill, more shouts, more curses. Only one more man made it to the rally point. Team KNIFE now had two more dead and one seriously wounded. Olivero took charge of that, leading the injured man up the hill to the casualty collection point near the LZ. It had taken fifteen minutes to inflict a further twenty casualties on the enemy, at the cost of 30 percent of their strength. If Captain Ramirez had had time to think, he would have realized that for all his cleverness he was in a losing game. But there wasn't time for thinking.

The BANNER men discouraged another group of the enemy with a few bursts of fire, but lost one of their number withdrawing up the hill. The next defense line was four hundred meters away. Tighter than the second, it was disagreeably close to their final defensive position. It was time to play their last card.

The enemy again closed in on empty terrain, and still didn't know what casualties they had inflicted on the evil spirits that appeared and killed and disappeared like something from a nightmare. Two of the men who occupied something akin to leadership positions were gone, one dead, the other gravely wounded, and now they stopped to regroup while the surviving leaders conferred.

For the soldiers, the situation was much the same. As soon as the casualties were identified, Ramirez rearranged his deployment to compensate, distantly thankful that he didn't have time to mourn his dead, that his training really did force him to focus on the problem at hand. The helicopter wasn't going to come in time. Or was it? Or did it matter? What did matter?

What he had to do was further reduce the enemy numbers so that an escape attempt had a decent chance at success. They had to run away, but they had to do some more killing first. Ramirez had been keeping his explosives in reserve. None of his men had yet fired or thrown a grenade, and this position was the one protected by their remaining claymore mines, each of them set to protect a rifleman's hole.

"Why are you waiting, eh?" Ramirez called downhill. "Come on, we are not finished with you yet! First we kill you, then we fuck your women!"

"They don't have women," Vega shouted. "They do it to each other. Come, fairies, it is time to die!"

And so they came. Like a puncher remorselessly closing on a boxer, cutting off the ring, still driven by anger, scarcely noting their losses, drawn to the voices and cursing them as they did so. But more carefully now, the enemy troops had learned. Moving from tree to tree, covering one another as they did so. Firing ahead to keep heads down.

"Something's happening down to the south, there. See the flashes?" Larson said. "Over at two o'clock on the mountainside."

"I see it." They'd spent over an hour trying to raise BANNER by flying and transmitting over all three exfiltration sites, and gotten nothing. Clark didn't like leaving the area, but had little choice. If that was what it might be, they had to get closer. Even with a clear line of sight, these little radios were good for less than ten miles.

"*Buster,*" he told the pilot. *Get there as fast as you can.*

Larson retracted his flaps and pushed the throttles forward.

It was called a fire-sack, a term borrowed from the Soviet Army, and perfectly descriptive of its function. The squad was spread out in a wide arc, every man in his hole, though four of the holes were occupied by one instead of two, and another was not occupied at all. In front of each hole were one or two claymores, faced convex side toward the enemy. The position was just inside a stand of trees and faced down across what must have been a rockfall or small landslide, an open space perhaps seventy meters wide, looking down on some fallen trees, and a few new ones. The noise and muzzle flashes of the enemy approached that line and stopped moving, though the firing did not abate at all.

"Okay, people," Ramirez said. "On command we get the hell out of here, back to the LZ, and from there down X-route two. But we gotta thin them down some more first."

The other side was talking, too, and finally doing so intelligently. They used names instead of places, just enough encoding to mask what they wanted to do, though they had again allowed themselves to follow terrain features instead of crossing them. Certainly they had courage, Ramirez thought; whatever sort of men they were, they didn't shrink from danger. If they'd had just a little training and one or two competent leaders, the fight would already have been over.

Chavez had other things on his mind. His weapon was flashless in addition to being noiseless, and the Ninja was using his goggles to pick out individual targets and then dropping them without a shred of remorse. He got one possible leader. It was almost too easy. The rattle of fire from the enemy line masked the sound of his own weapon. But he checked his ammo bag and realized that he had only two magazines and sixty rounds beyond what were in his weapon already. Captain Ramirez was playing it smart, but he was also playing it close.

Another head appeared from behind a tree, then an arm gesturing to someone else. Ding tracked in on it and loosed a single round. It caught the man in the throat, but didn't prevent a gurgling scream. Though Chavez didn't know it, that was the main leader of the enemy, and his scream galvanized them to action. All across the treeline fire lanced out at the light-fighters, and with a shout, the enemy attacked.

Ramirez let them get halfway across, then fired a grenade from his launcher. It was a phosphorus round, which created an intense, spidery white fountain of light. Instantly, every man triggered his claymore mines.

—"Oh, shit, there's KNIFE. Willie Pete and claymores." Clark shoved his antenna out the aircraft's window.

"KNIFE, this is VARIABLE; KNIFE, this is VARIABLE. Come in, over!" His attempt at help could not have come at a worse moment.

Thirty more men fell dead, and ten wounded under the scything fragments from the mines. Next, grenades were launched into the treeline, including all of the WP rounds, to start fires. Far enough away to avoid instant death, but too close to be untouched by the showering bits of burning phosphorus, some men caught fire, adding their screams to the cacophony of the night. Hand-thrown grenades were added to the field, killing yet more of the attackers. Then Ramirez keyed his radio again.

"Move out, move out now!" But he'd done the right thing once too often.

When the KNIFE team moved out from their positions, they were swept with automatic-weapons fire from men shooting on reflex. Those soldiers who had them tossed smoke and CS tear-gas grenades to conceal their departure, but the sparkling of the pyrotechnics merely gave the other side a point of aim, and each drew the fire from a dozen weapons. Two were killed, and another two wounded as a direct result of doing what they'd been taught to do. Ramirez had done a stellar job of maintaining control of his unit to this point, but it was here that he lost it. The radio earpiece started crackling with an unfamiliar voice.

"This is KNIFE," he said, standing erect. "VARIABLE, where the hell are you?"

"Overhead, we are overhead. What is your situation, over?"

"We're in deep shit, falling back to the LZ now, get down here, *get down here right now!*" Ramirez shouted for his men. "Get to the LZ, they're coming to get us!"

"Negative, negative. KNIFE, we cannot come in now. You must get clear, you must get clear. Acknowledge!" Clark told the radio. No reply. He repeated the instructions and again there was nothing.

* * *

And now there were only eight left of what had once been twenty-two men. Ramirez was carrying a wounded man, and his earpiece had fallen out as he ran for the LZ, two hundred meters up the hill, through one last stand of trees into the clearing where the helicopter would come.

But it didn't. Ramirez set his burden down, looking up at the sky with his eyes, then with his goggles, but there was no helicopter, no flash of strobe lights, no heat from turboshaft engines to light up the night sky. The captain yanked the earpiece out of the radio and screamed into it.

"VARIABLE, where the hell are you?"

"KNIFE, this is VARIABLE. We are orbiting your position in a fixed-wing aircraft. We cannot execute a pickup until tomorrow night. You must get clear, you must get clear. Acknowledge!"

"There's only eight of us left, there's only—" Ramirez stopped, and his humanity returned one last, lethal time. "Oh, my God." He hesitated, realizing that most of his men were gone, and he had been their commander, and he was responsible. That he wasn't, really, was something he would never learn.

The enemy was approaching now, approaching from three sides. There was only one way to escape. It was a preplanned route, but Ramirez looked down at the man he'd carried to the LZ and watched him die. He looked up again, looked round at his men, and didn't know what to do next. There wasn't time for training to work. A hundred meters away, the first of the enemy force emerged from the last line of trees and fired. His men returned it, but there were too many and the infantrymen were down to their last magazines.

Chavez saw it happening. He'd linked back up with Vega and León, to help a man whose leg was badly wounded. As he watched, a line of men swept across the LZ. He saw Ramirez drop prone, firing his weapon at the oncoming enemy, but there was nothing Ding and his friends could do, and they headed west, down the escape route. They didn't look back. They didn't need to. The sound told them enough. The chattering of the M-16s was answered by the louder fire of the AKs. A few more grenades went off. Men screamed and cursed, all of them in Spanish. And then all the fire was from AKs. The battle for this hill had ended.

"Does that mean what I think it means?" Larson asked.

"It means that some stateside REMF is going to die," Clark said quietly. There were tears in his eyes. He'd seen this happen once before, when his helicopter had gotten off in time and the other hadn't, and he'd been ashamed at the time and long thereafter that he had survived while others had not. "*Shit!*" He shook his head and got control of himself.

"KNIFE, this is VARIABLE. Do you read me, over? Reply by name. Say again, reply by name."

"Wait a minute," Chavez said. "This is Chavez. Who's on this net?"

"Listen fast, kid, 'cause your net is compromised. This is Clark. We met a while back. Head in the same direction you did on the practice night. Do you remember that?"

"Roger. I remember the way we headed then. We can do that."

"I'll be back for you tomorrow. Hang in there, kid. It ain't over yet. Repeat: I will be back for you. Now haul your ass out of there. Out."

"What was that all about?" Vega asked.

"We loop around east, down the hill to the north, then around east."

"And then what?" *Oso* demanded.

"How the fuck should I know?"

"Head back north," Clark ordered.

"What's an REMF?" Larson asked as he started the turn.

Clark's reply was so low as to be inaudible. "An REMF is a rear-echelon motherfucker, one of those useless, order-generating bastards who gets us line-animals killed. And one of them is going to pay for this, Larson. Now shut up and fly."

For another hour they continued their futile search for Team BANNER, then they headed back to Panama. That flight took two hours and fifteen minutes, during which Clark didn't say a word and Larson was afraid to. The pilot taxied the aircraft right into the hangar with the Pave Low, and the doors closed behind him. Ryan and Johns were waiting for them.

"Well?" Jack asked.

"We made contact with OMEN and FEATURE," Clark said. "Come on." He led them into an office with a table. There he spread out his map.

"What about the others?" Jack asked. Colonel Johns didn't have to. He already knew part of it from the look on Clark's face.

"OMEN will be right here tomorrow night. FEATURE will be here," Clark said, indicating two places marked on the map.

"Okay, we can handle that," Johns said.

"Goddammit!" Ryan growled. "What about the others?"

"We never made contact with BANNER. We watched the bad guys overrun KNIFE. Most of it," Clark corrected himself. "At least one man got away. I'm going in after him, on the ground." Clark turned to the pilot. "Larson, you'd better get a few hours. I need you bright-eyed and bushy-tailed in six hours."

"What about the weather?" he asked PJ.

"That fucking storm's jinking around like a Weasel on a SAM hunt. Nobody knows where the hell it's going, but it ain't there yet, and I've flown in weather before," Colonel Johns replied.

"Okay." The pilot walked off. There were some cots set in the next room. He landed on one and was asleep in a minute.

"Going in on the ground?" Ryan asked.

"What do you expect me to do—leave them there? Ain't we done enough of that?" Clark looked away. His eyes were red, and only PJ knew that it wasn't from strain and lack of sleep. "Sorry, Jack. There's some of our people there. I have to try. They'd try for me. It's cool, man. I know how to do it."

"How?" PJ asked.

"Larson and I'll fly in around noon, get a car and drive down. I told Chavez—that's the kid I talked to—to get around them and head east, down the mountain. We'll try to pick them up, drive 'em to the airport, and just fly them out."

"Just like that?" Ryan asked incredulously.

"Sure. Why not?"

"There's a difference between being brave and being an idiot," Ryan said.

"Who gives a fuck about being brave? It's my job." Clark walked off to get some sleep.

"You know what you're really afraid of?" Johns said when he'd left. "You're afraid of remembering the times that you could have done it and didn't. I can give you a play-by-play of every failure I've had in twenty-some years.'' The colonel was wearing his blue shirt with command wings and all the ribbons. He had quite a few.

Jack's eyes fixed on one, pale blue with five white stars. ''But you . . .''

''It's a nice thing to wear, and it's nice to have four-stars salute me first and treat me like I'm something special. But you know what matters? Those two guys I got out. One's a general now. The other one flies for Delta. They're both alive. They both have families. That's what matters, Mr. Ryan. The ones I didn't get out, they matter, too. Some of them are still there, because I wasn't good enough or fast enough or lucky enough. Or they weren't. Or something. I should have gotten them out. That's the job,'' Johns said quietly. ''That's what I do.''

We sent them in there, Jack told himself. *My agency sent them in there. And some of them are dead now, and we let somebody tell us not to do anything about it. And I'm supposed to be . . .*

''Might be dangerous going in tonight.''

''Possible. Looks that way.''

''You have three minis aboard your chopper,'' Ryan said after a moment. ''You only have two gunners.''

''I couldn't whistle another one up this fast and—''

''I'm a pretty fair shot,'' Jack told him.

28. Accounting

Cortez sat at the table, doing his sums. The Americans had done marvelously well. Nearly two hundred Cartel men had gone up the mountain. Ninety-six had returned alive, sixteen of those wounded. They'd even brought a live American down with them. He was badly hurt, still bleeding from four wounds, and he hadn't been well handled by the Colombian gunmen. The man was young and brave, biting off his screams, shaking with the effort to control himself. Such a courageous young man, this Green Beret. Cortez would not insult his bravery with questions. Besides, he was incoherent, and Cortez had other things to do.

There was a medical team here to treat ''friendly'' casualties. Cortez walked out to it and picked up a disposable syringe, filling it with morphine. He returned and stabbed the needle into a vein on the soldier's uninjured arm, pushing down on the plunger after it was in. The soldier relaxed at once, his pain extinguished by a wonderful, brief sensation of well-being. Then his breathing just stopped, and his life, too, was extinguished. Most unfortunate. Cortez could really have used men like this one, but they rarely worked for anything other than a flag. He walked over to his phone and called the proper number.

''*Jefe,* we eliminated one of the enemy forces last night. . . . Yes, *jefe,* there were ten of them as I suspected, and we got them all. We go after another team tonight. . . . There is one problem, *jefe*. The enemy fought well, and we took many casualties. I need more men for tonight's mission. *Sí,* thank you, *jefe*. That will do nicely. Send the men to Ríosucio, and have the leaders report to me this afternoon. I will brief them here. Oh? Yes, that will be excellent. We'll be waiting for you.''

With luck, Cortez thought, the next American team would fight equally well. With luck he could eliminate two-thirds of the Cartel's stable of gunmen in a single week. Along with their bosses, also tonight. He was on the downslope now, Cortez thought. He'd gambled dangerously and hard, but the tricky ones were behind him.

It was an early funeral. Greer had been a widower, and estranged from his wife long before that. The reason for the estrangement was next to the rectangular hole in Arlington, the simple white headstone of First Lieutenant Robert White Greer, USMC, his only son, who'd graduated from the Naval Academy and gone to Vietnam to die. Neither Moore nor Ritter had ever met the young man, and James had never kept a photo of him around the office. The former DDI had been a sentimental man but never a maudlin one. Yet he had long ago requested burial next to the grave of his son, and because of his rank and station an exception had been made and the place kept available for an event that for all men was as inevitable as it was untimely. He'd indeed been a sentimental man, but only in ways that mattered. Ritter thought that there were many explanations before his eyes. The way James had adopted several bright young people and brought them into the Agency, the interest he'd taken in their careers, the training and consideration he'd given them.

It was a small, quiet ceremony. James' few close friends were there, along with a much larger number of people from the government. Among the latter were the President—and, much to Bob Ritter's rage, Vice Admiral James A. Cutter, Jr. The President himself had spoken at the chapel service, noting the death of a man who had served his country continuously for more than fifty years, having enlisted in the U.S. Navy at seventeen, then entered the Academy, then reached two-star rank, achieving a third star for his flag after assuming his position at CIA. ''A standard of professionalism, integrity, and devotion to his country that few have equaled and none have excelled'' was how the President summarized the career of Vice Admiral James Greer.

And that bastard *Cutter sat right there in the front row as he said it, too,* Ritter told himself. He found it especially sickening as he watched the honor guard from the 3rd Infantry Regiment fold the flag that had been draped over the casket. There was no one to hand it to. Ritter had expected it to go to—

But where was Ryan? He moved his head, trying to look around. He hadn't noticed before because Jack hadn't come from Langley with the rest of the CIA delegation. The flag went to Judge Moore by default. Hands were shaken, words exchanged. Yes, it really was a mercy that he'd gone so rapidly at the end. Yes, men like this didn't appear every day. Yes, this was the end of the Greer line, and that was too bad, wasn't it? No, I never met his son, but I heard. . . . Ritter and Moore were in the Agency Cadillac ten minutes later, heading back up the George Washington Parkway.

''Where the hell was Ryan?'' the DCI asked.

''I don't know. I figured he'd drive himself in.''

Moore was not so much angered as upset by the impropriety. He still had the flag in his lap, holding it as gently as a newborn baby without knowing why—until he realized that if there really was a God, as the Baptist preachers of his youth had assured him, and if James had really had a soul, he held its best legacy in his hands.

It felt warm to the touch, and though he knew that it was merely his imagination or at most the residual heat absorbed from the morning sun, the energy radiating from the flag that James had served from his teens seemed to accuse him of treachery. They had just watched a funeral this morning, but two thousand miles away there were other people whom the Agency had sent to do a job and who would not receive even the empty reward of a grave amidst others of their kind.

"Bob, what the hell have we done?" Moore asked. "How did we ever get into this?"

"I don't know, Arthur. I just don't know."

"James really was lucky," the Director of Central Intelligence murmured. "At least he went out—"

"With a clear conscience?" Ritter looked out the window, unable to bring himself to face his boss. "Look, Arthur—" He stopped, not knowing what to say next. Ritter had been with the Agency since the fifties, had worked as a case officer, a supervisor, station chief, then head of section at Langley. He had lost case officers, had lost agents, but he'd never betrayed them. There was a first time for everything, he told himself. It had just come home to him in a very immediate way, however, that for every man there was also a first time for death, and that to meet that final accounting improperly was the ultimate cowardice, the ultimate failure of life. But what else could they do?

It was a short drive to Langley, and the car stopped before that question could be answered. They rode the elevator up. Moore walked to his office. Ritter walked to his. The secretaries hadn't returned yet. They were in a van. Ritter paced around his office until they arrived, then walked over to see Mrs. Cummings.

"Did Ryan call in or anything?"

"No, and I didn't see him at all. Do you know where he is?" Nancy asked.

"Sorry, I don't." Ritter walked back and on impulse called Ryan's home, where all he got was an answering machine. He checked his card file for Cathy's work number and got past the secretary to her.

"This is Bob Ritter. I need to know where Jack is."

"I don't know," Dr. Caroline Ryan replied guardedly. "He told me yesterday that he had to go out of town. He didn't say where."

A chill went across Ritter's face. "Cathy, I have to know. This is very important—I can't tell you how important. Please trust me. I have to know where he is."

"I *don't* know. You mean you don't, either?" There was alarm in her voice.

Ryan knows, Ritter realized.

"Look, Cathy, I'll track him down. Don't worry or anything, okay?" The effort to calm her down was wasted, but Ritter hung up as soon as he could. The DDO walked to Judge Moore's office. The flag was centered on the DCI's desk, still folded into its triangular section, called a cocked-hat. Judge Arthur Moore, Director of Central Intelligence, was sitting quietly, staring at it.

"Jack's gone. His wife says she doesn't know where. He knows, Arthur. He knows and he's off doing something."

"How could he have found out?"

"How the hell should I know?" Ritter thought for a moment, then waved at his boss. "Come on."

They walked into Ryan's office. Ritter opened the panel for Jack's wall safe and dialed in the proper combination, and nothing happened other than the fact that the warning light went on over the dial.

''Damn,'' Ritter said. ''I thought that was it.''

''James's combination?''

''Yeah. You know how he was, never did like the damned things, and he probably . . .'' Ritter looked around. He got it on the third try, pulling out the writing panel from the desk, and there it was.

''I thought I did dial the right one.'' He turned and tried again. This time the light was accompanied by the goddamned beeper. Ritter turned back and checked the number again. There was some more writing on the sheet. Ritter pulled the panel farther out.

''Oh, my God.''

Moore nodded and walked to the door. ''Nancy, tell security that it's us trying to work the safe. Looks like Jack changed the combination without telling us like he was supposed to.'' The DCI closed the door and turned back.

''He knows, Arthur.''

''Maybe. How do we check it out?''

A minute later they were in Ritter's office. He'd shredded all of his documents, but not his memory. You didn't forget the name of someone with the Medal of Honor. Then it was just a matter of flipping open his AUTOVON phone directory and calling the 1st Special Operations Wing at Eglin AFB.

''I need to talk to Colonel Paul Johns,'' Ritter told the sergeant who'd picked up the phone.

''Colonel Johns is off TDY somewhere, sir. I don't know where.''

''Who does?''

''The wing operations officer might, sir. This is a nonsecure line, sir,'' the sergeant reminded him.

''Give me his number.'' The sergeant did so, and Ritter's next call went out on, and to, a secure line.

''I need to find Colonel Johns,'' Ritter said after identifying himself.

''Sir, I have orders not to give that information out to anybody. That means nobody, sir.''

''Major, if he's down in Panama again, I need to know it. His life may depend on it. Something is happening that he needs to know about.''

''Sir, I have orders—''

''Stuff your orders, sonny. If you don't tell me, and that flight crew dies, it will be your fault! Now you make the call, Major, yes or no?''

The officer had never seen combat, and life-death decisions were theoretical matters to him—or had been until now.

''Sir, they're back where they were before. Same place, same crew. That's as far as I go, sir.''

''Thank you, Major. You did the right thing. You really did. Now I suggest that you make written note of this call and its content.'' Ritter hung up. The phone had been on speaker.

''Has to be Ryan,'' the DCI agreed. ''Now what do we do?''

''You tell me, Arthur.''

''How many more people are we going to kill, Bob?'' Moore asked. His greatest fear now was of mirrors, looking into them and seeing something less than the image he wanted to be there.

''You do understand the consequences?''

''Fuck the consequences,'' snorted the former chief judge of the Texas Court of Appeals.

Ritter nodded and punched a button on his phone. When he spoke, it was in his accustomed, decisive voice of command. ''I need everything CAPER has developed in the last two days.'' Another button. ''I want chief of Station Panama to call me in thirty minutes. Tell him to clear decks for the day—he's going to be busy.'' Ritter replaced the phone receiver in its cradle. They'd have to wait for a few minutes, but it wasn't the sort of occasion to wait in silence.

''Thank God,'' Ritter said after a moment.

Moore smiled for the first time this day. ''Me, too, Robert. Nice to be a man again, isn't it?''

The security police brought him in at gunpoint, the man in the tan suit. He said his name was Luna, and the briefcase he carried had already been searched for weapons. Clark recognized him.

''What the hell are you doing here, Tony?''

''Who's this?'' Ryan asked.

''Station chief for Panama,'' Clark answered. ''Tony, I hope you have a *very* good reason.''

''I have a telex for Dr. Ryan from Judge Moore.''

''What?''

Clark took Luna's arm and guided him into the office. He didn't have much time. He and Larson were to take off within minutes.

''This better not be some fucking joke,'' Clark announced.

''Hey, I'm delivering the mail, okay?'' Luna said. ''Now stop playing the macho game. I'm the spic here, remember?'' He handed Jack the first sheet.

TOP SECRET—EYES ONLY DDI

> IMPOSSIBLE TO REESTABLISH UPLINK TO SHOWBOAT TEAMS. TAKE WHATEVER ACTION YOU DEEM APPROPRIATE TO RETRIEVE ASSETS IN COUNTRY. TELL CLARK TO BE CAREFUL. THE ENCLOSED MIGHT BE OF HELP. C DOESN'T KNOW. GOOD LUCK. M/R.

''Nobody ever said they were stupid,'' Jack breathed as he handed the sheet to Clark. The heading was meant as a separate message in and of itself, one that had nothing to do with distribution or security. ''But does this mean what I think it does?''

''One less REMF to worry about. Make that two,'' Clark observed. He started flipping through the faxes. ''Holy shit!'' He set the pile down on the desk and paced a bit, staring out of the windows at the aircraft sitting in the hangar. ''Okay,'' he said to himself. Clark had never been one to dally over making plans. He spoke to Ryan for several minutes. Then, to Larson: ''Let's move ass, kid. We got a job to do.''

''Spare radios?'' Colonel Johns asked him as he left.

''Two spares, new batteries in all of 'em, and extra batteries,'' Clark replied.

''Nice to work with somebody's been around the block,'' PJ said. ''Check-six, Mr. Clark.''

''Always, Colonel Johns,'' Clark said as he headed to the door. ''See you in a few hours.''

The hangar doors opened. A small cart pulled the Beechcraft out into the sun, and the hangar doors closed. Ryan listened to the engines start up, and the sound diminished as the aircraft taxied away.

"What about us?" he asked Colonel Johns.

Captain Frances Montaigne came in. She looked as French as her ancestry, short, with raven-black hair. Not especially pretty, but Ryan's first impression was that she was a handful in bed—which stopped his thought processes cold as he wondered why that had occurred to him. It seemed odder still that she was a command pilot in a special-ops outfit.

"Weather's going dogshit on us, Colonel," she announced at once. "*Adele* is heading west again, doing twenty-five knots."

"Can't help the weather. Getting down and doing the snatch oughtn't to be too bad."

"Getting back might be kinda exciting, PJ," Montaigne observed darkly.

"One thing at a time, Francie. And we do have that alternate place to land."

"Colonel, even you aren't that crazy."

PJ turned to Ryan and shook his head. "Junior officers aren't what they used to be."

They stayed over water for most of the way down. Larson was as steady and confident as ever at the controls, but his eyes kept turning northeast. There was no mistaking it, the high, thin clouds that were the perennial harbinger of an approaching hurricane. Behind them was *Adele,* and she had already made another chapter in history. Born off the Cape Verdes, she'd streaked across the Atlantic at an average speed of seventeen knots, then stopped as soon as she'd entered the eastern Caribbean, lost power, gained it back, jinked north, west, even east once. There hadn't been one this crazy since *Joan,* years before. Small as hurricanes went, and nowhere near the brutal power of a *Camille, Adele* was still a dangerous storm with seventy-five-knot winds. The only people who flew near tropical cyclones were dedicated hurricane-hunter aircraft flown by people for whom merely mortal danger was boring. It was not a place for a twin-engine Beechcraft, even with Chuck Yeager at the controls. Larson was already making plans. In case the mission didn't go right, or the storm changed course yet again, he started picking fields to put down on, to refuel and head southeast around the gray maelstrom that was marching toward them. The air was smooth and still, deceptively so. The pilot wondered how many hours until it changed to something very different. And that was only one of the dangers he'd face.

Clark sat quietly in the right seat, staring forward, his face composed and inhumanly serene while his mind turned over faster than the Beech's twin props. In front of the windshield he kept seeing faces, some living, some dead. He remembered past combat actions, past dangers, past fears, past escapes in which those faces had played their parts. Most of all he remembered the lessons, some learned in classrooms and lectures, but the important ones had come from his own experience. John Terence Clark was not a man who forgot things. Gradually he refreshed his memory on all the important lessons for this day, the ones about being alone in unfriendly territory. Then came the faces who'd play their part today. He looked at them, a few feet before his eyes, saw the expressions he expected them to wear, measuring the faces to understand the people who wore them. Finally came the plan of the day. He contemplated what he wanted to do and balanced that against the probable objectives of the opposition. He considered alternative plans and things that might go awry. When all that was done, he made himself stop. You could quickly get to the point that imagination became an enemy. Each segment of the operation was locked into its own little box which he'd open one at a time. He'd trust to his experience and instinct. But part of him wondered if—when—those qualities would fail him.

Sooner or later, Clark admitted to himself. *But not today.*

He always told himself that.

PJ's mission briefing took two hours. He, Captain Willis, and Captain Montaigne worked out every detail—where they'd refuel, where the aircraft would orbit if something went wrong. Which routes to take if things went badly. Each crew member got full information. It was more than necessary; it was a moral obligation to the crew. They were risking their lives tonight. They had to know why. As always, Sergeant Zimmer had a few questions, and one important suggestion that was immediately incorporated in the plan. Then it was time to preflight the aircraft. Every system aboard each aircraft was fully checked out in a procedure that would last hours. Part of that was training for the new crewmen.

"What do you know about guns?" Zimmer asked Ryan.

"Never fired one of these babies." Ryan's hand stroked the handles of the minigun. A scaled-down version of the 20mm Vulcan cannon, it had a gang of six .30-caliber barrels that rotated clockwise under the power of an electrical motor, drawing shells from an enormous hopper to the left of the mount. It had two speed settings, 4,000 and 6,000 rounds per minute—66 or 100 rounds *per second.* The bullets were almost half tracers. The reason for that was psychological. The fire from the weapon looked like a laser beam from a science-fiction movie, the very embodiment of death. It also made a fine way to aim the weapon, since Zimmer assured him that the muzzle blast would be the most blinding thing short of staring into a noon sun. He checked Ryan out on the whole system: where the switches were, how to stand, how to aim.

"What do you know about combat, sir?"

"Depends on what you mean," Ryan replied.

"Combat is when people with guns are trying to kill you," Zimmer explained patiently. "It's dangerous."

"I know. I've been there a few times. Let's not dwell on that, okay? I'm already scared." Ryan looked over his gun, out the door of the aircraft, wondering why he'd been such a damned fool to volunteer for this. But what choice did he have? Could he just send these men off to danger? If he did, how did that make him different from Cutter? Jack looked around the interior of the aircraft. It seemed so large and strong and safe, sitting here on the concrete floor of the hangar. But it was an aircraft designed for life in the troubled air of an unfriendly sky. It was a helicopter: Ryan especially hated helicopters.

"The funny thing is, probably no sweat on the mission," Zimmer said after a moment. "Sir, we do our job right, it's just a flight in and a flight back out."

"That's what I'm scared of, Sarge," Ryan said, laughing mostly at himself.

They landed at Santagueda. Larson knew the man who ran the local flying service and talked him out of his Volkswagen Microvan. The two CIA officers drove north, and an hour later passed through the village of Anserma. They dallied here for half an hour, driving around until they found what they wanted to find: a few trucks heading in and out of a private dirt road and one expensive-looking car. CAPER had called it right, Clark saw, and it was the place he thought it was from the flight in. Having confirmed that, they moved out, heading north again for another hour and taking a side road into the mountains just outside of Vegas del Río. Clark had his nose buried in a map, and Larson found a hilltop switchback at which to stop. That's where the radio came out.

"KNIFE, this is VARIABLE, over." Nothing, despite five minutes of trying. Larson drove farther west, horsing the Microvan around cow paths as he struggled to find another high spot for Clark to try again. It was three in the afternoon, and their fifth attempt until they got a reply.

"KNIFE here. Over."

"Chavez, this is Clark. Where the hell are you?" Clark asked, in Spanish, of course.

"Let's talk awhile first."

"You're good, kid. We really could have used you in 3rd SOG."

"Why should I trust you? Somebody cut us off, man. Somebody decided to leave us here."

"It wasn't me."

"Glad to hear it," came the skeptical, bitter reply.

"Chavez, you're talking over a radio net that might be compromised. If you got a map, we're at the following set of coordinates," Clark told him. "There's two of us in a blue Volkswagen van. Check us out, take all the time you want."

"I already have!" the radio told him.

Clark's head spun around to see a man with an AK-47 twenty feet away.

"Let's be real cool, people," Sergeant Vega said. Three more men emerged from the treeline. One of them had a bloody bandage on his thigh. Chavez, too, had an AK slung over his shoulder, but he had held on to his silenced MP-5. He walked straight up to the van.

"Not bad, kid," Clark told him. "How'd you know?"

"UHF radio. You had to transmit from a high spot, right? The map says there's six of them. I heard you one other time, too, and I spotted you heading this way half an hour ago. Now what the fuck is going on?"

"First thing, let's get that casualty treated." Clark stepped out and handed Chavez his pistol, butt first. "I got a first-aid kit in the back."

The wounded man was Sergeant Juardo, a rifleman from the 10th Mountain at Fort Drum. Clark opened the back of the van and helped load him aboard, then uncovered the wound.

"You know what you're doing?" Vega asked.

"I used to be a SEAL," Clark replied, holding up his arm so that they could see the tattoo. Third Special Operations Group. Spent a lot of time in 'Nam, doing stuff that never made the TV news."

"What were you?"

"Came out a chief bosun's mate, E-7 to you." Clark examined the wound. It was bad to look at, but not life-threatening as long as the man didn't bleed out, which he'd managed not to do yet. So far it seemed that the infantrymen had done most of the right things. Clark ripped open an envelope and redusted the wound with sulfa. "You have any blood-expanders?"

"Here." Sergeant León passed over an IV bag. "None of us knows how to start one."

"It's not hard. Watch how I do it." Clark grabbed Juardo's upper arm hard and told him to make a fist. Then he stabbed the IV needle into the big vein inside the elbow. "See? Okay, I cheat. My wife's a nurse, and sometimes I get to practice at her hospital," Clark admitted. "How's it feel, kid?" he asked the patient.

"Nice to be sitting down," Juardo admitted.

"I don't want to give you a pain shot. We might need you awake. Think you can hack it?"

"You say so, man. Hey, Ding, you got any candy?"

Chavez tossed over his Tylenol bottle. "Last ones, Pablo. Make 'em last, man."

"Thanks, Ding."

"We have some sandwiches in the front," Larson said.

"Food!" Vega darted that way at once. A minute later the four soldiers were wolfing it down, along with a six-pack of Cokes that Larson had picked up on the way.

"Where'd you pick up the weapons?"

"Bad guys. We were just about out of ammo for our -16s, and I figured we might as well try to fit in, like."

"You're thinking good, kid," Clark told him.

"Okay, what's the plan?" Chavez asked.

"It's your call," Clark replied. "One of two things. We can drive you back to the airport and fly you out, take about three hours to get there, another three hours in the airplane, and it's over, you're back on U.S. territory."

"What else?"

"Chavez, how'd you like to get the fucker who did this to you?" Clark knew the answer before he'd asked the question.

Admiral Cutter was leaning back in his chair when the phone buzzed. He knew who it was from the line that was blinking. "Yes, Mr. President?"

"Come in here."

"On the way, sir."

Summer is as slow a season for the White House as for most government agencies. The President's calendar was fuller than usual with the ceremonial stuff that the politician in him loved and the executive in him abhorred. Shaking hands with "Miss Whole Milk," as he referred to the steady stream of visitors—though he occasionally wondered to himself if he'd ever meet a Miss Condom, what with the way sexual mores were changing of late. The burden was larger than most imagine. For each such visitor there was a sheet of paper, a few paragraphs of information so that the person would leave thinking that, gee, the President really knows what I'm all about. He's really *interested!* Pressing flesh and talking to ordinary people was an important and usually pleasurable part of the job, but not now, a week short of the convention, still behind in the goddamned polls, as every news network announced at least twice a week.

"What about Colombia?" the President asked as soon as the door was closed.

"Sir, you told me to shut it down. It's being shut down."

"Any problems with the Agency?"

"No, Mr. President."

"How exactly—"

"Sir, you told me you didn't want to know that."

"You're telling me it's something I shouldn't know?"

"I'm telling you, sir, that I am carrying out your instructions. The orders were given, and the orders are being complied with. I don't think you will object to the consequences."

"Really?"

Cutter relaxed a bit. "Sir, in a very real sense, the operation was a success. Drug shipments are down and will drop further in the next few months. I would suggest, sir, that you let the press talk about that for the moment. You can always point to it later. We've hurt them. With Operation TARPON we have something we can point to all we wish. With CAPER we have a way of continuing to gather intelligence information. We will have some dramatic arrests in a few months as well.''

"And how do you know that?''

"I've made those arrangements myself, sir.''

"And just how did you do that?'' the President asked, and stopped. "Something else I don't want to know?''

Cutter nodded.

"I assume that everything you've done is within the law,'' the President said for the benefit of the tape recorder he had running.

"You may make that assumption, sir.'' It was an artful reply in that it could mean anything, or nothing, depending on one's point of view. Cutter also knew about the tape recorder.

"And you're sure that your instructions are being carried out?''

"Of course, Mr. President.''

"Make sure again.''

It had taken far longer than the bearded consultant expected. Inspector O'Day held the printout in his hands, and it might as well have been Kurdish. The sheet was half covered with paragraphs entirely composed of ones and zeroes.

"Machine language,'' the consultant explained. "Whoever programmed this baby was a real pro. I recovered about forty percent of it. It's a transposition algorithm, just like I thought.''

"You told me that last night.''

"It ain't Russian. It takes in a message and enciphers it. No big deal, anybody can do that. What's really clever is that the system is based on an independent input signal that's unique to the individual transmission—over and above the encipherment algorithm that's already built into the system.''

"You want to explain that?''

"It means a very good computer lash-up—somewhere—governs how this baby operates. It can't be Russian. They don't have the hardware yet, unless they stole a really sexy one from us. Also, the input that adds the variable into the system probably comes from the NAVSTAR satellites. I'm guessing here, but I think it uses a very precise time mark to set the encryption key, one that's unique to each up-and-down transmission. Clever shit. That means NSA. The NAVSTAR satellites use atomic clocks to measure time with great precision, and the really sexy part of the system is also encrypted. Anyway, what we have here is a clever way of scrambling a signal in a way that you can't break or duplicate even if you know how it was done. Whoever set this baby up has access to everything we got. I used to consult with NSA, and never even heard of this puppy.''

"Okay, and when the disk is destroyed . . . ?''

"The link is gone, man. I mean, *gone*. If this is what it seems to be, you have an uplink facility that controls the algorithm, and ground stations that copy it down. You wipe this algorithm off, like somebody did, and the guys you used to be talking to can't communicate with you anymore, and nobody else can communicate with them either. Systems don't get any more secure than that.''

"You can tell all that? What else?''

"Half of what I just told you is informed speculation. I can't rebuild the algorithm. I can just tell you how it probably worked. The bit on the NAVSTAR is supposition, but good supposition. The transposition processing is partly recovered, and it has NSA written all over it. Whoever did it really knows how to write computer code. It's definitely ours. It's probably the most sophisticated machine code we have. Whoever got to use it must have some serious juice. And whoever it is, he scrubbed it. It can never be used again. Whatever operation it was used for must be over."

"Yeah," O'Day said, chilled by what he had just learned. "Good work."

"Now all you have to do is write a note to my prof and tell him why I missed an exam this morning."

"I'll have somebody do that," O'Day promised him on the way out the door. He headed for Dan Murray's office, and was surprised to see that he was out. The next stop was with Bill Shaw.

Half an hour later it was clear that a crime had probably been committed. The next question was what to do about it.

The helicopter took off light. Mission requirements were fairly complex—more so than in the previous insertions—and speed was important this time. As soon as the Pave Low got to cruising altitude, it tanked from the MC-130E. There was no banter this time.

Ryan sat in back, strapped into his place while the MH-53J bounced and buffeted in the wash of the tanker. He wore a green flight suit and a similarly green helmet. There was also a flak jacket. Zimmer had explained to him that it would stop a pistol round, probably, secondary fragments almost certainly, but that he shouldn't depend on it to stop a rifle bullet. One more thing to worry about. Once clear of the tanker for the first time—they'd have to tank again before making landfall—Jack turned around to look out the door. The clouds were nearly overhead now, the outlying reaches from *Adele*.

Juardo's wound complicated matters and changed plans somewhat. They loaded him into Clark's seat on the Beech, leaving him with a radio and spare batteries. Then Clark and the rest drove back toward Anserma. Larson was still checking the weather, which was changing on an hour-to-hour basis. He was due to take off in ninety minutes for his part of the mission.

"How you fixed for rounds?" Clark asked in the Microvan.

"All we need for the AKs," Chavez replied. "About sixty each for the subs. I never knew how useful a silenced gun was."

"They are nice. Grenades?"

"All of us?" Vega asked. "Five frags and two CS."

"What are we going into?" Ding asked next.

"It's a farmhouse outside Anserma."

"What's the security there like?"

"I don't know squat yet."

"Hey, wait a minute, what are you getting us into?" Vega demanded.

"Relax, Sarge. If it's too heavy to handle, we back off and leave. All I know is we're going in for a close look. Chavez and I can handle that. By the way, there's spare batteries in the bag down there. Need 'em?"

"Fuckin' A!" Chavez pulled out his night scope and replaced the batteries at once. "Who's in the house?"

"Two people we especially want. Number One is Félix Cortez," Clark said, giving some background. "He's the guy running the operation against the SHOWBOAT teams—that's the code name for this operation, in case nobody bothered to tell you. He also had a hand in the murder of the ambassador. I want his ass and I want it alive. Number Two is one Señor Escobedo. He's one of the big shots in the Cartel. A lot of people want his ass."

"Yeah," León said. "We ain't got no big shots yet."

"So far we've gotten five or six of the bastards. That was my end of the operation." Clark turned to look at Chavez. He had to say that to establish his credibility.

"But how, when—"

"We're not supposed to talk all that much, children," Clark told them. "You don't go around advertising about killing folks no matter who told you it was okay."

"Are you really that good?"

Clark just shook his head. "Sometimes. Sometimes not. If you guys weren't damned good, you wouldn't be here. And there are times when it's just pure dumb luck."

"We just walked into one," León said. "I don't even know what went wrong, but Captain Rojas just—"

"I know. I saw some pricks load his body into the back of a truck—"

León went rigid. "And what—"

"Did I do?" Clark asked. "There were three of them. I put them in the truck, too. Then I torched the truck. I'm not real proud of that, but I think I took some of the heat off you BANNER guys when I did. Wasn't much, but it was all I could do at the time."

"So who pulled the chopper back on us?"

"Same guy who chopped off the radio. I know who it is. After this is all over, I want his ass, too. You don't send people out in the field and then pull this crap on 'em."

"So what are you going to do?" Vega wanted to know.

"I'll slap him firmly on both wrists. Now listen, people, you worry about tonight. One job at a time. You're soldiers, not a bunch of teenage broads. Less talkin' and more thinkin'."

Chavez, Vega, and León took the cue. They started checking their gear. There was enough room in the van to strip and clean weapons. Clark pulled into Anserma at sundown. He found a quiet spot about a mile from the house and left the van. Clark took Vega's night goggles, and then he and Chavez went out to take a walk.

There had been farming here recently. Clark wondered what it had been, but that and the fact that it was close to the village meant that the trees had been thinned out for cooking fires. They were able to move fast. Half an hour later they could see the house, separated from the woods by two hundred meters of open ground.

"Not good," Clark observed from his place on the ground.

"I count six, all with AKs."

"Company," the CIA officer said, turning to see where the noise was coming from. It was a Mercedes, and therefore could have belonged to anyone in the Cartel. Two more cars came with it, one ahead and one behind. A total of six guards got out to check the area.

"Escobedo and LaTorre," Clark said from behind the binoculars. "Two big shots to see Colonel Cortez. I wonder why . . ."

"Too many, man," Chavez said.

"You notice there wasn't any password or anything?"

"So?"

"It's possible, if we play it right."

"But how . . ."

"Think creatively," Clark told him. "Back to the car." That took another twenty minutes. When they got there, Clark adjusted one of his radios.

"CAESAR, this is SNAKE, over."

The second refueling was accomplished within sight of the beach. They'd have to tank at least once more before heading back to Panama. The other alternative didn't seem especially likely at the moment. The good news was that Francie Montaigne was driving her Combat Talon with her usual aplomb, its four big propellers turning in a steady rhythm. Its radio operators were already talking to the surviving ground teams, taking that strain off the helicopter crew. For the first time in the mission, the air team was allowed to function as it had been trained. The MC-130E would coordinate the various pieces, coaching the Pave Low into the proper areas and away from possible threats in addition to keeping PJ's chopper filled up with gas.

In back, the ride had settled down. Ryan was up and walking around. Fear became boring after a while, and he even managed to use the Port-A-Pot without missing. The flight crew had accepted him at least as an approved interloper, and for some reason that meant a lot to him.

"Ryan, you hear me?" Johns asked.

Jack reached down to the mike button. "Yeah, Colonel."

"Your guy on the ground wants us to do something different."

"Like what?"

PJ told him. "It means another tanking, but otherwise we can hack it. Your call."

"You sure?"

"Special ops is what they pay us for."

"Okay, then. We want that bastard."

"Roger. Sergeant Zimmer, we'll be feet-dry in one minute. Systems check."

The flight engineer looked down his panel. "Roger that, PJ. Everything looks pretty solid to me, sir. Everything's green."

"Okay. First stop is Team OMEN. ETA is two-zero minutes. Ryan, you'd better grab hold of something. We're going to start nap-of-the-earth. I have to talk to our backup."

Jack didn't know what that meant. He found out as soon as they crossed the first range of coastal mountains. The Pave Low leapt up like a mad elevator, then the bottom dropped out as it cleared the summit. The helicopter was on computer-assisted-flight mode, taking a six-degree slope—it felt much worse than that—up and down the terrain features, and skimmed over the ground with bare feet of clearance. The aircraft was made to be safe, not comfortable. Ryan didn't feel much of either.

"First LZ in three minutes," Colonel Johns announced half an eternity later. "Let's go hot, Buck."

"Roger." Zimmer reached down on his console and flipped a toggle switch. "Switches hot. Guns are hot."

"Gunners, stand to. That means you, Ryan," PJ added.

"Thanks." Jack gasped without toggling his mike. He took position on the left side of the aircraft and hit the activation switch for the minigun, which started turning at once.

"ETA one minute," the copilot said. "I got a good strobe at eleven o'clock. Okay. OMEN, this is CAESAR, do you copy, over?"

Jack heard only one side of the conversation, but mentally thanked the flight crew for letting the guys in back know something.

"Roger, OMEN, say again your situation. . . . Roger that, we're coming in. Good strobe light. Thirty seconds. Get ready in back," Captain Willis told Ryan and the rest. "Safe guns, safe guns."

Jack held his thumbs clear of the switch and elevated the minigun at the sky. The helicopter took a big nose-up attitude as it came down. It stopped and hovered a foot off the ground, not quite touching.

"Buck, tell the captain to come forward immediately."

"Roger, PJ." Behind him, Ryan heard Zimmer run aft, then, through the soles of his feet, felt the troops race aboard. He kept his eyes outboard, looking over the rotating barrels of his gun until the helicopter took off, and even then he trained the mini down at the ground.

"Well, that wasn't so bad, was it?" Colonel Johns observed as he brought the aircraft back to a southerly heading. "Hell, I don't even know why they pay us for this. Where's that ground-pounder?"

"Hooking him up now, sir," Zimmer replied. "Got 'em all aboard. All clean, no casualties."

"Captain . . . ?"

"Yes, Colonel?"

"We got a job for your team if you think you're up to it."

"Let's hear it, sir."

The MC-130E Combat Talon was orbiting over Colombian territory, which made the crew a little nervous, since they didn't have permission. The main job now was to relay communications, and even with the sophisticated gear aboard the four-engine support aircraft, they couldn't handle it from over the ocean.

What they really needed was a good radar. The Pave Low/Combat Talon team was supposed to operate under supervision of an AWACS which, however, they hadn't brought along. Instead a lieutenant and a few NCOs were writing on maps and talking over secure radio circuits at the same time.

"CAESAR, say your fuel state," Captain Montaigne called.

"Looking good, CLAW. We're staying down in the valleys. Estimate we'll tank again in eight-zero minutes."

"Roger eight-zero minutes. Be advised negative hostile radio traffic at this time."

"Acknowledged." That was one possible problem. What if the Cartel had somebody in the Colombian Air Force? Sophisticated as both American aircraft were, a P-51 left over from the Second World War could easily kill both of them.

Clark was waiting for them. With two vehicles. Vega had stolen a farm truck big enough for their needs. It turned out that he was quite adept at rewiring ignition systems, a skill about whose acquisition he was vague. The helicopter touched down and the men ran out toward the strobe light that Chavez still had. Clark got their officer and briefed him quickly. The helicopter took off and headed north, helped by the twenty-knot wind blowing down the valley. Then it looped west, heading for the MC-130 and another midair refueling.

* * *

The Microvan and the truck drove back toward the farmhouse. Clark's mind was still racing. A really smart guy would have run the operation from inside the village, which would have been far tougher to approach. Cortez wanted to be far from anyone's view, but failed to consider his physical security requirements in military terms. Cortez was thinking like a spy, for whom security was secrecy, and not a line-animal, for whom security was a lot of guns and a clear field of fire. Everyone, he figured, had his limitations. Clark rode the back of the farm truck with the OMEN team group around him and his hand-drawn diagram of the objective. It was just like the old days, Clark thought, running missions on zero-minute notice. He hoped that these young light-fighters were as good as the animals in 3rd SOG. Even Clark, however, had limitations. The animals of 3rd SOG had been young then, too.

"Ten minutes, then," he concluded.

"All right," the captain agreed. "We haven't had much contact. We have all the weapons and ammo we need."

"So?" Escobedo asked.

"So we killed ten *norteamericanos* last night and we will kill ten more tonight."

"But the losses!" LaTorre objected.

"We are fighting highly skilled professional soldiers. Our men wiped them out, but the enemy fought bravely and well. Only one survived," Cortez said. "I have his body in the next room. He died here soon after they brought him in."

"How do you know that they are not close by?" Escobedo demanded. The idea of physical danger was something he'd allowed himself to forget.

"I know the location of every enemy group. They are waiting to be extracted by their helicopter support. They do not know that their helicopter has been withdrawn."

"How did you manage that?" LaTorre wondered aloud.

"Please permit me my methods. You hired me for my expertise. You should not be surprised when I demonstrate it."

"And now?"

"Our assault group—nearly two hundred men this time—should now be approaching the second American group. This one's code name is Team FEATURE," Félix added. "Our next question, of course, is which elements of the Cartel leadership are taking advantage of this—or perhaps I should say, which members are working with the Americans, using them for their own ends. As is often the case in such operations, both sides appear to be using the other."

"Oh?" It was Escobedo this time.

"*Sí, jefe*. And it should not surprise either of you that I have been able to identify those who have betrayed their comrades." He looked at both men, a thin smile on his lips.

There were only two road guards. Clark was back in the VW Microvan while OMEN raced through the woods to get to the objective. Vega and León had removed a side window, and now Vega, also in back, held it in place with his hand.

"Everybody ready?" Clark asked.

"Go!" Chavez replied.

"Here we go." Clark took the last turn in the road and slowed, taking the car right up to the two guards. They took their weapons off sling and assumed a more aggressive stance as he slowed the vehicle. "Excuse me, I am lost."

Clark knew, but he was in command, and the good commanders led from the front. They covered the two hundred yards to the house in thirty seconds.

"Door!" Clark said to Vega, who used his AK to blast off the hinges, then kicked it down. Clark dove through low, rolling when he hit, looking and seeing one man in the room. He had an AK, and fired it, but shot high. Clark dropped him with a silenced round in the face, then another as he fell. There was a doorway but no door to the next room. He gestured to Chavez, who tossed a CS grenade into it. They waited for it to go off, then both rushed the room, again diving in low.

There were three men. One, holding a pistol, took a step toward them. Clark and Chavez hit him in the chest and head. The other armed man, kneeling by the window, tried to turn about, but couldn't do it on his knees, and fell onto his side. Chavez was there in an instant, smashing his buttstock onto his forehead. Clark rushed the third man, slamming him against the block wall. León and Vega came in next, leapfrogging to the final door. That room was empty.

"Building is clear!" Vega shouted. "Hey, I—"

"Come on!" Clark dragged his man out the front. Chavez did the same, covered by León. Vega was slow in moving. They didn't know why until they were all outside.

Clark was already on his radio. "CAESAR, this is SNAKE. We got 'em. Let's get the fuck outa here."

"León," Vega said. "Look here."

"Tony," the sergeant said. The only other survivor from Ninja Hill had been a BANNER man. León walked over to Escobedo, who was still conscious. *"Motherfucker! You're fuckin' dead!"* León screamed, bringing his gun down.

"Stop!" Clark yelled at him. That almost didn't work, but Clark knocked him down, which did. "You're a soldier, goddammit, act like one! You and Vega—carry your friend on the chopper."

Team OMEN worked its way across the field. Several men, remarkably enough, weren't quite dead yet. That aberration was corrected with single rifle shots. The captain got his men together and counted them off with his finger.

"Good work," Clark told him. "You got everybody?"

"Yes!"

"Okay, here comes our ride."

The Pave Low swept in from the west this time, and again didn't quite touch the ground. *Just like the old days, Clark.* A helicopter that touched the ground could set off a mine. Not likely here, but PJ hadn't gotten old enough to be a colonel by overlooking any chances at all. He grabbed Escobedo—he'd gotten a good enough look by now to identify him—by the arm and propelled him to the ramp. One of the chopper crew met them there, did his count, and before Clark was sitting down with his charge, the MH-53J was moving up and north. He assigned a soldier to look after Señor Escobedo and went forward.

Sweet Jesus, Ryan thought. He'd counted eight bodies, and they'd just been the ones close to the helicopter. Jack switched off his gun motor and relaxed—and really did this time. Relaxation was a relative thing, he'd just learned. Being shot at really was worse than flying in the back of a goddamned helicopter. Amazing, he thought. A hand grabbed his shoulder.

"We got Cortez and Escobedo alive!" Clark shouted at him.

"Escobedo? What the hell was he—"

"You complaining?"

"What the hell can we do with him?" Jack asked.

"Well, I sure as shit couldn't just leave him there, could I?"

"But what—"

"If you want, I can give the bastard a flying lesson." Clark gestured toward the stern ramp. *If he learns to fly before he hits the ground, fine. . . .*

"No, goddammit, that's fucking murder!"

Clark grinned at him. "That gun next to you is not a negotiating tool, doc."

"Okay, people," PJ's voice came over the intercom before that conversation went any further. "One more stop and we call this one a day."

29. Fill-ups

It had started with the President's warning. Admiral Cutter wasn't used to having to make sure his orders had been carried out. In his naval career orders were things that you gave and that other people did, or that you did after being told to do so by others. He placed a call to the Agency and got Ritter and asked the question, the one that had to be an unnecessarily insulting one. Cutter knew that he'd already humiliated the man, and that to do so further was not a smart move—but what if the President had been right? That risk called for further action. Ritter's reaction was a troubling one. The irritation that should have been in his voice, wasn't. Instead he'd spoken like any other government bureaucrat saying that yes, the orders were being carried out, of course. Ritter was a cold, effective son of a bitch, but even that sort had its limits, beyond which emotion comes to the fore; Cutter knew that he'd reached and passed that point with the DDO. The anger just hadn't been there, and it ought to have been.

Something is wrong. The National Security Adviser told himself to relax. *Something might be wrong.* Maybe Ritter was playing mind games. Maybe even he'd seen that his course of action was the only proper one, Cutter speculated, and resigned himself to the inevitable. After all, Ritter liked being Deputy Director (Operations). That was his rice bowl, as the government saying went. Even the most important government officials had those. Even they were often uncomfortable with the idea of leaving behind the office and the secretary and the driver and most of all the title that designated them as Important People despite their meager salaries. Like the line from some movie or other, leaving the government meant entering the real world, and in the real world, people expected results to back up position papers and National Intelligence Estimates. How many people stayed in government service because of the security, the benefits, and the insulation from that "real" world? There were more of those, Cutter was sure, than of the ones who saw themselves as the honest servants of the people.

But even if that were likely, Cutter considered, it was not certain, and some further checking was in order. And so he placed his own call to Hurlburt Field and asked for Wing Operations.

"I need to talk to Colonel Johns."

"Colonel Johns is off post, sir, and cannot be reached."

"I need to know where he is."

"I do not have that information, sir."

"What do you mean, you don't have that information, Captain?" The real wing operations officer was off duty by now, and one of the helicopter pilots had drawn the duty for this evening.

"I mean I don't know, sir," the captain replied. He wanted to be a little more insolent in his answer to so stupid a question, but the call had come in on a secure line, and there was no telling who the hell was on the other end.

"Who does know?"

"I don't know that, sir, but I can try to find out."

Was this just some command fuck-up? Cutter asked himself. What if it wasn't?

"Are all your MC-130s in place, Captain?" Cutter asked.

"Three birds are off TDY somewhere or other, sir. Where they are is classified—I mean, sir, that where our aircraft happen to be is almost always classified. Besides, what with that hurricane chasing around south of here, we're getting ready to move a lot of our birds in case it heads this way."

Cutter could have demanded the information right then and there. But that would have meant identifying himself, and even then, he was talking to some twenty-something-year-old junior officer who might just say no because nobody had told him otherwise, and such a junior officer knew that he'd never be seriously punished for not taking initiative and doing something he'd been told not to do—at least not over a telephone line, secure or not. Such a demand would also have called attention to something in a way that he didn't want. . . .

"Very well," Cutter said finally and hung up. Then he called Andrews.

The first hint of trouble came from Larson, whose Beech was circling the FEATURE LZ. Juardo, still fighting the pain of his leg wound, was scanning out the side of the aircraft with his low-light goggles.

"Hey, man, I got some trucks on the ground down there at three o'clock. Like fifteen of 'em."

"Oh, that's just great," the pilot observed, and keyed his microphone.

"CLAW, this is LITTLE EYES, over."

"LITTLE EYES, this is CLAW," the Combat Talon answered.

"Be advised we have possible activity on the ground six klicks southeast of FEATURE. Say again we have trucks on the ground. No personnel are visible at this time. Recommend you warn FEATURE and CAESAR of possible intruders."

"Roger, copy."

"Christ, I hope they're slow tonight," Larson said over the intercom. "We're going down to take a look."

"You say so, man."

Larson extended his flaps and reduced power as much as he dared. There was precious little light, and flying low over mountains at night was not his idea of fun. Juardo looked down with his goggles, but the tree canopy was too heavy.

"I don't see anything."

"I wonder how long those trucks have been there. . . ."

There was a bright flash on the ground, perhaps five hundred meters below the summit. Then there were several more, small ones, like sparklers on the ground. Larson made another call:

"CLAW, this is LITTLE EYES. We have a possible firefight underway below FEATURE LZ."

"Roger."

* * *

"Roger, copy," PJ said to the MC-130. "Aircraft commander to crew: we have a possible firefight at the next LZ. We may have a hot pickup." At that moment something changed. The aircraft settled a touch and slowed. "Buck, what is that?"

"Uh-oh," the flight engineer said. "I think we have a P3 leak here. Possible pressure bleed leak, maybe a bad valve, number-two engine. I'm losing some N_f speed and some N_g, sir. T_5 is coming up a little." Ten feet over the flight engineer's head, a spring had broken, opening a valve wider than it was supposed to be. It released bleed air supposed to recirculate within the turboshaft engine. That reduced combustion in the engine, and was manifested in reduced N_f or free-power turbine speed, also in N_g power from the gas-producer turbine, and finally the loss of air volume resulted in increased tailpipe temperature, called T_5. Johns and Willis could see all this from their instruments, but they really depended on Sergeant Zimmer to tell them what the problem was. The engines belonged to him.

"Talk to me, Buck," Johns ordered.

"We just lost twenty-six-percent power in Number Two, sir. Can't fix it. Bad valve, shouldn't get much worse, though. Tailpipe temp ought to stabilize short of max-sustainable . . . maybe. Ain't an emergency yet, PJ. I'll keep an eye on it."

"Fine," the pilot growled. At the valve, not at Zimmer. This was not good news. Things had gone well tonight, too well. Like most combat veterans, Paul Johns was a suspicious man. What his mind went over now were power and weight considerations. He had to climb over those goddamned mountains in order to tank and fly back to Panama. . . .

But first he had a pickup to make.

"Give me a time."

"Four minutes," Captain Willis answered. "We'll be able to see it over that next ridge. Starting to mush on us, sir."

"Yeah, I can tell." Johns looked at his instruments. Number One was at 104 percent rated power. Number Two was just over 73 percent. Since they could accomplish their next segment of the mission despite the problem, it went onto the back burner for now. PJ dialed some more altitude into his autopilot. Climbing ridges would be getting harder now with greater weight on the airframe and less power to drag it around.

"It's a real fight, all right," Johns said a minute later. His night-vision systems showed lots of activity on the ground. Johns keyed his radio. "FEATURE, this is CAESAR, over." No answer.

"FEATURE, this is CAESAR, over." It took two more tries.

"CAESAR, this is FEATURE, we are under attack."

"Roger, FEATURE, I can see that, son. I make your position about three hundred meters down from the LZ. Get up the hill, we can cover. Say again, we can cover."

"We have close contact, CAESAR."

"Run for it. I repeat, run for it, we can cover you," PJ told him calmly. *Come on, kid. I've been here before. I know the drill. . . .* "Break contact now!"

"Roger. FEATURE, this is Six, head for the LZ. I repeat, head for the LZ now!" they heard him say. PJ keyed his intercom.

"Buck, let's go hot. Gunners to stations, we have a hot LZ here. There are friendlies on the ground. I say again: *there are friendlies on the ground, people*. So let's be goddamned careful with those fucking guns!"

Johns had wished a hundred times that he'd had one of these over Laos. The Pave Low carried over a thousand pounds of titanium armor which went, of course, over the engines, fuel cells, and transmission. The flight crew was protected by less effective Kevlar. The rest of the aircraft was less fortunate—a child could push a screwdriver through the aluminum skin—but those were the breaks. He orbited the LZ, a thousand feet higher and two thousand yards out, traveling in a clockwise circle to get a feel for things. Things didn't feel good.

"I don't like this, PJ," Zimmer told him over intercom. Sergeant Bean on the ramp gun felt the same way but didn't say anything. Ryan, who hadn't seen anything at any of the landing zones, also kept his mouth shut.

"They're moving, Buck."

"Looks like it."

"Okay, I'm spiraling in. AC to crew, we're heading in for a closer look. You may return fire directed at us, but nothing else until I say otherwise. I want to hear acknowledgments."

"Zimmer, acknowledge."

"Bean, acknowledge."

"Ryan, okay." *I can't see anything to shoot at anyway.*

It was worse than it looked. The attackers from the Cartel had chosen to approach the primary LZ from an unexpected direction. This took them right through the alternate extraction site selected by FEATURE, and the team had not had the time needed to prepare a full defensive network. Worst of all, some of the attackers were those who had survived the fight against KNIFE, and had learned a few things, like the way in which caution was sometimes improved by a speedy advance, not diminished by it. They also knew of the helicopter, but not enough. Had they known of its armament, the battle might have ended then and there, but they expected the rescue chopper to be unarmed because they had never really encountered any other sort. As usual in battle, the contest was defined by purpose and error, knowledge and ignorance. FEATURE was pulling back rapidly, leaving behind hastily arranged booby traps and claymores, but, as before, the casualties were less a warning to the attackers than a goad, and the Cartel's veterans of Ninja Hill were learning. Now they split into three distinct groups and began to envelop the hilltop LZ.

"I got a strobe," Willis said.

"FEATURE, this is CAESAR, confirm your LZ."

"CAESAR, FEATURE, do you have our strobe?"

"That's affirm. Coming in now. Get all your people in the open. I say again, get all your people where we can see them."

"We have three down we're bringing in. We're doing our best."

"Thirty seconds out," PJ told him.

"We'll be ready."

As before, the gunners heard half of the conversation, followed by their instructions: "AC to crew, I've ordered all friendlies into the open. Once we get a good count, I want you to hose down the area. Anything you can see is probably friendly. I want everything else suppressed hard. Ryan, that means beat the shit out of it."

"Roger," Jack replied.

"Fifteen seconds. Let's look sharp, people."

It came without warning. No one saw where it originated. The Pave Low was spiraling in steeply, but it could not wholly avoid flying over enemy troops. Six of them heard it approach and saw the black mass moving against the background of clouds. Simultaneously they aimed at the sky and let loose. The 7.62mm rounds lanced right through the floor of the helicopter. The sound was distinctive, like hail on a tin roof, and everyone who heard it knew immediately what it was. A scream confirmed it for the slow. Someone had been hit.

"PJ, we're taking fire," Zimmer said over the intercom circuit. As he said so, he trained his gun down and loosed a brief burst. Again the airframe vibrated. The line of tracers told the whole world what and where the Pave Low was, and more fire came in.

"Jesus!" Rounds hit the armored windshield. They didn't penetrate, but they left nicks, and their impacts sparked like fireflies. On instinct, Johns jinked to the right, away from the fire. That unmasked the left side of the aircraft.

Ryan was as scared as he had ever been. It seemed that there were a hundred, two hundred, a thousand muzzle flashes down there, all aimed straight at him. He wanted to cringe, but knew that his safest place was behind the thousand-plus-pound gun mount. The gun didn't really have much of a sight. He looked down the rotating barrels toward a particularly tight knot of flashes and depressed the trigger switch.

It felt like he was holding a jackhammer in his hands and sounded like a giant was ripping a canvas sail to bits. A gout of flame six feet long and three across erupted before his eyes, so bright that he could barely see through it, but the tight cylinder of tracers was impossible to miss, and it walked right into the flashes that were still sparkling on the ground. But not for long. He waved the gun around, assisted in the effort by the gyrations of the helicopter and the incredible vibration of the gun. The line of tracers wiggled and wavered over the target area for several seconds. By the time his thumbs came up, the sparkling of muzzle flashes had stopped.

"Son of a bitch," he said to himself, so surprised that he momentarily forgot about the danger. That wasn't the only incoming fire. Ryan selected another area and went to work, this time holding to short bursts, only a few hundred rounds each. Then the chopper turned fully away and he had no more targets.

On the flight deck, Willis and Johns scanned their instruments. They'd allowed themselves to be surprised. There was no critical damage to the aircraft. The flight controls, also protected by armor, engines, transmission, and fuel cells, were impervious to rifle fire. Or supposed to be.

"We got some people hurt back here," Zimmer reported. "Let's get it over with, PJ."

"Okay, Buck, I hear you." PJ brought the chopper back around, looping to the left now. "FEATURE, this is CAESAR, we're going to try that again." Even his voice had lost its icy calm. Combat hadn't changed very much, but he'd grown older.

"They're closing in. Move your ass, mister! We're all here, we're all here."

"Twenty seconds, son. AC to crew, we're going back in. Twenty seconds."

The helicopter stopped and pivoted in the air, not continuing its majestic sweep, and Johns hoped that those who were watching would be unprepared for that. He twisted the throttle control to max power and lowered his nose to dive in hard on the LZ. Two hundred meters out he brought the nose up and yanked the collective to slow down. It was his usual perfect maneuver. The Pave Low lost forward airspeed exactly at the right place—and dropped hard on the ground because of the reduced power from Number Two. Johns cringed when he felt it, half expecting it to set off a booby trap, but that didn't happen and he left it there.

It seemed to take forever. Minds and bodies pumped up with adrenaline have their own time, the sort that stops the ticking of watches. Ryan thought that he could see the rotor blades spinning individually at the top of his peripheral vision.

He wanted to look aft, wanted to see if the team had gotten aboard yet, but his area of responsibility was out the left-side gunner's door. He realized at once that he wasn't being paid to bring ammunition home. As soon as he was sure that there were no friendlies in front of him, he punched the gun switch and hosed down the treeline, sweeping his fire about a foot off the ground in a wide arc. On the other side, Zimmer was doing the same.

Aft, Clark was looking out the back door. Bean was on his minigun, and he couldn't shoot. This was where the friendlies were, and they moved toward the chopper, their legs pumping in what had to be a run, but seeming to be slow-motion. That was when the fire started from the trees.

Forward, Ryan was amazed that anyone could be alive in the area that he'd just hosed, but there it was. He saw a spark on the doorframe and knew it had to have been a bullet aimed right at him. Jack didn't cringe. There was no place to hide, and he knew that the side of the aircraft was getting hit far worse. He took an instant to look and see where the shooting was coming from, then trained on it and fired again. It seemed that the blast from the gun must push the aircraft sideways. The exhaust flames from the gun bored a hole through the dust kicked up by the spinning rotor, but still there were flashes of fire from the treeline.

Clark heard the screams inside and out over the low howl of the miniguns. He could feel the rounds hitting the side of the aircraft, and then saw two men fall just at the tail rotor of the helicopter while others were racing aboard.

"Shit!" He leapt to his feet and ran out the door, joined by Chavez and Vega. Clark lifted one of the fallen soldiers and dragged him toward the ramp. Chavez and Vega got the other. There was dust kicking up at their feet from the fire. Vega fell five feet from the ramp, taking his burden down with him. Clark tossed his soldier into the waiting hands of his team members and turned to assist. First he took the team member. When he turned, Chavez was struggling with Vega. Clark grabbed the man's shoulders and pushed backward, landing on the edge of the ramp. Ding grabbed *Oso*'s feet and swung them around, leaping over them to grab the base of the minigun as the helicopter started lifting off. Fire came straight through the door, but Bean now had a clear field for his weapon and swept it across the area.

It was slow getting off. The helicopter had several tons of new weight, was at over five thousand feet of altitude, and trying to fly with reduced power. Forward, PJ cursed the balky machine. The Pave Low struggled up a few feet, still taking fire.

On the ground around them the attackers were enraged that the men whom they wanted to kill were escaping, and ran for one last attempt to prevent it. They saw the helicopter as a trophy, some horrible apparition that had robbed them of success and their comrades of their lives, and each of them determined that this should not be. Over a hundred rifles were trained on the aircraft as it wavered, halfway between ground and flight.

Ryan felt the passage of several rounds—they were coming right through his door, going he knew not where, aiming for him and his gun. He was past fear. The flashes of rifle fire were places to aim, and that he did. One at a time he selected a target and touched his trigger, shifting rapidly from one to another. Safety, what there was of it, lay in eliminating the danger. There was no place to run, and he knew that the ability to respond was a luxury that everyone aboard the aircraft wanted, but only three of them had. He couldn't let them down. He moved the gun left to right and back again in a series of seconds that stretched out into hours, and he thought that he could hear each individual round the minigun spat out. His head jerked back when something hit his helmet, but he yanked it back and held the trigger down, spraying the area in one continuous blast of fire that changed as he realized that he had to bring his hands up and the muzzles down because the targets were dropping away. For one brief contradictory instant it seemed as if they and not he were getting away. Then it was over. For a moment, his hands wouldn't come off the gun. He tried to take a step back, but his hands wouldn't let go until he willed them to. Then they dropped to his side. Ryan shook his head to clear it. He was deafened by the noise from the minigun, and it took a few seconds before he started hearing the higher-frequency screams of wounded men. He looked around to see that the body of the aircraft was filled with the acidic smoke of the guns, but the rapidly increasing slipstream from forward flight was clearing it out. His eyes were still suffering from the gun flashes, and his legs were wobbly from the sudden fatigue that comes after violent action. He wanted to sit down, to go to sleep, to wake up in another place.

One of the screams was close by. It was Zimmer, only a few feet away, lying on his back and rolling around with his arms across his chest. Ryan went to see what the problem was.

Zimmer had taken three rounds in the chest. He was aspirating blood. It sprayed in a pink cloud from his mouth and nose. One round had shattered his right shoulder, but the serious ones were through the lungs. The man was bleeding to death before his eyes, Ryan knew at once. Was there a medic here? Might he do something?

"This is Ryan," he said over the intercom line. "Sergeant Zimmer is down. He's hit pretty bad."

"Buck!" PJ responded at once. "Buck, are you all right?"

Zimmer tried to answer but couldn't. His intercom line had been shot away. He shouted something Ryan couldn't understand, and Jack turned and screamed as loudly as he could at the rest of them, the others who didn't seem to care or know what the problem here was.

"Medic! Corpsman!" he added, not knowing what it was that Army troops said. Clark heard him and started heading that way.

"Come on, Zimmer, you're going to be all right," Jack told him. He remembered that much from his brief few months in the Marine Corps. Give them a reason to live. "We're going to fix this up and you're going to be all right. Hang in there, Sarge—it hurts, but you're going to be all right."

Clark was there a moment later. He stripped off the flight engineer's flak jacket, oblivious to the screech of pain that it caused from the wrecked shoulder. For Clark, too, it was too much a return to years past and things half-remembered. Somehow he'd forgotten just how scary, how awful this sort of thing was, and while he was recovering his senses more rapidly than most, the horror of having been helpless under fire and helpless with its aftermath had nearly overpowered him. And he was helpless now. He could see that from the placement of the wounds. Clark looked up at Ryan and shook his head.

"My kids!" Zimmer screamed. The sergeant had a reason to live, but the reason wasn't enough.

"Tell me about your kids," Ryan said. "Talk to me about your kids."

"Seven—I got seven kids—I gotta, I can't *die!* My kids—my kids need me."

"Hang in there, Sarge, we're going to get you out of here. You're going to make it," Ryan told him, tears clouding in his eyes at the shame of lying to a dying man.

"They need me!" His voice was weaker now as the blood was filling his throat and lungs.

Ryan looked up at Clark, hoping that there was something to be said. Some hope. Something. Clark just stared into Jack's face. He looked back down at Zimmer and took his hand, the uninjured one.

"Seven kids?" Jack asked.

"They need me," Zimmer whimpered, knowing now that he wouldn't be there, wouldn't see them grow and marry and have their own children, wouldn't be there to guide them, to protect them. He had failed to do what a father must do.

"I'll tell you something about your kids that you don't know, Zimmer," Ryan said to the dying man.

"Huh? What?" He looked confused, looked to Ryan for the answer to the great question of life. Jack didn't have that one, but told him what he could.

"They're all going to college, man." Ryan squeezed the hand as hard as he could. "You got my word, Zimmer, all your kids'll go to college. I will take care of that for you. Swear to God, man, I'll do it."

The sergeant's face changed a bit at that, but before Ryan could decide what emotion he beheld, the face changed again, and there was no emotion left. Ryan hit the intercom switch. "Zimmer's dead, Colonel."

"Roger." Ryan was offended by the coldness of the acknowledgment. He didn't hear what Johns was thinking: *God, oh God, what do I tell Carol and the kids?*

Ryan had Zimmer's head cradled on his lap. He disengaged himself slowly, resting the head down on the metal floor of the helicopter. Clark wrapped his burly arms around the younger man.

"I'm going to do it," Jack told him in a choking voice. "That wasn't a fucking lie. I am going to do it!"

"I know. He knew it too. He really did."

"You sure?" The tears had started, and it was hard for Jack to repeat the most important question of his life. "Are you really sure?"

"He knew what you said, Jack, and he believed you. What you did, doc, that was pretty good." Clark embraced Ryan in the way that men do only with their wives, their children, and those with whom they had faced death.

In the right-front seat, Colonel Johns put his grief away into a locked compartment that he would later open and experience to the full. But for now he had a mission to fly. Buck would surely understand that.

Cutter's jet arrived at Hurlburt Field well after dark. He was met by a car which took him to Wing Operations. He'd arrived entirely without warning, and strode into the Operations office like an evil spirit.

"Who the hell's in charge here?"

The sergeant at the desk recognized the President's National Security Adviser immediately from seeing him on television. "Right through that door, sir."

Cutter found a young captain dozing in his swivel chair. His eyes had cracked open just as the door did, and the twenty-nine-year-old officer jumped to his feet quite unsteadily.

"I want to know where Colonel Johns is," Vice Admiral Cutter told him quietly.

"Sir, that is information which I am not able to—"

"You know who the hell I am?"

"Yes, sir."

"Are you trying to say no to me, Captain?"

"Sir, I have my orders."

"Captain, I am countermanding all of your orders. Now, you answer my question and you do it right now." Cutter's voice was a few decibels higher now.

"Sir, I don't know where the—"

"Then you find somebody who does, and you get him here."

The captain was frightened enough that he took the route of least resistance. He called a major, who lived on post and was in the office in under eight minutes.

"What the hell is this?" the major said on the way through the door.

"Major, I am what's going on here," Cutter told him. "I want to know where Colonel Johns is. He's the goddamned CO of this outfit, isn't he?"

"Yessir!" *What the hell is this . . . ?*

"Are you telling me that the people of this unit don't know where their CO is?" Cutter was sufficiently amazed that his authority hadn't generated immediate compliance with his orders that he allowed himself to bluster off on a tangent.

"Sir, in Special Operations, we—"

"Is this a fucking Boy Scout camp or a military organization?" the Admiral shouted.

"Sir, this is a military organization," the major replied. "Colonel Johns is off TDY. I am under orders, sir, not to discuss his mission or his location with anyone without proper authority, and you are not on the list, sir. Those are my orders, Admiral."

Cutter was amazed and only got angrier. "Do you know what my job is and who I work for?" He hadn't had a junior officer talk to him like this in over a decade. And he'd broken that one's career like a matchstick.

"Sir, I have written orders on this matter. The President ain't on the list either, sir," the major said from the position of attention. *Fucking squid, calling the United States Air Force a Boy Scout camp! Well, fuck you and the horse you rode in on—Admiral, sir,* his face managed to communicate quite clearly.

Cutter had to soften his voice, had to regain control of his emotions. He could take care of this insolent punk at leisure. But for now he needed that information. He started, therefore, with an apology, man to man, as it were. "Major, you'll have to excuse me. This is a most important matter, and I can't explain to you why it is important or the issues involved here. I can say that this is a real life-or-death situation. Your Colonel Johns may be in a place where he needs help. The operation may be coming apart around him, and I really need to know. Your loyalty to your commander is laudable, and your devotion to duty is exemplary, but officers are supposed to exercise judgment. You have to do that now, Major. I am telling you that I need that information—and I need it now."

Reason succeeded where bluster had failed. "Admiral, the colonel went back down to Panama along with one of our MC-130s. I do not know why, and I don't know what they're doing. That is normal in a special-ops wing, sir. Practically everything we do is compartmented, and this one is tighter than most. What I just told you is everything I know, sir."

"Exactly where?"

"Howard, sir."

"Very well. How can I get in touch with them?"

"Sir, they're out of the net. I do not have that information. They can contact us but we can't contact them."

"That's crazy," Cutter objected.

"Not so, Admiral. We do that sort of thing all the time. With the MC-130 along, they're a self-contained unit. The Herky-bird takes maintenance and support personnel to sustain the operation, and unless they call us for something, they're completely independent of this base. In the event of a family emergency or something like that, we can try to contact them through Howard's base ops office, but we haven't had to do so in this case. I can try to open that channel now for you, if you wish, sir, but it might take a few hours."

"Thanks, but I can *be* there in a few hours."

"Weather's breaking down around that area, sir," the major warned him.

"That's okay." Cutter left the room and walked back to his car. His plane had already been refueled, and ten minutes later it was lifting off for Panama.

Johns was on an easier flight profile now, heading northeast down the great Andean valley that forms the spine of Colombia. The flight was smooth, but he had three concerns. First, he didn't have the necessary power to climb over the mountains to his west at his present aircraft weight. Second, he'd have to refuel in less than an hour. Third, the weather ahead was getting worse by the minute.

"CAESAR, this is CLAW, over."

"Roger, CLAW."

"When are we going to tank, sir?" Captain Montaigne asked.

"I want to get closer to the coast first, and maybe if we burn some more off I can head west some more to do it."

"Roger, but be advised that we're starting to get radar emissions, and somebody might just detect us. They're air-traffic radars, but this Herky-bird is big enough to give one a skin-paint, sir."

Damn! Somehow Johns had allowed himself to forget that.

"We got a problem here," PJ told Willis.

"Yeah. There's a pass about twenty minutes ahead that we might be able to climb over."

"How much?"

"Says eighty-one hundred on the charts. Drops down a lot lower farther up, but with the detection problem . . . and the weather. I don't know, Colonel."

"Let's find out how high we can take her," Johns said. He'd tried to go easy on the engines for the last half hour. Not now. He had to find out what he could do. PJ twisted the throttle control on the collective arm to full power, watching the gauge for Number Two as he did so. The needle didn't even reach 70 percent this time.

"The P3 leak is getting worse, boss," Willis told him.

"I see it." They worked to get maximum lift off the rotor, but though they didn't know it, that, too, had taken damage and was not delivering as much lift as it was supposed to. The Pave Low labored upward, reaching seventy-seven hundred feet, but that was where it stopped, and then it started descending, fighting every foot but gradually losing altitude.

"As we burn off more gas . . ." Willis said hopefully.

"Don't bet on it." PJ keyed his radio. "CLAW, CAESAR, we can't make it over the hills."

"Then we'll come to you."

"Negative, too soon. We have to tank closer to the coast."

"CAESAR, this is LITTLE EYES. I copy your problem. What sort of fuel you need for that monster?" Larson asked. He'd been pacing the helicopter since the pickup, in accordance with the plan.

"Son, right now I'd burn piss if I had enough."

"Can you make the coast?"

"That's affirmative. Close, but we ought to be able to make it."

"I can pick you an airfield one-zero-zero miles short of the coast that has all the avgas you need. I am also carrying a casualty who's bleeding and needs some medical help."

Johns and Willis looked at each other. "Where is it?"

"At current speed, about forty minutes. El Pindo. It's a little place for private birds. Ought to be deserted this time of night. They have ten-kay gallons of underground storage. It's a Shell concession and I've been in and out of there a bunch of times."

"Altitude?"

"Under five hundred. Nice, thick air for that rotor, Colonel."

"Let's do it," Willis said.

"CLAW, did you copy that?" Johns asked.

"That's affirm."

"That's what we're going to try. Break west. Stay close enough to maintain radio contact, but you are free to evade radar coverage."

"Roger, heading west," Montaigne replied.

In back, Ryan was sitting by his gun. There were eight wounded men in the helicopter, but two medics were working on them and Ryan was unable to offer any help better than that. Clark rejoined him.

"Okay, what are we going to do with Cortez and Escobedo?"

"Cortez we want, the other one, hell, I don't know. How do we explain kidnapping him?"

"What do you think we're going to do, put him on trial?" Clark asked over the din of the engines and the wind.

"Anything else is cold-blooded murder. He's a prisoner now, and killing prisoners is murder, remember?"

You're getting legal on me, Clark thought, but he knew that Ryan was right. Killing prisoners was contrary to the code.

"So we take him back?"

"That blows the operation," Ryan said. He knew he was talking too loudly for the subject. He was supposed to be quiet and thoughtful now, but the environment and the events of the evening defeated that. "Christ, I don't know what to do."

"Where are we going—I mean, where's this chopper going?"

"I don't know." Ryan keyed his intercom to ask. He was surprised by the answer and communicated it to Clark.

"Look, let me handle it. I got an idea. I'll take him out of here when we land. Larson and I will tidy that part of it up. I think I know what'll work."

"But—"

"You don't really want to know, do you?"

"You can't murder him!" Jack insisted.

"I won't," Clark said. Ryan didn't know how to read that answer. But it did offer a way out, and he took it.

Larson got there first. The airfield was poorly lit, only a few glow lights showing under the low ceiling, but he managed to get his aircraft down, and with his anticollision lights blinking, he guided the way to the fuel-service area. He'd barely stopped when the helicopter landed fifty yards away.

Larson was amazed. In the dim blue lights he could see numerous holes in the aircraft. A man in a flight suit ran out toward him. Larson met him and led him to the fuel hose. It was a long one, about an inch in diameter, used to fuel private aircraft. The power to the pumps was off, but Larson knew where the switch was, and he shot the door lock. He'd never done that before, but just like in the movies, five rounds removed the brass mechanism from the wooden frame of the door. A minute later, Sergeant Bean had the nozzle into one of the outrigger tanks. That was when Clark and Escobedo appeared. A soldier held a rifle to the latter's head while the CIA officers conferred.

"We're going back," Clark told the pilot.

"What?" Larson turned to see two soldiers taking Juardo out of the Beech and toward the helicopter.

"We're taking our friend here back home to Medellín. Couple of things we have to do first, though . . ."

"Oh, great." Larson walked back to his aircraft and climbed up on the wing to open his fuel caps. He had to wait fifteen minutes. The helicopter usually drank fuel through a far larger hose. When the crewman took the hose back, the chopper's rotor started turning again. Soon after that, it lifted off into the night. There was lightning ahead to the north, and Larson was just as happy that he wasn't flying there. He let Clark handle the fueling while he went inside to make a telephone call. The funny part was that he'd even make money off the deal. Except that there was nothing funny about anything that had happened during the preceding month.

"Okay," PJ said into the intercom. "That's the last pit stop, and we're heading for home."

"Engine temps aren't all that great," Willis said. The T-64-GE-7 engines were designed to burn aviation kerosene, not the more volatile and dangerous high-octane gas used by private planes. The manufacturer's warranty said that you could use that fuel for thirty hours before the burner cans were crisped down to ashes, but the warranty didn't say anything about bad valve springs and P3 loss.

"Looks like we're going to cool 'em down just fine," the colonel said, nodding at the weather ahead.

"Thinking positive again, are we, Colonel?" Willis said as coolly as he could manage. It wasn't just a thunderstorm there, it was a hurricane that stood between them and Panama. On the whole, it was something scarier than being shot at. You couldn't shoot *back* at a storm.

"CLAW, this is CAESAR, over," Johns called on his radio.

"I read you, CAESAR."

"How's the weather ahead look?"

"Bad, sir. Recommend that you head west, find a spot to climb over, and try to approach from the Pacific side."

Willis scanned the navigational display. "Uh-uh."

"CLAW, we just gained about five-kay pounds in weight. We, uh, looks like we need another way."

"Sir, the storm is moving west at fifteen knots, and your course to Panama takes you into the lower-right quadrant."

Headwinds all the way, PJ told himself.

"Give me a number."

"Estimated peak winds on your course home are seven-zero knots."

"Great!" Willis observed. "That makes us marginal for Panama, sir. Very damned marginal."

Johns nodded. The winds were bad enough. The rain that came with them would greatly reduce engine efficiency. His flight range might be less than half of what it should be . . . no way he could tank in the storm . . . the smart move would be to find a place to land and stay there, but he couldn't do that either. . . . Johns keyed his radio yet again.

"CLAW, this is CAESAR. We are heading for Alternate One."

"Are you out of your skull?" Francie Montaigne replied.

"I don't like it, sir," Willis said.

"Fine. You can testify to that effect someday. It's only a hundred miles off the coast, and if it doesn't work, we'll use the winds to slingshot us around. CLAW, I need a position check on Alternate One."

"You crazy fucker," Montaigne breathed. To her communications people: "Call up Alternate One. I need a position check and I need it now."

Murray was not having any fun at all. Though *Adele* wasn't really a major hurricane, Wegener had told him, it was more than he had ever expected to see. The seas had been forty feet, and though once *Panache* had looked like a white steel cliff alongside the dock, she now rode like a child's toy in a bathtub. The FBI agent had a scopolamine patch stuck to his head below and behind his ear to combat motion-sickness, but it wasn't fighting hard enough at the moment. But Wegener was just sitting in his bridge chair, smoking his pipe like the Old Man of the Sea while Murray held on to the grab-bar over his head, feeling like the man on the flying trapeze.

They were not in their programmed position. Wegener had explained to his visitor that there was only one place they could be. It moved, but that's where they had to be, and Murray was distantly thankful that the seas weren't quite as bad as they had been. He worked his way over to the door and looked out at the towering cylinder of cloud.

"*Panache,* this is CLAW, over," the speaker said. Wegener rose to take the mike.

"CLAW, this is *Panache*. Your signal is weak but readable, over."

"Position check, over."

Wegener gave it to the pilot, who sounded like a girl, he thought. Christ, they were everywhere now.

"CAESAR is inbound yours."

"Roger. Please advise CAESAR that conditions are below margins. I say again, it is not good down here at the moment."

"Roger, copy. Stand by." The voice came back two minutes later. "*Panache,* this is CLAW. CAESAR says he wants to try it. If he can't do it, he plans to HIFR. Can you handle that, over."

"That's affirmative, we can sure as hell try. Give me an ETA, over."

"Estimate six-zero minutes."

"Roger, we'll be ready. Keep us posted. Out." Wegener looked across his bridge. "Miss Walters, I have the conn. I want chiefs Oreza and Riley on the bridge, now."

"Captain has the conn," Ensign Walters said. She was disappointed. Here she was in the middle of a goddamned tropical storm and having the time of her young life. She wasn't even ill from it, though many of the crew were. So why couldn't the skipper let her keep the goddamned conn?

"Left standard rudder," Wegener ordered. "Come to new course three-three-five. All ahead two-thirds."

"Left standard rudder, aye, coming to new course three-three-five." The helmsman turned the wheel, then reached for the throttle controls. "Two thirds, sir."

"Very well. How you feel, Obrecki?" the skipper asked.

"Hell of a coaster, but I'm wondering when the ride is going to stop, sir." The youngster grinned, but didn't take his eyes off the compass.

"You're doing just fine. Let me know if you get tired, though."

"Aye aye, sir."

Oreza and Riley appeared a minute later. "What gives?" the former asked.

"We go to flight quarters in thirty minutes," the captain told them.

"Oh, fuck!" Riley observed. "Excuse me, Red, but . . . shit!"

"Okay, Master Chief, now that we've gotten that behind us, I'm depending on you to get it done," Wegener said sternly. Riley accepted the rebuke like the pro he was.

"Beg pardon, Cap'n, you'll get my best shot. Put the XO in the tower?"

Wegener nodded. The executive officer was the best man to command the evolution from the flight-control station. "Go get him." Riley left and Wegener turned to his quartermaster. "Portagee, I want you on the wheel when we go Hotel Corpin. I'll have the conn."

"Sir, there ain't no Hotel Corpin."

"That's why you're on the wheel. Relieve Obrecki in half an hour and get a feel for her. We gotta give him the best target we can."

"Jesus." Oreza looked out the windows. "You got it, Red."

Johns held the aircraft down, staying a scant five hundred feet above ground level. He disengaged the automatic flight controls, trusting more to his skill and instinct now, leaving the throttle to Willis and concentrating on his instruments as much as he could. It started in an instant. One moment they were flying in clear air, the next there was rain pelting the aircraft.

"This isn't so bad," Johns lied outrageously over the intercom.

"They even pay us to do it," Willis agreed with no small irony.

PJ checked the navigation display. The winds were from the northwest at the moment, slowing the helicopter somewhat, but that would change. His eyes flickered from the airspeed indicator to another one that worked off a Doppler-radar aimed at the ground. Satellite and inertial navigation systems told a computer display where he was and where he wanted to go, a red dot. Another screen held the display of a radar system that interrogated the storm ahead, showing the worst sections in red. He'd try to avoid those, but the yellow areas he had to fly through were bad enough.

"Shit!" Willis shouted. Both pilots yanked up on the collective and twisted to maximum power. They'd caught a downdraft. Both pairs of eyes locked onto the dial that gave them vertical velocity in feet per minute. For an instant they were headed down at over a thousand, less than thirty seconds of life for an aircraft at five hundred feet. But microbursts like that are localized phenomena. The helicopter bottomed out at two hundred and clawed its way back up. PJ decided that seven hundred feet was a safer cruise altitude at the moment. He said one word:

"Close."

Willis grunted by way of reply.

In back, men were strapped down to the floor. Ryan had already done that, and was holding on to his minigun mount as though it would make a difference. He could see out the open door—at nothing, really. Just a mass of gray darkness occasionally lit by lightning. The helicopter was jolting up and down, tossed like a child's kite by the moving masses of air, except that the helicopter weighed forty thousand pounds. But there was nothing he could do. His fate was in the hands of others, and nothing he knew or did mattered now. Even vomiting didn't make him feel any better, though he and others were doing that. He just wanted it to be over, and only intellect told him that he really did care how it ended—didn't he?

The buffeting continued, but the winds shifted as the helicopter penetrated the storm. They had started off from the northeast, but shifted with measurable speed counterclockwise, and were soon on the port quarter of the aircraft. That increased their ground speed. With an airspeed of one-fifty, they now had a ground speed of one-ninety and increasing.

"This is doing wonders for our fuel economy," Johns noted.

"Fifty miles," Willis replied.

"CAESAR, this is CLAW, over."

"Roger, CLAW, we are five-zero miles from Alternate One, and it's a little bumpy—" *A little bumpy, my ass,* Captain Montaigne thought, roller-coastering through lighter weather a hundred miles away "—otherwise okay," Johns reported. "If we cannot make the landing, I think we can try to slingshot out the other side and make for the Panamanian coast." Johns frowned as more water struck the windshield. Some was ingested into the engines at the same time.

"Flameout! We've lost Number Two."

"Restart it," Johns said, still trying to be cool. He lowered the nose and traded altitude for speed to get out of the heavy rain. That, too, was supposed to be a local phenomenon. Supposed to be.

"Working on it," Willis rasped.

"Losing power in Number One," Johns said. He twisted the throttle all the way and managed to get some of it back. His two-engine aircraft was now operating on one of its engines at 80 percent power. "Let's get Two back, Captain. We have a hundred foot per minute of 'down' right now."

"Working," Willis repeated. The rain eased a little, and Number Two started turning and burning again, but delivered only 40 percent. "I think the P3 loss just got worse. We got a shit sandwich here, Colonel. Forty miles. We're committed to Alternate One now."

"At least we have an option. I never could swim worth a damn." PJ's hands were sweaty now. He could feel them loose inside the handmade gloves. Intercom time: "AC to crew, we're about fifteen minutes out," he told them. "One-five minutes out."

Riley had assembled a group of ten, all experienced crewmen. Each had a safety line around his waist, and Riley checked every knot and buckle personally. Though all had life preservers on, finding a man overboard in these conditions would require a miracle from an especially loving God who had lots of things to keep Him busy tonight, Riley thought. Tie-down chains and more two-inch line was assembled and set in place, already secured to the deck wherever possible. He took the deck crew forward, standing them against the aft-facing wall of the superstructure. "All ready here," he said over the phone to the XO in flight control. To his people: "If any of you fuck up and go over the side, I'll fucking jump overboard an' strangle you myself!''

They were in a whirlpool of wind. According to the navigational display, they were now north of their target, traveling at nearly two hundred fifty knots. The buffet now was the worst it had been. One downburst hurled them down at the black waves until Johns stopped at a bare hundred feet. It was now to the point that the pilot wanted to throw up. He'd never flown in conditions like this, and it was worse than the manuals said it was. ''How far?''

''We should be there right now, sir!'' Willis said. ''Dead south.''

''Okay.'' Johns pushed the stick to the left. The sudden change of direction relative to the wind threatened to snap the helicopter over, but he held it and crabbed onto the new course. Two minutes later, they were in the clear.

''*Panache,* this is CAESAR, where the hell are you?''

''Lights on, everything, now!'' Wegener shouted when he heard the call. In a moment *Panache* was lit up like a Christmas tree.

''Goddamn if you don't look pretty down there!'' the voice said a few seconds later.

Adele was a small, weak, disorganized hurricane, now turning back into a tropical storm due to confused local weather conditions. That made her winds weaker than everyone had feared, but the eye was also small and disorganized, and the eye was what they needed now.

It is a common misconception that the eye of a hurricane is calm. It is not, though after experiencing the powerful winds in the innermost wall of clouds, the fifteen knots of breeze there seem like less than nothing to an observer. But the wind is unsteady and shifting, and the seas in the eye, though not as tall as those in the storm proper, are confused. Wegener had stationed his ship within a mile of the northwest edge of the eye, which was barely four miles across. The storm was moving at about fifteen knots. They had fifteen minutes to recover the helicopter. About the only good news was that the air was clear. No rain was falling, and the crew in the pilothouse could see the waves and allow for them.

Aft at flight control, the executive officer donned his headset and started talking.

''CAESAR, this is *Panache*. I am the flight-operations officer, and I will guide your approach. We have fifteen knots of wind, and the direction is variable. The ship is pitching and rolling in what looks like about fifteen-foot seas. We have about ten or fifteen minutes to do this, so there's not that much of a rush.'' That last sentence was merely aimed at making the helicopter's crew feel better. He wondered if anyone could bring this off.

''Skipper, a few more knots and I can hold her a little steadier,'' Portagee reported at the wheel.

''We can't run out of the eye.''

''I know that, sir, but I need a little more way on.''

Wegener went outside to look. The helicopter was visible now, its strobes blinking in the darkness as it circled the ship to allow the pilot to size things up. *If anything screws this up, it's going to be the roll,* Wegener realized. Portagee was right about the speed. ''Two-thirds,'' he called back inside.

''Christ, that's a little boat,'' Johns heard Willis breathe.

''Just so the oars ain't in the way.'' PJ took the helicopter down, circling one last time and coming to a straight course dead aft of the cutter. He leveled out at one hundred feet and found that he couldn't hover very well. He lacked the power, and the aircraft wavered left and right when he tried.

"Hold that damned boat steady!" he said over the radio circuit.

"We are trying, sir," the XO replied. "We have the wind off the port bow at the moment. I recommend you come in from the portside and stay at an angle to the deck all the way in."

"Roger, I can see why." Johns adjusted power one more time and moved in.

"Okay, let's move!" Riley told his men. They divided into three teams, one for each of the helicopter's wheel assemblies.

The deck, Johns saw, was not quite large enough for a fore-and-aft landing, but by angling his approach he could plant all six wheels on the black surface. He came in slowly, fifteen knots faster than the ship to start, and sloughing that off as he closed, but the wind shifted and turned the helicopter. Johns swore and turned fully away to try again.

"Sorry about that," he said. "I have some power problems here."

"Roger, take your time, sir," the XO replied.

PJ started again, a thousand yards out. The approach this time went well. He flared the aircraft a hundred yards aft to drop off excess speed, then flattened out and eased forward. His main gear touched just where he wanted, but the ship rolled hard and threw the aircraft to starboard. Instinctively PJ hit power and collective to lift free of the deck. He shouldn't have, and knew it even as he did so.

"This is hard," he said over the radio, managing not to curse as he brought the chopper back around.

"Shame we don't have more time to practice," the Coast Guard officer agreed. "That was a good, smooth approach. The ship just took a bad roll on us. Do that one more time, you'll be just fine."

"Okay, one more time." PJ came in again.

The ship was rolling twenty degrees left and right despite her stabilizers and bilge keels, but Johns fixed his eyes on the center of the target area, which wasn't rolling at all, just a fixed point in space. That had to be the trick, he told himself, pick the spot that isn't moving. Again he flared out to kill off speed and inched forward. Just as he approached the deck, his eyes shifted to where the nosewheels had to hit, and slammed the collective down. It felt almost as bad as a crash, but the collective held the chopper in place.

Riley was first up and rolled under the aircraft at the nosewheels. Another boatswain's mate followed with the tie-down chains. The master chief found a likely spot and hooked them in place, then shot his arm out and made a fist. Two men on the other end of the chains pulled them taut, and the chief rolled free and went down the portside to get to work on the main gear. It took several minutes. The Pave Low shifted twice before they had it secured, but soon they had two-inch line to back up the chains. By the time Riley was finished, it would have taken explosives to lift it from the deck. The deck crew entered the helicopter at the stern ramp and guided the passengers out. Riley counted fifteen people. He'd been told to expect more than that. Then he saw the bodies, and the men who were struggling with them.

Forward, Johns and Willis shut down their engines.

"CLAW, CAESAR is down. Return to base." Johns took off his helmet too soon to catch the reply, though Willis caught it.

"Roger. Out."

Johns looked around. He didn't feel like a pilot now. His aircraft was down. He was safe. It was time to get out and do something else. He couldn't get out his door without risking a fall overboard and . . . he'd allowed himself to forget Buck Zimmer. That door in his mind opened itself now. Well, he told himself, Buck would understand. The colonel stepped over the flight-engineer console. Ryan was still there, his flight suit speckled from his nausea. Johns knelt by the side of his sergeant. They'd served together on and off for over twenty years.

"He told me he has seven kids," Ryan said.

Johns' voice was too tired for any overt emotions. He spoke like a man a thousand years old, tired of life, tired of flying, tired of everything. "Yeah, cute ones. His wife is from Laos. Carol, her name is. Oh, God, Buck—why now?"

"Let me help," Jack said. Johns took the arms. Ryan got the legs. They had to wait in line. There were other bodies to be carried out, some dead, some only wounded, and they got the understandable priority. The soldiers, Jack saw, carried their own, helped by Sergeant Bean. The Coasties offered help, but it was declined—not unkindly, and the sailors understood the reason. Ryan and Johns also declined the assistance, the colonel because of the years with his friend, and the CIA officer because of a duty self-imposed. Riley and his men stayed behind briefly to collect packs and weapons. Then they, too, went below.

The bodies were set in a passageway for the time being. The wounded went to the crew's mess. Ryan and the Air Force officers were guided to the wardroom. There they found the man who'd started it all, months before, though none of them would ever understand how it had all happened. There was one more face, one which Jack recognized.

"Hi, Dan."

"Bad?" the FBI agent asked.

Jack didn't respond to that. "We got Cortez. I think he was wounded. He's probably in sick bay with a couple of soldiers keeping an eye on him."

"What got you?" Murray asked. He pointed to Jack's helmet.

Ryan took it off and saw a gouge where a 7.62 bullet had scraped away a quarter inch or so of fiberglass. Jack knew that he should have reacted to it, but that part of his life was four hundred miles behind him. Instead he sat down and stared at the deck and didn't say anything for a while. Two minutes later, Murray moved him onto a cot and covered him with a blanket.

Captain Montaigne had to fight the last two miles through high winds, but she was a particularly fine pilot and the Lockheed Hercules was a particularly fine aircraft. She touched down a little hard, but not too badly, and followed the guide jeep to her hangar. A man in civilian clothes was waiting there, along with some officers. As soon as she'd shut down, she walked out to meet them. She made them wait while she headed for the rest room, smiling through her fatigue that there was not a man in America who'd deny a lady a trip to the john. Her flight suit smelled horrible and her hair was a wreck, she saw in the mirror before she returned. They were waiting for her right outside the door.

"Captain, I want to know what you did tonight," the civilian asked—but he wasn't a civilian, she realized after a moment, though the prick certainly didn't deserve to be anything else. Montaigne didn't know everything that was behind all this, but she did know that much.

"I just flew a very long mission, sir. My crew and I are beat to hell."

"I want to talk to all of you about what you did."

"Sir, that is *my* crew. If there's any talking to be done, you'll talk to me!" she snapped back.

"What did you do?" Cutter demanded. He tried pretending it wasn't a girl. He didn't know that she was not pretending that he wasn't a man.

"Colonel Johns went in to rescue some special-ops troopers." She rubbed both hands across the back of her neck. "We got 'em—he got 'em, most of 'em, I suppose."

"Then where is he?"

Montaigne looked him right in the eye. "Sir, he had engine trouble. He couldn't climb out to us—couldn't get over the mountains. He flew right into the storm. He didn't fly out of it, sir. Anything else you want to know? I want to get showered, get some coffee down, and start thinking about search and rescue."

"The field's closed," the base commander said. "Nobody gets out for another ten hours. I think you need some rest, Captain."

"I think you're right, sir. Excuse me, I have to see to my crew. I'll have you the SAR coordinates in a few minutes. Somebody's gotta try," she added.

"Look, General, I want—" Cutter started to say.

"Mister, you leave that crew alone," said an Air Force one-star who was retiring soon anyway.

Larson landed at Medellín's city airport about the same time the MC-130 approached Panama. It had been a profane flight, Clark in the back with Escobedo, the latter's hands tied behind his back and a gun in his ribs. There had been many promises of death in the flight. Death to Clark, death to Larson and his girlfriend who worked for Avianca, death to many people. Clark just smiled through it all.

"So what do you do with me, eh? You kill me now?" he asked as the wheels locked in the down position. Finally, Clark responded.

"I suggested that we could give you a flying lesson out the back of the helicopter, but they wouldn't let me. So looks like we're going to have to let you go."

Escobedo didn't know how to answer. His bluster wasn't able to cope with the fact that they might not want to kill him. They just didn't have the courage to, Clark decided.

"I had Larson call ahead," he said.

"Larson, you motherless traitor, you think you will survive?"

Clark dug the pistol in Escobedo's ribs. "You don't bother the guy who's flying the goddamned airplane. If I were you, señor, I'd be very pleased to be coming home. We're even having you met at the airport."

"Met by whom?"

"By some of your friends," Clark said as the wheel squeaked down on the tarmac. Larson reversed his props to brake the aircraft. "Some of your fellow board members."

That's when he saw the real danger coming. "What did you tell them?"

"The truth," Larson answered. "That you were taking a flight out of the country under very strange circumstances, what with the storm and all. And, gee, what with all the odd happenings of the past few weeks, I thought that it was kind of a coincidence . . ."

"But I will tell them—"

"What?" Clark asked. "That we put our own lives at risk by delivering you back home? That it's all a trick? Sure, you tell them that."

The aircraft stopped but the engines didn't. Clark gagged the chieftain. Then he unbuckled Escobedo's seat belt and pulled him toward the door. A car was already there. Clark stepped down, his silenced automatic in Escobedo's back.

"You are not Larson," the man with the submachine gun said.

"I am his friend. He is flying. Here is your man. You should have something for us."

"You do not need to leave," said the man with the briefcase.

"This one has too many friends. It is best, I think, that we should leave."

"As you wish," the second one said. "But you have nothing to fear from us." He handed over the briefcase.

"Gracias, jefe," Clark said. They loved to be called that. He pushed Escobedo toward them.

"You should know better than to betray your friends," said the second one as Clark reentered the aircraft. The comment was aimed at the bound and gagged chieftain, whose eyes were very, very wide, staring back at Clark as he closed the door.

"Get us the hell out of here."

"Next stop, Venezuela," Larson said as he goosed the throttles.

"Then Gitmo. Think you can hack it?"

"I'll need some coffee, but they make it good down here." The aircraft lifted off and Larson thought, *Jesus, it's good to have this one behind us*. That was true for him, but not for everyone.

30. The Good of the Service

By the time Ryan awoke on his cot in the wardroom, they were out of the worst of it. The cutter managed to make a steady ten knots east, and with the storm heading northwest at fifteen, they were in moderate seas in six hours. Course was made northeast, and *Panache* increased to her best continuous speed of about twenty knots.

The soldiers were quartered with the cutter's enlisted crew, who treated them like visiting kings. By some miracle some liquor bottles were discovered—probably from the chiefs' quarters, but no one hazarded to ask—and swiftly emptied. Their uniforms was discarded and new clothing issued from ship's stores. The dead were placed in cold storage, which everyone understood was the only possible thing. There were five of them; two of them, including Zimmer, had died during the rescue. Eight men were wounded, one of them seriously, but the two Army medics, plus the cutter's independent-duty corpsman, were able to stabilize him. Mainly the soldiers slept and ate and slept some more during their brief cruise.

Cortez, who'd been wounded in the arm, was in the brig. Murray looked after him. After Ryan awoke, both men went below with a TV camera which was set up on a tripod, and the senior FBI executive started to ask some questions. It was soon apparent that Cortez had had nothing to do with the murder of Emil Jacobs, which was as surprising to Murray as it was reasonable on examination of the information.

It was a complication that neither man had actually expected, but one that might work in their favor, Ryan thought. He was the one who started asking the questions about Cortez's experience with the DGI. Cortez was wholly cooperative throughout. He'd betrayed one allegiance, and doing so to another came easily, especially with Jack's promise that he wouldn't be prosecuted if he cooperated. It was a promise that would be kept to the letter.

Cutter remained in Panama for another day. The search-and-rescue operation aimed at locating the downed helicopter was delayed by weather, and it was hardly surprising to him that nothing was found. The storm kept heading northwest and blew itself out on the Yucatan Peninsula, ending as a series of line squalls that caused half a dozen tornadoes in Texas several days later. Cutter didn't stay long enough for that. As soon as the weather permitted, he flew straight back to D.C. just hours after Captain Montaigne returned to Eglin Air Force Base, her crew sworn to secrecy that their commander had every reason to enforce.

Panache arrived at Guantánamo Naval Base thirty-six hours after taking the helicopter aboard. Captain Wegener had radioed for permission, claiming a machinery problem and wanting to get out of Hurricane *Adele*'s path. Several miles off, Colonel Johns started up their helicopter and flew it onto the base, where it was immediately rolled into a hangar. The cutter came alongside an hour later, showing moderate storm damage, some of which was quite real.

Clark and Larson met the ship at the dock. Their aircraft was also hidden away. Ryan and Murray joined them, and a squad of Marines went aboard the cutter to retrieve Félix Cortez. Some telephone calls were placed, and then it was time to decide what had to be done. There were no easy solutions, nothing that would be entirely legal. The soldiers were treated at the base hospital and flown the next day to Fort MacDill in Florida. The same day, Clark and Larson returned the aircraft to Washington, having stopped to refuel in the Bahamas. In Washington it was turned over to a small corporation that belongs to CIA. Larson went on leave, wondering if he should really marry the girl and raise a family. Of one thing he was certain: he would leave the Agency.

Predictably, one of the things that happened was quite unexpected, and would forever be a mystery to all but one.

Admiral Cutter had returned two days earlier, and was back in his regular routine. The President was off on a political trip, trying to reestablish himself in the polls before the convention started two weeks hence. That made easier what had been a very hectic few weeks for his National Security Adviser. One way or another, he decided, he'd had enough of this. He'd served this President well, done things that needed to be done, and was entitled to a reward. He thought a fleet command would be appropriate, preferably Commander-in-Chief Atlantic Fleet. Vice Admiral Painter, the current Assistant Chief of Naval Operations (Air Warfare), had been told to expect it, but it was the President's call to make, after all, and Cutter figured that he could have just about anything he wanted. After that, if the President was re-elected, maybe Chairman of the Joint Chiefs . . . It was something to think about over breakfast, which was at a civilized hour for a change. He'd even have time for a jog after his morning briefing from CIA. The doorbell rang at 7:15. Cutter answered it himself.

"Who are you?"

"Your regular briefing officer was taken ill, sir. I have the duty today," the man said. Forties, looked like one tough old field officer.

"Okay, come on." Cutter waved him into the study. The man sat down, glad to see that the Admiral had a TV and VCR in here.

"Okay, where do we start today?" Cutter asked after the door was closed.

"Gitmo, sir," the man said.

"What's happening in Cuba?"

"Actually, I have it on videotape, sir." The field officer inserted it in the unit and punched "play."

"What is this . . . ?" *Jesus Christ!* The tape played on for several minutes before the CIA officer stopped it.

"So what? That's the word of a traitor to his own country," Cutter said to answer the man's expectant smile.

"There's this, too." He held up a photograph of the two of them. "Personally, I'd love to see you in federal prison. That's what the FBI wants. They're going to arrest you later today. You can imagine the charges. Assistant Deputy Director Murray is running the case. He's probably meeting with a U.S. Magistrate right now—whatever the mechanics are. Personally I don't care about that."

"Then why—?"

"I'm a bit of a movie buff. Used to be in the Navy, too. In the movies at times like this, they always give a guy a chance to handle things himself—'for the good of the service,' they usually say. I wouldn't try running away. There's a team of FBI agents watching you, in case you haven't noticed. Given the way things work in this town—how long things take to get done—I don't suppose you'll be meeting them until ten or eleven. If you do, Admiral, then God help you. You'll get life. I only wish they could do something worse, but you'll get life in a federal pen, with some career hood sticking it up that tight little ass of yours when the guards aren't around. I wouldn't mind seeing that either. Anyway." He retrieved the videotape, tucking it in the briefcase along with the photograph that the Bureau really shouldn't have given him—and they'd told Ryan that he'd only use it to identify Cortez. "Good day, sir."

"But you've—"

"Done what? Nobody swore me to secrecy over this. What secrets have I revealed, Admiral? You were there for all of them."

"You're Clark, aren't you?"

"Excuse me? Who?" he said on his way out. Then he was gone.

Half an hour later, Pat O'Day saw Cutter jogging down the hill toward the George Washington Parkway. One nice thing about having the President out of town, the inspector thought, was that he didn't have to shake out of the rack at 4:30 to meet the bastard. He'd been here only forty minutes, spending a lot of time with his stretching exercises, and there he was. O'Day let him pass, then moved out, keeping up easily since the man was quite a bit older. But that wasn't all. . . .

O'Day followed him for a mile, then two, approaching the Pentagon. Cutter followed the jogging path between the road and the river. Perhaps he didn't feel well. He alternately jogged and walked. Maybe he's trying to see if he has a tail, O'Day thought, but . . . Then he started moving again.

Just opposite the beginning of the northern parking lot, Cutter got off the path, heading toward the road as though to cross it. The inspector had now closed to within fifty yards. Something was wrong. He didn't know what. It was . . .

. . . the way he was looking at the traffic. He wasn't looking for openings, O'Day realized too late. A bus was coming north, a D.C. transit bus, it had just come off the 14th Street Bridge and—

"Look out!" But the man wasn't listening for that sort of warning.

Brakes screeched. The bus tried to avoid the man, slamming into another car, then five more added their mass to the pileup. O'Day approached only because he was a cop, and cops are expected to do such things. Vice Admiral James A. Cutter, Jr., USN, was still in the road, thrown fifty feet by the collision.

He'd wanted it to look like an accident, O'Day thought, *but it wasn't.* The agent didn't notice a passerby in a cheap-bodied government car who came down the other side of the parkway, rubbernecking at the accident scene like many others, but with a look of satisfaction instead of horror at the sight.

Ryan was waiting at the White House. The President had flown home because of the death of his aide, but he was still President, and there was still work to be done, and if the DDI said that he needed to meet with the President, then it had to be important. The President was puzzled to see that along with Ryan were Al Trent and Sam Fellows, co-chairmen of the House Select Committee on Intelligence Oversight.

"Come on in," he said, guiding them regally into the Oval Office. "What's so important?"

"Mr. President, it has to do with some covert operations, especially one called SHOWBOAT."

"What's that?" the President asked, on guard. Ryan explained for a minute or so.

"Oh, that. Very well. SHOWBOAT was given to these two men personally by Judge Moore under his hazardous-operations rule."

"Dr. Ryan tells us that there are some other things we need to know about also. Other operations related to SHOWBOAT," Congressman Fellows said.

"I don't know about any of that."

"Yes, you do, Mr. President," Ryan said quietly. "You authorized it. It is my duty under the law to report on these matters to Congress. Before I do so, I felt it necessary to notify you. I asked the two congressmen here to witness my doing so."

"Mr. Trent, Mr. Fellows, could you please excuse me for a moment? There are some things going on that I don't know about. Will you allow me to question Dr. Ryan in private for a moment?"

Say no! Ryan wished as hard as he could, but one does not deny such requests to the President, and in a moment he and Ryan were alone.

"What are you hiding, Ryan?" the President asked. "I know you're hiding some things."

"Yes, sir, I am and I will. The identities of some of our people, CIA and military, who acted on what they thought was proper authority." Ryan explained further, wondering what of it the President knew and what he didn't. It was something he was sure he'd never fully know. Most of the really important secrets Cutter had taken to his grave. Ryan suspected what had happened there, but . . . but had decided to let that sleeping dog lie, too. *Was it possible to be connected with something like this,* he asked himself, *and not be corrupted by it?*

"What Cutter did, what you *say* he did—I didn't know. I'm sorry. I'm especially sorry about those soldiers."

"We got about half of them out, sir. I was there. That's the part I cannot forgive. Cutter deliberately cut them off with the intention of giving you a political—"

"I never authorized that!" he almost screamed.

"You allowed it to happen, sir." Ryan tried to look him straight in the eye, and on the moment of wavering, it was the President who looked away. "My God, sir, how could you do it?"

"The people want us to stop the flow of drugs."

"Then do it, do just what you tried to do, but do it in accordance with the law."

"It won't work that way."

"Why not?" Ryan asked. "Have the American people ever objected when we used force to protect our interests?"

"But what we had to do here could never be public."

"In that case, sir, all you needed to do was make the appropriate notification of the Congress and do it covertly. You got partial approval for the operation, politics would not necessarily have come into play, but in breaking the rules, sir, you took a national-security issue and made it into a political one."

"Ryan, you're smart and clever and good at what you do, but you're naïve."

Jack wasn't that naïve: "What are you asking me to do, sir?"

"How much does the Congress really need to know?"

"Are you asking me to lie for you, sir? You called me naïve, Mr. President. I had a man die in my arms two days ago, a sergeant in the Air Force who left seven children behind. Tell me, sir, am I naïve to let that weigh upon my thinking?"

"You can't talk to me that way."

"I take no pleasure in it, sir. But I will not lie for you."

"But you are willing to conceal the identities of people who—"

"Who followed your orders in good faith. Yes, Mr. President, I am willing to do that."

"What happens to the country, Jack?"

"I agree with you that we do not need another scandal, but that is a political question. On that, sir, you have to talk to the men outside. My function is to provide information for the government, and to perform certain tasks for the government. I am an instrument of policy. So were those people who died for their country, sir, and they had a right to expect that their lives would be given greater value by the government they served. They were people, Mr. President, young kids for the most part who went off to do a job because their country—you, sir—thought it important that they do so. What they didn't know was that there were enemies in Washington. They never suspected that, and that's why most of them died. Sir, the oath our people take when they put the uniform on requires them to bear 'true faith and allegiance' to their country. Isn't it written down somewhere that the country owes them the same thing? It's not the first time this has happened, but I wasn't part of it before, and I will not lie about it, sir, not to protect you or anyone else."

"I didn't know that, Jack. Honestly, I didn't know."

"Mr. President, I choose to believe that you are an honorable man. What you just said, sir, is that really an excuse?" Jack paused, and was fully answered by silence.

"Do you wish to meet with the congressmen before I brief them, sir?"

"Yes. Why don't you wait outside for us."

"Thank you, Mr. President."

Jack waited for an hour of discomfort before Trent and Fellows reappeared. They drove with him to Langley in silence, and the three walked into the office of the Director of Central Intelligence.

''Judge,'' Trent said, ''that may have been the greatest service you have ever done your country.''

''Under the circumstances—'' Moore paused. ''What else could I have done?''

''You could have left them to die, you could have warned the opposition that we were coming in,'' Jack said. ''In that case I wouldn't be here. And for that, Judge, I am in your debt. You could have stuck with the lie.''

''And live with myself?'' Moore smiled in a very strange way and shook his head.

''And the operations?'' Ryan asked. Exactly what had been discussed in the Oval Office he didn't know, and he told himself not to make any guesses.

''Never happened,'' Fellows said. ''Under the hazardous-operations rule, you have done what you needed to do—granted, a little late, but we have been notified. We don't need another scandal like this, and with the way things are going, the situation will settle itself. Politically it's shaky, but legally you can argue that it's all according to Hoyle.''

''The craziest part of all is, it almost worked,'' Trent observed. ''Your CAPER operation was brilliant, and I assume it'll be kept going.''

''It will. The whole operation did work,'' Ritter said for the first time. ''It really did. We did start a war within the Cartel, and Escobedo's killing was just the last act—or maybe not if it goes on further. With that many chieftains gone, maybe Colombia will be able to do a little better. We need that capability. We can't have it stripped away from us.''

''I agree,'' Ryan said. ''We need the capability, but you don't make public policy this way, damn it!''

''Jack, tell me what right and wrong is?'' Moore asked. ''You seem to be the expert today,'' he added without very much irony.

''This is supposed to be a democracy. We let the people know something, or at least we let *them* know.'' He waved at the congressmen. ''When a government decides to kill people who threaten its interests or its citizens, it doesn't have to be murder. Not always. I'm just not sure where the line is. But I don't have to be sure. Other people are supposed to tell us that.''

''Well, come January, it won't be us,'' Moore observed. ''It's agreed, then? It stays here. No political footballs?''

Trent and Fellows could scarcely have been further apart politically, the gay New Englander and the tough-minded Mormon from Arizona. They nodded agreement.

''No games on this,'' Trent said.

''It would just hurt the country,'' Fellows concurred.

''And what we've just done . . .'' Ryan murmured. *Whatever the hell it was . . .*

''You didn't do it,'' Trent said. ''The rest of us did.''

''Right,'' Jack snorted. ''Well, I'm gone soon, too.''

''Think so?'' Fellows asked.

''Not so, Dr. Ryan. We don't know who Fowler is going to appoint, probably some political lawyer he likes. I know the names on the list,'' Trent said.

''It sure as hell won't be me. He doesn't like me,'' Ryan said.

''He doesn't have to like you, and you're not going to be Director. But you will be here,'' Trent told him. *Deputy Director, maybe,* the congressman thought to himself.

"We'll see," Fellows said. "What if things turn out differently in November? Fowler may just screw it up yet."

"You have my word, Sam," Trent replied. "If that happens, it happens."

"There is one wild card, though," Ritter pointed out.

"I've already discussed that with Bill Shaw," Moore said. "It's funny. The only law he actually broke was illegal entry. None of the data he got out of her was technically classified. Amazing, isn't it?"

Ryan shook his head and left work early. He had an appointment with his attorney, who would soon be establishing an educational trust for seven kids living in Florida.

The infantrymen were cycled through Fort MacDill's special-operations center. Told that their operation had been a success, they were sworn to secrecy, given their promotions, and sent on to new postings. Except for one.

"Chavez?" a voice called.

"Yo, Mr. Clark."

"Buy you dinner?"

"There a good Mexican place around here?"

"Maybe I can find one."

"What's the occasion?"

"Let's talk jobs," Clark said. "There's an opening where I work. It pays better than what you do now. You'll have to go back to school for a couple of years, though."

"I've been thinkin' about that," Chavez replied. He'd been thinking that he was officer material. If he'd been in command instead of Ramirez, maybe—or maybe not. But he did want to find out.

"You're good, kid. I want you to work with me."

Chavez thought about that. At least he'd get a dinner out of the idea.

Captain Bronco Winters was dispatched to an F-15 squadron in Germany, where he distinguished himself and was soon a flight leader. He was a calmer young man now. He'd exorcised the demons of his mother's death. Winters would never look back. He'd had a job, and done it.

It was a cold, dismal fall after a hot, muggy summer in Washington. The political city emptied out for the presidential election, which shared that November with all of the House seats and a third of the Senate, plus hundreds of political-appointment slots in the executive branch. In the early fall, the FBI broke several Cuban-run spy rings, but strangely that was politically neutral. Although arresting a drug ring was a police success, arresting a spy ring was seen as a failure because of the existence of a spy ring in the first place. There was no political advantage except in the Cuban refugee community, whose votes might as well already have been cast anyway, since Fowler was talking about "opening a dialogue" with the Cuba they had left. The President regained the lead after his own convention, but ran a lackluster campaign and fired two key political advisers. But most of all, it was time for a change, and though it was close, J. Robert Fowler carried the election with a bare 2 percent advantage in the popular vote. Some called it a mandate; others called it a sloppy campaign on both sides. The latter was closer to the truth, Ryan thought after it was all over.

All over the city and its environs, displaced appointees made preparations to move home—wherever home was—or to move into law offices so that they could stay in the area. Congress hadn't changed very much, but Congress rarely did. Ryan remained in his office, wondering if he'd be confirmed as the next DDI. It was too soon to tell. One thing he did know was that the President was still President, and still a man of honor, whatever mistakes he'd made. Before he left, pardons would be issued to those who needed them. They'd go on the books, but no one was expected to notice, and after things were explained to the Fowler people—Trent would handle that—it wasn't expected that anyone ever would.

On the Saturday after the election, Dan Murray drove Moira Wolfe to Andrews Air Force Base, where a jet was waiting for them. It took just over three hours before they landed at Guantánamo. A leftover from the Spanish-American War, Gitmo, as it's called, is the only American military installation on Communist soil, a thorn stuck in Castro's side that rankled him as much as he rankled his oversized neighbor across the Florida Strait.

Moira was doing well at the Department of Agriculture, executive secretary to one of the department's top career executives. She was thinner now, but Murray wasn't concerned about that. She'd taken up walking for exercise, and was doing well with her psychological counseling. She was the last of the victims, and he hoped that this trip would help.

So this was the day, Cortez thought. He was surprised and disappointed at his fate, but resigned to it. He'd gambled greatly and lost greatly. He feared his fate, but he wouldn't let that show, not to Americans. They loaded him into the back of a sedan and drove toward the gate. He saw another car ahead of his, but made no special note of it.

And there it was, the tall barbed-wire fence, manned on one side by American Marines in their multicolor fatigues—they called them "utilities," Cortez had learned—and on the other by Cubans in their battle dress. Perhaps, just perhaps, Cortez thought, he might talk his way out of this. The car halted fifty meters from the gate. The corporal to his left pulled him out of the car and unlocked his handcuffs, lest he take them across and so enrich a Communist country. *Such trivial nonsense,* Félix thought.

"Come on, Pancho," the black corporal said. "Time to go home."

Even without the cuffs, both Marines grabbed him by the arms to help him walk to his mother country. There at the gate he saw two officers waiting for him, impassively for now. They would probably embrace him when he came across, which wouldn't mean a thing. In either case, Cortez was determined to meet his fate like a man. He straightened his back and smiled at those waiting for him as though they were family members waiting at the airport gate.

"Cortez," a man's voice called.

They stepped out of the guard shack, just inside the gate. He didn't know the man, but the woman . . .

Félix stopped, and the motion of the two Marines nearly toppled him. She just stood there, staring at him. She didn't speak a word, and Cortez didn't know what to say. The smile vanished from his lips. The look in her eyes made him shrink within himself. He'd never meant to hurt her. To use her, yes, of course, but never really . . .

"Come on, Pancho," the corporal said, heaving the man forward. They were just at the gate.

"Oh, by the way, this here's yours, Pancho," the corporal said, tucking a videocassette in his belt. "Welcome home, asshole." A final push.

"Welcome home, *Colonel,*" the senior of the two Cubans said. He embraced his former comrade and whispered: "You have much to answer for!"

But before they dragged him off, Félix turned one last time, seeing Moira, just standing there with the man he didn't know, and his last thought as he turned away was that once again she'd understood: silence was the greatest passion of all.

The Sum of All Fears

ACKNOWLEDGMENTS

As is always the case, there are people to thank.

Russ, for his excruciatingly patient education in physics (the mistakes are mine, not his);

Barry, for his insights;

Steve, for the mind-set;

Ralph, for his analysis;

John, for the law;

Fred, for the access;

Gerry, for his friendship;

Quite a few others who entertained my endless questions and ideas—even the dumb ones;

And all the men of goodwill who hope, as I do, that the corner may finally be turned, and were willing to talk about it.

For Mike and Peggy Rodgers, a sailor and his lady—
and all the men and women of the U.S. Armed Forces, because
the noblest of ideas have always been protected by warriors

Why, you may take the most gallant sailor, the most intrepid airman or the most audacious soldier, put them at a table together—what do you get? The sum of their fears.

—WINSTON CHURCHILL

[T]he two contenders met, with all their troops, on the field of Camlan to negotiate. Both sides were fully armed and desperately suspicious that the other side was going to try some ruse or stratagem. The negotiations were going along smoothly until one of the knights was stung by an asp and drew his sword to kill the reptile. The others saw the sword being drawn and immediately fell upon each other. A tremendous slaughter ensued. The chronicle . . . is quite specific about the point that the slaughter was excessive chiefly because the battle took place without preparations and premeditation.

—HERMAN KAHN, *On Thermonuclear War*

Prologue: Broken Arrow

"Like the wolf on the fold." In recounting the Syrian attack on the Israeli-held Golan Heights at 1400 local time on Saturday, the 6th of October, 1973, most commentators automatically recalled Lord Byron's famous line. There is also little doubt that that is precisely what the more literarily inclined Syrian commanders had in mind when they placed the final touches on the operations plans that would hurl more tanks and guns at the Israelis than any of Hitler's vaunted panzer generals had ever dreamed of having.

However, the sheep found by the Syrian Army that grim October day were more like big-horned rams in autumn rut than the more docile kind found in pastoral verse. Outnumbered by roughly nine to one, the two Israeli brigades on the Golan were crack units. The 7th Brigade held the northern Golan and scarcely budged, its defensive network a delicate balance of rigidity and flexibility. Individual strong-points held stubbornly, channeling the Syrian penetrations into rocky defiles where they could be pinched off and smashed by roving bands of Israeli armor which lay in wait behind the Purple Line. By the time reinforcements began arriving on the second day, the situation was still in hand—but barely. By the end of the fourth day, the Syrian tank army that had fallen upon the 7th lay a smoking ruin before it.

The Barak ("Thunderbolt") Brigade held the southern heights and was less fortunate. Here the terrain was less well suited to the defense, and here also the Syrians appear to have been more ably led. Within hours the Barak had been broken into several fragments. Though each piece would later prove to be as dangerous as a nest of vipers, the Syrian spearheads were quick to exploit the gaps and race toward their strategic objective, the Sea of Galilee. The situation that developed over the next thirty-six hours would prove to be the gravest test of Israeli arms since 1948.

Reinforcements began arriving on the second day. These had to be thrown into the battle area piecemeal—plugging holes, blocking roads, even rallying units that had broken under the desperate strain of combat and, for the first time in Israeli history, fled the field before the advancing Arabs. Only on the third day were the Israelis able to assemble their armored fist, first enveloping, then smashing the three deep Syrian penetrations. The changeover to offensive operations followed without pause. The Syrians were hurled back toward their own capital by a wrathful counter-attack, and surrendered a field littered with burned-out tanks and shattered men. At the end of this day the troopers of the Barak and the 7th heard over their unit radio nets a message from Israeli Defense Forces High Command:

YOU HAVE SAVED THE PEOPLE OF ISRAEL.

And so they had. Yet outside Israel, except for schools in which men learn the profession of arms, this epic battle is strangely unremembered. As in the Six Day War of 1967, the more freewheeling operations in the Sinai were the ones that attracted the excitement and admiration of the world: bridging the Suez, the Battle of the ''Chinese'' Farm, the encirclement of the Egyptian 3rd Army—this despite the fearful implications of the Golan fighting, which was far closer to home. Still, the survivors of those two brigades knew what they had done, and their officers could revel in the knowledge that among professional soldiers who know the measure of skill and courage that such a stand entails, their Battle for the Heights would be remembered with Thermopylae, Bastogne, and Gloucester Hill.

Each war knows many ironies, however, and the October War was no exception. As is true of most glorious defensive stands, this one was largely unnecessary. The Israelis had misread intelligence reports which, had they been acted on as little as twelve hours earlier, would have enabled them to execute pre-set plans and pour reserves onto the Heights hours before the onslaught commenced. Had they done so, there would have been no heroic stand. There would have been no need for their tankers and infantrymen to die in numbers so great that it would be weeks before the true casualty figures were released to a proud but grievously wounded nation. Had the information been acted upon, the Syrians would have been massacred before the Purple Line for all their lavish collection of tanks and guns—and there is little glory in massacres. This failure of intelligence has never been adequately explained. Did the fabled Mossad fail so utterly to discern the Arabs' plans? Or did Israeli political leaders fail to recognize the warnings they received? These questions received immediate attention in the world press, of course, most particularly in regard to Egypt's assault-crossing of the Suez, which breached the vaunted Bar-Lev Line.

Equally serious but less well appreciated was a more fundamental error made years earlier by the usually prescient Israeli general staff. For all its firepower, the Israeli Army was not heavily outfitted with tube artillery, particularly by Soviet standards. Instead of heavy concentrations of mobile field guns, the Israelis chose to depend heavily on large numbers of short-range mortars, and attack aircraft. This left Israeli gunners on the Heights outnumbered twelve to one, subject to crushing counter-battery fire, and unable to provide adequate support to the beleaguered defenders. That error cost many lives.

As is the case with most grave mistakes, this one was made by intelligent men, for the very best of reasons. The same attack-fighter that struck the Golan could rain steel and death on the Suez as little as an hour later. The IAF was the first modern air force to pay systematic attention to ''turn-around time.'' Its ground crewmen were trained to act much like a racing car's pit crew, and their speed and skill effectively doubled each plane's striking power, making the IAF a profoundly flexible and weighted instrument. And making a Phantom or a Skyhawk appear to be more valuable than a dozen mobile field guns.

What the Israeli planning officers had failed to take fully into account was the fact that the Soviets were the ones arming the Arabs, and, in doing so, would inculcate their clients with their own tactical philosophies. Intended to deal with NATO air power always deemed better than their own, Soviet surface-to-air missile (SAM) designers had always been among the world's best. *Russian* planners saw the coming October War as a splendid chance to test their newest tactical weapons and doctrine. They did not spurn it. The Soviets gave their Arab clients a SAM network such as the North Vietnamese or Warsaw Pact forces of the time dared not dream about, a nearly solid phalanx of interlocking missile batteries and radar systems deployed in depth, along with new mobile SAMs that could advance with the armored spearheads, extending the ''bubble'' of counter-air protection under which ground action could continue without interference. The officers and men who were to operate those systems had been painstakingly trained, many within the Soviet Union with the full benefit of everything the Soviets and Vietnamese had learned of American tactics and technology, which the Israelis were correctly expected to imitate. Of all the Arab soldiers in the October War, only these men would achieve their pre-war objectives. For two days they effectively neutralized the IAF. Had ground operations gone according to plan, that would have been enough.

And it is here that the story has its proper beginning. The situation on the Golan Heights was immediately evaluated as serious. The scarce and confused information coming in from the two stunned brigade staffs led Israeli High Command to believe that tactical control of the action had been lost. It seemed that their greatest nightmare had finally occurred: they had been caught fatally unready; their northern kibbutzim were vulnerable; their civilians, their *children* lay in the path of a Syrian armored force that by all rights could roll down from the Heights with the barest warning. The initial reaction of the staff operations officers was something close to panic.

But panic is something that good operations officers also plan for. In the case of a nation whose enemies' avowed objective was nothing short of physical annihilation, there was no defensive measure that could be called extreme. As early as 1968, the Israelis, like their American and NATO counterparts, had based their ultimate plan on the nuclear option. At 03:55 hours, local time, on October 7th, just fourteen hours after the actual fighting began, the alert orders for OPERATION JOSHUA were telexed to the IAF base outside Beersheba.

Israel did not have many nuclear weapons at the time—and denies having any to this date. Not that many would be needed, if it came to that. At Beersheba, in one of the countless underground bomb-storage bunkers, were twelve quite ordinary-looking objects, indistinguishable from the many other items designed to be attached to tactical aircraft except for the silver-red striped labels on their sides. No fins were attached, and there was nothing unusual in the streamlined shape of the burnished-brown aluminum skin, with barely visible seams and a few shackle points. There was a reason for that. To an unschooled or cursory observer, they might easily have been mistaken for fuel tanks or napalm canisters, and such objects hardly merit a second look. But each was a plutonium fission bomb with a nominal yield of 60 kilotons, quite enough to carve the heart out of a large city, or to kill thousands of troops in the field, or, with the addition of cobalt jackets—stored separately but readily attachable to the external skin—to poison a landscape to all kinds of life for years to come.

On this morning, activity at Beersheba was frantic. Reserve personnel were still streaming into the base from the previous day's devotions and family-visiting all over the small country. Those men on duty had been so for too long a time for the tricky job of arming aircraft with lethal ordnance. Even the newly arriving men had had precious little sleep. One team of ordnancemen, for security reasons not told the nature of their task, was arming a flight of A-4 Skyhawk strike-fighters with nuclear weapons under the eyes of two officers, known as "watchers," for that was their job, to keep visual track of everything that had to do with nuclear weapons. The bombs were wheeled under the centerline hardpoint of each of the four aircraft, lifted carefully by the hoisting arm, then shackled into place. The least exhausted of the ground crew might have noticed that the arming devices and tail fins had not yet been attached to the bombs. If so, they doubtless concluded that the officer assigned to that task was running late—as was nearly everything this cold and fateful morning. The nose of each weapon was filled with electronics gear. The actual exploder mechanism and capsule of nuclear material—collectively known as ''the physics package''—were already in the bombs, of course. The Israeli weapons, unlike American ones, were not designed to be carried by alert aircraft during time of peace, and they lacked the elaborate safeguards installed in American weapons by the technicians at the Pantex assembly plant, outside Amarillo, Texas. The fusing systems comprised two packages, one for attachment to the nose, and one integral with the tail fins. These were stored separately from the bombs themselves. All in all, the weapons were very unsophisticated by American or Soviet standards, in the same sense that a pistol is far less sophisticated than a machine gun, but, at close range, equally lethal.

Once the nose and fin packages were installed and activated, the only remaining activation procedure was the installation of a special arming panel within the cockpit of each fighter, and the attachment of the power plug from the aircraft to the bomb. At that point the bomb would be ''released to local control,'' placed in the hands of a young, aggressive pilot, whose job was then to loft it in a maneuver called The Idiot's Loop, which tossed the bomb on a ballistic path that would—probably—allow him and his aircraft to escape without harm when the bomb detonated.

Depending on the exigencies of the moment and the authorization of the ''watchers,'' Beersheba's senior ordnance officer had the option to attach the arming packages. Fortunately, this officer was not at all excited about the idea of having half-live ''nukes'' sitting about on a flight line that some lucky Arab might attack at any moment. A religious man, for all the dangers that faced his country on that cold dawn, he breathed a silent prayer of thanks when cooler heads prevailed in Tel Aviv, and gave the order to stand JOSHUA down. The senior pilots who would have flown the strike mission returned to their squadron ready-rooms and forgot what they had been briefed to do. The senior ordnance officer immediately ordered the bombs removed and returned to their place of safekeeping.

The bone-tired ground crew began removing the weapons just as other teams arrived on their own carts for the task of rearming the Skyhawks with Zuni rocket clusters. The strike order had been put up: *The Golan.* Hit the Syrian armored columns advancing on the Barak's sector of Purple Line from Kafr Shams. The ordnancemen jostled under the aircraft, two teams each trying to do their jobs, one team trying to remove bombs that they didn't know to be bombs at all, while the other hung Zunis on the wings.

There were more than four strike aircraft cycling through Beersheba, of course. The dawn's first mission over the Suez was just returning—what was left of it. The RF-4C Phantom reconnaissance aircraft had been lost, and its F-4E fighter escort limped in trailing fuel from perforated wing tanks and with one of its two engines disabled. The pilot had already radioed his warning in: there was some new kind of surface-to-air missile, maybe that new SA-6; its radar-tracking systems had not registered on the Phantom's threat-receiver; the recce bird had had no warning at all, and only luck had enabled him to evade the four targeted on his aircraft. That fact was flashed to IAF high command even before the aircraft touched down gingerly on the runway. The plane was directed to taxi down to the far end of the ramp, close to where the Skyhawks stood. The Phantom's pilot followed the jeep to the waiting fire-fighting vehicles, but just as it stopped, the left main tire blew out. The damaged strut collapsed as well, and 45,000 pounds of fighter dropped to the pavement like dishes from a collapsed table. Leaking fuel ignited, and a small but deadly fire enveloped the aircraft. An instant later, 20mm ammunition from the fighter's gun pod started cooking off, and one of the two crewmen was screaming within the mass of flames. Firefighters moved in with water-fog. The two ''watcher'' officers were the closest, and raced toward the flames to drag the pilot clear. All three were peppered by fragments from the exploding ammunition, while a fireman coolly made his way through the flames to the second crewman and carried him out, singed but alive. Other firemen collected the watchers and the pilot and loaded their bleeding bodies into an ambulance.

The nearby fire distracted the ordnancemen under the Skyhawks. One bomb, the one on aircraft number three, dropped a moment too soon, crushing the team supervisor's legs on the hoist. In the shrieking confusion of the moment, the team lost track of what was being done. The injured man was rushed to the base hospital while the three dismounted nuclear weapons were carted back to the storage bunker—in the chaos of an airbase on the first full day of a shooting war, the empty cradle on one of the carts somehow went unnoticed. The aircraft line chiefs arrived a moment later to begin abbreviated pre-flight checks as the jeep arrived from the ready shack. Four pilots jumped off it, each with a helmet in one hand and a tactical map in the other, each furiously eager to lash out at his country's enemies.

"What the hell's that?" snapped eighteen-year-old Lieutenant Mordecai Zadin. Called Motti by his friends, he had the gangling awkwardness of his age.

"Fuel tank, looks like," replied the line chief. He was a reservist who owned a garage in Haifa, a kindly, competent man of fifty years.

"Shit," the pilot replied, almost quivering with excitement. "I don't need extra fuel to go to the Golan and back!"

"I can take it off, but I'll need a few minutes." Motti considered that for a moment. A *sabra* from a northern kibbutz, a pilot for barely five months, he saw the rest of his comrades strapping into their aircraft. Syrians were attacking toward the home of his parents, and he had a sudden horror of being left behind on his first combat mission.

"Fuck it! You can strip it off when I get back." Zadin went up the ladder like a shot. The chief followed, strapping the pilot in place and checking the instruments over the pilot's shoulder.

"She's ready, Motti! Be careful."

"Have some tea for me when I get back." The youngster grinned with all the ferocity such a child could manage. The line chief slapped him on the helmet.

"You just bring my airplane back to me, *menchkin. Mazeltov.*"

The chief dropped down to the concrete and removed the ladder. He next gave the aircraft a last visual scan for anything amiss, as Motti got his engine turning. Zadin worked the flight controls and eased the throttle to full idle, checking fuel and engine-temperature gauges. Everything was where it should be. He looked over to the flight leader and waved his readiness. Motti pulled down the manual canopy, took a last look at the line chief, and fired off his farewell salute.

At eighteen, Zadin was not a particularly young pilot by IAF standards. Selected for his quick boy's reactions and aggressiveness, he'd been identified as a likely prospect four years earlier, and had fought hard for his place in the world's finest air force. Motti loved to fly, had wanted to fly ever since as a toddler he'd seen a Bf-109 training aircraft that an ironic fate had given Israel to start its air force. And he loved his Skyhawk. It was a pilot's aircraft. Not an electronicized monster like the Phantom, the A-4 was a small, responsive bird of prey that leaped at the twitch of his hand on the stick. Now he would fly combat. He was totally unafraid. It never occurred to him to fear for his life—like any teenager he was certain of his own immortality, and combat flyers are selected for their lack of human frailty. Yet he marked the day. Never had he seen so fine a dawn. He felt supernaturally alert, aware of everything: the rich wake-up coffee; the dusty smell of the morning air at Beersheba; now the manly scents of oil and leather in the cockpit; the idle static on his radio circuits; and the tingle of his hands on the control stick. He had never known such a day and it never occurred to Motti Zadin that fate would not give him another.

The four-plane formation taxied in perfect order to the end of runway zero-one. It seemed a good omen, taking off due north, toward an enemy only fifteen minutes away. On command of the flight leader—himself a mere twenty-one—all four pilots pushed their throttles to the stops, tripped their brakes, and dashed forward into the cool, calm morning air. In seconds all were airborne and climbing to five thousand feet, careful to avoid the civilian air traffic of Ben-Gurion International Airport, which in the mad scheme of life in the Middle East was still fully active.

The Captain gave his usual series of terse commands, just like a training flight: tuck it in, check engine, ordnance, electrical systems. Heads up for MiGs and friendlies. Make sure your IFF is squawking green. The fifteen minutes it took to fly from Beersheba to the Golan passed rapidly. Zadin's eyes strained to see the volcanic escarpment for which his older brother had died while taking it from the Syrians only six years before. The Syrians would not get it back, Motti told himself.

"Flight: turn right to heading zero-four-three. Targets are tank columns four kilometers east of the line. Heads up. Watch for SAMs and ground fire."

"Lead, four: I have tanks on the ground at one," Zadin reported coolly. "Look like our Centurions."

"Good eye, Four," the Captain replied. "They're friendly."

"I got a beeper, *I got launch warning!*" someone called. Eyes scanned the air for danger.

"*Shit!*" called an excited voice. "SAMs low at twelve coming up!"

"I see them. Flight, left and right, break NOW!" the Captain commanded.

The four Skyhawks scattered by elements. There were a dozen SA-2 missiles several kilometers off, like flying telephone poles, coming toward them at Mach-3. The SAMs split left and right too, but clumsily, and two exploded in a midair collision. Motti rolled right and hauled his stick into his belly, diving for the ground and cursing the extra wing weight. Good, the missiles were not able to track them down. He pulled level a bare hundred feet above the rocks, still heading toward the Syrians at four hundred knots, shaking the sky as he roared over the cheering, beleaguered troopers of the Barak.

The mission was a washout as a coherent strike, Motti already knew. It didn't matter. He'd get some Syrian tanks. He didn't have to know exactly whose, so long as they were Syrian. He saw another A-4 and formed up just as it began its firing run. He looked forward and saw them, the dome shapes of Syrian T-62s. Zadin toggled his arming switches without looking. The reflector gunsight appeared in front of his eyes.

"Uh-oh, more SAMs, coming in on the deck." It was the Captain's voice, still cool.

Motti's heart skipped a beat: a swarm of missiles, smaller ones—are these the SA-6s they told us about? he wondered quickly—was tracing over the rocks toward him. He checked his ESM gear; it had not sensed the attacking missiles. There was no warning beyond what his eyes told him. Instinctively Motti clawed for altitude in which to maneuver. Four missiles followed him up. Three kilometers away. He snap-rolled right, then spiraled down and left again. That fooled three of them, but the fourth followed him down. An instant later it exploded a bare thirty meters from his aircraft.

The Skyhawk felt as though it had been kicked aside ten meters or more. Motti struggled with the controls, getting back level just over the rocks. A quick look chilled him. Whole sections of his port wing were shredded. Warning beepers in his headset and flight instruments reported multiple disaster: hydraulics zeroing out, radio out, generator out. But he still had manual flight controls, and his weapons could fire from backup battery power. At that instant he saw his tormentors: a battery of SA-6 missiles, four launcher vehicles, a Straight Flush radar van, and a heavy truck full of reloads, all four kilometers away. His hawk's eyes could even see the Syrians struggling with the missiles, loading one onto a launcher rail.

They saw him, too, and then began a duel no less epic for its brevity.

Motti eased as far down as he dared with his buffeting controls and carefully centered the target in his reflector sight. He had forty-eight Zuni rockets. They fired in salvos of four. At two kilometers he opened fire into the target area. The Syrian missileers somehow managed to launch another SAM. There should have been no escape, but the SA-6 had a radar-proximity fuse, and the passing Zunis triggered it, exploding the SAM harmlessly half a kilometer away. Motti grinned savagely beneath his mask as he fired rockets and now 20-millimeter cannon fire into the mass of men and vehicles.

The third salvo hit, then four more as Zadin kicked rudder to drop his rockets all over the target area. The missile battery was transformed into an inferno of diesel fuel, missile propellant, and exploding warheads. A huge fireball loomed in his path, and Motti tore through it with a feral shout of glee, his enemies obliterated, his comrades avenged.

Zadin had but a moment of triumph. Great sheets of the aluminum which made up his aircraft's left wing were being ripped away by the four-hundred-knot slipstream. The A-4 began shuddering wildly. When Motti turned left for home, the wing collapsed entirely. The Skyhawk disintegrated in midair. It took only a few seconds before the teenaged warrior was smashed on the basaltic rocks of the Golan Heights, neither the first nor the last to die there. No other of his flight of four survived.

Of the SAM battery almost nothing was left. All six vehicles had been blasted to fragments. Of the ninety men who had manned them, the largest piece recovered was the headless torso of the battery commander. Both he and Zadin had served their countries well, but as is too often the case, conduct which in another time or place might have inspired the heroic verse of a Virgil or a Tennyson went unseen and unknown. Three days later Zadin's mother received the news by telegram, learning again that all Israel shared her grief, as if such a thing were possible for a woman who had lost two sons.

But the lingering footnote to this bit of unreported history was that the unarmed bomb broke loose from the disintegrating fighter and proceeded yet farther eastward, falling far from the fighter-bomber's wreckage to bury itself fifty meters from the home of a Druse farmer. It was not until three days later that the Israelis discovered that their bomb was missing, and not until the day after the October War ended that they were able to reconstruct the details of its loss. This left the Israelis with a problem insoluble even to their imaginations. The bomb was somewhere behind Syrian lines—but where? Which of the four aircraft had carried it? Where had it gone down? They could hardly ask the Syrians to search for it. And could they tell the Americans, from whom the "special nuclear material" had been adroitly and deniably obtained?

And so the bomb lay unknown, except to the Druse farmer, who simply covered it over with two meters of dirt and continued to farm his rocky patch.

1. The Longest Journey . . .

Arnold van Damm sprawled back in his executive swivel chair with all the elegance of a rag doll tossed into a corner. Jack had never seen him wear a coat except in the presence of the President, and not always then. At formal affairs that required black tie, Ryan wondered if Arnie needed a Secret Service agent standing by with a gun. The tie was loose in the unbuttoned collar, and he wondered if it had ever been tightly knotted. The sleeves on Arnie's L. L. Bean blue-striped shirt were rolled up, and grimy at the elbows because he usually read documents with his forearms planted on the chronically cluttered desk. But not when speaking to someone. For important conversations, the man leaned back, resting his feet on a desk drawer. Barely fifty, van Damm had thinning gray hair and a face as lined and careworn as an old map, but his pale blue eyes were always alert, and his mind keenly aware of everything that went on within or beyond his sight. It was a quality that went along with being the President's Chief of Staff.

He poured his Diet Coke into an oversized coffee mug that featured an emblem of the White House on one side and "Arnie" engraved on the other, and regarded the Deputy Director of Central Intelligence with a mixture of wariness and affection. "Thirsty?"

"I can handle a real Coke if you have one down there," Jack observed with a grin. Van Damm's left hand dropped below sight, and a red aluminum can appeared on a ballistic path that would have terminated in Ryan's lap had he not caught it. Opening the can under the circumstances was a tricky exercise, but Jack ostentatiously aimed the can at van Damm when he popped the top. Like the man or not, Ryan told himself, he had style. He was unaffected by his job except when he had to be. This was not such a time. Arnold van Damm acted important only for outsiders. Insiders didn't need an act.

"The Boss wants to know what the hell is going on over there," the Chief of Staff opened.

"So do I." Charles Alden, the President's National Security Advisor, entered the room. "Sorry I'm late, Arnie."

"So do we, gentlemen," Jack replied. "That hasn't changed in a couple of years. You want the best stuff we've got?"

"Sure," Alden said.

"Next time you fly to Moscow, look out for a large white rabbit with waistcoat and pocket watch. If he offers you a trip down a rabbit hole, take it and let me know what you find down there," Ryan said with mock gravity. "Look, I'm not one of those right-wing idiots who moans for a return to the Cold War, but then, at least, the Russians were predictable. The poor bastards are starting to act like we do now. They're unpredictable as hell. The funny part is, now I can understand what a pain in the ass we always were to the KGB. The political dynamic over there is changing on a daily basis. Narmonov is the sharpest political infighter in the world, but every time he goes to work, it's another crisis.''

''What sort of cat is he?'' van Damm asked. ''You've met the man.'' Alden had met Narmonov, but van Damm had not.

''Only once,'' Ryan cautioned.

Alden settled down in an armchair. ''Look, Jack, we've seen your file. So has the Boss. Hell, I've almost got him to respect you. Two Intelligence Stars, the submarine business, and, Jesus, the thing with Gerasimov. I've heard of still waters running deep, fella, but never this deep. No wonder Al Trent thinks you're so damned smart.'' The Intelligence Star was CIA's highest decoration for performance in the field. Jack actually had three. But the citation for the third was locked away in a very safe place, and was something so secret that even the new President didn't and would never know. ''So prove it. Talk to us.''

''He's one of those rare ones. He thrives on chaos. I've met docs like that. There are some, a rare few, who keep working in emergency rooms, doing trauma and like that, after everybody else burns out. Some people just groove to pressure and stress, Arnie. He's one of them. I don't think he really likes it, but he's good at it. He must have the physical constitution of a horse—''

''Most politicians do,'' van Damm observed.

''Lucky them. Anyway, does Narmonov really know where's he's going? I think the answer is both yes and no. He has some sort of idea where he's moving his country to, but how he gets there, and exactly where he's going to be when he arrives, that he doesn't know. That's the kind of balls the man has.''

''So, you like the guy.'' It was not a question.

''He could have snuffed my life out as easy as popping open this can of Coke, and he didn't. Yeah,'' Ryan admitted with a smile, ''that does compel me to like him a little. You'd have to be a fool not to admire the man. Even if we were still enemies, he'd still command respect.''

''So we're not enemies?'' Alden asked with a wry grin.

''How can we be?'' Jack asked in feigned surprise. ''The President says that's a thing of the past.''

The Chief of Staff grunted. ''Politicians talk a lot. That's what they're paid for. Will Narmonov make it?''

Ryan looked out the window in disgust, mainly at his own inability to answer the question. ''Look at it this way: Andrey Il'ych has got to be the most adroit political operator they've ever had. But he's doing a high-wire act. Sure, he's the best around, but remember when Karl Wallenda was the best high-wire guy around? He ended up as a red smear on the sidewalk because he had one bad day in a business where you only get one goof. Andrey Il'ych is in the same kind of racket. Will he make it? People have been asking that for eight years! We think so—I think so—but . . . but, hell, this is virgin ground, Arnie. We've never been here before. Neither has he. Even a goddamned weather forecaster has a data base to help him out. The two best Russian historians we have are Jake Kantrowitz at Princeton and Derek Andrews at Berkeley, and they're a hundred-eighty degrees apart at the moment. We just had them both into Langley two weeks ago. Personally I lean towards Jake's assessment, but our senior Russian analyst thinks Andrews is right. You pays your money and you takes your choice. That's the best we got. You want pontification, check the newspapers.''

Van Damm grunted and went on. ''Next hot spot?''

''The nationalities question is the big killer,'' Jack said. ''You don't need me to tell you that. How will the Soviet Union break up—what republics will leave—when and how, peacefully or violently? Narmonov is dealing with that on a daily basis. That problem is here to stay.''

"That's what I've been saying for about a year. How long to let things shake out?'' Alden wanted to know.

"Hey, I'm the guy who said East Germany would take at least a year to change over—I was the most optimistic guy in town at the time, and I was wrong by eleven months. Anything I or anyone else tells you is a wild-ass guess.''

"Other trouble spots?'' van Damm asked next.

"There's always the Middle East—'' Ryan saw the man's eyes light up.

"We want to move on that soon.''

"Then I wish you luck. We've been working on that since Nixon and Kissinger back during the '73 semifinals. It's chilled out quite a bit, but the fundamental problems are still there, and sooner or later it's going to be thawed. I suppose the good news is that Narmonov doesn't want any part of it. He may have to support his old friends, and selling them weapons is a big money-maker for him, but if things blow up, he won't push like they did in the old days. We learned that with Iraq. He might continue to pump weapons in—I think he won't, but it's a close call—but he will do nothing more than that to support an Arab attack on Israel. He won't move his ships, and he won't alert troops. I doubt he's willing even to back them if they rattle their sabers a little. Andrey Il'ych says those weapons are for defense, and I think he means it, despite the word we're getting from the Israelis.''

"That's solid?'' Alden asked. "State says different.''

"State's wrong,'' Ryan replied flatly.

"So does your boss,'' van Damm pointed out.

"In that case, sir, I must respectfully disagree with the DCI's assessment.''

Alden nodded. "Now I know why Trent likes you. You don't talk like a bureaucrat. How have you lasted so long, saying what you really think?''

"Maybe I'm the token.'' Ryan laughed, then turned serious. "Think about it. With all the ethnic crap he's dealing with, taking an active role bears as many dangers as advantages. No, he sells weapons for hard currency and only when the coast is clear. That's business, and that's as far as it goes.''

"So if we can find a way to settle things down . . . ?'' Alden mused.

"He might even help. At worst, he'll stand by the sidelines and bitch that he's not in the game. But tell me, how do you plan to settle things down?''

"Put a little pressure on Israel,'' van Damm replied simply.

"That's dumb for two reasons. It's wrong to pressure Israel until their security concerns are alleviated, and their security concerns will not be alleviated until some of the fundamental issues are settled first.''

"Like . . . ?''

"Like what is this conflict all about.'' *The one thing that everyone overlooks.*

"It's religious, but the damned fools believe in the same things!'' van Damm growled. "Hell, I read the Koran last month, and it's the same as what I learned in Sunday school.''

"That's true,'' Ryan agreed, "but so what? Catholics and Protestants both believe that Christ is the son of God, but that hasn't stopped Northern Ireland from blowing up. Safest place in the world to be Jewish. The friggin' Christians are so busy killing one another off that they don't have time to be anti-Semitic. Look, Arnie, however slight the religious differences in either place may appear to us, to *them* they appear big enough to kill over. That's as big as they need to be, pal.''

"True, I guess," the Chief of Staff agreed reluctantly. He thought for a moment. "Jerusalem, you mean?"

"Bingo." Ryan finished off his Coke and crushed the can before flipping it into van Damm's trash can for two. "The city is sacred to three religions—think of them as three tribes—but it physically belongs to only one of them. That one is at war with one of the others. The volatile nature of the region militates toward putting some armed troops in the place, but whose? Remember, some Islamic crazies shot up Mecca not that long ago. Now, if you put an Arab security force in Jerusalem, you create a security threat to Israel. If things stay as they are, with only an Israeli force, you offend the Arabs. Oh, and forget the UN. Israel won't like it because the Jews haven't made out all that well in the place. The Arabs won't like it because there's too many Christians. And we won't like it because the UN doesn't like us all that much. The only available international body is distrusted by everyone. Impasse."

"The President really wants to move on this," the Chief of Staff pointed out. *We have to do something to make it look like we're DOING SOMETHING.*

"Well, next time he sees the Pope, maybe he can ask for high-level intercession." Jack's irreverent grin froze momentarily. Van Damm thought he was cautioning himself against speaking badly of the President, whom he disliked. But then Ryan's face went blank. Arnie didn't know Jack well enough to recognize the look. "Wait a minute . . ."

The Chief of Staff chuckled. It wouldn't hurt for the President to see the Pope. It always looked good with the voters, and after that the President would have a well-covered dinner with B'nai B'rith to show that he liked all religions. In fact, as van Damm knew, the President went to church only for show now that his children were grown. That was one amusing aspect of life. The Soviet Union was turning back to religion in its search for societal values, but the American political left had turned away long ago and had no inclination to turn back, lest it should find the same values that the Russians were searching for. Van Damm had started off as a left-wing believer, but twenty-five years of hands-on experience in government had cured him of that. Now he distrusted ideologues of both wings with equal fervor. He was the sort to look for solutions whose only attraction was that they might actually work. His reverie on politics took him away from the discussion of the moment.

"You thinking about something, Jack?" Alden asked.

"You know, we're all 'people of the book,' aren't we?" Ryan asked, seeing the outline of a new thought in the fog.

"So?"

"And the Vatican is a real country, with real diplomatic status, but no armed forces . . . they're Swiss . . . and Switzerland is neutral, not even a member of the UN. The Arabs do their banking and carousing there . . . gee, I wonder if he'd go for it . . . ?" Ryan's face went blank again, and van Damm saw Jack's eyes center as the light bulb flashed on. It was always exciting to watch an idea being born, but less so when you didn't know what it was.

"Go for what? *Who* go for *what?*" the Chief of Staff asked with some annoyance. Alden just waited.

Ryan told them.

"I mean, a large part of this whole mess is over the Holy Places, isn't it? I could talk to some of my people at Langley. We have a really good—"

Van Damm leaned back in his chair. "What sort of contacts do you have? You mean talking to the Nuncio?"

Ryan shook his head. "The Nuncio is a good old guy, Cardinal Giancatti, but he's just here for show. You've been here long enough to know that, Arnie. You want to talk to folks who know stuff, you go to Father Riley at Georgetown. He taught me when I got my doctorate at G-Town. We're pretty tight. He's got a pipeline into the General."

"Who's that?"

"The Father General of the Society of Jesus. The head Jesuit, Spanish guy, his name is Francisco Alcalde. He and Father Tim taught together at St. Robert Bellarmine University in Rome. They're both historians, and Father Tim's his unofficial rep over here. You've never met Father Tim?"

"No. Is he worth it?"

"Oh, yeah. One of the best teachers I ever had. Knows D.C. inside and out. Good contacts back at the home office." Ryan grinned, but the joke was lost on van Damm.

"Can you set up a quiet lunch?" Alden asked. "Not here, someplace else."

"The Cosmos Club up in Georgetown. Father Tim belongs. The University Club is closer, but—"

"Right. Can he keep a secret?"

"A *Jesuit* keep a secret?" Ryan laughed. "You're not Catholic, are you?"

"How soon could you set it up?"

"Tomorrow or day after all right?"

"What about his loyalty?" van Damm asked out of a clear sky.

"Father Tim is an American citizen, and he's not a security risk. But he's also a priest, and he has taken vows to what he naturally considers an authority higher than the Constitution. You can trust the man to honor all his obligations, but don't forget what all those obligations are," Ryan cautioned. "You can't order him around, either."

"Set up the lunch. Sounds like I ought to meet the guy in any case. Tell him it's a get-acquainted thing," Alden said. "Make it soon. I'm free for lunch tomorrow and next day."

"Yes, sir." Ryan stood.

The Cosmos Club in Washington is located at the corner of Massachusetts and Florida avenues. The former manor house of Sumner Welles, Ryan thought it looked naked without about four hundred acres of rolling ground, a stable of thoroughbred horses, and perhaps a resident fox that the owner would hunt, but not too hard. These were surroundings the place had never possessed, and Ryan wondered why it had been built in this place in this style, so obviously at odds with the realities of Washington, but built by a man who had understood the workings of the city so consummately well. Chartered as a club of the intelligentsia—membership was based on "achievement" rather than money—it was known in Washington as a place of erudite conversation and the worst food in a town of undistinguished restaurants. Ryan led Alden into a small private room upstairs.

Father Timothy Riley, S.J., was waiting for them, a briar pipe clamped in his teeth as he paged through the morning's *Post*. A glass sat at his right hand, a skim of sherry at the bottom of it. Father Tim was wearing a rumpled shirt and a jacket that needed pressing, not the formal priest's uniform that he saved for important meetings and had been hand-tailored by one of the nicer shops on Wisconsin Avenue. But the white Roman collar was stiff and bright, and Jack had the sudden thought that despite all his years of Catholic education he didn't know what the things were made of. Starched cotton? Celluloid like the detachable collars of his grandfather's age? In either case, its evident rigidity must have been a reminder to its wearer of his place in this world, and the next.

"Hello, Jack!"

"Hi, Father. This is Charles Alden, Father Tim Riley." Handshakes were exchanged and places at the table selected. A waiter came in and took drink orders, closing the door as he left.

"How's the new job, Jack?" Riley asked.

"The horizons keep broadening," Ryan admitted. He left it at that. The priest would already know the problems Jack was having at Langley.

"We've had this idea about the Middle East, and Jack suggested that you'd be a good man to discuss it with," Alden said, getting everyone back to business. He had to stop when the waiter returned with drinks and menus. His discourse on the idea took several minutes.

"That's interesting," Riley said when it was all on the table.

"What's your read on the concept?" the National Security Advisor wanted to know.

"Interesting . . ." The priest was quiet for a moment.

"Will the Pope . . . ?" Ryan stopped Alden with a wave of the hand. Riley was not a man to be hurried when he was thinking. He was, after all, an historian, and they didn't have the urgency of medical doctors.

"It certainly is elegant," Riley observed after thirty seconds. "The Greeks will be a major problem, though."

"The Greeks? How so?" Ryan asked in surprise.

"The really contentious people right now are the Greek Orthodox. We and they are at each other's throats half the time over the most trivial administrative issues. You know, the rabbis and the imams are actually more cordial at the moment than the Christian priests are. That's the funny thing about religious people, it's hard to predict how they react. Anyway, the problems between the Greeks and Romans are mainly administrative—who gets custody over which site, that sort of thing. There was a big go-round over Bethlehem last year, who got to do the midnight mass in the Church of the Nativity. It is awfully disappointing, isn't it?"

"You're saying it won't work because two Catholic churches can't—"

"I said there could be a problem, Dr. Alden. I did not say that it wouldn't work." Riley lapsed back into silence for a moment. "You'll have to adjust the troika . . . but given the nature of the operation, I think we can get the right kind of cooperation. Co-opting the Greek Orthodox is something you'll have to do in any case. They and the Muslims get along very well, you know."

"How so?" Alden asked.

"Back when Mohammed was chased out of Mecca by the pre-Muslim pagans, he was granted asylum at the Monastery of St. Catherine in the Sinai—it's a Greek Orthodox shrine. They took care of him when he needed a friend. Mohammed was an honorable man; that monastery has enjoyed the protection of the Muslims ever since. Over a thousand years, and that place has never been troubled despite all the nasty things that have happened in the area. There is much to admire about Islam, you know. We in the West often overlook that because of the crazies who call themselves Muslims—as though we don't have the same problem in Christianity.

There is much nobility there, and they have a tradition of scholarship that commands respect. Except that nobody over here knows much about it,'' Riley concluded.

``Any other conceptual problems?'' Jack asked.

Father Tim laughed. ``The Council of Vienna! How did you forget that, Jack?''

``What?'' Alden sputtered in annoyance.

``Eighteen-fifteen. Everybody knows that! After the final settlement of the Napoleonic Wars, the Swiss had to promise never to export mercenaries. I'm sure we can finesse that. Excuse me, Dr. Alden. The Pope's guard detachment is composed of Swiss mercenaries. So was the French king's once—they all got killed defending King Louis and Marie Antoinette. Same thing nearly happened to the Pope's troops once, but they held the enemy off long enough for a small detachment to evacuate the Holy Father to a secure location, Castle Gandolfo, as I recall. Mercenaries used to be the main Swiss export, and they were feared wherever they went. The Swiss Guards of the Vatican are mostly for show now, of course, but once upon a time the need for them was quite real. In any case, Swiss mercenaries had such a ferocious reputation that a footnote of the Council of Vienna, which settled the Napoleonic Wars, compelled the Swiss to promise not to allow their people to fight anywhere but at home and the Vatican. But, as I just said, that is a trivial problem. The Swiss would be delighted to be seen helping solve this problem. It could only increase their prestige in a region where there is a lot of money.''

``Sure,'' Jack observed. ``Especially if we provide their equipment. M-1 tanks, Bradley fighting vehicles, cellular communications. . . .''

``Come on, Jack,'' Riley said.

``No, Father, the nature of the mission will demand some heavy weapons—for psychological impact if nothing else. You have to demonstrate that you're serious. Once you do that, then the rest of the force can wear the Michelangelo jump suits and carry their halberds and smile into the cameras—but you still need a Smith & Wesson to beat four aces, especially over there.''

Riley conceded the point. ``I like the elegance of the concept, gentlemen. It appeals to the noble. Everyone involved claims to believe in God by one name or another. By appealing to them in His name . . . hmm, that's the key, isn't it? The City of God. When do you need an answer?''

``It's not all that high-priority,'' Alden answered. Riley got the message. It was a matter of official White House interest, but was not something to be fast-tracked. Neither was it something to be buried on the bottom of someone's desk pile. It was, rather, a back-channel inquiry to be handled expeditiously and very quietly.

``Well, it has to go through the bureaucracy. The Vatican has the oldest continuously-operating bureaucracy in the world, remember.''

``That's why we're talking to you,'' Ryan pointed out. ``The General can cut through all the crap.''

``That's no way to talk about the princes of the church, Jack!'' Riley nearly exploded with laughter.

``I'm a Catholic, remember? I understand.''

``I'll drop them a line,'' Riley promised. *Today,* his eyes said.

``Quietly,'' Alden emphasized.

``Quietly,'' Riley agreed.

Ten minutes later Father Timothy Riley was back in his car for the short drive back to his office at Georgetown. Already his mind was at work. Ryan had guessed right about Father Tim's connections and their importance. Riley was composing his message in Attic Greek, the language of philosophers never spoken by more than fifty thousand people, but the language in which he'd studied Plato and Aristotle at Woodstock Seminary in Maryland all those years before.

Once in his office, he instructed his secretary to hold all calls, closed the door, and activated his personal computer. First he inserted a disk that allowed the use of Greek characters. Riley was not a skilled typist—having both a secretary and a computer rapidly erodes that skill—and it took him an hour to produce the document he needed. It was printed up as a double-spaced nine-page letter. Riley next opened a desk drawer and dialed in his code for a small but secure office safe that was concealed in what appeared to be a file drawer. Here, as Ryan had long suspected, was a cipher book, laboriously hand-printed by a young priest on the Father General's personal staff. Riley had to laugh. It just wasn't the sort of thing one associated with the priesthood. In 1944, when Admiral Chester Nimitz had suggested to Francis Cardinal Spellman, Catholic Vicar General for the U.S. military, that perhaps the Marianas Islands needed a new bishop, the Cardinal had produced his cipher book and used the communications network of the U.S. Navy to have a new bishop appointed. As with any other organization, the Catholic Church occasionally needed a secure communications link, and the Vatican cipher service had been around for centuries. In this case, the cipher key for this day was a lengthy passage from Aristotle's discourse on Being *qua* Being, with seven words removed and four grotesquely misspelled. A commercial encryption program handled the rest. Then he had to print out a new copy and set it aside. His computer was again switched off, erasing all record of the communiqué. Riley next faxed the letter to the Vatican and shredded all the hard copies. The entire exercise took three laborious hours, and when he informed his secretary that he was ready to get back to business, he knew that he'd have to work far into the night. Unlike an ordinary businessman, Riley didn't swear.

"I don't like this," Leary said quietly behind his binoculars.

"Neither do I," Paulson agreed. His view of the scene through the ten-power telescopic sight was less panoramic and far more focused. Nothing about the situation was pleasing. The subject was one the FBI had been chasing for more than ten years. Implicated in the deaths of two special agents of the Bureau and a United States Marshal, John Russell (a/k/a Matt Murphy, a/k/a Richard Burton, a/k/a/ Red Bear) had disappeared into the warm embrace of something called the Warrior Society of the Sioux Nation. There was little of the warrior about John Russell. Born in Minnesota far from the Sioux reservation, he'd been a petty felon whose one major conviction had landed him in a prison. It was there that he had discovered his ethnicity and begun thinking like his perverted image of a Native American—which to Paulson's way of thinking had more of Mikhail Bakunin in it than of Cochise or Toohoolhoolzote. Joining another prison-born group called the American Indian Movement, Russell had been involved in a half-dozen nihilistic acts, ending with the deaths of three federal officers, then vanished. But sooner or later they all screwed up, and today was John Russell's turn. Taking its chance to raise money by running drugs into Canada, the Warrior Society had made its mistake, and allowed its plans to be overheard by a federal informant.

They were in the ghostly remains of a farming town six miles from the Canadian border. The FBI Hostage Rescue Team, as usual without any hostages to rescue, was acting its role as the Bureau's premiere SWAT team. The ten men deployed on the mission under squad supervisor Dennis Black were under the administrative control of the Special Agent in Charge of the local field office. That was where the

Bureau's customary professionalism had come to a screeching halt. The local S-A-C had set up an elaborate ambush plan that had started badly and nearly ended in disaster, with three agents already in hospitals from the auto wrecks and two more with serious gunshot wounds. In return, one subject was known dead, and maybe another was wounded, but no one was sure at the moment. The rest—three or four; they were not sure of that either—were holed up in what had once been a motel. What they knew for sure was that either the motel had a still-working phone or, more likely, the subjects had a cellular "brick" and had called the media. What was happening now was of such magnificent confusion as to earn the admiration of Phineas T. Barnum. The local S-A-C was trying to salvage what remained of his professional reputation by using the media to his advantage. What he hadn't figured out yet was that handling network teams dispatched from as far away as Denver and Chicago wasn't quite the same thing as dealing with the local reporters fresh from journalism school. It was very hard to call the shots with the pros.

"Bill Shaw is going to have this guy's balls for brunch tomorrow," Leary observed quietly.

"That does us a whole lot of good," Paulson replied. A snort. "Besides, what balls?"

"What you got?" Black asked over the secure radio circuit.

"Movement, but no ID," Leary replied. "Bad light. These guys may be dumb, but they're not crazy."

"The subjects have asked for a TV reporter to come in with a camera, and the S-A-C has agreed."

"Dennis, have you—" Paulson nearly came off the scope at that.

"Yes, I have," Black replied. "He says he's in command." The Bureau's negotiator, a psychiatrist with hard-won expertise in these affairs, was still two hours away, and the S-A-C wanted something for the evening news. Black wanted to throttle the man, but he couldn't, of course.

"Can't arrest the guy for incompetence," Leary said, his hand over the microphone. *Well, the only thing these bastards don't have is a hostage. So why not give 'em one? That'll give the negotiator something to do.*

"Talk to me, Dennis," Paulson said next.

"Rules of Engagement are in force, on my authority," Supervisory Special Agent Black said. "The reporter is a female, twenty-eight, blond and blue, about five-six. Cameraman is a black guy, dark complexion, six-three. I told him where to walk. He's got brains, and he's playing ball."

"Roger that, Dennis."

"How long you been on the gun, Paulson?" Black asked next. The book said that a sniper could not stay fully alert on the gun for more than thirty minutes, at which point the observer and sniper exchanged positions. Dennis Black figured that someone had to play by the book.

"About fifteen minutes, Dennis. I'm okay . . . okay, I got the newsies."

They were very close, a mere hundred fifteen yards from the front door of the block building. The light was not good. The sun would set in another ninety minutes. It had been a blustery day. A hot southwesterly wind was ripping across the prairie. Dust stung the eyes. Worse, the wind was hitting over forty knots and was directly across his line of sight. That sort of wind could screw up his aim by as much as four inches.

"Team is standing by," Black advised. "We just got Compromise Authority."

"Well, at least he isn't a total asshole," Leary replied over the radio. He was too angry to care if the S-A-C heard that or not. More likely, the dumbass had just choked again.

Both sniper and observer wore ghillie suits. It had taken them two hours to get into position, but they were effectively invisible, their shaggy camouflage blending them in with the scrubby trees and prairie grass here. Leary watched the newsies approach. The girl was pretty, he thought, though her hair and makeup had to be suffering from the dry, harsh wind. The man on the camera looked like he could have played guard for the Vikings, maybe tough and fast enough to clear the way for that sensational new halfback, Tony Wills. Leary shook it off.

''The cameraman has a vest on. Girl doesn't.'' *You stupid bitch,* Leary thought. *I know Dennis told you what these bastards were all about.*

''Dennis said he was smart.'' Paulson trained the rifle on the building. ''Movement at the door!''

''Let's everyone try to be smart,'' Leary murmured.

''Subject One in sight,'' Paulson announced. ''Russell's coming out. Sniper One is on target.''

''Got him,'' three voices replied at once.

John Russell was an enormous man. Six-five, over two hundred fifty pounds of what had once been athletic but was now a frame running to fat and dissolution. He wore jeans, but was bare-chested with a headband securing his long black hair in place. His chest bore tattoos, some professionally done, but more of the prison spit-and-pencil variety. He was the sort of man police preferred to meet with gun in hand. He moved with the lazy arrogance that announced his willingness to depart from the rules.

''Subject One is carrying a large, blue-steel revolver,'' Leary told the rest of the team. *Looks like an N-Frame Smith.* . . . ''I, uh—Dennis, there's something odd about him . . .''

''What is it?'' Black asked immediately.

''Mike's right,'' Paulson said next, examining the face through his scope. There was a wildness to his eyes. ''He's on something, Dennis, he's doped up. Call those newsies back!'' But it was too late for that.

Paulson kept the sight on Russell's head. Russell wasn't a person now. He was a subject, a target. The team was now acting under the Compromise Authority rule. At least the S-A-C had done that right. It meant that if something went badly wrong, the HRT was free to take whatever action its leader deemed appropriate. Further, Paulson's special Sniper Rules of Engagement were explicit. If the subject appeared to threaten any agent or civilian with deadly force, then his right index finger would apply four pounds, three ounces of pressure to the precision set-trigger of the rifle in his grasp.

''Let's everybody be real cool, for Christ's sake,'' the sniper breathed. His Unertl telescopic sight had crosshairs and stadia marks. Automatically Paulson reestimated the range, then settled down while his brain tried to keep track of the gusting wind. The sight reticle was locked on Russell's head, right on the ear, which made a fine point of aim.

It was horridly comical to watch. The reporter smiling, moving the microphone back and forth. The burly cameraman aiming his minicam with its powerful single light running off the battery pack around the black man's waist. Russell was speaking forcefully, but neither Leary nor Paulson could hear a word he was saying against the wind. The look on his face was angry from the beginning, and did not improve. Soon his left hand balled into a fist, and his fingers started flexing around the grips of the revolver in his right. The wind buffeted the silk blouse close around the reporter's bra-less chest. Leary remembered that Russell had a reputation as a sexual athlete, supposedly on the brutal side. But there was a strange vacancy to his face. His expressions went from emotionless to passionate in what had to be a chemically induced whipsaw state that only added to the stress of being trapped by FBI agents. He calmed suddenly, but it wasn't a normal calm.

That asshole S-A-C, Leary swore at himself. *We ought to just back off and wait them out. The situation is stabilized. They're not going anywhere. We could negotiate by phone and just wait them out. . . .*

"Trouble!"

Russell's free hand grabbed the reporter's upper right arm. She tried to draw back, but possessed only a fraction of the strength required to do so. The cameraman moved. One hand came off the Sony. He was a big, strong man, and might have pulled it off, but his move only provoked Russell. The subject's gun hand moved.

"On target on target on target!" Paulson said urgently. *Stop, you asshole, STOP NOW!* He couldn't let the gun come up very far. His brain was racing, evaluating the situation. A large-frame Smith & Wesson, maybe a .44. It made big, bloody wounds. Maybe the subject was just punctuating his words, but Paulson didn't know or care what those words were. He was probably telling the black guy on the camera to stop; the gun seemed to be pointing more that way than at the girl, but the gun was still coming up and—

The crack of the rifle stopped time like a photograph. Paulson's finger had moved, seemingly of its own accord, but training had simply taken over. The rifle surged back in recoil, and the sniper's hand was already moving to work the bolt and load another round. The wind had chosen a bad moment to gust, throwing Paulson's aim off ever so slightly to the right. Instead of drilling through the center of Russell's head, the bullet struck well forward of the ear. On hitting bone, it fragmented. The subject's face was ripped explosively from the skull. Nose, eyes, and forehead vanished into a wet red mist. Only the mouth remained, and that was open and screaming, as blood vented from Russell's head as though from a clogged showerhead. Dying, but not dead, Russell jerked one round off at the cameraman before falling forward against the reporter. Then the cameraman was down, and the reporter was just standing there, not having had enough time even to be shocked by the blood and tissue on her clothing and face. Russell's hands clawed briefly at a face no longer there, then went still. Paulson's radio headset screamed "GO GO GO!" but he scarcely took note of it. He drove the second round into the chamber, and spotted a face in a window of the building. He recognized it from photographs. It was a subject, a bad guy. And there was a weapon there, looked like an old Winchester lever-action. It started moving. Paulson's second shot was better than the first, straight into the forehead of Subject Two, someone named William Ames.

Time started again. The HRT members raced in, dressed in their black Nomex coveralls and body armor. Two dragged the reporter away. Two more did the same with the cameraman, whose Sony was clasped securely to his chest. Another tossed an explosive flash-bang grenade through the broken window while Dennis Black and the remaining three team members dove through the open door. There were no other shots. Fifteen seconds later the radio crackled again.

"This is Team Leader. Building search complete. Two subjects down and dead. Subject Two is William Ames. Subject Three is Ernest Thorn, looks like he's been dead for a while from two in the chest. Subjects' weapons are neutralized. Site is secure. Repeat, site secure."

"Jesus!" It was Leary's first shooting involvement after ten years in the Bureau. Paulson got up to his knees after clearing his weapon, folded the rifle's bipod legs, then trotted toward the building. The local S-A-C beat him there, service automatic in hand, standing over the prone body of John Russell. It was just as well that the front of Russell's head was hidden. Every drop of blood he'd once had was now on the cracked cement sidewalk.

"Nice job!" the S-A-C told everyone. That was his last mistake in a day replete with them.

"You ignorant, shit-faced asshole!" Paulson pushed him against the painted block walls. "These people are dead because of you!" Leary jumped between them, pushing Paulson away from the surprised senior agent. Dennis Black appeared next, his face blank.

"Clean up your mess," he said, leading his men away before something else happened. "How's that newsie?"

The cameraman was lying on his back, the Sony at his eyes. The reporter was on her knees, vomiting. She had good cause. An agent had already wiped her face, but her expensive blouse was a red obscenity that would occupy her nightmares for weeks to come.

"You okay?" Dennis asked. "Turn that goddamned thing off!"

He set the camera down, switching off the light. The cameraman shook his head and felt at a spot just below the ribs. "Thanks for the advice, brother. Gotta send a letter to the people that make this vest. I really—" And his voice stopped. Finally the realization of what had happened took hold, and the shock started. "Oh God, oh, sweet merciful Jesus!"

Paulson walked to the Chevy Carryall and locked his rifle in the rigid guncase. Leary and one other agent stayed with him, telling him that he had done exactly the right thing. They'd do that until Paulson got over his stress period. It wasn't the sniper's first kill, but while they had all been different incidents, they were all the same, all things to be regretted. The aftermath to a real shooting does not include a commercial.

The reporter suffered the normal post-traumatic hysteria. She ripped off her blood-soaked blouse, forgetting that there was nothing under it. An agent wrapped a blanket around her and helped to steady her down. More news crews were converging on the scene, most heading toward the building. Dennis Black got his people together to clear their weapons and help with the two civilians. The reporter recovered in a few minutes. She asked if it had really been necessary, then learned that her cameraman had taken a shot that had been stopped by the Second Chance vest the Bureau had recommended to both of them, but which she had rejected. She next entered the elation phase, just as happy as she could be that she could still breathe. Soon the shock would return, but she was a bright journalist despite her youth and inexperience, and had already learned something important. Next time she'd listen when someone gave her good advice; the nightmares would merely punctuate the importance of the lesson. Within thirty minutes she was standing up without assistance, wearing her backup outfit, giving a level if brittle account of what had happened. But it was the tape footage that would impress the people at Black Rock, headquarters of CBS. The cameraman would get a personal letter from the head of the News Division. The footage had everything: drama, death, a courageous (and attractive) reporter, and would run as the lead piece for the evening news broadcast for this otherwise slow news day, to be repeated by all the network morning shows the next day. In each case the anchor would solemnly warn people that what they were about to see might disturb the sensitive—just to make sure that everyone understood that something especially juicy was about to screen. Since everyone had more than one chance to view the event, quite a few had their tape machines turning the second time around. One of them was the head of the Warrior Society. His name was Marvin Russell.

It had started innocently enough. His stomach was unsettled when he awoke. The morning jobs became a little more tiresome. He didn't feel quite himself. *You're over thirty,* he told himself. *You're not a boy anymore*. Besides, he'd always been vigorous. Maybe it was just a cold, a virus, the lingering effects of bad water, some stomach bug. He'd just work his way out of it. He added weight to his pack, took to carrying a loaded magazine in his rifle. He'd gotten lazy, that's all. That was easily remedied. He was nothing if not a determined man.

For a month or so, it worked. Sure, he was even more tired, but that was to be expected with the extra five kilos of weight he carried. He welcomed the additional fatigue as evidence of his warrior's virtue, went back to simpler foods, forced himself to adopt better sleep habits. It helped. The muscle aches were no different from the time he'd entered this demanding life, and he slept the dreamless sleep of the just. What had been tough became tougher still as his focused mind gave its orders to a recalcitrant body. Could he not defeat some invisible microbe? Had he not bested far larger and more formidable organisms? The thought was less a challenge than a petty amusement. As with most determined men, his competition was entirely within himself, the body resisting what the mind commanded.

But it never quite went away. Though his body became leaner and harder, the aches and the nausea persisted. He became annoyed with it, and the annoyance first surfaced in jokes. When his senior colleagues took note of his discomfort, he called it morning sickness, evoking gales of rough laughter. He bore the discomfort for another month, then found that it was necessary to lighten his load to maintain his place in front with the leaders. For the first time in his life, faint doubts appeared like wispy clouds in the clear sky of his determined self-image. It was no longer an amusement.

He stuck with it for still another month, never slacking in his routine except for the additional hour of sleep that he imposed on his otherwise tireless regimen. Despite this, his condition worsened—well, not exactly worsened, but did not improve a bit. Maybe it was merely the increasing years, he finally admitted to himself. He was, after all, only a man, however hard he worked to perfect his form. There was no disgrace in that, determined though he might have been to prevent it.

Finally he started grumbling about it. His comrades were understanding. All of them were younger than he, many having served their leader for five years or more. They revered him for his toughness, and if the toughness showed a few hairline cracks, what did it mean except that he was human after all, and all the more admirable because of it? One or two suggested home remedies, but finally a close friend and comrade told him that he was foolish indeed not to see one of the local doctors—his sister's husband was a good one, a graduate of British medical schools. Determined as he was to avoid this abnegation of his person, it was time to take what he knew to be good advice.

The doctor was as good as advertised. Sitting behind his desk in a laboratory coat the color of starched white, he took a complete medical history, then performed a preliminary examination. There was nothing overtly wrong. He talked about stress—something his patient needed no lectures about—and pointed out that over the years stress claimed an increasing heavy forfeit on those who bore it. He talked about good eating habits, how exercise could be overdone, how rest was important. He decided that the problem was a combination of various small things, including what was probably a small but annoying intestinal disorder, and prescribed a drug to ameliorate it. The doctor concluded his lecture with a soliloquy about patients who were too proud to do what was good for them, and how foolish they were. The patient nodded approvingly, according the physician deserved respect. He'd given not dissimilar lectures to his own subordinates, and was as determined as always to do things in exactly the right way.

The medication worked for a week or so. His stomach almost returned to normal. Certainly it improved, but he noted with annoyance that it wasn't quite the same as before. Or was it? It was, he admitted to himself, hard to remember such trivial things as how one felt on awakening. The mind, after all, concerned itself with the great ideas, like mission and purpose, and left the body to attend its own needs and leave the mind alone. The mind wasn't supposed to be bothered. The mind gave orders and expected them to be followed. It didn't need distractions like this. How could purpose exist with distractions? He'd determined his life's purpose long years before.

But it simply would not go away, and finally he had to return to the physician. A more careful examination was undertaken. He allowed his body to be poked and prodded, to have his blood drawn by a needle instead of the more violent instruments for which he had prepared himself. Maybe it was something almost serious, the physician told him, a low-order systemic infection, for example. There were drugs to treat that. Malaria, once pandemic to the region, for example, had similar but more serious debilitating effects, as did any number of maladies which had once been serious but were now easily defeated by the forces available to modern medicine. The tests would show what was wrong, and the doctor was determined to fix it. He knew of his patient's purpose in life, and shared it from a safer and more distant perspective.

He returned to the doctor's office two days later. Immediately he knew that something was wrong. He'd seen the same look often enough on the face of his intelligence officer. Something unexpected. Something to interfere with plans. The doctor began speaking slowly, searching for words, trying to find a way to make the message easier, but the patient would have none of that. He had chosen to live a dangerous life, and demanded the information as directly as he would have given it. The physician nodded respectfully, and replied in kind. The man took the news dispassionately. He was accustomed to disappointments of many kinds. He knew what lay at the end of every life, and had many times helped to deliver it to others. So. Now it lay in his path also, to be avoided if possible but there nonetheless, perhaps near, perhaps not. He asked what could be done, and the news was less bad than he had expected. The doctor did not insult him with words of comfort, but read his patient's mind and explained the facts of the matter. There were things to be done. They might succeed. They might not. Time would tell. His physical strength would help a great deal, as would his iron determination. A proper state of mind, the physician told him, was highly important. The patient almost smiled at that, but stopped himself. Better to show the courage of a stoic than the hope of a fool. And what was death, after all? Had he not lived a life dedicated to justice? To the will of God? Had he not sacrificed his life to a great and worthy purpose?

But that was the rub. He was not a man who planned on failure. He had selected a goal for his life, and years before determined to reach it regardless of cost to himself or others. On that altar he had sacrificed everything he might have been, the dreams of his dead parents, the education which they had hoped he would use for the betterment of himself and others, a normal, comfortable life with a woman who might bear him sons—all of that he had rejected in favor of a path of toil, danger, and utter determination to reach that single shining goal.

And now? Was it all for nothing? Was his life to end without meaning? Would he never see the day for which he had lived? Was God that cruel? All these thoughts paraded through his consciousness while his face remained neutral, his eyes guarded as always. No. He would not let that be. God could not have deserted him. He would see the day—or at least see it grow closer. His life would have meaning after all. It had not been all for nothing, nor would what future he might yet have be for nothing. On that, too, he was determined.

Ismael Qati would follow his doctor's orders, do what must be done to extend his time, and perhaps defeat this internal enemy, as insidious and contemptible as those outside. In the meantime he would redouble his efforts, push himself to the limits of physical endurance, ask his God for guidance, look for a sign of His will. As he had fought his other enemies, so would he fight this one, with courage and total dedication. He'd never known mercy in his life, after all, and he would not start showing it now. If he had to face death, the deaths of others paled even further than usual. But he would not lash out blindly. He would do what he had to do. He would carry on as before, waiting for the chance that his faith told him must lie somewhere beyond his sight, between himself and the end of his path. His determination had always been directed by intelligence. It was that which explained his effectiveness.

2. Labyrinths

The letter from Georgetown arrived in a Roman office, scarce minutes after transmission, where, as with any bureaucracy, the night clerk (what intelligence agencies call a watch officer) simply dropped it on the proper desk and went back to his studies for an exam on the metaphysical discourses of Aquinas. A young Jesuit priest named Hermann Schörner, private secretary to Francisco Alcalde, Father General of the Society of Jesus, arrived the next morning promptly at seven and began sorting the overnight mail. The fax from America was third from the top, and stopped the young cleric in his tracks. Cipher traffic was a routine part of his job, but was not all that common. The code prefix at the top of the communication indicated the originator and the priority. Father Schörner hurried through the rest of the mail and went immediately to work.

The procedure was an exact inversion of what Father Riley had done, except that Schörner's typing skills were excellent. He used an optical scanner to transcribe the text into a personal computer and punched up the decryption program. Irregularities on the facsimile copy caused some garbles, but that was easily fixed, and clear-text copy—still in Attic Greek, of course—slid out of the ink-jet printer. It had required merely twenty minutes, as opposed to Riley's three laborious hours. The young priest prepared morning coffee for himself and his boss, then read the letter with his second cup of the day. How extraordinary, Schörner reflected.

Reverend Francisco Alcalde was an elderly but uncommonly vigorous man. At sixty-six, he still played a fair game of tennis, and was known to ski with the Holy Father. A gaunt, wiry six-four, his thick mane of gray hair was brush-cut over deep-set owlish eyes. Alcalde was a man with solid intellectual credentials. The master of eleven languages, had he not been a priest he might have become the foremost medieval historian in Europe. But he was, before all things, a priest whose administrative duties chafed against his desire for both teaching and pastoral ministry. In a few years he would leave his post as Father General of Roman Catholicism's largest and most powerful order and find himself again as a university instructor, illuminating young minds and leaving campus to celebrate mass in a small working-class parish where he could concern himself with ordinary human needs. That, he thought, would be the final blessing of a life cluttered with so many of them. Not a perfect man, he frequently wrestled with the pride that attended his intellect, trying and not always succeeding to cultivate the humility necessary to his vocation. Well, he sighed, perfection was a goal never to be reached, and he smiled at the humor of it.

"*Guten Morgen, Hermann!*" he said, sweeping through the door.

"*Bongiorno,*" the German priest replied, then lapsed into Greek. "Something interesting this morning."

The bushy eyebrows twitched at the message, and he jerked his head toward the inner office. Schörner followed with the coffee.

"The tennis court is reserved for four o'clock," Schörner said as he poured his boss's cup.

"So you can humiliate me yet again?" It was occasionally joked that Schörner could turn professional, contributing his winnings to the Society, whose members were required to take a vow of poverty. "So, what is the message?"

"From Timothy Riley in Washington." Schörner handed it over.

Alcalde donned his reading glasses and read slowly. He left his coffee untouched and, on finishing the message, read through it again. Scholarship was his life, and Alcalde rarely spoke about something without reflection.

"Remarkable. I've heard of this Ryan fellow before . . . isn't he in intelligence?"

"Deputy Director of the American CIA. We educated him. Boston College and Georgetown. He's principally a bureaucrat, but he's been involved in several operations in the field. We don't know all of the details, but it would appear that none were improper. We have a small dossier on him. Father Riley speaks very highly of Dr. Ryan."

"So I see." Alcalde pondered that for a moment. He and Riley had been friends for thirty years. "He thinks this proposal may be genuine. And you, Hermann?"

"Potentially, it is a gift from God." The comment was delivered without irony.

"Indeed. But an urgent one. What of the American President?"

"I would guess that he has not yet been briefed, but soon will be. As to his character?" Schörner shrugged. "He could be a better man."

"Who of us could not?" Alcalde said, staring at the wall.

"Yes, Father."

"How is my calendar for today?" Schörner ran over the list from memory. "Very well . . . call Cardinal D'Antonio and tell him that I have something of importance. Fiddle the schedule as best you can. This is something that calls for immediate attention. Call Timothy, thank him for his message, and tell him that I am working on it.''

Ryan awoke reluctantly at five-thirty. The sun was an orange-pink glow that back-lit the trees, ten miles away on Maryland's eastern shore. His first considered course of action was to draw the shades. Cathy didn't have to go into Hopkins today, though it took him half the walk to the bathroom to remember why. His next action was to take two extra-strength Tylenol. He'd had too much to drink the previous night, and that, he reminded himself, was three days in a row. But what was the alternative? Sleep came increasingly hard to him, despite work hours that grew longer and fatigue that—

''Damn,'' he said, squinting at himself in the mirror. He looked terrible. He padded his way into the kitchen for coffee. Everything was better after coffee. His stomach contracted itself into a tight, resentful ball on seeing the wine bottles still sitting on the countertop. A bottle and a half, he reminded himself. Not two. He hadn't drunk two full bottles. One had already been opened. It wasn't that bad. Ryan flipped the switch for the coffee machine and headed for the garage. There he climbed into the station wagon and drove to the gate to get his paper. Not all that long ago he'd walked out to get it, but, hell, he told himself, he wasn't dressed. That was the reason. The car radio was set to an all-news station, and he got his first exposure to what the world was doing. The ball scores. The Orioles had lost again. Damn, and he was supposed to take little Jack to a game. He'd promised after the last Little League game he'd missed. And when, he asked himself, are you going to do that, next April? Damn.

Well, the whole season, practically, was ahead. School wasn't even out yet. He'd get to it. Sure. Ryan tossed the morning *Post* on the car seat and drove back to the house. The coffee was ready. First good news of the day. Ryan poured himself a mug and decided against breakfast. Again. That was bad, a part of his mind warned him. His stomach was in bad-enough shape already, and two mugs of straight-dripped coffee would not help. He forced his mind into the paper to stifle that voice.

It is not often appreciated how much intelligence services depend on the news media for their information. Part of it was functional. They were in much the same business, and the intelligence services didn't have the brain market cornered. More to the point, Ryan reflected, the newsies didn't pay people for information. Their confidential sources were driven either by conscience or anger to leak whatever information they let out, and that made for the best sort of information; any intelligence officer could tell you that. Nothing like anger or principle to get a person to leak all sorts of juicy stuff. Finally, though the media was replete with lazy people, quite a few smart ones were drawn by the better money that went with news-gathering. Ryan had learned which bylines to read slowly and carefully. And he noted the datelines, as well. As Deputy Director of the Central Intelligence Agency, he knew which department heads were strong and which were weak. The *Post* gave him better information, for example, than the German desk. The Middle East was still quiet. The Iraq business was finally settling out. The new arrangement over there was taking shape, at long last. *Now, if we could just do something about the Israeli side. . . .* It would be nice, he thought, to set that whole area to rest. And Ryan believed it possible. The East-West confrontation which had predated his birth was now a thing of history, and who would have believed that? Ryan refilled his mug without looking, something that even a hangover allowed him to do. And all in just a brief span of years—less time, in fact, than he had spent in the Agency. Damn. Who would have believed it?

Now that was so amazing that Ryan wondered how long people would be writing books about it. Generations, at least. The next week a KGB representative was coming into Langley to seek advice on parliamentary oversight. Ryan had counseled against letting him in—and the trip was being handled with the utmost secrecy—because the Agency still had Russians working for it, and the knowledge that KGB and CIA had instituted official contacts on anything would terrify them (equally true, Ryan admitted to himself, of Americans still in the employ of KGB . . . probably). It was an old friend coming over, Sergey Golovko. Friend, Ryan snorted, turning to the sports page. The problem with the morning paper was that it never had the results of last night's game. . . .

Jack's return to the bathroom was more civilized. He was awake now, though his stomach was even less happy with the world. Two antacid tablets helped that. And the Tylenol were working. He'd reinforce that with two more at work. By six-fifteen he was washed, shaved, and dressed. He kissed his still-sleeping wife on the way out—was rewarded by a vague *hmmm*—and opened the front door in time to see the car pulling up the driveway. It troubled Ryan vaguely that his driver had to awaken far earlier than he to get here on time. It bothered him a little more who his driver was.

"Morning, doc," John Clark said with a gruff smile. Ryan slid into the front seat. There was more leg room, and he thought it would insult the man to sit in back.

"Hi, John," Jack replied.

Tied it on again last night, eh, doc? Clark thought. *Damned fool. For someone as smart as you are, how can you be so dumb? Not getting the jogging in either, are you?* he wondered on seeing how tight the DDCI's belt looked. Well, he'd just have to learn, as Clark had learned, that late nights and too much booze were for dumb kids. John Clark had turned into a paragon of healthy virtue before reaching Ryan's age. He figured that it had saved his life at least once.

"Quiet night," Clark said next, heading out the driveway.

"That's nice." Ryan picked up the dispatch box and dialed in the code. He waited until the light flashed green before opening it. Clark was right, there wasn't much to be looked at. By the time they were halfway to Washington, he'd read everything and made a few notes.

"Going to see Carol and the kids tonight?" Clark asked as they passed over Maryland Route 3.

"Yeah, it is tonight, isn't it?"

"Yep."

It was a regular once-a-week routine. Carol Zimmer was the Laotian widow of Air Force sergeant Buck Zimmer, and Ryan had promised to take care of the family after Buck's death. Few people knew of it—fewer people knew of the mission on which Buck had died—but it gave Ryan great satisfaction. Carol now owned a 7-Eleven between Washington and Annapolis. It gave her family a steady and respectable income when added to her husband's pension, and, with the educational trust fund that Ryan had established, guaranteed that each of the eight would have a college degree when the time came—as it had already come for the eldest son. It would be a long haul to finish that up. The youngest was still in diapers.

"Those punks ever come back?" Jack asked.

Clark just turned and grinned. For several months after Carol had taken over the business, some local toughs had been hanging out at the store. They had objected to a Laotian woman and her mixed-race kids owning a business in the semirural area. Finally she had mentioned it to Clark. John had given them one warning, which they had been too dense to heed. Perhaps they'd mistaken him for an off-duty police officer, someone not to be taken too seriously. John and his Spanish-speaking friend had set things right, and after the gang leader had gotten out of the hospital, the punks had never come near the place. The local cops had been very understanding, and business had shown an immediate twenty-percent increase. *I wonder if that guy's knee ever came all the way back?* Clark wondered with a wistful smile. *Maybe now he'll take up an honest trade. . . .*

"How are the kids doing?"

"You know, it's kinda hard to get used to the idea of having one in college, doc. A little tough on Sandy, too . . . doc?"

"Yeah, John?"

"Pardon my saying so, but you look a little rocky. You want to back it off a little."

"That's what Cathy says." It occurred to Jack to tell Clark to mind his own business, but you didn't say that sort of thing to a man like Clark, and besides, he was a friend. And besides that, he was correct.

"Docs are usually right," John pointed out.

"I know. It's just a little—a little stressful at the office. Got some stuff happening, and—"

"Exercise beats the hell out of booze, man. You're one of the smartest guys I know. Act smart. End of advice." Clark shrugged and returned his attention to the morning traffic.

"You know, John, if you had decided to become a doc, you would have been very effective," Jack replied with a chuckle.

"How so?"

"With a bedside manner like yours, people would be afraid not to do what you said."

"I am the most even-tempered man I know," Clark protested.

"Right, no one's ever lived long enough for you to get really mad. They're dead by the time you're mildly annoyed."

And that was why Clark was Ryan's driver. Jack had engineered his transfer out of the Directorate of Operations to become a Security and Protective Officer. DCI Cabot had eliminated fully twenty percent of the field force, and people with paramilitary experience had been first on the block. Clark's expertise was too valuable to lose, and Ryan had bent two rules and outright evaded a third to accomplish this much, aided and abetted by Nancy Cummings and a friend in the Admin Directorate. Besides, Jack felt very safe around this man, and he was able to train the new kids in the SPO unit. He was even a superb driver, and as usual, he got Ryan into the basement garage right on time.

The Agency Buick slid into its spot, and Ryan got out, fiddling with his keys. The one for the executive elevator was on the end, and two minutes later, he arrived at the seventh floor, walking from the corridor to his office. The DDCI's office adjoins the long, narrow suite accorded the DCI, who was not at work yet. A small, surprisingly modest place for the number-two man in the country's premiere intelligence service, it overlooked the visitor-parking lot, beyond which was the thick stand of pines that separated the Agency compound from the George Washington Parkway and the Potomac River valley beyond. Ryan had kept Nancy Cummings from his previous and brief stint as Deputy Director (Intelligence). Clark took his seat in that office, going over dispatches that pertained to his duties, in preparation for the morning SPO conference—they concerned themselves with which terrorist group was making noise at the moment. No serious attempt had ever been made on a senior Agency executive, but history was not their institutional concern. The future was, and even CIA didn't have a particularly bright record for predicting that.

Ryan found his desk neatly piled with material too sensitive for the car's dispatch case, and prepped himself for the morning department-head meeting, which he co-chaired with the DCI. There was a drip-coffee machine in his office. Next to it was a clean but never-used mug that had once belonged to the man who'd brought him into the Agency, Vice Admiral James Greer. Nancy took care of that, and Ryan never began a day at Langley without thinking of his dead boss. So. He rubbed his hands across his face and eyes and went to work. What new and interesting things did the world hold in store this day?

The logger, like most of his trade, was a big, powerful man. Six-four and two hundred twenty pounds of former all-state defensive end, he'd joined the Marines instead of going to college—could have, he thought, could have taken the scholarship to Oklahoma or Pitt, but he'd decided against it. And he knew that he would never have wanted to leave Oregon for good. A college degree would have meant that. Maybe play pro ball, and then—turn into a "suit"? No. Since childhood he'd loved the outdoor life. He made a good living, raised his family in a friendly small town, lived a rough, healthy life, and was the best damned man in the company for dropping a tree straight and soft. He drew the special ones.

He yanked the string on the big, two-man chain saw. On a silent command, his helper took his end off the ground as the logger did the same. The tree had already been notched with a double-headed ax. They worked the saw in slowly and carefully. The logger kept one eye on the chain saw while the other watched the tree. There was an art to doing this just right. It was a point of honor with him that he didn't waste an inch of wood he didn't have to. Not like the guys down at the mill, though they'd told him that the mill wouldn't touch this baby. They pulled the saw after completing the first cut, and started the second without pausing for breath. This time it took four minutes. The logger was tensely alert now. He felt a puff of wind on his face and paused to make sure it was blowing the way he wanted. A tree, no matter how large, was a plaything for a stiff wind—especially when nearly cut in half. . . .

It was swaying at the top now . . . almost time. He backed the saw off and waved to his helper. *Watch my eyes, watch my hands!* The kid nodded seriously. About another foot would do it, the logger knew. They completed it very slowly. It abused the chain, but this was the dangerous part. Safety guys were monitoring the wind, and . . . now!

The logger brought the saw out and dropped it. The helper took the cue and backed off ten yards as his boss did the same. Both watched the base of the tree. If it kicked, that would tell them of the danger.

But it didn't. As always, it seemed so agonizingly slow. This was the part the Sierra Club liked to film, and the logger understood why. So slow, so agonizing, like the tree knew it was dying, and was trying not to, and losing, and the groan of the wood was a moan of despair. Well, yes, he thought, it did seem like that, but it was only a goddamned tree. The cut widened as he watched and the tree fell. The top was moving very fast now, but the danger was at the bottom, and that's what he continued to watch. As the trunk passed through the forty-five-degree mark, the wood parted completely. The body of the tree kicked then, moving over the stump about four feet, like the death rattle of a man. Then the noise. The immense swish of the top branches ripping through the air. He wondered quickly how fast the top was moving. Speed of sound, maybe? No, not that fast . . . and then—WHUMP! The tree actually bounced, but softly, when it hit the wet ground. Then it lay still. It was lumber now. That was always a little sad. It had been a pretty tree.

The Japanese official came over next, the logger was surprised to see. He touched the tree and murmured something that must have been a prayer. That amazed him, it seemed like something an Indian would do—interesting, the logger thought. He didn't know that Shinto was an animistic religion with many similarities to those of Native Americans. Talking to the spirit of the tree? Hmph. Next he came to the logger.

"You have great skill," the little Japanese said with an exquisitely polite bow.

"Thank you, sir." The logger nodded his head. It was the first Japanese he'd ever met. Seemed like a nice enough guy. And saying a prayer to the tree . . . that had class, the logger thought on reflection.

"A great pity to kill something so magnificent."

"Yeah, I guess it is. Is it true that you will put this in a church, like?"

"Oh, yes. We no longer have trees like this, and we need four huge beams. Twenty meters each. This one tree will do all of them, I hope," the man said, looking back at the fallen giant. "They must all come from a single tree. It is the tradition of the temple, you see."

"Ought to," the logger judged. "How old's the temple?"

"One thousand two hundred years. The old beams—they were damaged in the earthquake two years ago, and must be replaced very soon. With luck, these should last as long. I hope they will. It is a fine tree."

Under the supervision of the Japanese official, the fallen tree was cut into manageable segments—they weren't all that manageable. Quite a bit of special equipment had to be assembled to get this monster out, and Georgia-Pacific was charging a huge amount of money for the job. But that was not a problem. The Japanese, having selected the tree, paid without blinking. The representative even apologized for the fact that he didn't want the GP mill to work the tree. It was a religious thing, he explained slowly and clearly, and no insult to the American workers was intended. The senior GP executive nodded. That was okay with him. It was their tree now. They'd let it season for a little while before loading it on an American-flag timber carrier for the trip across the Pacific, where the log would be worked with skill and due religious ceremony—by hand, the GP man was amazed to hear—for its new and special purpose. That it would never reach Japan was something that none of them knew.

The term trouble-shooter was particularly awkward for a law-enforcement official, Murray thought. Of course, as he leaned back in the leather chair he could feel the 10mm Smith & Wesson automatic clipped to his waistband. He ought to have left it in his desk drawer, but he liked the feel of the beast. A revolver man for most of his career, he'd quickly come to love the compact power of the Smith. And Bill understood. For the first time in recent memory, the Director of the Federal Bureau of Investigation was a career cop who'd started his career on the street, busting bad guys. In fact, Murray and Shaw had started off in the same field division. Bill was slightly more skilled at the administrative side, but no one mistook him for a headquarters weenie. Shaw had first gotten high-level attention by staring down two armed bank robbers before the cavalry'd had time to arrive. He'd never fired his weapon in anger, of course—only a tiny percentage of FBI agents ever did—but he'd convinced those two hoods that he could drop both of them. There was steel under the gentlemanly velvet, and one hell of a brain. Which was why Dan Murray, a deputy assistant director, didn't mind working as Shaw's personal problem-solver.

"What the hell do we do with this guy?" Shaw asked with quiet disgust.

Murray had just finished his report on the Warrior Case. Dan sipped at his coffee and shrugged.

"Bill, the man is a genius with corruption cases—best we've ever had. He just doesn't know dick about the muscle end of the business. He got out of his depth with this one. Luckily enough, no permanent damage was done." And Murray was right. The newsies had treated the Bureau surprisingly well for saving the life of their reporter. What was truly amazing was the fact that the newsies had never quite understood that the reporter had had no place in that particular arena. As a result, they were grateful to the local S-A-C for letting the news team on the scene, and grateful to the Hostage Rescue Team for saving both of them when things had taken a dangerous turn. It wasn't the first time the Bureau had reaped a PR bonanza from a near-catastrophe. The FBI was more jealous of its public relations than any government agency, and Shaw's problem was simply that to fire S-A-C Walt Hoskins would look bad. Murray pressed on. "He's learned his lesson. Walt isn't stupid, Bill."

"And bagging the Governor last year was some coup, wasn't it?" Shaw grimaced. Hoskins *was* a genius at political corruption cases. A state governor was now contemplating life in a federal prison because of him. That was how Hoskins had become a Special-Agent-in-Charge in the first place. "You have something in mind, Dan?"

"ASAC Denver," Murray replied with a mischievous twinkle. "It's elegant. He goes from a little field office to head of corruption cases in a major field division. It's a promotion that takes him out of command and puts him back in what he's best at—and if the rumbles we're getting out of Denver are right, he'll have lots of work to do. Like maybe a senator and a congressman—maybe more. The preliminary indications on the water project look big. I mean *real* big, Bill: like twenty million bucks changing hands."

Shaw whistled respectfully at that. "All that for one senator and one congresscritter?"

"Like I said, maybe more. The latest thing is some environmental types being paid off—in government and out. Who do we have better at unraveling a ball of yarn that big? Walt's got a nose for this sort of thing. The man can't draw his gun without losing a few toes, but he's one hell of a bird dog." Murray closed the folder in his hands. "Anyway, you wanted me to look around and make a recommendation. Send him to Denver or retire him. Mike Delaney is willing to rotate back this way—his kid's going to start at GW this fall, and Mike wants to teach down at the Academy. That gives you the opening. It's all very neat and tidy, but it's your call, Director."

"Thank you, Mr. Murray," Director Shaw said gravely. Then his face broke into a grin. "Remember when all we had to worry about was chasing bank bandits? I *hate* this admin crap!"

"Maybe we shouldn't have caught so many," Dan agreed. "We'd still be working riverside Philly and having a beer with the troops at night. Why do people toast success? It just screws up your life.''

''We're both talking like old farts.''

''We both are old farts, Bill,'' Murray pointed out. ''But at least I don't travel around with a protective detail.''

''You son of a bitch!'' Shaw gagged and dribbled coffee down his necktie. ''Oh, Christ, Dan!'' he gasped, laughing. ''Look what you made me do.''

''Bad sign when a guy can't hold his coffee, Director.''

''Out! Get the orders cut before I bust you back to the street.''

''Oh, no, please, not that, anything but that!'' Murray stopped laughing and turned semiserious for a moment. ''What's Kenny doing now?''

''Just got his assignment to his submarine, USS *Maine*. Bonnie's doing fine with the baby—due in December. Dan?''

''Yeah, Bill?''

''Nice call on Hoskins. I needed an easy out on that. Thanks.''

''No problem, Bill. Walt will jump at it. I wish they were all this easy.''

''You following up on the Warrior Society?''

''Freddy Warder's working on it. We just might roll those bastards up in a few months.''

And both knew that would be nice. There were not many domestic terrorist groups left. Reducing their number by one more by the end of the year would be another major coup.

It was dawn in the Dakota badlands. Marvin Russell knelt on the hide of a bison, facing the sunrise. He wore jeans, but was bare-chested and barefoot. He was not a tall man, but there was no mistaking the power in him. During his first and only stint in prison—for burglary—he'd learned about pumping iron. It had begun merely as a hobby to work off surplus energy, had grown with the understanding that physical strength was the only form of self-defense that a man in the penitentiary could depend upon, and then blossomed into the attribute he'd come to associate with a warrior of the Sioux Nation. His five feet eight inches of height supported fully two hundred pounds of lean, hard muscle. His upper arms were the size of some men's upper legs. He had the waist of a ballerina and the shoulders of an NFL linebacker. He was also slightly mad, but Marvin Russell did not know that.

Life had not given him or his brother much of a chance. Their father had been an alcoholic who had worked occasionally and not well as an auto mechanic to provide money that he had transferred regularly and immediately to the nearest package store. Marvin's memories of childhood were bitter ones: shame for his father's nearly perpetual state of inebriation, and shame greater still for what his mother did while her husband was passed-out drunk in the living room. Food came from the government dole after the family had returned from Minnesota to the reservation. Schooling came from teachers who despaired of accomplishing anything. His neighborhood had been a scattered collection of government-built plain block houses that stood like specters in perpetual clouds of blowing prairie dust. Neither Russell boy had ever owned a baseball glove. Neither had known a Christmas as much other than a week or two when school was closed. Both had grown in a vacuum of neglect and learned to fend for themselves at an early age.

At first this had been a good thing, for self-reliance was the way of their people, but all children need direction, and direction was something the Russell parents had been unable to provide. The boys had learned to shoot and hunt before they'd learned to read. Often the dinner had been something brought home with .22-caliber holes in it. Almost as often, they had cooked the meals. Though not the only poor and neglected youth of their settlement, they had without doubt been at the bottom, and while some of the local kids had overcome their backgrounds, the leap from poverty to adequacy had been far too broad for them. From the time they had begun to drive—well before the legal age—they'd taken their father's dilapidated pickup a hundred miles or more on clear cool nights to distant towns where they might obtain some of the things their parents had been unable to provide. Surprisingly, the first time they'd been caught—by another Sioux holding a shotgun—they'd taken their whipping manfully and been sent home with bruises and a lecture. They'd learned from that. From that moment on, they'd only robbed whites.

In due course they'd been caught at that, also, red-handed inside a country store, by a tribal police officer. It was their misfortune that any crime committed on federal property was a federal case, and further that the new district court judge was a man with more compassion than perception. A hard lesson at that point might—or might not—have changed their path, but instead they'd gotten an administrative dismissal and counseling. A very serious young lady with a degree from the University of Wisconsin had explained to them over months that they could never have a beneficial self-image if they lived by stealing the goods of others. They would have more personal pride if they found something worthwhile to do. Emerging from that session wondering how the Sioux Nation had ever allowed itself to be overrun by white idiots, they learned to plan their crimes more carefully.

But not carefully enough, since the counselor could not have offered them the graduate-school expertise that the Russell boys might have received in a proper prison. And so they were caught, again, a year later, but this time off the reservation, and this time they found themselves dispatched to a year and a half of hard time because they'd been burglarizing a gun shop.

Prison had been the most frightening experience of their lives. Accustomed to land as open and vast as the Western sky, they'd spent over a year of their lives in a cage smaller than the federal government deemed appropriate for a badger in a zoo, and surrounded by people far worse than their most inflated ideas of their own toughness. Their first night on the blocks, they'd learned from screams that rape was not a crime inflicted exclusively on women. Needing protection, they had almost immediately been swept into the protective arms of their fellow Native American prisoners of the American Indian Movement.

They had never given much thought to their ancestry. Subliminally, they might have sensed that their peer group did not display the qualities they had seen on those occasions when the family TV had worked, and probably felt some vague shame that they had always been different. They'd learned to snicker at Western movies, of course, whose "Indian" actors were most often whites or Mexicans, mouthing words that reflected the thoughts of Hollywood scriptwriters who had about as much knowledge of the West as they had of Antarctica, but even there the messages had left a negative image of what they were and from what roots they had come. The American Indian Movement had changed all that. Everything was the White Man's fault. Espousing ideas that were a mix of trendy East Coast anthropology, a dash of Jean-Jacques Rousseau, more than a little John Ford Western (what else, after all, was the American cultural record?), and a great deal of misunderstood history, the Russell brothers came to understand that their ancestors were of noble stock, ideal hunter-warriors who had lived in harmony with nature and the gods. The fact that the Native Americans had lived in as peaceful a state as the Europeans—the word "Sioux" in Indian dialect means "snake," and was not an appellation assigned with affection—and that they had only begun roaming the Great Plains in the last decade of the 18th century were somehow left out, along with the vicious intertribal wars. Times had once been far better. They had been masters of their land, following the buffalo, hunting, living a healthy and satisfying life under the stars, and, occasionally, fighting short, heroic contests among themselves—rather like medieval jousts. Even the torture of captives was explained as an opportunity for warriors to display their stoic courage to their admiring if sadistic murderers.

Every man craves nobility of spirit, and it wasn't Marvin Russell's fault that the first such opportunity came from convicted felons. He and his brother learned about the gods of earth and sky, beliefs in which had been cruelly suppressed by false, white beliefs. They learned about the brotherhood of the plains, about how the whites had stolen what was rightfully theirs, had killed the buffalo which had been their livelihood, had divided, compressed, massacred, and finally imprisoned their people, leaving them little beyond alcoholism and despair. As with all successful lies, the cachet to this one was a large measure of truth.

Marvin Russell greeted the first orange limb of the sun, chanting something that might or might not have been authentic—no one really knew anymore, least of all him. But prison had not been an entirely negative experience. He'd arrived with a third-grade reading level, and left with high-school equivalency. Marvin Russell had not ever been a dullard, and it was not his fault either that he'd been betrayed by a public school system that had consigned him to failure before birth. He read books regularly, everything he could get on the history of his people. Not quite everything. He was highly selective in the editorial slant of the books he picked up. Anything in the least unfavorable to his people, of course, reflected the prejudice of whites. The Sioux had not been drunks before the whites arrived, had not lived in squalid little villages, had certainly not abused their children. That was all the invention of the white man.

But how to change things? he asked the sun. The glowing ball of gas was red with yet more blowing dust from this hot, dry summer, and the image that came to Marvin was of his brother's face. The stop-motion freeze-frame of the TV news. The local station had done things with the tape that the network had not. Every frame of the incident had been examined separately. The bullet striking John's face, two frames of his brother's face detaching itself from the head. Then the ghastly aftermath of the bullet's passage. The gunshot—damn that nigger and his vest!—and the hands coming up like something in a Roger Corman movie. He'd watched it five times, and each pixel of each image was so firmly fixed in his memory that he knew he'd never be able to forget it.

Just one more dead Indian. "Yes, I saw some good Indians," General William Tecumseh—a Native American name!—Sherman had said once. "They were dead." John Russell was dead, killed like so many without the chance for honorable combat, shot down like the animal a Native American was to whites. But more brutally than most. Marvin was sure the shot had been arranged with care. Cameras rolling. That wimp pussy reporter with her high-fashion clothes. She'd needed a lesson in what was what, and those FBI assassins had decided to give it to her. Just like the cavalry of old at Sand Creek and Wounded Knee and a hundred other nameless, forgotten battlefields.

And so Marvin Russell faced the sun, one of the gods of his people, and searched for answers. The answer wasn't here, the sun told him. His comrades were not reliable. John had died learning that. Trying to raise money with drugs! Using drugs! As though the whiskey the white man had used to destroy his people wasn't bad enough. The other "warriors" were creatures of their white-made environment. They didn't know that they'd already been destroyed by it. They called themselves Sioux warriors, but they were drunkards, petty criminals who had labored and failed to succeed even in that undemanding field. In a rare flash of honesty—how could one be dishonest before one of his gods?—Marvin admitted to himself that they were less than he. As his brother had been. Stupid to join their foolish quest for drug money. And ineffective. What had they ever accomplished? They'd killed an FBI agent and a United States Marshal, but that was long in the past. Since then? Since then they had merely talked about their one shining moment. But what sort of moment had it been? What had they accomplished? Nothing. The reservation was still there. The liquor was still there. The hopelessness was still there. Had anyone even noticed who they were and what they did? No. All they had accomplished was to anger the forces that continued to oppress them. So now the Warrior Society was hunted, even on its own reservation, living not like warriors at all, but like hunted animals. But they were supposed to be the hunters, the sun told him, not the prey.

Marvin was stirred by the thought. *He* was supposed to be the hunter. The whites were supposed to fear *him*. It had once been so, but was no more. He was supposed to be the wolf in the fold, but the white sheep had grown so strong that they didn't know there was such a thing as a wolf, and they hid behind formidable dogs who were not content to stay with the flocks, but hunted the wolves themselves until they and not the sheep were frightened, driven, nervous creatures, prisoners on their own range.

So he had to leave his range.

He had to find his brother wolves. He had to find wolves for whom the hunt was still real.

3. . . . A Single Sit

This was the day. His day. Captain Benjamin Zadin had enjoyed rapid career growth in the Israeli National Police. The youngest captain on the force, he was the last of three sons, the father of two sons of his own, David and Mordecai, and until very recently had been on the brink of suicide. The death of his beloved mother and the departure of his beautiful but adulterous wife had come within a single week, and that had only been two months before. Despite having done everything he'd ever planned on doing, he'd suddenly been faced with a life that seemed empty and pointless. His rank and pay, the respect of his subordinates, his demonstrated intelligence and clearheadedness in times of crisis and tension, his military record on dangerous and difficult border-patrol duty, they were all as nothing compared to an empty house of perverse memories.

Though Israel is regarded most often as "the Jewish state," that name disguises the fact that only a fraction of the country's population is actively religious. Benny

Zadin had never been so, despite the entreaties of his mother. Rather he'd enjoyed the swinging life-style of a modern hedonist, and not seen the inside of a *shul* since his Bar Mitzvah. He spoke and read Hebrew because he had to—it was the national language—but the rules of his heritage were to him a curious anachronism, a backward aspect of life in what was otherwise the most modern of countries. His wife had only accentuated that. One might measure the religious fervor of Israel, he'd often joked, by the swimming suits on its many beaches. His wife's background was Norwegian. A tall, skinny blonde, Elin Zadin looked about as Jewish as Eva Braun—that was their joke on the matter—and still enjoyed showing off her figure with the skimpiest of bikinis, and sometimes only half of that. Their marriage had been passionate and fiery. He'd known that she'd always had a wandering eye, of course, and had occasionally dallied himself, but her abrupt departure to another had surprised him—more than that, the manner of it had left him too stunned to weep or beg, had merely left him alone in a home that also contained several loaded weapons whose use, he knew, might easily have ended his pain. Only his sons had stopped that. He could not betray them as he'd been betrayed, he was too much of a man for that. But the pain had been—still was—very real.

Israel is too small a country for secrets. It was immediately noticed that Elin had taken up with another man, and the word had quickly made its way to Benny's station, where men could see from the hollow look around the eyes that their commander's spirit had been crushed. Some wondered how and when he would bounce back, but after a week the question had changed to whether he would do so at all. At that point, one of Zadin's squad sergeants had taken matters in hand. Appearing at his captain's front door on a Thursday evening, he'd brought with him Rabbi Israel Kohn. On that evening, Benjamin Zadin had rediscovered God. More than that, he told himself, surveying the Street of the Chain in Old Jerusalem, he knew again what it was to be a Jew. What had happened to him was God's punishment, no more, no less. Punishment for ignoring the words of his mother, punishment for his adultery, for the wild parties with his wife and others, for twenty years of evil thoughts and deeds while pretending to be a brave and upstanding commander of police and soldiers. But today he would change all that. Today he would break the law of man to expiate his sins against the Word of God.

It was early in the morning of what promised to be a blistering day, with a dry easterly wind blowing in from Arabia. He had forty men arrayed behind him, all of them armed with a mixture of automatic rifles, gas guns, and other arms that fired "rubber bullets," more accurately called missiles, made of ductile plastic that could knock a grown man down, and if the marksman were very careful, stop a heart from blunt trauma. His police were needed to allow the law to be broken—which was not the idea that Captain Zadin's immediate superiors had in mind—and to stop the interference of others willing to break a higher law to keep him from his job. That was the argument Rabbi Kohn had used, after all. Whose law was it? It was a question of metaphysics, something far too complicated for a simple police officer. What was far simpler, as the Rabbi had explained, was the idea that the site of Solomon's Temple was the spiritual home of Judaism and the Jews. The site on Temple Mount had been chosen by God, and if men had disputed that fact, it was of little account. It was time for Jews to reclaim what God had given them. A group of ten conservative and Hasidic rabbis would today stake out the place where the new temple would be reconstructed in precise accordance with the Holy Scriptures. Captain Zadin had orders to prevent their march through the Chain Gate, to stop them from doing their work, but he would ignore those orders, and his men would do as he commanded, protecting them from the Arabs who might be waiting with much the same intentions as he was supposed to have.

He was surprised that the Arabs were there so early. No better than animals, really, the people who'd killed David and Motti. His parents had told all of their sons what it had been like to be a Jew in Palestine in the 1930s, the attacks, the terror, the envy, the open hatred, how the British had refused to protect those who had fought with them in North Africa—against those who had allied themselves with the Nazis. The Jews could depend on no one but themselves and their God, and keeping faith with their God meant reestablishing His Temple on the rock where Abraham had forged the covenant between his people and their Lord. The government either didn't understand that or was willing to play politics with the destiny of the only country in the world where Jews were truly safe. His duty as a Jew superseded that, even if he'd not known it until quite recently.

Rabbi Kohn showed up at the appointed time. Alongside him was Rabbi Eleazar Goldmark, a tattooed survivor of Auschwitz, where he had learned the importance of faith while in the face of death itself. Both men held a bundle of stakes and surveyor's string. They'd make their measurements, and from this day forward a relay of men would guard the site, eventually forcing the government of Israel to clear the site of Muslim obscenities. An upwell of popular support throughout the country, and a flood of money from Europe and America, would allow the project to be completed in five years—and then no one would ever be able to talk about taking this land away from those to whom God Himself had deeded it.

"Shit," muttered someone behind Captain Zadin, but a turn and a look from his commander stifled whoever had blasphemed the moment of destiny.

Benny nodded to the two leading rabbis, who marched off. The police followed their captain, fifty meters behind. Zadin prayed for the safety of Kohn and Goldmark, but knew that the danger they faced was fully accepted, as Abraham had accepted the death of his son as a condition of God's Law.

But the faith that had brought Zadin to this moment had blinded him to what should have been the obvious fact that Israel was indeed a country too small for secrets, and that fellow Jews who viewed Kohn and Goldmark as simply another version of Iran's fundamentalist ayatollas knew of what was happening, and that as a result the word had gotten out. TV crews were assembled in the square at the foot of the Wailing Wall. Some wore the hard hats of construction workers in anticipation of the rain of stones that surely was coming. Perhaps that was all the better, Captain Zadin thought as he followed the rabbis to the top of Temple Mount. The world should know what was happening. Unconsciously he increased his pace to close on Kohn and Goldmark. Though they might accept the idea of martyrdom, his job was to protect them. His right hand went down to the holster at his hip and made sure the flap wasn't too tight. He might need that pistol soon.

The Arabs were there. It was a disappointment that there were so many, like fleas, like rats in a place they didn't belong. Just so long as they kept out of the way. They wouldn't, of course, and Zadin knew it. They were opposed to the Will of God. That was their misfortune.

Zadin's radio squawked, but he ignored it. It would just be his commander, asking him what the hell he was up to and ordering him to desist. Not today. Kohn and Goldmark strode fearlessly to the Arabs blocking their path. Zadin nearly wept at their courage and their faith, wondering how the Lord would show his favor to them, hoping that they would be allowed to live. Behind him, about half his men were truly with him, which was possible because Benny had worked his watch bill to make it so. He knew without looking that they were not using their Lexan shields; instead, safety switches on their shoulder weapons were now being flicked to the Off position. It was hard waiting for it, hard to anticipate the first cloud of stones that would be coming at any moment.

Dear God, please let them live, please protect them. Spare them as you spared Isaac.

Zadin was now less than fifty meters behind the two courageous rabbis, one Polish-born, a survivor of the infamous camps where his wife and child had died, where he had somehow kept his spirit and learned the importance of faith; the other American-born, a man who'd come to Israel, fought in her wars, and only then turned to God, as Benny himself had done so brief a span of days before.

The two were barely ten meters from the surly, dirty Arabs when it happened. The Arabs were the only ones who could see that their faces were serene, that they truly welcomed whatever the morning might hold for them, and only the Arabs saw the shock and the puzzlement on the face of the Pole, and the stunned pain on the American's at the realization of what fate had in mind.

On command, the leading row of Arabs, all of them teenagers with a lengthy history of confrontation, sat down. The hundred young men behind them did the same. Then the front row started clapping. And singing. Benny took a moment to comprehend it, though he was as fluent in Arabic as any Palestinian.

We shall overcome
We shall overcome
We shall overcome some day

The TV crews were immediately behind the police. Several of them laughed in surprise at the savage irony of it. One of them was CNN correspondent Pete Franks, who summed it up for everyone: *"Son of a BITCH!"* And in that moment Franks knew that the world had changed yet again. He'd been in Moscow for the first democratic meeting of the Supreme Soviet, in Managua the night the Sandinistas had lost their sure-thing election, and in Beijing to see the Goddess of Liberty destroyed. *And now* this? he thought. *The Arabs finally wised up. Holy shit.*

"I hope you have that tape rolling, Mickey."

"Are they singing what I think they're singing?"

"Sure as hell sounds like it. Let's get closer."

The leader of the Arabs was a twenty-year-old sociology student named Hashimi Moussa. His arm was permanently scarred from an Israeli club, and half his teeth were gone from a rubber bullet whose shooter had been especially angry on one particular day. No one questioned his courage. He'd had to prove that beyond doubt. He'd had to face death a dozen times before his position of leadership had been assured, but now he had it, and people listened to him, and he was able to activate an idea he'd cherished for five endless, patient years. It had taken three days to persuade them, then the fantastic good luck of a Jewish friend disgusted with the religious conservatives of his country who'd spoken a little too loudly about the plans of this day. Perhaps it was destiny, Hashimi thought, or the Will of Allah, or simply luck. Whatever it was, this was the moment he'd lived for since his fifteenth year, when he'd learned of Gandhi and King, and how they had defeated force with naked, passive courage. Persuading his people had meant stepping back from a warrior code that seemed part of their genes, but he'd done it. Now his beliefs would be put to the test.

All Benny Zadin saw was that his path was blocked. Rabbi Kohn said something to Rabbi Goldmark, but neither turned back to where the police were stopped, because to turn away was to admit defeat. Whether they were too shocked at what they saw or too angry, he would never learn. Captain Zadin turned to his men.

"Gas!" He'd planned this part in advance. The four men with gas guns were all religious men. They leveled their weapons and fired simultaneously into the crowd. The gas projectiles were dangerous and it was remarkable that no one was injured by them. In a few seconds, gray clouds of tear gas bloomed within the mass of sitting Arabs. But on command, each of them donned a mask to protect himself from it. This impeded their singing, but not their clapping or resolution, and it only enraged Captain Zadin further when the easterly wind blew the gas toward his men and away from the Arabs. Next, men with insulated gloves lifted the hot projectiles and threw them back toward the police. In a minute, they were able to remove their masks, and there was laughter in their singing now.

Next Zadin ordered the rubber bullets launched. He had six men armed with these weapons, and from a range of fifty meters they could force any man to run for cover. The first volley was perfect, hitting six of the Arabs in the front line. Two cried out in pain. One collapsed, but not one man moved from his place except to succor the injured. The next volley was aimed at heads not chests, and Zadin had the satisfaction of seeing a face explode in a puff of red.

The leader—Zadin recognized the face from earlier encounters—stood and gave a command the Israeli captain could not hear. But its significance became clear immediately. The singing became louder. Another volley of rubber bullets followed. One of his marksmen was very angry, the police commander saw. The Arab who'd taken one fully in the face now took another in the top of his head, and with it his body went limp in death. It should have warned Benny that he had already lost control of his men, but worse still was that he was losing control of himself.

Hashimi did not see the death of his comrade. The passion of the moment was overwhelming. The consternation on the faces of the two invading rabbis was manifest. He could not see the faces of the police behind their masks, but their actions, their movements, made their feelings clear. In a brilliant moment of clarity he knew that he was winning, and he shouted again to his people to redouble their efforts. This they did in the face of fire and death.

Captain Benjamin Zadin stripped off his helmet and walked forcefully toward the Arabs, past the rabbis who had suddenly been struck with incomprehensible indecision. Would the Will of God be upset by the discordant singing of some dirty savages?

"Uh-oh," Pete Franks observed, his eyes streaming from the gas that had blown over his face.

"I got it," the cameraman said without bidding, zooming his lens in on the advancing Israeli police commander. "Something is going to happen—this guy looks pissed, Pete!"

Oh, God, Franks thought. Himself a Jew, himself strangely at home in this barren but beloved land, he knew that history was occurring before his eyes yet again, was already composing his two or three minutes of verbal reporting that would overlay the tape his cameraman was recording for posterity, and was wondering if another Emmy might be in his future for doing his tough and dangerous job supremely well.

It happened quickly, much too quickly, as the captain strode directly to the Arab leader. Hashimi now knew that a friend was dead, his skull caved in by what was supposed to be a nonlethal weapon. He prayed silently for the soul of his comrade and hoped that Allah would understand the courage required to face death in this way. He would. Hashimi was sure of that. The Israeli approaching him was a face known to him. Zadin, the name was, a man who'd been there before often enough, just one more Israeli face most often hidden behind a Lexan mask and drawn gun, one more man unable to see Arabs as people, to whom a Muslim was the launcher for a rock or a Molotov cocktail. Well, today he'd learn different, Hashimi told himself. Today he'd see a man of courage and conviction.

Benny Zadin saw an animal, like a stubborn mule, like—what? He wasn't sure what he saw, but it wasn't a man, wasn't an Israeli. They'd changed tactics, that was all, and the tactics were womanly. They thought this would stand in the way of his purpose? Just as his wife had told him that she was leaving for the bed of a better man, that he could have the children, that his threats to beat her were empty words, that he couldn't do that, wasn't man enough to take charge of his own household. He saw that beautiful empty face and wondered why he hadn't taught her a lesson; she'd just stood there, not a meter away, staring at him, smiling—finally laughing at his inability to do what his manhood had commanded him to do, and, so, passive weakness had defeated strength.

But not this time.

"Move!" Zadin commanded in Arabic.

"No."

"I will kill you."

"You will not pass."

"Benny!" a levelheaded member of the police screamed. But it was too late for that. For Benjamin Zadin, the deaths of his brothers at Arab hands, the way his wife had left, and the way these people just sat in his way was too much. In one smooth motion he drew his service automatic and shot Hashimi in the forehead. The Arab youth fell forward, and the singing and clapping stopped. One of the other demonstrators started to move, but two others grabbed him and held him fast. Others began praying for their two dead comrades. Zadin turned his gun hand to one of these, but though his finger pressed on the trigger, something stopped him a gram short of the release pressure. It was the look in the eyes, the courage there, something other than defiance. Resolution, perhaps . . . and pity, for the look on Zadin's face was anguish that transcended pain, and the horror of what he had done crashed through his consciousness. He had broken faith with himself. He had killed in cold blood. He had taken the life of someone who had threatened no man's life. He had murdered. Zadin turned to the rabbis, looking for something, he knew not what, and whatever he sought simply was not there. As he turned away, the singing began again. Sergeant Moshe Levin came forward and took the captain's weapon.

"Come on, Benny, let's get you away from this place."

"What have I done?"

"It is done, Benny. Come with me."

Levin started to lead his commander away, but he had to turn and look at the morning's handiwork. Hashimi's body was slumped over, a pool of blood coursing down between the cobblestones. The sergeant knew that he had to do or say something. It wasn't supposed to be like this. His mouth hung open, and his face swung from side to side. In that moment, Hashimi's disciples knew that their leader had won.

they never recognized that Israeli legitimacy is based entirely on their moral position or they just didn't have the wit to care about it. Israel is now faced with an impossible ethical contradiction. If they really are a democracy that respects the rights of its citizens, they have to grant the Arabs broader rights. But that means playing hell with their political integrity, which depends on soothing their own extreme religious elements—and that crowd doesn't care a rat's ass about Arab rights, does it? But if they cave in to the religious zealots and stonewall, try to gloss over this thing, then they are not a democracy, and that imperils the political support from America without which they cannot survive economically or militarily. The same dilemma applies to us. Our support for Israel is based on their political legitimacy as a functioning liberal democracy, but that legitimacy just evaporated. A country whose police murder unarmed people has no legitimacy, Marcus. We can no more support an Israel that does things like this than we could have supported Somoza, Marcos, or any other tin-pot dictator—''

''Goddamn it, Charlie! Israel isn't—''

''I know that, Marcus. They're not. They're really not. But the only way they can prove that is to change, to become true to what they have always claimed to be. If they stonewall on this, Marcus, they're doomed. They'll lean on their political lobby and find out it isn't there anymore. If it goes that far, then they embarrass our government even more than it already is, and we'll be faced with the possible necessity of overtly cutting them off. We can't do that either. We must find another alternative.'' Alden turned back from the window. ''Ryan, that idea of yours is now on the front burner. I'll handle the President and State. The only way we can get Israel out of this is to find some kind of a peace plan that works. Call your friend at Georgetown and tell him it's no longer a study. Call it Project PILGRIMAGE. By tomorrow morning I need a good sketch of what we want to do and how we want to do it.''

''That's awful fast, sir,'' Ryan observed.

''Then don't let me stop you, Jack. If we don't move quickly on this, God only knows what might happen. You know Scott Adler at State?''

''We've talked a few times.''

''He's Brent Talbot's best man. I suggest you get together with him after you check with your friends. He can cover your backside on the State Department flank. We can't trust that bureaucracy to do anything fast. Better pack some bags, boy, you're going to be busy. I want facts, positions, and a gold-plated evaluation just as fast as you can generate it, and I want it done black as a coal mine.'' That last remark was aimed at Cabot. ''If this is going to work, we can't risk a single leak.''

''Yes, sir,'' Ryan said. Cabot just nodded.

Jack had never been in the faculty residence at Georgetown. It struck him as odd, but he shoved that thought aside as breakfast was served. Their table overlooked a parking lot.

''You were right, Jack,'' Riley observed. ''That was nothing to wake up to.''

''What's the word from Rome?''

''They like it,'' the President of Georgetown University replied simply.

''How much?'' Ryan asked.

''You're serious?''

''Alden told me two hours ago that this is now on the front burner.''

Riley accepted this news with a nod. ''Trying to save Israel, Jack?''

Ryan didn't know how much humor was in the question, and his physical state did not allow levity. "Father, all I'm doing is following up on something—you know, orders?"

"I am familiar with the term. Your timing was pretty good on floating this thing."

"Maybe so, but let's save the Nobel Prize for some other time, okay?"

"Finish your breakfast. We can still catch everybody over there before lunch, and you look pretty awful."

"I feel pretty awful," Ryan admitted.

"Everybody should stop drinking about forty," Riley observed. "After forty you really can't handle it anymore."

"You didn't," Jack noted.

"I'm a priest. I have to drink. What exactly are you looking for?"

"If we can get preliminary agreement from the major players, we want to get negotiations going ASAP, but this end of the equation has to be done very quietly. The President needs a quick evaluation of his options. That's what I'm doing."

"Will Israel play?"

"If they don't, they're fucked—excuse me, but that's exactly where things are."

"You're right, of course, but will they have the sense to recognize their position?"

"Father, all I do is gather and evaluate information. People keep asking me to tell fortunes, but I don't know how. What I do know is that what we saw on TV is going to ignite the biggest firestorm since Hiroshima, and we sure as hell have to try to do something before it burns up a whole region."

"Eat. I have to think for a few minutes, and I do that best when I'm chewing on something."

It was good advice, Ryan knew a few minutes later. The food soaked up the coffee acid in his stomach, and the energy from the food would help him get through the day. Inside an hour, he was on the move again, this time to the State Department. By lunch he was on his way home to pack, managing to nap for three hours along the way. He stopped back at Alden's White House office for a session that dragged far into the night. Alden had really taken charge there, and the skull session in his office covered a huge amount of ground. Before dawn Jack headed off to Andrews Air Force Base. He was able to call his wife from the VIP Lounge. Jack had hoped to take his son to a ball game over the weekend, but for him there wouldn't be a weekend. A final courier arrived from CIA, State, and the White House, delivering two hundred pages of data that he'd have to read on the way across the Atlantic.

4. Promised Land

The U.S. Air Force's Ramstein air base is set in a German valley, a fact which Ryan found slightly unsettling. His idea of a proper airport was one on land that was flat as far as the eye could see. He knew that it didn't make much of a difference, but it was one of the niceties of air travel to which he'd become accustomed. The base supported a full wing of F-16 fighter-bombers, each of which was stored in its own bombproof shelter which in its turn was surrounded by trees—the German people have a mania for green things that would impress the most ambitious American environmentalists. It was one of those remarkable cases in which the wishes of the tree-huggers coincided exactly with military necessity. Spotting the aircraft shelters from the air was extremely difficult, and some of the shelters—French-built—had trees planted on top of them, making camouflage both aesthetically and militarily pleasing. The base also housed a few large executive aircraft, including a converted 707 with "The United States of America" painted on it. Resembling a smaller version of the President's personal transport, it was known locally as "Miss Piggy," and was assigned to the use of the commander of USAF units in Europe. Ryan could not help but smile. Here were over seventy fighter aircraft tasked to the destruction of Soviet forces which were now drawing back from Germany, housed on an environmentally admirable facility, which was also home to a plane called Miss Piggy. The world was truly mad.

On the other hand, traveling Air Force guaranteed excellent hospitality and VIP treatment worthy of the name, in this case at an attractive edifice called the Cannon Hotel. The base commander, a full colonel, had met his VC-20B Gulfstream executive aircraft and whisked him off to his Distinguished Visitor's quarters where a slide-out drawer contained a nice collection of liquor bottles to help him to conquer jet lag with nine hours of drink-augmented sleep. That was just as well, because the available television service included a single channel. By the time he awoke at about six in the morning, local, he was almost in synch with the time zones, stiff and hungry, having almost survived another bout with travel shock. He hoped.

Jack didn't feel like jogging. That was what he told himself. In fact he knew that he couldn't have jogged half a mile with a gun to his head. And so he walked briskly. He soon found himself being passed by early-morning exercise nuts, many of whom had to be fighter pilots, they were so young and lean. Morning mist hung in the trees that were planted nearly to the edge of the blacktopped roads. It was much cooler than at home, with the still air disturbed every few minutes by the discordant roar of jet engines—"the sound of freedom"—the audible symbol of the military force that had guaranteed the peace of Europe for over forty years—now resented by the Germans, of course. Attitudes change as rapidly as the times. American power had achieved its goal and was becoming a thing of the past, at least as far as Germany was concerned. The inner-German border was gone. The fences and guard towers were down. The mines were gone. The plowed strip of dirt that had remained pristine for two generations to betray the footprints of defectors was now planted with grass and flowers. Locations in the East once examined in satellite photos or about which Western intelligence agencies had sought information at the cost of both money and blood were now walked over by camera-toting tourists, among whom were intelligence officers more shocked than bemused at the rapid changes that had come and gone like the sweep of a spring tide. *I knew that I was right about this place,* some thought. Or, *How did we ever blow that one so badly?*

Ryan shook his head. It was more than amazing. The question of the two Germanys had been the centerpiece of East-West conflict since before his birth, had appeared to be the one unchanging thing in the world, the subject of enough white papers and Special National Intelligence Estimates and news stories to fill the entire Pentagon with pulp. All the effort, all the examination of minutiae, the petty disputes—gone. Soon to be forgotten. Even scholarly historians would never have the energy to look at all the data that had been thought important—crucial, vital, worthy of men's lives—and was now little more than a vast footnote to the end of the Second World War. This base had been one such item. Designed to house the aircraft whose task it was to clear the skies of Russian planes and crush a Soviet attack, it was now an expensive anachronism whose residential apartments would soon house German families. Ryan wondered what they'd do with the aircraft shelters like that one there. . . . Wine cellars, maybe. The wine was pretty good.

"Halt!" Ryan stopped cold in his tracks and turned to see where the sound had come from. It was an Air Force security policeman—woman. Girl, actually, Ryan saw, though her M-16 rifle neither knew nor cared about plumbing fixtures.

"Did I do something wrong?"

"ID, please." The young lady was quite attractive, and quite professional. She also had a backup in the trees. Ryan handed over his CIA credentials.

"I've never seen one of these, sir."

"I came in last night on the VC-20. I'm staying over at the Inn, room 109. You can check with Colonel Parker's office."

"We're on security alert, sir," she said next, reaching for her radio.

"Just do your job, miss—excuse me, Sergeant Wilson. My plane doesn't leave till ten." Jack leaned against a tree to stretch. It was too nice a morning to get excited about anything, even if there were two armed people who didn't know who the hell he was.

"Roger." Sergeant Becky Wilson switched off her radio. "The Colonel's looking for you, sir."

"On the way back, I turn left at the Burger King?"

"That's right, sir." She handed his ID back with a smile.

"Thanks, Sarge. Sorry to bother you."

"You want a ride back, sir? The Colonel's waiting."

"I'd rather walk. He can wait, he's early." Ryan walked away from a buck sergeant who now had to ponder the importance of a man who kept her base commander sitting on the front step of the Cannon. It took ten brisk minutes, but Ryan's directional sense had not left him, despite the unfamiliar surroundings and a six-hour time differential.

"Morning, sir!" Ryan said as he vaulted the wall into the parking lot.

"I set up a little breakfast with COMUSAFE staff. We'd like your views on what's happening in Europe."

Jack laughed. "Great! I'm interested in hearing yours." Ryan walked off toward his room to dress. *What makes them think I know anything more than they do?* By the time his plane left, he'd learned four things he hadn't known. Soviet forces withdrawing from what had formerly been called East Germany were decidedly unhappy with the fact that there was no place for them to withdraw to. Elements of the former East German army were even less happy about their enforced retirement than Washington actually knew; they probably had allies among ex-members of the already de-established Stasi. Finally, though an even dozen members of the Red Army Faction had been apprehended in Eastern Germany, at least that many others had gotten the message and vanished before they, too, could be swept up by the *Bundeskriminalamt,* the German federal police. That explained the security alert at Ramstein, Ryan was told.

The VC-20B lifted off from the airfield just after ten in the morning, headed south. Those poor terrorists, he thought, devoting their lives and energy and intellect to something that was vanishing more swiftly than the German countryside below him. Like children whose mother had died. No friends now. They'd hidden out in Czechoslovakia and the German Democratic Republic, blissfully unaware of the coming demise of both communist states. Where would they hide now? Russia? No chance. Poland? That was a laugh. The world had changed under them, and was about to change again, Ryan thought with a wistful smile. Some more of their friends were about to watch the world change. Maybe, he corrected himself. Maybe . . .

''Hello, Sergey Nikolayevich,'' Ryan had said as the man had entered his office, a week before.

''Ivan Emmetovich,'' the Russian had replied, holding out his hand. Ryan remembered the last time they'd been this close, on the runway of Moscow's Sheremetyevo Airport. Golovko had held a gun in his hand then. It had not been a good day for either, but as usual, it was funny the way things had worked out. Golovko, for having nearly, but not quite, prevented the greatest defection in Soviet history, was now First Deputy Chairman of the Committee for State Security. Had he succeeded, he would not have gone quite so far, but for being very good, if not quite good enough, he'd been noticed by his own President, and his career had taken a leap upward. His security officer had camped in Nancy's office with John Clark, as Ryan had led Golovko into his.

''I am not impressed.'' Golovko looked around disapprovingly at the painted gypsum-board drywall. Ryan did have a single decent painting borrowed from a government warehouse, and, of course, the not-exactly-required photo of President Fowler over by the clothes tree on which Jack hung his coat.

''I do have a nicer view, Sergey Nikolayevich. Tell me, is the statue of Iron Feliks still in the middle of the square?''

''For the moment.'' Golovko smiled. ''Your Director is out of town, I gather.''

''Yes, the President decided that he needed some advice.''

''On what?'' Golovko asked with a crooked smile.

''Damned if I know,'' Ryan answered with a laugh. *Lots of things,* he didn't say.

''Difficult, is it not? For both of us.'' The new KGB Chairman was not a professional spook either—in fact that was not unusual. More often than not, the director of that grim agency had been a Party man, but the Party was becoming a thing of history also, and Narmonov had selected a computer expert who was supposed to bring new ideas into the Soviet Union's chief spy agency. That would make it more efficient. Ryan knew that Golovko had an IBM PC behind his desk in Moscow now.

''Sergey, I always used to say that if the world made sense, I'd be out of a job. So look what's happening. Want some coffee?''

''I would like that, Jack.'' A moment later he expressed approval of the brew.

''Nancy sets it up for me every morning. So. What can I do for you?''

''I have often heard that question, but never in such surroundings as this.'' There was a rumbling laugh from Ryan's guest. ''My God, Jack, do *you* ever wonder if this is all the result of some drug-induced dream?''

''Can't be. I cut myself shaving the other day and I didn't wake up.''

Golovko muttered something in Russian that Jack didn't catch, though his translators would when they went over the tapes.

''I am the one who reports to our parliamentarians on our activities. Your Director was kind enough to respond favorably to our request for advice.''

Ryan couldn't resist that opening: ''No problem, Sergey Nikolayevich. You can screen all your information through me. I'd be delighted to tell you how to present it.'' Golovko took it like a man.

"Thank you, but the Chairman might not understand." With jokes aside, it was time for business.

"We want a *quid pro quo.*" The fencing began.

"And that is?"

"Information on the terrorists you guys used to support."

"We cannot do that," Golovko said flatly.

"Sure you can."

Next Golovko waved the flag: "An intelligence service cannot betray confidences and continue to function."

"Really? Tell Castro that next time you see him," Ryan suggested.

"You're getting better at this, Jack."

"Thank you, Sergey. My government is most gratified indeed for your President's recent statement on terrorism. Hell, I like the guy personally. You know that. We're changing the world, man. Let's clean a few more messes up. You never approved of your government's support for those creeps."

"What makes you believe that?" the First Deputy Chairman asked.

"Sergey, you're a professional intelligence officer. There's no way you can personally approve the actions of undisciplined criminals. I feel the same way, of course, but in my case it's personal." Ryan leaned back with a hard look. He would always remember Sean Miller and the other members of the Ulster Liberation Army who'd made two earnest attempts to kill Jack Ryan and his family. Only three weeks earlier, after years exhausting every legal opportunity, after three writs to the Supreme Court, after demonstrations and appeals to the Governor of Maryland and the President of the United States for executive clemency, Miller and his colleagues had, one by one, walked into the gas chamber in Baltimore, and been carried out half an hour later, quite dead. *And may God have mercy on their souls,* Ryan thought. *If God has a strong enough stomach.* One chapter in his life was now closed for good.

"And the recent incident . . . ?"

"The Indians? That merely illustrates my case. Those 'revolutionaries' were dealing drugs to make money. They're going to turn on you, the people you used to fund. In a few years they're going to be more of a problem for you than they ever were for us." That was entirely correct, of course, and both men knew it. The terrorist-drug connection was something the Soviets were starting to worry about. Free enterprise was starting most rapidly of all in Russia's criminal sector. That was as troubling to Ryan as to Golovko. "What do you say?"

Golovko inclined his head to the side. "I will discuss it with the Chairman. He will approve."

"Remember what I said over in Moscow a couple of years back? Who needs diplomats to handle negotiations when you have real people to settle things?"

"I expected a quote from Kipling or something similarly poetic," the Russian observed dryly. "So how do you deal with your Congress?"

Jack chuckled. "Short version is, you tell them the truth."

"I needed to fly eleven thousand kilometers to hear you say that?"

"You select a handful of people in your parliament you can trust to keep their mouths shut, and whom the rest of parliament trust to be completely honest—that's the hard part—and you brief them into everything they need to know. You have to set up ground rules—"

"Ground rules?"

"A baseball term, Sergey. It means the special rules that apply to a specific playing field."

Golovko's eyes lit up. "Ah, yes, that is a useful term."

"Everyone has to agree on the rules, and you may never, ever break them." Ryan paused. He was talking like a college lecturer again, and it wasn't fair to speak that way to a fellow professional.

Golovko frowned. That was the hard part, of course: never, ever breaking the rules. The intelligence business wasn't often that cut and dried. And conspiracy was part of the Russian soul.

"It's worked for us," Ryan added.

Or has it? Ryan wondered. *Sergey knows if it has or not . . . well, he knows some things that I don't. He could tell me if we've had major leaks on the Hill since Peter Henderson . . . but at the same time he knows that we've penetrated so many of their operations despite their manic passion for the utmost secrecy.* Even the Soviets had admitted it publicly: the hemorrhage of defectors from KGB over the years had gutted scores of exquisitely planned operations against America and the West. In the Soviet Union as in America, secrecy was designed to shield failure as well as success.

"What it comes down to is trust," Ryan said after another moment. "The people in your parliament are patriots. If they didn't love their country, why would they put up with all the bullshit aspects of public life? It's the same here."

"Power," Golovko responded at once.

"No, not the smart ones, not the ones you will be dealing with. Oh, there'll be a few idiots. We have them here. They are not an endangered species. But there are always those who're smart enough to know that the power that comes with government service is an illusion. The duty that comes along with it is always greater in magnitude. No, Sergey, for the most part you'll be dealing with people as smart and honest as you are."

Golovko's head jerked at the compliment, one professional to another. He'd guessed right a few minutes earlier, Ryan was getting good at this. He started to think that he and Ryan were not really enemies any longer. Competitors, perhaps, but not enemies. There was more than professional respect between them now.

Ryan looked benignly at his visitor, smiling inwardly at having surprised him. And hoping that one of the people Golovko would select for oversight would be Oleg Kirilovich Kadishev, code name SPINNAKER. Known in the media as one of the most brilliant Soviet parliamentarians in a bumptious legislative body struggling to build a new country, his reputation for intelligence and integrity belied the fact that he'd been on the CIA payroll for several years, the best of all the agents recruited by Mary Pat Foley. The game goes on, Ryan thought. The rules were different. The world was different. But the game went on. Probably always would, Jack thought, vaguely sorry it was true. But, hell, America even spied on Israel—it was called "keeping an eye on things"; it was *never* called "running an operation." The oversight people in Congress would have leaked that in a minute. *Oh, Sergey, do you have a lot of new things to learn about!*

Lunch followed. Ryan took his guest to the executive dining room, where Golovko found the food somewhat better than KGB standards—something Ryan would not have believed. He also found that the top CIA executives wanted to meet him. The Directorate chiefs and their principal deputies all stood in line to shake his hand and be photographed. Finally there was a group photo before Golovko had taken the executive elevator back to his car. Then the people from Science and Technology, and Security had swept every inch of every corridor and room Golovko and his bodyguard had traveled. Finding nothing, they had swept again. And again. And once more until it was decided that he had not availed himself of the opportunity to play his own games. One of the S&T people had lamented the fact that it just wasn't the same anymore.

Ryan smiled, remembering the remark. Things were happening so goddamned fast. He settled back into the chair and tightened his seat belt. The VC-20 was approaching the Alps, and the air might be bumpy there.

"Want a paper, sir?" the attendant asked. It was a girl for a change, and a pretty one. Also married and pregnant. A pregnant staff sergeant. It made Ryan uneasy to be served by someone like that.

"What d'you have?"

"International Trib."

"Great!" Ryan took the paper—and nearly gasped. There it was, right on the front page. Some bonehead had leaked one of the photos. Golovko, Ryan, the directors of S&T, Ops, Admin, Records, and Intelligence, plunging through their lunches. None of the American identities were secret, of course, but even so. . . .

"Not a real good picture, sir," the sergeant noted with a grin. Ryan was unable to be unhappy.

"When are you due, Sarge?"

"Five more months, sir."

"Well, you'll be bringing your child into a much better world than the one either one of us was stuck with. Why don't you sit down and relax? I'm not liberated enough to be waited on by a pregnant lady."

The *International Herald-Tribune* is a joint venture of *The New York Times* and *The Washington Post.* The one sure way for Americans traveling in Europe to keep track of the ball scores and important comic strips, it had already broadened its distribution into what had been the Eastern Bloc to serve American businessmen and tourists who were flooding the former communist nations. The locals also used it, both as a way to hone their English skills and to keep track of what was happening in America, more than ever a fascination to people learning how to emulate something they'd been raised to hate. In addition it was as fine an information source as had ever been available in those countries. Soon everyone was buying it, and the American management of the paper was expanding operations to broaden its readership still further.

One such regular reader was Günther Bock. He lived in Sofia, Bulgaria, having left Germany—the eastern part—rather hurriedly some months before, after a warning tip from a former friend in the Stasi. With his wife, Petra, Bock had been a unit leader in the Baader-Meinhof Gang, and after that had been crushed by the West German police, in the Red Army Faction. Two near arrests by the *Bundeskriminalamt* had frightened him across the Czech border, and thence on to the DDR, where he had settled into a quiet semiretirement. With a new identity, new papers, a regular job—he never showed up, but the employment records were completely *in Ordnung*—he'd deemed himself safe. Neither he nor Petra had reckoned with the popular revolt that had overturned the government of the *Deutsche Demokratische Republik,* but they both decided that they could survive that change in anonymity. They'd never counted on a popular riot storming into Stasi headquarters, either. That event had resulted in the destruction of literally millions of documents. Many of the documents had not been destroyed, however. Many of the rioters had been agents of the *Bundesnachrichtendienst,* the West German intelligence agency, who'd been in the front ranks of the intruders and known exactly which rooms to savage. Within days, people from the RAF had started disappearing. It had been hard to tell at first. The DDR telephone system was so decrepit that getting phone calls through had never been easy, and for obvious security reasons the former associates had not lived in the same areas, but when another married couple had failed to make a rendezvous for dinner, Günther and Petra had sensed trouble. Too late. While the husband made rapid plans to leave the country, five heavily armed GSG-9 commandos had kicked down the flimsy door of the Bock apartment in East Berlin. They'd found Petra nursing one of her twin daughters, but whatever sympathy they might have felt at so touching a scene had been mitigated by the fact that Petra Bock had murdered three West German citizens, one quite brutally. Petra was now in a maximum-security prison, serving a life sentence in a country where ''life'' meant that you left prison in a casket or not at all. The twin daughters were the adopted children of a Munich police captain and his barren wife.

It was very odd, Günther thought, how much that stung him. After all, he was a revolutionary. He had plotted and killed for his cause. It was absurd that he would allow himself to be enraged by the imprisonment of his wife . . . and the loss of his children. But. But they had Petra's nose and eyes, and they'd smiled for him. They would not be taught to hate him, Günther knew. They'd never even be told who he and Petra had been. He'd dedicated himself to something larger and grander than mere corporeal existence. He and his colleagues had made a conscious and reasoned decision to build a better and more just world for the common man, and yet—and yet he and Petra had decided, also in a reasoned and conscious way, to bring into it children who would learn their parents' ways, to be the next generation of Bocks, to eat the fruits of their parents' heroic labor. Günther was enraged that this might not happen.

Worse still was his bewilderment. What *had* happened was quite impossible. *Unmöglich. Unglaublich.* The people, the common *Volk* of the DDR had risen up like revolutionaries themselves, forsaking their nearly perfect socialist state, opting instead to merge with the exploitative monstrosity crafted by the imperialist powers. They'd been seduced by Blaupunkt appliances and Mercedes automobiles, and—what? Günther Bock genuinely did not understand. Despite his inborn intelligence, the events did not connect into a comprehensible pattern. That the people of his country had examined ''scientific socialism'' and decided it did not work, and could never work—that was too great a leap of imagination for him to make. He'd committed too much of his life to Marxism ever to deny it. Without Marxism, after all, he was a criminal, a common murderer. Only his heroic revolutionary *ethos* elevated his activities above the acts of a thug. But his revolutionary *ethos* had been summarily rejected by his own chosen beneficiaries. That was simply impossible. *Unmöglich.*

It wasn't quite fair that so many impossible things piled one upon another. As he opened the paper he'd bought twenty minutes before at a kiosk seven blocks from his current residence, the photo on the front page caught his eye, as the paper's editor had fully intended.

CIA FETES KGB, the caption began.

''Was ist das denn für Quatsch?'' Günther muttered.

''In yet another remarkable turn in a remarkable time, the Central Intelligence Agency hosted the First Deputy Chairman of the KGB in a conference concerning 'issues of mutual concern' to the world's two largest intelligence empires. . . ." the story read. "Informed sources confirm that the newest area of East-West cooperation will include information-sharing on the increasingly close ties between international terrorists and the international drug trade. CIA and KGB will work together to . . ."

Bock set the paper down and stared out the window. He knew what it was to be a hunted animal. All revolutionaries did. It was the path he had chosen, along with Petra, and all their friends. The task was a clear one. They would test their cunning and skill against their enemies. The forces of light against the forces of darkness. Of course, it was the forces of light that had to run and hide, but that was a side issue. Sooner or later the situation would be reversed when the common people saw the truth and sided with the revolutionaries. Except for one little problem. The common people had chosen to go another way. And the terrorist world was rapidly running out of dark places in which the forces of light might hide.

He'd come to Bulgaria for two reasons. Of all the former East Bloc countries, Bulgaria was the most backward and because of it had managed the most orderly transition from communist rule. In fact, communists still ran the country, though under different names, and the country was still politically safe, or at least neutral. The Bulgarian intelligence apparat, once the source of designated killers for KGB whose hands had finally become too clean for such activity, was still peopled with reliable friends. *Reliable friends,* Günther thought. But the Bulgarians were still in the thrall of their Russian masters—associates, now—and if KGB were really cooperating with CIA . . . The number of safe places was being reduced by one more digit.

Günther Bock should have felt a chill at the increased personal danger. Instead his face flushed and pulsed with rage. As a revolutionary he'd often enough bragged that every hand in the world was turned against him—but whenever he'd said that, it had been with the inner realization that such was not and would never be the case. Now his boast was becoming reality. There were still places to run, still contacts he could trust. But how many? How soon before trusted associates would bend to the changes in the world? The Soviets had betrayed themselves and world socialism. The Germans. The Poles. The Czechs, the Hungarians, the Romanians. Who was next?

Couldn't they see? It was all a trap, some kind of incredible conspiracy of counterrevolutionary forces. A lie. They were casting away what could be—should be—was—the perfect social order of structured freedom from want, orderly efficiency, of fairness and equality. Of . . .

Could that all be a lie? Could it all have been a horrible mistake? Had he and Petra killed those cowering exploiters for nothing?

But it didn't matter, did it? Not to Günther Bock, not right now. He was soon to be hunted again. One more safe patch of ground was about to become a hunting preserve for his enemies. If the Bulgarians shared their papers with the Russians, if the Russians had a few men in the right office, with the right credentials and the right access, his address and new identity could already be on its way to Washington, and from there to BND headquarters, and in a week's time he might be sharing a cell close to Petra's.

Petra, with her light brown hair and laughing blue eyes. As brave a girl as any man could want. Seemingly cold to her victims, wonderfully warm to her comrades. So fine a mother she'd been to Erika and Ursel, so superior at that task as she'd been at every other she'd ever attempted. Betrayed by supposed friends, caged like an animal, robbed of her own offspring. His beloved Petra, comrade, lover, wife, believer. Robbed of her life. And now he was being driven farther from her. There had to be a way to change things back.

But first he had to get away.

Bock set the paper down and tidied up the kitchen. When things were clean and neat, he packed a single bag and left the apartment. The elevator had quit again, and he walked down the four flights to the street. Once there he caught a tram. In ninety minutes he was at the airport. His passport was a diplomatic one. In fact he had six of them carefully concealed in the lining of his Russian-made suitcase, and, ever the careful man, three of them were the numerical duplicates of others held by real Bulgarian diplomats, unknown to the Foreign Ministry office that kept the records. That guaranteed him free access to the most important ally of the international terrorist: air transport. Before time for lunch, his flight rotated off the tarmac, headed south.

Ryan's flight touched down at a military airport outside Rome just before noon, local time. By coincidence they rolled in right behind yet another VC-20B of the 89th Military Airlift Wing that had arrived only a few minutes earlier from Moscow. The black limousine on the apron was waiting for both aircraft.

Deputy Secretary of State Scott Adler greeted Ryan as he stepped off with an understated smile.

"Well?" Ryan asked through the airport sounds.

"It's a go."

"Damn," Ryan said as he took Adler's hand. "How many more miracles can we expect this year?"

"How many do you want?" Adler was a professional diplomat who'd worked his way up the Russian side of the State Department. Fluent in their language, well versed on their politics, past and present, he understood the Soviets as did few men in government—including Russians themselves. "You know the hard part about this?"

"Getting used to hearing *da* instead of *nyet*, right?"

"Takes all the fun out of negotiations. Diplomacy can really be a bitch when both sides are reasonable." Adler laughed as the car pulled off.

"Well, this ought to be a new experience for both of us," Jack observed soberly. He turned to watch "his" aircraft prepare for an immediate departure. He and Adler would be traveling together for the rest of the trip.

They sped toward central Rome with the usual heavy escort. The Red Brigade, so nearly exterminated a few years earlier, was back in business, and even if it hadn't been, the Italians were careful protecting foreign dignitaries. In the right-front seat was a serious-looking chap with a little Beretta squirt-gun. There were two lead cars, two chase cars, and enough cycles for a motorcross race. The speedy progress down the ancient streets of Rome made Ryan wish he were back in an airplane. Every Italian driver, it seemed, had ambitions to ride in the Formula One circuit. Jack would have felt safer in a car with Clark, driving an unobtrusive vehicle on a random path, but in his current position his security arrangements were ceremonial in addition to being practical. There was one other consideration, of course. . . .

"Nothing like a low profile," Jack muttered to Adler.

"Don't sweat it. Every time I've come here it's been the same way. First time?"

"Yep. First time in Rome. I wonder how I've ever missed coming here—always wanted to, the history and all."

"A lot of that," Adler agreed. "Think we might make a little more?"

Ryan turned to look at his colleague. Making history was a new thought to him. Not to mention a dangerous one. "That's not my job, Scott."

"If this does work, you know what'll happen."

"Frankly, I never bothered thinking about that."

"You ought to. No good deed ever goes unpunished."

"You mean Secretary Talbot . . . ?"

"No, not him. Definitely not my boss."

Ryan looked forward to see a truck scuttle out of the way of the motorcade. The Italian police officer riding on the extreme right of the motorcycle escort hadn't flinched a millimeter.

"I'm not in this for credit. I just had an idea, is all. Now I'm just the advance man."

Adler shook his head slightly and kept his peace. *Jesus, how did you ever last this long in government service?*

The striped jump suits of the Swiss Guards had been designed by Michelangelo. Like the red tunics of the British Guardsmen, they were anachronisms from a bygone era when it had made sense for soldiers to wear brightly colored uniforms, and also, like the Guardsmen uniforms, they were kept on more for their attractiveness to tourists than for any practical reason. The men and their weapons look so *quaint*. The Vatican guards carried halberds, evil-looking long-handled axes made originally for infantrymen to unhorse armored knights—as often as not by crippling the horse the enemy might be riding; horses didn't fight back very well, and war is ever a practical business. Once off his mount, an armored knight was dispatched with little more effort than that required to break up a lobster—and about as much remorse. People thought medieval weapons romantic somehow, Ryan told himself, but there was nothing romantic about what they were designed to do. A modern rifle might punch holes in some other fellow's anatomy. These were made to dismember. Both methods would kill, of course, but at least rifles made for neater burial.

The Swiss Guards had rifles, too, Swiss rifles made by SIG. Not all of them wore Renaissance costumes, and since the attempt on John Paul II, many of the guards had received additional training, quietly and unobtrusively, of course, since such training did not exactly fit the image of the Vatican. Ryan wondered what Vatican policy was on the use of deadly force, whether the chief of the guards chafed at the rules imposed from on high by people who certainly did not appreciate the nature of the threat and the need for decisive protective action. But they'd do their best within their constraints, grumbling among themselves and voicing their opinions when the time seemed right, just like everyone else in that business.

A bishop met them, an Irishman named Shamus O'Toole, whose thick red hair clashed horribly with his clothing. Ryan was first out of the car, and his first thought was a question: was he supposed to kiss O'Toole's ring or not? He didn't know. He hadn't met a real bishop since his confirmation—and it had been a long time since sixth grade in Baltimore. O'Toole deftly solved that problem by grasping Ryan's hand in a bearish grip.

"So many Irishmen in the world!" he said with a wide grin.

"Somebody has to keep things straight, Excellency."

"Indeed, indeed!" O'Toole greeted Adler next. Scott was Jewish and had no intentions of kissing anyone's ring. "Would you come with me, gentlemen?"

Bishop O'Toole let them into a building whose history might have justified three scholarly volumes, plus a picture book for its art and architecture. Jack barely noticed the two metal detectors they passed through on the third floor. Leonardo da Vinci might have done the job, so skillfully were they concealed in door frames. Just like the White House. The Swiss Guards didn't all wear uniforms. Some of the people prowling the halls in soft clothes were too young and too fit to be bureaucrats, but for all that the overall impression was a cross between visiting an old art museum and a cloister. The clerics wore cassocks, and the nuns—they were here in profusion also—were not wearing the semicivilian attire adopted by their American counterparts. Ryan and Adler were parked briefly in a waiting room, more to appreciate the surroundings than to inconvenience them, Jack was sure. A Titian madonna adorned the opposite wall, and Ryan admired it while Bishop O'Toole announced the visitors.

"God, I wonder if he ever did a small painting?" Ryan muttered. Adler chuckled.

"He did know how to capture a face and a look and a moment, didn't he? Ready?"

"Yeah," Ryan said. He felt oddly confident.

"Gentlemen!" O'Toole said from the open door. "Will you come this way, please?" They walked through yet another anteroom. This one had two secretarial desks, both unoccupied, and another set of doors that looked fourteen feet tall.

The office of Giovanni Cardinal D'Antonio would have been used in America for balls or formal occasions of state. The ceiling was frescoed, the walls covered with blue silk, and the floor's ancient hardwood accented with rugs large enough for an average living room. The furniture was probably the most recent in manufacture, and that looked to be at least two hundred years old, brocaded fabric taut over the cushions and gold leaf on the curved wooden legs. A silver coffee service told Ryan where to sit.

The Cardinal came toward them from his desk, smiling in the way that a king might have done a few centuries earlier to greet a favored minister. D'Antonio was a man of short stature, and clearly one who enjoyed good food. He must have been a good forty pounds overweight. The room air reported that he was a man who smoked, something he ought to have stopped, since he was rapidly approaching seventy years of age. The old, pudgy face had an earthy dignity to it. The son of a Sicilian fisherman, D'Antonio had mischievous brown eyes to suggest a roughness of character that fifty years of service to the Church had not wholly erased. Ryan knew his background and could easily see him pulling in nets at his father's side, back a very long time ago. The earthiness was also a useful disguise for a diplomat, and that's what D'Antonio was by profession, whatever his vocation might have been. A linguist like many Vatican officials, he was a man who had spent thirty years practicing his trade, and the lack of military power that had crippled his efforts at making the world change had merely taught him craftiness. In intelligence parlance he was an agent of influence, welcome in many settings, always ready to listen or offer advice. Of course he greeted Adler first.

"So good to see you again, Scott."

"Eminence, a pleasure as always." Adler took the offered hand and smiled his diplomat's smile.

"And you are Dr. Ryan. We have heard so many things about you."

"Thank you, Your Eminence."

"Please, please." D'Antonio waved both men to a sofa so beautiful that Ryan flinched at resting his weight on it. "Coffee?"

"Yes, thank you," Adler said for both of them. Bishop O'Toole did the pouring, then sat down to take notes. "So good of you to allow us in at such short notice."

"Nonsense." Ryan watched in no small amazement as the Cardinal reached inside his cassock and pulled out a cigar holder. A tool that looked like silver but was probably stainless steel performed the appropriate surgery on the largish brown tube, then D'Antonio lit it with a gold lighter. There wasn't even an apology about the sins of the flesh. It was as though the Cardinal had quietly flipped off the "dignity" switch to put his guests at ease. More likely, Ryan thought, he merely worked better with a cigar in his hand. Bismarck had felt the same way.

"You are familiar with the rough outlines of our concept," Adler opened.

"*Sì*. I must say that I find it very interesting. You know of course that the Holy Father proposed something along similar lines some time ago."

Ryan looked up at that. He hadn't.

"When that initiative first came out, I did a paper on its merits," Adler said. "The weak point was the inability to address security considerations, but in the aftermath of the Iraq situation, we have the opening. Also, you realize, of course, that our concept does not exactly—"

"Your concept is acceptable to us," D'Antonio said with a regal wave of his cigar. "How could it be otherwise?"

"That, Eminence, is precisely what we wanted to hear." Adler picked up his coffee. "You have no reservations?"

"You will find us highly flexible so long as there is genuine goodwill among the active parties. If there is total equality among the participants, we can agree unconditionally to your proposal." The old eyes sparkled. "But can you guarantee equality of treatment?"

"I believe we can," Adler said seriously.

"I think it should be possible, else we are all charlatans. What of the Soviets?"

"They will not interfere. In fact, we are hoping for open support. In any case, what with the distractions they already have—"

"Indeed. They will benefit from the diminution of the discord in the region, the stability on various markets, and general international goodwill."

Amazing, Ryan thought. *Amazing how matter-of-factly people have absorbed the changes in the world. As though they had been expected. They had not. Not by anyone. If anyone had suggested their possibility ten years earlier, he would have been institutionalized.*

"Quite so." The Deputy Secretary of State set down his cup. "Now, on the question of the announcement . . ."

Another wave of the cigar. "Of course you will want the Holy Father to make it."

"How very perceptive," Adler observed.

"I am not yet completely senile," the Cardinal replied. "And press leaks?"

"We would prefer none."

"That is easily accomplished in this city, but in yours? Who knows of this initiative?"

"Very few," Ryan said, opening his mouth for the first time since sitting down. "So far, so good."

"But on your next stop. . . ?" D'Antonio had not been informed of their next stop, but it was the obvious one.

"That might be a problem," Ryan said cautiously. "We'll see."

"The Holy Father and I will both be praying for your success."

"Perhaps this time your prayers will be answered," Adler said.

Fifty minutes later the VC-20B lifted off again. It soared upward across the Italian coast, then turned southwest to recross Italy on the way to its next destination.

"Jesus, that was fast," Jack observed when the seat belt light went off. He kept his buckled, of course. Adler lit a cigarette and blew smoke at the window on his side of the cabin.

"Jack, this is one of those situations where you do it fast or it doesn't get done." He turned and smiled. "They're rare, but they happen."

The cabin attendant—this one was a male—came aft and handed both men copies of a printout that had just arrived on the aircraft facsimile machine.

"What?" Ryan observed crossly. "What gives?"

In Washington people do not always have time to read the papers, at least not all the papers. To assist those in government service to see what the press is saying about things is an in-house daily press-summary sheet called *The Early Bird.* Early editions of all major American papers are flown to D.C. on regular airline flights, and before dawn they are vetted for stories relating to all manner of government operations. Relevant material is clipped and photocopied, then distributed by the thousands to various offices whose staff members then repeat the process by highlighting individual stories for their superiors. This process is particularly difficult in the White House, whose staff members are by definition interested in everything.

Dr. Elizabeth Elliot was Special Assistant to the President for National Security Affairs. The immediate subordinate to Dr. Charles Alden, whose title was the same, but without the "Special," Liz, also referred to as "E.E.," was dressed in a fashionable linen suit. Current fashions dictated that women's "power" clothing was not mannish but feminine, the idea being that since even the most obtuse of men would be able to tell the difference between themselves and women, there was little point in trying to conceal the truth. The truth was that Dr. Elliot was not physically unattractive and enjoyed dressing to emphasize the fact. Tall at five feet eight inches, and with a slender figure that long work hours and mediocre food sustained, she did not like playing second-fiddle to Charlie Alden. And besides, Alden was a Yalie. She'd most recently been Professor of Political Science at Bennington, and resented the fact that Yale was considered more prestigious by whatever authorities made such judgments.

Current work schedules at the White House were easier than those of only a few years earlier, at least in the national-security shop. President Fowler did not feel the need for a first-thing-in-the-morning intelligence briefing. The world situation was far more pacific than any of his predecessors had known, and Fowler's main problems were of the domestic political variety. Commentary on that could readily be had from watching morning TV news shows, something Fowler did by watching two or more TV sets at the same time, something that had infuriated his wife and still bemused his staffers. That fact meant that Dr. Alden didn't have to arrive until eight or so to get his morning briefing, after which he would brief the President at nine-thirty. President Fowler didn't like dealing directly with the briefing officers from CIA. As a result, it was E.E. who had to arrive just after six so that *she* could screen dispatches and message traffic, confer with the CIA watch officers (she didn't like them either), and their counterparts from State and Defense. She also got to read over *The Early Bird,* and to highlight items of interest for her boss, the estimable Dr. Charles Alden.

Like I'm a goddamned addle-brained simpering secretary, E.E. fumed.

Alden, she thought, was a logical contradiction. A liberal who talked tough, a skirt-chaser who supported women's rights, a kindly, considerate man who probably enjoyed using her like a goddamned functionary. That he was also a distinguished observer and an amazingly accurate forecaster of events, with an even dozen books—each of them thoughtful and perceptive—was beside the point. He was in *her* job. It had been promised to her while Fowler had still been a longshot candidate. The compromise that had placed Alden in his West Wing corner office and her in the basement was merely another of those acts that political figures use as excuses to violate their word without anything more than a perfunctory apology. The Vice President had demanded and gotten the concession at the convention; he'd also gotten what should have been her office on the main level for one of his own people, relegating her to this most prestigious of dungeons. In return for that, the Veep was a team player, and his tireless campaigning was widely regarded as having made the difference. The Vice President had delivered California, and without California, J. Robert Fowler would still be governor of Ohio. And so she had a twelve-by-fifteen office in the basement, playing secretary and/or administrative assistant to a goddamned Yalie who appeared once a month on the Sunday talk shows and hobnobbed with chiefs of state with her as lady-in-goddamned-waiting.

Dr. Elizabeth Elliot was in her normal early-morning mood, which was foul, as any White House regular could testify. She walked out of her office and into the White House Mess for a refill of her coffee cup. The strong drip coffee only made her mood the fouler, a thought that stopped her in her tracks and forced a self-directed smile she never bothered displaying for any of the security personnel who checked her pass every morning at the west ground-level entrance. They were just cops, after all, and cops were nothing to get excited about. Food was served by Navy stewards, and the only good thing about them was that they were largely minorities, many Filipinos in what she deemed a disgraceful carryover from America's colonial-exploitation period. The long-service secretaries and other support personnel were not political, hence mere bureaucrats of one description or another. The important people in this building were political. What little charm E.E. had was saved for them. The Secret Service agents observed her movements with about as much interest as they might have accorded the President's dog, if he'd had a dog, which he didn't. Both they and the professionals who ran the White House, despite the arrivals and departures of various self-inflated egos in human form, regarded her as just another of many politically elevated individuals who would depart in due course while the pros stayed on, faithfully doing their duty in accordance with their oaths of office. The White House caste system was an old one, with each regarding all the others as less than itself.

Elliot returned to her desk and set her coffee down to get a good stretch. The swivel chair was comfortable—the physical arrangements here were first-rate, far better than those at Bennington—but the endless weeks of early mornings and late nights had taken a physical toll in addition to that on her character. She told herself that she ought to return to working out. At least to walk. Many staffers took part of lunch to pace up and down the mall. The more energetic even jogged. Some female staffers took to jogging with military officers detailed to the building, especially the single ones, doubtless drawn to the short haircuts and simplistic mentalities that attached to uniformed service. But E.E. didn't have time for that, and so she settled for a stretch before sitting down with a muttered curse. Department head at America's most important women's college, and here she was playing secretary to a goddamned Yalie. But bitching didn't ever fix things, and she went back to work.

She was halfway through the *Bird,* and flipped to a new page as she picked up her yellow highlighting pen. The articles were unevenly set. Almost all were just crooked enough on the redacted pages to annoy, and E.E. was a pathologically neat person. At the top of page eleven was a small piece from the *Hartford Courant.* ALDEN PATERNITY CASE read the headline. Her coffee mug stopped in midflight.

What?

> Suit papers will be filed this week in New Haven by Ms. Marsha Blum, alleging that her newly born daughter was fathered by Professor Charles W. Alden, former Chairman of the Department of History at Yale, and currently National Security Advisor to President Fowler. Claiming a two-year relationship with Dr. Alden, Ms. Blum, herself a doctoral candidate in Russian history, is suing Alden for lack of child support. . . .

"That randy old goat," Elliot whispered to herself.

And it was true. That thought came to her in a blazing moment of clarity. It had to be. Alden's amorous adventures were already the subject of humorous columns in the *Post.* Charlie chased skirts, slacks, any garment that had a woman inside it.

Marsha Blum . . . Jewish? Probably. The jerk was banging one of his doctoral students. Knocked her up even. I wonder why she just didn't get an abortion and be done with it? I bet he dumped her, and she was so mad . . .

Oh, God, he's scheduled to fly to Saudi Arabia later today . . .

We can't *let that happen . . .*

The idiot. No warning, none. He didn't talk to anyone about it. He couldn't have. I would have heard. Secrets like that last about as long as they take to repeat in the lavatory. What if he hadn't even known himself? Could this Blum girl be that angry with Charlie? That resulted in a smirk. *Sure she could.*

Elliot lifted her phone . . . and paused for a moment. You didn't just call the President in his bedroom. Not for just anything. Especially not when you stood to make a personal gain from what happened.

On the other hand . . .

What would the Vice President say? Alden was really his man. But the VP was pretty strait-laced. Hadn't he warned Charlie to keep a lower profile on his womanizing? Yes, three months ago. The ultimate political sin. He'd gotten caught. Not with his hand in the cookie jar either. That brought out a short bark of a laugh. *Shtuping* one of his seminar girls! What an asshole! And this guy was telling the President how to conduct affairs of state. That almost unleashed a giggle.

Damage control.

The feminists would freak. They'd ignore the stupidity of the Blum girl for not taking care of her unwanted—was it?—pregnancy in the feminist way. After all, what was "pro-choice" all about? She'd made her choice, period. To the feminist community it was simply a case of a male turd who had exploited a sister and was now employed by a supposedly pro-feminist President.

The antiabortion crowd would also disapprove . . . even more violently. They'd recently done something intelligent, which struck Elizabeth Elliot as nothing short of miraculous. Two stoutly conservative senators were sponsoring legislation to compel "illegitimate fathers" to support their irregular offspring. If abortion was to be outlawed, it had finally occurred to those Neanderthals that someone had to do something about the unwanted children. Moreover, that crowd was on another morality kick, and they were kicking the Fowler Administration for a number of reasons already. To the right-wing nuts, Alden would just be another irresponsible lecher, a white one—so much the better—and one in an administration they loathed.

E.E. considered all the angles for several minutes, forcing herself to be dispassionate, examining the options, thinking it through from Alden's angle. What could he do? Deny it was his? Well, a genetic testing would establish that, and that was gutsball, something for which Alden probably didn't have the stomach. If he admitted it . . . well, clearly he couldn't marry the girl (the article said she was only twenty-four). Supporting the child would be an admission of paternity, a gross violation of academic integrity. After all, professors weren't supposed to bed their students. That it happened, as E.E. well knew, was besides the point. As with politics, the rule in academia was to avoid detection. What might be the subject of a hilarious anecdote over a faculty lunch table became infamy in the public press.

Charlie's gone, and what timing . . .

E.E. punched the number to the upstairs bedroom.

"The President, please. This is Dr. Elliot calling." A pause while the Secret Service agent asked if the President would take the call. *God, I hope I didn't catch him on the crapper!* But it was too late to worry about that.

The hand came off the mouthpiece at the other end of the circuit. Elliot heard the whirring sound of the President's shaver, then a gruff voice.

"What is it, Elizabeth?"

"Mr. President, we have a little problem I think you need to see right away."

"Right away?"

"Now, sir. It's potentially damaging. You'll want Arnie there also."

"It's not the proposal that we're—"

"No, Mr. President. Something else. I'm not kidding. It's potentially very serious."

"Okay, come on up in five minutes. I presume you can wait for me to brush my teeth?" A little presidential humor.

"Five minutes, sir."

The connection was broken. Elliot set the phone down slowly. Five minutes. She'd wanted more time than that. Quickly she took her makeup case from a desk drawer and hurried off to the nearest bathroom. A quick look in the mirror . . . no, first she had to take care of the morning coffee. Her stomach told her that an antacid tablet might be a good idea, too. She did that, then rechecked her hair and face. They'd do, she decided. Just some minor repairs to her cheek highlights. . . .

Elizabeth Elliot, Ph.D., walked stiffly back to her office and took another thirty seconds to compose herself before lifting *The Early Bird* and leaving for the elevator. It was already at the basement level, the door open. It was manned by a Secret Service agent who smiled good morning at the arrogant bitch only because he was inveterately polite, even to people like E.E.

"Where to?"

Dr. Elliot smiled most charmingly. "Going up," she told the surprised agent.

5. Changes and Guards

Ryan stayed in VIP quarters at the U.S. Embassy, waiting for the clock hands to move. He was taking Dr. Alden's place in Riyadh, but since he was visiting a prince, and princes don't like their calendars rearranged any more than the next man, he had to sit tight while the clock simulated Alden's flight time across the world to where Ryan was. After three hours he got tired of watching satellite TV, and took a walk, accompanied by a discreet security guard. Ordinarily Ryan would have availed himself of the man's services as a tour guide, but not today. Now he wanted his brain in neutral. It was his first time in Israel and he wanted his impressions to be his own while his mind played over what he'd been watching on TV.

It was hot here on the streets of Tel Aviv, and hotter still where he was going, of course. The streets were busy with people scurrying about shopping or pursuing business. There was the expected number of police about, but more discordant was the occasional civilian toting an Uzi sub-machine gun, doubtless on his—or her—way to or from a reserve meeting. It was the sort of thing to shock an American antigun nut (or warm the heart of a pro-gun nut). Ryan figured that the weapons display probably knocked the hell out of purse-snatching and street crime. Ordinary civil crime, he knew, was pretty rare here. But terrorist bombings and other less pleasant acts were not. And things were getting worse instead of better. That wasn't new either.

The Holy Land, sacred to Christians, Muslims, and Jews, he thought. Historically, it had the misfortune to be at the crossroads between Europe and Africa on one hand—the Roman, Greek, and Egyptian empires—and Asia on the other—the Babylonians, Assyrians, and Persians—and one constant fact in military history is that a crossroads is always contested by somebody. The rise of Christianity, followed 700 years later by the rise of Islam, hadn't changed matters very much, though it had redefined the teams somewhat and given wider religious significance to the crossroads already contested for three millennia. And that only made the wars all the more bitter.

It was easy to be cynical about it. The First Crusade, 1096, Ryan thought it was, had mainly been about extras. Knights and nobles were passionate people and produced more offspring than their castles and associated cathedrals could support. The son of a noble could hardly take up farming, and those not eliminated by childhood disease had to go *somewhere*. And when Pope Urban II had sent out his message that the infidels had overrun the land of Christ, it became possible for men to launch a war of aggression to reclaim land of religious importance *and* to find themselves fiefdoms to rule, peasants to oppress, and trade routes to the Orient on which to sit and charge their tolls. Whichever objective might have been the more important probably differed from one heart to another, but they all had known of both. Jack wondered how many different kinds of feet had trodden on these streets, and how they had reconciled their personal-political-commercial objectives with their putatively holy cause. Doubtless the same had been true of Muslims, of course, since three hundred years after Mohammed the venal had doubtless added their ranks to those of the devout, just as it had happened in Christianity. Stuck in the middle were the Jews, those not scattered by the Romans, or those who had found their way back. The Jews had probably been treated more brutally by the Christians back in the early second millennium, something else which had since changed, probably more than once.

Like a bone, an immortal bone fought over by endless packs of hungry dogs.

But the reason the bone was not ever destroyed, the reason the dogs kept coming back over the span of centuries was what the land represented. So much history. Scores of historical figures had been here, including the Son of God, as the Catholic part of Ryan believed. Beyond the significance of the very location, this narrow land bridge between continents and cultures, were thoughts and ideals and hopes that lived in the minds of men, somehow embodied in the sand and stones of a singularly unattractive place that only a scorpion could really love. Jack supposed that there were five great religions in the world, only three of which had really spread beyond their own point of origin. Those three had their home within a few miles of where he stood.

So, of course, this is where they fight wars.

The blasphemy was stunning. Monotheism had been born here, hadn't it? Starting with the Jews, and built upon by Christians and Muslims, here was the place where the idea had caught on. The Jewish people—Israelites seemed too strange a term—had defended their faith with stubborn ferocity for thousands of years, surviving everything the animists and pagans could throw at them, and then facing their sternest tests at the hands of religions grown on the ideas that they had defended. It hardly seemed fair—it wasn't fair at all, of course—but religious wars were the most barbaric of all. If one were fighting for God Himself, then one could do nearly anything. One's enemies in such a war were also fighting against God, a hateful and damnable thing. To dispute the authority of Authority itself—well, each soldier could see himself as God's own avenging sword. There could be no restraint. One's actions to chastise the enemy/sinner were sanctioned as thoroughly as anything could be. Rapine, plunder, slaughter, all the basest crimes of man would become something more than a right—made into a duty, a Holy Cause, not sins at all. Not just being paid to do terrible things, not just sinning because sin felt good, but being told that you could literally get away with anything, because God really was on your side. They even took it to the grave. In England, knights who had served in the Crusades were buried under stone effigies whose legs were crossed instead of sitting side by side—the mark of a holy crusader—so that all eternity could know that they'd served their time in God's name, wetting their swords in children's blood, raping anything that might have caught their lonely eyes, and stealing whatever wasn't set firmly in the ground. All sides. The Jews mainly as victims, but taking their part on the hilt end of the sword when they got the chance, because all men are alike in their virtues and vices.

The bastards must have loved it, Jack thought bleakly, watching a traffic cop settling a dispute at a busy corner. *There must have been some genuinely good men back then. What did they do? What did they think? I wonder what God thought?*

But Ryan wasn't a priest or a rabbi or an imam. Ryan was a senior intelligence officer, an instrument of his country, an observer and reporter of information. He continued looking around, and forgot about history for the moment.

The people were dressed for the oppressive heat, and the bustle of the streets made him think of Manhattan. So many of them had portable radios. He passed a sidewalk restaurant and saw no less than ten people listening to an hourly news broadcast. Jack had to smile at that. His kind of people. When driving his car, the radio was always tuned to an all-news D.C. station. The eyes he saw flickered about. The level of alertness was so pervasive that it took him a few moments to grasp it. Like the eyes of his own security guard. Looking for trouble. Well, that made sense. The incident on Temple Mount had not sparked a wave of violence, but such a wave was expected—it did not surprise Ryan that the people in his sight failed to recognize the greater threat to them that came from the absence of violence. Israel had a myopia of outlook that was not hard to comprehend. The Israelis, surrounded by countries that had every reason to see the Jewish state immolated, had elevated paranoia to an art form, and national security to an obsession. One thousand nine hundred years after Masada and the diaspora, they'd returned to a land they'd consecrated, fleeing oppression and genocide . . . only to invite more of the same. The difference was that they now held the sword, and had well and truly learned its use. But that, too, was a dead end. Wars were supposed to end in peace, but none of their wars had really ended. They'd stopped, been interrupted, no more than that. For Israel, peace had been nothing more than an intermission, time to bury the dead and train the next class of fighters. The Jews had fled from near-extermination at Christian hands, betting their existence on their ability to defeat Muslim nations that had at once voiced their desire to finish what Hitler had started. And God probably thought exactly what He had thought during the Crusades. Unfortunately, parting seas and fixing the sun in the sky seemed to be things of the Old Testament. Men were supposed to settle things now. But men didn't always do what they were supposed to do. When Thomas More had written *Utopia,* the state in which men acted morally in all cases, he had given both the place and the book the same title. The meaning of "Utopia" is "Noplace." Jack shook his head and turned a corner down another street of white-painted stucco buildings.

"Hello, Dr. Ryan."

The man was in his middle fifties, shorter than Jack, and more heavyset. He had a full beard, neatly trimmed, but speckled with gray, and looked less like a Jew than a unit commander in Sennacherib's Assyrian army. A broadsword or mace would not have been out of place in his hand. Had he not been smiling, Ryan would have wanted John Clark at his side.

"Hello, Avi. Fancy meeting you here."

General Abraham Ben Jakob was Ryan's counterpart in the Mossad, assistant director of the Israeli foreign-intelligence agency. A serious player in the intelligence trade, Avi had been a professional army officer until 1968, a paratrooper with extensive special-operations experience who'd been talent-scouted by Rafi Eitan and brought into the fold. His path had crossed Ryan's half a dozen times in the past few years, but always in Washington. Ryan had the utmost respect for Ben Jakob as a professional. He wasn't sure what Avi thought of him. General Ben Jakob was very effective at concealing his thoughts and feelings.

"What is the news from Washington, Jack?"

"All I know is what I saw on CNN at the embassy. Nothing official yet, and even if there were, you know the rules better than I do, Avi. Is there a good place to eat around here?"

That had already been planned, of course. Two minutes and a hundred yards later, they were in the back room of a quiet mom-and-pop place where both men's security guards could keep an eye on things. Ben Jakob ordered two Heinekens.

"Where you're going, they do not serve beer."

"Tacky, Avi. Very tacky," Ryan replied after his first sip.

"You are taking Alden's place in Riyadh, I understand."

"How could the likes of me ever take Dr. Alden's place anywhere?"

"You will be making your presentation about the same time Adler makes his. We are interested to hear it."

"In that case you will not mind waiting, I guess."

"No preview, not even one professional to another?"

"Especially not one professional to another." Jack drank his beer right out of the bottle. The menu, he saw, was in Hebrew. "Guess I'll have to let you order. . . . That damned fool!" *I've been left holding the bag before, but never one this big.*

"Alden." It was not a question. "He's *my* age. Good God, he should know that experienced women are both more reliable and more knowledgeable." Even in affairs of the heart, his terminology was professional.

"He might even pay more attention to his wife."

Ben Jakob grinned. "I keep forgetting how Catholic you are."

"That's not it, Avi. What lunatic wants more than *one* woman in his life?" Ryan asked deadpan.

"He's gone. That's the evaluation of our embassy." *But what does that mean?*

"Maybe so. Nobody asked me for an opinion. I really respect the guy. He gives the President good advice. He listens to us, and when he disagrees with the Agency, he generally has a good reason for doing so. He caught *me* short on something six months back. The man is brilliant. But playing around like that . . . well, I guess we all have our faults. What a damn-fool reason to lose a job like that. Can't keep his pants zipped." *And what timing,* Jack raged at himself.

"Such people cannot be in government service. They are too easy to compromise."

"The Russians are getting away from honey traps . . . and the girl was Jewish, wasn't she? One of yours, Avi?"

"*Doctor* Ryan! Would *I* do such a thing?" If a bear could laugh, it would have sounded like Avi Ben Jakob's outburst.

"Can't be your operation. There was evidently no attempt at blackmail." Jack nearly crossed the line with that one. The General's eyes narrowed.

"It was not our operation. You think us mad? Dr. Elliot will replace Alden."

Ryan looked up from his beer. He hadn't thought about that. *Oh, shit . . .*

"Both your friend and ours," Avi pointed out.

"How many government ministers have you disagreed with in the last twenty years, Avi?"

"None, of course."

Ryan snorted and finished off the bottle. "What was that you said earlier, the part about one professional to another, remember?"

"We both do the same thing. Sometimes, when we are very lucky, they listen to us."

"And some of the times they listen to us, we're the ones who're wrong. . . ."

General Ben Jakob didn't alter his steady, relaxed gaze into Ryan's face when he heard that. It was yet another sign of Ryan's growing maturity. He genuinely liked Ryan as a man and as a professional, but personal likes and dislikes had little place in the intelligence trade. Something fundamental was happening. Scott Adler had been to Moscow. Both he and Ryan had visited Cardinal D'Antonio in the Vatican. As originally planned, Ryan was supposed to backstop Adler here with the Israeli Foreign Ministry, but Alden's astounding *faux pas* had changed that.

Even for an intelligence professional, Avi Ben Jakob was a singularly well-informed man. Ryan waffled on the question of whether or not Israel was America's most dependable ally in the Middle East. That was to be expected from an historian, Avi judged. Whatever Ryan thought, most Americans did regard Israel that way, and as a result, Israelis heard more from inside the American government than any other country—more even than the British, who had a formal relationship with the American intelligence community.

Those sources had informed Ben Jakob's intelligence officers that Ryan was behind what was going on. That seemed incredibly unlikely. Jack was very bright, almost as smart as Alden, for example, but Ryan had also defined his own role as a servant, not a master, an implementer of policy, not a maker of it. Besides, the American President did not like Ryan, and had not hidden the fact from his inner circle. Elizabeth Elliot was reported to hate him, Avi knew. Something that had happened before the election, an imagined slight, a harsh word. Well, government ministers were notoriously touchy. *Not like Ryan and me,* General Ben Jakob thought. Both he and Ryan had faced death more than once, and perhaps that was their bond. They didn't have to agree on everything. There was respect between them.

Moscow, Rome, Tel Aviv, Riyadh. What could he deduce from that?

Scott Adler was Secretary of State Talbot's picked man, a highly skilled professional diplomat. Talbot was also bright. President Fowler might not have been terribly impressive, but he had selected superior cabinet officers and personal advisers. Except for Elliot, Avi corrected himself. Talbot used Deputy Secretary Adler to do his important advance work. And when Talbot himself entered formal negotiations, Adler was always at his side.

The most amazing thing, of course, was that not one of the Mossad's informants had a clue what was going on. *Something important in the Middle East,* they said. *Not sure what . . . I heard that Jack Ryan at the Agency had something to do with it. . . .* End of report.

It should have been infuriating, but Avi was used to that. Intelligence was a game where you never saw all the cards. Ben Jakob's brother was a pediatrician with similar problems. A sick child rarely told him what was wrong. Of course, his brother could always ask, or point, or probe. . . .

"Jack, I must tell my superiors something," General Ben Jakob said plaintively.

"Come on, General." Jack turned and waved for another beer. "Tell me, what the hell happened on the Mount?"

"The man was—is deranged. In the hospital they have a suicide watch on him. His wife had just left him, he came under the influence of a religious fanatic, and . . ." Ben Jakob shrugged. "It was terrible to see."

"That's true, Avi. Do you have any idea the political fix you're in now?"

"Jack, we've been dealing with this problem for—"

"I thought so. Avi, you are one very bright spook, but you do not know what's happening this time. You really don't."

"So tell me."

"I didn't mean that and you know it. What happened a couple days ago has changed things forever, General. You must know that."

"Changed to what?"

"You're going to have to wait. I have my orders, too."

"Does your country threaten us?"

"Threaten? That will never happen, Avi. How could it?" Ryan warned himself that he was talking too much. *This guy is good,* Jack reminded himself.

"But you cannot dictate policy to us."

Jack bit off his reply. "You're very clever, General, but I still have my orders. You have to wait. I'm sorry that your people in D.C. can't help you, but neither can I."

Ben Jakob changed tack yet again. "I'm even buying you a meal, and my country is not so rich as yours."

Jack laughed at his tone. "Good beer, too, and as you say, I can't do this where you say I'm going. If that's where I'm going. . . ."

"Your air crew has already filed the flight plan. I checked."

"So much for secrecy." Jack accepted the new bottle with a smile for the waiter. "Avi, let it rest for a while. Do you really think that we'd do anything to compromise your country's security?"

Yes! the General thought, but he couldn't say that of course. Instead he said nothing. But Ryan wasn't buying, and used the silence to change the course of the discussion himself.

"I hear you're a grandfather now."

"Yes. My daughter added to the gray in my beard. A daughter of her own. Leah."

"You have my word: Leah will have a secure country to grow up in, Avi."

"And who will see to that?" Ben Jakob asked.

"The same people who always have." Ryan congratulated himself for the answer. The poor guy really was desperate for information, and he was sad that Avi had made it so obvious. *Well, even the best of us can be pushed into corners. . . .*

Ben Jakob made a mental note to have the file on Ryan updated. The next time they met, he wanted to have better information. The General wasn't a man who enjoyed losing at anything.

Dr. Charles Alden contemplated his office. He wasn't leaving quite yet, of course. It would harm the Fowler Administration. His resignation, signed and sitting on the green desk blotter, was for the end of the month. But that was just for show. As of today, his duties were at an end. He'd show up, read the briefing papers, scribble his notes, but Elizabeth Elliot would do the briefs now. The President had been regretful, but his usual cool self. *Sorry to lose you, Charlie, really sorry, especially now, but I'm afraid there's just no other way. . . .* He'd managed to retain his dignity in the Oval Office despite the rage he'd felt. Even Arnie van Damm had been human enough to observe, "Oh, shit, Charlie!" Though enraged at the political damage to his boss, van Damm had at least mixed a little humanity and locker-room sympathy with his anger. But not Bob Fowler, champion of the poor and the helpless.

It was worse with Liz. That arrogant bitch, with her silence and her eloquent eyes. She'd get the credit for what he had done. She knew it, and was already basking in it.

The announcement would be made in the morning. It had already been leaked to the press. By whom was anyone's guess. Elliot, displaying her satisfaction? Arnie van Damm, in a rapid effort at damage control? One of a dozen others?

The transition from power to obscurity comes fast in Washington. The embarrassed look on the face of his secretary. The forced smiles of the other bureaucrats in the West Wing. But obscurity comes only after a blaze of publicity to announce the fact: like the flare of light from an exploding star, public death is preceded by dazzling fanfare. That was the media's job. The phone was ringing off the hook. There had been twenty of them waiting outside his house in the morning, cameras at the ready, sunlike lights blazing in his face. And knowing what it had to be even before the first question.

That foolish little bitch! With her cowlike eyes and cowlike udders and broad, cowlike hips. How could he have been so stupid! Professor Charles Winston Alden sat in his expensive chair and stared at his expensive desk. His head was bursting with a headache that he attributed to stress and anger. And he was right. But he failed to allow for the fact that his blood pressure was nearly double what it should have been, driven to new heights by the stress of the moment. He similarly failed to consider the fact that he had not taken his antihypertensive medication in the past week. A prototypical professor, he was always forgetting the little things while his methodical mind picked apart the most intricate of problems.

And so it came as a surprise. It started at an existing weakness in part of the Circle of Willis, the brain's own blood-beltway. Designed to get blood to any part of the brain, as a means of bypassing vessels that might become blocked with age, the vessel carried a huge amount of blood. Twenty years of high blood pressure, and twenty years of his taking his medication only when he remembered that he had an upcoming doctor's appointment, and the added stress of seeing his career stop with a demeaning personal disgrace, culminated in a rupture of the vessel on the right side of his head. What had been a searing migraine headache became death itself. Alden's eyes opened wide, and his hands flew up to grasp his skull as though to hold it together. It was too late for that. The rip widened, allowing more blood to escape. This both deprived important parts of his brain of the oxygen needed to function and further boosted intracranial pressure to the point that other brain cells were squeezed to extinction.

Though paralyzed, Alden did not lose consciousness for quite some time, and his brilliant mind recorded the event with remarkable clarity. Already unable to move, he knew that death was coming for him. *So close,* he thought, his mind racing to outrun death. *Thirty-five years to get here. All those books. All those seminars. The bright young students. The lecture circuit. The talk shows. The campaigns. All to get here. I was so close to accomplishing something important. Oh, God! To die* now, *to die like this!* But he knew that death was here, that he had to accept it. He hoped that someone would forgive him. He hadn't been a bad man, had he? He'd tried so hard to make a difference, to make the world a better place, and now on the brink of something really important . . . so much the better for everyone if this had happened while mounted on that foolish little cow . . . better still, he knew in one final moment, if his studies and his intellect had been his only pass—

Alden's disgrace and de facto firing determined the fact that his death would take long to discover. Instead of being buzzed by his secretary every few minutes, it took nearly an hour. Because she was intercepting all calls to him, none were forwarded. It would not have mattered in any case, though it would cause his secretary some guilt for weeks to come. Finally, when she was ready to leave for the day, she decided that she had to tell him so. She buzzed him over the intercom and got no response. Frowning, she paused, then buzzed him again. Still nothing. She next rose and walked to the door, knocking on it. Finally she opened it and screamed loudly enough that the Secret Service agents outside the Oval Office in the opposite corner of the building heard her. The first to arrive was Helen D'Agustino, one of the President's personal bodyguards, who'd been walking the corridors to loosen up after sitting most of the day.

"Shit!" And that fast her service revolver was out. She'd never seen so much blood in her life, all coming out of Alden's right ear and puddling on his desk. She shouted an alert over her radio transmitter. It had to be a head shot. Her sharp eyes swept the room, tracking over the front sight of her Model 19 Smith & Wesson. *Windows intact.* She darted across the room. *Nobody here. So, what then?*

Next she felt with her left hand for Alden's pulse on the carotid artery. Of course there was none, but training dictated that she had to check. Outside the room, all exits to the White House were blocked, guns were drawn, and visitors froze in their tracks. Secret Service agents were conducting a thorough check of the entire building.

"Goddamn!" Pete Connor observed as he entered the room.

"Sweep is complete!" a voice told both of them through their earpieces. "Building is clear. HAWK is secure." "Hawk" was the President's code name with the Secret Service. It displayed the agents' institutional sense of humor, both for its association with the President's name and its ironic dissonance with his politics.

"Ambulance is two minutes out!" the communications center added. They could get an ambulance faster than a helicopter.

"Stand easy, Daga," Connor said. "I think the man had a stroke."

"Move!" This was a Navy chief medical corpsman. The Secret Service agents were trained in first aid, of course, but the White House always had a medical team standing by, and the corpsman was first on the scene. He carried the sort of duffel bag carried by corpsmen in the field, but didn't bother opening it. There was just too much blood on the desk, he saw instantly, and the top of the puddle was congealing. The corpsman decided not to disturb the body—it was a potential crime scene, and the Secret Service guys had briefed him on that set of rules—most of the blood had come out Dr. Alden's right ear. There was a trickle from the left one also, and postmortem lividity was already starting in what parts of the face he could see. Diagnoses didn't come much easier than that.

"He's dead, probably been close to an hour, guys. Cerebral hemorrhage. Stroke. Isn't this guy a hypertensive?"

"Yeah, I think so," Special Agent D'Agustino said after a moment.

"You'll have to post him to be sure, but that's what he died of. Blowout."

A physician arrived next. He was a Navy captain, and confirmed his chief's observation.

"This is Connor, tell the ambulance to take it easy. PILGRIM is dead, looks like from natural causes. Repeat, PILGRIM is dead," the principal agent said over his radio.

The postmortem examination would check for many things, of course. Poison. Possible contamination of his food or water. But the White House environment was monitored on a continuous basis. D'Agustino and Connor shared a look. Yes, he had suffered from high blood pressure, and he sure as hell had had a bad day. Just about as bad as they get.

"How is he?" Heads turned. It was HAWK the President himself, with a literal ring of agents around him, pressing through the door. And Dr. Elliot behind him. D'Agustino made a mental note that they'd have to make up a new code name for her. She wondered if HARPY might suffice. Daga didn't like the bitch. No one on the Presidential Security Detail did. But they weren't paid to like her, or, for that matter, even to like the President.

"He's dead, Mr. President," the doctor said. "It appears he suffered a massive stroke."

The President took the news without a visible reaction. The Secret Service agents reminded themselves that he'd seen his wife through a multiyear battle against multiple sclerosis, finally losing her while still governor of Ohio. It must have drained the man, they thought, wanting it to be true. It must have stripped all of his emotions away. Certainly there were few emotions left in him. He made a clucking sound, and grimaced, and shook his head, and then he turned away.

Liz Elliot took his place, peering over the shoulder of an agent. Helen D'Agustino examined her face as Elliot pressed forward to get her look. Elliot liked to wear makeup, Daga knew, and she watched the new National Security Advisor pale beneath it. Certainly it was a horrible scene, D'Agustino knew. It looked as though a bucket of red paint had been spilled on the desk.

"Oh, God!" Dr. Elliot whispered.

"Out of the way, please!" called a new voice. It was an agent with a stretcher. He pushed Liz Elliot roughly out of the way. Daga noticed that she was too shocked to be angry at that, that her face was still very white, her eyes unfocused. She might think she's a tough bitch, Special Agent D'Agustino thought, but she's not as tough as she thinks. The thought gave the agent satisfaction.

Little weak at the knees, eh, Liz? Helen D'Agustino, one month out of the Secret Service Academy, had been out on a discreet surveillance when the subject—a counterfeiter—had "made" her and for some reason she'd never understood come out with a large automatic pistol. He'd even fired a round in her direction. No more than that, though. She'd earned her nickname, Daga, by drawing her S&W and landing three right in the poor bastard's ten-ring at a range of thirty-seven feet, just like a cardboard target at the range. Just that easy, too. She'd never even dreamed about it. And so Daga was one of the guys, a member of the Service pistol team when they'd outshot the Army's elite Delta Force commandos. Daga was tough. Clearly Liz Elliot was not, however arrogant she might be. *No guts, lady?* It did not occur to Special Agent Helen D'Agustino at that moment that Liz Elliot was HAWK's chief adviser for national security.

It had been a quiet meeting, the first such meeting that Günther Bock remembered. None of the blustering rhetoric so beloved of the revolutionary soldiers. His old comrade-in-arms, Ismael Qati, was normally a firebrand, eloquent in five languages, but Qati was subdued in every way, Bock saw. The ferocity of his smile was not there. The sweeping gestures that had always punctuated his words were more restrained, and Bock wondered if the man might not be feeling well.

"I grieved when I heard the news of your wife," Qati said, turning to personal matters for a moment.

"Thank you, my friend." Bock decided to put his best face on it: "It is a small thing compared to what your people have endured. There are always setbacks."

There were more than a few in this case, and both knew it. Their best weapon had always been solid intelligence information. But Bock's had dried up. The Red Army Faction had drawn for years on all sorts of information. Its own people within the West German government. Useful tidbits from the East German intelligence apparat, and all the Eastern Bloc clones of their common master, the KGB. Doubtless a good deal of their data had come from Moscow, routed through the smaller nations for political reasons that Bock had never questioned. After all, world socialism is itself a struggle with numerous tactical moves. *Used to be,* he corrected himself.

It was all gone now, the help upon which he'd been able to draw. The East Bloc intelligence services had turned on their revolutionary comrades like cur dogs. The Czechs and Hungarians had literally *sold* information on them to the West! The East Germans had given it away in the name of Greater German cooperation and brotherhood. East Germany—the German Democratic Republic—no longer existed. Now it was a mere appendage to capitalist Germany. And the Russians . . . Whatever indirect support they'd ever had from the Soviets was gone, possibly forever. With the demise of socialism in Europe, their sources within various government institutions had been rolled up, turned double agent, or simply stopped delivering, having lost their faith in a socialist future. At a stroke, the best and most useful weapon of the European revolutionary fighters had disappeared.

Fortunately, it was different here, different for Qati. The Israelis were as foolish as they were vicious. The one constant thing in the world, both Bock and Qati knew, was the inability of the Jews to make any kind of meaningful political initiative. Formidable as they were at the business of war, they had always been hopelessly inept at the business of peace. Added to that was their ability to dictate policy to their own masters as though they didn't want peace at all. Bock was not a student of world history, but he doubted that there was any precedent for such behavior as this. The ongoing revolt of both indigenous Israeli Arabs and Palestinian captives in the occupied territories was a bleeding sore on the soul of Israel. Once able to infiltrate Arab groups at will, Israeli police and domestic intelligence agencies were gradually being shut out, as popular support for this rebellion became more and more fixed in the minds of their enemies. At least Qati had an ongoing operation to command. Bock envied him that, however bad the tactical situation might be. Another perverse advantage for Qati was the efficiency of his enemy. Israeli intelligence had waged its shadow war against the Arab freedom fighters for two generations now. Over that time the foolish ones had died by the guns of Mossad officers. Those still alive, like Qati, were the survivors, the strong, clever, dedicated products of a Darwinian selection process.

"How are you dealing with informers?" Bock asked.

"We found one last week," Qati answered with a cruel smile. "He identified his case officer before he died. Now we have him under surveillance."

Bock nodded. Once the Israeli officer would merely have been assassinated, but Qati had learned. By watching him—very carefully and only intermittently—they might identify other infiltrators.

"And the Russians?" This question got a strong reaction.

"The pigs! They give us nothing of value. We are on our own. It has always been so." Qati's face showed what had today been rare animation. It came, then went, and the Arab's face lapsed back into enveloping fatigue.

"You seem tired, my friend."

"It has been a long day. For you also, I think."

Bock allowed himself a yawn and a stretch. "Until tomorrow?"

Qati rose with a nod, guiding his visitor to his room. Bock took his hand before retiring. They'd known each other for almost twenty years. Qati returned to the living room, and walked outside. His security people were in place and alert. Qati spoke with them briefly, as always, because loyalty resulted from attention to the needs of one's people. Then he too went to bed. He paused for evening prayers, of course. It troubled him vaguely that his friend Günther was an unbeliever. Brave, clever, dedicated though he was, he had no faith, and Qati did not understand how any man could carry on without that.

Carry on? Does he carry on at all? Qati asked himself as he lay down. His aching legs and arms at last knew rest, and though the pain in them didn't end, at least it changed. Bock was finished, wasn't he? Better for him if Petra had died at the hands of GSG-9. They must have wanted to kill her, those German commandos, but the rumor was that they they'd found her with a babe suckling on each breast, and you could not be a man and kill such a picture as that. Qati himself, for all his hatred for Israelis, could not do that. It would be an offense at God Himself. Petra, he thought, smiling in the dark. He'd taken her once, when Günther had been away. She'd been lonely, and he'd been hot-blooded from a successful operation in Lebanon, the killing of an Israeli adviser to the Christian militia, and so they'd shared their revolutionary fervor for two blazing hours.

Does Günther know? Did Petra tell him?

Perhaps she did. It wouldn't matter. Bock was not that sort of man, not like an Arab for whom it would have been a blood insult. Europeans were so casual about such things. It was a curiosity to Qati that they should be that way, but there were many curiosities in life. Bock was a true friend. Of that he was sure. The flame burned in Günther's soul as truly and brightly as it did in his own. It was sad that events in Europe had made life so hard on his friend. His woman caged. His children stolen. The very thought of it chilled Qati's blood. It was foolish of them to have brought children into the world. Qati had never married, and enjoyed the company of women rarely enough. In Lebanon ten years earlier, all those European girls, some in their teens even. He remembered with a quiet smile. Things no Arab girl would ever learn to do. So hot-blooded they'd been, wanting to show how dedicated they were. He knew that they had used him as surely as he'd used them. But Qati had been younger then, with a young man's passions.

Those passions were gone. He wondered if they would ever return. He hoped they would. He hoped mainly that he'd recover well enough that he'd have the energy for more than one thing. Treatment was going well, the doctor said. He was tolerating it much better than most. If he always felt tired, if the crippling bouts of nausea came from time to time, he mustn't be discouraged. That was normal—no, the normal way of things was not even so ''good'' as this. There was real hope, the doctor assured him on every visit. It wasn't merely the things any doctor would say to encourage his patient, the doctor had told him last week. He was truly doing well. He had a good chance. The important thing, Qati knew, was that he had something still to live for. He had purpose. That, he was sure, was the thing keeping him alive.

''What's the score?''

''Just carry on,'' Dr. Cabot replied over the secure satellite link. ''Charlie had a massive stroke at his desk.'' A pause. ''Maybe the best thing that could have happened to the poor bastard.''

''Liz Elliot taking over?''

''That's right.''

Ryan compressed his lips into a tight grimace, as though he'd just taken some particularly foul medicine. He checked his watch. Cabot had arisen early to make the call and give the instructions. He and his boss were not exactly friends, but the importance of this mission had overcome that. Maybe it would be the same with E.E., Ryan told himself.

"Okay, boss. I take off in ninety minutes, and we deliver our pitches simultaneously, as per the plan."

"Good luck, Jack."

"Thank you, Director." Ryan punched the Off button on the secure phone console. He walked out of the communications room and back to his room. His bag was already packed. All he had to do was knot his tie. The coat went over his shoulder. It was too hot here for that, and hotter still where he was going. He'd have to wear a coat there. It was expected, one of those curious rules of formal behavior that demanded the maximum discomfort to attain the proper degree of decorum. Ryan lifted his bag and left the room.

"Synchronize our watches?" Adler was waiting outside and chuckled.

"Hey, Scott, that isn't my idea!"

"It does make sense . . . kinda."

"I suppose. Well, I got an airplane to catch."

"Can't take off without you," Adler pointed out.

"One advantage to government service, isn't it?" Ryan looked up and down the corridor. It was empty, though he wondered if the Israelis had managed to bug it. If so, the Muzak might interfere with their bugs. "What do you think?"

"Even money."

"That good?"

"Yeah," Adler said with a grin. "This is the one, Jack. It was a good idea you had."

"Not just mine. I'll never get any credit for it anyway. Nobody'll ever know."

"We'll know. Let's get to work."

"Let me know how they react. Good luck, man."

"I think *mazeltov* is the proper expression." Adler took Ryan's hand. "Good flight."

The embassy limo took Ryan directly to the aircraft, whose engines were already turning. It had priority clearance to taxi, and was airborne in less than five minutes from the time he boarded. The VC-20B headed south, down the dagger-shape that was Israel, then east over the Gulf of Aqaba and into Saudi airspace.

As was his custom, Ryan stared out the window. His mind went over what he was supposed to do, but that had been rehearsed for over a week, and his brain could do that quietly while Ryan stared. The air was clear, the sky virtually cloudless as they flew over what was to all appearances a barren wasteland of sand and rock. What color there was came from stunted bushes too small to pick out individually, and had the general effect of an unshaven face. Jack knew that much of Israel looked exactly the same, as did the Sinai, where all those tank battles had been fought, and he found himself wondering why men chose to die for land like this. But they had, for almost as long as man had existed on the planet. Man's first organized wars had been fought here, and they hadn't stopped. At least not yet.

Riyadh, the capital of Saudi Arabia, is roughly in the center of that country, which is as large as all of America east of the Mississippi. The executive aircraft made a relatively fast descent, allowed by the modest amount of air traffic here, and the air was agreeably smooth as the pilot brought the aircraft low into the Riyadh International. In another few minutes the Gulfstream taxied toward the cargo terminal, and the attendant opened the forward door.

After two hours' exposure to air conditioning, Jack felt as though he'd stepped into a blast furnace. The shade temperature was over 110, and there was no shade. Worse, the sun reflected off the pavement, as though from a mirror, so intensely that Ryan's face stung from it. There to greet him was the deputy chief of mission at the embassy, and the usual security people. In a moment, he was sweating inside yet another embassy limo.

"Good flight?" the DCM asked.

"Not bad. Everything ready here?"

"Yes, sir."

It was nice to be called "sir," Jack thought. "Well, let's get on with it."

"My instructions are to accompany you as far as the door."

"That's right."

"You might be interested to know that we haven't had any press inquiries. D.C. has kept this one pretty quiet."

"That'll change in about five hours."

Riyadh was a clean city, though quite different from Western metropolises. The contrast with Israeli towns was remarkable. Nearly everything was new. Only two hours away, but that was by air. This place had never been the crossroads Palestine had been. The ancient trading routes had given the brutal heat of Arabia a wide berth, and though the coastal fishing and trading towns had known prosperity for millennia, the nomadic people of the interior had lived a stark existence, held together only by their Islamic faith, which was in turn anchored by the holy cities of Mecca and Medina. Two things had changed that. The British in the First World War had used this area as a diversion against Ottoman Turkey, drawing their forces here and away from sites which might have been of greater utility to their allies in Germany and Austria-Hungary. Then, in the 1930s, oil had been discovered. Oil in quantities so vast as to make Texas an apostrophe. With that, first the Arab world had changed, and then the whole world had soon followed.

From the first, the relationship between the Saudis and the West had been delicate. The Saudis were still a curious mixture of the primitive and the sophisticated. Some people on this peninsula were but a single generation from nomadic life that was little different from that of the wanderers of the Bronze Age. At the same time there was an admirable tradition of Koranic scholarship, a code that was harsh but scrupulously fair, and remarkably similar to the Talmudic traditions of Judaism. In a brief span of time these people had become accustomed to wealth beyond count or meaning. Viewed as comic wastrels by the "sophisticated" West, they were merely the newest entry in a long line of nouveau riche nations of which America had been a recent part. A nouveau riche himself, Ryan smiled at some of the buildings in sympathy. People with "old" money—earned by bumptious ancestors whose rough manners had long since been conveniently forgotten—were always uncomfortable around those who had made, not inherited, their comforts. As it was with individuals, so it was with nations. The Saudis and their Arab brethren were still learning how to be a nation, much less a rich and influential one, but the process was an exciting one for them and their friends. They'd had some easy lessons, and some very hard ones, most recently with their neighbors to the north. For the most part they had learned well, and now Ryan hoped that the next step would be as easily made. A nation achieves greatness by helping others to make peace, not by demonstrating prowess at war or commerce. To learn that, it had taken America from the time of Washington to the time of Theodore Roosevelt, whose Nobel Peace Prize adorned the wall in the White House room that still bore his name. *It took us almost a hundred twenty years,* Jack thought as the car turned and slowed. *Teddy got the Prize for arbitrating some little piss-ant border dispute, and we're asking these folks to help us settle the most dangerous flashpoint in the civilized world after merely fifty years of effective nationhood. What reason do we have to look down on these people?*

There is a choreography to occasions of state as delicate and as adamant as any ballet. The car—it used to be a carriage—arrives. The door is opened by a functionary—who used to be called a footman. The Official waits in dignified solitude while the Visitor alights from the car. The Visitor nods to the footman if he's polite, and Ryan was. Another, more senior, functionary first greets the Visitor, then conducts him to the Official. On both sides of the entryway are the official guards, who were in this case uniformed, armed soldiers. Photographers had been left out, for obvious reasons. Such affairs would be more comfortable in temperatures under a hundred degrees, but at least here there was shade from a canopy, as Ryan was conducted to his Official.

"Welcome to my country, Dr. Ryan." Prince Ali bin Sheik extended a firm hand to Jack.

"Thank you, Your Highness."

"Would you follow me?"

"Gladly, sir." *Before I melt.*

Ali led Jack and the DCM inside, where they parted ways. The building was a palace—Riyadh had quite a few palaces, since there were so many royal princes—but Ryan thought "working palace" might have been a more accurate term. It was smaller than the British counterparts Ryan had visited, and cleaner, Jack saw somewhat to his surprise. Probably because of the cleaner and dryer air of the region, which contrasted to the damp, sooty atmosphere of London. It was also air conditioned. The inside temperature could not have been far above eighty-five, which somehow seemed comfortable to Ryan. The Prince was dressed in flowing robes with a headdress held atop his head by a pair of circular—whats? Ryan wondered. He ought to have gotten briefed on that, Jack thought too late. Alden was supposed to have done this anyway. Charlie knew this area far better than he did, and—but Charlie Alden was dead, and Jack was carrying the ball.

Ali bin Sheik was referred to at State and CIA as a Prince-Without-Portfolio. Taller, thinner, and younger than Ryan, he advised the King of Saudi Arabia on foreign affairs and intelligence matters. Probably the Saudi intelligence service—British-trained—reported to him, but that was not as clear as it should have been, doubtless another legacy of the Brits, who took their secrecy far more seriously than Americans. Though the file on Ali was a thick one, it mainly dealt with his background. Educated at Cambridge, he'd become an Army officer, and continued his professional studies at Leavenworth and Carlisle Barracks in the United States. At Carlisle he'd been the youngest man in his class—a colonel at twenty-seven—to be a royal prince was career-enhancing—and finished third in a group whose top ten graduates had each gone on to command a division or equivalent post. The Army General who'd briefed Ryan on Ali remembered his classmate fondly as a young man of no mean intellectual gifts and superb command potential. Ali had played a major role in persuading the King to accept American aid during the Iraqi war. He was regarded as a serious player quick to make decisions and quicker still to express displeasure at having his time wasted, despite his courtly manners.

The Prince's office was easily identified by the two officers at the double doors. A third man opened them, bowing to both as they passed.

"I've heard much about you," Ali said casually.

"All good, I trust," Ryan replied, trying to be at ease.

Ali turned with an impish smile. "We have some mutual friends in Britain, Sir John. Do you keep current with your small-arms skills?"

"I really don't have the time, sir."

Ali waved Jack to a chair. "For some things one should make time."

Both sat, and things became formal. A servant appeared with a silver tray, and poured coffee for both men before withdrawing.

"I sincerely regret the news on Dr. Alden. For so fine a man to be brought down so foolishly . . . May God have mercy on his soul. At the same time, I have looked forward to meeting you for some time, Dr. Ryan."

Jack sipped at his coffee. It was thick, bitter, and hideously strong.

"Thank you, Your Highness. Thank you also for agreeing to see me in the place of a more senior official."

"The most effective efforts at diplomacy often begin informally. So how may I be of service?" Ali smiled and leaned back in his chair. The fingers of his left hand toyed with his beard. His eyes were as dark as flint, and though they seemed to gaze casually at his visitor, the atmosphere in the room was now businesslike. And that, Ryan saw, was fast enough.

"My country wishes to explore a means of—that is, the rough outline of a plan with which to alleviate tensions in this area."

"With Israel, of course. Adler, I presume, is delivering the same proposal to the Israelis at this moment?"

"Correct, Your Highness."

"That is dramatic," the Prince observed with an amused smile. "Do go on."

Jack began his pitch: "Sir, our foremost consideration in this matter must be the physical security of the State of Israel. Before either of us was born, America and other countries stood by and did very little to prevent the extermination of six million Jews. The guilt attending that infamy lies heavy on my country."

Ali nodded gravely before speaking. "I have never understood that. Perhaps you might have done better, but the strategic decisions made during the war by Roosevelt and Churchill were made in good faith. The issue with the shipload of Jews that nobody wanted prior to the outbreak of war, of course, is another issue entirely. I find it very strange indeed that your country did not grant asylum to those poor people. Fundamentally, however, no one saw what was coming, not the Jews, nor the Gentiles, and by the time it became clear what was happening, Hitler had physical control of Europe, and no direct intervention on your part was possible. Your leaders decided at that time that the best way to end the slaughter was to win the war as expeditiously as possible. That was logical. They might have made a political issue of the ongoing *Endlösung,* I believe the term was, but they decided that it would be ineffective from a practical point of view. That, in retrospect, was probably incorrect, but the decision was not made in malice." Ali paused to let his history lesson sink in for a moment. "In any case, we understand and conditionally accept the reasons behind your national goal to preserve the State of Israel. Our acceptance, as I am sure you will understand, is conditional upon your recognition of other people's rights. This part of the world is not composed of Jews and savages."

"And that, sir, is the basis of our proposal," Ryan replied. "If we can find a formula that recognizes those other rights, will you accept a plan in which America is the guarantor of Israeli security?'' Jack didn't have time to hold his breath for the reply.

''Of course. Have we not made that clear? Who else but America can guarantee the peace? If you must put troops in Israel to make them feel secure, if you must execute a treaty to formalize your guarantee, those are things we can accept, *but* what of Arab rights?''

''What is your view of how we should address those rights?'' Jack asked.

Prince Ali was stunned by the question. Was not Ryan's mission to present the American plan? He almost lapsed into anger, but Ali was too clever for that. It wasn't a trap he saw. It was a fundamental change in American policy.

''Dr. Ryan, you asked that question for a reason, but it was a rhetorical question nonetheless. I believe the answer to that question is yours to make.''

The answer took three minutes.

Ali shook his head sadly. ''That, Dr. Ryan, is something we would probably find acceptable, but the Israelis will never agree to it even though we might—more precisely, they would reject it for the very reason that we would accept it. They should agree to it, of course, but they will not.''

''Is it acceptable to your government, sir?''

''I must, of course, present it to others, but I think our response would be favorable.''

''Any objections at all?''

The Prince paused to finish his coffee. He stared over Ryan's head toward something on the far wall. ''We could offer several modifications, none of them really substantive to the central thesis of your scheme. Actually, I think the negotiations on those minor issues would be easily and quickly accomplished, since they are not matters of consequence to the other interested parties.''

''And who would be your choice for the Muslim representative?''

Ali leaned forward. ''That is simple. Anyone could tell you. The Imam of the Al-Aqusa Mosque is a distinguished scholar and linguist. His name is Ahmed bin Yussif. Ahmed is consulted by scholars throughout Islam for his opinions on matters of theology. Sunni, Shi'a, all defer to him on selected issues. He is even a Palestinian by birth.''

''That easy?'' Ryan closed his eyes and let out a breath. He'd guessed right on that one. Yussif was not exactly a political moderate, and had called for the expulsion of Israel from the West Bank. But he had also denounced terrorism per se on theological grounds. He wasn't quite perfect, but if the Muslims could live with him, he was perfect enough.

''You are very confident, Dr. Ryan.'' Ali shook his head. ''Too confident. I grant you that your plan is fairer than anything I or my government expected, but it will never happen.'' Ali paused again and fixed Ryan with his eyes. ''Now I must ask myself if this was ever a serious proposal, or merely something to give the appearance of fairness.''

''Your Highness, President Fowler addresses the United Nations General Assembly next Thursday. He will present this very plan then, live and in color. I am authorized to extend your government an invitation to the Vatican to negotiate the treaty formally.''

The Prince was sufficiently surprised by that that he lapsed into an Americanism: ''Do you really think you can bring this off?''

''Your Highness, we're going to give it one hell of a try.''

Ali rose and walked to his desk. There he lifted a phone, pushed a button and spoke rapidly and, to Ryan, incomprehensibly. Jack had a sudden, giddy moment of whimsy. The Arabic language, as with the Hebrew, went from right to left instead of left to right, and Ryan wondered how one's brain dealt with that.

Son of a BITCH, Jack thought to himself. *This just might work!*

Ali replaced the phone and turned to his visitor. "I think it is time for us to see His Majesty."

"That fast?"

"One advantage to our form of government is that when one government minister wishes access to another, it is merely a matter of calling a cousin or an uncle. We are a family business. I trust that your President is a man of his word."

"The UN speech is already written. I've seen it. He expects to take heat from the Israeli lobby at home. He's ready for that."

"I've seen them in action, Dr. Ryan. Even when we were fighting for our lives alongside American soldiers, they denied us weapons we needed for our own security. Do you think that will change?"

"Soviet communism is at an end. The Warsaw Pact is at an end. So many things that shaped the world I grew up in are gone, and gone forever. It's time to get rid of the rest of the turmoil in the world. You ask if we can do it—why not? Sir, the only constant factor in human existence is change." Jack knew that he was being outrageously confident, and wondered how Scott Adler was doing in Jerusalem. Adler wasn't a screamer, but he knew how to lay down the word. That hadn't been done with the Israelis for a long enough time that Jack didn't know when it had last been—or ever been—tried. But the President *was* committed to this. If the Israelis tried to stop it, they might just find out how lonely the world was.

"You forgot God, Dr. Ryan."

Jack smiled. "No, Your Highness. That's the point, isn't it?"

Prince Ali wanted to smile, but didn't. It wasn't time yet. He pointed to the door. "Our car is waiting."

At the New Cumberland Army Depot in Pennsylvania, the storage facility for standards and flags dating back to Revolutionary times, a brigadier general and a professional antiquarian laid flat on a table the dusty regimental colors once carried by the 10th United States Cavalry. The General wondered if some of the grit on the standard was left over from Colonel John Grierson's campaign against the Apaches. This standard would go to the regiment. It wouldn't see much use. Maybe once a year it would be taken out, but from this pattern a new one would be made. That this was happening at all was a curiosity. In an age of cutbacks, a new unit was forming. Not that the General objected. The 10th had a distinguished history, but had never gotten its fair shake from Hollywood, for example, which had made but a single movie about the Black regiments. For the 10th was one of four Black units—the 9th and 10th Cavalry, the 24th and 25th Infantry—each of which had played its part in settling the West. This regimental standard dated back to 1866. Its centerpiece was a buffalo, since the Indians who'd fought the troopers of the 10th thought their hair similar to the rough coat of an American bison. Black soldiers had been there at the defeat of Geronimo, and saved Teddy Roosevelt's ass on the charge up San Juan Hill, the General knew. It was about time that they got a little official recognition, and if the President had ordered it for political reasons, so what? The 10th had an honorable history, politics notwithstanding.

"Take a week," the civilian said. "I'll do this one personally. God, I wonder what Grierson would have thought of the TO & E for the Buffalos today!"

"It is substantial," the General allowed. He'd commanded the 11th Armored Cavalry Regiment a few years earlier. The Black Horse Cav was still in Germany, though he wondered how much longer that would last. But the historian was right. With 129 tanks, 228 armored personnel carriers, 24 self-propelled guns, 83 helicopters, and 5,000 troopers, a modern Armored Cavalry Regiment was in fact a reinforced brigade, fast-moving and very hard-hitting.

"Where are they going to be based?"

"The regiment will form up at Fort Stewart. After that, I'm not sure. Maybe it'll be the round-out for 18th Airborne Corps."

"Paint them brown, then?"

"Probably. The regiment knows about deserts, doesn't it?" The General felt the standard. Yeah, there was still grit in the fabric, from Texas, and New Mexico, and Arizona. He wondered if the troopers who had followed this standard knew that their outfit was being born anew. Maybe so.

6. Maneuvers

The Navy's change-of-command ceremony, little changed since the time of John Paul Jones, concluded on schedule at 11:24. It had been held two weeks earlier than expected, so that the departing skipper could more quickly assume the Pentagon duty that he would just as happily have avoided. Captain Jim Rosselli had brought USS *Maine* through the final eighteen months of her construction at General Dynamics' Electric Boat Division at Groton, Connecticut, through the launching and final outfitting, through builder's trials and acceptance trials, through commissioning, through shakedown and post-shakedown availability, through a day of practice missile shoots out of Port Canaveral, and through the Panama Canal for her trip to the missile-submarine base at Bangor, Washington. His last job had been to take the boat—*Maine* was huge, but in U.S. Navy parlance still a "boat"—on her first deterrence patrol into the Gulf of Alaska. That was over now, and, four days after returning his boat to port, he ended his association with the boat by turning her over to his relief, Captain Harry Ricks. It was slightly more complicated than that, of course. Missile submarines since the first, USS *George Washington*—long since converted to razor blades and other useful consumer items—had two complete crews, called "Blue" and "Gold." The idea was simply that the missile boats could spend more time at sea if the crews switched off duty. Though expensive, it worked very effectively. The "Ohio" class of fleet ballistic missile submarines was averaging over two-thirds of their time at sea, with continuing seventy-day patrols divided by twenty-five-day refit periods. Rosselli had, therefore, really given Ricks half of the command of the massive submarine, and full command of the "Gold" crew, which was now vacating the ship for the "Blue" crew, which would conduct the next patrol.

The ceremony concluded, Rosselli retired one last time to his stateroom. As the "plankowner" commanding officer, certain special souvenirs were his for the asking. A piece of teak decking material drilled for cribbage pegs was part of the tradition. That the skipper had never played cribbage in his life, after a single failed attempt, was beside the point. These traditions were not quite as old as Captain John Paul Jones, but were just as firm. His ball-cap, with *C.O.* and *Plankowner* emblazoned in gold on the back, would form part of his permanent collection, as would a ship's plaque, a photo signed by the entire crew, and various gifts from Electric Boat.

"God, I've wanted one of these!" Ricks said.

"They are pretty nice, Captain," Rosselli replied with a wistful smile. It really wasn't fair. Only the best of officers got to do what he'd done, of course. He'd had command of a fast-attack, USS *Honolulu,* whose reputation as a hot and lucky boat he had continued for his two-and-a-half-year tour as CO. Then he'd been given the Gold crew of USS *Tecumseh,* where he'd excelled yet again. This third—and most unusual—command tour had been necessarily abbreviated. His job had been to oversee the shipwrights at Groton, then get the boat "dialed in" for her first real team of COs. He'd only had the boat under way for—what? A hundred days, something like that. Just enough to get to know the girl.

"You're not making it any easier on yourself, Rosey," said the squadron commander, Captain (now a Rear Admiral Selectee) Bart Mancuso.

Rosselli tried to put humor in his voice. "Hey, Bart, one wop to another, show some pity, eh?"

"I hear ya', *paisan*. It isn't supposed to be easy."

Rosselli turned to Ricks. "Best crew I ever had. The XO is going to be one hell of a skipper when the time comes. The boat is fuckin' perfect. Everything works. The refit's a waste of time. The only thing on the gripe sheet that matters is the wiring in the wardroom pantry. Some yard electrician crossed a few cables, and the breakers aren't labeled right. Regs say we have to reset the wiring instead of relabeling the breakers. And that's it. *Nothing* else."

"Power plant?"

"Four-point-oh, people and equipment. You've seen the results of the ORSE, right?"

"Um-hum." Ricks nodded. The ship had scored almost perfectly on the Operational Reactor Safeguards Examination, which was the Holy Grail of the nuclear community.

"Sonar?"

"The equipment is the best in the fleet—we got the new upgrade before it became standard. I worked a deal with the guys at SubGru Two right before we commissioned. One of your old guys, Bart. Dr. Ron Jones. He's with Sonosystems, even rode for a week with us. The ray-path analyzer is like magic. Torpedo department needs a little work, but not much. I figure they can knock another thirty seconds off their average time. A young chief—matter of fact that department's pretty young across the board. Hasn't quite settled in yet, but they're not much slower than the guys I had on *Tecumseh,* and if I'd had a little more time I could have gotten them completely worked up."

"No sweat," Ricks observed comfortably. "Hell, Jim, I have to have something to do. How many contacts did you have on the patrol?"

"One Akula-class, the *Admiral Lunin*. Picked her up three times, never closer than sixty thousand yards. If he got a sniff of us—hell, he didn't. Never turned towards us. We held him for sixteen hours once. Had really good water, and, well''—Rosselli smiled—''I decided to trail him for a while, way the hell away, of course.''

''Once a fast-attack, always a fast-attack,'' Ricks said with a grin. He was a lifelong boomer driver, and the idea did not appeal to him, but what the hell, it wasn't a time to criticize.

''Nice profile you did on him,'' Mancuso put in, to show that he wasn't the least offended by Rosselli's action. ''Pretty good boat, isn't it?''

''The Akula? Too good. But not good enough,'' Rosselli said. ''I wouldn't start worrying until *we* find a way to track these mothers. I tried when I had *Honolulu,* against Richie Seitz on *Alabama*. He greased my ass for me. Only time that ever happened. I figure God could find an Ohio, but He'll have to have a good day.''

Rosselli wasn't kidding. The Ohio-class of missile submarines were more than just quiet. Their level of radiated noise was actually lower than the background noise level of the ocean, like a whisper at a rock concert. To hear them you had to get incredibly close, but to prevent that from happening, the Ohios had the best sonar systems yet devised. The Navy had done everything right with this class. The original contract had specified a maximum speed of 26–7 knots. The first Ohio had made 28.5. On builder's trials, *Maine* had made 29.1 due to a new and very slick super-polymer paint. The seven-bladed propeller enabled almost twenty knots without a hint of noisy cavitation, and the reactor plant operated in almost all regimes on natural convection circulation, obviating the need for potentially noisy feed-pumps. The Navy's mania for noise-control had reached its pinnacle in this class of submarine. Even the blades of the galley mixer were coated with vinyl to prevent metal-to-metal clatter. What Rolls-Royce was to cars, Ohio was to submarines.

Rosselli turned. ''Well, she's yours now, Harry.''

''You couldn't have set her up much better, Jim. Come on, the O-Club's open, and I'll buy you a beer.''

''Yeah,'' the former commanding officer observed with a husky voice. On the way out, members of the crew lined up to shake his hand one last time. By the time Rosselli got to the ladder, there were tears in his eyes. On the walk down the brow, they were running down his cheeks. Mancuso understood. It had been the same for him. A good CO developed a genuine love for his boat and his men, and for Rosselli it was worse still. He'd had his extra shots at command, more than even he had gotten, and that made the last one all the harder to leave. Like Mancuso, all Rosselli could look forward to now was a staff job, commanding a desk, nevermore to hold that godlike post of commanding officer of a ship of war. He'd be able to ride the boats, of course, to rate skippers, check ideas and tactics, but henceforth he'd be a tolerated visitor, never really welcome aboard. Most uncomfortable of all, he'd have to avoid revisiting his former command, lest the crew compare his command style to that of their new CO, possibly undermining the new man's command authority. It was, Mancuso reflected, like it must have been for immigrants, as it had been for his own ancestors, looking back one last time at Italy, knowing that they would never return to it, that their lives were irrevocably changed.

The three men climbed into Mancuso's staff car for the ride to the reception at the Officers Club. Rosselli set his souvenirs on the floor and extracted a handkerchief to wipe his eyes. *It isn't fair, just isn't fair. To leave command of a ship like this one to be a goddamned telephone operator at the NMCC. Joint service billet, my ass!* Rosselli blew his nose and contemplated the shore duty that the remainder of his active career held.

Mancuso looked away in quiet respect.

Ricks just shook his head. No need to get all that emotional about it. He was already making mental notes. The Torpedo Department wasn't up to speed yet, eh? Well, he'd do something about *that!* And the XO was supposed to be super-hot. Hmph. What skipper ever failed to praise his XO? If this guy thought he was ready for command, that meant an XO who might be a little *too* ready, and might not be totally supportive, might be feeling his oats. Ricks had had one of those already. Such XOs often needed some subtle reminders of who was boss. Ricks knew how to do that. The good news, the most important news, of course, was about the power plant. Ricks was a product of the Nuclear Navy's obsession with the nuclear power plant. It was something the Squadron Commander, Mancuso, was overly casual about, Ricks judged. The same was probably true of Rosselli. So, they'd passed their ORSE—so what? On *his* boats, the engineering crew had to be ready for an ORSE every goddamned day. One problem with these Ohios was that the systems worked so well people took things casually. That would be doubly true after maxing their ORSE. Complacency was the harbinger of disaster. And these fast-attack guys and their dumb mentality! *Tracking* an Akula, for God's sake! Even from sixty-K yards, what did this lunatic think he was doing?

Ricks' motto was that of the boomer community: WE HIDE WITH PRIDE (the less polite version was CHICKEN OF THE SEA). If they can't find you, they can't hurt you. Boomers weren't supposed to go around looking for trouble. Their job was to run from it. Missile submarines weren't actually combatant ships at all. That Mancuso didn't reprimand Rosselli on the spot was amazing to Ricks.

He had to consider that, however. Mancuso hadn't reprimanded Rosselli. He'd commended him.

Mancuso was his squadron commander, and did have those two Distinguished Service Medals. It wasn't exactly fair that Ricks was a boomer type stuck working for a fast-attack puke, but there it was. A charger himself, he was clearly a man who wanted aggressive skippers. And Mancuso was the guy who'd be doing his fitness reports. That was the central truth in the equation, wasn't it? Ricks was an ambitious man. He wanted command of a squadron, followed by a nice Pentagon tour, then he'd get his star as a Rear Admiral (Lower Half), then command of a Submarine Group—the one at Pearl would be nice; he liked Hawaii—after which he'd be very well suited for yet another Pentagon tour. Ricks was a man who'd mapped out his career path while still a lieutenant. So long as he did everything exactly by The Book, more exactly than anyone else, he'd stick to that path.

He hadn't quite planned on working for a fast-attack type, though. He'd have to adapt. Well, he knew how to do that. If that Akula showed up on his next patrol, he'd do what Rosselli had done—but better, of course. He had to. Mancuso would expect it, and Ricks knew that he was in direct competition with thirteen other SSBN COs. To get that squadron command, he had to be the best of fourteen. To be the best, he had to do things that would impress the squadron commander. Okay, so to keep his career path as straight as it had been for twenty years, he had to do a few new and different things. Ricks would have preferred not to, but career came first, didn't it? He knew that he was destined to have an Admiral's flag in the corner of his Pentagon office someday—someday soon. He'd make the adjustment. With an Admiral's flag came a staff, and a driver, and his own parking place in the acres of Pentagon blacktop, and further career-enhancing jobs that might, if he were very lucky, culminate in the E-Ring office of the CNO—better yet, Director of Naval Reactors, which was technically junior to the CNO, but carried with it eight full years in place. He knew himself better suited for that job, which was the one that set policy for the entire nuclear community. DNR wrote The Book. Everything he had to do was set forth in The Book. As the Bible was the path to salvation for Christian and Jew, The Book was the path to flag rank. Ricks knew The Book. Ricks was a brilliant engineer.

J. Robert Fowler was human after all, Ryan told himself. The conference was held upstairs, on the bedroom level of the White House, because the air conditioning in the West Wing was down for repairs, and the sun blasting through the windows of the Oval Office made that room uninhabitable. Instead they were using an upstairs sitting room, the one often delegated for the buffet line at those "informal" White House dinners that the President liked to have for "intimate" groups of fifty or so. The antique chairs were grouped around a largish dinner table in a room whose walls were decorated with a mural mélange of historical scenes. Moreover, it was a shirtsleeve environment. Fowler was a man uncomfortable with the trappings of his office. Once a federal prosecutor, an attorney who had not once defended a criminal before entering politics with both feet and never looking back, he'd grown up in an informal working environment and seemed to prefer a tie loose in his collar and sleeves rolled up to the elbow. It seemed so very odd to Ryan, who knew the President also to be priggish and stiff in his relationship with subordinates. Odder still, the President had walked into the room carrying the sports page from the *Baltimore Sun,* which he preferred to the local papers' sports coverage. President Fowler was a rabid football fan. The first NFL pre-season games were already history, and he was handicapping the teams for the coming season. The DDCI shrugged, leaving his coat on. There was as much complexity in this man as any other, Jack knew, and complexities were not predictable.

The President had discreetly cleared his calendar for this afternoon conference. Sitting at the head of the table, and directly under an air-conditioning vent, Fowler actually smiled a little as his guests took their places. At his left was G. Dennis Bunker, Secretary of Defense. Former CEO of Aerospace, Inc., Bunker was a former USAF fighter pilot who'd flown 100 missions in the early days of Vietnam, then left the service to found a company he'd ultimately built into a multibillion-dollar empire that sprawled across southern California. He'd sold that and all his other commercial holdings to take this job, keeping only one enterprise under his control—the San Diego Chargers. That retention had been the subject of considerable joshing during his confirmation hearings, and there was lighthearted speculation that Fowler liked Bunker mainly for his SecDef's love of football. Bunker was a rarity in the Fowler Administration, as close to a hawk as anyone here, a knowledgeable player in the defense area whose lectures to men in uniform were listened to. Though he'd left the Air Force as a captain, he'd left with three Distinguished Flying Crosses earned driving his F-105 fighter-bomber "downtown" into the environs of Hanoi. Dennis Bunker had seen the elephant. He could talk tactics with captains and strategy with generals. Both the uniforms and the politicians respected the SecDef, and that was rare.

Next to Bunker was Brent Talbot, Secretary of State. A former professor of political science at Northwestern University, Talbot was a longtime friend and ally of the President. Seventy years old, with regal white hair over a pale, intelligent face, Talbot was less an academic than an old-fashioned gentleman, albeit one with a killer instinct. After years of sitting on PFIAB—the President's Foreign Intelligence Advisory Board—and countless other commissions, he was in a place where he could make his impact felt. The archetypical outside-insider, he'd finally picked a winning horse in Fowler. He was also a man with genuine vision. The changes in the East-West relationship signaled to the SecState a historic opportunity to change the face of the world, and he wanted his name on the changes.

On the President's right was his Chief of Staff, Arnold van Damm. This was, after all, a political assembly, and political advice was of paramount import. Next to van Damm was Elizabeth Elliot, the new National Security Advisor. She looked rather severe today, Ryan noted, dressed in an expensive suit with a wispy cravat knotted around her pretty, thin neck. Beside her was Marcus Cabot, Director of Central Intelligence, and Ryan's immediate boss.

The second-rank people were farther away from the seat of power, of course. Ryan and Adler were at the far end of the table, both to separate them from the President and to allow their fuller visibility to the senior members of the conference when they began speaking.

"This your year, Dennis?" the President asked the SecDef.

"You bet it is!" Bunker said. "I've waited long enough, but with those two new linebackers, this year we're going to Denver."

"Then you'll meet the Vikings there," Talbot observed. "Dennis, you had the first draft pick, why didn't you take Tony Wills?"

"I have three good running backs. I needed linebackers, and that kid from Alabama is the best I've ever seen."

"You'll regret it," the Secretary of State pronounced. Tony Wills had been drafted from Northwestern. An academic All-American, Rhodes Scholar, winner of the Heisman Trophy, and the kid who had almost single-handedly resurrected Northwestern as a football school, Wills had been Talbot's prize student. By all accounts an exceptional young man, people were already talking about his future in politics. Ryan thought that premature, even in America's changing political landscape. "He'll kick your butt, third game of the season. And then again in the Super Bowl, if your team makes it that far, which I doubt, Dennis."

"We'll see," Bunker snorted.

The President laughed as he arranged his papers. Liz Elliot tried and failed to hide her disapproval, Jack noted from twenty feet away. Her papers were already arranged, her pen in its place to make notes, and her face impatient at the locker-room talk at her end of the table. Well, she had the job she'd angled for, even if it had taken a death—Ryan had heard the details by now—to get it for her.

"I think we'll call the meeting to order," President Fowler said. Noise in the room stopped cold. "Mr. Adler, could you fill us in on what happened on your trip?"

"Thank you, Mr. President. I would say that most of the pieces are in place. The Vatican agrees to the terms of our proposal unconditionally and is ready to host the negotiations at any time."

"How did Israel react?" Liz Elliot asked, to show that she was on top of things.

"Could have been better," Adler said neutrally. "They'll come, but I expect serious resistance."

"How serious?"

"Anything they can do to avoid being nailed down, they'll do. They are very uncomfortable with this idea."

"This was hardly unexpected, Mr. President," Talbot added.

"What about the Saudis?" Fowler asked Ryan.

"Sir, my read is that they'll play. Prince Ali was very optimistic. We spent an hour with the King, and his reaction was cautious but positive. Their concern is that the Israelis won't do it, no matter what pressure we put on them, and they are worried about being left hanging. Setting that aside for the moment, Mr. President, the Saudis appear quite willing to accept the plan as drafted, and to accept their participatory role in its implementation. They offered some modifications, which I outlined in my briefing sheet. As you can see, none of them are substantively troublesome. In fact, two of them look like genuine enhancements."

"The Soviets?"

"Scott handled that," Secretary Talbot replied. "They have signed off on the idea, but their read also is that Israel will not cooperate. President Narmonov cabled us day before yesterday that the plan is wholly compatible with his government's policy. They are willing to underwrite the plan to the extent that they will restrict arms sales to the other nations in the region to cover defensive needs only."

"Really?" Ryan blurted.

"That does clobber one of your predictions, doesn't it?" DCI Cabot noted with a chuckle.

"How so?" the President asked.

"Mr. President, arms sales to that area are a major cash cow for the Sovs. For them to reduce those sales will cost them billions in hard-currency earnings that they really need."

Ryan leaned back and whistled. "That is surprising."

"They also want to have a few people at the negotiations. That seems fair enough. The arms-sales aspect of the treaty—if we get that far—will be set up as a side-bar codicil between America and the Soviets."

Liz Elliot smiled at Ryan. She'd predicted that development.

"In return, the Soviets want some help on farm commodities, and a few trade credits," Talbot added. "It's cheap at the price. Soviet cooperation in this affair is hugely important to us, and the prestige associated with the treaty is important for them. It's a very equitable deal for the both of us. Besides, we have all that wheat lying around and doing nothing."

"So the only stumbling block is Israel?" Fowler asked the table. He was answered with nods. "How serious?"

"Jack," Cabot said, turning to his deputy, "how did Avi Ben Jakob react to things?"

"We had dinner the day before I flew to Saudi Arabia. He looked very unhappy. Exactly what he knew I do not know. I didn't give him very much to warn his government with, and—"

"What does 'not very much' mean, Ryan?" Elliot snapped down the table.

"Nothing," Ryan answered. "I told him to wait and see. Intelligence people don't like that. I would speculate that he knew something was up, but not what."

"The looks I got at the table over there were pretty surprised," Adler said to back Ryan up. "They expected something, but what I gave them wasn't it."

The Secretary of State leaned forward. "Mr. President, Israel has lived for two generations under the fiction that they and they alone are responsible for their national security. It's become almost a religious belief over there—and despite the fact that we give them vast amounts of arms and other grants every year, it is their government policy to live as though that idea were true. Their institutional fear is that once they mortgage their national security to the goodwill of others, they become vulnerable to the discontinuance of that goodwill.''

''You get tired of hearing that,'' Liz Elliot observed coldly.

Maybe you wouldn't if six million of your relatives got themselves turned into air pollution, Ryan thought to himself. *How the hell can we* not *be sensitive to memories of the Holocaust?*

''I think we can take it as given that a bilateral defense treaty between the United States and Israel will sail through the Senate,'' Arnie van Damm said, speaking for the first time.

''How quickly can we deploy the necessary units to Israeli territory?'' Fowler wanted to know.

''It would take roughly five weeks from the time you push the button, sir,'' the SecDef replied. ''The 10th Armored Cavalry Regiment is forming up right now. That's essentially a heavy brigade force, and it'll defeat—make that 'destroy'—any armored division the Arabs could throw at it. To that we'll add a Marine unit for show, and with the home-port deal at Haifa, we'll almost always have a carrier battle-group in the Eastern Med. Toss in the F-16 wing from Sicily, and you've got a sizable force. The military will like it, too. It gives them a big play area to train in. We'll use our base in the Negev the same way we use the National Training Center at Fort Irwin. The best way to keep that unit tight and ready is to train the hell out of it. It'll be expensive to run it that way, of course, but—''

''But we'll pay that price,'' Fowler said, cutting Bunker off gently. ''It's more than worth the expenditure, and we won't have any problems on the Hill keeping that funded, will we, Arnie?''

''Any congressman who bitches about this will have his career cut short,'' the Chief of Staff said confidently.

''So it's just a matter of eliminating Israeli opposition?'' Fowler went on.

''Correct, Mr. President,'' Talbot replied for the assembly.

''What's the best way to do that?'' This presidential question was rhetorical. That answer was already delineated. The current Israeli government, like all which had preceded it for a decade, was a shaky coalition of disparate interests. The right kind of shove from Washington would bring it down. ''What about the rest of the world?''

''The NATO countries will not be a problem. The rest of the U.N. will go along grudgingly,'' Elliot said before Talbot could speak. ''So long as the Saudis play ball on this, the Islamic world will fall into line. If Israel resists, they'll be as alone as they have ever been.''

''I don't like putting too much pressure on them,'' Ryan said.

''Dr. Ryan, that's not within your purview,'' Elliot said gently. A few heads moved slightly, and a few eyes narrowed, but no one rose to Jack's defense.

''That is true, Dr. Elliot,'' Ryan said after the awkward silence. ''It is also true that too much pressure might have an effect opposite from what the President intends. Then there is a moral dimension that needs to be considered.''

''Dr. Ryan, this is all about the moral dimension,'' the President said. ''The moral dimension is simply put: there has been enough war there, and it is time to put an end to it. Our plan is a means of doing that.''

Our plan, Ryan heard him say. Van Damm's eyes flickered for a moment, then went still. Jack realized that he was as alone here in this room as the President intended Israel to be. He looked down at his notes and kept his mouth shut. *Moral dimension, my ass!* Jack thought angrily. *This is about setting footprints in the sands of time, and about the political advantages of being seen as The Great Peacemaker.* But it wasn't a time for cynicism, and though the plan was no longer Ryan's, it was a worthy one.

"If we have to squeeze them, how do we go about it?" President Fowler asked lightly. "Nothing harsh, just to send a quiet and intelligible message."

"There's a major shipment of aircraft spares ready to go next week. They're replacing the radar systems on all their F-15 fighters," Secretary of Defense Bunker said. "There are other things, too, but that radar system is very important to them. It's brand-new. We're just installing it ourselves. The same is true for the F-16's new missile system. Their Air Force is their crown jewel. If we are forced to withhold that shipment for technical reasons, they'll get the signal loud and clear."

"Can it be done quietly?" Elliot asked.

"We can let them know that if they make noise, it won't help," van Damm said. "If the speech goes over well at the U.N., as it should, we might be able to obviate their congressional lobby."

"It might be preferable to sweeten the deal by allowing them to get more arms instead of crippling systems they already have." That was Ryan's last toss. Elliot slammed the door on the DDCI.

"We can't afford that."

The Chief of Staff agreed: "We can't possibly squeeze any more defense dollars out of the budget, even for Israel. The money just isn't there."

"I'd prefer to let them know ahead of time—if we really intend to squeeze them," the Secretary of State said.

Liz Elliot shook her head. "No. If they need to get the message, let them get it the hard way. They like to play tough. They ought to understand."

"Very well." The President made a last note on his pad. "We hold until the speech next week. I change the speech to include an invitation to enter formal negotiations in Rome starting two weeks from yesterday. We let Israel know that they either play ball or face the consequences, and that we're not kidding this time. We send that message as Secretary Bunker suggested, and do that by surprise. Anything else?"

"Leaks?" van Damm said quietly.

"What about Israel?" Elliot asked Scott Adler.

"I told them that this was highly sensitive, but—"

"Brent, get on the phone to their Foreign Minister, and tell them that if they start making noise prior to the speech, there will be major consequences."

"Yes, Mr. President."

"And as far as this group is concerned, there will be no leaks." That presidential command was aimed at the far end of the table. "Adjourned."

Ryan took his papers and walked outside. Marcus Cabot joined him in the hall after a moment.

"You should know when to keep your mouth shut, Jack."

"Look, Director, if we press them too hard—"

"We'll get what we want."

"I think it's wrong, and I think it's dumb. We'll get what we want. Okay, so it takes a few extra months, we'll still get it. We don't have to threaten them."

"The President wants it done that way." Cabot ended the discussion by walking off.

"Yes, sir," Jack responded to thin air.

The rest of the people filed out. Talbot gave Ryan a wink and a nod. The rest, except for Adler, avoided eye contact. Adler came over after a whisper from his boss.

"Nice try, Jack. You almost got yourself fired a few minutes ago."

That surprised Ryan. Wasn't he supposed to say what he thought? "Look, Scott, if I'm not allowed to—"

"You're not allowed to cross the President, not this one. You do not have the rank to make adverse advice stick. Brent was ready to make that point, but you got in the way—and you lost, and you didn't leave him any room to maneuver. So next time keep it zipped, okay?"

"Thanks for your support," Jack answered with an edge on his voice.

"You blew it, Jack. You said the right thing the wrong way. Learn from that, will you?" Adler paused. "The Boss also says 'well done' for your work in Riyadh. If you'd just learn when to shut up, he says, you'd be a lot more effective."

"Okay, thanks." Adler was right, of course. Ryan knew it.

"Where you headed?"

"Home. I don't have anything left to do today at the office."

"Come along with us. Brent wants to talk to you. We'll have a light dinner at my shop." Adler led Jack to the elevator.

"Well?" the President asked, still back in the room.

"I'd say it looks awfully good," van Damm said. "Especially if we can bring this one in before the elections."

"Be nice to hold a few extra seats," Fowler agreed. The first two years of his administration had not been easy. Budget problems, added to an economy that couldn't seem to decide what it wanted to do, had crippled his programs and saddled his tough managerial style with more question marks than exclamation points. The congressional elections in November would be the first real public response to their new President, and early poll numbers looked exceedingly iffy. It was the general way of things that the President's party lost seats in off-year elections, but this President could not afford to lose many. "Shame we have to pressure the Israelis, but . . ."

"Politically it'll be worth it—if we can bring the treaty off."

"We can," Elliot said, leaning against the doorframe. "If we make the time line, we can have the treaties out of the Senate by October 16th."

"You are one ambitious lady, Liz," Arnold noted. "Well, I have work to do. If you will excuse me, Mr. President?"

"See you tomorrow, Arnie."

Fowler walked over to the windows facing Pennsylvania Avenue. The blistering heat of early August rose in shimmers from the streets and sidewalks. Across the street in Lafayette Park, there remained two anti-nuclear-weapons signs. That garnered a smirk and a snort from Fowler. Didn't those dumb hippies know that nukes were a thing of the past? He turned.

"Join me for dinner, Elizabeth?"

Dr. Elliot smiled at her boss. "Love to, Bob."

The one good thing about his brother's involvement with drugs was that he had left nearly a hundred thousand dollars cash behind in a battered suitcase. Marvin Russell had taken that and driven to Minneapolis, where he'd bought presentable clothes, a decent set of luggage, and a ticket. One of the many things he'd learned in prison was the proper methodology for obtaining an alternate identity. He had three of them, complete with passports, that no cop knew anything about. He'd also learned about keeping a low profile. His clothes were presentable but not flashy. He purchased a standby ticket on a flight he expected to be underbooked, saving himself another few hundred dollars. That $91,545.00 had to last him a long time, and life got expensive where he was heading. Life also got very cheap, he knew, but not in terms of money. A warrior could face that, he decided early on.

After a layover in Frankfurt, he traveled on in a southerly direction. No fool, Russell had once participated in an international conference of sorts—he'd sacrificed a total identity-set for that trip, four years previously. At the conference he'd made a few contacts. Most important of all, he'd learned of contact procedures. The international terrorist community was a careful one. It had to be, with all the forces arrayed against it, and Russell did not know his luck—of the three contact numbers he remembered, one had long since been compromised and two Red Brigade members rolled quietly up with it. He used one of the others, and that number still worked. The contact had led him to a dinner meeting in Athens, where he'd been checked and cleared for further travel. Russell hurried back to his hotel—the local food did not agree with him—and sat down to wait for the phone to ring. To say he was nervous was an understatement. For all Marvin's caution, he knew that he was vulnerable. With not even a pocketknife to defend himself—traveling with weapons was far too dangerous—he was an easy mark for any cop who carried a gun. What if this contact line had been burned? If it had, he'd be arrested here, or summoned into a carefully prepared ambush from which he'd be lucky to escape alive. European cops weren't as mindful of constitutional rights as the Americans—but that thought died a rapid and quiet death. How kindly had the FBI treated his brother?

Damn! One more Sioux warrior shot down like a dog. Not even time to sing his Death Song. They'd pay for that. But only if he lived long enough, Marvin Russell corrected himself.

He sat by the window, the lights behind him extinguished, watching the traffic, watching for approaching police, waiting for the phone to ring. How would he make them pay? Russell asked himself. He didn't know, and really didn't care. Just so there was something he could do. The money belt was tight around his waist. One drawback of his physical condition was that there wasn't much slack in his waistline to take up. But he couldn't risk losing his money—without it, where the hell would he be? Keeping track of money was a pain in the ass, wasn't it? Marks in Germany. Drachmas or douche bags or something else here. Fortunately, you got your airline tickets with bucks. He traveled American-flag carriers mainly for that reason, certainly not because he liked the sight of the Stars and Stripes on the tailfins of the aircraft. The phone rang. Russell lifted it.

"Yes?"

"Tomorrow, nine-thirty, be in front of the hotel, ready to travel. Understood?"

"Nine-thirty. Yes." It clicked off before he could say more.

"Okay," Russell said to himself. He rose and moved toward the bed. The door was double-locked and chained, and he had a chair propped under the knob. Marvin pondered that. If he were being set up, they'd bag him like a duck in autumn right in front of the hotel, or maybe they'd take him away by car and spring the trap away from civilians . . . that was more likely, he judged. But certainly they wouldn't go to all the trouble of setting up a rendezvous and then kick in the door here. Probably not. Hard to predict what cops would do, wasn't it? So he slept in his jeans and shirt, the money belt securely wrapped around his waist. After all, he still had thieves to worry about. . . .

The sun rose about as early here as it did at home. Russell awoke with the first pink-orange glow. On checking in he'd requested an east-facing room. He said his prayers to the sun and prepared himself for travel. He had breakfast sent up—it cost a few extra drachmas, but what the hell?—and packed what few things he'd removed from his suitcase. By nine he was thoroughly ready and thoroughly nervous. If it was going to happen, it would happen in thirty minutes. He could easily be dead before lunch, dead in a foreign land, distant from the spirits of his people. Would they even send his body back to the Dakotas? Probably not. He'd just vanish from the face of the earth. The actions he ascribed to policemen were the same ones he would himself have taken, but what would be good tactics for a warrior were something else to cops, weren't they? Russell paced the room, looking out the window at the cars and the street vendors. Any one of those people selling trinkets or Cokes to the tourists could so easily be a police officer. No, more than one, more like ten. Cops didn't like fair fights, did they? They shot from ambush and attacked in gangs.

9:15. The numbers on the digital clock marched forward with a combination of sloth and alacrity that depended entirely on how often Russell turned to check them. It was time. He lifted his bags and left the room without a backward glance. It was a short walk to the elevator, which arrived quickly enough that it piqued Russell's paranoia yet again. A minute later he was in the lobby. A bellman offered to take his bags, but he declined the offer and made his way to the desk. The only thing left on his bill was breakfast, which he settled with his remaining local currency. He had a few minutes left over, and walked to the newsstand for a copy of anything that was in English. What was happening in the world? It was an odd moment of curiosity for Marvin, whose world was a constricted one of threats and responses and evasions. What was the world? he asked himself. It was what he could see at the time, little more than that, a bubble of space defined by what his senses reported to him. At home he could see distant horizons and a huge enveloping dome of sky. Here, reality was circumscribed by walls, and stretched a mere hundred feet from one horizon to another. He had a sudden attack of anxiety, knowing what it was to be a hunted animal, and struggled to fight it off. He checked his watch: 9:28. Time.

Russell walked outside to the cab stand, wondering what came next. He set his two bags down, looking about as casually as he could manage in the knowledge that guns might even now be aimed at his head. Would he die as John had died? A bullet in the head, no warning at all, not even the dignity an animal might have? That was no way to die, and the thought of it sickened him. Russell balled his hands into tight, powerful fists to control the trembling as a car approached. The driver was looking at him. This was it. He lifted his bags and walked to it.

"Mr. Drake?" It was the name under which Russell was currently traveling. The driver wasn't the one he'd met for dinner. Russell knew at once that he was dealing with pros, who compartmented everything. That was a good sign.

"That's me," Russell answered with a smile/grimace.

The driver got out and opened the trunk. Russell heaved the bags in, then walked to the passenger door and got in the front seat. If this were a trap, he could throttle the driver before he died. At least he'd accomplish that much.

Fifty meters away, Sergeant Spiridon Papanicolaou of the Hellenic National Police sat in an old Opel liveried as a taxi. Sitting there with an extravagant black mustache and munching on a breakfast roll, he looked like anything but a cop. He had a small automatic in the glove box, but like most European cops, he was not skilled in its use. The Nikon camera sitting in a clip holder under his seat was his only real weapon. His job was surveillance, actually working at the behest of the Ministry of Public Order. His memory for faces was photographic—the camera was for people lacking the talent of which he was justifiably proud. His method of operation was one that required great patience, but Papanicolaou had plenty of that. Whenever his superiors got wind of a possible terrorist operation in the Athens area, he prowled hotels and airports and docks. He wasn't the only such officer, but he was the best. He had a nose for it as his father had had a nose for where the fish were running. And he hated terrorists. In fact, he hated all variety of criminals, but terrorists were the worst of the lot, and he chafed at his government's off-again/on-again interest in running the murderous bastards out of his ancient and noble country. Currently the interest was on-again. A week earlier there had been a possible sighting report of someone from the PFLP near the Parthenon. Four men from his squad were at the airport. A few others were checking the cruise docks, but Papanicolaou liked to check the hotels. They had to stay somewhere. Never the best—they were too flashy. Never the worst—these bastards liked a modest degree of comfort. The middle sort, the comfortable family places on the secondary streets, with lots of college-age travelers whose rapid shuffling in and out made for difficulty in spotting one particular face. But Papanicolaou had his father's eyes. He could recognize a face from half a second's exposure at seventy meters.

And the driver of that blue Fiat was a "face." He couldn't remember if it had a name attached to it, but he remembered seeing the face somewhere. The "Unknown" file, probably, one of the hundreds of photographs in the files that came in from Interpol and the military-intelligence people whose lust for the blood of terrorists was even more frustrated by their government's policy. This was the country of Leonidas and Xenophon, Odysseus and Achilles. Greece—Hellas to the sergeant—was the home of epic warriors and the very birthplace of freedom and democracy, not a place for foreign scum to kill with impunity . . .

Who's the other one? Papanicolaou wondered. *Dresses like an American . . . odd features, though.* He raised the camera in one smooth motion, zoomed the lens to full magnification, and got off three rapid frames before putting it back down. The Fiat was moving . . . well, he'd see where it was going. The sergeant switched off his on-call light and headed out of the cab rank.

Russell settled back in the seat. He didn't bother with the seat belt. If he had to escape the car, he didn't want to be bothered. The driver was a good one, maneuvering in and out of traffic, which was lively here. He didn't say a word. That was fine with Russell, too. The American moved his head to the side and scanned forward, looking for a trap. His eyes flickered around the inside of the car. No obvious places to hide a weapon. No visible microphones or radio equipment. That didn't mean anything, but he looked anyway. Finally he pretended to relax and cocked his head in a direction from which he could look ahead and also behind by eyeing the right-side mirror. His hunter's instincts were taut and alert this morning. There was potential danger everywhere.

The driver took what seemed to be an aimless path. It was hard for Russell to be sure, of course. The streets of this city had predated chariots, much less automobiles, and later concessions made to wheeled vehicles had fallen short of making Athens a Los Angeles. Though the autos on the street were tiny ones, traffic seemed to be a constant, moving, anarchic logjam. He wanted to know where they were going, but there was no sense in asking. He would be unable to distinguish between a truthful answer and a lie—and even if he got a straight answer, it probably would not have meant anything to him. He was for better or worse committed to this course of action, Russell knew. It didn't make him feel any more comfortable, but to deny the truth of it was to lie to himself, and Russell was not that sort. The best he could do was to stay alert. That he did.

The airport, Papanicolaou thought. That was certainly convenient. In addition to his squadmates, there were at least twenty other officers there, armed with pistols and sub-machine guns. That should be easy. Just move a few of the plainclothes people in close while two heavily armed people in uniform strolled by, and take them down—he liked that American euphemism—quickly and cleanly. Off into a side room to see if they were what he thought, and if not—well, then his captain would fuss over them. Sorry, he'd say, but you fit a description we got from—whomever he might conveniently blame; maybe the French or Italians—and one cannot be too careful with international air travel. They would automatically upgrade whatever tickets the two people had to first-class ones. It almost always worked.

On the other hand, if that face was what Papanicolaou thought it was, well, then he'd have gotten his third terrorist of the year. Maybe even the fourth. Just because the other one dressed like an American didn't mean he had to be one. Four in just eight months—no, only seven months, the sergeant corrected himself. Not bad for one somewhat eccentric cop who liked to work alone. Papanicolaou allowed his car to close in slightly. He didn't want to lose these fish in traffic.

Russell counted a bunch of cabs. They had to cater to tourists mainly, or other people who didn't care to drive in the local traffic . . . *that's odd.* It took him a moment to figure why. Oh, sure, he thought, its dome light wasn't on. Only the driver. Most of the others had passengers, but even those without had their dome lights on. It must have been the on-duty light, he judged. But that one's was out. Russell's driver had it easy, taking the next right turn to head down toward what appeared to be something akin to a real highway. Most of the cabs failed to take the turn. Though Russell didn't know it, they were heading either toward museums or shopping areas. But the one with the light out followed them around the corner, fifty yards back.

"We're being followed," Marvin announced quietly. "You have a friend watching our back?"

"No." The driver's eyes immediately went up to the mirror. "Which one do you think it is?"

"I don't 'think,' sport. It's the taxi fifty yards back, right side, dirty-white, without the dome light on, I don't know the make of the car. He's made two turns with us. You should pay better attention," Russell added, wondering if this was the trap he feared. He figured he could kill the driver easily enough. A little guy with a skinny neck that he could wring as easily as he killed a mourning dove, yeah, it wouldn't be hard.

"Thank you. Yes, I should," the driver replied after identifying the cab. *And who might you be. . . ? We'll see.* He made another random turn. It followed.

"You are correct, my friend," the driver said thoughtfully. "How did you know?"

"I pay attention to things."

"So I see . . . this changes our plans somewhat." The driver's mind was racing. Unlike Russell, he knew that he hadn't been set up. Though he had been unable to establish his guest's bonafides, no intelligence or police officer would have given him that warning. Well, probably not, he corrected himself. But there was one way to check that. He was also angry at the Greeks. One of his comrades had disappeared off the streets of Piraeus in April, to turn up in Britain a few days later. That friend was now in Parkhurst Prison on the Isle of Wight. They'd once been able to operate in relative impunity in Greece, most often using the country as a safe transit point. He knew that doing actual operations here had been a mistake—just having the country as a sally-port had been quite valuable enough, an advantage not to be squandered—but that didn't mitigate his anger at the Greek police.

"It may be necessary to do something about this."

Russell's eyes went back to the driver. "I don't have a weapon."

"I do. I would prefer not to use it. How strong are you?"

By way of answering, Russell reached out his left hand and squeezed the driver's right knee.

"You have made your point," the driver said with a level voice. "If you cripple me, I cannot drive." *Now, how do we do this . . . ?* "Have you killed before?"

"Yes," Russell lied. He hadn't ever personally killed a man, but he'd killed enough other things. "I can do that."

The driver nodded and increased speed on his way out of town. He had to find . . .

Papanicolaou frowned. They were not heading to the airport. Too bad. Good thing he hadn't called it in. Well. He allowed himself to lay back, shielding himself with other vehicles. The paint job on the Fiat made it easy to spot, and as traffic thinned out, he could take it a little more casually. Maybe they were going to a safe house. If so, he'd have to be very careful, but also if so, he'd have a valuable piece of information. Identifying a safe house was about the best thing he could accomplish. Then the muscle boys could move in, or the intelligence squad could stake it out, identifying more and more faces, then assaulting the place in such a way as to arrest three or even more of the bastards. There could be a decoration and promotion at the end of this surveillance. Again he thought of making a radio call, but—but what did he really know? He was letting his excitement get away with him, wasn't he? He had a probable identification on a face without a name. Might his eyes have deceived him? Might the face be something other than what he thought? A common criminal, perhaps?

Spiridon Papanicolaou grumbled a curse at fate and luck, his trained eyes locked on the car. They were entering an old part of Athens, with narrow streets. Not a fashionable area, it was a working-class neighborhood with narrow streets, mainly empty. Those with jobs were at them. Housewives were at the local shops. Children played in parks. Quite a few people were taking their holidays on the islands, and the streets were emptier than one might have expected. The Fiat slowed suddenly and turned right into one of many anonymous sidestreets.

"Ready?"

"Yes."

The car stopped briefly. Russell had already removed his jacket and tie, still wondering if this could be the final act of the trap, but he didn't really care anymore. What would happen would happen. He flexed his hands as he walked back up the street.

Sergeant Spiridon Papanicolaou increased speed to approach the corner. If they were heading into this rabbit warren of narrow lanes, he could not maintain visual contact without getting closer. Well, if they identified him, he'd call for help. Police work was unpredictable, after all. As he approached the corner, he saw a man standing on the sidestreet, looking at a paper. Not either of the men he was shadowing. This one wasn't wearing a jacket, though his face was turned away, and the way he was standing there was like something in a movie. The sergeant smiled wryly at that—but the smile stopped at once.

As soon as Papanicolaou was fully onto the sidestreet, he saw the Fiat, no more than twenty meters away, and backing up rapidly toward him. The police officer stood on the brakes to stop his taxi, and started to think about reversing himself when an arm reached across his face. His hands came off the wheel to grab it, but the powerful hand gripped his chin, and another seized the back of his neck. His instinct to turn and see what was happening was answered by the way one hand wrenched his head to the left, and he saw the face of the American—but then he felt his vertebrae strain for a brief instant and snap with an audible sound that announced his death to Papanicolaou as surely and irrevocably as a bullet. Then he knew. The man did have odd features, like something else from a movie, like something . . .

Russell jumped out of the way and waved. The Fiat pulled forward again, then went into reverse and slammed hard into the taxi. The driver's head lolled forward atop its broken neck. Probably the man was dead already, Russell knew, but that wasn't a matter of concern. Yes, it was. He felt for a pulse, then made sure the neck was well and truly snapped—he worked it around to make sure the spine was severed, too—before moving to the Fiat. Russell smiled to himself as he got in. *Gee, that wasn't so hard . . .*

"He's dead. Let's get the hell out of here!"

"Are you sure?"

"I broke his neck like a toothpick. Yeah, he's dead, man. It was easy. Little pencil-neck of a guy."

"Like me, you mean?" The driver turned and grinned. He'd have to dump the car, of course, but the joy of their escape and the satisfaction of the killing was sufficient to the moment. And he had found a comrade, a worthy one. "Your name is?"

"Marvin."

"I am Ibrahim."

The President's speech was a triumph. The man did know how to deliver a good performance, Ryan told himself as the applause rippled across the General Assembly auditorium in New York. His gracious if rather cold smile thanked the assembled representatives of a hundred sixty or so countries. The cameras panned to the Israeli delegation, whose clapping was rather more perfunctory than that of the Arab states—there evidently hadn't been time to brief them. The Soviets outdid themselves, joining those who stood. Jack lifted the remote control and switched off the set before the ABC commentator could summarize what the President had said. Ryan had a draft of the speech on his desk, and had made notes of his own. Moments earlier the invitations had been telexed by the Vatican to all of the concerned foreign ministries. All would come to Rome in ten days. The draft treaty was ready for them. Quiet, rapid moves by a handful of ambassadors and deputy-assistant-secretaries of state had informed other governments of what was in the offing, and uniform approval had come back. The Israelis knew about that. The proper back-channel leaks had been allowed to percolate in the desired direction. If they stonewalled—well, Bunker had put a hold on that shipment of aircraft parts, and the Israelis had been too shocked to react yet. More accurately, they'd been told not to react if they ever wanted to see the new radar systems. There were already rumbles from the Israeli lobby, which had its own sources throughout the U.S. government, and was making discreet calls to key members of Congress. But Fowler had briefed the congressional leadership two days earlier, and the initial read on the Fowler Plan was highly favorable. The chairman and ranking member of the Senate Foreign Relations Committee had promised passage of both draft treaties in under a week. It was going to happen, Jack thought to himself. It might really work. Certainly it wouldn't hurt anything. All the goodwill America had generated in its own adventure in the Persian Gulf was on the line. The Arabs would see this as a fundamental change in U.S. policy—which it was—America was slapping Israel down. Israel would see it the same way, but that wasn't really true. The peace would be guaranteed the only way that was possible, by American military and political power. The demise of East-West confrontation had made it possible for America, acting in accord with the other major powers, to dictate a just peace. *What we think a just peace is,* Ryan corrected himself. *God, I hope this works out.*

It was too late for that, of course. It had, after all, been his idea, the Fowler Plan. They had to break the cycle, to find a way out of the trap. America was the only country trusted by both sides, a fact won with American blood on the one hand and vast amounts of money on the other. America had to guarantee the peace, and the peace had to be founded on something looking recognizably like justice to all concerned. The equation was both simple and complex. The principles could be expressed in a single short paragraph. The details of execution would take a small book. The monetary cost—well, the enabling legislation would sail through Congress despite the size of it. Saudi Arabia was actually underwriting a quarter of the cost, a concession won only four days earlier by Secretary Talbot. In return, the Saudis would be buying yet another installment of high-tech arms, which had been handled by Dennis Bunker. Those two had really handled their end superbly, Ryan knew. Whatever the President's faults, his two most important cabinet members—two close friends—were the best such team he'd ever seen in government service. And they'd served their President and their country well in the past week.

"This is going to work," Jack said quietly to himself in the privacy of his office. "Maybe, maybe, maybe." He checked his watch. He'd have a read on that in about three hours.

Qati faced his television with a frown. *Was it possible?* History said no, but—

But the Saudis had broken off their supply of money, seduced by the help America had given them against Iraq. And his organization had bet on the wrong horse in that one. Already his people were feeling the financial pinch, though they'd been careful to invest what funds they had received over the previous generation. Their Swiss and other European bankers had ensured a steady flow of money, and the pinch was more psychological than real, but to the Arab mind the psychological *was* real, just as it was to any politically astute mind.

The key to it, Qati knew, was whether or not the Americans would put real pressure on the Zionists. They'd never done so. They'd allowed the Israelis to attack an American warship and kill American sailors—and forgiven them before the bleeding had stopped, before the last victim had died. When American military forces had to fight for every dollar of funds from their own Congress, that same spineless body of political whores fell over itself giving arms to the Jews. America had never pressured Israel in any meaningful way. That was the key to his existence, wasn't it? So long as there was no peace in the Middle East, he had a mission: the destruction of the Jewish State. Without that—

But the problems in the Middle East predated his birth. They might go away, but only when—

But it was a time for truth, Qati told himself, stretching tired and sore limbs.

What prospects for destroying Israel did he have? Not from without. So long as America supported the Jews, and so long as the Arab states failed to unite. . . .

And the Russians? The cursed Russians had stood like begging dogs at the end of Fowler's speech.

It *was* possible. The thought was no less threatening to Qati than the first diagnosis of his cancer. He leaned back in his chair and closed his eyes. What if the Americans did pressure the Jews? What if the Russians did support this absurd new plan? What if the Israelis gave in to the pressure? What if the Palestinians found the concessions demanded of Israel to their taste? It could work. The Zionist state might continue to exist. The Palestinians might find contentment in their new land. A *modus vivendi* might evolve into being.

It would mean that his life had been to no purpose. It would mean that all the things he had worked for, all the sacrifice and self-denial had gone for nothing. His freedom fighters had fought and died for a generation . . . for a cause that might be forever lost.

Betrayed by his fellow Arabs, whose money and political support had sustained his men.

Betrayed by the Russians, whose support and arms had sustained his movement from its birth.

Betrayed by the Americans—the most perversely of all. For taking away their enemy.

Betrayed by Israel—for making something akin to a fair peace. It wasn't fair at all, of course. So long as a single Zionist lived on Arab lands, there would be no fairness.

Might he be betrayed by the Palestinians also? What if they came to accept this? Where would his dedicated fighters come from?

Betrayed by everyone?

No, God could not let that be. God was merciful, and gave his light to the faithful.

No, this could not really happen. It wasn't possible. Too many things had to fall into place for this hellish vision to become real. Had not there been so many peace plans for this region? So many visions. And where had they led? Even the Carter-Sadat-Begin talks in America, where the Americans had browbeaten their putative allies into serious concessions, had choked and died when Israel had utterly failed to consider an equitable settlement for the Palestinians. No, Qati was sure of that. Perhaps he could not depend on the Russians. Perhaps he could not depend on the Saudis. Certainly he could not depend on the Americans. But he could depend on Israel. The Jews were far too stupid, far too arrogant, far too shortsighted to see that their best hope for long-term security could only lie in an equitable peace. The irony struck him very hard, hard enough to garner a smile. It had to be God's plan, that his movement would be safeguarded by his bitterest enemies. Their obstinacy, their stiff Jewish necks would never bow to this. And if that was what was required for the war to continue, then the fact of it, and the irony of it, could only be a sign from God Himself that the cause guiding Qati and his men was indeed the Holy Cause they believed it to be.

"Never! Never will I bow to this infamy!" the Defense Minister shouted. It was a dramatic performance, even for him. He'd pounded the table hard enough to upset his water glass, and the puddle from it threatened to seep over the edge and into his lap. He studiously ignored it as his fierce blue eyes swept around the cabinet room.

"And what if Fowler is serious with his threats?"

"We'll break his career!" Defense said. "We can do that. We've jerked American politicians into line before!"

"More than we've been able to do here," the Foreign Minister observed *sotto voce* to his neighbor at the table.

"What was that?"

"I said it might not be possible in this case, Rafi." David Askenazi took a sip from his glass before going on. "Our ambassador in Washington tells me that his people on the Hill find real support for Fowler's plan. The Saudi Ambassador threw a major party last weekend for the congressional leadership. He performed well, our sources tell us. Right, Avi?"

"Correct, Minister," General Ben Jakob answered. His boss was out of the country at the moment, and he spoke for the Mossad. "The Saudis and the rest of the 'moderate' Gulf states are willing to end their declared state of war, to institute ministerial relations with us preparatory for full recognition at an unspecified later date, and to underwrite part of the American costs for stationing their troops and planes here—plus, I might add, picking up the entire cost of the peacekeeping force *and* the economic rehabilitation of our Palestinian friends."

"How do we say no to that?" the Foreign Minister inquired dryly. "Are you surprised at the support in the American Congress?"

"It's all a trick!" Defense insisted.

"If so, it's a damnably clever one," Ben Jakob said.

"You believe this twaddle, Avi? *You?*" Ben Jakob had been Rafi Mandel's best battalion commander in the Sinai, so many years before.

"I don't know, Rafi." The Deputy Director of the Mossad had never been more cognizant of his position as a deputy, and speaking in the name of his boss did not come easy.

"Your evaluation?" the Prime Minister asked gently. Someone at the table, he decided, had to be calm.

"The Americans are entirely sincere," Avi replied. "Their willingness to provide a physical guarantee—the mutual-defense treaty, and the stationing of troops—is genuine. From a strictly military point of—"

"*I* speak for the defense of Israel!" Mandel snarled.

Ben Jakob turned to stare his former commander down. "Rafi, you have always outranked me, but I've killed my share of enemies and you know it well." Avi paused for a moment to let that rest on the table. When he went on, his voice was quiet and measured and dispassionate as he allowed his reason to overcome emotions no less strong than Mandel's. "The American military units represent a serious commitment. We're talking about a twenty-five-percent increase in the striking power of our Air Force, and that tank unit is more powerful than our strongest brigade. Moreover, I do not see how that commitment can ever be withdrawn. For that to happen—our friends in America will never let it happen."

"We've been abandoned before!" Mandel pointed out coldly. "Our only defense is ourselves."

"Rafi," the Foreign Minister said. "My friend, where has that led us? You and I have fought together, too, and not merely in this room. Is there to be no end to it?"

"Better no treaty than a bad treaty!"

"I agree," the Prime Minister said. "But how bad will this treaty be?"

"We have all read the draft. I will propose some modest changes, but, my friends, I think it is time," the Foreign Minister said. "My advice to you is that we accept the Fowler Plan, with certain conditions." The Foreign Minister outlined them.

"Will the Americans grant those, Avi?"

"They'll complain about the cost, but our friends in their Congress will go along, whether President Fowler approves them or not. They will recognize our historic concessions, and they will wish to make us feel secure within our borders."

"Then I will resign!" Rafi Mandel shouted.

"No, Rafi, you will not," the Prime Minister said, growing a little tired of his histrionics. "If you resign, you cast yourself out. You want this seat someday, and you will never have it if you leave the cabinet now."

Mandel flushed crimson at that rebuke.

The Prime Minister looked around the room. "So what is the opinion of the government?"

Forty minutes later, Jack's phone rang. He lifted it, noting that it was his most secure line, the direct one that bypassed Nancy Cummings.

"Ryan." He listened for a minute and made some notes. "Thanks."

Next the DDCI rose and walked into Nancy's office, then turned left through the door into Marcus Cabot's more capacious room. Cabot was lying on the couch in the far corner. Like Judge Arthur Moore, his predecessor, Cabot liked to smoke the occasional cigar. His shoes were off, and he was reading over a file with striped tape on the borders. Just one more secret file in a building full of them. The folder dropped, and Cabot, looking like a pink, chubby volcano, eyed Ryan as he approached.

"What is it, Jack?"

"Just got a call from our friend in Israel. They're coming to Rome, and the cabinet voted to accept the treaty terms, with a few modifications."

"What are they?" Ryan handed over his notes. Cabot scanned them. "You and Talbot were right."

"Yeah, and I should have let him play the card instead of me."

"Good call, you predicted all but one." Cabot rose and slipped into his black loafers before walking to his desk. Here he lifted a phone. "Tell the President I'll meet him at the White House when he gets back from New York. I want Talbot and Bunker there also. Tell him it's a go." He set the phone back in the cradle. He grinned around the cigar in his teeth, trying to look like George Patton, who hadn't smoked to the best of Ryan's knowledge. "How about that?"

"How long you figure to finalize it?"

"With the advance work you and Adler did, plus the finishing work from Talbot and Bunker . . . ? Hmm. Give it two weeks. Won't go as fast as it did with Carter at Camp David, because too many professional diplomats are involved, but in fourteen days the President takes his seven-four-seven to Rome to sign the documents."

"You want me to go down with you to the White House?"

"No, I'll handle it."

"Okay." That wasn't unexpected. Ryan left the room the same way he'd come in.

7. The City of God

The cameras were in place. Air Force C-5B Galaxy transports had loaded the newest state-of-the-art ground-station vans at Andrews Air Force Base and flown them to Leonardo da Vinci Airport. This was less for the signing ceremony—if they got that far, commentators worried—than what wags called the pre-game show. The fully digital improved-definition equipment just coming on line, the producers felt, would better depict the art collections that litter Vatican walls as trees line national parks. Local carpenters and specialists from New York and Atlanta had worked around the clock to build the special booths from which the network anchors would broadcast. All three network morning news shows were originating from the Vatican. CNN was also there in force, as were NHK, BBC, and nearly every other television network in the world, all fighting for space in the grand piazza that sprawls before the church begun in 1503 by Bramante, carried on by Raphael, Michelangelo, and Bernini. A brief but violent windstorm had carried spray from the central fountain into the *Deutsche Welle* anchor booth and shorted out a hundred thousand marks' worth of equipment. Vatican officials had finally protested that there would be no room for the people to witness the event—for which they prayed—but by then it had been far too late. Someone remembered that in Roman times this had been the site of the Circus Maximus, and it was generally agreed that this was the grandest circus of recent years. Except that the Roman "circus" was mainly for chariot races.

The TV people enjoyed their stay in Rome. The crews for *Today* and *Good Morning America* were able, for once, to rise indecently late instead of before the paperboy, to begin their broadcasts after lunch—!!!—and finish in time for afternoon shopping, followed by dinner at one of Rome's many fine restaurants. Their research people scoured reference books for historical remote locations like the Colosseum—correctly called the Flavian Amphitheater, one careful back-room type discovered—where people waxed rhapsodic on the Roman substitute for NFL football: combat, to the death, man against man, man against beast, beast against Christian, and various other permutations thereof. But it was the Forum that was the symbolic focus for their time in Rome. Here were the ruins of Rome's civic center, where Cicero and Scipio had walked and talked and met with supporters and opponents, the place to which visitors had come for centuries. Eternal Rome, mother of a vast empire, playing yet another role on the world stage. In its center was the Vatican, just a handful of acres, really, but a sovereign country nonetheless. "How many divisions has the Pope?" a TV anchorman quoted Stalin, then rambled into a discourse on how the Church and its values had outlasted Marxism-Leninism to the extent that the Soviet Union had decided to open diplomatic relations with the Holy See, and had its own evening news, *Vremya,* originating from a booth less than fifty yards from his own.

Additional attention was given to the two other religions present in the negotiations. At the arrival ceremony, the Pope had recalled an incident from the earliest days of Islam: a commission of Catholic bishops had traveled to Arabia, essentially on an intelligence-gathering mission to see what Mohammed was up to. After a cordial first meeting, the senior Bishop had asked where he and his companions might celebrate mass. Mohammed had immediately offered the use of the mosque in which they stood. After all, the Prophet had observed, is this not a house consecrated to God? The Holy Father extended the same courtesy to the Israelis. In both cases there was some measure of discomfort to the more conservative churchmen present, but the Holy Father had swept that aside with a speech characteristically delivered in three languages.

''In the name of the God Whom we all know by different names, but Who is nevertheless the same God of all men, we offer our city to the service of men of goodwill. We share so many beliefs. We believe in a God of mercy and love. We believe in the spiritual nature of man. We believe in the paramount value of faith, and in the manifestation of that faith in charity and brotherhood. To our brothers from distant lands, we give you greetings and we offer our prayers that your faith will find a way to the justice and the peace of God to which all of our faiths direct us.''

''Wow,'' a morning-show anchor observed off-mike. ''I'm beginning to think this circus is serious.''

But coverage didn't stop there, of course. In the interest of fairness, balance, controversy, a proper understanding of events, and selling commercials, the TV coverage included the head of a Jewish paramilitary group who vociferously recalled Ferdinand and Isabella's expulsion of the Jews from Iberia, the czar's Black Hundreds, and, naturally, Hitler's Holocaust—which he emphasized further because of German reunification—and concluded that Jews were fools to trust anyone at all except the weapons in their own strong hands. From Qum, the Ayatolla Daryaei, the religious leader of Iran and long an enemy of everything Americans did, railed against all unbelievers, consigning each and every one to his personal version of hell, but translation made understanding difficult for American viewers, and his grandiloquent ranting was cut short. A self-styled ''charismatic Christian'' from the American South got the most air time. After first denouncing Roman Catholicism as the quintessential Anti-Christ, he repeated his renowned claim that God didn't even *hear* the prayers of the Jews, much less the infidel Muslims, whom he called Mohammedans as an unnecessary further insult.

But somehow those demagogues were ignored—more correctly, their views were. The TV networks received thousands of angry calls that such bigots were given air time at all. This delighted the TV executives, of course. It meant that people would return to the same show seeking further outrage. The American bigot immediately noticed a dip in his contribution envelopes. B'nai B'rith raced to condemn the off-the-reservation rabbi. The leader of the League of Islamic Nations, himself a distinguished cleric, denounced the radical imam as a heretic against the words of the Prophet, whom he quoted at length to make his point. The TV networks provided all of the countervailing commentary also, thus showing balance enough to pacify some viewers and enrage others.

Within a day, one newspaper column noted that the thousands of correspondents attending the conference had taken to calling it the Peace Bowl, in recognition of the circular configuration of the Piazza San Pietro. The more observant realized that this was evidence of the strain on reporters with a story to cover but nothing to report. Security at the conference was hermetically tight. Those participants who came and went were carried about by military aircraft via military air bases. Reporters and cameramen with their long lenses were kept as far from the action as possible, and for the most part travel was accomplished in darkness. The Swiss Guards of the Vatican, outfitted though they were in Renaissance jump suits, let not a mouse pass by their lines, and perversely when something significant did happen—the Swiss Defense Minister discreetly entered a remote doorway—no one noticed.

Polling information in numerous countries showed uniform hope that this would be the one. A world tired of discord and riding a euphoric wave of relief at recent changes in East-West relations somehow sensed that it was. Commentators warned that there had been no harder issue in recent history, but people the world over prayed in a hundred languages and a million churches for an end to this last and most dangerous dispute on the planet. To their credit, the TV networks reported that, too.

Professional diplomats, some of them the most certified of cynics who hadn't seen the inside of a church since childhood, felt the weight of such pressure as they had never known. Sketchy reports from Vatican custodial staffers spoke of solitary midnight walks down the nave of Saint Peter's, strolls along outside balconies on clear, starlit nights, long talks of some participants with the Holy Father. But nothing else. The highly paid TV anchors stared at one another in awkward silences. Print journalists struggled and stole any good idea they could find just so that they could produce some copy. Not since Carter's marathon stint at Camp David had such weighty negotiations proceeded with so little reportage.

And the world held its breath.

The old man wore a red fez trimmed with white. Not many continued the characteristic manner of dress, but this one kept to the way of his ancestors. Life was hard for the Druse, and the one solace he had lay in the religion he'd observed for all of his sixty-six years.

The Druse are members of a Middle Eastern religious sect combining aspects of Islam, Christianity, and Judaism, founded by Al-hakim bi'amrillahi, Caliph of Egypt in the 11th century, who had deemed himself the incarnation of God Himself. Living for the most part in Lebanon, Syria, and Israel, they occupy a precarious niche in the societies of all three nations. Unlike Muslim Israelis, they are allowed to serve in the armed forces of the Jewish state, a fact that does not engender trust for the Syrian Druse in the government that rules over them. While some Druse have risen to command in the Syrian Army, it was well remembered that one such officer, a colonel commanding a regiment, had been executed after the 1973 war for being forced off a strategic crossroads. Though in strictly military terms he'd fought bravely and well, and had been lucky to extract what remained of his command in good order, the loss of that crossroads had cost the Syrian Army a pair of tank brigades, and as a result the Colonel had been summarily executed . . . for being unlucky, and probably for being a Druse.

The old farmer didn't know all of the details behind that story, but knew enough. The Syrian Muslims had killed another Druse then, and more since. He accordingly trusted no one from the Syrian Army or government. But that did not mean that he had the least affection for Israel, either. In 1975 a long-barreled Israeli 175mm gun had scoured his area, searching for a Syrian ammunition depot, and the fragments from one stray round had mortally wounded his wife of forty years, adding loneliness to his surfeit of misery. What for Israel was a historical constant was for this simple farmer an immediate and deadly fact of life. Fate had decided that he should live between two armies, both of which regarded his physical existence as an annoying inconvenience. He was not a man who had ever asked much of life. He had a small holding of land which he farmed, a few sheep and goats, a simple house built of stones he'd carried from his rocky fields. All he wanted to do was live. It was not, he'd once thought, all that much to ask, but sixty-six turbulent years had proven him wrong and wrong again. He'd prayed for mercy from his God, and for justice, and for just a few comforts—he'd always known that wealth would never be his—so that his lot and that of his wife would be just a little easier. But that had never happened. Of the five children his wife had borne him, only one had survived into his teens, and that son had been conscripted into the Syrian Army in time for the 1973 war. His son had more luck than the entire family had known: when his BTR-60 personnel carrier had taken a hit from an Israeli tank, he'd been thrown out the top, losing only an eye and a hand in the process. Alive, but half-blinded, he'd married and given his father grandchildren as he lived a modestly successful life as a merchant and moneylender. Not much of a blessing, in contrast to what else had happened in his life, it seemed to the farmer the only joy he'd known.

The farmer grew his vegetables and grazed his few head of stock on his rocky patch close to the Syrian-Lebanese border. He didn't persevere, didn't really endure, and even survival was an overstatement of his existence. Life for the farmer was nothing more than a habit he could not break, an endless succession of increasingly weary days. When each spring his ewes produced new lambs, he prayed quietly that he'd not live to see them slaughtered—but he also resented the fact that these meek and foolish animals might outlast himself.

Another dawn. The farmer neither had nor needed an alarm clock. When the sky brightened, the bells on his sheep and goats started to clatter. His eyes opened, and he again became conscious of the pain in his limbs. He stretched in his bed, then rose slowly. In a few minutes he'd washed and scraped the gray stubble from his face, eaten his stale bread and strong, sweet coffee, and begun one more day of labor. The farmer did his gardening in the morning, before the heat of the day really took hold. He had a sizable garden, because selling off its surplus in the local market provided cash for the few things that he counted as luxuries. Even that was a struggle. The work punished his arthritic limbs, and keeping his animals away from the tender shoots was one more curse in his life, but the sheep and goats could also be sold for cash, and without that money he would long since have starved. The truth of the matter was that he ate adequately from the sweat of his wrinkled brow, and had he not been so lonely, he could have eaten more. As it was, solitude had made him parsimonious. Even his gardening tools were old. He trudged out to the field, the sun still low in the sky, to destroy the weeds that every day sprang up anew among his vegetables. If only someone could train a goat, he thought, echoing words of his father and grandfather. A goat that would eat the weeds but not the plants, that would be something. But a goat was no more intelligent than a clod of dirt, except when it came to doing mischief. The three-hour effort of lifting the mattock and tearing up the weeds began in the same corner of the garden, and he worked his way up one row and down the next with a steady pace that belied his age and infirmity.

Clunk.

What was that? The farmer stood up straight and wiped some sweat away. Halfway through the morning labor, beginning to look forward to the rest that came with attending to the sheep . . . Not a stone. He used his tool to pull the dirt away from—oh, that.

People often wonder at the process. Farmers the world over have joked of it since farming first began, the way that farm fields produce rocks. Stone fences along New England lanes attest to the superficially mysterious process. Water did it. Water falling as rain seeps into the soil. In the winter the water freezes into ice, which expands as it becomes a solid. As it expands, it pushes up rather than down, because pushing up is easier. That action moves rocks in the soil to the surface, and so fields grow rocks, something especially true on the Golan region of Syria, whose soil is a geologically recent construct of volcanism, and whose winters, surprisingly to many, can grow cold and frosty.

But this one was not a rock.

It was metallic, a sandy brown color, he saw, pulling the dirt away. Oh, yes, that day. The same day his son had been—

What do I do about this damned thing? the farmer asked himself. It was, of course, a bomb. He wasn't so foolish that he didn't know that much. How it had gotten here was a mystery, of course. He'd never seen any aircraft, Syrian or Israeli, drop bombs anywhere close to his farm, but that didn't matter. He could scarcely deny that it was here. To the farmer it might as well have been a rock, just a big brown rock, too big to dig out and carry off to the edge of the field, big enough to interrupt two rows of carrots. He didn't fear the thing. It had not gone off, after all, and that meant that it was broken. Proper bombs fell off airplanes and exploded when they hit the ground. This one had just dug its small crater, which he'd filled back up the next day, unmindful at the time of the injuries to his son.

Why couldn't it have just stayed two meters down, where it belonged? he asked himself. But that had never been the pattern of his life, had it? No, anything that could do him harm had found him, hadn't it? The farmer wondered why God had been so cruel to him. Had he not said all his prayers, followed all of the strict rules of the Druse? What had he ever asked for? Whose sins was he expiating?

Well. There was no sense asking such questions at this late date. For the moment, he had work to do. He continued his weeding, standing on the exposed tip of the bomb to get a few, and worked his way down the row. His son would visit in a day or two, allowing the old man to see and beam at his grandchildren, the one unqualified joy of his life. He'd ask his son's advice. His son had been a soldier, and understood such things.

It was the sort of week that any government employee hated. Something important was happening in a different time zone. There was a six-hour differential, and it seemed very strange to Jack that he was being afflicted with jet lag without having traveled anywhere.

"So how's it going over there?" Clark asked from the driver's seat.

"Damned well." Jack flipped through the documents. "The Saudis and Israelis actually agreed on something yesterday. They both wanted to change something, and both actually proposed the same change." Jack chuckled at that. It had to be accidental, and if they'd known, both sides would have changed their positions.

"That must have embarrassed the hell out of somebody!" Clark laughed aloud, thinking the same as his boss. It was still dark, and the one good thing about the early days was that the roads were empty. "You really liked the Saudis, didn't you?"

"Ever been over there?"

"Aside from the war, you mean? Lots of times, Jack. I staged into Iran from there back in '79 and '80, spent a lot of time with the Saudis, learned the language."

"What did you think of the place?" Jack asked.

"I liked it there. Got to know one guy pretty well, a major in their army—spook really, like me. Not much field experience, but a lot of book learning. He was smart enough to know that he had a lot to learn, and he listened when I told him stuff. Got invited to his house a coupla-three times. He had two sons, nice little kids. One's flying fighters now. Funny how they treat their women, though. Sandy'd never go for it." Clark paused as he changed lanes to pass a truck. "Professionally speaking, they were cooperative as hell. Anyway, what I saw I sort of liked. They're different from us, but so what? World ain't full of Americans."

"What about the Israelis?" Jack asked as he closed the document case.

"I've worked with them once or twice—well, more than that, doc, mainly in Lebanon. Their intelligence guys are real pros, cocky, arrogant bastards, but the ones I met had a lot to be cocky about. Fortress mentality, like—us-and-them mentality, y'know? Also understandable." Clark turned. "That's the big hangup, isn't it?"

"What do you mean?"

"Weaning them away from that. It can't be easy."

"It isn't. I wish they'd wake up to the way the world is now," Ryan growled.

"Doc, you have to understand. They all think like front-line grunts. What do you expect? Hell, man, their whole country is like a free-fire zone for the other side. They have the same way of thinking that us line animals had in 'Nam. There are two kinds of people—your people and everybody else." John Clark shook his head. "You know how many times I've tried to explain that to kids at the Farm? Basic survival mentality. The Israelis think that way 'cause they can't think any other way. The Nazis killed millions of Jews and we didn't do dick about it—well, okay, maybe we couldn't have done anything 'cause of the way things were at the time. Then again, I wonder if Hitler was all that hard a target if we woulda ever got serious about doing his ass.

"Anyway, I agree with you that they have to look beyond all that, but you gotta remember that we're asking one hell of a lot."

"Maybe you should have been along when I met with Avi," Jack observed with a yawn.

"General Ben Jakob? Supposed to be one tough, serious son of a bitch. His troops respect the man. That says a lot. Sorry I wasn't there, boss, but that two weeks of fishing was just about what I needed." Even line animals got vacations.

"I hear you, Mr. Clark."

"Hey, I gotta go down to Quantico this afternoon to requalify on pistol. If you don't mind me saying so, you look like you could use a little stress-relief, man. Why not come on down? I'll get a nice little Beretta for you to play with."

Jack thought about that. It sounded nice. In fact it sounded great. But. But he had too much work to do.

"No time, John."

"Aye aye, sir. You're not getting your exercise, you're drinking too goddamned much, and you look like shit, Dr. Ryan. That is my professional opinion."

About what Cathy told me last night, but Clark doesn't know just how bad it is. Jack stared out the window at the lights of houses whose government-worker occupants were just waking up.

"You're right. I have to do something about it, but today I just don't have the time."

"How about tomorrow at lunch we take a little run?"

"Lunch with the directorate chiefs," Jack evaded.

Clark shut up and concentrated on his driving. When would the poor, dumb bastard learn? Smart a guy as he was, he was letting the job eat him up.

The President awoke to find an unkempt mountain of blond hair on his chest and a thin, feminine arm flung across him. There were worse ways to awaken. He asked himself why he'd waited so long. She'd been clearly available to him for—God, for years. In her forties, but lithe and pretty, as much as any man could want, and the President was a man with a man's needs. His wife, Marian, had lingered for years, bravely fighting the MS that had ultimately stolen her life, but only after crushing what had once been a lively, charming, intelligent, bubbling personality, the light of his life, Fowler remembered. What personality he'd once had had largely been her creation, and it had died its own lingering death. A defense mechanism, he knew. All those endless months. He'd had to be strong for her, to provide for her the stoic reserve of energy without which she would have died so much sooner. But doing that had made an automaton of Bob Fowler. There was only so much personality, so much strength, so much courage a man contained, and as Marian's life had drained away, so had his humanity ebbed with it. And perhaps more than that, Fowler admitted to himself.

The perverse thing was that it had made him a better politician. His best years as governor and his presidential campaign had displayed the calm, dispassionate, intellectual reason that the voters had wanted, much to the surprise of pundits and mavens or whatever you called the commentators who thought they knew so much but never tried to find out themselves. It had also helped that his predecessor had run an unaccountably dumb campaign, but Fowler figured he would have won anyway.

The victory, almost two Novembers ago, had left him the first President since—Cleveland, wasn't it?—without a wife. And also without much of a personality. The Technocrat President, the editorial writers called him. That he was by profession a lawyer didn't seem to matter to the news media. Once they had a simple label that all could agree on, they made it truth whether it was accurate or not. The Ice Man.

If only Marian could have lived to see this. She'd known he wasn't made of ice. There were those who remembered what Bob Fowler had once been like, a passionate trial lawyer, advocate of civil rights, the scourge of organized crime. The man who cleaned up Cleveland. Not for very long, of course, for all such victories, like those in politics, were transitory. He remembered the birth of each of his children, the pride of fatherhood, the love of his wife for him and their two children, the quiet dinners in candlelit restaurants. He remembered meeting Marian at a high-school football game, and she'd loved the spectacle as much as he ever had. Thirty years of marriage which had begun while both were still in college, the last three of which had been an ongoing nightmare as the disease that had manifested itself in her late thirties had in her late forties taken a dramatic and downward turn and, finally, a death too long in coming but too soon in arriving, by which time he'd been too exhausted even to shed tears. And then the years of aloneness.

Well, perhaps that was over.

Thank God for the Secret Service, Fowler thought. In the governor's mansion in Columbus it would quickly have gotten out. But not here. Outside his door was a pair of armed agents, and down the hall that Army warrant officer with the leather briefcase called the Football, an appellation which did not please the President, but there were things even he could not change. His National Security Advisor could, in any case, share his bed, and the White House staffers kept the secret. That, he thought, was rather remarkable.

Fowler looked down at his lover. Elizabeth was undeniably pretty. Her skin was pale because her work habits denied her sunlight, but he preferred women with pale, fair skin. The covers were askew because of the previous night's gyrations, and he could examine her back; the skin was so smooth and soft. He felt her relaxed breath on his chest, and the way her left arm wrapped around him. He ran a hand down her back and was rewarded by a *hmmmmm* and a slight increase in pressure from the sleeping hug she gave him.

There was a discreet knock at the door. The President pulled the covers up and coughed. After a five-count, the door opened, and an agent came in with a coffee tray with some document printouts before withdrawing. Fowler knew he couldn't trust one of the ordinary staff *that* far, but the Secret Service really was the American version of the Praetorian Guard. The agent never betrayed his emotions, except for a good-morning nod at the Boss, as the agents referred to him. The devotion they gave him was almost slavish. Though well-educated men and women, they really did have a simple outlook on things, and Fowler knew that there was room in the world for such people. Someone, often someone quite skilled, had to carry out the decisions and orders of his or her superiors. The gun-toting agents were sworn to protect him, even to interpose their bodies between the President and any danger—the maneuver was called "catching the bullet"—and it amazed Fowler that such bright people could train themselves to do something so selflessly dumb. But it was to his benefit. As was their discretion. Well, the joke was that such good help was hard to come by. It was true: you had to be President to have that kind of servant.

Fowler reached for his coffee and poured a cup one-handed. He drank it black. After his first sip he used a remote-control to switch on a TV set. It was tuned to CNN, and the lead story—it was two in the afternoon there—was Rome, of course.

"Mmmmm." Elizabeth moved her head, and her hair swept across him. She always awoke slower than he. Fowler ran a finger down her spine, earning himself a last cuddle before her eyes opened. Her head came up with a violent start.

"Bob!"

"Yes?"

"Somebody's been here!" She pointed to the tray with the cups, and knew that Fowler hadn't fetched it himself.

"Coffee?"

"Bob!"

"Look, Elizabeth, the people outside the door know that you're here. What do you think we are hiding, and from whom are we hiding it? Hell, they probably have microphones in here." He'd never said that before. He didn't know for sure, and had studiously refrained from inquiring, but it was a logical thing to expect. The institutional paranoia of the Secret Service denied the agents the ability to trust Elizabeth or anyone else, except the President. Therefore, if she tried to kill him, they needed to know, so that the agents outside the door could burst in with their guns and save HAWK from his lover. There probably were microphones. Cameras, too? No, probably not cameras, but surely there had to be microphones. Fowler actually found that thought somewhat stimulating, a fact that editorial writers would never have believed. Not the Ice Man.

"My God!" Liz Elliot had never thought of that. She hoisted herself up, and her breasts dangled deliciously before his eyes. But Fowler was not that sort of morning person. Mornings were for work.

"I am the President, Elizabeth," Fowler pointed out as she disengaged herself. The idea of cameras occurred to her, too, and she quickly rearranged the bedclothes. Fowler smiled at the foolishness of it. "Coffee?" he asked again.

Elizabeth Elliot almost giggled. Here she was, in the President's bed, naked as a jaybird, with armed guards outside the door. But Bob had *let someone in the room!* The man was incredible. Had he even covered her up? She could ask, but decided not to, fearing that he might display his twisted sense of humor, which was at its best when it was slightly cruel. And yet. Had she ever had so good a lover as he? The first time—it must have been years, but he was so patient, so . . . respectful. So easy to manage. Elliot smiled her secret smile to herself. He could be directed to do exactly what she wanted, when she wanted it, and do it consummately well, for he loved to give pleasure to a woman. Why? she wondered. Perhaps he wanted to be remembered. He was a politician, after all, and what they all craved was a few lines in history books. Well, he'd have those, one way or another. Every President did, even Grant and Harding were remembered, and with what was happening. . . . Even here he craved being remembered, and so he did what the woman wanted, if the woman had the wit to ask.

"Turn the sound up," Liz said. Fowler complied at once, she was gratified to see. So eager to please, even in this. So why the hell had he let some servant in with the coffee! There was no understanding this man. He was already reading over the faxes from Rome.

"My dear, this is going to work. I hope your bags are packed, Elizabeth."

"Oh?"

"The Saudis and the Israelis actually agreed on the big one last night . . . according to Brent—God, this is amazing! He had separate solo sessions with both sides, and both of them suggested the same thing . . . and to keep them from knowing it, he simply cycled back and forth as he said it would probably be acceptable . . . then confirmed it on another round trip! Ha!" Fowler slapped the back of his hand on the page. "Brent is really delivering for us. And that Ryan guy, too. He's a pretentious pain in the ass, but that idea of his—"

"Come on, Bob! It wasn't even original. Ryan just repeated some things other people have been saying for years. It was new to Arnie, but Arnie's interests stop at the White House fence. Giving credit to Ryan for this is like saying he managed a nice sunset for you."

"Maybe," the President allowed. He thought there was more to the DDCI's concept-proposal than that, but it wasn't worth upsetting Elizabeth about. "Ryan did do a nice job with the Saudis, remember?"

"He'd be a lot more effective if he'd just keep his mouth shut. Fine, he gave the Saudis a good brief. That's not exactly a great moment in American foreign policy, is it? Giving briefs is his job. Brent and Dennis are the guys who really pulled it together, not Ryan."

"I suppose not. You're right, I guess. Brent and Dennis are the ones who got the final commitments to the conference . . . Brent says three more days, maybe four." The President handed the faxes over. It was time for him to rise and prepare for a day's work, but before he did he ran a hand over a particular curve in the sheet, just to let her know that . . .

"Stop that!" Liz giggled to make it sound playful. He did as told, of course. To ease the blow, she leaned over for a kiss, which was delivered, bad breath and all, just as requested.

"What gives?" a truck driver asked at the lumber terminal. Four enormous trailers sat in a line, away from the stacks of felled trees being prepared for shipment to Japan. "They were here last time, too."

"Going to Japan," the dispatcher observed, going over the trucker's manifest.

"So, what here ain't?"

"Something special. They're paying to have those logs kept that way, renting the trailers and everything. I hear the logs are being made into beams for a church or temple or something. Look close—they're chained together. Tied with a silk rope, too, but chains to make sure they stay together. Something about the tradition of the temple or something. Going to be a bitch of a rigging job to load them on the ship that way."

"Renting the trailers just to keep the logs in a special place? Chaining them together. Jeez! They got more money'n brains, don't they?"

"What do we care?" the dispatcher asked, tired of answering the same question every time a driver came through his office.

And they were sitting there. The idea, the dispatcher thought, was to let the logs season some. But whoever had thought that one up hadn't been thinking very clearly. This was the wettest summer on record in an area known for its precipitation, and the logs, which had been heavy with moisture when their parent tree had been felled, were merely soaking up more rain as it fell down across the yard. The stubs of branches trimmed off in the field hadn't helped much either. The rain just soaked into the exposed capillaries and proceeded into the trunk. The logs were probably heavier now than when they had been cut. Maybe they should throw a tarp over them, the dispatcher thought, but then they'd just be trapping the moisture in, and besides, the orders were to let them sit on the trailers. It was raining now. The yard was turning into a damned swamp, the mud churned by every passing truck and loading machine. Well, the Japanese probably had their own plans for seasoning and working the logs. Their orders precluded doing any real seasoning here, and it was their money. Even when they were loaded on the ship, they were supposed to be carried topside, the last items loaded on the MV *George McReady* for shipment across the Pacific. Sure as hell they'd get wet that way, too. If they got much wetter, the dispatcher thought, someone would have to be careful with them. If they got dropped into the river, they would scarcely float.

The farmer knew that his grandchildren were embarrassed by his backwardness. They resisted his hugs and kisses, probably complained a little before their father brought them out here, but he didn't mind. Children today lacked the respect of his generation. Perhaps that was a price for their greater opportunities. The cycle of the ages was breaking. His life had been little different from ten generations of ancestors, but his son was doing better despite his injuries, and his children would do better still. The boys were proud of their father. If their schoolmates commented adversely on their Druse religion, the boys could point out that their father had fought and bled against the hated Israelis, had even killed a few of the Zionists. The Syrian government was not totally ungrateful to its wounded veterans. The farmer's son had his own modest business, and government officials did not harass him, as they might otherwise have done. He'd married late, which was unusual for the area. His wife was pretty enough, and respectful—she treated the farmer well, possibly in gratitude for the fact that he had never shown an interest in moving into her small household. The farmer showed great pride in his grandchildren, strong, healthy boys, headstrong and rebellious as boys should be. The farmer's son was similarly proud, and was prospering. He and his father walked outside after the noon meal. The son looked at the garden that he'd once weeded, and felt pangs of guilt that his father was still working there every day. But hadn't he offered to take his father in? Hadn't he offered to give his father a little money? All such offers had been rejected. His father didn't have much, but he did have his stubborn pride.

"The garden looks very healthy this year."

"The rain has been good," the farmer agreed. "There are many new lambs. It has not been a bad year. And you?"

"My best year. Father, I wish you did not have to work so hard."

"Ah!" A wave of the hand. "What other life have I known? This is my place."

The courage of the man, the son thought. And the old man did have courage. He endured. Despite everything. He had not been able to give his son much, but he had passed along his stoic courage. When he'd found himself lying stunned on the Golan Heights, twenty meters from the smoking wreckage of the personnel carrier, he could have just lain down to die, the son knew, his eye put out, and his left hand a bloody mess that doctors would later have to remove. He could have just lain there on the ground and died, but he'd known that giving up was not something his father would have done. And so he'd risen and walked six kilometers to a battalion aid station, arriving there still carrying his rifle and accepting treatment only after making his report. He had a decoration for that, and his battalion commander had made life a little easier for him, giving him some money to start his little shop, making sure that local officials knew that he was to be treated with respect. The Colonel had given him the money, but his father had given him the courage. If only he would now accept a little help.

"My son, I need your advice."

That was something new. "Certainly, Father."

"Come, I will show you." He led his son into the garden, where the carrots were. With his foot, he scraped dirt off the—

"Stop!" the son nearly screamed. He took his father by the arm and pulled him back. "My God—how long has that been there?"

"Since the day you were hurt," the farmer answered.

The son's right hand went to his eyepatch, and for one horrid moment the terror of the day came back to him. The blinding flash, flying through the air, his dead comrades screaming as they burned to death. The Israelis had done that. One of their cannons had killed his mother, and now—this?

What was it? He commanded his father to stay put and walked back to see. He moved very carefully, as though he were traversing a minefield. His assignment in the Army had been with the combat engineers; though his unit had been committed to battle with the infantry, their job was supposed to have been laying a minefield. It was big, it looked like a thousand-kilo bomb. It had to be Israeli; he knew that from the color. He turned to look at his father.

"This has been here since then?"

"Yes. It made its own hole, and I filled it in. The frost must have brought it up. Is there danger? It is broken, no?"

"Father, these things never truly die. It is very dangerous. Big as it is, if it goes off it could destroy the house and you in it!"

The farmer gestured contempt for the thing. "If it wanted to explode, it would have done so when it fell."

"That is not true! You will listen to me on this. You will not come close to this cursed thing!"

"And what of my garden?" the farmer asked simply.

"I will find a way to have this removed. Then you can garden." The son considered that. It would be a problem. Not a small problem, either. The Syrian Army did not have a pool of skilled people to disarm unexploded bombs. Their method was to detonate them in place, which was eminently sensible, but his father would not long survive the destruction of his house. His wife would not easily tolerate having him in their own home, and he could not help his father rebuild, not with only one hand. The bomb had to be removed, but who would do that?

"You must promise me that you will not enter the garden!" the son announced sternly.

"As you say," the farmer replied. He had no intention of following his son's orders. "When can you have it removed?"

"I don't know. I need a few days to see what I can do."

The farmer nodded. Perhaps he'd follow his son's instructions after all, at least about not approaching this dead bomb. It had to be dead, of course, despite what his son had said. The farmer knew that much of fate. If the bomb had wanted to kill him, it would have happened by now. What other misfortune had avoided him?

The newsies finally got something to sink their teeth into the next day. Dimitrios Stavarkos, Patriarch of Constantinople, arrived by car—he refused to fly in helicopters—in broad daylight.

"A nun with a beard?" a cameraman asked over his hot mike as he zoomed in. The Swiss Guards at the door rendered honors, and Bishop O'Toole conducted the new visitor inside and out of view.

"Greek," the anchorman observed at once. "Greek Orthodox, must be a bishop or something. What's he doing here?" the anchor mused.

"What do we know about the Greek Orthodox Church?" his producer asked.

"They don't work for the Pope. They allow their priests to marry. The Israelis threw one of them in prison once for giving arms to the Arabs, I think," someone else observed over the line.

"So the Greeks get along with the Arabs, but not the Pope? What about the Israelis?"

"Don't know," the producer admitted. "Might be a good idea to find out."

"So now there are four religious groups involved."

"Is the Vatican really involved or did they just offer this place as neutral ground?" the Anchor asked. Like most anchormen, he was at his best when reading copy from a TelePrompTer.

"When has this happened before? If you want 'neutral,' you go to Geneva," the cameraman observed. He liked Geneva.

"What gives?" One of the researchers entered the booth. The producer filled her in.

"Where's that damned consultant?" the Anchor growled.

"Can you run the tape back?" the researcher asked. The control-room crew did that, and she freeze-framed the monitor.

"Dimitrios Stavarkos. He's the Patriarch of Constantinople—Istanbul to you,

Rick. He's the head of all the Orthodox churches, kind of like the Pope. The Greek, Russian, and Bulgarian Orthodox churches have their own heads, but they all defer to the Patriarch. Something like that."

"They allow their priests to marry, don't they?"

"Their priests, yes . . . but as I recall, if you become a bishop or higher, you have to be celibate—"

"Bummer," Rick observed.

"Stavarkos led the battle with the Catholics over the Church of the Nativity last year—won it, too, as I recall. He really pissed a few Catholic bishops off. What the hell is *he* doing here?"

"You're supposed to tell us that, Angie!" the Anchor noted crossly.

"Hold your water, Rick." Angie Miriles was tired of dealing with the airheaded prima donna. She sipped at her coffee for a minute or two and made her announcement. "I think I have this figured out."

"You mind filling us in?"

"Welcome!" Cardinal D'Antonio kissed Stavarkos on both cheeks. He found the man's beard distasteful, but that could not be helped. The Cardinal led the Patriarch into the conference room. There were sixteen people grouped around a table, and at the foot of it was an empty chair. Stavarkos took it.

"Thank you for joining us," said Secretary Talbot.

"One does not reject an invitation of this sort," the Patriarch replied.

"You've read the briefing material?" That had been delivered by messenger.

"It is very ambitious," Stavarkos allowed cautiously.

"Can you accept your role in the agreement?"

This was going awfully fast, the Patriarch thought. But— "Yes," he answered simply. "I require plenipotentiary authority over all Christian shrines in the Holy Land. If that is agreed to, then I will gladly join your agreement."

D'Antonio managed to keep his face impassive. He controlled his breathing and prayed rapidly for divine intervention. He'd never quite be able to decide whether he got it or not.

"It is very late in the day for such a sweeping demand." Heads turned. The speaker was Dmitriy Popov, First Deputy Foreign Minister of the Soviet Union. "It is also inconsiderate to seek unilateral advantage when everyone here has conceded so much. Would you stand in the way of the accord on that basis alone?"

Stavarkos was not accustomed to such direct rebukes.

"The question of Christian shrines is not of direct significance to the agreement, Your Holiness," Secretary Talbot observed. "We find your conditional willingness to participate disappointing."

"Perhaps I misunderstood the briefing material," Stavarkos allowed, covering his flanks. "Could you perhaps clarify what my status would be?"

"No way," the Anchor snorted.

"Why not?" Angela Miriles replied. "What else makes sense?"

"It's just too much."

"It is a lot," Miriles agreed, "but what else fits?"

"I'll believe it when I see it."

"You might not see it. Stavarkos doesn't much like the Roman Catholic Church. That battle they had last Christmas was a nasty one."

"How come we didn't report it, then?"

"Because we were too damned busy talking about the downturn in Christmas sales figures," *you asshole,* she didn't add.

"A separate commission, then?" Stavarkos didn't like that.

"The Metropolitan wishes to send his own representative," Popov said. Dmitriy Popov still believed in Marx rather than God, but the Russian Orthodox Church was *Russian,* and Russian participation in the agreement had to be real, however minor this point might appear. "I must say that I find this matter curious. Do we hold up the agreement on the issue of which Christian church is the most influential? Our purpose here is to defuse a potential flashpoint for war between Jews and Muslims, and the Christians stand in the way?" Popov asked the ceiling—a little theatrically, D'Antonio thought.

"This side issue is best left to a separate committee of Christian clerics," Cardinal D'Antonio finally allowed himself to say. "I pledge you my word before God that sectarian squabbles are at an end!"

I've heard that before, Stavarkos reminded himself—and yet. And yet, how could he allow himself to be so petty? He reminded himself also of what the Scriptures taught, and that he believed in every word of it. *I am making a fool of myself, and doing it before the Romans and the Russians!* An additional consideration was that the Turks merely tolerated his presence in Istanbul—Constantinople!—and this gave him the chance to earn immense prestige for his churches and his office.

"Please forgive me. I have allowed some regrettable incidents to color my better judgment. Yes, I will support this agreement, and I will trust my brethren to keep their word."

Brent Talbot leaned back in his chair and whispered his own prayer of thanks. Praying wasn't a habit with the Secretary of State, but here, in these surroundings, how could one avoid it?

"In that case, I believe we have an agreement." Talbot looked around the table, and one after another the heads nodded, some with enthusiasm, some with resignation. But they all nodded. They had reached an agreement.

"Mr. Adler, when will the documents be ready for initialing?" D'Antonio asked.

"Two hours, Your Eminence."

"Your Highness," Talbot said as he rose to his feet, "Your Eminences, Ministers—we have done it."

Strangely, they scarcely realized what they had done. The process had lasted for quite some time, and as with all such negotiations, the process had become reality, and the objective had become something separate from it. Now suddenly they were at the place they all intended to reach, and the wonder of the fact gave to them a sense of unreality that, for all their collective expertise at formulating and reaching foreign-policy goals, overcame their perceptions. Each of the participants stood, as Talbot did, and the movement, the stretch of legs, altered their perceptions somewhat. One by one they understood what they had done. More importantly, they understood that they had actually done it. The impossible had just happened.

David Askenazi walked around the table to Prince Ali, who had handled his country's part in the negotiations, and extended his hand. That wasn't good enough. The Prince gave the Minister a brotherly embrace.

"Before God, there will be peace between us, David."

"After all these years, Ali," replied the former Israeli tanker. As a lieutenant,

Askenazi had fought in the Suez in 1956, again as a captain in 1967, and his reserve battalion had reinforced the Golan in 1973. Both men were surprised by the applause that broke out. The Israeli burst into tears, embarrassing himself beyond belief.

"Do not be ashamed. Your personal courage is well known, Minister," Ali said graciously. "It is fitting that a soldier should make the peace, David."

"So many deaths. All those fine young boys who—on both sides, Ali. All those boys."

"But no more."

"Dmitriy, your help was extraordinary," Talbot told his Russian counterpart at the other end of the table.

"Remarkable what can happen when we cooperate, is it not?"

What occurred to Talbot had come already to Askenazi: "Two whole generations pissed away, Dmitriy. All that wasted time."

"We cannot recover lost time," Popov replied. "We can have the wit not to lose any more." The Russian smiled crookedly. "For moments like this, there should be vodka."

Talbot jerked his head toward Prince Ali. "We don't all drink."

"How can they live without vodka?" Popov chuckled.

"One of the mysteries of life, Dmitriy. We both have cables to send."

"Indeed we do, my friend."

To the fury of the correspondents in Rome, the first to break the story was a *Washington Post* reporter in Washington. It was inevitable. She had a source, an Air Force sergeant who did electronic maintenance on the VC-25A, the President's new military version of the Boeing 747. The sergeant had been prepped by the reporter. Everyone knew that the President was heading to Rome. It was just a question of when. As soon as the sergeant learned that she'd be heading out, she'd ostensibly called home to check that her good uniform was back from the cleaners. That she had called the wrong number was an honest mistake. It was just that the reporter had the same gag message on her answering machine. That was the story she'd use if she ever got caught, but she didn't in this case, and didn't ever expect to be.

An hour later, at the routine morning meeting between the President's press secretary and the White House correspondents, the *Post* reporter announced an "unconfirmed report" that Fowler was going to Rome—and did this mean that the treaty negotiations had reached an impasse or success? The press secretary was caught short by that. He'd just learned ten minutes before that he'd be flying to Rome, and as usual was sworn to total secrecy—an admonition that carried about as much weight as sunlight on a cloudy day. He allowed himself to be surprised by the question, though, and that surprised the man who had fully expected to engineer the leak—but only *after* lunch at the afternoon briefing. His "no comment" hadn't carried enough conviction, and the White House correspondents smelled the blood in the water. They all had edited copies of the President's appointments schedule, and sure enough, there were names to check with.

The President's aides were already making calls to cancel appointments and appearances. Even the President cannot allow important people to be inconvenienced without warning, and while those might keep secrets, not all of their assistants and secretaries can. It was a classic case of the phenomenon upon which a free press depends. People who know things cannot keep them inside. Especially secret things. Within an hour, confirmation was obtained from four widely separated sources:

President Fowler had canceled several days' worth of appointments. The President was going somewhere, and it wasn't Peoria. That was enough for all the TV networks to run bulletins timed to erase segments of various game shows with hastily written statements, which immediately cut to commercials, denying millions of people the knowledge of what the word or phrase was, but informing them of the best way to get their clothes clean despite deep grass stains.

It was late afternoon in Rome, a sultry, humid summer day, when the pool headquarters was told that three, only three, cameras—and no correspondents—would be permitted into the building whose outside had been subjected to weeks of careful scrutiny. In the "green room" trailers near each of the anchor booths, the network anchors on duty had makeup applied and hustled to their chairs, putting their earpieces in and waiting for word from their directors.

The picture that appeared simultaneously on the booth monitors and TV sets all over the world showed the conference room. In it was a large table all of whose seats were filled. At its head was the Pope, and before him was a folder of folio size, made of red calfskin—the reporters would never know of the momentary panic that had erupted when someone realized that he *didn't* know what kind of leather it was, and had to check with the supplier; fortunately, no one objected to the skin of a calf.

It had been agreed that no statement would be made here. Preliminary statements would be made in the capitals of each of the participants, and the really flowery speeches were being drafted for the formal signing ceremonies. A Vatican spokesman delivered a written release to all of the TV correspondents. It said in essence that a draft treaty concerning a final settlement of the Middle East dispute had been negotiated, and that the draft was ready for initialing by representatives of the interested nations. The formal treaty documents would be signed by the chiefs of state and/or foreign ministers in several days. The text of the treaty was not available for release, nor were its provisions. This did not exactly thrill the correspondents—mainly because they realized that the treaty details would be broken from the foreign ministries in the respective capitals of the concerned nations, to other reporters.

The red folder was passed from place to place. The order of the initialers, the Vatican statement pointed out, had been determined by lot, and it turned out that the Israeli Foreign Minister went first, followed by the Soviet, the Swiss, the American, the Saudi, and the Vatican representatives. Each used a fountain pen, and a curved blotter was applied to each set of initials by the priest who moved the document from place to place. It wasn't much of a ceremony, and it was swiftly accomplished. Handshakes came next, followed by a lengthy bit of mutual applause. And that was it.

"By God," Jack said, watching the TV picture change. He looked down to the fax of the treaty outline, and it was not very different from his original concept. The Saudis had made changes, as had the Israelis, the Soviets, the Swiss, and, of course, the State Department, but the original idea was his—except insofar as he himself had borrowed ideas from a multitude of others. There were few genuinely original ideas. What he'd really done had been to organize them, and pick an historically correct moment to make his comment. That was all. For all that, it was the proudest moment of his life. It was a shame that there was no one to congratulate him.

In the White House, President Fowler's best speechwriter was already working on the first draft of his speech. The American President would have primacy of place at the ceremony because it had been his idea, after all, his speech before the U.N. that had brought them all together in Rome. The Pope would speak—hell, they would all speak, the speechwriter thought, and for her that was a problem, since each speech had to be original and unrepetitive. She realized that she'd probably still be working on it while hopping the Atlantic on the -25A, pecking busily away on her laptop. But that, she knew, was what they paid her for, and Air Force One had a Laserjet printer.

Upstairs in the Oval Office the President was looking over his hastily revised schedule. A committee of new Eagle Scouts would have to be disappointed, as would the new Wisconsin Cheese Queen, or whatever the young lady's title was, and a multitude of business people whose importance in their own small ponds quite literally paled when they entered the side door into the President's workshop. His appointments secretary was getting the word out. Some people whose visits were genuinely important were being shoehorned into every spare minute of the next thirty-six hours. That would make the President's next day and a half as hectic as it ever got, but that, too, was part of the job.

"Well?" Fowler looked up to see Elizabeth Elliot grinning at him through the open door to the secretary's anteroom.

Well, this is what you wanted, isn't it? Your presidency will forever be remembered as the one in which the Middle East problems were settled once and for all. If—Liz admitted to herself in a rare moment of objective clarity—*it all works out, which is not a given in such disputes as this.*

"We have done a service to the whole world, Elizabeth." By "we" he actually meant "I," Elliot knew, but that was fair enough. It was Bob Fowler who'd endured the months of campaigning on top of his executive duties in Columbus, the endless speeches, kissing babies and kissing ass, stroking legions of reporters whose faces changed far more rapidly than their brutally repetitive questions. It was an endurance race to get into this one small room, this seat of executive power. It was a process that somehow did not break the men—pity it was still only men, Liz thought—who made it safely here. But the prize for all the effort, all the endless toil, was that the person who occupied it got to take the credit. It was a simple historical convention that people assumed the President was the one who directed things, who made the decisions. Because of that, the President was the one who got the kudos and the barbs. The President was responsible for what went well and for what went badly. Mostly that concerned domestic affairs, the blips in the unemployment figures, interest rates, inflation (wholesale and retail), and the all-powerful Leading Economic Indicators, but on rare occasions, something really important happened, something that changed the world. Reagan, Elliot admitted to herself, would be remembered by history as the guy who happened to be around when the Russians decided to cash in their chips on Marxism, and Bush was the man who collected that particular political pot. Nixon was the man who'd opened the door to China, and Carter the one who had come so tantalizingly close to doing what Fowler would now be remembered for. The American voters might select their political leaders for pocketbook issues, but history was made of more important stuff. What earned a man a few paragraphs in a general-history text and focused volumes of scholarly study were the fundamental changes in the shape of the political world. That was what really counted. Historians remembered the ones who shaped political events—Bismarck, not Edison—treating technical changes in society as though they were driven by political factors, and not the reverse, which, she judged, might have been equally likely. But historiography had its own rules and conventions that had little to do with reality, because reality was too large a thing to grasp, even for academics working years after events. Politicians played within those rules, and that suited them because following those rules meant that when something memorable happened, the historians would remember them.

"Service to the world?" Elliot responded after a lengthy pause. "Service to the world. I like the sound of that. They called Wilson the man who kept us out of war. You will be remembered as the one who put an end to war."

Fowler and Elliot both knew that scant months after being reelected on that platform, Wilson had led America into its first truly foreign war, the war to end all wars, optimists had called it, well before Holocaust and nuclear nightmares. But this time, both thought, it was more than mere optimism, and Wilson's transcendent vision of what the world could be was finally within the grasp of the political figures who made the world into the shape of their own choosing.

The man was a Druse, an unbeliever, but for all that he was respected. He bore the scars of his own battle with the Zionists. He'd gone into battle, and been decorated for his courage. He'd lost his mother to their inhuman weapons. And he'd supported the movement whenever asked. Qati was a man who had never lost touch with the fundamentals. As a boy he'd read the *Little Red Book* of Chairman Mao. That Mao was, of course, an infidel of the worst sort—he'd refused even to acknowledge the idea of a God and persecuted those who worshiped—was beside the point. The revolutionary was a fish who swam in a peasant sea, and maintaining the goodwill of those peasants—or in this case, a shopkeeper—was the foundation of whatever success he might enjoy. This Druse had contributed what money he could, had once sheltered a wounded freedom fighter in his home. Such debts were not forgotten. Qati rose from his desk to greet the man with a warm handshake and the perfunctory kisses.

"Welcome, my friend."

"Thank you for seeing me, Commander." The shopkeeper seemed very nervous, and Qati wondered what the problem was.

"Please, take a chair. Abdullah," he called, "would you bring coffee for our guest?"

"You are too kind."

"Nonsense. You are our comrade. Your friendship has not wavered in—how many years?"

The shopkeeper shrugged, smiling inwardly that this investment was about to pay off. He was frightened of Qati and his people—that was why he had never crossed them. He also kept Syrian authorities informed of what he'd done for them, because he was wary of those people, too. Mere survival in that part of the world was an art form, and a game of chance.

"I come to you for advice," he said after his first sip of coffee.

"Certainly." Qati leaned forward in his chair. "I am honored to be of help. What is the problem, my friend?"

"It is my father."

"How old is he now?" Qati asked. The farmer had occasionally given his men gifts also, most often a lamb. Just a peasant, and an infidel peasant at that, but he was one who shared his enemy with Qati and his men.

"Sixty-six—you know his garden?"

"Yes, I was there some years ago, soon after your mother was killed by the Zionists," Qati reminded him.

"In his garden there is an Israeli bomb."

"Bomb? You mean a shell."

"No, Commander, a bomb. What you can see of it is half a meter across."

"I see—and if the Syrians learn of it . . ."

"Yes. As you know, they explode such things in place. My father's house would be destroyed." The visitor held up his left forearm. "I cannot be of much help rebuilding it, and my father is too old to do it himself. I come here to ask how one might go about removing the damned thing."

"You have come to the right place. Do you know how long it has been there?"

"My father says that it fell the very day this happened to me." The shopkeeper gestured with his ruined arm again.

"Then surely Allah smiled on your family that day."

Some smile, the shopkeeper thought, nodding.

"You have been our most faithful friend. Of course we can help you. I have a man highly skilled in the business of disarming and removing Israeli bombs—and then he takes the guts from them and makes bombs for our use." Qati stopped and held up an admonishing finger. "You must never repeat that."

The visitor jerked somewhat in his chair. "For my part, Commander, you may kill all of them you wish, and if you can do it from a bomb the pigs dropped into my father's garden, I will pray for your safety and success."

"Please excuse me, my friend. No insult was intended. I must say such things, as you can understand." Qati's message was fully understood.

"I will never betray you," the shopkeeper announced forcefully.

"I know this." Now it was time to keep faith with the peasant sea. "Tomorrow I will send my man to your father's home. *Insh'Allah,*" he said, God willing.

"I am in your debt, Commander." *Sometime between now and the new year,* he hoped.

8. The Pandora Process

The converted Boeing 747 rotated off the Andrews runway just before sunset. President Fowler had had a bad day and a half of briefings and unbreakable appointments. He would have two more even worse; even presidents are subject to the vagaries of ordinary human existence, and in this case, the eight-hour flight to Rome was coupled with a six-hour time change. The jet lag would be a killer. Fowler was a seasoned-enough traveler to know that. To attenuate the worst of it, he'd fiddled with his sleep pattern yesterday and today so that he'd be sufficiently tired to sleep most of the way across, and the VC-25A had lavish accommodations to make the flight as comfortable as Boeing and the United States Air Force could arrange. An easy-riding aircraft, the -25A had its presidential accommodations in the very tip of the nose. The bed—actually a convertible sofa—was of decent size, and the mattress had been selected for his personal taste. The aircraft was also large enough that a proper separation between the press and the administration people was possible—nearly two hundred feet, in fact; the press was in a closed-off section in the tail—and while his press secretary was dealing with the reporters aft, Fowler was discreetly joined by his National Security Advisor. Pete Connor and Helen D'Agustino shared a look that an outsider might take to be blank, but which spoke volumes within the close fraternity of the Secret Service. The Air Force Security Policeman assigned to the door just stared at the aft bulkhead, trying not to smile.

"So, Ibrahim, what of our visitor?" Qati asked.

"He is strong, fearless, and quite cunning, but I don't know what possible use we have for him," Ibrahim Ghosn replied. He related the story of the Greek policeman.

"Broke his neck?" At least the man was not a plant . . . that is, if the policeman had really died, and this was not an elaborate ruse of the Americans, Greeks, Israelis, or God only knew who.

"Like a twig."

"His contacts in America?"

"They are few. He is hunted by their national police. His group, he says, killed three of them, and his brother was recently ambushed and murdered by them."

"He is ambitious in his choice of enemies. His education?"

"Poor in formal terms, but he is clever."

"Skills?"

"Few that are of use to us."

"He *is* an American," Qati pointed out. "How many of those have we had?"

Ghosn nodded. "That is true, Commander."

"The chance that he could be an infiltrator?"

"I would say slim, but we must be careful."

"In any case, I have something I need you to do." Qati explained about the bomb.

"Another one?" Ghosn was an expert at this task, but he was not exactly excited about being stuck with it. "I know the farm—that foolish old man. I know, I know, his son fought against the Israelis, and you like the cripple."

"That cripple saved the life of a comrade. Fazi would have bled to death had he not received shelter in that little shop. He didn't have to do that. That was at a time when the Syrians were angry with us."

"All right. I have nothing to do for the rest of the day. I need a truck and a few men."

"This new friend is strong, you say. Take him with you."

"As you say, Commander."

"And be careful!"

"*Insh'Allah.*" Ghosn was almost a graduate of the American University of Beirut—almost because one of his teachers had been kidnapped, and two others had used that as an excuse to leave the country. That had denied Ghosn the last nine credit hours needed for a degree in engineering. Not that he really needed it. He'd been at the top of his class, and learned well enough from the textbooks without having to listen to the explanations of instructors. He'd spent quite a bit of time in labs of his own making. Ghosn had never been a front-line soldier of the movement. Though he knew how to use small arms, his skills with explosives and electronic devices were too valuable to be risked. He was also youthful in appearance, handsome, and quite fair-skinned, as a result of which he traveled a lot. An advance man of sorts, he often surveyed sites for future operations, using his engineer's eye and memory to sketch maps, determine equipment needs, and provide technical support for the actual operations people, who treated him with far more respect than an outsider might have expected. Of his courage there was no doubt. He'd proven his bravery more than once, defusing unexploded bombs and shells that the Israelis had left in Lebanon, then reworking the explosives recovered into bombs of his own. Ibrahim Ghosn would have been a welcome addition to any one of a dozen professional organizations anywhere in the world. A gifted, if largely self-taught engineer, he was also a Palestinian whose family had evacuated Israel at the time of the country's founding, confidently expecting to return as soon as the Arab armies of the time erased the invaders quickly and easily. But that happy circumstance had not come about, and his childhood memories were of crowded, unsanitary camps where antipathy for Israel had been a creed as important as Islam. It could not have been otherwise. Disregarded by the Israelis as people who had voluntarily left their country, largely ignored by other Arab nations who might have made their lot easier but had not, Ghosn and those like him were mere pawns in a great game whose players had never agreed upon the rules. Hatred of Israel and its friends came as naturally as breathing, and finding ways to end the lives of such people was his task in life. It had never occurred to him to wonder why.

Ghosn got the keys for a Czech-built GAZ-66 truck. It wasn't as reliable as a Mercedes, but a lot easier to obtain—in this case it had been funneled to his organization through the Syrians years before. On the back was a home-built A-frame. Ghosn loaded the American in the cab with himself and the driver. Two other men rode on the loadbed as the truck pulled out of the camp.

Marvin Russell examined the terrain with the interest of a hunter in a new territory. The heat was oppressive, but really no worse than the Badlands during a bad summer wind, and the vegetation—or lack of it—wasn't all that different from the reservation of his youth. What appeared to others as bleak was just another dusty place to an American raised on one. Except here they didn't have the towering thunderstorms—and the tornados they spawned—of the American Plains. The hills were also higher than the rolling Badlands. Russell had never seen mountains before. Here he saw them, high and dry and hot enough to make a climber gasp. Most climbers, Marvin Russell thought. He could hack it. He was in shape, better shape than these Arabs.

The Arabs, on the other hand, seemed to be believers in guns. So many guns, mostly Russian AK-47s at first, but soon he was seeing heavy antiaircraft guns and the odd battery of surface-to-air missiles, tanks, and self-propelled field guns belonging to the Syrian Army. Ghosn noted his guest's interest and started explaining things.

"These are here to keep the Israelis out," he said, casting his explanation in accordance with his own beliefs. "Your country arms the Israelis and the Russians arm us." He didn't add that this was becoming increasingly tenuous.

"Ibrahim, have you been attacked?"

"Many times, Marvin. They send their aircraft. They send commando teams. They have killed thousands of my people. They drove us from our land, you see. We are forced to live in camps that—"

"Yeah, man. They're called reservations where I come from." That was something Ghosn didn't know about. "They came to our land, the land of our ancestors, killed off the buffalo, sent in their army, and massacred us. Mainly they attacked camps of women and children. We tried to fight back. We killed a whole regiment under General Custer at a place called the Little Big Horn—that's the name of a river—under a leader named Crazy Horse. But they didn't stop coming. Just too many of them, too many soldiers, too many guns, and they took the best of our land, and left us shit, man. They make us live like beggars. No, that's not right. Like animals, like we're not people, even, 'cause we look different, speak different, got a different religion. They did all that 'cause we were in a place they wanted to have, and they just moved us out, like sweepin' away the garbage.''

''I didn't know about that,'' Ghosn said, amazed that his were not the only people to be treated that way by the Americans and their Israeli vassals. ''When did it happen?''

''Hundred years ago. Actually started around 1865. We fought, man, we did the best we could, but we didn't have much of a chance. We didn't have friends, see? Didn't have friends like you got. Nobody gave us guns and tanks. So they killed off the bravest. Mainly they trapped the leaders and murdered them—Crazy Horse and Sitting Bull died like that. Then they squeezed us and starved us until we had to surrender. Left us dusty, shitty places to live, sent us enough food to keep us alive, but not enough to be strong. When some of us try to fight back, try to be men—well, I told you what they did to my brother. Shot him from ambush like he was an animal. Did it on television, even, so's people would know what happened when an Indian got too big for his britches.''

The man *was* a comrade, Ghosn realized. This was no infiltrator, and his story was no different from the story of a Palestinian. Amazing.

''So why did you come here, Marvin?''

''I had to leave before they got me, man. I ain't proud of it, but what else could I do—you want me to wait till they could ambush me?'' Russell shrugged. ''I figured I'd come someplace, find people like me, maybe learn a few things, learn how I could go back, maybe, teach my people how to fight back some.'' Russell shook his head. ''Hell, maybe it's all hopeless, but I ain't gonna give in—you understand that?''

''Yes, my friend, I understand. It has been so with my people since before I was born. But you, too, must understand: it is not hopeless. So long as you stand up and fight back, there is always hope. That is why they hunt you—because they fear you!''

''Hope you're right, man.'' Russell stared out the open window, and the dust stung his eyes, 7,000 miles from home. ''So, what are we doing?''

''When you fought the Americans, how did your warriors get weapons?''

''Mainly we took what they left behind.''

''So it is with us, Marvin.''

Fowler woke up about halfway across the Atlantic. Well, that was a first, he told himself. He'd never managed to do it in an airplane before. He wondered if any U.S. president had, or done it on the way to see the Pope, or with his National Security Advisor. He looked out the windows. It was bright this far north—the aircraft was close to Greenland—and he wondered for a moment if it were morning or still night. That was almost a metaphysical question on an airplane, of course, which changed the time far faster than a watch could.

Also metaphysical was his mission. This would be remembered. Fowler knew his history. This was something unique. It had never happened before. Perhaps it was the beginning of the process, perhaps the end of it, but what he was up to was simply expressed. He would put an end to war. J. Robert Fowler's name would be associated with this treaty. It was the initiative of his presidential administration.

His speech at the U.N. had called the nations of the world to the Vatican. His subordinates had run the negotiations. His name would be the first on the treaty documents. His armed forces would guarantee the peace. He had truly earned his place in history. That was immortality, the kind that all men wanted but few earned. Was it any wonder that he was excited? he asked himself with dispassionate reflectivity.

A president's greatest fear was gone now. He'd asked himself that question from the first moment, the first fleeting self-directed thought, while still a prosecutor chasing after the *capo* of the Cleveland family of the Cosa Nostra—*if you're the President, what if you have to push the button?* Could he have done it? Could he have decided that the security of his country required the deaths of thousands—millions—of other human beings? Probably not, he judged. He was too good a man for that. His job was to protect people, to show them the way, to lead them along a beneficial path. They might not always understand that he was right and they wrong, that his vision was the correct one, the logical one. Fowler knew himself to be cold and aloof on such matters, but he was always right. Of that he was certain. He had to be certain, of himself and his motivations. Were he ever wrong, he knew, his conviction would be mere arrogance, and he'd faced that charge often enough. The one thing he was unsure about was his ability to face a nuclear war.

But that was no longer an issue, was it? Though he'd never admit it publicly, Reagan and Bush had ended that chance, forcing the Soviets to face their own contradictions, and facing them, to change their ways. And it had all happened in peace, because men really were more logical than beasts. There would continue to be hot spots, but so long as he did his job right they would not get out of hand—and the trip he was making now would end the most dangerous problem remaining in the world, the one with which no recent administration could cope. What Nixon and Kissinger had failed to do, what had defied the valiant efforts of Carter, the halfhearted attempts of Reagan, and the well-meaning gambits of Bush and his own predecessor, what all had failed to do, Bob Fowler would accomplish. It was a thought in which to bask. Not only would he find his place in the history books, but he would also make the rest of his presidency that much easier to manage. This would also put the seal on his second term, a forty-five-state majority, solid control of Congress, and the remainder of his sweeping social programs. With historic accomplishments like this one came international prestige and immense domestic clout. It was power of the best kind, earned in the best way, and the sort that he could put to the best possible use. With a stroke of a pen—actually several pens, for that was the custom—Fowler became great, a giant among the good, and a good man among the powerful. Not once in a generation did a single man have such a moment as this. Maybe not once in a century. And no one could take it away.

The aircraft was traveling at 43,000 feet, moving at a ground speed of 633 knots. The placement of his cabin allowed him to look forward, as a president should look, and down at a world whose affairs he was managing so well. The ride was silky smooth, and Bob Fowler was going to make history. He looked over to Elizabeth, lying on her back, her right hand up around her head and the covers down at her waist, exposing her lovely chest to his eyes. While most of the rest of the passengers fidgeted in their seats, trying to get some sleep, he looked. Fowler didn't want to sleep right now. The President had never felt more like a man, a great man to be sure, but at this moment, just a man. His hand slid across her breasts. Elizabeth's eyes opened wide and she smiled, as though in her dreams she had read his thoughts.

* * *

Just like home, Russell thought to himself. The house was made of stones instead of block, and the roof was flat instead of peaked, but the dust was the same, and the pathetic little garden was the same. And the man might as easily have been a Sioux, the tiredness in his eyes, the bent back, the old, gnarled hands of one defeated by others.

"This must be the place," he said as the truck slowed.

"The old man's son fought the Israelis and was badly wounded. Both have been friends to us."

"You have to look out for your friends," Marvin agreed. The truck stopped, and Russell had to hop out to allow Ghosn to step down.

"Come along, I will introduce you."

It was all surprisingly formal to the American. He didn't understand a word, of course, but he didn't have to. The respect of his friend Ghosn for the old one was good to see. After a few more remarks the farmer looked at Russell and bowed his head, which embarrassed the American. Marvin took his hand gently and shook it in the manner of his people, muttering something that Ghosn translated. Then the farmer led them into his garden.

"Damn," Russell observed when he saw it.

"American Mark 84 2,000-pound bomb, it would appear. . . ." Ghosn said offhandedly, then knew he was wrong . . . the nose wasn't quite right . . . of course, the nose was crushed and distorted . . . but oddly so. . . . He thanked the farmer and waved him back to the truck. "First we must uncover it. Carefully, very carefully."

"I can handle that," Russell said. He went back to the truck and selected a folding shovel of a military design.

"We have people—"

The American cut Ghosn off. "Let me do it. I'll be careful."

"Do not touch it. Use the shovel to dig around it, but use your hands to remove the soil from the bomb itself. Marvin, I warn you, this is very dangerous."

"Better step back, then." Russell turned and grinned. He had to show this man that he was courageous. Killing the cop had been easy, no challenge at all. This was different.

"And leave my comrade in danger?" Ghosn asked rhetorically. He knew that this was the intelligent thing to do, what he would have done had his own people done the digging, because his skills were too valuable to be risked stupidly, but he could not show weakness in front of the American, could he? Besides, he could watch and see if the man was as courageous as he seemed.

Ghosn was not disappointed. Russell stripped to the waist and got on his knees to dig around the periphery of the bomb. He was even careful of the garden, far more so than Ghosn's men would have been. It took an hour until he'd dug a shallow pit around the device, piling up the soil in four neat mounds. Already Ghosn knew that there was something odd here. It was not a Mark 84. It had roughly the same size, but the shape was wrong, and the bombcase was . . . just wasn't right. The Mark 84 had a sturdy case made of cast steel, so that when the explosive filler detonated, the case would be transformed into a million razor-sharp fragments, the better to tear men to bits. But not this one. In two visible places the case was broken, and it wasn't quite thick enough for that kind of bomb. So what the hell was it?

Russell moved in closer and used his hands to pull the dirt off the surface of the bomb itself. He was careful and thorough. The American worked up a good sweat but didn't slacken his efforts even once. The muscles in his arm rippled, and Ghosn admired him for that. The man had a physical power like none he had ever seen. Even Israeli paratroopers didn't look so formidable. He'd excavated two or three tons of dirt, yet he barely showed the effort, his movements as steady and powerful as a machine.

"Stop for a minute," Ghosn said. "I must get my tools."

"Okay," Russell replied, sitting back and staring at the bomb.

Ghosn returned with a rucksack and a canteen, which he handed to the American.

"Thanks, man. It is a little warm here." Russell drank half a liter of water. "Now what?"

Ghosn took a paintbrush from the sack and began sweeping the last of the dirt from the weapon. "You should leave now," he warned.

"That's okay, Ibrahim. I'll stay if you don't mind."

"This is the dangerous part."

"You stayed by me, man," Russell pointed out.

"As you wish. I am now looking for the fuse."

"Not in the front?" Russell pointed to the nose of the bomb.

"Not there. There is usually one at the front—it appears to be missing; that's just a screw-on cap—one in the middle and one at the back."

"How come it don't have no fins on it?" Russell asked. "Don't bombs have fins on 'em, you know, like an arrow?"

"The fins were probably stripped off when it hit the ground. That's often how we find such bombs, because the fins come off and lie on the surface."

"Want me to uncover the back of the thing, then?"

"Very, very carefully, Marvin. Please."

"Okay, man." Russell moved around his friend and resumed pulling the dirt off the back end of the bombcase. Ghosn, he noted, was one cool son of a bitch. Marvin was as scared as he had ever been, this close to a shitload of explosives, but he could not and damned well would not show anything that looked like fear to this guy. Ibrahim might be a little pencil-necked geek, but the dude had real balls, dicking with a bomb like this. He noted that Ghosn was sweeping the dirt off like he was using the brush on a girl's tits, and made his own efforts just as cautious. Ten minutes later, he had uncovered the back.

"Ibrahim?"

"Yes, Marvin?" Ghosn said without looking.

"There ain't nothing here. The back's just a hole, man."

Ghosn lifted the brush from the case and turned to look. That was odd. But he had other things to do. "Thank you. You can stop now. I still have not found a fuse."

Russell backed off, sat on a mound of dirt, and proceeded to empty the rest of the canteen. On reflection he walked over to the truck. The three men there along with the farmer were just standing—the farmer watching in the open, the others observing more circumspectly behind the stone walls of the house. Russell tossed one man the empty canteen, and had a full one returned the same way. He gave a thumbs-up sign to all of them and walked back to the bomb.

"Back off for a minute and have a drink," Marvin said on his return.

"Good idea," Ghosn agreed, setting his brush down next to the bomb.

"Find anything?"

"A plug connection, nothing else." That was odd, too, Ghosn thought, pulling the top off the canteen. There were no stenciled markings, just a silver-and-red label block near the nose. Color codes were common on bombs, but he'd never seen that one before. So, what was this damned thing? Maybe a FAE or some kind of submunition canister? Something old and obsolete that he'd never seen before. It had come down in 1973, after all. Maybe something that had long since gone out of service. That was very bad news. If it were something he'd never seen before, it might have a fusing system that he didn't know. His manual for dealing with such things was Russian in origin, though printed in Arabic. Ghosn had long since committed it to memory, but there was no description for anything like this. And that was truly frightening. Ghosn took a long pull from the canteen and then poured a little across his face.

"Take it easy, man," Russell said, noticing the man's tension.

"This job is never easy, my friend, and it is always very frightening."

"You look pretty cool, Ibrahim." It wasn't a lie. While brushing the dirt off, he looked like a doctor, almost, doing something real hard, Russell thought, but doing it. The little fucker had balls, Marvin told himself again.

Ghosn turned and grinned. "That is all a lie. I am quite terrified. I truly hate doing this."

"You got a big pair, boy, and that's no shit."

"Thank you. Now I must return while I still can. You really should leave, you know."

Russell spat into the dirt. "Fuck it."

"That would be very difficult." Ghosn grinned. "And if you got a reaction from 'her,' you might not like it."

"I guess when these suckers come, the earth really does move!"

Ghosn knew enough of American idiom that he fell backwards and laughed uproariously. "Please, Marvin, do not say such things when I am working!" *I like this man!* Ghosn told himself. *We are too humorless a lot. I like this American!* He had to wait another few minutes before he calmed down enough to resume his work.

Another hour's brushing showed nothing. There were seams in the bombcase, even some sort of hatch . . . he'd never seen that before. But no fuse point. If there was one, it had to be underneath. Russell moved away some more dirt, allowing Ghosn to continue his search, but again, nothing. He decided to examine the back.

"There's a flashlight in my sack. . . ."

"Got it." Russell handed the light over.

Ghosn lay down on the dirt and contorted himself to look into the hole. It was dark, of course, and he switched on the light. . . . He saw electrical wiring, and something else, some sort of metal framework—latticework would be more accurate. He judged he could see perhaps eighty centimeters . . . and if this was a real bomb, there would not be so much empty space. So. So. Ghosn tossed the light to the American.

"We have just wasted five hours," he announced.

"Huh?"

"I don't know what this thing is, but it is not a bomb." He sat up and had a brief attack of the shakes, but it didn't last long.

"What is it, then?"

"Some kind of electronic sensing device, perhaps, a warning system. Maybe a camera pod—the lens assembly must be underneath. That doesn't matter. What is important is that it is no bomb."

"So now what?"

"We move it, take it back with us. It might be valuable. Perhaps something we can sell to the Russians or the Syrians."

"So the old guy was worried about nothing?"

"Correct." Ghosn rose and the two men walked back to the truck. "It is safe now," he told the farmer. Might as well tell him what he wanted to know, and why confuse him with the facts of the matter? The farmer kissed Ghosn's dirty hands, and those of the American, which further embarrassed Russell.

The driver pulled the truck around, and backed into the garden, careful to do as little damage to the rows of vegetables as possible. Russell watched as two men filled a half-dozen sandbags and hoisted them onto the truck. Next they put a sling around the bomb and began to crank it up with a winch. The bomb—or whatever it was—was heavier than expected, and Russell took over the hand winch, displaying his strength yet again as he cranked it up alone. The Arabs swung the A-frame forward, then he lowered the bomb into the nest made of sandbags. A few ropes secured it in place, and that was that.

The farmer would not let them leave. He brought out tea and bread, insisting on feeding the men before they left, and Ghosn accepted the man's hospitality with appropriate humility. Four lambs were added to the truck's load before they left.

"That was a good thing you did, man," Russell observed as they pulled off.

"Perhaps," Ghosn said tiredly. Stress was so much more tiring than actual labor, though the American seemed to handle both quite well. Two hours later they were back in the Bekaa Valley. The bomb—Ghosn didn't know what else to call it—was dropped unceremoniously in front of his workshop, and the party of five went to feast on fresh lamb. To Ghosn's surprise, the American had never had lamb before, and so was properly introduced to the traditional Arab delicacy.

"Got something interesting, Bill," Murray announced as he came into the Director's office.

"What's that, Danny?" Shaw looked up from his appointments schedule.

"A cop got himself killed over in Athens, and they think it was an American who did it." Murray filled Shaw in on the technical details.

"Broke his neck barehanded?" Bill asked.

"That's right. The cop was a skinny little guy," Murray said, "but . . ."

"Jesus. Okay, let's see." Murray handed the photo over. "We know this guy, Dan? It's not the best picture in the world."

"Al Denton thinks it might be Marvin Russell. He's playing computer games on the original slide. There were no prints or other forensic stuff. The car was registered to a third party who disappeared, probably never existed in the first place. The driver of the other vehicle is an unknown. Anyway, it fits Russell's description, short and powerful, and the cheekbones and coloration make him look like an Indian. Clothing is definitely American. So's the suitcase."

"So you think he skipped the country after we got his brother . . . smart move," Shaw judged. "He was supposed to be the bright one, wasn't he?"

"Smart enough to get teamed up with an Arab."

"Think so?" Shaw examined the other face. "Could be Greek, or anything Mediterranean. Skin's a little fair for an Arab, but it's a pretty ordinary face, and you said it's an unknown. Gut call, Dan?"

"Yep." Murray nodded. "I checked the file. A confidential informant told us a few years ago that Marvin made a trip east a few years back and made contacts with the PFLP. Athens is a convenient place to renew the association. Neutral ground.''

''Also a good place to make connections for a drug deal,'' Shaw suggested. ''What current info do we have on Brother Marvin?''

''Not much. Our best CI out there is back in the joint—had a brawl with a couple of reservation cops and came off second-best.''

Shaw grunted. The problem with Confidential Informants, of course, was that most of them were criminals who did illegal things and regularly ended up in jail. That both established their bonafides and made them temporarily useless. Such were the rules of the game. ''Okay,'' the FBI Director said. ''You want to do something. What is it?''

''With a little nudge, we can spring the CI on good-time rules and get him back into the Warrior Society. If this is a terrorist connection, we'd better start running some leads down. Ditto if it's for drugs. Interpol has already come up blank on the driver. No record of his face for either terrorist or drug connections. The Greeks have come to a blank wall. Information on the car didn't lead them anywhere. They have a dead sergeant, and all they got to go on is two faces with no names attached. Sending the photo to us was their last shot. They figured him for an American. . . .''

''Hotel?'' the Director asked, ever the investigator.

''Yeah, they identified that—that is, they know it's one of two places side by side. There were ten people with American passports who checked out that day, but they're both little places with lots of in-and-out, and they came up with nothing useful for identification purposes. The hotel staff is forgetful. That kind of a place. Who's to say that our friend even stayed there? The Greeks want us to do follow-up on the names from the hotel register,'' Murray concluded.

Bill Shaw handed the photo back. ''That's simple enough. Run with it.''

''Already being done.''

''Assuming we know that these two had anything to do with the killing. Well, you gotta go with your best guess. Okay: let the U.S. Attorney know that our CI has paid his debt to society. It's about time we ran those 'warriors' down once and for all.'' Shaw had won his spurs on counterterrorism, and that class of criminal was still his first hate.

''Yeah, I'll play up the drug connection on that. We ought to have him sprung in two weeks or so.''

''Fair enough, Dan.''

''When's the President get into Rome?'' Murray asked.

''Pretty soon. Really something, isn't it?''

''Bet your ass, man. Kenny'd better find himself another line of work soon. Peace is breaking out.''

Shaw grinned. ''Who woulda thunk it? We can always get him a badge and a gun so's he can earn an honest living.''

Presidential security was completed with a discreetly located flight of four Navy Tomcat fighters that had followed the VC-25A at a distance of five miles while a radar-surveillance aircraft made sure that nothing was approaching Air Force One. Normal commercial traffic was set aside, and the environs of the military airfield being used for the arrival had not so much been combed as strained. Already waiting on the pavement was the President's armored limousine, which had been flown in a few hours earlier by an Air Force C-141B, and enough Italian soldiers and police to discourage a regiment of terrorists. President Fowler emerged from his private washroom shaved and scrubbed pink, his tie exquisitely knotted, and smiling as brightly as Pete and Daga had ever seen. *As well he might,* Connor thought. The agent did not moralize as deeply as D'Agustino did. The President was a man, and as most presidents were, a lonely man—doubly so with the loss of his wife. Elliot might be an arrogant bitch, but she was undeniably attractive, and if that's what it took to allay the stress and pressure of the job, then that's what it took. The President had to relax, else the job would burn him up—as it had burned others up—and that was bad for the country. So long as HAWK didn't break any major laws, Connor and D'Agustino would protect both his privacy and his pleasures. Pete understood. Daga merely wished that he had better taste. E.E. had left the quarters a little earlier, and was dressed in something especially nice. She joined the President in the dining area just before landing for coffee and donuts. There was no denying that she was attractive, especially this morning. Maybe, Special Agent Helen D'Agustino thought, she was a good lay. Certainly she and the President were the best-rested people on the flight. The media pukes—the Secret Service has an institutional dislike for reporters—had squirmed and fidgeted in their seats throughout the flight, and looked rumpled despite their upbeat expressions. The most harried of all was the President's speechwriter, who'd worked through the night without pause except for coffee and head-calls and finally delivered the speech to Arnie van Damm a bare twenty minutes before touchdown. Fowler had run through it over breakfast and loved it.

"Callie, this is just wonderful!" The President beamed at the weary staff member, who had the literary elegance of a poet. Fowler amazed everyone in sight by giving the young lady—she was still on the sunny side of thirty—a hug that left tears in Callie Weston's eyes. "Get yourself some rest and enjoy Rome."

"A pleasure, Mr. President."

The aircraft came to a stop at the appointed place. The mobile stairs came immediately into place. A section of red carpet was rolled in place to lead from the stairs to the longer carpet that led in turn to the podium. The President and Prime Minister of Italy moved to their appointed places, along with the U.S. Ambassador and the usual hangers-on, including some exhausted protocol officers who'd had to plan this ceremony literally on the fly. The door of the aircraft was opened by an Air Force sergeant. Secret Service agents looked outside suspiciously for any sign of trouble, and caught glances from other agents of the advance team. When the President appeared, the Italian Air Force band played its arrival fanfare, different from the traditional American "Ruffles and Flourishes."

The President made his way down the steps alone, walking from reality to immortality, he reflected. Reporters noticed that his stride was bouncy and relaxed, and envied him the comfortable quarters where he could sleep in regal solitude. Sleep was the only sure cure for jet lag, and clearly the President had enjoyed a restful flight. The Brooks Brothers suit was newly pressed—Air Force One has all manner of amenities—his shoes positively sparkled, and his grooming was perfection itself. Fowler made his way to the U.S. Ambassador and his wife, who conducted him to the Italian President. The band struck up "The Star-Spangled Banner." Next came the traditional review of the assembled troops, and a brief arrival speech that only hinted at the eloquence that would soon follow. In all, it took twenty minutes before Fowler got into his car, along with the Ambassador, Dr. Elliot, and his personal bodyguards.

"First one of those I've ever enjoyed," was Fowler's evaluation of the ceremony. There was general agreement that the Italians had handled it with elegance.

"Elizabeth, I want you to stay close. There are a few aspects to the agreement that we need to go over. I need to see Brent, too. How's he doing?" Fowler asked the Ambassador.

"Tired but pretty happy with himself," Ambassador Coates replied. "The last negotiation session lasted over twenty hours."

"What's the local press saying?" E.E. asked.

"They're euphoric. They all are. This is a great day for the whole world." *It's happening on my turf, and I'll be there to see it!* Jed Coates said to himself. *Not often you get to see history made.*

"Well, that was nice."

The National Military Command Center—NMCC—is located in the D-Ring of the Pentagon near the River Entrance. One of the few such installations in government which actually looks like its Hollywood renditions, it is an arena roughly the size and proportions of a basketball court and two stories in height. NMCC is in essence the central telephone switchboard for the United States military. It is not the only one—the nearest alternate is at Fort Ritchie in the Maryland hills—since it is far too easy to destroy, but it is the most conveniently located of its type. It's a regular stop for VIPs who want to see the sexier parts of the Pentagon, much to the annoyance of the staff, for whom it's merely the place where they work.

Adjoining the NMCC is a smaller room in which one can see a set of IBM PC/AT personal computers—old ones with 5.25-inch floppy drives—that constitute the Hot Line, the direct communications link between the American and Soviet presidents. The NMCC "node" for the link was not the only one, but it was the primary downlink. That fact was not widely known in America, but it had been purposefully made known to the Soviets. Some form of direct communications between the two countries would be necessary even during an ongoing nuclear war, and letting the Soviets know that the only readily usable downlink was here might serve, some "experts" had judged three decades earlier, as a life-insurance policy for the area.

That, Captain James Rosselli, USN, thought, was just so much theoretician-generated horseshit. That no one had ever seriously questioned it was another example of all the horseshit that lay and stank within Washington in general and the Pentagon in particular. With all the nonsense that took place within the confines of Interstate 495, the Washington Beltway, it was just one more bit of data accepted as gospel, despite the fact that it didn't make a whole lot of sense. To "Rosey" Rosselli, Washington, D.C., was about 300 square miles surrounded by reality. He wondered if the laws of physics even applied inside the Beltway. He'd long since given up on the laws of logic.

Joint duty, Rosey grunted to himself. The most recent effort of Congress to reform the military—something it was singularly unable to do for itself, he groused—had prescribed that uniformed officers who aspired to flag rank—and which of them didn't?—had to spend some of their time in close association with peers from the other uniformed services. Rosselli had never been told how hanging around with a field-artillery man might make him a better submarine driver, but then no one else had evidently wondered about that. It was simply accepted as an article of faith that cross-pollination was good for something, and so the best and brightest officers were taken away from their professional specialties and dropped into things which they knew not the first thing about. Not that they'd ever learn how to do their new jobs, of course, but they might learn just enough to be dangerous, plus losing currency in what they were supposed to do. That was Congress's idea of military reform.

"Coffee, Cap'n?" an Army corporal asked.

"Better make it decaf," Rosey replied. *If my disposition gets any worse, I might start hurting people.*

Work here was career-enhancing. Rosselli knew that, and he also knew that being here was partly his fault. He'd majored in sub and minored in spook throughout his career. He'd already had a tour at the Navy's intelligence headquarters at Suitland, Maryland, near Andrews Air Force Base. At least this was a better commute—he'd gotten official housing at Bolling Air Force Base, and the trip to the Pentagon was a relatively simple hop across I-295/395 to his reserved parking place, another perk that came with duty in the NMCC, and one worth shedding blood for.

Once duty here had been relatively exciting. He remembered when the Soviets had splashed the Korean Airlines 747 and other incidents, and it must have been wonderfully chaotic during the Iraq War—that is, when the senior watch officer wasn't answering endless calls of "what's happening?" to anyone who'd managed to get the direct-line number. But now?

Now, as he had just watched on his desk TV, the President was about to defuse the world's biggest remaining diplomatic bomb, and soon Rosselli's work would mostly involve taking calls about collisions at sea, or crashed airplanes, or some dumbass soldier who'd gotten himself run over by a tank. Such things were serious, but not matters of great professional interest. So here he was. His paperwork was finished. That was something Jim Rosselli was good at—he'd learned how to shuffle papers in the Navy, and here he had a superb staff to help him with it—and the rest of the day was mainly involved with sitting and waiting for something to happen. The problem was that Rosselli was a do-er, not a wait-er, and who wanted a disaster to happen anyway?

"Gonna be a quiet day." This was Rosselli's XO, an Air Force F-15 pilot, Lieutenant Colonel Richard Barnes.

"I think you're right, Rocky." *Just what I wanted to hear!* Rosselli checked his watch. It was a twelve-hour shift, with five hours left to go. "Hell, it's getting to be a pretty quiet world."

"Ain't it the truth." Barnes turned back to the display screen. *Well, I got my two MiGs over the Persian Gulf. At least it hasn't been a complete waste of time.*

Rosselli stood and decided to walk around. The duty watch officers thought this was to look at what they were doing, to make sure they were doing something. One senior civilian ostentatiously continued doing the *Post* crossword. It was his "lunch" break and he preferred eating here to the mostly empty cafeterias. Here he could watch TV. Rosselli next wandered over to the left into the Hot Line room, and he was lucky for a change. A message was announced by the dinging of a little bell. The actual message received looked like random garbage, but the encryption machine changed that into cleartext Russian which a Marine translated:

> "So you think you know the real meaning of fear?
> Yeah, you think you do know, but I doubt it.
> When you sit in a shelter with bombs falling all over.
> And the houses around you are burning like torches.
> I agree that you experience horror and fright
> For such moments are dreadful, for as long as they last,

But the all-clear sounds—then it's okay—
You take a deep breath, the stress has passed by.
But real fear is a stone deep down in your chest.
You hear me? A stone. That's what it is, no more.

"Ilya Selvinskiy," the Marine Lieutenant said.

"Hmph?"

"Ilya Selvinskiy, Russian poet, did some famous work during the Second World War. I know this one, *Sprakh,* the title is, 'Fear.' It's very good." The young officer grinned. "My opposite number is pretty literate. So . . ." TRANSMISSION RECEIVED. THE REST OF THE POEM IS EVEN BETTER, ALEKSEY, the Lieutenant typed, STAND BY FOR REPLY.

"What do you send back?" Rosselli asked.

"Today . . . maybe a little Emily Dickinson. She was a morbid bitch, always talking about death and stuff. No, better yet—Edgar Allan Poe. They really like him over there. Hmmm, which one . . . ?" The Lieutenant opened a desk drawer and pulled out a volume.

"Don't you do it in advance?" Rosselli asked.

The Marine grinned up at his boss. "No, sir, that's cheating. We used to do it that way, but we changed things about two years ago, when things lightened up. Now it's sort of a game. He picks a poem, and I have to respond with a corresponding passage from an American poet. It helps pass the time, Cap'n. Good for language skills on both sides. Translating poetry is a bitch—good exercise." The Soviet side transmitted its messages in Russian, and the Americans in English, necessitating skilled translators at both ends.

"Much real business on the line?"

"Captain, I've never seen much more than test messages. Oh, when we have the SecState flying over, sometimes we check weather data. We even chatted a little about hockey when their national team came over to play with the NHL guys last August, but mainly it's duller than dirt, and that's why we trade poetry passages. Weren't for that, we'd all go nuts. Shame we can't talk like on CB or something, but the rules are the rules."

"Guess so. They say anything about the treaty stuff in Rome?"

"Not a word. We don't do that, sir."

"I see." Rosselli watched the Lieutenant pick a stanza from "Annabel Lee." He was surprised. Rosey had expected something from "The Raven." Nevermore . . .

The arrival day was one of rest and ceremony—and mystery. The treaty terms had still not been leaked, and news agencies, knowing that something "historic" had happened, were frantic to discover exactly what it was. To no avail. The chiefs of state of Israel, Saudi Arabia, Switzerland, the Soviet Union, the United States of America, and their host, Italy, arrayed themselves around a massive 15th-century table, punctuated with their chief diplomats and representatives of the Vatican and the Eastern Orthodox Church. In deference to the Saudis, toasts were offered in water or orange juice, which was the only discordant note of the evening. Soviet President Andrey Il'ych Narmonov was particularly effusive. His country's participation in the treaty was a matter of great importance, and the inclusion of the Russian Orthodox Church on the Commission for Christian Shrines would have major political import in Moscow. The dinner lasted three hours, after which the guests departed in view of the cameras on the far side of the avenue, and once more the newsies were thunderstruck by the fellowship. A jovial Fowler and Narmonov traveled together to the former's hotel and availed themselves for only the second time of the opportunity to discuss matters of bilateral interest.

"You have fallen behind in your deactivation of your missile forces," Fowler observed after pleasantries were dispensed with. He eased the blow by handing over a glass of wine.

"Thank you, Mr. President. As we told your people last week, our disposal facility has proven inadequate. We can't dismantle the damned things fast enough, and our nature-lovers in parliament are objecting to our method of neutralizing the propellant stocks."

Fowler smiled in sympathy. "I know the problem, Mr. President." The environmental movement had taken off in the Soviet Union the previous spring, with the Russian parliament passing a new set of laws modeled on—but much tougher than—American statutes. The amazing part was that the central Soviet government was abiding by the laws, but Fowler couldn't say that. The environmental nightmare inflicted on that country by more than seventy years of Marxism would take a generation of tough laws to fix. "Will this affect the deadline for fulfilling the treaty requirements?"

"You have my word, Robert," Narmonov said solemnly. "The missiles will be destroyed by 1st March even if I must blow them up myself."

"That is good enough for me, Andrey."

The reduction treaty, a carryover from the previous administration, mandated a fifty-percent reduction in intercontinental launchers by the coming spring. All of America's Minuteman-II missiles had been tagged for destruction, and the U.S. side of the treaty obligations was fully on track. As had been done under the Intermediate Nuclear Forces Treaty, the surplus missiles were dismantled to their component stages, which were either crushed or otherwise destroyed before witnesses. The news had covered the first few destructions, then grown tired of it. The missile silos, also under inspection, were stripped of their electronic equipment and, in the case of American structures, fifteen had already been declared surplus and sold—in four cases, farmers had purchased them and converted them to real silos. A Japanese conglomerate that had large holdings in North Dakota had further purchased a command bunker and made it into a wine cellar for the hunting lodge its executives used each fall.

American inspectors on the Soviet side reported that the Russians were trying mightily, but that the plant built for dismantlement of the Russian missiles had been poorly designed, as a result of which the Soviets were thirty percent behind schedule. Fully a hundred missiles were sitting on trailers outside the plant, the silos they'd left already destroyed by explosives. Though the Soviets had in each case removed and burned the guidance package in front of American inspectors, there were lingering intelligence evaluations that it was all a sham—the erector trailers, some argued, could elevate and fire the missiles. Suspicion of the Soviets was too hard a habit to break for some in the U.S. intelligence community, as was doubtless true of the Russians as well, Fowler thought.

"This treaty is a major step forward, Robert," Narmonov said after a sip from his wineglass—now that they were alone they could relax like gentlemen, the Russian thought with a sly grin. "You and your people are to be congratulated."

''Your help was crucial to its success, Andrey,'' Fowler replied graciously. It was a lie, but a politic one which both men understood. In fact it was not a lie, but neither man knew that.

''One less trouble spot for us to worry about. How blind we were!''

''That is true, my friend, but it is behind us. How are your people dealing with Germany?''

''The Army is not happy, as you might imagine—''

''Neither is mine.'' Fowler interrupted gently with his pronouncement. ''Soldiers are like dogs. Useful, of course, but they must know who the master is. Like dogs, they can be forgetful and must be reminded from time to time.''

Narmonov nodded thoughtfully as the translation came across. It was amazing how arrogant this man was. Just what his intelligence briefings had told him, the Soviet President noted. And patronizing, too. Well, the American had the luxury of a firm political system, Andrey Il'ych told himself. It allowed Fowler to be so sure of himself while he, Narmonov, had to struggle every day with a system not yet set in stone. Or even wood, the Russian thought bleakly. What a luxury indeed to be able to look on soldiers as dogs to be cowed. Didn't he know that dogs also had teeth? So strange the Americans were. Throughout communist rule in the Soviet Union, they had fretted about the political muscle of the Red Army—when in fact it had had none at all after Stalin's elimination of Tukhachevskiy. But now they discounted all such stories while the dissolution of the iron hand of Marxism-Leninism was allowing soldiers to think in ways that would have ended in execution only a few years earlier. Well, this was no time to disabuse the American of his illusions, was it?

''Tell me, Robert, this treaty idea—where exactly did it come from?'' Narmonov asked. He knew the truth and wanted to see Fowler's abilities as a liar.

''Many places, as with all such ideas,'' the President replied lightly. ''The moving force was Charles Alden—poor bastard. When the Israelis had that terrible incident, he activated his plan immediately and—well, it worked, didn't it?''

The Russian nodded again, and made his mental notes. Fowler lied with skill, evading the substance of the question to give a truthful but evasive answer. Khrushchev was right, as he'd already known. Politicians all the world over are not terribly different. It was something to remember about Fowler. He didn't like sharing credit, and was not above lying in the face of a peer, even over something so small as this. Narmonov was vaguely disappointed. Not that he'd expected anything else, but Fowler could have shown grace and humanity. He'd stood to lose nothing by it, after all. Instead he was as petty as any local Party *apparatchik. Tell me, Robert,* Narmonov asked behind a poker face that would have stood him well in Las Vegas, *what sort of man are you?*

''It is late, my friend,'' Narmonov observed. ''Tomorrow afternoon, then?''

Fowler stood. ''Tomorrow afternoon, Andrey.''

Bob Fowler escorted the Russian to the door and saw him off, then returned to his suite of rooms. Once there he pulled the handwritten checklist out of his pocket to make sure he'd asked all the questions.

''Well?''

''Well, the missile problem, he says, is exactly what our inspectors said it is. That ought to satisfy the guys at DIA.'' A grimace; it wouldn't. ''I think he's worried about his military.''

Dr. Elliot sat down. ''Anything else?''

The President poured her a glass of wine, then sat beside his National Security

Advisor. ''The normal pleasantries. He's a very busy, very worried man. Well, we knew that, didn't we?''

Liz swirled the wine around the glass and sniffed at it. She didn't like Italian wines, but this one wasn't bad. ''I've been thinking, Robert . . .''

''Yes, Elizabeth?''

''What happened to Charlie . . . we need to do something. It isn't fair that he should have disappeared like that. He's the guy who put this treaty on track, isn't he?''

''Well, yes,'' Fowler agreed, sipping at his own replenished glass. ''You're right, Elizabeth. It really was his effort.''

''I think we should let that out—quietly, of course. At the very least—''

''Yes, he should be remembered for something other than a pregnant grad student. That's very gracious of you, Elizabeth.'' Fowler tapped his glass against hers. ''You handle the media people. You're releasing the treaty details tomorrow before lunch?''

''That's right, about nine, I think.''

''Then after you're finished, take a few of the journalists aside and give it to them on background. Maybe Charlie will rest a little easier.''

''No problem, Mr. President,'' Liz agreed. Exorcising that particular demon came easily enough, didn't it? Was there anything she could not talk him into?

''Big day tomorrow.''

''The biggest, Bob, the biggest.'' Elliot leaned back and loosened the scarf from her throat. ''I never thought I'd ever have a moment like this.''

''I did,'' Fowler observed with a twinkle in his eye. There came a momentary pang of conscience. He'd expected to have it with someone else, but that was fate, wasn't it? Fate. The world was so strange. But he had no control over that, did he? And fate had decreed that he would be here at the moment in question, with Elizabeth. It wasn't his doing, was it? Therefore, he decided, there was no guilt, was there? How could there be guilt? He was making the world into a better, safer, more peaceful place. How could guilt attach to that?

Elliot closed her eyes as the President's hand caressed her offered neck. Never in her wildest dreams had she expected a moment like this.

The entire floor of the hotel was reserved for the President's party, and the two floors under it. Italian and American guards stood at all the entrances, and at various places in the buildings along the street. But the corridor outside the President's suite of rooms was the exclusive domain of the Presidential Protective Detail. Connor and D'Agustino made their own final check before retiring for the evening. A full squad of ten agents were in view, and another ten were behind various closed doors. Three of the visible agents had FAG-bags, black satchels across their chests. Officially called fast-action-gun bags, each contained an Uzi submachine gun which could be extracted and fired in about a second and a half. Anyone who got this far would find a warm reception.

''I see HAWK and HARPY are discussing affairs of state,'' Daga observed quietly.

''Helen, I didn't think you were so much of a prude,'' Pete Connor replied with a sly grin.

''None of my business, but in the old days people outside the door had to be eunuchs or something.''

''Keep talking like that and Santa will drop coal in your stocking.''

''I'd settle for that new automatic the FBI adopted,'' Daga said with a chuckle. ''They're like teenagers. It's unseemly.''

"Daga . . ."

"I know, he's the Boss, and he's a big boy, and we have to look the other way. Relax, Pete, you think I'm going to blab to a reporter?" She opened the door to the fire stairs and saw three agents, two of whom had their FAG-bags at the ready.

"And I was about to offer you a drink, too. . . ." Connor said deadpan. It was a joke. He and Daga were nondrinkers while on duty, and they were nearly always on duty. It wasn't that he had never thought about getting into her pants. He was divorced, as was she, but it would never have worked, and that was that. She knew it, too, and grinned at him.

"I could use one—the stuff they have here is what I was raised on. What a crummy job this is!" A final look down the corridor. "Everybody's in place, Pete. I think we can call it a night."

"You really like the ten-millimeter?"

"Fired one last week up at Greenbelt. Got a possible with my first string. It doesn't get much better than that, lover."

Connor stopped dead in his tracks and laughed. "Christ, Daga!"

"People might notice?" D'Agustino batted her eyes at him. "See what I mean, Pete?"

"God, who ever heard of a Guinea puritan?"

Helen D'Agustino elbowed the senior agent in the ribs and made her way to the elevator. Pete was right. She was turning into a damned prude, and she'd never ever been like that. A passionate woman whose single attempt at marriage had collapsed because one household wasn't large enough for two assertive egos—at least not two Italian ones—she knew she was allowing her prejudices to color her judgment. That was not a healthy thing, even over something both trivial and divorced from her job. What HAWK did on his own time was his business, but the look in his eyes. . . . He was infatuated with the bitch. Daga wondered if any president had allowed that to happen. Probably, she admitted. They were only men, after all, and all men sometimes thought from the testicles instead of the brain. That the President should become a lackey of such a shallow woman as this—that was what offended her. But that, she admitted to herself, was both odd and inconsistent. After all, women didn't come much more liberated than she was. So why, she asked herself, was it bothering her? It had been too long a day for that. She needed sleep, and knew that she'd only get five or six hours before she was on duty again. *Damn these overseas trips. . . .*

"So what is it?" Qati asked just after dawn. He'd been away the previous day, meeting some other guerrilla leaders, and also for a trip to the doctor, Ghosn knew, though he could not ask about that.

"Not sure," the engineer replied. "I'd guess a jamming pod, something like that."

"That's useful," the Commander said at once. Despite the rapprochement, or whatever the key phrase was, between East and West, business was still business. The Russians still had a military, and that military still had weapons. Countermeasures against those weapons were items of interest. Israeli equipment was particularly prized, since the Americans copied it. Even old equipment showed how the Israeli engineers thought through problems, and could provide useful clues to newer systems.

"Yes, we should be able to sell it to our Russian friends."

"How did the American work out?" Qati asked next.

"Quite well. I do like him, Ismael. I understand him better now." The engineer explained why. Qati nodded.

"What should we do with him, then?"

Ghosn shrugged. "Weapons training, perhaps? Let's see if he fits in with the men."

"Very well. I'll send him out this morning to see how well he knows combat skills. And you, how soon will you pick the thing apart?"

"I planned to do it today."

"Excellent. Do not let me stop you."

"How are you feeling, Commander?"

Qati frowned. He felt terrible, but he was telling himself that part of that was the possibility of some sort of treaty with the Israelis. Could it be real? Could it be possible? History said no, but there had been so many changes. . . . Some sort of agreement between the Zionists and the Saudis . . . well, after the Iraq business, what could he expect? The Americans had played their role, and now they were presenting some kind of bill. Disappointing, but hardly unexpected, and whatever the Americans were up to would divert attention away from the latest Israeli atrocity. That people calling themselves Arabs had been so womanly as to meekly accept fire and death. . . . Qati shook his head. You didn't fight that way. So the Americans would do something or other to neutralize the political impact of the Israeli massacre, and the Saudis were playing along like the lapdogs they were. Whatever was in the offing, it could hardly affect the Palestinian struggle. He should soon be feeling better, Qati told himself.

"It is of no account. Let me know when you've determined exactly what it is."

Ghosn took his dismissal and left. He was worried about his commander. The man was ill—he knew that much from his brother-in-law, but exactly how sick he didn't know. In any case, he had work to do.

The workshop was a disreputable-looking structure of plain wood walls and a roof of corrugated steel. Had it looked more sturdy, some Israeli F-16 pilot might have destroyed it years before.

The bomb—he still thought of it by that name—lay on the dirt floor. An A-frame like that used for auto or truck service stood over it, with a chain for moving the bomb if necessary, but yesterday two men had set it up in accordance with his instructions. Ghosn turned on the lights—he liked a brightly lit work area—and contemplated the . . . bomb.

Why do I keep calling it that? he asked himself. Ghosn shook his head. The obvious place to begin was the access door. It would not be easy. Impact with the ground had telescoped the bombcase, doubtless damaging the internal hinges . . . but he had all the time he wanted.

Ghosn selected a screwdriver from his toolbox and went to work.

President Fowler slept late. He was still fatigued from the flight, and . . . he almost laughed at himself in the mirror. Good Lord, three times in less than twenty-four hours . . . wasn't it? He tried to do the arithmetic in his head, but the effort defeated him before his morning coffee. In any case, three times in relatively short succession. He hadn't done *that* in quite a long time! But he'd also gotten his rest. His body was composed and relaxed after the morning shower, and the razor plowed through the cream on his face, revealing a man with younger, leaner features that matched the twinkle in his eyes. Three minutes later he selected a striped tie to go with the white shirt and gray suit. Not somber, but serious was the prescription for the day. He'd let the churchmen dazzle the cameras with their red silk. His speech would be all the more impressive if delivered by a well-turned-out businessman/politician, which was his political image, despite the fact that he'd never in his life run a private business of any sort. A serious man, Bob Fowler—with a common touch to be sure, but a serious man whom one could trust to do The Right Thing.

Well, I will sure as hell prove that today, the President of the United States told himself in yet another mirror as he checked his tie. His head turned at the knock on the door. "Come in."

"Good morning, Mr. President," said Special Agent Connor.

"How are you today, Pete?" Fowler asked, turning back to the mirror . . . the knot wasn't quite right, and he started afresh.

"Fine, thank you, sir. It's a mighty nice day outside."

"You people never get enough rest. Never get to see the sights, either. That's my fault, isn't it?" *There,* Fowler thought, *that's perfect.*

"It's okay, Mr. President. We're all volunteers. What do you want for breakfast, sir?"

"Good morning, Mr. President!" Dr. Elliot came in behind Connor. "This is the day!"

Bob Fowler turned with a smile. "It sure as hell is! Join me for breakfast, Elizabeth?"

"Love to. I have the morning brief—it's a nice short one for a change."

"Pete, breakfast for two . . . a big one. I'm hungry."

"Just coffee for me," Liz said to the servant. Connor caught the tone of her voice, but did not react beyond nodding before he left. "Bob, you look wonderful."

"So do you, Elizabeth." And so she did, in her most expensive suit, which was also serious-looking but just feminine enough. She took her seat and did the briefing.

"CIA says the Japanese are up to something," she said as she concluded.

"What?"

"They caught a whiff, Ryan says, of something in the next round of trade negotiations. The Prime Minister is quoted as saying something unkind."

"What exactly?"

" 'This is the last time we'll be cut out of our proper role on the world stage, and I'll make them pay for this,' " Dr. Elliot quoted. "Ryan thinks it's important."

"What do you think?"

"I think Ryan's being paranoid again. He's been cut out of this end of the treaty works, and he's trying to remind us how important he is. Marcus agrees with my assessment, but forwarded the report out of a fit of objectivity," Liz concluded with heavy irony.

"Cabot is something of a disappointment, isn't he?" Fowler observed as he looked over the briefing notes.

"He doesn't seem very effective at telling his people who the boss is. He's being captured by the bureaucracy over there, especially Ryan."

"You really don't like him, do you?" the President noted.

"He's arrogant. He's—"

"Elizabeth, he has a very impressive record. I don't much care for him either as a person, but as an intelligence officer he has done a lot of things very, very well."

"He's a throwback. He's James Bond—or thinks he is. Fine," Elliot admitted, "he's done some important things, but that sort of thing is history. We need someone now with a broader view."

"Congress won't go for it," the President said as breakfast was wheeled in. The food had been scanned for radioactives, checked for electronic devices, and sniffed for explosives—which, the President thought, put one hell of a strain on the dogs, who probably liked sausage as well as he did. ''We'll serve ourselves, thanks,'' the President dismissed the Navy steward before going on. ''They love him there, Congress loves the guy.'' He didn't have to add the fact that Ryan, as Deputy Director of Central Intelligence, was not merely a presidential appointee. He'd also been through a confirmation hearing in the U.S. Senate. Such people were not easily dismissed. There had to be a reason.

''I never have figured that out. Especially Trent. Of all the people to sign off on Ryan, why him?''

''Ask him,'' Fowler suggested as he buttered his pancakes.

''I have. He danced around the issue like the prima ballerina at the New York Ballet.'' The President laughed uproariously at that.

''Christ, woman, don't ever let *anybody* hear you say that!''

''Robert, we both support the estimable Mr. Trent's choice of sexual preference, but he is a prissy son of a bitch and we both know it.''

''True,'' Fowler had to agree. ''So what are you telling me, Elizabeth?''

''It's time for Cabot to put Ryan in his place.''

''How much of this is envy for Ryan's part in the treaty, Elizabeth?''

Elliot's eyes flared, but the President was looking at his plate. She took a deep breath before speaking and tried to decide if it were a goad or not. Probably not, but the President wasn't the sort to be impressed by emotions in matters like this. ''Bob, we've been through that. Ryan connected a few ideas that other people had already come up with. He's an intelligence officer, for God's sake! All they do is *report* what other people do.''

''He's done more than that.'' Fowler saw where this was going, but it was fun to play games with her.

''Fine, he's killed people! Is that what's special about him? James goddamned Bond! You even let them execute the ones who—''

''Elizabeth, those terrorists also killed seven Secret Service agents. My life depends on those people, and it would have been damned ungracious and just plain idiotic of me to commute the sentences of people who killed their colleagues.'' The President almost frowned at that—*So much for strongly held principle, eh, Bob?* a voice asked him—but managed to control himself.

''And now you can't do it at all, or people will say that you failed to do it once out of personal self-interest. You allowed yourself to be trapped and outmaneuvered,'' she pointed out. She had been goaded after all, Liz decided, and answered in kind, but Fowler wasn't buying.

''Elizabeth, I may be the only former prosecutor in America who doesn't believe in capital punishment, but . . . we do live in a democracy, and the people support the idea.'' He looked up from his meal. ''Those people were terrorists. I can't say I'm happy that I allowed them to be executed, but if anyone deserved it, they did. The time wasn't right to make a statement on that issue. Maybe in my second term. We have to wait for the right case. Politics is the art of the possible. That means one thing at a time, Elizabeth. You know that as well as I do.''

''If you don't do something, you'll wake up and find that Ryan is running CIA for you. He's able, I admit, but he's something from the past. He's the wrong person for the times we live in.''

God, you're an envious woman, Fowler thought. *But we all have our weaknesses.* It was time to stop playing with her, though. It wouldn't do to offend her too deeply.

"What do you have in mind?"

"We can ease him out."

"I'll think about it—Elizabeth, let's not spoil the day with a discussion like this one, okay? How do you plan to break the news of the treaty terms?"

Elliot leaned back and sipped at her coffee. She reproached herself for moving too soon and too passionately on this. She disliked Ryan greatly, but Bob was right. It wasn't the time, wasn't the place. She had all the time in the world to make her play, and she knew that she had to do it with skill.

"A copy of the treaty, I think."

"Can they read that fast?" Fowler laughed. The media was full of such illiterates.

"You should see the speculation. The lead *Times* piece was faxed in this morning. They're frantic. They'll eat it up. Besides, I ginned up some Cliffs Notes for them."

"However you want to do it," the President said as he finished off his sausage. He checked his watch. Timing was everything. There was a six-hour time difference between Rome and Washington. That meant the treaty could not be signed until two in the afternoon at the earliest, so as to catch the morning news shows. But the American people had to be prepped for the news, and that meant that the TV crews had to have the details of the treaty by three, Eastern Daylight Time, in order to absorb everything fully. Liz would break the news at nine, twenty minutes from now, he noted. "And you'll be playing up Charlie's part in it?"

"Right. It's only fair that he should get most of the credit."

And so much for Ryan's part in the process, Bob Fowler noted without comment. *Well, Charlie was the guy who really got it moving, wasn't he?* Fowler felt vaguely sorry for Ryan. Though he also thought the DDCI something from the past, he'd learned all that the man had done, and was impressed. Arnie van Damm thought a lot of Ryan also, and Arnie was the best judge of character in the administration. But Elizabeth was his National Security Advisor, and he could not have her and the DDCI at each other's throats, could he? No, he couldn't. It was that simple.

"Dazzle them, Elizabeth."

"Won't be hard." She smiled at him and left.

The task proved much harder than he'd expected. Ghosn thought about asking for help, but decided against it. Part of his aura in the organization was that he worked alone with these things except for the donkeywork, for which he would occasionally require a few strong backs.

The bomb/device/pod turned out to be of sturdier construction than he'd expected. Under the strong worklights, he took the time to wash it off with water and found a number of unexplained items. There were screw-in points which were plugged shut with slot-bolts. On removing one, he found yet another electrical lead. More surprising, the bombcase was thicker than he'd expected. He'd dismantled an Israeli jamming pod before, but though it had mostly been of aluminum construction, there had been several places where the case had been of fiberglass or plastic, which was transparent to electronic radiation.

He'd started on the access hatch, but found it nearly impossible to pry open and tried to find something easier. But there wasn't anything easier. Now he returned to the hatch, frustrated that several hours of work had led nowhere.

Ghosn sat back and lit a cigarette. *What are you?* he asked the object.

It was so much like a bomb, he realized. The heavy case—why hadn't he realized that it was so damned heavy, too heavy for a jamming pod . . . but it couldn't be a bomb, could it? No fuses, no detonator, what he had seen of the inside was electrical wiring and connectors. It *had to be* some kind of electronic device. He stubbed the cigarette out in the dirt and walked over to his workbench.

Ghosn had a wide variety of tools, one of which was a gasoline-powered rotary saw, useful for cutting steel. It was really a two-man tool, but he decided to use it alone, and to use it on the hatch, which had to be less sturdy than the case itself. He set the cutting depth to nine millimeters and started the tool, manhandling it onto the hatch. The sound of the saw was dreadful, more so as the diamond-edge of the blade bit into the steel, but the weight of the saw was sufficient to keep it from jerking off the bomb, and he slowly worked it down along the edge of the access hatch. It took twenty minutes for him to make the first cut. He stopped the saw and set it aside, then probed the cut with a bit of thin wire.

Finally! he told himself. He was through. He'd guessed right. The rest of the bombcase seemed to be . . . four centimeters or so, but the hatch was only a quarter of that. Ghosn was too happy to have accomplished *something* to ask himself why a jamming pod needed a full centimeter of hardened steel around it. Before starting again, he donned ear protection. His ears were ringing from the abuse of the first cut, and he didn't want a headache to make the job worse than it already was.

The "Special Report" graphics appeared on all the TV networks within seconds of one another. The network anchors who'd risen early—by the standards of their stint in Rome, that is—to receive their brief from Dr. Elliot raced to their booths literally breathless, and handed over their notes to their respective producers and researchers.

"I knew it," Angela Miriles said. "Rick, I *told* you!"

"Angie, I owe you lunch, dinner, and maybe breakfast in any restaurant you can name."

"I'll hold you to that." The chief researcher chuckled. The bastard could afford it.

"How do we do this?" the producer asked.

"I'm going to wing it. Give me two minutes and we're flying."

"Shit," Angie observed quietly to herself. Rick didn't like winging it. He did, however, like scooping the print reporters, and the timing of the event made that a gimme. *Take that,* New York Times*!* He sat still only long enough for makeup, then faced the cameras as the network's expert—some expert! Miriles thought to herself—joined Rick in the anchor booth.

"Five!" the assistant director said. "Four, three, two, one!" His hand jerked at the anchor.

"It's real," Rick announced. "In four hours, the President of the United States, along with the President of the Soviet Union, the King of Saudi Arabia, and the Prime Ministers of Israel and Switzerland, plus the chiefs of two major religious groups will sign a treaty that offers the hope for a complete settlement of the disputed areas of the Middle East. The details of the treaty are stunning." He went on for three uninterrupted minutes, speaking rapidly as though to race with his counterparts on the other networks.

"There has been nothing like this in living memory, yet another miracle—no, yet another milestone on the road to world peace. Dick?" The anchor turned to his expert commentator, a former ambassador to Israel.

"Rick, I've been reading this for half an hour now, and I still don't believe it. Maybe this is a miracle. We sure picked the right place for it. The concessions made by the Israeli government are stunning, but so are the guarantees that America is making to secure the peace. The secrecy of the negotiations is even more impressive. Had these details broken as recently as two days ago, the whole thing might have come apart before our eyes, but here and now, Rick, here and now, I believe it. It's real. You said it right. It's real. It's really happening, and in a few hours we'll see the world change once more.

"This would never have happened but for the unprecedented cooperation of the Soviet Union, and clearly we owe a vast debt of thanks to the embattled Soviet President, Andrey Narmonov."

"What do you make of the concession made by all the religious groups?"

"Just incredible. Rick, there have been religious wars in this region for virtually all of recorded history. But we should put in here that the architect of the treaty was the late Dr. Charles Alden. A senior administration official was generous in praise to the man who died only weeks ago, and died in disgrace. What a cruel irony it is that the man who really identified the basic problem in the region as the artificial incompatibility of the religions, all of which began in this one troubled region, that that man is not here to see his vision become reality. Alden was apparently the driving force behind this agreement, and one can only hope that history will remember that, despite the timing and circumstances of his death, it was Dr. Charles Alden of Yale who helped to make this miracle happen." The former Ambassador was also a Yalie, and a classmate of Charlie Alden.

"What of the others?" the anchor asked.

"Rick, when something of this magnitude happens—and it's darned rare when it does—there are always a lot of people who play their individual roles, and all of those roles are important. The Vatican Treaty was also the work of Secretary Brent Talbot, ably supported by Undersecretary Scott Adler, who is, by the way, a brilliant diplomatic technician and Talbot's right-hand man. At the same time, it was President Fowler who approved this initiative, who used muscle when that was needed, and who took Charlie's vision forward after his death. No president has ever had the political courage and dazzling vision to stake his political reputation on so wild a gambit. Had we failed on this, one can scarcely imagine the political fallout, but Fowler pulled it off. This is a great day for American diplomacy, a great day for East-West understanding, and perhaps the greatest moment for world peace in all of human history."

"I couldn't have said it better, Dick. What about the Senate, which has to approve the Vatican Treaty, and also the U.S.-Israeli Bilateral Defense Treaty?"

The commentator grinned and shook his head in overt amusement. "This will go through the United States Senate so fast that the President might smear the printer's ink on the bill. The only thing that can slow this up is the rhetoric you'll hear in the committee room and on the Senate floor."

"But the cost of stationing American troops—"

"Rick, we have a military for the purpose of preserving the peace. That's their job, and to do that job in this place, America will pay whatever it costs. This isn't a sacrifice for the American taxpayer. It's a privilege, an historic honor to place the seal of American strength on the peace of the world. Rick, this is what America is all about. Of course we'll do it."

"And that's it for now," Rick said, turning back to Camera One. "We'll be back in two and a half hours for live coverage of the signing of the Vatican Treaty. We now return you to New York. This is Rick Cousins reporting to you from the Vatican."

* * *

"Son of a bitch!" Ryan breathed. This time, unfortunately, the TV had awakened his wife, who was watching the events on the tube with interest.

"Jack, how much did you—" Cathy stood and went off to make the morning coffee. "I mean, you went over there, and you—"

"Honey, I was involved. I can't say how much." Jack knew he ought to have been angry at how credit for the first proposal had been assigned to Alden, but Charlie had been a good guy, even if he had displayed his share of human weaknesses, and Alden had pushed it along when it had needed a push. Besides, he told himself, history will find out a little, as it usually did. The real players knew. He knew. He was used to being in the background, to doing things that others didn't and couldn't know about. He turned to his wife and smiled.

And Cathy knew. She'd heard him speculating aloud a few months earlier. Jack didn't know that he murmured to himself when he shaved, and thought he didn't wake her up when he arose so early, but she'd never yet failed to see him off, even if she didn't open her eyes. Cathy liked the way he kissed her, thinking her asleep, and didn't want to spoil it. He was having trouble enough. Jack was hers, and the goodness of the man was no mystery to his wife.

It's not fair, the other Dr. Ryan told herself. *It was Jack's idea—at least part of it was.* How many other things didn't she know? It was a question Caroline Muller Ryan, M.D., F.A.C.S., rarely asked herself. But she could not pretend that Jack's nightmares weren't real. He had trouble sleeping, was drinking too much, and what sleep he had was littered with things she could never ask about. Part of that frightened her. What had her husband done? What guilt was he carrying?

Guilt? Cathy asked herself. Why had she asked herself that?

Ghosn pried the hatch off after three hours. He'd had to change a blade on the cutting tool, but the delay had mainly resulted from the fact that he ought to have asked for an extra hand but been too proud to do so. In any case it was done, and a prybar finished the job. The engineer took a worklight and looked into the thing. He found yet another mystery.

The inside of the device was a metal lattice-frame—titanium perhaps? he wondered—which held in place a cylindrical mass . . . secured with heavy bolts. Ghosn used his worklight to look around the cylinder and saw more wires, all connected to the cylinder. He caught the edge of a largish electronic device . . . some sort of radar transceiver, he thought. Aha! So it was some sort of . . . but why, then . . . ? Suddenly he knew that he was missing something . . . something big. But what? The markings on the cylinder were in Hebrew, and he didn't know that other Semitic language well, and he didn't understand the significance of these markings. The frame which held it, he saw, was partially designed as a shock-absorber . . . and it had worked admirably. The framing was grossly distorted, but the cylinder it held seemed largely intact. Damaged to be sure, but it had not split. . . . Whatever was inside the cylinder was supposed to be protected against shock. That made it delicate, and *that* meant it was some sort of delicate electronic device. So he came back to the idea that it was a jamming pod. Ghosn was too focused to realize that his mind had closed out other options; that his engineer's brain was so fixed on the task at hand that he was ignoring possibilities and the signals that presented them. Whatever it was, however, he had to get it out first. He next selected a wrench and went to work on the bolts securing the cylinder in place.

* * *

Fowler sat in a 16th-century chair, watching the protocol officers flutter around like pheasants unable to decide whether to walk or fly. People commonly thought that affairs like this one were run smoothly by professional stage-managers who planned everything in advance. Fowler knew better. Sure, things were smooth enough when there had been time enough—a few months—to work out all the details. But this affair had been set up with days, not months, of preparation, and the dozen or so protocol officers had scarcely decided who was the boss among themselves. Curiously, it was the Russian and the Swiss officers who were the calmest, and before the American President's eyes, it was they who huddled and worked out a quick alliance, then presented their plan—whatever it was—to the others, which they then put into play. Just like a good football squad, the President smiled to himself. The Vatican representative was too old for a job like this. The guy—a bishop, Fowler thought, maybe a monsignor—was over sixty and suffering from an anxiety attack that might just kill him. Finally the Russian took him aside for two quick minutes, nods were exchanged and a handshake, then people started moving as though they had a common purpose. Fowler decided that he'd have to find out the Russian's name. He looked like a real pro. More importantly, it was hugely entertaining to watch, and it relaxed the President at a moment when he needed the relaxation.

Finally—only five minutes late, and that was a miracle, Fowler thought with a suppressed grin—the various heads of state rose from their chairs, summoned like the members of a wedding party by the nervous mother-in-law-to-be, and told where to stand in line. More perfunctory handshakes were exchanged, along with a few jokes that suffered from the absence of translators. The Saudi King looked cross at the delays. As well he might, Fowler thought. The King probably had other things on his mind. Already there were death threats directed at him. But there was no fear on the man's face, Bob Fowler saw. He might be a humorless man, but he had the bearing and courage—and the class, the President admitted to himself—that went with his title. It had been he who'd first committed to the talks after two hours with Ryan. That was too bad, wasn't it? Ryan had filled in for Charlie Alden, taking his assignment on the fly and doing the job as though he'd prepared fully for it. The President frowned to himself at that. He'd allowed himself to forget just how frantic the initial maneuvers had been. Scott Adler in Moscow, Rome, and Jerusalem, and Jack Ryan in Rome and Riyadh. They'd done very well, and neither would ever get much credit. Such were the rules of history, President Fowler concluded. If they'd wanted credit, they ought to have tried for his job.

Two liveried Swiss Guards opened the immense bronze doors, revealing the corpulent form of Giovanni Cardinal D'Antonio. The sun-bright TV lights surrounded him with a man-made halo that nearly elicited a laugh from the President of the United States of America. The procession into the room began.

Whoever had built this thing, Ghosn thought, knew a thing or two about designing for brute force. It was odd, he thought. Israeli equipment always had a delicacy to it—no, wrong term. The Israelis were clever, efficient, elegant engineers. They made things as strong as they had to be, no more, no less. Even their ad hoc gear showed foresight and meticulous workmanship. But this one . . . this one was overengineered to a fare-thee-well. It had been hurriedly designed and assembled. It was almost crude, in fact. He was grateful for that. It made disassembly easier. No one had thought to include a self-destruct device that he'd have to figure out first—the Zionists were getting devilishly clever at that! One such subsystem had nearly killed Ghosn only five months earlier, but there was none here. The bolts holding the cylinder in place were jammed, but still straight, and that meant it was just a matter of having a big-enough wrench. He squirted penetrating oil onto each, and after waiting for fifteen minutes and two cigarettes, he attached the wrench to the first. The initial turns came hard, but soon the bolt allowed itself to be withdrawn. Five more to go.

It would be a long afternoon. The speeches came first. The Pope began, since he was the host, and his rhetoric was surprisingly muted, drawing quiet lessons from Scripture, again focusing on the similarities among the three religions present. Earphones gave each of the chiefs of state and religious figures simultaneous translations, which were quite unnecessary, as each of them had a written copy of the various speeches, and the men around the table struggled not to yawn, for speeches were only speeches, after all, and politicians have trouble listening to the words of others, even other chiefs of state. Fowler had the most trouble. He'd be going last. He surreptitiously checked his watch, keeping his face blank as he pondered the ninety minutes left to go.

It took another forty minutes, but finally all the bolts came out. Big, heavy, noncorrosive ones. This thing had been built to last, Ghosn thought, but that merely worked to his benefit. Now, to get the cylinder out. He took another careful look for possible antitamper devices—caution was the only defense in a job like his—and felt around the inside of the pod. The only thing connected was the radar transceiver; though there were three other plug connections, they were all vacant. In his fatigue, it did not strike Ghosn as odd that all three were facing him, easily accessible. The cylinder was jammed in place by the telescoped framing, but with the bolts removed, it was just a matter of applying enough force to drag it clear.

Andrey Il'ych Narmonov spoke briefly. His statement, Fowler thought, was simple and most dignified, showing remarkable modesty that was sure to elicit comment from the commentators.

Ghosn set an additional block and tackle on the A-frame. The cylinder, conveniently enough, had a hoist eye built into it. Thankfully the Israelis didn't like to waste energy any more than he did. The remainder of the pod was less heavy than he expected, but in a minute he had the cylinder hoisted to the point that its friction in its nesting frame was lifting the whole pod. That couldn't last. Ghosn sprayed more penetrating oil on the internal frame and waited for gravity to assert itself . . . but after a minute his patience wore thin and he found a gap large enough for a prybar and started levering the frame away from the cylinder walls one fraction of a millimeter at a time. Inside of four minutes there was a brief shriek of protesting metal and the pod fell free. Then it was just a matter of pulling on the chain and hoisting the cylinder free.

The cylinder was painted green, and had its own access hatch, which was not entirely surprising. Ghosn identified the type of wrench he needed and began work on the four bolts holding it in place. These bolts were tight but yielded quickly to his pressure. Ghosn was going faster now, and the excitement that always came near the end of the job took hold, despite the good sense that told him to relax.

* * *

Finally it was Fowler's turn.

The President of the United States walked to the lectern, a brown-leather folder in his hands. His shirt was starched stiff as plywood, and it was already chafing his neck, but he didn't care. This was the moment for which he had prepared his entire life. He looked straight into the camera, his face set in an expression serious but not grave, elated but not yet joyous, proud but not arrogant. He nodded to his peers.

"Holy Father, Your Majesty, Mr. President," Fowler began, "Messrs Prime Minister, and to all the people of our troubled but hopeful world:

"We have met in this ancient city, a city that has known war and peace for three thousand years and more, a city from which sprang one of the world's great civilizations, and is today home to a religious faith greater still. We have all come from afar, from deserts and from mountains, from sweeping European plains and from yet another city by a wide river, but unlike many foreigners who have visited this ancient city, we have all come in peace. We come with a single purpose—to bring an end to war and suffering, to bring the blessings of peace to one more troubled part of a world now emerging from a history bathed in blood but lit by the ideals that set us apart from the animals as a creation in the image of God." He looked down only to turn pages. Fowler knew how to give a speech. He'd had lots of practice over the previous thirty years, and he delivered this one as confidently as he'd addressed a hundred juries, measuring his words and his cadences, adding emotional content that belied his Ice Man image, using his voice like a musical instrument, something physical that was subordinate to and part of his intense personal will.

"This city, this Vatican state, is consecrated to the service of God and man, and today it has fulfilled that purpose better than at any time. For today, my fellow citizens of the world, today we have achieved another part of the dream that all men and women share wherever they may live. With the help of your prayers, through a vision given us so many centuries ago, we have come to see that peace is a better thing than war, a goal worthy of efforts even more mighty, demanding courage far greater than is required for the shedding of human blood. To turn away from war, to turn towards peace, is the measure of our strength.

"Today it is my honor, and a privilege that all of us share, to announce to the world a treaty to put a final end to the discord that has sadly defiled an area holy to us all. With this agreement, there will be a final solution based on justice, and faith, and the word of the God Whom we all know by different names, but Who knows each of us.

"This treaty recognizes the rights of all men and women in the region to security, and freedom of religion, to freedom of speech, to the basic dignity enshrined in the knowledge that all of us are God's creations, that each of us is unique, but that we are all equal in His sight. . . ."

The final hatch came open. Ghosn closed his eyes and whispered a fatigued prayer of thanks. He'd been at this for hours, skipping his noon meal. He set the hatch down, placing the bolts on the concave surface so that they wouldn't be lost. Ever the engineer, Ghosn was neat and tidy in everything he did. Inside the hatch was a plastic seal, still tight, he noted with admiration. That was a moisture and weather seal. And *that* definitely made it a sophisticated electronic device. Ghosn touched it gently. It wasn't pressurized. He used a small knife to cut the plastic and peeled it carefully aside. He looked for the first time into the cylinder, and it was as though a hand of ice suddenly gripped his heart. He was looking at a distorted sphere of yellow-gray . . . like dirty bread dough.

It was a bomb.

At least a self-destruct device. A very powerful one, fifty kilos of high explosive. . . .

Ghosn backed off; a sudden urge to urinate gripped his loins. The engineer fumbled for a smoke and lit it on the third attempt. How had he missed . . . what? What had he missed? Nothing. He'd been as careful as he always was. The Israelis hadn't killed him yet. Their design engineers were clever, but so was he.

Patience, he told himself. He commenced a new examination of the cylinder's exterior. There was the wire, still attached, from the radar device, and three additional plug points, all of them empty.

What do I know of this thing?

Radar transceiver, heavy case, access hatch . . . explosive sphere wired with . . .

Ghosn leaned forward again to examine the object. At regular and symmetrical intervals on the sphere were detonators . . . the wires from them were . . .

It isn't possible. No, it cannot be that!

Ghosn removed the detonators one by one, detaching the wires from each, and setting them down on a blanket, slowly and carefully, for detonators were the most twitchy things man made. The high explosive, on the other hand, was so safe to use that you could pinch off a piece and set it on fire to boil water. He used the knife to pry loose the surprisingly hard blocks.

"There is an ancient legend of Pandora, a woman of mythology given a box. Though told not to open it, she foolishly did so, admitting strife and war and death into our world. Pandora despaired at her deeds until she found, remaining alone in the bottom of the nearly empty box, the spirit of hope. We have seen all too much of war and strife, but now we have finally made use of hope. It has been a long road, a bloody road, a road marked with despair, but it has always been an upward road, because hope is humanity's collective vision of what can, should, and *must* be, and hope has led us to this point.

"That ancient legend may have its origin in paganism, but its truth is manifest today. On this day we put war and strife and unnecessary death back into the box. We close the box on conflict, leaving in our possession hope, Pandora's last and most important gift to all humanity. This day is the fulfillment of the dream of all mankind.

"On this day, we have accepted from the hands of God the gift of peace.

"Thank you." The President smiled warmly at the cameras and made his way to his chair amid the more-than-polite applause of his peers. It was time to sign the treaty. The moment was here, and after being the last speaker, Fowler would be the first to sign. The moment came quickly, and J. Robert Fowler became a man of history.

He was not going slowly now. He pulled the blocks away, knowing as he did so that he was being reckless and wasteful, but now he knew—thought he knew—what he had in his hands.

And there it was, a ball of metal, a shining nickel-plated sphere, not corroded or damaged by its years in the Druse's garden, protected by the plastic seal of the Israeli engineers. It was not a large object, not much larger than a ball that a child might play with. Ghosn knew what he would do next. He reached his hand all the way into the sundered mass of explosives, extending his fingers to the gleaming nickel surface.

Ghosn's fingertips brushed the ball of metal. It was warm to the touch.

"Allahu akhbar!"

9. Resolve

"This is interesting."

"It's a rather unique opportunity," Ryan agreed.

"How reliable—how trustworthy?" Cabot asked.

Ryan smiled at his boss. "Sir, that's always the question. You have to remember how the game works. You're never sure of anything—that is, what certainty you have generally takes years to acquire. This game only has a few rules, and nobody ever knows what the score is. In any case, this is a lot more than a defection." His name was Oleg Yurievich Lyalin—Cabot didn't know that yet—and he was a KGB "Illegal" who operated without the shield of diplomatic immunity and whose cover was that of a representative of a Soviet industrial concern. Lyalin ran a string of agents with the code name of THISTLE, and he was running it in Japan. "This guy is a real field-spook. He's got a better net going than the KGB *Rezident* in Tokyo, and his best source is right in the Japanese cabinet."

"And?"

"And he's offering us the use of his network."

"Is this as important as I'm starting to think it is . . . ?" the DCI asked his deputy.

"Boss, we rarely get a chance like this. We've never really run ops in Japan. We lack a sufficient number of Japanese-speaking people—even here on the inside to translate their documents—and our priorities have always been elsewhere. So just establishing the necessary infrastructure to conduct ops there would take years. But the Russians have been working in Japan since before the Bolsheviks took over. The reason is historical: the Japanese and the Russkies have fought wars for a long time, and they've always regarded Japan as a strategic rival—as a result of which they placed great emphasis on operations there even before Japanese technology became so important to them. What he is doing is essentially giving us the Russian business at a bargain price, the inventory, the accounts receivables, the physical plant, everything. It doesn't get much better than this."

"But what he's asking . . ."

"The money? So what? That's not a thousandth of a percent of what it's worth to our country," Jack pointed out.

"It's a million dollars a month!" Cabot protested. *Tax free!* the Director of Central Intelligence did not add.

Ryan managed not to laugh. "So the bastard's greedy, okay? Our trade deficit with Japan is how much at last count?" Jack inquired with a raised eyebrow. "He's offering us whatever we want for as long as we want it. All we have to do is arrange to pick him up and fly him and his family over whenever it becomes necessary. He doesn't want to retire to Moscow. He's forty-five, and that's the age when they get antsy. He has to rotate home in ten years—to what? He's lived in Japan almost continuously for thirteen years. He likes affluence. He likes cars, and VCRs, and not standing in line for potatoes. He likes us. About the only people he doesn't like is the Japanese—he doesn't like them at all. He figures he's not even betraying his country, 'cause he's not giving us anything he isn't feeding them, and part of the deal is that he does nothing against Mother Russia. Fine, I can live with that." Ryan chuckled for a moment. "It's capitalism. The man is starting an elite news service, and it's information we can really use."

"He's charging enough."

"Sir, it's worth it. The information he can give us will be worth billions in our trade negotiations, and billions in federal taxes as a result. Director, I used to be in the investment business, that's how I made my money. Investment opportunities like this come along about once every ten years. The Directorate of Operations wants to run with it. I agree. We'd have to be crazy to say no to this guy. His introductory package—well, you've had a chance to read it, right?"

The introductory package was the minutes of the last Japanese cabinet meeting, every word, grunt, and hiss. It was highly valuable for psychological analysis if nothing else. The nature of the exchange in the cabinet meetings could tell American analysts all sorts of things about how their government thought and reached decisions. That was data often inferred but never confirmed.

"It was most enlightening, especially what they said about the President. I didn't forward that. No sense getting him annoyed at a time like this. Okay—the operation is approved, Jack. How do we run things like this?"

"The code name we've selected is MUSHASHI. That's the name of a famous samurai dueling master, by the way. The operation will be called NIITAKA. We'll use Japanese names for the obvious reason"—Jack decided to explain; though Cabot was bright, he was new to the intelligence trade—"in the event of compromise or a leak from our side, we want it to appear that our source is Japanese, not Russian. Those names stay in this building. For outsiders who get let into this, we use a different code name. That one will be computer-generated and it'll change on a monthly basis."

"And the real name of the agent?"

"Director, it's your choice. You have the right to know it. I deliberately have not told you to this point because I wanted you to see the whole picture first. Historically it's evenly split, some directors want to know, and about the same number do not. It's a principle of intelligence operations that the fewer the number of people who know things, the less likely that there will be any sort of leak. Admiral Greer used to say the First Law of Intelligence Operations is that the likelihood of an operation's being burned was proportional to the *square* of the people in on the details. Your call, sir."

Cabot nodded thoughtfully. He decided to temporize. "You liked Greer, didn't you?"

"Like a father, sir. After I lost Dad in the plane crash, well, the Admiral sort of adopted me." *More like I adopted him,* Ryan thought. "On MUSHASHI, you'll probably want to think it through."

"And if the White House asks to know the details?" Cabot asked next.

"Director, despite what MUSHASHI thinks, his employers will regard what he is doing as high treason, and that's a capital crime over there. Narmonov is a good guy and all that, but the Soviets have executed forty people that we know of for espionage. That included TOP HAT, JOURNEYMAN, and a guy named Tolkachev, all of whom were highly productive agents for us. We tried to do a trade in all three cases, but they were popped before negotiations had a chance to get under way. The appeals process in the Soviet Union is still somewhat abbreviated,'' Ryan explained. ''The simple fact, sir, is that if this guy gets burned, he will probably be shot right in the head. That's why we take agent-identity so seriously. If we screw up, people die, *glasnost* notwithstanding. Most presidents understand that. One more thing.''

''Yes?''

''He's told us something else. He wants all his reports to be handled physically, not by cable. If we don't agree, he doesn't do business. Okay, technically that's no problem. We've done that before with agents of this caliber. The nature of his information is such that immediacy is not required. There's daily air service to and from Japan via United, Northwest, and even All Nippon Airways straight into Dulles International Airport.''

''But . . .'' Cabot's face twisted into a grimace.

''Yeah.'' Jack nodded. ''He doesn't trust our communications security. That scares me.''

''You don't think . . . ?''

''I don't know. We've had very limited success penetrating Soviet ciphers for the past few years. NSA assumes that they have the same problems with ours. Such assumptions are dangerous. We've had indications before that our signals are not fully secure, but this one comes from a very senior guy. I think we have to take this seriously.''

''Just how scary could this be?''

''Terrifying,'' Jack answered flatly. ''Director, for obvious reasons we have numerous communications systems. We have MERCURY right downstairs to handle all of our stuff. The rest of the government mainly uses stuff from NSA; Walker and Pelton compromised their systems a long time ago. Now, General Olson over at Fort Meade says they've fixed all that, but for expense reasons they have not fully adopted the TAPDANCE one-time systems that they've been playing with. We can warn NSA again—I think they'll ignore this warning also, but we have to do it—and on our end, I think it's time to act. For starters, sir, we need to think about a reexamination of MERCURY.'' That was the CIA's own communications nexus, located a few floors below the Director's office, and that used its own encrypting systems.

''Expensive,'' Cabot noted seriously. ''With our budget problems . . .''

''Not half as expensive as a systematic compromise of our message traffic is. Director, there is *nothing* as vital as secure communications links. Without that, it doesn't matter what else we have. Now, we've developed our own one-time system. All we need is authorization of funds to make it go.''

''Tell me about it. I haven't been briefed in.''

''Essentially it's our own version of the TAPDANCE. It's a one-time pad with transpositions stored on laser-disk CD ROM. The transpositions are generated from atmospheric radio noise, then superencrypted with noise from later in the day—atmospheric noise is pretty random, and by using two separate sets of the noise, and using a computer-generated random algorithm to mix the two, well, the mathematicians say that's as random as it gets. The transpositions are generated by computer and fed onto laser disks in realtime. We use a different disk for every day of the year. Each disk is unique, two copies only, one to the station, one in

MERCURY—no backups. The laser-disk reader we use at both ends looks normal, but has a beefed-up laser, and as it reads the transposition codes from the disk it also burns them right off the plastic. When the disk is used up, or the day ends—and the day will end first, since we're talking billions of characters per disk—the disk is destroyed by baking it in a microwave oven. That takes two minutes. It ought to be secure as hell. It can only be compromised at three stages: first, when the disks are manufactured; second, from disk-storage here; third, from disk-storage in each station. Compromise of one station does not compromise anyone else. We can't make the disks tamperproof—we've tried, and it would both cost too much and make them overly vulnerable to accidental damage. The downside of this is that it'll require us to hire and clear about twenty new communications technicians. The system is relatively cumbersome to use, hence the increased number of communicators. The main expense component is here. The field troops we've talked to actually prefer the new system because it's user-friendly."

"How much to set it up?"

"Fifty million dollars. We have to increase the size of MERCURY and set up the manufacturing facility. We have the space, but the machinery is expensive. From the time we get the money, we could have it up and running in maybe as little as three months."

"I see your point. It's probably worth doing, but getting the money . . . ?"

"With your permission, sir, I could talk to Mr. Trent about it."

"Hmm." Cabot stared down at his desk. "Okay, feel him out very gently. I'll bring this up with the President when he gets back. I'll trust you on MUSHASHI. You and who else know his real name?"

"The DO, Chief of Station Tokyo, and his case officer." The Director of Operations was Harry Wren, and if he was not quite Cabot's man, he was the man Cabot had picked for the job. Wren was on his way to Europe at the moment. A year ago Jack had thought the choice a mistake, but Wren was doing well. He'd also picked a superb deputy, actually a pair of them: the famous Ed and Mary Pat Foley, one of whom—Ryan could never decide which—would have been his choice for DO. Ed was the organization man, and Mary Pat was the cowboy side of the best husband-wife team the Agency had ever fielded. Making Mary Pat a senior executive would have been a worldwide first, and probably worth a few votes in Congress. She was pregnant again with her third, but that wasn't expected to slow Supergirl down. The Agency had its own day-care center, complete to cipher locks on the doors, a heavily armed response team of security officers, and the best play equipment Jack had ever seen.

"Sounds good, Jack. I'm sorry I faxed the President as soon as I did. I ought to have waited."

"No problem, sir. The information was thoroughly laundered."

"Let me know what Trent thinks about the funding."

"Yes, sir." Jack left for his office. He was getting good at this, the DDCI told himself. Cabot wasn't all that hard to manage.

Ghosn took his time to think. This was not a time for excitement, not a time for precipitous action. He sat down in the corner of his shop and chain-smoked his cigarettes for several hours, all the time staring at the gleaming metal ball that lay on the dirt floor. *How radioactive is it?* one part of his brain wondered almost continuously, but it was a little late for that. If that heavy sphere was giving off hard gammas, he was already dead, another part of his brain had already decided.

This was a time to think and evaluate. It required a supreme act of will for him to sit still, but he managed it.

For the first time in many years he was ashamed of his education. He had expertise both in electrical and mechanical engineering, but he'd hardly bothered cracking a book about their nuclear equivalent. What possible use could such a thing have had for him? he asked himself on the rare occasions that he'd considered acquiring knowledge in that area. Obviously none. As a result of that, he'd limited himself to broadening and deepening his knowledge in areas of direct interest: mechanical and electronic fusing systems, electronic countermeasure gear, the physical characteristics of explosives, the capabilities of explosive-sensing systems. He was a real expert on this last category of study. He read everything he could find on the instrumentation used in detecting explosives at airports and other areas of interest.

Number One, Ghosn told himself on lighting cigarette number fifty-four of the day, *every book I can find on nuclear materials, their physical and chemical properties; bomb technology, bomb physics; radiological signatures . . . the Israelis must know the bomb is missing—since 1973!* he thought in amazement. *Then why . . . ? Of course. The Golan Heights are volcanic in origin. The underlying rock and the soil in which those poor farmers tried to raise their vegetables were largely basaltic, and basalt had a relatively high background-radiation count . . . the bomb was buried two or three meters in rocky soil, and whatever emissions it gave off were lost in background count. . . .*

I'm safe*!* Ghosn realized.

Of course! If the weapon were that "hot," it would have been better shielded! Praise be to Allah for that!

Can I . . . can I? That was the question, wasn't it?

Why not?

"Why not?" Ghosn said aloud. "Why not. I have all the necessary pieces, damaged, but . . ."

Ghosn stubbed the cigarette out in the dirt next to all the others and rose. His body was racked by coughing—he knew that cigarettes were killing him . . . more dangerous than that . . . but they were good for thinking.

The engineer lifted the sphere. What to do with it? For the moment, he set it in the corner and covered it with a toolbox. Then he walked out of the building toward his jeep. The drive to headquarters took fifteen minutes.

"I need to see the Commander," Ghosn told the chief guard.

"He just retired for the evening," the guard said. The entire detail was becoming protective of their commander.

"He'll see me." Ghosn walked right past him and into the building.

Qati's quarters were on the second floor. Ghosn went up the steps, past another guard, and pulled open the bedroom door. He heard retching from the adjoining bathroom.

"Who the devil is it?" a cross voice asked. "I told you that I didn't want to be disturbed!"

"It's Ghosn. We need to talk."

"Can't it wait?" Qati appeared from the lighted doorway. His face was ashen. It came out as a question, not an order, and that told Ibrahim more than he'd ever known of his Commander's condition. Perhaps this would make him feel better.

"My friend, I need to show you something. I need to show it to you tonight." Ghosn strained to keep his voice level and unexcited.

"Is it that important?" Almost a moan.

''Yes.''

''Tell me about it.''

Ghosn just shook his head, tapping his ear as he did so. ''It's something interesting. That Israeli bomb has some new fusing systems. It nearly killed me. We need to warn our colleagues about it.''

''Bomb? I thought—'' Qati stopped himself. His face cleared for a moment and the Commander's expression formed a question. ''Tonight, you say?''

''I'll drive you over myself.''

Qati's strength of character prevailed. ''Very well. Let me get my clothes on.''

Ghosn waited downstairs. ''The Commander and I have to go see about something.''

''Mohammed!'' the chief guard called, but Ghosn cut him off.

''I'll take the Commander myself. There is no security problem at my shop.''

''But—''

''But you worry like an old woman! If the Israelis were that clever, you'd already be dead, and the Commander with you!'' It was too dark to see the expression on the guard's face, but Ghosn could feel the rage that radiated toward him from the man, an experienced front-line fighter.

''We'll see what the Commander says!''

''What's the problem now?'' Qati emerged from the door, tucking his shirt in.

''I'll drive you myself, Commander. We don't need a security force for this.''

''As you say, Ibrahim.'' Qati walked to the jeep and got in. Ghosn drove off past some astonished security guards.

''What exactly is this all about?''

''It's a bomb after all, not an electronics pod,'' the engineer replied.

''So? We've retrieved scores of the cursed things! What is this all about?''

''It is easier to show you.'' The engineer drove rapidly, watching the road. ''If you think I have wasted your time—when we are done, feel free to end my life.''

Qati's head turned at that. The thought had already occurred to him, but he was too good a leader for that. Ghosn might not be the material of a fighter, but he was an expert at what he did. His service to the organization was as valuable as any man's. The Commander endured the rest of the ride in silence, wishing the medicines he was taking allowed him to eat—no, to retain what he ate.

Fifteen minutes later, Ghosn parked his jeep fifty meters from the shop and led his Commander to the building by an indirect route. By this time Qati was thoroughly confused and more than a little angry. When the lights went on, he saw the bomb-case.

''So, what about it?''

''Come here.'' Ghosn led him to the corner. The engineer bent down and lifted the toolbox. ''Behold!''

''What is it?'' It looked like a small cannonball, a sphere of metal. Ghosn was enjoying this. Qati was angry, but that would soon change.

''It's plutonium.''

The Commander's head snapped around as though driven by a steel spring. ''What? What do—''

Ghosn held up his hand. He spoke softly but positively. ''What I am sure of, Commander, is that this is the explosive portion of an atomic bomb. An Israeli atomic bomb.''

''Impossible!'' the Commander whispered.

''Touch it,'' Ghosn suggested.

The Commander bent down and touched a finger to it. "It's warm, why?"

"From the decay of alpha particles. A form of radiation that is not harmful—here it is not, in any case. That is plutonium, the explosive element of an atomic bomb. It can be nothing else."

"You're sure?"

"Positive, absolutely positive. It can only be what I say it is." Ghosn walked over to the bombcase. "These"—he held up some tiny electronic parts—"they look like glass spiders, no? They are called kryton switches, they perform their function with total precision, and that kind of precision is necessary for only one application found inside a bombcase. These explosive blocks, the intact ones, note that some are hexagons, some are pentagons? That is necessary to make a perfect explosive sphere. A shaped charge, like that for an RPG, but the focus is inward. These explosive blocks are designed to crush that sphere to the size of a walnut."

"But it's metal! What you say is not possible."

"Commander, I do not know as much as I should of these matters, but I do know a little. When the explosives go off, they compress that metal sphere as though it were made of rubber. It *is* possible—you know what an RPG does to the metal on a tank, no? There is enough explosive here for a hundred RPG projectiles. They will crush the metal as I say. When it is compressed, the proximity of the atoms begins a nuclear chain-reaction. Think, Commander:

"The bomb fell into the old man's garden on the first day of the October War. The Israelis were frightened by the force of the Syrian attack, and they were immensely surprised by the effectiveness of the Russian rockets. The aircraft was shot down, and the bomb was lost. The exact circumstances don't matter. What matters, Ismael, is that we have the parts of a nuclear bomb." Ghosn pulled out another cigarette and lit it.

"Can you . . ."

"Possibly," the engineer said. Qati's face was suddenly cleared of the pain he'd known for over a month.

"Truly Allah is beneficent."

"Truly He is. Commander, we need to think about this, very carefully, very thoroughly. And security . . ."

Qati nodded. "Oh, yes. You did well to bring me here alone. For this matter we can trust no one . . . no one at all. . . ." Qati let his voice trail off, then turned to his man. "What do you need to do?"

"My first need is for information—books, Commander. And do you know where I must go to get them?"

"Russia?"

Ghosn shook his head. "Israel, Commander. Where else?"

Representative Alan Trent met with Ryan in a House hearing room. It was the one used for closed-door hearings, and was swept daily for bugs.

"How's life treating you, Jack?" the congressman asked.

"No special complaints, Al. The President had a good day."

"Indeed he did—the whole world did. The country owes you a debt of thanks, Dr. Ryan."

Jack's smile dripped with irony. "Let's not allow anybody to learn that, okay?"

Trent shrugged. "Rules of the game. You should be used to it by now. So. What brings you down on such short notice?"

"We have a new operation going. It's called NIITAKA." The DDCI explained on for several minutes. At a later date he would have to hand over some documentation. All that was required now was notification of the operation and its purpose.

"A million dollars a month. That's *all* he wants?" Trent laughed aloud.

"The Director was appalled," Jack reported.

"I've always liked Marcus, but he's a tightfisted son of a bitch. We've got two certified Japan-bashers on the oversight committee, Jack. It's going to be hard to rein them in with this stuff."

"Three, counting you, Al."

Trent looked very hurt. "Me, a Japan-basher? Just because there used to be two TV factories in my district, and a major auto-parts supplier has laid off half its people? Why the hell should I be the least bit angry about that? Let me see the cabinet minutes," the congressman commanded.

Ryan opened his case. "You can't copy them, you can't quote from them. Look, Al, this is a long-term op and—"

"Jack, I didn't just get into town from the chicken ranch, did I? You've turned into a humorless SOB. What's the problem?"

"Long hours," Jack explained as he handed the papers over. Al Trent was a speed reader, and flicked through the pages with indecent speed. His face went into neutral, and he turned back into what he was before all things, a cold, calculating politician. He was well to the left side of the spectrum, but unlike most of his ilk Trent let his ideology stop at the water's edge. He also saved his passion for the House floor and his bed at home. Elsewhere he was icily analytical.

"Fowler will go ballistic when he sees this. They are the most arrogant people. You've sat in on cabinet meetings. Ever hear stuff like this?" Trent asked.

"Only on political matters. I was surprised by the tone of the language, too, but it might just be a cultural thing, remember."

The congressman looked up briefly. "True. Beneath the patina of good manners, they can be wild and crazy folks, kind of like the Brits, but this is like Animal House. . . . Christ, Jack, this is explosive. Who recruited him?"

"The usual mating dance. He shows up at various receptions, and Chief of Station Tokyo caught a whiff, let it simmer for a few weeks, then made his move. The Russian handed over the packet and his contractual demands."

"Why Operation NIITAKA, by the way? I've heard that before somewhere, haven't I?"

"I picked it myself. When the Japanese strike force was heading for Pearl Harbor, the mission-execute signal was 'Climb Mount Niitaka.' Remember, you're the only guy here who knows that word. We're going onto a monthly-change identification cycle on this. This is hot enough that we're giving him the whole treatment."

"Right," Trent agreed. "What if this guy's an agent provocateur?"

"We've wondered about that. It's possible but unlikely. For KGB to do that—well, it kinda breaks the rules as they are understood now, doesn't it?"

"Wait!" Trent read over the last page again. "What the hell's this about communications?"

"What it is, is scary." Ryan explained what he wanted to do.

"Fifty million? You sure?"

"That's the one-time start-up costs. Then there's the new communicators. Total annual costs after start-up are about fifteen million."

"Pretty reasonable, actually." Trent shook his head. "NSA is quoting a much higher price to switch over to their system."

"They have a bigger infrastructure to worry about. That number I gave you ought to be solid. MERCURY is pretty small."

"How soon do you want it?" Trent knew that Ryan quoted hard budget numbers. It came from his business experience, Al knew, which was pretty thin in government service.

"Last week would be nice, sir."

Trent nodded. "I'll see what I can do. You want it 'black,' of course?"

"Like a cloudy midnight," Ryan answered.

"Goddamn it!" Trent swore. "I've *told* Olson about this. His technical weenies do their rain dance and he buys it every time. What if—"

"Yeah, what if all our communications are compromised." Jack did not make it a question. "Thank God for *glasnost,* eh?"

"Does Marcus understand the implications?"

"I explained it to him this morning. He understands. Al, Cabot may not have all the experience you or I would like, but he's a fast learner. I've had worse bosses."

"You're too loyal. Must be a lingering symptom of your time in the Marines," Trent observed. "You'd be a good director."

"Never happen."

"True. Now that Liz Elliot is National Security Advisor, you'll have to cover your ass. You know that."

"Yep."

"What in hell did you do to piss her off? Not that it's all that hard to do."

"It was back right after the convention," Ryan explained. "I was up in Chicago to brief Fowler. She caught me tired from a couple of long trips and she yanked my chain pretty hard. I yanked back."

"Learn to be nice to her," Trent suggested.

"Admiral Greer said that."

Trent handed the papers back to Ryan. "It is difficult, isn't it?"

"Sure is."

"Learn anyway. Best advice I can give you." *Probably a total waste of time, of course.*

"Yes, sir."

"Good timing on the request, by the way. The rest of the committee will be impressed as hell with the new operation. The Japan-bashers will put the word out to their friends on Appropriations that the Agency is really doing something useful. We'll have the money to you in two weeks if we're lucky. What the hell, fifty million bucks—chicken feed. Thanks for coming down."

Ryan locked his case and stood. "Always a pleasure."

Trent shook his hand. "You're a good man, Ryan. What a damned shame you're straight."

Jack laughed. "We all have our handicaps, Al."

Ryan returned to Langley to put the NIITAKA documents back in secure storage, and that ended his work for the day. He and Clark took the elevator down to the garage and left the building an hour early, something they did every two weeks or so. Forty minutes later they pulled into the parking lot of a 7-Eleven between Washington and Annapolis.

"Hello, Doc Ryan!" Carol Zimmer said from behind the register. One of her sons relieved her there, and she led Jack into the back room. John Clark checked out the store. He wasn't worried about Ryan's security, but he had some lingering worries about the way some local toughs felt about the Zimmer enterprise. He and

Chavez had taken care of that one gang leader, having done so in front of three of his minions, one of whom had tried to interfere. Chavez had shown mercy to that lad, who hadn't required an overnight stay at the local hospital. That, Clark judged, was a sign of Ding's growing maturity.

"How is business?" Jack asked in the back room.

"We up twenty-six 'rcent from this time las' year."

Carol Zimmer had been born in Laos less than forty years before, rescued from a hilltop fortress by an Air Force special-operations helicopter just as the North Vietnamese Army had overrun that last outpost of American power in Northern Laos. She'd been sixteen at the time, the last living child of a Hmong chieftain who'd served American interests, and his own—he'd been a willing agent—courageously and well, and to the death. She'd married Air Force sergeant Buck Zimmer, who'd died in yet another helicopter after yet another betrayal, and then Ryan had stepped in. He hadn't lost his business sense despite his years of government service. He'd selected a good site for the store, and as fate had it, they hadn't needed his educational trust fund for the first of the kids now in college. With a kind word from Ryan to Father Tim Riley, the lad had a full scholarship at Georgetown and was already dean's-listed in pre-med. Like most Asians, Carol had a reverence for learning that bordered on religious fanaticism, and which she passed on to all of her kids. She also ran her store with the mechanistic precision a Prussian sergeant expected of an infantry squad. Cathy Ryan could have performed a surgical procedure on the register counter. It was that clean. Jack smiled at the thought. Maybe Laurence Alvin Zimmer, Jr., would do just that.

Ryan looked over the books. His CPA certificate had lapsed, but he could still read a balance sheet.

"You eat dinnah with us?"

"Carol, I can't. I have to get home. My son has a Little League game tonight. Everything's okay? No problems—not even those punks?"

"They not come back. Mistah Clark scare them away fo' good!"

"If they ever come back, I want you to call me right away," Jack said seriously.

"Okay, okay. I learn lesson," she promised him.

"Fine. You take care." Ryan stood.

"Doc Ryan?"

"Yes?"

"Air Force say Buck die in accident. I never ask anybody, but I ask you: accident, no accident?"

"Carol, Buck lost his life doing his job, saving lives. I was there. So was Mr. Clark."

"The ones make Buck die . . . ?"

"You have nothing to fear from them," Ryan said evenly. "Nothing at all." Jack saw the recognition in her eyes. Though Carol had modest language skills, she'd caught what he'd meant by his answer.

"Thank you, Doc Ryan. I never ask again, but I must know."

"It's okay." He was surprised she'd waited so long.

The bulkhead-mounted speaker rattled. "Conn, sonar. I have a routine noise level bearing zero-four-seven, designate contact Sierra-5. No further information at this time. Will advise."

"Very well." Captain Ricks turned to the plotting table. "Tracking party, begin your TMA.'' The Captain looked around the room. Instruments showed a speed of seven knots, a depth of four hundred feet, and a course of three-zero-three. The contact was broad on his starboard beam.

The ensign commanding the tracking party immediately consulted the Hewlett-Packard minicomputer located in the starboard-after corner of the attack center. ''Okay,'' he announced, ''I have a trace angle . . . little shaky . . . computing now.'' That took the machine all of two seconds. ''Okay, I have a range gate . . . it's a convergence zone, range between three-five and four-five thousand yards if he's in CZ-1, five-five and six-one thousand yards for CZ-2.''

''It's almost too easy,'' the XO observed to the skipper.

''You're right, X, disable the computer,'' Ricks ordered.

Lieutenant Commander Wally Claggett, Executive Officer, ''Gold,'' USS *Maine,* walked back to the machine and switched it off. ''We have a casualty to the HP computer . . . looks like it'll take hours to fix,'' he announced. ''Pity.''

''Thanks a lot,'' Ensign Ken Shaw observed quietly to the quartermaster hunched next to him at the chart table.

''Be cool, Mr. Shaw,'' the petty officer whispered back. ''We'll take care o' ya. Don't need that thing now anyway, sir.''

''Let's keep it quiet in the attack center!'' Captain Ricks observed.

The submarine's course took her northwest. The sonar operators fed information to the attack center as she did so. Ten minutes later, the tracking party made its decision.

''Captain,'' Ensign Shaw announced. ''Estimate contact Sierra-5 is in the first CZ, range looks like three-nine thousand yards, course is generally southerly, speed between eight and ten knots.''

''You can do better than that!'' the CO announced sharply.

''Conn, sonar, Sierra-5 looks like Akula-class Soviet fast-attack, preliminary target ident is Akula number six, the *Admiral Lunin*. Stand by''—a moment's silence—''possible aspect change on Sierra-5, possible turn. Conn, we have a definite aspect change. Sierra-5 is now beam-on, definite beam-aspect on target.''

''Captain,'' the XO said, ''that maximizes the effectiveness of his towed array.''

''Right. Sonar, conn, I want a self-noise check.''

''Sonar aye, stand by, sir.'' Another few seconds. ''Conn, we're making some sort of noise . . . not sure what, rattle, like, maybe something in the after ballast tanks. Didn't show before, sir. Definitely aft . . . definitely metallic.''

''Conn, maneuvering room, we got something screwy back here. I can hear something from aft, maybe in the ballast tanks.''

''Captain,'' Shaw said next. ''Sierra-5 is now on a reciprocal heading. Target course is now southeasterly, roughly one-three-zero.''

''Maybe he can hear us,'' Ricks growled. ''I'm taking us up through the layer. Make your depth one hundred feet.''

''One hundred feet, aye,'' the diving officer responded immediately. ''Helm, five degrees up on the fairwater planes.''

''Five degrees up on the fairwater planes, aye. Sir, the fairwater planes are up five degrees, coming to one hundred feet.''

''Conn, maneuvering, the rattle has stopped. It stopped when we took the slight up-angle.''

The XO grunted next to the Captain. ''What the hell does that mean . . . ?''

''It probably means that some dumbass dockyard worker left his toolbox in the ballast tank. That happened to a friend of mine once.'' Ricks was truly angry now, but if you had to have such incidents, here was the place for them. "When we get above the layer, I want to go north and clear datum."

"Sir, I'd wait. We know where the CZ is. Let him slide out of it, then we can maneuver clear while he can't hear us. Let him think he's got us scoped before we start playing tricks. He probably thinks we don't have him. By maneuvering radically, we're tipping our hand."

Ricks considered that. "No, we've canceled the noise aft, we've probably dropped off his scopes already, and when we get above the layer, we can get lost in the surface noise and maneuver clear. His sonar isn't all that good. He doesn't even know what we are yet. He's just sniffing for something. This way we can put more distance between us."

"Aye aye," the XO responded neutrally.

Maine leveled off at one hundred feet, well above the thermocline layer, the boundary between relatively warm surface water and the cold deep water. It changed acoustical conditions drastically and, Ricks judged, should eliminate any chance that the Akula had him.

"Conn, sonar, contact lost on Sierra-5."

"Very well. I have the conn," Ricks announced.

"Captain has the conn," the officer of the deck acknowledged.

"Left ten degrees rudder, come to new course three-five-zero."

"Left ten degrees rudder, aye, coming to new course three-five-zero. Sir, my rudder is left ten degrees."

"Very well. Engine room, conn, make turns for ten knots."

"Engine room, aye, turns for ten knots. Building up slowly."

Maine steadied up on a northerly course and increased speed. It took several minutes for her towed-array sonar to straighten out and be useful again. During this time, the American submarine was somewhat blinded.

"Conn, maneuvering, we got that noise again!" the speaker announced.

"Slow to five—all ahead one-third!"

"All ahead one-third, aye. Sir, engine room answers all ahead one-third."

"Very well. Maneuvering, conn, what about that noise?"

"Still there, sir."

"We'll give it a minute," Ricks judged. "Sonar, conn, got anything on Sierra-5?"

"Negative, sir, holding no contacts at this time."

Ricks sipped at his coffee and watched the clock on the bulkhead for three minutes. "Maneuvering, conn, what about the noise?"

"Has not changed, sir. It's still there."

"Damn! X, bring her down a knot." Claggett did as he was told. The skipper was losing it, he realized. Not good. Another ten minutes passed. The worrisome noise aft attenuated but did not go away.

"Conn, sonar! Contact bearing zero-one-five, just appeared real sudden, like, it's Sierra-5, sir. Definite Akula-class, *Admiral Lunin*. Evaluate as direct-path contact, bow-on aspect. Probably just came up through the layer, sir."

"Does he have us?" Ricks asked.

"Probably yes, sir," the sonarman reported.

"Stop!" another voice announced. Commodore Mancuso walked into the room. "Okay, we conclude the exercise at this point. Will the officers please come with me?"

Everyone let out a collective breath as the lights went up. The room was set in a large square building shaped not at all like a submarine, though its various other rooms duplicated most of the important parts of an Ohio-class boomer. Mancuso led the attack-center crew into a conference room and closed the door.

''Bad tactical move, Captain.'' Bart Mancuso was not known for his diplomacy. ''XO, what advice was that you gave to your skipper?'' Claggett recited it word for word. ''Captain, why did you reject that advice?''

''Sir, I estimated that our acoustical advantage was sufficient to allow me to do that in such a way as to maximize separation from the target.''

''Wally?'' Mancuso turned to the skipper of the Red Team, Commander Wally Chambers, about to become the CO of USS *Key West*. Chambers had worked for Mancuso on *Dallas*, and had the makings of one hell of a fast-attack skipper. He had just proven that, in fact.

''It was too predictable, Captain. Moreover, by continuing course and changing depth course you presented the noise source to my towed array, and also gave me a hull-popping transient that ID'd you as a definite submarine contact. You would have been better off to turn bow-on, maintain depth, and slow down. All I had was a vague indication. If you'd slowed down, I would never have ID'd you. Since you didn't, I noted your hop on top the layer and sprinted in fast underneath as soon as I cleared the CZ. Captain, I didn't know I had you until you let me know, but you let me know, and you did let me get close. I floated my tail over the layer while I stayed right underneath it. There was a fairly good surface duct, and I had you at two-nine thousand yards. I could hear you, but you couldn't hear me. Then it was just a matter of continuing my sprint until I was close enough for a high-probability solution. I had you cold.''

''The point of the exercise was to show you what happened when you lost your acoustical advantage.'' Mancuso let that sink in before going on. ''Okay, so it wasn't fair, was it? Who ever said life was fair?''

''Akula's a good boat, but how good is its sonar?''

''We assume it's as good as a second-flight 688.''

No way, Ricks thought to himself. ''What other surprises can I expect?''

''Good question. The answer is that we don't know. And if you don't know, you assume they're as good as you are.''

No way, Ricks told himself.

Maybe even better, Mancuso didn't add.

''Okay,'' the Commodore told the assembled attack-center crew. ''Go over your own data and we do the wash-up in thirty minutes.''

Ricks watched Captain Mancuso exit the room, sharing a chuckle with Chambers. Mancuso was a smart, effective sub-driver, but he was still a damned fast-attack jockey who didn't belong in command of a boomer squadron because he simply didn't think the right way. Calling in his former shipmate from Atlantic Fleet, another fast-attack jockey—well, yeah, that's how it was done, but damn it! Ricks was sure he'd done the right thing.

It had been an unrealistic test. Ricks was sure of that. Hadn't Rosselli told the both of them that *Maine* was quiet as a black hole? Damn. This was his first chance to show the Commodore what he could do, and he'd been faked out of making a favorable impression by an artificial and unfair test, and some goofs from his people—the ones Rosselli had been so damned proud of.

''Mr. Shaw, let's see your TMA records.''

''Here, sir.'' Ensign Shaw, who'd graduated sub school at Groton less than two months before, was standing in the corner, the chart and his notes grasped tightly in his tense hands. Ricks snatched them away and spread them on a worktable. The Captain's eyes scanned the pages.

"Sloppy. You could have done this at least a minute faster."

"Yes, sir," Shaw replied. He didn't know how he might have gone faster, but the Captain said so, and the Captain was always right.

"That could have made the difference," Ricks told him, a muted but still nasty edge on his voice.

"Sorry, sir." That was Ensign Shaw's first real mistake. Ricks straightened, but still had to look up to meet Shaw's eyes. That didn't help his disposition either.

" 'Sorry' doesn't cut it, Mister. 'Sorry' endangers our ship and our mission. 'Sorry' gets people killed. 'Sorry' is what an unsatisfactory officer says. Do you understand me, Mr. Shaw?"

"Yes, sir."

"Fine." The word came out as a curse. "Let's make sure this never happens again."

The rest of the half hour was spent going over the records of the exercise. The officers left the room for a larger one, where they would relive the exercise, learning what the Red Team had seen and done. Lieutenant Commander Claggett slowed the Captain down.

"Skipper, you were a little hard on Shaw."

"What do you mean?" Ricks asked in annoyed surprise.

"He didn't make any mistakes. I couldn't have done the track more than thirty seconds faster myself. The quartermaster I had with him has been doing TMAs for five years. He's taught it at sub school. I kept an eye on both of them. They did okay."

"Are you saying the mistake was my fault?" Ricks asked in a deceptively gentle voice.

"Yes, sir," the XO replied honestly, as he had been taught to do.

"Is that a fact?" Ricks walked out the door without another word.

To say that Petra Hassler-Bock was unhappy was an understatement of epic proportions. A woman in her late thirties, she'd lived over fifteen years on the run, hiding from the West German police before things had simply become too dangerous, precipitating her escape to the East Zone—what had been the East Zone, the *Bundeskriminalamt* investigator smiled to himself. Amazingly, she'd thrived on it. Every photo in the thick file showed an attractive, vital, smiling woman with a girl's unlined face framed by pretty brown hair. This same face had coldly watched three people die, one after several days of knifework, the detective told himself. That murder had been part of an important political statement—it had been at the time of the vote on whether or not to allow the Americans to base their Pershing-2 and Cruise missiles in Germany, and the Red Army Faction had wanted to terrify people into seeing things their way. It hadn't worked, of course, though it had made the victim's death into a gothic exercise.

"Tell me, Petra, did you enjoy killing Wilhelm Manstein?" the detective asked.

"He was a pig," she answered defiantly. "An overweight, sweaty, whoremongering pig."

That was how they'd caught him, the detective knew. Petra had set up the kidnapping first by attracting his attention, then by establishing a brief but fiery relationship. Manstein had not been the most attractive example of German manhood, of course, but Petra's idea of women's liberation was rather more robust than the norm in Western countries. The nastiest members of Baader-Meinhof and the RAF had been the women. Perhaps it was a reaction to the *Kinder-Küche-Kirche* mind-set of German males, as some psychologists said, but the woman before him was the most coldly frightening assassin he'd ever met. The first body parts mailed to Manstein's family had been those which had offended her so greatly. Manstein had lived for ten days after that, the pathologist's report stated, providing noisy red entertainment for this still-young lady.

"Well, you took care of that, didn't you? I imagine Günther was somewhat unsettled by your passion, wasn't he? After all, you spent—what? Five nights with Herr Manstein before the kidnapping? Did you enjoy that part also, *mein Schatz?*" The insult scored, the detective saw. Petra had been attractive once, but no longer. Like a flower a day after cutting, she was no longer a living thing. Her skin was sallow, her eyes surrounded by dark rings, and she'd lost at least eight kilos. Defiance blazed out from her, but only briefly. "I expect you did, giving in to him, letting him 'do his thing.' You must have enjoyed it enough that he kept coming back. It wasn't just baiting him, was it? It could not have been just an act. Herr Manstein was a discerning philanderer. He had so much experience, and he only frequented the most skillful whores. Tell me, Petra, how did you acquire so much skill? Did you practice beforehand with Günther—or with others? All in the name of revolutionary justice, of course, or revolutionary *Kameradschaft, nicht wahr?* You are a worthless slut, Petra. Even whores have morals, but not you.

"And your beloved revolutionary cause," the detective sneered. *"Doch!* Such a cause. How does it feel to be rejected by the entire German *Volk?"* She stirred in her chair at that, but couldn't quite bring herself . . . "What's the matter, Petra, no heroic words now? You always talked about your visions of freedom and democracy, didn't you? Are you disappointed now that we have real democracy—and the people detest you and your kind! Tell me, Petra, what is it like to be rejected? Totally rejected. And you know it's true," the investigator added. "You know it's no joke. You watched the people in the street from your windows, didn't you, you and Günther? One of the demonstrations was right under your apartment, wasn't it? What did you think while you watched, Petra? What did you and Günther say to each other? Did you say it was a counterrevolutionary trick?" The detective shook his head, leaning forward to stare into those empty, lifeless eyes, enjoying his own work as she had done.

"Tell me, Petra, how do you explain the votes? Those were free elections. You know that, of course. Everything you stood for and worked for and murdered for—all a mistake, all for *nothing!* Well, it wasn't a total loss, was it? At least you got to make love to Wilhelm Manstein." The detective leaned back and lit a small cigar. He blew smoke up at the ceiling. "And now, Petra? I hoped you enjoyed that little tryst, *mein Schatz*. You will never leave this prison alive. Never, Petra. No one will ever feel pity for you, not even when you're confined to a wheelchair. Oh, no. They'll remember your crimes and tell themselves to leave you here with all the other vicious beasts. There is no hope for you. You will die in this building, Petra."

Petra Hassler-Bock's head jerked at that. Her eyes went wide for an instant as she thought to say something, but stopped short.

The detective went on conversationally. "We lost track of Günther, by the way. We nearly got him in Bulgaria—missed him by thirty hours. The Russians, you see, have been giving us their files on you and your friends. All those months you spent at those training camps. Well, in any case, Günther is still on the run. In

Lebanon, we think, probably holed up with your old friends in that ratpack. They're next,'' the detective told her. ''The Americans, the Russians, the Israelis, they're cooperating now, didn't you hear? It's part of this treaty business. Isn't *that* wonderful? I think we'll get Günther there . . . with luck he'll fight back or do something really foolish, and we can bring you a picture of his body. . . . Pictures, that's right! I almost forgot!

''I have something to show you,'' the investigator announced. He inserted a videocassette into a player and switched on the TV. It took a moment for the picture to settle down into what was plainly an amateur video taken with a hand-held camera. It showed twin girls, dressed in matching pink dirndl outfits, sitting side by side on a typical rug in a typical German apartment—everything was fully *in Ordnung,* even the magazines on the table were squared off. Then the action started.

''Komm, Erika. Komm, Ursel!'' a woman's voice urged, and both infants pulled themselves up on a coffee table and tottered toward her. The camera followed their halting, unstable steps into the woman's arms.

''Mutti, Mutti!'' they both said. The detective switched the TV off.

''They're talking and walking. *Ist das nicht wunderbar?* Their new mother loves them very much, Petra. Well, I thought you'd like to see that. That's all for today.'' The detective pressed a hidden button and a guard appeared to take the manacled prisoner back to her cell.

The cell was stark, a cubicle made of white-painted bricks. There was no outside window, and the door was of solid steel except for a spyhole and a slot for food trays. Petra didn't know about the TV camera that looked through what seemed to be yet another brick near the ceiling, but was really a small plastic panel transparent to red and infrared light. Petra Hassler-Bock retained her composure all the way to the cell, and until the door was slammed shut behind her.

Then she started coming apart.

Petra's hollow eyes stared at the floor—that was painted white also—too wide and horrified for tears at first, contemplating the nightmare that her life had become. It could not be real, part of her said with confidence that bordered on madness. All she'd believed in, all she'd worked for—gone! Günther, gone. The twins, gone. The cause, gone. Her life, gone.

The *Bundeskriminalamt* detectives interrogated her only for amusement. She knew that much. They had never seriously probed her for information, but there was a reason for that. She had nothing worthwhile to give them. They'd shown her copies of the files from Stasi headquarters. Nearly everything her erstwhile fraternal socialist brothers had had on her—far more than she had expected—was now in *West* German hands. Names, addresses, phone numbers, records dating back more than twenty years, things about herself that she'd forgotten, things about Günther that she'd never known. All in the hands of the BKA.

It was all over. All lost.

Petra gagged and started weeping. Even Erika and Ursel, her twins, the product of her own body, the physical evidence of her faith in the future, of her love for Günther. Taking their first steps in the apartment of strangers. Calling some stranger *Mutti,* mommy. The wife of a BKA captain—they'd told her that much. Petra wept for half an hour, not making noise, knowing that there had to be a microphone in the cell, this cursed white box that denied her sleep.

Everything lost.

Life—here? The first and only time she'd been in the exercise yard with other prisoners, they'd had to pull two of them off of her. She could remember their screams as the guards had taken her for medical treatment—whore, murderess, animal. . . . To live here for forty years or more, alone, always alone, waiting to go mad, waiting for her body to weaken and decay. For her life meant *life*. Of that she was certain. There would be no pity for her. The detective had made that clear. No pity at all. No friends. Lost and forgotten . . . except for the hate.

She made her decision calmly. In the manner of prisoners all over the world, she'd found a way of getting a piece of metal with an edge on it. It was, in fact, a segment of razor blade from the instrument with which she was allowed to shave her legs once a month. She removed it from its place of hiding, then pulled the sheet—also white—from the mattress. It was like any other, about ten centimeters thick, covered with heavy striped fabric. Its trim was a loop of fabric in which was inserted a ropelike stiffener, with the mattress fabric sewn tight around it to give the edge strength. With the razor edge she began detaching the trim from the mattress. It took three hours and not a small amount of blood, for the razor segment was small, and it cut her fingers many times, but finally she had two full meters of improvised rope. She turned one end of the rope into a noose. The free end of the rope she tied over the light fixture over the door. She had to stand on her chair to do that, but she'd have to stand on the chair in any case. It took three attempts to get the knot right. She didn't want too much length on the rope.

When she was satisfied with that, she proceeded without pause. Petra Hassler-Bock removed her dress and her bra. Next she knelt on the chair with her back to the door, getting its position and hers just right, placed the noose around her neck, and drew it tight. Then she drew up her legs, using her bra to secure them between her back and the door. She didn't want to flinch from this. She had to show her courage, her devotion. Without stopping for a prayer or lament, her hands pushed the chair away. Her body fell perhaps five centimeters before the improvised rope stopped her fall and drew tight. Her body rebelled against her will at this point. Her drawn-up legs fought against the bra holding them between the backs of her thighs and the metal door, but in fighting the restraint, they merely pushed Petra fractionally away from the door, and that increased the strangulation on her upper neck.

She was surprised by the pain. The noose fractured her larynx before sliding over it to a point under her jaw. Her eyes opened wide, staring at the white bricks of the far wall. That's when the panic hit her. Ideology has its limits. She couldn't die, didn't want to die, didn't want to—

Her fingers raced to her throat. It was a mistake. They fought to get under the mattress trim, but it was too thin, cutting so deeply into the soft flesh of her neck that she couldn't get a single finger under it. Still she fought, knowing that she had mere seconds before the blood loss to her brain . . . it was getting vague now, her vision was beginning to suffer. She couldn't see the lines of mortar between the even German-made brickwork on the far wall. Her hands kept trying, cutting into the surface blood vessels of her throat, drawing blood that only made the noose slick, able to sink in tighter, cutting off circulation through the carotid arteries even more. Her mouth opened wide and she tried to scream, no, she didn't want to die, didn't—needed help. Couldn't anyone hear her? Could no one help her? Too late, just two seconds, maybe only one, maybe not even that, the last remaining shred of consciousness told her that if she could just loosen the bra holding her legs, she could have stood and . . .

The detective watched the TV picture, saw her hands flutter toward the bra, searching limply for the clasp before they fell away, and twitched for a few more seconds, then stopped. *So close,* he thought. *So very close to saving herself.* It was a pity. She'd been a pretty girl, but she'd chosen to murder and torture, and she'd also chosen to die, and if she'd changed her mind at the end—didn't they all? Well, not quite all—that was merely renewed proof that the brutal ones were cowards after all, *nicht wahr?*

Aber natürlich.

"This television is broken," he said, switching it off. "Better get a new one to keep an eye on Prisoner Hassler-Bock."

"That will take about an hour," the guard supervisor said.

"That's fast enough." The detective removed the cassette from the same tape recorder he'd used to show the touching family scene. It went into his briefcase with the other. He locked the case and stood. There was no smile on his face, but there was a look of satisfaction. It wasn't his fault that the *Bundestag* and *Bundesrat* were unable to pass a simple and effective death-penalty statute. That was because of the Nazis, of course. Damned barbarians. But even barbarians were not total fools. They hadn't ripped up the autobahns after the war, had they? Of course not. So just because the Nazis had executed people—well, some of them had even been ordinary murderers whom any civilized government of the era would have executed. And if anyone merited death, Petra Hassler-Bock did. Murder by torture. Death by hanging. That, the detective figured, was fair enough. The Wilhelm Manstein murder case had been his from the start. He'd been there when the man's genitals had arrived by mail. He'd watched the pathologists examine the body, had attended the funeral, and he remembered the sleepless nights when he'd been unable to wash the horrid spectacles from his mind. Perhaps now he would. Justice had been slow, but it had come. With luck those two cute little girls would grow into proper citizens, and no one would ever know who and what their birth mother had once been.

The detective walked out of the prison toward his car. He didn't want to be near the prison when her body was discovered. Case closed.

"Hey, man."

"Marvin. I hear that you did well with weapons," Ghosn said to his friend.

"No big deal, man. I've been shooting since I was a kid. That's how you get dinner where I come from."

"You outshot our best instructor," the engineer pointed out.

"Your targets are a hell of a lot bigger than a rabbit, and they don't move. Hell, I used to hit jacks on the move with my .22. If you have to shoot what you eat, you learn right quick to hit what you aim at, boy. How'd you do with that bomb thing?" Marvin Russell asked.

"A lot of work for very little return," Ghosn replied.

"Maybe you can make a radio from all that electrical stuff," the American suggested.

"Perhaps something useful."

10. Last Stands

Flying west is always easier than flying east. The human body adjusts more easily to a longer day than a shorter one, and the combination of good food and good wine makes it all the easier. Air Force One had a sizable conference room that could be used for all manner of functions. In this case it was a dinner for senior administration officials and selected members of the press pool. The food, as usual, was superb. Air Force One may be the only aircraft in the world which serves something other than TV dinners. Its stewards shop daily for fresh foods which are most often prepared at six hundred knots at eight miles altitude, and more than one of the cooks had left military service to become executive chef at a country club or posh restaurant. Having cooked for the President of the United States of America looks good on any chef's résumé.

The wine in this case was from New York, a particularly good blush Chablis that the President was known to like, when he wasn't drinking beer. The converted 747 had three full cases stowed below. Two white-coated sergeants kept all the glasses filled as the courses came in and out. The atmosphere was relaxed, and the conversations all off the record, on deep background, and be careful or you'll never eat in here again.

"So, Mr. President," *The New York Times* asked. "How quickly do you think this will be implemented?"

"It is starting even as we speak. The Swiss Army representatives are already in Jerusalem to look things over. Secretary Bunker is meeting with the Israeli government to facilitate the arrival of American forces into the region. We expect to have things actually moving inside of two weeks."

"And the people who'll have to vacate their homes?" *The Chicago Tribune* continued the question.

"They will be seriously inconvenienced, but with our help the new homes will be constructed very rapidly. The Israelis have asked for and will get credits with which to purchase prefabricated housing made in America. We're also paying to set up a factory of that type for them to continue on their own. Many thousands of people will be relocated. That will be somewhat painful, but we're going to make it just as easy as we can."

"At the same time," Liz Elliot put in, "let's not forget that quality of life is more than having a roof over your head. Peace has a price, but it also has benefits. Those people will know real security for the first time in their lives."

"Excuse me, Mr. President," the *Tribune* reporter said with a raised glass. "That was not meant as criticism. I think we all agree that this treaty is a godsend." Heads nodded all around the table. "The way it is implemented is an important story, however, and our readers want to know about it."

"The relocations will be the hardest part," Fowler responded calmly. "We must salute the Israeli government for agreeing to it, and we must do the best we can to make the process just as painless as is humanly possible."

always faced a more rigorous revolutionary task because they lacked the ready-made sea of discontent from which Qati and his colleagues drew their recruits. That they had been less successful in their goals was due to objective circumstances, not a reflection on their intelligence or dedication.

Bock could have made a superb operations officer because he saw things clearly.

And now? Qati asked himself. That was a question, but one that would require time for contemplation. It was not a question for a hasty answer. He'd sleep on that one for several days . . . more like a week, the Commander promised himself as he tried to find sleep.

". . . I have the great privilege and high honor of introducing the President of the United States."

The assembled members of Congress stood as one person from their crowded seats in the House chamber. Arrayed in the front row were the members of the cabinet, the Joint Chiefs of Staff, and the Justices of the Supreme Court, who also rose. In the balconies were others, among them the Saudi and Israeli ambassadors sitting side-by-side for the first time in memory. The TV cameras panned the great room in which both history and infamy had been made. The applause echoed from wall to wall until hands grew red from it.

President Fowler rested his notes on the lectern. He turned to shake the hand of the Speaker of the House, the President Pro Tempore of the Senate, and his own Vice President, Roger Durling. In the euphoria of the moment no one would comment that Durling came last. Next he turned to smile and wave at the assembled multitude, and the noise increased yet again. Every gesture in Fowler's repertoire came into play. The one-hand wave, the two-hand wave, hands at shoulder level, and hands over the head. The response was truly bipartisan, and that was remarkable, Fowler noted. His most vociferous enemies in the House and Senate were assiduous in their enthusiasm, and he knew it to be genuine. There still was true patriotism in the Congress, much to the surprise of everyone. Finally, he waved for silence and the applause grudgingly subsided.

"My fellow Americans, I come to this house to report on recent events in Europe and the Middle East, and to lay before the United States Senate a pair of treaty documents which, I hope, will meet with your speedy and enthusiastic approval." More applause. "With these treaties the United States, operating in close cooperation with many other nations—some trusted old friends, and some valuable new ones—has helped to bring about peace in a region that has helped to give peace to the world, but which has known all too little peace itself.

"One can search all of human history. One can trace the evolution of the human spirit. All of human progress, all the shining lights that have lit our way up from barbarism, all the great and good men and women who have prayed and dreamed and hoped and worked for this moment—this moment, this opportunity, this culmination, is the last page in the history of human conflict. We have reached not a starting point, but a *stopping* point. We—" More applause interrupted the President. He was very slightly annoyed, having not planned for this interruption. Fowler smiled broadly, waving for silence.

"We have reached a stopping point. I have the honor to report to you that America has led the way on the road to justice and peace." Applause. "It is fitting that this should be so . . ."

"A little thick, isn't it?" Cathy Ryan asked.

"A little." Jack grunted in his chair and reached for his wine. "It's just how things go, babe. There are rules for this sort of thing just as there are for opera. You have to follow the formula. Besides, it is a major—hell, a colossal development. Peace is breaking out again.''

''When are you leaving?'' Cathy asked.

''Soon,'' Jack replied.

''Of course there is a price we must pay for this, but history demands responsibility from those who forge it,'' Fowler said on the TV. ''It is our task to guarantee the peace. We must send American men and women to protect the State of Israel. We are sworn to defend that small and courageous country against all enemies.''

''What enemies are they?'' Cathy asked.

''Syria isn't happy with the treaty as yet. Neither is Iran. As far as Lebanon goes, well, there isn't any Lebanon in any real sense of the word. It's just a place on the map where people die. Libya and all those terrorist groups. There are still enemies to be concerned about.'' Ryan finished off the glass and walked into the kitchen to refill it. It was a shame to waste good wine like this, Jack told himself. The way he was guzzling it, he might as well drink anything. . . .

''There will be a monetary cost as well,'' Fowler was saying as Ryan came back.

''Taxes are going up again,'' Cathy observed crossly.

''Well, what did you expect?'' *Fifty million of it is my fault, of course. A billion here, and a billion there . . .*

''Will this really make a difference?'' she asked.

''It should. We'll find out if all those religious leaders believe in what they say or if they're just bullshit artists. What we've done is to hoist them on their own petards, babe. . . . Make that 'principles,' '' Jack said after a moment. ''Either they work things out in accordance with their beliefs or they reveal themselves as charlatans.''

''And . . . ?''

''I don't think they're charlatans. I think they'll be faithful to what they've always said. They have to be.''

''And soon you won't have any real work to do, will you?''

Jack caught the hopeful note in her voice. ''I don't know about *that*.''

After the end of the President's speech came the commentary. Speaking in opposition was Rabbi Solomon Mendelev, an elderly New Yorker who was one of Israel's most fervent—some would say rabid—supporters. Oddly, he'd never actually traveled to Israel. Jack didn't know why that was true and made a mental note to find out why tomorrow. Mendelev led a small but effective segment of the Israeli lobby. He'd been nearly alone in voicing approval—well, understanding—of the shootings on Temple Mount. The rabbi had a beard, and wore a black yarmulke over what looked like a well-rumpled suit.

''This is a betrayal of the State of Israel,'' he said after receiving the first question. Surprisingly, he spoke with calm reason. ''In forcing Israel to return what was rightfully hers, the United States has betrayed the Jewish people's historic right to the land of their fathers, and also gravely compromised the physical security of the country. Israeli citizens will be forced from their homes at gunpoint, just as happened fifty years ago,'' he concluded ominously.

''Now wait a minute!'' another commentator responded heatedly.

''God, these people are passionate,'' Jack noted.

''I lost family members in the Holocaust,'' Mendelev said, his voice still reasonable. ''The whole point of the State of Israel is to give Jews a place where they can be safe.''

"But the President is sending American troops—"

"We sent American troops to Vietnam," Rabbi Mendelev pointed out. "And we made promises, and there was a treaty involved there also. Israel's only possible security is within defensible borders behind her own troops. What America has done is to bully that country into accepting an agreement. Fowler cut off defense supplies to Israel as a means of 'sending a message.' Well, the message was sent and received: either give in or be cut off. That is what happened. I can prove it, and I will testify before the Senate Foreign Relations Committee to prove it."

"Uh-oh," Jack observed quietly.

"Scott Adler, Deputy Secretary of State, personally delivered that message while John Ryan, the Deputy Director of the CIA, made his own pitch to Saudi Arabia. Ryan promised the Saudi King that America would bring Israel to heel. That's bad enough, but for Adler, a Jew, to do what he did. . . ." Mendelev shook his head.

"This guy's got some good sources."

"Is what he says true, Jack?" Cathy asked.

"Not exactly, but what we were doing over there was supposed to be secret. It wasn't supposed to be widely known that I was out of the country."

"I knew you were gone—"

"But not where to. It won't matter. He can make a little noise, but it won't matter."

The demonstrations began the next day. They'd bet everything on this. It was the last desperate throw. The two leaders were Russian Jews who'd only recently been allowed to leave a country that manifestly had little love for them. On arrival in their only true home, they'd been allowed to settle on the West Bank, that part of Palestine that had been taken from Jordan by force of arms in the Six Day War of 1967. Their prefabricated apartments—tiny by American standards but incomprehensibly luxurious by Russian ones—stood on one of the hundreds of rocky slopes that defined the region. It was new and strange to them, but it was home, and home is something people fight to defend. The son of Anatoliy—he'd renamed himself Nathan—was already a regular officer in the Israeli Army. The same was true of David's daughter. Their arrival into Israel so short a time before had seemed to all of them like salvation itself—and now they were being told to leave their homes? Again? Their lives had borne enough recent shocks. This was one too many.

The whole block of apartments was similarly occupied by Russian immigrants, and it was easy for Anatoliy and David to form a local *kollektiv* and get things properly organized. They found themselves an Orthodox rabbi—the only thing they didn't have in their small community—to provide religious guidance and began their march toward the Knesset behind a sea of flags and a holy Torah. Even in so small a country this took time, but the march was of such a nature as to attract the inevitable media coverage. By the time the sweating and weary marchers arrived at their destination, all the world knew of their trek and its purpose.

The Israeli Knesset is not the most sedate of the world's parliamentary bodies. The body of men and women ranges from the ultra-right to the ultra-left, with precious little room for a moderate middle. Voices are often raised, fists are often shaken or pounded on whatever surface presents itself, all beneath the black-and-white photo of Theodor Herzl, an Austrian whose ideal of Zionism in the mid-19th century was the guiding vision for what he hoped would be a safe homeland for his abused and mistreated people. The passion of the parliamentarians is such as to make many an observer wonder how it is possible, in a country where nearly everyone is a member of the Army Reserves and consequently has an automatic weapon in his (or her) closet, that some Knesset members have failed to be blasted to quivering fragments at their seats in the course of a spirited debate. What Theodor Herzl would have thought of the goings-on is anyone's guess. It was Israel's curse that the debates were too lively, the government too severely polarized both on political and religious grounds. Almost every religious subsect had its own special area of land and consequently its own parliamentary representation. It was a formula calculated to make France's often-fragmented assembly look well organized, and it had for a generation denied Israel a stable government with a coherent national policy.

The demonstrators, joined by many others, arrived an hour before debate was to begin on the question of the treaties. It was already possible—likely—that the government would fall, and the newly arrived citizens sent representatives to every member of the Knesset they could locate. Members who agreed with them came outside and gave fiery speeches denouncing the treaties.

"I don't like this," Liz Elliot observed, watching the TV in her office. The political furor in Israel was much stronger than she had expected, and Elliot had called Ryan in for an assessment of the situation.

"Well," the DDCI agreed, "it is the one thing we couldn't control, isn't it?"

"You're a big help, Ryan." On Elliot's desk was the polling data. Israel's most respected public-opinion firm had conducted a survey of five thousand people and found the numbers were 38 percent in favor of the treaty, 41 percent opposed, and 21 percent undecided. The numbers roughly matched the political makeup of the Knesset, whose right-wing elements slightly outnumbered the left, and whose precarious center was always fragmented into small groupings, all of which waited for a good offer from one side or the other that would magnify their political importance.

"Scott Adler went over this weeks ago. We knew going in that the Israeli government was shaky. For Christ's sake, when in the last twenty years has it *not* been shaky?"

"But if the Prime Minister cannot deliver . . ."

"Then it's back to Plan B. You wanted to put pressure on their government, didn't you? You'll get your wish." This was the one thing that hadn't been fully considered, Ryan thought, but the truth of the matter was that full consideration would not have helped. The Israeli government had been a model of anarchy in action for a generation. The treaty work had gone ahead on the assumption that once transformed into a *fait accompli,* the treaty would have to be ratified by the Knesset. Ryan had not been asked for an opinion on that, though he still thought it a fair assessment.

"The political officer at the embassy says that the balance of power may be the little party controlled by our friend Mendelev," Elliot noted, trying to be calm.

"Maybe so," Jack allowed.

"It's absurd!" Elliot snarled. "That little old fart hasn't even been there—"

"Some sort of religious thing. I checked. He doesn't want to go back until the Messiah arrives."

"Jesus!" the National Security Advisor exclaimed.

"Exactly. You got it." Ryan laughed and got a nasty look. "Look, Liz, the man has his personal religious beliefs. We may think they're a little off, but the Constitution demands that we both tolerate and *respect* them. That's the way we do things in this country, remember?"

Elliot waved her fist at the TV set. "But this crazy rabbi is screwing things up! Isn't there *anything* we can do about it?"

"Like what?" Jack asked quietly. There was more to her demeanor than panic.

"I don't know—*something*. . . ." Elliot allowed her voice to trail off, leaving an opening for her visitor.

Ryan leaned forward and waited until he had her full attention. "The historical precedent you're looking for, Dr. Elliot, is, 'Will no one rid me of this troublesome priest?' Now, if you're trying to tell me something, let's get it clear and in the open, shall we? Are you proposing that we interfere with the parliament of a friendly democratic country, or that we do something illegal within the borders of the United States of America?" A pause while her eyes focused a little more tightly. "Neither one of those things will happen, Dr. Elliot. We let them make up their own minds. If you even think of telling me to interfere with Israel's democratic processes, the President gets my resignation just as fast as I can drive down here to deliver it. If you're wishing out loud for us to hurt that little old guy in New York, remember that such wishes fall under at least two conspiracy statutes. My duty as an ordinary citizen, much less an official of the government of my country, is to report suspected violations of the law to the appropriate law-enforcement agencies." The look Ryan got after his pronouncement was venomous.

"Damn you! I never said—"

"You just fell into the most dangerous trap in government service, ma'am. You started to think that your wishes to make the world a better place supersede the principles under which our government is supposed to operate. I can't stop you from having such thoughts, but I can tell you that my agency will not be a party to it, not as long as I'm there." It sounded too much like a lecture, but Ryan felt that she needed it. She was entertaining the most dangerous of thoughts.

"I never said that!"

Bullshit. "Fine, you never said or thought that. I was mistaken. You have my apology. Let the Israelis decide to ratify the treaties or not. They have a democratic government. It is their right to decide. We have the right to nudge them in the right direction, to tell them that our continued level of aid is contingent upon their agreeing to it, but not to interfere directly with their governmental processes. There are some lines you may not cross, even if 'you' happen to be the U.S. government."

The National Security Advisor managed a smile. "Thank you for your views on the matter of proper government policy, Dr. Ryan. That will be all."

"Thank *you,* Dr. Elliot. My assessment, by the way, is that we should let things be. The treaty will be approved despite what you see here."

"Why?" Elliot managed not to hiss.

"The treaties are good for Israel in any objective sense. The people will realize that as soon as they've had a chance to digest the information and make their views known to their representatives. Israel *is* a democracy, and democracies generally do the smart thing. History, you see. Democracy has become popular in the world because it works. If we panic and take precipitous action, we'll only mess things up. If we let the process work as it's supposed to work, the right thing will probably happen."

"Probably?"

"There are no certainties in life; there are only probabilities," Ryan explained. Why didn't everyone understand that? he wondered to himself. "But interference has a higher probability of failure than doing nothing. Doing nothing at all is often the right thing. This is such a case. Let their system work. I think it will work. That is my opinion.''

''Thank you for your assessment,'' she said, turning away.

''A pleasure as always.''

Elliot waited until she heard the door close before turning to look. ''You arrogant prick, I'll break you for that,'' she promised.

Ryan climbed back into his car on West Executive Drive. *You went too far, man,* he told himself.

No, you didn't. She was *starting to think that way and you had to slam the door on it right there and then.*

It was the most dangerous thought that a person in government could have. He'd seen it before. Some dreadful thing happened to people in Washington, D.C. They arrived in the city, usually full of ideals, and those fine thoughts evaporated so rapidly in what was in fact a muggy and humid environment. Some called it being captured by the system. Ryan thought of it as a kind of environmental pollution. The very atmosphere of Washington corroded the soul.

And what makes you immune, Jack?

Ryan considered that, unmindful of the look Clark gave him in the mirror as they drove toward the river. What had made him different to this point was the fact that he had never given in, not even once . . . or had he? There were things he might have done differently. There were some things that hadn't worked out quite as well as he might have wished.

You're not different at all. You just think you are.

As long as I can face the question and the answers, then I am safe.

Sure.

''So?''

''So I can do many things,'' Ghosn replied. ''But not alone. I will need help.''

''And security?''

''That is an important question. I have to make a serious assessment of what the possibilities are. At that point I will know my precise requirements. I know I will need help in some areas, however.''

''Such as?'' the Commander asked.

''The explosives.''

''But you are an expert in such things,'' Qati objected.

''Commander, this task requires precision such as we have never been forced to face. We cannot use ordinary plastic explosives, for example, for the simple reason that they are plastic—they change shape. The explosive blocks I use must be as rigid as stone, must be shaped to a thousandth of a millimeter, and the shape must be determined mathematically. The theoretical side of that is something I could assimilate, but it will take months. I would rather devote my time to refabricating the nuclear material . . . and . . .''

''Yes?''

''I believe I can improve the bomb, Commander.''

''Improve? How?''

''If my initial readings are correct, this type of weapon can be adapted to become not a bomb but a trigger.''

''Trigger for what?'' Qati asked.

''A thermonuclear fusion bomb, a hydrogen bomb, Ismael. The yield of the weapon might be increased by a factor of ten, perhaps a hundred. We could destroy Israel, certainly a very large part of it.''

The Commander paused for a few breaths, assimilating that bit of information. When he spoke, he spoke softly. ''But you need help. Where might be the best place?''

''Günther may have some valuable contacts in Germany. If he can be trusted,'' Ghosn added.

''I have considered this. Günther can be trusted.'' Qati explained why.

''We are sure the story is real?'' Ghosn asked. ''I have no more faith in coincidences than you, Commander.''

''There was a photograph in a German newspaper. It appeared quite genuine.'' A German tabloid had managed to get a graphic black-and-white photo that showed the results of a hanging in all its ghastly splendor. The fact that Petra was nude above the waist had ensured its publication. Such an end for a terrorist murderer was too juicy to be denied to the German males, one of whom had been castrated by this woman.

''The problem is simply that we must minimize the number of people who know about this, else—excuse me, Ismael.''

''But we need some help. Yes, I understand that.'' Qati smiled. ''You are correct. It is time to discuss our plans with our friend. You propose to explode the bomb in Israel?''

''Where else? It is not my place to make such plans, but I assumed—''

''I have not thought about it. One thing at a time, Ibrahim. When are you leaving for Israel?''

''I planned to do so in the next week or so.''

''Let it wait until we see what this treaty business will do.'' Qati thought. ''Begin your studies. We will make haste slowly on this matter. First you must determine your requirements. We will then try to meet them in the most secure location we can arrange.''

It took forever, it seemed, but forever in political terms can be a time period ranging from five minutes to five years. In this case it took less than three days for the important part to happen. Fifty thousand more demonstrators arrived before the Knesset. Led by veterans of all of Israel's wars, the new crowd supported the treaties. There were more shouts and shaken fists, but for once there was no overt violence as the police managed to keep the two passionate groups separated. Instead they labored to outshout each other.

The cabinet met again in closed session, both ignoring and attending to the din outside their windows. The Defense Minister was surprisingly quiet during the discussion. On being asked, he agreed that the additional arms promised by the Americans would be hugely useful: forty-eight additional F-16 fighter-bombers; and for the first time, M-2/3 Bradley fighting vehicles, Hellfire antitank missiles, and access to the revolutionary new tank-gun technology America was developing. The Americans would underwrite most of the cost of building a high-tech training center in the Negev similar to their own National Training Center at Fort Irwin, California, where the 10th Cav unit would train constantly as the ''OpFor'' or opposing force against Israeli units. The Defense Minister knew the effect the NTC had had for the U.S. Army, which was at its highest state of professionalism since World War II. With the new matériel and training base, he judged that the real effectiveness of

Israel's defense forces would increase by fifty percent. To that he added the U.S. Air Force F-16 wing and the tank regiment, both of which, as spelled out in a secret codicil of the Mutual-Defense Treaty, chopped to Israeli command in time of emergency—a situation that was defined by Israel. That was totally unprecedented in American history, the Foreign Minister pointed out.

"So, is our national security degraded or enhanced by the treaties?" the Prime Minister asked.

"It is somewhat enhanced," the Defense Minister admitted.

"Then will you say so?"

Defense pondered that for a moment, his eyes boring in on the man seated at the head of the table. *Will you support me when I make my bid for the premiership?* his eyes asked.

The Prime Minister nodded.

"I will address the crowds. We can live with these treaties."

The speech did not pacify everyone, but it was enough to convince a third of the antitreaty demonstrators to depart. The crucial middle element in the Israeli parliament observed the events, consulted its conscience, and made its decision. The treaties were ratified by a slim margin. Even before the United States Senate had a chance to clear the treaties through the Armed Services and Foreign Relations committees, implementation of both agreements began.

11. Robosoldiers

They weren't supposed to look human. The Swiss Guards were all over 185 centimeters in height and not one weighed less than eighty-five kilograms, which translated to about six-one and a hundred eighty pounds for American tourists. Their physical fitness was manifest. The Guard encampment, just outside the city in what had been a Jewish settlement until less than two weeks before, had its own high-tech gymnasium, and the men were "encouraged" to pump iron until their exposed skin looked as taut as a drumhead. Their forearms, exposed below rolled-up sleeves, were thicker than the lower legs of most men, and already tanned brown beneath what were often sun-bleached blond hairs. Their mostly blue eyes were always hidden behind dark glasses in the case of the officers, and tinted Lexan shields for the rest.

They were outfitted in fatigues of an urban-camouflage pattern, a curious design of black, white, and several shades of gray that allowed them to blend in with the stones and whitewashed stucco of Jerusalem in a way that was eerily effective, especially at night. Their boots were the same, not the spit-shined elegance of parade soldiers. The helmets were Kevlar, covered with cloth of the same pattern. Over the fatigues went camouflaged flak jackets of American design that merely seemed to increase the physical bulk of the soldiers. Over the flak jackets came the web gear. Each man always carried four fragmentation grenades and two smokes, plus a one-liter canteen, first-aid packet, and ammo pouches for a light total load-out of about twelve kilos.

They traveled about the city in teams of five, one noncom and four privates per team, and twelve teams to each duty section. Each man carried a SIG assault rifle, two of which had grenade launchers slung underneath the barrel. The sergeant also carried a pistol, and two men in each team carried radios. The teams on patrol were in constant radio contact and regularly practiced mutual-support maneuvers.

Half of each duty section walked, while the other half moved about slowly and menacingly in American-built HMMWVs. Essentially an oversized jeep, each "hummer" had at least a pintle-mounted machine gun, and some had six-barreled miniguns plus Kevlar armor to protect the crews against the casual enemy. At the commanding note of their horns, everyone cleared a path.

At the command post were several armored fighting vehicles—English-built armored cars that could just barely navigate the streets of the ancient city. Always on duty at the post was a platoon-sized unit commanded by a captain. This was the emergency-response team. They were armed with heavy weapons, like the Swedish Carl Gustav M-2 recoilless, just the right thing for knocking a hole in any building. Supporting *them* was an engineer section with copious quantities of high explosives; the "sappers" ostentatiously practiced by knocking down those settlements which Israel had agreed to abandon. In fact, the entire regiment practiced its combat skills at those sites, and people were allowed to observe from a few hundred meters away in what was rapidly becoming a genuine tourist attraction. Already, Arab merchants were producing T-shirts with logos like ROBOSOLDIER! for anyone who cared to buy them. The commercial sense of the merchants was not unrewarded.

The Swiss Guards did not smile, nor did they speak to the casual interrogator, a facility that came easily to them. Journalists were encouraged to meet with the commanding officer, Colonel Jacques Schwindler, and were occasionally allowed to speak with lower ranks in barracks or at training exercises, but never on the street. Some contact with the locals was inevitable, of course. The soldiers were learning rudimentary Arabic, and English sufficed for everyone else. They occasionally issued traffic citations, though this was mainly a function of the local civil police force that was still forming up—with support from the Israelis who were phasing out of the function. More rarely a Swiss Guard would step into a street fight or other disturbance. Most often the mere sight of a five-man team would reduce people to respectful silence and docile civility. The mission of the Swiss was intimidation, and it didn't require many days for people to appreciate how good they were at it. At the same time, their operations depended most of all on something other than the physical.

On the right shoulder of each uniform was a patch. It was in the shape of a shield. The centerpiece was the white cross on red background of the Swiss, to demonstrate the origin of the soldiers. Around it were the Star and Crescent of Islam, the six-pointed Judaic Star of David, and the Christian Cross. There were three versions of the patch, so that each religious emblem had an equal chance of being on top. It was publicly known that the patches were distributed at random, and the symbology indicated that the Swiss flag protected them all equally.

The soldiers deferred always to religious leaders. Colonel Schwindler met daily with the religious troika which governed the city. It was believed that they alone made policy, but Schwindler was a clever, thoughtful man whose suggestions from the first had carried great weight with the Imam, the Rabbi, and the Patriarch. Schwindler had also traveled to the capitals of every Middle East nation. The Swiss had chosen well—he'd been known as the best colonel in their army. An honest and scrupulously fair man, he'd acquired an enviable reputation. Already on his office wall was a gold-mounted sword, a present from the King of Saudi Arabia. A stallion of equal magnificence was quartered at the Guard force encampment. Schwindler didn't know how to ride.

It was up to the troika to run the city. They had proven to be even more effective than anyone had dared to hope. Chosen for their piety and scholarship, each soon impressed the others. It had been agreed upon at once that each week there would be a public prayer service particular to one of the represented religions, and that each would attend, not actually participating, but demonstrating the respect that was at the foundation of their collective purpose. Originally suggested by the Imam, it had unexpectedly proven to be the most effective method of tempering their internal disagreements and also setting the example for the citizens of the city in their care. This was not to say that there were not disagreements. But those were invariably difficulties between two of the members, and in such cases the uninvolved third would mediate. It was in the interests of all to reach a peaceful and reasonable settlement. "The Lord God"—a phrase each of the three could use without prejudice—required their goodwill, and after a few initial teething problems, that goodwill prevailed. Over coffee, after concluding one dispute over scheduling access to one shrine or another, the Greek Patriarch noted with a chuckle that perhaps this was the first miracle he had ever witnessed. No, the Rabbi had replied, it was no miracle that men of God should have the conviction to obey their own religious principles. All at once? the Imam had asked with a smile, perhaps not a miracle, but certainly it had required over a millennium to achieve. Let us not begin a new dispute, the Greek had said with a rumbling laugh, over the settlement of another—now if you can only help me find a way to deal with my fellow Christians!

Outside on the streets, when clerics of one faith encountered those of another, greetings were exchanged to set an example for everyone. The Swiss Guards saluted each in their turn, and when speaking with the most senior, they would remove their glasses or helmets to show public respect.

That was the only humanity the Swiss Guards were allowed to demonstrate. It was said that they didn't even sweat.

"Scary sons of bitches," Ryan observed, standing in shirtsleeves at a corner. American tourists snapped pictures. Jews still looked a touch resentful. Arabs smiled. The Christians who'd largely been driven out of Jerusalem by increasing violence had barely started to return. Everyone got the hell out of their way as the five men moved briskly down the street, not quite marching, their helmeted heads turning left and right. "They really do look like robots."

"You know," Avi said, "there hasn't been a single attack on them since the first week. Not one."

"I wouldn't want to fool with them," Clark observed quietly.

In the first week, as though by Providence, an Arab youth had killed an elderly Israeli woman with a knife—it had been a street robbery rather than a crime with political significance—and had made the mistake of doing so in view of a Swiss private, who'd run him down and subdued him with a martial-arts blow right out of a movie. The Arab in question had been taken to the troika and given the choice of a trial by Israeli or Islamic law. He'd made the mistake of choosing the latter. After a week in an Israeli hospital to allow his injuries to heal, he'd faced a trial in accordance with the word of the Koran, chaired by Imam Ahmed bin Yussif. One day after that, he had been flown to Riyadh, Saudi Arabia, driven to a public square, and, after having had time to repent his misdeeds, publicly beheaded with a sword. Ryan wondered how you said *pour encourager les autres* in Hebrew, Greek, and

Arabic. Israelis had been amazed at the speed and severity of justice, but the Muslims had merely shrugged and pointed out that the Koran had its own stern criminal code, and that it had proven highly effective over the years.

"Your people are still a little unhappy with this, aren't they?"

Avi frowned. Ryan had faced him with the necessity of expressing his personal opinion or speaking the truth. "They'd feel safer with our paratroops here . . . man-to-man, Ryan?" Truth won out, as it had to with Avi.

"Sure."

"They'll learn. It will take a few more weeks, but they will learn. The Arabs like the Swiss, and the key to the peace on this street is how our Arab friends feel. Now, will you tell me something?" Clark's head moved fractionally at that.

"Maybe," Ryan answered, looking up the street.

"How much did you have to do with this?"

"Nothing at all," Jack replied with a neutral coldness that matched the pace of the soldiers. "It was Charlie Alden's idea, remember? I was just the messenger boy."

"So Elizabeth Elliot has told everyone." Avi didn't have to say any more.

"You wouldn't have asked the question unless you knew the answer, Avi. So why ask the question?"

"Artfully done." General Ben Jakob sat down and waved for the waiter. He ordered two beers before speaking again. Clark and the other bodyguard weren't drinking. "Your President pushed us too hard. Threatening us with withholding our arms. . . ."

"He could have gone a little easier, I suppose, but I do not make policy, Avi. Your people made it happen when they murdered those demonstrators. That reopened a part of our own history that we wish to forget. It neutralized your congressional lobby—a lot of those people were on the other side of our own civil-rights movement, remember. You forced us to move, Avi. You know that. Besides—" Ryan stopped abruptly.

"Yes?"

"Avi, this thing just might work. I mean, look around!" Jack said as the beers arrived. He was thirsty enough that a third of it disappeared in an instant.

"It is a slim possibility," Ben Jakob admitted.

"You get better intel from Syria than we do," Ryan pointed out. "I've heard that they've started saying nice things about the settlement—very quietly, I admit. Am I right?"

"If it's true." Avi grunted.

"You know the hard part about 'peace' intel?"

Ben Jakob's eyes were focused on a distant wall as he contemplated—what? "Believing it is possible?"

Jack nodded. "That's one area where we have the advantage over you guys, my friend. We've been through all that."

"True, but the Soviets never said—proclaimed—for two generations that they wanted to wipe you from the face of the earth. Tell the worthy President Fowler that such concerns are not so easily allayed."

Jack sighed. "I have. I did. Avi, I'm not your enemy."

"Neither are you my ally."

"Allies? We are now, General. The treaties are in force. General, my job is to provide information and analysis to my government. Policy is made by people senior to me, and smarter than me," Ryan added with deadpan irony.

"Oh? And who might they be?" General Ben Jakob smiled at the younger man. His voice dropped a few octaves. "You've been in the trade for what—not even ten years, Jack. The submarine business, what you did in Moscow, the role you played in the last election—"

Ryan tried to control his reaction but failed. "Jesus, Avi!" *How the hell did he find* that *out!*

"You cannot take the Lord's name in vain, Dr. Ryan," the deputy chief of the Mossad chided. "This is the City of God. Those Swiss chaps might shoot you. Tell the lovely Miss Elliot that if she pushes too hard, we still have friends in your media, and a story such as that . . ." Avi smiled.

"Avi, if your people mention that to Liz, she will not know what you are talking about."

"Rubbish!" General Ben Jakob snorted.

"You have my word on that, sir."

It was Brigadier Ben Jakob's turn to be surprised. "That is difficult to believe."

Jack finished off the beer. "Avi, I've said what I can. Has it ever occurred to you that your information may not have come from an entirely reliable source? I will tell you this: I have no personal knowledge of what you alluded to. If there was any kind of deal, I was kept out of it. Okay, I have reason to believe that something may have happened, and I can even speculate what it might have been, but if I ever have to sit in front of a judge and answer questions, all I can say is that I do not *know* anything. And you, my friend, cannot blackmail someone with something that person doesn't know about. You'd have to do a pretty good selling job just to convince them that something had happened in the first place."

"My God, what Moore and Ritter set up really was elegant, wasn't it?"

Ryan set down his empty glass. "Things like that never happen in real life, General. That's movie stuff. Look, Avi, maybe that report you have is a little on the thin side. The spectacular ones often are. Reality never quite keeps up with art, after all." It was a good play. Ryan grinned to carry the point.

"Dr. Ryan, in 1972 the Black September faction of the Palestine Liberation Organization contracted the Japanese Red Army to shoot up Ben Gurion Airport, which they did, killing off mainly American Protestant pilgrims from your island of Puerto Rico. The single terrorist taken alive by our security forces told his interrogators that his dead comrades and their victims would become a constellation of stars in the heavens. In prison he purportedly converted himself to Judaism, and even circumcised himself with his teeth, which speaks volumes for his flexibility," Brigadier General Avi Ben Jakob added matter-of-factly. "Do not ever tell me that there is something too mad to be true. I have been an intelligence officer for more than twenty years, and the only thing of which I am certain is that I have not yet seen it all."

"Avi, even I'm not that paranoid."

"You have never experienced a holocaust, Dr. Ryan."

"Oh? Cromwell and the Potato Famine don't count? Get off that horse, General. We're deploying the U.S. troops here. If it comes to that, there will be American blood on the Negev, or Golan, or whatever."

"And what if—"

"Avi, you ask what if. If *that* what-if ever happens, General, I will fly here myself. I used to be a Marine. You know I've been shot at before. There will be no second Holocaust. Not while I live. My countrymen will not let it happen ever again. Not my government, Avi, my countrymen. We will not let that happen. If

Americans have to die to help protect this country, then Americans will die to do so.''

''You said that to Vietnam.'' Clark's eyes flared at that one, Ben Jakob noticed. ''You have something to say?''

''General, I'm no high official, just a grunt with pretensions. But I got more combat time than anybody in this country of yours, and I'm telling you, sir, that what really scares me about this place is how you guys always fuck up the same way we did over there—we learned, you didn't. And what Dr. Ryan says is right. He'll come over. So will I, if it comes to that. I've killed my share of enemies, too,'' Clark told him in a low, quiet voice.

''Another Marine?'' Avi asked lightly, though he knew better.

''Close enough,'' Clark said. ''And I've kept current, as they say,'' he added with a smile.

''What about your associate?'' Avi motioned toward Chavez, who stood casually at the corner, eyeing the street.

''Good as I ever was. So're those kids in the Cav. But this war talk is all bullshit. You guys both know that. You want security, sir, you settle your domestic problems. Peace will follow that like a rainbow after a storm.''

''Learn from your mistakes. . . .''

''We had a four-thousand-mile buffer to fall back through, General. It isn't that far from here to the Med. You'd better learn from our mistakes. Good news is, you are better able to make a real peace than we ever were.''

''But to have it imposed—''

''Sir, if it works, you'll thank us. If it doesn't work, we have a lot of people to stand by you when the crap hits the fan.'' Clark noticed that Ding had moved casually from his post across the street, moving aimlessly, it seemed, like a tourist.

''Including you?''

''Bet your ass, General,'' Clark replied, alert now, watching the people on the street. What had Chavez spotted? What had he missed?

Who are they? Ghosn wondered. It took a second. *Brigadier General Abraham Ben Jakob, Deputy Director of the Mossad,* his brain answered after sorting through all the recognition photographs he'd memorized. *Talking to an American. I wonder who he is. . . .* Ghosn's head turned slowly and casually. The American would have several bodyguards . . . the one close by was obvious. A very serious fellow that one was, old . . . late forties, perhaps. It was the hardness—no, not hardness but alertness. One could control the face but not the eyes—ah, the man put sunglasses back on. More than one. Had to be more than one, plus Israeli security officers. Ghosn knew that he'd let his eyes linger a touch too long, but—

''Oops.'' A man had bumped into him, a fraction smaller and slighter than Ghosn. Dark complexion, possibly even a brother Arab, but he'd spoken in English. Contact was broken before Ghosn had time to realize that he'd been quickly and expertly frisked. ''Sorry.'' The man moved off. Ghosn didn't know, wasn't sure if it had been what it seemed to be or if he'd just been checked out by an Israeli, American, or other security officer. Well, he wasn't carrying a weapon, not even a pocketknife, just a shopping bag full of books.

Clark saw Ding give the all-clear sign, an ordinary gesture, like shooing an insect off his neck. Then why the eye-recognition from the target—anyone who took an interest in his protectee was a target—why had he stopped and looked? Clark turned around. There was a pretty girl just two tables away. Not Arab or Israeli, some sort of European, Germanic language, sounded like, maybe Dutch. Good-looking girl, and such girls attracted looks. Maybe he and the other two had just been between a looker and his lookee. Maybe. For a protective officer the balance between awareness and paranoia was impossible to draw even when you understood the tactical environment, and Clark had no such illusions here. On the other hand, they'd selected a random eatery on a random street, and the fact that Ryan was here, and that Ben Jakob and he had decided to look things over . . . nobody had intelligence that good, and nobody had enough troops to cover even a single city—except maybe the Russians in Moscow—to make the threat a real one. But why the eye-recognition?

Well. Clark recorded the face and it went into the memory hopper with all the hundreds of others.

Ghosn continued his own patrol. He'd purchased all the books he needed and was now observing the Swiss troops, how they moved, how tough they looked. Avi Ben Jakob, he thought. Missed opportunity. Targets like that one didn't appear every day. He continued down the rough, cobbled street, his eyes vacant as they appeared to scan at random. He'd take the next right, increase his pace, and try to get ahead of the Swiss before they made it to the next cross street. He both admired what he saw in them and regretted that he saw it.

"Nicely done," Ben Jakob observed to Clark. "Your subordinate is well trained."

"He shows promise." As Clark watched, Ding Chavez looped back to his lookout point across the street. "You know the face?"

"No. My people probably got a photograph. We'll check it out, but it was probably a young man with normal sexual drives," Ben Jakob jerked his head toward the Dutch girl, if that's what she was.

Clark was surprised the Israelis hadn't made a move. A shopping bag could contain anything. And "anything" had generally negative connotations in this environment. God, he hated this job. Looking out for himself was one thing. He typically used mobility, random paths, irregular pacing, always keeping an eye out for escape routes or ambush opportunities. But Ryan, while he might have had similar instincts—tactically speaking, the DDCI was pretty swift, Clark judged—had an overdeveloped sense of faith in the competence of his two bodyguards.

"So, Avi?" Ryan asked.

"Well, the first echelon of your cavalry troops is settling in. Our tank people like your Colonel Diggs. I must say I find their regimental crest rather odd—a bison is just a kind of wild cow, after all." Avi chuckled.

"As with a tank, Avi, you probably don't want to stand in front of one." Ryan wondered what would happen when the 10th Cav ran its first full-up training exercise with the Israelis. It was widely believed in the U.S. Army that the Israelis were overrated, and Diggs had a big reputation as a kick-ass tactician. "It looks like I can report to the President that the local situation is showing real signs of promise."

"There will be difficulties."

"Of course there will. Avi, the millennium doesn't arrive for a few more years," Jack noted. "But did you think things would go so smoothly so fast?"

"No, I didn't," Ben Jakob admitted. He fished out the cash to pay the check, and both men rose. Clark took his cue and went over to Chavez.

"Well?"

"Just that one guy. Heavy shopping bag, but it looked like books—textbooks, matter of fact. There was a sales slip still in one. Would you believe books on nuclear physics? The one title I saw was, anyway. Big, thick, heavy mother. Maybe he's a grad student or something, and that *is* one pretty lady over there, man."

"Let's keep our minds on business, Mr. Chavez."

"She's not my type, Mr. Clark."

"What do you think of the Swiss guys?"

"They look awful pretty for track-toads. I wouldn't want to play with them unless I picked the turf and the time, man." Chavez paused. "You notice the guy I frisked eyeballed them real hard?"

"No."

"He did . . . looked like he knew what he was—" Domingo Chavez paused. "I suppose people around here seen a lot of soldiers. Anyway, he gave 'em a professional sorta look. That's what I noticed first, not the way he eyeballed you and the doc. The guy had smart eyes, y'know what I mean?"

"What else?"

"Moved good, decent shape. Hands looked soft, though, not hard like a soldier. Too old for a college kid, but maybe not for a grad student." Chavez paused again. "Jesucristo! this is a paranoid business we're in, man. He was not carrying a weapon. His hands didn't look like he was a martial-arts type. He just came down the street looking at those Swiss grunts, eyeballed over where the doc and his friend were, then he just kept going. End of story." There were times when Chavez wished he'd opted to remain in the Army. He would have had his degree and his commission by now instead of cramming in night courses at George Mason while he played bodyguard to Ryan. At least the doc was a good guy, and working with Clark was . . . interesting. But this intelligence stuff was a strange life.

"Time to move," Clark advised.

"I got the point." Ding's hand checked the automatic clipped under his loose shirt. The Israeli guards were already moving up the street.

Ghosn caught them just as he'd planned. The Swiss had helped. An elderly Muslim cleric had stopped the squad sergeant to ask a question. There was a problem with translation. The imam didn't speak English, and the Swiss soldier's Arabic was still primitive. It was too good an opportunity to pass up.

"Excuse me," Ghosn said to the imam, "can I help with translation?" He absorbed the rapid-fire string of his native language and turned to the soldier.

"The imam is from Saudi Arabia. This is his first time in Jerusalem since he was a boy and he requires directions to the Troika's office."

On recognizing the seniority of the cleric, the sergeant removed his helmet and inclined his head respectfully. "Please tell him that we would be honored to escort him there."

"Ah, there you are!" another voice called. It was obviously an Israeli. His Arabic was accented but literate. "Good day, Sergeant," the man added in English.

"Greetings, Rabbi Ravenstein. You know this man?" the soldier asked.

"This is Imam Mohammed Al Faisal, a distinguished scholar and historian from Medina."

"Is it all I have been told?" Al Faisal asked Ravenstein directly.

"All that and more!" the rabbi replied.

"Excuse me?" Ghosn had to say.

"You are?" Ravenstein asked.

"A student. I was attempting to assist with the language problem."

"Ah, I see," Ravenstein said. "Very kind of you. Mohammed is here to look at a manuscript we uncovered at a dig. It's a scholarly Muslim commentary on a very old Torah, Tenth Century, a fantastic find. Sergeant, I can manage things from here, and thank you also, young man."

"Do you require escort, sir?" the sergeant asked. "We are heading that way."

"No, thank you, we are both too old to keep up with you."

"Very well." The sergeant saluted. "Good day."

The Swiss moved off. The few people who'd taken note of the brief encounter pointed and smiled.

"The commentary is by Al Qalda himself, and it seems to cite the work of Nuchem of Acre," Ravenstein said. "The state of preservation is incredible."

"Then I must see it!" The two scholars began walking down the street as rapidly as their aged legs would carry them, oblivious to everything around them.

Ghosn's face didn't change. He'd shown wonder and amusement for the benefit of the Swiss infantrymen now halfway down the block, themselves with a trailing escort of small children. His discipline allowed him to sidle off to the side, take another turn, and vanish down a narrow alley, but what he had just seen was far more depressing.

Mohammed Al Faisal was one of the five greatest Islamic scholars, a highly respected historian, and a distant member of the Saudi royal family despite his unpretentious nature. Except for his age—the man was nearing eighty—he might have been one of the members of the troika running Jerusalem—that and the fact that they'd wanted a scholar of Palestinian ancestry for political reasons. No friend of Israel, and one of the most conservative of the Saudi religious leaders, had he become enamored of the treaty also?

Worse still, the Swiss had treated the man with the utmost respect. Worst of all, the Israeli rabbi had done the same. The people in the streets, nearly all of them Palestinians, had watched it all with amusement and . . . what? Tolerance? Acceptance, as though it were the most natural thing in the world. The Israelis had long ago given lip-service to respect for their Arab neighbors, but that promise had not even been written on sand for all the permanence it had carried.

Ravenstein wasn't like that, of course. Another scholar, living in his own little world of dead things and ideas, he'd often counseled moderation in dealings with Arabs, and handled his archaeological digs with Muslim consultation . . . and now . . .

And now he was a psychological bridge between the Jewish world and the Arab one. People like that would continue doing what they had always done, but now it was not an aberration, was it?

Peace. It was possible. It could happen. It wasn't just another mad dream imposed on the region by outsiders. How quickly the ordinary people were adapting to it. Israelis were leaving their homes. The Swiss had already taken over one settlement and demolished several others. The Saudi commission was set up, and was beginning to work on restoring land parcels to their rightful owners. A great Arab university was planned for the outskirts of Jerusalem, to be built with Saudi money. It was moving so fast! Israelis were resisting, but less than he had expected. In another week, he'd heard from twenty people, tourists would flood the city—hotel bookings were arriving as rapidly as satellite phone links could deliver them. Already two enormous new hotels were being planned for the influx, and on the basis of increased tourism alone the Palestinians here would reap fantastic economic benefits. They were already proclaiming their total political victory over Israel, and had collectively decided to be magnanimous in their triumph—it made financial sense to be so, and the Palestinians had the most highly developed commercial sense in the Arab world.

But Israel would still survive.

Ghosn stopped at a street café, set down his bag, and ordered a glass of juice. He contemplated the narrow street as he waited. There were Jews and Muslims. Tourists would soon flood the place; the first wave had barely broken at local airports. Muslims, of course, to pray at the Dome of the Rock. Americans with their money, even Japanese, curious about a land even more ancient than their own. Prosperity would soon come to Palestine.

Prosperity was the handmaiden of peace, and the assassin of discontent.

But prosperity was not what Ibrahim Ghosn wanted for his people or his land. Ultimately, perhaps, but only after the other necessary preconditions had been met. He paid for his orange juice with American currency and walked off. Soon he was able to catch a cab. Ghosn had entered Israel from Egypt. He'd leave Jerusalem for Jordan, thence back to Lebanon. He had work to do, and he hoped the books he carried contained the necessary information.

Ben Goodley was a postdoctoral student from Harvard's Kennedy School of Government. A bright, good-looking academic of twenty-seven years, he was also possessed of enough ambition for the entire family after which the school had been named. His doctoral thesis had examined the folly of Vietnam from the intelligence side of the equation, and it had been sufficiently controversial that his professor had forwarded it to Liz Elliot for comment. The National Security Advisor's only beef with Goodley was that he was a man. Nobody was perfect.

"So exactly what sort of research do you want to do?" she asked him.

"Doctor, I hope to examine the nature of intelligence decisions as they relate to recent changes in Europe and the Middle East. The problem is getting FOI'd into certain areas."

"And what is your ultimate objective? I mean," Elliot said, "is it teaching, writing, government service, what?"

"Government service, of course. The historical environment demands, I think, that the right people take the right action. My thesis made it clear, didn't it, that we've been badly served by the intelligence community almost continuously since the 1960s. The whole institutional mind-set over there is geared in the wrong direction. At least"—he leaned back and tried to look comfortable—"that's how it often appears to an outsider."

"And why is that, do you think?"

"Recruiting is one problem. The way CIA, for example, selects people really determines how they obtain and analyze data. They create a gigantic self-fulfilling prophecy. Where's their objectivity, where's their ability to see trends? Did they predict 1989? Of course not. What are they missing now? Probably a lot of things. It might be nice," Goodley said, "to get a handle on the important issues before they become crisis items."

"I agree." Elliot watched the young man's shoulders drop as he discreetly let out a deep breath. She decided to play him just a little, just enough to let him know whom he'd be working for. "I wonder what we can do with you . . . ?" Elliot let her eyes trace across the far wall.

"Marcus Cabot has an opening for a research assistant. You'll need a security clearance, and you'll need to sign a very strict nondisclosure agreement. You cannot publish anything without having it cleared in advance."

"That's almost prior-restraint," Goodley pointed out. "What about the Constitutional issue?"

"Government must keep some secrets if it is to function. You may have access to some remarkable information. Is getting published your goal, or is it what you said? Public service does require some sacrifices."

"Well . . ."

"There will be some important openings at CIA in the next few years," Elliot promised.

"I see," Goodley said, quite truthfully. "I never intended to publish classified information of course."

"Of course," Elliot agreed. "I can handle that through my office, I suppose. I found your paper impressive. I want a mind like yours working for the government if you can agree to the necessary restrictions."

"In that case I guess I can accept them."

"Fine." Elliot smiled. "You are now a White House Fellow. My secretary will take you across the street to the security office. You have a bunch of forms to fill out."

"I already have a 'secret' clearance."

"You'll need more than that. You'll have to get a SAP/SAR clearance—that means 'special-access programs/special access required.' It normally takes a few months for that—"

"Months?" Goodley asked.

"I said 'usually.' We can fast-track part of that. I suggest you start apartment-hunting. The stipend is sufficient?"

"Quite sufficient."

"Fine. I'll call Marcus over at Langley. You'll want to meet him." Goodley beamed at the National Security Advisor. "Glad to have you on the team."

The new White House Fellow took his cue and stood. "I will try not to disappoint you."

Elliot watched him leave. It was so easy to seduce people, she knew. Sex was a useful tool for the task, but power and ambition were so much better. She'd already proven that. Elliot smiled to herself.

"An atomic bomb?" Bock asked.

"So it would seem," Qati replied.

"Who else knows?"

"Ghosn is the one who discovered it. Only he."

"Can it be used?" the German asked. *And why have you told me?*

"It was severely damaged and must be repaired. Ibrahim is now assembling the necessary information for evaluating the task. He thinks it possible."

Günther leaned back. "This is not some elaborate ruse? An Israeli trick, perhaps an American one?"

"If so, it is a very clever one," Qati said, then explained the circumstances of the discovery.

"Nineteen seventy-three . . . it does fit. I remember how close the Syrians came to destroying the Israelis. . . ." Bock was silent for a moment. He shook his head briefly. "How to use such a thing. . . ."

"That is the question, Günther."

"Too early to ask such a question. First, you must determine if the weapon can be repaired. Second, you must determine its explosive yield—no, before that you must determine its size, weight, and portability. That is the most important consideration. After that comes the yield—I will assume that—" He fell silent. "Assume? I know little of such weapons. They cannot be too heavy. They can be fired from artillery shells of less than twenty-centimeter diameter. I know that much."

"This one is much larger than that, my friend."

"You should not have told me this, Ismael. In a matter like this one, security is everything. You cannot trust anyone with knowledge such as this. People talk, people boast. There could be penetration agents in your organization."

"It was necessary. Ghosn knows that he will need some help. What contacts do you have in the DDR?"

"What sort?" Qati told him. "I know a few engineers, people who worked in the DDR nuclear program . . . it's a dead program, you know."

"How so?"

"Honecker was planning to build several reactors of the Russian sort. When Germany reunited, their environmental activists took one look at the design and—well, you can imagine. The Russian designs do not have a sterling reputation, do they?" Bock grunted. "As I keep telling you, the Russians are a backward people. Their reactor designs, one fellow told me, were mainly for production of nuclear material for weapons . . ."

"And . . ."

"And it is likely that there was a nuclear-weapons program within the DDR. Interesting, I never thought that through, did I?" Bock asked himself quietly. "What exactly do you want me to do?"

"I need you to travel to Germany and find some people—we would prefer merely one, for obvious reasons—to assist us."

Back to Germany? Bock asked himself. "I'll need—"

Qati tossed an envelope into his friend's lap. "Beirut has been a crossroads for centuries. Those travel documents are better than the real ones."

"You will need to move your location immediately," Bock said. "If I am caught, you will have to assume that they will get every bit of information I have. They broke Petra. They can break me or anyone else they wish."

"I will pray for your safety. In that envelope is a telephone number. When you return, we will be elsewhere."

"When do I leave?"

"Tomorrow."

12. Tinsmiths

"And I'll raise you a dime," Ryan said after taking his draw.

"You're bluffing," Chavez said after a sip of beer.

"I never bluff," Jack replied.

"Out." Clark tossed in his cards.

"They all say that," the Air Force sergeant observed. "See your dime and bump you a quarter."

"Call," Chavez said.

"Three jacks."

"Beats my eights," the sergeant groused.

"But not a straight, doc." Ding finished off his beer. "Gee, that puts me five bucks ahead."

"Never count your winnings at the table, son," Clark advised soberly.

"I never did like that song." Chavez grinned. "But I like this game."

"I thought soldiers were lousy gamblers," the Air Force sergeant observed sourly. He was three bucks down, and he was a real poker player. He got to practice against politicians all the time on long flights when they needed a good dealer.

"One of the first things they teach you at CIA is how to mark cards," Clark announced as he went for the next round of drinks.

"Always knew I should have taken the course at the Farm," Ryan said. He was about even, but every time he'd had a good hand, Chavez had held a better one. "Next time I'll let you play with my wife."

"She good?" Chavez asked.

"She's a surgeon. She deals seconds so smooth she can fool a professional mechanic. She plays with cards as a kind of dexterity exercise," Ryan explained with a grin. "I *never* let her deal."

"Mrs. Ryan would never do anything like that," Clark said when he sat back down.

"Your turn to deal," Ding said.

Clark started shuffling, something he also did fairly well. "So what you think, doc?"

"Jerusalem? Better than I hoped. How about you?"

"Last time I was there—'84, I think—God, it was like Olongapo in the P.I. You could smell it—the trouble, I mean. You couldn't actually see it, but, man, it was there. You could feel people watching you. Now? It's sure chilled out some. How about some five-card stud?" Clark asked.

"Dealer's choice," the sergeant agreed.

Clark dealt the hole cards, then the first set of up cards. "Nine of spades to the Air Force. Five of diamonds to our Latino friend. Queen of clubs to the doc, and the dealer gets—how about that? Dealer gets an ace. Ace bets a quarter."

"Well, John?" Ryan asked after the first round of bets.

"You do put a lot of faith in my powers of observation, Jack. We'll know for sure in a couple of months, but I'd say it looks all right." He dealt four more cards. "Possible straight—possible straight flush to the Air Force. Your bet, sir."

"Another quarter." The Air Force sergeant felt lucky. "The Israeli security guys have mellowed out some, too."

"How so?"

"Dr. Ryan, the Israelis really know about security. Every time we fly over here, they put a wall up around the bird, y'know? This time the wall wasn't so high. I talked to a couple of 'em and they say they're more relaxed—not officially, but personal, y'know? Used to be they hardly talked at all. Looked like a big difference to me, anyway."

Ryan smiled as he decided to fold. His eight, queen, and deuce weren't going anywhere. It never failed. You always got better data from sergeants than generals.

* * *

"What we have here," Ghosn said, flipping his book to the right page, "is essentially an Israeli copy of an American Mark-12 fission bomb. It's a boosted-fission design."

"What does that mean?" Qati asked.

"It means that tritium is squirted into the core just as the act of firing begins. That generates more neutrons and greatly increases the efficiency of the reaction. As a result, you need only a small amount of fissionable material . . ."

"But?" Qati heard the "but" coming.

Ghosn leaned back and stared at the core of the device. "But the mechanism to insert the boost material was destroyed by the impact. The kryton switches for the conventional explosives are no longer reliable and must be replaced. We have enough intact explosive blocks to determine their proper configuration, but manufacturing new ones will be very difficult. Unfortunately I cannot depend on simply reverse-engineering the entire weapon. I must duplicate the original design theoretically first, determine what it can and cannot do, then re-invent the processes for fabrication. Do you have any idea what the original cost for that was?"

"No," Qati admitted, sure that he was about to learn.

"More than what it cost to land people on the moon. The most brilliant minds in human history were part of this process: Einstein, Fermi, Bohr, Oppenheimer, Teller, Alvarez, von Neumann, Lawrence—a hundred others! The giants of physics in this century. Giants."

"You're telling me you cannot do it?"

Ghosn smiled. "No, Commander, I am telling you that I can. What is the work of genius the first time is the work of a tinsmith soon thereafter. It required genius the first time because it *was* the first time, and also because technology was so primitive. All the calculations had to be done manually at first, on big mechanical calculators. All the work on the first hydrogen bomb was done on the first primitive computers—Eniac, I think it was called. But today?" Ghosn laughed. It really was absurd. "A videogame has more computing power than Eniac ever did. I can run the calculations on a high-end personal computer in seconds and duplicate what took Einstein months. But the most important thing is that they did not really know if it was possible. It is, and I know *that!* Next, they made records of how they proceeded. Finally, I have a template, and though I cannot reverse-engineer it entirely, I can use this as a theoretical model.

"You know, given two or three years, I could do it all myself."

"Do you think we have two or three years?"

Ghosn shook his head. He'd already reported on what he saw in Jerusalem. "No, Commander. We surely do not."

Qati explained what he had ordered their German friend to do.

"That is good. Where do we move to?"

Berlin was once more the capital of Germany. It had been Bock's plan that this should be so, of course, but not that it should be this sort of Germany. He'd flown in from Italy—via Greece, and, before that, Syria—and cleared passport control with scarcely a wave. From that point, he'd simply rented a car and driven out of Berlin on highway E-74 north toward Greifswald.

Günther had rented a Mercedes-Benz. He rationalized this by telling himself that his cover was that of a businessman, and besides he hadn't rented the biggest one available. There were times when he thought he might as well have rented a bicycle. This road had been neglected by the DDR government, and now that the Federal Republic was fully in place, the highway was little more than a linear repair gang. It went without saying that the other side of the road was already fixed. His peripheral vision caught hundreds of big, powerful Benzes and BMWs streaking south toward Berlin as the capitalists from the West blazed about to reconquer economically what had collapsed under political betrayal.

Bock took his exit outside Greifswald, driving east through the town of Kemnitz. The attempts at road repair had not yet reached the secondary roads. After hitting half a dozen potholes Günther had to pull over and consult his map. He proceeded three kilometers, then made a series of turns, ending up on what had once been an upscale neighborhood of professionals. In the driveway of the house he sought was a Trabant. The grass was still neatly trimmed, of course, and the house was neatly arranged, down to the even curtains in the windows—this was Germany, after all—but there was an air of disrepair and depression not so much seen as felt. Bock parked his car a block away and walked an indirect route back to the house.

"I am here to see Herr Doktor Fromm," he told the woman, Frau Fromm, probably, who answered the door.

"Who may I say is calling?" she asked formally. She was in her middle forties, her skin tight over severe cheeks, with too many lines radiating from her dull blue eyes and tight, colorless lips. She examined the man on her front step with interest, and perhaps a little hope. Though Bock had no idea why this should be so, he took the chance to make use of it.

"An old friend." Bock smiled to reinforce the image. "May I surprise him?"

She wavered for a moment, then her face changed and good manners took hold. "Please come in."

Bock waited in the sitting room, and he realized that his impression was right—but why it was right struck him hard. The interior of the house reminded him of his own apartment in Berlin. The same specially made furniture that had once looked so good in contrast to what was available for ordinary citizens in the German Democratic Republic did not impress as it once had. Perhaps it was the Mercedes he'd driven up, Bock told himself as he heard footsteps approaching. But no. It was dust. Frau Fromm was not cleaning the house as a good German *Hausfrau* did. A sure sign that something was badly wrong.

"Yes?" Dr. Manfred Fromm said as a question before his eyes widened in delayed recognition. "Ah, so good to see you!"

"I wondered if you'd remember your old friend Hans," Bock said with a chuckle, stretching out his hand. "A long time, Manfred."

"A very long time indeed, *Junge!* Come to my study." The two men walked off under the inquisitive eyes of Frau Fromm. Dr. Fromm closed the door behind himself before speaking.

"I am sorry about your wife. It was unspeakable what happened."

"That is past. How are you doing?"

"You haven't heard? The Greens have attacked us. We're about to shut down."

Doktor Manfred Fromm was, on paper, the deputy assistant director of the Lubmin/Nord Nuclear Power Station. The station had been built twenty years earlier from the Soviet VVER Model 230 design, which, primitive as it was, had been adequate with an expert German operations team. Like all Soviet designs of the period, the reactor was a plutonium producer. But unlike Chernobyl it had a containment dome. It was neither terribly efficient nor especially unsafe, but did carry the benefit of producing weapons-grade nuclear material in addition to 816 megawatts of electrical power from its two functioning reactors.

"The Greens," Bock repeated quietly. "Them." The Green Party was a natural consequence of the German national spirit, which venerated all growing things on one hand, while trying very hard to kill them on the other. Formed from the extreme—or the consistent—elements of the environmental movement, it had fought against many things equally upsetting to the Communist Bloc. But where it had failed to prevent the deployment of theater nuclear weapons—and after their successful deployment had resulted in the INF Treaty, which had eliminated all such weapons on both sides of the line—it was now successfully raising the purest form of political hell in what had once been the German Democratic Republic. The nightmare of pollution in the East was now the obsession of the Greens, and number one on their hit list was the nuclear-power industry, which they called hideously unsafe. Bock reminded himself that the Greens had never truly been under proper political control. The party would never be a major power in German politics, and now it was being exploited by the same government that it had once annoyed. Whereas once the Greens had shrieked about the pollution of the Ruhr and the Rhein from Krupp, and howled about the deployment of NATO nuclear arms, now it was crusading in the East more fervently than Barbarossa had ever attempted in the Holy Land. Their incessant carping on the mess in the East was ensuring that socialism would not soon return to Germany. It was enough to make both men wonder if the Greens had not been a subtle capitalist ploy from the very beginning.

Fromm and the Bocks had met five years earlier. The Red Army Faction had come up with a plan to sabotage a West German reactor and wanted technical advice on how to do so most efficiently. Though never revealed to the public, their plan had been thwarted only at the last minute. Publicity on the BND's intelligence success would conversely have threatened Germany's own nuclear industry.

"Less than a year until they shut us down for good. I only go in to work three days a week now. I've been replaced by a 'technical expert' from the West. He lets me 'advise' him, of course," Fromm reported.

"There must be more, Manfred," Bock observed. Fromm had also been the chief engineer in Erich Honecker's most cherished military project. Though allies within the World Socialist Brotherhood, the Russians and the Germans could never have been true friends. The bad blood between the nations stretched back a thousand years, and while Germany had at least made a go of socialism, the Russians had failed completely. As a result, the East German military had never been anything like the much larger force in the West. To the last, the Russians had feared Germans, even those on their own side, before incomprehensibly allowing the country to be unified. Erich Honecker had decided that such distrust might have strategic ramifications, and had drawn plans to keep some of the plutonium produced at Greifswald and elsewhere. Manfred Fromm knew as much about nuclear bomb design as any Russian or American, even if he'd never quite been able to put his expertise into play. The plutonium stockpile secretly accumulated over ten years had been turned over to the Russians as a final gesture of Marxist fealty, lest the Federal German government get it. That last honorable act had resulted in angry recriminations—angry enough that one other cache of material had never been turned over. What connections Fromm and his colleagues had once had with the Soviets were completely gone.

"Oh, I have a fine offer." Fromm lifted a manila envelope on his cluttered desk. "They want me to go to Argentina. My counterparts in the West have been there for years, along with most of the chaps I worked with."

"What do they offer?"

Fromm snorted. "One million D-Mark per year until the project is completed. No difficulties with taxes, numbered account, all the normal enticements," Fromm said with an emotionless voice. And that, of course, was quite impossible. Fromm could no more work for fascists than he could breathe water. His grandfather, one of the original Spartacists, had died in one of the first labor camps soon after Hitler's accession to power. His father had been part of the communist underground and a player in a spy ring, had somehow survived the war despite the systematic hunting of the Gestapo and the *Sicherheitsdienst,* and been an honored local Party member to the day of his death. Fromm had learned Marxism-Leninism while he'd learned to walk, and the elimination of his profession had not enamored him of the new political system which he'd been educated to despise. He'd lost his job, had never fulfilled his prime ambition, and was now being treated like an office boy by some pink-cheeked engineer's assistant from Göttingen. Worst of all, his wife wanted him to take the job in Argentina and was making a further hell of his life so long as he refused to consider it. Finally he had to ask his question. "Why are you here, Günther? The entire country is looking for you, and despite that fine disguise, you are in danger here."

Bock smiled confidently. "Isn't it amazing what new hair and glasses can do for you?"

"That does not answer my question."

"I have friends who need your skills."

"What friends might those be?" Fromm asked dubiously.

"They are politically acceptable to me and to you. I have not forgotten Petra," Bock replied.

"That was a good plan we put together, wasn't it? What went wrong?"

"We had a spy among us. Because of her they changed the security arrangements at the plant three days before we were supposed to go in."

"A Green?"

Günther allowed himself a bitter smile. "*Ja.* She had second thoughts about possible civilian casualties and damage to the environment. Well, she is now part of the environment." Petra had done the shooting, her husband remembered. There was nothing worse than a spy, and it was fitting that Petra should have done the execution.

"Part of the environment, you say? How poetic." It was Fromm's first attempt at levity, and about as successful as all his attempts. Manfred Fromm was a singularly humorless man.

"I cannot offer you money. In fact, I cannot tell you anything else. You must decide on the basis of what I have already said." Bock didn't have a gun, but he did have a knife. He wondered if Manfred knew the alternatives he faced. Probably not. Despite his ideological purity, Fromm was a technocrat, and narrowly focused.

"When do we leave?"

"Are you being watched?"

"No. I had to travel to Switzerland for the 'business offer.' Such things cannot be discussed in this country, even if it is united and happy," he explained. "I made my own travel arrangements. No, I do not think I am being watched."

"Then we can leave at once. You need not pack anything."

"What do I tell my wife?" Fromm asked, then wondered why he'd bothered. It wasn't as though his marriage was a happy one.

"That is your concern."

"Let me pack some things. It's easier that way. How long . . . ?"

"I do not know."

It took half an hour. Fromm explained to his wife that he was going to be away for a few days for further business discussions. She gave him a hopeful kiss. Argentina might be nice, and nicer still to be able to live *well* somewhere. Perhaps this old friend had been able to talk sense into him. He drove a Mercedes, after all. Perhaps he knew what the future really held.

Three hours later Bock and Fromm boarded a flight to Rome. After an hour's layover, their next stop was Turkey, and from there to Damascus, where they checked into a hotel to get some needed rest.

If anything, Ghosn told himself, Marvin Russell was even more formidable-looking than he'd been before. What little excess weight he'd carried had sweated off, and his daily fitness exercises with the soldiers of the movement had only added to an already muscular physique, while the sun had bronzed him until he might almost have been mistaken for an Arab. The one discordant note was his religion. His comrades reported that he was a true pagan, an unbeliever, who prayed to the sun, of all things. It disquieted the Muslims, but people were working, gently, to show him the true faith of Islam, and it was reported that he listened respectfully. It was also reported that he was a dead shot with any weapon to any range; that he was the most lethal hand-to-hand fighter they'd ever encountered—he'd nearly crippled an instructor—and that he had field-craft skills that would impress a fox. A clever, cunning, natural warrior was the overall assessment. Aside from his religious eccentricities, the others liked and admired him.

"Marvin, if you get any tougher you will frighten me!" Ghosn chuckled at his American friend.

"Ibrahim, this is the best thing I've ever done, coming here. I never knew that there were other folks who been fucked over like my people, man—but you guys are better at fighting back. You guys got real balls." Ghosn blinked at that—this from a man who'd snapped a policeman's neck like a twig. "I really want to help, man, any way I can."

"There is always a place for a true warrior." If his language skills improved, he'd make a fine instructor, Ghosn thought. "Well, I must be off."

"Where you going?"

"A place we have east of here." It was to the north. "Some special work I must do."

"That thing we dug up?" Russell asked casually. Almost too casually, Ghosn thought, but that was not possible, was it? Caution was one thing. Paranoia was another.

"Something else. Sorry, my friend, but we must take our security seriously."

Marvin nodded. "It's cool, man. That's what killed my brother, fucking up security. See ya' when you get back."

Ghosn left for his car and drove out of the camp. He took the Damascus road for an hour. Foreigners so often failed to appreciate how small the Middle East was—the important parts, at least. The drive from Jerusalem to Damascus, for example, would have been a mere two hours on decent roads, though the two cities were the proverbial worlds apart politically . . . or had been, Ghosn reminded himself. He'd heard of some ominous rumblings from Syria of late. Was even that government tiring of the struggle? It was easy to call that an impossibility, but that word no longer had its prior meaning.

Five kilometers outside Damascus he spotted the other car waiting at the prescribed place. He drove past it for two thousand meters, scanning for surveillance before he decided it was safe to turn around. A minute later he pulled over close to it. The two men got out as they'd been directed to do, and their driver, a member of the Organization, simply drove away.

"Good morning, Günther."

"And to you, Ibrahim. This is my friend Manfred." Both men got into the back of the car, and the engineer drove off at once.

Ghosn eyed the newcomer in the mirror. Older than Bock, thinner, with deep-sunk eyes. He was poorly dressed for the environment and sweating like a pig. Ibrahim handed back a plastic water bottle. The newcomer wiped off the top with his handkerchief before drinking. *Arabs not sanitary enough for you?* Ghosn wondered. Well, that was not his concern, was it?

The drive to the new location took two hours. Ghosn deliberately took a circuitous route despite the fact that the sun would keep a careful observer informed of their direction. He didn't know what sort of training this Manfred fellow had, and while it was prudent to assume he knew every skill there was, it was also prudent to employ every trick in the book. By the time they arrived at their destination, only a trained reconnaissance soldier would have been able to duplicate the route.

Qati had chosen well. Until a few months earlier it had been a command center for Hezbollah. Dug into the side of a steep hillside, the corrugated-iron roof was covered with earth and planted with the sparse local shrubbery. Only a skilled man who knew exactly what he was looking for could ever have spotted it, and that was unlikely. Hezbollah was particularly adept at routing out informers in its midst. A dirt track ran right past it to an abandoned farm whose land was too played-out even for opium and hashish production, which was the major cash crop in the area. Inside the structure was about a hundred square meters of concrete-floored shade, even with room to park a few vehicles. The only bad news was that this place would be a deathtrap in case of an earthquake, Ghosn told himself, not an unknown occurrence in the region. He pulled the car in between two posts, out of sight. On leaving the car, he dropped camouflage netting behind it. Yes, Qati had chosen well.

The hardest balance, as always, was choosing between the two aspects of security. On the one hand, the more people who knew anything was happening, the worse it was. On the other, some people were necessary just to provide a guard force. Qati had brought most of his personal guard, ten men of known loyalty and skill. They knew Ghosn and Bock by sight, and their leader came forward to meet Manfred.

"This is our new friend," Ghosn told the man, who looked closely at the German's face and walked away.

"Was gibt's hier?" Fromm asked in tense German.

"What we have here," Ghosn answered in English, "is very interesting."

Manfred took his lesson from that.

"Kommen Sie mit, bitte." Ghosn led them to a wall with a door in it. A man with a rifle stood outside of it, which made much better sense than a lock. The engineer nodded to the guard, who nodded curtly back. Ghosn led them into the room and pulled a cord to turn on the fluorescent lighting. There was a large metal worktable covered with a tarp. Ghosn removed the tarp without further comment. He was tiring of the drama in any case. It was time for real work.

"Gott im Himmel!"

"I've never seen it myself," Bock admitted. "So that is what it looks like?"

Fromm put on some glasses and peered over the mechanism for perhaps a minute before looking up. "American design, but not American manufacture." He pointed. "Wrong sort of wiring. Crude device, thirty years—no, older than that in design, but not in fabrication. These circuit boards are . . . 1960s, perhaps early '70s. Soviet? From the cache in Azerbaijan, perhaps?"

Ghosn merely shook his head.

"Israeli? *Ist das möglich?"* That question got a nod.

"More than possible, my friend. It is here."

"Gravity bomb. Tritium injection into the pit to boost yield—fifty to seventy kilotons, I'd guess—radar and impact fusing. It has actually been dropped, but did not go off. Why?"

"Apparently it was never armed. Everything we recovered is before you," Ghosn answered. He was already impressed with Manfred.

Fromm ran his fingers inside the bombcase, searching for connectors. "You're correct. How interesting." There was a long pause. "You know that it can probably be repaired . . . and even . . ."

"Even what?" Ghosn asked, knowing the answer.

"This design can be converted into a triggering device."

"For what?" Bock asked.

"For a hydrogen bomb," Ghosn answered. "I suspected that."

"Awfully heavy, nothing like the efficiency of a modern design. As they say, crude but effective. . . ." Fromm looked up. "You want my help to repair it, then?"

"Will you help?" Ghosn asked.

"Ten years—more, twenty years I have studied and thought. . . . How will it be used?"

"Does that trouble you?"

"It will not be used in Germany?"

"Of course not," Ghosn answered almost in annoyance. What quarrel did the Organization really have with the Germans, after all?

Something in Bock's mind, however, went *click*. He closed his eyes for a moment to engrave the thought in his memory.

"Yes, I will help."

"You will be well paid," Ghosn promised him. He saw a moment later that this was a mistake. But that didn't matter, did it?

"I do not do such things for money! You think I am a mercenary?" Fromm asked indignantly.

"Excuse me. I meant no insult. A skilled worker is someone to be rewarded for his time. We are not beggars, you know."

Neither am I, Fromm almost said before his good sense intervened. These were not the Argentines, were they? They were not fascists, not capitalists, they were revolutionary comrades who had also fallen upon bad political times . . . though he was sure their fiscal situation was highly favorable indeed. The Soviets had never *given* arms to the Arabs. It had all been sold for hard currency, even under Brezhnev and Andropov, and if that had been good enough for the Soviets when they still held the true faith . . . then . . .

"Forgive me. I merely stated a fact, and I did not mean to insult you, either. I know you are not beggars. You are revolutionary soldiers, freedom fighters, and I will be honored to assist you in any way I can.'' He waved his hand. ''You may feel free to pay me whatever you think fair''—it would be plenty, more than a mere million D-Mark!—''but please understand that I do not sell myself for money.''

''It is a pleasure to meet an honorable man,'' Ghosn said with a satisfied look.

Bock thought they had both laid it on rather thick, but kept his peace. He already suspected how Fromm would be paid.

''So,'' Ghosn said next. ''Where do we begin?''

''First, we think. I need paper and a pencil.''

''And who might you be?'' Ryan asked.

''Ben Goodley, sir.''

''Boston?'' Ryan asked. The accent was quite distinctive.

''Yes, sir. Kennedy School. I'm a postdoctoral Fellow and, well, now I'm a White House Fellow also.''

''Nancy?'' Ryan turned to his secretary.

''The Director has him on your calendar, Dr. Ryan.''

''Okay, Dr. Goodley,'' Ryan said with a smile, ''come on in.'' Clark took his seat after sizing the new guy up.

''Want some coffee?''

''You have decaf?'' Goodley asked.

''You want to work here, boy, you'd better get used to the real stuff. Grab a seat. Sure you don't want any?''

''I'll pass, sir.''

''Okay.'' Ryan poured his customary mug and sat down behind his desk. ''So what are you doing in this puzzle palace?''

''The short version is, looking for a job. I did my dissertation on intelligence operations, their history and prospects. I need to see some things to finish my work at Kennedy, then I want to find out if I can do the real thing.''

Jack nodded. That sounded familiar enough. ''Clearances?''

''TS, SAP/SAR. Those are new. I already had a 'secret' because some of my work at Kennedy involved going into some presidential archives, mainly in D.C., but some of the stuff in Boston is still sensitive. I even was part of the team that FOI'd a lot of stuff from the Cuban Missile Crisis.''

''Dr. Nicholas Bledsoe, his work?''

''That's right.''

''I didn't buy all of Nick's conclusions, but that was a hell of a piece of research.'' Jack raised his mug in salute.

Goodley had written nearly half of that monograph, including the conclusions. ''What did you take issue with—if I may ask?''

''Khrushchev's action was fundamentally irrational. I think—and the record bears this out—that his placing the missiles there was impulsive rather than reasoned.''

''I disagree. The paper pointed out that the principal Soviet concern was our IRBMs in Europe, especially the ones in Turkey. It seems logical to conclude that it was all a ploy to reach a stable situation regarding theater forces.''

''Your paper didn't report on everything,'' Jack said.

''Such as?'' Goodley asked, hiding his annoyance.

''Such as the intel we were getting from Penkovskiy and others. Those documents are still classified and will remain so for another twenty years.''

''Isn't fifty years a long time?''

''Sure is,'' Ryan agreed. ''But there's a reason. Some of that information is still

. . . well, not exactly current, but it would reveal some tricks we don't want revealed.''

''Isn't that just a *little* extreme?'' Goodley asked as dispassionately as he could manage.

''Let's say we had Agent BANANA operating back then. Okay, he's dead now—died of old age, say—but maybe Agent PEAR was recruited by him, and he's still working. If the Sovs find out who BANANA was, that might give them a clue. Also you have to think about certain methods of message-transfer. People have been playing baseball for a hundred fifty years, but a change-up is still a change-up. I used to think the same way you do, Ben. You learn that most of the things that are done here are done for a reason.''

Captured by the system, Goodley thought.

''By the way, you did notice that Khrushchev's last batch of tapes pretty much proved Nick Bledsoe wrong on some of his points—one other thing.''

''Yes?''

''Let's say that John Kennedy had hard intel in the spring of 1961, really good stuff that Khrushchev wanted to change the system. In '58 he'd effectively gutted the Red Army, and he was trying to reform the Party. Let's say that Kennedy had hard stuff on that, and he was told by a little bird that if he cut the Russkies a little slack, maybe we could have had a rapprochement in the '60s. *Glasnost,* say, thirty years early. Let's say all that happened, and the President blew the call, decided for political reasons that it was disadvantageous to cut Nikita a little slack. . . . *That* would mean that the 1960s were all a great big mistake. Vietnam, everything, all a gigantic screwup.''

''I don't believe it. I've been through the archives. It's not consistent with everything we know about—''

''Consistency in a politician?'' Ryan interrupted. ''There's a revolutionary concept.''

''If you're saying that really happened—''

''It was a hypothetical,'' Jack said with a raised eyebrow. Hell, he thought, the information was all out there for anyone who wanted to pull it together. That it had never been done was just another manifestation of a wider and more troubling problem. But the part that worried him was right in this building. He'd leave history to historians . . . until, someday, he decided to rejoin their professional ranks. *And when will that be, Jack?*

''Nobody'd ever believe it.''

''Most people believe that Lyndon Johnson lost the New Hampshire primary to Eugene McCarthy because of the Tet Offensive, too. Welcome to the world of intelligence, Dr. Goodley. You know what's the hard part of recognizing the truth?'' Jack asked.

''What's that?''

''Knowing that something just bit you on the ass. It's not as easy as you think.''

''And the breakup of the Warsaw Pact?''

''Case in point,'' Ryan agreed. ''We had all kinds of indicators, and we all blew the call. Well, that's not true, exactly. A lot of the youngsters in the DI—Directorate of Intelligence,'' Jack explained unnecessarily, which struck Goodley as patronizing, ''were making noise, but the section chiefs pooh-poohed it.''

''And you, sir?''

''If the Director's agreeable, we can let you see some of that. Most of it, in fact. The majority of our agents and field officers got faked out of their jockstraps, too.

We all could have done better, and that's as true of me as it is of anybody else. If I have a weakness, it's that I have too tactical a focus.''

''Trees instead of the forest?''

''Yep,'' Ryan admitted. ''That's the big trap here, but knowing about it doesn't always help a whole hell of a lot.''

''I guess that's why they sent me over,'' Goodley observed.

Jack grinned. ''Hell, that's not terribly different from how I got started here. Welcome aboard. Where do you want to start, Dr. Goodley?''

Ben already had a good idea on that, of course. If Ryan could not see it coming, that was not his problem, was it?

''So where do you get the computers?'' Bock asked. Fromm was closeted away with his paper and pencils.

''Israel for a start, maybe Jordan or Turkey,'' Ghosn replied.

''This will be rather expensive,'' Bock warned.

''I have already checked out the computer-controlled machine tools. Yes, they are expensive.'' *But not that expensive.* It occurred to Ghosn that he had access to hard-currency assets that might boggle the mind of this unbeliever. ''We will see what your friend requires. Whatever it is, we will get it.''

13. Process

Why did I ever accept this job? .

Roger Durling was a proud man. The upset winner of what was supposed to have been a secure Senate seat, then the youngest governor in the history of California, he knew pride to be a weakness, but he also knew that there was much to justify his.

I could have waited a few years, maybe returned to the Senate and earned *my way into the White House instead of cutting a deal and delivering the election to Fowler . . . in return for this.*

''This'' was Air Force Two, the radio call sign for whatever aircraft the Vice President rode on. The implicit contrast with ''Air Force One'' made just one more joke that attached to what was putatively the second most important political post in the United States, though not as earthily apt as John Nance Garner's observation: ''A pitcher of warm spit.'' The whole office of Vice President, Durling judged, was one of the few mistakes made by the Founding Fathers. It had once been worse. Originally the Vice President was supposed to have been the losing candidate who, after losing, would patriotically take his place in a government not his and preside over the Senate, setting aside petty political differences to serve the country. How James Madison had ever been that foolish was something scholars had never really examined, but the mistake had been corrected quickly enough by the 12th Amendment in 1803. Even in an age when gentlemen preparing for a duel referred to each other as ''sir,'' that was something that pressed selflessness too far. And so the law had been changed, and the Vice President was now an appendage instead of a defeated enemy. That so many Vice Presidents had succeeded to the top job was less a matter of design than happenstance. That so many had done well—Andrew Johnson, Theodore Roosevelt, Harry Truman—was miraculous.

It was in any case a chance he would never have. Bob Fowler was physically healthy and politically as secure as any President had been since . . . Eisenhower? Durling wondered. Maybe even FDR. The important, almost co-equal role for the Vice President that Carter had initiated with Walter Mondale—something largely ignored but highly constructive—was a thing of the past. Fowler did not need Durling anymore. The President had made that quite clear.

And so Durling was relegated to subsidiary—not even secondary—duties. Fowler got to fly about in a converted 747 dedicated to his use alone. Roger Durling got whatever aircraft might be available, in this case one of the VC-20B Gulfstreams that were used by anyone who had the right credentials. Senators and House members on junkets got them if they were on the right committees, or if the President sensed a need to stroke their egos.

You're being petty, Durling told himself. *By being petty, you justify all the crap you have to put up with.*

His misjudgment had been at least as great as Madison's, the Vice President told himself as the aircraft taxied out. In deciding that a political figure would place country above his own ambition, Madison had merely been optimistic. Durling, on the other hand, had ignored an evident political reality, that the real difference in importance between President and Vice President was far greater than the difference between Fowler and any of a dozen committee chairmen in the House or Senate. The President had to deal with Congress to get any work done. He didn't *need* to deal with his Vice President.

How had he allowed himself to get here? That earned an amused grunt, though the question had occurred to Durling a thousand times. Patriotism, of course, or at least the political version of it. He'd delivered California, and without California he and Fowler would both still be governors. The one substantive concession he'd gotten—the accession of Charlie Alden to the post of National Security Advisor—had been for naught, but he had been the deciding factor in changing the Presidency from one party to another. And his reward for that was drawing every crap detail in the executive branch, delivering speeches that would rarely make the news, though those of various cabinet officials did, speeches to keep faithful the party faithful, speeches to float new ideas—usually bad ones, and rarely his own—and wait for lightning to strike himself instead of the President. Today he was going out to talk about the need to raise taxes to pay for the peace in the Middle East. What a marvelous political opportunity! he thought. Roger Durling would outline the need for new taxes in St. Louis before a convention of purchasing managers, and he was sure the applause would be deafening.

But he had accepted the job, had given his word to perform the duties of the office, and if he did any less, then what would he be?

The aircraft rolled unevenly past the hangars and various aircraft, including NEACP, the 747 configured as the National Emergency Airborne Command Post, known as "Kneecap," or more dramatically as "The Doomsday Plane." Always within two flying hours of wherever the President might be (a real headache when the President visited Russia or China), it was the only safe place the President might occupy in a nuclear crisis—but that didn't really matter anymore, did it? Durling saw people shuffling in and out of the aircraft. Funding hadn't been reduced on that yet—well, it was part of the President's personal fleet—and it was still kept ready for a rapid departure. He wondered how soon that might change. Everything else had.

"We're ready for departure. All buckled, sir?" the sergeant-attendant asked.

"You bet! Let's get this show on the road," Durling replied with a smile. On Air Force One, he knew, people often showed their confidence in the aircraft and the crew by not buckling. More evidence that his airplane was second-best, but he could hardly growl at the sergeant for being a pro, and to this man Roger Durling was important. The Vice President reflected that this made the sergeant E-6 in the U.S. Air Force a more honorable man than most of the people in politics, but that wasn't much of a surprise, was it?

"That's a roger."

"*Again?*" Ryan asked.

"Yes, sir," the voice on the other end of the phone said.

"Okay, give me a few minutes."

"Yes, sir."

Ryan finished off his coffee and walked off toward Cabot's office. He was surprised to see Goodley in there again. The youngster was keeping his distance from the Director's cigar smoke, and even Jack thought that Marcus was overdoing the Patton act or whatever the hell Cabot thought he was trying to look like.

"What is it, Jack?"

"CAMELOT," Jack replied with visible annoyance. "Those White House pukes have bowed out again. They want me to join in instead."

"Well, are you that tied up?"

"Sir, we talked about that four months ago. It's important for the people at the White House to—"

"The President and his people are busy on some things," the DCI explained tiredly.

"Sir, these things are scheduled weeks in advance, and it's the fourth straight time that—"

"I *know*, Jack."

Ryan stood his ground. "Director, somebody has to explain to them how important this is."

"I've tried, dammit!" Cabot shot back. He had done so, Jack knew.

"Have you tried working through Secretary Talbot, or maybe Dennis Bunker?" Jack asked. *At least the President listens to them,* Jack didn't add.

He didn't have to. Cabot got the message. "Look, Jack, we can't give orders to the President. We can only give advice. He doesn't always take it. You're pretty good at this, anyway. Dennis likes playing with you."

"Fine, sir, but it's not my job—do they even *read* the washup notes?"

"Charlie Alden did. I suppose Liz Elliot does too."

"I bet," Ryan observed icily, ignoring Goodley's presence. "Sir, they are being irresponsible."

"That's a little strong, Jack."

"It's a little true, Director," Ryan said as calmly as he could.

"Can I ask what CAMELOT is?" Ben Goodley asked.

"It's a game," Cabot answered. "Crisis-management, usually."

"Oh, like SAGA and GLOBAL?"

"Yeah," Ryan said. "The President never plays. The reason is that we cannot risk knowledge of how he would act in a given situation—and yes, that is overly

Byzantine, but it's always been that way. Instead, the National Security Advisor or some other senior staff member takes his place, and the President is supposed to be briefed on how it goes. Except that President Fowler thinks that he doesn't have to bother, and now his people are starting to act the same dumb way.'' Jack was sufficiently annoyed that he used the words ''President Fowler'' and ''dumb'' in the same sentence.

''Well, I mean, is it really necessary?'' Goodley asked. ''Sounds like an anachronism to me.''

''You have car insurance, Ben?'' Jack asked.

''Yes, sure.''

''Ever have an auto accident?''

''Not one that was my fault,'' Goodley replied.

''Then why bother with insurance?'' Jack answered the question: ''Because it's *insurance,* right? You don't expect to need it, you never want to need it, but because you *might* need it, you spend the money—or time, in this case—to have it.''

The Presidential Scholar made a dismissive gesture. ''Come on, it's a different thing altogether.''

''That's right. In a car it's just your ass.'' Ryan stopped the sermon. ''Okay, Director, I'm off for the rest of the day.''

''Your objections and recommendations are noted, Jack. I will bring them up at my first opportunity—oh, before you leave, about NIITAKA . . .''

Ryan stopped in his tracks and stared down at Cabot. ''Sir, Mr. Goodley is not cleared for that word, much less that file.''

''We are not discussing the substance of the case. When will the people downstairs''—Ryan was grateful he didn't say MERCURY—''be ready for the, uh, modified operations? I want to improve data-transfer.''

''Six weeks. Until then we have to use the other methods we discussed.''

The Director of Central Intelligence nodded. ''Very well. The White House is very interested in that, Jack. Good job to all concerned.''

''Glad to hear that, sir. See you tomorrow.'' Jack walked out.

''NIITAKA?'' Goodley asked after the door closed. ''Sounds Japanese.''

''Sorry, Goodley. You can forget that word at your earliest opportunity.'' Cabot had spoken it only to remind Ryan of his place, and the honorable part of the man already regretted having done so.

''Yes, sir. May I ask an unrelated question?''

''Sure.''

''Is Ryan as good as people say?''

Cabot stubbed out the remains of his cigar, to the relief of his visitor. ''He's got quite a record.''

''Really? I've heard that. You know, that's the whole reason I'm here, to examine the personality types that really make a difference. I mean, how does someone grow into the job? Ryan's skyrocketed up the ladder here. I'd be very interested in seeing how he managed to do that.''

''He's done it by being right a lot more often than he's wrong, by making some tough calls, and with some field jobs that even I can hardly believe,'' Cabot said after a moment's consideration. ''And you can never, ever reveal that to anyone, Dr. Goodley.''

''I understand, sir. Could I see his record, his personnel file?''

The DCI's eyebrows arched. ''Everything you see in there is classified. Anything you try to write about it—''

"Excuse me, but I know that, sir. Everything I write is subject to security review. I signed off on that. It's important that I learn how a person really fits in here, and Ryan would seem to be an ideal case study for examining how that process happens. I mean, that's why the White House sent me over here," Goodley pointed out. "I'm supposed to report to them on what I find."

Cabot was silent for a moment. "I suppose that's okay, then."

Ryan's car arrived at the Pentagon's River Entrance. He was met by an Air Force one-star and conducted inside, bypassing the metal detector. Two minutes later he was in one of many subterranean rooms that lie under and around this ugliest of official buildings.

"Hello, Jack," Dennis Bunker called from the far end of the room.

"Mr. Secretary." Jack nodded as he took his National Security Advisor's chair. The game started immediately. "What seems to be the problem?"

"Aside from the fact that Liz Elliot has decided not to grace us with her presence?" The Secretary of Defense chuckled, then went serious. "There has been an attack on one of our cruisers in the Eastern Med. The information is still sketchy, but the ship has been severely damaged and may be sinking. We presume heavy casualties."

"What do we know?" Jack asked, settling into the game. He put on a color-coded name tag that identified which part he was playing. A card hanging from the ceiling over his chair had the same purpose.

"Not much." Bunker looked up as a Navy lieutenant entered the room.

"Sir, USS *Kidd* reports that *Valley Forge* exploded and sank five minutes ago as a result of the initial damage. There are no more than twenty survivors, and rescue operations are under way."

"What is the cause of the loss?" Ryan asked.

"Unknown, sir. *Kidd* was thirty miles from *Valley Forge* at the time of the incident. Her helo is on the scene now. Commander Sixth Fleet has brought all his ships to full-alert status. USS *Theodore Roosevelt* is launching aircraft to sweep the area."

"I know the CAG on *TR*, Robby Jackson," Ryan said to nobody in particular. Not that it mattered. *Theodore Roosevelt* was actually in Norfolk, and Robby was still preparing for his next cruise. The names in the war game were generic, and personal knowledge of the players didn't matter since they were not supposed to be real people. But if it were real, Robby was Commander Air Group on USS *Theodore Roosevelt,* and his would be the first plane off the cats. It was well to remember that though this might be a game, its purpose was deadly serious. "Background information?" Jack asked. He didn't remember all of the pre-brief on the scenario being played out.

"CIA reports a possible mutiny in the Soviet Union by Red Army units in Kazakhstan, and disturbances in two Navy bases there also," the game narrator, a Navy commander, reported.

"Soviet units in the vicinity of *Valley Forge?*" Bunker asked.

"Possibly a submarine," the naval officer answered.

"Flash Message," the wall speaker announced. "USS *Kidd* reports that it has destroyed an inbound surface-to-surface missile with its Close-In Weapons System. Superficial damage to the ship, no casualties."

Jack walked to the corner to pour himself a cup of coffee. He smiled as he did so. These games were fun, he admitted to himself. He really did enjoy them. They were also realistic. He'd been swept away from a normal day's routine, dumped in a stuffy room, given confused and fragmented information, and had no idea at all what the hell was supposed to be going on. That was reality. The old joke: How do crisis-managers resemble mushrooms? They're kept in the dark and fed horseshit.

"Sir, we have an incoming HOTLINE message . . ."

Okay, Ryan thought, *it's* that *kind of game today. The Pentagon must have come up with the scenario. Let's see if it's still possible to blow the world up. . . .*

"More concrete?" Qati asked.

"Much more concrete," Fromm answered. "The machines each weigh several tons, and they must be totally stable. The room must be totally stable, and totally sealed. It must be clean like a hospital—no, much better than any hospital you have ever seen." Fromm looked down at his list. *Not cleaner than a* German *hospital, of course.* "Next, electrical power. We'll need three large backup generators, and at least two UPSs—"

"What?" Qati asked.

"Un-interruptible power supplies," Ghosn translated. "We'll keep one of the backup generators turning at all times, of course?"

"Correct," Fromm answered. "Since this is a primitive operation, we'll try not to use more than one machine at a time. The real problem with electricity is ensuring a secure circuit. So, we take the line current through the UPSs to protect against spikes. The computer systems on the milling machines are highly sensitive.

"Next!" Fromm said. "Skilled operators."

"That will be highly difficult," Ghosn observed.

The German smiled, amazing everyone present. "Not so. It will be easier than you think."

"Really?" Qati asked. *Good news from this infidel?*

"We'll need perhaps five highly trained men, but you have them in the region, I am sure."

"Where? There is no machine shop in the region that—"

"Certainly there is. People here wear spectacles, do they not?"

"But—"

"Of course!" Ghosn said, rolling his eyes in amazement.

"The degree of precision, you see," Fromm explained to Qati, "is no different from what is required for eyeglasses. The machines are very similar in design, just larger, and what we are attempting to do is simply to produce precise and predictable curves in a rigid material. Nuclear bombs are produced to exacting specifications. So are spectacles. Our desired object is larger, but the principle is the same, and with the proper machinery it is merely a matter of scale, not of substance. So: can you obtain skilled lens-makers?"

"I don't see why not," Qati replied, hiding his annoyance.

"They must be highly skilled," Fromm said like a schoolmaster. "The best you can find, people with long experience, preferably with training in Germany or England."

"There will be a security problem," Ghosn said quietly.

"Oh? Why is that?" Fromm asked with a feigned bafflement that struck both of the others as the summit of arrogance.

"Quite so," Qati agreed.

"Next, we need sturdy tables on which to mount the machines."

* * *

Halfway point, Lieutenant Commander Walter Claggett told himself. In forty-five more days, USS *Maine* would surface outside Juan de Fuca Straits, link up with the tugboat, and follow Little Toot into Bangor, where she would then tie up and begin the handoff process to the "Blue" crew for the next deterrence-patrol cycle. *And not a moment too soon.*

Walter Claggett—friends called him Dutch, a nickname that had originated at the Naval Academy for a reason he no longer remembered; Claggett was Black—was thirty-six years old, and it had been made known to him before sailing that he was being "deep-dipped" for early selection to commander and had a chance for an early crack at a fast-attack boat. That was fine with him. His two attempts at marriage had both ended in failure, which was not uncommon for submariners—thankfully, there were no kids involved in either union—and the Navy was his life. He was just as happy to spend all of his time at sea, saving his carousing time for those not really brief intervals on the beach. To be at sea, to slide through black water in control of a majestic ship of war, that was the best of all things to Walter Claggett. The company of good men, respect truly earned in a most demanding profession, the acquired ability to know every time what the right thing to do was, the relaxed banter in the wardroom, the responsibility he had to counsel his men—Claggett relished every aspect of his career.

It was just his commanding officer he couldn't stand.

How the hell did Captain Harry Ricks ever make it this far? he asked himself for the twentieth time this week. The man was brilliant. He could have designed a submarine reactor system on the back of an envelope, or maybe even in his head during a rare daydream. He knew things about submarine design that Electric Boat's shipwrights had never even thought about. He could discuss the ins and outs of periscope design with the Navy's chief optics expert, and knew more about satellite-navigation aids than NASA or TRW or whoever the hell was running *that* program. Surely he knew more about the guidance packages on their Trident-II D-5 sea-launched ballistic missiles than anyone this side of Lockheed's Missile Systems Division. Over dinner two weeks earlier, he'd recited a whole page from the maintenance manual. From a technical point of view, Ricks might have been the most thoroughly prepared officer in the United States Navy.

Harry Ricks was the quintessential product of the Nuclear Navy. As an engineer he was unequaled. The technical aspects of his job were almost instinctive to him. Claggett was good, and knew it; he also knew that he'd never be as good as Harry Ricks.

It's just that he doesn't know dick about submarining or submariners, Claggett reflected bleakly. It was incredible, but true, that Ricks had little feeling for seamanship and none at all for sailors.

"Sir," Claggett said slowly, "this is a very good chief. He's young, but he's sharp."

"He can't keep control of his people," Ricks replied.

"Captain, I don't know what you mean by that."

"His training methods aren't what they're supposed to be."

"He is a little unconventional, but he has cut six seconds off the average reload time. The fish are all fully functional, even the one that came over from the beach bad. The compartment is completely squared away. What more can we ask of the man?"

"I don't ask. I direct. I order. I expect things to be done my way, the right way. And they will be done that way,'' Ricks observed in a dangerously quiet voice.

It made no sense at all to cross the skipper on issues like this, especially when he posed them in this way, but Claggett's job as executive officer was to stand between the crew and the captain, especially when the captain was wrong.

''Sir, I must respectfully disagree. I think we look at results, and the results here are just about perfect. A good chief is one who stretches the envelope, and this one hasn't stretched it very far. If you slap him down, it will have a negative effect on him and his department.''

''X, I expect support from all my officers, and especially from you.''

Claggett sat straight up in his chair as though from a blow. He managed to speak calmly. ''Captain, you have my support and my loyalty. It is not my job to be a robot. I'm supposed to offer alternatives. At least,'' he added, ''that's what they told me at PXO School.'' Claggett regretted the last sentence even before it was spoken, but somehow it had come out anyway. The CO's cabin was quite small, and immediately got smaller still.

That was a very foolish thing to say, Lieutenant *Commander Walter Martin Claggett,* Ricks thought with a blank look.

''Next, the reactor drills,'' Ricks said.

''Another one? So soon?'' *For Christ's sake, the last one was friggin'* PERFECT. *Almost perfect,* Claggett corrected himself. *The kids might have saved ten or fifteen seconds somewhere.* The Executive Officer didn't know where that might have been, though.

''Proficiency means every day, X.''

''Indeed it does, sir, but they are proficient. I mean, the ORSE we ran right before Captain Rosselli left missed setting the squadron record by a whisker, and the last drill we ran beat *that!*''

''No matter how good drill results are, always demand better. That way you always *get* better. Next ORSE, I want the squadron record, X.''

He wants the Navy record, the world record, maybe even a certificate from God, Claggett thought. *More than that, he wants it on* his *record.*

The growler phone on the bulkhead rattled. Ricks lifted it.

''Commanding Officer . . . yes, on the way.'' He hung up. ''Sonar contact.''

Claggett was out the door in two seconds, the Captain right behind him.

''What is it?'' Claggett asked first. As executive officer, he was also the approach officer for tactical engagements.

''Took me a couple minutes to recognize it,'' the leading sonarman reported. ''Real fluky contact. I think it's a 688, bearing about one-nine-five. Direct-path contact, sir.''

''Playback,'' Ricks ordered. The sonarman took over another screen—his had grease-pencil marks on it and he didn't want to remove those yet—and ran the display back a few minutes.

''See here, Cap'n? Real fluky . . . right about here it started firming up. That's when I called in.''

The Captain stabbed his finger on the screen. ''You should have had it there, petty officer. That's two minutes wasted. Pay closer attention next time.''

''Aye aye, Cap'n.'' What else could a twenty-three-year-old sonarman second-class say? Ricks left the sonar room. Claggett followed, patting the sonar operator on the shoulder as he went.

Goddamn it, Captain!

"Course two-seven-zero, speed five, depth five hundred even. We're under the layer," the Officer of the Deck reported. "Holding contact Sierra-Eleven at bearing one-nine-five, broad on the port beam. Fire-control tracking party is manned. We have fish in tubes one, three, and four. Tube two is empty for service. Doors closed, tubes dry."

"Tell me about Sierra-Eleven," Ricks ordered.

"Direct-path contact. He's below the layer, range unknown."

"Environmental conditions?"

"Flat calm on the roof, a moderate layer at about one hundred feet. We have good isothermal water around us. Sonar conditions are excellent."

"First read on Sierra-Eleven is over ten thousand yards." It was Ensign Shaw on the tracking party.

"Conn, Sonar, we evaluate contact Sierra-Eleven as a definite 688-class, US fast-attack. I can guestimate speed at about fourteen-fifteen knots, sir."

"Whoa!" Claggett observed to Ricks. "We picked up a Los Angeles at 10-K plus! That's gonna piss somebody off . . ."

"Sonar, conn, I want data, not guesses," Ricks said.

"Cap'n, he did well to pick that contact out of the background," Claggett said very quietly. Summer in the Gulf of Alaska meant fishing boats and baleen whales, both in large numbers, making noise and cluttering up sonar displays. "That's one hell of a good sonarman in there."

"We pay him to be good, X. We don't award medals for doing an adequate job. I want a playback later to see if there might have been a sniff earlier that he missed."

Anybody can find something on playback, Claggett thought to himself.

"Conn, Sonar, I'm getting a very faint blade-count . . . seems to indicate fourteen knots, plus or minus one, sir."

"Very well. That's better, Sonar."

"Uh, Captain . . . may be a little closer than ten thousand . . . not much, but a little. Track is firming up . . . best estimate now nine-five hundred yards, course roughly three-zero-five," Shaw reported next, waiting for the sky to fall.

"So he's not over ten thousand yards off now?"

"No, sir, looks like nine-five hundred."

"Let me know when you change your mind again," Ricks replied. "Drop speed to four knots."

"Reduce speed four knots, aye," the OOD acknowledged.

"Let him get ahead of us?" Claggett asked.

"Yep." The Captain nodded.

"We have a firing solution," the weapons officer said. The XO checked his watch. It didn't get much better than this.

"Very well. Glad to hear it," Ricks replied.

"Speed is now four knots."

"Okay, we have him. Sierra-Eleven is at bearing two-zero-one, range nine-one hundred yards, course three-zero-zero, speed fifteen."

"Dead meat," Claggett said. *Of course he's making it easy by going that fast.*

"True enough. This will look good on the patrol report."

"That's tricky," Ryan observed. "I don't like the way this is going."

"Neither do I," Bunker agreed. "I recommend weapons release to the *TR* battle group."

"I agree, and will so advise the President." Ryan placed the call. Under the rules for this game, the President was supposed to be on Air Force One, somewhere over the Pacific, returning from an unspecified country on the Pacific Rim. The President's decision-making role was being played by a committee elsewhere in the Pentagon. Jack made his recommendation and waited for the reply.

"Only in self-defense, Dennis."

"Bullshit," Bunker said quietly. "He listens to me."

Jack grinned. "I agree, but not this time. No offensive action, you may act only to defend the ships in the group."

The SecDef turned to the action officer: "Forward that to *Theodore Roosevelt.* Tell them I expect full combat air patrols. Anything over two hundred miles I want reported to me. Under two hundred, the battle-group commander is free to act at discretion. For submarines, the bubble radius is fifty—five-zero—miles. Inside that, prosecute to kill."

"That's creative," Jack said.

"We have that attack on *Valley Forge.*" The best estimate at the moment was that it had been a surprise missile attack from a Soviet submarine. It appeared that some units of the Russian fleet were acting independently, or at least under orders not emanating from Moscow. Then things got worse.

"HOTLINE message. There has just been a ground-force attack on a Strategic Rocket Regiment . . . SS-18 base in Central Asia."

"Launch all the ready bombers right now! Jack, tell the President that I just gave the order."

"Comm-link failure," the wall speaker said. "Radio contact with Air Force One has been interrupted."

"Tell me more!" Jack demanded.

"That's all we have, sir."

"Where's the Vice President now?" Ryan asked.

"He's aboard Kneecap Alternate, six hundred miles south of Bermuda. Kneecap Prime is four hundred miles ahead of Air Force One, preparing to land in Alaska for the transfer."

"Close enough to Russia that an intercept is possible . . . but not likely . . . have to be a one-way mission," Bunker thought aloud. "Unless they strayed over a Soviet warship with SAMs. . . . Vice President is temporarily in charge."

"Sir, I—"

"That's my call to make, Jack. The President is either out of the loop or has had his comm links compromised. SecDef says that the Vice President is in charge until the comm links are reestablished and validated by code-word authentication. Forces are now at DEFCON-ONE on my authority."

One thing about Dennis Bunker, Ryan thought, the man never stopped being a fighter jock. He makes decisions and sticks to them. He was usually right, too, as he was here.

Ryan's file was a thick one. Almost five inches, Goodley saw in the privacy of his seventh-floor cubbyhole. Half an inch of that was background and security-clearance forms. The academic record was fairly impressive, especially his doctoral work in history at Georgetown University. Georgetown wasn't Harvard, of course, but it was a fairly respectable institution, Goodley told himself. His first Agency job had been as part of Admiral James Greer's Junior Varsity program, and his first report, "Agents and Agencies," had dealt with terrorism. Odd coincidence, Goodley thought, given what had happened later.

The documents on Ryan's encounter in London occupied thirty double-space pages, mainly police-report summaries and a few news photos. Goodley started making notes. *Cowboy,* he wrote first of all. Running into things like that. The academic shook his head. Twenty minutes later, he read over the executive summary of Ryan's second CIA report, the one which confidently predicted that the terrorists would probably never operate in America—delivered days before the attack on his family.

Guessed wrong there, didn't you, Ryan? Goodley chuckled to himself. As bright as they said he was, he made mistakes like everyone else. . . .

He'd made a few while working in England, too. He hadn't predicted Chernenko's succession of Andropov, though he had predicted Narmonov was the coming man well in advance of nearly everyone, except Kantrowitz up at Princeton, who'd been the first to see star quality in Andrey Il'ych. Goodley reminded himself that he'd been an undergraduate then, bedding that girl at Wellesley, Debra Frost . . . wonder what ever happened to her . . . ?

"Son of a bitch . . ." Ben whispered a few minutes later. "Son of a *bitch.*"

Red October, a Soviet ballistic missile submarine . . . defected. Ryan was one of the first to suspect it. . . . Ryan, an analyst at London Station had . . . run the operation at sea! *Killed* a Russian sailor. That was the cowboy part again. Couldn't just arrest the guy, had to shoot him down like something in a movie. . . .

Goddamn! A Russian ballistic-missile defected . . . *and they kept it quiet . . . oh, the boat was later sunk in deep water.*

Back to London after that for a few more months before rotating home to be Greer's special assistant and heir-apparent. Some interesting work with the arms-control people. . . .

That can't be right. The KGB Chairman was killed in a plane crash. . . .

Goodley was taking furious notes now. Liz Elliot could not have known any of this, could she?

You're not looking for good stuff about Ryan, the White House Fellow reminded himself. Elliot had never really said that, of course, but she had made herself clear in a way that he'd understood . . . or thought he'd understood, Goodley corrected himself. He suddenly realized just how dangerous a game this might be.

Ryan kills people. He'd shot and killed at least three. You didn't get that from talking to the man. Life wasn't a Western. People didn't carry revolvers with notches cut in the handles. Goodley didn't feel a chill over his skin, but he did remind himself that Ryan was someone to be regarded warily. He'd never before met someone who had killed other men, and was not foolish enough to regard such people as heroic or somehow more than other men, but it was something to keep in mind, wasn't it?

There were blank spots around the time of James Greer's death, he noted . . . wasn't that the time when all that stuff was happening down in Colombia? He made some notes. Ryan had been acting DDI then, but just after Fowler took over, Judge Arthur Moore and Robert Ritter had retired to make way for the new presidential administration, and Ryan had been confirmed by the Senate as Deputy Director of Central Intelligence. So much for his work record. Goodley closed that portion and opened up the personal and financial side. . . .

"Bad call . . ." Ryan said. Twenty minutes too late.

"I think you're right."

"Too late. What did we do wrong?"

"I'm not sure," Bunker replied. "Tell the *TR* group to disengage and pull back, maybe?"

Ryan stared at the map on the far wall. "Maybe, but we've backed Andrey Il'ych into a corner . . . we have to let him out."

"How? How do we do that without cornering ourselves?"

"I think there was a problem with this scenario . . . not sure what, though. . . ."

"Let's rattle his cage hard," Ricks thought aloud.

"Like how, Cap'n?" Claggett asked.

"Status on Tube Two?"

"Empty, it was down for maintenance inspection," the weapons officer replied.

"Is it okay?"

"Yes, sir, completed the inspection half an hour before we got the contact."

"Okay . . ." Ricks grinned. "I want a water slug out of tube two. Let's give him a real launch transient to wake him up!"

Damn! Claggett thought. It was almost something Mancuso or Rosselli would have done. Almost . . . "Sir, that's kind of a noisy way to do it. We can shake him up enough with a 'Tango' call on the Gertrude."

"Weps, we have a solution on Sierra-Eleven?" *Mancuso wants aggressive skippers, well, I'll show him aggressive—*

"Yes, sir!" the weapons officer snapped back at once.

"Firing Point Procedures. Prepare to fire a water slug on Tube Two."

"Sir, I confirm torpedo tube two is empty. Weapons in tubes one, three, and four are secure." A call was made to the torpedo room to reconfirm what the electronic displays announced. In the torpedo room, the chief made a look through the small glass port to make certain that they wouldn't be launching anything.

"Tube Two is empty by visual inspection. High-pressure air is online," the chief called over the communications circuit. "We are ready to shoot."

"Open outer door."

"Open outer door, aye. Outer door is open."

"Weps?"

"Locked in."

"Match generated bearings and . . . SHOOT!"

The weapons officer pushed the proper button. USS *Maine* shuddered with the sudden pulse of high-pressure air out of the torpedo tube and into the sea.

Aboard USS *Omaha,* six thousand yards away, a sonarman had been trying for the past few minutes to decide if the trace on his screen was something other than clutter when a dot appeared on the screen.

"Conn, Sonar, transient, transient. Mechanical Transient bearing zero-eight-eight, dead aft!"

"What the hell?" the Officer of the Deck said. He was the boat's navigator, in the third week of duty in the new post. "What's back there?"

"Transient, transient—launch transient bearing zero-eight-eight! I say again, LAUNCH TRANSIENT DEAD AFT!"

"All ahead flank!" the suddenly pale Lieutenant said a touch too loudly. "Battle stations! Stand by the five-inch room." He lifted the command phone for the Captain, but the general alarm was already sounding, and the Commanding Officer ran barefoot into the attack center, his coveralls still open.

"What the fuck is going on?"

"Sir, we had a launch transient dead aft—Sonar, conn, what else do you have?"

"Nothing, sir, nothing after the transient. That was a launch-transient, HP air into the water, but . . . sounded a little funny, sir. I show nothing in the water."

"Right full rudder!" the OOD ordered, ignoring the Captain. He hadn't been relieved yet, and conning the boat was his responsibility. "Make your depth one hundred feet. Five-inch room, launch a decoy now-now-now!"

"Right full rudder, aye. Sir, my rudder is right full, no course given. Speed twenty knots and accelerating," helmsman said.

"Very well. Come to course zero-one-zero."

"Aye, coming to new course zero-one-zero!"

"Who's in this area?" the CO asked in a relaxed voice, though he didn't feel relaxed.

"*Maine*'s around here somewhere," the navigator answered.

"Harry Ricks." *That asshole,* he didn't say. It would have been bad for discipline. "Sonar, talk to me!"

"Conn, Sonar, there is nothing in the water. If there was a torpedo, I'd have it, sir."

"Nav, drop speed to one-third."

"Aye, all ahead one-third."

"I think we scared the piss out of him," Ricks observed, hovering over the sonar display. Seconds after the simulated launch, the 688 on the scope had floored his power plant, and now there was also the gurgling sound of a decoy.

"Just backed off on the power, sir, blade count is coming down."

"Yeah, he knows there's nothing after him, now. We'll give him a call on the Gertrude."

"That dumbass! Doesn't he know that there may be an Akula around here?" the Commanding Officer of USS *Omaha* growled.

"We don't show him, sir, just a bunch of fishing boats."

"Okay. Secure from general quarters. We'll let *Maine* have her little laugh." He grimaced. "My fault. We should have been trolling along at ten instead of fifteen knots. Make it so."

"Aye, sir. Where to?"

"The boomer ought to have a feel for what's north of here. Go southeast."

"Right."

"Nice reaction, Nav. We might have evaded the fish. Lessons?"

"You said it, sir. We were going too fast."

"Learn from your Captain's mistake, Mr. Auburn."

"Always, sir."

The skipper punched the younger man's shoulder on the way out.

Thirty-six thousand yards away, the *Admiral Lunin* was drifting at three knots just over the thermocline layer, her towed-array sonar drooping under it.

"Well?" her Captain asked.

"We have this burst of noise at one-three-zero," the sonar officer said, pointing to the display, "and nothing else. Fifteen seconds later, we have another burst of noise here . . . ahead of the first. The signature appears to be an American Los Angeles class going to full power, then slowing and disappearing off our screens."

"An exercise, Yevgeniy . . . the first transient was an American missile submarine . . . an Ohio-class. What do you think of that?'' Captain First Rank Valentin Borissovich Dubinin asked.

''No one has ever detected an Ohio in deep water. . . .''

''For all things there is a first time.''

''And now?''

''We will hover and wait. The Ohio is quieter than a sleeping whale, but at least we know now that there is one in the area. We will not chase after it. Very foolish of the Americans to make noise in this way. I've never seen that happen before.''

''The game has changed, Captain,'' the sonar officer observed. It had changed quite a lot. He didn't have to say ''Comrade Captain'' anymore.

''Indeed it has, Yevgeniy. Now it is a true game. No one need get hurt, and we can test our skills as in the Olympics.''

''Critique?''

''I would have closed a little before shooting, sir,'' the weapons officer said. ''Even money he might have evaded that one.''

''Agreed, but we were only trying to shake him up,'' Ricks said comfortably.

Then what was the purpose of that exercise? Dutch Claggett wondered. *Oh, of course, to show how aggressive you are.*

''I guess we accomplished that,'' the XO said to support his captain. There were grins all around the control room. Boomers and fast-attack subs often played games, mostly pre-planned. As usual, the Ohio had won this one, too. They'd known that *Omaha* was around, of course, and that she was looking for a Russian Akula that the P-3s had lost off the Aleutians a few days before. But the Russian ''Shark'' class sub was nowhere to be heard.

''OOD, take her south. We went and made a datum with that launch transient. We'll clear datum back down where *Omaha* was.''

''Aye aye, sir.''

''Well done, people.'' Ricks walked back to his cabin.

''New course?''

''South,'' Dubinin said. ''He'll clear datum by going into the area already swept by the Los Angeles. We'll maintain position just over the layer, leave our 'tail' under it, and try to reacquire.'' There wasn't much chance, the Captain knew, but fortune still favored the bold. Or something like that. The submarine was due to go back to port in another week, and supposedly the new sonar array she was due to receive during her scheduled overhaul was a major improvement over the current one. He'd been here south of Alaska for three weeks. The submarine he'd detected, USS *Maine* or USS *Nevada,* if his intelligence reports were correct, would finish this patrol, refit, conduct another, refit again, then yet another patrol in February, which coincided with his deployment schedule after his overhaul. So the next time he was back, he'd be up against the same captain, and this one had made a mistake. After the refit, *Admiral Lunin* would be quieter, and would have better sonar, and Dubinin was starting to wonder when he'd be able to play his game against the Americans. . . . Wouldn't it be nice, he thought. All the time he'd spent to get here, the wonderful years learning his trade in Northern Fleet under Marko Ramius. What a pity, for such a brilliant officer to have died in an accident. But duty at sea was dangerous, always had been, always would be. Marko had got his crew off before scuttling. . . . Dubinin shook his head. Today he might have gotten assistance from the Americans. Might? Would have, just as an American ship would get one from a Soviet. The changes in his country and the world made Dubinin feel much better about his job. It had always been a demanding game of skill, but its deadly purpose had changed. Oh, yes, the American missile submarines still had their rockets pointed at his country, and Soviet rockets were pointed at America, but perhaps they would be gone soon. Until they were, he'd continue to do his job, and it seemed ironic indeed that just as the Soviet Navy was on the threshold of becoming competitive—the Akula class was roughly equal with an early Los Angeles class in a mechanical sense—the need for it was diminishing. Like a friendly game of cards, perhaps? he asked himself. Not a bad simile. . . .

"Speed, Captain?"

Dubinin considered that. "Assume a range of twenty nautical miles and a target speed of five knots. We'll do seven knots, I think. That way we can remain very quiet and perhaps still catch him . . . every two hours we'll turn to maximize the capacity of the sonar. . . . Yes, that is the plan." *Next time, Yevgeniy, we'll have two new officer sonar operators to back you up,* Dubinin reminded himself. The drawdown of the Soviet submarine force had released a lot of young officers who were now getting specialist training. The submarine's complement of officers would double, and even more than the new equipment, that would make a difference in his abilities to hunt.

"We blew it," Bunker said. "I blew it. I gave the President bad advice."

"You're not the only one," Ryan admitted as he stretched. "But was that scenario realistic—I mean, really realistic?"

It turned out that the whole thing had been a ploy by a hard-pressed Soviet leader trying to get control over his military, and doing so by making it look as though some renegades had taken action.

"Not likely, but possible."

"All things are possible," Jack observed. "What do you suppose their war games say about us?"

Bunker laughed. "Nothing good, I'm sure."

At the end, America had had to accept the loss of its cruiser, USS *Valley Forge,* in return for the Charlie-class submarine that USS *Kidd*'s helicopter had found and sunk. That was not regarded as an even trade, rather like losing a rook to the other fellow's knight. Soviet forces had gone on alert in Eastern Germany, and the weaker NATO forces had been unsure of their ability to deal with them. As a result, the Soviets had won a concession on the troop-pullback schedule. Ryan thought the whole scenario contrived, but they often were, and the point in any case was to see how to manage an unlikely crisis. Here they had done badly, moving too rapidly in nonessential areas, and too slowly on the ones that mattered, but which had not been recognized in time.

The lesson, as always, was: Don't make mistakes. That was something known by any first-grader, of course, and all men made mistakes, but the difference between a first-grader and a senior official was that official mistakes carried far more weight. That fact was an entirely different lesson, and one often not learned.

14. Revelation

''So what have you found?''

''He's a most interesting man,'' Goodley replied. ''He's done some things at CIA that are hardly believable.''

''I know about the submarine business, and the defection of the KGB head. What else?'' Liz Elliot asked.

''He's rather well liked in the international intelligence community, like Sir Basil Charleston over in England—well, it's easy to see why they like him—but the same is true in the NATO countries, especially in France. Ryan stumbled across something that enabled the DGSE to bag a bunch of *Action Directe* people,'' Goodley explained. He was somewhat uncomfortable with his role of designated informer.

The National Security Advisor didn't like to be kept waiting, but there was no sense in pressing the young scholar, was there? Her face took on a wry smile. ''Am I to assume that you have started admiring the man?''

''He's done fine work, but he's made his mistakes, too. His estimate on the fall of East Germany and the progress of reunification was way off.'' He had not managed to learn that everyone else was, as well. Goodley himself had guessed almost exactly right on this issue up at the Kennedy School, and the paper he'd published in an obscure journal was something else that had earned him attention at the White House. The White House Fellow stopped again.

''And . . . ?'' Elliot prodded.

''And there are some troubling aspects in his personal life.''

Finally! ''And those are?''

''Ryan was investigated by the SEC for possible insider-stock trading before he entered CIA employ. It seems there was a computer-software company about to get a Navy contract. Ryan found out about it before anyone else and made a real killing. The SEC found out—the reason is that the company executives themselves were also investigated—and examined Ryan's records. He got off on a technicality.''

''Explain,'' Liz ordered.

''In order to cover their own backsides, the company officials arranged to have something published in a defense trade paper, just a little filler item, not even two column inches, but it was enough to show that the information upon which they and Ryan operated was technically in the public domain. That made it legal. What's more interesting is what Ryan did with the money after attention was called to it. He cut it out of his brokerage account—that's in a blind-trust arrangement now with four different money-managers.'' Goodley stopped. ''You know what Ryan's worth now?''

''No, what is it?''

''Over fifteen million dollars. He's by far the richest guy at the Agency. His holdings are somewhat undervalued. I'd say he's worth closer to twenty myself, but he's been using the same accounting method since before he joined CIA, and you can't critique him there. How you figure net worth is kind of metaphysical, isn't it? Accountants have different ways of doing things. Anyway, what he did with that windfall: he split it off to a separate account. Then a short while ago it all moved out into an educational trust fund."

"His kids?"

"No," Goodley answered. "The beneficiaries—no, let me back up. He used part of the money to set up a convenience store—a 7-Eleven—for a widow and her children. The rest of the money is set aside in T-Bills and a few blue-chip stocks to educate her children."

"Who is she?"

"Her name is Carol Zimmer. Laotian by birth, she's the widow of an Air Force sergeant who got killed in a training accident. Ryan has been looking after the family. He even signed out of his office to attend the birth of the newest child—a girl, by the way. Ryan visits the family periodically," Goodley concluded.

"I see." She didn't, but that is what one says. "Any professional connection?"

"Not really. Mrs. Zimmer, as I said, was Laotian. Her father was one of those tribal chieftains that CIA supported against the North Vietnamese. The whole group was wiped out. I haven't discovered how she managed to escape. She married an Air Force sergeant and came to America. He died in an accident somewhere, rather recently. There is nothing in Ryan's file to show any previous connection to the family at all. The Laos connection is possible—to CIA, I mean—but Ryan wasn't in government employ then, he was an undergrad in college. There's nothing in the file to show a connection of any kind. Just one day, a few months before the last presidential election, he set up this trust fund, and ever since he visits them on the average of once a week. Oh, there was one other thing."

"What's that?"

"I cross-referenced this from another file. There was some trouble at the 7-Eleven, some local punks were bothering the Zimmer family. Ryan's principal bodyguard is a CIA officer named Clark. He used to be a field officer, and now is a protective guy. I wasn't able to get his file," Goodley explained. "Anyway, this Clark guy evidently assaulted a couple of gang kids. Sent one to the hospital. I checked a newspaper clipping. It was in the news, a little item—concerned citizen sort of thing. Clark and another CIA guy—the paper identified them as federal employees, no CIA connection—were supposedly accosted by four street toughs. This Clark guy must be a piece of work. The gang leader had his knee broken and was hospitalized. One other was just knocked unconscious, and the rest just stood there and wet their pants. The local cops treated it as a gang problem—well, a former gang problem. No formal charges were pressed."

"What else do you know about this Clark?"

"I've seen him a few times. Big guy, late forties, quiet, actually seems kind of shy. But he moves—you know what he moves like? I took karate courses once. The instructor was a former Green Beret, Vietnam veteran, all that stuff. Like that. He moves like an athlete, fluid, economical, but it's his eyes. They're always moving around. He looks at you sideways and decides if you're a threat or not a threat. . . ." Goodley paused. At that moment he realized what Clark really was. Whatever else he was, Ben Goodley was no fool. "That is one dangerous guy."

"What?" Liz Elliot didn't know what he was talking about.

"Excuse me. I learned that from the karate teacher up at Cambridge. The really dangerous ones don't seem dangerous. You just sort of lose track of them in the room. My teacher, he was mugged on the subway station right there by Harvard. I mean, they tried to mug him. He left three kids bleeding on the bricks. They thought he was just a janitor or something—he's an African-American, about fifty now, I guess. Looks like a janitor or something the way he dresses, not dangerous at all. That's what Clark is like, just like my old *sensei*. . . . Interesting,'' Goodley said. ''Well, he's a SPO, and they're supposed to be good at their job.

''I speculate that Ryan found out that some punks were bothering Mrs. Zimmer, and had his bodyguard straighten things out. The Anne Arundel County police thought it was just fine.''

''Conclusions?''

''Ryan has done some very good work, but he's blown some big ones, too. Fundamentally, he's a creature of the past. He's still a Cold War guy. He's got problems with the Administration, like a few days ago when you didn't attend the CAMELOT game. He doesn't think you take your jobs seriously, thinks that not playing those war games is irresponsible.''

''He said that?''

''Almost a direct quote, I was in the room with Cabot when he came in and bitched.''

Elliot shook her head. ''That's a Cold Warrior talking. If the President does his job right, and if I do my job right, there won't be any crises to manage. That's the whole point, isn't it?''

''And so far, you guys seem to be doing all right,'' Goodley observed.

The National Security Advisor ignored the remark, looking at her notes.

The walls were in place, and weather-sealed with plastic sheeting. The air-conditioning system was already running, removing both humidity and dust from the air. Fromm was at work with the machine-tool tables. Table was too pedestrian a term. They were designed to hold several tons each, and had screw jacks on each sturdy leg. The German was leveling each machine with the aid of spirit-levels built into the frames.

''Perfect,'' he said after three hours of work. It had to be perfect. Now it was. Under each table was a full meter of reinforced concrete footings. Once leveled, the legs were bolted into place so that each was a solid part of the earth.

''The tools must be so rigid?'' Ghosn asked. Fromm shook his head.

''Quite the reverse. The tools float on a cushion of air.''

''But you said they weigh over a ton each!'' Qati objected.

''Floating them on an air cushion is trivial—you've seen photographs of hovercraft weighing a hundred tons. Floating them is necessary to dampen out vibrations from the earth.''

''What tolerances are we seeking?'' Ghosn asked.

''Roughly what one needs for an astronomical telescope,'' the German replied.

''But the original bombs—''

Fromm cut Ghosn off. ''The original American bombs on Hiroshima and Nagasaki were crude embarrassments. They wasted almost all of their reaction mass, especially the Hiroshima weapon—you would not manufacture so crude a weapon any more than you would design a bomb with a burning gunpowder fuse, eh?

''In any case, you cannot use such a wasteful design,'' Fromm went on. ''After the first bombs, the American engineers had to face the problem that they had limited supplies of fissile material. That few kilos of plutonium over there is the most expensive material in the world. The plant needed to make it though nuclear bombardment costs billions, then comes the additional cost of separation, another plant, and another billion. Only America had the money to do the initial project. Everyone in the world *knew* about nuclear fission—it was no secret, what real secrets are there in physics, eh?—but only America had the money and resources to make the attempt. And the people,'' Fromm added. ''What people they had! So the first bombs—they made three, by the way—were designed to use all the available material, and because the main criterion was reliability, they were made to be crude but effective. And they required the largest aircraft in the world to carry them.

''*Also* . . . then the war was won, and bomb-design became a professional study and not a frantic wartime project, *ja?* The plutonium reactor they have at Hanford turned out only a few tens of kilos of plutonium per year at the time, and the Americans had to learn to use the material more efficiently. The Mark-12 bomb was one of the first really advanced designs, and the Israelis improved it somewhat. That bomb has five times the yield of the Hiroshima device for less than a fifth of the reaction mass—twenty-fivefold improvement in efficiency, *ja?* And we can improve that by almost a factor of ten.

''Now a really expert design team with the proper facilities could advance that by another factor of . . . perhaps four. Modern warheads are the most elegant, the most fascinating—''

''Two megatons?'' Ghosn asked. Was it possible?

''We cannot do it here,'' Fromm said, the sorrow manifest in his voice. ''The available information is insufficient. The physics are straightforward, but there are engineering concerns, and there are no published articles to aid us in the bomb-design process. Remember that warhead tests are being carried out even today to make the bombs smaller and yet more efficient. One must experiment in this field as with any other, and we cannot experiment. Nor do we have the time or money to train technicians to execute the design. I *could* come up with a theoretical design for a megaton-plus device, but in truth it would have only a fifty-percent likelihood of success. Perhaps a little more, but it would not be a practical undertaking without a proper experimental-test program.''

''What can you do?'' Qati asked.

''I can make this into a weapon with a nominal yield of between four hundred and five hundred kilotons. It will be roughly a cubic meter in size and weigh roughly five hundred kilos.'' Fromm paused to read the looks on their faces. ''It will not be an elegant device, and it will be overly bulky and heavy. It will also be quite powerful.'' It would be far more clever in design than anything American or Russian technicians had managed in the first fifteen years of the nuclear age, and that, Fromm thought, wasn't bad at all.

''Explosive containment?'' Ghosn asked.

''Yes.'' This young Arab was very clever, Fromm thought. ''The first bombs used massive steel cases. Ours will use explosives—bulky but light, and just as effective. We will squirt tritium into the core at the moment of ignition. As in the original Israeli design, that will generate large quantities of neutrons to boost the fission reaction; that reaction in turn will blast additional neutrons into another tritium supply, causing a fusion reaction. The energy budget is roughly fifty kilotons from the primary and four hundred from the secondary.''

''How much tritium?'' While not a difficult substance to obtain in small amounts—watchmakers and gunsight manufacturers used it, but only in microscopic quantities—Ghosn knew supplies over ten miligrams were virtually unobtainable, as he had just discovered himself. Tritium—not plutonium despite what Fromm had said—was the most expensive commercially available material on the planet. You could get tritium, but not plutonium.

"I have fifty grams," Fromm announced smugly. "Far more than we can actually use."

"Fifty *grams!*" Ghosn exclaimed. *"Fifty?"*

"Our reactor complex was manufacturing special nuclear material for our own bomb project. When the socialist government fell, it was decided to give the plutonium to the Soviets—loyalty to the world socialist cause, you see. The Soviets didn't see things that way. Their reaction"—Fromm paused—"they called it . . . well, I will leave that to your imagination. Their reaction was so strong that I decided to hide our tritium production. As you know it is very valuable commercially—my insurance policy, you might call it."

"Where?"

"In the basement of my home, concealed in some nickel-hydrogen batteries."

Qati didn't like that, not one small bit. The Arab chieftain was not a well man, the German could see, and that did not help him conceal his feelings.

"I need to return to Germany in any case to get the machine tools," he said.

"You have them?"

"Five kilometers from my home is the Karl Marx Astrophysical Institute. We were supposed to manufacture astronomical telescopes there, visual and X-ray telescopes. Alas, it never opened. Such a fine 'cover' wasted, eh? In the machine shop, in crates marked *Astrophysical Instruments,* are six high-precision, five-axis machines—the finest sort," Fromm observed with a wolfish grin. "Cincinnati Milacron, from the United States of America. Precisely what the Americans use at their Oak Ridge, Rocky Flats, and Pantex fabrication plants."

"What about operators?" Ghosn asked.

"We were training twenty of them, sixteen men and four women, each with a university degree. . . . No, that would be too dangerous. It is not really necessary in any case. The machines are 'user-friendly,' as they say. We could do the work ourselves, but that would take too much time. Any skilled lensmaker—even a master gunsmith, as a matter of fact—can operate them. What was the business of Nobel Prize winners fifty years ago is now the work of a competent machinist," Fromm said. "Such is the nature of progress, *ja?*"

"It could be, then again it could not," Yevgeniy said. He'd been on duty for twenty hours straight, and only six hours of fitful sleep separated that from yet another, longer stint.

Finding it, if that indeed was what they'd done, had taken all of Dubinin's skill. He'd guessed that the American missile sub had headed south, and that her cruising speed was on the order of five knots. Next came environmental considerations. He'd had to stay close, within direct-path range, not allowing himself to come into a sonar convergence zone. The CZs were annular—donut—shaped areas around a vessel. Sound that went downward from a point within the convergence zone was refracted by the water temperature and pressure, traveling back and forth to the surface on a helical path at semiregular intervals that in turn depended on environmental conditions. By staying out of them, relative to where he thought his target was, he could evade one means of detection. To do that meant that he had to stay within theoretical direct-path distance, the area in which sound simply traveled radially from its source. To accomplish that without detection, he had to remain on the top side of the thermocline layer—he figured that the American would remain under it—while allowing his towed-array sonar to hang below it. In this way his own engine-plant noises would probably be deflected away from the American submarine.

Dubinin's tactical problem lay in his disadvantages. The American submarine was quieter than his, and possessed both better sonars and better sonar-operators. Senior Lieutenant Yevgeniy Nikolayevich Rykov was a very bright young officer, but he was the only sonar expert aboard who might fairly be matched against his American counterparts, and the boy was burning himself out. Captain Dubinin's only advantage lay in himself. He was a fine tactician, and knew it. And his American counterpart was not, Dubinin thought, and didn't know it. There was a final disadvantage. By staying on top of the layer, he made counterdetection by an American patrol aircraft easier, but Dubinin was willing to run that risk. What lay before him was a prize such as no Russian submarine commander had ever grasped.

Both Captain and Lieutenant stared at a "waterfall" display, looking not at a strobe of light, but instead a disjointed, barely visible vertical line that wasn't as bright as it should have been. The American Ohio-class was quieter than the background noise of the ocean, and both men wondered if somehow environmental conditions were showing them the acoustical shadow of that most sophisticated of missile submarines. It was just as likely, Dubinin thought, that fatigue was playing hallucinatory games with both of their minds.

"We need a transient," Rykov said, reaching for his tea. "A dropped tool, a slammed hatch . . . a mistake, a mistake. . . ."

I could ping him . . . I could duck below the layer and hit him with a blast of active sonar energy and find out . . . NO! Dubinin turned away and nearly swore at himself. *Patience, Valentin. They are patient, we must be patient.*

"Yevgeniy Nikolay'ch, you look weary."

"I can rest in Petropavlovsk, Captain. I will sleep for a week, and see my wife—well, I will not sleep entirely for that week," he said with an exhausted grin. The Lieutenant's face was illuminated by the yellow glow of the screen. "But I will not turn away from a chance like this one!"

"There will be no accidental transients."

"I know, Captain. Those damned American crews . . . I *know* it's him, I *know* it's an Ohio! What *else* could it be?"

"Imagination, Yevgeniy, imagination and too large a wish on our part."

Lieutenant Rykov turned. "I think my captain knows better than that!"

"I think my lieutenant is right." *Such a game this is! Ship against ship, mind against mind. Chess in three dimensions, played in an ever-changing physical environment.* And the Americans were the masters of the game. Dubinin knew that. Better equipment, better crews, better training. Of course the Americans knew that too, and two generations of advantage had generated arrogance rather than innovation . . . not in all, but certainly in some. A clever commander in the missile submarine would be doing things differently. . . . *If* I *had such a submarine, not all the world could find me!*

"Twelve more hours, then we must break contact and turn for home."

"Too bad," Rykov observed, not meaning it. Six weeks at sea was enough for him.

* * *

"Make your depth six-zero feet," the Officer of the Deck said.

"Make my depth six-zero feet, aye," the Diving Officer replied. "Ten degrees up on the fairwater planes."

The missile-firing drill had just begun. A regular occurrence, it was intended both to ensure the competence of the crew and desensitize them to their primary war-fighting mission, the launch of twenty-four UGM-93 Trident-II D-5 missiles, each with ten Mark 5 re-entry vehicles of 400 kilotons nominal yield. A total of two hundred forty warheads with a total net yield of 96 megatons. But there was more to it than that, since nuclear weapons depended on the interlocking logic of several physical laws. Small weapons employed their yield with greater efficiencies than larger ones. Most important of all, the Mark 5 RV had a demonstrated accuracy of ±50 meters CEP ("Circular Error Probable"), meaning that after a flight of over four thousand nautical miles, half the warheads would land within 164.041 *feet* of their targets, and nearly all the rest within 300 feet. The "miss" distance was far smaller than the crater to be expected from such a warhead, as a result of which the D-5 missile was the first sea-launched ballistic missile with counterforce capability. It was designed for a disarming first-strike. Given the normal two-at-one targeting, *Maine* could eliminate 120 Soviet missiles and/or missile-control bunkers, roughly ten percent of the current Soviet ICBM force, which was itself configured for a counterforce mission.

In the missile-control center—MCC—aft of the cavernous missile room, a senior chief petty officer lit up his panel. All twenty-four birds were on line. On-board navigation equipment fed data into each missile-guidance system. It would be updated in a few minutes from orbiting navigation satellites. To hit a target, the missile had to know not only where the target was, but also where the missile itself was starting from. The NAVSTAR Global Positioning System could do that with a tolerance of less than five meters. The senior chief watched status lights change as missiles were interrogated by his computers and reported their readiness.

Around the submarine, water pressure on the hull diminished at a rate of 2.2 tons per square foot for every 100 feet of rise toward the surface. *Maine*'s hull expanded slightly as the pressure was relieved, and there was a tiny amount of noise as steel relaxed from the compression.

It was only a groan, scarcely audible even over the sonar systems and seductively close to the call of a whale. Rykov was so drunk with fatigue that had it come a few minutes later he would have missed it, but though his daydreams were getting the best of him, his mind retained enough of its sharpness to take note of the sound.

"Captain . . . hull-popping noise . . . right there!" His finger stabbed the screen, just at the bottom of the shadow he and Dubinin had been examining. "He's coming shallow."

Dubinin raced into the control room. "Stand by to change depth." He put on a headset that connected him to Lieutenant Rykov.

"Yevgeniy Nikolay'ch, this must be done well and done quickly. I will drop below the layer just as the American goes over it."

"No, Captain, you can wait. His array will hang below briefly, as ours would do!"

"Damn!" Dubinin almost laughed. "Forgive me, Lieutenant. For that, a bottle of Starka." Which was the best Russian-made vodka.

"My wife and I will drink your health . . . I'm getting an angle reading. . . . Estimate target five degrees depression from our array. . . . Captain, if I can hold him, the moment we lose him through the layer—"

"Yes, a quick range estimate!" It would be crude, but it would be something. Dubinin rasped quick orders to his tracking officer.

"Two degrees . . . hull noises are gone . . . this is very hard to hold, but he's occulting the background a little more now—GONE! He's through the layer now!"

"One, two, three . . ." Dubinin counted. The American must be doing a missile drill, or coming up to receive communications, in any case he'd go to twenty meters depth, and his towed array . . . five hundred meters long . . . speed five knots, and . . . Now!

"Helm, down five degrees on the bow planes. We're going just below the layer. *Starpom,* make note of outside water temperature. Gently, helm, gently . . ."

Admiral Lunin dipped her bow and slid below the undulating border that marked the difference between relatively warm surface water and colder deep water.

"Range?" Dubinin asked his tracking officer.

"Estimate between five and nine thousand meters, Captain! Best I can do with the data."

"Well done, Kolya! Splendid."

"We're below the layer now, water temperature down five degrees!" the *Starpom* called.

"Bow planes to zero, level out."

"Planes to zero, Captain . . . zero angle on the boat."

Had there been enough overhead room, Dubinin would have leaped off his feet. He'd just done what no other Soviet submarine commander—and if his intelligence information was right, only a handful of Americans—had ever done. He'd established contact with and *tracked* an American Ohio-class fleet ballistic-missile submarine. In a war situation he'd be able to fire off ranging pings with his active sonar and launch torpedoes. He'd stalked the world's most elusive game, and was close enough for a killing shot. His skin tingled from the excitement of the moment. Nothing in the world could match this feeling. Nothing at all.

"Ryl nepravo," he said next. "Right rudder, new course three-zero-zero. Increase speed slowly to ten knots."

"But, Captain . . ." his *Starpom*—executive officer—said.

"We're breaking contact. He'll continue this drill for at least thirty minutes. It is very unlikely that we can evade counterdetection when he concludes it. Better to leave now. We do not want him to know what we have done. We will meet this one again. In any case our mission is accomplished. We have tracked him, and we got close enough to launch our attack. At Petropavlovsk, men, there will be much drinking, and your captain will do the buying! Now let's clear the area quietly so that he will not know that we were ever here."

Captain Robert Jefferson Jackson wished he was younger, wished that his hair was still completely black, that he could again be a young "nugget" fresh from Pensacola, ready to take his first hop in one of the forbidding fighter aircraft that sat like enormous birds of prey along the flight line at Oceana Naval Air Station. That all twenty-four of the F-14D Tomcats in the immediate area were his was not as satisfying as the knowledge that *one* was his and his alone. Instead, as Commander Air Group, he "owned" two Tomcat squadrons, two more of F/A-18 Hornets, one of A-6E Intruder medium-attack aircraft, another of S-3 submarine hunters, and finally the less glamorous tankers, electronic-warfare Prowlers, and rescue/ASW helicopters. A total of seventy-eight birds with an aggregate value of . . . what? A billion dollars? Much more if you considered replacement cost. Then there were the three thousand men who flew and serviced the aircraft, each of whom was beyond price, of course. He was responsible for all of it. It was much more fun to be a new fighter pilot who drove his personal airplane and left the worrying to management. Robby was now management, the guy the kids talked about in their cabins on the ship. They didn't want to be called into his office, because that was like going to see the Principal. They didn't really like flying with him, because (A) he was too old to be good at it anymore (they thought), and (B) he'd tell them whatever he thought they were doing wrong (fighter pilots do not often admit mistakes, except among themselves).

There was a certain irony to it. His previous job had been in the Pentagon, pushing papers. He'd prayed and lusted for release from that job, whose main excitement every day was finding a decent parking spot. Then he'd gotten command of his air wing—and been stuck with more admin crap than he'd ever faced in his life. At least he got to fly twice a week—if he was lucky. Today was such a day. His command master chief petty officer gave him a grin on the way out the door.

"Mind the store, Master Chief."

"Roger that, skipper. It'll be here when you get back."

Jackson stopped in his tracks. "You *can* have someone steal all the paperwork."

"I'll see what I can do, sir."

A staff car took him to the flight line. Jackson was already in his Nomex flight suit, an old smelly one whose olive-drab color was faded from many washings, and threadbare at the elbows and seat from years of use. He could and should have gotten a new one, but pilots are superstitious creatures; Robby and this flight suit had been through a lot together.

"Hey, skipper!" called one of his squadron commanders.

Commander Bud Sanchez was shorter than Jackson. His olive skin and Bismarck mustache accentuated bright eyes and a grin right out of a toothpaste commercial. Sanchez, Commanding Officer of VF-1, would fly Jackson's wing today. They'd flown together when Jackson had commanded VF-41 off the *John F. Kennedy*. "Your bird is all dialed in. Ready to kick a little ass?"

"Who's the opposition today?"

"Some jarheads out of Cherry Point in -18-Deltas. We got a Hummer already orbiting a hundred miles out, and the exercise is BARCAP against low-level intruders." BARCAP meant Barrier Combat Air Patrol. The mission was to prevent attacking aircraft from crossing a line that they were not supposed to cross. "Up to some heavy ACM? Those Marines sounded a little cocky over the phone."

"The Marine I can't take ain't been born yet," Robby said as he pulled his helmet off the rack. It bore his call sign, Spade.

"Hey, you RIOs," Sanchez called, "quit holdin' hands and let's get it on!"

"On the way, Bud." Michael "Lobo" Alexander came from around the lockers, followed by Jackson's radar-intercept officer, Henry "Shredder" Walters. Both were under thirty, both lieutenants. In the locker room, people talked by call sign rather than rank. Robby loved the fellowship of squadron life as much as he loved his country.

Outside, the plane captains—petty officers—who were responsible for maintaining the aircraft walked the officers to their respective birds and helped them aboard. (On the dangerous area of a carrier flight deck, pilots are led virtually by the hand by enlisted men, lest they get lost or hurt.) Jackson's bird had a double-zero ID number on the nose. Under the cockpit was painted ''CAPT R.J. Jackson 'SPADE' '' to make sure that everyone knew that this was the CAG's bird. Under that was a flag representing a MiG-29 fighter aircraft that an Iraqi had mistakenly flown too close to Jackson's Tomcat not so long before. There hadn't been much to it—the other pilot had forgotten, once, to check his ''six'' and paid the price—but a kill was a kill, and kills were what fighter pilots lived for.

Five minutes later, all four men were strapped in, and engines were turning.

''How are you this morning, Shredder?'' Jackson asked over his intercom.

''Ready to waste some Marines, skipper. Lookin' good back here. Is this thing gonna fly today?''

''Guess it's time to find out.'' Jackson switched to radio. ''Bud, this is Spade, ready here.''

''Roger, Spade, you have the lead.'' Both pilots looked around, got an all-clear from their plane captains, and looked around again.

''Spade has the lead.'' Jackson tripped his brakes. ''Rolling now.''

''Hello, *mein Schatz,*'' Manfred Fromm said to his wife.

Traudl rushed forward to embrace him. ''Where have you been?''

''That I cannot say,'' Fromm replied with a knowing twinkle in his eye. He hummed a few bars from Lloyd Webber's ''Don't Cry for Me, Argentina.''

''I knew you would see,'' Traudl beamed at him.

''You must not talk of this.'' To confirm her suspicion he handed her a wad of banknotes, five packets of ten thousand D-Marks each. *That should keep the mercenary bitch quiet and happy,* Manfred Fromm told himself. ''And I will only be here overnight. I had some business to do, and of course—''

''Of course, Manfred.'' She hugged him again, the money in her hands. ''If only you had called!''

Arrangements had been absurdly easy to make. A ship outbound for Latakia, Syria, was sailing from Rotterdam in seventy hours. He and Bock had arranged for a commercial trucking company to load the machine tools into a small cargo container which would be loaded on the ship and unloaded onto a Syrian dock in six more days. It would have been faster to send the tools by air, or even by rail to a Greek or Italian port for faster transshipment by sea, but Rotterdam was the world's busiest port, with overworked customs officials whose main task was searching for drug shipments. Sniffer dogs could go over that particular container to their hearts' content.

Fromm let his wife go into the kitchen to make coffee. It would take a few minutes, and that was all he needed. He walked down into his basement. In the corner, as far from the water heater as was possible, was an orderly pile of lumber, on top of which were four black metal boxes. Each weighed about ten kilograms, about twenty-five pounds. Fromm carried one at a time—on the second trip, he got a pair of gloves from his bureau drawer to protect his hands—and placed them in the trunk of his rented BMW. By the time the coffee was ready, his task was complete.

''You have a fine tan,'' Traudl observed, carrying the tray out from the kitchen. In her mind she'd already spent about a quarter of the money her husband had given her. So Manfred had seen the light. She'd known he would, sooner or later. Better that it should be sooner. She'd be especially nice to him tonight.

* * *

"Günther?"

Bock didn't like leaving Fromm to his own devices, but he also had a task to perform. This was a far greater risk. It was, he told himself, a high-risk operational concept, even if the real dangers were in the planning stage, which was both an oddity and a relief.

Erwin Keitel lived on a pension, and not an especially comfortable one at that. Its necessity came from two facts. First, he was a former Lieutenant Colonel in the East German Stasi, the intelligence and counterintelligence arm of the defunct German Democratic Republic; second, he had liked his work of thirty-two years. Whereas most of his former colleagues had acknowledged the changes in their country and for the most part put their German identity ahead of whatever ideology they'd once held—and told literally everything they knew to the *Bundesnachrichtendienst*—Keitel had decided that he was not going to work for capitalists. That made him one of the "politically unemployed" citizens of the united Germany. His pension was a matter of convenience. The new German government honored, after a fashion, pre-existing government obligations. It was at the least politically expedient, and what Germany now was, was a matter of daily struggling with facts that were not and could not be reconciled. It was easier to give Keitel a pension than to leave him on the official dole, which was deemed more demeaning than a pension. By the government, that is. Keitel didn't see things quite that way. If the world made any sense at all, he thought, he would have been executed or exiled—exactly where he might have been exiled to, Keitel didn't know. He'd begun to consider going over to the Russians—he'd had good contacts in the KGB—but that thought had died a quick death. The Soviets had washed their hands of everything to do with the DDR, fearing treachery from people whose allegiance to world socialism—or whatever the hell the Russians stood for now, Keitel had no idea—was somewhat less than their allegiance to their new country. Keitel took his seat beside Bock's in the corner booth of a quiet *Gasthaus* in what had formerly been East Berlin.

"This is very dangerous, my friend."

"I am aware of that, Erwin." Bock waved for two liter glasses of beer. Service was quicker than it had been a few years before, but both men ignored that.

"I cannot tell you how I feel about what they did to Petra," Keitel said after the girl left them.

"Do you know exactly what happened?" Bock asked in a level and emotionless voice.

"The detective who ran the case visited her in prison—he did so quite often—not for interrogation. They made a conscious effort to push her over the edge. You must understand, Günther, courage in a man or a woman is a finite quality. It was not weakness on her part. Anyone can break. It is simply a matter of time. They watched her die," the retired colonel said.

"Oh?" Bock's face didn't change, but his knuckles went white on the stein handle.

"There was a television camera hidden in her cell. They have her suicide on videotape. They watched her do it, and did nothing to stop her."

Bock didn't say anything, and the room was too dim to see how pale his face went. It was as though a hot blast from a furnace swept over him, followed by one from the North Pole. He closed his eyes for a brief second to get control of himself.

Petra would not have wished him to be governed by emotion at a time like this. He opened his eyes to look at his friend.

"Is that a fact?"

"I know the name of the detective. I know his address. I still have friends," Keitel assured Bock.

"Yes, Erwin, I am sure you do. I need your help to do something."

"Anything."

"You know, of course, what brought us to this."

"That depends on how you mean it," Keitel said. "The people disappointed me in the way they allowed themselves to be seduced, but the common people always lack the discipline to know what is good for them. The real cause of our national misfortune. . . ."

"Precisely—the Americans and the Russians."

"Mein lieber Günther, even a united Germany cannot—"

"Yes, it can. If we are to remake the world into our image, Erwin, both of our oppressors must be damaged severely."

"But how?"

"There is a way. Can you believe me that much, just for now?"

Keitel drained his beer and sat back. He'd helped train Bock. At fifty-six, it was too late for him to change his ideas of the world, and he was still a fine judge of character. Bock was a man such as himself. Günther had been a careful, ruthless, and very effective clandestine operator.

"What of our detective friend?"

Bock shook his head. "As much satisfaction as that might give me, no. This is not a time for personal revenge. We have a movement and a country to save." *More than one, in fact,* Bock thought, but this was not the time for that. What was taking shape in his mind was a grand stroke, a breathtaking maneuver that might—he was too intellectually honest to say *would,* even to himself—change the world into a more malleable shape. Exactly what would happen after that, who could say? That would not matter at all if he and his friends were unable to take the first bold step.

"How long have we known each other—fifteen years, twenty?" Keitel smiled. *"Aber natürlich.* Of course I can trust you."

"How many others can we trust?"

"How many do we need?"

"No more than ten, but we will need a total of ten."

Keitel's face went blank. *Eight men we can trust absolutely . . . ?*

"That is too many for safety, Günther. What sort of men?" Bock told him. "I know where to start. It should be possible . . . men of my age . . . and some younger, of your age. The physical skills you require are not difficult to obtain, but remember that much of this is beyond our control."

"As some of my friends say, that is in God's hands," Günther said with a smirk.

"Barbarians," Keitel snorted. "I have never liked them."

"Ja, doch, they don't even let a man have a beer." Bock smiled. "But they are strong, Erwin, they are determined, and they are faithful to the cause."

"Whose cause is that?"

"One we both share at the moment. How much time do you need?"

"Two weeks. I can be reached—"

"No." Bock shook his head. "Too risky. Can you travel, are you being watched?"

"Watch me? All of my subordinates have changed allegiance, and the BND knows that the KGB will have nothing to do with me. They would not waste the assets to watch me. I am a gelding, you see?"

"Some gelding, Erwin." Bock handed over some cash. "We will meet in Cyprus in two weeks. Make sure you are not followed."

"I will—I do. I have not forgotten how, my friend."

Fromm awoke at dawn. He dressed at leisure, trying not to wake Traudl. She'd been more of a wife in the past twelve hours than in the preceding twelve months, and his conscience told him that their nearly failed marriage had not been entirely her fault. He was surprised to find breakfast waiting on the table for him.

"When will you be back?"

"I'm not sure. Probably several months."

"That long?"

"*Mein Schatz,* the reason I am there is that they need what I know, and I am being well paid." He made a mental note to have Qati send additional funds. So long as money kept coming in, she'd not be nervous.

"It is not possible for me to join you?" Traudl asked, showing real affection for her man.

"It is no place for a woman." Which was honest enough that his conscience allowed itself to relax a little. He finished his coffee. "I must be off."

"Hurry back."

Manfred Fromm kissed his wife and walked out the door. The BMW was not affected in the least by the fifty kilos of weight in the trunk. He waved to Traudl one last time before driving off. He gave the house a final look in the mirror, thinking, correctly, that he might not see it again.

His next stop was the Karl Marx Astrophysical Institute. The single-story buildings were already showing their neglect, and it surprised him that vandals had not broken windows. The truck was already there. Fromm used his keys to let himself into the machine shop. The tools were still there, still in hermetically sealed crates, and the crates were still marked *Astrophysical Instruments*. It was just a matter of signing some forms he'd typed up the previous afternoon. The truck driver knew how to operate the propane-fueled forklift, and drove each crate into the container. Fromm took the batteries from the trunk of his car and set them in a final, small box, which was loaded on last. It took the driver an additional half hour to chain things down in place, and then he drove off. He and "Herr Professor Fromm" would meet again outside Rotterdam.

Fromm rendezvoused with Bock in Greifswald. They drove west in the latter's car—Bock was a better driver.

"How was home?"

"Traudl liked the money a great deal," Fromm reported.

"We'll send her more, at regular intervals . . . every two weeks, I think."

"Good. I was going to ask Qati about that."

"We take care of our friends," Bock observed as they passed over what had once been a border crossing. Now it was merely green.

"How long for the fabrication process?"

"Three months . . . maybe four. We could go faster," Fromm said apologetically, "but remember that I have never actually done this with real material, only in simulation. There is absolutely no margin for error. It will be complete by the middle of January. At that point, it is yours to use." Fromm wondered, of course, what plans Bock and the others had for it, but that was not really his concern, was it? *Doch.*

15. Development

Ghosn could only shake his head. He knew objectively that it resulted from the sweeping political changes in Europe, the effective elimination of borders attendant to the economic unification, the collapse of the Warsaw Pact and headlong rush to join in the new European family. Even so, the hardest part of getting these five machine tools out of Germany and into his valley had been finding a suitable truck at Latakia, and that had actually been rather difficult, since negotiating the road into where his shop lay had incomprehensibly been overlooked by everyone—including, he thought with some satisfaction, the German. Fromm was now observing closely as a gang of men labored to move the last of the five tools onto its table. Arrogant as he may have been, Fromm was an expert technologist. Even the tables had been built to exactly the right size, with ten centimeters of extra space around each tool so that one could rest his notebook. The backup generators and UPSs were in place and tested. It was just a matter of getting the tools set up and fully calibrated, which would take about a week.

Bock and Qati were observing the whole procedure from the far end of the building, careful to keep out of the way.

"I have the beginnings of an operational plan," Günther said.

"You do not intend the bomb for Israel, then?" Qati asked. He was the one who would approve or disapprove the plan. He would, however, listen to his German friend. "Can you tell me of it yet?"

"Yes." Bock did so.

"Interesting. What of security?"

"One problem is our friend Manfred—more properly, his wife. She knows his skills, and she knows he is away somewhere."

"I would have thought that killing her carries more risks than rewards."

"Ordinarily it would appear so, but all of Fromm's fellow experts are also away—with their wives in most cases. Were she merely to disappear, it would be assumed by the neighbors that she'd joined her husband. His absence risks a comment by her, however casual it might be, that Manfred is off doing something. Someone might notice."

"Does she actually know what his former job was?"

"Manfred is very security-conscious, but we must assume that she does. What woman does not?"

"Go on," Qati said tiredly.

"Discovery of her body will force the police to search for her husband, and that is also a problem. She must disappear. Then it will seem that she has joined her husband."

"Instead of the other way around," Qati observed with a rare smile, "at the end of the project."

"Quite so."

"What sort of woman is she?"

"A shrew, a money-grabber, not a believer," Bock, an atheist, said, somewhat to Qati's amusement.

"How will you do it?"

Bock explained briefly. "It will also validate the reliability of our people for that part of the operation. I'll leave the details to my friends."

"Trickery? One cannot be overly careful in an enterprise like this one."

"If you wish, a videotape of the elimination? Something unequivocal?" Bock had done that before.

"It is barbaric," Qati said. "But regrettably necessary."

"I will take care of that when I go to Cyprus."

"You'll need security for that trip, my friend."

"Yes, thank you, I think I will." Bock knew what that meant. If his capture looked imminent—well, he was in a profession that entailed serious risks, and Qati had to be careful. Günther's own operational proposal made that all the more imperative.

"The tools all have levelers for the air plates," Ghosn said in annoyance, fifteen meters away. "Very good ones—why all the trouble with the table?"

"My young friend, this is something we can only do one time. Do you wish to take any chances at all?"

Ghosn nodded. The man was right, even if he was a patronizing son of a bitch. "And the tritium?"

"In those batteries. I've kept them in a cool place. You release the tritium by heating them. The procedure for recovering the tritium is delicate but straightforward."

"Ah, yes, I know how to do that." Ghosn remembered such lab experiments from university.

Fromm handed him a copy of the manual for the first tool. "Now, we both have new things to learn so that we can teach the operators."

Captain Dubinin sat in the office of the Master Shipwright of the yard. Known variously as Shipyard Number 199, Leninskaya Komsomola, or simply Komsomol'sk, it was the yard at which the *Admiral Lunin* had been built. Himself a former submarine commander, the man preferred the title Master Shipwright to Superintendent and had changed the title on his office door accordingly on taking the job two years earlier. He was a traditionalist, but also a brilliant engineer. Today he was a happy man.

"While you were gone, I got hold of something wonderful!"

"What might that be, Admiral?"

"The prototype for a new reactor feed pump. It's big, cumbersome, and a cast-iron bastard to install and maintain, but it's—"

"Quiet?"

"As a thief," the Admiral said with a smile. "It reduces the radiated noise of your current pump by a factor of fifty."

"Indeed? Who did we steal that from?"

The Master Shipwright laughed at that. "You don't need to know, Valentin Borissovich. Now, I have a question for you: I have heard that you did something very clever ten days ago."

Dubinin smiled. "Admiral, that is something which I cannot—"

"Yes, you can. I spoke with your squadron commander. Tell me, how close did you get to USS *Nevada?*"

"I think it was actually *Maine,*" Dubinin said. The intelligence types disagreed, but he went with his instincts. "About eight thousand meters. We identified him from a mechanical transient made during an exercise, then I proceeded to stalk on the basis of a couple of wild guesses—"

"Rubbish! Humility can be overdone, Captain. Go on."

"And after tracking what we thought was our target, he confirmed it with a hull transient. I think he came up to conduct a rocket-firing drill. At that point, given our operational schedule and the tactical situation, I elected to break contact while it was possible to do so without counterdetection."

"That was your cleverest move of all," the Master Shipwright said, pointing a finger at his guest. "You could not have decided better, because the next time you go out, you will be the most quiet submarine we've ever put to sea."

"They still have the advantage over us," Dubinin pointed out honestly.

"That is true, but for once the advantage will be less than the difference between one commander and another, which is as it should be. We both studied under Marko Ramius. If only he were here to see this!"

Dubinin nodded agreement. "Yes, given current political circumstances it is truly a game of skill, not one of malice anymore."

"Would that I were young enough to play," the Master Shipwright said.

"And the new sonar?"

"This is our design from the Severomorsk Laboratory, a large-aperture array, roughly a forty-percent improvement in sensitivity. On the whole, you will be the equal of an American Los Angeles class in nearly all regimes."

Except crew, Dubinin didn't say. It would be years before his country had the ability to train men as the Western navies did, and by that time Dubinin would no longer have command at sea—*but!* In three months time he'd have the best ship that his nation had ever given one of its captains. If he were able to cajole his squadron commander into giving him a larger officer complement, he could beach the more inept of his conscripts and begin a really effective training regimen for the rest. Training and leading the crew was his job. He was the commanding officer of *Admiral Lunin*. He took credit for what went well and blame for what went badly. Ramius had taught him that from the first day aboard the first submarine. His fate was in his own hands, and what man could ask for more than that?

Next year, USS Maine, *when the bitterly cold storms of winter sweep across the North Pacific, we will meet again.*

"Not a single contact," Captain Ricks said in the wardroom.

"Except for *Omaha.*" LCDR Claggett looked over some paperwork. "And he was in too much of a hurry."

"Ivan doesn't even try anymore. Like he's gone out of business." It was almost a lament from the Navigator.

"Why even try to find us?" Ricks observed. "Hell, aside from that Akula that got lost . . ."

"We did track the guy a while back," Nav pointed out.

"Maybe next time we'll get some hull shots," a lieutenant observed lightly from behind a magazine. There was general laughter. Some of the more extreme fast-attack skippers had on very rare occasions maneuvered close enough to some Soviet submarines to take flash photographs of their hulls. But that was a thing of the past.

The Russians were a lot better at the submarine game than they'd been only ten years earlier. Being number two did make one try harder.

"Now, the next engineering drill," Ricks said.

The Executive Officer noted that the faces around the table didn't change. The officers were learning not to groan or roll their eyes. Ricks had a very limited sense of humor.

"Hello, Robby!" Joshua Painter got up from his swivel chair and walked over to shake hands with his visitor.

"Morning, sir."

"Grab a seat." A steward served coffee to both men. "How's the wing look?"

"I think we'll be ready on time, sir."

Admiral Joshua Painter, USN, was Supreme Allied Commander Atlantic, Commander-in-Chief Atlantic, and Commander-in-Chief U.S. Atlantic Fleet—they paid him only one salary for the three jobs, though he did have three staffs to do his thinking for him. A career aviator—mainly fighters—he had reached the summit of his career. He would not be selected for Chief of Naval Operations. Someone with fewer politically rough edges would get that job, but Painter was content. Under the rather eccentric organization of the armed services, the CNO and other service chiefs merely advised the Secretary of Defense. The SecDef was the one who gave the orders to the area CINCs—commanders-in-chief. SACLANT-CINCLANT-CINCLANTFLT might have been an awkward, cumbersome, and generally bloated command, but it was a *command*. Painter owned real ships, real airplanes, and real Marines, had the authority to tell them where to go and what to do. Two complete fleets, 2nd and 6th, came under his authority: seven aircraft carriers, a battleship—though an aviator, Painter rather liked battleships; his grandfather had commanded one—over a hundred destroyers and cruisers, sixty submarines, a division and a half of Marines, thousands of combat aircraft. The fact of the matter was that only one country in the world had more combat power than Joshua Painter did, and that country was no longer a serious strategic threat in these days of international amity. He no longer had to look forward to the possibility of war. Painter was a happy man. A man who'd flown missions over Vietnam, he'd seen American power go from its post–World War II peak to its nadir in the 1970s, then bounce back again until America once more was the most powerful country on earth. He'd played his part in the best of times and the worst of times, and now the best of times were better still. Robby Jackson was one of the men to whom his Navy would be turned over.

"What's this I heard about Soviet pilots in Libya again?" Jackson asked.

"Well, they never really left, did they?" Painter asked rhetorically. "Our friend wants their newest weapons, and he's paying with hard cash. They need the cash. It's business. That's simple enough."

"You'd think he'd learn," Robby observed with a shake of the head.

"Well, maybe he will . . . soon. It must be real lonely being the last of the hotheads. Maybe that's why he's loading up while he still can. That's what the intel people say."

"And the Russians?"

"Quite a lot of instructors and technical people there on contract, especially aviators and SAM types."

"Nice to know. If our friend tries anything, he's got some good stuff to hide behind."

"Not good enough to stop you, Robby."

"Good enough to make me write some letters." Jackson had written enough of those. As a CAG, he could look forward on this cruise—as with every other he'd ever taken—to deaths in his air wing. To the best of his knowledge, no carrier had ever sailed for a deployment, whether in peace or war, without some fatalities, and as the "owner" of the air wing, the deaths were his responsibility. *Wouldn't it be nice to be the first,* Jackson thought. Aside from the fact that it would look good on his record, not having to tell a wife or a set of parents that Johnny had lost his life in service of his country . . . possible, but not likely, Robby told himself. Naval aviation was too dangerous. Past forty now, knowing that immortality was something between a myth and a joke, he had already found himself staring at the pilots in the squadron ready rooms and wondering which of the handsome, proud young faces would not be around when *TR* again made landfall at the Virginia Capes, whose pretty, pregnant wife would find a chaplain and another aviator on her doorstep just before lunch, along with a squadron wife to hold her hand when the world ended in distant fire and blood. A possible clash with Libyans was just one more threat in a universe where death was a permanent resident. He'd gotten too old for this life, Jackson admitted quietly to himself. Still as fine a fighter pilot as any—he was too mature to call himself the world's best anymore, except over drinks—the sadder aspects of the life were catching up, and it would soon be time to move on, if he were lucky, to an admiral's flag, just flying occasionally to show he still knew how and trying to make the good decisions that would minimize the unwanted visits.

"Problems?" Painter asked.

"Spares," Captain Jackson replied. "It's getting harder to keep all the birds up."

"Doing the best we can."

"Yes, sir, I know. Going to get worse, too, if I'm reading the papers right." Like maybe three carriers would be retired, along with their air wings. Didn't people ever learn?

"Every time we've won a war we've been punished for it," CINCLANT said. "At least winning this one didn't cost us a whole lot. Don't worry, there'll be a place for you when the time comes. You're my best wing commander, Captain."

"Thank you, sir. I don't mind hearing things like that."

Painter laughed. "Neither did I."

"There is a saying in English," Golovko observed. " 'With friends like these, who has need of enemies?' What else do we know?"

"It would appear that they turned over their entire supply of plutonium," the man said. A representative of the weapons research and design institute at Sarova, south of Gorkiy, he was less a weapons engineer than a scientist who kept track of what people outside the Soviet Union were up to. "I ran the calculations myself. It is theoretically possible that they developed more of the material, but what they turned over to us slightly exceeds our own production of plutonium from plants of similar design here in the Soviet Union. I think we got it all from them."

"I have read all that. Why are you here now?"

"The original study overlooked something."

"And what might that be?" the First Deputy Chairman of the Committee for State Security asked.

"Tritium."

"And that is?" Golovko didn't remember. He was not an expert on nuclear materials, being more grounded in diplomatic and intelligence operations.

The man from Sarova hadn't taught basic physics in years. "Hydrogen is the simplest of materials. An atom of hydrogen contains a proton, which is positively charged, and an electron, which is negatively charged. If you add a neutron—that has no electrical charge—to the hydrogen atom, you get deuterium. Add another, and you get tritium. It has three times the atomic weight of hydrogen because of the additional neutrons. In simple terms, neutrons are the stuff of atomic weapons. When you liberate them from their host atoms, they radiate outward, bombarding other atomic nuclei, releasing more neutrons. That causes a chain reaction, releasing vast amounts of energy. Tritium is useful because the hydrogen atom is not supposed to contain any neutrons at all, much less two of them. It is unstable, and tends to break down at a fixed rate. The half-life of tritium is 12.3 years," he explained. "Thus, if you insert tritium in a fission device, the additional neutrons it adds to the initial fission reaction accelerate or 'boost' the fission in the plutonium or uranium reaction mass by a factor of between five and forty, allowing a far more efficient use of the heavy fission materials like plutonium or enriched uranium. Secondly, additional amounts of tritium placed in the proper location nearby the fission device—called a 'primary' in this case—begin a fusion reaction. There are other ways of doing this, of course. The chemicals of choice are lithium-deuteride and lithium-hydride, which is more stable, but tritium is still extremely useful for certain weapons applications."

"And how does one make tritium?"

"Essentially by placing large quantities of lithium-aluminum in a nuclear reactor and allowing the thermal neutron flux—that's an engineering term for the back-and-forth traffic of the particles—to irradiate and transform lithium to tritium by capture of some of the neutrons. It turns up as small, faceted bubbles inside the metal. I believe that the Germans also manufactured tritium at their Greifswald plant."

"Why? What evidence do you have?"

"We analyzed the plutonium they sent us. Plutonium has two isotopes, Plutonium-239 and -240. From the relative proportions, you can determine the neutron flux in the reactor. The German sample has too little 240. Something was attenuating the neutron flux. That something was probably—almost certainly—tritium."

"You are certain of that?"

"The physics involved here are complex but straightforward. In fact you can in many cases identify the plant that produced a plutonium sample by examining the ratio of various materials. My team and I are quite certain of our conclusions."

"Those plants were under international inspection, yes? Are there no controls on the production of tritium?"

"The Germans managed to circumvent some of the plutonium inspections, and there are no international controls on tritium at all. Even if there were such controls, concealing tritium production would be child's play."

Golovko swore under his breath. "How much?"

The scientist shrugged. "Impossible to say. The plant is being completely shut down. We no longer have access to it."

"Doesn't tritium have other uses?"

"Oh, yes. It's commercially very valuable. It's phosphorescent—glows in the dark. People use it for watch dials, gunsights, instrument faces, all manner of applications. It is commercially very valuable, on the order of fifty thousand American dollars per gram.''

Golovko was surprised at himself for the digression. ''Back up for a moment, please. You tell me that our Fraternal Socialist Comrades in the German Democratic Republic were working not only to make their own atomic bombs, but also hydrogen bombs?''

''Yes, that is likely.''

''And one element of this plan is unaccounted for?''

''Also correct—possibly correct,'' the man corrected himself.

''Likely?'' It was like extracting an admission from a child, the First Deputy Chairman thought.

''*Da*. In their place, given the directives they received from Erich Honecker, it is certainly something I would have done. It was, moreover, technically quite simple to do. After all, we gave them the reactor technology.''

''What in hell were we thinking about?'' Golovko muttered to himself.

''Yes, we made the same mistake with the Chinese, didn't we?''

''Didn't anyone—'' The engineer cut him off.

''Of course there were warnings voiced. From my institute and the one at Kyshtym. No one listened. It was judged politically expedient to make this technology available to our allies.'' The last word was delivered evenly.

''And you think we should do something?''

''I suppose we could ask our colleagues in the Foreign Ministry, but it would be worthwhile to get something substantive done. So I decided to come here.''

''You think, then, that the Germans—the new Germans, I mean—might have a supply of fissionable material and this tritium from which they might make their own nuclear arsenal?''

''That is a real possibility. There are, as you know, a sizable number of German nuclear scientists who are mainly working in South America at the moment. The best of all possible worlds for them. They are doing what may well be weapons-related research twelve thousand kilometers from home, learning that which they need to learn at a distant location, and on someone else's payroll. If that is indeed the case, are they doing so merely as a business venture? I suppose that is a possibility, but it would seem more likely that their government has some knowledge of the affair. Since their government has taken no action to stop them, one must assume that their government approves of that activity. The most likely reason for their government to approve is the possible application of the knowledge they are acquiring for German national interests.''

Golovko frowned. His visitor had just strung three possibilities into a threat. He was thinking like an intelligence officer, and an especially paranoid one at that. But those were often the best kind.

''What else do you have?''

''Thirty possible names.'' He handed a file over. ''We've spoken with our people—those who helped the Germans set up the Greifswald plant, I mean. Based on their recollections, these are the people most likely to be part of the project, if any. Half a dozen of them are remembered as being very clever indeed, good enough to work with us at Sarova.''

''Any of them make overt inquiries into—''

''No, and not necessary. Physics is physics. Fission is fission. Laws of science do not respect rules of classification. You cannot conceal nature, and that's exactly what we're dealing with here. If these people can operate a reactor, then the best of them can design nuclear weapons, given the necessary materials—and our reactor design *gave* them the ability to generate the proper materials. I think it is something you need to look into—to see what they did, and what they have. In any case, that is my advice."

"I have some very good people in Directorate T of the First Chief Directorate," Golovko said. "After we digest this information, some of them will come to speak with you." Sarova was only a few hours away by train.

"Yes, I've met with some of your technology analysts. A few of them are very good indeed. I hope you still have good contacts in Germany."

Golovko didn't answer that. He had many contacts still in Germany, but how many of them had been doubled? He'd recently done a reliability assessment of former penetration agents in the Stasi, and concluded that none could be trusted—more properly, that those who could be trusted were no longer in positions of any use, and even those . . . He decided on the spot to make this an all-Russian operation.

"If they have the materials, how soon might they fabricate weapons?"

"Given their level of technical expertise, and the fact that they've had access to American systems under NATO, there is no reason whatever why they could not have homemade weapons already in their inventory. They would not be crude weapons, either. In their position, and given the special nuclear materials, I could easily have produced two-stage weapons within months of unification. More sophisticated three-stage weapons . . . maybe another year."

"Where would you do it?"

"In East Germany, of course. Better security. Exactly where?" The man thought for a minute. "Look for a place with extremely precise machine tools, the sort associated with high-precision optical instruments. The X-ray telescope we just orbited was a direct spinoff of H-Bomb research. Management of X-rays, you see, is very important in a multistage weapon. We learned much of American bomb technology from open-source papers on focusing X-rays for astrophysical observations. As I said, it's physics. It cannot be hidden, only discovered; once discovered, it is open for all who have the intelligence and the desire to make use of it."

"That is so wonderfully reassuring," Golovko observed crossly. But who could he be angry with—this man for speaking the truth, or Nature for being so easy to discover? "Excuse me, Professor. Thank you very much indeed for taking the time to bring this to our attention."

"My father is a mathematics teacher. He has lived his entire life in Kiev. He remembers the Germans."

Golovko saw the man out the door, then walked back to stare out the window. *Why did we ever let them unify?* he asked himself. *Do they still want land?* Lebensraum? *Do they still want to be the dominant European power? Or are you being paranoid, Sergey?* He was paid to be paranoid, of course. Golovko sat down and lifted his phone.

"It is a small thing, and if it is necessary nothing more needs to be said," Keitel replied to the question.

"And the men?"

"I have what I need, and they are reliable. All have worked overseas, mainly in Africa. All are experienced. Three colonels, six lieutenant colonels, two majors—all of them retired like me."

"Reliability is all-important," Bock reminded the man.

"I know that, Günther. Each of these men would have been a general someday. Each has impeccable Party credentials. Why do you think they were retired, eh? Our New Germany cannot trust them."

"Agent-provocateurs?"

"I am the intelligence officer here," Keitel reminded his friend. "I do not tell you your job. Don't you tell me mine. Please, my friend, either you trust me or you do not. That choice is yours."

"I know that, Erwin. Forgive me. This operation is most important."

"And I know that, Günther."

"How soon can you do it?"

"Five days—I'd prefer that we take longer, but I am prepared to move quickly. The problem, of course, is disposing of the body in a suitable manner."

Bock nodded. That was something he'd never had to worry about. The Red Army Faction had rarely had to worry about that—except in the case of the turncoat Green woman who'd blown that one operation. But that one had been happenstance rather than design. Burying her in a national forest had been done—out of humor actually, not that he had thought of it, putting her back into the ecology she'd loved so much. It had been Petra's idea.

"How will I deliver the videotape to you?"

"Someone will meet you here. Not me, someone else. Stay at the same hotel two weeks from today. You will be met. Conceal the tape cassette in a book."

"Very well." Keitel thought Bock was overdoing things. Cloak-and-dagger was such a game that amateurs enjoyed playing it more than the professionals, for whom it was merely the job. Why not simply put the thing in a box and wrap it in plastic like a movie cassette? "I will soon need some funding."

Bock handed over an envelope. "A hundred thousand marks."

"That will do nicely. Two weeks from today." Keitel left Bock to pay the bill and walked off.

Günther ordered another beer, staring off to the sea, cobalt blue under a clear sky. Ships were passing out on the horizon—one was a naval vessel, whose he couldn't tell at that distance, and the rest were simply merchantmen plying their trade from one unknown port to another.

On a day like this, a warm sun and a cool ocean breeze. Not far away was a beach of powdery white sand where children and lovers could enjoy the water. He thought of Petra and Erika and Ursel. No one passing by could tell from his face. The overt emotions of his loss were behind him. He'd wept and raged enough to exorcise them, but within him were the higher emotions of cold fury and revenge. So fine a day it was, and he had no one with whom to enjoy it. Whatever fine days might come later would find him just as alone. There would never be another Petra for him. He might find a girl here to use, just as some sort of biological exercise, but that wouldn't change things. He would be alone for the remainder of his life. It was not a pleasant thought. No love, no children, no personal future. Around him the terrace bar was about half full of people, mainly Europeans, mainly on vacation with their families, smiling and laughing as they drank their beer or wine or other local concoctions, thinking ahead to the entertainments the night might hold, the intimate dinners, and the cool cotton sheets that would follow, the laughter and the affection—all the things that the world had denied Günther Bock.

He hated them all, sitting there alone, his eyes sweeping over the scene as he might have done a zoo, watching the animals. Bock detested them for their laughter and their smiles . . . and their futures. It wasn't fair. He'd had a purpose in life, a goal to strive for. They had jobs. Fifty or so weeks per year they left their homes and drove to their workplaces and did whatever unimportant thing it was that they did, and came home, and like good Europeans saved their money for the annual fling in the Aegean, or Majorca, or America, or someplace where there was sun and clean air and a beach. Pointless though their lives might have been, they had the happiness that life had denied to the solitary man sitting in the shade of a white umbrella, staring out to sea again and sipping at his beer. It was not fair, not the least bit fair. He had devoted his life to their welfare—and they had the life that he'd hoped to give them, while he had less than nothing.

Except his mission.

Bock decided that he would not lie to himself on this issue any more than he did on others. He hated them. Hated them all. If he didn't have a future, why should they? If happiness was a stranger to him, why should it be their companion? He hated them because they had rejected him and Petra, and Qati, and all the rest who fought against injustice and oppression. In doing that, they had chosen the bad over the good—and for that one was damned. He was more than they were, Bock knew, he was better than they could ever hope to be. He could look down on all of them and their pointless little lives, and whatever he did to them—for them, he still tried to believe—was for him alone to decide. If some of them were hurt, that was too bad. They were not really people. They were empty shadows of what could have been people if they'd lived lives of purpose. They had not cast him out, they'd cast themselves out, seeking the happiness that came from . . . whatever lives they led. The lazy way. Like cattle. Bock imagined them, heads down in feeding troughs, making contented barnyard noises while he surveyed them. If some had to die—and some *did* have to die—should it trouble him? Not at all, Günther decided.

"*Mister* President . . ."

"Yes, Elizabeth?" Fowler replied with a chuckle.

"When's the last time someone told you how good a lover you are?"

"I sure don't hear that in the Cabinet Room." Fowler was speaking to the top of her head, which nestled on his chest. Her left arm was wrapped around his chest, while his left hand stroked her blond hair. The fact of the matter, the President thought, was that he was indeed pretty good at this. He had patience, which he judged the most important talent for the business. Liberation and equal-rights issues notwithstanding, it was a man's job to make a woman feel cherished and respected. "Not in the Press Room either."

"Well, you're hearing it from your National Security Advisor."

"Thank you, Dr. Elliot." Both had a good laugh. Elizabeth moved up to kiss him, dragging her breast along his chest to do so. "Bob, you don't know what you mean to me."

"Oh, I think I might," the President allowed.

Elliot shook her head. "All those dry years in academe. Never had time, always too busy. I was so tied up with being a professor. So much time wasted. . . ." A sigh.

"Well, I hope I was worth waiting for, dear."

"You were, and you are." She rolled over, resting her head on his shoulder and drawing his hand across her chest until it rested on a convenient spot. His other hand found a similar place, and her hands held his in place.

What do I say next? Liz asked herself. She had spoken the truth. Bob Fowler was a gentle, patient, and talented lover. It was also true that on hearing such a thing, any man, even a president, was under control. *Nothing, for a while,* she decided. There was time to enjoy him further, and time to examine her own feelings, her eyes open and staring at a dark rectangle on the wall that was a fine oil painting whose artist she'd never bothered to note, some sweeping Western landscape of where the plains ended at the Front Range of the Rockies. His hands moved gently, not quite arousing her again, but giving her subtle waves of pleasure which she accepted passively, occasionally adjusting the position of her head to show that she was still awake.

She was starting to love the man. Wasn't that odd? She paused, wondering if it was or wasn't. There was much to like and admire in him. There was also much to confuse. He was an irreconcilable mixture of coldness and warmth, and his sense of humor defied understanding. He cared deeply about many things, but his depth of feeling seemed always motivated by a logical understanding of issues and principles rather than true passion. He was often befuddled—genuinely so—that others didn't share his feelings on issues, in the same way that teachers of mathematics were never angered, but saddened and puzzled that others failed to see the beauty and symmetry of their calculations. Fowler was also capable of remarkable cruelty and total ruthlessness, both delivered without a trace of rancor. People stood in his way, and if he could destroy them, he did. It was like the line in *The Godfather*. It was never personal, just business. Perhaps he'd learned that from the *mafiosi* he'd sent to prison, Liz wondered. The same man could treat his true followers with a matter-of-fact coldness that rewarded efficiency and loyalty with . . . how could she describe it? The gratitude of an accountant.

And yet he was also a wonderfully tender man in bed. Liz frowned at the wall. There was no understanding him, was there?

"Did you see that report from Japan?" the President asked, getting to business just as Elliot was on the verge of a conclusion.

"Ummm, glad you brought that up. Something disturbing came into the office the other day."

"About what?" Fowler showed his interest by moving his hands in a more deliberate fashion, as though to coax information out of her that she'd been waiting to reveal for some time.

"Ryan," Liz replied.

"Him again? What is it?"

"The reports we heard about improper financial dealings were true, but it looks like he weaseled out of them on a technicality. It would have been enough to keep him out of this Administration, but since he's grandfathered in from before—"

"There are technicalities and technicalities. What other thing do you have?"

"Sexual impropriety, and possibly using Agency personnel to settle personal scores."

"Sexual impropriety . . . disgraceful. . . ."

Elliot giggled. He liked that. "There might be a child involved." Fowler did not like that. He was a very seriously committed man on the issue of children's rights. His hands stopped moving.

"What do we know?"

"Not enough. It should be looked at, though," Liz said, coaxing his hands back into motion.

"Okay, have the FBI do a quiet investigation," the President said, ending the issue, he thought.

"That won't work."

"Why?"

"Ryan has a very close relationship with the Bureau. They might balk on those grounds, might smooth the thing over."

"Bill Shaw isn't like that. He's as good a cop as I've ever met—even *I* can't make him do things, and that's the way it should be." Logic and principle again. The man was impossible to predict.

"Shaw worked personally on the Ryan Case—the terrorist thing, I mean. Prior personal involvement by the head of the investigative agency . . . ?"

"True," Fowler admitted. It would look bad. Conflict of interest and all that.

"And Shaw's personal troubleshooter is that Murray fellow. He and Ryan are pretty tight."

A grunt. "So, what then?"

"Somebody from the Attorney General's office, I think."

"Why not Secret Service?" Fowler asked, knowing the answer, but wondering if she did.

"Then it looks like it's a witch-hunt."

"Good point. Okay, the A.G.'s office. Call Greg tomorrow."

"Okay, Bob." Time to change subjects. She brought one of his hands to her face and kissed it. "You know, at times like this I really miss cigarettes."

"Smoke after sex?" he asked with a harder embrace.

"When you make love to me, Bob, I smoke during sex. . . ." She turned to stare into his eyes.

"Maybe I should think about relighting the fire?"

"They say," the National Security Advisor purred, moving to kiss him again, "they say the President of the United States is the most powerful man in the world."

"I do my best, Elizabeth."

Half an hour later Elliot decided that it was true. She was starting to love him. Then she wondered what he felt for her. . . .

16. Fueling the Fire

"*Guten Abend, Frau Fromm,*" the man said.

"And you are?"

"Peter Wiegler, from the *Berliner Tageblatt*. I wonder if I might speak with you briefly."

"About what?" she asked.

"*Aber* . . ." He gestured at the rain he was standing in. She remembered that she was civilized after all, even to a journalist.

"Yes, of course, please come in."

"Thank you." He came in out of the rain and removed his coat, which she hung on a peg. He was a captain in the KGB's First Chief (Foreign) Directorate, a promising young officer of thirty years, handsome, gifted in languages, the holder of a master's degree in psychology, and another in engineering. He already had

Traudl Fromm figured out. The new Audi parked outside was comfortable but not luxurious, her clothing—also new—very presentable but not overpowering. She was proud and moderately greedy, but also parsimonious. Curious, but guarded. She was hiding something, also smart enough to know that turning him away would generate more suspicion than whatever explanation she might have. He took his seat on an overstuffed chair and waited for the next move. She didn't offer coffee. She hoped the encounter would be a short one. He wondered if this third person on his list of ten names might be something worth reporting to Moscow Center.

"Your husband is associated with the Greifswald-Nord Nuclear Power Station?"

"He was. As you know, it is being closed down."

"Quite so. I would like to know what you and he think of that. Is Dr. Fromm at home?"

"No, he is not," she answered uncomfortably. "Wiegler" didn't react visibly.

"Really? May I ask where he is?"

"He is away on business."

"Perhaps I might come back in a few days, then?"

"Perhaps. You might call ahead?" It was the way she said it that the KGB officer noticed. She was hiding something, and the Captain knew that it had to be something—

There was another knock at the door. Traudl Fromm went to answer it.

"Guten Abend, Frau Fromm," a voice said. "We bring a message from Manfred."

The Captain heard the voice, and something inside his head went on alert. He told himself not to react. This was Germany, and everything was *in Ordnung*. Besides, he might learn something. . . .

"I, ah, have a guest at the moment," Traudl answered.

The next statement was delivered in a whisper. The Captain heard approaching steps, and took his time before turning to look. It was a fatal error.

The face he saw might as easily have come from one of the endless World War II movies that he'd grown up on, just that it lacked the black-and-silver-trimmed uniform of an SS officer. It was a stern, middle-aged face with light blue eyes entirely devoid of emotion. A professional face that measured his as quickly as he—

It was time to—

"Hello. I was just about to leave."

"Who is he?" Traudl didn't get a chance to answer.

"I'm a reporter with—" It was too late. A pistol appeared from nowhere. *"Was gibt's hier?"* he demanded.

"Where is your car?" the man behind the gun asked.

"I parked it down the street. I—"

"All those spaces right in front? Reporters are lazy. Who are you?"

"I'm a reporter with the—"

"I think not."

"This one, too," the one in back said. The Captain remembered the face from somewhere. . . . He told himself not to panic. That, too, was a mistake.

"Listen closely. You will be going on a short trip. If you cooperate, you will be returned here within three hours. If you do not cooperate, things will go badly for you. *Verstehen Sie?"*

They had to be intelligence officers, the Captain thought, making a correct guess.

And they had to be German, and that meant that they would play by the rules, he told himself, making the last mistake of what had been a promising career.

The courier arrived from Cyprus right on schedule, handing off his package to another man at one of five pre-selected transfer points, all of which had been under surveillance for twelve hours. The second man walked two blocks and started up his Yamaha motorcycle, tearing off into the countryside just as fast as he could in an area where motorcyclists were all certifiably mad. Two hours after that, he delivered the package, certain that he had not been followed, and kept going another thirty minutes before circling back to his point of origin.

Günther Bock took the package and was annoyed to see that it was to all appearances a movie cassette—*Chariots of Fire*—rather than the hollowed-out book he'd requested. Perhaps Erwin was delivering a message along with the cassette. Bock inserted it in a player and switched it on, catching the first few minutes of the feature movie, which was subtitled in French. Soon, he realized that Keitel's message was on what intelligence professionals really did. He fast-forwarded through ninety minutes of the film before the picture changed.

What?

''*Who* are you?'' an off-camera voice asked harshly.

''I am Peter Wiegler, I am a reporter with—'' The rest was a scream. The equipment used was crude, just an electrical cord ripped off a lamp or appliance, the insulation trimmed off the free end to expose a few centimeters of copper. Few understood just how effective crude instruments could be, especially if the user possessed some degree of sophistication. The man who called himself Peter Wiegler screamed as though his throat would split from the effort. He'd already bitten through his lower lip in previous efforts to keep silent. The only good thing about using electricity was that it wasn't especially bloody, just noisy.

''You must understand that you are being foolish. Your courage is impressive, but wasted here. Courage only has use when there is hope of rescue. We've already searched your car. We have your passports. We know that you are not German. So, what are you? Pole, Russian, what?''

The young man opened his eyes and took a long breath before speaking. ''I am an investigative reporter with the *Berliner Tageblatt.*'' They hit him again with the electric cord, and this time he passed out. Bock watched a man's back approach the victim and check his eyes and pulse. The torturer appeared to be wearing a chemical-warfare-protective suit of rubberized fabric, but without the hood and gloves. It must have been awfully hot, Bock thought.

''Obviously a trained intelligence officer. Probably Russian. Not circumcised, and his dental work is stainless steel, not especially well done. That means an East Bloc service, of course. Too bad, this lad is quite brave.'' The voice was admirably clinical, Bock thought.

''What drugs do we have?'' another voice asked.

''A rather good tranquilizer. Now?''

''Now. Not too much.''

''Very well.'' The man went off-camera, then returned with a syringe. He grasped the victim's upper arm, then injected the drug into a vein inside the elbow. It took three minutes before the KGB man regained consciousness, just enough for the rush of drugs to assault his higher brain functions.

''Sorry we had to do that to you. You have passed the test,'' the voice said, this time in Russian.

"What test—" The answer was in Russian, just two words before his brain took hold and stopped him. "Why did you ask me in Russian?"

"Because that was what we wished to know. Good night."

The victim's eyes went wide as a small-caliber pistol appeared, was placed against his chest, and fired. The camera withdrew a bit to show more of the room. A plastic sheet—actually three of them—covered the floor to catch blood and other droppings under the metal chair. The bullet wound was speckled with black powder marks and bulged outward from the intrusion of gun-gasses below the skin. There wasn't much bleeding. Heart wounds never produced much. In a few more seconds the body stopped quivering.

"We could have taken more time to ascertain additional information, but we have what we need, as I will explain later." It was Keitel's voice, off-camera.

"Now, Traudl . . ."

They brought her in front of the camera, hands bound in front of her, her mouth gagged with the same bandaging tape, her eyes wide in terror, naked. She was trying to say something around the gag, but no one there had been interested. The tape was a day and a half old, of course. Günther could tell that from the TV that was playing in the corner, tuned to an evening news broadcast. The entire performance was a professional *tour de force* designed to meet his requirements.

Bock could almost hear the man thinking, *Now, how do we do this?* Günther momentarily regretted the instructions he'd given Keitel. But the evidence had to be positive. Magicians and other experts in illusion regularly consulted with intelligence agencies—but some things could not be faked, and he had to be sure that he could trust Keitel to do terrible and dangerous things. It was an objective necessity that this be graphic.

Another man looped a rope over a ceiling beam and hauled her hands up, then the first pressed his pistol into her armpit and fired a single shot. At least he wasn't a sadist, Bock thought. Such people were not reliable. It was quite sad to watch in any case. The bullet had punctured her heart, but she was too excited to die quickly, struggling for more than half a minute, eyes still wide, fighting for breath, still trying to speak, probably begging for help, asking why. . . . After she went limp, one checked the pulse at her neck, then lowered her slowly to the floor. They'd been as gentle about it as they could have been under the circumstances. The shooter spoke without facing the camera.

"I hope you are satisfied. I did not enjoy this."

"You weren't supposed to," Bock said to the television set.

The Russian was taken off the chair and laid beside Traudl Fromm. While the bodies were dismembered, Keitel's voice spoke. It was a useful diversion, as the visual scene simply got more horrible. Bock was not squeamish about many things, but it troubled his psyche when human bodies were abused after death. Necessary or not, it seemed gratuitous to him.

"The Russian is undoubtedly an intelligence officer, as you have seen. His automobile was a rental from Berlin, and is being driven tomorrow to Magdeburg, where it will be turned in. It was parked down the street, normal procedure for a professional, of course, but a giveaway in the event of capture. In the car we found a list of names, all of them in the DDR nuclear-power industry. It would seem that our Russian comrades have suddenly become interested in Honecker's bomb project. A pity we didn't have another few years to follow up on that, no? I regret the complication involved, but it took us several days to set up arrangements for disposing of the bodies, and we had no idea Frau Fromm had her 'guest' when we knocked on the door. At that point, of course, it was too late. Besides, with the rain we had ideal conditions for the kidnapping.'' Two men were working on each body. All wore the protective suits, and now they had their hoods and masks on, doubtless to protect them from the smell as much as to protect their identity. As in a slaughterhouse, sawdust was applied in buckets full to soak up the copious amounts of blood being spilled. Bock knew from experience just how messy murders could be. They worked quickly as Keitel's voice-over went on, using powered industrial cutting tools. Arms and legs had been removed from the torsos, and then the heads were removed and held up to the camera. No one could fake this. Keitel's men had truly murdered two human beings. The dismemberment in front of a playing television made that absolutely certain, and would doubtless also make disposal easier. The pieces were assembled neatly for wrapping in plastic. One of the men started brushing the blood-soaked sawdust into a pile for yet another plastic bag.

''The body parts will be burned at two widely separated locations. This will be accomplished long before you get the tape. That ends our message. We await further instructions.'' And the tape returned to the dramatization of the 1920 Olympics—or was it 1924? Bock wondered. Not that it mattered, of course.

''Yes, Colonel?''

''One of my officers has failed to check in.'' The Colonel was from Directorate T, the technical branch of the First Chief Directorate. The holder of a doctor's degree in engineering, his personal specialty was missile systems. He had worked in America and France, ferreting out the secrets of various military weapons before being promoted to his current job.

''Details?''

''Captain Yevgeniy Stepanovich Feodorov, age thirty, married, one child, a fine young officer on the Major's List. He was one of the three I sent into Germany at your direction to check out their nuclear facilities. He's one of my best.''

''How long?'' Golovko asked.

''Six days. He flew into Berlin via Paris last week. He had German papers, good ones from downstairs, and a list of ten names to investigate. His instructions were to maintain a low profile unless he discovered something important, in which case he was to make contact with Station Berlin—what's left of it, I mean. We scheduled a periodic check-in, of course. He didn't make it, and after twenty-four hours, I got the alert.''

''Could it be that he's just careless?''

''Not this boy,'' the Colonel said flatly. ''Does the name mean anything to you?''

''Feodorov . . . wasn't his father . . . ?''

''Stefan Yurievich, yes. Yevgeniy is his youngest son.''

''Good God, Stefan taught *me,*'' Golovko said. ''Possibility of . . . ?''

''Defection?'' The Colonel shook his head angrily. ''Not a chance. His wife is in the chorus with the opera. No—they met in university and married young over the objections of both sets of parents. It's a love match like we all wish we had. She's a stunningly beautiful girl, voice like an angel. Only a *zhopnik* would walk away from her. Then there's the child. He is by all reports a good father.'' Golovko saw where this was leading.

''Arrested, then?''

''I haven't heard a whisper. Perhaps you might arrange to have that checked. I fear the worst.'' The Colonel frowned and stared down at the rug. He didn't want to be the one who broke the news to Natalia Feodorova.

"Hard to believe," Golovko said.

"Sergey Nikolay'ch, if your suspicions are correct, then this program we were tasked to investigate is a matter of grave importance to them, is it not? We may have confirmed something in the most expensive way possible."

General Lieutenant Sergey Nikolayevich Golovko was silent for several seconds. *It's not supposed to be like this,* he told himself. *The intelligence business is supposed to be civilized. Killing each other's officers is a thing of the distant past. We don't* do *that sort of thing anymore, haven't done it in years . . . decades. . . .*

"None of the alternatives are credible, are they?"

The Colonel shook his head. "No. But the most credible is that our man stumbled into something both real and extremely sensitive. Sensitive enough to kill for. A secret nuclear-weapons program is that sensitive, is it not?"

"Arguably, yes." The Colonel was showing the sort of loyalty to his people that KGB expected, Golovko noted. He was also thinking over the alternatives and presenting his best estimate of the situation.

"Have you sent your technical people to Sarova yet?"

"Day after tomorrow. My best man was sick, just got out of the hospital—broke his leg in a fall down some stairs."

"Have him carried there if necessary. I want a worst-case estimate of plutonium production at the DDR power stations. Send another man to Kyshtym to back-check the people at Sarova. Pull in the other people you sent to Germany. We'll restart the investigation more carefully. Two-man teams, and the backup man is to be armed . . . that is dangerous," Golovko said on reflection.

"General, it takes a lot of time and money to train my field people. I will need two years to replace Feodorov, two whole years. You can't just pull an officer out of another branch and drop him into this line of work. These people must understand what they are looking for. Assets like that should be protected."

"You are correct. I will clear it with the Chairman and send experienced officers . . . maybe some people from the Academy . . . credential them like German police officials?"

"I like that, Sergey Nikolay'ch."

"Good man, Pavel Ivan'ch. And on Feodorov?"

"Maybe he'll turn up. Thirty days before he's declared missing, then I'll have to see his wife. Very well, I'll pull my people in and start planning the next phase of the operation. When will I have a list of the escort officers?"

"Tomorrow morning."

"Very well, General, thank you for your time."

Golovko shook the man's hand and remained standing until the door closed. He had ten minutes until his next appointment.

"Damn," he said to his desk top.

"More delays?"

Fromm did not quite manage to hide his disgust. "We are saving time! The material we will be working on has machining characteristics similar to stainless steel. We must also manufacture blanks for the casting process. Here."

Fromm unfolded his working drawings.

"We have here a folded cylinder of plutonium. Around the plutonium is a cylinder of beryllium, which is a godsend for our purposes. It is very light, very stiff, an X-ray window, and a neutron reflector. Unfortunately, it is also rather difficult to machine. We must use cubic boron-nitride tools, essentially an analog to industrial diamond. Steel or carbon tools would have results you do not wish to contemplate. We also have health considerations.''

''Beryllium is not toxic,'' Ghosn said. ''I checked.''

''True, but the dust resulting from the matching process converts to beryllium oxide, which when inspired converts again to beryllium hydroxide, and *that* causes berylliosis, which is uniformly fatal.'' Fromm paused, staring at Ghosn like a schoolmaster before going on.

''Now, around the beryllium is a cylinder of tungsten-rhenium, which we need for its density. We will purchase twelve kilograms in powder form, which we will sinter into cylindrical segments. You know sintering? That is heating it just hot enough to form. Melting and casting is too difficult, and not necessary for our purposes. Around that goes the explosive-lens assembly. And this is just the primary, Ghosn, not even a quarter of our total energy budget.''

''And the precision required . . .''

''Exactly. Think of this as the world's largest ring or necklace. What we produce must be as finely finished as the most beautiful piece of jewelry you have ever seen—or perhaps a precision optical instrument.''

''The tungsten-rhenium?''

''Available from any major electrical concern. It's used in special filaments for vacuum tubes, numerous other applications, and it's far easier to work than pure tungsten.''

''Beryllium—oh, yes, it's used in gyroscopes and other instruments . . . thirty kilograms.''

''Twenty-five . . . yes, get thirty. You have no idea how lucky we are.''

''How so?''

''The Israeli plutonium is gallium-stabilized. Plutonium has four phase-transformations below melting point, and has the curious habit, in certain temperature regimes, of changing its density by a factor of over twenty percent. It is a multistate metal.''

''In other words, a subcritical mass can—''

''Exactly,'' Fromm said. ''What appears to be a subcritical mass can under certain circumstances convert itself into criticality. It will not explode, but the gamma- and neutron-flux would be lethal within a radius of . . . oh, anywhere from ten to thirty meters, depending on circumstances. That was discovered during the Manhattan Project. They were—no, not lucky. They were brilliant scientists, and as soon as they had a gram or so of plutonium, it was decided to investigate its properties. Had they waited, or simply assumed that they knew more than they did—well . . .''

''I had no idea,'' Ghosn admitted. *Merciful God . . .*

''Not everything is in books, my young friend, or should I say, not all the books have all the information. In any case, with the addition of gallium, the plutonium is a stable mass. It is actually quite safe to work, as long as we take the proper precautions.''

''So we start by machining out stainless-steel blanks to these specifications, then make our casting-molds—investment casting, of course.''

Fromm nodded. ''Correct. Very good, *mein Junge.*''

''Then when the casting is done, we will machine the bomb material. . . . I see. Well, we seem to have good machinists.''

They'd ''drafted''—that was the term they used—ten men, all Palestinians, from local optical shops, and trained them on the use of the machine tools.

The tools were all that Fromm had said they were. Two years earlier they'd been totally state-of-the-art, identical to the equipment used in the American Y-12 fabrication plant at Oak Ridge, Tennessee. Tolerances were measured by laser interferometry, and the rotating tool heads were computer-controlled in three dimensions through five axes of movement. Instructions were passed to the computers via touch-screens. The design itself had been done on a minicomputer and drawn out on an expensive drafting machine.

Ghosn and Fromm brought the machinists in and set them to work on their first task, making the stainless-steel blank for the plutonium primary that would ignite the thermonuclear fire.

"Now," Fromm said, "for the explosive lenses. . . ."

"I've heard much about you," Bock said.

"I hope it was good," Marvin Russell replied with a guarded smile.

My first Indian, Bock thought quickly. He was oddly disappointed. Except for the cheekbones, he might have easily been mistaken for any Caucasian, and even those could seem like a Slav with perhaps a taste of Tatar in his background. . . . What color there was had come mainly from the sun. The rest of the man was formidable enough, the size and obvious strength.

"I hear you killed a police officer in Greece by snapping his neck."

"I don't know why people make a big deal about that," Russell said with weary honesty. "He was a scrawny little fuck, and I know how to take care of myself."

Bock smiled and nodded. "I understand how you feel, but your method was impressive in any case. I have heard good things about you, Mr. Russell, and—"

"Just call me Marvin. Everybody else does."

Bock smiled. "As you wish, Marvin. I am Günther. Particularly your skill with weapons."

"It's no big deal," Russell said, genuinely puzzled. "Anybody can learn to shoot."

"How do you like it here?"

"I like it a lot. These people—I mean, they have heart, y'know? They ain't quitters. They work real hard at what they do. I admire that. And what they done for me, Gunther, it's like family, man."

"We are a family, Marvin. We share everything, good and bad. We all have the same enemies."

"Yeah, I seen that."

"We may need your help for something, Marvin. It's for something fairly important."

"Okay," Russell replied simply.

"What do you mean?"

"I mean 'yes,' Gunther."

"You haven't even asked what it is," the German pointed out.

"Okay." Marvin smiled. "So tell me."

"We need you to go back to America in a few months. How dangerous is that for you?"

"Depends. I've done time—in prison, I mean. You know that. My fingerprints are on file with the cops, but they don't have a picture of me—I mean, the one they have is pretty old. I've changed since then. They're looking for me up in the Dakotas, probably. If you send me there, it might be a little tricky."

"Nowhere near there, Marvin."

"Then it shouldn't be much of a problem, dependin' on what you need me to do."

"How do you feel about killing people—Americans, I mean." Bock watched his face for a reaction.

"Americans." Marvin snorted. "Hey, man, *I'm* a fuckin' American, okay? My country ain't what you think. *They* stole my country from me, just like what happened to these guys here, okay? It ain't just here shit like that happened, okay? You want me to do some people for you, yeah, I can do that, if you got a reason. I mean, I don't kill for fun, I ain't no psycho, but you got a reason, sure, I can do it."

"Maybe more than one—"

"I heard you when you said 'people,' Günther. I ain't so stupid that I think 'people' means one guy. You just make sure some cops, maybe even some FBI guys are in there, yeah, I'll help kill all you want. One thing you need to know, though."

"What's that?"

"The other side ain't dumb. They got my brother, remember. They're serious dudes."

"We also are serious," Bock assured him.

"I seen that, man. What can you tell me about the job?"

"What do you mean, Marvin?" Bock asked as casually as he could.

"I mean I grew up there, man, remember? I know stuff that maybe you don't. Okay, you got security and all that, and you ain't gonna tell me anything now. Fine, that's no problem. But you might need my help later on. These guys here are okay, they're smart and all, but they don't know dick about America—I mean, not what you need to get around and stuff. You go huntin', you gotta know the ground. I know the ground."

"That is why we want your help," Bock assured him, as though he'd already thought that part all the way through. Actually he had not, and now he was wondering just how useful this man might be.

Andrey Il'ych Narmonov saw himself as the captain of the world's largest ship of state. That was the good news. The bad news was that the ship had a leaky bottom, a broken rudder, and uncertain engines. Not to mention a mutinous crew. His office in the Kremlin was large, with room to pace about, something he found himself doing all too much of late. That, he thought, was a sign of an uncertain man, and the President of the Union of Soviet Socialist Republics could not afford that, especially when he had an important guest.

Union of Sovereign *Soviet Republics,* he thought. Though the official name-change had not yet been approved, that was how his people were starting to think. *That's the problem.*

The ship of state was breaking up. There was no precedent for it. The dissolution of the British Empire was the example that many liked to use, but that wasn't quite right, was it? Nor was any other example. The Soviet Union of old had been a unique political creation. What was now happening in the Soviet Union was also entirely without precedent. What had once been exhilarating to him was now more than frightening. He was the one who had to make the hard decisions, and he had no historical model to follow. He was completely on his own, as alone as any man had ever been, with a task larger than any man had ever faced. Lauded in the West as a consummate political tactician, he thought of it himself as an endless succession of crises. *Wasn't it Gladstone?* he thought. *Wasn't it he who described his job as being the man on a raft in the rapids, fending off rocks with a pole? How apt, how apt indeed.* Narmonov and his country were being swept along by overwhelming forces of history, somewhere down that river was an immense cataract, a falls that could destroy everything . . . but he was too busy with the pole and the rocks to look so far ahead. That was what being a political tactician meant. He devoted all his creative energy to day-to-day survival, and was losing sight of the next week . . . even the day after tomorrow. . . .

"Andrey Il'ych, you are growing thin," Oleg Kirilovich Kadishev observed from his leather seat.

"The walking is good for my heart," the President replied wryly.

"Then perhaps you will join our Olympic team?"

Narmonov stopped for a moment. "It would be nice indeed to compete merely against foreigners. *They* think I am brilliant. Alas, our own people know better."

"What can I do to help my President?"

"I need your help, the help of those on the right."

It was Kadishev's turn to smile. The press—Western as well as Soviet—never got that straight. The *left* wing in the Soviet Union was that of the communist hard-liners. For over eighty years, reform in that country had always come from the right. All the men executed by Stalin for wanting to allow the merest bit of personal freedom had always been denounced as *Right*-Deviationists. But self-styled progressives in the West were always on the political left, and they called *their* reactionary enemies "conservatives" and generally identified them as being on the political *right.* It seemed too great a stretch of imagination for Western journalists to adjust their ideological polarity to a different political reality. The newly liberated Soviet journalists had merely aped their Western colleagues and used the foreign descriptions to muddle what was already a chaotic political scene. The same was true of "progressive" Western politicians, of course, who were championing so many of the experiments of the Soviet Union in their own countries—all the experiments which had been taken to the limit and proven to be something worse than mere failures. Perhaps the blackest humor available in all the world was the carping from leftist elements in the West, some of whom were already observing that the *backward* Russians had failed because they had proven unable to covert socialism into a humanistic government—whereas *advanced* Western governments could accomplish just that (of course, Karl Marx himself had said that, hadn't he?). Such people were, Kadishev thought with a bemused shake of his head, no less idealistic than the members of the first Revolutionary Soviets, and just as addlebrained. The Russians had merely taken the revolutionary ideals to their logical limits, and found there only emptiness and disaster. Now that they were turning back—a move that called for political and moral courage such as the world had rarely seen—the West *still* didn't understand what was happening! *Khrushchev was right all along,* the parliamentarian thought. *Politicians are the same all over the world.*

Mostly idiots.

"Andrey Il'ych, we do not always agree on methods, but we *have* always agreed on goals. I know you are having trouble with our friends on the other side."

"*And* with your side," President Narmonov pointed out more sharply than he should have.

"And with my side, it is true," Kadishev admitted casually. "Andrey Il'ych, do you say that we must agree with you on everything?"

Narmonov turned, his eyes momentarily angry and wide. "Please, not that, not today."

"How may we help you?" *Losing control of your emotions, Comrade President? A bad sign, my friend. . . .*

"I need your support on the ethnic issue. We cannot have the entire Union break apart."

Kadishev shook his head forcefully. "*That* is inevitable. Letting the Balts and the Azeris go eliminates many problems."

"We need the Azerbaijani oil. If we let that go, our economic situation worsens. If we let the Balts go, the momentum will strip away half of our country."

"Half our population, true, but scarcely twenty percent of our land. And most of our problems," Kadishev said again.

"And what of the people who leave? We throw them into chaos and civil war. How many will die, how many deaths on our conscience, eh?" the President demanded.

"Which is a normal consequence of decolonization. We cannot prevent it. By attempting to, we merely keep the civil war within our own borders. *That* forces us to place too much power into the hands of the security forces, and that is too dangerous. I don't trust the Army any more than you do."

"The Army will not launch a coup. There are no Bonapartists in the Red Army."

"You have greater confidence in their fealty than I do. I think they see a unique historical opportunity. The Party has held the military down since the Tukhachevskiy business. Soldiers have long memories, and they may be thinking that this is their chance."

"Those people are all dead! And their children with them," Narmonov countered angrily. It had been over fifty years, after all. Those few with direct memory of the purges were in wheelchairs or living on pensions.

"But not their grandchildren, and there is institutional memory to consider as well." Kadishev leaned back and considered a new thought that had sprung almost fully formed into his head. *Might that be possible . . . ?*

"They have concerns, yes, and those concerns are little different from my own. We differ on how to deal with the problem, not on the issue of control. While I am not sure of their judgment, I *am* sure of their loyalty."

"Perhaps you are correct, but I am not so sanguine."

"With your help we can present a united front to the forces of early dissolution. That will discourage them. That will allow us to get through a few years of normalization, and then we can consider an orderly departure for the republics with a genuine commonwealth—association, whatever you wish to call it—to keep us associated economically while being separate politically."

The man is desperate, Kadishev saw. *He really is collapsing under the strain. The man who moves about the political arena like a Central Army hockey forward is showing signs of fatigue . . . will he survive without my help?*

Probably, Kadishev judged. Probably. That was too bad, the younger man thought. Kadishev was the de facto leader of the forces on the "left," the forces that wanted to break up the entire country and the government that went with it, yanking the remaining nation—based on the Russian Federation—into the 21st century by its throat. If Narmonov fell . . . if he found himself unable to continue, then who . . .

Why, me, of course.

Would the Americans support him?

How could they fail to support Agent SPINNAKER *of their own Central Intelligence Agency?*

Kadishev had been working for the Americans since his recruitment by Mary Patricia Foley some six years before. He didn't think of it as treason. He was working for the betterment of his country, and saw himself as succeeding. He'd fed the Americans information on the internal workings of the Soviet government, some of it highly valuable, some material they could as easily have gotten from their own reporters. He knew that they regarded him as their most valuable source of political intelligence in the Soviet Union, especially now that he controlled fully forty percent of the votes in the country's bumptious new parliament, the Congress of People's Deputies. *Thirty-nine percent,* he told himself. *One must be honest.* Perhaps another eight percent could be his if he made the proper move. There were many shades of political loyalty among the twenty-five hundred members. Genuine democrats, Russian nationalists of both democratic and socialist stripe, radicals of both left and right. There was also a cautious middle of politicians, some genuinely concerned about what course their country might take, others merely seeking to conserve their personal political status. How many could he appeal to? How many could he win over?

Not quite enough . . .

But there was one more card he could play, wasn't there?

Da. If he had the audacity to play it.

"Andrey Il'ych," he said in a conciliatory voice, "you ask me to depart from an important principle so that I can help you reach a goal we share—but to do so by a route that I distrust. This is a very difficult matter. I am not even sure that I can deliver the support you require. My comrades might well turn their backs on me." It only agitated the man further.

"Rubbish! I know how well they trust you and your judgment."

They are not the only ones who trust me, Kadishev told himself.

As with most investigations, this one was done mainly with paper. Ernest Wellington was a young attorney, and an ambitious one. As a law-school graduate and a member of the bar, he could have applied to the FBI and learned the business of investigation properly, but he considered himself a lawyer rather than a cop, besides which he enjoyed politics, and the FBI prided itself on avoiding political wrangling wherever possible. Wellington had no such inhibitions. He enjoyed politics, considered it the life's blood of government service, and knew it to be the path to speedy advancement both within and without the government. The contacts he was making now would make his value to any of a hundred "connected" law firms jump fivefold, plus making him a known name within the Department of Justice. Soon he would be in the running for a "special-assistant" job. After that—in five years or so—he'd have a crack at a section chief's office . . . maybe even U.S. Attorney in a major city, or head of a special DoJ strike force. That opened the door to political life, where Ernest Wellington could be a real player in the Great Game of Washington. All in all, it was heady wine indeed for an ambitious man of twenty-seven years, an honors graduate from Harvard Law who'd ostentatiously turned down lucrative offers from prestigious firms, preferring instead to devote his early professional years to public service.

Wellington had a pile of paper on his desk. His office was in what was almost an attic in the Justice Department's building on the Mall, and the view from the single window was of the parking lot that rested in the center of the Depression-era structure. It was small, and the air conditioning was faulty, but it was private. It is little appreciated that lawyers avoid time in court as assiduously as the boastful avoid genuine tests of ability. Had he taken the jobs offered by the New York corporate firms—the best such offer was for over $100,000 per year—his real function would have been that of proofreader, really a glorified secretary, examining contracts for typos and possible loopholes. Early life in the Justice Department was little different. Whereas in a real prosecutorial office he might have been tossed alive into a courtroom environment to sink or swim, here at headquarters he examined records, looking for inconsistencies, nuances, possible technical violations of the law, as though he were an editor for a particularly good mystery writer. Wellington started making his notes.

John Patrick Ryan. Deputy to the Director of Central Intelligence, nominated by the President—politics at work—and confirmed less than two years previously. Prior to that acting Deputy Director (Intelligence), following the death of Vice Admiral James Greer. Prior to that, Special Assistant to DDI Greer, and sometime special representative of the Directorate of Intelligence over in England. Ryan had been an instructor in history at the Naval Academy, a graduate student at Georgetown University, and a broker at the Baltimore office of Merrill Lynch. Also, briefly, a second lieutenant in the United States Marine Corps. Clearly a man who enjoyed career changes, Wellington thought, noting all the important dates.

Personal wealth. The requisite financial statement was in the file, near the top. Ryan was worth quite a bit. Where had it come from? That analysis took several hours. In his days as a broker, J. P. Ryan had been a real cowboy. He'd bet over a hundred thousand dollars on the Chicago and North Western Railroad at the time of the employee takeover, and reaped . . . over six million from it. That was his one really big score—sixty-to-one opportunities were not all that common, were they?—but some of the others were also noteworthy. On hitting a personal net worth of eight million, he'd called it quits and gone to Georgetown for his doctorate in history. Continued to play the market on an amateur basis—that wasn't quite right, was it?—until joining government service. His portfolio was now managed by a multiplicity of investment counselors . . . their accounting methods were unusually conservative. Ryan's net worth looked to be twenty million, maybe a little more. The accounts were managed on a blind basis. All Ryan saw was quarterly earnings statements. There were ways around that, of course, but it was all strictly legal. Proving impropriety was virtually impossible unless they put a wiretap on the line of his brokers, and that was not something easily accomplished.

He had been investigated by the SEC, but that had actually been a spinoff of the SEC's look at the firm he'd bought into. The summary sheet noted in clipped bureaucratese that no technical violation had been made, but Wellington observed that this judgment was more technical than substantive. Ryan had balked at signing a consent order—understandably—and the government had not pressed him on the issue. That was less understandable, but explainable, since Ryan had not been the actual target of the investigation; someone had decided that it had all probably been a coincidence. Ryan had, however, broken that money out of his main account . . . *Gentleman's Agreement?* Wellington wrote on his legal pad. Perhaps. If asked, Ryan would respond that he'd done it out of an overscrupulous sense of guilt. The money had gone into T-Bills, rolled over automatically for years and untouched until it had all been used to . . . *I see. That's interesting. . . .*

Why an educational trust fund? Who was Carol Zimmer? What interest did Ryan have in her children? Timing? Significance?

It was amazing, as always, that so much paper could show so little. Perhaps, Wellington mused, that was the real point of government paperwork, to give the appearance of substance while saying as little as possible. He chuckled. That was also the point of most legal papers, wasn't it? For two hundred dollars per hour, lawyers loved to quibble over the placement of commas and other weighty matters. He paused, recycling his brain. He had missed something very obvious.

Ryan was not liked by the Fowler Administration. *Why,* then, had he been nominated for DDCI. Politics? But politics was the reason you selected people unqualified for . . . Did Ryan have any political connections at all? The file didn't show any. Wellington riffled through the papers and found a letter signed by Alan Trent and Sam Fellows of the House Select Committee. *That* was an odd couple, a gay and a Mormon. Ryan had sailed through confirmation much more easily than Marcus Cabot, even easier than Bunker and Talbot, the President's two star cabinet members. Part of that was because he was a second-level man, but that didn't explain it all. That meant political connections, and very fine ones. Why? What connections? Trent and Fellows . . . *what the hell could* those *two ever agree on?*

It was certain that Fowler and his people didn't like Ryan, else the Attorney General would not have personally placed Wellington on the case. Case? Was that the right term for his activities? If there was a *case,* why wasn't this being handled by the FBI? Politics, obviously. Ryan had worked closely with the FBI on several things . . . but . . .

William Connor Shaw, Director of the Federal Bureau of Investigation, was celebrated as the most honest man in government. Politically naive, of course, but the man dripped integrity, and that wasn't all so bad a quality in a police agency, was it? Congress thought so. There was even talk of eliminating special prosecutors, the FBI had become so clean, especially after the special prosecutor had bungled the . . . but the Bureau was being segregated from this one.

This was an interesting case, wasn't it? A man could win his spurs on something like this.

17. Processing

The days were shorter now, Jack told himself. It wasn't that he was all that late, just that the days were shortening. The earth's orbit around the sun, and the way the axis of rotation was not perpendicular with the plane of the . . . ecliptic? Something like that. His driver dropped him off in front of the door, and he walked tiredly in, wondering when the last day had been, outside of the weekends, when he'd seen his house in daylight and not outlined by electric lights. About the only good news was that he didn't bring work home—but that wasn't quite true either, was it? He brought no documents home, but it was less easy to clear out his mind than to clear off his desk.

Ryan heard the sounds of a normal house, the TV tuned to Nickelodeon. The washing machine was making noise. Have to have that fixed. He walked into the family room to announce himself.

''Daddy!'' Jack Jr. ran over to deliver a hug followed by a plaintive look. ''Daddy, you promised to take me to a baseball game!''

Oh, shit . . . The kids were back in school, and there couldn't be more than a dozen home games left up in Baltimore. He had to, had to, had to . . . *When?* When could he break loose? The new communications center project was only half done, and that was his baby, and the contractor was a week behind, and he had to get that back on line if it was going to be ready when it was supposed to be. . . .

''I'm going to try, Jack,'' Ryan promised his son, who was too young to understand about any obligation beyond a father's promise.

''Daddy, you promised!''

''I know.'' *Shit!* Jack made a mental note. He had to do something about that.

''Bedtime,'' Cathy announced. ''Tomorrow's a schoolday.''

Ryan hugged and kissed both of his children, but the exercise in affection merely left an empty spot in his conscience. What sort of a father was he turning into? Jack Jr.'s First Communion was next April or May, and who could say if he'd be home for that? Better find out the date so that he could schedule it now. Try to schedule it now. Jack reminded himself that little things like promises to his kids were—

Little things?

God, how did this ever happen? Where has my life gone?

He watched the kids head to their rooms, then himself headed to the kitchen. His dinner was in the oven. He set the plate on the breakfast counter before walking to the refrigerator. He was buying wine in boxes now. It was much more convenient, and his taste in wine was getting far less selective of late. The cardboard boxes held a Mylar bag full of—Australian, wasn't it? About where California wines had been twenty years earlier. The vintage in question was very fruity, to mask its inadequacies, and had the proper alcohol content, which was what he was mainly after anyway. Jack looked at the wall clock. If he were very lucky, he might get six and a half, maybe seven hours of sleep before a new day started. He needed the wine to sleep. At the office, he lived on coffee, and his system was becoming saturated with caffeine. Once he'd been able to nap at his desk, but no longer. By eleven in the morning his system was wired, and by late afternoon his body played a strange melody of fatigue and alertness that sometimes left him wondering if he were going a little mad. Well, as long as he asked himself that question. . . .

A few minutes later he finished his dinner. Pity the oven had dried it out. Cathy had done this one herself. He'd been—he'd planned to be home at a decent hour, but . . . It was always something, wasn't it? When he stood, there was a twinge of discomfort from his stomach. On the way into the family room he opened the closet door to pull a packet of antacid tablets from his coat pocket. These he chewed and washed down with wine, starting off his third glass in less than thirty minutes at home.

Cathy wasn't there, though she'd left some papers on the table next to her customary chair. Jack listened and thought he heard a shower running. Fine. He took the cable controller and flipped to CNN for another news-fix. The lead story was something about Jerusalem.

Ryan settled back into his chair and allowed himself a smile. It was working. The story was about the resurgence of tourism. Shopowners were loading up in anticipation of their biggest Christmas in a decade. Jesus, explained a Jew who'd opted to stay in the town of Bethlehem, was after all a nice Jewish boy from a good family. His Arab partner toured the camera crew through the store. *Arab partner?* Jack thought. *Well, why not?*

It's worth it, Ryan told himself. *You helped bring that about.* You *helped make that happen. You have saved lives, and if nobody else knows, the hell with it. You know. God knows. Isn't that enough?*

No, Jack told himself in a quiet flash of honesty.

So what if the idea had not been completely original? What idea ever was? It had been his thought that had brought it together, his contacts that had gotten the Vatican on board, his. . . . He deserved something for it, some recognition, enough for a little footnote in some history book, but would he get it?

Jack snorted into his wine. No chance. Liz Elliot, that clever bitch, telling everybody that it was Charlie Alden who'd done it. If Jack ever tried to set the record straight, he'd look like a swine stealing credit from a dead man—and a good man, despite his mistake with that Blum girl. *Cheer up, Jack. You're still alive. You have a wife, you have kids.*

It still wasn't fair, was it? Fair? Why had he ever expected life to be fair? Was he turning into another one of *them?* Ryan asked himself. Another Liz Elliot, another grasping, small-minded ass with an ego-size inversely proportionate to her character. He'd so often worried and wondered about the process, how a person might be corrupted. He'd feared the overt methods, deciding that a cause or a mission was *so* vital that you might lose perspective on the important things, like the value of a single human life, even the life of an enemy. He hadn't lost that, not ever, and knew that he never would. It was the subtler things that were wearing at him. He was turning into a functionary, worrying about credit and status and influence.

He closed his eyes to remind himself of what he already had: a wife, two kids, financial independence, accomplishments that no one could ever take away.

You are *turning into one of them. . . .*

He'd fought—he had *killed*—to defend his family. Maybe Elliot was offended by that, but in quiet moments like this, Jack remembered the times with a thin, grim smile. Not two hundred yards from where he now sat, he'd drilled three rounds into a terrorist's chest, coldly and efficiently—steel on target!—validating all the things they'd taught him at Quantico. That his heart had been beating a thousand times per second, that he'd come close to wetting his pants, that he'd had to swallow back his vomit, were small things. He'd done what he had to do, and because of that his wife and children were alive. He was a man who'd proven his manhood in every possible way—winning and marrying a wonderful girl, fathering two God-sent children, defending all of them with skill and courage. Every time fate had presented its challenge, Jack had met it and gotten the job done.

Yeah, he told himself, smiling at the TV. *Screw Liz Elliot.* That was a humorous thought. Who, he asked himself, would want to? That cold, skinny bitch, with her arrogance and . . . what else? Ryan's mind paused, seeking the answer to the question. What else? She was weak, wasn't she? Weak and timid. Beneath all the bluster and the hardness, what was really in there? Probably not much. He'd seen that sort of National Security Advisor before. Cutter, unwilling to face the music. Liz Elliot. Who'd want to screw her? Not very smart, and nothing in there to back up what smarts she did have. Good thing for her that the President had Bunker and Talbot to fall back on.

You're better than all of them. It was a satisfying thought to accompany the end of this glass of wine. *Why not have another? This stuff really isn't all that bad, is it?*

When Ryan returned, he saw Cathy was back also, going over her patient notes in the high-backed chair she liked.

"Want a glass of wine, honey?"

Dr. Caroline Ryan shook her head. "I have two procedures tomorrow."

Jack came around to take his place in the other chair, almost not glancing at his wife, but he caught her out the corner of his eye.

"Wow."

Cathy looked up from her paperwork to grin at him. Her face was nicely made up. Jack wondered how she'd managed not to mess her hair up in the shower.

"Where did you get that?"

"Out of a catalog."

"Whose, Fredericks?"

Dr. Caroline Muller Ryan, M.D., F.A.C.S., was dressed in a black peignoir that was a masterpiece of revelation and concealment. He couldn't tell what held the robe portion in place. Underneath was something filmy and . . . very nice. The color was odd, though, Cathy's nighties were all white. He'd never forgotten the wonderful white one she'd worn on their wedding night. Not that she'd been a virgin at the time, but somehow that white silk had made her so . . . that, too, was a memory that would never go away, Jack told himself. She'd never worn it since, saying that like her wedding dress, it was something to be used only once. What have I done to earn this wonderful girl? Jack asked himself.

"To what do I owe this honor?" Jack asked.

"I've been thinking."

"About what?"

"Well, Little Jack is seven. Sally is ten. I want another one."

"Another what?" Jack set his glass down.

"Another baby, you dope!"

"Why?" her husband asked.

"Because I can, and because I want one. I'm sorry," she went on with a soft smile, "if that bothers you. The exercise, I mean."

"I think I can handle that."

"I have to get up at four-thirty," Cathy said next. "My first procedure is before seven."

"So?"

"So." She rose and walked over to her husband. Cathy bent down to kiss him on the cheek. "See me upstairs."

Ryan sat still for a minute or two, gunning down the rest of his drink, switching off the TV, and smiling to himself. He checked to make sure the house was locked and the security system armed. He stopped off in the bathroom to brush his teeth. A surreptitious check of her vanity drawer revealed a thermometer and a little index card with dates and temperatures on it. So. She wasn't kidding. She'd been thinking about this and, typically, keeping it to herself. Well, that was okay, wasn't it? Yeah.

Jack entered the bedroom and paused to hang up his clothes, donning a bathrobe before joining his wife at the bedside. She rose to wrap her arms around his neck, and he kissed her.

"You sure about this, babe?"

"Does it bother you?"

"Cathy, to please you—anything you want that I can get or give, honey. Anything."

I wish you'd cut back on the drinking, Cathy didn't say. It wasn't the time. She felt his hands through the peignoir. Jack had strong but gentle hands that now traced her figure through the outfit. It was cheap and tarty, but every woman was entitled to look cheap and tarty once in a while, even an associate professor of ophthalmologic surgery at The Wilmer Eye Institute of the Johns Hopkins Hospital. Jack's mouth tasted like toothpaste and cheap white wine, but the rest of him smelled like a man, the man who'd made her life into a dream—mostly a dream. He was working too hard, drinking too much, not sleeping enough. But underneath all that was her man. And they didn't come any better, weaknesses, absences, and all.

Cathy made the proper noises when Jack's hands found the buttons. He got the message, but his fingers were clumsy. Annoying, the buttons were small and in those damned little fabric loops, but behind the buttons and the fabric were her breasts, and that fact ensured that he would not stop. Cathy took in a deep breath and smelled her favorite dusting powder. She didn't like perfume. A woman generated all the smells a man needed, she thought. There. Now his hands found her bare, smooth and still young skin. Thirty-six was not old, not too old for one more child. One more was all she craved, one more time to feel a new life growing within her. She'd accept the stomach upsets, the compressed bladder, the odd discomfort that merely gave detail to the wonder and the miracle of new life. The pain of birth—it was not fun, not at all, but to be able to do it, to have Jack at her side as he'd done with Sally and Little Jack, it was the most profound act of love that she had ever known. It was what being a woman meant, to be able to bring life to the world, to give a man the only kind of immortality that was, as he gave it to her.

And besides, she thought with a suppressed giggle, getting pregnant beat the hell out of jogging as a form of exercise.

Jack's hands removed her garment completely and eased her onto the bed. He was good at this, always had been, from their first nervous time, and at that moment she'd known that he would ask for her hand . . . after he'd sampled the other parts. Another giggle of past and present as his hands slid over skin that was now both hot and cold to the touch. And when he'd asked, when he'd worked up the courage, she'd seen the fear in his eyes, the terror at the possibility of rejection, when she was the one who had worried—even cried once—for a week that he might not ask, might change his mind, might find someone else. From before their first lovemaking, Cathy had known. This was the one. Jack was the man with whom she would share her life, whose children she would bear, whom she would love to the grave, maybe beyond if the priests were right. It wasn't his size or his strength, not even the bravery he'd had to show twice in her sight—and, she suspected, more than that in other places she'd never know about—it was his goodness, his gentleness, and a strength that only the perceptive knew about. Her husband was in some ways ordinary, in others unique, but in all ways a man, with all the strengths and few of the weaknesses. . . .

And tonight he would give her another child. Her cycle, predictable as always, was confirmed by her morning temperature. Well, she admitted, it was mainly a statistical probability, but a very high probability in her case. Mustn't get too clinical, not with Jack, and not at a time like this.

Her skin was on fire now. Jack was *so* good at this. His kisses both gentle and passionate, his hands so wonderfully skilled. He was wrecking her hair, but that didn't matter. Surgical caps made perms a waste of time and money. Through the scent of the dusting powder now came the more significant smells of a woman who was nearly ready. Ordinarily she was more of a participant in these episodes, but tonight she was letting Jack take complete charge, searching over her silky skin for the . . . interesting parts. He liked that occasionally. He also liked it when she played a more active role. More than one way to do this. It came almost as a surprise. Cathy arched her back and whimpered the first time, not really saying anything. It wasn't necessary. They'd been married long enough that he knew all the signals. She kissed him hard and wantonly, digging her nails into his shoulders. That signal meant *now!*

But nothing happened.

She took his hand, kissed it, and moved it down so that he would know that she was ready.

He seemed unusually tense. Okay, she was rushing him . . . why not let . . . after all, she'd let him take charge, and if she changed now. . . . She moved the hand back to her breast and was not disappointed. Cathy paid closer attention to him now. Tried to. His skills in exciting her were unchanged. She cried out again, kissed him hard, gasping a little, letting him know that he was the one, that her world centered on him as his centered on her. But still his back and shoulders were tense and knotted. What was the matter?

Her hands moved again, running over his chest, pulling playfully on the black hairs. That always set him off . . . especially as her hands followed the hairy trail down to . . .

What?

"Jack, what's wrong?" It seemed forever before she heard him speak.

"I don't know." Jack rolled over, away from his wife, onto his back, and his eyes stared in the ceiling.

"Tired?"

"I guess that's it." Jack slurred the words. "Sorry, honey."

Damn damn damn! But before she could think to say something else, his eyes closed.

It's the hours he's working, and all that drinking. But it wasn't fair! This was the day, this was the moment, and—

You're being selfish.

Cathy rose from the bed and collected her peignoir from the floor. She hung it up neatly before getting another that was fit to sleep in and heading into the bathroom.

He's a man, not a machine. He's tired. He's been working too goddamned hard. Everyone has a bad day. Sometimes he wants it and you're *not in the mood, and sometimes that makes him a little mad, and it's not his fault and it's not your fault. You have a wonderful marriage, but not a perfect one. Jack's as good a man as you have ever known, but he is not perfect either.*

But I wanted . . .

I want another baby, and the timing is so right, right now!

Cathy's eyes filled with tears of disappointment. She knew she was being unfair. But she was still disappointed. And a little angry.

"Well, Commodore, I can't knock the service."

"Hell, Ron, you expect me to have an old shipmate pick up a rental?"

"As a matter of fact, yes."

Mancuso snorted. His driver tossed the bags into the back of the Navy Plymouth while he and Jones let themselves into the back.

"How's the family?"

''Great, thank you, Commodore—''

''You can call me Bart now, Dr. Jones. Besides, I just screened for Admiral.''

''All right!'' Dr. Ron Jones observed. ''Bart. I like that. Just don't call me Indy. Let's see, the family. Kim's back in school for her doctorate. The kids are all in school—day-care, whatever—and I'm turning into a damned businessman.''

''Entrepreneur, I believe, is the correct term,'' Mancuso observed.

''Okay, be technical. Yeah, I own a big piece of the company. But I still get my hands dirty. I got a business guy to do the accounting bullshit. I still like to do real work. Last month I was down at AUTEC on the *Tennessee* checking out a new system.'' Jones looked at the driver. ''Okay to talk here?''

''Petty Officer Vincent is cleared higher than I am. Isn't that right?''

''Yes, sir, Admiral's always right, sir,'' the driver observed as he headed off toward Bangor.

''You got a problem, Bart.''

''How big?''

''A unique problem, skipper,'' Jones said, lapsing back to the time when he and Mancuso had done some interesting things aboard USS *Dallas*. ''It's never happened before.''

Mancuso read his eyes. ''Got pictures of the kids?''

Jones nodded. ''You bet. How are Mike and Dominic doing?''

''Well, Mike's looking at the Air Force Academy.''

''Tell him the oxygen rots your brain.''

''Dominic's thinking CalTech.''

''No kidding? Hell, I can help him out.''

The rest of the drive occupied itself with small talk. Mancuso swept into his office and closed the soundproof door behind Jones after ordering coffee from his steward.

''What's the problem, Ron?''

Jones hesitated just a fraction before answering. ''I think somebody was tracking *Maine*.''

''Track an Ohio? Come on.''

''Where is she now?''

''Heading back out to sea, as a matter of fact. Blue Crew is embarked. She links up with a 688 when she clears the strait for some noise checks, then clears to her patrol area.'' Mancuso could discuss almost anything with Jones. His company consulted on the sonar technology for all submarines and antisubmarine platforms in the U.S. fleet, and that necessarily included a lot of operational information.

''Got any Gold Crew guys on base now?''

''The Captain's off on vacation. XO's here, Dutch Claggett. Know him?''

''Wasn't he on the *Norfolk?* Black guy, right?''

''That's right.''

''I've heard good stuff about him. He did a nice job on a carrier group on his command quals. I was riding a P-3 when he kicked their ass.''

''You heard right. He's being deep-dipped. This time next year he'll be taking command of a fast-attack.''

''Who's his skipper?''

''Harry Ricks. Heard of him, too?''

Jones looked at the floor and muttered something. ''I got a new guy working for me, retired chief whose last tour was with Ricks. Is he as bad as I hear?''

"Ricks is a super engineer," Mancuso said. "I mean it. He's a genius at that stuff."

"Fine, skipper, so are you, but does Ricks know how to drive?"

"Want some coffee, Ron?" Mancuso gestured at the pot.

"You might want Commander Claggett here, sir." Jones rose and got his own coffee. "Since when have you turned diplomat?"

"Command responsibilities, Ron. I never told outsiders about the crazy stuff you did on *Dallas*."

Jones turned and laughed. "Okay, you got me there. I have the sonar analysis in my briefcase. I need to see his course tracks, depth records, that stuff. I think there's a good chance *Maine* had a trailer, and that, Bart, is no shit."

Mancuso lifted his phone. "Find Lieutenant Commander Claggett. I need him in my office at once. Thank you. Ron, how sure—"

"I did the analysis myself. One of my people looked it over and caught a whiff. I spent fifty hours massaging the data. One chance in three, maybe more, that she was being trailed."

Bart Mancuso set his coffee cup down. "That's really hard to believe."

"I know. That very fact may be skewing my analysis. It is kinda incredible."

It was an article of faith in the United States Navy that its fleet ballistic-missile submarines had never, not ever, not once been tracked while on deterrence patrol. As with most articles of faith, however, it had caveats.

The location of American missile-sub bases was not a secret. Even the United Parcel Service deliverymen who dropped off packages knew what to look for. In its quest for cost-efficiency, the Navy mainly used civilian security officers—"rentacops"—at its bases. Except that Marines were used wherever there were nuclear weapons. Wherever you saw Marines, there were nukes about. That was called a security measure. The missile boats themselves were unmistakably different from the smaller fast-attack subs. The ship names were on the Navy register, and the sailors of those ships wore ballcaps identifying them by name and hull number. With knowledge available to anyone, the Soviets knew where to station their own fast-attack boats to catch the American "boomers" on the way out to sea.

At first this had not been a problem. The first classes of Soviet fast-attack submarines had been equipped with "Helen Keller" sonars that could neither see nor hear, and the boats themselves had been noisier than unmuffled automobiles. All that had changed with the advent of the Victor-III class, which approximated a late American 594-class in radiated noise levels, and began to approach adequacy in sonar performance. Victor-IIIs had occasionally turned up at the Juan de Fuca Strait—and elsewhere—waiting for a U.S. missile sub to deploy, and in some cases, since harbor entrances are typically restricted waters, they had established contact and held on tight. That occasionally had included active sonar-lashing, both unnerving and annoying to American sub crews. As a result, U.S. fast-attack subs often accompanied missile submarines to sea. Their mission was to force the Soviet subs off. This was accomplished by the simple expedient of offering an additional target for sonar, confusing the tactical situation, or sometimes by forcing the Russian submarine off-track by ramming—called "shouldering," to defuse that most obscene of marine terms. In fact, American boomers had been tracked, only in shallow water, only near well-known harbors, and only for brief periods of time. As soon as the American subs reached deep water, their tactics were to increase speed to degrade the trailing sub's sonar performance, to maneuver evasively, and then go quiet. At that point—every time—the American submarine broke contact. The Soviet sub lost its track, and became the prey instead of the hunter. Missile submarines typically had highly drilled torpedo departments, and the more aggressive skippers would have all four of their tubes loaded with Mark 48 torpedoes with solutions set on the now-blinded Soviet sub as they watched them wander away in vulnerable befuddlement.

The simple fact was that American missile submarines were invulnerable in their patrol areas. When fast-attack boats were sent in to hunt them, care had to be given to operating depths—much like traffic control for commercial aircraft—lest an inadvertent ramming occur. American fast-attack boats, even the most advanced 688-class, had rarely tracked missile submarines, and the cases where Ohios had been tracked could be counted on the fingers of one hand. Nearly all involved a grievous mistake made by the missile-boat skippers, the ultimate ''black mark in the copybook,'' and even then only a very good and very lucky fast-attack skipper had managed to pull it off—and never ever without being counterdetected. *Omaha* had one of the best drivers in the Pacific Fleet, and he had failed to find *Maine* despite having some good intelligence data provided—better than anything a Soviet commander would ever get.

''Good morning, sir,'' Dutch Claggett said on his way through the door. ''I was right down the hall at personnel.''

''Commander, this is Dr. Ron Jones.''

''This the Jonesy you like to brag on, sir?'' Claggett took the civilian's hand.

''None of those stories are true,'' Jones said.

Claggett stopped cold when he saw the looks. ''Somebody die or something?''

''Grab a seat,'' Mancuso said. ''Ron thinks you might have been tracked on your last patrol.''

''Bullshit,'' Claggett observed. ''Excuse me, sir.''

''You're pretty confident,'' Jones said.

''*Maine* is the best submarine we own, Dr. Jones. We are a black hole. We don't radiate sound, we suck it in from around us.''

''You know the party line, Commander. Now, can we talk business?'' Ron unlocked his briefcase and pulled out a heavy sheaf of computer printouts. ''Right around the halfway point in your patrol.''

''Okay, yeah, that's when we snuck up behind *Omaha.*''

''I'm not talking about that. *Omaha* was in front of you,'' Jones said, flipping to the right page.

''I still don't believe it, but I'll look at what you got.''

The computer pages were essentially a graphic printout of two ''waterfall'' sonar displays. They bore time and true-bearing references. A separate set showed environmental data, mainly water temperature.

''You had a lot of clutter to worry about,'' Jones said, pointing to notations on the pages. ''Fourteen fishing boats, half a dozen deep-draft merchant ships, and I see the humpbacks were up to thin out the krill. So your sonar crew was busy, maybe a little overloaded. You also had a pretty hard layer.''

''All that's right,'' Claggett allowed.

''What's this?'' Jones pointed to a blossom of noise on the display.

''Well, we were tracking *Omaha,* and the Captain decided to rattle their cage with a water slug.''

''No shit?'' Jones asked. ''Well, that explains his reaction. I guess they changed their underwear and headed north. You never would have pulled that off on me, by the way.''

''Think so?''

''Yeah, I think so,'' Jones replied. ''I always paid real good attention to what was aft of us. I've been out on Ohios, Commander, okay? You can be tracked. Anybody can. It isn't just the platform. Now, look here.''

The printout was a computer-generated cacophony of dots that seemed for the most part to show nothing but random noise, as though a convention of ants had walked across the pages for hours. As with all truly random events, this one had irregularities, places where for one reason or another the ants had never trod, or places where a large number had congregated and then dispersed.

''This line of bearing,'' Jones said. ''This pattern comes back eight times, and it comes back only when the layer thins out.''

Commander Claggett frowned. ''Eight, you say? These two could be reverbs from the fishing boats, or really distant CZ-contacts.'' He flipped through the pages. Claggett knew his sonar. ''This is thin.''

''That's why your people didn't catch it, either aboard or here. But that's why I got the contract to back-check your people,'' Jones said. ''Who was out there?''

''Commodore?'' Claggett asked, and got a nod. ''There was an Akula-class out there somewhere. The P-3s lost him south of Kodiak, so he was within maybe six hundred miles of us. That doesn't mean this is him.''

''Which one?''

''Admiral Lunin,'' Claggett answered.

''Captain Dubinin?''

''Jesus, you *are* cleared pretty good,'' Mancuso noted. ''They say he's very good.''

''Ought to be, we have a mutual friend. Is Commander Claggett cleared for that?''

''No. Sorry, Dutch, but that is really black.''

''He ought to be cleared for that,'' Jones said. ''This secrecy crap goes way too far, Bart.''

''Rules are rules.''

''Yeah, sure. Anyway, this is the one that twigged me. Last page.'' Ron flipped through to the end. ''You were coming up to antenna depth . . .''

''Yeah, practice on the missiles.''

''You made some hull noises.''

''We came up fast, and the hull's made of steel, not elastic,'' Claggett said in some annoyance. ''So?''

''So your hull went up through the layer faster than your 'tail' did. Your towed array caught this.''

Claggett and Mancuso both went very quiet. What they saw was a fuzzy vertical line, but the line was in a frequency range that denoted a Soviet submarine's acoustical signature. It was by no means conclusive evidence, but it, like all the other things Jones had notated, was dead aft of *Maine's* course.

''Now, if I was a betting man, which I'm not, of course, I'd give you two-to-one that while you were underneath the layer, someone might have been tooling along just over top, letting his tail hang under it. He caught your hull transient, saw you were going shallow, and ducked under the layer just as you came over it. Cute move, but your big up-angle meant that your tail stayed down longer than it should have, and that's where this signature came from.''

"But there's nothing after that."

"Nothing at all," Jones admitted. "It never came back. From there on to the end of the tapes, nothing but random noise and otherwise-identified contacts."

"It's pretty thin, Ron," Mancuso said, standing up to straighten his back.

"I know. That's why I flew out. In writing it would never sell."

"What do you know about Russian sonar that we don't?"

"Getting better . . . approaching where we were, oh, ten or twelve years ago. They pay more attention to broad-band than we do—that's changing now. I sold the Pentagon on taking another look at the broad-band integration system Texas Instrument's been working on. Commander, what you said before about being a black hole. It cuts both ways. You can't *see* a black hole, but you *can* detect it. What if you track an Ohio by what should be there but isn't?"

"Background noise?"

"Yep." Jones nodded. "You make a hole in it. You make a black spot where there's no noise. If he can really isolate a line of bearing on his gear, and if he's got really good filters, and one dynamite sonar operator, I think it's possible—*if* something else cues you in."

"That's *real* thin."

Jones granted that observation. "But it's not impossible. I ran the numbers. It's not good, but it's not impossible. Moreover, we can track below ambient now. Maybe they can, too. I'm hearing they've started turning out a new large-aperture tail—the one designed by the guys outside Murmansk. Good as a BQR-15 used to be."

"I don't believe it," Mancuso said.

"I do, skipper. It's not new technology. What do we know about *Lunin?*"

"She's in overhaul right now. Let's see." Mancuso turned to look at the polar-projection chart on his office wall. "If that was him, then if he headed straight back to base . . . it's *possible,* technically speaking, but you're assuming a hell of a lot."

"I'm saying that this bird was just in the neighborhood when you fired that water slug, that you headed south, and so did he, that you gave him a hull transient which he reacted to, and then he broke contact on his own. The data is thin, but it fits—maybe, I grant you, *maybe*. That's what they pay me for, guys."

"I commended Ricks for rattling *Omaha*'s cage like that," Mancuso said after a moment. "I want aggressive skippers."

Jones chuckled to break the tension in the room. "I wonder why, Bart?"

"Dutch knows about that job we had on the beach, that pickup we did."

"That was a little exciting," Jones admitted.

"One chance in three. . . ."

"The probability increases if you assume the other skipper is smart. Dubinin had a great teacher."

"What are you two talking about?" Lieutenant Commander Claggett asked in some exasperation.

"You know we have all sorts of data on the Russian Typhoon class, lots more on their torpedoes. Ever wonder how we got all that data, Commander?"

"Ron, goddamn it!"

"I didn't break any rules, skipper, and besides, he needs to know."

"I can't do that and you know it."

"Fine, Bart." Jones paused. "Commander, you may speculate on how we got all that information in one great big lump. You might even guess right."

Claggett had heard a few rumbles, like why the Eight-Ten dock at Norfolk had been closed so long a few years before. There was a story floated about, spoken only in submarine wardrooms far at sea and well below the surface, that somehow the U.S. Navy had gotten its hands on a Russian missile sub, how a very strange reactor had turned up at the Navy's nuclear-power school in Idaho for tests and then had disappeared, how complete drawings *and* some hardware from Soviet torpedoes had magically appeared in Groton, and how two night missile shots out of Vandenberg Air Force Base had not appeared to be American missiles at all. Lots of operational intelligence had come into the fleet, very good stuff, stuff that sounded like it had come from someone who knew what the hell he was talking about—not always the case with intelligence information—on Soviet submarine tactics and training. Claggett needed only look at Mancuso's uniform to see the ribbon that denoted a Distinguished Service Medal, America's highest peacetime decoration. The ribbon had a star on it, indicating a second such award. Mancuso was rather young for a squadron command, and very young indeed to be selected for Rear Admiral (Lower Half). And here was a former enlisted man who'd sailed with Mancuso, and now called him *Bart*. He nodded to Dr. Jones.

"I get the picture. Thanks."

"You're saying operator error?"

Jones frowned. He didn't know all that much about Harry Ricks. "Mainly bad luck. Call it good luck, even. Nothing bad happened, and we've learned something. We know more about the Akula than we used to. A weird set of circumstances came together. Won't happen again in a hundred years, maybe. Your skipper was a victim of circumstance, and the other guy—if there was another guy there—was very damned sharp. Hey, the important thing about mistakes is that you learn from them, right?"

"Harry gets back in ten days," Mancuso said. "Can you be back here then?"

"Sorry," Jones said with a shake of the head. "I'm going to be in England. I'm going out on HMS *Turbulent* for a few days of hide 'n' seek. The Brits have a new processor that we need to look at, and I drew the duty."

"You're not going to ask me to present this to the CO, are you, sir?" Claggett asked after a minute's reflection.

"No, Dutch . . . you trying to tell me something?"

It was Claggett's turn to look unhappy. "Sir, he's my boss, and he's not a bad boss, but he is a little positive in his thinking."

That was artfully done, Jones thought. *Not a bad boss . . . a little positive. He just called his skipper an idiot in a way that no one could ever call disloyal.* Ron wondered what sort of hyper-nuc-engineer this Ricks was. The good news was that this XO had his act together. And a smart skipper listened to his XO.

"Skipper, how's Mr. Chambers doing?"

"Just took over *Key West*. Got a kid you trained as his leading sonarman. Billy Zerwinski, just made chief, I hear."

"Oh, yeah? Good for him. I figured Mr. Chambers was going places, but Billy Z as a chief? What is my Navy coming to?"

"This is taking forever," Qati observed sourly. His skin was pasty white. The man was suffering again from his drug treatment.

"That is false," Fromm replied sternly. "I told you several months, and it will be several months. The first time this was done, it took three years and the resources of the world's richest nation. I will do it for you in an eighth of that time, and on a shoestring budget. In a few days we'll start to work on the rhodium. That will be much easier.''

''And the plutonium?'' Ghosn asked.

''That will be the last metal work—you know why, of course.''

''Yes, Herr Fromm, and we must be extremely careful, since when you work with a critical mass you must be careful that it does not become critical while you are forming it,'' Ghosn replied, allowing his exacerbation to show for a change. He was tired. He'd been at work for eighteen hours now, supervising the workers. ''And the tritium?''

''Last of all. Again the obvious reason. It is relatively unstable, and we want the tritium we use to be as pure as possible.''

''Quite so.'' Ghosn yawned, barely having heard the answer to his question, and not troubling himself to wonder why Fromm had answered as he had.

For his part Fromm made a mental note. Palladium. He needed a small quantity of palladium. How had he forgotten that? He grunted to himself. Long hours, miserable climate, surly workers and associates. A small price to pay, of course, for this opportunity. He was doing what only a handful of men had ever done, and he was doing it in such a way as to equal the work of Fermi and the rest in 1944–5. It was not often that a man could measure himself against the giants and come off well in the comparison. He found himself wondering idly what the weapon would be used for, but admitted to himself that he didn't care, not really. Well, he had other work to do.

The German walked across the room to where the milling machines were. Here another team of technicians were at work. The beryllium piece now on the machine had the most intricate shape and had been the hardest to program, with concave, convex, and other complex curves. The machine was computer-controlled, of course, but was kept under constant observation through the Lexan panels that isolated the machining area from the outside world. The area was ventilated upwards into an electrostatic air-cleaner. There was no sense in just dumping the metallic dust into the external air—in fact, doing so constituted a major security hazard. Over the electrostatic collection plates was a solid two meters of earth. Beryllium was not radioactive, but plutonium was, and plutonium would presently be worked on this very same machine. The beryllium was both necessary to the device and good practice for later tasks.

The milling machine was everything Fromm had hoped for when he'd ordered it several years before. The computer-driven tools were monitored by lasers, producing a degree of perfection that could not have been achieved so quickly as recently as five years ago. The surface of the beryllium was jeweled from the machining, already looking like the finish on a particularly fine rifle bolt, and this was only the first stage of machining. The data readout on the machine showed tolerances measured in angstroms. The toolhead was spinning at 25,000 rpm, not so much grinding as burning off irregularities. Separate instruments kept a computer eye on the work being done, both measuring tolerances and waiting for the toolhead to show signs of wear, at which point the machine would automatically stop and replace the tool with a fresh one. Technology was wonderful. What had once been the work of specially trained master machinists overseen by Nobel Prize winners was now being done by microchips.

The actual casing for the device was already fabricated. Ellipsoidal in shape, it was 98 centimeters in length by 52 in extreme breadth. Made of steel one centimeter in thickness, it had to be strong, but not grossly so, just enough to hold a vacuum. Also ready for installation were curved blocks of polyethylene and polyurethane foam, because a device of this sort required the special properties of both the strongest and the flimsiest materials. They had gotten ahead of themselves in some areas, of course, but there was no sense in wasting time or idle hands. On another machine, workers were practicing yet again on a stainless-steel blank that simulated the folded-cylinder plutonium reaction-mass primary. It was their seventh such practice session. Despite the sophistication of the machines, the first two had gone badly, as expected. By number five they had figured most of the process out, and the sixth attempt had been good enough to work—but not good enough for Fromm. The German had a simple mental model for the overall task, one formulated by America's National Aeronautics and Space Administration to describe the first moon landing. In order for the device to perform as desired, a complex series of individual events had to take place in an inhumanly precise sequence. He viewed the process as a walk through a series of gates. The wider the gates were, the easier it would be to walk through them quickly. Plus/minus tolerances reflected slight closure of the individual gates. Fromm wanted zero tolerances. He wanted every single part of the weapon to match his design criteria as exactly as the available technology made possible. The closer to perfection he could get, the more likely it was that the device would perform exactly as he predicted . . . or even better, part of him thought. Unable to experiment, unable to find empirical solutions to complex theoretical problems, he'd overengineered the weapon, provided an energy budget that was several orders of magnitude beyond what was really necessary for the projected yield. That explained the vast quantity of tritium he planned to use, more than five times what was really needed in a theoretical sense. That carried its own problems, of course. His tritium supply was several years old, and some parts of it had decayed into ^{3}He, a decidedly undesirable isotope of helium, but by filtering the tritium through palladium he'd separate the tritium out, ensuring a proper total yield. American and Soviet bombmakers could get away with far less of it, because of their extensive experimentation, but Fromm had his own advantage. He did not have to concern himself with a long shelf-life for his device, and that was a luxury that his Soviet and American counterparts did not have. It was the only advantage he had over them, and Fromm planned to make full use of it. As with most parts of bomb design, it was an advantage that cut both ways, but Fromm knew he had full control over the device. *Palladium,* he told himself. *Mustn't forget that.* But he had plenty of time.

"Finished." The head of the team waved for Fromm to look. The stainless-steel blank came off the machine easily, and he handed it to Fromm. It was thirty centimeters in length. The shape was complex, what one would get from taking a large water tumbler and bending its top outside and down toward the base. It would not hold water because of a hole in the center of what might have been the bottom—actually it would, Fromm told himself a second later, just in the wrong way. The blank weighed about three kilograms, and every surface was mirror-smooth. He held it up to the light to check for imperfections and irregularities. His eyes were not that good. The quality of the finish was easier to understand mathematically than visually. The surface, so said the machine, was accurate to a thousandth of a micron, or a fraction of a single wavelength of light.

"It is a jewel," Ghosn observed, standing behind Fromm. The machinist beamed.

"Adequate," was Fromm's judgment. He looked at the machinist. "When you've made five more equally as good, I will be satisfied. Every metal segment must be of this quality. Begin another,'' he told the machinist. Fromm handed the blank to Ghosn and walked away.

''Infidel,'' the machinist growled under his breath.

''Yes, he is,'' Ghosn agreed. ''But he is the most skilled man I have ever met.''

''I'd rather work for a Jew.''

''This is magnificent work,'' Ghosn said to change the subject.

''I would not have believed it possible to polish metal so precisely. This machine is incredible. I could make anything with it.''

''That is good. Make another of these,'' Ghosn told him with a smile.

''As you say.''

Ghosn walked to Qati's room. The Commander was looking at a plate of simple foods, but unable to touch it for fear of retching.

''Perhaps this will make you feel better,'' Ghosn told him.

''That is?'' Qati said, taking it.

''That is what the plutonium will look like.''

''Like glass . . .''

''Smoother than that. Smooth enough for a laser mirror. I could tell you the accuracy of the surface, but you've never seen anything that small in your life anyway. Fromm is a genius.''

''He's an arrogant, overbearing—''

''Yes, Commander, he is all of that, but he is exactly the man we need. I could never have done this myself. Perhaps, given a year or two, perhaps I might have been able to rework that Israeli bomb into something that would work—the problems were far more complex than I knew only a few weeks ago. But this Fromm . . . what I am learning from him! By the time we are finished, I *will* be able to do it again on my own!''

''Really?''

''Commander, do you know what engineering is?'' Ghosn asked. ''It is like cooking. If you have the right recipe, the right book, and the right ingredients, anyone can do it. Certainly this task is a hard one, but the principle holds. You must know how to use the various mathematical formulae, but they are all in books also. It is merely a question of education. With computers, the proper tools—and a good teacher, which this Fromm bastard is . . .''

''Then why haven't more—''

''The hard part is getting the ingredients, specifically the plutonium or U-235. That requires a nuclear reactor plant of a specific type or the new centrifuge technology. Either represents a vast investment, and one which is difficult to conceal. It also explains the remarkable security measures taken in the handling and transport of bombs and their components. The oft-told tale that bombs are hard to make is a lie.''

18. Progress

Wellington had three men working for him. Each was an experienced investigator, accustomed to politically sensitive cases which demanded the utmost discretion. His job was to identify likely areas of field investigation, then to examine and correlate the information they returned to his office in the Justice Department. The tricky part was to gather the information without notice going back to the target of the probe, and Wellington correctly thought that that part of the task would be particularly difficult with a target like Ryan. The DDCI was nothing if not perceptive. His previous job had qualified him as a man who could hear the grass grow and read tea leaves with the best of them. That meant going slow . . . but not too slow. It also seemed likely to the young attorney that the purpose of his investigation was not to produce data suitable for a grand jury, which gave him quite a bit more leeway than he might otherwise have had. He doubted that Ryan could have been so foolish as to have actually broken any law. The SEC rules had been grazed, perhaps bent, but on inspection of the SEC investigation documents, it was clear that Ryan's action had, arguably, been made in good faith and full expectation that he had not violated any statute. That judgment might have been technical on Ryan's part, but the law *was* technical. The Securities and Exchange Commission could have pushed, and might even have gotten an indictment, but they would never have gotten a conviction . . . maybe they could have muscled him into a settlement and/or a consent decree, but Wellington doubted that also. They'd suggested it as a sign of good faith, and he had answered with a flat *no*. Ryan was not a man to tolerate being pushed around. This man had killed people. That didn't frighten Wellington in any way. It was merely an indicator of the man's strength of character. Ryan was a tough, formidable son of a bitch who met things head-on when he had to.

That's his weakness, Wellington told himself.

He prefers to meet things head-on. He lacks subtlety. It was a common failing of the honest, and a grievous weakness in a political environment.

Ryan had political protectors, however. Trent and Fellows were nothing if not canny political craftsmen.

What an interesting tactical problem. . . .

Wellington saw his task as twofold: to get something that could be used against Ryan, and something that would also neutralize his political allies.

Carol Zimmer. Wellington closed one file and opened another.

There was a photograph from the Immigration and Naturalization Service. That one was years old—she'd been a child-bride in the most literal sense of the word when she'd first come to America, a tiny little thing with a doll's face. A more recent photo taken by his field investigator showed a mature woman still short of forty, her face now showing some lines where once there had been the smoothness of china. If anything she was more beautiful than before. The timid, almost hunted look in the first photo—understandable, since it had been taken after her escape from Laos—had been replaced by that of a woman secure in her life. She had a cute smile, Wellington told himself.

The lawyer remembered a classmate in law school, Cynthia Yu. *Damn, hadn't she been quite a lay . . . same sort of eyes, almost, the Oriental coquette. . . .*

Might that *be it?*

Something that simple?

Ryan was married: Wife, Caroline Muller Ryan, M.D., eye surgeon. Photo: a quintessential Wasp, except that she was Catholic, slender and attractive, mother of two.

Well, just because a man has a pretty wife . . .

Ryan had established an educational trust fund. . . . Wellington opened another file. In it was a Xerox copy of the document.

Ryan, he saw, had done it alone, through a lawyer—not his regular lawyer! A D.C. guy. And Caroline Ryan had not signed the papers . . . did she even know about it? The information on his desk suggested that she did not.

Wellington next checked the birth records on the newest Zimmer child. Her husband had been killed in a "routine training accident" . . . the timing was equivocal. She might have gotten pregnant the very week her husband had been killed. Then again, she might not have. It was her seventh child—eighth? You couldn't tell with those, could you? Gestation could be nine months, or less. First kids were usually late. Later kids, as often as not, were early. Birth weight of the child . . . five pounds seven ounces . . . less than average, but she was an Asian, and they were small . . . did they have smaller-than-normal babies? Wellington made his notes, recognizing that he had a series of maybes and not a single fact.

But, hell, was he really looking for facts?

The two punks. Ryan's bodyguards, Clark and Chavez, had mangled one of them. His investigator had checked that out with the Anne Arundel County Police Department. The local cops had signed off on Clark's story. The punks in question had long but minor records, a few summary probations, a few sessions with youth counselors. The cops were delighted at the way things had turned out. "Okay with me if he'd shot that worthless little fucker," a police sergeant had said with a laugh recorded on the investigator's tape cassette. "That Clark guy looked like one very serious dude. His sidekick ain't much different. If those punks were dumb enough to hassle them, hey, it's a tough world, y'know? Two other gang members confirmed the story the way the good guys told it, and that's a closed case, man."

But *why* had Ryan set his two bodyguards on them?

He's killed to protect his family, hasn't he? This is not a guy who tolerates danger to his . . . friends . . . family . . . lovers?

It is *possible.*

"Hmm . . ." Wellington observed to himself. The DDCI is getting a little on the side. Nothing illegal, just unsavory. Also out of character for the saintly Dr. John Patrick Ryan. When his lover is annoyed by some local gang members, he simply sics his bodyguards on them, like a mafia *capo* might do, as a lordly public service that no cop would ever bother fooling with.

Might that be enough?

No.

He needed something more. Evidence, some sort of evidence. Not good enough for a grand jury . . . but good enough for—what? To launch an official investigation. Of course. Such investigations were never really secret, were they? A few whispers, a few rumors. Easily done. But first Wellington needed something to hang his hat on.

''There are those who say this could be a preview of the Super Bowl: Three weeks into the NFL season, the Metrodome. Both teams are two and oh. Both teams look like the class of their respective conferences. The San Diego Chargers take on the Minnesota Vikings.''

''You know, Tony Wills's rookie season has started even more spectacularly than his college career. Only two games, and he has three hundred six yards rushing in forty-six carries—that's six-point-seven yards every time he touches the ball, and he did *that* against the Bears and the Falcons, two fine rushing defenses,'' the color man observed. ''Can anybody stop Tony Wills?''

''And a hundred twenty-five yards in his nine pass receptions. It's no wonder that they call this kid the franchise.''

''Plus his doctorate from Oxford University.'' The color man laughed. ''Academic All-American, Rhodes Scholar, the man who singlehandedly put Northwestern University back on the map with two trips to the Rose Bowl. You suppose he's faster than a speeding bullet?''

''We'll find out. That rookie middle linebacker for the Chargers, Maxim Bradley, is the best thing I've seen since Dick Butkus came out of Illinois, the best middle linebacker Alabama ever turned out—and that's the school of Leroy Jordan, Cornelius Bennett, and quite a few other all-pros. They don't call him the Secretary of Defense for nothing.'' It was already the biggest joke in the NFL, referring to the team owner, Dennis Bunker, the real SecDef.

''Tim, I think we got us a ball game!''

''I should be there,'' Brent Talbot observed. ''Dennis is.''

''If I tried to keep him away from his games, he'd resign,'' President Fowler said. ''Besides, he used his own plane.'' Dennis Bunker owned his own small jet, and though he allowed others to fly him around, he still maintained a current commercial pilot's license. It was one of the reasons the military respected him. He could try his hand at almost anything that flew, having once been a distinguished combat flyer.

''What's the spread on this one?''

''Vikings by three,'' the President answered. ''That's just because of the home field. The teams are pretty even. I saw Wills against the Falcons last week. He's some kid.''

''Tony's all of that. A wonderful boy. Smart, marvelous attitude, spends a lot of time with kids.''

''How about we get him to be a spokesman for the antidrug campaign?''

''He already does that in Chicago. I can call him if you want.''

Fowler turned. ''Do it, Brent.''

Behind them Pete Connor and Helen D'Agustino relaxed on a couch. President Fowler knew them both to be football fans, and the President's TV room was large and comfortable.

''Anybody want a beer?'' Fowler asked. He could not watch a ball game without a beer.

''I'll get it,'' D'Agustino said, heading for the refrigerator in the next room. It was the most curious thing about this most complex of men, ''Daga'' thought to herself. The man looked, dressed, walked, and acted like a patrician. He was a genuine intellectual, with the arrogance to match. But in front of a TV watching a football game—Fowler watched baseball only when his presidential duties required it—he was Joe Six-Pack, with a bowl of popcorn and a glass of beer, or two, or three. Of course, even here, his "anybody want a beer?" was a command. His bodyguards could not drink on duty, and Talbot never touched the stuff. Daga got herself a Diet Coke.

"Thank you," Fowler said when she handed the glass to her President. He was even more polite at football games. Perhaps, D'Agustino thought, because it was something he and his wife had done. She hoped that was true. It gave the man the humanity that he needed above all things.

"Wow! Bradley hit Wills hard enough that we heard it up here." On the screen, both men got up and traded what looked like an emotional exchange but was probably a mutual laugh.

"Might as well get acquainted fast, Tim. They'll be seeing a lot of each other. Second and seven from the thirty-one, both teams just getting loosened up. That Bradley's a smart linebacker. He played off the center and filled the hole like he knew what was coming."

"He certainly reads his keys well for a rook, and that Viking center made the Pro Bowl last year," the color guy pointed out.

"Great ass on that Bradley kid," Daga pointed out quietly.

"This women's lib stuff is going too far, Helen," Pete said with a grin. He shifted positions on the couch to get his service revolver out of his kidney.

Günther Bock and Marvin Russell stood on the sidewalk just outside the White House grounds among a crowd of a hundred or so tourists, most of whom aimed cameras at the executive mansion. They'd arrived in the city the previous evening, and tomorrow they'd tour the Capitol. Both wore ballcaps to protect them from what still felt like a summer sun. Bock had a camera draped around his neck on a Mickey Mouse strap. He snapped a few photos, mainly to blend in with the rest of the tourists. The real observations came from his trained eye. This was a much harder target than people realized. The buildings around the White House were all large enough that sharpshooters were provided with excellent perches concealed by the stonework. He knew that he was probably under surveillance right now, but they couldn't have the time or money to compare his likeness to every photo they had on their books, and he'd taken the trouble to alter his appearance enough to dispense with that worry.

The President's helicopter flew in and landed only a hundred meters from where he stood. A man with a man-portable SAM might stand a good chance of taking it out—except for the practical considerations. To be there at the right time was much harder than it seemed. The ideal way would be to have a small truck, perhaps one with a hole cut in the roof so that the missileer could stand, fire, and attempt his escape. Except for the riflemen who certainly perched on the surrounding buildings, and Bock had no illusions that such snipers would miss their targets. Americans had invented sharpshooting, and their President would have the services of the best. Doubtless some of the people in this crowd of tourists were also Secret Service agents, and it was unlikely that he'd spot them.

The bomb could be driven here and detonated in a truck . . . depending on the protective measures that Ghosn had warned him about. Similarly, he might be able to deliver the weapon by truck to the immediate vicinity of the Capitol Building, perhaps at the time of the President's State of the Union Address . . . if the weapon were ready on time. That they weren't sure of, and there was also the question of shipping it here—three weeks it would take. Latakia to Rotterdam, then transshipment to an American port. Baltimore was the closest major port. Norfolk/Newport News was next. Both handled lots of containerized shipping. They could fly it in, but airborne cargo was often X-rayed, and they could not risk that.

The idea was to catch the President on a weekend. It almost had to be a weekend for everything else to work. Everything else. Bock knew that he was violating one of his most important operational precepts—simplicity. But for this to have a chance of working, he had to arrange more than one incident, and he had to do it on a weekend. But the American President was in the White House only about half the time on weekends, and his movements between Washington, Ohio, and other places were unpredictable. The simplest security measure available to the President of the United States was the one they used: his movement schedule, as well known as it might have been, was irregular and its precise details were often closely held. Bock needed at least a week's lead-time to set up his other arrangements—and that was optimistic—but it would be nearly impossible to get that seven days. It would actually have been simpler to plan a simple assassination with conventional weapons. A small aircraft, for example, might be armed with SA-7 missiles . . . probably not. The President's helicopter undoubtedly had the best infrared jammers available. . . .

One chance. You get only one chance.

What if we are patient? What if we simply sit on the bomb for a year and bring it into the country for the next *State of the Union speech?* Getting the bomb close enough to the Capitol Building to destroy it and everyone in it should not be hard. He'd heard—and would see tomorrow—that the Capitol was a building of classical construction—lots of stone, but little structural ironwork . . . perhaps all they needed was patience.

But that wouldn't happen. Qati would not allow it. There was both the question of security and the more important consideration that Qati thought himself a dying man, and dying men were not known for their patience.

And would it work in any case? How well did the Americans guard the areas where the President's presence was predictable well in advance? Were their radiological sensors in the area?

You'd put them there, wouldn't you?

Only one chance. You'll never be able to repeat this.

At least one week's advance notice or you'll never achieve anything beyond mass murder.

Must be a place without the likely presence of radiological sensors. That eliminated Washington.

Bock started walking away from the black iron fence. His face did not betray the anger he felt.

"Back to the hotel?" Russell asked.

"Yes, why not?" Both men were still tired from their traveling anyway.

"Good, wanted to catch the ball game. You know, that's about the only thing Fowler and I see eye to eye on?"

"Hmph? What's that?"

"Football." Russell laughed. "You know? Football. Okay, I'll teach it t'ya."

Fifteen minutes later they were in their room. Russell switched the TV to the local NBC channel.

* * *

''That was some drive, Tom. The Vikings had to convert six third-downs, and two of them required measurements.''

''And one was a bad spot,'' President Fowler said.

''Ref didn't think so.'' Talbot chuckled.

''They're holding Tony Wills to barely three yards a carry, and one of those was his twenty-yard break on the reverse that caught the Chargers napping.''

''A lot of work for three points, Tim, but they did get the three.''

''And now the Chargers get their chance at offense. The Vikings defense is a little iffy, with two of their starters out with minor injuries. I bet they're sorry to miss this one.''

The Chargers' quarterback took his first snap, faded back five steps, and hurled the ball toward his flanker, slanting across the middle, but a hand tipped the ball and it ended up in the surprised face of the Vikings' free safety, who pulled it in and fell at the forty.

Bock found the game exciting in a distant sort of way, but almost totally incomprehensible. Russell tried to explain, but it didn't really help very much. Günther consoled himself with a beer, stretching out on the bed while his mind rolled over what he'd seen. Bock knew what he wanted his plan to accomplish, but the exact details—especially here in America—were looking harder than expected. If only—

''What was that they said?''

''The Secretary of Defense,'' Russell answered.

''A joke?''

Marvin turned. ''Sort of a joke. That's what they call the middle linebacker, Maxim Bradley, from the University of Alabama. But the real one owns the team. Dennis Bunker—there he is.'' The camera showed Bunker in one of the stadium's sky-boxes.

How remarkable, Bock thought.

''What is this Super Bowl they talked about?''

''That's the championship game. They have a playoff series of the most successful teams, and the last one is called the Super Bowl.''

''Like the World Cup, you mean?''

''Yeah, something like that. 'Cept we do it every year. This year—actually next year, end of January—it's in the new stadium they built at Denver. The Skydome, I think they call it.''

''They expect these two teams to go there?''

Russell shrugged. ''That's the talk. The regular season is sixteen weeks, man, then three weeks of playoffs, then another week wait for the Super Bowl.''

''Who goes to this last game?''

''Lots of people. Hey, man, it's *the* game. Everybody wants to go to it. Getting tickets is a mother. These two teams are the best bet to go all the way, but it's real unpredictable, y'know?''

''President Fowler is a football enthusiast?''

''That's what they say. He's supposed to go to a lot of Redskin games right here in D.C.''

''What about security?'' Bock asked.

''It's tough. They put him in one of the special boxes. Figure they have it rigged with bulletproof glass or something.''

How very foolish, Bock thought. Of course, a stadium was easier to secure than it might seem to the casual observer. A heavy crew-served weapon could be fired only from an entrance ramp, and watching those was relatively easy. On the other hand . . .

Bock closed his eyes. He was thinking in an unorganized way, vacillating between conventional and unconventional approaches to the problem. He was also allowing himself to focus on the wrong thing. Killing the American President was desirable but not essential. What *was* essential was to kill the largest possible number of people in the most spectacular way imaginable, then to coordinate with other activities in order to foment . . .

Think! Concentrate on the real mission.

''The television coverage for these games is most impressive,'' Bock observed after a minute.

''Yeah, they make a big deal of that. Satellite vans, all that stuff.'' Russell was concentrating on the game. The Vikings had scored something called a touchdown, and the score was now ten to nothing, but it seemed now that the other team was moving rapidly in the other direction.

''Has the game ever been seriously disrupted?''

Marvin turned. ''Huh? Oh, during the war with Iraq, they had really tight security—and you remember the movie, right?''

''Movie?'' Bock asked.

''*Black Sunday,* I think it was—some Middle East guys tried to blow up the place.'' Russell laughed. ''Already been done, man. In Hollywood, anyway. They used a blimp. Anyway, during the Super Bowl when we were fighting Iraq, they wouldn't let the TV blimp come near the place.''

''Is there a game at Denver today?''

''No, that's tomorrow night, Broncos and the Seahawks. Won't be much of a game. The Broncos are rebuilding this year.''

''I see.'' Bock left the room and arranged for the concierge to get them tickets to Denver in the morning.

Cathy got up to see him off. She even fixed breakfast. Her solicitude over the past few days had not made her husband feel any better. Quite the reverse. But he couldn't say anything about it, could he? Even the way she overdid it, straightening his tie and kissing him on the way out the door. The smile, the loving look, all for a husband who couldn't get it up, Jack thought on his way out to the car. The same sort of smothering attention you might give to some poor bastard in a wheelchair.

''Morning, doc.''

''Hello, John.''

''Catch the Vikings-Chargers game yesterday?''

''No, I, uh, took my son to see the Orioles. They lost six to one.'' Success was following Jack everywhere, but at least he'd kept his word to his son. That was something, wasn't it?

''Twenty-four to twenty-one in overtime. God, that Wills kid is incredible. They held him to ninety-six yards, but when he had to deliver, he popped it for twenty yards and set up the field goal,'' Clark reported.

''You have money on the game?''

''Five bucks at the office, but it was a three-point spread. The education fund won that one.''

It gave Ryan something to chuckle about. Gambling was as illegal at CIA as it was in every other government office, but a serious attempt to enforce a ban on football betting might have started a revolution—the same was true at the FBI, Jack was sure, which enforced interstate gambling statutes—and the semiofficial system was that half-point betting spreads were not allowed. All "pushes" (odds-caused ties) forfeited into the Agency's in-house charity, the Education Aid Fund. It was something that even the Agency's own Inspector General winked at—in fact, he liked to lay money on games as much as the next guy.

"Looks like you at least got some sleep, Jack," Clark noted as they made their way toward Route 50.

"Eight hours," Jack said. He'd wanted another chance the previous night, but Cathy had said no. *You're too tired, Jack. That's all it is. You're working too hard, and I want you to take it easy, okay?*

Like I'm a goddamned stud horse that's been overworked.

"Good for you," Clark said. "Or maybe your wife insisted, eh?"

Ryan stared ahead at the road. "Where's the box?"

"Here."

Ryan unlocked it and started looking at the weekend's dispatches.

They caught an early direct flight from Washington National to Denver's Stapleton International. It was a clear day most of the way across the country. Bock got a window seat and looked at the country, his first time in America. As were most Europeans, he was surprised, almost awed by the sheer size and diversity. The wooded hills of Appalachia; the flat farmlands of Kansas, speckled with the immense circular signature of the traveling irrigation systems; the stunning way the plains ended and the Rockies began within easy sight of Denver. No doubt Marvin would say something when they arrived about how this had all been property of his people. What rubbish. They'd been nomadic barbarians, following the herds of bison, or whatever had once been there before civilization arrived. America might be his enemy, but it was a civilized country, and all the more dangerous for it. By the time the aircraft landed, he was squirming with his need for a smoke. Ten minutes after landing they'd rented a car and were examining a map. Bock's head was dizzy from the lack of oxygen here. Nearly fifteen hundred meters of altitude, he realized. It was a wonder that people could play American football here.

They'd landed behind the morning rush hour, and driving to the stadium was simple. Southwest of the city, the new Skydome was a distinctive structure located on an immense plot of ground to allow ample room for parking. He parked the car close to a ticket window and decided that the simple approach would be best.

"Can I get two tickets for tonight's match?" he asked the attendant.

"Sure, we have a few hundred left. Where do you want them?"

"I don't know the stadium at all, I'm afraid."

"You must be new here," the lady observed with a friendly smile. "All we got's in the upper deck, Section Sixty-six and Sixty-eight."

"Two, please. Is cash all right?"

"Sure is. Where are you from?"

"Denmark," Bock replied.

"Really? Well, welcome to Denver! Hope you enjoy the game."

"Can I look around to see where my seat is?"

"Technically, no, but nobody really minds."

"Thank you." Bock smiled back at the simpering fool.

"They had seats for tonight?" Marvin Russell asked. "I'll be damned."

"Come, we will see where they are."

Bock walked through the nearest open gate, just a few meters from the big ABC vans that carried the satellite equipment for the evening broadcast. He took the time to notice that the stadium was hard-wired for the equipment. So the TV vans would always be in the same place, just by Gate 5. Inside, he saw a team of technicians setting up their equipment, then he headed up the nearest ramp, deliberately heading in the wrong direction.

The stadium had to seat sixty thousand people, perhaps a little more. It had three primary levels, called lower, mezzanine, and upper, plus two complete ranks of enclosed boxes, some of which looked quite luxurious. Structurally it was quite impressive. Massive reinforced-concrete construction, all the upper decks were cantilevered. There were no pillars to block a spectator's view. A fine stadium. A superb target. Beyond the parking lot to the north were endless hectares of low-rise apartment buildings. To the east was a government office center. The stadium was not in the city center, but that couldn't be helped. Bock found and took his seat, orienting himself with the compass and the TV equipment. The latter was quite easy. An ABC banner was being hung below one of the press boxes.

"Hey!"

"Yes?" Bock looked down at a security guard.

"You're not supposed to be here."

"Sorry." He held up his tickets. "I just bought them, and I wanted to see where my seats were so that I would know where to park. I've never seen an American football game," he added, heavy on the accent. Americans, he'd heard, were always nice to people with European accents.

"You want to park in Area A or B. Try to arrive early, like before five. You want to beat the rush-hour traffic. It can be a bear out there."

Günther bobbed his head. "Thank you. I'll be leaving now."

"No problem, sir. It's no big deal. I mean, it's the insurance, y'know? You have people wandering around, they might get hurt and sue."

Bock and Russell left. They circled the bottom level, just so that Günther could be sure he had the configuration memorized. Then that became unnecessary when he found a stadium diagram printed on a small card.

"Seen what you wanted?" Marvin asked when they got back to the car.

"Yes, possibly."

"You know, that's pretty subtle," the American mused aloud.

"What do you mean?"

"Dickin' with the TV. The really dumb thing about revolutionaries is that they overlook the psychological stuff. You don't have to kill a lot of people, just pissin' them off, scarin' them, that's enough, isn't it?"

Bock stopped at the parking-lot exit and looked at his companion. "You have learned much, my friend."

"This is pretty hot stuff," Ryan said, leafing through the pages.

"I didn't know it was that bad," Mary Patricia Foley agreed.

"How are you feeling?"

The senior field officer's eyes twinkled. "Clyde has dropped. Waiting for my water to break."

Jack looked up. "Clyde?"

"That's what I'm calling him—her—whatever."

"Doing your exercises?"

"Rocky Balboa should be in the shape I'm in. Ed's got the nursery all painted up. The crib is put back together. All ready, Jack."

"How much time will you be taking off?"

"Four weeks, maybe six."

"I may want you to go over some of this at home," Ryan said, lingering on page two.

"Long as you pay me." Mary Pat laughed.

"What do you think, MP?"

"I think SPINNAKER is the best source we have. If he says it, it's probably true."

"We haven't caught a whiff of this anywhere else. . . ."

"That's why you recruit good penetration agents."

"True," Ryan had to agree.

The report from Agent SPINNAKER wasn't quite earthshaking, but it was like the first rumble that got people worrying about a major quake. Since the Russians had taken the cork out of the bottle, the Soviet Union had developed an instant case of political schizophrenia. Wrong term, Ryan reflected. Multiple-personality disorder, perhaps. There were five identifiable political areas: the true-believing communists, who thought that any divergence from the True Path was a mistake (the Forward-to-the-Past crowd, some called them); the progressive socialists, who wanted to create socialism with a human face (something that had singularly failed in Massachusetts, Jack thought wryly); the middle-of-the-roaders, who wanted some free-market capitalism backed up with a solid safety net (or craved the worst of both worlds, as any economist could say); the reformists, who wanted a thin net and a lot of capitalism (but no one knew what capitalism was yet, except for a rapidly expanding criminal sector); and on the far right, those who wanted a right-wing authoritarian government (which was what had put communism in place over seventy years before). The groups on the extreme ends of the spectrum had perhaps ten percent in the Congress of People's Deputies. The remaining eighty percent of the votes were fairly evenly split among the three vaguely centrist positions. Naturally enough, various issues scrambled allegiances—environmentalism was particularly hot and divisive—and the biggest wild card was the incipient breakup of the republics that had always chafed under Russian rule, all the more so because of the political *coda* imposed from Moscow. Finally, each of the five groupings had its own political subsets. For example, there was currently a lot of talk from the political right of inviting the most likely Romanov heir-presumptive back to Moscow—not to take over, but merely to accept a semiofficial apology for the murder of his ancestors. Or so the cover story went. Whoever had come up with that idea, Jack thought, was either the most naive son of a bitch since Alice went down the rabbit hole or a politician with a dangerously simplistic mind-set. The good news, CIA's Station Paris reported, was that the Prince of all the Russians had a better feel for politics and his own safety than his sponsors did.

The bad news was that the political and economic situation in the Soviet Union looked utterly hopeless. SPINNAKER's report merely made it look more ominous. Andrey Il'ych Narmonov was desperate, running out of options, running out of allies, running out of ideas, running out of time, and running out of maneuvering room. He was, the report said, overly concerned with his waffling on the nationalities problem, to the point that he was trying to strengthen his hold on the security apparatus—MVD, KGB, and the military—so that he could keep the empire together by force. But the military, SPINNAKER said, was both unhappy with that mission, and unhappy with the halfhearted way Narmonov planned to implement it.

There had been speculation about the Soviet military and its supposed political ambitions since the time of Lenin. It wasn't new. Stalin had taken a scythe through his officer corps in the late 1930s; it was generally agreed that Marshal Tukhashevskiy had not really posed a political threat, that it had been yet another case of Stalin's malignant paranoia. Khrushchev had done the same in the late '50s, but without the mass executions; that had been done because Khrushchev had wanted to save money on tanks and depend on nuclear arms instead. Narmonov had retired quite a few generals and colonels also; in this case, the move had been exclusively one of economizing on military expense across the board. But this time also, the military reductions had been accompanied by a political renaissance. For the first time there was a true political opposition movement in the country, and the fact of the matter was that the Soviet Army had all the guns. To counter that worrisome possibility, the KGB's Third Chief Directorate had existed for generations—KGB officers who wore military uniforms and whose mission it was to keep an eye on everything. But the Third Chief Directorate was a mere shadow of what it had been. The military had persuaded Narmonov to remove it as a precondition to its own goal of a truly professional force, loyal to the country and the new constitution.

Historians invariably deemed the age in which they lived to be one of transition. For once they were right, Jack thought. If this were not an age of transition, then it was hard to imagine what the hell was. In the case of the Soviets, they were poised between two political and economic worlds, teetering, not quite balanced, not quite sure which way they would go. And that made their political situation dangerously vulnerable to . . . what? Jack asked himself.

Damned near anything.

SPINNAKER said Narmonov was being pressured to make a deal with the military, which, he said, was part of the Forward-to-the-Past mob. Group One. The danger existed, he said, that the Soviet Union would revert to a quasi-military state that repressed its progressive elements; that Narmonov had lost his nerve.

"He says he's had one-on-one meetings with Andrey Il'ych," Mary Pat pointed out. "Intel doesn't come any better than that."

"Also true," Jack replied. "It is worrisome, isn't it?"

"I'm not really concerned about a reversion to Marxist rule. . . . What worries me—"

"Yeah, I know. Civil war." *Civil war in a country with thirty thousand nuclear warheads. There's a cheery thought.*

"Our position has been to cut Narmonov as much slack as he needs, but if our guy is right, that might be the wrong policy."

"What's Ed think?"

"Same as me. We trust Kadishev. I recruited him. Ed and I have seen every report he's ever sent in. He delivers. He's smart, well placed, very perceptive, ballsy son of a gun. When's the last time he gave us bad stuff?"

"I don't know that he ever has," Jack replied.

"Neither do I, Jack."

Ryan leaned back in his chair. "Christ, I just love these easy calls. . . . I don't know, MP. The time I met Narmonov . . . that is one tough, smart, agile son of a bitch. He's got real brass ones." Jack stopped. *More than you can say for yourself, boy.*

"We all have our limitations. Even the brass ones go soft." Mrs. Foley smiled.

wrong metaphor. People run out of steam. Stress, hours, time in the saddle. grinds us all down. Why do you think I'm taking time off? Being pregnant me a great excuse. Having a newborn isn't exactly a picnic, but I get a month off the fundamentals, real-life instead of the stuff we do here every day. That's advantage we have over men, doc. You guys can't break away like we women n. That may be Andrey Il'ych's problem. Who can he turn to for advice? Where an he go for help? He's been there a long time. He's dealing with a deteriorating situation, and he's running out of gas. That's what SPINNAKER tells us, and it is consistent with the facts.''

''Except that we haven't heard anything like this from anyone else.''

''But he's our best guy for the inside stuff.''

''Which completes the circularity of the argument, Mary Pat.''

''Doc, you have the report, and you have my opinion,'' Mrs. Foley pointed out.

''Yes, ma'am.'' Jack set the document on his desk.

''What are you going to tell them?'' ''Them'' was the top row of the executive branch: Fowler, Elliot, Talbot.

''I guess I go with your evaluation. I'm not entirely comfortable with it, but I don't have anything to counter your position with. Besides, the last time I went against you, turned out I was the one who blew the call.''

''You know, you're a pretty good boss.''

''And you're pretty good at letting me down easy.''

''We all have bad days,'' Mrs. Foley said as she got awkwardly to her feet. ''Let me waddle back to my office.''

Jack rose also and walked to open the door for her. ''When are you due?''

She smiled back at him. ''October thirty-first—Halloween, but I'm always late, and they're always big ones.''

''You take care of yourself.'' Jack watched her leave, then walked in to see the Director.

''You'd better look this over.''

''Narmonov? I heard another SPINNAKER came in.''

''You heard right, sir.''

''Who's doing the writeup?''

''I will,'' Jack said. ''I want to do some cross-checking first, though.''

''I go down tomorrow. I'd like to have it then.''

''I'll have it done tonight.''

''Good. Thanks, Jack.''

This is the place, Günther told himself halfway into the first quarter. The stadium accommodated sixty-two thousand seven hundred twenty paying fans. Bock figured another thousand or so people selling snacks and beverages. The game was not supposed to be an important one, but it was clear that Americans were as serious about their football as Europeans were. There was a surprising number of people with multicolored paint on their faces—the local team colors, of course. Several were actually stripped to the waist and had their chests painted up like football sweaters, complete with the huge numbers the Americans used. Various exhortatory banners hung from the rails at the front of the upper decks. There were women on the playing field selected for their dancing ability and other physical attributes, leading the fans in cheers. Bock learned about a curious kind of demonstration called The Wave.

He also learned about the sovereignty of American television. This large raucous been in one also, and their introduction had been one of harsh words. The difference was that he tended to forget slights—most of them, anyway—and she did not; and she had the ear of the President. Because of her, his role in the Vatican Treaty would never be known. The one thing he had done that was untainted by his work at the Agency—Ryan was proud of what he'd done in CIA, but knew that it was narrowly political or strategic, aimed at the betterment of his own country, while the Vatican Treaty had been for the betterment of the whole world. That one proud insight. Gone, credited to others. Jack didn't want sole credit. It had not been exclusively his work, but he did want fair mention as one of the players. Was that asking too much? Fourteen-hour days, much of it spent in cars, the three times he'd risked his life for his country—for what? So that some political bitch from Bennington could tear up his evaluations.

Liz, you wouldn't even be *there except for me and what I did, and neither would your boss, the Ice Man, Jonathan Robert Fowler of Ohio!*

But they could not know that. Jack had given his word. Given his word to what? For what?

The worst part of all, it was now affecting him in a way that was both new and totally unexpected. He'd disappointed his wife again this night. It was incomprehensible to him. Like throwing a light switch and getting no light, like turning the key to start the car and—

Like not being a man. That was the simple description.

I am *a man. I've done all the things a man can do.*

Try explaining that to your wife, chump!

I've fought for my family, for my country, killed for my family and my country. I've won respect among the best of men. I've done things that can never be known and kept the secrets that had to be kept. I've served as well as any man can.

So why are you looking out at the water at two in the morning, ace?

I've made a difference! Jack's mind raged.

Who knows? Who cares?

But what of my friends?

A whole lot of good they do you—besides, what friends? When's the last time you saw Skip Tyler or Robby Jackson? Your friends at Langley—why not confide your problems to them?

Dawn came as a surprise, but not so much a surprise as that he'd actually slept, sitting alone in the living room. Jack rose, feeling the aches in his muscles unhelped by whatever number of hours he'd not been awake. It hadn't been sleep, he told himself on the way to the bathroom. It was just that he hadn't been awake. Sleep was rest, and he felt singularly unrested, with a pounding headache from the cheap wine of the previous night. The only good news—if that's what it was—was that Cathy didn't get up. Jack fixed his own coffee and was waiting at the door when Clark drove up.

"Another great weekend, I see," the man said as Ryan got into the car.

"*Et tu,* John?"

"Look, Deputy Director, you want to take a swing at me, go right ahead. You looked like shit a couple of months back and you're getting worse instead of better. When's the last time you took a vacation, got away for more than a day or two, you know, maybe pretended you were a real person instead of some fuckin' government ticket-puncher who's afraid that if he leaves nobody'll notice?"

"Clark, you do have a way of brightening my mornings."

"Hey, man, I'm just a SPO, but don't bitch if I take the 'protective' part seriously, 'kay?'' John pulled the car over and parked it. ''Doc, I've seen this before. People burn out. You're burning out. You're burning the candle both ends and the middle. That's hard to do when you're in your twenties, and you ain't in your twenties anymore, in case nobody bothered telling you.''

''I'm quite aware of the infirmities that come with age.'' Ryan tried a wry smile to show that it wasn't that big a deal, that Clark was overdoing it.

It didn't work. Suddenly it occurred to John that his wife hadn't been at the door. Trouble at home? Well, he couldn't ask about that, could he? What he saw in Ryan's face was bad enough. It wasn't just fatigue. He was tiring from within, all the shit he was taking from up the chain of command, the strain of backstopping Director Cabot on damned near everything that went out the front door. Cabot—not a bad guy, he meant well, but the truth of the matter was that he just didn't know what the hell he was doing. So Congress depended on Ryan, and the Operations and Intelligence Directorates depended on Ryan for leadership and coordination. He couldn't escape his responsibilities, and didn't have the good sense to realize that some were really things he could leave to others. The directorate chiefs could have taken up more of the slack, but they were letting Ryan do it all. A strong bark from the Deputy Director's office could have set that right, but would Cabot back him up—or would those White House pukes take it as a sign that Jack was trying a takeover?

Fuckin' politics! Clark thought as he pulled back onto the road. Office politics, political politics. And something was wrong at home, too. Clark didn't know what, but he knew it was something.

Doc, you're too damned good a man for this!

''Can I lay a piece of advice on you?''

''Go ahead,'' Jack replied, looking through dispatches.

''Take two weeks, go to Disney World, Club Med, find a beach and walk it. Get the hell out of town for a while.''

''The kids are in school.''

''So take them out of school, for Christ's sake! Better yet, maybe, leave them and get away, you and your wife. No, you're not that kind. Take them to see Mickey.''

''I can't. They're in school—''

''They're in *grammar* school, not graduate school, doc. Missing two weeks of long division and learning to spell 'squirrel' won't stunt their intellectual growth. You need to get away, recharge the batteries, smell the fucking roses!''

''Too much work, John.''

''You listen to me! You know how many friends I've buried? You know how many people I went out with who never got the chance to have a wife and kids and a nice house on the water? A lot, pal, a whole lot, never came close to having what you have. You got all that, and you're trying very damned hard to end up dead—and that's what's gonna happen, doc. One way or another, give it maybe ten years.''

''I have a job to do!''

''It ain't important enough to wreck your fucking life for, you dumbass! Can't you see that?''

''And then who runs the shop?''

''Sir, you might be hard to replace when you're at your best, but the shape you're in now, that Goodley kid can do your job at least as well as you can.'' And that, Clark saw, scored for points. ''Just how effective do you think you are right now?''

''Will you do me a favor and just drive the car.'' There was another SPINNAKER report waiting for him, according to coded phrases in the morning dispatches, along with one from NIITAKA. This would be a busy day.

Just what he needed, Jack thought to himself, closing his eyes for a moment's rest.

It got worse. Ryan was surprised to find himself at work, more surprised that fatigue had defeated morning coffee and allowed him to sleep for forty minutes or so on the way in. He accepted Clark's told-you-so look and made his way up to the 7th floor. A messenger brought in the two important files, along with a note that Director Cabot was going to be late. The guy was keeping banker's hours. Spies were supposed to work harder, Jack thought. *I sure as hell do.*

NIITAKA came first. The Japanese, the report said, were planning to renege on a rare trade concession made only six months earlier. It would be explained away as "unfortunate and unforeseen" circumstances, part of which might be true, Ryan thought as he read down the page—the Japanese had as many domestic political problems as everyone else—but there was something else: they were going to coordinate something in Mexico . . . something to do with the state visit of their Prime Minister to Washington the coming February. Instead of buying American farm goods, they were opting to buy them cheaper from Mexico, playing that off against reduced tariff barriers into that country. That was the plan, in any case. They weren't sure they could get the concession from Mexico, and they were planning . . .

. . . a bribe?

"Jesus," Ryan breathed. The Mexican Institutional Revolutionary Party—PRI—didn't exactly have an exemplary record for integrity, but this . . . ? It would be handled in face-to-face talks in Mexico City. If they got the concession, trading access to Mexican markets to opening Japan to Mexican foodstuffs, then the amount of American foodstuffs they had committed to buy the previous February would be reduced. It made good business sense. Japan would get food a little cheaper than they could in America while at the same time opening up a new market. Their excuse to American farmers would have to do with agricultural chemicals that their food-and-drug agency would decide, much to everyone's surprise, not to like for reasons of public health.

The bribe was fully in proportion to the magnitude of the target. Twenty-five million dollars, to be paid in a roundabout, quasi-legal fashion. When the Mexican President left office the following year, he would head a new corporation that . . . no, they would buy out a corporation he already owned for fair market value, and the new ownership would keep him on, while inflating the value of the business and paying his impressive salary in return for his obvious expertise at public relations.

"Nice separation," Ryan said aloud. It was almost comical, and the funny part was that it might even be legal in America if someone hired a sharp-enough lawyer. Maybe not even that much. Plenty of people from State and Commerce had hired themselves out to Japanese interests immediately after leaving government service.

Except for one little thing: what Ryan held in his hand was evidence of conspiracy. In one way they were foolish: the Japanese thought that some councils were sacrosanct, that some words spoken aloud would never be heard outside the four enclosing walls that heard them. They didn't know that a certain cabinet member had a certain mistress who in turn had a personal beef that matched her ability to loosen a man's tongue; and that America now had access to all that information, courtesy of a KGB officer. . . .

"Think, boy."

If they could get harder evidence, and give that over to Fowler. . . . But how? You couldn't exactly cite the report of a spy in court . . . a Russian national, a KGB officer working in a third country.

But they weren't talking about an open court with rules of evidence, were they? Fowler could discuss this in his own face-to-face meet with their PM.

Ryan's phone rang. "Yes, Nancy?"

"The Director just called in. He's got the flu."

"Lucky him. Thanks. Flu, my ass," Ryan said after hanging up. The man was lazy.

. . . Fowler could play it one of two ways: (1) face-to-face, tell him that we know what he's up to and we won't stand for it, that we will inform the proper congressional people and . . . or, (2) just leak it to the press.

Option 2 would have all sorts of evil consequences, not the least of which would be in Mexico. Fowler didn't like the Mexican President, and liked the PRI even less. Whatever you said about Fowler, he was an honest man who loathed corruption in all its forms.

Option 1 . . . Ryan had to report this to Al Trent, didn't he? He had to let Trent know about the new operation, but Trent had his personal ax to grind on trade issues, and Fowler would worry that he might be leaky on this issue. On the other hand, could he legally *not* tell Trent? Ryan lifted his phone again.

"Nancy, could you tell the general counsel that I need to see him? Thanks."

Next came SPINNAKER. *What,* Ryan thought, *does Mr. Kadishev have to say today . . . ?*

"Dear God in heaven." Ryan forced himself to relax. He read through the complete report, then stopped and read through it again. He picked up his phone and punched the button to speed-dial Mary Pat Foley.

But the phone just rang for thirty seconds until someone picked it up.

"Yes?"

"Who is this?"

"Who is this?"

"This is Deputy Director Ryan. Where's Mary Pat?"

"In labor, sir. Sorry, I didn't know who you were," the man's voice went on. "Ed's with her, of course."

"Okay, thanks." Ryan hung up. "Shit!" On the other hand, he couldn't be angry about that, could he? He got up and walked out to his secretary's office.

"Nancy, Mary Pat's in labor," Jack told Mrs. Cummings.

"Oh, wonderful—well, not wonderful, it's not all that much fun," Nancy observed. "Flowers?"

"Yeah, something nice—you know that stuff better than I do. Put it on my American Express."

"Wait until we're sure everything's okay?"

"Yeah, right." Ryan returned to his office. "Now what?" he asked himself.

You know what you have to do. The only question is whether or not you really want to do it.

Jack lifted his phone again and punched yet another speed-dial button.

"Elizabeth Elliot," she said, picking up her direct line, the one known only to a handful of government insiders.

"Jack Ryan."

The cold voice grew yet colder. "What is it?"

"I need to see the President."

"What about?" she asked.

"Not over the phone."

"It's a secure phone, Ryan!"

"Not secure enough. When can I come over? It's important."

"How important?"

"Important enough to bump his appointment schedule, Liz!" Ryan snapped back. "You think I'm playing games here?"

"Calm down and wait." Ryan heard pages turning. "Be here in forty minutes. You can have fifteen minutes. I'll fix the schedule."

"Thank you, Dr. Elliot." Ryan managed not to slam the phone down. *Goddamn that woman!* Ryan got up again. Clark was back in Nancy's office. "Warm the car up."

"Where to?" Clark asked, rising.

"Downtown." Jack turned. "Nancy, call the Director. Tell him I have to get something to the Boss, and, with all due respect, he should get his tail in here." That would be inconvenient. Cabot's place was an hour away, in fox country.

"Yes, sir." One of the few things he could depend on was Nancy Cummings' professionalism.

"I need three copies of this. Make one more for the Director and return the original to secure storage."

"Take two minutes," Nancy said.

"Fine." Jack walked off to the washroom. Looking in the mirror, he saw that Clark was as right as ever. He really did look like hell. But that couldn't be helped. "Ready?"

"If you are, doc." Clark was already holding the documents in a zipped leather case.

The perversity of life did not abate this Monday morning. Somewhere around the I-66 cutoff, some fool had managed to cause an accident, and that backed traffic up. What should have been a ten- or fifteen-minute drive took thirty-five. Even senior government officials have to deal with D.C. traffic. The Agency car pulled into West Executive Drive barely on time. Jack managed not to run into the west entrance to the White House only because someone might notice. Reporters used this entrance, too. A minute later he was in Liz Elliot's corner office.

"What gives?" the National Security Advisor asked.

"I'd prefer to go over this just once. We have a report from a penetration agent that you're not going to like very much."

"You have to tell me something," Elliot pointed out, reasonably for once.

"Narmonov, his military, and nukes."

She nodded. "Let's go." It was a short walk down two corridors, past eight Secret Service agents who guarded the President's office like a pack of very respectful wolves.

"I hope this is good," President Fowler said without rising. "I'm missing a budget brief for this."

"Mr. President, we have a very highly placed penetration agent inside the Soviet government," Ryan began.

"I know that. I have asked you not to reveal his name to me, as you recall."

"Yes, sir," Ryan said. "I'm going to tell you his name now. Oleg Kirilovich Kadishev. We call him SPINNAKER. He was recruited some years ago by Mary Patricia Foley when she and her husband were in Moscow."

"Why did you give me that?" Fowler asked.

"So that you can evaluate what he says. You've seen his reports before under the code names RESTORATIVE and PIVOT."

"PIVOT . . . ? That's the one back in September that talked about problems with Narmonov's—I mean, that he was having trouble with his security apparatus."

"Correct, Mr. President." *Good for you,* Ryan thought. *You remember what we send down.* It was not always so, Ryan knew.

"I gather his problems are worsening or you would not be here. Go on," Fowler ordered, leaning back in his chair.

"Kadishev says he had a meeting with Narmonov last week—late last week—"

"Wait a minute. Kadishev—he's a member of their parliament, head of one of the opposition groups, right?"

"Also correct, sir. He has a lot of one-on-ones with Narmonov, and that's why he's so valuable to us."

"Fine, I can see that."

"In their most recent meeting, he says, Narmonov said that his problems are indeed getting worse. He's allowed his military and security forces to increase their internal clout, but it would seem that this is not enough. There may be opposition to the arms-reduction-treaty implementation. According to this report, the Soviet military wants to hold on to all of its SS-18s instead of eliminating six regiments of them as agreed. Our man says that Narmonov may be ready to give in to them on that point. Sir, that would be treaty violation, and that's why I'm here."

"How important is it?" Liz Elliot asked. "The technical side, I mean."

"Okay, we've never been able to make this very clear. Secretary Bunker understands, but Congress has never quite figured it out: since we're in the process of reducing nuclear arms by a little more than half, we've changed the nuclear equation. When both sides had ten thousand RVs it was pretty clear to everyone that nuclear war was a difficult—virtually impossible—thing to win. With so many warheads to hit, you'd never get them all, and there would always be enough left to launch a crippling counterattack.

"But with the reductions, the calculus changes. Now, depending on the mix of forces, such an attack becomes theoretically possible, and that's why the mix of forces was so carefully spelled out in the treaty documents."

"You're saying that the reduction makes things more dangerous rather than less?" Fowler asked.

"No, sir, not exactly. I've said all along—I consulted with the treaty team back some years ago, back when Ernie Allen was running it—that the net strategic improvement from a fifty-percent reduction was illusory, mere symbolism."

"Oh, *come* on," Elliot observed scathingly. "It's a reduction by half of—"

"Dr. Elliot, if you ever bothered to sit in on the CAMELOT games you'd understand this a little better." Ryan turned away before he noticed her reaction to this rebuke. Fowler noticed her flush briefly and almost smiled in amusement at her discomfort at being cut down in front of her lover. The President returned his attention to Ryan, sure that he and Elizabeth would speak further on the matter.

"This issue gets very technical. If you don't believe me, ask Secretary Bunker or General Fremont out at SAC Headquarters. The deciding factor is the mix of forces, not the number. If they hold on to those extra SS-18 regiments, the mix is changed to the point at which the Soviets have a genuine advantage. The effect on the treaty is substantive, not merely numerical. But there's more."

"Okay," the President said.

"According to this report, there appears to be some collusion between the military and the KGB. As you know, while the Soviet military owns and maintains the strategic launchers, the warheads have always been under KGB control. Kadishev thinks that those two agencies are getting a little too cozy, and further that security on the warheads might be problematic.''

''Meaning what?''

''Meaning that an inventory of tactical warheads is being withheld.''

''Missing nukes?''

''Small ones. It's possible, he says.''

''In other words,'' Fowler said, ''their military may be blackmailing Narmonov, and it's possible that they are holding some small weapons as their trump cards?''

Not bad, Mr. President. ''Correct, sir.''

Fowler was quiet for thirty seconds or so, turning that over in his head as he stared into space. ''How reliable is this Kadishev?''

''Mr. President, he's been in our employ for five years. His advice has been very valuable to us, and to the best of our knowledge he's never misled us.''

''Possible that he's been turned?'' Elliot asked.

''Possible but not likely. We have ways of dealing with that. There are prearranged code phrases which warn us of trouble. Good-news phrases accompany each report, and did in this case also.''

''What about confirming the report through other sources?''

''Sorry, Dr. Elliot, but we have nothing to confirm this.''

''You came down here with an unconfirmed report?'' Elliot asked.

''That is correct,'' Ryan admitted, not knowing how tired he looked. ''There aren't too many agents who could make me do that, but this is one of them.''

''What can you do to confirm that?'' Fowler asked.

''We can make discreet inquiries through our own networks, and with your permission we can have careful discussions with some foreign services. The Brits have someone in the Kremlin who's giving them some really good stuff. I know Sir Basil Charleston, and I can make approaches, but that means revealing something of what we know. You don't do something like this on the old-boy net. At this level you have to make a real *quid pro quo*. We never do that without getting executive approval.''

''I can understand that. Give me a day to think about it. Does Marcus know about this?''

''No, Mr. President. He has the flu. Ordinarily I would not have come here without consulting with the Director first, but I figured you would want to know about this quickly.''

''You've said previously that the Soviet military was more politically reliable than this,'' Elliot observed.

''Also correct, Dr. Elliot. Action such as Kadishev reports is completely unprecedented. Historically, our worries about political ambition within the Soviet military have been as groundless as they've been continuous. It would seem that this may have changed. The possibility of a de facto alliance between the military and the KGB is most disturbing.''

''So you were wrong before?'' Elliot pressed.

''That is a possibility,'' Ryan admitted.

''And now?'' Fowler asked.

''Mr. President, what do you want me to say? Might I be wrong on this also? Yes, I may. Am I sure this report is accurate? No, I am not, but the import of the information compels me to bring it to your attention.''

"I'm less concerned with the missile issue than with the missing warheads," Elliot said. "If Narmonov is facing real blackmail . . . wow."

"Kadishev is a potential political rival to Narmonov," Fowler noted speculatively. "Why confide in him?"

"You meet regularly with the congressional leadership, sir. So does he. The political dynamic in the Congress of People's Deputies is more confused than on the Hill. Moreover, there's genuine respect between the two. Kadishev has supported Narmonov more often than he's opposed the man. They may be rivals, but there is also a commonality of views on many key issues."

"Okay, I want this information confirmed any way you can, and as quickly as you can."

"Yes, Mr. President."

"How's Goodley working out?" Elliot asked.

"He's a bright kid. He's got a good feel for the Eastern Bloc. I read over a paper he did up at the Kennedy School a while back, and it was better than what our people did at the time."

"Get him in on this. A fresh mind might be useful," Liz opined.

Jack shook his head emphatically. "This is too sensitive for him."

"Goodley is that Presidential Fellow you told me about? Is he that good, Elizabeth?" Fowler wanted to know.

"I think so."

"My authority, Ryan, let him in," the President ordered.

"Yes, sir."

"Anything else?"

"Sir, if you have a minute, we did have something else come in about Japan." Jack explained further for a few minutes.

"Is that a fact . . . ?" Fowler smiled in his clever way. "What do you think of them?"

"I think they like to play games," Ryan answered. "I do not envy the folks who have to negotiate with them."

"How can we find out if this is true?"

"It comes from a good source. It's another one we guard closely."

"Wouldn't it be nice if . . . how would we find out if the deal is struck?"

"I don't know, Mr. President."

"I could ram something like that right down his throat. I'm getting tired of this trade impasse, and I'm tired of being lied to. Find a way to do it."

"We'll try, Mr. President."

"Thanks for coming in." The President didn't rise or extend his hand. Ryan stood and left.

"What do you think?" Fowler asked as he scanned over the report.

"It confirms what Talbot says about Narmonov's vulnerability . . . but worse."

"I agree. Ryan looks harried."

"He shouldn't be playing both sides of the street."

"Hmph?" the President grunted without looking up.

"I have a preliminary report from the investigation Justice has been running. It looks as though he is playing around, as we suspected, and there is a kid involved. She's the widow of an Air Force guy who died in a training accident. Ryan has spent a lot of money to take care of the family, and his wife doesn't know."

"I don't need that sort of scandal, not another womanizer on top of Charlie's affairs.'' *Good thing they haven't found out about us,* he didn't have to say. That was, in any case, a different matter. Alden had been a married man. Ryan still was. Fowler was not. That made it different. ''How sure are you of this? You said a preliminary report?''

''That's right.''

''Firm it up and let me know what you find out.''

Liz nodded and went on. ''This thing with the Soviet military . . . scary.''

''Very scary,'' Fowler agreed. ''We'll talk about it over lunch.''

''And that is the halfway point,'' Fromm said. ''Might I ask a favor?''

''What favor is that?'' Ghosn asked, hoping that it was not to go back to Germany for time with his wife. That might be sticky.

''I have not had a drink in two months.''

Ibrahim smiled. ''You understand that I am not permitted such things.''

''But do the same rules apply to me?'' The German smiled. ''I am an infidel, after all.''

Ghosn laughed heartily. ''Quite true. I'll talk to Günther about it.''

''Thank you. Tomorrow, we begin on the plutonium.''

''It will take so long?''

''Yes, that and the explosive blocks. We are precisely on schedule.''

''That is good to know.'' *January 12th was the day.*

''Who do we have good in the KGB?'' Ryan asked himself back in his office. The big problem with SPINNAKER's report was that much, maybe most, of the KGB was loyal to Narmonov. The part that might not be was the Second Chief Directorate, which concerned itself with the country's internal security. The First Chief—a/k/a Foreign—Directorate definitely was, especially with Golovko in his position as First Deputy Chairman to keep an eye on things. That man was a pro, and reasonably nonpolitical. Ryan had a wild thought that a direct call might—no, he'd have to set up a meet . . . but where?

No, that was too dangerous.

''You want me?'' It was Goodley, sticking his head through Jack's door. Ryan waved him in.

''Want a promotion?''

''What do you mean?''

''I mean that at the direction of the President of the United States you are in on something that I think you're not ready for.'' Jack handed him the SPINNAKER report. ''Read.''

''Why me, and why did you say—''

''I also said you did a nice job predicting the breakup of the Pact. It was better than anything we did in-house, by the way.''

''You mind if I say that you're a strange guy to work with?''

''How do you mean that?'' Jack asked.

''You don't like my attitude, but you commend my work.''

Ryan leaned back in his chair and closed his eyes. ''Ben, believe it or not, I am not always right. I make mistakes. I've made some whoppers even, but I am smart enough to know that, and because I'm that smart, I look for people with opposing views to backstop me. That's a good habit to get into. I learned it from Admiral Greer. If you learn anything from your time here, Dr. Goodley, learn that. We can't afford fuckups here. They happen anyway, but we still can't afford them. That paper you did at Kennedy was better than what I did. It's theoretically possible that you might again one day be right when I am wrong. Fair enough?''

''Yes, sir,'' Goodley replied quietly, surprised at the statement. Of course he'd be right when Ryan was wrong. That's why he was here.

''Read.''

''Mind if I smoke?''

Jack's eyes opened. ''You a smoker?''

''I quit a couple of years ago, but since I've been here . . .''

''Try to break that habit, but before you do, give me one.''

They both lit up and puffed away in silence, Goodley reading over the report, Ryan watching his eyes. The Presidential Fellow looked up.

''Damn.''

''Good first reaction. Now, what do you think?''

''It's plausible.''

Ryan shook his head. ''That's what I just told the President an hour ago. I'm not sure, but I had to take it to him.''

''What do you want me to do?''

''I want to play on this a little. The DI's Russian people will chew on it for a couple of days. I want you and me to do our own analysis, but I want a different spin on it.''

''Meaning what?''

''Meaning that you think it's plausible, and I have my doubts. Therefore, you will look for reasons it might not be true, and I'll look for reasons that it is.'' Jack paused. ''The Intelligence Directorate will play this conventionally. They're too organized down there. I don't want that.''

''But you want me to—''

''I want you to exercise that brain. I think you're smart, Ben. I want you to prove it. That's an order, by the way.''

Goodley considered that. He wasn't accustomed to getting or taking orders. ''I don't know that I can do that.''

''Why not?''

''It's contrary to my views. It's not the way I see this, it's—''

''Your beef with me and a lot of people here is the corporate mind of CIA, right? Part of that is correct, we do have a corporate mind, and there are drawbacks to that. It's also true that your way of thinking has its own pitfalls. If you can prove to me that you are no more a prisoner of your views than I try to be of mine, then you have a future here. Objectivity isn't easy. You have to exercise it.''

It was a very clever challenge, Goodley thought. He wondered next if he'd perhaps misjudged the DDCI.

''Will Russell cooperate?''

''Yes, Ismael, he will,'' Bock said, sipping at a beer. He'd gotten a case of a good German export brew for Fromm, and kept a few for himself. ''He thinks we'll be setting off a large conventional bomb to eliminate television coverage of the game.''

''Clever, but not actually intelligent,'' Qati observed. He wanted a beer himself, but could not ask. Besides, he told himself, it would probably upset his stomach, and he'd actually enjoyed three consecutive days of relative health.

"His outlook is limited to tactical matters, yes. On tactical matters he is quite useful, however. His assistance will be crucial to that phase of the operation."

"Fromm is working out well."

"As I thought he would. It really is a pity that he will not see it to fruition. The same with the machinists?"

"Unfortunately, yes." Qati frowned. Not a man who blanched at the sight of blood, neither was he one to kill unnecessarily. He'd had to kill people for reasons of security before, though never this many. It was almost becoming a habit. But, he asked himself, why worry about a few when you plan to kill so many more?

"Have you planned for the consequences of failure or discovery?" Bock asked.

"Yes, I have," Qati replied with a sly smile, followed by an explanation.

"That is ingenious. Good to plan for every contingency."

"I thought you'd like it."

21. Connectivity

It took two weeks, but something finally came back. A KGB officer in the employ of CIA nosed around and heard something: there might be an ongoing operation about nuclear weapons in Germany. Something being run out of Moscow Center. Golovko himself was overseeing things. People working in KGB Station Berlin were cut out of it. End of report.

"Well?" Ryan asked Goodley. "What do you think?"

"It fits the SPINNAKER report. If the story about a fluky inventory of tactical nukes is correct, it certainly makes sense that it would have something to do with the pullbacks of their forward-deployed forces. Things get lost in transit all the time. I lost two boxes of books when I moved down here myself."

"I'd like to think that people take closer care of nuclear weapons than that," Ryan said dryly, noting that Goodley still had a hell of a lot to learn. "What else?"

"I've been looking for data to counter the report. The Soviet reason for their inability to deactivate the SS-18s on schedule is that the factory they built for the purpose is inadequate. Our on-site inspectors can't decide if it's true or not—engineering question. I find it hard to believe that if the Russians actually built the thing—and, hell, they've been building SS-18s for quite a while, haven't they?—they should be able to design a place to dismantle them safely. They say the problem is in the fueling systems, and the wording of the treaty documents. The -18 uses storable liquids and has a pressurized body—that is, the missile structure depends on pressurization to remain rigid. They can defuel in the silos, but then they can't extract the birds without damaging them, and the treaty requires that they be taken intact to the disposal facility. But the disposal facility isn't designed right for defueling, they say. Something about a design flaw and possible environmental contamination. The storable liquids are nasty, they say, and you have to take all sorts of precautions to keep from poisoning people, and the facility is only three kilometers from a city, etc., etc.'' Goodley paused. ''The explanation is plausible, but you have to wonder how people could have screwed up so badly.''

''Structural problem,'' Jack said. ''They have trouble placing facilities out in the boonies for the simple reason that there few people have cars, and getting people from their homes to their place of work is more complicated there than here. It's subtle stuff like that that drives us crazy trying to figure the Russians out.''

''On the other hand, they can point to a basic mistake like that and try to explain all kinds of things away.''

''Very good, Ben,'' Jack observed. ''Now you're thinking like a real spook.''

''This is a crazy place to work.''

''Storable liquids are nasty, by the way. Corrosive, reactive, toxic. Remember all the problems we had with the Titan-II missiles?''

''No,'' Goodley admitted.

''Maintenance of the things is a bastard. You have to take all sorts of precautions, despite which you routinely get leaks. The leaks corrode things, injure the maintenance people. . . .''

''Have we exchanged positions on this?'' Ben asked lightly.

Ryan smiled, eyes closed. ''I'm not sure.''

''We're supposed to have better data than this. We're supposed to be able to find things out.''

''Yeah, I thought that way once myself. People expect us to know everything there is about every rock, puddle, and personality in the whole world.'' His eyes opened. ''We don't. Never have. Never will. Disappointing, isn't it? The all-pervasive CIA. We have a fairly important question here, and all we have are probabilities, not certainties. How is the President supposed to make a decision if we can't give him facts instead of possibly learned opinions? I've said it before—in writing, even. What we provide people with, most of the time, is official guesses. You know, it's embarrassing to have to send something like this out.'' Jack's eyes fell on the Directorate of Intelligence report. Their teams of Russian experts had chewed on SPINNAKER for a week and decided that it was probably true but could represent a misunderstanding.

Jack's eyes closed again, and he wished his headache would go away. ''That's our structural problem. We look at various probabilities. If you give people a firm opinion, you run the risk of being wrong. Guess what? People remember when you're wrong a lot more often than when you're right. So the tendency is to include all the possibilities. It's intellectually honest, even. Hell of a good dodge. Problem is, it doesn't give people what they think they need. On the user end, people as often as not need probabilities rather than certainties, but they don't always know that. It can drive you crazy, Ben. The outside bureaucracies ask for things we often as not cannot deliver, and our inside bureaucracy doesn't like sticking its neck out on the line any more than anyone else. Welcome to the real world of intelligence.''

''I never figured you for a cynic.''

''I'm not a cynic. I'm a realist. Some things we know. Some things we don't. The people here are not robots. They're just people looking for answers and finding more questions instead. We have a lot of good people in this building, but bureaucracy mutes individual voices, and facts are discovered more often by individuals than committees.'' There was a knock on the door. ''Come in.''

''Dr. Ryan, your secretary isn't—''

''She's having a late lunch.''

"I have something for you, sir." The man handed the envelope over. Ryan signed for it and dismissed the messenger.

"Good old All Nippon Airlines," Ryan said after opening the envelope. It was another NIITAKA report. He snapped upright in his chair. "Holy shit!"

"Problem?" Goodley asked.

"You're not cleared for this."

"What seems to be the problem?" Narmonov asked.

Golovko was in the uncomfortable position of having to announce a major success with unpleasant consequences. "President, we have for some time been working on a project to penetrate American cipher systems. We've had some successes, particularly with their diplomatic systems. This is a message that was sent to several of their embassies. We've recovered all of it."

"And?"

"Who sent this out?"

"Look, Jack," Cabot said, "Liz Elliot took the last SPINNAKER seriously, and she wants State's opinion."

"Well, that's just great. What we've learned from it is that KGB has penetrated our diplomatic ciphers. NIITAKA read the same cable that our Ambassador got. So now Narmonov knows what we're worried about."

"The White House will say that it's not all that bad. Does it really hurt that he knows what our concerns are?" the Director asked.

"The short version is—yes, it does. Sir, you realize that I didn't know about this cable, and how do I read it? I get the text from a KGB officer in Tokyo. Jesus Christ, did we send this inquiry out to Upper Volta, too?"

"They got it all?"

Jack's voice turned to acid. "Care to check the translation?"

"Go see Olson."

"On the way."

Forty minutes later, Ryan and Clark breezed into the outer office of Lieutenant General Ronald Olson, Director of the National Security Agency. Located at Fort Meade, Maryland, between Washington and Baltimore, it had the atmosphere of another Alcatraz, but without the pleasant view of San Francisco Bay. The main building was surrounded by a double fence patrolled by dogs at night—something even CIA didn't bother with, considering it overly theatrical—as physical evidence of their mania for security. NSA's job was to make and break ciphers, to record and interpret every bit of electronic noise on the planet. Jack left his driver reading a *Newsweek* as he strode into the top-floor office of the man who ran this particular outfit, which was several times the size of CIA.

"Ron, you got one big problem."

"What, exactly?"

Jack handed over the NIITAKA dispatch. "I've warned you about this."

"When did this go out?"

"Seventy-two hours ago."

"Out of Foggy Bottom, right?"

"Correct. It was read in Moscow precisely eight hours later."

"Meaning that someone in State might have leaked it, and their embassy could have sent it over by satellite," Olson said. "Or it could have leaked from a cipher clerk or any one of fifty foreign-service officers. . . ."

"Or it could mean that they've broken the whole encoding system."

"STRIPE is secure, Jack."

"Ron, why haven't you just expanded TAPDANCE?"

"Get me the funding and I will."

"This agent has warned us before that they've penetrated our cipher systems. They're reading our mail, Ron, and this is a pretty good piece of evidence."

The General stood his ground. "It's equivocal and you know it."

"Well, our guy is saying that he wants personal assurance from the Director that we haven't, don't, and will never use comm links to transmit his material. As proof of that necessity, he sends us this, which he got at some significant hazard to his own ass." Jack paused. "How many people use this system?"

"STRIPE is exclusively for the State Department. Similar systems are used by the Defense Department. More or less the same machine, slightly different keying systems. The Navy especially likes it. It's very user-friendly," Olson said.

"General, we've had the random-pad technology available for over three years. Your first version, TAPDANCE, used tape cassettes. We're moving over to CD-ROM. It works, it's easy to use. We'll have our systems up and running in another couple of weeks."

"And you want us to copy it?"

"Looks sensible to me."

"You know what my people will say if we copy a system from CIA?" Olson asked.

"Goddamn it! We stole the idea from you, remember?"

"Jack, we're working on something similar, easier to use, little bit more secure. There are problems, but my back-room boys are almost ready to try it out."

Almost ready, Ryan thought. *That means anywhere from three months to three years.*

"General, I'm putting you on official notice. We have indications that your communications links are compromised."

"And?"

"And I will make that report to Congress and the President as well."

"It's much more likely that there's someone at State who leaked this. Further, it is possible that you're the victim of disinformation. What does this agent give us?" the NSA Director asked.

"Some very useful material—us and Japan."

"But nothing on the Soviet Union?"

Jack hesitated before answering, but there was no question of Olson's loyalty. Or his intelligence. "Correct."

"And you're saying that you're certain this *isn't* a false-flag operation? I repeat—certain?"

"You know better than that, Ron. What's certain in this business?"

"Before I request a couple hundred million dollars' worth of funding, I need something better than this. It's happened before, and we've done it, too—if the other side has something you can't break, get them to change it. Make it appear that they're penetrated."

"That might have been true fifty years ago, but not anymore."

"Repeat, I need better evidence before I go to see Trent. We can't slap something together as quickly as you can with MERCURY. We have to make thousands of the goddamned things. Supporting that is complex and costly as hell. I need hard evidence before I stick my neck out that far."

"Fair enough, General. I've had my say."

"Jack, we'll look into it. I have a tiger team that does that, and I'll have them examining the problem tomorrow morning. I appreciate your concern. We're friends, remember?"

"Sorry, Ron. Long hours."

"Maybe you need some time off. You look tired."

"That's what everybody tells me."

Ryan's next stop was at the FBI.

"I heard," Dan Murray said. "That bad?"

"I think so. Ron Olson isn't so sure." Jack didn't have to explain. Of all the possible disasters for a government to face short of war, none was worse than leaky communications links. Literally everything depended on secure methods of moving information from one place to another. Wars had been won and lost on the basis of a single message that had been leaked to the other side. One of America's most stunning foreign-policy coups, the Washington Naval Treaty, had been the direct result of the State Department's ability to read the cipher traffic between all of the participating diplomats and their governments. A government that had no secrets could not function.

"Well, there's the Walkers, Pelton, the others. . . ." Murray observed. The KGB had been remarkably successful at recruiting people within the American communications agencies. Cipher clerks held the most sensitive jobs in the embassies, but were so poorly paid and regarded that they were still called "clerks," not even "technicians." Some resented that. Some resented it enough that they had decided that they could make money from what they knew. They all learned eventually that intelligence agencies pay poorly (except for CIA, which rewarded treason with real money), but by then it was always too late to turn back. From Walker the Russians had learned how American cipher machines were designed and how their keying systems worked. The basics of the cipher machines hadn't really changed all that much in the preceding ten years. Improved technology had made them more efficient and much more reliable than their stepping-switch and pin-disc ancestors, but they all worked on a mathematical area called Complexity Theory, which had been developed by telephone engineers sixty years earlier to predict the working of large switching systems. And the Russians had some of the best mathematical theorists in the world. It was believed by many that knowledge of the structure of cipher machines might enable a really clever mathematician to crack a whole system. Had some unknown Russian made a theoretical breakthrough? If so . . .

"We have to assume there are more we haven't caught. Add that to their technical expertise, and I'm really worried."

"Doesn't affect the Bureau directly, thank God." Most of the FBI encrypted communications were voice links, and though they could be broken, the data recovered was both too time-sensitive and further disguised by the use of code names and slang that mostly concealed what agents were up to. Besides which, the opposition had real limits on how many things they could examine.

"Can you have your people do some scratching around?"

"Oh, yeah. You're going up the chain on this?"

"I think I have to, Dan."

"You're bucking a couple of major bureaucracies."

Ryan leaned against the doorframe. "My cause is just, isn't it?"

"You never learn, do you?" Murray shook his head and laughed.

* * *

"Those bastard Americans!" Narmonov raged.

"What's the problem now, Andrey Il'ych?"

"Oleg Kirilovich, have you any idea what it is like dealing with a suspicious foreign country?"

"Not yet," Kadishev answered. "I only deal with suspicious domestic elements." The effective abolition of the Politburo had perversely eliminated the apprenticeship period during which an up-and-coming Soviet political figure might learn the international version of statecraft. Now they were no better off than Americans were. And that, Kadishev reminded himself, was something to keep in mind. "What seems to be the problem?"

"This must be kept absolutely secret, my young friend."

"Understood."

"The Americans have circulated a memorandum around their embassies to make discreet inquiries concerning my political vulnerability."

"Indeed?" Kadishev did not allow himself to react beyond the single word. He was immediately struck by the dichotomy of the situation. His report had had the proper effect on the American government, but the fact that Narmonov knew of it made his discovery as an American agent possible. Wasn't that interesting? he asked himself in a moment of clear objectivity. His maneuvers were now a genuine gamble, with a downside as enormous as the upside. Such things were to be expected, weren't they? He was not gambling a month's wages. "How do we know this?" he asked after a moment's reflection.

"That I cannot reveal."

"I understand." *Damn! Well, he is confiding in me . . . though that might be a clever ploy on Andrey Il'ych's part, mightn't it?* "But we are sure of it?"

"Quite sure."

"How can I help?"

"I need your help, Oleg. Again, I ask for it."

"This business with the Americans concerns you greatly, then?"

"Of course it does!"

"I can understand that it is something to be considered, but what real interest do they have in our domestic politics?"

"You know the answer to that."

"True."

"I need your help," Narmonov repeated.

"I must discuss this with my colleagues."

"Quickly, if you please."

"Yes." Kadishev took his leave and walked out to his car. He drove himself, which was unusual for a senior Soviet politician. Times had changed. Such officials now had to be men of the people, and that meant that the reserved center lanes of the broad Moscow streets were gone, along with most of the other traditional perks. That was too bad, Kadishev thought, but without the other changes that made it necessary, he'd still be a lonely voice in some distant *oblast* instead of the leader of a major faction in the Congress of People's Deputies. So he was willing to do without the dacha in the woods east of Moscow, and the luxury apartment, and the chauffeur-driven, handmade limousine, and all the other things that had once attached to the rulers of this vast and unhappy country. He drove to his legislative office, where at least he had a reserved parking place. Once behind the closed door of his office, he composed a brief letter on his personal typewriter. This he folded into a pocket. There was work to do this day. He walked down the street to the immense lobby of the Congress, and checked his coat. The attendant was female. She took his coat and handed him a numbered token. He thanked her politely. As she took the coat to its numbered hook, the attendant removed the note from the inside pocket and tucked it into the pocket of her own jacket. Four hours later it arrived in the American Embassy.

"Panic attack?" Fellows asked.

"You might call it that, gentlemen," Ryan said.

"Okay, tell us about the problem." Trent sipped at his tea.

"We've had more indications that our communications links may be penetrated."

"Again?" Trent rolled his eyes.

"Come on, Al, we've heard that song before," Fellows grumbled. "Details, Jack, details."

Ryan went through the data.

"And what's the White House think?"

"I don't know yet. I'm heading up the street after I leave here. Frankly I'd rather discuss it with you guys first, and I had to come down on some other stuff anyway." Jack went on to describe the SPINNAKER report on Narmonov's problems.

"How long have you had this?"

"A couple of weeks—"

"Why haven't we heard it?" Trent demanded.

"Because we've been running around in circles trying to confirm it," Jack answered.

"And?"

"Al, we've been unable to confirm directly. There are indications that the KGB is up to something. There seems to be a very discreet operation in Germany, looking for some lost tactical nukes."

"Good Lord!" Fellows noted. "What do you mean by 'lost'?"

"We're not sure. If it ties in with SPINNAKER, well, maybe there's been some creative accounting on the part of the Soviet Army."

"Your opinion?"

"I don't know, guys, I just don't know. Our analysis people are about evenly divided—those that are willing to offer an opinion."

"We know their army isn't real happy," Fellows said slowly. "The loss of funding, loss of prestige, loss of units and billets . . . but *that* unhappy?"

"Pleasant thought," Trent added. "A power struggle in a country with all those nukes. . . . How reliable has SPINNAKER been?"

"Very. Five years of devoted service."

"He's a member of their parliament, right?" Fellows asked.

"Correct."

"Evidently a very senior one to get stuff like this . . . that's okay, I don't think either one of us wants to know his name," Fellows added.

Trent nodded. "Probably somebody we've met." *Good guess, Al,* Jack didn't say. "You're taking this seriously also?"

"Yes, sir, and also trying very hard to confirm it."

"Anything new on NIITAKA?" Trent asked.

"Sir, I—"

"I heard from up the street that there's something to do with Mexico," Al Trent said next. "The President evidently wants my support on something. You are cleared to tell us. Honest, Jack, the President has authorized it."

It was a technical rules violation, but Ryan had never known Trent to break his word. He went through that report also.

"Those little bastards!" Trent breathed. "You know how many votes it cost me to roll over on that trade deal, and now they're planning to *break* it! So you're saying we've been rolled again?"

"A possibility, sir."

"Sam? The farmers in your district use all those nasty agricultural chemicals. Might cost 'em."

"Al, free trade is an important principle," Fellows said.

"So's keeping your goddamned word!"

"No argument, Al." Fellows started thinking about how many of his farmers might lose expected export income from a flipflop on the deal that he'd fought for on the floor of the House. "How can we confirm this one?"

"Not sure yet."

"Bug his airplane?" Trent suggested with a chuckle. "If we can confirm this, I'd like to be there when Fowler shoves it up his ass! God *damn* it! I lost *votes* over this!" That he'd carried his district 58–42 was, for the moment, beside the point. "Well, the President wants us to back him up on this one. Problems from your side of the aisle, Sam?"

"Probably not."

"I'd just as soon stay clear of the political side of this, gentlemen. I'm just here as a messenger, remember?"

"Jack Ryan, last of the virgins." Trent laughed. "Good report, thanks for coming down. Let us know if the President wants us to authorize the new and improved TAPDANCE."

"He'll never try. You're looking at two or three hundred million bucks, and bucks are tight," Fellows noted. "I want to see better data before we spring for it. We've dropped too much money down these black holes."

"All I can say, Congressman, is that I'm taking it very seriously. So is the FBI."

"And Ron Olson?" Trent asked.

"He's circling his wagons."

"You'll have a better chance if he asks," Fellows told Ryan.

"I know. Well, at least we'll have our system up and running in three more weeks. We've started turning out the first set of discs and doing preliminary tests now."

"How so?"

"We use a computer to look for nonrandomness. The big one, the Cray YMP. We brought in a consultant from MIT's Artificial Intelligence Laboratory to do a new kind of type-token program. In another week—ten days, call it—we'll know if the system is what we expect it to be. Then we'll start sending the hardware out."

"I really hope you're wrong on this," Trent said as the meeting closed.

"So do I, man, but my instincts say otherwise."

"And how much is it going to cost?" Fowler asked over lunch.

"From what I gather, two or three hundred million."

"No. We've got budget problems enough."

"I agree," Liz Elliot said. "But I wanted to discuss it with you first. It's Ryan's idea. Olson at NSA says he's full of it, says the systems are secure, but Ryan's really crazed about this new encoding system. You know he pushed the same thing through for the Agency—even went to Congress directly.''

''Oh, really?'' Fowler looked up from his plate. ''He didn't go through OMB? What gives?''

''Bob, he delivered his pitch for the new NSA system to Trent and Fellows before he came to see me!''

''Who the hell does he think he is!''

''I keep telling you, Bob.''

''He's out, Elizabeth. Out. O-U-T. Get moving on it.''

''Okay, I think I know how to do it.''

Circumstances made it easy. One of Ernest Wellington's investigators had been staking out the 7-Eleven for a week. The Zimmer family business was just off U.S. Route 50 between Washington and Annapolis, and was adjacent to a large housing development from which it drew much of its business. The investigator parked his van at the end of a street that gave him both a view of the business building and the family house which was only fifty yards away from it. The van was a typical covert-surveillance vehicle, custom-built by one of several specialty firms. The roof vent concealed a sophisticated periscope, whose two lenses were connected respectively to a TV camera and a 35mm Canon. The investigator had a cooler full of soft drinks, a large thermos of coffee and a chemical toilet. He thought of the cramped van as his own personal space vehicle, and some of its high-tech gadgetry was at least as good as NASA had installed on the Shuttle.

''Bingo!'' the radio crackled. ''Subject vehicle is taking the exit. Breaking off now.''

The man in the van lifted his own microphone. ''Roger, out.''

Clark had noticed the Mercury two days earlier. One of the problems with commuting was that the same vehicles kept showing up from time to time, and he'd decided that's all it was. It never got close, and never followed them off the main road. In this case, as he took the exit, it didn't follow. Clark shifted his attention to other matters. He hadn't noticed that the guy was using a microphone . . . but those new cellular things had you talking into the visor, and—wasn't technology wonderful? A good chase car need not tip himself off anymore. He pulled into the 7-Eleven parking lot, his eyes scanning for trouble. He saw none. Clark and Ryan exited the car at the same instant. Clark's topcoat was unbuttoned, as was his suit jacket, the easier to allow access to the Beretta 10mm pistol riding on his right hip. The sun was setting, casting a lovely orange glow in the western sky, and it was unseasonably warm, shirtsleeve weather that made him regret the raincoat he was wearing. D.C.-area weather was as predictably unpredictable as anywhere in the world.

''Hello, Dr. Ryan,'' one of the Zimmer kids said. ''Mom's over at the house.''

''Okay.'' Ryan walked back outside and headed for the flagstone walk to the Zimmer residence. He spotted Carol in the back, with her youngest on the new swing set. Clark trailed, alert as ever, seeing nothing but still-green lawns and parked cars, a few kids throwing a football. Such temperate weather in the beginning of December worried Clark. He believed it heralded a bastard of a winter.

''Hi, Carol!'' Jack called. Mrs. Zimmer was closely observing her youngest in the swing seat.

"Doc Ryan, you like the new swing set?"

Jack nodded a little guiltily. He should have helped get it together. He was an expert on assembling toys. He leaned over. "How's the little munchkin?"

"She won't get out, and it's dinnertime," Carol said. "You help?"

"How's everyone else?"

"Peter accepted in college, too! Full scholarship MIT."

"Great!" Jack gave her a congratulatory hug. *What's the old joke? "The doctor is five and the lawyer is three?" God, wouldn't Buck be proud of how these kids are turning out?* It was little more than the normal Asian obsession with education, of course, the same thing that had stood Jewish-Americans in such good stead. If an opportunity presents itself, grab it by the throat. He bent down to the newest Zimmer, who held her arms up for her Uncle Jack.

"Come on, Jackie." He picked her up and got a kiss for his trouble. Ryan looked up when he heard the noise.

"Gotcha." It's a simple trick, and an effective one. Even if you know it's coming, you can't do much to prevent it. The van had several buttons which, when pressed, beeped the horn. It was a sound the human brain recognized as a danger signal, and one instinctively looked toward whatever direction it had come from to see if there was any cause for concern. The investigator hit the nearest one, and, sure enough, Ryan looked up toward the sound, with an armful of kid. He'd caught the hug for the woman, and the kiss from the kid, and now he had a full-face shot on the 1200-speed film in his camera to back up the videotape. That simple. He had the goods on this Ryan guy. Amazing that a man with such a lovely wife would feel the need to screw around, but that was life, wasn't it? A CIA bodyguard to keep everything nice and secure. A kid involved, too. *What a shit,* the man thought as the motor-drive whirred away on the Canon.

"You stay for dinnah! This time you stay. We celebrate Peter scholarship."

"Can't say no to that one, doc," Clark observed.

"Okay." Ryan carried Jacqueline Theresa Zimmer into the house. Neither he nor Clark noticed that the van parked fifty yards away pulled off a few minutes later.

It was the most delicate part of the process. The plutonium was set into cerium sulfide ceramic crucibles. The crucibles were carried to the electric furnace. Fromm closed and locked the door. A vacuum pump evacuated the enclosure and replaced argon.

"Air has oxygen," Fromm explained. "Argon is an inert gas. We take no chances. Plutonium is highly reactive and pyrophoric. The ceramic crucibles are also inert and nonreactive. We use more than one crucible to avoid the possibility of forming a critical mass and starting a premature atomic reaction."

"The phase-transformations?" Ghosn asked.

"Correct."

"How long?" This question from Qati.

"Two hours. We take our time in this part. On removal from the furnace, the crucibles will be covered, of course, and we make the pour in an inert-gas enclosure. Now you know why we needed this sort of furnace."

"No danger when you make the pour?"

Fromm shook his head. "None at all, so long as we are careful. The configuration of the mold absolutely prevents forming a critical mass. I've done this many times in simulation. There have been accidents, but those invariably involved larger masses of fissile material and took place before all the hazards of handling plutonium were fully understood. No, we will move slowly and carefully. Pretend it is gold," Fromm concluded.

"The machining process?"

"Three weeks, and two more of assembly and testing of the components."

"The tritium extraction?" Ghosn asked.

Fromm bent down to look into the furnace. "I'll do that right before completion, and that will conclude the exercise."

"See any resemblance?" the investigator asked.

"Hard to tell," Wellington thought. "In any case, he sure seems to like the little tyke. Cute enough. I watched them build the swing set last weekend. The little one—name's Jackie, by the way, Jacqueline Theresa—"

"Oh? That's interesting." Wellington made a note.

"Anyway, the little one loves the damned thing."

"Seems right fond of Mr. Ryan, also."

"You suppose he really is the father?"

"Possible," Wellington said, watching the videotape and comparing the picture there with the still shots. "Light wasn't very good."

"I can have the back-room boys enhance it. Take a few days for the tape, though. They have to do it frame by frame."

"I think that's a good idea. We want this to be solid."

"It will be. So what's going to happen to him?"

"He'll be encouraged to leave government service, I suppose."

"You know, if we were private citizens, you might call this blackmail, invasion of privacy. . . ."

"But we're not, and it isn't. This guy holds a security clearance, and it appears that his personal life isn't what it should be."

"I suppose that's not our fault, is it?"

"Exactly."

22. Repercussions

"Damn it, Ryan, you can't do that!"

"Do what?" Jack responded.

"You went over my head to the Hill."

"What do you mean? All I did was suggest to Trent and Fellows that there might be a problem. I'm supposed to do that."

"It's not confirmed," the Director insisted.

"So, what ever is fully confirmed?"

"Look at this." Cabot handed over a new file.

"This is SPINNAKER. Why haven't I seen it yet?"

''Just read it!'' Cabot snapped back.

''Confirms the leak . . .'' It was a short one, and Jack raced through it. ''Except he thinks it's a leak in the Moscow Embassy. Like a code clerk, maybe.''

''Pure speculation on his part—all he really says is that he wants his reports transported by hand now. That's the only definite thing this tells us.''

Cabot dodged. ''I know we've done that before.''

''Yes, we have,'' Ryan admitted. It would even be easier now with the direct air service from New York to Moscow.

''What's the rat line look like now?''

Ryan frowned at that. Cabot liked to use Agency jargon, though the term ''rat line,'' meaning the chain of people and methods that transported a document from agent to case officer, had actually gone out of favor. ''It's a fairly simple one. Kadishev leaves his messages in a coat pocket. The checkroom attendant at their Congress retrieves the messages and gets them off to one of our people by brush-pass. Simple and direct. Also rather fast. I've never been comfortable with it, but it works.''

''So now we have two top agents who're unhappy with our communications systems, and I have to fly all the way to Japan—personally—to meet with one.''

''It's not all that unusual for an agent to want to meet a high Agency official, Director. These people get twitchy, and knowing that some higher-up cares about them is what they need.''

''It'll waste a whole week of my time!'' Cabot objected.

''You have to go to Korea in late January anyway,'' Ryan pointed out. ''Catch our friend on the way back. He's not demanding to see you immediately, just soon.'' Ryan returned to the SPINNAKER report, wondering why Cabot allowed himself to be sidetracked by irrelevancies. The reason, of course, was that the man was a dilettante, and a lazy one, who disliked losing arguments.

The new report said that Narmonov was very worried indeed that the West would find out just how desperate his situation with the Soviet military and KGB was. There was no further information on missing nuclear weapons, but plenty on new changes in parliamentary loyalties. The report gave Ryan the impression of having been slapped together. He decided to have Mary Pat look at it. Of all the people in the Agency, she was the only one who really understood the guy.

''I presume you're taking it to the President.''

''Yes, I think I have to.''

''If I may make a suggestion, remember to tell him that we have not really confirmed anything Kadishev has said.''

Cabot looked up. ''So?''

''So it's true, Director. When you single-source something, especially something that's apparently highly important, you tell people that.''

''I believe this guy.''

''I'm not so sure.''

''The Russian department buys it,'' Cabot noted.

''True, they've signed off on it, but I'd feel a hell of a lot better if we had independent confirmation,'' Jack said.

''Do you have any firm basis to doubt this information?''

''Nothing I can show to you, no. It's just that we ought to have been able to confirm something by now.''

''So you expect me to go all the way down to the White House, present this, and then admit that it might be wrong?'' Cabot stamped out his cigar, much to Jack's relief.

''Yes, sir.''

''I won't do that!''

''You have to do that, sir. You have to do that because it happens to be true. It's the rule.''

''Jack, it can get slightly tedious when you tell me what the rules of this place are. I am the Director, you know.''

''Look, Marcus,'' Ryan said, trying to keep the exasperation out of his voice, ''what we have with this guy is some really hot information, something which, if true, could affect the way we deal with the Soviets. But it is not confirmed. It just comes from one person, okay? What if he's wrong? What if he misunderstands something? What if he's lying, even?''

''Do we have any reason to believe that?''

''None at all, Director, but on something this important—is it prudent or reasonable to affect our government's policy on the basis of a short letter from a single person?'' That was always the best way to get to Marcus Cabot, prudence and reason.

''I hear what you're saying, Jack. Okay. My car is waiting. I'll be back in a couple of hours.''

Cabot grabbed his coat and walked out to the executive elevator. His Agency car was waiting. As Director of Central Intelligence he got a pair of bodyguards, one driving and the other in the front-passenger seat. Otherwise he had to deal with traffic the same as everyone else. Ryan, he thought on the drive down the George Washington Parkway, was becoming a pain in the ass. Okay, so he himself was new here. Okay, so he was inexperienced. Okay, so he liked to leave day-to-day stuff to his subordinates. He was the Director, after all, and didn't need to deal with every little damned thing. He was getting tired of having the rules of conduct explained to him once or twice a week, tired of having Ryan go over his head, tired of having analysis explained to him every time something really juicy came in. By the time he entered the White House, Cabot was quite annoyed.

''Morning, Marcus,'' Liz Elliot said in her office.

''Good morning. We have another SPINNAKER report. President needs to go over it.''

''So, what's Kadishev up to?''

''Who told you his name?'' the DCI growled.

''Ryan—didn't you know?''

''Goddamn it!'' Cabot swore. ''He didn't tell me that.''

''Sit down, Marcus. We have a few minutes. How happy are you with Ryan?''

''Sometimes he forgets who's the Director and who's the Deputy.''

''He is a little on the arrogant side, isn't he?''

''Slightly,'' Cabot agreed frostily.

''He's good at what he does—within limitations—but personally I'm getting a little tired of his attitude.''

''I know what you mean. He likes telling me what I have to do—with this, for example.''

''Oh, he doesn't trust your judgment?'' the National Security Advisor asked, selecting her needle with care.

Cabot looked up. ''Yeah, that's the attitude he conveys.''

"Well, we weren't able to change everything from the previous administration. Of course, he *is* a pro at this. . . ." Her voice trailed off.

"And I'm not?" Cabot demanded.

"Of course you are, Marcus, you know I never meant it that way!"

"Sorry, Liz. You're right. Sometimes he rubs me the wrong way. That's all."

"Let's go see the Boss."

"How solid is this?" President Fowler asked five minutes later.

"As you've already heard, this agent has been working for us over five years, and his information has invariably been accurate."

"Have you confirmed it?"

"Not completely," Cabot replied. "It's unlikely that we can, but our Russian department believes it, and so do I."

"Ryan had his doubts."

Cabot was getting a little tired of hearing about Ryan. "I do not, Mr. President. I think Ryan is trying to impress us with his new views on the Soviet government, trying to show us that he's not a cold-warrior anymore." Again Cabot had dwelt on irrelevancies, Elliot thought to herself.

Fowler's eyes shifted. "Elizabeth?"

"It's certainly plausible that the Soviet security apparatus is trying to stake out an improved position," her voice purred at its most reasonable timbre. "They're unhappy with the liberalization, they're unhappy with their loss of power, and they're unhappy with what they think is a failure of leadership on Narmonov's part. This information, therefore, is consistent with a lot of other facts we have. I think we should believe it."

"If this is true, then we have to ease off on our support for Narmonov. We cannot be party to a reversion to more centralized rule, particularly if it results from elements who so clearly dislike us."

"Agreed," Liz said. "Better to lose Narmonov. If he can't break their military to his will, then someone else will have to. Of course, we have to give him a fair chance . . . how we do that is rather tricky. We don't want to dump the country into the hands of their military, do we?"

"Are you kidding?" Fowler observed.

They stood on a catwalk inside the massive boat-shed where the Trident submarines were prepared for sea, watching the crew of USS *Georgia* load up for their next cruise.

"Talked his way out of it, Bart?" Jones asked.

"His explanation made a lot of sense, Ron."

"When's the last time you caught me wrong?"

"For all things there is a first time."

"Not this one, skipper," Dr. Jones said quietly. "I got a feeling."

"Okay, I want you to spend some more time on the simulator with his sonar troops."

"Fair enough." Jones was quiet for a few seconds. "You know, it might be fun to go out, just one more time. . . ."

Mancuso turned. "You volunteering?"

"No. Kim might not understand my being away for three months. Two weeks is long enough. Too long, as a matter of fact. I'm getting very domesticated, Bart, getting old and respectable. Not young and bright-eyed like those kids."

"What do you think of them?"

"The sonar guys? They're good. So's the tracking party. The guy Ricks replaced was Jim Rosselli, right?"

"That's right."

"He trained them well. Can we go off the record?"

"Sure."

"Ricks is not a good skipper. He's too tough on the troops, demands too much, too hard to satisfy. Not like you were at all, Bart."

Mancuso dodged the compliment. "We all have different styles."

"I know that, but I wouldn't want to sail with him. One of his chiefs asked for a transfer off. So did half a dozen petty officers."

"They all had family problems." Mancuso had approved all the transfers, including the young chief torpedoman.

"No, they didn't," Jones said. "They needed excuses, and they used them."

"Ron, look, I'm the squadron commander, okay? I can only evaluate my COs on the basis of performance. Ricks didn't get here by being a loser."

"You look from the top down. I look from the bottom up. From my perspective, this man is not a good skipper. I wouldn't say that to anybody else, but we were shipmates. Okay, I was a peon, just a lowly E-6, but you never treated me that way. You were a good boss. Ricks isn't. The crew doesn't like him, does not have confidence in him."

"Damn it, Ron, I can't allow stuff like that to affect my judgment."

"Yeah, I know. Annapolis, old school tie—ring, whatever matters to you Canoe U. grads. You have to approach it a different way. Like I said, I wouldn't talk this way with anybody else. If I was on that boat, I'd try to transfer off."

"I sailed with some skippers I didn't like. It's mainly a matter of style."

"You say so, Commodore." Jones paused. "Just remember one thing, okay? There's lots of ways to impress a senior officer, but there's only one way to impress a crew."

Fromm insisted that they take their time. The mold had long since cooled and was now broken open in the inert atmosphere of the first machine tool. The roughly formed metal mass was set in place. Fromm personally checked the computer codes that told the machine what it had to do and punched the first button. The robotic system activated. The moving arm selected the proper toolhead, secured it on the rotating spindle, and maneuvered itself into place. The enclosed area was flooded with argon gas, and Freon began spraying on the plutonium to keep everything to the proper isothermal heat environment. Fromm touched the computer screen, selecting the initial program. The spindle started turning, reaching over a thousand RPM, and approached the plutonium mass with a motion that was neither human nor mechanistic, but something else entirely, like a caricature of a man's action. As they watched from behind the Lexan shield, the first shavings of the silvery metal thread peeled off the main mass.

"How much are we losing?" Ghosn asked.

"Oh, the total will be less than twenty grams," Fromm estimated. "It's nothing to worry about." Fromm looked at another gauge, the one that measured relative pressures. The machine tool was totally isolated from the rest of the room, with the pressure inside its enclosure marginally less than outside. The fact that argon gas was heavier than air would keep oxygen away from the plutonium. That prevented possible combustion. Combustion would generate plutonium dust, which was every bit as lethal as Fromm had told them. A toxic heavy metal, the additional hazard of radioactivity—mainly low-energy alphas—merely made death more rapid and marginally less pleasant. The machinists moved in to take over supervision of the process. They had worked out extremely well, Fromm thought. The skills they'd brought with them had grown with remarkable speed under his tutelage. They were nearly as good as the men he'd trained in Germany, despite their lack of formal education. There was much to be said for practical instead of theoretical work.

"How long?" Qati asked.

"How many times do I have to tell you? We are precisely on schedule. This phase of the project is the most time-consuming. The product we are now producing must be perfect. Absolutely perfect. If this part of the device fails to function, nothing else will."

"That's true of everything we've done!" Ghosn pointed out.

"Correct, my young friend, but this is the easiest thing to get wrong. The metal is hard to work, and the metallic phase transformations make it all the more delicate. Now, let's see those explosive blocks."

Ghosn was right. Everything had to work. The explosives had been almost entirely his problem after Fromm had set the design specifications. They'd taken normal TNT and added a stiffener, a plastic that made the material quite rigid, but without affecting its chemical properties. Normally explosives are plastic and easily malleable by their nature. That property had to be eliminated, since the shape of the blocks was crucial to the way in which their explosive energy was delivered. Ghosn had shaped six hundred such blocks, each a segment of a full ellipsoid. Seventy of them would nest together exactly, forming an explosive ring with an outside diameter of 35 centimeters. Each block had a squib fired from kryton switches. The wires leading from the power supply to the switches all had to be of exactly the same length. Fromm lifted one of the blocks.

"You say that these are all identical?" Fromm asked.

"Completely. I followed your directions exactly."

"Pick seventy at random. I'll take one of the stainless-steel blanks, and we will test your work."

The spot was already prepared, of course. It was, in fact, the eroded crater from an American-made Mark 84 bomb dropped by an Israeli F-4 Phantom some years before. Qati's men had erected a prefabricated structure of timber posts and beams whose roof was three layers of sandbags. Camouflage netting had been added to reduce the chance of notice. Test assembly took three hours, and an electronic strain-gauge was inserted in the steel blank and a wire run to the next crater down—two hundred meters away—where Fromm waited with an oscilloscope. They were finished just before dusk.

"Ready," Ghosn said.

"Proceed," Fromm replied, concentrating on his scope.

Ibrahim pressed the button. The structure disintegrated before their eyes. A few sandbags survived, flying through the air, but mainly there was a shower of dirt. On the O-scope, the peak pressure was frozen in place well before the *crump* of the blast wave passed over their heads. Bock and Qati were somewhat disappointed in the physical effects of the explosion, most of which had been attenuated by the sandbags. Was such a small detonation enough to ignite a nuclear device?

"Well?" Ghosn asked as a man ran off to the newly deepened crater.

"Ten percent off," Fromm said, looking up. Then he smiled. "Ten percent too much."

"What does that mean?" Qati demanded, suddenly worried that they'd done something wrong.

"It means that my young student has learned his lessons well." Fifteen minutes later, they were sure. It took two men to find it, and half an hour to remove the tungsten casing from the core. What had been a nearly solid steel mass as big around as a man's fist was now a distorted cylinder no wider than a cigar. Had it been plutonium, a nuclear reaction would have taken place. Of that the German was sure. Fromm hefted it in his hand and presented it to Ibrahim.

"Herr Ghosn," he said formally. "You have a gift with explosives. You are a fine engineer. In the DDR it took us three attempts to get it right. You have done it in one."

"How many more?"

Fromm nodded. "Very good. We shall do another tomorrow. We will test all the stainless-steel blanks, of course."

"That is why we made them," Ghosn agreed.

On the way back, Bock ran over his own calculations. According to Fromm, the force of the final explosion would be more than four hundred fifty thousand tons of TNT. He therefore based his estimates on a mere four hundred thousand. Bock was always conservative on casualty estimates. The stadium and all in it would be vaporized. No, he corrected himself. That wasn't really true. There was nothing magical about this weapon. It was merely a large explosive device. The stadium and all in it would be totally destroyed, but there would be a great deal of rubble flung ballistically hundreds, perhaps thousands of meters. The ground nearest the device would be pulverized down to pieces of molecular size. Dust particles would then be sucked up into the fireball. Bits of the bomb-assembly residue would affix themselves to the rising, boiling dust. That's what fallout was, he'd learned, dirt with bomb residue attached. The nature of the blast—being set off at ground level—would maximize the fallout, which would be borne downwind. The majority would fall within thirty kilometers of the blast site. The remainder would be a plaything of the winds, to fall over Chicago or St. Louis or maybe even Washington. How many would die from that?

Good question. He estimated roughly two hundred thousand from the blast itself, certainly no more than that. Another fifty to one hundred thousand from secondary effects, that number including long-term deaths from cancers which would take years to manifest themselves. As Qati had noted earlier, the actual death count was somewhat disappointing. It was so easy to think of nuclear bombs as magical engines of destruction, but they were not. They were merely highly powerful bombs with some interesting secondary effects. It also made for the finest terrorist weapon yet conceived.

Terrorist? Bock asked himself. *Is that what I am?*

It was, of course, in the eye of the beholder. Bock had long since decided his measure of respect for the judgment of others. This event would be the best expression of it.

"John, I need an idea," Ryan said.

"What's that?" Clark asked.

"I've drawn a blank. The Japanese Prime Minister is going to be in Mexico in February, then he's flying up here to see the President. We want to know what he's going to be saying on his airplane."

"I don't have the legs to dress up as a stew, doc. Besides, I've never learned to do the tea ceremony, either." The field officer turned SPO paused and turned serious. "Bug an airplane . . . ? That sounds like a real technical challenge."

"What do you know about this?"

John examined his coffee. "I've placed intelligence-gathering devices before, but always on the ground. With an aircraft you have lots of ambient noise to worry about. You also have to sweat where your subject intends to sit. Finally, with a presidential aircraft you need to worry about security. The technical side is probably the hardest," he decided. "The greatest personal threat to the guy is probably at home—unless he's going to stopover at Detroit, right? Mexico City. Okay, people speak Spanish there, and my Spanish is pretty good. I'd take Ding down with me, of course. . . . What sort of aircraft will he be using?"

"I checked. He'll be flying a JAL 747. The upper deck behind the cockpit is laid out as his conference room. They put in beds, too. That's where he'll be. Their PM likes to kibbitz with the drivers. He's pretty smart about traveling, sleeps as much as he can to handle the jet lag."

Clark nodded. "People have to wipe the windows. Not like he's got an air force base to handle all the ground-service requirements like we do it. If JAL flies into there regularly, they'll have Mexican ground crews. I'll check out data on the 747. . . . Like I said, that's the easy part. I can probably talk my way there. Might even get Ding to head down with a good set of papers and get a job. That would make it easier. I presume this has executive approval?"

"The President said 'find a way.' He'll have to approve the final op-plan."

"I need to talk to the S&T guys." Clark referred to the CIA's Directorate of Science and Technology. "The real problem is noise. . . . How fast, doc?"

"Fast, John."

"Okay." Clark rose. "Gee, I get to be a field-spook again. I'll be over in the new building. It may take me a few days to figure if it's possible or not. This mean I can't go on the U.K. trip?"

"Bother you?" Jack asked.

"Nope. Just as soon stay home."

"Fair enough. I get to do some Christmas shopping at Hamleys."

"You know how lucky you are to have 'em little? All my girls want now is clothes, and I can't pick girl clothes worth a damn." Clark lived in horror of buying women's clothing.

"Sally has her doubts now, but little Jack still believes."

Clark shook his head. "After you stop believing in Santa Claus, the whole world just goes downhill."

"Ain't it the truth?"

23. Opinions

"Jack, you look bloody awful," Sir Basil Charleston observed.

"If one more person tells me that, I'm going to waste him."

"Bad flight?"

"Bumpy as hell all the way across. Didn't sleep much." As the even-darker-than-usual circles under his eyes proclaimed.

"Well, we'll see if lunch helps."

"It is a pretty day," Ryan noted as they walked up Westminster Bridge Road toward Parliament. It was a rare early-winter English day with a blue, cloudless sky. A brisk wind swept down the Thames, but Ryan didn't mind. He had a heavy coat and a scarf around his neck, and the frigid blast on his face woke him up. "Trouble at the office, Bas?"

"Found a bug, a bloody bug, two floors down from my office! The whole building's being swept."

"Things are tough all over. KGB?"

"Not sure," Charleston said as they crossed the bridge. "Trouble with the façade, you see, bloody thing began crumbling—same as happened to Scotland Yard a few years ago. The workers replacing it found an unexplained wire and followed it. . . . Our Russian friends have not cut back on their activities, and there are other services as well. See anything like that in your shop?"

"No. It helps that we're more isolated than Century House." Jack meant that the British Secret Intelligence Service was in so densely populated an area—there was a nearby apartment block, for example—that a very low-power bug could get data out. That was less likely at the Agency's Langley headquarters, which sat alone on a large wooded campus. In addition to that, the newer construction had allowed installation of elaborate protections against internal radio sources. "You should do what we've done and install wave guides."

"That would cost a bloody fortune, which we do not have at the moment."

"What the hell, it gives us a chance to take a walk. If anyone can bug us out here, we've already lost."

"It never ends, does it? We win the Cold War, but it never ever ends."

"Which Greek was it? The one whose personal hell was rolling a big rock up a hill, and every time he got it there the son of a bitch rolled down the other side."

"Sisyphus . . . ? Tantalus, perhaps? Long time since I bade farewell to Oxford, Sir John. In either case, you're right. Get to the top of one hill and all you see is another damned hill." They continued walking down the embankment, away from Parliament, but toward lunch. Meetings like this one had rules. You couldn't get down to business until after the small talk and a pregnant pause. In this case, there were some off-season American tourists snapping pictures. Charleston and Ryan walked around to avoid them.

"We have a problem, Bas."

"What's that?" Charleston said without turning. Behind them were three security officers. Two more preceded them.

Jack didn't turn either. "We have a guy inside the Kremlin. Spends some time with Narmonov. Says Andrey Il'ych is worried about a military/KGB coup. Says that they might renege on the strategic-arms treaty. Also says that some tactical nuclear devices may be missing from their inventories in Germany."

"Indeed? That's cheery news. How good is your source?"

"Extremely good."

"Well, I can only say it's news to me, Dr. Ryan."

"How good is your guy?" Jack asked.

"Quite good."

"Nothing like this?"

"Some rumbles, of course. I mean, Narmonov does have a full plate, doesn't he? Ever since that dreadful affair with the Balts, and the Georgians, *and* his Muslims. What is it you Yanks say, 'one-armed paperhanger'? He's that busy and more. He's had to make a deal with his security forces, but a *coup d'état?*" Charleston shood his head. "No. The tea leaves don't appear that way to us."

"That's precisely what our agent is telling us. What about the nuclear thing?"

"I'm afraid our chap isn't well-placed for that sort of information. More the civilian side, you see." And that, Jack knew, was as far as Basil would go. "How seriously are you taking this?"

"Very seriously. I have to. This agent has been giving us good stuff for a lot of years."

"One of Mrs. Foley's recruits?" Charleston asked with a chuckle. "What a marvelous young lady. I understand she recently delivered another child?"

"Little girl, Emily Sarah, looks just like her mom." Jack thought he'd dodged the first question rather adroitly. "Mary Pat will be back at work right after New Year."

"Ah, yes, you do have that fortress nursery on your grounds, don't you?"

"One of the smartest investments we ever made. Wish I'd thought of it."

"You Americans!" Sir Basil laughed. "Missing nuclear weapons. Yes, I suppose one must take that very seriously indeed. Possible collusion between the Army and KGB and a tactical-nuclear trump. Quite frightening, I must say, but we have not heard a whisper. Rather a difficult secret to keep, wouldn't you say? I mean, blackmail doesn't work terribly well unless people know they're being blackmailed."

"We've also caught a rumble that KGB is running some nuclear-oriented operation in Germany. That's all, just a rumble."

"Yes, we've heard that too," Charleston said as they turned to walk down the brow to the *Tattersall Castle,* an old paddle steamer long since converted to a restaurant.

"And?"

"And we've run our own op. It seems that Erich Honecker had his own little Manhattan Project under way. Fortunately it died in the womb. Ivan was quite upset to learn of it. The DDR returned a goodly supply of plutonium to their former socialist colleagues just before the change. I speculate that KGB is investigating the same thing."

"Why didn't you tell us?" *Jesus, Bas,* Jack thought. *You guys just don't forget, do you?*

"Nothing to tell, Jack." Charleston nodded at the headwaiter, who took them to a table well aft. The security officers situated themselves between their charges and the rest of luncheoning humanity. "Our German friends have been very forthcoming. The project, they say, has been quashed, completely and for all time. We've had our technical people over everything, and they confirmed everything our German colleagues told us."

"When was this?"

"Several months ago. Ever eat here, Jack?" Charleston asked as the waiter appeared.

"Not this one, a few of the other ferryboats." Basil ordered a pint of bitter. Jack decided on a lager. They watched the waiter withdraw. "The KGB op is more recent."

"Interesting. Could be the same thing, you know, could be that they had the same interests we had and were just a little slower to move."

"On nukes?" Ryan shook his head. "Our Russian friends are pretty smart, Bas, and they pay much closer attention to nuclear issues than we do. It's one of the things I admire about them."

"Yes, they did learn their lesson from China, didn't they?" Charleston set his menu down and waved for the waiter to bring the drinks. "You think this is a serious matter, then?"

"Sure do."

"Your judgment is generally rather good, Jack. Thank you," Basil told the waiter. Both men made their orders. "You think we should poke about?"

"I think that might be a good idea."

"Very well. What else can you tell me?"

"I'm afraid that's it, Bas."

"Your source must be very good indeed." Sir Basil sipped at his beer. "I think you have reservations."

"I do, but . . . hell, Basil, when do we not have reservations?"

"Any contrary data?"

"None, just that we've been totally unable to confirm. Our source is good enough that we may not be able to confirm elsewhere. That's why I came over. Your guy must be pretty good, too, judging by what you've sent us. Whoever he is, he might be the best chance to back our guy up."

"And if we can't confirm?"

"Then probably we'll go with it anyway." Ryan didn't like that.

"And your reservations?"

"Probably don't matter. Two reasons. Number one, I'm not sure myself whether to sign off on this or not. Number two, not everyone cares what I think."

"And that's why you've not received credit for your work on the treaty?"

Ryan grinned rather tiredly, having not had much sleep in the preceding thirty-six hours. "I refuse to be surprised by that, and I won't ask how you pulled that one out of the hat."

"But?"

"But I wish somebody would leak it to the press or something!" Ryan allowed himself a laugh.

"I'm afraid we don't do that here. I've only leaked it to one person."

"PM?"

"His Royal Highness. You're having dinner with him tonight, correct? I reckoned he might like to know."

Jack thought about that. The Prince of Wales wouldn't let it go any further. Ryan could never have told him . . . but . . . "Thanks, pal."

"We all crave recognition in one way or another. You and I are both denied it as a matter of course. Not really fair, but there you are. In this case I broke one of my own rules, and if you ask why, I'll tell you: what you did was bloody marvelous, Jack. If there were justice in the world, Her Majesty would enter you in the Order of Merit."

"You can't tell her, Basil. She just might do it all on her own."

"She might indeed, and that would let out the little secret, mightn't it?" Dinner arrived, and they had to wait again.

"It wasn't just me. You know that Charlie Alden did a lot of good work. So did Talbot, Bunker, Scott Adler, a bunch of others."

"Your modesty is as comprehensive as ever, Dr. Ryan."

"Does that mean 'stupid,' Bas?" Ryan got a smile instead of an answer. The Brits were good at that.

* * *

Fromm would never have believed it. They'd made five stainless-steel blanks to duplicate the size and configuration of the plutonium. Ghosn had made all the necessary explosive blocks. They'd tested the explosives on all five blanks, and in every case the explosives had done their job. This was one very talented young man. Of course he'd had exact plans to follow, and Fromm had generated them with the help of a fine computer, but even so, getting something so difficult right the first time was hardly the norm in engineering.

The plutonium was now through the first part of the machining process. It actually looked rather good, like a high-quality steel forging machined to be part of an automotive engine. That was a good beginning. The robot arm of the milling machine removed the plutonium from its spindle and set it in an enclosed box. The box was, of course, filled with argon gas. The arm sealed it and moved it to a door, then Fromm removed it from the machine enclosure and walked over to the air-bearing lathe. The process was reverse-duplicated. He slid the box into the enclosure. Vacuum pumps were activated and while the air was sucked out the top of the enclosure, argon gas was added at the bottom. When the internal atmosphere was totally inert, the robot arm of this tool opened the box and extracted the plutonium. The next programmed set of movements set it precisely on a new spindle. The degree of precision was hugely important. Under Fromm's supervision, the spindle was activated, building its speed up slowly to fifteen thousand RPM.

"It would appear that—no!" Fromm swore. He'd thought he'd gotten it perfect. The spindle slowed back down, and a tiny adjustment was made. Fromm took his time checking the balance, then powered it up again. This time it was perfect. He took the RPMs all the way to twenty-five thousand and there was no jitter at all.

"You men did the first machining very nicely," Fromm said over his shoulder.

"How much mass did we lose?" Ghosn asked.

"Eighteen-point-five-two-seven grams." Fromm switched the spindle off and stood. "I can scarcely praise our workers enough. I suggest that we wait until tomorrow to begin final polishing. It is foolish to rush about. We're all tired, and I think dinner is called for."

"As you say, Herr Fromm."

"Manfred," the German said, surprising the younger man. "Ibrahim, we must talk."

"Outside?" Ghosn led the German out the door. Night was falling.

"We mustn't kill these men. They are too valuable. What if this opportunity presents itself again?"

"But you agreed . . ."

"I never expected things would go this well. The schedule I worked up assumed that you and I—no, I shall be honest, that *I* would have to supervise everything. You, Ibrahim, have astounded me with your skill. What we have done here is to have assembled a superb team. We must keep this team together!"

And where else will we get ten kilos of plutonium? Ghosn wanted to ask.

"Manfred, I think you are correct. I will discuss this with the Commander. You must remember—"

"Security. *Ich weiss es schon.* We can take no chances at this stage. I merely entreat you, as a matter of justice—of professional recognition, *ja?*—that consideration must be given. Do you understand?"

"Quite well, Manfred, I agree with you." The German was acquiring humanity, Ghosn thought. A pity it came so late. "In any case, I also agree with your desire for a decent dinner before we begin the final phase. Tonight there is fresh lamb, and we've obtained some German beer. Bitburger, I hope you like it."

"A good regional lager. A pity, Ibrahim, that your religion denies it to you."

"On this night," Ghosn said, "I hope Allah will forgive me for indulging." Just as well, Ibrahim thought, to earn the infidel's confidence.

"Jack, it would appear that you are working too hard."

"It's the commute, sir. Two or three hours a day in a car."

"Find a place closer?" His Royal Highness suggested gently.

"Give up Peregrine Cliff?" Ryan shook his head. "Then what about Cathy and Johns Hopkins? Then there's the kids, taking them out of school. No, that's no solution."

"You doubtless recall that the first time we met, you commented rather forcefully on my physical and psychological condition. I rather doubt that I looked as dreadful as you do now." The Prince had received more than one bit of information from Sir Basil Charleston, Jack noted, as a result of which there was no alcohol being served with dinner.

"It blows hot and cold at work. At the moment, it's blowing rather hot."

"Truman, then? 'If you can't stand the heat, get out of the kitchen'?"

"Yes, sir, something like that, but it'll cool off. Just that we have some things happening now. It's like that. When you were driving your ship, it was like that, too, wasn't it?"

"That was much healthier work. I also had a far shorter distance to commute. About fifteen feet, as a matter of fact," he added with a chuckle.

Ryan laughed rather tiredly. "Must be nice. For me it's that far to see my secretary."

"And the family?"

There was no sense in lying. "Could be better. My work doesn't help."

"Something is troubling you, Jack. It's quite obvious, you know."

"Too much stress. I've been hitting the booze too hard, not enough exercise. The usual. It'll get better, just I've had a longer than usual stretch of bad times at the office. I appreciate your concern, sir, but I'll be all right." Jack almost convinced himself that it was true. Almost.

"As you say."

"And I must say that's the best dinner I've had in a very long time. So, when's the next time you're coming over to our side of the pond?" Ryan asked, grateful for the chance to change subjects.

"Late spring. A breeder in Wyoming will have some horses for me. Polo ponies, actually."

"You gotta be crazy to play that game. Lacrosse on horses."

"Well, it gives me a chance to enjoy the countryside. Magnificent place, Wyoming. I plan to tour Yellowstone also."

"Never been there," Jack said.

"Perhaps you could come with us, then? I might even teach you how to ride."

"Maybe," Jack allowed, wondering how he'd look on a horse, and wondering how the hell he'd be able to get away from the office for a week. "Just so you don't wave one of those hammers at me."

"Mallet, Jack, mallet. I shan't try to involve you in polo. You'd probably end up killing some unfortunate horse. I presume you'll be able to find the time."

"I can sure try. If I'm lucky, the world will settle down a little by then."

"It's settled down quite a bit, thanks in large part to your work."

"Sir, Basil may have placed a little too much emphasis on what I did. I was just one cog in the machine."

"Modesty can be overdone. I find it disappointing that you failed to receive any recognition," the Prince observed.

"That's life, isn't it?" Jack was surprised at how it came out. For once he'd been unable to hide his feelings completely.

"I thought as much. Yes, Jack, that's life, and life is not always fair. Have you thought perhaps about changing your line of work—take leave, perhaps?"

Jack grinned. "Come on, I don't look all that bad. They need me at the office."

His Royal Highness became very serious. "Jack, are we friends?"

Ryan sat upright in his chair. "I don't have all that many, but you're one of them."

"Do you trust my judgment?"

"Yes, sir, I do."

"Get out. Leave. You can always come back to it. A person of your talents never really leaves. You know that. I don't like the way you look. You've been at it too long. Have you any idea how lucky you are that you *can* leave? You have a degree of freedom I do not. Use it."

"Nice try, man. If you were in my position, you wouldn't leave. Same reason, even. I'm not a quitter. Neither are you. It's that simple."

"Pride can be a destructive force," the Prince pointed out.

Jack leaned forward. "It's not pride. It's fact. They do need me. I wish they didn't, but they do. Problem is, they don't know it."

"Is the new Director that bad?"

"Marcus is not a bad person, but he's lazy. He likes his position better than he likes his duties. I don't suppose that's a problem limited to the American government, is it? I know better. So do you. Duty comes first. Maybe you're stuck with your job because you were born into it, but I'm just as stuck with mine because I'm the guy best able to do it."

"Do they listen to you?" His Highness asked sharply.

Jack shrugged. "Not always. Hell, sometimes I'm wrong, but there has to be somebody there who does the right thing, at least tries to. That's me, sir. That's why I can't bug out. You know that just as well as I do."

"Even if it harms you?"

"Correct."

"Your sense of duty is admirable, Sir John."

"I had a couple of good teachers. You didn't run and hide when you knew you were a target. You could have done that—"

"No, I could not have done so. If I had—"

"The bad guys would have won," Jack finished the thought. "My problem isn't very different, is it? I learned part of this from you. Surprised?" Jack asked.

"Yes," he admitted.

"You don't run away from things. Neither do I."

"Your verbal maneuvering is as skillful as ever."

"See? I haven't lost it yet." Jack was rather pleased with himself.

"I will insist that you bring the family out to Wyoming with us."

"You can always go over my head—talk to Cathy."

His Highness laughed. "Perhaps I will. Flying back tomorrow?"

"Yes, sir. I'm going to hit Hamleys for some toys."

"Get yourself some sleep, Jack. We'll have this argument again next year."

It was five hours earlier in Washington. Liz Elliot stared across her desk at Bob Holtzman, who covered the White House. Like the permanent staffers here, Holtzman had seen them come and go, outlasting them all. His greater experience in the building was something of a paradox. Though necessarily cut out of the really good stuff—Holtzman knew that there were some secrets he'd never see until years too late to make a story of them; that was the work of historians—his skill at reading nuances and catching whiffs would have earned him a senior place at any intelligence agency. But his paper paid much better than any government agency, especially since he'd also penned a few best-selling books on life at the highest levels of government.

"This is deep background?"

"That's right," the National Security Advisor said.

Holtzman nodded and made his notes. That set the rules. No direct quotes. Elizabeth Elliot could be referred to as an "administration official," or in the plural as "sources within." He looked up from his notebook—tape recorders were also out for this sort of interview—and waited. Liz Elliot liked her drama. She was a bright woman, somewhat elitist—not an uncommon trait in White House officialdom—and definitely the person closest to the President, if he was reading the signals right. But that was none of the public's business. The probable love affair between the President and his National Security Advisor was no longer a complete secret. The White House staffers were as discreet as ever—more, in fact. He found it odd that they should be so. Fowler was not the most lovable of men. Perhaps they felt sympathy for what had to be a lonely man. The circumstances of his wife's death were well known, and had probably added a percentage point of sympathy votes in the last election. Maybe the staffers thought he'd change with a steady romance in his life. Maybe they were just being good professionals. (That distinguished them from political appointees, Holtzman thought. Nothing was sacred to them.) Maybe Fowler and Elliot were just being very careful. In any case, the White House press had discussed it off and on at The Confidential Source, the bar at the National Press Club building, just two blocks away, and it had been decided that Fowler's love life was not properly a matter of public interest so long as it did not injure his job performance. After all, his foreign-policy performance was pretty good. Euphoria from the Vatican Treaty and its stunningly favorable aftermath had never gone away. You couldn't slam a president who was doing so fine a job.

"We may have a problem with the Russians," Elliot began.

"Oh?" Holtzman was caught by surprise for once.

"We have reason to believe that Narmonov is having considerable difficulty dealing with his senior military commanders. That could have effects on final compliance with the arms treaty."

"How so?"

"We have reason to believe that the Soviets will resist elimination of some of their SS-18 stocks. They're already behind in destruction of the missiles."

Reason to believe. Twice. Holtzman thought about that for a moment. A very sensitive source, probably a spy rather than an intercept. "They say that there's a problem with the destruct facility. The inspectors we have over there seem to believe them."

"Possibly the factory was designed with—what do you call it? Creative incompetence."

"What's the Agency say?" Holtzman asked, scribbling his notes just as fast as he could.

"They gave us the initial report, but so far they've been unable to get us a real opinion."

"What about Ryan? He's pretty good on the Soviets."

"Ryan's turning into a disappointment," Liz said. "As a matter of fact—and this is something you can't say, you can't use his name—we have a little investigation going that's turned up some disturbing data."

"Like?"

"Like I think we're getting skewed data. Like I think a senior Agency official is having an affair with a person of foreign birth, and there may be a child involved."

"Ryan?"

The National Security Advisor shook her head. "Can't confirm or deny. Remember the rules."

"I won't forget," Holtzman replied, hiding his annoyance. Did she think she was dealing with Jimmy Olsen?

"The problem is, it looks like he knows we don't like what he's telling us, and as a result he's trying to put a spin on the data to please us. This is a time when we really need good stuff from Langley, but we're not getting it."

Holtzman nodded thoughtfully. That was not exactly a new problem at Langley, but Ryan wasn't that sort, was he? The reporter set that aside. "And Narmonov?"

"If what we're getting is in any way correct, he may be on the way out, whether from the right or the left, we can't say. It may be that he's losing it."

"That's solid?"

"It appears so. The part about blackmail from his security forces is very disturbing. But with our problems at Langley . . ." Liz held up her hands.

"Just when things were going so well, too. I guess you're having problems with Cabot?"

"He's learning his job pretty well. If he had better support, he'd be okay."

"How worried are you?" Holtzman asked.

"Very much so. This is a time when we need good intel, but we're not getting it. How the hell can we figure out what to do about Narmonov unless we get good information. So what do we get?" Liz asked in exasperation. "Our hero is running around doing stuff that really doesn't concern his agency—he's gone over people's heads to the Hill on some things—doing a Chicken Little act on one thing while at the same time he's not getting Cabot good analysis on what appears to be a major issue. Of course, he has his distractions. . . ."

Our hero, Holtzman thought, *What an interesting choice of words. She really hates the guy, doesn't she.* Holtzman knew the fact, but not the reason. There was no reason for her to be jealous of him. Ryan had never shown great ambition, at least not in a political sense. He was a pretty good man, by all accounts. The reporter remembered his one public *faux pas,* a confrontation with Al Trent which, Holtzman was certain, must have been staged. Ryan and Trent got along very well now by all accounts. What could possibly have been important enough to stage something like that? Ryan had two intelligence stars—what for, Holtzman had never been able to find out. Just rumors, five different versions of four different stories, probably all of them false. Ryan wasn't all that popular with the press. The reason was that he had never really leaked anything. He took secrecy a little too seriously. On the other hand, he didn't try to curry favor either, and Holtzman respected anyone who avoided that. Of one thing he was sure: he had gravely underestimated the antipathy for Ryan in the Fowler Administration.

I'm being manipulated. That was as obvious as a peacock in a barnyard. Very cleverly, of course. The bit about the Russians was probably genuine. The Central Intelligence Agency's inability to get vital information to the White House wasn't exactly new either, was it? That was probably true also. So where was the lie? Or was there a lie at all? Maybe they just wanted to get truthful but sensitive information out . . . in the normal way. It wasn't the first time he'd learned things in the northwest-corner office of the White House West Wing.

Could Holtzman *not* do a story on this?

Not hardly, Bobby boy, the reporter told himself.

The ride home was smooth as silk. Ryan caught as much sleep as he could, while the sergeant who took care of the cabin read through assembly instructions for some of the toys Jack had picked up.

"Yo, Sarge." The pilot was back in the cabin for a stretch. "Whatcha doin'?"

"Well, Maj, our DV here picked up some stuff for the kiddies." The NCO handed over a page of directions. Tab-1 into Slot-A, use ⅞ths bolt, tighten with a wrench, using . . .

"I think I'd rather tinker with broke engines."

"Roger that," the sergeant agreed. "This guy's got some bad times ahead."

24. Revelation

"I don't like being used," Holtzman said, leaning back with his hands clasped at the base of his neck.

He sat in the conference room with his managing editor, another long-term Washington-watcher who'd won his spurs in the feeding frenzy that had ended the presidency of Richard Nixon. Those had been heady times. It had given the entire American media a taste for blood that had never gone away. The only good part about it, Holtzman thought, was that they didn't cozy up to anyone now. Any politician was a potential target for the righteous wrath of America's investigatorial priesthood. The fact of it was healthy, though the extent of it occasionally was not.

"That's beside the point. Who does? So what do we know is true?" the editor asked.

"We have to believe her that the White House isn't getting good data. That's nothing new at CIA, though it's not as bad as it used to be. The fact of the matter is that Agency performance has improved somewhat—well, there is the problem that Cabot has lopped off a lot of heads. We also have to believe what she says about Narmonov and his military."

"And Ryan?"

"I've met him at social functions, never officially. He's actually a fairly nice guy, good sense of humor. He must have a hell of a record. Two Intelligence

Stars—what for, we do not know. He fought Cabot on downsizing the Operations Directorate, evidently saved a few jobs. He's moved up very fast. Al Trent likes him despite that run-in they had a few years ago. There's gotta be a story in that, but Trent flatly refused to discuss it the only time I asked him. Supposedly they kissed and made up, and I believe that like I believe in the Easter Bunny.''

''Is he the sort to play around?'' the editor asked next.

''What sort is that? You expect they're issued a scarlet 'A' for their shirts?''

''Very clever, Bob. So what the hell are you asking me?''

''Do we run a story on this or not?''

The editor's eyes widened in surprise. ''Are you kidding? How can we *not* run a story on this?''

''I just don't like being used.''

''We've been through that! I don't either. Granted that it's obvious in this case, but it's still an important story, and if we don't run it, then the *Times* will. How soon will you have it ready?''

''Soon,'' Holtzman promised. Now he knew why he'd declined a promotion to assistant managing editor. He didn't need the money; his book income absolved him of the necessity of working at all. He liked being a journalist, still had his idealism, still cared about what he did. It was a further blessing, he thought, that he was absolved of the necessity of making executive decisions.

The new feed-water pump was everything the Master Shipwright had promised on the installation side, Captain Dubinin noted. They'd practically had to dismantle a whole compartment to get it in, plus torch a hole through the submarine's double hull. He could still look up and see sky through what should have been a curved steel overhead, something very unnerving indeed for a submarine officer. They had to make sure that the pump worked satisfactorily before they welded shut the ''soft patch'' through which it had arrived. It could have been worse. This submarine had a steel hull. Those Soviet submarines made of titanium were the devil to weld shut.

The pump/steam–generator room was immediately aft of the reactor compartment. In fact the reactor vessel abutted the bulkhead on the forward side, and the pump assembly on the after side. The pump circulated water in and out of the reactor. The saturated steam went into the steam-generator, where it ran through an interface. There its heat caused water in the ''outside'' or nonradioactive loop to flash to steam, which then turned the submarine's turbine engines (in turn driving the propeller through reduction gears). The ''inner loop'' steam, with most of its energy lost, then ran through a condenser that was cooled by seawater from outside the hull, and was pumped as water back into the bottom of the reactor vessel for reheating to continue the cycle. The steam-generator and condenser were actually the same large structure, and the same multistage pump handled all of the circulation. This one mechanical object was the acoustical Achilles' heel of all nuclear-powered ships. The pump had to exchange vast quantities of water that was ''hot'' both thermally and radioactively. Doing that much mechanical work had always meant making a large amount of noise. Until now.

''It's an ingenious design,'' Dubinin said.

''It should be. The Americans spent ten years perfecting it for their missile submarines, then decided not to use it. The design team was crushed.''

The Captain grunted. The new American reactor designs were able to use natural convection-circulation. One more technical advantage. They were so damnably

"What's the problem?" The Second Officer moved two steps to the panel and flipped on the deck floods.

"Well, we still have one of them."

"One of—" The junior officer looked down. "Oh. The other three . . ."

The First Officer shook his head. How could you describe the power of mere water? "That's strong chain, too, the wave snapped it like yarn. Impressive."

The Second Officer picked up the phone and punched a button. "Bosun, our deck cargo just got swept over the side. I need a damage check on the front of the superstructure." He didn't have to say that the check should be done from inside the structure.

An hour later it was clear that they'd been lucky. The single strike from the deck cargo had landed right on a portion of the superstructure backed by sturdy steel beams. Damage was minor, some welding and painting to be done. That didn't change the fact that someone would have to cut down a new tree. Three of the four logs were gone, and that Japanese temple would have to wait.

The three logs, still chained together, were already well aft of the *George M.* They were still green, and started soaking up seawater, making them heavier still.

Cathy Ryan watched her husband's car pull out of the driveway. She was now past the stage of feeling bad for him. Now she was hurt. He wouldn't talk about it—that is, he didn't try to explain himself, didn't apologize, tried to pretend that . . . what? And then part of the time he said he didn't feel well, was too tired. Cathy wanted to talk it over, but didn't know how to begin. The male ego was a fragile thing, Dr. Caroline Ryan knew, and this had to be its most fragile spot. It had to be a combination of stress and fatigue and booze. Jack wasn't a machine. He was wearing down. She'd seen the symptoms months earlier. As much the commute as anything else. Two and a half, sometimes three hours every day in the car. The fact that he had a driver was something, but not much. Three more hours a day that he was away, thinking, working, not home where he belonged.

Am I helping or hurting? she asked herself. *Is part of it my fault?*

Cathy walked into the bathroom and looked at herself in the mirror. Okay, she wasn't a pink-cheeked kid anymore. There were worry lines around her mouth and squint lines around her eyes. She should have her spectacle prescription looked at. She was starting to get headaches during procedures, and she knew it could be a problem with her eyes—she was, after all, an ophthalmic surgeon—but like everyone else she was short of time and was putting off having her eyes looked at by another member of The Wilmer Eye Institute staff. Which was pretty dumb, she admitted to herself. She still had rather pretty eyes. At least the color didn't change, even though their refractive error might suffer from all the close work that her job mandated.

She was still quite slim. Wouldn't hurt to sweat off three or four pounds—better yet, to transfer that weight into her breasts. She was a small-breasted woman from a small-breasted family in a world that rewarded women for having udders to rival Elsie the Borden cow. Her usual joke that bust size was inversely proportional to brain size was a defense mechanism. She craved larger ones as a man always wanted a larger penis, but God or the gene pool had not chosen to give her those, and she would *not* submit to the vain ignominy of surgery—besides which she didn't like the numbers on that kind of surgery. Too many silicone-implant cases developed complications.

The rest of her . . . her hair, of course, was always a mess, but surgical discipline absolutely prevented her from paying great attention to that. It was still blond and short and very fine, and when Jack took the time to notice, he liked her hair. Her face was still pretty, despite the squint lines and worry lines. Her legs had always been pretty nice, and with all the walking she did at Hopkins/Wilmer, they had actually firmed up slightly. Cathy concluded that her looks were not the sort to make dogs bark when she passed. She was, in fact, still rather attractive. At least the other docs at the hospital thought so. Some of her senior medical students positively swooned over her, she liked to think. Certainly no one fought to escape her rounds.

She was also a good mother. Though Sally and Little Jack were still asleep, she never failed to look after them. Especially with Jack gone so much, Cathy filled in, even to the point of playing catch with her son during T-ball season (that was something that made her husband uncomfortably guilty whenever he learned of it). She cooked good meals when she had the time. Whatever the house needed, she either did herself or "contracted out"—Jack's phrase—to others.

She still loved her husband, and she let him know it. She had a good sense of humor, Cathy thought. She didn't let most things bother her. She never failed to touch Jack whenever the opportunity presented itself; she was a doctor, with a delicate touch. She talked to him, asked what he thought of something or other, let him know that she cared about him, cared about his opinions on things. There could be no doubt in his mind that he was still her man in every way. In fact, she loved him in every way a wife could. Cathy concluded that she wasn't doing anything wrong.

So why didn't he—couldn't he . . . ?

The face in the mirror was more puzzled than hurt, she thought. *What else can I do?* she asked it.

Nothing.

Cathy tried to set that aside. A new day was beginning. She had to get the kids ready for school. That meant setting breakfast up before they awoke. This part of life wasn't fair, of course. She was a surgeon, a professor of surgery, as a matter of fact, but the simple facts of life also said she was a mother, with mother's duties that her husband did not share, at least not on the early morning of a workday. So much for women's lib. She got into her robe and walked down to the kitchen. It could have been worse. Both kids liked oatmeal, and actually preferred the flavored instant kind. She boiled the water for it, then turned the range to low heat while she walked back to wake the little ones up. Ten minutes later Sally and Little Jack were washed and dressed on their way to the kitchen. Sally arrived first, setting the TV to the Disney Channel in time for Mousercise. Cathy took her ten minutes of peace to look at the morning paper and drink her coffee.

On the bottom right-hand side of the front page was an article about Russia. *Well, maybe that's one of the things that's bothering Jack.* She decided to read it. Maybe she could talk to him, find out why he was so . . . distracted? Was it just that, maybe?

". . . disappointed with the ability of CIA to deliver data on the problem. There are further rumors of an underway investigation. An administration official confirms the rumors that a senior CIA official is suspected of financial misconduct and also of sexual improprieties. The name of this official has not been revealed, but he is reportedly very senior and responsible for coordinating information for the administration. . . ."

Sexual improprieties? What did that mean? Who was it?

He.

Very senior and responsible for . . .

That was Jack. That was her husband. That was the phrase they used for someone at his level. In a quiet moment of total clarity, she knew that it had to be.

Jack . . . playing around? My Jack?

It wasn't possible.

Was it?

His inability to perform, his tiredness, the drinking, the distractions? Was it possible that the reason he didn't . . . someone else was exciting him?

It wasn't possible. Not Jack. Not her Jack.

But why else . . . ? She was still attractive—everyone thought so. She was still a good wife—there was no doubt of that. Jack wasn't ill. She would have caught any gross symptoms; she was a doctor, and a good one, and she knew she would not have missed anything important. She went out of her way to be nice to Jack, to talk to him, to let him know that she loved him, and . . .

Perhaps it wasn't *likely,* but was it *possible?*

Yes.

No. Cathy set the paper down and sipped at her coffee. Not possible. Not her Jack.

It was the last hour of the last leg in the manufacturing process. Ghosn and Fromm watched the lathe with what looked like detachment, but was in both cases barely controlled excitement. The Freon liquid being sprayed on the rotating metal prevented their seeing the product whose final manufacture was under way. That didn't help, even though both knew that seeing would not have helped in the least. The part of the plutonium mass being machined was hidden from their sight by other metal, and even if *that* had been otherwise, they both knew that their eyes were too coarse an instrument to detect imperfections. Both watched the machine readout of the computer systems. Tolerances indicated by the machine were well within the twelve angstroms specified by Herr Doktor Fromm. They had to believe the computer, didn't they?

"Just a few more centimeters," Ghosn said as Bock and Qati joined them.

"You've never explained the Secondary part of the unit," the Commander said. He'd taken to calling the bomb "the unit."

Fromm turned, not really grateful for the distraction, though he knew he should be. "What do you wish to know?"

"I understand how the Primary works, but not the Secondary," Qati said simply and reasonably.

"Very well. The theoretical side of this is quite straightforward once you understand the principle. That was the difficult part, you see, discovering the principle. It was thought at first that making the Secondary work was simply a matter of temperature—that is what distinguishes the center of a star, *ja?* Actually it is not, the first theoreticians overlooked the matter of pressure. That is rather strange in retrospect, but pioneering work is often that way. The key to making the Secondary work is managing the energy in such a way as to convert energy into pressure at the same time you use its vast heat, and also to change its direction by ninety degrees. That is no small task when you are talking about redirecting seventy kilotons of energy," Fromm said smugly. "However, the belief that to make the Secondary function is a matter of great theoretical difficulty, that is a fiction. The real insight Ulam and Teller had was a simple one, as most great insights are.

Pressure *is* temperature. What they discovered—the secret—is that there is no secret. Once you understand the principles involved, what remains is just a question of engineering. Making the bomb work is computationally, not technically, demanding. The difficult part is to make the weapon portable. That is pure engineering,'' Fromm said again.

''Soda straws?'' Bock asked, knowing that his countryman wanted to be asked about that. He was a smug bastard.

''I cannot know for sure, but I believe this to be my personal innovation. The material is perfect. It is light, it is hollow, and it is easily twisted into the proper configuration.'' Fromm walked over to the assembly table and returned with one. ''The base material is polyethylene, and as you see, we have coated the outside with copper and the inside with rhodium. The length of the 'straw' is sixty centimeters, and the inside diameter is just under three millimeters. Many thousands of them surround the Secondary, in bundles twisted one hundred eighty degrees into a geometric shape called a helix. A helix is a useful shape. It can direct energy while retaining its ability to radiate heat in all directions.''

Inside every engineer, Qati thought, was a frustrated teacher. ''But what do they do?''

''*Also* . . . the first emission off the Primary is massive gamma radiation. Just behind that are the X-rays. In both cases we are talking about high-energy photons, quantum particles which carry energy but which have no mass—''

''Light waves,'' Bock said, remembering his *Gymnasium* physics. Fromm nodded.

''Correct. Extremely energetic light waves of a different—higher—frequency. Now, we have this vast amount of energy radiating from the Primary. Some we can reflect or warp toward the Secondary by use of the channels we have built. Most is lost, of course, but the fact is that we will have so much energy at our fingertips that we need only a small fraction of it. The X-rays sweep down the straws. Much of their energy is absorbed by the metallic coatings, while the oblique surfaces reflect some further down, allowing further energy absorption. The polyethylene also absorbs a good deal of energy. And what do you suppose happens?''

''Absorb that much energy, and it must explode, of course,'' Bock said before Qati could.

''Very good, Herr Bock. When the straws explode—actually they convert into plasma, but having split straws, we will not split hairs, eh?—the plasma expands radially to their axes, thus converting the axial energy from the Primary into radial energy imploding on the Secondary.''

The light bulb went on in Qati's head. ''Brilliant—but you lose half of the energy, that part expanding outward.''

''Yes and no. It still makes an energy barrier, and that is what we need. Next, the uranium fins around the body of the Secondary are also converted to plasma—from the same energy flux, but more slowly than the straws due to their mass. This plasma has far greater density, and is pressed inward. Within the actual Secondary casing, there is two centimeters of vacuum, since that space will be evacuated. So we have a 'running start' for the plasma that is racing inward.''

''So you use the energy from the Primary, redirected into a right-angle turn to perform the same function on the Secondary that is first done by chemical explosives?'' Qati saw.

''Excellent, Commander!'' Fromm replied, just patronizingly enough to be noticed. ''We now have a relatively heavy mass of plasma pressing inward. The vacuum gap gives it room to accelerate before slamming into the Secondary. This compresses the Secondary. The secondary assembly is lithium-deuteride and lithium-hydride, both doped with tritium, surrounded by uranium 238. This assembly is crushed violently by the imploding plasma. It is also being bombarded by neutrons from the Primary, of course. The combination of heat, pressure, and neutron bombardment causes the lithium to fission into tritium. The tritium immediately begins the fusion process, generating vast quantities of high-energy neutrons along with the liberated energy. The neutrons attack the U-238, causing a fast-fission reaction, adding to the overall Secondary yield.''

''The key, as Herr Fromm said,'' Ghosn explained, ''is managing the energy.''

''Straws,'' Bock noted.

''Yes, I said the same thing,'' Ghosn said. ''It is truly brilliant. Like building a bridge from paper.''

''And the yield from the Secondary?'' Qati asked. He didn't really understand the physics, but he did understand the final number.

''The Primary will generate approximately seventy kilotons. The Secondary will generate roughly four hundred sixty-five kilotons. The numbers are approximate because of possible irregularities within the weapon, and also because we cannot test to measure actual effects.''

''How confident are you in the performance of the weapon?''

''Totally,'' Fromm said.

''But without testing, you said . . .''

''Commander, I knew from the beginning that a proper test program was not possible. That is the same problem we had in the DDR. For that reason the design is overengineered, in some cases by a factor of forty percent, in others by a factor of more than one hundred. You must understand that an American, British, French, or even Soviet weapon of the same yield would not be a fifth the size of our 'unit.' Such refinements of size and efficiency can come only from extensive testing. The physics of the device are entirely straightforward. Engineering refinements come only from practice. As Herr Ghosn said, building a bridge. The Roman bridges of antiquity were very inefficient structures. By modern standards they use far too much stone, and as a result far too much labor to build them, *ja?* Over the years we have learned to build bridges more efficiently, using fewer materials and less labor to perform the same task. But do not forget that some Roman bridges still stand. They are still bridges, even if they are inefficient. This bomb design, though inefficient and wasteful of materials, is still a bomb, and it *will* work as I say.''

Heads turned as the beeper on the lathe went off. An indicator light blinked green. The task was finished. Fromm walked over, telling the technicians to flush the Freon out of the system. Five minutes later the object of so much loving care was visible. The manipulator arm brought it into view. It was finished.

''Excellent,'' Fromm said. ''We will carefully examine the plutonium, and then we will commence assembly. *Meine Herren,* the difficult part is behind us.'' He thought that called for a beer, and made another mental note that he hadn't gotten the palladium yet. Details, details. But that's what engineering was.

''What gives, Dan?'' Ryan asked over his secure phone. He had missed the morning paper at home only to find the offending article waiting on his desk as part of *The Bird.*

"It sure as hell didn't come from here, Jack. It must be in your house."

"Well, I just tore our security director a brand-new asshole. He says he doesn't have anything going. What the hell does a 'very senior' official mean?"

"It means that this Holtzman guy got carried away with his adjectives. Look, Jack, I've already gone too far. I'm not supposed to discuss ongoing investigations, remember?"

"I'm not concerned about that. Somebody just leaked material that comes from a closely held source. If the world made any sense, we'd bring Holtzman in for questioning!" Ryan snarled into the phone.

"You want to rein in a little, boy?"

The DDCI looked up from the phone and commanded himself to take a deep breath. It wasn't Holtzman's fault, was it? "Okay, I just simmered down."

"Whatever investigation is under way, it isn't the Bureau running it."

"No shit?"

"You have my word on it," Murray said.

"That's fair enough, Dan." Ryan calmed down further. If it wasn't the FBI and it wasn't his own in-house security arm, then that part of the story was probably fiction.

"Who could have leaked it?"

Jack barked out a laugh. "Could have? Ten or fifteen people on the Hill. Maybe five in the White House, twenty—maybe forty here."

"So the other part could just be camouflage, or somebody who wants a score settled." Murray did not make it a question. He figured at least a third of all press leaks were aimed at settling grudges in one way or another. "The source is sensitive?"

"This phone isn't all that secure, remember?"

"Gotcha. Look, I can approach Holtzman quietly and informally. He's a good guy, responsible, a pro. We can talk to him off the record and let him know that he may be endangering people and methods."

"I have to go to Marcus for that."

"And I have to talk to Bill, but Bill will play ball."

"Okay, I'll talk to my Director. I'll be back." Ryan hung up and walked again to the Director's office.

"I've seen it," Director Cabot said.

"The Bureau doesn't know about this investigation, and neither do our people. From that we can surmise that the scandal part of the story is pure bull, but somebody's been leaking the take from SPINNAKER, and that sort of thing gets agents killed."

"What do you suggest?" the DCI asked.

"Dan Murray and I approach Holtzman informally and let him know that he's stepping on sensitive toes. We ask him to back off."

"Ask?"

"Ask. You don't give orders to reporters. Not unless you sign their paychecks, anyway," Jack corrected himself. "I've never actually done this, but Dan has. It was his idea."

"I have to go upstairs on this," Cabot said.

"Goddamn it, Marcus, we *are* upstairs!"

"Dealing with the press—it has to be decided elsewhere."

"Super—get in your car and drive down and make sure you ask very nicely." Ryan turned and stormed out before Cabot had a chance to flush at the insult.

By the time he'd walked the few yards to his private office, Jack's hands were quivering. *Can't he back me up on* anything? Nothing was going right lately. Jack pounded once on his desk, and the pain brought things back under control. Clark's little operation, that seemed to be heading in the right direction. That was one thing, and one thing was better than nothing.

Not much better. Jack looked at the photo of his wife and kids.

"Goddamn it," he swore to himself. He couldn't get that guy to back him up on anything, he'd become a lousy father to his kids, and sure as hell he was no great shakes as a husband lately.

Liz Elliot read the front-page article with no small degree of satisfaction. Holtzman had delivered exactly what she had expected. Reporters were so easy to manipulate. It opened a whole new world for her, she had belatedly realized. With Marcus Cabot being so weak, and no one within the CIA bureaucracy to back him up, she would have effective control of that, as well. Wasn't that something?

Removing Ryan from his post was now more than a mere exercise in spite, as desirable as so simple a motive might have been. Ryan was the one who had said no to a few White House requests, who occasionally went directly to Congress on internal matters . . . who prevented her from having closer contact with the Agency. With him out of the way, she could give orders—couched as "suggestions"—to Cabot, who would then carry them out with a total absence of resistance. Dennis Bunker would still have Defense and his dumb football team. Brent Talbot would have the State Department. Elizabeth Elliot would have control of the National Security apparatus—because she also had the ear, and all the other important parts, of the President. Her phone beeped.

"Director Cabot is here."

"Send him in," Liz said. She stood and walked toward the door. "Good morning, Marcus."

"Hello, Dr. Elliot."

"What brings you down?" she asked, waving him to a seat on the couch.

"This newspaper article."

"I saw it," the National Security Advisor said sympathetically.

"Whoever leaked this might have endangered a valuable source."

"I know. Somebody at your end? I mean, what is this about an in-house investigation?"

"It isn't us."

"Really?" Dr. Elliot leaned back and played with her blue silk cravat. "Who, then?"

"We don't know, Liz." Cabot looked even more uncomfortable than she had expected. Maybe, she thought playfully, he thought he was the target of the investigation . . . ? There was an interesting idea. "We want to talk to Holtzman."

"What do you mean?"

"I mean we and the FBI talk to him, informally of course, to let him know that he may be doing something irresponsible."

"Who came up with that, Marcus?"

"Ryan and Murray."

"Really?" She paused, as though considering the matter. "I don't think that's a good idea. You know how reporters are. If you have to stroke them, you have to stroke them properly . . . hmm. I can handle that if you wish."

"This really is serious. SPINNAKER is very important to us." Cabot tended to repeat himself when he got excited.

"I know it. Ryan was pretty clear in his briefing, back when you were ill. You still haven't confirmed his reports?"

Cabot shook his head. "No. Jack went off to England to ask the Brits to nose around, but we don't expect anything for a while."

"What do you want me to tell Holtzman?"

"Tell him that he may be jeopardizing a highly important source. The man could die over this, and the political fallout might be very serious," Cabot concluded.

"Yes, it could have undesired effects on their political scene, couldn't it?"

"If SPINNAKER is right, then they're in for a huge political shakeup. Revealing that we know what we know could jeopardize him. Remember that—"

Elliot interrupted. "That Kadishev is our main fallback position. Yes. And if he gets 'burned,' then we might have no fallback position. You've made yourself very clear, Marcus. Thank you. I'll work on this myself."

"That should be quite satisfactory," Cabot said after a moment's pause.

"Fine. Anything else I need to know this morning?"

"No, that's why I came down."

"I think it's time to show you something. Something we've been working on here. Pretty sensitive," she added. Marcus got the message.

"What is it?" the DCI asked guardedly.

"This is absolutely confidential." Elliot pulled a large manila envelope from her desk. "I mean absolutely, Marcus. It doesn't leave the building, okay?"

"Agreed." The DCI was already interested.

Liz opened the envelope and handed over some photographs. Cabot looked them over.

"Who's the woman?"

"Carol Zimmer. She's the widow of an Air Force crewman who got himself killed somehow or other." Elliot filled in some additional details.

"Ryan, screwing around? I'll be damned."

"Any chance we could get more information from inside the Agency?"

"If you mean accomplishing that without any suspicion on his part, it would be very difficult." Cabot shook his head. "His two SPOs, Clark and Chavez, no way. They're very tight. Good friends, I mean."

"Ryan's friendly with bodyguards? You serious?" Elliot was surprised. It was like being solicitous toward furniture.

"Clark's an old field officer. Chavez is a new kid, working as a SPO while he finishes his college degree, looking to be a field officer. I've seen the files. Clark'll retire in a few more years, and keeping him around as a SPO is just a matter of being decent. He's done some really interesting things. Good man, good officer."

Elliot didn't like that, but from what Cabot said, it seemed that it couldn't be helped. "We want Ryan eased out."

"That might not be easy. They really like him on the Hill."

"You just said he's insubordinate."

"It won't wash on the Hill. You know that. You want him fired, the President just has to ask for his resignation."

But that wouldn't wash on the Hill either, Liz thought, and it seemed immediately clear that Marcus Cabot wouldn't be much help. She hadn't really expected that he would be. Cabot was too soft.

"We can handle it entirely from this end if you want."

"Probably a good idea. If it became known at Langley that I had a hand in this, it might look like spite. Can't have that," Cabot demurred. "Bad for morale."

"Okay." Liz stood, and so did Cabot. "Thanks for coming down."

Two minutes later she was back in her chair, her feet propped up on a drawer. This was going *so* well. Exactly as planned. *I'm getting good at this. . . .*

"So?"

"This was published in a Washington paper today," Golovko said. It was seven in the evening in Moscow, the sky outside dark and cold as only Moscow could get cold. That he had to report on something in an American newspaper did not warm the night very much.

Andrey Il'ych Narmonov took the translation from the First Deputy Chairman and read through it. Finished, he tossed the two pages contemptuously onto his desk top. "What rubbish is this?"

"Holtzman is a very important Washington reporter. He has access to very senior officials in the Fowler Administration."

"And he probably writes a good deal of fiction, just as our reporters do."

"We think not. We think the tone of the report indicates that he was given the data by someone in the White House."

"Indeed?" Narmonov pulled out a handkerchief and blew his nose, cursing the cold that the sudden weather change had brought with it. If there was anything for which he did not have time, it was an illness, even a minor one. "I don't believe it. I've told Fowler personally about the difficulty with the missile destruction, and the rest of this political twaddle is just that. You know that I've had to deal with uniformed hotheads—those fools who went off on their own in the Baltic region. So do the Americans. It's incredible to me that they should take such nonsense seriously. Surely their intelligence services tell them the truth—and the truth is what I've told Fowler myself!"

"Comrade President." Golovko paused for a beat. *Comrade* was too hard a habit to break. "Just as we have political elements who distrust the Americans, so they have elements who continue to hate and distrust us. Changes between us have come and gone very rapidly. Too rapidly for many to assimilate. I find it plausible that there might be American political officials who believe this report."

"Fowler is vain, he is far weaker as a man than he would like people to know, he is personally insecure—but he is not a fool, and only a fool would believe this, particularly after meeting me and talking with me." Narmonov handed the translation back to Golovko.

"My analysts believe otherwise. We think it possible that the Americans really believe this."

"Thank them for their opinion. I disagree."

"If the Americans are getting a report saying this, it means that they have a spy within our government."

"I have no doubt that they have such people—after all, we do also, do we not?—but I do not believe it in this case. The reason is simple, no spy could have reported something which I did not say, correct? I have not said this to anyone. It is not true. What do you do to a spy who lies to us?"

"My President, it is not something we look upon kindly," Golovko assured him.

"That is doubtless true of the Americans also." Narmonov paused for a moment, then smiled. "Do you know what this could be?"

"We are always open to ideas."

"Think like a politician. This could easily be a sign of some sort of power play within their government. Our involvement would then be merely incidental."

Golovko thought about that. "We have heard that there is—that Ryan, their Deputy Director, is unloved by Fowler. . . ."

"Ryan, ah, yes, I remember him. A worthy adversary, Sergey Nikolay'ch?"

"He is that."

"And an honorable one. He gave his word to me that one time, and he kept his word."

Definitely something a politician would remember, Golovko thought.

"Why are they unhappy with him?" Narmonov asked.

"Reportedly a clash of personalities."

"That I can believe. Fowler and his vanity." Narmonov held up his hands. "There you have it. Perhaps I might have made a good intelligence analyst?"

"The finest," Golovko agreed. He had to agree, of course. Moreover, his President had said something that his own people had not examined fully. He left the august presence of his chief of state with a troubled expression. The defection of KGB Chairman Gerasimov a few years ago—an event that Ryan had himself engineered, if Golovko read the signs correctly—had inevitably crippled KGB's overseas operations. Six complete networks in America had collapsed, along with eight more in Western Europe. Replacement networks were only now beginning to take their place. That left major holes in KGB's ability to penetrate American government operations. The only good news was that they were starting to read a noteworthy fraction of American diplomatic and military communications—as much as four or five percent in a good month. But code-breaking was no substitute for penetration agents. There was something very strange going on here. Golovko didn't know what it was. Perhaps his President was right. Perhaps this was merely the ripples from an internal power-play. But it could also have been something else. The fact that Golovko didn't know what it was did not help matters.

"Just made it back in time," Clark said. "Did they sweep the wheels today?"

"If it's Wednesday. . . ." Jack replied. Every week his official car was examined for possible electronic bugs.

"Can we talk about it, then?"

"Yes."

"Chavez was right. It's easy, just a matter of dropping a nice little *mordida* on the right guy. The regular maintenance man will be taken sick that day, the two of us get tapped to service the 747. I get to play maid, scrub the sinks and the crappers, replenish the bar, the whole thing. You'll have the official evaluation on your desk tomorrow, but the short version is, yeah, we can do it, and the likelihood of discovery is minimal."

"You know the downside?"

"Oh, yeah. Major International Incident. I get early retirement. That's okay, Jack. I can retire whenever I want. It would be a shame for Ding, though. That kid is showing real promise."

"And if you're discovered?"

"I say in my best Spanish that some Japanese reporter asked me to do it, and paid me a lot of pesos to do it. That's the hook, Jack. They won't make a big deal about it if they think it's one of their own. Looks too bad, loss of face and all that."

"John, you're a tricky, underhanded son of a bitch."

"Just want to serve my country, sir." Clark started laughing. A few minutes later he took the turn. "Hope we're not too late."

"It was a long one at the office."

"I saw that thing in the paper. What are we doing about it?"

"The White House will be talking to Holtzman, telling him to lay off."

"Somebody dipping his pen in the company inkwell?"

"Not that we know about, same with the FBI."

"Camouflage for the real story, eh?"

"Looks that way."

"What bullshit," Clark observed as he pulled into the parking place.

It turned out that Carol was in her home, cleaning up after dinner. The Zimmer family Christmas tree was up. Clark began ferrying the presents in. Jack had picked some of them up in England; Clark and Nancy Cummings had helped to wrap them—Ryan was hopeless at wrapping presents. Unfortunately, they'd walked into the house just in time to hear crying.

"No problem, Dr. Ryan," one of the kids told him in the kitchen. "Jackie had a little accident. Mom's in the bathroom."

"Okay." Ryan walked that way, careful to announce his presence.

"Okay, okay, come in," Carol said.

Jack saw Carol leaning over the bathtub. Jacqueline was crying in the piteous monotone of a child who knows that she has misbehaved. There was a pile of kids' clothes on the tile floor, and the air positively reeked of crushed flowers. "What happened?"

"Jackie think my perfume is same as her toy perfume, pour whole bottle." Carol looked up from scrubbing.

Ryan lifted the little girl's shirt. "You're not kidding."

"Whole bottle—expensive! Bad girl!"

Jacqueline's crying increased in pitch. She'd probably had her backside smacked already. Ryan was just as happy not to have seen that. He disciplined his own kids as necessary, but didn't like to see other people smack theirs. That was one of several weak spots in his character. Even after Carol lifted her youngest out of the tub, the smell had not gone away.

"Wow, it is pretty strong, isn't it?" Jack picked Jackie up, which didn't mute her crying very much.

"Eighty dollar!" Carol said, but her anger was now gone. She had ample experience with small children, and knew that they were expected to do mischief. Jack carried the little one out to the living room. Her attitude changed when she saw the stack of presents.

"You too nice," her mother noted.

"Hey, I just happened to be doing some shopping, okay?"

"You no come here Christmas, you have you own family."

"I know, Carol, but I can't let Christmas go by without stopping in." Clark came in with a final pile. These were his, Jack saw. Good man, Clark.

"We have nothing for you," Carol Zimmer said.

"Sure you do. Jackie gave me a good hug."

"What about me?" John asked.

Jack handed Jackie over. It was funny. Quite a few men were wary of John Clark on the basis of looks alone, but the Zimmer kids thought of him as a big teddy bear. A few minutes later they drove away.

"Nice of you to do that, John," Ryan said as they drove off.

"No big deal. Hey, man, you know how much fun it was to shop for little kids?

Who the hell wants to buy his kid a Bali bra—that's what Maggie wanted, put it on her list—a sexy bra, for Christ's sake. How the hell can a father walk into a department store and buy something like that for his own daughter?''

''They get a little big for Barbie Dolls.''

''More's the pity, doc, more's the pity.''

Jack turned and chuckled. ''That bra—''

''Yeah, Jack, if I ever find out, he's dog meat.''

Ryan had to laugh at that, but he knew he could afford to laugh. His little girl wasn't dating yet. That would be hard, watching her leave with someone else, beyond his protective reach. Harder still for a man like John Clark.

''Regular time tomorrow?''

''Yep.''

''See ya' then, doc.''

Ryan walked into his house at 8:55. His dinner was in its usual place. He poured his usual glass of wine, took a sip, then removed his coat and hung it in the closet before walking upstairs to change clothes. He caught Cathy going the other way and smiled at her. He didn't kiss her. He was just too tired. That was the problem. If he could only get time to relax. Clark was right, just a few days off to unwind. That's all he needed, Jack told himself as he changed.

Cathy opened the closet door to get some medical files she'd left in her own topcoat. She almost turned away when she noticed something, not sure what it was. Cathy Ryan leaned in, puzzled, then caught it. Where was it? Her nose searched left and right in a way that might have appeared comical except for the look on her face when she found it. Jack's camel-hair coat, the expensive one she'd gotten for him last year.

It wasn't her perfume.

26. Integration

The assembly had begun with the purchase of additional instruments. An entire day was spent attaching one heavy block of spent uranium to the inside of the far end of the case.

''This is tedious, I know,'' Fromm said almost apologetically. ''In America and elsewhere there are special jigs, specially designed tools, people assemble many individual weapons of the same design, all advantages that we do not have.''

''And here everything must be just as exact. Commander,'' Ghosn added.

''My young friend is correct. The physics are the same for all of us.''

''Then don't let us stop you,'' Qati said.

Fromm went immediately back to work. Part of him was already counting the money he'd receive, but most concerned itself with the job at hand. Only half of the machinists had actually worked on the bomb's physics package itself. The rest had been employed entirely with manufacturing other fittings, most of which could be called cradles. These would hold the bomb components in place, and were mainly made from stainless steel for strength and compactness. Each was set in place according to a precise sequence, as the bomb was more complex than most machines, and required assembly according to a rigid set of instructions. Here again the process was made simpler by the quality of the design and the precision of the machine tools. Even the machinists were amazed that the parts all fit, and they murmured among themselves that whatever Fromm might be—and on this subject their speculation had been wide-ranging and colorful—he was an inhumanly skilled designer. The hardest part was installing the various uranium blocks. Installation of the lighter and milder materials went much more smoothly.

"The procedure for the tritium transfer?" Ghosn asked.

"We'll leave that for last, of course," Fromm said, backing off from checking a measurement.

"Just heat the battery to release the gas, correct?"

"Yes," Fromm said with a nod, "but—no, no, not that way!"

"What did I do wrong?"

"This must twist in," Fromm told the machinist. He stepped forward to demonstrate. "Like that, do you see?"

"Yes, thank you."

"The elliptical reflectors hang on these—"

"Yes, thank you, I know."

"Very good."

Fromm waved to Ghosn. "Come over here. You see how this works now?" Fromm pointed to two series of elliptical surfaces which nested together one after the other—there was a total of nineteen—each made of a different material. "The energy off the Primary impacts the first set of these surfaces, destroying each in its turn, but in the process . . ."

"Yes, it is always more clear to see the physical model than to extract it from a sheet of figures." This portion of the weapon derived its utility from the fact that light waves have no mass but do carry momentum. They were not "light" waves at all, technically speaking, but since the energy was all in the form of photons, the same principle held. The energy would immolate each of the elliptical surfaces, but in the process each surface would transfer a small but reliable percentage of the energy in another direction, adding to the energy already headed that way from the Primary itself.

"Your energy budget is lavish, Herr Fromm," Ghosn observed not for the first time.

The German shrugged. "Yes, it must be. If you cannot test, you must overengineer. The first American bomb—the one used on Hiroshima—was an untested design. It was wasteful of materials and disgustingly inefficient, but it was overengineered. And it did work. With a proper test program . . ." With a proper test program he could measure the empirical effects, determine exactly what the necessary energy budget was, and how well he managed it, determine the exact performance of each component, improve those that needed improvement, and reduce the size of those which were too large or too massive for the task at hand, just as the Americans, and Russians, and British, and French had done over a period of decades, constantly refining their designs, making them more and more efficient, and because of that, smaller, lighter, simpler, more reliable, less expensive. This, Fromm thought, was the ultimate engineering discipline, and he was immeasurably grateful that he had finally gotten the chance to try his hand at it. This design was crude and heavy, no masterpiece of design. It would function—of that he was certain—but with time he could have done so much better. . . .

"Yes, I see. A man of your skill could reduce this entire unit to the size of a large bucket."

It was a vast compliment. "Thank you, Herr Ghosn. Probably not that small, but small enough for the nose of a rocket."

"If our Iraqi brothers had taken the time . . ."

"Indeed, there would be no Israel. But they were foolish, were they not?"

"They were impatient," Ibrahim said, silently cursing them for it.

"One must be cold and clearheaded about such things. Such decisions must be made on the basis of logic, not emotion."

"Indeed."

Achmed was feeling very poorly indeed. He'd made his excuses and taken his leave, heading off to see the Commander's own physician, as per orders from Qati. Achmed had little experience of doctors. It was, he thought, something to be avoided if possible. He'd seen combat action and seen death and wounds, but never to himself. Even that was preferable to his current situation. One could understand injury from a bullet or a grenade, but what had made him ill so quickly and unexpectedly?

The doctor listened to his description of his condition, asked a few questions that were not entirely foolish, and noted that Achmed was a smoker—that had earned the fighter a headshake and a cluck, as though cigarettes had anything to do with his situation. What rubbish, Achmed thought. Didn't he run six kilometers each day—or had, until very recently?

The physical examination came next. The doctor placed a stethoscope on his chest and listened. Instantly, Achmed noted, the doctor's eyes became guarded in a way not unlike the expression of a courageous fighter who didn't wish to betray his feelings.

"Breathe in," the physician ordered. Achmed did so. "Now, out slowly."

The stethoscope moved. "Again, please." The procedure was repeated six more times, front and back.

"Well?" Achmed asked when the examination was finished.

"I don't know. I want to take you to see someone who understands these lung problems better."

"I have no time for that."

"You have time for this. I will talk to your Commander if necessary."

Achmed managed not to grumble. "Very well."

It was a measure of Ryan's own situation that he took no note of it, or more correctly that he was grateful for the diminished attention his wife accorded him. It helped. It took some of the pressure off. Maybe she understood that he just needed to be left alone for a while. He'd make it up to her, Jack promised himself. He sure as hell would, when he got it all back together. He was sure of that, or told himself that he was, though a distant part of his mind was less sure and announced the fact to a consciousness that preferred not to listen. He tried to cut back on the drinking, but with the reduced demands he could, he decided, get a little more sleep, and the wine helped him sleep. In the spring, when things warmed up, he'd get back into a healthier routine. Yeah, that was it. He'd jog. He'd take the time at work, at lunch he'd get outside with the rest of the local sweat squad and run around the perimeter road inside the CIA enclosure. Clark would be a good trainer for this. Clark was a rock. Better him than Chavez, who was disgustingly fit and singularly unsympathetic to those who failed to keep in good shape—doubtless a carryover from his time in the infantry, Ryan thought. Ding would learn as he got closer to thirty. That number was the great equalizer, when you stopped being young and had to face the fact that everything had limits.

Christmas could have gone better, he thought, sitting at his desk. But it had been in the middle of the week, which meant that the kids were home two full weeks. It also meant that Cathy had to miss time at work, and that was a little hard on her. She liked her work, and as much as she loved the kids, and as fine a mother as she was, she resented the time away from Hopkins and her patients. Strictly speaking, it wasn't fair for her, Jack admitted to himself. She, too, was a professional and a fine one, despite which she was the one who always got tapped with kid duty while he never got relief from his work. But there were thousands of eye surgeons, and even a few hundred professors of eye surgery, but there was only one DDCI, and that was that. Not fair, perhaps, but a fact.

So much the better if he were able to accomplish something, Ryan told himself. Letting Elizabeth Elliot handle that damned newsie had been a mistake. Not that he'd expected much else from Marcus Cabot. The man was a drone. It really was that simple. He enjoyed the prestige that went with his post, but he didn't *do* anything. Ryan got most of the work, none of the credit, and all of the blame. Maybe that would change. He had the Mexican operation fully in hand, had taken that over entirely from the Directorate of Operations, and, by God, he'd get the credit for this. Maybe then things would get better. He pulled out the file for the operation and decided that he'd go over every detail, check every possible contingency. This one would work, and he'd make those White House bastards respect him.

''Go to your room!'' Cathy shouted at Little Jack. Both an order and an admission of failure. Then she walked out of the room, tears in her eyes. She was acting stupidly, shouting at the kids when she should be confronting her own husband. *But how?* What could she say? What if—what if it were true? Then what? She kept telling herself that it couldn't be, but that was too hard to believe. How else to explain it? Jack had never failed at anything in his life. She remembered with pride the fact that he'd risked his life for her and the children. She'd been terrified, the breath frozen in her throat, walking along the beach, watching her man advance toward men with guns, with his life and others in the balance. How could a man who had done that betray his own wife? It didn't make any sense.

But what other explanation was there? Didn't he find her exciting anymore? If so, why not? Wasn't she pretty enough? Didn't she do everything—and more—that a wife could? The simple rejection was bad enough—but to be set aside, to know that his energy and vigor was serving some other, unknown woman with cheap perfume was more than she could bear.

She had to confront him, had to get it into the open, had to find out.

How? she asked herself. That was the question. Could she discuss it with someone at Hopkins . . . a psychiatrist, perhaps? Get professional advice . . . ?

And risk having it get out, risk having her shame widely known? Caroline Ryan, Associate Professor, pretty, bright Cathy Ryan can't even hold on to her own husband? What do you suppose she did wrong? her friends would whisper when she was elsewhere. Sure, they'd all say that it couldn't be *her* fault, but then they'd pause and look embarrassed, and after a moment they'd wonder aloud what she might have done differently, why she hadn't noticed the signals, because, after all, a failed marriage was rarely the work of a single partner, and Jack wasn't really the sort to play around, was he? The embarrassment of it would be worse than anything in her life, she thought, forgetting for the moment times that had been far worse.

It didn't make any sense. But she didn't know what to do about it, though at the same time she knew that doing nothing was probably the worst thing of all. Was it all a trap? Did she have any choices at all?

"What's the matter, Mommy?" Sally asked, a Barbie in her hands.

"Nothing, honey, just leave Mommy alone for a little while, okay?"

"Jack says he's sorry and can he come out of his room?"

"Yes, if he promises to be good."

"Okay!" Sally ran out of the room.

Was it that simple? Cathy wondered. She could forgive him almost anything. Could she forgive him this? Not because she would want to forgive him. Because there was more to it than her pride. There were also the kids, and kids needed a father, even a neglectful one. Was her pride more important than their needs? The other side of that—what sort of household would they have if Mom and Dad didn't get along? Wasn't that even more destructive? After all, she could always find . . .

. . . another Jack?

She started crying again. She cried for herself, for her own inability to make a decision, for the injury to her character. It was the sort of weeping that did nothing for the problem except make it worse. Part wanted him gone. Part wanted him back. No part knew what to do.

"You understand that this is strictly confidential," the investigator said rather than asked. The man before him was short and overweight, with soft, pink hands. The Bismarck mustache was obviously an affectation to make him look manly. In fact he didn't look terribly impressive at all until you took a close look at his face. Those dark eyes didn't miss a thing.

"Doctors are accustomed to confidentiality," Bernie Katz replied, handing the credentials back. "Make it fast. I have rounds in twenty minutes."

The investigator thought that his assignment did have a certain elegance to it, though he wasn't sure that he approved. The problem was that playing around wasn't exactly a felony, though it did usually disqualify a man from a high security clearance. After all, if a man could break a promise made in a church, then why not one made merely of paper?

Bernie Katz leaned back, waiting as patiently as he was able, which wasn't very patient. He was a surgeon, accustomed to doing things and making his own decisions, not waiting for others. One hand twirled at his mustache as he rocked in the chair.

"How well do you know Dr. Caroline Ryan?"

"Cathy? I've worked with her on and off for eleven years."

"What can you tell me about her?"

"She's a brilliant surgeon, technically speaking, exceptional judgment, superbly skilled. She's one of the best instructors we have on staff. She's also a good friend. What seems to be the problem here?" Katz's eyes narrowed on his visitor.

"Sorry, I'm the guy asking the questions."

"Yeah, I can tell. Get on with it," Katz said coldly, examining the man, watching body language, expression, demeanor. He didn't like what he saw.

"Has she made any comments lately . . . I mean, trouble at home, that sort of thing?"

"You do understand, I hope, that I am a physician, and things said to me are privileged."

"Is Cathy Ryan your patient?" the man asked.

"I've examined her in the past. We all do that here."

"Are you a psychiatrist?"

Katz nearly growled back an answer. Like most surgeons he had a temper. "You know the answer to that."

The investigator looked up from his notes and spoke matter-of-factly. "In that case privilege does not apply. Now, could you answer the question, please?"

"No."

"No, what?"

"No, she has made no such comments to the best of my knowledge."

"Comments on her husband, his behavior, changes in the way he's acting?"

"No. I know Jack pretty well, too. I really like the guy. He's evidently a good husband. They have two great kids, and you know the story on what happened to them some years back as well as I do, right?"

"Correct, but people change."

"Not them." Katz's comment had the finality of a death sentence.

"You seem quite certain."

"I'm a doctor. I live by my judgment. What you are alleging is crap."

"I'm alleging nothing," the investigator said, knowing it was a lie, and knowing that Katz knew it for a lie. He'd judged the man correctly from the first moment. Katz was a hotheaded, passionate man unlikely to keep any secret he deemed unworthy of being kept. Probably one hell of a doctor, too.

"I return to my original question. Has Caroline Ryan acted in any way different from, say, a year ago?"

"She's a year older. They have kids, the kids are growing up, and kids can be a bother. I have a few of my own. Okay, so she's gained a pound or two, maybe—not a bad thing, she tries to be too thin—and she's a little tireder than she ought to be. She has a long commute, and work is hard here, especially for a mother with kids."

"That's all, you think?"

"Hey, I'm an eye-cutter, not a marriage counselor. Not my field."

"Why did you say you're not a marriage counselor? I never brought that up, did I?"

Clever son of a bitch, aren't you? Katz thought, letting go of his mustache. *Degree in psychology, maybe . . . more likely self-taught. Cops were pretty good at reading people. Reading me, even?* "Trouble at home for a married person generally means a troubled marriage," Katz said slowly. "No, there has been no such comment."

"You're sure?"

"Quite sure."

"Okay, thank you for your time, Dr. Katz. Sorry to have bothered you." He handed over a card. "If you hear anything like that, I'd appreciate it if you called me."

"What gives?" Katz asked. "If you want my cooperation, I want an answer. I don't spy on people for the fun of it."

"Doctor, her husband holds a very high and very sensitive government position. We routinely keep an eye on such people for reasons of national security. You do the same thing, even if you don't think much about it. If a surgeon shows up with liquor on his breath, for example, you take note of it and you take action, correct?''

''That doesn't happen here, ever,'' Katz assured him.

''But you would take note of such a thing if it did happen.''

''You bet we would.''

''Glad to hear it. As you know, John Ryan has access to all sorts of highly sensitive information. Were we not to keep an eye on such people, we would be irresponsible. We've—this is a highly sensitive matter, Dr. Katz.''

''I understand that.''

''We've had indications that her husband might be acting . . . irregularly. We have to check that out. Understand? We *have* to.''

''Okay.''

''That's all we ask.''

''Very well.''

''Thank you for your cooperation, sir.'' The investigator shook hands and left.

Katz managed not to flush until the man was gone. He didn't really know Jack all that well. They'd met at parties perhaps five or six times, traded a few jokes, talked about baseball or the weather or maybe international relations. Jack had never begged off on an answer, had never said *I can't discuss that* or anything. Pleasant-enough guy, Bernie thought. A good father by all accounts. But he didn't *know* the man at all.

Katz did, however, know Cathy as well as he knew any other doctor. She was a thoroughly wonderful person. If one of his kids should ever need eye surgery, she was one of the three people in the world whom he would trust to do the fix, and that was the highest compliment he could pay to anyone. She'd backed him up on cases and procedures, and he had backed her up. When one needed advice, it was the other who got asked. They were friends, and associates. If they'd ever decided to leave the Hopkins/Wilmer faculty, they would have set up an office together, because a medical partnership is even harder to maintain than a good marriage. He might have married her, Katz thought, if he'd had the chance. She would have been an easy girl to love. She had to be a good mother. She drew a disproportionate number of kids as patients because in some cases the surgeon needed small hands, and hers were small, dainty, and supremely skillful. She lavished attention on her little patients. The floor nurses loved her for it. Everyone loved her, as a matter of fact. Her surgical team was extremely loyal to her. They didn't come any better than Cathy.

Trouble at home? Jack's playing around behind her back . . . hurting my *friend?*

''That worthless son of a bitch.''

He was late again, Cathy saw. After nine this time. Couldn't he ever get home at a decent hour?

And if not, why not?

''Hi, Cath,'' he said on his way through to the bedroom. ''Sorry I'm late.''

When he was out of sight, she walked toward the closet and opened the door to check the coat. Nothing. He'd had it cleaned the very next day, claiming that it had been spotted. It had been spotted, Cathy remembered, but, but, but . . .

What to do?

She almost started crying again.

Cathy was back in her chair when Jack came through on his way toward the kitchen. He didn't notice the look, didn't notice the silence. His wife stayed in her place, not really seeing the television picture her eyes were fixed on while her mind kept going over and over it, searching for an answer but finding only more anger.

She needed advice. She didn't want her marriage to end, did she? She could feel the process by which emotion and anger were taking over from reason and love. She knew that she ought to be worried about that, ought to resist the process, but she found herself unable to do either as the anger simply fed on itself. Cathy walked quietly into the kitchen and got herself a drink. She didn't have any procedures tomorrow. It was okay to have one drink. Again she looked over at her husband, and again he didn't notice. Didn't notice her? *Why* didn't he notice her? She'd put up with so much. Okay, the time they'd spent in England had been all right, she'd had a fairly good time teaching on staff at Guy's Hospital; it hadn't hurt her tenure at Hopkins a bit. But the other stuff—he was away so damned much! All that time back and forth to Russia when he was messed up with the arms treaty, so many other things, playing spy or something, leaving her at home with the kids, forcing her to lose time at work. She'd missed a couple of good procedures for that reason, when she'd been unable to get a sitter and had been forced to stick Bernie with something that she ought to have done.

And what had Jack been up to all that time? She had once accepted the fact that she couldn't even ask. What *had* he been doing? Maybe having a good laugh? A little fling with some sultry female agent somewhere? Like in the movies. There he was, in some exotic setting, a quiet, darkly lit bar, having a meeting with some agent, and one thing might have led to another. . . .

Cathy settled back in front of the TV and gulped at her drink. She nearly sputtered it back out. She wasn't accustomed to drinking bourbon straight.

This is all a mistake.

It seemed as though there were a war within her mind, the forces of good on one side, and the forces of evil on the other—or was it the forces of naiveté and those of reality? She didn't know, and she was too upset to judge.

Well, it didn't matter for tonight, did it? She was having her period, and even if Jack had asked—which he wouldn't, she knew—she'd say no. Why should he ask if he was getting it somewhere else? Why should she say yes if he was? Why get the leavings? Why be second-string?

She sipped more carefully at her drink this time.

Need to get advice, need to talk to somebody! *But who?*

Maybe Bernie, she decided. She could trust Bernie. Soon as she got back. Two days.

"That takes care of the preliminaries."

"Sure does, boss," the coach said. "How goes the Pentagon, Dennis?"

"Not as much fun as you're having, Paul."

"That's the choice, isn't it? Fun or importance?"

"Everybody all right?"

"Yes, sir! We're pretty healthy for this far into the season, and we have the bye this week to get everybody up to speed. I want another crack at those Vikings."

"So do I," Secretary Bunker said from his E-Ring office. "Think we can really stop Tony Wills this time?"

"We can sure try. Isn't he one great kid? I haven't seen running like that since Gayle Sayers. Defensing him is a bitch, though."

"Let's not try to think too far ahead. I want to be in Denver in a few weeks."

"We play 'em one at a time, Dennis, you know that. Just we don't know who we're playing yet. I'd prefer L.A. We can handle them easy enough,'' the coach thought. ''Then we'll probably have to handle Miami in the division game. That'll be harder, but we can do it.''

''I think so, too.''

''I have films to look at.''

''Fair enough. Just remember, one at a time—but three more wins.''

''You tell the President to come on out to Denver. We'll be there to see him. This is San Diego's year. The Chargers go all the way.''

Dubinin watched the water invade the graving dock as the sluices were opened. *Admiral Lunin* was ready. The new sonar array was rolled up on its spool inside the teardrop-shaped fairing that sat atop the rudder post. The seven-bladed screw of manganese-bronze had been inspected and polished. The hull was restored to full watertight integrity. His submarine was ready for sea.

As was the crew. He'd gotten rid of eighteen conscript sailors and replaced them with eighteen new officers. The radical downsizing of the Soviet submarine fleet had eliminated a large number of officer billets. It would have been a waste of skilled manpower to return them to civilian life—besides which there were not enough jobs for them—and as a result they'd been retrained and assigned to the remaining submarines as technical experts. His sonar department would now be almost exclusively officers—two *michmaniy* would assist with the maintenance—and all of them were genuine experts. Surprisingly, there was little grumbling among them. The Akula-class had what was for Soviet submarines very comfortable accommodations, but more important than that was the fact that the new members of the wardroom had been fully briefed on their mission, and what the boat had done—probably done, Dubinin corrected himself—on the previous cruise. It was the sort of thing that appealed to the sportsman in them. This was for the submariner the ultimate test of skill. For that they would do their best.

Dubinin would do the same. Pulling in a lot of old professional debts, and leaning heavily on the yard's Master Shipwright, he'd performed miracles during the refit. Bedding had all been replaced. The ship had been scrubbed surgically clean and repainted with bright, airy colors. Dubinin had worked with the local supply officers and obtained the best food he could find. A well-fed crew was a happy crew, and men responded to a commander who worked hard for them. That was the whole point of the new professional spirit in the Soviet Navy. Valentin Borissovich Dubinin had learned his trade from the best teacher his Navy had ever had, and he was determined that he would be the new Marko Ramius. He had the best ship, had the best crew, and he would on this cruise set the standard for the Soviet Pacific Fleet.

He would also have to be lucky, of course.

''That's the hardware,'' Fromm said. ''From now on . . .''

''Yes, from now on we are assembling the actual device. I see you've changed the design somewhat . . . ?''

''Yes. Two tritium reservoirs. I prefer the shorter injection piping. Mechanically it is no different. The timing is not critical, and the pressurization ensures that it will function properly.''

''Also makes loading the tritium easier,'' Ghosn observed. ''That's why you did it.''

''Correct.''

The inside of the device made Ghosn think of the half-assembled body of some alien airplane. There was the delicacy and precision of aircraft parts, but the almost baffling configuration in which they were placed. Something from a science-fiction movie, Ghosn thought, whimsical for a brief moment . . . but then this was science fiction, or had been until recently. The first public discussion of nuclear weapons had been in H. G. Wells, hadn't it? That hadn't been so long ago.

"Commander, I saw your doctor," Achmed said in the far corner.

"And—you still look ill, my friend," Qati noted. "What is the problem?"

"He wants me to see another doctor in Damascus."

Qati instantly did not like that. Did not like it at all. But Achmed was a comrade who had served the movement for years. How could he say no to someone who had twice saved his life, once stopping a bullet himself to do so?

"You know that what goes on here. . . ."

"Commander, I will die before I speak of this place. Even though I know nothing of this—this project. I will die first."

There was no doubting the man, and Qati knew what it was to be seriously ill at a young and healthy age. He could not deny the man medical care while he himself regularly visited a physician. How could his men respect him if he did such a thing?

"Two men will go with you. I will select them."

"Thank you, Commander. Please forgive my weakness."

"Weakness?" Qati grabbed the man by the shoulder. "You are the strongest among us! We need you back, and we need you healthy! Go tomorrow."

Achmed nodded and withdrew to another place, embarrassed and shamed by his illness. His Commander, he knew, faced death. It had to be cancer, he had so often visited the physician. Whatever it was, the Commander had not let it stop him. There was courage, he thought.

"Break for the night?" Ghosn asked.

Fromm shook his head. "No, let's take another hour or two to assemble the explosive bed. We should be able to get part of it in place before we're too weary." Both men looked up as Qati approached.

"Still on schedule?"

"Herr Qati, whatever arrangements you have in mind, we will be ready a day early. Ibrahim saved us that day with his work on the explosives." The German held one of the small hexagonal blocks. The squibs were already in place, the wire trailing off. Fromm looked at the other two, then bent down, setting the first block in its nesting place. Fromm made sure the block was exactly in place, then attached a numbered tag on the wire and draped it into a plastic tray that held a number of dividers, like the trays of a toolbox. Qati attached the wire to a terminal, checking three times to make sure the number on the wire was the same as that on the terminal. Fromm watched also. The process took four minutes. The electrical components had already been pre-tested. They could not be tested again. The first part of the bomb was now live.

27. Data Fusion

"I've had my say, Bart," Jones said on the way to the airport.

"That bad?"

"The crew hates him—the training they just went through didn't help. Hey, I was there, okay? I was in with the sonar guys, in the simulator, and he was there, and I wouldn't want to work for him. He almost yelled at me."

"Oh?" That surprised Mancuso.

"Yeah, he said something that I didn't like—something plain wrong, skipper—and I called him on it, and you should have seen his reaction. Shit, I thought he'd have a stroke or something. And he was wrong, Bart. It was my tape. He was hassling his people for not cueing on something that wasn't there, okay? It was one of my trick tapes, and they saw that it was bogus, but he didn't and he started raisin' hell. That's a good sonar department. He doesn't know how to use it, but he sure likes to kibbitz like he does. Anyway, after he left, the guys started talking, okay? That isn't the only bunch he gives a hard time to. I hear the engineers are going nuts trying to keep this clown happy. Is it true they maxed an ORSE?"

Mancuso nodded, despite the fact he didn't like hearing this. "They came within a whisker of setting a record."

"Well, the guy doesn't want a record, he wants a perfect. He wants to redefine what perfect is. I'm telling you, man, if I was stuck on that boat, after the first cruise the first thing up through the hatch would be my seabag. I'd fuckin' *desert* before I worked for that guy!" Jones paused. He'd gone too far. "I caught the signal his XO gave you, I even thought he might have been a little out of line, maybe. I was wrong. That's one very loyal XO. Ricks hates one of his JOs, the kid does tracking-party duty. The quartermaster who's breaking him in—Ensign Shaw, I think his name is—says he's a real good kid, but the skipper's riding him like a broke-down horse."

"Great, what am I supposed to do about it?"

"Beats me, Bart. I retired as an E-6, remember?" *Relieve the son of a bitch,* Jones thought, though he knew better. You could only relieve for cause.

"I'll talk to him," Mancuso promised.

"You know, I heard about skippers like that. Never did believe the stories. Guess I got spoiled working for you," Dr. Jones observed as they approached the terminal. "You haven't changed a bit, you know that? You still listen when somebody talks at you."

"You have to listen, Ron. You can't know it all yourself."

"I got news: not everyone knows that. I got one more suggestion."

"Don't let him go hunting?"

"If I were in your position, I wouldn't." Jones opened the door. "I don't want to rain on the parade, skipper. That's my professional observation. He isn't up to the game. Ricks is nothing near the captain you used to be."

Used to be. A singularly poor choice of words, Mancuso thought, but it was true. It was a hell of a lot easier to run a boat than to run a squadron, and a hell of a lot more fun, too.

"Better hustle if you want to catch that flight." Mancuso held out his hand.

"Skipper, always a pleasure."

Mancuso watched him walk into the terminal. Jones had never once given him bad advice, and if anything he'd gotten smarter. A pity he hadn't stayed in and gone for a commission. That wasn't true, the Commodore thought next. Ron would have made one hell of a CO, but he would never have had a chance. The system didn't allow it, and that was that.

The driver headed back without being told, leaving Mancuso in his rear seat with his thoughts. The system hadn't changed enough. He'd come up the old way, power school, an engineer tour before he got command. There was too much engineering in the Navy, not enough leadership. He'd made the transition, as did most of the skippers—but not all. Too many people made it through who thought that other people were just numbers, machines to be fixed, things to order, who measured people by numbers that were more easily understood than real results. Jim Rosselli wasn't like that. Neither was Bart Mancuso, but Harry Ricks was.

So. Now what the hell do I do?

First and foremost, he had no basis for relieving Ricks. Had the story come from anyone except Jones, he would have dismissed it as personality clashes. Jones was too reliable an observer for that. Mancuso considered what he'd been told and matched it with the higher-than-usual rate of transfer requests, the rather equivocal words he'd heard from Dutch Claggett. The XO was in a very touchy spot. Already selected for command . . . one bad word from Ricks and he'd lose that; against that possibility he had his loyalty to the Navy. His job demanded loyalty to his CO even while the Navy demanded truth. It was an impossible position for Claggett, and he'd done all that he could.

The responsibility was Mancuso's. He was the squadron commander. The boats were his. The skippers and crews were his. He rated the COs. That was it, wasn't it?

But was it right? All he had was anecdotal information and coincidence. What if Jones was just pissed off at the guy? What if the transfer requests had just been a statistical blip?

Dodging the issue, Bart. They pay you to make the tough decisions. Ensigns and chiefs get the easy ones. Senior captains are supposed to know what to do. That was one of the Navy's more entertaining fictions.

Mancuso lifted his carphone. "I want *Maine*'s XO in my office in thirty minutes."

"Yes, sir," his yeoman responded.

Mancuso closed his eyes and dozed for the rest of the ride. Nothing like a catnap to clear the mind. It had always worked on USS *Dallas*.

Hospital food, Cathy thought. Even at Hopkins it was still hospital food. There had to be a special school somewhere for hospital chefs. The curriculum would be devoted to eliminating whatever fresh ideas they had, along with any skills they might have with spices, knowledge of recipes. . . . About the only thing they couldn't ruin was the Jell-O.

"Bernie, I need some advice."

"What's the problem, Cath?" He knew already what it had to be, just from the look on her face and the tone of her voice. He waited as sympathetically as he could. Cathy was a proud woman, as she had every right to be. This had to be dreadfully hard on her.

"It's Jack." The words came out rapidly, as though by a spasm, then stopped again.

The pain Katz saw in her eyes was more than he could bear. "You think he's . . ."

"What? No—I mean—how, why did you . . . ?"

"Cathy, I'm not supposed to do this, but you're too important a friend for that. Screw the rules! Look, I had a guy in here last week, asking about you and Jack."

The hurt only got worse. "What do you mean? Who was here? Where from?"

"Government guy, some kind of investigator. Cathy, I'm sorry, but he asked me if there—if you had said anything about trouble at home. This guy was checking up on Jack, and he wanted to know if I knew anything that you were saying."

"What did you say?"

"I told him I didn't know anything. I told him that you're one of the best people I know. You are, Cathy. You're not alone. You have friends, and if there is anything I can do—that any of us can do—to help you, we will help you. Cathy, you're like family. You're probably feeling very hurt, and you're probably feeling very embarrassed. That is stupid, Cathy, that is very stupid. You know it's stupid, don't you?" Those pretty blue eyes were covered in tears, Katz saw, and in this moment he craved the chance to kill Jack Ryan, maybe do it on a table with a very sharp, very small surgical knife. "Cathy, being alone doesn't help. This is what friends are really for. You are not alone."

"I just can't believe it, Bernie. I just *can't.*"

"Come on, let's talk in my office, where it's private. Food's crummy today anyway." Katz got her out of there, and he was sure that no one noticed. Two minutes later they were in his private office. He moved a stack of case files from the only other chair and sat her in it.

"He's just been acting different lately."

"Do you really think it's possible that Jack is fooling around?" It took half a minute. Katz watched her eyes go up and down, finally staying down as she faced reality.

"It's possible. Yes."

Bastard! "Have you talked to him about it?" Katz kept his voice low and reasonable, but not dispassionate. She needed a friend now, and friends had to share pain to be useful.

A shake of the head. "No, I don't know how."

"You know that you have to do that."

"Yeah." Not so much a word as a gasp.

"It's not going to be easy. Remember," Katz said with gentle hope in his voice, "it could all be a mistake. Just some crazy misunderstanding." Which Bernie Katz didn't believe for a moment.

She looked up, and her eyes were streaming now. "Bernie, is there something wrong with me?"

"No!" Katz managed not to shout. "Cathy, if there's a better person in this hospital than you, goddamn if I've ever met them! There is *nothing* wrong with you! You hear me? Whatever the hell this is, it is *not your fault!*"

"Bernie, I want another baby, I don't want to lose Jack—"

"Then if you really think that, you have to win him back."

"I *can't!* He isn't, he doesn't—" She broke down completely.

Katz learned then and there that anger has few limits. Having to keep it in, being denied a target, didn't help, but Cathy needed a friend more than she needed anything else.

''Dutch, this whole conversation is off the record.''

Lieutenant Commander Claggett was instantly on guard. ''As you say, Commodore.''

''Tell me about Captain Ricks.''

''Sir, he's my CO.''

''I'm aware of that, Dutch,'' Mancuso said. ''I'm the squadron commander. If there's a problem with one of my skippers, there's a problem with one of my boats. Those boats cost a billion a copy, and I have to know about the problems. Is that clear, Commander?''

''Yes, sir.''

''Talk. That's an order.''

Dutch Claggett sat ramrod straight and spoke rapidly. ''Sir, he couldn't lead a three-year-old to the crapper. He treats the troops like they're robots. He demands a lot, but he never praises even when the guys put out. That's not the way I was taught to officer. He doesn't listen, sir. He doesn't listen to me, doesn't listen to the troops. Okay, fine, he's the CO. He owns the boat, but a smart skipper listens.''

''That's the reason for the transfers?''

''Yes, sir. He gave the chief torpedoman a bad time—I think he was wrong. Chief Getty was showing some initiative. He had the weapons on line, he had his people well trained, but Captain Ricks didn't like the way he did it and came down on him. I counseled against it, but the CO didn't listen. So Getty put in for transfer, and the skipper was glad to get rid of him, and endorsed it.''

''Do you have confidence in him?'' Mancuso asked.

''Technically he's very good. Engineering-wise, he's brilliant. He just doesn't know people and he doesn't know tactics.''

''He told me he wants to prove otherwise. Can he?''

''Sir, you're going too far now. I don't know that I have the right to answer that.''

Mancuso knew it was true, but pressed on anyway. ''You're supposed to be qualified for command, Dutch. Get used to making some hard calls.''

''Can he do it? Yes, sir. We have a good boat and a good crew. What he can't do the rest of us will do for him.''

The Commodore nodded and went silent for a moment. ''If you have any trouble with your next FitRep, I want to know about it. I think you may be a better XO than he's entitled to, Commander.''

''Sir, he's not a bad guy. I hear he's a good father and all that. His wife's a sweetie. It's just that he never learned to handle people, and nobody ever bothered teaching him right. Despite that he is a capable officer. If he'd only give an inch on the humanity side, he'd be a real star.''

''Are you comfortable with your op-orders?''

''If we sniff out an Akula to go in and track him—safe distance and all that. Am I comfortable? Hell, yes. Come on, Commodore, we're so quiet there's not a thing to worry about. I was surprised Washington approved this thing, and all, but that's bureaucratic stuff. The short version is, anybody can drive this boat. Okay, maybe Cap'n Ricks isn't perfect, but unless our boat breaks, Popeye could do the mission.''

* * *

They put the Secondary assembly in before the Primary. The collection of lithium compounds was contained in a metal cylinder roughly the size of a 105mm artillery casing, 65 centimeters high and 11 centimeters in diameter. It even had a rim machined on the bottom end so that it would fit in exactly the right spot. There was a small curved tube at the bottom that attached to what would soon be the tritium reservoir. On the outside of the casing were the fins made of spent uranium 238. They looked like rows of thick, black soda crackers, Fromm thought. Their mission, of course, was to be immolated to plasma. Beneath the cylinder were the first bundles of ''soda straws''—even Fromm was calling them that now, though they actually were not; they were of the wrong diameter. Sixty centimeters in length, each bundle of a hundred was held together by thin but strong plastic spacers, and the bottom of each had been given a half-turn to make each bundle into a helix, a shape rather like that of a spiral staircase. The hard part in this segment of the design was to arrange the helixes to nest together perfectly. Seemingly trivial, it had taken fully two days for Fromm to figure out, but as with all aspects of his design, the pieces all fit into proper place until that portion of the design seemed a perfectly assembled mass of . . . soda straws. It almost made the German laugh. With tape measure, micrometer, and an expert eye—gradation marks had been machined into many of the parts, a small detail that had impressed Ghosn very greatly indeed. When Fromm was satisfied, they went on. First came the plastic foam blocks, each cut to precise specifications. They fit into the elliptical bombcase. Ghosn and Fromm were now doing all the work. Slowly, carefully, they eased the first block into place within the flanges on the interior of the case. The straw bundles came next, one at a time, nesting perfectly with those immediately under them. At every step both men stopped to check the work. Fromm and Ghosn both checked the work, checked the plans, checked the work again, and checked the plans again.

For Bock and Qati, watching a few meters away, it was the most tedious thing they had ever seen.

''The people who do this work in America and Russia must die of boredom,'' the German said quietly.

''Perhaps.''

''Next bundle, number thirty-six,'' Fromm said.

''Thirty-six,'' Ghosn replied, examining the three tags on the next batch of a hundred straws. ''Bundle thirty-six.''

''Thirty-six,'' Fromm agreed, looking at the tags. He took it and maneuvered it into place. It fit perfectly, Qati saw, coming closer. The German's skilled hands moved it slightly, so that the slits on its plastic jigs dropped into the slots on the jigs directly underneath. When Fromm was satisfied, Ghosn looked.

''Correct position,'' Ibrahim said for what must have been the hundredth time of the day.

''I agree,'' Fromm announced, and both men wired it firmly into place.

''Like assembling a gun,'' Qati whispered to Günther as he walked away from the worktable.

''No.'' Bock shook his head. ''Worse than that. More like a child's toy.'' The two men looked at each other and started laughing.

''Enough of that!'' Fromm said in annoyance. ''This is serious work! We need silence! Next bundle, number thirty-seven!''

''Thirty-seven,'' Ghosn dutifully replied.

Bock and Qati walked out of the room together.

"Watching a woman having a baby cannot be as dreadful as this!" Qati raged when they got outside.

Bock lit a cigarette. "It isn't. I know. Women move faster than this."

"Indeed, that is unskilled labor." Qati laughed again. The humor vanished, and the Commander became serious. "It's a pity."

"Yes, it is. They have all served us well. When?"

"Very soon." Qati paused. "Günther, your part in the plan . . . it is very dangerous."

Bock took a long pull on his cigarette, blowing the smoke out into the chilled air. "It is my plan, is it not? I know the risks."

"I do not approve of suicidal plans," Qati observed after a moment.

"Nor do I. It is dangerous, but I expect to survive. Ismael, if we wanted a safe life, we would be working in offices—and we would never have met. What binds us is the danger and the mission. I've lost my Petra, my daughters, but I still have my mission. I do not say that this is enough, but is it not more than most men have?" Günther looked up at the stars. "I have thought often of this, my friend. How does one change the world? Not in safety. The safe ones, the timid ones, they benefit from our work. They rage at life, but they lack the courage to act. We are the ones who act. We take the risks, we face the danger, we deny ourselves for others. It is our task. My friend, it is far too late to have second thoughts."

"Günther, it is easier for me. I am a dying man."

"I know." He turned to look at his friend. "We're all dying men. We've cheated death, you and I. Eventually death will win, and the death we face lies not in bed. You chose this path, and so did I. Can we turn back now?"

"I cannot, but facing death is a hard thing."

"That is true." Günther flipped his cigarette into the dirt. "But at least we have the privilege of knowing. The little people do not. In choosing not to act, they choose not to know. That is their choice. One can either be an agent of destiny or a victim of it. Everyone has that choice." Bock led his friend back in. "We have made ours."

"Bundle thirty-eight!" Fromm commanded as they entered.

"Thirty-eight," Ghosn acknowledged.

"Yes, Commodore?"

"Sit down, Harry, we need to talk over some things."

"Well, I have the crew all ready. The sonar troops are hot."

Mancuso looked at his subordinate. *At what point,* he wondered, *does a positive can-do attitude become a lie?* "I'm a little concerned with the transfer rate from your ship."

Ricks didn't go defensive. "Well, we had some guys with family concerns. No sense holding on to people whose minds are in the wrong place. A statistical blip. I had it happen once before."

I bet you did. "How's morale?" Mancuso asked next.

"You've seen the results of our drills and exams. That must tell you something," Captain Ricks replied.

Clever son of a bitch. "Okay, let me make it clear, Harry. You had a run-in with Dr. Jones."

"So?"

"So I talked with him about it."

"How formal is this?"

"Informal as you like, Harry."

"Fine. Your Jones fellow is a pretty good technician, but he seems to have forgotten the fact that he left the Navy as an enlisted man. If he wants to talk to me as an equal, it would help if he'd bothered to accomplish something."

"That man has a doctor's degree in physics from CalTech, Harry."

Ricks took on a puzzled expression. "So?"

"So he's one of the smartest people I know, and he was the best enlisted man I ever met."

"That's fine, but if enlisted were as smart as officers, we'd pay them more." It was the supreme arrogance of the statement that angered Bart Mancuso.

"Captain, when I was driving *Dallas,* and Jones talked, I listened. If life had worked out a little different, he'd be on his XO tour right now and on his way to command of a fast-attack. Ron would have made a superb CO."

Ricks dismissed that. "We'll never know that, will we? I always figured that those who can, do. Those who can't make excuses. Okay, fine, he's a good technician. I don't dispute that. He did good work with my sonar department, and I'm grateful for that, but let's not get too excited. There are lots of technicians, and lots of contractors."

This was going nowhere, Mancuso saw. It was time to lay the law down. "Look, Harry, I'm catching rumbles about morale on your boat. I see that many transfer requests, and it tells me there might be a problem. So I nose around, and my impression is confirmed. You have a problem whether you know it or not."

"That, sir, is bullshit. It's like the alcohol-counseling weenies. People with no drinking problem say they have no drinking problem, but the counselors say that denial of a problem is the first indication there is one. It's a circular argument. If I had a morale problem on my boat, performance figures would show it. But they *don't.* My record is pretty clear. I drive submarines for a living. I've been in the top one percent of the top one percent since I put this suit on. Okay, my style isn't the same as the next guy's. I don't kiss butt, and I don't mollycoddle. I demand performance, and I get it. You show me one hard indicator that I'm not doing it right, and I'll listen, but until you do, sir, it isn't broke, and I'm not going to try and fix it."

Bartolomeo Vito Mancuso, Captain (Rear Admiral selectee), United States Navy, did not come out of his chair only because his mainly Sicilian ancestry had been somewhat diluted in America. In the old country, he was instantly sure, his great-great-grandfather would have leveled his *lupara* and blown a wide, bloody hole through Ricks' chest for that. Instead he kept his face impassive and coldly decided on the spot that Ricks would never get beyond captain's rank. It was in his power to do that. He had a large collection of COs working for him. Only the top two, maybe the top three, would screen for flag rank. Ricks would be rated no higher than fourth in that group. It might be dishonest, Mancuso told himself in a moment of dispassionate integrity, but it was still the right thing to do. This man could not be trusted with command higher than he now held, and he had probably come too far already. It would be so easy. Ricks would object loudly and passionately to being rated fourth in a group of fourteen, but Mancuso would simply say, *Sorry, Harry—I'm not saying there's anything wrong with you, just that Andy, Bill, and Chuck are a little better. Just bad luck to be in a squadron of aces, Harry. I have to make an honest call, and they're just a whisker better.*

Ricks was just fast enough to realize that he had crossed over a line, that there really were no "off-the-record" talks in the Navy. He had defied his squadron commander, a man already on the fast track, a man trusted and believed by the Pentagon and the OP-02 bureaucracy.

"Sir, excuse me for being so positive. It's just that nobody likes to be called down when—"

Mancuso smiled as he cut the man off. "No problem, Harry. We Italians tend to be a little passionate, too." *Too late, Harry. . . .*

"Maybe you're right. Let me think it over. Besides, if I tangle with that Akula, I'll show you what my people can do."

Little late to talk about "my people," fella. But Mancuso had to give him the chance, didn't he? Not much of a chance, but a little one. If there were a miracle, then he might reconsider. *Might,* Bart told himself, *if this arrogant little prick decides to kiss my ass at the main gate at noon on the Fourth of July while the marching band passes by.*

"Sessions like this are supposed to be uncomfortable for everybody," the squadron commander said. Ricks would end up as an engineering expert, and a good one, once Mancuso got rid of him, and there was no disgrace in topping out as a captain, was there? Not for a good man, anyway.

"Nothing else?" Golovko asked.

"Not a thing," the Colonel replied.

"And our officer?"

"I saw his widow two days ago. I told her that he was dead, but that we were unable to recover the body. She took the news badly. It is a hard thing to see so lovely a face in tears," the man reported quietly.

"What about the pension, other arrangements?"

"I am seeing to it myself."

"Good, those damned paper-pushers don't seem to care about anyone or anything. If there's a problem, let me know."

"I have nothing more to suggest from the technical-intelligence side," the Colonel went on. "Can you follow up elsewhere?"

"We're still rebuilding our network inside their defense ministry. Preliminary indications are that there is nothing, that the new Germany has disavowed the whole DDR project," Golovko said. "There is a hint that American and British agencies have made similar inquiries and come away satisfied."

"It is unlikely, I think, that German nuclear weapons would be a matter of immediate concern to the Americans or the English."

"True. We are carrying on, but I do not expect to find anything. I think this is an empty hole."

"In that case, Sergey Nikolayevich, why was our man murdered?"

"We still don't *know* that, damn it!"

"Yes, I suppose he might now be working for the Argentineans. . . ."

"Colonel, remember your place!"

"I have not forgotten it. Nor have I forgotten that when someone troubles to murder an intelligence officer there is a good reason for it."

"But there's nothing there! At least three intelligence services are looking. Our people in Argentina are still working—"

"Oh, yes, the Cubans?"

"Correct, that was their area of responsibility, and we can scarcely depend on their assistance now, can we?"

The Colonel closed his eyes. What had KGB come to? "I still think we should press on."

"Your recommendation is noted. The operation is not over."

Exactly what he could do now, Golovko thought after the man left, exactly what new avenues he should explore . . . he didn't know. He had a goodly percentage of his field force sniffing for leads, but as yet there was nothing. This miserable profession was so much like police work, wasn't it?

Marvin Russell went over his requirements. Certainly these were generous people. He still had almost all of the money he'd brought over. He'd even offered to make use of it, but Qati would have none of that. He had a briefcase in which were forty thousand dollars in crisp twenties and fifties, and on setting himself up in America he'd take in a direct bank transfer from an English bank. His tasks were fairly simple. First he needed new identities for himself and the others. That was child's play. Even doing the driver's licenses was not difficult if you had the right hardware, and he'd be purchasing that for cash. He'd even be able to set the equipment up in the safe house. Now, exactly why he had to do hotel reservations in addition to setting up the safe house was another question. These characters sure liked to keep things complicated.

On the way to the airport he'd taken a day to stop at a good tailor shop—Beirut might have been at war, but life still went on. By the time he boarded the British Airways jet for Heathrow he looked quite distinguished. Three very nice suits—two of them packed. A conservative haircut, expensive shoes that cramped his feet.

"Magazine, sir?" the stew asked.

"Thank you." Russell smiled.

"American?"

"That's right. Going home."

"It must be rather difficult in Lebanon."

"Did get kind of exciting, yes."

"Drink?"

"A beer would be very nice." Russell grinned. He was even getting the businessman lingo down. The plane was not even a third full, and it seemed like this stewardess was going to adopt him. Maybe it was the tan, Russell thought.

"There you go, sir. Will you be staying long in London?"

" 'Fraid not. Connecting to Chicago. Two-hour layover."

"That is too bad." She even looked disappointed for him. The Brits, Russell thought, sure were nice people. Almost as hospitable as those Arabs.

The last bundle went in just after three in the morning, local time. Fromm didn't alter his demeanor a dot. He checked this one as carefully as he had checked the first, fixing it in place only after he was fully satisfied. Then he stood straight up and stretched.

"Enough!"

"I agree, Manfred."

"This time tomorrow we'll have the assembly finished. What remains is simple, not fourteen hours' work."

"In that case, let's get some sleep." On the way out of the building, Ghosn gave the Commander a wink.

Qati watched them depart, then walked over to the senior guard. "Where's Achmed?"

"Went to see the doctor, remember?"

"Hmmm. When's he back?"

"Tomorrow, maybe the day after, I'm not sure."

"Very well. We will have a special job for you soon."

The guard watched the men walking away from the building and nodded dispassionately. "Where do you want us to excavate the hole?"

28. Contractual Obligations

Jet lag could be a real bitch, Marvin thought. Russell had left O'Hare in a rented Mercury and driven west to a motel just east of Des Moines. He surprised the clerk by paying cash for his room, explaining that his wallet and credit cards had been stolen. He had an obviously brand-new wallet to support that statement, besides which the clerk honored cash as readily as any businessman. Sleep came easily that night. He awoke just after five, after a good ten hours of slumber, had himself a big American breakfast—as hospitable as people were in Lebanon, they didn't know how to eat; he wondered how they managed to live without bacon—and set off for Colorado. By lunch he was halfway across Nebraska, and going over his plans and requirements again. Dinner found him in the town of Roggen, an hour northeast of Denver, which was close enough. Stiff from travel, he found yet another motel and crashed for the night. This time he was able to watch and enjoy some American TV, including a recap of the NFL season on ESPN. It was surprising how much he'd missed football. Almost as surprising as how much he'd missed having a drink whenever he wanted. That craving was fixed with a bottle of Jack Daniel's he'd gotten along the way. By midnight he was feeling pretty mellow, looking around at his surroundings, glad to be back in America, and also glad for the reason he was back. It was time for some payback. Russell had not forgotten who had once owned Colorado, and hadn't forgotten the massacre at Sand Creek.

It should have been expected. Things had gone too smoothly, and reality does not often allow perfection. A small mistake in one of the fittings for the Primary had been detected, and that fitting had to be removed and remachined, a process that set them back by thirty hours, of which forty minutes had been required for the machining and the rest for disassembly and reassembly of the weapon. Fromm, who should have been philosophical, had been livid during the whole procedure, and insisted on doing the fix himself. Then had come the laborious replacement of the explosive blocks, all the more onerous for having already been done once.

"Only three millimeters," Ghosn noted. Just a mistaken setting on one of the controls. Since it had been a manual job, the computers hadn't caught it. One of Fromm's figures had been misread, and the first visual inspection of the assembly hadn't caught it. "And we had that extra day."

Fromm merely grumbled behind his protective mask as he and Ghosn lifted the plutonium assembly and gently set it in place. Five minutes later it was clear that they had it correctly located. The bars of tungsten-rhenium next fit into their own places, then the beryllium segments, and finally, the heavy depleted-uranium hemisphere that separated the Primary from the Secondary. Fifty more explosive blocks and they were done. Fromm ordered a pause—what they had just accomplished was heavy work, and he wanted a short rest. The machinists were already gone, their services no longer required.

"We should have been done by now," the German said quietly.

"It is unreasonable to expect perfection, Manfred."

"The ignorant bastard couldn't read!"

"The number on the plans was smudged." *And that was your fault,* Ghosn did not have to say.

"Then he should have asked!"

"As you say, Manfred. You pick a poor time to be impatient. We are on schedule."

The young Arab just didn't understand, Fromm knew. The culmination of his life's ambitions, and it should have been done by now! "Come on."

It required ten additional hours until the seventieth and last explosive block sat in its resting place. Ghosn attached its wire lead to the proper terminal, and that was that. He extended his hand to the German, who took it.

"Congratulations, Herr Doktor Fromm."

"*Ja.* Thank you, Herr Ghosn. Now we only need to weld the case shut, draw the vacuum—oh, excuse me, the tritium. How did I forget that? Who does the welding?" Manfred asked.

"I will. I'm very good at that." The top half of the bombcase had a wide flange to ensure the safety of that procedure, and it had already been checked for a perfect fit. The machinists had not merely handled the precise work on the explosive part of the device. Every single part—except for the single mistrimmed fitting—had been cut and shaped to Fromm's specifications, and the bombcase had already been checked. It fit as tightly as the back of a watch.

"Doing the tritium is easy."

"Yes, I know." Ghosn motioned for the German to go outside. "You are fully satisfied with the design and the assembly?"

"Completely," Fromm said confidently. "It will function exactly as I predict."

"Excellent," Qati said, waiting outside with one of his bodyguards.

Fromm turned, noting the Commander's presence, along with one of his ubiquitous guards. Dirty, scruffy people, but he had to admire them, Fromm told himself as he turned to look at the darkened valley. There was a quarter-moon, and he could just make out the landscape. So dry and harsh it was. Not these people's fault that they looked as they did. The land here was hard. But the sky was clear. Fromm looked up at the stars on this cloudless night. More stars than one could see in Germany, especially the Eastern part, with all its air pollution, and he thought about astrophysics, the path he might have taken, so closely related to the path he had.

Ghosn stood behind the German. He turned to Qati and nodded. The Commander made the same gesture to his bodyguard, whose name was Abdullah.

"Just the tritium remains," Fromm said, his back to them.

"Yes," Ghosn said. "I can do that myself."

Fromm was about to say that there was one more thing. He let it wait a moment, and didn't pay attention to Abdullah's footsteps. There was no sound at all as the guard removed a silenced pistol from his belt and pointed it at Fromm's head from a range of one meter. Fromm began to turn, to make sure that Ghosn knew about the tritium, but he never made it around. Abdullah had his orders. It was supposed to be merciful, as it had been for the machinists. It was a pity that it had been necessary at all, Qati thought, but it was necessary, and that was that. None of that mattered to Abdullah, who merely followed his orders, squeezing on the trigger smoothly and expertly until the round fired. The bullet entered the back of Fromm's skull, soon thereafter exiting through his forehead. The German dropped in a crumpled mass. Blood fountained out, but sideways, without reaching Abdullah's clothing. The guard waited until the blood flow stopped, then summoned two comrades to carry the body to the waiting truck. He'd be buried with the machinists. That, at least, was fitting, Qati thought. All the experts in the same place.

"A pity," Ghosn observed quietly.

"Yes, but do you really think we would have further use of him?"

Ibrahim shook his head. "No. He would have been a liability. We could not trust him. An infidel and a mercenary. He fulfilled his contract."

"And the device?"

"It will work. I have checked the numbers twenty times. It is far better than anything I might have designed."

"What's this about tritium?"

"In the batteries. I only need to heat them up and bleed off the gas. Then the gas is pumped into the two reservoirs. You know the rest."

Qati grunted. "You have explained it, but I do not know it."

"This part of the job is work for a high-school chemistry lab, no more than that. Simple."

"Why did Fromm leave it for last?"

Ghosn shrugged. "Something has to be last. This is an easy task rather than a hard one. Perhaps that is why. I can do it now if you wish."

"Good."

Qati watched the procedure. One after another, Ghosn loaded the batteries into the furnace, which he set for very low heat. A metal tube and a vacuum pump drew off the gas emitted by each in turn. It took less than an hour.

"Fromm lied to us," Ghosn observed when he was done.

"What?" Qati asked in alarm.

"Commander, there is almost fifteen percent more tritium than he promised. So much the better."

The next step was even simpler. Ghosn carefully checked that each reservoir was air- and pressure-tight—it was the sixth such test; the young engineer had learned from his German teacher—then transferred the tritium gas. The valves were closed and locked shut with cotter pins, so that any vibration in transit could not open them.

"Finished," Ghosn announced. The guards lifted the top of the bombcase and lowered it into place from an overhead winch. It fit precisely into place. Ghosn took an hour to weld it shut. Another test confirmed that the bombcase was pressure-tight. He next attached a Leybold vacuum pump to the case.

"What exactly do you need to achieve?"

"A millionth of an atmosphere is what we specified."

"Can you do that? Won't it harm—"

Ghosn spoke not unlike Fromm, surprising the both of them. "Commander, please? All that presses in is *air*. It does not crush you, and it will not crush this steel case, will it? It will take a few hours, and we can also test the integrity of the bombcase again.'' Which had also been done five times. Even without being welded, the case held well. Now one piece of metal, it would be as perfect as the mission required. ''We can get some sleep. It doesn't hurt the pump to run.''

''When will it be ready to transport?''

''In the morning. When is the ship leaving?''

''Two days.''

''There you have it.'' Ghosn smiled broadly. ''Time to spare.''

First, Marvin visited the local branch of Colorado Federal Bank and Trust Company. He amazed and delighted the branch vice president by placing a call to England and having five hundred thousand dollars transferred by wire. Computers made things so much easier. In seconds he had confirmation that Mr. Robert Friend was every bit as substantial as he claimed to be.

''Can you recommend a good local realtor?'' Russell asked the very solicitous banker.

''Right down the street, third door on the right. I'll have your checks ready when you get back.'' The banker watched him leave and placed a rapid phone call to his wife, who worked in the real-estate office. She was waiting for him at the door.

''Mr. Friend, welcome to Roggen!''

''Thank you, good to be back.''

''You've been away?''

''Spent some time in Saudi Arabia,'' Russell/Friend explained. ''But I missed my winters.''

''What are you looking for?''

''Oh, a medium-sized ranch, place where I might raise some beef.''

''House, barns?''

''Yeah, a good-sized house. Not that big, don't need it—there's just me, you see—say about three thousand square feet. I can go smaller for good land.''

''You originally from around here?''

''The Dakotas, actually, but I need to be close to Denver for the transportation—air travel, I mean. I do a lot of that. My old homestead is too far from things.''

''Will you want help to run your ranch?''

''Yeah, I'll need that, say a place big enough for two hands—maybe a couple. I really should have a place closer to town, but, damn it, I just want a place where I can eat my own beef.''

''I know what you mean,'' the realtor agreed. ''I have a couple of places you might like.''

''Then let's go see them.'' Russell smiled at the lady.

The second one was perfect. Just off Exit 50, five hundred acres, a nice old farmhouse with a new kitchen, a two-car garage, and three sturdy outbuildings. There was clear land in all directions, a pond with some trees half a mile from the house, and plenty of room for the cattle that Russell would never see.

''This one's been on the market for five months. The owner's estate is asking four hundred,'' the realtor said, ''but we can probably get them to go for three-fifty.''

''Okay,'' Russell said, checking access to Interstate 76. ''Tell them if they sign the contract this week, I'll make a fifty-thousand cash deposit, settlement in, oh, say four or five weeks. No problem on financing. I'll pay cash for the whole thing when I get the rest of my funds transferred. But—I want to start moving in immediately. God, I hate living in hotels, done way too much of that. You think we get all that done?''

The realtor beamed at him. ''I think I can guarantee it.''

''Great. So, how did the Broncos do this year?''

''Eight and eight. They're rebuilding. My husband and I have season tickets. You going to try and get tickets for the Super Bowl?''

''I'd sure like to.''

''Going to be pretty hard,'' the realtor warned him.

''I'll find a way.'' An hour and one telephone call later, the realtor took a cashier's check for fifty thousand dollars from her banker husband. Russell had directions to the local furniture and appliance store. After an hour there, Marvin purchased a white Ford van from the local dealership and drove it to the ranch. He parked it in one of the barns. He'd be keeping the rental for a while. He would spend one more night in the motel, then settle into his new house. He did not feel any sense of accomplishment. There was much left to do.

Cathy Ryan found herself paying closer attention to the newspapers now. They were good for reporting scandals and leaks, and she now had the interest in such things that she had lacked before, especially for the by-line of Robert Holtzman. Unfortunately, the new articles on the problems at CIA were more general, concentrating mainly on changes within the Soviet Union that she had difficulty understanding. It just wasn't an area in which she had much interest—as Jack didn't much care about the developments in eye surgery that his wife was very excited about. Finally there did come a piece about financial impropriety and a ''very senior official.'' That was the second such item and she realized that if it was Jack, she had all the investigatorial documents there in her own home. It was a Sunday, and Jack was away at work again, leaving her at home with the kids again. The kids enjoyed this chilly morning in front of the TV. Cathy Ryan went into the financial files.

They were a disaster. Money management was another thing that failed to interest Dr. Caroline Ryan, and Jack assumed the duties more or less by default, just as cooking fell into her domain. She didn't even know the filing system, and was certain that Jack never expected her to wade into this colossal mess of documents. Along the way, she learned that the blind trust that managed their stock portfolio was doing rather well at the moment. Ordinarily, she just saw the year-end earnings statements. Money didn't interest her very much. The house was paid off. The kids' education funds were already set up. The Ryan family actually lived off the combined income of the two Doctors Ryan, which allowed their investments to grow, while complicating their annual taxes, which was also something that Jack—CPA certification or not—took care of, with the aid of the family's attorney. The most recent statement of net worth drew a gasp. Cathy decided to add the money managers to the Christmas-card list. But that was not what she was after. She found it at two-thirty in the afternoon. The file was simply marked ''Zimmer,'' and was naturally enough in the last drawer she got to.

The Zimmer file was several inches thick. She sat cross-legged on the floor before opening it, her head already aching from eyestrain and the Tylenol which she should have taken but hadn't. The first document was a letter from Jack to an attorney—not their regular attorney, the one who did their wills and taxes and other routine work—instructing him to set up an educational trust fund for seven children, a number which had been changed to eight several months later, Cathy saw. The trust fund had been set up with an initial investment of over half a million dollars, and managed as a stock portfolio through the same managers who did part of the Ryan family account. Cathy was surprised to see that Jack did actually make recommendations for this account, something that he did not do for his own. He hadn't lost his touch, either. The yield from the Zimmer portfolio was twenty-three percent. Another hundred thousand dollars had been invested in a business—a Sub-Chapter-S corporation, she saw, whatever that was—with Southland Corporation as—oh, she realized, a 7-Eleven. It was a Maryland corporation, with the address given as . . .

That's only a few miles from here! It was, in fact, right off of Route 50, and that meant that Jack passed it twice a day on his way to and from work.

How convenient!

So who the hell was Carol Zimmer?

Medical bills? Obstetrics?

Dr. Marsha Rosen! *I know her!* Had Cathy not been on the faculty at Hopkins, she would have used Marsha Rosen for her own pregnancies; Rosen was a Yale graduate with a very fine reputation.

A baby? Jacqueline Zimmer? Jacqueline? Cathy thought, her face flushed scarlet. Then the tears began streaming down her cheeks.

You bastard! You can't give me a baby, but you gave one to her, didn't you!

She checked the date, then searched her memory. Jack hadn't been home that day until very late. She remembered, because she'd had to cancel out on a dinner party over at . . .

He was there! He was there for the delivery, wasn't he! What more proof do I need? The triumph of the discovery changed at once into black despair.

The world could end so easily, Cathy thought. Just a slip of paper could do it, and that was it. It was over.

Is it over?

How could it not be? Even if he still wanted—did she want him?

What about the kids? Cathy asked herself. She closed the file and replaced it without rising. "You're a doctor," she said to herself. "You're supposed to think before you act."

The kids needed a father. But what sort of father was he? Gone thirteen or fourteen hours a day, sometimes seven days a week. He managed to take his son to one—just one!—baseball game despite constant pleas. He was lucky to make half of Little Jack's T-Ball games. He missed *every* school affair, the Christmas plays, all the other things. Cathy had been half surprised that he'd been home Christmas morning. The night before, assembling the toys, he'd gotten drunk again, and she hadn't even bothered trying to attract him. What was the point? His present to her . . . well, it was nice enough, but the sort of thing a man could get in a few minutes of shopping, no big deal—

Shopping.

Cathy rose and checked through the mail on Jack's desk. His credit card bills were sitting in the pile. She opened one and found a bunch of entries from . . . Hamleys, in London. Six hundred dollars? But he'd only gotten one thing for Little Jack, and two small items for Sally. Six hundred dollars!

Christmas shopping for two *families, Jack?*

"Just how much more evidence do you need, Cathy girl?" she asked herself aloud again. "Oh God oh God oh God . . ."

She didn't move for a very long time, nor did she see or hear anything outside of her own misery. Only the mother in her kept subconscious track of the sound of the kids in the playroom.

Jack got home just before seven that evening, actually rather pleased with himself to be an hour early, and further pleased that he had the Mexico operation set in concrete now. All he had to do was take it to the White House, and then after he got it approved—Fowler would go for this; risks and all, distaste for covert operations and all, this was too juicy for the politician in him to turn down—and after Clark and Chavez brought it off, his stock would go up. And things would change. Things would get better. He would get things straightened out. For starters, he'd plan a vacation. It was time for one. A week off, maybe two, and if some CIA puke showed up with daily briefing documents, Ryan would kill the son of a bitch. He wanted freedom from the job, and he'd get it. Two good weeks. Take the kids out of school and go see Mickey, just as Clark had suggested. He'd make the reservations tomorrow.

"I'm home!" Jack announced. Silence. That was odd. He went downstairs and found the kids in front of the TV. They were doing too damned much of that, but that was their father's fault. He'd change that, too. He'd cut back on his hours. It was time Marcus held up his end instead of working banker's hours and leaving Jack with all the goddamned work.

"Where's Mommy?"

"I don't know," Sally said without turning away from the green slime and orange guck.

Ryan walked back upstairs and into the bedroom to change. Still no sign of his wife. He found her carrying a basket of wash. Jack stood in her path, leaning forward to kiss her, but she leaned back and shook her head. Okay, that was no big thing.

"What's for dinner, babe?" he inquired lightly.

"I don't know. Why don't you fix something?" It was her tone, the snappy way she fired back without provocation.

"What did I do?" Jack asked. He was already surprised, but he hadn't had time enough to grasp her demeanor. The look in her eyes was an alien thing, and when she answered to this question, her voice made him shrivel.

"Nothing, Jack, you haven't done anything at all." She pushed past him with the basket and disappeared around the corner.

He just stood there, flat against the wall, his mouth open, not knowing what to say, and not understanding why his wife had suddenly decided to despise him.

It took only a day and a half from Latakia to Piraeus. Bock had found a ship heading to the right port, eliminating the need to transship at Rotterdam. Qati disliked deviation from the plan, but a careful check of shipping schedules showed that the five days saved might be important, and he agreed to it. He and Ghosn watched the gantry crane lift up the cargo container and move it onto the deck of the *Carmen Vita,* a Greek-flag container ship on the Mediterranean run. She would sail on the evening tide, and arrive in the United States in eleven days. They could have chartered a jet aircraft and done this, Qati thought, but it would have been too dangerous. Eleven days. He'd be able to see his physician again, and still have time to fly to America and make certain that all the arrangements were satisfactory. The workers secured the container box in place. It would be well protected, in the center of the ship, with other boxes atop it, and well aft so that winter storms would not buffet it directly. The two men retired to a waterfront bar and waited for the ship to sail, then flew to Damascus and drove from there to their headquarters. The bomb shop was already gone—mothballed would have been a more accurate term. The power cables had been cut, and dirt pushed over all the entrances. If someone ever drove a heavy truck over the concealed roof there would be a major surprise, but that was unlikely. It *was* possible that they might use the facility again, and against that slim possibility was the inconvenience of removing the machines to another burial place. Simply covering the facility over was the most logical alternative.

Russell flew to Chicago to catch the first round of playoff games. He took with him a camera, an expensive Nikon F4, and burned up two rolls of ASA-100 color prints photographing the ABC trucks—the *Monday Night Football* team was doing this particular wild-card game—before catching a cab back to the airport. He was lucky enough on the flight that he caught part of the game on the radio during the drive from Stapleton International to his new house off Interstate 76. The Bears pulled it out in overtime, 23–20. That meant that Chicago would have the honor of losing the following week to the Vikings in the Metrodome. Minnesota had a bye during the first week of wild-card games. Tony Wills' pulled groin would be fully healed, and that rookie, the announcer pointed out, had barely missed making two thousand rushing yards in his first NFL season, plus eight hundred yards as a receiver. Russell managed to catch nearly all of the AFC game because it was played on the West Coast. There were no surprises, but it was still football.

USS *Maine* left the shed without incident. Tugs turned her around, pointing the submarine down the channel, and continued to stand by if assistance were required. Captain Ricks stood atop the sail, actually aft of the cockpit, leaning against rails set in the very top of the structure. Lieutenant Commander Claggett stood his watch in the control room. The navigator actually did the work, using the periscope to mark positions, which a quartermaster dutifully checked off on the chart, ensuring that the submarine was in the center of the channel and headed in the proper direction. The trip to sea was a fairly lengthy one. Throughout the boat, men continued to stow gear. Those not actually on watch settled into their bunks and tried to nap. Soon *Maine* would be on her regular six-hour watch cycle. The sailors all made the conscious effort to get their minds from land-mode into at-sea-mode. Families and friends might as well have been on another planet. For the next two months their entire world was contained within the steel hull of their submarine.

Mancuso watched the sailing as he always did for each of his boats. It was a shame, he decided, that there was no way to get Ricks off the boat. But there was no such way. He'd meet with Group in a few days to go over routine business. At that meeting he'd express his misgivings about Ricks. He would not be able to go too far this first time, just to let Group know that he had his doubts about the "Gold" CO. The quasi-political nature of the exercise grated on Mancuso, who liked things in the open and aboveboard, the Navy Way. But the Navy Way had its own rules of behavior, and in the absence of substantive cause for action, all he could do now was express concern with Ricks and his way of running things. Besides, Group was headed by yet another hyper-engineering type who would probably have a little too much sympathy with Harry.

Mancuso tried to find an emotion for the moment, but failed. The slate-gray shape diminished in the distance, gliding across the oily-calm waters of the harbor, heading out for her fifth deterrence patrol, as U.S. Navy submarines had been doing for over thirty years. Business as usual, world changes and all, that's all it was. *Maine* sailed out to keep the peace through the threat of the most inhuman force known to man. The Commodore shook his head. What a hell of a way to run a railroad. That was why he'd always been a fast-attack man. But it worked, had worked, probably would continue to work for a lot more years, Bart told himself, and while not every boomer skipper was another Mush Morton, they'd all brought their boats back. He got into his navy-blue official car and told the driver to take him back to the office. Paperwork beckoned.

At least the kids didn't notice. Jack took some comfort in that. Kids lived as spectators in a highly complex world which required years of schooling to appreciate, as a result of which they took note mainly of the parts that they understood, and that did not include a mom and dad who simply didn't talk. It wouldn't last forever, of course, but it might last long enough for things to be smoothed over. Probably would, Jack thought. Sure it would.

He didn't know what was wrong, nor did he know what to do about it. What he ought to have done, of course, was get home at a decent hour, maybe take her out to dinner at a nice place and—but that was not possible with two kids in school. Getting a sitter in the middle of the week and this far out of town was impractical. Another option was simply to get home and pay closer attention to his wife, leading to a—

But he couldn't depend on his ability to do that, and one more failure could only make things worse.

He looked up from his desk, out at the pines that lay beyond the CIA boundary fence. The symmetry was perfect. His work was messing up his family life, and now his family life was messing up his work. So now he had nothing at all that he could do properly. Wasn't that nice? Ryan got up from his desk and left the office, wandering to the nearest kiosk. Once there he purchased his first pack of cigarettes in . . . five years? Six? Whatever, he stripped off the cellophane top and tapped one out. One luxury of having a private office was that he could smoke without interference—CIA had become just like all government offices in that respect; for the most part, people could smoke only in the rest rooms. He pretended not to see the disapproving look on Nancy's face on his way back in, then went rooting in his desk for an ashtray before lighting up.

It was, he decided a minute later—just as the initial dizziness hit him—one of the dependable pleasures of life. Alcohol was another. You ingested these substances and you got the desired result, which explained their popularity in spite of the dangers to health that everyone knew about. Alcohol and nicotine, the two things that make intolerable life into something else. While they shortened it.

Wasn't that just great? Ryan almost laughed at his incredible stupidity. Just what else of himself would he destroy? But did it matter?

His work mattered. That he was sure of. That was what had landed him in this mess, one way or another. That was the prime destructive factor in his life, but he could no more leave that than he could change anything else.

"Nancy, please ask Mr. Clark to come in."

John appeared two minutes later. "Aw, hell, doc!" he observed almost immediately. "Now, what's the wife gonna say?"

"Not a thing."

"Bet you're wrong on that." Clark turned to open a window for ventilation. He'd quit a long time before. It was the one vice that he feared. It had killed his father. "What do you want?"

"How's the hardware?"

"Waiting for your go-ahead to build it."

"Go," Jack said simply.

"You got a go-mission order?"

"No, but I don't need it. We'll call it part of the feasibility study. How long to slap things together?"

"Three days, they say. We'll need some cooperation from the Air Force."

"What about the computer side?"

"That program has already been validated. They've taken tapes from six different aircraft and smoothed out the noise. It's never taken them more than two or three hours to do an hour of tape."

"Mexico City to D.C. is . . ."

"Depending on weather, just under four hours, max. Doing the full tape will be an overnighter," Clark estimated. "The President's schedule is what?"

"Arrival ceremony is Monday afternoon. The first business session is the following morning. State dinner Tuesday night."

"You going?"

Ryan shook his head. "No, we're going to the one a week earlier—geez, that's not too far off, is it? I'll call the 89th Wing at Andrews. They do training hops all the time. Getting your team aboard won't be hard."

"I have three capture teams selected. They're all ex-Air Force and -Navy elint spooks," Clark said. "They know the business."

"Okay, run with it."

"You got it, doc."

Jack watched him leave and lit up another.

29. Crossroads

MV *Carmen Vita* cleared the Strait of Gibraltar right on schedule, her Pielstick diesels driving her at a constant nineteen knots. The crew of forty officers and men (this ship did not have any women in the crew, though three of the officers had their wives with them) settled down for the normal sailing routine of watch-keeping and maintenance. They were seven days out from the Virginia Capes. On her deck and stowed below were a goodly number of standard-sized container boxes. These actually came in two sizes, and they were all loaded with various types of cargo which the captain and crew neither knew nor cared very much about. The whole point of containerization was that the ship was used exclusively as a contract-hauler, much as a trucker was used by various businesses. All the ship's crew needed to worry about was the weight of the containers, and that always seemed to work out rather uniformly, since the containers themselves were always loaded to reflect what a commercial truck could legally pull along a public highway.

The ship's southerly routing also made for a fairly sedate and uneventful passage. The really bitter winter storms followed a more northerly track, and the ship's master, a native of India, was happy for it. A youngish man for such a substantial command—he was only thirty-seven—he knew that good weather made for a fast and fuel-efficient voyage. He aspired to a larger and more sumptuous ship, and by keeping *Carmen Vita* on schedule and under budget, he'd get that in due course.

It was the tenth day in a row that Clark hadn't seen Mrs. Ryan. John Clark had a good memory for such things, honed by years of field operations of one sort or another in which one stayed alive by keeping track of everything whether it seemed important or not. He'd never seen her more than twice in a row. Jack worked an inconvenient schedule—but so did she, with early-morning surgery at least twice a week . . . and she was awake this morning. He saw her head through the kitchen window, sitting at a table, probably drinking coffee and reading the paper or watching TV. But she hadn't even turned her head to look at her husband when he left, had she? Ordinarily she got up to kiss him goodbye like any wife. Ten days in a row.

Not a good sign, was it? What was the problem? Jack came out to the car, his face dark and looking down. There was the grimace again.

"Morning, doc!" Clark greeted him cheerily.

"Hi, John," was the subdued reply. He hadn't brought his paper again, either. He started reading from the dispatch box as usual, and by the time they reached the the D.C. Beltway, he'd just be staring, a grim thousand-yard stare in his eyes as he lit a continuous chain of cigarettes. Clark decided that he just couldn't stand it anymore:

"Problem at home, doc?" he asked quietly, watching the road.

"Yeah, but it's my problem."

"Guess so. The kids are okay?"

"It's not the kids, John. Leave it, okay?"

"Right." Clark concentrated on his driving while Ryan went through the message traffic.

What the hell is the problem? Be analytical, Clark told himself, *think it through.* His boss had been depressed for over a month now, but it had really gotten worse—the news article, that thing from Holtzman? A family problem, not involving the kids. That meant trouble with the wife. He made a mental note to recheck that piece and any subsequent pieces when he got into the office. Seventy minutes after picking Ryan up—traffic was light this morning—he headed for CIA's rather impressive library and got the staff there busy. It wasn't hard for them. The Agency kept a special file for all the pieces that concerned it, arranged in folders by the authors' by-lines. The problem, Clark thought, was immediately clear.

Holtzman had talked about financial and sexual misconduct. Right after that article came out . . .

"Aw, shit," Clark whispered to himself. He made copies of the various recent pieces—there were four of them—and went for a walk to clear his head. One nice thing about being a SPO, especially a SPO assigned to Ryan, was that he had very little work to do. Ryan was a homebody while in Langley. He didn't really move around all that much. As he took a quick walking tour of the grounds, he reread the news articles and made another connection. The Sunday piece. Ryan had gone home early that day. He'd been upbeat, talking about getting away right after the Mexican job, taking John's advice for a trip to Florida—but the next morning he'd looked like a corpse. And he wasn't bringing the paper out with him. His wife must have been reading it, and something had gone very bad between Ryan and his wife. That seemed reasonably clear. Clear enough for Clark.

Clark came back into the building, going through the normal routine of passing through the computer-controlled gates, then setting off to locate Chavez, who was in the New Headquarters Building. John found him in an office, going over schedules.

"Ding, get your coat." Ten minutes later they were on the D.C. Beltway. Chavez was checking a map.

"Okay," Chavez said. "I have it. Broadway and Monument, up from the harbor."

Russell was dressed in coveralls. The photos of the ABC vans in Chicago had turned out very well, and he'd had a lab in Boulder blow them up to poster size. These he compared to his van—it was exactly the same model of utility van—to make precise measurements. What came next wasn't easy. He'd purchased a dozen large sheets of semirigid plastic, and he began carving them to make an exact match of the ABC logo. As he finished each, he taped it to the side of his van and used a marker pencil to scribe in the letters. It required six attempts to get it right, and Russell next used the knife to make reference marks on the van. It seemed a pity to score the paint on the van, but he reminded himself that the van would be blown up anyway, and there was no sense in getting sentimental about a truck. On the whole, he was proud of his artistic talents. He hadn't had a chance to exercise them since he'd learned a trade in the prison shop, many years before. When the logo was painted on, black letters on the white-painted truck, nobody would be able to tell the difference.

The next job of the day was to drive to the local motor-vehicle agency to get commercial tags for the van. He explained that he would use it for his electronics business, installing and servicing commercial phone systems. He walked out with temporary tags, and they promised delivery of the real ones in four working days, which struck Russell as unnecessarily efficient. Getting the license was even easier. The international licensing documents that Ghosn had provided to go along with his passport were honored by the State of Colorado, after he passed a written test, and he had a photo-certified license card to go along with the tags. His only "mistake" was messing up one of the forms, but the clerk let him sign a fresh one while Russell dumped the first in the trash can. Or appeared to. The blank form slid into the pocket of his parka.

Johns Hopkins Hospital is not located in the best of neighborhoods. As compensation for that fact the Baltimore City Police guarded it in a way that reminded Clark of his time in Vietnam. He found a parking place on Broadway, just across from the main entrance. Then he and Chavez went in, walking around the marble statue of Jesus which both found rather admirable in size and execution. The large complex—Hopkins is a vast facility—made finding the right part difficult, but ten minutes later they were sitting outside The Wilmer Eye Institute office of Associate Professor Caroline M. Ryan, M.D., F.A.C.S. Clark relaxed and read a magazine while Chavez cast his lecherous dark eyes on the receptionist whom Mrs. Ryan evidently rated. The other Dr. Ryan, as Clark thought of her, showed up at 12:35 with an armful of documents. She gave the two CIA officers a *who-are-you* look and breezed into her office without a word. It didn't take much of a look on his part either.

She'd always appeared to him a very attractive and dignified female. Not now. Her face, if anything, was in worse shape than her husband's. This really was getting out of hand, John thought. Clark gave it a ten-count and just walked past the open-mouthed receptionist to begin his newest career, marriage counselor.

"What is this?" Cathy asked. "I don't have any appointments today."

"Ma'am, I need a few minutes of your time."

"Who are you? Are you going to ask me about Jack?"

"Ma'am, my name is Clark." He reached into his shirt pocket and pulled out the card-sized CIA photo-pass, attached as most were to a metal chain that went around his neck. "There may be some things you need to know about."

Cathy's eyes went hard almost at once, the anger taking over from the hurt. "I know," she said. "I've heard it all."

"No, ma'am, I think that you do not know. This isn't a good place to talk. May I invite you to lunch?"

"Around here? The streets aren't all that—"

"Safe?" Clark smiled to show just how absurd her observation was.

For the first time Caroline Ryan applied a professional eye to her visitor. He was about Jack's height but bulkier. Whereas she had once found her husband's face manly, Clark's was rugged. His hands looked large and powerful, and his body language proclaimed that he could deal with anything. More impressive was his demeanor. The man could have intimidated almost anyone, she realized, but he was going out of his way to appear gentlemanly, and succeeding, like the ballplayers who sometimes came here to see the kids. *Teddy bear* was what she thought. Not because he was, but because he wanted to be.

"There's a place right down Monument Street."

"Fine." Clark turned and lifted her overcoat from the clothes tree. He held it almost daintily for her to put it on. Chavez joined them outside. He was much smaller than Clark, but more overtly dangerous, like a gang kid who was trying to smooth off his edges. Chavez, she saw, took the lead as they walked outside, preceding them up the sidewalk in a way that was almost comical. The streets here were not what she thought safe—at least not for a woman walking alone, though that was more a problem at night than during the day—but Chavez moved like a man in battle. That, she thought, was interesting. They found the small restaurant quickly, and Clark steered everyone into a corner booth. Both the men had their backs to the wall so that they could stare outward at any incoming threat. Both had their coats unbuttoned, though they both seemed outwardly relaxed.

"Who exactly are you?" she asked. The whole affair was like something from a bad movie.

"I'm your husband's driver," John replied. "I'm a field officer, paramilitary type. I've been with the Agency for almost twenty years."

"You're not supposed to tell people stuff like that."

Clark just shook his head. "Ma'am, we haven't even started breaking laws yet. Now I'm mainly a Security and Protective Officer, a SPO. Ding Chavez here is also a SPO."

"Hello, Doctor Ryan. My real name is Domingo." He held out his hand. "I work with your husband also. John and I drive him around and protect him on trips and stuff."

"You're both carrying guns?"

Ding almost looked embarrassed. "Yes, ma'am."

With that, the adventurous part of the meeting ended, Cathy thought. Two obviously very tough men were trying to charm her. They had even succeeded. But that didn't change her problem. She was about to say something, but Clark started off first.

"Ma'am, there seems to be a problem between you and your husband. I don't know what it is—I think I know some of it—but I do know that it's hurting the guy. That's bad for the Agency."

"Gentlemen, I appreciate your concern, but this is a private matter."

"Yes, ma'am," Clark responded in his eerily polite voice. He reached into his pocket and pulled out Xerox copies of the Holtzman articles. "Is this the problem?"

"That's not any of your . . ." Her mouth clamped shut.

"I thought so. Ma'am, none of this is true. I mean, the sexual impropriety part. That's definitely not true. Your husband hardly goes anywhere without one of us. Because of where he works and who he is, he has to sign out for every place he goes to—like a doctor on call, okay? If you want I can get you copies of his itinerary for as far back as you want."

"That can't be legal."

"No, it probably isn't," Clark agreed. "So?"

She so wanted to believe, Cathy thought, but she couldn't, and it was best to tell them why. "Look, your loyalty to Jack is very impressive—but I *know,* okay? I went through the financial records, and I know about that Zimmer woman, and I know about the kid!"

"What exactly do you know?"

"I know that Jack was there for the delivery. I know about the money, and how he tried to hide it from me and everybody else. I know that he's being investigated by the government."

"What do you mean?"

"A government investigator was here at Hopkins! I know that!"

"Dr. Ryan, there is no such investigation at CIA, and no investigation at the FBI, either. That's a fact."

"Then who was here?"

"I'm afraid I don't know that," Clark answered. It wasn't entirely true, but Clark figured this lie was not pertinent to the matter at hand.

"Look, I know about Carol Zimmer," she said again.

"What do you know?" Clark repeated quietly. The response he got surprised him.

The answer almost came out as a scream. "Jack's playing around, and she's the one! And there's a kid involved, and Jack is spending so much time with her that he doesn't have any time for me and he can't even—" She stopped, at the point of sobbing.

Clark waited for her to settle down. His eyes didn't leave her face for an instant, and he saw it all as clearly as though it had been printed on a page. Ding merely looked embarrassed. He wasn't old enough to understand.

"Will you hear me through?"

"Sure, why not? It's over, the only reason I haven't just walked out is the kids. So go ahead, make your pitch. Tell me that he still loves me and all that. He doesn't have the guts to talk about it to me himself, but I'm sure he had something to do with this," she concluded bitterly.

"First of all, he does not know we are here. If he finds out, I'll probably lose my job, but that's no big thing. I have my retirement. Besides, I'm about to break bigger rules than that one. Where do I begin?" Clark paused before going on.

"Carol Zimmer is a widow. Her husband was Chief Master Sergeant Buck Zimmer, U.S. Air Force. He died in the line of duty. As a matter of fact, he died in your husband's arms. I know. I was there. Buck took five rounds in the chest. Both lungs. It took him five or six minutes to die. He left behind seven children—eight, if you count the one his wife was carrying. Buck didn't know about that one when he died. Carol was waiting to surprise him.

"Sergeant Zimmer was the crew chief on an Air Force special-operations helicopter. We took that aircraft into a foreign country to rescue a group of U.S. Army soldiers who were conducting a covert mission."

"I was one of 'em, ma'am," Ding announced, somewhat to Clark's displeasure. "I wouldn't be here if the doc hadn't put it out on the line."

"The soldiers had been deliberately cut off from support from this end of the operation—"

"Who?"

"He's dead now," Clark answered in a way that left no doubt at all. "Your husband uncovered what was an illegal operation. He and Dan Murray of the FBI set up the rescue mission. It was a bad one, really tough. We were very lucky to get it done. I'm surprised you haven't noticed something—nightmares, maybe?"

"He doesn't sleep well—well, yes, sometimes he . . ."

"Dr. Ryan missed having a bullet take his head off by . . . oh, maybe two inches, maybe three. We had to rescue a squad of soldiers off a hilltop, and they were under attack. Jack worked one machine gun. Buck Zimmer had another one. Buck took hits as we lifted out, went down hard. Jack and I tried to help him, but I don't even think you Hopkins guys could have done very much. It wasn't real pretty. He died—" Clark stopped for a moment, and Cathy could see that he wasn't faking the pain. "He was talking about his kids. Worried about 'em, like any man would be. Your husband held Zimmer in his arms and promised him that he would look after them, that he'd see they were all educated, that he would take care of the family. Ma'am, I've been in this business a long time, back before you learned how to drive a car, okay? I've never seen anything better than what Jack did.

"After we got back, Jack did what he promised. I mean, of course. I'm not surprised he kept it a secret from you. There are aspects to the total operation that I do not know myself. But this much I do know: that man gives his word, he keeps it. I helped. We got the family moved up here from Florida. He set them up a little business. One of the kids is already in college, at Georgetown, and the second-oldest is already accepted into MIT. I forgot to tell you, Carol Zimmer—well, Carol ain't her name. She was born in Laos. Zimmer got her out when everything went to hell there, married her, and they started punching out kids like movie tickets. Anyway, she's a typical Asian mom. She thinks education is a gift from God Himself, and those kids really study hard. They all think your husband's a saint. We stop in to see them at least once a week, every week."

"I want to believe you," Cathy said. "What about the baby?"

"You mean when it was born? Yeah, we were both there. My wife was the coach for the delivery—Jack didn't think it was right for him to be in the room, and I've never been there for one. It kind of scares me," Clark admitted. "So we waited in the usual place with all the other wimps. If you want, I can introduce you to the Zimmer family. You can also confirm the story through Dan Murray at the FBI, if you think that is necessary."

"Won't that get you into trouble?" Cathy knew at once that she could trust Murray. He was strait-laced on moral issues; it came from being a cop.

"I will definitely lose my job. I suppose they could prosecute me—technically I have just committed a federal felony—but I doubt it would go that far. Ding would lose his job, too, because he hasn't had the sense to keep his mouth shut like I told him to."

"Shit," Ding commented, then looked embarrassed. "Excuse me, ma'am. John, this is a matter of honor. 'Cept for the doc, I'd be fertilizer on some Colombian hilltop. I owe him my life. That counts more than a job, *'mano.*"

Clark handed over an index card. "These are the dates of the operation. You may remember that when Admiral Greer died, Jack didn't make the funeral."

"Yes! Bob Ritter called me, and—"

"That's when it was. You can verify all of this with Mr. Murray."

"God!" It all hit her at once.

"Yes, ma'am. All the garbage in these articles. It's all a lie."

"Who's doing it?"

"I don't know, but I am going to find out. Doctor, I've been watching your guy come apart for the past six months. I've seen it happen before, in combat—I spent quite some time in Vietnam—but this has been worse. That Vatican Treaty, the way the Middle East is settling down. Jack had a big part in that, but he isn't getting any credit at all. Exactly what part he played, I'm not sure. He's pretty good at keeping secrets. That's part of his problem. He keeps it all inside. You do that too much and it's like cancer, like acid or something. It eats you up. It's eating him up, and this crap in the papers has made it a lot worse.

"All I can say, doc, is this: I don't know a better man than your husband, and I've been around the block a few times. He's put it on the line more than the times you know about, but there's people around who don't like him very much, and those people are trying to get him in a way that he can't deal with. It's typical, dirty, underhanded crap, but Jack's not the kind of guy who can deal with that. He plays by the rules, you see. So it's eating him up."

Cathy was weeping now. Clark handed her a handkerchief.

"I figured you should know. If you think it's necessary, I want you to check it out as much as you think you have to. That's your decision, and I want you to make the call without worrying about me or Ding or anybody else, okay? I'll take you to see Carol Zimmer and the kids. If I lose my job—the hell with it. I've been in the business too damned long anyway."

"Christmas presents?"

"For the Zimmer kids? Yeah, I helped wrap them. Your husband can't wrap presents worth a damn, but I suppose you know that. I even delivered some of my own. My two are too grown for fun presents, and they're great kids, the Zimmers. It's nice being an uncle," John added with a genuine smile.

"All a lie?"

"I don't know about the financial stuff, just the other things. And they tried to get at him through you, judging by what you just said."

The tears stopped at that moment. Cathy wiped her eyes and looked up. "You're right. You said you don't know who's doing this?"

"I'm planning to find out," Clark promised her. Her demeanor had changed completely. This was some broad.

"I want you to let me know. And I want to meet the Zimmer family."

"When do you get off work?"

"I have to make a few phone calls and some notes—say an hour?"

"I can squeeze that in, but I may have to leave early. They have a 7-Eleven about ten miles from your place."

"I know it's close, but not exactly where."

"You can follow me down."

"Let's go." Cathy led them out, or tried to. Chavez beat her out the door, and held the point all the way back to the hospital. He and Clark decided to stay outside and get some air, then spotted two youths sitting on their car.

It was strange, John Clark thought as he crossed the street. At the beginning Caroline Ryan had been the angry one, angry and betrayed. He'd been the voice of understanding. Now she was feeling much better—though worse in another way—but he had absorbed all of her anger. It was a little too much to bear, and there in front of him was an outlet for it.

"Off the car, punk!"

"Christ, John!" Ding said behind him.

"Says who!" the youth said, hardly turning to see the man approaching. He got his head around just in time to see the hand grasp his shoulder. Then the world rotated and the brick wall of a building approached his face very rapidly. Fortunately, his boom-box absorbed most of the impact, which however had a negative effect on the boom-box.

"Motherfucker!" the kid snarled, coming out with a knife. His companion was six feet away, and also had a knife out.

Clark just smiled at them. "Who's first?"

The thought of avenging his appliance died a quick death. Both youths knew danger when they saw it.

"You lucky I don't have my gun, man!"

"You can leave the knives, too."

"You a cop?"

"No, I am not a policeman," Clark said, walking over with his hand out. Chavez backed him up, his coat opened, as both youths noticed. They dropped their knives and started walking away.

"What the hell is—"

Clark turned to see a policeman approaching, with a large dog. Both were fully alert. John pulled out his CIA pass. "I didn't like their attitude."

Chavez handed the knives over. "They dropped these, sir."

"You really should leave that sort of thing to us."

"Yes, sir," Clark agreed. "You're right. Nice dog you have there."

The cop pocketed the knives. "Have a good one," he said, wondering what the hell this had been about.

"You, too, officer." Clark paused and turned to Chavez. "Goddamn, that felt good."

"Ready to go to Mexico, John?"

"Yeah. I just hate leaving unfinished business behind, you know?"

"So who's trying to fuck him over?"

"Not sure."

"Bull," Ding observed.

"Won't be sure until I talk to Holtzman."

"You say so, man. I like her," he added. "That's some lady."

"Yeah, she is. Just what he needs to set things straight."

"You think she'll call that Murray guy?"

"Does it matter?"

"No." Chavez looked up the street. "A question of honor, Mr. C."

"I knew you'd understand, Ding."

Jacqueline Zimmer was a beautiful child, Cathy thought, holding her. She wanted another, must have another. Jack would give her one, maybe another girl if they were lucky.

"We hear so much 'bout you!" Carol said. "You doctor?"

"Yes, I teach doctors, I'm a professor of surgery."

"My oldes' son must meet you. He want to be doctor. He student at Georgetown."

"Maybe I can help him a little. Can I ask you a question?"

"Yes."

"Your husband . . ."

"Buck? He die. I don't know all the things, just that he die—on duty, yes? Is secret thing. Very hard for me," Carol said soberly, but without overt grief. She was over that now. "Buck was a very good man. So your husban'. You be nice to him," Mrs. Zimmer added.

"Oh, I will," Cathy promised. "Now, we have to make this a secret?"

"What secret?"

"Jack doesn't know that I know about you."

"Oh? I know there are many secret, but—okay, I un'erstan'. I keep this secret, too."

"I will talk to Jack about that. I think you should come to our house and meet our children. But for now, we keep the secret?"

"Yes, okay. We surprise him?"

"Right." Cathy smiled as she handed the child back. "I will see you again, soon."

"Feel better, doc?" Clark asked her out in the parking lot.

"Thank you . . ."

"Call me John."

"Thanks, John." It was the warmest smile since his kids' at Christmas.

"Anytime."

Clark drove west on Route 50. Cathy turned east for home. Her knuckles were white on the steering wheel of her car. The anger was back now. For the most part she was angry at herself. How could she have thought that of Jack? She'd been very foolish, very small, and so disgustingly selfish. But it wasn't really her fault. Someone else had invaded their household, she decided as she pulled into the garage. She was on the phone almost immediately. She had to do one more thing. She had to be completely certain.

"Hi, Dan."

"Cathy! How's the eye business, kid?" Murray asked.

"Got a question for you."

"Shoot."

She'd already decided how to do it. "There's a problem with Jack. . . ."

Murray's voice became guarded. "What is it?"

"He's having nightmares," Cathy said. It wasn't a lie, but what followed was. "Something about a helicopter, and Buck somebody . . . I can't ask him about it, but—"

Murray cut her off. "Cathy, I can't talk about it over the phone. That's a business matter, kid."

"Really?"

"Really, Cathy. It's something I know about, but I cannot discuss it with you. I'm sorry, but that's the way it has to be. It's business."

Cathy went on with a touch of alarm in her voice. "It's not something that's happening now—I mean—"

"It's way in the past, Cathy. That's all I can say. If you think Jack needs professional help, then I can make a few calls and—"

"No, I don't think so. It was really bad a few months ago, but it does seem to be getting better. I was just worried that it might be something at the office. . . ."

"All behind him, Cathy. Honest."

"You sure, Dan?"

"Positive. I would not kid around on something like this."

And that, Cathy knew, was that. Dan was every bit as honest as Jack was. "Thanks, Dan. Thanks a lot," she said in her best medical voice, the one that revealed nothing at all.

"Anytime, Cathy." By the time he hung up, Murray wondered if he'd just been had in some way. No, he decided, there was no way she could have found out about that.

Had he seen the other end of the disconnected phone line, he would have been surprised to discover how wrong he was. Cathy sat alone in the kitchen, crying one last time. She'd had to check, there had not been a choice to purge all the emotions from her soul, but now she was completely certain that Clark had spoken the truth; that someone was trying to hurt her husband, that whoever it was was willing to use his wife and his family against him. *Who could ever hate a man so much that they would try that?* she wondered.

Whoever it was was her enemy. Whoever it was had attacked her and her family just as coldly as those terrorists had done, but much more cravenly.

Whoever it was would pay for that.

"Where have you been?"

"Sorry, doc. I had some errands to run." Clark had come back through the S&T office. "Here."

"What's this?" Ryan took the bottle. It was an expensive container of Chivas Regal in a ceramic bottle. The sort you couldn't see through.

"That's our transceiver. They made up four of them. Nice job, isn't it? Here's the pickup." Clark handed over a green stick, almost the thickness of a cocktail straw, but not quite. "It'll look like a plastic doodad to hold the flowers in place. We decided to use three of them. The techies say they can multiplex the outbound transmissions, and for some reason or other they can crunch the computer time down to one-to-one. They also say that if we had another few months to play with the comm links, we could almost real-time the whole thing."

"What we have is enough," Jack said. Here and now "almost" was better than perfect too late. "I've funded enough research projects."

"I agree. What about the test flights?"

"Tomorrow, ten o'clock."

"Super." Clark stood. "Hey, doc, how about you call it a day? You look wasted."

"I think you're right. Give me another hour and I'm out of here."
"Fair enough."

Russell met them at Atlanta. They'd come across through Mexico City, thence through Miami, where the customs people were very interested in drugs, but not particularly interested in Greek businessmen who opened their bags without being asked. Russell, who was now Robert Friend of Roggen, Colorado—with the driver's license to prove it—shook hands with both of them and helped to collect their baggage.
"Weapons?" Qati asked.
"Not here, man. I have everything you need at home."
"Any problems?"
"Not one." Russell was silent for a moment. "Maybe there is one."
"What?" Ghosn asked with concealed alarm. Being on foreign soil always made him nervous, and this was his first trip to America.
"Cold as hell where we're going, guys. You might want to get some decent coats."
"That can wait," the Commander decided. He was feeling very bad now. The latest batch of chemotherapy had denied him food for nearly two days, and as much as he craved nourishment, his stomach rebelled at the mere sight of it in one of the airport fast-food stands. "What about our flight?"
"Hour and a half. How about you get some sweaters, okay? Follow me. I'm not foolin' about the weather. It's like zero where we're going."
"Zero? That is not so—" Ghosn stopped. "You mean below zero, centigrade?"
Russell stopped for a second. "Oh. Yeah, that's right. Zero here means something different. Zero's cold, guys, okay?"
"As you say," Qati agreed. Half an hour later they had thick woolen sweaters to go under their thin raincoats. The mostly empty Delta flight to Denver left on time. Three hours later they walked off their last jetway for a while. Ghosn had never seen so much snow in his life.
"I can hardly breathe," Qati said.
"It'll take you a day to get used to the altitude. You guys go get the luggage. I'll get the car and warm it up for you."
"If he's betrayed us," Qati said as Russell walked away, "we'll know it in the next few minutes."
"He has not," Ghosn replied. "He is a strange man, but a faithful one."
"He is an infidel, a pagan."
"That is true, but he also listened to an imam in my presence. At least he was polite. I tell you, he is faithful."
"We will see," Qati said, walking tiredly and breathlessly to the baggage-claim level. Both men looked around as they moved, searching for eyes. That was always the giveaway, the eyes that fixed on you. It was hard even for the most professional of men to keep from looking at their targets.
They collected their luggage without incident, and Marvin was waiting. He could not stop the blast of air from hitting them, and thin as the air was, it was also colder than either had ever experienced. The heat of the car was welcome indeed.
"How go the preparations?"
"Everything is on schedule, Commander," Russell said. He drove off. The Arabs were quietly impressed by the vast open space, the broad interstate highway—they found the speed-limit signs very strange—and the obvious wealth in the area. They

were also impressed with Russell, who had manifestly done quite well. Both men rested easier that he had not betrayed them. It was not that Qati had actually expected it, rather that he knew that his vulnerability increased as they got closer to the final part of the plan. That, he knew, was normal.

The farm was of a good size. Russell had thoughtfully overheated it somewhat, but what Qati noted most of all was its obvious defensibility, with a clear field of fire in all directions. He got them inside and carried the bags for them.

"You guys have to be pretty tired," Marvin observed. "Why don't you just bed down? You're safe here, okay?" Qati took the advice. Ghosn did not. He and Russell went to the kitchen. Ibrahim was happy to learn that Marvin was a skilled cook.

"What is this meat?"

"Venison—deer meat. I know you can't eat pork, but you got any problems with deer?" the American asked.

Ghosn shook his head. "No, but I have never had it."

"It's okay, I promise. I found this at a local store this morning. Native-American soul food, man. This is good mule deer. There's a game-rancher around here who grows them commercially. I can try you out on beefalo, too."

"What the devil is that?"

"Beefalo? Another thing you can only get around here. It's a cross between beef cattle and buffalo. Buffalo is what my people used to eat, man, biggest damned cow you're ever gonna see!" Russell grinned. "Good lean meat, healthy and everything. But venison's the best, Ismael."

"You must not call me that," Ghosn said tiredly. It had been a twenty-seven-hour day for him, counting the time zones.

"I got the IDs for you and the Commander." Russell pulled the envelopes from a drawer and tossed them on the table. "Names are exactly what you wanted, see? We just have to do the photos and put them on the cards. I have the equipment to do it."

"Was this hard to get?"

Marvin laughed. "Naw, it's standard commercial stuff. I used my own license form as a master, ginned up the copies, then I got the hardware to do first-class dupes. Lots of companies use photo-passes, and the equipment is standardized. Three hours' work. I figure we have all day tomorrow and day after to go over everything."

"Excellent, Marvin."

"You want a drink?"

"Alcohol, you mean?"

"Hey, man, I saw you have a beer with that German guy—what was his name?"

"Herr Fromm, you mean."

"Come on, it's not as bad as eatin' pork, is it?"

"Thank you, but I will pass on that—is that how you say it?"

" 'Pass on the drink'?—yeah, that's fine, man. How's that Fromm guy doing?" Marvin asked casually, looking at the meat. It was almost done.

"Doing well," Ghosn answered just as casually. "He went off to see his wife."

"Exactly what were you guys working on, anyway?" Russell poured himself a shot of Jack Daniel's.

"He helped us with the explosives, some special tricks, you see. He's an expert in the field."

"Great."

* * *

It was the first hopeful sign in a few days, maybe a few weeks, Ryan thought. Dinner was fine, all the better to make it home in time to have it with the kids. Cathy had evidently gotten home from work at a reasonable hour and had taken the time to fix a good one. Best of all, they'd talked over dinner, not about very much, but they'd talked. Afterwards Jack had helped her clean up. Finally the kids went off to bed, and they were alone.

"I'm sorry I snapped at you," Cathy said.

"It's okay, I guess I deserved it." Ryan was willing to say almost anything to calm things down.

"No, I was wrong, Jack. I was feeling bitchy, and I had cramps, and my back hurt. What's wrong with you is that you're working too hard and drinking too much." She came over to kiss him. "Smoking, Jack?"

He was amazed. He hadn't expected to be kissed. More than that, he expected an explosion if she discovered that he'd smoked. "Sorry, babe. Bad day at the office. I wimped."

Cathy held his hands. "Jack, I want you to cut back on the drinking, and get your rest. That's your problem, that and the stress. We'll worry about the smoking later, just so you don't smoke around the kids. I haven't been very sympathetic, and I've been a little wrong myself, but you have to clean up your act. What you've been doing is bad for you, and bad for us."

"I know."

"Go to bed. You need sleep more than anything else."

Being married to a physician had its drawbacks. Chief among those was that you couldn't argue with one. Jack kissed her on the cheek and did as he was told.

30. East Room

Clark arrived at the house at the proper time and had to do something unusual. He waited. After a couple of minutes he was ready to knock on the door, but then it opened. Dr. Ryan (male) came out partway, then stopped and turned to kiss Dr. Ryan (female), who watched him walk off, and, after his back was fully turned, fired off a beaming smile at the car.

All right! Clark thought. Maybe he did have a new career set up. Jack also looked fairly decent, and Clark told him so as soon as he got in the car.

"Yeah, well, I got sent to bed early." Jack chuckled, tossing his paper on the front seat. "Forgot to have a drink, too."

"Couple more days like that and you just might be human again."

"Maybe you're right." But he still lit up a cigarette, somewhat to Clark's annoyance. Then he realized just how smart Caroline Ryan was. One thing at a time. Damn, Clark told himself, that *is* some broad.

"I'm set up for the test flight. Ten o'clock."

"Good. It is nice to put you to some real work, John. Playing SPO must be boring as hell," Ryan said, opening the dispatch box.

"It has its moments, sir," Clark replied, pulling onto Falcon's Nest Road. It was another quiet day on the dispatches, and soon Ryan had his head buried in the morning *Post*.

Three hours later, Clark and Chavez arrived at Andrews Air Force Base. A pair of VC-20Bs had already been scheduled for routine training flights. The pilots and crews of the 89th Military Airlift—"The President's"—Wing had a strict regimen for maintaining proficiency. The two aircraft took off a few minutes apart and headed east to perform various familiarization maneuvers to acquaint two new copilots with air-traffic control procedures—which the drivers already knew backwards and forwards, of course, but that was beside the point.

In the back, an Air Force technical sergeant was doing his own training, playing with the sophisticated communications equipment that the plane carried. He occasionally looked aft to see that civilian, whoever the hell he was, talking into a flower pot, or just into a little green stick. There are some things, the sergeant thought, that a guy just isn't supposed to understand. He was entirely correct.

Two hours later the two Gulfstreams landed back at Andrews and rolled to a halt at the VIP terminal. Clark gathered up his gear and walked out to meet another civilian who'd been aboard the other aircraft. The pair walked off to their car, already talking.

"I could understand part of what you were saying—clear, I mean," Chavez reported. "Say about a third of it, maybe a little less."

"Okay, we'll see what the techies can do with it." The drive back to Langley took thirty-five minutes, and from there Clark and Chavez drove back into Washington for a late lunch.

Bob Holtzman had gotten the call the previous evening. It had come on his unlisted home line. A curt, short message, it had also piqued his interest. At two in the afternoon he walked into a small Mexican place in Georgetown called Esteban's. Most of the business crowd had gone, leaving the place about a third full, mainly with kids from Georgetown University. A wave from the back told him where to go.

"Hello," Holtzman said, sitting down.

"You Holtzman?"

"That's right," the reporter said. "And you are?"

"Two friendly guys," the older one said. "Join us for lunch?"

"Okay." The younger one got up and started feeding quarters into a jukebox that played Mexican music. In a moment it was certain that his tape recorder wouldn't have a chance of working.

"What do you want to see me about?"

"You've been writing some pieces on the Agency," the older one started off. "The target of your articles is the Deputy Director, Dr. John Ryan."

"I never said that," Holtzman replied.

"Whoever leaked all that shit to you lied. It's a setup."

"Says who?"

"Just how honest a reporter are you?"

"What do you mean?" Holtzman asked.

"If I tell you something totally off the record, will you print it?"

"That depends on the nature of the information. What exactly is your intention?"

"What I mean, Mr. Holtzman, is that I can prove to you that you've been lied to, but the proof of that can never be revealed. It would endanger some people. It would also prove that somebody's been using you to grind an ax or two. I want to know who that person is."

"You know that I can never reveal a source. That violates our code of ethics."

"Ethics in a reporter," the man said just loudly enough to be heard over the music. "I like that. Do you also protect sources who lie to you?"

"No, we don't do that."

"Okay, then I'm going to tell you a little story, but the condition is that you may never, ever reveal what I am going to tell you. Will you honor such a condition?"

"What if I find out you are misleading me?"

"Then you will be free to print it. Fair enough?" Clark got a nod. "Just remember, I will be very unhappy if you ever print it, 'cuz I ain't lying. One more thing, you can't ever use what I am going to tell you as a lead to do your own digging."

"That's asking a lot."

"You make the call, Mr. Holtzman. You have the reputation of an honest reporter, and a pretty smart one. There are some things that can't be reported—well, that's going too far. Let's say that there are things that have to remain secret for a very long time. Like years. What I'm getting at is this: you've been used. You have been conned into printing lies in order to hurt someone. Now, I'm not a reporter, but if I were, that would bother me. It would bother me because it's wrong, and it would bother me because someone took me for a sucker."

"You have it figured out. Okay, I agree to your conditions."

"Fair enough." Clark told his story. It took ten minutes.

"What about the mission? Where exactly did the man die?"

"Sorry, pal. And you can forget about finding that one out. Less than ten people can answer that." Clark's lie was a clever one. "If you even manage to figure out who they are, they won't talk—they can't. Not too many people voluntarily leak information about breaking laws."

"And the Zimmer woman?"

"You can check out most of that story. Where she lives, the family business, where the kid was born, who was there, who the doctor was."

Holtzman checked his notes. "There's something really, really big behind all this, isn't there?"

Clark just stared at him. "All I want is a name."

"What will you do with it?"

"Nothing that concerns you."

"What will Ryan do with it?"

"He doesn't know we're here."

"Bullshit."

"That, Mr. Holtzman, is the truth."

Bob Holtzman had been a reporter a very long time. He'd been lied to by experts. He'd been the target of very organized and well-planned lies, had been the instrument of political vendettas. He didn't like that part of his job, not in the least. The contempt he felt for politicians came mainly from their willingness to break any rule. Whenever a politician broke his word, told the most outrageous of lies, took money from a contributor and left the room at once to perform a service for that contributor, it was called "just politics." That was wrong, and Holtzman knew it. There was still in him something of the idealist who had graduated from

Columbia's journalism school, and though life had made him a cynic, he was one of those few people in Washington who remembered his ideals and occasionally mourned for them.

"Assuming I can verify this story you've told, what's in it for me?"

"Maybe just satisfaction. Maybe nothing more than that. I honestly doubt there will be any more, but if there is, I'll let you know."

"Just satisfaction?" Holtzman asked.

"Ever want to get even with a bully?" Clark asked lightly.

The reporter brushed that aside. "What do you do at the Agency?"

Clark smiled. "I'm really not supposed to talk about that."

"Once upon a time, the story goes, a very senior Soviet official defected, right off the tarmac at Moscow airport."

"I've heard that story. If you ever printed it . . ."

"Yes, it would fuck up relations, wouldn't it?" Holtzman observed.

"How long have you had it?"

"Since right before the last election. The President asked me not to run it."

"Fowler, you mean?"

"No, the one Fowler beat."

"And you played ball." Clark was impressed.

"The man had a family, a wife and a daughter. Were they killed in a plane crash, like the press release said?"

"You ever going to print this?"

"I can't, not for a lot of years, but someday I'm going to do a book. . . ."

"They got out, too," Clark said. "You're looking at the guy who got them out of the country."

"I don't believe in coincidences."

"The wife's name is Maria. The daughter's name is Katryn."

Holtzman didn't react, but he knew that only a handful of people in the Agency could possibly have known the details to that one. He'd just asked his own trick question and gotten the right answer.

"Five years from today I want the details of the bust-out."

Clark was quiet for a moment. Well, if the reporter was willing to break a rule, then Clark had to play ball, too. "That's fair. Okay, you have a deal."

"Jesus Christ, John!" Chavez said.

"The man needs a *quid pro quo*."

"How many people inside know the details?"

"Of the operation? Not many. My end . . . if you mean all the details, maybe twenty, and only five of them are still in the Agency. Ten of them are not Agency employees."

"Then who?"

"That would give too much away."

"Air Force Special Ops," Holtzman said. "Or maybe the Army, Task Force 160, those crazy guys at Fort Campbell, the ones who went into Iraq the first night—"

"You can speculate all you want, but I'm not going to say anything. I will say this, when I tell you my end, I want to know how the hell you figured out that we even had this operation."

"People like to talk," Holtzman said simply.

"True enough. Do we have a deal, sir?"

"If I can verify what you've told me, if I'm sure I've been lied to, yes, I will reveal the source. You have to promise that it will never get to the press."

Jesus, this is like diplomacy, Clark reflected. "Agreed. I'll call you in two days. For what it's worth, you're the first reporter I've ever talked to."

"So, what do you think?" Holtzman asked with a grin.

"I think I ought to stick with spooks." John paused. "You might have been a pretty good one."

"I am a pretty good one."

"Just how heavy is this thing?" Russell asked.

"Seven hundred kilos." Ghosn did the mental arithmetic. "Three quarters of a ton—your ton, that is."

"Okay," Russell said. "The truck'll handle that. How do we get it from the truck into my truck?" The question turned Ghosn pale.

"I had not considered that."

"How was it loaded on?"

"The box is set on a wooden . . . platform?"

"You mean a pallet? They put it in with a forklift?"

"Yes," Ghosn said, "that is correct."

"You're lucky. Come on, I'll show you." Russell led the man out into the cold. Two minutes later he saw that one of the barns had a concrete loading dock and a rusty, propane-powered forklift. The only bad news was that the dirt path leading up to it was covered with snow and frozen mud. "How delicate is the bomb?"

"Bombs can be very delicate, Marvin," Ghosn pointed out.

Russell had a good laugh at that one. "Yeah, I guess so."

It was fully ten hours earlier in Syria. Dr. Vladimir Moiseyevich Kaminiskiy had just started work, early as was his custom. A professor at Moscow State University, he'd been sent to Syria to teach in his specialty, which was respiratory problems. It was not a specialty to make a man an optimist. Much of what he saw in the Soviet Union and also here in Syria was lung cancer, a disease as preventable as it was lethal.

His first case of the day had been referred by a Syrian practitioner whom he admired—the man was French-trained and very thorough—and also one who only referred interesting cases.

On entering the examining room, Kaminiskiy found a fit-looking man in his early thirties. A closer look showed someone with a gray, drawn face. His first impression was, *cancer,* but Kaminiskiy was a careful man. It could be something else, something contagious. His examination took longer than he'd expected, necessitating several X-ray films, and some additional tests, but he was called back to the Soviet Embassy before the results arrived.

It required all of Clark's patience, but he let it go almost three days on the assumption that Holtzman didn't get right on the case. John left his house at eight-thirty in the evening and drove to a gas station. There he told the attendant to fill up the car—he hated pumping it himself—and walked over to the pay phone.

"Yeah," Holtzman said, answering his unlisted line.

Clark didn't identify himself. "You have a chance to run the facts down?"

"Yeah, as a matter of fact. Got most of 'em, anyway. Looks like you were right. Really is annoying when people lie to you, isn't it?"

"Who?"

"I call her Liz. The President calls her Elizabeth. Want a freebie?" Holtzman added.

"Sure."

"Call this evidence of good faith on my part. Fowler and she are getting it on. Nobody's reported it because we figure it's not the public's business."

"Good for you," Clark observed. "Thanks. I owe you one."

"Five years, man."

"I'll be around." Clark hung up. *So,* John thought. *I thought that's who it was.* He dropped another quarter in the phone. He got lucky on the first try. It was a woman's voice.

"Hello?"

"Dr. Caroline Ryan?"

"Yes, who's this?"

"The name you wanted, ma'am, is Elizabeth Elliot. The President's National Security Advisor." Clark decided not to add the other part. It was not relevant to the situation, was it?

"You're sure?"

"Yes."

"Thank you." The line clicked off.

Cathy had sent Jack to bed early again. The man was being sensible. Well, that wasn't a surprise, was it? she thought. After all, he married me.

The timing could have been a little better. A few days earlier she had planned to skip the official dinner, claiming work as an excuse, but now . . .

How do I do this . . . ?

"Morning, Bernie," Cathy Ryan said as she scrubbed her hands, as usual, all the way to the elbows.

"Hi, Cath. How's it going?"

"A lot better, Bernie."

"Really?" Dr. Katz started scrubbing.

"Really."

"Glad to hear it," Katz observed dubiously.

Cathy finished, shutting off the water with taps from her elbows. "Bernie, it turns out I overreacted rather badly."

"What about the guy who came to see me?" Katz asked, his head down.

"It was not true. I can't explain now, maybe some other time. Need a favor."

"Sure, what?"

"The cornea replacement I have scheduled for Wednesday, can you take it?"

"What gives?"

"Jack and I have to go to a formal dinner in the White House tomorrow night. State dinner for the Prime Minister of Finland, would you believe? The procedure is straightforward, no complications I know about. I can have you the file this afternoon. Jenkins is going to do the procedure—I'm just supposed to ride shotgun." Jenkins was a bright young resident.

"Okay, I'll do it."

"Okay, thanks. Owe you one," Cathy said on her way through the door.

The *Carmen Vita* pulled into Hampton Roads barely an hour late. She turned to port and proceeded south past the Navy piers. The captain and pilot rode the portside bridge wing, noting the carrier that was even now departing from the pier with a few hundred wives and children waving goodbye to USS *Theodore Roosevelt*. Two cruisers, two destroyers, and a frigate were already moving. They, the pilot explained, were the screening ships for "The Stick," as *TR* was called by her crew. The Indian-born captain grunted and returned to business. Half an hour later the container ship approached her pier at the end of Terminal Boulevard. Three tugs took their position and eased the *Carmen Vita* alongside. The ship had barely been tied up when the gantry cranes started moving cargo.

"Roggen, Colorado?" the trucker asked. He flipped open his large book map and looked on I-76 for the right place. "Okay, I see it."

"How fast?" Russell asked.

"From the time I leave here? Eighteen hundred miles. Oh, two days, maybe forty hours if I'm lucky. Gonna cost you."

"How much?" Russell asked. The trucker told him. "Cash all right?"

"Cash is fine. I knock ten percent off for that," the trucker said. The IRS never found out about cash transactions.

"Half in advance." Russell peeled off the bills. "Half on delivery, a grand bonus if you break forty hours."

"Sounds good to me. What about the box?"

"You bring that right back here. We'll be getting more stuff in a month," Russell lied. "We can make this a sort of regular run for you."

"Sounds good to me."

Russell returned to his friends, and together they watched the unloading process from the comfort of a block building with a large coffee urn.

Teddy Roosevelt cleared the harbor in record time, bending on twenty knots before they reached the sea buoy. Already the aircraft were orbiting overhead, first among them the F-14 Tomcat fighters that had lifted off from Oceana Naval Air Station. As soon as there was sea room, the carrier came into the northerly wind to commence flight operations. The first plane down had the Double-Zero number of the CAG, Captain Robby Jackson. His Tomcat caught a gust over the fantail, and as a result caught the number-two wire when it landed—"trapped"—somewhat to Jackson's annoyance. The next aircraft, flown by Commander Rafael Sanchez, made a perfect trap on the #3 arrester wire. Both aircraft taxied out of harm's way. Jackson left the fighter and immediately sprinted to his place on Vulture's Row, high up on the carrier's island structure, so that he could observe the arrival of the rest of his aircraft. This was how a deployment started, with the CAG and squadron commanders watching their troops land. Each trap would be recorded on videotape for critiques. The cruise had not gotten off to a very good start, Jackson noted as he sipped his first mug of shipboard coffee. He'd missed his customary "OK" grade, as the Air Boss had informed him with a twinkling eye.

"Hey, skipper, how my kids doing?" Sanchez asked, taking his seat behind Robby.

"Not bad. I see you kept your record going, Bud."

"It's not hard, Captain. You just keep an eye on the wind as you turn in. I saw that gust you took. Guess I should have warned you."

"Pride goeth before the fall, Commander," Robby observed. Sanchez had seventeen consecutive OKs. Maybe he could see the wind, Jackson thought. Seventy uneventful minutes later, *TR* turned back east, taking the great-circle route for the Strait of Gibraltar.

* * *

The trucker made sure the container box was firmly secured to the bed of his truck, then climbed into the cab of his Kenworth diesel tractor. He started his engine and waved to Russell, who waved back.

"I still think we should follow him," Ghosn said.

"He'd notice and wonder why," Marvin replied. "And if something goes wrong, what would you do, fill in the hole it makes in the highway? You didn't follow the ship, did you?"

"True." Ghosn looked at Qati and shrugged. Then they walked off to their car for the drive to Charlotte, from which they would fly directly to Denver.

Jack was ready early, as he usually was, but Cathy took her time. It was so unusual for her to look in a mirror and see hair that looked like it belonged to a real woman, as opposed to a surgeon who didn't give a damn. That had entailed the waste of two hours, but there were prices that one had to pay. Before she went downstairs, Cathy took two suitcases out from her closet and set them in the middle of the bedroom.

"Here, can you do this?" she asked her husband.

"Sure, babe." Ryan took the gold necklace and clasped it around her neck. It was one he'd given her on the Christmas before Little Jack was born. Some good memories went along with this necklace, Jack remembered. Then he stood back. "Turn around."

Cathy did as she was told. Her evening dress was royal-blue silk that caught and reflected light like glass. Jack Ryan was not a man who understood women's fashions—figuring the Russians out came more easily to him—but he approved whatever the new rules were. The rich blue of the dress and the gold jewelry she wore with it set off the blush of her fair skin and the buttery yellow of her hair. "Nice," Jack said. "All ready, babe?"

"Sure am, Jack." She smiled back at him. "Go warm the car up."

Cathy watched him head out into the garage, then said a few words to the sitter. She put on her fur—surgeons typically have little use for animal-rights activists—and followed Jack a minute later. Jack backed out of the garage and headed off.

Clark had to laugh to himself. Ryan still didn't know beans about countersurveillance techniques. He watched the taillights of the car diminish, then disappear entirely around the bend of the road before heading into the Ryan driveway.

"You're Mr. Clark?" the sitter asked.

"That's right."

"They're in the bedroom." The sitter pointed.

"Thank you." Clark returned a minute later. Typical woman, he thought, they all overpack. Even Caroline Ryan wasn't perfect. "Good night."

"Night." The sitter was already entranced with the TV.

It takes just under an hour to drive from Annapolis, Maryland, into Central D.C. Ryan missed having an official car, but his wife had insisted that they drive themselves. They turned off of Pennsylvania Avenue, through the gate into East Executive Drive, where uniformed police directed them to a parking place. Their wagon looked a little humble mixed in with Caddys and Lincolns, but that was all right with Jack. The Ryans walked up the gentle slope to the East Entrance, where Secret Service personnel checked their invitations against the guest list, and checked them off. Jack's car keys set off the metal detector, evoking an embarrassed smile.

No matter how many times one goes there, there is always something magical about visiting the White House, especially at night. Ryan led his wife westward. They handed off their coats and took their numbered token right next to the White House's own small theater, then continued. At the chicane turn there were the usual three social reporters, women in their sixties who stared you in the face while making their notes and generally looked like the witches from *Macbeth* with their open-mouth, drooly smiles. Officers from all the military services decked out in their full-dress—what Ryan used to call "Headwaiter"—uniforms waited in files to provide escort duty. As usual the Marines looked best with their scarlet sashes, and a disgustingly good-looking captain motioned them up the stairs to the main level. Jack noted the admiring glance cast at his wife and decided to smile about it.

At the top of the marble stairs another officer, this one a female Army lieutenant, directed them into the East Room. They were announced into the room—as though anyone were listening—and a liveried usher approached at once with a silver tray of drinks.

"You're driving, Jack," Cathy whispered. Jack took a Perrier and a twist. Cathy got champagne.

The East Room of the White House is the size of a small gymnasium. The walls are ivory-white, its false columns decorated with gold leaf. There was a string quartet in one corner, along with a grand piano that was being played, rather well, Ryan thought, by an Army sergeant. Half the people were already here, the men in black tie and the women in dresses. Perhaps there were people who were totally comfortable at such affairs, Ryan told himself, but he wasn't one of them. He started circulating, and soon found Defense Secretary Bunker and his wife, Charlotte.

"Hello, Jack."

"Hi, Dennis, you know my wife?"

"Caroline," Cathy said, sticking her hand out.

"So, what do you think about the game?"

Jack laughed. "Sir, I know how you and Brent Talbot have been fighting over this. I was born in Baltimore. Somebody stole our team."

"You didn't lose that much, did you? This is our year."

"But the Vikings say the same thing."

"They were lucky to get past New York."

"The Raiders gave you a brief scare, as I recall."

"They got lucky," Bunker grumbled. "We buried 'em in the second half."

Caroline Ryan and Charlotte Bunker traded a woman-to-woman look: *Football!* Cathy turned, and there she was. Mrs. Bunker made off while the boys talked about boy things.

Cathy took a deep breath. She wondered if this was the right time and the right place, but she could no more have stopped herself now than she could have given up surgery. She left Jack facing the other way, and headed across the floor in a line as direct as a falcon's.

Dr. Elizabeth Elliot was dressed almost identically to Dr. Caroline Ryan. The cuts and pleats were a little different, but the expensive garments were close enough to make a fashion editor wonder if they had shopped at the same store. A triple string of pearls graced her neck, and she was talking with two others. Her head turned as she saw the approaching shape.

"Hello, Dr. Elliot. You remember me?" Cathy asked with a warm smile.

"No. Should I?"

"Caroline Ryan. That help?"

"Sorry," Liz replied, knowing at once who she was, but not knowing anything else that might be of interest. "Do you know Bob and Libby Holtzman?"

"I've read your material," Cathy said, taking Holtzman's extended hand.

"It's always nice to hear that." Holtzman noted the delicacy of her touch and could feel the guilt shoot up his arm. Was this the woman whose marriage he had attacked? "This is Libby."

"You're a reporter, too," Cathy observed. Libby Holtzman was taller than she, and dressed in an outfit that emphasized her ample bosom. One of hers is worth both of mine, Cathy noted, managing not to sigh. Libby had the sort of bust on which men yearn to lay their heads.

"You operated on a cousin of mine a year or so ago," Libby Holtzman said. "Her mom says you're the best surgeon in the world."

"All doctors love to hear that." Cathy decided that she would like Mrs. Holtzman, despite her physical handicap.

"I know you're a surgeon, but where have we met?" Liz Elliot asked with the offhand interest she might have shown a dog breeder.

"Bennington. In my freshman year, you taught PoliSci 101."

"Is that a fact? I'm surprised you remember." She made it clear that she did not.

"Yes. Well, you know how it is." Cathy smiled. "Freshman Pre-Med is a real bear. We really have to concentrate on the important stuff. So the unimportant courses are all throwaways, easy A's."

Elliot's expression didn't change. "I was never an easy grader."

"Sure you were. It was just a matter of repeating it all back to you." Cathy smiled even more broadly.

Bob Holtzman was tempted to take a step back, but managed not to move at all. His wife's eyes went a touch wider, having caught the signals more quickly than her husband. A war had just begun. It would be nastier than most.

"What ever happened to Dr. Brooks?"

"Who?" Liz asked.

Cathy turned to the Holtzmans. "Times really were different back in the '70s, weren't they? Dr. Elliot just had her master's, and the PoliSci department was—well, kind of radical. You know, the fashionable kind." She turned back. "Surely you haven't forgotten Dr. Brooks and Dr. Hemmings! Where was that house you shared with them?"

"I don't remember." Liz told herself to maintain control. This would all be over soon. But she couldn't walk away.

"Wasn't it on that three-way corner, a few blocks from the campus . . . ? We used to call them the Marx Brothers," Cathy explained with a giggle. "Brooks never wore socks—in Vermont, remember; he must have gotten terrible colds from that—and Hemmings never washed his hair. That was some department. Of course, Dr. Brooks went off to Berkeley, and then you went out there, too, to finish your doctorate. I guess you liked working under him. Tell me, how is Bennington now?"

"Just as nice as ever."

"I never get back there for the alum meetings," Cathy said.

"I haven't been back there myself in over a year," Liz replied.

"What ever happened to Dr. Brooks?" Cathy asked again.

"He teaches at Vassar now, I think."

"Oh, you've kept track of him? Still trying to bed every skirt in sight, too, I bet. Radical-chic. How often do you see him?"

"Not in a couple of years."

"We never understood what you saw in them," Cathy observed.

"Come now, Caroline, none of us were virgins back then."

Cathy sipped at her champagne. "That's true, times were different, and we did lots of very dumb things. But I got lucky. Jack made an honest woman of me."

Zing! Libby Holtzman thought.

"Some of us haven't had time."

"I don't know how you manage without a family. I don't think I could handle the loneliness."

"At least I never have to worry about an unfaithful husband," Liz observed icily, finding her own weapon, not knowing it wasn't loaded anymore.

Cathy looked amused. "Yes, I suppose some women have to worry about that. But I don't, thank God."

"How can any woman be sure?"

"Only a fool is unsure. If you know your man," Cathy explained, "you know what he can and cannot do."

"And you really feel that secure?" Liz asked.

"Of course."

"They say the wife is always the last to know."

Cathy's head cocked to one side. "Is this a philosophical discussion or are you trying to say something to my face instead of behind my back?"

Jesus! Bob Holtzman felt that he was a spectator at a prizefight.

"Did I give you that impression? Oh, I'm so sorry, Caroline."

"That's okay, Liz."

"Excuse me, but I prefer—"

"I go by 'professor,' too; you know, medical doctor, Johns Hopkins, and all that."

"I thought you were an *associate* professor."

Dr. Ryan nodded. "That's right. I got offered a full professorship at the University of Virginia, but that meant moving away from the house we like, moving the kids out of school, and, of course, there's the problem with Jack's career. So I turned it down."

"I guess you are pretty tied down."

"I do have responsibilities, and I like working at Hopkins. We're doing some pioneer work, and it's good to be where the action is. It must have been much easier for you to come to Washington, what with nothing to hold you anywhere—and besides, what's new in political science?"

"I'm quite satisfied with my life, thank you."

"I'm sure you are," Cathy replied, seeing the chink and knowing how to exploit it. "You can always tell when a person is happy in their work."

"And you, Professor?"

"Life couldn't be much better. As a matter of fact, there's only one real difference between us," Caroline Ryan said.

"And that is?"

". . . I don't know where my wife wandered off to. There's yours with Liz Elliot and the Holtzmans. I wonder what they're talking about?" Bunker said. . . .

"At home, at night, I sleep with a man," Cathy said sweetly. "And the nice thing about it is that I never have to change the batteries."

. . . Jack turned to see his wife and Elizabeth Elliot, whose pearl necklace seemed to turn brown before his eyes, she went so pale. His wife was shorter than the National Security Advisor, and she looked like a pixie next to Libby Holtzman, but whatever the hell had just happened, Cathy was holding her ground like a momma-bear on her kill, her eyes locked on the taller Elliot. He moved over to see what the problem was.

"Hi, honey."

"Hello, Jack," Cathy said, her eyes fixed on her target. "Do you know Bob and Libby?"

"Hi." Ryan shook hands with both, catching looks from them that he could only guess at. Mrs. Holtzman seemed about to explode, but then she took a breath and controlled herself.

"You're the lucky guy who married this woman?" Libby asked. That comment made Elliot turn away first from the confrontation.

"Actually she's the one who married me, I think," Jack said after a further moment's confusion.

"If you'll excuse me," Elliot said, departing from the battlefield as gracefully as she could. Cathy took Jack's arm and steered him toward the corner with the piano.

"What in the *hell* was that all about?" Libby Holtzman asked her husband. She thought she knew most of it already. Her successful struggle not to laugh aloud had nearly strangled her.

"What it's about, my dear, is that I broke an ethical rule. And you know something?"

"You did the right thing," Libby announced. "The Marx Brothers? 'Three-way corner.' Liz Elliot, the Queen Radical WASP. My God."

"Jack, I have a terrible headache, I mean, a really terrible one," Cathy whispered to her husband.

"That bad?"

She nodded. "Can we get out of here before I get nauseous?"

"Cathy, you don't just walk out of these things," Jack pointed out.

"Sure, you do."

"What were you and Liz talking about?"

"I don't think I like her very much."

"You're not the only one. Okay." Jack headed for the door with Cathy on his arm. The Army captain at the stairs was very understanding. Five minutes later they were outside. Jack helped his wife into the car and headed back up the drive toward Pennsylvania.

"Go straight," Cathy said.

"But—"

"Go straight, Jack." It was her surgeon's voice. The one that told people what to do. Ryan pulled past Lafayette Park. "Now left."

"Where are we supposed to be going?"

"Now turn right—and left into the driveway."

"But—"

"Jack, please?" Cathy said softly.

The doorman of the Hay Adams Hotel helped Caroline from the car. Jack handed the keys to the parking attendant, then followed his wife in. He watched the concierge hand her a key, then she breezed off to the elevators. He followed her onto and off the elevator, and from there to a corner suite.

"What gives, Cathy?"

"Jack, there's been too much work, too much kids, and not enough us. Tonight, my darling, there is time for us." She wrapped her arms around his neck, and there was nothing for her husband to do but kiss her. She put the key in his hand. "Now get the door open before we scare somebody."

"But what about—"

"Jack, shut up. Please," she added.

"Yes, dear." Ryan led his wife into the room.

Cathy was gratified to see that her instructions had been carried out as perfectly as the staff of this most excellent of hotels could arrange. A light dinner was set on the table, along with a chilled bottle of Moët. She draped her coat on the sofa in confidence that everything else was as it should be.

"Could you pour the champagne? I'll be back in a moment. You might want to take your coat off and relax," she said over her shoulder on the way into the bedroom.

"Sure," Jack said to himself. He didn't know what was going on, or what Cathy had in mind, but he didn't really care all that much either. After dropping his dinner jacket atop his wife's mink, he peeled the foil off the champagne, then twisted off the wire, and gently worked the cork free. He poured two glasses and set the bottle back in the silver bucket. He decided to trust the wine untasted, then walked to look out the window at the White House. Jack didn't hear her come back into the room. He felt it, felt the air change somehow. When he turned, she was standing there in the doorway.

It was the second time she'd worn it, the floor-length gown of white silk. The first time had been their honeymoon. Cathy walked barefoot across the carpet to her husband, gliding through space like an apparition.

"Your headache must have gone away."

"I'm still thirsty, though," Cathy said, smiling up at Jack's face.

"I think I can handle that." Jack lifted the glass and held it to her lips. She took a single sip, then moved it to his.

"Hungry?"

"No."

She leaned against him, taking both his hands in hers. "I love you, Jack. Shall we?"

Jack turned her around, and walked behind, his hands at her waist. The bed, he saw, was turned down, and the light out, though the glare from the floodlit White House washed in through the windows.

"Remember the first time, the first night we were married?"

Jack chuckled. "I remember both, Cathy."

"This is going to be another first time, Jack." She reached behind him and flipped off the cummerbund. Her husband took the cue. When he was naked, she embraced him as fiercely as she could manage, and the silk of her nightgown rustled against his skin. "Lie down."

"You're more beautiful than ever, Cathy."

"I wouldn't want anyone to steal you from me." Cathy joined him on the bed. He was ready, and so was she. Caroline pulled the nightgown up to her waist and mounted him, then let it fall down around her. His hands found her breasts. She held them in place, rocking up and down on him, knowing that he couldn't last very long, but neither could she.

No man should be so lucky, Jack told himself, straining, trying to control himself, and though he failed miserably, he was rewarded with a smile that nearly broke his heart.

"Not bad," Cathy said a minute later, kissing his hands.

"Out of practice."

"The night is young," she said as she lay down beside him, "and that's the best I've had in a while, too. Now, are you hungry?"

Ryan looked around the room. "I, uh . . ."

"Wait." She left the bed and returned with a bathrobe with the hotel monogram. "I want you to stay warm."

Dinner passed in silence. There was nothing that needed to be said, and for the following hour they silently pretended that they were both in their twenties again, young enough to experiment in love, to explore it like a new and wonderful place where every turn in the road revealed something never before seen. It had been far too long, Jack told himself, but he dismissed the thought from a mind that for once was untroubled. Dessert was finished, and he poured the last of the champagne.

"I have to stop drinking." *But not tonight.*

Cathy finished off her glass and set it on the table. "It wouldn't hurt you to stop, but you're not an alcoholic. We proved that last week. You needed rest, and you got your rest. And now, I want more of you."

"If there's any left."

Cathy stood and took his hand. "There's plenty more where that came from."

This time Jack did the leading. Once in the bedroom, he reached down and pulled the nightgown over her head, then tossed his robe on the floor next to it.

The first kiss lasted for some eternal period of time. He lifted her in his arms and laid her on the bed, joining her a moment later. The urgency had not passed for either of them. Soon he was atop her, feeling her warmth under and around him. He did better this time, controlling himself until her back arched and her face took on the curious look of pain that every man wants to give his wife. At the end, his arms reached under her and lifted her off the bed, up against his chest. Cathy loved it when he did that, loved her man's strength almost as much as his goodness. And then it was over, and he lay at her side. Cathy pulled him against her, his face to her regrettably flat chest.

"There never was anything wrong with you," she whispered into his ear. She was not surprised by what came next. She knew the man so well, though she'd been foolish enough to forget the fact. She hoped that she'd be able to forgive herself for that. Jack's whole body shook with his sobs. Cathy held him fast to her, feeling his tears on her breasts. Such a fine, strong man.

"I've been a lousy husband, and a lousy father."

Her cheek came down on the top of his head. "Neither one of us has set any records lately, Jack, but that's over, isn't it?"

"Yeah." He kissed her breast. "How did I ever find you?"

"You won me, Jack. In the great lottery of life, you got me. I got you. Do you think that married people always deserve each other? All the ones I see at work who just can't make it. Maybe they just don't try, maybe they just forget."

"Forget?"

What I almost forgot. " 'For richer, for poorer; for better, for worse; in sickness and in health, as long as we both shall live.' Remember? I made the promise, too. Jack, I know how good you can be, and that's plenty good enough. I was so bitchy to you last week. . . . I'm sorry for all the terrible things I did. But that's all over."

Presently the weeping stopped. "Thanks, babe."

"Thank you, Jack." She ran a finger down his back.

"You mean?" His head moved back to see her face. He got another smile, the gentle kind that a woman saved for her husband.

"I think so. Maybe this one will be another girl."
"That might be nice."
"Go to sleep."
"In a minute." Jack rose to head for the bathroom, then into the sitting room before coming back. Ten minutes later he was still. Cathy rose to put her nightie back on, and on her way back from the bathroom she canceled the wake-up call that Jack had just ordered. It was her turn to stare out the windows at the home of the President. The world had never seemed prettier. Now, if she could just get Jack to quit working for those people. . . .

The truck made a fuel stop outside of Lexington, Kentucky. The driver paused ten minutes to load up on coffee and pancakes—he found breakfasts best for staying awake on the road—then pressed on. The thousand-dollar bonus sounded pretty good, and to be sure of it he had to cross the Mississippi before the rush hour in St. Louis.

31. Dancers

Ryan knew it was too late when the traffic woke him up and he saw that the windows were flooded with light. A look at his watch showed eight-fifteen. That almost set off a panic attack, but it was too late to panic, wasn't it? Jack rose from the bed and walked into the sitting room to see his wife already working on her morning coffee.
"Don't you have to work today?"
"I was supposed to assist with a procedure that started a few minutes ago, but Bernie is covering for me. I think you ought to put some clothes on, though."
"How do I get to work?"
"John'll be here at nine."
"Right." Ryan walked off to shower and shave. On the way, he looked in the closet and noted that a suit, shirt, and tie were waiting for him. His wife had certainly planned this one carefully. He had to smile. Jack had never thought of his wife as a master—mistress?—of conspiracy. By eight-forty he was washed and shaved.
"You know I have an appointment right across the street at eleven."
"No, I didn't. Say hi to that Elliot bitch for me." Cathy smiled.
"You don't like her, either?" he asked.
"Not much there to like. She was a crummy college teacher. She's not as smart as she thinks. Major ego problems."
"I've noticed. She doesn't like me very much."
"I did get that impression. We had a little fight yesterday. I think I won," Cathy observed.
"What was it all about anyway?"
"Oh, just a girl-to-girl thing." Cathy paused. "Jack . . . ?"

"Yeah, babe?"

"I think it's time for you to leave."

Ryan examined his breakfast plate. "I think you may be right. I have a couple more things to do . . . but when they're done . . ."

"How long?" she asked.

"Two months at the outside. I can't just leave, babe. I'm a presidential appointee. I had to be confirmed by the Senate, remember? You can't just walk away from that—it's like desertion if you do. There are rules you have to follow."

Cathy nodded. She'd won her point already. "I understand, Jack. Two months is good enough. What would you like to do?"

"I could get a research job almost anywhere, Center for Strategic and International Studies, Heritage, maybe the Johns Hopkins Center for Advanced International Studies. I had this talk in England with Basil. When you get to my level, you're never really gone. Hmph. I might even write another book. . . ."

"We'll start off with a nice long vacation, soon as the kids are out of school."

"I thought . . . ?"

"I won't be too pregnant then, Jack."

"You really think it happened last night?"

Her eyes arched wickedly. "The timing was just about right, and you had two chances, didn't you? What's the matter? You feel used?"

Her husband smiled. "I've been used worse."

"See me tonight?"

"Did I ever tell you how much I like that nightie?"

"My wedding dress? It's a little formal, but it did have the desired effect. Shame we don't have more time now, isn't it?"

Jack decided he'd better get out of here while he still could. "Yeah, babe, but I have work to do, and so do you."

"Awww," Cathy observed playfully.

"I can't tell the President that I was late because I was boffing my wife across the street." Jack came to his wife and kissed her. "Thanks, honey."

"A pleasure, Jack."

Ryan emerged from the front door to see Clark waiting in the drive-through. He got right in.

"Morning, doc."

"Hi, John. You only made one mistake."

"What's that?"

"Cathy knew your name. How?"

"You don't need to know," Clark replied, handing over the dispatch box. "Hell, sometimes I like to sack in myself, y'know?"

"I'm sure you broke some kind of law."

"Yeah, right." Clark headed out. "When do we get the go-ahead on the Mexico job?"

"That's what I'm going into the White House for."

"Eleven?"

"Right."

It was gratifying to see that the CIA could in fact operate without his presence. Ryan arrived on the seventh floor to see that everyone was at work. Even Marcus was where he belonged.

"Ready for your trip?" Jack asked the Director.

"Yeah, heading off tonight. Station Japan is setting up the meet with Lyalin."

"Marcus, please remember that he is Agent MUSHASHI, and his information is NIITAKA. Using his real name, even here, is a bad habit to get into."

"Yeah, Jack. You're heading down to see the President soon for the Mexico thing?"

"That's right."

"I like the way you set that thing up."

"Thanks, Marcus, but the credit goes to Clark and Chavez. Open to a suggestion?" Jack asked.

"Go ahead."

"Put them back in Operations?"

"If they bring this one off, the President will go along with it. So will I."

"Fair enough." That, Jack thought, was pretty easy. He wondered why.

Dr. Kaminiskiy went over the films and swore at himself for his error of the previous day. It hardly seemed possible, but—

But it wasn't possible. Not here. Was it? He had to run some additional tests, but first he spent an hour tracking down his Syrian colleague. The patient was moved to another hospital, one with a laminar room. Even if Kaminiskiy were wrong, this man had to be totally isolated.

Russell fired up the forklift and took several minutes to figure out the controls. He wondered what the previous owner had needed with one, but there was no point in that. There was enough remaining pressure in the propane tanks that he didn't have to worry about that either. He walked back to the house.

The people here in Colorado were friendly enough. Already, the local newspaper distributors had set up the delivery boxes at the end of the drive. Russell had the morning paper to read with his coffee. A moment later he realized how good a thing that was.

"Uh-oh," he observed quietly.

"What is the problem, Marvin?"

"I've never seen this before. The Vikings fans are planning a convoy . . . over a thousand cars and buses. Damn," he noted. "That'll screw the roads up." He turned to see the extended weather forecast.

"What do you mean?"

"They have to come down I-76 to get to Denver. That might mess things up some. We want to arrive about noon, maybe a little later . . . about the same time the convoy is supposed to arrive. . . ."

"Convoy—what do you mean? Convoy defending against what?" Qati asked.

"Not a real convoy," Russell explained. "More like a, uh, a motorcade. The fans from Minnesota have a big deal laid on. Tell you what, let's get a motel room for us. One close to the airport. When's our flight?" He paused. "Jesus, I really haven't been thinking very clear, have I?"

"What do you mean?" Ghosn asked again.

"Weather," Russell replied. "This is Colorado, and it is January. What if we get another snowstorm?" He scanned the page. *Uh-oh . . .*

"For driving, you mean?"

"That's right. Look, what we ought to do is get rooms reserved, one of the motels right by the airport, say. We can go down the night before . . . or I'll get the rooms for two—no, three nights, so there won't be any suspicion. Christ, I hope there's vacancies.'' Russell walked to the phone and flipped open the Yellow Pages right next to it. It took him four tries to find a room with twin doubles in a little independent place a mile from the airport. This he had to guarantee with a credit card that he'd managed not to use until now. He didn't like having to do that. One more bit of paper for his trail.

''Good morning, Liz.'' Ryan walked into the office and sat down. ''How are you today?''

The National Security Advisor didn't like being baited any more than the next person. She'd had a little battle with this bastard's wife—in front of reporters!—and taken her lumps publicly. Whether Ryan had had anything to do with it or not, he must have had a good laugh about it last night. Worse than that, what that skinny little bitch had said also went after Bob Fowler, didn't it? The President had thought so on being told last night.

''You ready for the brief?''

''Sure am.''

''Come on.'' She'd let Bob handle this.

Helen D'Agustino watched the two officials enter the Oval Office. She'd heard the story, of course. A Secret Service agent had heard the whole thing, and the vicious putdown administered to Dr. Elliot had already been the subject of a few discreet chuckles.

''Good morning, Mr. President,'' she heard Ryan say as the door closed.

''Morning, Ryan. Okay, let's hear it.''

''Sir, what we plan to do is actually fairly simple. Two CIA officers will be in Mexico, at the airport, covered as airline maintenance personnel. They'll do the normal stuff, emptying ashtrays, cleaning the johns. Before they leave they will place fresh flower arrangements in the upstairs lounge. Concealed in the arrangements will be microphones like this one.'' Ryan pulled the plastic spike from his pocket and handed it over. ''These will transmit what they pick up to a second transmitter, concealed in a bottle. That device will broadcast a multichannel EHF—that's extremely high frequency—signal out of the aircraft. A series of three other aircraft will fly parallel courses with the 747 to receive that signal. An additional receiver with a tape recorder attached will be concealed on the 747, both as a backup to the air-to-air links and as a cover for the operation. If it's located, the bugs will seem to be something done by the news people accompanying the Prime Minister. We don't expect that, of course. We'll have people at Dulles to recover our gadgets. In either case, the electronic transmission will be processed and the transcripts presented to you a few hours after the aircraft lands.''

''Very well. What are the chances for success?'' Chief of Staff Arnold van Damm asked. He had to be there, of course. This was more an exercise in politics than statecraft. The downside political risk was serious, just as the reward for success would be more than noteworthy.

''Sir, there are no guarantees for operations of this kind. If something is said, it is likely that we'll know what it is, but he might not even discuss the matter at all. The equipment has all been tested. It works. The field officer running this operation is well experienced. He's done touchy ones before.''

''Like?'' van Damm asked.

''Like getting Gerasimov's wife and daughter out a few years ago.'' Ryan explained on for a minute or so.

''Is the operation worth the risk?'' Fowler asked.

That surprised Ryan quite a bit. "Sir, that decision is yours to make."

"But I asked you for an opinion."

"Yes, Mr. President, it is. The take we've been getting from NIITAKA shows a considerable degree of arrogance on their part. Something like this might have the net effect of shocking them into playing honest ball with us."

"You approve of our policy of dealing with Japan?" van Damm asked, just as surprised as Ryan had been a moment earlier.

"My approval or disapproval is beside the point, but the answer to your question is, yes."

The Chief of Staff was openly amazed. "But the previous administration—how come you never told us?"

"You never asked, Arnie. I don't make government policy, remember? I'm a spook. I do what you tell me to do, as long as it's legal."

"You're satisfied on the legality of the operation?" Fowler asked with a barely suppressed smile.

"Mr. President, you're the lawyer, not me. If I do not know the legal technicalities—and I don't—I must assume that you, as an officer of the court, are not ordering me to break the law."

"That's the best dance number I've seen since the Kirov Ballet was in Kennedy Center last summer," van Damm observed with a laugh.

"Ryan, you know all the moves. You have my approval," Fowler said after a brief pause. "If we get what we expect, then what?"

"We have to go over that with the State Department guys," Liz Elliot announced.

"That is potentially dangerous," Ryan observed. "The Japanese have been hiring a lot of the people from the trade-negotiation section. We have to assume that they have people inside."

"Commercial espionage?" Fowler asked.

"Sure, why not? NIITAKA has never given us hard evidence of that, but if I were a bureaucrat looking to leave government service and make half a mill' a year representing them—like a lot of them do—how would I present myself to them as a potentially valuable asset? I'd do it the same way a Soviet official or spook presents bonafides to us. You deliver something juicy up-front. That's illegal, but we're not devoting any assets to looking at the problem. For that reason, wide dissemination of the information from this operation is very dangerous. Obviously you'll want the opinion of Secretary Talbot and a few others, but I'd be really careful how much farther you spread it. Also, remember that if you tell the PM that you know what he said—and if he knows he only said it in one place—you run the risk of compromising this intelligence-gathering technique." The President accepted that without anything more than a raised eyebrow.

"Make it look like a leak in Mexico?" van Damm asked.

"That's the obvious ploy," Ryan agreed.

"And if I confront him with it directly?" Fowler asked.

"Kind of hard to beat a straight flush, Mr. President. And if this were ever to leak, Congress would go ballistic. That's one of my problems. I'm required to discuss this operation with Al Trent and Sam Fellows. Sam will play ball, but Al has political reasons to dislike the Japanese."

"I could order you not to tell him. . . ."

"Sir, that's one law I may not break for any reason."

"I might have to give you that order," Fowler observed.

Ryan was surprised again. Both he and the President knew what the consequences of that order would be. Just what Cathy had in mind. It might, in fact, be a fine excuse to leave government service.

"Well, maybe that won't be necessary. I'm tired of playing patty-cake with these people. They made an agreement, and they're going to keep it or have to deal with a very irate president. Worse than that, the idea that someone can suborn the president of a country in so venal a way is contemptible. Goddamn it! I hate corruption."

"Right on, boss," van Damm commented. "Besides, the voters will like it."

"That bastard," Fowler went on after a moment. Ryan couldn't tell how much of this was real and how much feigned. "He tells me he's coming over to work out a few details, get acquainted some more, and what he's really planning is to welsh on a deal. Well, we'll see about that. I guess it's time he learned about hardball." The discourse stopped. "Ryan, I missed you last night."

"My wife got a headache, sir. Had to leave. Sorry."

"Feeling all right now?"

"Yes, sir, thank you."

"Turn your people loose."

Ryan stood. "Will do, Mr. President."

Van Damm followed him out and walked him to the West Entrance. "Nice job, Jack."

"Gee, they going to start liking me?" Jack asked wryly. The meeting had gone much too well.

"I don't know what happened last night, but Liz is really pissed at your wife."

"They talked about something, but I don't know what."

"Jack, you want it straight?" van Damm asked.

Ryan knew that the friendly walk to the door was just too convenient, and the symbolism was explicit enough, wasn't it? "When, Arnie?"

"I'd like to say it's just business and not personal, but it is personal. I'm sorry, Jack, but it happens. The President will give you a glowing sendoff."

"Nice of him," Jack replied matter-of-factly.

"I tried, Jack. You know I like you. These things happen."

"I'll go quietly. But—"

"I know. No back-shots on the way out or after you're gone. You'll be asked in periodically, maybe draw some special missions, liaison stuff. You get an honorable discharge. On that, Jack, you have my word of honor, and the President's. He's not a bad guy, Jack, really he isn't. He's a tough-minded son of a bitch and a good politician, but he's as honest as any man I know. It's just that your way of thinking and his way of thinking are different—and he's the President."

Jack could have said that the mark of intellectual honesty is the solicitation of opposing points of view. Instead he said, "Like I said, I'll go quietly. I've been doing this long enough. It's time to relax a little, smell the roses and play with the kids."

"Good man." Van Damm patted his arm. "You bring this job off and your going-away statement from the Boss will sparkle. We'll have Callie Weston write it, even."

"You stroke like a pro, Arnie." Ryan shook his hand and walked off to his car. Van Damm would have been surprised to see the smile on his face.

"Do you have to do it that way?"

"Elizabeth, ideological differences notwithstanding, he has served his country well. I disagree with him on a lot of things, but he's never lied to me, and he's always tried to give me good advice,'' Fowler replied, looking at the plastic-stick microphone. He suddenly wondered if it was working.

''I *told* you what happened last night.''

''You got your wish. He's on the way out. At this level you do not throw people out the door. You do it in a civilized and honorable way. Anything else is small-minded and decidedly stupid politically. I agree with you that he's a dinosaur, but even dinosaurs get a nice spot in the museums.''

''But—''

''That's all. Okay, you had words with his wife last night. I'm sorry about that, but what kind of person penalizes someone for what their wife did?''

''Bob, I have a right to expect your support!''

Fowler didn't like that, but responded reasonably. ''And you have it, Elizabeth. Now, this is neither the time nor the place for this sort of discussion.''

Marcus Cabot arrived at Andrews Air Force Base just after lunch for his flight to Korea. The arrangements were more luxurious than they looked. The aircraft was a U.S. Air Force C-141B Starlifter, an aircraft with four engines and an oddly serpentlike fuselage. Loaded into the cargo area, he saw, was essentially a house trailer complete with kitchen, living and bed rooms. It was also heavily insulated—the C-141 is a noisy aircraft, especially aft. He went out the front door to meet the flight crew. The pilot, he saw, was a blond captain of thirty years. There were, in fact, two complete flight crews. The flight would be long, with a fueling stop at Travis Air Force Base in California, followed by three midair ''tankings'' over the Pacific. It would also be singularly boring, and he would sleep through it as much as possible. He wondered if government service was really worth it, and the knowledge that Ryan would soon be gone—Arnold van Damm had gotten the word to him—didn't improve his outlook. The Director of Central Intelligence strapped himself in and started to read through his briefing documents. An Air Force noncom offered him a glass of wine, which he started on as the aircraft taxied off the ramp.

John Clark and Domingo Chavez boarded their own flight later that afternoon for Mexico City. It was better, the senior man thought, to get settled in and acclimated. Mexico City was yet another high-altitude metropolis whose thin air was made all the worse by air pollution. Their mission gear was carefully packed away, and they expected no trouble with customs clearance. Neither carried a weapon, of course, as this sort of mission did not require it.

The truck pulled off the Interstate exactly thirty-eight hours and forty minutes after leaving the cargo terminal at Norfolk. That was the easy part. It took fifteen minutes and all the driver's skill to back his rig up to the concrete loading dock outside the barn. A warm sun had thawed the ground into a six-inch-deep layer of gooey mud that almost prevented him from completing the maneuver, but on the third try he made it. The driver jumped down and walked back toward the dock.

''How do you open this thing?'' Russell asked.

''I'll show you.'' The driver paused to scrape the mud off his boots, then worked the latch on the container. ''Need help unloading?''

''No, I'll do it myself. There's coffee over in the house.''

''Thank you, sir. I could use a cup.''

''Well, that was easy enough,'' Russell said to Qati as they watched the man go ight here, sir.'' The sonarman pointed to a line on the display. Though it l fuzzy, it was in fact composed of discrete yellow dots in a specific frequency , and as the time scale moved vertically upward, more dots kept appearing, r only in that they seemed to form a vague and fuzzy line. The only change line was a slight drift in direction. ''I can't tell you what it is yet.''

ell me what it isn't.''

ain't no surface contact, and I don't think it's random noise either, sir.'' The officer traced it all the way to the top of the tube with a grease pencil. ''Right here, I decided it might actually be something.''

/hat else you got?''

ierra-15 over here is a merchant, heading southeast and way the hell away us—that's a third-CZ contact we been trackin' since before turn of the last , and that's about it, Mr. Pitney. I guess it's too bumpy topside for the men to be out this far.''

utenant Pitney tapped the screen. ''Call it Sierra-16, and I'll get a track started. s the water?''

)eep channel seems very good today, sir. Surface noise is a little tough, though. one's tough to hold.''

(eep an eye on it.''

ye aye.'' The sonarman turned back to his scope.

eutenant Jeff Pitney returned to the control room, lifted the growler phone, and hed the button for the Captain's cabin. ''Gator here, Cap'n. We have a possible contact bearing two-nine-five, very faint. Our friend might be back, sir. . . . sir.'' Pitney hung up and hit the 1-MC speaker system. ''Man the fire-control ing party.''

ptain Ricks appeared a minute later, wearing sneakers and his blue coveralls. irst stop was to control, to check course, speed, and depth. Then he went into r.

Let's see it.''

Damn thing just faded on me again, sir,'' the sonarman said sheepishly. He a piece of toilet paper—there was a roll over each scope—to erase the previous , and penciled in another. ''I think we have something here, sir.''

I hope you didn't interrupt my sleep for nothing,'' Ricks noted. Lieutenant y caught the look the two other sonarmen exchanged at that.

Coming back, sir. You know, if this is an Akula, we should be getting a little p noise in this spectrum over here. . . .''

Intelligence says he's coming out of overhaul. Ivan is learning how to make ı quieter,'' Ricks said.

Guess so . . . slow drift to the north, call the current bearing two-nine-seven.'' ı men knew that figure could be off by ten degrees either way. Even with the mously expensive system on *Maine,* really long-distance bearings were pretty ıe.

Anybody else around?'' Pitney asked.

Omaha is supposed to be around somewhere south of Kodiak. Wrong direction. not her. Sure it's not a surface contact?''

No way, Cap'n. If it was diesel, I'd know it, and if it was steam, I'd know , too. There's no pounding from surface noise. Has to be a submerged contact, 'n. Only thing makes sense.''

Pitney, we're on two-eight-one?''

Yessir.''

away. Marvin opened the doors and saw a single large box wi four sides, along with arrows to show which side was up, champagne glass to tell the illiterate it was delicate. It was als pallet. Marvin removed the fasteners that held it in place, thei The task of removing the bomb and putting it inside the ba another minute. Russell shut the forklift down, then draped a the time the trucker came back, the cargo box was again clo:

"Well, you got your bonus," Marvin told him, handing o

The driver riffled through the bills. Now he got to drive the but first he'd hit the nearest truck stop for eight hours of sleej business with you, sir. You said you might have another job so?"

"That's right."

"Here's how you reach me." The trucker handed over his

"Heading right back?"

"After I get some sack time. I just heard on the radio t tomorrow night. A big one, they say."

"That time of year, isn't it?"

"Sure is. You have a good one, sir."

"Be careful, man," Russell said, shaking his hand one mo

"It's a mistake to let him go," Ghosn observed to the Con

"I think not. The only face he has really seen is Marvin's,

"True."

"Have you checked it?" Qati asked.

"There is no damage to the packing box. I will do a n tomorrow. I would say that we are almost ready."

"Yes."

"You want the good news or the bad news?" Jack asked.

"Good first," Cathy said.

"They're asking me to resign my position."

"What's the bad news?"

"Well, you never really leave. They'll want me to come ba consult, stuff like that."

"Is that what you want?"

"This work does get in your blood, Cathy. Would you like to just be a doc with an office and patients and glasses to prescril

"How much?"

"Couple times a year, probably. Special areas I happen to Nothing regular."

"Okay, that's fair—and, no, I couldn't give up teaching soon?"

"Well, I have two things I have to finish up with. Then we ha for the job. . . ." *How about the Foleys,* Jack thought. *But wh*

"Conn, sonar."

"Conn, aye," the navigator answered.

"Sir, I got a possible contact bearing two-nine-five, very coming back."

"On the way." It was a short five steps into the sonar room.

"Come left to two-six-five. We'll set up a better baseline for the target-motion analysis, try to get a range estimate before we turn in."

Turn in, Pitney thought. *Jesus, boomers aren't supposed to do this stuff.* He gave the order anyway, of course.

"Where's the layer?"

"One-five-zero feet, sir. Judging by the surface noise, there's twenty-five-footers up there," the sonarman added.

"So he's probably staying deep to smooth the ride out."

"Damn, lost him again . . . we'll see what happens when the tail straightens back out. . . ."

Ricks leaned his head out of the sonar room and spoke a single word: "Coffee." It never occurred to him that the sonarmen might like some, too.

It took five more minutes of waiting before the dots started appearing again in the right place.

"Okay, he's back. I think," the sonarman added. "Bearing looks like three-zero-two now."

Ricks walked out to the plotting table. Ensign Shaw was doing his calculations along with a quartermaster. "Has to be a hundred-thousand-plus yards. I'm assuming a northeasterly course from the bearing drift, speed of less than ten. Has to be a hundred-K yards or more." That was good, fast work, Shaw and the petty officer thought.

Ricks nodded curtly and went back to sonar.

"Firming up, getting some stuff on the fifty-hertz line now. Starting to smell like Mr. Akula, maybe."

"You must have a pretty good channel."

"Right, Captain, pretty good and improving a little. That storm's gonna change it when the turbulence gets down to our depth, sir."

Ricks went into control again: "Mr. Shaw?"

"Best estimate is one-one-five-K yards, course northeasterly, speed five knots, maybe one or two more, sir. If his speed's much higher than that, the range is awfully far."

"Okay, I want us to come around very gently, come right to zero-eight-zero."

"Aye aye, sir. Helm, right five degrees rudder, come to new course zero-eight-zero."

"Right five degrees rudder, aye. Sir, my rudder is right five degrees, coming to new course zero-eight-zero."

"Very well."

Slowly, so as not to make too great a bend in the towed array, USS *Maine* reversed course. It took three minutes before she settled down on the new course, doing something no U.S. fleet ballistic-missile submarine had ever done before. Lieutenant Commander Claggett appeared in the control room soon thereafter.

"How long you figure he's going to hold this course?" he asked Ricks.

"What would you do?"

"I think I'd troll along in a ladder pattern," Dutch answered, "and my drift would be south instead of north, reverse of how we do it in the Barents Sea, right? Interval between sweeps will be determined by the performance of his tail. That's one hard piece of intel we can develop, but depending on how that number looks, we'll have to be real careful how we trail him, won't we?"

"Well, I can't approach to less than thirty thousand yards under any circumstances. So . . . we'll close to fifty-K until we have a better feel for him, then ease

"In this movie the objective was to kill the entire stadium?" Ghosn asked very quietly.

"Huh—oh, yeah, that's right." Russell was loading the dishes into the dishwasher. "Not like we're doing." He turned. "Hey, don't feel bad. Just taking out the TV coverage is going to piss people off like you wouldn't believe. And this stadium is covered, okay? That blimp-thing wouldn't work. You'd need like a nuke or something to do the same thing."

"There's an idea," Ghosn observed with a chuckle, wondering what reaction he'd get.

"Some idea. Yeah, you might start a real nuclear war—shit, man, guess whose people lives up in the Dakotas, where all those SAC bases are? I don't think I could play that kind of a game." Russell dumped in the detergent and started the wash cycle. "What exactly do you have in that thing, anyway?"

"A very compact and powerful high-explosive compound. It will do some damage to the stadium, of course."

"I figured that. Well, taking out the TV won't be hard—that's delicate shit, y'know?—and just doing that—man, I'm telling you, it's going to have an effect like you wouldn't believe."

"I agree, Marvin, but I would like to hear your reasoning on this," Qati said.

"We've never had a really destructive terrorist act over here. This one will change things. People won't feel safe. They'll install checkpoints and security stuff everywhere. It'll really piss people off, make people think. Maybe they'll see what the real problems are. That's the whole point, isn't it?"

"Correct, Marvin," Qati replied.

"Can I help you with the painting?" Ghosn asked. He might get curious, Ibrahim thought, and they couldn't have that.

"I'd appreciate it."

"You must promise to turn the heat on," the engineer observed with a smile.

"Depend on it, man, or else the paint won't dry right. I guess this is kinda cold for ya."

"Your people must be very hard to live in such a place."

Russell reached for his coat and gloves. "Hey, man, it's our place, y'know?"

"Do you really expect to find him?" the *Starpom* asked.

"I think we have a fine chance," Dubinin replied, leaning over the chart. "He'll be somewhere in here, well away from the coastal waters—too many fishermen with nets there—and north of this area."

"Excellent, Captain, only two million square kilometers to search."

"And we will cover only two-thirds of that. I said a fine chance, not a certainty. In three or four more years, we'll have the RPV the designers are working on, and we can send our sonar receptors down into the deep sound channel." Dubinin referred to the next step in submarine technology, a robot minisub which would be controlled from the mother ship by a fiber-optic cable. It would carry both sensors and weapons, and by diving very deep it could find out if sonar conditions in the thousand-to-two-thousand-meter regime were really as good as the theorists suggested. That would change the game radically.

"Anything on the turbulence sensors?"

"Negative, Captain," a lieutenant answered.

"I wonder if those things are worth the trouble," the executive officer groused.

"They worked the last time."

"We had calm seas overhead then. How often are the seas calm in the North Pacific in winter?"

"It could still tell us something. We must use every trick we have. Why are you not optimistic?"

"Even Ramius only tracked an Ohio once, and that was on builder's trials, when they had the shaft problem. And even then, he only held the contact for—what? Seventy minutes."

"We had this one before."

"True enough, Captain." The *Starpom* tapped a pencil on the chart.

Dubinin thought about his intelligence briefing on the enemy—old habits were hard to break. Harrison Sharpe Ricks, Captain, Naval Academy, in his second missile-submarine command, reportedly a brilliant engineer and technician, a likely candidate for higher command. A hard and demanding taskmaster, highly regarded in his Navy. He'd made a mistake before, and was unlikely to make another, Dubinin told himself.

"Fifty thousand yards, exactly," Ensign Shaw reported.

"This guy's not doing any Crazy Ivans," Claggett thought for the first time.

"He's not expecting to be hunted himself, is he?" Ricks asked.

"I guess not, but his tail's not as good as he thinks it is." The Akula was doing a ladder-search pattern. The long legs were on a roughly southwest-to-northeast vector, and at the end of each he shifted down southeast to the next leg, with an interval between search legs of about fifty thousand yards, twenty-five nautical miles. That gave a notional range of about thirteen miles to the Russian's towed-array sonar. At least, Claggett thought, that's what the intelligence guys would have said.

"You know, I think we'll hold at fifty-K yards, just to play it on the safe side," Ricks announced after a moment's reflection. "This guy is a lot quieter than I expected."

"Plant noises are down quite a bit, aren't they? If this guy was creeping instead of trying to cover ground. . . ." Claggett was pleased that his Captain was speaking like his conservative-engineer self again. He wasn't especially surprised. When push came to shove, Ricks reverted to type, but that was all right with the XO, who didn't think it was especially prudent to play fast-attack with a billion-dollar boomer.

"We could still hold him at forty, thirty-five tops."

"Think so? How much will his tail's performance improve with a slower speed?"

"Good point. It'll be some, but intelligence calls it a thin-line array like ours . . . probably not all that much. Even so, we're getting a good profile on this bird, aren't we?" Ricks asked rhetorically. He'd get a gold star in his copybook for this.

"So, what do you think, MP?" Jack asked Mrs. Foley. He held the translation in his hand. She'd opted for the original Russian-language document.

"Hey, I recruited him, Jack. He's my boy."

Ryan checked his watch; it was just about time. Sir Basil Charleston was nothing if not punctual. His secure direct-line phone rang right on the hour.

"Ryan."

"Bas here."

"What gives, man?"

''That thing we talked out, we had our chap look into it. Nothing at all, my boy.''

''Not even that our impressions were incorrect?'' Jack asked, his eyes screwed tightly shut as though to keep the news out.

''Correct, Jack, not even that. I admit I find that slightly curious, but it is plausible, if not likely, that our chap should not know this.''

''Thanks for trying, pal. We owe you one.''

''Sorry we could not be of help.'' The line went dead.

It was the worst possible news, Ryan thought. He stared briefly at the ceiling.

''The Brits have been unable to confirm or deny SPINNAKER's allegations,'' Jack announced. ''What's that leave us with?''

''It's really like this?'' Ben Goodley asked. ''It all comes down to *opinion?''*

''Ben, if we were really that smart at reading fortunes, we'd be *making* fortunes in the stock market,'' Ryan said gruffly.

''But you did!'' Goodley pointed out.

''I got lucky on a few hot issues.'' Ryan dismissed the observation. ''Mary Pat, what do you think?''

Mrs. Foley looked tired, but then she had an infant to worry about. Jack thought he should tell her to take it easier. ''I have to back up my agent, Jack. You know that. He's our best source of political intelligence. He gets in to see Narmonov alone. That's why he's so valuable, and that's why his stuff has always been hard to back up—but it's never been wrong, has it?''

''The scary part is that he's starting to convince me.''

''Why scary, Dr. Ryan?''

Jack lit a cigarette. '' 'Cause I know Narmonov. That man could have made me disappear one cold night outside o' Moscow. We cut a deal, shook on it, and that was that. Takes a very confident man to do something like that. If he has lost that confidence, then . . . then the whole thing could come apart, rapidly and unpredictably. Can you think of anything scarier than that?'' Ryan's eyes swept the room.

''Not hardly,'' agreed the head of the Intelligence Directorate's Russian Department. ''I think we have to go with it.''

''So do I,'' Mary Pat agreed.

''Ben?'' Jack asked. ''You believed this guy from the beginning. What he says backs up your position from up at Harvard.''

Dr. Benjamin Goodley didn't like being cornered like that. He had learned a hard but important lesson in his months in CIA: it was one thing to form an opinion in an academic community, to discuss options around the lunch tables in the Harvard faculty club, but it was different here. From these opinions national policy was made. And that, he realized, was what being captured by the system actually meant.

''I hate to say this, but I've changed my mind. There may be a dynamic here we haven't examined.''

''What might that be?'' the head of the Russian Department asked.

''Just consider this abstractly. If Narmonov goes down, who replaces him?''

''Kadishev is one of the possibilities, say one chance in three or so,'' Mary Pat answered.

''In academia—hell, anywhere—isn't that a conflict of interest?''

''M.P.?'' Ryan asked, shifting his eyes.

''Okay, so what? When has he ever lied to us before?''

Goodley decided to run with it, pretending this was an academic discussion. ''Mrs. Foley, I was detailed to look for indications that SPINNAKER was wrong. I've checked everything I've had access to. The only thing I've found is a slight change in the tone of his reports over the last few months. The way he uses language is subtly different. His statements are more positive, less speculative in some areas. Now, that may fit his reports—the content of them, I mean—but . . . but there may be some meaning in that.''

''You're basing your evaluation on how he dots his *i*'s?'' the Russian expert demanded with a snort. ''Kid, we don't do that sort of work here.''

''Well, I have to take this one downtown,'' Ryan said. ''I have to tell the President that we think he's right. I want to get Andrews and Kantrowitz in here to backstop us—objections?'' There were none. ''Okay, thank you. Ben, could you stay for a moment? Mary Pat, take a long weekend. That's an order.''

''She's colicky, and I haven't been getting much sleep,'' Mrs. Foley explained.

''So have Ed take the night duty,'' Jack suggested.

''Ed doesn't have tits. I nurse, remember?''

''M.P., has it ever occurred to you that nursing is a conspiracy of lazy men?'' Ryan asked with a grin.

The baleful look in her eyes concealed her good humor. ''Yeah, at about two every morning. See you Monday.''

Goodley got back in his chair after the other two left. ''Okay, you can yell at me now.''

Jack waved for him to light up. ''What do you mean?''

''For bringing up a dumb idea.''

''Dumb idea, my ass. You were the first to suggest it. You've been doing good work.''

''I haven't found beans,'' the Harvard scholar grumbled.

''No, but you've been looking in all the right places.''

''If this stuff was for-real, how likely is it that you'd be able to confirm through other sources?'' Goodley asked.

''A little better than even money, maybe sixty percent, tops. Mary Pat was right. This guy's been giving us stuff we can't always get somewhere else. But you're also correct: he stands to profit from being right. I have to run this one down to the White House before the weekend starts. Then I'm going to call Jake Kantrowitz and Eric Andrews and get them to fly in here for a look-see next week. Got any particular plans for the weekend?'' Jack asked.

''No.''

''You do now. I want you to sweep through all your notes and do us a position paper, a good one.'' Ryan tapped his desk. ''I want it here Monday morning.''

''Why?''

''Because you're intellectually honest, Ben. When you look at something, you really look.''

''But you never agree with my conclusions!'' Goodley objected.

''Not very often, but your supporting data is first-rate. Nobody's right all the time. Nobody's wrong all the time, either. The process is important, the intellectual discipline, and you have that locked down pretty tight, Dr. Goodley. I hope you like living in Washington. I'm going to offer you a permanent position here. We're setting up a special group in the DI. Their mission will be to take contrarian positions, an in-house Team-B that reports directly to the DDI. You'll be the number-two man in the Russian Section. Think you can handle it? Think carefully, Ben,'' Jack added hastily. ''You'll take a lot of heat from the A-Team. Long hours, mediocre pay, and not a hell of a lot of satisfaction at the end of the day. But you'll

"Here is my latest report," Agent MUSHASHI said, handing over the envelope.

"Our President is most impressed with the quality of your information," Cabot replied.

"As I am impressed with the salary."

"So, what can I do for you?"

"I wanted to be sure that you are taking me seriously," Lyalin said.

"We do that," Marcus assured him. *Does this fellow think we pay in the millions for the fun of it?* He wondered. It was Cabot's first face-to-face with an agent. Though he'd been briefed to expect a conversation just like this one, it still came as a surprise.

"I plan to defect in a year, with my family. What exactly will you do for me?"

"Well, we will debrief you at length, then assist you in finding a comfortable place to live and work."

"Where?"

"Anywhere you wish, within reason." Cabot managed to conceal his exasperation. This was work for a junior case officer.

"What do you mean, 'within reason'?"

"We won't let you live right across the street from the Russian Embassy. What exactly do you have in mind?"

"I don't know yet."

Then why did you bring this up? "What sort of climate do you like?"

"Warm, I think."

"Well, there's Florida, lots of sun."

"I will think about that." The man paused. "You do not lie to me?"

"Mr. Lyalin, we take good care of our guests."

"Okay. I will continue to send you information." And with that, the man simply got up and left.

Marcus Cabot managed not to swear, but the look he gave to the station chief ignited a laugh.

"First time you've done a touchy-feely, right?"

"You mean that's all?" Cabot could scarcely believe it.

"Director, this is a funny business. Crazy as it sounds, what you just did was very important," Sam Yamata said. "Now he knows that we really care about him. Bringing up the President was a good move, by the way."

"You say so." Cabot opened the envelope and started reading. "Good Lord!"

"More on the Prime Minister's trip?"

"Yes, the details we didn't get before. Which bank, payoffs to other officials. We may not even need to bug the airplane. . . ."

"Bug an airplane?" Yamata asked.

"You never heard me say that."

The station chief nodded. "How could I? You were never here."

"I need to get this off to Washington fast."

Yamata checked his watch. "We'll never catch the direct flight in time."

"Then we'll fax it secure."

"We're not set up for that. Not on the Agency side, I mean."

"How about the NSA guys?"

"They have it, Director, but we've been warned about the security of their systems."

"The President needs this. It has to go out. Do it, my authority."

"Yes, sir."

33. Passages

It was nice to wake up at a decent hour—eight o'clock—at home on a Saturday. Without a headache. That was something he hadn't done in months. He fully planned to spend the day at home doing precisely nothing more than shave, and he planned that only because he'd be going to mass that evening. Ryan soon learned that on Saturday mornings his children were glued to the TV set, watching various cartoons, including something concerning turtles that he'd heard about but never seen. On reflection, he decided to pass on it this morning also.

"How are you this morning?" he asked Cathy on his way into the kitchen.

"Not bad at all. I—oh, damn!"

The noise she heard was the distinctive trilling of the secure phone. Jack ran into the library to catch it.

"Yeah?"

"Dr. Ryan, this is the ops room. Swordsman," the watch officer said.

"Okay." Jack hung up. "Damn."

"What's the matter?" Cathy asked from the doorway.

"I have to go in. By the way, I have to be in tomorrow, too."

"Jack, come on—"

"Look, babe, there are a couple of things I have to do before I leave. One's happening right about now—and you can forget that, okay?—and I have to be in on it."

"Where do you have to go this time?"

"Just into the office. I don't have any overseas stuff planned at all, as a matter of fact."

"Supposed to snow tonight, maybe a big one."

"Great. Well, I can always stay over."

"I'm going to be so happy when you leave that goddamned place for good."

"Can you stick with me just a couple months more?"

" 'Couple of months'?"

"April first, I'm out of there. Deal?"

"Jack, it's not that I don't like what you do, just that—"

"Yeah, the hours. Me, too. I'm used to the idea of leaving now, turning into a normal person again. I gotta change."

Cathy bowed to the inevitable and went back to the kitchen. Jack dressed casually. On weekends you didn't have to wear a suit. He decided that he could even dispense with a tie, and also that he'd drive himself. Thirty minutes later he was on the road.

It was a gloriously clear afternoon over the Strait of Gibraltar. Europe to the north, Africa to the south. The narrow passage had once been a mountain range, the geologists said, and the Mediterranean a dry basin until the Atlantic had broken in. This would have been the perfect place to watch from, too, thirty thousand feet up.

And best of all, he would not have had to worry about commercial air traffic back then. Now he had to listen to the guard circuit make sure some airliner didn't blunder into his path. Or the other way around, which was actually more honest.

"There's our company," Robby Jackson observed.

"Never seen her before, sir," Lieutenant Walters said.

"Her" was the Soviet carrier *Kuznetzov,* the first real carrier in the Russian Fleet. Sixty-five thousand tons, thirty fixed-wing aircraft, ten or so helicopters. Escorting her were the cruisers *Slava* and *Marshal Ustinov,* plus what looked like one Sovremenny- and two Udaloy-class destroyers. They were coming east in a compressed tactical formation, and were two hundred forty miles behind the *TR* battle group. Half a day back, Robby thought, or half an hour, depending on how you looked at it.

"We give 'em a flyby?" Walters asked.

"Nope, why piss 'em off?"

"Looks like they're in a hurry," the RIO said, looking through a pair of binoculars. "I'd say about twenty-five knots."

"Maybe they're just trying to clear the strait as quick as they can."

"I doubt that, skipper. What do you suppose they're here for?"

"Same as us, according to intel. Train, show the flag, make friends and influence people."

"Didn't you have a run-in once . . . ?"

"Yeah, a Forger put a heat-seeker up my ass a few years back. Got my Tom back all right, though." Robby paused for a moment. "They said it was an accident, supposedly the pilot was punished."

"Believe it?"

Jackson gave the Russian battle group a last look. "Yeah, as a matter of fact."

"First time I saw a picture of that thing I said to myself, there's a Navy Cross that hasn't happened yet."

"Chill out, Shredder. Okay, we seen 'em. Let's head back." Robby moved the stick to turn back east. This he did in a leisurely maneuver rather than the hard-bank-and-pull a younger fighter jock might try. Why stress the airframe unnecessarily? Jackson would have thought if he'd bothered to think about it. In the backseat, Lieutenant Henry "Shredder" Walters thought the CAG was just turning into an old guy.

Not that old. Captain Jackson was as alert as ever. His seat was jacked up about as far as it would go, because Robby was on the short side. This gave him a good field of view. His eyes swept in a constant pattern left-right, up-down, and in to look at his instruments about once a minute. His main concern was commercial air traffic, and also private planes, since this was a weekend, and people liked to orbit the Rock to take pictures. A civilian in a Learjet, Robby thought, could be more dangerous than a loose Sidewinder. . . .

"Jesus! Coming up at nine!"

Captain Jackson's head snapped to the left. Fifty feet away was a MiG-29 Fulcrum-N, the new naval variant of the Russian air-superiority fighter. The visored face of the pilot was staring at him. Robby saw that four missiles were hanging on the wings. The Tomcat had only two at the moment.

"Came up from underneath," Shredder reported.

"Clever of him." Robby took the news with equanimity. The Russian pilot waved. Robby returned the gesture.

"Damn, if he wanted to—"

"Shredder, will you cool it? I've been playing games with Ivan for almost twenty years. I've intercepted more Bears than you've had pussy. We're not tactical. I just wanted to fly back here and get a look at their formation. Ivan over there decided to come up to look at us. He's being neighborly about it." Robby edged his stick forward, taking his aircraft down a few feet. He wanted to eyeball the Russian's underside. No extra fuel tanks, just the four missiles, AA-11 "Archers," NATO called them. The tail hook looked flimsier than the one the Americans had on their planes, and he remembered reports of landing problems the Russians had experienced. Well, carrier aviation was new to them, wasn't it? They'd spend years learning all the lessons. Other than that, the aircraft looked impressive. Newly painted, the pleasant gray the Russians used instead of the high-tech infrared-suppressive gray that the U.S. Navy had adopted a few years ago. The Russian version was prettier; the USN paint was more effective in concealment, though it did give the planes a painfully leprous appearance. He memorized the tail number to report to the wing intelligence troops. He couldn't see any of the pilot. The helmet and visor covered his face, and he wore gloves. Fifty-foot closure was a little tight, but not that big a deal. Probably the Russian was trying to show him that he was good, but not crazy. That was fair enough. Robby came back up level and waved to thank the Russian for holding a steady line. Again the gesture was returned.

What's your name, boy? Robby thought. He also wondered what the Russian thought about the victory flag painted under the cockpit, under which was printed in small letters, MiG-29, 17-1-91. *Let's not get too cocky over there.*

The 747 landed after its long trans-Pacific flight, much to the relief of the flight crew, Clark was sure. Twelve-hour flights must have been a bitch, the CIA officer was sure, especially flying into a smog-filled bowl at the end of it. The aircraft taxied out, then turned and finally stopped at a space marked by a military band, several rows of soldiers and civilians, and the customary red carpet.

"You know, after that much time in an airplane I'm too dogshit to do anything intelligent," Chavez observed quietly.

"So remember never to run for president," Clark replied.

"Right, Mr. C."

The stairs were rolled up, and presently the door opened. The band struck up something or other—the two CIA officers were too far away to hear it clearly. The normal TV crews flitted about. The arriving Japanese Prime Minister was met by the Mexican Foreign Minister, listened to a brief speech, made a brief one of his own, walked past the troops who'd been standing in place for ninety minutes, then did the first sensible thing of the day. He got into a limo and drove off to his embassy for a shower—or more likely, Clark thought, a hot bath. The way the Japs did it was probably the perfect cure for air travel, a long soak in hundred-plus degree water. It was sure to take the wrinkles out of the skin and the stiffness out of the muscles, John thought. Pity that Americans hadn't learned that one. Ten minutes after the last dignitary left, and the troops marched off, and the carpet was rolled back up, the maintenance people were summoned to the aircraft.

The pilot spoke briefly with the head mechanic. One of the big Pratt and Whitney engines was running just a hair warm. Other than that, he had no beefs at all. Then the flight crew departed for a rest. Three security people took station around the outside of the aircraft. Two more paced the interior. Clark and Chavez entered, showing their passes to Mexican and Japanese officials, and went to work. Ding started in the washrooms, taking his time because he'd been told the Japanese were particular about having spotless latrines. It required only one sniff of the air inside the airplane to note that Japanese citizens were allowed to smoke. Each ashtray had to be checked, and more than half of those required emptying and cleaning. Newspapers and magazines were collected. Other cleaning staff handled the vacuuming.

Forward, Clark checked the booze locker. Half the people aboard must have arrived with hangovers, he decided. There were some serious drinkers aboard. He was also gratified to see that the technical people at Langley had guessed right on the brand of scotch that JAL liked to serve. Finally he went up to the lounge area behind the cockpit. It exactly matched the computer mock-up he'd examined for hours prior to coming down. By the time he'd finished his cleaning duties, he was sure that bringing this one off would be a snap. He helped Ding with the trash bags and left the aircraft in time to catch a dinner. On the way out to his car, he passed a note to a CIA officer from Station Mexico.

"Goddamn it!" Ryan swore. "This came in through State?"

"Correct, sir. Director Cabot's orders to use a fax line. He wanted to save transcription time."

"Didn't Sam Yamata bother to explain about datelines and time zones?"

" 'Fraid not."

There was no sense swearing further at the man from the Japan Department. Ryan read through the pages again. "Well, what do you think?"

"I think the Prime Minister is walking into an ambush."

"Isn't that too damned bad?" Ryan observed. "Messenger this down to the White House. The President's going to want it PDQ."

"Right." The man left. Ryan dialed up operations next. "How's Clark doing?" Jack asked without preamble.

"Okay, he says. He's ready to make the plant. The monitor aircraft are all standing by. We know of no changes in the PM's schedule."

"Thanks."

"How long are you going to be in?"

Jack looked outside. The snow had already started. "Maybe all night."

It was developing into a big one. The eastbound cold-weather storm from the Midwest was linking into a low-pressure area coming up the coast. The really big snowstorms in the D.C. area always came in from the south, and the National Weather Service was saying six-to-eight inches. That prediction was up from two-to-four only a few hours earlier. He could leave work right now, then try to fight his way back in the morning, or he could stay. Staying, unfortunately, looked like the best option.

Golovko was also in his office, though the time in Moscow was eight hours ahead of Washington. That fact did not contribute to Sergey's humor, which was poor.

"Well?" he asked the man from the communications-intelligence watch staff.

"We got lucky. This document was sent by facsimile printer from the U.S. Embassy Tokyo to Washington." He handed the sheet over.

The slick thermal paper was covered mainly with gibberish, some discrete but disordered letters, and even more black-and-white hash from the random noise, but perhaps as much as twenty percent was legible English, including two complete sentences and one full paragraph.

"Well?" Golovko asked again.

"When I delivered it to the Japanese section for comment, they handed me this." Another document was passed. "I've marked the paragraph."

Golovko read the Russian-language paragraph, then compared it to the English—

"It's a fucking translation. How was our document sent in?"

"By embassy courier. It wasn't transmitted because two of the crypto machines in Tokyo were being repaired, and the *Rezident* decided it was unimportant enough to wait. It ended up in the embassy bag. So they are not reading our ciphers, but they got this anyway."

"Who's working this case? Lyalin? Yes," Golovko said, almost to himself. He next called the senior watch officer for the First Chief Directorate. "Colonel, this is Golovko. I want a Flash-priority to *Rezident* Tokyo. Lyalin to report to Moscow immediately."

"What's the problem?"

"The problem is we have another leak."

"Lyalin is a very effective officer. I know the material he's sending back."

"So do the Americans. Get that message off at once. Then I want everything we have from THISTLE on my desk." Golovko hung up and looked at the Major standing in front of his desk. "That mathematician who figured this all out—good God, I wish we'd had him five years ago!"

"He spent ten years devising this theory on ordering chaos. If it's ever made public, he'll win the Planck Medal. He took the work of Mandelbrot at Harvard University in America and MacKenzie at Cambridge, and—"

"I will take your word for it, Major. The last time you tried to explain this witchcraft to me I merely got a headache. How is the work going?"

"We grow stronger every day. The only thing we cannot break is the new CIA system that's starting to come on line. It seems to use a new principle. We're working on it."

President Fowler boarded the Marine VH-3 helicopter before the snow got too bad. Painted a shiny olive-drab on the bottom, with white on top, and little else in the way of markings, it was his personal bird, with the call sign Marine-One. Elizabeth Elliot boarded just behind him, the press corps noted. Pretty soon they'd have to break the story on the two, some thought. Or maybe the President would do the job for them by marrying the bitch.

The pilot, a Marine lieutenant colonel, brought the twin-turbine engines to full power, then eased up on the collective, rising slowly and turning northwest. He was almost instantly on instruments, which he didn't like. Flying blind and on instruments didn't trouble him. Flying blind and on instruments with the President aboard did. Flying in snow was about the worst thing there was. All external visual references were gone. Staring out the windshield could turn the most seasoned airman into a disoriented and airsick feather-merchant in a matter of seconds. As a result, he spent far more time scanning his instruments. The chopper had all manner of safety features, including collision-avoidance radar, plus having the undivided attention of two senior air-traffic controllers. In some perverse ways, this was a safe way to fly. In clear air some lunatic with a Cessna might just try to perform a midair with Marine-One, and maneuvering to avoid such things was a regular drill for the Colonel, both in the air and in the aircraft simulator at Anacostia Naval Air Station.

"Wind's picking up faster than I 'spected," the copilot, a major, observed. "May get a little bumpy when we hit the mountains."

"Sounds good to me."

"Let's get some dinner first."

Oleg Yurievich Lyalin boarded his flight to Moscow with mixed feelings. The summons was not all that irregular. It was troublesome that it had come so soon after his meeting with the CIA Director, but that was probably happenstance. More likely it had to do with the information he'd been delivering to Moscow about the Japanese Prime Minister's trip to America. One surprise he had not told CIA concerned Japanese overtures to the Soviet Union to trade high technology for oil and lumber. That deal would have upset the Americans greatly only a few years earlier, and marked the culmination of a five-year project that Lyalin had worked on. He settled into his airline seat and allowed himself to relax. He had never betrayed his country, after all, had he?

The satellite uplink trucks were in two batches. There were eleven network vehicles, all parked just at the stadium wall. Two hundred meters away were thirty-one more, smaller Ku-band uplinks for what looked like regional TV stations, as opposed to the bigger networks' vans. The first storm had passed, and what looked like a tank division's worth of heavy equipment was sweeping up the snow from the stadium's enormous parking lot.

There was the spot, Ghosn thought, right next to the ABC "A" unit. There was a good twenty meters of open space. The absence of security astounded him. He counted only three police cars, just enough to keep drunks away from men trying to get their work done. So secure the Americans felt. They'd tamed the Russians, crushed Iraq, intimidated Iran, pacified his own people, and now they were as totally relaxed as a people could be. They must love their comforts, Ibrahim told himself. Even their stadia had roofs and heat to keep the elements out.

"Gonna knock those things over like dominoes," Marvin observed from the driver's seat.

"Indeed we will," Ghosn agreed.

"See what I told you about security?"

"I was wrong to doubt you, my friend."

"Never hurts to be careful." Russell started another drive around the perimeter. "We'll come in this gate right here, and just drive right up." The headlights of the van illuminated the few flakes of this second storm. It was too cold to snow a lot, Russell had explained. This Canadian air mass was heading south. It would warm up as it hit Texas, dropping its moisture there instead of on Denver, which had half a meter, Ghosn estimated. The men who cleared the roads were quite efficient. As with everything else, the Americans liked their conveniences. Cold weather—build a stadium with a roof. Snow on the highways—get rid of it. Palestinians—buy them off. Though his face didn't show it, he had never hated America more than at this moment. Their power and their arrogance showed in everything they did. They protected themselves against everything, no matter how big or small, knew that they did, and proclaimed it to themselves and the whole world.

Oh, God, to bring them down!

The fire was agreeably warm. The President's cabin at Camp David was in the classic American pattern, heavy logs laid one atop the other, though on the inside, they were reinforced with Kevlar fiber, and the windows were made of rugged polycarbonate to stop a bullet. The furniture was an even more curious mix of ultramodern and old-comfortable. Before the couch he sat on were three printers for the major news services because his predecessors liked to see the wire copy, and there were three full-sized televisions, one of which was usually tuned to CNN. But not tonight. Tonight it was on Cinemax. Half a mile away was a discreetly-sited antenna farm that tracked all of the commercial satellites, along with most of the military ones, a benefit of which was access to every commercial satellite channel—even the X-rated ones, which Fowler didn't bother with—creating the world's most expensive and exclusive cable system.

Fowler poured himself a beer. It was a bottle of Dortmunder Union, a popular German brew that the Air Force flew over—being President did carry some useful and unofficial perks. Liz Elliot drank a French white while the President's left hand toyed with her hair.

The movie was a sappy comedic romance that appealed to Bob Fowler. The female lead, in fact, reminded him of Liz in looks and mannerisms. A little too snappy, a little too domineering, but not without redeeming social value. Now that Ryan was gone—well, on the way to be gone—maybe things would settle down.

"We've certainly done well, haven't we?"

"Yes, we have, Bob." She paused for a sip of wine. "You were right about Ryan. Better to let him go honorably." *So long as he's gone, along with that little shrew he married.*

"I'm glad to hear you say that. He's not a bad guy, just old-fashioned. Out of date."

"Obsolete," Liz added.

"Yeah," the President agreed. "Why are we talking about him?"

"I can think of better things." She turned her face into his hand and kissed it.

"So can I," the President murmured as he set his glass down.

"The roads are covered," Cathy reported. "I think you made the right decision."

"Yeah, there was just a bad one on the Parkway just outside the gate. I'll be home tomorrow night. I can always steal one of the four-by-fours they have downstairs."

"Where's John?"

"He's not here right now."

"Oh," Cathy observed. *And what might he be up to?*

"While I'm here, I might as well get some work done. Call you in the morning."

"Okay, 'bye."

"That's one aspect of this place that I won't miss," Jack told Goodley. "Okay, what have you developed?"

"We've been able to verify all the meetings through September."

"You look like you're ready to drop. How long have you been up?"

"Since yesterday, I guess."

"Must be nice to be still in your twenties. Grab a piece of the couch outside," Ryan ordered.

"What about you?"

"I want to read over this stuff again." Jack tapped the file on his desk. "You're not into this one yet. Go get some Zs."

"See you in the morning."

The door closed behind Goodley. Jack started to read through the NIITAKA documents, but soon lost concentration. He locked the file in his desk and found a piece of his own couch, but sleep wouldn't come. After a few minutes of staring at the ceiling, Ryan decided that he might as well stare at something less boring. He switched on the TV. Jack worked the controller to catch a news broadcast, but he hit the wrong button and found himself staring at the tail end of a commercial on Channel 20, an independent Washington station. He almost corrected the mistake when the movie came back. It took a moment. Gregory Peck and Ava Gardner . . . black and white . . . Australia.

"Oh, yeah," Ryan said to himself. It was *On the Beach*. He hadn't seen that in years, a Cold War classic from . . . Nevil Shute, wasn't it? A Gregory Peck movie was always worth the trouble. Fred Astaire, too.

The aftermath of a nuclear war. Jack was surprised at how tired he was. He'd been getting his rest lately, and . . .

. . . he went to sleep, but not all the way. As sometimes happened to him, the movie entered his mind, though the dream was in color, and that was better than the black-and-white print on the TV, his mind decided, then decided further to watch the movie in its entirety. From the inside. Jack Ryan began to take over various roles. He drove Fred Astaire's Ferrari in the bloody and last Australian Grand Prix. He sailed to San Francisco in the USS *Sawfish,* SSN-623 (except, part of his mind objected, that 623 was the number of a different submarine, USS *Nathan Hale,* wasn't it?). And the Morse signal, the Coke bottle on the windowshade, that wasn't very funny at all, because it meant that he and his wife would have to have that cup of tea, and he really didn't want to do that because it meant he had to put the pill in the baby's formula so that he could be sure that the baby would die and his wife wasn't up to it—understandable, his doctor was a wife—and he had to take the responsibility because he was the one who always did and wasn't it a shame that he had to leave Ava Gardner on the beach watching him sail so that he and his men could die at home if they made it which they probably wouldn't and the streets were so empty now. Cathy and Sally and Little Jack were all dead and it was all his fault because he made them take their pills so that they wouldn't die of something else that was even worse but that was still dumb and wrong even though there wasn't much of a choice was there so instead why not use a gun to do it and

"What the fuck!" Jack snapped upright as though driven by a steel spring. He looked at his hands, which were shaking rather badly, until they realized that his mind was under conscious control now. "You just had a nightmare, boy, and this one wasn't the helicopter with Buck and John.

"It was worse."

Ryan reached for his cigarettes and lit one, standing up after he did so. The snow was still coming down. The scrapers weren't keeping pace with it, down on the parking lot. It took time to shake one of these off, watching his family die like that. So many of the goddamned things. *I've gotta get away from this place!* There were just too many memories, and not all of them were good. The wrong call he'd made before the attack on his family, the time in the submarine, being left on the runway at Sheremetyevo Airport and looking at good old Sergey Nikolayevich from the wrong side of a pistol, and worst of all that helicopter ride out of Colombia. It was just too much. It was time to leave. Fowler and even Liz Elliot were doing him a favor, weren't they?

Whether they knew it or not.

Such a nice world lay out there. He'd done his part. He'd made parts of it a little better, and had helped others to do more. The movie he'd just lived in, hell, it might have come to pass in one way or another. But not now. It was clean and white out there, the lights over the parking lot just illuminating it enough, so much better than it usually looked. He'd done his part. Now it was someone else's turn to try his or her hand at the easier stuff.

"Yeah." Jack blew his smoke out at the window. First, he'd have to break this habit again. Cathy would insist. And then? Then an extended vacation, this coming summer, maybe go back to England—maybe by ship instead of flying? Take the time to drive around Europe, maybe blow the whole summer. Be a free man again. Walk the beach. But then he'd have to get a job, do something. Annapolis—no, that was out. Some private group? Maybe teach? Georgetown, maybe?

"Espionage 101." He chuckled to himself. That was it, he'd teach how to do all the illegal stuff.

"How the hell did James Greer ever last so long in this crummy racket?" How had he handled the stress? That was one lesson he'd never passed on.

"You still need sleep, man," he reminded himself. This time he made sure the TV was off.

34. Placement

Ryan was surprised to see that the snow hadn't stopped. The walkway outside his top-floor office window had almost two feet piled up, and the maintenance crews had failed completely to keep up with things through the night. High winds were blowing and drifting snow across the roads and parking lots more quickly than it could be removed, and even the snow that they did manage to move simply found another inconvenient place to blow over. It had been years since a storm like this had hit the Washington area. The local citizenry was already beyond panic into desperation, Jack thought. Cabin fever would already be setting in. Food stocks would not easily be replaced. Already some husbands and some wives were looking at their spouses and wondering how hard to cook they might be. . . . It was one thing to laugh about as he went to get water for his coffee machine. He grabbed Ben Goodley's shoulder on the way out of the office.

"Shake it loose, Dr. Goodley."

The eyes opened slowly. "What time is it?"

"Seven-twenty. What part of New England are you from originally?"

"New Hampshire, up north, place called Littleton."

"Well, take a look out the window and it might remind you of home."

By the time Jack returned with fresh water, the younger man was standing at the windows. "Looks like about a foot and a half out there, maybe a little more. So, what's the big deal? Where I come from this is called a flurry."

"In D.C. it's called The Ice Age. I'll have coffee ready in a few minutes." Ryan decided to call the security desk of the lobby. "What's the situation?"

"People calling in saying they can't make it. But what the hell—most of the night staff couldn't get out. The G.W. Parkway is closed. So's the Beltway on the Maryland side, and the Wilson Bridge—again."

"Outstanding. Okay, this is important, so listen up—that means anybody who makes it in is probably KGB-trained. Shoot 'em." Goodley could hear the laughter on the phone from ten feet away. "Keep me posted on the weather situation. And reserve me a four-by-four, the GMC, in case I have to go somewhere." Jack hung up and looked at Goodley. "Rank hath its privileges. Besides, we have a couple of them."

"What about people who have to get in?"

Jack watched the coffee start to come out of the machine. "If the Beltway and G.W. are closed, that means that two-thirds of our people can't get in. Now you know why the Russians have invested so much money in weather-control programs."

"Doesn't anybody down here—"

"No, people down here pretend that snow is something that happens on ski slopes. If it doesn't stop soon, it'll be Wednesday before anything starts moving in this town."

"It's really that bad here?"

"You'll see for yourself, Ben."

"And I left my cross-country skis up in Boston."

"We didn't hit that hard," the Major objected.

"Major, the breaker board seems to disagree with you," the crew chief replied. He pushed the breaker back in position. The small black plastic tab hesitated for a moment, then popped right back out. "No radio because of this one, and no hydraulics 'cause of that one. I'm afraid we're grounded for a while, sir."

The metering pins for the landing gear had arrived at two in the morning, on the second attempt. The first, aborted, attempts had been by car, until someone had decided that only a military vehicle could make it. The parts had arrived by HMMWV, and even that had been held up by the various stopped cars on the highways between Washington and Camp David. Repairs on the helicopter were supposed to have started in another hour or so—it was not a difficult job—but suddenly they were more complicated.

"Well?" the Major asked.

"Probably a couple of loose wires in there. I gotta pull the whole board, sir, inspect the whole thing. That's a whole day's work at best. Better tell 'em to warm up a backup aircraft."

The Major looked outside. This was not a day he wanted to fly anyway. "We're not supposed to go back until tomorrow morning. When'll it be fixed?"

"If I start now . . . say around midnight."

"Get breakfast first. I'll take care of the backup bird."

"Roge-o, Major."

"I'll have them run some power out here for a heater, and a radio, too." The Major knew the crew chief was from San Diego.

The Major trudged back to the cabin. The helicopter pad was on a high spot, and the wind was trying very hard to blow it clear of snow. As a result there was only six inches to worry about. Down below, the drifts were as much as three feet deep. The grunts out walking the woods must be having a fine time, he thought.

"How bad?" the pilot asked, shaving.

"Circuit panel is acting up. The chief says he needs all day to get it back on line."

"We didn't hit that hard," the Colonel objected.

"I already said that. Want me to make the call?"

"Yeah, go ahead. Have you checked the threat board?"

"The world's at peace, Colonel, sir. I checked."

The "threat board" was mainly an expression. The alert level of the government agencies that dealt with various problems depended on the expected level of danger in the world. The greater the possible danger, the more assets were kept ready to deal with them. At the moment there was no perceived threat to the United States of America, and that meant that only a single aircraft was kept ready to backstop the President's VH-3. The Major placed the call to Anacostia.

"Yeah, let's keep dash-two warm. Dash-one is down with electrical problems . . . no, we can handle it here. Oughta be back on line by midnight. Right. 'Bye." The Major hung up just in time for Pete Connor to enter their cabin.

"What gives?"

"Bird's broke," the Colonel replied.

"I didn't think we hit that hard," Connor objected.

"Well, that makes it official," the Major observed. "The only one who thinks we did hit that hard's the friggin' airplane."

"The backup's on alert status," the Colonel said as he finished shaving. "Sorry, Pete. Electrical problem, maybe had nothing to do with the touchdown. The backup can be here in thirty-five minutes. Our threat board is blank. Anything we need to know about?"

Connor shook his head. "No, Ed. We know of no particular threat."

"I can bring the backup bird here, but it means exposing it to the weather. We can take better care of it down at Anacostia. That's your call, sir."

"You can leave it down there."

"The Boss still wants to watch the game up here, right?"

"Correct. We all get a day off. Lift off for D.C. tomorrow about six-thirty. Problem with that?"

"No, ought to be fixed before then."

"Okay." Connor left and walked back to his cabin.

"What's it like out there?" Daga asked.

"About how it looks," Pete said. "The chopper's broke."

"I wish they'd be more careful," Special Agent Helen D'Agustino observed as she brushed her hair.

"Not their fault." Connor lifted the phone to the Secret Service command center, located a few blocks west of the White House. "This is Connor. The chopper is down with a mechanical problem. Backup is being kept at Anacostia because of weather conditions. Anything on the board I need to know about?"

"No, sir," the junior agent responded. On his status board, in LED characters he could see that the President of the United States—designated POTUS on his display—was shown to be at Camp David. The First Lady of the United States—FLOTUS—space was blank. The Vice President was at his official residence on the ground of the U.S. Naval Observatory off Massachusetts Avenue, Northwest, along with his family. "Everything's nice and calm, far as we know."

"How are the roads down there?" Pete asked.

"Bad. Every Carryall we have is out retrieving people."

"Thank God for Chevrolet." Like the FBI, the Secret Service used the big Chevy four-wheel-drive trucks to get around. Heavily armored and with roughly the fuel-efficiency of a tank, the Carryall was able to do things that only a tank could excel. "Okay, it's nice and snug up here."

"I bet the Marines are freezing their *cojones* off."

"What about Dulles?"

"The Prime Minister is due in at eighteen hundred. The guys say Dulles has one runway open now. They expect to have everything clear by afternoon. Storm's slacking off a little here, finally. You know, the funny thing . . ."

"Yeah." Connor didn't need to hear the rest. The funny thing was that weather like this made the job of the Secret Service easier. "Okay, you know where to reach us."

"Right. See ya tomorrow, Pete."

Connor looked outside when he heard the noise. A Marine was driving a snowplow, trying to clear the paths between the cabins. Two more were working on the roads. It seemed rather odd. The equipment was painted in the Pentagon's woodland camouflage pattern of greens and browns, but the Marines were in their whites. There were even white pullover covers for their M-16A2 rifles. Anyone who tried to get in here today would find, too late, that the perimeter guard force was totally invisible, and these Marines were all combat veterans. At times like this, even the Secret Service could relax, and that came rarely enough. There came a knock on the door. Daga got it.

"Morning papers, ma'am." A Marine corporal handed them over.

"You know," D'Agustino observed after she closed the door, "sometimes I think the guys who deliver these things are the only people you can really depend on."

"What about the Marines?" Pete asked with a laugh.

"Oh, them, too."

"Aspect change in Sierra-16!" the sonarman called. "Target is coming left."

"Very well," Dutch Claggett replied. "Mr. Pitney, you have the conn."

"Aye aye, sir, I have the conn," the navigator said as the XO went into the sonar room. The fire-control tracking party perked up, waiting to restart their calculations.

"Right there, sir." The sonarman tapped the screen with his pencil. "Looks like a beam aspect now. Conn, sonar, bearing is now one-seven-zero, target is coming left. Radiated noise level is constant, estimate target speed is unchanged."

"Very well, thank you."

It was the third such turn they had tracked. Claggett's estimation appeared to be correct. The Russian was conducting a very methodical, very conservative—and very smart—search pattern of this patrol area, just like the 688s did in looking for Russian subs. The interval between the rungs of this ladder seemed to be about forty thousand yards.

"X, that new feed pump they have is a beaut," the sonarman observed. "His plant noise is way the hell down, and the sucker's doing ten knots according to the tracking party."

"Couple more years and we're going to have to worry about these guys."

"Transient, transient—mechanical transient on Sierra-16, bearing is now one-six-four, still drifting left. Speed constant." The petty officer circled the noise blip on the screen. "Maybe, sir, but they still got a lot to learn."

"Range to target is now four-eight thousand yards."

"Mr. Pitney, let's open the range some. Bring her right," the executive officer commanded.

"Aye, helm, left five degrees rudder, come to new course two-zero-four."

"Turning for another leg?" Captain Ricks asked as he entered sonar.

"Yeah, looks like the legs are pretty regular, Cap'n."

"Methodical son of a bitch, isn't he?"

"Turned within two minutes of our estimate," Claggett replied. "I just ordered us right to maintain distance."

"Fair enough." Ricks was actually enjoying this. He hadn't been aboard a fast-attack boat since his first assistant-department-head tour. Playing tag with Russian submarines was something he had not done in the past fifteen years. On the rare occasions he'd heard them at all, his action had always been the same: track long enough to determine the other sub's course, then turn perpendicular to it and head away until it faded back to random noise.

Necessarily, the game was changing somewhat. It wasn't as easy as it used to be. The Russian subs were getting quieter. What had been an annoying trend a few years ago was rapidly turning into something genuinely troubling. And maybe we just had to change the way we do business. . . .

"You know, X, what if this becomes the standard tactic?"

"What do you mean, Cap'n?"

"I mean, as quiet as these guys are getting, maybe this is the smart move."

"Huh?" Claggett was lost.

"If you're tracking the guy, at least you always know where he is. You can even launch a SLOT buoy and call in assets to help you dispose of him. Think about it. They're getting pretty quiet. If you break off as soon as you detect the guy, what's to say you don't blunder into him again? So instead, we track at a nice, safe distance and just keep an eye on him."

"Uh, Captain, that's fine as far as it goes, but what if the other guy gets a sniff of us, or what if he just reverses course and boogies backwards at high speed?"

"Good point. So we trail on his quarter instead of just off his stern . . . that will make an accidental closure less likely. Banging straight aft for a trailer is a logical defensive measure, but he can't go punching holes all over the ocean, can he?"

Jesus, this guy is trying to develop tactics. . . . "Sir, let me know if you sell that one to OP-02."

"Instead of trailing dead aft, I'm going to hold off his northern quarter now. It gives us better performance off the tail anyway. It should actually be safer."

That part of it made sense, Claggett thought. "You say so, Cap'n. Maintain fifty-K yards?"

"Yes, we still want to be a little cautious."

The second storm, as predicted, hadn't done very much, Ghosn saw. There was a light dusting—that seemed to be the term they used—on the vehicles and parking lot. Hardly enough to bother with, it duplicated the most severe winter storm he'd ever seen in Lebanon.

"How about some breakfast?" Marvin asked. "I hate to work on an empty stomach."

The man was remarkable, Ibrahim thought. He was completely free of jitters. Either very brave or . . . something else. Ghosn considered that. He'd killed the Greek policeman without a blink, had taught a brutal lesson to one of the organization's combat instructors, shown his prowess with firearms, and been completely contemptuous of danger when they'd uncovered the Israeli bomb. There was something missing in this man, he concluded. The man was fearless, and such men were not normal. It wasn't that he was able to control his fear as most soldiers learned to do. Fear simply wasn't there. Was it merely a case of trying to impress people?

Or was it real? Probably real, Ghosn thought, and if it were, this man was truly mad, and therefore more dangerous than useful. It made things easier for Ghosn to think that.

The motel didn't offer room service from its small coffee shop. All three walked out into the cold to get their breakfasts. Along the way, Russell picked up a paper to read about the game.

Qati and Ghosn only needed a brief look to find one more reason to hate Americans. They ate eggs with bacon or ham, and pancakes with sausage—in all three cases, products of the most unclean of animals, the pig. Both men found the sight and smell of pork products repulsive. Marvin didn't help when he ordered some as unconsciously as he'd ordered coffee. The Commander, Ghosn noted, ordered oatmeal, and halfway through breakfast he went suddenly pale and left the table.

"What's the matter with him anyway? Sick?" Russell asked.

"Yes, Marvin, he is quite ill." Ghosn looked at the greasy bacon on Russell's plate and knew the smell of it had set Qati's stomach off.

"I hope he's able to drive."

"That will not be a problem." Ghosn wondered if that were true. Of course it was, he told himself, the Commander had been through tougher times—but such bluster was for others, not for times like this. No, because there had never been such a time as this, the Commander would do what must be done. Russell paid for the breakfast with cash, leaving a large tip because the waitress looked like a Native American.

Qati was pale when they got back to the rooms, and wiping his face after a long bout of nausea.

"Can I get you something, man?" Russell asked. "Milk, something good for your stomach?"

"Not now, Marvin, thank you."

"You say so, man." Russell opened his paper. There was nothing to do for the next few hours but wait. The morning line on the game, he saw, was Minnesota by six and a half. He decided that if anyone asked, he'd take the Vikings and give the points.

Special Agent Walter Hoskins, Assistant Special Agent in Charge (Corruption and Racketeering), of the Denver Field Division, knew that he would miss the game despite the fact that his wife had given him a ticket for Christmas. This he had sold to the S-A-C for two hundred dollars. Hoskins had work to do. A confidential informant had scored at the annual NFL Commissioner's party last night. That party—like the ones preceding the Kentucky Derby—always attracted the rich, powerful, and important. This one had been no exception. Both U.S. Senators from Colorado and California, a gaggle of congressmen, the states' governors, and approximately three hundred others had attended. His CI had been at the table with Colorado's governor, senators, and the congresswoman from the third district, all of whom were targets of his corruption case. Liquor had flowed, and in the *vino* had been the usual amount of *veritas*. A deal had been made last night. The dam would be built. The payoffs had been agreed upon. Even the head of the Sierra Club's local branch had been in on it. In return for a large donation from the contractor and a new park to be authorized by the Governor, the environmentalists would mute their objections to the project. The sad part, Hoskins thought, was that the area really needed the water project. It would be good for everyone, including the local fishermen. What made it illegal was that bribes were being made. He would have his choice of five federal statutes to apply to the case, the nastiest of which was the RICO law, the Racketeer-Influenced and Corrupt Organization Act that had been passed over twenty years before without a thought about its possible scope of coverage. He already had one governor in a federal penitentiary, and to that he would add four more elected officials. The scandal would rip Colorado state politics asunder. The confidential informant in question was the Governor's personal aide, an idealistic young woman who had decided eight months earlier that enough was enough. Women were always best for wearing a wire, especially if they had large breasts, as this one did. The mike went right in the bra, and the geometry of the location made for good sound quality. It was also a safe spot because the Governor had already sampled her charms and found them lacking. The old saw was right: hell really did have no fury like a woman scorned.

"Well?" Murray asked, annoyed to have to be in his office on another Sunday. He'd had to ride the subway in, and now that was broken down. He might be stuck all day here.

"Dan, we have enough to prosecute already, but I want to wait until the money gets passed to do the bust. My CI really delivered for us. I'm doing the transcript myself right now."

"Can you fax it?"

"Soon as I'm done. Dan, we've got them all by the ass, all of 'em."

"Walt, we just might put up a statue to you," Murray said, forgetting his annoyance. Like most career cops he loathed public corruption almost as much as he loathed kidnappers.

"Dan, the transfer here is the best thing that ever happened to me." Hoskins laughed into the phone. "Maybe I'll run for one of the vacant Senate seats."

"Colorado could do worse," Dan observed. *Just so you don't carry a gun anywhere,* Murray thought unkindly. He knew that was unfair. Though Walt wasn't worth beans on the muscle end of the business, the other side of his assessment the previous year had also been correct: Hoskins was a brilliant investigator, a chessmaster to equal Bill Shaw, even. Walt just couldn't bring down a bust worth a damn. Well, Murray corrected himself, this one wouldn't be very hard. Politicians hid behind lawyers and press spokesmen, not guns. "What about the U.S. Attorney?"

"He's a good, sharp kid, Dan. He's on the team. Backup from the Department of Justice won't hurt, but the fact of the matter is that this guy can do it if he has to."

"Okay. Shoot me the transcript when it's done." Murray switched buttons on his phone, calling Shaw's home in Chevy Chase.

"Yeah."

"Bill, Dan here," Murray said over the secure phone. "Hoskins scored last night. Says he's got it all on tape—all five principal subjects cut the deal over their roast beef."

"You realize that we might have to promote the guy now?" the FBI Director noted with a chuckle.

"So make him a deputy assistant director," Dan suggested.

"That hasn't kept you out of trouble. Do I need to come in?"

"Not really. What's it like there?"

"I'm thinking of putting up a ski-jump in the driveway. Roads really look bad."

"I took the Metro in, then it shut down—ice on the tracks or something."

"Washington, D.C., the City that Panics," Shaw replied. "Okay, I plan to relax and watch the game, Mr. Murray."

"And I, Mr. Shaw, will forgo my personal pleasures and work for the greater glory of the Bureau."

"Good, I like dedication in my subordinates. Besides, I got my grandson here," Shaw reported, watching his daughter-in-law feed him from a bottle.

"How is Kenny Junior?"

"Oh, we just might make an agent out of him. Unless you really need me, Dan. . . ."

"Bill, enjoy the kid, just remember to hand him back when he messes the diapers."

"Right. Keep me posted on this. I'll have to take this to the President myself, you know."

"You expect problems there?"

"No. He's a standup guy on corruption stuff."

"I'll be back." Murray walked out of his office toward communications. He found Inspector Pat O'Day heading the same way.

"Were those your sled dogs I saw in the drive-thru, Pat?"

"Some of us drive decent cars." O'Day had a four-wheel-drive pickup. "The 9th Street barrier is frozen in the up position, by the way. I've told 'em to leave the other one down."

"What are you in for?"

"I have the watch in the command center. My relief lives out in Frederick. I don't expect to see him until half-past Thursday. I-270 is closed until spring, I think."

"Christ, this is a wimpy town when it snows."

"Tell me about it." O'Day's last field assignment had been in Wyoming, and he still missed the hunting out there.

Murray told the communications staff that the inbound fax from Denver was code-word material. Nobody would get to see it but him for the moment.

"I can't match this one," Goodley said just after lunch.

"Which one?"

"The first one that shook us up—no, excuse me, the second one. I cannot reconcile Narmonov's and SPINNAKER's schedules."

"That doesn't necessarily mean anything."

"I know. The odd thing is, remember what I said about linguistic differences in his reports?"

"Yeah, but remember my Russian is pretty thin. I can't catch nuances like you can."

"This is the first place it shows up, and it's also the first one where I can't satisfy myself that they definitely met." Goodley paused. "I think I might have something here."

"Remember that you have to sell it to our Russian department."

"That's not going to be easy."

"That's right," Ryan agreed. "Back it up with something, Ben."

One of the security guys helped Clark with the case of bottles. He restocked the bar supplies, then headed to the upper level with the remaining four bottles of Chivas. Chavez tagged behind with the flowers. John Clark put the bottles in their places and looked around the compartment to be sure that everything was in order.

He fussed with a few minor items to show that he was being sincere. The bottle with the transceiver in it had a cracked top. That should make sure that nobody tried to open it, he thought. Clever of the S&T guys, he thought. The simple things usually worked best.

The flower arrangements had to be fastened in place. They were mainly white roses, nice ones, Chavez thought, and the little green sticks that held them in place looked like they belonged. Ding next went downstairs and looked at the forward washrooms. In the trash bin of one he dropped a very small, Japanese-made tape recorder, making sure beforehand that it was operating properly. He met Clark at the base of the spiral stairs and then both left the aircraft. The advance security people were just starting to arrive as they disappeared into the terminal's lower level.

Once inside, both men found a locked room and used it to change clothes. They emerged dressed like businessmen, hair recombed, both wearing sunglasses.

"They always this easy, Mr. C?"

"Nope." Both men walked to the opposite side of the terminal. This put them half a mile from the JAL 747, but with a direct line of sight to it. They could also see a Gulfstream-IV business jet liveried as a private aircraft. It was supposed to take off right before the Japanese aircraft, but would head on a diverging course. Clark took a Sony Walkman from his briefcase, inserted a tape cassette, and donned the earphones. In fact, he heard the murmurs of the security men on the aircraft, and the tape was recording their words as his eyes scanned a paperback book. It was a pity that he couldn't understand Japanese, Clark thought. As with most covert operations, the main component was sitting around and doing precisely nothing while he waited for something to happen. He looked up to see the red carpet being rolled out again, and the troops forming up, and a lectern being set up. It must have been a real pain in the ass for the people who had to handle these things, he thought.

Things picked up rapidly. The President of Mexico personally accompanied the Japanese Prime Minister to the aircraft, shaking his hand warmly at the base of the stairs. That might have been evidence right there, Clark thought. There was elation that the job was going well, but sadness that such things as this really happened. The party went up the stairs, the door closed, the stairs were hauled off, and the 747 started its engines.

Clark heard the conversation pick up in the airplane's upstairs lounge. Then sound quality went immediately to hell when the engines fired up. Clark watched the Gulfstream begin taxiing off. The 747 began rolling two minutes later. It made sense. You had to be careful sending aircraft into the sky behind a jumbo. The big wide-bodies left behind wake turbulence that could be very dangerous. The two CIA officers remained in the observation lounge until the JAL airliner lifted off, and then their job was done.

Aloft, the Gulfstream climbed out to its cruising altitude of forty-one thousand feet on a heading of zero-two-six, inbound to New Orleans. The pilot eased off on the throttle somewhat, coached by the men in the back. Off to their right, the 747 was leveling off at the same altitude, on a course of zero-three-one. Inside the bigger aircraft, the supposed bottle of scotch was pointed out a window, and its EHF transmissions were scattering out toward the Gulfstream's receptors. The very favorable data-bandwidth of the system guaranteed a good signal, and no less than ten tape recorders were at work, two for each separate side-band channel. The pilot eased his course as far east as he dared until the two aircraft were over the water, then he turned back left as a second aircraft, this one an EC-135 that had struggled to get out of Tinker Air Force Base in Oklahoma, took up station thirty miles east and two thousand feet below the larger Boeing product.

The first aircraft landed at New Orleans, unloaded its men and equipment, refueled, then lifted off to head back to Mexico City.

Clark was at the embassy. One of his additions to the operation was a Japanese-speaker from the Agency's Intelligence Directorate. Reasoning that his test reception would be useful to determine the effectiveness of the system, he had further decided that it would be better still to get an immediate read on what was being said. Clark thought that this was a reasonable demonstration of operational initiative. The linguist took his time, listening to the taped conversation three times before he started typing. He generated less than two pages. It annoyed him that Clark was reading over his shoulder.

" 'I wish it was this easy to make a deal with the opposition in the Diet,' " Clark read aloud. " 'We merely must take care of some of his associates also.' "

"Looks to me that we got what we want," the linguist observed.

"Where's your communications guy?" Clark asked the Station Chief.

"I can do it myself." It was, indeed, easy enough. The Station Chief transcribed the two typed pages into a computer. Attached to the computer was a small machine that looked like a video-disc machine. On the large disc were literally billions of random digital numbers. Each letter he typed was randomly transformed into something else and transmitted to the MERCURY room at Langley. Here the incoming signal was recorded. A communications technician selected the proper description disc from the secure library, slid it into his own machine, and pressed a button. Within seconds a laster printer generated two pages of cleartext message. This was sealed in an envelope and handed to a messenger, who made for the seventh-floor office of the Deputy Director.

"Dr. Ryan, the dispatch you were waiting for."

"Thank you." Jack signed for it. "Dr. Goodley, you're going to have to excuse me for a moment."

"No problem." Ben went back to his pile of papers.

Ryan pulled the dispatch out and read it slowly and carefully twice. Then he picked up the phone and asked for a secure line to Camp David.

"Command center," a voice answered.

"This is Dr. Ryan at Langley. I need to talk to the Boss."

"Wait one, sir," the Navy chief petty officer replied. Ryan lit a cigarette.

"This is the President," a new voice said.

"Mr. President, this is Ryan. I have a fragment of conversation off the 747."

"So soon?"

"It was made before engine startup, sir. We have an unidentified voice—we think it's the PM—saying that he made the deal." Jack read off three lines verbatim.

"That son of a bitch," Fowler breathed. "You know, with evidence like that I could prosecute a guy."

"I thought you'd want this fast, sir. I can fax you the initial transcript. The full one will take until twenty-one hundred or so."

"It'll be nice to have something to read after the game. Okay, send it up." The line went dead.

"You're welcome, sir," Jack said into the phone.

* * *

"It is time," Ghosn said.

"Okay." Russell stood up and got into his heavy coat. It would be a really cold one outside. The predicted high temperature was six above, and they were not there yet. A bitter northeast wind was sweeping down out of Nebraska, where it was even colder. The only good thing about that was the clear sky it brought. Denver is also a city with a smog problem made all the worse by winter-temperature inversions. But today the sky was literally cloudless, and to the west Marvin could see streams of snow being blown off the Front Range peaks like white banners. Surely it was auspicious, and the clear weather meant that the flight out of Stapleton would not be delayed as he had feared a few days before. He started the engine of the van, rehearsing his lines and going over the plan as he allowed the vehicle to heat. Marvin turned to look at the cargo. Almost a ton of super-high explosives, Ibrahim had said. That would really piss people off. Next he got into the rental car and started that one, too, flipping the heater all the way on. Shame that Commander Qati felt so bad. Maybe it was nerves, Russell thought.

A few minutes later they came out. Ghosn got in next to Marvin. He was nervous, too.

"Ready, man?"

"Yes."

"Okay." Russell dropped the van into reverse and backed out of the parking place. He pulled forward, checking that the rental car was following, then headed off the parking lot onto the highway.

The drive to the stadium required only a few uneventful minutes. The police were out in force, and he saw that Ghosn was eyeing them very carefully. Marvin was not concerned. The cops were only there for traffic control, after all, and they were just standing around, since the traffic had scarcely begun. It was almost six hours till game time. He turned off the road onto the parking lot at the media entrance, and there was a cop he had to talk to. Qati had already broken off, and was now circling a few blocks away. Marvin stopped the van and rolled his window down.

"Howdy," he said to the cop.

Officer Peter Dawkins of the Denver City Police was already cold despite the fact that he was a native Coloradan. He was supposed to guard the media and VIP gate, a post he'd been stuck with only because he was a very junior officer. The senior guys were in warmer spots.

"Who are you?" Dawkins asked.

"Tech staff," Russell replied. "This is the media gate, right?"

"Yeah, but you're not on my list." There was a limited number of available spaces in the VIP lot, and Dawkins couldn't just let anyone in.

"Tape machine broke in the A unit over there," Russell explained with a wave. "We had to bring down a backup."

"Nobody told me," the police officer observed.

"Nobody told me either until six last night. We had to bring the goddamned thing down from Omaha." Russell waved his clipboard rather vaguely. In the back, Ghosn was scarcely breathing.

"Why didn't they fly it down?"

" 'Cause FedEx don't work on Sunday, man, and the damned thing's too big to get through the door of a Lear. I ain't complaining, man. I'm Chicago tech staff, okay? I'm Network. I get triple-time-and-a-half for this shit, away from home, special event, weekend overtime."

"That sounds pretty decent," Dawkins observed.

"Better'n a week's normal pay, man. Keep talking, officer." Russell grinned. "This is a buck and a quarter a minute, y'know?"

"You must have a hell of a union."

"We sure do." Marvin laughed.

"You know where to take it?"

"No problem, sir." Russell pulled off. Ghosn let out a long breath as the van started moving again. He'd listened to every word, sure that something would go disastrously wrong.

Dawkins watched the van pull away. He checked his watch and made a notation of his own on his clipboard. For some reason the Captain wanted him to keep track of who arrived when. It didn't make sense to Dawkins, but the Captain's ideas didn't always make sense, did they? It took a moment for him to realize that the ABC van had Colorado tags. That was odd, he thought, as a Lincoln Town Car pulled up. This one was on his list. It was the President of the NFL's American Conference. The VIPs were supposed to be pretty early, probably, Dawkins thought, so they could settle into their sky boxes and start their drinking early. He'd also drawn security at the President's party the night before and watched every rich clown in Colorado get sloppy drunk, along with various politicians and other Very Important People—mostly assholes, the young cop thought, having watched them—from all over America. He supposed that Hemingway was right after all: the rich just have more money.

Two hundred yards away, Russell parked the van, set the brake, and left the engine on. Ghosn went in back. The game was scheduled to start at 4:20 local time. Major affairs always ran late, Ibrahim judged. He'd assumed a start time of 4:30. To that he added another half hour, setting T-Zero at 5:00, Rocky Mountain Standard Time. Arbitrary numbers always had zeroes in them, after all, and the actual time of the detonation had been set weeks before: precisely on the first hour after game start.

The device did not have a very sophisticated antitamper device. There was a crude one set on each access door, but there hadn't been time to do anything complicated, and that, Ghosn thought, was a good thing. The gusting northeast wind was rocking the van, and a delicate tumbler switch might not have been a good idea after all.

For that matter, he realized rather belatedly, just slamming the door closed on the van might have . . . *What* else *have you failed to consider?* he wondered. Ghosn reminded himself that all such moments brought up the most frightening of thoughts. He swiftly ran over everything he had done to this point. Everything had been checked a hundred times and more. It was ready. Of course it was ready. Hadn't he spent months of careful preparation for this?

The engineer made a last check of his test circuits. All were fine. The cold had not affected the batteries that badly. He connected the wires to the timer—or tried to. His hands were stiff from the cold, and quivered from the emotion of the moment. Ghosn stopped. He took a moment to get control of himself and attached them on the second try, screwing down the nut to hold them firmly in place.

And that, he decided, was that. Ghosn closed the access door, which set the simple tamper switch, and backed away from the device. No, he said to himself. It is no longer a "device."

"That it?" Russell asked.

"Yes, Marvin," Ghosn answered quietly. He moved forward into the passenger seat.

"Then let's leave." Marvin watched the younger man get out and reached across to lock the door. Then he exited the van and locked his. They walked west, past the big network uplink vans with their huge dish antennas. They had to be worth millions each, Marvin thought, and every one would be wrecked, along with the TV weenies, just like the ones who had made a sporting event of his brother's death. Killing them didn't worry him a bit, not one little bit. In a moment the bulk of the stadium shielded them from the wind. They continued across the parking lot, past the ranks of early-arriving fans and the cars which were pulling onto the lot, many of them from Minnesota, full of fans dressed warmly, carrying peanuts and wearing hats, some of them adorned with horns.

Qati and the rental car were on a sidestreet. He simply slid over from the driver's seat, allowing Marvin to get behind the wheel. Traffic was now becoming thick, and, to avoid the worst of it, Russell took an alternate route he'd scouted out the previous day.

"You know, it really is a shame, messing with the game like this."

"What do you mean?" Qati asked.

"This is the fifth time the Vikings have made it to the Super Bowl. This time it looks like they're going to win. That Wills kid they have running for them is the best since Sayers, and because of us nobody'll see it happen. Too bad." Russell shook his head and grinned at the irony of it all. Neither Qati nor Ghosn bothered to reply, but Russell hadn't expected them to. They just didn't have much sense of humor, did they? The motel parking lot was nearly empty. Everyone staying there must have been a fan of one sort or another, Marvin thought as he opened the door.

"All packed?"

"Yes." Ghosn traded a look with the Commander. It was too bad, but it could not be helped.

The room hadn't been made up yet, but that was no big thing. Marvin went into the bathroom, closing the door behind him. When the American emerged, he saw that both Arabs were standing.

"Ready?"

"Yes," Qati said. "Could you get my bag down, Marvin?"

"Sure." Russell turned and reached for the suitcase that lay on the metal shelf. He didn't hear the steel bar that struck the back of his neck. His short but powerful frame dropped to the cheap all-weather carpet on the floor. Qati had struck hard, but not hard enough to kill, the Commander realized. He was weakening by the day. Ghosn helped him move the body back into the bathroom, where they laid him faceup. The motel was a cheap one, and the bathroom was small, too small for their purposes. They'd hoped to set him in the tub, but there wasn't room for both men to stand. Instead, Qati simply knelt by the American's side. Ghosn shrugged his disappointment and reached for a towel from the rack.

He wrapped the towel around Russell's neck. The man was more stunned than unconscious, and his hands were beginning to move. Ghosn had to move quickly. Qati handed him the steak knife that he'd removed from the coffee shop after dinner the previous night. Ghosn took it and cut deeply into the side of Russell's neck, just below the right ear. Blood shot out as though from a hose, and Ibrahim pushed the towel back down to keep it from splashing on his clothes. Then he did the same thing to the carotid artery on the left side. Both men held the towel down, almost as though to stanch the blood flow.

It was at that moment that Marvin's eyes came completely open. There was no comprehension in them, there was no time for him to understand what was happening. His arms moved, but each man used all his weight to hold them down and prevented the American from accomplishing anything. He didn't speak, though his mouth opened, and, after a last accusing look at Ghosn, the eyes went dreamy for a moment, then rolled back. By this time Qati and Ghosn were leaning back to avoid the blood that now filled the grooves between the bathroom tiles. Ibrahim pulled back the towel. The blood was trickling out now, and was not a concern. The towel was quite sodden, however. He tossed it into the tub. Qati handed him another.

"I hope God will be merciful to him," Ghosn said quietly.

"He was a pagan." It was too late for recriminations.

"Is it his fault that he never met a godly man?"

"Wash," Qati said. There were two sinks outside the bathroom. Each man lathered his hands thoroughly, checking his clothes for any sign of blood. There was none.

"What will happen to this place when the bomb goes off?" Qati asked.

Ghosn thought about that. "This close . . . it will be outside the fireball, but—" He walked to the windows and pulled the drapes back a few centimeters. The stadium was readily visible, and a direct line of sight made it easy to say what would happen. "The thermal pulse will set it afire, and then the blast wave will flatten the building. The whole building will be consumed."

"You're sure?"

"Completely. The effects of the bomb are easy to predict."

"Good." Qati removed all the travel documents and identification he and Ghosn had used to this point. They'd have to clear customs inspection, and they had already tempted fate enough. The surplus documents they tossed in a trash can. Ghosn got both bags and took them out to the car. They checked the room once more. Qati got into the car. Ghosn closed the door for the last time, leaving the Do Not Disturb card on the knob. It was a short drive to the airport, and their flight left in two hours.

The parking lot filled up rapidly. By three hours before game time, much to Dawkins' surprise, the VIP lot was filled. Already the pre-game show had begun. He could see a team wandering around the lot with a minicam, interviewing the Vikings fans, who had converted one entire half of the parking lot into a giant tailgate party. There were white vapor trails rising from charcoal grills. Dawkins knew that the Vikings fans were slightly nutty, but this was ridiculous. All they had to do was walk inside. They could have any manner of food and drink, and consume it in 68-degree air, sitting on a cushioned seat, but no—they were proclaiming their toughness in air that couldn't be much more than 5 degrees Fahrenheit. Dawkins was a skier and had worked his way through college as a ski patrol at one of the Aspen slopes. He knew cold and he knew the value of warmth. You couldn't impress cold air with anything. The air and wind simply didn't notice.

"How are things going, Pete?"

Dawkins turned. "No problems, Sarge. Everybody on the list is checked off."

"I'll spell you for a few minutes. Go inside and warm up for a while. You can get coffee at the security booth just inside the gate."

"Thanks." Dawkins knew that he'd need something. He was going to be stuck outside for the whole game, patrolling the lot to make sure nobody tried to steal something. Plainclothes officers were on the lookout for pickpockets and ticket scalpers, but most of them would get to go inside and watch the game. All Dawkins had was a radio. That was to be expected, he thought. He had less than three years on the force. He was still almost a rookie. The young officer walked up the slope toward the stadium, right past the ABC minivan he'd checked through. He looked inside and saw the Sony tape machine. Funny, it didn't seem to be hooked up to anything. He wondered where those two techies were, but getting coffee was more important. Even polypropylene underwear had its limits, and Dawkins was as cold as he had ever remembered.

Qati and Ghosn returned the car to the rental agency and took the courtesy bus to the terminal, where they checked in their bags for the flight, then headed in to check their flight's status. Here they learned that the American MD-80 for Dallas–Fort Worth was delayed. Weather in Texas, the clerk at the desk explained. There was ice on the runways from the storm that had just skirted past Denver the previous night.

"I must make my connection to Mexico. Can you book me through another city?" Ghosn asked.

"We have one leaving for Miami, same departure time as your flight to Dallas. I can book you a connecting flight in Miami." The ticket agent tapped the data into her terminal. "There's a one-hour layover. Oh, okay, it's only a fifteen-minute difference into Mexico City."

"Could you do that, please? I must make my connection."

"Both tickets?"

"Yes, excuse me."

"No problem." The young lady smiled at her computer. Ghosn wondered if she'd survive the event. The huge glass windows faced the stadium, and even at this distance the blast wave . . . maybe, he thought, if she ducked fast enough. But she'd already be blinded from the flash. Such pretty dark eyes, too. A pity. "Here you go. I'll make sure they switch the bags over," she promised him. That Ghosn took with a grain of salt.

"Thank you."

"The gate is that way." She pointed.

"Thank you once more."

The ticket agent watched them head off. The young one was pretty cute, she thought, but his big brother—or boss? she wondered—looked like a sourpuss. Maybe he didn't like to fly.

"Well?" Qati asked.

"The connecting flight roughly duplicates our schedule. We've lost a quarter hour buffer time in Mexico. The weather problem is localized. There should be no further difficulty."

The terminal was very nearly empty. Those people who wished to leave Denver were evidently waiting for later flights so that they might watch the game on TV, and the same appeared to be true of arriving flights, Ibrahim saw. There were scarcely twenty people in the departure lounge.

"Okay, I can't reconcile the schedules here either," Goodley said. "In fact, I'd almost say we have a smoking gun."

"How so?" Ryan asked.

"Narmonov was only in Moscow two days last week, Monday and Friday. Tuesday, Wednesday, and Thursday he was in Latvia, Lithuania, the Western Ukraine, and then a trip down to Volgograd for some local politicking. Friday's out because of when the message came over, right? But Monday, our friend was in the Congress building practically all day. I don't think they met last week, but the letter infers that they did. I think we got a lie here."

"Show me," Jack said.

Goodley spread his data out on Ryan's desk. Together they went over the dates and itineraries.

"Well, isn't that interesting," Jack said after a few minutes. "That son of a bitch."

"Persuasive?" Goodley wanted to know.

"Completely?" The Deputy Director shook his head. "No."

"Why not?"

"It's possible that our data is incorrect. It's possible that they met on the sly, maybe last Sunday when Andrey Il'ych was out at his dacha. One swallow doesn't make a spring," Jack said with a nod toward the snow outside. "We need to make a detailed check on this before it goes any farther, but what you've uncovered here is very, very interesting, Ben."

"But, damn it—"

"Ben, you go slow on stuff like this," Jack explained. "You don't toss out the work of a valuable agent on the basis of equivocal data, and this is equivocal, isn't it?"

"Technically, yes. You think he's been turned?"

"Doubled, you mean?" Ryan grinned. "You're picking up on the jargon, Dr. Goodley. You answer the question for me."

"Well, if he'd been doubled on us, no, he wouldn't send this sort of data. They wouldn't want to send us this kind of signal unless elements within the KGB—"

"Think it through, Ben," Jack cautioned.

"Oh, yeah. It compromises them, too, doesn't it? You're right, it's not likely. If he'd been turned, the data should be different."

"Exactly. If you're right, and if he's been misleading us, the most likely explanation is the one you came up with. He stands to profit from the political demise of Narmonov. It helps to think like a cop in this business. Who profits—who has motive, that's the test you apply here. Best person to look at this is Mary Pat."

"Call her in?" Goodley asked.

"Day like this?"

Qati and Ghosn boarded the flight on the first call, taking their first-class seats and strapping in. Ten minutes later the aircraft pulled back from the gate and taxied out to the end of the runway. They'd made a smart move, Ghosn thought. The flight to Dallas had still not been called. Two minutes after that, the airliner lifted off and soon turned southeast toward the warmer climes of Florida.

The maid was having a bad day already. Most of the guests had left late and she was way behind on her schedule. She clucked with disappointment at seeing the keep-out card on one doorknob, but it was not on the other, connecting room, and she thought it might be a mistake. The flip side of the card was the green Make Up

Room NOW message, and guests often made that mistake. First she went into the unmarked one. It was easy. Only one of the beds had been used. She stripped off the linen and replaced it with the speed that came from doing the same job more than fifty times per day. Then she checked out the bathroom, replaced the soiled towels, put a new bar of soap in the holder, and emptied the trash can into the bag that hung from her cart. Then she had to make a decision—whether to make up the other room or not. The card on the knob said no, but if they didn't want it, why didn't they do the same thing for this room? It was worth a look at least. If anything obviously important was laid out, she'd stay clear. The maid looked through the open connecting door and saw two ordinarily messed-up beds. No clothing was on the floors. In fact, the room was as neat today as it had been the day before. She stuck her head through the door and looked back toward the wash area. Nothing remarkable there either. She decided to clean it, too. The maid got behind her cart and turned it to push through the door. Again she did the beds, then headed back to—

How had she missed that before? A man's legs. What? She walked forward and—

It took the manager over a minute to calm her down enough to understand what she was saying. Thank God, he thought, that there were no guests on that side of the motel now; all were off to see the game. The young man took a deep breath and walked outside, past the coffee shop and around to the back side of the motel. The door had closed automatically, but his passkey fixed that.

"My God," he said simply. At least he'd been prepared for it. The manager was no fool. He didn't touch anything, but rather walked into the connecting room and out that door. The desk phone in his office had all the emergency numbers printed on a small card. He punched up the second one.

"Police."

"I want to report a murder," the manager said as calmly as he could manage.

President Fowler set the fax down on the corner table and shook his head. "It really is unbelievable that he'd try something so blatant."

"What are you going to do about it?" Liz asked.

"Well, we have to verify it, of course, but I think we'll be able to do that. Brent is flying back from the game tonight. I'll want him in my office early for his advice, but I figure we'll just confront him with it. If he doesn't like it, that's just too damned bad. This is Mafia stuff."

"You really do have a thing about this, don't you?"

Fowler opened a bottle of beer. "Once a prosecutor, always a prosecutor. A hood is a hood is a hood."

The JAL 747 touched down at Dulles International Airport three minutes early. Out of deference to the weather, and with the approval of the Japanese Ambassador, the arrival ceremony was abbreviated. Besides, the sign of a really important arrival in Washington was informality. It was one of the local folkways that the Ambassador had explained to the current Prime Minister's predecessor. After a brief but sincere greeting from Deputy Secretary of State Scott Adler, the official party was loaded into all the four-wheel-drive vehicles that the embassy had been able to assemble on such short notice, and headed off to the Madison Hotel, a few blocks from the White House. The President, he learned, was at Camp David, and would be coming back to Washington the following morning. The Japanese Prime Minister, still suffering from the lingering effects of travel, decided to get a few more hours of sleep. He'd not yet taken off his coat when another cleanup crew boarded the aircraft yet again. One man retrieved the unused liquor, including one bottle with a cracked neck. Another emptied the wastebaskets of the various washrooms into a large trash bag. They were soon on their way to Langley. All of the chase aircraft except the first landed at Andrews Air Force Base, where the flight crews also began their mandated rest periods—in this case at the base officers' club. The recordings started their trip to Langley by car, arriving later than the tape recorder from Dulles. It turned out that the machine off the 747 had the best sound quality, and the technicians started on that tape first.

The Gulfstream returned to Mexico City, also on time. The aircraft rolled out to the general-aviation terminal and the flight crew of three—it was an Air Force crew, though no one knew that—walked into the terminal for dinner. Since they were Air Force, it was time for some crew rest. Clark was still at the embassy, and planned to catch the first quarter at least before heading back to D.C. and all that damned snow.

''Be careful or you're going to fall asleep during the game,'' the National Security Advisor warned.

''It's only my second beer, Elizabeth,'' Fowler replied.

There was a cooler next to the sofa, and a large silver tray of munchies. Elliot still found it quite incredible. J. Robert Fowler, President of the United States, so intelligent and hard-minded in every possible way, but a rabid football fan, sitting here like Archie Bunker, waiting for the kickoff.

''I found one, but the other one's a son of a bitch,'' the crew chief reported. ''Can't seem to figure this one out, Colonel.''

''Come on inside and warm up,'' the pilot said. ''You've been out here too long anyway.''

''Some kind of drug deal, I'll bet you,'' the junior detective said.

''Then it's amateurs,'' his partner observed. The photographer had snapped his customary four rolls of film, and now the coroner's men were lifting the body into the plastic bag for transport to the morgue. There could be little doubt on the cause of death. It was a particularly brutal murder. It seemed that the killers—there had to be two, the senior man already thought—had to have held the man's arms down before they slashed his throat, and then they had watched him bleed out while using the towel to keep their clothes clean. Maybe they were paying off a debt somehow or other. Perhaps this guy had done a rip-off, or there was some old grudge that they had settled. This was clearly not a crime of passion; it was far too cruel and calculated for that.

The detectives noted their good luck, however. The victim's wallet had still been in his pocket. They had all his ID, and better than that, they had two complete sets of other ID, all of which were now being checked out. The motel records had noted the license numbers of both vehicles associated with these rooms, and those also were being checked on the motor-vehicle-records computer.

''The guy's an Indian,'' the coroner's rep said as they picked him up. ''Native American, I mean.''

''I've seen the face somewhere before,'' the junior detective thought. ''Wait a minute.'' Something caught his eye. He unbuttoned the man's shirt, revealing the top of a tattoo.

''He's done time,'' the senior man said. The tattoo on the man's chest was a crude one, spit-and-pencil, and it showed something that he'd seen before. . . . ''Wait a minute . . . this means something . . .''

''Warrior Society!''

''You're right. The Feds had something out on—oh, yeah, remember? The shooting up in North Dakota last year?'' The senior man thought for a second. ''When we get the information from the license, make sure they send it right off to Washington. Okay, you can take him out now.'' The body was lifted and carried out. ''Bring in the maid and the manager.''

Inspector Pat O'Day had the good luck of drawing watch duty in the FBI's command center, Room 5005 of the Hoover Building. The room was oddly shaped, roughly triangular, with the desks of the command staff in the angle, and screens on the long wall. The quiet day they were having—there was adverse weather across half the country, and adverse weather is more of an obstacle to crime than any police agency—meant that one of the screens was showing the teams lining up for the coin toss in Denver. Just as the Vikings won the toss and elected to receive, a young lady from communications walked in with a couple of faxes from the Denver P.D.

''A murder case, sir. They think we might know who this is.''

The quality of photographs on driver's licenses is not the sort to impress a professional anything, and blowing them up—then sending them via fax—didn't improve matters very much. He had to stare at it for a few seconds, and almost decided that he didn't know the face until he remembered some things from his time in Wyoming.

''I've seen this guy before . . . Indian . . . Marvin Russell?'' He turned to another agent. ''Stan, have you ever seen this guy?''

''Nope.''

O'Day looked over the rest of the faxes. Whoever he was, he was dead, with a slashed throat, the Denver cops said. ''Probable drug-related killing'' was the initial read from the Denver homicide guys. Well, that made sense, didn't it? John Russell had been part of a drug deal. The other initial data was that there had been other IDs at the scene of the crime, but that the licenses had been fakes—very good ones, the notes said. However, they had a truck registered to the victim, and also a car at the scene was a rental that had been signed out to Robert Friend, which was the name on the victim's license. The Denver P.D. was now looking for the vehicles, and he wanted to know if the Bureau had anything useful on the victim and any likely associates.

''Get back to 'em, and tell 'em to fax us the photos from the other IDs they found.''

''Yes, sir.''

Pat watched the teams get onto the field for the kickoff, then lifted the phone. ''Dan? Pat. You want to come on down here? I think an old friend of ours just might have turned up dead. . . . No, not that kind of friend.''

Murray showed up just in time for the kickoff, which took precedence over the faxes. Minnesota got the ball out to the twenty-four-yard line, and their offense went to work. The network immediately had the screen covered with all sorts of useless information so that the fans couldn't see the players.

"This look like Marvin Russell to you?" Pat asked.

"Sure as hell does. Where is he?"

O'Day waved at the TV screen. "Would you believe Denver? They found him about ninety minutes ago with his throat cut. Local P.D. thinks it's drug-related."

"Well, that's what did his brother in. What else?" Murray took the faxes from O'Day's hand.

Tony Wills got the first handoff, taking the ball five yards off tackle—almost breaking it for more. On second down, both men saw Wills catch a swing pass for twenty yards.

"That kid is really something," Pat said. "I remember seeing a game where Jimmy Brown . . ."

Bob Fowler had just started his third beer of the afternoon, wishing he'd been at the game instead of being stuck here. Of course, the Secret Service would have gone ape, and the security at the game would have to have been beefed up to the point that people would still be trying to get in. That was not a good political move, was it? Liz Elliot, sitting next to the President, flipped one of the other TVs to HBO to catch a movie. She donned a set of headphones so that she could hear it without disturbing the Commander-in-Chief. It just made no sense at all, she thought, none. How this man could get so enthusiastic about something as dumb as a little-boys' game. . . .

Pete Dawkins finished his pre-game duties by pulling a chain across his gate. Anyone who wanted to get in now would have to use one of the two gates that were still open, but guarded. At the last Super Bowl a very clever gang of thieves had prowled the parking lot and come away with two hundred thousand dollars' worth of goods from the parked cars—mainly tape decks and radios—and that was not going to happen in Denver. He started his patrol, along with three other officers. By agreement, they'd circulate all around the lot instead of sticking to specific areas. It was too cold for that. Moving around would at least keep them warm. Dawkins' legs felt as stiff as cardboard, and moving would loosen them up. He didn't really expect to stop any crimes. What car thief would be so dumb as to prowl around in zero-degree weather? Soon he found himself in the area the Minnesota fans had occupied. They were certainly well organized. The tailgate parties had all ended on time. The lawn chairs were all stowed away, and they'd done a very effective job of cleaning up the area. Except for a few puddles of frozen coffee, you could hardly tell that they had done something here. Maybe the Minnesota fans weren't such idiots after all.

Dawkins had a radio plugged into his ear. Listening to a game on the radio was like having sex with your clothes on, but at least he knew what the cheers were about. Minnesota scored first. Wills took it in by sweeping left end from fifteen yards out. The Vikings' first drive had taken only seven plays and four minutes fifty seconds. Minnesota sounded pretty tough today.

"God, Dennis must be sick," Fowler observed. Liz didn't hear him, concentrating instead on her movie. The Secretary of Defense immediately had cause to feel sicker. The kickoff was fielded at the five, and the reserve running back who handled that duty for the Chargers made it all the way to the forty—but there he fumbled and a Viking fell on the ball.

* * *

"They say Marvin was a clever little bastard. Look at the numbers on the other licenses. Except for the first couple of digits, they're the same as his. . . . I bet he got—well, somebody got—one of his ID machines," Murray said.

"Passports and everything," O'Day replied, watching Tony Wills do it again for eight yards. "If they don't figure a way to key on that kid, this game's going to be a blowout."

"What kind of passports?"

"They didn't say. I've asked for more information. They'll fax the photos when they get back into the office."

In Denver the computers were humming. The rental car company was identified, and a check of their system revealed that the car had been returned to Stapleton International Airport just a few hours earlier. That made a really hot trail, and the detectives drove directly there from the motel after taking initial statements from the first pair of "witnesses." The descriptions of the other two matched the photos on the passports. These were on their way to police headquarters. Already, they knew, the FBI was yelling for information. That made it sound more and more like a major drug case. Both detectives wondered where the victim's van was.

Dawkins finished his first circuit of the stadium just as Minnesota made its second touchdown. Again it was Wills, this time a four-yard pass out of the backfield. The guy already had fifty-one yards rushing and two receptions. Dawkins found himself looking at the ABC van he'd checked through. Why the Colorado tags? They said they were from Chicago, and that they had brought the tape widget in from Omaha. But the truck was painted like an official network truck. The local TV stations were not network-owned. They all showed network affiliation, but the big letters on them were for the local call-letters for the stations. Something to ask the sarge about. Dawkins circled the entry on his clipboard and wrote a question mark next to it. He walked inside to the security booth.

"Where's the sarge?"

"Out walking the lot," the officer at the booth replied. "The dumbass has twenty bet on the Chargers. I don't think he can take it."

"I'll see if I can get him to lay a little more," Dawkins replied with a grin. "Which way did he go?"

"North, I think."

"Thanks."

The Vikings kicked off again, with the score 14–0. The same return man took the kick, this time three yards deep in the end zone. He ignored the safety man's advice to down the ball and went up the middle like a shot. Breaking one tackle at the sixteen, he took advantage of a picture-book block and broke for the sidelines. Fifteen yards later it was clear that only the kicker had a chance, but the kicker was slow. At one hundred three yards, it was the longest kick return in Super Bowl history. The point after was good, and the game was now 14–7.

"Feeling better, Dennis?" the Secretary of State asked the Secretary of Defense.

Bunker set his coffee down. He had decided not to drink. He wanted to be stone sober when he accepted the Lombardi Trophy from the Commissioner.

"Yeah, now we just have to figure a way to stop your boy."

"Good luck."

"He's a great kid, Brent. Goddamn if he can't run."

"He isn't just an athlete. Kid's got brains, and a good heart."

"Brent, if you educated him, I know he's smart," Bunker said generously. "I just wish he'd pull a hamstring right about now."

Dawkins found his sergeant a few minutes later. "Something funny here," he said.

"What's that?"

"This truck—little white van on the east end of the row of big satellite trucks, 'ABC' painted on it. Colorado commercial tags, but supposedly it's from Chicago or maybe Omaha. I check 'em through, said they had a tape deck to replace a broken one, but when I walked past it a few minutes ago, it wasn't hooked up, and the guys who brought it in were gone."

"What are you telling me?" the sergeant asked.

"I think it might be a good idea to check it out."

"Okay, call it in. I'll give it a walk-past." The sergeant looked at the clipboard to check the tag number. "I was headed off to help out the Wells Fargo guys at the loading dock. You take that for me, okay?"

"Sure, Sarge." Dawkins headed off.

The watch supervisor lifted his Motorola radio. "Lieutenant Vernon, this is Sergeant Yankevich, could you meet me down at the TV place?"

Yankevich started walking back south around the stadium. He had his own personal radio, but it lacked an earpiece. San Diego stopped the Vikings on downs. Minnesota punted—a good one that required a fair catch at the Chargers' thirty. Well, maybe his team could get the game even. Somebody ought to shoot that Wills kid, he thought angrily.

Officer Dawkins walked to the north end of the stadium and saw a Wells Fargo armored car parked at the lower-level loading dock. One man was trying to sling out bags of what had to be coins.

"What's the problem?"

"The driver's beat his knee up, he's off having it fixed. Can you give me a hand?"

"Inside or outside?" Dawkins asked.

"You hand them out, okay? Be careful, they're heavy mothers."

"Gotcha." Dawkins hopped inside. The interior of the armored truck was lined with shelves holding innumerable bags of mainly quarters, it looked like. He lifted one, and it was as heavy as he'd been told. The police officer stuck his clipboard in his belt and went to work, handing them out to the loading dock, where the guard set them on a two-wheel handtruck. Trust the sarge to stick him with this.

Yankevich met the Lieutenant at the media entrance. Both walked over to the truck in question. The Lieutenant looked inside. "A big box with 'Sony' written on it . . . wait a minute. Says it's a commercial videotape machine."

Sergeant Yankevich filled his boss in on what Dawkins had told him. "It's probably nothing, but—"

"Yeah—but. Let me find the ABC guy. I'm also going to call the bomb squad. Stay here and keep an eye on the thing."

"I have a Slim Jim in my car. If you want I can get in easy enough." Every cop knows how to break into cars.

"I don't think so. We'll let the bomb guys think it over—besides, it's probably just what it looks like. If they came down to replace a broke tapedeck—well, maybe the broken one was fixed and they decided they didn't need it.''

''Okay, Lieutenant.'' Yankevich walked inside to get another cup of coffee to keep warm, then returned to the out-of-doors he loved so much. The sun was setting behind the Rockies, and even in zero weather with a bitter wind, it was always something beautiful to watch. The police sergeant walked past the network uplink vans to watch the glowing orange ball dip through one of the blowing snow clouds. Some things were better than football. When the last edge of the sun dipped below the ridgeline, he turned back, deciding to take another look at the box inside the truck. He would not make it.

35. Three Shakes

The timer just outside the bombcase reached 5:00:00, and things began to happen.

First, high-voltage capacitors began to charge, and small pyrotechnics adjacent to the tritium reservoirs at both ends of the bomb fired. These drove pistons, forcing the tritium down narrow metal tubes. One tube led into the Primary, the other into the Secondary. There was no hurry here, and the objective was to mix the various collections of lithium-deuteride with the fusion-friendly tritium atoms. Elapsed time was ten seconds.

At 5:00:10, the timer sent out a second signal.

Time Zero.

The capacitors discharged, sending an impulse down a wire into a divider network. The length of the first wire was 50 centimeters. This took one and two-thirds nanoseconds. The impulse entered a dividing network using krytron switches—each of them a small and exceedingly fast device using self-ionized and radioactive krypton gas to time its discharges with remarkable precision. Using pulse-compression to build their amperage, the dividing network split the impulse into seventy different wires, each of which was exactly one meter in length. The relayed impulses required three-tenths of a shake (three nanoseconds) to transit this distance. The wires all had to be of the same length, of course, because all of the seventy explosive blocks were supposed to detonate at the same instant. With the krytrons and the simple expedient of cutting each wire to the same length, this was easy to achieve.

The impulses reached the detonators simultaneously. Each explosive block had three separate detonators, and none of them failed to function. The detonators were small wire filaments, sufficiently thin that the arriving current exploded each. The impulse was transferred into the explosive blocks, and the physical detonation process began 4.4 nanoseconds after the signal was transmitted by the timer. The result was not an explosion, but an *im*plosion, since the explosive force was mainly focused inward.

The high-explosives blocks were actually very sophisticated laminates of two materials, each laced with dust from light and heavy metals. The outer layer in each case was a relatively slow explosive with a detonation speed of just over seven thousand meters per second. The explosive wave in each expanded radially from the detonator, quickly reaching the edge of the block. Since the blocks were detonated from the outside-in, the blast front traveled inward through the blocks. The border between the slow and fast explosives contained bubbles—called voids—which began to change the shockwave from spherical-shaped to a planar, or flat wave, which was focused again to match exactly its metallic target, called "drivers."

The "driver" in each case was a piece of carefully shaped tungsten-rhenium. These were hit by a force wave traveling at more than nine thousand eight hundred meters (six miles) per second. Inside the tungsten-rhenium was a one-centimeter layer of beryllium. Beyond that was a one-millimeter thickness of uranium 235, which though thin weighed almost as much as the far thicker beryllium. The entire metallic mass was driving across a vacuum, and since the explosion was focused on a central point, the actual closing speed of opposite segments of the bomb was 18,600 meters (or 11.5 miles) per second.

The central aiming point of the explosives and the metallic projectiles was a ten-kilogram (22-pound) mass of radioactive plutonium 239. It was shaped like a glass tumbler whose top had been bent outwards and down toward the bottom, creating two parallel walls of metal. Ordinarily denser than lead, the plutonium was compressed further by the million-atmospheres pressure of the implosion. This had to be done very quickly. The plutonium 239 mass also included a small but troublesome quantity of plutonium 240, which was even less stable and prone to pre-ignition. The outer and inner surfaces were slammed together and driven in turn toward the geometric center of the weapon.

The final external act came from a device called a "zipper." Operating off the third signal from the still-intact electronic timer, the zipper was a miniature particle accelerator, a very compact minicyclotron that looked remarkably like a hand-held hair-dryer. This fired deuterium atoms at a beryllium target. Neutrons traveling ten percent of the speed of light were generated in vast numbers and traveled down a metal tube into the center of the Primary, called the Pit. The neutrons were timed to arrive just as the plutonium reached half of its peak density.

Ordinarily a material weighing roughly twice an equivalent mass of lead, the plutonium was already ten times denser than that and still accelerating inward. The bombardment of neutrons entered a mass of still-compressing plutonium.

Fission.

The plutonium atom has an atomic weight of 239, that being the combined number of neutrons and protons in the atomic nucleus. What began happened at literally millions of places at once, but each event was precisely the same. An invading "slow" neutron passed close enough to a plutonium nucleus to fall under the Strong Nuclear Force that holds atomic nuclei together. The neutron was pulled into the atom's center, changing the energy state of the host nucleus and kicking it into an unstable state. The once symmetrical atomic nucleus began gyrating wildly and was torn apart by force fluctuations. In most cases a neutron or proton disappeared entirely, converted to energy in homage to Einstein's law $E = MC^2$. The energy that resulted from the disappearance of the particles was released in the form of gamma and X-radiation, or any of thirty or so other but less important routes. Finally, the atomic nucleus released two or three additional neutrons. This was the important part. The process that had required only one neutron to start released two or three more, each traveling at over ten percent of the speed of light—20,000 miles per second—through space occupied by a plutonium mass two hundred times the density of water. The majority of the newly liberated atomic particles found targets to hit.

A chain reaction merely means that the process builds on itself, that the energy released is sufficient to continue the process without outside assistance. The fission of the plutonium proceeded in steps called "doublings." The energy liberated by each step was double that of the preceding one, and that of each subsequent step was doubled again. What began as a trivial amount of energy and just a handful of freed particles doubled and redoubled, and the interval between steps was measured in fractions of nanoseconds. The rate of increase—that is, the acceleration of the chain reaction—is called the "Alpha," and is the most important variable in the fission process. An Alpha of 1,000 means that the number of doublings per microsecond is a vast number, 2^{1000}—the number 2 multiplied by itself one *thousand* times. At peak fission—between 2^{50} and 2^{53}—the bomb would be generating 10 billion billion watts of power, one hundred thousand times the electrical-generating capacity of the entire world. Fromm had designed the bomb to do just that—and that was only ten percent of the weapon's total designed output. The Secondary had yet to be affected. No part of it had yet been touched by the forces only a few inches away.

But the fission process had scarcely begun.

Some of the gamma rays, traveling at the speed of light, were outside the bombcase while the plutonium was still being compressed by the explosives. Even nuclear reactions take time. Other gamma rays started to impact on the Secondary. The majority of the gammas streaked through a gas cloud that only a few microseconds earlier had been the chemical explosive blocks, heating it far beyond the temperatures chemicals alone could achieve. Made up of very light atoms like carbon and oxygen, this cloud emitted a vast quantity of low-frequency "soft" X-rays. To this point, the device was functioning exactly as Fromm and Ghosn had planned.

The fission process was seven nanoseconds—0.7 shakes—old when something went wrong.

Radiation from the fissioning plutonium blazed in on the tritium-impregnated lithium-deuteride that occupied the geometric center of the Pit. The reason Manfred Fromm had left the tritium extraction to last lay in his basic engineer's conservatism. Tritium is an unstable gas, with a half-life of 12.3 years, meaning that a quantity of pure tritium will, after that time, be composed half of tritium and half of ^{3}He. Called "helium-three," ^{3}He is a form of that second-lightest of elements whose nucleus lacks an extra neutron, and craves another. By filtering the gas through a thin block of palladium, the ^{3}He would have been easily separated out, but Ghosn hadn't known about that. As a result, more than a fifth of the tritium was the wrong material. It could hardly have been a worse material.

The intense bombardment from the adjacent fission reaction seared the lithium compound. Normally a material half the density of salt, it was compressed to a metallic state that exceeded the density of earth's core. What began was actually a fusion reaction, though a small one, releasing huge quantities of new neutrons, and also changing many of the lithium atoms into more tritium, which broke down—"fused"—under the intense pressure to release yet more neutrons. The additional neutrons generated were supposed to invade the plutonium mass, boosting the alpha and causing at least a doubling of the weapon's unboosted fission yield. This had been the first method of increasing the power of the second-generation nuclear weapons. But the presence of ^{3}He poisoned the reaction, trapping nearly a quarter of the high-energy neutrons in uselessly stable helium atoms.

For several more nanoseconds, this did not matter. The plutonium was still increasing its reaction rate, still doubling, still increasing its Alpha at a rate only expressable numerically.

Energy was now flooding into the Secondary. The metallically coated straws flashed to plasma, pressing inward on the secondary. Radiant energy in quantities not found on the surface of the sun vaporized but also reflected off elliptical surfaces, delivering yet more energy to the Secondary assembly, called the *Holraum*. The plasma from the immolated straws pounded inward toward the second reservoir of lithium compounds. The dense uranium 238 fins just outside the Secondary pit also flashed to dense plasma, driving inward through the vacuum, then striking and compressing the tubular containment of more ^{238}U around the central container which held the largest quantity of lithium-deuteride/tritium. The forces were immense, and the structure was pounded with a degree of pressure greater than that of a healthy stellar core.

But not enough.

The Primary's reaction had already slackened. Starved of neutrons by the presence of the ^{3}He poison, the bomb's explosive force began to blow apart the reaction mass as soon as the physical forces reached their balance. The chain reaction reached a moment of stability, at last unable to sustain its geometric rate of growth; the last two chain-reaction doublings were lost entirely, and what should have been a total Primary yield of seventy thousand tons of TNT was halved, halved again, and in fact ended with a total yield of eleven thousand two hundred tons of high explosive.

Fromm's design had been as perfect as the circumstances and materials allowed. An equivalent weapon less than a quarter the size was possible, but his specifications were more than adequate. A massive safety factor in the energy budget had been planned for. Even a thirty-kiloton yield would have been enough to ignite the "spark plug" in the Secondary to start a massive fusion "burn," but thirty-KT was not reached. The bomb was technically called a "fizzle."

But it was a fizzle equivalent to eleven thousand two hundred tons of TNT. That could be represented by a cube of high explosives seventy-five feet high, seventy-five feet long, and seventy-five feet thick, as much as could be carried by nearly four hundred trucks, or one medium-sized ship—but conventional explosives could never have detonated with anything approaching this deadly efficiency; in fact, a conventional explosion of this magnitude is a practical impossibility. For all that, it was still a fizzle.

As yet no perceptible physical effects had even left the bombcase, much less the truck. The steel case remained largely intact, though that would rapidly change. Gamma radiation had already escaped, along with X-rays, but these were invisible. Visible light had not yet emerged from the plasma cloud that had only three "shakes" before been over a thousand pounds of exquisitely designed hardware . . . and yet, everything that was to happen had already taken place. All that remained now was the distribution of the energy already released by natural laws which neither knew nor cared about the purposes of their manipulators.

36. Weapons Effects

Sergeant Ed Yankevich should have been the first to notice what was happening. His eyes were on the van, and he was walking in that direction, scarcely forty feet away, but the human nervous system works in milliseconds and no faster.

The fizzle had just ended when the first radiation reached the police officer. These were gamma rays, which are actually photons, the same stuff that light waves are made of, but far more energetic. They were already attacking the body of the truck as well, causing the sheet steel to fluoresce like neon. Immediately behind the gammas were X-rays, also composed of photons but less energetic. The difference was lost on Yankevich, who would be the first to die. The intense radiation was most readily absorbed by his bones, which rapidly heated to incandescence, while at the same time the neurons of his brain were simultaneously excited as though each had become a flash bulb. In fact, Sergeant Yankevich was unable to notice a thing. He literally disintegrated, exploded from within by the tiny fraction of energy his body was able to absorb as the rest raced through him. But the gammas and X-rays were heading in all possible directions at the speed of light, and their next effect was one no one had anticipated.

Adjacent to the van, whose body was now being reduced to molecular bits of metal, was ABC's "A" satellite unit. Inside were several people who would have no more time to sense their fate than Sergeant Yankevich. The same was true of the elaborate and expensive electrical equipment in the van. But at the rear of this vehicle, pointing south and upward, was a large parabolic-dish antenna, not unlike the kind used for radar. In the center of this, like the stamen of a flower, was the wave guide, essentially a metal tube with a square cross-section whose inside dimensions roughly approximated the wavelength of the signal it was now broadcasting to a satellite 22,600 miles over the equator.

The wave-guide of the A unit, and soon thereafter each of the eleven trucks lined up west of it, was struck by the gammas and X-rays. In the process, electrons were blasted off the atoms of the metal—in some cases the guides were lined with gold plate, which accentuated the process—which gave up their energy at once in the form of photons. These photons formed waves whose frequency was roughly that of the satellite uplink transmitters. There was one difference: the uplink trucks were in no case transmitting as much as one thousand watts of radio-frequency—RF—energy, and in most cases far less than that. The energy transfer from the A unit's wave guide, however, released nearly a million watts of energy in one brief, orgasmic pulse that ended in less than a microsecond as the antenna and the associated truck were also vaporized by the searing energy front. Next to go was the ABC "B" unit, then TWI. NHK, which was sending the Super Bowl to Japan, was the fourth van in the line. There were eight more. All were destroyed. This process took approximately fifteen "shakes." The satellites to which they transmitted were a long distance away. It would take the energy roughly an eighth of a second to span the distance, a relative eternity.

Next to emerge from the explosion—the truck was now part of it—was light and heat energy. The first blast of light escaped just before the expanding fireball blocked it. The second installment escaped soon thereafter, radiating in all directions. This generated the two-phase pulse which is characteristic of nuclear detonations.

The next energy effect was blast. This was actually a secondary effect. The air absorbed much of the soft X-rays and was burned into an opaque mass which stopped further electromagnetic radiation, transforming it into mechanical energy that expanded at several times the speed of sound, but before that energy had a chance to damage anything, more distant events were already under way.

The primary ABC video link was actually by fiber-optic cable—a high-quality landline—but the cable ran through the A van and was cut even before the stadium itself was damaged. The backup link was through the Telstar 301 satellite, and the Pacific Coast was serviced by Telstar 302. ABC used the Net-1 and Net-2 primary links on each bird. Also using Telstar 301 was Trans World International, which represented the NFL's worldwide rights and distributed the game to most of Europe, plus Israel and Egypt. TWI sent the same video signal to all its European clients, and also provided facilities for separate audio uplinks in the various European languages, which usually meant more than one audio link per country. Spain, for example, accounted for five dialects, each of which had its own audio sideband-channel. NHK, broadcasting to Japan, used both the JISO-F2R satellite and its regular full-time link, Westar 4, which was owned and operated by Hughes Aerospace. Italian TV used Major Path 1 of the Teleglobe satellite (owned by the Intelsat conglomerate) to feed its own viewers, plus those in Dubai and whatever Israelis didn't like the play-by-play through TWI and Telstar. Teleglobe's Major Path 2 was delegated to serve most of South America. Also present, either right at the stadium or a short distance away, were CNN, ABC's own news division, CBS Newsnet, and ESPN. Local Denver stations had their own satellite trucks on the scene, their uses mainly rented to outsiders.

There was a total of thirty-seven active satellite uplink trucks using either microwave or Ku-band transmitters to generate a total of 48 active video, and 168 active audio signals, all feeding over a billion sports fans in seventy-one countries when the gamma and X-ray flux struck. In most cases the impact generated a signal in the wave guides, but in six trucks, the traveling-wave tubes themselves were illuminated first and put out a gigantic pulse on exactly the proper frequencies. Even that was beside the point, however. Resonances and otherwise inconsequential irregularities within the wave guides meant that wide segments of the satellite frequencies were all covered with the noise-spike. All but two of the communications satellites orbiting over the Western Hemisphere were being worked by the TV crews at Denver. What happened to them is expressed simply. Their sensitive antennas were designed to receive billionths of watts. Instead, they were suddenly bombarded with between one and ten thousand times that on numerous separate channels. That surge overloaded an equal number of the front-end amplifiers inside the satellites. The computer software running the satellites took note of this and began to activate isolation switches to protect the sensitive equipment from the spike. Had the incident affected merely one such receiver, service would have been restored at once and nothing further would have happened, but commercial communications satellites are immensely expensive artifacts, costing hundreds of millions of dollars to build and hundreds of millions more to launch into orbit. When more than five amplifiers recorded spikes, the software automatically began shutting circuits down, lest possibly serious damage to the entire satellite result. When twenty or more were affected, the software took the further step of deactivating all onboard circuits, and next firing off an emergency signal to its command ground station to say that something very serious had just happened. The safety software on the satellites were all customized variations of a single, very conservative program designed to safeguard billions of dollars' worth of nearly irreplaceable assets. In a brief flicker of time, a sizable fraction of the world's satellite communications dropped out of existence. Cable television and telecommunications systems all ceased, even before the technicians who managed their operations knew that something had gone disastrously wrong.

Pete Dawkins was resting for a moment. He thought of it as protecting the armored truck. The Wells Fargo guard was off delivering another few hundred pounds of quarters, and the police officer was sitting, his back against the shelves full of coin bags, listening to his radio. The Chargers were coming up to the line for a third-and-five at the Vikings' forty-seven. At that moment, the darkening sky outside turned incandescent yellow, then red—not the friendly, gentle red of a sunset, but a searing violet that was far brighter than that color could possibly have been. His mind barely had time to register that fact when it was assaulted by a million other things at once. The earth rose beneath him. The armored car was tossed up and sideways like a toy kicked by a child. The open rear door was slammed shut as if struck by a cannon. The body of the truck sheltered him from the shockwave—as did the body of the stadium, though Dawkins had not the time to realize it. Even so, he was nearly blinded by the flash that did reach him, and deafened by the overpressure wave that swept across him like the crushing hand of a giant. Had Dawkins been less disoriented, he might have thought *earthquake,* but even that idea did not occur to him. Survival did. The noise had not stopped, nor had the shaking, when he realized that he was trapped inside a vehicle whose fuel tank contained perhaps as much as fifty gallons of gasoline. He blinked his eyes clear and started crawling out the shattered windshield toward the brightest spot he could see. He did not notice that the backs of his hands looked worse than any sunburn he'd ever had. He did not realize that he could not hear a thing. All he cared about was getting to the light.

Outside Moscow, in a bunker under sixty meters of concrete, is the national headquarters of *Voyska PVO,* the Soviet air-defense service. A new facility, it was designed much like its Western counterparts in the form of a theater, since this configuration allowed the maximum number of people to see the data displayed on the large wall that was required for the map displays which were needed for their duties. It was 03:00:13 local time, according to the digital clock over the display, 00:00:13 Zulu (Greenwich Mean) Time, 19:00:13 in Washington, D.C.

On duty was Lieutenant General Ivan Grigoriyevich Kuropatkin, a former—he would have said "current"—fighter pilot, now fifty-one years of age. The third-ranking man at this post, he was taking his place in the normal duty rotation. Though as a very senior officer he could have opted for more convenient hours, the new Soviet military was to be founded on professionalism, and professional officers, he thought, led by example. Arrayed around him were his usual battle staff, composed of colonels, majors, plus a leavening of captains and lieutenants for menial work.

The job of *Voyska PVO* was to defend the Soviet Union against attack. In the missile age and in the absence of an effective defense against ballistic missiles—both sides were still working on that—his duties were more to warn than defend. Kuropatkin didn't like that, but neither could he change it. In geosynchronous orbit over the coast of Peru was a pair of satellites, called Eagle-I and -II, whose task it was to watch the United States and spot a missile launch just as soon as the missiles left their silos. The same satellites could also spot an SLBM launch from the Gulf of Alaska, though their coverage that far north was somewhat dependent on weather which, at the moment, was vile. The display from the orbiting Eagles was in the infrared spectrum, which mainly measured heat. The display was presented as the camera perceived it, without borderlines or other computer-generated data which, the Russian designers thought, simply cluttered the display unnecessarily. Kuropatkin was not looking up, but rather at a junior officer who seemed to be doing a calculation of some sort, when something caught his eye. His gaze shifted automatically, entirely without conscious thought, and it took fully a second for him to realize why.

There was a white dot in the center of the display.

"*Nichevo* . . ." He shook that off at once. "Isolate and zoom in!" he ordered loudly. The Colonel working the controls was sitting right next to him, and was already doing just that.

"Central United States, General. Double-flash thermal signature, that is a probable nuclear detonation," the Colonel said mechanically, his professional judgment overpowering his intellectual denial.

"Coordinates."

"Working, General." The distance from the Center to the satellite ensured a delay in getting things to happen. By the time the satellite's telescopic lens started moving in, the thermal signature from the fireball was expanding rapidly. Kuropatkin's immediate impression was that this could not possibly be a mistake, and as hot as that image was, what materialized in the pit of his stomach was a fist of ice.

"Central U.S., looks like the city of *Densva*."

"Denver, what the hell's in Denver?" Kuropatkin demanded. "Find out."

"Yes, General."

Kuropatkin was already reaching for a telephone. This line was a direct link to the Ministry of Defense and also the residence of the Soviet President. He spoke quickly but clearly.

"Attention: This is Lieutenant General Kuropatkin at PVO Moscow Center. We have just registered a nuclear detonation in the United States. I repeat: we have just registered a nuclear detonation in the United States."

One voice on the line swore. That would be President Narmonov's watch staff.

The other voice, that of the Defense Ministry's senior watch officer, was more reasoned. "How sure are you of this?"

"Double-flash signature," Kuropatkin replied, astounded at his own coolness. "I'm watching the fireball expansion now. This *is* a nuclear event. I will call in more data as soon as I have it—what?" he asked a junior officer.

"General, Eagle-II just took one hell of an energy spike, four of the SHF links just shut down momentarily, and another is gone completely," a major said, leaning over the General's desk.

"What happened, what was it?"

"I don't know."

"Find out."

The picture went blank just as San Diego was coming up for their third-and-five at the forty-seven. Fowler finished off his fourth beer of the afternoon and set the glass down in annoyance. Damned TV people. Someone probably tripped over a plug, and he'd miss a play or two in what looked like one hell of a game. He ought to have gone to this one, despite the advice of the Secret Service. He glanced over to see what Elizabeth was watching, but her screen had suddenly gone blank as well. Had one of the Marines driven over the cable with a snowplow? Good help certainly was hard to come by, the President grumped. But no, that wasn't right. The ABC affiliate—Baltimore's Channel 13, WJZ—put up its "Network Difficulty—Please Stand By" graphic, whereas Elizabeth's channel was just random noise now. How very odd. Like any male TV viewer, Fowler picked up the TV controller and changed channels. CNN was off the air, too, but the local Baltimore and Washington stations were not. He'd just started wondering what that meant when a phone started ringing. It had an unusually atonal, strident sound, and was one of the four kept on the lower shelf of the coffee table that sat right in front of his couch. He reached down for it before he realized which one it was, and that delayed understanding caused his skin to go cold. It was the red phone, the one from North American Aerospace Defense Command at Cheyenne Mountain, Colorado.

"This is the President," Fowler said in a gruff, suddenly frightened voice.

"Mr. President, this is Major General Joe Borstein. I am the senior NORAD watch officer. Sir, we have just registered a nuclear detonation in the Central United States."

"What?" the President said after two or three seconds' pause.

"Sir, there's been a nuclear explosion. We're checking the exact location now, but it appears to have been in the Denver area."

"Are you sure?" the President asked, fighting to keep calm.

"We're rechecking our instruments now, sir, but, yes, we're pretty sure. Sir, we don't know what happened or how it got there, but there was a nuclear explosion. I urge you to get to a place of safety at once while we try and figure out what's going on."

Fowler looked up. Neither TV picture had changed and now alarm klaxons were erupting all over the presidential compound.

Offutt Air Force Base, just outside Omaha, Nebraska, was once known as Fort Crook. The former cavalry post had a splendid if somewhat anachronistic collection of red brick dwellings for its most senior officers, in the rear of which was stabling for the horses they no longer needed, and in front of which was a flat parade ground of sufficient size to exercise a regiment of cavalry. About a mile from that was the headquarters of the Strategic Air Command, a much more modern building with its own antique, a B-17 Flying Fortress of World War II, sitting outside. Also outside the building but below ground was the new command post, completed in 1989. A capacious room, local wags joked that it had been built because Hollywood's rendition of such rooms was better than the one SAC had originally built for itself, and the Air Force had decided to alter its reality to fit a fictional image.

Major General Chuck Timmons, Deputy Chief of Staff (Operations), had availed himself of the opportunity to stand his watch here instead of in his upstairs office, and had in fact been watching the Super Bowl out of one eye on one of the eight large-screen TVs, but on two of the others had been real-time imagery from the Defense Support Program Satellites, called the DSPS birds, and he had caught the double-flash at Denver just as fast as everyone else. Timmons dropped the pencil he'd been working with. Behind his battle-staff seat were several glassed-in rooms—

there were two levels of such rooms—which contained the fifty or so support personnel who kept SAC operating around the clock. Timmons lifted his phone and punched the button for the senior intelligence officer.

"I see it, sir."

"Possible mistake?"

"Negative, sir, test circuitry says the bird's working just fine."

"Keep me posted." Timmons turned to his deputy. "Get the boss in here. Beep everybody, I want a full emergency-action team and a full battle-staff—and I want it now!" To his operations officer: "Get Looking Glass up now! I want the alert wings postured for takeoff, and I want an immediate alert flashed to everybody."

In the glassed-in room behind the General and to his left, a sergeant pushed a few buttons. Though SAC had long since ceased keeping aircraft in the air around the clock, thirty percent of SAC's aircraft were typically kept on alert status at any time. The order out to the alert wings was sent by landline and used a computer-generated voice because it had been decided that a human might get excited and slur his words. The orders took perhaps twenty seconds to be transmitted, and the operations officers at the alert wings were galvanized to action.

At the moment, that meant two wings, the 416th Bomb Wing at Griffiss Air Force Base, Rome, New York, which flew the B-52, and the 384th, which flew the B-1B out of nearby McConnell Air Force Base in Kansas. At the latter, crewmen in their ready rooms, nearly all of whom had also been watching the Super Bowl, raced out the door to waiting vehicles which took them to their guarded aircraft. The first man from each crew of four slapped the emergency-startup button that was part of the nosewheel assembly, then ran farther aft to sprint up the ladder into the aircraft. Even before the crews were strapped in, the engines were starting up. The ground crews yanked off the red-flagged safety pins. Rifle-armed sentries got out of the way of the aircraft, training their weapons outward to engage any possible threat. To this point, no one knew that this was anything more than a particularly ill-timed drill.

At McConnell, the first aircraft to move was the wing commander's personal B-1B. An athletic forty-five, the Colonel also had the advantage of having his aircraft parked closest to the alert shack. As soon as all four of his engines were turning and the way cleared, he tripped his brakes and began to taxi his aircraft toward the end of the runway. That took two minutes, and on reaching the spot, he was told to wait.

At Offutt, the alert KC-135 was under no such restrictions. Called "Looking Glass," the converted—and twenty-five-year-old—Boeing 707 had aboard a general officer and a complete if downsized battle-staff. It was just lifting off into the falling darkness. Onboard radios and command links were just coming on line, and the officer aboard hadn't yet learned what all the hubbub was about. Behind him on the ground, three more additional and identical aircraft were being prepped for departure.

"What gives, Chuck?" CINC-SAC said as he came in. He was wearing casual clothes, and his shoes were not tied yet.

"Nuclear detonation at Denver, also some trouble on satellite communications links that we just found out about. I've postured the alert aircraft. Looking Glass just lifted off. Still don't know what the hell's going on, but Denver just blew up."

"Get 'em off," the Commander-in-Chief Strategic Air Commander ordered.

Timmons gestured to a communications officer, who relayed the order. Twenty seconds later, the first B-1B roared down the runway at McConnell.

It was not a time for niceties. A Marine captain pushed open the door into the President's cabin and tossed two white parkas at Fowler and Elliot even before the first Secret Service agent showed up.

"Right now, sir!" he urged. "Chopper's still broke, sir."

"Where to?" Pete Connor arrived with his overcoat unbuttoned, just in time to hear what the Marine had said.

"Command post, 'less you say different. Chopper's broke," the captain said yet again. "Come on, sir!" he nearly screamed at the President.

"Bob!" Elliot said in some alarm. She didn't know what the President had heard over the phone, merely that he looked pale and sick. Both donned their parkas and came outside. They saw that a full squad of Marines lay in the snow, their loaded rifles pointed outward. Six more stood around the Hummer, whose engine was screaming in neutral.

At Anacostia Naval Air Station in Washington, the crew of Marine Two—it wouldn't be Marine One until the President got aboard—was just lifting off amid a worrisome cloud of snow, but in a few seconds they were above the ground effect and able to see fairly well. The pilot, a major, turned his aircraft northwest, wondering what the hell was happening. The only people who knew anything knew merely that they didn't know very much. For a few minutes this would not matter. As with any organization, responses to a sudden emergency were planned beforehand and had been thoroughly rehearsed both to get things done and to attenuate the panic that might come from indecision mixed with danger.

"What the hell is going on in Denver that I need to know about?" General Kuropatkin asked in his hole outside Moscow.

"Nothing I know of," his intelligence officer replied honestly.

That's a big help, the General thought. He lifted the phone to the Soviet military intelligence agency, the GRU.

"Operations/Watch Center," a voice answered.

"This is General Kuropatkin at PVO Moscow."

"I know the reason for your call," the GRU Colonel assured him.

"What is happening at Denver? Is there a nuclear-weapons storage facility, anything like that?"

"No, General. Rocky Mountain Arsenal is near there. That is a storage center for chemical weapons, in the process of being deactivated. It's turning into a depot for the American reserve army—they call it the National Guard—tanks and mechanized equipment. Outside Denver is Rocky Flats. They used to fabricate weapons components there, but—"

"Where exactly?" Kuropatkin asked.

"Northwest of the city. I believe the explosion is in the southern part of Denver, General."

"Correct. Go on."

"Rocky Flats is also in the process of deactivation. To the best of our knowledge, there are no more weapons components to be found there."

"Do they transport weapons through there? I *must know something!"* The General was finally getting excited.

"I have nothing more to tell you. We're as much in the dark as you. Perhaps KGB has more, but we do not."

You couldn't shoot a man for honesty, Kuropatkin knew. He switched lines again. Like most professional soldiers, he had little use for spies, but the next call was a necessity.

"State Security, command center," a male voice said.

"American department, the duty watch officer."

"Stand by." There was the usual chirping and clicking, and a female voice answered next. "American desk."

"This is Lieutenant General Kuropatkin at PVO Moscow Center," the man said yet again. "I need to know what, if anything, is happening in the Central United States, the city of Denver."

"Very little, I would imagine. Denver is a major city, and a large administrative center for the American government, the second-largest after Washington, in fact. It is a Sunday evening there, and very little should be happening at the moment." Kuropatkin heard pages riffling. "Oh, yes."

"Yes, what?"

"The final game in the championship-elimination series of American-rules football. It is being played in the new Denver city stadium which, I believe, is an enclosed structure."

Kuropatkin managed not to curse the woman for that irrelevancy. "I don't need *that*. Is there any civil unrest, any sort of disturbance or ongoing problem? A weapons-storage facility, a secret base of some sort that I don't know about?"

"General, everything we have on such subjects is available to you. What is the nature of your inquiry?"

"Woman, there has been a nuclear explosion there."

"In Denver?"

"Yes!"

"Where, exactly?" she asked, cooler than the General was.

"Stand by." Kuropatkin turned. "I need coordinates on the explosion and I need them now!"

"Thirty-nine degrees forty minutes north latitude, one hundred five degrees six minutes west longitude. Those numbers are approximate," the Lieutenant on the satellite desk added. "Our resolution isn't very good in the infrared spectrum, General." Kuropatkin relayed the numbers.

"Wait," the woman's voice said. "I need to fetch a map."

Andrey Il'ych Narmonov was asleep. It was now 3:10 in the morning in Moscow. The phone woke him, and an instant later his bedroom door opened. Narmonov nearly panicked at the second event. No one ever entered his bedroom without permission. It was KGB Major Pavel Khrulev, the assistant chief of the President's personal security detail.

"My President, there is an emergency. You must come with me at once."

"What is the matter, Pasha?"

"There has been a nuclear explosion in America."

"What—who?"

"That is all I know. We must go at once to the command bunker. The car is waiting. Don't bother getting dressed." Khrulev tossed him a robe.

* * *

Ryan stubbed out his cigarette, still annoyed at the "Technical Difficulty—Please Stand By" sign that was keeping him from watching the game. Goodley came in with a couple cans of Coke. Dinner was already ordered.

"What gives?" Goodley asked.

"Picture went out." Ryan took his Coke and popped it open.

At SAC Headquarters, a lieutenant colonel at the far left side of the third row of battle-staff seats consulted the TV-controller card. The room had eight TV displays, arranged in two horizontal rows of four. One could call up more than fifty individual displays, and the woman was an intelligence officer whose first instinct was to check the new channels. A quick manipulation of her controller showed that both CNN and its subsidiary CNN Headline News were off the air. She knew that they used different satellite circuits, and that piqued her curiosity, perhaps the most important aspect of intelligence work. The system also allowed access to other cable channels, and she started going through them. HBO was off the air. Showtime was off the air. ESPN was off the air. She checked her directory and concluded that at least four satellites were not functioning. At that point the Colonel got up and walked over to CINC-SAC.

"Sir, there's something very odd here," she said.

"What's that?" CINC-SAC said without turning.

"At least four commercial satellites appear to be down. That includes a Telstar, an Intelsat, and a Hughes bird. They're all down, sir."

That notification caused CINC-SAC to turn. "What else can you tell me?"

"Sir, NORAD reports that the explosion was in the Denver metropolitan area, very close to the Skydome, where they were playing the Super Bowl. SecState and SecDef were both at the game, sir."

"Christ, you're right," CINC-SAC realized instantly.

At Andrews Air Force Base, the National Emergency Airborne Command Post—NEACP, pronounced "Kneecap"—was positioned on the ramp with two of its four engines turning, waiting for someone to arrive so that the crew could take off.

Captain Jim Rosselli had barely been on duty for an hour when this nightmare arrived. He sat in the NMCC Crisis Management Room, wishing a flag officer were here. That was not to be. While there had once been a general or admiral in the National Military Command Center at all times, the thaw between East and West and the downsizing of the Pentagon now meant that a senior officer was always on call, but the day-to-day administrative work was handled by captains and colonels. It could have been worse, Rosselli thought. At least he knew what it was to have lots of nuclear weapons at his disposal.

"What the *fuck* is going on?" Lieutenant Colonel Richard Barnes asked the wall. He knew that Rosselli didn't know.

"Rocky, can we save that for another time?" Rosselli asked calmly. His voice was dead-level. One might never have known from looking at or listening to the Captain that he was excited, but the former submarine commander's hands were so moist that by rubbing them on his trousers he'd already created a damp spot that their navy-blue color made invisible.

"You got it, Jim."

"Call General Wilkes, let's get him in here."

"Right." Barnes punched a button on the secure phone, calling Brigadier General Paul Wilkes, a former bomber pilot who lived in official housing on Bolling Air Force Base, just across the Potomac from National Airport.

"Yeah," Wilkes said gruffly.

"Barnes here, sir. We need you in the NMCC immediately." That was all the Colonel had to say. "Immediately" is a word that has special meaning for an aviator.

"On the way." Wilkes hung up and muttered further: "Thank God for four-wheel-drive." He struggled into an olive-drab winter parka and headed out the door without bothering with boots. His personal car was a Toyota Land Cruiser that he liked for driving the back country. It started at once, and he backed out, struggling across roads not yet plowed.

The Presidential Crisis Room at Camp David was an anachronistic leftover from the bad old days, or so Bob Fowler had thought on first seeing it over a year before. Constructed during the Eisenhower Administration, it had been designed to resist nuclear attack in an age when the accuracy of a missile was measured in miles rather than yards. Blasted into the living granite rock of the Catoctin Mountains of western Maryland, it had a solid sixty feet of overhead protection, and until 1975 or so had been a highly secure and survivable shelter. About thirty feet wide and forty deep, with a ten-foot ceiling, it contained a staff of twelve, mostly Navy communications types, of whom six were enlisted men. The equipment was not quite as modern as that on NEACP or certain other facilities that the President might use. He sat at a console that looked like 1960s NASA in configuration. There was even an ashtray built into the desk top. In front of him was a bank of television sets. The chair was a comfortable one, even if the situation decidedly was not. Elizabeth Elliot took the one next to his.

"Okay," President J. Robert Fowler said, "what the hell is going on?"

The senior briefing officer, he saw, was a Navy lieutenant commander. That was not very promising.

"Sir, your helicopter is down with a mechanical problem. A second Marine helo is on its way here now to get you to Kneecap. We have CINC-SAC and CINC-NORAD on line. These buttons here give you direct lines to all the other CINCs." By this, the naval officer meant the Commanders-in-Chief of major joint-service commands: CINCLANT was Commander-in-Chief Atlantic, Admiral Joshua Painter, USN; there was a corresponding CINC-PAC in charge of Pacific area forces, and both were traditionally Navy posts. CINC-SOUTH was in Panama, CINC-CENT in Bahrain, CINC-FOR—heading Forces Command—was at Fort McPherson in Atlanta, Georgia, all three of which were traditionally Army posts. There were others as well, including SACEUR, Supreme Allied Commander Europe, the chief NATO military officer, who at the moment was an Air Force four-star general. Under the existing command system, the service chiefs actually had no command authority. Instead, they advised the Secretary of Defense, who in turn advised the President. Presidential orders were issued from the President through the SecDef directly to the CINCs.

But the SecDef . . .

Fowler looked for the button labeled NORAD and pushed it.

"This is the President. I am in my Camp David communications room."

"Mr. President, this is still Major General Borstein. CINC-NORAD is not here, sir. He was in Denver for the Super Bowl. Mr. President, it is my duty to advise you that our instruments put the detonation either at or very near the Skydome stadium in Denver. It would appear very likely that Secretaries Bunker and Talbot are both dead, along with CINC-NORAD.''

''Yes,'' Fowler said. There was no emotion in his voice. He'd already reached that conclusion.

''The Vice-CINC is traveling at the moment. I will be the senior NORAD officer for the next few hours until someone more senior manages to get back.''

''Very well. Now: What the hell is going on?''

''Sir, we do not know. The detonation was not preceded by anything unusual. There was not—I repeat, sir, *not*—a ballistic inbound track prior to the explosion. We are trying to contact the air controllers at Stapleton International Airport to have them check their radar tapes for a possible airborne delivery vehicle. We didn't see anything coming in on any of our scopes.''

''Would you have seen an inbound aircraft?''

''Not necessarily, sir,'' General Borstein replied. ''It's a good system, but there are ways to beat it, especially if you use a single aircraft. In any case, Mr. President, there are some things we need to do at once. Can we talk about that for a moment?''

''Yes.''

''Sir, on my own command authority as acting-CINC-NORAD, I have placed my command on DEFCON-ONE alert. As you know, NORAD has that authority, and also nuclear-release authority for defensive purposes only.''

''You will not release any nuclear weapons without my authorization,'' Fowler said forcefully.

''Sir, the only nukes we have in our inventory are in storage,'' Borstein said. His voice was admirably mechanical, the other uniformed people thought. ''I propose that we next initiate a conference call with CINC-SAC.''

''Do it,'' Fowler ordered. It happened instantly.

''Mr. President, this in CINC-SAC,'' General Peter Fremont, USAF, announced. His voice was all business.

''What the hell is going on?''

''Sir, we do not know that, but there are some things we should do immediately.''

''Go on.''

''Sir, I recommend that we immediately place all of our strategic forces on a higher alert level. I recommend DEFCON-TWO. If we are dealing with a nuclear attack, we should posture our forces to maximum readiness. That will enable us to respond to an attack with the greatest possible effect. It could also have the effect of deterring whoever got this thing under way, in the event that he might have—or we could give him—second thoughts.

''If I can add to that, sir, we should also increase our readiness across the board. If for no other reason, the availability of military units to provide assistance and to reduce possible civilian panic might be very useful. I recommend DEFCON-THREE for conventional forces.''

''Better to do that selectively, Robert,'' Liz Elliot said.

''I heard that—who is it?'' Borstein asked.

''This the National Security Advisor,'' Liz said, a touch too loudly. She was as pale as her white silk blouse. Fowler was still under control. Elliot was struggling to do the same.

''We have not met, Dr. Elliot. Unfortunately, our command-and-control systems do not allow us to do that selectively—at least not very fast. By sending out the alert now, however, we can activate all the units we need, then select the units we need to do things while they come on line. That will save us at least an hour. That is my recommendation.''

''I concur in that,'' General Fremont added at once.

''Very well, do it,'' Fowler said. It sounded reasonable enough.

The communications were handled through separate channels. CINC-SAC handled the strategic forces. The first Emergency Action Message used the same robotic voice that had already scrambled the alerted SAC wings. While the SAC bomber bases already knew that they were being alerted, the DEFCON-TWO notice made it official and far more ominous. Fiber-optic landlines carried a similar notice to the Navy's Extremely Low Frequency radio system located in Michigan's Upper Peninsula region. This signal had to be sent out by mechanical Morse. The nature of this radio system was such that it could only send out its characters very slowly, rather like the speed of a novice typist, and it acted as a cueing system, telling submarines to come to the surface for a more detailed message to be delivered by satellite radios.

At King's Bay, Georgia; Charleston, South Carolina; and Groton, Connecticut, and at three other locations in the Pacific, signals by landline and satellite link were received by the duty staffs of the missile submarine squadrons, most of them aboard submarine tenders. Of America's thirty-six missile submarines in service at the moment, nineteen were at sea, on ''deterrence patrol,'' as it was called. Two were in yard-overhaul status, and were totally unavailable for duty. The rest were tied up alongside tenders, except for USS *Ohio,* which was in the boatshed at Bangor. All had reduced crews aboard, though not one had her CO aboard this Sunday evening. That didn't really matter. The ''boomers'' all had two crews, and in every case one of the two commanding officers assigned to each boat was within thirty minutes of his command. All carried beepers, which went off almost simultaneously. The duty crews aboard each submarine began preparations for immediate sortie. The Command Duty Officer on each boomer was an officer who had passed the stringent test required before a submariner could be ''qualified for command.'' Their operational orders were clear: when this sort of alert came, they had to get to sea just as fast as possible. Most thought it a drill, but drills for strategic forces were a serious business. Already, tugboats were lighting up their diesels to help the slate-gray hulls away from the tenders. Deck crews were removing safety lines and stanchions, as men who'd been aboard the tenders scrambled down the ladders to their various ships. Aboard, division officers and assistants checked their rosters to see who was aboard and who was not. The fact of the matter was that these warships, like all warships, were overmanned. They could easily sail and operate with half a crew if they had to. DEFCON-TWO meant that they had to.

Captain Rosselli and the NMCC staff handled the conventional forces. Pre-set recordings went directly to the individual units. In the Army that meant division level. In the Air Force it was at the wing level, and in the Navy it was at the squadron level. The conventional forces were going to DEFCON-THREE. Captain Rosselli and Colonel Barnes handled voice lines to higher command levels. Even when talking to three-star officers with no less than twenty-five years of service each, it was necessary to tell every single one that: *No, sir, this is not repeat not a drill.*

American military units all over the world went instantly on alert. As was to be expected, those units which ordinarily maintained high alert levels responded the most quickly. One of these was the Berlin Brigade.

37. Human Effects

"Captain, we have an Emergency Action Message on the ELF."

"What?" Ricks asked, turning away from the chart table.

"Emergency Action Message, Captain." The communications officer handed over the brief code group.

"Great time for a drill." Ricks shook his head and said, "Battle Stations. Alert-One."

A petty officer immediately activated the 1-MC and made the announcement. "General Quarters, General Quarters, all hands man your battle stations." Next came an electronic alarm sure to end the most captivating of dreams.

"Mr. Pitney," Ricks said over the noise. "Antenna depth."

"Aye, Captain. Diving officer, make your depth six-zero feet."

"Make my depth six-zero feet, aye. Helm, ten degrees up on the fairwater planes."

"Ten degrees up on the fairwater planes, aye." The young crewman—helm duty is typically given to very junior men—pulled back on the aircraftlike wheel. "Sir, my planes are up ten degrees."

"Very well."

Barely had that been done when people flooded into the control room. The Chief of the Boat—*Maine*'s senior enlisted man—took his battle station at the air-manifold panel. He was the submarine's senior Diving Officer. Lieutenant Commander Claggett entered the conn to back the Captain up. Pitney, the boat's navigator, was already at his post, which was conning officer. Various enlisted men took their seats at weapons consoles. Aft, officers and men assumed their positions as different as the Missile Control Center—MCC—which monitored the status of *Maine*'s twenty-four Trident missiles, and the auxiliary equipment room, which was mainly concerned with the ship's backup diesel engine.

In the control room, the IC—internal communications—man of the watch called off the compartments as they reported in as manned and ready.

"What gives?" Claggett asked Ricks. The Captain merely handed over the brief EAM slip.

"Drill?"

"I suppose. Why not?" Ricks asked. "It's a Sunday, right?"

"Still bumpy up on the roof?"

As though on cue, *Maine* started taking rolls. The depth gauge showed 290 feet, and the massive submarine suddenly rocked 10 degrees to starboard. Throughout the vessel, men rolled their eyes and grumbled. There was scarcely a man aboard who hadn't lost it at least once. This was the perfect environment for motion sickness. With no outside references—submarines are conspicuously short of windows and portholes—the eyes saw something that clearly was not moving while the inner ears reported that movement was definitely taking place. The same thing that had affected nearly all of the Apollo astronauts began to affect these sailors. Unconsciously, men shook their heads sharply, as though to repel a bothersome insect. They uniformly hoped that whatever the hell they were up to—no one from Ricks on down knew as yet what was happening—they'd soon be able to get back where they belonged—four hundred feet, where the ship's motion was imperceptible.

"Level at six-zero feet, sir."

"Very well," Pitney replied.

"Conn, sonar, contact lost on Sierra-16. Surface noise is screwing us all up."

"What's the last position?" Ricks asked.

"Last bearing was two-seven-zero, estimated range four-nine thousand yards," Ensign Shaw replied.

"Okay. Run up the UHF antenna. Up 'scope," he also ordered the quartermaster of the watch. *Maine* was taking 20-degree rolls now, and Ricks wanted to see why. The quartermaster rotated the red-and-white control wheel, and the oiled cylinder hissed up on hydraulic power.

"Wow," the Captain said as he put his hands on the handles. He could feel the power of the sea slapping the exposed top of the instrument. He bent down to look.

"We have a UHF signal coming in now, sir," the communications officer reported.

"That's nice," Ricks said. "I'd call that thirty-foot seas, people, mostly rollers, some are breaking over. Well, we can shoot through that if we have to," he added almost as a joke. After all, this had to be a drill.

"How's the sky?" Claggett asked.

"Overcast—no stars." Ricks stood back and slapped the handles up. "Down 'scope." He turned to Claggett. "X, we want to get back tracking our friend just as soon as we can."

"Aye, Cap'n."

Ricks was about to lift the phone to MCC. He wanted to tell the missile-control crew that he wanted this drill over just as fast as they could arrange it. The communications officer was in the compartment before he could push the proper button.

"Captain, this isn't a drill."

"What do you mean?" Ricks noticed that the Lieutenant didn't look very happy.

"DEFCON-TWO, sir." He handed over the message.

"What?" Ricks scanned the message, which was brief and chillingly to the point. "What the hell's going on?" He handed it off to Dutch Claggett.

"DEFCON-TWO? We've never been at DEFCON-TWO, not as long as I've been in . . . I remember a DEFCON-THREE once, but I was a plebe then. . . ."

Around the compartment, men traded glances. The American military has five alert levels, numbered five through one. DEFCON-FIVE was denoted normal peacetime operations. FOUR was slightly higher, calling for increased manning of certain posts, keeping more people—mainly meaning pilots and soldiers—close to their airplanes or tanks, as the case might be. DEFCON-THREE was far more serious. At that point units were fully manned for operational deployment. At DEFCON-TWO units began to deploy, and this level was saved for the imminent threat of war. DEFCON-ONE was a level to which American forces had never been called.

At that point, war was to be considered something more than a threat. Weapons were loaded and aimed in anticipation of orders to shoot.

But the entire DEFCON system was more haphazard than one might imagine. Submarines generally kept a higher-than-normal state of alert as a part of routine operations. Missile submarines, always ready to launch their birds in a matter of minutes, were effectively at DEFCON-TWO all the time. The notice from the FLTSATCOM merely made it official, and a lot more ominous.

"What else?" Ricks asked communications.

"That's it, sir."

"Any news come in, any threat warning?"

"Sir, we got the usual news broadcast yesterday. I was planning to get the next one in about five hours—you know, so we'd have the Super Bowl score." The Lieutenant paused. "Sir, there was nothing in the news, and nothing official about any crisis."

"So what the hell is going on?" Ricks asked rhetorically. "Well, that doesn't really matter, does it?"

"Captain," Claggett said, "for starters, I think we need to break off from our friend at two-seven-zero."

"Yeah. Bring her around northeast, X. He's not due for another turn soon, and that'll open the range pretty fast, then we'll head north to open further."

Claggett looked at the chart, mainly as a matter of habit to see that the water was deep. It was. They were, in fact, astride the great-circle route from Seattle to Japan. On command, USS *Maine* turned to port. A right turn would have been just as easy, but this way they would immediately start opening the range on the Akula which they'd been tracking for several days. In a minute this put the submarine broadside-to the thirty-footers rolling just a few feet over their heads and made the submarine's sail almost exactly that, a target for the natural forces at work. The boat took a 40-degree roll. All over the submarine, men braced and grabbed for loose gear.

"Take her down a little, Captain?" Claggett asked.

"In a few minutes. Let's see if there's any follow-up on the satellite channel."

Three pieces of what had once been one of the most magnificent evergreen trees in Oregon had now been in the North Pacific for several weeks. The logs had still been green and heavy when they'd fallen off the MV *George McReady*. Since becoming just another entry in the flotsam on the sea, they'd soaked in more water, and the heavy steel chain that held them together changed what should have been a slightly positive buoyancy into neutral buoyancy. They could not quite get to the surface, at least not in these weather conditions. The pounding of the seas defeated every attempt at rising to the sunlight—of which there was none at the moment—and they hovered like blimps, turning slowly as the sea struggled mightily to break their chains.

A junior sonarman aboard *Maine* heard something, something at zero-four-one, almost dead ahead. It was an odd sound, he thought, metallic, like a tinkle but deeper. Not a ship, he thought, not a biologic. It was almost lost in the surface noise, and wouldn't settle down on bearing. . . .

"Shit!" He keyed his microphone. "Conn, sonar—sonar contact close aboard!"

"What?" Ricks dashed into sonar.

"Don't know what, but it's close, sir!"

"Where?"

"Can't tell, like both sides of the bow—not a ship, I don't know what the hell it is, sir!'' The petty officer checked off the pip on his screen while his ears strained to identify the sound. ''Not a point source—it's *close,* sir!''

''But—'' Ricks stopped, turned, and shouted on reflex: ''Emergency dive!'' He knew it was too late for that.

The entire length of USS *Maine* reverberated like a base drum as one of the logs struck the fiberglass dome over the bow sonar array.

There were three sections of what had once been a single tree. The first hit axially just on the edge of the sonar dome, doing very little damage because the submarine was only doing a few knots, and everything about her hull was built for strength. The noise was bad enough. The first log was shunted aside, but there were two more, and the center one tapped the hull once just outside the control room.

The helmsman responded at once to the Captain's command, pushing his control yoke all the way to the stops. The stern of the submarine rose at once, into the path of the logs. *Maine* had a cruciform stern. There was a rudder both above and below the propeller shaft. To the left and right were the stern planes, which operated like the stabilizers of an aircraft. On the outer surface of each was another vertical structure that looked like an auxiliary rudder, but was in fact a fitting for sonar sensors. The chain between two of the logs fouled on that. Two logs were outboard, and one inboard. The inboard one was just long enough to reach the spinning propeller. The resulting noise was the worst anyone had ever heard. *Maine*'s seven-bladed screw was made of manganese-bronze alloy that had been shaped into its nearly perfect configuration over a period of seven months. It was immensely strong, but not this strong. Its scimitar-shaped blades struck the logs one after another, like a slow, inefficient saw. Each impact gouged or dented the outboard edges. The officer in the maneuvering room, aft, had already decided to stop the shaft before the order to do so arrived. Outside the hull, not a hundred feet from his post, he heard the screams of abused metal as the sonar fitting was wrenched off the starboard stern plane; along with it went the additional fitting that held the submarine's towed-array sonar. At that point the logs, one of them now badly splintered, fell off into the submarine's wake, and the worst of the noise stopped.

''What the fuck was that?'' Ricks nearly screamed.

''Tail's gone, sir. We just lost the tail,'' a sonarman said. ''Right-side lateral array is damaged, sir.'' Ricks was already out of the room. The petty officer was talking to himself.

''Conn, maneuvering room,'' a speaker was saying. ''Something just pounded the hell out of our screw. I'm checking for damage to the shaft now.''

''Stern planes are damaged, sir. Very sluggish on the controls,'' the helmsman said. The Chief of the Boat pulled the youngster off the seat and took his place. Slowly and carefully, the Master Chief worked the control wheel.

''Damaged hydraulics, feels like. The trim tabs''—these were electrically powered—''look okay.'' He worked the wheel left and right. ''Rudder is okay, sir.''

''Lock the stern planes in neutral. Ten degrees up on the fairwater planes.'' This order came from the XO.

''Aye.''

''So, what was it?'' Dubinin asked.

''Metallic—an enormous mechanical transient, bearing zero-five-one.'' The officer tapped the blazing mark on his screen. ''Low frequency as you see, like a drum . . . but this noise here, much higher pitch. I heard that on my phones, sounded like a machine gun. Wait a minute . . .'' Senior Lieutenant Rykov said, thinking rapidly. "The frequency—I mean the interval of the impulses—that was a blade-rate, that was a propeller . . . only thing it could be. . . ."

"And now?" the Captain asked.

"Gone completely."

"I want the entire sonar crew on duty." Captain Dubinin returned to control. "Come about, new course zero-four-zero. Speed ten."

Getting a Soviet Army truck was simplicity itself. They'd stolen it, along with a staff car. It was just after midnight in Berlin, and since it was a Sunday night, the streets were empty. Berlin is as lively a city as any in the world, but Monday there is a workday, and work is something that Germans take seriously. What little traffic there was came from people late to leave their local *Gasthaus*, or perhaps a few workers whose jobs required round-the-clock manning. What mattered was that traffic was agreeably light, allowing them to get to their destination right on time.

There used to be a wall, Günther Bock thought. On one side was the American Berlin detachment, and on the other a Soviet detachment, each with a small but heavily used exercise area adjacent to their barracks. The wall was gone now, leaving nothing but grass between two mechanized forces. The staff car pulled up to the Soviet gate. The sentry there was a senior sergeant of twenty years with pimples on his face and an untidy uniform. His eyes went a little wide when he saw the three stars on Keitel's shoulder boards.

"Stand at attention!" Keitel roared in perfect Russian. The boy complied at once. "I am here from Army Command to conduct an unannounced readiness inspection. You will not report our arrival to anyone. Is that clear?"

"Yes, Colonel!"

"Carry on—and clean up that filthy uniform before I come back through here or you'll find yourself on the Chinese border! Move!" Keitel ordered Bock, who was sitting at the wheel.

"Zu Befehl, Herr Oberst," Bock replied after he moved off. It was funny, actually. There were a few humorous aspects to all this, Bock thought. A few. But you had to have the right sense of humor for it.

The regimental headquarters was in an old building once used by Hitler's Wehrmacht that the Russians had used more than they had maintained. It did have the usual garden outside, and in the summer one could see the flowers arranged to duplicate the unit's patch. This one was a Guards Tank Regiment, though one with a history to which its soldiers paid little attention, judging by the sentry at the gate. Bock pulled right up to the door. Keitel and the rest dismounted from their vehicles and walked into the front door like gods in a bad mood.

"Who's the duty officer of this whorehouse?" Keitel bellowed. A corporal just pointed. Corporals do not dispute the orders of staff-grade officers. The duty officer, they found, was a major, perhaps thirty years of age.

"What is this?" the young officer asked.

"I am Colonel Ivanenko of the Inspectorate. *This* is an unannounced operational-readiness inspection. Hit your alarm!" The Major walked two steps and punched a button that set off sirens all over the camp area.

"Next, call your regimental commander, and get his drunken ass over here! What is your readiness state, Major?" Keitel demanded without giving the man a chance to take a breath. The junior officer stopped in midreach for the phone, not knowing which order he was supposed to follow first. *"Well?"*

"Our readiness is in accordance with unit norms, Colonel Ivanenko."

"You have a chance to prove that." Keitel turned to one of the others. "Take this child's name!"

Less than two thousand meters away, they could see lights going on at the American base in what had so recently been West Berlin.

"They're having a drill also," Keitel/Ivanenko observed. "Splendid. We'd better be faster than they are," he added.

"What is this?" The regimental commander, also a colonel, arrived without his buttons done.

"*This* looks like a sorry spectacle!" Keitel boomed. "*This* is an unannounced readiness inspection. You have a regiment to lead, Colonel. I suggest you get to it without asking any further questions."

"But—"

"But *what?*" Keitel demanded. "*Don't you know what a readiness inspection* is?"

There was one thing about dealing with Russians, Keitel thought. They were arrogant, overbearing, and they hated Germans, however much they protested otherwise. On the other hand, when browbeaten, they were predictable. Even though his rank insignia was no higher than this man's, he had a louder voice, and that was all he needed.

"I'll show you what my boys can do."

"We'll be outside to watch," Keitel assured him.

"Dr. Ryan, you'd better get down here." The line clicked off.

"Okay," Jack said. He grabbed his cigarettes and walked down to room 7-F-27, the CIA's Operations Center. Located on the north side of the building, it was the counterpart to operations rooms in many other government agencies. In the center of the twenty-by-thirty-foot room, once you got past the cipher lock on the door, was a large circular table with a lazy-Susan bookcase in the center and six seats around it. The seats had overhead plaques to designate their functions: Senior Duty Officer, Press, Africa—Latin America, Europe—USSR, Near-East—Terrorism, and South Asia—East Asia—Pacific. The wall clocks showed the time in Moscow, Beijing, Beirut, Tripoli, and, of course, Greenwich Mean. There was an adjacent conference room that looked down on the CIA's internal courtyard.

"What gives?" Jack asked, arriving with Goodley in his wake.

"According to NORAD a nuclear device just went off in Denver."

"I hope that's a fucking joke!" Jack replied. That, too, was a reflex. Before the man had a chance to respond, Ryan's stomach turned over. Nobody made jokes like that one.

"I wish it were," the Senior Duty Officer replied.

"What do we know?"

"Not much."

"Anything? Threat board?" Jack asked. Again it was reflexive. If there had been anything, he would have heard it by now. "Okay—where's Marcus?"

"Coming home in the C-141, somewhere between Japan and the Aleutians. You're it, sir," the SDO pointed out, quietly thanking a beneficent God that it wasn't himself. "President's at Camp David. SecDef and SecState—"

"Dead?" Ryan asked.

"It would appear so, sir."

Ryan closed his eyes. "Holy Jesus. The Vice President?"

"At his official residence. We've only been going about three minutes. The

NMCC watch officer is a Captain James Rosselli. General Wilkes is on the way in. DIA's on line. They—I mean the President just ordered DEFCON-TWO on our strategic forces.''

''Anything from the Russians?''

''Nothing unusual at all. There's a regional air-defense exercise under way in Eastern Siberia. That's all.''

''Okay, alert all the stations. Put the word out that I want to hear anything they might have—anything. They are to hit every source they can just as fast as they can.'' Jack paused one more time. ''How sure are we that this really happened?''

''Sir, two DSPS satellites copied the flash. We have a KH-11 that's going to be overhead in about twenty minutes, and I've directed NPIC to put every camera they have on Denver. NORAD says it's a definite nuclear detonation, but there's no word on yield or damage. The explosion seems to be in the immediate area of the stadium—like *Black Sunday,* sir, but real. This is definitely not a drill, not if we're jacking the strategic forces to DEFCON-TWO, sir.''

''Inbound ballistic track? Aircraft delivery?''

''Negative on the first, there was no launch warning, and no ballistic radar track.''

''What about a FOBS?'' Goodley asked. A weapon could be delivered by satellite. That was the purpose of a Fractional-Orbital Bombardment System.

''They would have caught that,'' the SDO replied. ''I already asked. On the aircraft side, they don't know yet. They're trying to check air-traffic-control tapes.''

''So we don't know jack shit.''

''Correct.''

''President check in with us yet?'' Ryan asked.

''No, but we have an open line there. He has the National Security Advisor there also.''

''Most likely scenario?''

''I'd say terrorism.''

Ryan nodded. ''So would I. I'm taking over the conference room. Okay, I want DO, DI, DS&T in here immediately. If you need choppers to fetch them in, order 'em.'' Ryan walked into the room, leaving the door open.

''Christ,'' Goodley said. ''You sure you want me here?''

''Yes, and when you have an idea, you say it out loud. I forgot about FOBS.'' Jack lifted the phone and punched the FBI button.

''Command Center.''

''This is CIA, Deputy Director Ryan speaking. Who is this?''

''Inspector Pat O'Day. I have Deputy Assistant Director Murray here also. You're on speaker, sir.''

''Talk to me, Dan.'' Jack put his phone on speaker also. A watch officer handed him a cup of coffee.

''We don't know anything. No heads-up at all, Jack. Thinking terrorists?''

''At the moment it seems the most plausible alternative.''

''How sure are you of that?''

''Sure?'' Ryan shook his head at the phone, Goodley saw. ''What's 'sure' mean, Dan?''

''I hear you. We're still trying to figure out what happened here, too. I can't even get CNN on the TV to work.''

''What?''

''One of my communications people says the satellites are all out,'' Murray explained. ''Didn't you know that?''

"No." Jack pointed for Goodley to get back into the Ops Center and find out. "If that's true, it could scratch the terrorism idea. Jesus, that's scary!"

"It's true, Jack. We've checked."

"They think ten commercial commosats are nonfunctional," Goodley said. "All the defense birds are on line, though. Our commlinks are okay."

"Find the most senior S&T guy you can find—or one of our commo people—and ask him what could snuff out satellites. Move!" Jack ordered. "Where's Shaw?"

"On his way in. Going to be a while the way the roads are."

"Dan, I'll give you everything I get here."

"It'll be a two-way street." The line went dead.

The most horrible thing was that Ryan didn't know what to do next. It was his job to gather data and forward it to the President, but he had no data. What information there was would come in through military circuits. CIA had failed again, Ryan told himself. Someone had done something to his country and he hadn't warned anyone. People were dead because his agency had failed in its mission. Ryan was Deputy Director, the man who really ran the shop for the political drone placed over his head. The failure was personal. A million people dead, maybe, and there he was, all alone in an elegant little conference room staring at a wall with nothing on it. He hunted a line to NORAD and punched it.

"NORAD," a disembodied voice answered.

"This is the CIA Operations Center, Deputy Director Ryan speaking. I need information."

"We do not have much, sir. We think the bomb exploded in the immediate vicinity of the Skydome. We are trying to estimate yield, but nothing yet. A helicopter has been dispatched from Lowry Air Force Base."

"Will you keep us posted?"

"Yes, sir."

"Thank you." That was a big help, Ryan thought. Now he knew that someone else didn't know anything.

There was nothing magical about a mushroom cloud, Battalion Chief Mike Callaghan of the Denver City Fire Department knew. He'd seen one before, as a rookie firefighter. It had been a fire in the Burlington yards just outside the city, in 1968. A propane tank-car had let go, right next to another trainload of bombs en route to the Navy's munitions terminal at Oakland, California. The chief back then had had the good sense to pull his men back when the tank ruptured, and from a quarter mile away they'd watched a hundred tons of bombs go off in a hellish firecracker series. There had been a mushroom then also. A large mass of hot air rose, roiling as it went into an annular shape. It created an updraft, drawing air upward into its donut-shaped center, making the stem of the mushroom. . . .

But this one was much larger.

He was behind the wheel of his red-painted command car, following the first alarm, three Seagrave pumper units, an aerial ladder truck, and two ambulances. It was a pitiful first response. Callaghan lifted his radio and ordered a general alarm. Next he ordered his men to approach from upwind.

Christ, what had happened here?

It couldn't be that . . . most of the city was still intact.

Chief Callaghan didn't know much, but he knew there was a fire to fight and people to rescue. As his car turned off the last sidestreet onto the boulevard leading to the stadium, he saw the main smoke mass. The parking lot, of course. It had to be. The mushroom cloud was blowing rapidly southwest toward the mountains. The parking lot was a mass of fire and flame from burning gasoline and oil and auto parts. A powerful gust of wind cleared the smoke briefly, just enough that he could see that there had been a stadium here . . . a few sections were still . . . not intact, but you could tell what they were—had been only a few minutes before. Callaghan shut that out. He had a fire to fight. He had people to rescue. The first pump unit pulled up at a hydrant. They had good water here. The stadium was fully sprinklered, and that system fed off two 36-inch, high-pressure mains that gridded around the complex.

He parked his car next to the first big Seagrave and left it to climb on top of the fire engine. Some heavy structural material—the stadium roof, he supposed—was in the parking lot to his right. More had landed a quarter mile away in the mercifully empty parking lot of a shopping center. Callaghan used his portable radio to order the next wave of rescue units to check both the shopping center and the residential area that lay beyond it. The smaller fires would have to wait. There were people in the stadium who needed help, but his firefighters would have to fight through two hundred yards of burning cars to get to them. . . .

Just then he looked up to see a blue Air Force rescue helicopter. The UH-1N landed thirty yards away. Callaghan ran over toward it. The officer inside the back, he saw, was an Army major.

"Callaghan," he said. "Battalion chief."

"Griggs," the Major replied. "You need a look-around?"

"Right."

" 'Kay." The Major spoke into his headset and the helicopter lifted off. Callaghan grabbed a seat belt but didn't strap in.

It didn't take long. What appeared to be a wall of smoke from street level became discrete pillars of black and gray smoke from overhead. Perhaps half of the cars had ignited. He could use one of the driving lanes to get closer in, but some of the way was blocked by wrecked and burning cars. The chopper made a single circuit, bouncing through the roiled, hot air. Looking down, Callaghan could see a mass of melted asphalt, some of it still glowing red. The only spot not giving off smoke was the south end of the stadium itself, which seemed to glisten, though he didn't know why. What they could see appeared to be a crater whose dimensions were hard to judge, since they could only catch bits and pieces of it at a time. It took a long look to determine that parts of the stadium structure remained standing, perhaps four or five sections, Callaghan thought. There had to be people in there.

"Okay, I've seen enough," Callaghan told Griggs. The officer handed him a headset so that they could speak coherently.

"What is this?"

"Just what it looks like, far as I can tell," Griggs replied. "What do you need?"

"Heavy-lift and rigging equipment. There are probably people in what's left of the stadium. We gotta get in to them. But what about the—what about radiation?"

The Major shrugged. "I don't know. When I leave here, I'm picking up a team from Rocky Flats. I work at the Arsenal, and I know a little about this, but the specialists are at Rocky Flats. There's a NEST team there. I need to get them down here ASAP. Okay, I'll call the guard people at the Arsenal, we can get the heavy equipment down here fast. Keep your people to windward. Keep your people at this end. Do not attempt to approach from any other direction, okay?"

"Right."

"Set up a decontamination station right there where your engines are. When people come out, hose them down—strip them and hose them down. Understand?" the Major asked as the chopper touched down. "Then get them to the nearest hospital. Upwind—remember that everything has to go northeast into the wind, so you know you're safe."

"What about fallout?"

"I'm no expert, but I'll give you the best I got. Looks like it was a small one. Not much fallout. The suction from the fireball and the surface wind should have driven most of the radioactive shit away from here. Not all, but most. It should be okay for an hour or so—exposure, I mean. By that time I'll have the NEST guys here and they can tell you for sure. Best I can do for now, Chief. Good luck."

Callaghan jumped out and ran clear. The chopper lifted right off, heading northwest for Rocky Flats.

"Well?" Kuropatkin asked.

"General, we measure yield by the initial and residual heat emissions. There is something odd about this, but my best figure is between one hundred fifty and two hundred kilotons." The Major showed his commander the calculations.

"What's odd about it?"

"The energy from the initial flash was low. That might mean some clouds were in the way. The residual heat is quite high. This was a major detonation, comparable to a very large tactical warhead or a small strategic one."

"Here's the target book," a lieutenant said. It was just that, a clothbound quarto-sized volume whose thick pages were actually foldout maps. It was intended for use in strike-damage evaluation. The map of the Denver area had a plastic overlay that showed the targeting of Soviet strategic missiles. A total of eight birds were detailed on the city, five SS-18s and three SS-19s, totaling no fewer than sixty-four warheads and twenty megatons of yield. Someone, Kuropatkin reflected, thought Denver a worthy target.

"We're assuming a ground-burst?" Kuropatkin asked.

"Correct," the Major replied. He used a compass to draw a circle centered on the stadium complex. "A two-hundred-kiloton device would have a lethal blast radius this wide. . . ."

The map was color-coded. Hard-to-kill structures were colored brown. Dwellings were yellow. Green denoted commercial and other buildings deemed easy targets to destroy. The stadium, he saw, was green, as was nearly everything immediately around it. Well inside the lethal radius were hundreds of houses and low-rise apartment buildings.

"How many in the stadium?"

"I called KGB for an estimate," the Lieutenant said. "It's an enclosed structure—with a roof. The Americans like their comforts. Total capacity is over sixty thousand."

"My God," General Kuropatkin breathed. "Sixty thousand there . . . at least another hundred thousand inside this radius. The Americans must be insane by now." *And if they think* we *did it. . . .*

"Well?" Borstein asked.

"I ran the numbers three times. Best guess, one-fifty-KT, sir," the Captain said.

Borstein rubbed his face. "Christ. Casualty count?"

"Two hundred-K, based on computer modeling and a quick look at the maps we have on file,'' she answered. ''Sir, if somebody's thinking terrorist device, they're wrong. It's too big for that.''

Borstein activated the conference line to the President and CINC-SAC.

''We have some early numbers here.''

''Okay, I'm waiting,'' the President said. He stared at the speaker as though it were a person.

''Initial yield estimates look like one hundred fifty kilotons.''

''That big?'' General Fremont's voice asked.

''We checked the numbers three times.''

''Casualties?'' CINC-SAC asked next.

''On the order of two hundred thousand initial dead. Add fifty more to that from delayed effects.''

President Fowler recoiled backwards as though slapped across the face. For the past five minutes he had denied as much as he could. This most important of denials had just vanished. Two hundred thousand people dead. His citizens, the people he'd sworn to preserve, protect, and defend.

''What else?'' his voice asked.

''I didn't catch that,'' Borstein said.

Fowler took a deep breath and spoke again. ''What else do you have?''

''Sir, our impression here is that the yield is awfully high for a terrorist device.''

''I'd have to concur in that,'' CINC-SAC said. ''An IND—an improvised nuclear device, that is, what we'd expect from unsophisticated terrorists—should not be much more than twenty-KT. This sounds like a multistage weapon.''

''Multistage?'' Elliot said toward the speaker.

''A thermonuclear device,'' General Borstein replied. ''An H-Bomb.''

''Ryan here, who's this?''

''Major Fox, sir, at NORAD. We have an initial feel for yield and casualties.'' The Major read off the bomb numbers.

''Too big for a terrorist weapon,'' said an officer from the Directorate of Science and Technology.

''That's what we think, sir.''

''Casualties?'' Ryan asked.

''Probable prompt-kill number is two hundred thousand or so. That includes the people at the stadium.''

I have to wake up, Ryan told himself, his eyes screwed tightly shut. *This has to be a fucking nightmare, and I'm going to wake up from it.* But he opened his eyes, and nothing had changed at all.

Robby Jackson was sitting in the cabin of the carrier's skipper, Captain Ernie Richards. They had been half-listening to the game, but mainly discussing tactics for an upcoming war game. The *Theodore Roosevelt* battle group would approach Israel from the west, simulating an attacking enemy. The enemy in this case was the Russians. It seemed highly unlikely, of course, but you had to set some rules for the game. The Russians, in this case, were going to be clever. The battle group would be broken up to resemble a loose assembly of merchant ships instead of a tactical formation. The first attack wave would be fighters and attack-bombers squawking ''international'' on their IFF boxes, and would try to approach Ben-Gurion International Airport in the guise of peaceful airliners, the better to get inside

Israeli airspace unannounced. Jackson's operations people had already purloined airliner schedules and were examining the time factors, the better to make their first attack seem as plausible as possible. The odds against them were long. It was not expected that *TR* could do much more than annoy the IAF and the new USAF contingent. But Jackson liked long odds.

"Turn up the radio, Rob. I forgot what the score is."

Jackson leaned across the table and turned the dial, but got music. The carrier had her own on-board TV system, and was also radio-tuned to the U.S. Armed Forces network. "Maybe the antenna broke," the Air Wing Commander observed.

Richards laughed. "At a time like this? I could have a mutiny aboard."

"That would look good on the old fit-rep, wouldn't it?" Someone knocked at the door. "Come!" Richards said. It was a yeoman.

"Flash-traffic, sir." The petty officer handed the clipboard over.

"Anything important?" Robby asked.

Richards just handed the message over. Then he lifted the growler phone and punched up the bridge. "General quarters."

"What the hell?" Jackson murmured. "DEFCON-THREE—why, for Christ's sake?"

Ernie Richards, a former attack pilot, had a reputation as something of a character. He'd reinstituted the traditional Navy practice of bugle calls to announce drills. In this case, the 1-MC speaker system blared forth the opening bars of John Williams' frantic call to arms in *Star Wars,* followed by the usual electronic gonging.

"Let's go, Rob." Both men started running down to the Combat Information Center.

"What can you tell me?" Andrey Il'ych Narmonov asked.

"The bomb had a force of nearly two hundred kilotons. That means a large device, a hydrogen bomb," General Kuropatkin said. "The death count will be well over one hundred thousand dead. We also have indications of a strong electromagnetic pulse that struck one of our early-warning satellites."

"What could account for that?" The questioner here was one of Narmonov's military advisers.

"We do not know."

"Do we have any nuclear weapons unaccounted for?" Kuropatkin heard his President ask.

"Absolutely not," a third voice replied.

"Anything else?"

"With your permission, I would like to order *Voyska PVO* to a higher alert level. We already have a training exercise under way in Eastern Siberia."

"Is that provocative?" Narmonov asked.

"No, it is totally defensive. Our interceptors cannot harm anyone more than a few hundred kilometers from our own borders. For the moment I will keep all my aircraft within Soviet airspace."

"Very well, you may proceed."

In his underground control center, Kuropatkin merely pointed to another officer, who lifted a phone. The Soviet air-defense system had already been prepped, of course; inside a minute radio messages were being broadcast, and long-range search radars came on all over the country's periphery. Both the messages and the radar signals were immediately detected by National Security Agency assets, both on the ground and in orbit.

"Anything else I should do?" Narmonov asked his advisers.

A Foreign Ministry official spoke for all of them. "I think doing nothing is probably best. When Fowler wishes to speak with us, he will do so. He has trouble enough without our interfering."

The American Airlines MD-80 landed at Miami International Airport and taxied over to the terminal. Qati and Ghosn rose from their first-class seats and left the aircraft. Their bags would be transferred automatically to the connecting flight, not that either one particularly cared about that, of course. Both men were nervous, but less so than one might have expected. Death was something both had accepted as an overt possibility for this mission. If they survived, so much the better. Ghosn didn't panic until he realized that there was no unusual activity at all. There should have been some, he thought. He found a bar and looked for the usual elevated television set. It was tuned to a local station. There was no game coverage. He debated asking a question, but decided not to. It was a good decision. He had only to wait a minute before he overheard another voice asking what the score was.

"It was fourteen-seven Vikings," another voice answered. "Then the goddamned signal was lost."

"When?"

"About ten minutes ago. Funny they don't have it back yet."

"Earthquake, like the Series game in San Francisco?"

"Your guess is as good as mine, man," the bartender replied.

Ghosn stood and left for the walk back to the departure lounge.

"What does CIA have?" Fowler asked.

"Nothing at the moment, sir. We're collecting data, but you know everything that we—wait a minute." Ryan took the message form that the Senior Duty Officer handed him. "Sir, I have a flash here from NSA. The Russian air-defense system just went to a higher alert level. Radars are all coming on, and there's a lot of radio chatter."

"What does that mean?" Liz Elliot asked.

"It means that they want to increase their ability to protect themselves. PVO isn't a threat to anybody unless they're approaching or inside Soviet airspace."

"But *why* would they do it?" Elliot asked again.

"Maybe they're afraid somebody will attack them."

"Goddamn it, Ryan!" the President shouted.

"Mr. President, excuse me. That was not a flippant remark. It is literally true. *Voyska PVO* is a defense system like our NORAD. Our air-defense and warning systems are now at a higher alert status. So are theirs. It's a defensive move only. They have to know that we've had this event. When there's trouble of this sort, it's natural to activate your own defenses, just as we have done."

"It's potentially disturbing," General Borstein said at NORAD HQ. "Ryan, you forget we *have* been attacked. They have not. Now, before they've even bothered to call us, they're jacking up their alert levels. I find that a little worrisome."

"Ryan, what about those reports that we got about missing Soviet nuclear weapons?" Fowler asked. "Could that fit into this situation?"

"What missing nukes?" CINC-SAC demanded. "Why the hell didn't I hear about that?"

"What kind of nukes?" Borstein asked a second later.

"That was an unconfirmed report from a penetration agent. There are no details,"

Ryan answered, then realized he had to press on. "The sum of the information received is this: We've been told that Narmonov has political problems with his military; that they are unhappy with the way he's doing things; that in the ongoing pullback from Germany, an unspecified number of nuclear weapons—probably tactical ones—have turned up missing; that KGB is conducting an operation to determine what, if anything, is missing. Supposedly Narmonov is personally concerned that he might be the target of political blackmail, and that the blackmail could have a nuclear dimension. *But,* and I must emphasize the *but,* we have been totally unable to confirm these reports despite repeated attempts, and we are examining the possibility that our agent is lying to us."

"Why didn't you tell us that?" Fowler asked.

"Mr. President, we're in the process of formulating our assessment now. The work is still ongoing, sir, I mean, we've been doing it over the weekend."

"Well, it sure as hell wasn't one of ours," General Fremont said heatedly. "And it's no goddamned terrorist bomb, it's too goddamned big for that. *Now* you tell us that the Russians may have a short inventory. That's more than disturbing, Ryan."

"And it could explain the increased alert level at PVO," Borstein added ominously.

"Are you two telling me," the President asked, "that this could have been a Soviet device?"

"There aren't all that many nuclear powers around," Borstein replied first. "And the yield of this device is just too damned big for amateurs."

"Wait a minute." Jack jumped in again. "You have to remember that the facts we have here are very thin. There is a difference between information and speculation. You have to remember that."

"How big are Soviet tactical nuclear weapons?" Liz Elliot wanted to know.

CINC-SAC handled that one: "A lot like ours. They have little one-kiloton ones for artillery rounds, and they have warheads up to five hundred-KT left over from the SS-20s they did away with."

"In other words the yield of this explosion falls into the range of the Soviet warhead types that we have heard are missing?"

"Correct, Dr. Elliot," General Fremont replied.

At Camp David, Elizabeth Elliot leaned back in her chair and turned to the President. She spoke too softly for the speakerphone to catch her words.

"Robert, you were supposed to be at that game, along with Brent and Dennis."

It was strange that he hadn't had that thought enter his mind yet, Fowler told himself. He, too, leaned back. "No," he replied. "I cannot believe that the Russians would attempt such a thing."

"What was that?" a voice on the speaker asked.

"Wait a minute," the President said too quietly.

"Mr. President, I didn't catch what you said."

"I said, wait a minute!" Fowler shouted. He put his hand over the speaker for a moment. "Elizabeth, it's our job to get control of this situation and we will. Let's try to put this personal stuff aside for the moment."

"Mr. President, I want you on Kneecap just as fast as you can get there," CINC-SAC said. "This situation could be very serious indeed."

"If we're going to get control, Robert, we must do it quickly."

Fowler turned to the naval officer standing behind him. "When's the chopper due in?"

"Twenty-five minutes, sir, then thirty more to get you to Andrews for Kneecap."

"Almost an hour . . ." Fowler looked at the wall clock, as people do when they know what time it is, know what time it will take to do something, and look at the clock anyway. "The radio links on the chopper aren't enough for this. Tell the chopper to take Vice President Durling to Kneecap. General Fremont?"

"Yes, Mr. President."

"You have extra Kneecaps there, don't you?"

"Yes, I do, sir."

"I'm sending the Vice President up on the primary. You send a spare down here. You can land it at Hagerstown, can't you?"

"Yes, sir, we can use the Fairchild-Republic airfield, where they used to build the A-10s."

"Okay, do that. It'll take me an hour to get to Andrews, and I cannot afford to waste an hour. It's my job to settle this thing down, and I need that hour."

"That, sir, is a mistake," Fremont said in the coldest voice he had. It would take two hours to get the aircraft to central Maryland.

"That may be, but it's what I'm going to do. This is not a time for me to run away."

Behind the President, Pete Connor and Helen D'Agustino traded a baleful look. They had no illusions on what would happen if there were a nuclear attack on the United States. Mobility was the President's best defense, and he had just thrown that away.

The radio message from Camp David went out at once. The presidential helicopter was just crossing the Washington Beltway when it turned and went back southeast. It landed on the grounds of the U.S. Naval Observatory. Vice President Roger Durling and his entire family jumped aboard. They didn't even bother strapping in. Secret Service agents, with their Uzi sub-machine guns out, knelt inside the aircraft. All Durling knew was what the Secret Service detail had told him. Durling told himself that he had to relax, that he had to keep his head. He looked at his youngest child, a boy only four years old. To be that age again, he'd thought only the day before, to be that age again and be able to grow up in a world where the chance of a major war no longer existed. All the horrors of his youth, the Cuban Missile Crisis that had marked his freshman year in college, his service as a platoon leader in the 82nd Airborne, a year of which had been in Vietnam. War experience made Durling a most unusual liberal politician. He hadn't run from it. He'd taken his chances and remembered having two men die in his arms. Just yesterday he'd looked at his son and thanked God that he wouldn't have to know any of that.

And now, this. His son still didn't know anything more than that they were getting a surprise helicopter ride, and he loved to fly. His wife knew more, and there were tears streaming from her eyes as she stared back at him.

The Marine VH-3 touched down within fifty yards of the aircraft. The first Secret Service agent leaped off and saw a platoon of Air Force security police marking the way to the stairs. The Vice President was practically dragged toward them, while a burly agent picked up his young son and ran the distance. Two minutes later, before people had even strapped in, the pilot of the National Emergency Airborne Command Post—Kneecap—firewalled his engines and roared down runway Zero-

One Left. He headed east for the Atlantic Ocean, where a KC-10 tanker was already orbiting to top off the Boeing's tanks.

''We have a major problem here,'' Ricks said in the maneuvering room. *Maine* had just tried to move. At any speed over three knots, the propeller screeched like a banshee. The shaft was slightly bent, but they'd live with that for a while. ''All seven blades must be damaged. If we try for anything over three we make noise. Over five and we'll lose the shaft bearings in a matter of minutes. The outboard motor can give us two or three knots, but that's noisy too. Comments?'' There were none. No one aboard doubted Ricks' engineering expertise. ''Options?''

''Kinda thin, aren't they?'' Dutch Claggett observed.

Maine had to stay near the surface. At this alert level, she had to be ready to launch in minutes. Ordinarily they could have gone to a deeper depth, if for no other reason than to reduce the horrible motion the ship was taking right now from surface turbulence, but her reduced speed made coming up too time-consuming.

''How close is *Omaha?*'' the chief engineer asked.

''Probably within a hundred miles, and there's P-3s at Kodiak—but we still have that Akula out there to worry about,'' Claggett said. ''Sir, we can hang tough right here and wait it out.''

''No, we have a hurt boomer. We need some kind of support.''

''That means radiating,'' the XO pointed out.

''We'll use a SLOT buoy.''

''At two knots through the water, that doesn't buy us much, sir. Captain, radiating is a mistake.''

Ricks looked at his chief engineer, who said, ''I like the idea of having a friend around.''

''So do I,'' the Captain said. It didn't take long. The buoy was on the surface in seconds and immediately began broadcasting a short message in UHF. It was programmed to continue broadcasting for hours.

''We're going to have a nationwide panic on our hands,'' Fowler said. That was not his most penetrating observation. He had a growing panic in his own command center, and knew it. ''Is there anything coming out of Denver?''

''Nothing on any commercial TV or radio channel that I know of,'' a voice at NORAD replied.

''Okay, you people stand by.'' Fowler searched his panel for another button.

''FBI Command Center. Inspector O'Day speaking.''

''This is the President,'' Fowler said unnecessarily. It was a direct line and the light on the FBI panel was neatly labeled. ''Who's in charge down there?''

''I am Deputy Assistant Director Murray, Mr. President. I'm the senior man at the moment.''

''How are your communications?''

''They're okay, sir. We have access to the military commsats.''

''One thing we have to worry about is a nationwide panic. To prevent that, I want you to send people to all the TV network headquarters. I want your people to explain to them that they may not broadcast anything about this. If necessary, you are directed to use force to prevent it.''

Murray didn't like that. ''Mr. President, that is against—''

"I know the law, okay? I used to be a prosecutor. This is necessary to preserve life and order, and it will be done, Mr. Murray. That is a Presidential Order. Get to it."

"Yes, sir."

38. First Contacts

The various communications-satellite operators were fiercely independent companies and very often ruthless competitors, but they were not enemies. Between them were agreements informally called treaties. There was always the possibility that one satellite or another could go down, whether from an internal breakdown or collision with space debris that was becoming a real worry for them. Accordingly, there were mutual-assistance agreements specifying that in the event one operator lost a bird, his associates would take up the slack, just as newspapers in the same city traditionally agreed to share printing facilities in the event of a fire or natural disaster. To back up these agreements, there were open phone lines between the various corporate headquarters. Intelsat was the first to call Telstar.

"Bert, we just had two birds go down," Intelsat's duty engineer reported in a slightly shaken voice. "What gives?"

"Shit, we just lost three, and Westar 4 and Teleglobe are down, too. We've had complete system failures here. Running checks now—you?"

"Same here, Bert. Any ideas?"

"None. We're talking like nine birds down, Stacy. Fuck!" The man paused. "Ideas? Wait a minute, getting something . . . okay, it's software. We're interrogating 301 now . . . they got spiked . . . Jesus! 301 got spiked on over a hundred freqs! Somebody just tried to zorch us."

"That's how it looks here, too. But who?"

"Sure as hell wasn't a hacker . . . this would take megawatts to do that on just one channel."

"Bert, that's exactly what I'm getting. Phone links, everything spiked at once. You in any hurry to light them back up?"

"You kidding me? I got a billion worth of hardware up there. Till I find out what the hell clobbered them, they stay down. I've got my senior VP on the way in now. The Pres was out in Denver," Bert added.

"Mine, too, but my chief engineer is snowed in. Damned if I'm going to put my ass on the line. I think we should cooperate on this, Bert."

"No arguments with me, Stace. I'll whistle up Fred Kent at Hughes and see what he thinks. It'll take a while for us to review everything and do full systems checks. I'm staying down until I know—and I mean *know*—what happened here. We got an industry to protect, man."

"Agreed. I won't light back up without talking to you."

"Keep me posted on anything you find out?"

"You got it, Bert. I'll be back to you in an hour one way or another."

* * *

The Soviet Union is a vast country, by far the largest in the world both in area and in the expanse of its borders. All of those borders are guarded, since both the current country and all its precursors have been invaded many times. Border defenses include the obvious—troop concentrations, airfields, and radar posts—and the subtle, like radio reception antennas. The latter were designed to listen in on radio and other electronic emissions. The information was passed on by landline or microwave links to Moscow Center, the headquarters of the Committee for State Security, the KGB, at #2 Dzerzhinskiy Square. The KGB's Eighth Chief Directorate is tasked to communications intelligence and communications security. It has a long and distinguished history that has benefited from another traditional Russian strength, a fascination with theoretical mathematics. The relationship between ciphers and mathematics is a logical one, and the most recent manifestation of this was the work of a bearded, thirtyish gnome of a man who was fascinated with the work of Benoit Mandelbrot at Harvard University, the man who had effectively invented fractal geometry. Uniting this work with that of MacKenzie's work on Chaos Theory at Cambridge University in England, the young Russian genius had invented a genuinely new theoretical way of looking at mathematical formulae. It was generally conceded by that handful of people who understood what he was talking about that his work was easily worth a Planck Medal. It was an historical accident that his father happened to be a General in the KGB's Chief Border Guards Directorate, and that as a result the Committee for State Security had taken immediate note of his work. The mathematician now had everything a grateful Motherland could offer, and someday he'd probably have that Planck Medal also.

He'd needed two years to make his theoretical breakthrough into something practical, but fifteen months earlier he'd made his first "recovery" from the U.S. State Department's most secure cipher, called STRIPE. Six months after that he'd proven conclusively that it was similar in structure to everything the U.S. military used. Cross-checking with another team of cryptanalysts who had access to the work of the Walker spy ring, and the even more serious work done by Pelton, what had resulted only six months earlier was a systematic penetration of American encryption systems. It was still not perfect. Daily keying procedures occasionally proved impossible to break. Sometimes they went as much as a week without recovering one message, but they'd gone as many as three days recovering over half of what they received, and their results were improving by the month. Indeed, the main problem seemed to be that they didn't have the computer hardware to do all the work they should have been able to do, and the Eighth Directorate was busily training more linguists to handle the message traffic they were receiving.

Sergey Nikolayevich Golovko had been awakened from a sound sleep and driven to his office to add his name to the people all over the world shocked into frightened sobriety. A First Chief Directorate man all of his life, his job was to examine the collective American mind and advise his President on what was going on. The decrypts flooding onto his desk were the most useful tool.

He had no less than thirty such messages which bore one of two messages. All strategic forces were being ordered to Defense Condition Two, and all conventional forces were coming to Defense Condition Three. The American President was panicking, KGB's First Deputy Chairman thought. There was no other explanation. *Was it possible that he thought the Soviet Union had committed this infamy?* That was the most frightening thought of his life.

"Another one, naval one." The messenger dropped it on his desk.

Golovko needed only one look. "Flash this to the Navy immediately." He had to call his President with the rest. Golovko lifted the phone.

For once the Soviet bureaucracy worked quickly. Minutes later, an extremely low-frequency signal went out, and the submarine *Admiral Lunin* went to the surface to copy the full message. Captain Dubinin read it as the printer generated it.

AMERICAN SUBMARINE USS MAINE REPORTS LOCATION AS 50D-55M-09SN 153D-01M-23SW. PROPELLER DISABLED BY COLLISION OF UNKNOWN CAUSE. Dubinin left the communications room and made for the chart table.

"Where were we when we copied that transient?"

"Here, Captain, and the bearing was here." The navigator traced the line with his pencil.

Dubinin just shook his head. He handed the message over. "Look at this."

"What do you suppose he's doing?"

"He'll be close to the surface. So . . . we'll go up, just under the layer, and we'll move quickly. Surface noise will play hell with his sonar. Fifteen knots."

"You suppose he was following us?"

"Took you long enough to realize that, didn't it?" Dubinin measured the distance to the target. "Very proud, this one. We'll see about that. You know how the Americans boast of taking hull photographs? Now, my young lieutenant, now it will be our turn!"

"What does this mean?" Narmonov asked the First Deputy Chairman.

"The Americans have been attacked by forces unknown, and the attack was serious, causing major loss of life. It is to be expected that they will increase their military readiness. A major consideration will be the maintenance of public order," Golovko replied over the secure phone line.

"And?"

"And, unfortunately, all their strategic weapons happen to be aimed at the *Rodina*."

"But we had no part in this!" the Soviet President objected.

"Correct. You see, such responses are automatic. They are planned in advance and become almost reflexive moves. Once attacked, you become highly cautious. Countermoves are planned in advance so that you may act rapidly while applying your intellectual capacities to an analysis of the problem without additional and unnecessary distractions."

The Soviet President turned to his Defense Minister. "So, what should we do?"

"I advise an increase in our alert status. Defensive-only, of course. Whoever conducted this attack might, after all, attempt to strike us also."

"Approved," Narmonov said bluntly. "Highest peacetime alert."

Golovko frowned at his telephone receiver. His choice of words had been exquisitely correct: reflexive. "May I make a suggestion?"

"Yes," the Defense Minister said.

"If it is possible, perhaps it would be well to tell our forces the reason for the alert. It might lessen the shock of the order."

"It's a needless complication," Defense thought.

"The Americans have not done this," Golovko said urgently, "and that was almost certainly a mistake. Please consider the state of mind of people suddenly taken from ordinary peacetime operations to an elevated state of alert. It will only require a few additional words. Those few words could be important."

''Good idea,'' Narmonov thought. ''Make it so,'' he ordered Defense.

''We will soon hear from the Americans on the Hot Line,'' Narmonov said. ''What will they say?''

''That is hard to guess, but whatever it is, we should have a reply ready for them, just to settle things down, to make sure they know we had nothing to do with it.''

Narmonov nodded. That made good sense. ''Start working on it.''

The Soviet defense-communications agency operators grumbled at the signal they'd been ordered to dispatch. For ease of transmission, the meat of the signal should have been contained in a single five-letter code group that could be transmitted, decrypted, and comprehended instantly by all recipients, but that was not possible now. The additional sentences had to be edited down to keep the transmission from being too long. A major did this, got it approved by his boss, a major general, and sent it out over no less than thirty communications links. The message was further altered to apply to specific military services.

The *Admiral Lunin* had only been on her new course for five minutes when a second ELF signal arrived. The communications officer fairly ran into the control room with it.

GENERAL ALERT LEVEL TWO. THERE HAS BEEN A NUCLEAR DETONATION OF UNKNOWN ORIGIN IN THE UNITED STATES. AMERICAN STRATEGIC AND CONVENTIONAL FORCES HAVE BEEN ALERTED FOR POSSIBLE WAR. ALL NAVAL FORCES WILL SORTIE AT ONCE. TAKE ALL NECESSARY PROTECTIVE MEASURES.

''Has the world gone mad?'' the Captain asked the message. He got no reply. ''That's all?''

''That is all, no cueing to put the antenna up.''

''These are not proper instructions,'' Dubinin objected. '' 'All necessary protective measures'? What do they mean by that? Protecting ourselves, protecting the Motherland—what the hell do they mean?''

''Captain,'' the *Starpom* said, ''General Alert Two carries its own rules of action.''

''I know that,'' Dubinin said, ''but do they apply here?''

''Why else would the signal have been sent?''

A Level Two General Alert was something unprecedented for the Soviet Military. It meant that the rules of action were not those of a war, but not those of peace either. Though Dubinin, like every other Soviet ship captain, fully understood his duties, the implications of the order seemed far too frightening. The thought passed, however. He was a naval officer. He had his orders. Whoever had given those orders must have understood the situation better than he. The commanding officer of the *Admiral Lunin* stood erect and turned to his second in command.

''Increase speed to twenty-five knots. Battle stations.''

It happened just as fast as men could move. The New York FBI office, set in the Jacob Javits Federal Office Building on the southern end of Manhattan, dispatched its men north, and the light Sunday traffic made it easy. The unmarked but powerful cars screamed uptown to the various network headquarters buildings. The same thing happened in Atlanta, where agents left the Martin Luther King Building for CNN Headquarters. In each case, no fewer than three agents marched into the master control rooms and laid down the law: Nothing from Denver would go out. In no case did the network employees know why this was so, so busy were they trying to reestablish contact. The same thing happened in Colorado, where, under the direction of Assistant Special-Agent-in-Charge Walter Hoskins, the local field division's agents invaded all the network affiliates, and the local phone company, where they cut all long-distance lines over the furious objections of the Bell employees. But Hoskins had made one mistake. It came from the fact that he didn't watch much television.

KOLD was an independent station that was also trying to become a superstation. Like TBS, WWOR, and a few others, it had its own satellite link to cover a wide viewing area. A daring financial gamble, it had not yet paid off for the investors who were running the station on a highly leveraged shoestring out of an old and almost windowless building northeast of the city. The station used one of the Anik-series Canadian satellites and reached Alaska, Canada, and the North-Central U.S. reasonably well with its programming, which was mainly old network shows.

The KOLD building had once been Denver's first network television station, and was constructed in the pattern originally required by the Federal Communications Commission in the 1930s: monolithic reinforced concrete, fit to survive an enemy bomb attack—the specifications predated nuclear weapons. The only windows were in the executive offices on the south side of the building. It was ten minutes after the event that someone passed by the open door of the program manager. He stopped cold, turned and ran back to the newsroom. In another minute a cameraman entered onto the freight elevator that ran all the way to the roof. The picture, hard-wired into the control room and then sent out on a Ku-band transmitter to the Anik satellite, which was untouched by earlier events, broke into the reruns of *The Adventures of Dobie Gillis* across Alaska, Montana, North Dakota, Idaho, and three Canadian provinces. In Calgary, Alberta, a reporter for a local paper who'd never got over her crush on Dwayne Hickman was startled by the picture and the voice-over, and called her city desk. Her breathless report went out at once on the Reuters wire. Soon thereafter, CBC uplinked the video to Europe on one of their unaffected Anik satellites.

By that time the Denver FBI had a pair of men entering the KOLD building. They laid down the law to a news crew that protested about the First Amendment of the U.S. Constitution, which argument carried less weight than the men with guns who shut the power down to their transmitter. The FBI agents at least apologized as they did so. They needn't have bothered. What had been a fool's errand from the beginning was already an exercise in futility.

"So, what the hell is going on?" Richards asked his staff.

"We have no idea, sir. No reason was given for the alert," the communications officer said lamely.

"Well, it leaves us between two chairs, doesn't it?" This was a rhetorical question. The *TR* battle group was just passing Malta, and was now in range of targets in the Soviet Union. That required "The Stick's" A-6E Intruders to take off, climb rapidly to cruising altitude, and top off their tanks soon thereafter, but at that point they had the gas to make it all the way to their targets on or near the Kerch Peninsula. Only a year before, U.S. Navy carriers, though carrying a sizable complement of thermonuclear bombs, had not been part of the SIOP. This acronym, pronounced "Sy-Op," stood for "Single Integrated Operations Plan," and was the master blueprint for dismantling the Soviet Union. The drawdown of strategic missiles—mostly land-based ones for the United States—had radically reduced the number of available warheads, and, like planners everywhere, the Joint Strategic Targeting Staff, co-located with headquarters SAC, tried to make up for the shortfall in any way they could. As a result, whenever an aircraft carrier was in range of Soviet targets, it assumed its SIOP tasking. In the case of USS *Theodore Roosevelt,* it meant that about the time the ship passed east of Malta, she became not a conventional-theater force, but a nuclear-strategic force. To fulfill this mission, *TR* carried fifty B-61-Mod-8 nuclear gravity bombs in a special, heavily-guarded magazine. The B-61 had FUFO—for ''full fusing option,'' more commonly called ''dial-a-yield''—that selected an explosive power ranging from ten to five hundred kilotons. The bombs were twelve feet long, less than a foot in diameter, weighed a mere seven hundred pounds, and were nicely streamlined to cut air resistance. Each A-6E could carry two of them, with all of its other hard-points occupied by auxiliary fuel tanks to allow a combat radius of more than a thousand miles. Ten of them were the explosive equivalent of a whole squadron of Minuteman missiles. Their assigned targets were naval, on the principle that people most often kill friends, or at least associates, rather than total strangers. One assigned SIOP mission, for example, was to reduce the Nikolayev Shipyard on the Dniepr River to a radioactive puddle. Which was, incidentally, where the Soviet carrier *Kuznetzov* had been built.

The Captain's additional problem was that his battle group commander, an admiral, had taken the chance to fly into Naples for a conference with the Commander of the United States Sixth Fleet. Richards was on his own.

''Where's our friend?'' *Roosevelt*'s CO asked.

''About two hundred fifty miles back,'' the operations officer said. ''Close.''

''Let's get the plus-fives right up, skipper,'' Jackson said. ''I'll take two and orbit right about here to watch the back door.'' He tapped the chart.

''Play it cool, Rob.''

''No sweat, Ernie.'' Jackson walked to a phone. ''Who's up?'' he asked the VF-1 ready room. ''Good.'' Jackson went off to get his flight suit and helmet.

''Gentlemen,'' Richards said as Jackson left, ''since we are now east of Malta, we are now part of the SIOP, therefore a strategic and not a conventional asset, and DEFCON-TWO applies to us. If anyone here needs a refresher on the DEFCON-TWO Rules of Engagement, you'd better do it fast. Anything that might be construed as a threat to us may be engaged and destroyed on my authority as battle group commander. Questions?''

''Sir, we don't know what is happening,'' the ops officer pointed out.

''Yeah. We'll try to think first, but, people, let's get our collective act together. Something bad is happening, and we're at DEFCON-TWO.''

It was a fine, clear night on the flight deck. Jackson briefed Commander Sanchez and their respective RIOs, then the plane captains for the two Tomcats sitting on the waist cats walked the flight crews out to them. Jackson and Walters got aboard. The plane captain helped strap both in, then disappeared downward and removed the ladder. Captain Jackson ran through the start-up sequence, watching his engine instruments come into normal idle. The F-14D was currently armed with four radar-homing Phoenix missiles and four infrared Sidewinders.

''Ready back there, Shredder?'' Jackson asked.

''Let's do it, Spade,'' Walter replied.

Robby pushed his throttles to the stops, then jerked them around the detent and into afterburner, and signaled his readiness to the catapult officer, who looked down the deck to make sure it was clear. The officer fired off a salute to the aircraft.

Jackson blinked his flying lights in reply, dropping his hand to the stick and pulling his head back against the rest. A second later the cat officer's lighted wand touched the deck. A petty officer hit the firing button, and steam jetted into the catapult machinery.

For all his years at this business, his senses never quite seemed to be fast enough. The acceleration of the catapult nearly jerked his eyeballs around inside their sockets. The dim glow lights of the deck vanished behind him. The back of the aircraft settled and they were off. Jackson made sure he was actually flying before taking the aircraft out of burner, then he retracted his gear and flaps and started a slow climb to altitude. He was just through a thousand feet when ''Bud'' Sanchez and ''Lobo'' Alexander pulled alongside.

''There go the radars,'' Shredder said, taking note of his instruments. The entire *TR* battle group shut down every emission in a matter of seconds. Now no one would be able to track them from their own electronic noise.

Jackson settled down. Whatever this was, he told himself, it couldn't be all that bad, could it? It was a beautifully clear night, and the higher he got, the clearer it became through the panoramic canopy of his fighter. The stars were discrete pinpricks of light, and their twinkling ceased almost entirely as they reached thirty thousand feet. He could see the distant strobes of commercial aircraft, and the coastlines of half a dozen countries. A night like this, he thought, could make a poet of a peasant. It was for moments like these that he'd become a pilot. He turned west, with Sanchez on his wing. There were some clouds that way, he realized at once. He couldn't see all that many stars.

''Okay,'' Jackson ordered, ''let's get a quick picture.''

The Radar Intercept Officer activated his systems. The F-14D had just been fitted with a new Hughes-built radar called an LPI, for ''low probability of intercept.'' Though using less power than the AWG-9 system it had replaced, the LPI combined greater sensitivity with a far lower chance of being picked up by another aircraft's threat receiver. It also had vastly improved look-down performance.

''There they are,'' Walters reported. ''Nice circular formation.''

''They have anything up?''

''Everything I see has a transponder on.''

'' 'Kay—we'll be on station in another few minutes.''

Fifty miles behind them, an E-2C Hawkeye airborne-early-warning bird was coming off the number-two catapult. Behind it, two KA-6 tankers were firing up, along with more fighters. The tankers would soon arrive at Jackson's station to top off his fuel tanks, enabling the CAG to stay aloft for four more hours. The E-2C was the most important. It climbed out at full military power, turning south to take station fifty miles from its mother ship. As soon as it reached twenty-five thousand, its surveillance radar switched on, and the onboard crew of three operators began cataloging their contacts. Their data was sent by digital link back to the carrier and also to the group air-warfare officer aboard the Aegis cruiser, USS *Thomas Gates,* whose call sign was ''Stetson.''

''Nothing much, skipper.''

''Okay, we're on station. Let's orbit and searchlight around.'' Jackson turned his aircraft into a shallow right turn, with Sanchez in close formation.

The Hawkeye spotted them first. They were almost directly under Jackson and his two Tomcats, and out of the detection cone of their radars for the moment.

''Stetson, this is Falcon-Two, we have four bogies on the deck, bearing two-eight-one, one hundred miles out.'' The reference was for *TR*'s position.

''IFF?''

"Negative, their speed is four hundred, altitude seven hundred, course one-three-five."

"Amplify," the AWO said.

"They're in a loose finger-four, Stetson," the Hawkeye controller said. "Estimate we have tactical fighters here."

"I got something," Shredder reported to Jackson a moment later. "On the deck, looks like two—no, four aircraft, heading southeast."

"Whose?"

"Not ours."

In *TR*'s combat information center, no one as yet had a clue what was going on, but the group intelligence staff was doing its best to find out. What they had learned to this point was that most satellite news channels seemed to be down, though all military satellite links were up and running. A further electronic sweep of the satellite spectrum showed that a lot of video circuits were unaccountably inactive, as were the satellite phone links. So addicted were the communications people to the high-tech channels, that it required the services of a third-class radioman to suggest sweeping shortwave bands. The first they found was BBC. The news flash was recorded and raced into CIC. The voice spoke with the quiet assurance that the British Broadcasting Corporation was known for:

"Reuters reports a nuclear detonation in the Central United States. The Denver, Color*ay*do"—the Brits have trouble pronouncing some American state names—"television station, KOLD, broadcast via satellite a picture of a mushroom cloud over Denver, along with a voice report of a massive explosion. Station KOLD is now off the air, and attempts to reach Denver by telephone have not yet been successful. There has as yet been no official comment whatever on this incident."

"Holy Christ," someone said for all of them. Captain Richards looked around the room at his staff.

"Well, now we know why we're at DEFCON-TWO. Let's get some more fighters up. F-18s forward of us, -14s aft. I want four A-6s loaded with B-61s and briefed on SIOP targets. One squadron of -18s loaded with antiship missiles, and start planning an Alpha Strike on the *Kuznetzov* battle group."

"Captain," a talker called. "Falcon reports four inbound tactical aircraft."

Richards had only to turn around to see the main tactical display, a radarscope full three feet across. The four new contacts showed up as inverted V-shapes with course vectors. Closest point of approach was less than twenty miles, easily within range of air-to-surface missiles.

"Have Spade ID those bandits right now!"

". . . close and identify," was the order from the Hawkeye control aircraft.

"Roger," Jackson acknowledged. "Bud, go loose."

"Roger." Commander Sanchez eased his stick to the left to open the distance between his fighter and Jackson's. Called the "Loose Deuce," the formation enabled the aircraft to be mutually supporting and also impossible to attack simultaneously. As he split off, both aircraft tipped down and dove at full dry power. In a few seconds they were through Mach-One.

"Boresighted," Shredder told his driver. "I'm activating the TV system."

The Tomcat was built with a simple identification device. It was a television camera with a ten-power telescopic lens that worked equally well in daylight and darkness. Lieutenant Walters was able to slave the TV into the radar system, and in a few seconds he had four dots that grew rapidly as the Tomcats overtook them. "Twin rudder configuration."

"Falcon, this is Spade. Inform Stick we have visual but no ID, and we are closing."

Major Pyotr Arabov was no tenser than usual. An instructor pilot, he was teaching three Libyans the intricacies of night overwater navigation. They had turned over the Italian island of Pantelleria thirty minutes earlier, and were now inbound for Tripoli and home. Formation flying at night was difficult for the three Libyans, though each had over three hundred hours in type, and overwater flying was the most dangerous of all. Fortunately they had picked a good night for it. The star-filled sky gave them a good horizon reference. Better to learn the easy way first, Arabov thought, and at this altitude. A true tactical profile, at one hundred meters and higher speed on a cloudy night could be exceedingly dangerous. He was not any more impressed with the airmanship of these Libyans than the U.S. Navy had been on several occasions, but they did seem willing to learn, and that was something. Besides, their oil-rich country, having learned its own lessons from the Iraqis, had decided that if it were to have an air force at all, it had better have a properly trained one. That meant the Soviet Union could sell a lot more of its MiG-29s, despite the fact that sales in the Israel area were now severely curtailed. It also meant that Major Arabov was being paid partly in hard currency.

The instructor pilot looked left and right to see that the formation was—well, not exactly tight, but close enough. The aircraft were behaving sluggishly with two fuel tanks under each wing. Each fuel tank had stabilizing fins, and looked rather like bombs, actually.

"They're carrying something, skipper. MiG-29s, for sure."

"Right." Jackson checked the display himself, then keyed his radio. "Stick, this is Spade, over."

"Go ahead." The digital radio circuit allowed Jackson to recognize Captain Richards' voice.

"Stick, we have ID on the bogies. Four MiG-two-niners. They appear to have underwing cargo. Course, speed, and altitude unchanged." There was a brief pause.

"Splash the bandits."

Jackson's head snapped up. "Say again, Stick."

"Spade, this is Stick: Splash the bandits. Acknowledge."

He called them "bandits," Jackson thought. *And he knows more than I do.*

"Roger, engaging now. Out." Jackson keyed his radio again. "Bud, follow me in."

"Shit!" Shredder observed. "Recommend we target two Phoenix, left pair and right pair."

"Do it," Jackson replied, setting the weapons switch on the top of his stick to the AIM-54 setting. Lieutenant Walters programmed the missiles to keep their radars quiet until they were merely a mile out.

"Ready. Range is sixteen-thousand. Birds are in acquisition."

Jackson's heads-up display showed the correct symbology. A beeping tone in his headset told him that the first missile was ready to fire. He squeezed the trigger once, waited a second, then squeezed again.

"Shit!" Michael "Lobo" Alexander observed, half a mile away.

"You know better than that!" Sanchez snarled back at him.

"Sky is clear. I don't see anything else around us."

Jackson closed his eyes to save as much of his vision as possible from the yellow-white exhaust flames of the missiles. They rapidly pulled away, accelerating to over three thousand miles per hour, almost a mile per second. Jackson watched them home in as he positioned his aircraft for another shot if the Phoenixes failed to function properly.

Arabov made another instrument check. There was nothing unusual. His threat receivers showed only air-search radars, though one reading had disappeared a few minutes earlier. Other than that, this was an exceedingly routine training mission, proceeding straight and level on a direct course toward a fixed point. His threat receivers had not detected the LPI radar which had been tracking him and his flight of four over the past five minutes. It was able, however, to detect the powerful homing radar in a Phoenix missile.

A bright red warning light flashed on, and a screeching sound abused his hearing. Arabov looked down to check his instruments. They seemed to be functioning, but this wasn't—his next move was to turn his head. He just had time to see a half-moon of yellow light and a ghostly, starlit smoke trail, then a flash.

The Phoenix targeted on the right-hand pair exploded just a few feet from them. The one-hundred-thirty-five-pound warhead filled their air with high-speed fragments which shredded both MiGs. The same happened to the left-hand pair. The air was filled with an incandescent cloud of exploding jet fuel and airplane parts. Three pilots were killed directly by the explosion. Arabov was rocketed out of the disintegrating fighter by his ejection seat, whose parachute opened a scant two hundred feet over the water. Already unconscious from the unexpected shock of ejection, the Russian Major was saved by systems that anticipated his injuries. An inflatable collar held his head above water, a UHF radio began screaming for the nearest rescue helicopter, and a powerful blue-white strobe light started flashing in the darkness. Around him were a few thin patches of burning fuel and nothing else.

Jackson watched the entire process. He'd probably set an all-time one-shot record. Four aircraft on one missile salvo. But there had been no skill involved. As with his Iraqi victim, they hadn't known he was there. Any new nugget right out of the RAG could have done this. It was murder, not war—what war? he asked, was there a war?—and he didn't even know why.

"Splash four MiGs," he said over the radio. "Stick, this is Spade, splash four. Returning to CAP station, we need some gas."

"Roger, Spade, tankers are overhead now. We copy you splashed four."

"Uh, Spade, what the fuck is going on?" Lieutenant Walters asked.

"I wish I knew, Shredder." *Did I just fire the first shot in a war?* What *war?*

Despite his earlier screaming, the Guards tank regiment was about as sharp a Russian unit as Keitel had ever seen. Their T-80 main battle tanks looked slightly toylike with their reactive armor panels festooned on turret and hull, but they were also low-slung dangerous-looking vehicles whose enormously long 125mm guns left no doubt as to their identity and purpose. The supposed inspection team was moving about in groups of three. Keitel had the most dangerous mission, as he was with the regimental commander. Keitel—"Colonel Ivanenko"—checked his watch as he walked behind the real Colonel.

Just two hundred meters away, Günther Bock and two other ex-Stasi officers approached a tank crew. They were boarding their vehicle as the officers approached.

"Stop!" one ordered.

"Yes, Colonel," the junior sergeant who commanded the tank replied.

"Step down. We are going to inspect your vehicle."

The commander, gunner, and driver assembled in front of their vehicle while the other crews boarded theirs. Bock waited for the neighboring tanks to button up, then shot all three Russians with his silenced automatic. The three bodies were tossed under the tank. Bock took the gunner's seat and looked around for the controls he'd been briefed on. Not twelve hundred meters away, parked at right angles to his tank, were over fifty American M1A1 tanks whose crews were also boarding their vehicles.

"Power coming on," the driver reported over the intercom. The diesel engine roared to life along with all the others.

Bock flipped the loading switch to Armor-Piercing Fin-Stabilized Discarding-Sabot round and punched the load button. Automatically, the breech to the tank's main gun dropped open, and first the shell, then the propellant charge were rammed home, and the breech shut by itself. That, Bock thought, was easy enough. Next he depressed the gunsight and selected an American tank. It was easy to spot. The American tank park was lit up like any parking lot so that trespassers might easily be spotted. The laser gave him a range display, and Bock elevated the gun to the proper stadimeter line. The wind he estimated as zero. It was a calm night. Bock checked his watch and waited for the sweep hand to reach the twelve. Then he squeezed the triggers. Bock's T-80 rocked backwards, along with three others. Two-thirds of a second later, the shell struck the turret of the American tank. The results were impressive. He'd struck the ammo compartment in the rear of the turret. The forty rounds of ammunition ignited at once. Blowout panels vented most of it straight up, but the protective fire-doors inside the vehicle had already been blown out by the shell, and the crew incinerated in their seats as their two-million-dollar tank turned into a mottled green-and-brown volcano, along with two others.

One hundred meters to the north, the regimental commander froze in midsentence, turning toward the noise in disbelief.

"What's going on?" he managed to shout before Keitel shot him in the back of the head.

Bock had already fired his second round into the engine box of another tank, and was loading a third. Seven M1A1s were burning before the first American gunner got a round loaded. The huge turret swung around while tank commanders screamed orders at their drivers and gunners. Bock saw the operating turret and swung toward it. His round missed wide to the left, but struck another Abrams behind the first. The American shot also missed high because the gunner was excited. His second round was instantly loaded, and the American exploded a T-80 two down from Bock's. Günther decided to leave this American alone.

"We're under attack—commence firing commence firing!" the "Soviet" tank commanders screamed into their own command circuits.

Keitel ran to the command vehicle. "I am Colonel Ivanenko. Your commander is dead—get moving! Take those crazy bastards out while we still have a regiment left!"

The operations officer hesitated, having not the slightest idea what was happening, only able to hear the gunfire. But the orders came from a colonel. He lifted his radio, dialed up the battalion command circuit, and relayed the instruction.

There was the expected moment's hesitation. At least ten American tanks were now burning, but four were shooting back. Then the entire Soviet line opened fire, and three of the active American tanks were blown apart. Those shielded by the front row began firing off smoke and maneuvering, mainly backwards, as the Soviet tanks started to roll. Keitel watched in admiration as the Soviet T-80s moved out. Seven of them remained still, of which four were burning. Two more blew up before they crossed the line where once a wall had stood.

It was worth it, Keitel thought, just for this moment. Whatever Günther had in mind, it was worth it to see the Russians and Americans killing each other.

Admiral Joshua Painter arrived at CINCLANT headquarters just in time to catch the dispatch from *Theodore Roosevelt.*

"Who's in command there?"

"Sir, the battle group commander flew into Naples. Senior officer in the group is Captain Richards," Fleet Intelligence replied. "He said he had four MiGs inbound and armed, and since we're at DEFCON-TWO, he splashed them as a potential threat to the group."

"Whose MiGs?"

"Could be from the *Kuznetzov* group, sir."

"Wait a minute—you said DEFCON-TWO?"

"*TR*'s east of Malta now, sir, SIOP applies," Fleet Operations pointed out.

"Does anybody know what's going on?"

"I sure as hell don't," the Fleet Intelligence Officer replied honestly.

"Get me Richards on a voice line." Painter stopped. "What's the fleet status?"

"Everything alongside has orders to prepare to get under way, sir. That's automatic."

"But why are we *at* DEFCON-THREE here?"

"Sir, they haven't told us that."

"Fabulous." Painter pulled the sweater over his head and yelled for coffee.

"*Roosevelt* on line two, sir," the intercom called. Painter punched the button and put the phone on speaker.

"This is CINCLANT."

"Richards here, sir."

"What's going on?"

"Sir, we're fifteen minutes into a DEFCON-TWO alert here. We had a flight of MiG-29s inbound and I ordered them splashed."

"Why?"

"They appeared to be armed, sir, and we copied a radio transmission about the explosion."

Painter went instantly cold. "What explosion?"

"Sir, BBC reports a nuclear detonation in Denver. The local TV station that originated the report, they say, is now off the air. With that kind of information, I took the shot. I'm senior officer present. It's my battle group here. Sir, unless you have some more questions, I have things to do here."

Painter knew he had to get out of the man's way. "Use your head, Ernie. Use your goddamned head."

"Aye aye, sir. Out." The line went dead.

"Nuclear explosion?" Fleet Intelligence asked.

Painter had a hot line to the National Military Command Center. He activated it. "This is CINCLANT."

"Captain Rosselli, sir."

"Have we had a nuclear explosion?"

"That's affirmative, sir. In the Denver area, NORAD estimates yield in the low hundreds and high casualties. That's all we know. We haven't got the word out to everyone yet."

"Well, here's something else for you to know: *Theodore Roosevelt* just intercepted and splashed four MiG-29s inbound. Keep me posted. Unless otherwise directed, I'm putting everything to sea."

Bob Fowler was into his third cup of coffee already. He was cursing himself for having drunk those four strong German beers like he was Archie Bunker or something, and one of his fears was that the people here would notice the alcohol on his breath. Intellect told him that his thought processes might be somewhat affected by the alcohol intake, but he'd had the drinks over a period of hours, and natural processes plus the coffee either already had or soon would purge it from his system entirely.

For the first time, he was grateful for the death of his wife, Marian. He'd been there at the bedside, had watched his beloved wife die. He knew what grief and tragedy were, and however dreadful the deaths of all those people in Denver might be, he told himself, he had to step back from it, had to set it aside, had to concentrate on preventing the death of anyone else.

So far, Fowler told himself, things had gone well. He had moved quickly to cut off the spread of the news. A nationwide panic was something that he didn't need. His military services were at a higher level of alert that would either prevent or deter an additional attack for some indefinite period of time.

"Okay," he said on the conference line to NORAD and SAC. "Let's summarize what has happened to this point."

NORAD answered: "Sir, we've had a single nuclear detonation in the hundred-kiloton range. There has as yet been no report from the scene. Our forces are moving to a high state of alert. Satellite communications are down—"

"Why?" Elizabeth Elliot asked in a voice more brittle than Fowler's. "What could have done that?"

"We don't know. A nuclear detonation in space might, from EMP effects—that's electromagnetic pulse. When a nuclear device explodes at high altitude, most of its energy is released in the form of electromagnetic radiation. The Russians know more about the practical effects of such explosions than we do; they have more empirical data from their tests at Novaya Zemlya back in the 1960s. But we have no evidence of such an explosion, and we should have noticed it. Therefore a nuclear attack on satellites is most unlikely. Next possibility is a massive blast of electromagnetic energy from a ground source. Now, the Russians *have* pumped a lot of money into microwave weapons-research. They have a ship in the Eastern Pacific with lots of antennas aboard. It's the *Yuri Gagarin*. She's classed as a space-event-support ship, and she has four enormous high-gain antennas. That ship is currently three hundred miles off the coast of Peru, well within sight of the injured satellites. Supposedly the ship is supporting operations for the *Mir* space station. Aside from that, we're out of guesses. I have an officer talking with Hughes Aerospace right now to see what their thinking is.

"Okay, we're still trying to get ATC tapes from Stapleton to see if an aircraft might have delivered the bomb, and we are awaiting word from rescue and other teams dispatched to the site of the explosion. That's all I have."

"We have two wings fully in the air and more coming on line as we speak,"

CINC-SAC said next. ''All my missile wings are alerted. My Vice-CINC is in the air in Looking Glass Auxiliary West, and another Kneecap is about to take off for where you are, sir.''

''Anything happening in the Soviet Union?''

''Their air-defense people are increasing their alert level, as we have already discussed,'' General Borstein replied. ''We're getting other radio activity, but nothing we can classify yet. There is no indication of an attack on the United States.''

''Okay.'' The President let out a breath. Things were bad, but not out of control. All he had to do was get things settled down, and then he could go forward. ''I'm going to open the direct line to Moscow.''

''Very well, sir,'' NORAD replied.

A Navy chief yeoman was two seats away from President Fowler. His computer terminal was already lit up. ''You want to slide down here, Mr. President,'' the chief said. ''I can't cross-deck my display to your screen.''

Fowler crab-walked his swivel chair the eight feet to the chief's place.

''Sir, the way this works is, I type in what you say here, and it's relayed directly through the NMCC computers in the Pentagon—all they do is encipher it—but when the Russians reply, it arrives in the Hot Line room in Russian, is translated there, and then sent here from the Pentagon. There's a backup at Fort Ritchie in case something goes wrong in D.C. We have landline and two separate satellite links. Sir, I can type about as fast as you can speak.'' The chief yeoman's name tag read *Orontia,* and Fowler couldn't decide what his ancestry was. He was a good twenty pounds overweight, but he sounded relaxed and competent. Fowler would settle for that. Chief Orontia also had a pack of cigarettes sitting next to his keyboard. The President stole one, ignoring the no-smoking signs that hung on every wall. Orontia lit it with a Zippo.

''All ready, sir.'' Chief Pablo Orontia looked sideways at his Commander-in-Chief. His gaze didn't betray the fact that he'd been born in Pueblo, Colorado, and still had family there. The President would settle things down, that was his job. Orontia's job, he reasoned, was to do his best to help the man. Orontia had served his country in two wars and many other crises, mainly as an admiral's yeoman on carriers, and now he turned off his feelings as he had trained himself to do.

''Dear President Narmonov . . .''

Captain Rosselli watched the first for-real transmission of the Hot Line since his arrival in Washington. The message was put up on the IBM-PC/AT and encrypted, then the computer operator hit the return button to transmit it. He really should be back at his desk, Jim thought, but what went through here might be vital to what he was doing.

> AS YOU HAVE PROBABLY BEEN TOLD, THERE HAS BEEN A MAJOR EXPLOSION IN THE CENTRAL PART OF MY COUNTRY. I HAVE BEEN TOLD THAT IT WAS A NUCLEAR EXPLOSION, AND THAT THE LOSS OF LIFE IS SEVERE, President Narmonov read, with his advisers at his side.

''About what one would expect,'' Narmonov said. ''Send our reply.''

''Jesus, that was fast!'' the Army Colonel on duty remarked and began his translation. A Marine sergeant typed the English version, which was automatically linked to Camp David, Fort Ritchie, and the State Department. The computers printed out hard copy that was sent almost as fast to SAC, NORAD, and the intelligence agencies via facsimile printer.

> AUTHENTICATOR: TIMETABLE TIMETABLE TIMETABLE
> REPLY FROM MOSCOW
> PRESIDENT FOWLER:
> WE HAVE NOTED THE EVENT. PLEASE ACCEPT OUR DEEPEST SYMPATHY AND THAT OF THE SOVIET PEOPLE. HOW IS SUCH AN ACCIDENT POSSIBLE?

''Accident?'' Fowler asked.

''That was awfully fast, Robert,'' Elliot observed at once. ''Too damned fast. His English isn't very good. The message had to be translated, and you take time to read things like this. Their reply must have been canned—made up in advance . . . what does that mean?'' Liz asked, almost talking to herself, as Fowler formulated his next message. *What's going on here? Who is doing this, and why . . . ?*

> PRESIDENT NARMONOV:
> I REGRET TO INFORM YOU THAT THIS WAS NOT AN ACCIDENT. THERE IS NO AMERICAN NUCLEAR DEVICE WITHIN A HUNDRED MILES, NOR WERE ANY US WEAPONS IN TRANSIT IN THE AREA. THIS WAS A DELIBERATE ACT BY UNKNOWN FORCES.

''Well, that's no surprise,'' Narmonov said. He congratulated himself for correctly predicting the first message from America. ''Send the next reply,'' he told the communicator. To his advisers: ''Fowler is an arrogant man, with the weaknesses of arrogance, but he is no fool. He will be very emotional about this. We must settle him down, calm him. If he can keep control of himself, his intelligence will allow him to maintain control of the matter.''

''My President,'' said Golovko, who had just arrived in the command center. ''I think this is a mistake.''

''What do you mean?'' Narmonov asked in some surprise.

''It is a mistake to tailor your words to what you think of the man, his character, and his mental state. People change under stress. The man at the other end of that telephone line may not be the same man whom you met in Rome.''

The Soviet President dismissed that idea. ''Nonsense. People like that never change. We have enough of them here. I've been dealing with people like Fowler all my life.''

> PRESIDENT FOWLER:
> IF THIS IS IN FACT A DELIBERATE ACT THEN IT IS A CRIME WHOLLY WITHOUT PRECEDENT IN HUMAN HISTORY. WHAT MADMAN WOULD DO SUCH A THING AND TO WHAT PURPOSE? SUCH ACTION MIGHT ALL TOO EASILY LEAD TO GLOBAL CATASTROPHE. YOU MUST BELIEVE THAT THE SOVIET UNION HAD NOTHING TO DO WITH THIS INFAMOUS ACT.

''Too fast, Robert,'' Elliot said. '' 'You must believe'? What is this guy trying to say?''

''Elizabeth, you're reading too much into this,'' Fowler replied.

"These responses are *canned,* Robert! Canned. He's answering too fast. He had them prepared in advance. That means something."

"Like what?"

"Like we were supposed to be *at the game,* Robert! It looks to me like these were tailored for somebody else—like Durling. What if the bomb was supposed to get you, too, along with Brent and Dennis?"

"I have to set that aside, I told you that!" Fowler said angrily. He paused and took a deep breath. He could not allow himself to get angry. He had to stay calm. "Look, Elizabeth—"

"You *can't* set that aside! You have to consider that possibility, because if it was planned, that tells us something about what is going on."

"Dr. Elliot is right," NORAD said over the open phone line. "Mr. President, you are entirely correct to distance yourself from this event in an emotional sense, but you have to consider all possible aspects of the operational concept that may be at work here."

"I am compelled to agree with that," CINC-SAC added.

"So, what do I do?" Fowler asked.

"Sir," NORAD said, "I don't like this 'you must believe' stuff either. It might be a good idea to let him know that we're ready to defend ourselves."

"Yeah," General Fremont agreed. "He knows that, anyway, if his people are doing their job right."

"But what if he takes our alert level as a threat?"

"They won't, sir," NORAD assured him. "It's just how anybody would do business in a case like this. Their senior military leadership is very professional."

Dr. Elliot stirred at that remark, Fowler noted. "Okay, I'll tell him we've alerted our forces, but that we don't have any evil intentions."

> PRESIDENT NARMONOV:
> WE HAVE NO REASON TO SUSPECT SOVIET INVOLVEMENT IN THIS INCIDENT. HOWEVER, WE MUST ACT PRUDENTLY. WE HAVE BEEN THE VICTIM OF A VICIOUS ATTACK, AND MUST TAKE ACTION TO PROTECT OURSELVES AGAINST ANOTHER. ACCORDINGLY I HAVE PLACED OUR ARMED FORCES ON A PRECAUTIONARY ALERT. THIS IS ALSO NECESSARY FOR THE MAINTENANCE OF PUBLIC ORDER, AND TO ASSIST IN RESCUE OPERATIONS. YOU HAVE MY PERSONAL ASSURANCE THAT WE WILL TAKE NO OFFENSIVE ACTION WITHOUT JUST CAUSE.

"That's reassuring," Narmonov said dryly. "Nice of him to let us know about the alert."

"We know," Golovko said, "and he must know that we already know."

"He does not know that we know the extent of his alert," the Defense Minister said. "He cannot know that we are reading their codes. The alert level of their forces is more than precautionary. The American strategic forces have not been at this readiness status since 1962."

"Really?" Narmonov asked.

"General, that is not technically true," Golovko said urgently. "Their ordinary level of readiness is very high for American strategic forces, even when their military posture is Defense Condition Five. The change to which you refer is inconsequential."

"Is this true?" Narmonov asked.

The Defense Minister shrugged. "It depends on how you look at it. Their land-based rocket force is always at a higher level of alert than ours because of the lower maintenance requirements of their rockets. The same is true of their submarines, which spend far more time at sea than ours do. The technical difference may be small, but the psychological difference is not. The increased level of alert tells their people that something horrible is under way. I think that is significant.''

''I do not,'' Golovko shot back.

Marvelous, Narmonov thought, *two of my most important advisers cannot agree on something this important. . . .*

''We need to reply,'' the Foreign Minister said.

> PRESIDENT FOWLER:
>
> WE HAVE NOTED YOUR INCREASED ALERT STATUS. SINCE MOST OF YOUR WEAPONS ARE IN FACT POINTED AT THE SOVIET UNION WE MUST ALSO TAKE PRECAUTIONS. I SUGGEST THAT IT IS VITAL THAT NEITHER OF OUR TWO COUNTRIES TAKE ANY ACTION THAT MIGHT SEEM PROVOCATIVE.

''That's the first time he didn't have it canned,'' Elliot said. ''First he says 'I didn't do it,' now he says we better not provoke him. What's he really thinking?''

Ryan looked over the faxes of all six messages. He handed them to Goodley. ''Tell me what you think.''

''Pure vanilla. Looks like everyone is playing a very cautious game, and that's what they should be doing. We alert our forces as a precaution and they do the same. Fowler's said that we have no reason to think they did it—that's good. Narmonov says both sides should play it cool on provoking the other side—that's good, too. So far, so good,'' Ben Goodley thought.

''I agree,'' the Senior Duty Officer said.

''That makes it unanimous,'' Jack said. *Thank God, Bob, I didn't know you had it in you.*

Rosselli walked back to his desk. Okay, things appeared to be more or less under control.

''Where the hell have you been?'' Rocky Barnes asked.

''Hot Line room, things appear to be fairly cool.''

''Not anymore, Jim.''

General Paul Wilkes was almost there. It had taken nearly twenty minutes to get from his house onto I-295 and from there to I-395, a total distance of less than five miles. Snowplows had barely touched this road, and now it was cold enough that what had been salted was freezing to ice anyway. Worst of all, those few D.C. drivers who were venturing out were showing their customary driving skill. Even those with four-wheel-drives were acting as though the additional traction made them immune to the laws of physics. Wilkes had just passed over South Capitol Street, and was now heading downhill toward the Maine Avenue exit. To his left, some maniac in a Toyota was passing him, and then came right, to head for the exit into downtown D.C. The Toyota skidded sideways on a patch of ice that front-wheel drive didn't master. There was no chance to avoid it. Wilkes broadsided the car at about fifteen miles per hour.

''The hell with it,'' he said aloud. He didn't have time for this. The General backed up a few feet and started to maneuver around before the driver even got out.

He didn't check his mirror. As he changed lanes, he was rear-ended by a tractor-trailer doing about twenty-five. It was enough to drive the General's car over the concrete divider and into the face of another car. Wilkes was killed instantly.

39. Echoes

Elizabeth Elliot stared blankly at the far wall as she sipped her coffee. It was the only thing that made sense. All the warnings they'd had and ignored. It all fit. The Soviet military was making a power-play and targeting Bob Fowler had to be part of it. *We should have been there,* she thought. *He wanted to go to the game, and everyone expected him to, because Dennis Bunker owned one of the teams.* I *would have been there, too. I could be dead now. If they wanted to kill Bob, then they also wanted to kill me. . . .*

> PRESIDENT NARMONOV:
> I AM GRATIFIED THAT WE AGREE ON THE NECESSITY FOR CAUTION AND REASON. I MUST NOW CONFER WITH MY ADVISERS SO THAT WE MAY ASCERTAIN THE CAUSE OF THIS HORRIBLE EVENT, AND ALSO TO BEGIN RESCUE OPERATIONS. I WILL KEEP YOU INFORMED.

The reply that came back was almost immediate.

> PRESIDENT FOWLER:
> WE WILL STAND BY.

''That's simple enough,'' the President said, looking at the screen.

''Think so?'' Elliot asked.

''What do you mean?''

''Robert, we've had a nuclear explosion at a location that you were supposed to be at. That's number one. Number two: we've had reports of missing Soviet nuclear weapons. Number three: how do we really know that it's Narmonov at the other end of this computer modem?'' Liz asked.

''What?''

''Our best intelligence suggests the possibility of a *coup d'état* in Russia, doesn't it? But we're acting now as though such intelligence did not exist *even though* we've had what very easily could be a tactical nuclear weapon—exactly what we think is missing—explode over here. We are not considering all of the potential dimensions here.'' Dr. Elliot turned to the speakerphone. ''General Borstein, how hard is it to get a nuclear device into the United States?''

''With our border controls, it's child's play,'' NORAD replied. ''What are you saying, Dr. Elliot?''

''I'm saying that we've had hard intel for some time now that Narmonov is in political trouble—that his military is acting up, *and* that there's a nuclear dimension. Okay, what if they stage a coup? A Sunday evening—Monday morning—is good timing because everyone's asleep. We always assumed that the nuclear element was for domestic blackmail—but what if the operation was more clever than that? What if they figured they could decapitate our government in order to prevent our interference with their coup? Okay, the bomb goes off, and Durling is on Kneecap—just like he is right now—and they're talking to him. They can predict what we're going to think, and they pre-plan their statements over the Hot Line. We go on automatic alert, and so do they—you see? We *can't* interfere with the coup in any way."

"Mr. President, before you evaluate that possibility, I think you need some outside advice from the intelligence community," CINC-SAC said.

Another phone lit up. The yeoman got it.

"For you, Mr. President, NMCC."

"Who is this?" Fowler asked.

"Sir, this is Captain Jim Rosselli at the National Military Command Center. We have two reports of contact between U.S. and Soviet forces. USS *Theodore Roosevelt* reports that they have splashed—that means shot down, sir—a flight of four inbound Russian MiG-29 aircraft—"

"What? Why?"

"Sir, under the Rules of Engagement, the captain of a ship has the right to take defense action to protect his command. *Theodore Roosevelt* is now at DEFCON-TWO, and as the alert level changes, you get more latitude in what you can do, and when you can take action. Sir, the second is as follows: there is an unconfirmed report of shots being exchanged between Russian and American tanks in Berlin. SACEUR says the radio message stopped—I mean, it was cut off, sir. Before that, a U.S. Army captain reported that Soviet tanks were attacking the Berlin Brigade at its base in southern Berlin, and that a tank battalion of ours was just about wiped out, sir. They were attacked in their lager by Soviet forces stationed just across from them. Those two things—the reports, I mean, were almost simultaneous. The reported times were just two minutes apart, Mr. President. We're trying to reestablish contact with Berlin right now, going through SACEUR at Mons, Belgium."

"Christ," Fowler observed. "Elizabeth, does this fit into your scenario?"

"It could show that they're not kidding, that they are serious about not being interfered with."

Most of the American forces had escaped out of the lager. The senior officer on the scene had decided on the spot to turn and run for cover in the woods and residential streets around the brigade base. He was a lieutenant colonel, the brigade executive officer. The Colonel commanding the brigade was nowhere to be found, and the XO was now considering his options. The brigade had two mechanized infantry battalions and one of tanks. From the last, only nine of fifty-two M1A1s had gotten away. He could see the glow from the rest of them, still burning in their lager.

A DEFCON-THREE alert out of nowhere, and then minutes later, this. Over forty tanks and a hundred men lost, shot down without warning. Well, he'd see about that.

The Berlin Brigade had been in place since long before his birth, and scattered throughout its encampment were defensive positions. The Colonel dispatched his remaining tanks and ordered his Bradley fighting vehicles to volley-fire their TOW-2 missiles.

The Russian tanks had overrun the tank lager and stopped. They had no further orders. Battalion commanders were not yet in control of their formations, left behind by the mad dash of the T-80s across the line, and the regimental commander was nowhere to be found. Without orders, the tank companies stopped, sitting still, looking for targets. The regimental executive officer was also missing, and when the senior battalion commander realized this, his tank dashed off to the headquarters vehicle, since he was the next-senior officer in the regiment. It was amazing, he thought. First the readiness drill, next the flash alert from Moscow, and then the Americans had started shooting. He hadn't a clue what was going on. Even the barracks and administrative buildings were still lit up, he realized. Someone would have to get those lights off. His T-80 was back-lit as though on a target range.

''Command tank, two o'clock, skylined, moving left to right,'' a sergeant told a corporal.

''Identified,'' the gunner replied over the intercom.

''Fire.''

''On the way.'' The corporal squeezed his trigger. The seal-cap blew off the missile tube, and the TOW-2 blasted out, trailing behind a thin control wire. The target was about twenty-five hundred meters away. The gunner kept his crosshairs on target, guiding the antitank missile to its target. It took eight seconds, and the gunner had the satisfaction of seeing detonation right in the center of the turret.

''Target,'' the Bradley commander said, indicating a direct hit. ''Cease fire. Now let's find another one of these fuckers . . . ten o'clock, tank, coming around the PX!''

The turret came left. ''Identified!''

''Okay, what does CIA make of this?'' Fowler asked.

''Sir, again all we have is scattered and unconnected information,'' Ryan replied.

''*Roosevelt* has a Soviet carrier battle group a few hundred miles behind them, and they carry MiG-29s,'' Admiral Painter said.

''They're even closer to Libya, and our friend the Colonel has a hundred of the same aircraft.''

''Flying over water at midnight?'' Painter asked. ''When's the last time you heard of the Libyans doing that—and twenty-some miles from one of our battle groups!''

''What about Berlin?'' Liz Elliot asked.

''We don't know!'' Ryan stopped and took a deep breath. ''Remember that we just don't know much.''

''Ryan, what if SPINNAKER was right?'' Elliot asked.

''What do you mean?''

''What if there is a military coup going on right now over there, and they set a bomb off over here to keep us from interfering, to decapitate us?''

''That's totally crazy,'' Jack answered. ''Risk a war? Why do it? What would we do if there were a coup? Attack at once?''

''Their military might expect us to,'' Elliot pointed out.

''Disagree. I think SPINNAKER might have been lying to us from the beginning on this issue.''

''Are you making this up?'' Fowler asked. It was coming home to the President now that he might actually have been the real target of the bomb, that Elizabeth's theoretical model for the Russian plan was the only thing that made sense.

"No, sir!" Ryan snapped back indignantly. "I'm the *hawk* here, remember? The Russian military is too smart to pull something like this. It's too big a gamble."

"Then explain the attacks on our forces!" Elliot said.

"We don't know for sure that there have been attacks on our forces."

"So now you think our people are lying?" Fowler asked.

"Mr. President, you are not thinking this through. Okay, let's assume that there is an ongoing coup in the Soviet Union—I don't accept that hypothesis, but let's assume it, okay? The purpose, you say, for exploding the bomb over here is to keep us from interfering. Fine. Then why attack our military forces if they want us to sit on our hands?"

"To show that they're serious," Elliot fired back.

"That's crazy! It's tantamount to telling us they *did* explode the bomb here. Do you think they would expect us not to respond to a nuclear attack?" Ryan demanded, then answered his own question: *"It does not make sense!"*

"Then give me something that does," Fowler said.

"Mr. President, we are in the very earliest stages of a crisis. The information we have coming in now is scattered and confused. Until we know more, trying to put a spin on it is dangerous."

Fowler's face bore down on the speakerphone. "Your job is to tell me what's going on, not to give me lessons in crisis-management. When you have something I can use, get back to me!"

"What in the hell are they thinking?" Ryan asked.

"Is there something I don't know here?" Goodley asked. The young academic looked as alarmed as Ryan felt.

"Why should you be any different from the rest of us?" Jack snapped back, and regretted it. "Welcome to crisis-management. Nobody knows crap, and you're expected to make good decisions anyway. Except it's not possible, it just isn't."

"The thing with the carrier scares me," the S&T man observed.

"Wrong. If we only splashed four aircraft, it's only a handful of people," Ryan pointed out. "Land combat is something else. If we really have a battle going on in Berlin, that's the scary one, almost as bad as an attack on some of our strategic assets. Let's see if we can get hold of SACEUR."

The nine surviving M1A1 tanks were racing north along a Berlin avenue, along with a platoon of Bradley fighting vehicles. Streetlights were on, heads sticking out windows, and it was instantly apparent to the few onlookers that whatever was happening wasn't a drill. All the tanks had the speed governors removed from their engines, and they could all have been arrested in America for violating the national interstate highway limit. One mile north of their camp, they turned east. Leading the formation was a senior NCO who knew Berlin well—this was his third tour in the once-divided city—well enough that he had a perfect spot in mind, if the Russians hadn't got there first. There was a construction site. A memorial to the Wall and its victims was going up after a long competition. It overlooked the Russian and American compounds which were soon to be vacated, and bulldozers had pushed up a high berm of dirt for the sculpture that would sit atop it. But it wasn't there yet, just a thick dirt ramp. The Soviet tanks were milling about on their objective, probably waiting for their infantry to show up or something. They were taking TOW hits from the Bradleys and returning fire into the woods.

"Christ, they're going to kill those Bradley guys," the unit commander—a captain whose tank was the last survivor of his company—said. "Okay, find your spots." That took another minute. Then the tanks were hull-down, just their guns and the tops of turrets showing. "Straight down the line! Commence firing, fire at will."

All nine tanks fired at once. The range was just over two thousand meters, and now the element of surprise was with someone else. Five Russian tanks died with the first volley, and six more in the second, as the Abrams tanks went into rapid fire.

In the trees with the Bradleys, the brigade XO watched the north end of the Russian line crumple. That was the only word for it, he thought. The tank crews were all combat vets, and now they had the edge. The northernmost Russian battalion tried to reorient itself, but one of his Bradleys had evidently scored on its commander, and there was confusion there. Why the Russians hadn't pressed home the attack was one question that floated about the rear of his brain, but that was something to save for the after-action report. Right now he saw that they had screwed up, and that was a good thing for him and his men.

"Sir, I've got Seventh Army." A sergeant handed him a microphone.

'What's happening over there?"

"General, this Lieutenant Colonel Ed Long, we just got our ass attacked by the regiment across town from us. No warning at all, they just came into our kazerne like Jeb Stuart. We've got 'em stopped, but I've lost most of my tanks. We need some help here."

"Losses?"

"Sir, I've lost over forty tanks, eight Bradleys, and at least two hundred men."

"Opposition?"

"One regiment of tanks. Nothing else yet, but they have lots of friends, sir. I could sure use some myself."

"I'll see what I can do."

General Kuropatkin checked his status board. Every radar system that was not down for repair was now operating. Satellite information told him that two SAC bases were empty. That meant their aircraft were now airborne and flying toward the Soviet Union along with KC-135 tankers. Their missile fields would also be at full alert. His Eagle satellites would give launch-warning, announcing that his country had thirty minutes left to live. Thirty minutes, the General thought. Thirty minutes and the reason of the American President were all that stood between life and death for his country.

"Air activity picking up over Germany," a colonel said. "We show some American fighters coming out from Ramstein and Bitburg, heading east. Total of eight aircraft."

"What do we have on the American Stealth fighters?"

"There is a squadron—eighteen of them—at Ramstein. Supposedly the Americans are demonstrating them for possible sale to their NATO allies."

"They could all be in the air right now," Kuropatkin noted, "carrying nuclear weapons, for that matter."

"Correct, they can easily carry two B-61-type weapons each. With high-altitude cruise, they could be over Moscow before we knew it. . . ."

"And with their bombsights . . . they could lay their weapons exactly on any target they wish . . . two and a half hours from the time they lift off . . . my God."

In the weapon's earth-penetration mode, it could be placed close enough to eliminate the President's shelter. Kuropatkin lifted his phone. "I need to talk to the President."

"Yes, General, what is it?" Narmonov asked.

"We have indications of American air activity over Germany."

"There's more than that. A Guards regiment in Berlin reports being under attack by American troops."

"That's mad."

And the report came in not five minutes after my friend Fowler promised not to do anything provocative. "Speak quickly, I have enough business here already."

"President Narmonov. Two weeks ago a squadron of American F-117A Stealth fighters arrived at their Ramstein air base, ostensibly for demonstration to their NATO allies. The Americans said they want to sell them. Each of those aircraft can carry two half-megaton weapons."

"Yes?"

"I cannot detect them. They are virtually invisible to everything we have."

"What are you telling me?"

"From the time they leave their bases, then refuel, they can be over Moscow in less than three hours. We would have no more warning than Iraq had."

"Are they truly that effective?"

"One reason we left so many people in Iraq was to observe closely what the Americans are capable of. Our people never saw that American plane on a radar-scope, neither ours nor the French scopes Saddam had. Yes, they are that good."

"But why would they wish to do such a thing?" Narmonov demanded.

"Why would they attack our regiment in Berlin?" the Defense Minister asked in reply.

"I thought this place was proof against anything in their arsenal."

"Not against a nuclear gravity bomb delivered with high accuracy. We are only one hundred meters down here," Defense said. *In the old battle between warhead and armor, warhead always wins. . . .*

"Back to Berlin," Narmonov said. "Do we know what's happening there?"

"No, what we have has come from junior officers only."

"Get someone in there to find out. Tell our people to fall back if they can do so safely—and take defensive action only. Do you object to that?"

"No, that is prudent."

The National Photographic Intelligence Center, NPIC, is located at the Washington Navy Yard, in one of several windowless buildings housing highly sensitive government activities. At the moment they had a total of three KH-11 photographic and two KH-12 "Lacrosse" radar-imaging satellites in orbit. At 00:26:46 Zulu Time, one of the -11s came within optical range of Denver. All of its cameras zoomed in on the city, especially its southern suburbs. The images were downlinked in real-time to Fort Belvoir, Virginia, and sent from there to NPIC by fiber-optic cable. At NPIC, they were recorded in two-inch videotape. Analysis started immediately.

This aircraft was a DC-10. Qati and Ghosn again availed themselves of first-class seating, pleased and amazed at their good luck. The word had gotten out only minutes before the flight was called. As soon as the report had gone out on the Reuters wire, it had been inevitable. AP and UPI had instantly picked it up, and all television stations subscribed to the wire services. Surprised that the networks had not yet put out their own special bulletins, the local affiliates ran with it anyway. The one thing about it that had surprised Qati was the silence. As the word spread like a wave through the terminal building, what lay behind it was not shouting and panic, but an eerie silence that allowed one to hear the flight calls and other background noises normally submerged by the cacophony of voices in such public areas. So the Americans faced tragedy and death, the Commander thought. The lack of passion surprised him.

It was soon behind him in any case. The DC-10 accelerated down the runway and lifted off. A few minutes later it was over international waters, heading toward a neutral country and safety. One more connection, both men thought in a silence of their own. One more connection, and they would disappear completely. Who would have expected such luck?

"The infrared emissions are remarkable," the photoanalyst thought aloud. It was his first nuclear detonation. "I have damage and secondary fires up to a mile from the stadium. Not much of the stadium itself. Too much smoke and IR interference. Next pass, if we're lucky, we ought to have some visible-light imagery."

"What can you tell us about casualty count?" Ryan asked.

"What I have is inconclusive. Mainly the visible-light shots show smoke that's obscuring everything. Infrared levels are very impressive. Lots of fires immediately around the stadium itself. Cars, I guess, gas tanks cooking off."

Jack turned to the senior Science and Technology officer. "Who do we have up in the photo section?"

"Nobody," S&T replied. "Weekend, remember? We let NPIC handle weekend work unless we expect something hot."

"Who's the best guy?"

"Andy Davis, but he lives in Manassas. He'll never make it in."

"Goddamn it." Ryan picked up the phone again. "Send us the best ten photos you have," he told NPIC.

"You'll have them in two or three minutes."

"How about someone to evaluate the bomb effects?"

"I can do that," S&T said. "Ex-Air Force. I used to work intel for SAC."

"Run with it."

The nine Abrams tanks had by now accounted for nearly thirty of the Russian T-80s. The Soviets had pulled south to find cover of their own. Their return fire had killed three more of the M1A1s, but now the odds were a lot more even. The Captain commanding the tank detachment sent his Bradleys east to conduct reconnaissance. As with their first dash, there were people watching them, but for the most part they did this from windows now unlit. The streetlights worried one Bradley commander, who took a rifle and began shooting them out, to the horror of Berliners who had the courage to watch.

"*Was nun?*" Keitel asked. What now?

"Now we get the devil away from here and disappear. Our work is done," Bock replied, turning the wheel to the left. A northerly escape route seemed best. They'd dump the car and truck, change their clothes, and vanish. They might even survive all this, Bock thought. Wouldn't that be something? But his main thought was that he'd avenged his Petra. It had been the Americans and Russians who'd brought her death about. Germans had only been the pawns of the great players, and the great players were paying now, Bock told himself, were paying now and would pay more. Revenge wasn't so cold a dish after all, was it?

"Russian staff car," the gunner said, "and a GAZ truck."

"Chain gun." The track commander took his time identifying the inbound targets. "Wait."

"I *love* killin' officers. . . ." The gunner centered the sight for his 25mm cannon. "On target, Sarge."

For all his experience as a terrorist, Bock was not a soldier. He took the dark, square shape two blocks away for a large truck. His plan had worked. The American alert, so perfectly timed, could only mean that Qati and Ghosn had done their job exactly as he'd envisioned five months earlier. His eyes shifted as he saw what looked like a flash bulb and a streak of light that went over his head.

"Fire—hose 'em!"

The gunner had his selector switch on rapid fire. The 25-millimeter chain gun was wonderfully accurate, and the tracers allowed you to walk fire right into the target. The first long burst hit the truck. There might, he reasoned, be armed soldiers in the truck. The initial rounds went into the engine block, shattering it into fragments, then, as the vehicle surged forward, the next burst swept through the cab and cargo area. The truck collapsed on two flattened front tires and ground to a halt, the wheel rims digging grooves in the asphalt. By that time the gunner had shifted fire and put a short burst through the staff car. This target merely lost control and slammed into a parked BMW. Just to make sure, the gunner hit the car again, and then the truck. Someone actually got out of the truck, probably wounded already from the way he moved. Two more 25mm rounds fixed that.

The track commander moved immediately. One does not linger where one has killed. Two minutes later they found another surveillance spot. Police cars were racing down the streets, their blue lights flashing. One of them stopped a few hundred meters from the Bradley, backed up and raced off, the track commander saw. Well, he'd always known German cops were smart.

Five minutes after the Bradley departed for another block, the first Berliner, an exceedingly courageous physician, came out his front door and went to the staff car. Both men were dead, each torso ripped to shreds by the cannon shells, though both faces were intact except for the splashed blood. The truck was an even greater mess. One of the men there might have survived for a few minutes, but by the time the doctor got there, it was far too late. He found it odd that they all wore Russian officers' uniforms. Not knowing what else to do, he called the police. Only later did he realize how disproportionate his understanding of the events outside his home had been.

"They weren't kidding about the infrared signature. This must have been some bomb," the S&T guy observed. "Damage is a little funny, though . . . hmph."

"What do you mean, Ted?" Ryan asked.

"I mean the ground damage ought to be worse than this . . . must be shadows and reflections." He looked up. "Sorry. Shockwaves don't go through things—like a hill, I mean. There must have been reflections and shadows here, that's all. These houses here ought not to be there anymore."

"I still don't know what you mean," Ryan said.

"There are always anomalies in cases like this. I'll get back to you when I have this figured out, okay?" Ted Ayres asked.

Walter Hoskins sat in his office because he didn't know what else to do, and as most senior man present, he had to answer the phones. All he needed to do was turn to see what the stadium was. The pall of smoke was only five miles away through his windows, one of which was cracked. Part of him wondered if he should send a team down there, but he had no such orders. He turned his chair to look that way again, amazed that the window was almost intact. After all, it was supposed to have been a nuclear bomb, and it was only five miles. The remains of the cloud were now over the front range of the Rockies, still intact enough that you could tell what it had been, and behind it like a wake was another black plume of fires from the bomb area, The destruction must be . . .

. . . not enough. Not enough? What a crazy thought. With nothing else to do, Hoskins lifted the phone and dialed up Washington. "Give me Murray."

"Yeah, Walt."

"How busy are you?"

"Not very, as a matter of fact. How is it at your end?"

"We have the TV stations and phones shut down. I hope the President will be there when I have to explain that one to the judge."

"Walt, this isn't the time—"

"Not why I called."

"Well, then you want to tell me?"

"I can see it from here, Dan," Hoskins said in a voice that was almost dreamy.

"How bad is it?"

"All I see is the smoke, really. The mushroom cloud is over the mountains now, all orange, like. Sunset, it's high enough to catch the sunset, I guess. I can see lots of little fires. They're lighting up the smoke from the stadium area. Dan?"

"Yeah, Walt?" Dan responded. The man seemed to be in shock, Murray thought.

"Something odd."

"What's that?"

"My windows aren't broken. I'm only like five miles from there, and only one of my windows is cracked, even. Odd, isn't it?" Hoskins paused. "I have some stuff here that you said you wanted, pictures and stuff." Hoskins leafed through the documents that had been set in his In basket. "Marvin Russell sure picked a busy day to die. Anyway, I have the passport stuff you wanted. Important?"

"It can wait."

"Okay." Hoskins hung up.

"Walt's losing it, Pat," Murray observed.

"You blame him?" O'Day asked.

Dan shook his head. "No."

"If this gets worse . . ." Pat observed.

"How far out is your family?"

"Not far enough."

"Five miles," Murray said quietly.

"What?"

"Walt said that his office is just five miles away, he can see it from there. His windows aren't broken, even."

''Bullshit,'' O'Day replied. ''He must really be out of it. Five miles, that's less than nine thousand yards.''

''What do you mean?''

''NORAD said the bomb was a hundred-kiloton range. That'll break windows over a hell of a long distance. Only takes half a pound or so of overpressure to do a window.''

''How do you know?''

''Used to be in the Navy—intelligence, remember? I had to evaluate the damage distances for Russian tactical nukes once. A hundred-kiloton bomb at nine thousand yards won't sink you, but it'll wreck everything topside, scorch paint, start small fires. Bad news, man.''

''Curtains, like?''

''Ought to,'' O'Day thought aloud. ''Yeah, regular curtains would light up, especially if they're dark ones.''

''Walt's not so far out of it that he'd miss a fire in his office. . . .'' Murray lifted his phone to Langley.

''Yeah, what is it, Dan?'' Jack said into the speaker.

''What number do you have on the size of the explosion?''

''According to NORAD, one-fifty, maybe two hundred kilotons, size of a big tactical weapon or a small strategic one,'' Ryan said. ''Why?'' On the other side of the table, the S&T officer looked up from the photos.

''I just talked to my ASAC Denver. He can see the stadium area from his office—five miles, Jack. He's only got one cracked window.''

''Bull,'' S&T noted.

''What do you mean?'' Ryan asked.

''Five miles, that's eight thousand meters,'' Ted Ayres pointed out. ''The thermal pulse alone should fry the place, and the shock wave would sure as hell blow a plate-glass window out.''

Murray heard that. ''Yeah, that's what a guy here just said. Hey, my guy might be a little out of it—shock, I mean—but he'd notice a fire next to his desk, don't you think?''

''Do we have anything from people on the scene yet?'' Jack asked Ayres.

''No, the NEST team is on the way, but the imagery tells us a lot, Jack.''

''Dan, how quick can you get somebody to the scene?'' Ryan asked.

''I'll find out.''

''Hoskins.''

''Dan Murray, Walt. Get some people down there fast as you can. You stay put to coordinate.''

''Okay.''

Hoskins gave the proper orders, wondering just how badly he might be endangering his people. Then, with nothing else to do, he looked over the file on his desk. Marvin Russell, he thought, yet another criminal who died of dumb. Drug dealers. Didn't they ever learn?

Roger Durling was grateful when the Kneecap aircraft disengaged from the tanker. The converted 747 had the usual pussycat ride, but not when in close proximity to a KC-10 tanker. It was something only his son enjoyed. Aboard in the conference room were an Air Force brigadier, a Navy captain, a Marine major, and four other field- and staff-grade officers. All the data the President got came to Kneecap automatically, including the Hot Line transcripts.

"You know, what they're saying is okay, but it sure as hell would be nice to know what everyone's thinking."

"What if this really is a Russian attack?" the General asked.

"Why would they do it?"

"You've heard the chatter between the President and CIA, sir."

"Yeah, but that Ryan guy's right," Durling said. "None of this makes any sense."

"So who ever said the world had to make sense? What about the contact in the Med and Berlin?"

"Forward-deployed forces. We go on alert, and they go on alert, and they're close to each other, and someone goofs. You know, like Gavrilo Prinzip shooting the Archduke. An accident happens and then things just slide down the chute."

"That's why we have the Hot Line, Mr. Vice President."

"True," Durling conceded. "And so far it seems to be working."

They made the first fifty yards easily, but then it got harder, and soon it went from hard to impossible. Callaghan had a total of fifty firefighters trying to fight their way on, with a hundred more in support. On reflection, he had a continuous water spray over every man and woman. If nothing else, he reasoned, it would wash whatever fallout or dust or whatever the hell was out here off his people and into the sewer drains—that which didn't freeze first, that is. The men in front were coated with ice that made a translucent layer on their turn-out coats.

The biggest problem was the cars. They'd been tossed about like toys, lying on their sides or tops, leaking gasoline that collected into burning puddles that were being supplied faster than they burned off. Callaghan ordered a truck in. One at a time, his men ran cables to the frames of the wrecked cars, and the truck dragged them clear, but this was horribly time-consuming. It would take forever to get into the stadium. And there were people in there. He was sure of it. There had to be. Callaghan just stood there, out of the water spray, guilty that he was warmer than his people. He turned when he heard the roar of a large diesel engine.

"Hello." It was a man wearing the uniform of a U.S. Army colonel. The name tag on his parka read *Lyle*. "I hear you need heavy equipment."

"What you got?"

"I have three engineer tanks, M728s, just rolling in now. Got something else, too."

"What's that?"

"A hundred MOPP suits, you know, chemical warfare gear. It ain't perfect, but it's better than what your people got on. Warmer, too. Why don't you pull your people off and get them outfitted. Truck's over there." The Colonel pointed.

Callaghan hesitated for a moment, but decided that he couldn't turn this offer down. He called his people off and pulled them back to don the military gear. Colonel Lyle tossed him an outfit.

"The water fog's a good idea, ought to keep dust and stuff down. So, what do you want us to do?"

"You can't tell from here, but there is still some structure in there. I think there might be survivors. I have to find out. Can you help us get through these cars?"

"Sure." The Colonel lifted his own radio and ordered the first vehicle in. The M728, Callaghan saw, was essentially a tank with a dozer blade on the front, and a big A-frame and winch on the back of the turret. There was even an odd-looking short-barreled gun.

''This isn't going to be very neat. Can you live with that?''

''Screw neat—get in there!''

''Okay.'' Lyle picked up the interphone at the left rear of the vehicle. ''Make a hole,'' he ordered.

The driver revved up the diesel just as the first firemen returned. He made a sincere effort to avoid the fire hoses—even so he split eight two-and-a-half-inch lines. The blade dropped and the tank crashed into the mass of burning cars at twenty miles per hour. It made a hole, all right, about thirty feet deep. Then the tank backed off and started widening it.

''Jesus,'' Callaghan observed. ''What do you know about radiation stuff?''

''Not much. I checked with the NEST guys before I drove down. They ought to be here any time. Until then . . .'' Lyle shrugged. ''You really think there's live ones in there?''

''Part of the structure is still there. I saw it from the chopper.''

''No shit?''

''Yeah, I saw it.''

''But that's crazy. The NORAD guys say it was a big one.''

''What?'' Callaghan shouted over the noise of the tank.

''The bomb, it was supposed to be a big one. There shouldn't even be a parking lot here.''

''You mean this was a *little* one?'' Callaghan looked at the man as though he were crazy.

''Hell, yes!'' Lyle stopped for a moment. ''If there's people in there . . .'' He ran to the back of the tank and grabbed the phone. A moment later the M728 stopped.

''What's the matter?''

''If there are survivors, hell, we might squash one this way. I just told him to take it easier. Goddamn, you're right. And I thought you were crazy.''

''What do you mean?'' Callaghan shouted again, waving his firefighters to put their spray on the tank also.

''There may be survivors in there. This bomb was a hell of a lot smaller than they told me on the phone.''

''*Maine,* this is Sea Devil One-Three,'' the P-3C Orion called. ''We're about forty minutes out from your position. What seems to be the problem?''

''We have screw and shaft damage, and we have an Akula in the neighborhood, last fix five-zero thousand yards southwest,'' Ricks answered.

''Roger that. We'll see if we can drive him off for you. We'll report when we get on station. Out.''

''Captain, we can do three knots, let's do that, north, open as much as we can,'' Claggett said.

Ricks shook his head. ''No, we'll stay quiet.''

''Sir, our friend out there must have copied the collision transient. He will be coming this way. We've lost our best sonar. Smart move is to evade as best we can.''

''No, the smart move is to stay covert.''

''Then at least launch a MOSS.''

''That makes sense, sir,'' the weapons officer thought.

"Okay, program it to sound like we are now, and give it a southerly course."

"Right." *Maine*'s number-three torpedo tube was loaded with a MOSS, a Mobile Submarine Simulator. Essentially a modified torpedo itself, the MOSS contained a sonar transducer connected to a noise generator, instead of a warhead. It would radiate the sound of an Ohio-class submarine, and was designed to simulate a damaged one. Since shaft damage was one of the few reasons that an Ohio might make noise, that option was already programmed in. The weapons officer selected the proper noise track, and launched the weapon a few minutes later. The MOSS sped off to the south, and two thousand yards away, it began radiating.

The skies had cleared over Charleston, South Carolina. What had fallen as snow in Virginia and Maryland had been mainly sleet here. The afternoon sun had removed most of that, returning the antebellum city to its normally pristine state. As the Admiral commanding Submarine Group Six watched from the tender, two of his ballistic-missile submarines started down the Cooper River for the sea and safety. He wasn't the only one to watch. One hundred ninety miles over his head, a Soviet reconnaissance satellite made its pass, continuing up the coast to Norfolk, where the sky was also clearing. The satellite downlinked its pictures to the Russian intelligence center on Cuba's western tip. From there it was immediately relayed by communications satellite. Most of the Russian satellites used high-polar orbits, and had not been affected by the EMP. The imagery was in Moscow in a matter of seconds.

"Yes?" the Defense Minister asked.

"We have imagery of three American naval bases. Missile submarines at Charleston and King's Bay are putting to sea."

"Thank you." The Defense Minister replaced the phone. Another threat. He relayed it at once to President Narmonov.

"What does that mean?"

"It means that the military action taken by the Americans is not merely defensive. Some of the submarines in question carry the Trident D-5 missile, which has first-strike capability. You'll recall how interested the Americans were in forcing us to eliminate our SS-18s?"

"Yes, and they are removing a large number of their Minutemen," Narmonov said. "So?"

"So they don't *need* land-based missiles to make a first strike. They can do it from submarines. We cannot. We depend on our land-based ICBMs for that."

"And what of our SS-18s?"

"We're removing the warheads from some of them even as we speak, and if they ever get that damned deactivation facility working, we'll be in full compliance with the treaty—we are now, in fact, just the damned Americans don't admit it." The Defense Minister paused. Narmonov wasn't getting it. "In other words, while we have eliminated some of our most accurate missiles, the Americans still have theirs. We are at a strategic disadvantage."

"I have not had much sleep, and my thinking is not at its best," Narmonov said testily. "You *agreed* to this treaty document only a year ago, and now you're telling me that we are threatened by it?"

They're all the same, the Defense Minister thought. *They never listen, they never really pay attention. Tell them something a hundred times and they just don't hear you!*

"The elimination of so many missiles and warheads changes the correlation of forces—"

"Rubbish! We're still equal in every way!" President Narmonov objected.

"That is not the question. The important factor is the relationship between the number of launchers—and their relative vulnerability—and the number of warheads available to both sides. We can still strike first and eliminate the American land-based missile force with our land-based missiles. That is why they were so willing to remove half of theirs. But the majority of their warheads are at sea, and now, for the first time, such sea-based missiles are totally adequate for a disarming first strike."

"Kuropatkin," Narmonov said, "are you hearing this?"

"Yes, I am. The Defense Minister is correct. The additional dimension, if I may say it, is that the reduction in the number of launchers has changed the overall ratio of launchers-to-warheads. For the first time in a generation, a truly disarming first-strike is possible, especially if the Americans are able to decapitate our government with their first strike."

"And they could do that with the Stealth fighters they put in Germany," Defense concluded the statement.

"Wait a minute. Are you telling me that Fowler blew up his own city as an excuse to attack us? What madness is this?" Now the Soviet President began to understand fear.

The Defense Minister spoke slowly and clearly. "Whoever detonated that weapon is beside the point. If Fowler begins to think that it was our doing, he has the ability to act against us. Comrade President, you must understand this: technically speaking, our country is on the edge of annihilation. Less than thirty minutes separate their land-based missiles from us. Twenty minutes for their sea-based ones, and as little as two hours from those goddamned invisible tactical bombers, which would be the most advantageous opening move. All that separates us from destruction is the mental state of President Fowler."

"I understand." The Soviet President was quiet for half a minute. He stared off at the status board on the far wall. When he spoke, his voice showed the anger that comes from fright. "What do you propose we should do—attack the Americans? I will not do such a thing."

"Of course not, but we would be well advised to place our strategic forces on full alert. The Americans will take note of this and realize that a disarming attack is not possible, and we can settle this affair down long enough for reason to take hold."

"Golovko?"

The First Deputy Chairman of the KGB shrank from the inquiry. "We know that they are at full alert status. It is possible that our doing the same will provoke them."

"If we do not, we present ourselves as a much more inviting target." The Defense Minister was inhumanly calm, perhaps the only man in the room who was fully in control of himself. "We know that the American President is under great stress, that he has lost many thousands of his citizens. He might lash out without thinking. He is much less likely to do so if he knows that we are in a position to respond in kind. We do not dare to show weakness at a time like this. Weakness always invites attack."

Narmonov looked around the room for a dissenting opinion. There was none. "Make it so," he told Defense.

* * *

''We still haven't heard anything from Denver,'' Fowler said, rubbing his eyes.

''I wouldn't expect much,'' General Borstein replied.

NORAD's command post is literally inside of a mountain. The entrance tunnel had a series of steel blast-doors. The structures inside were designed to survive anything that could be aimed at them. Shock-absorbing springs and bags of compressed air isolated the people and machines from the granite floors. Overhead were steel roofs to stop any rock fragments that might be blasted free by a near-miss. Borstein didn't expect to survive an attack. There was a whole regiment of Soviet SS-18 Mod 4s tasked to the destruction of this post and a few others. Instead of ten or more MIRVs, they carried a single *twenty-five*-megaton warhead whose only plausible military mission was to turn Cheyenne Mountain into Cheyenne Lake. That was a pleasant thought. Borstein was a fighter pilot by trade. He'd started off in the F-100, called the ''Hun'' by its drivers, graduated from there to F-4 Phantoms, and commanded an F-15 squadron in Europe. He'd always been a tactical guy, stick and rudder, scarf and goggles: kick the tires, light the fires, first one up's the leader. Borstein frowned at the thought. Even he wasn't old enough to remember those days. His job was continental air defense, to keep people from blowing his country up. He'd failed. A nearby piece of America was blown up, along with his boss, and he didn't know why or how or who. Borstein was not a man accustomed to failure, but failure was what he saw on his map display.

''General!'' a major called to him.

''What is it?''

''Picking up some radio and microwave chatter. First guess is that Ivan's alerting his missile regiments. Ditto in some naval bases. Flash traffic outbound from Moscow.''

''Christ!'' Borstein lifted his phone again.

''Never done it?'' Elliot asked.

''Strange but true,'' Borstein said. ''Even during the Cuban Missile Crisis, the Russians never put their ICBMs on alert.''

''I don't believe it,'' Fowler snorted. ''Never?''

''The General's right,'' Ryan said. ''The reason is that their telephone system historically has been in pretty bad shape. I guess they've finally gotten it fixed enough—''

''What do you mean?''

''Mr. President, God is in the details. You send alert messages by voice—we do it that way, and so do the Soviets. The Russian phone system stinks, and you don't want to use a fluky system for orders of that importance. That's why they've been investing so much money in fixing it up, just as we have invested a lot in our command-and-control systems. They use a lot of fiber-optic cable now, just like we do, plus a whole new set of microwave relays. That's how we're catching it,'' Jack explained. ''Scatter off the microwave repeaters.''

''Another couple of years, they'll be fully fiber-optic and we wouldn't have known,'' General Fremont added. ''I don't like this.''

''Neither do I,'' Ryan said, ''but we're at DEFCON-TWO also, aren't we?''

''They don't know that. We didn't tell them that,'' Liz Elliot said.

''Unless they're reading our mail. I've told you we have reports that they've penetrated our cipher systems.''

''NSA says you're crazy.''

"Maybe I am, but NSA's been wrong before, too."

"What do you think Narmonov's mental state is?"

As scared as I am? Ryan wondered. "Sir, there's no telling that."

"And we don't even know if it's really him," Elliot put in.

"Liz, I reject your hypothesis," Jack snapped over the conference line. "The only thing you have to support it comes from my agency, and we have our doubts about it." *Christ, I'm sorry I ever took that report in,* he told himself.

"Cut that out, Ryan!" Fowler snarled back. "I need facts, not arguments now, okay?"

"Sir, as I keep pointing out, we do not as yet have sufficient information on which to base any decision."

"Balls," the Colonel next to General Fremont said.

"What do you mean?" CINC-SAC turned away from the speakerphone.

"Dr. Elliot is right, sir. What she said earlier makes sense."

"Mr. President," they heard a voice say. "We have a Hot Line transmission coming in."

> PRESIDENT FOWLER:
>
> WE HAVE JUST RECEIVED A REPORT THAT A US ARMY UNIT IN BERLIN HAS ATTACKED A SOVIET UNIT WITHOUT WARNING. CASUALTIES ARE REPORTED SEVERE. PLEASE EXPLAIN WHAT IS HAPPENING.

"Oh, shit," Ryan said, looking at the fax.

"I need opinions, people," Fowler said over the conference line.

"The best thing is to say that we have no knowledge of this incident," Elliot said. "If we admit knowledge, we have to assume some responsibility."

"This is a singularly bad time to lie," Ryan said forcefully. Even he thought he was overdoing it. *They won't listen to you if you shout, Jack, boy. . . .*

"Tell that to Narmonov," Elliot shot back. "They attacked us, remember?"

"So the reports say, but—"

"Ryan, are you saying our people lied?" Borstein snarled from Cheyenne Mountain.

"No, General, but at times like this the news is chancy, and you know that as well as I do!"

"If we deny knowledge, we can avoid taking a stand that we might have to back down from, and we avoid challenging them for the moment," the National Security Advisor insisted. "Why are they bringing this up now?" she asked.

"Mr. President, you used to be a prosecutor," Ryan said. "You know how unreliable eyewitness accounts can be. Narmonov could be asking that question in good faith. My advice is to answer it honestly." Jack turned to Goodley, who gave him a thumbs-up.

"Robert, we're not dealing with civilians, we're dealing with professional soldiers, and they ought to be good observers. Narmonov is accusing us of something we didn't do," Elliot countered. "Soviet troops do not initiate combat operations without orders. Therefore he must know that his accusation is false. If we admit knowledge, we will appear to admit his charge is true. I don't know what game he's playing—whoever that is at the other end of the line—but if we simply say we don't know what he's talking about, we buy ourselves time."

"I strongly disagree with that," Jack said as calmly as he could manage.

PRESIDENT NARMONOV:

AS YOU KNOW, I AM MAINLY CONCERNED WITH EVENTS WITHIN OUR OWN BORDERS. I HAVE AS YET NO INFORMATION FROM BERLIN. THANK YOU FOR YOUR INQUIRY. I JUST ORDERED MY PEOPLE TO CHECK INTO IT.

"Opinions?"

"The bastard's lying through his teeth," the Defense Minister said. "Their communications system is too good for that."

"Robert, Robert, why do you lie when I know you are lying . . . ?" Narmonov said, his head down. The Soviet President now had his own questions to ask. Over the past two or three months his contacts with America had grown slightly cold. When he asked for some additional credits, he was put off. The Americans were insisting on full compliance with the arms-reduction agreement even though they knew what the problem was, and even though he'd given Fowler his word face-to-face that everything would be done. What had changed? Why had Fowler retreated from his promises? What the hell was he doing now?

"It's more than just a lie, more than just this lie," the Defense Minister observed after a moment.

"What do you mean?"

"He has emphasized again that his interest is in rescue of casualties in the Denver area, but we know he has placed his strategic forces on full alert. Why has he not told us of this?"

"Because he is afraid of provoking us . . . ?" Narmonov asked. His words seemed rather hollow even to himself.

"Possibly," Defense admitted. "But they do not know the success we've had reading their codes. Perhaps they think they have concealed this from us."

"No," Kuropatkin said in his command center. "I must disagree with that. We could hardly fail to see some of these indicators. They should know that we are aware of some aspects of their strategic alert."

"But not all." The Defense Minister turned to stare at Narmonov. "We must face the possibility that the American President is no longer rational."

"The first time?" Fowler asked.

Elizabeth Elliot nodded. She was quite pale now. "It's not widely known, Robert, but it is true. The Russians have never placed their Strategic Rocket Forces on alert. Until now."

"Why now?" the President asked.

"Robert, the only thing that makes sense is that it isn't Narmonov over there."

"But how can we be sure?"

"We can't. All we have is this computer link. There's no voice link, no visual link."

"Dear God."

40. Collisions

''Ryan, how do we know it's really Narmonov over there?''

''Mr. President, who else would it be?''

''Goddamn it, Ryan! You're the one who brought me the reports!''

''Mr. President, you have to settle down,'' Jack said in a voice that wasn't particularly calm. ''Yes, I brought you that information, and I also told you it was unconfirmed, and I just told you a few minutes ago that we have reason to believe that it may not ever have been true at all.''

''Can't you see your own data? You're the one who warned us that there might be some missing nukes!'' Elliot pointed out. ''Well, they turned up—they turned up here, right where we were supposed to be!''

Christ, she's even more rattled than he is, Helen D'Agustino told herself. She traded a look with Pete Connor, who was pasty-white. *This is going too fast.*

''Look, Liz, I keep telling you that our information is too damned thin. We don't have enough to make any kind of informed judgment here.''

''But why have they gone on nuclear alert?''

''For the same reason that we have!'' Ryan shouted back. ''Maybe if both sides would back off—''

''Ryan, don't tell me what to do,'' Fowler said quietly. ''What I want from you is information. We make the decisions here.''

Jack turned away from the speakerphone. Now he was losing it, Goodley thought, now Ryan was pale and sick-looking. The Deputy Director of Central Intelligence stared out the windows at the CIA courtyard and the largely empty building beyond. He took a few deep breaths and turned back.

''Mr. President,'' Jack said under taut control, ''our opinion is that President Narmonov is in control of the Soviet government. We do not know the origin of the explosion in Denver, but there is no information in our possession that would lead us to believe that it was a Soviet weapon. Our opinion is that for the Soviets to undertake such an operation would be lunacy, and even if their military were in control—after a coup about which we have no information at all, sir—such a miscalculation is unlikely to the point of—the likelihood is so low as to approach zero, sir. That is CIA's position.''

''And Kadishev?'' Fowler asked.

''Sir, we have evidence just developed yesterday and today to suggest that his reports may be false. We cannot confirm one of the meetings that should—''

''*One?* You can't confirm *one* meeting?'' Elliot asked.

''Will you let me talk?'' Jack snarled, losing it again. ''Damn it, it was Goodley who did this work, not me!'' He paused for a breath. ''Dr. Goodley noted some subtle differences in the nature of the reports and decided to check up on them. All of Kadishev's reports supposedly came from face-to-face meetings with Narmonov.

In one case we cannot reconcile the schedules of both men. We cannot be sure they met in that case at all. If they didn't meet, then Kadishev is a liar.''

''I suppose you've considered the possibility that they met in secret?'' Elliot inquired acidly. ''Or do you think that a subject like this would be handled as a routine business matter! Do you think he'd be discussing a possible coup in a routine scheduled meeting!''

''I keep telling you that his information has never been confirmed, not by us, not by the Brits, not by anybody.''

''Ryan, would you expect that a conspiracy leading to a military coup, especially in a country like the Soviet Union, would be handled in the utmost secrecy?'' Fowler asked.

''Of course.''

''Then would you necessarily expect to have it confirmed by other sources?'' Fowler asked, talking like a lawyer in a courtroom.

''No, sir,'' Ryan admitted.

''Then this is the best information we have, isn't it?''

''Yes, Mr. President, if it's true.''

''You say that you have no firm evidence to confirm it?''

''Correct, Mr. President.''

''But you have no hard information to contradict it either, do you?''

''Sir, we have reasons—''

''Answer my question!''

Ryan's right hand compressed into a tight, white fist. ''No, Mr. President, nothing hard.''

''And for the past few years he's given us good, reliable information?''

''Yes, sir.''

''So, based on the record of Mr. Kadishev, this is the best available information?''

''Yes, sir.''

''Thank you. I suggest, Dr. Ryan, that you try to develop additional information. When you get it, I'll listen to it.'' The line clicked off.

Jack stood slowly. His legs were stiff and sore from the stress of the moment. He took one step to the window and lit a cigarette. ''I blew it,'' he told the world. ''Oh, Christ, I've blown it. . . .''

''Not your fault, Jack,'' Goodley offered.

Jack spun around. ''That'll look real good on my fucking tombstone, won't it? 'It wasn't his fault' the fucking world blew up!''

''Come on, Jack, it's not that bad.''

''Think so? Did you hear their voices?''

The Soviet carrier *Kuznetzov* didn't launch aircraft in the manner of U.S. carriers. Rather, it had a ski-jump bow configuration. The first MiG-29 raced forward from its starting point and went up the angled ramp and into the air. This manner of takeoff was hard on pilots and aircraft, but it worked. Another aircraft followed, and both turned to head east. They'd barely gotten to altitude when the flight leader noted a buzz in his headphones.

''Sounds like an emergency beeper on the guard frequency,'' he said to his wingman. ''Sounds like one of ours.''

''*Da,* east-southeast. It is one of ours. Who do you suppose it is?''

''I have no idea.'' The flight leader passed this information on to *Kuznetzov* and received instructions to investigate.

* * *

"This is Falcon-Two," the Hawkeye reported. "We have two inbounds from the Russkie carrier, fast movers, bearing three-one-five and two-five-zero miles from Stick."

Captain Richards looked at the tactical display. "Spade, this is Stick. Close and warn them off."

"Roger," Jackson replied. He'd just topped his fuel tanks off. Jackson could stay up for another three hours or so, and he still carried six missiles.

" 'Warn them off'?" Lieutenant Walters asked.

"Shredder, I don't know what's going on either." Jackson brought the stick around. Sanchez did the same, again splitting out to a wide interval.

The two pairs of aircraft flew on reciprocal courses at a closing speed of just under a thousand miles per hour. Four minutes later both Tomcats went active on their radars. Ordinarily that would have alerted the Russians to the fact that American fighters were in the area, and that the area might not be totally healthy. But the new American radars were stealthy and were not picked up.

It turned out that this didn't matter. A few seconds later the Russians activated their own radar systems.

"Two fighters coming in toward us!"

The Russian flight leader checked his own radar display and frowned. The two MiGs were only supposed to be guarding their own task force. The alert had come in, and the fighters went up. Now he was on what might be a rescue mission and had no particular desire to play foolish games with American aircraft, especially at night. He knew that the Americans knew he was about. His threat receiver did detect the emanations from their airborne early-warning aircraft.

"Come right," he ordered. "Down to one thousand meters to look for that beeper." He'd leave his radar on, however, to show that he didn't wish to be trifled with.

"They're evading to the left, going down."

"Bud, you have the lead," Jackson said. Sanchez had the most missiles. Robby would cover his tail.

"Stick, this is Falcon-Two, both inbounds are breaking south and diving for the deck."

As Richards watched, the course vectors changed on both inbound aircraft. Their course tracks were not actually converging with the *Roosevelt* group at the moment, though they would be coming fairly close.

"What are they up to?"

"Well, they don't know where we are, do they?" the Operations Officer pointed out. "Their radars are on, though."

"Looking for us, then?"

"That would be my guess."

"Well, now we know where the other four came from." Captain Richards picked up the mike to talk to Jackson and Sanchez.

"Splash 'em," was the order. Robby took high cover. Sanchez went down, pulling behind and below both MiGs.

"I've lost the Americans."

"Forget them! We're looking for a rescue beeper, remember?" The flight leader craned his neck. "Is that a strobe light? On the surface at two o'clock . . . ?"

"I have it."

"Follow me down!"

"Evading, down and right!" Bud called. "Engaging now."

He was a bare two thousand yards aft of the MiGs. Sanchez selected a Sidewinder and lined his aircraft up on the "south guy," the trailing wingman. As the Tomcat continued to close, the pilot got the warbling tone in his earphones and triggered off his missile. The AIM-9M Sidewinder leaped off its launch rail, straight into the starboard engine of the MiG-29, which exploded. Barely had that happened when Sanchez triggered off a second 'Winder.

"Splash one."

"What the hell!" The flight leader caught the flash out the corner of his eye and turned to see his wingman's aircraft heading down before a trail of yellow. He wrenched his stick left, his throttle hand punching the flare/chaff-release button as his eyes searched the darkness for his attacker.

Sanchez's second missile missed right. It didn't matter. He was still tracking, and the MiG's turn brought the target right into the path of his 20mm cannon. One quick burst detached part of the MiG's wing. The pilot barely ejected in time. Sanchez watched the chute deploy. A minute later, as he orbited overhead, he saw that both Russians seemed to have survived the incidents. That was fine with Bud.

"Splash two. Stick, we have two good chutes on the splashes . . . wait a minute, there's three strobes down there," Jackson called. He gave the position, and almost instantly a helicopter lifted off from *Theodore Roosevelt*.

"Spade, is it supposed to be this easy?" Walters asked.

"I thought the Russians were smarter than this myself," the Captain admitted. "This is like first day of duck season."

Ten minutes later *Kuznetzov* made a radio call for its two MiGs and got no reply.

The Air Force helicopter returned from Rocky Flats. Major Griggs alighted with five men, all of them dressed in protective gear. Two of them ran to find Chief Callaghan close to the M728 engineer tanks.

"Ten more minutes if we're lucky," Colonel Lyle shouted from atop the lead tank.

"Who's in charge here?" one of the NEST team asked.

"Who are you?"

"Parsons, team leader." Laurence Parsons was the head of the on-duty Nuclear Emergency Search Team, yet another failure for this day. Their job was to locate nuclear devices before they went off. Three such teams were kept on duty around the clock, one just outside Washington, another in Nevada, and the third, recently activated at Rocky Flats to help make up for the retirement of the Energy Department's weapons-fabrication facility outside Denver. It had been anticipated, of course, that they wouldn't always be able to get there in time. He held a radiation counter in his hand, and didn't like what he saw. "How long have your people been here?"

"About half an hour, maybe forty minutes."

"Ten more minutes, I want everybody away from here. You're taking Rems here, Chief."

"What do you mean? The Major said the fallout is all—"

"What you're getting is from neutron activation. It's hot here!"

Callaghan cringed at the thought. His life was being attacked by something he couldn't see or feel. "There may be people inside. We're almost there."

"Then do it fast! I mean *fast!*" Parsons and his team started moving back to the helicopter. They had their own work to do. At the chopper they met a man in civilian clothes.

"Who the fuck are you?" Parsons demanded.

"FBI! What happened here?"

"Take a guess!"

"Washington needs information!"

"Larry, it's hotter here than it is at the stadium!" another NEST team member reported.

"Makes sense," Parsons said. "Ground burst." He pointed. "Far side, downwind side. In-close was shielded some."

"What can you tell me?" the FBI agent asked.

"Not much," Parsons said over the sound of the turning rotor. "Ground burst, yield under twenty KT, all I got."

"It's dangerous here?"

"Hell, yes! Set up—where, where?"

"How about at the Aurora Presbyterian Hospital, two miles upwind?" a NESTer suggested. "Across from Aurora Mall. Ought to be okay there."

"You know where that is?" Parsons asked.

"Yes!"

"Then move out! Ken, you tell these people to get the hell out of here, it's twenty percent hotter here than in close. We have to get samples. Ken, you make sure they clear the area in ten minutes—fifteen max. Drag them out if you have to. Start here!"

"Right."

The FBI agent ducked as the helicopter lifted off. The NEST team member began running down the line of fire trucks, waving for them to get away. The agent decided to do the same. After a few minutes he got in his car and headed northeast.

"Shit, I forgot about the neutrons," Major Griggs said.

"Thanks a lot!" Callaghan screamed over the sound of the tank.

"It's okay, they cut it off at a hundred. A hundred won't really hurt anybody."

Callaghan heard the sound of the engines pulling away. "What about the people inside?" The chief found the interphone at the back of the tank. "Listen up, we have ten minutes and we gotta get the hell out of here. Lean on it!"

"You got it, man," the tank commander replied. "Better get clear. I'll give you a ten count."

Callaghan ran to the side. Colonel Lyle jumped off and did the same. Inside the vehicle, the driver backed off ten yards, took the engine to the red line, and slipped the brake. The M728 crushed five vehicles, slamming them aside. The tank was moving at perhaps a mile per hour, but it didn't stop. Its treads ripped up the asphalt, then it was through.

The area immediately next to the stadium structure was amazingly intact. Most of the wreckage from the roof and upper wall had been thrown hundreds of yards, but here there were only small piles of brick and concrete fragments. Too much for a wheeled vehicle, but clear enough that men could walk. Firefighters advanced and sprayed everything. The asphalt was still very hot, and the water steamed off it. Callaghan ran in front of the tank, waving for his men to go left and right.

* * *

"You know what this looks like?" a NEST team member said as the helicopter circled the ruined stadium.

"Yeah, Chernobyl. They had firemen there, too." Parsons turned away from that thought. "Head downwind," he told the pilot. "Andy, what do you make this?"

"Ground burst, and this wasn't any hundred-KT weapon, Larry, not even twenty-five."

"What screwed up NORAD's estimate, do you think?"

"The parking lot. Asphalt, plus all those burning cars—it's the perfect black-body material—it's even *black,* for God's sake! I'm surprised the thermal pulse didn't look bigger than that—and everything around here is white from the snow 'n' ice, right? They got a megareflection plus a huge energy contrast."

"Makes sense, Andy," Parsons agreed. "Terrorists?"

"That's my bet for now, Larry. But we gotta get some residue to be sure."

The sounds of battle had died down. The Bradley commander heard scattered firing and guessed that the Russians had pulled back partway, maybe all the way to their own kazerne. It made sense, both sides' tanks had been badly mauled, and it was now a battle for infantrymen and their fighting vehicles. Foot soldiers, he knew, were smarter than tankers. It came from wearing a shirt instead of a foot of iron. Vulnerability made you think. He changed position yet again. It was odd how this worked, though he'd practiced the maneuver often enough. The vehicle ran close to a corner, and a man would dismount to peer around it.

"Nothin', Sarge. It's all—wait!" Something moving, 'bout two miles down the street. . . ." The soldier raised a pair of glasses. "BDRM! The missile kind."

Okay, the sergeant thought, *that'll be the reconnaissance element for the next wave*. His job was entirely straightforward. Reconnaissance was a two-part job. His job was both to find the enemy and to prevent the enemy from finding things.

"Another one!"

"Get ready to move. Traverse right, targets to the right," he added for the gunner.

"Ready, Sarge."

"Go!" The Bradley's armored body rocked backwards as a vehicle leaped into the intersection. The gunner brought his turret around. It looked like a small-bore shooting gallery. There were two BDRM armored scout cars heading straight toward them. The gunner engaged the leader, exploding the antitank missile launcher on top. The BDRM veered to the left and rammed some parked cars. Already the gunner shifted fire to the second, which jerked right to evade, but the street was too narrow for that. The chain gun was a nice compromise between a machine gun and a cannon. The gunner was able to walk his tracers into the target, and had the satisfaction of watching it explode. But—

"Back fast—now!" the sergeant screamed into the intercom. There had been a third BDRM back there. The Bradley retreated the way it had come. Barely had it gotten behind the buildings when a missile streaked down the street it had crossed, trailing a thin wire behind it. The missile exploded a few hundred meters away.

"Time to leave, turn us around," the track commander said. Then he activated his radio. "This is Delta Three-Three. We have contact with reconnaissance vehicles. Two destroyed, but the third one spotted us. We got more friends coming in, sir."

* * *

"General, we've pushed them back across the line, I can hold out against what's here, but if more gets in to us, we're screwed," Colonel Long said. "Sir, we need help here!"

"Okay, I'll have some air to you in ten minutes. Fast-movers on the way now."

"That's a start, but I need more than that, sir."

SACEUR turned to his operations officer. "What's ready?"

"Second of the 11th Cav, sir. They're moving out of their kazerne right now."

"What's between them and Berlin?"

"Russians? Not much. If they move fast. . . ."

"Move 'em out." SACEUR walked back to his desk and lifted the phone for Washington.

"Yes, what is it?" Fowler asked.

"Sir, it appears that the Russians are bringing reinforcements into Berlin. I have just ordered the 2nd Squadron, 11th Armored Cav to move toward Berlin to reinforce. I also have aircraft heading in now to assess the situation."

"Do you have any idea what they're up to?"

"None, sir, it makes no damned sense at all, but we still have people being killed. What are the Russians telling you, Mr. President?"

"They're asking why we attacked them, General."

"Are they nuts?" *Or is it something else?* SACEUR wondered. *Something really frightening?*

"General." It was a woman's voice, probably that Elliot woman, SACEUR thought. "I want to be very clear on this. Are you sure that the Soviets initiated the attack?"

"Yes, ma'am!" SACEUR replied heatedly. "The commander of the Berlin Brigade is probably dead. The XO is Lieutenant Colonel Edward Long. I know the kid, he's good. He says the Russians opened fire on the brigade without warning while they were responding to the alert you sent out from D.C. They didn't even have their tubes loaded. I repeat, ma'am, the Russians are the ones who started shooting, and that's definite. Now, do I have your permission to reinforce?"

"What happens if you don't?" Fowler asked.

"In that case, Mr. President, you have about five thousand letters to write."

"Look, okay, send in the reinforcements. Tell Berlin to take no offensive action. We're trying to get things settled down."

"I wish you luck, Mr. President, but right now I have a command to run."

> PRESIDENT NARMONOV:
>
> WE HAVE RECEIVED WORD FROM EUROPE THAT A SOVIET TANK REGIMENT LAUNCHED AN ATTACK ON OUR BERLIN BRIGADE WITHOUT WARNING. I JUST TALKED TO OUR COMMANDER AND HE CONFIRMS THAT THIS IS TRUE.
>
> WHAT IS HAPPENING? WHY DID YOUR TROOPS ATTACK OUR TROOPS?

"Have we heard anything from Berlin yet?" Narmonov asked.

The Defense Minister shook his head. "No, the lead reconnaissance elements should just be getting in now. Radio communications are a disaster. Our VHF radios work poorly in cities because they are line-of-sight only. What we're getting is fragmented, mainly tactical communications between subunit commanders. We have not established contact with the regimental commander. He may be dead. After all,'' Defense pointed out, ''the Americans like to go after commanders first.''

''So we really do not know what is going on?''

''No, but I am *certain* that no Soviet commander would open fire on Americans without just cause!''

Golovko closed his eyes and swore under his breath. Now the Defense Minister was showing the strain.

''Sergey Nikolay'ch?'' Narmonov asked.

''We have nothing more to report from KGB. You may expect that all of the American land-based missiles are fully on alert, as are all their submarine missiles at sea. We estimate that the American missile submarines in port will all have sortied in a matter of hours.''

''And our missile submarines?''

''One is leaving the dock now. The rest are preparing to do so. It will take most of the day to get them all out.''

''Why are we so slow?'' Narmonov demanded.

''The Americans have two complete crews for their boats. We have only one. It's simply easier for them to surge them out this way.''

''So you are telling me that their strategic forces are totally ready, or nearly so, and ours are not?''

''All of our land-based rockets are fully prepared.''

''President Narmonov, your reply to the Americans . . . ?''

''What do I say now?'' Andrey Il'ych asked.

A colonel entered the room. ''Report from Berlin.'' He handed it to the Defense Minister.

''The Americans are in the eastern part of the city. The first wave of scout cars was taken under fire. Four vehicles, the officer commanding was killed in one of them. We've returned fire and gotten two American vehicles . . . no contact as yet with our regiment.'' The Defense Minister looked at the other one. ''Carrier *Kuznetzov* reports that he launched a two-plane patrol. They detected a rescue radio signal and went to investigate. Contact was then lost. They have an American carrier battle group four hundred kilometers away, and request instructions.''

''What does that mean?''

The Defense Minister checked the times on the second dispatch. ''If our planes are not back by now, they are nearly out of fuel. We must assume they were lost, cause unknown, but the close proximity of the American carrier is troubling. . . . What the *hell* are they doing?''

PRESIDENT FOWLER:

I AM CERTAIN THAT NO SOVIET COMMANDER WOULD ATTACK AMERICAN TROOPS WITHOUT ORDERS, AND THERE WERE NO SUCH ORDERS. WE HAVE SENT ADDITIONAL TROOPS INTO BERLIN TO INVESTIGATE AND THEY WERE ATTACKED BY YOUR FORCES IN THE EASTERN PART OF THE CITY, WELL AWAY FROM YOUR ENCAMPMENT. WHAT ARE YOU DOING?

''What the hell is he talking about? What am *I* doing? What the hell is he doing!'' Fowler growled. A light came on. It was the CIA. The President pushed the button, adding a new line to his conference call.

''That depends on who 'he' is,'' Elliot warned.

''Yes, what is it?''

"Mr. President, what we have here is simple confusion."

"Ryan! We don't want analysis, we want information. Do you have any?" Liz shouted.

"The Soviets are sortieing their ships out of the Northern Fleet ports. One missile submarine is supposed to be heading out."

"So their land-based missiles are fully alerted?"

"Correct."

"And they're adding to their submarine missile force also?"

"Yes, Mr. President."

"Do you have any good news?"

"Sir, the news is that there is no real news right now, and you're—"

"Listen, Ryan. One last time: I want information from you and nothing else. You brought me that Kadishev stuff and now you're saying it was all wrong. So why should I believe you now?"

"Sir, when I gave it to you I told you it was not confirmed!"

"I think we may have confirmation now," Liz pointed out. "General Borstein, if they're fully on line, what exactly is the threat?"

"The fastest thing they can get to us is an ICBM. Figure one regiment of SS-18s targeted on the Washington area, and most of the others targeted on our missile fields in the Dakotas, plus the sub bases at Charleston, King's Bay, Bangor, and the rest. Warning time will be twenty-five minutes."

"And we will be targets here?" Liz asked.

"That is a reasonable assumption, Dr. Elliot."

"So they will try to use SS-18s to finish what the first weapon missed?"

"If that was their work, yes."

"General Fremont, how far out is the backup Kneecap?"

"Dr. Elliot, it took off about ten minutes ago. It'll be at Hagerstown in ninety-five minutes. They have some good tail winds." CINC-SAC regretted that addition almost at once.

"So if they are thinking about an attack, and they launch it within the next hour and a half, we're dead here?"

"Yes."

"Elizabeth, it's our job to prevent that, remember?" Fowler said quietly.

The National Security Advisor looked over at the President. Her face might have been made of glass, so brittle it looked. It wasn't supposed to be like this. She was the chief adviser to the most powerful man in the world, in a place of ultimate safety, guarded by dedicated servants, but less than thirty minutes from the time some faceless, nameless Russian made a decision, perhaps one already made, she'd be dead. Dead, a few ashes in the wind, certainly no more than that. Everything she'd worked for, all the books and classes and seminars would have ended in a blinding, annihilating flash.

"Robert, we don't even know who we're talking to," she said in an uneven voice.

"Back to their message, Mr. President," General Fremont said. " 'Additional troops to investigate.' Sir, that sounds like reinforcements."

A rookie fireman found the first survivor, crawling up the concrete ramp from the basement loading dock. It was amazing he'd made it. His hands had second-degree burns, and the crawl had ground bits of glass and concrete and Lord knew what into his injuries. The firefighter lifted the man—it was a cop—and carried him off to the evacuation point. The two remaining fire engines sprayed both men with water, then they were ordered to strip, and they were hosed again. The police officer was semiconscious, but tore a sheet of paper off the clipboard he'd been holding, and all during the ambulance ride he was trying to tell the fireman something, but the firefighter was too cold, too tired, and much too scared to pay attention. He'd done his job, and might have lost his life in the process. It was altogether too much for a twenty-year-old, who simply stared at the wet floor of the ambulance and shivered inside his blanket.

The entranceway had been topped with a pre-stressed concrete lintel. That had been shattered by the blast, with one piece blocking the way in. A soldier from the tank snaked a cable from the turret-mounted winch around the largest of the remaining blocks. As he did this, Chief Callaghan kept staring at his watch. It was too late to stop now in any case. He had to see this through if he died in the process.

The cable went taut, pulling the concrete fragment clear. Miraculously, the remainder of the entranceway did not collapse. Callaghan led the way through the rubbled opening, with Colonel Lyle behind him.

The emergency lights were on, and it seemed that every sprinkler head had gone off. This part of the stadium was where the main came into the structure, Callaghan remembered, and that explained the falling water. There were other sounds, the kind that came from people. Callaghan went into a men's room and found two women, both sitting in the water, both of their coats sprinkled with their own vomit.

"Get 'em out of here!" he shouted to his men. "Go both ways, give it a quick check, and get back here fast as you can!" Callaghan checked all the toilet stalls. They were unoccupied. Another look at the room showed nothing else. They'd come all this way for two women in the wrong bathroom. Just two. The chief looked at Colonel Lyle, but there really wasn't anything to say. Both men walked out into the concourse.

It took Callaghan a moment to realize it, even though it was right there, an entrance to the stadium's lower level. Whereas only a short time before the view would have been of the stadium south side, and the roof, what he now saw was the mountains, still outlined in orange by a distant setting sun. The opening called to him, and as though in a trance, he walked up the ramp.

It was a scene from hell. Somehow this section had been shielded one way or another from the blast. But not the thermal pulse. There were perhaps three hundred seats, still largely intact, still with people in them. What had once been people. They were burned black, charcoaled like overdone meat, worse than any fire victim he'd ever seen in nearly thirty years of fighting fires. At least three hundred, still sitting there, looking at where the field had been.

"Come on, Chief," Colonel Lyle said, pulling him away. The man collapsed, and Lyle saw him vomiting inside his gas mask. The Colonel got it off him and pulled him clear. "Time to leave. It's all over here. You've done your job." It turned out that four more people were still alive. The firemen loaded them on the engine deck of the tank, which drove off at once to the evacuation point. The remaining firefighters there washed everything off and departed, too.

Perhaps the only good luck of the day, Larry Parsons thought, was the snow cover. It had attenuated the thermal damage to the adjacent buildings. Instead of hundreds of house fires, there were only a few. Better, the afternoon sun of the previous day had been just intense enough to form a crust on the yards and roofs around the stadium. Parsons was looking for material on that crust. He and his men searched with scintillometers. The almost incredible fact of the matter was that while a nuclear bomb converted much of its mass into energy, the total mass lost in the process was minuscule. Aside from that, matter is very hard to destroy, and he was searching for residue from the device. This was easier than one might have thought. The material was dark, on a flat white surface, and it was also highly radioactive. He had a choice of six very hot spots, two miles downrange of the stadium. Parsons had taken the hottest. Dressed in his lead-coated protective suit, he was trudging across a snow-covered lawn. Probably an elderly couple, he thought. No kids had built a snowman or lain down to make angels. The rippling sound of the counter grew larger . . . there.

The residue was hardly larger in size than dust particles, but there were many of them, probably pulverized gravel and paving material from the parking lot, Parsons thought. If he were very lucky, it had been sucked up through the center of the fireball, and bomb residue had affixed itself to it. If he were lucky. Parsons scooped up a trowel's worth and slid it into a plastic bag. This he tossed to his teammate, who dropped the bag into a lead bucket.

"Very hot stuff, Larry!"

"I know. Let me get one more." He scooped up another sample and bagged it as well. Then he lifted his radio.

"Parsons here. You got anything?"

"Yeah, three nice ones, Larry. Enough, I think, for an assay."

"Meet me at the chopper."

"On the way."

Parsons and his partner walked off, ignoring the wide eyes watching from behind windows. Those people were not his concern for the moment. Thank God, he thought, that they hadn't bothered him with questions. The helicopter sat in the middle of a street, its rotor still turning.

"Where to?" Andy Bowler asked.

"We're going to the command center—shopping center. Should be nice and cold there. You take the samples back and run them through the spectrometer."

"You should come along."

"Can't," Parsons said with a shake of the head. "I have to call into D.C. This isn't what they told us. Somebody goofed, and I gotta tell them. Have to use a landline for that."

The conference room had at least forty phone lines routed into it, one of which was Ryan's direct line. The electronic warble caught his attention. Jack pushed the flashing button and lifted the receiver.

"Ryan."

"Jack, what's going on?" Cathy Ryan asked her husband. There was alarm but not panic in her voice.

"What do you mean?"

"The local TV station says an atomic bomb went off in Denver. Is there a war, Jack?"

"Cathy, I can't—no, honey, there's no war going on, okay?"

"Jack, they showed a picture. Is there anything I need to know?"

"You know almost everything I know. Something happened. We don't know what exactly, and we're trying to find out. The President's at Camp David with the National Security Advisor and—"

"Elliot?"

"Yes. They're talking to the Russians right now. Honey, I have work to do."

"Should I take the children somewhere?"

The proper thing, and the honorable and dramatic thing, Jack told himself, was to tell his wife to stay home, that they had to share the risks with everyone else, but the fact was there was no place of safety that he knew. Ryan looked out the window, wondering what the hell he should say.

"No."

"Liz Elliot is advising the President?"

"That's right."

"Jack, she's a small, weak person. Maybe she's smart, but inside she's weak."

"I know. Cathy, I really have things to do here."

"Love you."

"And I love you, too, babe. 'Bye." Jack replaced the receiver. "The word's out," he announced, "pictures and all."

"Jack!" It was the Senior Duty Officer. "AP just sent out a flash: shooting in Berlin between U.S. and Soviet forces. Reuters is reporting the explosion in Denver."

Ryan got on the phone to Murray. "You have the wire services?"

"Jack, I knew this wouldn't work."

"What do you mean?"

"The President told us to shut the networks down. I guess we goofed somewhere."

"Super. You should have refused that one, Dan."

"I tried, okay?"

There were just too many redundancies, too many nodes. Two satellites serving the United States were still up and operating, and so was nearly all of the microwave-repeater system that had preceded them. The networks didn't merely run out of New York and Atlanta. NBC's Los Angeles bureau, after a surreptitious call from Rockefeller Center, took over for that network. CBS and ABC accomplished the same out of Washington and Chicago, respectively. The irate reporters also let the public know that FBI agents were "holding hostage" the network news headquarters people in the most heinous abuse yet of the First Amendment. ABC was outraged that its crew had been killed, but that was a small thing compared to the scope of the story. The proverbial cat was out of the bag, and phone lines at the White House press office lit up. Many reporters had the direct number to Camp David as well. There was no statement from the President. That only made things worse. The CBS affiliate in Omaha, Nebraska, had only to drive past SAC headquarters to note the beefed-up guard force and the empty flight line. Those pictures would be on nationwide in a matter of minutes, but it was the local news teams who did the best and the worst work. There is scarcely a city or town in America that lacks a National Guard armory or a base for reservists. Concealing the activity at all of them was tantamount to concealing a sunrise, and the wire-service printers reported activity everywhere. All that was needed to punctuate those reports was the few minutes of tape from KOLD in Denver, running almost continuously now, to explain what was going on, and why.

The phones at the Aurora Presbyterian were all being used. Parsons knew that he could have forced his way onto one, but it was easier to run across the street to a largely deserted shopping center. He found an FBI agent there, wearing a blue ''raid'' jacket that proclaimed his identity in large block letters.

''You the guy from the stadium?'' Parsons' headgear was gone, but he still wore the metallic coat and pants.

''Yeah.''

''I need a phone.''

''Save your quarters.'' They were standing outside a men's clothing store. The door had alarm tape on it, but looked cheap. The agent pulled out his service pistol and fired five rounds, shattering the glass. ''After you, pal.''

Parsons ran to the counter and lifted the store phone, dialing his headquarters in Washington. Nothing happened.

''Where are you calling?''

''D.C.''

''The long-distance lines are down.''

''What do you mean? The phone company shouldn't be hurt from this.''

''We did it. Orders from Washington,'' the agent explained.

''What fucking idiot ordered that?''

''The President.''

''Outstanding. I gotta get a call out.''

''Wait.'' The agent took the phone and called his own office.

''Hoskins.''

''This is Larry Parsons, NEST team leader. Can you relay something to Washington?''

''Sure.''

''The bomb was a ground burst, less than fifteen kilotons. We have samples of the residue, and it's on the way to Rocky Flats for spectroscopy. You know how to get that out?''

''Yes, I can do that.''

''Okay.'' Parsons hung up.

''You have pieces from the bomb?'' the FBI agent asked incredulously.

''Sounds crazy, doesn't it? That's what fallout is, bomb residue that gets attached to dirt particles.''

''So what?''

''So we can figure out a lot from that. Come on,'' he told the agent. Both men ran back across the street toward the hospital. An FBI agent, Parsons decided, was a useful fellow to have around.

''Jack, got something from Denver, came in through Walt Hoskins. The bomb was a ground burst, fifty or so kilotons. The NEST guys have residue and they're going to test it.''

Ryan took his notes. ''Casualty count?''

''Didn't say.''

''Fifty kilotons,'' the S&T man observed. ''Low for what the satellites said, but possible. Still, too goddamned big for an IND.''

The F-16C wasn't exactly ideal for this mission, but it was fast. Four had left Ramstein only twenty minutes earlier. Put aloft by the initial DEFCON-THREE alert, they'd come east to what they still referred to as the inner-German border. They'd not even arrived there when new orders had sent them toward the southern end of Berlin to get a look at what was happening at the Berlin Brigade's kazerne. Four F-15s from Bitburg joined for top cover. All eight USAF fighters were loaded for air-to-air missions only, with two extra fuel tanks each in the place of bombs for the F-16s, and conformal fuel cells for the Eagles. From ten thousand feet they could see the flashes and explosion on the ground. The flight of four broke into two elements of two each, and went down for a closer look, while the Eagles orbited overhead. The problem, it was later decided, was twofold. First, the pilots were simply too surprised at the turn of events to consider all the possibilities; adding to this was the fact that American aircraft losses over Iraq had been so minor as to make the pilots forget that this was a different place.

The Russian tank regiment had both SA-8 and SA-11 missiles, plus the normal complement of Shilka 23mm flak vehicles. The antiair company commander had waited for this moment, not illuminating his radars, playing it smart, as the Iraqis had singularly failed to do. He waited until the American aircraft were under a thousand meters before giving his order.

Barely had their threat receivers come on when a swarm of missiles rose from the eastern edge of the Russian encampment. The Eagles, high up, had a much better chance at evasion. The F-16 Fighting Falcons, descending right into the SAM trap, had almost none. Two were blotted out in a matter of seconds. The second pair dodged the first wave of SAMs, but one was caught in the frag pattern of a second-wave SA-11 it almost but not quite evaded. That pilot ejected successfully, but died when he landed too hard on the roof of an apartment building. The fourth F-16 escaped by skimming the rooftops and screaming west on full burner. Two of the Eagles joined him. A total of five American aircraft crashed into the city. Only one of the pilots lived. The escaping aircraft radioed the news to Commander U.S. Air Forces Europe at Ramstein. Already he had twelve F-16s arming up with heavy ordnance. The next wave would be different.

> PRESIDENT NARMONOV:
> WE SENT SOME AIRCRAFT INTO BERLIN TO INVESTIGATE THE SITUATION THERE. THEY WERE SHOT DOWN WITHOUT WARNING BY SOVIET MISSILES. WHY WAS THIS DONE?

"What does this mean?"

" 'Shot down without warning'? There's a *battle* under way, and that's why the aircraft were sent there! The regiment has antiaircraft troops," the Defense Minister explained. "They only have short-range, low-altitude rockets. If the Americans were just looking from a safe height—ten thousand meters—we couldn't even have touched them. They must have been lower, probably trying to support their troops with an air attack. That's the only way we could have gotten them."

"But we have no information?"

"No, we have not established contact yet."

"We will not answer this one."

"That is a mistake," Golovko said.

"This situation is dangerous enough already," Narmonov said angrily. "We do not know what is going on there. How can I respond when he claims to have information which I do not?"

"If you do not respond, you appear to admit the incident."

"We admit nothing!" the Defense Minister shouted. "We could not even have done this unless they were attacking us, and we don't know whether it really happened or not.''

''So tell them that,'' Golovko suggested. ''Perhaps if they understand that we are as confused as they, they will also understand that—''

''But they won't understand, and they won't believe. They've already accused us of launching this attack, and they won't believe that we have no control over the area.''

Narmonov retreated to a corner table and poured himself a cup of tea, while the intelligence and defense advisers traded—arguments? Was that the right word? The Soviet President looked up at the ceiling. This command center dated back to Stalin. A spur off one of the Moscow subway lines built by Lazar Kaganovich, Stalin's pet Jewish anti-Semite and his most trusted henchman, it was fully a hundred meters down, but now his people told him that it was not truly a place of safety after all.

What was Fowler thinking? Narmonov asked himself. The man was undoubtedly shaken by the murder of so many American citizens, but how could it be possible that he was thinking that the Soviets were responsible? And what was actually happening? A battle in Berlin, a possible clash between naval forces in the Mediterranean, all unrelated—or were they?

Did it matter? Narmonov stared at a picture on the wall and realized that, no, it did not matter. He and Fowler were both politicians for whom appearances had more weight than reality, and perceptions more importance than facts. The American had lied to him in Rome over a trivial matter. Was he lying now? If he were, then none of the past ten years of progress mattered at all, did they? It had all been for nothing.

''How do wars begin?'' Narmonov asked himself quietly in the corner. In history, wars of conquest were started by strong men who wished to grow stronger still. But the time for men of imperial ambition had passed. The last such criminal had died not so long before. All that had changed in the 20th century. The First World War had been started—how? A tubercular assassin had killed a buffoon so unloved that his own family had ignored the funeral. An overbearing diplomatic note had prompted Czar Nikolay II to leap to the defense of people he hadn't loved, and then the timetables had begun. Nikolay had the last chance, Narmonov remembered. The last of the Czars had held in his hand the chance to stop it all, but hadn't. If only he'd known what his decision for war would mean, he might have found the strength to stop it, but in his fear and his weakness he'd signed the mobilization order that had ended one age and begun another. That war had begun because small, frightened men feared war less than showing weakness.

Fowler is such a man, Narmonov told himself. *Proud, arrogant, a man who lied in a small thing lest I think less of him. He will be angered by the deaths. He will fear additional deaths, but he will fear displaying weakness even more. My country is at the mercy of such a man.*

It was an elegant trap Narmonov was in. The irony of it might have evoked a tight, bitter smile, but instead the Soviet President set down his tea, for his stomach would take no more hot, bitter liquid. He could not afford to show weakness either, could he? That would only encourage Fowler to yet more irrationality. Part of Andrey Il'ych Narmonov asked if what he thought of Jonathan Robert Fowler might also apply to himself. . . . But he had to reply. To do nothing would display weakness, wouldn't it?

* * *

"No answer?" Fowler asked the chief yeoman.

"No, sir, nothing yet." Orontia's eyes were locked on the computer screen.

"My God," the President muttered. "All those people dead."

And I could have been one of them, Liz Elliot thought, the idea coming back to her like waves on a beach, crashing in, ebbing away only to crash back again. *Someone wanted to kill us, and I am part of that "us." And we don't know who or why. . . .*

"We can't let this go any farther."

We don't even know what we are trying to stop. Who is doing this? Why are they doing it? Liz looked over at the clock and calculated the time to the arrival of the Kneecap aircraft. *We should have gone out on the first one. Why didn't we think to have it fly to Hagerstown to pick us up! We're stuck here in a perfect target, and if they want to kill us, this time they'll get us, won't they?*

"How can we stop it?" Liz asked. "He's not even answering us."

Sea Devil One-Three, a P-3C Orion antisubmarine aircraft out of Kodiak Naval Air Station, was buffeting through the winds at low altitude, about five hundred feet. It laid the first line of ten DIFAR sonobuoys ten miles southwest of *Maine*'s position. In the back, the sonar operators were strapped tightly into their high-backed seats, most with a vomit bag close by as they tried to make sense of their displays. It took several minutes for things to firm up.

"Christ, that's my boat," Jim Rosselli said. He dialed Bangor and asked for Commodore Mancuso.

"Bart, what gives?"

"*Maine* reported a collision, shaft and screw damage. There's a P-3 riding shotgun on her right now, and we have *Omaha* heading toward her flat-out. That's the good news. The bad news is that *Maine* was tracking an Akula at the time."

"She was *what?*"

"Harry sold me and OP-02 on the idea, Jim. Too late to worry about it now. It should be okay. The Akula was way off. You heard what Harry did to *Omaha* last year, right?"

"Yeah, I thought he stripped a gear."

"Look, it should be okay. I'm surging my boats right now, Jim. Unless you need me for something else, I'm kinda busy."

"Right." Rosselli hung up.

"What gives?" Rocky Barnes asked.

Rosselli handed over the message. "My old sub, disabled in the Gulf of Alaska, and there's a Russian prowling around."

"Hey, they're quiet, right? You told me that. The Russians don't even know where they are."

"Yeah."

"Cheer up, Jim. I probably knew some of those F-16 drivers who got snuffed over Berlin."

"Where the hell is Wilkes? He should have been here by now," Rosselli said. "He's got a good car."

"No tellin', man. What the fuck is going on?"

"I don't know, Rocky."

"We've got a long one coming in," Chief Orontia said. "Here it comes."

PRESIDENT FOWLER:

WE HAVE NO INFORMATION FROM BERLIN ON THE MATTER TO WHICH YOU REFER. COMMUNICATIONS HAVE BROKEN DOWN. MY ORDERS HAVE GONE OUT TO OUR TROOPS, AND IF THEY HAVE GOTTEN THEM THEN THEY WILL TAKE NO ACTION EXCEPT IN SELF-DEFENSE. PERHAPS THEY FELT THEMSELVES TO BE UNDER ATTACK BY YOUR AIRCRAFT AND ACTED TO DEFEND THEMSELVES. IN ANY CASE WE ARE TRYING EVEN NOW TO REESTABLISH CONTACT WITH THE TROOPS, BUT OUR FIRST ATTEMPT TO REACH THEM WAS STOPPED BY AMERICAN TROOPS WHO WERE WELL OUTSIDE THEIR CAMP. YOU ACCUSE US OF HAVING OPENED FIRE, YET I HAVE TOLD YOU THAT OUR FORCES HAVE NO SUCH ORDERS, AND THE ONLY DEFINITE WORD WE HAVE TELLS US THAT YOUR FORCES WERE WELL INTO OUR ZONE OF THE CITY WHEN THEY STRUCK.

MR. PRESIDENT, I CANNOT RECONCILE YOUR WORDS WITH THE FACTS WE HAVE. I MAKE NO ACCUSATION, BUT I KNOW OF NOTHING MORE THAT I CAN SAY TO ASSURE YOU THAT SOVIET FORCES HAVE TAKEN NO ACTION WHATEVER AGAINST AMERICAN FORCES.

YOU HAVE TOLD US THAT YOUR ALERTING OF YOUR FORCES IS DEFENSIVE ONLY, BUT WE HAVE INDICATIONS THAT YOUR STRATEGIC FORCES ARE IN A VERY HIGH STATE OF ALERT. YOU SAY YOU HAVE NO REASON TO BELIEVE THAT WE ARE TO BLAME FOR THIS INFAMY, YET YOUR MOST ALERT FORCES ARE THOSE ARRAYED AGAINST MY COUNTRY. WHAT DO YOU WISH ME TO THINK? YOU ASK FOR PROOF OF OUR GOOD INTENTIONS, BUT ALL OF YOUR ACTIONS APPEAR TO LACK THEM.

"He's blustering," Liz Elliot observed at once. "Whoever it is over there is rattled. Good, we may get the upper hand here yet."

"Good?" CINC-SAC asked. "You realize that this frightened person you're talking about has a whole lot of missiles pointing at us. I don't read it that way, Dr. Elliot. I think we have an angry man here. He's thrown our inquiries right back in our face."

"What do you mean, General?"

"He says he knows we're alerted. Okay, that's no surprise, but he also says that those weapons are pointed at him. He's accusing us of threatening him now—with nukes, Mr. President. That matters a hell of a lot more than the piss-ant business in Berlin."

"I agree," General Borstein added. "He's trying to bluster us, sir. We asked about a couple of lost airplanes, and we get all this tossed back at us."

Fowler punched up CIA again. "Ryan, you got the latest one?"

"Yes, sir."

"What do you make of Narmonov's mental state?"

"Sir, he's a little angry right now, and also very concerned about our defensive posture. He's trying to find a way out of this."

"I don't read it that way. He's rattled."

"Well, who the hell isn't?" Jack asked. "Of *course* he's rattled, the same as everyone else."

"Look, Ryan, we are in control up here."

"I never said otherwise, Liz," Jack replied, biting off what he really thought. "This is a grave situation, and he's as concerned as we are. He's trying to figure out what's happening the same as everyone else. The problem is nobody really knows anything."

"Well, whose fault is that? That is your job, isn't it?" Fowler asked testily.

"Yes, Mr. President, and we're working on it. A lot of people are."

"Robert, does this sound like Narmonov? You've met the man, you've spent time with him."

"Elizabeth, I just don't know."

"It's the only thing that makes sense. . . ."

"Liz, who says that any of this has to make sense?" Ryan asked.

"This weapon was a big one, right, General Borstein?"

"That's what our instruments tell us, yes."

"Who has bombs that large?"

"Us, the Russians, the Brits, the French. Maybe the Chinese have weapons like this, but we don't think so; theirs are big and clunky. Israel has warheads in this range. That's it. India, Pakistan, South Africa all probably have fission weapons, but not large enough for this."

"Ryan, is that correct information?" Elliot asked.

"Yes, it is."

"So if it wasn't Britain, France or Israel, then who the hell was it?"

"Goddamn it, Liz! *We don't know,* okay? We do not know, and this isn't a fucking Sherlock Holmes mystery. Eliminating who it wasn't doesn't tell us who it was! You can't convert the absence of information into a conclusion."

"Does CIA know everybody who has weapons of this type?" Fowler asked.

"Yes, sir, we think we do."

"How confident are you in that?"

"Until today I would have bet my life on it."

"So again you are not telling me the truth, are you?" Fowler observed coldly.

Jack stood from his chair. "Sir, you may be the President of the United States, but don't you ever accuse me of lying again! My wife just called here to ask if she should take the kids somewhere, and if you think I'd be so goddamned dumb as to play games at a time like this, you, sir, are the one who needs help!"

"Thank you, Ryan, that will be all." The line clicked off.

"Jesus!" the Senior Duty Officer observed.

Jack looked around the room for a wastebasket. He just made it in time. Ryan fell to his knees and vomited into it. He reached for a can of Coke and washed his mouth out, spitting back into the basket. No one spoke until he rose.

"They just don't understand," Jack said quietly. He stretched, then lit a cigarette. "They just don't understand.

"You see, this is all very simple. There is a difference between not knowing anything and understanding that you don't know. We have a crisis, and all the players are reverting to type. The President is thinking like a lawyer, trying to be cool, doing what he knows how to do, running down the evidence and trying to make a case, interrogating the witnesses, trying to reduce everything, playing that game. Liz is fixed on the fact that she might have been blown up, can't set that aside. Well." Ryan shrugged. "I guess I can understand that. I've been there, too. She's a political scientist, looking for a theoretical model. She's feeding that to the President. She has a real elegant model, but it's based on crap, isn't it, Ben?"

"You left out something, Jack," Goodley pointed out.

Ryan shook his head. "No, Ben, I just haven't gotten there yet. Because I can't control my *fucking* temper, they won't listen to me now. I should have known, I had my warning—I even saw it coming—but I let my temper get the best of me again. And you know the funny part? If it wasn't for me, Fowler would still be in Columbus, Ohio, and Elliot would be teaching shiny young faces at Bennington." Jack walked to the window again. It was dark outside, and the lighted room made it into a mirror.

"What are you talking about?"

"That, gentlemen, is a secret. Maybe that's what they'll put on the stone: Here lies John Patrick Ryan. He tried to do the right thing—and look what happened. I wonder if Cathy and the kids will make it. . . ."

"Come on, it's not that bad," the Senior Duty Officer observed, but all the others in the room felt the chill.

Jack turned. "Isn't it? Don't you see where this is heading? They're not listening to anybody. They're not listening. They might listen to Dennis Bunker or Brent Talbot, but they're both air pollution, little bits of fallout somewhere over Colorado. I'm the closest thing in town to an adviser right now, and I got myself tossed out."

41. The Field of Camlan

The *Admiral Lunin* was going too fast for safety. Captain Dubinin knew that, but chances like this did not come along often. This was, in fact, the first, and the Captain wondered if it might also be the last. Why were the Americans on a full-blown nuclear alert—yes, of course, a possible nuclear explosion in their country was a grave matter, but could they be so mad as to assume that a Soviet had done such a thing?

"Get me a polar projection chart," he said to a quartermaster. Dubinin knew what he would see, but it wasn't a time for remembrance, it was a time for hard facts. The meter-square sheet of hard paper was on the table a moment later. Dubinin took a pair of dividers and walked them from *Maine*'s estimated position to Moscow, and to the strategic rocket fields in the central part of his country.

"Yes." It could hardly be more clear, could it?

"What is it, Captain?" the *Starpom* asked.

"USS *Maine*, according to our intelligence estimates, is in the northernmost patrol sector of the missile submarines based at Bangor. That makes good sense, doesn't it?"

"Yes, Captain, based on what little we know of their patrol patterns."

"She carries the D-5 rocket, twenty-four of them, eight or so warheads per rocket. . . ." He paused. There had been a time when he'd been able to do such calculations in his head instantly.

"One hundred ninety-two, Captain," the executive officer said for him.

"Correct, thank you. That includes nearly all of our SS-18s, less those being deactivated by treaty, and the CEP accuracy of the D-5 makes it likely that those one hundred ninety-two warheads will destroy roughly one hundred sixty of their targets, which, in turn, accounts for more than a fifth of our total warhead count, and our most accurate warheads at that. Remarkable, isn't it?'' Dubinin asked quietly.

''You really think they're that good?''

''The Americans demonstrated their marksmanship ability over Iraq, didn't they? I for one have never doubted the quality of their weapons.''

''Captain, we know that the American D-5 submarine rockets are the most likely first-strike tool . . .''

''Continue the thought.''

The *Starpom* looked at the chart. ''Of course. This is the closest one.''

''Indeed. USS *Maine* is the point of the lance aimed at our country.'' Dubinin tapped the chart with his dividers. ''If the Americans launch an attack, the first rockets will fly from this point, and nineteen minutes after that, they will hit. I wonder if our comrades in the Strategic Rocket Forces can respond that quickly . . . ?''

''But, Captain, what can we do about this?'' the executive officer asked dubiously.

Dubinin pulled the chart off the table and slid it back into its open drawer. ''Nothing. Not a thing. We cannot attack preemptively without orders or grave provocation, can we? According to our best intelligence, he can launch his rockets at intervals of fifteen seconds, probably less, really. The manual becomes less important in war, doesn't it? Say four minutes from the first to the last. You have to do a ladder-north strike pattern to avoid warhead fratricide. That doesn't matter, if you examine the physics of the event. I looked at that while I was at Frunze, you know. Since our rockets are liquid-fueled, they cannot launch while the attack is under way. Even if their electronic components can withstand the electromagnetic effects, they are too fragile structurally to tolerate the physical forces. So unless we can launch with confidence before the enemy warheads fall, our tactics are to ride it out and launch a few minutes later. For our part here, if he can launch in four minutes, that means we have to be within six thousand meters, hear the first launch transient, and fire our own torpedo immediately to have any hope of stopping him from firing his last rocket, don't we?''

''A difficult task.''

The Captain shook his head. ''An impossible task. The only thing that makes sense is for us to eliminate him before he receives his launch order, but we cannot do that without orders, and we have no such orders.''

''So, what do we do?''

''Not very much we can do.'' Dubinin leaned over the chart table. ''Let's assume that he's truly disabled, and that we have an accurate position fix. We still have to detect him. If his engine plant is down at minimums, hearing him will be nearly impossible, especially if he's up against the surface noise. If we go active, what's to stop him from launching a torpedo against us? If he does that, we can fire back—and hope to survive, ourselves. Our weapon might even hit him, but then again it might not. If he does not shoot as soon as he hears our active sonar . . . maybe we can close enough that we can intimidate him, force him down. We'll lose him again when he goes under the layer . . . but if we can force him down . . . and then stay atop the layer, blasting away with our active sonar . . . perhaps we can keep him from going to missile-firing depth.'' Dubinin frowned mightily. ''Not an especially brilliant plan, is it? If one of them suggested it''—he waved to the junior officers conning the ship—"I'd tear a strip off their young backs. But I don't see anything better. Do you?"

"Captain, that makes us exceedingly vulnerable to attack." The idea was more accurately described as suicidal, the *Starpom* thought, though he was sure Dubinin knew that.

"Yes, it does, but if that is what is required to prevent this bastard from getting to firing depth, it is exactly what I propose to do. I see no alternative."

PRESIDENT NARMONOV:

PLEASE UNDERSTAND THE POSITION WE ARE IN. THE WEAPON WHICH DESTROYED DENVER WAS OF SUCH A SIZE AND TYPE AS TO MAKE IT VERY UNLIKELY THAT THIS CRIME WAS COMMITTED BY TERRORISTS, YET WE HAVE TAKEN NO ACTION WHATEVER TO RETALIATE AGAINST ANYONE. WERE YOUR COUNTRY ATTACKED, YOU TOO WOULD ALERT YOUR STRATEGIC FORCES. WE HAVE SIMILARLY ALERTED OURS, ALONG WITH OUR CONVENTIONAL FORCES. FOR TECHNICAL REASONS IT WAS NECESSARY TO INITIATE A GLOBAL ALERT INSTEAD OF A MORE SELECTIVE ONE. BUT AT NO TIME HAVE I ISSUED ANY INSTRUCTIONS TO COMMENCE OFFENSIVE OPERATIONS. OUR ACTIONS TO THIS POINT HAVE BEEN DEFENSIVE ONLY, AND HAVE SHOWN CONSIDERABLE RESTRAINT.

WE HAVE NO EVIDENCE TO SUGGEST THAT YOUR COUNTRY HAS INITIATED ACTION AGAINST OUR HOMELAND, BUT WE HAVE BEEN INFORMED THAT YOUR TROOPS IN BERLIN HAVE ATTACKED OURS, AND HAVE ALSO ATTACKED AIRCRAFT ATTEMPTING TO INSPECT THE AREA. WE ARE SIMILARLY INFORMED THAT SOVIET AIRCRAFT HAVE APPROACHED AN AMERICAN CARRIER GROUP IN THE MEDITERRANEAN.

PRESIDENT NARMONOV, I URGE YOU TO RESTRAIN YOUR FORCES. IF WE CAN END THE PROVOCATIONS, WE CAN END THIS CRISIS, BUT I CANNOT TELL MY PEOPLE NOT TO DEFEND THEMSELVES.

" 'Restrain your forces'? Goddamn it," the Defense Minister swore. "We haven't *done* anything! He's accusing *us* of provoking *him! His* tanks have invaded East Berlin, *his* fighter-bombers have attacked our forces there, and he just confirmed the fact that his carrier aircraft have attacked ours! And this arrogant madman now says that we must not provoke him! What does he expect us to do—run away everywhere we see an American?"

"That might be the most prudent thing we can do," Golovko observed.

"Run like a thief from a policeman?" Defense asked sarcastically. "You ask that we should do that?"

"I suggest it as a possibility to be considered." The First Deputy Chairman of KGB stood his ground bravely, Narmonov thought.

"The important part of this message is the second sentence," the Foreign Minister pointed out. His analysis was all the more chilling for its matter-of-fact tone. "They say that they do not believe this was a terrorist attack. Who is left as a likely attacker, then? He goes on to say that America has not yet retaliated against anyone *yet*. The subsequent statement that they have no evidence to suggest that we perpetrated this infamy is, I think, rather hollow when juxtaposed with the first paragraph."

"And running away will only make it more clear to him that we are the ones who started this," Defense added.

" 'More clear'?" Golovko asked.

"I must agree with that," Narmonov said, looking up from his chair. "I must assume now that Fowler is not rational. This communiqué is not well reasoned. He is accusing us, quite explicitly."

"What of the nature of the explosion?" Golovko asked the Defense Minister.

"A weapon of that size is indeed too large for terrorists. Our studies indicate that a first- or even second-generation fission device might be achievable, but the maximum yield for such a device is certainly less than a hundred—probably less than forty kilotons. Our instruments tell us that this device was well over a hundred. That means a third-generation fission weapon or more likely a multistage fusion device. To do that is not the work of amateurs."

"So, then, who could have done it?" Narmonov asked.

Golovko looked over to his President. "I have no idea. We did uncover a possible DDR bomb project. They were producing plutonium, as you all know, but we have good reason to believe that the project never truly got under way. We've looked at ongoing projects in South America. They are not to this point either. Israel has such capabilities, but what reason would they have to do this? Attack their own guardian? If China were to do something like this, they would more likely attack us. We have the land and resources they need, and America has much more value to them as a trading partner than as an enemy. No, for this to be a project of a nation-state means that only one of a handful has the ability to do it, and the problems of operational security are virtually insurmountable. Andrey Il'ych, if you *directed* KGB to do this, we probably could not. The type of individual necessary for such a mission—by that I mean the skill, intelligence, dedication—are not qualities which you find in a psychotic; murder on this scale, likely to bring about such a crisis as this, would require a diseased personality. KGB has no such people, for the obvious reason."

"So you are telling me that you have no information and that you can find no sensible hypothesis to explain the events of this morning?"

"That is the case, Comrade President. I wish I could report something else, but I cannot."

"What sort of advice is Fowler getting?"

"I don't know," Golovko admitted. "Secretaries Talbot and Bunker are both dead. Both were watching the football match—Defense Secretary Bunker was the owner of one of the teams, in fact. The Director of CIA is either still in Japan or on his way back from there."

"The Deputy Director is Ryan, correct?"

"That is true."

"I know him. He is not a fool."

"No, he is not, but he is also being dismissed. Fowler dislikes him, and we have learned that Ryan has been asked to resign. Therefore, I cannot say who is advising President Fowler, except for Elizabeth Elliot, the National Security Advisor, with whom our Ambassador is not impressed."

"You tell me, then, that this weak, vain man is probably not getting good advice from anyone?"

"Yes."

"That explains much." Narmonov leaned back and closed his eyes. "So I am the only one who can give him good advice, but he probably thinks I am the one who killed his city. Splendid." It was perhaps the most penetrating analysis of the night, but wrong.

PRESIDENT FOWLER:

FIRST OF ALL, I HAVE DISCUSSED THIS MATTER WITH MY MILITARY COMMANDERS AND HAVE BEEN ASSURED THAT NO SOVIET ATOMIC WARHEAD IS MISSING.

SECOND, WE HAVE MET, YOU AND I, AND I HOPE YOU KNOW THAT I WOULD NEVER HAVE GIVEN SUCH A CRIMINAL ORDER AS THIS.

THIRD, ALL OF OUR ORDERS TO OUR MILITARY FORCES HAVE BEEN OF A DEFENSIVE NATURE. I HAVE AUTHORIZED NO OFFENSIVE ACTION WHATEVER.

FOURTH, I HAVE ALSO MADE INQUIRIES WITH OUR INTELLIGENCE SERVICES, AND I REGRET TO INFORM YOU THAT WE TOO HAVE NO IDEA WHO COULD HAVE COMMITTED THIS INHUMAN ACT. WE WILL WORK TO CHANGE THAT, AND ANY INFORMATION WE DEVELOP WILL BE SENT TO YOU AT ONCE.

MR. PRESIDENT, I WILL GIVE NO FURTHER ORDERS TO MY FORCES OF ANY KIND UNLESS PROVOKED. THE SOVIET MILITARY IS IN A DEFENSIVE POSTURE AND WILL REMAIN SO.

''Oh, God,'' Elliot rasped. ''How many lies do we have here?'' Her finger traced down the computer screen.

''One, we know that they have missing warheads. That is a lie.

''Two, why is he stressing the fact that it's really him that you two met in Rome? Why bother doing that unless he thinks that we suspect it's *not* Narmonov at all? The real guy wouldn't do that, he wouldn't have to, would he? Probably a lie.

''Three, we know that they've attacked us in Berlin. That's a lie.

''Four, he brings up the KGB for the first time. I wonder why. What if they actually have a cover plan . . . after intimidating us—beautiful, after intimidating us, they offer us their cover plan, and we have to buy it.

''Five, now he's warning us not to provoke him. They're in a 'defensive posture,' eh? Some posture.'' Liz paused. ''Robert, this is spin-control pure and simple. He's trying to fake us out.''

''That's the way I read it, too. Comments, anyone?''

''The nonprovocation statement is troubling,'' CINC-SAC replied. General Fremont was watching his status boards. He now had ninety-six bombers in the air, and over a hundred tankers. His missile fields were on line. The Defense Support Program satellites had their Cassegrain-focus telescopic cameras zoomed in on the Soviet missile fields instead of on wide-field scanning mode. ''Mr. President, there is something we need to discuss right about now.''

''What is that, General?''

Fremont spoke in his best calm-professional voice. ''Sir, the builddown of the respective strategic-missile forces on both sides has affected the calculus of a nuclear strike. Before, when we had over a thousand ICBMs, neither we nor the Soviets ever expected that a disarming first-strike was a real strategic possibility. It just demanded too much. Things are different now. Improvements in missile technology plus the reduction in the number of fixed high-value targets now means that such a strike is a theoretical possibility. Add to that Soviet delays in deactivating their older SS-18s to comply with the strategic-arms treaty, and we have what may well be a strategic posture on their part in which such a strike may be an attractive option. Remember that we've been reducing our missile stocks faster than they. Now, I know that Narmonov gave you a personal assurance that he'd be fully in compliance with the treaty in four more weeks, but those missile regiments are still active as far as we can tell.

''Now,'' Fremont went on, ''if that intelligence you have that Narmonov was being threatened by his military is correct—well, sir, the situation is pretty clear, isn't it?''

''Make it clearer, General,'' Fowler said so quietly that CINC-SAC barely heard him.

''Sir, what if Dr. Elliot is right, what if they really expected you to be at the game? Along with Secretary Bunker, I mean. The way our command-and-control works, that would have severely crippled us. I'm not saying they would have attacked, but certainly they would have been in a position, while denying responsibility for the Denver explosion, to—well, to announce their change in government in such a way as to prevent us, by simple intimidation, from acting against them. That's bad enough. But they've missed their target, so to speak, haven't they? Okay, now what are they thinking? They may be thinking that you suspect that they've done this thing, and that you're angry enough to retaliate in one way or another. If they're thinking that, sir, they might also be thinking that their best way of protecting themselves is to disarm us quickly. Mr. President, I'm not saying that they are thinking that way, but that they might be.'' And a cold evening grew colder still.

''And how do we stop them from launching, General?'' Fowler asked.

''Sir, the only thing that will keep them from launching is the certainty that the strike will not work. That's particularly true if we're dealing with their military. They're good. They're smart. They're rational. They think before they act, like all good soldiers. If they know we're ready to shoot at the first hint of an attack, then that attack becomes militarily futile, and it will not be initiated.''

''That's good advice, Robert,'' Elliot said.

''What's NORAD think?'' Fowler asked. The President didn't think to consider that he was asking a two-star general to evaluate the opinion of a four-star.

''Mr. President, if we are to get some rationality back into this situation, that would appear to be the way to do it.''

''Very well. General Fremont, what do you propose?''

''Sir, at this point, we can advance our strategic-forces readiness to DEFCON-ONE. The code word for that is SNAPCOUNT. At that point we are at maximum readiness.''

''Won't that provoke them?''

''Mr. President, no, it should not. Two reasons. First, we are already at a high state of alert, they know it, and while they are clearly concerned, they have not objected in any way. That's the one sign of rationality we've seen to this point. Second, they won't know until we tell them that we've upped things a notch. We don't have to tell them until they do something provocative.''

Fowler sipped at his newest cup of coffee. He'd have to visit the bathroom soon, he realized.

''General, I'm going to hold off on that. Let me think that one over for a few minutes.''

''Very well, sir.'' Fremont's voice did not reveal any overt disappointment, but a thousand miles from Camp David, CINC-SAC turned to look at his Deputy Chief of Staff (Operations).

''What is it?'' Parsons asked. There was nothing more for him to do at the moment. Having made his urgent phone call, and having decided to let his fellow

NEST team members handle the lab work, he'd decided to assist the doctors. He'd brought instruments to evaluate the radiation exposure to the firefighters and handful of survivors, something in which the average physician has little expertise. The situation was not especially cheerful. Of the seven people who had survived the explosion at the stadium, five already showed signs of extreme radiation sickness. Parsons evaluated their exposures at anywhere from four hundred to over a thousand Rems. Six hundred was the maximum exposure normally compatible with survival, though with heroic treatment higher exposures had been survived. If one called living another year or two with three or four varieties of cancer breaking out in one's body "survival." The last one, fortunately, seemed to have the least. He was still cold, though his hands and face were badly burned, but he hadn't vomited yet. He was also quite deaf.

It was a young man, Parsons saw. The clothing in the bag next to his bed included a handgun and a badge—a cop. He also held something in his hand, and when the boy looked up, he saw the FBI agent standing next to the NEST leader.

Officer Pete Dawkins was deep in shock, nearly insensate. His shaking came both from being cold and wet and from the aftermath of more terror than any man had ever faced and survived. His mind had divided itself into three or four separate areas, all of which were operating along different paths and at different speeds, and none of them were particularly sane or coherent. What held part of one such area together was training. While Parsons ran some sort of instrument over the clothing he'd worn only a short time before, Dawkins' damaged eyes saw standing next to him another man in a blue plastic windbreaker. On the sleeves and over the chest were printed "FBI." The young officer sprang upwards, disconnecting himself from the IV line. That caused both a doctor and a nurse to push him back down, but Dawkins fought them with the strength of madness, holding out his hand to the agent.

Special Agent Bill Clinton was also badly shaken. Only the vagaries of scheduling had saved his life. He, too, had had a ticket for the game, but he'd had to give it to another member of his squad. From that misfortune, which had enraged the young agent only four days earlier, his life had been spared. What he'd seen at the stadium had stunned him. His exposure to radiation—only forty Rems, according to Parsons—terrified him, but Clinton, too, was a cop, and he took the paper from Dawkins' hand.

It was, he saw, a list of cars. One was circled and had a question-mark scribbled next to the license plate.

"What's this mean?" Clinton asked, leaning past a nurse who was trying to restart Dawkins' IV line.

"Van," the man gasped, not hearing, but knowing the question. "Got in . . . asked Sarge to check it out, but—south side, by the TV trucks. ABC van, little one, two guys, I let them in. Not on my list."

"South side, does that mean anything?" Clinton asked Parsons.

"That's where it was." Parsons leaned down. "What did they look like, the two men?" He gestured at the paper, and then pointed at himself and Clinton.

"White, both thirties, ordinary . . . said they came from Omaha . . . with a tape machine. Thought it was funny they came from Omaha . . . told Sergeant Yankevich . . . went to check it out right before."

"Look," a doctor said, "this man is in very bad shape, and I have to—"

"Back off," Clinton said.

"Did you look in the truck?"

Dawkins only stared. Parsons grabbed a piece of paper and drew a truck on it, stabbing at the picture with his pencil.

Dawkins nodded, on the edge of consciousness. "Big box, three feet, 'Sony' printed on it—they said it was a tape deck. Truck from Omaha . . . but—" He pointed at the list.

Clinton looked. "Colorado tags!"

"I let it in," Dawkins said just before he collapsed.

"Three-foot box . . ." Parsons said quietly.

"Come on." Clinton ran out of the emergency room. The nearest phone was at the admitting desk. All four were being used. Clinton took one right out of the hand of an admitting clerk, hung up, and cleared the line.

"What are you doing!"

"Shut up!" the agent commanded. "I need Hoskins. . . . Walt, this is Clinton at the hospital. I need you to run a tag number. Colorado E-R-P-five-two-zero. Suspicious van at the stadium. Two men were driving it, white, thirties, ordinary-looking. The witness is a cop, but now he's passed out."

"Okay. Who's with you?"

"Parsons, the NEST guy."

"Get down here—no, stay put, but keep this line open." Hoskins put that line on hold, then dialed another from memory. It was for the Colorado Department of Motor Vehicles. "This is the FBI, I need a quick tag check. Your computer up?"

"Yes, sir," a female voice assured him.

"Edward Robert Paul Five Two Zero." Hoskins looked down at his desk. Why did that sound familiar?

"Very well." Hoskins heard the tapping. "Here we go, that's a brand-new van registered to Mr. Robert Friend of Roggen. You need the license number for Mr. Friend?"

"Christ," Hoskins said.

"Excuse me, sir?" He read off the number. "That's correct."

"Can you check two other license numbers?"

"Surely." He read them off. "First one's an incorrect number . . . so's the second—wait a minute, these numbers are just like—"

"I know. Thank you." Hoskins set the phone down. "Okay, Walt, think fast. . . ." First he needed more information from Clinton.

"Murray."

"Dan, this is Walt Hoskins. Something just came in you need to know."

"Shoot."

"Our friend Marvin Russell parked a van at the stadium. The NEST guy says that the place where he parked it is pretty close to where the bomb went off. There was at least one—no, wait a minute—okay. There was one other guy in there with him, and the other one must have been driving the rental car. Okay. Inside the van was a large box. The van was painted up like an ABC vehicle, but Russell was found dead a couple miles away. So he must have dropped off the van and left. Dan, this looks like how the bomb might have gotten there."

"What else do you have, Walt?"

"I have passport photos and other ID for two other people."

"Fax 'em."

"On the way." Hoskins left for the communications room. On the way he grabbed another agent. "Get the Denver homicide guys who're working the Russell case—wherever they are, get 'em on the phone real fast."

"Thinking terrorism again?" Pat O'Day asked. "I thought the bomb was too big for that."

"Russell was a suspected terrorist, and we think he might—shit!" Murray exclaimed.

"What's that, Dan?"

"Tell Records I want the photos from Athens that're in the Russell file." The Deputy Assistant Director waited for the call to be made. "We had an inquiry from the Greeks, one of their officers got murdered and they sent us some photos. I thought at the time it might be Marvin, but . . . there was somebody else in there, a car, I think. We had him in profile, I think. . . ."

"Fax coming in from Denver," a woman announced.

"Bring it over," Murray commanded.

"Here's page one." The rest arrived rapidly.

"Airline ticket . . . connecting ticket. Pat—"

O'Day took it. "I'll run it down."

"Shit, look at this!"

"Familiar face?"

"It looks like . . . Ismael Qati, maybe? I don't know the other one."

"Mustache and hair are wrong, Dan," O'Day said, turning away from his phone. "A little thin, too. Better call Records to see what they have current on the mutt. You don't want to jump too fast, man."

"Right." Murray lifted his phone.

"Good news, Mr. President," Borstein said from inside Cheyenne Mountain. "We have a KH-11 pass coming up through the Central Soviet Union. It's almost dawn there now, clear weather for a change, and we'll get a look at some missile fields. The bird's already programmed. NPIC is real-timing it into here and Offutt also."

"But not here," Fowler groused. Camp David had never been set up for that, a remarkable oversight, Fowler thought. It did go into Kneecap, which was where he should have gone when he'd had the chance. "Well, tell me what you see."

"Will do, sir, this ought to be very useful for us," Borstein promised.

"Coming up now, sir," a new voice said. "Sir, this is Major Costello, NORAD intel. We couldn't have timed this much better. The bird is going to sweep very close to four regiments, south to north, at Zhangiz Tobe, Alyesk, Uzhur, and Gladkaya, all but the last are SS-18 bases. Gladkaya is SS-11s, old birds. Sir, Alyesk is one of the places they're supposed to be deactivating but haven't yet. . . ."

The morning sky was clear at Alyesk. First light was beginning to brighten the northeastern horizon, but none of the soldiers of the Strategic Rocket Forces bothered to look. They were weeks behind schedule and their current orders were to correct that deficiency. That such orders were nearly impossible was beside the point. At each of the forty launch silos was a heavy articulated truck. The SS-18s—the Russians actually called them RS-20s, for Rocket, Strategic, Number 20—were old ones, more than eleven years, in fact, which was why the Soviets had agreed to eliminate them. Powered by liquid-fueled motors, the fuels and oxidizers in question were dangerous, corrosive chemicals—unsymmetrical dimethyl hydrazine and nitrogen tetroxide—and the fact that they were called ''storable'' liquids was a relative statement. They were more stable than cryogenic fuels insofar as they did not require refrigeration, but they were toxic to the point of nearly instant lethality to human contact, and they were necessarily highly reactive. One safeguard was the encapsulation of the missiles in steel capsules which were loaded like immense rifle cartridges into the silos, a Soviet design innovation that protected the delicate silo instrumentation from the chemicals. That the Soviets bothered with such systems at all was not—as American intelligence officers carped—to take advantage of their higher energy impulse, but rather a result of the fact that the Soviets had lagged in developing a reliable and powerful solid fuel for its missiles, a situation only recently remedied with the new SS-25. Though undeniably large and powerful, the SS-18—given the ominous NATO code name of SATAN—was an ill-tempered, pitiless bitch to maintain, and the crews were delighted to be rid of them. More than one Strategic Rocket Forces soldier had been killed in maintenance and training accidents, just as Americans had lost men with its counterpart U.S. missile, the Titan-II. All of the Aleysk birds were tagged for elimination, and that was the reason for the presence of the men and the transporter trucks. But first the warheads had to be removed. The Americans could watch the missiles in the destruction process, but the warheads were still the most secret of artifacts. Under the watchful eyes of a colonel, the nose shroud was removed from Rocket Number 31 by a small crane, exposing the MIRVs. Each of the conically shaped multiple independently targetable re-entry vehicles was about 40 centimeters in width at the bottom, tapering to a needle point 150 centimeters above its base. Each also represented about half a megaton of three-stage thermonuclear device. The soldiers treated the MIRVs with all the respect they so clearly deserved.

''Okay, getting some pictures now,'' Fowler heard Major Costello say. ''Not much activity . . . sir, we're isolating on just a few of the silos, the ones that we can see the best—there's woods all over there, Mr. President, but because of the angle of the satellite we know which ones we can see clearly . . . okay, there's one, Tobe Silo Zero-Five . . . nothing unusual . . . the command bunker is right there . . . I can see guards patrolling around . . . more than usual . . .I see five—seven people—we can get them real good in infrared, it's cold there, sir. Nothing else. Nothing else unusual, sir . . . good. Okay, coming up on Alyesk now—Jeez!''

''What is it?''

''Sir, we're looking at four silos on four different cameras. . . .''

''Those are service trucks,'' General Fremont said from the SAC command center. ''Service trucks at all four. Silo doors are open, Mr. President.''

''What does that mean?''

Costello took the question: ''Mr. President, these are all -18 Mod 2s, fairly old ones. They were supposed to be deactivated by now, but they haven't been. We now have five silos in sight, sir, and all five have service trucks there. I can see two with people standing around, doing something to the missiles.''

''What's a service truck?'' Liz Elliot asked.

''Those are the trucks they use to transport the missiles. They also have all the tools you use to work on them. There's one truck per bird—actually more than one. It's a big semi-truck, like a hook 'n' ladder truck, actually, with storage bins built in for all the tools and stuff—Jim, they look like they pulled the shroud—yeah!

There are the warheads, it's lit up, and they're doing something to the RVs . . . I wonder what?''

Fowler nearly exploded. It was like listening to a football game on the radio, and— ''What does all this mean!''

''Sir, we can't tell . . . coming up to Uzhur now. Not much activity, Uzhur has the new mark of the -18, the Mod 5 . . . no trucks, I can see sentries again. Mr. President, I would estimate that we have more than the usual number of sentries around. Gladkaya next . . . that'll take a couple of minutes. . . .''

''Why are the trucks there?'' Fowler asked.

''Sir, all I can say is that they appear to be working on the birds.''

''Goddamn it! Doing what!'' Fowler screamed into the speakerphone.

The reply was very different from the cool voice of a few minutes earlier. ''Sir, there's no way we can tell that.''

''Then tell me what you *do* know!''

''Mr. President, as I already said, these missiles are old ones, they're maintenance-intensive, and they were scheduled for destruction, but they're overdue for that. We observed increased site security at all three SS-18 regiments, but at Alyesk every bird we saw had a truck and a maintenance crew there, and the silos were all open. That's all we can tell from these pictures, sir.''

''Mr. President,'' General Borstein said, ''Major Costello has told you everything he can.''

''General, you told me that we'd get something useful from this. *What* did we get?''

''Sir, it may be significant that there's all that work going on at Alyesk.''

''But you don't know what the work is!''

''No, sir, we don't,'' Borstein admitted rather sheepishly.

''Could they be readying those missiles for launch?''

''Yes, sir, that is a possibility.''

''My God.''

''Robert,'' the National Security Advisor said, ''I am getting very frightened.''

''Elizabeth, we don't have time for this.'' Fowler collected himself. ''We must maintain control of ourselves, and control of the situation. We must. We must convince Narmonov—''

''Robert, don't you *see!* It's *not him!* That's the only thing that makes *sense*. We don't know who we're dealing with!''

''What can we do about it?''

''I don't know!''

''Well, whoever it is, they don't want a nuclear war. Nobody would. It's too crazy,'' the President assured her, sounding almost like a parent.

''Are you sure of that? Robert, are you really sure? They tried to kill *us!''*

''Even if that's true, we have to set it aside.''

''But we *can't*. If they were willing to try once, they will be willing to try again! Don't you see?''

Just a few feet behind him, Helen D'Agustino realized that she'd read Liz Elliot correctly the previous summer. She was as much a coward as a bully. And now whom did the President have to advise him? Fowler rose from his chair and headed for the bathroom. Pete Connor trailed along as far as the door, because even Presidents are not allowed to make that trip alone. ''Daga'' looked down on Dr. Elliot. Her face was—what? the Secret Service agent asked herself. It was beyond fear. Agent D'Agustino was every bit as frightened herself, but she didn't—that was unfair, wasn't it? Nobody was asking her for advice, nobody was asking her to make sense of this mess. Clearly, none of it made sense at all. It simply didn't. At least no one was asking her about it, but that wasn't her job. It was Liz Elliot's job.

"I got a contact here," one of the sonar operators said aboard Sea Devil One-Three. "Buoy three, bearing two-one-five . . . blade count now . . . single screw—nuclear submarine contact! Not American, screw's not American."

"Got him on four," another sonarman said. "This dude's hauling ass, blade count shows over twenty, maybe twenty-five knots, bearing my buoy is three-zero-zero."

"Okay," the Tacco said, "I have a posit. Can you give me drift?"

"Bearing now two-one-zero!" the first one responded. "This guy is moving!"

Two minutes later it was clear the contact was heading straight for USS *Maine*.

"Is this possible?" Jim Rosselli asked. The radio message had gone from Kodiak straight to the NMCC. The commander of the patrol squadron didn't know what to do and was screaming for instructions. The report came in the form of a RED ROCKET, copied off also to CINCPAC, who would also be requesting direction from above.

"What do you mean?" Barnes asked.

"He's heading straight for where *Maine* is. How the hell could he know where she is?"

"How'd we find out?"

"SLOT buoy, radio—oh, no, that asshole hasn't maneuvered clear?"

"Kick this to the President?" Colonel Barnes asked.

"I guess." Rosselli lifted the phone.

"This is the President."

"Sir, this is Captain Jim Rosselli at the National Military Command Center. We have a disabled submarine in the Gulf of Alaska, USS *Maine,* an Ohio-class missile boat. Sir, she has prop damage and cannot maneuver. There is a Soviet attack submarine heading straight toward her, about ten miles out. We have a P-3C Orion ASW aircraft that is now tracking the Russian. Sir, he requests instructions."

"I thought they can't track our missile submarines."

"Sir, nobody can, but in this case they must have DF—I mean used direction-finders to locate the sub when she radioed for help. *Maine* is a missile submarine, part of SIOP, and is under DEFCON-TWO Rules of Engagement. Therefore, so is the Orion that's riding shotgun for her. Sir, they want to know what to do."

"How important is *Maine?*" Fowler asked.

General Fremont took that. "Sir, that sub is part of the SIOP, a big part, over two hundred warheads, very accurate ones. If the Russians can take her out, they've hurt us badly."

"How badly?"

"Sir, it makes one hell of a hole in our war plan. *Maine* carries the D-5 missile, and they are tasked counterforce. They're supposed to attack missile fields and selected command-and-control assets. If something happens to her, it would take literally hours to patch up that hole in the plan."

"Captain Rosselli, you're Navy, right?"

"Yes, Mr. President—sir, I have to tell you that I was CO of *Maine*'s Gold Crew until a few months ago."

"How soon before we have to make a decision?"

"Sir, the Akula is inbound at twenty-five knots, currently about twenty thousand yards from our boat. Technically speaking, they're within torpedo range right now."

"What are my options?"

"You can order an attack or not order an attack," Rosselli replied.

"General Fremont?"

"Mr. President—no, Captain Rosselli?"

"Yes, General?"

"How sure are you that the Russians are boring straight in on our boat?"

"The signal is quite positive on that, sir."

"Mr. President, I think we have to protect our assets. The Russians won't be real pleased with an attack on one of their boats, but it's an attack boat, not a strategic asset. If they challenge us on this, we can explain it. What I want to know is why they ordered the boat in this way. They must know that it would alarm us."

"Captain Rosselli, you have my authorization for the aircraft to engage and destroy the submarine."

"Aye aye, sir." Rosselli lifted the other phone. "GRAY BEAR, this is MARBLEHEAD"—the current code name for the NMCC—"National Command Authority approves I repeat *approves* your request. Acknowledge."

"MARBLEHEAD, this is GRAY BEAR, we copy request to engage is approved."

"That's affirmative."

"Roger. Out."

The Orion turned in. Even the pilots were feeling the effects of the weather now. Technically it was still light, but the low ceiling and heavy seas made it seem that they were flying down an immense and bumpy corridor. That was the bad news. The good news was that their contact was acting dumb, running very fast, below the layer, and almost impossible to miss. The Tacco in back coached him in along the Akula's course. Sticking out the tail of the converted Lockheed Electra airliner was a sensitive device called a magnetic anomaly detector. It reported on variations in the earth's magnetic field, such as those caused by the metallic mass of a submarine.

"Madman madman madman, smoke away!" the system operator called. He pushed a button to release a smoke float. In front, the pilot immediately turned left to set up another run. This he did, then a third, turning left each time.

"Okay, how's this look back there?" the pilot asked.

"Solid contact, nuclear-powered sub, positive Russian. I say let's do it this time."

"Fair enough," the pilot observed.

"Jesus!" the copilot muttered.

"Open the doors."

"Coming open now. Safeties off, release is armed, weapon is hot."

"Okay, I have it set," the Tacco said. "Clear to drop."

It was too easy. The pilot lined up on the smoke floats, which were almost perfectly in a row. He passed over the first, then the second, then the third. . . .

"Dropping now-now-now! Torp away!" The pilot added power and climbed a few hundred feet.

The Mark 50 ASW torpedo dropped clear, retarded by a small parachute that automatically released when the fish hit the water. The new and very sophisticated weapon was powered by an almost noiseless propulsion instead of a propeller, and had been programmed to stay covert until it reached the target depth of five hundred feet.

It was just about time to slow down, Dubinin thought, another few thousand meters. His gamble, he felt, had been a good one. It seemed a wholly reasonable supposition that the American missile submarine would stay near the surface. If he'd guessed right, then by racing in just below the layer—he was running at one hundred ten meters—surface noise would keep the Americans from hearing him and he could conduct the remainder of the search more covertly. He was about to congratulate himself for a good tactical decision.

"Torpedo sonar on the starboard bow!" Lieutenant Rykov screamed from sonar.

"Rudder left! Ahead flank! Where is the torpedo?"

Rykov: "Depression angle fifteen! Below us!"

"Emergency surface! Full rise on the planes! New course three-zero-zero!" Dubinin dashed into sonar.

"What the hell?"

Rykov was pale. "I can't hear screws . . . just that damned sonar . . . looking away—no, it's in acquisition now!"

Dubinin turned: "Countermeasures—three—now!"

"Cans away!"

Admiral Lunin's countermeasures operators rapidly fired off three 15-centimeter cans of gas-generating material. These filled the water with bubbles, making a target for the torpedo, but one that didn't move. The Mark 50 had already sensed the submarine's presence and was turning in.

"Coming through one hundred meters," the *Starpom* called. "Speed twenty-eight knots."

"Level off at fifteen, but don't be afraid of broaching."

"Understood! Twenty-nine knots."

"Lost it, the curve in the towed array just ruined our reception." Rykov's hands went up in frustration.

"Then we must be patient," Dubinin said. It wasn't much of a joke, but the sonar crew loved him for it.

"The Orion just engaged the inbound, sir, just picked up an ultrasonic sonar, very faint, bearing two-four-zero. It's one of ours, it's a Mark 50, sir."

"That ought to take care of him," Ricks observed. "Thank God."

"Passing through fifty meters, leveling out, ten degrees on the planes. Speed thirty-one."

"Countermeasures didn't work . . . ," Rykov said. The towed array was straightening out, and the torpedo was still back there.

"No propeller noises?"

"None . . . I should be able to hear them even at this speed."

"Must be one of their new ones. . . ."

"The Mark 50? It's supposed to be a very clever little fish."

"We will see about that. Yevgeniy, remember the surface action?" Dubinin smiled.

The *Starpom* did a superb job of maintaining control, but the thirty-foot seas guaranteed that the submarine would broach—break the surface—as the waves and troughs swept overhead. The torpedo was a scant three hundred meters behind when the Akula leveled out. The American Mark 50 antisubmarine torpedo was not a smart weapon, but a "brilliant" one. It had identified and ignored the countermeasures Dubinin had ordered only minutes before and, using a powerful ultrasonic sonar, was now looking for the sub in order to conclude its mission. But here physical laws intervened in favor of the Russians. It is widely believed that sonar reflects off the metal hull of a ship, but this is not true. Rather, sonar reflects off the air inside a submarine, or more precisely off the border of water and air through which the sound energy cannot pass. The Mark 50 was programmed to identify these air-water boundaries as ships. As the torpedo rocketed after its prey, it began to see immense ship-shapes stretching as far as its sonar could reach. Those were waves. Though the weapon had been programmed to ignore a flat surface and thus avoid a problem called "surface capture," its designers had not addressed the problem of a heavy, rolling sea. The Mark 50 selected the nearest such shape, raced toward it—

—and sprang into clear air like a leaping salmon. It crashed into the back of the next wave, reacquired the same immense target shape—

—and leaped again. This time the torpedo hit at a slight angle. Dynamic forces caused it to turn and race north inside the body of a wave, sensing huge ships both left and right. It turned left, springing into the air yet again, but this time it hit the next wave hard enough to detonate its contact fuse.

"That was close!" Rykov said.

"No, not close, perhaps a thousand meters, but probably more." The Captain leaned into the control room. "Slow to five knots, down to thirty meters."

"We hit it?"

"I don't know, sir," the operator said. "He went shallow in a hurry, and the fish went charging up after him, circled around some—" The sonarman traced his finger on the display. "Then it exploded here, close to where the Akula disappeared into the surface noise. Can't say—no breakup noises, sir, I have to call it a miss."

"Bearing and distance to the target?" Dubinin asked.

"Roughly nine thousand meters, bearing zero-five-zero," the *Starpom* replied. "What is the plan now, Captain?"

"We will locate and destroy the target," said Captain First Rank Valentin Borissovich Dubinin.

"But—"

"We have been attacked. Those bastards tried to kill us!"

"That was an aerial weapon," the executive officer pointed out.

"I heard no airplane. We have been attacked. We will defend ourselves."

"Well?"

Inspector Pat O'Day was making furious notes. American Airlines, like all the major carriers, had its ticket information on computer. With a ticket number and flight numbers, he could track anyone down. "Okay," he told the woman on the other end. "Wait a minute." O'Day turned. "Dan, there were only six first-class tickets on that flight from Denver to Dallas–Fort Worth, the flight was nearly empty—but it hasn't taken off yet because of ice and snow in Dallas. We have the names for two other first-class passengers who changed to a Miami flight. Now, the Dallas connection was for Mexico City. The two who changed through Miami were also booked on a DC-10 out of Miami into Mexico City. That plane's off, one hour out of Mexico."

"Turn it around?"

"They say they can't because of fuel."

"One hour—Christ!" Murray swore.

O'Day ran a large hand over his face. As scared as everyone else in America—more so, since everyone in the command center had informed reason to be frightened—Inspector Patrick Sean O'Day was trying mightily to set everything aside and concentrate on whatever he had at hand. It was too slim and too circumstantial to be considered hard evidence as yet. He'd seen too many coincidences in his twenty years with the Bureau. He'd also seen major cases break on thinner stuff than this. You ran with what you had, and they had this.

"Dan, I—"

A messenger came in from the Records Division. She handed over two files to Murray. The Deputy Assistant Director opened the Russell file first, rummaging for the Athens photo. Next he took out the most recent photo of Ismael Qati. He set both next to the passport photos just faxed in from Denver.

"What do you think, Pat?"

"The passport one of this guy still looks thin for Mr. Qati . . . cheekbones and eyes are right, mustache isn't. He's losing hair, too, if this is him. . . ."

"Go with the eyes?"

"The eyes are right, Dan, the nose—yeah, it's him. Who's this other mutt?"

"No name, just these frames from Athens. Fair skin, dark hair, well-groomed. Haircut's right, hairline is right." He checked the descriptive data on the license and passport. "Height, little guy, build—it fits, Pat."

"I agree, I agree about eighty percent worth, man. Who's the Legal Attaché in Mexico City?"

"Bernie Montgomery—shit! He's in town to meet with Bill."

"Try Langley?"

"Yeah." Murray lifted his CIA line. "Where's Ryan?"

"Right here, Dan. What gives?"

"We have something. First, a guy named Marvin Russell, Sioux Indian, member of the Warrior Society, he dropped out of sight last year, somewhere in Europe, we thought. He turned up with his throat cut in Denver today. There were two people with him, they flew out. One, we have a picture but no name. The other may be Ismael Qati."

That bastard! "Where are they?"

"We think they're aboard an American Airlines flight from Miami to Mexico City, first-class tickets, about an hour out from the terminal."

"And you think there's a connection?"

"A vehicle registered to Marvin Russell, a/k/a Robert Friend of Roggen, Colorado, was on the stadium grounds. We have fake IDs from two people, probably Qati and the unknown subject, recovered from the murder scene. There's plenty enough to arrest on suspicion of murder."

Yeah, Jack thought. Had the situation not been so horrible, Ryan would have laughed at that. "Murder, eh? You going to try and make the arrest?"

"Unless you have a better idea."

Ryan was quiet for a moment. "Maybe I do. Hold on for a minute." He lifted another phone and dialed the United States Embassy in Mexico City. "This is Ryan calling for the Station Chief. Tony? Jack Ryan here. Is Clark still there? Good, put him on.''

''Jesus, Jack, what the hell is—'' Ryan cut him off.

''Shut up, John. I have something for you to do. We have two people coming in to the airport there on an American flight from Miami, due in about an hour. We'll fax you the photos in a few minutes. We think they might be involved in this.''

''So it's a terrorist gig?''

''Best thing we have, John. We want those two, and we want them fast.''

''Might be a problem from the local cops, Jack,'' Clark warned. ''I can't exactly have a shoot-out down here.''

''Is the Ambassador in?''

''I think so.''

''Transfer me over and stand by.''

''Right.''

''Ambassador's office,'' a female voice said.

''This is CIA Headquarters, and I need the Ambassador right now!''

''Surely.'' The secretary was a cool one, Ryan thought.

''Yeah, what is it?''

''Mr. Ambassador, this is Jack Ryan, Deputy Director of CIA—''

''This is an open phone line.''

''I know that! Shut up and listen. There are two people coming into Mexico City airport in an American Airlines flight from Miami. We need to pick them up and get them back here just as fast as we can.''

''Our people?''

''No, we think they're terrorists.''

''That means arresting them, clearing it through the local legal system and—''

''We don't have time for that!''

''Ryan, we can't strong-arm these people, they won't stand for it.''

''Mr. Ambassador, I want you to call the President of Mexico right now, and I want you to tell him that we need his cooperation—it's life-and-death, okay? If he doesn't agree immediately, I want you to tell him this, and I need you to write it down. Tell him that we know about his retirement plan. Okay? Use those exact words, *We know about his retirement plan.''*

''What does that mean?''

''It means that you say exactly that, do you understand?''

''Look, I don't like playing games and—''

''Mr. Ambassador, if you do not do exactly what I'm telling you, I will have one of my people render you unconscious and then have the DCM make the call.''

''You can't threaten me like that!''

''I just did, pal, and if you think I'm kidding, you just fucking try me!''

''Temper, Jack,'' Ben Goodley cautioned.

Ryan looked away from the phone. ''Sir, excuse me. It's very tense here, okay, we've had a nuclear device go off in Denver, and this may be the best lead we have. Look, there isn't time for niceties. Please. Play along with me. Please.''

''Very well.''

Ryan let out a breath. ''Okay. Tell him also that one of our people, a Mr. Clark, will be at the airport security office in a few minutes. Mr. Ambassador, I cannot emphasize enough how important this is. Please do it now.''

''I'll do it. You'd better calm down up there,'' the career foreign-service officer advised.

"We're trying very hard, sir. Please have your secretary transfer me back to the Station Chief. Thank you." Ryan looked over to Goodley. "Just hit me over the fucking head if you feel the need, Ben."

"Clark."

"We're faxing some photos down, along with their names and seat assignments. Okay, you are to check in with the airport security boss before you grab 'em. You still have the airplane down there?"

"Right."

"When you have 'em, get 'em aboard, and get 'em the hell up here."

"Okay, Jack. We're on it."

Ryan killed the line and picked up on Murray. "Fax the data you have to our Station Chief Mexico. I have two field officers on the scene, good ones, Clark and Chavez."

"Clark?" Murray asked as he handed the fax information to Pat O'Day. "The same one who—"

"That's the man."

"I wish him luck."

The tactical problem was complex. Dubinin had an antisubmarine aircraft overhead and could not afford to make a single mistake. Somewhere ahead was an American missile submarine that he fully intended to destroy. He had ordered it to protect himself, the Captain reasoned. He had been fired upon with a live weapon. That changed matters greatly. He really should radio fleet command for instructions, or at least to announce his intentions, but with an aircraft overhead that was suicide, and he'd brushed close enough to death for one day. The attack on *Admiral Lunin* could only mean that the Americans were planning an attack on his country. They'd violated their favorite international hobbyhorse—the seas were free for the passage of all. They'd attacked him in international waters before he was close enough to commit a hostile act. Someone, therefore, thought there was a state of war. Fine, Dubinin thought. So be it.

The submarine's towed-array sonar was drooping well below the level of the boat, and the sonar crewmen were now concentrating as they never had.

"Contact," Lieutenant Rykov called. "Sonar contact, bearing one-one-three, single screw . . . noisy, sounds like a damaged submarine. . . ."

"You're certain it's not a surface contact?"

"Positive . . . surface traffic is well south of this track because of the storms. The sound is definitely characteristic of a submarine power plant . . . noisy, as though from some damage . . . southerly drift . . . bearing one-one-five now."

Valentin Borissovich turned to shout into the control room: "Estimated distance to target's reported position?"

"Seven thousand meters!"

"Long, long shot . . . southerly drift . . . speed?"

"Difficult to tell . . . less than six knots, certainly . . . there's a blade-rate there, but it's faint and I can't read it."

"We may not get more than one shot," Dubinin whispered to himself. He went back to control. "Weapons! Set up a torpedo on a course of one-one-five, initial search depth seventy meters, activation point . . . four thousand meters."

"Very well." The Lieutenant made the proper adjustments to his board. "Set for tube one . . . weapon is hot, ready! Outer door is closed, Captain."

Dubinin turned to look at the executive officer. Ordinarily a very sober man—

he scarcely drank even at ceremonial dinners—the *Starpom* nodded approval. The Captain didn't need it, but was grateful for it even so.

"Open outer door."

"Outer door is open." The weapons officer flipped the plastic cover off the firing switch.

"Fire."

The Lieutenant stabbed the button home. "Weapon is free."

"Conn, sonar! Transient, transient, bearing one-seven-five—*torpedo in the water bearing one-nine-five!*"

"All ahead full!" Ricks shouted to the helm.

"Captain!" Claggett screamed. "Belay that order!"

"What?" The youngster at the helm was all of nineteen and had never heard a captain's order countermanded. "What do I do, sir?"

"Captain, if you goose the engines like that, we lose the shaft in about fifteen seconds!"

"Shit, you're right." Ricks was pink beneath the red battle lights in the control room. "Tell the engine room, best safe speed, helm, right ten degrees rudder, come north, new course zero-zero-zero."

"Right ten degrees rudder, aye." The boy's voice quavered as he turned the wheel. Fear is as contagious as plague. "Sir, my rudder is right ten degrees, coming to new course zero-zero-zero."

Ricks swallowed and nodded. "Very well."

"Conn, sonar, bearing to torpedo is now bearing one-nine-zero, torpedo going left to right, torpedo is not pinging at this time."

"Thank you," Claggett replied.

"Without our tail, we're going to lose track of it real quick."

"That's true, sir. Captain, how about we let the Orion know what's going on?"

"Good idea, run up the antenna."

"Sea Devil One-Three, this is *Maine*."

"*Maine*, this is One-Three, we are still evaluating that torpedo we dropped and—"

"One-Three, we have a torpedo in the water one-eight-zero. You missed the guy. Start another search pattern south of us. I think this bird is engaging our MOSS."

"Roger, on the way." The Tacco informed Kodiak that there was a for-real battle going on now.

"Mr. President," Ryan said, "we may have some useful information here, sir." Jack was sitting down in front of the speakerphone, his hands flat on the table and wet enough to leave marks on the Formica top, Goodley saw. For all that, he envied Ryan's ability to control himself.

"What might that be?" Fowler asked harshly.

Ryan's head dropped at the tone of the reply. "Sir, the FBI has just informed us that they have information on two, possibly three, confirmed terrorist suspects in Denver today. Two of them are believed to be on an airliner inbound to Mexico. I have people in the area, and we're going to try and pick them up, sir."

"Wait a minute," Fowler said. "We *know* that this wasn't a terrorist act."

"Ryan, this is General Fremont. How was this information developed?"

"I don't know all the details, but they have information on an automobile—a truck, I think, a van, that was at the site. They've checked the tag number and the owner—the owner turned up dead, and we ran the other two down by their airline tickets and—"

"Hold it!" CINC-SAC cut Ryan off. "How the *hell* can anyone know that—a survivor from the bomb site? For Christ's sake, man, this was a hundred-kiloton weapon—"

"Uh, General, the best number we have now—it came from the FBI—is fifty-KT, and—"

"The FBI?" Borstein said from NORAD. "What the hell do they know about this? Anyway, a fifty-kiloton weapon wouldn't leave any survivors for over a mile around. Mr. President, that cannot be good information."

"Mr. President, this is the NMCC," Ryan heard on the same line. "We just received a message from Kodiak. That Soviet submarine is attacking USS *Maine*. There is a torpedo in the water, *Maine* is attempting to evade."

Jack heard something, he wasn't sure what, over the speakerphone.

"Sir," Fremont said at once, "this is a very ominous development."

"I understand that, General," the President said just loudly enough to hear. "General–SNAPCOUNT."

"What the hell's that?" Goodley asked quietly.

"Mr. President, that is a mistake. We have a solid piece of information here. You wanted information from us and now we have it!" Ryan barked rapidly, almost losing it again. His hands went from flat to fists. Jack struggled with himself again, and regained control. "Sir, this is a real indicator."

"Ryan, it looks to me like you've been lying and misleading me all day," Fowler said in a voice that hardly sounded human at all. The line went dead for the last time.

The final alert signal was sent out simultaneously over dozens of circuits. The duplication of channels, their known function, the brevity of the message, and the identical encipherment pattern told the Soviets much, even before the receipted signal was input into their computers. When the single word came out, it was reprinted in the Kremlin command center only seconds later. Golovko took the dispatch off the machine.

"SNAPCOUNT," he said simply.

"What is that?" President Narmonov asked.

"A code word." Golovko's mouth went white for a moment. "It's a term from American football, I think. It means the set of numbers used before the—the quarterback takes the ball to begin a play."

"I don't understand," Narmonov said.

"Once the Americans had the code word COCKEDPISTOL to denote complete strategic readiness. The meaning is unambiguous to anyone, yes?" The KGB's Deputy Chairman went on as though in a dream: "This word, to an American, would mean much the same thing. I can only conclude that—"

"Yes."

42. Asp and Sword

PRESIDENT NARMONOV:

I SEND THIS TO YOU, OR YOUR SUCCESSOR, AS A WARNING.

WE HAVE JUST RECEIVED A REPORT THAT A SOVIET SUBMARINE IS EVEN NOW ATTACKING AN AMERICAN MISSILE SUBMARINE. AN ATTACK ON OUR STRATEGIC ASSETS WILL NOT BE TOLERATED, AND WILL BE INTERPRETED AS THE PRECURSOR TO AN ATTACK AGAINST THE UNITED STATES.

I MUST FURTHER ADVISE YOU THAT OUR STRATEGIC FORCES ARE AT THEIR MAXIMUM STATE OF READINESS. WE ARE PREPARED TO DEFEND OURSELVES.

IF YOU ARE SERIOUS IN YOUR PROTESTATIONS OF INNOCENCE, I URGE YOU TO CEASE ALL AGGRESSIVE ACTS WHILE THERE IS STILL TIME.

" 'Successor'? What the hell does *that* mean?" Narmonov turned away for a moment, then looked at Golovko. "What is happening here? Is Fowler ill? Is he mad? What goes on here? What's this submarine business?" When he finished talking, his mouth remained open like that of a hooked fish. The Soviet President was gulping his breaths now.

"We had a report of a disabled American missile submarine in the eastern Pacific, and sent a submarine to investigate, but that submarine has no authorization to attack," the Defense Minister said.

"Are there any circumstances under which our men might do this?"

"None. Without authorization from Moscow, they may act only in self-defense." The Defense Minister looked away, unable to bear the gaze of his President. He had no wish to speak again, but neither did he have a choice. "I no longer think this is a controllable situation."

"Mr. President." It was an Army warrant officer. He opened his briefcase—"the football"—and removed a ring binder. The first divider was bordered in red. Fowler flipped to it. The page read:

SIOP
MAJOR ATTACK OPTION
****SKYFALL****

"So, what the hell is SNAPCOUNT?" Goodley asked.

"That's as high as alerts go, Ben. That means the pistol is cocked and pointed, and you can feel the pressure on the trigger."

"How the hell did we—"

"Drop it, Ben! However the fuck we got here, we *are* here." Ryan stood and started walking around. "We better start thinking very fast, people."

The senior duty officer started: "We have to make Fowler understand—"

"He can't understand," Goodley said harshly. "He can't understand if he isn't listening."

"State and Defense are out—they're both dead," Ryan pointed out.

"Vice President—Kneecap."

"Very good, Ben . . . do we have a button for that . . . yes!" Ryan pushed it.

"Kneecap."

"This is CIA, DDCI Ryan speaking. I need to talk to the Vice President."

"Wait one, sir." It turned out to be a short "one."

"This is Roger Durling. Hello, Ryan."

"Hello, Mr. Vice President. We have a problem here," Jack announced.

"What went wrong? We've been copying the Hot Line messages. They were kinda tense but okay until about twenty minutes ago. What the hell went wrong?"

"Sir, the President is convinced that there has been a *coup d'état* in the Soviet Union."

"What? Whose fault is that?"

"Mine, sir," Ryan admitted. "I'm the jerk who delivered the information. Please set that aside. The President isn't listening to me."

Jack was amazed to hear a brief, bitter laugh. "Yeah, Bob doesn't listen to me very much either."

"Sir, we have to get to him. We now have information that this may have been a terrorist incident."

"What information is that?" Jack ran it down in about a minute. "That's thin," Durling observed.

"It may be thin, sir, but it's all we got, and it's a goddamned sight better than anything else we've got in."

"Okay, stop for a minute. Right now I want your evaluation of the situation."

"Sir, my best read is that the President is wrong, it *is* Andrey Il'ych Narmonov over there. It's approaching dawn in Moscow. President Narmonov is suffering from sleep deprivation, he's just as scared as we are—and from that last message he's wondering if President Fowler is crazy or not. That is a bad combination. We have reports of isolated contact between Soviet and American forces. Christ knows what really happened, but both sides are reading it as aggressive acts. What's really happening is simple chaos—forward-deployed forces bumping, but they're shooting because of alert levels on both sides. It's cascading on itself."

"Agreed, I agree with all of that. Go on."

"Somebody has to back down and do it very fast. Sir, you have to talk to the President. He won't even take my calls now. Talbot and Bunker are both dead, and there's nobody else he'll listen to."

"What about Arnie van Damm?"

"Fuck!" Ryan snarled. How had he forgotten Arnie? "Where is he?"

"I don't know. I can have the Secret Service find out real fast. What about Liz?"

"She's the one who came up with the brilliant idea that Narmonov isn't there."

"Bitch," Durling observed. He'd worked so hard and wasted so much political capital to get Charlie Alden into that job. "Okay, I'll try to get through to him. Stand by."

"Right."

"The Vice President is calling, sir. Line Six."

Fowler punched the button. "Make it fast, Roger."

"Bob, you need to get this thing back under control."

"What do you think I've been trying to do!"

Durling was sitting in a high-backed leather chair. He closed his eyes. The tone of the answer said it all. "Bob, you have made things worse instead of better. You have to step back from this for a moment. Take a deep breath, walk around the room—think! There is no reason to expect that the Russians did this. Now, I just talked to CIA, and they said—"

"Ryan, you mean?"

"Yes, he just filled me in and—"

"Ryan's been lying to me."

"Bullshit, Bob." Durling kept his voice level and reasonable. He called it his country-doctor voice. "He's too much of a pro for that."

"Roger, I know you mean well, but I don't have time for psychoanalysis. We have what may be a nuclear strike about to be launched on us. The good news, I suppose, is that you'll survive. I wish you luck, Roger. Wait—there's a Hot Line message coming in."

PRESIDENT FOWLER:

THIS IS ANDREY IL'YCH NARMONOV COMMUNICATING TO YOU.

THE SOVIET UNION HAS TAKEN NO AGGRESSIVE ACTS AGAINST THE UNITED STATES. NONE AT ALL. WE HAVE NO INTEREST IN HARMING YOUR COUNTRY. WE WISH TO BE LEFT ALONE AND TO LIVE IN PEACE.

I HAVE AUTHORIZED NO ACTION WHATEVER AGAINST ANY AMERICAN FORCES OR CITIZENS, YET YOU THREATEN US. IF YOU ATTACK US, WE MUST THEN ATTACK YOU ALSO, AND MILLIONS WILL DIE. WILL IT ALL BE AN ACCIDENT?

THE CHOICE IS YOURS. I CANNOT STOP YOU FROM ACTING IRRATIONALLY. I HOPE THAT YOU WILL REGAIN CONTROL OF YOURSELF. TOO MANY LIVES ARE AT RISK FOR EITHER OF US TO ACT IRRATIONALLY.

"At least we're still getting these," Goodley noted.

"Yeah, it just makes things so much better. It's going to set him off," Ryan announced. "This one's really going to do it. You can't tell an irrational person that he's losing it. . . ."

"Ryan, this is Durling." Ryan fairly leaped at the button.

"Yes, Mr. Vice President."

"He didn't—he didn't listen, and then this new one came in, and he reacted rather badly to it."

"Sir, can you open a channel to SAC?"

"No, I'm afraid not. They're on a conference call with NORAD and Camp David. Part of the problem, Jack, the President knows he's vulnerable there and he's afraid—well . . ."

"Yeah, everyone's afraid, aren't we?"

There was silence for a moment, and Ryan wondered if Durling felt guilty for being in a place of relative safety.

At Rocky Flats, the residue samples were loaded into a gamma-ray spectrometer. It had taken longer than expected, due to a minor equipment problem. The operators stood behind a shield and used lead-lined rubber gloves and yard-long tongs to move the samples out of the lead bucket, then waited for the technician to activate the machine.

"Okay—this is a hot one, all right."

The machine had two displays, one on a cathode-ray tube, with a backup paper printout. It measured the energy of the photoelectrons generated by the gamma radiation within the instrument. The precise energy state of these electrons identified both the element and the isotope of the source. These showed as lines or spikes on the graphic display. The relative intensity of the various energy lines—shown as the height of the spike—determined the proportions. A more precise measurement would require insertion of the sample in a small reactor for reactivation, but this system was good enough for the moment.

The technician flipped to the beta channel. ''Whoa, look at that tritium line! What did you say the yield on this thing was?''

''Under fifteen.''

''Well, it had a shitload of tritium, doc—look at that!'' The technician—he was a master's candidate—made a notation on his pad and switched back to the gamma channel. ''Okay . . . plutonium, we've got some 239, 240; neptunium, americium, gadolinium, curium, promethium, uranium—some U-235, some 238 . . . I—this was a sophisticated beast, guys.''

''Fizzle,'' one of the NESTers said, reading the numbers. ''We're looking at the remains of fizzle. This was not an IND. All that tritium. . . . Christ, this was supposed to be a two-stager, that's too much for a boosted fission weapon—it's a fucking H-Bomb!''

The technician adjusted his dials to fine-tune the display. ''Look at the 239/240 mix. . . .''

''Get the book!''

Sitting on the shelf opposite the spectrometer was a three-inch binder of red vinyl.

''Savannah River,'' the technician said. ''They've always had that gadolinium problem. . . . Hanford does it another way . . . they always seem to generate too much promethium.''

''Are you crazy?''

''Trust me,'' the technician said. ''My thesis is on contamination problems at the plutonium plants. Here's the numbers!'' He read them off.

A NESTer flipped to the index, then back to a page. ''It's close! Close! Say the gadolinium again!''

''Zero point zero five eight times ten to the minus 7, plus or minus point zero zero two.''

''Holy Mary Mother of God!'' The man turned the book around.

''Savannah River. . . . That's not possible.''

''Nineteen sixty-eight. It was a vintage year. It's our stuff. It's our fucking plutonium.''

The senior NESTer blinked his disbelief away. ''Okay, let me call D.C.''

''Can't,'' the technician said as he refined his readings. ''The long-distance lines are all down.''

''Where's Larry?''

''Aurora Presbyterian, working with the FBI guys. I put the number on a Post-it over the phone in the corner. I think he's working D.C. through them.''

''Murray.''

''Hoskins—I just heard from Rocky Flats. Dan, this sounds nuts: the NEST team says the weapon used American plutonium. I asked him to confirm it, and he did—said he asked the same thing. The plutonium came from the DOE plant at Savannah River, turned out in February 1968, K Reactor. They have chapter and verse, he says they can even tell you what part of K Reactor—sounds like bullshit to me, too, but he's the friggin' expert."

"Walt, how the hell am I going to get anybody to believe that?"

"Dan, that's what the man told me."

"I need to talk to him."

"The phone lines are down, remember? I can get him in here in a few minutes."

"Do that, and do it fast."

"Yeah, Dan?"

"Jack, the NEST team just reported into our Denver office. The material in the bomb was American."

"What?"

"Listen, Jack, we've all said that, okay? The NEST team got fallout samples and analyzed them, and they say the uranium—no, plutonium—came from Savannah River, 1968. I have the NEST team leader coming in to the Denver Field Division now. The long-distance lines are down, but I can patch through our system and you can talk to him directly."

Ryan looked at the Science and Technology officer. "Tell me what you think."

"Savannah River, they've had problems there, like a thousand-pound MUF."

"Muff?"

"M-U-F, acronym: material unaccounted for. Lost material."

"Terrorists," Ryan said positively.

"Starting to make sense," S&T agreed.

"Oh, God, and he won't listen to me now!" Well, there was still Durling.

"That's hard to believe," the Vice President said.

"Sir, it's hard data, checked by the NEST team at Rocky Flats, it's hard, scientific data. It may sound nuts, but it's objective fact." *I hope, oh God, I hope*. Durling could hear Ryan thinking it. "Sir, this was definitely not a Russian weapon—that's the important thing. We are *certain* it was not a Soviet weapon. Tell the President right now!"

"Will do." Durling nodded to the Air Force communications sergeant.

"Yes, Roger," the President said.

"Sir, we've just received some important information."

"What now?" The President sounded tired unto death.

"It came to me from CIA, but they got it from the FBI. The NEST team has identified the bomb material as definitely not Russian. They think the bomb material is American."

"That is crazy!" Borstein announced. "We do not have any missing weapons. We take damned good care of those things!"

"Roger, you got that from Ryan, didn't you?"

"Yes, Bob, I did."

Durling heard a long sigh over the line. "Thank you."

The Vice President's hand trembled as he lifted the other phone. "He didn't buy it."

"He's *got* to buy it, sir, it's *true!*"

"I'm out of ideas here. You were right, Jack, he's not listening to anyone now."

"New Hot Line message, sir."
PRESIDENT NARMONOV, Jack read:

> YOU ACCUSE ME OF IRRATIONALITY. WE HAVE TWO HUNDRED THOUSAND DEAD, AN ATTACK ON OUR FORCES IN BERLIN, AN ATTACK ON OUR NAVY BOTH IN THE MEDITERRANEAN AND THE PACIFIC. . . .

"He's close to doing it. Goddamn it! We've got the information he needs to stop this thing in its tracks and—"

"I'm out of ideas," Durling said over the speakerphone. "These damned messages over the Hot Line are making things worse instead of better, and—"

"That seems to be the key problem, doesn't it?" Ryan looked up. "Ben, you good driving in snow?"

"Yeah, but—"

"Come on!" Ryan raced out of the room. They caught an elevator to the first floor and Jack ran into the security room. "Keys to the car!"

"Here, sir!" A very frightened young man tossed them over. The CIA's security force kept its vehicles just off the VIP lot. The blue GMC Jimmy four-wheel-drive was unlocked.

"Where are we going?" Goodley asked as he got into the driver's-side door.

"Pentagon, River Entrance—and get us there fast."

"What was it?" The torpedo had circled something but not exploded, and finally run out of fuel.

"Not enough mass to set off the magnetic exploder—too small to hit directly . . . must have been a decoy," Dubinin said. "Where's that original intercept?" A sailor handed it over. " *'Propeller disabled by collision,'* Goddamn it! We were tracking a bad power plant, not a damaged screw." The Captain smashed his fist down on the chart table hard enough to draw blood. "Come north, go active!"

"Oh, shit, conn, sonar, we have an active low-frequency sonar bearing one-nine-zero."

"Warm up the weapons!"

"Sir, if we deploy the outboard we'll get another two or three knots," Claggett said.

"Too noisy!" Ricks snapped back.

"Sir, we're up in the surface noise. The high-freqs from the outboard motor won't matter much up here. His active sonar is low-freq, and that active stuff's liable to detect us whether we're noisy or not. What we need now is distance, sir, if he gets too close the Orion can't engage to support us."

"We have to take him out."

"Bad move, sir. We're on SNAPCOUNT status now, if we have to shoot, that takes priority. Putting a unit in the water will tell us just where to look. Captain, we need distance to keep out of his active sonar, and we can't risk a shot."

"*No!* Weapons officer, set it up!"

"Aye, sir."

"Communications, tell the Orion to get us some help!"

"Here's the last one, Colonel."

"Well, that was fast enough," the regimental commander said.

"The boys are getting lots of practice," the Major standing next to him observed as the tenth and final RV was lifted off the SS-18 at Alyesk. "Be careful there, Sergeant."

It was ice that did it. A few minutes earlier some snow had blown into the missile capsule. The shuffling of boots had crushed and melted it, but then the subzero temperatures had refrozen it into an invisible, paper-thin skim of ice. The sergeant was in the process of stepping back off the fold-down catwalk when he slipped, and his wrench went flying. It bounced off the railing, twirling like a baton for a moment. The sergeant grabbed for it but missed, and it went down.

"Run!" the Colonel screamed. The sergeant needed no encouragement. The corporal on the crane swung the warhead clear and himself jumped from the vehicle. They all knew to go upwind.

The wrench nearly made it all the way down, but it struck an interior fitting and went sideways, gouging the skin of the first stage in two places. The missile skin was also the missile tankage, and both the fuel and oxidizer were released. The two chemicals formed small clouds—only a few grams of each were leaking—but the chemicals were hypergolic. They ignited on contact. That happened two minutes after the wrench began its fall.

The explosion was a powerful one. It knocked the Colonel down, over two hundred meters from the silo. He instinctively rolled behind a thick pine tree as the crushing overpressure wave swept by. He looked a moment later to see the silo topped by a pillar of flame. His men had all made it—a miracle, he thought. His next thought reflected the humor that so often accompanies an escape from death: *Well, that's one less missile for the Americans to bother us about!*

The Defense Support Program Satellite already had its sensor focused on the Russian missile fields. The energy bloom was unmistakable. The signal was downlinked to Alice Springs in Australia, and from there back up to a USAF communications satellite, which relayed it to North America. It took just over half a second.

"Possible launch—possible launch at Alyesk!"

In that moment everything changed for Major General Joe Borstein. His eyes focused on the real-time display, and his first thought was that it had happened, despite everything, all the changes, all the progress, all the treaties, somehow it had happened, and he was watching it and he would be there to watch it all happen until the SS-18 with his name on it landed on Cheyenne Mountain. This wasn't dropping bombs on the Paul Doumer Bridge, or hassling fighters over Germany. This was the end of life.

Borstein's voice was the sound of sandpaper. "I only see one . . . where's the bird?"

"No bird no bird no bird," a female captain announced. "The bloom is too big, more like an explosion. No bird, no bird. This is not a launch, I repeat this is *not* a launch."

Borstein saw that his hands were shaking. They hadn't done that the time he'd been shot down, nor the time he'd crashed at Edwards, nor the times he'd driven airplanes through weather too foul for hailstones. He looked around at his people and saw in their faces the same thing he'd just felt in the pit of his stomach. Somehow it had been like watching a dreadfully scary movie to this point, but it was not a movie now. He lifted the phone to SAC and switched off the input to the Gold Phone line to Camp David.

"Pete, did you copy that?"

"I sure did, Joe."

"We, uh, we better settle this thing down, Pete. The President's losing it."

CINC-SAC paused for a beat before responding. "I almost lost it, but I just got it back."

"Yeah, I hear you, Pete."

"What the hell was that?"

Borstein flipped the switch back on. "Mr. President, that was an explosion, we think, in the Alyesk missile fields. We, uh, sure had a scare there for a moment, but there is no bird in the air—say again, Mr. President, there are no birds flying now. That was a definite false alarm."

"What does it mean?"

"Sir, I do not know that. Perhaps—they were servicing the missiles, sir, and maybe they had an accident. It's happened before—we had the same problem with the Titan-II."

"General Borstein is correct," CINC-SAC confirmed soberly. "That's why we got rid of the Titan-II . . . Mr. President?"

"Yes, General?"

"Sir, I recommend we try to cool things down some more, sir."

"And just how do we do that?" Fowler wanted to know. "What if that was related to their alert activity?"

The ride down the George Washington Parkway was uneventful. Though covered with snow, Goodley had maintained a steady forty miles per hour in four-wheel drive, and not lost control once, getting around abandoned cars like a race-car driver at Daytona. He pulled into the River/Mall Entrance to the Pentagon. The civilian guard there was backed up by a soldier now, whose M-16 rifle was undoubtedly loaded.

"CIA!" Goodley said.

"Wait." Ryan handed over his badge. "In the slot. I think it'll work here."

Goodley did as he was told. Ryan's high-level badge had the right electronic code for this security device. The gate went up, and the road barrier went down, clearing the way. The soldier nodded. If the pass worked, everything had to be okay, right?

"Right up to the first set of doors."

"Park it?"

"Leave it! You come in with me."

Security inside the River Entrance was also beefed up. Jack tried to pass through the metal detector, but was stopped by pocket change that he then threw on the floor in a rage. "NMCC?"

"Come with me, sir."

The entrance to the National Military Command Center was barred by a wall of bullet-resistant glass, behind which was a black female sergeant armed with a revolver.

"CIA—I have to get in." Ryan held his badge against the black pad, and again it worked.

"Who are you, sir?" a Navy petty officer asked.

"DDCI. You take me to whoever's running this."

"Follow me, sir. The man you want to see is Captain Rosselli."

"*Captain?* No flag officer?"

"General Wilkes got lost, sir. We don't know where the hell he is." The enlisted man turned through a door.

Ryan saw a Navy captain and an Air Force lieutenant colonel, a status board, and a gang of multiple-line phones. "You Rosselli?"

"That's right—and you?"

"Jack Ryan, DDCI."

"You picked a bad place to come to, pal," Colonel Barnes observed.

"Anything changed?"

"Well, we just had what looked like a missile launch in Russia—"

"Jesus!"

"No bird came up, maybe an explosion in the hole. You have anything we need to know?"

"I need a line into the FBI command center and I need to talk to both of you."

"That's crazy," Rosselli said two minutes later.

"Maybe so." Ryan lifted the line. "Dan, Jack here."

"Where the hell are you, Jack? I just called Langley."

"Pentagon. What do you have on the bomb?"

"Stand by, I have a patch through to Dr. Larry Parsons. He's the NEST boss. He's on now."

"Okay, this is Ryan, Deputy Director of CIA. Talk to me."

"The bomb was made of American plutonium. That's definite. They've rechecked the sample four times. Savannah River Plant, February 1968, K Reactor."

"You're sure?" Jack asked, wishing very hard that the answer would be affirmative.

"Positive. Crazy as it sounds, it was our stuff."

"What else?"

"Murray tells me you have had problems with the yield estimate. Okay, I've been there, okay? This was a small device, less than fifteen—that's *one-five* kiloton yield. There are survivors from the scene—not many, but I've seen them myself, okay? I'm not sure what screwed up the initial estimate, but I have *been* there and I'm telling you it was a little one. It also seems to have been a fizzle. We're trying to ascertain more about that now—but this is the important part, okay? The bomb material was definitely American in origin. One hundred percent sure."

Rosselli leaned over to make sure that this phone line was a secure one into FBI headquarters. "Wait a minute. Sir, this is Captain Jim Rosselli, U.S. Navy. I have a master's in nuclear physics. Just to make sure this is what I'm hearing, I want you to give me the 239/240 proportions, okay?"

"Wait a minute and I will. . . . Okay, 239 was nine eight point nine three; 240 is zero point four five. You want the trace elements also?"

"No, that'll do it. Thank you, sir." Rosselli looked up and spoke quietly. "Either he's telling the truth or he's one smart fuckin' liar."

"Captain, I'm glad you agree. I need you to do something."

"What's that?"

"I need to get on the Hot Line."

"I can't allow that."

"Captain, have you been keeping track of the messages?"

"No, Rocky, and I haven't had time. We've got three separate battles going on and—"

"Let's go look."

Ryan hadn't been in there before, which struck him as odd. The printed copies of the messages were being kept on a clipboard. There were six people in the room, and they all looked ashen.

"Christ, Ernie—" Rosselli observed.

"Anything lately?" Jack asked.

"Nothing since the President sent one out twenty minutes ago."

"It was going fine when I was here right after—oh, my God. . . ." Rosselli observed as he got to the bottom.

"The President has lost it," Jack said. "He refuses to take information from me and he refuses to listen to Vice President Durling. Now this is real simple, okay? I know President Narmonov. He knows me. With what the FBI just gave us, what you just heard, Captain, I think I might be able to accomplish something. If not—"

"Sir, that is not possible," Rosselli replied.

"Why?" Jack asked. Though his heart was racing, he forced himself to control his breathing. He had to be cool be cool be cool now.

"Sir, the whole point of this link is that the only two people on it are—"

"One of them, maybe both now, is not playing with a full deck. Captain, you can see where we are. I can't force you to do this. I'm asking you to think. You just used your head a moment ago. Use it again," Ryan said calmly.

"Sir, they'll lock us up for doing this," the Link supervisor said.

"You have to be alive to be locked up," Jack said. "We are at SNAPCOUNT right now. You people know how serious this is. Captain Rosselli, you are the senior officer present, and you make the call."

"I see everything you put on that machine before it's transmitted."

"Fair enough. Can I type it myself?"

"Yes. You type, and it's crossloaded and encrypted before it goes out."

A Marine sergeant made room for him. Jack sat down and lit a cigarette, ignoring the signs prohibiting the vice.

ANDREY IL'YCH, Ryan tapped in slowly, THIS IS JACK RYAN. DO YOU STILL MAKE YOUR OWN FIRES IN THE DACHA?

"Okay?"

Rosselli nodded to the NCO sitting next to Ryan. "Transmit."

"What is this?" the Defense Minister asked. Four men hovered over the terminal. A Soviet Army major translated.

"Something's wrong here," the communications officer said. "This is—"

"Send back, 'Do you remember who it was who bandaged your knee?' "

"What?"

"Send it!" Narmonov said.

They waited for two minutes.

YOUR BODYGUARD ANATOLIY ASSISTED ME, BUT MY TROUSERS WERE RUINED.

"It's Ryan."

"Make sure," Golovko said.

The translator looked at his screen. "It says, *'And our friend is doing well?'* "

Ryan typed: HE RECEIVED AN HONORABLE BURIAL AT CAMP DAVID.

"What the hell?" Rosselli asked.

"There's not twenty people in the world who know this. He's making sure it's really me," Jack said. His fingers were poised over the keys.

"That looks like bullshit."

"Okay, fine, it's bullshit, but does it *hurt* anything?" Ryan demanded.
"Send it."

"What the hell is this?" Fowler shouted. "Who's doing this—"

"Sir, we have an incoming from the President. He's ordering us to—"
"Ignore it," Jack said coldly.
"Goddamn it, I can't!"
"Captain, the President has lost control. If you allow him to shut me off, your family, my family, a whole lot of people are going to die. Captain, your oath is to the Constitution, not the President. Now you look over those messages again and tell me that I'm wrong!"
"From Moscow," the translator said. " *'Ryan, what is happening?'* "

PRESIDENT NARMONOV:
WE HAVE BEEN THE VICTIMS OF A TERRORIST ACT. THERE WAS MUCH CONFUSION HERE, BUT WE NOW HAVE POSITIVE EVIDENCE AS TO THE ORIGIN OF THE WEAPON.
WE ARE CERTAIN THAT THE WEAPON WAS NOT SOVIET. I REPEAT WE ARE CERTAIN THE WEAPON WAS NOT SOVIET.
WE ARE NOW ATTEMPTING TO APPREHEND THE TERRORISTS. WE MAY HAVE THEM WITHIN THE NEXT FEW MINUTES.

"Send back, 'Why has your President accused us of this?' "
There was another pause of two minutes.

PRESIDENT NARMONOV:
WE HAVE BEEN THE VICTIMS OF GREAT CONFUSION HERE. WE HAVE HAD SOME INTELLIGENCE REPORTS OF POLITICAL TURMOIL IN THE SOVIET UNION. THESE REPORTS WERE FALSE, BUT THEY CONFUSED US GREATLY. IN ADDITION, THE OTHER INCIDENTS HAVE HAD AN INCENDIARY EFFECT ON BOTH SIDES.

"That's true enough."

"Pete, you get people in there just as fast as you can and arrest this man!"
Connor couldn't say no to that despite the look he received from Helen D'Agustino. He called Secret Service headquarters and relayed the message.

"He asks, *'What you—what* do *you suggest?'* "

I ASK THAT YOU TRUST US AND ALLOW US TO TRUST YOU. WE BOTH MUST BACK AWAY FROM THIS. I SUGGEST THAT BOTH YOU AND WE REDUCE THE ALERT LEVELS OF STRATEGIC FORCES AND GIVE ORDERS TO ALL TROOPS TO EITHER HOLD IN PLACE OR WITHDRAW AWAY FROM ANY SOVIET OR AMERICAN UNIT IN CLOSE PROXIMITY, AND IF POSSIBLE THAT ALL SHOOTING BE STOPPED IMMEDIATELY.

"Well?" Ryan asked.
"Send it."

* * *

"Can it be a trick?" the Defense Minister asked. "Can it *not* be a trick?"

"Golovko?"

"I believe that it is Ryan, and I believe he is sincere—but can he persuade his President?"

President Narmonov walked away for a moment, thinking of history, thinking of Nikolay II. "If we stand our forces down . . . ?"

"Then they can strike us, and our ability to retaliate is cut in half!"

"Is half enough?" Narmonov asked, seeing the escape hatch, leaning toward it, praying for the opening to be real. "Is half enough to destroy them?"

"Well . . ." Defense nodded. "Certainly, we have more than double the amount we need to destroy them. We call it overkill."

"Sir, the Soviet reply reads: '*Ryan:*

" '*On my order, being sent out as you read this, Soviet strategic forces are standing down. We will maintain our defensive alert for the moment, but we will stand down our offensive forces to a lower alert level which is still higher than peacetime standards. If you match our move, I propose a phased mutual stand-down over the next five hours.*' "

Jack's head went down on the keyboard, actually placing some characters on the screen.

"Could I have a glass of water? My throat's a little dry."

"Mr. President?" Fremont said.

"Yes, General."

"Sir, however this happened, I think it's a good idea."

Part of Bob Fowler wanted to hurl his coffee cup into the wall, but he stopped himself. It didn't matter, did it? It did, but not that way.

"What do you recommend?"

"Sir, just to make sure, we wait until we see evidence of a stand-down. When we do, we can back off ourselves. For starters—right now—we can rescind SNAPCOUNT without any real degradation of our readiness."

"General Borstein?"

"Sir, I concur in that," said the voice from NORAD.

"General Fremont: Approved."

"Thank you, Mr. President. We'll get right on it." General Peter Fremont, United States Air Force, Commander-in-Chief Strategic Air Command, turned to his Deputy Chief of Staff (Operations). "Keep the alert going, posture the birds, but keep them on the ground. Let's get those missiles uncocked."

"Contact . . . bearing three-five-two . . . range seven thousand six hundred meters." They'd been waiting several minutes for that.

"Set it up. No wires, activation point four thousand meters out." Dubinin looked up. He didn't know why the aircraft overhead hadn't already executed another attack.

"Set!" the weapons officer called a moment later.

"Fire!" Dubinin ordered.

''Captain, message coming in on the ELF,'' the communications officer said over the squawk box.

''That's the message that announces the end of the world.'' The Captain sighed. ''Well, we fired our shots, didn't we?'' It would have been nice to think that their action would save lives, but he knew better. It would enable the Soviet forces to kill more Americans, which wasn't quite the same thing. Everything about nuclear weapons was evil, wasn't it?

''Go deep?''

Dubinin shook his head. ''No, they seem to have more trouble with the surface turbulence than I expected. We may actually be safer here. Come right to zero-nine-zero. Suspend pinging. Increase speed to ten knots.''

Another squawk: ''We have the message—five-letter group: 'Cease all hostilities'!''

''Antenna depth, quickly!''

The Mexican police proved to be extremely cooperative, and the literate Spanish of Clark and Chavez hadn't hurt very much. Four plainclothes detectives from the Federal Police waited with the CIA officers in the lounge while four more uniformed officers with light automatic weapons took unobtrusive positions nearby.

''We don't have enough people to do this properly,'' the senior *Federal* worried.

''Better to do it off the airplane,'' Clark said.

''*Muy bien, Señor*. You think they may be armed?''

''Actually, no, I don't. Guns can be dangerous when you're traveling.''

''Has this something to do with—Denver?''

Clark turned and nodded. ''We think so.''

''It will be interesting to see what such men look like.'' The detective meant the eyes, of course. He'd seen the photographs.

The DC-10 pulled up to the gate and cut power to its three engines. The jetway moved a few feet to mate with the forward door.

''They travel first class,'' John said unnecessarily.

''*Sí*. The airline says there are fifteen first-class passengers, and they've been told to hold the rest. You will see, Señor Clark, we know our business.''

''I have no doubt of that. Forgive me if I gave that impression, *Teniente*.''

''You are CIA, no?''

''I am not permitted to say.''

''Then of course you are. What will you do with them?''

''We will speak,'' Clark said simply.

The gate attendant opened the door to the jetway. Two Federal Police officers took their places left and right of the door, their jackets open. Clark prayed there would be no gunplay. The people started walking out, and the usual greetings were called from the waiting area.

''Bingo,'' Clark said quietly. The police lieutenant straightened his tie to signal the men at the door. They made it easy, the last two first-class passengers to come out. Qati looked sick and pale, Clark noticed. Maybe it had been a bad flight. He stepped over the rope barrier. Chavez did the same, smiling and calling to a passenger who looked at them in open puzzlement.

''Ernesto!'' John said, running up to him.

''I'm afraid I'm the wrong—''

Clark went right past the man from Miami.

Ghosn was slow to react, dulled by the flight from America, relaxed by the thought that they had escaped. By the time he started to move, he was tackled from behind. Another policeman placed a gun against the back of his head, and he was handcuffed before they hauled him to his feet.

''Well, I'll be a son of a bitch,'' Chavez said. ''You're the guy with the books! We've met before, sweetheart.''

''Qati,'' John said to the other one. They'd already been patted down. Neither was armed. ''I've wanted to meet you for years.''

Clark took out their tickets. The police would collect their luggage. The police moved them out very quickly. The business and tourist passengers would not know that anything untoward had happened until they were told by family members in a few minutes.

''Very smooth, Lieutenant,'' John said to the senior officer.

''As I said, we know our business.''

''Could you have your people phone the embassy and tell them that we got 'em both alive.''

''Of course.''

The eight men waited in a small room while the bags were collected. There could be evidence in them, and there wasn't that much of a hurry. The Mexican police lieutenant examined their faces closely, but saw nothing more or less human than what he'd seen in the faces of a hundred murderers. It was vaguely disappointing, even though he was a good-enough cop to know better. The luggage was searched, but aside from some prescription drugs—they were checked and determined not to be narcotics—there was nothing unusual. The police borrowed a courtesy van for the drive to the Gulfstream.

''I hope you have enjoyed your stay in Mexico,'' the lieutenant said in parting.

''What the hell is going on?'' the pilot asked. Though in civilian clothes, she was an Air Force major.

''Let me explain it like this,'' Clark said. ''You Air Scouts are going to drive the airplane to Andrews. Mr. Chavez and I are going to interview these two gentlemen in back. You will not look, not hear, not think about anything that's going on in back.''

''What—''

''That was a *thought,* Major. I do not want you to have any *thoughts* about this. Do I have to explain myself again?''

''No, sir.''

''Then let's get the hell out of here.''

The pilot and copilot went forward. The two communications technicians sat at their consoles and drew the curtain between themselves and the main cabin.

Clark turned to see his two guests exchanging looks. That was no good. He removed Qati's tie and wrapped it around his eyes. Chavez did the same to his charge. Next both were gagged, and Clark went forward to find some earplugs. Finally, they set both men in seats as far apart as the airplane's cabin allowed. John let the plane take off before he did anything else. The fact was that he despised torture, but he needed information now, and he was prepared to do anything to get it.

''Torpedo in the water!''

''Christ, he's dead aft of us!'' Ricks turned. ''Best possible speed, come left to two-seven-zero! XO, take the return shot!''

"Aye! Snapshot," Claggett said. "One-eight-zero, activation point three thousand, initial search depth two hundred."

"Ready!"

"Match and shoot!"

"Three fired, sir." It was a standard tactic. The torpedo fired on the reciprocal heading would at least force the other guy to cut the control wires to his weapon. Ricks was already in sonar.

"Missed the launch transient, sir, and didn't catch the fish very soon either. Surface noise. . . ."

"Take her deep?" Ricks asked Claggett.

"This surface noise may be our best friend."

"Okay, Dutch . . . you were right before, I should have dropped the outboard."

"ELF message sir—SNAPCOUNT is canceled, sir."

"Canceled?" Ricks asked incredulously.

"Canceled, yes, sir."

"Well, isn't that good news," Claggett said.

"Now what?" the Tacco asked himself. The message in his hand made no sense at all.

"Sir, we finally got the bastard."

"Run your track."

"Sir, he fired at *Maine*!"

"I know, but I can't engage."

"That's crazy, sir."

"Sure as hell is," the tactical officer agreed.

"Speed?"

"Six knots, sir—maneuvering says the shaft bearings are pretty bad, sir."

"If we try any more . . ." Ricks frowned.

Claggett nodded. ". . . the whole thing comes apart. I think it's about time for some countermeasures."

"Do it."

"Five-inch room, launch a spread." Claggett turned back. "We're not going fast enough to make a turn very useful."

"I figure it's about even money."

"Could be worse. Why the hell do you think they canceled SNAPCOUNT?" the XO asked, staring at the sonar scope.

"X, I guess the danger of war is over. . . . I haven't handled this well, have I?"

"Shit, skipper, who would have known?"

Ricks turned. "Thanks, X."

"The torpedo is now active, ping-and-listen mode, bearing one-six-zero."

"Torpedo, American Mark 48, bearing three-four-five, just went active!"

"Ahead full, maintain course," Dubinin ordered.

"Countermeasures?" the *Starpom* asked.

The Captain shook his head. "No, no—we're at the edge of its acquisition range . . . and that would just give it a reason to turn this way. The surface conditions will help. We're not supposed to have battles in heavy weather," Dubinin pointed out. "It's hard on the instruments."

"Captain, I have the satellite signal—it's an all-forces message, 'Disengage and withdraw from any hostile forces, take action only for self-defense.' "

"I'm going to be court-martialed," Valentin Borissovich Dubinin observed quietly.

"You did nothing wrong, you reacted correctly at every—"

"Thank you. I hope you will testify to that effect."

"Change in signal—change in aspect, torpedo just turned west away from us," Lieutenant Rykov said. "The first programmed turn must have been to the right."

"Thank God it wasn't to the left. I think we've survived. Now, if only our weapon can miss. . . ."

"Sir, it's continuing to close. The torpedo is probably in acquisition—continuous pinging now."

"Less than two thousand yards," Ricks said.

"Yeah," Claggett agreed.

"Try some more countermeasures—hell, go continuous on them." The tactical situation was getting worse. *Maine* was not moving quickly enough to make an evasive course worthwhile. The countermeasures filled the sea with bubbles, and while they might draw the Russian torpedo into a turn—their only real hope—the sad fact of the matter was that as the fish penetrated the bubbles it would find *Maine* with its sonar again. Perhaps a continuous set of such false targets would saturate the seeker. That was their best shot right now.

"Let's keep her near the surface," Ricks added. Claggett looked at him and nodded in understanding.

"Not working, sir . . . sir, I've lost the fish aft, in the baffles now."

"Surface the ship," Ricks called. "Emergency blow!"

"Surface capture?"

"And now I'm out of ideas, X."

"Come left, parallel to the seas?"

"Okay, you do it."

Claggett went into control. "Up 'scope!" He took a quick look and checked the submarine's course. "Come right to new course zero-five-five!"

USS *Maine* surfaced for the last time into thirty-five-foot seas and nearly total darkness. Her circular hull wallowed in the rolling waves, and she was slow to turn.

The countermeasures were a mistake. Though the Russian torpedo was pinging, it was mainly a wake-follower. Its seeker head tracked bubbles, and the string of countermeasures made for a perfect trail, which suddenly stopped. When *Maine* surfaced, the submarine left the bubble stream. Again the factors involved were technical. The surface turbulence confused the wake-following software and the torpedo began its programmed circular search pattern, just under the surface. On its third circuit it found an unusually hard echo amid the confusing shapes over its head. The torpedo turned to close, now activating its magnetic-influence fusing system. The Russian weapon was less sophisticated than the American Mark 50. It could not go higher than twenty meters of depth and so was not drawn up to the surface. The active magnetic field it generated was cast out like an invisible spider-web, and when that net was disturbed by the presence of a metallic mass—

The thousand-kilo warhead exploded fifty feet from *Maine*'s already crippled stern. The twenty-thousand-ton warship shook as though rammed.

An alarm sounded instantly: *"Flooding flooding flooding in the engine room!"*

Ricks lifted the phone. "How bad?"

"Get everybody off, sir!"

"Abandon ship! Break out the survival gear! Send out message: damaged and sinking, give our position!"

"Captain Rosselli! Flash traffic coming in."

Ryan looked up. He'd had his drink, followed by something colder and carbonated. Whatever the message was, the naval officer could handle it.

"You Mr. Ryan?" a man in a suit asked. Two more were behind him.

"Dr. Ryan, yeah."

"Secret Service, sir, the President ordered us to come here and arrest you."

Jack laughed at that. "What for?"

The agent looked instantly uncomfortable. "He didn't say, sir."

"I'm not a cop, but my dad was. I don't think you can arrest me without a charge. The law, you know? The Constitution. 'Preserve, protect, and defend.' "

The agent was in an instant quandary. He had orders from someone he had to obey, but he was too professional to violate the law. "Sir, the President said . . ."

"Well, tell you what. I'll just sit right here, and you can talk to the President on that phone and find out. I'm not going anywhere." Jack lit another cigarette and lifted another phone.

"Hello?"

"Hey, babe."

"Jack! What's going on?"

"It's okay. It got a little tense, but we have it under control now, Cath, I'm afraid I'm going to be stuck here for a while, but it's okay, Cathy, honest."

"Sure?"

"You worry about that new baby, not about anything else. That's an order."

"I'm late, Jack. Just a day, but—"

"Good." Ryan leaned back in his chair, closed his eyes, and smiled blissfully. "You want it to be a girl, eh?"

"Yes."

"Then I guess I do, too. Honey, I'm still busy here, but, honest, you can relax. Have to run. 'Bye." He replaced the phone. "Glad I remembered to do that."

"Sir, the President wants to talk to you." The senior agent handed the phone toward Ryan.

What makes you think I want to talk to him? Jack nearly asked. But that would have been unprofessional. He took the phone. "Ryan here, sir."

"Tell me what you know," Fowler said curtly.

"Mr. President, if you give me about fifteen minutes, I can do a better job. Dan Murray at FBI knows everything I do, and I have to make contact with two officers. Is that okay, sir?"

"Very well."

"Thank you, Mr. President." Ryan handed the phone back and placed a call to the CIA Operations Center. "This is Ryan. Did Clark make the pickup?"

"Sir, this is an unsecure line."

"I don't care—answer the question."

"Yes, sir, they're flying back now. We don't have a comm link to the aircraft. It's Air Force, sir."

"Who's the best guy to evaluate the explosion?"

"Wait." The Senior Duty Officer passed that along to the Science and Technology man. "He says Dr. Lowell at Lawrence-Livermore."

"Get him moving. The nearest air base is probably Travis. Get him something fast." Ryan hung that line up and turned to the senior Hot Line officer.

"There's a VC-20 just took off from Mexico City inbound for Andrews. I have two officers and two—two other people aboard. I need to establish a comm link to the aircraft. Get someone to set that up, please."

"Can't do it here, sir, but you can in the conference room on the other side."

Ryan stood. "Come with me?" he said to the Secret Service agents.

It could hardly have been more bitter, Qati thought, but a moment later he realized that this wasn't true. He had faced death for a year now, and death by any cause was still death. Had he escaped—but he had not escaped.

"Okay, let's talk."

"I do not understand," Qati said in Arabic.

"I have a little trouble with that accent," Clark replied, feeling very clever. "I learned the language from a Saudi. Please speak slowly."

Qati allowed himself to be shaken momentarily by the use of his native tongue. He decided to reply in English to show his own cleverness. "I will never tell you a thing."

"Sure you will."

Qati knew that he had to resist as long as he could. It would be worth the price.

43. The Revenge of Moedred

Dubinin had little choice in the matter. As soon as he was certain that the American torpedo was dead, he ran up his satellite antenna and broadcast his report. The American Orion dropped active sonobuoys all around him but did not attack, confirming his impression that he had committed a crime little different from murder. As soon as the signal was receipted, he turned about and headed for the direction of the explosion. A seaman could do nothing else.

> PRESIDENT FOWLER:
> I REGRET TO INFORM YOU THAT A SOVIET SUBMARINE, AFTER BEING ATTACKED, COUNTERATTACKED AN AMERICAN SUBMARINE, POSSIBLY DAMAGING IT. IT WOULD APPEAR THAT THIS HAPPENED SHORTLY BEFORE I BROADCAST MY DISENGAGEMENT ORDER. I OFFER NO EXCUSE FOR THIS MISTAKE. THE INCIDENT WILL BE INVESTIGATED, AND IF THE FACTS WARRANT, THE CAPTAIN OF OUR SUBMARINE WILL BE PUNISHED SEVERELY.

"Well?"

"Mr. President, I think we acknowledge, thank the man, and let this one slide, sir," Jack replied.

"I agree. Thank you." The line went dead again.

"That was my boat!" Rosselli snarled.

"Yeah," Ryan said. "Sorry to hear it. I've spent time aboard subs, with Bart Mancuso, as a matter of fact. Know him?"

"He's the squadron commander out at Bangor."

Ryan turned. "Oh? I didn't know. I'm sorry, Captain, but what else can we do?"

"I know," Rosselli said quietly. "With luck maybe they can get the crew off. . . ."

Jackson was nearly out of fuel and ready to turn back. *Theodore Roosevelt* had an Alpha Strike spotted and ready to take off when the new orders came in. The battle group immediately increased speed to open the distance between the American and Russian formations. It didn't seem to Jackson like running away. The Hawkeye called a warning that the Russian ships had turned west—perhaps into the wind to launch aircraft. But though four fighters were aloft, they orbited the battle group, which continued west. Their search radars were up, but their missile radars went down. That, he knew, was a hopeful sign.

And so, Robby told himself, *so ends my second war, if that's what it was. . . .* He brought his Tomcat around, with Sanchez on his wing. Four more F-14s would orbit here, just to keep an eye on things for the next few hours.

Jackson trapped just in time to see a rescue helicopter landing forward. By the time he dismounted the aircraft, three people were in the ship's hospital. He headed down to see who they were and what had been going on. A few minutes later he knew that he wouldn't be painting any more victory flags on his aircraft. Not for something like this.

Berlin settled down much more quickly than anyone imagined. The relief column of the 11th Armored Cavalry Regiment had gone only thirty kilometers when the halt order arrived, and it pulled off the autobahn to wait. Inside Berlin itself, the American brigade got the word first, and pulled back into the western portion of the kazerne. Russians probed forward with dismounted infantry to see what was happening, but without orders to renew the attack, they remained tensely in place. Soon the area was flooded with police cars, much to the bemusement of the soldiers. Twenty minutes after the Americans began moving, communications were reestablished with Moscow, and the Russians pulled farther back into their defensive positions. A number of unexplained bodies were found, including the regimental commander and his executive officer, plus three tank crews, all of whom had been killed with small-arms fire. But the most important discovery was made by a Berlin policeman, who was first to examine the truck and staff car ripped apart by 25mm cannon slugs from a Bradley. The "Russians" were all dead, but none had identity disks. The policeman immediately called for assistance, which was dispatched at once. Two of the faces looked familiar to the cop, though he couldn't remember why.

"Jack."

"Hi, Arnie, grab a seat."

"What happened, Jack?"

Ryan shook his head. His mental state was one of giddiness. His reason told him that sixty thousand people had died, but despite that, the relief at having stopped something a hundred times worse had left him in a slightly drunken condition. "Not really sure yet, Arnie. You know the important part."

"The President sounds like hell."

A grunt. "You ought to have heard him a couple hours ago. He lost it, Arnie."

"That bad?"

Jack nodded. "That bad." A pause. "Maybe anybody would have, maybe you just can't expect a guy to deal with this, but—but that's his job, man."

"You know, he once told me that he was most grateful for Reagan and the others because of the changes, the fact that something like this wasn't really possible anymore."

"Listen, man, as long as those goddamned things exist, it's possible."

"You advocating disarmament?" van Damm asked.

Ryan looked up again. The giddiness was gone now. "I got the stars out of my eyes a long time ago. What I'm saying is, if it's possible, you damned well think about it. He didn't. He didn't even look at the war games we ran. He was just so sure it would never happen. Well, it did, didn't it?"

"How did Liz do?"

"Don't ask. The Boss needed good advice, and he didn't get any from her."

"And you?"

"He didn't listen to me, and that's partly my fault, I guess."

"Hey, it's over."

Jack nodded again. "Yeah."

"Ryan, call for you."

Jack took the phone. "Ryan here. Yeah, okay. Go slower." He listened for several minutes, making notes. "Thanks, John."

"What was that?"

"A confession. Is the helicopter ready?"

"At the pad. On the other side," one of the Secret Service men said.

The helicopter was a VH-60. Ryan climbed aboard and strapped in, along with van Damm and three agents. The chopper lifted off at once. The sky was clearing. The wind was still lively, but there were stars to be seen in the west.

"Where's the Vice President?" van Damm asked.

"Kneecap," an agent replied. "He stays up six more hours till we're sure this is over."

Jack didn't even hear. He had his ear-protectors in, and took the chance to lean back and stare into space. The helicopter even had a bar, he saw. What a nice way to travel.

"They wanted to start a nuclear war?" Chavez asked.

"That's what they said." Clark washed his hands. It wasn't that bad. He'd broken only four of Qati's fingers. It was the way you worked the broken bones that really mattered. Ghosn—they now knew his name—had taken a little more, but both stories were almost identical.

"I heard it, too, man, but—"

"Yeah. Ambitious fuckers, weren't they?" Clark put some ice cubes into a bag and walked back to rest it on Qati's hand. He had his information now, and he was not a sadist. The sensible thing, he thought, was to toss their asses out of the airplane here and now, but that wasn't his job either. Both terrorists were manacled to their seats. Clark took a chair in the back so that he could keep an eye on both. Their luggage was there also. He decided to rummage through it now that he had the time.

* * *

"Hello, Ryan," the President said from his chair. "Hi, Arnie."

"Bad day, Bob," van Damm offered.

"Very." The man had aged. It seemed a cliché, but it was true. His skin was sallow, the eyes sitting at the bottom of dark-rimmed wells. Though he was normally a carefully groomed man, Fowler's hair was askew. "Ryan, you have them?"

"Yes, sir, two of our field officers grabbed them in Mexico City. Their names are Ismael Qati and Ibrahim Ghosn. You know who Qati is. We've been after that guy for a long time. He had a piece of the Beirut bombing, two aircraft incidents, lots of other things, mainly to do with Israel. Ghosn is one of his people, evidently an engineer by profession. They were somehow able to fabricate the weapon."

"Whose sponsorship?" the President asked.

"We—our man, that is—had to sweat that out of them. Sir, that's a technical violation—"

Fowler's eyes flared into life. "I forgive them! Get on with it."

"Sir, they say the, uh, operation was bankrolled and supported by the Ayatolla Mahmoud Haji Daryaei."

"Iran." Not a question, a statement. Fowler's eyes became more animated.

"Correct. As you know, Iran isn't exactly pleased with how our actions in the Gulf worked out, and—sir, according to our people, this is what they said:

"It was a two-part plan. Part one was the bomb in Denver. Part two was an incident in Berlin. They had another guy working with them, Günther Bock, former Red Army Faction guy, his wife was arrested by the Germans last year and she later hanged herself. The objective, Mr. President, was to drive us and the Russians into a nuclear exchange—or at the least to so screw up our relations that the situation in the Gulf would revert to chaos. That would serve Iranian interests—or so Daryaei supposedly thinks."

"How did they get the weapon?"

"They say it's Israeli—was Israeli," Ryan corrected himself. "Evidently it got lost in 1973. We have to check that with the Israelis, but it makes sense. The plutonium came from Savannah River, and it's probably part of the big MUF they had some years back. We've long suspected that the first generation of Israeli nukes was fabricated from material obtained over here."

Fowler stood. "You're telling me that this fucking *mullah* did this—and killing a hundred thousand Americans wasn't *enough? He wanted to start a nuclear war, too!*"

"That is the information, sir."

"Where is he?"

"As a matter of fact, Mr. President, we know quite a lot about him. He has supported several terrorist groups, as you know. He was the loudest Islamic voice against the Vatican Treaty, but he lost a lot of prestige when it started working, and that did not improve his disposition very much. Daryaei lives in Qum in Iran. His political faction is losing some of its power, and there's already been an attempt on his life."

"Is their story plausible?"

"Yes, Mr. President, it is."

"You think Daryaei capable of such a thing?"

"On the record, sir, I would have to say that he is. Yes."

"He lives in Qum?"

"Correct. It's a city with a religious history, very important to the Shi'a branch of Islam. I don't know the exact population, certainly more than a hundred thousand."

"Where in Qum does he live?"

"That's the problem. He moves around a lot. He was nearly killed last year, and he learned from that. Never sleeps in the same place twice, so we hear. He stays in the same part of the city, but I can't give you a location better than plus or minus a mile or so."

"He did this?"

"So it would seem, Mr. President. That's our best data."

"But you can't localize him better than a mile."

"Yes, sir."

Fowler contemplated that for a few seconds before speaking, but when he did, Ryan's blood turned to ice.

"That's close enough."

PRESIDENT NARMONOV:
WE HAVE APPREHENDED THE TERRORISTS AND DETERMINED THE EXTENT OF THE OPERATION. . . .

"Is this possible?"

"Yes, I would say so," Golovko replied. "Daryaei is a fanatic. He loathes the Americans."

"Those *barbarians* tried to bait us into—"

"Let them handle it," Golovko advised. "It is they who suffered the worst losses."

"You know what he will wish to do?"

"Yes, Comrade President, as do you."

PRESIDENT FOWLER:
PENDING EXAMINATION OF THE EVIDENCE I WILL ACCEPT YOUR LAST COMMUNICATION AS FACT. WE WASH OUR HANDS OF THIS. WHATEVER ACTION YOU FEEL IS NECESSARY, WE WILL NOT OBJECT NOW OR IN THE FUTURE. THESE MADMEN WERE WILLING TO DESTROY US BOTH. TO HELL WITH THEM.

"Christ, Andruska," Ryan murmured. *That's a clear statement!* The President read the message off the screen without a word.

Ryan had been under the impression that Narmonov had kept control of his emotions, but now the reverse seemed to be true. Fowler sat rock-steady in his chair, surveying the room with calm eyes.

"The world will learn a lesson from this," Fowler said. "I'll make sure that nobody ever does this again."

Another phone line went off. "Mr. President, FBI, sir."

"Yes?"

"Mr. President, this is Murray, we've just had a flash from the *Bundeskriminalamt*—that's the German Federal Criminal Police—that they've found the body of one Günther Bock in eastern Berlin, dressed in the uniform of a Russian army colonel. There were nine others similarly dressed, one of whom is believed to be a former colonel in the Stasi. The data we got from Qati and the other one is confirmed on that side, sir."

"Murray, I want an opinion. Are you confident in the confessions?"

"Sir, generally speaking, when we bag these guys they sing like canaries. It's not the Mafia, there's no law of *omertà*."

"Thank you, Mr. Murray." Fowler looked up at Ryan. "Well?"

"Sounds like we got good stuff from them."

"So we agree for once." Fowler punched his SAC button. "General Fremont?"

"Yes, Mr. President?"

"How quickly can you re-target a missile. I want to attack a city in Iran."

"What?"

"I'll let Deputy Director Ryan explain."

"Those sons of bitches." Fremont spoke for everyone in the room.

"Yes, General, and I intend to get the man who did this, and get him in a way that will send a message that nobody will ever forget. The leader of Iran has committed an act of war against the United States of America. I intend to reply exactly in proportion to his act. I want a missile targeted on Qum. How long will that take?"

"Ten minutes at least, sir, let me, uh, check with my operations people." CINC-SAC flipped off his microphone switch. "Christ."

"Pete," the Deputy Chief of Staff (Operations) said, "the man is right. That fucker almost killed us all—us and the Russians! For *profit,* for political *profit!*"

"I don't like it."

"You have to re-target the bird. I suggest a Minuteman-III out of Minot. The three RVs'll flatten the place. I'll need ten minutes."

Fremont nodded.

"Mr. President, you can wait."

"No, I'm not going to wait. Ryan, you know what they did, you know why they did it. It was an act of war—"

"An act of terrorism, sir."

"State-sponsored terrorism is war—your own position paper from six years ago said that!"

Jack had not known that Fowler'd read it, and being hoist on his own petard came as a surprise. "Well, yes, sir, I did say that, but—"

"That *holy man* tried to kill—*did* kill thousands of Americans, and tried to trick us and the Russians into killing two *hundred million* more! He almost succeeded."

"Yes, sir, that is also true, but—" Fowler cut him off with a raised hand and continued to speak in the placid voice of a man whose decision had been made.

"It was an act of war. I will reply in kind. That's decided. I'm the President. I'm the Commander-in-Chief. I am the one who evaluates and acts upon the safety and security of the United States. I decide what the military of this country does. This man slaughtered thousands of our citizens, and used a nuclear weapon to do it. I have decided that I will reply in kind. Under the Constitution, that is my right, and my duty."

"Mr. President," van Damm spoke. "The American people—"

Fowler's anger appeared, but only briefly. *"The American people will* demand *that I act!* But that's not the only reason. I must act. I must reply to this—just to make sure it never happens again!"

"Please think it through, sir."

"Arnold, I have."

Ryan looked over at Pete Connors and Helen D'Agustino. Both concealed their feelings with marvelous skill. The rest of the room approved of Fowler's purpose, and Jack already knew that he was not the one to reason with the man. He looked at the clock and wondered what would come next.

"Mr. President, this is General Fremont."

"I'm here, General."

"Sir, we have re-targeted a Minuteman-III missile in North Dakota for the target specified. I—sir, have you thought this through?"

"General, I am your Commander-in-Chief. Is the missile readied for launch?"

"Sir, the launch sequence will take about a minute from the time you give the order."

"The order is given."

"Sir, it's not that simple. I need an ID check. You've been briefed on the procedure, sir."

Fowler reached for his wallet and removed a plastic card, much like a credit card. On it were ten different eight-number groups. Only Fowler knew which one he was supposed to read.

"Three-Three-Six-Zero-Four-Two-Zero-Nine."

"Sir, I confirm your identification code. Next, Mr. President, the order must be confirmed."

"What?"

"Sir, the two-man rule applies. In the event of an overt attack, I can be the second man, but since that is not the case, someone on my list must confirm the order."

"I have my Chief of Staff right here."

"Sir, negative on that, the rule is that to be on the list you must be an elected official or one approved by Congress—the Senate, that is—like a cabinet secretary."

"I'm on the list," Jack said.

"Is that Dr. Ryan, DDCI?"

"Correct, General."

"Deputy Director Ryan, this is CINC-SAC," Fremont said in a voice that oddly mimicked the robotic one used to issue SAC orders. "Sir, I have received a nuclear-launch order. I need you to confirm that order, but first I also need to verify your identity, sir. Could you please read your identification code?"

Jack reached for his own ID card and read off his code group. Ryan could hear Fremont or one of his people flipping through the pages of a book.

"Sir, I confirm your identification as Dr. John Patrick Ryan, Deputy Director of Central Intelligence."

Jack looked at Fowler. If he didn't do it, the President would just get someone else. It really was that simple, wasn't it? And was Fowler wrong—was he really wrong?

"It's my responsibility, Jack," Fowler said, standing at Ryan's side, resting his hand on Jack's shoulder. "You're just confirming it."

"Dr. Ryan, CINC-SAC here, I repeat, sir, I have a nuclear-launch order from the President, and I require confirmation, sir."

Ryan looked at his President, then leaned down to the microphone. He struggled for the breath to speak. "CINC-SAC, this is John Patrick Ryan. I am DDCI." Jack paused, then went on quickly:

"Sir, I do *not* confirm this order. I repeat, General, this is *not* a valid launch order. Acknowledge at once!"

"Sir, I copy negative approval of the order."

"That is correct," Jack said, his voice growing stronger. "General, it is my duty to inform you that in my opinion the President is not, I repeat *not* in command of his faculties. I urge you to consider that if another launch order is attempted." Jack rested his hands on the desk, took a deep breath, and snapped back erect.

Fowler was slow to react, but when he did, he pressed his face against Jack's. "Ryan, I order you—"

Jack's emotions exploded one last time: "To do what? To kill a hundred thousand people—and why?"

"What they tried to do—"

"What you damned near *let* them do!" Ryan jabbed a finger into the President's chest. "You're the one who fucked up! You're the one who took us to the edge—and now the real reason you're willing to slaughter a whole city is because you're mad, because your pride is hurt, and you want to get even. You want to show them that nobody can push *you* around! *That's the reason, isn't it? ISN'T IT?"* Fowler went white. Ryan lowered his voice. "You need a better reason than that to kill people. I know. I've had to do that. I *have* killed people. You want this man killed, we can do it, but I'm not going to help you kill a hundred thousand others just to take out the one man you want."

Ryan stepped back. He dropped his ID card on the desk and walked from the room.

"Jesus!" Chuck Timmons observed. They'd heard the entire exchange over the hot mike. Everyone in SAC headquarters had.

"Yeah," Fremont said. "Thank Him. But first deactivate that missile!" The Commander-in-Chief Strategic Air Command had to think for a moment. He couldn't remember if Congress was in session or not, but that was beside the point. He ordered his communications officer to place a call to the chairmen and ranking minority members of the Senate and House armed-services committees. When all four were on line, they'd stage a conference call with the Vice President, who was still aboard Kneecap.

"Jack?" Ryan turned.

"Yeah, Arnie?"

"Why?"

"That's why they have a two-man rule. There are a hundred thousand people in that city—probably more, I can't recall how big it is." Jack looked into the cold clear sky. "Not on my conscience. If we need Daryaei dead, there are other ways." Ryan blew smoke into the wind. "And that fucker'll be just as dead."

"I think you were right. I want you to know that."

Jack turned. "Thank you, sir." A long pause. "Where's Liz, by the way?"

"Back in the cabin, under sedation. She didn't cut the mustard, did she?"

"Arnie, today nobody did. Mainly we were lucky. You can tell the President that I'm resigning effective—oh, Friday, I guess. Good a day as any. Someone else'll have to decide on the replacement."

The President's Chief of Staff was quiet for a moment, then brought things back to the main issue. "You know what you've just started here, don't you?"

"Constitutional crisis, Arnie?" Jack flipped the butt into the snow. "Not my first, Arnie, not my first. I need to ride that chopper back to Andrews."

"I'll take care of it."

* * *

They'd just crossed into U.S. territory when a thought struck John Clark. Qati's bags had those medications. One was Prednisone, and another was Compazine. Prednisone was a steroid . . . often used to mitigate the adverse effects of—he got up from his seat and looked at Qati. Though still blindfolded, the man was different from the most recent photos he'd seen of the man, thinner, his hair was—the man had cancer, Clark thought. What did that mean? He got on the radio and called that information ahead.

The Gulfstream was a few minutes later getting in. Ryan was awakened on the couch in the VIP lounge on the south side of the Andrews complex. Murray was next to him, still awake. Three FBI vehicles were there. Clark, Chavez, Qati, and Ghosn were loaded into them, and the convoy of four-wheel-drives headed into D.C.

''What are we going to do with them?'' Murray asked.

''I have an idea, but we need to do something first.''

''What, exactly?''

''You have an interrogation room at the Hoover Building?''

''No, Buzzard's Point, the Washington Field Office,'' Murray said. ''Did your guy Mirandize them?''

''Yeah, I told him he had to do that, right before he started cutting their balls off.'' Ryan turned as he heard a loud noise. Kneecap was landing on the same Runway Zero-One it had left ten or so hours before. They must have shut down the strategic systems quicker than expected, Jack thought.

The *Admiral Lunin* surfaced amid the flares and smoke floats dropped by the P-3. It was much too far for a rescue aircraft to come out, at least in this weather. The seas hadn't moderated, and the light was bad, but Dubinin's was the only ship in the area, and he did the best he could to start rescue operations.

The interrogation room was ten by ten, with a cheap table and five equally cheap chairs. There was no two-way mirror. That trick had been around far too long. Instead, two fiber-optic cables ran out of the room and into cameras, one from a light switch, and the other from what looked like a nail hole in the doorframe.

Both terrorists were set in place, looking somewhat the worse for wear. The broken fingers both sported offended the professional ethic of the FBI, but Murray decided to pass on that. Clark and Chavez went off for coffee.

''As you see,'' Ryan told them, ''you failed. Washington is still here.''

''And Denver?'' Ghosn asked. ''I know about Denver.''

''Yes, you did manage to do something there, but the guilty parties have already paid.''

''What do you mean?'' Qati asked.

''I mean that Qum isn't there anymore. Your friend Daryaei is now explaining his misdeeds to Allah.''

They were just too tired, Ryan thought. Fatigue was the worst enemy of men, even worse than the dull pain in his hand. Qati didn't show horror at all. His next error was worse.

''You have made an enemy of all Islam. All that you have done to make peace in the region will be *as nothing!* because of this.''

"Was that your objective?" Ryan asked in considerable surprise, drawing on the two hours of sleep he'd had. "Was *that* what you wanted to do? Oh, my God!"

"Your god?" Qati spat.

"What of Marvin Russell?" Murray asked.

"We killed him. He was merely an infidel," Qati said.

Murray looked at Ghosn. "This is true? Wasn't he a guest in your camp?"

"He was with us for some months, yes. The fool's help was indispensable."

"And you murdered him."

"Yes, along with two hundred thousand others."

"Tell me," Jack said, "isn't there a line in the Koran that goes something like, 'If a man shall enter your tent and eat your salt, even though he be an infidel, you will protect him'?"

"You quote poorly—and what do you care of the Koran?"

"You might be surprised."

44. The Breeze of Evening

Ryan's next call was to Arnie van Damm. He explained what he had learned.

"My God! They were willing to—"

"Yeah, and it almost worked," Ryan said huskily. "Clever, weren't they?"

"I'll tell him."

"I have to report this, Arnie. I have to tell the Vice President."

"I understand."

"One more thing."

"What's that?"

The request he made was approved largely because no one had a better idea. After the two terrorists had had their hands treated, they were bedded down separately in FBI holding cells.

"What do you think, Dan?"

"It's—Christ, Jack, where are the words for something like this?"

"The man's got cancer," Clark said. "He figures that if he has to die—why not a bunch of others? Dedicated son of a bitch, isn't he?"

"What are you going to do?" Murray asked.

"We don't have a federal death-penalty statute, do we?"

"No, neither does Colorado, as a matter of fact." Murray took a moment to understand where Ryan was heading. "Oh."

Golovko had considerable trouble tracking Ryan down with his phone call. The report on his desk from Dr. Moiseyev, sitting there amid all the other things, had dumbfounded him, but on learning Jack's plans, it was easy to set the rendezvous.

Perhaps the only good news of the week was the rescue. The *Admiral Lunin* pulled into Kodiak harbor at dawn. Alongside the pier, she off-loaded her guests. Of the *Maine*'s crew of one hundred fifty-seven, perhaps a hundred had gotten off before the submarine was claimed by the sea. Dubinin and his crew had rescued eighty-one of them, and recovered eleven bodies, one of which was Captain Harry Ricks. Professionals regarded it as an incredible feat of seamanship, though the news media failed to cover the story until the Soviet submarine had put back to sea. Among the first to call home was Ensign Ken Shaw.

Joining them on the trip out of Andrews was Dr. Woodrow Lowell of the Lawrence-Livermore Laboratory, a bearded, bearish man, known to his friends as Red because of his hair. He'd spent six hours in Denver reviewing the damage patterns.

''I have a question,'' Jack said to him. ''How was it the yield estimates were so far off? That almost made us think the Russians did it.''

''It was a parking lot,'' Lowell replied. ''It was made of macadam, a mixture of gravel and asphalt. The energy from the bomb liberated various complex hydrocarbons from the upper layer of the pavement and ignited it—like a great big fuel-air explosive bomb. The water vapor there—from the snow that flashed away—caused another reaction that released more energy. What resulted was a flame-front double the diameter of the nuclear fireball. Add to that the fact that snow cover reflected a lot of the energy, and you got a huge augmentation of the apparent energy released. It would have fooled anybody. Then afterwards, the pavement had another effect. It radiated residual heat very rapidly. The short version is, the energy signature was much larger than the actual yield justified. Now, you want the real bad news?'' Lowell asked.

''Okay.''

''The bomb was a fizzle.''

''What do you mean?''

''I mean it should have been much larger, and we don't know why. The bomb residue was lousy with tritium. The design yield was at least ten times what it actually delivered.''

''You mean?''

''Yeah, if this thing had worked . . .''

''We *were* lucky, weren't we?''

''If you want to call that luck, yeah.''

Somehow Jack slept for most of the flight.

The aircraft landed the next morning at Beersheba. Israeli military personnel met the aircraft and convoyed everyone to Jerusalem. The press had found out some of what was happening, but not enough to be a bother, not on a secure Israeli Air Force base. That would come later. Prince Ali bin Sheik was waiting outside the VIP building.

''Your Highness.'' Jack nodded to him. ''Thank you for coming.''

''How could I not?'' Ali handed over a newspaper.

Jack scanned the headline. ''I didn't think that would stay secret very long.''

''It's true, then?''

''Yes, sir.''

''And you stopped it?''

''Stopped it?'' Ryan shrugged. ''I just wouldn't—it was a lie, Ali. I was lucky I guessed—no, that's not true. I didn't know that until later. It's just that I couldn't put my name to it, that's all. Your Highness, that's not important now. There are some things I have to do. Sir, will you help us?''

"With anything, my friend."

"Ivan Emmettovich!" Golovko called. And to Ali, "Your Royal Highness."

"Sergey Nikolay'ch. Avi." The Russian walked up with Avi Ben Jakob at his side.

"Jack," John Clark said. "You guys want to get to a better spot? One mortar round sure would waste a lot of top spooks, y'know?"

"Come with me," Avi said, then led them inside. Golovko briefed them on what he had.

"The man is still alive?" Ben Jakob asked.

"Suffering all the pains of hell, but yes, for another few days."

"I cannot go to Damascus," Avi said.

"You never told us you lost a nuke," Ryan said.

"What do you mean?"

"You know what I mean. The press doesn't have that yet, but they will in another day or two. Avi, you never told us there was something lost out there! Do you know what that might have meant to us?" Ryan asked.

"We assumed that it had broken up. We tried to search for it, but—"

"Geology," Dr. Lowell said. "The Golan Heights are volcanic, lots of basaltic rock, makes for a high background count, and that means it's hard to track in on a hot spot—but you still should have told us. We have some tricks at Livermore we might have used, stuff not too many people know about."

"I am sorry, but it is done," General Ben Jakob said. "You fly to Damascus, then?"

They used Prince Ali's plane for that, a personal Boeing 727 whose flight crew, Jack learned, was exclusively composed of former drivers from the President's Wing. It was nice to travel first class. The mission was covert, and the Syrians cooperated. Representatives from the U.S., Soviet, and Saudi embassies attended a brief meeting at the Syrian Foreign Ministry, and then they went off to the hospital.

He'd been a powerful man, Jack could see, but he was wasting away like dead, rotting meat. Despite the oxygen line under his nose, his skin was almost blue. All his visitors had to wear protective gear, and Ryan was careful to keep back. Ali handled the interrogation.

"You know why I am here?"

The man nodded.

"As you hope to see Allah, you will tell me what you know."

The armored column of the 10th Armored Cavalry Regiment ran from the Negev to the border of Lebanon. Overhead was a full squadron of F-16s, and another of Tomcats from the USS *Theodore Roosevelt*. The Syrian Army was also deployed in force, though its air force was staying out of the way. The Middle East had taken its lesson on American air power. The display of force was massive and unequivocal. The word was out: nobody would get in the way. The vehicles drove deep into the small, abused country, finally onto a valley road. The spot had been marked on the map by a dying man anxious to save what remained of his soul, and only an hour's work was needed to determine the exact location. Army engineers found the entrance and checked for booby-traps, then waved the others in.

"God Almighty," Dr. Lowell said, swinging a powerful light around the darkened room. More engineers swept the room, checking for wires on the machines, and carefully checking every drawer of every table and desk before the rest were allowed farther than the door. Then Lowell went to work. There was a set of plans that he took outside to read in the light.

"You know," he said after fifteen minutes of total silence, "I never really appreciated how easy this was. We've had this illusion that you really needed to—" He stopped. "Illusion, that's the right word."

"What are you telling me?"

"It was supposed to be a five-hundred-kiloton device."

"If it had gone off right, we would have known it had to be the Russians," Jack said. "No one could have stopped it. We wouldn't be here now."

"Yeah, I think we have to adjust our threat estimate some."

"Doc, we think we found something," an Army officer said. Dr. Lowell went inside, then returned to don protective clothing.

"So large as that?" Golovko asked, staring at the plans.

"Clever people. Do you know how hard it was for me to persuade the President that—excuse me. I didn't, did I? If this had been a big one, I would have believed the report."

"And what report is that?" Golovko asked.

"Can we conduct a little business?"

"If you wish."

"You're holding someone we want," Jack said.

"Lyalin?"

"Yes."

"He betrayed his country. He will suffer for it."

"Sergey, first, he gave us nothing that we could use against you. That was his deal. We only got the take from THISTLE, his Japanese network. Second, except for him and what he gave us, we might not be here now. Turn him loose."

"In return for what?"

"We have an agent who told us that Narmonov was being blackmailed by your military, and that your military was using some missing tactical nuclear weapons to make it stick. That's why we suspected that the weapon might have been yours."

"But that's a lie!"

"He was very convincing," Ryan replied. "I almost believed it myself. The President and Dr. Elliot did believe it, and that's why things got so bad on us. I'll gladly hang this bastard out to dry, but it's betraying a confidence . . . remember our conversation in my office, Sergey? If you want that name, you have to pay."

"That man we will shoot," Golovko promised.

"No, you can't."

"What do you mean?"

"We've cut him off, and all I said was that he lied to us. If he gave us stuff that wasn't true, even in your country it does not constitute espionage, does it? Better not to kill him. You'll understand, if we can make this deal."

The First Deputy Chairman considered that for a moment. "You can have Lyalin—three days. You have my word, Jack."

"Our man has the codename of SPINNAKER. Oleg Kirilovich—"

"Kadishev? *Kadishev!*"

"You think you're disappointed? You ought to see it from my side."

"This is the truth—no games now, Ryan?"

"On that, sir, you have my word of honor. I wouldn't mind seeing him shot, but he's a politician, and in this case he really didn't commit espionage, did he? Do something creative with him. Make him dogcatcher somewhere,'' Jack suggested.

Golovko nodded. ''It will be done.''

''A pleasure doing business with you, Sergey. A shame about Lyalin.''

''What do you mean?'' Golovko asked.

''The stuff he was giving us—both of us—it's really too valuable to lose. . . .''

''We do not do business to that degree, Ryan, but I admire your sense of humor.''

Dr. Lowell emerged from the structure just then, carrying a lead bucket.

''What's in there?''

''I think it's some plutonium. Want to take a closer look? You could end up like our friend in Damascus.'' Lowell handed the bucket to a soldier, and to the engineer commander he said, ''Move everything out, box it, ship it. I want to examine everything. Make sure you move everything out.''

''Yes, sir,'' the Colonel said. ''And the sample?''

Four hours later they were in Dimona, the Israeli nuclear ''research'' facility, where there was another gamma-ray spectrometer. While technicians ran the test, Lowell went over the plans again, shaking his head. To Ryan the drawings looked like the diagram of a computer chip or something similarly incomprehensible.

''It's big, clunky. Ours are less than a quarter this size . . . but you know how long it took us to build something of this size and yield?'' Lowell looked up. ''Ten years. They did it in a cave in five months. How's that for progress, Dr. Ryan?''

''I didn't know. We always figured a terrorists' device—but what went wrong?''

''Probably something with the tritium. We had two fizzles back in the fifties, helium contamination. Not too many people know about that. That's my best guess. The design needs some further looking at—we'll computer-model it—but on gross examination, it looks like a fairly competent—oh, thank you.'' Lowell took the spectrometry printout from the Israeli technician. He shook his head and spoke very softly:

''Savannah River, K Reactor, 1968—it was a *very* good year.''

''This is the one? You're sure?''

''Yeah, this is the one. The Israelis told me the type of weapon they lost, the mass of plutonium—except for the scraps, it's all here.'' Lowell tapped the design sheets. ''That's it, that's all of it,'' he said.

''Until the next time,'' Lowell added.

Always a student of the law and its administration, Deputy Assistant Director Daniel E. Murray observed the proceedings with interest. Rather odd that they used priests instead of lawyers, of course, but damn if it didn't work. The trial took just a day. It was scrupulously fair and admirably swift. The sentence didn't bother Murray, either.

They flew to Riyadh aboard Prince Ali's aircraft, leaving the USAF transport at Beersheba. There would be no indecent haste in the administration of sentence. There had to be time for prayer and reconciliation, and no one wanted to treat this any differently from a more pedestrian case. It also gave time for people to sit and reflect, and in Ryan's case to meet with another surprise. Prince Ali brought him in to Ryan's accommodations.

''I am Mahmoud Haji Daryaei,'' the man said unnecessarily. Jack knew his face well enough from the CIA file. He also knew that the last time Daryaei had spoken with an American, the ruler of Iran had been Mohammed Reza Pahlavi.

"What can I do for you?" Ryan asked. Ali handled the translation for both of them.

"Is it true? What I have been told, I wish to know that it is true."

"Yes, sir, it is true."

"Why should I believe you?" The man was approaching seventy years of age, with a deeply lined face and black, angry eyes.

"Then why did you ask the question?"

"Insolence does not please me."

"Attacks against American citizens do not please me," Ryan answered.

"I had nothing to do with this, you know that."

"I do now, yes. Will you answer a question? If they had asked for your help, would you have given it?"

"No," Daryaei said.

"Why should I believe that?"

"To slaughter so many people, even unbelievers, is a crime before God."

"Besides," Ryan added, "you know how we would react to such a thing."

"You accuse me of the ability to do such a thing?"

"You accuse us of such things regularly. But in this case you were mistaken."

"You hate me."

"I have no love for you," Jack admitted readily. "You are the enemy of my country. You have supported those who kill my fellow citizens. You have taken pleasure in the deaths of people whom you have never met."

"And yet you refused to allow your President to kill me."

"That is incorrect. I refused to allow my President to destroy the city."

"Why?"

"If you truly think yourself a man of God, how can you ask such a question?"

"You are an unbeliever!"

"Wrong. I believe, just as you do, but in a different way. Are we so different? Prince Ali doesn't think so. Does peace between us frighten you so much as that? Or do you fear gratitude more than hate? In any case, you asked why, and I will answer. I was asked to assist in the deaths of innocent people. I could not live with that on my conscience. It was as simple as that. Even the deaths of those I should perhaps consider unbelievers. Is that so hard for you to understand?"

Prince Ali said something that he didn't bother to translate, perhaps a quote from the Koran. It sounded stylized and poetic. Whatever it was, Daryaei nodded and spoke one last time to Ryan.

"I will consider this. Goodbye."

Durling settled into the chair for the first time. Arnold van Damm sat across the room.

"You handled matters well."

"Was there anything else we could have done?"

"I suppose not. It's today, then?"

"Right."

"Ryan's handling it?" Durling asked, looking through the summary sheets.

"Yes, it seemed the best thing to do."

"I want to see him when he gets back."

"Didn't you know? He resigned. As of today, he's out," van Damm said.

"The hell you say!"

"He's out," Arnie reiterated.

Durling shook his finger at the man. "Before you leave, you tell him that I want him in my office."

"Yes, Mr. President."

The executions were at noon on Saturday, six days after the bomb exploded. The people gathered, Ghosn and Qati were led out into the market square. They were given time to pray. It was a first for Jack, being a spectator at something like this. Murray just stood, his face set. Clark and Chavez, along with a gaggle of security personnel, were mainly watching the crowd.

"It just seems so inconsequential," Ryan said as the event got under way.

"It is not! The world will learn from this," Prince Ali said solemnly. "Many will learn. This is justice happening. That is the lesson."

"Some lesson." Ryan turned to look at his companions atop the building. He'd had time to reflect, and all he saw was—what? Ryan didn't know. He'd done his job, but what had it all meant? "The deaths of sixty thousand people who never should have died put an end to wars that need never have been? Is that how history is made, Ali?"

"All men die, Jack. *Insh-Allah,* never again in numbers so great. You stopped it, you prevented something worse. What you did, my friend . . . the blessings of God go with you."

"I would have confirmed the launch order," Avi said, his voice uncomfortable in its frankness. "And then? I would have blown my brains out, perhaps? Who can say? Of this I am certain: I would not have had the courage to say no."

"Nor I," Golovko said.

Ryan said nothing as he looked back down at the square. He'd missed the first one, but that was all right.

Even though Qati knew it was coming, it didn't matter. As with so many things in life, it was all controlled by reflex. A soldier prodded his side with a sword, barely enough to break the skin. Instantly, Qati's back arched, his neck extended itself in an involuntary flinch. The Captain of the Saudi Special Forces already had his sword moving. He must have practiced, Jack realized a moment later, because the head was removed with a single stroke as deceptively powerful as a ballet master's. Qati's head landed a meter or so away, and then the body flopped down, blood spraying from the severed vessels. He could see the arms and legs tightening against the restraints, but that, too, was mere reflex. The blood pumped out in a steady rhythm as Qati's heart continued to work, striving to preserve a life already departed. Finally that, too, stopped, and all that was left of Qati were separated parts and a dark stain on the ground. The Saudi Captain wiped the sword clean on what looked like a bolt of silk, replaced it in the golden scabbard, and walked into a path the crowd made for him.

The crowd did not exult. In fact, there was no noise at all. Perhaps a collective intake of breath, a few murmured prayers from the more devout among those present; for whose souls the prayers were offered only they and their God could say. At once those in the front row began to depart. A few from inside the crowd who'd been denied a view came to the fence line, but they stayed there for only a moment before going about their business. After the prescribed interval, the body parts would be collected and given a proper burial in accordance with the religion that each of them had defiled.

Jack didn't know what emotion he was supposed to feel. He'd seen enough death. He knew that much. But these deaths did not touch his heart at all, and now he wondered and worried a little about that.

"You asked me how history is made, Jack," Ali said. "You have just seen it."

"What do you mean?"

"You do not need us to tell you," Golovko said.

The men who started a war, or tried to, executed like criminals in the market square, Jack thought. *Not a bad precedent.*

"Maybe you're right, maybe it will make people think twice before the next time." *That's an idea whose time has come.*

"In all our countries," Ali said, "the sword is the symbol of justice . . . an anachronism, perhaps, from a time when men acted as men. But a sword still has a use."

"Certainly it is precise," Golovko observed.

"So, Jack, you have fully left government service?" Ali asked after a moment. Ryan turned away from the scene, just as everyone else had done.

"Yes, Your Highness."

"And those foolish 'ethics' laws no longer apply. Good." Ali turned. The Special Forces officer appeared as though by magic. The salute he gave Prince Ali was the sort to impress Kipling. The sword came next. The scabbard was wrought gold encrusted with jewels. The hilt was gold and ivory, and you could see where parts of it had been worn down by generations of strong hands. Manifestly the weapon of a king.

"This is three hundred years old," Ali said, turning to Ryan. "It has been carried in peace and war by my ancestors. It even has a name—*Breeze of Evening* is the best I can do in English. It means more than that, of course. We wish you to have it, Dr. Ryan, as a reminder of those who died—and those who did not, because of you. It has killed many times. His Majesty believes that the sword has killed enough."

Ryan took the scimitar from the Prince's hand. The gold scabbard was nicked and abraded by generations of sandstorms and battles, but Ryan saw that his reflection was not so terribly distorted as he might have feared. The blade, he saw, on drawing it partway, was mirror-bright, still rippled from the Damascus smith who'd shaped the steel into its fearful and effective purpose. Such a dichotomy, Ryan thought, smiling without knowing it, that something so beautiful could have so terrible a purpose. Such irony. And yet—

He'd keep the sword, hang it in a place of honor, look at it from time to time to remind himself of what it and he had done. And just maybe—

"Killed enough?" Ryan slid the sword back into its sheath and let it fall to his side. "Yes, Your Highness. I think we all have."

Afterword

Now that the tale is told, a few things need to be made clear. All of the material in this novel relating to weapons technology and fabrication is readily available in any one of dozens of books. For reasons which I hope will be obvious to the reader, certain technical details have been altered, sacrificing plausibility in the interests of obscurity. This was done to salve my conscience, *not* in any reasonable expectation that it matters a damn.

The Manhattan Project of World War II still represents the most remarkable congregation of scientific talent in human history, never equaled, and perhaps never to be exceeded. The vastly expensive project broke new scientific ground and produced numerous additional discoveries. Modern computer theory, for example, largely grew from bomb-related research, and the first huge mainframe computers were mainly used for bomb design.

I was first bemused, then stunned, as my research revealed just how easy such a project might be today. It is generally known that nuclear secrets are not as secure as we would like—in fact the situation is worse than even well-informed people appreciate. What required billions of dollars in the 1940s is much less expensive today. A modern personal computer has far more power and reliability than the first Eniac, and the "hydrocodes" which enable a computer to test and validate a weapon's design are easily duplicated. The exquisite machine tools used to fabricate parts can be had for the asking. When I asked explicitly for specifications for the very machines used at Oak Ridge and elsewhere, they arrived Federal Express the next day. Some highly specialized items designed specifically for bomb manufacture may now be found in stereo speakers. The fact of the matter is that a sufficiently wealthy individual could, over a period of from five to ten years, produce a multistage thermonuclear device. Science is all in the public domain, and allows few secrets.

Delivery of such a device is child's play. I could base that statement on "extensive conversations" with various police and security agencies, but it doesn't take long for a person to say, "Are you kidding?" I heard that phrase more than once. Probably no country—certainly no liberal democracy—can secure its borders against such a threat.

So that's the problem. What might be the solution? For starters, international controls over the traffic in nuclear materials and technology ought to be made something more than the joke they currently are. Nuclear weapons cannot be uninvented, and I personally think that nuclear power is a safe and environmentally benign alternative to the use of fossil fuels, but any tool must be used with care, and this tool admits of abuses too fearful for us to ignore.

—Peregrine Cliff, February 1991